TARZAN SUPER PACK

by Edgar Rice Burroughs

TARZAN OF THE APES

OUT TO SEA

I had this story from one who had no business to tell it to me, or to any other. I may credit the seductive influence of an old vintage upon the narrator for the beginning of it, and my own skeptical incredulity during the days that followed for the balance of the strange tale.

When my convivial host discovered that he had told me so much, and that I was prone to doubtfulness, his foolish pride assumed the task the old vintage had commenced, and so he unearthed written evidence in the form of musty manuscript, and dry official records of the British Colonial Office to support many of the salient features of his remarkable narrative.

I do not say the story is true, for I did not witness the happenings which it portrays, but the fact that in the telling of it to you I have taken fictitious names for the principal characters quite sufficiently evidences the sincerity of my own belief that it *may* be true.

The yellow, mildewed pages of the diary of a man long dead, and the records of the Colonial Office dovetail perfectly with the narrative of my convivial host, and so I give you the story as I painstakingly pieced it out from these several various agencies.

If you do not find it credible you will at least be as one with me in acknowledging that it is unique, remarkable, and interesting.

From the records of the Colonial Office and from the dead man's diary we learn that a certain young English nobleman, whom we shall call John Clayton, Lord Greystoke, was commissioned to make a peculiarly delicate investigation of conditions in a British West Coast African Colony from whose simple native inhabitants another European power was known to be recruiting soldiers for its native army, which it used solely for the forcible collection of rubber and ivory from the savage tribes along the Congo and the Aruwimi. The natives of the British Colony complained that many of their young men were enticed away through the medium of fair and glowing promises, but that few if any ever returned to their families.

The Englishmen in Africa went even further, saying that these poor blacks were held in virtual slavery, since after their terms of enlistment expired their ignorance was imposed upon by their white officers, and they were told that they had yet several years to serve.

And so the Colonial Office appointed John Clayton to a new post in British West Africa, but his confidential instructions centered on a thorough investigation of the unfair treatment of black British subjects by the officers of a friendly European power. Why he was sent, is, however, of little moment to this story, for he never made an investigation, nor, in fact, did he ever reach his destination.

Clayton was the type of Englishman that one likes best to associate with the noblest monuments of historic achievement upon a thousand victorious battlefields—a strong, virile man —mentally, morally, and physically.

In stature he was above the average height; his eyes were gray, his features regular and strong; his carriage that of perfect, robust health influenced by his years of army training.

Political ambition had caused him to seek transference from the army to the Colonial Office and so we find him, still young, entrusted with a delicate and important commission in the service of the Queen.

When he received this appointment he was both elated and appalled. The preferment seemed to him in the nature of a well-merited reward for painstaking and intelligent service, and as a stepping stone to posts of greater importance and responsibility; but, on the other hand, he had been married to the Hon. Alice Rutherford for scarce a three months, and it was the thought of taking this fair young girl into the dangers and isolation of tropical Africa that appalled him.

For her sake he would have refused the appointment, but she would not have it so. Instead she insisted that he accept, and, indeed, take her with him.

There were mothers and brothers and sisters, and aunts and cousins to express various opinions on the subject, but as to what they severally advised history is silent.

We know only that on a bright May morning in 1888, John, Lord Greystoke, and Lady Alice sailed from Dover on their way to Africa.

A month later they arrived at Freetown where they chartered a small sailing vessel, the Fuwalda, which was to bear them to their final destination.

And here John, Lord Greystoke, and Lady Alice, his wife, vanished from the eyes and from the knowledge of men.

Two months after they weighed anchor and cleared from the port of Freetown a half dozen British war vessels were scouring the south Atlantic for trace of them or their little vessel, and it was almost immediately that the wreckage was found upon the shores of St. Helena which convinced the world that the Fuwalda had gone down with all on board, and hence the search was stopped ere it had scarce begun; though hope lingered in longing hearts for many years.

The Fuwalda, a barkentine of about one hundred tons, was a vessel of the type often seen in coastwise trade in the far southern Atlantic, their crews composed of the off scourings of the sea—unhanged murderers and cutthroats of every race and every nation.

The Fuwalda was no exception to the rule. Her officers were swarthy bullies, hating and hated by their crew. The captain, while a competent seaman, was a brute in his treatment of his men. He knew, or at least he used, but two arguments in his dealings with them—a belaying pin and a revolver—nor is it likely that the motley aggregation he signed would have understood aught else.

So it was that from the second day out from Freetown John Clayton and his young wife witnessed scenes upon the deck of the Fuwalda such as they had believed were never enacted outside the covers of printed stories of the sea.

It was on the morning of the second day that the first link was forged in what was destined to form a chain of circumstances ending in a life for one then unborn such as has never been paralleled in the history of man.

Two sailors were washing down the decks of the Fuwalda, the first mate was on duty, and the captain had stopped to speak with John Clayton and Lady Alice.

The men were working backwards toward the little party who were facing away from the sailors. Closer and closer they came, until one of them was directly behind the captain. In another moment he would have passed by and this strange narrative would never have been recorded.

But just that instant the officer turned to leave Lord and Lady Greystoke, and, as he did so, tripped against the sailor and sprawled headlong upon the deck, overturning the water- pail so that he was drenched in its dirty contents.

For an instant the scene was ludicrous; but only for an instant. With a volley of awful oaths, his face suffused with the scarlet of mortification and rage, the captain regained his feet, and with a terrific blow felled the sailor to the deck.

The man was small and rather old, so that the brutality of the act was thus accentuated. The other seaman, however, was neither old nor small—a huge bear of a man, with fierce black mustachios, and a great bull neck set between massive shoulders.

As he saw his mate go down he crouched, and, with a low snarl, sprang upon the captain crushing him to his knees with a single mighty blow.

From scarlet the officer's face went white, for this was mutiny; and mutiny he had met and subdued before in his brutal career. Without waiting to rise he whipped a revolver from his pocket, firing point blank at the great mountain of muscle towering before him; but, quick as he was, John Clayton was almost as quick, so that the bullet which was intended for the sailor's heart lodged in the sailor's leg instead, for Lord Greystoke had struck down the captain's arm as he had seen the weapon flash in the sun.

Words passed between Clayton and the captain, the former making it plain that he was disgusted with the brutality displayed toward the crew, nor would he countenance anything further of the kind while he and Lady Greystoke remained passengers.

The captain was on the point of making an angry reply, but, thinking better of it, turned on his heel and black and scowling, strode aft.

He did not care to antagonize an English official, for the Queen's mighty arm wielded a punitive instrument which he could appreciate, and which he feared—England's far-reaching navy.

The two sailors picked themselves up, the older man assisting his wounded comrade to rise. The big fellow, who was known among his mates as Black Michael, tried his leg gingerly, and, finding that it bore his weight, turned to Clayton with a word of gruff thanks.

Though the fellow's tone was surly, his words were evidently well meant. Ere he had scarce finished his little speech he had turned and was limping off toward the forecastle with the very apparent intention of forestalling any further conversation.

They did not see him again for several days, nor did the captain accord them more than the surliest of grunts when he was forced to speak to them.

They took their meals in his cabin, as they had before the unfortunate occurrence; but the captain was careful to see that his duties never permitted him to eat at the same time.

The other officers were coarse, illiterate fellows, but little above the villainous crew they bullied, and were only too glad to avoid social intercourse with the polished English noble and his lady, so that the Claytons were left very much to themselves.

This in itself accorded perfectly with their desires, but it also rather isolated them from the life of the little ship so that they were unable to keep in touch with the daily happenings which were to culminate so soon in bloody tragedy.

There was in the whole atmosphere of the craft that undefinable something which presages disaster. Outwardly, to the knowledge of the Claytons, all went on as before upon the little vessel; but that there was an undertow leading them toward some unknown danger both felt, though they did not speak of it to each other.

On the second day after the wounding of Black Michael, Clayton came on deck just in time to see the limp body of one of the crew being carried below by four of his fellows while the first mate, a heavy belaying pin in his hand, stood glowering at the little party of sullen sailors.

Clayton asked no questions—he did not need to—and the following day, as the great lines of a British battleship grew out of the distant horizon, he half determined to demand that he and Lady Alice be put aboard her, for his fears were steadily increasing that nothing but harm could result from remaining on the lowering, sullen Fuwalda.

Toward noon they were within speaking distance of the British vessel, but when Clayton had nearly decided to ask the captain to put them aboard her, the obvious ridiculousness of such a request became suddenly apparent. What reason could he give the officer commanding her majesty's ship for desiring to go back in the direction from which he had just come!

What if he told them that two insubordinate seamen had been roughly handled by their officers? They would but laugh in their sleeves and attribute his reason for wishing to leave the ship to but one thing—cowardice.

John Clayton, Lord Greystoke, did not ask to be transferred to the British man-of-war. Late in the afternoon he saw her upper works fade below the far horizon, but not before he learned that which confirmed his greatest fears, and caused him to curse the false pride which had restrained him from seeking safety for his young wife a few short hours before, when safety was within reach—a safety which was now gone forever.

It was mid-afternoon that brought the little old sailor, who had been felled by the captain a few days before, to where Clayton and his wife stood by the ship's side watching the ever diminishing outlines of the great battleship. The old fellow was polishing brasses, and as he came edging along until close to Clayton he said, in an undertone:

"'Ell's to pay, sir, on this 'ere craft, an' mark my word for it, sir. 'Ell's to pay."

"What do you mean, my good fellow?" asked Clayton.

"Wy, hasn't ye seen wats goin' on? Hasn't ye 'eard that devil's spawn of a capting an' is mates knockin' the bloomin' lights outen 'arf the crew?

"Two busted 'eads yeste'day, an' three to-day. Black Michael's as good as new agin an' 'e's not the bully to stand fer it, not 'e; an' mark my word for it, sir."

"You mean, my man, that the crew contemplates mutiny?" asked Clayton.

"Mutiny!" exclaimed the old fellow. "Mutiny! They means murder, sir, an' mark my word for it, sir."

"When?"

"Hit's comin', sir; hit's comin' but I'm not a-sayin' wen, an' I've said too damned much now, but ye was a good sort t'other day an' I thought it no more'n right to warn ye. But keep a still tongue in yer 'ead an' when ye 'ear shootin' git below an' stay there.

"That's all, only keep a still tongue in yer 'ead, or they'll put a pill between yer ribs, an' mark my word for it, sir," and the old fellow went on with his polishing, which carried him away from where the Claytons were standing.

"Deuced cheerful outlook, Alice," said Clayton.

"You should warn the captain at once, John. Possibly the trouble may yet be averted," she said.

"I suppose I should, but yet from purely selfish motives I am almost prompted to 'keep a still tongue in my 'ead.' Whatever they do now they will spare us in recognition of my stand for this fellow Black Michael, but should they find that I had betrayed them there would be no mercy shown us, Alice."

"You have but one duty, John, and that lies in the interest of vested authority. If you do not warn the captain you are as much a party to whatever follows as though you had helped to plot and carry it out with your own head and hands."

"You do not understand, dear," replied Clayton. "It is of you I am thinking—there lies my first duty. The captain has brought this condition upon himself, so why then should I risk subjecting my wife to unthinkable horrors in a probably futile attempt to save him from his own brutal folly? You have no conception, dear, of what would follow were this pack of cutthroats to gain control of the Fuwalda."

"Duty is duty, John, and no amount of sophistries may change it. I would be a poor wife for an English lord were I to be responsible for his shirking a plain duty. I realize the danger which must follow, but I can face it with you."

"Have it as you will then, Alice," he answered, smiling. "Maybe we are borrowing trouble. While I do not like the looks of things on board this ship, they may not be so bad after all, for it is possible that the 'Ancient Mariner' was but voicing the desires of his wicked old heart rather than speaking of real facts.

"Mutiny on the high sea may have been common a hundred years ago, but in this good year 1888 it is the least likely of happenings.

"But there goes the captain to his cabin now. If I am going to warn him I might as well get the beastly job over for I have little stomach to talk with the brute at all."

So saying he strolled carelessly in the direction of the companionway through which the captain had passed, and a moment later was knocking at his door.

"Come in," growled the deep tones of that surly officer.

And when Clayton had entered, and closed the door behind him:

"Well?"

"I have come to report the gist of a conversation I heard to-day, because I feel that, while there may be nothing to it, it is as well that you be forearmed. In short, the men contemplate mutiny and murder."

"It's a lie!" roared the captain. "And if you have been interfering again with the discipline of this ship, or meddling in affairs that don't concern you you can take the consequences, and be damned. I don't care whether you are an English lord or not. I'm captain of this here ship, and from now on you keep your meddling nose out of my business."

The captain had worked himself up to such a frenzy of rage that he was fairly purple of face, and he shrieked the last words at the top of his voice, emphasizing his remarks by a loud thumping of the table with one huge fist, and shaking the other in Clayton's face.

Greystoke never turned a hair, but stood eying the excited man with level gaze.

"Captain Billings," he drawled finally, "if you will pardon my candor, I might remark that you are something of an ass."

Whereupon he turned and left the captain with the same indifferent ease that was habitual with him, and which was more surely calculated to raise the ire of a man of Billings' class than a torrent of invective.

So, whereas the captain might easily have been brought to regret his hasty speech had Clayton attempted to conciliate him, his temper was now irrevocably set in the mold in which Clayton had left it, and the last chance of their working together for their common good was gone.

"Well, Alice," said Clayton, as he rejoined his wife, "I might have saved my breath. The fellow proved most ungrateful. Fairly jumped at me like a mad dog.

"He and his blasted old ship may hang, for aught I care; and until we are safely off the thing I shall spend my energies in looking after our own welfare. And I rather fancy the first step to that end should be to go to our cabin and look over my revolvers. I am sorry now that we packed the larger guns and the ammunition with the stuff below."

They found their quarters in a bad state of disorder. Clothing from their open boxes and bags strewed the little apartment, and even their beds had been torn to pieces.

"Evidently someone was more anxious about our belongings than we," said Clayton. "Let's have a look around, Alice, and see what's missing."

A thorough search revealed the fact that nothing had been taken but Clayton's two revolvers and the small supply of ammunition he had saved out for them.

"Those are the very things I most wish they had left us," said Clayton, "and the fact that they wished for them and them alone is most sinister."

"What are we to do, John?" asked his wife. "Perhaps you were right in that our best chance lies in maintaining a neutral position.

"If the officers are able to prevent a mutiny, we have nothing to fear, while if the mutineers are victorious our one slim hope lies in not having attempted to thwart or antagonize them."

"Right you are, Alice. We'll keep in the middle of the road."

As they started to straighten up their cabin, Clayton and his wife simultaneously noticed the corner of a piece of paper protruding from beneath the door of their quarters. As Clayton stooped to reach for it he was amazed to see it move further into the room, and then he realized that it was being pushed inward by someone from without.

Quickly and silently he stepped toward the door, but, as he reached for the knob to throw it open, his wife's hand fell upon his wrist.

"No, John," she whispered. "They do not wish to be seen, and so we cannot afford to see them. Do not forget that we are keeping to the middle of the road."

Clayton smiled and dropped his hand to his side. Thus they stood watching the little bit of white paper until it finally remained at rest upon the floor just inside the door.

Then Clayton stooped and picked it up. It was a bit of grimy, white paper roughly folded into a ragged square. Opening it they found a crude message printed almost illegibly, and with many evidences of an unaccustomed task.

Translated, it was a warning to the Claytons to refrain from reporting the loss of the revolvers, or from repeating what the old sailor had told them—to refrain on pain of death.

"I rather imagine we'll be good," said Clayton with a rueful smile. "About all we can do is to sit tight and wait for whatever may come."

THE SAVAGE HOME

Nor did they have long to wait, for the next morning as Clayton was emerging on deck for his accustomed walk before breakfast, a shot rang out, and then another, and another.

The sight which met his eyes confirmed his worst fears. Facing the little knot of officers was the entire motley crew of the Fuwalda, and at their head stood Black Michael.

At the first volley from the officers the men ran for shelter, and from points of vantage behind masts, wheel-house and cabin they returned the fire of the five men who represented the hated authority of the ship.

Two of their number had gone down before the captain's revolver. They lay where they had fallen between the combatants. But then the first mate lunged forward upon his face, and at a cry of command from Black Michael the mutineers charged the remaining four. The crew had been able to muster but six firearms, so most of them were armed with boat hooks, axes, hatchets and crowbars.

The captain had emptied his revolver and was reloading as the charge was made. The second mate's gun had jammed, and so there were but two weapons opposed to the mutineers as they bore down upon the officers, who now started to give back before the infuriated rush of their men.

Both sides were cursing and swearing in a frightful manner, which, together with the reports of the firearms and the screams and groans of the wounded, turned the deck of the Fuwalda to the likeness of a madhouse.

Before the officers had taken a dozen backward steps the men were upon them. An ax in the hands of a burly Negro cleft the captain from forehead to chin, and an instant later the others were down: dead or wounded from dozens of blows and bullet wounds.

Short and grisly had been the work of the mutineers of the Fuwalda, and through it all John Clayton had stood leaning carelessly beside the companionway puffing meditatively upon his pipe as though he had been but watching an indifferent cricket match.

As the last officer went down he thought it was time that he returned to his wife lest some members of the crew find her alone below.

Though outwardly calm and indifferent, Clayton was inwardly apprehensive and wrought up, for he feared for his wife's safety at the hands of these ignorant, half-brutes into whose hands fate had so remorselessly thrown them.

As he turned to descend the ladder he was surprised to see his wife standing on the steps almost at his side.

"How long have you been here, Alice?"

"Since the beginning," she replied. "How awful, John. Oh, how awful! What can we hope for at the hands of such as those?"

"Breakfast, I hope," he answered, smiling bravely in an attempt to allay her fears.

"At least," he added, "I'm going to ask them. Come with me, Alice. We must not let them think we expect any but courteous treatment."

The men had by this time surrounded the dead and wounded officers, and without either partiality or compassion proceeded to throw both living and dead over the sides of the vessel. With equal heartlessness they disposed of their own dead and dying.

Presently one of the crew spied the approaching Claytons, and with a cry of: "Here's two more for the fishes," rushed toward them with uplifted ax.

But Black Michael was even quicker, so that the fellow went down with a bullet in his back before he had taken a half dozen steps.

With a loud roar, Black Michael attracted the attention of the others, and, pointing to Lord and Lady Greystoke, cried:

"These here are my friends, and they are to be left alone. D'ye understand?

"I'm captain of this ship now, an' what I says goes," he added, turning to Clayton. "Just keep to yourselves, and nobody'll harm ye," and he looked threateningly on his fellows.

The Claytons heeded Black Michael's instructions so well that they saw but little of the crew and knew nothing of the plans the men were making.

Occasionally they heard faint echoes of brawls and quarreling among the mutineers, and on two occasions the vicious bark of firearms rang out on the still air. But Black Michael was a fit leader for this band of cutthroats, and, withal held them in fair subjection to his rule.

On the fifth day following the murder of the ship's officers, land was sighted by the lookout. Whether island or mainland, Black Michael did not know, but he announced to Clayton that if investigation showed that the place was habitable he and Lady Greystoke were to be put ashore with their belongings.

"You'll be all right there for a few months," he explained, "and by that time we'll have been able to make an inhabited coast somewhere and scatter a bit. Then I'll see that yer gover'ment's notified where you be an' they'll soon send a man- o'war to fetch ye off.

"It would be a hard matter to land you in civilization without a lot o' questions being asked, an' none o' us here has any very convincin' answers up our sleeves."

Clayton remonstrated against the inhumanity of landing them upon an unknown shore to be left to the mercies of savage beasts, and, possibly, still more savage men.

But his words were of no avail, and only tended to anger Black Michael, so he was forced to desist and make the best he could of a bad situation.

About three o'clock in the afternoon they came about off a beautiful wooded shore opposite the mouth of what appeared to be a land-locked harbor.

Black Michael sent a small boat filled with men to sound the entrance in an effort to determine if the Fuwalda could be safely worked through the entrance.

In about an hour they returned and reported deep water through the passage as well as far into the little basin.

Before dark the barkentine lay peacefully at anchor upon the bosom of the still, mirror-like surface of the harbor.

The surrounding shores were beautiful with semitropical verdure, while in the distance the country rose from the ocean in hill and tableland, almost uniformly clothed by primeval forest.

No signs of habitation were visible, but that the land might easily support human life was evidenced by the abundant bird and animal life of which the watchers on the Fuwalda's deck caught occasional glimpses, as well as by the shimmer of a little river which emptied into the harbor, insuring fresh water in plenitude.

As darkness settled upon the earth, Clayton and Lady Alice still stood by the ship's rail in silent contemplation of their future abode. From the dark shadows of the mighty forest came the wild calls of savage beasts—the deep roar of the lion, and, occasionally, the shrill scream of a panther.

The woman shrank closer to the man in terror-stricken anticipation of the horrors lying in wait for them in the awful blackness of the nights to come, when they should be alone upon that wild and lonely shore.

Later in the evening Black Michael joined them long enough to instruct them to make their preparations for landing on the morrow. They tried to persuade him to take them to some more hospitable coast near enough to civilization so that they might hope to fall into friendly hands. But no pleas, or threats, or promises of reward could move him.

"I am the only man aboard who would not rather see ye both safely dead, and, while I know that's the sensible way to make sure of our own necks, yet Black Michael's not the man to forget a favor. Ye saved my life once, and in return I'm goin' to spare yours, but that's all I can do.

"The men won't stand for any more, and if we don't get ye landed pretty quick they may even change their minds about giving ye that much show. I'll put all yer stuff ashore with ye as well as cookin' utensils an' some old sails for tents, an' enough grub to last ye until ye can find fruit and game.

"With yer guns for protection, ye ought to be able to live here easy enough until help comes. When I get safely hid away I'll see to it that the British gover'ment learns about where ye be; for the life of me I couldn't tell 'em exactly where, for I don't know myself. But they'll find ye all right."

After he had left them they went silently below, each wrapped in gloomy forebodings.

Clayton did not believe that Black Michael had the slightest intention of notifying the British government of their whereabouts, nor was he any too sure but that some treachery was contemplated for the following day when they should be on shore with the sailors who would have to accompany them with their belongings.

Once out of Black Michael's sight any of the men might strike them down, and still leave Black Michael's conscience clear.

And even should they escape that fate was it not but to be faced with far graver dangers? Alone, he might hope to survive for years; for he was a strong, athletic man.

But what of Alice, and that other little life so soon to be launched amidst the hardships and grave dangers of a primeval world?

The man shuddered as he meditated upon the awful gravity, the fearful helplessness, of their situation. But it was a merciful Providence which prevented him from foreseeing the hideous reality which awaited them in the grim depths of that gloomy wood.

Early next morning their numerous chests and boxes were hoisted on deck and lowered to waiting small boats for transportation to shore.

There was a great quantity and variety of stuff, as the Claytons had expected a possible five to eight years' residence in their new home. Thus, in addition to the many necessities they had brought, there were also many luxuries.

Black Michael was determined that nothing belonging to the Claytons should be left on board. Whether out of compassion for them, or in furtherance of his own self-interests, it would be difficult to say.

There was no question but that the presence of property of a missing British official upon a suspicious vessel would have been a difficult thing to explain in any civilized port in the world.

So zealous was he in his efforts to carry out his intentions that he insisted upon the return of Clayton's revolvers to him by the sailors in whose possession they were.

Into the small boats were also loaded salt meats and biscuit, with a small supply of potatoes and beans, matches, and cooking vessels, a chest of tools, and the old sails which Black Michael had promised them.

As though himself fearing the very thing which Clayton had suspected, Black Michael accompanied them to shore, and was the last to leave them when the small boats, having filled the ship's casks with fresh water, were pushed out toward the waiting Fuwalda.

As the boats moved slowly over the smooth waters of the bay, Clayton and his wife stood silently watching their departure—in the breasts of both a feeling of impending disaster and utter hopelessness.

And behind them, over the edge of a low ridge, other eyes watched—close set, wicked eyes, gleaming beneath shaggy brows.

As the Fuwalda passed through the narrow entrance to the harbor and out of sight behind a projecting point, Lady Alice threw her arms about Clayton's neck and burst into uncontrolled sobs.

Bravely had she faced the dangers of the mutiny; with heroic fortitude she had looked into the terrible future; but now that the horror of absolute solitude was upon them, her overwrought nerves gave way, and the reaction came.

He did not attempt to check her tears. It were better that nature have her way in relieving these long-pent emotions, and it was many minutes before the girl—little more than a child she was—could again gain mastery of herself.

"Oh, John," she cried at last, "the horror of it. What are we to do? What are we to do?"

"There is but one thing to do, Alice," and he spoke as quietly as though they were sitting in their snug living room at home, "and that is work. Work must be our salvation. We must not give ourselves time to think, for in that direction lies madness.

"We must work and wait. I am sure that relief will come, and come quickly, when once it is apparent that the Fuwalda has been lost, even though Black Michael does not keep his word to us."

"But John, if it were only you and I," she sobbed, "we could endure it I know; but—"

"Yes, dear," he answered, gently, "I have been thinking of that, also; but we must face it, as we must face whatever comes, bravely and with the utmost confidence in our ability to cope with circumstances whatever they may be.

"Hundreds of thousands of years ago our ancestors of the dim and distant past faced the same problems which we must face, possibly in these same primeval forests. That we are here today evidences their victory.

"What they did may we not do? And even better, for are we not armed with ages of superior knowledge, and have we not the means of protection, defense, and sustenance which science has given us, but of which they were totally ignorant? What they accomplished, Alice, with instruments and weapons of stone and bone, surely that may we accomplish also."

"Ah, John, I wish that I might be a man with a man's philosophy, but I am but a woman, seeing with my heart rather than my head, and all that I can see is too horrible, too unthinkable to put into words.

"I only hope you are right, John. I will do my best to be a brave primeval woman, a fit mate for the primeval man."

Clayton's first thought was to arrange a sleeping shelter for the night; something which might serve to protect them from prowling beasts of prey.

He opened the box containing his rifles and ammunition, that they might both be armed against possible attack while at work, and then together they sought a location for their first night's sleeping place.

A hundred yards from the beach was a little level spot, fairly free of trees; here they decided eventually to build a permanent house, but for the time being they both thought it best to construct a little platform in the trees out of reach of the larger of the savage beasts in whose realm they were.

To this end Clayton selected four trees which formed a rectangle about eight feet square, and cutting long branches from other trees he constructed a framework around them, about ten feet from the ground, fastening the ends of the branches securely to the trees by means of rope, a quantity of which Black Michael had furnished him from the hold of the Fuwalda.

Across this framework Clayton placed other smaller branches quite close together. This platform he paved with the huge fronds of elephant's ear which grew in profusion about them, and over the fronds he laid a great sail folded into several thicknesses.

Seven feet higher he constructed a similar, though lighter platform to serve as roof, and from the sides of this he suspended the balance of his sailcloth for walls.

When completed he had a rather snug little nest, to which he carried their blankets and some of the lighter luggage.

It was now late in the afternoon, and the balance of the daylight hours were devoted to the building of a rude ladder by means of which Lady Alice could mount to her new home.

All during the day the forest about them had been filled with excited birds of brilliant plumage, and dancing, chattering monkeys, who watched these new arrivals and their wonderful nest building operations with every mark of keenest interest and fascination.

Notwithstanding that both Clayton and his wife kept a sharp lookout they saw nothing of larger animals, though on two occasions they had seen their little simian neighbors come screaming and chattering from the near-by ridge, casting frightened glances back over their little shoulders, and evincing as plainly as though by speech that they were fleeing some terrible thing which lay concealed there.

Just before dusk Clayton finished his ladder, and, filling a great basin with water from the near-by stream, the two mounted to the comparative safety of their aerial chamber.

As it was quite warm, Clayton had left the side curtains thrown back over the roof, and as they sat, like Turks, upon their blankets, Lady Alice, straining her eyes into the darkening shadows of the wood, suddenly reached out and grasped Clayton's arms.

"John," she whispered, "look! What is it, a man?"

As Clayton turned his eyes in the direction she indicated, he saw silhouetted dimly against the shadows beyond, a great figure standing upright upon the ridge.

For a moment it stood as though listening and then turned slowly, and melted into the shadows of the jungle.

"What is it, John?"

"I do not know, Alice," he answered gravely, "it is too dark to see so far, and it may have been but a shadow cast by the rising moon."

"No, John, if it was not a man it was some huge and grotesque mockery of man. Oh, I am afraid."

He gathered her in his arms, whispering words of courage and love into her ears.

Soon after, he lowered the curtain walls, tying them securely to the trees so that, except for a little opening toward the beach, they were entirely enclosed.

As it was now pitch dark within their tiny aerie they lay down upon their blankets to try to gain, through sleep, a brief respite of forgetfulness.

Clayton lay facing the opening at the front, a rifle and a brace of revolvers at his hand.

Scarcely had they closed their eyes than the terrifying cry of a panther rang out from the jungle behind them. Closer and closer it came until they could hear the great beast directly beneath them. For an hour or more they heard it sniffing and clawing at the trees which supported their platform, but at last it roamed away across the beach, where Clayton could see it clearly in the brilliant moonlight—a great, handsome beast, the largest he had ever seen.

During the long hours of darkness they caught but fitful snatches of sleep, for the night noises of a great jungle teeming with myriad animal life kept their overwrought nerves on edge, so that a hundred times they were startled to wakefulness by piercing screams, or the stealthy moving of great bodies beneath them.

LIFE AND DEATH

Morning found them but little, if at all refreshed, though it was with a feeling of intense relief that they saw the day dawn.

As soon as they had made their meager breakfast of salt pork, coffee and biscuit, Clayton commenced work upon their house, for he realized that they could hope for no safety and no peace of mind at night until four strong walls effectually barred the jungle life from them.

The task was an arduous one and required the better part of a month, though he built but one small room. He constructed his cabin of small logs about six inches in diameter, stopping the chinks with clay which he found at the depth of a few feet beneath the surface soil.

At one end he built a fireplace of small stones from the beach. These also he set in clay and when the house had been entirely completed he applied a coating of the clay to the entire outside surface to the thickness of four inches.

In the window opening he set small branches about an inch in diameter both vertically and horizontally, and so woven that they formed a substantial grating that could withstand the strength of a powerful animal. Thus they obtained air and proper ventilation without fear of lessening the safety of their cabin.

The A-shaped roof was thatched with small branches laid close together and over these long jungle grass and palm fronds, with a final coating of clay.

15

The door he built of pieces of the packing-boxes which had held their belongings, nailing one piece upon another, the grain of contiguous layers running transversely, until he had a solid body some three inches thick and of such great strength that they were both moved to laughter as they gazed upon it.

Here the greatest difficulty confronted Clayton, for he had no means whereby to hang his massive door now that he had built it. After two days' work, however, he succeeded in fashioning two massive hardwood hinges, and with these he hung the door so that it opened and closed easily.

The stuccoing and other final touches were added after they moved into the house, which they had done as soon as the roof was on, piling their boxes before the door at night and thus having a comparatively safe and comfortable habitation.

The building of a bed, chairs, table, and shelves was a relatively easy matter, so that by the end of the second month they were well settled, and, but for the constant dread of attack by wild beasts and the ever growing loneliness, they were not uncomfortable or unhappy.

At night great beasts snarled and roared about their tiny cabin, but, so accustomed may one become to oft repeated noises, that soon they paid little attention to them, sleeping soundly the whole night through.

Thrice had they caught fleeting glimpses of great man-like figures like that of the first night, but never at sufficiently close range to know positively whether the half-seen forms were those of man or brute.

The brilliant birds and the little monkeys had become accustomed to their new acquaintances, and as they had evidently never seen human beings before they presently, after their first fright had worn off, approached closer and closer, impelled by that strange curiosity which dominates the wild creatures of the forest and the jungle and the plain, so that within the first month several of the birds had gone so far as even to accept morsels of food from the friendly hands of the Claytons.

One afternoon, while Clayton was working upon an addition to their cabin, for he contemplated building several more rooms, a number of their grotesque little friends came shrieking and scolding through the trees from the direction of the ridge. Ever as they fled they cast fearful glances back of them, and finally they stopped near Clayton jabbering excitedly to him as though to warn him of approaching danger.

At last he saw it, the thing the little monkeys so feared— the man-brute of which the Claytons had caught occasional fleeting glimpses.

It was approaching through the jungle in a semi-erect position, now and then placing the backs of its closed fists upon the ground—a great anthropoid ape, and, as it advanced, it emitted deep guttural growls and an occasional low barking sound.

Clayton was at some distance from the cabin, having come to fell a particularly perfect tree for his building operations. Grown careless from months of continued safety, during which time he had seen no dangerous animals during the daylight hours, he had left his rifles and revolvers all within the little cabin, and now that he saw the great ape crashing through the underbrush directly toward him, and from a direction which practically cut him off from escape, he felt a vague little shiver play up and down his spine.

He knew that, armed only with an ax, his chances with this ferocious monster were small indeed—and Alice; O God, he thought, what will become of Alice?

There was yet a slight chance of reaching the cabin. He turned and ran toward it, shouting an alarm to his wife to run in and close the great door in case the ape cut off his retreat.

Lady Greystoke had been sitting a little way from the cabin, and when she heard his cry she looked up to see the ape springing with almost incredible swiftness, for so large and awkward an animal, in an effort to head off Clayton.

With a low cry she sprang toward the cabin, and, as she entered, gave a backward glance which filled her soul with terror, for the brute had intercepted her husband, who now stood at bay grasping his ax with both hands ready to swing it upon the infuriated animal when he should make his final charge.

"Close and bolt the door, Alice," cried Clayton. "I can finish this fellow with my ax."

But he knew he was facing a horrible death, and so did she.

The ape was a great bull, weighing probably three hundred pounds. His nasty, close-set eyes gleamed hatred from beneath his shaggy brows, while his great canine fangs were bared in a horrid snarl as he paused a moment before his prey.

Over the brute's shoulder Clayton could see the doorway of his cabin, not twenty paces distant, and a great wave of horror and fear swept over him as he saw his young wife emerge, armed with one of his rifles.

She had always been afraid of firearms, and would never touch them, but now she rushed toward the ape with the fearlessness of a lioness protecting its young.

"Back, Alice," shouted Clayton, "for God's sake, go back."

But she would not heed, and just then the ape charged, so that Clayton could say no more.

The man swung his ax with all his mighty strength, but the powerful brute seized it in those terrible hands, and tearing it from Clayton's grasp hurled it far to one side.

With an ugly snarl he closed upon his defenseless victim, but ere his fangs had reached the throat they thirsted for, there was a sharp report and a bullet entered the ape's back between his shoulders.

Throwing Clayton to the ground the beast turned upon his new enemy. There before him stood the terrified girl vainly trying to fire another bullet into the animal's body; but she did not understand the mechanism of the firearm, and the hammer fell futilely upon an empty cartridge.

Almost simultaneously Clayton regained his feet, and without thought of the utter hopelessness of it, he rushed forward to drag the ape from his wife's prostrate form.

With little or no effort he succeeded, and the great bulk rolled inertly upon the turf before him—the ape was dead. The bullet had done its work.

A hasty examination of his wife revealed no marks upon her, and Clayton decided that the huge brute had died the instant he had sprung toward Alice.

Gently he lifted his wife's still unconscious form, and bore her to the little cabin, but it was fully two hours before she regained consciousness.

Her first words filled Clayton with vague apprehension. For some time after regaining her senses, Alice gazed wonderingly about the interior of the little cabin, and then, with a satisfied sigh, said:

"O, John, it is so good to be really home! I have had an awful dream, dear. I thought we were no longer in London, but in some horrible place where great beasts attacked us."

"There, there, Alice," he said, stroking her forehead, "try to sleep again, and do not worry your head about bad dreams."

That night a little son was born in the tiny cabin beside the primeval forest, while a leopard screamed before the door, and the deep notes of a lion's roar sounded from beyond the ridge.

Lady Greystoke never recovered from the shock of the great ape's attack, and, though she lived for a year after her baby was born, she was never again outside the cabin, nor did she ever fully realize that she was not in England.

Sometimes she would question Clayton as to the strange noises of the nights; the absence of servants and friends, and the strange rudeness of the furnishings within her room, but, though he made no effort to deceive her, never could she grasp the meaning of it all.

In other ways she was quite rational, and the joy and happiness she took in the possession of her little son and the constant attentions of her husband made that year a very happy one for her, the happiest of her young life.

That it would have been beset by worries and apprehension had she been in full command of her mental faculties Clayton well knew; so that while he suffered terribly to see her so, there were times when he was almost glad, for her sake, that she could not understand.

Long since had he given up any hope of rescue, except through accident. With unremitting zeal he had worked to beautify the interior of the cabin.

Skins of lion and panther covered the floor. Cupboards and bookcases lined the walls. Odd vases made by his own hand from the clay of the region held beautiful tropical flowers. Curtains of grass and bamboo covered the windows, and, most arduous task of all, with his meager assortment of tools he had fashioned lumber to neatly seal the walls and ceiling and lay a smooth floor within the cabin.

That he had been able to turn his hands at all to such unaccustomed labor was a source of mild wonder to him. But he loved the work because it was for her and the tiny life that had come to cheer them, though adding a hundredfold to his responsibilities and to the terribleness of their situation.

During the year that followed, Clayton was several times attacked by the great apes which now seemed to continually infest the vicinity of the cabin; but as he never again ventured outside without both rifle and revolvers he had little fear of the huge beasts.

He had strengthened the window protections and fitted a unique wooden lock to the cabin door, so that when he hunted for game and fruits, as it was constantly necessary for him to do to insure sustenance, he had no fear that any animal could break into the little home.

At first he shot much of the game from the cabin windows, but toward the end the animals learned to fear the strange lair from whence issued the terrifying thunder of his rifle.

In his leisure Clayton read, often aloud to his wife, from the store of books he had brought for their new home. Among these were many for little children—picture books, primers, readers—for they had known that their little child would be old enough for such before they might hope to return to England.

At other times Clayton wrote in his diary, which he had always been accustomed to keep in French, and in which he recorded the details of their strange life. This book he kept locked in a little metal box.

A year from the day her little son was born Lady Alice passed quietly away in the night. So peaceful was her end that it was hours before Clayton could awake to a realization that his wife was dead.

The horror of the situation came to him very slowly, and it is doubtful that he ever fully realized the enormity of his sorrow and the fearful responsibility that had devolved upon him with the care of that wee thing, his son, still a nursing babe.

The last entry in his diary was made the morning following her death, and there he recites the sad details in a matter-of-fact way that adds to the pathos of it; for it breathes a tired apathy born of long sorrow and hopelessness, which even this cruel blow could scarcely awake to further suffering:

My little son is crying for nourishment—O Alice, Alice, what shall I do?

And as John Clayton wrote the last words his hand was destined ever to pen, he dropped his head wearily upon his outstretched arms where they rested upon the table he had built for her who lay still and cold in the bed beside him.

For a long time no sound broke the deathlike stillness of the jungle midday save the piteous wailing of the tiny man-child.

THE APES

In the forest of the table-land a mile back from the ocean old Kerchak the Ape was on a rampage of rage among his people.

The younger and lighter members of his tribe scampered to the higher branches of the great trees to escape his wrath; risking their lives upon branches that scarce supported their weight rather than face old Kerchak in one of his fits of uncontrolled anger.

The other males scattered in all directions, but not before the infuriated brute had felt the vertebra of one snap between his great, foaming jaws.

A luckless young female slipped from an insecure hold upon a high branch and came crashing to the ground almost at Kerchak's feet.

With a wild scream he was upon her, tearing a great piece from her side with his mighty teeth, and striking her viciously upon her head and shoulders with a broken tree limb until her skull was crushed to a jelly.

And then he spied Kala, who, returning from a search for food with her young babe, was ignorant of the state of the mighty male's temper until suddenly the shrill warnings of her fellows caused her to scamper madly for safety.

But Kerchak was close upon her, so close that he had almost grasped her ankle had she not made a furious leap far into space from one tree to another—a perilous chance which apes seldom if ever take, unless so closely pursued by danger that there is no alternative.

She made the leap successfully, but as she grasped the limb of the further tree the sudden jar loosened the hold of the tiny babe where it clung frantically to her neck, and she saw the little thing hurled, turning and twisting, to the ground thirty feet below.

With a low cry of dismay Kala rushed headlong to its side, thoughtless now of the danger from Kerchak; but when she gathered the wee, mangled form to her bosom life had left it.

With low moans, she sat cuddling the body to her; nor did Kerchak attempt to molest her. With the death of the babe his fit of demoniacal rage passed as suddenly as it had seized him.

Kerchak was a huge king ape, weighing perhaps three hundred and fifty pounds. His forehead was extremely low and receding, his eyes bloodshot, small and close set to his coarse, flat nose; his ears large and thin, but smaller than most of his kind.

His awful temper and his mighty strength made him supreme among the little tribe into which he had been born some twenty years before.

Now that he was in his prime, there was no simian in all the mighty forest through which he roved that dared contest his right to rule, nor did the other and larger animals molest him.

Old Tantor, the elephant, alone of all the wild savage life, feared him not—and he alone did Kerchak fear. When Tantor trumpeted, the great ape scurried with his fellows high among the trees of the second terrace.

The tribe of anthropoids over which Kerchak ruled with an iron hand and bared fangs, numbered some six or eight families, each family consisting of an adult male with his females and their young, numbering in all some sixty or seventy apes.

Kala was the youngest mate of a male called Tublat, meaning broken nose, and the child she had seen dashed to death was her first; for she was but nine or ten years old.

Notwithstanding her youth, she was large and powerful—a splendid, clean-limbed animal, with a round, high forehead, which denoted more intelligence than most of her kind possessed. So, also, she had a great capacity for mother love and mother sorrow.

But she was still an ape, a huge, fierce, terrible beast of a species closely allied to the gorilla, yet more intelligent; which, with the strength of their cousin, made her kind the most fearsome of those awe-inspiring progenitors of man.

When the tribe saw that Kerchak's rage had ceased they came slowly down from their arboreal retreats and pursued again the various occupations which he had interrupted.

The young played and frolicked about among the trees and bushes. Some of the adults lay prone upon the soft mat of dead and decaying vegetation which covered the ground, while others turned over pieces of fallen branches and clods of earth in search of the small bugs and reptiles which formed a part of their food.

Others, again, searched the surrounding trees for fruit, nuts, small birds, and eggs.

They had passed an hour or so thus when Kerchak called them together, and, with a word of command to them to follow him, set off toward the sea.

They traveled for the most part upon the ground, where it was open, following the path of the great elephants whose comings and goings break the only roads through those tangled mazes of bush, vine, creeper, and tree. When they walked it was with a rolling, awkward motion, placing the knuckles of their closed hands upon the ground and swinging their ungainly bodies forward.

But when the way was through the lower trees they moved more swiftly, swinging from branch to branch with the agility of their smaller cousins, the monkeys. And all the way Kala carried her little dead baby hugged closely to her breast.

It was shortly after noon when they reached a ridge overlooking the beach where below them lay the tiny cottage which was Kerchak's goal.

He had seen many of his kind go to their deaths before the loud noise made by the little black stick in the hands of the strange white ape who lived in that wonderful lair, and Kerchak had made up his brute mind to own that death-dealing contrivance, and to explore the interior of the mysterious den.

He wanted, very, very much, to feel his teeth sink into the neck of the queer animal that he had learned to hate and fear, and because of this, he came often with his tribe to reconnoiter, waiting for a time when the white ape should be off his guard.

Of late they had quit attacking, or even showing themselves; for every time they had done so in the past the little stick had roared out its terrible message of death to some member of the tribe.

Today there was no sign of the man about, and from where they watched they could see that the cabin door was open. Slowly, cautiously, and noiselessly they crept through the jungle toward the little cabin.

There were no growls, no fierce screams of rage—the little black stick had taught them to come quietly lest they awaken it.

On, on they came until Kerchak himself slunk stealthily to the very door and peered within. Behind him were two males, and then Kala, closely straining the little dead form to her breast.

Inside the den they saw the strange white ape lying half across a table, his head buried in his arms; and on the bed lay a figure covered by a sailcloth, while from a tiny rustic cradle came the plaintive wailing of a babe.

Noiselessly Kerchak entered, crouching for the charge; and then John Clayton rose with a sudden start and faced them.

The sight that met his eyes must have frozen him with horror, for there, within the door, stood three great bull apes, while behind them crowded many more; how many he never knew, for his revolvers were hanging on the far wall beside his rifle, and Kerchak was charging.

When the king ape released the limp form which had been John Clayton, Lord Greystoke, he turned his attention toward the little cradle; but Kala was there before him, and when he would have grasped the child she snatched it herself, and before he could intercept her she had bolted through the door and taken refuge in a high tree.

As she took up the little live baby of Alice Clayton she dropped the dead body of her own into the empty cradle; for the wail of the living had answered the call of universal motherhood within her wild breast which the dead could not still.

High up among the branches of a mighty tree she hugged the shrieking infant to her bosom, and soon the instinct that was as dominant in this fierce female as it had been in the breast of his tender and beautiful mother—the instinct of mother love—reached out to the tiny man-child's half-formed understanding, and he became quiet.

Then hunger closed the gap between them, and the son of an English lord and an English lady nursed at the breast of Kala, the great ape.

In the meantime the beasts within the cabin were warily examining the contents of this strange lair.

Once satisfied that Clayton was dead, Kerchak turned his attention to the thing which lay upon the bed, covered by a piece of sailcloth.

Gingerly he lifted one corner of the shroud, but when he saw the body of the woman beneath he tore the cloth roughly from her form and seized the still, white throat in his huge, hairy hands.

A moment he let his fingers sink deep into the cold flesh, and then, realizing that she was already dead, he turned from her, to examine the contents of the room; nor did he again molest the body of either Lady Alice or Sir John.

The rifle hanging upon the wall caught his first attention; it was for this strange, death-dealing thunder-stick that he had yearned for months; but now that it was within his grasp he scarcely had the temerity to seize it.

Cautiously he approached the thing, ready to flee precipitately should it speak in its deep roaring tones, as he had heard it speak before, the last words to those of his kind who, through ignorance or rashness, had attacked the wonderful white ape that had borne it.

Deep in the beast's intelligence was something which assured him that the thunder-stick was only dangerous when in the hands of one who could manipulate it, but yet it was several minutes ere he could bring himself to touch it.

Instead, he walked back and forth along the floor before it, turning his head so that never once did his eyes leave the object of his desire.

Using his long arms as a man uses crutches, and rolling his huge carcass from side to side with each stride, the great king ape paced to and fro, uttering deep growls, occasionally punctuated with the ear-piercing scream, than which there is no more terrifying noise in all the jungle.

Presently he halted before the rifle. Slowly he raised a huge hand until it almost touched the shining barrel, only to withdraw it once more and continue his hurried pacing.

It was as though the great brute by this show of fearlessness, and through the medium of his wild voice, was endeavoring to bolster up his courage to the point which would permit him to take the rifle in his hand.

Again he stopped, and this time succeeded in forcing his reluctant hand to the cold steel, only to snatch it away almost immediately and resume his restless beat.

Time after time this strange ceremony was repeated, but on each occasion with increased confidence, until, finally, the rifle was torn from its hook and lay in the grasp of the great brute.

Finding that it harmed him not, Kerchak began to examine it closely. He felt of it from end to end, peered down the black depths of the muzzle, fingered the sights, the breech, the stock, and finally the trigger.

During all these operations the apes who had entered sat huddled near the door watching their chief, while those outside strained and crowded to catch a glimpse of what transpired within.

Suddenly Kerchak's finger closed upon the trigger. There was a deafening roar in the little room and the apes at and beyond the door fell over one another in their wild anxiety to escape.

Kerchak was equally frightened, so frightened, in fact, that he quite forgot to throw aside the author of that fearful noise, but bolted for the door with it tightly clutched in one hand.

As he passed through the opening, the front sight of the rifle caught upon the edge of the inswung door with sufficient force to close it tightly after the fleeing ape.

When Kerchak came to a halt a short distance from the cabin and discovered that he still held the rifle, he dropped it as he might have dropped a red hot iron, nor did he again attempt to recover it—the noise was too much for his brute nerves; but he was now quite convinced that the terrible stick was quite harmless by itself if left alone.

It was an hour before the apes could again bring themselves to approach the cabin to continue their investigations, and when they finally did so, they found to their chagrin that the door was closed and so securely fastened that they could not force it.

The cleverly constructed latch which Clayton had made for the door had sprung as Kerchak passed out; nor could the apes find means of ingress through the heavily barred windows.

After roaming about the vicinity for a short time, they started back for the deeper forests and the higher land from whence they had come.

Kala had not once come to earth with her little adopted babe, but now Kerchak called to her to descend with the rest, and as there was no note of anger in his voice she dropped lightly from branch to branch and joined the others on their homeward march.

Those of the apes who attempted to examine Kala's strange baby were repulsed with bared fangs and low menacing growls, accompanied by words of warning from Kala.

When they assured her that they meant the child no harm she permitted them to come close, but would not allow them to touch her charge.

It was as though she knew that her baby was frail and delicate and feared lest the rough hands of her fellows might injure the little thing.

Another thing she did, and which made traveling an onerous trial for her. Remembering the death of her own little one, she clung desperately to the new babe, with one hand, whenever they were upon the march.

The other young rode upon their mothers' backs; their little arms tightly clasping the hairy necks before them, while their legs were locked beneath their mothers' armpits.

Not so with Kala; she held the small form of the little Lord Greystoke tightly to her breast, where the dainty hands clutched the long black hair which covered that portion of her body. She had seen one child fall from her back to a terrible death, and she would take no further chances with this.

THE WHITE APE

Tenderly Kala nursed her little waif, wondering silently why it did not gain strength and agility as did the little apes of other mothers. It was nearly a year from the time the little fellow came into her possession before he would walk alone, and as for climbing—my, but how stupid he was!

Kala sometimes talked with the older females about her young hopeful, but none of them could understand how a child could be so slow and backward in learning to care for itself. Why, it could not even find food alone, and more than twelve moons had passed since Kala had come upon it.

Had they known that the child had seen thirteen moons before it had come into Kala's possession they would have considered its case as absolutely hopeless, for the little apes of their own tribe were as far advanced in two or three moons as was this little stranger after twenty-five.

Tublat, Kala's husband, was sorely vexed, and but for the female's careful watching would have put the child out of the way.

"He will never be a great ape," he argued. "Always will you have to carry him and protect him. What good will he be to the tribe? None; only a burden."

"Let us leave him quietly sleeping among the tall grasses, that you may bear other and stronger apes to guard us in our old age."

"Never, Broken Nose," replied Kala. "If I must carry him forever, so be it."

And then Tublat went to Kerchak to urge him to use his authority with Kala, and force her to give up little Tarzan, which was the name they had given to the tiny Lord Greystoke, and which meant "White-Skin."

But when Kerchak spoke to her about it Kala threatened to run away from the tribe if they did not leave her in peace with the child; and as this is one of the inalienable rights of the jungle folk, if they be dissatisfied among their own people, they bothered her no more, for Kala was a fine clean-limbed young female, and they did not wish to lose her.

As Tarzan grew he made more rapid strides, so that by the time he was ten years old he was an excellent climber, and on the ground could do many wonderful things which were beyond the powers of his little brothers and sisters.

In many ways did he differ from them, and they often marveled at his superior cunning, but in strength and size he was deficient; for at ten the great anthropoids were fully grown, some of them towering over six feet in height, while little Tarzan was still but a half-grown boy.

Yet such a boy!

From early childhood he had used his hands to swing from branch to branch after the manner of his giant mother, and as he grew older he spent hour upon hour daily speeding through the tree tops with his brothers and sisters.

He could spring twenty feet across space at the dizzy heights of the forest top, and grasp with unerring precision, and without apparent jar, a limb waving wildly in the path of an approaching tornado.

He could drop twenty feet at a stretch from limb to limb in rapid descent to the ground, or he could gain the utmost pinnacle of the loftiest tropical giant with the ease and swiftness of a squirrel.

Though but ten years old he was fully as strong as the average man of thirty, and far more agile than the most practiced athlete ever becomes. And day by day his strength was increasing.

His life among these fierce apes had been happy; for his recollection held no other life, nor did he know that there existed within the universe aught else than his little forest and the wild jungle animals with which he was familiar.

He was nearly ten before he commenced to realize that a great difference existed between himself and his fellows. His little body, burned brown by exposure, suddenly caused him feelings of intense shame, for he realized that it was entirely hairless, like some low snake, or other reptile.

He attempted to obviate this by plastering himself from head to foot with mud, but this dried and fell off. Besides it felt so uncomfortable that he quickly decided that he preferred the shame to the discomfort.

In the higher land which his tribe frequented was a little lake, and it was here that Tarzan first saw his face in the clear, still waters of its bosom.

It was on a sultry day of the dry season that he and one of his cousins had gone down to the bank to drink. As they leaned over, both little faces were mirrored on the placid pool; the fierce and terrible features of the ape beside those of the aristocratic scion of an old English house.

Tarzan was appalled. It had been bad enough to be hairless, but to own such a countenance! He wondered that the other apes could look at him at all.

That tiny slit of a mouth and those puny white teeth! How they looked beside the mighty lips and powerful fangs of his more fortunate brothers!

And the little pinched nose of his; so thin was it that it looked half starved. He turned red as he compared it with the beautiful broad nostrils of his companion. Such a generous nose! Why it spread half across his face! It certainly must be fine to be so handsome, thought poor little Tarzan.

But when he saw his own eyes; ah, that was the final blow —a brown spot, a gray circle and then blank whiteness! Frightful! not even the snakes had such hideous eyes as he.

So intent was he upon this personal appraisement of his features that he did not hear the parting of the tall grass behind him as a great body pushed itself stealthily through the jungle; nor did his companion, the ape, hear either, for he was drinking and the noise of his sucking lips and gurgles of satisfaction drowned the quiet approach of the intruder.

Not thirty paces behind the two she crouched—Sabor, the huge lioness—lashing her tail. Cautiously she moved a great padded paw forward, noiselessly placing it before she lifted the next. Thus she advanced; her belly low, almost touching the surface of the ground—a great cat preparing to spring upon its prey.

Now she was within ten feet of the two unsuspecting little playfellows—carefully she drew her hind feet well up beneath her body, the great muscles rolling under the beautiful skin.

So low she was crouching now that she seemed flattened to the earth except for the upward bend of the glossy back as it gathered for the spring.

No longer the tail lashed—quiet and straight behind her it lay.

An instant she paused thus, as though turned to stone, and then, with an awful scream, she sprang.

Sabor, the lioness, was a wise hunter. To one less wise the wild alarm of her fierce cry as she sprang would have seemed a foolish thing, for could she not more surely have fallen upon her victims had she but quietly leaped without that loud shriek?

But Sabor knew well the wondrous quickness of the jungle folk and their almost unbelievable powers of hearing. To them the sudden scraping of one blade of grass across another was as effectual a warning as her loudest cry, and Sabor knew that she could not make that mighty leap without a little noise.

Her wild scream was not a warning. It was voiced to freeze her poor victims in a paralysis of terror for the tiny fraction of an instant which would suffice for her mighty claws to sink into their soft flesh and hold them beyond hope of escape.

So far as the ape was concerned, Sabor reasoned correctly. The little fellow crouched trembling just an instant, but that instant was quite long enough to prove his undoing.

Not so, however, with Tarzan, the man-child. His life amidst the dangers of the jungle had taught him to meet emergencies with self-confidence, and his higher intelligence resulted in a quickness of mental action far beyond the powers of the apes.

So the scream of Sabor, the lioness, galvanized the brain and muscles of little Tarzan into instant action.

Before him lay the deep waters of the little lake, behind him certain death; a cruel death beneath tearing claws and rending fangs.

Tarzan had always hated water except as a medium for quenching his thirst. He hated it because he connected it with the chill and discomfort of the torrential rains, and he feared it for the thunder and lightning and wind which accompanied them.

The deep waters of the lake he had been taught by his wild mother to avoid, and further, had he not seen little Neeta sink beneath its quiet surface only a few short weeks before never to return to the tribe?

But of the two evils his quick mind chose the lesser ere the first note of Sabor's scream had scarce broken the quiet of the jungle, and before the great beast had covered half her leap Tarzan felt the chill waters close above his head.

He could not swim, and the water was very deep; but still he lost no particle of that self-confidence and resourcefulness which were the badges of his superior being.

Rapidly he moved his hands and feet in an attempt to scramble upward, and, possibly more by chance than design, he fell into the stroke that a dog uses when swimming, so that within a few seconds his nose was above water and he found that he could keep it there by continuing his strokes, and also make progress through the water.

He was much surprised and pleased with this new acquirement which had been so suddenly thrust upon him, but he had no time for thinking much upon it.

He was now swimming parallel to the bank and there he saw the cruel beast that would have seized him crouching upon the still form of his little playmate.

The lioness was intently watching Tarzan, evidently expecting him to return to shore, but this the boy had no intention of doing.

Instead he raised his voice in the call of distress common to his tribe, adding to it the warning which would prevent would-be rescuers from running into the clutches of Sabor.

Almost immediately there came an answer from the distance, and presently forty or fifty great apes swung rapidly and majestically through the trees toward the scene of tragedy.

In the lead was Kala, for she had recognized the tones of her best beloved, and with her was the mother of the little ape who lay dead beneath cruel Sabor.

Though more powerful and better equipped for fighting than the apes, the lioness had no desire to meet these enraged adults, and with a snarl of hatred she sprang quickly into the brush and disappeared.

Tarzan now swam to shore and clambered quickly upon dry land. The feeling of freshness and exhilaration which the cool waters had imparted to him, filled his little being with grateful surprise, and ever after he lost no opportunity to take a daily plunge in lake or stream or ocean when it was possible to do so.

For a long time Kala could not accustom herself to the sight; for though her people could swim when forced to it, they did not like to enter water, and never did so voluntarily.

The adventure with the lioness gave Tarzan food for pleasurable memories, for it was such affairs which broke the monotony of his daily life—otherwise but a dull round of searching for food, eating, and sleeping.

The tribe to which he belonged roamed a tract extending, roughly, twenty-five miles along the seacoast and some fifty miles inland. This they traversed almost continually, occasionally remaining for months in one locality; but as they moved through the trees with great speed they often covered the territory in a very few days.

Much depended upon food supply, climatic conditions, and the prevalence of animals of the more dangerous species; though Kerchak often led them on long marches for no other reason than that he had tired of remaining in the same place.

At night they slept where darkness overtook them, lying upon the ground, and sometimes covering their heads, and more seldom their bodies, with the great leaves of the elephant's ear. Two or three might lie cuddled in each other's arms for additional warmth if the night were chill, and thus Tarzan had slept in Kala's arms nightly for all these years.

That the huge, fierce brute loved this child of another race is beyond question, and he, too, gave to the great, hairy beast all the affection that would have belonged to his fair young mother had she lived.

When he was disobedient she cuffed him, it is true, but she was never cruel to him, and was more often caressing him than chastising him.

Tublat, her mate, always hated Tarzan, and on several occasions had come near ending his youthful career.

Tarzan on his part never lost an opportunity to show that he fully reciprocated his foster father's sentiments, and whenever he could safely annoy him or make faces at him or hurl insults upon him from the safety of his mother's arms, or the slender branches of the higher trees, he did so.

His superior intelligence and cunning permitted him to invent a thousand diabolical tricks to add to the burdens of Tublat's life.

Early in his boyhood he had learned to form ropes by twisting and tying long grasses together, and with these he was forever tripping Tublat or attempting to hang him from some overhanging branch.

By constant playing and experimenting with these he learned to tie rude knots, and make sliding nooses; and with these he and the younger apes amused themselves. What Tarzan did they tried to do also, but he alone originated and became proficient.

One day while playing thus Tarzan had thrown his rope at one of his fleeing companions, retaining the other end in his grasp. By accident the noose fell squarely about the running ape's neck, bringing him to a sudden and surprising halt.

Ah, here was a new game, a fine game, thought Tarzan, and immediately he attempted to repeat the trick. And thus, by painstaking and continued practice, he learned the art of roping.

Now, indeed, was the life of Tublat a living nightmare. In sleep, upon the march, night or day, he never knew when that quiet noose would slip about his neck and nearly choke the life out of him.

Kala punished, Tublat swore dire vengeance, and old Kerchak took notice and warned and threatened; but all to no avail.

Tarzan defied them all, and the thin, strong noose continued to settle about Tublat's neck whenever he least expected it.

The other apes derived unlimited amusement from Tublat's discomfiture, for Broken Nose was a disagreeable old fellow, whom no one liked, anyway.

In Tarzan's clever little mind many thoughts revolved, and back of these was his divine power of reason.

If he could catch his fellow apes with his long arm of many grasses, why not Sabor, the lioness?

It was the germ of a thought, which, however, was destined to mull around in his conscious and subconscious mind until it resulted in magnificent achievement.

But that came in later years.

TARZAN SUPER PACK

JUNGLE BATTLES

The wanderings of the tribe brought them often near the closed and silent cabin by the little land-locked harbor. To Tarzan this was always a source of never-ending mystery and pleasure.

He would peek into the curtained windows, or, climbing upon the roof, peer down the black depths of the chimney in vain endeavor to solve the unknown wonders that lay within those strong walls.

His child-like imagination pictured wonderful creatures within, and the very impossibility of forcing entrance added a thousandfold to his desire to do so.

He could clamber about the roof and windows for hours attempting to discover means of ingress, but to the door he paid little attention, for this was apparently as solid as the walls.

It was in the next visit to the vicinity, following the adventure with old Sabor, that, as he approached the cabin, Tarzan noticed that from a distance the door appeared to be an independent part of the wall in which it was set, and for the first time it occurred to him that this might prove the means of entrance which had so long eluded him.

He was alone, as was often the case when he visited the cabin, for the apes had no love for it; the story of the thunder-stick having lost nothing in the telling during these ten years had quite surrounded the white man's deserted abode with an atmosphere of weirdness and terror for the simians.

The story of his own connection with the cabin had never been told him. The language of the apes had so few words that they could talk but little of what they had seen in the cabin, having no words to accurately describe either the strange people or their belongings, and so, long before Tarzan was old enough to understand, the subject had been forgotten by the tribe.

Only in a dim, vague way had Kala explained to him that his father had been a strange white ape, but he did not know that Kala was not his own mother.

On this day, then, he went directly to the door and spent hours examining it and fussing with the hinges, the knob and the latch. Finally he stumbled upon the right combination, and the door swung creakingly open before his astonished eyes.

For some minutes he did not dare venture within, but finally, as his eyes became accustomed to the dim light of the interior he slowly and cautiously entered.

In the middle of the floor lay a skeleton, every vestige of flesh gone from the bones to which still clung the mildewed and moldered remnants of what had once been clothing. Upon the bed lay a similar gruesome thing, but smaller, while in a tiny cradle near-by was a third, a wee mite of a skeleton.

To none of these evidences of a fearful tragedy of a long dead day did little Tarzan give but passing heed. His wild jungle life had inured him to the sight of dead and dying animals, and had he known that he was looking upon the remains of his own father and mother he would have been no more greatly moved.

The furnishings and other contents of the room it was which riveted his attention. He examined many things minutely—strange tools and weapons, books, paper, clothing— what little had withstood the ravages of time in the humid atmosphere of the jungle coast.

He opened chests and cupboards, such as did not baffle his small experience, and in these he found the contents much better preserved.

Among other things he found a sharp hunting knife, on the keen blade of which he immediately proceeded to cut his finger. Undaunted he continued his experiments, finding that he could hack and hew splinters of wood from the table and chairs with this new toy.

For a long time this amused him, but finally tiring he continued his explorations. In a cupboard filled with books he came across one with brightly colored pictures—it was a child's illustrated alphabet—

A is for Archer Who shoots with a bow. B is for Boy, His first name is Joe.

The pictures interested him greatly.

EDGAR RICE BURROUGHS

There were many apes with faces similar to his own, and further over in the book he found, under "M," some little monkeys such as he saw daily flitting through the trees of his primeval forest. But nowhere was pictured any of his own people; in all the book was none that resembled Kerchak, or Tublat, or Kala.

At first he tried to pick the little figures from the leaves, but he soon saw that they were not real, though he knew not what they might be, nor had he any words to describe them.

The boats, and trains, and cows and horses were quite meaningless to him, but not quite so baffling as the odd little figures which appeared beneath and between the colored pictures—some strange kind of bug he thought they might be, for many of them had legs though nowhere could he find one with eyes and a mouth. It was his first introduction to the letters of the alphabet, and he was over ten years old.

Of course he had never before seen print, or ever had spoken with any living thing which had the remotest idea that such a thing as a written language existed, nor ever had he seen anyone reading.

So what wonder that the little boy was quite at a loss to guess the meaning of these strange figures.

Near the middle of the book he found his old enemy, Sabor, the lioness, and further on, coiled Histah, the snake.

Oh, it was most engrossing! Never before in all his ten years had he enjoyed anything so much. So absorbed was he that he did not note the approaching dusk, until it was quite upon him and the figures were blurred.

He put the book back in the cupboard and closed the door, for he did not wish anyone else to find and destroy his treasure, and as he went out into the gathering darkness he closed the great door of the cabin behind him as it had been before he discovered the secret of its lock, but before he left he had noticed the hunting knife lying where he had thrown it upon the floor, and this he picked up and took with him to show to his fellows.

He had taken scarce a dozen steps toward the jungle when a great form rose up before him from the shadows of a low bush. At first he thought it was one of his own people but in another instant he realized that it was Bolgani, the huge gorilla.

So close was he that there was no chance for flight and little Tarzan knew that he must stand and fight for his life; for these great beasts were the deadly enemies of his tribe, and neither one nor the other ever asked or gave quarter.

Had Tarzan been a full-grown bull ape of the species of his tribe he would have been more than a match for the gorilla, but being only a little English boy, though enormously muscular for such, he stood no chance against his cruel antagonist. In his veins, though, flowed the blood of the best of a race of mighty fighters, and back of this was the training of his short lifetime among the fierce brutes of the jungle.

He knew no fear, as we know it; his little heart beat the faster but from the excitement and exhilaration of adventure. Had the opportunity presented itself he would have escaped, but solely because his judgment told him he was no match for the great thing which confronted him. And since reason showed him that successful flight was impossible he met the gorilla squarely and bravely without a tremor of a single muscle, or any sign of panic.

In fact he met the brute midway in its charge, striking its huge body with his closed fists and as futilely as he had been a fly attacking an elephant. But in one hand he still clutched the knife he had found in the cabin of his father, and as the brute, striking and biting, closed upon him the boy accidentally turned the point toward the hairy breast. As the knife sank deep into its body the gorilla shrieked in pain and rage.

But the boy had learned in that brief second a use for his sharp and shining toy, so that, as the tearing, striking beast dragged him to earth he plunged the blade repeatedly and to the hilt into its breast.

The gorilla, fighting after the manner of its kind, struck terrific blows with its open hand, and tore the flesh at the boy's throat and chest with its mighty tusks.

For a moment they rolled upon the ground in the fierce frenzy of combat. More and more weakly the torn and bleeding arm struck home with the long sharp blade, then the little figure stiffened with a spasmodic jerk, and Tarzan, the young Lord Greystoke, rolled unconscious upon the dead and decaying vegetation which carpeted his jungle home.

A mile back in the forest the tribe had heard the fierce challenge of the gorilla, and, as was his custom when any danger threatened, Kerchak called his people together, partly for mutual protection against a common enemy, since this gorilla might be but one of a party of several, and also to see that all members of the tribe were accounted for.

It was soon discovered that Tarzan was missing, and Tublat was strongly opposed to sending assistance. Kerchak himself had no liking for the strange little waif, so he listened to Tublat, and, finally, with a shrug of his shoulders, turned back to the pile of leaves on which he had made his bed.

But Kala was of a different mind; in fact, she had not waited but to learn that Tarzan was absent ere she was fairly flying through the matted branches toward the point from which the cries of the gorilla were still plainly audible.

Darkness had now fallen, and an early moon was sending its faint light to cast strange, grotesque shadows among the dense foliage of the forest.

Here and there the brilliant rays penetrated to earth, but for the most part they only served to accentuate the Stygian blackness of the jungle's depths.

Like some huge phantom, Kala swung noiselessly from tree to tree; now running nimbly along a great branch, now swinging through space at the end of another, only to grasp that of a farther tree in her rapid progress toward the scene of the tragedy her knowledge of jungle life told her was being enacted a short distance before her.

The cries of the gorilla proclaimed that it was in mortal combat with some other denizen of the fierce wood. Suddenly these cries ceased, and the silence of death reigned throughout the jungle.

Kala could not understand, for the voice of Bolgani had at last been raised in the agony of suffering and death, but no sound had come to her by which she possibly could determine the nature of his antagonist.

That her little Tarzan could destroy a great bull gorilla she knew to be improbable, and so, as she neared the spot from which the sounds of the struggle had come, she moved more warily and at last slowly and with extreme caution she traversed the lowest branches, peering eagerly into the moon- splashed blackness for a sign of the combatants.

Presently she came upon them, lying in a little open space full under the brilliant light of the moon—little Tarzan's torn and bloody form, and beside it a great bull gorilla, stone dead.

With a low cry Kala rushed to Tarzan's side, and gathering the poor, blood-covered body to her breast, listened for a sign of life. Faintly she heard it—the weak beating of the little heart.

Tenderly she bore him back through the inky jungle to where the tribe lay, and for many days and nights she sat guard beside him, bringing him food and water, and brushing the flies and other insects from his cruel wounds.

Of medicine or surgery the poor thing knew nothing. She could but lick the wounds, and thus she kept them cleansed, that healing nature might the more quickly do her work.

At first Tarzan would eat nothing, but rolled and tossed in a wild delirium of fever. All he craved was water, and this she brought him in the only way she could, bearing it in her own mouth.

No human mother could have shown more unselfish and sacrificing devotion than did this poor, wild brute for the little orphaned waif whom fate had thrown into her keeping.

At last the fever abated and the boy commenced to mend. No word of complaint passed his tight set lips, though the pain of his wounds was excruciating.

A portion of his chest was laid bare to the ribs, three of which had been broken by the mighty blows of the gorilla. One arm was nearly severed by the giant fangs, and a great piece had been torn from his neck, exposing his jugular vein, which the cruel jaws had missed but by a miracle.

With the stoicism of the brutes who had raised him he endured his suffering quietly, preferring to crawl away from the others and lie huddled in some clump of tall grasses rather than to show his misery before their eyes.

Kala, alone, he was glad to have with him, but now that he was better she was gone longer at a time, in search of food; for the devoted animal had scarcely eaten enough to support her own life while Tarzan had been so low, and was in consequence, reduced to a mere shadow of her former self.

THE LIGHT OF KNOWLEDGE

After what seemed an eternity to the little sufferer he was able to walk once more, and from then on his recovery was so rapid that in another month he was as strong and active as ever.

During his convalescence he had gone over in his mind many times the battle with the gorilla, and his first thought was to recover the wonderful little weapon which had transformed him from a hopelessly outclassed weakling to the superior of the mighty terror of the jungle.

Also, he was anxious to return to the cabin and continue his investigations of its wondrous contents.

So, early one morning, he set forth alone upon his quest. After a little search he located the clean-picked bones of his late adversary, and close by, partly buried beneath the fallen leaves, he found the knife, now red with rust from its exposure to the dampness of the ground and from the dried blood of the gorilla.

He did not like the change in its former bright and gleaming surface; but it was still a formidable weapon, and one which he meant to use to advantage whenever the opportunity presented itself. He had in mind that no more would he run from the wanton attacks of old Tublat.

In another moment he was at the cabin, and after a short time had again thrown the latch and entered. His first concern was to learn the mechanism of the lock, and this he did by examining it closely while the door was open, so that he could learn precisely what caused it to hold the door, and by what means it released at his touch.

He found that he could close and lock the door from within, and this he did so that there would be no chance of his being molested while at his investigation.

He commenced a systematic search of the cabin; but his attention was soon riveted by the books which seemed to exert a strange and powerful influence over him, so that he could scarce attend to aught else for the lure of the wondrous puzzle which their purpose presented to him.

Among the other books were a primer, some child's readers, numerous picture books, and a great dictionary. All of these he examined, but the pictures caught his fancy most, though the strange little bugs which covered the pages where there were no pictures excited his wonder and deepest thought.

Squatting upon his haunches on the table top in the cabin his father had built—his smooth, brown, naked little body bent over the book which rested in his strong slender hands, and his great shock of long, black hair falling about his well-shaped head and bright, intelligent eyes—Tarzan of the apes, little primitive man, presented a picture filled, at once, with pathos and with promise—an allegorical figure of the primordial groping through the black night of ignorance toward the light of learning.

His little face was tense in study, for he had partially grasped, in a hazy, nebulous way, the rudiments of a thought which was destined to prove the key and the solution to the puzzling problem of the strange little bugs.

In his hands was a primer opened at a picture of a little ape similar to himself, but covered, except for hands and face, with strange, colored fur, for such he thought the jacket and trousers to be. Beneath the picture were three little bugs—

Boy.

And now he had discovered in the text upon the page that these three were repeated many times in the same sequence.

Another fact he learned—that there were comparatively few individual bugs; but these were repeated many times, occasionally alone, but more often in company with others.

Slowly he turned the pages, scanning the pictures and the text for a repetition of the combination B-O-Y. Presently he found it beneath a picture of another little ape and a strange animal which went upon four legs like the jackal and resembled him not a little. Beneath this picture the bugs appeared as:

A boy and a dog

There they were, the three little bugs which always accompanied the little ape.

And so he progressed very, very slowly, for it was a hard and laborious task which he had set himself without knowing it—a task which might seem to you or me impossible—learning to read without having the slightest knowledge of letters or written language, or the faintest idea that such things existed.

He did not accomplish it in a day, or in a week, or in a month, or in a year; but slowly, very slowly, he learned after he had grasped the possibilities which lay in those little bugs, so that by the time he was fifteen he knew the various combinations of letters which stood for every pictured figure in the little primer and in one or two of the picture books.

Of the meaning and use of the articles and conjunctions, verbs and adverbs and pronouns he had but the faintest conception.

One day when he was about twelve he found a number of lead pencils in a hitherto undiscovered drawer beneath the table, and in scratching upon the table top with one of them he was delighted to discover the black line it left behind it.

He worked so assiduously with this new toy that the table top was soon a mass of scrawly loops and irregular lines and his pencil-point worn down to the wood. Then he took another pencil, but this time he had a definite object in view.

He would attempt to reproduce some of the little bugs that scrambled over the pages of his books.

It was a difficult task, for he held the pencil as one would grasp the hilt of a dagger, which does not add greatly to ease in writing or to the legibility of the results.

But he persevered for months, at such times as he was able to come to the cabin, until at last by repeated experimenting he found a position in which to hold the pencil that best permitted him to guide and control it, so that at last he could roughly reproduce any of the little bugs.

Thus he made a beginning of writing.

Copying the bugs taught him another thing—their number; and though he could not count as we understand it, yet he had an idea of quantity, the base of his calculations being the number of fingers upon one of his hands.

His search through the various books convinced him that he had discovered all the different kinds of bugs most often repeated in combination, and these he arranged in proper order with great ease because of the frequency with which he had perused the fascinating alphabet picture book.

His education progressed; but his greatest finds were in the inexhaustible storehouse of the huge illustrated dictionary, for he learned more through the medium of pictures than text, even after he had grasped the significance of the bugs.

When he discovered the arrangement of words in alphabetical order he delighted in searching for and finding the combinations with which he was familiar, and the words which followed them, their definitions, led him still further into the mazes of erudition.

By the time he was seventeen he had learned to read the simple, child's primer and had fully realized the true and wonderful purpose of the little bugs.

No longer did he feel shame for his hairless body or his human features, for now his reason told him that he was of a different race from his wild and hairy companions. He was a M-A-N, they were A-P-E-S, and the little apes which scurried through the forest top were M-O-N-K-E-Y-S. He knew, too, that old Sabor was a L-I-O-N-E-S-S, and Histah a S-N-A-K-E, and Tantor an E-L-E-P-H-A-N-T. And so he learned to read. From then on his progress was rapid. With the help of the great dictionary and the active intelligence of a healthy mind endowed by inheritance with more than ordinary reasoning powers he shrewdly guessed at much which he could not really understand, and more often than not his guesses were close to the mark of truth.

There were many breaks in his education, caused by the migratory habits of his tribe, but even when removed from his books his active brain continued to search out the mysteries of his fascinating avocation.

Pieces of bark and flat leaves and even smooth stretches of bare earth provided him with copy books whereon to scratch with the point of his hunting knife the lessons he was learning.

Nor did he neglect the sterner duties of life while following the bent of his inclination toward the solving of the mystery of his library.

He practiced with his rope and played with his sharp knife, which he had learned to keep keen by whetting upon flat stones.

The tribe had grown larger since Tarzan had come among them, for under the leadership of Kerchak they had been able to frighten the other tribes from their part of the jungle so that they had plenty to eat and little or no loss from predatory incursions of neighbors.

Hence the younger males as they became adult found it more comfortable to take mates from their own tribe, or if they captured one of another tribe to bring her back to Kerchak's band and live in amity with him rather than attempt to set up new establishments of their own, or fight with the redoubtable Kerchak for supremacy at home.

Occasionally one more ferocious than his fellows would attempt this latter alternative, but none had come yet who could wrest the palm of victory from the fierce and brutal ape.

Tarzan held a peculiar position in the tribe. They seemed to consider him one of them and yet in some way different. The older males either ignored him entirely or else hated him so vindictively that but for his wondrous agility and speed and the fierce protection of the huge Kala he would have been dispatched at an early age.

Tublat was his most consistent enemy, but it was through Tublat that, when he was about thirteen, the persecution of his enemies suddenly ceased and he was left severely alone, except on the occasions when one of them ran amuck in the throes of one of those strange, wild fits of insane rage which attacks the males of many of the fiercer animals of the jungle. Then none was safe.

On the day that Tarzan established his right to respect, the tribe was gathered about a small natural amphitheater which the jungle had left free from its entangling vines and creepers in a hollow among some low hills.

The open space was almost circular in shape. Upon every hand rose the mighty giants of the untouched forest, with the matted undergrowth banked so closely between the huge trunks that the only opening into the little, level arena was through the upper branches of the trees.

Here, safe from interruption, the tribe often gathered. In the center of the amphitheater was one of those strange earthen drums which the anthropoids build for the queer rites the sounds of which men have heard in the fastnesses of the jungle, but which none has ever witnessed.

Many travelers have seen the drums of the great apes, and some have heard the sounds of their beating and the noise of the wild, weird revelry of these first lords of the jungle, but Tarzan, Lord Greystoke, is, doubtless, the only human being who ever joined in the fierce, mad, intoxicating revel of the Dum-Dum.

From this primitive function has arisen, unquestionably, all the forms and ceremonials of modern church and state, for through all the countless ages, back beyond the uttermost ramparts of a dawning humanity our fierce, hairy forebears danced out the rites of the Dum-Dum to the sound of their earthen drums, beneath the bright light of a tropical moon in the depth of a mighty jungle which stands unchanged today as it stood on that long forgotten night in the dim, unthinkable vistas of the long dead past when our first shaggy ancestor swung from a swaying bough and dropped lightly upon the soft turf of the first meeting place.

On the day that Tarzan won his emancipation from the persecution that had followed him remorselessly for twelve of his thirteen years of life, the tribe, now a full hundred strong, trooped silently through the lower terrace of the jungle trees and dropped noiselessly upon the floor of the amphitheater.

The rites of the Dum-Dum marked important events in the life of the tribe—a victory, the capture of a prisoner, the killing of some large fierce denizen of the jungle, the death or accession of a king, and were conducted with set ceremonialism.

Today it was the killing of a giant ape, a member of another tribe, and as the people of Kerchak entered the arena two mighty bulls were seen bearing the body of the vanquished between them.

They laid their burden before the earthen drum and then squatted there beside it as guards, while the other members of the community curled themselves in grassy nooks to sleep until the rising moon should give the signal for the commencement of their savage orgy.

For hours absolute quiet reigned in the little clearing, except as it was broken by the discordant notes of brilliantly feathered parrots, or the screeching and twittering of the thousand jungle birds flitting ceaselessly amongst the vivid orchids and flamboyant blossoms which festooned the myriad, moss-covered branches of the forest kings.

At length as darkness settled upon the jungle the apes commenced to bestir themselves, and soon they formed a great circle about the earthen drum. The females and young squatted in a thin line at the outer periphery of the circle, while just in front of them ranged the adult males. Before the drum sat three old females, each armed with a knotted branch fifteen or eighteen inches in length.

Slowly and softly they began tapping upon the resounding surface of the drum as the first faint rays of the ascending moon silvered the encircling tree tops.

As the light in the amphitheater increased the females augmented the frequency and force of their blows until presently a wild, rhythmic din pervaded the great jungle for miles in every direction. Huge, fierce brutes stopped in their hunting, with up-pricked ears and raised heads, to listen to the dull booming that betokened the Dum-Dum of the apes.

Occasionally one would raise his shrill scream or thunderous roar in answering challenge to the savage din of the anthropoids, but none came near to investigate or attack, for the great apes, assembled in all the power of their numbers, filled the breasts of their jungle neighbors with deep respect.

As the din of the drum rose to almost deafening volume Kerchak sprang into the open space between the squatting males and the drummers.

Standing erect he threw his head far back and looking full into the eye of the rising moon he beat upon his breast with his great hairy paws and emitted his fearful roaring shriek.

One—twice—thrice that terrifying cry rang out across the teeming solitude of that unspeakably quick, yet unthinkably dead, world.

Then, crouching, Kerchak slunk noiselessly around the open circle, veering far away from the dead body lying before the altar-drum, but, as he passed, keeping his little, fierce, wicked, red eyes upon the corpse.

Another male then sprang into the arena, and, repeating the horrid cries of his king, followed stealthily in his wake. Another and another followed in quick succession until the jungle reverberated with the now almost ceaseless notes of their bloodthirsty screams.

It was the challenge and the hunt.

When all the adult males had joined in the thin line of circling dancers the attack commenced.

Kerchak, seizing a huge club from the pile which lay at hand for the purpose, rushed furiously upon the dead ape, dealing the corpse a terrific blow, at the same time emitting the growls and snarls of combat. The din of the drum was now increased, as well as the frequency of the blows, and the warriors, as each approached the victim of the hunt and delivered his bludgeon blow, joined in the mad whirl of the Death Dance.

Tarzan was one of the wild, leaping horde. His brown, sweat-streaked, muscular body, glistening in the moonlight, shone supple and graceful among the uncouth, awkward, hairy brutes about him.

None was more stealthy in the mimic hunt, none more ferocious than he in the wild ferocity of the attack, none who leaped so high into the air in the Dance of Death.

As the noise and rapidity of the drumbeats increased the dancers apparently became intoxicated with the wild rhythm and the savage yells. Their leaps and bounds increased, their bared fangs dripped saliva, and their lips and breasts were flecked with foam.

For half an hour the weird dance went on, until, at a sign from Kerchak, the noise of the drums ceased, the female drummers scampering hurriedly through the line of dancers toward the outer rim of squatting spectators. Then, as one, the males rushed headlong upon the thing which their terrific blows had reduced to a mass of hairy pulp.

Flesh seldom came to their jaws in satisfying quantities, so a fit finale to their wild revel was a taste of fresh killed meat, and it was to the purpose of devouring their late enemy that they now turned their attention.

Great fangs sunk into the carcass tearing away huge hunks, the mightiest of the apes obtaining the choicest morsels, while the weaker circled the outer edge of the fighting, snarling pack awaiting their chance to dodge in and snatch a dropped tidbit or filch a remaining bone before all was gone.

Tarzan, more than the apes, craved and needed flesh. Descended from a race of meat eaters, never in his life, he thought, had he once satisfied his appetite for animal food; and so now his agile little body wormed its way far into the mass of struggling, rending apes in an endeavor to obtain a share which his strength would have been unequal to the task of winning for him.

At his side hung the hunting knife of his unknown father in a sheath self-fashioned in copy of one he had seen among the pictures of his treasure-books.

At last he reached the fast disappearing feast and with his sharp knife slashed off a more generous portion than he had hoped for, an entire hairy forearm, where it protruded from beneath the feet of the mighty Kerchak, who was so busily engaged in perpetuating the royal prerogative of gluttony that he failed to note the act of LESE-MAJESTE.

So little Tarzan wriggled out from beneath the struggling mass, clutching his grisly prize close to his breast.

Among those circling futilely the outskirts of the banqueters was old Tublat. He had been among the first at the feast, but had retreated with a goodly share to eat in quiet, and was now forcing his way back for more.

So it was that he spied Tarzan as the boy emerged from the clawing, pushing throng with that hairy forearm hugged firmly to his body.

Tublat's little, close-set, bloodshot, pig-eyes shot wicked gleams of hate as they fell upon the object of his loathing. In them, too, was greed for the toothsome dainty the boy carried.

But Tarzan saw his arch enemy as quickly, and divining what the great beast would do he leaped nimbly away toward the females and the young, hoping to hide himself among them. Tublat, however, was close upon his heels, so that he had no opportunity to seek a place of concealment, but saw that he would be put to it to escape at all.

Swiftly he sped toward the surrounding trees and with an agile bound gained a lower limb with one hand, and then, transferring his burden to his teeth, he climbed rapidly upward, closely followed by Tublat.

Up, up he went to the waving pinnacle of a lofty monarch of the forest where his heavy pursuer dared not follow him. There he perched, hurling taunts and insults at the raging, foaming beast fifty feet below him.

And then Tublat went mad.

With horrifying screams and roars he rushed to the ground, among the females and young, sinking his great fangs into a dozen tiny necks and tearing great pieces from the backs and breasts of the females who fell into his clutches.

In the brilliant moonlight Tarzan witnessed the whole mad carnival of rage. He saw the females and the young scamper to the safety of the trees. Then the great bulls in the center of the arena felt the mighty fangs of their demented fellow, and with one accord they melted into the black shadows of the overhanging forest.

There was but one in the amphitheater beside Tublat, a belated female running swiftly toward the tree where Tarzan perched, and close behind her came the awful Tublat.

It was Kala, and as quickly as Tarzan saw that Tublat was gaining on her he dropped with the rapidity of a falling stone, from branch to branch, toward his foster mother.

Now she was beneath the overhanging limbs and close above her crouched Tarzan, waiting the outcome of the race.

She leaped into the air grasping a low-hanging branch, but almost over the head of Tublat, so nearly had he distanced her. She should have been safe now but there was a rending, tearing sound, the branch broke and precipitated her full upon the head of Tublat, knocking him to the ground.

Both were up in an instant, but as quick as they had been Tarzan had been quicker, so that the infuriated bull found himself facing the man-child who stood between him and Kala.

Nothing could have suited the fierce beast better, and with a roar of triumph he leaped upon the little Lord Greystoke. But his fangs never closed in that nut brown flesh.

A muscular hand shot out and grasped the hairy throat, and another plunged a keen hunting knife a dozen times into the broad breast. Like lightning the blows fell, and only ceased when Tarzan felt the limp form crumple beneath him.

As the body rolled to the ground Tarzan of the Apes placed his foot upon the neck of his lifelong enemy and, raising his eyes to the full moon, threw back his fierce young head and voiced the wild and terrible cry of his people.

One by one the tribe swung down from their arboreal retreats and formed a circle about Tarzan and his vanquished foe. When they had all come Tarzan turned toward them.

"I am Tarzan," he cried. "I am a great killer. Let all respect Tarzan of the Apes and Kala, his mother. There be none among you as mighty as Tarzan. Let his enemies beware."

Looking full into the wicked, red eyes of Kerchak, the young Lord Greystoke beat upon his mighty breast and screamed out once more his shrill cry of defiance.

THE TREE-TOP HUNTER

The morning after the Dum-Dum the tribe started slowly back through the forest toward the coast.

The body of Tublat lay where it had fallen, for the people of Kerchak do not eat their own dead.

The march was but a leisurely search for food. Cabbage palm and gray plum, pisang and scitamine they found in abundance, with wild pineapple, and occasionally small mammals, birds, eggs, reptiles, and insects. The nuts they cracked between their powerful jaws, or, if too hard, broke by pounding between stones.

Once old Sabor, crossing their path, sent them scurrying to the safety of the higher branches, for if she respected their number and their sharp fangs, they on their part held her cruel and mighty ferocity in equal esteem.

Upon a low-hanging branch sat Tarzan directly above the majestic, supple body as it forged silently through the thick jungle. He hurled a pineapple at the ancient enemy of his people. The great beast stopped and, turning, eyed the taunting figure above her.

With an angry lash of her tail she bared her yellow fangs, curling her great lips in a hideous snarl that wrinkled her bristling snout in serried ridges and closed her wicked eyes to two narrow slits of rage and hatred.

With back-laid ears she looked straight into the eyes of Tarzan of the Apes and sounded her fierce, shrill challenge. And from the safety of his overhanging limb the ape-child sent back the fearsome answer of his kind.

For a moment the two eyed each other in silence, and then the great cat turned into the jungle, which swallowed her as the ocean engulfs a tossed pebble.

But into the mind of Tarzan a great plan sprang. He had killed the fierce Tublat, so was he not therefore a mighty fighter? Now would he track down the crafty Sabor and slay her likewise. He would be a mighty hunter, also.

At the bottom of his little English heart beat the great desire to cover his nakedness with *clothes* for he had learned from his picture books that all *men* were so covered, while *monkeys* and *apes* and every other living thing went naked.

Clothes therefore, must be truly a badge of greatness; the insignia of the superiority of *man* over all other animals, for surely there could be no other reason for wearing the hideous things.

Many moons ago, when he had been much smaller, he had desired the skin of Sabor, the lioness, or Numa, the lion, or Sheeta, the leopard to cover his hairless body that he might no longer resemble hideous Histah, the snake; but now he was proud of his sleek skin for it betokened his descent from a mighty race, and the conflicting desires to go naked in prideful proof of his ancestry, or to conform to the customs of his own kind and wear hideous and uncomfortable apparel found first one and then the other in the ascendency.

As the tribe continued their slow way through the forest after the passing of Sabor, Tarzan's head was filled with his great scheme for slaying his enemy, and for many days thereafter he thought of little else.

On this day, however, he presently had other and more immediate interests to attract his attention.

Suddenly it became as midnight; the noises of the jungle ceased; the trees stood motionless as though in paralyzed expectancy of some great and imminent disaster. All nature waited—but not for long.

Faintly, from a distance, came a low, sad moaning. Nearer and nearer it approached, mounting louder and louder in volume.

The great trees bent in unison as though pressed earthward by a mighty hand. Farther and farther toward the ground they inclined, and still there was no sound save the deep and awesome moaning of the wind.

Then, suddenly, the jungle giants whipped back, lashing their mighty tops in angry and deafening protest. A vivid and blinding light flashed from the whirling, inky clouds above. The deep cannonade of roaring thunder belched forth its fearsome challenge. The deluge came—all hell broke loose upon the jungle.

The tribe shivering from the cold rain, huddled at the bases of great trees. The lightning, darting and flashing through the blackness, showed wildly waving branches, whipping streamers and bending trunks.

Now and again some ancient patriarch of the woods, rent by a flashing bolt, would crash in a thousand pieces among the surrounding trees, carrying down numberless branches and many smaller neighbors to add to the tangled confusion of the tropical jungle.

Branches, great and small, torn away by the ferocity of the tornado, hurtled through the wildly waving verdure, carrying death and destruction to countless unhappy denizens of the thickly peopled world below.

For hours the fury of the storm continued without surcease, and still the tribe huddled close in shivering fear. In constant danger from falling trunks and branches and paralyzed by the vivid flashing of lightning and the bellowing of thunder they crouched in pitiful misery until the storm passed.

The end was as sudden as the beginning. The wind ceased, the sun shone forth—nature smiled once more.

The dripping leaves and branches, and the moist petals of gorgeous flowers glistened in the splendor of the returning day. And, so—as Nature forgot, her children forgot also. Busy life went on as it had been before the darkness and the fright.

But to Tarzan a dawning light had come to explain the mystery of *clothes*. How snug he would have been beneath the heavy coat of Sabor! And so was added a further incentive to the adventure.

For several months the tribe hovered near the beach where stood Tarzan's cabin, and his studies took up the greater portion of his time, but always when journeying through the forest he kept his rope in readiness, and many were the smaller animals that fell into the snare of the quick thrown noose.

Once it fell about the short neck of Horta, the boar, and his mad lunge for freedom toppled Tarzan from the overhanging limb where he had lain in wait and from whence he had launched his sinuous coil.

The mighty tusker turned at the sound of his falling body, and, seeing only the easy prey of a young ape, he lowered his head and charged madly at the surprised youth.

Tarzan, happily, was uninjured by the fall, alighting catlike upon all fours far outspread to take up the shock. He was on his feet in an instant and, leaping with the agility of the monkey he was, he gained the safety of a low limb as Horta, the boar, rushed futilely beneath.

Thus it was that Tarzan learned by experience the limitations as well as the possibilities of his strange weapon.

He lost a long rope on this occasion, but he knew that had it been Sabor who had thus dragged him from his perch the outcome might have been very different, for he would have lost his life, doubtless, into the bargain.

It took him many days to braid a new rope, but when, finally, it was done he went forth purposely to hunt, and lie in wait among the dense foliage of a great branch right above the well-beaten trail that led to water.

Several small animals passed unharmed beneath him. He did not want such insignificant game. It would take a strong animal to test the efficacy of his new scheme.

At last came she whom Tarzan sought, with lithe sinews rolling beneath shimmering hide; fat and glossy came Sabor, the lioness.

Her great padded feet fell soft and noiseless on the narrow trail. Her head was high in ever alert attention; her long tail moved slowly in sinuous and graceful undulations.

Nearer and nearer she came to where Tarzan of the Apes crouched upon his limb, the coils of his long rope poised ready in his hand.

Like a thing of bronze, motionless as death, sat Tarzan. Sabor passed beneath. One stride beyond she took—a second, a third, and then the silent coil shot out above her.

For an instant the spreading noose hung above her head like a great snake, and then, as she looked upward to detect the origin of the swishing sound of the rope, it settled about her neck. With a quick jerk Tarzan snapped the noose tight about the glossy throat, and then he dropped the rope and clung to his support with both hands.

Sabor was trapped.

With a bound the startled beast turned into the jungle, but Tarzan was not to lose another rope through the same cause as the first. He had learned from experience. The lioness had taken but half her second bound when she felt the rope tighten about her neck; her body turned completely over in the air and she fell with a heavy crash upon her back. Tarzan had fastened the end of the rope securely to the trunk of the great tree on which he sat.

Thus far his plan had worked to perfection, but when he grasped the rope, bracing himself behind a crotch of two mighty branches, he found that dragging the mighty, struggling, clawing, biting, screaming mass of iron-muscled fury up to the tree and hanging her was a very different proposition.

The weight of old Sabor was immense, and when she braced her huge paws nothing less than Tantor, the elephant, himself, could have budged her.

The lioness was now back in the path where she could see the author of the indignity which had been placed upon her. Screaming with rage she suddenly charged, leaping high into the air toward Tarzan, but when her huge body struck the limb on which Tarzan had been, Tarzan was no longer there.

Instead he perched lightly upon a smaller branch twenty feet above the raging captive. For a moment Sabor hung half across the branch, while Tarzan mocked, and hurled twigs and branches at her unprotected face.

Presently the beast dropped to the earth again and Tarzan came quickly to seize the rope, but Sabor had now found that it was only a slender cord that held her, and grasping it in her huge jaws severed it before Tarzan could tighten the strangling noose a second time.

Tarzan was much hurt. His well-laid plan had come to naught, so he sat there screaming at the roaring creature beneath him and making mocking grimaces at it.

Sabor paced back and forth beneath the tree for hours; four times she crouched and sprang at the dancing sprite above her, but might as well have clutched at the illusive wind that murmured through the tree tops.

At last Tarzan tired of the sport, and with a parting roar of challenge and a well-aimed ripe fruit that spread soft and sticky over the snarling face of his enemy, he swung rapidly through the trees, a hundred feet above the ground, and in a short time was among the members of his tribe.

Here he recounted the details of his adventure, with swelling chest and so considerable swagger that he quite impressed even his bitterest enemies, while Kala fairly danced for joy and pride.

MAN AND MAN

Tarzan of the Apes lived on in his wild, jungle existence with little change for several years, only that he grew stronger and wiser, and learned from his books more and more of the strange worlds which lay somewhere outside his primeval forest.

To him life was never monotonous or stale. There was always Pisah, the fish, to be caught in the many streams and the little lakes, and Sabor, with her ferocious cousins to keep one ever on the alert and give zest to every instant that one spent upon the ground.

Often they hunted him, and more often he hunted them, but though they never quite reached him with those cruel, sharp claws of theirs, yet there were times when one could scarce have passed a thick leaf between their talons and his smooth hide.

Quick was Sabor, the lioness, and quick were Numa and Sheeta, but Tarzan of the Apes was lightning.

With Tantor, the elephant, he made friends. How? Ask not. But this is known to the denizens of the jungle, that on many moonlight nights Tarzan of the Apes and Tantor, the elephant, walked together, and where the way was clear Tarzan rode, perched high upon Tantor's mighty back.

Many days during these years he spent in the cabin of his father, where still lay, untouched, the bones of his parents and the skeleton of Kala's baby. At eighteen he read fluently and understood nearly all he read in the many and varied volumes on the shelves.

Also could he write, with printed letters, rapidly and plainly, but script he had not mastered, for though there were several copy books among his treasure, there was so little written English in the cabin that he saw no use for bothering with this other form of writing, though he could read it, laboriously.

Thus, at eighteen, we find him, an English lordling, who could speak no English, and yet who could read and write his native language. Never had he seen a human being other than himself, for the little area traversed by his tribe was watered by no greater river to bring down the savage natives of the interior.

High hills shut it off on three sides, the ocean on the fourth. It was alive with lions and leopards and poisonous snakes. Its untouched mazes of matted jungle had as yet invited no hardy pioneer from the human beasts beyond its frontier.

But as Tarzan of the Apes sat one day in the cabin of his father delving into the mysteries of a new book, the ancient security of his jungle was broken forever.

At the far eastern confine a strange cavalcade strung, in single file, over the brow of a low hill.

In advance were fifty black warriors armed with slender wooden spears with ends hard baked over slow fires, and long bows and poisoned arrows. On their backs were oval shields, in their noses huge rings, while from the kinky wool of their heads protruded tufts of gay feathers.

Across their foreheads were tattooed three parallel lines of color, and on each breast three concentric circles. Their yellow teeth were filed to sharp points, and their great protruding lips added still further to the low and bestial brutishness of their appearance.

Following them were several hundred women and children, the former bearing upon their heads great burdens of cooking pots, household utensils and ivory. In the rear were a hundred warriors, similar in all respects to the advance guard.

That they more greatly feared an attack from the rear than whatever unknown enemies lurked in their advance was evidenced by the formation of the column; and such was the fact, for they were fleeing from the white man's soldiers who had so harassed them for rubber and ivory that they had turned upon their conquerors one day and massacred a white officer and a small detachment of his black troops.

For many days they had gorged themselves on meat, but eventually a stronger body of troops had come and fallen upon their village by night to revenge the death of their comrades.

That night the black soldiers of the white man had had meat a-plenty, and this little remnant of a once powerful tribe had slunk off into the gloomy jungle toward the unknown, and freedom.

But that which meant freedom and the pursuit of happiness to these savage blacks meant consternation and death to many of the wild denizens of their new home.

For three days the little cavalcade marched slowly through the heart of this unknown and untracked forest, until finally, early in the fourth day, they came upon a little spot near the banks of a small river, which seemed less thickly overgrown than any ground they had yet encountered.

Here they set to work to build a new village, and in a month a great clearing had been made, huts and palisades erected, plantains, yams and maize planted, and they had taken up their old life in their new home. Here there were no white men, no soldiers, nor any rubber or ivory to be gathered for cruel and thankless taskmasters.

Several moons passed by ere the blacks ventured far into the territory surrounding their new village. Several had already fallen prey to old Sabor, and because the jungle was so infested with these fierce and bloodthirsty cats, and with lions and leopards, the ebony warriors hesitated to trust themselves far from the safety of their palisades.

But one day, Kulonga, a son of the old king, Mbonga, wandered far into the dense mazes to the west. Warily he stepped, his slender lance ever ready, his long oval shield firmly grasped in his left hand close to his sleek ebony body.

At his back his bow, and in the quiver upon his shield many slim, straight arrows, well smeared with the thick, dark, tarry substance that rendered deadly their tiniest needle prick.

Night found Kulonga far from the palisades of his father's village, but still headed westward, and climbing into the fork of a great tree he fashioned a rude platform and curled himself for sleep.

Three miles to the west slept the tribe of Kerchak.

Early the next morning the apes were astir, moving through the jungle in search of food. Tarzan, as was his custom, prosecuted his search in the direction of the cabin so that by leisurely hunting on the way his stomach was filled by the time he reached the beach.

The apes scattered by ones, and twos, and threes in all directions, but ever within sound of a signal of alarm.

Kala had moved slowly along an elephant track toward the east, and was busily engaged in turning over rotted limbs and logs in search of succulent bugs and fungi, when the faintest shadow of a strange noise brought her to startled attention.

For fifty yards before her the trail was straight, and down this leafy tunnel she saw the stealthy advancing figure of a strange and fearful creature.

It was Kulonga.

Kala did not wait to see more, but, turning, moved rapidly back along the trail. She did not run; but, after the manner of her kind when not aroused, sought rather to avoid than to escape.

Close after her came Kulonga. Here was meat. He could make a killing and feast well this day. On he hurried, his spear poised for the throw.

At a turning of the trail he came in sight of her again upon another straight stretch. His spear hand went far back the muscles rolled, lightning-like, beneath the sleek hide. Out shot the arm, and the spear sped toward Kala.

A poor cast. It but grazed her side.

With a cry of rage and pain the she-ape turned upon her tormentor. In an instant the trees were crashing beneath the weight of her hurrying fellows, swinging rapidly toward the scene of trouble in answer to Kala's scream.

As she charged, Kulonga unslung his bow and fitted an arrow with almost unthinkable quickness. Drawing the shaft far back he drove the poisoned missile straight into the heart of the great anthropoid.

With a horrid scream Kala plunged forward upon her face before the astonished members of her tribe.

Roaring and shrieking the apes dashed toward Kulonga, but that wary savage was fleeing down the trail like a frightened antelope.

He knew something of the ferocity of these wild, hairy men, and his one desire was to put as many miles between himself and them as he possibly could.

They followed him, racing through the trees, for a long distance, but finally one by one they abandoned the chase and returned to the scene of the tragedy.

None of them had ever seen a man before, other than Tarzan, and so they wondered vaguely what strange manner of creature it might be that had invaded their jungle.

On the far beach by the little cabin Tarzan heard the faint echoes of the conflict and knowing that something was seriously amiss among the tribe he hastened rapidly toward the direction of the sound.

When he arrived he found the entire tribe gathered jabbering about the dead body of his slain mother.

Tarzan's grief and anger were unbounded. He roared out his hideous challenge time and again. He beat upon his great chest with his clenched fists, and then he fell upon the body of Kala and sobbed out the pitiful sorrowing of his lonely heart.

To lose the only creature in all his world who ever had manifested love and affection for him was the greatest tragedy he had ever known.

What though Kala was a fierce and hideous ape! To Tarzan she had been kind, she had been beautiful.

Upon her he had lavished, unknown to himself, all the reverence and respect and love that a normal English boy feels for his own mother. He had never known another, and so to Kala was given, though mutely, all that would have belonged to the fair and lovely Lady Alice had she lived.

After the first outburst of grief Tarzan controlled himself, and questioning the members of the tribe who had witnessed the killing of Kala he learned all that their meager vocabulary could convey.

It was enough, however, for his needs. It told him of a strange, hairless, black ape with feathers growing upon its head, who launched death from a slender branch, and then ran, with the fleetness of Bara, the deer, toward the rising sun.

Tarzan waited no longer, but leaping into the branches of the trees sped rapidly through the forest. He knew the windings of the elephant trail along which Kala's murderer had flown, and so he cut straight through the jungle to intercept the black warrior who was evidently following the tortuous detours of the trail.

At his side was the hunting knife of his unknown sire, and across his shoulders the coils of his own long rope. In an hour he struck the trail again, and coming to earth examined the soil minutely.

In the soft mud on the bank of a tiny rivulet he found footprints such as he alone in all the jungle had ever made, but much larger than his. His heart beat fast. Could it be that he was trailing a MAN—one of his own race?

There were two sets of imprints pointing in opposite directions. So his quarry had already passed on his return along the trail. As he examined the newer spoor a tiny particle of earth toppled from the outer edge of one of the footprints to the bottom of its shallow depression—ah, the trail was very fresh, his prey must have but scarcely passed.

Tarzan swung himself to the trees once more, and with swift noiselessness sped along high above the trail.

He had covered barely a mile when he came upon the black warrior standing in a little open space. In his hand was his slender bow to which he had fitted one of his death dealing arrows.

Opposite him across the little clearing stood Horta, the boar, with lowered head and foam flecked tucks, ready to charge.

Tarzan looked with wonder upon the strange creature beneath him—so like him in form and yet so different in face and color. His books had portrayed the NEGRO, but how different had been the dull, dead print to this sleek thing of ebony, pulsing with life.

As the man stood there with taut drawn bow Tarzan recognized him not so much the NEGRO as the ARCHER of his picture book—

A stands for Archer

How wonderful! Tarzan almost betrayed his presence in the deep excitement of his discovery.

But things were commencing to happen below him. The sinewy black arm had drawn the shaft far back; Horta, the boar, was charging, and then the black released the little poisoned arrow, and Tarzan saw it fly with the quickness of thought and lodge in the bristling neck of the boar.

Scarcely had the shaft left his bow ere Kulonga had fitted another to it, but Horta, the boar, was upon him so quickly that he had no time to discharge it. With a bound the black leaped entirely over the rushing beast and turning with incredible swiftness planted a second arrow in Horta's back.

Then Kulonga sprang into a near-by tree.

Horta wheeled to charge his enemy once more; a dozen steps he took, then he staggered and fell upon his side. For a moment his muscles stiffened and relaxed convulsively, then he lay still.

Kulonga came down from his tree.

With a knife that hung at his side he cut several large pieces from the boar's body, and in the center of the trail he built a fire, cooking and eating as much as he wanted. The rest he left where it had fallen.

Tarzan was an interested spectator. His desire to kill burned fiercely in his wild breast, but his desire to learn was even greater. He would follow this savage creature for a while and know from whence he came. He could kill him at his leisure later, when the bow and deadly arrows were laid aside.

When Kulonga had finished his repast and disappeared beyond a near turning of the path, Tarzan dropped quietly to the ground. With his knife he severed many strips of meat from Horta's carcass, but he did not cook them.

He had seen fire, but only when Ara, the lightning, had destroyed some great tree. That any creature of the jungle could produce the red-and-yellow fangs which devoured wood and left nothing but fine dust surprised Tarzan greatly, and why the black warrior had ruined his delicious repast by plunging it into the blighting heat was quite beyond him. Possibly Ara was a friend with whom the Archer was sharing his food.

But, be that as it may, Tarzan would not ruin good meat in any such foolish manner, so he gobbled down a great quantity of the raw flesh, burying the balance of the carcass beside the trail where he could find it upon his return.

And then Lord Greystoke wiped his greasy fingers upon his naked thighs and took up the trail of Kulonga, the son of Mbonga, the king; while in far-off London another Lord Greystoke, the younger brother of the real Lord Greystoke's father, sent back his chops to the club's CHEF because they were underdone, and when he had finished his repast he dipped his finger-ends into a silver bowl of scented water and dried them upon a piece of snowy damask.

All day Tarzan followed Kulonga, hovering above him in the trees like some malign spirit. Twice more he saw him hurl his arrows of destruction—once at Dango, the hyena, and again at Manu, the monkey. In each instance the animal died almost instantly, for Kulonga's poison was very fresh and very deadly.

Tarzan thought much on this wondrous method of slaying as he swung slowly along at a safe distance behind his quarry. He knew that alone the tiny prick of the arrow could not so quickly dispatch these wild things of the jungle, who were often torn and scratched and gored in a frightful manner as they fought with their jungle neighbors, yet as often recovered as not.

No, there was something mysterious connected with these tiny slivers of wood which could bring death by a mere scratch. He must look into the matter.

That night Kulonga slept in the crotch of a mighty tree and far above him crouched Tarzan of the Apes.

When Kulonga awoke he found that his bow and arrows had disappeared. The black warrior was furious and frightened, but more frightened than furious. He searched the ground below the tree, and he searched the tree above the ground; but there was no sign of either bow or arrows or of the nocturnal marauder.

Kulonga was panic-stricken. His spear he had hurled at Kala and had not recovered; and, now that his bow and arrows were gone, he was defenseless except for a single knife. His only hope lay in reaching the village of Mbonga as quickly as his legs would carry him.

That he was not far from home he was certain, so he took the trail at a rapid trot.

From a great mass of impenetrable foliage a few yards away emerged Tarzan of the Apes to swing quietly in his wake.

Kulonga's bow and arrows were securely tied high in the top of a giant tree from which a patch of bark had been removed by a sharp knife near to the ground, and a branch half cut through and left hanging about fifty feet higher up. Thus Tarzan blazed the forest trails and marked his caches.

As Kulonga continued his journey Tarzan closed on him until he traveled almost over the black's head. His rope he now held coiled in his right hand; he was almost ready for the kill.

The moment was delayed only because Tarzan was anxious to ascertain the black warrior's destination, and presently he was rewarded, for they came suddenly in view of a great clearing, at one end of which lay many strange lairs.

Tarzan was directly over Kulonga, as he made the discovery. The forest ended abruptly and beyond lay two hundred yards of planted fields between the jungle and the village.

Tarzan must act quickly or his prey would be gone; but Tarzan's life training left so little space between decision and action when an emergency confronted him that there was not even room for the shadow of a thought between.

So it was that as Kulonga emerged from the shadow of the jungle a slender coil of rope sped sinuously above him from the lowest branch of a mighty tree directly upon the edge of the fields of Mbonga, and ere the king's son had taken a half dozen steps into the clearing a quick noose tightened about his neck.

So quickly did Tarzan of the Apes drag back his prey that Kulonga's cry of alarm was throttled in his windpipe. Hand over hand Tarzan drew the struggling black until he had him hanging by his neck in mid-air; then Tarzan climbed to a larger branch drawing the still threshing victim well up into the sheltering verdure of the tree.

Here he fastened the rope securely to a stout branch, and then, descending, plunged his hunting knife into Kulonga's heart. Kala was avenged.

Tarzan examined the black minutely, for he had never seen any other human being. The knife with its sheath and belt caught his eye; he appropriated them. A copper anklet also took his fancy, and this he transferred to his own leg.

He examined and admired the tattooing on the forehead and breast. He marveled at the sharp filed teeth. He investigated and appropriated the feathered headdress, and then he prepared to get down to business, for Tarzan of the Apes was hungry, and here was meat; meat of the kill, which jungle ethics permitted him to eat.

How may we judge him, by what standards, this ape-man with the heart and head and body of an English gentleman, and the training of a wild beast?

Tublat, whom he had hated and who had hated him, he had killed in a fair fight, and yet never had the thought of eating Tublat's flesh entered his head. It could have been as revolting to him as is cannibalism to us.

But who was Kulonga that he might not be eaten as fairly as Horta, the boar, or Bara, the deer? Was he not simply another of the countless wild things of the jungle who preyed upon one another to satisfy the cravings of hunger?

Suddenly, a strange doubt stayed his hand. Had not his books taught him that he was a man? And was not The Archer a man, also?

Did men eat men? Alas, he did not know. Why, then, this hesitancy! Once more he essayed the effort, but a qualm of nausea overwhelmed him. He did not understand.

All he knew was that he could not eat the flesh of this black man, and thus hereditary instinct, ages old, usurped the functions of his untaught mind and saved him from transgressing a worldwide law of whose very existence he was ignorant.

Quickly he lowered Kulonga's body to the ground, removed the noose, and took to the trees again.

THE FEAR-PHANTOM

From a lofty perch Tarzan viewed the village of thatched huts across the intervening plantation.

He saw that at one point the forest touched the village, and to this spot he made his way, lured by a fever of curiosity to behold animals of his own kind, and to learn more of their ways and view the strange lairs in which they lived.

His savage life among the fierce wild brutes of the jungle left no opening for any thought that these could be aught else than enemies. Similarity of form led him into no erroneous conception of the welcome that would be accorded him should he be discovered by these, the first of his own kind he had ever seen.

Tarzan of the Apes was no sentimentalist. He knew nothing of the brotherhood of man. All things outside his own tribe were his deadly enemies, with the few exceptions of which Tantor, the elephant, was a marked example.

And he realized all this without malice or hatred. To kill was the law of the wild world he knew. Few were his primitive pleasures, but the greatest of these was to hunt and kill, and so he accorded to others the right to cherish the same desires as he, even though he himself might be the object of their hunt.

His strange life had left him neither morose nor bloodthirsty. That he joyed in killing, and that he killed with a joyous laugh upon his handsome lips betokened no innate cruelty. He killed for food most often, but, being a man, he sometimes killed for pleasure, a thing which no other animal does; for it has remained for man alone among all creatures to kill senselessly and wantonly for the mere pleasure of inflicting suffering and death.

And when he killed for revenge, or in self-defense, he did that also without hysteria, for it was a very businesslike proceeding which admitted of no levity.

So it was that now, as he cautiously approached the village of Mbonga, he was quite prepared either to kill or be killed should he be discovered. He proceeded with unwonted stealth, for Kulonga had taught him great respect for the little sharp splinters of wood which dealt death so swiftly and unerringly.

At length he came to a great tree, heavy laden with thick foliage and loaded with pendant loops of giant creepers. From this almost impenetrable bower above the village he crouched, looking down upon the scene below him, wondering over every feature of this new, strange life.

There were naked children running and playing in the village street. There were women grinding dried plantain in crude stone mortars, while others were fashioning cakes from the powdered flour. Out in the fields he could see still other women hoeing, weeding, or gathering.

All wore strange protruding girdles of dried grass about their hips and many were loaded with brass and copper anklets, armlets and bracelets. Around many a dusky neck hung curiously coiled strands of wire, while several were further ornamented by huge nose rings.

Tarzan of the Apes looked with growing wonder at these strange creatures. Dozing in the shade he saw several men, while at the extreme outskirts of the clearing he occasionally caught glimpses of armed warriors apparently guarding the village against surprise from an attacking enemy.

He noticed that the women alone worked. Nowhere was there evidence of a man tilling the fields or performing any of the homely duties of the village.

Finally his eyes rested upon a woman directly beneath him.

Before her was a small cauldron standing over a low fire and in it bubbled a thick, reddish, tarry mass. On one side of her lay a quantity of wooden arrows the points of which she dipped into the seething substance, then laying them upon a narrow rack of boughs which stood upon her other side.

Tarzan of the Apes was fascinated. Here was the secret of the terrible destructiveness of The Archer's tiny missiles. He noted the extreme care which the woman took that none of the matter should touch her hands, and once when a particle spattered upon one of her fingers he saw her plunge the member into a vessel of water and quickly rub the tiny stain away with a handful of leaves.

Tarzan knew nothing of poison, but his shrewd reasoning told him that it was this deadly stuff that killed, and not the little arrow, which was merely the messenger that carried it into the body of its victim.

How he should like to have more of those little death-dealing slivers. If the woman would only leave her work for an instant he could drop down, gather up a handful, and be back in the tree again before she drew three breaths.

As he was trying to think out some plan to distract her attention he heard a wild cry from across the clearing. He looked and saw a black warrior standing beneath the very tree in which he had killed the murderer of Kala an hour before.

The fellow was shouting and waving his spear above his head. Now and again he would point to something on the ground before him.

The village was in an uproar instantly. Armed men rushed from the interior of many a hut and raced madly across the clearing toward the excited sentry. After them trooped the old men, and the women and children until, in a moment, the village was deserted.

Tarzan of the Apes knew that they had found the body of his victim, but that interested him far less than the fact that no one remained in the village to prevent his taking a supply of the arrows which lay below him.

Quickly and noiselessly he dropped to the ground beside the cauldron of poison. For a moment he stood motionless, his quick, bright eyes scanning the interior of the palisade.

No one was in sight. His eyes rested upon the open doorway of a nearby hut. He would take a look within, thought Tarzan, and so, cautiously, he approached the low thatched building.

For a moment he stood without, listening intently. There was no sound, and he glided into the semi-darkness of the interior.

Weapons hung against the walls—long spears, strangely shaped knives, a couple of narrow shields. In the center of the room was a cooking pot, and at the far end a litter of dry grasses covered by woven mats which evidently served the owners as beds and bedding. Several human skulls lay upon the floor.

Tarzan of the Apes felt of each article, hefted the spears, smelled of them, for he "saw" largely through his sensitive and highly trained nostrils. He determined to own one of these long, pointed sticks, but he could not take one on this trip because of the arrows he meant to carry.

As he took each article from the walls, he placed it in a pile in the center of the room. On top of all he placed the cooking pot, inverted, and on top of this he laid one of the grinning skulls, upon which he fastened the headdress of the dead Kulonga.

Then he stood back, surveyed his work, and grinned. Tarzan of the Apes enjoyed a joke.

But now he heard, outside, the sounds of many voices, and long mournful howls, and mighty wailing. He was startled. Had he remained too long? Quickly he reached the doorway and peered down the village street toward the village gate.

The natives were not yet in sight, though he could plainly hear them approaching across the plantation. They must be very near.

Like a flash he sprang across the opening to the pile of arrows. Gathering up all he could carry under one arm, he overturned the seething cauldron with a kick, and disappeared into the foliage above just as the first of the returning natives entered the gate at the far end of the village street. Then he turned to watch the proceeding below, poised like some wild bird ready to take swift wing at the first sign of danger.

The natives filed up the street, four of them bearing the dead body of Kulonga. Behind trailed the women, uttering strange cries and weird lamentation. On they came to the portals of Kulonga's hut, the very one in which Tarzan had wrought his depredations.

Scarcely had half a dozen entered the building ere they came rushing out in wild, jabbering confusion. The others hastened to gather about. There was much excited gesticulating, pointing, and chattering; then several of the warriors approached and peered within.

Finally an old fellow with many ornaments of metal about his arms and legs, and a necklace of dried human hands depending upon his chest, entered the hut.

It was Mbonga, the king, father of Kulonga.

For a few moments all was silent. Then Mbonga emerged, a look of mingled wrath and superstitious fear writ upon his hideous countenance. He spoke a few words to the assembled warriors, and in an instant the men were flying through the little village searching minutely every hut and corner within the palisades.

Scarcely had the search commenced than the overturned cauldron was discovered, and with it the theft of the poisoned arrows. Nothing more they found, and it was a thoroughly awed and frightened group of savages which huddled around their king a few moments later.

Mbonga could explain nothing of the strange events that had taken place. The finding of the still warm body of Kulonga—on the very verge of their fields and within easy earshot of the village—knifed and stripped at the door of his father's home, was in itself sufficiently mysterious, but these last awesome discoveries within the village, within the dead Kulonga's own hut, filled their hearts with dismay, and conjured in their poor brains only the most frightful of superstitious explanations.

They stood in little groups, talking in low tones, and ever casting affrighted glances behind them from their great rolling eyes.

Tarzan of the Apes watched them for a while from his lofty perch in the great tree. There was much in their demeanor which he could not understand, for of superstition he was ignorant, and of fear of any kind he had but a vague conception.

The sun was high in the heavens. Tarzan had not broken fast this day, and it was many miles to where lay the toothsome remains of Horta the boar.

So he turned his back upon the village of Mbonga and melted away into the leafy fastness of the forest.

"KING OF THE APES"

It was not yet dark when he reached the tribe, though he stopped to exhume and devour the remains of the wild boar he had cached the preceding day, and again to take Kulonga's bow and arrows from the tree top in which he had hidden them.

It was a well-laden Tarzan who dropped from the branches into the midst of the tribe of Kerchak.

With swelling chest he narrated the glories of his adventure and exhibited the spoils of conquest.

Kerchak grunted and turned away, for he was jealous of this strange member of his band. In his little evil brain he sought for some excuse to wreak his hatred upon Tarzan.

EDGAR RICE BURROUGHS

The next day Tarzan was practicing with his bow and arrows at the first gleam of dawn. At first he lost nearly every bolt he shot, but finally he learned to guide the little shafts with fair accuracy, and ere a month had passed he was no mean shot; but his proficiency had cost him nearly his entire supply of arrows.

The tribe continued to find the hunting good in the vicinity of the beach, and so Tarzan of the Apes varied his archery practice with further investigation of his father's choice though little store of books.

It was during this period that the young English lord found hidden in the back of one of the cupboards in the cabin a small metal box. The key was in the lock, and a few moments of investigation and experimentation were rewarded with the successful opening of the receptacle.

In it he found a faded photograph of a smooth faced young man, a golden locket studded with diamonds, linked to a small gold chain, a few letters and a small book.

Tarzan examined these all minutely.

The photograph he liked most of all, for the eyes were smiling, and the face was open and frank. It was his father.

The locket, too, took his fancy, and he placed the chain about his neck in imitation of the ornamentation he had seen to be so common among the black men he had visited. The brilliant stones gleamed strangely against his smooth, brown hide.

The letters he could scarcely decipher for he had learned little or nothing of script, so he put them back in the box with the photograph and turned his attention to the book.

This was almost entirely filled with fine script, but while the little bugs were all familiar to him, their arrangement and the combinations in which they occurred were strange, and entirely incomprehensible.

Tarzan had long since learned the use of the dictionary, but much to his sorrow and perplexity it proved of no avail to him in this emergency. Not a word of all that was writ in the book could he find, and so he put it back in the metal box, but with a determination to work out the mysteries of it later on.

Little did he know that this book held between its covers the key to his origin—the answer to the strange riddle of his strange life. It was the diary of John Clayton, Lord Greystoke—kept in French, as had always been his custom.

Tarzan replaced the box in the cupboard, but always thereafter he carried the features of the strong, smiling face of his father in his heart, and in his head a fixed determination to solve the mystery of the strange words in the little black book.

At present he had more important business in hand, for his supply of arrows was exhausted, and he must needs journey to the black men's village and renew it.

Early the following morning he set out, and, traveling rapidly, he came before midday to the clearing. Once more he took up his position in the great tree, and, as before, he saw the women in the fields and the village street, and the cauldron of bubbling poison directly beneath him.

For hours he lay awaiting his opportunity to drop down unseen and gather up the arrows for which he had come; but nothing now occurred to call the villagers away from their homes. The day wore on, and still Tarzan of the Apes crouched above the unsuspecting woman at the cauldron.

Presently the workers in the fields returned. The hunting warriors emerged from the forest, and when all were within the palisade the gates were closed and barred.

Many cooking pots were now in evidence about the village. Before each hut a woman presided over a boiling stew, while little cakes of plantain, and cassava puddings were to be seen on every hand.

Suddenly there came a hail from the edge of the clearing.

Tarzan looked.

It was a party of belated hunters returning from the north, and among them they half led, half carried a struggling animal.

As they approached the village the gates were thrown open to admit them, and then, as the people saw the victim of the chase, a savage cry rose to the heavens, for the quarry was a man.

As he was dragged, still resisting, into the village street, the women and children set upon him with sticks and stones, and Tarzan of the Apes, young and savage beast of the jungle, wondered at the cruel brutality of his own kind.

Sheeta, the leopard, alone of all the jungle folk, tortured his prey. The ethics of all the others meted a quick and merciful death to their victims.

Tarzan had learned from his books but scattered fragments of the ways of human beings.

When he had followed Kulonga through the forest he had expected to come to a city of strange houses on wheels, puffing clouds of black smoke from a huge tree stuck in the roof of one of them—or to a sea covered with mighty floating buildings which he had learned were called, variously, ships and boats and steamers and craft.

He had been sorely disappointed with the poor little village of the blacks, hidden away in his own jungle, and with not a single house as large as his own cabin upon the distant beach.

He saw that these people were more wicked than his own apes, and as savage and cruel as Sabor, herself. Tarzan began to hold his own kind in low esteem.

Now they had tied their poor victim to a great post near the center of the village, directly before Mbonga's hut, and here they formed a dancing, yelling circle of warriors about him, alive with flashing knives and menacing spears.

In a larger circle squatted the women, yelling and beating upon drums. It reminded Tarzan of the Dum-Dum, and so he knew what to expect. He wondered if they would spring upon their meat while it was still alive. The Apes did not do such things as that.

The circle of warriors about the cringing captive drew closer and closer to their prey as they danced in wild and savage abandon to the maddening music of the drums. Presently a spear reached out and pricked the victim. It was the signal for fifty others.

Eyes, ears, arms and legs were pierced; every inch of the poor writhing body that did not cover a vital organ became the target of the cruel lancers.

The women and children shrieked their delight.

The warriors licked their hideous lips in anticipation of the feast to come, and vied with one another in the savagery and loathsomeness of the cruel indignities with which they tortured the still conscious prisoner.

Then it was that Tarzan of the Apes saw his chance. All eyes were fixed upon the thrilling spectacle at the stake. The light of day had given place to the darkness of a moonless night, and only the fires in the immediate vicinity of the orgy had been kept alight to cast a restless glow upon the restless scene.

Gently the lithe boy dropped to the soft earth at the end of the village street. Quickly he gathered up the arrows—all of them this time, for he had brought a number of long fibers to bind them into a bundle.

Without haste he wrapped them securely, and then, ere he turned to leave, the devil of capriciousness entered his heart. He looked about for some hint of a wild prank to play upon these strange, grotesque creatures that they might be again aware of his presence among them.

Dropping his bundle of arrows at the foot of the tree, Tarzan crept among the shadows at the side of the street until he came to the same hut he had entered on the occasion of his first visit.

Inside all was darkness, but his groping hands soon found the object for which he sought, and without further delay he turned again toward the door.

He had taken but a step, however, ere his quick ear caught the sound of approaching footsteps immediately without. In another instant the figure of a woman darkened the entrance of the hut.

Tarzan drew back silently to the far wall, and his hand sought the long, keen hunting knife of his father. The woman came quickly to the center of the hut. There she paused for an instant feeling about with her hands for the thing she sought. Evidently it was not in its accustomed place, for she explored ever nearer and nearer the wall where Tarzan stood.

So close was she now that the ape-man felt the animal warmth of her naked body. Up went the hunting knife, and then the woman turned to one side and soon a guttural "ah" proclaimed that her search had at last been successful.

Immediately she turned and left the hut, and as she passed through the doorway Tarzan saw that she carried a cooking pot in her hand.

He followed closely after her, and as he reconnoitered from the shadows of the doorway he saw that all the women of the village were hastening to and from the various huts with pots and kettles. These they were filling with water and placing over a number of fires near the stake where the dying victim now hung, an inert and bloody mass of suffering.

Choosing a moment when none seemed near, Tarzan hastened to his bundle of arrows beneath the great tree at the end of the village street. As on the former occasion he overthrew the cauldron before leaping, sinuous and catlike, into the lower branches of the forest giant.

Silently he climbed to a great height until he found a point where he could look through a leafy opening upon the scene beneath him.

The women were now preparing the prisoner for their cooking pots, while the men stood about resting after the fatigue of their mad revel. Comparative quiet reigned in the village.

Tarzan raised aloft the thing he had pilfered from the hut, and, with aim made true by years of fruit and coconut throwing, launched it toward the group of savages.

Squarely among them it fell, striking one of the warriors full upon the head and felling him to the ground. Then it rolled among the women and stopped beside the half-butchered thing they were preparing to feast upon.

All gazed in consternation at it for an instant, and then, with one accord, broke and ran for their huts.

It was a grinning human skull which looked up at them from the ground. The dropping of the thing out of the open sky was a miracle well aimed to work upon their superstitious fears.

Thus Tarzan of the Apes left them filled with terror at this new manifestation of the presence of some unseen and unearthly evil power which lurked in the forest about their village.

Later, when they discovered the overturned cauldron, and that once more their arrows had been pilfered, it commenced to dawn upon them that they had offended some great god by placing their village in this part of the jungle without propitiating him. From then on an offering of food was daily placed below the great tree from whence the arrows had disappeared in an effort to conciliate the mighty one.

But the seed of fear was deep sown, and had he but known it, Tarzan of the Apes had laid the foundation for much future misery for himself and his tribe.

That night he slept in the forest not far from the village, and early the next morning set out slowly on his homeward march, hunting as he traveled. Only a few berries and an occasional grub worm rewarded his search, and he was half famished when, looking up from a log he had been rooting beneath, he saw Sabor, the lioness, standing in the center of the trail not twenty paces from him.

The great yellow eyes were fixed upon him with a wicked and baleful gleam, and the red tongue licked the longing lips as Sabor crouched, worming her stealthy way with belly flattened against the earth.

Tarzan did not attempt to escape. He welcomed the opportunity for which, in fact, he had been searching for days past, now that he was armed with something more than a rope of grass.

Quickly he unslung his bow and fitted a well-daubed arrow, and as Sabor sprang, the tiny missile leaped to meet her in mid-air. At the same instant Tarzan of the Apes jumped to one side, and as the great cat struck the ground beyond him another death-tipped arrow sunk deep into Sabor's loin.

With a mighty roar the beast turned and charged once more, only to be met with a third arrow full in one eye; but this time she was too close to the ape-man for the latter to sidestep the onrushing body.

Tarzan of the Apes went down beneath the great body of his enemy, but with gleaming knife drawn and striking home. For a moment they lay there, and then Tarzan realized that the inert mass lying upon him was beyond power ever again to injure man or ape.

With difficulty he wriggled from beneath the great weight, and as he stood erect and gazed down upon the trophy of his skill, a mighty wave of exultation swept over him.

With swelling breast, he placed a foot upon the body of his powerful enemy, and throwing back his fine young head, roared out the awful challenge of the victorious bull ape.

The forest echoed to the savage and triumphant paean. Birds fell still, and the larger animals and beasts of prey slunk stealthily away, for few there were of all the jungle who sought for trouble with the great anthropoids.

And in London another Lord Greystoke was speaking to HIS kind in the House of Lords, but none trembled at the sound of his soft voice.

Sabor proved unsavory eating even to Tarzan of the Apes, but hunger served as a most efficacious disguise to toughness and rank taste, and ere long, with well-filled stomach, the ape-man was ready to sleep again. First, however, he must remove the hide, for it was as much for this as for any other purpose that he had desired to destroy Sabor.

Deftly he removed the great pelt, for he had practiced often on smaller animals. When the task was finished he carried his trophy to the fork of a high tree, and there, curling himself securely in a crotch, he fell into deep and dreamless slumber.

What with loss of sleep, arduous exercise, and a full belly, Tarzan of the Apes slept the sun around, awakening about noon of the following day. He straightway repaired to the carcass of Sabor, but was angered to find the bones picked clean by other hungry denizens of the jungle.

Half an hour's leisurely progress through the forest brought to sight a young deer, and before the little creature knew that an enemy was near a tiny arrow had lodged in its neck.

So quickly the virus worked that at the end of a dozen leaps the deer plunged headlong into the undergrowth, dead. Again did Tarzan feast well, but this time he did not sleep.

Instead, he hastened on toward the point where he had left the tribe, and when he had found them proudly exhibited the skin of Sabor, the lioness.

"Look!" he cried, "Apes of Kerchak. See what Tarzan, the mighty killer, has done. Who else among you has ever killed one of Numa's people? Tarzan is mightiest amongst you for Tarzan is no ape. Tarzan is—" But here he stopped, for in the language of the anthropoids there was no word for man, and Tarzan could only write the word in English; he could not pronounce it.

The tribe had gathered about to look upon the proof of his wondrous prowess, and to listen to his words. Only Kerchak hung back, nursing his hatred and his rage.

Suddenly something snapped in the wicked little brain of the anthropoid. With a frightful roar the great beast sprang among the assemblage.

Biting, and striking with his huge hands, he killed and maimed a dozen ere the balance could escape to the upper terraces of the forest.

Frothing and shrieking in the insanity of his fury, Kerchak looked about for the object of his greatest hatred, and there, upon a near-by limb, he saw him sitting.

"Come down, Tarzan, great killer," cried Kerchak. "Come down and feel the fangs of a greater! Do mighty fighters fly to the trees at the first approach of danger?" And then Kerchak emitted the volleying challenge of his kind.

Quietly Tarzan dropped to the ground. Breathlessly the tribe watched from their lofty perches as Kerchak, still roaring, charged the relatively puny figure.

Nearly seven feet stood Kerchak on his short legs. His enormous shoulders were bunched and rounded with huge muscles. The back of his short neck was as a single lump of iron sinew which bulged beyond the base of his skull, so that his head seemed like a small ball protruding from a huge mountain of flesh.

His back-drawn, snarling lips exposed his great fighting fangs, and his little, wicked, blood-shot eyes gleamed in horrid reflection of his madness.

Awaiting him stood Tarzan, himself a mighty muscled animal, but his six feet of height and his great rolling sinews seemed pitifully inadequate to the ordeal which awaited them.

His bow and arrows lay some distance away where he had dropped them while showing Sabor's hide to his fellow apes, so that he confronted Kerchak now with only his hunting knife and his superior intellect to offset the ferocious strength of his enemy.

As his antagonist came roaring toward him, Lord Greystoke tore his long knife from its sheath, and with an answering challenge as horrid and bloodcurdling as that of the beast he faced, rushed swiftly to meet the attack. He was too shrewd to allow those long hairy arms to encircle him, and just as their bodies were about to crash together, Tarzan of the Apes grasped one of the huge wrists of his assailant, and, springing lightly to one side, drove his knife to the hilt into Kerchak's body, below the heart.

Before he could wrench the blade free again, the bull's quick lunge to seize him in those awful arms had torn the weapon from Tarzan's grasp.

Kerchak aimed a terrific blow at the ape-man's head with the flat of his hand, a blow which, had it landed, might easily have crushed in the side of Tarzan's skull.

The man was too quick, and, ducking beneath it, himself delivered a mighty one, with clenched fist, in the pit of Kerchak's stomach.

The ape was staggered, and what with the mortal wound in his side had almost collapsed, when, with one mighty effort he rallied for an instant—just long enough to enable him to wrest his arm free from Tarzan's grasp and close in a terrific clinch with his wiry opponent.

Straining the ape-man close to him, his great jaws sought Tarzan's throat, but the young lord's sinewy fingers were at Kerchak's own before the cruel fangs could close on the sleek brown skin.

Thus they struggled, the one to crush out his opponent's life with those awful teeth, the other to close forever the windpipe beneath his strong grasp while he held the snarling mouth from him.

The greater strength of the ape was slowly prevailing, and the teeth of the straining beast were scarce an inch from Tarzan's throat when, with a shuddering tremor, the great body stiffened for an instant and then sank limply to the ground.

Kerchak was dead.

Withdrawing the knife that had so often rendered him master of far mightier muscles than his own, Tarzan of the Apes placed his foot upon the neck of his vanquished enemy, and once again, loud through the forest rang the fierce, wild cry of the conqueror.

And thus came the young Lord Greystoke into the kingship of the Apes.

MAN'S REASON

There was one of the tribe of Tarzan who questioned his authority, and that was Terkoz, the son of Tublat, but he so feared the keen knife and the deadly arrows of his new lord that he confined the manifestation of his objections to petty disobediences and irritating mannerisms; Tarzan knew, however, that he but waited his opportunity to wrest the kingship from him by some sudden stroke of treachery, and so he was ever on his guard against surprise.

For months the life of the little band went on much as it had before, except that Tarzan's greater intelligence and his ability as a hunter were the means of providing for them more bountifully than ever before. Most of them, therefore, were more than content with the change in rulers.

Tarzan led them by night to the fields of the black men, and there, warned by their chief's superior wisdom, they ate only what they required, nor ever did they destroy what they could not eat, as is the way of Manu, the monkey, and of most apes.

So, while the blacks were wroth at the continued pilfering of their fields, they were not discouraged in their efforts to cultivate the land, as would have been the case had Tarzan permitted his people to lay waste the plantation wantonly.

During this period Tarzan paid many nocturnal visits to the village, where he often renewed his supply of arrows. He soon noticed the food always standing at the foot of the tree which was his avenue into the palisade, and after a little, he commenced to eat whatever the blacks put there.

When the awe-struck savages saw that the food disappeared overnight they were filled with consternation and dread, for it was one thing to put food out to propitiate a god or a devil, but quite another thing to have the spirit really come into the village and eat it. Such a thing was unheard of, and it clouded their superstitious minds with all manner of vague fears.

Nor was this all. The periodic disappearance of their arrows, and the strange pranks perpetrated by unseen hands, had wrought them to such a state that life had become a veritable burden in their new home, and now it was that Mbonga and his head men began to talk of abandoning the village and seeking a site farther on in the jungle.

Presently the black warriors began to strike farther and farther south into the heart of the forest when they went to hunt, looking for a site for a new village.

More often was the tribe of Tarzan disturbed by these wandering huntsmen. Now was the quiet, fierce solitude of the primeval forest broken by new, strange cries. No longer was there safety for bird or beast. Man had come.

Other animals passed up and down the jungle by day and by night—fierce, cruel beasts—but their weaker neighbors only fled from their immediate vicinity to return again when the danger was past.

With man it is different. When he comes many of the larger animals instinctively leave the district entirely, seldom if ever to return; and thus it has always been with the great anthropoids. They flee man as man flees a pestilence.

For a short time the tribe of Tarzan lingered in the vicinity of the beach because their new chief hated the thought of leaving the treasured contents of the little cabin forever. But when one day a member of the tribe discovered the blacks in great numbers on the banks of a little stream that had been their watering place for generations, and in the act of clearing a space in the jungle and erecting many huts, the apes would remain no longer; and so Tarzan led them inland for many marches to a spot as yet undefiled by the foot of a human being.

Once every moon Tarzan would go swinging rapidly back through the swaying branches to have a day with his books, and to replenish his supply of arrows. This latter task was becoming more and more difficult, for the blacks had taken to hiding their supply away at night in granaries and living huts.

This necessitated watching by day on Tarzan's part to discover where the arrows were being concealed.

Twice had he entered huts at night while the inmates lay sleeping upon their mats, and stolen the arrows from the very sides of the warriors. But this method he realized to be too fraught with danger, and so he commenced picking up solitary hunters with his long, deadly noose, stripping them of weapons and ornaments and dropping their bodies from a high tree into the village street during the still watches of the night.

These various escapades again so terrorized the blacks that, had it not been for the monthly respite between Tarzan's visits, in which they had opportunity to renew hope that each fresh incursion would prove the last, they soon would have abandoned their new village.

The blacks had not as yet come upon Tarzan's cabin on the distant beach, but the ape-man lived in constant dread that, while he was away with the tribe, they would discover and despoil his treasure. So it came that he spent more and more time in the vicinity of his father's last home, and less and less with the tribe. Presently the members of his little community began to suffer on account of his neglect, for disputes and quarrels constantly arose which only the king might settle peaceably.

At last some of the older apes spoke to Tarzan on the subject, and for a month thereafter he remained constantly with the tribe.

The duties of kingship among the anthropoids are not many or arduous.

In the afternoon comes Thaka, possibly, to complain that old Mungo has stolen his new wife. Then must Tarzan summon all before him, and if he finds that the wife prefers her new lord he commands that matters remain as they are, or possibly that Mungo give Thaka one of his daughters in exchange.

Whatever his decision, the apes accept it as final, and return to their occupations satisfied.

Then comes Tana, shrieking and holding tight her side from which blood is streaming. Gunto, her husband, has cruelly bitten her! And Gunto, summoned, says that Tana is lazy and will not bring him nuts and beetles, or scratch his back for him.

So Tarzan scolds them both and threatens Gunto with a taste of the death-bearing slivers if he abuses Tana further, and Tana, for her part, is compelled to promise better attention to her wifely duties.

And so it goes, little family differences for the most part, which, if left unsettled would result finally in greater factional strife, and the eventual dismemberment of the tribe.

But Tarzan tired of it, as he found that kingship meant the curtailment of his liberty. He longed for the little cabin and the sun-kissed sea—for the cool interior of the well-built house, and for the never-ending wonders of the many books.

As he had grown older, he found that he had grown away from his people. Their interests and his were far removed. They had not kept pace with him, nor could they understand aught of the many strange and wonderful dreams that passed through the active brain of their human king. So limited was their vocabulary that Tarzan could not even talk with them of the many new truths, and the great fields of thought that his reading had opened up before his longing eyes, or make known ambitions which stirred his soul.

Among the tribe he no longer had friends as of old. A little child may find companionship in many strange and simple creatures, but to a grown man there must be some semblance of equality in intellect as the basis for agreeable association.

Had Kala lived, Tarzan would have sacrificed all else to remain near her, but now that she was dead, and the playful friends of his childhood grown into fierce and surly brutes he felt that he much preferred the peace and solitude of his cabin to the irksome duties of leadership amongst a horde of wild beasts.

The hatred and jealousy of Terkoz, son of Tublat, did much to counteract the effect of Tarzan's desire to renounce his kingship among the apes, for, stubborn young Englishman that he was, he could not bring himself to retreat in the face of so malignant an enemy.

That Terkoz would be chosen leader in his stead he knew full well, for time and again the ferocious brute had established his claim to physical supremacy over the few bull apes who had dared resent his savage bullying.

Tarzan would have liked to subdue the ugly beast without recourse to knife or arrows. So much had his great strength and agility increased in the period following his maturity that he had come to believe that he might master the redoubtable Terkoz in a hand to hand fight were it not for the terrible advantage the anthropoid's huge fighting fangs gave him over the poorly armed Tarzan.

The entire matter was taken out of Tarzan's hands one day by force of circumstances, and his future left open to him, so that he might go or stay without any stain upon his savage escutcheon.

It happened thus:

The tribe was feeding quietly, spread over a considerable area, when a great screaming arose some distance east of where Tarzan lay upon his belly beside a limpid brook, attempting to catch an elusive fish in his quick, brown hands.

With one accord the tribe swung rapidly toward the frightened cries, and there found Terkoz holding an old female by the hair and beating her unmercifully with his great hands.

As Tarzan approached he raised his hand aloft for Terkoz to desist, for the female was not his, but belonged to a poor old ape whose fighting days were long over, and who, therefore, could not protect his family.

Terkoz knew that it was against the laws of his kind to strike this woman of another, but being a bully, he had taken advantage of the weakness of the female's husband to chastise her because she had refused to give up to him a tender young rodent she had captured.

When Terkoz saw Tarzan approaching without his arrows, he continued to belabor the poor woman in a studied effort to affront his hated chieftain.

Tarzan did not repeat his warning signal, but instead rushed bodily upon the waiting Terkoz.

Never had the ape-man fought so terrible a battle since that long-gone day when Bolgani, the great king gorilla had so horribly manhandled him ere the new-found knife had, by accident, pricked the savage heart.

Tarzan's knife on the present occasion but barely offset the gleaming fangs of Terkoz, and what little advantage the ape had over the man in brute strength was almost balanced by the latter's wonderful quickness and agility.

In the sum total of their points, however, the anthropoid had a shade the better of the battle, and had there been no other personal attribute to influence the final outcome, Tarzan of the Apes, the young Lord Greystoke, would have died as he had lived—an unknown savage beast in equatorial Africa.

But there was that which had raised him far above his fellows of the jungle—that little spark which spells the whole vast difference between man and brute—Reason. This it was which saved him from death beneath the iron muscles and tearing fangs of Terkoz.

Scarcely had they fought a dozen seconds ere they were rolling upon the ground, striking, tearing and rending—two great savage beasts battling to the death.

Terkoz had a dozen knife wounds on head and breast, and Tarzan was torn and bleeding—his scalp in one place half torn from his head so that a great piece hung down over one eye, obstructing his vision.

But so far the young Englishman had been able to keep those horrible fangs from his jugular and now, as they fought less fiercely for a moment, to regain their breath, Tarzan formed a cunning plan. He would work his way to the other's back and, clinging there with tooth and nail, drive his knife home until Terkoz was no more.

The maneuver was accomplished more easily than he had hoped, for the stupid beast, not knowing what Tarzan was attempting, made no particular effort to prevent the accomplishment of the design.

But when, finally, he realized that his antagonist was fastened to him where his teeth and fists alike were useless against him, Terkoz hurled himself about upon the ground so violently that Tarzan could but cling desperately to the leaping, turning, twisting body, and ere he had struck a blow the knife was hurled from his hand by a heavy impact against the earth, and Tarzan found himself defenseless.

During the rollings and squirmings of the next few minutes, Tarzan's hold was loosened a dozen times until finally an accidental circumstance of those swift and everchanging evolutions gave him a new hold with his right hand, which he realized was absolutely unassailable.

His arm was passed beneath Terkoz's arm from behind and his hand and forearm encircled the back of Terkoz's neck. It was the half-Nelson of modern wrestling which the untaught ape-man had stumbled upon, but superior reason showed him in an instant the value of the thing he had discovered. It was the difference to him between life and death.

And so he struggled to encompass a similar hold with the left hand, and in a few moments Terkoz's bull neck was creaking beneath a full-Nelson.

There was no more lunging about now. The two lay perfectly still upon the ground, Tarzan upon Terkoz's back. Slowly the bullet head of the ape was being forced lower and lower upon his chest.

Tarzan knew what the result would be. In an instant the neck would break. Then there came to Terkoz's rescue the same thing that had put him in these sore straits—a man's reasoning power.

"If I kill him," thought Tarzan, "what advantage will it be to me? Will it not rob the tribe of a great fighter? And if Terkoz be dead, he will know nothing of my supremacy, while alive he will ever be an example to the other apes."

"*Ka-goda?*" hissed Tarzan in Terkoz's ear, which, in ape tongue, means, freely translated: "Do you surrender?"

For a moment there was no reply, and Tarzan added a few more ounces of pressure, which elicited a horrified shriek of pain from the great beast.

"*Ka-goda?*" repeated Tarzan.

"*Ka-goda!*" cried Terkoz.

"Listen," said Tarzan, easing up a trifle, but not releasing his hold. "I am Tarzan, King of the Apes, mighty hunter, mighty fighter. In all the jungle there is none so great.

"You have said: '*Ka-goda*' to me. All the tribe have heard. Quarrel no more with your king or your people, for next time I shall kill you. Do you understand?"

"*Huh*," assented Terkoz.

"And you are satisfied?"

"*Huh*," said the ape.

Tarzan let him up, and in a few minutes all were back at their vocations, as though naught had occurred to mar the tranquility of their primeval forest haunts.

But deep in the minds of the apes was rooted the conviction that Tarzan was a mighty fighter and a strange creature. Strange because he had had it in his power to kill his enemy, but had allowed him to live—unharmed.

That afternoon as the tribe came together, as was their wont before darkness settled on the jungle, Tarzan, his wounds washed in the waters of the stream, called the old males about him.

"You have seen again to-day that Tarzan of the Apes is the greatest among you," he said.

"*Huh*," they replied with one voice, "Tarzan is great."

"Tarzan," he continued, "is not an ape. He is not like his people. His ways are not their ways, and so Tarzan is going back to the lair of his own kind by the waters of the great lake which has no farther shore. You must choose another to rule you, for Tarzan will not return."

And thus young Lord Greystoke took the first step toward the goal which he had set—the finding of other white men like himself.

HIS OWN KIND

The following morning, Tarzan, lame and sore from the wounds of his battle with Terkoz, set out toward the west and the seacoast.

He traveled very slowly, sleeping in the jungle at night, and reaching his cabin late the following morning.

For several days he moved about but little, only enough to gather what fruits and nuts he required to satisfy the demands of hunger.

In ten days he was quite sound again, except for a terrible, half-healed scar, which, starting above his left eye ran across the top of his head, ending at the right ear. It was the mark left by Terkoz when he had torn the scalp away.

During his convalescence Tarzan tried to fashion a mantle from the skin of Sabor, which had lain all this time in the cabin. But he found the hide had dried as stiff as a board, and as he knew naught of tanning, he was forced to abandon his cherished plan.

Then he determined to filch what few garments he could from one of the black men of Mbonga's village, for Tarzan of the Apes had decided to mark his evolution from the lower orders in every possible manner, and nothing seemed to him a more distinguishing badge of manhood than ornaments and clothing.

To this end, therefore, he collected the various arm and leg ornaments he had taken from the black warriors who had succumbed to his swift and silent noose, and donned them all after the way he had seen them worn.

About his neck hung the golden chain from which depended the diamond encrusted locket of his mother, the Lady Alice. At his back was a quiver of arrows slung from a leathern shoulder belt, another piece of loot from some vanquished black.

About his waist was a belt of tiny strips of rawhide fashioned by himself as a support for the home-made scabbard in which hung his father's hunting knife. The long bow which had been Kulonga's hung over his left shoulder.

The young Lord Greystoke was indeed a strange and war-like figure, his mass of black hair falling to his shoulders behind and cut with his hunting knife to a rude bang upon his forehead, that it might not fall before his eyes.

His straight and perfect figure, muscled as the best of the ancient Roman gladiators must have been muscled, and yet with the soft and sinuous curves of a Greek god, told at a glance the wondrous combination of enormous strength with suppleness and speed.

A personification, was Tarzan of the Apes, of the primitive man, the hunter, the warrior.

With the noble poise of his handsome head upon those broad shoulders, and the fire of life and intelligence in those fine, clear eyes, he might readily have typified some demigod of a wild and warlike bygone people of his ancient forest.

But of these things Tarzan did not think. He was worried because he had not clothing to indicate to all the jungle folks that he was a man and not an ape, and grave doubt often entered his mind as to whether he might not yet become an ape.

Was not hair commencing to grow upon his face? All the apes had hair upon theirs but the black men were entirely hairless, with very few exceptions.

True, he had seen pictures in his books of men with great masses of hair upon lip and cheek and chin, but, nevertheless, Tarzan was afraid. Almost daily he whetted his keen knife and scraped and whittled at his young beard to eradicate this degrading emblem of apehood.

And so he learned to shave—rudely and painfully, it is true—but, nevertheless, effectively.

When he felt quite strong again, after his bloody battle with Terkoz, Tarzan set off one morning towards Mbonga's village. He was moving carelessly along a winding jungle trail, instead of making his progress through the trees, when suddenly he came face to face with a black warrior.

The look of surprise on the savage face was almost comical, and before Tarzan could unsling his bow the fellow had turned and fled down the path crying out in alarm as though to others before him.

Tarzan took to the trees in pursuit, and in a few moments came in view of the men desperately striving to escape.

There were three of them, and they were racing madly in single file through the dense undergrowth.

Tarzan easily distanced them, nor did they see his silent passage above their heads, nor note the crouching figure squatted upon a low branch ahead of them beneath which the trail led them.

Tarzan let the first two pass beneath him, but as the third came swiftly on, the quiet noose dropped about the black throat. A quick jerk drew it taut.

There was an agonized scream from the victim, and his fellows turned to see his struggling body rise as by magic slowly into the dense foliage of the trees above.

With frightened shrieks they wheeled once more and plunged on in their efforts to escape.

Tarzan dispatched his prisoner quickly and silently; removed the weapons and ornaments, and—oh, the greatest joy of all—a handsome deerskin breechcloth, which he quickly transferred to his own person.

Now indeed was he dressed as a man should be. None there was who could now doubt his high origin. How he should have liked to have returned to the tribe to parade before their envious gaze this wondrous finery.

Taking the body across his shoulder, he moved more slowly through the trees toward the little palisaded village, for he again needed arrows.

As he approached quite close to the enclosure he saw an excited group surrounding the two fugitives, who, trembling with fright and exhaustion, were scarce able to recount the uncanny details of their adventure.

Mirando, they said, who had been ahead of them a short distance, had suddenly come screaming toward them, crying that a terrible white and naked warrior was pursuing him. The three of them had hurried toward the village as rapidly as their legs would carry them.

Again Mirando's shrill cry of mortal terror had caused them to look back, and there they had seen the most horrible sight—their companion's body flying upwards into the trees, his arms and legs beating the air and his tongue protruding from his open mouth. No other sound did he utter nor was there any creature in sight about him.

The villagers were worked up into a state of fear bordering on panic, but wise old Mbonga affected to feel considerable skepticism regarding the tale, and attributed the whole fabrication to their fright in the face of some real danger.

"You tell us this great story," he said, "because you do not dare to speak the truth. You do not dare admit that when the lion sprang upon Mirando you ran away and left him. You are cowards."

Scarcely had Mbonga ceased speaking when a great crashing of branches in the trees above them caused the blacks to look up in renewed terror. The sight that met their eyes made even wise old Mbonga shudder, for there, turning and twisting in the air, came the dead body of Mirando, to sprawl with a sickening reverberation upon the ground at their feet.

With one accord the blacks took to their heels; nor did they stop until the last of them was lost in the dense shadows of the surrounding jungle.

Again Tarzan came down into the village and renewed his supply of arrows and ate of the offering of food which the blacks had made to appease his wrath.

Before he left he carried the body of Mirando to the gate of the village, and propped it up against the palisade in such a way that the dead face seemed to be peering around the edge of the gatepost down the path which led to the jungle.

Then Tarzan returned, hunting, always hunting, to the cabin by the beach.

It took a dozen attempts on the part of the thoroughly frightened blacks to reenter their village, past the horrible, grinning face of their dead fellow, and when they found the food and arrows gone they knew, what they had only too well feared, that Mirando had seen the evil spirit of the jungle.

That now seemed to them the logical explanation. Only those who saw this terrible god of the jungle died; for was it not true that none left alive in the village had ever seen him? Therefore, those who had died at his hands must have seen him and paid the penalty with their lives.

As long as they supplied him with arrows and food he would not harm them unless they looked upon him, so it was ordered by Mbonga that in addition to the food offering there should also be laid out an offering of arrows for this Munan- go-Keewati, and this was done from then on.

If you ever chance to pass that far off African village you will still see before a tiny thatched hut, built just without the village, a little iron pot in which is a quantity of food, and beside it a quiver of well-daubed arrows.

When Tarzan came in sight of the beach where stood his cabin, a strange and unusual spectacle met his vision.

On the placid waters of the landlocked harbor floated a great ship, and on the beach a small boat was drawn up.

But, most wonderful of all, a number of white men like himself were moving about between the beach and his cabin.

Tarzan saw that in many ways they were like the men of his picture books. He crept closer through the trees until he was quite close above them.

There were ten men, swarthy, sun-tanned, villainous looking fellows. Now they had congregated by the boat and were talking in loud, angry tones, with much gesticulating and shaking of fists.

Presently one of them, a little, mean-faced, black-bearded fellow with a countenance which reminded Tarzan of Pamba, the rat, laid his hand upon the shoulder of a giant who stood next him, and with whom all the others had been arguing and quarreling.

The little man pointed inland, so that the giant was forced to turn away from the others to look in the direction indicated. As he turned, the little, mean-faced man drew a revolver from his belt and shot the giant in the back.

The big fellow threw his hands above his head, his knees bent beneath him, and without a sound he tumbled forward upon the beach, dead.

The report of the weapon, the first that Tarzan had ever heard, filled him with wonderment, but even this unaccustomed sound could not startle his healthy nerves into even a semblance of panic.

The conduct of the white strangers it was that caused him the greatest perturbation. He puckered his brows into a frown of deep thought. It was well, thought he, that he had not given way to his first impulse to rush forward and greet these white men as brothers.

They were evidently no different from the black men—no more civilized than the apes—no less cruel than Sabor.

For a moment the others stood looking at the little, mean- faced man and the giant lying dead upon the beach.

Then one of them laughed and slapped the little man upon the back. There was much more talk and gesticulating, but less quarreling.

Presently they launched the boat and all jumped into it and rowed away toward the great ship, where Tarzan could see other figures moving about upon the deck.

When they had clambered aboard, Tarzan dropped to earth behind a great tree and crept to his cabin, keeping it always between himself and the ship.

Slipping in at the door he found that everything had been ransacked. His books and pencils strewed the floor. His weapons and shields and other little store of treasures were littered about.

As he saw what had been done a great wave of anger surged through him, and the new made scar upon his forehead stood suddenly out, a bar of inflamed crimson against his tawny hide.

Quickly he ran to the cupboard and searched in the far recess of the lower shelf. Ah! He breathed a sigh of relief as he drew out the little tin box, and, opening it, found his greatest treasures undisturbed.

The photograph of the smiling, strong-faced young man, and the little black puzzle book were safe.

What was that?

His quick ear had caught a faint but unfamiliar sound.

Running to the window Tarzan looked toward the harbor, and there he saw that a boat was being lowered from the great ship beside the one already in the water. Soon he saw many people clambering over the sides of the larger vessel and dropping into the boats. They were coming back in full force.

For a moment longer Tarzan watched while a number of boxes and bundles were lowered into the waiting boats, then, as they shoved off from the ship's side, the ape-man snatched up a piece of paper, and with a pencil printed on it for a few moments until it bore several lines of strong, well-made, almost letter-perfect characters.

This notice he stuck upon the door with a small sharp splinter of wood. Then gathering up his precious tin box, his arrows, and as many bows and spears as he could carry, he hastened through the door and disappeared into the forest.

When the two boats were beached upon the silvery sand it was a strange assortment of humanity that clambered ashore.

Some twenty souls in all there were, fifteen of them rough and villainous appearing seamen.

The others of the party were of different stamp.

One was an elderly man, with white hair and large rimmed spectacles. His slightly stooped shoulders were draped in an ill-fitting, though immaculate, frock coat, and a shiny silk hat added to the incongruity of his garb in an African jungle.

The second member of the party to land was a tall young man in white ducks, while directly behind came another elderly man with a very high forehead and a fussy, excitable manner.

After these came a huge Negress clothed like Solomon as to colors. Her great eyes rolled in evident terror, first toward the jungle and then toward the cursing band of sailors who were removing the bales and boxes from the boats.

The last member of the party to disembark was a girl of about nineteen, and it was the young man who stood at the boat's prow to lift her high and dry upon land. She gave him a brave and pretty smile of thanks, but no words passed between them.

In silence the party advanced toward the cabin. It was evident that whatever their intentions, all had been decided upon before they left the ship; and so they came to the door, the sailors carrying the boxes and bales, followed by the five who were of so different a class. The men put down their burdens, and then one caught sight of the notice which Tarzan had posted.

"Ho, mates!" he cried. "What's here? This sign was not posted an hour ago or I'll eat the cook."

The others gathered about, craning their necks over the shoulders of those before them, but as few of them could read at all, and then only after the most laborious fashion, one finally turned to the little old man of the top hat and frock coat.

"Hi, perfesser," he called, "step for'rd and read the bloomin' notis."

Thus addressed, the old man came slowly to where the sailors stood, followed by the other members of his party. Adjusting his spectacles he looked for a moment at the placard and then, turning away, strolled off muttering to himself: "Most remarkable—most remarkable!"

"Hi, old fossil," cried the man who had first called on him for assistance, "did je think we wanted of you to read the bloomin' notis to yourself? Come back here and read it out loud, you old barnacle."

The old man stopped and, turning back, said: "Oh, yes, my dear sir, a thousand pardons. It was quite thoughtless of me, yes—very thoughtless. Most remarkable—most remarkable!"

Again he faced the notice and read it through, and doubtless would have turned off again to ruminate upon it had not the sailor grasped him roughly by the collar and howled into his ear.

"Read it out loud, you blithering old idiot."

"Ah, yes indeed, yes indeed," replied the professor softly, and adjusting his spectacles once more he read aloud:

This is the house of Tarzan, the killer of beasts and many black men. Do not harm the things which are Tarzan's. Tarzan watches. Tarzan of the apes.

"Who the devil is Tarzan?" cried the sailor who had before spoken.

"He evidently speaks English," said the young man.

"But what does 'Tarzan of the Apes' mean?" cried the girl.

"I do not know, Miss Porter," replied the young man, "unless we have discovered a runaway simian from the London Zoo who has brought back a European education to his jungle home. What do you make of it, Professor Porter?" he added, turning to the old man.

Professor Archimedes Q. Porter adjusted his spectacles.

"Ah, yes, indeed; yes indeed—most remarkable, most remarkable!" said the professor; "but I can add nothing further to what I have already remarked in elucidation of this truly momentous occurrence," and the professor turned slowly in the direction of the jungle.

"But, papa," cried the girl, "you haven't said anything about it yet."

"Tut, tut, child; tut, tut," responded Professor Porter, in a kindly and indulgent tone, "do not trouble your pretty head with such weighty and abstruse problems," and again he wandered slowly off in still another direction, his eyes bent upon the ground at his feet, his hands clasped behind him beneath the flowing tails of his coat.

"I reckon the daffy old bounder don't know no more'n we do about it," growled the rat-faced sailor.

"Keep a civil tongue in your head," cried the young man, his face paling in anger, at the insulting tone of the sailor. "You've murdered our officers and robbed us. We are absolutely in your power, but you'll treat Professor Porter and Miss Porter with respect or I'll break that vile neck of yours with my bare hands—guns or no guns," and the young fellow stepped so close to the rat-faced sailor that the latter, though he bore two revolvers and a villainous looking knife in his belt, slunk back abashed.

"You damned coward," cried the young man. "You'd never dare shoot a man until his back was turned. You don't dare shoot me even then," and he deliberately turned his back full upon the sailor and walked nonchalantly away as if to put him to the test.

The sailor's hand crept slyly to the butt of one of his revolvers; his wicked eyes glared vengefully at the retreating form of the young Englishman. The gaze of his fellows was upon him, but still he hesitated. At heart he was even a greater coward than Mr. William Cecil Clayton had imagined.

Two keen eyes had watched every move of the party from the foliage of a nearby tree. Tarzan had seen the surprise caused by his notice, and while he could understand nothing of the spoken language of these strange people their gestures and facial expressions told him much.

The act of the little rat-faced sailor in killing one of his comrades had aroused a strong dislike in Tarzan, and now that he saw him quarreling with the fine-looking young man his animosity was still further stirred.

Tarzan had never seen the effects of a firearm before, though his books had taught him something of them, but when he saw the rat-faced one fingering the butt of his revolver he thought of the scene he had witnessed so short a time before, and naturally expected to see the young man murdered as had been the huge sailor earlier in the day.

So Tarzan fitted a poisoned arrow to his bow and drew a bead upon the rat-faced sailor, but the foliage was so thick that he soon saw the arrow would be deflected by the leaves or some small branch, and instead he launched a heavy spear from his lofty perch.

Clayton had taken but a dozen steps. The rat-faced sailor had half drawn his revolver; the other sailors stood watching the scene intently.

Professor Porter had already disappeared into the jungle, whither he was being followed by the fussy Samuel T. Philander, his secretary and assistant.

Esmeralda, the Negress, was busy sorting her mistress' baggage from the pile of bales and boxes beside the cabin, and Miss Porter had turned away to follow Clayton, when something caused her to turn again toward the sailor.

And then three things happened almost simultaneously. The sailor jerked out his weapon and leveled it at Clayton's back, Miss Porter screamed a warning, and a long, metal-shod spear shot like a bolt from above and passed entirely through the right shoulder of the rat-faced man.

The revolver exploded harmlessly in the air, and the seaman crumpled up with a scream of pain and terror.

Clayton turned and rushed back toward the scene. The sailors stood in a frightened group, with drawn weapons, peering into the jungle. The wounded man writhed and shrieked upon the ground.

Clayton, unseen by any, picked up the fallen revolver and slipped it inside his shirt, then he joined the sailors in gazing, mystified, into the jungle.

"Who could it have been?" whispered Jane Porter, and the young man turned to see her standing, wide-eyed and wondering, close beside him.

"I dare say Tarzan of the Apes is watching us all right," he answered, in a dubious tone. "I wonder, now, who that spear was intended for. If for Snipes, then our ape friend is a friend indeed."

"By jove, where are your father and Mr. Philander? There's someone or something in that jungle, and it's armed, whatever it is. Ho! Professor! Mr. Philander!" young Clayton shouted. There was no response.

"What's to be done, Miss Porter?" continued the young man, his face clouded by a frown of worry and indecision.

"I can't leave you here alone with these cutthroats, and you certainly can't venture into the jungle with me; yet someone must go in search of your father. He is more than apt to wandering off aimlessly, regardless of danger or direction, and Mr. Philander is only a trifle less impractical than he. You will pardon my bluntness, but our lives are all in jeopardy here, and when we get your father back something must be done to impress upon him the dangers to which he exposes you as well as himself by his absent-mindedness."

"I quite agree with you," replied the girl, "and I am not offended at all. Dear old papa would sacrifice his life for me without an instant's hesitation, provided one could keep his mind on so frivolous a matter for an entire instant. There is only one way to keep him in safety, and that is to chain him to a tree. The poor dear is SO impractical."

"I have it!" suddenly exclaimed Clayton. "You can use a revolver, can't you?"

"Yes. Why?"

"I have one. With it you and Esmeralda will be comparatively safe in this cabin while I am searching for your father and Mr. Philander. Come, call the woman and I will hurry on. They can't have gone far."

Jane did as he suggested and when he saw the door close safely behind them Clayton turned toward the jungle.

Some of the sailors were drawing the spear from their wounded comrade and, as Clayton approached, he asked if he could borrow a revolver from one of them while he searched the jungle for the professor.

The rat-faced one, finding he was not dead, had regained his composure, and with a volley of oaths directed at Clayton refused in the name of his fellows to allow the young man any firearms.

This man, Snipes, had assumed the role of chief since he had killed their former leader, and so little time had elapsed that none of his companions had as yet questioned his authority.

Clayton's only response was a shrug of the shoulders, but as he left them he picked up the spear which had transfixed Snipes, and thus primitively armed, the son of the then Lord Greystoke strode into the dense jungle.

Every few moments he called aloud the names of the wanderers. The watchers in the cabin by the beach heard the sound of his voice growing ever fainter and fainter, until at last it was swallowed up by the myriad noises of the primeval wood.

When Professor Archimedes Q. Porter and his assistant, Samuel T. Philander, after much insistence on the part of the latter, had finally turned their steps toward camp, they were as completely lost in the wild and tangled labyrinth of the matted jungle as two human beings well could be, though they did not know it.

It was by the merest caprice of fortune that they headed toward the west coast of Africa, instead of toward Zanzibar on the opposite side of the dark continent.

When in a short time they reached the beach, only to find no camp in sight, Philander was positive that they were north of their proper destination, while, as a matter of fact they were about two hundred yards south of it.

It never occurred to either of these impractical theorists to call aloud on the chance of attracting their friends' attention. Instead, with all the assurance that deductive reasoning from a wrong premise induces in one, Mr. Samuel T. Philander grasped Professor Archimedes Q. Porter firmly by the arm and hurried the weakly protesting old gentleman off in the direction of Cape Town, fifteen hundred miles to the south.

When Jane and Esmeralda found themselves safely behind the cabin door the Negress's first thought was to barricade the portal from the inside. With this idea in mind she turned to search for some means of putting it into execution; but her first view of the interior of the cabin brought a shriek of terror to her lips, and like a frightened child the huge woman ran to bury her face on her mistress' shoulder.

Jane, turning at the cry, saw the cause of it lying prone upon the floor before them—the whitened skeleton of a man. A further glance revealed a second skeleton upon the bed.

"What horrible place are we in?" murmured the awe-struck girl. But there was no panic in her fright.

At last, disengaging herself from the frantic clutch of the still shrieking Esmeralda, Jane crossed the room to look into the little cradle, knowing what she should see there even before the tiny skeleton disclosed itself in all its pitiful and pathetic frailty.

What an awful tragedy these poor mute bones proclaimed! The girl shuddered at thought of the eventualities which might lie before herself and her friends in this ill-fated cabin, the haunt of mysterious, perhaps hostile, beings.

Quickly, with an impatient stamp of her little foot, she endeavored to shake off the gloomy forebodings, and turning to Esmeralda bade her cease her wailing.

"Stop, Esmeralda, stop it this minute!" she cried. "You are only making it worse."

She ended lamely, a little quiver in her own voice as she thought of the three men, upon whom she depended for protection, wandering in the depth of that awful forest.

Soon the girl found that the door was equipped with a heavy wooden bar upon the inside, and after several efforts the combined strength of the two enabled them to slip it into place, the first time in twenty years.

Then they sat down upon a bench with their arms about one another, and waited.

AT THE MERCY OF THE JUNGLE

After Clayton had plunged into the jungle, the sailors —mutineers of the Arrow—fell into a discussion of their next step; but on one point all were agreed—that they should hasten to put off to the anchored Arrow, where they could at least be safe from the spears of their unseen foe. And so, while Jane Porter and Esmeralda were barricading themselves within the cabin, the cowardly crew of cutthroats were pulling rapidly for their ship in the two boats that had brought them ashore.

So much had Tarzan seen that day that his head was in a whirl of wonder. But the most wonderful sight of all, to him, was the face of the beautiful white girl.

Here at last was one of his own kind; of that he was positive. And the young man and the two old men; they, too, were much as he had pictured his own people to be.

But doubtless they were as ferocious and cruel as other men he had seen. The fact that they alone of all the party were unarmed might account for the fact that they had killed no one. They might be very different if provided with weapons.

Tarzan had seen the young man pick up the fallen revolver of the wounded Snipes and hide it away in his breast; and he had also seen him slip it cautiously to the girl as she entered the cabin door.

He did not understand anything of the motives behind all that he had seen; but, somehow, intuitively he liked the young man and the two old men, and for the girl he had a strange longing which he scarcely understood. As for the big black woman, she was evidently connected in some way to the girl, and so he liked her, also.

For the sailors, and especially Snipes, he had developed a great hatred. He knew by their threatening gestures and by the expression upon their evil faces that they were enemies of the others of the party, and so he decided to watch closely.

Tarzan wondered why the men had gone into the jungle, nor did it ever occur to him that one could become lost in that maze of undergrowth which to him was as simple as is the main street of your own home town to you.

When he saw the sailors row away toward the ship, and knew that the girl and her companion were safe in his cabin, Tarzan decided to follow the young man into the jungle and learn what his errand might be. He swung off rapidly in the direction taken by Clayton, and in a short time heard faintly in the distance the now only occasional calls of the Englishman to his friends.

Presently Tarzan came up with the white man, who, almost fagged, was leaning against a tree wiping the perspiration from his forehead. The ape-man, hiding safe behind a screen of foliage, sat watching this new specimen of his own race intently.

At intervals Clayton called aloud and finally it came to Tarzan that he was searching for the old man.

Tarzan was on the point of going off to look for them himself, when he caught the yellow glint of a sleek hide moving cautiously through the jungle toward Clayton.

It was Sheeta, the leopard. Now, Tarzan heard the soft bending of grasses and wondered why the young white man was not warned. Could it be he had failed to note the loud warning? Never before had Tarzan known Sheeta to be so clumsy.

No, the white man did not hear. Sheeta was crouching for the spring, and then, shrill and horrible, there rose from the stillness of the jungle the awful cry of the challenging ape, and Sheeta turned, crashing into the underbrush.

Clayton came to his feet with a start. His blood ran cold. Never in all his life had so fearful a sound smote upon his ears. He was no coward; but if ever man felt the icy fingers of fear upon his heart, William Cecil Clayton, eldest son of Lord Greystoke of England, did that day in the fastness of the African jungle.

The noise of some great body crashing through the underbrush so close beside him, and the sound of that bloodcurdling shriek from above, tested Clayton's courage to the limit; but he could not know that it was to that very voice he owed his life, nor that the creature who hurled it forth was his own cousin—the real Lord Greystoke.

The afternoon was drawing to a close, and Clayton, disheartened and discouraged, was in a terrible quandary as to the proper course to pursue; whether to keep on in search of Professor Porter, at the almost certain risk of his own death in the jungle by night, or to return to the cabin where he might at least serve to protect Jane from the perils which confronted her on all sides.

He did not wish to return to camp without her father; still more, he shrank from the thought of leaving her alone and unprotected in the hands of the mutineers of the Arrow, or to the hundred unknown dangers of the jungle.

Possibly, too, he thought, the professor and Philander might have returned to camp. Yes, that was more than likely. At least he would return and see, before he continued what seemed to be a most fruitless quest. And so he started, stumbling back through the thick and matted underbrush in the direction that he thought the cabin lay.

To Tarzan's surprise the young man was heading further into the jungle in the general direction of Mbonga's village, and the shrewd young ape-man was convinced that he was lost.

To Tarzan this was scarcely incomprehensible; his judgment told him that no man would venture toward the village of the cruel blacks armed only with a spear which, from the awkward way in which he carried it, was evidently an unaccustomed weapon to this white man. Nor was he following the trail of the old men. That, they had crossed and left long since, though it had been fresh and plain before Tarzan's eyes.

Tarzan was perplexed. The fierce jungle would make easy prey of this unprotected stranger in a very short time if he were not guided quickly to the beach.

Yes, there was Numa, the lion, even now, stalking the white man a dozen paces to the right.

Clayton heard the great body paralleling his course, and now there rose upon the evening air the beast's thunderous roar. The man stopped with upraised spear and faced the brush from which issued the awful sound. The shadows were deepening, darkness was settling in.

God! To die here alone, beneath the fangs of wild beasts; to be torn and rended; to feel the hot breath of the brute on his face as the great paw crushed down up his breast!

For a moment all was still. Clayton stood rigid, with raised spear. Presently a faint rustling of the bush apprised him of the stealthy creeping of the thing behind. It was gathering for the spring. At last he saw it, not twenty feet away—the long, lithe, muscular body and tawny head of a huge black-maned lion.

The beast was upon its belly, moving forward very slowly. As its eyes met Clayton's it stopped, and deliberately, cautiously gathered its hind quarters behind it.

In agony the man watched, fearful to launch his spear, powerless to fly.

He heard a noise in the tree above him. Some new danger, he thought, but he dared not take his eyes from the yellow green orbs before him. There was a sharp twang as of a broken banjo-string, and at the same instant an arrow appeared in the yellow hide of the crouching lion.

With a roar of pain and anger the beast sprang; but, somehow, Clayton stumbled to one side, and as he turned again to face the infuriated king of beasts, he was appalled at the sight which confronted him. Almost simultaneously with the lion's turning to renew the attack a half-naked giant dropped from the tree above squarely on the brute's back.

With lightning speed an arm that was banded layers of iron muscle encircled the huge neck, and the great beast was raised from behind, roaring and pawing the air—raised as easily as Clayton would have lifted a pet dog.

The scene he witnessed there in the twilight depths of the African jungle was burned forever into the Englishman's brain.

The man before him was the embodiment of physical perfection and giant strength; yet it was not upon these he depended in his battle with the great cat, for mighty as were his muscles, they were as nothing by comparison with Numa's. To his agility, to his brain and to his long keen knife he owed his supremacy.

His right arm encircled the lion's neck, while the left hand plunged the knife time and again into the unprotected side behind the left shoulder. The infuriated beast, pulled up and backwards until he stood upon his hind legs, struggled impotently in this unnatural position.

Had the battle been of a few seconds' longer duration the outcome might have been different, but it was all accomplished so quickly that the lion had scarce time to recover from the confusion of its surprise ere it sank lifeless to the ground.

Then the strange figure which had vanquished it stood erect upon the carcass, and throwing back the wild and handsome head, gave out the fearsome cry which a few moments earlier had so startled Clayton.

Before him he saw the figure of a young man, naked except for a loin cloth and a few barbaric ornaments about arms and legs; on the breast a priceless diamond locket gleaming against a smooth brown skin.

The hunting knife had been returned to its homely sheath, and the man was gathering up his bow and quiver from where he had tossed them when he leaped to attack the lion.

Clayton spoke to the stranger in English, thanking him for his brave rescue and complimenting him on the wondrous strength and dexterity he had displayed, but the only answer was a steady stare and a faint shrug of the mighty shoulders, which might betoken either disparagement of the service rendered, or ignorance of Clayton's language.

When the bow and quiver had been slung to his back the wild man, for such Clayton now thought him, once more drew his knife and deftly carved a dozen large strips of meat from the lion's carcass. Then, squatting upon his haunches, he proceeded to eat, first motioning Clayton to join him.

The strong white teeth sank into the raw and dripping flesh in apparent relish of the meal, but Clayton could not bring himself to share the uncooked meat with his strange host; instead he watched him, and presently there dawned upon him the conviction that this was Tarzan of the Apes, whose notice he had seen posted upon the cabin door that morning.

If so he must speak English.

Again Clayton attempted speech with the ape-man; but the replies, now vocal, were in a strange tongue, which resembled the chattering of monkeys mingled with the growling of some wild beast.

No, this could not be Tarzan of the Apes, for it was very evident that he was an utter stranger to English.

When Tarzan had completed his repast he rose and, pointing a very different direction from that which Clayton had been pursuing, started off through the jungle toward the point he had indicated.

Clayton, bewildered and confused, hesitated to follow him, for he thought he was but being led more deeply into the mazes of the forest; but the ape-man, seeing him disinclined to follow, returned, and, grasping him by the coat, dragged him along until he was convinced that Clayton understood what was required of him. Then he left him to follow voluntarily.

The Englishman, finally concluding that he was a prisoner, saw no alternative open but to accompany his captor, and thus they traveled slowly through the jungle while the sable mantle of the impenetrable forest night fell about them, and the stealthy footfalls of padded paws mingled with the breaking of twigs and the wild calls of the savage life that Clayton felt closing in upon him.

Suddenly Clayton heard the faint report of a firearm—a single shot, and then silence.

In the cabin by the beach two thoroughly terrified women clung to each other as they crouched upon the low bench in the gathering darkness.

The Negress sobbed hysterically, bemoaning the evil day that had witnessed her departure from her dear Maryland, while the white girl, dry eyed and outwardly calm, was torn by inward fears and forebodings. She feared not more for herself than for the three men whom she knew to be wandering in the abysmal depths of the savage jungle, from which she now heard issuing the almost incessant shrieks and roars, barkings and growlings of its terrifying and fearsome denizens as they sought their prey.

And now there came the sound of a heavy body brushing against the side of the cabin. She could hear the great padded paws upon the ground outside. For an instant, all was silence; even the bedlam of the forest died to a faint murmur. Then she distinctly heard the beast outside sniffing at the door, not two feet from where she crouched. Instinctively the girl shuddered, and shrank closer to the black woman.

"Hush!" she whispered. "Hush, Esmeralda," for the woman's sobs and groans seemed to have attracted the thing that stalked there just beyond the thin wall.

A gentle scratching sound was heard on the door. The brute tried to force an entrance; but presently this ceased, and again she heard the great pads creeping stealthily around the cabin. Again they stopped—beneath the window on which the terrified eyes of the girl now glued themselves.

"God!" she murmured, for now, silhouetted against the moonlit sky beyond, she saw framed in the tiny square of the latticed window the head of a huge lioness. The gleaming eyes were fixed upon her in intent ferocity.

"Look, Esmeralda!" she whispered. "For God's sake, what shall we do? Look! Quick! The window!"

Esmeralda, cowering still closer to her mistress, took one frightened glance toward the little square of moonlight, just as the lioness emitted a low, savage snarl.

The sight that met the poor woman's eyes was too much for the already overstrung nerves.

"Oh, Gaberelle!" she shrieked, and slid to the floor an inert and senseless mass.

For what seemed an eternity the great brute stood with its forepaws upon the sill, glaring into the little room. Presently it tried the strength of the lattice with its great talons.

The girl had almost ceased to breathe, when, to her relief, the head disappeared and she heard the brute's footsteps leaving the window. But now they came to the door again, and once more the scratching commenced; this time with increasing force until the great beast was tearing at the massive panels in a perfect frenzy of eagerness to seize its defenseless victims.

Could Jane have known the immense strength of that door, built piece by piece, she would have felt less fear of the lioness reaching her by this avenue.

Little did John Clayton imagine when he fashioned that crude but mighty portal that one day, twenty years later, it would shield a fair American girl, then unborn, from the teeth and talons of a man-eater.

For fully twenty minutes the brute alternately sniffed and tore at the door, occasionally giving voice to a wild, savage cry of baffled rage. At length, however, she gave up the attempt, and Jane heard her returning toward the window, beneath which she paused for an instant, and then launched her great weight against the timeworn lattice.

The girl heard the wooden rods groan beneath the impact; but they held, and the huge body dropped back to the ground below.

Again and again the lioness repeated these tactics, until finally the horrified prisoner within saw a portion of the lattice give way, and in an instant one great paw and the head of the animal were thrust within the room.

Slowly the powerful neck and shoulders spread the bars apart, and the lithe body protruded farther and farther into the room.

As in a trance, the girl rose, her hand upon her breast, wide eyes staring horror-stricken into the snarling face of the beast scarce ten feet from her. At her feet lay the prostrate form of the Negress. If she could but arouse her, their combined efforts might possibly avail to beat back the fierce and bloodthirsty intruder.

Jane stooped to grasp the black woman by the shoulder. Roughly she shook her.

"Esmeralda! Esmeralda!" she cried. "Help me, or we are lost."

Esmeralda opened her eyes. The first object they encountered was the dripping fangs of the hungry lioness.

With a horrified scream the poor woman rose to her hands and knees, and in this position scurried across the room, shrieking: "O Gaberelle! O Gaberelle!" at the top of her lungs.

Esmeralda weighed some two hundred and eighty pounds, and her extreme haste, added to her extreme corpulency, produced a most amazing result when Esmeralda elected to travel on all fours.

For a moment the lioness remained quiet with intense gaze directed upon the flitting Esmeralda, whose goal appeared to be the cupboard, into which she attempted to propel her huge bulk; but as the shelves were but nine or ten inches apart, she only succeeded in getting her head in; whereupon, with a final screech, which paled the jungle noises into insignificance, she fainted once again.

With the subsidence of Esmeralda the lioness renewed her efforts to wriggle her huge bulk through the weakening lattice.

The girl, standing pale and rigid against the farther wall, sought with ever-increasing terror for some loophole of escape. Suddenly her hand, tight-pressed against her bosom, felt the hard outline of the revolver that Clayton had left with her earlier in the day.

Quickly she snatched it from its hiding-place, and, leveling it full at the lioness's face, pulled the trigger.

There was a flash of flame, the roar of the discharge, and an answering roar of pain and anger from the beast.

Jane Porter saw the great form disappear from the window, and then she, too, fainted, the revolver falling at her side.

But Sabor was not killed. The bullet had but inflicted a painful wound in one of the great shoulders. It was the surprise at the blinding flash and the deafening roar that had caused her hasty but temporary retreat.

In another instant she was back at the lattice, and with renewed fury was clawing at the aperture, but with lessened effect, since the wounded member was almost useless.

She saw her prey—the two women—lying senseless upon the floor. There was no longer any resistance to be overcome. Her meat lay before her, and Sabor had only to worm her way through the lattice to claim it.

Slowly she forced her great bulk, inch by inch, through the opening. Now her head was through, now one great forearm and shoulder.

Carefully she drew up the wounded member to insinuate it gently beyond the tight pressing bars.

A moment more and both shoulders through, the long, sinuous body and the narrow hips would glide quickly after.

It was on this sight that Jane Porter again opened her eyes.

THE FOREST GOD

When Clayton heard the report of the firearm he fell into an agony of fear and apprehension. He knew that one of the sailors might be the author of it; but the fact that he had left the revolver with Jane, together with the overwrought condition of his nerves, made him morbidly positive that she was threatened with some great danger. Perhaps even now she was attempting to defend herself against some savage man or beast.

What were the thoughts of his strange captor or guide Clayton could only vaguely conjecture; but that he had heard the shot, and was in some manner affected by it was quite evident, for he quickened his pace so appreciably that Clayton, stumbling blindly in his wake, was down a dozen times in as many minutes in a vain effort to keep pace with him, and soon was left hopelessly behind.

Fearing that he would again be irretrievably lost, he called aloud to the wild man ahead of him, and in a moment had the satisfaction of seeing him drop lightly to his side from the branches above.

For a moment Tarzan looked at the young man closely, as though undecided as to just what was best to do; then, stooping down before Clayton, he motioned him to grasp him about the neck, and, with the white man upon his back, Tarzan took to the trees.

The next few minutes the young Englishman never forgot. High into bending and swaying branches he was borne with what seemed to him incredible swiftness, while Tarzan chafed at the slowness of his progress.

From one lofty branch the agile creature swung with Clayton through a dizzy arc to a neighboring tree; then for a hundred yards maybe the sure feet threaded a maze of interwoven limbs, balancing like a tightrope walker high above the black depths of verdure beneath.

From the first sensation of chilling fear Clayton passed to one of keen admiration and envy of those giant muscles and that wondrous instinct or knowledge which guided this forest god through the inky blackness of the night as easily and safely as Clayton would have strolled a London street at high noon.

Occasionally they would enter a spot where the foliage above was less dense, and the bright rays of the moon lit up before Clayton's wondering eyes the strange path they were traversing.

At such times the man fairly caught his breath at sight of the horrid depths below them, for Tarzan took the easiest way, which often led over a hundred feet above the earth.

And yet with all his seeming speed, Tarzan was in reality feeling his way with comparative slowness, searching constantly for limbs of adequate strength for the maintenance of this double weight.

Presently they came to the clearing before the beach. Tarzan's quick ears had heard the strange sounds of Sabor's efforts to force her way through the lattice, and it seemed to Clayton that they dropped a straight hundred feet to earth, so quickly did Tarzan descend. Yet when they struck the ground it was with scarce a jar; and as Clayton released his hold on the ape-man he saw him dart like a squirrel for the opposite side of the cabin.

The Englishman sprang quickly after him just in time to see the hind quarters of some huge animal about to disappear through the window of the cabin.

As Jane opened her eyes to a realization of the imminent peril which threatened her, her brave young heart gave up at last its final vestige of hope. But then to her surprise she saw the huge animal being slowly drawn back through the window, and in the moonlight beyond she saw the heads and shoulders of two men.

As Clayton rounded the corner of the cabin to behold the animal disappearing within, it was also to see the ape-man seize the long tail in both hands, and, bracing himself with his feet against the side of the cabin, throw all his mighty strength into the effort to draw the beast out of the interior.

Clayton was quick to lend a hand, but the ape-man jabbered to him in a commanding and peremptory tone something which Clayton knew to be orders, though he could not understand them.

At last, under their combined efforts, the great body was slowly dragged farther and farther outside the window, and then there came to Clayton's mind a dawning conception of the rash bravery of his companion's act.

For a naked man to drag a shrieking, clawing man-eater forth from a window by the tail to save a strange white girl, was indeed the last word in heroism.

Insofar as Clayton was concerned it was a very different matter, since the girl was not only of his own kind and race, but was the one woman in all the world whom he loved.

Though he knew that the lioness would make short work of both of them, he pulled with a will to keep it from Jane Porter. And then he recalled the battle between this man and the great, black-maned lion which he had witnessed a short time before, and he commenced to feel more assurance.

Tarzan was still issuing orders which Clayton could not understand.

He was trying to tell the stupid white man to plunge his poisoned arrows into Sabor's back and sides, and to reach the savage heart with the long, thin hunting knife that hung at Tarzan's hip; but the man would not understand, and Tarzan did not dare release his hold to do the things himself, for he knew that the puny white man never could hold mighty Sabor alone, for an instant.

Slowly the lioness was emerging from the window. At last her shoulders were out.

And then Clayton saw an incredible thing. Tarzan, racking his brains for some means to cope single-handed with the infuriated beast, had suddenly recalled his battle with Terkoz; and as the great shoulders came clear of the window, so that the lioness hung upon the sill only by her forepaws, Tarzan suddenly released his hold upon the brute.

With the quickness of a striking rattler he launched himself full upon Sabor's back, his strong young arms seeking and gaining a full-Nelson upon the beast, as he had learned it that other day during his bloody, wrestling victory over Terkoz.

With a roar the lioness turned completely over upon her back, falling full upon her enemy; but the black-haired giant only closed tighter his hold.

Pawing and tearing at earth and air, Sabor rolled and threw herself this way and that in an effort to dislodge this strange antagonist; but ever tighter and tighter drew the iron bands that were forcing her head lower and lower upon her tawny breast.

Higher crept the steel forearms of the ape-man about the back of Sabor's neck. Weaker and weaker became the lioness's efforts.

At last Clayton saw the immense muscles of Tarzan's shoulders and biceps leap into corded knots beneath the silver moonlight. There was a long sustained and supreme effort on the ape-man's part—and the vertebrae of Sabor's neck parted with a sharp snap.

In an instant Tarzan was upon his feet, and for the second time that day Clayton heard the bull ape's savage roar of victory. Then he heard Jane's agonized cry:

"Cecil—Mr. Clayton! Oh, what is it? What is it?"

Running quickly to the cabin door, Clayton called out that all was right, and shouted to her to open the door. As quickly as she could she raised the great bar and fairly dragged Clayton within.

"What was that awful noise?" she whispered, shrinking close to him.

"It was the cry of the kill from the throat of the man who has just saved your life, Miss Porter. Wait, I will fetch him so you may thank him."

The frightened girl would not be left alone, so she accompanied Clayton to the side of the cabin where lay the dead body of the lioness.

Tarzan of the Apes was gone.

Clayton called several times, but there was no reply, and so the two returned to the greater safety of the interior.

"What a frightful sound!" cried Jane, "I shudder at the mere thought of it. Do not tell me that a human throat voiced that hideous and fearsome shriek."

"But it did, Miss Porter," replied Clayton; "or at least if not a human throat that of a forest god."

And then he told her of his experiences with this strange creature—of how twice the wild man had saved his life—of the wondrous strength, and agility, and bravery—of the brown skin and the handsome face.

"I cannot make it out at all," he concluded. "At first I thought he might be Tarzan of the Apes; but he neither speaks nor understands English, so that theory is untenable."

"Well, whatever he may be," cried the girl, "we owe him our lives, and may God bless him and keep him in safety in his wild and savage jungle!"

"Amen," said Clayton, fervently.

"For the good Lord's sake, ain't I dead?"

The two turned to see Esmeralda sitting upright upon the floor, her great eyes rolling from side to side as though she could not believe their testimony as to her whereabouts.

And now, for Jane Porter, the reaction came, and she threw herself upon the bench, sobbing with hysterical laughter.

"MOST REMARKABLE"

Several miles south of the cabin, upon a strip of sandy beach, stood two old men, arguing.

Before them stretched the broad Atlantic. At their backs was the Dark Continent. Close around them loomed the impenetrable blackness of the jungle.

Savage beasts roared and growled; noises, hideous and weird, assailed their ears. They had wandered for miles in search of their camp, but always in the wrong direction. They were as hopelessly lost as though they suddenly had been transported to another world.

At such a time, indeed, every fiber of their combined intellects must have been concentrated upon the vital question of the minute—the life-and-death question to them of retracing their steps to camp.

Samuel T. Philander was speaking.

"But, my dear professor," he was saying, "I still maintain that but for the victories of Ferdinand and Isabella over the fifteenth-century Moors in Spain the world would be today a thousand years in advance of where we now find ourselves. The Moors were essentially a tolerant, broad-minded, liberal race of agriculturists, artisans and merchants—the very type of people that has made possible such civilization as we find today in America and Europe—while the Spaniards—"

"Tut, tut, dear Mr. Philander," interrupted Professor Porter; "their religion positively precluded the possibilities you suggest. Moslemism was, is, and always will be, a blight on that scientific progress which has marked—"

"Bless me! Professor," interjected Mr. Philander, who had turned his gaze toward the jungle, "there seems to be someone approaching."

Professor Archimedes Q. Porter turned in the direction indicated by the nearsighted Mr. Philander.

"Tut, tut, Mr. Philander," he chided. "How often must I urge you to seek that absolute concentration of your mental faculties which alone may permit you to bring to bear the highest powers of intellectuality upon the momentous problems which naturally fall to the lot of great minds? And now I find you guilty of a most flagrant breach of courtesy in interrupting my learned discourse to call attention to a mere quadruped of the genus *felis*. As I was saying, Mr.—"

"Heavens, Professor, a lion?" cried Mr. Philander, straining his weak eyes toward the dim figure outlined against the dark tropical underbrush.

"Yes, yes, Mr. Philander, if you insist upon employing slang in your discourse, a 'lion.' But as I was saying—"

"Bless me, Professor," again interrupted Mr. Philander; "permit me to suggest that doubtless the Moors who were conquered in the fifteenth century will continue in that most regrettable condition for the time being at least, even though we postpone discussion of that world calamity until we may attain the enchanting view of yon *felis carnivora* which distance proverbially is credited with lending."

In the meantime the lion had approached with quiet dignity to within ten paces of the two men, where he stood curiously watching them.

The moonlight flooded the beach, and the strange group stood out in bold relief against the yellow sand.

"Most reprehensible, most reprehensible," exclaimed Professor Porter, with a faint trace of irritation in his voice. "Never, Mr. Philander, never before in my life have I known one of these animals to be permitted to roam at large from its cage. I shall most certainly report this outrageous breach of ethics to the directors of the adjacent zoological garden."

"Quite right, Professor," agreed Mr. Philander, "and the sooner it is done the better. Let us start now."

Seizing the professor by the arm, Mr. Philander set off in the direction that would put the greatest distance between themselves and the lion.

They had proceeded but a short distance when a backward glance revealed to the horrified gaze of Mr. Philander that the lion was following them. He tightened his grip upon the protesting professor and increased his speed.

"As I was saying, Mr. Philander," repeated Professor Porter.

Mr. Philander took another hasty glance rearward. The lion also had quickened his gait, and was doggedly maintaining an unvarying distance behind them.

"He is following us!" gasped Mr. Philander, breaking into a run.

"Tut, tut, Mr. Philander," remonstrated the professor, "this unseemly haste is most unbecoming to men of letters. What will our friends think of us, who may chance to be upon the street and witness our frivolous antics? Pray let us proceed with more decorum."

Mr. Philander stole another observation astern.

The lion was bounding along in easy leaps scarce five paces behind.

Mr. Philander dropped the professor's arm, and broke into a mad orgy of speed that would have done credit to any varsity track team.

"As I was saying, Mr. Philander—" screamed Professor Porter, as, metaphorically speaking, he himself "threw her into high." He, too, had caught a fleeting backward glimpse of cruel yellow eyes and half open mouth within startling proximity of his person.

With streaming coat tails and shiny silk hat Professor Archimedes Q. Porter fled through the moonlight close upon the heels of Mr. Samuel T. Philander.

Before them a point of the jungle ran out toward a narrow promontory, and it was for the heaven of the trees he saw there that Mr. Samuel T. Philander directed his prodigious leaps and bounds; while from the shadows of this same spot peered two keen eyes in interested appreciation of the race.

It was Tarzan of the Apes who watched, with face a-grin, this odd game of follow-the-leader.

He knew the two men were safe enough from attack in so far as the lion was concerned. The very fact that Numa had foregone such easy prey at all convinced the wise forest craft of Tarzan that Numa's belly already was full.

The lion might stalk them until hungry again; but the chances were that if not angered he would soon tire of the sport, and slink away to his jungle lair.

Really, the one great danger was that one of the men might stumble and fall, and then the yellow devil would be upon him in a moment and the joy of the kill would be too great a temptation to withstand.

So Tarzan swung quickly to a lower limb in line with the approaching fugitives; and as Mr. Samuel T. Philander came panting and blowing beneath him, already too spent to struggle up to the safety of the limb, Tarzan reached down and, grasping him by the collar of his coat, yanked him to the limb by his side.

Another moment brought the professor within the sphere of the friendly grip, and he, too, was drawn upward to safety just as the baffled Numa, with a roar, leaped to recover his vanishing quarry.

For a moment the two men clung panting to the great branch, while Tarzan squatted with his back to the stem of the tree, watching them with mingled curiosity and amusement.

It was the professor who first broke the silence.

"I am deeply pained, Mr. Philander, that you should have evinced such a paucity of manly courage in the presence of one of the lower orders, and by your crass timidity have caused me to exert myself to such an unaccustomed degree in order that I might resume my discourse. As I was saying, Mr. Philander, when you interrupted me, the Moors—"

"Professor Archimedes Q. Porter," broke in Mr. Philander, in icy tones, "the time has arrived when patience becomes a crime and mayhem appears garbed in the mantle of virtue. You have accused me of cowardice. You have insinuated that you ran only to overtake me, not to escape the clutches of the lion. Have a care, Professor Archimedes Q. Porter! I am a desperate man. Goaded by long-suffering patience the worm will turn."

"Tut, tut, Mr. Philander, tut, tut!" cautioned Professor Porter; "you forget yourself."

"I forget nothing as yet, Professor Archimedes Q. Porter; but, believe me, sir, I am tottering on the verge of forgetfulness as to your exalted position in the world of science, and your gray hairs."

The professor sat in silence for a few minutes, and the darkness hid the grim smile that wreathed his wrinkled countenance. Presently he spoke.

"Look here, Skinny Philander," he said, in belligerent tones, "if you are lookin' for a scrap, peel off your coat and come on down on the ground, and I'll punch your head just as I did sixty years ago in the alley back of Porky Evans' barn."

"Ark!" gasped the astonished Mr. Philander. "Lordy, how good that sounds! When you're human, Ark, I love you; but somehow it seems as though you had forgotten how to be human for the last twenty years."

The professor reached out a thin, trembling old hand through the darkness until it found his old friend's shoulder.

"Forgive me, Skinny," he said, softly. "It hasn't been quite twenty years, and God alone knows how hard I have tried to be 'human' for Jane's sake, and yours, too, since He took my other Jane away."

Another old hand stole up from Mr. Philander's side to clasp the one that lay upon his shoulder, and no other message could better have translated the one heart to the other.

They did not speak for some minutes. The lion below them paced nervously back and forth. The third figure in the tree was hidden by the dense shadows near the stem. He, too, was silent—motionless as a graven image.

"You certainly pulled me up into this tree just in time," said the professor at last. "I want to thank you. You saved my life."

"But I didn't pull you up here, Professor," said Mr. Philander. "Bless me! The excitement of the moment quite caused me to forget that I myself was drawn up here by some outside agency—there must be someone or something in this tree with us."

"Eh?" ejaculated Professor Porter. "Are you quite positive, Mr. Philander?"

"Most positive, Professor," replied Mr. Philander, "and," he added, "I think we should thank the party. He may be sitting right next to you now, Professor."

"Eh? What's that? Tut, tut, Mr. Philander, tut, tut!" said Professor Porter, edging cautiously nearer to Mr. Philander.

Just then it occurred to Tarzan of the Apes that Numa had loitered beneath the tree for a sufficient length of time, so he raised his young head toward the heavens, and there rang out upon the terrified ears of the two old men the awful warning challenge of the anthropoid.

The two friends, huddled trembling in their precarious position on the limb, saw the great lion halt in his restless pacing as the blood-curdling cry smote his ears, and then slink quickly into the jungle, to be instantly lost to view.

"Even the lion trembles in fear," whispered Mr. Philander.

"Most remarkable, most remarkable," murmured Professor Porter, clutching frantically at Mr. Philander to regain the balance which the sudden fright had so perilously endangered. Unfortunately for them both, Mr. Philander's center of equilibrium was at that very moment hanging upon the ragged edge of nothing, so that it needed but the gentle impetus supplied by the additional weight of Professor Porter's body to topple the devoted secretary from the limb.

For a moment they swayed uncertainly, and then, with mingled and most unscholarly shrieks, they pitched headlong from the tree, locked in frenzied embrace.

It was quite some moments ere either moved, for both were positive that any such attempt would reveal so many breaks and fractures as to make further progress impossible.

At length Professor Porter made an attempt to move one leg. To his surprise, it responded to his will as in days gone by. He now drew up its mate and stretched it forth again.

"Most remarkable, most remarkable," he murmured.

"Thank God, Professor," whispered Mr. Philander, fervently, "you are not dead, then?"

"Tut, tut, Mr. Philander, tut, tut," cautioned Professor Porter, "I do not know with accuracy as yet."

With infinite solicitude Professor Porter wiggled his right arm—joy! It was intact. Breathlessly he waved his left arm above his prostrate body—it waved!

"Most remarkable, most remarkable," he said.

"To whom are you signaling, Professor?" asked Mr. Philander, in an excited tone.

Professor Porter deigned to make no response to this puerile inquiry. Instead he raised his head gently from the ground, nodding it back and forth a half dozen times.

"Most remarkable," he breathed. "It remains intact."

Mr. Philander had not moved from where he had fallen; he had not dared the attempt. How indeed could one move when one's arms and legs and back were broken?

One eye was buried in the soft loam; the other, rolling sidewise, was fixed in awe upon the strange gyrations of Professor Porter.

"How sad!" exclaimed Mr. Philander, half aloud. "Concussion of the brain, superinducing total mental aberration. How very sad indeed! and for one still so young!"

Professor Porter rolled over upon his stomach; gingerly he bowed his back until he resembled a huge tom cat in proximity to a yelping dog. Then he sat up and felt of various portions of his anatomy.

"They are all here," he exclaimed. "Most remarkable!"

Whereupon he arose, and, bending a scathing glance upon the still prostrate form of Mr. Samuel T. Philander, he said:

"Tut, tut, Mr. Philander; this is no time to indulge in slothful ease. We must be up and doing."

Mr. Philander lifted his other eye out of the mud and gazed in speechless rage at Professor Porter. Then he attempted to rise; nor could there have been any more surprised than he when his efforts were immediately crowned with marked success.

He was still bursting with rage, however, at the cruel injustice of Professor Porter's insinuation, and was on the point of rendering a tart rejoinder when his eyes fell upon a strange figure standing a few paces away, scrutinizing them intently.

Professor Porter had recovered his shiny silk hat, which he had brushed carefully upon the sleeve of his coat and replaced upon his head. When he saw Mr. Philander pointing to something behind him he turned to behold a giant, naked but for a loin cloth and a few metal ornaments, standing motionless before him.

"Good evening, sir!" said the professor, lifting his hat.

For reply the giant motioned them to follow him, and set off up the beach in the direction from which they had recently come.

"I think it the better part of discretion to follow him," said Mr. Philander.

"Tut, tut, Mr. Philander," returned the professor. "A short time since you were advancing a most logical argument in substantiation of your theory that camp lay directly south of us. I was skeptical, but you finally convinced me; so now I am positive that toward the south we must travel to reach our friends. Therefore I shall continue south."

"But, Professor Porter, this man may know better than either of us. He seems to be indigenous to this part of the world. Let us at least follow him for a short distance."

"Tut, tut, Mr. Philander," repeated the professor. "I am a difficult man to convince, but when once convinced my decision is unalterable. I shall continue in the proper direction, if I have to circumambulate the continent of Africa to reach my destination."

Further argument was interrupted by Tarzan, who, seeing that these strange men were not following him, had returned to their side.

Again he beckoned to them; but still they stood in argument.

Presently the ape-man lost patience with their stupid ignorance. He grasped the frightened Mr. Philander by the shoulder, and before that worthy gentleman knew whether he was being killed or merely maimed for life, Tarzan had tied one end of his rope securely about Mr. Philander's neck.

"Tut, tut, Mr. Philander," remonstrated Professor Porter; "it is most unbeseeming in you to submit to such indignities."

But scarcely were the words out of his mouth ere he, too, had been seized and securely bound by the neck with the same rope. Then Tarzan set off toward the north, leading the now thoroughly frightened professor and his secretary.

In deathly silence they proceeded for what seemed hours to the two tired and hopeless old men; but presently as they topped a little rise of ground they were overjoyed to see the cabin lying before them, not a hundred yards distant.

Here Tarzan released them, and, pointing toward the little building, vanished into the jungle beside them.

"Most remarkable, most remarkable!" gasped the professor. "But you see, Mr. Philander, that I was quite right, as usual; and but for your stubborn willfulness we should have escaped a series of most humiliating, not to say dangerous accidents. Pray allow yourself to be guided by a more mature and practical mind hereafter when in need of wise counsel."

Mr. Samuel T. Philander was too much relieved at the happy outcome to their adventure to take umbrage at the professor's cruel fling. Instead he grasped his friend's arm and hastened him forward in the direction of the cabin.

It was a much-relieved party of castaways that found itself once more united. Dawn discovered them still recounting their various adventures and speculating upon the identity of the strange guardian and protector they had found on this savage shore.

Esmeralda was positive that it was none other than an angel of the Lord, sent down especially to watch over them.

"Had you seen him devour the raw meat of the lion, Esmeralda," laughed Clayton, "you would have thought him a very material angel."

"There was nothing heavenly about his voice," said Jane Porter, with a little shudder at recollection of the awful roar which had followed the killing of the lioness.

"Nor did it precisely comport with my preconceived ideas of the dignity of divine messengers," remarked Professor Porter, "when the—ah—gentleman tied two highly respectable and erudite scholars neck to neck and dragged them through the jungle as though they had been cows."

BURIALS

As it was now quite light, the party, none of whom had eaten or slept since the previous morning, began to bestir themselves to prepare food.

The mutineers of the Arrow had landed a small supply of dried meats, canned soups and vegetables, crackers, flour, tea, and coffee for the five they had marooned, and these were hurriedly drawn upon to satisfy the craving of long-famished appetites.

The next task was to make the cabin habitable, and to this end it was decided to at once remove the gruesome relics of the tragedy which had taken place there on some bygone day.

Professor Porter and Mr. Philander were deeply interested in examining the skeletons. The two larger, they stated, had belonged to a male and female of one of the higher white races.

The smallest skeleton was given but passing attention, as its location, in the crib, left no doubt as to its having been the infant offspring of this unhappy couple.

As they were preparing the skeleton of the man for burial, Clayton discovered a massive ring which had evidently encircled the man's finger at the time of his death, for one of the slender bones of the hand still lay within the golden bauble.

Picking it up to examine it, Clayton gave a cry of astonishment, for the ring bore the crest of the house of Greystoke.

At the same time, Jane discovered the books in the cupboard, and on opening the fly-leaf of one of them saw the name, *John Clayton, London*. In a second book which she hurriedly examined was the single name, *Greystoke*.

"Why, Mr. Clayton," she cried, "what does this mean? Here are the names of some of your own people in these books."

"And here," he replied gravely, "is the great ring of the house of Greystoke which has been lost since my uncle, John Clayton, the former Lord Greystoke, disappeared, presumably lost at sea."

"But how do you account for these things being here, in this savage African jungle?" exclaimed the girl.

"There is but one way to account for it, Miss Porter," said Clayton. "The late Lord Greystoke was not drowned. He died here in this cabin and this poor thing upon the floor is all that is mortal of him."

"Then this must have been Lady Greystoke," said Jane reverently, indicating the poor mass of bones upon the bed.

"The beautiful Lady Alice," replied Clayton, "of whose many virtues and remarkable personal charms I often have heard my mother and father speak. Poor woman," he murmured sadly.

With deep reverence and solemnity the bodies of the late Lord and Lady Greystoke were buried beside their little African cabin, and between them was placed the tiny skeleton of the baby of Kala, the ape.

As Mr. Philander was placing the frail bones of the infant in a bit of sail cloth, he examined the skull minutely. Then he called Professor Porter to his side, and the two argued in low tones for several minutes.

"Most remarkable, most remarkable," said Professor Porter.

"Bless me," said Mr. Philander, "we must acquaint Mr. Clayton with our discovery at once."

"Tut, tut, Mr. Philander, tut, tut!" remonstrated Professor Archimedes Q. Porter. "'Let the dead past bury its dead.'"

And so the white-haired old man repeated the burial service over this strange grave, while his four companions stood with bowed and uncovered heads about him.

From the trees Tarzan of the Apes watched the solemn ceremony; but most of all he watched the sweet face and graceful figure of Jane Porter.

In his savage, untutored breast new emotions were stirring. He could not fathom them. He wondered why he felt so great an interest in these people—why he had gone to such pains to save the three men. But he did not wonder why he had torn Sabor from the tender flesh of the strange girl.

Surely the men were stupid and ridiculous and cowardly. Even Manu, the monkey, was more intelligent than they. If these were creatures of his own kind he was doubtful if his past pride in blood was warranted.

But the girl, ah—that was a different matter. He did not reason here. He knew that she was created to be protected, and that he was created to protect her.

He wondered why they had dug a great hole in the ground merely to bury dry bones. Surely there was no sense in that; no one wanted to steal dry bones.

Had there been meat upon them he could have understood, for thus alone might one keep his meat from Dango, the hyena, and the other robbers of the jungle.

When the grave had been filled with earth the little party turned back toward the cabin, and Esmeralda, still weeping copiously for the two she had never heard of before today, and who had been dead twenty years, chanced to glance toward the harbor. Instantly her tears ceased.

"Look at them low down white trash out there!" she shrilled, pointing toward the Arrow. "They-all's a desecrating us, right here on this here perverted island."

And, sure enough, the Arrow was being worked toward the open sea, slowly, through the harbor's entrance.

"They promised to leave us firearms and ammunition," said Clayton. "The merciless beasts!"

"It is the work of that fellow they call Snipes, I am sure," said Jane. "King was a scoundrel, but he had a little sense of humanity. If they had not killed him I know that he would have seen that we were properly provided for before they left us to our fate."

"I regret that they did not visit us before sailing," said Professor Porter. "I had proposed requesting them to leave the treasure with us, as I shall be a ruined man if that is lost."

Jane looked at her father sadly.

"Never mind, dear," she said. "It wouldn't have done any good, because it is solely for the treasure that they killed their officers and landed us upon this awful shore."

"Tut, tut, child, tut, tut!" replied Professor Porter. "You are a good child, but inexperienced in practical matters," and Professor Porter turned and walked slowly away toward the jungle, his hands clasped beneath his long coat tails and his eyes bent upon the ground.

His daughter watched him with a pathetic smile upon her lips, and then turning to Mr. Philander, she whispered:

"Please don't let him wander off again as he did yesterday. We depend upon you, you know, to keep a close watch upon him."

"He becomes more difficult to handle each day," replied Mr. Philander, with a sigh and a shake of his head. "I presume he is now off to report to the directors of the Zoo that one of their lions was at large last night. Oh, Miss Jane, you don't know what I have to contend with."

"Yes, I do, Mr. Philander; but while we all love him, you alone are best fitted to manage him; for, regardless of what he may say to you, he respects your great learning, and, therefore, has immense confidence in your judgment. The poor dear cannot differentiate between erudition and wisdom."

Mr. Philander, with a mildly puzzled expression on his face, turned to pursue Professor Porter, and in his mind he was revolving the question of whether he should feel complimented or aggrieved at Miss Porter's rather backhanded compliment.

Tarzan had seen the consternation depicted upon the faces of the little group as they witnessed the departure of the Arrow; so, as the ship was a wonderful novelty to him in addition, he determined to hasten out to the point of land at the north of the harbor's mouth and obtain a nearer view of the boat, as well as to learn, if possible, the direction of its flight.

Swinging through the trees with great speed, he reached the point only a moment after the ship had passed out of the harbor, so that he obtained an excellent view of the wonders of this strange, floating house.

There were some twenty men running hither and thither about the deck, pulling and hauling on ropes.

A light land breeze was blowing, and the ship had been worked through the harbor's mouth under scant sail, but now that they had cleared the point every available shred of canvas was being spread that she might stand out to sea as handily as possible.

Tarzan watched the graceful movements of the ship in rapt admiration, and longed to be aboard her. Presently his keen eyes caught the faintest suspicion of smoke on the far northern horizon, and he wondered over the cause of such a thing out on the great water.

About the same time the look-out on the Arrow must have discerned it, for in a few minutes Tarzan saw the sails being shifted and shortened. The ship came about, and presently he knew that she was beating back toward land.

A man at the bows was constantly heaving into the sea a rope to the end of which a small object was fastened. Tarzan wondered what the purpose of this action might be.

At last the ship came up directly into the wind; the anchor was lowered; down came the sails. There was great scurrying about on deck.

A boat was lowered, and in it a great chest was placed. Then a dozen sailors bent to the oars and pulled rapidly toward the point where Tarzan crouched in the branches of a tree.

In the stern of the boat, as it drew nearer, Tarzan saw the rat-faced man.

It was but a few minutes later that the boat touched the beach. The men jumped out and lifted the great chest to the sand. They were on the north side of the point so that their presence was concealed from those at the cabin.

The men argued angrily for a moment. Then the rat-faced one, with several companions, ascended the low bluff on which stood the tree that concealed Tarzan. They looked about for several minutes.

"Here is a good place," said the rat-faced sailor, indicating a spot beneath Tarzan's tree.

"It is as good as any," replied one of his companions. "If they catch us with the treasure aboard it will all be confiscated anyway. We might as well bury it here on the chance that some of us will escape the gallows to come back and enjoy it later."

The rat-faced one now called to the men who had remained at the boat, and they came slowly up the bank carrying picks and shovels.

"Hurry, you!" cried Snipes.

"Stow it!" retorted one of the men, in a surly tone. "You're no admiral, you damned shrimp."

"I'm Cap'n here, though, I'll have you to understand, you swab," shrieked Snipes, with a volley of frightful oaths.

"Steady, boys," cautioned one of the men who had not spoken before. "It ain't goin' to get us nothing by fightin' amongst ourselves."

"Right enough," replied the sailor who had resented Snipes' autocratic tones; "but it ain't a-goin' to get nobody nothin' to put on airs in this bloomin' company neither."

"You fellows dig here," said Snipes, indicating a spot beneath the tree. "And while you're diggin', Peter kin be a-makin' of a map of the location so's we kin find it again. You, Tom, and Bill, take a couple more down and fetch up the chest."

"Wot are you a-goin' to do?" asked he of the previous altercation. "Just boss?"

"Git busy there," growled Snipes. "You didn't think your Cap'n was a-goin' to dig with a shovel, did you?"

The men all looked up angrily. None of them liked Snipes, and this disagreeable show of authority since he had murdered King, the real head and ringleader of the mutineers, had only added fuel to the flames of their hatred.

"Do you mean to say that you don't intend to take a shovel, and lend a hand with this work? Your shoulder's not hurt so all-fired bad as that," said Tarrant, the sailor who had before spoken.

"Not by a damned sight," replied Snipes, fingering the butt of his revolver nervously.

"Then, by God," replied Tarrant, "if you won't take a shovel you'll take a pickax."

With the words he raised his pick above his head, and, with a mighty blow, he buried the point in Snipes' brain.

For a moment the men stood silently looking at the result of their fellow's grim humor. Then one of them spoke.

"Served the skunk jolly well right," he said.

One of the others commenced to ply his pick to the ground. The soil was soft and he threw aside the pick and grasped a shovel; then the others joined him. There was no further comment on the killing, but the men worked in a better frame of mind than they had since Snipes had assumed command.

When they had a trench of ample size to bury the chest, Tarrant suggested that they enlarge it and inter Snipes' body on top of the chest.

"It might 'elp fool any as 'appened to be diggin' 'ereabouts," he explained.

The others saw the cunning of the suggestion, and so the trench was lengthened to accommodate the corpse, and in the center a deeper hole was excavated for the box, which was first wrapped in sailcloth and then lowered to its place, which brought its top about a foot below the bottom of the grave. Earth was shovelled in and tramped down about the chest until the bottom of the grave showed level and uniform.

Two of the men rolled the rat-faced corpse unceremoniously into the grave, after first stripping it of its weapons and various other articles which the several members of the party coveted for their own.

They then filled the grave with earth and tramped upon it until it would hold no more.

The balance of the loose earth was thrown far and wide, and a mass of dead undergrowth spread in as natural a manner as possible over the new-made grave to obliterate all signs of the ground having been disturbed.

Their work done the sailors returned to the small boat, and pulled off rapidly toward the Arrow.

The breeze had increased considerably, and as the smoke upon the horizon was now plainly discernible in considerable volume, the mutineers lost no time in getting under full sail and bearing away toward the southwest.

Tarzan, an interested spectator of all that had taken place, sat speculating on the strange actions of these peculiar creatures.

Men were indeed more foolish and more cruel than the beasts of the jungle! How fortunate was he who lived in the peace and security of the great forest!

Tarzan wondered what the chest they had buried contained. If they did not want it why did they not merely throw it into the water? That would have been much easier.

Ah, he thought, but they do want it. They have hidden it here because they intend returning for it later.

Tarzan dropped to the ground and commenced to examine the earth about the excavation. He was looking to see if these creatures had dropped anything which he might like to own. Soon he discovered a spade hidden by the underbrush which they had laid upon the grave.

He seized it and attempted to use it as he had seen the sailors do. It was awkward work and hurt his bare feet, but he persevered until he had partially uncovered the body. This he dragged from the grave and laid to one side.

Then he continued digging until he had unearthed the chest. This also he dragged to the side of the corpse. Then he filled in the smaller hole below the grave, replaced the body and the earth around and above it, covered it over with underbrush, and returned to the chest.

Four sailors had sweated beneath the burden of its weight — Tarzan of the Apes picked it up as though it had been an empty packing case, and with the spade slung to his back by a piece of rope, carried it off into the densest part of the jungle.

He could not well negotiate the trees with his awkward burden, but he kept to the trails, and so made fairly good time.

For several hours he traveled a little north of east until he came to an impenetrable wall of matted and tangled vegetation. Then he took to the lower branches, and in another fifteen minutes he emerged into the amphitheater of the apes, where they met in council, or to celebrate the rites of the Dum-Dum.

Near the center of the clearing, and not far from the drum, or altar, he commenced to dig. This was harder work than turning up the freshly excavated earth at the grave, but Tarzan of the Apes was persevering and so he kept at his labor until he was rewarded by seeing a hole sufficiently deep to receive the chest and effectually hide it from view.

Why had he gone to all this labor without knowing the value of the contents of the chest?

Tarzan of the Apes had a man's figure and a man's brain, but he was an ape by training and environment. His brain told him that the chest contained something valuable, or the men would not have hidden it. His training had taught him to imitate whatever was new and unusual, and now the natural curiosity, which is as common to men as to apes, prompted him to open the chest and examine its contents.

But the heavy lock and massive iron bands baffled both his cunning and his immense strength, so that he was compelled to bury the chest without having his curiosity satisfied.

By the time Tarzan had hunted his way back to the vicinity of the cabin, feeding as he went, it was quite dark.

Within the little building a light was burning, for Clayton had found an unopened tin of oil which had stood intact for twenty years, a part of the supplies left with the Claytons by Black Michael. The lamps also were still useable, and thus the interior of the cabin appeared as bright as day to the astonished Tarzan.

He had often wondered at the exact purpose of the lamps. His reading and the pictures had told him what they were, but he had no idea of how they could be made to produce the wondrous sunlight that some of his pictures had portrayed them as diffusing upon all surrounding objects.

As he approached the window nearest the door he saw that the cabin had been divided into two rooms by a rough partition of boughs and sailcloth.

In the front room were the three men; the two older deep in argument, while the younger, tilted back against the wall on an improvised stool, was deeply engrossed in reading one of Tarzan's books.

Tarzan was not particularly interested in the men, however, so he sought the other window. There was the girl. How beautiful her features! How delicate her snowy skin!

She was writing at Tarzan's own table beneath the window. Upon a pile of grasses at the far side of the room lay the Negress asleep.

For an hour Tarzan feasted his eyes upon her while she wrote. How he longed to speak to her, but he dared not attempt it, for he was convinced that, like the young man, she would not understand him, and he feared, too, that he might frighten her away.

At length she arose, leaving her manuscript upon the table. She went to the bed upon which had been spread several layers of soft grasses. These she rearranged.

Then she loosened the soft mass of golden hair which crowned her head. Like a shimmering waterfall turned to burnished metal by a dying sun it fell about her oval face; in waving lines, below her waist it tumbled.

Tarzan was spellbound. Then she extinguished the lamp and all within the cabin was wrapped in Cimmerian darkness.

Still Tarzan watched. Creeping close beneath the window he waited, listening, for half an hour. At last he was rewarded by the sounds of the regular breathing within which denotes sleep.

Cautiously he intruded his hand between the meshes of the lattice until his whole arm was within the cabin. Carefully he felt upon the desk. At last he grasped the manuscript upon which Jane Porter had been writing, and as cautiously withdrew his arm and hand, holding the precious treasure.

Tarzan folded the sheets into a small parcel which he tucked into the quiver with his arrows. Then he melted away into the jungle as softly and as noiselessly as a shadow.

EDGAR RICE BURROUGHS

THE JUNGLE TOLL

Early the following morning Tarzan awoke, and his first thought of the new day, as the last of yesterday, was of the wonderful writing which lay hidden in his quiver.

Hurriedly he brought it forth, hoping against hope that he could read what the beautiful white girl had written there the preceding evening.

At the first glance he suffered a bitter disappointment; never before had he so yearned for anything as now he did for the ability to interpret a message from that golden-haired divinity who had come so suddenly and so unexpectedly into his life.

What did it matter if the message were not intended for him? It was an expression of her thoughts, and that was sufficient for Tarzan of the Apes.

And now to be baffled by strange, uncouth characters the like of which he had never seen before! Why, they even tipped in the opposite direction from all that he had ever examined either in printed books or the difficult script of the few letters he had found.

Even the little bugs of the black book were familiar friends, though their arrangement meant nothing to him; but these bugs were new and unheard of.

For twenty minutes he pored over them, when suddenly they commenced to take familiar though distorted shapes. Ah, they were his old friends, but badly crippled.

Then he began to make out a word here and a word there. His heart leaped for joy. He could read it, and he would.

In another half hour he was progressing rapidly, and, but for an exceptional word now and again, he found it very plain sailing.

Here is what he read:

West coast of Africa, about 10x degrees south latitude. (So Mr. Clayton says.) February 3 (?), 1909.
Dearest Hazel:
It seems foolish to write you a letter that you may never see, but I simply must tell somebody of our awful experiences since we sailed from Europe on the ill-fated Arrow.

If we never return to civilization, as now seems only too likely, this will at least prove a brief record of the events which led up to our final fate, whatever it may be.

As you know, we were supposed to have set out upon a scientific expedition to the Congo. Papa was presumed to entertain some wondrous theory of an unthinkably ancient civilization, the remains of which lay buried somewhere in the Congo valley. But after we were well under sail the truth came out.

It seems that an old bookworm who has a book and curio shop in Baltimore discovered between the leaves of a very old Spanish manuscript a letter written in 1550 detailing the adventures of a crew of mutineers of a Spanish galleon bound from Spain to South America with a vast treasure of "doubloons" and "pieces of eight," I suppose, for they certainly sound weird and piraty.

The writer had been one of the crew, and the letter was to his son, who was, at the very time the letter was written, master of a Spanish merchantman.

Many years had elapsed since the events the letter narrated had transpired, and the old man had become a respected citizen of an obscure Spanish town, but the love of gold was still so strong upon him that he risked all to acquaint his son with the means of attaining fabulous wealth for them both.

The writer told how when but a week out from Spain the crew had mutinied and murdered every officer and man who opposed them; but they defeated their own ends by this very act, for there was none left competent to navigate a ship at sea.

They were blown hither and thither for two months, until sick and dying of scurvy, starvation, and thirst, they had been wrecked on a small islet.

The galleon was washed high upon the beach where she went to pieces; but not before the survivors, who numbered but ten souls, had rescued one of the great chests of treasure.

This they buried well up on the island, and for three years they lived there in constant hope of being rescued.

One by one they sickened and died, until only one man was left, the writer of the letter.

The men had built a boat from the wreckage of the galleon, but having no idea where the island was located they had not dared to put to sea.

When all were dead except himself, however, the awful loneliness so weighed upon the mind of the sole survivor that he could endure it no longer, and choosing to risk death upon the open sea rather than madness on the lonely isle, he set sail in his little boat after nearly a year of solitude.

Fortunately he sailed due north, and within a week was in the track of the Spanish merchantmen plying between the West Indies and Spain, and was picked up by one of these vessels homeward bound.

The story he told was merely one of shipwreck in which all but a few had perished, the balance, except himself, dying after they reached the island. He did not mention the mutiny or the chest of buried treasure.

The master of the merchantman assured him that from the position at which they had picked him up, and the prevailing winds for the past week he could have been on no other island than one of the Cape Verde group, which lie off the West Coast of Africa in about 16x or 17x north latitude.

His letter described the island minutely, as well as the location of the treasure, and was accompanied by the crudest, funniest little old map you ever saw; with trees and rocks all marked by scrawly X's to show the exact spot where the treasure had been buried.

When papa explained the real nature of the expedition, my heart sank, for I know so well how visionary and impractical the poor dear has always been that I feared that he had again been duped; especially when he told me he had paid a thousand dollars for the letter and map.

To add to my distress, I learned that he had borrowed ten thousand dollars more from Robert Canler, and had given his notes for the amount.

Mr. Canler had asked for no security, and you know, dearie, what that will mean for me if papa cannot meet them. Oh, how I detest that man!

We all tried to look on the bright side of things, but Mr. Philander, and Mr. Clayton—he joined us in London just for the adventure—both felt as skeptical as I.

Well, to make a long story short, we found the island and the treasure—a great iron-bound oak chest, wrapped in many layers of oiled sailcloth, and as strong and firm as when it had been buried nearly two hundred years ago.

It was *simply filled* with gold coin, and was so heavy that four men bent underneath its weight.

The horrid thing seems to bring nothing but murder and misfortune to those who have anything to do with it, for three days after we sailed from the Cape Verde Islands our own crew mutinied and killed every one of their officers.

Oh, it was the most terrifying experience one could imagine—I cannot even write of it.

They were going to kill us too, but one of them, the leader, named King, would not let them, and so they sailed south along the coast to a lonely spot where they found a good harbor, and here they landed and have left us.

They sailed away with the treasure to-day, but Mr. Clayton says they will meet with a fate similar to the mutineers of the ancient galleon, because King, the only man aboard who knew aught of navigation, was murdered on the beach by one of the men the day we landed.

I wish you could know Mr. Clayton; he is the dearest fellow imaginable, and unless I am mistaken he has fallen very much in love with me.

He is the only son of Lord Greystoke, and some day will inherit the title and estates. In addition, he is wealthy in his own right, but the fact that he is going to be an English Lord makes me very sad—you know what my sentiments have always been relative to American girls who married titled foreigners. Oh, if he were only a plain American gentleman!

But it isn't his fault, poor fellow, and in everything except birth he would do credit to my country, and that is the greatest compliment I know how to pay any man.

We have had the most weird experiences since we were landed here. Papa and Mr. Philander lost in the jungle, and chased by a real lion.

Mr. Clayton lost, and attacked twice by wild beasts. Esmeralda and I cornered in an old cabin by a perfectly awful man-eating lioness. Oh, it was simply "terrific," as Esmeralda would say.

But the strangest part of it all is the wonderful creature who rescued us. I have not seen him, but Mr. Clayton and papa and Mr. Philander have, and they say that he is a perfectly god-like white man tanned to a dusky brown, with the strength of a wild elephant, the agility of a monkey, and the bravery of a lion.

He speaks no English and vanishes as quickly and as mysteriously after he has performed some valorous deed, as though he were a disembodied spirit.

Then we have another weird neighbor, who printed a beautiful sign in English and tacked it on the door of his cabin, which we have preempted, warning us to destroy none of his belongings, and signing himself "Tarzan of the Apes."

We have never seen him, though we think he is about, for one of the sailors, who was going to shoot Mr. Clayton in the back, received a spear in his shoulder from some unseen hand in the jungle.

The sailors left us but a meager supply of food, so, as we have only a single revolver with but three cartridges left in it, we do not know how we can procure meat, though Mr. Philander says that we can exist indefinitely on the wild fruit and nuts which abound in the jungle.

I am very tired now, so I shall go to my funny bed of grasses which Mr. Clayton gathered for me, but will add to this from day to day as things happen.

Lovingly,

Jane Porter.

To Hazel Strong, Baltimore, Md.

Tarzan sat in a brown study for a long time after he finished reading the letter. It was filled with so many new and wonderful things that his brain was in a whirl as he attempted to digest them all.

So they did not know that he was Tarzan of the Apes. He would tell them.

In his tree he had constructed a rude shelter of leaves and boughs, beneath which, protected from the rain, he had placed the few treasures brought from the cabin. Among these were some pencils.

He took one, and beneath Jane Porter's signature he wrote:

I am Tarzan of the Apes

He thought that would be sufficient. Later he would return the letter to the cabin.

In the matter of food, thought Tarzan, they had no need to worry—he would provide, and he did.

The next morning Jane found her missing letter in the exact spot from which it had disappeared two nights before. She was mystified; but when she saw the printed words beneath her signature, she felt a cold, clammy chill run up her spine. She showed the letter, or rather the last sheet with the signature, to Clayton.

"And to think," she said, "that uncanny thing was probably watching me all the time that I was writing—oh! It makes me shudder just to think of it."

"But he must be friendly," reassured Clayton, "for he has returned your letter, nor did he offer to harm you, and unless I am mistaken he left a very substantial memento of his friendship outside the cabin door last night, for I just found the carcass of a wild boar there as I came out."

From then on scarcely a day passed that did not bring its offering of game or other food. Sometimes it was a young deer, again a quantity of strange, cooked food—cassava cakes pilfered from the village of Mbonga—or a boar, or leopard, and once a lion.

Tarzan derived the greatest pleasure of his life in hunting meat for these strangers. It seemed to him that no pleasure on earth could compare with laboring for the welfare and protection of the beautiful white girl.

Some day he would venture into the camp in daylight and talk with these people through the medium of the little bugs which were familiar to them and to Tarzan.

But he found it difficult to overcome the timidity of the wild thing of the forest, and so day followed day without seeing a fulfillment of his good intentions.

The party in the camp, emboldened by familiarity, wandered farther and yet farther into the jungle in search of nuts and fruit.

Scarcely a day passed that did not find Professor Porter straying in his preoccupied indifference toward the jaws of death. Mr. Samuel T. Philander, never what one might call robust, was worn to the shadow of a shadow through the ceaseless worry and mental distraction resultant from his Herculean efforts to safeguard the professor.

A month passed. Tarzan had finally determined to visit the camp by daylight.

It was early afternoon. Clayton had wandered to the point at the harbor's mouth to look for passing vessels. Here he kept a great mass of wood, high piled, ready to be ignited as a signal should a steamer or a sail top the far horizon.

Professor Porter was wandering along the beach south of the camp with Mr. Philander at his elbow, urging him to turn his steps back before the two became again the sport of some savage beast.

The others gone, Jane and Esmeralda had wandered into the jungle to gather fruit, and in their search were led farther and farther from the cabin.

Tarzan waited in silence before the door of the little house until they should return. His thoughts were of the beautiful white girl. They were always of her now. He wondered if she would fear him, and the thought all but caused him to relinquish his plan.

He was rapidly becoming impatient for her return, that he might feast his eyes upon her and be near her, perhaps touch her. The ape-man knew no god, but he was as near to worshipping his divinity as mortal man ever comes to worship. While he waited he passed the time printing a message to her; whether he intended giving it to her he himself could not have told, but he took infinite pleasure in seeing his thoughts expressed in print—in which he was not so uncivilized after all. He wrote:

I am Tarzan of the Apes. I want you. I am yours. You are mine. We live here together always in my house. I will bring you the best of fruits, the tenderest deer, the finest meats that roam the jungle. I will hunt for you. I am the greatest of the jungle fighters. I will fight for you. I am the mightiest of the jungle fighters. You are Jane Porter, I saw it in your letter. When you see this you will know that it is for you and that Tarzan of the Apes loves you.

As he stood, straight as a young Indian, by the door, waiting after he had finished the message, there came to his keen ears a familiar sound. It was the passing of a great ape through the lower branches of the forest.

For an instant he listened intently, and then from the jungle came the agonized scream of a woman, and Tarzan of the Apes, dropping his first love letter upon the ground, shot like a panther into the forest.

Clayton, also, heard the scream, and Professor Porter and Mr. Philander, and in a few minutes they came panting to the cabin, calling out to each other a volley of excited questions as they approached. A glance within confirmed their worst fears.

Jane and Esmeralda were not there.

Instantly, Clayton, followed by the two old men, plunged into the jungle, calling the girl's name aloud. For half an hour they stumbled on, until Clayton, by merest chance, came upon the prostrate form of Esmeralda.

He stopped beside her, feeling for her pulse and then listening for her heartbeats. She lived. He shook her.

"Esmeralda!" he shrieked in her ear. "Esmeralda! For God's sake, where is Miss Porter? What has happened? Esmeralda!"

Slowly Esmeralda opened her eyes. She saw Clayton. She saw the jungle about her.

"Oh, Gaberelle!" she screamed, and fainted again.

By this time Professor Porter and Mr. Philander had come up.

"What shall we do, Mr. Clayton?" asked the old professor. "Where shall we look? God could not have been so cruel as to take my little girl away from me now."

"We must arouse Esmeralda first," replied Clayton. "She can tell us what has happened. Esmeralda!" he cried again, shaking the black woman roughly by the shoulder.

"O Gaberelle, I want to die!" cried the poor woman, but with eyes fast closed. "Let me die, dear Lord, don't let me see that awful face again."

"Come, come, Esmeralda," cried Clayton.

"The Lord isn't here; it's Mr. Clayton. Open your eyes."

Esmeralda did as she was bade.

"O Gaberelle! Thank the Lord," she said.

"Where's Miss Porter? What happened?" questioned Clayton.

"Ain't Miss Jane here?" cried Esmeralda, sitting up with wonderful celerity for one of her bulk. "Oh, Lord, now I remember! It must have took her away," and the Negress commenced to sob, and wail her lamentations.

"What took her away?" cried Professor Porter.

"A great big giant all covered with hair."

"A gorilla, Esmeralda?" questioned Mr. Philander, and the three men scarcely breathed as he voiced the horrible thought.

"I thought it was the devil; but I guess it must have been one of them gorilephants. Oh, my poor baby, my poor little honey," and again Esmeralda broke into uncontrollable sobbing.

Clayton immediately began to look about for tracks, but he could find nothing save a confusion of trampled grasses in the close vicinity, and his woodcraft was too meager for the translation of what he did see.

All the balance of the day they sought through the jungle; but as night drew on they were forced to give up in despair and hopelessness, for they did not even know in what direction the thing had borne Jane.

It was long after dark ere they reached the cabin, and a sad and grief-stricken party it was that sat silently within the little structure.

Professor Porter finally broke the silence. His tones were no longer those of the erudite pedant theorizing upon the abstract and the unknowable; but those of the man of action— determined, but tinged also by a note of indescribable hopelessness and grief which wrung an answering pang from Clayton's heart.

"I shall lie down now," said the old man, "and try to sleep. Early to-morrow, as soon as it is light, I shall take what food I can carry and continue the search until I have found Jane. I will not return without her."

His companions did not reply at once. Each was immersed in his own sorrowful thoughts, and each knew, as did the old professor, what the last words meant—Professor Porter would never return from the jungle.

At length Clayton arose and laid his hand gently upon Professor Porter's bent old shoulder.

"I shall go with you, of course," he said.

"I knew that you would offer—that you would wish to go, Mr. Clayton; but you must not. Jane is beyond human assistance now. What was once my dear little girl shall not lie alone and friendless in the awful jungle.

"The same vines and leaves will cover us, the same rains beat upon us; and when the spirit of her mother is abroad, it will find us together in death, as it has always found us in life.

"No; it is I alone who may go, for she was my daughter— all that was left on earth for me to love."

"I shall go with you," said Clayton simply.

The old man looked up, regarding the strong, handsome face of William Cecil Clayton intently. Perhaps he read there the love that lay in the heart beneath—the love for his daughter.

He had been too preoccupied with his own scholarly thoughts in the past to consider the little occurrences, the chance words, which would have indicated to a more practical man that these young people were being drawn more and more closely to one another. Now they came back to him, one by one.

"As you wish," he said.

"You may count on me, also," said Mr. Philander.

"No, my dear old friend," said Professor Porter. "We may not all go. It would be cruelly wicked to leave poor Esmeralda here alone, and three of us would be no more successful than one.

"There be enough dead things in the cruel forest as it is. Come—let us try to sleep a little."

THE CALL OF THE PRIMITIVE

From the time Tarzan left the tribe of great anthropoids in which he had been raised, it was torn by continual strife and discord. Terkoz proved a cruel and capricious king, so that, one by one, many of the older and weaker apes, upon whom he was particularly prone to vent his brutish nature, took their families and sought the quiet and safety of the far interior.

But at last those who remained were driven to desperation by the continued truculence of Terkoz, and it so happened that one of them recalled the parting admonition of Tarzan:

"If you have a chief who is cruel, do not do as the other apes do, and attempt, any one of you, to pit yourself against him alone. But, instead, let two or three or four of you attack him together. Then, if you will do this, no chief will dare to be other than he should be, for four of you can kill any chief who may ever be over you."

And the ape who recalled this wise counsel repeated it to several of his fellows, so that when Terkoz returned to the tribe that day he found a warm reception awaiting him.

There were no formalities. As Terkoz reached the group, five huge, hairy beasts sprang upon him.

At heart he was an arrant coward, which is the way with bullies among apes as well as among men; so he did not remain to fight and die, but tore himself away from them as quickly as he could and fled into the sheltering boughs of the forest.

Two more attempts he made to rejoin the tribe, but on each occasion he was set upon and driven away. At last he gave it up, and turned, foaming with rage and hatred, into the jungle.

For several days he wandered aimlessly, nursing his spite and looking for some weak thing on which to vent his pent anger.

It was in this state of mind that the horrible, man-like beast, swinging from tree to tree, came suddenly upon two women in the jungle.

He was right above them when he discovered them. The first intimation Jane Porter had of his presence was when the great hairy body dropped to the earth beside her, and she saw the awful face and the snarling, hideous mouth thrust within a foot of her.

One piercing scream escaped her lips as the brute hand clutched her arm. Then she was dragged toward those awful fangs which yawned at her throat. But ere they touched that fair skin another mood claimed the anthropoid.

The tribe had kept his women. He must find others to replace them. This hairless white ape would be the first of his new household, and so he threw her roughly across his broad, hairy shoulders and leaped back into the trees, bearing Jane away.

Esmeralda's scream of terror had mingled once with that of Jane, and then, as was Esmeralda's manner under stress of emergency which required presence of mind, she swooned.

But Jane did not once lose consciousness. It is true that that awful face, pressing close to hers, and the stench of the foul breath beating upon her nostrils, paralyzed her with terror; but her brain was clear, and she comprehended all that transpired.

With what seemed to her marvelous rapidity the brute bore her through the forest, but still she did not cry out or struggle. The sudden advent of the ape had confused her to such an extent that she thought now that he was bearing her toward the beach.

For this reason she conserved her energies and her voice until she could see that they had approached near enough to the camp to attract the succor she craved.

She could not have known it, but she was being borne farther and farther into the impenetrable jungle.

The scream that had brought Clayton and the two older men stumbling through the undergrowth had led Tarzan of the Apes straight to where Esmeralda lay, but it was not Esmeralda in whom his interest centered, though pausing over her he saw that she was unhurt.

For a moment he scrutinized the ground below and the trees above, until the ape that was in him by virtue of training and environment, combined with the intelligence that was his by right of birth, told his wondrous woodcraft the whole story as plainly as though he had seen the thing happen with his own eyes.

And then he was gone again into the swaying trees, following the high-flung spoor which no other human eye could have detected, much less translated.

At boughs' ends, where the anthropoid swings from one tree to another, there is most to mark the trail, but least to point the direction of the quarry; for there the pressure is downward always, toward the small end of the branch, whether the ape be leaving or entering a tree. Nearer the center of the tree, where the signs of passage are fainter, the direction is plainly marked.

Here, on this branch, a caterpillar has been crushed by the fugitive's great foot, and Tarzan knows instinctively where that same foot would touch in the next stride. Here he looks to find a tiny particle of the demolished larva, ofttimes not more than a speck of moisture.

Again, a minute bit of bark has been upturned by the scraping hand, and the direction of the break indicates the direction of the passage. Or some great limb, or the stem of the tree itself has been brushed by the hairy body, and a tiny shred of hair tells him by the direction from which it is wedged beneath the bark that he is on the right trail.

Nor does he need to check his speed to catch these seemingly faint records of the fleeing beast.

To Tarzan they stand out boldly against all the myriad other scars and bruises and signs upon the leafy way. But strongest of all is the scent, for Tarzan is pursuing up the wind, and his trained nostrils are as sensitive as a hound's.

There are those who believe that the lower orders are specially endowed by nature with better olfactory nerves than man, but it is merely a matter of development.

Man's survival does not hinge so greatly upon the perfection of his senses. His power to reason has relieved them of many of their duties, and so they have, to some extent, atrophied, as have the muscles which move the ears and scalp, merely from disuse.

The muscles are there, about the ears and beneath the scalp, and so are the nerves which transmit sensations to the brain, but they are under-developed because they are not needed.

Not so with Tarzan of the Apes. From early infancy his survival had depended upon acuteness of eyesight, hearing, smell, touch, and taste far more than upon the more slowly developed organ of reason.

The least developed of all in Tarzan was the sense of taste, for he could eat luscious fruits, or raw flesh, long buried with almost equal appreciation; but in that he differed but slightly from more civilized epicures.

Almost silently the ape-man sped on in the track of Terkoz and his prey, but the sound of his approach reached the ears of the fleeing beast and spurred it on to greater speed.

Three miles were covered before Tarzan overtook them, and then Terkoz, seeing that further flight was futile, dropped to the ground in a small open glade, that he might turn and fight for his prize or be free to escape unhampered if he saw that the pursuer was more than a match for him.

He still grasped Jane in one great arm as Tarzan bounded like a leopard into the arena which nature had provided for this primeval-like battle.

When Terkoz saw that it was Tarzan who pursued him, he jumped to the conclusion that this was Tarzan's woman, since they were of the same kind—white and hairless—and so he rejoiced at this opportunity for double revenge upon his hated enemy.

To Jane the strange apparition of this god-like man was as wine to sick nerves.

From the description which Clayton and her father and Mr. Philander had given her, she knew that it must be the same wonderful creature who had saved them, and she saw in him only a protector and a friend.

But as Terkoz pushed her roughly aside to meet Tarzan's charge, and she saw the great proportions of the ape and the mighty muscles and the fierce fangs, her heart quailed. How could any vanquish such a mighty antagonist?

Like two charging bulls they came together, and like two wolves sought each other's throat. Against the long canines of the ape was pitted the thin blade of the man's knife.

Jane—her lithe, young form flattened against the trunk of a great tree, her hands tight pressed against her rising and falling bosom, and her eyes wide with mingled horror, fascination, fear, and admiration—watched the primordial ape battle with the primeval man for possession of a woman—for her.

As the great muscles of the man's back and shoulders knotted beneath the tension of his efforts, and the huge biceps and forearm held at bay those mighty tusks, the veil of centuries of civilization and culture was swept from the blurred vision of the Baltimore girl.

When the long knife drank deep a dozen times of Terkoz' heart's blood, and the great carcass rolled lifeless upon the ground, it was a primeval woman who sprang forward with outstretched arms toward the primeval man who had fought for her and won her.

And Tarzan?

He did what no red-blooded man needs lessons in doing. He took his woman in his arms and smothered her upturned, panting lips with kisses.

For a moment Jane lay there with half-closed eyes. For a moment—the first in her young life—she knew the meaning of love.

But as suddenly as the veil had been withdrawn it dropped again, and an outraged conscience suffused her face with its scarlet mantle, and a mortified woman thrust Tarzan of the Apes from her and buried her face in her hands.

Tarzan had been surprised when he had found the girl he had learned to love after a vague and abstract manner a willing prisoner in his arms. Now he was surprised that she repulsed him.

He came close to her once more and took hold of her arm. She turned upon him like a tigress, striking his great breast with her tiny hands.

Tarzan could not understand it.

A moment ago and it had been his intention to hasten Jane back to her people, but that little moment was lost now in the dim and distant past of things which were but can never be again, and with it the good intentions had gone to join the impossible.

Since then Tarzan of the Apes had felt a warm, lithe form close pressed to his. Hot, sweet breath against his cheek and mouth had fanned a new flame to life within his breast, and perfect lips had clung to his in burning kisses that had seared a deep brand into his soul—a brand which marked a new Tarzan.

Again he laid his hand upon her arm. Again she repulsed him. And then Tarzan of the Apes did just what his first ancestor would have done.

He took his woman in his arms and carried her into the jungle.

Early the following morning the four within the little cabin by the beach were awakened by the booming of a cannon. Clayton was the first to rush out, and there, beyond the harbor's mouth, he saw two vessels lying at anchor.

One was the Arrow and the other a small French cruiser. The sides of the latter were crowded with men gazing shoreward, and it was evident to Clayton, as to the others who had now joined him, that the gun which they had heard had been fired to attract their attention if they still remained at the cabin.

Both vessels lay at a considerable distance from shore, and it was doubtful if their glasses would locate the waving hats of the little party far in between the harbor's points.

Esmeralda had removed her red apron and was waving it frantically above her head; but Clayton, still fearing that even this might not be seen, hurried off toward the northern point where lay his signal pyre ready for the match.

It seemed an age to him, as to those who waited breathlessly behind, ere he reached the great pile of dry branches and underbrush.

As he broke from the dense wood and came in sight of the vessels again, he was filled with consternation to see that the Arrow was making sail and that the cruiser was already under way.

Quickly lighting the pyre in a dozen places, he hurried to the extreme point of the promontory, where he stripped off his shirt, and, tying it to a fallen branch, stood waving it back and forth above him.

But still the vessels continued to stand out; and he had given up all hope, when the great column of smoke, rising above the forest in one dense vertical shaft, attracted the attention of a lookout aboard the cruiser, and instantly a dozen glasses were leveled on the beach.

Presently Clayton saw the two ships come about again; and while the Arrow lay drifting quietly on the ocean, the cruiser steamed slowly back toward shore.

At some distance away she stopped, and a boat was lowered and dispatched toward the beach.

As it was drawn up a young officer stepped out.

"Monsieur Clayton, I presume?" he asked.

"Thank God, you have come!" was Clayton's reply. "And it may be that it is not too late even now."

"What do you mean, Monsieur?" asked the officer.

Clayton told of the abduction of Jane Porter and the need of armed men to aid in the search for her.

"MON DIEU!" exclaimed the officer, sadly. "Yesterday and it would not have been too late. Today and it may be better that the poor lady were never found. It is horrible, Monsieur. It is too horrible."

Other boats had now put off from the cruiser, and Clayton, having pointed out the harbor's entrance to the officer, entered the boat with him and its nose was turned toward the little landlocked bay, into which the other craft followed.

Soon the entire party had landed where stood Professor Porter, Mr. Philander and the weeping Esmeralda.

Among the officers in the last boats to put off from the cruiser was the commander of the vessel; and when he had heard the story of Jane's abduction, he generously called for volunteers to accompany Professor Porter and Clayton in their search.

Not an officer or a man was there of those brave and sympathetic Frenchmen who did not quickly beg leave to be one of the expedition.

The commander selected twenty men and two officers, Lieutenant D'Arnot and Lieutenant Charpentier. A boat was dispatched to the cruiser for provisions, ammunition, and carbines; the men were already armed with revolvers.

Then, to Clayton's inquiries as to how they had happened to anchor off shore and fire a signal gun, the commander, Captain Dufranne, explained that a month before they had sighted the Arrow bearing southwest under considerable canvas, and that when they had signaled her to come about she had but crowded on more sail.

They had kept her hull-up until sunset, firing several shots after her, but the next morning she was nowhere to be seen. They had then continued to cruise up and down the coast for several weeks, and had about forgotten the incident of the recent chase, when, early one morning a few days before the lookout had described a vessel laboring in the trough of a heavy sea and evidently entirely out of control.

As they steamed nearer to the derelict they were surprised to note that it was the same vessel that had run from them a few weeks earlier. Her forestaysail and mizzen spanker were set as though an effort had been made to hold her head up into the wind, but the sheets had parted, and the sails were tearing to ribbons in the half gale of wind.

In the high sea that was running it was a difficult and dangerous task to attempt to put a prize crew aboard her; and as no signs of life had been seen above deck, it was decided to stand by until the wind and sea abated; but just then a figure was seen clinging to the rail and feebly waving a mute signal of despair toward them.

Immediately a boat's crew was ordered out and an attempt was successfully made to board the Arrow.

The sight that met the Frenchmen's eyes as they clambered over the ship's side was appalling.

A dozen dead and dying men rolled hither and thither upon the pitching deck, the living intermingled with the dead. Two of the corpses appeared to have been partially devoured as though by wolves.

The prize crew soon had the vessel under proper sail once more and the living members of the ill-starred company carried below to their hammocks.

The dead were wrapped in tarpaulins and lashed on deck to be identified by their comrades before being consigned to the deep.

None of the living was conscious when the Frenchmen reached the Arrow's deck. Even the poor devil who had waved the single despairing signal of distress had lapsed into unconsciousness before he had learned whether it had availed or not.

It did not take the French officer long to learn what had caused the terrible condition aboard; for when water and brandy were sought to restore the men, it was found that there was none, nor even food of any description.

He immediately signalled to the cruiser to send water, medicine, and provisions, and another boat made the perilous trip to the Arrow.

When restoratives had been applied several of the men regained consciousness, and then the whole story was told. That part of it we know up to the sailing of the Arrow after the murder of Snipes, and the burial of his body above the treasure chest.

It seems that the pursuit by the cruiser had so terrorized the mutineers that they had continued out across the Atlantic for several days after losing her; but on discovering the meager supply of water and provisions aboard, they had turned back toward the east.

With no one on board who understood navigation, discussions soon arose as to their whereabouts; and as three days' sailing to the east did not raise land, they bore off to the north, fearing that the high north winds that had prevailed had driven them south of the southern extremity of Africa.

They kept on a north-northeasterly course for two days, when they were overtaken by a calm which lasted for nearly a week. Their water was gone, and in another day they would be without food.

Conditions changed rapidly from bad to worse. One man went mad and leaped overboard. Soon another opened his veins and drank his own blood.

When he died they threw him overboard also, though there were those among them who wanted to keep the corpse on board. Hunger was changing them from human beasts to wild beasts.

Two days before they had been picked up by the cruiser they had become too weak to handle the vessel, and that same day three men died. On the following morning it was seen that one of the corpses had been partially devoured.

All that day the men lay glaring at each other like beasts of prey, and the following morning two of the corpses lay almost entirely stripped of flesh.

The men were but little stronger for their ghoulish repast, for the want of water was by far the greatest agony with which they had to contend. And then the cruiser had come.

When those who could had recovered, the entire story had been told to the French commander; but the men were too ignorant to be able to tell him at just what point on the coast the professor and his party had been marooned, so the cruiser had steamed slowly along within sight of land, firing occasional signal guns and scanning every inch of the beach with glasses.

They had anchored by night so as not to neglect a particle of the shore line, and it had happened that the preceding night had brought them off the very beach where lay the little camp they sought.

The signal guns of the afternoon before had not been heard by those on shore, it was presumed, because they had doubtless been in the thick of the jungle searching for Jane Porter, where the noise of their own crashing through the underbrush would have drowned the report of a far distant gun.

By the time the two parties had narrated their several adventures, the cruiser's boat had returned with supplies and arms for the expedition.

Within a few minutes the little body of sailors and the two French officers, together with Professor Porter and Clayton, set off upon their hopeless and ill-fated quest into the untracked jungle.

HEREDITY

When Jane realized that she was being borne away a captive by the strange forest creature who had rescued her from the clutches of the ape she struggled desperately to escape, but the strong arms that held her as easily as though she had been but a day-old babe only pressed a little more tightly.

So presently she gave up the futile effort and lay quietly, looking through half-closed lids at the faces of the man who strode easily through the tangled undergrowth with her.

The face above her was one of extraordinary beauty.

A perfect type of the strongly masculine, unmarred by dissipation, or brutal or degrading passions. For, though Tarzan of the Apes was a killer of men and of beasts, he killed as the hunter kills, dispassionately, except on those rare occasions when he had killed for hate—though not the brooding, malevolent hate which marks the features of its own with hideous lines.

When Tarzan killed he more often smiled than scowled, and smiles are the foundation of beauty.

One thing the girl had noticed particularly when she had seen Tarzan rushing upon Terkoz—the vivid scarlet band upon his forehead, from above the left eye to the scalp; but now as she scanned his features she noticed that it was gone, and only a thin white line marked the spot where it had been.

As she lay more quietly in his arms Tarzan slightly relaxed his grip upon her.

Once he looked down into her eyes and smiled, and the girl had to close her own to shut out the vision of that handsome, winning face.

Presently Tarzan took to the trees, and Jane, wondering that she felt no fear, began to realize that in many respects she had never felt more secure in her whole life than now as she lay in the arms of this strong, wild creature, being borne, God alone knew where or to what fate, deeper and deeper into the savage fastness of the untamed forest.

When, with closed eyes, she commenced to speculate upon the future, and terrifying fears were conjured by a vivid imagination, she had but to raise her lids and look upon that noble face so close to hers to dissipate the last remnant of apprehension.

No, he could never harm her; of that she was convinced when she translated the fine features and the frank, brave eyes above her into the chivalry which they proclaimed.

On and on they went through what seemed to Jane a solid mass of verdure, yet ever there appeared to open before this forest god a passage, as by magic, which closed behind them as they passed.

Scarce a branch scraped against her, yet above and below, before and behind, the view presented naught but a solid mass of inextricably interwoven branches and creepers.

As Tarzan moved steadily onward his mind was occupied with many strange and new thoughts. Here was a problem the like of which he had never encountered, and he felt rather than reasoned that he must meet it as a man and not as an ape.

The free movement through the middle terrace, which was the route he had followed for the most part, had helped to cool the ardor of the first fierce passion of his new found love.

Now he discovered himself speculating upon the fate which would have fallen to the girl had he not rescued her from Terkoz.

He knew why the ape had not killed her, and he commenced to compare his intentions with those of Terkoz.

True, it was the order of the jungle for the male to take his mate by force; but could Tarzan be guided by the laws of the beasts? Was not Tarzan a Man? But what did men do? He was puzzled; for he did not know.

He wished that he might ask the girl, and then it came to him that she had already answered him in the futile struggle she had made to escape and to repulse him.

But now they had come to their destination, and Tarzan of the Apes with Jane in his strong arms, swung lightly to the turf of the arena where the great apes held their councils and danced the wild orgy of the Dum-Dum.

Though they had come many miles, it was still but midafternoon, and the amphitheater was bathed in the half light which filtered through the maze of encircling foliage.

The green turf looked soft and cool and inviting. The myriad noises of the jungle seemed far distant and hushed to a mere echo of blurred sounds, rising and falling like the surf upon a remote shore.

A feeling of dreamy peacefulness stole over Jane as she sank down upon the grass where Tarzan had placed her, and as she looked up at his great figure towering above her, there was added a strange sense of perfect security.

As she watched him from beneath half-closed lids, Tarzan crossed the little circular clearing toward the trees upon the further side. She noted the graceful majesty of his carriage, the perfect symmetry of his magnificent figure and the poise of his well-shaped head upon his broad shoulders.

What a perfect creature! There could be naught of cruelty or baseness beneath that godlike exterior. Never, she thought had such a man strode the earth since God created the first in his own image.

With a bound Tarzan sprang into the trees and disappeared. Jane wondered where he had gone. Had he left her there to her fate in the lonely jungle?

She glanced nervously about. Every vine and bush seemed but the lurking-place of some huge and horrible beast waiting to bury gleaming fangs into her soft flesh. Every sound she magnified into the stealthy creeping of a sinuous and malignant body.

How different now that he had left her!

For a few minutes that seemed hours to the frightened girl, she sat with tense nerves waiting for the spring of the crouching thing that was to end her misery of apprehension.

She almost prayed for the cruel teeth that would give her unconsciousness and surcease from the agony of fear.

She heard a sudden, slight sound behind her. With a cry she sprang to her feet and turned to face her end.

There stood Tarzan, his arms filled with ripe and luscious fruit.

Jane reeled and would have fallen, had not Tarzan, dropping his burden, caught her in his arms. She did not lose consciousness, but she clung tightly to him, shuddering and trembling like a frightened deer.

Tarzan of the Apes stroked her soft hair and tried to comfort and quiet her as Kala had him, when, as a little ape, he had been frightened by Sabor, the lioness, or Histah, the snake.

Once he pressed his lips lightly upon her forehead, and she did not move, but closed her eyes and sighed.

She could not analyze her feelings, nor did she wish to attempt it. She was satisfied to feel the safety of those strong arms, and to leave her future to fate; for the last few hours had taught her to trust this strange wild creature of the forest as she would have trusted but few of the men of her acquaintance.

As she thought of the strangeness of it, there commenced to dawn upon her the realization that she had, possibly, learned something else which she had never really known before—love. She wondered and then she smiled.

And still smiling, she pushed Tarzan gently away; and looking at him with a half-smiling, half-quizzical expression that made her face wholly entrancing, she pointed to the fruit upon the ground, and seated herself upon the edge of the earthen drum of the anthropoids, for hunger was asserting itself.

Tarzan quickly gathered up the fruit, and, bringing it, laid it at her feet; and then he, too, sat upon the drum beside her, and with his knife opened and prepared the various fruits for her meal.

Together and in silence they ate, occasionally stealing sly glances at one another, until finally Jane broke into a merry laugh in which Tarzan joined.

"I wish you spoke English," said the girl.

Tarzan shook his head, and an expression of wistful and pathetic longing sobered his laughing eyes.

Then Jane tried speaking to him in French, and then in German; but she had to laugh at her own blundering attempt at the latter tongue.

"Anyway," she said to him in English, "you understand my German as well as they did in Berlin."

Tarzan had long since reached a decision as to what his future procedure should be. He had had time to recollect all that he had read of the ways of men and women in the books at the cabin. He would act as he imagined the men in the books would have acted were they in his place.

Again he rose and went into the trees, but first he tried to explain by means of signs that he would return shortly, and he did so well that Jane understood and was not afraid when he had gone.

Only a feeling of loneliness came over her and she watched the point where he had disappeared, with longing eyes, awaiting his return. As before, she was appraised of his presence by a soft sound behind her, and turned to see him coming across the turf with a great armful of branches.

Then he went back again into the jungle and in a few minutes reappeared with a quantity of soft grasses and ferns.

Two more trips he made until he had quite a pile of material at hand.

Then he spread the ferns and grasses upon the ground in a soft flat bed, and above it leaned many branches together so that they met a few feet over its center. Upon these he spread layers of huge leaves of the great elephant's ear, and with more branches and more leaves he closed one end of the little shelter he had built.

Then they sat down together again upon the edge of the drum and tried to talk by signs.

The magnificent diamond locket which hung about Tarzan's neck, had been a source of much wonderment to Jane. She pointed to it now, and Tarzan removed it and handed the pretty bauble to her.

She saw that it was the work of a skilled artisan and that the diamonds were of great brilliancy and superbly set, but the cutting of them denoted that they were of a former day. She noticed too that the locket opened, and, pressing the hidden clasp, she saw the two halves spring apart to reveal in either section an ivory miniature.

One was of a beautiful woman and the other might have been a likeness of the man who sat beside her, except for a subtle difference of expression that was scarcely definable.

She looked up at Tarzan to find him leaning toward her gazing on the miniatures with an expression of astonishment. He reached out his hand for the locket and took it away from her, examining the likenesses within with unmistakable signs of surprise and new interest. His manner clearly denoted that he had never before seen them, nor imagined that the locket opened.

This fact caused Jane to indulge in further speculation, and it taxed her imagination to picture how this beautiful ornament came into the possession of a wild and savage creature of the unexplored jungles of Africa.

Still more wonderful was how it contained the likeness of one who might be a brother, or, more likely, the father of this woodland demi-god who was even ignorant of the fact that the locket opened.

Tarzan was still gazing with fixity at the two faces. Presently he removed the quiver from his shoulder, and emptying the arrows upon the ground reached into the bottom of the bag-like receptacle and drew forth a flat object wrapped in many soft leaves and tied with bits of long grass.

Carefully he unwrapped it, removing layer after layer of leaves until at length he held a photograph in his hand.

Pointing to the miniature of the man within the locket he handed the photograph to Jane, holding the open locket beside it.

The photograph only served to puzzle the girl still more, for it was evidently another likeness of the same man whose picture rested in the locket beside that of the beautiful young woman.

Tarzan was looking at her with an expression of puzzled bewilderment in his eyes as she glanced up at him. He seemed to be framing a question with his lips.

The girl pointed to the photograph and then to the miniature and then to him, as though to indicate that she thought the likenesses were of him, but he only shook his head, and then shrugging his great shoulders, he took the photograph from her and having carefully rewrapped it, placed it again in the bottom of his quiver.

For a few moments he sat in silence, his eyes bent upon the ground, while Jane held the little locket in her hand, turning it over and over in an endeavor to find some further clue that might lead to the identity of its original owner.

At length a simple explanation occurred to her.

The locket had belonged to Lord Greystoke, and the likenesses were of himself and Lady Alice.

This wild creature had simply found it in the cabin by the beach. How stupid of her not to have thought of that solution before.

But to account for the strange likeness between Lord Greystoke and this forest god—that was quite beyond her, and it is not strange that she could not imagine that this naked savage was indeed an English nobleman.

At length Tarzan looked up to watch the girl as she examined the locket. He could not fathom the meaning of the faces within, but he could read the interest and fascination upon the face of the live young creature by his side.

She noticed that he was watching her and thinking that he wished his ornament again she held it out to him. He took it from her and taking the chain in his two hands he placed it about her neck, smiling at her expression of surprise at his unexpected gift.

Jane shook her head vehemently and would have removed the golden links from about her throat, but Tarzan would not let her. Taking her hands in his, when she insisted upon it, he held them tightly to prevent her.

At last she desisted and with a little laugh raised the locket to her lips.

Tarzan did not know precisely what she meant, but he guessed correctly that it was her way of acknowledging the gift, and so he rose, and taking the locket in his hand, stooped gravely like some courtier of old, and pressed his lips upon it where hers had rested.

It was a stately and gallant little compliment performed with the grace and dignity of utter unconsciousness of self. It was the hall-mark of his aristocratic birth, the natural outcropping of many generations of fine breeding, an hereditary instinct of graciousness which a lifetime of uncouth and savage training and environment could not eradicate.

It was growing dark now, and so they ate again of the fruit which was both food and drink for them; then Tarzan rose, and leading Jane to the little bower he had erected, motioned her to go within.

For the first time in hours a feeling of fear swept over her, and Tarzan felt her draw away as though shrinking from him.

Contact with this girl for half a day had left a very diferent Tarzan from the one on whom the morning's sun had risen.

Now, in every fiber of his being, heredity spoke louder than training.

He had not in one swift transition become a polished gentleman from a savage ape-man, but at last the instincts of the former predominated, and over all was the desire to please the woman he loved, and to appear well in her eyes.

So Tarzan of the Apes did the only thing he knew to assure Jane of her safety. He removed his hunting knife from its sheath and handed it to her hilt first, again motioning her into the bower.

The girl understood, and taking the long knife she entered and lay down upon the soft grasses while Tarzan of the Apes stretched himself upon the ground across the entrance.

And thus the rising sun found them in the morning.

When Jane awoke, she did not at first recall the strange events of the preceding day, and so she wondered at her odd surroundings—the little leafy bower, the soft grasses of her bed, the unfamiliar prospect from the opening at her feet.

Slowly the circumstances of her position crept one by one into her mind. And then a great wonderment arose in her heart—a mighty wave of thankfulness and gratitude that though she had been in such terrible danger, yet she was unharmed.

She moved to the entrance of the shelter to look for Tarzan. He was gone; but this time no fear assailed her for she knew that he would return.

In the grass at the entrance to her bower she saw the imprint of his body where he had lain all night to guard her. She knew that the fact that he had been there was all that had permitted her to sleep in such peaceful security.

With him near, who could entertain fear? She wondered if there was another man on earth with whom a girl could feel so safe in the heart of this savage African jungle. Even the lions and panthers had no fears for her now.

She looked up to see his lithe form drop softly from a near-by tree. As he caught her eyes upon him his face lighted with that frank and radiant smile that had won her confidence the day before.

As he approached her Jane's heart beat faster and her eyes brightened as they had never done before at the approach of any man.

He had again been gathering fruit and this he laid at the entrance of her bower. Once more they sat down together to eat.

Jane commenced to wonder what his plans were. Would he take her back to the beach or would he keep her here? Suddenly she realized that the matter did not seem to give her much concern. Could it be that she did not care!

She began to comprehend, also, that she was entirely contented sitting here by the side of this smiling giant eating delicious fruit in a sylvan paradise far within the remote depths of an African jungle—that she was contented and very happy.

She could not understand it. Her reason told her that she should be torn by wild anxieties, weighted by dread fears, cast down by gloomy forebodings; but instead, her heart was singing and she was smiling into the answering face of the man beside her.

When they had finished their breakfast Tarzan went to her bower and recovered his knife. The girl had entirely forgotten it. She realized that it was because she had forgotten the fear that prompted her to accept it.

Motioning her to follow, Tarzan walked toward the trees at the edge of the arena, and taking her in one strong arm swung to the branches above.

The girl knew that he was taking her back to her people, and she could not understand the sudden feeling of loneliness and sorrow which crept over her.

For hours they swung slowly along.

Tarzan of the Apes did not hurry. He tried to draw out the sweet pleasure of that journey with those dear arms about his neck as long as possible, and so he went far south of the direct route to the beach.

Several times they halted for brief rests, which Tarzan did not need, and at noon they stopped for an hour at a little brook, where they quenched their thirst, and ate.

So it was nearly sunset when they came to the clearing, and Tarzan, dropping to the ground beside a great tree, parted the tall jungle grass and pointed out the little cabin to her.

She took him by the hand to lead him to it, that she might tell her father that this man had saved her from death and worse than death, that he had watched over her as carefully as a mother might have done.

But again the timidity of the wild thing in the face of human habitation swept over Tarzan of the Apes. He drew back, shaking his head.

The girl came close to him, looking up with pleading eyes. Somehow she could not bear the thought of his going back into the terrible jungle alone.

Still he shook his head, and finally he drew her to him very gently and stooped to kiss her, but first he looked into her eyes and waited to learn if she were pleased, or if she would repulse him.

Just an instant the girl hesitated, and then she realized the truth, and throwing her arms about his neck she drew his face to hers and kissed him—unashamed.

"I love you—I love you," she murmured.

From far in the distance came the faint sound of many guns. Tarzan and Jane raised their heads.

From the cabin came Mr. Philander and Esmeralda.

From where Tarzan and the girl stood they could not see the two vessels lying at anchor in the harbor.

Tarzan pointed toward the sounds, touched his breast and pointed again. She understood. He was going, and something told her that it was because he thought her people were in danger.

Again he kissed her.

"Come back to me," she whispered. "I shall wait for you—always."

He was gone—and Jane turned to walk across the clearing to the cabin.

Mr. Philander was the first to see her. It was dusk and Mr. Philander was very near sighted.

"Quickly, Esmeralda!" he cried. "Let us seek safety within; it is a lioness. Bless me!"

Esmeralda did not bother to verify Mr. Philander's vision. His tone was enough. She was within the cabin and had slammed and bolted the door before he had finished pronouncing her name. The "Bless me" was startled out of Mr. Philander by the discovery that Esmeralda, in the exuberance of her haste, had fastened him upon the same side of the door as was the close-approaching lioness.

He beat furiously upon the heavy portal.

"Esmeralda! Esmeralda!" he shrieked. "Let me in. I am being devoured by a lion."

Esmeralda thought that the noise upon the door was made by the lioness in her attempts to pursue her, so, after her custom, she fainted.

Mr. Philander cast a frightened glance behind him.

Horrors! The thing was quite close now. He tried to scramble up the side of the cabin, and succeeded in catching a fleeting hold upon the thatched roof.

For a moment he hung there, clawing with his feet like a cat on a clothesline, but presently a piece of the thatch came away, and Mr. Philander, preceding it, was precipitated upon his back.

At the instant he fell a remarkable item of natural history leaped to his mind. If one feigns death lions and lionesses are supposed to ignore one, according to Mr. Philander's faulty memory.

So Mr. Philander lay as he had fallen, frozen into the horrid semblance of death. As his arms and legs had been extended stiffly upward as he came to earth upon his back the attitude of death was anything but impressive.

Jane had been watching his antics in mild-eyed surprise. Now she laughed—a little choking gurgle of a laugh; but it was enough. Mr. Philander rolled over upon his side and peered about. At length he discovered her.

"Jane!" he cried. "Jane Porter. Bless me!"

He scrambled to his feet and rushed toward her. He could not believe that it was she, and alive.

"Bless me!" Where did you come from? Where in the world have you been? How—"

"Mercy, Mr. Philander," interrupted the girl, "I can never remember so many questions."

"Well, well," said Mr. Philander. "Bless me! I am so filled with surprise and exuberant delight at seeing you safe and well again that I scarcely know what I am saying, really. But come, tell me all that has happened to you."

THE VILLAGE OF TORTURE

As the little expedition of sailors toiled through the dense jungle searching for signs of Jane Porter, the futility of their venture became more and more apparent, but the grief of the old man and the hopeless eyes of the young Englishman prevented the kind hearted D'Arnot from turning back.

He thought that there might be a bare possibility of finding her body, or the remains of it, for he was positive that she had been devoured by some beast of prey. He deployed his men into a skirmish line from the point where Esmeralda had been found, and in this extended formation they pushed their way, sweating and panting, through the tangled vines and creepers. It was slow work. Noon found them but a few miles inland. They halted for a brief rest then, and after pushing on for a short distance further one of the men discovered a well-marked trail.

It was an old elephant track, and D'Arnot after consulting with Professor Porter and Clayton decided to follow it.

The path wound through the jungle in a northeasterly direction, and along it the column moved in single file.

Lieutenant D'Arnot was in the lead and moving at a quick pace, for the trail was comparatively open. Immediately behind him came Professor Porter, but as he could not keep pace with the younger man D'Arnot was a hundred yards in advance when suddenly a half dozen black warriors arose about him.

D'Arnot gave a warning shout to his column as the blacks closed on him, but before he could draw his revolver he had been pinioned and dragged into the jungle.

His cry had alarmed the sailors and a dozen of them sprang forward past Professor Porter, running up the trail to their officer's aid.

They did not know the cause of his outcry, only that it was a warning of danger ahead. They had rushed past the spot where D'Arnot had been seized when a spear hurled from the jungle transfixed one of the men, and then a volley of arrows fell among them.

Raising their rifles they fired into the underbrush in the direction from which the missiles had come.

By this time the balance of the party had come up, and volley after volley was fired toward the concealed foe. It was these shots that Tarzan and Jane Porter had heard.

Lieutenant Charpentier, who had been bringing up the rear of the column, now came running to the scene, and on hearing the details of the ambush ordered the men to follow him, and plunged into the tangled vegetation.

In an instant they were in a hand-to-hand fight with some fifty black warriors of Mbonga's village. Arrows and bullets flew thick and fast.

Queer African knives and French gun butts mingled for a moment in savage and bloody duels, but soon the natives fled into the jungle, leaving the Frenchmen to count their losses.

Four of the twenty were dead, a dozen others were wounded, and Lieutenant D'Arnot was missing. Night was falling rapidly, and their predicament was rendered doubly worse when they could not even find the elephant trail which they had been following.

There was but one thing to do, make camp where they were until daylight. Lieutenant Charpentier ordered a clearing made and a circular abatis of underbrush constructed about the camp.

This work was not completed until long after dark, the men building a huge fire in the center of the clearing to give them light to work by.

When all was safe as possible against attack of wild beasts and savage men, Lieutenant Charpentier placed sentries about the little camp and the tired and hungry men threw themselves upon the ground to sleep.

The groans of the wounded, mingled with the roaring and growling of the great beasts which the noise and firelight had attracted, kept sleep, except in its most fitful form, from the tired eyes. It was a sad and hungry party that lay through the long night praying for dawn.

The blacks who had seized D'Arnot had not waited to participate in the fight which followed, but instead had dragged their prisoner a little way through the jungle and then struck the trail further on beyond the scene of the fighting in which their fellows were engaged.

They hurried him along, the sounds of battle growing fainter and fainter as they drew away from the contestants until there suddenly broke upon D'Arnot's vision a good-sized clearing at one end of which stood a thatched and palisaded village.

It was now dusk, but the watchers at the gate saw the approaching trio and distinguished one as a prisoner ere they reached the portals.

A cry went up within the palisade. A great throng of women and children rushed out to meet the party.

And then began for the French officer the most terrifying experience which man can encounter upon earth—the reception of a white prisoner into a village of African cannibals.

To add to the fiendishness of their cruel savagery was the poignant memory of still crueler barbarities practiced upon them and theirs by the white officers of that arch hypocrite, Leopold II of Belgium, because of whose atrocities they had fled the Congo Free State—a pitiful remnant of what once had been a mighty tribe.

They fell upon D'Arnot tooth and nail, beating him with sticks and stones and tearing at him with claw-like hands. Every vestige of clothing was torn from him, and the merciless blows fell upon his bare and quivering flesh. But not once did the Frenchman cry out in pain. He breathed a silent prayer that he be quickly delivered from his torture.

But the death he prayed for was not to be so easily had. Soon the warriors beat the women away from their prisoner. He was to be saved for nobler sport than this, and the first wave of their passion having subsided they contented themselves with crying out taunts and insults and spitting upon him.

Presently they reached the center of the village. There D'Arnot was bound securely to the great post from which no live man had ever been released.

A number of the women scattered to their several huts to fetch pots and water, while others built a row of fires on which portions of the feast were to be boiled while the balance would be slowly dried in strips for future use, as they expected the other warriors to return with many prisoners. The festivities were delayed awaiting the return of the warriors who had remained to engage in the skirmish with the white men, so that it was quite late when all were in the village, and the dance of death commenced to circle around the doomed officer.

Half fainting from pain and exhaustion, D'Arnot watched from beneath half-closed lids what seemed but the vagary of delirium, or some horrid nightmare from which he must soon awake.

The bestial faces, daubed with color—the huge mouths and flabby hanging lips—the yellow teeth, sharp filed—the rolling, demon eyes—the shining naked bodies—the cruel spears. Surely no such creatures really existed upon earth—he must indeed be dreaming.

The savage, whirling bodies circled nearer. Now a spear sprang forth and touched his arm. The sharp pain and the feel of hot, trickling blood assured him of the awful reality of his hopeless position.

Another spear and then another touched him. He closed his eyes and held his teeth firm set—he would not cry out.

He was a soldier of France, and he would teach these beasts how an officer and a gentleman died.

Tarzan of the Apes needed no interpreter to translate the story of those distant shots. With Jane Porter's kisses still warm upon his lips he was swinging with incredible rapidity through the forest trees straight toward the village of Mbonga.

He was not interested in the location of the encounter, for he judged that that would soon be over. Those who were killed he could not aid, those who escaped would not need his assistance.

It was to those who had neither been killed or escaped that he hastened. And he knew that he would find them by the great post in the center of Mbonga village.

Many times had Tarzan seen Mbonga's black raiding parties return from the northward with prisoners, and always were the same scenes enacted about that grim stake, beneath the flaring light of many fires.

He knew, too, that they seldom lost much time before consummating the fiendish purpose of their captures. He doubted that he would arrive in time to do more than avenge.

On he sped. Night had fallen and he traveled high along the upper terrace where the gorgeous tropic moon lighted the dizzy pathway through the gently undulating branches of the tree tops.

Presently he caught the reflection of a distant blaze. It lay to the right of his path. It must be the light from the camp fire the two men had built before they were attacked—Tarzan knew nothing of the presence of the sailors.

So sure was Tarzan of his jungle knowledge that he did not turn from his course, but passed the glare at a distance of a half mile. It was the camp fire of the Frenchmen.

In a few minutes more Tarzan swung into the trees above Mbonga's village. Ah, he was not quite too late! Or, was he? He could not tell. The figure at the stake was very still, yet the black warriors were but pricking it.

Tarzan knew their customs. The death blow had not been struck. He could tell almost to a minute how far the dance had gone.

In another instant Mbonga's knife would sever one of the victim's ears—that would mark the beginning of the end, for very shortly after only a writhing mass of mutilated flesh would remain.

There would still be life in it, but death then would be the only charity it craved.

The stake stood forty feet from the nearest tree. Tarzan coiled his rope. Then there rose suddenly above the fiendish cries of the dancing demons the awful challenge of the ape-man.

The dancers halted as though turned to stone.

The rope sped with singing whir high above the heads of the blacks. It was quite invisible in the flaring lights of the camp fires.

D'Arnot opened his eyes. A huge black, standing directly before him, lunged backward as though felled by an invisible hand.

Struggling and shrieking, his body, rolling from side to side, moved quickly toward the shadows beneath the trees.

The blacks, their eyes protruding in horror, watched spellbound.

Once beneath the trees, the body rose straight into the air, and as it disappeared into the foliage above, the terrified negroes, screaming with fright, broke into a mad race for the village gate.

D'Arnot was left alone.

He was a brave man, but he had felt the short hairs bristle upon the nape of his neck when that uncanny cry rose upon the air.

As the writhing body of the black soared, as though by unearthly power, into the dense foliage of the forest, D'Arnot felt an icy shiver run along his spine, as though death had risen from a dark grave and laid a cold and clammy finger on his flesh.

As D'Arnot watched the spot where the body had entered the tree he heard the sounds of movement there.

The branches swayed as though under the weight of a man's body—there was a crash and the black came sprawling to earth again,—to lie very quietly where he had fallen.

Immediately after him came a white body, but this one alighted erect.

D'Arnot saw a clean-limbed young giant emerge from the shadows into the firelight and come quickly toward him.

What could it mean? Who could it be? Some new creature of torture and destruction, doubtless.

D'Arnot waited. His eyes never left the face of the advancing man. Nor did the other's frank, clear eyes waver beneath D'Arnot's fixed gaze.

D'Arnot was reassured, but still without much hope, though he felt that that face could not mask a cruel heart.

Without a word Tarzan of the Apes cut the bonds which held the Frenchman. Weak from suffering and loss of blood, he would have fallen but for the strong arm that caught him.

He felt himself lifted from the ground. There was a sensation as of flying, and then he lost consciousness.

THE SEARCH PARTY

When dawn broke upon the little camp of Frenchmen in the heart of the jungle it found a sad and disheartened group.

As soon as it was light enough to see their surroundings Lieutenant Charpentier sent men in groups of three in several directions to locate the trail, and in ten minutes it was found and the expedition was hurrying back toward the beach.

It was slow work, for they bore the bodies of six dead men, two more having succumbed during the night, and several of those who were wounded required support to move even very slowly.

Charpentier had decided to return to camp for reinforcements, and then make an attempt to track down the natives and rescue D'Arnot.

It was late in the afternoon when the exhausted men reached the clearing by the beach, but for two of them the return brought so great a happiness that all their suffering and heartbreaking grief was forgotten on the instant.

As the little party emerged from the jungle the first person that Professor Porter and Cecil Clayton saw was Jane, standing by the cabin door.

With a little cry of joy and relief she ran forward to greet them, throwing her arms about her father's neck and bursting into tears for the first time since they had been cast upon this hideous and adventurous shore.

Professor Porter strove manfully to suppress his own emotions, but the strain upon his nerves and weakened vitality were too much for him, and at length, burying his old face in the girl's shoulder, he sobbed quietly like a tired child.

Jane led him toward the cabin, and the Frenchmen turned toward the beach from which several of their fellows were advancing to meet them.

Clayton, wishing to leave father and daughter alone, joined the sailors and remained talking with the officers until their boat pulled away toward the cruiser whither Lieutenant Charpentier was bound to report the unhappy outcome of his adventure.

Then Clayton turned back slowly toward the cabin. His heart was filled with happiness. The woman he loved was safe.

He wondered by what manner of miracle she had been spared. To see her alive seemed almost unbelievable.

As he approached the cabin he saw Jane coming out. When she saw him she hurried forward to meet him.

"Jane!" he cried, "God has been good to us, indeed. Tell me how you escaped—what form Providence took to save you for—us."

He had never before called her by her given name. Forty-eight hours before it would have suffused Jane with a soft glow of pleasure to have heard that name from Clayton's lips—now it frightened her.

"Mr. Clayton," she said quietly, extending her hand, "first let me thank you for your chivalrous loyalty to my dear father. He has told me how noble and self-sacrificing you have been. How can we repay you!"

Clayton noticed that she did not return his familiar salutation, but he felt no misgivings on that score. She had been through so much. This was no time to force his love upon her, he quickly realized.

"I am already repaid," he said. "Just to see you and Professor Porter both safe, well, and together again. I do not think that I could much longer have endured the pathos of his quiet and uncomplaining grief.

"It was the saddest experience of my life, Miss Porter; and then, added to it, there was my own grief—the greatest I have ever known. But his was so hopeless—his was pitiful. It taught me that no love, not even that of a man for his wife may be so deep and terrible and self-sacrificing as the love of a father for his daughter."

The girl bowed her head. There was a question she wanted to ask, but it seemed almost sacrilegious in the face of the love of these two men and the terrible suffering they had endured while she sat laughing and happy beside a godlike creature of the forest, eating delicious fruits and looking with eyes of love into answering eyes.

But love is a strange master, and human nature is still stranger, so she asked her question.

"Where is the forest man who went to rescue you? Why did he not return?"

"I do not understand," said Clayton. "Whom do you mean?"

"He who has saved each of us—who saved me from the gorilla."

"Oh," cried Clayton, in surprise. "It was he who rescued you? You have not told me anything of your adventure, you know."

"But the wood man," she urged. "Have you not seen him? When we heard the shots in the jungle, very faint and far away, he left me. We had just reached the clearing, and he hurried off in the direction of the fighting. I know he went to aid you."

Her tone was almost pleading—her manner tense with suppressed emotion. Clayton could not but notice it, and he wondered, vaguely, why she was so deeply moved—so anxious to know the whereabouts of this strange creature.

Yet a feeling of apprehension of some impending sorrow haunted him, and in his breast, unknown to himself, was implanted the first germ of jealousy and suspicion of the ape-man, to whom he owed his life.

"We did not see him," he replied quietly. "He did not join us." And then after a moment of thoughtful pause: "Possibly he joined his own tribe—the men who attacked us." He did not know why he had said it, for he did not believe it.

The girl looked at him wide eyed for a moment.

"No!" she exclaimed vehemently, much too vehemently he thought. "It could not be. They were savages."

Clayton looked puzzled.

"He is a strange, half-savage creature of the jungle, Miss Porter. We know nothing of him. He neither speaks nor understands any European tongue—and his ornaments and weapons are those of the West Coast savages."

Clayton was speaking rapidly.

"There are no other human beings than savages within hundreds of miles, Miss Porter. He must belong to the tribes which attacked us, or to some other equally savage—he may even be a cannibal."

Jane blanched.

"I will not believe it," she half whispered. "It is not true. You shall see," she said, addressing Clayton, "that he will come back and that he will prove that you are wrong. You do not know him as I do. I tell you that he is a gentleman."

Clayton was a generous and chivalrous man, but something in the girl's breathless defense of the forest man stirred him to unreasoning jealousy, so that for the instant he forgot all that they owed to this wild demi-god, and he answered her with a half sneer upon his lip.

"Possibly you are right, Miss Porter," he said, "but I do not think that any of us need worry about our carrion-eating acquaintance. The chances are that he is some half-demented castaway who will forget us more quickly, but no more surely, than we shall forget him. He is only a beast of the jungle, Miss Porter."

The girl did not answer, but she felt her heart shrivel within her.

She knew that Clayton spoke merely what he thought, and for the first time she began to analyze the structure which supported her newfound love, and to subject its object to a critical examination.

Slowly she turned and walked back to the cabin. She tried to imagine her wood-god by her side in the saloon of an ocean liner. She saw him eating with his hands, tearing his food like a beast of prey, and wiping his greasy fingers upon his thighs. She shuddered.

She saw him as she introduced him to her friends—uncouth, illiterate—a boor; and the girl winced.

She had reached her room now, and as she sat upon the edge of her bed of ferns and grasses, with one hand resting upon her rising and falling bosom, she felt the hard outlines of the man's locket.

She drew it out, holding it in the palm of her hand for a moment with tear-blurred eyes bent upon it. Then she raised it to her lips, and crushing it there buried her face in the soft ferns, sobbing.

"Beast?" she murmured. "Then God make me a beast; for, man or beast, I am yours."

She did not see Clayton again that day. Esmeralda brought her supper to her, and she sent word to her father that she was suffering from the reaction following her adventure.

The next morning Clayton left early with the relief expedition in search of Lieutenant D'Arnot. There were two hundred armed men this time, with ten officers and two surgeons, and provisions for a week.

They carried bedding and hammocks, the latter for transporting their sick and wounded.

It was a determined and angry company—a punitive expedition as well as one of relief. They reached the sight of the skirmish of the previous expedition shortly after noon, for they were now traveling a known trail and no time was lost in exploring.

From there on the elephant-track led straight to Mbonga's village. It was but two o'clock when the head of the column halted upon the edge of the clearing.

Lieutenant Charpentier, who was in command, immediately sent a portion of his force through the jungle to the opposite side of the village. Another detachment was dispatched to a point before the village gate, while he remained with the balance upon the south side of the clearing.

It was arranged that the party which was to take its position to the north, and which would be the last to gain its station should commence the assault, and that their opening volley should be the signal for a concerted rush from all sides in an attempt to carry the village by storm at the first charge.

For half an hour the men with Lieutenant Charpentier crouched in the dense foliage of the jungle, waiting the signal. To them it seemed like hours. They could see natives in the fields, and others moving in and out of the village gate.

At length the signal came—a sharp rattle of musketry, and like one man, an answering volley tore from the jungle to the west and to the south.

The natives in the field dropped their implements and broke madly for the palisade. The French bullets mowed them down, and the French sailors bounded over their prostrate bodies straight for the village gate.

So sudden and unexpected the assault had been that the whites reached the gates before the frightened natives could bar them, and in another minute the village street was filled with armed men fighting hand to hand in an inextricable tangle.

For a few moments the blacks held their ground within the entrance to the street, but the revolvers, rifles and cutlasses of the Frenchmen crumpled the native spearmen and struck down the black archers with their bows halfdrawn.

Soon the battle turned to a wild rout, and then to a grim massacre; for the French sailors had seen bits of D'Arnot's uniform upon several of the black warriors who opposed them.

They spared the children and those of the women whom they were not forced to kill in self-defense, but when at length they stopped, parting, blood covered and sweating, it was because there lived to oppose them no single warrior of all the savage village of Mbonga.

Carefully they ransacked every hut and corner of the village, but no sign of D'Arnot could they find. They questioned the prisoners by signs, and finally one of the sailors who had served in the French Congo found that he could make them understand the bastard tongue that passes for language between the whites and the more degraded tribes of the coast, but even then they could learn nothing definite regarding the fate of D'Arnot.

Only excited gestures and expressions of fear could they obtain in response to their inquiries concerning their fellow; and at last they became convinced that these were but evidences of the guilt of these demons who had slaughtered and eaten their comrade two nights before.

At length all hope left them, and they prepared to camp for the night within the village. The prisoners were herded into three huts where they were heavily guarded. Sentries were posted at the barred gates, and finally the village was wrapped in the silence of slumber, except for the wailing of the native women for their dead.

The next morning they set out upon the return march. Their original intention had been to burn the village, but this idea was abandoned and the prisoners were left behind, weeping and moaning, but with roofs to cover them and a palisade for refuge from the beasts of the jungle.

Slowly the expedition retraced its steps of the preceding day. Ten loaded hammocks retarded its pace. In eight of them lay the more seriously wounded, while two swung beneath the weight of the dead.

Clayton and Lieutenant Charpentier brought up the rear of the column; the Englishman silent in respect for the other's grief, for D'Arnot and Charpentier had been inseparable friends since boyhood.

Clayton could not but realize that the Frenchman felt his grief the more keenly because D'Arnot's sacrifice had been so futile, since Jane had been rescued before D'Arnot had fallen into the hands of the savages, and again because the service in which he had lost his life had been outside his duty and for strangers and aliens; but when he spoke of it to Lieutenant Charpentier, the latter shook his head.

"No, Monsieur," he said, "D'Arnot would have chosen to die thus. I only grieve that I could not have died for him, or at least with him. I wish that you could have known him better, Monsieur. He was indeed an officer and a gentleman—a title conferred on many, but deserved by so few.

"He did not die futilely, for his death in the cause of a strange American girl will make us, his comrades, face our ends the more bravely, however they may come to us."

Clayton did not reply, but within him rose a new respect for Frenchmen which remained undimmed ever after.

It was quite late when they reached the cabin by the beach. A single shot before they emerged from the jungle had announced to those in camp as well as on the ship that the expedition had been too late—for it had been prearranged that when they came within a mile or two of camp one shot was to be fired to denote failure, or three for success, while two would have indicated that they had found no sign of either D'Arnot or his black captors.

So it was a solemn party that awaited their coming, and few words were spoken as the dead and wounded men were tenderly placed in boats and rowed silently toward the cruiser.

Clayton, exhausted from his five days of laborious marching through the jungle and from the effects of his two battles with the blacks, turned toward the cabin to seek a mouthful of food and then the comparative ease of his bed of grasses after two nights in the jungle.

By the cabin door stood Jane.

"The poor lieutenant?" she asked. "Did you find no trace of him?"

"We were too late, Miss Porter," he replied sadly.

"Tell me. What had happened?" she asked.

"I cannot, Miss Porter, it is too horrible."

"You do not mean that they had tortured him?" she whispered.

"We do not know what they did to him *before* they killed him," he answered, his face drawn with fatigue and the sorrow he felt for poor D'Arnot and he emphasized the word before.

"*Before* they killed him! What do you mean? They are not—? They are not—?"

She was thinking of what Clayton had said of the forest man's probable relationship to this tribe and she could not frame the awful word.

"Yes, Miss Porter, they were—cannibals," he said, almost bitterly, for to him too had suddenly come the thought of the forest man, and the strange, unaccountable jealousy he had felt two days before swept over him once more.

And then in sudden brutality that was as unlike Clayton as courteous consideration is unlike an ape, he blurted out:

"When your forest god left you he was doubtless hurrying to the feast."

He was sorry ere the words were spoken though he did not know how cruelly they had cut the girl. His regret was for his baseless disloyalty to one who had saved the lives of every member of his party, and offered harm to none.

The girl's head went high.

"There could be but one suitable reply to your assertion, Mr. Clayton," she said icily, "and I regret that I am not a man, that I might make it." She turned quickly and entered the cabin.

Clayton was an Englishman, so the girl had passed quite out of sight before he deduced what reply a man would have made.

"Upon my word," he said ruefully, "she called me a liar. And I fancy I jolly well deserved it," he added thoughtfully. "Clayton, my boy, I know you are tired out and unstrung, but that's no reason why you should make an ass of yourself. You'd better go to bed."

But before he did so he called gently to Jane upon the opposite side of the sailcloth partition, for he wished to apologize, but he might as well have addressed the Sphinx. Then he wrote upon a piece of paper and shoved it beneath the partition.

Jane saw the little note and ignored it, for she was very angry and hurt and mortified, but—she was a woman, and so eventually she picked it up and read it.

My Dear Miss Porter:

I had no reason to insinuate what I did. My only excuse is that my nerves must be unstrung—which is no excuse at all.

Please try and think that I did not say it. I am very sorry. I would not have hurt *you*, above all others in the world. Say that you forgive me.

Wm. Cecil Clayton.

"He did think it or he never would have said it," reasoned the girl, "but it cannot be true—oh, I know it is not true!"

One sentence in the letter frightened her: "I would not have hurt *you* above all others in the world."

A week ago that sentence would have filled her with delight, now it depressed her.

She wished she had never met Clayton. She was sorry that she had ever seen the forest god. No, she was glad. And there was that other note she had found in the grass before the cabin the day after her return from the jungle, the love note signed by Tarzan of the Apes.

Who could be this new suitor? If he were another of the wild denizens of this terrible forest what might he not do to claim her?

"Esmeralda! Wake up," she cried.

"You make me so irritable, sleeping there peacefully when you know perfectly well that the world is filled with sorrow."

"Gaberelle!" screamed Esmeralda, sitting up. "What is it now? A hipponocerous? Where is he, Miss Jane?"

"Nonsense, Esmeralda, there is nothing. Go back to sleep. You are bad enough asleep, but you are infinitely worse awake."

"Yes honey, but what's the matter with you, precious? You acts sort of disgranulated this evening."

"Oh, Esmeralda, I'm just plain ugly to-night," said the girl. "Don't pay any attention to me—that's a dear."

"Yes, honey; now you go right to sleep. Your nerves are all on edge. What with all these ripotamuses and man eating geniuses that Mister Philander been telling about—Lord, it ain't no wonder we all get nervous prosecution."

Jane crossed the little room, laughing, and kissing the faithful woman, bid Esmeralda good night.

BROTHER MEN

When D'Arnot regained consciousness, he found himself lying upon a bed of soft ferns and grasses beneath a little "A" shaped shelter of boughs.

At his feet an opening looked out upon a green sward, and at a little distance beyond was the dense wall of jungle and forest.

He was very lame and sore and weak, and as full consciousness returned he felt the sharp torture of many cruel wounds and the dull aching of every bone and muscle in his body as a result of the hideous beating he had received.

Even the turning of his head caused him such excruciating agony that he lay still with closed eyes for a long time.

He tried to piece out the details of his adventure prior to the time he lost consciousness to see if they would explain his present whereabouts—he wondered if he were among friends or foes.

At length he recollected the whole hideous scene at the stake, and finally recalled the strange white figure in whose arms he had sunk into oblivion.

D'Arnot wondered what fate lay in store for him now. He could neither see nor hear any signs of life about him.

The incessant hum of the jungle—the rustling of millions of leaves—the buzz of insects—the voices of the birds and monkeys seemed blended into a strangely soothing purr, as though he lay apart, far from the myriad life whose sounds came to him only as a blurred echo.

At length he fell into a quiet slumber, nor did he awake again until afternoon.

Once more he experienced the strange sense of utter bewilderment that had marked his earlier awakening, but soon he recalled the recent past, and looking through the opening at his feet he saw the figure of a man squatting on his haunches.

The broad, muscular back was turned toward him, but, tanned though it was, D'Arnot saw that it was the back of a white man, and he thanked God.

The Frenchman called faintly. The man turned, and rising, came toward the shelter. His face was very handsome—the handsomest, thought D'Arnot, that he had ever seen.

Stooping, he crawled into the shelter beside the wounded officer, and placed a cool hand upon his forehead.

D'Arnot spoke to him in French, but the man only shook his head—sadly, it seemed to the Frenchman.

Then D'Arnot tried English, but still the man shook his head. Italian, Spanish and German brought similar discouragement.

D'Arnot knew a few words of Norwegian, Russian, Greek, and also had a smattering of the language of one of the West Coast negro tribes—the man denied them all.

After examining D'Arnot's wounds the man left the shelter and disappeared. In half an hour he was back with fruit and a hollow gourd-like vegetable filled with water.

D'Arnot drank and ate a little. He was surprised that he had no fever. Again he tried to converse with his strange nurse, but the attempt was useless.

Suddenly the man hastened from the shelter only to return a few minutes later with several pieces of bark and—wonder of wonders—a lead pencil.

Squatting beside D'Arnot he wrote for a minute on the smooth inner surface of the bark; then he handed it to the Frenchman.

D'Arnot was astonished to see, in plain print-like characters, a message in English:

I am Tarzan of the Apes. Who are you? Can you read this language?

D'Arnot seized the pencil—then he stopped. This strange man wrote English—evidently he was an Englishman.

"Yes," said D'Arnot, "I read English. I speak it also. Now we may talk. First let me thank you for all that you have done for me."

The man only shook his head and pointed to the pencil and the bark.

"*Mon Dieu!*" cried D'Arnot. "If you are English why is it then that you cannot speak English?"

And then in a flash it came to him—the man was a mute, possibly a deaf mute.

So D'Arnot wrote a message on the bark, in English.

I am Paul d'Arnot, Lieutenant in the navy of France. I thank you for what you have done for me. You have saved my life, and all that I have is yours. May I ask how it is that one who writes English does not speak it?

Tarzan's reply filled D'Arnot with still greater wonder:

I speak only the language of my tribe—the great apes who were Kerchak's; and a little of the languages of Tantor, the elephant, and Numa, the lion, and of the other folks of the jungle I understand. With a human being I have never spoken, except once with Jane Porter, by signs. This is the first time I have spoken with another of my kind through written words.

D'Arnot was mystified. It seemed incredible that there lived upon earth a full-grown man who had never spoken with a fellow man, and still more preposterous that such a one could read and write.

He looked again at Tarzan's message—" except once, with Jane Porter." That was the American girl who had been carried into the jungle by a gorilla.

A sudden light commenced to dawn on D'Arnot—this then was the "gorilla." He seized the pencil and wrote:

Where is Jane Porter?

And Tarzan replied, below:

Back with her people in the cabin of Tarzan of the Apes.

She is not dead then? Where was she? What happened to her?

She is not dead. She was taken by Terkoz to be his wife; but Tarzan of the Apes took her away from Terkoz and killed him before he could harm her.

None in all the jungle may face Tarzan of the Apes in battle, and live. I am Tarzan of the Apes—mighty fighter.

D'Arnot wrote:

I am glad she is safe. It pains me to write, I will rest a while.

And then Tarzan:

Yes, rest. When you are well I shall take you back to your people.

For many days D'Arnot lay upon his bed of soft ferns. The second day a fever had come and D'Arnot thought that it meant infection and he knew that he would die.

An idea came to him. He wondered why he had not thought of it before.

He called Tarzan and indicated by signs that he would write, and when Tarzan had fetched the bark and pencil, D'Arnot wrote:

Can you go to my people and lead them here? I will write a message that you may take to them, and they will follow you.

Tarzan shook his head and taking the bark, wrote:

I had thought of that—the first day; but I dared not. The great apes come often to this spot, and if they found you here, wounded and alone, they would kill you.

D'Arnot turned on his side and closed his eyes. He did not wish to die; but he felt that he was going, for the fever was mounting higher and higher. That night he lost consciousness.

For three days he was in delirium, and Tarzan sat beside him and bathed his head and hands and washed his wounds.

On the fourth day the fever broke as suddenly as it had come, but it left D'Arnot a shadow of his former self, and very weak. Tarzan had to lift him that he might drink from the gourd.

The fever had not been the result of infection, as D'Arnot had thought, but one of those that commonly attack whites in the jungles of Africa, and either kill or leave them as suddenly as D'Arnot's had left him.

Two days later, D'Arnot was tottering about the amphitheater, Tarzan's strong arm about him to keep him from falling.

They sat beneath the shade of a great tree, and Tarzan found some smooth bark that they might converse.

D'Arnot wrote the first message:

What can I do to repay you for all that you have done for me?

And Tarzan, in reply:

Teach me to speak the language of men.

And so D'Arnot commenced at once, pointing out familiar objects and repeating their names in French, for he thought that it would be easier to teach this man his own language, since he understood it himself best of all.

It meant nothing to Tarzan, of course, for he could not tell one language from another, so when he pointed to the word man which he had printed upon a piece of bark he learned from D'Arnot that it was pronounced *homme*, and in the same way he was taught to pronounce ape, *Singe* and tree, *Arbre*.

He was a most eager student, and in two more days had mastered so much French that he could speak little sentences such as: "That is a tree," "this is grass," "I am hungry," and the like, but D'Arnot found that it was difficult to teach him the French construction upon a foundation of English.

The Frenchman wrote little lessons for him in English and had Tarzan repeat them in French, but as a literal translation was usually very poor French Tarzan was often confused.

D'Arnot realized now that he had made a mistake, but it seemed too late to go back and do it all over again and force Tarzan to unlearn all that he had learned, especially as they were rapidly approaching a point where they would be able to converse.

On the third day after the fever broke Tarzan wrote a message asking D'Arnot if he felt strong enough to be carried back to the cabin. Tarzan was as anxious to go as D'Arnot, for he longed to see Jane again.

It had been hard for him to remain with the Frenchman all these days for that very reason, and that he had unselfishly done so spoke more glowingly of his nobility of character than even did his rescuing the French officer from Mbonga's clutches.

D'Arnot, only too willing to attempt the journey, wrote:

But you cannot carry me all the distance through this tangled forest.

Tarzan laughed.

"*Mais oui*," he said, and D'Arnot laughed aloud to hear the phrase that he used so often glide from Tarzan's tongue.

So they set out, D'Arnot marveling as had Clayton and Jane at the wondrous strength and agility of the apeman.

Mid-afternoon brought them to the clearing, and as Tarzan dropped to earth from the branches of the last tree his heart leaped and bounded against his ribs in anticipation of seeing Jane so soon again.

No one was in sight outside the cabin, and D'Arnot was perplexed to note that neither the cruiser nor the Arrow was at anchor in the bay.

An atmosphere of loneliness pervaded the spot, which caught suddenly at both men as they strode toward the cabin.

Neither spoke, yet both knew before they opened the closed door what they would find beyond.

Tarzan lifted the latch and pushed the great door in upon its wooden hinges. It was as they had feared. The cabin was deserted.

The men turned and looked at one another. D'Arnot knew that his people thought him dead; but Tarzan thought only of the woman who had kissed him in love and now had fled from him while he was serving one of her people.

A great bitterness rose in his heart. He would go away, far into the jungle and join his tribe. Never would he see one of his own kind again, nor could he bear the thought of returning to the cabin. He would leave that forever behind him with the great hopes he had nursed there of finding his own race and becoming a man among men.

And the Frenchman? D'Arnot? What of him? He could get along as Tarzan had. Tarzan did not want to see him more. He wanted to get away from everything that might remind him of Jane.

As Tarzan stood upon the threshold brooding, D'Arnot had entered the cabin. Many comforts he saw that had been left behind. He recognized numerous articles from the cruiser —a camp oven, some kitchen utensils, a rifle and many rounds of ammunition, canned foods, blankets, two chairs and a cot—and several books and periodicals, mostly American.

"They must intend returning," thought D'Arnot.

He walked over to the table that John Clayton had built so many years before to serve as a desk, and on it he saw two notes addressed to Tarzan of the Apes.

One was in a strong masculine hand and was unsealed. The other, in a woman's hand, was sealed.

"Here are two messages for you, Tarzan of the Apes," cried D'Arnot, turning toward the door; but his companion was not there.

D'Arnot walked to the door and looked out. Tarzan was nowhere in sight. He called aloud but there was no response.

"*Mon Dieu!*" exclaimed D'Arnot, "he has left me. I feel it. He has gone back into his jungle and left me here alone."

And then he remembered the look on Tarzan's face when they had discovered that the cabin was empty—such a look as the hunter sees in the eyes of the wounded deer he has wantonly brought down.

The man had been hard hit—D'Arnot realized it now— but why? He could not understand.

The Frenchman looked about him. The loneliness and the horror of the place commenced to get on his nerves—already weakened by the ordeal of suffering and sickness he had passed through.

To be left here alone beside this awful jungle—never to hear a human voice or see a human face—in constant dread of savage beasts and more terribly savage men—a prey to solitude and hopelessness. It was awful.

And far to the east Tarzan of the Apes was speeding through the middle terrace back to his tribe. Never had he traveled with such reckless speed. He felt that he was running away from himself—that by hurtling through the forest like a frightened squirrel he was escaping from his own thoughts. But no matter how fast he went he found them always with him.

He passed above the sinuous body of Sabor, the lioness, going in the opposite direction—toward the cabin, thought Tarzan.

What could D'Arnot do against Sabor—or if Bolgani, the gorilla, should come upon him—or Numa, the lion, or cruel Sheeta?

Tarzan paused in his flight.

"What are you, Tarzan?" he asked aloud. "An ape or a man?"

"If you are an ape you will do as the apes would do— leave one of your kind to die in the jungle if it suited your whim to go elsewhere.

"If you are a man, you will return to protect your kind. You will not run away from one of your own people, because one of them has run away from you."

D'Arnot closed the cabin door. He was very nervous. Even brave men, and D'Arnot was a brave man, are sometimes frightened by solitude.

He loaded one of the rifles and placed it within easy reach. Then he went to the desk and took up the unsealed letter addressed to Tarzan.

Possibly it contained word that his people had but left the beach temporarily. He felt that it would be no breach of ethics to read this letter, so he took the enclosure from the envelope and read:

To Tarzan of the Apes:
We thank you for the use of your cabin, and are sorry that you did not permit us the pleasure of seeing and thanking you in person.

We have harmed nothing, but have left many things for you which may add to your comfort and safety here in your lonely home.

If you know the strange white man who saved our lives so many times, and brought us food, and if you can converse with him, thank him, also, for his kindness.

We sail within the hour, never to return; but we wish you and that other jungle friend to know that we shall always thank you for what you did for strangers on your shore, and that we should have done infinitely more to reward you both had you given us the opportunity. Very respectfully,

Wm. Cecil Clayton.

"'Never to return,'" muttered D'Arnot, and threw himself face downward upon the cot.

An hour later he started up listening. Something was at the door trying to enter.

D'Arnot reached for the loaded rifle and placed it to his shoulder.

Dusk was falling, and the interior of the cabin was very dark; but the man could see the latch moving from its place.

He felt his hair rising upon his scalp.

Gently the door opened until a thin crack showed something standing just beyond.

D'Arnot sighted along the blue barrel at the crack of the door—and then he pulled the trigger.

LOST TREASURE

When the expedition returned, following their fruitless endeavor to succor D'Arnot, Captain Dufranne was anxious to steam away as quickly as possible, and all save Jane had acquiesced.

"No," she said, determinedly, "I shall not go, nor should you, for there are two friends in that jungle who will come out of it some day expecting to find us awaiting them.

"Your officer, Captain Dufranne, is one of them, and the forest man who has saved the lives of every member of my father's party is the other.

"He left me at the edge of the jungle two days ago to hasten to the aid of my father and Mr. Clayton, as he thought, and he has stayed to rescue Lieutenant D'Arnot; of that you may be sure.

"Had he been too late to be of service to the lieutenant he would have been back before now—the fact that he is not back is sufficient proof to me that he is delayed because Lieutenant D'Arnot is wounded, or he has had to follow his captors further than the village which your sailors attacked."

"But poor D'Arnot's uniform and all his belongings were found in that village, Miss Porter," argued the captain, "and the natives showed great excitement when questioned as to the white man's fate."

"Yes, Captain, but they did not admit that he was dead and as for his clothes and accouterments being in their possession—why more civilized peoples than these poor savage negroes strip their prisoners of every article of value whether they intend killing them or not.

"Even the soldiers of my own dear South looted not only the living but the dead. It is strong circumstantial evidence, I will admit, but it is not positive proof."

"Possibly your forest man, himself was captured or killed by the savages," suggested Captain Dufranne.

The girl laughed.

"You do not know him," she replied, a little thrill of pride setting her nerves a-tingle at the thought that she spoke of her own.

"I admit that he would be worth waiting for, this superman of yours," laughed the captain. "I most certainly should like to see him."

"Then wait for him, my dear captain," urged the girl, "for I intend doing so."

The Frenchman would have been a very much surprised man could he have interpreted the true meaning of the girl's words.

They had been walking from the beach toward the cabin as they talked, and now they joined a little group sitting on camp stools in the shade of a great tree beside the cabin.

Professor Porter was there, and Mr. Philander and Clayton, with Lieutenant Charpentier and two of his brother officers, while Esmeralda hovered in the background, ever and anon venturing opinions and comments with the freedom of an old and much-indulged family servant.

The officers arose and saluted as their superior approached, and Clayton surrendered his camp stool to Jane.

"We were just discussing poor Paul's fate," said Captain Dufranne. "Miss Porter insists that we have no absolute proof of his death—nor have we. And on the other hand she maintains that the continued absence of your omnipotent jungle friend indicates that D'Arnot is still in need of his services, either because he is wounded, or still is a prisoner in a more distant native village."

"It has been suggested," ventured Lieutenant Charpentier, "that the wild man may have been a member of the tribe of blacks who attacked our party—that he was hastening to aid *them*—his own people."

Jane shot a quick glance at Clayton.

"It seems vastly more reasonable," said Professor Porter.

"I do not agree with you," objected Mr. Philander. "He had ample opportunity to harm us himself, or to lead his people against us. Instead, during our long residence here, he has been uniformly consistent in his role of protector and provider."

"That is true," interjected Clayton, "yet we must not overlook the fact that except for himself the only human beings within hundreds of miles are savage cannibals. He was armed precisely as are they, which indicates that he has maintained relations of some nature with them, and the fact that he is but one against possibly thousands suggests that these relations could scarcely have been other than friendly."

"It seems improbable then that he is not connected with them," remarked the captain; "possibly a member of this tribe."

"Otherwise," added another of the officers, "how could he have lived a sufficient length of time among the savage denizens of the jungle, brute and human, to have become proficient in woodcraft, or in the use of African weapons."

"You are judging him according to your own standards, gentlemen," said Jane. "An ordinary white man such as any of you—pardon me, I did not mean just that—rather, a white man above the ordinary in physique and intelligence could never, I grant you, have lived a year alone and naked in this tropical jungle; but this man not only surpasses the average white man in strength and agility, but as far transcends our trained athletes and 'strong men' as they surpass a day-old babe; and his courage and ferocity in battle are those of the wild beast."

"He has certainly won a loyal champion, Miss Porter," said Captain Dufranne, laughing. "I am sure that there be none of us here but would willingly face death a hundred times in its most terrifying forms to deserve the tributes of one even half so loyal—or so beautiful."

"You would not wonder that I defend him," said the girl, "could you have seen him as I saw him, battling in my behalf with that huge hairy brute.

"Could you have seen him charge the monster as a bull might charge a grizzly—absolutely without sign of fear or hesitation—you would have believed him more than human.

"Could you have seen those mighty muscles knotting under the brown skin—could you have seen them force back those awful fangs—you too would have thought him invincible.

"And could you have seen the chivalrous treatment which he accorded a strange girl of a strange race, you would feel the same absolute confidence in him that I feel."

"You have won your suit, my fair pleader," cried the captain. "This court finds the defendant not guilty, and the cruiser shall wait a few days longer that he may have an opportunity to come and thank the divine Portia."

"For the Lord's sake honey," cried Esmeralda. "You all don't mean to tell ME that you're going to stay right here in this here land of carnivable animals when you all got the opportunity to escapade on that boat? Don't you tell me *that*, honey."

"Why, Esmeralda! You should be ashamed of yourself," cried Jane. "Is this any way to show your gratitude to the man who saved your life twice?"

"Well, Miss Jane, that's all jest as you say; but that there forest man never did save us to stay here. He done save us so we all could get *away* from here. I expect he be mighty peevish when he find we ain't got no more sense than to stay right here after he done give us the chance to get away.

"I hoped I'd never have to sleep in this here geological garden another night and listen to all them lonesome noises that come out of that jumble after dark."

"I don't blame you a bit, Esmeralda," said Clayton, "and you certainly did hit it off right when you called them 'lonesome' noises. I never have been able to find the right word for them but that's it, don't you know, lonesome noises."

"You and Esmeralda had better go and live on the cruiser," said Jane, in fine scorn. "What would you think if you *had* to live all of your life in that jungle as our forest man has done?"

"I'm afraid I'd be a blooming bounder as a wild man," laughed Clayton, ruefully. "Those noises at night make the hair on my head bristle. I suppose that I should be ashamed to admit it, but it's the truth."

"I don't know about that," said Lieutenant Charpentier. "I never thought much about fear and that sort of thing—never tried to determine whether I was a coward or brave man; but the other night as we lay in the jungle there after poor D'Arnot was taken, and those jungle noises rose and fell around us I began to think that I was a coward indeed. It was not the roaring and growling of the big beasts that affected me so much as it was the stealthy noises—the ones that you heard suddenly close by and then listened vainly for a repetition of—the unaccountable sounds as of a great body moving almost noiselessly, and the knowledge that you didn't *know* how close it was, or whether it were creeping closer after you ceased to hear it? It was those noises—and the eyes.

"*Mon Dieu!* I shall see them in the dark forever—the eyes that you see, and those that you don't see, but feel—ah, they are the worst."

All were silent for a moment, and then Jane spoke.

"And he is out there," she said, in an awe-hushed whisper. "Those eyes will be glaring at him to-night, and at your comrade Lieutenant D'Arnot. Can you leave them, gentlemen, without at least rendering them the passive succor which remaining here a few days longer might insure them?"

"Tut, tut, child," said Professor Porter. "Captain Dufranne is willing to remain, and for my part I am perfectly willing, perfectly willing—as I always have been to humor your childish whims."

"We can utilize the morrow in recovering the chest, Professor," suggested Mr. Philander.

"Quite so, quite so, Mr. Philander, I had almost forgotten the treasure," exclaimed Professor Porter. "Possibly we can borrow some men from Captain Dufranne to assist us, and one of the prisoners to point out the location of the chest."

"Most assuredly, my dear Professor, we are all yours to command," said the captain.

And so it was arranged that on the next day Lieutenant Charpentier was to take a detail of ten men, and one of the mutineers of the Arrow as a guide, and unearth the treasure; and that the cruiser would remain for a full week in the little harbor. At the end of that time it was to be assumed that D'Arnot was truly dead, and that the forest man would not return while they remained. Then the two vessels were to leave with all the party.

Professor Porter did not accompany the treasure-seekers on the following day, but when he saw them returning empty-handed toward noon, he hastened forward to meet them —his usual preoccupied indifference entirely vanished, and in its place a nervous and excited manner.

"Where is the treasure?" he cried to Clayton, while yet a hundred feet separated them.

Clayton shook his head.

"Gone," he said, as he neared the professor.

"Gone! It cannot be. Who could have taken it?" cried Professor Porter.

"God only knows, Professor," replied Clayton. "We might have thought the fellow who guided us was lying about the location, but his surprise and consternation on finding no chest beneath the body of the murdered Snipes were too real to be feigned. And then our spades showed us that *something* had been buried beneath the corpse, for a hole had been there and it had been filled with loose earth."

"But who could have taken it?" repeated Professor Porter.

"Suspicion might naturally fall on the men of the cruiser," said Lieutenant Charpentier, "but for the fact that sub-lieutenant Janviers here assures me that no men have had shore leave—that none has been on shore since we anchored here except under command of an officer. I do not know that you would suspect our men, but I am glad that there is now no chance for suspicion to fall on them," he concluded.

"It would never have occurred to me to suspect the men to whom we owe so much," replied Professor Porter, graciously. "I would as soon suspect my dear Clayton here, or Mr. Philander."

The Frenchmen smiled, both officers and sailors. It was plain to see that a burden had been lifted from their minds.

"The treasure has been gone for some time," continued Clayton. "In fact the body fell apart as we lifted it, which indicates that whoever removed the treasure did so while the corpse was still fresh, for it was intact when we first uncovered it."

"There must have been several in the party," said Jane, who had joined them. "You remember that it took four men to carry it."

"By jove!" cried Clayton. "That's right. It must have been done by a party of blacks. Probably one of them saw the men bury the chest and then returned immediately after with a party of his friends, and carried it off."

"Speculation is futile," said Professor Porter sadly. "The chest is gone. We shall never see it again, nor the treasure that was in it."

Only Jane knew what the loss meant to her father, and none there knew what it meant to her.

Six days later Captain Dufranne announced that they would sail early on the morrow.

Jane would have begged for a further reprieve, had it not been that she too had begun to believe that her forest lover would return no more.

In spite of herself she began to entertain doubts and fears. The reasonableness of the arguments of these disinterested French officers commenced to convince her against her will.

That he was a cannibal she would not believe, but that he was an adopted member of some savage tribe at length seemed possible to her.

She would not admit that he could be dead. It was impossible to believe that that perfect body, so filled with triumphant life, could ever cease to harbor the vital spark—as soon believe that immortality were dust.

As Jane permitted herself to harbor these thoughts, others equally unwelcome forced themselves upon her.

If he belonged to some savage tribe he had a savage wife —a dozen of them perhaps—and wild, half-caste children. The girl shuddered, and when they told her that the cruiser would sail on the morrow she was almost glad.

It was she, though, who suggested that arms, ammunition, supplies and comforts be left behind in the cabin, ostensibly for that intangible personality who had signed himself Tarzan of the Apes, and for D'Arnot should he still be living, but really, she hoped, for her forest god—even though his feet should prove of clay.

And at the last minute she left a message for him, to be transmitted by Tarzan of the Apes.

She was the last to leave the cabin, returning on some trivial pretext after the others had started for the boat.

She kneeled down beside the bed in which she had spent so many nights, and offered up a prayer for the safety of her primeval man, and crushing his locket to her lips she murmured:

"I love you, and because I love you I believe in you. But if I did not believe, still should I love. Had you come back for me, and had there been no other way, I would have gone into the jungle with you—forever."

THE OUTPOST OF THE WORLD

With the report of his gun D'Arnot saw the door fly open and the figure of a man pitch headlong within onto the cabin floor.

The Frenchman in his panic raised his gun to fire again into the prostrate form, but suddenly in the half dusk of the open door he saw that the man was white and in another instant realized that he had shot his friend and protector, Tarzan of the Apes.

With a cry of anguish D'Arnot sprang to the ape-man's side, and kneeling, lifted the latter's head in his arms—calling Tarzan's name aloud.

There was no response, and then D'Arnot placed his ear above the man's heart. To his joy he heard its steady beating beneath.

Carefully he lifted Tarzan to the cot, and then, after closing and bolting the door, he lighted one of the lamps and examined the wound.

The bullet had struck a glancing blow upon the skull. There was an ugly flesh wound, but no signs of a fracture of the skull.

D'Arnot breathed a sigh of relief, and went about bathing the blood from Tarzan's face.

Soon the cool water revived him, and presently he opened his eyes to look in questioning surprise at D'Arnot.

The latter had bound the wound with pieces of cloth, and as he saw that Tarzan had regained consciousness he arose and going to the table wrote a message, which he handed to the ape-man, explaining the terrible mistake he had made and how thankful he was that the wound was not more serious.

Tarzan, after reading the message, sat on the edge of the couch and laughed.

"It is nothing," he said in French, and then, his vocabulary failing him, he wrote:

You should have seen what Bolgani did to me, and Kerchak, and Terkoz, before I killed them—then you would laugh at such a little scratch.

D'Arnot handed Tarzan the two messages that had been left for him.

Tarzan read the first one through with a look of sorrow on his face. The second one he turned over and over, searching for an opening—he had never seen a sealed envelope before. At length he handed it to D'Arnot.

The Frenchman had been watching him, and knew that Tarzan was puzzled over the envelope. How strange it seemed that to a full-grown white man an envelope was a mystery. D'Arnot opened it and handed the letter back to Tarzan.

Sitting on a camp stool the ape-man spread the written sheet before him and read:

To Tarzan of the Apes:

Before I leave let me add my thanks to those of Mr. Clayton for the kindness you have shown in permitting us the use of your cabin.

That you never came to make friends with us has been a great regret to us. We should have liked so much to have seen and thanked our host.

There is another I should like to thank also, but he did not come back, though I cannot believe that he is dead.

I do not know his name. He is the great white giant who wore the diamond locket upon his breast.

If you know him and can speak his language carry my thanks to him, and tell him that I waited seven days for him to return.

Tell him, also, that in my home in America, in the city of Baltimore, there will always be a welcome for him if he cares to come.

I found a note you wrote me lying among the leaves beneath a tree near the cabin. I do not know how you learned to love me, who have never spoken to me, and I am very sorry if it is true, for I have already given my heart to another.

But know that I am always your friend,
Jane Porter.

Tarzan sat with gaze fixed upon the floor for nearly an hour. It was evident to him from the notes that they did not know that he and Tarzan of the Apes were one and the same.

"I have given my heart to another," he repeated over and over again to himself.

Then she did not love him! How could she have pretended love, and raised him to such a pinnacle of hope only to cast him down to such utter depths of despair!

Maybe her kisses were only signs of friendship. How did he know, who knew nothing of the customs of human beings?

Suddenly he arose, and, bidding D'Arnot good night as he had learned to do, threw himself upon the couch of ferns that had been Jane Porter's.

D'Arnot extinguished the lamp, and lay down upon the cot.

For a week they did little but rest, D'Arnot coaching Tarzan in French. At the end of that time the two men could converse quite easily.

One night, as they were sitting within the cabin before retiring, Tarzan turned to D'Arnot.

"Where is America?" he said.

D'Arnot pointed toward the northwest.

"Many thousands of miles across the ocean," he replied. "Why?"

"I am going there."

D'Arnot shook his head.

"It is impossible, my friend," he said.

Tarzan rose, and, going to one of the cupboards, returned with a well-thumbed geography.

Turning to a map of the world, he said:

"I have never quite understood all this; explain it to me, please."

When D'Arnot had done so, showing him that the blue represented all the water on the earth, and the bits of other colors the continents and islands, Tarzan asked him to point out the spot where they now were.

D'Arnot did so.

"Now point out America," said Tarzan.

And as D'Arnot placed his finger upon North America, Tarzan smiled and laid his palm upon the page, spanning the great ocean that lay between the two continents.

"You see it is not so very far," he said; "scarce the width of my hand."

D'Arnot laughed. How could he make the man understand?

Then he took a pencil and made a tiny point upon the shore of Africa.

"This little mark," he said, "is many times larger upon this map than your cabin is upon the earth. Do you see now how very far it is?"

Tarzan thought for a long time.

"Do any white men live in Africa?" he asked.

"Yes."

"Where are the nearest?"

D'Arnot pointed out a spot on the shore just north of them.

"So close?" asked Tarzan, in surprise.

"Yes," said D'Arnot; "but it is not close."

"Have they big boats to cross the ocean?"

"Yes."

"We shall go there to-morrow," announced Tarzan.

Again D'Arnot smiled and shook his head.

"It is too far. We should die long before we reached them."

"Do you wish to stay here then forever?" asked Tarzan.

"No," said D'Arnot.

"Then we shall start to-morrow. I do not like it here longer. I should rather die than remain here."

"Well," answered D'Arnot, with a shrug, "I do not know, my friend, but that I also would rather die than remain here. If you go, I shall go with you."

"It is settled then," said Tarzan. "I shall start for America to-morrow."

"How will you get to America without money?" asked D'Arnot.

"What is money?" inquired Tarzan.

It took a long time to make him understand even imperfectly.

"How do men get money?" he asked at last.

"They work for it."

"Very well. I will work for it, then."

"No, my friend," returned D'Arnot, "you need not worry about money, nor need you work for it. I have enough money for two—enough for twenty. Much more than is good for one man and you shall have all you need if ever we reach civilization."

So on the following day they started north along the shore. Each man carrying a rifle and ammunition, beside bedding and some food and cooking utensils.

The latter seemed to Tarzan a most useless encumbrance, so he threw his away.

"But you must learn to eat cooked food, my friend," remonstrated D'Arnot. "No civilized men eat raw flesh."

"There will be time enough when I reach civilization," said Tarzan. "I do not like the things and they only spoil the taste of good meat."

For a month they traveled north. Sometimes finding food in plenty and again going hungry for days.

They saw no signs of natives nor were they molested by wild beasts. Their journey was a miracle of ease.

Tarzan asked questions and learned rapidly. D'Arnot taught him many of the refinements of civilization—even to the use of knife and fork; but sometimes Tarzan would drop them in disgust and grasp his food in his strong brown hands, tearing it with his molars like a wild beast.

Then D'Arnot would expostulate with him, saying:

"You must not eat like a brute, Tarzan, while I am trying to make a gentleman of you. *Mon Dieu!* Gentlemen do not thus—it is terrible."

Tarzan would grin sheepishly and pick up his knife and fork again, but at heart he hated them.

On the journey he told D'Arnot about the great chest he had seen the sailors bury; of how he had dug it up and carried it to the gathering place of the apes and buried it there.

"It must be the treasure chest of Professor Porter," said D'Arnot. "It is too bad, but of course you did not know."

Then Tarzan recalled the letter written by Jane to her friend—the one he had stolen when they first came to his cabin, and now he knew what was in the chest and what it meant to Jane.

"To-morrow we shall go back after it," he announced to D'Arnot.

"Go back?" exclaimed D'Arnot. "But, my dear fellow, we have now been three weeks upon the march. It would require three more to return to the treasure, and then, with that enormous weight which required, you say, four sailors to carry, it would be months before we had again reached this spot."

"It must be done, my friend," insisted Tarzan. "You may go on toward civilization, and I will return for the treasure. I can go very much faster alone."

"I have a better plan, Tarzan," exclaimed D'Arnot. "We shall go on together to the nearest settlement, and there we will charter a boat and sail back down the coast for the treasure and so transport it easily. That will be safer and quicker and also not require us to be separated. What do you think of that plan?"

"Very well," said Tarzan. "The treasure will be there whenever we go for it; and while I could fetch it now, and catch up with you in a moon or two, I shall feel safer for you to know that you are not alone on the trail. When I see how helpless you are, D'Arnot, I often wonder how the human race has escaped annihilation all these ages which you tell me about. Why, Sabor, single handed, could exterminate a thousand of you."

D'Arnot laughed.

"You will think more highly of your genus when you have seen its armies and navies, its great cities, and its mighty engineering works. Then you will realize that it is mind, and not muscle, that makes the human animal greater than the mighty beasts of your jungle.

"Alone and unarmed, a single man is no match for any of the larger beasts; but if ten men were together, they would combine their wits and their muscles against their savage enemies, while the beasts, being unable to reason, would never think of combining against the men. Otherwise, Tarzan of the Apes, how long would you have lasted in the savage wilderness?"

"You are right, D'Arnot," replied Tarzan, "for if Kerchak had come to Tublat's aid that night at the Dum-Dum, there would have been an end of me. But Kerchak could never think far enough ahead to take advantage of any such opportunity. Even Kala, my mother, could never plan ahead. She simply ate what she needed when she needed it, and if the supply was very scarce, even though she found plenty for several meals, she would never gather any ahead.

"I remember that she used to think it very silly of me to burden myself with extra food upon the march, though she was quite glad to eat it with me, if the way chanced to be barren of sustenance."

"Then you knew your mother, Tarzan?" asked D'Arnot, in surprise.

"Yes. She was a great, fine ape, larger than I, and weighing twice as much."

"And your father?" asked D'Arnot.

"I did not know him. Kala told me he was a white ape, and hairless like myself. I know now that he must have been a white man."

D'Arnot looked long and earnestly at his companion.

"Tarzan," he said at length, "it is impossible that the ape, Kala, was your mother. If such a thing can be, which I doubt, you would have inherited some of the characteristics of the ape, but you have not—you are pure man, and, I should say, the offspring of highly bred and intelligent parents. Have you not the slightest clue to your past?"

"Not the slightest," replied Tarzan.

"No writings in the cabin that might have told something of the lives of its original inmates?"

"I have read everything that was in the cabin with the exception of one book which I know now to be written in a language other than English. Possibly you can read it."

Tarzan fished the little black diary from the bottom of his quiver, and handed it to his companion.

D'Arnot glanced at the title page.

"It is the diary of John Clayton, Lord Greystoke, an English nobleman, and it is written in French," he said.

Then he proceeded to read the diary that had been written over twenty years before, and which recorded the details of the story which we already know—the story of adventure, hardships and sorrow of John Clayton and his wife Alice, from the day they left England until an hour before he was struck down by Kerchak.

D'Arnot read aloud. At times his voice broke, and he was forced to stop reading for the pitiful hopelessness that spoke between the lines.

Occasionally he glanced at Tarzan; but the ape-man sat upon his haunches, like a carven image, his eyes fixed upon the ground.

Only when the little babe was mentioned did the tone of the diary alter from the habitual note of despair which had crept into it by degrees after the first two months upon the shore.

Then the passages were tinged with a subdued happiness that was even sadder than the rest.

One entry showed an almost hopeful spirit.

To-day our little boy is six months old. He is sitting in Alice's lap beside the table where I am writing—a happy, healthy, perfect child.

Somehow, even against all reason, I seem to see him a grown man, taking his father's place in the world—the second John Clayton—and bringing added honors to the house of Greystoke.

There—as though to give my prophecy the weight of his endorsement—he has grabbed my pen in his chubby fists and with his inkbegrimed little fingers has placed the seal of his tiny finger prints upon the page.

And there, on the margin of the page, were the partially blurred imprints of four wee fingers and the outer half of the thumb.

When D'Arnot had finished the diary the two men sat in silence for some minutes.

"Well! Tarzan of the Apes, what think you?" asked D'Arnot. "Does not this little book clear up the mystery of your parentage?

"Why man, you are Lord Greystoke."

"The book speaks of but one child," he replied. "Its little skeleton lay in the crib, where it died crying for nourishment, from the first time I entered the cabin until Professor Porter's party buried it, with its father and mother, beside the cabin.

"No, that was the babe the book speaks of—and the mystery of my origin is deeper than before, for I have thought much of late of the possibility of that cabin having been my birthplace. I am afraid that Kala spoke the truth," he concluded sadly.

D'Arnot shook his head. He was unconvinced, and in his mind had sprung the determination to prove the correctness of his theory, for he had discovered the key which alone could unlock the mystery, or consign it forever to the realms of the unfathomable.

A week later the two men came suddenly upon a clearing in the forest.

In the distance were several buildings surrounded by a strong palisade. Between them and the enclosure stretched a cultivated field in which a number of negroes were working.

The two halted at the edge of the jungle.

Tarzan fitted his bow with a poisoned arrow, but D'Arnot placed a hand upon his arm.

"What would you do, Tarzan?" he asked.

"They will try to kill us if they see us," replied Tarzan. "I prefer to be the killer."

"Maybe they are friends," suggested D'Arnot.

"They are black," was Tarzan's only reply.

And again he drew back his shaft.

"You must not, Tarzan!" cried D'Arnot. "White men do not kill wantonly. *Mon Dieu*! but you have much to learn.

"I pity the ruffian who crosses you, my wild man, when I take you to Paris. I will have my hands full keeping your neck from beneath the guillotine."

Tarzan lowered his bow and smiled.

"I do not know why I should kill the blacks back there in my jungle, yet not kill them here. Suppose Numa, the lion, should spring out upon us, I should say, then, I presume: Good morning, Monsieur Numa, how is Madame Numa; eh?"

"Wait until the blacks spring upon you," replied D'Arnot, "then you may kill them. Do not assume that men are your enemies until they prove it."

"Come," said Tarzan, "let us go and present ourselves to be killed," and he started straight across the field, his head high held and the tropical sun beating upon his smooth, brown skin.

Behind him came D'Arnot, clothed in some garments which had been discarded at the cabin by Clayton when the officers of the French cruiser had fitted him out in more presentable fashion.

Presently one of the blacks looked up, and beholding Tarzan, turned, shrieking, toward the palisade.

In an instant the air was filled with cries of terror from the fleeing gardeners, but before any had reached the palisade a white man emerged from the enclosure, rifle in hand, to discover the cause of the commotion.

What he saw brought his rifle to his shoulder, and Tarzan of the Apes would have felt cold lead once again had not D'Arnot cried loudly to the man with the leveled gun:

"Do not fire! We are friends!"

"Halt, then!" was the reply.

"Stop, Tarzan!" cried D'Arnot. "He thinks we are enemies."

Tarzan dropped into a walk, and together he and D'Arnot advanced toward the white man by the gate.

The latter eyed them in puzzled bewilderment.

"What manner of men are you?" he asked, in French.

"White men," replied D'Arnot. "We have been lost in the jungle for a long time."

The man had lowered his rifle and now advanced with outstretched hand.

"I am Father Constantine of the French Mission here," he said, "and I am glad to welcome you."

"This is Monsieur Tarzan, Father Constantine," replied D'Arnot, indicating the ape-man; and as the priest extended his hand to Tarzan, D'Arnot added: "and I am Paul D'Arnot, of the French Navy."

Father Constantine took the hand which Tarzan extended in imitation of the priest's act, while the latter took in the superb physique and handsome face in one quick, keen glance.

And thus came Tarzan of the Apes to the first outpost of civilization.

For a week they remained there, and the ape-man, keenly observant, learned much of the ways of men; meanwhile black women sewed white duck garments for himself and D'Arnot so that they might continue their journey properly clothed.

THE HEIGHT OF CIVILIZATION

Another month brought them to a little group of buildings at the mouth of a wide river, and there Tarzan saw many boats, and was filled with the timidity of the wild thing by the sight of many men.

Gradually he became accustomed to the strange noises and the odd ways of civilization, so that presently none might know that two short months before, this handsome Frenchman in immaculate white ducks, who laughed and chatted with the gayest of them, had been swinging naked through primeval forests to pounce upon some unwary victim, which, raw, was to fill his savage belly.

The knife and fork, so contemptuously flung aside a month before, Tarzan now manipulated as exquisitely as did the polished D'Arnot.

So apt a pupil had he been that the young Frenchman had labored assiduously to make of Tarzan of the Apes a polished gentleman in so far as nicety of manners and speech were concerned.

"God made you a gentleman at heart, my friend," D'Arnot had said; "but we want His works to show upon the exterior also."

As soon as they had reached the little port, D'Arnot had cabled his government of his safety, and requested a three- months' leave, which had been granted.

He had also cabled his bankers for funds, and the enforced wait of a month, under which both chafed, was due to their inability to charter a vessel for the return to Tarzan's jungle after the treasure.

During their stay at the coast town "Monsieur Tarzan" became the wonder of both whites and blacks because of several occurrences which to Tarzan seemed the merest of nothings.

Once a huge black, crazed by drink, had run amuck and terrorized the town, until his evil star had led him to where the black-haired French giant lolled upon the veranda of the hotel.

Mounting the broad steps, with brandished knife, the Negro made straight for a party of four men sitting at a table sipping the inevitable absinthe.

Shouting in alarm, the four took to their heels, and then the black spied Tarzan.

With a roar he charged the ape-man, while half a hundred heads peered from sheltering windows and doorways to witness the butchering of the poor Frenchman by the giant black.

Tarzan met the rush with the fighting smile that the joy of battle always brought to his lips.

As the Negro closed upon him, steel muscles gripped the black wrist of the uplifted knife-hand, and a single swift wrench left the hand dangling below a broken bone.

With the pain and surprise, the madness left the black man, and as Tarzan dropped back into his chair the fellow turned, crying with agony, and dashed wildly toward the native village.

On another occasion as Tarzan and D'Arnot sat at dinner with a number of other whites, the talk fell upon lions and lion hunting.

Opinion was divided as to the bravery of the king of beasts —some maintaining that he was an arrant coward, but all agreeing that it was with a feeling of greater security that they gripped their express rifles when the monarch of the jungle roared about a camp at night.

D'Arnot and Tarzan had agreed that his past be kept secret, and so none other than the French officer knew of the ape-man's familiarity with the beasts of the jungle.

"Monsieur Tarzan has not expressed himself," said one of the party. "A man of his prowess who has spent some time in Africa, as I understand Monsieur Tarzan has, must have had experiences with lions—yes?"

"Some," replied Tarzan, dryly. "Enough to know that each of you are right in your judgment of the characteristics of the lions—you have met. But one might as well judge all blacks by the fellow who ran amuck last week, or decide that all whites are cowards because one has met a cowardly white.

"There is as much individuality among the lower orders, gentlemen, as there is among ourselves. Today we may go out and stumble upon a lion which is over-timid—he runs away from us. To-morrow we may meet his uncle or his twin brother, and our friends wonder why we do not return from the jungle. For myself, I always assume that a lion is ferocious, and so I am never caught off my guard."

"There would be little pleasure in hunting," retorted the first speaker, "if one is afraid of the thing he hunts."

D'Arnot smiled. Tarzan afraid!

"I do not exactly understand what you mean by fear," said Tarzan. "Like lions, fear is a different thing in different men, but to me the only pleasure in the hunt is the knowledge that the hunted thing has power to harm me as much as I have to harm him. If I went out with a couple of rifles and a gun bearer, and twenty or thirty beaters, to hunt a lion, I should not feel that the lion had much chance, and so the pleasure of the hunt would be lessened in proportion to the increased safety which I felt."

"Then I am to take it that Monsieur Tarzan would prefer to go naked into the jungle, armed only with a jackknife, to kill the king of beasts," laughed the other, good naturedly, but with the merest touch of sarcasm in his tone.

"And a piece of rope," added Tarzan.

Just then the deep roar of a lion sounded from the distant jungle, as though to challenge whoever dared enter the lists with him.

"There is your opportunity, Monsieur Tarzan," bantered the Frenchman.

"I am not hungry," said Tarzan simply.

The men laughed, all but D'Arnot. He alone knew that a savage beast had spoken its simple reason through the lips of the ape-man.

"But you are afraid, just as any of us would be, to go out there naked, armed only with a knife and a piece of rope," said the banterer. "Is it not so?"

"No," replied Tarzan. "Only a fool performs any act without reason."

"Five thousand francs is a reason," said the other. "I wager you that amount you cannot bring back a lion from the jungle under the conditions we have named—naked and armed only with a knife and a piece of rope."

Tarzan glanced toward D'Arnot and nodded his head.

"Make it ten thousand," said D'Arnot.

"Done," replied the other.

Tarzan arose.

"I shall have to leave my clothes at the edge of the settlement, so that if I do not return before daylight I shall have something to wear through the streets."

"You are not going now," exclaimed the wagerer—"at night?"

"Why not?" asked Tarzan. "Numa walks abroad at night —it will be easier to find him."

"No," said the other, "I do not want your blood upon my hands. It will be foolhardy enough if you go forth by day."

"I shall go now," replied Tarzan, and went to his room for his knife and rope.

The men accompanied him to the edge of the jungle, where he left his clothes in a small storehouse.

But when he would have entered the blackness of the undergrowth they tried to dissuade him; and the wagerer was most insistent of all that he abandon his foolhardy venture.

"I will accede that you have won," he said, "and the ten thousand francs are yours if you will but give up this foolish attempt, which can only end in your death."

Tarzan laughed, and in another moment the jungle had swallowed him.

The men stood silent for some moments and then slowly turned and walked back to the hotel veranda.

Tarzan had no sooner entered the jungle than he took to the trees, and it was with a feeling of exultant freedom that he swung once more through the forest branches.

This was life! Ah, how he loved it! Civilization held nothing like this in its narrow and circumscribed sphere, hemmed in by restrictions and conventionalities. Even clothes were a hindrance and a nuisance.

At last he was free. He had not realized what a prisoner he had been.

How easy it would be to circle back to the coast, and then make toward the south and his own jungle and cabin.

Now he caught the scent of Numa, for he was traveling up wind. Presently his quick ears detected the familiar sound of padded feet and the brushing of a huge, fur-clad body through the undergrowth.

Tarzan came quietly above the unsuspecting beast and silently stalked him until he came into a little patch of moonlight.

Then the quick noose settled and tightened about the tawny throat, and, as he had done it a hundred times in the past, Tarzan made fast the end to a strong branch and, while the beast fought and clawed for freedom, dropped to the ground behind him, and leaping upon the great back, plunged his long thin blade a dozen times into the fierce heart.

Then with his foot upon the carcass of Numa, he raised his voice in the awesome victory cry of his savage tribe.

For a moment Tarzan stood irresolute, swayed by conflicting emotions of loyalty to D'Arnot and a mighty lust for the freedom of his own jungle. At last the vision of a beautiful face, and the memory of warm lips crushed to his dissolved the fascinating picture he had been drawing of his old life.

The ape-man threw the warm carcass of Numa across his shoulders and took to the trees once more.

The men upon the veranda had sat for an hour, almost in silence.

They had tried ineffectually to converse on various subjects, and always the thing uppermost in the mind of each had caused the conversation to lapse.

"*Mon Dieu,*" said the wagerer at length, "I can endure it no longer. I am going into the jungle with my express and bring back that mad man."

"I will go with you," said one.

"And I"–"And I"–"And I," chorused the others.

As though the suggestion had broken the spell of some horrid nightmare they hastened to their various quarters, and presently were headed toward the jungle—each one heavily armed.

"God! What was that?" suddenly cried one of the party, an Englishman, as Tarzan's savage cry came faintly to their ears.

"I heard the same thing once before," said a Belgian, "when I was in the gorilla country. My carriers said it was the cry of a great bull ape who has made a kill."

D'Arnot remembered Clayton's description of the awful roar with which Tarzan had announced his kills, and he half smiled in spite of the horror which filled him to think that the uncanny sound could have issued from a human throat —from the lips of his friend.

As the party stood finally near the edge of the jungle, debating as to the best distribution of their forces, they were startled by a low laugh near them, and turning, beheld advancing toward them a giant figure bearing a dead lion upon its broad shoulders.

Even D'Arnot was thunderstruck, for it seemed impossible that the man could have so quickly dispatched a lion with the pitiful weapons he had taken, or that alone he could have borne the huge carcass through the tangled jungle.

The men crowded about Tarzan with many questions, but his only answer was a laughing depreciation of his feat.

To Tarzan it was as though one should eulogize a butcher for his heroism in killing a cow, for Tarzan had killed so often for food and for self-preservation that the act seemed anything but remarkable to him. But he was indeed a hero in the eyes of these men—men accustomed to hunting big game.

Incidentally, he had won ten thousand francs, for D'Arnot insisted that he keep it all.

This was a very important item to Tarzan, who was just commencing to realize the power which lay beyond the little pieces of metal and paper which always changed hands when human beings rode, or ate, or slept, or clothed themselves, or drank, or worked, or played, or sheltered themselves from the rain or cold or sun.

It had become evident to Tarzan that without money one must die. D'Arnot had told him not to worry, since he had more than enough for both, but the ape-man was learning many things and one of them was that people looked down upon one who accepted money from another without giving something of equal value in exchange.

Shortly after the episode of the lion hunt, D'Arnot succeeded in chartering an ancient tub for the coastwise trip to Tarzan's land-locked harbor.

It was a happy morning for them both when the little vessel weighed anchor and made for the open sea.

The trip to the beach was uneventful, and the morning after they dropped anchor before the cabin, Tarzan, garbed once more in his jungle regalia and carrying a spade, set out alone for the amphitheater of the apes where lay the treasure.

Late the next day he returned, bearing the great chest upon his shoulder, and at sunrise the little vessel worked through the harbor's mouth and took up her northward journey.

Three weeks later Tarzan and D'Arnot were passengers on board a French steamer bound for Lyons, and after a few days in that city D'Arnot took Tarzan to Paris.

The ape-man was anxious to proceed to America, but D'Arnot insisted that he must accompany him to Paris first, nor would he divulge the nature of the urgent necessity upon which he based his demand.

One of the first things which D'Arnot accomplished after their arrival was to arrange to visit a high official of the police department, an old friend; and to take Tarzan with him.

Adroitly D'Arnot led the conversation from point to point until the policeman had explained to the interested Tarzan many of the methods in vogue for apprehending and identifying criminals.

Not the least interesting to Tarzan was the part played by finger prints in this fascinating science.

"But of what value are these imprints," asked Tarzan, "when, after a few years the lines upon the fingers are entirely changed by the wearing out of the old tissue and the growth of new?"

"The lines never change," replied the official. "From infancy to senility the fingerprints of an individual change only in size, except as injuries alter the loops and whorls. But if imprints have been taken of the thumb and four fingers of both hands one must needs lose all entirely to escape identification."

"It is marvelous," exclaimed D'Arnot. "I wonder what the lines upon my own fingers may resemble."

"We can soon see," replied the police officer, and ringing a bell he summoned an assistant to whom he issued a few directions.

The man left the room, but presently returned with a little hardwood box which he placed on his superior's desk.

"Now," said the officer, "you shall have your fingerprints in a second."

He drew from the little case a square of plate glass, a little tube of thick ink, a rubber roller, and a few snowy white cards.

Squeezing a drop of ink onto the glass, he spread it back and forth with the rubber roller until the entire surface of the glass was covered to his satisfaction with a very thin and uniform layer of ink.

"Place the four fingers of your right hand upon the glass, thus," he said to D'Arnot. "Now the thumb. That is right. Now place them in just the same position upon this card, here, no—a little to the right. We must leave room for the thumb and the fingers of the left hand. There, that's it. Now the same with the left."

"Come, Tarzan," cried D'Arnot, "let's see what your whorls look like."

Tarzan complied readily, asking many questions of the officer during the operation.

"Do fingerprints show racial characteristics?" he asked. "Could you determine, for example, solely from fingerprints whether the subject was Negro or Caucasian?"

"I think not," replied the officer.

"Could the finger prints of an ape be detected from those of a man?"

"Probably, because the ape's would be far simpler than those of the higher organism."

"But a cross between an ape and a man might show the characteristics of either progenitor?" continued Tarzan.

"Yes, I should think likely," responded the official; "but the science has not progressed sufficiently to render it exact enough in such matters. I should hate to trust its findings further than to differentiate between individuals. There it is absolute. No two people born into the world probably have ever had identical lines upon all their digits. It is very doubtful if any single fingerprint will ever be exactly duplicated by any finger other than the one which originally made it."

"Does the comparison require much time or labor?" asked D'Arnot.

"Ordinarily but a few moments, if the impressions are distinct."

D'Arnot drew a little black book from his pocket and commenced turning the pages.

Tarzan looked at the book in surprise. How did D'Arnot come to have his book?

Presently D'Arnot stopped at a page on which were five tiny little smudges.

He handed the open book to the policeman.

"Are these imprints similar to mine or Monsieur Tarzan's or can you say that they are identical with either?" The officer drew a powerful glass from his desk and examined all three specimens carefully, making notations meanwhile upon a pad of paper.

Tarzan realized now what was the meaning of their visit to the police officer.

The answer to his life's riddle lay in these tiny marks.

With tense nerves he sat leaning forward in his chair, but suddenly he relaxed and dropped back, smiling.

D'Arnot looked at him in surprise.

"You forget that for twenty years the dead body of the child who made those fingerprints lay in the cabin of his father, and that all my life I have seen it lying there," said Tarzan bitterly.

The policeman looked up in astonishment.

"Go ahead, captain, with your examination," said D'Arnot, "we will tell you the story later—provided Monsieur Tarzan is agreeable."

Tarzan nodded his head.

"But you are mad, my dear D'Arnot," he insisted. "Those little fingers are buried on the west coast of Africa."

"I do not know as to that, Tarzan," replied D'Arnot. "It is possible, but if you are not the son of John Clayton then how in heaven's name did you come into that God forsaken jungle where no white man other than John Clayton had ever set foot?"

"You forget—Kala," said Tarzan.

"I do not even consider her," replied D'Arnot.

The friends had walked to the broad window overlooking the boulevard as they talked. For some time they stood there gazing out upon the busy throng beneath, each wrapped in his own thoughts.

"It takes some time to compare finger prints," thought D'Arnot, turning to look at the police officer.

To his astonishment he saw the official leaning back in his chair hastily scanning the contents of the little black diary.

D'Arnot coughed. The policeman looked up, and, catching his eye, raised his finger to admonish silence. D'Arnot turned back to the window, and presently the police officer spoke.

"Gentlemen," he said.

Both turned toward him.

"There is evidently a great deal at stake which must hinge to a greater or lesser extent upon the absolute correctness of this comparison. I therefore ask that you leave the entire matter in my hands until Monsieur Desquerc, our expert returns. It will be but a matter of a few days."

"I had hoped to know at once," said D'Arnot. "Monsieur Tarzan sails for America tomorrow."

"I will promise that you can cable him a report within two weeks," replied the officer; "but what it will be I dare not say. There are resemblances, yet—well, we had better leave it for Monsieur Desquerc to solve."

THE GIANT AGAIN

A taxicab drew up before an oldfashioned residence upon the outskirts of Baltimore.

A man of about forty, well built and with strong, regular features, stepped out, and paying the chauffeur dismissed him.

A moment later the passenger was entering the library of the old home.

"Ah, Mr. Canler!" exclaimed an old man, rising to greet him.

"Good evening, my dear Professor," cried the man, extending a cordial hand.

"Who admitted you?" asked the professor.

"Esmeralda."

"Then she will acquaint Jane with the fact that you are here," said the old man.

"No, Professor," replied Canler, "for I came primarily to see you."

"Ah, I am honored," said Professor Porter.

"Professor," continued Robert Canler, with great deliberation, as though carefully weighing his words, "I have come this evening to speak with you about Jane."

"You know my aspirations, and you have been generous enough to approve my suit."

Professor Archimedes Q. Porter fidgeted in his armchair. The subject always made him uncomfortable. He could not understand why. Canler was a splendid match.

"But Jane," continued Canler, "I cannot understand her. She puts me off first on one ground and then another. I have always the feeling that she breathes a sigh of relief every time I bid her good-by."

"Tut, tut," said Professor Porter. "Tut, tut, Mr. Canler. Jane is a most obedient daughter. She will do precisely as I tell her."

"Then I can still count on your support?" asked Canler, a tone of relief marking his voice.

"Certainly, sir; certainly, sir," exclaimed Professor Porter. "How could you doubt it?"

"There is young Clayton, you know," suggested Canler. "He has been hanging about for months. I don't know that Jane cares for him; but beside his title they say he has inherited a very considerable estate from his father, and it might not be strange,—if he finally won her, unless—" and Canler paused.

"Tut—tut, Mr. Canler; unless—what?"

"Unless, you see fit to request that Jane and I be married at once," said Canler, slowly and distinctly.

"I have already suggested to Jane that it would be desirable," said Professor Porter sadly, "for we can no longer afford to keep up this house, and live as her associations demand."

"What was her reply?" asked Canler.

"She said she was not ready to marry anyone yet," replied Professor Porter, "and that we could go and live upon the farm in northern Wisconsin which her mother left her.

"It is a little more than self-supporting. The tenants have always made a living from it, and been able to send Jane a trifle beside, each year. She is planning on our going up there the first of the week. Philander and Mr. Clayton have already gone to get things in readiness for us."

"Clayton has gone there?" exclaimed Canler, visibly chagrined. "Why was I not told? I would gladly have gone and seen that every comfort was provided."

"Jane feels that we are already too much in your debt, Mr. Canler," said Professor Porter.

Canler was about to reply, when the sound of footsteps came from the hall without, and Jane entered the room.

"Oh, I beg your pardon!" she exclaimed, pausing on the threshold. "I thought you were alone, papa."

"It is only I, Jane," said Canler, who had risen, "won't you come in and join the family group? We were just speaking of you."

"Thank you," said Jane, entering and taking the chair Canler placed for her. "I only wanted to tell papa that Tobey is coming down from the college tomorrow to pack his books. I want you to be sure, papa, to indicate all that you can do without until fall. Please don't carry this entire library to Wisconsin, as you would have carried it to Africa, if I had not put my foot down."

"Was Tobey here?" asked Professor Porter.

"Yes, I just left him. He and Esmeralda are exchanging religious experiences on the back porch now."

"Tut, tut, I must see him at once!" cried the professor. "Excuse me just a moment, children," and the old man hastened from the room.

As soon as he was out of earshot Canler turned to Jane.

"See here, Jane," he said bluntly. "How long is this thing going on like this? You haven't refused to marry me, but you haven't promised either. I want to get the license tomorrow, so that we can be married quietly before you leave for Wisconsin. I don't care for any fuss or feathers, and I'm sure you don't either."

The girl turned cold, but she held her head bravely.

"Your father wishes it, you know," added Canler.

"Yes, I know."

She spoke scarcely above a whisper.

"Do you realize that you are buying me, Mr. Canler?" she said finally, and in a cold, level voice. "Buying me for a few paltry dollars? Of course you do, Robert Canler, and the hope of just such a contingency was in your mind when you loaned papa the money for that hair-brained escapade, which but for a most mysterious circumstance would have been surprisingly successful.

"But you, Mr. Canler, would have been the most surprised. You had no idea that the venture would succeed. You are too good a businessman for that. And you are too good a businessman to loan money for buried treasure seeking, or to loan money without security—unless you had some special object in view.

"You knew that without security you had a greater hold on the honor of the Porters than with it. You knew the one best way to force me to marry you, without seeming to force me.

"You have never mentioned the loan. In any other man I should have thought that the prompting of a magnanimous and noble character. But you are deep, Mr. Robert Canler. I know you better than you think I know you.

"I shall certainly marry you if there is no other way, but let us understand each other once and for all."

While she spoke Robert Canler had alternately flushed and paled, and when she ceased speaking he arose, and with a cynical smile upon his strong face, said:

"You surprise me, Jane. I thought you had more self-control —more pride. Of course you are right. I am buying you, and I knew that you knew it, but I thought you would prefer to pretend that it was otherwise. I should have thought your self respect and your Porter pride would have shrunk from admitting, even to yourself, that you were a bought woman. But have it your own way, dear girl," he added lightly. "I am going to have you, and that is all that interests me."

Without a word the girl turned and left the room.

Jane was not married before she left with her father and Esmeralda for her little Wisconsin farm, and as she coldly bid Robert Canler goodby as her train pulled out, he called to her that he would join them in a week or two.

At their destination they were met by Clayton and Mr. Philander in a huge touring car belonging to the former, and quickly whirled away through the dense northern woods toward the little farm which the girl had not visited before since childhood.

The farmhouse, which stood on a little elevation some hundred yards from the tenant house, had undergone a complete transformation during the three weeks that Clayton and Mr. Philander had been there.

The former had imported a small army of carpenters and plasterers, plumbers and painters from a distant city, and what had been but a dilapidated shell when they reached it was now a cosy little two-story house filled with every modern convenience procurable in so short a time.

"Why, Mr. Clayton, what have you done?" cried Jane Porter, her heart sinking within her as she realized the probable size of the expenditure that had been made.

"S-sh," cautioned Clayton. "Don't let your father guess. If you don't tell him he will never notice, and I simply couldn't think of him living in the terrible squalor and sordidness which Mr. Philander and I found. It was so little when I would like to do so much, Jane. For his sake, please, never mention it."

"But you know that we can't repay you," cried the girl. "Why do you want to put me under such terrible obligations?"

"Don't, Jane," said Clayton sadly. "If it had been just you, believe me, I wouldn't have done it, for I knew from the start that it would only hurt me in your eyes, but I couldn't think of that dear old man living in the hole we found here. Won't you please believe that I did it just for him and give me that little crumb of pleasure at least?"

"I do believe you, Mr. Clayton," said the girl, "because I know you are big enough and generous enough to have done it just for him—and, oh Cecil, I wish I might repay you as you deserve—as you would wish."

"Why can't you, Jane?"

"Because I love another."

"Canler?"

"No."

"But you are going to marry him. He told me as much before I left Baltimore."

The girl winced.

"I do not love him," she said, almost proudly.

"Is it because of the money, Jane?"

She nodded.

"Then am I so much less desirable than Canler? I have money enough, and far more, for every need," he said bitterly.

"I do not love you, Cecil," she said, "but I respect you. If I must disgrace myself by such a bargain with any man, I prefer that it be one I already despise. I should loathe the man to whom I sold myself without love, whomsoever he might be. You will be happier," she concluded, "alone—with my respect and friendship, than with me and my contempt."

He did not press the matter further, but if ever a man had murder in his heart it was William Cecil Clayton, Lord Greystoke, when, a week later, Robert Canler drew up before the farmhouse in his purring six cylinder.

A week passed; a tense, uneventful, but uncomfortable week for all the inmates of the little Wisconsin farmhouse.

Canler was insistent that Jane marry him at once.

At length she gave in from sheer loathing of the continued and hateful importuning.

It was agreed that on the morrow Canler was to drive to town and bring back the license and a minister.

Clayton had wanted to leave as soon as the plan was announced, but the girl's tired, hopeless look kept him. He could not desert her.

Something might happen yet, he tried to console himself by thinking. And in his heart, he knew that it would require but a tiny spark to turn his hatred for Canler into the blood lust of the killer.

Early the next morning Canler set out for town.

In the east smoke could be seen lying low over the forest, for a fire had been raging for a week not far from them, but the wind still lay in the west and no danger threatened them.

About noon Jane started off for a walk. She would not let Clayton accompany her. She wanted to be alone, she said, and he respected her wishes.

In the house Professor Porter and Mr. Philander were immersed in an absorbing discussion of some weighty scientific problem. Esmeralda dozed in the kitchen, and Clayton, heavy-eyed after a sleepless night, threw himself down upon the couch in the living room and soon dropped into a fitful slumber.

To the east the black smoke clouds rose higher into the heavens, suddenly they eddied, and then commenced to drift rapidly toward the west.

On and on they came. The inmates of the tenant house were gone, for it was market day, and none was there to see the rapid approach of the fiery demon.

Soon the flames had spanned the road to the south and cut off Canler's return. A little fluctuation of the wind now carried the path of the forest fire to the north, then blew back and the flames nearly stood still as though held in leash by some master hand.

Suddenly, out of the northeast, a great black car came careening down the road.

With a jolt it stopped before the cottage, and a black-haired giant leaped out to run up onto the porch. Without a pause he rushed into the house. On the couch lay Clayton. The man started in surprise, but with a bound was at the side of the sleeping man.

Shaking him roughly by the shoulder, he cried:

"My God, Clayton, are you all mad here? Don't you know you are nearly surrounded by fire? Where is Miss Porter?"

Clayton sprang to his feet. He did not recognize the man, but he understood the words and was upon the veranda in a bound.

"Scott!" he cried, and then, dashing back into the house, "Jane! Jane! where are you?"

In an instant Esmeralda, Professor Porter and Mr. Philander had joined the two men.

"Where is Miss Jane?" cried Clayton, seizing Esmeralda by the shoulders and shaking her roughly.

"Oh, Gaberelle, Mister Clayton, she done gone for a walk."

"Hasn't she come back yet?" and, without waiting for a reply, Clayton dashed out into the yard, followed by the others. "Which way did she go?" cried the black-haired giant of Esmeralda.

"Down that road," cried the frightened woman, pointing toward the south where a mighty wall of roaring flames shut out the view.

"Put these people in the other car," shouted the stranger to Clayton. "I saw one as I drove up—and get them out of here by the north road.

"Leave my car here. If I find Miss Porter we shall need it. If I don't, no one will need it. Do as I say," as Clayton hesitated, and then they saw the lithe figure bound away cross the clearing toward the northwest where the forest still stood, untouched by flame.

In each rose the unaccountable feeling that a great responsibility had been raised from their shoulders; a kind of implicit confidence in the power of the stranger to save Jane if she could be saved.

"Who was that?" asked Professor Porter.

"I do not know," replied Clayton. "He called me by name and he knew Jane, for he asked for her. And he called Esmeralda by name."

"There was something most startlingly familiar about him," exclaimed Mr. Philander, "And yet, bless me, I know I never saw him before."

"Tut, tut!" cried Professor Porter. "Most remarkable! Who could it have been, and why do I feel that Jane is safe, now that he has set out in search of her?"

"I can't tell you, Professor," said Clayton soberly, "but I know I have the same uncanny feeling."

"But come," he cried, "we must get out of here ourselves, or we shall be shut off," and the party hastened toward Clayton's car.

When Jane turned to retrace her steps homeward, she was alarmed to note how near the smoke of the forest fire seemed, and as she hastened onward her alarm became almost a panic when she perceived that the rushing flames were rapidly forcing their way between herself and the cottage.

At length she was compelled to turn into the dense thicket and attempt to force her way to the west in an effort to circle around the flames and reach the house.

In a short time the futility of her attempt became apparent and then her one hope lay in retracing her steps to the road and flying for her life to the south toward the town.

The twenty minutes that it took her to regain the road was all that had been needed to cut off her retreat as effectually as her advance had been cut off before.

A short run down the road brought her to a horrified stand, for there before her was another wall of flame. An arm of the main conflagration had shot out a half mile south of its parent to embrace this tiny strip of road in its implacable clutches.

Jane knew that it was useless again to attempt to force her way through the undergrowth.

She had tried it once, and failed. Now she realized that it would be but a matter of minutes ere the whole space between the north and the south would be a seething mass of billowing flames.

Calmly the girl kneeled down in the dust of the roadway and prayed for strength to meet her fate bravely, and for the delivery of her father and her friends from death.

Suddenly she heard her name being called aloud through the forest:

"Jane! Jane Porter!" It rang strong and clear, but in a strange voice.

"Here!" she called in reply. "Here! In the roadway!"

Then through the branches of the trees she saw a figure swinging with the speed of a squirrel.

A veering of the wind blew a cloud of smoke about them and she could no longer see the man who was speeding toward her, but suddenly she felt a great arm about her. Then she was lifted up, and she felt the rushing of the wind and the occasional brush of a branch as she was borne along.

She opened her eyes.

Far below her lay the undergrowth and the hard earth.

About her was the waving foliage of the forest.

From tree to tree swung the giant figure which bore her, and it seemed to Jane that she was living over in a dream the experience that had been hers in that far African jungle.

Oh, if it were but the same man who had borne her so swiftly through the tangled verdure on that other day! but that was impossible! Yet who else in all the world was there with the strength and agility to do what this man was now doing?

She stole a sudden glance at the face close to hers, and then she gave a little frightened gasp. It was he!

"My forest man!" she murmured, "No, I must be delerious!"

"Yes, your man, Jane Porter. Your savage, primeval man come out of the jungle to claim his mate—the woman who ran away from him," he added almost fiercely.

"I did not run away," she whispered. "I would only consent to leave when they had waited a week for you to return."

They had come to a point beyond the fire now, and he had turned back to the clearing.

Side by side they were walking toward the cottage. The wind had changed once more and the fire was burning back upon itself—another hour like that and it would be burned out.

"Why did you not return?" she asked.

"I was nursing D'Arnot. He was badly wounded."

"Ah, I knew it!" she exclaimed.

"They said you had gone to join the blacks—that they were your people."

He laughed.

"But you did not believe them, Jane?"

"No;—what shall I call you?" she asked. "What is your name?"

"I was Tarzan of the Apes when you first knew me," he said.

"Tarzan of the Apes!" she cried—" and that was your note I answered when I left?"

"Yes, whose did you think it was?"

"I did not know; only that it could not be yours, for Tarzan of the Apes had written in English, and you could not understand a word of any language."

Again he laughed.

"It is a long story, but it was I who wrote what I could not speak—and now D'Arnot has made matters worse by teaching me to speak French instead of English.

"Come," he added, "jump into my car, we must overtake your father, they are only a little way ahead."

As they drove along, he said:

"Then when you said in your note to Tarzan of the Apes that you loved another—you might have meant me?"

"I might have," she answered, simply.

"But in Baltimore—Oh, how I have searched for you—they told me you would possibly be married by now. That a man named Canler had come up here to wed you. Is that true?"

"Yes."

"Do you love him?"

"No."

"Do you love me?"

She buried her face in her hands.

"I am promised to another. I cannot answer you, Tarzan of the Apes," she cried.

"You have answered. Now, tell me why you would marry one you do not love."

"My father owes him money."

Suddenly there came back to Tarzan the memory of the letter he had read—and the name Robert Canler and the hinted trouble which he had been unable to understand then.

He smiled.

"If your father had not lost the treasure you would not feel forced to keep your promise to this man Canler?"

"I could ask him to release me."

"And if he refused?"

"I have given my promise."

He was silent for a moment. The car was plunging along the uneven road at a reckless pace, for the fire showed threateningly at their right, and another change of the wind might sweep it on with raging fury across this one avenue of escape.

Finally they passed the danger point, and Tarzan reduced their speed.

"Suppose I should ask him?" ventured Tarzan.

"He would scarcely accede to the demand of a stranger," said the girl. "Especially one who wanted me himself."

"Terkoz did," said Tarzan, grimly.

Jane shuddered and looked fearfully up at the giant figure beside her, for she knew that he meant the great anthropoid he had killed in her defense.

"This is not the African jungle," she said. "You are no longer a savage beast. You are a gentleman, and gentlemen do not kill in cold blood."

"I am still a wild beast at heart," he said, in a low voice, as though to himself.

Again they were silent for a time.

"Jane," said the man, at length, "if you were free, would you marry me?"

She did not reply at once, but he waited patiently.

The girl was trying to collect her thoughts.

What did she know of this strange creature at her side? What did he know of himself? Who was he? Who, his parents?

Why, his very name echoed his mysterious origin and his savage life.

He had no name. Could she be happy with this jungle waif? Could she find anything in common with a husband whose life had been spent in the tree tops of an African wilderness, frolicking and fighting with fierce anthropoids; tearing his food from the quivering flank of fresh-killed prey, sinking his strong teeth into raw flesh, and tearing away his portion while his mates growled and fought about him for their share?

Could he ever rise to her social sphere? Could she bear to think of sinking to his? Would either be happy in such a horrible misalliance?

"You do not answer," he said. "Do you shrink from wounding me?"

"I do not know what answer to make," said Jane sadly. "I do not know my own mind."

"You do not love me, then?" he asked, in a level tone.

"Do not ask me. You will be happier without me. You were never meant for the formal restrictions and conventionalities of society—civilization would become irksome to you, and in a little while you would long for the freedom of your old life—a life to which I am as totally unfitted as you to mine."

"I think I understand you," he replied quietly. "I shall not urge you, for I would rather see you happy than to be happy myself. I see now that you could not be happy with—an ape."

There was just the faintest tinge of bitterness in his voice.

"Don't," she remonstrated. "Don't say that. You do not understand."

But before she could go on a sudden turn in the road brought them into the midst of a little hamlet. Before them stood Clayton's car surrounded by the party he had brought from the cottage.

CONCLUSION

At the sight of Jane, cries of relief and delight broke from every lip, and as Tarzan's car stopped beside the other, Professor Porter caught his daughter in his arms.

For a moment no one noticed Tarzan, sitting silently in his seat.

Clayton was the first to remember, and, turning, held out his hand.

"How can we ever thank you?" he exclaimed. "You have saved us all. You called me by name at the cottage, but I do not seem to recall yours, though there is something very familiar about you. It is as though I had known you well under very different conditions a long time ago."

Tarzan smiled as he took the proffered hand.

"You are quite right, Monsieur Clayton," he said, in French. "You will pardon me if I do not speak to you in English. I am just learning it, and while I understand it fairly well I speak it very poorly."

"But who are you?" insisted Clayton, speaking in French this time himself.

"Tarzan of the Apes."

Clayton started back in surprise.

"By Jove!" he exclaimed. "It is true."

And Professor Porter and Mr. Philander pressed forward to add their thanks to Clayton's, and to voice their surprise and pleasure at seeing their jungle friend so far from his savage home.

The party now entered the modest little hostelry, where Clayton soon made arrangements for their entertainment.

They were sitting in the little, stuffy parlor when the distant chugging of an approaching automobile caught their attention.

Mr. Philander, who was sitting near the window, looked out as the car drew in sight, finally stopping beside the other automobiles.

"Bless me!" said Mr. Philander, a shade of annoyance in his tone. "It is Mr. Canler. I had hoped, er—I had thought or—er—how very happy we should be that he was not caught in the fire," he ended lamely.

"Tut, tut! Mr. Philander," said Professor Porter. "Tut, tut! I have often admonished my pupils to count ten before speaking. Were I you, Mr. Philander, I should count at least a thousand, and then maintain a discreet silence."

"Bless me, yes!" acquiesced Mr. Philander. "But who is the clerical appearing gentleman with him?"

Jane blanched.

Clayton moved uneasily in his chair.

Professor Porter removed his spectacles nervously, and breathed upon them, but replaced them on his nose without wiping.

The ubiquitous Esmeralda grunted.

Only Tarzan did not comprehend.

Presently Robert Canler burst into the room.

"Thank God!" he cried. "I feared the worst, until I saw your car, Clayton. I was cut off on the south road and had to go away back to town, and then strike east to this road. I thought we'd never reach the cottage."

No one seemed to enthuse much. Tarzan eyed Robert Canler as Sabor eyes her prey.

Jane glanced at him and coughed nervously.

"Mr. Canler," she said, "this is Monsieur Tarzan, an old friend."

Canler turned and extended his hand. Tarzan rose and bowed as only D'Arnot could have taught a gentleman to do it, but he did not seem to see Canler's hand.

Nor did Canler appear to notice the oversight.

"This is the Reverend Mr. Tousley, Jane," said Canler, turning to the clerical party behind him. "Mr. Tousley, Miss Porter."

Mr. Tousley bowed and beamed.

Canler introduced him to the others.

"We can have the ceremony at once, Jane," said Canler. "Then you and I can catch the midnight train in town."

Tarzan understood the plan instantly. He glanced out of half-closed eyes at Jane, but he did not move.

The girl hesitated. The room was tense with the silence of taut nerves.

All eyes turned toward Jane, awaiting her reply.

"Can't we wait a few days?" she asked. "I am all unstrung. I have been through so much today."

Canler felt the hostility that emanated from each member of the party. It made him angry.

"We have waited as long as I intend to wait," he said roughly. "You have promised to marry me. I shall be played with no longer. I have the license and here is the preacher. Come Mr. Tousley; come Jane. There are plenty of witnesses —more than enough," he added with a disagreeable inflection; and taking Jane Porter by the arm, he started to lead her toward the waiting minister.

But scarcely had he taken a single step ere a heavy hand closed upon his arm with a grip of steel.

Another hand shot to his throat and in a moment he was being shaken high above the floor, as a cat might shake a mouse.

Jane turned in horrified surprise toward Tarzan.

And, as she looked into his face, she saw the crimson band upon his forehead that she had seen that other day in far distant Africa, when Tarzan of the Apes had closed in mortal combat with the great anthropoid—Terkoz.

She knew that murder lay in that savage heart, and with a little cry of horror she sprang forward to plead with the ape-man. But her fears were more for Tarzan than for Canler. She realized the stern retribution which justice metes to the murderer.

Before she could reach them, however, Clayton had jumped to Tarzan's side and attempted to drag Canler from his grasp.

With a single sweep of one mighty arm the Englishman was hurled across the room, and then Jane laid a firm white hand upon Tarzan's wrist, and looked up into his eyes.

"For my sake," she said.

The grasp upon Canler's throat relaxed.

Tarzan looked down into the beautiful face before him.

"Do you wish this to live?" he asked in surprise.

"I do not wish him to die at your hands, my friend," she replied. "I do not wish you to become a murderer."

Tarzan removed his hand from Canler's throat.

"Do you release her from her promise?" he asked. "It is the price of your life."

Canler, gasping for breath, nodded.

"Will you go away and never molest her further?"

Again the man nodded his head, his face distorted by fear of the death that had been so close.

Tarzan released him, and Canler staggered toward the door. In another moment he was gone, and the terror-stricken preacher with him.

Tarzan turned toward Jane.

"May I speak with you for a moment, alone," he asked.

The girl nodded and started toward the door leading to the narrow veranda of the little hotel. She passed out to await Tarzan and so did not hear the conversation which followed.

"Wait," cried Professor Porter, as Tarzan was about to follow.

The professor had been stricken dumb with surprise by the rapid developments of the past few minutes.

"Before we go further, sir, I should like an explanation of the events which have just transpired. By what right, sir, did you interfere between my daughter and Mr. Canler? I had promised him her hand, sir, and regardless of our personal likes or dislikes, sir, that promise must be kept."

"I interfered, Professor Porter," replied Tarzan, "because your daughter does not love Mr. Canler—she does not wish to marry him. That is enough for me to know."

"You do not know what you have done," said Professor Porter. "Now he will doubtless refuse to marry her."

"He most certainly will," said Tarzan, emphatically.

"And further," added Tarzan, "you need not fear that your pride will suffer, Professor Porter, for you will be able to pay the Canler person what you owe him the moment you reach home."

"Tut, tut, sir!" exclaimed Professor Porter. "What do you mean, sir?"

"Your treasure has been found," said Tarzan.

"What—what is that you are saying?" cried the professor. "You are mad, man. It cannot be."

"It is, though. It was I who stole it, not knowing either its value or to whom it belonged. I saw the sailors bury it, and, ape-like, I had to dig it up and bury it again elsewhere. When D'Arnot told me what it was and what it meant to you I returned to the jungle and recovered it. It had caused so much crime and suffering and sorrow that D'Arnot thought it best not to attempt to bring the treasure itself on here, as had been my intention, so I have brought a letter of credit instead.

"Here it is, Professor Porter," and Tarzan drew an envelope from his pocket and handed it to the astonished professor, "two hundred and forty-one thousand dollars. The treasure was most carefully appraised by experts, but lest there should be any question in your mind, D'Arnot himself bought it and is holding it for you, should you prefer the treasure to the credit."

"To the already great burden of the obligations we owe you, sir," said Professor Porter, with trembling voice, "is now added this greatest of all services. You have given me the means to save my honor."

Clayton, who had left the room a moment after Canler, now returned.

"Pardon me," he said. "I think we had better try to reach town before dark and take the first train out of this forest. A native just rode by from the north, who reports that the fire is moving slowly in this direction."

This announcement broke up further conversation, and the entire party went out to the waiting automobiles.

Clayton, with Jane, the professor and Esmeralda occupied Clayton's car, while Tarzan took Mr. Philander in with him.

"Bless me!" exclaimed Mr. Philander, as the car moved off after Clayton. "Who would ever have thought it possible! The last time I saw you you were a veritable wild man, skipping about among the branches of a tropical African forest, and now you are driving me along a Wisconsin road in a French automobile. Bless me! But it is most remarkable."

"Yes," assented Tarzan, and then, after a pause, "Mr. Philander, do you recall any of the details of the finding and burying of three skeletons found in my cabin beside that African jungle?"

"Very distinctly, sir, very distinctly," replied Mr. Philander.

"Was there anything peculiar about any of those skeletons?"

Mr. Philander eyed Tarzan narrowly.

"Why do you ask?"

"It means a great deal to me to know," replied Tarzan. "Your answer may clear up a mystery. It can do no worse, at any rate, than to leave it still a mystery. I have been entertaining a theory concerning those skeletons for the past two months, and I want you to answer my question to the best of your knowledge—were the three skeletons you buried all human skeletons?"

"No," said Mr. Philander, "the smallest one, the one found in the crib, was the skeleton of an anthropoid ape."

"Thank you," said Tarzan.

In the car ahead, Jane was thinking fast and furiously. She had felt the purpose for which Tarzan had asked a few words with her, and she knew that she must be prepared to give him an answer in the very near future.

He was not the sort of person one could put off, and somehow that very thought made her wonder if she did not really fear him.

And could she love where she feared?

She realized the spell that had been upon her in the depths of that far-off jungle, but there was no spell of enchantment now in prosaic Wisconsin.

Nor did the immaculate young Frenchman appeal to the primal woman in her, as had the stalwart forest god.

Did she love him? She did not know—now.

She glanced at Clayton out of the corner of her eye. Was not here a man trained in the same school of environment in which she had been trained—a man with social position and culture such as she had been taught to consider as the prime essentials to congenial association?

Did not her best judgment point to this young English nobleman, whose love she knew to be of the sort a civilized woman should crave, as the logical mate for such as herself?

Could she love Clayton? She could see no reason why she could not. Jane was not coldly calculating by nature, but training, environment and heredity had all combined to teach her to reason even in matters of the heart.

That she had been carried off her feet by the strength of the young giant when his great arms were about her in the distant African forest, and again today, in the Wisconsin woods, seemed to her only attributable to a temporary mental reversion to type on her part—to the psychological appeal of the primeval man to the primeval woman in her nature.

If he should never touch her again, she reasoned, she would never feel attracted toward him. She had not loved him, then. It had been nothing more than a passing hallucination, super-induced by excitement and by personal contact.

Excitement would not always mark their future relations, should she marry him, and the power of personal contact eventually would be dulled by familiarity.

Again she glanced at Clayton. He was very handsome and every inch a gentleman. She should be very proud of such a husband.

And then he spoke—a minute sooner or a minute later might have made all the difference in the world to three lives —but chance stepped in and pointed out to Clayton the psychological moment.

"You are free now, Jane," he said. "Won't you say yes—I will devote my life to making you very happy."

"Yes," she whispered.

That evening in the little waiting room at the station Tarzan caught Jane alone for a moment.

"You are free now, Jane," he said, "and _I_ have come across the ages out of the dim and distant past from the lair of the primeval man to claim you—for your sake I have become a civilized man—for your sake I have crossed oceans and continents—for your sake I will be whatever you will me to be. I can make you happy, Jane, in the life you know and love best. Will you marry me?"

For the first time she realized the depths of the man's love —all that he had accomplished in so short a time solely for love of her. Turning her head she buried her face in her arms.

What had she done? Because she had been afraid she might succumb to the pleas of this giant, she had burned her bridges behind her—in her groundless apprehension that she might make a terrible mistake, she had made a worse one.

And then she told him all—told him the truth word by word, without attempting to shield herself or condone her error.

"What can we do?" he asked. "You have admitted that you love me. You know that I love you; but I do not know the ethics of society by which you are governed. I shall leave the decision to you, for you know best what will be for your eventual welfare."

"I cannot tell him, Tarzan," she said. "He too, loves me, and he is a good man. I could never face you nor any other honest person if I repudiated my promise to Mr. Clayton. I shall have to keep it—and you must help me bear the burden, though we may not see each other again after tonight."

The others were entering the room now and Tarzan turned toward the little window.

But he saw nothing outside—within he saw a patch of greensward surrounded by a matted mass of gorgeous tropical plants and flowers, and, above, the waving foliage of mighty trees, and, over all, the blue of an equatorial sky.

In the center of the greensward a young woman sat upon a little mound of earth, and beside her sat a young giant. They ate pleasant fruit and looked into each other's eyes and smiled. They were very happy, and they were all alone.

His thoughts were broken in upon by the station agent who entered asking if there was a gentleman by the name of Tarzan in the party.

"I am Monsieur Tarzan," said the ape-man.

"Here is a message for you, forwarded from Baltimore; it is a cablegram from Paris."

Tarzan took the envelope and tore it open. The message was from D'Arnot.

It read:

Fingerprints prove you Greystoke. Congratulations. D'ARNOT.

As Tarzan finished reading, Clayton entered and came toward him with extended hand.

Here was the man who had Tarzan's title, and Tarzan's estates, and was going to marry the woman whom Tarzan loved—the woman who loved Tarzan. A single word from Tarzan would make a great difference in this man's life.

It would take away his title and his lands and his castles, and—it would take them away from Jane Porter also. "I say, old man," cried Clayton, "I haven't had a chance to thank you for all you've done for us. It seems as though you had your hands full saving our lives in Africa and here.

"I'm awfully glad you came on here. We must get better acquainted. I often thought about you, you know, and the remarkable circumstances of your environment.

"If it's any of my business, how the devil did you ever get into that bally jungle?"

"I was born there," said Tarzan, quietly. "My mother was an Ape, and of course she couldn't tell me much about it. I never knew who my father was."

THE RETURN OF TARZAN

THE AFFAIR ON THE LINER

"Magnifique!" ejaculated the Countess de Coude, beneath her breath.

"Eh?" questioned the count, turning toward his young wife. "What is it that is magnificent?" and the count bent his eyes in various directions in quest of the object of her admiration.

"Oh, nothing at all, my dear," replied the countess, a slight flush momentarily coloring her already pink cheek. "I was but recalling with admiration those stupendous skyscrapers, as they call them, of New York," and the fair countess settled herself more comfortably in her steamer chair, and resumed the magazine which "nothing at all" had caused her to let fall upon her lap.

Her husband again buried himself in his book, but not without a mild wonderment that three days out from New York his countess should suddenly have realized an admiration for the very buildings she had but recently characterized as horrid.

Presently the count put down his book. "It is very tiresome, Olga," he said. "I think that I shall hunt up some others who may be equally bored, and see if we cannot find enough for a game of cards."

"You are not very gallant, my husband," replied the young woman, smiling, "but as I am equally bored I can forgive you. Go and play at your tiresome old cards, then, if you will."

When he had gone she let her eyes wander slyly to the figure of a tall young man stretched lazily in a chair not far distant.

"*Magnifique!*" she breathed once more.

The Countess Olga de Coude was twenty. Her husband forty. She was a very faithful and loyal wife, but as she had had nothing whatever to do with the selection of a husband, it is not at all unlikely that she was not wildly and passionately in love with the one that fate and her titled Russian father had selected for her. However, simply because she was surprised into a tiny exclamation of approval at sight of a splendid young stranger it must not be inferred therefrom that her thoughts were in any way disloyal to her spouse. She merely admired, as she might have admired a particularly fine specimen of any species. Furthermore, the young man was unquestionably good to look at.

As her furtive glance rested upon his profile he rose to leave the deck. The Countess de Coude beckoned to a passing steward. "Who is that gentleman?" she asked.

"He is booked, madam, as Monsieur Tarzan, of Africa," replied the steward.

"Rather a large estate," thought the girl, but now her interest was still further aroused.

As Tarzan walked slowly toward the smoking-room he came unexpectedly upon two men whispering excitedly just without. He would have vouchsafed them not even a passing thought but for the strangely guilty glance that one of them shot in his direction. They reminded Tarzan of melodramatic villains he had seen at the theaters in Paris. Both were very dark, and this, in connection with the shrugs and stealthy glances that accompanied their palpable intriguing, lent still greater force to the similarity.

Tarzan entered the smoking-room, and sought a chair a little apart from the others who were there. He felt in no mood for conversation, and as he sipped his absinth he let his mind run rather sorrowfully over the past few weeks of his life. Time and again he had wondered if he had acted wisely in renouncing his birthright to a man to whom he owed nothing. It is true that he liked Clayton, but—ah, but that was not the question. It was not for William Cecil Clayton, Lord Greystoke, that he had denied his birth. It was for the woman whom both he and Clayton had loved, and whom a strange freak of fate had given to Clayton instead of to him.

That she loved him made the thing doubly difficult to bear, yet he knew that he could have done nothing less than he did do that night within the little railway station in the far Wisconsin woods. To him her happiness was the first consideration of all, and his brief experience with civilization and civilized men had taught him that without money and position life to most of them was unendurable.

Jane Porter had been born to both, and had Tarzan taken them away from her future husband it would doubtless have plunged her into a life of misery and torture. That she would have spurned Clayton once he had been stripped of both his title and his estates never for once occurred to Tarzan, for he credited to others the same honest loyalty that was so inherent a quality in himself. Nor, in this instance, had he erred. Could any one thing have further bound Jane Porter to her promise to Clayton it would have been in the nature of some such misfortune as this overtaking him.

Tarzan's thoughts drifted from the past to the future. He tried to look forward with pleasurable sensations to his return to the jungle of his birth and boyhood; the cruel, fierce jungle in which he had spent twenty of his twenty-two years. But who or what of all the myriad jungle life would there be to welcome his return? Not one. Only Tantor, the elephant, could he call friend. The others would hunt him or flee from him as had been their way in the past.

Not even the apes of his own tribe would extend the hand of fellowship to him.

If civilization had done nothing else for Tarzan of the Apes, it had to some extent taught him to crave the society of his own kind, and to feel with genuine pleasure the congenial warmth of companionship. And in the same ratio had it made any other life distasteful to him. It was difficult to imagine a world without a friend—without a living thing who spoke the new tongues which Tarzan had learned to love so well. And so it was that Tarzan looked with little relish upon the future he had mapped out for himself.

As he sat musing over his cigarette his eyes fell upon a mirror before him, and in it he saw reflected a table at which four men sat at cards. Presently one of them rose to leave, and then another approached, and Tarzan could see that he courteously offered to fill the vacant chair, that the game might not be interrupted. He was the smaller of the two whom Tarzan had seen whispering just outside the smoking-room.

It was this fact that aroused a faint spark of interest in Tarzan, and so as he speculated upon the future he watched in the mirror the reflection of the players at the table behind him. Aside from the man who had but just entered the game Tarzan knew the name of but one of the other players. It was he who sat opposite the new player, Count Raoul de Coude, whom at over-attentive steward had pointed out as one of the celebrities of the passage, describing him as a man high in the official family of the French minister of war.

Suddenly Tarzan's attention was riveted upon the picture in the glass. The other swarthy plotter had entered, and was standing behind the count's chair. Tarzan saw him turn and glance furtively about the room, but his eyes did not rest for a sufficient time upon the mirror to note the reflection of Tarzan's watchful eyes. Stealthily the man withdrew something from his pocket. Tarzan could not discern what the object was, for the man's hand covered it.

Slowly the hand approached the count, and then, very deftly, the thing that was in it was transferred to the count's pocket. The man remained standing where he could watch the Frenchman's cards. Tarzan was puzzled, but he was all attention now, nor did he permit another detail of the incident to escape him.

The play went on for some ten minutes after this, until the count won a considerable wager from him who had last joined the game, and then Tarzan saw the fellow back of the count's chair nod his head to his confederate. Instantly the player arose and pointed a finger at the count.

"Had I known that monsieur was a professional card sharp I had not been so ready to be drawn into the game," he said.

Instantly the count and the two other players were upon their feet.

De Coude's face went white.

"What do you mean, sir?" he cried. "Do you know to whom you speak?"

"I know that I speak, for the last time, to one who cheats at cards," replied the fellow.

The count leaned across the table, and struck the man full in the mouth with his open palm, and then the others closed in between them.

"There is some mistake, sir," cried one of the other players. "Why, this is Count de Coude, of France." "If I am mistaken," said the accuser, "I shall gladly apologize; but before I do so first let monsieur le count explain the extra cards which I saw him drop into his side pocket."

And then the man whom Tarzan had seen drop them there turned to sneak from the room, but to his annoyance he found the exit barred by a tall, gray-eyed stranger.

"Pardon," said the man brusquely, attempting to pass to one side.

"Wait," said Tarzan.

"But why, monsieur?" exclaimed the other petulantly. "Permit me to pass, monsieur."

"Wait," said Tarzan. "I think that there is a matter in here that you may doubtless be able to explain."

The fellow had lost his temper by this time, and with a low oath seized Tarzan to push him to one side. The ape-man but smiled as he twisted the big fellow about and, grasping him by the collar of his coat, escorted him back to the table, struggling, cursing, and striking in futile remonstrance. It was Nikolas Rokoff's first experience with the muscles that had brought their savage owner victorious through encounters with Numa, the lion, and Terkoz, the great bull ape.

The man who had accused De Coude, and the two others who had been playing, stood looking expectantly at the count. Several other passengers had drawn toward the scene of the altercation, and all awaited the denouement.

"The fellow is crazy," said the count. "Gentlemen, I implore that one of you search me."

"The accusation is ridiculous." This from one of the players.

"You have but to slip your hand in the count's coat pocket and you will see that the accusation is quite serious," insisted the accuser. And then, as the others still hesitated to do so: "Come, I shall do it myself if no other will," and he stepped forward toward the count.

"No, monsieur," said De Coude. "I will submit to a search only at the hands of a gentleman."

"It is unnecessary to search the count. The cards are in his pocket. I myself saw them placed there."

All turned in surprise toward this new speaker, to behold a very well-built young man urging a resisting captive toward them by the scruff of his neck.

"It is a conspiracy," cried De Coude angrily. "There are no cards in my coat," and with that he ran his hand into his pocket. As he did so tense silence reigned in the little group. The count went dead white, and then very slowly he withdrew his hand, and in it were three cards.

He looked at them in mute and horrified surprise, and slowly the red of mortification suffused his face. Expressions of pity and contempt tinged the features of those who looked on at the death of a man's honor.

"It is a conspiracy, monsieur." It was the gray-eyed stranger who spoke. "Gentlemen," he continued, "monsieur le count did not know that those cards were in his pocket. They were placed there without his knowledge as he sat at play. From where I sat in that chair yonder I saw the reflection of it all in the mirror before me. This person whom I just intercepted in an effort to escape placed the cards in the count's pocket."

De Coude had glanced from Tarzan to the man in his grasp.

"*Mon Dieu*, Nikolas!" he cried. "You?"

Then he turned to his accuser, and eyed him intently for a moment.

"And you, monsieur, I did not recognize you without your beard. It quite disguises you, Paulvitch. I see it all now. It is quite clear, gentlemen."

"What shall we do with them, monsieur?" asked Tarzan. "Turn them over to the captain?"

"No, my friend," said the count hastily. "It is a personal matter, and I beg that you will let it drop. It is sufficient that I have been exonerated from the charge. The less we have to do with such fellows, the better. But, monsieur, how can I thank you for the great kindness you have done me? Permit me to offer you my card, and should the time come when I may serve you, remember that I am yours to command."

Tarzan had released Rokoff, who, with his confederate, Paulvitch, had hastened from the smoking-room. Just as he was leaving, Rokoff turned to Tarzan. "Monsieur will have ample opportunity to regret his interference in the affairs of others."

Tarzan smiled, and then, bowing to the count, handed him his own card.

The count read:

M. *Jean C. Tarzan*

"Monsieur Tarzan," he said, "may indeed wish that he had never befriended me, for I can assure him that he has won the enmity of two of the most unmitigated scoundrels in all Europe. Avoid them, monsieur, by all means."

"I have had more awe-inspiring enemies, my dear count," replied Tarzan with a quiet smile, "yet I am still alive and unworried. I think that neither of these two will ever find the means to harm me."

"Let us hope not, monsieur," said De Coude; "but yet it will do no harm to be on the alert, and to know that you have made at least one enemy today who never forgets and never forgives, and in whose malignant brain there are always hatching new atrocities to perpetrate upon those who have thwarted or offended him. To say that Nikolas Rokoff would be to place a wanton affront upon his satanic majesty."

That night as Tarzan entered his cabin he found a folded note upon the floor that had evidently been pushed beneath the door. He opened it and read:

M. Tarzan:

Doubtless you did not realize the gravity of your offense, or you would not have done the thing you did today. I am willing to believe that you acted in ignorance and without any intention to offend a stranger. For this reason I shall gladly permit you to offer an apology, and on receiving your assurances that you will not again interfere in affairs that do not concern you, I shall drop the matter.

Otherwise—but I am sure that you will see the wisdom of adopting the course I suggest. Very respectfully, *Nikolas Rokoff.*

Tarzan permitted a grim smile to play about his lips for a moment, then he promptly dropped the matter from his mind, and went to bed.

In a nearby cabin the Countess de Coude was speaking to her husband.

"Why so grave, my dear Raoul?" she asked. "You have been as glum as could be all evening. What worries you?"

"Olga, Nikolas is on board. Did you know it?"

"Nikolas!" she exclaimed. "But it is impossible, Raoul. It cannot be. Nikolas is under arrest in Germany."

"So I thought myself until I saw him today—him and that other arch scoundrel, Paulvitch. Olga, I cannot endure his persecution much longer. No, not even for you. Sooner or later I shall turn him over to the authorities. In fact, I am half minded to explain all to the captain before we land. On a French liner it were an easy matter, Olga, permanently to settle this Nemesis of ours."

"Oh, no, Raoul!" cried the countess, sinking to her knees before him as he sat with bowed head upon a divan. "Do not do that. Remember your promise to me. Tell me, Raoul, that you will not do that. Do not even threaten him, Raoul."

De Coude took his wife's hands in his, and gazed upon her pale and troubled countenance for some time before he spoke, as though he would wrest from those beautiful eyes the real reason which prompted her to shield this man.

"Let it be as you wish, Olga," he said at length. "I cannot understand. He has forfeited all claim upon your love, loyalty, or respect. He is a menace to your life and honor, and the life and honor of your husband. I trust you may never regret championing him."

"I do not champion him, Raoul," she interrupted vehemently. "I believe that I hate him as much as you do, but—Oh, Raoul, blood is thicker than water."

"I should today have liked to sample the consistency of his," growled De Coude grimly. "The two deliberately attempted to besmirch my honor, Olga," and then he told her of all that had happened in the smoking-room. "Had it not been for this utter stranger, they had succeeded, for who would have accepted my unsupported word against the damning evidence of those cards hidden on my person? I had almost begun to doubt myself when this Monsieur Tarzan dragged your precious Nikolas before us, and explained the whole cowardly transaction."

"Monsieur Tarzan?" asked the countess, in evident surprise.

"Yes. Do you know him, Olga?"

"I have seen him. A steward pointed him out to me."

"I did not know that he was a celebrity," said the count.

Olga de Coude changed the subject. She discovered suddenly that she might find it difficult to explain just why the steward had pointed out the handsome Monsieur Tarzan to her. Perhaps she flushed the least little bit, for was not the count, her husband, gazing at her with a strangely quizzical expression. "Ah," she thought, "a guilty conscience is a most suspicious thing."

FORGING BONDS OF HATE AND—?

It was not until late the following afternoon that Tarzan saw anything more of the fellow passengers into the midst of whose affairs his love of fair play had thrust him. And then he came most unexpectedly upon Rokoff and Paulvitch at a moment when of all others the two might least appreciate his company.

They were standing on deck at a point which was temporarily deserted, and as Tarzan came upon them they were in heated argument with a woman. Tarzan noted that she was richly appareled, and that her slender, well-modeled figure denoted youth; but as she was heavily veiled he could not discern her features.

The men were standing on either side of her, and the backs of all were toward Tarzan, so that he was quite close to them without their being aware of his presence. He noticed that Rokoff seemed to be threatening, the woman pleading; but they spoke in a strange tongue, and he could only guess from appearances that the girl was afraid.

Rokoff's attitude was so distinctly filled with the threat of physical violence that the ape-man paused for an instant just behind the trio, instinctively sensing an atmosphere of danger. Scarcely had he hesitated ere the man seized the woman roughly by the wrist, twisting it as though to wring a promise from her through torture. What would have happened next had Rokoff had his way we may only conjecture, since he did not have his way at all. Instead, steel fingers gripped his shoulder, and he was swung unceremoniously around, to meet the cold gray eyes of the stranger who had thwarted him on the previous day.

"*Sapristi!*" screamed the infuriated Rokoff. "What do you mean? Are you a fool that you thus again insult Nikolas Rokoff?"

"This is my answer to your note, monsieur," said Tarzan, in a low voice. And then he hurled the fellow from him with such force that Rokoff lunged sprawling against the rail.

"Name of a name!" shrieked Rokoff. "Pig, but you shall die for this," and, springing to his feet, he rushed upon Tarzan, tugging the meanwhile to draw a revolver from his hip pocket. The girl shrank back in terror.

"Nikolas!" she cried. "Do not—oh, do not do that. Quick, monsieur, fly, or he will surely kill you!" But instead of flying Tarzan advanced to meet the fellow. "Do not make a fool of yourself, monsieur," he said.

Rokoff, who was in a perfect frenzy of rage at the humiliation the stranger had put upon him, had at last succeeded in drawing the revolver. He had stopped, and now he deliberately raised it to Tarzan's breast and pulled the trigger. The hammer fell with a futile click on an empty chamber—the ape-man's hand shot out like the head of an angry python; there was a quick wrench, and the revolver sailed far out across the ship's rail, and dropped into the Atlantic.

For a moment the two men stood there facing one another. Rokoff had regained his self-possession. He was the first to speak.

"Twice now has monsieur seen fit to interfere in matters which do not concern him. Twice he has taken it upon himself to humiliate Nikolas Rokoff. The first offense was overlooked on the assumption that monsieur acted through ignorance, but this affair shall not be overlooked. If monsieur does not know who

Nikolas Rokoff is, this last piece of effrontery will insure that monsieur later has good reason to remember him."

"That you are a coward and a scoundrel, monsieur," replied Tarzan, "is all that I care to know of you," and he turned to ask the girl if the man had hurt her, but she had disappeared. Then, without even a glance toward Rokoff and his companion, he continued his stroll along the deck.

Tarzan could not but wonder what manner of conspiracy was on foot, or what the scheme of the two men might be. There had been something rather familiar about the appearance of the veiled woman to whose rescue he had just come, but as he had not seen her face he could not be sure that he had ever seen her before. The only thing about her that he had particularly noticed was a ring of peculiar workmanship upon a finger of the hand that Rokoff had seized, and he determined to note the fingers of the women passengers he came upon thereafter, that he might discover the identity of her whom Rokoff was persecuting, and learn if the fellow had offered her further annoyance.

Tarzan had sought his deck chair, where he sat speculating on the numerous instances of human cruelty, selfishness, and spite that had fallen to his lot to witness since that day in the jungle four years since that his eyes had first fallen upon a human being other than himself—the sleek, black Kulonga, whose swift spear had that day found the vitals of Kala, the great she-ape, and robbed the youth, Tarzan, of the only mother he had ever known.

He recalled the murder of King by the rat-faced Snipes; the abandonment of Professor Porter and his party by the mutineers of the ARROW; the cruelty of the black warriors and women of Mbonga to their captives; the petty jealousies of the civil and military officers of the West Coast colony that had afforded him his first introduction to the civilized world.

"*Mon Dieu!*" he soliloquized, "but they are all alike. Cheating, murdering, lying, fighting, and all for things that the beasts of the jungle would not deign to possess—money to purchase the effeminate pleasures of weaklings. And yet withal bound down by silly customs that make them slaves to their unhappy lot while firm in the belief that they be the lords of creation enjoying the only real pleasures of existence. In the jungle one would scarcely stand supinely aside while another took his mate. It is a silly world, an idiotic world, and Tarzan of the Apes was a fool to renounce the freedom and the happiness of his jungle to come into it."

Presently, as he sat there, the sudden feeling came over him that eyes were watching from behind, and the old instinct of the wild beast broke through the thin veneer of civilization, so that Tarzan wheeled about so quickly that the eyes of the young woman who had been surreptitiously regarding him had not even time to drop before the gray eyes of the ape-man shot an inquiring look straight into them. Then, as they fell, Tarzan saw a faint wave of crimson creep swiftly over the now half-averted face.

He smiled to himself at the result of his very uncivilized and ungallant action, for he had not lowered his own eyes when they met those of the young woman. She was very young, and equally good to look upon. Further, there was something rather familiar about her that set Tarzan to wondering where he had seen her before. He resumed his former position, and presently he was aware that she had arisen and was leaving the deck. As she passed, Tarzan turned to watch her, in the hope that he might discover a clew to satisfy his mild curiosity as to her identity.

Nor was he disappointed entirely, for as she walked away she raised one hand to the black, waving mass at the nape of her neck—the peculiarly feminine gesture that admits cognizance of appraising eyes behind her—and Tarzan saw upon a finger of this hand the ring of strange workmanship that he had seen upon the finger of the veiled woman a short time before.

So it was this beautiful young woman Rokoff had been persecuting. Tarzan wondered in a lazy sort of way whom she might be, and what relations one so lovely could have with the surly, bearded Russian.

After dinner that evening Tarzan strolled forward, where he remained until after dark, in conversation with the second officer, and when that gentleman's duties called him elsewhere Tarzan lolled lazily by the rail watching the play of the moonlight upon the gently rolling waters. He was half hidden by a davit, so that two men who approached along the deck did not see him, and as they passed Tarzan caught enough of their conversation to cause him to fall in behind them, to follow and learn what deviltry they were up to. He had recognized the voice as that of Rokoff, and had seen that his companion was Paulvitch.

Tarzan had overheard but a few words: "And if she screams you may choke her until—" But those had been enough to arouse the spirit of adventure within him, and so he kept the two men in sight as they walked, briskly now, along the deck. To the smoking-room he followed them, but they merely halted at the doorway long enough, apparently, to assure themselves that one whose whereabouts they wished to establish was within.

Then they proceeded directly to the first-class cabins upon the promenade deck. Here Tarzan found greater difficulty in escaping detection, but he managed to do so successfully. As they halted before one of the polished hardwood doors, Tarzan slipped into the shadow of a passageway not a dozen feet from them.

To their knock a woman's voice asked in French: "Who is it?"

"It is I, Olga—Nikolas," was the answer, in Rokoff's now familiar guttural. "May I come in?"

"Why do you not cease persecuting me, Nikolas?" came the voice of the woman from beyond the thin panel. "I have never harmed you."

"Come, come, Olga," urged the man, in propitiary tones; "I but ask a half dozen words with you. I shall not harm you, nor shall I enter your cabin; but I cannot shout my message through the door."

Tarzan heard the catch click as it was released from the inside. He stepped out from his hiding-place far enough to see what transpired when the door was opened, for he could not but recall the sinister words he had heard a few moments before upon the deck, "And if she screams you may choke her."

Rokoff was standing directly in front of the door. Paulvitch had flattened himself against the paneled wall of the corridor beyond. The door opened. Rokoff half entered the room, and stood with his back against the door, speaking in a low whisper to the woman, whom Tarzan could not see. Then Tarzan heard the woman's voice, level, but loud enough to distinguish her words.

"No, Nikolas," she was saying, "it is useless. Threaten as you will, I shall never accede to your demands. Leave the room, please; you have no right here. You promised not to enter."

"Very well, Olga, I shall not enter; but before I am done with you, you shall wish a thousand times that you had done at once the favor I have asked. In the end I shall win anyway, so you might as well save trouble and time for me, and disgrace for yourself and your—"

"Never, Nikolas!" interrupted the woman, and then Tarzan saw Rokoff turn and nod to Paulvitch, who sprang quickly toward the doorway of the cabin, rushing in past Rokoff, who held the door open for him. Then the latter stepped quickly out. The door closed. Tarzan heard the click of the lock as Paulvitch turned it from the inside. Rokoff remained standing before the door, with head bent, as though to catch the words of the two within. A nasty smile curled his bearded lip.

Tarzan could hear the woman's voice commanding the fellow to leave her cabin. "I shall send for my husband," she cried. "He will show you no mercy."

Paulvitch's sneering laugh came through the polished panels.

"The purser will fetch your husband, madame," said the man. "In fact, that officer has already been notified that you are entertaining a man other than your husband behind the locked door of your cabin."

"Bah!" cried the woman. "My husband will know!"

"Most assuredly your husband will know, but the purser will not; nor will the newspaper men who shall in some mysterious way hear of it on our landing. But they will think it a fine story, and so will all your friends when they read of it at breakfast on—let me see, this is Tuesday—yes, when they read of it at breakfast next Friday morning. Nor will it detract from the interest they will all feel when they learn that the man whom madame entertained is a Russian servant—her brother's valet, to be quite exact."

"Alexis Paulvitch," came the woman's voice, cold and fearless, "you are a coward, and when I whisper a certain name in your ear you will think better of your demands upon me and your threats against me, and then you will leave my cabin quickly, nor do I think that ever again will you, at least, annoy me," and there came a moment's silence in which Tarzan could imagine the woman leaning toward the scoundrel and whispering the thing she had hinted at into his ear. Only a moment of silence, and then a startled oath from the man—the scuffling of feet—a woman's scream—and silence.

But scarcely had the cry ceased before the ape-man had leaped from his hiding-place. Rokoff started to run, but Tarzan grasped him by the collar and dragged him back. Neither spoke, for both felt instinctively that murder was being done in that room, and Tarzan was confident that Rokoff had had no intention that his confederate should go that far—he felt that the man's aims were deeper than that—deeper and even more sinister than brutal, cold-blooded murder. Without hesitating to question those within, the ape-man threw his giant shoulder against the frail panel, and in a shower of splintered wood he entered the cabin, dragging Rokoff after him. Before him, on a couch, the woman lay, and on top of her was Paulvitch, his fingers gripping the fair throat, while his victim's hands beat futilely at his face, tearing desperately at the cruel fingers that were forcing the life from her.

The noise of his entrance brought Paulvitch to his feet, where he stood glowering menacingly at Tarzan. The girl rose falteringly to a sitting posture upon the couch. One hand was at her throat, and her breath came in little gasps. Although disheveled and very pale, Tarzan recognized her as the young woman whom he had caught staring at him on deck earlier in the day.

"What is the meaning of this?" said Tarzan, turning to Rokoff, whom he intuitively singled out as the instigator of the outrage. The man remained silent, scowling. "Touch the button, please," continued the ape-man; "we will have one of the ship's officers here—this affair has gone quite far enough."

"No, no," cried the girl, coming suddenly to her feet. "Please do not do that. I am sure that there was no real intention to harm me. I angered this person, and he lost control of himself, that is all. I would not care to have the matter go further, please, monsieur," and there was such a note of pleading in her voice that Tarzan could not press the matter, though his better judgment warned him that there was something afoot here of which the proper authorities should be made cognizant.

"You wish me to do nothing, then, in the matter?" he asked.

"Nothing, please," she replied.

"You are content that these two scoundrels should continue persecuting you?"

She did not seem to know what answer to make, and looked very troubled and unhappy. Tarzan saw a malicious grin of triumph curl Rokoff's lip. The girl evidently was in fear of these two—she dared not express her real desires before them.

"Then," said Tarzan, "I shall act on my own responsibility. To you," he continued, turning to Rokoff, "and this includes your accomplice, I may say that from now on to the end of the voyage I shall take it upon myself to keep an eye on you, and should there chance to come to my notice any act of either one of you that might even remotely annoy this young woman you shall be called to account for it directly to me, nor shall the calling or the accounting be pleasant experiences for either of you.

"Now get out of here," and he grabbed Rokoff and Paulvitch each by the scruff of the neck and thrust them forcibly through the doorway, giving each an added impetus down the corridor with the toe of his boot. Then he turned back to the stateroom and the girl. She was looking at him in wide-eyed astonishment.

"And you, madame, will confer a great favor upon me if you will but let me know if either of those rascals troubles you further."

"Ah, monsieur," she answered, "I hope that you will not suffer for the kind deed you attempted. You have made a very wicked and resourceful enemy, who will stop at nothing to satisfy his hatred. You must be very careful indeed, Monsieur—"

"Pardon me, madame, my name is Tarzan."

"Monsieur Tarzan. And because I would not consent to notify the officers, do not think that I am not sincerely grateful to you for the brave and chivalrous protection you rendered me. Good night, Monsieur

Tarzan. I shall never forget the debt I owe you," and, with a most winsome smile that displayed a row of perfect teeth, the girl curtsied to Tarzan, who bade her good night and made his way on deck.

It puzzled the man considerably that there should be two on board—this girl and Count de Coude—who suffered indignities at the hands of Rokoff and his companion, and yet would not permit the offenders to be brought to justice. Before he turned in that night his thoughts reverted many times to the beautiful young woman into the evidently tangled web of whose life fate had so strangely introduced him. It occurred to him that he had not learned her name. That she was married had been evidenced by the narrow gold band that encircled the third finger of her left hand. Involuntarily he wondered who the lucky man might be.

Tarzan saw nothing further of any of the actors in the little drama that he had caught a fleeting glimpse of until late in the afternoon of the last day of the voyage. Then he came suddenly face to face with the young woman as the two approached their deck chairs from opposite directions. She greeted him with a pleasant smile, speaking almost immediately of the affair he had witnessed in her cabin two nights before. It was as though she had been perturbed by a conviction that he might have construed her acquaintance with such men as Rokoff and Paulvitch as a personal reflection upon herself.

"I trust monsieur has not judged me," she said, "by the unfortunate occurrence of Tuesday evening. I have suffered much on account of it—this is the first time that I have ventured from my cabin since; I have been ashamed," she concluded simply.

"One does not judge the gazelle by the lions that attack it," replied Tarzan. "I had seen those two work before—in the smoking-room the day prior to their attack on you, if I recollect it correctly, and so, knowing their methods, I am convinced that their enmity is a sufficient guarantee of the integrity of its object. Men such as they must cleave only to the vile, hating all that is noblest and best."

"It is very kind of you to put it that way," she replied, smiling. "I have already heard of the matter of the card game. My husband told me the entire story. He spoke especially of the strength and bravery of Monsieur Tarzan, to whom he feels that he owes an immense debt of gratitude."

"Your husband?" repeated Tarzan questioningly.

"Yes. I am the Countess de Coude."

"I am already amply repaid, madame, in knowing that I have rendered a service to the wife of the Count de Coude."

"Alas, monsieur, I already am so greatly indebted to you that I may never hope to settle my own account, so pray do not add further to my obligations," and she smiled so sweetly upon him that Tarzan felt that a man might easily attempt much greater things than he had accomplished, solely for the pleasure of receiving the benediction of that smile.

He did not see her again that day, and in the rush of landing on the following morning he missed her entirely, but there had been something in the expression of her eyes as they parted on deck the previous day that haunted him. It had been almost wistful as they had spoken of the strangeness of the swift friendships of an ocean crossing, and of the equal ease with which they are broken forever.

Tarzan wondered if he should ever see her again.

WHAT HAPPENED IN THE RUE MAULE

On his arrival in Paris, Tarzan had gone directly to the apartments of his old friend, D'Arnot, where the naval lieutenant had scored him roundly for his decision to renounce the title and estates that were rightly his from his father, John Clayton, the late Lord Greystoke.

"You must be mad, my friend," said D'Arnot, "thus lightly to give up not alone wealth and position, but an opportunity to prove beyond doubt to all the world that in your veins flows the noble blood of two of England's most honored houses—instead of the blood of a savage she-ape. It is incredible that they could have believed you—Miss Porter least of all.

"Why, I never did believe it, even back in the wilds of your African jungle, when you tore the raw meat of your kills with mighty jaws, like some wild beast, and wiped your greasy hands upon your thighs. Even then, before there was the slightest proof to the contrary, I knew that you were mistaken in the belief that Kala was your mother.

"And now, with your father's diary of the terrible life led by him and your mother on that wild African shore; with the account of your birth, and, final and most convincing proof of all, your own baby finger prints upon the pages of it, it seems incredible to me that you are willing to remain a nameless, penniless vagabond."

"I do not need any better name than Tarzan," replied the ape-man; "and as for remaining a penniless vagabond, I have no intention of so doing. In fact, the next, and let us hope the last, burden that I shall be forced to put upon your unselfish friendship will be the finding of employment for me."

"Pooh, pooh!" scoffed D'Arnot. "You know that I did not mean that. Have I not told you a dozen times that I have enough for twenty men, and that half of what I have is yours? And if I gave it all to you, would it represent even the tenth part of the value I place upon your friendship, my Tarzan? Would it repay the services you did me in Africa? I do not forget, my friend, that but for you and your wondrous bravery I had died at the stake in the village of Mbonga's cannibals. Nor do I forget that to your self-sacrificing devotion I owe the fact that I recovered from the terrible wounds I received at their hands—I discovered later something of what it meant to you to remain with me in the amphitheater of apes while your heart was urging you on to the coast.

"When we finally came there, and found that Miss Porter and her party had left, I commenced to realize something of what you had done for an utter stranger. Nor am I trying to repay you with money, Tarzan. It is that just at present you need money; were it sacrifice that I might offer you it were the same—my friendship must always be yours, because our tastes are similar, and I admire you. That I cannot command, but the money I can and shall."

"Well," laughed Tarzan, "we shall not quarrel over the money. I must live, and so I must have it; but I shall be more contented with something to do. You cannot show me your friendship in a more convincing manner than to find employment for me—I shall die of inactivity in a short while. As for my birthright—it is in good hands. Clayton is not guilty of robbing me of it. He truly believes that he is the real Lord Greystoke, and the chances are that he will make a better English lord than a man who was born and raised in an African jungle. You know that I am but half civilized even now. Let me see red in anger but for a moment, and all the instincts of the savage beast that I really am, submerge what little I possess of the milder ways of culture and refinement.

"And then again, had I declared myself I should have robbed the woman I love of the wealth and position that her marriage to Clayton will now insure to her. I could not have done that—could I, Paul?

"Nor is the matter of birth of great importance to me," he went on, without waiting for a reply. "Raised as I have been, I see no worth in man or beast that is not theirs by virtue of their own mental or physical prowess. And so I am as happy to think of Kala as my mother as I would be to try to picture the poor, unhappy little English girl who passed away a year after she bore me. Kala was always kind to me in her fierce and savage way. I must have nursed at her hairy breast from the time that my own mother died. She fought for me against the wild denizens of the forest, and against the savage members of our tribe, with the ferocity of real mother love.

"And I, on my part, loved her, Paul. I did not realize how much until after the cruel spear and the poisoned arrow of Mbonga's black warrior had stolen her away from me. I was still a child when that occurred, and I threw myself upon her dead body and wept out my anguish as a child might for his own mother. To you, my friend, she would have appeared a hideous and ugly creature, but to me she was beautiful—so gloriously does love transfigure its object. And so I am perfectly content to remain forever the son of Kala, the she-ape."

"I do not admire you the less for your loyalty," said D'Arnot, "but the time will come when you will be glad to claim your own. Remember what I say, and let us hope that it will be as easy then as it is now. You must bear in mind that Professor Porter and Mr. Philander are the only people in the world who can swear that the little skeleton found in the cabin with those of your father and mother was that of an infant anthropoid ape, and not the offspring of Lord and Lady Greystoke. That evidence is most important. They are both old men. They may not live many years longer. And then, did it not occur to you that once Miss Porter knew the truth she would break her engagement with Clayton? You might easily have your title, your estates, and the woman you love, Tarzan. Had you not thought of that?"

Tarzan shook his head. "You do not know her," he said. "Nothing could bind her closer to her bargain than some misfortune to Clayton. She is from an old southern family in America, and southerners pride themselves upon their loyalty."

Tarzan spent the two following weeks renewing his former brief acquaintance with Paris. In the daytime he haunted the libraries and picture galleries. He had become an omnivorous reader, and the world of possibilities that were opened to him in this seat of culture and learning fairly appalled him when he contemplated the very infinitesimal crumb of the sum total of human knowledge that a single individual might hope to acquire even after a lifetime of study and research; but he learned what he could by day, and threw himself into a search for relaxation and amusement at night. Nor did he find Paris a whit less fertile field for his nocturnal avocation.

If he smoked too many cigarettes and drank too much absinth it was because he took civilization as he found it, and did the things that he found his civilized brothers doing. The life was a new and alluring one, and in addition he had a sorrow in his breast and a great longing which he knew could never be fulfilled, and so he sought in study and in dissipation—the two extremes—to forget the past and inhibit contemplation of the future.

He was sitting in a music hall one evening, sipping his absinth and admiring the art of a certain famous Russian dancer, when he caught a passing glimpse of a pair of evil black eyes upon him. The man turned and was lost in the crowd at the exit before Tarzan could catch a good look at him, but he was confident that he had seen those eyes before and that they had been fastened on him this evening through no passing accident. He had had the uncanny feeling for some time that he was being watched, and it was in response to this animal instinct that was strong within him that he had turned suddenly and surprised the eyes in the very act of watching him.

Before he left the music hall the matter had been forgotten, nor did he notice the swarthy individual who stepped deeper into the shadows of an opposite doorway as Tarzan emerged from the brilliantly lighted amusement hall.

Had Tarzan but known it, he had been followed many times from this and other places of amusement, but seldom if ever had he been alone. Tonight D'Arnot had had another engagement, and Tarzan had come by himself.

As he turned in the direction he was accustomed to taking from this part of Paris to his apartments, the watcher across the street ran from his hiding-place and hurried on ahead at a rapid pace.

Tarzan had been wont to traverse the Rue Maule on his way home at night. Because it was very quiet and very dark it reminded him more of his beloved African jungle than did the noisy and garish streets surrounding it. If you are familiar with your Paris you will recall the narrow, forbidding precincts of the Rue Maule. If you are not, you need but ask the police about it to learn that in all Paris there is no street to which you should give a wider berth after dark.

On this night Tarzan had proceeded some two squares through the dense shadows of the squalid old tenements which line this dismal way when he was attracted by screams and cries for help from the third floor of an opposite building. The voice was a woman's. Before the echoes of her first cries had died Tarzan was bounding up the stairs and through the dark corridors to her rescue.

At the end of the corridor on the third landing a door stood slightly ajar, and from within Tarzan heard again the same appeal that had lured him from the street. Another instant found him in the center of a dimly-lighted room. An oil lamp burned upon a high, old-fashioned mantel, casting its dim rays over a dozen repulsive figures. All but one were men. The other was a woman of about thirty. Her face, marked by low passions and dissipation, might once have been lovely. She stood with one hand at her throat, crouching against the farther wall.

"Help, monsieur," she cried in a low voice as Tarzan entered the room; "they were killing me."

As Tarzan turned toward the men about him he saw the crafty, evil faces of habitual criminals. He wondered that they had made no effort to escape. A movement behind him caused him to turn. Two things his eyes saw, and one of them caused him considerable wonderment. A man was sneaking stealthily from the room, and in the brief glance that Tarzan had of him he saw that it was Rokoff. But the other thing that he saw was of more immediate interest. It was a great brute of a fellow tiptoeing upon him from behind with a huge bludgeon in his hand, and then, as the man and his confederates saw that he was discovered, there was a concerted rush upon Tarzan from all sides. Some of the men drew knives. Others picked up chairs, while the fellow with the bludgeon raised it high above his head in a mighty swing that would have crushed Tarzan's head had it ever descended upon it.

But the brain, and the agility, and the muscles that had coped with the mighty strength and cruel craftiness of Terkoz and Numa in the fastness of their savage jungle were not to be so easily subdued as these apaches of Paris had believed.

Selecting his most formidable antagonist, the fellow with the bludgeon, Tarzan charged full upon him, dodging the falling weapon, and catching the man a terrific blow on the point of the chin that felled him in his tracks.

Then he turned upon the others. This was sport. He was reveling in the joy of battle and the lust of blood. As though it had been but a brittle shell, to break at the least rough usage, the thin veneer of his civilization fell from him, and the ten burly villains found themselves penned in a small room with a wild and savage beast, against whose steel muscles their puny strength was less than futile.

At the end of the corridor without stood Rokoff, waiting the outcome of the affair. He wished to be sure that Tarzan was dead before he left, but it was not a part of his plan to be one of those within the room when the murder occurred.

The woman still stood where she had when Tarzan entered, but her face had undergone a number of changes with the few minutes which had elapsed. From the semblance of distress which it had worn when Tarzan first saw it, it had changed to one of craftiness as he had wheeled to meet the attack from behind; but the change Tarzan had not seen.

Later an expression of surprise and then one of horror superseded the others. And who may wonder. For the immaculate gentleman her cries had lured to what was to have been his death had been suddenly metamorphosed into a demon of revenge. Instead of soft muscles and a weak resistance, she was looking upon a veritable Hercules gone mad.

"*Mon Dieu!*" she cried; "he is a beast!" For the strong, white teeth of the ape-man had found the throat of one of his assailants, and Tarzan fought as he had learned to fight with the great bull apes of the tribe of Kerchak.

He was in a dozen places at once, leaping hither and thither about the room in sinuous bounds that reminded the woman of a panther she had seen at the zoo. Now a wrist-bone snapped in his iron grip, now a shoulder was wrenched from its socket as he forced a victim's arm backward and upward.

With shrieks of pain the men escaped into the hallway as quickly as they could; but even before the first one staggered, bleeding and broken, from the room, Rokoff had seen enough to convince him that Tarzan would not be the one to lie dead in that house this night, and so the Russian had hastened to a nearby den and telephoned the police that a man was committing murder on the third floor of Rue Maule, 27. When the officers arrived they found three men groaning on the floor, a frightened woman lying upon a filthy bed, her face buried in her arms, and what appeared to be a well-dressed young gentleman standing in the center of the room awaiting the reenforcements which he had thought the footsteps of the officers hurrying up the stairway had announced—but they were mistaken in the last; it was a wild beast that looked upon them through those narrowed lids and steel-gray eyes. With the smell of blood the last vestige of civilization had deserted Tarzan, and now he stood at bay, like a lion surrounded by hunters, awaiting the next overt act, and crouching to charge its author.

"What has happened here?" asked one of the policemen.

Tarzan explained briefly, but when he turned to the woman for confirmation of his statement he was appalled by her reply.

"He lies!" she screamed shrilly, addressing the policeman. "He came to my room while I was alone, and for no good purpose. When I repulsed him he would have killed me had not my screams attracted these gentlemen, who were passing the house at the time. He is a devil, monsieurs; alone he has all but killed ten men with his bare hands and his teeth."

So shocked was Tarzan by her ingratitude that for a moment he was struck dumb. The police were inclined to be a little skeptical, for they had had other dealings with this same lady and her lovely coterie of gentlemen friends. However, they were policemen, not judges, so they decided to place all the inmates of the room under arrest, and let another, whose business it was, separate the innocent from the guilty.

But they found that it was one thing to tell this well-dressed young man that he was under arrest, but quite another to enforce it.

"I am guilty of no offense," he said quietly. "I have but sought to defend myself. I do not know why the woman has told you what she has. She can have no enmity against me, for never until I came to this room in response to her cries for help had I seen her."

"Come, come," said one of the officers; "there are judges to listen to all that," and he advanced to lay his hand upon Tarzan's shoulder. An instant later he lay crumpled in a corner of the room, and then, as his comrades rushed in upon the ape-man, they experienced a taste of what the apaches had but recently gone through. So quickly and so roughly did he handle them that they had not even an opportunity to draw their revolvers.

During the brief fight Tarzan had noted the open window and, beyond, the stem of a tree, or a telegraph pole—he could not tell which. As the last officer went down, one of his fellows succeeded in drawing his revolver and, from where he lay on the floor, fired at Tarzan. The shot missed, and before the man could fire again Tarzan had swept the lamp from the mantel and plunged the room into darkness.

The next they saw was a lithe form spring to the sill of the open window and leap, panther-like, onto the pole across the walk. When the police gathered themselves together and reached the street their prisoner was nowhere to be seen.

They did not handle the woman and the men who had not escaped any too gently when they took them to the station; they were a very sore and humiliated detail of police. It galled them to think that it would be necessary to report that a single unarmed man had wiped the floor with the whole lot of them, and then escaped them as easily as though they had not existed.

The officer who had remained in the street swore that no one had leaped from the window or left the building from the time they entered until they had come out. His comrades thought that he lied, but they could not prove it.

When Tarzan found himself clinging to the pole outside the window, he followed his jungle instinct and looked below for enemies before he ventured down. It was well he did, for just beneath stood a policeman. Above, Tarzan saw no one, so he went up instead of down.

The top of the pole was opposite the roof of the building, so it was but the work of an instant for the muscles that had for years sent him hurtling through the treetops of his primeval forest to carry him across the little space between the pole and the roof. From one building he went to another, and so on, with much climbing, until at a cross street he discovered another pole, down which he ran to the ground.

For a square or two he ran swiftly; then he turned into a little all-night cafe and in the lavatory removed the evidences of his over-roof promenade from hands and clothes. When he emerged a few moments later it was to saunter slowly on toward his apartments.

Not far from them he came to a well-lighted boulevard which it was necessary to cross. As he stood directly beneath a brilliant arc light, waiting for a limousine that was approaching to pass him, he heard his name called in a sweet feminine voice. Looking up, he met the smiling eyes of Olga de Coude as she leaned forward upon the back seat of the machine. He bowed very low in response to her friendly greeting. When he straightened up the machine had borne her away.

"Rokoff and the Countess de Coude both in the same evening," he soliloquized; "Paris is not so large, after all."

THE COUNTESS EXPLAINS

"Your Paris is more dangerous than my savage jungles, Paul," concluded Tarzan, after narrating his adventures to his friend the morning following his encounter with the apaches and police in the Rue Maule. "Why did they lure me there? Were they hungry?"

D'Arnot feigned a horrified shudder, but he laughed at the quaint suggestion.

"It is difficult to rise above the jungle standards and reason by the light of civilized ways, is it not, my friend?" he queried banteringly.

"Civilized ways, forsooth," scoffed Tarzan. "Jungle standards do not countenance wanton atrocities. There we kill for food and for self-preservation, or in the winning of mates and the protection of the young. Always, you see, in accordance with the dictates of some great natural law. But here! Faugh, your civilized man is more brutal than the brutes. He kills wantonly, and, worse than that, he utilizes a noble sentiment, the brotherhood of man, as a lure to entice his unwary victim to his doom. It was in answer to an appeal from a fellow being that I hastened to that room where the assassins lay in wait for me.

"I did not realize, I could not realize for a long time afterward, that any woman could sink to such moral depravity as that one must have to call a would-be rescuer to death. But it must have been so—the sight of Rokoff there and the woman's later repudiation of me to the police make it impossible to place any other construction upon her acts. Rokoff must have known that I frequently passed through the Rue Maule. He lay in wait for me—his entire scheme worked out to the last detail, even to the woman's story in case a hitch should occur in the program such as really did happen. It is all perfectly plain to me."

"Well," said D'Arnot, "among other things, it has taught you what I have been unable to impress upon you—that the Rue Maule is a good place to avoid after dark."

"On the contrary," replied Tarzan, with a smile, "it has convinced me that it is the one worth-while street in all Paris. Never again shall I miss an opportunity to traverse it, for it has given me the first real entertainment I have had since I left Africa."

"It may give you more than you will relish even without another visit," said D'Arnot. "You are not through with the police yet, remember. I know the Paris police well enough to assure you that they will not soon forget what you did to them. Sooner or later they will get you, my dear Tarzan, and then they will lock the wild man of the woods up behind iron bars. How will you like that?"

"They will never lock Tarzan of the Apes behind iron bars," replied he, grimly.

There was something in the man's voice as he said it that caused D'Arnot to look up sharply at his friend. What he saw in the set jaw and the cold, gray eyes made the young Frenchman very apprehensive for this great child, who could recognize no law mightier than his own mighty physical prowess. He saw that something must be done to set Tarzan right with the police before another encounter was possible.

"You have much to learn, Tarzan," he said gravely. "The law of man must be respected, whether you relish it or no. Nothing but trouble can come to you and your friends should you persist in defying the police. I can explain it to them once for you, and that I shall do this very day, but hereafter you must obey the law. If its representatives say 'Come,' you must come; if they say 'Go,' you must go. Now we shall go to my great friend in the department and fix up this matter of the Rue Maule. Come!"

Together they entered the office of the police official a half hour later. He was very cordial. He remembered Tarzan from the visit the two had made him several months prior in the matter of finger prints.

When D'Arnot had concluded the narration of the events which had transpired the previous evening, a grim smile was playing about the lips of the policeman. He touched a button near his hand, and as he waited for the clerk to respond to its summons he searched through the papers on his desk for one which he finally located.

"Here, Joubon," he said as the clerk entered. "Summon these officers—have them come to me at once," and he handed the man the paper he had sought. Then he turned to Tarzan.

"You have committed a very grave offense, monsieur," he said, not unkindly, "and but for the explanation made by our good friend here I should be inclined to judge you harshly. I am, instead, about to do a rather unheard-of-thing. I have summoned the officers whom you maltreated last night. They shall hear Lieutenant D'Arnot's story, and then I shall leave it to their discretion to say whether you shall be prosecuted or not.

"You have much to learn about the ways of civilization. Things that seem strange or unnecessary to you, you must learn to accept until you are able to judge the motives behind them. The officers whom you attacked were but doing their duty. They had no discretion in the matter. Every day they risk their lives in the protection of the lives or property of others. They would do the same for you. They are very brave men, and they are deeply mortified that a single unarmed man bested and beat them.

"Make it easy for them to overlook what you did. Unless I am gravely in error you are yourself a very brave man, and brave men are proverbially magnanimous."

Further conversation was interrupted by the appearance of the four policemen. As their eyes fell on Tarzan, surprise was writ large on each countenance.

"My children," said the official, "here is the gentleman whom you met in the Rue Maule last evening. He has come voluntarily to give himself up. I wish you to listen attentively to Lieutenant D'Arnot, who will tell you a part of the story of monsieur's life. It may explain his attitude toward you of last night. Proceed, my dear lieutenant."

D'Arnot spoke to the policemen for half an hour. He told them something of Tarzan's wild jungle life. He explained the savage training that had taught him to battle like a wild beast in self-preservation. It became plain to them that the man had been guided by instinct rather than reason in his attack upon them. He had not understood their intentions. To him they had been little different from any of the various forms of life he had been accustomed to in his native jungle, where practically all were his enemies.

"Your pride has been wounded," said D'Arnot, in conclusion. "It is the fact that this man overcame you that hurts the most. But you need feel no shame. You would not make apologies for defeat had you been penned in that small room with an African lion, or with the great Gorilla of the jungles.

"And yet you were battling with muscles that have time and time again been pitted, and always victoriously, against these terrors of the dark continent. It is no disgrace to fall beneath the superhuman strength of Tarzan of the Apes."

And then, as the men stood looking first at Tarzan and then at their superior the ape-man did the one thing which was needed to erase the last remnant of animosity which they might have felt for him. With outstretched hand he advanced toward them.

"I am sorry for the mistake I made," he said simply. "Let us be friends." And that was the end of the whole matter, except that Tarzan became a subject of much conversation in the barracks of the police, and increased the number of his friends by four brave men at least.

On their return to D'Arnot's apartments the lieutenant found a letter awaiting him from an English friend, William Cecil Clayton, Lord Greystoke. The two had maintained a correspondence since the birth of their friendship on that ill-fated expedition in search of Jane Porter after her theft by Terkoz, the bull ape.

"They are to be married in London in about two months," said D'Arnot, as he completed his perusal of the letter. Tarzan did not need to be told who was meant by "they." He made no reply, but he was very quiet and thoughtful during the balance of the day.

That evening they attended the opera. Tarzan's mind was still occupied by his gloomy thoughts. He paid little or no attention to what was transpiring upon the stage. Instead he saw only the lovely vision of a beautiful American girl, and heard naught but a sad, sweet voice acknowledging that his love was returned. And she was to marry another!

He shook himself to be rid of his unwelcome thoughts, and at the same instant he felt eyes upon him. With the instinct that was his by virtue of training he looked up squarely into the eyes that were looking at him, to find that they were shining from the smiling face of Olga, Countess de Coude. As Tarzan returned her bow he was positive that there was an invitation in her look, almost a plea. The next intermission found him beside her in her box.

"I have so much wished to see you," she was saying. "It has troubled me not a little to think that after the service you rendered to both my husband and myself no adequate explanation was ever made you of what must have seemed ingratitude on our part in not taking the necessary steps to prevent a repetition of the attacks upon us by those two men."

"You wrong me," replied Tarzan. "My thoughts of you have been only the most pleasant. You must not feel that any explanation is due me. Have they annoyed you further?"

"They never cease," she replied sadly. "I feel that I must tell some one, and I do not know another who so deserves an explanation as you. You must permit me to do so. It may be of service to you, for I know Nikolas Rokoff quite well enough to be positive that you have not seen the last of him. He will find some means to be revenged upon you. What I wish to tell you may be of aid to you in combating any scheme of revenge he may harbor. I cannot tell you here, but tomorrow I shall be at home to Monsieur Tarzan at five."

"It will be an eternity until tomorrow at five," he said, as he bade her good night. From a corner of the theater Rokoff and Paulvitch saw Monsieur Tarzan in the box of the Countess de Coude, and both men smiled.

At four-thirty the following afternoon a swarthy, bearded man rang the bell at the servants' entrance of the palace of the Count de Coude. The footman who opened the door raised his eyebrows in recognition as he saw who stood without. A low conversation passed between the two.

At first the footman demurred from some proposition that the bearded one made, but an instant later something passed from the hand of the caller to the hand of the servant. Then the latter turned and led the visitor by a roundabout way to a little curtained alcove off the apartment in which the countess was wont to serve tea of an afternoon.

A half hour later Tarzan was ushered into the room, and presently his hostess entered, smiling, and with outstretched hands.

"I am so glad that you came," she said.

"Nothing could have prevented," he replied.

For a few moments they spoke of the opera, of the topics that were then occupying the attention of Paris, of the pleasure of renewing their brief acquaintance which had had its inception under such odd circumstances, and this brought them to the subject that was uppermost in the minds of both.

"You must have wondered," said the countess finally, "what the object of Rokoff's persecution could be. It is very simple. The count is intrusted with many of the vital secrets of the ministry of war. He often has in his possession papers that foreign powers would give a fortune to possess—secrets of state that their agents would commit murder and worse than murder to learn.

"There is such a matter now in his possession that would make the fame and fortune of any Russian who could divulge it to his government. Rokoff and Paulvitch are Russian spies. They will stop at nothing to procure this information. The affair on the liner—I mean the matter of the card game—was for the purpose of blackmailing the knowledge they seek from my husband.

"Had he been convicted of cheating at cards, his career would have been blighted. He would have had to leave the war department. He would have been socially ostracized. They intended to hold this club over him—the price of an avowal on their part that the count was but the victim of the plot of enemies who wished to besmirch his name was to have been the papers they seek.

"You thwarted them in this. Then they concocted the scheme whereby my reputation was to be the price, instead of the count's. When Paulvitch entered my cabin he explained it to me. If I would obtain the information for them he promised to go no farther, otherwise Rokoff, who stood without, was to notify the purser that I was entertaining a man other than my husband behind the locked doors of my cabin. He was to tell every one he met on the boat, and when we landed he was to have given the whole story to the newspaper men.

"Was it not too horrible? But I happened to know something of Monsieur Paulvitch that would send him to the gallows in Russia if it were known by the police of St. Petersburg. I dared him to carry out his plan, and then I leaned toward him and whispered a name in his ear. Like that"—and she snapped her fingers—" he flew at my throat as a madman. He would have killed me had you not interfered."

"The brutes!" muttered Tarzan.

"They are worse than that, my friend," she said.

"They are devils. I fear for you because you have gained their hatred. I wish you to be on your guard constantly. Tell me that you will, for my sake, for I should never forgive myself should you suffer through the kindness you did me."

"I do not fear them," he replied. "I have survived grimmer enemies than Rokoff and Paulvitch." He saw that she knew nothing of the occurrence in the Rue Maule, nor did he mention it, fearing that it might distress her.

"For your own safety," he continued, "why do you not turn the scoundrels over to the authorities? They should make quick work of them."

She hesitated for a moment before replying.

"There are two reasons," she said finally. "One of them it is that keeps the count from doing that very thing. The other, my real reason for fearing to expose them, I have never told—only Rokoff and I know it. I wonder," and then she paused, looking intently at him for a long time.

"And what do you wonder?" he asked, smiling.

"I was wondering why it is that I want to tell you the thing that I have not dared tell even to my husband. I believe that you would understand, and that you could tell me the right course to follow. I believe that you would not judge me too harshly."

"I fear that I should prove a very poor judge, madame," Tarzan replied, "for if you had been guilty of murder I should say that the victim should be grateful to have met so sweet a fate."

"Oh, dear, no," she expostulated; "it is not so terrible as that. But first let me tell you the reason the count has for not prosecuting these men; then, if I can hold my courage, I shall tell you the real reason that I dare not. The first is that Nikolas Rokoff is my brother. We are Russians. Nikolas has been a bad man since I can remember. He was cashiered from the Russian army, in which he held a captaincy. There was a scandal for a time, but after a while it was partially forgotten, and my father obtained a position for him in the secret service.

"There have been many terrible crimes laid at Nikolas' door, but he has always managed to escape punishment. Of late he has accomplished it by trumped-up evidence convicting his victims of treason against the czar, and the Russian police, who are always only too ready to fasten guilt of this nature upon any and all, have accepted his version and exonerated him."

"Have not his attempted crimes against you and your husband forfeited whatever rights the bonds of kinship might have accorded him?" asked Tarzan. "The fact that you are his sister has not deterred him from seeking to besmirch your honor. You owe him no loyalty, madame."

"Ah, but there is that other reason. If I owe him no loyalty though he be my brother, I cannot so easily disavow the fear I hold him in because of a certain episode in my life of which he is cognizant.

"I might as well tell you all," she resumed after a pause, "for I see that it is in my heart to tell you sooner or later. I was educated in a convent. While there I met a man whom I supposed to be a gentleman. I knew little or nothing about men and less about love. I got it into my foolish head that I loved this man, and at his urgent request I ran away with him. We were to have been married.

"I was with him just three hours. All in the daytime and in public places—railroad stations and upon a train. When we reached our destination where we were to have been married, two officers stepped up to my escort as we descended from the train, and placed him under arrest. They took me also, but when I had told my story they did not detain me, other than to send me back to the convent under the care of a matron. It seemed that the man who had wooed me was no gentleman at all, but a deserter from the army as well as a fugitive from civil justice. He had a police record in nearly every country in Europe.

"The matter was hushed up by the authorities of the convent. Not even my parents knew of it. But Nikolas met the man afterward, and learned the whole story. Now he threatens to tell the count if I do not do just as he wishes me to."

Tarzan laughed. "You are still but a little girl. The story that you have told me cannot reflect in any way upon your reputation, and were you not a little girl at heart you would know it. Go to your husband tonight, and tell him the whole story, just as you have told it to me. Unless I am much mistaken he will laugh at you for your fears, and take immediate steps to put that precious brother of yours in prison where he belongs."

"I only wish that I dared," she said; "but I am afraid. I learned early to fear men. First my father, then Nikolas, then the fathers in the convent. Nearly all my friends fear their husbands—why should I not fear mine?"

"It does not seem right that women should fear men," said Tarzan, an expression of puzzlement on his face. "I am better acquainted with the jungle folk, and there it is more often the other way around, except among the black men, and they to my mind are in most ways lower in the scale than the beasts. No, I cannot understand why civilized women should fear men, the beings that are created to protect them. I should hate to think that any woman feared me."

"I do not think that any woman would fear you, my friend," said Olga de Coude softly. "I have known you but a short while, yet though it may seem foolish to say it, you are the only man I have ever known whom I think that I should never fear—it is strange, too, for you are very strong. I wondered at the ease with which you handled Nikolas and Paulvitch that night in my cabin. It was marvellous." As Tarzan was leaving her a short time later he wondered a little at the clinging pressure of her hand at parting, and the firm insistence with which she exacted a promise from him that he would call again on the morrow.

The memory of her half-veiled eyes and perfect lips as she had stood smiling up into his face as he bade her good-by remained with him for the balance of the day. Olga de Coude was a very beautiful woman, and Tarzan of the Apes a very lonely young man, with a heart in him that was in need of the doctoring that only a woman may provide.

As the countess turned back into the room after Tarzan's departure, she found herself face to face with Nikolas Rokoff.

"How long have you been here?" she cried, shrinking away from him.

"Since before your lover came," he answered, with a nasty leer.

"Stop!" she commanded. "How dare you say such a thing to me—your sister!"

"Well, my dear Olga, if he is not your lover, accept my apologies; but it is no fault of yours that he is not. Had he one-tenth the knowledge of women that I have you would be in his arms this minute. He is a stupid fool, Olga. Why, your every word and act was an open invitation to him, and he had not the sense to see it."

The woman put her hands to her ears.

"I will not listen. You are wicked to say such things as that. No matter what you may threaten me with, you know that I am a good woman. After tonight you will not dare to annoy me, for I shall tell Raoul all. He will understand, and then, Monsieur Nikolas, beware!"

"You shall tell him nothing," said Rokoff. "I have this affair now, and with the help of one of your servants whom I may trust it will lack nothing in the telling when the time comes that the details of the sworn evidence shall be poured into your husband's ears. The other affair served its purpose well—we now have something tangible to work on, Olga. A real *affair*—and you a trusted wife. Shame, Olga," and the brute laughed.

So the countess told her count nothing, and matters were worse than they had been. From a vague fear her mind was transferred to a very tangible one. It may be, too, that conscience helped to enlarge it out of all proportion.

THE PLOT THAT FAILED

For a month Tarzan was a regular and very welcome devotee at the shrine of the beautiful Countess de Coude. Often he met other members of the select little coterie that dropped in for tea of an afternoon. More often Olga found devices that would give her an hour of Tarzan alone.

For a time she had been frightened by what Nikolas had insinuated. She had not thought of this big, young man as anything more than friend, but with the suggestion implanted by the evil words of her brother she had grown to speculate much upon the strange force which seemed to attract her toward the gray-eyed stranger. She did not wish to love him, nor did she wish his love.

She was much younger than her husband, and without having realized it she had been craving the haven of a friendship with one nearer her own age. Twenty is shy in exchanging confidences with forty. Tarzan was but two years her senior. He could understand her, she felt. Then he was clean and honorable and chivalrous. She was not afraid of him. That she could trust him she had felt instinctively from the first.

From a distance Rokoff had watched this growing intimacy with malicious glee. Ever since he had learned that Tarzan knew that he was a Russian spy there had been added to his hatred for the ape-man a great fear that he would expose him. He was but waiting now until the moment was propitious for a master stroke. He wanted to rid himself forever of Tarzan, and at the same time reap an ample revenge for the humiliations and defeats that he had suffered at his hands.

Tarzan was nearer to contentment than he had been since the peace and tranquility of his jungle had been broken in upon by the advent of the marooned Porter party. He enjoyed the pleasant social intercourse with Olga's friends, while the friendship which had sprung up between the fair countess and himself was a source of never-ending delight. It broke in upon and dispersed his gloomy thoughts, and served as a balm to his lacerated heart.

Sometimes D'Arnot accompanied him on his visits to the De Coude home, for he had long known both Olga and the count. Occasionally De Coude dropped in, but the multitudinous affairs of his official position and the never-ending demands of politics kept him from home usually until late at night.

Rokoff spied upon Tarzan almost constantly, waiting for the time that he should call at the De Coude palace at night, but in this he was doomed to disappointment. On several occasions Tarzan accompanied the countess to her home after the opera, but he invariably left her at the entrance—much to the disgust of the lady's devoted brother.

Finding that it seemed impossible to trap Tarzan through any voluntary act of his own, Rokoff and Paulvitch put their heads together to hatch a plan that would trap the ape-man in all the circumstantial evidence of a compromising position.

For days they watched the papers as well as the movements of De Coude and Tarzan. At length they were rewarded. A morning paper made brief mention of a smoker that was to be given on the following evening by the German minister. De Coude's name was among those of the invited guests. If he attended this meant that he would be absent from his home until after midnight.

On the night of the banquet Paulvitch waited at the curb before the residence of the German minister, where he could scan the face of each guest that arrived. He had not long to wait before De Coude descended from his car and passed him. That was enough. Paulvitch hastened back to his quarters, where Rokoff awaited him. There they waited until after eleven, then Paulvitch took down the receiver of their telephone. He called a number.

"The apartments of Lieutenant D'Arnot?" he asked, when he had obtained his connection.

"A message for Monsieur Tarzan, if he will be so kind as to step to the telephone."

For a minute there was silence.

"Monsieur Tarzan?"

"Ah, yes, monsieur, this is Francois—in the service of the Countess de Coude. Possibly monsieur does poor Francois the honor to recall him—yes?

"Yes, monsieur. I have a message, an urgent message from the countess. She asks that you hasten to her at once—she is in trouble, monsieur.

"No, monsieur, poor Francois does not know. Shall I tell madame that monsieur will be here shortly?

"Thank you, monsieur. The good God will bless you."

Paulvitch hung up the receiver and turned to grin at Rokoff.

"It will take him thirty minutes to get there. If you reach the German minister's in fifteen, De Coude should arrive at his home in about forty-five minutes. It all depends upon whether the fool will remain fifteen minutes after he finds that a trick has been played upon him; but unless I am mistaken Olga will be loath to let him go in so short a time as that. Here is the note for De Coude. Hasten!"

Paulvitch lost no time in reaching the German minister's. At the door he handed the note to a footman. "This is for the Count de Coude. It is very urgent. You must see that it is placed in his hands at once," and he dropped a piece of silver into the willing hand of the servant. Then he returned to his quarters.

A moment later De Coude was apologizing to his host as he tore open the envelope. What he read left his face white and his hand trembling.

Monsieur Le Count De Coude:
One who wishes to save the honor of your name takes this means to warn you that the sanctity of your home is this minute in jeopardy.

A certain man who for months has been a constant visitor there during your absence is now with your wife. If you go at once to your countess' boudoir you will find them together.

A Friend.

Twenty minutes after Paulvitch had called Tarzan, Rokoff obtained a connection with Olga's private line. Her maid answered the telephone which was in the countess' boudoir.

"But madame has retired," said the maid, in answer to Rokoff's request to speak with her.

"This is a very urgent message for the countess' ears alone," replied Rokoff. "Tell her that she must arise and slip something about her and come to the telephone. I shall call up again in five minutes." Then he hung up his receiver. A moment later Paulvitch entered.

"The count has the message?" asked Rokoff.

"He should be on his way to his home by now," replied Paulvitch.

"Good! My lady will be sitting in her boudoir, very much in negligee, about now. In a minute the faithful Jacques will escort Monsieur Tarzan into her presence without announcing him. It will take a few minutes for explanations. Olga will look very alluring in the filmy creation that is her night-dress, and the clinging robe which but half conceals the charms that the former does not conceal at all. Olga will be surprised, but not displeased.

"If there is a drop of red blood in the man the count will break in upon a very pretty love scene in about fifteen minutes from now. I think we have planned marvelously, my dear Alexis. Let us go out and drink to the very good health of Monsieur Tarzan in some of old Plancon's unparalleled absinth; not forgetting that the Count de Coude is one of the best swordsmen in Paris, and by far the best shot in all France."

When Tarzan reached Olga's, Jacques was awaiting him at the entrance.

"This way, Monsieur," he said, and led the way up the broad, marble staircase. In another moment he had opened a door, and, drawing aside a heavy curtain, obsequiously bowed Tarzan into a dimly lighted apartment. Then Jacques vanished.

Across the room from him Tarzan saw Olga seated before a little desk on which stood her telephone. She was tapping impatiently upon the polished surface of the desk. She had not heard him enter.

"Olga," he said, "what is wrong?"

She turned toward him with a little cry of alarm.

"Jean!" she cried. "What are you doing here? Who admitted you? What does it mean?"

Tarzan was thunderstruck, but in an instant he realized a part of the truth.

"Then you did not send for me, Olga?"

"Send for you at this time of night? *Mon Dieu!* Jean, do you think that I am quite mad?"

"Francois telephoned me to come at once; that you were in trouble and wanted me."

"Francois? Who in the world is Francois?"

"He said that he was in your service. He spoke as though I should recall the fact."

"There is no one by that name in my employ. Some one has played a joke upon you, Jean," and Olga laughed.

"I fear that it may be a most sinister 'joke,' Olga," he replied. "There is more back of it than humor."

"What do you mean? You do not think that—"

"Where is the count?" he interrupted.

"At the German ambassador's."

"This is another move by your estimable brother. Tomorrow the count will hear of it. He will question the servants. Everything will point to—to what Rokoff wishes the count to think."

"The scoundrel!" cried Olga. She had arisen, and come close to Tarzan, where she stood looking up into his face. She was very frightened. In her eyes was an expression that the hunter sees in those of a poor, terrified doe—puzzled—questioning. She trembled, and to steady herself raised her hands to his broad shoulders. "What shall we do, Jean?" she whispered. "It is terrible. Tomorrow all Paris will read of it—he will see to that."

Her look, her attitude, her words were eloquent of the age-old appeal of defenseless woman to her natural protector—man. Tarzan took one of the warm little hands that lay on his breast in his own strong one. The act was quite involuntary, and almost equally so was the instinct of protection that threw a sheltering arm around the girl's shoulders.

The result was electrical. Never before had he been so close to her. In startled guilt they looked suddenly into each other's eyes, and where Olga de Coude should have been strong she was weak, for she crept closer into the man's arms, and clasped her own about his neck. And Tarzan of the Apes? He took the panting figure into his mighty arms, and covered the hot lips with kisses.

Raoul de Coude made hurried excuses to his host after he had read the note handed him by the ambassador's butler. Never afterward could he recall the nature of the excuses he made. Everything was quite a blur to him up to the time that he stood on the threshold of his own home. Then he became very cool, moving quietly and with caution. For some inexplicable reason Jacques had the door open before he was halfway to the steps. It did not strike him at the time as being unusual, though afterward he remarked it.

Very softly he tiptoed up the stairs and along the gallery to the door of his wife's boudoir. In his hand was a heavy walking stick—in his heart, murder.

Olga was the first to see him. With a horrified shriek she tore herself from Tarzan's arms, and the ape-man turned just in time to ward with his arm a terrific blow that De Coude had aimed at his head. Once, twice, three times the heavy stick fell with lightning rapidity, and each blow aided in the transition of the ape-man back to the primordial.

With the low, guttural snarl of the bull ape he sprang for the Frenchman. The great stick was torn from his grasp and broken in two as though it had been matchwood, to be flung aside as the now infuriated beast charged for his adversary's throat. Olga de Coude stood a horrified spectator of the terrible scene which ensued during the next brief moment, then she sprang to where Tarzan was murdering her husband—choking the life from him—shaking him as a terrier might shake a rat.

Frantically she tore at his great hands. "Mother of God!" she cried. "You are killing him, you are killing him! Oh, Jean, you are killing my husband!"

Tarzan was deaf with rage. Suddenly he hurled the body to the floor, and, placing his foot upon the upturned breast, raised his head. Then through the palace of the Count de Coude rang the awesome challenge of the bull ape that has made a kill. From cellar to attic the horrid sound searched out the servants, and left them blanched and trembling. The woman in the room sank to her knees beside the body of her husband, and prayed.

Slowly the red mist faded from before Tarzan's eyes. Things began to take form—he was regaining the perspective of civilized man. His eyes fell upon the figure of the kneeling woman. "Olga," he whispered. She looked up, expecting to see the maniacal light of murder in the eyes above her. Instead she saw sorrow and contrition.

"Oh, Jean!" she cried. "See what you have done. He was my husband. I loved him, and you have killed him."

Very gently Tarzan raised the limp form of the Count de Coude and bore it to a couch. Then he put his ear to the man's breast.

"Some brandy, Olga," he said.

She brought it, and together they forced it between his lips. Presently a faint gasp came from the white lips. The head turned, and De Coude groaned.

"He will not die," said Tarzan. "Thank God!"

"Why did you do it, Jean?" she asked.

"I do not know. He struck me, and I went mad. I have seen the apes of my tribe do the same thing. I have never told you my story, Olga. It would have been better had you known it—this might not have happened. I never saw my father. The only mother I knew was a ferocious she-ape. Until I was fifteen I had never seen a human being. I was twenty before I saw a white man. A little more than a year ago I was a naked beast of prey in an African jungle.

"Do not judge me too harshly. Two years is too short a time in which to attempt to work the change in an individual that it has taken countless ages to accomplish in the white race."

"I do not judge at all, Jean. The fault is mine. You must go now—he must not find you here when he regains consciousness. Good-by."

It was a sorrowful Tarzan who walked with bowed head from the palace of the Count de Coude.

Once outside his thoughts took definite shape, to the end that twenty minutes later he entered a police station not far from the Rue Maule. Here he soon found one of the officers with whom he had had the encounter several weeks previous. The policeman was genuinely glad to see again the man who had so roughly handled him. After a moment of conversation Tarzan asked if he had ever heard of Nikolas Rokoff or Alexis Paulvitch.

"Very often, indeed, monsieur. Each has a police record, and while there is nothing charged against them now, we make it a point to know pretty well where they may be found should the occasion demand. It is only the same precaution that we take with every known criminal. Why does monsieur ask?"

"They are known to me," replied Tarzan. "I wish to see Monsieur Rokoff on a little matter of business. If you can direct me to his lodgings I shall appreciate it."

A few minutes later he bade the policeman adieu, and, with a slip of paper in his pocket bearing a certain address in a semirespectable quarter, he walked briskly toward the nearest taxi stand.

Rokoff and Paulvitch had returned to their rooms, and were sitting talking over the probable outcome of the evening's events. They had telephoned to the offices of two of the morning papers from which they momentarily expected representatives to hear the first report of the scandal that was to stir social Paris on the morrow.

A heavy step sounded on the stairway. "Ah, but these newspaper men are prompt," exclaimed Rokoff, and as a knock fell upon the door of their room: "Enter, monsieur."

The smile of welcome froze upon the Russian's face as he looked into the hard, gray eyes of his visitor.

"Name of a name!" he shouted, springing to his feet, "What brings you here!"

"Sit down!" said Tarzan, so low that the men could barely catch the words, but in a tone that brought Rokoff to his chair, and kept Paulvitch in his.

"You know what has brought me here," he continued, in the same low tone. "It should be to kill you, but because you are Olga de Coude's brother I shall not do that—now.

"I shall give you a chance for your lives. Paulvitch does not count much—he is merely a stupid, foolish little tool, and so I shall not kill him so long as I permit you to live. Before I leave you two alive in this room you will have done two things. The first will be to write a full confession of your connection with tonight's plot—and sign it.

"The second will be to promise me upon pain of death that you will permit no word of this affair to get into the newspapers. If you do not do both, neither of you will be alive when I pass next through that doorway. Do you understand?" And, without waiting for a reply: "Make haste; there is ink before you, and paper and a pen."

Rokoff assumed a truculent air, attempting by bravado to show how little he feared Tarzan's threats. An instant later he felt the ape-man's steel fingers at his throat, and Paulvitch, who attempted to dodge them and reach the door, was lifted completely off the floor, and hurled senseless into a corner. When Rokoff commenced to blacken about the face Tarzan released his hold and shoved the fellow back into his chair. After a moment of coughing Rokoff sat sullenly glaring at the man standing opposite him. Presently Paulvitch came to himself, and limped painfully back to his chair at Tarzan's command.

"Now write," said the ape-man. "If it is necessary to handle you again I shall not be so lenient."

Rokoff picked up a pen and commenced to write.

"See that you omit no detail, and that you mention every name," cautioned Tarzan.

Presently there was a knock at the door. "Enter," said Tarzan.

A dapper young man came in. "I am from the *Matin*," he announced. "I understand that Monsieur Rokoff has a story for me."

"Then you are mistaken, monsieur," replied Tarzan. "You have no story for publication, have you, my dear Nikolas."

Rokoff looked up from his writing with an ugly scowl upon his face.

"No," he growled, "I have no story for publication—now."

"Nor ever, my dear Nikolas," and the reporter did not see the nasty light in the ape-man's eye; but Nikolas Rokoff did.

"Nor ever," he repeated hastily.

"It is too bad that monsieur has been troubled," said Tarzan, turning to the newspaper man. "I bid monsieur good evening," and he bowed the dapper young man out of the room, and closed the door in his face.

An hour later Tarzan, with a rather bulky manuscript in his coat pocket, turned at the door leading from Rokoff's room.

"Were I you I should leave France," he said, "for sooner or later I shall find an excuse to kill you that will not in any way compromise your sister."

A DUEL

D'Arnot was asleep when Tarzan entered their apartments after leaving Rokoff's. Tarzan did not disturb him, but the following morning he narrated the happenings of the previous evening, omitting not a single detail.

"What a fool I have been," he concluded. "De Coude and his wife were both my friends. How have I returned their friendship? Barely did I escape murdering the count. I have cast a stigma on the name of a good woman. It is very probable that I have broken up a happy home."

"Do you love Olga de Coude?" asked D'Arnot.

"Were I not positive that she does not love me I could not answer your question, Paul; but without disloyalty to her I tell you that I do not love her, nor does she love me. For an instant we were the victims of a sudden madness—it was not love—and it would have left us, unharmed, as suddenly as it had come upon us even though De Coude had not returned. As you know, I have had little experience of women. Olga de Coude is very beautiful; that, and the dim light and the seductive surroundings, and the appeal of the defenseless for protection, might have been resisted by a more civilized man, but my civilization is not even skin deep—it does not go deeper than my clothes.

"Paris is no place for me. I will but continue to stumble into more and more serious pitfalls. The man-made restrictions are irksome. I feel always that I am a prisoner. I cannot endure it, my friend, and so I think that I shall go back to my own jungle, and lead the life that God intended that I should lead when He put me there."

"Do not take it so to heart, Jean," responded D'Arnot. "You have acquitted yourself much better than most 'civilized' men would have under similar circumstances. As to leaving Paris at this time, I rather think that Raoul de Coude may be expected to have something to say on that subject before long."

Nor was D'Arnot mistaken. A week later on Monsieur Flaubert was announced about eleven in the morning, as D'Arnot and Tarzan were breakfasting. Monsieur Flaubert was an impressively polite gentleman. With many low bows he delivered Monsieur le Count de Coude's challenge to Monsieur Tarzan. Would monsieur be so very kind as to arrange to have a friend meet Monsieur Flaubert at as early an hour as convenient, that the details might be arranged to the mutual satisfaction of all concerned?

Certainly. Monsieur Tarzan would be delighted to place his interests unreservedly in the hands of his friend, Lieutenant D'Arnot. And so it was arranged that D'Arnot was to call on Monsieur Flaubert at two that afternoon, and the polite Monsieur Flaubert, with many bows, left them.

When they were again alone D'Arnot looked quizzically at Tarzan.

"Well?" he said.

"Now to my sins I must add murder, or else myself be killed," said Tarzan. "I am progressing rapidly in the ways of my civilized brothers."

"What weapons shall you select?" asked D'Arnot. "De Coude is accredited with being a master with the sword, and a splendid shot."

"I might then choose poisoned arrows at twenty paces, or spears at the same distance," laughed Tarzan. "Make it pistols, Paul."

"He will kill you, Jean."

"I have no doubt of it," replied Tarzan. "I must die some day."

"We had better make it swords," said D'Arnot. "He will be satisfied with wounding you, and there is less danger of a mortal wound." "Pistols," said Tarzan, with finality.

D'Arnot tried to argue him out of it, but without avail, so pistols it was.

D'Arnot returned from his conference with Monsieur Flaubert shortly after four.

"It is all arranged," he said. "Everything is satisfactory. Tomorrow morning at daylight—there is a secluded spot on the road not far from Etamps. For some personal reason Monsieur Flaubert preferred it. I did not demur."

"Good!" was Tarzan's only comment. He did not refer to the matter again even indirectly. That night he wrote several letters before he retired. After sealing and addressing them he placed them all in an envelope addressed to D'Arnot. As he undressed D'Arnot heard him humming a music-hall ditty.

The Frenchman swore under his breath. He was very unhappy, for he was positive that when the sun rose the next morning it would look down upon a dead Tarzan. It grated upon him to see Tarzan so unconcerned.

"This is a most uncivilized hour for people to kill each other," remarked the ape-man when he had been routed out of a comfortable bed in the blackness of the early morning hours. He had slept well, and so it seemed that his head scarcely touched the pillow ere his man deferentially aroused him. His remark was addressed to D'Arnot, who stood fully dressed in the doorway of Tarzan's bedroom.

D'Arnot had scarcely slept at all during the night. He was nervous, and therefore inclined to be irritable. "I presume you slept like a baby all night," he said.

Tarzan laughed. "From your tone, Paul, I infer that you rather harbor the fact against me. I could not help it, really."

"No, Jean; it is not that," replied D'Arnot, himself smiling. "But you take the entire matter with such infernal indifference—it is exasperating. One would think that you were going out to shoot at a target, rather than to face one of the best shots in France."

Tarzan shrugged his shoulders. "I am going out to expiate a great wrong, Paul. A very necessary feature of the expiation is the marksmanship of my opponent. Wherefore, then, should I be dissatisfied? Have you not yourself told me that Count de Coude is a splendid marksman?"

"You mean that you hope to be killed?" exclaimed D'Arnot, in horror.

"I cannot say that I hope to be; but you must admit that there is little reason to believe that I shall not be killed."

Had D'Arnot known the thing that was in the ape-man's mind—that had been in his mind almost from the first intimation that De Coude would call him to account on the field of honor—he would have been even more horrified than he was.

In silence they entered D'Arnot's great car, and in similar silence they sped over the dim road that leads to Etamps. Each man was occupied with his own thoughts. D'Arnot's were very mournful, for he was genuinely fond of Tarzan. The great friendship which had sprung up between these two men whose lives and training had been so widely different had but been strengthened by association, for they were both men to whom the same high ideals of manhood, of personal courage, and of honor appealed with equal force. They could understand one another, and each could be proud of the friendship of the other.

Tarzan of the Apes was wrapped in thoughts of the past; pleasant memories of the happier occasions of his lost jungle life. He recalled the countless boyhood hours that he had spent cross-legged upon the table in his dead father's cabin, his little brown body bent over one of the fascinating picture books from which, unaided, he had gleaned the secret of the printed language long before the sounds of human speech fell upon his ears. A smile of contentment softened his strong face as he thought of that day of days that he had had alone with Jane Porter in the heart of his primeval forest.

Presently his reminiscences were broken in upon by the stopping of the car—they were at their destination. Tarzan's mind returned to the affairs of the moment. He knew that he was about to die, but there was no fear of death in him. To a denizen of the cruel jungle death is a commonplace. The first law of nature compels them to cling tenaciously to life—to fight for it; but it does not teach them to fear death.

D'Arnot and Tarzan were first upon the field of honor. A moment later De Coude, Monsieur Flaubert, and a third gentleman arrived. The last was introduced to D'Arnot and Tarzan; he was a physician.

D'Arnot and Monsieur Flaubert spoke together in whispers for a brief time. The Count de Coude and Tarzan stood apart at opposite sides of the field. Presently the seconds summoned them. D'Arnot and Monsieur Flaubert had examined both pistols. The two men who were to face each other a moment later stood silently while Monsieur Flaubert recited the conditions they were to observe.

They were to stand back to back. At a signal from Monsieur Flaubert they were to walk in opposite directions, their pistols hanging by their sides. When each had proceeded ten paces D'Arnot was to give the final signal—then they were to turn and fire at will until one fell, or each had expended the three shots allowed.

While Monsieur Flaubert spoke Tarzan selected a cigarette from his case, and lighted it. De Coude was the personification of coolness—was he not the best shot in France?

Presently Monsieur Flaubert nodded to D'Arnot, and each man placed his principal in position.

"Are you quite ready, gentlemen?" asked Monsieur Flaubert.

"Quite," replied De Coude.

Tarzan nodded. Monsieur Flaubert gave the signal. He and D'Arnot stepped back a few paces to be out of the line of fire as the men paced slowly apart. Six! Seven! Eight! There were tears in D'Arnot's eyes. He loved Tarzan very much. Nine! Another pace, and the poor lieutenant gave the signal he so hated to give. To him it sounded the doom of his best friend.

Quickly De Coude wheeled and fired. Tarzan gave a little start. His pistol still dangled at his side. De Coude hesitated, as though waiting to see his antagonist crumple to the ground. The Frenchman was too experienced a marksman not to know that he had scored a hit. Still Tarzan made no move to raise his pistol. De Coude fired once more, but the attitude of the ape-man—the utter indifference that was so apparent in every line of the nonchalant ease of his giant figure, and the even unruffled puffing of his cigarette—had disconcerted the best marksman in France. This time Tarzan did not start, but again De Coude knew that he had hit.

Suddenly the explanation leaped to his mind—his antagonist was coolly taking these terrible chances in the hope that he would receive no staggering wound from any of De Coude's three shots. Then he would take his own time about shooting De Coude down deliberately, coolly, and in cold blood. A little shiver ran up the Frenchman's spine. It was fiendish—diabolical. What manner of creature was this that could stand complacently with two bullets in him, waiting for the third?

And so De Coude took careful aim this time, but his nerve was gone, and he made a clean miss. Not once had Tarzan raised his pistol hand from where it hung beside his leg.

For a moment the two stood looking straight into each other's eyes. On Tarzan's face was a pathetic expression of disappointment. On De Coude's a rapidly growing expression of horror—yes, of terror.

He could endure it no longer.

"Mother of God! Monsieur—shoot!" he screamed.

But Tarzan did not raise his pistol. Instead, he advanced toward De Coude, and when D'Arnot and Monsieur Flaubert, misinterpreting his intention, would have rushed between them, he raised his left hand in a sign of remonstrance.

"Do not fear," he said to them, "I shall not harm him."

It was most unusual, but they halted. Tarzan advanced until he was quite close to De Coude.

"There must have been something wrong with monsieur's pistol," he said. "Or monsieur is unstrung. Take mine, monsieur, and try again," and Tarzan offered his pistol, butt foremost, to the astonished De Coude.

"MON DIEU, monsieur!" cried the latter. "Are you mad?"

"No, my friend," replied the ape-man; "but I deserve to die. It is the only way in which I may atone for the wrong I have done a very good woman. Take my pistol and do as I bid."

"It would be murder," replied De Coude. "But what wrong did you do my wife? She swore to me that—"

"I do not mean that," said Tarzan quickly. "You saw all the wrong that passed between us. But that was enough to cast a shadow upon her name, and to ruin the happiness of a man against whom I had no enmity. The fault was all mine, and so I hoped to die for it this morning. I am disappointed that monsieur is not so wonderful a marksman as I had been led to believe."

"You say that the fault was all yours?" asked De Coude eagerly.

"All mine, monsieur. Your wife is a very pure woman. She loves only you. The fault that you saw was all mine. The thing that brought me there was no fault of either the Countess de Coude or myself. Here is a paper which will quite positively demonstrate that," and Tarzan drew from his pocket the statement Rokoff had written and signed.

De Coude took it and read. D'Arnot and Monsieur Flaubert had drawn near. They were interested spectators of this strange ending of a strange duel. None spoke until De Coude had quite finished, then he looked up at Tarzan.

"You are a very brave and chivalrous gentleman," he said. "I thank God that I did not kill you."

De Coude was a Frenchman. Frenchmen are impulsive. He threw his arms about Tarzan and embraced him. Monsieur Flaubert embraced D'Arnot. There was no one to embrace the doctor. So possibly it was pique which prompted him to interfere, and demand that he be permitted to dress Tarzan's wounds.

"This gentleman was hit once at least," he said. "Possibly thrice."

"Twice," said Tarzan. "Once in the left shoulder, and again in the left side—both flesh wounds, I think." But the doctor insisted upon stretching him upon the sward, and tinkering with him until the wounds were cleansed and the flow of blood checked.

One result of the duel was that they all rode back to Paris together in D'Arnot's car, the best of friends. De Coude was so relieved to have had this double assurance of his wife's loyalty that he felt no rancor at all toward Tarzan. It is true that the latter had assumed much more of the fault than was rightly his, but if he lied a little he may be excused, for he lied in the service of a woman, and he lied like a gentleman.

The ape-man was confined to his bed for several days. He felt that it was foolish and unnecessary, but the doctor and D'Arnot took the matter so to heart that he gave in to please them, though it made him laugh to think of it.

"It is droll," he said to D'Arnot. "To lie abed because of a pin prick! Why, when Bolgani, the king gorilla, tore me almost to pieces, while I was still but a little boy, did I have a nice soft bed to lie on? No, only the damp, rotting vegetation of the jungle. Hidden beneath some friendly bush I lay for days and weeks with only Kala to nurse me—poor, faithful Kala, who kept the insects from my wounds and warned off the beasts of prey.

"When I called for water she brought it to me in her own mouth—the only way she knew to carry it. There was no sterilized gauze, there was no antiseptic bandage—there was nothing that would not have driven our dear doctor mad to have seen. Yet I recovered—recovered to lie in bed because of a tiny scratch that one of the jungle folk would scarce realize unless it were upon the end of his nose."

But the time was soon over, and before he realized it Tarzan found himself abroad again. Several times De Coude had called, and when he found that Tarzan was anxious for employment of some nature he promised to see what could be done to find a berth for him.

It was the first day that Tarzan was permitted to go out that he received a message from De Coude requesting him to call at the count's office that afternoon.

He found De Coude awaiting him with a very pleasant welcome, and a sincere congratulation that he was once more upon his feet. Neither had ever mentioned the duel or the cause of it since that morning upon the field of honor.

"I think that I have found just the thing for you, Monsieur Tarzan," said the count. "It is a position of much trust and responsibility, which also requires considerably physical courage and prowess. I cannot imagine a man better fitted than you, my dear Monsieur Tarzan, for this very position. It will necessitate travel, and later it may lead to a very much better post—possibly in the diplomatic service.

"At first, for a short time only, you will be a special agent in the service of the ministry of war. Come, I will take you to the gentleman who will be your chief. He can explain the duties better than I, and then you will be in a position to judge if you wish to accept or no."

De Coude himself escorted Tarzan to the office of General Rochere, the chief of the bureau to which Tarzan would be attached if he accepted the position. There the count left him, after a glowing description to the general of the many attributes possessed by the ape-man which should fit him for the work of the service.

A half hour later Tarzan walked out of the office the possessor of the first position he had ever held. On the morrow he was to return for further instructions, though General Rochere had made it quite plain that Tarzan might prepare to leave Paris for an almost indefinite period, possibly on the morrow.

It was with feelings of the keenest elation that he hastened home to bear the good news to D'Arnot. At last he was to be of some value in the world. He was to earn money, and, best of all, to travel and see the world.

He could scarcely wait to get well inside D'Arnot's sitting room before he burst out with the glad tidings. D'Arnot was not so pleased.

"It seems to delight you to think that you are to leave Paris, and that we shall not see each other for months, perhaps. Tarzan, you are a most ungrateful beast!" and D'Arnot laughed.

"No, Paul; I am a little child. I have a new toy, and I am tickled to death."

And so it came that on the following day Tarzan left Paris en route for Marseilles and Oran.

THE DANCING GIRL OF SIDI AISSA

Tarzan's first mission did not bid fair to be either exciting or vastly important. There was a certain lieutenant of *spahis* whom the government had reason to suspect of improper relations with a great European power. This Lieutenant Gernois, who was at present stationed at Sidibel-Abbes, had recently been attached to the general staff, where certain information of great military value had come into his possession in the ordinary routine of his duties. It was this information which the government suspected the great power was bartering for with the officer.

It was at most but a vague hint dropped by a certain notorious Parisienne in a jealous mood that had caused suspicion to rest upon the lieutenant. But general staffs are jealous of their secrets, and treason so serious a thing that even a hint of it may not be safely neglected. And so it was that Tarzan had come to Algeria in the guise of an American hunter and traveler to keep a close eye upon Lieutenant Gernois.

He had looked forward with keen delight to again seeing his beloved Africa, but this northern aspect of it was so different from his tropical jungle home that he might as well have been back in Paris for all the heart thrills of homecoming that he experienced. At Oran he spent a day wandering through the narrow, crooked alleys of the Arab quarter enjoying the strange, new sights. The next day found him at Sidi-bel-Abbes, where he presented his letters of introduction to both civil and military authorities—letters which gave no clew to the real significance of his mission.

Tarzan possessed a sufficient command of English to enable him to pass among Arabs and Frenchmen as an American, and that was all that was required of it. When he met an Englishman he spoke French in order that he might not betray himself, but occasionally talked in English to foreigners who understood that tongue, but could not note the slight imperfections of accent and pronunciation that were his.

Here he became acquainted with many of the French officers, and soon became a favorite among them. He met Gernois, whom he found to be a taciturn, dyspeptic-looking man of about forty, having little or no social intercourse with his fellows.

For a month nothing of moment occurred. Gernois apparently had no visitors, nor did he on his occasional visits to the town hold communication with any who might even by the wildest flight of imagination be construed into secret agents of a foreign power. Tarzan was beginning to hope that, after all, the rumor might have been false, when suddenly Gernois was ordered to Bou Saada in the Petit Sahara far to the south.

A company of SPAHIS and three officers were to relieve another company already stationed there. Fortunately one of the officers, Captain Gerard, had become an excellent friend of Tarzan's, and so when the ape-man suggested that he should embrace the opportunity of accompanying him to Bou Saada, where he expected to find hunting, it caused not the slightest suspicion.

At Bouira the detachment detrained, and the balance of the journey was made in the saddle. As Tarzan was dickering at Bouira for a mount he caught a brief glimpse of a man in European clothes eying him from the doorway of a native coffeehouse, but as Tarzan looked the man turned and entered the little, low-ceilinged mud hut, and but for a haunting impression that there had been something familiar about the face or figure of the fellow, Tarzan gave the matter no further thought.

The march to Aumale was fatiguing to Tarzan, whose equestrian experiences hitherto had been confined to a course of riding lessons in a Parisian academy, and so it was that he quickly sought the comforts of a bed in the Hotel Grossat, while the officers and troops took up their quarters at the military post.

Although Tarzan was called early the following morning, the company of *Spahis* was on the march before he had finished his breakfast. He was hurrying through his meal that the soldiers might not get too far in advance of him when he glanced through the door connecting the dining room with the bar.

To his surprise, he saw Gernois standing there in conversation with the very stranger he had seen in the coffee-house at Bouira the day previous. He could not be mistaken, for there was the same strangely familiar attitude and figure, though the man's back was toward him.

As his eyes lingered on the two, Gernois looked up and caught the intent expression on Tarzan's face. The stranger was talking in a low whisper at the time, but the French officer immediately interrupted him, and the two at once turned away and passed out of the range of Tarzan's vision.

This was the first suspicious occurrence that Tarzan had ever witnessed in connection with Gernois' actions, but he was positive that the men had left the barroom solely because Gernois had caught Tarzan's eyes upon them; then there was the persistent impression of familiarity about the stranger to further augment the ape-man's belief that here at length was something which would bear watching.

A moment later Tarzan entered the barroom, but the men had left, nor did he see aught of them in the street beyond, though he found a pretext to ride to various shops before he set out after the column which had now considerable start of him. He did not overtake them until he reached Sidi Aissa shortly after noon, where the soldiers had halted for an hour's rest. Here he found Gernois with the column, but there was no sign of the stranger.

It was market day at Sidi Aissa, and the numberless caravans of camels coming in from the desert, and the crowds of bickering Arabs in the market place, filled Tarzan with a consuming desire to remain for a day that he might see more of these sons of the desert. Thus it was that the company of *Spahis* marched on that afternoon toward Bou Saada without him. He spent the hours until dark wandering about the market in company with a youthful Arab, one Abdul, who had been recommended to him by the innkeeper as a trustworthy servant and interpreter.

Here Tarzan purchased a better mount than the one he had selected at Bouira, and, entering into conversation with the stately Arab to whom the animal had belonged, learned that the seller was Kadour ben Saden, sheik of a desert tribe far south of Djelfa. Through Abdul, Tarzan invited his new acquaintance to dine with him. As the three were making their way through the crowds of marketers, camels, donkeys, and horses that filled the market place with a confusing babel of sounds, Abdul plucked at Tarzan's sleeve.

"Look, master, behind us," and he turned, pointing at a figure which disappeared behind a camel as Tarzan turned. "He has been following us about all afternoon," continued Abdul.

"I caught only a glimpse of an Arab in a dark-blue burnoose and white turban," replied Tarzan. "Is it he you mean?"

"Yes. I suspected him because he seems a stranger here, without other business than following us, which is not the way of the Arab who is honest, and also because he keeps the lower part of his face hidden, only his eyes showing. He must be a bad man, or he would have honest business of his own to occupy his time."

"He is on the wrong scent then, Abdul," replied Tarzan, "for no one here can have any grievance against me. This is my first visit to your country, and none knows me. He will soon discover his error, and cease to follow us."

"Unless he be bent on robbery," returned Abdul.

"Then all we can do is wait until he is ready to try his hand upon us," laughed Tarzan, "and I warrant that he will get his bellyful of robbing now that we are prepared for him," and so he dismissed the subject from his mind, though he was destined to recall it before many hours through a most unlooked-for occurrence.

Kadour ben Saden, having dined well, prepared to take leave of his host. With dignified protestations of friendship, he invited Tarzan to visit him in his wild domain, where the antelope, the stag, the boar, the panther, and the lion might still be found in sufficient numbers to tempt an ardent huntsman.

On his departure the ape-man, with Abdul, wandered again into the streets of Sidi Aissa, where he was soon attracted by the wild din of sound coming from the open doorway of one of the numerous *Cafes Maures*. It was after eight, and the dancing was in full swing as Tarzan entered. The room was filled to repletion with Arabs. All were smoking, and drinking their thick, hot coffee.

Tarzan and Abdul found seats near the center of the room, though the terrific noise produced by the musicians upon their Arab drums and pipes would have rendered a seat farther from them more acceptable to the quiet-loving ape-man. A rather good-looking Ouled-Nail was dancing, and, perceiving Tarzan's European clothes, and scenting a generous gratuity, she threw her silken handkerchief upon his shoulder, to be rewarded with a franc.

When her place upon the floor had been taken by another the bright-eyed Abdul saw her in conversation with two Arabs at the far side of the room, near a side door that let upon an inner court, around the gallery of which were the rooms occupied by the girls who danced in this cafe.

At first he thought nothing of the matter, but presently he noticed from the corner of his eye one of the men nod in their direction, and the girl turn and shoot a furtive glance at Tarzan. Then the Arabs melted through the doorway into the darkness of the court.

When it came again the girl's turn to dance she hovered close to Tarzan, and for the ape-man alone were her sweetest smiles. Many an ugly scowl was cast upon the tall European by swarthy, dark-eyed sons of the desert, but neither smiles nor scowls produced any outwardly visible effect upon him. Again the girl cast her handkerchief upon his shoulder, and again was she rewarded with a franc piece. As she was sticking it upon her forehead, after the custom of her kind, she bent low toward Tarzan, whispering a quick word in his ear.

"There are two without in the court," she said quickly, in broken French, "who would harm m'sieur. At first I promised to lure you to them, but you have been kind, and I cannot do it. Go quickly, before they find that I have failed them. I think that they are very bad men."

Tarzan thanked the girl, assuring her that he would be careful, and, having finished her dance, she crossed to the little doorway and went out into the court. But Tarzan did not leave the cafe as she had urged.

For another half hour nothing unusual occurred, then a surly-looking Arab entered the cafe from the street. He stood near Tarzan, where he deliberately made insulting remarks about the European, but as they were in his native tongue Tarzan was entirely innocent of their purport until Abdul took it upon himself to enlighten him.

"This fellow is looking for trouble," warned Abdul. "He is not alone. In fact, in case of a disturbance, nearly every man here would be against you. It would be better to leave quietly, master."

"Ask the fellow what he wants," commanded Tarzan.

"He says that 'the dog of a Christian' insulted the Ouled-Nail, who belongs to him. He means trouble, m'sieur."

"Tell him that I did not insult his or any other Ouled-Nail, that I wish him to go away and leave me alone. That I have no quarrel with him, nor has he any with me."

"He says," replied Abdul, after delivering this message to the Arab, "that besides being a dog yourself that you are the son of one, and that your grandmother was a hyena. Incidentally you are a liar."

The attention of those near by had now been attracted by the altercation, and the sneering laughs that followed this torrent of invective easily indicated the trend of the sympathies of the majority of the audience.

Tarzan did not like being laughed at, neither did he relish the terms applied to him by the Arab, but he showed no sign of anger as he arose from his seat upon the bench. A half smile played about his lips, but of a sudden a mighty fist shot into the face of the scowling Arab, and back of it were the terrible muscles of the ape-man.

At the instant that the man fell a half dozen fierce plainsmen sprang into the room from where they had apparently been waiting for their cue in the street before the cafe. With cries of "Kill the unbeliever!" and "Down with the dog of a Christian!" they made straight for Tarzan. A number of the younger Arabs in the audience sprang to their feet to join in the assault upon the unarmed white man. Tarzan and Abdul were rushed back toward the end of the room by the very force of numbers opposing them. The young Arab remained loyal to his master, and with drawn knife fought at his side.

With tremendous blows the ape-man felled all who came within reach of his powerful hands. He fought quietly and without a word, upon his lips the same half smile they had worn as he rose to strike down the man who had insulted him. It seemed impossible that either he or Abdul could survive the sea of wicked-looking swords and knives that surrounded them, but the very numbers of their assailants proved the best bulwark of their safety. So closely packed was the howling, cursing mob that no weapon could be wielded to advantage, and none of the Arabs dared use a firearm for fear of wounding one of his compatriots.

Finally Tarzan succeeded in seizing one of the most persistent of his attackers. With a quick wrench he disarmed the fellow, and then, holding him before them as a shield, he backed slowly beside Abdul toward the little door which led into the inner courtyard. At the threshold he paused for an instant, and, lifting the struggling Arab above his head, hurled him, as though from a catapult, full in the faces of his on-pressing fellows.

Then Tarzan and Abdul stepped into the semidarkness of the court. The frightened Ouled-Nails were crouching at the tops of the stairs which led to their respective rooms, the only light in the courtyard coming from the sickly candles which each girl had stuck with its own grease to the woodwork of her door-frame, the better to display her charms to those who might happen to traverse the dark inclosure.

Scarcely had Tarzan and Abdul emerged from the room ere a revolver spoke close at their backs from the shadows beneath one of the stairways, and as they turned to meet this new antagonist, two muffled figures sprang toward them, firing as they came. Tarzan leaped to meet these two new assailants. The foremost lay, a second later, in the trampled dirt of the court, disarmed and groaning from a broken wrist. Abdul's knife found the vitals of the second in the instant that the fellow's revolver missed fire as he held it to the faithful Arab's forehead.

The maddened horde within the cafe were now rushing out in pursuit of their quarry. The Ouled-Nails had extinguished their candles at a cry from one of their number, and the only light within the yard came feebly from the open and half-blocked door of the cafe. Tarzan had seized a sword from the man who had fallen before Abdul's knife, and now he stood waiting for the rush of men that was coming in search of them through the darkness.

Suddenly he felt a light hand upon his shoulder from behind, and a woman's voice whispering, "Quick, m'sieur; this way. Follow me."

"Come, Abdul," said Tarzan, in a low tone, to the youth; "we can be no worse off elsewhere than we are here."

The woman turned and led them up the narrow stairway that ended at the door of her quarters. Tarzan was close beside her. He saw the gold and silver bracelets upon her bare arms, the strings of gold coin that depended from her hair ornaments, and the gorgeous colors of her dress. He saw that she was a Ouled-Nail, and instinctively he knew that she was the same who had whispered the warning in his ear earlier in the evening.

As they reached the top of the stairs they could hear the angry crowd searching the yard beneath.

"Soon they will search here," whispered the girl. "They must not find you, for, though you fight with the strength of many men, they will kill you in the end. Hasten; you can drop from the farther window of my room to the street beyond. Before they discover that you are no longer in the court of the buildings you will be safe within the hotel."

But even as she spoke, several men had started up the stairway at the head of which they stood. There was a sudden cry from one of the searchers. They had been discovered. Quickly the crowd rushed for the stairway. The foremost assailant leaped quickly upward, but at the top he met the sudden sword that he had not expected—the quarry had been unarmed before.

With a cry, the man toppled back upon those behind him. Like tenpins they rolled down the stairs. The ancient and rickety structure could not withstand the strain of this unwonted weight and jarring. With a creaking and rending of breaking wood it collapsed beneath the Arabs, leaving Tarzan, Abdul, and the girl alone upon the frail platform at the top.

"Come!" cried the Ouled-Nail. "They will reach us from another stairway through the room next to mine. We have not a moment to spare."

Just as they were entering the room Abdul heard and translated a cry from the yard below for several to hasten to the street and cut off escape from that side.

"We are lost now," said the girl simply.

"We?" questioned Tarzan.

"Yes, m'sieur," she responded; "they will kill me as well. Have I not aided you?"

This put a different aspect on the matter. Tarzan had rather been enjoying the excitement and danger of the encounter. He had not for an instant supposed that either Abdul or the girl could suffer except through accident, and he had only retreated just enough to keep from being killed himself. He had had no intention of running away until he saw that he was hopelessly lost were he to remain.

Alone he could have sprung into the midst of that close-packed mob, and, laying about him after the fashion of Numa, the lion, have struck the Arabs with such consternation that escape would have been easy. Now he must think entirely of these two faithful friends.

He crossed to the window which overlooked the street. In a minute there would be enemies below. Already he could hear the mob clambering the stairway to the next quarters—they would be at the door beside him in another instant. He put a foot upon the sill and leaned out, but he did not look down. Above him, within arm's reach, was the low roof of the building. He called to the girl. She came and stood beside him. He put a great arm about her and lifted her across his shoulder.

"Wait here until I reach down for you from above," he said to Abdul. "In the meantime shove everything in the room against that door—it may delay them long enough." Then he stepped to the sill of the narrow window with the girl upon his shoulders. "Hold tight," he cautioned her. A moment later he had clambered to the roof above with the ease and dexterity of an ape. Setting the girl down, he leaned far over the roof's edge, calling softly to Abdul. The youth ran to the window.

"Your hand," whispered Tarzan. The men in the room beyond were battering at the door. With a sudden crash it fell splintering in, and at the same instant Abdul felt himself lifted like a feather onto the roof above. They were not a moment too soon, for as the men broke into the room which they had just quitted a dozen more rounded the corner in the street below and came running to a spot beneath the girl's window.

THE FIGHT IN THE DESERT

As the three squatted upon the roof above the quarters of the Ouled-Nails they heard the angry cursing of the Arabs in the room beneath. Abdul translated from time to time to Tarzan.

"They are berating those in the street below now," said Abdul, "for permitting us to escape so easily. Those in the street say that we did not come that way—that we are still within the building, and that those above, being too cowardly to attack us, are attempting to deceive them into believing that we have escaped. In a moment they will have fighting of their own to attend to if they continue their brawling."

Presently those in the building gave up the search, and returned to the cafe. A few remained in the street below, smoking and talking.

Tarzan spoke to the girl, thanking her for the sacrifice she had made for him, a total stranger.

"I liked you," she said simply. "You were unlike the others who come to the cafe. You did not speak coarsely to me—the manner in which you gave me money was not an insult."

"What shall you do after tonight?" he asked. "You cannot return to the cafe. Can you even remain with safety in Sidi Aissa?"

"Tomorrow it will be forgotten," she replied. "But I should be glad if it might be that I need never return to this or another cafe. I have not remained because I wished to; I have been a prisoner."

"A prisoner!" ejaculated Tarzan incredulously.

"A slave would be the better word," she answered. "I was stolen in the night from my father's *douar* by a band of marauders. They brought me here and sold me to the Arab who keeps this cafe. It has been nearly two years now since I saw the last of mine own people. They are very far to the south. They never come to Sidi Aissa."

"You would like to return to your people?" asked Tarzan. "Then I shall promise to see you safely so far as Bou Saada at least. There we can doubtless arrange with the commandant to send you the rest of the way."

"Oh, m'sieur," she cried, "how can I ever repay you! You cannot really mean that you will do so much for a poor Ouled-Nail. But my father can reward you, and he will, for is he not a great sheik? He is Kadour ben Saden."

"Kadour ben Saden!" ejaculated Tarzan. "Why, Kadour ben Saden is in Sidi Aissa this very night. He dined with me but a few hours since."

"My father in Sidi Aissa?" cried the amazed girl. "Allah be praised then, for I am indeed saved."

"Hssh!" cautioned Abdul. "Listen."

From below came the sound of voices, quite distinguishable upon the still night air. Tarzan could not understand the words, but Abdul and the girl translated.

"They have gone now," said the latter. "It is you they want, m'sieur. One of them said that the stranger who had offered money for your slaying lay in the house of Akmed din Soulef with a broken wrist, but that he had offered a still greater reward if some would lay in wait for you upon the road to Bou Saada and kill you."

"It is he who followed m'sieur about the market today," exclaimed Abdul. "I saw him again within the cafe—him and another; and the two went out into the inner court after talking with this girl here. It was they who attacked and fired upon us, as we came out of the cafe. Why do they wish to kill you, m'sieur?"

"I do not know," replied Tarzan, and then, after a pause: "Unless—" But he did not finish, for the thought that had come to his mind, while it seemed the only reasonable solution of the mystery, appeared at the same time quite improbable. Presently the men in the street went away. The courtyard and the cafe were deserted. Cautiously Tarzan lowered himself to the sill of the girl's window. The room was empty. He returned to the roof and let Abdul down, then he lowered the girl to the arms of the waiting Arab.

From the window Abdul dropped the short distance to the street below, while Tarzan took the girl in his arms and leaped down as he had done on so many other occasions in his own forest with a burden in his arms. A little cry of alarm was startled from the girl's lips, but Tarzan landed in the street with but an imperceptible jar, and lowered her in safety to her feet.

She clung to him for a moment.

"How strong m'sieur is, and how active," she cried. "El Adrea, the black lion, himself is not more so."

"I should like to meet this *El Adrea* of yours," he said. "I have heard much about him."

"And you come to the *douar* of my father you shall see him," said the girl. "He lives in a spur of the mountains north of us, and comes down from his lair at night to rob my father's *douar*. With a single blow of his mighty paw he crushes the skull of a bull, and woe betide the belated wayfarer who meets El Adrea abroad at night."

Without further mishap they reached the hotel. The sleepy landlord objected strenuously to instituting a search for Kadour ben Saden until the following morning, but a piece of gold put a different aspect on the matter, so that a few moments later a servant had started to make the rounds of the lesser native hostelries where it might be expected that a desert sheik would find congenial associations. Tarzan had felt it necessary to find the girl's father that night, for fear he might start on his homeward journey too early in the morning to be intercepted.

They had waited perhaps half an hour when the messenger returned with Kadour ben Saden. The old sheik entered the room with a questioning expression upon his proud face.

"Monsieur has done me the honor to—" he commenced, and then his eyes fell upon the girl. With outstretched arms he crossed the room to meet her. "My daughter!" he cried. "Allah is merciful!" and tears dimmed the martial eyes of the old warrior.

When the story of her abduction and her final rescue had been told to Kadour ben Saden he extended his hand to Tarzan.

"All that is Kadour ben Saden's is thine, my friend, even to his life," he said very simply, but Tarzan knew that those were no idle words.

It was decided that although three of them would have to ride after practically no sleep, it would be best to make an early start in the morning, and attempt to ride all the way to Bou Saada in one day. It would have been comparatively easy for the men, but for the girl it was sure to be a fatiguing journey.

She, however, was the most anxious to undertake it, for it seemed to her that she could not quickly enough reach the family and friends from whom she had been separated for two years.

It seemed to Tarzan that he had not closed his eyes before he was awakened, and in another hour the party was on its way south toward Bou Saada. For a few miles the road was good, and they made rapid progress, but suddenly it became only a waste of sand, into which the horses sank fetlock deep at nearly every step. In addition to Tarzan, Abdul, the sheik, and his daughter were four of the wild plainsmen of the sheik's tribe who had accompanied him upon the trip to Sidi Aissa. Thus, seven guns strong, they entertained little fear of attack by day, and if all went well they should reach Bou Saada before nightfall.

A brisk wind enveloped them in the blowing sand of the desert, until Tarzan's lips were parched and cracked. What little he could see of the surrounding country was far from alluring—a vast expanse of rough country, rolling in little, barren hillocks, and tufted here and there with clumps of dreary shrub. Far to the south rose the dim lines of the Saharan Atlas range. How different, thought Tarzan, from the gorgeous Africa of his boyhood!

Abdul, always on the alert, looked backward quite as often as he did ahead. At the top of each hillock that they mounted he would draw in his horse and, turning, scan the country to the rear with utmost care. At last his scrutiny was rewarded.

"Look!" he cried. "There are six horsemen behind us."

"Your friends of last evening, no doubt, monsieur," remarked Kadour ben Saden dryly to Tarzan.

"No doubt," replied the ape-man. "I am sorry that my society should endanger the safety of your journey. At the next village I shall remain and question these gentlemen, while you ride on. There is no necessity for my being at Bou Saada tonight, and less still why you should not ride in peace."

"If you stop we shall stop," said Kadour ben Saden. "Until you are safe with your friends, or the enemy has left your trail, we shall remain with you. There is nothing more to say."

Tarzan nodded his head. He was a man of few words, and possibly it was for this reason as much as any that Kadour ben Saden had taken to him, for if there be one thing that an Arab despises it is a talkative man.

All the balance of the day Abdul caught glimpses of the horsemen in their rear. They remained always at about the same distance. During the occasional halts for rest, and at the longer halt at noon, they approached no closer.

"They are waiting for darkness," said Kadour ben Saden.

And darkness came before they reached Bou Saada. The last glimpse that Abdul had of the grim, white-robed figures that trailed them, just before dusk made it impossible to distinguish them, had made it apparent that they were rapidly closing up the distance that intervened between them and their intended quarry. He whispered this fact to Tarzan, for he did not wish to alarm the girl. The ape-man drew back beside him.

"You will ride ahead with the others, Abdul," said Tarzan. "This is my quarrel. I shall wait at the next convenient spot, and interview these fellows."

"Then Abdul shall wait at thy side," replied the young Arab, nor would any threats or commands move him from his decision.

"Very well, then," replied Tarzan. "Here is as good a place as we could wish. Here are rocks at the top of this hillock. We shall remain hidden here and give an account of ourselves to these gentlemen when they appear."

They drew in their horses and dismounted. The others riding ahead were already out of sight in the darkness. Beyond them shone the lights of Bou Saada. Tarzan removed his rifle from its boot and loosened his revolver in its holster. He ordered Abdul to withdraw behind the rocks with the horses, so that they should be shielded from the enemies' bullets should they fire. The young Arab pretended to do as he was bid, but when he had fastened the two animals securely to a low shrub he crept back to lie on his belly a few paces behind Tarzan.

The ape-man stood erect in the middle of the road, waiting. Nor did he have long to wait. The sound of galloping horses came suddenly out of the darkness below him, and a moment later he discerned the moving blotches of lighter color against the solid background of the night.

"Halt," he cried, "or we fire!"

The white figures came to a sudden stop, and for a moment there was silence. Then came the sound of a whispered council, and like ghosts the phantom riders dispersed in all directions. Again the desert lay still about him, yet it was an ominous stillness that foreboded evil.

Abdul raised himself to one knee. Tarzan cocked his jungle-trained ears, and presently there came to him the sound of horses walking quietly through the sand to the east of him, to the west, to the north, and to the south. They had been surrounded. Then a shot came from the direction in which he was looking, a bullet whirred through the air above his head, and he fired at the flash of the enemy's gun.

Instantly the soundless waste was torn with the quick staccato of guns upon every hand. Abdul and Tarzan fired only at the flashes—they could not yet see their foemen. Presently it became evident that the attackers were circling their position, drawing closer and closer in as they began to realize the paltry numbers of the party which opposed them.

But one came too close, for Tarzan was accustomed to using his eyes in the darkness of the jungle night, than which there is no more utter darkness this side the grave, and with a cry of pain a saddle was emptied.

"The odds are evening, Abdul," said Tarzan, with a low laugh.

But they were still far too one-sided, and when the five remaining horsemen whirled at a signal and charged full upon them it looked as if there would be a sudden ending of the battle. Both Tarzan and Abdul sprang to the shelter of the rocks, that they might keep the enemy in front of them. There was a mad clatter of galloping hoofs, a volley of shots from both sides, and the Arabs withdrew to repeat the maneuver; but there were now only four against the two.

For a few moments there came no sound from out of the surrounding blackness. Tarzan could not tell whether the Arabs, satisfied with their losses, had given up the fight, or were waiting farther along the road to waylay them as they proceeded on toward Bou Saada. But he was not left long in doubt, for now all from one direction came the sound of a new charge. But scarcely had the first gun spoken ere a dozen shots rang out behind the Arabs. There came the wild shouts of a new party to the controversy, and the pounding of the feet of many horses from down the road to Bou Saada.

The Arabs did not wait to learn the identity of the oncomers. With a parting volley as they dashed by the position which Tarzan and Abdul were holding, they plunged off along the road toward Sidi Aissa. A moment later Kadour ben Saden and his men dashed up.

The old sheik was much relieved to find that neither Tarzan nor Abdul had received a scratch. Not even had their horses been wounded. They sought out the two men who had fallen before Tarzan's shots, and, finding that both were dead, left them where they lay.

"Why did you not tell me that you contemplated ambushing those fellows?" asked the sheik in a hurt tone. "We might have had them all if the seven of us had stopped to meet them."

"Then it would have been useless to stop at all," replied Tarzan, "for had we simply ridden on toward Bou Saada they would have been upon us presently, and all could have been engaged. It was to prevent the transfer of my own quarrel to another's shoulders that Abdul and I stopped off to question them. Then there is your daughter—I could not be the cause of exposing her needlessly to the marksmanship of six men."

Kadour ben Saden shrugged his shoulders. He did not relish having been cheated out of a fight.

The little battle so close to Bou Saada had drawn out a company of soldiers. Tarzan and his party met them just outside the town. The officer in charge halted them to learn the significance of the shots.

"A handful of marauders," replied Kadour ben Saden. "They attacked two of our number who had dropped behind, but when we returned to them the fellows soon dispersed. They left two dead. None of my party was injured."

This seemed to satisfy the officer, and after taking the names of the party he marched his men on toward the scene of the skirmish to bring back the dead men for purposes of identification, if possible.

Two days later, Kadour ben Saden, with his daughter and followers, rode south through the pass below Bou Saada, bound for their home in the far wilderness. The sheik had urged Tarzan to accompany him, and the girl had added her entreaties to those of her father; but, though he could not explain it to them, Tarzan's duties loomed particularly large after the happenings of the past few days, so that he could not think of leaving his post for an instant. But he promised to come later if it lay within his power to do so, and they had to content themselves with that assurance.

During these two days Tarzan had spent practically all his time with Kadour ben Saden and his daughter. He was keenly interested in this race of stern and dignified warriors, and embraced the opportunity which their friendship offered to learn what he could of their lives and customs. He even commenced to acquire the rudiments of their language under the pleasant tutorage of the brown-eyed girl. It was with real regret that he saw them depart, and he sat his horse at the opening to the pass, as far as which he had accompanied them, gazing after the little party as long as he could catch a glimpse of them.

Here were people after his own heart! Their wild, rough lives, filled with danger and hardship, appealed to this half-savage man as nothing had appealed to him in the midst of the effeminate civilization of the great cities he had visited. Here was a life that excelled even that of the jungle, for here he might have the society of men—real men whom he could honor and respect, and yet be near to the wild nature that he loved. In his head revolved an idea that when he had completed his mission he would resign and return to live for the remainder of his life with the tribe of Kadour ben Saden.

Then he turned his horse's head and rode slowly back to Bou Saada.

The front of the Hotel du Petit Sahara, where Tarzan stopped in Bou Saada, is taken up with the bar, two dining-rooms, and the kitchens. Both of the dining-rooms open directly off the bar, and one of them is reserved for the use of the officers of the garrison. As you stand in the barroom you may look into either of the dining-rooms if you wish.

It was to the bar that Tarzan repaired after speeding Kadour ben Saden and his party on their way. It was yet early in the morning, for Kadour ben Saden had elected to ride far that day, so that it happened that when Tarzan returned there were guests still at breakfast.

As his casual glance wandered into the officers' dining-room, Tarzan saw something which brought a look of interest to his eyes. Lieutenant Gernois was sitting there, and as Tarzan looked a white-robed Arab approached and, bending, whispered a few words into the lieutenant's ear. Then he passed on out of the building through another door.

In itself the thing was nothing, but as the man had stooped to speak to the officer, Tarzan had caught sight of something which the accidental parting of the man's burnoose had revealed—he carried his left arm in a sling.

NUMA "EL ADREA"

On the same day that Kadour ben Saden rode south the diligence from the north brought Tarzan a letter from D'Arnot which had been forwarded from Sidi-bel-Abbes. It opened the old wound that Tarzan would have been glad to have forgotten; yet he was not sorry that D'Arnot had written, for one at least of his subjects could never cease to interest the ape-man. Here is the letter:

My Dear Jean:
Since last I wrote you I have been across to London on a matter of business. I was there but three days. The very first day I came upon an old friend of yours—quite unexpectedly—in Henrietta Street. Now you never in the world would guess whom. None other than Mr. Samuel T. Philander. But it is true. I can see your look of incredulity. Nor is this all. He insisted that I return to the hotel with him, and there I found the others—Professor Archimedes Q. Porter, Miss Porter, and that enormous black woman, Miss Porter's maid—Esmeralda, you will recall. While I was there Clayton came in. They are to be married soon, or rather sooner, for I rather suspect that we shall receive announcements almost any day. On account of his father's death it is to be a very quiet affair—only blood relatives.

While I was alone with Mr. Philander the old fellow became rather confidential. Said Miss Porter had already postponed the wedding on three different occasions. He confided that it appeared to him that she was not particularly anxious to marry Clayton at all; but this time it seems that it is quite likely to go through.

Of course they all asked after you, but I respected your wishes in the matter of your true origin, and only spoke to them of your present affairs.

Miss Porter was especially interested in everything I had to say about you, and asked many questions. I am afraid I took a rather unchivalrous delight in picturing your desire and resolve to go back eventually to your native jungle. I was sorry afterward, for it did seem to cause her real anguish to contemplate the awful dangers to which you wished to return. "And yet," she said, "I do not know. There are more unhappy fates than the grim and terrible jungle presents to Monsieur Tarzan. At least his conscience will be free from remorse. And there are moments of quiet and restfulness by day, and vistas of exquisite beauty. You may find it strange that I should say it, who experienced such terrifying experiences in that frightful forest, yet at times I long to return, for I cannot but feel that the happiest moments of my life were spent there."

There was an expression of ineffable sadness on her face as she spoke, and I could not but feel that she knew that I knew her secret, and that this was her way of transmitting to you a last tender message from a heart that might still enshrine your memory, though its possessor belonged to another.

Clayton appeared nervous and ill at ease while you were the subject of conversation. He wore a worried and harassed expression. Yet he was very kindly in his expressions of interest in you. I wonder if he suspects the truth about you?

Tennington came in with Clayton. They are great friends, you know. He is about to set out upon one of his interminable cruises in that yacht of his, and was urging the entire party to accompany him. Tried to inveigle me into it, too. Is thinking of circumnavigating Africa this time. I told him that his precious toy would take him and some of his friends to the bottom of the ocean one of these days if he didn't get it out of his head that she was a liner or a battleship.

I returned to Paris day before yesterday, and yesterday I met the Count and Countess de Coude at the races. They inquired after you. De Coude really seems quite fond of you. Doesn't appear to harbor the least ill will. Olga is as beautiful as ever, but a trifle subdued. I imagine that she learned a lesson through her acquaintance with you that will serve her in good stead during the balance of her life. It is fortunate for her, and for De Coude as well, that it was you and not another man more sophisticated.

Had you really paid court to Olga's heart I am afraid that there would have been no hope for either of you.

She asked me to tell you that Nikolas had left France. She paid him twenty thousand francs to go away, and stay. She is congratulating herself that she got rid of him before he tried to carry out a threat he recently made her that he should kill you at the first opportunity. She said that she should hate to think that her brother's blood was on your hands, for she is very fond of you, and made no bones in saying so before the count. It never for a moment seemed to occur to her that there might be any possibility of any other outcome of a meeting between you and Nikolas. The count quite agreed with her in that. He added that it would take a regiment of Rokoffs to kill you. He has a most healthy respect for your prowess.

Have been ordered back to my ship. She sails from Havre in two days under sealed orders. If you will address me in her care, the letters will find me eventually. I shall write you as soon as another opportunity presents.

Your sincere friend,

Paul D'arnot.

"I fear," mused Tarzan, half aloud, "that Olga has thrown away her twenty thousand francs."

He read over that part of D'Arnot's letter several times in which he had quoted from his conversation with Jane Porter. Tarzan derived a rather pathetic happiness from it, but it was better than no happiness at all.

The following three weeks were quite uneventful. On several occasions Tarzan saw the mysterious Arab, and once again he had been exchanging words with Lieutenant Gernois; but no amount of espionage or shadowing by Tarzan revealed the Arab's lodgings, the location of which Tarzan was anxious to ascertain.

Gernois, never cordial, had kept more than ever aloof from Tarzan since the episode in the dining-room of the hotel at Aumale. His attitude on the few occasions that they had been thrown together had been distinctly hostile.

That he might keep up the appearance of the character he was playing, Tarzan spent considerable time hunting in the vicinity of Bou Saada. He would spend entire days in the foothills, ostensibly searching for gazelle, but on the few occasions that he came close enough to any of the beautiful little animals to harm them he invariably allowed them to escape without so much as taking his rifle from its boot. The ape-man could see no sport in slaughtering the most harmless and defenseless of God's creatures for the mere pleasure of killing.

In fact, Tarzan had never killed for "pleasure," nor to him was there pleasure in killing. It was the joy of righteous battle that he loved—the ecstasy of victory. And the keen and successful hunt for food in which he pitted his skill and craftiness against the skill and craftiness of another; but to come out of a town filled with food to shoot down a soft-eyed, pretty gazelle—ah, that was crueller than the deliberate and cold-blooded murder of a fellow man. Tarzan would have none of it, and so he hunted alone that none might discover the sham that he was practicing.

And once, probably because of the fact that he rode alone, he was like to have lost his life. He was riding slowly through a little ravine when a shot sounded close behind him, and a bullet passed through the cork helmet he wore. Although he turned at once and galloped rapidly to the top of the ravine, there was no sign of any enemy, nor did he see aught of another human being until he reached Bou Saada.

"Yes," he soliloquized, in recalling the occurrence, "Olga has indeed thrown away her twenty thousand francs."

That night he was Captain Gerard's guest at a little dinner.

"Your hunting has not been very fortunate?" questioned the officer.

"No," replied Tarzan; "the game hereabout is timid, nor do I care particularly about hunting game birds or antelope. I think I shall move on farther south, and have a try at some of your Algerian lions."

"Good!" exclaimed the captain. "We are marching toward Djelfa on the morrow. You shall have company that far at least. Lieutenant Gernois and I, with a hundred men, are ordered south to patrol a district in which the marauders are giving considerable trouble. Possibly we may have the pleasure of hunting the lion together—what say you?"

Tarzan was more than pleased, nor did he hesitate to say so; but the captain would have been astonished had he known the real reason of Tarzan's pleasure. Gernois was sitting opposite the ape-man. He did not seem so pleased with his captain's invitation.

"You will find lion hunting more exciting than gazelle shooting," remarked Captain Gerard, "and more dangerous."

"Even gazelle shooting has its dangers," replied Tarzan. "Especially when one goes alone. I found it so today. I also found that while the gazelle is the most timid of animals, it is not the most cowardly."

He let his glance rest only casually upon Gernois after he had spoken, for he did not wish the man to know that he was under suspicion, or surveillance, no matter what he might think. The effect of his remark upon him, however, might tend to prove his connection with, or knowledge of, certain recent happenings. Tarzan saw a dull red creep up from beneath Gernois' collar. He was satisfied, and quickly changed the subject.

When the column rode south from Bou Saada the next morning there were half a dozen Arabs bringing up the rear.

"They are not attached to the command," replied Gerard in response to Tarzan's query. "They merely accompany us on the road for companionship."

Tarzan had learned enough about Arab character since he had been in Algeria to know that this was no real motive, for the Arab is never overfond of the companionship of strangers, and especially of French soldiers. So his suspicions were aroused, and he decided to keep a sharp eye on the little party that trailed behind the column at a distance of about a quarter of a mile. But they did not come close enough even during the halts to enable him to obtain a close scrutiny of them.

He had long been convinced that there were hired assassins on his trail, nor was he in great doubt but that Rokoff was at the bottom of the plot. Whether it was to be revenge for the several occasions in the past that Tarzan had defeated the Russian's purposes and humiliated him, or was in some way connected with his mission in the Gernois affair, he could not determine. If the latter, and it seemed probable since the evidence he had had that Gernois suspected him, then he had two rather powerful enemies to contend with, for there would be many opportunities in the wilds of Algeria, for which they were bound, to dispatch a suspected enemy quietly and without attracting suspicion.

After camping at Djelfa for two days the column moved to the southwest, from whence word had come that the marauders were operating against the tribes whose *douars* were situated at the foot of the mountains.

The little band of Arabs who had accompanied them from Bou Saada had disappeared suddenly the very night that orders had been given to prepare for the morrow's march from Djelfa. Tarzan made casual inquiries among the men, but none could tell him why they had left, or in what direction they had gone. He did not like the looks of it, especially in view of the fact that he had seen Gernois in conversation with one of them some half hour after Captain Gerard had issued his instructions relative to the new move. Only Gernois and Tarzan knew the direction of the proposed march. All the soldiers knew was that they were to be prepared to break camp early the next morning. Tarzan wondered if Gernois could have revealed their destination to the Arabs.

Late that afternoon they went into camp at a little oasis in which was the *douar* of a sheik whose flocks were being stolen, and whose herdsmen were being killed. The Arabs came out of their goatskin tents, and surrounded the soldiers, asking many questions in the native tongue, for the soldiers were themselves natives. Tarzan, who, by this time, with the assistance of Abdul, had picked up quite a smattering of Arab, questioned one of the younger men who had accompanied the sheik while the latter paid his respects to Captain Gerard.

No, he had seen no party of six horsemen riding from the direction of Djelfa. There were other oases scattered about—possibly they had been journeying to one of these. Then there were the marauders in the mountains above—they often rode north to Bou Saada in small parties, and even as far as Aumale and Bouira. It might indeed have been a few marauders returning to the band from a pleasure trip to one of these cities.

Early the next morning Captain Gerard split his command in two, giving Lieutenant Gernois command of one party, while he headed the other. They were to scour the mountains upon opposite sides of the plain.

"And with which detachment will Monsieur Tarzan ride?" asked the captain. "Or maybe it is that monsieur does not care to hunt marauders?"

"Oh, I shall be delighted to go," Tarzan hastened to explain. He was wondering what excuse he could make to accompany Gernois. His embarrassment was short-lived, and was relieved from a most unexpected source. It was Gernois himself who spoke.

"If my captain will forego the pleasure of Monsieur Tarzan's company for this once, I shall esteem it an honor indeed to have monsieur ride with me today," he said, nor was his tone lacking in cordiality. In fact, Tarzan imagined that he had overdone it a trifle, but, even so, he was both astounded and pleased, hastening to express his delight at the arrangement.

And so it was that Lieutenant Gernois and Tarzan rode off side by side at the head of the little detachment of *Spahis*. Gernois' cordiality was short-lived. No soone had they ridden out of sight of Captain Gerard and his men than he lapsed once more into his accustomed taciturnity. As they advanced the ground became rougher. Steadily it ascended toward the mountains, into which they filed through a narrow canon close to noon. By the side of a little rivulet Gernois called the midday halt. Here the men prepared and ate their frugal meal, and refilled their canteens.

After an hour's rest they advanced again along the canon, until they presently came to a little valley, from which several rocky gorges diverged. Here they halted, while Gernois minutely examined the surrounding heights from the center of the depression.

"We shall separate here," he said, "several riding into each of these gorges," and then he commenced to detail his various squads and issue instructions to the non-commissioned officers who were to command them. When he had done he turned to Tarzan. "Monsieur will be so good as to remain here until we return."

Tarzan demurred, but the officer cut him short. "There may be fighting for one of these sections," he said, "and troops cannot be embarrassed by civilian noncombatants during action."

"But, my dear lieutenant," expostulated Tarzan, "I am most ready and willing to place myself under command of yourself or any of your sergeants or corporals, and to fight in the ranks as they direct. It is what I came for."

"I should be glad to think so," retorted Gernois, with a sneer he made no attempt to disguise. Then shortly: "You are under my orders, and they are that you remain here until we return. Let that end the matter," and he turned and spurred away at the head of his men. A moment later Tarzan found himself alone in the midst of a desolate mountain fastness.

The sun was hot, so he sought the shelter of a nearby tree, where he tethered his horse, and sat down upon the ground to smoke. Inwardly he swore at Gernois for the trick he had played upon him. A mean little revenge, thought Tarzan, and then suddenly it occurred to him that the man would not be such a fool as to antagonize him through a trivial annoyance of so petty a description. There must be something deeper than this behind it. With the thought he arose and removed his rifle from its boot. He looked to its loads and saw that the magazine was full. Then he inspected his revolver. After this preliminary precaution he scanned the surrounding heights and the mouths of the several gorges—he was determined that he should not be caught napping.

The sun sank lower and lower, yet there was no sign of returning SPAHIS. At last the valley was submerged in shadow Tarzan was too proud to go back to camp until he had given the detachment ample time to return to the valley, which he thought was to have been their rendezvous. With the closing in of night he felt safer from attack, for he was at home in the dark. He knew that none might approach him so cautiously as to elude those alert and sensitive ears of his; then there were his eyes, too, for he could see well at night; and his nose, if they came toward him from up-wind, would apprise him of the approach of an enemy while they were still a great way off.

So he felt that he was in little danger, and thus lulled to a sense of security he fell asleep, with his back against the tree.

He must have slept for several hours, for when he was suddenly awakened by the frightened snorting and plunging of his horse the moon was shining full upon the little valley, and there, not ten paces before him, stood the grim cause of the terror of his mount.

Superb, majestic, his graceful tail extended and quivering, and his two eyes of fire riveted full upon his prey, stood Numa El Adrea, the black lion. A little thrill of joy tingled through Tarzan's nerves. It was like meeting an old friend after years of separation. For a moment he sat rigid to enjoy the magnificent spectacle of this lord of the wilderness.

But now Numa was crouching for the spring. Very slowly Tarzan raised his gun to his shoulder. He had never killed a large animal with a gun in all his life—heretofore he had depended upon his spear, his poisoned arrows, his rope, his knife, or his bare hands. Instinctively he wished that he had his arrows and his knife—he would have felt surer with them.

Numa was lying quite flat upon the ground now, presenting only his head. Tarzan would have preferred to fire a little from one side, for he knew what terrific damage the lion could do if he lived two minutes, or even a minute after he was hit. The horse stood trembling in terror at Tarzan's back. The ape-man took a cautious step to one side—Numa but followed him with his eyes. Another step he took, and then another. Numa had not moved. Now he could aim at a point between the eye and the ear.

His finger tightened upon the trigger, and as he fired Numa sprang. At the same instant the terrified horse made a last frantic effort to escape—the tether parted, and he went careening down the canon toward the desert.

No ordinary man could have escaped those frightful claws when Numa sprang from so short a distance, but Tarzan was no ordinary man. From earliest childhood his muscles had been trained by the fierce exigencies of his existence to act with the rapidity of thought. As quick as was EL ADREA, Tarzan of the Apes was quicker, and so the great beast crashed against a tree where he had expected to feel the soft flesh of man, while Tarzan, a couple of paces to the right, pumped another bullet into him that brought him clawing and roaring to his side.

Twice more Tarzan fired in quick succession, and then *El Adrea* lay still and roared no more. It was no longer Monsieur Jean Tarzan; it was Tarzan of the Apes that put a savage foot upon the body of his savage kill, and, raising his face to the full moon, lifted his mighty voice in the weird and terrible challenge of his kind—a bull ape had made his kill. And the wild things in the wild mountains stopped in their hunting, and trembled at this new and awful voice, while down in the desert the children of the wilderness came out of their goatskin tents and looked toward the mountains, wondering what new and savage scourge had come to devastate their flocks.

A half mile from the valley in which Tarzan stood, a score of white-robed figures, bearing long, wicked-looking guns, halted at the sound, and looked at one another with questioning eyes. But presently, as it was not repeated, they took up their silent, stealthy way toward the valley.

Tarzan was now confident that Gernois had no intention of returning for him, but he could not fathom the object that had prompted the officer to desert him, yet leave him free to return to camp. His horse gone, he decided that it would be foolish to remain longer in the mountains, so he set out toward the desert.

He had scarcely entered the confines of the canon when the first of the white-robed figures emerged into the valley upon the opposite side. For a moment they scanned the little depression from behind sheltering bowlders, but when they had satisfied themselves that it was empty they advanced across it. Beneath the tree at one side they came upon the body of El Adrea. With muttered exclamations they crowded about it. Then, a moment later, they hurried down the canon which Tarzan was threading a brief distance in advance of them. They moved cautiously and in silence, taking advantage of shelter, as men do who are stalking man.

THROUGH THE VALLEY OF THE SHADOW

As Tarzan walked down the wild canon beneath the brilliant African moon the call of the jungle was strong upon him. The solitude and the savage freedom filled his heart with life and buoyancy. Again he was Tarzan of the Apes—every sense alert against the chance of surprise by some jungle enemy—yet treading lightly and with head erect, in proud consciousness of his might.

The nocturnal sounds of the mountains were new to him, yet they fell upon his ears like the soft voice of a half-forgotten love. Many he intuitively sensed—ah, there was one that was familiar indeed; the distant coughing of Sheeta, the leopard; but there was a strange note in the final wail which made him doubt. It was a panther he heard.

Presently a new sound—a soft, stealthy sound—obtruded itself among the others. No human ears other than the ape-man's would have detected it. At first he did not translate it, but finally he realized that it came from the bare feet of a number of human beings. They were behind him, and they were coming toward him quietly. He was being stalked.

In a flash he knew why he had been left in that little valley by Gernois; but there had been a hitch in the arrangements—the men had come too late. Closer and closer came the footsteps. Tarzan halted and faced them, his rifle ready in his hand. Now he caught a fleeting glimpse of a white burnoose. He called aloud in French, asking what they would of him. His reply was the flash of a long gun, and with the sound of the shot Tarzan of the Apes plunged forward upon his face.

The Arabs did not rush out immediately; instead, they waited to be sure that their victim did not rise. Then they came rapidly from their concealment, and bent over him. It was soon apparent that he was not dead. One of the men put the muzzle of his gun to the back of Tarzan's head to finish him, but another waved him aside. "If we bring him alive the reward is to be greater," explained the latter. So they bound his hands and feet, and, picking him up, placed him on the shoulders of four of their number. Then the march was resumed toward the desert. When they had come out of the mountains they turned toward the south, and about daylight came to the spot where their horses stood in care of two of their number.

From here on their progress was more rapid. Tarzan, who had regained consciousness, was tied to a spare horse, which they evidently had brought for the purpose. His wound was but a slight scratch, which had furrowed the flesh across his temple. It had stopped bleeding, but the dried and clotted blood smeared his face and clothing. He had said no word since he had fallen into the hands of these Arabs, nor had they addressed him other than to issue a few brief commands to him when the horses had been reached.

For six hours they rode rapidly across the burning desert, avoiding the oases near which their way led. About noon they came to a DOUAR of about twenty tents. Here they halted, and as one of the Arabs was releasing the alfa-grass ropes which bound him to his mount they were surrounded by a mob of men, women, and children. Many of the tribe, and more especially the women, appeared to take delight in heaping insults upon the prisoner, and some had even gone so far as to throw stones at him and strike him with sticks, when an old sheik appeared and drove them away.

"Ali-ben-Ahmed tells me," he said, "that this man sat alone in the mountains and slew El Adrea. What the business of the stranger who sent us after him may be, I know not, and what he may do with this man when we turn him over to him, I care not; but the prisoner is a brave man, and while he is in our hands he shall be treated with the respect that be due one who hunts *the lord with the large head* alone and by night—and slays him."

Tarzan had heard of the respect in which Arabs held a lion-killer, and he was not sorry that chance had played into his hands thus favorably to relieve him of the petty tortures of the tribe. Shortly after this he was taken to a goat-skin tent upon the upper side of the *douar*. There he was fed, and then, securely bound, was left lying on a piece of native carpet, alone in the tent.

He could see a guard sitting before the door of his frail prison, but when he attempted to force the stout bonds that held him he realized that any extra precaution on the part of his captors was quite unnecessary; not even his giant muscles could part those numerous strands.

Just before dusk several men approached the tent where he lay, and entered it. All were in Arab dress, but presently one of the number advanced to Tarzan's side, and as he let the folds of cloth that had hidden the lower half of his face fall away the ape-man saw the malevolent features of Nikolas Rokoff. There was a nasty smile on the bearded lips. "Ah, Monsieur Tarzan," he said, "this is indeed a pleasure. But why do you not rise and greet your guest?" Then, with an ugly oath, "Get up, you dog!" and, drawing back his booted foot, he kicked Tarzan heavily in the side. "And here is another, and another, and another," he continued, as he kicked Tarzan about the face and side. "One for each of the injuries you have done me."

The ape-man made no reply—he did not even deign to look upon the Russian again after the first glance of recognition. Finally the sheik, who had been standing a mute and frowning witness of the cowardly attack, intervened.

"Stop!" he commanded. "Kill him if you will, but I will see no brave man subjected to such indignities in my presence. I have half a mind to turn him loose, that I may see how long you would kick him then."

This threat put a sudden end to Rokoff's brutality, for he had no craving to see Tarzan loosed from his bonds while he was within reach of those powerful hands.

"Very well," he replied to the Arab; "I shall kill him presently."

"Not within the precincts of my *douar*," returned the sheik. "When he leaves here he leaves alive. What you do with him in the desert is none of my concern, but I shall not have the blood of a Frenchman on the hands of my tribe on account of another man's quarrel—they would send soldiers here and kill many of my people, and burn our tents and drive away our flocks."

"As you say," growled Rokoff. "I'll take him out into the desert below the *douar*, and dispatch him."

"You will take him a day's ride from my country," said the sheik, firmly, "and some of my children shall follow you to see that you do not disobey me—otherwise there may be two dead Frenchmen in the desert."

Rokoff shrugged. "Then I shall have to wait until the morrow—it is already dark."

"As you will," said the sheik. "But by an hour after dawn you must be gone from my *douar*. I have little liking for unbelievers, and none at all for a coward."

Rokoff would have made some kind of retort, but he checked himself, for he realized that it would require but little excuse for the old man to turn upon him. Together they left the tent. At the door Rokoff could not resist the temptation to turn and fling a parting taunt at Tarzan. "Sleep well, monsieur," he said, "and do not forget to pray well, for when you die tomorrow it will be in such agony that you will be unable to pray for blaspheming."

No one had bothered to bring Tarzan either food or water since noon, and consequently he suffered considerably from thirst. He wondered if it would be worth while to ask his guard for water, but after making two or three requests without receiving any response, he decided that it would not.

Far up in the mountains he heard a lion roar. How much safer one was, he soliloquized, in the haunts of wild beasts than in the haunts of men. Never in all his jungle life had he been more relentlessly tracked down than in the past few months of his experience among civilized men. Never had he been any nearer death.

Again the lion roared. It sounded a little nearer. Tarzan felt the old, wild impulse to reply with the challenge of his kind. His kind? He had almost forgotten that he was a man and not an ape. He tugged at his bonds. God, if he could but get them near those strong teeth of his. He felt a wild wave of madness sweep over him as his efforts to regain his liberty met with failure.

Numa was roaring almost continually now. It was quite evident that he was coming down into the desert to hunt. It was the roar of a hungry lion. Tarzan envied him, for he was free. No one would tie him with ropes and slaughter him like a sheep. It was that which galled the ape-man. He did not fear to die, no—it was the humiliation of defeat before death, without even a chance to battle for his life.

It must be near midnight, thought Tarzan. He had several hours to live. Possibly he would yet find a way to take Rokoff with him on the long journey. He could hear the savage lord of the desert quite close by now. Possibly he sought his meat from among the penned animals within the *douar*.

For a long time silence reigned, then Tarzan's trained ears caught the sound of a stealthily moving body. It came from the side of the tent nearest the mountains—the back. Nearer and nearer it came. He waited, listening intently, for it to pass. For a time there was silence without, such a terrible silence that Tarzan was surprised that he did not hear the breathing of the animal he felt sure must be crouching close to the back wall of his tent.

There! It is moving again. Closer it creeps. Tarzan turns his head in the direction of the sound. It is very dark within the tent. Slowly the back rises from the ground, forced up by the head and shoulders of a body that looks all black in the semi-darkness. Beyond is a faint glimpse of the dimly starlit desert. A grim smile plays about Tarzan's lips. At least Rokoff will be cheated. How mad he will be! And death will be more merciful than he could have hoped for at the hands of the Russian.

Now the back of the tent drops into place, and all is darkness again—whatever it is is inside the tent with him. He hears it creeping close to him—now it is beside him. He closes his eyes and waits for the mighty paw.

Upon his upturned face falls the gentle touch of a soft hand groping in the dark, and then a girl's voice in a scarcely audible whisper pronounces his name.

"Yes, it is I," he whispers in reply. "But in the name of Heaven who are you?"

"The Ouled-Nail of Sisi Aissa," came the answer. While she spoke Tarzan could feel her working about his bonds. Occasionally the cold steel of a knife touched his flesh. A moment later he was free.

"Come!" she whispered.

On hands and knees he followed her out of the tent by the way she had come. She continued crawling thus flat to the ground until she reached a little patch of shrub. There she halted until he gained her side. For a moment he looked at her before he spoke.

"I cannot understand," he said at last. "Why are you here? How did you know that I was a prisoner in that tent? How does it happen that it is you who have saved me?"

She smiled. "I have come a long way tonight," she said, "and we have a long way to go before we shall be out of danger. Come; I shall tell you all about as we go."

Together they rose and set off across the desert in the direction of the mountains.

"I was not quite sure that I should ever reach you," she said at last. "El Adrea is abroad tonight, and after I left the horses I think he winded me and was following—I was terribly frightened."

"What a brave girl," he said. "And you ran all that risk for a stranger—an alien—an unbeliever?"

She drew herself up very proudly.

"I am the daughter of the Sheik Kabour ben Saden," she answered. "I should be no fit daughter of his if I would not risk my life to save that of the man who saved mine while he yet thought that I was but a common Ouled-Nail."

"Nevertheless," he insisted, "you are a very brave girl. But how did you know that I was a prisoner back there?"

"Achmet-din-Taieb, who is my cousin on my father's side, was visiting some friends who belong to the tribe that captured you. He was at the *douar* when you were brought in. When he reached home he was telling us about the big Frenchman who had been captured by Ali-ben-Ahmed for another Frenchman who wished to kill him. From the description I knew that it must be you. My father was away. I tried to persuade some of the men to come and save you, but they would not do it, saying: 'Let the unbelievers kill one another if they wish. It is none of our affair, and if we go and interfere with Ali-ben-Ahmed's plans we shall only stir up a fight with our own people.'

"So when it was dark I came alone, riding one horse and leading another for you. They are tethered not far from here. By morning we shall be within my father's *douar*. He should be there himself by now—then let them come and try to take Kadour ben Saden's friend."

For a few moments they walked on in silence.

"We should be near the horses," she said. "It is strange that I do not see them here."

Then a moment later she stopped, with a little cry of consternation.

"They are gone!" she exclaimed. "It is here that I tethered them."

Tarzan stooped to examine the ground. He found that a large shrub had been torn up by the roots. Then he found something else. There was a wry smile on his face as he rose and turned toward the girl.

"El Adrea has been here. From the signs, though, I rather think that his prey escaped him. With a little start they would be safe enough from him in the open."

There was nothing to do but continue on foot. The way led them across a low spur of the mountains, but the girl knew the trail as well as she did her mother's face. They walked in easy, swinging strides, Tarzan keeping a hand's breadth behind the girl's shoulder, that she might set the pace, and thus be less fatigued. As they walked they talked, occasionally stopping to listen for sounds of pursuit.

It was now a beautiful, moonlit night. The air was crisp and invigorating. Behind them lay the interminable vista of the desert, dotted here and there with an occasional oasis. The date palms of the little fertile spot they had just left, and the circle of goatskin tents, stood out in sharp relief against the yellow sand—a phantom paradise upon a phantom sea. Before them rose the grim and silent mountains. Tarzan's blood leaped in his veins. This was life! He looked down upon the girl beside him—a daughter of the desert walking across the face of a dead world with a son of the jungle. He smiled at the thought. He wished that he had had a sister, and that she had been like this girl. What a bully chum she would have been!

They had entered the mountains now, and were progressing more slowly, for the trail was steeper and very rocky.

For a few minutes they had been silent. The girl was wondering if they would reach her father's *douar* before the pursuit had overtaken them. Tarzan was wishing that they might walk on thus forever. If the girl were only a man they might. He longed for a friend who loved the same wild life that he loved. He had learned to crave companionship, but it was his misfortune that most of the men he knew preferred immaculate linen and their clubs to nakedness and the jungle. It was, of course, difficult to understand, yet it was very evident that they did.

The two had just turned a projecting rock around which the trail ran when they were brought to a sudden stop. There, before them, directly in the middle of the path, stood Numa, El Adrea, the black lion. His green eyes looked very wicked, and he bared his teeth, and lashed his bay-black sides with his angry tail. Then he roared—the fearsome, terror-inspiring roar of the hungry lion which is also angry.

"Your knife," said Tarzan to the girl, extending his hand. She slipped the hilt of the weapon into his waiting palm. As his fingers closed upon it he drew her back and pushed her behind him. "Walk back to the desert as rapidly as you can. If you hear me call you will know that all is well, and you may return."

"It is useless," she replied, resignedly. "This is the end."

"Do as I tell you," he commanded. "Quickly! He is about to charge." The girl dropped back a few paces, where she stood watching for the terrible sight that she knew she should soon witness.

The lion was advancing slowly toward Tarzan, his nose to the ground, like a challenging bull, his tail extended now and quivering as though with intense excitement.

The ape-man stood, half crouching, the long Arab knife glistening in the moonlight. Behind him the tense figure of the girl, motionless as a carven statue. She leaned slightly forward, her lips parted, her eyes wide. Her only conscious thought was wonder at the bravery of the man who dared face with a puny knife the lord with the large head. A man of her own blood would have knelt in prayer and gone down beneath those awful fangs without resistance. In either case the result would be the same—it was inevitable; but she could not repress a thrill of admiration as her eyes rested upon the heroic figure before her. Not a tremor in the whole giant frame—his attitude as menacing and defiant as that of El Adrea himself.

The lion was quite close to him now—but a few paces intervened—he crouched, and then, with a deafening roar, he sprang.

JOHN CALDWELL, LONDON

As Numa El Adrea launched himself with widespread paws and bared fangs he looked to find this puny man as easy prey as the score who had gone down beneath him in the past. To him man was a clumsy, slow-moving, defenseless creature—he had little respect for him.

But this time he found that he was pitted against a creature as agile and as quick as himself. When his mighty frame struck the spot where the man had been he was no longer there.

The watching girl was transfixed by astonishment at the ease with which the crouching man eluded the great paws. And now, O Allah! He had rushed in behind El Adrea's shoulder even before the beast could turn, and had grasped him by the mane. The lion reared upon his hind legs like a horse—Tarzan had known that he would do this, and he was ready. A giant arm encircled the black-maned throat, and once, twice, a dozen times a sharp blade darted in and out of the bay-black side behind the left shoulder.

Frantic were the leaps of Numa—awful his roars of rage and pain; but the giant upon his back could not be dislodged or brought within reach of fangs or talons in the brief interval of life that remained to the lord with the large head. He was quite dead when Tarzan of the Apes released his hold and arose. Then the daughter of the desert witnessed a thing that terrified her even more than had the presence of El Adrea. The man placed a foot upon the carcass of his kill, and, with his handsome face raised toward the full moon, gave voice to the most frightful cry that ever had smote upon her ears.

With a little cry of fear she shrank away from him—she thought that the fearful strain of the encounter had driven him mad. As the last note of that fiendish challenge died out in the diminishing echoes of the distance the man dropped his eyes until they rested upon the girl.

Instantly his face was lighted by the kindly smile that was ample assurance of his sanity, and the girl breathed freely once again, smiling in response.

"What manner of man are you?" she asked. "The thing you have done is unheard of. Even now I cannot believe that it is possible for a lone man armed only with a knife to have fought hand to hand with El Adrea and conquered him, unscathed—to have conquered him at all. And that cry—it was not human. Why did you do that?"

Tarzan flushed. "It is because I forget," he said, "sometimes, that I am a civilized man. When I kill it must be that I am another creature." He did not try to explain further, for it always seemed to him that a woman must look with loathing upon one who was yet so nearly a beast.

Together they continued their journey. The sun was an hour high when they came out into the desert again beyond the mountains. Beside a little rivulet they found the girl's horses grazing. They had come this far on their way home, and with the cause of their fear no longer present had stopped to feed.

With little trouble Tarzan and the girl caught them, and, mounting, rode out into the desert toward the *douar* of Sheik Kadour ben Saden.

No sign of pursuit developed, and they came in safety about nine o'clock to their destination. The sheik had but just returned. He was frantic with grief at the absence of his daughter, whom he thought had been again abducted by the marauders. With fifty men he was already mounted to go in search of her when the two rode into the *douar*.

His joy at the safe return of his daughter was only equaled by his gratitude to Tarzan for bringing her safely to him through the dangers of the night, and his thankfulness that she had been in time to save the man who had once saved her.

No honor that Kadour ben Saden could heap upon the ape-man in acknowledgment of his esteem and friendship was neglected. When the girl had recited the story of the slaying of El Adrea Tarzan was surrounded by a mob of worshiping Arabs—it was a sure road to their admiration and respect.

The old sheik insisted that Tarzan remain indefinitely as his guest. He even wished to adopt him as a member of the tribe, and there was for some time a half-formed resolution in the ape-man's mind to accept and remain forever with these wild people, whom he understood and who seemed to understand him. His friendship and liking for the girl were potent factors in urging him toward an affirmative decision.

Had she been a man, he argued, he should not have hesitated, for it would have meant a friend after his own heart, with whom he could ride and hunt at will; but as it was they would be hedged by the conventionalities that are even more strictly observed by the wild nomads of the desert than by their more civilized brothers and sisters. And in a little while she would be married to one of these swarthy warriors, and there would be an end to their friendship. So he decided against the sheik's proposal, though he remained a week as his guest.

When he left, Kadour ben Saden and fifty white-robed warriors rode with him to Bou Saada. While they were mounting in the *douar* of Kadour ben Saden the morning of their departure, the girl came to bid farewell to Tarzan.

"I have prayed that you would remain with us," she said simply, as he leaned from his saddle to clasp her hand in farewell, "and now I shall pray that you will return." There was an expression of wistfulness in her beautiful eyes, and a pathetic droop at the corners of her mouth. Tarzan was touched.

"Who knows?" and then he turned and rode after the departing Arabs.

Outside Bou Saada he bade Kadour ben Saden and his men good-by, for there were reasons which made him wish to make his entry into the town as secret as possible, and when he had explained them to the sheik the latter concurred in his decision. The Arabs were to enter Bou Saada ahead of him, saying nothing as to his presence with them. Later Tarzan would come in alone, and go directly to an obscure native inn.

Thus, making his entrance after dark, as he did, he was not seen by any one who knew him, and reached the inn unobserved. After dining with Kadour ben Saden as his guest, he went to his former hotel by a roundabout way, and, coming in by a rear entrance, sought the proprietor, who seemed much surprised to see him alive.

Yes, there was mail for monsieur; he would fetch it. No, he would mention monsieur's return to no one. Presently he returned with a packet of letters. One was an order from his superior to lay off on his present work, and hasten to Cape Town by the first steamer he could get. His further instructions would be awaiting him there in the hands of another agent whose name and address were given. That was all—brief but explicit. Tarzan arranged to leave Bou Saada early the next morning. Then he started for the garrison to see Captain Gerard, whom the hotel man had told him had returned with his detachment the previous day.

He found the officer in his quarters. He was filled with surprise and pleasure at seeing Tarzan alive and well.

"When Lieutenant Gernois returned and reported that he had not found you at the spot that you had chosen to remain while the detachment was scouting, I was filled with alarm. We searched the mountain for days. Then came word that you had been killed and eaten by a lion. As proof your gun was brought to us. Your horse had returned to camp the second day after your disappearance. We could not doubt. Lieutenant Gernois was grief-stricken—he took all the blame upon himself. It was he who insisted on carrying on the search himself. It was he who found the Arab with your gun. He will be delighted to know that you are safe."

"Doubtless," said Tarzan, with a grim smile.

"He is down in the town now, or I should send for him," continued Captain Gerard. "I shall tell him as soon as he returns."

Tarzan let the officer think that he had been lost, wandering finally into the *douar* of Kadour ben Saden, who had escorted him back to Bou Saada. As soon as possible he bade the good officer adieu, and hastened back into the town. At the native inn he had learned through Kadour ben Saden a piece of interesting information. It told of a black-bearded white man who went always disguised as an Arab. For a time he had nursed a broken wrist. More recently he had been away from Bou Saada, but now he was back, and Tarzan knew his place of concealment. It was for there he headed.

Through narrow, stinking alleys, black as Erebus, he groped, and then up a rickety stairway, at the end of which was a closed door and a tiny, unglazed window. The window was high under the low eaves of the mud building. Tarzan could just reach the sill. He raised himself slowly until his eyes topped it. The room within was lighted, and at a table sat Rokoff and Gernois. Gernois was speaking.

"Rokoff, you are a devil!" he was saying. "You have hounded me until I have lost the last shred of my honor. You have driven me to murder, for the blood of that man Tarzan is on my hands. If it were not that that other devil's spawn, Paulvitch, still knew my secret, I should kill you here tonight with my bare hands."

Rokoff laughed. "You would not do that, my dear lieutenant," he said. "The moment I am reported dead by assassination that dear Alexis will forward to the minister of war full proof of the affair you so ardently long to conceal; and, further, will charge you with my murder. Come, be sensible. I am your best friend. Have I not protected your honor as though it were my own?"

Gernois sneered, and spat out an oath.

"Just one more little payment," continued Rokoff, "and the papers I wish, and you have my word of honor that I shall never ask another cent from you, or further information."

"And a good reason why," growled Gernois. "What you ask will take my last cent, and the only valuable military secret I hold. You ought to be paying me for the information, instead of taking both it and money, too."

"I am paying you by keeping a still tongue in my head," retorted Rokoff. "But let's have done. Will you, or will you not? I give you three minutes to decide. If you are not agreeable I shall send a note to your commandant tonight that will end in the degradation that Dreyfus suffered—the only difference being that he did not deserve it."

For a moment Gernois sat with bowed head. At length he arose. He drew two pieces of paper from his blouse.

"Here," he said hopelessly. "I had them ready, for I knew that there could be but one outcome." He held them toward the Russian.

Rokoff's cruel face lighted in malignant gloating. He seized the bits of paper.

"You have done well, Gernois," he said. "I shall not trouble you again—unless you happen to accumulate some more money or information," and he grinned.

"You never shall again, you dog!" hissed Gernois. "The next time I shall kill you. I came near doing it tonight. For an hour I sat with these two pieces of paper on my table before me ere I came here—beside them lay my loaded revolver. I was trying to decide which I should bring. Next time the choice shall be easier, for I already have decided. You had a close call tonight, Rokoff; do not tempt fate a second time."

Then Gernois rose to leave. Tarzan barely had time to drop to the landing and shrink back into the shadows on the far side of the door. Even then he scarcely hoped to elude detection. The landing was very small, and though he flattened himself against the wall at its far edge he was scarcely more than a foot from the doorway. Almost immediately it opened, and Gernois stepped out. Rokoff was behind him. Neither spoke. Gernois had taken perhaps three steps down the stairway when he halted and half turned, as though to retrace his steps.

Tarzan knew that discovery would be inevitable. Rokoff still stood on the threshold a foot from him, but he was looking in the opposite direction, toward Gernois. Then the officer evidently reconsidered his decision, and resumed his downward course. Tarzan could hear Rokoff's sigh of relief. A moment later the Russian went back into the room and closed the door.

Tarzan waited until Gernois had had time to get well out of hearing, then he pushed open the door and stepped into the room. He was on top of Rokoff before the man could rise from the chair where he sat scanning the paper Gernois had given him. As his eyes turned and fell upon the ape-man's face his own went livid.

"You!" he gasped.

"I," replied Tarzan.

"What do you want?" whispered Rokoff, for the look in the ape-man's eyes frightened him. "Have you come to kill me? You do not dare. They would guillotine you. You do not dare kill me."

"I dare kill you, Rokoff," replied Tarzan, "for no one knows that you are here or that I am here, and Paulvitch would tell them that it was Gernois. I heard you tell Gernois so. But that would not influence me, Rokoff. I would not care who knew that I had killed you; the pleasure of killing you would more than compensate for any punishment they might inflict upon me. You are the most despicable cur of a coward, Rokoff, I have ever heard of. You should be killed. I should love to kill you," and Tarzan approached closer to the man.

Rokoff's nerves were keyed to the breaking point. With a shriek he sprang toward an adjoining room, but the ape-man was upon his back while his leap was yet but half completed. Iron fingers sought his throat—the great coward squealed like a stuck pig, until Tarzan had shut off his wind. Then the ape-man dragged him to his feet, still choking him. The Russian struggled futilely—he was like a babe in the mighty grasp of Tarzan of the Apes.

Tarzan sat him in a chair, and long before there was danger of the man's dying he released his hold upon his throat. When the Russian's coughing spell had abated Tarzan spoke to him again.

"I have given you a taste of the suffering of death," he said. "But I shall not kill—this time. I am sparing you solely for the sake of a very good woman whose great misfortune it was to have been born of the same woman who gave birth to you. But I shall spare you only this once on her account. Should I ever learn that you have again annoyed her or her husband—should you ever annoy me again—should I hear that you have returned to France or to any French posession, I shall make it my sole business to hunt you down and complete the choking I commenced tonight." Then he turned to the table, on which the two pieces of paper still lay. As he picked them up Rokoff gasped in horror.

Tarzan examined both the check and the other. He was amazed at the information the latter contained. Rokoff had partially read it, but Tarzan knew that no one could remember the salient facts and figures it held which made it of real value to an enemy of France.

"These will interest the chief of staff," he said, as he slipped them into his pocket. Rokoff groaned. He did not dare curse aloud.

The next morning Tarzan rode north on his way to Bouira and Algiers. As he had ridden past the hotel Lieutenant Gernois was standing on the veranda. As his eyes discovered Tarzan he went white as chalk. The ape-man would have been glad had the meeting not occurred, but he could not avoid it. He saluted the officer as he rode past. Mechanically Gernois returned the salute, but those terrible, wide eyes followed the horseman, expressionless except for horror. It was as though a dead man looked upon a ghost.

At Sidi Aissa Tarzan met a French officer with whom he had become acquainted on the occasion of his recent sojourn in the town.

"You left Bou Saada early?" questioned the officer. "Then you have not heard about poor Gernois."

"He was the last man I saw as I rode away," replied Tarzan. "What about him?"

"He is dead. He shot himself about eight o'clock this morning."

Two days later Tarzan reached Algiers. There he found that he would have a two days' wait before he could catch a ship bound for Cape Town. He occupied his time in writing out a full report of his mission. The secret papers he had taken from Rokoff he did not inclose, for he did not dare trust them out of his own possession until he had been authorized to turn them over to another agent, or himself return to Paris with them.

As Tarzan boarded his ship after what seemed a most tedious wait to him, two men watched him from an upper deck. Both were fashionably dressed and smooth shaven. The taller of the two had sandy hair, but his eyebrows were very black. Later in the day they chanced to meet Tarzan on deck, but as one hurriedly called his companion's attention to something at sea their faces were turned from Tarzan as he passed, so that he did not notice their features. In fact, he had paid no attention to them at all.

Following the instructions of his chief, Tarzan had booked his passage under an assumed name—John Caldwell, London. He did not understand the necessity of this, and it caused him considerable speculation. He wondered what role he was to play in Cape Town.

"Well," he thought, "thank Heaven that I am rid of Rokoff. He was commencing to annoy me. I wonder if I am really becoming so civilized that presently I shall develop a set of nerves. He would give them to me if any one could, for he does not fight fair. One never knows through what new agency he is going to strike. It is as though Numa, the lion, had induced Tantor, the elephant, and Histah, the snake, to join him in attempting to kill me. I would then never have known what minute, or by whom, I was to be attacked next. But the brutes are more chivalrous than man—they do not stoop to cowardly intrigue."

At dinner that night Tarzan sat next to a young woman whose place was at the captain's left. The officer introduced them.

Miss Strong! Where had he heard the name before? It was very familiar. And then the girl's mother gave him the clew, for when she addressed her daughter she called her Hazel.

Hazel Strong! What memories the name inspired. It had been a letter to this girl, penned by the fair hand of Jane Porter, that had carried to him the first message from the woman he loved. How vividly he recalled the night he had stolen it from the desk in the cabin of his long-dead father, where Jane Porter had sat writing it late into the night, while he crouched in the darkness without. How terror-stricken she would have been that night had she known that the wild jungle beast squatted outside her window, watching her every move.

And this was Hazel Strong—Jane Porter's best friend!

SHIPS THAT PASS

Let us go back a few months to the little, windswept platform of a railway station in northern Wisconsin. The smoke of forest fires hangs low over the surrounding landscape, its acrid fumes smarting the eyes of a little party of six who stand waiting the coming of the train that is to bear them away toward the south.

Professor Archimedes Q. Porter, his hands clasped beneath the tails of his long coat, paces back and forth under the ever-watchful eye of his faithful secretary, Mr. Samuel T. Philander. Twice within the past few minutes he has started absent-mindedly across the tracks in the direction of a near-by swamp, only to be rescued and dragged back by the tireless Mr. Philander.

Jane Porter, the professor's daughter, is in strained and lifeless conversation with William Cecil Clayton and Tarzan of the Apes. Within the little waiting room, but a bare moment before, a confession of love and a renunciation had taken place that had blighted the lives and happiness of two of the party, but William Cecil Clayton, Lord Greystoke, was not one of them.

Behind Miss Porter hovered the motherly Esmeralda. She, too, was happy, for was she not returning to her beloved Maryland? Already she could see dimly through the fog of smoke the murky headlight of the oncoming engine. The men began to gather up the hand baggage. Suddenly Clayton exclaimed.

"By Jove! I've left my ulster in the waiting-room," and hastened off to fetch it.

"Good-bye, Jane," said Tarzan, extending his hand. "God bless you!"

"Good-bye," replied the girl faintly. "Try to forget me—no, not that—I could not bear to think that you had forgotten me."

"There is no danger of that, dear," he answered. "I wish to Heaven that I might forget. It would be so much easier than to go through life always remembering what might have been. You will be happy, though; I am sure you shall—you must be. You may tell the others of my decision to drive my car on to New York—I don't feel equal to bidding Clayton good-bye. I want always to remember him kindly, but I fear that I am too much of a wild beast yet to be trusted too long with the man who stands between me and the one person in all the world I want."

As Clayton stooped to pick up his coat in the waiting room his eyes fell on a telegraph blank lying face down upon the floor. He stooped to pick it up, thinking it might be a message of importance which some one had dropped. He glanced at it hastily, and then suddenly he forgot his coat, the approaching train—everything but that terrible little piece of yellow paper in his hand. He read it twice before he could fully grasp the terrific weight of meaning that it bore to him.

When he had picked it up he had been an English nobleman, the proud and wealthy possessor of vast estates—a moment later he had read it, and he knew that he was an untitled and penniless beggar. It was D'Arnot's cablegram to Tarzan, and it read:

Finger prints prove you Greystoke. Congratulations.
D'arnot.

He staggered as though he had received a mortal blow. Just then he heard the others calling to him to hurry—the train was coming to a stop at the little platform. Like a man dazed he gathered up his ulster. He would tell them about the cablegram when they were all on board the train. Then he ran out upon the platform just as the engine whistled twice in the final warning that precedes the first rumbling jerk of coupling pins. The others were on board, leaning out from the platform of a Pullman, crying to him to hurry. Quite five minutes elapsed before they were settled in their seats, nor was it until then that Clayton discovered that Tarzan was not with them.

"Where is Tarzan?" he asked Jane Porter. "In another car?"

"No," she replied; "at the last minute he determined to drive his machine back to New York. He is anxious to see more of America than is possible from a car window. He is returning to France, you know."

Clayton did not reply. He was trying to find the right words to explain to Jane Porter the calamity that had befallen him—and her. He wondered just what the effect of his knowledge would be on her. Would she still wish to marry him—to be plain Mrs. Clayton? Suddenly the awful sacrifice which one of them must make loomed large before his imagination. Then came the question: Will Tarzan claim his own? The ape-man had known the contents of the message before he calmly denied knowledge of his parentage! He had admitted that Kala, the ape, was his mother! Could it have been for love of Jane Porter?

There was no other explanation which seemed reasonable. Then, having ignored the evidence of the message, was it not reasonable to assume that he meant never to claim his birthright? If this were so, what right had he, William Cecil Clayton, to thwart the wishes, to balk the self-sacrifice of this strange man? If Tarzan of the Apes could do this thing to save Jane Porter from unhappiness, why should he, to whose care she was intrusting her whole future, do aught to jeopardize her interests?

And so he reasoned until the first generous impulse to proclaim the truth and relinquish his titles and his estates to their rightful owner was forgotten beneath the mass of sophistries which self-interest had advanced. But during the balance of the trip, and for many days thereafter, he was moody and distraught. Occasionally the thought obtruded itself that possibly at some later day Tarzan would regret his magnanimity, and claim his rights.

Several days after they reached Baltimore Clayton broached the subject of an early marriage to Jane.

"What do you mean by early?" she asked.

"Within the next few days. I must return to England at once—I want you to return with me, dear."

"I can't get ready so soon as that," replied Jane. "It will take a whole month, at least."

She was glad, for she hoped that whatever called him to England might still further delay the wedding. She had made a bad bargain, but she intended carrying her part loyally to the bitter end—if she could manage to secure a temporary reprieve, though, she felt that she was warranted in doing so. His reply disconcerted her.

"Very well, Jane," he said. "I am disappointed, but I shall let my trip to England wait a month; then we can go back together."

But when the month was drawing to a close she found still another excuse upon which to hang a postponement, until at last, discouraged and doubting, Clayton was forced to go back to England alone.

The several letters that passed between them brought Clayton no nearer to a consummation of his hopes than he had been before, and so it was that he wrote directly to Professor Porter, and enlisted his services. The old man had always favored the match. He liked Clayton, and, being of an old southern family, he put rather an exaggerated value on the advantages of a title, which meant little or nothing to his daughter.

Clayton urged that the professor accept his invitation to be his guest in London, an invitation which included the professor's entire little family—Mr. Philander, Esmeralda, and all. The Englishman argued that once Jane was there, and home ties had been broken, she would not so dread the step which she had so long hesitated to take.

So the evening that he received Clayton's letter Professor Porter announced that they would leave for London the following week.

But once in London Jane Porter was no more tractable than she had been in Baltimore. She found one excuse after another, and when, finally, Lord Tennington invited the party to cruise around Africa in his yacht, she expressed the greatest delight in the idea, but absolutely refused to be married until they had returned to London. As the cruise was to consume a year at least, for they were to stop for indefinite periods at various points of interest, Clayton mentally anathematized Tennington for ever suggesting such a ridiculous trip.

It was Lord Tennington's plan to cruise through the Mediterranean, and the Red Sea to the Indian Ocean, and thus down the East Coast, putting in at every port that was worth the seeing.

And so it happened that on a certain day two vessels passed in the Strait of Gibraltar. The smaller, a trim white yacht, was speeding toward the east, and on her deck sat a young woman who gazed with sad eyes upon a diamondstudded locket which she idly fingered. Her thoughts were far away, in the dim, leafy fastness of a tropical jungle—and her heart was with her thoughts.

She wondered if the man who had given her the beautiful bauble, that had meant so much more to him than the intrinsic value which he had not even known could ever have meant to him, was back in his savage forest.

And upon the deck of the larger vessel, a passenger steamer passing toward the east, the man sat with another young woman, and the two idly speculated upon the identity of the dainty craft gliding so gracefully through the gentle swell of the lazy sea.

When the yacht had passed the man resumed the conversation that her appearance had broken off.

"Yes," he said, "I like America very much, and that means, of course, that I like Americans, for a country is only what its people make it. I met some very delightful people while I was there. I recall one family from your own city, Miss Strong, whom I liked particularly—Professor Porter and his daughter."

"Jane Porter!" exclaimed the girl. "Do you mean to tell me that you know Jane Porter? Why, she is the very best friend I have in the world. We were little children together—we have known each other for ages."

"Indeed!" he answered, smiling. "You would have difficulty in persuading any one of the fact who had seen either of you."

"I'll qualify the statement, then," she answered, with a laugh. "We have known each other for two ages—hers and mine. But seriously we are as dear to each other as sisters, and now that I am going to lose her I am almost heartbroken."

"Going to lose her?" exclaimed Tarzan. "Why, what do you mean? Oh, yes, I understand. You mean that now that she is married and living in England, you will seldom if ever see her."

"Yes," replied she; "and the saddest part of it all is that she is not marrying the man she loves. Oh, it is terrible. Marrying from a sense of duty! I think it is perfectly wicked, and I told her so. I have felt so strongly on the subject that although I was the only person outside of blood relations who was to have been asked to the wedding I would not let her invite me, for I should not have gone to witness the terrible mockery. But Jane Porter is peculiarly positive. She has convinced herself that she is doing the only honorable thing that she can do, and nothing in the world will ever prevent her from marrying Lord Greystoke except Greystoke himself, or death."

"I am sorry for her," said Tarzan.

"And I am sorry for the man she loves," said the girl, "for he loves her. I never met him, but from what Jane tells me he must be a very wonderful person. It seems that he was born in an African jungle, and brought up by fierce, anthropoid apes. He had never seen a white man or woman until Professor Porter and his party were marooned on the coast right at the threshold of his tiny cabin. He saved them from all manner of terrible beasts, and accomplished the most wonderful feats imaginable, and then to cap the climax he fell in love with Jane and she with him, though she never really knew it for sure until she had promised herself to Lord Greystoke."

"Most remarkable," murmured Tarzan, cudgeling his brain for some pretext upon which to turn the subject. He delighted in hearing Hazel Strong talk of Jane, but when he was the subject of the conversation he was bored and embarrassed. But he was soon given a respite, for the girl's mother joined them, and the talk became general.

The next few days passed uneventfully. The sea was quiet. The sky was clear. The steamer plowed steadily on toward the south without pause. Tarzan spent quite a little time with Miss Strong and her mother. They whiled away their hours on deck reading, talking, or taking pictures with Miss Strong's camera. When the sun had set they walked.

One day Tarzan found Miss Strong in conversation with a stranger, a man he had not seen on board before. As he approached the couple the man bowed to the girl and turned to walk away.

"Wait, Monsieur Thuran," said Miss Strong; "you must meet Mr. Caldwell. We are all fellow passengers, and should be acquainted."

The two men shook hands. As Tarzan looked into the eyes of Monsieur Thuran he was struck by the strange familiarity of their expression.

"I have had the honor of monsieur's acquaintance in the past, I am sure," said Tarzan, "though I cannot recall the circumstances."

Monsieur Thuran appeared ill at ease.

"I cannot say, monsieur," he replied. "It may be so. I have had that identical sensation myself when meeting a stranger."

"Monsieur Thuran has been explaining some of the mysteries of navigation to me," explained the girl.

Tarzan paid little heed to the conversation that ensued—he was attempting to recall where he had met Monsieur Thuran before. That it had been under peculiar circumstances he was positive. Presently the sun reached them, and the girl asked Monsieur Thuran to move her chair farther back into the shade. Tarzan happened to be watching the man at the time, and noticed the awkward manner in which he handled the chair—his left wrist was stiff. That clew was sufficient—a sudden train of associated ideas did the rest.

Monsieur Thuran had been trying to find an excuse to make a graceful departure. The lull in the conversation following the moving of their position gave him an opportunity to make his excuses. Bowing low to Miss Strong, and inclining his head to Tarzan, he turned to leave them.

"Just a moment," said Tarzan. "If Miss Strong will pardon me I will accompany you. I shall return in a moment, Miss Strong."

Monsieur Thuran looked uncomfortable. When the two men had passed out of the girl's sight, Tarzan stopped, laying a heavy hand on the other's shoulder.

"What is your game now, Rokoff?" he asked.

"I am leaving France as I promised you," replied the other, in a surly voice.

"I see you are," said Tarzan; "but I know you so well that I can scarcely believe that your being on the same boat with me is purely a coincidence. If I could believe it the fact that you are in disguise would immediately disabuse my mind of any such idea."

"Well," growled Rokoff, with a shrug, "I cannot see what you are going to do about it. This vessel flies the English flag. I have as much right on board her as you, and from the fact that you are booked under an assumed name I imagine that I have more right."

"We will not discuss it, Rokoff. All I wanted to say to you is that you must keep away from Miss Strong—she is a decent woman."

Rokoff turned scarlet.

"If you don't I shall pitch you overboard," continued Tarzan. "Do not forget that I am just waiting for some excuse." Then he turned on his heel, and left Rokoff standing there trembling with suppressed rage.

He did not see the man again for days, but Rokoff was not idle. In his stateroom with Paulvitch he fumed and swore, threatening the most terrible of revenges.

"I would throw him overboard tonight," he cried, "were I sure that those papers were not on his person. I cannot chance pitching them into the ocean with him. If you were not such a stupid coward, Alexis, you would find a way to enter his stateroom and search for the documents."

Paulvitch smiled. "You are supposed to be the brains of this partnership, my dear Nikolas," he replied. "Why do you not find the means to search Monsieur Caldwell's stateroom—eh?"

Two hours later fate was kind to them, for Paulvitch, who was ever on the watch, saw Tarzan leave his room without locking the door. Five minutes later Rokoff was stationed where he could give the alarm in case Tarzan returned, and Paulvitch was deftly searching the contents of the ape-man's luggage.

He was about to give up in despair when he saw a coat which Tarzan had just removed. A moment later he grasped an official envelope in his hand. A quick glance at its contents brought a broad smile to the Russian's face.

When he left the stateroom Tarzan himself could not have told that an article in it had been touched since he left it—Paulvitch was a past master in his chosen field. When he handed the packet to Rokoff in the seclusion of their stateroom the larger man rang for a steward, and ordered a pint of champagne.

"We must celebrate, my dear Alexis," he said.

"It was luck, Nikolas," explained Paulvitch. "It is evident that he carries these papers always upon his person—just by chance he neglected to transfer them when he changed coats a few minutes since. But there will be the deuce to pay when he discovers his loss. I am afraid that he will immediately connect you with it. Now that he knows that you are on board he will suspect you at once."

"It will make no difference whom he suspects—after to-night," said Rokoff, with a nasty grin.

After Miss Strong had gone below that night Tarzan stood leaning over the rail looking far out to sea. Every night he had done this since he had come on board—sometimes he stood thus for an hour. And the eyes that had been watching his every movement since he had boarded the ship at Algiers knew that this was his habit.

Even as he stood there this night those eyes were on him. Presently the last straggler had left the deck. It was a clear night, but there was no moon—objects on deck were barely discernible.

From the shadows of the cabin two figures crept stealthily upon the ape-man from behind. The lapping of the waves against the ship's sides, the whirring of the propeller, the throbbing of the engines, drowned the almost soundless approach of the two.

They were quite close to him now, and crouching low, like tacklers on a gridiron. One of them raised his hand and lowered it, as though counting off seconds—one—two—three! As one man the two leaped for their victim. Each grasped a leg, and before Tarzan of the Apes, lightning though he was, could turn to save himself he had been pitched over the low rail and was falling into the Atlantic.

Hazel Strong was looking from her darkened port across the dark sea. Suddenly a body shot past her eyes from the deck above. It dropped so quickly into the dark waters below that she could not be sure of what it was—it might have been a man, she could not say. She listened for some outcry from above—for the always-fearsome call, "Man overboard!" but it did not come. All was silence on the ship above—all was silence in the sea below.

The girl decided that she had but seen a bundle of refuse thrown overboard by one of the ship's crew, and a moment later sought her berth.

THE WRECK OF THE LADY ALICE

The next morning at breakfast Tarzan's place was vacant. Miss Strong was mildly curious, for Mr. Caldwell had always made it a point to wait that he might breakfast with her and her mother. As she was sitting on deck later Monsieur Thuran paused to exchange a half dozen pleasant words with her. He seemed in most excellent spirits—his manner was the extreme of affability. As he passed on Miss Strong thought what a very delightful man was Monsieur Thuran.

The day dragged heavily. She missed the quiet companionship of Mr. Caldwell—there had been something about him that had made the girl like him from the first; he had talked so entertainingly of the places he had seen—the peoples and their customs—the wild beasts; and he had always had a droll way of drawing striking comparisons between savage animals and civilized men that showed a considerable knowledge of the former, and a keen, though somewhat cynical, estimate of the latter.

When Monsieur Thuran stopped again to chat with her in the afternoon she welcomed the break in the day's monotony. But she had begun to become seriously concerned in Mr. Caldwell's continued absence; somehow she constantly associated it with the start she had had the night before, when the dark object fell past her port into the sea. Presently she broached the subject to Monsieur Thuran. Had he seen Mr. Caldwell today? He had not. Why?

"He was not at breakfast as usual, nor have I seen him once since yesterday," explained the girl.

Monsieur Thuran was extremely solicitous.

"I did not have the pleasure of intimate acquaintance with Mr. Caldwell," he said. "He seemed a most estimable gentleman, however. Can it be that he is indisposed, and has remained in his stateroom? It would not be strange."

"No," replied the girl, "it would not be strange, of course; but for some inexplicable reason I have one of those foolish feminine presentiments that all is not right with Mr. Caldwell. It is the strangest feeling—it is as though I knew that he was not on board the ship."

Monsieur Thuran laughed pleasantly. "Mercy, my dear Miss Strong," he said; "where in the world could he be then? We have not been within sight of land for days."

"Of course, it is ridiculous of me," she admitted. And then: "But I am not going to worry about it any longer; I am going to find out where Mr. Caldwell is," and she motioned to a passing steward.

"That may be more difficult than you imagine, my dear girl," thought Monsieur Thuran, but aloud he said: "By all means."

"Find Mr. Caldwell, please," she said to the steward, "and tell him that his friends are much worried by his continued absence."

"You are very fond of Mr. Caldwell?" suggested Monsieur Thuran.

"I think he is splendid," replied the girl. "And mamma is perfectly infatuated with him. He is the sort of man with whom one has a feeling of perfect security—no one could help but have confidence in Mr. Caldwell."

A moment later the steward returned to say that Mr. Caldwell was not in his stateroom. "I cannot find him, Miss Strong, and"—he hesitated—" I have learned that his berth was not occupied last night. I think that I had better report the matter to the captain."

"Most assuredly," exclaimed Miss Strong. "I shall go with you to the captain myself. It is terrible! I know that something awful has happened. My presentiments were not false, after all."

It was a very frightened young woman and an excited steward who presented themselves before the captain a few moments later. He listened to their stories in silence—a look of concern marking his expression as the steward assured him that he had sought for the missing passenger in every part of the ship that a passenger might be expected to frequent.

"And are you sure, Miss Strong, that you saw a body fall overboard last night?" he asked.

"There is not the slightest doubt about that," she answered. "I cannot say that it was a human body—there was no outcry. It might have been only what I thought it was—a bundle of refuse. But if Mr. Caldwell is not found on board I shall always be positive that it was he whom I saw fall past my port."

The captain ordered an immediate and thorough search of the entire ship from stem to stern—no nook or cranny was to be overlooked. Miss Strong remained in his cabin, waiting the outcome of the quest. The captain asked her many questions, but she could tell him nothing about the missing man other than what she had herself seen during their brief acquaintance on shipboard. For the first time she suddenly realized how very little indeed Mr. Caldwell had told her about himself or his past life. That he had been born in Africa and educated in Paris was about all she knew, and this meager information had been the result of her surprise that an Englishman should speak English with such a marked French accent.

"Did he ever speak of any enemies?" asked the captain.

"Never."

"Was he acquainted with any of the other passengers?"

"Only as he had been with me—through the circumstance of casual meeting as fellow shipmates."

"Er—was he, in your opinion, Miss Strong, a man who drank to excess?"

"I do not know that he drank at all—he certainly had not been drinking up to half an hour before I saw that body fall overboard," she answered, "for I was with him on deck up to that time."

"It is very strange," said the captain. "He did not look to me like a man who was subject to fainting spells, or anything of that sort. And even had he been it is scarcely credible that he should have fallen completely over the rail had he been taken with an attack while leaning upon it—he would rather have fallen inside, upon the deck. If he is not on board, Miss Strong, he was thrown overboard—and the fact that you heard no outcry would lead to the assumption that he was dead before he left the ship's deck—murdered."

The girl shuddered.

It was a full hour later that the first officer returned to report the outcome of the search.

"Mr. Caldwell is not on board, sir," he said.

"I fear that there is something more serious than accident here, Mr. Brently," said the captain. "I wish that you would make a personal and very careful examination of Mr. Caldwell's effects, to ascertain if there is any clew to a motive either for suicide or murder—sift the thing to the bottom."

"Aye, aye, sir!" responded Mr. Brently, and left to commence his investigation.

Hazel Strong was prostrated. For two days she did not leave her cabin, and when she finally ventured on deck she was very wan and white, with great, dark circles beneath her eyes. Waking or sleeping, it seemed that she constantly saw that dark body dropping, swift and silent, into the cold, grim sea.

Shortly after her first appearance on deck following the tragedy, Monsieur Thuran joined her with many expressions of kindly solicitude.

"Oh, but it is terrible, Miss Strong," he said. "I cannot rid my mind of it."

"Nor I," said the girl wearily. "I feel that he might have been saved had I but given the alarm."

"You must not reproach yourself, my dear Miss Strong," urged Monsieur Thuran. "It was in no way your fault. Another would have done as you did. Who would think that because something fell into the sea from a ship that it must necessarily be a man? Nor would the outcome have been different had you given an alarm. For a while they would have doubted your story, thinking it but the nervous hallucination of a woman—had you insisted it would have been too late to have rescued him by the time the ship could have been brought to a stop, and the boats lowered and rowed back miles in search of the unknown spot where the tragedy had occurred. No, you must not censure yourself. You have done more than any other of us for poor Mr. Caldwell—you were the only one to miss him. It was you who instituted the search."

The girl could not help but feel grateful to him for his kind and encouraging words. He was with her often—almost constantly for the remainder of the voyage—and she grew to like him very much indeed. Monsieur Thuran had learned that the beautiful Miss Strong, of Baltimore, was an American heiress—a very wealthy girl in her own right, and with future prospects that quite took his breath away when he contemplated them, and since he spent most of his time in that delectable pastime it is a wonder that he breathed at all.

It had been Monsieur Thuran's intention to leave the ship at the first port they touched after the disappearance of Tarzan. Did he not have in his coat pocket the thing he had taken passage upon this very boat to obtain? There was nothing more to detain him here. He could not return to the Continent fast enough, that he might board the first express for St. Petersburg.

But now another idea had obtruded itself, and was rapidly crowding his original intentions into the background. That American fortune was not to be sneezed at, nor was its possessor a whit less attractive.

"*Sapristi!* but she would cause a sensation in St. Petersburg." And he would, too, with the assistance of her inheritance.

After Monsieur Thuran had squandered a few million dollars, he discovered that the vocation was so entirely to his liking that he would continue on down to Cape Town, where he suddenly decided that he had pressing engagements that might detain him there for some time.

Miss Strong had told him that she and her mother were to visit the latter's brother there—they had not decided upon the duration of their stay, and it would probably run into months.

She was delighted when she found that Monsieur Thuran was to be there also.

"I hope that we shall be able to continue our acquaintance," she said. "You must call upon mamma and me as soon as we are settled."

Monsieur Thuran was delighted at the prospect, and lost no time in saying so. Mrs. Strong was not quite so favorably impressed by him as her daughter.

"I do not know why I should distrust him," she said to Hazel one day as they were discussing him. "He seems a perfect gentleman in every respect, but sometimes there is something about his eyes—a fleeting expression which I cannot describe, but which when I see it gives me a very uncanny feeling."

The girl laughed. "You are a silly dear, mamma," she said.

"I suppose so, but I am sorry that we have not poor Mr. Caldwell for company instead."

"And I, too," replied her daughter.

Monsieur Thuran became a frequent visitor at the home of Hazel Strong's uncle in Cape Town. His attentions were very marked, but they were so punctiliously arranged to meet the girl's every wish that she came to depend upon him more and more. Did she or her mother or a cousin require an escort—was there a little friendly service to be rendered, the genial and ubiquitous Monsieur Thuran was always available. Her uncle and his family grew to like him for his unfailing courtesy and willingness to be of service. Monsieur Thuran was becoming indispensable. At length, feeling the moment propitious, he proposed. Miss Strong was startled. She did not know what to say.

"I had never thought that you cared for me in any such way," she told him. "I have looked upon you always as a very dear friend. I shall not give you my answer now. Forget that you have asked me to be your wife. Let us go on as we have been—then I can consider you from an entirely different angle for a time. It may be that I shall discover that my feeling for you is more than friendship. I certainly have not thought for a moment that I loved you."

This arrangement was perfectly satisfactory to Monsieur Thuran. He deeply regretted that he had been hasty, but he had loved her for so long a time, and so devotedly, that he thought that every one must know it.

"From the first time I saw you, Hazel," he said, "I have loved you. I am willing to wait, for I am certain that so great and pure a love as mine will be rewarded. All that I care to know is that you do not love another. Will you tell me?"

"I have never been in love in my life," she replied, and he was quite satisfied. On the way home that night he purchased a steam yacht, and built a million-dollar villa on the Black Sea.

The next day Hazel Strong enjoyed one of the happiest surprises of her life—she ran face to face upon Jane Porter as she was coming out of a jeweler's shop.

"Why, Jane Porter!" she exclaimed. "Where in the world did you drop from? Why, I can't believe my own eyes."

"Well, of all things!" cried the equally astonished Jane. "And here I have been wasting whole reams of perfectly good imagination picturing you in Baltimore—the very idea!" And she threw her arms about her friend once more, and kissed her a dozen times.

By the time mutual explanations had been made Hazel knew that Lord Tennington's yacht had put in at Cape Town for at least a week's stay, and at the end of that time was to continue on her voyage—this time up the West Coast—and so back to England. "Where," concluded Jane, "I am to be married."

"Then you are not married yet?" asked Hazel.

"Not yet," replied Jane, and then, quite irrelevantly, "I wish England were a million miles from here."

Visits were exchanged between the yacht and Hazel's relatives. Dinners were arranged, and trips into the surrounding country to entertain the visitors. Monsieur Thuran was a welcome guest at every function. He gave a dinner himself to the men of the party, and managed to ingratiate himself in the good will of Lord Tennington by many little acts of hospitality.

Monsieur Thuran had heard dropped a hint of something which might result from this unexpected visit of Lord Tennington's yacht, and he wanted to be counted in on it. Once when he was alone with the Englishman he took occasion to make it quite plain that his engagement to Miss Strong was to be announced immediately upon their return to America. "But not a word of it, my dear Tennington—not a word of it."

"Certainly, I quite understand, my dear fellow," Tennington had replied. "But you are to be congratulated—ripping girl, don't you know—really."

The next day it came. Mrs. Strong, Hazel, and Monsieur Thuran were Lord Tennington's guests aboard his yacht. Mrs. Strong had been telling them how much she had enjoyed her visit at Cape Town, and that she regretted that a letter just received from her attorneys in Baltimore had necessitated her cutting her visit shorter than they had intended.

"When do you sail?" asked Tennington.

"The first of the week, I think," she replied. "Indeed?" exclaimed Monsieur Thuran. "I am very fortunate. I, too, have found that I must return at once, and now I shall have the honor of accompanying and serving you."

"That is nice of you, Monsieur Thuran," replied Mrs. Strong. "I am sure that we shall be glad to place ourselves under your protection." But in the bottom of her heart was the wish that they might escape him. Why, she could not have told.

"By Jove!" ejaculated Lord Tennington, a moment later. "Bully idea, by Jove!"

"Yes, Tennington, of course," ventured Clayton; "it must be a bully idea if you had it, but what the deuce is it? Goin' to steam to China via the south pole?"

"Oh, I say now, Clayton," returned Tennington, "you needn't be so rough on a fellow just because you didn't happen to suggest this trip yourself—you've acted a regular bounder ever since we sailed.

"No, sir," he continued, "it's a bully idea, and you'll all say so. It's to take Mrs. Strong and Miss Strong, and Thuran, too, if he'll come, as far as England with us on the yacht. Now, isn't that a corker?"

"Forgive me, Tenny, old boy," cried Clayton. "It certainly IS a corking idea—I never should have suspected you of it. You're quite sure it's original, are you?"

"And we'll sail the first of the week, or any other time that suits your convenience, Mrs. Strong," concluded the big-hearted Englishman, as though the thing were all arranged except the sailing date.

"Mercy, Lord Tennington, you haven't even given us an opportunity to thank you, much less decide whether we shall be able to accept your generous invitation," said Mrs. Strong.

"Why, of course you'll come," responded Tennington. "We'll make as good time as any passenger boat, and you'll be fully as comfortable; and, anyway, we all want you, and won't take no for an answer."

And so it was settled that they should sail the following Monday.

Two days out the girls were sitting in Hazel's cabin, looking at some prints she had had finished in Cape Town. They represented all the pictures she had taken since she had left America, and the girls were both engrossed in them, Jane asking many questions, and Hazel keeping up a perfect torrent of comment and explanation of the various scenes and people.

"And here," she said suddenly, "here's a man you know. Poor fellow, I have so often intended asking you about him, but I never have been able to think of it when we were together." She was holding the little print so that Jane did not see the face of the man it portrayed.

"His name was John Caldwell," continued Hazel. "Do you recall him? He said that he met you in America. He is an Englishman."

"I do not recollect the name," replied Jane. "Let me see the picture." "The poor fellow was lost overboard on our trip down the coast," she said, as she handed the print to Jane.

"Lost over—Why, Hazel, Hazel—don't tell me that he is dead—drowned at sea! Hazel! Why don't you say that you are joking!" And before the astonished Miss Strong could catch her Jane Porter had slipped to the floor in a swoon.

After Hazel had restored her chum to consciousness she sat looking at her for a long time before either spoke.

"I did not know, Jane," said Hazel, in a constrained voice, "that you knew Mr. Caldwell so intimately that his death could prove such a shock to you."

"John Caldwell?" questioned Miss Porter. "You do not mean to tell me that you do not know who this man was, Hazel?"

"Why, yes, Jane; I know perfectly well who he was—his name was John Caldwell; he was from London."

"Oh, Hazel, I wish I could believe it," moaned the girl. "I wish I could believe it, but those features are burned so deep into my memory and my heart that I should recognize them anywhere in the world from among a thousand others, who might appear identical to any one but me."

"What do you mean, Jane?" cried Hazel, now thoroughly alarmed. "Who do you think it is?"

"I don't think, Hazel. I know that that is a picture of Tarzan of the Apes."

"Jane!"

"I cannot be mistaken. Oh, Hazel, are you sure that he is dead? Can there be no mistake?"

"I am afraid not, dear," answered Hazel sadly. "I wish I could think that you are mistaken, but now a hundred and one little pieces of corroborative evidence occur to me that meant nothing to me while I thought that he was John Caldwell, of London. He said that he had been born in Africa, and educated in France."

"Yes, that would be true," murmured Jane Porter dully.

"The first officer, who searched his luggage, found nothing to identify John Caldwell, of London. Practically all his belongings had been made, or purchased, in Paris. Everything that bore an initial was marked either with a 'T' alone, or with 'J. C. T.' We thought that he was traveling incognito under his first two names—the J. C. standing for John Caldwell."

"Tarzan of the Apes took the name Jean C. Tarzan," said Jane, in the same lifeless monotone. "And he is dead! Oh! Hazel, it is horrible! He died all alone in this terrible ocean! It is unbelievable that that brave heart should have ceased to beat—that those mighty muscles are quiet and cold forever! That he who was the personification of life and health and manly strength should be the prey of slimy, crawling things, that—" But she could go no further, and with a little moan she buried her head in her arms, and sank sobbing to the floor.

For days Miss Porter was ill, and would see no one except Hazel and the faithful Esmeralda. When at last she came on deck all were struck by the sad change that had taken place in her. She was no longer the alert, vivacious American beauty who had charmed and delighted all who came in contact with her. Instead she was a very quiet and sad little girl—with an expression of hopeless wistfulness that none but Hazel Strong could interpret.

The entire party strove their utmost to cheer and amuse her, but all to no avail. Occasionally the jolly Lord Tennington would wring a wan smile from her, but for the most part she sat with wide eyes looking out across the sea.

With Jane Porter's illness one misfortune after another seemed to attack the yacht. First an engine broke down, and they drifted for two days while temporary repairs were being made. Then a squall struck them unaware, that carried overboard nearly everything above deck that was portable. Later two of the seamen fell to fighting in the forecastle, with the result that one of them was badly wounded with a knife, and the other had to be put in irons. Then, to cap the climax, the mate fell overboard at night, and was drowned before help could reach him. The yacht cruised about the spot for ten hours, but no sign of the man was seen after he disappeared from the deck into the sea.

Every member of the crew and guests was gloomy and depressed after these series of misfortunes. All were apprehensive of worse to come, and this was especially true of the seamen who recalled all sorts of terrible omens and warnings that had occurred during the early part of the voyage, and which they could now clearly translate into the precursors of some grim and terrible tragedy to come.

Nor did the croakers have long to wait. The second night after the drowning of the mate the little yacht was suddenly wracked from stem to stern. About one o'clock in the morning there was a terrific impact that threw the slumbering guests and crew from berth and bunk. A mighty shudder ran through the frail craft; she lay far over to starboard; the engines stopped. For a moment she hung there with her decks at an angle of forty-five degrees—then, with a sullen, rending sound, she slipped back into the sea and righted.

Instantly the men rushed upon deck, followed closely by the women. Though the night was cloudy, there was little wind or sea, nor was it so dark but that just off the port bow a black mass could be discerned floating low in the water.

"A derelict," was the terse explanation of the officer of the watch.

Presently the engineer hurried on deck in search of the captain.

"That patch we put on the cylinder head's blown out, sir," he reported, "and she's makin' water fast for'ard on the port bow."

An instant later a seaman rushed up from below.

"My Gawd!" he cried. "Her whole bleedin' bottom's ripped out. She can't float twenty minutes."

"Shut up!" roared Tennington. "Ladies, go below and get some of your things together. It may not be so bad as that, but we may have to take to the boats. It will be safer to be prepared. Go at once, please. And, Captain Jerrold, send some competent man below, please, to ascertain the exact extent of the damage. In the meantime I might suggest that you have the boats provisioned."

The calm, low voice of the owner did much to reassure the entire party, and a moment later all were occupied with the duties he had suggested. By the time the ladies had returned to the deck the rapid provisioning of the boats had been about completed, and a moment later the officer who had gone below had returned to report. But his opinion was scarcely needed to assure the huddled group of men and women that the end of the *Lady Alice* was at hand.

"Well, sir?" said the captain, as his officer hesitated.

"I dislike to frighten the ladies, sir," he said, "but she can't float a dozen minutes, in my opinion. There's a hole in her you could drive a bally cow through, sir."

For five minutes the *Lady Alice* had been settling rapidly by the bow. Already her stern loomed high in the air, and foothold on the deck was of the most precarious nature. She carried four boats, and these were all filled and lowered away in safety. As they pulled rapidly from the stricken little vessel Jane Porter turned to have one last look at her. Just then there came a loud crash and an ominous rumbling and pounding from the heart of the ship—her machinery had broken loose, and was dashing its way toward the bow, tearing out partitions and bulkheads as it went—the stern rose rapidly high above them; for a moment she seemed to pause there—a vertical shaft protruding from the bosom of the ocean, and then swiftly she dove headforemost beneath the waves.

In one of the boats the brave Lord Tennington wiped a tear from his eye—he had not seen a fortune in money go down forever into the sea, but a dear, beautiful friend whom he had loved.

At last the long night broke, and a tropical sun smote down upon the rolling water. Jane Porter had dropped into a fitful slumber—the fierce light of the sun upon her upturned face awoke her. She looked about her. In the boat with her were three sailors, Clayton, and Monsieur Thuran. Then she looked for the other boats, but as far as the eye could reach there was nothing to break the fearful monotony of that waste of waters—they were alone in a small boat upon the broad Atlantic.

BACK TO THE PRIMITIVE

As Tarzan struck the water, his first impulse was to swim clear of the ship and possible danger from her propellers. He knew whom to thank for his present predicament, and as he lay in the sea, just supporting himself by a gentle movement of his hands, his chief emotion was one of chagrin that he had been so easily bested by Rokoff.

He lay thus for some time, watching the receding and rapidly diminishing lights of the steamer without it ever once occurring to him to call for help. He never had called for help in his life, and so it is not strange that he did not think of it now. Always had he depended upon his own prowess and resourcefulness, nor had there ever been since the days of Kala any to answer an appeal for succor. When it did occur to him it was too late.

There was, thought Tarzan, a possible one chance in a hundred thousand that he might be picked up, and an even smaller chance that he would reach land, so he determined that to combine what slight chances there were, he would swim slowly in the direction of the coast—the ship might have been closer in than he had known.

His strokes were long and easy—it would be many hours before those giant muscles would commence to feel fatigue. As he swam, guided toward the east by the stars, he noticed that he felt the weight of his shoes, and so he removed them. His trousers went next, and he would have removed his coat at the same time but for the precious papers in its pocket. To assure himself that he still had them he slipped his hand in to feel, but to his consternation they were gone.

Now he knew that something more than revenge had prompted Rokoff to pitch him overboard—the Russian had managed to obtain possession of the papers Tarzan had wrested from him at Bou Saada. The ape-man swore softly, and let his coat and shirt sink into the Atlantic. Before many hours he had divested himself of his remaining garments, and was swimming easily and unencumbered toward the east.

The first faint evidence of dawn was paling the stars ahead of him when the dim outlines of a low-lying black mass loomed up directly in his track. A few strong strokes brought him to its side—it was the bottom of a wave-washed derelict. Tarzan clambered upon it—he would rest there until daylight at least. He had no intention to remain there inactive—a prey to hunger and thirst. If he must die he preferred dying in action while making some semblance of an attempt to save himself.

The sea was quiet, so that the wreck had only a gently undulating motion, that was nothing to the swimmer who had had no sleep for twenty hours. Tarzan of the Apes curled up upon the slimy timbers, and was soon asleep.

The heat of the sun awoke him early in the forenoon. His first conscious sensation was of thirst, which grew almost to the proportions of suffering with full returning consciousness; but a moment later it was forgotten in the joy of two almost simultaneous discoveries. The first was a mass of wreckage floating beside the derelict in the midst of which, bottom up, rose and fell an overturned lifeboat; the other was the faint, dim line of a far-distant shore showing on the horizon in the east.

Tarzan dove into the water, and swam around the wreck to the lifeboat. The cool ocean refreshed him almost as much as would a draft of water, so that it was with renewed vigor that he brought the smaller boat alongside the derelict, and, after many herculean efforts, succeeded in dragging it onto the slimy ship's bottom. There he righted and examined it—the boat was quite sound, and a moment later floated upright alongside the wreck. Then Tarzan selected several pieces of wreckage that might answer him as paddles, and presently was making good headway toward the far-off shore.

It was late in the afternoon by the time he came close enough to distinguish objects on land, or to make out the contour of the shore line. Before him lay what appeared to be the entrance to a little, landlocked harbor. The wooded point to the north was strangely familiar. Could it be possible that fate had thrown him up at the very threshold of his own beloved jungle! But as the bow of his boat entered the mouth of the harbor the last shred of doubt was cleared away, for there before him upon the farther shore, under the shadows of his primeval forest, stood his own cabin—built before his birth by the hand of his long-dead father, John Clayton, Lord Greystoke.

With long sweeps of his giant muscles Tarzan sent the little craft speeding toward the beach. Its prow had scarcely touched when the ape-man leaped to shore—his heart beat fast in joy and exultation as each long-familiar object came beneath his roving eyes—the cabin, the beach, the little brook, the dense jungle, the black, impenetrable forest. The myriad birds in their brilliant plumage—the gorgeous tropical blooms upon the festooned creepers falling in great loops from the giant trees.

Tarzan of the Apes had come into his own again, and that all the world might know it he threw back his young head, and gave voice to the fierce, wild challenge of his tribe. For a moment silence reigned upon the jungle, and then, low and weird, came an answering challenge—it was the deep roar of Numa, the lion; and from a great distance, faintly, the fearsome answering bellow of a bull ape.

Tarzan went to the brook first, and slaked his thirst. Then he approached his cabin. The door was still closed and latched as he and D'Arnot had left it. He raised the latch and entered. Nothing had been disturbed; there were the table, the bed, and the little crib built by his father—the shelves and cupboards just as they had stood for ever twenty-three years—just as he had left them nearly two years before.

His eyes satisfied, Tarzan's stomach began to call aloud for attention—the pangs of hunger suggested a search for food. There was nothing in the cabin, nor had he any weapons; but upon a wall hung one of his old grass ropes. It had been many times broken and spliced, so that he had discarded it for a better one long before. Tarzan wished that he had a knife. Well, unless he was mistaken he should have that and a spear and bows and arrows before another sun had set—the rope would take care of that, and in the meantime it must be made to procure food for him. He coiled it carefully, and, throwing it about his shoulder, went out, closing the door behind him.

Close to the cabin the jungle commenced, and into it Tarzan of the Apes plunged, wary and noiseless—once more a savage beast hunting its food. For a time he kept to the ground, but finally, discovering no spoor indicative of nearby meat, he took to the trees. With the first dizzy swing from tree to tree all the old joy of living swept over him. Vain regrets and dull heartache were forgotten. Now was he living. Now, indeed, was the true happiness of perfect freedom his. Who would go back to the stifling, wicked cities of civilized man when the mighty reaches of the great jungle offered peace and liberty? Not he.

While it was yet light Tarzan came to a drinking place by the side of a jungle river. There was a ford there, and for countless ages the beasts of the forest had come down to drink at this spot. Here of a night might always be found either Sabor or Numa crouching in the dense foliage of the surrounding jungle awaiting an antelope or a water buck for their meal. Here came Horta, the boar, to water, and here came Tarzan of the Apes to make a kill, for he was very empty.

On a low branch he squatted above the trail. For an hour he waited. It was growing dark. A little to one side of the ford in the densest thicket he heard the faint sound of padded feet, and the brushing of a huge body against tall grasses and tangled creepers. None other than Tarzan might have heard it, but the ape-man heard and translated—it was Numa, the lion, on the same errand as himself. Tarzan smiled.

Presently he heard an animal approaching warily along the trail toward the drinking place. A moment more and it came in view—it was Horta, the boar. Here was delicious meat—and Tarzan's mouth watered. The grasses where Numa lay were very still now—ominously still. Horta passed beneath Tarzan—a few more steps and he would be within the radius of Numa's spring. Tarzan could imagine how old Numa's eyes were shining—how he was already sucking in his breath for the awful roar which would freeze his prey for the brief instant between the moment of the spring and the sinking of terrible fangs into splintering bones.

But as Numa gathered himself, a slender rope flew through the air from the low branches of a near-by tree. A noose settled about Horta's neck. There was a frightened grunt, a squeal, and then Numa saw his quarry dragged backward up the trail, and, as he sprang, Horta, the boar, soared upward beyond his clutches into the tree above, and a mocking face looked down and laughed into his own.

Then indeed did Numa roar. Angry, threatening, hungry, he paced back and forth beneath the taunting ape-man. Now he stopped, and, rising on his hind legs against the stem of the tree that held his enemy, sharpened his huge claws upon the bark, tearing out great pieces that laid bare the white wood beneath.

And in the meantime Tarzan had dragged the struggling Horta to the limb beside him. Sinewy fingers completed the work the choking noose had commenced. The ape-man had no knife, but nature had equipped him with the means of tearing his food from the quivering flank of his prey, and gleaming teeth sank into the succulent flesh while the raging lion looked on from below as another enjoyed the dinner that he had thought already his.

It was quite dark by the time Tarzan had gorged himself. Ah, but it had been delicious! Never had he quite accustomed himself to the ruined flesh that civilized men had served him, and in the bottom of his savage heart there had constantly been the craving for the warm meat of the fresh kill, and the rich, red blood.

He wiped his bloody hands upon a bunch of leaves, slung the remains of his kill across his shoulder, and swung off through the middle terrace of the forest toward his cabin, and at the same instant Jane Porter and William Cecil Clayton arose from a sumptuous dinner upon the *Lady Alice*, thousands of miles to the east, in the Indian Ocean.

Beneath Tarzan walked Numa, the lion, and when the ape-man deigned to glance downward he caught occasional glimpses of the baleful green eyes following through the darkness. Numa did not roar now—instead, he moved stealthily, like the shadow of a great cat; but yet he took no step that did not reach the sensitive ears of the ape-man.

Tarzan wondered if he would stalk him to his cabin door. He hoped not, for that would mean a night's sleep curled in the crotch of a tree, and he much preferred the bed of grasses within his own abode. But he knew just the tree and the most comfortable crotch, if necessity demanded that he sleep out. A hundred times in the past some great jungle cat had followed him home, and compelled him to seek shelter in this same tree, until another mood or the rising sun had sent his enemy away.

But presently Numa gave up the chase and, with a series of blood-curdling moans and roars, turned angrily back in search of another and an easier dinner. So Tarzan came to his cabin unattended, and a few moments later was curled up in the mildewed remnants of what had once been a bed of grasses. Thus easily did Monsieur Jean C. Tarzan slough the thin skin of his artificial civilization, and sink happy and contented into the deep sleep of the wild beast that has fed to repletion. Yet a woman's "yes" would have bound him to that other life forever, and made the thought of this savage existence repulsive.

Tarzan slept late into the following forenoon, for he had been very tired from the labors and exertion of the long night and day upon the ocean, and the jungle jaunt that had brought into play muscles that he had scarce used for nearly two years. When he awoke he ran to the brook first to drink. Then he took a plunge into the sea, swimming about for a quarter of an hour. Afterward he returned to his cabin, and breakfasted off the flesh of Horta. This done, he buried the balance of the carcass in the soft earth outside the cabin, for his evening meal.

Once more he took his rope and vanished into the jungle. This time he hunted nobler quarry—man; although had you asked him his own opinion he could have named a dozen other denizens of the jungle which he considered far the superiors in nobility of the men he hunted. Today Tarzan was in quest of weapons. He wondered if the women and children had remained in Mbonga's village after the punitive expedition from the French cruiser had massacred all the warriors in revenge for D'Arnot's supposed death. He hoped that he should find warriors there, for he knew not how long a quest he should have to make were the village deserted.

The ape-man traveled swiftly through the forest, and about noon came to the site of the village, but to his disappointment found that the jungle had overgrown the plantain fields and that the thatched huts had fallen in decay. There was no sign of man. He clambered about among the ruins for half an hour, hoping that he might discover some forgotten weapon, but his search was without fruit, and so he took up his quest once more, following up the stream, which flowed from a southeasterly direction. He knew that near fresh water he would be most likely to find another settlement.

As he traveled he hunted as he had hunted with his ape people in the past, as Kala had taught him to hunt, turning over rotted logs to find some toothsome vermin, running high into the trees to rob a bird's nest, or pouncing upon a tiny rodent with the quickness of a cat. There were other things that he ate, too, but the less detailed the account of an ape's diet, the better—and Tarzan was again an ape, the same fierce, brutal anthropoid that Kala had taught him to be, and that he had been for the first twenty years of his life.

Occasionally he smiled as he recalled some friend who might even at the moment be sitting placid and immaculate within the precincts of his select Parisian club—just as Tarzan had sat but a few months before; and then he would stop, as though turned suddenly to stone as the gentle breeze carried to his trained nostrils the scent of some new prey or a formidable enemy.

That night he slept far inland from his cabin, securely wedged into the crotch of a giant tree, swaying a hundred feet above the ground. He had eaten heartily again—this time from the flesh of Bara, the deer, who had fallen prey to his quick noose.

Early the next morning he resumed his journey, always following the course of the stream. For three days he continued his quest, until he had come to a part of the jungle in which he never before had been. Occasionally upon the higher ground the forest was much thinner, and in the far distance through the trees he could see ranges of mighty mountains, with wide plains in the foreground. Here, in the open spaces, were new game—countless antelope and vast herds of zebra. Tarzan was entranced—he would make a long visit to this new world.

On the morning of the fourth day his nostrils were suddenly surprised by a faint new scent. It was the scent of man, but yet a long way off. The ape-man thrilled with pleasure. Every sense was on the alert as with crafty stealth he moved quickly through the trees, up-wind, in the direction of his prey. Presently he came upon it—a lone warrior treading softly through the jungle.

Tarzan followed close above his quarry, waiting for a clearer space in which to hurl his rope. As he stalked the unconscious man, new thoughts presented themselves to the ape-man—thoughts born of the refining influences of civilization, and of its cruelties. It came to him that seldom if ever did civilized man kill a fellow being without some pretext, however slight. It was true that Tarzan wished this man's weapons and ornaments, but was it necessary to take his life to obtain them?

The longer he thought about it, the more repugnant became the thought of taking human life needlessly; and thus it happened that while he was trying to decide just what to do, they had come to a little clearing, at the far side of which lay a palisaded village of beehive huts.

As the warrior emerged from the forest, Tarzan caught a fleeting glimpse of a tawny hide worming its way through the matted jungle grasses in his wake—it was Numa, the lion. He, too, was stalking the black man. With the instant that Tarzan realized the native's danger his attitude toward his erstwhile prey altered completely—now he was a fellow man threatened by a common enemy.

Numa was about to charge—there was little time in which to compare various methods or weigh the probable results of any. And then a number of things happened, almost simultaneously—the lion sprang from his ambush toward the retreating black—Tarzan cried out in warning—and the black turned just in time to see Numa halted in mid-flight by a slender strand of grass rope, the noosed end of which had fallen cleanly about his neck.

The ape-man had acted so quickly that he had been unable to prepare himself to withstand the strain and shock of Numa's great weight upon the rope, and so it was that though the rope stopped the beast before his mighty talons could fasten themselves in the flesh of the black, the strain overbalanced Tarzan, who came tumbling to the ground not six paces from the infuriated animal. Like lightning Numa turned upon this new enemy, and, defenseless as he was, Tarzan of the Apes was nearer to death that instant than he ever before had been. It was the black who saved him. The warrior realized in an instant that he owed his life to this strange white man, and he also saw that only a miracle could save his preserver from those fierce yellow fangs that had been so near to his own flesh.

With the quickness of thought his spear arm flew back, and then shot forward with all the force of the sinewy muscles that rolled beneath the shimmering ebon hide. True to its mark the iron-shod weapon flew, transfixing Numa's sleek carcass from the right groin to beneath the left shoulder. With a hideous scream of rage and pain the brute turned again upon the black. A dozen paces he had gone when Tarzan's rope brought him to a stand once more—then he wheeled again upon the ape-man, only to feel the painful prick of a barbed arrow as it sank half its length in his quivering flesh. Again he stopped, and by this time Tarzan had run twice around the stem of a great tree with his rope, and made the end fast.

The black saw the trick, and grinned, but Tarzan knew that Numa must be quickly finished before those mighty teeth had found and parted the slender cord that held him. It was a matter of but an instant to reach the black's side and drag his long knife from its scabbard. Then he signed the warrior to continue to shoot arrows into the great beast while he attempted to close in upon him with the knife; so as one tantalized upon one side, the other sneaked cautiously in upon the other. Numa was furious. He raised his voice in a perfect frenzy of shrieks, growls, and hideous moans, the while he reared upon his hind legs in futile attempt to reach first one and then the other of his tormentors.

But at length the agile ape-man saw his chance, and rushed in upon the beast's left side behind the mighty shoulder. A giant arm encircled the tawny throat, and a long blade sank once, true as a die, into the fierce heart. Then Tarzan arose, and the black man and the white looked into each other's eyes across the body of their kill—and the black made the sign of peace and friendship, and Tarzan of the Apes answered in kind.

FROM APE TO SAVAGE

The noise of their battle with Numa had drawn an excited horde of savages from the nearby village, and a moment after the lion's death the two men were surrounded by lithe, ebon warriors, gesticulating and jabbering—a thousand questions that drowned each ventured reply.

And then the women came, and the children—eager, curious, and, at sight of Tarzan, more questioning than ever. The ape-man's new friend finally succeeded in making himself heard, and when he had done talking the men and women of the village vied with one another in doing honor to the strange creature who had saved their fellow and battled single-handed with fierce Numa.

At last they led him back to their village, where they brought him gifts of fowl, and goats, and cooked food. When he pointed to their weapons the warriors hastened to fetch spear, shield, arrows, and a bow. His friend of the encounter presented him with the knife with which he had killed Numa. There was nothing in all the village he could not have had for the asking.

How much easier this was, thought Tarzan, than murder and robbery to supply his wants. How close he had been to killing this man whom he never had seen before, and who now was manifesting by every primitive means at his command friendship and affection for his would-be slayer. Tarzan of the Apes was ashamed. Hereafter he would at least wait until he knew men deserved it before he thought of killing them.

The idea recalled Rokoff to his mind. He wished that he might have the Russian to himself in the dark jungle for a few minutes. There was a man who deserved killing if ever any one did. And if he could have seen Rokoff at that moment as he assiduously bent every endeavor to the pleasant task of ingratiating himself into the affections of the beautiful Miss Strong, he would have longed more than ever to mete out to the man the fate he deserved.

Tarzan's first night with the savages was devoted to a wild orgy in his honor. There was feasting, for the hunters had brought in an antelope and a zebra as trophies of their skill, and gallons of the weak native beer were consumed. As the warriors danced in the firelight, Tarzan was again impressed by the symmetry of their figures and the regularity of their features—the flat noses and thick lips of the typical West Coast savage were entirely missing. In repose the faces of the men were intelligent and dignified, those of the women ofttimes prepossessing.

It was during this dance that the ape-man first noticed that some of the men and many of the women wore ornaments of gold—principally anklets and armlets of great weight, apparently beaten out of the solid metal. When he expressed a wish to examine one of these, the owner removed it from her person and insisted, through the medium of signs, that Tarzan accept it as a gift. A close scrutiny of the bauble convinced the ape-man that the article was of virgin gold, and he was surprised, for it was the first time that he had ever seen golden ornaments among the savages of Africa, other than the trifling baubles those near the coast had purchased or stolen from Europeans. He tried to ask them from whence the metal came, but he could not make them understand.

When the dance was done Tarzan signified his intention to leave them, but they almost implored him to accept the hospitality of a great hut which the chief set apart for his sole use. He tried to explain that he would return in the morning, but they could not understand. When he finally walked away from them toward the side of the village opposite the gate, they were still further mystified as to his intentions.

Tarzan, however, knew just what he was about. In the past he had had experience with the rodents and vermin that infest every native village, and, while he was not overscrupulous about such matters, he much preferred the fresh air of the swaying trees to the fetid atmosphere of a hut.

The natives followed him to where a great tree overhung the palisade, and as Tarzan leaped for a lower branch and disappeared into the foliage above, precisely after the manner of Manu, the monkey, there were loud exclamations of surprise and astonishment. For half an hour they called to him to return, but as he did not answer them they at last desisted, and sought the sleeping-mats within their huts.

Tarzan went back into the forest a short distance until he had found a tree suited to his primitive requirements, and then, curling himself in a great crotch, he fell immediately into a deep sleep.

The following morning he dropped into the village street as suddenly as he had disappeared the preceding night. For a moment the natives were startled and afraid, but when they recognized their guest of the night before they welcomed him with shouts and laughter. That day he accompanied a party of warriors to the nearby plains on a great hunt, and so dexterous did they find this white man with their own crude weapons that another bond of respect and admiration was thereby wrought.

For weeks Tarzan lived with his savage friends, hunting buffalo, antelope, and zebra for meat, and elephant for ivory. Quickly he learned their simple speech, their native customs, and the ethics of their wild, primitive tribal life. He found that they were not cannibals—that they looked with loathing and contempt upon men who ate men.

Busuli, the warrior whom he had stalked to the village, told him many of the tribal legends—how, many years before, his people had come many long marches from the north; how once they had been a great and powerful tribe; and how the slave raiders had wrought such havoc among them with their death-dealing guns that they had been reduced to a mere remnant of their former numbers and power.

"They hunted us down as one hunts a fierce beast," said Busuli. "There was no mercy in them. When it was not slaves they sought it was ivory, but usually it was both. Our men were killed and our women driven away like sheep. We fought against them for many years, but our arrows and spears could not prevail against the sticks which spit fire and lead and death to many times the distance that our mightiest warrior could place an arrow. At last, when my father was a young man, the Arabs came again, but our warriors saw them a long way off, and Chowambi, who was chief then, told his people to gather up their belongings and come away with him—that he would lead them far to the south until they found a spot to which the Arab raiders did not come.

"And they did as he bid, carrying all their belongings, including many tusks of ivory. For months they wandered, suffering untold hardships and privations, for much of the way was through dense jungle, and across mighty mountains, but finally they came to this spot, and although they sent parties farther on to search for an even better location, none has ever been found."

"And the raiders have never found you here?" asked Tarzan.

"About a year ago a small party of Arabs and Manyuema stumbled upon us, but we drove them off, killing many. For days we followed them, stalking them for the wild beasts they are, picking them off one by one, until but a handful remained, but these escaped us."

As Busuli talked he fingered a heavy gold armlet that encircled the glossy hide of his left arm. Tarzan's eyes had been upon the ornament, but his thoughts were elsewhere. Presently he recalled the question he had tried to ask when he first came to the tribe—the question he could not at that time make them understand. For weeks he had forgotten so trivial a thing as gold, for he had been for the time a truly primeval man with no thought beyond today. But of a sudden the sight of gold awakened the sleeping civilization that was in him, and with it came the lust for wealth. That lesson Tarzan had learned well in his brief experience of the ways of civilized man. He knew that gold meant power and pleasure. He pointed to the bauble.

"From whence came the yellow metal, Busuli?" he asked.

The black pointed toward the southeast.

"A moon's march away—maybe more," he replied.

"Have you been there?" asked Tarzan.

"No, but some of our people were there years ago, when my father was yet a young man. One of the parties that searched farther for a location for the tribe when first they settled here came upon a strange people who wore many ornaments of yellow metal. Their spears were tipped with it, as were their arrows, and they cooked in vessels made all of solid metal like my armlet.

"They lived in a great village in huts that were built of stone and surrounded by a great wall. They were very fierce, rushing out and falling upon our warriors before ever they learned that their errand was a peaceful one. Our men were few in number, but they held their own at the top of a little rocky hill, until the fierce people went back at sunset into their wicked city. Then our warriors came down from their hill, and, after taking many ornaments of yellow metal from the bodies of those they had slain, they marched back out of the valley, nor have any of us ever returned.

"They are wicked people—neither white like you nor black like me, but covered with hair as is Bolgani, the gorilla. Yes, they are very bad people indeed, and Chowambi was glad to get out of their country."

"And are none of those alive who were with Chowambi, and saw these strange people and their wonderful city?" asked Tarzan.

"Waziri, our chief, was there," replied Busuli. "He was a very young man then, but he accompanied Chowambi, who was his father."

So that night Tarzan asked Waziri about it, and Waziri, who was now an old man, said that it was a long march, but that the way was not difficult to follow. He remembered it well.

"For ten days we followed this river which runs beside our village. Up toward its source we traveled until on the tenth day we came to a little spring far up upon the side of a lofty mountain range. In this little spring our river is born. The next day we crossed over the top of the mountain, and upon the other side we came to a tiny rivulet which we followed down into a great forest. For many days we traveled along the winding banks of the rivulet that had now become a river, until we came to a greater river, into which it emptied, and which ran down the center of a mighty valley.

"Then we followed this large river toward its source, hoping to come to more open land. After twenty days of marching from the time we had crossed the mountains and passed out of our own country we came again to another range of mountains. Up their side we followed the great river, that had now dwindled to a tiny rivulet, until we came to a little cave near the mountain-top. In this cave was the mother of the river.

"I remember that we camped there that night, and that it was very cold, for the mountains were high. The next day we decided to ascend to the top of the mountains, and see what the country upon the other side looked like, and if it seemed no better than that which we had so far traversed we would return to our village and tell them that they had already found the best place in all the world to live.

"And so we clambered up the face of the rocky cliffs until we reached the summit, and there from a flat mountain-top we saw, not far beneath us, a shallow valley, very narrow; and upon the far side of it was a great village of stone, much of which had fallen and crumbled into decay."

The balance of Waziri's story was practically the same as that which Busuli had told.

"I should like to go there and see this strange city," said Tarzan, "and get some of their yellow metal from its fierce inhabitants."

"It is a long march," replied Waziri, "and I am an old man, but if you will wait until the rainy season is over and the rivers have gone down I will take some of my warriors and go with you."

And Tarzan had to be contented with that arrangement, though he would have liked it well enough to have set off the next morning—he was as impatient as a child. Really Tarzan of the Apes was but a child, or a primeval man, which is the same thing in a way.

The next day but one a small party of hunters returned to the village from the south to report a large herd of elephant some miles away. By climbing trees they had had a fairly good view of the herd, which they described as numbering several large tuskers, a great many cows and calves, and full-grown bulls whose ivory would be worth having.

The balance of the day and evening was filled with preparation for a great hunt—spears were overhauled, quivers were replenished, bows were restrung; and all the while the village witch doctor passed through the busy throngs disposing of various charms and amulets designed to protect the possessor from hurt, or bring him good fortune in the morrow's hunt.

At dawn the hunters were off. There were fifty sleek, black warriors, and in their midst, lithe and active as a young forest god, strode Tarzan of the Apes, his brown skin contrasting oddly with the ebony of his companions. Except for color he was one of them. His ornaments and weapons were the same as theirs—he spoke their language—he laughed and joked with them, and leaped and shouted in the brief wild dance that preceded their departure from the village, to all intent and purpose a savage among savages. Nor, had he questioned himself, is it to be doubted that he would have admitted that he was far more closely allied to these people and their life than to the Parisian friends whose ways, apelike, he had successfully mimicked for a few short months.

But he did think of D'Arnot, and a grin of amusement showed his strong white teeth as he pictured the immaculate Frenchman's expression could he by some means see Tarzan as he was that minute. Poor Paul, who had prided himself on having eradicated from his friend the last traces of wild savagery. "How quickly have I fallen!" thought Tarzan; but in his heart he did not consider it a fall—rather, he pitied the poor creatures of Paris, penned up like prisoners in their silly clothes, and watched by policemen all their poor lives, that they might do nothing that was not entirely artificial and tiresome.

A two hours' march brought them close to the vicinity in which the elephants had been seen the previous day. From there on they moved very quietly indeed searching for the spoor of the great beasts. At length they found the well-marked trail along which the herd had passed not many hours before. In single file they followed it for about half an hour. It was Tarzan who first raised his hand in signal that the quarry was at hand—his sensitive nose had warned him that the elephants were not far ahead of them.

The blacks were skeptical when he told them how he knew.

"Come with me," said Tarzan, "and we shall see."

With the agility of a squirrel he sprang into a tree and ran nimbly to the top. One of the blacks followed more slowly and carefully. When he had reached a lofty limb beside the ape-man the latter pointed to the south, and there, some few hundred yards away, the black saw a number of huge black backs swaying back and forth above the top of the lofty jungle grasses. He pointed the direction to the watchers below, indicating with his fingers the number of beasts he could count.

Immediately the hunters started toward the elephants. The black in the tree hastened down, but Tarzan stalked, after his own fashion, along the leafy way of the middle terrace.

It is no child's play to hunt wild elephants with the crude weapons of primitive man. Tarzan knew that few native tribes ever attempted it, and the fact that his tribe did so gave him no little pride—already he was commencing to think of himself as a member of the little community. As Tarzan moved silently through the trees he saw the warriors below creeping in a half circle upon the still unsuspecting elephants. Finally they were within sight of the great beasts. Now they singled out two large tuskers, and at a signal the fifty men rose from the ground where they had lain concealed, and hurled their heavy war spears at the two marked beasts. There was not a single miss; twenty-five spears were embedded in the sides of each of the giant animals. One never moved from the spot where it stood when the avalanche of spears struck it, for two, perfectly aimed, had penetrated its heart, and it lunged forward upon its knees, rolling to the ground without a struggle.

The other, standing nearly head-on toward the hunters, had not proved so good a mark, and though every spear struck not one entered the great heart. For a moment the huge bull stood trumpeting in rage and pain, casting about with its little eyes for the author of its hurt. The blacks had faded into the jungle before the weak eyes of the monster had fallen upon any of them, but now he caught the sound of their retreat, and, amid a terrific crashing of underbrush and branches, he charged in the direction of the noise.

It so happened that chance sent him in the direction of Busuli, whom he was overtaking so rapidly that it was as though the black were standing still instead of racing at full speed to escape the certain death which pursued him. Tarzan had witnessed the entire performance from the branches of a nearby tree, and now that he saw his friend's peril he raced toward the infuriated beast with loud cries, hoping to distract him.

But it had been as well had he saved his breath, for the brute was deaf and blind to all else save the particular object of his rage that raced futilely before him. And now Tarzan saw that only a miracle could save Busuli, and with the same unconcern with which he had once hunted this very man he hurled himself into the path of the elephant to save the black warrior's life.

He still grasped his spear, and while Tantor was yet six or eight paces behind his prey, a sinewy white warrior dropped as from the heavens, almost directly in his path. With a vicious lunge the elephant swerved to the right to dispose of this temerarious foeman who dared intervene between himself and his intended victim; but he had not reckoned on the lightning quickness that could galvanize those steel muscles into action so marvelously swift as to baffle even a keener eyesight than Tantor's.

And so it happened that before the elephant realized that his new enemy had leaped from his path Tarzan had driven his iron-shod spear from behind the massive shoulder straight into the fierce heart, and the colossal pachyderm had toppled to his death at the feet of the ape-man.

Busuli had not beheld the manner of his deliverance, but Waziri, the old chief, had seen, and several of the other warriors, and they hailed Tarzan with delight as they swarmed about him and his great kill. When he leaped upon the mighty carcass, and gave voice to the weird challenge with which he announced a great victory, the blacks shrank back in fear, for to them it marked the brutal Bolgani, whom they feared fully as much as they feared Numa, the lion; but with a fear with which was mixed a certain uncanny awe of the manlike thing to which they attributed supernatural powers.

But when Tarzan lowered his raised head and smiled upon them they were reassured, though they did not understand. Nor did they ever fully understand this strange creature who ran through the trees as quickly as Manu, yet was even more at home upon the ground than themselves; who was except as to color like unto themselves, yet as powerful as ten of them, and singlehanded a match for the fiercest denizens of the fierce jungle.

When the remainder of the warriors had gathered, the hunt was again taken up and the stalking of the retreating herd once more begun; but they had covered a bare hundred yards when from behind them, at a great distance, sounded faintly a strange popping.

For an instant they stood like a group of statuary, intently listening. Then Tarzan spoke.

"Guns!" he said. "The village is being attacked."

"Come!" cried Waziri. "The Arab raiders have returned with their cannibal slaves for our ivory and our women!"

THE IVORY RAIDERS

Waziri's warriors marched at a rapid trot through the jungle in the direction of the village. For a few minutes, the sharp cracking of guns ahead warned them to haste, but finally the reports dwindled to an occasional shot, presently ceasing altogether. Nor was this less ominous than the rattle of musketry, for it suggested but a single solution to the little band of rescuers—that the illy garrisoned village had already succumbed to the onslaught of a superior force.

The returning hunters had covered a little more than three miles of the five that had separated them from the village when they met the first of the fugitives who had escaped the bullets and clutches of the foe. There were a dozen women, youths, and girls in the party, and so excited were they that they could scarce make themselves understood as they tried to relate to Waziri the calamity that had befallen his people.

"They are as many as the leaves of the forest," cried one of the women, in attempting to explain the enemy's force. "There are many Arabs and countless Manyuema, and they all have guns. They crept close to the village before we knew that they were about, and then, with many shouts, they rushed in upon us, shooting down men, and women, and children. Those of us who could fled in all directions into the jungle, but more were killed. I do not know whether they took any prisoners or not—they seemed only bent upon killing us all. The Manyuema called us many names, saying that they would eat us all before they left our country—that this was our punishment for killing their friends last year. I did not hear much, for I ran away quickly."

The march toward the village was now resumed, more slowly and with greater stealth, for Waziri knew that it was too late to rescue—their only mission could be one of revenge. Inside the next mile a hundred more fugitives were met. There were many men among these, and so the fighting strength of the party was augmented.

Now a dozen warriors were sent creeping ahead to reconnoiter. Waziri remained with the main body, which advanced in a thin line that spread in a great crescent through the forest. By the chief's side walked Tarzan.

Presently one of the scouts returned. He had come within sight of the village.

"They are all within the palisade," he whispered.

"Good!" said Waziri. "We shall rush in upon them and slay them all," and he made ready to send word along the line that they were to halt at the edge of the clearing until they saw him rush toward the village—then all were to follow.

"Wait!" cautioned Tarzan. "If there are even fifty guns within the palisade we shall be repulsed and slaughtered. Let me go alone through the trees, so that I may look down upon them from above, and see just how many there be, and what chance we might have were we to charge. It were foolish to lose a single man needlessly if there be no hope of success. I have an idea that we can accomplish more by cunning than by force. Will you wait, Waziri?"

"Yes," said the old chief. "Go!"

So Tarzan sprang into the trees and disappeared in the direction of the village. He moved more cautiously than was his wont, for he knew that men with guns could reach him quite as easily in the treetops as on the ground. And when Tarzan of the Apes elected to adopt stealth, no creature in all the jungle could move so silently or so completely efface himself from the sight of an enemy.

In five minutes he had wormed his way to the great tree that overhung the palisade at one end of the village, and from his point of vantage looked down upon the savage horde beneath. He counted fifty Arabs and estimated that there were five times as many Manyuema. The latter were gorging themselves upon food and, under the very noses of their white masters, preparing the gruesome feast which is the *piece de resistance* that follows a victory in which the bodies of their slain enemies fall into their horrid hands.

The ape-man saw that to charge that wild horde, armed as they were with guns, and barricaded behind the locked gates of the village, would be a futile task, and so he returned to Waziri and advised him to wait; that he, Tarzan, had a better plan.

But a moment before one of the fugitives had related to Waziri the story of the atrocious murder of the old chief's wife, and so crazed with rage was the old man that he cast discretion to the winds. Calling his warriors about him, he commanded them to charge, and, with brandishing spears and savage yells, the little force of scarcely more than a hundred dashed madly toward the village gates. Before the clearing had been half crossed the Arabs opened up a withering fire from behind the palisade.

With the first volley Waziri fell. The speed of the chargers slackened. Another volley brought down a half dozen more. A few reached the barred gates, only to be shot in their tracks, without the ghost of a chance to gain the inside of the palisade, and then the whole attack crumpled, and the remaining warriors scampered back into the forest. As they ran the raiders opened the gates, rushing after them, to complete the day's work with the utter extermination of the tribe. Tarzan had been among the last to turn back toward the forest, and now, as he ran slowly, he turned from time to time to speed a well-aimed arrow into the body of a pursuer.

Once within the jungle, he found a little knot of determined blacks waiting to give battle to the oncoming horde, but Tarzan cried to them to scatter, keeping out of harm's way until they could gather in force after dark.

"Do as I tell you," he urged, "and I will lead you to victory over these enemies of yours. Scatter through the forest, picking up as many stragglers as you can find, and at night, if you think that you have been followed, come by roundabout ways to the spot where we killed the elephants today. Then I will explain my plan, and you will find that it is good. You cannot hope to pit your puny strength and simple weapons against the numbers and the guns of the Arabs and the Manyuema."

They finally assented. "When you scatter," explained Tarzan, in conclusion, "your foes will have to scatter to follow you, and so it may happen that if you are watchful you can drop many a Manyuema with your arrows from behind some great trees."

They had barely time to hasten away farther into the forest before the first of the raiders had crossed the clearing and entered it in pursuit of them.

Tarzan ran a short distance along the ground before he took to the trees. Then he raced quickly to the upper terrace, there doubling on his tracks and making his way rapidly back toward the village. Here he found that every Arab and Manyuema had joined in the pursuit, leaving the village deserted except for the chained prisoners and a single guard.

The sentry stood at the open gate, looking in the direction of the forest, so that he did not see the agile giant that dropped to the ground at the far end of the village street. With drawn bow the ape-man crept stealthily toward his unsuspecting victim. The prisoners had already discovered him, and with wide eyes filled with wonder and with hope they watched their would-be rescuer. Now he halted not ten paces from the unconscious Manyuema. The shaft was drawn back its full length at the height of the keen gray eye that sighted along its polished surface. There was a sudden twang as the brown fingers released their hold, and without a sound the raider sank forward upon his face, a wooden shaft transfixing his heart and protruding a foot from his black chest.

Then Tarzan turned his attention to the fifty women and youths chained neck to neck on the long slave chain. There was no releasing of the ancient padlocks in the time that was left him, so the ape-man called to them to follow him as they were, and, snatching the gun and cartridge belt from the dead sentry, he led the now happy band out through the village gate and into the forest upon the far side of the clearing.

It was a slow and arduous march, for the slave chain was new to these people, and there were many delays as one of their number would stumble and fall, dragging others down with her. Then, too, Tarzan had been forced to make a wide detour to avoid any possibility of meeting with returning raiders. He was partially guided by occasional shots which indicated that the Arab horde was still in touch with the villagers; but he knew that if they would but follow his advice there would be but few casualties other than on the side of the marauders.

Toward dusk the firing ceased entirely, and Tarzan knew that the Arabs had all returned to the village. He could scarce repress a smile of triumph as he thought of their rage on discovering that their guard had been killed and their prisoners taken away. Tarzan had wished that he might have taken some of the great store of ivory the village contained, solely for the purpose of still further augmenting the wrath of his enemies; but he knew that that was not necessary for its salvation, since he already had a plan mapped out which would effectually prevent the Arabs leaving the country with a single tusk. And it would have been cruel to have needlessly burdened these poor, overwrought women with the extra weight of the heavy ivory.

It was after midnight when Tarzan, with his slow-moving caravan, approached the spot where the elephants lay. Long before they reached it they had been guided by the huge fire the natives had built in the center of a hastily improvised *boma*, partially for warmth and partially to keep off chance lions.

When they had come close to the encampment Tarzan called aloud to let them know that friends were coming. It was a joyous reception the little party received when the blacks within the *boma* saw the long file of fettered friends and relatives enter the firelight. These had all been given up as lost forever, as had Tarzan as well, so that the happy blacks would have remained awake all night to feast on elephant meat and celebrate the return of their fellows, had not Tarzan insisted that they take what sleep they could, against the work of the coming day.

At that, sleep was no easy matter, for the women who had lost their men or their children in the day's massacre and battle made night hideous with their continued wailing and howling. Finally, however, Tarzan succeeded in silencing them, on the plea that their noise would attract the Arabs to their hiding-place, when all would be slaughtered.

When dawn came Tarzan explained his plan of battle to the warriors, and without demur one and all agreed that it was the safest and surest way in which to rid themselves of their unwelcome visitors and be revenged for the murder of their fellows.

First the women and children, with a guard of some twenty old warriors and youths, were started southward, to be entirely out of the zone of danger. They had instructions to erect temporary shelter and construct a protecting *boma* of thorn bush; for the plan of campaign which Tarzan had chosen was one which might stretch out over many days, or even weeks, during which time the warriors would not return to the new camp.

Two hours after daylight a thin circle of black warriors surrounded the village. At intervals one was perched high in the branches of a tree which could overlook the palisade. Presently a Manyuema within the village fell, pierced by a single arrow. There had been no sound of attack—none of the hideous war-cries or vainglorious waving of menacing spears that ordinarily marks the attack of savages—just a silent messenger of death from out of the silent forest.

The Arabs and their followers were thrown into a fine rage at this unprecedented occurrence. They ran for the gates, to wreak dire vengeance upon the foolhardy perpetrator of the outrage; but they suddenly realized that they did not know which way to turn to find the foe. As they stood debating with many angry shouts and much gesticulating, one of the Arabs sank silently to the ground in their very midst—a thin arrow protruding from his heart.

Tarzan had placed the finest marksmen of the tribe in the surrounding trees, with directions never to reveal themselves while the enemy was faced in their direction. As a black released his messenger of death he would slink behind the sheltering stem of the tree he had selected, nor would he again aim until a watchful eye told him that none was looking toward his tree.

Three times the Arabs started across the clearing in the direction from which they thought the arrows came, but each time another arrow would come from behind to take its toll from among their number. Then they would turn and charge in a new direction. Finally they set out upon a determined search of the forest, but the blacks melted before them, so that they saw no sign of an enemy.

But above them lurked a grim figure in the dense foliage of the mighty trees—it was Tarzan of the Apes, hovering over them as if he had been the shadow of death. Presently a Manyuema forged ahead of his companions; there was none to see from what direction death came, and so it came quickly, and a moment later those behind stumbled over the dead body of their comrade—the inevitable arrow piercing the still heart.

It does not take a great deal of this manner of warfare to get upon the nerves of white men, and so it is little to be wondered at that the Manyuema were soon panic-stricken. Did one forge ahead an arrow found his heart; did one lag behind he never again was seen alive; did one stumble to one side, even for a bare moment from the sight of his fellows, he did not return—and always when they came upon the bodies of their dead they found those terrible arrows driven with the accuracy of superhuman power straight through the victim's heart. But worse than all else was the hideous fact that not once during the morning had they seen or heard the slightest sign of an enemy other than the pitiless arrows.

When finally they returned to the village it was no better. Every now and then, at varying intervals that were maddening in the terrible suspense they caused, a man would plunge forward dead. The blacks besought their masters to leave this terrible place, but the Arabs feared to take up the march through the grim and hostile forest beset by this new and terrible enemy while laden with the great store of ivory they had found within the village; but, worse yet, they hated to leave the ivory behind.

Finally the entire expedition took refuge within the thatched huts—here, at least, they would be free from the arrows. Tarzan, from the tree above the village, had marked the hut into which the chief Arabs had gone, and, balancing himself upon an overhanging limb, he drove his heavy spear with all the force of his giant muscles through the thatched roof. A howl of pain told him that it had found a mark. With this parting salute to convince them that there was no safety for them anywhere within the country, Tarzan returned to the forest, collected his warriors, and withdrew a mile to the south to rest and eat. He kept sentries in several trees that commanded a view of the trail toward the village, but there was no pursuit.

An inspection of his force showed not a single casualty—not even a minor wound; while rough estimates of the enemies' loss convinced the blacks that no fewer than twenty had fallen before their arrows. They were wild with elation, and were for finishing the day in one glorious rush upon the village, during which they would slaughter the last of their foemen. They were even picturing the various tortures they would inflict, and gloating over the suffering of the Manyuema, for whom they entertained a peculiar hatred, when Tarzan put his foot down flatly upon the plan.

"You are crazy!" he cried. "I have shown you the only way to fight these people. Already you have killed twenty of them without the loss of a single warrior, whereas, yesterday, following your own tactics, which you would now renew, you lost at least a dozen, and killed not a single Arab or Manyuema. You will fight just as I tell you to fight, or I shall leave you and go back to my own country."

They were frightened when he threatened this, and promised to obey him scrupulously if he would but promise not to desert them.

"Very well," he said. "We shall return to the elephant *boma* for the night. I have a plan to give the Arabs a little taste of what they may expect if they remain in our country, but I shall need no help. Come! If they suffer no more for the balance of the day they will feel reassured, and the relapse into fear will be even more nerve-racking than as though we continued to frighten them all afternoon."

So they marched back to their camp of the previous night, and, lighting great fires, ate and recounted the adventures of the day until long after dark. Tarzan slept until midnight, then he arose and crept into the Cimmerian blackness of the forest. An hour later he came to the edge of the clearing before the village. There was a camp-fire burning within the palisade. The ape-man crept across the clearing until he stood before the barred gates. Through the interstices he saw a lone sentry sitting before the fire.

Quietly Tarzan went to the tree at the end of the village street. He climbed softly to his place, and fitted an arrow to his bow. For several minutes he tried to sight fairly upon the sentry, but the waving branches and flickering firelight convinced him that the danger of a miss was too great—he must touch the heart full in the center to bring the quiet and sudden death his plan required.

He had brought, besides, his bow, arrows, and rope, the gun he had taken the previous day from the other sentry he had killed. Caching all these in a convenient crotch of the tree, he dropped lightly to the ground within the palisade, armed only with his long knife. The sentry's back was toward him. Like a cat Tarzan crept upon the dozing man. He was within two paces of him now—another instant and the knife would slide silently into the fellow's heart.

Tarzan crouched for a spring, for that is ever the quickest and surest attack of the jungle beast—when the man, warned, by some subtle sense, sprang to his feet and faced the ape-man.

THE WHITE CHIEF OF THE WAZIRI

When the eyes of the black Manyuema savage fell upon the strange apparition that confronted him with menacing knife they went wide in horror. He forgot the gun within his hands; he even forgot to cry out—his one thought was to escape this fearsome-looking white savage, this giant of a man upon whose massive rolling muscles and mighty chest the flickering firelight played.

But before he could turn Tarzan was upon him, and then the sentry thought to scream for aid, but it was too late. A great hand was upon his windpipe, and he was being borne to the earth. He battled furiously but futilely—with the grim tenacity of a bulldog those awful fingers were clinging to his throat. Swiftly and surely life was being choked from him. His eyes bulged, his tongue protruded, his face turned to a ghastly purplish hue—there was a convulsive tremor of the stiffening muscles, and the Manyuema sentry lay quite still.

The ape-man threw the body across one of his broad shoulders and, gathering up the fellow's gun, trotted silently up the sleeping village street toward the tree that gave him such easy ingress to the palisaded village. He bore the dead sentry into the midst of the leafy maze above.

First he stripped the body of cartridge belt and such ornaments as he craved, wedging it into a convenient crotch while his nimble fingers ran over it in search of the loot he could not plainly see in the dark. When he had finished he took the gun that had belonged to the man, and walked far out upon a limb, from the end of which he could obtain a better view of the huts. Drawing a careful bead on the beehive structure in which he knew the chief Arabs to be, he pulled the trigger. Almost instantly there was an answering groan. Tarzan smiled. He had made another lucky hit.

Following the shot there was a moment's silence in the camp, and then Manyuema and Arab came pouring from the huts like a swarm of angry hornets; but if the truth were known they were even more frightened than they were angry. The strain of the preceding day had wrought upon the fears of both black and white, and now this single shot in the night conjured all manner of terrible conjectures in their terrified minds.

When they discovered that their sentry had disappeared, their fears were in no way allayed, and as though to bolster their courage by warlike actions, they began to fire rapidly at the barred gates of the village, although no enemy was in sight. Tarzan took advantage of the deafening roar of this fusillade to fire into the mob beneath him.

No one heard his shot above the din of rattling musketry in the street, but some who were standing close saw one of their number crumple suddenly to the earth. When they leaned over him he was dead. They were panic-stricken, and it took all the brutal authority of the Arabs to keep the Manyuema from rushing helter-skelter into the jungle—anywhere to escape from this terrible village.

After a time they commenced to quiet down, and as no further mysterious deaths occurred among them they took heart again. But it was a short-lived respite, for just as they had concluded that they would not be disturbed again Tarzan gave voice to a weird moan, and as the raiders looked up in the direction from which the sound seemed to come, the ape-man, who stood swinging the dead body of the sentry gently to and fro, suddenly shot the corpse far out above their heads.

With howls of alarm the throng broke in all directions to escape this new and terrible creature who seemed to be springing upon them. To their fear-distorted imaginations the body of the sentry, falling with wide-sprawled arms and legs, assumed the likeness of a great beast of prey. In their anxiety to escape, many of the blacks scaled the palisade, while others tore down the bars from the gates and rushed madly across the clearing toward the jungle.

For a time no one turned back toward the thing that had frightened them, but Tarzan knew that they would in a moment, and when they discovered that it was but the dead body of their sentry, while they would doubtless be still further terrified, he had a rather definite idea as to what they would do, and so he faded silently away toward the south, taking the moonlit upper terrace back toward the camp of the Waziri.

Presently one of the Arabs turned and saw that the thing that had leaped from the tree upon them lay still and quiet where it had fallen in the center of the village street. Cautiously he crept back toward it until he saw that it was but a man. A moment later he was beside the figure, and in another had recognized it as the corpse of the Manyuema who had stood on guard at the village gate.

His companions rapidly gathered around at his call, and after a moment's excited conversation they did precisely what Tarzan had reasoned they would. Raising their guns to their shoulders, they poured volley after volley into the tree from which the corpse had been thrown—had Tarzan remained there he would have been riddled by a hundred bullets.

When the Arabs and Manyuema discovered that the only marks of violence upon the body of their dead comrade were giant finger prints upon his swollen throat they were again thrown into deeper apprehension and despair. That they were not even safe within a palisaded village at night came as a distinct shock to them. That an enemy could enter into the midst of their camp and kill their sentry with bare hands seemed outside the bounds of reason, and so the superstitious Manyuema commenced to attribute their ill luck to supernatural causes; nor were the Arabs able to offer any better explanation.

With at least fifty of their number flying through the black jungle, and without the slightest knowledge of when their uncanny foemen might resume the cold-blooded slaughter they had commenced, it was a desperate band of cut-throats that waited sleeplessly for the dawn. Only on the promise of the Arabs that they would leave the village at daybreak, and hasten onward toward their own land, would the remaining Manyuema consent to stay at the village a moment longer. Not even fear of their cruel masters was sufficient to overcome this new terror.

And so it was that when Tarzan and his warriors returned to the attack the next morning they found the raiders prepared to march out of the village. The Manyuema were laden with stolen ivory. As Tarzan saw it he grinned, for he knew that they would not carry it far. Then he saw something which caused him anxiety—a number of the Manyuema were lighting torches in the remnant of the camp-fire. They were about to fire the village.

Tarzan was perched in a tall tree some hundred yards from the palisade. Making a trumpet of his hands, he called loudly in the Arab tongue: "Do not fire the huts, or we shall kill you all! Do not fire the huts, or we shall kill you all!"

A dozen times he repeated it. The Manyuema hesitated, then one of them flung his torch into the campfire. The others were about to do the same when an Arab sprung upon them with a stick, beating them toward the huts. Tarzan could see that he was commanding them to fire the little thatched dwellings. Then he stood erect upon the swaying branch a hundred feet above the ground, and, raising one of the Arab guns to his shoulder, took careful aim and fired. With the report the Arab who was urging on his men to burn the village fell in his tracks, and the Manyuema threw away their torches and fled from the village. The last Tarzan saw of them they were racing toward the jungle, while their former masters knelt upon the ground and fired at them.

But however angry the Arabs might have been at the insubordination of their slaves, they were at least convinced that it would be the better part of wisdom to forego the pleasure of firing the village that had given them two such nasty receptions. In their hearts, however, they swore to return again with such force as would enable them to sweep the entire country for miles around, until no vestige of human life remained.

They had looked in vain for the owner of the voice which had frightened off the men who had been detailed to put the torch to the huts, but not even the keenest eye among them had been able to locate him. They had seen the puff of smoke from the tree following the shot that brought down the Arab, but, though a volley had immediately been loosed into its foliage, there had been no indication that it had been effective.

Tarzan was too intelligent to be caught in any such trap, and so the report of his shot had scarcely died away before the ape-man was on the ground and racing for another tree a hundred yards away. Here he again found a suitable perch from which he could watch the preparations of the raiders. It occurred to him that he might have considerable more fun with them, so again he called to them through his improvised trumpet.

"Leave the ivory!" he cried. "Leave the ivory! Dead men have no use for ivory!"

Some of the Manyuema started to lay down their loads, but this was altogether too much for the avaricious Arabs. With loud shouts and curses they aimed their guns full upon the bearers, threatening instant death to any who might lay down his load. They could give up firing the village, but the thought of abandoning this enormous fortune in ivory was quite beyond their conception—better death than that.

And so they marched out of the village of the Waziri, and on the shoulders of their slaves was the ivory ransom of a score of kings. Toward the north they marched, back toward their savage settlement in the wild and unknown country which lies back from the Kongo in the uttermost depths of The Great Forest, and on either side of them traveled an invisible and relentless foe.

Under Tarzan's guidance the black Waziri warriors stationed themselves along the trail on either side in the densest underbrush. They stood at far intervals, and, as the column passed, a single arrow or a heavy spear, well aimed, would pierce a Manyuema or an Arab. Then the Waziri would melt into the distance and run ahead to take his stand farther on. They did not strike unless success were sure and the danger of detection almost nothing, and so the arrows and the spears were few and far between, but so persistent and inevitable that the slow-moving column of heavy-laden raiders was in a constant state of panic—panic at the uncertainty of who the next would be to fall, and when.

It was with the greatest difficulty that the Arabs prevented their men a dozen times from throwing away their burdens and fleeing like frightened rabbits up the trail toward the north. And so the day wore on—a frightful nightmare of a day for the raiders—a day of weary but well-repaid work for the Waziri. At night the Arabs constructed a rude *boma* in a little clearing by a river, and went into camp.

At intervals during the night a rifle would bark close above their heads, and one of the dozen sentries which they now had posted would tumble to the ground. Such a condition was insupportable, for they saw that by means of these hideous tactics they would be completely wiped out, one by one, without inflicting a single death upon their enemy. But yet, with the persistent avariciousness of the white man, the Arabs clung to their loot, and when morning came forced the demoralized Manyuema to take up their burdens of death and stagger on into the jungle.

For three days the withering column kept up its frightful march. Each hour was marked by its deadly arrow or cruel spear. The nights were made hideous by the barking of the invisible gun that made sentry duty equivalent to a death sentence.

On the morning of the fourth day the Arabs were compelled to shoot two of their blacks before they could compel the balance to take up the hated ivory, and as they did so a voice rang out, clear and strong, from the jungle: "Today you die, oh, Manyuema, unless you lay down the ivory. Fall upon your cruel masters and kill them! You have guns, why do you not use them? Kill the Arabs, and we will not harm you. We will take you back to our village and feed you, and lead you out of our country in safety and in peace. Lay down the ivory, and fall upon your masters—we will help you. Else you die!"

As the voice died down the raiders stood as though turned to stone. The Arabs eyed their Manyuema slaves; the slaves looked first at one of their fellows, and then at another—they were but waiting for some one to take the initiative. There were some thirty Arabs left, and about one hundred and fifty blacks. All were armed—even those who were acting as porters had their rifles slung across their backs.

The Arabs drew together. The sheik ordered the Manyuema to take up the march, and as he spoke he cocked his rifle and raised it. But at the same instant one of the blacks threw down his load, and, snatching his rifle from his back, fired point-black at the group of Arabs. In an instant the camp was a cursing, howling mass of demons, fighting with guns and knives and pistols. The Arabs stood together, and defended their lives valiantly, but with the rain of lead that poured upon them from their own slaves, and the shower of arrows and spears which now leaped from the surrounding jungle aimed solely at them, there was little question from the first what the outcome would be. In ten minutes from the time the first porter had thrown down his load the last of the Arabs lay dead.

When the firing had ceased Tarzan spoke again to the Manyuema:

"Take up our ivory, and return it to our village, from whence you stole it. We shall not harm you."

For a moment the Manyuema hesitated. They had no stomach to retrace that difficult three days' trail. They talked together in low whispers, and one turned toward the jungle, calling aloud to the voice that had spoken to them from out of the foliage.

"How do we know that when you have us in your village you will not kill us all?" he asked.

"You do not know," replied Tarzan, "other than that we have promised not to harm you if you will return our ivory to us. But this you do know, that it lies within our power to kill you all if you do not return as we direct, and are we not more likely to do so if you anger us than if you do as we bid?"

"Who are you that speaks the tongue of our Arab masters?" cried the Manyuema spokesman. "Let us see you, and then we shall give you our answer."

Tarzan stepped out of the jungle a dozen paces from them.

"Look!" he said. When they saw that he was white they were filled with awe, for never had they seen a white savage before, and at his great muscles and giant frame they were struck with wonder and admiration.

"You may trust me," said Tarzan. "So long as you do as I tell you, and harm none of my people, we shall do you no hurt. Will you take up our ivory and return in peace to our village, or shall we follow along your trail toward the north as we have followed for the past three days?"

The recollection of the horrid days that had just passed was the thing that finally decided the Manyuema, and so, after a short conference, they took up their burdens and set off to retrace their steps toward the village of the Waziri. At the end of the third day they marched into the village gate, and were greeted by the survivors of the recent massacre, to whom Tarzan had sent a messenger in their temporary camp to the south on the day that the raiders had quitted the village, telling them that they might return in safety.

It took all the mastery and persuasion that Tarzan possessed to prevent the Waziri falling on the Manyuema tooth and nail, and tearing them to pieces, but when he had explained that he had given his word that they would not be molested if they carried the ivory back to the spot from which they had stolen it, and had further impressed upon his people that they owed their entire victory to him, they finally acceded to his demands, and allowed the cannibals to rest in peace within their palisade.

That night the village warriors held a big palaver to celebrate their victories, and to choose a new chief. Since old Waziri's death Tarzan had been directing the warriors in battle, and the temporary command had been tacitly conceded to him. There had been no time to choose a new chief from among their own number, and, in fact, so remarkably successful had they been under the ape-man's generalship that they had had no wish to delegate the supreme authority to another for fear that what they already had gained might be lost. They had so recently seen the results of running counter to this savage white man's advice in the disastrous charge ordered by Waziri, in which he himself had died, that it had not been difficult for them to accept Tarzan's authority as final.

The principal warriors sat in a circle about a small fire to discuss the relative merits of whomever might be suggested as old Waziri's successor. It was Busuli who spoke first:

"Since Waziri is dead, leaving no son, there is but one among us whom we know from experience is fitted to make us a good king. There is only one who has proved that he can successfully lead us against the guns of the white man, and bring us easy victory without the loss of a single life. There is only one, and that is the white man who has led us for the past few days," and Busuli sprang to his feet, and with uplifted spear and half-bent, crouching body commenced to dance slowly about Tarzan, chanting in time to his steps: "Waziri, king of the Waziri; Waziri, killer of Arabs; Waziri, king of the Waziri."

One by one the other warriors signified their acceptance of Tarzan as their king by joining in the solemn dance. The women came and squatted about the rim of the circle, beating upon tom-toms, clapping their hands in time to the steps of the dancers, and joining in the chant of the warriors. In the center of the circle sat Tarzan of the Apes—Waziri, king of the Waziri, for, like his predecessor, he was to take the name of his tribe as his own.

Faster and faster grew the pace of the dancers, louder and louder their wild and savage shouts. The women rose and fell in unison, shrieking now at the tops of their voices. The spears were brandishing fiercely, and as the dancers stooped down and beat their shields upon the hard-tramped earth of the village street the whole sight was as terribly primeval and savage as though it were being staged in the dim dawn of humanity, countless ages in the past.

As the excitement waxed the ape-man sprang to his feet and joined in the wild ceremony. In the center of the circle of glittering black bodies he leaped and roared and shook his heavy spear in the same mad abandon that enthralled his fellow savages. The last remnant of his civilization was forgotten—he was a primitive man to the fullest now; reveling in the freedom of the fierce, wild life he loved, gloating in his kingship among these wild blacks.

Ah, if Olga de Coude had but seen him then—could she have recognized the well-dressed, quiet young man whose well-bred face and irreproachable manners had so captivated her but a few short months ago? And Jane Porter! Would she have still loved this savage warrior chieftain, dancing naked among his naked savage subjects? And D'Arnot! Could D'Arnot have believed that this was the same man he had introduced into half a dozen of the most select clubs of Paris? What would his fellow peers in the House of Lords have said had one pointed to this dancing giant, with his barbaric headdress and his metal ornaments, and said: "There, my lords, is John Clayton, Lord Greystoke."

And so Tarzan of the Apes came into a real kingship among men—slowly but surely was he following the evolution of his ancestors, for had he not started at the very bottom?

THE LOTTERY OF DEATH

Jane Porter had been the first of those in the lifeboat to awaken the morning after the wreck of the *Lady Alice*. The other members of the party were asleep upon the thwarts or huddled in cramped positions in the bottom of the boat.

When the girl realized that they had become separated from the other boats she was filled with alarm. The sense of utter loneliness and helplessness which the vast expanse of deserted ocean aroused in her was so depressing that, from the first, contemplation of the future held not the slightest ray of promise for her. She was confident that they were lost—lost beyond possibility of succor.

Presently Clayton awoke. It was several minutes before he could gather his senses sufficiently to realize where he was, or recall the disaster of the previous night. Finally his bewildered eyes fell upon the girl.

"Jane!" he cried. "Thank God that we are together!"

"Look," said the girl dully, indicating the horizon with an apathetic gesture. "We are all alone."

Clayton scanned the water in every direction.

"Where can they be?" he cried. "They cannot have gone down, for there has been no sea, and they were afloat after the yacht sank—I saw them all."

He awoke the other members of the party, and explained their plight.

"It is just as well that the boats are scattered, sir," said one of the sailors. "They are all provisioned, so that they do not need each other on that score, and should a storm blow up they could be of no service to one another even if they were together, but scattered about the ocean there is a much better chance that one at least will be picked up, and then a search will be at once started for the others. Were we together there would be but one chance of rescue, where now there may be four."

They saw the wisdom of his philosophy, and were cheered by it, but their joy was short-lived, for when it was decided that they should row steadily toward the east and the continent, it was discovered that the sailors who had been at the only two oars with which the boat had been provided had fallen asleep at their work, and allowed both to slip into the sea, nor were they in sight anywhere upon the water.

During the angry words and recriminations which followed the sailors nearly came to blows, but Clayton succeeded in quieting them; though a moment later Monsieur Thuran almost precipitated another row by making a nasty remark about the stupidity of all Englishmen, and especially English sailors.

"Come, come, mates," spoke up one of the men, Tompkins, who had taken no part in the altercation, "shootin' off our bloomin' mugs won't get us nothin'. As Spider 'ere said afore, we'll all bloody well be picked up, anyway, sez 'e, so wot's the use o' squabblin'? Let's eat, sez I."

"That's not a bad idea," said Monsieur Thuran, and then, turning to the third sailor, Wilson, he said: "Pass one of those tins aft, my good man."

"Fetch it yerself," retorted Wilson sullenly. "I ain't a-takin' no orders from no—furriner—you ain't captain o' this ship yet."

The result was that Clayton himself had to get the tin, and then another angry altercation ensued when one of the sailors accused Clayton and Monsieur Thuran of conspiring to control the provisions so that they could have the lion's share.

"Some one should take command of this boat," spoke up Jane Porter, thoroughly disgusted with the disgraceful wrangling that had marked the very opening of a forced companionship that might last for many days. "It is terrible enough to be alone in a frail boat on the Atlantic, without having the added misery and danger of constant bickering and brawling among the members of our party. You men should elect a leader, and then abide by his decisions in all matters. There is greater need for strict discipline here than there is upon a well-ordered ship."

She had hoped before she voiced her sentiments that it would not be necessary for her to enter into the transaction at all, for she believed that Clayton was amply able to cope with every emergency, but she had to admit that so far at least he had shown no greater promise of successfully handling the situation than any of the others, though he had at least refrained from adding in any way to the unpleasantness, even going so far as to give up the tin to the sailors when they objected to its being opened by him.

The girl's words temporarily quieted the men, and finally it was decided that the two kegs of water and the four tins of food should be divided into two parts, one-half going forward to the three sailors to do with as they saw best, and the balance aft to the three passengers.

Thus was the little company divided into two camps, and when the provisions had been apportioned each immediately set to work to open and distribute food and water. The sailors were the first to get one of the tins of "food" open, and their curses of rage and disappointment caused Clayton to ask what the trouble might be.

"Trouble!" shrieked Spider. "Trouble! It's worse than trouble—it's death! This—-tin is full of coal oil!"

Hastily now Clayton and Monsieur Thuran tore open one of theirs, only to learn the hideous truth that it also contained, not food, but coal oil. One after another the four tins on board were opened. And as the contents of each became known howls of anger announced the grim truth—there was not an ounce of food upon the boat.

"Well, thank Gawd it wasn't the water," cried Thompkins. "It's easier to get along without food than it is without water. We can eat our shoes if worse comes to worst, but we couldn't drink 'em."

As he spoke Wilson had been boring a hole in one of the water kegs, and as Spider held a tin cup he tilted the keg to pour a draft of the precious fluid. A thin stream of blackish, dry particles filtered slowly through the tiny aperture into the bottom of the cup. With a groan Wilson dropped the keg, and sat staring at the dry stuff in the cup, speechless with horror.

"The kegs are filled with gunpowder," said Spider, in a low tone, turning to those aft. And so it proved when the last had been opened.

"Coal oil and gunpowder!" cried Monsieur Thuran. "SAPRISTI! What a diet for shipwrecked mariners!"

With the full knowledge that there was neither food nor water on board, the pangs of hunger and thirst became immediately aggravated, and so on the first day of their tragic adventure real suffering commenced in grim earnest, and the full horrors of shipwreck were upon them.

As the days passed conditions became horrible. Aching eyes scanned the horizon day and night until the weak and weary watchers would sink exhausted to the bottom of the boat, and there wrest in dream-disturbed slumber a moment's respite from the horrors of the waking reality.

The sailors, goaded by the remorseless pangs of hunger, had eaten their leather belts, their shoes, the sweatbands from their caps, although both Clayton and Monsieur Thuran had done their best to convince them that these would only add to the suffering they were enduring.

Weak and hopeless, the entire party lay beneath the pitiless tropic sun, with parched lips and swollen tongues, waiting for the death they were beginning to crave. The intense suffering of the first few days had become deadened for the three passengers who had eaten nothing, but the agony of the sailors was pitiful, as their weak and impoverished stomachs attempted to cope with the bits of leather with which they had filled them. Tompkins was the first to succumb. Just a week from the day the *Lady Alice* went down the sailor died horribly in frightful convulsions.

For hours his contorted and hideous features lay grinning back at those in the stern of the little boat, until Jane Porter could endure the sight no longer. "Can you not drop his body overboard, William?" she asked.

Clayton rose and staggered toward the corpse. The two remaining sailors eyed him with a strange, baleful light in their sunken orbs. Futilely the Englishman tried to lift the corpse over the side of the boat, but his strength was not equal to the task.

"Lend me a hand here, please," he said to Wilson, who lay nearest him.

"Wot do you want to throw 'im over for?" questioned the sailor, in a querulous voice.

"We've got to before we're too weak to do it," replied Clayton. "He'd be awful by tomorrow, after a day under that broiling sun."

"Better leave well enough alone," grumbled Wilson. "We may need him before tomorrow."

Slowly the meaning of the man's words percolated into Clayton's understanding. At last he realized the fellow's reason for objecting to the disposal of the dead man.

"God!" whispered Clayton, in a horrified tone. "You don't mean—"

"W'y not?" growled Wilson. "Ain't we gotta live? He's dead," he added, jerking his thumb in the direction of the corpse. "He won't care."

"Come here, Thuran," said Clayton, turning toward the Russian. "We'll have something worse than death aboard us if we don't get rid of this body before dark."

Wilson staggered up menacingly to prevent the contemplated act, but when his comrade, Spider, took sides with Clayton and Monsieur Thuran he gave up, and sat eying the corpse hungrily as the three men, by combining their efforts, succeeded in rolling it overboard.

All the balance of the day Wilson sat glaring at Clayton, in his eyes the gleam of insanity. Toward evening, as the sun was sinking into the sea, he commenced to chuckle and mumble to himself, but his eyes never left Clayton.

After it became quite dark Clayton could still feel those terrible eyes upon him. He dared not sleep, and yet so exhausted was he that it was a constant fight to retain consciousness. After what seemed an eternity of suffering his head dropped upon a thwart, and he slept. How long he was unconscious he did not know—he was awakened by a shuffling noise quite close to him. The moon had risen, and as he opened his startled eyes he saw Wilson creeping stealthily toward him, his mouth open and his swollen tongue hanging out.

The slight noise had awakened Jane Porter at the same time, and as she saw the hideous tableau she gave a shrill cry of alarm, and at the same instant the sailor lurched forward and fell upon Clayton. Like a wild beast his teeth sought the throat of his intended prey, but Clayton, weak though he was, still found sufficient strength to hold the maniac's mouth from him.

At Jane Porter's scream Monsieur Thuran and Spider awoke. On seeing the cause of her alarm, both men crawled to Clayton's rescue, and between the three of them were able to subdue Wilson and hurl him to the bottom of the boat. For a few minutes he lay there chattering and laughing, and then, with an awful scream, and before any of his companions could prevent, he staggered to his feet and leaped overboard.

The reaction from the terrific strain of excitement left the weak survivors trembling and prostrated. Spider broke down and wept; Jane Porter prayed; Clayton swore softly to himself; Monsieur Thuran sat with his head in his hands, thinking. The result of his cogitation developed the following morning in a proposition he made to Spider and Clayton.

"Gentlemen," said Monsieur Thuran, "you see the fate that awaits us all unless we are picked up within a day or two. That there is little hope of that is evidenced by the fact that during all the days we have drifted we have seen no sail, nor the faintest smudge of smoke upon the horizon.

"There might be a chance if we had food, but without food there is none. There remains for us, then, but one of two alternatives, and we must choose at once. Either we must all die together within a few days, or one must be sacrificed that the others may live. Do you quite clearly grasp my meaning?"

Jane Porter, who had overheard, was horrified. If the proposition had come from the poor, ignorant sailor, she might possibly have not been so surprised; but that it should come from one who posed as a man of culture and refinement, from a gentleman, she could scarcely credit.

"It is better that we die together, then," said Clayton.

"That is for the majority to decide," replied Monsieur Thuran. "As only one of us three will be the object of sacrifice, we shall decide. Miss Porter is not interested, since she will be in no danger."

"How shall we know who is to be first?" asked Spider.

EDGAR RICE BURROUGHS

"It may be fairly fixed by lot," replied Monsieur Thuran. "I have a number of franc pieces in my pocket. We can choose a certain date from among them—the one to draw this date first from beneath a piece of cloth will be the first."

"I shall have nothing to do with any such diabolical plan," muttered Clayton; "even yet land may be sighted or a ship appear—in time."

"You will do as the majority decide, or you will be 'the first' without the formality of drawing lots," said Monsieur Thuran threateningly. "Come, let us vote on the plan; I for one am in favor of it. How about you, Spider?" "And I," replied the sailor.

"It is the will of the majority," announced Monsieur Thuran, "and now let us lose no time in drawing lots. It is as fair for one as for another. That three may live, one of us must die perhaps a few hours sooner than otherwise."

Then he began his preparation for the lottery of death, while Jane Porter sat wide-eyed and horrified at thought of the thing that she was about to witness. Monsieur Thuran spread his coat upon the bottom of the boat, and then from a handful of money he selected six franc pieces. The other two men bent close above him as he inspected them. Finally he handed them all to Clayton.

"Look at them carefully," he said. "The oldest date is eighteen-seventy-five, and there is only one of that year."

Clayton and the sailor inspected each coin. To them there seemed not the slightest difference that could be detected other than the dates. They were quite satisfied. Had they known that Monsieur Thuran's past experience as a card sharp had trained his sense of touch to so fine a point that he could almost differentiate between cards by the mere feel of them, they would scarcely have felt that the plan was so entirely fair. The 1875 piece was a hair thinner than the other coins, but neither Clayton nor Spider could have detected it without the aid of a micrometer.

"In what order shall we draw?" asked Monsieur Thuran, knowing from past experience that the majority of men always prefer last chance in a lottery where the single prize is some distasteful thing—there is always the chance and the hope that another will draw it first. Monsieur Thuran, for reasons of his own, preferred to draw first if the drawing should happen to require a second adventure beneath the coat.

And so when Spider elected to draw last he graciously offered to take the first chance himself. His hand was under the coat for but a moment, yet those quick, deft fingers had felt of each coin, and found and discarded the fatal piece. When he brought forth his hand it contained an 1888 franc piece. Then Clayton drew. Jane Porter leaned forward with a tense and horrified expression on her face as the hand of the man she was to marry groped about beneath the coat. Presently he withdrew it, a franc piece lying in the palm. For an instant he dared not look, but Monsieur Thuran, who had leaned nearer to see the date, exclaimed that he was safe.

Jane Porter sank weak and trembling against the side of the boat. She felt sick and dizzy. And now, if Spider should not draw the 1875 piece she must endure the whole horrid thing again.

The sailor already had his hand beneath the coat. Great beads of sweat were standing upon his brow. He trembled as though with a fit of ague. Aloud he cursed himself for having taken the last draw, for now his chances for escape were but three to one, whereas Monsieur Thuran's had been five to one, and Clayton's four to one.

The Russian was very patient, and did not hurry the man, for he knew that he himself was quite safe whether the 1875 piece came out this time or not. When the sailor withdrew his hand and looked at the piece of money within, he dropped fainting to the bottom of the boat. Both Clayton and Monsieur Thuran hastened weakly to examine the coin, which had rolled from the man's hand and lay beside him. It was not dated 1875. The reaction from the state of fear he had been in had overcome Spider quite as effectually as though he had drawn the fated piece.

But now the whole proceeding must be gone through again. Once more the Russian drew forth a harmless coin. Jane Porter closed her eyes as Clayton reached beneath the coat. Spider bent, wide-eyed, toward the hand that was to decide his fate, for whatever luck was Clayton's on this last draw, the opposite would be Spider's. Then William Cecil Clayton, Lord Greystoke, removed his hand from beneath the coat, and with a coin tight pressed within his palm where none might see it, he looked at Jane Porter. He did not dare open his hand.

"Quick!" hissed Spider. "My Gawd, let's see it."

Clayton opened his fingers. Spider was the first to see the date, and ere any knew what his intention was he raised himself to his feet, and lunged over the side of the boat, to disappear forever into the green depths beneath—the coin had not been the 1875 piece.

The strain had exhausted those who remained to such an extent that they lay half unconscious for the balance of the day, nor was the subject referred to again for several days. Horrible days of increasing weakness and hopelessness. At length Monsieur Thuran crawled to where Clayton lay.

"We must draw once more before we are too weak even to eat," he whispered.

Clayton was in such a state that he was scarcely master of his own will. Jane Porter had not spoken for three days. He knew that she was dying. Horrible as the thought was, he hoped that the sacrifice of either Thuran or himself might be the means of giving her renewed strength, and so he immediately agreed to the Russian's proposal.

They drew under the same plan as before, but there could be but one result—Clayton drew the 1875 piece.

"When shall it be?" he asked Thuran.

The Russian had already drawn a pocketknife from his trousers, and was weakly attempting to open it.

"Now," he muttered, and his greedy eyes gloated upon the Englishman.

"Can't you wait until dark?" asked Clayton. "Miss Porter must not see this thing done. We were to have been married, you know."

A look of disappointment came over Monsieur Thuran's face.

"Very well," he replied hesitatingly. "It will not be long until night. I have waited for many days—I can wait a few hours longer."

"Thank you, my friend," murmured Clayton. "Now I shall go to her side and remain with her until it is time. I would like to have an hour or two with her before I die."

When Clayton reached the girl's side she was unconscious—he knew that she was dying, and he was glad that she should not have to see or know the awful tragedy that was shortly to be enacted. He took her hand and raised it to his cracked and swollen lips. For a long time he lay caressing the emaciated, clawlike thing that had once been the beautiful, shapely white hand of the young Baltimore belle.

It was quite dark before he knew it, but he was recalled to himself by a voice out of the night. It was the Russian calling him to his doom.

"I am coming, Monsieur Thuran," he hastened to reply.

Thrice he attempted to turn himself upon his hands and knees, that he might crawl back to his death, but in the few hours that he had lain there he had become too weak to return to Thuran's side.

"You will have to come to me, monsieur," he called weakly. "I have not sufficient strength to gain my hands and knees."

"SAPRISTI!" muttered Monsieur Thuran. "You are attempting to cheat me out of my winnings."

Clayton heard the man shuffling about in the bottom of the boat. Finally there was a despairing groan. "I cannot crawl," he heard the Russian wail. "It is too late. You have tricked me, you dirty English dog."

"I have not tricked you, monsieur," replied Clayton. "I have done my best to rise, but I shall try again, and if you will try possibly each of us can crawl halfway, and then you shall have your 'winnings.'"

Again Clayton exerted his remaining strength to the utmost, and he heard Thuran apparently doing the same. Nearly an hour later the Englishman succeeded in raising himself to his hands and knees, but at the first forward movement he pitched upon his face.

A moment later he heard an exclamation of relief from Monsieur Thuran.

"I am coming," whispered the Russian.

Again Clayton essayed to stagger on to meet his fate, but once more he pitched headlong to the boat's bottom, nor, try as he would, could he again rise. His last effort caused him to roll over on his back, and there he lay looking up at the stars, while behind him, coming ever nearer and nearer, he could hear the laborious shuffling, and the stertorous breathing of the Russian.

It seemed that he must have lain thus an hour waiting for the thing to crawl out of the dark and end his misery. It was quite close now, but there were longer and longer pauses between its efforts to advance, and each forward movement seemed to the waiting Englishman to be almost imperceptible.

Finally he knew that Thuran was quite close beside him. He heard a cackling laugh, something touched his face, and he lost consciousness.

THE CITY OF GOLD

The very night that Tarzan of the Apes became chief of the Waziri the woman he loved lay dying in a tiny boat two hundred miles west of him upon the Atlantic. As he danced among his naked fellow savages, the firelight gleaming against his great, rolling muscles, the personification of physical perfection and strength, the woman who loved him lay thin and emaciated in the last coma that precedes death by thirst and starvation.

The week following the induction of Tarzan into the kingship of the Waziri was occupied in escorting the Manyuema of the Arab raiders to the northern boundary of Waziri in accordance with the promise which Tarzan had made them. Before he left them he exacted a pledge from them that they would not lead any expeditions against the Waziri in the future, nor was it a difficult promise to obtain. They had had sufficient experience with the fighting tactics of the new Waziri chief not to have the slightest desire to accompany another predatory force within the boundaries of his domain.

Almost immediately upon his return to the village Tarzan commenced making preparations for leading an expedition in search of the ruined city of gold which old Waziri had described to him. He selected fifty of the sturdiest warriors of his tribe, choosing only men who seemed anxious to accompany him on the arduous march, and share the dangers of a new and hostile country.

The fabulous wealth of the fabled city had been almost constantly in his mind since Waziri had recounted the strange adventures of the former expedition which had stumbled upon the vast ruins by chance. The lure of adventure may have been quite as powerful a factor in urging Tarzan of the Apes to undertake the journey as the lure of gold, but the lure of gold was there, too, for he had learned among civilized men something of the miracles that may be wrought by the possessor of the magic yellow metal. What he would do with a golden fortune in the heart of savage Africa it had not occurred to him to consider—it would be enough to possess the power to work wonders, even though he never had an opportunity to employ it.

So one glorious tropical morning Waziri, chief of the Waziri, set out at the head of fifty clean-limbed ebon warriors in quest of adventure and of riches. They followed the course which old Waziri had described to Tarzan. For days they marched—up one river, across a low divide; down another river; up a third, until at the end of the twenty-fifth day they camped upon a mountainside, from the summit of which they hoped to catch their first view of the marvelous city of treasure.

Early the next morning they were climbing the almost perpendicular crags which formed the last, but greatest, natural barrier between them and their destination. It was nearly noon before Tarzan, who headed the thin line of climbing warriors, scrambled over the top of the last cliff and stood upon the little flat table-land of the mountaintop.

On either hand towered mighty peaks thousands of feet higher than the pass through which they were entering the forbidden valley. Behind him stretched the wooded valley across which they had marched for many days, and at the opposite side the low range which marked the boundary of their own country.

But before him was the view that centered his attention. Here lay a desolate valley—a shallow, narrow valley dotted with stunted trees and covered with many great bowlders. And on the far side of the valley lay what appeared to be a mighty city, its great walls, its lofty spires, its turrets, minarets, and domes showing red and yellow in the sunlight. Tarzan was yet too far away to note the marks of ruin—to him it appeared a wonderful city of magnificent beauty, and in imagination he peopled its broad avenues and its huge temples with a throng of happy, active people.

For an hour the little expedition rested upon the mountain-top, and then Tarzan led them down into the valley below. There was no trail, but the way was less arduous than the ascent of the opposite face of the mountain had been. Once in the valley their progress was rapid, so that it was still light when they halted before the towering walls of the ancient city.

The outer wall was fifty feet in height where it had not fallen into ruin, but nowhere as far as they could see had more than ten or twenty feet of the upper courses fallen away. It was still a formidable defense. On several occasions Tarzan had thought that he discerned things moving behind the ruined portions of the wall near to them, as though creatures were watching them from behind the bulwarks of the ancient pile. And often he felt the sensation of unseen eyes upon him, but not once could he be sure that it was more than imagination.

That night they camped outside the city. Once, at midnight, they were awakened by a shrill scream from beyond the great wall. It was very high at first, descending gradually until it ended in a series of dismal moans. It had a strange effect upon the blacks, almost paralyzing them with terror while it lasted, and it was an hour before the camp settled down to sleep once more. In the morning the effects of it were still visible in the fearful, sidelong glances that the Waziri continually cast at the massive and forbidding structure which loomed above them.

It required considerable encouragement and urging on Tarzan's part to prevent the blacks from abandoning the venture on the spot and hastening back across the valley toward the cliffs they had scaled the day before. But at length, by dint of commands, and threats that he would enter the city alone, they agreed to accompany him.

For fifteen minutes they marched along the face of the wall before they discovered a means of ingress. Then they came to a narrow cleft about twenty inches wide. Within, a flight of concrete steps, worn hollow by centuries of use, rose before them, to disappear at a sharp turning of the passage a few yards ahead.

Into this narrow alley Tarzan made his way, turning his giant shoulders sideways that they might enter at all. Behind him trailed his black warriors. At the turn in the cleft the stairs ended, and the path was level; but it wound and twisted in a serpentine fashion, until suddenly at a sharp angle it debouched upon a narrow court, across which loomed an inner wall equally as high as the outer. This inner wall was set with little round towers alternating along its entire summit with pointed monoliths. In places these had fallen, and the wall was ruined, but it was in a much better state of preservation than the outer wall.

Another narrow passage led through this wall, and at its end Tarzan and his warriors found themselves in a broad avenue, on the opposite side of which crumbling edifices of hewn granite loomed dark and forbidding. Upon the crumbling debris along the face of the buildings trees had grown, and vines wound in and out of the hollow, staring windows; but the building directly opposite them seemed less overgrown than the others, and in a much better state of preservation. It was a massive pile, surmounted by an enormous dome. At either side of its great entrance stood rows of tall pillars, each capped by a huge, grotesque bird carved from the solid rock of the monoliths.

As the ape-man and his companions stood gazing in varying degrees of wonderment at this ancient city in the midst of savage Africa, several of them became aware of movement within the structure at which they were looking. Dim, shadowy shapes appeared to be moving about in the semi-darkness of the interior. There was nothing tangible that the eye could grasp—only an uncanny suggestion of life where it seemed that there should be no life, for living things seemed out of place in this weird, dead city of the long-dead past.

Tarzan recalled something that he had read in the library at Paris of a lost race of white men that native legend described as living in the heart of Africa. He wondered if he were not looking upon the ruins of the civilization that this strange people had wrought amid the savage surroundings of their strange and savage home. Could it be possible that even now a remnant of that lost race inhabited the ruined grandeur that had once been their progenitor? Again he became conscious of a stealthy movement within the great temple before him. "Come!" he said, to his Waziri. "Let us have a look at what lies behind those ruined walls."

His men were loath to follow him, but when they saw that he was bravely entering the frowning portal they trailed a few paces behind in a huddled group that seemed the personification of nervous terror. A single shriek such as they had heard the night before would have been sufficient to have sent them all racing madly for the narrow cleft that led through the great walls to the outer world.

As Tarzan entered the building he was distinctly aware of many eyes upon him. There was a rustling in the shadows of a near-by corridor, and he could have sworn that he saw a human hand withdrawn from an embrasure that opened above him into the domelike rotunda in which he found himself.

The floor of the chamber was of concrete, the walls of smooth granite, upon which strange figures of men and beasts were carved. In places tablets of yellow metal had been set in the solid masonry of the walls.

When he approached closer to one of these tablets he saw that it was of gold, and bore many hieroglyphics. Beyond this first chamber there were others, and back of them the building branched out into enormous wings. Tarzan passed through several of these chambers, finding many evidences of the fabulous wealth of the original builders. In one room were seven pillars of solid gold, and in another the floor itself was of the precious metal. And all the while that he explored, his blacks huddled close together at his back, and strange shapes hovered upon either hand and before them and behind, yet never close enough that any might say that they were not alone.

The strain, however, was telling upon the nerves of the Waziri. They begged Tarzan to return to the sunlight. They said that no good could come of such an expedition, for the ruins were haunted by the spirits of the dead who had once inhabited them.

"They are watching us, O king," whispered Busuli. "They are waiting until they have led us into the innermost recesses of their stronghold, and then they will fall upon us and tear us to pieces with their teeth. That is the way with spirits. My mother's uncle, who is a great witch doctor, has told me all about it many times."

Tarzan laughed. "Run back into the sunlight, my children," he said. "I will join you when I have searched this old ruin from top to bottom, and found the gold, or found that there is none. At least we may take the tablets from the walls, though the pillars are too heavy for us to handle; but there should be great storerooms filled with gold—gold that we can carry away upon our backs with ease. Run on now, out into the fresh air where you may breathe easier."

Some of the warriors started to obey their chief with alacrity, but Busuli and several others hesitated to leave him—hesitated between love and loyalty for their king, and superstitious fear of the unknown. And then, quite unexpectedly, that occurred which decided the question without the necessity for further discussion. Out of the silence of the ruined temple there rang, close to their ears, the same hideous shriek they had heard the previous night, and with horrified cries the black warriors turned and fled through the empty halls of the age-old edifice.

Behind them stood Tarzan of the Apes where they had left him, a grim smile upon his lips—waiting for the enemy he fully expected was about to pounce upon him. But again silence reigned, except for the faint suggestion of the sound of naked feet moving stealthily in near-by places.

Then Tarzan wheeled and passed on into the depths of the temple. From room to room he went, until he came to one at which a rude, barred door still stood, and as he put his shoulder against it to push it in, again the shriek of warning rang out almost beside him. It was evident that he was being warned to refrain from desecrating this particular room. Or could it be that within lay the secret to the treasure stores?

At any rate, the very fact that the strange, invisible guardians of this weird place had some reason for wishing him not to enter this particular chamber was sufficient to treble Tarzan's desire to do so, and though the shrieking was repeated continuously, he kept his shoulder to the door until it gave before his giant strength to swing open upon creaking wooden hinges.

Within all was black as the tomb. There was no window to let in the faintest ray of light, and as the corridor upon which it opened was itself in semi-darkness, even the open door shed no relieving rays within. Feeling before him upon the floor with the butt of his spear, Tarzan entered the Stygian gloom. Suddenly the door behind him closed, and at the same time hands clutched him from every direction out of the darkness.

The ape-man fought with all the savage fury of self-preservation backed by the herculean strength that was his. But though he felt his blows land, and his teeth sink into soft flesh, there seemed always two new hands to take the place of those that he fought off. At last they dragged him down, and slowly, very slowly, they overcame him by the mere weight of their numbers. And then they bound him—his hands behind his back and his feet trussed up to meet them. He had heard no sound except the heavy breathing of his antagonists, and the noise of the battle. He knew not what manner of creatures had captured him, but that they were human seemed evident from the fact that they had bound him.

Presently they lifted him from the floor, and half dragging, half pushing him, they brought him out of the black chamber through another doorway into an inner courtyard of the temple. Here he saw his captors. There must have been a hundred of them—short, stocky men, with great beards that covered their faces and fell upon their hairy breasts.

The thick, matted hair upon their heads grew low over their receding brows, and hung about their shoulders and their backs. Their crooked legs were short and heavy, their arms long and muscular. About their loins they wore the skins of leopards and lions, and great necklaces of the claws of these same animals depended upon their breasts. Massive circlets of virgin gold adorned their arms and legs. For weapons they carried heavy, knotted bludgeons, and in the belts that confined their single garments each had a long, wicked-looking knife.

But the feature of them that made the most startling impression upon their prisoner was their white skins—neither in color nor feature was there a trace of the negroid about them. Yet, with their receding foreheads, wicked little close-set eyes, and yellow fangs, they were far from prepossessing in appearance.

During the fight within the dark chamber, and while they had been dragging Tarzan to the inner court, no word had been spoken, but now several of them exchanged grunting, monosyllabic conversation in a language unfamiliar to the ape-man, and presently they left him lying upon the concrete floor while they trooped off on their short legs into another part of the temple beyond the court.

As Tarzan lay there upon his back he saw that the temple entirely surrounded the little inclosure, and that on all sides its lofty walls rose high above him. At the top a little patch of blue sky was visible, and, in one direction, through an embrasure, he could see foliage, but whether it was beyond or within the temple he did not know.

About the court, from the ground to the top of the temple, were series of open galleries, and now and then the captive caught glimpses of bright eyes gleaming from beneath masses of tumbling hair, peering down upon him from above.

The ape-man gently tested the strength of the bonds that held him, and while he could not be sure it seemed that they were of insufficient strength to withstand the strain of his mighty muscles when the time came to make a break for freedom; but he did not dare to put them to the crucial test until darkness had fallen, or he felt that no spying eyes were upon him.

He had lain within the court for several hours before the first rays of sunlight penetrated the vertical shaft; almost simultaneously he heard the pattering of bare feet in the corridors about him, and a moment later saw the galleries above fill with crafty faces as a score or more entered the courtyard.

For a moment every eye was bent upon the noonday sun, and then in unison the people in the galleries and those in the court below took up the refrain of a low, weird chant. Presently those about Tarzan began to dance to the cadence of their solemn song. They circled him slowly, resembling in their manner of dancing a number of clumsy, shuffling bears; but as yet they did not look at him, keeping their little eyes fixed upon the sun.

For ten minutes or more they kept up their monotonous chant and steps, and then suddenly, and in perfect unison, they turned toward their victim with upraised bludgeons and emitting fearful howls, the while they contorted their features into the most diabolical expressions, they rushed upon him.

At the same instant a female figure dashed into the midst of the bloodthirsty horde, and, with a bludgeon similar to their own, except that it was wrought from gold, beat back the advancing men.

LA

For a moment Tarzan thought that by some strange freak of fate a miracle had saved him, but when he realized the ease with which the girl had, single-handed, beaten off twenty gorilla-like males, and an instant later, as he saw them again take up their dance about him while she addressed them in a singsong monotone, which bore every evidence of rote, he came to the conclusion that it was all but a part of the ceremony of which he was the central figure.

After a moment or two the girl drew a knife from her girdle, and, leaning over Tarzan, cut the bonds from his legs. Then, as the men stopped their dance, and approached, she motioned to him to rise. Placing the rope that had been about his legs around his neck, she led him across the courtyard, the men following in twos.

Through winding corridors she led, farther and farther into the remoter precincts of the temple, until they came to a great chamber in the center of which stood an altar. Then it was that Tarzan translated the strange ceremony that had preceded his introduction into this holy of holies.

He had fallen into the hands of descendants of the ancient sun worshippers. His seeming rescue by a votaress of the high priestess of the sun had been but a part of the mimicry of their heathen ceremony—the sun looking down upon him through the opening at the top of the court had claimed him as his own, and the priestess had come from the inner temple to save him from the polluting hands of worldlings—to save him as a human offering to their flaming deity.

And had he needed further assurance as to the correctness of his theory he had only to cast his eyes upon the brownish-red stains that caked the stone altar and covered the floor in its immediate vicinity, or to the human skulls which grinned from countless niches in the towering walls.

The priestess led the victim to the altar steps. Again the galleries above filled with watchers, while from an arched doorway at the east end of the chamber a procession of females filed slowly into the room. They wore, like the men, only skins of wild animals caught about their waists with rawhide belts or chains of gold; but the black masses of their hair were incrusted with golden headgear composed of many circular and oval pieces of gold ingeniously held together to form a metal cap from which depended at each side of the head, long strings of oval pieces falling to the waist.

The females were more symmetrically proportioned than the males, their features were much more perfect, the shapes of their heads and their large, soft, black eyes denoting far greater intelligence and humanity than was possessed by their lords and masters.

Each priestess bore two golden cups, and as they formed in line along one side of the altar the men formed opposite them, advancing and taking each a cup from the female opposite. Then the chant began once more, and presently from a dark passageway beyond the altar another female emerged from the cavernous depths beneath the chamber.

The high priestess, thought Tarzan. She was a young woman with a rather intelligent and shapely face. Her ornaments were similar to those worn by her votaries, but much more elaborate, many being set with diamonds. Her bare arms and legs were almost concealed by the massive, bejeweled ornaments which covered them, while her single leopard skin was supported by a close-fitting girdle of golden rings set in strange designs with innumerable small diamonds. In the girdle she carried a long, jeweled knife, and in her hand a slender wand in lieu of a bludgeon.

As she advanced to the opposite side of the altar she halted, and the chanting ceased. The priests and priestesses knelt before her, while with wand extended above them she recited a long and tiresome prayer. Her voice was soft and musical—Tarzan could scarce realize that its possessor in a moment more would be transformed by the fanatical ecstasy of religious zeal into a wild-eyed and bloodthirsty executioner, who, with dripping knife, would be the first to drink her victim's red, warm blood from the little golden cup that stood upon the altar.

As she finished her prayer she let her eyes rest for the first time upon Tarzan. With every indication of considerable curiosity she examined him from head to foot. Then she addressed him, and when she had finished stood waiting, as though she expected a reply.

"I do not understand your language," said Tarzan. "Possibly we may speak together in another tongue?" But she could not understand him, though he tried French, English, Arab, Waziri, and, as a last resort, the mongrel tongue of the West Coast.

She shook her head, and it seemed that there was a note of weariness in her voice as she motioned to the priests to continue with the rites. These now circled in a repetition of their idiotic dance, which was terminated finally at a command from the priestess, who had stood throughout, still looking intently upon Tarzan.

At her signal the priests rushed upon the ape-man, and, lifting him bodily, laid him upon his back across the altar, his head hanging over one edge, his legs over the opposite. Then they and the priestesses formed in two lines, with their little golden cups in readiness to capture a share of the victim's lifeblood after the sacrificial knife had accomplished its work.

In the line of priests an altercation arose as to who should have first place. A burly brute with all the refined intelligence of a gorilla stamped upon his bestial face was attempting to push a smaller man to second place, but the smaller one appealed to the high priestess, who in a cold peremptory voice sent the larger to the extreme end of the line. Tarzan could hear him growling and rumbling as he went slowly to the inferior station.

Then the priestess, standing above him, began reciting what Tarzan took to be an invocation, the while she slowly raised her thin, sharp knife aloft. It seemed ages to the ape-man before her arm ceased its upward progress and the knife halted high above his unprotected breast.

Then it started downward, slowly at first, but as the incantation increased in rapidity, with greater speed. At the end of the line Tarzan could still hear the grumbling of the disgruntled priest. The man's voice rose louder and louder. A priestess near him spoke in sharp tones of rebuke. The knife was quite near to Tarzan's breast now, but it halted for an instant as the high priestess raised her eyes to shoot her swift displeasure at the instigator of this sacrilegious interruption.

There was a sudden commotion in the direction of the disputants, and Tarzan rolled his head in their direction in time to see the burly brute of a priest leap upon the woman opposite him, dashing out her brains with a single blow of his heavy cudgel. Then that happened which Tarzan had witnessed a hundred times before among the wild denizens of his own savage jungle. He had seen the thing fall upon Kerchak, and

Tublat, and Terkoz; upon a dozen of the other mighty bull apes of his tribe; and upon Tantor, the elephant; there was scarce any of the males of the forest that did not at times fall prey to it. The priest went mad, and with his heavy bludgeon ran amuck among his fellows.

His screams of rage were frightful as he dashed hither and thither, dealing terrific blows with his giant weapon, or sinking his yellow fangs into the flesh of some luckless victim. And during it the priestess stood with poised knife above Tarzan, her eyes fixed in horror upon the maniacal thing that was dealing out death and destruction to her votaries.

Presently the room was emptied except for the dead and dying on the floor, the victim upon the altar, the high priestess, and the madman. As the cunning eyes of the latter fell upon the woman they lighted with a new and sudden lust. Slowly he crept toward her, and now he spoke; but this time there fell upon Tarzan's surprised ears a language he could understand; the last one that he would ever have thought of employing in attempting to converse with human beings—the low guttural barking of the tribe of great anthropoids—his own mother tongue. And the woman answered the man in the same language.

He was threatening—she attempting to reason with him, for it was quite evident that she saw that he was past her authority. The brute was quite close now—creeping with clawlike hands extended toward her around the end of the altar. Tarzan strained at the bonds which held his arms pinioned behind him. The woman did not see—she had forgotten her prey in the horror of the danger that threatened herself. As the brute leaped past Tarzan to clutch his victim, the ape-man gave one superhuman wrench at the thongs that held him. The effort sent him rolling from the altar to the stone floor on the opposite side from that on which the priestess stood; but as he sprang to his feet the thongs dropped from his freed arms, and at the same time he realized that he was alone in the inner temple—the high priestess and the mad priest had disappeared.

And then a muffled scream came from the cavernous mouth of the dark hole beyond the sacrificial altar through which the priestess had entered the temple. Without even a thought for his own safety, or the possibility for escape which this rapid series of fortuitous circumstances had thrust upon him, Tarzan of the Apes answered the call of the woman in danger. With a little bound he was at the gaping entrance to the subterranean chamber, and a moment later was running down a flight of age-old concrete steps that led he knew not where.

The faint light that filtered in from above showed him a large, low-ceiled vault from which several doorways led off into inky darkness, but there was no need to thread an unknown way, for there before him lay the objects of his search—the mad brute had the girl upon the floor, and gorilla-like fingers were clutching frantically at her throat as she struggled to escape the fury of the awful thing upon her.

As Tarzan's heavy hand fell upon his shoulder the priest dropped his victim, and turned upon her would-be rescuer. With foam-flecked lips and bared fangs the mad sun-worshiper battled with the tenfold power of the maniac. In the blood lust of his fury the creature had undergone a sudden reversion to type, which left him a wild beast, forgetful of the dagger that projected from his belt—thinking only of nature's weapons with which his brute prototype had battled.

But if he could use his teeth and hands to advantage, he found one even better versed in the school of savage warfare to which he had reverted, for Tarzan of the Apes closed with him, and they fell to the floor tearing and rending at one another like two bull apes; while the primitive priestess stood flattened against the wall, watching with wide, fear-fascinated eyes the growing, snapping beasts at her feet.

At last she saw the stranger close one mighty hand upon the throat of his antagonist, and as he forced the bruteman's head far back rain blow after blow upon the upturned face. A moment later he threw the still thing from him, and, arising, shook himself like a lion. He placed a foot upon the carcass before him, and raised his head to give the victory cry of his kind, but as his eyes fell upon the opening above him leading into the temple of human sacrifice he thought better of his intended act.

The girl, who had been half paralyzed by fear as the two men fought, had just commenced to give thought to her probable fate now that, though released from the clutches of a madman, she had fallen into the hands of one whom but a moment before she had been upon the point of killing. She looked about for some means of escape. The black mouth of a diverging corridor was near at hand, but as she turned to dart into it the ape-man's eyes fell upon her, and with a quick leap he was at her side, and a restraining hand was laid upon her arm.

"Wait!" said Tarzan of the Apes, in the language of the tribe of Kerchak.

The girl looked at him in astonishment.

"Who are you," she whispered, "who speaks the language of the first man?"

"I am Tarzan of the Apes," he answered in the vernacular of the anthropoids.

"What do you want of me?" she continued. "For what purpose did you save me from Tha?"

"I could not see a woman murdered?" It was a half question that answered her.

"But what do you intend to do with me now?" she continued.

"Nothing," he replied, "but you can do something for me—you can lead me out of this place to freedom." He made the suggestion without the slightest thought that she would accede. He felt quite sure that the sacrifice would go on from the point where it had been interrupted if the high priestess had her way, though he was equally positive that they would find Tarzan of the Apes unbound and with a long dagger in his hand a much less tractable victim than Tarzan disarmed and bound.

The girl stood looking at him for a long moment before she spoke.

"You are a very wonderful man," she said. "You are such a man as I have seen in my daydreams ever since I was a little girl. You are such a man as I imagine the forbears of my people must have been—the great race of people who built this mighty city in the heart of a savage world that they might wrest from the bowels of the earth the fabulous wealth for which they had sacrificed their far-distant civilization.

"I cannot understand why you came to my rescue in the first place, and now I cannot understand why, having me within your power, you do not wish to be revenged upon me for having sentenced you to death—for having almost put you to death with my own hand."

"I presume," replied the ape-man, "that you but followed the teachings of your religion. I cannot blame *you* for that, no matter what I may think of your creed. But who are you—what people have I fallen among?"

"I am La, high priestess of the Temple of the Sun, in the city of Opar. We are descendants of a people who came to this savage world more than ten thousand years ago in search of gold. Their cities stretched from a great sea under the rising sun to a great sea into which the sun descends at night to cool his flaming brow. They were very rich and very powerful, but they lived only a few months of the year in their magnificent palaces here; the rest of the time they spent in their native land, far, far to the north.

"Many ships went back and forth between this new world and the old. During the rainy season there were but few of the inhabitants remained here, only those who superintended the working of the mines by the black slaves, and the merchants who had to stay to supply their wants, and the soldiers who guarded the cities and the mines.

"It was at one of these times that the great calamity occurred. When the time came for the teeming thousands to return none came. For weeks the people waited. Then they sent out a great galley to learn why no one came from the mother country, but though they sailed about for many months, they were unable to find any trace of the mighty land that had for countless ages borne their ancient civilization—it had sunk into the sea.

"From that day dated the downfall of my people. Disheartened and unhappy, they soon became a prey to the black hordes of the north and the black hordes of the south. One by one the cities were deserted or overcome. The last remnant was finally forced to take shelter within this mighty mountain fortress. Slowly we have dwindled in power, in civilization, in intellect, in numbers, until now we are no more than a small tribe of savage apes.

"In fact, the apes live with us, and have for many ages. We call them the first men—we speak their language quite as much as we do our own; only in the rituals of the temple do we make any attempt to retain our mother tongue. In time it will be forgotten, and we will speak only the language of the apes; in time we will no longer banish those of our people who mate with apes, and so in time we shall descend to the very beasts from which ages ago our progenitors may have sprung."

"But why are you more human than the others?" asked the man.

"For some reason the women have not reverted to savagery so rapidly as the men. It may be because only the lower types of men remained here at the time of the great catastrophe, while the temples were filled with the noblest daughters of the race. My strain has remained clearer than the rest because for countless ages my foremothers were high priestesses—the sacred office descends from mother to daughter. Our husbands are chosen for us from the noblest in the land. The most perfect man, mentally and physically, is selected to be the husband of the high priestess."

"From what I saw of the gentlemen above," said Tarzan, with a grin, "there should be little trouble in choosing from among them."

The girl looked at him quizzically for a moment.

"Do not be sacrilegious," she said. "They are very holy men—they are priests."

"Then there are others who are better to look upon?" he asked.

"The others are all more ugly than the priests," she replied.

Tarzan shuddered at her fate, for even in the dim light of the vault he was impressed by her beauty.

"But how about myself?" he asked suddenly. "Are you going to lead me to liberty?"

"You have been chosen by The Flaming God as his own," she answered solemnly. "Not even I have the power to save you—should they find you again. But I do not intend that they shall find you. You risked your life to save mine. I may do no less for you. It will be no easy matter—it may require days; but in the end I think that I can lead you beyond the walls. Come, they will look here for me presently, and if they find us together we shall both be lost—they would kill me did they think that I had proved false to my god."

"You must not take the risk, then," he said quickly. "I will return to the temple, and if I can fight my way to freedom there will be no suspicion thrown upon you."

But she would not have it so, and finally persuaded him to follow her, saying that they had already remained in the vault too long to prevent suspicion from falling upon her even if they returned to the temple.

"I will hide you, and then return alone," she said, "telling them that I was long unconscious after you killed Tha, and that I do not know whither you escaped."

And so she led him through winding corridors of gloom, until finally they came to a small chamber into which a little light filtered through a stone grating in the ceiling.

"This is the Chamber of the Dead," she said. "None will think of searching here for you—they would not dare. I will return after it is dark. By that time I may have found a plan to effect your escape."

She was gone, and Tarzan of the Apes was left alone in the Chamber of the Dead, beneath the long-dead city of Opar.

THE CASTAWAYS

Clayton dreamed that he was drinking his fill of water, pure, delightful drafts of fresh water. With a start he gained consciousness to find himself wet through by torrents of rain that were falling upon his body and his upturned face. A heavy tropical shower was beating down upon them. He opened his mouth and drank. Presently he was so revived and strengthened that he was enabled to raise himself upon his hands. Across his legs lay Monsieur Thuran. A few feet aft Jane Porter was huddled in a pitiful little heap in the bottom of the boat—she was quite still. Clayton knew that she was dead.

After infinite labor he released himself from Thuran's pinioning body, and with renewed strength crawled toward the girl. He raised her head from the rough boards of the boat's bottom. There might be life in that poor, starved frame even yet. He could not quite abandon all hope, and so he seized a water-soaked rag and squeezed the precious drops between the swollen lips of the hideous thing that had but a few short days before glowed with the resplendent life of happy youth and glorious beauty.

For some time there was no sign of returning animation, but at last his efforts were rewarded by a slight tremor of the half-closed lids. He chafed the thin hands, and forced a few more drops of water into the parched throat. The girl opened her eyes, looking up at him for a long time before she could recall her surroundings.

"Water?" she whispered. "Are we saved?"

"It is raining," he explained. "We may at least drink. Already it has revived us both."

"Monsieur Thuran?" she asked. "He did not kill you. Is he dead?"

"I do not know," replied Clayton. "If he lives and this rain revives him—" But he stopped there, remembering too late that he must not add further to the horrors which the girl already had endured.

But she guessed what he would have said.

"Where is he?" she asked.

Clayton nodded his head toward the prostrate form of the Russian. For a time neither spoke.

"I will see if I can revive him," said Clayton at length.

"No," she whispered, extending a detaining hand toward him. "Do not do that—he will kill you when the water has given him strength. If he is dying, let him die. Do not leave me alone in this boat with that beast."

Clayton hesitated. His honor demanded that he attempt to revive Thuran, and there was the possibility, too, that the Russian was beyond human aid. It was not dishonorable to hope so. As he sat fighting out his battle he presently raised his eyes from the body of the man, and as they passed above the gunwale of the boat he staggered weakly to his feet with a little cry of joy.

"Land, Jane!" he almost shouted through his cracked lips. "Thank God, land!"

The girl looked, too, and there, not a hundred yards away, she saw a yellow beach, and, beyond, the luxurious foliage of a tropical jungle.

"Now you may revive him," said Jane Porter, for she, too, had been haunted with the pangs of conscience which had resulted from her decision to prevent Clayton from offering succor to their companion.

It required the better part of half an hour before the Russian evinced sufficient symptoms of returning consciousness to open his eyes, and it was some time later before they could bring him to a realization of their good fortune. By this time the boat was scraping gently upon the sandy bottom.

Between the refreshing water that he had drunk and the stimulus of renewed hope, Clayton found strength to stagger through the shallow water to the shore with a line made fast to the boat's bow. This he fastened to a small tree which grew at the top of a low bank, for the tide was at flood, and he feared that the boat might carry them all out to sea again with the ebb, since it was quite likely that it would be beyond his strength to get Jane Porter to the shore for several hours. Next he managed to stagger and crawl toward the near-by jungle, where he had seen evidences of profusion of tropical fruit. His former experience in the jungle of Tarzan of the Apes had taught him which of the many growing things were edible, and after nearly an hour of absence he returned to the beach with a little armful of food.

The rain had ceased, and the hot sun was beating down so mercilessly upon her that Jane Porter insisted on making an immediate attempt to gain the land. Still further invigorated by the food Clayton had brought, the three were able to reach the half shade of the small tree to which their boat was moored. Here, thoroughly exhausted, they threw themselves down to rest, sleeping until dark.

For a month they lived upon the beach in comparative safety. As their strength returned the two men constructed a rude shelter in the branches of a tree, high enough from the ground to insure safety from the larger beasts of prey. By day they gathered fruits and trapped small rodents; at night they lay cowering within their frail shelter while savage denizens of the jungle made hideous the hours of darkness.

They slept upon litters of jungle grasses, and for covering at night Jane Porter had only an old ulster that belonged to Clayton, the same garment that he had worn upon that memorable trip to the Wisconsin woods.

Clayton had erected a frail partition of boughs to divide their arboreal shelter into two rooms—one for the girl and the other for Monsieur Thuran and himself.

From the first the Russian had exhibited every trait of his true character—selfishness, boorishness, arrogance, cowardice, and lust. Twice had he and Clayton come to blows because of Thuran's attitude toward the girl. Clayton dared not leave her alone with him for an instant. The existence of the Englishman and his fiancee was one continual nightmare of horror, and yet they lived on in hope of ultimate rescue.

Jane Porter's thoughts often reverted to her other experience on this savage shore. Ah, if the invincible forest god of that dead past were but with them now. No longer would there be aught to fear from prowling beasts, or from the bestial Russian. She could not well refrain from comparing the scant protection afforded her by Clayton with what she might have expected had Tarzan of the Apes been for a single instant confronted by the sinister and menacing attitude of Monsieur Thuran. Once, when Clayton had gone to the little stream for water, and Thuran had spoken coarsely to her, she voiced her thoughts.

"It is well for you, Monsieur Thuran," she said, "that the poor Monsieur Tarzan who was lost from the ship that brought you and Miss Strong to Cape Town is not here now."

"You knew the pig?" asked Thuran, with a sneer.

"I knew the man," she replied. "The only real man, I think, that I have ever known."

There was something in her tone of voice that led the Russian to attribute to her a deeper feeling for his enemy than friendship, and he grasped at the suggestion to be further revenged upon the man whom he supposed dead by besmirching his memory to the girl.

"He was worse than a pig," he cried. "He was a poltroon and a coward. To save himself from the righteous wrath of the husband of a woman he had wronged, he perjured his soul in an attempt to place the blame entirely upon her. Not succeeding in this, he ran away from France to escape meeting the husband upon the field of honor. That is why he was on board the ship that bore Miss Strong and myself to Cape Town. I know whereof I speak, for the woman in the case is my sister. Something more I know that I have never told another—your brave Monsieur Tarzan leaped overboard in an agony of fear because I recognized him, and insisted that he make reparation to me the following morning—we could have fought with knives in my stateroom."

Jane Porter laughed. "You do not for a moment imagine that one who has known both Monsieur Tarzan and you could ever believe such an impossible tale?"

"Then why did he travel under an assumed name?" asked Monsieur Thuran.

"I do not believe you," she cried, but nevertheless the seed of suspicion was sown, for she knew that Hazel Strong had known her forest god only as John Caldwell, of London.

A scant five miles north of their rude shelter, all unknown to them, and practically as remote as though separated by thousands of miles of impenetrable jungle, lay the snug little cabin of Tarzan of the Apes. While farther up the coast, a few miles beyond the cabin, in crude but well-built shelters, lived a little party of eighteen souls—the occupants of the three boats from the *Lady Alice* from which Clayton's boat had become separated.

Over a smooth sea they had rowed to the mainland in less than three days. None of the horrors of shipwreck had been theirs, and though depressed by sorrow, and suffering from the shock of the catastrophe and the unaccustomed hardships of their new existence there was none much the worse for the experience.

All were buoyed by the hope that the fourth boat had been picked up, and that a thorough search of the coast would be quickly made. As all the firearms and ammunition on the yacht had been placed in Lord Tennington's boat, the party was well equipped for defense, and for hunting the larger game for food.

Professor Archimedes Q. Porter was their only immediate anxiety. Fully assured in his own mind that his daughter had been picked up by a passing steamer, he gave over the last vestige of apprehension concerning her welfare, and devoted his giant intellect solely to the consideration of those momentous and abstruse scientific problems which he considered the only proper food for thought in one of his erudition. His mind appeared blank to the influence of all extraneous matters.

"Never," said the exhausted Mr. Samuel T. Philander, to Lord Tennington, "never has Professor Porter been more difficult—er—I might say, impossible. Why, only this morning, after I had been forced to relinquish my surveillance for a brief half hour he was entirely missing upon my return. And, bless me, sir, where do you imagine I discovered him? A half mile out in the ocean, sir, in one of the lifeboats, rowing away for dear life. I do not know how he attained even that magnificent distance from shore, for he had but a single oar, with which he was blissfully rowing about in circles.

"When one of the sailors had taken me out to him in another boat the professor became quite indignant at my suggestion that we return at once to land. 'Why, Mr. Philander,' he said, 'I am surprised that you, sir, a man of letters yourself, should have the temerity so to interrupt the progress of science. I had about deduced from certain astronomic phenomena I have had under minute observation during the past several tropic nights an entirely new nebular hypothesis which will unquestionably startle the scientific world. I wish to consult a very excellent monograph on Laplace's hypothesis, which I understand is in a certain private collection in New York City. Your interference, Mr. Philander, will result in an irreparable delay, for I was just rowing over to obtain this pamphlet.' And it was with the greatest difficulty that I persuaded him to return to shore, without resorting to force," concluded Mr. Philander.

Miss Strong and her mother were very brave under the strain of almost constant apprehension of the attacks of savage beasts. Nor were they quite able to accept so readily as the others the theory that Jane, Clayton, and Monsieur Thuran had been picked up safely.

Jane Porter's Esmeralda was in a constant state of tears at the cruel fate which had separated her from her "po, li'le honey."

Lord Tennington's great-hearted good nature never deserted him for a moment. He was still the jovial host, seeking always for the comfort and pleasure of his guests. With the men of his yacht he remained the just but firm commander—there was never any more question in the jungle than there had been on board the *Lady Alice* as to who was the final authority in all questions of importance, and in all emergencies requiring cool and intelligent leadership.

Could this well-organized and comparatively secure party of castaways have seen the ragged, fear-haunted trio a few miles south of them they would scarcely have recognized in them the formerly immaculate members of the little company that had laughed and played upon the *Lady Alice*. Clayton and Monsieur Thuran were almost naked, so torn had their clothes been by the thorn bushes and tangled vegetation of the matted jungle through which they had been compelled to force their way in search of their ever more difficult food supply.

Jane Porter had of course not been subjected to these strenuous expeditions, but her apparel was, nevertheless, in a sad state of disrepair.

Clayton, for lack of any better occupation, had carefully saved the skin of every animal they had killed. By stretching them upon the stems of trees, and diligently scraping them, he had managed to save them in a fair condition, and now that his clothes were threatening to cover his nakedness no longer, he commenced to fashion a rude garment of them, using a sharp thorn for a needle, and bits of tough grass and animal tendons in lieu of thread.

The result when completed was a sleeveless garment which fell nearly to his knees. As it was made up of numerous small pelts of different species of rodents, it presented a rather strange and wonderful appearance, which, together with the vile stench which permeated it, rendered it anything other than a desirable addition to a wardrobe. But the time came when for the sake of decency he was compelled to don it, and even the misery of their condition could not prevent Jane Porter from laughing heartily at sight of him.

Later, Thuran also found it necessary to construct a similar primitive garment, so that, with their bare legs and heavily bearded faces, they looked not unlike reincarnations of two prehistoric progenitors of the human race. Thuran acted like one.

Nearly two months of this existence had passed when the first great calamity befell them. It was prefaced by an adventure which came near terminating abruptly the sufferings of two of them—terminating them in the grim and horrible manner of the jungle, forever.

Thuran, down with an attack of jungle fever, lay in the shelter among the branches of their tree of refuge. Clayton had been into the jungle a few hundred yards in search of food. As he returned Jane Porter walked to meet him. Behind the man, cunning and crafty, crept an old and mangy lion. For three days his ancient thews and sinews had proved insufficient for the task of providing his cavernous belly with meat. For months he had eaten less and less frequently, and farther and farther had he roamed from his accustomed haunts in search of easier prey. At last he had found nature's weakest and most defenseless creature—in a moment more Numa would dine.

Clayton, all unconscious of the lurking death behind him, strode out into the open toward Jane. He had reached her side, a hundred feet from the tangled edge of jungle when past his shoulder the girl saw the tawny head and the wicked yellow eyes as the grasses parted, and the huge beast, nose to ground, stepped softly into view.

So frozen with horror was she that she could utter no sound, but the fixed and terrified gaze of her fear-widened eyes spoke as plainly to Clayton as words. A quick glance behind him revealed the hopelessness of their situation. The lion was scarce thirty paces from them, and they were equally as far from the shelter. The man was armed with a stout stick—as efficacious against a hungry lion, he realized, as a toy pop-gun charged with a tethered cork.

Numa, ravenous with hunger, had long since learned the futility of roaring and moaning as he searched for prey, but now that it was as surely his as though already he had felt the soft flesh beneath his still mighty paw, he opened his huge jaws, and gave vent to his long-pent rage in a series of deafening roars that made the air tremble.

"Run, Jane!" cried Clayton. "Quick! Run for the shelter!" But her paralyzed muscles refused to respond, and she stood mute and rigid, staring with ghastly countenance at the living death creeping toward them.

Thuran, at the sound of that awful roar, had come to the opening of the shelter, and as he saw the tableau below him he hopped up and down, shrieking to them in Russian.

"Run! Run!" he cried. "Run, or I shall be left all alone in this horrible place," and then he broke down and commenced to weep. For a moment this new voice distracted the attention of the lion, who halted to cast an inquiring glance in the direction of the tree. Clayton could endure the strain no longer. Turning his back upon the beast, he buried his head in his arms and waited.

The girl looked at him in horror. Why did he not do something? If he must die, why not die like a man—bravely; beating at that terrible face with his puny stick, no matter how futile it might be. Would Tarzan of the Apes have done thus? Would he not at least have gone down to his death fighting heroically to the last?

Now the lion was crouching for the spring that would end their young lives beneath cruel, rending, yellow fangs. Jane Porter sank to her knees in prayer, closing her eyes to shut out the last hideous instant. Thuran, weak from fever, fainted.

Seconds dragged into minutes, long minutes into an eternity, and yet the beast did not spring. Clayton was almost unconscious from the prolonged agony of fright—his knees trembled—a moment more and he would collapse.

Jane Porter could endure it no longer. She opened her eyes. Could she be dreaming?

"William," she whispered; "look!"

Clayton mastered himself sufficiently to raise his head and turn toward the lion. An ejaculation of surprise burst from his lips. At their very feet the beast lay crumpled in death. A heavy war spear protruded from the tawny hide. It had entered the great back above the right shoulder, and, passing entirely through the body, had pierced the savage heart.

Jane Porter had risen to her feet; as Clayton turned back to her she staggered in weakness. He put out his arms to save her from falling, and then drew her close to him—pressing her head against his shoulder, he stooped to kiss her in thanksgiving.

Gently the girl pushed him away.

"Please do not do that, William," she said. "I have lived a thousand years in the past brief moments. I have learned in the face of death how to live. I do not wish to hurt you more than is necessary; but I can no longer bear to live out the impossible position I have attempted because of a false sense of loyalty to an impulsive promise I made you.

"The last few seconds of my life have taught me that it would be hideous to attempt further to deceive myself and you, or to entertain for an instant longer the possibility of ever becoming your wife, should we regain civilization."

"Why, Jane," he cried, "what do you mean? What has our providential rescue to do with altering your feelings toward me? You are but unstrung—tomorrow you will be yourself again."

"I am more nearly myself this minute than I have been for over a year," she replied. "The thing that has just happened has again forced to my memory the fact that the bravest man that ever lived honored me with his love. Until it was too late I did not realize that I returned it, and so I sent him away. He is dead now, and I shall never marry. I certainly could not wed another less brave than he without harboring constantly a feeling of contempt for the relative cowardice of my husband. Do you understand me?"

"Yes," he answered, with bowed head, his face mantling with the flush of shame.

And it was the next day that the great calamity befell.

THE TREASURE VAULTS OF OPAR

It was quite dark before La, the high priestess, returned to the Chamber of the Dead with food and drink for Tarzan. She bore no light, feeling with her hands along the crumbling walls until she gained the chamber. Through the stone grating above, a tropic moon served dimly to illuminate the interior.

Tarzan, crouching in the shadows at the far side of the room as the first sound of approaching footsteps reached him, came forth to meet the girl as he recognized that it was she.

"They are furious," were her first words. "Never before has a human sacrifice escaped the altar. Already fifty have gone forth to track you down. They have searched the temple—all save this single room."

"Why do they fear to come here?" he asked.

"It is the Chamber of the Dead. Here the dead return to worship. See this ancient altar? It is here that the dead sacrifice the living—if they find a victim here. That is the reason our people shun this chamber. Were one to enter he knows that the waiting dead would seize him for their sacrifice."

"But you?" he asked.

"I am high priestess—I alone am safe from the dead. It is I who at rare intervals bring them a human sacrifice from the world above. I alone may enter here in safety."

"Why have they not seized me?" he asked, humoring her grotesque belief.

She looked at him quizzically for a moment. Then she replied:

"It is the duty of a high priestess to instruct, to interpret—according to the creed that others, wiser than herself, have laid down; but there is nothing in the creed which says that she must believe. The more one knows of one's religion the less one believes—no one living knows more of mine than I."

"Then your only fear in aiding me to escape is that your fellow mortals may discover your duplicity?"

"That is all—the dead are dead; they cannot harm—or help. We must therefore depend entirely upon ourselves, and the sooner we act the better it will be. I had difficulty in eluding their vigilance but now in bringing you this morsel of food. To attempt to repeat the thing daily would be the height of folly. Come, let us see how far we may go toward liberty before I must return."

She led him back to the chamber beneath the altar room. Here she turned into one of the several corridors leading from it. In the darkness Tarzan could not see which one. For ten minutes they groped slowly along a winding passage, until at length they came to a closed door. Here he heard her fumbling with a key, and presently came the sound of a metal bolt grating against metal. The door swung in on scraping hinges, and they entered.

"You will be safe here until tomorrow night," she said.

Then she went out, and, closing the door, locked it behind her.

Where Tarzan stood it was dark as Erebus. Not even his trained eyes could penetrate the utter blackness. Cautiously he moved forward until his out-stretched hand touched a wall, then very slowly he traveled around the four walls of the chamber.

Apparently it was about twenty feet square. The floor was of concrete, the walls of the dry masonry that marked the method of construction above ground. Small pieces of granite of various sizes were ingeniously laid together without mortar to construct these ancient foundations.

The first time around the walls Tarzan thought he detected a strange phenomenon for a room with no windows but a single door. Again he crept carefully around close to the wall. No, he could not be mistaken! He paused before the center of the wall opposite the door. For a moment he stood quite motionless, then he moved a few feet to one side. Again he returned, only to move a few feet to the other side.

Once more he made the entire circuit of the room, feeling carefully every foot of the walls. Finally he stopped again before the particular section that had aroused his curiosity. There was no doubt of it! A distinct draft of fresh air was blowing into the chamber through the intersection of the masonry at that particular point—and nowhere else.

Tarzan tested several pieces of the granite which made up the wall at this spot, and finally was rewarded by finding one which lifted out readily. It was about ten inches wide, with a face some three by six inches showing within the chamber. One by one the ape-man lifted out similarly shaped stones. The wall at this point was constructed entirely, it seemed, of these almost perfect slabs. In a short time he had removed some dozen, when he reached in to test the next layer of masonry. To his surprise, he felt nothing behind the masonry he had removed as far as his long arm could reach.

It was a matter of but a few minutes to remove enough of the wall to permit his body to pass through the aperture. Directly ahead of him he thought he discerned a faint glow—scarcely more than a less impenetrable darkness. Cautiously he moved forward on hands and knees, until at about fifteen feet, or the average thickness of the foundation walls, the floor ended abruptly in a sudden drop. As far out as he could reach he felt nothing, nor could he find the bottom of the black abyss that yawned before him, though, clinging to the edge of the floor, he lowered his body into the darkness to its full length.

Finally it occurred to him to look up, and there above him he saw through a round opening a tiny circular patch of starry sky. Feeling up along the sides of the shaft as far as he could reach, the ape-man discovered that so much of the wall as he could feel converged toward the center of the shaft as it rose. This fact precluded possibility of escape in that direction.

As he sat speculating on the nature and uses of this strange passage and its terminal shaft, the moon topped the opening above, letting a flood of soft, silvery light into the shadowy place. Instantly the nature of the shaft became apparent to Tarzan, for far below him he saw the shimmering surface of water. He had come upon an ancient well—but what was the purpose of the connection between the well and the dungeon in which he had been hidden?

As the moon crossed the opening of the shaft its light flooded the whole interior, and then Tarzan saw directly across from him another opening in the opposite wall. He wondered if this might not be the mouth of a passage leading to possible escape. It would be worth investigating, at least, and this he determined to do.

Quickly returning to the wall he had demolished to explore what lay beyond it, he carried the stones into the passageway and replaced them from that side. The deep deposit of dust which he had noticed upon the blocks as he had first removed them from the wall had convinced him that even if the present occupants of the ancient pile had knowledge of this hidden passage they had made no use of it for perhaps generations.

The wall replaced, Tarzan turned to the shaft, which was some fifteen feet wide at this point. To leap across the intervening space was a small matter to the ape-man, and a moment later he was proceeding along a narrow tunnel, moving cautiously for fear of being precipitated into another shaft such as he had just crossed.

He had advanced some hundred feet when he came to a flight of steps leading downward into Stygian gloom. Some twenty feet below, the level floor of the tunnel recommenced, and shortly afterward his progress was stopped by a heavy wooden door which was secured by massive wooden bars upon the side of Tarzan's approach. This fact suggested to the ape-man that he might surely be in a passageway leading to the outer world, for the bolts, barring progress from the opposite side, tended to substantiate this hypothesis, unless it were merely a prison to which it led.

Along the tops of the bars were deep layers of dust—a further indication that the passage had lain long unused. As he pushed the massive obstacle aside, its great hinges shrieked out in weird protest against this unaccustomed disturbance. For a moment Tarzan paused to listen for any responsive note which might indicate that the unusual night noise had alarmed the inmates of the temple; but as he heard nothing he advanced beyond the doorway.

Carefully feeling about, he found himself within a large chamber, along the walls of which, and down the length of the floor, were piled many tiers of metal ingots of an odd though uniform shape. To his groping hands they felt not unlike double-headed bootjacks. The ingots were quite heavy, and but for the enormous number of them he would have been positive that they were gold; but the thought of the fabulous wealth these thousands of pounds of metal would have represented were they in reality gold, almost convinced him that they must be of some baser metal.

At the far end of the chamber he discovered another barred door, and again the bars upon the inside renewed the hope that he was traversing an ancient and forgotten passageway to liberty. Beyond the door the passage ran straight as a war spear, and it soon became evident to the ape-man that it had already led him beyond the outer walls of the temple. If he but knew the direction it was leading him! If toward the west, then he must also be beyond the city's outer walls.

With increasing hopes he forged ahead as rapidly as he dared, until at the end of half an hour he came to another flight of steps leading upward. At the bottom this flight was of concrete, but as he ascended his naked feet felt a sudden change in the substance they were treading. The steps of concrete had given place to steps of granite. Feeling with his hands, the ape-man discovered that these latter were evidently hewed from rock, for there was no crack to indicate a joint.

For a hundred feet the steps wound spirally up, until at a sudden turning Tarzan came into a narrow cleft between two rocky walls. Above him shone the starry sky, and before him a steep incline replaced the steps that had terminated at its foot. Up this pathway Tarzan hastened, and at its upper end came out upon the rough top of a huge granite bowlder.

A mile away lay the ruined city of Opar, its domes and turrets bathed in the soft light of the equatorial moon. Tarzan dropped his eyes to the ingot he had brought away with him. For a moment he examined it by the moon's bright rays, then he raised his head to look out upon the ancient piles of crumbling grandeur in the distance.

"Opar," he mused, "Opar, the enchanted city of a dead and forgotten past. The city of the beauties and the beasts. City of horrors and death; but—city of fabulous riches." The ingot was of virgin gold.

The bowlder on which Tarzan found himself lay well out in the plain between the city and the distant cliffs he and his black warriors had scaled the morning previous. To descend its rough and precipitous face was a task of infinite labor and considerable peril even to the ape-man; but at last he felt the soft soil of the valley beneath his feet, and without a backward glance at Opar he turned his face toward the guardian cliffs, and at a rapid trot set off across the valley.

The sun was just rising as he gained the summit of the flat mountain at the valley's western boundary. Far beneath him he saw smoke arising above the tree-tops of the forest at the base of the foothills.

"Man," he murmured. "And there were fifty who went forth to track me down. Can it be they?"

Swiftly he descended the face of the cliff, and, dropping into a narrow ravine which led down to the far forest, he hastened onward in the direction of the smoke. Striking the forest's edge about a quarter of a mile from the point at which the slender column arose into the still air, he took to the trees. Cautiously he approached until there suddenly burst upon his view a rude *boma*, in the center of which, squatted about their tiny fires, sat his fifty black Waziri. He called to them in their own tongue:

"Arise, my children, and greet thy king!"

With exclamations of surprise and fear the warriors leaped to their feet, scarcely knowing whether to flee or not. Then Tarzan dropped lightly from an overhanging branch into their midst. When they realized that it was indeed their chief in the flesh, and no materialized spirit, they went mad with joy.

"We were cowards, oh, Waziri," cried Busuli. "We ran away and left you to your fate; but when our panic was over we swore to return and save you, or at least take revenge upon your murderers. We were but now preparing to scale the heights once more and cross the desolate valley to the terrible city."

"Have you seen fifty frightful men pass down from the cliffs into this forest, my children?" asked Tarzan.

"Yes, Waziri," replied Busuli. "They passed us late yesterday, as we were about to turn back after you. They had no woodcraft. We heard them coming for a mile before we saw them, and as we had other business in hand we withdrew into the forest and let them pass. They were waddling rapidly along upon short legs, and now and then one would go upon all fours like Bolgani, the gorilla. They were indeed fifty frightful men, Waziri."

When Tarzan had related his adventures and told them of the yellow metal he had found, not one demurred when he outlined a plan to return by night and bring away what they could carry of the vast treasure; and so it was that as dusk fell across the desolate valley of Opar fifty ebon warriors trailed at a smart trot over the dry and dusty ground toward the giant bowlder that loomed before the city.

If it had seemed a difficult task to descend the face of the bowlder, Tarzan soon found that it would be next to impossible to get his fifty warriors to the summit. Finally the feat was accomplished by dint of herculean efforts upon the part of the ape-man. Ten spears were fastened end to end, and with one end of this remarkable chain attached to his waist, Tarzan at last succeeded in reaching the summit.

Once there, he drew up one of his blacks, and in this way the entire party was finally landed in safety upon the bowlder's top. Immediately Tarzan led them to the treasure chamber, where to each was allotted a load of two ingots, for each about eighty pounds.

By midnight the entire party stood once more at the foot of the bowlder, but with their heavy loads it was mid-forenoon ere they reached the summit of the cliffs. From there on the homeward journey was slow, as these proud fighting men were unaccustomed to the duties of porters. But they bore their burdens uncomplainingly, and at the end of thirty days entered their own country.

Here, instead of continuing on toward the northwest and their village, Tarzan guided them almost directly west, until on the morning of the thirty-third day he bade them break camp and return to their own village, leaving the gold where they had stacked it the previous night.

"And you, Waziri?" they asked.

"I shall remain here for a few days, my children," he replied. "Now hasten back to thy wives and children."

When they had gone Tarzan gathered up two of the ingots and, springing into a tree, ran lightly above the tangled and impenetrable mass of undergrowth for a couple of hundred yards, to emerge suddenly upon a circular clearing about which the giants of the jungle forest towered like a guardian host. In the center of this natural amphitheater, was a little flat-topped mound of hard earth.

Hundreds of times before had Tarzan been to this secluded spot, which was so densely surrounded by thorn bushes and tangled vines and creepers of huge girth that not even Sheeta, the leopard, could worm his sinuous way within, nor Tantor, with his giant strength, force the barriers which protected the council chamber of the great apes from all but the harmless denizens of the savage jungle.

Fifty trips Tarzan made before he had deposited all the ingots within the precincts of the amphitheater. Then from the hollow of an ancient, lightning-blasted tree he produced the very spade with which he had uncovered the chest of Professor Archimedes Q. Porter which he had once, apelike, buried in this selfsame spot. With this he dug a long trench, into which he laid the fortune that his blacks had carried from the forgotten treasure vaults of the city of Opar.

That night he slept within the amphitheater, and early the next morning set out to revisit his cabin before returning to his Waziri. Finding things as he had left them, he went forth into the jungle to hunt, intending to bring his prey to the cabin where he might feast in comfort, spending the night upon a comfortable couch.

For five miles toward the south he roamed, toward the banks of a fair-sized river that flowed into the sea about six miles from his cabin. He had gone inland about half a mile when there came suddenly to his trained nostrils the one scent that sets the whole savage jungle aquiver—Tarzan smelled man.

The wind was blowing off the ocean, so Tarzan knew that the authors of the scent were west of him. Mixed with the man scent was the scent of Numa. Man and lion. "I had better hasten," thought the ape-man, for he had recognized the scent of whites. "Numa may be a-hunting."

When he came through the trees to the edge of the jungle he saw a woman kneeling in prayer, and before her stood a wild, primitive-looking white man, his face buried in his arms. Behind the man a mangy lion was advancing slowly toward this easy prey. The man's face was averted; the woman's bowed in prayer. He could not see the features of either.

Already Numa was about to spring. There was not a second to spare. Tarzan could not even unsling his bow and fit an arrow in time to send one of his deadly poisoned shafts into the yellow hide. He was too far away to reach the beast in time with his knife. There was but a single hope—a lone alternative. And with the quickness of thought the ape-man acted.

A brawny arm flew back—for the briefest fraction of an instant a huge spear poised above the giant's shoulder—and then the mighty arm shot out, and swift death tore through the intervening leaves to bury itself in the heart of the leaping lion. Without a sound he rolled over at the very feet of his intended victims—dead.

For a moment neither the man nor the woman moved. Then the latter opened her eyes to look with wonder upon the dead beast behind her companion. As that beautiful head went up Tarzan of the Apes gave a gasp of incredulous astonishment. Was he mad? It could not be the woman he loved! But, indeed, it was none other.

And the woman rose, and the man took her in his arms to kiss her, and of a sudden the ape-man saw red through a bloody mist of murder, and the old scar upon his forehead burned scarlet against his brown hide.

There was a terrible expression upon his savage face as he fitted a poisoned shaft to his bow. An ugly light gleamed in those gray eyes as he sighted full at the back of the unsuspecting man beneath him.

For an instant he glanced along the polished shaft, drawing the bowstring far back, that the arrow might pierce through the heart for which it was aimed.

But he did not release the fatal messenger. Slowly the point of the arrow drooped; the scar upon the brown forehead faded; the bowstring relaxed; and Tarzan of the Apes, with bowed head, turned sadly into the jungle toward the village of the Waziri.

THE FIFTY FRIGHTFUL MEN

For several long minutes Jane Porter and William Cecil Clayton stood silently looking at the dead body of the beast whose prey they had so narrowly escaped becoming.

The girl was the first to speak again after her outbreak of impulsive avowal.

"Who could it have been?" she whispered.

"God knows!" was the man's only reply.

"If it is a friend, why does he not show himself?" continued Jane. "Wouldn't it be well to call out to him, and at least thank him?"

Mechanically Clayton did her bidding, but there was no response.

Jane Porter shuddered. "The mysterious jungle," she murmured. "The terrible jungle. It renders even the manifestations of friendship terrifying."

"We had best return to the shelter," said Clayton. "You will be at least a little safer there. I am no protection whatever," he added bitterly.

"Do not say that, William," she hastened to urge, acutely sorry for the wound her words had caused. "You have done the best you could. You have been noble, and self-sacrificing, and brave. It is no fault of yours that you are not a superman. There is only one other man I have ever known who could have done more than you. My words were ill chosen in the excitement of the reaction—I did not wish to wound you. All that I wish is that we may both understand once and for all that I can never marry you—that such a marriage would be wicked."

"I think I understand," he replied. "Let us not speak of it again—at least until we are back in civilization."

The next day Thuran was worse. Almost constantly he was in a state of delirium. They could do nothing to relieve him, nor was Clayton over-anxious to attempt anything. On the girl's account he feared the Russian—in the bottom of his heart he hoped the man would die. The thought that something might befall him that would leave her entirely at the mercy of this beast caused him greater anxiety than the probability that almost certain death awaited her should she be left entirely alone upon the outskirts of the cruel forest.

The Englishman had extracted the heavy spear from the body of the lion, so that when he went into the forest to hunt that morning he had a feeling of much greater security than at any time since they had been cast upon the savage shore. The result was that he penetrated farther from the shelter than ever before.

To escape as far as possible from the mad ravings of the fever-stricken Russian, Jane Porter had descended from the shelter to the foot of the tree—she dared not venture farther. Here, beside the crude ladder Clayton had constructed for her, she sat looking out to sea, in the always surviving hope that a vessel might be sighted.

Her back was toward the jungle, and so she did not see the grasses part, or the savage face that peered from between. Little, bloodshot, close-set eyes scanned her intently, roving from time to time about the open beach for indications of the presence of others than herself. Presently another head appeared, and then another and another. The man in the shelter commenced to rave again, and the heads disappeared as silently and as suddenly as they had come. But soon they were thrust forth once more, as the girl gave no sign of perturbation at the continued wailing of the man above.

One by one grotesque forms emerged from the jungle to creep stealthily upon the unsuspecting woman. A faint rustling of the grasses attracted her attention. She turned, and at the sight that confronted her staggered to her feet with a little shriek of fear. Then they closed upon her with a rush. Lifting her bodily in his long, gorilla-like arms, one of the creatures turned and bore her into the jungle. A filthy paw covered her mouth to stifle her screams. Added to the weeks of torture she had already undergone, the shock was more than she could withstand. Shattered nerves collapsed, and she lost consciousness. When she regained her senses she found herself in the thick of the primeval forest. It was night. A huge fire burned brightly in the little clearing in which she lay. About it squatted fifty frightful men. Their heads and faces were covered with matted hair. Their long arms rested upon the bent knees of their short, crooked legs. They were gnawing, like beasts, upon unclean food. A pot boiled upon the edge of the fire, and out of it one of the creatures would occasionally drag a hunk of meat with a sharpened stick.

When they discovered that their captive had regained consciousness, a piece of this repulsive stew was tossed to her from the foul hand of a nearby feaster. It rolled close to her side, but she only closed her eyes as a qualm of nausea surged through her.

For many days they traveled through the dense forest. The girl, footsore and exhausted, was half dragged, half pushed through the long, hot, tedious days. Occasionally, when she would stumble and fall, she was cuffed and kicked by the nearest of the frightful men. Long before they reached their journey's end her shoes had been discarded—the soles entirely gone. Her clothes were torn to mere shreds and tatters, and through the pitiful rags her once white and tender skin showed raw and bleeding from contact with the thousand pitiless thorns and brambles through which she had been dragged.

The last two days of the journey found her in such utter exhaustion that no amount of kicking and abuse could force her to her poor, bleeding feet. Outraged nature had reached the limit of endurance, and the girl was physically powerless to raise herself even to her knees.

As the beasts surrounded her, chattering threateningly the while they goaded her with their cudgels and beat and kicked her with their fists and feet, she lay with closed eyes, praying for the merciful death that she knew alone could give her surcease from suffering; but it did not come, and presently the fifty frightful men realized that their victim was no longer able to walk, and so they picked her up and carried her the balance of the journey.

Late one afternoon she saw the ruined walls of a mighty city looming before them, but so weak and sick was she that it inspired not the faintest shadow of interest. Wherever they were bearing her, there could be but one end to her captivity among these fierce half brutes.

At last they passed through two great walls and came to the ruined city within. Into a crumbling pile they bore her, and here she was surrounded by hundreds more of the same creatures that had brought her; but among them were females who looked less horrible. At sight of them the first faint hope that she had entertained came to mitigate her misery. But it was short-lived, for the women offered her no sympathy, though, on the other hand, neither did they abuse her.

After she had been inspected to the entire satisfaction of the inmates of the building she was borne to a dark chamber in the vaults beneath, and here upon the bare floor she was left, with a metal bowl of water and another of food.

For a week she saw only some of the women whose duty it was to bring her food and water. Slowly her strength was returning—soon she would be in fit condition to offer as a sacrifice to The Flaming God. Fortunate indeed it was that she could not know the fate for which she was destined.

As Tarzan of the Apes moved slowly through the jungle after casting the spear that saved Clayton and Jane Porter from the fangs of Numa, his mind was filled with all the sorrow that belongs to a freshly opened heart wound.

He was glad that he had stayed his hand in time to prevent the consummation of the thing that in the first mad wave of jealous wrath he had contemplated. Only the fraction of a second had stood between Clayton and death at the hands of the ape-man. In the short moment that had elapsed after he had recognized the girl and her companion and the relaxing of the taut muscles that held the poisoned shaft directed at the Englishman's heart, Tarzan had been swayed by the swift and savage impulses of brute life.

He had seen the woman he craved—his woman—his mate—in the arms of another. There had been but one course open to him, according to the fierce jungle code that guided him in this other existence; but just before it had become too late the softer sentiments of his inherent chivalry had risen above the flaming fires of his passion and saved him. A thousand times he gave thanks that they had triumphed before his fingers had released that polished arrow.

As he contemplated his return to the Waziri the idea became repugnant. He did not wish to see a human being again. At least he would range alone through the jungle for a time, until the sharp edge of his sorrow had become blunted. Like his fellow beasts, he preferred to suffer in silence and alone.

That night he slept again in the amphitheater of the apes, and for several days he hunted from there, returning at night. On the afternoon of the third day he returned early. He had lain stretched upon the soft grass of the circular clearing for but a few moments when he heard far to the south a familiar sound. It was the passing through the jungle of a band of great apes—he could not mistake that. For several minutes he lay listening. They were coming in the direction of the amphitheater.

Tarzan arose lazily and stretched himself. His keen ears followed every movement of the advancing tribe. They were upwind, and presently he caught their scent, though he had not needed this added evidence to assure him that he was right.

As they came closer to the amphitheater Tarzan of the Apes melted into the branches upon the other side of the arena. There he waited to inspect the newcomers. Nor had he long to wait.

Presently a fierce, hairy face appeared among the lower branches opposite him. The cruel little eyes took in the clearing at a glance, then there was a chattered report returned to those behind. Tarzan could hear the words. The scout was telling the other members of the tribe that the coast was clear and that they might enter the amphitheater in safety.

First the leader dropped lightly upon the soft carpet of the grassy floor, and then, one by one, nearly a hundred anthropoids followed him. There were the huge adults and several young. A few nursing babes clung close to the shaggy necks of their savage mothers.

Tarzan recognized many members of the tribe. It was the same into which he had come as a tiny babe. Many of the adults had been little apes during his boyhood. He had frolicked and played about this very jungle with them during their brief childhood. He wondered if they would remember him—the memory of some apes is not overlong, and two years may be an eternity to them.

From the talk which he overheard he learned that they had come to choose a new king—their late chief had fallen a hundred feet beneath a broken limb to an untimely end.

Tarzan walked to the end of an overhanging limb in plain view of them. The quick eyes of a female caught sight of him first. With a barking guttural she called the attention of the others. Several huge bulls stood erect to get a better view of the intruder. With bared fangs and bristling necks they advanced slowly toward him, with deep-throated, ominous growls.

"Karnath, I am Tarzan of the Apes," said the ape-man in the vernacular of the tribe. "You remember me. Together we teased Numa when we were still little apes, throwing sticks and nuts at him from the safety of high branches."

The brute he had addressed stopped with a look of half-comprehending, dull wonderment upon his savage face.

"And Magor," continued Tarzan, addressing another, "do you not recall your former king—he who slew the mighty Kerchak? Look at me! Am I not the same Tarzan—mighty hunter—invincible fighter—that you all knew for many seasons?"

The apes all crowded forward now, but more in curiosity than threatening. They muttered among themselves for a few moments.

"What do you want among us now?" asked Karnath.

"Only peace," answered the ape-man.

Again the apes conferred. At length Karnath spoke again.

"Come in peace, then, Tarzan of the Apes," he said.

And so Tarzan of the Apes dropped lightly to the turf into the midst of the fierce and hideous horde—he had completed the cycle of evolution, and had returned to be once again a brute among brutes.

There were no greetings such as would have taken place among men after a separation of two years. The majority of the apes went on about the little activities that the advent of the ape-man had interrupted, paying no further attention to him than as though he had not been gone from the tribe at all.

One or two young bulls who had not been old enough to remember him sidled up on all fours to sniff at him, and one bared his fangs and growled threateningly—he wished to put Tarzan immediately into his proper place. Had Tarzan backed off, growling, the young bull would quite probably have been satisfied, but always after Tarzan's station among his fellow apes would have been beneath that of the bull which had made him step aside.

But Tarzan of the Apes did not back off. Instead, he swung his giant palm with all the force of his mighty muscles, and, catching the young bull alongside the head, sent him sprawling across the turf. The ape was up and at him again in a second, and this time they closed with tearing fingers and rending fangs—or at least that had been the intention of the young bull; but scarcely had they gone down, growling and snapping, than the ape-man's fingers found the throat of his antagonist.

Presently the young bull ceased to struggle, and lay quite still. Then Tarzan released his hold and arose—he did not wish to kill, only to teach the young ape, and others who might be watching, that Tarzan of the Apes was still master.

The lesson served its purpose—the young apes kept out of his way, as young apes should when their betters were about, and the old bulls made no attempt to encroach upon his prerogatives. For several days the she-apes with young remained suspicious of him, and when he ventured too near rushed upon him with wide mouths and hideous roars. Then Tarzan discreetly skipped out of harm's way, for that also is a custom among the apes—only mad bulls will attack a mother. But after a while even they became accustomed to him.

He hunted with them as in days gone by, and when they found that his superior reason guided him to the best food sources, and that his cunning rope ensnared toothsome game that they seldom if ever tasted, they came again to look up to him as they had in the past after he had become their king. And so it was that before they left the amphitheater to return to their wanderings they had once more chosen him as their leader.

The ape-man felt quite contented with his new lot. He was not happy—that he never could be again, but he was at least as far from everything that might remind him of his past misery as he could be. Long since he had given up every intention of returning to civilization, and now he had decided to see no more his black friends of the Waziri. He had foresworn humanity forever. He had started life an ape—as an ape he would die.

He could not, however, erase from his memory the fact that the woman he loved was within a short journey of the stamping-ground of his tribe; nor could he banish the haunting fear that she might be constantly in danger. That she was illy protected he had seen in the brief instant that had witnessed Clayton's inefficiency. The more Tarzan thought of it, the more keenly his conscience pricked him.

Finally he came to loathe himself for permitting his own selfish sorrow and jealousy to stand between Jane Porter and safety. As the days passed the thing preyed more and more upon his mind, and he had about determined to return to the coast and place himself on guard over Jane Porter and Clayton, when news reached him that altered all his plans and sent him dashing madly toward the east in reckless disregard of accident and death.

Before Tarzan had returned to the tribe, a certain young bull, not being able to secure a mate from among his own people, had, according to custom, fared forth through the wild jungle, like some knight-errant of old, to win a fair lady from some neighboring community.

He had but just returned with his bride, and was narrating his adventures quickly before he should forget them. Among other things he told of seeing a great tribe of strange-looking apes.

"They were all hairy-faced bulls but one," he said, "and that one was a she, lighter in color even than this stranger," and he chucked a thumb at Tarzan.

The ape-man was all attention in an instant. He asked questions as rapidly as the slow-witted anthropoid could answer them.

"Were the bulls short, with crooked legs?"

"They were."

"Did they wear the skins of Numa and Sheeta about their loins, and carry sticks and knives?"

"They did."

"And were there many yellow rings about their arms and legs?"

"Yes."

"And the she one—was she small and slender, and very white?"

"Yes."

"Did she seem to be one of the tribe, or was she a prisoner?"

"They dragged her along—sometimes by an arm—sometimes by the long hair that grew upon her head; and always they kicked and beat her. Oh, but it was great fun to watch them."

"God!" muttered Tarzan.

"Where were they when you saw them, and which way were they going?" continued the ape-man.

"They were beside the second water back there," and he pointed to the south. "When they passed me they were going toward the morning, upward along the edge of the water."

"When was this?" asked Tarzan.

"Half a moon since."

Without another word the ape-man sprang into the trees and fled like a disembodied spirit eastward in the direction of the forgotten city of Opar.

HOW TARZAN CAME AGAIN TO OPAR

When Clayton returned to the shelter and found Jane Porter was missing, he became frantic with fear and grief. He found Monsieur Thuran quite rational, the fever having left him with the surprising suddenness which is one of its peculiarities. The Russian, weak and exhausted, still lay upon his bed of grasses within the shelter.

When Clayton asked him about the girl he seemed surprised to know that she was not there.

"I have heard nothing unusual," he said. "But then I have been unconscious much of the time."

Had it not been for the man's very evident weakness, Clayton should have suspected him of having sinister knowledge of the girl's whereabouts; but he could see that Thuran lacked sufficient vitality even to descend, unaided, from the shelter. He could not, in his present physical condition, have harmed the girl, nor could he have climbed the rude ladder back to the shelter.

Until dark the Englishman searched the nearby jungle for a trace of the missing one or a sign of the trail of her abductor. But though the spoor left by the fifty frightful men, unversed in woodcraft as they were, would have been as plain to the densest denizen of the jungle as a city street to the Englishman, yet he crossed and recrossed it twenty times without observing the slightest indication that many men had passed that way but a few short hours since.

As he searched, Clayton continued to call the girl's name aloud, but the only result of this was to attract Numa, the lion. Fortunately the man saw the shadowy form worming its way toward him in time to climb into the branches of a tree before the beast was close enough to reach him. This put an end to his search for the balance of the afternoon, as the lion paced back and forth beneath him until dark.

Even after the beast had left, Clayton dared not descend into the awful blackness beneath him, and so he spent a terrifying and hideous night in the tree. The next morning he returned to the beach, relinquishing the last hope of succoring Jane Porter.

During the week that followed, Monsieur Thuran rapidly regained his strength, lying in the shelter while Clayton hunted food for both. The men never spoke except as necessity demanded. Clayton now occupied the section of the shelter which had been reserved for Jane Porter, and only saw the Russian when he took food or water to him, or performed the other kindly offices which common humanity required.

When Thuran was again able to descend in search of food, Clayton was stricken with fever. For days he lay tossing in delirium and suffering, but not once did the Russian come near him. Food the Englishman could not have eaten, but his craving for water amounted practically to torture. Between the recurrent attacks of delirium, weak though he was, he managed to reach the brook once a day and fill a tiny can that had been among the few appointments of the lifeboat.

Thuran watched him on these occasions with an expression of malignant pleasure—he seemed really to enjoy the suffering of the man who, despite the just contempt in which he held him, had ministered to him to the best of his ability while he lay suffering the same agonies. At last Clayton became so weak that he was no longer able to descend from the shelter. For a day he suffered for water without appealing to the Russian, but finally, unable to endure it longer, he asked Thuran to fetch him a drink. The Russian came to the entrance to Clayton's room, a dish of water in his hand. A nasty grin contorted his features.

"Here is water," he said. "But first let me remind you that you maligned me before the girl—that you kept her to yourself, and would not share her with me—"

Clayton interrupted him. "Stop!" he cried. Stop! What manner of cur are you that you traduce the character of a good woman whom we believe dead! God! I was a fool ever to let you live—you are not fit to live even in this vile land."

"Here is your water," said the Russian. "All you will get," and he raised the basin to his lips and drank; what was left he threw out upon the ground below. Then he turned and left the sick man.

Clayton rolled over, and, burying his face in his arms, gave up the battle.

The next day Thuran determined to set out toward the north along the coast, for he knew that eventually he must come to the habitations of civilized men—at least he could be no worse off than he was here, and, furthermore, the ravings of the dying Englishman were getting on his nerves. So he stole Clayton's spear and set off upon his journey. He would have killed the sick man before he left had it not occurred to him that it would really have been a kindness to do so.

That same day he came to a little cabin by the beach, and his heart filled with renewed hope as he saw this evidence of the proximity of civilization, for he thought it but the outpost of a nearby settlement. Had he known to whom it belonged, and that its owner was at that very moment but a few miles inland, Nikolas Rokoff would have fled the place as he would a pestilence. But he did not know, and so he remained for a few days to enjoy the security and comparative comforts of the cabin. Then he took up his northward journey once more.

In Lord Tennington's camp preparations were going forward to build permanent quarters, and then to send out an expedition of a few men to the north in search of relief.

As the days had passed without bringing the longed-for succor, hope that Jane Porter, Clayton, and Monsieur Thuran had been rescued began to die. No one spoke of the matter longer to Professor Porter, and he was so immersed in his scientific dreaming that he was not aware of the elapse of time.

Occasionally he would remark that within a few days they should certainly see a steamer drop anchor off their shore, and that then they should all be reunited happily. Sometimes he spoke of it as a train, and wondered if it were being delayed by snowstorms.

"If I didn't know the dear old fellow so well by now," Tennington remarked to Miss Strong, "I should be quite certain that he was—er—not quite right, don't you know." "If it were not so pathetic it would be ridiculous," said the girl, sadly. "I, who have known him all my life, know how he worships Jane; but to others it must seem that he is perfectly callous to her fate. It is only that he is so absolutely impractical that he cannot conceive of so real a thing as death unless nearly certain proof of it is thrust upon him."

"You'd never guess what he was about yesterday," continued Tennington. "I was coming in alone from a little hunt when I met him walking rapidly along the game trail that I was following back to camp. His hands were clasped beneath the tails of his long black coat, and his top hat was set firmly down upon his head, as with eyes bent upon the ground he hastened on, probably to some sudden death had I not intercepted him.

"'Why, where in the world are you bound, professor?' I asked him. 'I am going into town, Lord Tennington,' he said, as seriously as possible, 'to complain to the postmaster about the rural free delivery service we are suffering from here. Why, sir, I haven't had a piece of mail in weeks. There should be several letters for me from Jane. The matter must be reported to Washington at once.'

"And would you believe it, Miss Strong," continued Tennington, "I had the very deuce of a job to convince the old fellow that there was not only no rural free delivery, but no town, and that he was not even on the same continent as Washington, nor in the same hemisphere.

"When he did realize he commenced to worry about his daughter—I think it is the first time that he really has appreciated our position here, or the fact that Miss Porter may not have been rescued."

"I hate to think about it," said the girl, "and yet I can think of nothing else than the absent members of our party."

"Let us hope for the best," replied Tennington. "You yourself have set us each a splendid example of bravery, for in a way your loss has been the greatest."

"Yes," she replied; "I could have loved Jane Porter no more had she been my own sister."

Tennington did not show the surprise he felt. That was not at all what he meant. He had been much with this fair daughter of Maryland since the wreck of the *Lady Alice*, and it had recently come to him that he had grown much more fond of her than would prove good for the peace of his mind, for he recalled almost constantly now the confidence which Monsieur Thuran had imparted to him that he and Miss Strong were engaged. He wondered if, after all, Thuran had been quite accurate in his statement. He had never seen the slightest indication on the girl's part of more than ordinary friendship.

"And then in Monsieur Thuran's loss, if they are lost, you would suffer a severe bereavement," he ventured.

She looked up at him quickly. "Monsieur Thuran had become a very dear friend," she said. "I liked him very much, though I have known him but a short time."

"Then you were not engaged to marry him?" he blurted out. "Heavens, no!" she cried. "I did not care for him at all in that way."

There was something that Lord Tennington wanted to say to Hazel Strong—he wanted very badly to say it, and to say it at once; but somehow the words stuck in his throat. He started lamely a couple of times, cleared his throat, became red in the face, and finally ended by remarking that he hoped the cabins would be finished before the rainy season commenced.

But, though he did not know it, he had conveyed to the girl the very message he intended, and it left her happy—happier than she had ever before been in all her life.

Just then further conversation was interrupted by the sight of a strange and terrible-looking figure which emerged from the jungle just south of the camp. Tennington and the girl saw it at the same time. The Englishman reached for his revolver, but when the half-naked, bearded creature called his name aloud and came running toward them he dropped his hand and advanced to meet it.

None would have recognized in the filthy, emaciated creature, covered by a single garment of small skins, the immaculate Monsieur Thuran the party had last seen upon the deck of the *Lady Alice*.

Before the other members of the little community were apprised of his presence Tennington and Miss Strong questioned him regarding the other occupants of the missing boat.

"They are all dead," replied Thuran. "The three sailors died before we made land. Miss Porter was carried off into the jungle by some wild animal while I was lying delirious with fever. Clayton died of the same fever but a few days since. And to think that all this time we have been separated by but a few miles—scarcely a day's march. It is terrible!"

How long Jane Porter lay in the darkness of the vault beneath the temple in the ancient city of Opar she did not know. For a time she was delirious with fever, but after this passed she commenced slowly to regain her strength. Every day the woman who brought her food beckoned to her to arise, but for many days the girl could only shake her head to indicate that she was too weak.

But eventually she was able to gain her feet, and then to stagger a few steps by supporting herself with one hand upon the wall. Her captors now watched her with increasing interest. The day was approaching, and the victim was gaining in strength.

Presently the day came, and a young woman whom Jane Porter had not seen before came with several others to her dungeon. Here some sort of ceremony was performed—that it was of a religious nature the girl was sure, and so she took new heart, and rejoiced that she had fallen among people upon whom the refining and softening influences of religion evidently had fallen. They would treat her humanely—of that she was now quite sure.

And so when they led her from her dungeon, through long, dark corridors, and up a flight of concrete steps to a brilliant courtyard, she went willingly, even gladly—for was she not among the servants of God? It might be, of course, that their interpretation of the supreme being differed from her own, but that they owned a god was sufficient evidence to her that they were kind and good.

But when she saw a stone altar in the center of the courtyard, and dark-brown stains upon it and the nearby concrete of the floor, she began to wonder and to doubt. And as they stooped and bound her ankles, and secured her wrists behind her, her doubts were turned to fear. A moment later, as she was lifted and placed supine across the altar's top, hope left her entirely, and she trembled in an agony of fright.

During the grotesque dance of the votaries which followed, she lay frozen in horror, nor did she require the sight of the thin blade in the hands of the high priestess as it rose slowly above her to enlighten her further as to her doom.

As the hand began its descent, Jane Porter closed her eyes and sent up a silent prayer to the Maker she was so soon to face—then she succumbed to the strain upon her tired nerves, and swooned.

Day and night Tarzan of the Apes raced through the primeval forest toward the ruined city in which he was positive the woman he loved lay either a prisoner or dead.

In a day and a night he covered the same distance that the fifty frightful men had taken the better part of a week to traverse, for Tarzan of the Apes traveled along the middle terrace high above the tangled obstacles that impede progress upon the ground.

The story the young bull ape had told made it clear to him that the girl captive had been Jane Porter, for there was not another small white "she" in all the jungle. The "bulls" he had recognized from the ape's crude description as the grotesque parodies upon humanity who inhabit the ruins of Opar. And the girl's fate he could picture as plainly as though he were an eyewitness to it. When they would lay her across that trim altar he could not guess, but that her dear, frail body would eventually find its way there he was confident.

But, finally, after what seemed long ages to the impatient ape-man, he topped the barrier cliffs that hemmed the desolate valley, and below him lay the grim and awful ruins of the now hideous city of Opar. At a rapid trot he started across the dry and dusty, bowlder-strewn ground toward the goal of his desires.

Would he be in time to rescue? He hoped against hope. At least he could be revenged, and in his wrath it seemed to him that he was equal to the task of wiping out the entire population of that terrible city. It was nearly noon when he reached the great bowlder at the top of which terminated the secret passage to the pits beneath the city. Like a cat he scaled the precipitous sides of the frowning granite *kopje*. A moment later he was running through the darkness of the long, straight tunnel that led to the treasure vault. Through this he passed, then on and on until at last he came to the well-like shaft upon the opposite side of which lay the dungeon with the false wall.

As he paused a moment upon the brink of the well a faint sound came to him through the opening above. His quick ears caught and translated it—it was the dance of death that preceded a sacrifice, and the singsong ritual of the high priestess. He could even recognize the woman's voice. Could it be that the ceremony marked the very thing he had so hastened to prevent? A wave of horror swept over him. Was he, after all, to be just a moment too late? Like a frightened deer he leaped across the narrow chasm to the continuation of the passage beyond. At the false wall he tore like one possessed to demolish the barrier that confronted him—with giant muscles he forced the opening, thrusting his head and shoulders through the first small hole he made, and carrying the balance of the wall with him, to clatter resoundingly upon the cement floor of the dungeon.

With a single leap he cleared the length of the chamber and threw himself against the ancient door. But here he stopped. The mighty bars upon the other side were proof even against such muscles as his. It needed but a moment's effort to convince him of the futility of endeavoring to force that impregnable barrier. There was but one other way, and that led back through the long tunnels to the bowlder a mile beyond the city's walls, and then back across the open as he had come to the city first with his Waziri.

He realized that to retrace his steps and enter the city from above ground would mean that he would be too late to save the girl, if it were indeed she who lay upon the sacrificial altar above him. But there seemed no other way, and so he turned and ran swiftly back into the passageway beyond the broken wall. At the well he heard again the monotonous voice of the high priestess, and, as he glanced aloft, the opening, twenty feet above, seemed so near that he was tempted to leap for it in a mad endeavor to reach the inner courtyard that lay so near.

If he could but get one end of his grass rope caught upon some projection at the top of that tantalizing aperture! In the instant's pause and thought an idea occurred to him. He would attempt it. Turning back to the tumbled wall, he seized one of the large, flat slabs that had composed it. Hastily making one end of his rope fast to the piece of granite, he returned to the shaft, and, coiling the balance of the rope on the floor beside him, the ape-man took the heavy slab in both hands, and, swinging it several times to get the distance and the direction fixed, he let the weight fly up at a slight angle, so that, instead of falling straight back into the shaft again, it grazed the far edge, tumbling over into the court beyond.

Tarzan dragged for a moment upon the slack end of the rope until he felt that the stone was lodged with fair security at the shaft's top, then he swung out over the black depths beneath. The moment his full weight came upon the rope he felt it slip from above. He waited there in awful suspense as it dropped in little jerks, inch by inch. The stone was being dragged up the outside of the masonry surrounding the top of the shaft—would it catch at the very edge, or would his weight drag it over to fall upon him as he hurtled into the unknown depths below?

THROUGH THE FOREST PRIMEVAL

For a brief, sickening moment Tarzan felt the slipping of the rope to which he clung, and heard the scraping of the block of stone against the masonry above.

Then of a sudden the rope was still—the stone had caught at the very edge. Gingerly the ape-man clambered up the frail rope. In a moment his head was above the edge of the shaft. The court was empty. The inhabitants of Opar were viewing the sacrifice. Tarzan could hear the voice of La from the nearby sacrificial court. The dance had ceased. It must be almost time for the knife to fall; but even as he thought these things he was running rapidly toward the sound of the high priestess' voice.

Fate guided him to the very doorway of the great roofless chamber. Between him and the altar was the long row of priests and priestesses, awaiting with their golden cups the spilling of the warm blood of their victim. La's hand was descending slowly toward the bosom of the frail, quiet figure that lay stretched upon the hard stone. Tarzan gave a gasp that was almost a sob as he recognized the features of the girl he loved. And then the scar upon his forehead turned to a flaming band of scarlet, a red mist floated before his eyes, and, with the awful roar of the bull ape gone mad, he sprang like a huge lion into the midst of the votaries.

Seizing a cudgel from the nearest priest, he laid about him like a veritable demon as he forged his rapid way toward the altar. The hand of La had paused at the first noise of interruption. When she saw who the author of it was she went white. She had never been able to fathom the secret of the strange white man's escape from the dungeon in which she had locked him. She had not intended that he should ever leave Opar, for she had looked upon his giant frame and handsome face with the eyes of a woman and not those of a priestess.

In her clever mind she had concocted a story of wonderful revelation from the lips of the flaming god himself, in which she had been ordered to receive this white stranger as a messenger from him to his people on earth. That would satisfy the people of Opar, she knew. The man would be satisfied, she felt quite sure, to remain and be her husband rather than to return to the sacrificial altar.

But when she had gone to explain her plan to him he had disappeared, though the door had been tightly locked as she had left it. And now he had returned—materialized from thin air—and was killing her priests as though they had been sheep. For the moment she forgot her victim, and before she could gather her wits together again the huge white man was standing before her, the woman who had lain upon the altar in his arms.

"One side, La," he cried. "You saved me once, and so I would not harm you; but do not interfere or attempt to follow, or I shall have to kill you also."

As he spoke he stepped past her toward the entrance to the subterranean vaults.

"Who is she?" asked the high priestess, pointing at the unconscious woman.

"She is mine," said Tarzan of the Apes.

For a moment the girl of Opar stood wide-eyed and staring. Then a look of hopeless misery suffused her eyes—tears welled into them, and with a little cry she sank to the cold floor, just as a swarm of frightful men dashed past her to leap upon the ape-man.

But Tarzan of the Apes was not there when they reached out to seize him. With a light bound he had disappeared into the passage leading to the pits below, and when his pursuers came more cautiously after they found the chamber empty, they but laughed and jabbered to one another, for they knew that there was no exit from the pits other than the one through which he had entered. If he came out at all he must come this way, and they would wait and watch for him above.

And so Tarzan of the Apes, carrying the unconscious Jane Porter, came through the pits of Opar beneath the temple of The Flaming God without pursuit. But when the men of Opar had talked further about the matter, they recalled to mind that this very man had escaped once before into the pits, and, though they had watched the entrance he had not come forth; and yet today he had come upon them from the outside. They would again send fifty men out into the valley to find and capture this desecrater of their temple.

After Tarzan reached the shaft beyond the broken wall, he felt so positive of the successful issue of his flight that he stopped to replace the tumbled stones, for he was not anxious that any of the inmates should discover this forgotten passage, and through it come upon the treasure chamber. It was in his mind to return again to Opar and bear away a still greater fortune than he had already buried in the amphitheater of the apes.

On through the passageways he trotted, past the first door and through the treasure vault; past the second door and into the long, straight tunnel that led to the lofty hidden exit beyond the city. Jane Porter was still unconscious.

At the crest of the great bowlder he halted to cast a backward glance toward the city. Coming across the plain he saw a band of the hideous men of Opar. For a moment he hesitated. Should he descend and make a race for the distant cliffs, or should he hide here until night? And then a glance at the girl's white face determined him. He could not keep her here and permit her enemies to get between them and liberty. For aught he knew they might have been followed through the tunnels, and to have foes before and behind would result in almost certain capture, since he could not fight his way through the enemy burdened as he was with the unconscious girl.

To descend the steep face of the bowlder with Jane Porter was no easy task, but by binding her across his shoulders with the grass rope he succeeded in reaching the ground in safety before the Oparians arrived at the great rock. As the descent had been made upon the side away from the city, the searching party saw nothing of it, nor did they dream that their prey was so close before them.

By keeping the *kopje* between them and their pursuers, Tarzan of the Apes managed to cover nearly a mile before the men of Opar rounded the granite sentinel and saw the fugitive before them. With loud cries of savage delight, they broke into a mad run, thinking doubtless that they would soon overhaul the burdened runner; but they both underestimated the powers of the ape-man and overestimated the possibilities of their own short, crooked legs.

By maintaining an easy trot, Tarzan kept the distance between them always the same. Occasionally he would glance at the face so near his own. Had it not been for the faint beating of the heart pressed so close against his own, he would not have known that she was alive, so white and drawn was the poor, tired face.

And thus they came to the flat-topped mountain and the barrier cliffs. During the last mile Tarzan had let himself out, running like a deer that he might have ample time to descend the face of the cliffs before the Oparians could reach the summit and hurl rocks down upon them. And so it was that he was half a mile down the mountainside ere the fierce little men came panting to the edge.

With cries of rage and disappointment they ranged along the cliff top shaking their cudgels, and dancing up and down in a perfect passion of anger. But this time they did not pursue beyond the boundary of their own country. Whether it was because they recalled the futility of their former long and irksome search, or after witnessing the ease with which the ape-man swung along before them, and the last burst of speed, they realized the utter hopelessness of further pursuit, it is difficult to say; but as Tarzan reached the woods that began at the base of the foothills which skirted the barrier cliffs they turned their faces once more toward Opar.

Just within the forest's edge, where he could yet watch the cliff tops, Tarzan laid his burden upon the grass, and going to the near-by rivulet brought water with which he bathed her face and hands; but even this did not revive her, and, greatly worried, he gathered the girl into his strong arms once more and hurried on toward the west.

Late in the afternoon Jane Porter regained consciousness. She did not open her eyes at once—she was trying to recall the scenes that she had last witnessed. Ah, she remembered now. The altar, the terrible priestess, the descending knife. She gave a little shudder, for she thought that either this was death or that the knife had buried itself in her heart and she was experiencing the brief delirium preceding death. And when finally she mustered courage to open her eyes, the sight that met them confirmed her fears, for she saw that she was being borne through a leafy paradise in the arms of her dead love. "If this be death," she murmured, "thank God that I am dead."

"You spoke, Jane!" cried Tarzan. "You are regaining consciousness!"

"Yes, Tarzan of the Apes," she replied, and for the first time in months a smile of peace and happiness lighted her face.

"Thank God!" cried the ape-man, coming to the ground in a little grassy clearing beside the stream. "I was in time, after all."

"In time? What do you mean?" she questioned.

"In time to save you from death upon the altar, dear," he replied. "Do you not remember?" "Save me from death?" she asked, in a puzzled tone. "Are we not both dead, my Tarzan?"

He had placed her upon the grass by now, her back resting against the stem of a huge tree. At her question he stepped back where he could the better see her face.

"Dead!" he repeated, and then he laughed. "You are not, Jane; and if you will return to the city of Opar and ask them who dwell there they will tell you that I was not dead a few short hours ago. No, dear, we are both very much alive."

"But both Hazel and Monsieur Thuran told me that you had fallen into the ocean many miles from land," she urged, as though trying to convince him that he must indeed be dead. "They said that there was no question but that it must have been you, and less that you could have survived or been picked up."

"How can I convince you that I am no spirit?" he asked, with a laugh. "It was I whom the delightful Monsieur Thuran pushed overboard, but I did not drown—I will tell you all about it after a while—and here I am very much the same wild man you first knew, Jane Porter."

The girl rose slowly to her feet and came toward him.

"I cannot even yet believe it," she murmured. "It cannot be that such happiness can be true after all the hideous things that I have passed through these awful months since the *Lady Alice* went down."

She came close to him and laid a hand, soft and trembling, upon his arm.

"It must be that I am dreaming, and that I shall awaken in a moment to see that awful knife descending toward my heart—kiss me, dear, just once before I lose my dream forever."

Tarzan of the Apes needed no second invitation. He took the girl he loved in his strong arms, and kissed her not once, but a hundred times, until she lay there panting for breath; yet when he stopped she put her arms about his neck and drew his lips down to hers once more.

"Am I alive and a reality, or am I but a dream?" he asked.

"If you are not alive, my man," she answered, "I pray that I may die thus before I awaken to the terrible realities of my last waking moments."

For a while both were silent—gazing into each others' eyes as though each still questioned the reality of the wonderful happiness that had come to them. The past, with all its hideous disappointments and horrors, was forgotten—the future did not belong to them; but the present—ah, it was theirs; none could take it from them. It was the girl who first broke the sweet silence.

"Where are we going, dear?" she asked. "What are we going to do?"

"Where would you like best to go?" he asked. "What would you like best to do?"

"To go where you go, my man; to do whatever seems best to you," she answered.

"But Clayton?" he asked. For a moment he had forgotten that there existed upon the earth other than they two. "We have forgotten your husband."

"I am not married, Tarzan of the Apes," she cried. "Nor am I longer promised in marriage. The day before those awful creatures captured me I spoke to Mr. Clayton of my love for you, and he understood then that I could not keep the wicked promise that I had made. It was after we had been miraculously saved from an attacking lion." She paused suddenly and looked up at him, a questioning light in her eyes. "Tarzan of the Apes," she cried, "it was you who did that thing? It could have been no other."

He dropped his eyes, for he was ashamed.

"How could you have gone away and left me?" she cried reproachfully.

"Don't, Jane!" he pleaded. "Please don't! You cannot know how I have suffered since for the cruelty of that act, or how I suffered then, first in jealous rage, and then in bitter resentment against the fate that I had not deserved. I went back to the apes after that, Jane, intending never again to see a human being." He told her then of his life since he had returned to the jungle—of how he had dropped like a plummet from a civilized Parisian to a savage Waziri warrior, and from there back to the brute that he had been raised.

She asked him many questions, and at last fearfully of the things that Monsieur Thuran had told her—of the woman in Paris. He narrated every detail of his civilized life to her, omitting nothing, for he felt no shame, since his heart always had been true to her. When he had finished he sat looking at her, as though waiting for her judgment, and his sentence.

"I knew that he was not speaking the truth," she said. "Oh, what a horrible creature he is!"

"You are not angry with me, then?" he asked.

And her reply, though apparently most irrelevant, was truly feminine.

"Is Olga de Coude very beautiful?" she asked.

And Tarzan laughed and kissed her again. "Not one-tenth so beautiful as you, dear," he said.

She gave a contented little sigh, and let her head rest against his shoulder. He knew that he was forgiven.

That night Tarzan built a snug little bower high among the swaying branches of a giant tree, and there the tired girl slept, while in a crotch beneath her the ape-man curled, ready, even in sleep, to protect her.

It took them many days to make the long journey to the coast. Where the way was easy they walked hand in hand beneath the arching boughs of the mighty forest, as might in a far-gone past have walked their primeval forbears. When the underbrush was tangled he took her in his great arms, and bore her lightly through the trees, and the days were all too short, for they were very happy. Had it not been for their anxiety to reach and succor Clayton they would have drawn out the sweet pleasure of that wonderful journey indefinitely.

On the last day before they reached the coast Tarzan caught the scent of men ahead of them—the scent of black men. He told the girl, and cautioned her to maintain silence. "There are few friends in the jungle," he remarked dryly.

In half an hour they came stealthily upon a small party of black warriors filing toward the west. As Tarzan saw them he gave a cry of delight—it was a band of his own Waziri. Busuli was there, and others who had accompanied him to Opar. At sight of him they danced and cried out in exuberant joy. For weeks they had been searching for him, they told him.

The blacks exhibited considerable wonderment at the presence of the white girl with him, and when they found that she was to be his woman they vied with one another to do her honor. With the happy Waziri laughing and dancing about them they came to the rude shelter by the shore.

There was no sign of life, and no response to their calls. Tarzan clambered quickly to the interior of the little tree hut, only to emerge a moment later with an empty tin. Throwing it down to Busuli, he told him to fetch water, and then he beckoned Jane Porter to come up.

Together they leaned over the emaciated thing that once had been an English nobleman. Tears came to the girl's eyes as she saw the poor, sunken cheeks and hollow eyes, and the lines of suffering upon the once young and handsome face.

"He still lives," said Tarzan. "We will do all that can be done for him, but I fear that we are too late."

When Busuli had brought the water Tarzan forced a few drops between the cracked and swollen lips. He wetted the hot forehead and bathed the pitiful limbs.

Presently Clayton opened his eyes. A faint, shadowy smile lighted his countenance as he saw the girl leaning over him. At sight of Tarzan the expression changed to one of wonderment.

"It's all right, old fellow," said the ape-man. "We've found you in time. Everything will be all right now, and we'll have you on your feet again before you know it."

The Englishman shook his head weakly. "It's too late," he whispered. "But it's just as well. I'd rather die."

"Where is Monsieur Thuran?" asked the girl.

"He left me after the fever got bad. He is a devil. When I begged for the water that I was too weak to get he drank before me, threw the rest out, and laughed in my face." At the thought of it the man was suddenly animated by a spark of vitality. He raised himself upon one elbow. "Yes," he almost shouted; "I will live. I will live long enough to find and kill that beast!" But the brief effort left him weaker than before, and he sank back again upon the rotting grasses that, with his old ulster, had been the bed of Jane Porter.

"Don't worry about Thuran," said Tarzan of the Apes, laying a reassuring hand on Clayton's forehead. "He belongs to me, and I shall get him in the end, never fear."

For a long time Clayton lay very still. Several times Tarzan had to put his ear quite close to the sunken chest to catch the faint beating of the wornout heart. Toward evening he aroused again for a brief moment.

"Jane," he whispered. The girl bent her head closer to catch the faint message. "I have wronged you—and him," he nodded weakly toward the ape-man. "I loved you so—it is a poor excuse to offer for injuring you; but I could not bear to think of giving you up. I do not ask your forgiveness. I only wish to do now the thing I should have done over a year ago." He fumbled in the pocket of the ulster beneath him for something that he had discovered there while he lay between the paroxysms of fever. Presently he found it—a crumpled bit of yellow paper. He handed it to the girl, and as she took it his arm fell limply across his chest, his head dropped back, and with a little gasp he stiffened and was still. Then Tarzan of the Apes drew a fold of the ulster across the upturned face.

For a moment they remained kneeling there, the girl's lips moving in silent prayer, and as they rose and stood on either side of the now peaceful form, tears came to the ape-man's eyes, for through the anguish that his own heart had suffered he had learned compassion for the suffering of others.

Through her own tears the girl read the message upon the bit of faded yellow paper, and as she read her eyes went very wide. Twice she read those startling words before she could fully comprehend their meaning.

Finger prints prove you Greystoke. Congratulations.
D'ARNOT.

She handed the paper to Tarzan. "And he has known it all this time," she said, "and did not tell you?"

"I knew it first, Jane," replied the man. "I did not know that he knew it at all. I must have dropped this message that night in the waiting room. It was there that I received it."

"And afterward you told us that your mother was a she-ape, and that you had never known your father?" she asked incredulously.

"The title and the estates meant nothing to me without you, dear," he replied. "And if I had taken them away from him I should have been robbing the woman I love—don't you understand, Jane?" It was as though he attempted to excuse a fault.

She extended her arms toward him across the body of the dead man, and took his hands in hers.

"And I would have thrown away a love like that!" she said.

THE PASSING OF THE APE-MAN

The next morning they set out upon the short journey to Tarzan's cabin. Four Waziri bore the body of the dead Englishman. It had been the ape-man's suggestion that Clayton be buried beside the former Lord Greystoke near the edge of the jungle against the cabin that the older man had built.

Jane Porter was glad that it was to be so, and in her heart of hearts she wondered at the marvelous fineness of character of this wondrous man, who, though raised by brutes and among brutes, had the true chivalry and tenderness which only associates with the refinements of the highest civilization.

They had proceeded some three miles of the five that had separated them from Tarzan's own beach when the Waziri who were ahead stopped suddenly, pointing in amazement at a strange figure approaching them along the beach. It was a man with a shiny silk hat, who walked slowly with bent head, and hands clasped behind him underneath the tails of his long, black coat.

At sight of him Jane Porter uttered a little cry of surprise and joy, and ran quickly ahead to meet him. At the sound of her voice the old man looked up, and when he saw who it was confronting him he, too, cried out in relief and happiness. As Professor Archimedes Q. Porter folded his daughter in his arms tears streamed down his seamed old face, and it was several minutes before he could control himself sufficiently to speak.

When a moment later he recognized Tarzan it was with difficulty that they could convince him that his sorrow had not unbalanced his mind, for with the other members of the party he had been so thoroughly convinced that the ape-man was dead it was a problem to reconcile the conviction with the very lifelike appearance of Jane's "forest god." The old man was deeply touched at the news of Clayton's death.

"I cannot understand it," he said. "Monsieur Thuran assured us that Clayton passed away many days ago."

"Thuran is with you?" asked Tarzan.

"Yes; he but recently found us and led us to your cabin. We were camped but a short distance north of it. Bless me, but he will be delighted to see you both."

"And surprised," commented Tarzan.

A short time later the strange party came to the clearing in which stood the ape-man's cabin. It was filled with people coming and going, and almost the first whom Tarzan saw was D'Arnot.

"Paul!" he cried. "In the name of sanity what are you doing here? Or are we all insane?"

It was quickly explained, however, as were many other seemingly strange things. D'Arnot's ship had been cruising along the coast, on patrol duty, when at the lieutenant's suggestion they had anchored off the little landlocked harbor to have another look at the cabin and the jungle in which many of the officers and men had taken part in exciting adventures two years before. On landing they had found Lord Tennington's party, and arrangements were being made to take them all on board the following morning, and carry them back to civilization.

Hazel Strong and her mother, Esmeralda, and Mr. Samuel T. Philander were almost overcome by happiness at Jane Porter's safe return. Her escape seemed to them little short of miraculous, and it was the consensus of opinion that it could have been achieved by no other man than Tarzan of the Apes. They loaded the uncomfortable ape-man with eulogies and attentions until he wished himself back in the amphitheater of the apes.

All were interested in his savage Waziri, and many were the gifts the black men received from these friends of their king, but when they learned that he might sail away from them upon the great canoe that lay at anchor a mile off shore they became very sad.

As yet the newcomers had seen nothing of Lord Tennington and Monsieur Thuran. They had gone out for fresh meat early in the day, and had not yet returned.

"How surprised this man, whose name you say is Rokoff, will be to see you," said Jane Porter to Tarzan.

"His surprise will be short-lived," replied the ape-man grimly, and there was that in his tone that made her look up into his face in alarm. What she read there evidently confirmed her fears, for she put her hand upon his arm, and pleaded with him to leave the Russian to the laws of France.

"In the heart of the jungle, dear," she said, "with no other form of right or justice to appeal to other than your own mighty muscles, you would be warranted in executing upon this man the sentence he deserves; but with the strong arm of a civilized government at your disposal it would be murder to kill him now. Even your friends would have to submit to your arrest, or if you resisted it would plunge us all into misery and unhappiness again. I cannot bear to lose you again, my Tarzan. Promise me that you will but turn him over to Captain Dufranne, and let the law take its course—the beast is not worth risking our happiness for."

He saw the wisdom of her appeal, and promised. A half hour later Rokoff and Tennington emerged from the jungle. They were walking side by side. Tennington was the first to note the presence of strangers in the camp. He saw the black warriors palavering with the sailors from the cruiser, and then he saw a lithe, brown giant talking with Lieutenant D'Arnot and Captain Dufranne.

"Who is that, I wonder," said Tennington to Rokoff, and as the Russian raised his eyes and met those of the ape-man full upon him, he staggered and went white.

"*Sapristi!*" he cried, and before Tennington realized what he intended he had thrown his gun to his shoulder, and aiming point-blank at Tarzan pulled the trigger. But the Englishman was close to him—so close that his hand reached the leveled barrel a fraction of a second before the hammer fell upon the cartridge, and the bullet that was intended for Tarzan's heart whirred harmlessly above his head.

Before the Russian could fire again the ape-man was upon him and had wrested the firearm from his grasp. Captain Dufranne, Lieutenant D'Arnot, and a dozen sailors had rushed up at the sound of the shot, and now Tarzan turned the Russian over to them without a word. He had explained the matter to the French commander before Rokoff arrived, and the officer gave immediate orders to place the Russian in irons and confine him on board the cruiser.

Just before the guard escorted the prisoner into the small boat that was to transport him to his temporary prison Tarzan asked permission to search him, and to his delight found the stolen papers concealed upon his person.

The shot had brought Jane Porter and the others from the cabin, and a moment after the excitement had died down she greeted the surprised Lord Tennington. Tarzan joined them after he had taken the papers from Rokoff, and, as he approached, Jane Porter introduced him to Tennington.

"John Clayton, Lord Greystoke, my lord," she said.

The Englishman looked his astonishment in spite of his most herculean efforts to appear courteous, and it required many repetitions of the strange story of the ape-man as told by himself, Jane Porter, and Lieutenant D'Arnot to convince Lord Tennington that they were not all quite mad.

At sunset they buried William Cecil Clayton beside the jungle graves of his uncle and his aunt, the former Lord and Lady Greystoke. And it was at Tarzan's request that three volleys were fired over the last resting place of "a brave man, who met his death bravely."

Professor Porter, who in his younger days had been ordained a minister, conducted the simple services for the dead. About the grave, with bowed heads, stood as strange a company of mourners as the sun ever looked down upon. There were French officers and sailors, two English lords, Americans, and a score of savage African braves.

Following the funeral Tarzan asked Captain Dufranne to delay the sailing of the cruiser a couple of days while he went inland a few miles to fetch his "belongings," and the officer gladly granted the favor.

Late the next afternoon Tarzan and his Waziri returned with the first load of "belongings," and when the party saw the ancient ingots of virgin gold they swarmed upon the ape-man with a thousand questions; but he was smilingly obdurate to their appeals—he declined to give them the slightest clew as to the source of his immense treasure. "There are a thousand that I left behind," he explained, "for every one that I brought away, and when these are spent I may wish to return for more."

The next day he returned to camp with the balance of his ingots, and when they were stored on board the cruiser Captain Dufranne said he felt like the commander of an old-time Spanish galleon returning from the treasure cities of the Aztecs. "I don't know what minute my crew will cut my throat, and take over the ship," he added.

The next morning, as they were preparing to embark upon the cruiser, Tarzan ventured a suggestion to Jane Porter.

"Wild beasts are supposed to be devoid of sentiment," he said, "but nevertheless I should like to be married in the cabin where I was born, beside the graves of my mother and my father, and surrounded by the savage jungle that always has been my home."

"Would it be quite regular, dear?" she asked. "For if it would I know of no other place in which I should rather be married to my forest god than beneath the shade of his primeval forest."

And when they spoke of it to the others they were assured that it would be quite regular, and a most splendid termination of a remarkable romance. So the entire party assembled within the little cabin and about the door to witness the second ceremony that Professor Porter was to solemnize within three days.

D'Arnot was to be best man, and Hazel Strong bridesmaid, until Tennington upset all the arrangements by another of his marvelous "ideas."

"If Mrs. Strong is agreeable," he said, taking the bridesmaid's hand in his, "Hazel and I think it would be ripping to make it a double wedding."

The next day they sailed, and as the cruiser steamed slowly out to sea a tall man, immaculate in white flannel, and a graceful girl leaned against her rail to watch the receding shore line upon which danced twenty naked, black warriors of the Waziri, waving their war spears above their savage heads, and shouting farewells to their departing king.

"I should hate to think that I am looking upon the jungle for the last time, dear," he said, "were it not that I know that I am going to a new world of happiness with you forever," and, bending down, Tarzan of the Apes kissed his mate upon her lips.

THE BEASTS OF TARZAN

KIDNAPPED

"The entire affair is shrouded in mystery," said D'Arnot. "I have it on the best of authority that neither the police nor the special agents of the general staff have the faintest conception of how it was accomplished. All they know, all that anyone knows, is that Nikolas Rokoff has escaped."

John Clayton, Lord Greystoke—he who had been "Tarzan of the Apes"—sat in silence in the apartments of his friend, Lieutenant Paul D'Arnot, in Paris, gazing meditatively at the toe of his immaculate boot.

His mind revolved many memories, recalled by the escape of his arch-enemy from the French military prison to which he had been sentenced for life upon the testimony of the ape-man.

He thought of the lengths to which Rokoff had once gone to compass his death, and he realized that what the man had already done would doubtless be as nothing by comparison with what he would wish and plot to do now that he was again free.

Tarzan had recently brought his wife and infant son to London to escape the discomforts and dangers of the rainy season upon their vast estate in Uziri—the land of the savage Waziri warriors whose broad African domains the ape-man had once ruled.

He had run across the Channel for a brief visit with his old friend, but the news of the Russian's escape had already cast a shadow upon his outing, so that though he had but just arrived he was already contemplating an immediate return to London.

"It is not that I fear for myself, Paul," he said at last. "Many times in the past have I thwarted Rokoff's designs upon my life; but now there are others to consider. Unless I misjudge the man, he would more quickly strike at me through my wife or son than directly at me, for he doubtless realizes that in no other way could he inflict greater anguish upon me. I must go back to them at once, and remain with them until Rokoff is recaptured—or dead."

As these two talked in Paris, two other men were talking together in a little cottage upon the outskirts of London. Both were dark, sinister-looking men.

One was bearded, but the other, whose face wore the pallor of long confinement within doors, had but a few days' growth of black beard upon his face. It was he who was speaking.

"You must needs shave off that beard of yours, Alexis," he said to his companion. "With it he would recognize you on the instant. We must separate here in the hour, and when we meet again upon the deck of the *Kincaid*, let us hope that we shall have with us two honoured guests who little anticipate the pleasant voyage we have planned for them.

"In two hours I should be upon my way to Dover with one of them, and by tomorrow night, if you follow my instructions carefully, you should arrive with the other, provided, of course, that he returns to London as quickly as I presume he will.

"There should be both profit and pleasure as well as other good things to reward our efforts, my dear Alexis. Thanks to the stupidity of the French, they have gone to such lengths to conceal the fact of my escape for these many days that I have had ample opportunity to work out every detail of our little adventure so carefully that there is little chance of the slightest hitch occurring to mar our prospects. And now good-bye, and good luck!"

Three hours later a messenger mounted the steps to the apartment of Lieutenant D'Arnot.

"A telegram for Lord Greystoke," he said to the servant who answered his summons. "Is he here?"

The man answered in the affirmative, and, signing for the message, carried it within to Tarzan, who was already preparing to depart for London.

Tarzan tore open the envelope, and as he read his face went white.

"Read it, Paul," he said, handing the slip of paper to D'Arnot. "It has come already."

The Frenchman took the telegram and read:

"Jack stolen from the garden through complicity of new servant. Come at once.—JANE."

As Tarzan leaped from the roadster that had met him at the station and ran up the steps to his London town house he was met at the door by a dry-eyed but almost frantic woman.

Quickly Jane Porter Clayton narrated all that she had been able to learn of the theft of the boy.

The baby's nurse had been wheeling him in the sunshine on the walk before the house when a closed taxicab drew up at the corner of the street. The woman had paid but passing attention to the vehicle, merely noting that it discharged no passenger, but stood at the kerb with the motor running as though waiting for a fare from the residence before which it had stopped.

Almost immediately the new houseman, Carl, had come running from the Greystoke house, saying that the girl's mistress wished to speak with her for a moment, and that she was to leave little Jack in his care until she returned.

The woman said that she entertained not the slightest suspicion of the man's motives until she had reached the doorway of the house, when it occurred to her to warn him not to turn the carriage so as to permit the sun to shine in the baby's eyes.

As she turned about to call this to him she was somewhat surprised to see that he was wheeling the carriage rapidly toward the corner, and at the same time she saw the door of the taxicab open and a swarthy face framed for a moment in the aperture.

Intuitively, the danger to the child flashed upon her, and with a shriek she dashed down the steps and up the walk toward the taxicab, into which Carl was now handing the baby to the swarthy one within.

Just before she reached the vehicle, Carl leaped in beside his confederate, slamming the door behind him. At the same time the chauffeur attempted to start his machine, but it was evident that something had gone wrong, as though the gears refused to mesh, and the delay caused by this, while he pushed the lever into reverse and backed the car a few inches before again attempting to go ahead, gave the nurse time to reach the side of the taxicab.

Leaping to the running-board, she had attempted to snatch the baby from the arms of the stranger, and here, screaming and fighting, she had clung to her position even after the taxicab had got under way; nor was it until the machine had passed the Greystoke residence at good speed that Carl, with a heavy blow to her face, had succeeded in knocking her to the pavement.

Her screams had attracted servants and members of the families from residences near by, as well as from the Greystoke home. Lady Greystoke had witnessed the girl's brave battle, and had herself tried to reach the rapidly passing vehicle, but had been too late.

That was all that anyone knew, nor did Lady Greystoke dream of the possible identity of the man at the bottom of the plot until her husband told her of the escape of Nikolas Rokoff from the French prison where they had hoped he was permanently confined.

As Tarzan and his wife stood planning the wisest course to pursue, the telephone bell rang in the library at their right. Tarzan quickly answered the call in person.

"Lord Greystoke?" asked a man's voice at the other end of the line.

"Yes."

"Your son has been stolen," continued the voice, "and I alone may help you to recover him. I am conversant with the plot of those who took him. In fact, I was a party to it, and was to share in the reward, but now they are trying to ditch me, and to be quits with them I will aid you to recover him on condition that you will not prosecute me for my part in the crime. What do you say?"

"If you lead me to where my son is hidden," replied the ape-man, "you need fear nothing from me."

"Good," replied the other. "But you must come alone to meet me, for it is enough that I must trust you. I cannot take the chance of permitting others to learn my identity."

"Where and when may I meet you?" asked Tarzan.

The other gave the name and location of a public-house on the water-front at Dover—a place frequented by sailors.

"Come," he concluded, "about ten o'clock tonight. It would do no good to arrive earlier. Your son will be safe enough in the meantime, and I can then lead you secretly to where he is hidden. But be sure to come alone, and under no circumstances notify Scotland Yard, for I know you well and shall be watching for you.

"Should any other accompany you, or should I see suspicious characters who might be agents of the police, I shall not meet you, and your last chance of recovering your son will be gone."

Without more words the man rang off.

Tarzan repeated the gist of the conversation to his wife. She begged to be allowed to accompany him, but he insisted that it might result in the man's carrying out his threat of refusing to aid them if Tarzan did not come alone, and so they parted, he to hasten to Dover, and she, ostensibly to wait at home until he should notify her of the outcome of his mission.

Little did either dream of what both were destined to pass through before they should meet again, or the far-distant—but why anticipate?

For ten minutes after the ape-man had left her Jane Clayton walked restlessly back and forth across the silken rugs of the library. Her mother heart ached, bereft of its firstborn. Her mind was in an anguish of hopes and fears.

Though her judgment told her that all would be well were her Tarzan to go alone in accordance with the mysterious stranger's summons, her intuition would not permit her to lay aside suspicion of the gravest dangers to both her husband and her son.

The more she thought of the matter, the more convinced she became that the recent telephone message might be but a ruse to keep them inactive until the boy was safely hidden away or spirited out of England. Or it might be that it had been simply a bait to lure Tarzan into the hands of the implacable Rokoff.

With the lodgment of this thought she stopped in wide-eyed terror. Instantly it became a conviction. She glanced at the great clock ticking the minutes in the corner of the library.

It was too late to catch the Dover train that Tarzan was to take. There was another, later, however, that would bring her to the Channel port in time to reach the address the stranger had given her husband before the appointed hour.

Summoning her maid and chauffeur, she issued instructions rapidly. Ten minutes later she was being whisked through the crowded streets toward the railway station.

It was nine-forty-five that night that Tarzan entered the squalid "pub" on the water-front in Dover. As he passed into the evil-smelling room a muffled figure brushed past him toward the street.

"Come, my lord!" whispered the stranger.

The ape-man wheeled about and followed the other into the ill-lit alley, which custom had dignified with the title of thoroughfare. Once outside, the fellow led the way into the darkness, nearer a wharf, where high-piled bales, boxes, and casks cast dense shadows. Here he halted.

"Where is the boy?" asked Greystoke.

"On that small steamer whose lights you can just see yonder," replied the other.

In the gloom Tarzan was trying to peer into the features of his companion, but he did not recognize the man as one whom he had ever before seen. Had he guessed that his guide was Alexis Paulvitch he would have realized that naught but treachery lay in the man's heart, and that danger lurked in the path of every move.

"He is unguarded now," continued the Russian. "Those who took him feel perfectly safe from detection, and with the exception of a couple of members of the crew, whom I have furnished with enough gin to silence them effectually for hours, there is none aboard the *Kincaid*. We can go aboard, get the child, and return without the slightest fear."

Tarzan nodded.

"Let's be about it, then," he said.

His guide led him to a small boat moored alongside the wharf. The two men entered, and Paulvitch pulled rapidly toward the steamer. The black smoke issuing from her funnel did not at the time make any suggestion to Tarzan's mind. All his thoughts were occupied with the hope that in a few moments he would again have his little son in his arms.

At the steamer's side they found a monkey-ladder dangling close above them, and up this the two men crept stealthily. Once on deck they hastened aft to where the Russian pointed to a hatch.

"The boy is hidden there," he said. "You had better go down after him, as there is less chance that he will cry in fright than should he find himself in the arms of a stranger. I will stand on guard here."

So anxious was Tarzan to rescue the child that he gave not the slightest thought to the strangeness of all the conditions surrounding the *Kincaid*. That her deck was deserted, though she had steam up, and from the volume of smoke pouring from her funnel was all ready to get under way made no impression upon him.

With the thought that in another instant he would fold that precious little bundle of humanity in his arms, the ape-man swung down into the darkness below. Scarcely had he released his hold upon the edge of the hatch than the heavy covering fell clattering above him.

Instantly he knew that he was the victim of a plot, and that far from rescuing his son he had himself fallen into the hands of his enemies. Though he immediately endeavoured to reach the hatch and lift the cover, he was unable to do so.

Striking a match, he explored his surroundings, finding that a little compartment had been partitioned off from the main hold, with the hatch above his head the only means of ingress or egress. It was evident that the room had been prepared for the very purpose of serving as a cell for himself.

There was nothing in the compartment, and no other occupant. If the child was on board the *Kincaid* he was confined elsewhere.

For over twenty years, from infancy to manhood, the ape-man had roamed his savage jungle haunts without human companionship of any nature. He had learned at the most impressionable period of his life to take his pleasures and his sorrows as the beasts take theirs.

So it was that he neither raved nor stormed against fate, but instead waited patiently for what might next befall him, though not by any means without an eye to doing the utmost to succour himself. To this end he examined his prison carefully, tested the heavy planking that formed its walls, and measured the distance of the hatch above him.

And while he was thus occupied there came suddenly to him the vibration of machinery and the throbbing of the propeller.

The ship was moving! Where to and to what fate was it carrying him?

And even as these thoughts passed through his mind there came to his ears above the din of the engines that which caused him to go cold with apprehension.

Clear and shrill from the deck above him rang the scream of a frightened woman.

MAROONED

As Tarzan and his guide had disappeared into the shadows upon the dark wharf the figure of a heavily veiled woman had hurried down the narrow alley to the entrance of the drinking-place the two men had just quitted.

Here she paused and looked about, and then as though satisfied that she had at last reached the place she sought, she pushed bravely into the interior of the vile den.

A score of half-drunken sailors and wharf-rats looked up at the unaccustomed sight of a richly gowned woman in their midst. Rapidly she approached the slovenly barmaid who stared half in envy, half in hate, at her more fortunate sister.

"Have you seen a tall, well-dressed man here, but a minute since," she asked, "who met another and went away with him?"

The girl answered in the affirmative, but could not tell which way the two had gone. A sailor who had approached to listen to the conversation vouchsafed the information that a moment before as he had been about to enter the "pub" he had seen two men leaving it who walked toward the wharf.

"Show me the direction they went," cried the woman, slipping a coin into the man's hand.

The fellow led her from the place, and together they walked quickly toward the wharf and along it until across the water they saw a small boat just pulling into the shadows of a nearby steamer.

"There they be," whispered the man.

"Ten pounds if you will find a boat and row me to that steamer," cried the woman.

"Quick, then," he replied, "for we gotta go it if we're goin' to catch the *Kincaid* afore she sails. She's had steam up for three hours an' jest been a-waitin' fer that one passenger. I was a-talkin' to one of her crew 'arf an hour ago."

As he spoke he led the way to the end of the wharf where he knew another boat lay moored, and, lowering the woman into it, he jumped in after and pushed off. The two were soon scudding over the water.

At the steamer's side the man demanded his pay and, without waiting to count out the exact amount, the woman thrust a handful of bank-notes into his outstretched hand. A single glance at them convinced the fellow that he had been more than well paid. Then he assisted her up the ladder, holding his skiff close to the ship's side against the chance that this profitable passenger might wish to be taken ashore later.

But presently the sound of the donkey engine and the rattle of a steel cable on the hoisting-drum proclaimed the fact that the *Kincaid*'s anchor was being raised, and a moment later the waiter heard the propellers revolving, and slowly the little steamer moved away from him out into the channel.

As he turned to row back to shore he heard a woman's shriek from the ship's deck.

"That's wot I calls rotten luck," he soliloquized. "I might jest as well of 'ad the whole bloomin' wad."

When Jane Clayton climbed to the deck of the *Kincaid* she found the ship apparently deserted. There was no sign of those she sought nor of any other aboard, and so she went about her search for her husband and the child she hoped against hope to find there without interruption.

Quickly she hastened to the cabin, which was half above and half below deck. As she hurried down the short companion-ladder into the main cabin, on either side of which were the smaller rooms occupied by the officers, she failed to note the quick closing of one of the doors before her. She passed the full length of the main room, and then retracing her steps stopped before each door to listen, furtively trying each latch.

All was silence, utter silence there, in which the throbbing of her own frightened heart seemed to her overwrought imagination to fill the ship with its thunderous alarm.

One by one the doors opened before her touch, only to reveal empty interiors. In her absorption she did not note the sudden activity upon the vessel, the purring of the engines, the throbbing of the propeller. She had reached the last door upon the right now, and as she pushed it open she was seized from within by a powerful, dark-visaged man, and drawn hastily into the stuffy, ill-smelling interior.

The sudden shock of fright which the unexpected attack had upon her drew a single piercing scream from her throat; then the man clapped a hand roughly over the mouth.

"Not until we are farther from land, my dear," he said. "Then you may yell your pretty head off."

Lady Greystoke turned to look into the leering, bearded face so close to hers. The man relaxed the pressure of his fingers upon her lips, and with a little moan of terror as she recognized him the girl shrank away from her captor.

"Nikolas Rokoff! M. Thuran!" she exclaimed.

"Your devoted admirer," replied the Russian, with a low bow.

"My little boy," she said next, ignoring the terms of endearment—" where is he? Let me have him. How could you be so cruel—even as you—Nikolas Rokoff—cannot be entirely devoid of mercy and compassion? Tell me where he is. Is he aboard this ship? Oh, please, if such a thing as a heart beats within your breast, take me to my baby!"

"If you do as you are bid no harm will befall him," replied Rokoff. "But remember that it is your own fault that you are here. You came aboard voluntarily, and you may take the consequences. I little thought," he added to himself, "that any such good luck as this would come to me."

He went on deck then, locking the cabin-door upon his prisoner, and for several days she did not see him. The truth of the matter being that Nikolas Rokoff was so poor a sailor that the heavy seas the *Kincaid* encountered from the very beginning of her voyage sent the Russian to his berth with a bad attack of sea-sickness.

During this time her only visitor was an uncouth Swede, the *Kincaid*'s unsavoury cook, who brought her meals to her. His name was Sven Anderssen, his one pride being that his patronymic was spelt with a double "s."

The man was tall and raw-boned, with a long yellow moustache, an unwholesome complexion, and filthy nails. The very sight of him with one grimy thumb buried deep in the lukewarm stew, that seemed, from the frequency of its repetition, to constitute the pride of his culinary art, was sufficient to take away the girl's appetite.

His small, blue, close-set eyes never met hers squarely. There was a shiftiness of his whole appearance that even found expression in the cat-like manner of his gait, and to it all a sinister suggestion was added by the long slim knife that always rested at his waist, slipped through the greasy cord that supported his soiled apron. Ostensibly it was but an implement of his calling; but the girl could never free herself of the conviction that it would require less provocation to witness it put to other and less harmless uses.

His manner toward her was surly, yet she never failed to meet him with a pleasant smile and a word of thanks when he brought her food to her, though more often than not she hurled the bulk of it through the tiny cabin port the moment that the door closed behind him.

During the days of anguish that followed Jane Clayton's imprisonment, but two questions were uppermost in her mind—the whereabouts of her husband and her son. She fully believed that the baby was aboard the *Kincaid*, provided that he still lived, but whether Tarzan had been permitted to live after having been lured aboard the evil craft she could not guess.

She knew, of course, the deep hatred that the Russian felt for the Englishman, and she could think of but one reason for having him brought aboard the ship—to dispatch him in comparative safety in revenge for his having thwarted Rokoff's pet schemes, and for having been at last the means of landing him in a French prison.

Tarzan, on his part, lay in the darkness of his cell, ignorant of the fact that his wife was a prisoner in the cabin almost above his head.

The same Swede that served Jane brought his meals to him, but, though on several occasions Tarzan had tried to draw the man into conversation, he had been unsuccessful. He had hoped to learn through this fellow whether his little son was aboard the *Kincaid*, but to every question upon this or kindred subjects the fellow returned but one reply, "Ay tank it blow purty soon purty hard." So after several attempts Tarzan gave it up.

For weeks that seemed months to the two prisoners the little steamer forged on they knew not where. Once the *Kincaid* stopped to coal, only immediately to take up the seemingly interminable voyage.

Rokoff had visited Jane Clayton but once since he had locked her in the tiny cabin. He had come gaunt and hollow-eyed from a long siege of sea-sickness. The object of his visit was to obtain from her her personal cheque for a large sum in return for a guarantee of her personal safety and return to England.

"When you set me down safely in any civilized port, together with my son and my husband," she replied, "I will pay you in gold twice the amount you ask; but until then you shall not have a cent, nor the promise of a cent under any other conditions."

"You will give me the cheque I ask," he replied with a snarl, "or neither you nor your child nor your husband will ever again set foot within any port, civilized or otherwise."

"I would not trust you," she replied. "What guarantee have I that you would not take my money and then do as you pleased with me and mine regardless of your promise?"

"I think you will do as I bid," he said, turning to leave the cabin. "Remember that I have your son—if you chance to hear the agonized wail of a tortured child it may console you to reflect that it is because of your stubbornness that the baby suffers—and that it is your baby."

"You would not do it!" cried the girl. "You would not—could not be so fiendishly cruel!"

"It is not I that am cruel, but you," he returned, "for you permit a paltry sum of money to stand between your baby and immunity from suffering."

The end of it was that Jane Clayton wrote out a cheque of large denomination and handed it to Nikolas Rokoff, who left her cabin with a grin of satisfaction upon his lips.

The following day the hatch was removed from Tarzan's cell, and as he looked up he saw Paulvitch's head framed in the square of light above him.

"Come up," commanded the Russian. "But bear in mind that you will be shot if you make a single move to attack me or any other aboard the ship."

The ape-man swung himself lightly to the deck. About him, but at a respectful distance, stood a half-dozen sailors armed with rifles and revolvers. Facing him was Paulvitch.

Tarzan looked about for Rokoff, who he felt sure must be aboard, but there was no sign of him.

"Lord Greystoke," commenced the Russian, "by your continued and wanton interference with M. Rokoff and his plans you have at last brought yourself and your family to this unfortunate extremity. You have only yourself to thank. As you may imagine, it has cost M. Rokoff a large amount of money to finance this expedition, and, as you are the sole cause of it, he naturally looks to you for reimbursement.

"Further, I may say that only by meeting M. Rokoff's just demands may you avert the most unpleasant consequences to your wife and child, and at the same time retain your own life and regain your liberty."

"What is the amount?" asked Tarzan. "And what assurance have I that you will live up to your end of the agreement? I have little reason to trust two such scoundrels as you and Rokoff, you know."

The Russian flushed.

"You are in no position to deliver insults," he said. "You have no assurance that we will live up to our agreement other than my word, but you have before you the assurance that we can make short work of you if you do not write out the cheque we demand.

"Unless you are a greater fool than I imagine, you should know that there is nothing that would give us greater pleasure than to order these men to fire. That we do not is because we have other plans for punishing you that would be entirely upset by your death."

"Answer one question," said Tarzan. "Is my son on board this ship?"

"No," replied Alexis Paulvitch, "your son is quite safe elsewhere; nor will he be killed until you refuse to accede to our fair demands. If it becomes necessary to kill you, there will be no reason for not killing the child, since with you gone the one whom we wish to punish through the boy will be gone, and he will then be to us only a constant source of danger and embarrassment. You see, therefore, that you may only save the life of your son by saving your own, and you can only save your own by giving us the cheque we ask."

"Very well," replied Tarzan, for he knew that he could trust them to carry out any sinister threat that Paulvitch had made, and there was a bare chance that by conceding their demands he might save the boy.

That they would permit him to live after he had appended his name to the cheque never occurred to him as being within the realms of probability. But he was determined to give them such a battle as they would never forget, and possibly to take Paulvitch with him into eternity. He was only sorry that it was not Rokoff.

He took his pocket cheque-book and fountain-pen from his pocket.

"What is the amount?" he asked.

Paulvitch named an enormous sum. Tarzan could scarce restrain a smile.

Their very cupidity was to prove the means of their undoing, in the matter of the ransom at least. Purposely he hesitated and haggled over the amount, but Paulvitch was obdurate. Finally the ape-man wrote out his cheque for a larger sum than stood to his credit at the bank.

As he turned to hand the worthless slip of paper to the Russian his glance chanced to pass across the starboard bow of the *Kincaid*. To his surprise he saw that the ship lay within a few hundred yards of land. Almost down to the water's edge ran a dense tropical jungle, and behind was higher land clothed in forest.

Paulvitch noted the direction of his gaze.

"You are to be set at liberty here," he said.

Tarzan's plan for immediate physical revenge upon the Russian vanished. He thought the land before him the mainland of Africa, and he knew that should they liberate him here he could doubtless find his way to civilization with comparative ease.

Paulvitch took the cheque.

"Remove your clothing," he said to the ape-man. "Here you will not need it."

Tarzan demurred.

Paulvitch pointed to the armed sailors. Then the Englishman slowly divested himself of his clothing.

A boat was lowered, and, still heavily guarded, the ape-man was rowed ashore. Half an hour later the sailors had returned to the *Kincaid*, and the steamer was slowly getting under way.

As Tarzan stood upon the narrow strip of beach watching the departure of the vessel he saw a figure appear at the rail and call aloud to attract his attention.

The ape-man had been about to read a note that one of the sailors had handed him as the small boat that bore him to the shore was on the point of returning to the steamer, but at the hail from the vessel's deck he looked up.

He saw a black-bearded man who laughed at him in derision as he held high above his head the figure of a little child. Tarzan half started as though to rush through the surf and strike out for the already moving steamer; but realizing the futility of so rash an act he halted at the water's edge.

Thus he stood, his gaze riveted upon the *Kincaid* until it disappeared beyond a projecting promontory of the coast.

From the jungle at his back fierce bloodshot eyes glared from beneath shaggy overhanging brows upon him.

Little monkeys in the tree-tops chattered and scolded, and from the distance of the inland forest came the scream of a leopard.

But still John Clayton, Lord Greystoke, stood deaf and unseeing, suffering the pangs of keen regret for the opportunity that he had wasted because he had been so gullible as to place credence in a single statement of the first lieutenant of his arch-enemy.

"I have at least," he thought, "one consolation—the knowledge that Jane is safe in London. Thank Heaven she, too, did not fall into the clutches of those villains."

Behind him the hairy thing whose evil eyes had been watching his as a cat watches a mouse was creeping stealthily toward him.

Where were the trained senses of the savage ape-man?

Where the acute hearing?

Where the uncanny sense of scent?

BEASTS AT BAY

Slowly Tarzan unfolded the note the sailor had thrust into his hand, and read it. At first it made little impression on his sorrow-numbed senses, but finally the full purport of the hideous plot of revenge unfolded itself before his imagination.

"This will explain to you," (the note read) "the exact nature of my intentions relative to your offspring and to you.

"You were born an ape. You lived naked in the jungles—to your own we have returned you; but your son shall rise a step above his sire. It is the immutable law of evolution.

"The father was a beast, but the son shall be a man—he shall take the next ascending step in the scale of progress. He shall be no naked beast of the jungle, but shall wear a loincloth and copper anklets, and, perchance, a ring in his nose, for he is to be reared by men—a tribe of savage cannibals.

"I might have killed you, but that would have curtailed the full measure of the punishment you have earned at my hands.

"Dead, you could not have suffered in the knowledge of your son's plight; but living and in a place from which you may not escape to seek or succour your child, you shall suffer worse than death for all the years of your life in contemplation of the horrors of your son's existence.

"This, then, is to be a part of your punishment for having dared to pit yourself against

N. R.

"P.S.—The balance of your punishment has to do with what shall presently befall your wife—that I shall leave to your imagination."

As he finished reading, a slight sound behind him brought him back with a start to the world of present realities.

Instantly his senses awoke, and he was again Tarzan of the Apes.

As he wheeled about, it was a beast at bay, vibrant with the instinct of self-preservation, that faced a huge bull-ape that was already charging down upon him.

The two years that had elapsed since Tarzan had come out of the savage forest with his rescued mate had witnessed slight diminution of the mighty powers that had made him the invincible lord of the jungle. His great estates in Uziri had claimed much of his time and attention, and there he had found ample field for the practical use and retention of his almost superhuman powers; but naked and unarmed to do battle with the shaggy, bull-necked beast that now confronted him was a test that the ape-man would scarce have welcomed at any period of his wild existence.

But there was no alternative other than to meet the rage-maddened creature with the weapons with which nature had endowed him.

Over the bull's shoulder Tarzan could see now the heads and shoulders of perhaps a dozen more of these mighty fore-runners of primitive man.

He knew, however, that there was little chance that they would attack him, since it is not within the reasoning powers of the anthropoid to be able to weigh or appreciate the value of concentrated action against an enemy—otherwise they would long since have become the dominant creatures of their haunts, so tremendous a power of destruction lies in their mighty thews and savage fangs.

With a low snarl the beast now hurled himself at Tarzan, but the ape-man had found, among other things in the haunts of civilized man, certain methods of scientific warfare that are unknown to the jungle folk.

Whereas, a few years since, he would have met the brute rush with brute force, he now sidestepped his antagonist's headlong charge, and as the brute hurtled past him swung a mighty right to the pit of the ape's stomach.

With a howl of mingled rage and anguish the great anthropoid bent double and sank to the ground, though almost instantly he was again struggling to his feet.

Before he could regain them, however, his white-skinned foe had wheeled and pounced upon him, and in the act there dropped from the shoulders of the English lord the last shred of his superficial mantle of civilization.

Once again he was the jungle beast revelling in bloody conflict with his kind. Once again he was Tarzan, son of Kala the she-ape.

His strong, white teeth sank into the hairy throat of his enemy as he sought the pulsing jugular.

Powerful fingers held the mighty fangs from his own flesh, or clenched and beat with the power of a steam-hammer upon the snarling, foam-flecked face of his adversary.

In a circle about them the balance of the tribe of apes stood watching and enjoying the struggle. They muttered low gutturals of approval as bits of white hide or hairy bloodstained skin were torn from one contestant or the other. But they were silent in amazement and expectation when they saw the mighty white ape wriggle upon the back of their king, and, with steel muscles tensed beneath the armpits of his antagonist, bear down mightily with his open palms upon the back of the thick bullneck, so that the king ape could but shriek in agony and flounder helplessly about upon the thick mat of jungle grass.

As Tarzan had overcome the huge Terkoz that time years before when he had been about to set out upon his quest for human beings of his own kind and colour, so now he overcame this other great ape with the same wrestling hold upon which he had stumbled by accident during that other combat. The little audience of fierce anthropoids heard the creaking of their king's neck mingling with his agonized shrieks and hideous roaring.

Then there came a sudden crack, like the breaking of a stout limb before the fury of the wind. The bullet-head crumpled forward upon its flaccid neck against the great hairy chest—the roaring and the shrieking ceased.

The little pig-eyes of the onlookers wandered from the still form of their leader to that of the white ape that was rising to its feet beside the vanquished, then back to their king as though in wonder that he did not arise and slay this presumptuous stranger.

They saw the new-comer place a foot upon the neck of the quiet figure at his feet and, throwing back his head, give vent to the wild, uncanny challenge of the bull-ape that has made a kill. Then they knew that their king was dead.

Across the jungle rolled the horrid notes of the victory cry. The little monkeys in the tree-tops ceased their chattering. The harsh-voiced, brilliant-plumed birds were still. From afar came the answering wail of a leopard and the deep roar of a lion.

It was the old Tarzan who turned questioning eyes upon the little knot of apes before him. It was the old Tarzan who shook his head as though to toss back a heavy mane that had fallen before his face—an old habit dating from the days that his great shock of thick, black hair had fallen about his shoulders, and often tumbled before his eyes when it had meant life or death to him to have his vision unobstructed.

The ape-man knew that he might expect an immediate attack on the part of that particular surviving bull-ape who felt himself best fitted to contend for the kingship of the tribe. Among his own apes he knew that it was not unusual for an entire stranger to enter a community and, after having dispatched the king, assume the leadership of the tribe himself, together with the fallen monarch's mates.

On the other hand, if he made no attempt to follow them, they might move slowly away from him, later to fight among themselves for the supremacy. That he could be king of them, if he so chose, he was confident; but he was not sure he cared to assume the sometimes irksome duties of that position, for he could see no particular advantage to be gained thereby.

One of the younger apes, a huge, splendidly muscled brute, was edging threateningly closer to the ape-man. Through his bared fighting fangs there issued a low, sullen growl.

Tarzan watched his every move, standing rigid as a statue. To have fallen back a step would have been to precipitate an immediate charge; to have rushed forward to meet the other might have had the same result, or it might have put the bellicose one to flight—it all depended upon the young bull's stock of courage.

To stand perfectly still, waiting, was the middle course. In this event the bull would, according to custom, approach quite close to the object of his attention, growling hideously and baring slavering fangs. Slowly he would circle about the other, as though with a chip upon his shoulder; and this he did, even as Tarzan had foreseen.

It might be a bluff royal, or, on the other hand, so unstable is the mind of an ape, a passing impulse might hurl the hairy mass, tearing and rending, upon the man without an instant's warning.

As the brute circled him Tarzan turned slowly, keeping his eyes ever upon the eyes of his antagonist. He had appraised the young bull as one who had never quite felt equal to the task of overthrowing his former king, but who one day would have done so. Tarzan saw that the beast was of wondrous proportions, standing over seven feet upon his short, bowed legs.

His great, hairy arms reached almost to the ground even when he stood erect, and his fighting fangs, now quite close to Tarzan's face, were exceptionally long and sharp. Like the others of his tribe, he differed in several minor essentials from the apes of Tarzan's boyhood.

At first the ape-man had experienced a thrill of hope at sight of the shaggy bodies of the anthropoids—a hope that by some strange freak of fate he had been again returned to his own tribe; but a closer inspection had convinced him that these were another species.

As the threatening bull continued his stiff and jerky circling of the ape-man, much after the manner that you have noted among dogs when a strange canine comes among them, it occurred to Tarzan to discover if the language of his own tribe was identical with that of this other family, and so he addressed the brute in the language of the tribe of Kerchak.

"Who are you," he asked, "who threatens Tarzan of the Apes?"

The hairy brute looked his surprise.

"I am Akut," replied the other in the same simple, primal tongue which is so low in the scale of spoken languages that, as Tarzan had surmised, it was identical with that of the tribe in which the first twenty years of his life had been spent.

"I am Akut," said the ape. "Molak is dead. I am king. Go away or I shall kill you!"

"You saw how easily I killed Molak," replied Tarzan. "So I could kill you if I cared to be king. But Tarzan of the Apes would not be king of the tribe of Akut. All he wishes is to live in peace in this country. Let us be friends. Tarzan of the Apes can help you, and you can help Tarzan of the Apes."

"You cannot kill Akut," replied the other. "None is so great as Akut. Had you not killed Molak, Akut would have done so, for Akut was ready to be king."

For answer the ape-man hurled himself upon the great brute who during the conversation had slightly relaxed his vigilance.

In the twinkling of an eye the man had seized the wrist of the great ape, and before the other could grapple with him had whirled him about and leaped upon his broad back.

Down they went together, but so well had Tarzan's plan worked out that before ever they touched the ground he had gained the same hold upon Akut that had broken Molak's neck.

Slowly he brought the pressure to bear, and then as in days gone by he had given Kerchak the chance to surrender and live, so now he gave to Akut—in whom he saw a possible ally of great strength and resource—the option of living in amity with him or dying as he had just seen his savage and heretofore invincible king die.

"Ka-Goda?" whispered Tarzan to the ape beneath him.

It was the same question that he had whispered to Kerchak, and in the language of the apes it means, broadly, "Do you surrender?"

Akut thought of the creaking sound he had heard just before Molak's thick neck had snapped, and he shuddered.

He hated to give up the kingship, though, so again he struggled to free himself; but a sudden torturing pressure upon his vertebra brought an agonized "ka-goda!" from his lips.

Tarzan relaxed his grip a trifle.

"You may still be king, Akut," he said. "Tarzan told you that he did not wish to be king. If any question your right, Tarzan of the Apes will help you in your battles."

The ape-man rose, and Akut came slowly to his feet. Shaking his bullet head and growling angrily, he waddled toward his tribe, looking first at one and then at another of the larger bulls who might be expected to challenge his leadership.

But none did so; instead, they drew away as he approached, and presently the whole pack moved off into the jungle, and Tarzan was left alone once more upon the beach.

The ape-man was sore from the wounds that Molak had inflicted upon him, but he was inured to physical suffering and endured it with the calm and fortitude of the wild beasts that had taught him to lead the jungle life after the manner of all those that are born to it.

His first need, he realized, was for weapons of offence and defence, for his encounter with the apes, and the distant notes of the savage voices of Numa the lion, and Sheeta, the panther, warned him that his was to be no life of indolent ease and security.

It was but a return to the old existence of constant bloodshed and danger—to the hunting and the being hunted. Grim beasts would stalk him, as they had stalked him in the past, and never would there be a moment, by savage day or by cruel night, that he might not have instant need of such crude weapons as he could fashion from the materials at hand.

Upon the shore he found an out-cropping of brittle, igneous rock. By dint of much labour he managed to chip off a narrow sliver some twelve inches long by a quarter of an inch thick. One edge was quite thin for a few inches near the tip. It was the rudiment of a knife.

With it he went into the jungle, searching until he found a fallen tree of a certain species of hardwood with which he was familiar. From this he cut a small straight branch, which he pointed at one end.

Then he scooped a small, round hole in the surface of the prostrate trunk. Into this he crumbled a few bits of dry bark, minutely shredded, after which he inserted the tip of his pointed stick, and, sitting astride the bole of the tree, spun the slender rod rapidly between his palms.

After a time a thin smoke rose from the little mass of tinder, and a moment later the whole broke into flame. Heaping some larger twigs and sticks upon the tiny fire, Tarzan soon had quite a respectable blaze roaring in the enlarging cavity of the dead tree.

Into this he thrust the blade of his stone knife, and as it became superheated he would withdraw it, touching a spot near the thin edge with a drop of moisture. Beneath the wetted area a little flake of the glassy material would crack and scale away.

Thus, very slowly, the ape-man commenced the tedious operation of putting a thin edge upon his primitive hunting-knife.

He did not attempt to accomplish the feat all in one sitting. At first he was content to achieve a cutting edge of a couple of inches, with which he cut a long, pliable bow, a handle for his knife, a stout cudgel, and a goodly supply of arrows.

These he cached in a tall tree beside a little stream, and here also he constructed a platform with a roof of palm-leaves above it.

When all these things had been finished it was growing dusk, and Tarzan felt a strong desire to eat.

He had noted during the brief incursion he had made into the forest that a short distance up-stream from his tree there was a much-used watering place, where, from the trampled mud of either bank, it was evident beasts of all sorts and in great numbers came to drink. To this spot the hungry ape-man made his silent way.

Through the upper terrace of the tree-tops he swung with the grace and ease of a monkey. But for the heavy burden upon his heart he would have been happy in this return to the old free life of his boyhood.

Yet even with that burden he fell into the little habits and manners of his early life that were in reality more a part of him than the thin veneer of civilization that the past three years of his association with the white men of the outer world had spread lightly over him—a veneer that only hid the crudities of the beast that Tarzan of the Apes had been.

Could his fellow-peers of the House of Lords have seen him then they would have held up their noble hands in holy horror.

Silently he crouched in the lower branches of a great forest giant that overhung the trail, his keen eyes and sensitive ears strained into the distant jungle, from which he knew his dinner would presently emerge.

Nor had he long to wait.

Scarce had he settled himself to a comfortable position, his lithe, muscular legs drawn well up beneath him as the panther draws his hindquarters in preparation for the spring, than Bara, the deer, came daintily down to drink.

But more than Bara was coming. Behind the graceful buck came another which the deer could neither see nor scent, but whose movements were apparent to Tarzan of the Apes because of the elevated position of the ape-man's ambush.

He knew not yet exactly the nature of the thing that moved so stealthily through the jungle a few hundred yards behind the deer; but he was convinced that it was some great beast of prey stalking Bara for the selfsame purpose as that which prompted him to await the fleet animal. Numa, perhaps, or Sheeta, the panther.

In any event, Tarzan could see his repast slipping from his grasp unless Bara moved more rapidly toward the ford than at present.

Even as these thoughts passed through his mind some noise of the stalker in his rear must have come to the buck, for with a sudden start he paused for an instant, trembling, in his tracks, and then with a swift bound dashed straight for the river and Tarzan. It was his intention to flee through the shallow ford and escape upon the opposite side of the river.

Not a hundred yards behind him came Numa.

Tarzan could see him quite plainly now. Below the ape-man Bara was about to pass. Could he do it? But even as he asked himself the question the hungry man launched himself from his perch full upon the back of the startled buck.

In another instant Numa would be upon them both, so if the ape-man were to dine that night, or ever again, he must act quickly.

Scarcely had he touched the sleek hide of the deer with a momentum that sent the animal to its knees than he had grasped a horn in either hand, and with a single quick wrench twisted the animal's neck completely round, until he felt the vertebrae snap beneath his grip.

The lion was roaring in rage close behind him as he swung the deer across his shoulder, and, grasping a foreleg between his strong teeth, leaped for the nearest of the lower branches that swung above his head.

With both hands he grasped the limb, and, at the instant that Numa sprang, drew himself and his prey out of reach of the animal's cruel talons.

There was a thud below him as the baffled cat fell back to earth, and then Tarzan of the Apes, drawing his dinner farther up to the safety of a higher limb, looked down with grinning face into the gleaming yellow eyes of the other wild beast that glared up at him from beneath, and with taunting insults flaunted the tender carcass of his kill in the face of him whom he had cheated of it.

With his crude stone knife he cut a juicy steak from the hindquarters, and while the great lion paced, growling, back and forth below him, Lord Greystoke filled his savage belly, nor ever in the choicest of his exclusive London clubs had a meal tasted more palatable.

The warm blood of his kill smeared his hands and face and filled his nostrils with the scent that the savage carnivora love best.

And when he had finished he left the balance of the carcass in a high fork of the tree where he had dined, and with Numa trailing below him, still keen for revenge, he made his way back to his tree-top shelter, where he slept until the sun was high the following morning.

SHEETA

The next few days were occupied by Tarzan in completing his weapons and exploring the jungle. He strung his bow with tendons from the buck upon which he had dined his first evening upon the new shore, and though he would have preferred the gut of Sheeta for the purpose, he was content to wait until opportunity permitted him to kill one of the great cats.

He also braided a long grass rope—such a rope as he had used so many years before to tantalize the ill-natured Tublat, and which later had developed into a wondrous effective weapon in the practised hands of the little ape-boy.

A sheath and handle for his hunting-knife he fashioned, and a quiver for arrows, and from the hide of Bara a belt and loin-cloth. Then he set out to learn something of the strange land in which he found himself. That it was not his old familiar west coast of the African continent he knew from the fact that it faced east—the rising sun came up out of the sea before the threshold of the jungle.

But that it was not the east coast of Africa he was equally positive, for he felt satisfied that the *Kincaid* had not passed through the Mediterranean, the Suez Canal, and the Red Sea, nor had she had time to round the Cape of Good Hope. So he was quite at a loss to know where he might be.

Sometimes he wondered if the ship had crossed the broad Atlantic to deposit him upon some wild South American shore; but the presence of Numa, the lion, decided him that such could not be the case.

As Tarzan made his lonely way through the jungle paralleling the shore, he felt strong upon him a desire for companionship, so that gradually he commenced to regret that he had not cast his lot with the apes. He had seen nothing of them since that first day, when the influences of civilization were still paramount within him.

Now he was more nearly returned to the Tarzan of old, and though he appreciated the fact that there could be little in common between himself and the great anthropoids, still they were better than no company at all.

Moving leisurely, sometimes upon the ground and again among the lower branches of the trees, gathering an occasional fruit or turning over a fallen log in search of the larger bugs, which he still found as palatable as of old, Tarzan had covered a mile or more when his attention was attracted by the scent of Sheeta up-wind ahead of him.

Now Sheeta, the panther, was one of whom Tarzan was exceptionally glad to fall in with, for he had it in mind not only to utilize the great cat's strong gut for his bow, but also to fashion a new quiver and loin-cloth from pieces of his hide. So, whereas the ape-man had gone carelessly before, he now became the personification of noiseless stealth.

Swiftly and silently he glided through the forest in the wake of the savage cat, nor was the pursuer, for all his noble birth, one whit less savage than the wild, fierce thing he stalked.

As he came closer to Sheeta he became aware that the panther on his part was stalking game of his own, and even as he realized this fact there came to his nostrils, wafted from his right by a vagrant breeze, the strong odour of a company of great apes.

The panther had taken to a large tree as Tarzan came within sight of him, and beyond and below him Tarzan saw the tribe of Akut lolling in a little, natural clearing. Some of them were dozing against the boles of trees, while others roamed about turning over bits of bark from beneath which they transferred the luscious grubs and beetles to their mouths.

Akut was the closest to Sheeta.

The great cat lay crouched upon a thick limb, hidden from the ape's view by dense foliage, waiting patiently until the anthropoid should come within range of his spring.

Tarzan cautiously gained a position in the same tree with the panther and a little above him. In his left hand he grasped his slim stone blade. He would have preferred to use his noose, but the foliage surrounding the huge cat precluded the possibility of an accurate throw with the rope.

Akut had now wandered quite close beneath the tree wherein lay the waiting death. Sheeta slowly edged his hind paws along the branch still further beneath him, and then with a hideous shriek he launched himself toward the great ape. The barest fraction of a second before his spring another beast of prey above him leaped, its weird and savage cry mingling with his.

As the startled Akut looked up he saw the panther almost above him, and already upon the panther's back the white ape that had bested him that day near the great water.

The teeth of the ape-man were buried in the back of Sheeta's neck and his right arm was round the fierce throat, while the left hand, grasping a slender piece of stone, rose and fell in mighty blows upon the panther's side behind the left shoulder.

Akut had just time to leap to one side to avoid being pinioned beneath these battling monsters of the jungle.

With a crash they came to earth at his feet. Sheeta was screaming, snarling, and roaring horribly; but the white ape clung tenaciously and in silence to the thrashing body of his quarry.

Steadily and remorselessly the stone knife was driven home through the glossy hide—time and again it drank deep, until with a final agonized lunge and shriek the great feline rolled over upon its side and, save for the spasmodic jerking of its muscles, lay quiet and still in death.

Then the ape-man raised his head, as he stood over the carcass of his kill, and once again through the jungle rang his wild and savage victory challenge.

Akut and the apes of Akut stood looking in startled wonder at the dead body of Sheeta and the lithe, straight figure of the man who had slain him.

Tarzan was the first to speak.

He had saved Akut's life for a purpose, and, knowing the limitations of the ape intellect, he also knew that he must make this purpose plain to the anthropoid if it were to serve him in the way he hoped.

"I am Tarzan of the Apes," he said, "Mighty hunter. Mighty fighter. By the great water I spared Akut's life when I might have taken it and become king of the tribe of Akut. Now I have saved Akut from death beneath the rending fangs of Sheeta.

"When Akut or the tribe of Akut is in danger, let them call to Tarzan thus"—and the ape-man raised the hideous cry with which the tribe of Kerchak had been wont to summon its absent members in times of peril.

"And," he continued, "when they hear Tarzan call to them, let them remember what he has done for Akut and come to him with great speed. Shall it be as Tarzan says?"

"Huh!" assented Akut, and from the members of his tribe there rose a unanimous "Huh."

Then, presently, they went to feeding again as though nothing had happened, and with them fed John Clayton, Lord Greystoke.

He noticed, however, that Akut kept always close to him, and was often looking at him with a strange wonder in his little bloodshot eyes, and once he did a thing that Tarzan during all his long years among the apes had never before seen an ape do—he found a particularly tender morsel and handed it to Tarzan.

As the tribe hunted, the glistening body of the ape-man mingled with the brown, shaggy hides of his companions. Oftentimes they brushed together in passing, but the apes had already taken his presence for granted, so that he was as much one of them as Akut himself.

If he came too close to a she with a young baby, the former would bare her great fighting fangs and growl ominously, and occasionally a truculent young bull would snarl a warning if Tarzan approached while the former was eating. But in those things the treatment was no different from that which they accorded any other member of the tribe.

Tarzan on his part felt very much at home with these fierce, hairy progenitors of primitive man. He skipped nimbly out of reach of each threatening female—for such is the way of apes, if they be not in one of their occasional fits of bestial rage—and he growled back at the truculent young bulls, baring his canine teeth even as they. Thus easily he fell back into the way of his early life, nor did it seem that he had ever tasted association with creatures of his own kind.

For the better part of a week he roamed the jungle with his new friends, partly because of a desire for companionship and partially through a well-laid plan to impress himself indelibly upon their memories, which at best are none too long; for Tarzan from past experience knew that it might serve him in good stead to have a tribe of these powerful and terrible beasts at his call.

When he was convinced that he had succeeded to some extent in fixing his identity upon them he decided to again take up his exploration. To this end he set out toward the north early one day, and, keeping parallel with the shore, travelled rapidly until almost nightfall.

When the sun rose the next morning he saw that it lay almost directly to his right as he stood upon the beach instead of straight out across the water as heretofore, and so he reasoned that the shore line had trended toward the west. All the second day he continued his rapid course, and when Tarzan of the Apes sought speed, he passed through the middle terrace of the forest with the rapidity of a squirrel.

That night the sun set straight out across the water opposite the land, and then the ape-man guessed at last the truth that he had been suspecting.

Rokoff had set him ashore upon an island.

He might have known it! If there was any plan that would render his position more harrowing he should have known that such would be the one adopted by the Russian, and what could be more terrible than to leave him to a lifetime of suspense upon an uninhabited island?

Rokoff doubtless had sailed directly to the mainland, where it would be a comparatively easy thing for him to find the means of delivering the infant Jack into the hands of the cruel and savage foster-parents, who, as his note had threatened, would have the upbringing of the child.

Tarzan shuddered as he thought of the cruel suffering the little one must endure in such a life, even though he might fall into the hands of individuals whose intentions toward him were of the kindest. The ape-man had had sufficient experience with the lower savages of Africa to know that even there may be found the cruder virtues of charity and humanity; but their lives were at best but a series of terrible privations, dangers, and sufferings.

Then there was the horrid after-fate that awaited the child as he grew to manhood. The horrible practices that would form a part of his life-training would alone be sufficient to bar him forever from association with those of his own race and station in life.

A cannibal! His little boy a savage man-eater! It was too horrible to contemplate.

The filed teeth, the slit nose, the little face painted hideously. Tarzan groaned. Could he but feel the throat of the Russ fiend beneath his steel fingers!

And Jane!

What tortures of doubt and fear and uncertainty she must be suffering. He felt that his position was infinitely less terrible than hers, for he at least knew that one of his loved ones was safe at home, while she had no idea of the whereabouts of either her husband or her son.

It is well for Tarzan that he did not guess the truth, for the knowledge would have but added a hundredfold to his suffering.

As he moved slowly through the jungle his mind absorbed by his gloomy thoughts, there presently came to his ears a strange scratching sound which he could not translate.

Cautiously he moved in the direction from which it emanated, presently coming upon a huge panther pinned beneath a fallen tree.

As Tarzan approached, the beast turned, snarling, toward him, struggling to extricate itself; but one great limb across its back and the smaller entangling branches pinioning its legs prevented it from moving but a few inches in any direction.

The ape-man stood before the helpless cat fitting an arrow to his bow that he might dispatch the beast that otherwise must die of starvation; but even as he drew back the shaft a sudden whim stayed his hand.

Why rob the poor creature of life and liberty, when it would be so easy a thing to restore both to it! He was sure from the fact that the panther moved all its limbs in its futile struggle for freedom that its spine was uninjured, and for the same reason he knew that none of its limbs were broken.

Relaxing his bowstring, he returned the arrow to the quiver and, throwing the bow about his shoulder, stepped closer to the pinioned beast.

On his lips was the soothing, purring sound that the great cats themselves made when contented and happy. It was the nearest approach to a friendly advance that Tarzan could make in the language of Sheeta.

The panther ceased his snarling and eyed the ape-man closely. To lift the tree's great weight from the animal it was necessary to come within reach of those long, strong talons, and when the tree had been removed the man would be totally at the mercy of the savage beast; but to Tarzan of the Apes fear was a thing unknown.

Having decided, he acted promptly.

Unhesitatingly, he stepped into the tangle of branches close to the panther's side, still voicing his friendly and conciliatory purr. The cat turned his head toward the man, eyeing him steadily—questioningly. The long fangs were bared, but more in preparedness than threat.

Tarzan put a broad shoulder beneath the bole of the tree, and as he did so his bare leg pressed against the cat's silken side, so close was the man to the great beast.

Slowly Tarzan extended his giant thews.

The great tree with its entangling branches rose gradually from the panther, who, feeling the encumbering weight diminish, quickly crawled from beneath. Tarzan let the tree fall back to earth, and the two beasts turned to look upon one another.

A grim smile lay upon the ape-man's lips, for he knew that he had taken his life in his hands to free this savage jungle fellow; nor would it have surprised him had the cat sprung upon him the instant that it had been released.

But it did not do so. Instead, it stood a few paces from the tree watching the ape-man clamber out of the maze of fallen branches.

Once outside, Tarzan was not three paces from the panther. He might have taken to the higher branches of the trees upon the opposite side, for Sheeta cannot climb to the heights to which the ape-man can go; but something, a spirit of bravado perhaps, prompted him to approach the panther as though to discover if any feeling of gratitude would prompt the beast to friendliness.

As he approached the mighty cat the creature stepped warily to one side, and the ape-man brushed past him within a foot of the dripping jaws, and as he continued on through the forest the panther followed on behind him, as a hound follows at heel.

For a long time Tarzan could not tell whether the beast was following out of friendly feelings or merely stalking him against the time he should be hungry; but finally he was forced to believe that the former incentive it was that prompted the animal's action.

Later in the day the scent of a deer sent Tarzan into the trees, and when he had dropped his noose about the animal's neck he called to Sheeta, using a purr similar to that which he had utilized to pacify the brute's suspicions earlier in the day, but a trifle louder and more shrill.

It was similar to that which he had heard panthers use after a kill when they had been hunting in pairs.

Almost immediately there was a crashing of the underbrush close at hand, and the long, lithe body of his strange companion broke into view.

At sight of the body of Bara and the smell of blood the panther gave forth a shrill scream, and a moment later two beasts were feeding side by side upon the tender meat of the deer.

For several days this strangely assorted pair roamed the jungle together.

When one made a kill he called the other, and thus they fed well and often.

On one occasion as they were dining upon the carcass of a boar that Sheeta had dispatched, Numa, the lion, grim and terrible, broke through the tangled grasses close beside them.

With an angry, warning roar he sprang forward to chase them from their kill. Sheeta bounded into a near-by thicket, while Tarzan took to the low branches of an overhanging tree.

Here the ape-man unloosed his grass rope from about his neck, and as Numa stood above the body of the boar, challenging head erect, he dropped the sinuous noose about the maned neck, drawing the stout strands taut with a sudden jerk. At the same time he called shrilly to Sheeta, as he drew the struggling lion upward until only his hind feet touched the ground.

Quickly he made the rope fast to a stout branch, and as the panther, in answer to his summons, leaped into sight, Tarzan dropped to the earth beside the struggling and infuriated Numa, and with a long sharp knife sprang upon him at one side even as Sheeta did upon the other.

The panther tore and rent Numa upon the right, while the ape-man struck home with his stone knife upon the other, so that before the mighty clawing of the king of beasts had succeeded in parting the rope he hung quite dead and harmless in the noose.

And then upon the jungle air there rose in unison from two savage throats the victory cry of the bull-ape and the panther, blended into one frightful and uncanny scream.

As the last notes died away in a long-drawn, fearsome wail, a score of painted warriors, drawing their long war-canoe upon the beach, halted to stare in the direction of the jungle and to listen.

MUGAMBI

By the time that Tarzan had travelled entirely about the coast of the island, and made several trips inland from various points, he was sure that he was the only human being upon it.

Nowhere had he found any sign that men had stopped even temporarily upon this shore, though, of course, he knew that so quickly does the rank vegetation of the tropics erase all but the most permanent of human monuments that he might be in error in his deductions.

The day following the killing of Numa, Tarzan and Sheeta came upon the tribe of Akut. At sight of the panther the great apes took to flight, but after a time Tarzan succeeded in recalling them.

It had occurred to him that it would be at least an interesting experiment to attempt to reconcile these hereditary enemies. He welcomed anything that would occupy his time and his mind beyond the filling of his belly and the gloomy thoughts to which he fell prey the moment that he became idle.

To communicate his plan to the apes was not a particularly difficult matter, though their narrow and limited vocabulary was strained in the effort; but to impress upon the little, wicked brain of Sheeta that he was to hunt with and not for his legitimate prey proved a task almost beyond the powers of the ape-man.

Tarzan, among his other weapons, possessed a long, stout cudgel, and after fastening his rope about the panther's neck he used this instrument freely upon the snarling beast, endeavouring in this way to impress upon its memory that it must not attack the great, shaggy manlike creatures that had approached more closely once they had seen the purpose of the rope about Sheeta's neck.

That the cat did not turn and rend Tarzan is something of a miracle which may possibly be accounted for by the fact that twice when it turned growling upon the ape-man he had rapped it sharply upon its sensitive nose, inculcating in its mind thereby a most wholesome fear of the cudgel and the ape-beasts behind it.

EDGAR RICE BURROUGHS

It is a question if the original cause of his attachment for Tarzan was still at all clear in the mind of the panther, though doubtless some subconscious suggestion, superinduced by this primary reason and aided and abetted by the habit of the past few days, did much to compel the beast to tolerate treatment at his hands that would have sent it at the throat of any other creature.

Then, too, there was the compelling force of the manmind exerting its powerful influence over this creature of a lower order, and, after all, it may have been this that proved the most potent factor in Tarzan's supremacy over Sheeta and the other beasts of the jungle that had from time to time fallen under his domination.

Be that as it may, for days the man, the panther, and the great apes roamed their savage haunts side by side, making their kills together and sharing them with one another, and of all the fierce and savage band none was more terrible than the smooth-skinned, powerful beast that had been but a few short months before a familiar figure in many a London drawing room.

Sometimes the beasts separated to follow their own inclinations for an hour or a day, and it was upon one of these occasions when the ape-man had wandered through the tree-tops toward the beach, and was stretched in the hot sun upon the sand, that from the low summit of a near-by promontory a pair of keen eyes discovered him.

For a moment the owner of the eyes looked in astonishment at the figure of the savage white man basking in the rays of that hot, tropic sun; then he turned, making a sign to some one behind him. Presently another pair of eyes were looking down upon the ape-man, and then another and another, until a full score of hideously trapped, savage warriors were lying upon their bellies along the crest of the ridge watching the white-skinned stranger.

They were down wind from Tarzan, and so their scent was not carried to him, and as his back was turned half toward them he did not see their cautious advance over the edge of the promontory and down through the rank grass toward the sandy beach where he lay.

Big fellows they were, all of them, their barbaric headdresses and grotesquely painted faces, together with their many metal ornaments and gorgeously coloured feathers, adding to their wild, fierce appearance.

Once at the foot of the ridge, they came cautiously to their feet, and, bent half-double, advanced silently upon the unconscious white man, their heavy war-clubs swinging menacingly in their brawny hands.

The mental suffering that Tarzan's sorrowful thoughts induced had the effect of numbing his keen, perceptive faculties, so that the advancing savages were almost upon him before he became aware that he was no longer alone upon the beach.

So quickly, though, were his mind and muscles wont to react in unison to the slightest alarm that he was upon his feet and facing his enemies, even as he realized that something was behind him. As he sprang to his feet the warriors leaped toward him with raised clubs and savage yells, but the foremost went down to sudden death beneath the long, stout stick of the ape-man, and then the lithe, sinewy figure was among them, striking right and left with a fury, power, and precision that brought panic to the ranks of the blacks.

For a moment they withdrew, those that were left of them, and consulted together at a short distance from the ape-man, who stood with folded arms, a half-smile upon his handsome face, watching them. Presently they advanced upon him once more, this time wielding their heavy war-spears. They were between Tarzan and the jungle, in a little semicircle that closed in upon him as they advanced.

There seemed to the ape-man but slight chance to escape the final charge when all the great spears should be hurled simultaneously at him; but if he had desired to escape there was no way other than through the ranks of the savages except the open sea behind him.

His predicament was indeed most serious when an idea occurred to him that altered his smile to a broad grin. The warriors were still some little distance away, advancing slowly, making, after the manner of their kind, a frightful din with their savage yells and the pounding of their naked feet upon the ground as they leaped up and down in a fantastic war dance.

271

Then it was that the ape-man lifted his voice in a series of wild, weird screams that brought the blacks to a sudden, perplexed halt. They looked at one another questioningly, for here was a sound so hideous that their own frightful din faded into insignificance beside it. No human throat could have formed those bestial notes, they were sure, and yet with their own eyes they had seen this white man open his mouth to pour forth his awful cry.

But only for a moment they hesitated, and then with one accord they again took up their fantastic advance upon their prey; but even then a sudden crashing in the jungle behind them brought them once more to a halt, and as they turned to look in the direction of this new noise there broke upon their startled visions a sight that may well have frozen the blood of braver men than the Wagambi.

Leaping from the tangled vegetation of the jungle's rim came a huge panther, with blazing eyes and bared fangs, and in his wake a score of mighty, shaggy apes lumbering rapidly toward them, half erect upon their short, bowed legs, and with their long arms reaching to the ground, where their horny knuckles bore the weight of their ponderous bodies as they lurched from side to side in their grotesque advance.

The beasts of Tarzan had come in answer to his call.

Before the Wagambi could recover from their astonishment the frightful horde was upon them from one side and Tarzan of the Apes from the other. Heavy spears were hurled and mighty war-clubs wielded, and though apes went down never to rise, so, too, went down the men of Ugambi.

Sheeta's cruel fangs and tearing talons ripped and tore at the black hides. Akut's mighty yellow tusks found the jugular of more than one sleek-skinned savage, and Tarzan of the Apes was here and there and everywhere, urging on his fierce allies and taking a heavy toll with his long, slim knife.

In a moment the blacks had scattered for their lives, but of the score that had crept down the grassy sides of the promontory only a single warrior managed to escape the horde that had overwhelmed his people.

This one was Mugambi, chief of the Wagambi of Ugambi, and as he disappeared in the tangled luxuriousness of the rank growth upon the ridge's summit only the keen eyes of the ape-man saw the direction of his flight.

Leaving his pack to eat their fill upon the flesh of their victims—flesh that he could not touch—Tarzan of the Apes pursued the single survivor of the bloody fray. Just beyond the ridge he came within sight of the fleeing black, making with headlong leaps for a long war-canoe that was drawn well up upon the beach above the high tide surf.

Noiseless as the fellow's shadow, the ape-man raced after the terror-stricken black. In the white man's mind was a new plan, awakened by sight of the war-canoe. If these men had come to his island from another, or from the mainland, why not utilize their craft to make his way to the country from which they had come? Evidently it was an inhabited country, and no doubt had occasional intercourse with the mainland, if it were not itself upon the continent of Africa.

A heavy hand fell upon the shoulder of the escaping Mugambi before he was aware that he was being pursued, and as he turned to do battle with his assailant giant fingers closed about his wrists and he was hurled to earth with a giant astride him before he could strike a blow in his own defence.

In the language of the West Coast, Tarzan spoke to the prostrate man beneath him.

"Who are you?" he asked.

"Mugambi, chief of the Wagambi," replied the black.

"I will spare your life," said Tarzan, "if you will promise to help me to leave this island. What do you answer?"

"I will help you," replied Mugambi. "But now that you have killed all my warriors, I do not know that even I can leave your country, for there will be none to wield the paddles, and without paddlers we cannot cross the water."

Tarzan rose and allowed his prisoner to come to his feet. The fellow was a magnificent specimen of manhood—a black counterpart in physique of the splendid white man whom he faced.

"Come!" said the ape-man, and started back in the direction from which they could hear the snarling and growling of the feasting pack. Mugambi drew back.

"They will kill us," he said.

"I think not," replied Tarzan. "They are mine."

Still the black hesitated, fearful of the consequences of approaching the terrible creatures that were dining upon the bodies of his warriors; but Tarzan forced him to accompany him, and presently the two emerged from the jungle in full view of the grisly spectacle upon the beach. At sight of the men the beasts looked up with menacing growls, but Tarzan strode in among them, dragging the trembling Wagambi with him.

As he had taught the apes to accept Sheeta, so he taught them to adopt Mugambi as well, and much more easily; but Sheeta seemed quite unable to understand that though he had been called upon to devour Mugambi's warriors he was not to be allowed to proceed after the same fashion with Mugambi. However, being well filled, he contented himself with walking round the terror-stricken savage, emitting low, menacing growls the while he kept his flaming, baleful eyes riveted upon the black.

Mugambi, on his part, clung closely to Tarzan, so that the ape-man could scarce control his laughter at the pitiable condition to which the chief's fear had reduced him; but at length the white took the great cat by the scruff of the neck and, dragging it quite close to the Wagambi, slapped it sharply upon the nose each time that it growled at the stranger.

At the sight of the thing—a man mauling with his bare hands one of the most relentless and fierce of the jungle carnivora—Mugambi's eyes bulged from their sockets, and from entertaining a sullen respect for the giant white man who had made him prisoner, the black felt an almost worshipping awe of Tarzan.

The education of Sheeta progressed so well that in a short time Mugambi ceased to be the object of his hungry attention, and the black felt a degree more of safety in his society.

To say that Mugambi was entirely happy or at ease in his new environment would not be to adhere strictly to the truth. His eyes were constantly rolling apprehensively from side to side as now one and now another of the fierce pack chanced to wander near him, so that for the most of the time it was principally the whites that showed.

Together Tarzan and Mugambi, with Sheeta and Akut, lay in wait at the ford for a deer, and when at a word from the ape-man the four of them leaped out upon the affrighted animal the black was sure that the poor creature died of fright before ever one of the great beasts touched it.

Mugambi built a fire and cooked his portion of the kill; but Tarzan, Sheeta, and Akut tore theirs, raw, with their sharp teeth, growling among themselves when one ventured to encroach upon the share of another.

It was not, after all, strange that the white man's ways should have been so much more nearly related to those of the beasts than were the savage blacks. We are, all of us, creatures of habit, and when the seeming necessity for schooling ourselves in new ways ceases to exist, we fall naturally and easily into the manners and customs which long usage has implanted ineradicably within us.

Mugambi from childhood had eaten no meat until it had been cooked, while Tarzan, on the other hand, had never tasted cooked food of any sort until he had grown almost to manhood, and only within the past three or four years had he eaten cooked meat. Not only did the habit of a lifetime prompt him to eat it raw, but the craving of his palate as well; for to him cooked flesh was spoiled flesh when compared with the rich and juicy meat of a fresh, hot kill.

That he could, with relish, eat raw meat that had been buried by himself weeks before, and enjoy small rodents and disgusting grubs, seems to us who have been always "civilized" a revolting fact; but had we learned in childhood to eat these things, and had we seen all those about us eat them, they would seem no more sickening to us now than do many of our greatest dainties, at which a savage African cannibal would look with repugnance and turn up his nose.

For instance, there is a tribe in the vicinity of Lake Rudolph that will eat no sheep or cattle, though its next neighbors do so. Near by is another tribe that eats donkey-meat—a custom most revolting to the surrounding tribes that do not eat donkey. So who may say that it is nice to eat snails and frogs' legs and oysters, but disgusting to feed upon grubs and beetles, or that a raw oyster, hoof, horns, and tail, is less revolting than the sweet, clean meat of a fresh-killed buck?

The next few days Tarzan devoted to the weaving of a barkcloth sail with which to equip the canoe, for he despaired of being able to teach the apes to wield the paddles, though he did manage to get several of them to embark in the frail craft which he and Mugambi paddled about inside the reef where the water was quite smooth.

During these trips he had placed paddles in their hands, when they attempted to imitate the movements of him and Mugambi, but so difficult is it for them long to concentrate upon a thing that he soon saw that it would require weeks of patient training before they would be able to make any effective use of these new implements, if, in fact, they should ever do so.

There was one exception, however, and he was Akut. Almost from the first he showed an interest in this new sport that revealed a much higher plane of intelligence than that attained by any of his tribe. He seemed to grasp the purpose of the paddles, and when Tarzan saw that this was so he took much pains to explain in the meagre language of the anthropoid how they might be used to the best advantage.

From Mugambi Tarzan learned that the mainland lay but a short distance from the island. It seemed that the Wagambi warriors had ventured too far out in their frail craft, and when caught by a heavy tide and a high wind from offshore they had been driven out of sight of land. After paddling for a whole night, thinking that they were headed for home, they had seen this land at sunrise, and, still taking it for the mainland, had hailed it with joy, nor had Mugambi been aware that it was an island until Tarzan had told him that this was the fact.

The Wagambi chief was quite dubious as to the sail, for he had never seen such a contrivance used. His country lay far up the broad Ugambi River, and this was the first occasion that any of his people had found their way to the ocean.

Tarzan, however, was confident that with a good west wind he could navigate the little craft to the mainland. At any rate, he decided, it would be preferable to perish on the way than to remain indefinitely upon this evidently uncharted island to which no ships might ever be expected to come.

And so it was that when the first fair wind rose he embarked upon his cruise, and with him he took as strange and fearsome a crew as ever sailed under a savage master.

Mugambi and Akut went with him, and Sheeta, the panther, and a dozen great males of the tribe of Akut.

A HIDEOUS CREW

The war-canoe with its savage load moved slowly toward the break in the reef through which it must pass to gain the open sea. Tarzan, Mugambi, and Akut wielded the paddles, for the shore kept the west wind from the little sail.

Sheeta crouched in the bow at the ape-man's feet, for it had seemed best to Tarzan always to keep the wicked beast as far from the other members of the party as possible, since it would require little or no provocation to send him at the throat of any than the white man, whom he evidently now looked upon as his master.

In the stern was Mugambi, and just in front of him squatted Akut, while between Akut and Tarzan the twelve hairy apes sat upon their haunches, blinking dubiously this way and that, and now and then turning their eyes longingly back toward shore.

All went well until the canoe had passed beyond the reef. Here the breeze struck the sail, sending the rude craft lunging among the waves that ran higher and higher as they drew away from the shore.

With the tossing of the boat the apes became panic-stricken. They first moved uneasily about, and then commenced grumbling and whining. With difficulty Akut kept them in hand for a time; but when a particularly large wave struck the dugout simultaneously with a little squall of wind their terror broke all bounds, and, leaping to their feet, they all but overturned the boat before Akut and Tarzan together could quiet them. At last calm was restored, and eventually the apes became accustomed to the strange antics of their craft, after which no more trouble was experienced with them.

The trip was uneventful, the wind held, and after ten hours' steady sailing the black shadows of the coast loomed close before the straining eyes of the ape-man in the bow. It was far too dark to distinguish whether they had approached close to the mouth of the Ugambi or not, so Tarzan ran in through the surf at the closest point to await the dawn.

The dugout turned broadside the instant that its nose touched the sand, and immediately it rolled over, with all its crew scrambling madly for the shore. The next breaker rolled them over and over, but eventually they all succeeded in crawling to safety, and in a moment more their ungainly craft had been washed up beside them.

The balance of the night the apes sat huddled close to one another for warmth; while Mugambi built a fire close to them over which he crouched. Tarzan and Sheeta, however, were of a different mind, for neither of them feared the jungle night, and the insistent craving of their hunger sent them off into the Stygian blackness of the forest in search of prey.

Side by side they walked when there was room for two abreast. At other times in single file, first one and then the other in advance. It was Tarzan who first caught the scent of meat—a bull buffalo—and presently the two came stealthily upon the sleeping beast in the midst of a dense jungle of reeds close to a river.

Closer and closer they crept toward the unsuspecting beast, Sheeta upon his right side and Tarzan upon his left nearest the great heart. They had hunted together now for some time, so that they worked in unison, with only low, purring sounds as signals.

For a moment they lay quite silent near their prey, and then at a sign from the ape-man Sheeta sprang upon the great back, burying his strong teeth in the bull's neck. Instantly the brute sprang to his feet with a bellow of pain and rage, and at the same instant Tarzan rushed in upon his left side with the stone knife, striking repeatedly behind the shoulder.

One of the ape-man's hands clutched the thick mane, and as the bull raced madly through the reeds the thing striking at his life was dragged beside him. Sheeta but clung tenaciously to his hold upon the neck and back, biting deep in an effort to reach the spine.

For several hundred yards the bellowing bull carried his two savage antagonists, until at last the blade found his heart, when with a final bellow that was half-scream he plunged headlong to the earth. Then Tarzan and Sheeta feasted to repletion.

After the meal the two curled up together in a thicket, the man's black head pillowed upon the tawny side of the panther. Shortly after dawn they awoke and ate again, and then returned to the beach that Tarzan might lead the balance of the pack to the kill.

When the meal was done the brutes were for curling up to sleep, so Tarzan and Mugambi set off in search of the Ugambi River. They had proceeded scarce a hundred yards when they came suddenly upon a broad stream, which the Negro instantly recognized as that down which he and his warriors had paddled to the sea upon their ill-starred expedition.

The two now followed the stream down to the ocean, finding that it emptied into a bay not over a mile from the point upon the beach at which the canoe had been thrown the night before.

Tarzan was much elated by the discovery, as he knew that in the vicinity of a large watercourse he should find natives, and from some of these he had little doubt but that he should obtain news of Rokoff and the child, for he felt reasonably certain that the Russian would rid himself of the baby as quickly as possible after having disposed of Tarzan.

He and Mugambi now righted and launched the dugout, though it was a most difficult feat in the face of the surf which rolled continuously in upon the beach; but at last they were successful, and soon after were paddling up the coast toward the mouth of the Ugambi. Here they experienced considerable difficulty in making an entrance against the combined current and ebb tide, but by taking advantage of eddies close in to shore they came about dusk to a point nearly opposite the spot where they had left the pack asleep.

Making the craft fast to an overhanging bough, the two made their way into the jungle, presently coming upon some of the apes feeding upon fruit a little beyond the reeds where the buffalo had fallen. Sheeta was not anywhere to be seen, nor did he return that night, so that Tarzan came to believe that he had wandered away in search of his own kind.

Early the next morning the ape-man led his band down to the river, and as he walked he gave vent to a series of shrill cries. Presently from a great distance and faintly there came an answering scream, and a half-hour later the lithe form of Sheeta bounded into view where the others of the pack were clambering gingerly into the canoe.

The great beast, with arched back and purring like a contented tabby, rubbed his sides against the ape-man, and then at a word from the latter sprang lightly to his former place in the bow of the dugout.

When all were in place it was discovered that two of the apes of Akut were missing, and though both the king ape and Tarzan called to them for the better part of an hour, there was no response, and finally the boat put off without them. As it happened that the two missing ones were the very same who had evinced the least desire to accompany the expedition from the island, and had suffered the most from fright during the voyage, Tarzan was quite sure that they had absented themselves purposely rather than again enter the canoe.

As the party were putting in for the shore shortly after noon to search for food a slender, naked savage watched them for a moment from behind the dense screen of verdure which lined the river's bank, then he melted away up-stream before any of those in the canoe discovered him.

Like a deer he bounded along the narrow trail until, filled with the excitement of his news, he burst into a native village several miles above the point at which Tarzan and his pack had stopped to hunt.

"Another white man is coming!" he cried to the chief who squatted before the entrance to his circular hut. "Another white man, and with him are many warriors. They come in a great war-canoe to kill and rob as did the black-bearded one who has just left us."

Kaviri leaped to his feet. He had but recently had a taste of the white man's medicine, and his savage heart was filled with bitterness and hate. In another moment the rumble of the war-drums rose from the village, calling in the hunters from the forest and the tillers from the fields.

Seven war-canoes were launched and manned by paint-daubed, befeathered warriors. Long spears bristled from the rude battle-ships, as they slid noiselessly over the bosom of the water, propelled by giant muscles rolling beneath glistening, ebony hides.

There was no beating of tom-toms now, nor blare of native horn, for Kaviri was a crafty warrior, and it was in his mind to take no chances, if they could be avoided. He would swoop noiselessly down with his seven canoes upon the single one of the white man, and before the guns of the latter could inflict much damage upon his people he would have overwhelmed the enemy by force of numbers.

Kaviri's own canoe went in advance of the others a short distance, and as it rounded a sharp bend in the river where the swift current bore it rapidly on its way it came suddenly upon the thing that Kaviri sought.

So close were the two canoes to one another that the black had only an opportunity to note the white face in the bow of the oncoming craft before the two touched and his own men were upon their feet, yelling like mad devils and thrusting their long spears at the occupants of the other canoe.

But a moment later, when Kaviri was able to realize the nature of the crew that manned the white man's dugout, he would have given all the beads and iron wire that he possessed to have been safely within his distant village. Scarcely had the two craft come together than the frightful apes of Akut rose, growling and barking, from the bottom of the canoe, and, with long, hairy arms far outstretched, grasped the menacing spears from the hands of Kaviri's warriors.

The blacks were overcome with terror, but there was nothing to do other than to fight. Now came the other war-canoes rapidly down upon the two craft. Their occupants were eager to join the battle, for they thought that their foes were white men and their native porters.

They swarmed about Tarzan's craft; but when they saw the nature of the enemy all but one turned and paddled swiftly upriver. That one came too close to the ape-man's craft before its occupants realized that their fellows were pitted against demons instead of men. As it touched Tarzan spoke a few low words to Sheeta and Akut, so that before the attacking warriors could draw away there sprang upon them with a blood-freezing scream a huge panther, and into the other end of their canoe clambered a great ape.

At one end the panther wrought fearful havoc with his mighty talons and long, sharp fangs, while Akut at the other buried his yellow canines in the necks of those that came within his reach, hurling the terror-stricken blacks overboard as he made his way toward the centre of the canoe.

Kaviri was so busily engaged with the demons that had entered his own craft that he could offer no assistance to his warriors in the other. A giant of a white devil had wrested his spear from him as though he, the mighty Kaviri, had been but a new-born babe. Hairy monsters were overcoming his fighting men, and a black chieftain like himself was fighting shoulder to shoulder with the hideous pack that opposed him.

Kaviri battled bravely against his antagonist, for he felt that death had already claimed him, and so the least that he could do would be to sell his life as dearly as possible; but it was soon evident that his best was quite futile when pitted against the superhuman brawn and agility of the creature that at last found his throat and bent him back into the bottom of the canoe.

Presently Kaviri's head began to whirl—objects became confused and dim before his eyes—there was a great pain in his chest as he struggled for the breath of life that the thing upon him was shutting off for ever. Then he lost consciousness.

When he opened his eyes once more he found, much to his surprise, that he was not dead. He lay, securely bound, in the bottom of his own canoe. A great panther sat upon its haunches, looking down upon him.

Kaviri shuddered and closed his eyes again, waiting for the ferocious creature to spring upon him and put him out of his misery of terror.

After a moment, no rending fangs having buried themselves in his trembling body, he again ventured to open his eyes. Beyond the panther kneeled the white giant who had overcome him.

The man was wielding a paddle, while directly behind him Kaviri saw some of his own warriors similarly engaged. Back of them again squatted several of the hairy apes.

Tarzan, seeing that the chief had regained consciousness, addressed him.

"Your warriors tell me that you are the chief of a numerous people, and that your name is Kaviri," he said.

"Yes," replied the black.

"Why did you attack me? I came in peace."

"Another white man 'came in peace' three moons ago," replied Kaviri; "and after we had brought him presents of a goat and cassava and milk, he set upon us with his guns and killed many of my people, and then went on his way, taking all of our goats and many of our young men and women."

"I am not as this other white man," replied Tarzan. "I should not have harmed you had you not set upon me. Tell me, what was the face of this bad white man like? I am searching for one who has wronged me. Possibly this may be the very one."

"He was a man with a bad face, covered with a great, black beard, and he was very, very wicked—yes, very wicked indeed."

"Was there a little white child with him?" asked Tarzan, his heart almost stopped as he awaited the black's answer.

"No, bwana," replied Kaviri, "the white child was not with this man's party—it was with the other party."

"Other party!" exclaimed Tarzan. "What other party?"

"With the party that the very bad white man was pursuing. There was a white man, woman, and the child, with six Mosula porters. They passed up the river three days ahead of the very bad white man. I think that they were running away from him."

A white man, woman, and child! Tarzan was puzzled. The child must be his little Jack; but who could the woman be—and the man? Was it possible that one of Rokoff's confederates had conspired with some woman—who had accompanied the Russian—to steal the baby from him?

If this was the case, they had doubtless purposed returning the child to civilization and there either claiming a reward or holding the little prisoner for ransom.

But now that Rokoff had succeeded in chasing them far inland, up the savage river, there could be little doubt but that he would eventually overhaul them, unless, as was still more probable, they should be captured and killed by the very cannibals farther up the Ugambi, to whom, Tarzan was now convinced, it had been Rokoff's intention to deliver the baby.

As he talked to Kaviri the canoes had been moving steadily up-river toward the chief's village. Kaviri's warriors plied the paddles in the three canoes, casting sidelong, terrified glances at their hideous passengers. Three of the apes of Akut had been killed in the encounter, but there were, with Akut, eight of the frightful beasts remaining, and there was Sheeta, the panther, and Tarzan and Mugambi.

Kaviri's warriors thought that they had never seen so terrible a crew in all their lives. Momentarily they expected to be pounced upon and torn asunder by some of their captors; and, in fact, it was all that Tarzan and Mugambi and Akut could do to keep the snarling, ill-natured brutes from snapping at the glistening, naked bodies that brushed against them now and then with the movements of the paddlers, whose very fear added incitement to the beasts.

At Kaviri's camp Tarzan paused only long enough to eat the food that the blacks furnished, and arrange with the chief for a dozen men to man the paddles of his canoe.

Kaviri was only too glad to comply with any demands that the ape-man might make if only such compliance would hasten the departure of the horrid pack; but it was easier, he discovered, to promise men than to furnish them, for when his people learned his intentions those that had not already fled into the jungle proceeded to do so without loss of time, so that when Kaviri turned to point out those who were to accompany Tarzan, he discovered that he was the only member of his tribe left within the village.

Tarzan could not repress a smile.

"They do not seem anxious to accompany us," he said; "but just remain quietly here, Kaviri, and presently you shall see your people flocking to your side."

Then the ape-man rose, and, calling his pack about him, commanded that Mugambi remain with Kaviri, and disappeared in the jungle with Sheeta and the apes at his heels.

For half an hour the silence of the grim forest was broken only by the ordinary sounds of the teeming life that but adds to its lowering loneliness. Kaviri and Mugambi sat alone in the palisaded village, waiting.

Presently from a great distance came a hideous sound. Mugambi recognized the weird challenge of the ape-man. Immediately from different points of the compass rose a horrid semicircle of similar shrieks and screams, punctuated now and again by the blood-curdling cry of a hungry panther.

BETRAYED

The two savages, Kaviri and Mugambi, squatting before the entrance to Kaviri's hut, looked at one another—Kaviri with ill-concealed alarm.

"What is it?" he whispered.

"It is Bwana Tarzan and his people," replied Mugambi. "But what they are doing I know not, unless it be that they are devouring your people who ran away."

Kaviri shuddered and rolled his eyes fearfully toward the jungle. In all his long life in the savage forest he had never heard such an awful, fearsome din.

Closer and closer came the sounds, and now with them were mingled the terrified shrieks of women and children and of men. For twenty long minutes the blood-curdling cries continued, until they seemed but a stone's throw from the palisade. Kaviri rose to flee, but Mugambi seized and held him, for such had been the command of Tarzan.

A moment later a horde of terrified natives burst from the jungle, racing toward the shelter of their huts. Like frightened sheep they ran, and behind them, driving them as sheep might be driven, came Tarzan and Sheeta and the hideous apes of Akut.

Presently Tarzan stood before Kaviri, the old quiet smile upon his lips.

"Your people have returned, my brother," he said, "and now you may select those who are to accompany me and paddle my canoe."

Tremblingly Kaviri tottered to his feet, calling to his people to come from their huts; but none responded to his summons.

"Tell them," suggested Tarzan, "that if they do not come I shall send my people in after them."

Kaviri did as he was bid, and in an instant the entire population of the village came forth, their wide and frightened eyes rolling from one to another of the savage creatures that wandered about the village street.

Quickly Kaviri designated a dozen warriors to accompany Tarzan. The poor fellows went almost white with terror at the prospect of close contact with the panther and the apes in the narrow confines of the canoes; but when Kaviri explained to them that there was no escape—that Bwana Tarzan would pursue them with his grim horde should they attempt to run away from the duty—they finally went gloomily down to the river and took their places in the canoe.

It was with a sigh of relief that their chieftain saw the party disappear about a headland a short distance up-river.

For three days the strange company continued farther and farther into the heart of the savage country that lies on either side of the almost unexplored Ugambi. Three of the twelve warriors deserted during that time; but as several of the apes had finally learned the secret of the paddles, Tarzan felt no dismay because of the loss.

As a matter of fact, he could have travelled much more rapidly on shore, but he believed that he could hold his own wild crew together to better advantage by keeping them to the boat as much as possible. Twice a day they landed to hunt and feed, and at night they slept upon the bank of the mainland or on one of the numerous little islands that dotted the river.

Before them the natives fled in alarm, so that they found only deserted villages in their path as they proceeded. Tarzan was anxious to get in touch with some of the savages who dwelt upon the river's banks, but so far he had been unable to do so.

Finally he decided to take to the land himself, leaving his company to follow after him by boat. He explained to Mugambi the thing that he had in mind, and told Akut to follow the directions of the black.

"I will join you again in a few days," he said. "Now I go ahead to learn what has become of the very bad white man whom I seek."

At the next halt Tarzan took to the shore, and was soon lost to the view of his people.

The first few villages he came to were deserted, showing that news of the coming of his pack had travelled rapidly; but toward evening he came upon a distant cluster of thatched huts surrounded by a rude palisade, within which were a couple of hundred natives.

The women were preparing the evening meal as Tarzan of the Apes poised above them in the branches of a giant tree which overhung the palisade at one point.

The ape-man was at a loss as to how he might enter into communication with these people without either frightening them or arousing their savage love of battle. He had no desire to fight now, for he was upon a much more important mission than that of battling with every chance tribe that he should happen to meet with.

At last he hit upon a plan, and after seeing that he was concealed from the view of those below, he gave a few hoarse grunts in imitation of a panther. All eyes immediately turned upward toward the foliage above.

It was growing dark, and they could not penetrate the leafy screen which shielded the ape-man from their view. The moment that he had won their attention he raised his voice to the shriller and more hideous scream of the beast he personated, and then, scarce stirring a leaf in his descent, dropped to the ground once again outside the palisade, and, with the speed of a deer, ran quickly round to the village gate.

Here he beat upon the fibre-bound saplings of which the barrier was constructed, shouting to the natives in their own tongue that he was a friend who wished food and shelter for the night.

Tarzan knew well the nature of the black man. He was aware that the grunting and screaming of Sheeta in the tree above them would set their nerves on edge, and that his pounding upon their gate after dark would still further add to their terror.

That they did not reply to his hail was no surprise, for natives are fearful of any voice that comes out of the night from beyond their palisades, attributing it always to some demon or other ghostly visitor; but still he continued to call.

"Let me in, my friends!" he cried. "I am a white man pursuing the very bad white man who passed this way a few days ago. I follow to punish him for the sins he has committed against you and me.

"If you doubt my friendship, I will prove it to you by going into the tree above your village and driving Sheeta back into the jungle before he leaps among you. If you will not promise to take me in and treat me as a friend I shall let Sheeta stay and devour you."

For a moment there was silence. Then the voice of an old man came out of the quiet of the village street.

"If you are indeed a white man and a friend, we will let you come in; but first you must drive Sheeta away."

"Very well," replied Tarzan. "Listen, and you shall hear Sheeta fleeing before me."

The ape-man returned quickly to the tree, and this time he made a great noise as he entered the branches, at the same time growling ominously after the manner of the panther, so that those below would believe that the great beast was still there.

When he reached a point well above the village street he made a great commotion, shaking the tree violently, crying aloud to the panther to flee or be killed, and punctuating his own voice with the screams and mouthings of an angry beast.

Presently he raced toward the opposite side of the tree and off into the jungle, pounding loudly against the boles of trees as he went, and voicing the panther's diminishing growls as he drew farther and farther away from the village.

A few minutes later he returned to the village gate, calling to the natives within.

"I have driven Sheeta away," he said. "Now come and admit me as you promised."

For a time there was the sound of excited discussion within the palisade, but at length a half-dozen warriors came and opened the gates, peering anxiously out in evident trepidation as to the nature of the creature which they should find waiting there. They were not much relieved at sight of an almost naked white man; but when Tarzan had reassured them in quiet tones, protesting his friendship for them, they opened the barrier a trifle farther and admitted him.

When the gates had been once more secured the self-confidence of the savages returned, and as Tarzan walked up the village street toward the chief's hut he was surrounded by a host of curious men, women, and children.

From the chief he learned that Rokoff had passed up the river a week previous, and that he had horns growing from his forehead, and was accompanied by a thousand devils. Later the chief said that the very bad white man had remained a month in his village.

Though none of these statements agreed with Kaviri's, that the Russian was but three days gone from the chieftain's village and that his following was much smaller than now stated, Tarzan was in no manner surprised at the discrepancies, for he was quite familiar with the savage mind's strange manner of functioning.

What he was most interested in knowing was that he was upon the right trail, and that it led toward the interior. In this circumstance he knew that Rokoff could never escape him.

After several hours of questioning and cross-questioning the ape-man learned that another party had preceded the Russian by several days—three whites—a man, a woman, and a little man-child, with several Mosulas.

Tarzan explained to the chief that his people would follow him in a canoe, probably the next day, and that though he might go on ahead of them the chief was to receive them kindly and have no fear of them, for Mugambi would see that they did not harm the chief's people, if they were accorded a friendly reception.

"And now," he concluded, "I shall lie down beneath this tree and sleep. I am very tired. Permit no one to disturb me."

The chief offered him a hut, but Tarzan, from past experience of native dwellings, preferred the open air, and, further, he had plans of his own that could be better carried out if he remained beneath the tree. He gave as his reason a desire to be close at hand should Sheeta return, and after this explanation the chief was very glad to permit him to sleep beneath the tree.

Tarzan had always found that it stood him in good stead to leave with natives the impression that he was to some extent possessed of more or less miraculous powers. He might easily have entered their village without recourse to the gates, but he believed that a sudden and unaccountable disappearance when he was ready to leave them would result in a more lasting impression upon their childlike minds, and so as soon as the village was quiet in sleep he rose, and, leaping into the branches of the tree above him, faded silently into the black mystery of the jungle night.

All the balance of that night the ape-man swung rapidly through the upper and middle terraces of the forest. When the going was good there he preferred the upper branches of the giant trees, for then his way was better lighted by the moon; but so accustomed were all his senses to the grim world of his birth that it was possible for him, even in the dense, black shadows near the ground, to move with ease and rapidity. You or I walking beneath the arcs of Main Street, or Broadway, or State Street, could not have moved more surely or with a tenth the speed of the agile ape-man through the gloomy mazes that would have baffled us entirely.

At dawn he stopped to feed, and then he slept for several hours, taking up the pursuit again toward noon.

Twice he came upon natives, and, though he had considerable difficulty in approaching them, he succeeded in each instance in quieting both their fears and bellicose intentions toward him, and learned from them that he was upon the trail of the Russian.

Two days later, still following up the Ugambi, he came upon a large village. The chief, a wicked-looking fellow with the sharp-filed teeth that often denote the cannibal, received him with apparent friendliness.

The ape-man was now thoroughly fatigued, and had determined to rest for eight or ten hours that he might be fresh and strong when he caught up with Rokoff, as he was sure he must do within a very short time.

The chief told him that the bearded white man had left his village only the morning before, and that doubtless he would be able to overtake him in a short time. The other party the chief had not seen or heard of, so he said.

Tarzan did not like the appearance or manner of the fellow, who seemed, though friendly enough, to harbour a certain contempt for this half-naked white man who came with no followers and offered no presents; but he needed the rest and food that the village would afford him with less effort than the jungle, and so, as he knew no fear of man, beast, or devil, he curled himself up in the shadow of a hut and was soon asleep.

Scarcely had he left the chief than the latter called two of his warriors, to whom he whispered a few instructions. A moment later the sleek, black bodies were racing along the river path, up-stream, toward the east.

In the village the chief maintained perfect quiet. He would permit no one to approach the sleeping visitor, nor any singing, nor loud talking. He was remarkably solicitous lest his guest be disturbed.

Three hours later several canoes came silently into view from up the Ugambi. They were being pushed ahead rapidly by the brawny muscles of their black crews. Upon the bank before the river stood the chief, his spear raised in a horizontal position above his head, as though in some manner of predetermined signal to those within the boats.

And such indeed was the purpose of his attitude—which meant that the white stranger within his village still slept peacefully.

In the bows of two of the canoes were the runners that the chief had sent forth three hours earlier. It was evident that they had been dispatched to follow and bring back this party, and that the signal from the bank was one that had been determined upon before they left the village.

In a few moments the dugouts drew up to the verdure-clad bank. The native warriors filed out, and with them a half-dozen white men. Sullen, ugly-looking customers they were, and none more so than the evil-faced, black-bearded man who commanded them.

"Where is the white man your messengers report to be with you?" he asked of the chief.

"This way, bwana," replied the native. "Carefully have I kept silence in the village that he might be still asleep when you returned. I do not know that he is one who seeks you to do you harm, but he questioned me closely about your coming and your going, and his appearance is as that of the one you described, but whom you believed safe in the country which you called Jungle Island.

"Had you not told me this tale I should not have recognized him, and then he might have gone after and slain you. If he is a friend and no enemy, then no harm has been done, bwana; but if he proves to be an enemy, I should like very much to have a rifle and some ammunition."

"You have done well," replied the white man, "and you shall have the rifle and ammunition whether he be a friend or enemy, provided that you stand with me."

"I shall stand with you, bwana," said the chief, "and now come and look upon the stranger, who sleeps within my village."

So saying, he turned and led the way toward the hut, in the shadow of which the unconscious Tarzan slept peacefully.

Behind the two men came the remaining whites and a score of warriors; but the raised forefingers of the chief and his companion held them all to perfect silence.

As they turned the corner of the hut, cautiously and upon tiptoe, an ugly smile touched the lips of the white as his eyes fell upon the giant figure of the sleeping ape-man.

The chief looked at the other inquiringly. The latter nodded his head, to signify that the chief had made no mistake in his suspicions. Then he turned to those behind him and, pointing to the sleeping man, motioned for them to seize and bind him.

A moment later a dozen brutes had leaped upon the surprised Tarzan, and so quickly did they work that he was securely bound before he could make half an effort to escape.

Then they threw him down upon his back, and as his eyes turned toward the crowd that stood near, they fell upon the malign face of Nikolas Rokoff.

A sneer curled the Russian's lips. He stepped quite close to Tarzan.

"Pig!" he cried. "Have you not learned sufficient wisdom to keep away from Nikolas Rokoff?"

Then he kicked the prostrate man full in the face.

"That for your welcome," he said.

"Tonight, before my Ethiop friends eat you, I shall tell you what has already befallen your wife and child, and what further plans I have for their futures."

EDGAR RICE BURROUGHS

THE DANCE OF DEATH

Through the luxuriant, tangled vegetation of the Stygian jungle night a great lithe body made its way sinuously and in utter silence upon its soft padded feet. Only two blazing points of yellow-green flame shone occasionally with the reflected light of the equatorial moon that now and again pierced the softly sighing roof rustling in the night wind.

Occasionally the beast would stop with high-held nose, sniffing searchingly. At other times a quick, brief incursion into the branches above delayed it momentarily in its steady journey toward the east. To its sensitive nostrils came the subtle unseen spoor of many a tender four-footed creature, bringing the slaver of hunger to the cruel, drooping jowl.

But steadfastly it kept on its way, strangely ignoring the cravings of appetite that at another time would have sent the rolling, fur-clad muscles flying at some soft throat.

All that night the creature pursued its lonely way, and the next day it halted only to make a single kill, which it tore to fragments and devoured with sullen, grumbling rumbles as though half famished for lack of food.

It was dusk when it approached the palisade that surrounded a large native village. Like the shadow of a swift and silent death it circled the village, nose to ground, halting at last close to the palisade, where it almost touched the backs of several huts. Here the beast sniffed for a moment, and then, turning its head upon one side, listened with up-pricked ears.

What it heard was no sound by the standards of human ears, yet to the highly attuned and delicate organs of the beast a message seemed to be borne to the savage brain. A wondrous transformation was wrought in the motionless mass of statuesque bone and muscle that had an instant before stood as though carved out of the living bronze.

As if it had been poised upon steel springs, suddenly released, it rose quickly and silently to the top of the palisade, disappearing, stealthily and catlike, into the dark space between the wall and the back of an adjacent hut.

In the village street beyond women were preparing many little fires and fetching cooking-pots filled with water, for a great feast was to be celebrated ere the night was many hours older. About a stout stake near the centre of the circling fires a little knot of black warriors stood conversing, their bodies smeared with white and blue and ochre in broad and grotesque bands. Great circles of colour were drawn about their eyes and lips, their breasts and abdomens, and from their clay-plastered coiffures rose gay feathers and bits of long, straight wire.

The village was preparing for the feast, while in a hut at one side of the scene of the coming orgy the bound victim of their bestial appetites lay waiting for the end. And such an end!

Tarzan of the Apes, tensing his mighty muscles, strained at the bonds that pinioned him; but they had been re-enforced many times at the instigation of the Russian, so that not even the ape-man's giant brawn could budge them.

Death!

Tarzan had looked the Hideous Hunter in the face many a time, and smiled. And he would smile again tonight when he knew the end was coming quickly; but now his thoughts were not of himself, but of those others—the dear ones who must suffer most because of his passing.

Jane would never know the manner of it. For that he thanked Heaven; and he was thankful also that she at least was safe in the heart of the world's greatest city. Safe among kind and loving friends who would do their best to lighten her misery.

But the boy!

Tarzan writhed at the thought of him. His son! And now he—the mighty Lord of the Jungle—he, Tarzan, King of the Apes, the only one in all the world fitted to find and save the child from the horrors that

Rokoff's evil mind had planned—had been trapped like a silly, dumb creature. He was to die in a few hours, and with him would go the child's last chance of succour.

Rokoff had been in to see and revile and abuse him several times during the afternoon; but he had been able to wring no word of remonstrance or murmur of pain from the lips of the giant captive.

So at last he had given up, reserving his particular bit of exquisite mental torture for the last moment, when, just before the savage spears of the cannibals should for ever make the object of his hatred immune to further suffering, the Russian planned to reveal to his enemy the true whereabouts of his wife whom he thought safe in England.

Dusk had fallen upon the village, and the ape-men could hear the preparations going forward for the torture and the feast. The dance of death he could picture in his mind's eye—for he had seen the thing many times in the past. Now he was to be the central figure, bound to the stake.

The torture of the slow death as the circling warriors cut him to bits with the fiendish skill, that mutilated without bringing unconsciousness, had no terrors for him. He was inured to suffering and to the sight of blood and to cruel death; but the desire to live was no less strong within him, and until the last spark of life should flicker and go out, his whole being would remain quick with hope and determination. Let them relax their watchfulness but for an instant, he knew that his cunning mind and giant muscles would find a way to escape—escape and revenge.

As he lay, thinking furiously on every possibility of self-salvation, there came to his sensitive nostrils a faint and a familiar scent. Instantly every faculty of his mind was upon the alert. Presently his trained ears caught the sound of the soundless presence without—behind the hut wherein he lay. His lips moved, and though no sound came forth that might have been appreciable to a human ear beyond the walls of his prison, yet he realized that the one beyond would hear. Already he knew who that one was, for his nostrils had told him as plainly as your eyes or mine tell us of the identity of an old friend whom we come upon in broad daylight.

An instant later he heard the soft sound of a fur-clad body and padded feet scaling the outer wall behind the hut and then a tearing at the poles which formed the wall. Presently through the hole thus made slunk a great beast, pressing its cold muzzle close to his neck.

It was Sheeta, the panther.

The beast snuffed round the prostrate man, whining a little. There was a limit to the interchange of ideas which could take place between these two, and so Tarzan could not be sure that Sheeta understood all that he attempted to communicate to him. That the man was tied and helpless Sheeta could, of course, see; but that to the mind of the panther this would carry any suggestion of harm in so far as his master was concerned, Tarzan could not guess.

What had brought the beast to him? The fact that he had come augured well for what he might accomplish; but when Tarzan tried to get Sheeta to gnaw his bonds asunder the great animal could not seem to understand what was expected of him, and, instead, but licked the wrists and arms of the prisoner.

Presently there came an interruption. Some one was approaching the hut. Sheeta gave a low growl and slunk into the blackness of a far corner. Evidently the visitor did not hear the warning sound, for almost immediately he entered the hut—a tall, naked, savage warrior.

He came to Tarzan's side and pricked him with a spear. From the lips of the ape-man came a weird, uncanny sound, and in answer to it there leaped from the blackness of the hut's farthermost corner a bolt of fur-clad death. Full upon the breast of the painted savage the great beast struck, burying sharp talons in the black flesh and sinking great yellow fangs in the ebon throat.

There was a fearful scream of anguish and terror from the black, and mingled with it was the hideous challenge of the killing panther. Then came silence—silence except for the rending of bloody flesh and the crunching of human bones between mighty jaws.

The noise had brought sudden quiet to the village without. Then there came the sound of voices in consultation.

High-pitched, fear-filled voices, and deep, low tones of authority, as the chief spoke. Tarzan and the panther heard the approaching footsteps of many men, and then, to Tarzan's surprise, the great cat rose from across the body of its kill, and slunk noiselessly from the hut through the aperture through which it had entered.

The man heard the soft scraping of the body as it passed over the top of the palisade, and then silence. From the opposite side of the hut he heard the savages approaching to investigate.

He had little hope that Sheeta would return, for had the great cat intended to defend him against all comers it would have remained by his side as it heard the approaching savages without.

Tarzan knew how strange were the workings of the brains of the mighty carnivora of the jungle—how fiendishly fearless they might be in the face of certain death, and again how timid upon the slightest provocation. There was doubt in his mind that some note of the approaching blacks vibrating with fear had struck an answering chord in the nervous system of the panther, sending him slinking through the jungle, his tail between his legs.

The man shrugged. Well, what of it? He had expected to die, and, after all, what might Sheeta have done for him other than to maul a couple of his enemies before a rifle in the hands of one of the whites should have dispatched him!

If the cat could have released him! Ah! that would have resulted in a very different story; but it had proved beyond the understanding of Sheeta, and now the beast was gone and Tarzan must definitely abandon hope.

The natives were at the entrance to the hut now, peering fearfully into the dark interior. Two in advance held lighted torches in their left hands and ready spears in their right. They held back timorously against those behind, who were pushing them forward.

The shrieks of the panther's victim, mingled with those of the great cat, had wrought mightily upon their poor nerves, and now the awful silence of the dark interior seemed even more terribly ominous than had the frightful screaming.

Presently one of those who was being forced unwillingly within hit upon a happy scheme for learning first the precise nature of the danger which menaced him from the silent interior. With a quick movement he flung his lighted torch into the centre of the hut. Instantly all within was illuminated for a brief second before the burning brand was dashed out against the earth floor.

There was the figure of the white prisoner still securely bound as they had last seen him, and in the centre of the hut another figure equally as motionless, its throat and breasts horribly torn and mangled.

The sight that met the eyes of the foremost savages inspired more terror within their superstitious breasts than would the presence of Sheeta, for they saw only the result of a ferocious attack upon one of their fellows.

Not seeing the cause, their fear-ridden minds were free to attribute the ghastly work to supernatural causes, and with the thought they turned, screaming, from the hut, bowling over those who stood directly behind them in the exuberance of their terror.

For an hour Tarzan heard only the murmur of excited voices from the far end of the village. Evidently the savages were once more attempting to work up their flickering courage to a point that would permit them to make another invasion of the hut, for now and then came a savage yell, such as the warriors give to bolster up their bravery upon the field of battle.

But in the end it was two of the whites who first entered, carrying torches and guns. Tarzan was not surprised to discover that neither of them was Rokoff. He would have wagered his soul that no power on earth could have tempted that great coward to face the unknown menace of the hut.

When the natives saw that the white men were not attacked they, too, crowded into the interior, their voices hushed with terror as they looked upon the mutilated corpse of their comrade. The whites tried in vain to elicit an explanation from Tarzan; but to all their queries he but shook his head, a grim and knowing smile curving his lips.

At last Rokoff came.

His face grew very white as his eyes rested upon the bloody thing grinning up at him from the floor, the face set in a death mask of excruciating horror.

"Come!" he said to the chief. "Let us get to work and finish this demon before he has an opportunity to repeat this thing upon more of your people."

The chief gave orders that Tarzan should be lifted and carried to the stake; but it was several minutes before he could prevail upon any of his men to touch the prisoner.

At last, however, four of the younger warriors dragged Tarzan roughly from the hut, and once outside the pall of terror seemed lifted from the savage hearts.

A score of howling blacks pushed and buffeted the prisoner down the village street and bound him to the post in the centre of the circle of little fires and boiling cooking-pots.

When at last he was made fast and seemed quite helpless and beyond the faintest hope of succour, Rokoff's shrivelled wart of courage swelled to its usual proportions when danger was not present.

He stepped close to the ape-man, and, seizing a spear from the hands of one of the savages, was the first to prod the helpless victim. A little stream of blood trickled down the giant's smooth skin from the wound in his side; but no murmur of pain passed his lips.

The smile of contempt upon his face seemed to infuriate the Russian. With a volley of oaths he leaped at the helpless captive, beating him upon the face with his clenched fists and kicking him mercilessly about the legs.

Then he raised the heavy spear to drive it through the mighty heart, and still Tarzan of the Apes smiled contemptuously upon him.

Before Rokoff could drive the weapon home the chief sprang upon him and dragged him away from his intended victim.

"Stop, white man!" he cried. "Rob us of this prisoner and our death-dance, and you yourself may have to take his place."

The threat proved most effective in keeping the Russian from further assaults upon the prisoner, though he continued to stand a little apart and hurl taunts at his enemy. He told Tarzan that he himself was going to eat the ape-man's heart. He enlarged upon the horrors of the future life of Tarzan's son, and intimated that his vengeance would reach as well to Jane Clayton.

"You think your wife safe in England," said Rokoff. "Poor fool! She is even now in the hands of one not even of decent birth, and far from the safety of London and the protection of her friends. I had not meant to tell you this until I could bring to you upon Jungle Island proof of her fate.

"Now that you are about to die the most unthinkably horrid death that it is given a white man to die—let this word of the plight of your wife add to the torments that you must suffer before the last savage spear-thrust releases you from your torture."

The dance had commenced now, and the yells of the circling warriors drowned Rokoff's further attempts to distress his victim.

The leaping savages, the flickering firelight playing upon their painted bodies, circled about the victim at the stake.

To Tarzan's memory came a similar scene, when he had rescued D'Arnot from a like predicament at the last moment before the final spear-thrust should have ended his sufferings. Who was there now to rescue him? In all the world there was none able to save him from the torture and the death.

The thought that these human fiends would devour him when the dance was done caused him not a single qualm of horror or disgust. It did not add to his sufferings as it would have to those of an ordinary white man, for all his life Tarzan had seen the beasts of the jungle devour the flesh of their kills.

Had he not himself battled for the grisly forearm of a great ape at that long-gone Dum-Dum, when he had slain the fierce Tublat and won his niche in the respect of the Apes of Kerchak?

The dancers were leaping more closely to him now. The spears were commencing to find his body in the first torturing pricks that prefaced the more serious thrusts.

It would not be long now. The ape-man longed for the last savage lunge that would end his misery.

And then, far out in the mazes of the weird jungle, rose a shrill scream.

For an instant the dancers paused, and in the silence of the interval there rose from the lips of the fast-bound white man an answering shriek, more fearsome and more terrible than that of the jungle-beast that had roused it.

For several minutes the blacks hesitated; then, at the urging of Rokoff and their chief, they leaped in to finish the dance and the victim; but ere ever another spear touched the brown hide a tawny streak of green-eyed hate and ferocity bounded from the door of the hut in which Tarzan had been imprisoned, and Sheeta, the panther, stood snarling beside his master.

For an instant the blacks and the whites stood transfixed with terror. Their eyes were riveted upon the bared fangs of the jungle cat.

Only Tarzan of the Apes saw what else there was emerging from the dark interior of the hut.

CHIVALRY OR VILLAINY

From her cabin port upon the *Kincaid*, Jane Clayton had seen her husband rowed to the verdure-clad shore of Jungle Island, and then the ship once more proceeded upon its way.

For several days she saw no one other than Sven Anderssen, the *Kincaid*'s taciturn and repellent cook. She asked him the name of the shore upon which her husband had been set.

"Ay tank it blow purty soon purty hard," replied the Swede, and that was all that she could get out of him.

She had come to the conclusion that he spoke no other English, and so she ceased to importune him for information; but never did she forget to greet him pleasantly or to thank him for the hideous, nauseating meals he brought her.

Three days from the spot where Tarzan had been marooned the *Kincaid* came to anchor in the mouth of a great river, and presently Rokoff came to Jane Clayton's cabin.

"We have arrived, my dear," he said, with a sickening leer. "I have come to offer you safety, liberty, and ease. My heart has been softened toward you in your suffering, and I would make amends as best I may.

"Your husband was a brute—you know that best who found him naked in his native jungle, roaming wild with the savage beasts that were his fellows. Now I am a gentleman, not only born of noble blood, but raised gently as befits a man of quality.

"To you, dear Jane, I offer the love of a cultured man and association with one of culture and refinement, which you must have sorely missed in your relations with the poor ape that through your girlish infatuation you married so thoughtlessly. I love you, Jane. You have but to say the word and no further sorrows shall afflict you—even your baby shall be returned to you unharmed."

Outside the door Sven Anderssen paused with the noonday meal he had been carrying to Lady Greystoke. Upon the end of his long, stringy neck his little head was cocked to one side, his close-set eyes were half closed, his ears, so expressive was his whole attitude of stealthy eavesdropping, seemed truly to be cocked forward—even his long, yellow, straggly moustache appeared to assume a sly droop.

As Rokoff closed his appeal, awaiting the reply he invited, the look of surprise upon Jane Clayton's face turned to one of disgust. She fairly shuddered in the fellow's face.

"I would not have been surprised, M. Rokoff," she said, "had you attempted to force me to submit to your evil desires, but that you should be so fatuous as to believe that I, wife of John Clayton, would come to you willingly, even to save my life, I should never have imagined. I have known you for a scoundrel, M. Rokoff; but until now I had not taken you for a fool."

Rokoff's eyes narrowed, and the red of mortification flushed out the pallor of his face. He took a step toward the girl, threateningly.

"We shall see who is the fool at last," he hissed, "when I have broken you to my will and your plebeian Yankee stubbornness has cost you all that you hold dear—even the life of your baby—for, by the bones of St. Peter, I'll forego all that I had planned for the brat and cut its heart out before your very eyes. You'll learn what it means to insult Nikolas Rokoff."

Jane Clayton turned wearily away.

"What is the use," she said, "of expatiating upon the depths to which your vengeful nature can sink? You cannot move me either by threats or deeds. My baby cannot judge yet for himself, but I, his mother, can foresee that should it have been given him to survive to man's estate he would willingly sacrifice his life for the honour of his mother. Love him as I do, I would not purchase his life at such a price. Did I, he would execrate my memory to the day of his death."

Rokoff was now thoroughly angered because of his failure to reduce the girl to terror. He felt only hate for her, but it had come to his diseased mind that if he could force her to accede to his demands as the price of her life and her child's, the cup of his revenge would be filled to brimming when he could flaunt the wife of Lord Greystoke in the capitals of Europe as his mistress.

Again he stepped closer to her. His evil face was convulsed with rage and desire. Like a wild beast he sprang upon her, and with his strong fingers at her throat forced her backward upon the berth.

At the same instant the door of the cabin opened noisily. Rokoff leaped to his feet, and, turning, faced the Swede cook.

Into the fellow's usually foxy eyes had come an expression of utter stupidity. His lower jaw drooped in vacuous harmony. He busied himself in arranging Lady Greystoke's meal upon the tiny table at one side of her cabin.

The Russian glared at him.

"What do you mean," he cried, "by entering here without permission? Get out!"

The cook turned his watery blue eyes upon Rokoff and smiled vacuously.

"Ay tank it blow purty soon purty hard," he said, and then he began rearranging the few dishes upon the little table.

"Get out of here, or I'll throw you out, you miserable blockhead!" roared Rokoff, taking a threatening step toward the Swede.

Anderssen continued to smile foolishly in his direction, but one ham-like paw slid stealthily to the handle of the long, slim knife that protruded from the greasy cord supporting his soiled apron.

Rokoff saw the move and stopped short in his advance. Then he turned toward Jane Clayton.

"I will give you until tomorrow," he said, "to reconsider your answer to my offer. All will be sent ashore upon one pretext or another except you and the child, Paulvitch and myself. Then without interruption you will be able to witness the death of the baby."

He spoke in French that the cook might not understand the sinister portent of his words. When he had done he banged out of the cabin without another look at the man who had interrupted him in his sorry work.

When he had gone, Sven Anderssen turned toward Lady Greystoke—the idiotic expression that had masked his thoughts had fallen away, and in its place was one of craft and cunning.

"Hay tank Ay ban a fool," he said. "Hay ben the fool. Ay savvy Franch."

Jane Clayton looked at him in surprise.

"You understood all that he said, then?"

Anderssen grinned.

"You bat," he said.

"And you heard what was going on in here and came to protect me?"

"You bane good to me," explained the Swede. "Hay treat me like darty dog. Ay help you, lady. You yust vait—Ay help you. Ay ban Vast Coast lots times."

"But how can you help me, Sven," she asked, "when all these men will be against us?"

"Ay tank," said Sven Anderssen, "it blow purty soon purty hard," and then he turned and left the cabin.

Though Jane Clayton doubted the cook's ability to be of any material service to her, she was nevertheless deeply grateful to him for what he already had done. The feeling that among these enemies she had one friend brought the first ray of comfort that had come to lighten the burden of her miserable apprehensions throughout the long voyage of the *Kincaid*.

She saw no more of Rokoff that day, nor of any other until Sven came with her evening meal. She tried to draw him into conversation relative to his plans to aid her, but all that she could get from him was his stereotyped prophecy as to the future state of the wind. He seemed suddenly to have relapsed into his wonted state of dense stupidity.

However, when he was leaving her cabin a little later with the empty dishes he whispered very low, "Leave on your clothes an' roll up your blankets. Ay come back after you purty soon."

He would have slipped from the room at once, but Jane laid her hand upon his sleeve.

"My baby?" she asked. "I cannot go without him."

"You do wot Ay tal you," said Anderssen, scowling. "Ay ban halpin' you, so don't you gat too fonny."

When he had gone Jane Clayton sank down upon her berth in utter bewilderment. What was she to do? Suspicions as to the intentions of the Swede swarmed her brain. Might she not be infinitely worse off if she gave herself into his power than she already was?

No, she could be no worse off in company with the devil himself than with Nikolas Rokoff, for the devil at least bore the reputation of being a gentleman.

She swore a dozen times that she would not leave the *Kincaid* without her baby, and yet she remained clothed long past her usual hour for retiring, and her blankets were neatly rolled and bound with stout cord, when about midnight there came a stealthy scratching upon the panels of her door.

Swiftly she crossed the room and drew the bolt. Softly the door swung open to admit the muffled figure of the Swede. On one arm he carried a bundle, evidently his blankets. His other hand was raised in a gesture commanding silence, a grimy forefinger upon his lips.

He came quite close to her.

"Carry this," he said. "Do not make some noise when you see it. It ban you kid."

Quick hands snatched the bundle from the cook, and hungry mother arms folded the sleeping infant to her breast, while hot tears of joy ran down her cheeks and her whole frame shook with the emotion of the moment.

"Come!" said Anderssen. "We got no time to vaste."

He snatched up her bundle of blankets, and outside the cabin door his own as well. Then he led her to the ship's side, steadied her descent of the monkey-ladder, holding the child for her as she climbed to the waiting boat below. A moment later he had cut the rope that held the small boat to the steamer's side, and, bending silently to the muffled oars, was pulling toward the black shadows up the Ugambi River.

Anderssen rowed on as though quite sure of his ground, and when after half an hour the moon broke through the clouds there was revealed upon their left the mouth of a tributary running into the Ugambi. Up this narrow channel the Swede turned the prow of the small boat.

Jane Clayton wondered if the man knew where he was bound. She did not know that in his capacity as cook he had that day been rowed up this very stream to a little village where he had bartered with the natives for such provisions as they had for sale, and that he had there arranged the details of his plan for the adventure upon which they were now setting forth.

Even though the moon was full, the surface of the small river was quite dark. The giant trees overhung its narrow banks, meeting in a great arch above the centre of the river. Spanish moss dropped from the gracefully bending limbs, and enormous creepers clambered in riotous profusion from the ground to the loftiest branch, falling in curving loops almost to the water's placid breast.

Now and then the river's surface would be suddenly broken ahead of them by a huge crocodile, startled by the splashing of the oars, or, snorting and blowing, a family of hippos would dive from a sandy bar to the cool, safe depths of the bottom.

From the dense jungles upon either side came the weird night cries of the carnivora—the maniacal voice of the hyena, the coughing grunt of the panther, the deep and awful roar of the lion. And with them strange, uncanny notes that the girl could not ascribe to any particular night prowler—more terrible because of their mystery.

Huddled in the stern of the boat she sat with her baby strained close to her bosom, and because of that little tender, helpless thing she was happier tonight than she had been for many a sorrow-ridden day.

Even though she knew not to what fate she was going, or how soon that fate might overtake her, still was she happy and thankful for the moment, however brief, that she might press her baby tightly in her arms. She could scarce wait for the coming of the day that she might look again upon the bright face of her little, black-eyed Jack.

Again and again she tried to strain her eyes through the blackness of the jungle night to have but a tiny peep at those beloved features, but only the dim outline of the baby face rewarded her efforts. Then once more she would cuddle the warm, little bundle close to her throbbing heart.

It must have been close to three o'clock in the morning that Anderssen brought the boat's nose to the shore before a clearing where could be dimly seen in the waning moonlight a cluster of native huts encircled by a thorn *boma*.

At the village gate they were admitted by a native woman, the wife of the chief whom Anderssen had paid to assist him. She took them to the chief's hut, but Anderssen said that they would sleep without upon the ground, and so, her duty having been completed, she left them to their own devices.

The Swede, after explaining in his gruff way that the huts were doubtless filthy and vermin-ridden, spread Jane's blankets on the ground for her, and at a little distance unrolled his own and lay down to sleep.

It was some time before the girl could find a comfortable position upon the hard ground, but at last, the baby in the hollow of her arm, she dropped asleep from utter exhaustion. When she awoke it was broad daylight.

About her were clustered a score of curious natives—mostly men, for among the aborigines it is the male who owns this characteristic in its most exaggerated form. Instinctively Jane Clayton drew the baby more closely to her, though she soon saw that the blacks were far from intending her or the child any harm.

In fact, one of them offered her a gourd of milk—a filthy, smoke-begrimed gourd, with the ancient rind of long-curdled milk caked in layers within its neck; but the spirit of the giver touched her deeply, and her face lightened for a moment with one of those almost forgotten smiles of radiance that had helped to make her beauty famous both in Baltimore and London.

She took the gourd in one hand, and rather than cause the giver pain raised it to her lips, though for the life of her she could scarce restrain the qualm of nausea that surged through her as the malodorous thing approached her nostrils.

It was Anderssen who came to her rescue, and taking the gourd from her, drank a portion himself, and then returned it to the native with a gift of blue beads.

The sun was shining brightly now, and though the baby still slept, Jane could scarce restrain her impatient desire to have at least a brief glance at the beloved face. The natives had withdrawn at a command from their chief, who now stood talking with Anderssen, a little apart from her.

As she debated the wisdom of risking disturbing the child's slumber by lifting the blanket that now protected its face from the sun, she noted that the cook conversed with the chief in the language of the Negro.

What a remarkable man the fellow was, indeed! She had thought him ignorant and stupid but a short day before, and now, within the past twenty-four hours, she had learned that he spoke not only English but French as well, and the primitive dialect of the West Coast.

She had thought him shifty, cruel, and untrustworthy, yet in so far as she had reason to believe he had proved himself in every way the contrary since the day before. It scarce seemed credible that he could be serving her from motives purely chivalrous. There must be something deeper in his intentions and plans than he had yet disclosed.

She wondered, and when she looked at him—at his close-set, shifty eyes and repulsive features, she shuddered, for she was convinced that no lofty characteristics could be hid behind so foul an exterior.

As she was thinking of these things the while she debated the wisdom of uncovering the baby's face, there came a little grunt from the wee bundle in her lap, and then a gurgling coo that set her heart in raptures.

The baby was awake! Now she might feast her eyes upon him.

Quickly she snatched the blanket from before the infant's face; Anderssen was looking at her as she did so.

He saw her stagger to her feet, holding the baby at arm's length from her, her eyes glued in horror upon the little chubby face and twinkling eyes.

Then he heard her piteous cry as her knees gave beneath her, and she sank to the ground in a swoon.

THE SWEDE

As the warriors, clustered thick about Tarzan and Sheeta, realized that it was a flesh-and-blood panther that had interrupted their dance of death, they took heart a trifle, for in the face of all those circling spears even the mighty Sheeta would be doomed.

Rokoff was urging the chief to have his spearmen launch their missiles, and the black was upon the instant of issuing the command, when his eyes strayed beyond Tarzan, following the gaze of the ape-man.

With a yell of terror the chief turned and fled toward the village gate, and as his people looked to see the cause of his fright, they too took to their heels—for there, lumbering down upon them, their huge forms exaggerated by the play of moonlight and camp fire, came the hideous apes of Akut.

The instant the natives turned to flee the ape-man's savage cry rang out above the shrieks of the blacks, and in answer to it Sheeta and the apes leaped growling after the fugitives. Some of the warriors turned to battle with their enraged antagonists, but before the fiendish ferocity of the fierce beasts they went down to bloody death.

Others were dragged down in their flight, and it was not until the village was empty and the last of the blacks had disappeared into the bush that Tarzan was able to recall his savage pack to his side. Then it was that he discovered to his chagrin that he could not make one of them, not even the comparatively intelligent Akut, understand that he wished to be freed from the bonds that held him to the stake.

In time, of course, the idea would filter through their thick skulls, but in the meanwhile many things might happen—the blacks might return in force to regain their village; the whites might readily pick them all off with their rifles from the surrounding trees; he might even starve to death before the dull-witted apes realized that he wished them to gnaw through his bonds.

As for Sheeta—the great cat understood even less than the apes; but yet Tarzan could not but marvel at the remarkable characteristics this beast had evidenced. That it felt real affection for him there seemed little doubt, for now that the blacks were disposed of it walked slowly back and forth about the stake, rubbing its sides against the ape-man's legs and purring like a contented tabby. That it had gone of its own volition to bring the balance of the pack to his rescue, Tarzan could not doubt. His Sheeta was indeed a jewel among beasts.

Mugambi's absence worried the ape-man not a little. He attempted to learn from Akut what had become of the black, fearing that the beasts, freed from the restraint of Tarzan's presence, might have fallen upon the man and devoured him; but to all his questions the great ape but pointed back in the direction from which they had come out of the jungle.

The night passed with Tarzan still fast bound to the stake, and shortly after dawn his fears were realized in the discovery of naked black figures moving stealthily just within the edge of the jungle about the village. The blacks were returning.

With daylight their courage would be equal to the demands of a charge upon the handful of beasts that had routed them from their rightful abodes. The result of the encounter seemed foregone if the savages could curb their superstitious terror, for against their overwhelming numbers, their long spears and poisoned arrows, the panther and the apes could not be expected to survive a really determined attack.

That the blacks were preparing for a charge became apparent a few moments later, when they commenced to show themselves in force upon the edge of the clearing, dancing and jumping about as they waved their spears and shouted taunts and fierce warcries toward the village.

These manoeuvres Tarzan knew would continue until the blacks had worked themselves into a state of hysterical courage sufficient to sustain them for a short charge toward the village, and even though he doubted that they would reach it at the first attempt, he believed that at the second or the third they would swarm through the gateway, when the outcome could not be aught than the extermination of Tarzan's bold, but unarmed and undisciplined, defenders.

Even as he had guessed, the first charge carried the howling warriors but a short distance into the open—a shrill, weird challenge from the ape-man being all that was necessary to send them scurrying back to the bush. For half an hour they pranced and yelled their courage to the sticking-point, and again essayed a charge.

This time they came quite to the village gate, but when Sheeta and the hideous apes leaped among them they turned screaming in terror, and again fled to the jungle.

Again was the dancing and shouting repeated. This time Tarzan felt no doubt they would enter the village and complete the work that a handful of determined white men would have carried to a successful conclusion at the first attempt.

To have rescue come so close only to be thwarted because he could not make his poor, savage friends understand precisely what he wanted of them was most irritating, but he could not find it in his heart to place blame upon them. They had done their best, and now he was sure they would doubtless remain to die with him in a fruitless effort to defend him.

The blacks were already preparing for the charge. A few individuals had advanced a short distance toward the village and were exhorting the others to follow them. In a moment the whole savage horde would be racing across the clearing.

Tarzan thought only of the little child somewhere in this cruel, relentless wilderness. His heart ached for the son that he might no longer seek to save—that and the realization of Jane's suffering were all that weighed upon his brave spirit in these that he thought his last moments of life. Succour, all that he could hope for, had come to him in the instant of his extremity—and failed. There was nothing further for which to hope.

The blacks were half-way across the clearing when Tarzan's attention was attracted by the actions of one of the apes. The beast was glaring toward one of the huts. Tarzan followed his gaze. To his infinite relief and delight he saw the stalwart form of Mugambi racing toward him.

The huge black was panting heavily as though from strenuous physical exertion and nervous excitement. He rushed to Tarzan's side, and as the first of the savages reached the village gate the native's knife severed the last of the cords that bound Tarzan to the stake.

In the street lay the corpses of the savages that had fallen before the pack the night before. From one of these Tarzan seized a spear and knob stick, and with Mugambi at his side and the snarling pack about him, he met the natives as they poured through the gate.

EDGAR RICE BURROUGHS

Fierce and terrible was the battle that ensued, but at last the savages were routed, more by terror, perhaps, at sight of a black man and a white fighting in company with a panther and the huge fierce apes of Akut, than because of their inability to overcome the relatively small force that opposed them.

One prisoner fell into the hands of Tarzan, and him the ape-man questioned in an effort to learn what had become of Rokoff and his party. Promised his liberty in return for the information, the black told all he knew concerning the movements of the Russian.

It seemed that early in the morning their chief had attempted to prevail upon the whites to return with him to the village and with their guns destroy the ferocious pack that had taken possession of it, but Rokoff appeared to entertain even more fears of the giant white man and his strange companions than even the blacks themselves.

Upon no conditions would he consent to returning even within sight of the village. Instead, he took his party hurriedly to the river, where they stole a number of canoes the blacks had hidden there. The last that had been seen of them they had been paddling strongly up-stream, their porters from Kaviri's village wielding the blades.

So once more Tarzan of the Apes with his hideous pack took up his search for the ape-man's son and the pursuit of his abductor.

For weary days they followed through an almost uninhabited country, only to learn at last that they were upon the wrong trail. The little band had been reduced by three, for three of Akut's apes had fallen in the fighting at the village. Now, with Akut, there were five great apes, and Sheeta was there—and Mugambi and Tarzan.

The ape-man no longer heard rumors even of the three who had preceded Rokoff—the white man and woman and the child. Who the man and woman were he could not guess, but that the child was his was enough to keep him hot upon the trail. He was sure that Rokoff would be following this trio, and so he felt confident that so long as he could keep upon the Russian's trail he would be winning so much nearer to the time he might snatch his son from the dangers and horrors that menaced him.

In retracing their way after losing Rokoff's trail Tarzan picked it up again at a point where the Russian had left the river and taken to the brush in a northerly direction. He could only account for this change on the ground that the child had been carried away from the river by the two who now had possession of it.

Nowhere along the way, however, could he gain definite information that might assure him positively that the child was ahead of him. Not a single native they questioned had seen or heard of this other party, though nearly all had had direct experience with the Russian or had talked with others who had.

It was with difficulty that Tarzan could find means to communicate with the natives, as the moment their eyes fell upon his companions they fled precipitately into the bush. His only alternative was to go ahead of his pack and waylay an occasional warrior whom he found alone in the jungle.

One day as he was thus engaged, tracking an unsuspecting savage, he came upon the fellow in the act of hurling a spear at a wounded white man who crouched in a clump of bush at the trail's side. The white was one whom Tarzan had often seen, and whom he recognized at once.

Deep in his memory was implanted those repulsive features—the close-set eyes, the shifty expression, the drooping yellow moustache.

Instantly it occurred to the ape-man that this fellow had not been among those who had accompanied Rokoff at the village where Tarzan had been a prisoner. He had seen them all, and this fellow had not been there. There could be but one explanation—he it was who had fled ahead of the Russian with the woman and the child—and the woman had been Jane Clayton. He was sure now of the meaning of Rokoff's words.

The ape-man's face went white as he looked upon the pasty, vice-marked countenance of the Swede. Across Tarzan's forehead stood out the broad band of scarlet that marked the scar where, years before, Terkoz had torn a great strip of the ape-man's scalp from his skull in the fierce battle in which Tarzan had sustained his fitness to the kingship of the apes of Kerchak.

The man was his prey—the black should not have him, and with the thought he leaped upon the warrior, striking down the spear before it could reach its mark. The black, whipping out his knife, turned to do battle with this new enemy, while the Swede, lying in the bush, witnessed a duel, the like of which he had never dreamed to see—a half-naked white man battling with a half-naked black, hand to hand with the crude weapons of primeval man at first, and then with hands and teeth like the primordial brutes from whose loins their forebears sprung.

For a time Anderssen did not recognize the white, and when at last it dawned upon him that he had seen this giant before, his eyes went wide in surprise that this growling, rending beast could ever have been the well-groomed English gentleman who had been a prisoner aboard the *Kincaid*.

An English nobleman! He had learned the identity of the *Kincaid*'s prisoners from Lady Greystoke during their flight up the Ugambi. Before, in common with the other members of the crew of the steamer, he had not known who the two might be.

The fight was over. Tarzan had been compelled to kill his antagonist, as the fellow would not surrender.

The Swede saw the white man leap to his feet beside the corpse of his foe, and placing one foot upon the broken neck lift his voice in the hideous challenge of the victorious bull-ape.

Anderssen shuddered. Then Tarzan turned toward him. His face was cold and cruel, and in the grey eyes the Swede read murder.

"Where is my wife?" growled the ape-man. "Where is the child?"

Anderssen tried to reply, but a sudden fit of coughing choked him. There was an arrow entirely through his chest, and as he coughed the blood from his wounded lung poured suddenly from his mouth and nostrils.

Tarzan stood waiting for the paroxysm to pass. Like a bronze image—cold, hard, and relentless—he stood over the helpless man, waiting to wring such information from him as he needed, and then to kill.

Presently the coughing and haemorrhage ceased, and again the wounded man tried to speak. Tarzan knelt near the faintly moving lips.

"The wife and child!" he repeated. "Where are they?"

Anderssen pointed up the trail.

"The Russian—he got them," he whispered.

"How did you come here?" continued Tarzan. "Why are you not with Rokoff?"

"They catch us," replied Anderssen, in a voice so low that the ape-man could just distinguish the words. "They catch us. Ay fight, but my men they all run away. Then they get me when Ay ban vounded. Rokoff he say leave me here for the hyenas. That vas vorse than to kill. He tak your vife and kid."

"What were you doing with them—where were you taking them?" asked Tarzan, and then fiercely, leaping close to the fellow with fierce eyes blazing with the passion of hate and vengeance that he had with difficulty controlled, "What harm did you do to my wife or child? Speak quick before I kill you! Make your peace with God! Tell me the worst, or I will tear you to pieces with my hands and teeth. You have seen that I can do it!"

A look of wide-eyed surprise overspread Anderssen's face.

"Why," he whispered, "Ay did not hurt them. Ay tried to save them from that Russian. Your vife was kind to me on the *Kincaid*, and Ay hear that little baby cry sometimes. Ay got a vife an' kid for my own by Christiania an' Ay couldn't bear for to see them separated an' in Rokoff's hands any more. That vas all. Do Ay look like Ay ban here to hurt them?" he continued after a pause, pointing to the arrow protruding from his breast.

There was something in the man's tone and expression that convinced Tarzan of the truth of his assertions. More weighty than anything else was the fact that Anderssen evidently seemed more hurt than frightened. He knew he was going to die, so Tarzan's threats had little effect upon him; but it was quite apparent that he wished the Englishman to know the truth and not to wrong him by harbouring the belief that his words and manner indicated that he had entertained.

The ape-man instantly dropped to his knees beside the Swede.

"I am sorry," he said very simply. "I had looked for none but knaves in company with Rokoff. I see that I was wrong. That is past now, and we will drop it for the more important matter of getting you to a place of comfort and looking after your wounds. We must have you on your feet again as soon as possible."

The Swede, smiling, shook his head.

"You go on an' look for the vife an' kid," he said. "Ay ban as gude as dead already; but"—he hesitated—" Ay hate to think of the hyenas. Von't you finish up this job?"

Tarzan shuddered. A moment ago he had been upon the point of killing this man. Now he could no more have taken his life than he could have taken the life of any of his best friends.

He lifted the Swede's head in his arms to change and ease his position.

Again came a fit of coughing and the terrible haemorrhage. After it was over Anderssen lay with closed eyes.

Tarzan thought that he was dead, until he suddenly raised his eyes to those of the ape-man, sighed, and spoke—in a very low, weak whisper.

"Ay tank it blow purty soon purty hard!" he said, and died.

TAMBUDZA

Tarzan scooped a shallow grave for the *Kincaid*'s cook, beneath whose repulsive exterior had beaten the heart of a chivalrous gentleman. That was all he could do in the cruel jungle for the man who had given his life in the service of his little son and his wife.

Then Tarzan took up again the pursuit of Rokoff. Now that he was positive that the woman ahead of him was indeed Jane, and that she had again fallen into the hands of the Russian, it seemed that with all the incredible speed of his fleet and agile muscles he moved at but a snail's pace.

It was with difficulty that he kept the trail, for there were many paths through the jungle at this point—crossing and crisscrossing, forking and branching in all directions, and over them all had passed natives innumerable, coming and going. The spoor of the white men was obliterated by that of the native carriers who had followed them, and over all was the spoor of other natives and of wild beasts.

It was most perplexing; yet Tarzan kept on assiduously, checking his sense of sight against his sense of smell, that he might more surely keep to the right trail. But, with all his care, night found him at a point where he was positive that he was on the wrong trail entirely.

He knew that the pack would follow his spoor, and so he had been careful to make it as distinct as possible, brushing often against the vines and creepers that walled the jungle-path, and in other ways leaving his scent-spoor plainly discernible.

As darkness settled a heavy rain set in, and there was nothing for the baffled ape-man to do but wait in the partial shelter of a huge tree until morning; but the coming of dawn brought no cessation of the torrential downpour.

For a week the sun was obscured by heavy clouds, while violent rain and wind storms obliterated the last remnants of the spoor Tarzan constantly though vainly sought.

During all this time he saw no signs of natives, nor of his own pack, the members of which he feared had lost his trail during the terrific storm. As the country was strange to him, he had been unable to judge his course accurately, since he had had neither sun by day nor moon nor stars by night to guide him.

When the sun at last broke through the clouds in the fore-noon of the seventh day, it looked down upon an almost frantic ape-man.

For the first time in his life, Tarzan of the Apes had been lost in the jungle. That the experience should have befallen him at such a time seemed cruel beyond expression. Somewhere in this savage land his wife and son lay in the clutches of the arch-fiend Rokoff.

What hideous trials might they not have undergone during those seven awful days that nature had thwarted him in his endeavours to locate them? Tarzan knew the Russian, in whose power they were, so well that he could not doubt but that the man, filled with rage that Jane had once escaped him, and knowing that Tarzan might be close upon his trail, would wreak without further loss of time whatever vengeance his polluted mind might be able to conceive.

But now that the sun shone once more, the ape-man was still at a loss as to what direction to take. He knew that Rokoff had left the river in pursuit of Anderssen, but whether he would continue inland or return to the Ugambi was a question.

The ape-man had seen that the river at the point he had left it was growing narrow and swift, so that he judged that it could not be navigable even for canoes to any great distance farther toward its source. However, if Rokoff had not returned to the river, in what direction had he proceeded?

From the direction of Anderssen's flight with Jane and the child Tarzan was convinced that the man had purposed attempting the tremendous feat of crossing the continent to Zanzibar; but whether Rokoff would dare so dangerous a journey or not was a question.

Fear might drive him to the attempt now that he knew the manner of horrible pack that was upon his trail, and that Tarzan of the Apes was following him to wreak upon him the vengeance that he deserved.

At last the ape-man determined to continue toward the northeast in the general direction of German East Africa until he came upon natives from whom he might gain information as to Rokoff's whereabouts.

The second day following the cessation of the rain Tarzan came upon a native village the inhabitants of which fled into the bush the instant their eyes fell upon him. Tarzan, not to be thwarted in any such manner as this, pursued them, and after a brief chase caught up with a young warrior. The fellow was so badly frightened that he was unable to defend himself, dropping his weapons and falling upon the ground, wide-eyed and screaming as he gazed on his captor.

It was with considerable difficulty that the ape-man quieted the fellow's fears sufficiently to obtain a coherent statement from him as to the cause of his uncalled-for terror.

From him Tarzan learned, by dint of much coaxing, that a party of whites had passed through the village several days before. These men had told them of a terrible white devil that pursued them, warning the natives against it and the frightful pack of demons that accompanied it.

The black had recognized Tarzan as the white devil from the descriptions given by the whites and their black servants. Behind him he had expected to see a horde of demons disguised as apes and panthers.

In this Tarzan saw the cunning hand of Rokoff. The Russian was attempting to make travel as difficult as possible for him by turning the natives against him in superstitious fear.

The native further told Tarzan that the white man who had led the recent expedition had promised them a fabulous reward if they would kill the white devil. This they had fully intended doing should the opportunity present itself; but the moment they had seen Tarzan their blood had turned to water, as the porters of the white men had told them would be the case.

Finding the ape-man made no attempt to harm him, the native at last recovered his grasp upon his courage, and, at Tarzan's suggestion, accompanied the white devil back to the village, calling as he went for his fellows to return also, as "the white devil has promised to do you no harm if you come back right away and answer his questions."

One by one the blacks straggled into the village, but that their fears were not entirely allayed was evident from the amount of white that showed about the eyes of the majority of them as they cast constant and apprehensive sidelong glances at the ape-man.

The chief was among the first to return to the village, and as it was he that Tarzan was most anxious to interview, he lost no time in entering into a palaver with the black.

The fellow was short and stout, with an unusually low and degraded countenance and apelike arms. His whole expression denoted deceitfulness.

Only the superstitious terror engendered in him by the stories poured into his ears by the whites and blacks of the Russian's party kept him from leaping upon Tarzan with his warriors and slaying him forthwith, for he and his people were inveterate maneaters. But the fear that he might indeed be a devil, and that out there in the jungle behind him his fierce demons waited to do his bidding, kept M'ganwazam from putting his desires into action.

Tarzan questioned the fellow closely, and by comparing his statements with those of the young warrior he had first talked with he learned that Rokoff and his safari were in terror-stricken retreat in the direction of the far East Coast.

Many of the Russian's porters had already deserted him. In that very village he had hanged five for theft and attempted desertion. Judging, however, from what the Waganwazam had learned from those of the Russian's blacks who were not too far gone in terror of the brutal Rokoff to fear even to speak of their plans, it was apparent that he would not travel any great distance before the last of his porters, cooks, tent-boys, gun-bearers, askari, and even his headman, would have turned back into the bush, leaving him to the mercy of the merciless jungle.

M'ganwazam denied that there had been any white woman or child with the party of whites; but even as he spoke Tarzan was convinced that he lied. Several times the ape-man approached the subject from different angles, but never was he successful in surprising the wily cannibal into a direct contradiction of his original statement that there had been no women or children with the party.

Tarzan demanded food of the chief, and after considerable haggling on the part of the monarch succeeded in obtaining a meal. He then tried to draw out others of the tribe, especially the young man whom he had captured in the bush, but M'ganwazam's presence sealed their lips.

At last, convinced that these people knew a great deal more than they had told him concerning the whereabouts of the Russian and the fate of Jane and the child, Tarzan determined to remain overnight among them in the hope of discovering something further of importance.

When he had stated his decision to the chief he was rather surprised to note the sudden change in the fellow's attitude toward him. From apparent dislike and suspicion M'ganwazam became a most eager and solicitous host.

Nothing would do but that the ape-man should occupy the best hut in the village, from which M'ganwazam's oldest wife was forthwith summarily ejected, while the chief took up his temporary abode in the hut of one of his younger consorts.

Had Tarzan chanced to recall the fact that a princely reward had been offered the blacks if they should succeed in killing him, he might have more quickly interpreted M'ganwazam's sudden change in front.

To have the white giant sleeping peacefully in one of his own huts would greatly facilitate the matter of earning the reward, and so the chief was urgent in his suggestions that Tarzan, doubtless being very much fatigued after his travels, should retire early to the comforts of the anything but inviting palace.

As much as the ape-man detested the thought of sleeping within a native hut, he had determined to do so this night, on the chance that he might be able to induce one of the younger men to sit and chat with him before the fire that burned in the centre of the smoke-filled dwelling, and from him draw the truths he sought. So Tarzan accepted the invitation of old M'ganwazam, insisting, however, that he much preferred sharing a hut with some of the younger men rather than driving the chief's old wife out in the cold.

The toothless old hag grinned her appreciation of this suggestion, and as the plan still better suited the chief's scheme, in that it would permit him to surround Tarzan with a gang of picked assassins, he readily assented, so that presently Tarzan had been installed in a hut close to the village gate.

As there was to be a dance that night in honour of a band of recently returned hunters, Tarzan was left alone in the hut, the young men, as M'ganwazam explained, having to take part in the festivities.

As soon as the ape-man was safely installed in the trap, M'Ganwazam called about him the young warriors whom he had selected to spend the night with the white devil!

None of them was overly enthusiastic about the plan, since deep in their superstitious hearts lay an exaggerated fear of the strange white giant; but the word of M'ganwazam was law among his people, so not one dared refuse the duty he was called upon to perform.

As M'ganwazam unfolded his plan in whispers to the savages squatting about him the old, toothless hag, to whom Tarzan had saved her hut for the night, hovered about the conspirators ostensibly to replenish the supply of firewood for the blaze about which the men sat, but really to drink in as much of their conversation as possible.

Tarzan had slept for perhaps an hour or two despite the savage din of the revellers when his keen senses came suddenly alert to a suspiciously stealthy movement in the hut in which he lay. The fire had died down to a little heap of glowing embers, which accentuated rather than relieved the darkness that shrouded the interior of the evil-smelling dwelling, yet the trained senses of the ape-man warned him of another presence creeping almost silently toward him through the gloom.

He doubted that it was one of his hut mates returning from the festivities, for he still heard the wild cries of the dancers and the din of the tom-toms in the village street without. Who could it be that took such pains to conceal his approach?

As the presence came within reach of him the ape-man bounded lightly to the opposite side of the hut, his spear poised ready at his side.

"Who is it," he asked, "that creeps upon Tarzan of the Apes, like a hungry lion out of the darkness?"

"Silence, bwana!" replied an old cracked voice. "It is Tambudza—she whose hut you would not take, and thus drive an old woman out into the cold night."

"What does Tambudza want of Tarzan of the Apes?" asked the ape-man.

"You were kind to me to whom none is now kind, and I have come to warn you in payment of your kindness," answered the old hag.

"Warn me of what?"

"M'ganwazam has chosen the young men who are to sleep in the hut with you," replied Tambudza. "I was near as he talked with them, and heard him issuing his instructions to them. When the dance is run well into the morning they are to come to the hut.

"If you are awake they are to pretend that they have come to sleep, but if you sleep it is M'ganwazam's command that you be killed. If you are not then asleep they will wait quietly beside you until you do sleep, and then they will all fall upon you together and slay you. M'ganwazam is determined to win the reward the white man has offered."

"I had forgotten the reward," said Tarzan, half to himself, and then he added, "How may M'ganwazam hope to collect the reward now that the white men who are my enemies have left his country and gone he knows not where?"

"Oh, they have not gone far," replied Tambudza. "M'ganwazam knows where they camp. His runners could quickly overtake them—they move slowly."

"Where are they?" asked Tarzan.

"Do you wish to come to them?" asked Tambudza in way of reply.

Tarzan nodded.

"I cannot tell you where they lie so that you could come to the place yourself, but I could lead you to them, bwana."

In their interest in the conversation neither of the speakers had noticed the little figure which crept into the darkness of the hut behind them, nor did they see it when it slunk noiselessly out again.

It was little Buulaoo, the chief's son by one of his younger wives—a vindictive, degenerate little rascal who hated Tambudza, and was ever seeking opportunities to spy upon her and report her slightest breach of custom to his father.

"Come, then," said Tarzan quickly, "let us be on our way."

This Buulaoo did not hear, for he was already legging it up the village street to where his hideous sire guzzled native beer, and watched the evolutions of the frantic dancers leaping high in the air and cavorting wildly in their hysterical capers.

So it happened that as Tarzan and Tambudza sneaked warily from the village and melted into the Stygian darkness of the jungle two lithe runners took their way in the same direction, though by another trail.

When they had come sufficiently far from the village to make it safe for them to speak above a whisper, Tarzan asked the old woman if she had seen aught of a white woman and a little child.

"Yes, bwana," replied Tambudza, "there was a woman with them and a little child—a little white piccaninny. It died here in our village of the fever and they buried it!"

A BLACK SCOUNDREL

When Jane Clayton regained consciousness she saw Anderssen standing over her, holding the baby in his arms. As her eyes rested upon them an expression of misery and horror overspread her countenance.

"What is the matter?" he asked. "You ban sick?"

"Where is my baby?" she cried, ignoring his questions.

Anderssen held out the chubby infant, but she shook her head.

"It is not mine," she said. "You knew that it was not mine. You are a devil like the Russian."

Anderssen's blue eyes stretched in surprise.

"Not yours!" he exclaimed. "You tole me the kid aboard the *Kincaid* ban your kid."

"Not this one," replied Jane dully. "The other. Where is the other? There must have been two. I did not know about this one."

"There vasn't no other kid. Ay tank this ban yours. Ay am very sorry."

Anderssen fidgeted about, standing first on one foot and then upon the other. It was perfectly evident to Jane that he was honest in his protestations of ignorance of the true identity of the child.

Presently the baby commenced to crow, and bounce up and down in the Swede's arms, at the same time leaning forward with little hands out-reaching toward the young woman.

She could not withstand the appeal, and with a low cry she sprang to her feet and gathered the baby to her breast.

For a few minutes she wept silently, her face buried in the baby's soiled little dress. The first shock of disappointment that the tiny thing had not been her beloved Jack was giving way to a great hope that after all some miracle had occurred to snatch her baby from Rokoff's hands at the last instant before the *Kincaid* sailed from England.

Then, too, there was the mute appeal of this wee waif alone and unloved in the midst of the horrors of the savage jungle. It was this thought more than any other that had sent her mother's heart out to the innocent babe, while still she suffered from disappointment that she had been deceived in its identity.

"Have you no idea whose child this is?" she asked Anderssen.

The man shook his head.

"Not now," he said. "If he ain't ban your kid, Ay don' know whose kid he do ban. Rokoff said it was yours. Ay tank he tank so, too.

"What do we do with it now? Ay can't go back to the *Kincaid*. Rokoff would have me shot; but you can go back. Ay take you to the sea, and then some of these black men they take you to the ship—eh?"

"No! no!" cried Jane. "Not for the world. I would rather die than fall into the hands of that man again. No, let us go on and take this poor little creature with us. If God is willing we shall be saved in one way or another."

So they again took up their flight through the wilderness, taking with them a half-dozen of the Mosulas to carry provisions and the tents that Anderssen had smuggled aboard the small boat in preparation for the attempted escape.

The days and nights of torture that the young woman suffered were so merged into one long, unbroken nightmare of hideousness that she soon lost all track of time. Whether they had been wandering for days or years she could not tell. The one bright spot in that eternity of fear and suffering was the little child whose tiny hands had long since fastened their softly groping fingers firmly about her heart.

In a way the little thing took the place and filled the aching void that the theft of her own baby had left. It could never be the same, of course, but yet, day by day, she found her mother-love, enveloping the waif more closely until she sometimes sat with closed eyes lost in the sweet imagining that the little bundle of humanity at her breast was truly her own.

For some time their progress inland was extremely slow. Word came to them from time to time through natives passing from the coast on hunting excursions that Rokoff had not yet guessed the direction of their flight. This, and the desire to make the journey as light as possible for the gently bred woman, kept Anderssen to a slow advance of short and easy marches with many rests.

The Swede insisted upon carrying the child while they travelled, and in countless other ways did what he could to help Jane Clayton conserve her strength. He had been terribly chagrined on discovering the mistake he had made in the identity of the baby, but once the young woman became convinced that his motives were truly chivalrous she would not permit him longer to upbraid himself for the error that he could not by any means have avoided.

At the close of each day's march Anderssen saw to the erection of a comfortable shelter for Jane and the child. Her tent was always pitched in the most favourable location. The thorn *boma* round it was the strongest and most impregnable that the Mosula could construct.

Her food was the best that their limited stores and the rifle of the Swede could provide, but the thing that touched her heart the closest was the gentle consideration and courtesy which the man always accorded her.

That such nobility of character could lie beneath so repulsive an exterior never ceased to be a source of wonder and amazement to her, until at last the innate chivalry of the man, and his unfailing kindliness and sympathy transformed his appearance in so far as Jane was concerned until she saw only the sweetness of his character mirrored in his countenance.

They had commenced to make a little better progress when word reached them that Rokoff was but a few marches behind them, and that he had at last discovered the direction of their flight. It was then that Anderssen took to the river, purchasing a canoe from a chief whose village lay a short distance from the Ugambi upon the bank of a tributary.

Thereafter the little party of fugitives fled up the broad Ugambi, and so rapid had their flight become that they no longer received word of their pursuers. At the end of canoe navigation upon the river, they abandoned their canoe and took to the jungle. Here progress became at once arduous, slow, and dangerous.

The second day after leaving the Ugambi the baby fell ill with fever. Anderssen knew what the outcome must be, but he had not the heart to tell Jane Clayton the truth, for he had seen that the young woman had come to love the child almost as passionately as though it had been her own flesh and blood.

As the baby's condition precluded farther advance, Anderssen withdrew a little from the main trail he had been following and built a camp in a natural clearing on the bank of a little river.

Here Jane devoted her every moment to caring for the tiny sufferer, and as though her sorrow and anxiety were not all that she could bear, a further blow came with the sudden announcement of one of the Mosula porters who had been foraging in the jungle adjacent that Rokoff and his party were camped quite close to them, and were evidently upon their trail to this little nook which all had thought so excellent a hiding-place.

This information could mean but one thing, and that they must break camp and fly onward regardless of the baby's condition. Jane Clayton knew the traits of the Russian well enough to be positive that he would separate her from the child the moment that he recaptured them, and she knew that separation would mean the immediate death of the baby.

As they stumbled forward through the tangled vegetation along an old and almost overgrown game trail the Mosula porters deserted them one by one.

The men had been staunch enough in their devotion and loyalty as long as they were in no danger of being overtaken by the Russian and his party. They had heard, however, so much of the atrocious disposition of Rokoff that they had grown to hold him in mortal terror, and now that they knew he was close upon them their timid hearts would fortify them no longer, and as quickly as possible they deserted the three whites.

Yet on and on went Anderssen and the girl. The Swede went ahead, to hew a way through the brush where the path was entirely overgrown, so that on this march it was necessary that the young woman carry the child.

All day they marched. Late in the afternoon they realized that they had failed. Close behind them they heard the noise of a large safari advancing along the trail which they had cleared for their pursuers.

When it became quite evident that they must be overtaken in a short time Anderssen hid Jane behind a large tree, covering her and the child with brush.

"There is a village about a mile farther on," he said to her. "The Mosula told me its location before they deserted us. Ay try to lead the Russian off your trail, then you go on to the village. Ay tank the chief ban friendly to white men—the Mosula tal me he ban. Anyhow, that was all we can do.

"After while you get chief to tak you down by the Mosula village at the sea again, an' after a while a ship is sure to put into the mouth of the Ugambi. Then you be all right. Gude-by an' gude luck to you, lady!"

"But where are you going, Sven?" asked Jane. "Why can't you hide here and go back to the sea with me?"

"Ay gotta tal the Russian you ban dead, so that he don't luke for you no more," and Anderssen grinned.

"Why can't you join me then after you have told him that?" insisted the girl.

Anderssen shook his head.

"Ay don't tank Ay join anybody any more after Ay tal the Russian you ban dead," he said.

"You don't mean that you think he will kill you?" asked Jane, and yet in her heart she knew that that was exactly what the great scoundrel would do in revenge for his having been thwarted by the Swede. Anderssen did not reply, other than to warn her to silence and point toward the path along which they had just come.

"I don't care," whispered Jane Clayton. "I shall not let you die to save me if I can prevent it in any way. Give me your revolver. I can use that, and together we may be able to hold them off until we can find some means of escape."

"It won't work, lady," replied Anderssen. "They would only get us both, and then Ay couldn't do you no good at all. Think of the kid, lady, and what it would be for you both to fall into Rokoff's hands again. For his sake you must do what Ay say. Here, take my rifle and ammunition; you may need them."

He shoved the gun and bandoleer into the shelter beside Jane. Then he was gone.

She watched him as he returned along the path to meet the oncoming safari of the Russian. Soon a turn in the trail hid him from view.

Her first impulse was to follow. With the rifle she might be of assistance to him, and, further, she could not bear the terrible thought of being left alone at the mercy of the fearful jungle without a single friend to aid her.

She started to crawl from her shelter with the intention of running after Anderssen as fast as she could. As she drew the baby close to her she glanced down into its little face.

How red it was! How unnatural the little thing looked. She raised the cheek to hers. It was fiery hot with fever!

With a little gasp of terror Jane Clayton rose to her feet in the jungle path. The rifle and bandoleer lay forgotten in the shelter beside her. Anderssen was forgotten, and Rokoff, and her great peril.

All that rioted through her fear-mad brain was the fearful fact that this little, helpless child was stricken with the terrible jungle-fever, and that she was helpless to do aught to allay its sufferings—sufferings that were sure to coming during ensuing intervals of partial consciousness.

Her one thought was to find some one who could help her—some woman who had had children of her own—and with the thought came recollection of the friendly village of which Anderssen had spoken. If she could but reach it—in time!

There was no time to be lost. Like a startled antelope she turned and fled up the trail in the direction Anderssen had indicated.

From far behind came the sudden shouting of men, the sound of shots, and then silence. She knew that Anderssen had met the Russian.

A half-hour later she stumbled, exhausted, into a little thatched village. Instantly she was surrounded by men, women, and children. Eager, curious, excited natives plied her with a hundred questions, no one of which she could understand or answer.

All that she could do was to point tearfully at the baby, now wailing piteously in her arms, and repeat over and over, "Fever—fever—fever."

The blacks did not understand her words, but they saw the cause of her trouble, and soon a young woman had pulled her into a hut and with several others was doing her poor best to quiet the child and allay its agony.

The witch doctor came and built a little fire before the infant, upon which he boiled some strange concoction in a small earthen pot, making weird passes above it and mumbling strange, monotonous chants. Presently he dipped a zebra's tail into the brew, and with further mutterings and incantations sprinkled a few drops of the liquid over the baby's face.

After he had gone the women sat about and moaned and wailed until Jane thought that she should go mad; but, knowing that they were doing it all out of the kindness of their hearts, she endured the frightful waking nightmare of those awful hours in dumb and patient suffering.

It must have been well toward midnight that she became conscious of a sudden commotion in the village. She heard the voices of the natives raised in controversy, but she could not understand the words.

Presently she heard footsteps approaching the hut in which she squatted before a bright fire with the baby on her lap. The little thing lay very still now, its lids, half-raised, showed the pupils horribly upturned.

Jane Clayton looked into the little face with fear-haunted eyes. It was not her baby—not her flesh and blood—but how close, how dear the tiny, helpless thing had become to her. Her heart, bereft of its own, had gone out to this poor, little, nameless waif, and lavished upon it all the love that had been denied her during the long, bitter weeks of her captivity aboard the *Kincaid*.

She saw that the end was near, and though she was terrified at contemplation of her loss, still she hoped that it would come quickly now and end the sufferings of the little victim.

The footsteps she had heard without the hut now halted before the door. There was a whispered colloquy, and a moment later M'ganwazam, chief of the tribe, entered. She had seen but little of him, as the women had taken her in hand almost as soon as she had entered the village.

M'ganwazam, she now saw, was an evil-appearing savage with every mark of brutal degeneracy writ large upon his bestial countenance. To Jane Clayton he looked more gorilla than human. He tried to converse with her, but without success, and finally he called to some one without.

In answer to his summons another Negro entered—a man of very different appearance from M'ganwazam—so different, in fact, that Jane Clayton immediately decided that he was of another tribe. This man acted as interpreter, and almost from the first question that M'ganwazam put to her, Jane felt an intuitive conviction that the savage was attempting to draw information from her for some ulterior motive.

She thought it strange that the fellow should so suddenly have become interested in her plans, and especially in her intended destination when her journey had been interrupted at his village.

Seeing no reason for withholding the information, she told him the truth; but when he asked if she expected to meet her husband at the end of the trip, she shook her head negatively.

Then he told her the purpose of his visit, talking through the interpreter.

"I have just learned," he said, "from some men who live by the side of the great water, that your husband followed you up the Ugambi for several marches, when he was at last set upon by natives and killed. Therefore I have told you this that you might not waste your time in a long journey if you expected to meet your husband at the end of it; but instead could turn and retrace your steps to the coast."

Jane thanked M'ganwazam for his kindness, though her heart was numb with suffering at this new blow. She who had suffered so much was at last beyond reach of the keenest of misery's pangs, for her senses were numbed and calloused.

With bowed head she sat staring with unseeing eyes upon the face of the baby in her lap. M'ganwazam had left the hut. Sometime later she heard a noise at the entrance—another had entered. One of the women sitting opposite her threw a faggot upon the dying embers of the fire between them.

With a sudden flare it burst into renewed flame, lighting up the hut's interior as though by magic.

The flame disclosed to Jane Clayton's horrified gaze that the baby was quite dead. How long it had been so she could not guess.

A choking lump rose to her throat, her head drooped in silent misery upon the little bundle that she had caught suddenly to her breast.

For a moment the silence of the hut was unbroken. Then the native woman broke into a hideous wail.

A man coughed close before Jane Clayton and spoke her name.

With a start she raised her eyes to look into the sardonic countenance of Nikolas Rokoff.

ESCAPE

For a moment Rokoff stood sneering down upon Jane Clayton, then his eyes fell to the little bundle in her lap. Jane had drawn one corner of the blanket over the child's face, so that to one who did not know the truth it seemed but to be sleeping.

"You have gone to a great deal of unnecessary trouble," said Rokoff, "to bring the child to this village. If you had attended to your own affairs I should have brought it here myself.

"You would have been spared the dangers and fatigue of the journey. But I suppose I must thank you for relieving me of the inconvenience of having to care for a young infant on the march.

"This is the village to which the child was destined from the first. M'ganwazam will rear him carefully, making a good cannibal of him, and if you ever chance to return to civilization it will doubtless afford you much food for thought as you compare the luxuries and comforts of your life with the details of the life your son is living in the village of the Waganwazam.

"Again I thank you for bringing him here for me, and now I must ask you to surrender him to me, that I may turn him over to his foster parents." As he concluded Rokoff held out his hands for the child, a nasty grin of vindictiveness upon his lips.

To his surprise Jane Clayton rose and, without a word of protest, laid the little bundle in his arms.

"Here is the child," she said. "Thank God he is beyond your power to harm."

Grasping the import of her words, Rokoff snatched the blanket from the child's face to seek confirmation of his fears. Jane Clayton watched his expression closely.

She had been puzzled for days for an answer to the question of Rokoff's knowledge of the child's identity. If she had been in doubt before the last shred of that doubt was wiped away as she witnessed the terrible anger of the Russian as he looked upon the dead face of the baby and realized that at the last moment his dearest wish for vengeance had been thwarted by a higher power.

Almost throwing the body of the child back into Jane Clayton's arms, Rokoff stamped up and down the hut, pounding the air with his clenched fists and cursing terribly. At last he halted in front of the young woman, bringing his face down close to hers.

"You are laughing at me," he shrieked. "You think that you have beaten me—eh? I'll show you, as I have shown the miserable ape you call 'husband,' what it means to interfere with the plans of Nikolas Rokoff.

"You have robbed me of the child. I cannot make him the son of a cannibal chief, but"—and he paused as though to let the full meaning of his threat sink deep—" I can make the mother the wife of a cannibal, and that I shall do—after I have finished with her myself."

If he had thought to wring from Jane Clayton any sign of terror he failed miserably. She was beyond that. Her brain and nerves were numb to suffering and shock.

To his surprise a faint, almost happy smile touched her lips. She was thinking with thankful heart that this poor little corpse was not that of her own wee Jack, and that—best of all—Rokoff evidently did not know the truth.

She would have liked to have flaunted the fact in his face, but she dared not. If he continued to believe that the child had been hers, so much safer would be the real Jack wherever he might be. She had, of course, no knowledge of the whereabouts of her little son—she did not know, even, that he still lived, and yet there was the chance that he might.

It was more than possible that without Rokoff's knowledge this child had been substituted for hers by one of the Russian's confederates, and that even now her son might be safe with friends in London, where there were many, both able and willing, to have paid any ransom which the traitorous conspirator might have asked for the safe release of Lord Greystoke's son.

She had thought it all out a hundred times since she had discovered that the baby which Anderssen had placed in her arms that night upon the *Kincaid* was not her own, and it had been a constant and gnawing source of happiness to her to dream the whole fantasy through in its every detail.

No, the Russian must never know that this was not her baby. She realized that her position was hopeless—with Anderssen and her husband dead there was no one in all the world with a desire to succour her who knew where she might be found.

Rokoff's threat, she realized, was no idle one. That he would do, or attempt to do, all that he had promised, she was perfectly sure; but at the worst it meant but a little earlier release from the hideous anguish that she had been enduring. She must find some way to take her own life before the Russian could harm her further.

Just now she wanted time—time to think and prepare herself for the end. She felt that she could not take the last, awful step until she had exhausted every possibility of escape. She did not care to live unless she might find her way back to her own child, but slight as such a hope appeared she would not admit its impossibility until the last moment had come, and she faced the fearful reality of choosing between the final alternatives—Nikolas Rokoff on one hand and self-destruction upon the other.

"Go away!" she said to the Russian. "Go away and leave me in peace with my dead. Have you not brought sufficient misery and anguish upon me without attempting to harm me further? What wrong have I ever done you that you should persist in persecuting me?"

"You are suffering for the sins of the monkey you chose when you might have had the love of a gentleman—of Nikolas Rokoff," he replied. "But where is the use in discussing the matter? We shall bury the child here, and you will return with me at once to my own camp. Tomorrow I shall bring you back and turn you over to your new husband—the lovely M'ganwazam. Come!"

He reached out for the child. Jane, who was on her feet now, turned away from him.

"I shall bury the body," she said. "Send some men to dig a grave outside the village."

Rokoff was anxious to have the thing over and get back to his camp with his victim. He thought he saw in her apathy a resignation to her fate. Stepping outside the hut, he motioned her to follow him, and a moment later, with his men, he escorted Jane beyond the village, where beneath a great tree the blacks scooped a shallow grave.

Wrapping the tiny body in a blanket, Jane laid it tenderly in the black hole, and, turning her head that she might not see the mouldy earth falling upon the pitiful little bundle, she breathed a prayer beside the grave of the nameless waif that had won its way to the innermost recesses of her heart.

Then, dry-eyed but suffering, she rose and followed the Russian through the Stygian blackness of the jungle, along the winding, leafy corridor that led from the village of M'ganwazam, the black cannibal, to the camp of Nikolas Rokoff, the white fiend.

Beside them, in the impenetrable thickets that fringed the path, rising to arch above it and shut out the moon, the girl could hear the stealthy, muffled footfalls of great beasts, and ever round about them rose the deafening roars of hunting lions, until the earth trembled to the mighty sound.

The porters lighted torches now and waved them upon either hand to frighten off the beasts of prey. Rokoff urged them to greater speed, and from the quavering note in his voice Jane Clayton knew that he was weak from terror.

The sounds of the jungle night recalled most vividly the days and nights that she had spent in a similar jungle with her forest god—with the fearless and unconquerable Tarzan of the Apes. Then there had been no thoughts of terror, though the jungle noises were new to her, and the roar of a lion had seemed the most awe-inspiring sound upon the great earth.

How different would it be now if she knew that he was somewhere there in the wilderness, seeking her! Then, indeed, would there be that for which to live, and every reason to believe that succour was close at hand—but he was dead! It was incredible that it should be so.

There seemed no place in death for that great body and those mighty thews. Had Rokoff been the one to tell her of her lord's passing she would have known that he lied. There could be no reason, she thought, why M'ganwazam should have deceived her. She did not know that the Russian had talked with the savage a few minutes before the chief had come to her with his tale.

At last they reached the rude *boma* that Rokoff's porters had thrown up round the Russian's camp. Here they found all in turmoil. She did not know what it was all about, but she saw that Rokoff was very angry, and from bits of conversation which she could translate she gleaned that there had been further desertions while he had been absent, and that the deserters had taken the bulk of his food and ammunition.

When he had done venting his rage upon those who remained he returned to where Jane stood under guard of a couple of his white sailors. He grasped her roughly by the arm and started to drag her toward his tent. The girl struggled and fought to free herself, while the two sailors stood by, laughing at the rare treat.

Rokoff did not hesitate to use rough methods when he found that he was to have difficulty in carrying out his designs. Repeatedly he struck Jane Clayton in the face, until at last, half-conscious, she was dragged within his tent.

Rokoff's boy had lighted the Russian's lamp, and now at a word from his master he made himself scarce. Jane had sunk to the floor in the middle of the enclosure. Slowly her numbed senses were returning to her and she was commencing to think very fast indeed. Quickly her eyes ran round the interior of the tent, taking in every detail of its equipment and contents.

Now the Russian was lifting her to her feet and attempting to drag her to the camp cot that stood at one side of the tent. At his belt hung a heavy revolver. Jane Clayton's eyes riveted themselves upon it. Her palm itched to grasp the huge butt. She feigned again to swoon, but through her half-closed lids she waited her opportunity.

It came just as Rokoff was lifting her upon the cot. A noise at the tent door behind him brought his head quickly about and away from the girl. The butt of the gun was not an inch from her hand. With a single, lightning-like move she snatched the weapon from its holster, and at the same instant Rokoff turned back toward her, realizing his peril.

She did not dare fire for fear the shot would bring his people about him, and with Rokoff dead she would fall into hands no better than his and to a fate probably even worse than he alone could have imagined. The memory of the two brutes who stood and laughed as Rokoff struck her was still vivid.

As the rage and fear-filled countenance of the Slav turned toward her Jane Clayton raised the heavy revolver high above the pasty face and with all her strength dealt the man a terrific blow between the eyes.

Without a sound he sank, limp and unconscious, to the ground. A moment later the girl stood beside him—for a moment at least free from the menace of his lust.

Outside the tent she again heard the noise that had distracted Rokoff's attention. What it was she did not know, but, fearing the return of the servant and the discovery of her deed, she stepped quickly to the camp table upon which burned the oil lamp and extinguished the smudgy, evil-smelling flame.

In the total darkness of the interior she paused for a moment to collect her wits and plan for the next step in her venture for freedom.

About her was a camp of enemies. Beyond these foes a black wilderness of savage jungle peopled by hideous beasts of prey and still more hideous human beasts.

There was little or no chance that she could survive even a few days of the constant dangers that would confront her there; but the knowledge that she had already passed through so many perils unscathed, and that somewhere out in the faraway world a little child was doubtless at that very moment crying for her, filled her with determination to make the effort to accomplish the seemingly impossible and cross that awful land of horror in search of the sea and the remote chance of succour she might find there.

Rokoff's tent stood almost exactly in the centre of the *boma*. Surrounding it were the tents and shelters of his white companions and the natives of his safari. To pass through these and find egress through the *boma* seemed a task too fraught with insurmountable obstacles to warrant even the slightest consideration, and yet there was no other way.

To remain in the tent until she should be discovered would be to set at naught all that she had risked to gain her freedom, and so with stealthy step and every sense alert she approached the back of the tent to set out upon the first stage of her adventure.

Groping along the rear of the canvas wall, she found that there was no opening there. Quickly she returned to the side of the unconscious Russian. In his belt her groping fingers came upon the hilt of a long hunting-knife, and with this she cut a hole in the back wall of the tent.

Silently she stepped without. To her immense relief she saw that the camp was apparently asleep. In the dim and flickering light of the dying fires she saw but a single sentry, and he was dozing upon his haunches at the opposite side of the enclosure.

Keeping the tent between him and herself, she crossed between the small shelters of the native porters to the *boma* wall beyond.

Outside, in the darkness of the tangled jungle, she could hear the roaring of lions, the laughing of hyenas, and the countless, nameless noises of the midnight jungle.

For a moment she hesitated, trembling. The thought of the prowling beasts out there in the darkness was appalling. Then, with a sudden brave toss of her head, she attacked the thorny *boma* wall with her delicate hands. Torn and bleeding though they were, she worked on breathlessly until she had made an opening through which she could worm her body, and at last she stood outside the enclosure.

Behind her lay a fate worse than death, at the hands of human beings.

Before her lay an almost certain fate—but it was only death—sudden, merciful, and honourable death.

Without a tremor and without regret she darted away from the camp, and a moment later the mysterious jungle had closed about her.

ALONE IN THE JUNGLE

Tambudza, leading Tarzan of the Apes toward the camp of the Russian, moved very slowly along the winding jungle path, for she was old and her legs stiff with rheumatism.

So it was that the runners dispatched by M'ganwazam to warn Rokoff that the white giant was in his village and that he would be slain that night reached the Russian's camp before Tarzan and his ancient guide had covered half the distance.

The guides found the white man's camp in a turmoil. Rokoff had that morning been discovered stunned and bleeding within his tent. When he had recovered his senses and realized that Jane Clayton had escaped, his rage was boundless.

Rushing about the camp with his rifle, he had sought to shoot down the native sentries who had allowed the young woman to elude their vigilance, but several of the other whites, realizing that they were already in a precarious position owing to the numerous desertions that Rokoff's cruelty had brought about, seized and disarmed him.

Then came the messengers from M'ganwazam, but scarce had they told their story and Rokoff was preparing to depart with them for their village when other runners, panting from the exertions of their swift flight through the jungle, rushed breathless into the firelight, crying that the great white giant had escaped from M'ganwazam and was already on his way to wreak vengeance against his enemies.

Instantly confusion reigned within the encircling *boma*. The blacks belonging to Rokoff's safari were terror-stricken at the thought of the proximity of the white giant who hunted through the jungle with a fierce pack of apes and panthers at his heels.

Before the whites realized what had happened the superstitious fears of the natives had sent them scurrying into the bush—their own carriers as well as the messengers from M'ganwazam—but even in their haste they had not neglected to take with them every article of value upon which they could lay their hands.

Thus Rokoff and the seven white sailors found themselves deserted and robbed in the midst of a wilderness.

The Russian, following his usual custom, berated his companions, laying all the blame upon their shoulders for the events which had led up to the almost hopeless condition in which they now found themselves; but the sailors were in no mood to brook his insults and his cursing.

In the midst of this tirade one of them drew a revolver and fired point-blank at the Russian. The fellow's aim was poor, but his act so terrified Rokoff that he turned and fled for his tent.

As he ran his eyes chanced to pass beyond the *boma* to the edge of the forest, and there he caught a glimpse of that which sent his craven heart cold with a fear that almost expunged his terror of the seven men at his back, who by this time were all firing in hate and revenge at his retreating figure.

What he saw was the giant figure of an almost naked white man emerging from the bush.

Darting into his tent, the Russian did not halt in his flight, but kept right on through the rear wall, taking advantage of the long slit that Jane Clayton had made the night before.

The terror-stricken Muscovite scurried like a hunted rabbit through the hole that still gaped in the *boma*'s wall at the point where his own prey had escaped, and as Tarzan approached the camp upon the opposite side Rokoff disappeared into the jungle in the wake of Jane Clayton.

As the ape-man entered the *boma* with old Tambudza at his elbow the seven sailors, recognizing him, turned and fled in the opposite direction. Tarzan saw that Rokoff was not among them, and so he let them go their way—his business was with the Russian, whom he expected to find in his tent. As to the sailors, he was sure that the jungle would exact from them expiation for their villainies, nor, doubtless, was he wrong, for his were the last white man's eyes to rest upon any of them.

Finding Rokoff's tent empty, Tarzan was about to set out in search of the Russian when Tambudza suggested to him that the departure of the white man could only have resulted from word reaching him from M'ganwazam that Tarzan was in his village.

"He has doubtless hastened there," argued the old woman. "If you would find him let us return at once."

Tarzan himself thought that this would probably prove to be the fact, so he did not waste time in an endeavour to locate the Russian's trail, but, instead, set out briskly for the village of M'ganwazam, leaving Tambudza to plod slowly in his wake.

His one hope was that Jane was still safe and with Rokoff. If this was the case, it would be but a matter of an hour or more before he should be able to wrest her from the Russian.

He knew now that M'ganwazam was treacherous and that he might have to fight to regain possession of his wife. He wished that Mugambi, Sheeta, Akut, and the balance of the pack were with him, for he realized that single-handed it would be no child's play to bring Jane safely from the clutches of two such scoundrels as Rokoff and the wily M'ganwazam.

To his surprise he found no sign of either Rokoff or Jane in the village, and as he could not trust the word of the chief, he wasted no time in futile inquiry. So sudden and unexpected had been his return, and so quickly had he vanished into the jungle after learning that those he sought were not among the Waganwazam, that old M'ganwazam had no time to prevent his going.

Swinging through the trees, he hastened back to the deserted camp he had so recently left, for here, he knew, was the logical place to take up the trail of Rokoff and Jane.

Arrived at the *boma*, he circled carefully about the outside of the enclosure until, opposite a break in the thorny wall, he came to indications that something had recently passed into the jungle. His acute sense of smell told him that both of those he sought had fled from the camp in this direction, and a moment later he had taken up the trail and was following the faint spoor.

Far ahead of him a terror-stricken young woman was slinking along a narrow game-trail, fearful that the next moment would bring her face to face with some savage beast or equally savage man. As she ran on, hoping against hope that she had hit upon the direction that would lead her eventually to the great river, she came suddenly upon a familiar spot.

At one side of the trail, beneath a giant tree, lay a little heap of loosely piled brush—to her dying day that little spot of jungle would be indelibly impressed upon her memory. It was where Anderssen had hidden her—where he had given up his life in the vain effort to save her from Rokoff.

At sight of it she recalled the rifle and ammunition that the man had thrust upon her at the last moment. Until now she had forgotten them entirely. Still clutched in her hand was the revolver she had snatched from Rokoff's belt, but that could contain at most not over six cartridges—not enough to furnish her with food and protection both on the long journey to the sea.

With bated breath she groped beneath the little mound, scarce daring to hope that the treasure remained where she had left it; but, to her infinite relief and joy, her hand came at once upon the barrel of the heavy weapon and then upon the bandoleer of cartridges.

As she threw the latter about her shoulder and felt the weight of the big game-gun in her hand a sudden sense of security suffused her. It was with new hope and a feeling almost of assured success that she again set forward upon her journey.

That night she slept in the crotch of a tree, as Tarzan had so often told her that he was accustomed to doing, and early the next morning was upon her way again. Late in the afternoon, as she was about to cross a little clearing, she was startled at the sight of a huge ape coming from the jungle upon the opposite side.

The wind was blowing directly across the clearing between them, and Jane lost no time in putting herself downwind from the huge creature. Then she hid in a clump of heavy bush and watched, holding the rifle ready for instant use.

To her consternation she saw that the apes were pausing in the centre of the clearing. They came together in a little knot, where they stood looking backward, as though in expectation of the coming of others of their tribe. Jane wished that they would go on, for she knew that at any moment some little, eddying gust of wind might carry her scent down to their nostrils, and then what would the protection of her rifle amount to in the face of those gigantic muscles and mighty fangs?

Her eyes moved back and forth between the apes and the edge of the jungle toward which they were gazing until at last she perceived the object of their halt and the thing that they awaited. They were being stalked.

Of this she was positive, as she saw the lithe, sinewy form of a panther glide noiselessly from the jungle at the point at which the apes had emerged but a moment before.

Quickly the beast trotted across the clearing toward the anthropoids. Jane wondered at their apparent apathy, and a moment later her wonder turned to amazement as she saw the great cat come quite close to the apes, who appeared entirely unconcerned by its presence, and, squatting down in their midst, fell assiduously to the business of preening, which occupies most of the waking hours of the cat family.

If the young woman was surprised by the sight of these natural enemies fraternizing, it was with emotions little short of fear for her own sanity that she presently saw a tall, muscular warrior enter the clearing and join the group of savage beasts assembled there.

At first sight of the man she had been positive that he would be torn to pieces, and she had half risen from her shelter, raising her rifle to her shoulder to do what she could to avert the man's terrible fate.

Now she saw that he seemed actually conversing with the beasts—issuing orders to them.

Presently the entire company filed on across the clearing and disappeared in the jungle upon the opposite side.

With a gasp of mingled incredulity and relief Jane Clayton staggered to her feet and fled on away from the terrible horde that had just passed her, while a half-mile behind her another individual, following the same trail as she, lay frozen with terror behind an ant-hill as the hideous band passed quite close to him.

This one was Rokoff; but he had recognized the members of the awful aggregation as allies of Tarzan of the Apes. No sooner, therefore, had the beasts passed him than he rose and raced through the jungle as fast as he could go, in order that he might put as much distance as possible between himself and these frightful beasts.

So it happened that as Jane Clayton came to the bank of the river, down which she hoped to float to the ocean and eventual rescue, Nikolas Rokoff was but a short distance in her rear.

Upon the bank the girl saw a great dugout drawn half-way from the water and tied securely to a near-by tree.

This, she felt, would solve the question of transportation to the sea could she but launch the huge, unwieldy craft. Unfastening the rope that had moored it to the tree, Jane pushed frantically upon the bow of the heavy canoe, but for all the results that were apparent she might as well have been attempting to shove the earth out of its orbit.

She was about winded when it occurred to her to try working the dugout into the stream by loading the stern with ballast and then rocking the bow back and forth along the bank until the craft eventually worked itself into the river.

There were no stones or rocks available, but along the shore she found quantities of driftwood deposited by the river at a slightly higher stage. These she gathered and piled far in the stern of the boat, until at last, to her immense relief, she saw the bow rise gently from the mud of the bank and the stern drift slowly with the current until it again lodged a few feet farther down-stream.

Jane found that by running back and forth between the bow and stern she could alternately raise and lower each end of the boat as she shifted her weight from one end to the other, with the result that each time she leaped to the stern the canoe moved a few inches farther into the river.

As the success of her plan approached more closely to fruition she became so wrapped in her efforts that she failed to note the figure of a man standing beneath a huge tree at the edge of the jungle from which he had just emerged.

He watched her and her labours with a cruel and malicious grin upon his swarthy countenance.

The boat at last became so nearly free of the retarding mud and of the bank that Jane felt positive that she could pole it off into deeper water with one of the paddles which lay in the bottom of the rude craft. With this end in view she seized upon one of these implements and had just plunged it into the river bottom close to the shore when her eyes happened to rise to the edge of the jungle.

As her gaze fell upon the figure of the man a little cry of terror rose to her lips. It was Rokoff.

He was running toward her now and shouting to her to wait or he would shoot—though he was entirely unarmed it was difficult to discover just how he intended making good his threat.

Jane Clayton knew nothing of the various misfortunes that had befallen the Russian since she had escaped from his tent, so she believed that his followers must be close at hand.

However, she had no intention of falling again into the man's clutches. She would rather die at once than that that should happen to her. Another minute and the boat would be free.

Once in the current of the river she would be beyond Rokoff's power to stop her, for there was no other boat upon the shore, and no man, and certainly not the cowardly Rokoff, would dare to attempt to swim the crocodile-infested water in an effort to overtake her.

Rokoff, on his part, was bent more upon escape than aught else. He would gladly have forgone any designs he might have had upon Jane Clayton would she but permit him to share this means of escape that she had discovered. He would promise anything if she would let him come aboard the dugout, but he did not think that it was necessary to do so.

He saw that he could easily reach the bow of the boat before it cleared the shore, and then it would not be necessary to make promises of any sort. Not that Rokoff would have felt the slightest compunction in ignoring any promises he might have made the girl, but he disliked the idea of having to sue for favour with one who had so recently assaulted and escaped him.

Already he was gloating over the days and nights of revenge that would be his while the heavy dugout drifted its slow way to the ocean.

Jane Clayton, working furiously to shove the boat beyond his reach, suddenly realized that she was to be successful, for with a little lurch the dugout swung quickly into the current, just as the Russian reached out to place his hand upon its bow.

His fingers did not miss their goal by a half-dozen inches. The girl almost collapsed with the reaction from the terrific mental, physical, and nervous strain under which she had been labouring for the past few minutes. But, thank Heaven, at last she was safe!

Even as she breathed a silent prayer of thanksgiving, she saw a sudden expression of triumph lighten the features of the cursing Russian, and at the same instant he dropped suddenly to the ground, grasping firmly upon something which wriggled through the mud toward the water.

Jane Clayton crouched, wide-eyed and horror-stricken, in the bottom of the boat as she realized that at the last instant success had been turned to failure, and that she was indeed again in the power of the malignant Rokoff.

For the thing that the man had seen and grasped was the end of the trailing rope with which the dugout had been moored to the tree.

DOWN THE UGAMBI

Halfway between the Ugambi and the village of the Waganwazam, Tarzan came upon the pack moving slowly along his old spoor. Mugambi could scarce believe that the trail of the Russian and the mate of his savage master had passed so close to that of the pack.

It seemed incredible that two human beings should have come so close to them without having been detected by some of the marvellously keen and alert beasts; but Tarzan pointed out the spoor of the two he trailed, and at certain points the black could see that the man and the woman must have been in hiding as the pack passed them, watching every move of the ferocious creatures.

It had been apparent to Tarzan from the first that Jane and Rokoff were not travelling together. The spoor showed distinctly that the young woman had been a considerable distance ahead of the Russian at first, though the farther the ape-man continued along the trail the more obvious it became that the man was rapidly overhauling his quarry.

At first there had been the spoor of wild beasts over the footprints of Jane Clayton, while upon the top of all Rokoff's spoor showed that he had passed over the trail after the animals had left their records upon the ground. But later there were fewer and fewer animal imprints occurring between those of Jane's and the Russian's feet, until as he approached the river the ape-man became aware that Rokoff could not have been more than a few hundred yards behind the girl.

He felt they must be close ahead of him now, and, with a little thrill of expectation, he leaped rapidly forward ahead of the pack. Swinging swiftly through the trees, he came out upon the river-bank at the very point at which Rokoff had overhauled Jane as she endeavoured to launch the cumbersome dugout.

In the mud along the bank the ape-man saw the footprints of the two he sought, but there was neither boat nor people there when he arrived, nor, at first glance, any sign of their whereabouts.

It was plain that they had shoved off a native canoe and embarked upon the bosom of the stream, and as the ape-man's eye ran swiftly down the course of the river beneath the shadows of the overarching trees he saw in the distance, just as it rounded a bend that shut it off from his view, a drifting dugout in the stern of which was the figure of a man.

Just as the pack came in sight of the river they saw their agile leader racing down the river's bank, leaping from hummock to hummock of the swampy ground that spread between them and a little promontory which rose just where the river curved inward from their sight.

To follow him it was necessary for the heavy, cumbersome apes to make a wide detour, and Sheeta, too, who hated water. Mugambi followed after them as rapidly as he could in the wake of the great white master.

A half-hour of rapid travelling across the swampy neck of land and over the rising promontory brought Tarzan, by a short cut, to the inward bend of the winding river, and there before him upon the bosom of the stream he saw the dugout, and in its stern Nikolas Rokoff.

Jane was not with the Russian.

At sight of his enemy the broad scar upon the ape-man's brow burned scarlet, and there rose to his lips the hideous, bestial challenge of the bull-ape.

Rokoff shuddered as the weird and terrible alarm fell upon his ears. Cowering in the bottom of the boat, his teeth chattering in terror, he watched the man he feared above all other creatures upon the face of the earth as he ran quickly to the edge of the water.

Even though the Russian knew that he was safe from his enemy, the very sight of him threw him into a frenzy of trembling cowardice, which became frantic hysteria as he saw the white giant dive fearlessly into the forbidding waters of the tropical river.

With steady, powerful strokes the ape-man forged out into the stream toward the drifting dugout. Now Rokoff seized one of the paddles lying in the bottom of the craft, and, with terrorwide eyes still glued upon the living death that pursued him, struck out madly in an effort to augment the speed of the unwieldy canoe.

And from the opposite bank a sinister ripple, unseen by either man, moving steadily toward the half-naked swimmer.

Tarzan had reached the stern of the craft at last. One hand upstretched grasped the gunwale. Rokoff sat frozen with fear, unable to move a hand or foot, his eyes riveted upon the face of his Nemesis.

Then a sudden commotion in the water behind the swimmer caught his attention. He saw the ripple, and he knew what caused it.

At the same instant Tarzan felt mighty jaws close upon his right leg. He tried to struggle free and raise himself over the side of the boat. His efforts would have succeeded had not this unexpected interruption galvanized the malign brain of the Russian into instant action with its sudden promise of deliverance and revenge.

Like a venomous snake the man leaped toward the stern of the boat, and with a single swift blow struck Tarzan across the head with the heavy paddle. The ape-man's fingers slipped from their hold upon the gunwale.

There was a short struggle at the surface, and then a swirl of waters, a little eddy, and a burst of bubbles soon smoothed out by the flowing current marked for the instant the spot where Tarzan of the Apes, Lord of the Jungle, disappeared from the sight of men beneath the gloomy waters of the dark and forbidding Ugambi.

Weak from terror, Rokoff sank shuddering into the bottom of the dugout. For a moment he could not realize the good fortune that had befallen him—all that he could see was the figure of a silent, struggling white man disappearing beneath the surface of the river to unthinkable death in the slimy mud of the bottom.

Slowly all that it meant to him filtered into the mind of the Russian, and then a cruel smile of relief and triumph touched his lips; but it was short-lived, for just as he was congratulating himself that he was now comparatively safe to proceed upon his way to the coast unmolested, a mighty pandemonium rose from the river-bank close by.

As his eyes sought the authors of the frightful sound he saw standing upon the shore, glaring at him with hate-filled eyes, a devil-faced panther surrounded by the hideous apes of Akut, and in the forefront of them a giant black warrior who shook his fist at him, threatening him with terrible death.

The nightmare of that flight down the Ugambi with the hideous horde racing after him by day and by night, now abreast of him, now lost in the mazes of the jungle far behind for hours and once for a whole day, only to reappear again upon his trail grim, relentless, and terrible, reduced the Russian from a strong and robust man to an emaciated, white-haired, fear-gibbering thing before ever the bay and the ocean broke upon his hopeless vision.

Past populous villages he had fled. Time and again warriors had put out in their canoes to intercept him, but each time the hideous horde had swept into view to send the terrified natives shrieking back to the shore to lose themselves in the jungle.

Nowhere in his flight had he seen aught of Jane Clayton. Not once had his eyes rested upon her since that moment at the river's brim his hand had closed upon the rope attached to the bow of her dugout and he had believed her safely in his power again, only to be thwarted an instant later as the girl snatched up a heavy express rifle from the bottom of the craft and levelled it full at his breast.

Quickly he had dropped the rope then and seen her float away beyond his reach, but a moment later he had been racing up-stream toward a little tributary in the mouth of which was hidden the canoe in which he and his party had come thus far upon their journey in pursuit of the girl and Anderssen.

What had become of her?

There seemed little doubt in the Russian's mind, however, but that she had been captured by warriors from one of the several villages she would have been compelled to pass on her way down to the sea. Well, he was at least rid of most of his human enemies.

But at that he would gladly have had them all back in the land of the living could he thus have been freed from the menace of the frightful creatures who pursued him with awful relentlessness, screaming and growling at him every time they came within sight of him. The one that filled him with the greatest terror was the panther—the flaming-eyed, devil-faced panther whose grinning jaws gaped wide at him by day, and whose fiery orbs gleamed wickedly out across the water from the Cimmerian blackness of the jungle nights.

The sight of the mouth of the Ugambi filled Rokoff with renewed hope, for there, upon the yellow waters of the bay, floated the *Kincaid* at anchor. He had sent the little steamer away to coal while he had gone up the river, leaving Paulvitch in charge of her, and he could have cried aloud in his relief as he saw that she had returned in time to save him.

Frantically he alternately paddled furiously toward her and rose to his feet waving his paddle and crying aloud in an attempt to attract the attention of those on board. But loud as he screamed his cries awakened no answering challenge from the deck of the silent craft.

Upon the shore behind him a hurried backward glance revealed the presence of the snarling pack. Even now, he thought, these manlike devils might yet find a way to reach him even upon the deck of the steamer unless there were those there to repel them with firearms.

What could have happened to those he had left upon the *Kincaid?* Where was Paulvitch? Could it be that the vessel was deserted, and that, after all, he was doomed to be overtaken by the terrible fate that he had been flying from through all these hideous days and nights? He shivered as might one upon whose brow death has already laid his clammy finger.

Yet he did not cease to paddle frantically toward the steamer, and at last, after what seemed an eternity, the bow of the dugout bumped against the timbers of the *Kincaid.* Over the ship's side hung a monkey-ladder, but as the Russian grasped it to ascend to the deck he heard a warning challenge from above, and, looking up, gazed into the cold, relentless muzzle of a rifle.

After Jane Clayton, with rifle levelled at the breast of Rokoff, had succeeded in holding him off until the dugout in which she had taken refuge had drifted out upon the bosom of the Ugambi beyond the man's reach, she had lost no time in paddling to the swiftest sweep of the channel, nor did she for long days and weary nights cease to hold her craft to the most rapidly moving part of the river, except when during the hottest hours of the day she had been wont to drift as the current would take her, lying prone in the bottom of the canoe, her face sheltered from the sun with a great palm leaf.

Thus only did she gain rest upon the voyage; at other times she continually sought to augment the movement of the craft by wielding the heavy paddle.

Rokoff, on the other hand, had used little or no intelligence in his flight along the Ugambi, so that more often than not his craft had drifted in the slow-going eddies, for he habitually hugged the bank farthest from that along which the hideous horde pursued and menaced him.

Thus it was that, though he had put out upon the river but a short time subsequent to the girl, yet she had reached the bay fully two hours ahead of him. When she had first seen the anchored ship upon the quiet water, Jane Clayton's heart had beat fast with hope and thanksgiving, but as she drew closer to the craft and saw that it was the *Kincaid,* her pleasure gave place to the gravest misgivings.

It was too late, however, to turn back, for the current that carried her toward the ship was much too strong for her muscles. She could not have forced the heavy dugout upstream against it, and all that was left her was to attempt either to make the shore without being seen by those upon the deck of the *Kincaid,* or to throw herself upon their mercy—otherwise she must be swept out to sea.

She knew that the shore held little hope of life for her, as she had no knowledge of the location of the friendly Mosula village to which Anderssen had taken her through the darkness of the night of their escape from the *Kincaid.*

With Rokoff away from the steamer it might be possible that by offering those in charge a large reward they could be induced to carry her to the nearest civilized port. It was worth risking—if she could make the steamer at all.

The current was bearing her swiftly down the river, and she found that only by dint of the utmost exertion could she direct the awkward craft toward the vicinity of the *Kincaid.* Having reached the decision to board the steamer, she now looked to it for aid, but to her surprise the decks appeared to be empty and she saw no sign of life aboard the ship.

The dugout was drawing closer and closer to the bow of the vessel, and yet no hail came over the side from any lookout aboard. In a moment more, Jane realized, she would be swept beyond the steamer, and then, unless they lowered a boat to rescue her, she would be carried far out to sea by the current and the swift ebb tide that was running.

The young woman called loudly for assistance, but there was no reply other than the shrill scream of some savage beast upon the jungle-shrouded shore. Frantically Jane wielded the paddle in an effort to carry her craft close alongside the steamer.

For a moment it seemed that she should miss her goal by but a few feet, but at the last moment the canoe swung close beneath the steamer's bow and Jane barely managed to grasp the anchor chain.

Heroically she clung to the heavy iron links, almost dragged from the canoe by the strain of the current upon her craft. Beyond her she saw a monkey-ladder dangling over the steamer's side. To release her hold upon the chain and chance clambering to the ladder as her canoe was swept beneath it seemed beyond the pale of possibility, yet to remain clinging to the anchor chain appeared equally as futile.

Finally her glance chanced to fall upon the rope in the bow of the dugout, and, making one end of this fast to the chain, she succeeded in drifting the canoe slowly down until it lay directly beneath the ladder. A moment later, her rifle slung about her shoulders, she had clambered safely to the deserted deck.

Her first task was to explore the ship, and this she did, her rifle ready for instant use should she meet with any human menace aboard the *Kincaid*. She was not long in discovering the cause of the apparently deserted condition of the steamer, for in the forecastle she found the sailors, who had evidently been left to guard the ship, deep in drunken slumber.

With a shudder of disgust she clambered above, and to the best of her ability closed and made fast the hatch above the heads of the sleeping guard. Next she sought the galley and food, and, having appeased her hunger, she took her place on deck, determined that none should board the *Kincaid* without first having agreed to her demands.

For an hour or so nothing appeared upon the surface of the river to cause her alarm, but then, about a bend upstream, she saw a canoe appear in which sat a single figure. It had not proceeded far in her direction before she recognized the occupant as Rokoff, and when the fellow attempted to board he found a rifle staring him in the face.

When the Russian discovered who it was that repelled his advance he became furious, cursing and threatening in a most horrible manner; but, finding that these tactics failed to frighten or move the girl, he at last fell to pleading and promising.

Jane had but a single reply for his every proposition, and that was that nothing would ever persuade her to permit Rokoff upon the same vessel with her. That she would put her threats into action and shoot him should he persist in his endeavour to board the ship he was convinced.

So, as there was no other alternative, the great coward dropped back into his dugout and, at imminent risk of being swept to sea, finally succeeded in making the shore far down the bay and upon the opposite side from that on which the horde of beasts stood snarling and roaring.

Jane Clayton knew that the fellow could not alone and unaided bring his heavy craft back up-stream to the *Kincaid*, and so she had no further fear of an attack by him. The hideous crew upon the shore she thought she recognized as the same that had passed her in the jungle far up the Ugambi several days before, for it seemed quite beyond reason that there should be more than one such a strangely assorted pack; but what had brought them down-stream to the mouth of the river she could not imagine.

Toward the day's close the girl was suddenly alarmed by the shouting of the Russian from the opposite bank of the stream, and a moment later, following the direction of his gaze, she was terrified to see a ship's boat approaching from up-stream, in which, she felt assured, there could be only members of the *Kincaid's* missing crew—only heartless ruffians and enemies.

IN THE DARKNESS OF THE NIGHT

When Tarzan of the Apes realized that he was in the grip of the great jaws of a crocodile he did not, as an ordinary man might have done, give up all hope and resign himself to his fate.

Instead, he filled his lungs with air before the huge reptile dragged him beneath the surface, and then, with all the might of his great muscles, fought bitterly for freedom. But out of his native element the ape-man was too greatly handicapped to do more than excite the monster to greater speed as it dragged its prey swiftly through the water.

Tarzan's lungs were bursting for a breath of pure fresh air. He knew that he could survive but a moment more, and in the last paroxysm of his suffering he did what he could to avenge his own death.

His body trailed out beside the slimy carcass of his captor, and into the tough armour the ape-man attempted to plunge his stone knife as he was borne to the creature's horrid den.

His efforts but served to accelerate the speed of the crocodile, and just as the ape-man realized that he had reached the limit of his endurance he felt his body dragged to a muddy bed and his nostrils rise above the water's surface. All about him was the blackness of the pit—the silence of the grave.

For a moment Tarzan of the Apes lay gasping for breath upon the slimy, evil-smelling bed to which the animal had borne him. Close at his side he could feel the cold, hard plates of the creatures coat rising and falling as though with spasmodic efforts to breathe.

For several minutes the two lay thus, and then a sudden convulsion of the giant carcass at the man's side, a tremor, and a stiffening brought Tarzan to his knees beside the crocodile. To his utter amazement he found that the beast was dead. The slim knife had found a vulnerable spot in the scaly armour.

Staggering to his feet, the ape-man groped about the reeking, oozy den. He found that he was imprisoned in a subterranean chamber amply large enough to have accommodated a dozen or more of the huge animals such as the one that had dragged him thither.

He realized that he was in the creature's hidden nest far under the bank of the stream, and that doubtless the only means of ingress or egress lay through the submerged opening through which the crocodile had brought him.

His first thought, of course, was of escape, but that he could make his way to the surface of the river beyond and then to the shore seemed highly improbable. There might be turns and windings in the neck of the passage, or, most to be feared, he might meet another of the slimy inhabitants of the retreat upon his journey outward.

Even should he reach the river in safety, there was still the danger of his being again attacked before he could effect a safe landing. Still there was no alternative, and, filling his lungs with the close and reeking air of the chamber, Tarzan of the Apes dived into the dark and watery hole which he could not see but had felt out and found with his feet and legs.

The leg which had been held within the jaws of the crocodile was badly lacerated, but the bone had not been broken, nor were the muscles or tendons sufficiently injured to render it useless. It gave him excruciating pain, that was all.

But Tarzan of the Apes was accustomed to pain, and gave it no further thought when he found that the use of his legs was not greatly impaired by the sharp teeth of the monster.

Rapidly he crawled and swam through the passage which inclined downward and finally upward to open at last into the river bottom but a few feet from the shore line. As the ape-man reached the surface he saw the heads of two great crocodiles but a short distance from him. They were making rapidly in his direction, and with a superhuman effort the man struck out for the overhanging branches of a near-by tree.

Nor was he a moment too soon, for scarcely had he drawn himself to the safety of the limb than two gaping mouths snapped venomously below him. For a few minutes Tarzan rested in the tree that had proved the means of his salvation. His eyes scanned the river as far down-stream as the tortuous channel would permit, but there was no sign of the Russian or his dugout.

When he had rested and bound up his wounded leg he started on in pursuit of the drifting canoe. He found himself upon the opposite of the river to that at which he had entered the stream, but as his quarry was upon the bosom of the water it made little difference to the ape-man upon which side he took up the pursuit.

To his intense chagrin he soon found that his leg was more badly injured than he had thought, and that its condition seriously impeded his progress. It was only with the greatest difficulty that he could proceed faster than a walk upon the ground, and in the trees he discovered that it not only impeded his progress, but rendered travelling distinctly dangerous.

From the old negress, Tambudza, Tarzan had gathered a suggestion that now filled his mind with doubts and misgivings. When the old woman had told him of the child's death she had also added that the white woman, though grief-stricken, had confided to her that the baby was not hers.

Tarzan could see no reason for believing that Jane could have found it advisable to deny her identity or that of the child; the only explanation that he could put upon the matter was that, after all, the white woman who had accompanied his son and the Swede into the jungle fastness of the interior had not been Jane at all.

The more he gave thought to the problem, the more firmly convinced he became that his son was dead and his wife still safe in London, and in ignorance of the terrible fate that had overtaken her first-born.

After all, then, his interpretation of Rokoff's sinister taunt had been erroneous, and he had been bearing the burden of a double apprehension needlessly—at least so thought the ape-man. From this belief he garnered some slight surcease from the numbing grief that the death of his little son had thrust upon him.

And such a death! Even the savage beast that was the real Tarzan, inured to the sufferings and horrors of the grim jungle, shuddered as he contemplated the hideous fate that had overtaken the innocent child.

As he made his way painfully towards the coast, he let his mind dwell so constantly upon the frightful crimes which the Russian had perpetrated against his loved ones that the great scar upon his forehead stood out almost continuously in the vivid scarlet that marked the man's most relentless and bestial moods of rage. At times he startled even himself and sent the lesser creatures of the wild jungle scampering to their hiding places as involuntary roars and growls rumbled from his throat.

Could he but lay his hand upon the Russian!

Twice upon the way to the coast bellicose natives ran threateningly from their villages to bar his further progress, but when the awful cry of the bull-ape thundered upon their affrighted ears, and the great white giant charged bellowing upon them, they had turned and fled into the bush, nor ventured thence until he had safely passed.

Though his progress seemed tantalizingly slow to the ape-man whose idea of speed had been gained by such standards as the lesser apes attain, he made, as a matter of fact, almost as rapid progress as the drifting canoe that bore Rokoff on ahead of him, so that he came to the bay and within sight of the ocean just after darkness had fallen upon the same day that Jane Clayton and the Russian ended their flights from the interior.

The darkness lowered so heavily upon the black river and the encircling jungle that Tarzan, even with eyes accustomed to much use after dark, could make out nothing a few yards from him. His idea was to search the shore that night for signs of the Russian and the woman who he was certain must have preceded Rokoff down the Ugambi. That the *Kincaid* or other ship lay at anchor but a hundred yards from him he did not dream, for no light showed on board the steamer.

Even as he commenced his search his attention was suddenly attracted by a noise that he had not at first perceived—the stealthy dip of paddles in the water some distance from the shore, and about opposite the point at which he stood. Motionless as a statue he stood listening to the faint sound.

Presently it ceased, to be followed by a shuffling noise that the ape-man's trained ears could interpret as resulting from but a single cause—the scraping of leather-shod feet upon the rounds of a ship's monkey-ladder. And yet, as far as he could see, there was no ship there—nor might there be one within a thousand miles.

As he stood thus, peering out into the darkness of the cloud-enshrouded night, there came to him from across the water, like a slap in the face, so sudden and unexpected was it, the sharp staccato of an exchange of shots and then the scream of a woman.

Wounded though he was, and with the memory of his recent horrible experience still strong upon him, Tarzan of the Apes did not hesitate as the notes of that frightened cry rose shrill and piercing upon the still night air. With a bound he cleared the intervening bush—there was a splash as the water closed about him—and then, with powerful strokes, he swam out into the impenetrable night with no guide save the memory of an illusive cry, and for company the hideous denizens of an equatorial river.

The boat that had attracted Jane's attention as she stood guard upon the deck of the *Kincaid* had been perceived by Rokoff upon one bank and Mugambi and the horde upon the other. The cries of the Russian had brought the dugout first to him, and then, after a conference, it had been turned toward the *Kincaid*, but before ever it covered half the distance between the shore and the steamer a rifle had spoken from the latter's deck and one of the sailors in the bow of the canoe had crumpled and fallen into the water.

After that they went more slowly, and presently, when Jane's rifle had found another member of the party, the canoe withdrew to the shore, where it lay as long as daylight lasted.

The savage, snarling pack upon the opposite shore had been directed in their pursuit by the black warrior, Mugambi, chief of the Wagambi. Only he knew which might be foe and which friend of their lost master.

Could they have reached either the canoe or the *Kincaid* they would have made short work of any whom they found there, but the gulf of black water intervening shut them off from farther advance as effectually as though it had been the broad ocean that separated them from their prey.

Mugambi knew something of the occurrences which had led up to the landing of Tarzan upon Jungle Island and the pursuit of the whites up the Ugambi. He knew that his savage master sought his wife and child who had been stolen by the wicked white man whom they had followed far into the interior and now back to the sea.

He believed also that this same man had killed the great white giant whom he had come to respect and love as he had never loved the greatest chiefs of his own people. And so in the wild breast of Mugambi burned an iron resolve to win to the side of the wicked one and wreak vengeance upon him for the murder of the ape-man.

But when he saw the canoe come down the river and take in Rokoff, when he saw it make for the *Kincaid*, he realized that only by possessing himself of a canoe could he hope to transport the beasts of the pack within striking distance of the enemy.

So it happened that even before Jane Clayton fired the first shot into Rokoff's canoe the beasts of Tarzan had disappeared into the jungle.

After the Russian and his party, which consisted of Paulvitch and the several men he had left upon the *Kincaid* to attend to the matter of coaling, had retreated before her fire, Jane realized that it would be but a temporary respite from their attentions which she had gained, and with the conviction came a determination to make a bold and final stroke for freedom from the menacing threat of Rokoff's evil purpose.

With this idea in view she opened negotiations with the two sailors she had imprisoned in the forecastle, and having forced their consent to her plans, upon pain of death should they attempt disloyalty, she released them just as darkness closed about the ship.

With ready revolver to compel obedience, she let them up one by one, searching them carefully for concealed weapons as they stood with hands elevated above their heads. Once satisfied that they were unarmed, she set them to work cutting the cable which held the *Kincaid* to her anchorage, for her bold plan was nothing less than to set the steamer adrift and float with her out into the open sea, there to trust to the mercy of the elements, which she was confident would be no more merciless than Nikolas Rokoff should he again capture her.

There was, too, the chance that the *Kincaid* might be sighted by some passing ship, and as she was well stocked with provisions and water—the men had assured her of this fact—and as the season of storm was well over, she had every reason to hope for the eventual success of her plan.

The night was deeply overcast, heavy clouds riding low above the jungle and the water—only to the west, where the broad ocean spread beyond the river's mouth, was there a suggestion of lessening gloom.

It was a perfect night for the purposes of the work in hand.

Her enemies could not see the activity aboard the ship nor mark her course as the swift current bore her outward into the ocean. Before daylight broke the ebb-tide would have carried the *Kincaid* well into the Benguela current which flows northward along the coast of Africa, and, as a south wind was prevailing, Jane hoped to be out of sight of the mouth of the Ugambi before Rokoff could become aware of the departure of the steamer.

Standing over the labouring seamen, the young woman breathed a sigh of relief as the last strand of the cable parted and she knew that the vessel was on its way out of the maw of the savage Ugambi.

With her two prisoners still beneath the coercing influence of her rifle, she ordered them upon deck with the intention of again imprisoning them in the forecastle; but at length she permitted herself to be influenced by their promises of loyalty and the arguments which they put forth that they could be of service to her, and permitted them to remain above.

For a few minutes the *Kincaid* drifted rapidly with the current, and then, with a grinding jar, she stopped in midstream. The ship had run upon a low-lying bar that splits the channel about a quarter of a mile from the sea.

For a moment she hung there, and then, swinging round until her bow pointed toward the shore, she broke adrift once more.

At the same instant, just as Jane Clayton was congratulating herself that the ship was once more free, there fell upon her ears from a point up the river about where the *Kincaid* had been anchored the rattle of musketry and a woman's scream—shrill, piercing, fear-laden.

The sailors heard the shots with certain conviction that they announced the coming of their employer, and as they had no relish for the plan that would consign them to the deck of a drifting derelict, they whispered together a hurried plan to overcome the young woman and hail Rokoff and their companions to their rescue.

It seemed that fate would play into their hands, for with the reports of the guns Jane Clayton's attention had been distracted from her unwilling assistants, and instead of keeping one eye upon them as she had intended doing, she ran to the bow of the *Kincaid* to peer through the darkness toward the source of the disturbance upon the river's bosom.

Seeing that she was off her guard, the two sailors crept stealthily upon her from behind.

The scraping upon the deck of the shoes of one of them startled the girl to a sudden appreciation of her danger, but the warning had come too late.

As she turned, both men leaped upon her and bore her to the deck, and as she went down beneath them she saw, outlined against the lesser gloom of the ocean, the figure of another man clamber over the side of the *Kincaid*.

After all her pains her heroic struggle for freedom had failed. With a stifled sob she gave up the unequal battle.

ON THE DECK OF THE KINCAID

When Mugambi had turned back into the jungle with the pack he had a definite purpose in view. It was to obtain a dugout wherewith to transport the beasts of Tarzan to the side of the *Kincaid*. Nor was he long in coming upon the object which he sought.

Just at dusk he found a canoe moored to the bank of a small tributary of the Ugambi at a point where he had felt certain that he should find one.

Without loss of time he piled his hideous fellows into the craft and shoved out into the stream. So quickly had they taken possession of the canoe that the warrior had not noticed that it was already occupied. The huddled figure sleeping in the bottom had entirely escaped his observation in the darkness of the night that had now fallen.

But no sooner were they afloat than a savage growling from one of the apes directly ahead of him in the dugout attracted his attention to a shivering and cowering figure that trembled between him and the great anthropoid. To Mugambi's astonishment he saw that it was a native woman. With difficulty he kept the ape from her throat, and after a time succeeded in quelling her fears.

It seemed that she had been fleeing from marriage with an old man she loathed and had taken refuge for the night in the canoe she had found upon the river's edge.

Mugambi did not wish her presence, but there she was, and rather than lose time by returning her to the shore the black permitted her to remain on board the canoe.

As quickly as his awkward companions could paddle the dugout down-stream toward the Ugambi and the *Kincaid* they moved through the darkness. It was with difficulty that Mugambi could make out the shadowy form of the steamer, but as he had it between himself and the ocean it was much more apparent than to one upon either shore of the river.

As he approached it he was amazed to note that it seemed to be receding from him, and finally he was convinced that the vessel was moving down-stream. Just as he was about to urge his creatures to renewed efforts to overtake the steamer the outline of another canoe burst suddenly into view not three yards from the bow of his own craft.

At the same instant the occupants of the stranger discovered the proximity of Mugambi's horde, but they did not at first recognize the nature of the fearful crew. A man in the bow of the oncoming boat challenged them just as the two dugouts were about to touch.

For answer came the menacing growl of a panther, and the fellow found himself gazing into the flaming eyes of Sheeta, who had raised himself with his forepaws upon the bow of the boat, ready to leap in upon the occupants of the other craft.

Instantly Rokoff realized the peril that confronted him and his fellows. He gave a quick command to fire upon the occupants of the other canoe, and it was this volley and the scream of the terrified native woman in the canoe with Mugambi that both Tarzan and Jane had heard.

Before the slower and less skilled paddlers in Mugambi's canoe could press their advantage and effect a boarding of the enemy the latter had turned swiftly down-stream and were paddling for their lives in the direction of the *Kincaid*, which was now visible to them.

The vessel after striking upon the bar had swung loose again into a slow-moving eddy, which returns up-stream close to the southern shore of the Ugambi only to circle out once more and join the downward flow a hundred yards or so farther up. Thus the *Kincaid* was returning Jane Clayton directly into the hands of her enemies.

It so happened that as Tarzan sprang into the river the vessel was not visible to him, and as he swam out into the night he had no idea that a ship drifted so close at hand. He was guided by the sounds which he could hear coming from the two canoes.

As he swam he had vivid recollections of the last occasion upon which he had swum in the waters of the Ugambi, and with them a sudden shudder shook the frame of the giant.

But, though he twice felt something brush his legs from the slimy depths below him, nothing seized him, and of a sudden he quite forgot about crocodiles in the astonishment of seeing a dark mass loom suddenly before him where he had still expected to find the open river.

So close was it that a few strokes brought him up to the thing, when to his amazement his outstretched hand came in contact with a ship's side.

As the agile ape-man clambered over the vessel's rail there came to his sensitive ears the sound of a struggle at the opposite side of the deck.

Noiselessly he sped across the intervening space.

The moon had risen now, and, though the sky was still banked with clouds, a lesser darkness enveloped the scene than that which had blotted out all sight earlier in the night. His keen eyes, therefore, saw the figures of two men grappling with a woman.

That it was the woman who had accompanied Anderssen toward the interior he did not know, though he suspected as much, as he was now quite certain that this was the deck of the *Kincaid* upon which chance had led him.

But he wasted little time in idle speculation. There was a woman in danger of harm from two ruffians, which was enough excuse for the ape-man to project his giant thews into the conflict without further investigation.

The first that either of the sailors knew that there was a new force at work upon the ship was the falling of a mighty hand upon a shoulder of each. As if they had been in the grip of a fly-wheel, they were jerked suddenly from their prey.

"What means this?" asked a low voice in their ears.

They were given no time to reply, however, for at the sound of that voice the young woman had sprung to her feet and with a little cry of joy leaped toward their assailant.

"Tarzan!" she cried.

The ape-man hurled the two sailors across the deck, where they rolled, stunned and terrified, into the scuppers upon the opposite side, and with an exclamation of incredulity gathered the girl into his arms.

Brief, however, were the moments for their greeting.

Scarcely had they recognized one another than the clouds above them parted to show the figures of a half-dozen men clambering over the side of the *Kincaid* to the steamer's deck.

Foremost among them was the Russian. As the brilliant rays of the equatorial moon lighted the deck, and he realized that the man before him was Lord Greystoke, he screamed hysterical commands to his followers to fire upon the two.

Tarzan pushed Jane behind the cabin near which they had been standing, and with a quick bound started for Rokoff. The men behind the Russian, at least two of them, raised their rifles and fired at the charging ape-man; but those behind them were otherwise engaged—for up the monkey-ladder in their rear was thronging a hideous horde.

First came five snarling apes, huge, manlike beasts, with bared fangs and slavering jaws; and after them a giant black warrior, his long spear gleaming in the moonlight.

Behind him again scrambled another creature, and of all the horrid horde it was this they most feared—Sheeta, the panther, with gleaming jaws agape and fiery eyes blazing at them in the mightiness of his hate and of his blood lust.

The shots that had been fired at Tarzan missed him, and he would have been upon Rokoff in another instant had not the great coward dodged backward between his two henchmen, and, screaming in hysterical terror, bolted forward toward the forecastle.

For the moment Tarzan's attention was distracted by the two men before him, so that he could not at the time pursue the Russian. About him the apes and Mugambi were battling with the balance of the Russian's party.

Beneath the terrible ferocity of the beasts the men were soon scampering in all directions—those who still lived to scamper, for the great fangs of the apes of Akut and the tearing talons of Sheeta already had found more than a single victim.

Four, however, escaped and disappeared into the forecastle, where they hoped to barricade themselves against further assault. Here they found Rokoff, and, enraged at his desertion of them in their moment of peril, no less than at the uniformly brutal treatment it had been his wont to accord them, they gloated upon the opportunity now offered them to revenge themselves in part upon their hated employer.

Despite his prayers and grovelling pleas, therefore, they hurled him bodily out upon the deck, delivering him to the mercy of the fearful things from which they had themselves just escaped.

Tarzan saw the man emerge from the forecastle—saw and recognized his enemy; but another saw him even as soon.

It was Sheeta, and with grinning jaws the mighty beast slunk silently toward the terror-stricken man.

When Rokoff saw what it was that stalked him his shrieks for help filled the air, as with trembling knees he stood, as one paralyzed, before the hideous death that was creeping upon him.

Tarzan took a step toward the Russian, his brain burning with a raging fire of vengeance. At last he had the murderer of his son at his mercy. His was the right to avenge.

Once Jane had stayed his hand that time that he sought to take the law into his own power and mete to Rokoff the death that he had so long merited; but this time none should stay him.

His fingers clenched and unclenched spasmodically as he approached the trembling Russ, beastlike and ominous as a brute of prey.

Presently he saw that Sheeta was about to forestall him, robbing him of the fruits of his great hate.

He called sharply to the panther, and the words, as if they had broken a hideous spell that had held the Russian, galvanized him into sudden action. With a scream he turned and fled toward the bridge.

After him pounced Sheeta the panther, unmindful of his master's warning voice.

Tarzan was about to leap after the two when he felt a light touch upon his arm. Turning, he found Jane at his elbow.

"Do not leave me," she whispered. "I am afraid."

Tarzan glanced behind her.

All about were the hideous apes of Akut. Some, even, were approaching the young woman with bared fangs and menacing guttural warnings.

The ape-man warned them back. He had forgotten for the moment that these were but beasts, unable to differentiate his friends and his foes. Their savage natures were roused by their recent battle with the sailors, and now all flesh outside the pack was meat to them.

Tarzan turned again toward the Russian, chagrined that he should have to forgo the pleasure of personal revenge—unless the man should escape Sheeta. But as he looked he saw that there could be no hope of that. The fellow had retreated to the end of the bridge, where he now stood trembling and wide-eyed, facing the beast that moved slowly toward him.

The panther crawled with belly to the planking, uttering uncanny mouthings. Rokoff stood as though petrified, his eyes protruding from their sockets, his mouth agape, and the cold sweat of terror clammy upon his brow.

Below him, upon the deck, he had seen the great anthropoids, and so had not dared to seek escape in that direction. In fact, even now one of the brutes was leaping to seize the bridge-rail and draw himself up to the Russian's side.

Before him was the panther, silent and crouched.

Rokoff could not move. His knees trembled. His voice broke in inarticulate shrieks. With a last piercing wail he sank to his knees—and then Sheeta sprang.

Full upon the man's breast the tawny body hurtled, tumbling the Russian to his back.

As the great fangs tore at the throat and chest, Jane Clayton turned away in horror; but not so Tarzan of the Apes. A cold smile of satisfaction touched his lips. The scar upon his forehead that had burned scarlet faded to the normal hue of his tanned skin and disappeared.

Rokoff fought furiously but futilely against the growling, rending fate that had overtaken him. For all his countless crimes he was punished in the brief moment of the hideous death that claimed him at the last.

After his struggles ceased Tarzan approached, at Jane's suggestion, to wrest the body from the panther and give what remained of it decent human burial; but the great cat rose snarling above its kill, threatening even the master it loved in its savage way, so that rather than kill his friend of the jungle, Tarzan was forced to relinquish his intentions.

All that night Sheeta, the panther, crouched upon the grisly thing that had been Nikolas Rokoff. The bridge of the *Kincaid* was slippery with blood. Beneath the brilliant tropic moon the great beast feasted until, when the sun rose the following morning, there remained of Tarzan's great enemy only gnawed and broken bones.

Of the Russian's party, all were accounted for except Paulvitch. Four were prisoners in the *Kincaid's* forecastle. The rest were dead.

With these men Tarzan got up steam upon the vessel, and with the knowledge of the mate, who happened to be one of those surviving, he planned to set out in quest of Jungle Island; but as the morning dawned there came with it a heavy gale from the west which raised a sea into which the mate of the *Kincaid* dared not venture. All that day the ship lay within the shelter of the mouth of the river; for, though night witnessed a lessening of the wind, it was thought safer to wait for daylight before attempting the navigation of the winding channel to the sea.

Upon the deck of the steamer the pack wandered without let or hindrance by day, for they had soon learned through Tarzan and Mugambi that they must harm no one upon the *Kincaid*; but at night they were confined below.

Tarzan's joy had been unbounded when he learned from his wife that the little child who had died in the village of M'ganwazam was not their son. Who the baby could have been, or what had become of their own, they could not imagine, and as both Rokoff and Paulvitch were gone, there was no way of discovering.

There was, however, a certain sense of relief in the knowledge that they might yet hope. Until positive proof of the baby's death reached them there was always that to buoy them up.

It seemed quite evident that their little Jack had not been brought aboard the *Kincaid*. Anderssen would have known of it had such been the case, but he had assured Jane time and time again that the little one he had brought to her cabin the night he aided her to escape was the only one that had been aboard the *Kincaid* since she lay at Dover.

PAULVITCH PLOTS REVENGE

As Jane and Tarzan stood upon the vessel's deck recounting to one another the details of the various adventures through which each had passed since they had parted in their London home, there glared at them from beneath scowling brows a hidden watcher upon the shore.

Through the man's brain passed plan after plan whereby he might thwart the escape of the Englishman and his wife, for so long as the vital spark remained within the vindictive brain of Alexander Paulvitch none who had aroused the enmity of the Russian might be entirely safe.

Plan after plan he formed only to discard each either as impracticable, or unworthy the vengeance his wrongs demanded. So warped by faulty reasoning was the criminal mind of Rokoff's lieutenant that he could not grasp the real truth of that which lay between himself and the ape-man and see that always the fault had been, not with the English lord, but with himself and his confederate.

And at the rejection of each new scheme Paulvitch arrived always at the same conclusion—that he could accomplish naught while half the breadth of the Ugambi separated him from the object of his hatred.

But how was he to span the crocodile-infested waters? There was no canoe nearer than the Mosula village, and Paulvitch was none too sure that the *Kincaid* would still be at anchor in the river when he returned should he take the time to traverse the jungle to the distant village and return with a canoe. Yet there was no other way, and so, convinced that thus alone might he hope to reach his prey, Paulvitch, with a parting scowl at the two figures upon the *Kincaid*'s deck, turned away from the river.

Hastening through the dense jungle, his mind centred upon his one fetich—revenge—the Russian forgot even his terror of the savage world through which he moved.

Baffled and beaten at every turn of Fortune's wheel, reacted upon time after time by his own malign plotting, the principal victim of his own criminality, Paulvitch was yet so blind as to imagine that his greatest happiness lay in a continuation of the plottings and schemings which had ever brought him and Rokoff to disaster, and the latter finally to a hideous death.

As the Russian stumbled on through the jungle toward the Mosula village there presently crystallized within his brain a plan which seemed more feasible than any that he had as yet considered.

He would come by night to the side of the *Kincaid*, and once aboard, would search out the members of the ship's original crew who had survived the terrors of this frightful expedition, and enlist them in an attempt to wrest the vessel from Tarzan and his beasts.

In the cabin were arms and ammunition, and hidden in a secret receptacle in the cabin table was one of those infernal machines, the construction of which had occupied much of Paulvitch's spare time when he had stood high in the confidence of the Nihilists of his native land.

That was before he had sold them out for immunity and gold to the police of Petrograd. Paulvitch winced as he recalled the denunciation of him that had fallen from the lips of one of his former comrades ere the poor devil expiated his political sins at the end of a hempen rope.

But the infernal machine was the thing to think of now. He could do much with that if he could but get his hands upon it. Within the little hardwood case hidden in the cabin table rested sufficient potential destructiveness to wipe out in the fraction of a second every enemy aboard the *Kincaid*.

Paulvitch licked his lips in anticipatory joy, and urged his tired legs to greater speed that he might not be too late to the ship's anchorage to carry out his designs.

All depended, of course, upon when the *Kincaid* departed. The Russian realized that nothing could be accomplished beneath the light of day. Darkness must shroud his approach to the ship's side, for should he be sighted by Tarzan or Lady Greystoke he would have no chance to board the vessel.

The gale that was blowing was, he believed, the cause of the delay in getting the *Kincaid* under way, and if it continued to blow until night then the chances were all in his favour, for he knew that there was little likelihood of the ape-man attempting to navigate the tortuous channel of the Ugambi while darkness lay upon the surface of the water, hiding the many bars and the numerous small islands which are scattered over the expanse of the river's mouth.

It was well after noon when Paulvitch came to the Mosula village upon the bank of the tributary of the Ugambi. Here he was received with suspicion and unfriendliness by the native chief, who, like all those who came in contact with Rokoff or Paulvitch, had suffered in some manner from the greed, the cruelty, or the lust of the two Muscovites.

When Paulvitch demanded the use of a canoe the chief grumbled a surly refusal and ordered the white man from the village. Surrounded by angry, muttering warriors who seemed to be but waiting some slight pretext to transfix him with their menacing spears the Russian could do naught else than withdraw.

A dozen fighting men led him to the edge of the clearing, leaving him with a warning never to show himself again in the vicinity of their village.

Stifling his anger, Paulvitch slunk into the jungle; but once beyond the sight of the warriors he paused and listened intently. He could hear the voices of his escort as the men returned to the village, and when he was sure that they were not following him he wormed his way through the bushes to the edge of the river, still determined some way to obtain a canoe.

Life itself depended upon his reaching the *Kincaid* and enlisting the survivors of the ship's crew in his service, for to be abandoned here amidst the dangers of the African jungle where he had won the enmity of the natives was, he well knew, practically equivalent to a sentence of death.

A desire for revenge acted as an almost equally powerful incentive to spur him into the face of danger to accomplish his design, so that it was a desperate man that lay hidden in the foliage beside the little river searching with eager eyes for some sign of a small canoe which might be easily handled by a single paddle.

Nor had the Russian long to wait before one of the awkward little skiffs which the Mosula fashion came in sight upon the bosom of the river. A youth was paddling lazily out into midstream from a point beside the village. When he reached the channel he allowed the sluggish current to carry him slowly along while he lolled indolently in the bottom of his crude canoe.

All ignorant of the unseen enemy upon the river's bank the lad floated slowly down the stream while Paulvitch followed along the jungle path a few yards behind him.

A mile below the village the black boy dipped his paddle into the water and forced his skiff toward the bank. Paulvitch, elated by the chance which had drawn the youth to the same side of the river as that along which he followed rather than to the opposite side where he would have been beyond the stalker's reach, hid in the brush close beside the point at which it was evident the skiff would touch the bank of the slow-moving stream, which seemed jealous of each fleeting instant which drew it nearer to the broad and muddy Ugambi where it must for ever lose its identity in the larger stream that would presently cast its waters into the great ocean.

Equally indolent were the motions of the Mosula youth as he drew his skiff beneath an overhanging limb of a great tree that leaned down to implant a farewell kiss upon the bosom of the departing water, caressing with green fronds the soft breast of its languorous love.

And, snake-like, amidst the concealing foliage lay the malevolent Russ. Cruel, shifty eyes gloated upon the outlines of the coveted canoe, and measured the stature of its owner, while the crafty brain weighed the chances of the white man should physical encounter with the black become necessary.

Only direct necessity could drive Alexander Paulvitch to personal conflict; but it was indeed dire necessity which goaded him on to action now.

There was time, just time enough, to reach the *Kincaid* by nightfall. Would the black fool never quit his skiff? Paulvitch squirmed and fidgeted. The lad yawned and stretched. With exasperating deliberateness he examined the arrows in his quiver, tested his bow, and looked to the edge upon the hunting-knife in his loin-cloth.

Again he stretched and yawned, glanced up at the river-bank, shrugged his shoulders, and lay down in the bottom of his canoe for a little nap before he plunged into the jungle after the prey he had come forth to hunt.

Paulvitch half rose, and with tensed muscles stood glaring down upon his unsuspecting victim. The boy's lids drooped and closed. Presently his breast rose and fell to the deep breaths of slumber. The time had come!

The Russian crept stealthily nearer. A branch rustled beneath his weight and the lad stirred in his sleep. Paulvitch drew his revolver and levelled it upon the black. For a moment he remained in rigid quiet, and then again the youth relapsed into undisturbed slumber.

The white man crept closer. He could not chance a shot until there was no risk of missing. Presently he leaned close above the Mosula. The cold steel of the revolver in his hand insinuated itself nearer and nearer to the breast of the unconscious lad. Now it stopped but a few inches above the strongly beating heart.

But the pressure of a finger lay between the harmless boy and eternity. The soft bloom of youth still lay upon the brown cheek, a smile half parted the beardless lips. Did any qualm of conscience point its disquieting finger of reproach at the murderer?

To all such was Alexander Paulvitch immune. A sneer curled his bearded lip as his forefinger closed upon the trigger of his revolver. There was a loud report. A little hole appeared above the heart of the sleeping boy, a little hole about which lay a blackened rim of powder-burned flesh.

The youthful body half rose to a sitting posture. The smiling lips tensed to the nervous shock of a momentary agony which the conscious mind never apprehended, and then the dead sank limply back into that deepest of slumbers from which there is no awakening.

The killer dropped quickly into the skiff beside the killed. Ruthless hands seized the dead boy heartlessly and raised him to the low gunwale. A little shove, a splash, some widening ripples broken by the sudden surge of a dark, hidden body from the slimy depths, and the coveted canoe was in the sole possession of the white man—more savage than the youth whose life he had taken.

Casting off the tie rope and seizing the paddle, Paulvitch bent feverishly to the task of driving the skiff downward toward the Ugambi at top speed.

Night had fallen when the prow of the bloodstained craft shot out into the current of the larger stream. Constantly the Russian strained his eyes into the increasing darkness ahead in vain endeavour to pierce the black shadows which lay between him and the anchorage of the *Kincaid*.

Was the ship still riding there upon the waters of the Ugambi, or had the ape-man at last persuaded himself of the safety of venturing forth into the abating storm? As Paulvitch forged ahead with the current he asked himself these questions, and many more beside, not the least disquieting of which were those which related to his future should it chance that the *Kincaid* had already steamed away, leaving him to the merciless horrors of the savage wilderness.

In the darkness it seemed to the paddler that he was fairly flying over the water, and he had become convinced that the ship had left her moorings and that he had already passed the spot at which she had lain earlier in the day, when there appeared before him beyond a projecting point which he had but just rounded the flickering light from a ship's lantern.

Alexander Paulvitch could scarce restrain an exclamation of triumph. The *Kincaid* had not departed! Life and vengeance were not to elude him after all.

He stopped paddling the moment that he descried the gleaming beacon of hope ahead of him. Silently he drifted down the muddy waters of the Ugambi, occasionally dipping his paddle's blade gently into the current that he might guide his primitive craft to the vessel's side.

As he approached more closely the dark bulk of a ship loomed before him out of the blackness of the night. No sound came from the vessel's deck. Paulvitch drifted, unseen, close to the *Kincaid*'s side. Only the momentary scraping of his canoe's nose against the ship's planking broke the silence of the night.

Trembling with nervous excitement, the Russian remained motionless for several minutes; but there was no sound from the great bulk above him to indicate that his coming had been noted.

Stealthily he worked his craft forward until the stays of the bowsprit were directly above him. He could just reach them. To make his canoe fast there was the work of but a minute or two, and then the man raised himself quietly aloft.

A moment later he dropped softly to the deck. Thoughts of the hideous pack which tenanted the ship induced cold tremors along the spine of the cowardly prowler; but life itself depended upon the success of his venture, and so he was enabled to steel himself to the frightful chances which lay before him.

No sound or sign of watch appeared upon the ship's deck. Paulvitch crept stealthily toward the forecastle. All was silence. The hatch was raised, and as the man peered downward he saw one of the *Kincaid*'s crew reading by the light of the smoky lantern depending from the ceiling of the crew's quarters.

Paulvitch knew the man well, a surly cut-throat upon whom he figured strongly in the carrying out of the plan which he had conceived. Gently the Russ lowered himself through the aperture to the rounds of the ladder which led into the forecastle.

He kept his eyes turned upon the reading man, ready to warn him to silence the moment that the fellow discovered him; but so deeply immersed was the sailor in the magazine that the Russian came, unobserved, to the forecastle floor.

There he turned and whispered the reader's name. The man raised his eyes from the magazine—eyes that went wide for a moment as they fell upon the familiar countenance of Rokoff's lieutenant, only to narrow instantly in a scowl of disapproval.

"The devil!" he ejaculated. "Where did you come from? We all thought you were done for and gone where you ought to have gone a long time ago. His lordship will be mighty pleased to see you."

Paulvitch crossed to the sailor's side. A friendly smile lay on the Russian's lips, and his right hand was extended in greeting, as though the other might have been a dear and long lost friend. The sailor ignored the proffered hand, nor did he return the other's smile.

"I've come to help you," explained Paulvitch. "I'm going to help you get rid of the Englishman and his beasts—then there will be no danger from the law when we get back to civilization. We can sneak in on them while they sleep—that is Greystoke, his wife, and that black scoundrel, Mugambi. Afterward it will be a simple matter to clean up the beasts. Where are they?"

"They're below," replied the sailor; "but just let me tell you something, Paulvitch. You haven't got no more show to turn us men against the Englishman than nothing. We had all we wanted of you and that other beast. He's dead, an' if I don't miss my guess a whole lot you'll be dead too before long. You two treated us like dogs, and if you think we got any love for you you better forget it."

"You mean to say that you're going to turn against me?" demanded Paulvitch.

The other nodded, and then after a momentary pause, during which an idea seemed to have occurred to him, he spoke again.

"Unless," he said, "you can make it worth my while to let you go before the Englishman finds you here."

"You wouldn't turn me away in the jungle, would you?" asked Paulvitch. "Why, I'd die there in a week."

"You'd have a chance there," replied the sailor. "Here, you wouldn't have no chance. Why, if I woke up my maties here they'd probably cut your heart out of you before the Englishman got a chance at you at all. It's mighty lucky for you that I'm the one to be awake now and not none of the others."

"You're crazy," cried Paulvitch. "Don't you know that the Englishman will have you all hanged when he gets you back where the law can get hold of you?"

"No, he won't do nothing of the kind," replied the sailor. "He's told us as much, for he says that there wasn't nobody to blame but you and Rokoff—the rest of us was just tools. See?"

For half an hour the Russian pleaded or threatened as the mood seized him. Sometimes he was upon the verge of tears, and again he was promising his listener either fabulous rewards or condign punishment; but the other was obdurate. (condign: of equal value)

He made it plain to the Russian that there were but two plans open to him—either he must consent to being turned over immediately to Lord Greystoke, or he must pay to the sailor, as a price for permission to quit the *Kincaid* unmolested, every cent of money and article of value upon his person and in his cabin.

"And you'll have to make up your mind mighty quick," growled the man, "for I want to turn in. Come now, choose—his lordship or the jungle?"

"You'll be sorry for this," grumbled the Russian.

"Shut up," admonished the sailor. "If you get funny I may change my mind, and keep you here after all."

Now Paulvitch had no intention of permitting himself to fall into the hands of Tarzan of the Apes if he could possibly avoid it, and while the terrors of the jungle appalled him they were, to his mind, infinitely preferable to the certain death which he knew he merited and for which he might look at the hands of the ape-man.

"Is anyone sleeping in my cabin?" he asked.

EDGAR RICE BURROUGHS

The sailor shook his head. "No," he said; "Lord and Lady Greystoke have the captain's cabin. The mate is in his own, and there ain't no one in yours."

"I'll go and get my valuables for you," said Paulvitch.

"I'll go with you to see that you don't try any funny business," said the sailor, and he followed the Russian up the ladder to the deck.

At the cabin entrance the sailor halted to watch, permitting Paulvitch to go alone to his cabin. Here he gathered together his few belongings that were to buy him the uncertain safety of escape, and as he stood for a moment beside the little table on which he had piled them he searched his brain for some feasible plan either to ensure his safety or to bring revenge upon his enemies.

And presently as he thought there recurred to his memory the little black box which lay hidden in a secret receptacle beneath a false top upon the table where his hand rested.

The Russian's face lighted to a sinister gleam of malevolent satisfaction as he stooped and felt beneath the table top. A moment later he withdrew from its hiding-place the thing he sought. He had lighted the lantern swinging from the beams overhead that he might see to collect his belongings, and now he held the black box well in the rays of the lamplight, while he fingered at the clasp that fastened its lid.

The lifted cover revealed two compartments within the box. In one was a mechanism which resembled the works of a small clock. There also was a little battery of two dry cells. A wire ran from the clockwork to one of the poles of the battery, and from the other pole through the partition into the other compartment, a second wire returning directly to the clockwork.

Whatever lay within the second compartment was not visible, for a cover lay over it and appeared to be sealed in place by asphaltum. In the bottom of the box, beside the clockwork, lay a key, and this Paulvitch now withdrew and fitted to the winding stem.

Gently he turned the key, muffling the noise of the winding operation by throwing a couple of articles of clothing over the box. All the time he listened intently for any sound which might indicate that the sailor or another were approaching his cabin; but none came to interrupt his work.

When the winding was completed the Russian set a pointer upon a small dial at the side of the clockwork, then he replaced the cover upon the black box, and returned the entire machine to its hiding-place in the table.

A sinister smile curled the man's bearded lips as he gathered up his valuables, blew out the lamp, and stepped from his cabin to the side of the waiting sailor.

"Here are my things," said the Russian; "now let me go."

"I'll first take a look in your pockets," replied the sailor. "You might have overlooked some trifling thing that won't be of no use to you in the jungle, but that'll come in mighty handy to a poor sailorman in London. Ah! just as I feared," he ejaculated an instant later as he withdrew a roll of bank-notes from Paulvitch's inside coat pocket.

The Russian scowled, muttering an imprecation; but nothing could be gained by argument, and so he did his best to reconcile himself to his loss in the knowledge that the sailor would never reach London to enjoy the fruits of his thievery.

It was with difficulty that Paulvitch restrained a consuming desire to taunt the man with a suggestion of the fate that would presently overtake him and the other members of the *Kincaid*'s company; but fearing to arouse the fellow's suspicions, he crossed the deck and lowered himself in silence into his canoe.

A minute or two later he was paddling toward the shore to be swallowed up in the darkness of the jungle night, and the terrors of a hideous existence from which, could he have had even a slight foreknowledge of what awaited him in the long years to come, he would have fled to the certain death of the open sea rather than endure it.

The sailor, having made sure that Paulvitch had departed, returned to the forecastle, where he hid away his booty and turned into his bunk, while in the cabin that had belonged to the Russian there ticked on and on through the silences of the night the little mechanism in the small black box which held for the unconscious sleepers upon the ill-starred *Kincaid* the coming vengeance of the thwarted Russian.

THE LAST OF THE KINCAID

Shortly after the break of day Tarzan was on deck noting the condition of the weather. The wind had abated. The sky was cloudless. Every condition seemed ideal for the commencement of the return voyage to Jungle Island, where the beasts were to be left. And then—home!

The ape-man aroused the mate and gave instructions that the *Kincaid* sail at the earliest possible moment. The remaining members of the crew, safe in Lord Greystoke's assurance that they would not be prosecuted for their share in the villainies of the two Russians, hastened with cheerful alacrity to their several duties.

The beasts, liberated from the confinement of the hold, wandered about the deck, not a little to the discomfiture of the crew in whose minds there remained a still vivid picture of the savagery of the beasts in conflict with those who had gone to their deaths beneath the fangs and talons which even now seemed itching for the soft flesh of further prey.

Beneath the watchful eyes of Tarzan and Mugambi, however, Sheeta and the apes of Akut curbed their desires, so that the men worked about the deck amongst them in far greater security than they imagined.

At last the *Kincaid* slipped down the Ugambi and ran out upon the shimmering waters of the Atlantic. Tarzan and Jane Clayton watched the verdure-clad shore-line receding in the ship's wake, and for once the ape-man left his native soil without one single pang of regret.

No ship that sailed the seven seas could have borne him away from Africa to resume his search for his lost boy with half the speed that the Englishman would have desired, and the slow-moving *Kincaid* seemed scarce to move at all to the impatient mind of the bereaved father.

Yet the vessel made progress even when she seemed to be standing still, and presently the low hills of Jungle Island became distinctly visible upon the western horizon ahead.

In the cabin of Alexander Paulvitch the thing within the black box ticked, ticked, ticked, with apparently unending monotony; but yet, second by second, a little arm which protruded from the periphery of one of its wheels came nearer and nearer to another little arm which projected from the hand which Paulvitch had set at a certain point upon the dial beside the clockwork. When those two arms touched one another the ticking of the mechanism would cease—for ever.

Jane and Tarzan stood upon the bridge looking out toward Jungle Island. The men were forward, also watching the land grow upward out of the ocean. The beasts had sought the shade of the galley, where they were curled up in sleep. All was quiet and peace upon the ship, and upon the waters.

Suddenly, without warning, the cabin roof shot up into the air, a cloud of dense smoke puffed far above the *Kincaid*, there was a terrific explosion which shook the vessel from stem to stern.

Instantly pandemonium broke loose upon the deck. The apes of Akut, terrified by the sound, ran hither and thither, snarling and growling. Sheeta leaped here and there, screaming out his startled terror in hideous cries that sent the ice of fear straight to the hearts of the *Kincaid*'s crew.

Mugambi, too, was trembling. Only Tarzan of the Apes and his wife retained their composure. Scarce had the debris settled than the ape-man was among the beasts, quieting their fears, talking to them in low, pacific tones, stroking their shaggy bodies, and assuring them, as only he could, that the immediate danger was over.

An examination of the wreckage showed that their greatest danger, now, lay in fire, for the flames were licking hungrily at the splintered wood of the wrecked cabin, and had already found a foothold upon the lower deck through a great jagged hole which the explosion had opened.

By a miracle no member of the ship's company had been injured by the blast, the origin of which remained for ever a total mystery to all but one—the sailor who knew that Paulvitch had been aboard the *Kincaid* and in his cabin the previous night. He guessed the truth; but discretion sealed his lips. It would, doubtless, fare none too well for the man who had permitted the arch enemy of them all aboard the ship in the watches of the night, where later he might set an infernal machine to blow them all to kingdom come. No, the man decided that he would keep this knowledge to himself.

As the flames gained headway it became apparent to Tarzan that whatever had caused the explosion had scattered some highly inflammable substance upon the surrounding woodwork, for the water which they poured in from the pump seemed rather to spread than to extinguish the blaze.

Fifteen minutes after the explosion great, black clouds of smoke were rising from the hold of the doomed vessel. The flames had reached the engine-room, and the ship no longer moved toward the shore. Her fate was as certain as though the waters had already closed above her charred and smoking remains.

"It is useless to remain aboard her longer," remarked the ape-man to the mate. "There is no telling but there may be other explosions, and as we cannot hope to save her, the safest thing which we can do is to take to the boats without further loss of time and make land."

Nor was there other alternative. Only the sailors could bring away any belongings, for the fire, which had not yet reached the forecastle, had consumed all in the vicinity of the cabin which the explosion had not destroyed.

Two boats were lowered, and as there was no sea the landing was made with infinite ease. Eager and anxious, the beasts of Tarzan sniffed the familiar air of their native island as the small boats drew in toward the beach, and scarce had their keels grated upon the sand than Sheeta and the apes of Akut were over the bows and racing swiftly toward the jungle. A half-sad smile curved the lips of the ape-man as he watched them go.

"Good-bye, my friends," he murmured. "You have been good and faithful allies, and I shall miss you."

"They will return, will they not, dear?" asked Jane Clayton, at his side.

"They may and they may not," replied the ape-man. "They have been ill at ease since they were forced to accept so many human beings into their confidence. Mugambi and I alone affected them less, for he and I are, at best, but half human. You, however, and the members of the crew are far too civilized for my beasts—it is you whom they are fleeing. Doubtless they feel that they cannot trust themselves in the close vicinity of so much perfectly good food without the danger that they may help themselves to a mouthful some time by mistake."

Jane laughed. "I think they are just trying to escape you," she retorted. "You are always making them stop something which they see no reason why they should not do. Like little children they are doubtless delighted at this opportunity to flee from the zone of parental discipline. If they come back, though, I hope they won't come by night."

"Or come hungry, eh?" laughed Tarzan.

For two hours after landing the little party stood watching the burning ship which they had abandoned. Then there came faintly to them from across the water the sound of a second explosion. The *Kincaid* settled rapidly almost immediatel thereafter, and sank within a few minutes.

The cause of the second explosion was less a mystery than that of the first, the mate attributing it to the bursting of the boilers when the flames had finally reached them; but what had caused the first explosion was a subject of considerable speculation among the stranded company.

JUNGLE ISLAND AGAIN

The first consideration of the party was to locate fresh water and make camp, for all knew that their term of existence upon Jungle Island might be drawn out to months, or even years.

Tarzan knew the nearest water, and to this he immediately led the party. Here the men fell to work to construct shelters and rude furniture while Tarzan went into the jungle after meat, leaving the faithful Mugambi and the Mosula woman to guard Jane, whose safety he would never trust to any member of the *Kincaid*'s cut-throat crew.

Lady Greystoke suffered far greater anguish than any other of the castaways, for the blow to her hopes and her already cruelly lacerated mother-heart lay not in her own privations but in the knowledge that she might now never be able to learn the fate of her first-born or do aught to discover his whereabouts, or ameliorate his condition—a condition which imagination naturally pictured in the most frightful forms.

For two weeks the party divided the time amongst the various duties which had been allotted to each. A daylight watch was maintained from sunrise to sunset upon a bluff near the camp—a jutting shoulder of rock which overlooked the sea. Here, ready for instant lighting, was gathered a huge pile of dry branches, while from a lofty pole which they had set in the ground there floated an improvised distress signal fashioned from a red undershirt which belonged to the mate of the *Kincaid*.

But never a speck upon the horizon that might be sail or smoke rewarded the tired eyes that in their endless, hopeless vigil strained daily out across the vast expanse of ocean.

It was Tarzan who suggested, finally, that they attempt to construct a vessel that would bear them back to the mainland. He alone could show them how to fashion rude tools, and when the idea had taken root in the minds of the men they were eager to commence their labours.

But as time went on and the Herculean nature of their task became more and more apparent they fell to grumbling, and to quarrelling among themselves, so that to the other dangers were now added dissension and suspicion.

More than before did Tarzan now fear to leave Jane among the half brutes of the *Kincaid*'s crew; but hunting he must do, for none other could so surely go forth and return with meat as he. Sometimes Mugambi spelled him at the hunting; but the black's spear and arrows were never so sure of results as the rope and knife of the ape-man.

Finally the men shirked their work, going off into the jungle by twos to explore and to hunt. All this time the camp had had no sight of Sheeta, or Akut and the other great apes, though Tarzan had sometimes met them in the jungle as he hunted.

And as matters tended from bad to worse in the camp of the castaways upon the east coast of Jungle Island, another camp came into being upon the north coast.

Here, in a little cove, lay a small schooner, the Cowrie, whose decks had but a few days since run red with the blood of her officers and the loyal members of her crew, for the Cowrie had fallen upon bad days when it had shipped such men as Gust and Momulla the Maori and that arch-fiend Kai Shang of Fachan.

There were others, too, ten of them all told, the scum of the South Sea ports; but Gust and Momulla and Kai Shang were the brains and cunning of the company. It was they who had instigated the mutiny that they might seize and divide the catch of pearls which constituted the wealth of the Cowrie's cargo.

It was Kai Shang who had murdered the captain as he lay asleep in his berth, and it had been Momulla the Maori who had led the attack upon the officer of the watch.

Gust, after his own peculiar habit, had found means to delegate to the others the actual taking of life. Not that Gust entertained any scruples on the subject, other than those which induced in him a rare regard for his own personal safety. There is always a certain element of risk to the assassin, for victims of deadly assault are seldom prone to die quietly and considerately. There is always a certain element of risk to go so far as to dispute the issue with the murderer. It was this chance of dispute which Gust preferred to forgo.

But now that the work was done the Swede aspired to the position of highest command among the mutineers. He had even gone so far as to appropriate and wear certain articles belonging to the murdered captain of the Cowrie—articles of apparel which bore upon them the badges and insignia of authority.

Kai Shang was peeved. He had no love for authority, and certainly not the slightest intention of submitting to the domination of an ordinary Swede sailor.

The seeds of discontent were, therefore, already planted in the camp of the mutineers of the Cowrie at the north edge of Jungle Island. But Kai Shang realized that he must act with circumspection, for Gust alone of the motley horde possessed sufficient knowledge of navigation to get them out of the South Atlantic and around the cape into more congenial waters where they might find a market for their ill-gotten wealth, and no questions asked.

The day before they sighted Jungle Island and discovered the little land-locked harbour upon the bosom of which the Cowrie now rode quietly at anchor, the watch had discovered the smoke and funnels of a warship upon the southern horizon.

The chance of being spoken and investigated by a man-of-war appealed not at all to any of them, so they put into hiding for a few days until the danger should have passed.

And now Gust did not wish to venture out to sea again. There was no telling, he insisted, but that the ship they had seen was actually searching for them. Kai Shang pointed out that such could not be the case since it was impossible for any human being other than themselves to have knowledge of what had transpired aboard the Cowrie.

But Gust was not to be persuaded. In his wicked heart he nursed a scheme whereby he might increase his share of the booty by something like one hundred per cent. He alone could sail the Cowrie, therefore the others could not leave Jungle Island without him; but what was there to prevent Gust, with just sufficient men to man the schooner, slipping away from Kai Shang, Momulla the Maori, and some half of the crew when opportunity presented?

It was for this opportunity that Gust waited. Some day there would come a moment when Kai Shang, Momulla, and three or four of the others would be absent from camp, exploring or hunting. The Swede racked his brain for some plan whereby he might successfully lure from the sight of the anchored ship those whom he had determined to abandon.

To this end he organized hunting party after hunting party, but always the devil of perversity seemed to enter the soul of Kai Shang, so that wily celestial would never hunt except in the company of Gust himself.

One day Kai Shang spoke secretly with Momulla the Maori, pouring into the brown ear of his companion the suspicions which he harboured concerning the Swede. Momulla was for going immediately and running a long knife through the heart of the traitor.

It is true that Kai Shang had no other evidence than the natural cunning of his own knavish soul—but he imagined in the intentions of Gust what he himself would have been glad to accomplish had the means lain at hand.

But he dared not let Momulla slay the Swede, upon whom they depended to guide them to their destination. They decided, however, that it would do no harm to attempt to frighten Gust into acceding to their demands, and with this purpose in mind the Maori sought out the self-constituted commander of the party.

When he broached the subject of immediate departure Gust again raised his former objection—that the warship might very probably be patrolling the sea directly in their southern path, waiting for them to make the attempt to reach other waters.

Momulla scoffed at the fears of his fellow, pointing out that as no one aboard any warship knew of their mutiny there could be no reason why they should be suspected.

"Ah!" exclaimed Gust, "there is where you are wrong. There is where you are lucky that you have an educated man like me to tell you what to do. You are an ignorant savage, Momulla, and so you know nothing of wireless."

The Maori leaped to his feet and laid his hand upon the hilt of his knife.

"I am no savage," he shouted.

"I was only joking," the Swede hastened to explain. "We are old friends, Momulla; we cannot afford to quarrel, at least not while old Kai Shang is plotting to steal all the pearls from us. If he could find a man to navigate the Cowrie he would leave us in a minute. All his talk about getting away from here is just because he has some scheme in his head to get rid of us."

"But the wireless," asked Momulla. "What has the wireless to do with our remaining here?"

"Oh yes," replied Gust, scratching his head. He was wondering if the Maori were really so ignorant as to believe the preposterous lie he was about to unload upon him. "Oh yes! You see every warship is equipped with what they call a wireless apparatus. It lets them talk to other ships hundreds of miles away, and it lets them listen to all that is said on these other ships. Now, you see, when you fellows were shooting up the Cowrie you did a whole lot of loud talking, and there isn't any doubt but that that warship was a-lyin' off south of us listenin' to it all. Of course they might not have learned the name of the ship, but they heard enough to know that the crew of some ship was mutinying and killin' her officers. So you see they'll be waiting to search every ship they sight for a long time to come, and they may not be far away now."

When he had ceased speaking the Swede strove to assume an air of composure that his listener might not have his suspicions aroused as to the truth of the statements that had just been made.

Momulla sat for some time in silence, eyeing Gust. At last he rose.

"You are a great liar," he said. "If you don't get us on our way by tomorrow you'll never have another chance to lie, for I heard two of the men saying that they'd like to run a knife into you and that if you kept them in this hole any longer they'd do it."

"Go and ask Kai Shang if there is not a wireless," replied Gust. "He will tell you that there is such a thing and that vessels can talk to one another across hundreds of miles of water. Then say to the two men who wish to kill me that if they do so they will never live to spend their share of the swag, for only I can get you safely to any port."

So Momulla went to Kai Shang and asked him if there was such an apparatus as a wireless by means of which ships could talk with each other at great distances, and Kai Shang told him that there was.

Momulla was puzzled; but still he wished to leave the island, and was willing to take his chances on the open sea rather than to remain longer in the monotony of the camp.

"If we only had someone else who could navigate a ship!" wailed Kai Shang.

That afternoon Momulla went hunting with two other Maoris. They hunted toward the south, and had not gone far from camp when they were surprised by the sound of voices ahead of them in the jungle.

They knew that none of their own men had preceded them, and as all were convinced that the island was uninhabited, they were inclined to flee in terror on the hypothesis that the place was haunted—possibly by the ghosts of the murdered officers and men of the Cowrie.

But Momulla was even more curious than he was superstitious, and so he quelled his natural desire to flee from the supernatural. Motioning his companions to follow his example, he dropped to his hands and knees, crawling forward stealthily and with quakings of heart through the jungle in the direction from which came the voices of the unseen speakers.

Presently, at the edge of a little clearing, he halted, and there he breathed a deep sigh of relief, for plainly before him he saw two flesh-and-blood men sitting upon a fallen log and talking earnestly together.

One was Schneider, mate of the *Kincaid*, and the other was a seaman named Schmidt.

"I think we can do it, Schmidt," Schneider was saying. "A good canoe wouldn't be hard to build, and three of us could paddle it to the mainland in a day if the wind was right and the sea reasonably calm. There ain't no use waiting for the men to build a big enough boat to take the whole party, for they're sore now and sick of working like slaves all day long. It ain't none of our business anyway to save the Englishman. Let him look out for himself, says I." He paused for a moment, and then eyeing the other to note the effect of his next words, he continued, "But we might take the woman. It would be a shame to leave a nice-lookin' piece like she is in such a Gott-forsaken hole as this here island."

Schmidt looked up and grinned.

"So that's how she's blowin', is it?" he asked. "Why didn't you say so in the first place? Wot's in it for me if I help you?"

"She ought to pay us well to get her back to civilization," explained Schneider, "an' I tell you what I'll do. I'll just whack up with the two men that helps me. I'll take half an' they can divide the other half—you an' whoever the other bloke is. I'm sick of this place, an' the sooner I get out of it the better I'll like it. What do you say?"

"Suits me," replied Schmidt. "I wouldn't know how to reach the mainland myself, an' know that none o' the other fellows would, so's you're the only one that knows anything of navigation you're the fellow I'll tie to."

Momulla the Maori pricked up his ears. He had a smattering of every tongue that is spoken upon the seas, and more than a few times had he sailed on English ships, so that he understood fairly well all that had passed between Schneider and Schmidt since he had stumbled upon them.

He rose to his feet and stepped into the clearing. Schneider and his companion started as nervously as though a ghost had risen before them. Schneider reached for his revolver. Momulla raised his right hand, palm forward, as a sign of his pacific intentions.

"I am a friend," he said. "I heard you; but do not fear that I will reveal what you have said. I can help you, and you can help me." He was addressing Schneider. "You can navigate a ship, but you have no ship. We have a ship, but no one to navigate it. If you will come with us and ask no questions we will let you take the ship where you will after you have landed us at a certain port, the name of which we will give you later. You can take the woman of whom you speak, and we will ask no questions either. Is it a bargain?"

Schneider desired more information, and got as much as Momulla thought best to give him. Then the Maori suggested that they speak with Kai Shang. The two members of the *Kincaid's* company followed Momulla and his fellows to a point in the jungle close by the camp of the mutineers. Here Momulla hid them while he went in search of Kai Shang, first admonishing his Maori companions to stand guard over the two sailors lest they change their minds and attempt to escape. Schneider and Schmidt were virtually prisoners, though they did not know it.

Presently Momulla returned with Kai Shang, to whom he had briefly narrated the details of the stroke of good fortune that had come to them. The Chinaman spoke at length with Schneider, until, notwithstanding his natural suspicion of the sincerity of all men, he became quite convinced that Schneider was quite as much a rogue as himself and that the fellow was anxious to leave the island.

These two premises accepted there could be little doubt that Schneider would prove trustworthy in so far as accepting the command of the Cowrie was concerned; after that Kai Shang knew that he could find means to coerce the man into submission to his further wishes.

When Schneider and Schmidt left them and set out in the direction of their own camp, it was with feelings of far greater relief than they had experienced in many a day. Now at last they saw a feasible plan for leaving the island upon a seaworthy craft. There would be no more hard labour at ship-building, and no risking their lives upon a crudely built makeshift that would be quite as likely to go to the bottom as it would to reach the mainland.

Also, they were to have assistance in capturing the woman, or rather women, for when Momulla had learned that there was a black woman in the other camp he had insisted that she be brought along as well as the white woman.

As Kai Shang and Momulla entered their camp, it was with a realization that they no longer needed Gust. They marched straight to the tent in which they might expect to find him at that hour of the day, for though it would have been more comfortable for the entire party to remain aboard the ship, they had mutually decided that it would be safer for all concerned were they to pitch their camp ashore.

Each knew that in the heart of the others was sufficient treachery to make it unsafe for any member of the party to go ashore leaving the others in possession of the Cowrie, so not more than two or three men at a time were ever permitted aboard the vessel unless all the balance of the company was there too.

As the two crossed toward Gust's tent the Maori felt the edge of his long knife with one grimy, calloused thumb. The Swede would have felt far from comfortable could he have seen this significant action, or read what was passing amid the convolutions of the brown man's cruel brain.

Now it happened that Gust was at that moment in the tent occupied by the cook, and this tent stood but a few feet from his own. So that he heard the approach of Kai Shang and Momulla, though he did not, of course, dream that it had any special significance for him.

Chance had it, though, that he glanced out of the doorway of the cook's tent at the very moment that Kai Shang and Momulla approached the entrance to his, and he thought that he noted a stealthiness in their movements that comported poorly with amicable or friendly intentions, and then, just as they two slunk within the interior, Gust caught a glimpse of the long knife which Momulla the Maori was then carrying behind his back.

The Swede's eyes opened wide, and a funny little sensation assailed the roots of his hairs. Also he turned almost white beneath his tan. Quite precipitately he left the cook's tent. He was not one who required a detailed exposition of intentions that were quite all too obvious.

As surely as though he had heard them plotting, he knew that Kai Shang and Momulla had come to take his life. The knowledge that he alone could navigate the Cowrie had, up to now, been sufficient assurance of his safety; but quite evidently something had occurred of which he had no knowledge that would make it quite worth the while of his co-conspirators to eliminate him.

Without a pause Gust darted across the beach and into the jungle. He was afraid of the jungle; uncanny noises that were indeed frightful came forth from its recesses—the tangled mazes of the mysterious country back of the beach.

But if Gust was afraid of the jungle he was far more afraid of Kai Shang and Momulla. The dangers of the jungle were more or less problematical, while the danger that menaced him at the hands of his companions was a perfectly well-known quantity, which might be expressed in terms of a few inches of cold steel, or the coil of a light rope. He had seen Kai Shang garrotte a man at Pai-sha in a dark alleyway back of Loo Kotai's place. He feared the rope, therefore, more than he did the knife of the Maori; but he feared them both too much to remain within reach of either. Therefore he chose the pitiless jungle.

THE LAW OF THE JUNGLE

In Tarzan's camp, by dint of threats and promised rewards, the ape-man had finally succeeded in getting the hull of a large skiff almost completed. Much of the work he and Mugambi had done with their own hands in addition to furnishing the camp with meat.

Schneider, the mate, had been doing considerable grumbling, and had at last openly deserted the work and gone off into the jungle with Schmidt to hunt. He said that he wanted a rest, and Tarzan, rather than add to the unpleasantness which already made camp life almost unendurable, had permitted the two men to depart without a remonstrance.

Upon the following day, however, Schneider affected a feeling of remorse for his action, and set to work with a will upon the skiff. Schmidt also worked good-naturedly, and Lord Greystoke congratulated himself that at last the men had awakened to the necessity for the labour which was being asked of them and to their obligations to the balance of the party.

It was with a feeling of greater relief than he had experienced for many a day that he set out that noon to hunt deep in the jungle for a herd of small deer which Schneider reported that he and Schmidt had seen there the day before.

The direction in which Schneider had reported seeing the deer was toward the south-west, and to that point the ape-man swung easily through the tangled verdure of the forest.

And as he went there approached from the north a half-dozen ill-featured men who went stealthily through the jungle as go men bent upon the commission of a wicked act.

They thought that they travelled unseen; but behind them, almost from the moment they quitted their own camp, a tall man crept upon their trail. In the man's eyes were hate and fear, and a great curiosity. Why went Kai Shang and Momulla and the others thus stealthily toward the south? What did they expect to find there? Gust shook his low-browed head in perplexity. But he would know. He would follow them and learn their plans, and then if he could thwart them he would—that went without question.

At first he had thought that they searched for him; but finally his better judgment assured him that such could not be the case, since they had accomplished all they really desired by chasing him out of camp. Never would Kai Shang or Momulla go to such pains to slay him or another unless it would put money into their pockets, and as Gust had no money it was evident that they were searching for someone else.

Presently the party he trailed came to a halt. Its members concealed themselves in the foliage bordering the game trail along which they had come. Gust, that he might the better observe, clambered into the branches of a tree to the rear of them, being careful that the leafy fronds hid him from the view of his erstwhile mates.

He had not long to wait before he saw a strange white man approach carefully along the trail from the south.

At sight of the newcomer Momulla and Kai Shang arose from their places of concealment and greeted him. Gust could not overhear what passed between them. Then the man returned in the direction from which he had come.

He was Schneider. Nearing his camp he circled to the opposite side of it, and presently came running in breathlessly. Excitedly he hastened to Mugambi.

"Quick!" he cried. "Those apes of yours have caught Schmidt and will kill him if we do not hasten to his aid. You alone can call them off. Take Jones and Sullivan—you may need help—and get to him as quick as you can. Follow the game trail south for about a mile. I will remain here. I am too spent with running to go back with you," and the mate of the *Kincaid* threw himself upon the ground, panting as though he was almost done for.

Mugambi hesitated. He had been left to guard the two women. He did not know what to do, and then Jane Clayton, who had heard Schneider's story, added her pleas to those of the mate.

"Do not delay," she urged. "We shall be all right here. Mr. Schneider will remain with us. Go, Mugambi. The poor fellow must be saved."

Schmidt, who lay hidden in a bush at the edge of the camp, grinned. Mugambi, heeding the commands of his mistress, though still doubtful of the wisdom of his action, started off toward the south, with Jones and Sullivan at his heels.

No sooner had he disappeared than Schmidt rose and darted north into the jungle, and a few minutes later the face of Kai Shang of Fachan appeared at the edge of the clearing. Schneider saw the Chinaman, and motioned to him that the coast was clear.

Jane Clayton and the Mosula woman were sitting at the opening of the former's tent, their backs toward the approaching ruffians. The first intimation that either had of the presence of strangers in camp was the sudden appearance of a half-dozen ragged villains about them.

"Come!" said Kai Shang, motioning that the two arise and follow him.

Jane Clayton sprang to her feet and looked about for Schneider, only to see him standing behind the newcomers, a grin upon his face. At his side stood Schmidt. Instantly she saw that she had been made the victim of a plot.

"What is the meaning of this?" she asked, addressing the mate.

"It means that we have found a ship and that we can now escape from Jungle Island," replied the man.

"Why did you send Mugambi and the others into the jungle?" she inquired.

"They are not coming with us—only you and I, and the Mosula woman."

"Come!" repeated Kai Shang, and seized Jane Clayton's wrist.

One of the Maoris grasped the black woman by the arm, and when she would have screamed struck her across the mouth.

Mugambi raced through the jungle toward the south. Jones and Sullivan trailed far behind. For a mile he continued upon his way to the relief of Schmidt, but no signs saw he of the missing man or of any of the apes of Akut.

At last he halted and called aloud the summons which he and Tarzan had used to hail the great anthropoids. There was no response. Jones and Sullivan came up with the black warrior as the latter stood voicing his weird call. For another half-mile the black searched, calling occasionally.

Finally the truth flashed upon him, and then, like a frightened deer, he wheeled and dashed back toward camp. Arriving there, it was but a moment before full confirmation of his fears was impressed upon him. Lady Greystoke and the Mosula woman were gone. So, likewise, was Schneider.

When Jones and Sullivan joined Mugambi he would have killed them in his anger, thinking them parties to the plot; but they finally succeeded in partially convincing him that they had known nothing of it.

As they stood speculating upon the probable whereabouts of the women and their abductor, and the purpose which Schneider had in mind in taking them from camp, Tarzan of the Apes swung from the branches of a tree and crossed the clearing toward them.

His keen eyes detected at once that something was radically wrong, and when he had heard Mugambi's story his jaws clicked angrily together as he knitted his brows in thought.

What could the mate hope to accomplish by taking Jane Clayton from a camp upon a small island from which there was no escape from the vengeance of Tarzan? The ape-man could not believe the fellow such a fool, and then a slight realization of the truth dawned upon him.

Schneider would not have committed such an act unless he had been reasonably sure that there was a way by which he could quit Jungle Island with his prisoners. But why had he taken the black woman as well? There must have been others, one of whom wanted the dusky female.

"Come," said Tarzan, "there is but one thing to do now, and that is to follow the trail."

As he finished speaking a tall, ungainly figure emerged from the jungle north of the camp. He came straight toward the four men. He was an entire stranger to all of them, not one of whom had dreamed that another human being than those of their own camp dwelt upon the unfriendly shores of Jungle Island.

It was Gust. He came directly to the point.

"Your women were stolen," he said. "If you want ever to see them again, come quickly and follow me. If we do not hurry the Cowrie will be standing out to sea by the time we reach her anchorage."

"Who are you?" asked Tarzan. "What do you know of the theft of my wife and the black woman?"

"I heard Kai Shang and Momulla the Maori plot with two men of your camp. They had chased me from our camp, and would have killed me. Now I will get even with them. Come!"

Gust led the four men of the *Kincaid's* camp at a rapid trot through the jungle toward the north. Would they come to the sea in time? But a few more minutes would answer the question.

And when at last the little party did break through the last of the screening foliage, and the harbour and the ocean lay before them, they realized that fate had been most cruelly unkind, for the Cowrie was already under sail and moving slowly out of the mouth of the harbour into the open sea.

What were they to do? Tarzan's broad chest rose and fell to the force of his pent emotions. The last blow seemed to have fallen, and if ever in all his life Tarzan of the Apes had had occasion to abandon hope it was now that he saw the ship bearing his wife to some frightful fate moving gracefully over the rippling water, so very near and yet so hideously far away.

In silence he stood watching the vessel. He saw it turn toward the east and finally disappear around a headland on its way he knew not whither. Then he dropped upon his haunches and buried his face in his hands.

It was after dark that the five men returned to the camp on the east shore. The night was hot and sultry. No slightest breeze ruffled the foliage of the trees or rippled the mirror-like surface of the ocean. Only a gentle swell rolled softly in upon the beach.

Never had Tarzan seen the great Atlantic so ominously at peace. He was standing at the edge of the beach gazing out to sea in the direction of the mainland, his mind filled with sorrow and hopelessness, when from the jungle close behind the camp came the uncanny wail of a panther.

There was a familiar note in the weird cry, and almost mechanically Tarzan turned his head and answered. A moment later the tawny figure of Sheeta slunk out into the half-light of the beach. There was no moon, but the sky was brilliant with stars. Silently the savage brute came to the side of the man. It had been long since Tarzan had seen his old fighting companion, but the soft purr was sufficient to assure him that the animal still recalled the bonds which had united them in the past.

The ape-man let his fingers fall upon the beast's coat, and as Sheeta pressed close against his leg he caressed and fondled the wicked head while his eyes continued to search the blackness of the waters.

Presently he started. What was that? He strained his eyes into the night. Then he turned and called aloud to the men smoking upon their blankets in the camp. They came running to his side; but Gust hesitated when he saw the nature of Tarzan's companion.

"Look!" cried Tarzan. "A light! A ship's light! It must be the Cowrie. They are becalmed." And then with an exclamation of renewed hope, "We can reach them! The skiff will carry us easily."

Gust demurred. "They are well armed," he warned. "We could not take the ship—just five of us."

"There are six now," replied Tarzan, pointing to Sheeta, "and we can have more still in a half-hour. Sheeta is the equivalent of twenty men, and the few others I can bring will add full a hundred to our fighting strength. You do not know them."

The ape-man turned and raised his head toward the jungle, while there pealed from his lips, time after time, the fearsome cry of the bull-ape who would summon his fellows.

Presently from the jungle came an answering cry, and then another and another. Gust shuddered. Among what sort of creatures had fate thrown him? Were not Kai Shang and Momulla to be preferred to this great white giant who stroked a panther and called to the beasts of the jungle?

In a few minutes the apes of Akut came crashing through the underbrush and out upon the beach, while in the meantime the five men had been struggling with the unwieldy bulk of the skiff's hull.

By dint of Herculean efforts they had managed to get it to the water's edge. The oars from the two small boats of the *Kincaid*, which had been washed away by an off-shore wind the very night that the party had landed, had been in use to support the canvas of the sailcloth tents. These were hastily requisitioned, and by the time Akut and his followers came down to the water all was ready for embarkation.

Once again the hideous crew entered the service of their master, and without question took up their places in the skiff. The four men, for Gust could not be prevailed upon to accompany the party, fell to the oars, using them paddle-wise, while some of the apes followed their example, and presently the ungainly skiff was moving quietly out to sea in the direction of the light which rose and fell gently with the swell.

A sleepy sailor kept a poor vigil upon the Cowrie's deck, while in the cabin below Schneider paced up and down arguing with Jane Clayton. The woman had found a revolver in a table drawer in the room in which she had been locked, and now she kept the mate of the *Kincaid* at bay with the weapon.

The Mosula woman kneeled behind her, while Schneider paced up and down before the door, threatening and pleading and promising, but all to no avail. Presently from the deck above came a shout of warning and a shot. For an instant Jane Clayton relaxed her vigilance, and turned her eyes toward the cabin skylight. Simultaneously Schneider was upon her.

The first intimation the watch had that there was another craft within a thousand miles of the Cowrie came when he saw the head and shoulders of a man poked over the ship's side. Instantly the fellow sprang to his feet with a cry and levelled his revolver at the intruder. It was his cry and the subsequent report of the revolver which threw Jane Clayton off her guard.

Upon deck the quiet of fancied security soon gave place to the wildest pandemonium. The crew of the Cowrie rushed above armed with revolvers, cutlasses, and the long knives that many of them habitually wore;

but the alarm had come too late. Already the beasts of Tarzan were upon the ship's deck, with Tarzan and the two men of the *Kincaid's* crew.

In the face of the frightful beasts the courage of the mutineers wavered and broke. Those with revolvers fired a few scattering shots and then raced for some place of supposed safety. Into the shrouds went some; but the apes of Akut were more at home there than they.

Screaming with terror the Maoris were dragged from their lofty perches. The beasts, uncontrolled by Tarzan who had gone in search of Jane, loosed in the full fury of their savage natures upon the unhappy wretches who fell into their clutches.

Sheeta, in the meanwhile, had felt his great fangs sink into but a singular jugular. For a moment he mauled the corpse, and then he spied Kai Shang darting down the companionway toward his cabin.

With a shrill scream Sheeta was after him—a scream which awoke an almost equally uncanny cry in the throat of the terror-stricken Chinaman.

But Kai Shang reached his cabin a fraction of a second ahead of the panther, and leaping within slammed the door—just too late. Sheeta's great body hurtled against it before the catch engaged, and a moment later Kai Shang was gibbering and shrieking in the back of an upper berth.

Lightly Sheeta sprang after his victim, and presently the wicked days of Kai Shang of Fachan were ended, and Sheeta was gorging himself upon tough and stringy flesh.

A moment scarcely had elapsed after Schneider leaped upon Jane Clayton and wrenched the revolver from her hand, when the door of the cabin opened and a tall and half-naked white man stood framed within the portal.

Silently he leaped across the cabin. Schneider felt sinewy fingers at his throat. He turned his head to see who had attacked him, and his eyes went wide when he saw the face of the ape-man close above his own.

Grimly the fingers tightened upon the mate's throat. He tried to scream, to plead, but no sound came forth. His eyes protruded as he struggled for freedom, for breath, for life.

Jane Clayton seized her husband's hands and tried to drag them from the throat of the dying man; but Tarzan only shook his head.

"Not again," he said quietly. "Before have I permitted scoundrels to live, only to suffer and to have you suffer for my mercy. This time we shall make sure of one scoundrel—sure that he will never again harm us or another," and with a sudden wrench he twisted the neck of the perfidious mate until there was a sharp crack, and the man's body lay limp and motionless in the ape-man's grasp. With a gesture of disgust Tarzan tossed the corpse aside. Then he returned to the deck, followed by Jane and the Mosula woman.

The battle there was over. Schmidt and Momulla and two others alone remained alive of all the company of the Cowrie, for they had found sanctuary in the forecastle. The others had died, horribly, and as they deserved, beneath the fangs and talons of the beasts of Tarzan, and in the morning the sun rose on a grisly sight upon the deck of the unhappy Cowrie; but this time the blood which stained her white planking was the blood of the guilty and not of the innocent.

Tarzan brought forth the men who had hidden in the forecastle, and without promises of immunity from punishment forced them to help work the vessel—the only alternative was immediate death.

A stiff breeze had risen with the sun, and with canvas spread the Cowrie set in toward Jungle Island, where a few hours later, Tarzan picked up Gust and bid farewell to Sheeta and the apes of Akut, for here he set the beasts ashore to pursue the wild and natural life they loved so well; nor did they lose a moment's time in disappearing into the cool depths of their beloved jungle.

That they knew that Tarzan was to leave them may be doubted—except possibly in the case of the more intelligent Akut, who alone of all the others remained upon the beach as the small boat drew away toward the schooner, carrying his savage lord and master from him.

And as long as their eyes could span the distance, Jane and Tarzan, standing upon the deck, saw the lonely figure of the shaggy anthropoid motionless upon the surf-beaten sands of Jungle Island.

It was three days later that the Cowrie fell in with H.M. sloop-of-war Shorewater, through whose wireless Lord Greystoke soon got in communication with London. Thus he learned that which filled his and his wife's heart with joy and thanksgiving—little Jack was safe at Lord Greystoke's town house.

It was not until they reached London that they learned the details of the remarkable chain of circumstances that had preserved the infant unharmed.

It developed that Rokoff, fearing to take the child aboard the Kincaid by day, had hidden it in a low den where nameless infants were harboured, intending to carry it to the steamer after dark.

His confederate and chief lieutenant, Paulvitch, true to the long years of teaching of his wily master, had at last succumbed to the treachery and greed that had always marked his superior, and, lured by the thoughts of the immense ransom that he might win by returning the child unharmed, had divulged the secret of its parentage to the woman who maintained the foundling asylum. Through her he had arranged for the substitution of another infant, knowing full well that never until it was too late would Rokoff suspect the trick that had been played upon him.

The woman had promised to keep the child until Paulvitch returned to England; but she, in turn, had been tempted to betray her trust by the lure of gold, and so had opened negotiations with Lord Greystoke's solicitors for the return of the child.

Esmeralda, the old Negro nurse whose absence on a vacation in America at the time of the abduction of little Jack had been attributed by her as the cause of the calamity, had returned and positively identified the infant.

The ransom had been paid, and within ten days of the date of his kidnapping the future Lord Greystoke, none the worse for his experience, had been returned to his father's home.

And so that last and greatest of Nikolas Rokoff's many rascalities had not only miserably miscarried through the treachery he had taught his only friend, but it had resulted in the arch-villain's death, and given to Lord and Lady Greystoke a peace of mind that neither could ever have felt so long as the vital spark remained in the body of the Russian and his malign mind was free to formulate new atrocities against them.

Rokoff was dead, and while the fate of Paulvitch was unknown, they had every reason to believe that he had succumbed to the dangers of the jungle where last they had seen him—the malicious tool of his master.

And thus, in so far as they might know, they were to be freed for ever from the menace of these two men—the only enemies which Tarzan of the Apes ever had had occasion to fear, because they struck at him cowardly blows, through those he loved.

It was a happy family party that were reunited in Greystoke House the day that Lord Greystoke and his lady landed upon English soil from the deck of the Shorewater.

Accompanying them were Mugambi and the Mosula woman whom he had found in the bottom of the canoe that night upon the bank of the little tributary of the Ugambi.

The woman had preferred to cling to her new lord and master rather than return to the marriage she had tried to escape.

Tarzan had proposed to them that they might find a home upon his vast African estates in the land of the Waziri, where they were to be sent as soon as opportunity presented itself.

Possibly we shall see them all there amid the savage romance of the grim jungle and the great plains where Tarzan of the Apes loves best to be.

Who knows?

THE SON OF TARZAN

CHAPTER 1

The long boat of the *Marjorie W.* was floating down the broad Ugambi with ebb tide and current. Her crew were lazily enjoying this respite from the arduous labor of rowing up stream. Three miles below them lay the *Marjorie W.* herself, quite ready to sail so soon as they should have clambered aboard and swung the long boat to its davits. Presently the attention of every man was drawn from his dreaming or his gossiping to the northern bank of the river. There, screaming at them in a cracked falsetto and with skinny arms outstretched, stood a strange apparition of a man.

"Wot the 'ell?" ejaculated one of the crew.

"A white man!" muttered the mate, and then: "Man the oars, boys, and we'll just pull over an' see what he wants."

When they came close to the shore they saw an emaciated creature with scant white locks tangled and matted. The thin, bent body was naked but for a loin cloth. Tears were rolling down the sunken pock-marked cheeks. The man jabbered at them in a strange tongue.

"Rooshun," hazarded the mate. "Savvy English?" he called to the man.

He did, and in that tongue, brokenly and haltingly, as though it had been many years since he had used it, he begged them to take him with them away from this awful country. Once on board the *Marjorie W.* the stranger told his rescuers a pitiful tale of privation, hardships, and torture, extending over a period of ten years. How he happened to have come to Africa he did not tell them, leaving them to assume he had forgotten the incidents of his life prior to the frightful ordeals that had wrecked him mentally and physically. He did not even tell them his true name, and so they knew him only as Michael Sabrov, nor was there any resemblance between this sorry wreck and the virile, though unprincipled, Alexis Paulvitch of old.

It had been ten years since the Russian had escaped the fate of his friend, the arch-fiend Rokoff, and not once, but many times during those ten years had Paulvitch cursed the fate that had given to Nicholas Rokoff death and immunity from suffering while it had meted to him the hideous terrors of an existence infinitely worse than the death that persistently refused to claim him.

Paulvitch had taken to the jungle when he had seen the beasts of Tarzan and their savage lord swarm the deck of the Kincaid, and in his terror lest Tarzan pursue and capture him he had stumbled on deep into the jungle, only to fall at last into the hands of one of the savage cannibal tribes that had felt the weight of Rokoff's evil temper and cruel brutality. Some strange whim of the chief of this tribe saved Paulvitch from death only to plunge him into a life of misery and torture. For ten years he had been the butt of the village, beaten and stoned by the women and children, cut and slashed and disfigured by the warriors; a victim of often recurring fevers of the most malignant variety. Yet he did not die. Smallpox laid its hideous clutches upon him; leaving him unspeakably branded with its repulsive marks. Between it and the attentions of the tribe the countenance of Alexis Paulvitch was so altered that his own mother could not have recognized in the pitiful mask he called his face a single familiar feature. A few scraggly, yellow-white locks had supplanted the thick, dark hair that had covered his head. His limbs were bent and twisted, he walked with a shuffling, unsteady gait, his body doubled forward. His teeth were gone--knocked out by his savage masters. Even his mentality was but a sorry mockery of what it once had been.

They took him aboard the *Marjorie W.*, and there they fed and nursed him. He gained a little in strength; but his appearance never altered for the better--a human derelict, battered and wrecked, they had found him; a human derelict, battered and wrecked, he would remain until death claimed him. Though still in his thirties, Alexis Paulvitch could easily have passed for eighty. Inscrutable Nature had demanded of the accomplice a greater penalty than his principal had paid.

In the mind of Alexis Paulvitch there lingered no thoughts of revenge--only a dull hatred of the man whom he and Rokoff had tried to break, and failed. There was hatred, too, of the memory of Rokoff, for Rokoff had led him into the horrors he had undergone. There was hatred of the police of a score of cities from which he had had to flee. There was hatred of law, hatred of order, hatred of everything. Every moment of the man's waking life was filled with morbid thought of hatred~he had become mentally as he was physically in outward appearance, the personification of the blighting emotion of Hate. He had little or nothing to do with the men who had rescued him. He was too weak to work and too morose for company, and so they quickly left him alone to his own devices.

The *Marjorie W.* had been chartered by a syndicate of wealthy manufacturers, equipped with a laboratory and a staff of scientists, and sent out to search for some natural product which the manufacturers who footed the bills had been importing from South America at an enormous cost. What the product was none on board the *Marjorie W.* knew except the scientists, nor is it of any moment to us, other than that it led the ship to a certain island off the coast of Africa after Alexis Paulvitch had been taken aboard.

The ship lay at anchor off the coast for several weeks. The monotony of life aboard her became trying for the crew. They went often ashore, and finally Paulvitch asked to accompany them~he too was tiring of the blighting sameness of existence upon the ship.

The island was heavily timbered. Dense jungle ran down almost to the beach. The scientists were far inland, prosecuting their search for the valuable commodity that native rumor upon the mainland had led them to believe might be found here in marketable quantity. The ship's company fished, hunted, and explored. Paulvitch shuffled up and down the beach, or lay in the shade of the great trees that skirted it. One day, as the men were gathered at a little distance inspecting the body of a panther that had fallen to the gun of one of them who had been hunting inland, Paulvitch lay sleeping beneath his tree. He was awakened by the touch of a hand upon his shoulder. With a start he sat up to see a huge, anthropoid ape squatting at his side, inspecting him intently. The Russian was thoroughly frightened. He glanced toward the sailors~they were a couple of hundred yards away. Again the ape plucked at his shoulder, jabbering plaintively. Paulvitch saw no menace in the inquiring gaze, or in the attitude of the beast. He got slowly to his feet. The ape rose at his side.

Half doubled, the man shuffled cautiously away toward the sailors. The ape moved with him, taking one of his arms. They had come almost to the little knot of men before they were seen, and by this time Paulvitch had become assured that the beast meant no harm. The animal evidently was accustomed to the association of human beings. It occurred to the Russian that the ape represented a certain considerable money value, and before they reached the sailors he had decided he should be the one to profit by it.

When the men looked up and saw the oddly paired couple shuffling toward them they were filled with amazement, and started on a run toward the two. The ape showed no sign of fear. Instead he grasped each sailor by the shoulder and peered long and earnestly into his face. Having inspected them all he returned to Paulvitch's side, disappointment written strongly upon his countenance and in his carriage.

The men were delighted with him. They gathered about, asking Paulvitch many questions, and examining his companion. The Russian told them that the ape was his~nothing further would he offer—but kept harping continually upon the same theme, "The ape is mine. The ape is mine." Tiring of Paulvitch, one of the men essayed a pleasantry. Circling about behind the ape he prodded the anthropoid in the back with a pin. Like a flash the beast wheeled upon its tormentor, and, in the briefest instant of turning, the placid, friendly animal was metamorphosed to a frenzied demon of rage. The broad grin that had sat upon the sailor's face as he perpetrated his little joke froze to an expression of terror. He attempted to dodge the long arms that reached for him; but, failing, drew a long knife that hung at his belt. With a single wrench the ape tore the weapon from the man's grasp and flung it to one side, then his yellow fangs were buried in the sailor's shoulder.

With sticks and knives the man's companions fell upon the beast, while Paulvitch danced around the cursing snarling pack mumbling and screaming pleas and threats. He saw his visions of wealth rapidly dissipating before the weapons of the sailors.

The ape, however, proved no easy victim to the superior numbers that seemed fated to overwhelm him. Rising from the sailor who had precipitated the battle he shook his giant shoulders, freeing himself from two of the men that were clinging to his back, and with mighty blows of his open palms felled one after another of his attackers, leaping hither and thither with the agility of a small monkey.

The fight had been witnessed by the captain and mate who were just landing from the *Marjorie W.*, and Paulvitch saw these two now running forward with drawn revolvers while the two sailors who had brought them ashore trailed at their heels. The ape stood looking about him at the havoc he had wrought, but whether he was awaiting a renewal of the attack or was deliberating which of his foes he should exterminate first Paulvitch could not guess. What he could guess, however, was that the moment the two officers came within firing distance of the beast they would put an end to him in short order unless something were done and done quickly to prevent. The ape had made no move to attack the Russian but even so the man was none too sure of what might happen were he to interfere with the savage beast, now thoroughly aroused to bestial rage, and with the smell of new spilled blood fresh in its nostrils. For an instant he hesitated, and then again there rose before him the dreams of affluence which this great anthropoid would doubtless turn to realities once Paulvitch had landed him safely in some great metropolis like London.

The captain was shouting to him now to stand aside that he might have a shot at the animal; but instead Paulvitch shuffled to the ape's side, and though the man's hair quivered at its roots he mastered his fear and laid hold of the ape's arm.

"Come!" he commanded, and tugged to pull the beast from among the sailors, many of whom were now sitting up in wide eyed fright or crawling away from their conqueror upon hands and knees.

Slowly the ape permitted itself to be led to one side, nor did it show the slightest indication of a desire to harm the Russian. The captain came to a halt a few paces from the odd pair.

"Get aside, Sabrov!" he commanded. "I'll put that brute where he won't chew up any more able seamen."

"It wasn't his fault, captain," pleaded Paulvitch. "Please don't shoot him. The men started it—they attacked him first. You see, he's perfectly gentle—and he's mine—he's mine—he's mine! I won't let you kill him," he concluded, as his half-wrecked mentality pictured anew the pleasure that money would buy in London—money that he could not hope to possess without some such windfall as the ape represented.

The captain lowered his weapon. "The men started it, did they?" he repeated. "How about that?" and he turned toward the sailors who had by this time picked themselves from the ground, none of them much the worse for his experience except the fellow who had been the cause of it, and who would doubtless nurse a sore shoulder for a week or so.

"Simpson done it," said one of the men. "He stuck a pin into the monk from behind, and the monk got him—which served him bloomin' well right—an' he got the rest of us, too, for which I can't blame him, since we all jumped him to once."

The captain looked at Simpson, who sheepishly admitted the truth of the allegation, then he stepped over to the ape as though to discover for himself the sort of temper the beast possessed, but it was noticeable that he kept his revolver cocked and leveled as he did so. However, he spoke soothingly to the animal who squatted at the Russian's side looking first at one and then another of the sailors. As the captain approached him the ape half rose and waddled forward to meet him. Upon his countenance was the same strange, searching expression that had marked his scrutiny of each of the sailors he had first encountered. He came quite close to the officer and laid a paw upon one of the man's shoulders, studying his face intently for a long moment, then came the expression of disappointment accompanied by what was almost a human sigh, as he turned away to peer in the same curious fashion into the faces of the mate and the two sailors who had arrived with the officers. In each instance he sighed and passed on, returning at length to Paulvitch's side, where he squatted down once more; thereafter evincing little or no interest in any of the other men, and apparently forgetful of his recent battle with them.

When the party returned aboard the *Marjorie W.*, Paulvitch was accompanied by the ape, who seemed anxious to follow him. The captain interposed no obstacles to the arrangement, and so the great anthropoid was tacitly admitted to membership in the ship's company. Once aboard he examined each new face minutely, evincing the same disappointment in each instance that had marked his scrutiny of the others. The officers and scientists aboard often discussed the beast, but they were unable to account satisfactorily for the strange ceremony with which he greeted each new face. Had he been discovered upon the mainland, or any other place than the almost unknown island that had been his home, they would have concluded that he had formerly been a pet of man; but that theory was not tenable in the face of the isolation of his uninhabited island. He seemed continually to be searching for someone, and during the first days of the return voyage from the island he was often discovered nosing about in various parts of the ship; but after he had seen and examined each face of the ship's company, and explored every corner of the vessel he lapsed into utter indifference of all about him. Even the Russian elicited only casual interest when he brought him food. At other times the ape appeared merely to tolerate him. He never showed affection for him, or for anyone else upon the *Marjorie W.*, nor did he at any time evince any indication of the savage temper that had marked his resentment of the attack of the sailors upon him at the time that he had come among them.

Most of his time was spent in the eye of the ship scanning the horizon ahead, as though he were endowed with sufficient reason to know that the vessel was bound for some port where there would be other human beings to undergo his searching scrutiny. All in all, Ajax, as he had been dubbed, was considered the most remarkable and intelligent ape that any one aboard the *Marjorie W.* ever had seen. Nor was his intelligence the only remarkable attribute he owned. His stature and physique were, for an ape, awe inspiring. That he was old was quite evident, but if his age had impaired his physical or mental powers in the slightest it was not apparent.

And so at length the *Marjorie W.* came to England, and there the officers and the scientists, filled with compassion for the pitiful wreck of a man they had rescued from the jungles, furnished Paulvitch with funds and bid him and his Ajax Godspeed.

Upon the dock and all through the journey to London the Russian had his hands full with Ajax. Each new face of the thousands that came within the anthropoid's ken must be carefully scrutinized, much to the horror of many of his victims; but at last, failing, apparently, to discover whom he sought, the great ape relapsed into morbid indifference, only occasionally evincing interest in a passing face.

In London, Paulvitch went directly with his prize to a certain famous animal trainer. This man was much impressed with Ajax with the result that he agreed to train him for a lion's share of the profits of exhibiting him, and in the meantime to provide for the keep of both the ape and his owner.

And so came Ajax to London, and there was forged another link in the chain of strange circumstances that were to affect the lives of many people.

CHAPTER 2

Mr. Harold Moore was a bilious-countenanced, studious young man. He took himself very seriously, and life, and his work, which latter was the tutoring of the young son of a British nobleman. He felt that his charge was not making the progress that his parents had a right to expect, and he was now conscientiously explaining this fact to the boy's mother.

"It's not that he isn't bright," he was saying; "if that were true I should have hopes of succeeding, for then I might bring to bear all my energies in overcoming his obtuseness; but the trouble is that he is exceptionally intelligent, and learns so quickly that I can find no fault in the matter of the preparation of his lessons. What concerns me, however, is that fact that he evidently takes no interest whatever in the subjects we are studying. He merely accomplishes each lesson as a task to be rid of as quickly as possible and I am sure that no lesson ever again enters his mind until the hours of study and recitation once more arrive. His sole interests seem to be feats of physical prowess and the reading of everything that he can get hold of relative to savage beasts and the lives and customs of uncivilized peoples; but particularly do stories of animals appeal to him. He will sit for hours together poring over the work of some African explorer, and upon two occasions I have found him setting up in bed at night reading Carl Hagenbeck's book on men and beasts."

The boy's mother tapped her foot nervously upon the hearth rug.

"You discourage this, of course?" she ventured.

Mr. Moore shuffled embarrassedly.

"I—ah—essayed to take the book from him," he replied, a slight flush mounting his sallow cheek; "but—ah—your son is quite muscular for one so young."

"He wouldn't let you take it?" asked the mother.

"He would not," confessed the tutor. "He was perfectly good natured about it; but he insisted upon pretending that he was a gorilla and that I was a chimpanzee attempting to steal food from him. He leaped upon me with the most savage growls I ever heard, lifted me completely above his head, hurled me upon his bed, and after going through a pantomime indicative of choking me to death he stood upon my prostrate form and gave voice to a most fearsome shriek, which he explained was the victory cry of a bull ape. Then he carried me to the door, shoved me out into the hall and locked me from his room."

For several minutes neither spoke again. It was the boy's mother who finally broke the silence.

"It is very necessary, Mr. Moore," she said, "that you do everything in your power to discourage this tendency in Jack, he—"; but she got no further. A loud "Whoop!" from the direction of the window brought them both to their feet. The room was upon the second floor of the house, and opposite the window to which their attention had been attracted was a large tree, a branch of which spread to within a few feet of the sill. Upon this branch now they both discovered the subject of their recent conversation, a tall, well-built boy, balancing with ease upon the bending limb and uttering loud shouts of glee as he noted the terrified expressions upon the faces of his audience.

The mother and tutor both rushed toward the window but before they had crossed half the room the boy had leaped nimbly to the sill and entered the apartment with them.

"'The wild man from Borneo has just come to town,'" he sang, dancing a species of war dance about his terrified mother and scandalized tutor, and ending up by throwing his arms about the former's neck and kissing her upon either cheek.

"Oh, Mother," he cried, "there's a wonderful, educated ape being shown at one of the music halls. Willie Grimsby saw it last night. He says it can do everything but talk. It rides a bicycle, eats with knife and fork, counts up to ten, and ever so many other wonderful things, and can I go and see it too? Oh, please, Mother—please let me."

Patting the boy's cheek affectionately, the mother shook her head negatively. "No, Jack," she said; "you know I do not approve of such exhibitions."

"I don't see why not, Mother," replied the boy. "All the other fellows go and they go to the Zoo, too, and you'll never let me do even that. Anybody'd think I was a girl—or a mollycoddle. Oh, Father," he exclaimed, as the door opened to admit a tall gray-eyed man. "Oh, Father, can't I go?"

"Go where, my son?" asked the newcomer.

"He wants to go to a music hall to see a trained ape," said the mother, looking warningly at her husband.

"Who, Ajax?" questioned the man.

The boy nodded.

"Well, I don't know that I blame you, my son," said the father, "I wouldn't mind seeing him myself. They say he is very wonderful, and that for an anthropoid he is unusually large. Let's all go, Jane—what do you say?" And he turned toward his wife, but that lady only shook her head in a most positive manner, and turning to Mr. Moore asked him if it was not time that he and Jack were in the study for the morning recitations. When the two had left she turned toward her husband.

"John," she said, "something must be done to discourage Jack's tendency toward anything that may excite the cravings for the savage life which I fear he has inherited from you. You know from your own experience how strong is the call of the wild at times. You know that often it has necessitated a stern struggle on your part to resist the almost insane desire which occasionally overwhelms you to plunge once again into the jungle life that claimed you for so many years, and at the same time you know, better than any other, how frightful a fate it would be for Jack, were the trail to the savage jungle made either alluring or easy to him."

"I doubt if there is any danger of his inheriting a taste for jungle life from me," replied the man, "for I cannot conceive that such a thing may be transmitted from father to son. And sometimes, Jane, I think that in your solicitude for his future you go a bit too far in your restrictive measures. His love for animals—his desire, for example, to see this trained ape—is only natural in a healthy, normal boy of his age. Just because he wants to see Ajax is no indication that he would wish to marry an ape, and even should he, far be it from you Jane to have the right to cry 'shame!'" and John Clayton, Lord Greystoke, put an arm about his wife, laughing good-naturedly down into her upturned face before he bent his head and kissed her. Then, more seriously, he continued: "You have never told Jack anything concerning my early life, nor have you permitted me to, and in this I think that you have made a mistake. Had I been able to tell him of the experiences of Tarzan of the Apes I could doubtless have taken much of the glamour and romance from jungle life that naturally surrounds it in the minds of those who have had no experience of it. He might then have profited by my experience, but now, should the jungle lust ever claim him, he will have nothing to guide him but his own impulses, and I know how powerful these may be in the wrong direction at times."

But Lady Greystoke only shook her head as she had a hundred other times when the subject had claimed her attention in the past.

"No, John," she insisted, "I shall never give my consent to the implanting in Jack's mind of any suggestion of the savage life which we both wish to preserve him from."

It was evening before the subject was again referred to and then it was raised by Jack himself. He had been sitting, curled in a large chair, reading, when he suddenly looked up and addressed his father.

"Why," he asked, coming directly to the point, "can't I go and see Ajax?"

"Your mother does not approve," replied his father.

"Do you?"

"That is not the question," evaded Lord Greystoke. "It is enough that your mother objects."

"I am going to see him," announced the boy, after a few moments of thoughtful silence. "I am not different from Willie Grimsby, or any other of the fellows who have been to see him. It did not harm them and it will not harm me. I could go without telling you; but I would not do that. So I tell you now, beforehand, that I am going to see Ajax."

There was nothing disrespectful or defiant in the boy's tone or manner. His was merely a dispassionate statement of facts. His father could scarce repress either a smile or a show of the admiration he felt for the manly course his son had pursued.

"I admire your candor, Jack," he said. "Permit me to be candid, as well. If you go to see Ajax without permission, I shall punish you. I have never inflicted corporal punishment upon you, but I warn you that should you disobey your mother's wishes in this instance, I shall."

"Yes, sir," replied the boy; and then: "I shall tell you, sir, when I have been to see Ajax."

Mr. Moore's room was next to that of his youthful charge, and it was the tutor's custom to have a look into the boy's each evening as the former was about to retire. This evening he was particularly careful not to neglect his duty, for he had just come from a conference with the boy's father and mother in which it had been impressed upon him that he must exercise the greatest care to prevent Jack visiting the music hall where Ajax was being shown. So, when he opened the boy's door at about half after nine, he was greatly excited, though not entirely surprised to find the future Lord Greystoke fully dressed for the street and about to crawl from his open bed room window.

Mr. Moore made a rapid spring across the apartment; but the waste of energy was unnecessary, for when the boy heard him within the chamber and realized that he had been discovered he turned back as though to relinquish his planned adventure.

"Where were you going?" panted the excited Mr. Moore.

"I am going to see Ajax," replied the boy, quietly.

"I am astonished," cried Mr. Moore; but a moment later he was infinitely more astonished, for the boy, approaching close to him, suddenly seized him about the waist, lifted him from his feet and threw him face downward upon the bed, shoving his face deep into a soft pillow.

"Be quiet," admonished the victor, "or I'll choke you."

Mr. Moore struggled; but his efforts were in vain. Whatever else Tarzan of the Apes may or may not have handed down to his son he had at least bequeathed him almost as marvelous a physique as he himself had possessed at the same age. The tutor was as putty in the boy's hands. Kneeling upon him, Jack tore strips from a sheet and bound the man's hands behind his back. Then he rolled him over and stuffed a gag of the same material between his teeth, securing it with a strip wound about the back of his victim's head. All the while he talked in a low, conversational tone.

"I am Waja, chief of the Waji," he explained, "and you are Mohammed Dubn, the Arab sheik, who would murder my people and steal my ivory," and he dexterously trussed Mr. Moore's hobbled ankles up behind to meet his hobbled wrists. "Ah—ha! Villain! I have you in me power at last. I go; but I shall return!" And the son of Tarzan skipped across the room, slipped through the open window, and slid to liberty by way of the down spout from an eaves trough.

Mr. Moore wriggled and struggled about the bed. He was sure that he should suffocate unless aid came quickly. In his frenzy of terror he managed to roll off the bed. The pain and shock of the fall jolted him back to something like sane consideration of his plight. Where before he had been unable to think intelligently because of the hysterical fear that had claimed him he now lay quietly searching for some means of escape from his dilemma. It finally occurred to him that the room in which Lord and Lady Greystoke had been sitting when he left them was directly beneath that in which he lay upon the floor. He knew that some time had elapsed since he had come up stairs and that they might be gone by this time, for it seemed to him that he had struggled about the bed, in his efforts to free himself, for an eternity. But the best that he could do was to attempt to attract attention from below, and so, after many failures, he managed to work himself into a position in which he could tap the toe of his boot against the floor. This he proceeded to do at short intervals, until, after what seemed a very long time, he was rewarded by hearing footsteps ascending the stairs, and presently a knock upon the door. Mr. Moore tapped vigorously with his toe—he could not reply in any other way. The knock was repeated after a moment's silence. Again Mr. Moore tapped. Would they never open the door! Laboriously he rolled in the direction of succor. If he could get his back against the door he could then tap upon its base, when surely he must be heard. The knocking was repeated a little louder, and finally a voice called: "Mr. Jack!"

It was one of the house men—Mr. Moore recognized the fellow's voice. He came near to bursting a blood vessel in an endeavor to scream "come in" through the stifling gag. After a moment the man knocked again, quite loudly and again called the boy's name. Receiving no reply he turned the knob, and at the same instant a sudden recollection filled the tutor anew with numbing terror—he had, himself, locked the door behind him when he had entered the room.

He heard the servant try the door several times and then depart. Upon which Mr. Moore swooned.

In the meantime Jack was enjoying to the full the stolen pleasures of the music hall. He had reached the temple of mirth just as Ajax's act was commencing, and having purchased a box seat was now leaning breathlessly over the rail watching every move of the great ape, his eyes wide in wonder. The trainer was not slow to note the boy's handsome, eager face, and as one of Ajax's biggest hits consisted in an entry to one or more boxes during his performance, ostensibly in search of a long-lost relative, as the trainer explained, the man realized the effectiveness of sending him into the box with the handsome boy, who, doubtless, would be terror stricken by proximity to the shaggy, powerful beast.

When the time came, therefore, for the ape to return from the wings in reply to an encore the trainer directed its attention to the boy who chanced to be the sole occupant of the box in which he sat. With a spring the huge anthropoid leaped from the stage to the boy's side; but if the trainer had looked for a laughable scene of fright he was mistaken. A broad smile lighted the boy's features as he laid his hand upon the shaggy arm of his visitor. The ape, grasping the boy by either shoulder, peered long and earnestly into his face, while the latter stroked his head and talked to him in a low voice.

Never had Ajax devoted so long a time to an examination of another as he did in this instance. He seemed troubled and not a little excited, jabbering and mumbling to the boy, and now caressing him, as the trainer had never seen him caress a human being before. Presently he clambered over into the box with him and snuggled down close to the boy's side. The audience was delighted; but they were still more delighted when the trainer, the period of his act having elapsed, attempted to persuade Ajax to leave the box. The ape would not budge. The manager, becoming excited at the delay, urged the trainer to greater haste, but when the latter entered the box to drag away the reluctant Ajax he was met by bared fangs and menacing growls.

The audience was delirious with joy. They cheered the ape. They cheered the boy, and they hooted and jeered at the trainer and the manager, which luckless individual had inadvertently shown himself and attempted to assist the trainer.

Finally, reduced to desperation and realizing that this show of mutiny upon the part of his valuable possession might render the animal worthless for exhibition purposes in the future if not immediately subdued, the trainer had hastened to his dressing room and procured a heavy whip. With this he now returned to the box; but when he had threatened Ajax with it but once he found himself facing two infuriated enemies instead of one, for the boy had leaped to his feet, and seizing a chair was standing ready at the ape's side to defend his new found friend. There was no longer a smile upon his handsome face. In his gray eyes was an expression which gave the trainer pause, and beside him stood the giant anthropoid growling and ready.

What might have happened, but for a timely interruption, may only be surmised; but that the trainer would have received a severe mauling, if nothing more, was clearly indicated by the attitudes of the two who faced him.

It was a pale-faced man who rushed into the Greystoke library to announce that he had found Jack's door locked and had been able to obtain no response to his repeated knocking and calling other than a strange tapping and the sound of what might have been a body moving about upon the floor.

Four steps at a time John Clayton took the stairs that led to the floor above. His wife and the servant hurried after him. Once he called his son's name in a loud voice; but receiving no reply he launched his great weight, backed by all the undiminished power of his giant muscles, against the heavy door. With a snapping of iron butts and a splintering of wood the obstacle burst inward.

At its foot lay the body of the unconscious Mr. Moore, across whom it fell with a resounding thud. Through the opening leaped Tarzan, and a moment later the room was flooded with light from a dozen electric bulbs.

It was several minutes before the tutor was discovered, so completely had the door covered him; but finally he was dragged forth, his gag and bonds cut away, and a liberal application of cold water had hastened returning consciousness.

"Where is Jack?" was John Clayton's first question, and then; "Who did this?" as the memory of Rokoff and the fear of a second abduction seized him.

Slowly Mr. Moore staggered to his feet. His gaze wandered about the room. Gradually he collected his scattered wits. The details of his recent harrowing experience returned to him.

"I tender my resignation, sir, to take effect at once," were his first words. "You do not need a tutor for your son—what he needs is a wild animal trainer."

"But where is he?" cried Lady Greystoke.

"He has gone to see Ajax."

It was with difficulty that Tarzan restrained a smile, and after satisfying himself that the tutor was more scared than injured, he ordered his closed car around and departed in the direction of a certain well-known music hall.

CHAPTER 3

As the trainer, with raised lash, hesitated an instant at the entrance to the box where the boy and the ape confronted him, a tall broad-shouldered man pushed past him and entered. As his eyes fell upon the newcomer a slight flush mounted the boy's cheeks.

"Father!" he exclaimed.

The ape gave one look at the English lord, and then leaped toward him, calling out in excited jabbering. The man, his eyes going wide in astonishment, stopped as though turned to stone.

"Akut!" he cried.

The boy looked, bewildered, from the ape to his father, and from his father to the ape. The trainer's jaw dropped as he listened to what followed, for from the lips of the Englishman flowed the gutturals of an ape that were answered in kind by the huge anthropoid that now clung to him.

And from the wings a hideously bent and disfigured old man watched the tableau in the box, his pock-marked features working spasmodically in varying expressions that might have marked every sensation in the gamut from pleasure to terror.

"Long have I looked for you, Tarzan," said Akut. "Now that I have found you I shall come to your jungle and live there always."

The man stroked the beast's head. Through his mind there was running rapidly a train of recollection that carried him far into the depths of the primeval African forest where this huge, man-like beast had fought shoulder to shoulder with him years before. He saw the black Mugambi wielding his deadly knob-stick, and beside them, with bared fangs and bristling whiskers, Sheeta the terrible; and pressing close behind the savage and the savage panther, the hideous apes of Akut. The man sighed. Strong within him surged the jungle lust that he had thought dead. Ah! if he could go back even for a brief month of it, to feel again the brush of leafy branches against his naked hide; to smell the musty rot of dead vegetation—frankincense and myrrh to the jungle born; to sense the noiseless coming of the great carnivora upon his trail; to hunt and to be hunted; to kill! The picture was alluring. And then came another picture—a sweet-faced woman, still young and beautiful; friends; a home; a son. He shrugged his giant shoulders.

"It cannot be, Akut," he said; "but if you would return, I shall see that it is done. You could not be happy here—I may not be happy there."

The trainer stepped forward. The ape bared his fangs, growling.

"Go with him, Akut," said Tarzan of the Apes. "I will come and see you tomorrow."

The beast moved sullenly to the trainer's side. The latter, at John Clayton's request, told where they might be found. Tarzan turned toward his son.

"Come!" he said, and the two left the theater. Neither spoke for several minutes after they had entered the limousine. It was the boy who broke the silence.

"The ape knew you," he said, "and you spoke together in the ape's tongue. How did the ape know you, and how did you learn his language?"

And then, briefly and for the first time, Tarzan of the Apes told his son of his early life—of the birth in the jungle, of the death of his parents, and of how Kala, the great she ape had suckled and raised him from infancy almost to manhood. He told him, too, of the dangers and the horrors of the jungle; of the great beasts that stalked one by day and by night; of the periods of drought, and of the cataclysmic rains; of hunger; of cold; of intense heat; of nakedness and fear and suffering. He told him of all those things that seem most horrible to the creature of civilization in the hope that the knowledge of them might expunge from the lad's mind any inherent desire for the jungle. Yet they were the very things that made the memory of the jungle what it was to Tarzan—that made up the composite jungle life he loved. And in the telling he forgot one thing—the principal thing—that the boy at his side, listening with eager ears, was the son of Tarzan of the Apes.

After the boy had been tucked away in bed—and without the threatened punishment—John Clayton told his wife of the events of the evening, and that he had at last acquainted the boy with the facts of his jungle life. The mother, who had long foreseen that her son must some time know of those frightful years during which his father had roamed the jungle, a naked, savage beast of prey, only shook her head, hoping against hope that the lure she knew was still strong in the father's breast had not been transmitted to his son.

Tarzan visited Akut the following day, but though Jack begged to be allowed to accompany him he was refused. This time Tarzan saw the pock-marked old owner of the ape, whom he did not recognize as the wily Paulvitch of former days. Tarzan, influenced by Akut's pleadings, broached the question of the ape's purchase; but Paulvitch would not name any price, saying that he would consider the matter.

When Tarzan returned home Jack was all excitement to hear the details of his visit, and finally suggested that his father buy the ape and bring it home. Lady Greystoke was horrified at the suggestion. The boy was insistent. Tarzan explained that he had wished to purchase Akut and return him to his jungle home, and to this the mother assented. Jack asked to be allowed to visit the ape, but again he was met with flat refusal. He had the address, however, which the trainer had given his father, and two days later he found the opportunity to elude his new tutor—who had replaced the terrified Mr. Moore—and after a considerable search through a section of London which he had never before visited, he found the smelly little quarters of the pock-marked old man. The old fellow himself replied to his knocking, and when he stated that he had come to see Ajax, opened the door and admitted him to the little room which he and the great ape occupied. In former years Paulvitch had been a fastidious scoundrel; but ten years of hideous life among the cannibals of Africa had eradicated the last vestige of niceness from his habits. His apparel was wrinkled and soiled. His hands were unwashed, his few straggling locks uncombed. His room was a jumble of filthy disorder. As the boy entered he saw the great ape squatting upon the bed, the coverlets of which were a tangled wad of filthy blankets and ill-smelling quilts. At sight of the youth the ape leaped to the floor and shuffled forward. The man, not recognizing his visitor and fearing that the ape meant mischief, stepped between them, ordering the ape back to the bed.

"He will not hurt me," cried the boy. "We are friends, and before, he was my father's friend. They knew one another in the jungle. My father is Lord Greystoke. He does not know that I have come here. My mother forbid my coming; but I wished to see Ajax, and I will pay you if you will let me come here often and see him."

At the mention of the boy's identity Paulvitch's eyes narrowed. Since he had first seen Tarzan again from the wings of the theater there had been forming in his deadened brain the beginnings of a desire for revenge. It is a characteristic of the weak and criminal to attribute to others the misfortunes that are the result of their own wickedness, and so now it was that Alexis Paulvitch was slowly recalling the events of his past life and as he did so laying at the door of the man whom he and Rokoff had so assiduously attempted to ruin and murder all the misfortunes that had befallen him in the failure of their various schemes against their intended victim.

He saw at first no way in which he could, with safety to himself, wreak vengeance upon Tarzan through the medium of Tarzan's son; but that great possibilities for revenge lay in the boy was apparent to him, and so he determined to cultivate the lad in the hope that fate would play into his hands in some way in the future. He told the boy all that he knew of his father's past life in the jungle and when he found that the boy had been kept in ignorance of all these things for so many years, and that he had been forbidden visiting the zoological gardens; that he had had to bind and gag his tutor to find an opportunity to come to the music hall and see Ajax, he guessed immediately the nature of the great fear that lay in the hearts of the boy's parents—that he might crave the jungle as his father had craved it.

And so Paulvitch encouraged the boy to come and see him often, and always he played upon the lad's craving for tales of the savage world with which Paulvitch was all too familiar. He left him alone with Akut much, and it was not long until he was surprised to learn that the boy could make the great beast understand him—that he had actually learned many of the words of the primitive language of the anthropoids.

During this period Tarzan came several times to visit Paulvitch. He seemed anxious to purchase Ajax, and at last he told the man frankly that he was prompted not only by a desire upon his part to return the beast to the liberty of his native jungle; but also because his wife feared that in some way her son might learn the whereabouts of the ape and through his attachment for the beast become imbued with the roving instinct which, as Tarzan explained to Paulvitch, had so influenced his own life.

The Russian could scarce repress a smile as he listened to Lord Greystoke's words, since scarce a half hour had passed since the time the future Lord Greystoke had been sitting upon the disordered bed jabbering away to Ajax with all the fluency of a born ape.

It was during this interview that a plan occurred to Paulvitch, and as a result of it he agreed to accept a certain fabulous sum for the ape, and upon receipt of the money to deliver the beast to a vessel that was sailing south from Dover for Africa two days later. He had a double purpose in accepting Clayton's offer. Primarily, the money consideration influenced him strongly, as the ape was no longer a source of revenue to him, having consistently refused to perform upon the stage after having discovered Tarzan. It was as though the beast had suffered himself to be brought from his jungle home and exhibited before thousands of curious spectators for the sole purpose of searching out his long lost friend and master, and, having found him, considered further mingling with the common herd of humans unnecessary. However that may be, the fact remained that no amount of persuasion could influence him even to show himself upon the music hall stage, and upon the single occasion that the trainer attempted force the results were such that the unfortunate man considered himself lucky to have escaped with his life. All that saved him was the accidental presence of Jack Clayton, who had been permitted to visit the animal in the dressing room reserved for him at the music hall, and had immediately interfered when he saw that the savage beast meant serious mischief.

And after the money consideration, strong in the heart of the Russian was the desire for revenge, which had been growing with constant brooding over the failures and miseries of his life, which he attributed to Tarzan; the latest, and by no means the least, of which was Ajax's refusal to longer earn money for him. The ape's refusal he traced directly to Tarzan, finally convincing himself that the ape man had instructed the great anthropoid to refuse to go upon the stage.

Paulvitch's naturally malign disposition was aggravated by the weakening and warping of his mental and physical faculties through torture and privation. From cold, calculating, highly intelligent perversity it had deteriorated into the indiscriminating, dangerous menace of the mentally defective. His plan, however, was sufficiently cunning to at least cast a doubt upon the assertion that his mentality was wandering. It assured him first of the competence which Lord Greystoke had promised to pay him for the deportation of the ape, and then of revenge upon his benefactor through the son he idolized. That part of his scheme was crude and brutal—it lacked the refinement of torture that had marked the master strokes of the Paulvitch of old, when he had worked with that virtuoso of villainy, Nikolas Rokoff—but it at least assured Paulvitch of immunity from responsibility, placing that upon the ape, who would thus also be punished for his refusal longer to support the Russian.

Everything played with fiendish unanimity into Paulvitch's hands. As chance would have it, Tarzan's son overheard his father relating to the boy's mother the steps he was taking to return Akut safely to his jungle home, and having overheard he begged them to bring the ape home that he might have him for a play-fellow. Tarzan would not have been averse to this plan; but Lady Greystoke was horrified at the very thought of it. Jack pleaded with his mother; but all unavailingly. She was obdurate, and at last the lad appeared to acquiesce in his mother's decision that the ape must be returned to Africa and the boy to school, from which he had been absent on vacation.

He did not attempt to visit Paulvitch's room again that day, but instead busied himself in other ways. He had always been well supplied with money, so that when necessity demanded he had no difficulty in collecting several hundred pounds. Some of this money he invested in various strange purchases which he managed to smuggle into the house, undetected, when he returned late in the afternoon.

The next morning, after giving his father time to precede him and conclude his business with Paulvitch, the lad hastened to the Russian's room. Knowing nothing of the man's true character the boy dared not take him fully into his confidence for fear that the old fellow would not only refuse to aid him, but would report the whole affair to his father. Instead, he simply asked permission to take Ajax to Dover. He explained that it would relieve the old man of a tiresome journey, as well as placing a number of pounds in his pocket, for the lad purposed paying the Russian well.

"You see," he went on, "there will be no danger of detection since I am supposed to be leaving on an afternoon train for school. Instead I will come here after they have left me on board the train. Then I can take Ajax to Dover, you see, and arrive at school only a day late. No one will be the wiser, no harm will be done, and I shall have had an extra day with Ajax before I lose him forever."

The plan fitted perfectly with that which Paulvitch had in mind. Had he known what further the boy contemplated he would doubtless have entirely abandoned his own scheme of revenge and aided the boy whole heartedly in the consummation of the lad's, which would have been better for Paulvitch, could he have but read the future a few short hours ahead.

That afternoon Lord and Lady Greystoke bid their son good-bye and saw him safely settled in a first-class compartment of the railway carriage that would set him down at school in a few hours. No sooner had they left him, however, than he gathered his bags together, descended from the compartment and sought a cab stand outside the station. Here he engaged a cabby to take him to the Russian's address. It was dusk when he arrived. He found Paulvitch awaiting him. The man was pacing the floor nervously. The ape was tied with a stout cord to the bed. It was the first time that Jack had ever seen Ajax thus secured. He looked questioningly at Paulvitch. The man, mumbling, explained that he believed the animal had guessed that he was to be sent away and he feared he would attempt to escape.

Paulvitch carried another piece of cord in his hand. There was a noose in one end of it which he was continually playing with. He walked back and forth, up and down the room. His pock-marked features were working horribly as he talked silent to himself. The boy had never seen him thus—it made him uneasy. At last Paulvitch stopped on the opposite side of the room, far from the ape.

"Come here," he said to the lad. "I will show you how to secure the ape should he show signs of rebellion during the trip."

The lad laughed. "It will not be necessary," he replied. "Ajax will do whatever I tell him to do."

The old man stamped his foot angrily. "Come here, as I tell you," he repeated. "If you do not do as I say you shall not accompany the ape to Dover—I will take no chances upon his escaping."

Still smiling, the lad crossed the room and stood before the Russ.

"Turn around, with your back toward me," directed the latter, "that I may show you how to bind him quickly."

The boy did as he was bid, placing his hands behind him when Paulvitch told him to do so. Instantly the old man slipped the running noose over one of the lad's wrists, took a couple of half hitches about his other wrist, and knotted the cord.

The moment that the boy was secured the attitude of the man changed. With an angry oath he wheeled his prisoner about, tripped him and hurled him violently to the floor, leaping upon his breast as he fell. From the bed the ape growled and struggled with his bonds. The boy did not cry out—a trait inherited from his savage sire whom long years in the jungle following the death of his foster mother, Kala the great ape, had taught that there was none to come to the succor of the fallen.

Paulvitch's fingers sought the lad's throat. He grinned down horribly into the face of his victim.

"Your father ruined me," he mumbled. "This will pay him. He will think that the ape did it. I will tell him that the ape did it. That I left him alone for a few minutes, and that you sneaked in and the ape killed you. I will throw your body upon the bed after I have choked the life from you, and when I bring your father he will see the ape squatting over it," and the twisted fiend cackled in gloating laughter. His fingers closed upon the boy's throat.

Behind them the growling of the maddened beast reverberated against the walls of the little room. The boy paled, but no other sign of fear or panic showed upon his countenance. He was the son of Tarzan. The fingers tightened their grip upon his throat. It was with difficulty that he breathed, gaspingly. The ape lunged against the stout cord that held him. Turning, he wrapped the cord about his hands, as a man might have done, and surged heavily backward. The great muscles stood out beneath his shaggy hide. There was a rending as of splintered wood—the cord held, but a portion of the footboard of the bed came away.

At the sound Paulvitch looked up. His hideous face went white with terror—the ape was free.

With a single bound the creature was upon him. The man shrieked. The brute wrenched him from the body of the boy. Great fingers sunk into the man's flesh. Yellow fangs gaped close to his throat—he struggled, futilely—and when they closed, the soul of Alexis Paulvitch passed into the keeping of the demons who had long been awaiting it.

The boy struggled to his feet, assisted by Akut. For two hours under the instructions of the former the ape worked upon the knots that secured his friend's wrists. Finally they gave up their secret, and the boy was free. Then he opened one of his bags and drew forth some garments. His plans had been well made. He did not consult the beast, which did all that he directed. Together they slunk from the house, but no casual observer might have noted that one of them was an ape.

CHAPTER 4

The killing of the friendless old Russian, Michael Sabrov, by his great trained ape, was a matter for newspaper comment for a few days. Lord Greystoke read of it, and while taking special precautions not to permit his name to become connected with the affair, kept himself well posted as to the police search for the anthropoid.

As was true of the general public, his chief interest in the matter centered about the mysterious disappearance of the slayer. Or at least this was true until he learned, several days subsequent to the tragedy, that his son Jack had not reported at the public school en route for which they had seen him safely ensconced in a railway carriage. Even then the father did not connect the disappearance of his son with the mystery surrounding the whereabouts of the ape. Nor was it until a month later that careful investigation revealed the fact that the boy had left the train before it pulled out of the station at London, and the cab driver had been found who had driven him to the address of the old Russian, that Tarzan of the Apes realized that Akut had in some way been connected with the disappearance of the boy.

Beyond the moment that the cab driver had deposited his fare beside the curb in front of the house in which the Russian had been quartered there was no clue. No one had seen either the boy or the ape from that instant—at least no one who still lived. The proprietor of the house identified the picture of the lad as that of one who had been a frequent visitor in the room of the old man. Aside from this he knew nothing. And there, at the door of a grimy, old building in the slums of London, the searchers came to a blank wall—baffled.

The day following the death of Alexis Paulvitch a youth accompanying his invalid grandmother, boarded a steamer at Dover. The old lady was heavily veiled, and so weakened by age and sickness that she had to be wheeled aboard the vessel in an invalid chair.

The boy would permit none but himself to wheel her, and with his own hands assisted her from the chair to the interior of their stateroom—and that was the last that was seen of the old lady by the ship's company until the pair disembarked. The boy even insisted upon doing the work of their cabin steward, since, as he explained, his grandmother was suffering from a nervous disposition that made the presence of strangers extremely distasteful to her.

Outside the cabin—and none there was aboard who knew what he did in the cabin—the lad was just as any other healthy, normal English boy might have been. He mingled with his fellow passengers, became a prime favorite with the officers, and struck up numerous friendships among the common sailors. He was generous and unaffected, yet carried an air of dignity and strength of character that inspired his many new friends with admiration as well as affection for him.

Among the passengers there was an American named Condon, a noted blackleg and crook who was "wanted" in a half dozen of the larger cities of the United States. He had paid little attention to the boy until on one occasion he had seen him accidentally display a roll of bank notes. From then on Condon cultivated the youthful Briton. He learned, easily, that the boy was traveling alone with his invalid grandmother, and that their destination was a small port on the west coast of Africa, a little below the equator; that their name was Billings, and that they had no friends in the little settlement for which they were bound. Upon the point of their purpose in visiting the place Condon found the boy reticent, and so he did not push the matter—he had learned all that he cared to know as it was.

Several times Condon attempted to draw the lad into a card game; but his victim was not interested, and the black looks of several of the other men passengers decided the American to find other means of transferring the boy's bank roll to his own pocket.

At last came the day that the steamer dropped anchor in the lee of a wooded promontory where a score or more of sheet-iron shacks making an unsightly blot upon the fair face of nature proclaimed the fact that civilization had set its heel. Straggling upon the outskirts were the thatched huts of natives, picturesque in their primeval savagery, harmonizing with the background of tropical jungle and accentuating the squalid hideousness of the white man's pioneer architecture.

The boy, leaning over the rail, was looking far beyond the man-made town deep into the God-made jungle. A little shiver of anticipation tingled his spine, and then, quite without volition, he found himself gazing into the loving eyes of his mother and the strong face of the father which mirrored, beneath its masculine strength, a love no less than the mother's eyes proclaimed. He felt himself weakening in his resolve. Nearby one of the ship's officers was shouting orders to a flotilla of native boats that was approaching to lighter the consignment of the steamer's cargo destined for this tiny post.

"When does the next steamer for England touch here?" the boy asked.

"The Emanuel ought to be along most any time now," replied the officer. "I figgered we'd find her here," and he went on with his bellowing remarks to the dusty horde drawing close to the steamer's side.

The task of lowering the boy's grandmother over the side to a waiting canoe was rather difficult. The lad insisted on being always at her side, and when at last she was safely ensconced in the bottom of the craft that was to bear them shoreward her grandson dropped catlike after her. So interested was he in seeing her comfortably disposed that he failed to notice the little package that had worked from his pocket as he assisted in lowering the sling that contained the old woman over the steamer's side, nor did he notice it even as it slipped out entirely and dropped into the sea.

Scarcely had the boat containing the boy and the old woman started for the shore than Condon hailed a canoe upon the other side of the ship, and after bargaining with its owner finally lowered his baggage and himself aboard. Once ashore he kept out of sight of the two-story atrocity that bore the legend "Hotel" to lure unsuspecting wayfarers to its multitudinous discomforts. It was quite dark before he ventured to enter and arrange for accommodations.

In a back room upon the second floor the lad was explaining, not without considerable difficulty, to his grandmother that he had decided to return to England upon the next steamer. He was endeavoring to make it plain to the old lady that she might remain in Africa if she wished but that for his part his conscience demanded that he return to his father and mother, who doubtless were even now suffering untold sorrow because of his absence; from which it may be assumed that his parents had not been acquainted with the plans that he and the old lady had made for their adventure into African wilds.

Having come to a decision the lad felt a sense of relief from the worry that had haunted him for many sleepless nights. When he closed his eyes in sleep it was to dream of a happy reunion with those at home. And as he dreamed, Fate, cruel and inexorable, crept stealthily upon him through the dark corridor of the squalid building in which he slept—Fate in the form of the American crook, Condon.

Cautiously the man approached the door of the lad's room. There he crouched listening until assured by the regular breathing of those within that both slept. Quietly he inserted a slim, skeleton key in the lock of the door. With deft fingers, long accustomed to the silent manipulation of the bars and bolts that guarded other men's property, Condon turned the key and the knob simultaneously. Gentle pressure upon the door swung it slowly inward upon its hinges. The man entered the room, closing the door behind him. The moon was temporarily overcast by heavy clouds. The interior of the apartment was shrouded in gloom. Condon groped his way toward the bed. In the far corner of the room something moved—moved with a silent stealthiness which transcended even the trained silence of the burglar. Condon heard nothing. His attention was riveted upon the bed in which he thought to find a young boy and his helpless, invalid grandmother.

The American sought only the bank roll. If he could possess himself of this without detection, well and good; but were he to meet resistance he was prepared for that too. The lad's clothes lay across a chair beside the bed. The American's fingers felt swiftly through them—the pockets contained no roll of crisp, new notes. Doubtless they were beneath the pillows of the bed. He stepped closer toward the sleeper; his hand was already half way beneath the pillow when the thick cloud that had obscured the moon rolled aside and the room was flooded with light. At the same instant the boy opened his eyes and looked straight into those of Condon. The man was suddenly conscious that the boy was alone in the bed. Then he clutched for his victim's throat. As the lad rose to meet him Condon heard a low growl at his back, then he felt his wrists seized by the boy, and realized that beneath those tapering, white fingers played muscles of steel.

He felt other hands at his throat, rough hairy hands that reached over his shoulders from behind. He cast a terrified glance backward, and the hairs of his head stiffened at the sight his eyes revealed, for grasping him from the rear was a huge, man-like ape. The bared fighting fangs of the anthropoid were close to his throat. The lad pinioned his wrists. Neither uttered a sound. Where was the grandmother? Condon's eyes swept the room in a single all-inclusive glance. His eyes bulged in horror at the realization of the truth which that glance revealed. In the power of what creatures of hideous mystery had he placed himself! Frantically he fought to beat off the lad that he might turn upon the fearsome thing at his back. Freeing one hand he struck a savage blow at the lad's face. His act seemed to unloose a thousand devils in the hairy creature clinging to his throat. Condon heard a low and savage snarl. It was the last thing that the American ever heard in this life. Then he was dragged backward upon the floor, a heavy body fell upon him, powerful teeth fastened themselves in his jugular, his head whirled in the sudden blackness which rims eternity—a moment later the ape rose from his prostrate form; but Condon did not know—he was quite dead.

The lad, horrified, sprang from the bed to lean over the body of the man. He knew that Akut had killed in his defense, as he had killed Michael Sabrov; but here, in savage Africa, far from home and friends what would they do to him and his faithful ape? The lad knew that the penalty of murder was death. He even knew that an accomplice might suffer the death penalty with the principal. Who was there who would plead for them? All would be against them. It was little more than a half-civilized community, and the chances were that they would drag Akut and him forth in the morning and hang them both to the nearest tree—he had read of such things being done in America, and Africa was worse even and wilder than the great West of his mother's native land. Yes, they would both be hanged in the morning!

Was there no escape? He thought in silence for a few moments, and then, with an exclamation of relief, he struck his palms together and turned toward his clothing upon the chair. Money would do anything! Money would save him and Akut! He felt for the bank roll in the pocket in which he had been accustomed to carry it. It was not there! Slowly at first and at last frantically he searched through the remaining pockets of his clothing. Then he dropped upon his hands and knees and examined the floor. Lighting the lamp he moved the bed to one side and, inch by inch, he felt over the entire floor. Beside the body of Condon he hesitated, but at last he nerved himself to touch it. Rolling it over he sought beneath it for the money. Nor was it there. He guessed that Condon had entered their room to rob; but he did not believe that the man had had time to possess himself of the money; however, as it was nowhere else, it must be upon the body of the dead man. Again and again he went over the room, only to return each time to the corpse; but no where could he find the money.

He was half-frantic with despair. What were they to do? In the morning they would be discovered and killed. For all his inherited size and strength he was, after all, only a little boy—a frightened, homesick little boy—reasoning faultily from the meager experience of childhood. He could think of but a single glaring fact—they had killed a fellow man, and they were among savage strangers, thirsting for the blood of the first victim whom fate cast into their clutches. This much he had gleaned from penny-dreadfuls.

And they must have money!

Again he approached the corpse. This time resolutely. The ape squatted in a corner watching his young companion. The youth commenced to remove the American's clothing piece by piece, and, piece by piece, he examined each garment minutely. Even to the shoes he searched with painstaking care, and when the last article had been removed and scrutinized he dropped back upon the bed with dilated eyes that saw nothing in the present—only a grim tableau of the future in which two forms swung silently from the limb of a great tree.

How long he sat thus he did not know; but finally he was aroused by a noise coming from the floor below. Springing quickly to his feet he blew out the lamp, and crossing the floor silently locked the door. Then he turned toward the ape, his mind made up.

Last evening he had been determined to start for home at the first opportunity, to beg the forgiveness of his parents for this mad adventure. Now he knew that he might never return to them. The blood of a fellow man was upon his hands—in his morbid reflections he had long since ceased to attribute the death of Condon to the ape. The hysteria of panic had fastened the guilt upon himself. With money he might have bought justice; but penniless!—ah, what hope could there be for strangers without money here?

But what had become of the money? He tried to recall when last he had seen it. He could not, nor, could he, would he have been able to account for its disappearance, for he had been entirely unconscious of the falling of the little package from his pocket into the sea as he clambered over the ship's side into the waiting canoe that bore him to shore.

Now he turned toward Akut. "Come!" he said, in the language of the great apes.

Forgetful of the fact that he wore only a thin pajama suit he led the way to the open window. Thrusting his head out he listened attentively. A single tree grew a few feet from the window. Nimbly the lad sprang to its bole, clinging cat-like for an instant before he clambered quietly to the ground below. Close behind him came the great ape. Two hundred yards away a spur of the jungle ran close to the straggling town. Toward this the lad led the way. None saw them, and a moment later the jungle swallowed them, and John Clayton, future Lord Greystoke, passed from the eyes and the knowledge of men.

It was late the following morning that a native houseman knocked upon the door of the room that had been assigned to Mrs. Billings and her grandson. Receiving no response he inserted his pass key in the lock, only to discover that another key was already there, but from the inside. He reported the fact to Herr Skopf, the proprietor, who at once made his way to the second floor where he, too, pounded vigorously upon the door. Receiving no reply he bent to the key hole in an attempt to look through into the room beyond. In so doing, being portly, he lost his balance, which necessitated putting a palm to the floor to maintain his equilibrium. As he did so he felt something soft and thick and wet beneath his fingers. He raised his open palm before his eyes in the dim light of the corridor and peered at it. Then he gave a little shudder, for even in the semi-darkness he saw a dark red stain upon his hand. Leaping to his feet he hurled his shoulder against the door. Herr Skopf is a heavy man—or at least he was then—I have not seen him for several years. The frail door collapsed beneath his weight, and Herr Skopf stumbled precipitately into the room beyond.

Before him lay the greatest mystery of his life. Upon the floor at his feet was the dead body of a strange man. The neck was broken and the jugular severed as by the fangs of a wild beast. The body was entirely naked, the clothing being strewn about the corpse. The old lady and her grandson were gone. The window was open. They must have disappeared through the window for the door had been locked from the inside.

But how could the boy have carried his invalid grandmother from a second story window to the ground? It was preposterous. Again Herr Skopf searched the small room. He noticed that the bed was pulled well away from the wall—why? He looked beneath it again for the third or fourth time. The two were gone, and yet his judgment told him that the old lady could not have gone without porters to carry her down as they had carried her up the previous day.

Further search deepened the mystery. All the clothing of the two was still in the room—if they had gone then they must have gone naked or in their night clothes. Herr Skopf shook his head; then he scratched it. He was baffled. He had never heard of Sherlock Holmes or he would have lost no time in invoking the aid of that celebrated sleuth, for here was a real mystery: An old woman—an invalid who had to be carried from the ship to her room in the hotel—and a handsome lad, her grandson, had entered a room on the second floor of his hostelry the day before. They had had their evening meal served in their room—that was the last that had been seen of them. At nine the following morning the corpse of a strange man had been the sole occupant of that room. No boat had left the harbor in the meantime—there was not a railroad within hundreds of miles—there was no other white settlement that the two could reach under several days of arduous marching accompanied by a well-equipped safari. They had simply vanished into thin air, for the native he had sent to inspect the ground beneath the open window had just returned to report that there was no sign of a footstep there, and what sort of creatures were they who could have dropped that distance to the soft turf without leaving spoor? Herr Skopf shuddered. Yes, it was a great mystery—there was something uncanny about the whole thing—he hated to think about it, and he dreaded the coming of night.

It was a great mystery to Herr Skopf—and, doubtless, still is.

CHAPTER 5

Captain Armand Jacot of the Foreign Legion sat upon an outspread saddle blanket at the foot of a stunted palm tree. His broad shoulders and his close-cropped head rested in luxurious ease against the rough bole of the palm. His long legs were stretched straight before him overlapping the meager blanket, his spurs buried in the sandy soil of the little desert oasis. The captain was taking his ease after a long day of weary riding across the shifting sands of the desert.

Lazily he puffed upon his cigarette and watched his orderly who was preparing his evening meal. Captain Armand Jacot was well satisfied with himself and the world. A little to his right rose the noisy activity of his troop of sun-tanned veterans, released for the time from the irksome trammels of discipline, relaxing tired muscles, laughing, joking, and smoking as they, too, prepared to eat after a twelve-hour fast. Among them, silent and taciturn, squatted five white-robed Arabs, securely bound and under heavy guard.

It was the sight of these that filled Captain Armand Jacot with the pleasurable satisfaction of a duty well-performed. For a long, hot, gaunt month he and his little troop had scoured the places of the desert waste in search of a band of marauders to the sin-stained account of which were charged innumerable thefts of camels, horses, and goats, as well as murders enough to have sent the whole unsavory gang to the guillotine several times over.

A week before, he had come upon them. In the ensuing battle he had lost two of his own men, but the punishment inflicted upon the marauders had been severe almost to extinction. A half dozen, perhaps, had escaped; but the balance, with the exception of the five prisoners, had expiated their crimes before the nickel jacketed bullets of the legionaries. And, best of all, the ring leader, Achmet ben Houdin, was among the prisoners.

From the prisoners Captain Jacot permitted his mind to traverse the remaining miles of sand to the little garrison post where, upon the morrow, he should find awaiting him with eager welcome his wife and little daughter. His eyes softened to the memory of them, as they always did. Even now he could see the beauty of the mother reflected in the childish lines of little Jeanne's face, and both those faces would be smiling up into his as he swung from his tired mount late the following afternoon. Already he could feel a soft cheek pressed close to each of his—velvet against leather.

His reverie was broken in upon by the voice of a sentry summoning a non-commissioned officer. Captain Jacot raised his eyes. The sun had not yet set; but the shadows of the few trees huddled about the water hole and of his men and their horses stretched far away into the east across the now golden sand. The sentry was pointing in this direction, and the corporal, through narrowed lids, was searching the distance. Captain Jacot rose to his feet. He was not a man content to see through the eyes of others. He must see for himself. Usually he saw things long before others were aware that there was anything to see—a trait that had won for him the sobriquet of Hawk. Now he saw, just beyond the long shadows, a dozen specks rising and falling among the sands. They disappeared and reappeared, but always they grew larger. Jacot recognized them immediately. They were horsemen—horsemen of the desert. Already a sergeant was running toward him. The entire camp was straining its eyes into the distance. Jacot gave a few terse orders to the sergeant who saluted, turned upon his heel and returned to the men. Here he gathered a dozen who saddled their horses, mounted and rode out to meet the strangers. The remaining men disposed themselves in readiness for instant action. It was not entirely beyond the range of possibilities that the horsemen riding thus swiftly toward the camp might be friends of the prisoners bent upon the release of their kinsmen by a sudden attack. Jacot doubted this, however, since the strangers were evidently making no attempt to conceal their presence. They were galloping rapidly toward the camp in plain view of all. There might be treachery lurking beneath their fair appearance; but none who knew The Hawk would be so gullible as to hope to trap him thus.

The sergeant with his detail met the Arabs two hundred yards from the camp. Jacot could see him in conversation with a tall, white-robed figure—evidently the leader of the band. Presently the sergeant and this Arab rode side by side toward camp. Jacot awaited them. The two reined in and dismounted before him.

"Sheik Amor ben Khatour," announced the sergeant by way of introduction.

Captain Jacot eyed the newcomer. He was acquainted with nearly every principal Arab within a radius of several hundred miles. This man he never had seen. He was a tall, weather beaten, sour looking man of sixty or more. His eyes were narrow and evil. Captain Jacot did not relish his appearance.

"Well?" he asked, tentatively.

The Arab came directly to the point.

"Achmet ben Houdin is my sister's son," he said. "If you will give him into my keeping I will see that he sins no more against the laws of the French."

Jacot shook his head. "That cannot be," he replied. "I must take him back with me. He will be properly and fairly tried by a civil court. If he is innocent he will be released."

"And if he is not innocent?" asked the Arab.

"He is charged with many murders. For any one of these, if he is proved guilty, he will have to die."

The Arab's left hand was hidden beneath his burnous. Now he withdrew it disclosing a large goatskin purse, bulging and heavy with coins. He opened the mouth of the purse and let a handful of the contents trickle into the palm of his right hand—all were pieces of good French gold. From the size of the purse and its bulging proportions Captain Jacot concluded that it must contain a small fortune. Sheik Amor ben Khatour dropped the spilled gold pieces one by one back into the purse. Jacot was eyeing him narrowly. They were alone. The sergeant, having introduced the visitor, had withdrawn to some little distance—his back was toward them. Now the sheik, having returned all the gold pieces, held the bulging purse outward upon his open palm toward Captain Jacot.

"Achmet ben Houdin, my sister's son, *might* escape tonight," he said. "Eh?"

Captain Armand Jacot flushed to the roots of his close-cropped hair. Then he went very white and took a half-step toward the Arab. His fists were clenched. Suddenly he thought better of whatever impulse was moving him.

"Sergeant!" he called. The non-commissioned officer hurried toward him, saluting as his heels clicked together before his superior.

"Take this black dog back to his people," he ordered. "See that they leave at once. Shoot the first man who comes within range of camp tonight."

Sheik Amor ben Khatour drew himself up to his full height. His evil eyes narrowed. He raised the bag of gold level with the eyes of the French officer.

"You will pay more than this for the life of Achmet ben Houdin, my sister's son," he said. "And as much again for the name that you have called me and a hundred fold in sorrow in the bargain."

"Get out of here!" growled Captain Armand Jacot, "before I kick you out."

All of this happened some three years before the opening of this tale. The trail of Achmet ben Houdin and his accomplices is a matter of record—you may verify it if you care to. He met the death he deserved, and he met it with the stoicism of the Arab.

A month later little Jeanne Jacot, the seven-year-old daughter of Captain Armand Jacot, mysteriously disappeared. Neither the wealth of her father and mother, or all the powerful resources of the great republic were able to wrest the secret of her whereabouts from the inscrutable desert that had swallowed her and her abductor.

A reward of such enormous proportions was offered that many adventurers were attracted to the hunt. This was no case for the modern detective of civilization, yet several of these threw themselves into the search—the bones of some are already bleaching beneath the African sun upon the silent sands of the Sahara.

Two Swedes, Carl Jenssen and Sven Malbihn, after three years of following false leads at last gave up the search far to the south of the Sahara to turn their attention to the more profitable business of ivory poaching. In a great district they were already known for their relentless cruelty and their greed for ivory. The natives feared and hated them. The European governments in whose possessions they worked had long sought them; but, working their way slowly out of the north they had learned many things in the no-man's-land south of the Sahara which gave them immunity from capture through easy avenues of escape that were unknown to those who pursued them. Their raids were sudden and swift. They seized ivory and retreated into the trackless wastes of the north before the guardians of the territory they raped could be made aware of their presence. Relentlessly they slaughtered elephants themselves as well as stealing ivory from the natives. Their following consisted of a hundred or more renegade Arabs and Negro slaves—a fierce, relentless band of cut-throats. Remember them—Carl Jenssen and Sven Malbihn, yellow-bearded, Swedish giants—for you will meet them later.

In the heart of the jungle, hidden away upon the banks of a small unexplored tributary of a large river that empties into the Atlantic not so far from the equator, lay a small, heavily palisaded village. Twenty palm-thatched, beehive huts sheltered its black population, while a half-dozen goat skin tents in the center of the clearing housed the score of Arabs who found shelter here while, by trading and raiding, they collected the cargoes which their ships of the desert bore northward twice each year to the market of Timbuktu.

Playing before one of the Arab tents was a little girl of ten—a black-haired, black-eyed little girl who, with her nut-brown skin and graceful carriage looked every inch a daughter of the desert. Her little fingers were busily engaged in fashioning a skirt of grasses for a much-disheveled doll which a kindly disposed slave had made for her a year or two before. The head of the doll was rudely chipped from ivory, while the body was a rat skin stuffed with grass. The arms and legs were bits of wood, perforated at one end and sewn to the rat skin torso. The doll was quite hideous and altogether disreputable and soiled, but Meriem thought it the most beautiful and adorable thing in the whole world, which is not so strange in view of the fact that it was the only object within that world upon which she might bestow her confidence and her love.

Everyone else with whom Meriem came in contact was, almost without exception, either indifferent to her or cruel. There was, for example, the old black hag who looked after her, Mabunu—toothless, filthy and ill tempered. She lost no opportunity to cuff the little girl, or even inflict minor tortures upon her, such as pinching, or, as she had twice done, searing the tender flesh with hot coals. And there was The Sheik, her father. She feared him more than she did Mabunu. He often scolded her for nothing, quite habitually terminating his tirades by cruelly beating her, until her little body was black and blue.

But when she was alone she was happy, playing with Geeka, or decking her hair with wild flowers, or making ropes of grasses. She was always busy and always singing—when they left her alone. No amount of cruelty appeared sufficient to crush the innate happiness and sweetness from her full little heart. Only when The Sheik was near was she quiet and subdued. Him she feared with a fear that was at times almost hysterical terror. She feared the gloomy jungle too—the cruel jungle that surrounded the little village with chattering monkeys and screaming birds by day and the roaring and coughing and moaning of the carnivora by night. Yes, she feared the jungle; but so much more did she fear The Sheik that many times it was in her childish head to run away, out into the terrible jungle forever rather than longer to face the ever present terror of her father.

As she sat there this day before The Sheik's goatskin tent, fashioning a skirt of grasses for Geeka, The Sheik appeared suddenly approaching. Instantly the look of happiness faded from the child's face. She shrunk aside in an attempt to scramble from the path of the leathern-faced old Arab; but she was not quick enough. With a brutal kick the man sent her sprawling upon her face, where she lay quite still, tearless but trembling. Then, with an oath at her, the man passed into the tent. The old, black hag shook with appreciative laughter, disclosing an occasional and lonesome yellow fang.

When she was sure The Sheik had gone, the little girl crawled to the shady side of the tent, where she lay quite still, hugging Geeka close to her breast, her little form racked at long intervals with choking sobs. She dared not cry aloud, since that would have brought The Sheik upon her again. The anguish in her little heart was not alone the anguish of physical pain; but that infinitely more pathetic anguish—of love denied a childish heart that yearns for love.

Little Meriem could scarce recall any other existence than that of the stern cruelty of The Sheik and Mabunu. Dimly, in the back of her childish memory there lurked a blurred recollection of a gentle mother; but Meriem was not sure but that even this was but a dream picture induced by her own desire for the caresses she never received, but which she lavished upon the much loved Geeka. Never was such a spoiled child as Geeka. Its little mother, far from fashioning her own conduct after the example set her by her father and nurse, went to the extreme of indulgence. Geeka was kissed a thousand times a day. There was play in which Geeka was naughty; but the little mother never punished. Instead, she caressed and fondled; her attitude influenced solely by her own pathetic desire for love.

Now, as she pressed Geeka close to her, her sobs lessened gradually, until she was able to control her voice, and pour out her misery into the ivory ear of her only confidante.

"Geeka loves Meriem," she whispered. "Why does The Sheik, my father, not love me, too? Am I so naughty? I try to be good; but I never know why he strikes me, so I cannot tell what I have done which displeases him. Just now he kicked me and hurt me so, Geeka; but I was only sitting before the tent making a skirt for you. That must be wicked, or he would not have kicked me for it. But why is it wicked, Geeka? Oh dear! I do not know, I do not know. I wish, Geeka, that I were dead. Yesterday the hunters brought in the body of El Adrea. El Adrea was quite dead. No more will he slink silently upon his unsuspecting prey. No more will his great head and his maned shoulders strike terror to the hearts of the grass eaters at the drinking ford by night. No more will his thundering roar shake the ground. El Adrea is dead. They beat his body terribly when it was brought into the village; but El Adrea did not mind. He did not feel the blows, for he was dead. When I am dead, Geeka, neither shall I feel the blows of Mabunu, or the kicks of The Sheik, my father. Then shall I be happy. Oh, Geeka, how I wish that I were dead!"

If Geeka contemplated a remonstrance it was cut short by sounds of altercation beyond the village gates. Meriem listened. With the curiosity of childhood she would have liked to have run down there and learn what it was that caused the men to talk so loudly. Others of the village were already trooping in the direction of the noise. But Meriem did not dare. The Sheik would be there, doubtless, and if he saw her it would be but another opportunity to abuse her, so Meriem lay still and listened.

Presently she heard the crowd moving up the street toward The Sheik's tent. Cautiously she stuck her little head around the edge of the tent. She could not resist the temptation, for the sameness of the village life was monotonous, and she craved diversion. What she saw was two strangers—white men. They were alone, but as they approached she learned from the talk of the natives that surrounded them that they possessed a considerable following that was camped outside the village. They were coming to palaver with The Sheik.

The old Arab met them at the entrance to his tent. His eyes narrowed wickedly when they had appraised the newcomers. They stopped before him, exchanging greetings. They had come to trade for ivory they said. The Sheik grunted. He had no ivory. Meriem gasped. She knew that in a near-by hut the great tusks were piled almost to the roof. She poked her little head further forward to get a better view of the strangers. How white their skins! How yellow their great beards!

Suddenly one of them turned his eyes in her direction. She tried to dodge back out of sight, for she feared all men; but he saw her. Meriem noticed the look of almost shocked surprise that crossed his face. The Sheik saw it too, and guessed the cause of it.

"I have no ivory," he repeated. "I do not wish to trade. Go away. Go now."

He stepped from his tent and almost pushed the strangers about in the direction of the gates. They demurred, and then The Sheik threatened. It would have been suicide to have disobeyed, so the two men turned and left the village, making their way immediately to their own camp.

The Sheik returned to his tent; but he did not enter it. Instead he walked to the side where little Meriem lay close to the goat skin wall, very frightened. The Sheik stooped and clutched her by the arm. Viciously he jerked her to her feet, dragged her to the entrance of the tent, and shoved her viciously within. Following her he again seized her, beating her ruthlessly.

"Stay within!" he growled. "Never let the strangers see thy face. Next time you show yourself to strangers I shall kill you!"

With a final vicious cuff he knocked the child into a far corner of the tent, where she lay stifling her moans, while The Sheik paced to and fro muttering to himself. At the entrance sat Mabunu, muttering and chuckling.

In the camp of the strangers one was speaking rapidly to the other.

"There is no doubt of it, Malbihn," he was saying. "Not the slightest; but why the old scoundrel hasn't claimed the reward long since is what puzzles me."

"There are some things dearer to an Arab, Jenssen, than money," returned the first speaker—"revenge is one of them."

"Anyhow it will not harm to try the power of gold," replied Jenssen.

Malbihn shrugged.

"Not on The Sheik," he said. "We might try it on one of his people; but The Sheik will not part with his revenge for gold. To offer it to him would only confirm his suspicions that we must have awakened when we were talking to him before his tent. If we got away with our lives, then, we should be fortunate."

"Well, try bribery, then," assented Jenssen.

But bribery failed—grewsomely. The tool they selected after a stay of several days in their camp outside the village was a tall, old headman of The Sheik's native contingent. He fell to the lure of the shining metal, for he had lived upon the coast and knew the power of gold. He promised to bring them what they craved, late that night.

Immediately after dark the two white men commenced to make arrangements to break camp. By midnight all was prepared. The porters lay beside their loads, ready to swing them aloft at a moment's notice. The armed askaris loitered between the balance of the safari and the Arab village, ready to form a rear guard for the retreat that was to begin the moment that the head man brought that which the white masters awaited.

Presently there came the sound of footsteps along the path from the village. Instantly the askaris and the whites were on the alert. More than a single man was approaching. Jenssen stepped forward and challenged the newcomers in a low whisper.

"Who comes?" he queried.

"Mbeeda," came the reply.

Mbeeda was the name of the traitorous head man. Jenssen was satisfied, though he wondered why Mbeeda had brought others with him. Presently he understood. The thing they fetched lay upon a litter borne by two men. Jenssen cursed beneath his breath. Could the fool be bringing them a corpse? They had paid for a living prize!

The bearers came to a halt before the white men.

"This has your gold purchased," said one of the two. They set the litter down, turned and vanished into the darkness toward the village. Malbihn looked at Jenssen, a crooked smile twisting his lips. The thing upon the litter was covered with a piece of cloth.

"Well?" queried the latter. "Raise the covering and see what you have bought. Much money shall we realize on a corpse—especially after the six months beneath the burning sun that will be consumed in carrying it to its destination!"

"The fool should have known that we desired her alive," grumbled Malbihn, grasping a corner of the cloth and jerking the cover from the thing that lay upon the litter.

At sight of what lay beneath both men stepped back—involuntary oaths upon their lips—for there before them lay the dead body of Mbeeda, the faithless head man.

Five minutes later the safari of Jenssen and Malbihn was forcing its way rapidly toward the west, nervous askaris guarding the rear from the attack they momentarily expected.

CHAPTER 6

His first night in the jungle was one which the son of Tarzan held longest in his memory. No savage carnivora menaced him. There was never a sign of hideous barbarian. Or, if there were, the boy's troubled mind took no cognizance of them. His conscience was harassed by the thought of his mother's suffering. Self-blame plunged him into the depths of misery. The killing of the American caused him little or no remorse. The fellow had earned his fate. Jack's regret on this score was due mainly to the effect which the death of Condon had had upon his own plans. Now he could not return directly to his parents as he had planned. Fear of the primitive, borderland law, of which he had read highly colored, imaginary tales, had thrust him into the jungle a fugitive. He dared not return to the coast at this point—not that he was so greatly influenced through personal fear as from a desire to shield his father and mother from further sorrow and from the shame of having their honored name dragged through the sordid degradation of a murder trial.

With returning day the boy's spirits rose. With the rising sun rose new hope within his breast. He would return to civilization by another way. None would guess that he had been connected with the killing of the stranger in the little out-of-the-way trading post upon a remote shore.

Crouched close to the great ape in the crotch of a tree the boy had shivered through an almost sleepless night. His light pajamas had been but little protection from the chill dampness of the jungle, and only that side of him which was pressed against the warm body of his shaggy companion approximated to comfort.

And so he welcomed the rising sun with its promise of warmth as well as light—the blessed sun, dispeller of physical and mental ills.

He shook Akut into wakefulness.

"Come," he said. "I am cold and hungry. We will search for food, out there in the sunlight," and he pointed to an open plain, dotted with stunted trees and strewn with jagged rock.

The boy slid to the ground as he spoke, but the ape first looked carefully about, sniffing the morning air. Then, satisfied that no danger lurked near, he descended slowly to the ground beside the boy."

"Numa, and Sabor his mate, feast upon those who descend first and look afterward, while those who look first and descend afterward live to feast themselves." Thus the old ape imparted to the son of Tarzan the boy's first lesson in jungle lore. Side by side they set off across the rough plain, for the boy wished first to be warm. The ape showed him the best places to dig for rodents and worms; but the lad only gagged at the thought of devouring the repulsive things. Some eggs they found, and these he sucked raw, as also he ate roots and tubers which Akut unearthed. Beyond the plain and across a low bluff they came upon water—brackish, ill-smelling stuff in a shallow water hole, the sides and bottom of which were trampled by the feet of many beasts. A herd of zebra galloped away as they approached.

The lad was too thirsty by now to cavil at anything even remotely resembling water, so he drank his fill while Akut stood with raised head, alert for any danger. Before the ape drank he cautioned the boy to be watchful; but as he drank he raised his head from time to time to cast a quick glance toward a clump of bushes a hundred yards away upon the opposite side of the water hole. When he had done he rose and spoke to the boy, in the language that was their common heritage—the tongue of the great apes.

"There is no danger near?" he asked.

"None," replied the boy. "I saw nothing move while you drank."

"Your eyes will help you but little in the jungle," said the ape.

"Here, if you would live, you must depend upon your ears and your nose but most upon your nose. When we came down to drink I knew that no danger lurked near upon this side of the water hole, for else the zebras would have discovered it and fled before we came; but upon the other side toward which the wind blows danger might lie concealed. We could not smell it for its scent is being blown in the other direction, and so I bent my ears and eyes down wind where my nose cannot travel."

"And you found—nothing?" asked the lad, with a laugh.

"I found Numa crouching in that clump of bushes where the tall grasses grow," and Akut pointed.

"A lion?" exclaimed the boy. "How do you know? I can see nothing."

"Numa is there, though," replied the great ape. "First I heard him sigh. To you the sigh of Numa may sound no different from the other noises which the wind makes among the grasses and the trees; but later you must learn to know the sigh of Numa. Then I watched and at last I saw the tall grasses moving at one point to a force other than the force of the wind. See, they are spread there upon either side of Numa's great body, and as he breathes—you see? You see the little motion at either side that is not caused by the wind—the motion that none of the other grasses have?"

The boy strained his eyes—better eyes than the ordinary boy inherits—and at last he gave a little exclamation of discovery.

"Yes," he said, "I see. He lies there," and he pointed. "His head is toward us. Is he watching us?"

"Numa is watching us," replied Akut, "but we are in little danger, unless we approach too close, for he is lying upon his kill. His belly is almost full, or we should hear him crunching the bones. He is watching us in silence merely from curiosity. Presently he will resume his feeding or he will rise and come down to the water for a drink. As he neither fears or desires us he will not try to hide his presence from us; but now is an excellent time to learn to know Numa, for you must learn to know him well if you would live long in the jungle. Where the great apes are many Numa leaves us alone. Our fangs are long and strong, and we can fight; but when we are alone and he is hungry we are no match for him. Come, we will circle him and catch his scent. The sooner you learn to know it the better; but keep close to the trees, as we go around him, for Numa often does that which he is least expected to do. And keep your ears and your eyes and your nose open. Remember always that there may be an enemy behind every bush, in every tree and amongst every clump of jungle grass. While you are avoiding Numa do not run into the jaws of Sabor, his mate. Follow me," and Akut set off in a wide circle about the water hole and the crouching lion.

The boy followed close upon his heels, his every sense upon the alert, his nerves keyed to the highest pitch of excitement. This was life! For the instant he forgot his resolutions of a few minutes past to hasten to the coast at some other point than that at which he had landed and make his way immediately back to London. He thought now only of the savage joy of living, and of pitting one's wits and prowess against the wiles and might of the savage jungle brood which haunted the broad plains and the gloomy forest aisles of the great, untamed continent. He knew no fear. His father had had none to transmit to him; but honor and conscience he did have and these were to trouble him many times as they battled with his inherent love of freedom for possession of his soul.

They had passed but a short distance to the rear of Numa when the boy caught the unpleasant odor of the carnivore. His face lighted with a smile. Something told him that he would have known that scent among a myriad of others even if Akut had not told him that a lion lay near. There was a strange familiarity—a weird familiarity in it that made the short hairs rise at the nape of his neck, and brought his upper lip into an involuntary snarl that bared his fighting fangs. There was a sense of stretching of the skin about his ears, for all the world as though those members were flattening back against his skull in preparation for deadly combat. His skin tingled. He was aglow with a pleasurable sensation that he never before had known. He was, upon the instant, another creature—wary, alert, ready. Thus did the scent of Numa, the lion, transform the boy into a beast.

He had never seen a lion—his mother had gone to great pains to prevent it. But he had devoured countless pictures of them, and now he was ravenous to feast his eyes upon the king of beasts in the flesh. As he trailed Akut he kept an eye cocked over one shoulder, rearward, in the hope that Numa might rise from his kill and reveal himself. Thus it happened that he dropped some little way behind Akut, and the next he knew he was recalled suddenly to a contemplation of other matters than the hidden Numa by a shrill scream of warning from the Ape. Turning his eyes quickly in the direction of his companion, the boy saw that, standing in the path directly before him, which sent tremors of excitement racing along every nerve of his body. With body half-merging from a clump of bushes in which she must have lain hidden stood a sleek and beautiful lioness. Her yellow-green eyes were round and staring, boring straight into the eyes of the boy. Not ten paces separated them. Twenty paces behind the lioness stood the great ape, bellowing instructions to the boy and hurling taunts at the lioness in an evident effort to attract her attention from the lad while he gained the shelter of a near-by tree.

But Sabor was not to be diverted. She had her eyes upon the lad. He stood between her and her mate, between her and the kill. It was suspicious. Probably he had ulterior designs upon her lord and master or upon the fruits of their hunting. A lioness is short tempered. Akut's bellowing annoyed her. She uttered a little rumbling growl, taking a step toward the boy.

"The tree!" screamed Akut.

The boy turned and fled, and at the same instant the lioness charged. The tree was but a few paces away. A limb hung ten feet from the ground, and as the boy leaped for it the lioness leaped for him. Like a monkey he pulled himself up and to one side. A great forepaw caught him a glancing blow at the hips—just grazing him. One curved talon hooked itself into the waist band of his pajama trousers, ripping them from him as the lioness sped by. Half-naked the lad drew himself to safety as the beast turned and leaped for him once more.

Akut, from a near-by tree, jabbered and scolded, calling the lioness all manner of foul names. The boy, patterning his conduct after that of his preceptor, unstoppered the vials of his invective upon the head of

which from little careless remarks dropped at home he knew his father possessed. That would
better at least than a lifetime of the cramped and cloying restrictions of civilization.

s rather contented than otherwise as he made his way in the direction of the coast, for while
liberty and the savage pleasures of the wild his conscience was at the same time clear, for he
as doing all that lay in his power to return to his parents. He rather looked forward, too, to
nen again—creatures of his own kind—for there had been many occasions upon which he had
r companionship than that of the old ape. The affair with the blacks still rankled in his heart.

hed them in such innocent good fellowship and with such childlike assurance of a hospitable
he reception which had been accorded him had proved a shock to his boyish ideals. He no
pon the black man as his brother; but rather as only another of the innumerable foes of the
gle—a beast of prey which walked upon two feet instead of four.

cks were his enemies there were those in the world who were not. There were those who
lcome him with open arms; who would accept him as a friend and brother, and with whom
nctuary from every enemy. Yes, there were always white men. Somewhere along the coast
pths of the jungle itself there were white men. To them he would be a welcome visitor. They
him. And there were also the great apes—the friends of his father and of Akut. How glad they
ive the son of Tarzan of the Apes! He hoped that he could come upon them before he found
pon the coast. He wanted to be able to tell his father that he had known his old friends of
e had hunted with them, that he had joined with them in their savage life, and their fierce,
nies—the strange ceremonies of which Akut had tried to tell him. It cheered him immensely
ese happy meetings. Often he rehearsed the long speech which he would make to the apes,
ld tell them of the life of their former king since he had left them.

he would play at meeting with white men. Then he would enjoy their consternation at sight
boy trapped in the war togs of a black warrior and roaming the jungle with only a great ape
a.

ys passed, and with the traveling and the hunting and the climbing the boy's muscles
is agility increased until even phlegmatic Akut marvelled at the prowess of his pupil. And
his great strength and revelling in it, became careless. He strode through the jungle, his
, defying danger. Where Akut took to the trees at the first scent of Numa, the lad laughed
king of beasts and walked boldly past him. Good fortune was with him for a long time. The
well-fed, perhaps, or the very boldness of the strange creature which invaded their domain
ith surprise that thoughts of attack were banished from their minds as they stood,
hing his approach and his departure. Whatever the cause, however, the fact remains that
ns the boy passed within a few paces of some great lion without arousing more than a

s are necessarily alike in character or temper. They differ as greatly as do individuals of the
cause ten lions act similarly under similar conditions one cannot say that the eleventh lion
he chances are that he will not. The lion is a creature of high nervous development. He
he reasons. Having a nervous system and brains he is the possessor of temperament, which
ly by extraneous causes. One day the boy met the eleventh lion. The former was walking
n upon which grew little clumps of bushes. Akut was a few yards to the left of the lad who
scover the presence of Numa.

lled the boy, laughing. "Numa lies hid in the bushes to my right. Take to the trees. Akut!
an, will protect you," and the boy, laughing, kept straight along his way which led close
n which Numa lay concealed.

d to him to come away, but the lad only flourished his spear and executed an improvised
y his contempt for the king of beasts. Closer and closer to the dread destroyer he came,

the enemy, until in realization of the futility of words as weapons he bethought himself of something heavier to hurl. There was nothing but dead twigs and branches at hand, but these he flung at the upturned, snarling face of Sabor just as his father had before him twenty years ago, when as a boy he too had taunted and tantalized the great cats of the jungle.

The lioness fretted about the bole of the tree for a short time; but finally, either realizing the uselessness of her vigil, or prompted by the pangs of hunger, she stalked majestically away and disappeared in the brush that hid her lord, who had not once shown himself during the altercation.

Freed from their retreats Akut and the boy came to the ground, to take up their interrupted journey once more. The old ape scolded the lad for his carelessness.

"Had you not been so intent upon the lion behind you you might have discovered the lioness much sooner than you did,"

"But you passed right by her without seeing her," retorted the boy.

Akut was chagrined.

"It is thus," he said, "that jungle folk die. We go cautiously for a lifetime, and then, just for an instant, we forget, and—" he ground his teeth in mimicry of the crunching of great jaws in flesh. "It is a lesson," he resumed. "You have learned that you may not for too long keep your eyes and your ears and your nose all bent in the same direction."

That night the son of Tarzan was colder than he ever had been in all his life. The pajama trousers had not been heavy; but they had been much heavier than nothing. And the next day he roasted in the hot sun, for again their way led much across wide and treeless plains.

It was still in the boy's mind to travel to the south, and circle back to the coast in search of another outpost of civilization. He had said nothing of this plan to Akut, for he knew that the old ape would look with displeasure upon any suggestion that savored of separation.

For a month the two wandered on, the boy learning rapidly the laws of the jungle; his muscles adapting themselves to the new mode of life that had been thrust upon them. The thews of the sire had been transmitted to the son—it needed only the hardening of use to develop them. The lad found that it came quite naturally to him to swing through the trees. Even at great heights he never felt the slightest dizziness, and when he had caught the knack of the swing and the release, he could hurl himself through space from branch to branch with even greater agility than the heavier Akut.

And with exposure came a toughening and hardening of his smooth, white skin, browning now beneath the sun and wind. He had removed his pajama jacket one day to bathe in a little stream that was too small to harbor crocodiles, and while he and Akut had been disporting themselves in the cool waters a monkey had dropped down from the over hanging trees, snatched up the boy's single remaining article of civilized garmenture, and scampered away with it.

For a time Jack was angry; but when he had been without the jacket for a short while he began to realize that being half-clothed is infinitely more uncomfortable than being entirely naked. Soon he did not miss his clothing in the least, and from that he came to revel in the freedom of his unhampered state. Occasionally a smile would cross his face as he tried to imagine the surprise of his schoolmates could they but see him now. They would envy him. Yes, how they would envy him. He felt sorry for them at such times, and again as he thought of them amid luxuries and comforts of their English homes, happy with their fathers and mothers, a most uncomfortable lump would arise into the boy's throat, and he would see a vision of his mother's face through a blur of mist that came unbidden to his eyes. Then it was that he urged Akut onward, for now they were headed westward toward the coast. The old ape thought that they were searching for a tribe of his own kind, nor did the boy disabuse his mind of this belief. It would do to tell Akut of his real plans when they had come within sight of civilization.

One day as they were moving slowly along beside a river they came unexpectedly upon a native village. Some children were playing beside the water. The boy's heart leaped within his breast at sight of them—for over a month he had seen no human being. What if these were naked savages? What if their skins were black? Were they not creatures fashioned in the mold of their Maker, as was he? They were his brothers and sisters! He started toward them. With a low warning Akut laid a hand upon his arm to hold him back. The boy shook himself free, and with a shout of greeting ran forward toward the ebon players.

The sound of his voice brought every head erect. Wide eyes viewed him for an instant, and then, with screams of terror, the children turned and fled toward the village. At their heels ran their mothers, and from the village gate, in response to the alarm, came a score of warriors, hastily snatched spears and shields ready in their hands.

At sight of the consternation he had wrought the boy halted. The glad smile faded from his face as with wild shouts and menacing gestures the warriors ran toward him. Akut was calling to him from behind to turn and flee, telling him that the blacks would kill him. For a moment he stood watching them coming, then he raised his hand with the palm toward them in signal for them to halt, calling out at the same time that he came as a friend—that he had only wanted to play with their children. Of course they did not understand a word that he addressed to them, and their answer was what any naked creature who had run suddenly out of the jungle upon their women and children might have expected—a shower of spears. The missiles struck all about the boy, but none touched him. Again his spine tingled and the short hairs lifted at the nape of his neck and along the top of his scalp. His eyes narrowed. Sudden hatred flared in them to wither the expression of glad friendliness that had lighted them but an instant before. With a low snarl, quite similar to that of a baffled beast, he turned and ran into the jungle. There was Akut awaiting him in a tree. The ape urged him to hasten in flight, for the wise old anthropoid knew that they two, naked and unarmed, were no match for the sinewy black warriors who would doubtless make some sort of search for them through the jungle.

But a new power moved the son of Tarzan. He had come with a boy's glad and open heart to offer his friendship to these people who were human beings like himself. He had been met with suspicion and spears. They had not even listened to him. Rage and hatred consumed him. When Akut urged speed he held back. He wanted to fight, yet his reason made it all too plain that it would be but a foolish sacrifice of his life to meet these armed men with his naked hands and his teeth—already the boy thought of his teeth, of his fighting fangs, when possibility of combat loomed close.

Moving slowly through the trees he kept his eyes over his shoulder, though he no longer neglected the possibilities of other dangers which might lurk on either hand or ahead—his experience with the lioness did not need a repetition to insure the permanency of the lesson it had taught. Behind he could hear the savages advancing with shouts and cries. He lagged further behind until the pursuers were in sight. They did not see him, for they were not looking among the branches of the trees for human quarry. The lad kept just ahead of them. For a mile perhaps they continued the search, and then they turned back toward the village. Here was the boy's opportunity, that for which he had been waiting, while the hot blood of revenge coursed through his veins until he saw his pursuers through a scarlet haze.

When they turned back he turned and followed them. Akut was no longer in sight. Thinking that the boy followed he had gone on further ahead. He had no wish to tempt fate within range of those deadly spears. Slinking silently from tree to tree the boy dogged the footsteps of the returning warriors. At last one dropped behind his fellows as they followed a narrow path toward the village. A grim smile lit the lad's face. Swiftly he hurried forward until he moved almost above the unconscious black—stalking him as Sheeta, the panther, stalked his prey, as the boy had seen Sheeta do on many occasions.

Suddenly and silently he leaped forward and downward upon the broad shoulders of his prey. In the instant of contact his fingers sought and found the man's throat. The weight of the boy's body hurled the black heavily to the ground, the knees in his back knocking the breath from him as he struck. Then a set of strong, white teeth fastened themselves in his neck, and muscular fingers closed tighter upon his wind-pipe. For a time the warrior struggled frantically, throwing himself about in an effort to dislodge his antagonist;

but all the while he was weakening and all the while the grim and s tenaciously to him, and dragged him slowly into the bush to one side c

Hidden there at last, safe from the prying eyes of searchers, should t him, the lad choked the life from the body of his victim. At last he kne by limp relaxation, that the warrior was dead. Then a strange desire se and thrilled. Involuntarily he leaped to his feet and placed one foot u expanded. He raised his face toward the heavens and opened his mou seemed screaming within him for outward expression, but no sound pa a full minute, his face turned toward the sky, his breast heaving to the p of vengeance.

The silence which marked the first great kill of the son of Tarzan wa the hideous victory cry of the bull ape had marked the kills of his migh

CHAPTER 7

Akut, discovering that the boy was not close behind him, turned back a short distance in return when he was brought to a sudden and startl moving through the trees toward him. It was the boy, yet could it be? In back hung an oblong shield such as the black warriors who had attacke and arm were bands of iron and brass, while a loin cloth was twisted ab thrust through its folds.

When the boy saw the ape he hastened forward to exhibit his trophies. of his newly won possessions. Boastfully he recounted the details of his

"With my bare hands and my teeth I killed him," he said. "I would ha chose to be my enemies. And now that I have a spear I shall show Num; a foe. Only the white men and the great apes, Akut, are our friends. The avoid or kill. This have I learned of the jungle."

They made a detour about the hostile village, and resumed their jour much pride in his new weapons and ornaments. He practiced continuall object ahead hour by hour as they traveled their loitering way, until h youthful muscles may attain to speedily. All the while his training went longer was there a single jungle spoor but was an open book to the ke indefinite spoor that elude the senses of civilized man and are only parti; came to be familiar friends of the eager boy. He could differentiate the in by scent, and he could tell, too, whether an animal was approaching or waning strength of its effluvium. Nor did he need the evidence of his eyes lions or four up wind,—a hundred yards away or half a mile.

Much of this had Akut taught him, but far more was instinctive know inherited from his father. He had come to love the jungle life. The const the many deadly foes that lurked by day and by night along the pathway o to the spirit of adventure which breathes strong in the heart of every rec Yet, though he loved it, he had not let his selfish desires outweigh the s to a realization of the moral wrong which lay beneath the adventurous Africa. His love of father and mother was strong within him, too strong to was undoubtedly causing them days of sorrow. And so he held tight to hi the coast where he might communicate with them and receive funds for sure that he could now persuade his parents to let him spend at least

African estate be something

And so he he enjoyed th knew that he meeting whit longed for ot He had appr welcome tha longer looke bloodthirsty

But if the always would he might fin or even in h would befrie would be to r a trading po: the jungle, th primeval cer to dwell upo in which he

At other ti of a naked w as his compa

And so th developed a the boy, rea proud head in the face o lions he met so filled the round-eyed, on many oc warning gro

But no tw human fam will do likev thinks, ther is affected v across a sm; was the first

"Run, Ak I, the son o beside the l

The ape s war dance t

until, with a sudden, angry growl, the lion rose from his bed not ten paces from the youth. A huge fellow he was, this lord of the jungle and the desert. A shaggy mane clothed his shoulders. Cruel fangs armed his great jaws. His yellow-green eyes blazed with hatred and challenge.

The boy, with his pitifully inadequate spear ready in his hand, realized quickly that this lion was different from the others he had met; but he had gone too far now to retreat. The nearest tree lay several yards to his left—the lion could be upon him before he had covered half the distance, and that the beast intended to charge none could doubt who looked upon him now. Beyond the lion was a thorn tree—only a few feet beyond him. It was the nearest sanctuary but Numa stood between it and his prey.

The feel of the long spear shaft in his hand and the sight of the tree beyond the lion gave the lad an idea—a preposterous idea—a ridiculous, forlorn hope of an idea; but there was no time now to weigh chances—there was but a single chance, and that was the thorn tree. If the lion charged it would be too late—the lad must charge first, and to the astonishment of Akut and none the less of Numa, the boy leaped swiftly toward the beast. Just for a second was the lion motionless with surprise and in that second Jack Clayton put to the crucial test an accomplishment which he had practiced at school.

Straight for the savage brute he ran, his spear held butt foremost across his body. Akut shrieked in terror and amazement. The lion stood with wide, round eyes awaiting the attack, ready to rear upon his hind feet and receive this rash creature with blows that could crush the skull of a buffalo.

Just in front of the lion the boy placed the butt of his spear upon the ground, gave a mighty spring, and, before the bewildered beast could guess the trick that had been played upon him, sailed over the lion's head into the rending embrace of the thorn tree—safe but lacerated.

Akut had never before seen a pole-vault. Now he leaped up and down within the safety of his own tree, screaming taunts and boasts at the discomfited Numa, while the boy, torn and bleeding, sought some position in his thorny retreat in which he might find the least agony. He had saved his life; but at considerable cost in suffering. It seemed to him that the lion would never leave, and it was a full hour before the angry brute gave up his vigil and strode majestically away across the plain. When he was at a safe distance the boy extricated himself from the thorn tree; but not without inflicting new wounds upon his already tortured flesh.

It was many days before the outward evidence of the lesson he had learned had left him; while the impression upon his mind was one that was to remain with him for life. Never again did he uselessly tempt fate.

He took long chances often in his after life; but only when the taking of chances might further the attainment of some cherished end—and, always thereafter, he practiced pole-vaulting.

For several days the boy and the ape lay up while the former recovered from the painful wounds inflicted by the sharp thorns. The great anthropoid licked the wounds of his human friend, nor, aside from this, did they receive other treatment, but they soon healed, for healthy flesh quickly replaces itself.

When the lad felt fit again the two continued their journey toward the coast, and once more the boy's mind was filled with pleasurable anticipation.

And at last the much dreamed of moment came. They were passing through a tangled forest when the boy's sharp eyes discovered from the lower branches through which he was traveling an old but well-marked spoor—a spoor that set his heart to leaping—the spoor of man, of white men, for among the prints of naked feet were the well defined outlines of European made boots. The trail, which marked the passage of a good-sized company, pointed north at right angles to the course the boy and the ape were taking toward the coast.

Doubtless these white men knew the nearest coast settlement. They might even be headed for it now. At any rate it would be worth while overtaking them if even only for the pleasure of meeting again creatures of his own kind. The lad was all excitement; palpitant with eagerness to be off in pursuit. Akut demurred. He wanted nothing of men. To him the lad was a fellow ape, for he was the son of the king of apes. He tried to dissuade the boy, telling him that soon they should come upon a tribe of their own folk where some day when he was older the boy should be king as his father had before him. But Jack was obdurate. He insisted that he wanted to see white men again. He wanted to send a message to his parents. Akut listened and as he listened the intuition of the beast suggested the truth to him—the boy was planning to return to his own kind.

The thought filled the old ape with sorrow. He loved the boy as he had loved the father, with the loyalty and faithfulness of a hound for its master. In his ape brain and his ape heart he had nursed the hope that he and the lad would never be separated. He saw all his fondly cherished plans fading away, and yet he remained loyal to the lad and to his wishes. Though disconsolate he gave in to the boy's determination to pursue the safari of the white men, accompanying him upon what he believed would be their last journey together.

The spoor was but a couple of days old when the two discovered it, which meant that the slow-moving caravan was but a few hours distant from them whose trained and agile muscles could carry their bodies swiftly through the branches above the tangled undergrowth which had impeded the progress of the laden carriers of the white men.

The boy was in the lead, excitement and anticipation carrying him ahead of his companion to whom the attainment of their goal meant only sorrow. And it was the boy who first saw the rear guard of the caravan and the white men he had been so anxious to overtake.

Stumbling along the tangled trail of those ahead a dozen heavily laden blacks who, from fatigue or sickness, had dropped behind were being prodded by the black soldiers of the rear guard, kicked when they fell, and then roughly jerked to their feet and hustled onward. On either side walked a giant white man, heavy blonde beards almost obliterating their countenances. The boy's lips formed a glad cry of salutation as his eyes first discovered the whites—a cry that was never uttered, for almost immediately he witnessed that which turned his happiness to anger as he saw that both the white men were wielding heavy whips brutally upon the naked backs of the poor devils staggering along beneath loads that would have overtaxed the strength and endurance of strong men at the beginning of a new day.

Every now and then the rear guard and the white men cast apprehensive glances rearward as though momentarily expecting the materialization of some long expected danger from that quarter. The boy had paused after his first sight of the caravan, and now was following slowly in the wake of the sordid, brutal spectacle. Presently Akut came up with him. To the beast there was less of horror in the sight than to the lad, yet even the great ape growled beneath his breath at useless torture being inflicted upon the helpless slaves. He looked at the boy. Now that he had caught up with the creatures of his own kind, why was it that he did not rush forward and greet them? He put the question to his companion.

"They are fiends," muttered the boy. "I would not travel with such as they, for if I did I should set upon them and kill them the first time they beat their people as they are beating them now; but," he added, after a moment's thought, "I can ask them the whereabouts of the nearest port, and then, Akut, we can leave them."

The ape made no reply, and the boy swung to the ground and started at a brisk walk toward the safari. He was a hundred yards away, perhaps, when one of the whites caught sight of him. The man gave a shout of alarm, instantly levelling his rifle upon the boy and firing. The bullet struck just in front of its mark, scattering turf and fallen leaves against the lad's legs. A second later the other white and the black soldiers of the rear guard were firing hysterically at the boy.

Jack leaped behind a tree, unhit. Days of panic ridden flight through the jungle had filled Carl Jenssen and Sven Malbihn with jangling nerves and their native boys with unreasoning terror. Every new note from behind sounded to their frightened ears the coming of The Sheik and his bloodthirsty entourage. They were in a blue funk, and the sight of the naked white warrior stepping silently out of the jungle through which the enemy, until in realization of the futility of words as weapons he bethought himself of something heavier to hurl. There was nothing but dead twigs and branches at hand, but these he flung at the upturned, snarling face of Sabor just as his father had before him twenty years ago, when as a boy he too had taunted and tantalized the great cats of the jungle.

The lioness fretted about the bole of the tree for a short time; but finally, either realizing the uselessness of her vigil, or prompted by the pangs of hunger, she stalked majestically away and disappeared in the brush that hid her lord, who had not once shown himself during the altercation.

Freed from their retreats Akut and the boy came to the ground, to take up their interrupted journey once more. The old ape scolded the lad for his carelessness.

"Had you not been so intent upon the lion behind you you might have discovered the lioness much sooner than you did,"

"But you passed right by her without seeing her," retorted the boy.

Akut was chagrined.

"It is thus," he said, "that jungle folk die. We go cautiously for a lifetime, and then, just for an instant, we forget, and—" he ground his teeth in mimicry of the crunching of great jaws in flesh. "It is a lesson," he resumed. "You have learned that you may not for too long keep your eyes and your ears and your nose all bent in the same direction."

That night the son of Tarzan was colder than he ever had been in all his life. The pajama trousers had not been heavy; but they had been much heavier than nothing. And the next day he roasted in the hot sun, for again their way led much across wide and treeless plains.

It was still in the boy's mind to travel to the south, and circle back to the coast in search of another outpost of civilization. He had said nothing of this plan to Akut, for he knew that the old ape would look with displeasure upon any suggestion that savored of separation.

For a month the two wandered on, the boy learning rapidly the laws of the jungle; his muscles adapting themselves to the new mode of life that had been thrust upon them. The thews of the sire had been transmitted to the son—it needed only the hardening of use to develop them. The lad found that it came quite naturally to him to swing through the trees. Even at great heights he never felt the slightest dizziness, and when he had caught the knack of the swing and the release, he could hurl himself through space from branch to branch with even greater agility than the heavier Akut.

And with exposure came a toughening and hardening of his smooth, white skin, browning now beneath the sun and wind. He had removed his pajama jacket one day to bathe in a little stream that was too small to harbor crocodiles, and while he and Akut had been disporting themselves in the cool waters a monkey had dropped down from the over hanging trees, snatched up the boy's single remaining article of civilized garmenture, and scampered away with it.

For a time Jack was angry; but when he had been without the jacket for a short while he began to realize that being half-clothed is infinitely more uncomfortable than being entirely naked. Soon he did not miss his clothing in the least, and from that he came to revel in the freedom of his unhampered state. Occasionally a smile would cross his face as he tried to imagine the surprise of his schoolmates could they but see him now. They would envy him. Yes, how they would envy him. He felt sorry for them at such times, and again as he thought of them amid luxuries and comforts of their English homes, happy with their fathers and mothers, a most uncomfortable lump would arise into the boy's throat, and he would see a vision of his mother's face through a blur of mist that came unbidden to his eyes. Then it was that he urged Akut onward, for now they were headed westward toward the coast. The old ape thought that they were searching for a tribe of his own kind, nor did the boy disabuse his mind of this belief. It would do to tell Akut of his real plans when they had come within sight of civilization.

One day as they were moving slowly along beside a river they came unexpectedly upon a native village. Some children were playing beside the water. The boy's heart leaped within his breast at sight of them—for over a month he had seen no human being. What if these were naked savages? What if their skins were black? Were they not creatures fashioned in the mold of their Maker, as was he? They were his brothers and sisters! He started toward them. With a low warning Akut laid a hand upon his arm to hold him back. The boy shook himself free, and with a shout of greeting ran forward toward the ebon players.

The sound of his voice brought every head erect. Wide eyes viewed him for an instant, and then, with screams of terror, the children turned and fled toward the village. At their heels ran their mothers, and from the village gate, in response to the alarm, came a score of warriors, hastily snatched spears and shields ready in their hands.

At sight of the consternation he had wrought the boy halted. The glad smile faded from his face as with wild shouts and menacing gestures the warriors ran toward him. Akut was calling to him from behind to turn and flee, telling him that the blacks would kill him. For a moment he stood watching them coming, then he raised his hand with the palm toward them in signal for them to halt, calling out at the same time that he came as a friend—that he had only wanted to play with their children. Of course they did not understand a word that he addressed to them, and their answer was what any naked creature who had run suddenly out of the jungle upon their women and children might have expected—a shower of spears. The missiles struck all about the boy, but none touched him. Again his spine tingled and the short hairs lifted at the nape of his neck and along the top of his scalp. His eyes narrowed. Sudden hatred flared in them to wither the expression of glad friendliness that had lighted them but an instant before. With a low snarl, quite similar to that of a baffled beast, he turned and ran into the jungle. There was Akut awaiting him in a tree. The ape urged him to hasten in flight, for the wise old anthropoid knew that they two, naked and unarmed, were no match for the sinewy black warriors who would doubtless make some sort of search for them through the jungle.

But a new power moved the son of Tarzan. He had come with a boy's glad and open heart to offer his friendship to these people who were human beings like himself. He had been met with suspicion and spears. They had not even listened to him. Rage and hatred consumed him. When Akut urged speed he held back. He wanted to fight, yet his reason made it all too plain that it would be but a foolish sacrifice of his life to meet these armed men with his naked hands and his teeth—already the boy thought of his teeth, of his fighting fangs, when possibility of combat loomed close.

Moving slowly through the trees he kept his eyes over his shoulder, though he no longer neglected the possibilities of other dangers which might lurk on either hand or ahead—his experience with the lioness did not need a repetition to insure the permanency of the lesson it had taught. Behind he could hear the savages advancing with shouts and cries. He lagged further behind until the pursuers were in sight. They did not see him, for they were not looking among the branches of the trees for human quarry. The lad kept just ahead of them. For a mile perhaps they continued the search, and then they turned back toward the village. Here was the boy's opportunity, that for which he had been waiting, while the hot blood of revenge coursed through his veins until he saw his pursuers through a scarlet haze.

When they turned back he turned and followed them. Akut was no longer in sight. Thinking that the boy followed he had gone on further ahead. He had no wish to tempt fate within range of those deadly spears. Slinking silently from tree to tree the boy dogged the footsteps of the returning warriors. At last one dropped behind his fellows as they followed a narrow path toward the village. A grim smile lit the lad's face. Swiftly he hurried forward until he moved almost above the unconscious black—stalking him as Sheeta, the panther, stalked his prey, as the boy had seen Sheeta do on many occasions.

Suddenly and silently he leaped forward and downward upon the broad shoulders of his prey. In the instant of contact his fingers sought and found the man's throat. The weight of the boy's body hurled the black heavily to the ground, the knees in his back knocking the breath from him as he struck. Then a set of strong, white teeth fastened themselves in his neck, and muscular fingers closed tighter upon his wind-pipe. For a time the warrior struggled frantically, throwing himself about in an effort to dislodge his antagonist;

but all the while he was weakening and all the while the grim and silent thing he could not see clung tenaciously to him, and dragged him slowly into the bush to one side of the trail.

Hidden there at last, safe from the prying eyes of searchers, should they miss their fellow and return for him, the lad choked the life from the body of his victim. At last he knew by the sudden struggle, followed by limp relaxation, that the warrior was dead. Then a strange desire seized him. His whole being quivered and thrilled. Involuntarily he leaped to his feet and placed one foot upon the body of his kill. His chest expanded. He raised his face toward the heavens and opened his mouth to voice a strange, weird cry that seemed screaming within him for outward expression, but no sound passed his lips—he just stood there for a full minute, his face turned toward the sky, his breast heaving to the pent emotion, like an animate statue of vengeance.

The silence which marked the first great kill of the son of Tarzan was to typify all his future kills, just as the hideous victory cry of the bull ape had marked the kills of his mighty sire.

CHAPTER 7

Akut, discovering that the boy was not close behind him, turned back to search for him. He had gone but a short distance in return when he was brought to a sudden and startled halt by sight of a strange figure moving through the trees toward him. It was the boy, yet could it be? In his hand was a long spear, down his back hung an oblong shield such as the black warriors who had attacked them had worn, and upon ankle and arm were bands of iron and brass, while a loin cloth was twisted about the youth's middle. A knife was thrust through its folds.

When the boy saw the ape he hastened forward to exhibit his trophies. Proudly he called attention to each of his newly won possessions. Boastfully he recounted the details of his exploit.

"With my bare hands and my teeth I killed him," he said. "I would have made friends with them but they chose to be my enemies. And now that I have a spear I shall show Numa, too, what it means to have me for a foe. Only the white men and the great apes, Akut, are our friends. Them we shall seek, all others must we avoid or kill. This have I learned of the jungle."

They made a detour about the hostile village, and resumed their journey toward the coast. The boy took much pride in his new weapons and ornaments. He practiced continually with the spear, throwing it at some object ahead hour by hour as they traveled their loitering way, until he gained a proficiency such as only youthful muscles may attain to speedily. All the while his training went on under the guidance of Akut. No longer was there a single jungle spoor but was an open book to the keen eyes of the lad, and those other indefinite spoor that elude the senses of civilized man and are only partially appreciable to his savage cousin came to be familiar friends of the eager boy. He could differentiate the innumerable species of the herbivora by scent, and he could tell, too, whether an animal was approaching or departing merely by the waxing or waning strength of its effluvium. Nor did he need the evidence of his eyes to tell him whether there were two lions or four up wind,—a hundred yards away or half a mile.

Much of this had Akut taught him, but far more was instinctive knowledge—a species of strange intuition inherited from his father. He had come to love the jungle life. The constant battle of wits and senses against the many deadly foes that lurked by day and by night along the pathway of the wary and the unwary appealed to the spirit of adventure which breathes strong in the heart of every red-blooded son of primordial Adam. Yet, though he loved it, he had not let his selfish desires outweigh the sense of duty that had brought him to a realization of the moral wrong which lay beneath the adventurous escapade that had brought him to Africa. His love of father and mother was strong within him, too strong to permit unalloyed happiness which was undoubtedly causing them days of sorrow. And so he held tight to his determination to find a port upon the coast where he might communicate with them and receive funds for his return to London. There he felt sure that he could now persuade his parents to let him spend at least a portion of his time upon those

African estates which from little careless remarks dropped at home he knew his father possessed. That would be something, better at least than a lifetime of the cramped and cloying restrictions of civilization.

And so he was rather contented than otherwise as he made his way in the direction of the coast, for while he enjoyed the liberty and the savage pleasures of the wild his conscience was at the same time clear, for he knew that he was doing all that lay in his power to return to his parents. He rather looked forward, too, to meeting white men again—creatures of his own kind—for there had been many occasions upon which he had longed for other companionship than that of the old ape. The affair with the blacks still rankled in his heart. He had approached them in such innocent good fellowship and with such childlike assurance of a hospitable welcome that the reception which had been accorded him had proved a shock to his boyish ideals. He no longer looked upon the black man as his brother; but rather as only another of the innumerable foes of the bloodthirsty jungle—a beast of prey which walked upon two feet instead of four.

But if the blacks were his enemies there were those in the world who were not. There were those who always would welcome him with open arms; who would accept him as a friend and brother, and with whom he might find sanctuary from every enemy. Yes, there were always white men. Somewhere along the coast or even in the depths of the jungle itself there were white men. To them he would be a welcome visitor. They would befriend him. And there were also the great apes—the friends of his father and of Akut. How glad they would be to receive the son of Tarzan of the Apes! He hoped that he could come upon them before he found a trading post upon the coast. He wanted to be able to tell his father that he had known his old friends of the jungle, that he had hunted with them, that he had joined with them in their savage life, and their fierce, primeval ceremonies—the strange ceremonies of which Akut had tried to tell him. It cheered him immensely to dwell upon these happy meetings. Often he rehearsed the long speech which he would make to the apes, in which he would tell them of the life of their former king since he had left them.

At other times he would play at meeting with white men. Then he would enjoy their consternation at sight of a naked white boy trapped in the war togs of a black warrior and roaming the jungle with only a great ape as his companion.

And so the days passed, and with the traveling and the hunting and the climbing the boy's muscles developed and his agility increased until even phlegmatic Akut marvelled at the prowess of his pupil. And the boy, realizing his great strength and revelling in it, became careless. He strode through the jungle, his proud head erect, defying danger. Where Akut took to the trees at the first scent of Numa, the lad laughed in the face of the king of beasts and walked boldly past him. Good fortune was with him for a long time. The lions he met were well-fed, perhaps, or the very boldness of the strange creature which invaded their domain so filled them with surprise that thoughts of attack were banished from their minds as they stood, round-eyed, watching his approach and his departure. Whatever the cause, however, the fact remains that on many occasions the boy passed within a few paces of some great lion without arousing more than a warning growl.

But no two lions are necessarily alike in character or temper. They differ as greatly as do individuals of the human family. Because ten lions act similarly under similar conditions one cannot say that the eleventh lion will do likewise—the chances are that he will not. The lion is a creature of high nervous development. He thinks, therefore he reasons. Having a nervous system and brains he is the possessor of temperament, which is affected variously by extraneous causes. One day the boy met the eleventh lion. The former was walking across a small plain upon which grew little clumps of bushes. Akut was a few yards to the left of the lad who was the first to discover the presence of Numa.

"Run, Akut," called the boy, laughing. "Numa lies hid in the bushes to my right. Take to the trees. Akut! I, the son of Tarzan, will protect you," and the boy, laughing, kept straight along his way which led close beside the brush in which Numa lay concealed.

The ape shouted to him to come away, but the lad only flourished his spear and executed an improvised war dance to show his contempt for the king of beasts. Closer and closer to the dread destroyer he came, until, with a sudden, angry growl, the lion rose from his bed not ten paces from the youth. A huge fellow he was, this lord of the jungle and the desert. A shaggy mane clothed his shoulders. Cruel fangs armed his great jaws. His yellow-green eyes blazed with hatred and challenge.

The boy, with his pitifully inadequate spear ready in his hand, realized quickly that this lion was different from the others he had met; but he had gone too far now to retreat. The nearest tree lay several yards to his left—the lion could be upon him before he had covered half the distance, and that the beast intended to charge none could doubt who looked upon him now. Beyond the lion was a thorn tree—only a few feet beyond him. It was the nearest sanctuary but Numa stood between it and his prey.

The feel of the long spear shaft in his hand and the sight of the tree beyond the lion gave the lad an idea—a preposterous idea—a ridiculous, forlorn hope of an idea; but there was no time now to weigh chances—there was but a single chance, and that was the thorn tree. If the lion charged it would be too late—the lad must charge first, and to the astonishment of Akut and none the less of Numa, the boy leaped swiftly toward the beast. Just for a second was the lion motionless with surprise and in that second Jack Clayton put to the crucial test an accomplishment which he had practiced at school.

Straight for the savage brute he ran, his spear held butt foremost across his body. Akut shrieked in terror and amazement. The lion stood with wide, round eyes awaiting the attack, ready to rear upon his hind feet and receive this rash creature with blows that could crush the skull of a buffalo.

Just in front of the lion the boy placed the butt of his spear upon the ground, gave a mighty spring, and, before the bewildered beast could guess the trick that had been played upon him, sailed over the lion's head into the rending embrace of the thorn tree—safe but lacerated.

Akut had never before seen a pole-vault. Now he leaped up and down within the safety of his own tree, screaming taunts and boasts at the discomfited Numa, while the boy, torn and bleeding, sought some position in his thorny retreat in which he might find the least agony. He had saved his life; but at considerable cost in suffering. It seemed to him that the lion would never leave, and it was a full hour before the angry brute gave up his vigil and strode majestically away across the plain. When he was at a safe distance the boy extricated himself from the thorn tree; but not without inflicting new wounds upon his already tortured flesh.

It was many days before the outward evidence of the lesson he had learned had left him; while the impression upon his mind was one that was to remain with him for life. Never again did he uselessly tempt fate.

He took long chances often in his after life; but only when the taking of chances might further the attainment of some cherished end—and, always thereafter, he practiced pole-vaulting.

For several days the boy and the ape lay up while the former recovered from the painful wounds inflicted by the sharp thorns. The great anthropoid licked the wounds of his human friend, nor, aside from this, did they receive other treatment, but they soon healed, for healthy flesh quickly replaces itself.

When the lad felt fit again the two continued their journey toward the coast, and once more the boy's mind was filled with pleasurable anticipation.

And at last the much dreamed of moment came. They were passing through a tangled forest when the boy's sharp eyes discovered from the lower branches through which he was traveling an old but well-marked spoor—a spoor that set his heart to leaping—the spoor of man, of white men, for among the prints of naked feet were the well defined outlines of European made boots. The trail, which marked the passage of a good-sized company, pointed north at right angles to the course the boy and the ape were taking toward the coast.

Doubtless these white men knew the nearest coast settlement. They might even be headed for it now. At any rate it would be worth while overtaking them if even only for the pleasure of meeting again creatures of his own kind. The lad was all excitement; palpitant with eagerness to be off in pursuit. Akut demurred. He wanted nothing of men. To him the lad was a fellow ape, for he was the son of the king of apes. He tried to dissuade the boy, telling him that soon they should come upon a tribe of their own folk where some day when he was older the boy should be king as his father had before him. But Jack was obdurate. He insisted that he wanted to see white men again. He wanted to send a message to his parents. Akut listened and as he listened the intuition of the beast suggested the truth to him—the boy was planning to return to his own kind.

The thought filled the old ape with sorrow. He loved the boy as he had loved the father, with the loyalty and faithfulness of a hound for its master. In his ape brain and his ape heart he had nursed the hope that he and the lad would never be separated. He saw all his fondly cherished plans fading away, and yet he remained loyal to the lad and to his wishes. Though disconsolate he gave in to the boy's determination to pursue the safari of the white men, accompanying him upon what he believed would be their last journey together.

The spoor was but a couple of days old when the two discovered it, which meant that the slow-moving caravan was but a few hours distant from them whose trained and agile muscles could carry their bodies swiftly through the branches above the tangled undergrowth which had impeded the progress of the laden carriers of the white men.

The boy was in the lead, excitement and anticipation carrying him ahead of his companion to whom the attainment of their goal meant only sorrow. And it was the boy who first saw the rear guard of the caravan and the white men he had been so anxious to overtake.

Stumbling along the tangled trail of those ahead a dozen heavily laden blacks who, from fatigue or sickness, had dropped behind were being prodded by the black soldiers of the rear guard, kicked when they fell, and then roughly jerked to their feet and hustled onward. On either side walked a giant white man, heavy blonde beards almost obliterating their countenances. The boy's lips formed a glad cry of salutation as his eyes first discovered the whites—a cry that was never uttered, for almost immediately he witnessed that which turned his happiness to anger as he saw that both the white men were wielding heavy whips brutally upon the naked backs of the poor devils staggering along beneath loads that would have overtaxed the strength and endurance of strong men at the beginning of a new day.

Every now and then the rear guard and the white men cast apprehensive glances rearward as though momentarily expecting the materialization of some long expected danger from that quarter. The boy had paused after his first sight of the caravan, and now was following slowly in the wake of the sordid, brutal spectacle. Presently Akut came up with him. To the beast there was less of horror in the sight than to the lad, yet even the great ape growled beneath his breath at useless torture being inflicted upon the helpless slaves. He looked at the boy. Now that he had caught up with the creatures of his own kind, why was it that he did not rush forward and greet them? He put the question to his companion.

"They are fiends," muttered the boy. "I would not travel with such as they, for if I did I should set upon them and kill them the first time they beat their people as they are beating them now; but," he added, after a moment's thought, "I can ask them the whereabouts of the nearest port, and then, Akut, we can leave them."

The ape made no reply, and the boy swung to the ground and started at a brisk walk toward the safari. He was a hundred yards away, perhaps, when one of the whites caught sight of him. The man gave a shout of alarm, instantly levelling his rifle upon the boy and firing. The bullet struck just in front of its mark, scattering turf and fallen leaves against the lad's legs. A second later the other white and the black soldiers of the rear guard were firing hysterically at the boy.

Jack leaped behind a tree, unhit. Days of panic ridden flight through the jungle had filled Carl Jenssen and Sven Malbihn with jangling nerves and their native boys with unreasoning terror. Every new note from behind sounded to their frightened ears the coming of The Sheik and his bloodthirsty entourage. They were in a blue funk, and the sight of the naked white warrior stepping silently out of the jungle through which they had just passed had been sufficient shock to let loose in action all the pent nerve energy of Malbihn, who had been the first to see the strange apparition. And Malbihn's shout and shot had set the others going.

When their nervous energy had spent itself and they came to take stock of what they had been fighting it developed that Malbihn alone had seen anything clearly. Several of the blacks averred that they too had obtained a good view of the creature but their descriptions of it varied so greatly that Jenssen, who had seen nothing himself, was inclined to be a trifle skeptical. One of the blacks insisted that the thing had been eleven feet tall, with a man's body and the head of an elephant. Another had seen *three* immense Arabs with huge, black beards; but when, after conquering their nervousness, the rear guard advanced upon the enemy's position to investigate they found nothing, for Akut and the boy had retreated out of range of the unfriendly guns.

Jack was disheartened and sad. He had not entirely recovered from the depressing effect of the unfriendly reception he had received at the hands of the blacks, and now he had found an even more hostile one accorded him by men of his own color.

"The lesser beasts flee from me in terror," he murmured, half to himself, "the greater beasts are ready to tear me to pieces at sight. Black men would kill me with their spears or arrows. And now white men, men of my own kind, have fired upon me and driven me away. Are all the creatures of the world my enemies? Has the son of Tarzan no friend other than Akut?"

The old ape drew closer to the boy.

"There are the great apes," he said. "They only will be the friends of Akut's friend. Only the great apes will welcome the son of Tarzan. You have seen that men want nothing of you. Let us go now and continue our search for the great apes—our people."

The language of the great apes is a combination of monosyllabic gutturals, amplified by gestures and signs. It may not be literally translated into human speech; but as near as may be this is what Akut said to the boy.

The two proceeded in silence for some time after Akut had spoken. The boy was immersed in deep thought—bitter thoughts in which hatred and revenge predominated. Finally he spoke: "Very well, Akut," he said, "we will find our friends, the great apes."

The anthropoid was overjoyed; but he gave no outward demonstration of his pleasure. A low grunt was his only response, and a moment later he had leaped nimbly upon a small and unwary rodent that had been surprised at a fatal distance from its burrow. Tearing the unhappy creature in two Akut handed the lion's share to the lad.

CHAPTER 8

A year had passed since the two Swedes had been driven in terror from the savage country where The Sheik held sway. Little Meriem still played with Geeka, lavishing all her childish love upon the now almost hopeless ruin of what had never, even in its palmiest days, possessed even a slight degree of loveliness. But to Meriem, Geeka was all that was sweet and adorable. She carried to the deaf ears of the battered ivory head all her sorrows all her hopes and all her ambitions, for even in the face of hopelessness, in the clutches of the dread authority from which there was no escape, little Meriem yet cherished hopes and ambitions. It is true that her ambitions were rather nebulous in form, consisting chiefly of a desire to escape with Geeka to some remote and unknown spot where there were no Sheiks, no Mabunus—where El Adrea could find no entrance, and where she might play all day surrounded only by flowers and birds and the harmless little monkeys playing in the tree tops.

The Sheik had been away for a long time, conducting a caravan of ivory, skins, and rubber far into the north. The interim had been one of great peace for Meriem. It is true that Mabunu had still been with her, to pinch or beat her as the mood seized the villainous old hag; but Mabunu was only one. When The Sheik was there also there were two of them, and The Sheik was stronger and more brutal even than Mabunu. Little Meriem often wondered why the grim old man hated her so. It is true that he was cruel and unjust to all with whom he came in contact, but to Meriem he reserved his greatest cruelties, his most studied injustices.

Today Meriem was squatting at the foot of a large tree which grew inside the palisade close to the edge of the village. She was fashioning a tent of leaves for Geeka. Before the tent were some pieces of wood and small leaves and a few stones. These were the household utensils. Geeka was cooking dinner. As the little girl played she prattled continuously to her companion, propped in a sitting position with a couple of twigs. She was totally absorbed in the domestic duties of Geeka—so much so that she did not note the gentle swaying of the branches of the tree above her as they bent to the body of the creature that had entered them stealthily from the jungle.

In happy ignorance the little girl played on, while from above two steady eyes looked down upon her—unblinking, unwavering. There was none other than the little girl in this part of the village, which had been almost deserted since The Sheik had left long months before upon his journey toward the north.

And out in the jungle, an hour's march from the village, The Sheik was leading his returning caravan homeward.

A year had passed since the white men had fired upon the lad and driven him back into the jungle to take up his search for the only remaining creatures to whom he might look for companionship—the great apes. For months the two had wandered eastward, deeper and deeper into the jungle. The year had done much for the boy—turning his already mighty muscles to thews of steel, developing his woodcraft to a point where it verged upon the uncanny, perfecting his arboreal instincts, and training him in the use of both natural and artificial weapons.

He had become at last a creature of marvelous physical powers and mental cunning. He was still but a boy, yet so great was his strength that the powerful anthropoid with which he often engaged in mimic battle was no match for him. Akut had taught him to fight as the bull ape fights, nor ever was there a teacher better fitted to instruct in the savage warfare of primordial man, or a pupil better equipped to profit by the lessons of a master.

As the two searched for a band of the almost extinct species of ape to which Akut belonged they lived upon the best the jungle afforded. Antelope and zebra fell to the boy's spear, or were dragged down by the two powerful beasts of prey who leaped upon them from some overhanging limb or from the ambush of the undergrowth beside the trail to the water hole or the ford.

The pelt of a leopard covered the nakedness of the youth; but the wearing of it had not been dictated by any prompting of modesty. With the rifle shots of the white men showering about him he had reverted to the savagery of the beast that is inherent in each of us, but that flamed more strongly in this boy whose father had been raised a beast of prey. He wore his leopard skin at first in response to a desire to parade a trophy of his prowess, for he had slain the leopard with his knife in a hand-to-hand combat. He saw that the skin was beautiful, which appealed to his barbaric sense of ornamentation, and when it stiffened and later commenced to decompose because of his having no knowledge of how to cure or tan it was with sorrow and regret that he discarded it. Later, when he chanced upon a lone, black warrior wearing the counterpart of it, soft and clinging and beautiful from proper curing, it required but an instant to leap from above upon the shoulders of the unsuspecting black, sink a keen blade into his heart and possess the rightly preserved hide.

There were no after-qualms of conscience. In the jungle might is right, nor does it take long to inculcate this axiom in the mind of a jungle dweller, regardless of what his past training may have been. That the black would have killed him had he had the chance the boy knew full well. Neither he nor the black were any more sacred than the lion, or the buffalo, the zebra or the deer, or any other of the countless creatures who roamed, or slunk, or flew, or wriggled through the dark mazes of the forest. Each had but a single life, which was sought by many. The greater number of enemies slain the better chance to prolong that life. So the boy smiled and donned the finery of the vanquished, and went his way with Akut, searching, always searching for the elusive anthropoids who were to welcome them with open arms. And at last they found them. Deep in the jungle, buried far from sight of man, they came upon such another little natural arena as had witnessed the wild ceremony of the Dum-Dum in which the boy's father had taken part long years before.

First, at a great distance, they heard the beating of the drum of the great apes. They were sleeping in the safety of a huge tree when the booming sound smote upon their ears. Both awoke at once. Akut was the first to interpret the strange cadence.

"The great apes!" he growled. "They dance the Dum-Dum. Come, Korak, son of Tarzan, let us go to our people."

Months before Akut had given the boy a name of his own choosing, since he could not master the man given name of Jack. Korak is as near as it may be interpreted into human speech. In the language of the apes it means Killer. Now the Killer rose upon the branch of the great tree where he had been sleeping with his back braced against the stem. He stretched his lithe young muscles, the moonlight filtering through the foliage from above dappling his brown skin with little patches of light.

The ape, too, stood up, half squatting after the manner of his kind. Low growls rumbled from the bottom of his deep chest—growls of excited anticipation. The boy growled in harmony with the ape. Then the anthropoid slid softly to the ground. Close by, in the direction of the booming drum, lay a clearing which they must cross. The moon flooded it with silvery light. Half-erect, the great ape shuffled into the full glare of the moon. At his side, swinging gracefully along in marked contrast to the awkwardness of his companion, strode the boy, the dark, shaggy coat of the one brushing against the smooth, clear hide of the other. The lad was humming now, a music hall air that had found its way to the forms of the great English public school that was to see him no more. He was happy and expectant. The moment he had looked forward to for so long was about to be realized. He was coming into his own. He was coming home. As the months had dragged or flown along, retarded or spurred on as privation or adventure predominated, thoughts of his own home, while oft recurring, had become less vivid. The old life had grown to seem more like a dream than a reality, and the balking of his determination to reach the coast and return to London had finally thrown the hope of realization so remotely into the future that it too now seemed little more than a pleasant but hopeless dream.

Now all thoughts of London and civilization were crowded so far into the background of his brain that they might as well have been non-existent. Except for form and mental development he was as much an ape as the great, fierce creature at his side.

In the exuberance of his joy he slapped his companion roughly on the side of the head. Half in anger, half in play the anthropoid turned upon him, his fangs bared and glistening. Long, hairy arms reached out to seize him, and, as they had done a thousand times before, the two clinched in mimic battle, rolling upon the sward, striking, growling and biting, though never closing their teeth in more than a rough pinch. It was wondrous practice for them both. The boy brought into play wrestling tricks that he had learned at school, and many of these Akut learned to use and to foil. And from the ape the boy learned the methods that had been handed down to Akut from some common ancestor of them both, who had roamed the teeming earth when ferns were trees and crocodiles were birds.

But there was one art the boy possessed which Akut could not master, though he did achieve fair proficiency in it for an ape—boxing. To have his bull-like charges stopped and crumpled with a suddenly planted fist upon the end of his snout, or a painful jolt in the short ribs, always surprised Akut. It angered him too, and at such times his mighty jaws came nearer to closing in the soft flesh of his friend than at any other, for he was still an ape, with an ape's short temper and brutal instincts; but the difficulty was in catching his tormentor while his rage lasted, for when he lost his head and rushed madly into close quarters with the boy he discovered that the stinging hail of blows released upon him always found their mark and effectually stopped him—effectually and painfully. Then he would withdraw growling viciously, backing away with grinning jaws distended, to sulk for an hour or so.

Tonight they did not box. Just for a moment or two they wrestled playfully, until the scent of Sheeta, the panther, brought them to their feet, alert and wary. The great cat was passing through the jungle in front of them. For a moment it paused, listening. The boy and the ape growled menacingly in chorus and the carnivore moved on.

Then the two took up their journey toward the sound of the Dum-Dum. Louder and louder came the beating of the drum. Now, at last, they could hear the growling of the dancing apes, and strong to their nostrils came the scent of their kind. The lad trembled with excitement. The hair down Akut's spine stiffened—the symptoms of happiness and anger are often similar.

Silently they crept through the jungle as they neared the meeting place of the apes. Now they were in the trees, worming their way forward, alert for sentinels. Presently through a break in the foliage the scene burst upon the eager eyes of the boy. To Akut it was a familiar one; but to Korak it was all new. His nerves tingled at the savage sight. The great bulls were dancing in the moonlight, leaping in an irregular circle about the flat-topped earthen drum about which three old females sat beating its resounding top with sticks worn smooth by long years of use.

Akut, knowing the temper and customs of his kind, was too wise to make their presence known until the frenzy of the dance had passed. After the drum was quiet and the bellies of the tribe well-filled he would hail them. Then would come a parley, after which he and Korak would be accepted into membership by the community. There might be those who would object; but such could be overcome by brute force, of which he and the lad had an ample surplus. For weeks, possibly months, their presence might cause ever decreasing suspicion among others of the tribe; but eventually they would become as born brothers to these strange apes.

He hoped that they had been among those who had known Tarzan, for that would help in the introduction of the lad and in the consummation of Akut's dearest wish, that Korak should become king of the apes. It was with difficulty, however, that Akut kept the boy from rushing into the midst of the dancing anthropoids—an act that would have meant the instant extermination of them both, since the hysterical frenzy into which the great apes work themselves during the performance of their strange rites is of such a nature that even the most ferocious of the carnivora give them a wide berth at such times.

As the moon declined slowly toward the lofty, foliaged horizon of the amphitheater the booming of the drum decreased and lessened were the exertions of the dancers, until, at last, the final note was struck and the huge beasts turned to fall upon the feast they had dragged hither for the orgy.

From what he had seen and heard Akut was able to explain to Korak that the rites proclaimed the choosing of a new king, and he pointed out to the boy the massive figure of the shaggy monarch, come into his kingship, no doubt, as many human rulers have come into theirs—by the murder of his predecessor.

When the apes had filled their bellies and many of them had sought the bases of the trees to curl up in sleep Akut plucked Korak by the arm.

"Come," he whispered. "Come slowly. Follow me. Do as Akut does."

Then he advanced slowly through the trees until he stood upon a bough overhanging one side of the amphitheater. Here he stood in silence for a moment. Then he uttered a low growl. Instantly a score of apes leaped to their feet. There savage little eyes sped quickly around the periphery of the clearing. The king ape was the first to see the two figures upon the branch. He gave voice to an ominous growl. Then he took a few lumbering steps in the direction of the intruders. His hair was bristling. His legs were stiff, imparting a halting, jerky motion to his gait. Behind him pressed a number of bulls.

He stopped just a little before he came beneath the two—just far enough to be beyond their spring. Wary king! Here he stood rocking himself to and fro upon his short legs, baring his fangs in hideous grinnings, rumbling out an ever increasing volume of growls, which were slowly but steadily increasing to the proportions of roars. Akut knew that he was planning an attack upon them. The old ape did not wish to fight. He had come with the boy to cast his lot with the tribe.

"I am Akut," he said. "This is Korak. Korak is the son of Tarzan who was king of the apes. I, too, was king of the apes who dwelt in the midst of the great waters. We have come to hunt with you, to fight with you. We are great hunters. We are mighty fighters. Let us come in peace."

The king ceased his rocking. He eyed the pair from beneath his beetling brows. His bloodshot eyes were savage and crafty. His kingship was very new and he was jealous of it. He feared the encroachments of two strange apes. The sleek, brown, hairless body of the lad spelled "man," and man he feared and hated.

"Go away!" he growled. "Go away, or I will kill you."

The eager lad, standing behind the great Akut, had been pulsing with anticipation and happiness. He wanted to leap down among these hairy monsters and show them that he was their friend, that he was one of them. He had expected that they would receive him with open arms, and now the words of the king ape filled him with indignation and sorrow. The blacks had set upon him and driven him away. Then he had turned to the white men—to those of his own kind—only to hear the ping of bullets where he had expected words of cordial welcome. The great apes had remained his final hope. To them he looked for the companionship man had denied him. Suddenly rage overwhelmed him.

The king ape was almost directly beneath him. The others were formed in a half circle several yards behind the king. They were watching events interestedly. Before Akut could guess his intention, or prevent, the boy leaped to the ground directly in the path of the king, who had now succeeded in stimulating himself to a frenzy of fury.

"I am Korak!" shouted the boy. "I am the Killer. I came to live among you as a friend. You want to drive me away. Very well, then, I shall go; but before I go I shall show you that the son of Tarzan is your master, as his father was before him—that he is not afraid of your king or you."

For an instant the king ape had stood motionless with surprise. He had expected no such rash action upon the part of either of the intruders. Akut was equally surprised. Now he shouted excitedly for Korak to come back, for he knew that in the sacred arena the other bulls might be expected to come to the assistance of their king against an outsider, though there was small likelihood that the king would need assistance. Once those mighty jaws closed upon the boy's soft neck the end would come quickly. To leap to his rescue would mean death for Akut, too; but the brave old ape never hesitated. Bristling and growling, he dropped to the sward just as the king ape charged.

The beast's hands clutched for their hold as the animal sprang upon the lad. The fierce jaws were wide distended to bury the yellow fangs deeply in the brown hide. Korak, too, leaped forward to meet the attack; but leaped crouching, beneath the outstretched arms. At the instant of contact the lad pivoted on one foot, and with all the weight of his body and the strength of his trained muscles drove a clenched fist into the bull's stomach. With a gasping shriek the king ape collapsed, clutching futilely for the agile, naked creature nimbly sidestepping from his grasp.

Howls of rage and dismay broke from the bull apes behind the fallen king, as with murder in their savage little hearts they rushed forward upon Korak and Akut; but the old ape was too wise to court any such unequal encounter. To have counseled the boy to retreat now would have been futile, and Akut knew it. To delay even a second in argument would have sealed the death warrants of them both. There was but a single hope and Akut seized it. Grasping the lad around the waist he lifted him bodily from the ground, and turning ran swiftly toward another tree which swung low branches above the arena. Close upon their heels swarmed the hideous mob; but Akut, old though he was and burdened by the weight of the struggling Korak, was still fleeter than his pursuers.

With a bound he grasped a low limb, and with the agility of a little monkey swung himself and the boy to temporary safety. Nor did he hesitate even here; but raced on through the jungle night, bearing his burden to safety. For a time the bulls pursued; but presently, as the swifter outdistanced the slower and found themselves separated from their fellows they abandoned the chase, standing roaring and screaming until the jungle reverberated to their hideous noises. Then they turned and retraced their way to the amphitheater.

When Akut felt assured that they were no longer pursued he stopped and released Korak. The boy was furious.

"Why did you drag me away?" he cried. "I would have taught them! I would have taught them all! Now they will think that I am afraid of them."

"What they think cannot harm you," said Akut. "You are alive. If I had not brought you away you would be dead now and so would I. Do you not know that even Numa slinks from the path of the great apes when there are many of them and they are mad?"

CHAPTER 9

It was an unhappy Korak who wandered aimlessly through the jungle the day following his inhospitable reception by the great apes. His heart was heavy from disappointment. Unsatisfied vengeance smoldered in his breast. He looked with hatred upon the denizens of his jungle world, bearing his fighting fangs and growling at those that came within radius of his senses. The mark of his father's early life was strong upon him and enhanced by months of association with beasts, from whom the imitative faculty of youth had absorbed a countless number of little mannerisms of the predatory creatures of the wild.

He bared his fangs now as naturally and upon as slight provocation as Sheeta, the panther, bared his. He growled as ferociously as Akut himself. When he came suddenly upon another beast his quick crouch bore a strange resemblance to the arching of a cat's back. Korak, the killer, was looking for trouble. In his heart of hearts he hoped to meet the king ape who had driven him from the amphitheater. To this end he insisted upon remaining in the vicinity; but the exigencies of the perpetual search for food led them several miles further away during day.

They were moving slowly down wind, and warily because the advantage was with whatever beast might chance to be hunting ahead of them, where their scent-spoor was being borne by the light breeze. Suddenly the two halted simultaneously. Two heads were cocked upon one side. Like creatures hewn from solid rock they stood immovable, listening. Not a muscle quivered. For several seconds they remained thus, then Korak advanced cautiously a few yards and leaped nimbly into a tree. Akut followed close upon his heels. Neither had made a noise that would have been appreciable to human ears at a dozen paces.

Stopping often to listen they crept forward through the trees. That both were greatly puzzled was apparent from the questioning looks they cast at one another from time to time. Finally the lad caught a glimpse of a palisade a hundred yards ahead, and beyond it the tops of some goatskin tents and a number of thatched huts. His lip upcurled in a savage snarl. Blacks! How he hated them. He signed to Akut to remain where he was while he advanced to reconnoiter.

Woe betide the unfortunate villager whom The Killer came upon now. Slinking through the lower branches of the trees, leaping lightly from one jungle giant to its neighbor where the distance was not too great, or swinging from one hand hold to another Korak came silently toward the village. He heard a voice beyond the palisade and toward that he made his way. A great tree overhung the enclosure at the very point from which the voice came. Into this Korak crept. His spear was ready in his hand. His ears told him of the proximity of a human being. All that his eyes required was a single glance to show him his target. Then, lightning like, the missile would fly to its goal. With raised spear he crept among the branches of the tree glaring narrowly downward in search of the owner of the voice which rose to him from below.

At last he saw a human back. The spear hand flew to the limit of the throwing position to gather the force that would send the iron shod missile completely through the body of the unconscious victim. And then The Killer paused. He leaned forward a little to get a better view of the target. Was it to insure more perfect aim, or had there been that in the graceful lines and the childish curves of the little body below him that had held in check the spirit of murder running riot in his veins?

He lowered his spear cautiously that it might make no noise by scraping against foliage or branches. Quietly he crouched in a comfortable position along a great limb and there he lay with wide eyes looking down in

EDGAR RICE BURROUGHS

wonder upon the creature he had crept upon to kill—looking down upon a little girl, a little nut brown maiden. The snarl had gone from his lip. His only expression was one of interested attention—he was trying to discover what the girl was doing. Suddenly a broad grin overspread his face, for a turn of the girl's body had revealed Geeka of the ivory head and the rat skin torso—Geeka of the splinter limbs and the disreputable appearance. The little girl raised the marred face to hers and rocking herself backward and forward crooned a plaintive Arab lullaby to the doll. A softer light entered the eyes of The Killer. For a long hour that passed very quickly to him Korak lay with gaze riveted upon the playing child. Not once had he had a view of the girl's full face. For the most part he saw only a mass of wavy, black hair, one brown little shoulder exposed upon the side from where her single robe was caught beneath her arm, and a shapely knee protruding from beneath her garment as she sat cross legged upon the ground. A tilt of the head as she emphasized some maternal admonition to the passive Geeka revealed occasionally a rounded cheek or a piquant little chin. Now she was shaking a slim finger at Geeka, reprovingly, and again she crushed to her heart this only object upon which she might lavish the untold wealth of her childish affections.

Korak, momentarily forgetful of his bloody mission, permitted the fingers of his spear hand to relax a little their grasp upon the shaft of his formidable weapon. It slipped, almost falling; but the occurrence recalled The Killer to himself. It reminded him of his purpose in slinking stealthily upon the owner of the voice that had attracted his vengeful attention. He glanced at the spear, with its well-worn grip and cruel, barbed head. Then he let his eyes wander again to the dainty form below him. In imagination he saw the heavy weapon shooting downward. He saw it pierce the tender flesh, driving its way deep into the yielding body. He saw the ridiculous doll drop from its owner's arms to lie sprawled and pathetic beside the quivering body of the little girl. The Killer shuddered, scowling at the inanimate iron and wood of the spear as though they constituted a sentient being endowed with a malignant mind.

Korak wondered what the girl would do were he to drop suddenly from the tree to her side. Most likely she would scream and run away. Then would come the men of the village with spears and guns and set upon him. They would either kill him or drive him away. A lump rose in the boy's throat. He craved the companionship of his own kind, though he scarce realized how greatly. He would have liked to slip down beside the little girl and talk with her, though he knew from the words he had overheard that she spoke a language with which he was unfamiliar. They could have talked by signs a little. That would have been better than nothing. Too, he would have been glad to see her face. What he had glimpsed assured him that she was pretty; but her strongest appeal to him lay in the affectionate nature revealed by her gentle mothering of the grotesque doll.

At last he hit upon a plan. He would attract her attention, and reassure her by a smiling greeting from a greater distance. Silently he wormed his way back into the tree. It was his intention to hail her from beyond the palisade, giving her the feeling of security which he imagined the stout barricade would afford.

He had scarcely left his position in the tree when his attention was attracted by a considerable noise upon the opposite side of the village. By moving a little he could see the gate at the far end of the main street. A number of men, women and children were running toward it. It swung open, revealing the head of a caravan upon the opposite side. In trooped the motley organization—black slaves and dark hued Arabs of the northern deserts; cursing camel drivers urging on their vicious charges; overburdened donkeys, waving sadly pendulous ears while they endured with stoic patience the brutalities of their masters; goats, sheep and horses. Into the village they all trooped behind a tall, sour, old man, who rode without greetings to those who shrunk from his path directly to a large goatskin tent in the center of the village. Here he spoke to a wrinkled hag.

Korak, from his vantage spot, could see it all. He saw the old man asking questions of the black woman, and then he saw the latter point toward a secluded corner of the village which was hidden from the main street by the tents of the Arabs and the huts of the natives in the direction of the tree beneath which the little girl played. This was doubtless her father, thought Korak. He had been away and his first thought upon returning was of his little daughter. How glad she would be to see him! How she would run and throw herself into his arms, to be crushed to his breast and covered with his kisses. Korak sighed. He thought of his own father and mother far away in london.

He returned to his place in the tree above the girl. If he couldn't have happiness of this sort himself he wanted to enjoy the happiness of others. Possibly if he made himself known to the old man he might be permitted to come to the village occasionally as a friend. It would be worth trying. He would wait until the old Arab had greeted his daughter, then he would make his presence known with signs of peace.

The Arab was striding softly toward the girl. In a moment he would be beside her, and then how surprised and delighted she would be! Korak's eyes sparkled in anticipation—and now the old man stood behind the little girl. His stern old face was still unrelaxed. The child was yet unconscious of his presence. She prattled on to the unresponsive Geeka. Then the old man coughed. With a start the child glanced quickly up over her shoulder. Korak could see her full face now. It was very beautiful in its sweet and innocent childishness—all soft and lovely curves. He could see her great, dark eyes. He looked for the happy love light that would follow recognition; but it did not come. Instead, terror, stark, paralyzing terror, was mirrored in her eyes, in the expression of her mouth, in the tense, cowering attitude of her body. A grim smile curved the thin, cruel lip of the Arab. The child essayed to crawl away; but before she could get out of his reach the old man kicked her brutally, sending her sprawling upon the grass. Then he followed her up to seize and strike her as was his custom.

Above them, in the tree, a beast crouched where a moment before had been a boy—a beast with dilating nostrils and bared fangs—a beast that trembled with rage.

The Sheik was stooping to reach for the girl when The Killer dropped to the ground at his side. His spear was still in his left hand but he had forgotten it. Instead his right fist was clenched and as The Sheik took a backward step, astonished by the sudden materialization of this strange apparition apparently out of clear air, the heavy fist landed full upon his mouth backed by the weight of the young giant and the terrific power of his more than human muscles.

Bleeding and senseless The Sheik sank to earth. Korak turned toward the child. She had regained her feet and stood wide eyed and frightened, looking first into his face and then, horror struck, at the recumbent figure of The Sheik. In an involuntary gesture of protection The Killer threw an arm about the girl's shoulders and stood waiting for the Arab to regain consciousness. For a moment they remained thus, when the girl spoke.

"When he regains his senses he will kill me," she said, in Arabic.

Korak could not understand her. He shook his head, speaking to her first in English and then in the language of the great apes; but neither of these was intelligible to her. She leaned forward and touched the hilt of the long knife that the Arab wore. Then she raised her clasped hand above her head and drove an imaginary blade into her breast above her heart. Korak understood. The old man would kill her. The girl came to his side again and stood there trembling. She did not fear him. Why should she? He had saved her from a terrible beating at the hands of The Sheik. Never, in her memory, had another so befriended her. She looked up into his face. It was a boyish, handsome face, nut-brown like her own. She admired the spotted leopard skin that circled his lithe body from one shoulder to his knees. The metal anklets and armlets adorning him aroused her envy. Always had she coveted something of the kind; but never had The Sheik permitted her more than the single cotton garment that barely sufficed to cover her nakedness. No furs or silks or jewelry had there ever been for little Meriem.

And Korak looked at the girl. He had always held girls in a species of contempt. Boys who associated with them were, in his estimation, mollycoddles. He wondered what he should do. Could he leave her here to be abused, possibly murdered, by the villainous old Arab? No! But, on the other hand, could he take her into the jungle with him? What could he accomplish burdened by a weak and frightened girl? She would scream at her own shadow when the moon came out upon the jungle night and the great beasts roamed, moaning and roaring, through the darkness.

He stood for several minutes buried in thought. The girl watched his face, wondering what was passing in his mind. She, too, was thinking of the future. She feared to remain and suffer the vengeance of The Sheik. There was no one in all the world to whom she might turn, other than this half-naked stranger who had dropped miraculously from the clouds to save her from one of The Sheik's accustomed beatings. Would her new friend leave her now? Wistfully she gazed at his intent face. She moved a little closer to him, laying a slim, brown hand upon his arm. The contact awakened the lad from his absorption. He looked down at her, and then his arm went about her shoulder once more, for he saw tears upon her lashes.

"Come," he said. "The jungle is kinder than man. You shall live in the jungle and Korak and Akut will protect you."

She did not understand his words, but the pressure of his arm drawing her away from the prostrate Arab and the tents was quite intelligible. One little arm crept about his waist and together they walked toward the palisade. Beneath the great tree that had harbored Korak while he watched the girl at play he lifted her in his arms and throwing her lightly across his shoulder leaped nimbly into the lower branches. Her arms were about his neck and from one little hand Geeka dangled down his straight youngback.

And so Meriem entered the jungle with Korak, trusting, in her childish innocence, the stranger who had befriended her, and perhaps influenced in her belief in him by that strange intuitive power possessed by woman. She had no conception of what the future might hold. She did not know, nor could she have guessed the manner of life led by her protector. Possibly she pictured a distant village similar to that of The Sheik in which lived other white men like the stranger. That she was to be taken into the savage, primeval life of a jungle beast could not have occurred to her. Had it, her little heart would have palpitated with fear. Often had she wished to run away from the cruelties of The Sheik and Mabunu; but the dangers of the jungle always had deterred her.

The two had gone but a short distance from the village when the girl spied the huge proportions of the great Akut. With a half-stifled scream she clung more closely to Korak, and pointed fearfully toward the ape.

Akut, thinking that The Killer was returning with a prisoner, came growling toward them—a little girl aroused no more sympathy in the beast's heart than would a full-grown bull ape. She was a stranger and therefore to be killed. He bared his yellow fangs as he approached, and to his surprise The Killer bared his likewise, but he bared them at Akut, and snarled menacingly.

"Ah," thought Akut, "The Killer has taken a mate," and so, obedient to the tribal laws of his kind, he left them alone, becoming suddenly absorbed in a fuzzy caterpillar of peculiarly succulent appearance. The larva disposed of, he glanced from the corner of an eye at Korak. The youth had deposited his burden upon a large limb, where she clung desperately to keep from falling.

"She will accompany us," said Korak to Akut, jerking a thumb in the direction of the girl. "Do not harm her. We will protect her."

Akut shrugged. To be burdened by the young of man was in no way to his liking. He could see from her evident fright at her position on the branch, and from the terrified glances she cast in his direction that she was hopelessly unfit. By all the ethics of Akut's training and inheritance the unfit should be eliminated; but if The Killer wished this there was nothing to be done about it but to tolerate her. Akut certainly didn't want her—of that he was quite positive. Her skin was too smooth and hairless. Quite snake-like, in fact, and her face was most unattractive. Not at all like that of a certain lovely she he had particularly noticed among the apes in the amphitheater the previous night. Ah, there was true feminine beauty for one!—a great, generous mouth; lovely, yellow fangs, and the cutest, softest side whiskers! Akut sighed. Then he rose, expanded his great chest and strutted back and forth along a substantial branch, for even a puny thing like this she of Korak's might admire his fine coat and his graceful carriage.

But poor little Meriem only shrank closer to Korak and almost wished that she were back in the village of The Sheik where the terrors of existence were of human origin, and so more or less familiar. The hideous ape frightened her. He was so large and so ferocious in appearance. His actions she could only interpret as a menace, for how could she guess that he was parading to excite admiration? Nor could she know of the bond of fellowship which existed between this great brute and the godlike youth who had rescued her from the Sheik.

Meriem spent an evening and a night of unmitigated terror. Korak and Akut led her along dizzy ways as they searched for food. Once they hid her in the branches of a tree while they stalked a near-by buck. Even her natural terror of being left alone in the awful jungle was submerged in a greater horror as she saw the man and the beast spring simultaneously upon their prey and drag it down, as she saw the handsome face of her preserver contorted in a bestial snarl; as she saw his strong, white teeth buried in the soft flesh of the kill.

When he came back to her blood smeared his face and hands and breast and she shrank from him as he offered her a huge hunk of hot, raw meat. He was evidently much disturbed by her refusal to eat, and when, a moment later, he scampered away into the forest to return with fruit for her she was once more forced to alter her estimation of him. This time she did not shrink, but acknowledged his gift with a smile that, had she known it, was more than ample payment to the affection starved boy.

The sleeping problem vexed Korak. He knew that the girl could not balance herself in safety in a tree crotch while she slept, nor would it be safe to permit her to sleep upon the ground open to the attacks of prowling beasts of prey. There was but a single solution that presented itself—he must hold her in his arms all night. And that he did, with Akut braced upon one side of her and he upon the other, so that she was warmed by the bodies of them both.

She did not sleep much until the night was half spent; but at last Nature overcame her terrors of the black abyss beneath and the hairy body of the wild beast at her side, and she fell into a deep slumber which outlasted the darkness. When she opened her eyes the sun was well up. At first she could not believe in the reality of her position. Her head had rolled from Korak's shoulder so that her eyes were directed upon the hairy back of the ape. At sight of it she shrank away. Then she realized that someone was holding her, and turning her head she saw the smiling eyes of the youth regarding her. When he smiled she could not fear him, and now she shrank closer against him in natural revulsion toward the rough coat of the brute upon her other side.

Korak spoke to her in the language of the apes; but she shook her head, and spoke to him in the language of the Arab, which was as unintelligible to him as was ape speech to her. Akut sat up and looked at them. He could understand what Korak said but the girl made only foolish noises that were entirely unintelligible and ridiculous. Akut could not understand what Korak saw in her to attract him. He looked at her long and steadily, appraising her carefully, then he scratched his head, rose and shook himself.

His movement gave the girl a little start—she had forgotten Akut for the moment. Again she shrank from him. The beast saw that she feared him, and being a brute enjoyed the evidence of the terror his brutishness inspired. Crouching, he extended his huge hand stealthily toward her, as though to seize her. She shrank still further away. Akut's eyes were busy drinking in the humor of the situation—he did not see the narrowing eyes of the boy upon him, nor the shortening neck as the broad shoulders rose in a characteristic attitude of preparation for attack. As the ape's fingers were about to close upon the girl's arm the youth rose suddenly with a short, vicious growl. A clenched fist flew before Meriem's eyes to land full upon the snout of the astonished Akut. With an explosive bellow the anthropoid reeled backward and tumbled from the tree.

Korak stood glaring down upon him when a sudden swish in the bushes close by attracted his attention. The girl too was looking down; but she saw nothing but the angry ape scrambling to his feet. Then, like a bolt from a cross bow, a mass of spotted, yellow fur shot into view straight for Akut's back. It was Sheeta, the leopard.

CHAPTER 10

As the leopard leaped for the great ape Meriem gasped in surprise and horror—not for the impending fate of the anthropoid, but at the act of the youth who but for an instant before had angrily struck his strange companion; for scarce had the carnivore burst into view than with drawn knife the youth had leaped far out above him, so that as Sheeta was almost in the act of sinking fangs and talons in Akut's broad back The Killer landed full upon the leopard's shoulders.

The cat halted in mid air, missed the ape by but a hair's breadth, and with horrid snarlings rolled over upon its back, clutching and clawing in an effort to reach and dislodge the antagonist biting at its neck and knifing it in the side.

Akut, startled by the sudden rush from his rear, and following hoary instinct, was in the tree beside the girl with an agility little short of marvelous in so heavy a beast. But the moment that he turned to see what was going on below him brought him as quickly to the ground again. Personal differences were quickly forgotten in the danger which menaced his human companion, nor was he a whit less eager to jeopardize his own safety in the service of his friend than Korak had been to succor him.

The result was that Sheeta presently found two ferocious creatures tearing him to ribbons. Shrieking, snarling and growling, the three rolled hither and thither among the underbrush, while with staring eyes the sole spectator of the battle royal crouched trembling in the tree above them hugging Geeka frantically to her breast.

It was the boy's knife which eventually decided the battle, and as the fierce feline shuddered convulsively and rolled over upon its side the youth and the ape rose and faced one another across the prostrate carcass. Korak jerked his head in the direction of the little girl in the tree.

"Leave her alone," he said; "she is mine."

Akut grunted, blinked his blood-shot eyes, and turned toward the body of Sheeta. Standing erect upon it he threw out his great chest, raised his face toward the heavens and gave voice to so horrid a scream that once again the little girl shuddered and shrank. It was the victory cry of the bull ape that has made a kill. The boy only looked on for a moment in silence; then he leaped into the tree again to the girl's side. Akut presently rejoined them. For a few minutes he busied himself licking his wounds, then he wandered off to hunt his breakfast.

For many months the strange life of the three went on unmarked by any unusual occurrences. At least without any occurrences that seemed unusual to the youth or the ape; but to the little girl it was a constant nightmare of horrors for days and weeks, until she too became accustomed to gazing into the eyeless sockets of death and to the feel of the icy wind of his shroud-like mantle. Slowly she learned the rudiments of the only common medium of thought exchange which her companions possessed—the language of the great apes. More quickly she perfected herself in jungle craft, so that the time soon came when she was an important factor in the chase, watching while the others slept, or helping them to trace the spoor of whatever prey they might be stalking. Akut accepted her on a footing which bordered upon equality when it was necessary for them to come into close contact; but for the most part he avoided her. The youth always was kind to her, and if there were many occasions upon which he felt the burden of her presence he hid it from her. Finding that the night damp and chill caused her discomfort and even suffering, Korak constructed a tight little shelter high among the swaying branches of a giant tree. Here little Meriem slept in comparative warmth and safety, while The Killer and the ape perched upon near-by branches, the former always before the entrance to the lofty domicile, where he best could guard its inmate from the dangers of arboreal enemies. They were too high to feel much fear of Sheeta; but there was always Histah, the snake, to strike terror to one's soul, and the great baboons who lived near-by, and who, while never attacking always bared their fangs and barked at any of the trio when they passed near them.

After the construction of the shelter the activities of the three became localized. They ranged less widely, for there was always the necessity of returning to their own tree at nightfall. A river flowed near by. Game and fruit were plentiful, as were fish also. Existence had settled down to the daily humdrum of the wild—the search for food and the sleeping upon full bellies. They looked no further ahead than today. If the youth thought of his past and of those who longed for him in the distant metropolis it was in a detached and impersonal sort of way as though that other life belonged to another creature than himself. He had given up hope of returning to civilization, for since his various rebuffs at the hands of those to whom he had looked for friendship he had wandered so far inland as to realize that he was completely lost in the mazes of the jungle.

Then, too, since the coming of Meriem he had found in her that one thing which he had most missed before in his savage, jungle life—human companionship. In his friendship for her there was appreciable no trace of sex influence of which he was cognizant. They were friends—companions—that was all. Both might have been boys, except for the half tender and always masterful manifestation of the protective instinct which was apparent in Korak's attitude.

The little girl idolized him as she might have idolized an indulgent brother had she had one. Love was a thing unknown to either; but as the youth neared manhood it was inevitable that it should come to him as it did to every other savage, jungle male.

As Meriem became proficient in their common language the pleasures of their companionship grew correspondingly, for now they could converse and aided by the mental powers of their human heritage they amplified the restricted vocabulary of the apes until talking was transformed from a task into an enjoyable pastime. When Korak hunted, Meriem usually accompanied him, for she had learned the fine art of silence, when silence was desirable. She could pass through the branches of the great trees now with all the agility and stealth of The Killer himself. Great heights no longer appalled her. She swung from limb to limb, or she raced through the mighty branches, surefooted, lithe, and fearless. Korak was very proud of her, and even old Akut grunted in approval where before he had growled in contempt.

A distant village of blacks had furnished her with a mantle of fur and feathers, with copper ornaments, and weapons, for Korak would not permit her to go unarmed, or unversed in the use of the weapons he stole for her. A leather thong over one shoulder supported the ever present Geeka who was still the recipient of her most sacred confidences. A light spear and a long knife were her weapons of offense or defense. Her body, rounding into the fulness of an early maturity, followed the lines of a Greek goddess; but there the similarity ceased, for her face was beautiful.

As she grew more accustomed to the jungle and the ways of its wild denizens fear left her. As time wore on she even hunted alone when Korak and Akut were prowling at a great distance, as they were sometimes forced to do when game was scarce in their immediate vicinity. Upon these occasions she usually confined her endeavors to the smaller animals though sometimes she brought down a deer, and once even Horta, the boar—a great tusker that even Sheeta might have thought twice before attacking.

In their stamping grounds in the jungle the three were familiar figures. The little monkeys knew them well, often coming close to chatter and frolic about them. When Akut was by, the small folk kept their distance, but with Korak they were less shy and when both the males were gone they would come close to Meriem, tugging at her ornaments or playing with Geeka, who was a never ending source of amusement to them. The girl played with them and fed them, and when she was alone they helped her to pass the long hours until Korak's return.

Nor were they worthless as friends. In the hunt they helped her locate her quarry. Often they would come racing through the trees to her side to announce the near presence of antelope or giraffe, or with excited warnings of the proximity of Sheeta or Numa. Luscious, sun-kissed fruits which hung far out upon the frail bough of the jungle's waving crest were brought to her by these tiny, nimble allies. Sometimes they played tricks upon her; but she was always kind and gentle with them and in their wild, half-human way they were kind to her and affectionate. Their language being similar to that of the great apes Meriem could converse with them though the poverty of their vocabulary rendered these exchanges anything but feasts of reason.

For familiar objects they had names, as well as for those conditions which induced pain or pleasure, joy, sorrow, or rage. These root words were so similar to those in use among the great anthropoids as to suggest that the language of the Manus was the mother tongue. Dreams, aspirations, hopes, the past, the sordid exchange. Dreams, aspirations, hopes, the past, the future held no place in the conversation of Manu, the monkey. All was of the present—particularly of filling his belly and catching lice.

Poor food was this to nourish the mental appetite of a girl just upon the brink of womanhood. And so, finding Manu only amusing as an occasional playfellow or pet, Meriem poured out her sweetest soul thoughts into the deaf ears of Geeka's ivory head. To Geeka she spoke in Arabic, knowing that Geeka, being but a doll, could not understand the language of Korak and Akut, and that the language of Korak and Akut being that of male apes contained nothing of interest to an Arab doll.

Geeka had undergone a transformation since her little mother had left the village of The Sheik. Her garmenture now reflected in miniature that of Meriem. A tiny bit of leopard skin covered her ratskin torso from shoulder to splinter knee. A band of braided grasses about her brow held in place a few gaudy feathers from the parakeet, while other bits of grass were fashioned into imitations of arm and leg ornaments of metal. Geeka was a perfect little savage; but at heart she was unchanged, being the same omnivorous listener as of yore. An excellent trait in Geeka was that she never interrupted in order to talk about herself. Today was no exception. She had been listening attentively to Meriem for an hour, propped against the bole of a tree while her lithe, young mistress stretched catlike and luxurious along a swaying branch before her.

"Little Geeka," said Meriem, "our Korak has been gone for a long time today. We miss him, little Geeka, do we not? It is dull and lonesome in the great jungle when our Korak is away. What will he bring us this time, eh? Another shining band of metal for Meriem's ankle? Or a soft, doeskin loin cloth from the body of a black she? He tells me that it is harder to get the possessions of the shes, for he will not kill them as he does the males, and they fight savagely when he leaps upon them to wrest their ornaments from them. Then come the males with spears and arrows and Korak takes to the trees. Sometimes he takes the she with him and high among the branches divests her of the things he wishes to bring home to Meriem. He says that the blacks fear him now, and at first sight of him the women and children run shrieking to their huts; but he follows them within, and it is not often that he returns without arrows for himself and a present for Meriem. Korak is mighty among the jungle people—our Korak, Geeka—no, MY Korak!"

Meriem's conversation was interrupted by the sudden plunge of an excited little monkey that landed upon her shoulders in a flying leap from a neighboring tree.

"Climb!" he cried. "Climb! The Mangani are coming."

Meriem glanced lazily over her shoulder at the excited disturber of her peace.

"Climb, yourself, little Manu," she said. "The only Mangani in our jungle are Korak and Akut. It is they you have seen returning from the hunt. Some day you will see your own shadow, little Manu, and then you will be frightened to death."

But the monkey only screamed his warning more lustily before he raced upward toward the safety of the high terrace where Mangani, the great ape, could not follow. Presently Meriem heard the sound of approaching bodies swinging through the trees. She listened attentively. There were two and they were great apes—Korak and Akut. To her Korak was an ape—a Mangani, for as such the three always described themselves. Man was an enemy, so they did not think of themselves as belonging any longer to the same genus. Tarmangani, or great white ape, which described the white man in their language, did not fit them all. Gomangani—great black ape, or Negro—described none of them so they called themselves plain Mangani.

Meriem decided that she would feign slumber and play a joke on Korak. So she lay very still with eyes tightly closed. She heard the two approaching closer and closer. They were in the adjoining tree now and must have discovered her, for they had halted. Why were they so quiet? Why did not Korak call out his customary greeting? The quietness was ominous. It was followed presently by a very stealthy sound—one of them was creeping upon her. Was Korak planning a joke upon his own account? Well, she would fool him.

Cautiously she opened her eyes the tiniest bit, and as she did so her heart stood still. Creeping silently toward her was a huge bull ape that she never before had seen. Behind him was another like him.

With the agility of a squirrel Meriem was upon her feet and at the same instant the great bull lunged for her. Leaping from limb to limb the girl fled through the jungle while close behind her came the two great apes. Above them raced a bevy of screaming, chattering monkeys, hurling taunts and insults at the Mangani, and encouragement and advice to the girl.

From tree to tree swung Meriem working ever upward toward the smaller branches which would not bear the weight of her pursuers. Faster and faster came the bull apes after her. The clutching fingers of the foremost were almost upon her again and again, but she eluded them by sudden bursts of speed or reckless chances as she threw herself across dizzy spaces.

Slowly she was gaining her way to the greater heights where safety lay, when, after a particularly daring leap, the swaying branch she grasped bent low beneath her weight, nor whipped upward again as it should have done. Even before the rending sound which followed Meriem knew that she had misjudged the strength of the limb. It gave slowly at first. Then there was a ripping as it parted from the trunk. Releasing her hold Meriem dropped among the foliage beneath, clutching for a new support. She found it a dozen feet below the broken limb. She had fallen thus many times before, so that she had no particular terror of a fall—it was the delay which appalled her most, and rightly, for scarce had she scrambled to a place of safety than the body of the huge ape dropped at her side and a great, hairy arm went about her waist.

Almost at once the other ape reached his companion's side. He made a lunge at Meriem; but her captor swung her to one side, bared his fighting fangs and growled ominously. Meriem struggled to escape. She struck at the hairy breast and bearded cheek. She fastened her strong, white teeth in one shaggy forearm. The ape cuffed her viciously across the face, then he had to turn his attention to his fellow who quite evidently desired the prize for his own.

The captor could not fight to advantage upon the swaying bough, burdened as he was by a squirming, struggling captive, so he dropped quickly to the ground beneath. The other followed him, and here they fought, occasionally abandoning their duel to pursue and recapture the girl who took every advantage of her captors' preoccupation in battle to break away in attempted escape; but always they overtook her, and first one and then the other possessed her as they struggled to tear one another to pieces for the prize.

Often the girl came in for many blows that were intended for a hairy foe, and once she was felled, lying unconscious while the apes, relieved of the distraction of detaining her by force, tore into one another in fierce and terrible combat.

Above them screamed the little monkeys, racing hither and thither in a frenzy of hysterical excitement. Back and forth over the battle field flew countless birds of gorgeous plumage, squawking their hoarse cries of rage and defiance. In the distance a lion roared.

The larger bull was slowly tearing his antagonist to pieces. They rolled upon the ground biting and striking. Again, erect upon their hind legs they pulled and tugged like human wrestlers; but always the giant fangs found their bloody part to play until both combatants and the ground about them were red with gore.

Meriem, through it all, lay still and unconscious upon the ground. At last one found a permanent hold upon the jugular of the other and thus they went down for the last time. For several minutes they lay with scarce a struggle. It was the larger bull who arose alone from the last embrace. He shook himself. A deep growl rumbled from his hairy throat. He waddled back and forth between the body of the girl and that of his vanquished foe. Then he stood upon the latter and gave tongue to his hideous challenge. The little monkeys broke, screaming, in all directions as the terrifying noise broke upon their ears. The gorgeous birds took wing and fled. Once again the lion roared, this time at a greater distance.

The great ape waddled once more to the girl's side. He turned her over upon her back, and stooping commenced to sniff and listen about her face and breast. She lived. The monkeys were returning. They came in swarms, and from above hurled down insults upon the victor.

The ape showed his displeasure by baring his teeth and growling up at them. Then he stooped and lifting the girl to his shoulder waddled off through the jungle. In his wake followed the angry mob.

CHAPTER 11

Korak, returning from the hunt, heard the jabbering of the excited monkeys. He knew that something was seriously amiss. Histah, the snake, had doubtless coiled his slimy folds about some careless Manu. The youth hastened ahead. The monkeys were Meriem's friends. He would help them if he could. He traveled rapidly along the middle terrace. In the tree by Meriem's shelter he deposited his trophies of the hunt and called aloud to her. There was no answer. He dropped quickly to a lower level. She might be hiding from him.

Upon a great branch where Meriem often swung at indolent ease he saw Geeka propped against the tree's great bole. What could it mean? Meriem had never left Geeka thus alone before. Korak picked up the doll and tucked it in his belt. He called again, more loudly; but no Meriem answered his summons. In the distance the jabbering of the excited Manus was growing less distinct.

Could their excitement be in any way connected with Meriem's disappearance? The bare thought was enough. Without waiting for Akut who was coming slowly along some distance in his rear, Korak swung rapidly in the direction of the chattering mob. But a few minutes sufficed to overtake the rearmost. At sight of him they fell to screaming and pointing downward ahead of them, and a moment later Korak came within sight of the cause of their rage.

The youth's heart stood still in terror as he saw the limp body of the girl across the hairy shoulders of a great ape. That she was dead he did not doubt, and in that instant there arose within him a something which he did not try to interpret nor could have hade he tried; but all at once the whole world seemed centered in that tender, graceful body, that frail little body, hanging so pitifully limp and helpless across the bulging shoulders of the brute.

He knew then that little Meriem was his world—his sun, his moon, his stars—with her going had gone all light and warmth and happiness. A groan escaped his lips, and after that a series of hideous roars, more bestial than the beasts', as he dropped plummet-like in mad descent toward the perpetrator of this hideous crime.

The bull ape turned at the first note of this new and menacing voice, and as he turned a new flame was added to the rage and hatred of The Killer, for he saw that the creature before him was none other than the king ape which had driven him away from the great anthropoids to whom he had looked for friendship and asylum.

Dropping the body of the girl to the ground the bull turned to battle anew for possession of his expensive prize; but this time he looked for an easy conquest. He too recognized Korak. Had he not chased him away from the amphitheater without even having to lay a fang or paw upon him? With lowered head and bulging shoulders he rushed headlong for the smooth-skinned creature who was daring to question his right to his prey.

They met head on like two charging bulls, to go down together tearing and striking. Korak forgot his knife. Rage and bloodlust such as his could be satisfied only by the feel of hot flesh between rending fangs, by the gush of new life blood against his bare skin, for, though he did not realize it, Korak, The Killer, was fighting for something more compelling than hate or revenge—he was a great male fighting another male for a she of his own kind.

So impetuous was the attack of the man-ape that he found his hold before the anthropoid could prevent him—a savage hold, with strong jaws closed upon a pulsing jugular, and there he clung, with closed eyes, while his fingers sought another hold upon the shaggy throat.

It was then that Meriem opened her eyes. At the sight before her they went wide.

"Korak!" she cried. "Korak! My Korak! I knew that you would come. Kill him, Korak! Kill him!" And with flashing eyes and heaving bosom the girl, coming to her feet, ran to Korak's side to encourage him. Nearby lay The Killer's spear, where he had flung it as he charged the ape. The girl saw it and snatched it up. No faintness overcame her in the face of this battle primeval at her feet. For her there was no hysterical reaction from the nerve strain of her own personal encounter with the bull. She was excited; but cool and entirely unafraid. Her Korak was battling with another Mangani that would have stolen her; but she did not seek the safety of an overhanging bough there to watch the battle from afar, as would a she Mangani. Instead she placed the point of Korak's spear against the bull ape's side and plunged the sharp point deep into the savage heart. Korak had not needed her aid, for the great bull had been already as good as dead, with the blood gushing from his torn jugular; but Korak rose smiling with a word of approbation for his helper.

How tall and fine she was! Had she changed suddenly within the few hours of his absence, or had his battle with the ape affected his vision? He might have been looking at Meriem through new eyes for the many startling and wonderful surprises his gaze revealed. How long it had been since he had found her in her father's village, a little Arab girl, he did not know, for time is of no import in the jungle and so he had kept no track of the passing days. But he realized, as he looked upon her now, that she was no longer such a little girl as he had first seen playing with Geeka beneath the great tree just within the palisade. The change must have been very gradual to have eluded his notice until now. And what was it that had caused him to realize it so suddenly? His gaze wandered from the girl to the body of the dead bull. For the first time there flashed to his understanding the explanation of the reason for the girl's attempted abduction. Korak's eyes went wide and then they closed to narrow slits of rage as he stood glaring down upon the abysmal brute at his feet. When next his glance rose to Meriem's face a slow flush suffused his own. Now, indeed, was he looking upon her through new eyes—the eyes of a man looking upon a maid.

Akut had come up just as Meriem had speared Korak's antagonist. The exultation of the old ape was keen. He strutted, stiff-legged and truculent about the body of the fallen enemy. He growled and upcurved his long, flexible lip. His hair bristled. He was paying no attention to Meriem and Korak. Back in the uttermost recesses of his little brain something was stirring—something which the sight and smell of the great bull had aroused. The outward manifestation of the germinating idea was one of bestial rage; but the inner sensations were pleasurable in the extreme. The scent of the great bull and the sight of his huge and hairy figure had wakened in the heart of Akut a longing for the companionship of his own kind. So Korak was not alone undergoing a change.

And Meriem? She was a woman. It is woman's divine right to love. Always she had loved Korak. He was her big brother. Meriem alone underwent no change. She was still happy in the companionship of her Korak. She still loved him—as a sister loves an indulgent brother—and she was very, very proud of him. In all the jungle there was no other creature so strong, so handsome, or so brave.

Korak came close to her. There was a new light in his eyes as she looked up into them; but she did not understand it. She did not realize how close they were to maturity, nor aught of all the difference in their lives the look in Korak's eyes might mean.

"Meriem," he whispered and his voice was husky as he laid a brown hand upon her bare shoulder. "Meriem!" Suddenly he crushed her to him. She looked up into his face, laughing, and then he bent and kissed her full upon the mouth. Even then she did not understand. She did not recall ever having been kissed before. It was very nice. Meriem liked it. She thought it was Korak's way of showing how glad he was that the great ape had not succeeded in running away with her. She was glad too, so she put her arms about The Killer's neck and kissed him again and again. Then, discovering the doll in his belt she transferred it to her own possession, kissing it as she had kissed Korak.

Korak wanted her to say something. He wanted to tell her how he loved her; but the emotion of his love choked him and the vocabulary of the Mangani was limited.

There came a sudden interruption. It was from Akut—a sudden, low growl, no louder than those he had been giving vent to the while he pranced about the dead bull, nor half so loud in fact; but of a timbre that bore straight to the perceptive faculties of the jungle beast ingrained in Korak. It was a warning. Korak looked quickly up from the glorious vision of the sweet face so close to his. Now his other faculties awoke. His ears, his nostrils were on the alert. Something was coming!

The Killer moved to Akut's side. Meriem was just behind them. The three stood like carved statues gazing into the leafy tangle of the jungle. The noise that had attracted their attention increased, and presently a great ape broke through the underbrush a few paces from where they stood. The beast halted at sight of them. He gave a warning grunt back over his shoulder, and a moment later coming cautiously another bull appeared. He was followed by others—both bulls and females with young, until two score hairy monsters stood glaring at the three. It was the tribe of the dead king ape. Akut was the first to speak. He pointed to the body of the dead bull.

"Korak, mighty fighter, has killed your king," he grunted. "There is none greater in all the jungle than Korak, son of Tarzan. Now Korak is king. What bull is greater than Korak?" It was a challenge to any bull who might care to question Korak's right to the kingship. The apes jabbered and chattered and growled among themselves for a time. At last a young bull came slowly forward rocking upon his short legs, bristling, growling, terrible.

The beast was enormous, and in the full prime of his strength. He belonged to that almost extinct species for which white men have long sought upon the information of the natives of the more inaccessible jungles. Even the natives seldom see these great, hairy, primordial men.

Korak advanced to meet the monster. He, too, was growling. In his mind a plan was revolving. To close with this powerful, untired brute after having just passed through a terrific battle with another of his kind would have been to tempt defeat. He must find an easier way to victory. Crouching, he prepared to meet the charge which he knew would soon come, nor did he have long to wait. His antagonist paused only for sufficient time to permit him to recount for the edification of the audience and the confounding of Korak a brief resume of his former victories, of his prowess, and of what he was about to do to this puny Tarmangani. Then he charged.

With clutching fingers and wide opened jaws he came down upon the waiting Korak with the speed of an express train. Korak did not move until the great arms swung to embrace him, then he dropped low beneath them, swung a terrific right to the side of the beast's jaw as he side-stepped his rushing body, and swinging quickly about stood ready over the fallen ape where he sprawled upon the ground.

It was a surprised anthropoid that attempted to scramble to its feet. Froth flecked its hideous lips. Red were the little eyes. Blood curdling roars tumbled from the deep chest. But it did not reach its feet. The Killer stood waiting above it, and the moment that the hairy chin came upon the proper level another blow that would have felled an ox sent the ape over backward.

Again and again the beast struggled to arise, but each time the mighty Tarmangani stood waiting with ready fist and pile driver blow to bowl him over. Weaker and weaker became the efforts of the bull. Blood smeared his face and breast. A red stream trickled from nose and mouth. The crowd that had cheered him on at first with savage yells, now jeered him—their approbation was for the Tarmangani.

"Kagoda?" inquired Korak, as he sent the bull down once more.

Again the stubborn bull essayed to scramble to his feet. Again The Killer struck him a terrific blow. Again he put the question, kagoda—have you had enough?

For a moment the bull lay motionless. Then from between battered lips came the single word: "Kagoda!"

"Then rise and go back among your people," said Korak. "I do not wish to be king among people who once drove me from them. Keep your own ways, and we will keep ours. When we meet we may be friends, but we shall not live together."

An old bull came slowly toward The Killer.

"You have killed our king," he said. "You have defeated him who would have been king. You could have killed him had you wished. What shall we do for a king?"

Korak turned toward Akut.

"There is your king," he said. But Akut did not want to be separated from Korak, although he was anxious enough to remain with his own kind. He wanted Korak to remain, too. He said as much.

The youth was thinking of Meriem—of what would be best and safest for her. If Akut went away with the apes there would be but one to watch over and protect her. On the other hand were they to join the tribe he would never feel safe to leave Meriem behind when he went out to hunt, for the passions of the ape-folk are not ever well controlled. Even a female might develop an insane hatred for the slender white girl and kill her during Korak's absence.

"We will live near you," he said, at last. "When you change your hunting ground we will change ours, Meriem and I, and so remain near you; but we shall not dwell among you."

Akut raised objections to this plan. He did not wish to be separated from Korak. At first he refused to leave his human friend for the companionship of his own kind; but when he saw the last of the tribe wandering off into the jungle again and his glance rested upon the lithe figure of the dead king's young mate as she cast admiring glances at her lord's successor the call of blood would not be denied. With a farewell glance toward his beloved Korak he turned and followed the she ape into the labyrinthine mazes of the wood.

After Korak had left the village of the blacks following his last thieving expedition, the screams of his victim and those of the other women and children had brought the warriors in from the forest and the river. Great was the excitement and hot was the rage of the men when they learned that the white devil had again entered their homes, frightened their women and stolen arrows and ornaments and food.

Even their superstitious fear of this weird creature who hunted with a huge bull ape was overcome in their desire to wreak vengeance upon him and rid themselves for good and all of the menace of his presence in the jungle.

And so it was that a score of the fleetest and most doughty warriors of the tribe set out in pursuit of Korak and Akut but a few minutes after they had left the scene of The Killer's many depredations.

The youth and the ape had traveled slowly and with no precautions against a successful pursuit. Nor was their attitude of careless indifference to the blacks at all remarkable. So many similar raids had gone unpunished that the two had come to look upon the Negroes with contempt. The return journey led them straight up wind. The result being that the scent of their pursuers was borne away from them, so they proceeded upon their way in total ignorance of the fact that tireless trackers but little less expert in the mysteries of woodcraft than themselves were dogging their trail with savage insistence.

The little party of warriors was led by Kovudoo, the chief; a middle-aged savage of exceptional cunning and bravery. It was he who first came within sight of the quarry which they had followed for hours by the mysterious methods of their almost uncanny powers of observation, intuition, and even scent.

Kovudoo and his men came upon Korak, Akut and Meriem after the killing of the king ape, the noise of the combat having led them at last straight to their quarry. The sight of the slender white girl had amazed the savage chief and held him gazing at the trio for a moment before ordering his warriors to rush out upon their prey. In that moment it was that the great apes came and again the blacks remained awestruck witnesses to the palaver, and the battle between Korak and the young bull.

But now the apes had gone, and the white youth and the white maid stood alone in the jungle. One of Kovudoo's men leaned close to the ear of his chief. "Look!" he whispered, and pointed to something that dangled at the girl's side. "When my brother and I were slaves in the village of The Sheik my brother made that thing for The Sheik's little daughter—she played with it always and called it after my brother, whose name is Geeka. Just before we escaped some one came and struck down The Sheik, stealing his daughter away. If this is she The Sheik will pay you well for her return."

Korak's arm had again gone around the shoulders of Meriem. Love raced hot through his young veins. Civilization was but a half-remembered state—London as remote as ancient Rome. In all the world there were but they two—Korak, The Killer, and Meriem, his mate. Again he drew her close to him and covered her willing lips with his hot kisses. And then from behind him broke a hideous bedlam of savage war cries and a score of shrieking blacks were upon them.

Korak turned to give battle. Meriem with her own light spear stood by his side. An avalanche of barbed missiles flew about them. One pierced Korak's shoulder, another his leg, and he went down.

Meriem was unscathed for the blacks had intentionally spared her. Now they rushed forward to finish Korak and made good the girl's capture; but as they came there came also from another point in the jungle the great Akut and at his heels the huge bulls of his new kingdom.

Snarling and roaring they rushed upon the black warriors when they saw the mischief they had already wrought. Kovudoo, realizing the danger of coming to close quarters with these mighty ape-men, seized Meriem and called upon his warriors to retreat. For a time the apes followed them, and several of the blacks were badly mauled and one killed before they succeeded in escaping. Nor would they have gotten off thus easily had Akut not been more concerned with the condition of the wounded Korak than with the fate of the girl upon whom he had always looked as more or less of an interloper and an unquestioned burden.

Korak lay bleeding and unconscious when Akut reached his side. The great ape tore the heavy spears from his flesh, licked the wounds and then carried his friend to the lofty shelter that Korak had constructed for Meriem. Further than this the brute could do nothing. Nature must accomplish the rest unaided or Korak must die.

He did not die, however. For days he lay helpless with fever, while Akut and the apes hunted close by that they might protect him from such birds and beasts as might reach his lofty retreat. Occasionally Akut brought him juicy fruits which helped to slake his thirst and allay his fever, and little by little his powerful constitution overcame the effects of the spear thrusts. The wounds healed and his strength returned. All during his rational moments as he had lain upon the soft furs which lined Meriem's nest he had suffered more acutely from fears for Meriem than from the pain of his own wounds. For her he must live. For her he must regain his strength that he might set out in search of her. What had the blacks done to her? Did she still live, or had they sacrificed her to their lust for torture and human flesh? Korak almost trembled with terror as the most hideous possibilities of the girl's fate suggested themselves to him out of his knowledge of the customs of Kovudoo's tribe.

The days dragged their weary lengths along, but at last he had sufficiently regained his strength to crawl from the shelter and make his way unaided to the ground. Now he lived more upon raw meat, for which he was entirely dependent on Akut's skill and generosity. With the meat diet his strength returned more rapidly, and at last he felt that he was fit to undertake the journey to the village of the blacks.

CHAPTER 12

Two tall, bearded white men moved cautiously through the jungle from their camp beside a wide river. They were Carl Jenssen and Sven Malbihn, but little altered in appearance since the day, years before, that they and their safari had been so badly frightened by Korak and Akut as the former sought haven with them.

Every year had they come into the jungle to trade with the natives, or to rob them; to hunt and trap; or to guide other white men in the land they knew so well. Always since their experience with The Sheik had they operated at a safe distance from his territory.

Now they were closer to his village than they had been for years, yet safe enough from discovery owing to the uninhabited nature of the intervening jungle and the fear and enmity of Kovudoo's people for The Sheik, who, in time past, had raided and all but exterminated the tribe.

This year they had come to trap live specimens for a European zoological garden, and today they were approaching a trap which they had set in the hope of capturing a specimen of the large baboons that frequented the neighborhood. As they approached the trap they became aware from the noises emanating from its vicinity that their efforts had been crowned with success. The barking and screaming of hundreds of baboons could mean naught else than that one or more of their number had fallen a victim to the allurements of the bait.

The extreme caution of the two men was prompted by former experiences with the intelligent and doglike creatures with which they had to deal. More than one trapper has lost his life in battle with enraged baboons who will hesitate to attack nothing upon one occasion, while upon another a single gun shot will disperse hundreds of them.

Heretofore the Swedes had always watched near-by their trap, for as a rule only the stronger bulls are thus caught, since in their greediness they prevent the weaker from approaching the covered bait, and when once within the ordinary rude trap woven on the spot of interlaced branches they are able, with the aid of their friends upon the outside, to demolish their prison and escape. But in this instance the trappers had utilized a special steel cage which could withstand all the strength and cunning of a baboon. It was only necessary, therefore, to drive away the herd which they knew were surrounding the prison and wait for their boys who were even now following them to the trap.

As they came within sight of the spot they found conditions precisely as they had expected. A large male was battering frantically against the steel wires of the cage that held him captive. Upon the outside several hundred other baboons were tearing and tugging in his aid, and all were roaring and jabbering and barking at the top of their lungs.

But what neither the Swedes nor the baboons saw was the half-naked figure of a youth hidden in the foliage of a nearby tree. He had come upon the scene at almost the same instant as Jenssen and Malbihn, and was watching the activities of the baboons with every mark of interest.

Korak's relations with the baboons had never been over friendly. A species of armed toleration had marked their occasional meetings. The baboons and Akut had walked stiff legged and growling past one another, while Korak had maintained a bared fang neutrality. So now he was not greatly disturbed by the predicament of their king. Curiosity prompted him to tarry a moment, and in that moment his quick eyes caught the unfamiliar coloration of the clothing of the two Swedes behind a bush not far from him. Now he was all alertness. Who were these interlopers? What was their business in the jungle of the Mangani? Korak slunk noiselessly around them to a point where he might get their scent as well as a better view of them, and scarce had he done so when he recognized them—they were the men who had fired upon him years before. His eyes blazed. He could feel the hairs upon his scalp stiffen at the roots. He watched them with the intentness of a panther about to spring upon its prey.

He saw them rise and, shouting, attempt to frighten away the baboons as they approached the cage. Then one of them raised his rifle and fired into the midst of the surprised and angry herd. For an instant Korak thought that the baboons were about to charge, but two more shots from the rifles of the white men sent them scampering into the trees. Then the two Europeans advanced upon the cage. Korak thought that they were going to kill the king. He cared nothing for the king but he cared less for the two white men. The king had never attempted to kill him—the white men had. The king was a denizen of his own beloved jungle—the white men were aliens. His loyalty therefore was to the baboon against the human. He could speak the language of the baboon—it was identical to that of the great apes. Across the clearing he saw the jabbering horde watching.

Raising his voice he shouted to them. The white men turned at the sound of this new factor behind them. They thought it was another baboon that had circled them; but though they searched the trees with their eyes they saw nothing of the now silent figure hidden by the foliage. Again Korak shouted.

"I am The Killer," he cried. "These men are my enemies and yours. I will help you free your king. Run out upon the strangers when you see me do so, and together we will drive them away and free your king."

And from the baboons came a great chorus: "We will do what you say, Korak."

Dropping from his tree Korak ran toward the two Swedes, and at the same instant three hundred baboons followed his example. At sight of the strange apparition of the half-naked white warrior rushing upon them with uplifted spear Jenssen and Malbihn raised their rifles and fired at Korak; but in the excitement both missed and a moment later the baboons were upon them. Now their only hope of safety lay in escape, and dodging here and there, fighting off the great beasts that leaped upon their backs, they ran into the jungle. Even then they would have died but for the coming of their men whom they met a couple of hundred yards from the cage.

Once the white men had turned in flight Korak gave them no further attention, turning instead to the imprisoned baboon. The fastenings of the door that had eluded the mental powers of the baboons, yielded their secret immediately to the human intelligence of The Killer, and a moment later the king baboon stepped forth to liberty. He wasted no breath in thanks to Korak, nor did the young man expect thanks. He knew that none of the baboons would ever forget his service, though as a matter of fact he did not care if they did. What he had done had been prompted by a desire to be revenged upon the two white men. The baboons could never be of service to him. Now they were racing in the direction of the battle that was being waged between their fellows and the followers of the two Swedes, and as the din of battle subsided in the distance, Korak turned and resumed his journey toward the village of Kovudoo.

On the way he came upon a herd of elephants standing in an open forest glade. Here the trees were too far apart to permit Korak to travel through the branches—a trail he much preferred not only because of its freedom from dense underbrush and the wider field of vision it gave him but from pride in his arboreal ability. It was exhilarating to swing from tree to tree; to test the prowess of his mighty muscles; to reap the pleasurable fruits of his hard won agility. Korak joyed in the thrills of the highflung upper terraces of the great forest, where, unhampered and unhindered, he might laugh down upon the great brutes who must keep forever to the darkness and the gloom of the musty soil.

But here, in this open glade where Tantor flapped his giant ears and swayed his huge bulk from side to side, the ape-man must pass along the surface of the ground—a pygmy amongst giants. A great bull raised his trunk to rattle a low warning as he sensed the coming of an intruder. His weak eyes roved hither and thither but it was his keen scent and acute hearing which first located the ape-man. The herd moved restlessly, prepared for fight, for the old bull had caught the scent of man.

"Peace, Tantor," called The Killer. "It is I, Korak, Tarmangani."

The bull lowered his trunk and the herd resumed their interrupted meditations. Korak passed within a foot of the great bull. A sinuous trunk undulated toward him, touching his brown hide in a half caress. Korak slapped the great shoulder affectionately as he went by. For years he had been upon good terms with Tantor and his people. Of all the jungle folk he loved best the mighty pachyderm—the most peaceful and at the same time the most terrible of them all. The gentle gazelle feared him not, yet Numa, lord of the jungle, gave him a wide berth. Among the younger bulls, the cows and the calves Korak wound his way. Now and then another trunk would run out to touch him, and once a playful calf grasped his legs and upset him.

The afternoon was almost spent when Korak arrived at the village of Kovudoo. There were many natives lolling in shady spots beside the conical huts or beneath the branches of the several trees which had been left standing within the enclosure. Warriors were in evidence upon hand. It was not a good time for a lone enemy to prosecute a search through the village. Korak determined to await the coming of darkness. He was a match for many warriors; but he could not, unaided, overcome an entire tribe—not even for his beloved Meriem. While he waited among the branches and foliage of a near-by tree he searched the village constantly with his keen eyes, and twice he circled it, sniffing the vagrant breezes which puffed erratically from first one point of the compass and then another. Among the various stenches peculiar to a native village the ape-man's sensitive nostrils were finally rewarded by cognizance of the delicate aroma which marked the presence of her he sought. Meriem was there—in one of those huts! But which one he could not know without closer investigation, and so he waited, with the dogged patience of a beast of prey, until night had fallen.

The camp fires of the blacks dotted the gloom with little points of light, casting their feeble rays in tiny circles of luminosity that brought into glistening relief the naked bodies of those who lay or squatted about them. It was then that Korak slid silently from the tree that had hidden him and dropped lightly to the ground within the enclosure.

Keeping well in the shadows of the huts he commenced a systematic search of the village—ears, eyes and nose constantly upon the alert for the first intimation of the near presence of Meriem. His progress must of necessity be slow since not even the keen-eared curs of the savages must guess the presence of a stranger within the gates. How close he came to a detection on several occasions The Killer well knew from the restless whining of several of them.

It was not until he reached the back of a hut at the head of the wide village street that Korak caught again, plainly, the scent of Meriem. With nose close to the thatched wall Korak sniffed eagerly about the structure—tense and palpitant as a hunting hound. Toward the front and the door he made his way when once his nose had assured him that Meriem lay within; but as he rounded the side and came within view of the entrance he saw a burly Negro armed with a long spear squatting at the portal of the girl's prison. The fellow's back was toward him, his figure outlined against the glow of cooking fires further down the street. He was alone. The nearest of his fellows were beside a fire sixty or seventy feet beyond. To enter the hut Korak must either silence the sentry or pass him unnoticed. The danger in the accomplishment of the former alternative lay in the practical certainty of alarming the warriors near by and bringing them and the balance of the village down upon him. To achieve the latter appeared practically impossible. To you or me it would have been impossible; but Korak, The Killer, was not as you or I.

There was a good twelve inches of space between the broad back of the black and the frame of the doorway. Could Korak pass through behind the savage warrior without detection? The light that fell upon the glistening ebony of the sentry's black skin fell also upon the light brown of Korak's. Should one of the many further down the street chance to look long in this direction they must surely note the tall, light-colored, moving figure; but Korak depended upon their interest in their own gossip to hold their attention fast where it already lay, and upon the firelight near them to prevent them seeing too plainly at a distance into the darkness at the village end where his work lay.

Flattened against the side of the hut, yet not arousing a single warning rustle from its dried thatching, The Killer came closer and closer to the watcher. Now he was at his shoulder. Now he had wormed his sinuous way behind him. He could feel the heat of the naked body against his knees. He could hear the man breathe. He marveled that the dull-witted creature had not long since been alarmed; but the fellow sat there as ignorant of the presence of another as though that other had not existed.

Korak moved scarcely more than an inch at a time, then he would stand motionless for a moment. Thus was he worming his way behind the guard when the latter straightened up, opened his cavernous mouth in a wide yawn, and stretched his arms above his head. Korak stood rigid as stone. Another step and he would be within the hut. The black lowered his arms and relaxed. Behind him was the frame work of the doorway. Often before had it supported his sleepy head, and now he leaned back to enjoy the forbidden pleasure of a cat nap.

But instead of the door frame his head and shoulders came in contact with the warm flesh of a pair of living legs. The exclamation of surprise that almost burst from his lips was throttled in his throat by steel-thewed fingers that closed about his windpipe with the suddenness of thought. The black struggled to arise—to turn upon the creature that had seized him—to wriggle from its hold; but all to no purpose. As he had been held in a mighty vise of iron he could not move. He could not scream. Those awful fingers at his throat but closed more and more tightly. His eyes bulged from their sockets. His face turned an ashy blue. Presently he relaxed once more—this time in the final dissolution from which there is no quickening. Korak propped the dead body against the door frame. There it sat, lifelike in the gloom. Then the ape-man turned and glided into the Stygian darkness of the hut's interior.

"Meriem!" he whispered.

"Korak! My Korak!" came an answering cry, subdued by fear of alarming her captors, and half stifled by a sob of joyful welcome.

The youth knelt and cut the bonds that held the girl's wrists and ankles. A moment later he had lifted her to her feet, and grasping her by the hand led her towards the entrance. Outside the grim sentinel of death kept his grisly vigil. Sniffing at his dead feet whined a mangy native cur. At sight of the two emerging from the hut the beast gave an ugly snarl and an instant later as it caught the scent of the strange white man it raised a series of excited yelps. Instantly the warriors at the near-by fire were attracted. They turned their heads in the direction of the commotion. It was impossible that they should fail to see the white skins of the fugitives.

Korak slunk quickly into the shadows at the hut's side, drawing Meriem with him; but he was too late. The blacks had seen enough to arouse their suspicions and a dozen of them were now running to investigate. The yapping cur was still at Korak's heels leading the searchers unerringly in pursuit. The youth struck viciously at the brute with his long spear; but, long accustomed to dodging blows, the wily creature made a most uncertain target.

Other blacks had been alarmed by the running and shouting of their companions and now the entire population of the village was swarming up the street to assist in the search. Their first discovery was the dead body of the sentry, and a moment later one of the bravest of them had entered the hut and discovered the absence of the prisoner. These startling announcements filled the blacks with a combination of terror and rage; but, seeing no foe in evidence they were enabled to permit their rage to get the better of their terror, and so the leaders, pushed on by those behind them, ran rapidly around the hut in the direction of the yapping of the mangy cur. Here they found a single white warrior making away with their captive, and recognizing him as the author of numerous raids and indignities and believing that they had him cornered and at a disadvantage, they charged savagely upon him.

Korak, seeing that they were discovered, lifted Meriem to his shoulders and ran for the tree which would give them egress from the village. He was handicapped in his flight by the weight of the girl whose legs would but scarce bear her weight, to say nothing of maintaining her in rapid flight, for the tightly drawn bonds that had been about her ankles for so long had stopped circulation and partially paralyzed her extremities.

Had this not been the case the escape of the two would have been a feat of little moment, since Meriem was scarcely a whit less agile than Korak, and fully as much at home in the trees as he. But with the girl on his shoulder Korak could not both run and fight to advantage, and the result was that before he had covered half the distance to the tree a score of native curs attracted by the yelping of their mate and the yells and shouts of their masters had closed in upon the fleeing white man, snapping at his legs and at last succeeding in tripping him. As he went down the hyena-like brutes were upon him, and as he struggled to his feet the blacks closed in.

A couple of them seized the clawing, biting Meriem, and subdued her—a blow upon the head was sufficient. For the ape-man they found more drastic measures would be necessary.

Weighted down as he was by dogs and warriors he still managed to struggle to his feet. To right and left he swung crushing blows to the faces of his human antagonists—to the dogs he paid not the slightest attention other than to seize the more persistent and wring their necks with a single quick movement of the wrist.

A knob stick aimed at him by an ebon Hercules he caught and wrested from his antagonist, and then the blacks experienced to the full the possibilities for punishment that lay within those smooth flowing muscles beneath the velvet brown skin of the strange, white giant. He rushed among them with all the force and ferocity of a bull elephant gone mad. Hither and thither he charged striking down the few who had the temerity to stand against him, and it was evident that unless a chance spear thrust brought him down he would rout the entire village and regain his prize. But old Kovudoo was not to be so easily robbed of the ransom which the girl represented, and seeing that their attack which had up to now resulted in a series of individual combats with the white warrior, he called his tribesmen off, and forming them in a compact body about the girl and the two who watched over her bid them do nothing more than repel the assaults of the ape-man.

Again and again Korak rushed against this human barricade bristling with spear points. Again and again he was repulsed, often with severe wounds to caution him to greater wariness. From head to foot he was red with his own blood, and at last, weakening from the loss of it, he came to the bitter realization that alone he could do no more to succor his Meriem.

Presently an idea flashed through his brain. He called aloud to the girl. She had regained consciousness now and replied.

"Korak goes," he shouted; "but he will return and take you from the Gomangani. Good-bye, my Meriem. Korak will come for you again."

"Good-bye!" cried the girl. "Meriem will look for you until you come."

Like a flash, and before they could know his intention or prevent him, Korak wheeled, raced across the village and with a single leap disappeared into the foliage of the great tree that was his highroad to the village of Kovudoo. A shower of spears followed him, but their only harvest was a taunting laugh flung back from out the darkness of the jungle.

CHAPTER 13

Meriem, again bound and under heavy guard in Kovudoo's own hut, saw the night pass and the new day come without bringing the momentarily looked for return of Korak. She had no doubt but that he would come back and less still that he would easily free her from her captivity. To her Korak was little short of omnipotent. He embodied for her all that was finest and strongest and best in her savage world. She gloried in his prowess and worshipped him for the tender thoughtfulness that always had marked his treatment of her. No other within the ken of her memory had ever accorded her the love and gentleness that was his daily offering to her. Most of the gentler attributes of his early childhood had long since been forgotten in the fierce battle for existence which the customs of the mysterious jungle had forced upon him. He was more often savage and bloodthirsty than tender and kindly. His other friends of the wild looked for no gentle tokens of his affection. That he would hunt with them and fight for them was sufficient. If he growled and showed his fighting fangs when they trespassed upon his inalienable rights to the fruits of his kills they felt no anger toward him—only greater respect for the efficient and the fit—for him who could not only kill but protect the flesh of his kill.

But toward Meriem he always had shown more of his human side. He killed primarily for her. It was to the feet of Meriem that he brought the fruits of his labors. It was for Meriem more than for himself that he squatted beside his flesh and growled ominously at whosoever dared sniff too closely to it. When he was cold in the dark days of rain, or thirsty in a prolonged drouth, his discomfort engendered first of all thoughts of Meriem's welfare—after she had been made warm, after her thirst had been slaked, then he turned to the affair of ministering to his own wants.

The softest skins fell gracefully from the graceful shoulders of his Meriem. The sweetest-scented grasses lined her bower where other soft, furry pelts made hers the downiest couch in all the jungle.

What wonder then that Meriem loved her Korak? But she loved him as a little sister might love a big brother who was very good to her. As yet she knew naught of the love of a maid for a man.

So now as she lay waiting for him she dreamed of him and of all that he meant to her. She compared him with The Sheik, her father, and at thought of the stern, grizzled, old Arab she shuddered. Even the savage blacks had been less harsh to her than he. Not understanding their tongue she could not guess what purpose they had in keeping her a prisoner. She knew that man ate man, and she had expected to be eaten; but she had been with them for some time now and no harm had befallen her. She did not know that a runner had been dispatched to the distant village of The Sheik to barter with him for a ransom. She did not know, nor did Kovudoo, that the runner had never reached his destination—that he had fallen in with the safari of Jenssen and Malbihn and with the talkativeness of a native to other natives had unfolded his whole mission to the black servants of the two Swedes. These had not been long in retailing the matter to their masters, and the result was that when the runner left their camp to continue his journey he had scarce passed from sight before there came the report of a rifle and he rolled lifeless into the underbrush with a bullet in his back.

A few moments later Malbihn strolled back into the encampment, where he went to some pains to let it be known that he had had a shot at a fine buck and missed. The Swedes knew that their men hated them, and that an overt act against Kovudoo would quickly be carried to the chief at the first opportunity. Nor were they sufficiently strong in either guns or loyal followers to risk antagonizing the wily old chief.

Following this episode came the encounter with the baboons and the strange, white savage who had allied himself with the beasts against the humans. Only by dint of masterful maneuvering and the expenditure of much power had the Swedes been able to repulse the infuriated apes, and even for hours afterward their camp was constantly besieged by hundreds of snarling, screaming devils.

The Swedes, rifles in hand, repelled numerous savage charges which lacked only efficient leadership to have rendered them as effective in results as they were terrifying in appearance. Time and time again the two men thought they saw the smooth-skinned body of the wild ape-man moving among the baboons in the forest, and the belief that he might head a charge upon them proved most disquieting. They would have given much for a clean shot at him, for to him they attributed the loss of their specimen and the ugly attitude of the baboons toward them.

"The fellow must be the same we fired on several years ago," said Malbihn. "That time he was accompanied by a gorilla. Did you get a good look at him, Carl?"

"Yes," replied Jenssen. "He was not five paces from me when I fired at him. He appears to be an intelligent looking European—and not much more than a lad. There is nothing of the imbecile or degenerate in his features or expression, as is usually true in similar cases, where some lunatic escapes into the woods and by living in filth and nakedness wins the title of wild man among the peasants of the neighborhood. No, this fellow is of different stuff—and so infinitely more to be feared. As much as I should like a shot at him I hope he stays away. Should he ever deliberately lead a charge against us I wouldn't give much for our chances if we happened to fail to bag him at the first rush."

But the white giant did not appear again to lead the baboons against them, and finally the angry brutes themselves wandered off into the jungle leaving the frightened safari in peace.

The next day the Swedes set out for Kovudoo's village bent on securing possession of the person of the white girl whom Kovudoo's runner had told them lay captive in the chief's village. How they were to accomplish their end they did not know. Force was out of the question, though they would not have hesitated to use it had they possessed it. In former years they had marched rough shod over enormous areas, taking toll by brute force even when kindliness or diplomacy would have accomplished more; but now they were in bad straits—so bad that they had shown their true colors scarce twice in a year and then only when they came upon an isolated village, weak in numbers and poor in courage.

Kovudoo was not as these, and though his village was in a way remote from the more populous district to the north his power was such that he maintained an acknowledged suzerainty over the thin thread of villages which connected him with the savage lords to the north. To have antagonized him would have spelled ruin for the Swedes. It would have meant that they might never reach civilization by the northern route. To the west, the village of The Sheik lay directly in their path, barring them effectually. To the east the trail was unknown to them, and to the south there was no trail. So the two Swedes approached the village of Kovudoo with friendly words upon their tongues and deep craft in their hearts.

Their plans were well made. There was no mention of the white prisoner—they chose to pretend that they were not aware that Kovudoo had a white prisoner. They exchanged gifts with the old chief, haggling with his plenipotentiaries over the value of what they were to receive for what they gave, as is customary and proper when one has no ulterior motives. Unwarranted generosity would have aroused suspicion.

During the palaver which followed they retailed the gossip of the villages through which they had passed, receiving in exchange such news as Kovudoo possessed. The palaver was long and tiresome, as these native ceremonies always are to Europeans. Kovudoo made no mention of his prisoner and from his generous offers of guides and presents seemed anxious to assure himself of the speedy departure of his guests. It was Malbihn who, quite casually, near the close of their talk, mentioned the fact that The Sheik was dead. Kovudoo evinced interest and surprise.

"You did not know it?" asked Malbihn. "That is strange. It was during the last moon. He fell from his horse when the beast stepped in a hole. The horse fell upon him. When his men came up The Sheik was quite dead."

Kovudoo scratched his head. He was much disappointed. No Sheik meant no ransom for the white girl. Now she was worthless, unless he utilized her for a feast or—a mate. The latter thought aroused him. He spat at a small beetle crawling through the dust before him. He eyed Malbihn appraisingly. These white men were peculiar. They traveled far from their own villages without women. Yet he knew they cared for women. But how much did they care for them?—that was the question that disturbed Kovudoo.

"I know where there is a white girl," he said, unexpectedly. "If you wish to buy her she may be had cheap."

Malbihn shrugged. "We have troubles enough, Kovudoo," he said, "without burdening ourselves with an old she-hyena, and as for paying for one—" Malbihn snapped his fingers in derision.

"She is young," said Kovudoo, "and good looking."

The Swedes laughed. "There are no good looking white women in the jungle, Kovudoo," said Jenssen. "You should be ashamed to try to make fun of old friends."

Kovudoo sprang to his feet. "Come," he said, "I will show you that she is all I say."

Malbihn and Jenssen rose to follow him and as they did so their eyes met, and Malbihn slowly drooped one of his lids in a sly wink. Together they followed Kovudoo toward his hut. In the dim interior they discerned the figure of a woman lying bound upon a sleeping mat.

Malbihn took a single glance and turned away. "She must be a thousand years old, Kovudoo," he said, as he left the hut.

"She is young," cried the savage. "It is dark in here. You cannot see. Wait, I will have her brought out into the sunlight," and he commanded the two warriors who watched the girl to cut the bonds from her ankles and lead her forth for inspection.

Malbihn and Jenssen evinced no eagerness, though both were fairly bursting with it—not to see the girl but to obtain possession of her. They cared not if she had the face of a marmoset, or the figure of pot-bellied Kovudoo himself. All that they wished to know was that she was the girl who had been stolen from The Sheik several years before. They thought that they would recognize her for such if she was indeed the same, but even so the testimony of the runner Kovudoo had sent to The Sheik was such as to assure them that the girl was the one they had once before attempted to abduct.

As Meriem was brought forth from the darkness of the hut's interior the two men turned with every appearance of disinterestedness to glance at her. It was with difficulty that Malbihn suppressed an ejaculation of astonishment. The girl's beauty fairly took his breath from him; but instantly he recovered his poise and turned to Kovudoo.

"Well?" he said to the old chief.

"Is she not both young and good looking?" asked Kovudoo.

"She is not old," replied Malbihn; "but even so she will be a burden. We did not come from the north after wives—there are more than enough there for us."

Meriem stood looking straight at the white men. She expected nothing from them—they were to her as much enemies as the black men. She hated and feared them all. Malbihn spoke to her in Arabic.

"We are friends," he said. "Would you like to have us take you away from here?"

Slowly and dimly as though from a great distance recollection of the once familiar tongue returned to her.

"I should like to go free," she said, "and go back to Korak."

"You would like to go with us?" persisted Malbihn.

"No," said Meriem.

Malbihn turned to Kovudoo. "She does not wish to go with us," he said.

"You are men," returned the black. "Can you not take her by force?"

"It would only add to our troubles," replied the Swede. "No, Kovudoo, we do not wish her; though, if you wish to be rid of her, we will take her away because of our friendship for you."

Now Kovudoo knew that he had made a sale. They wanted her. So he commenced to bargain, and in the end the person of Meriem passed from the possession of the black chieftain into that of the two Swedes in consideration of six yards of Amerikan, three empty brass cartridge shells and a shiny, new jack knife from New Jersey. And all but Meriem were more than pleased with the bargain.

Kovudoo stipulated but a single condition and that was that the Europeans were to leave his village and take the girl with them as early the next morning as they could get started. After the sale was consummated he did not hesitate to explain his reasons for this demand. He told them of the strenuous attempt of the girl's savage mate to rescue her, and suggested that the sooner they got her out of the country the more likely they were to retain possession of her.

Meriem was again bound and placed under guard, but this time in the tent of the Swedes. Malbihn talked to her, trying to persuade her to accompany them willingly. He told her that they would return her to her own village; but when he discovered that she would rather die than go back to the old sheik, he assured her that they would not take her there, nor, as a matter of fact, had they had an intention of so doing. As he talked with the girl the Swede feasted his eyes upon the beautiful lines of her face and figure. She had grown tall and straight and slender toward maturity since he had seen her in The Sheik's village on that long gone day. For years she had represented to him a certain fabulous reward. In his thoughts she had been but the personification of the pleasures and luxuries that many francs would purchase. Now as she stood before him pulsing with life and loveliness she suggested other seductive and alluring possibilities. He came closer to her and laid his hand upon her. The girl shrank from him. He seized her and she struck him heavily in the mouth as he sought to kiss her. Then Jenssen entered the tent.

"Malbihn!" he almost shouted. "You fool!"

Sven Malbihn released his hold upon the girl and turned toward his companion. His face was red with mortification.

"What the devil are you trying to do?" growled Jenssen. "Would you throw away every chance for the reward? If we maltreat her we not only couldn't collect a sou, but they'd send us to prison for our pains. I thought you had more sense, Malbihn."

"I'm not a wooden man," growled Malbihn.

"You'd better be," rejoined Jenssen, "at least until we have delivered her over in safety and collected what will be coming to us."

"Oh, hell," cried Malbihn. "What's the use? They'll be glad enough to have her back, and by the time we get there with her she'll be only too glad to keep her mouth shut. Why not?"

"Because I say not," growled Jenssen. "I've always let you boss things, Sven; but here's a case where what I say has got to go—because I'm right and you're wrong, and we both know it."

"You're getting damned virtuous all of a sudden," growled Malbihn. "Perhaps you think I have forgotten about the inn keeper's daughter, and little Celella, and that nigger at—"

"Shut up!" snapped Jenssen. "It's not a matter of virtue and you are as well aware of that as I. I don't want to quarrel with you, but so help me God, Sven, you're not going to harm this girl if I have to kill you to prevent it. I've suffered and slaved and been nearly killed forty times in the last nine or ten years trying to accomplish what luck has thrown at our feet at last, and now I'm not going to be robbed of the fruits of success because you happen to be more of a beast than a man. Again I warn you, Sven—" and he tapped the revolver that swung in its holster at his hip.

Malbihn gave his friend an ugly look, shrugged his shoulders, and left the tent. Jenssen turned to Meriem. "If he bothers you again, call me," he said. "I shall always be near."

The girl had not understood the conversation that had been carried on by her two owners, for it had been in Swedish; but what Jenssen had just said to her in Arabic she understood and from it grasped an excellent idea of what had passed between the two. The expressions upon their faces, their gestures, and Jenssen's final tapping of his revolver before Malbihn had left the tent had all been eloquent of the seriousness of their altercation. Now, toward Jenssen she looked for friendship, and with the innocence of youth she threw herself upon his mercy, begging him to set her free, that she might return to Korak and her jungle life; but she was doomed to another disappointment, for the man only laughed at her roughly and told her that if she tried to escape she would be punished by the very thing that he had just saved her from.

All that night she lay listening for a signal from Korak. All about the jungle life moved through the darkness. To her sensitive ears came sounds that the others in the camp could not hear—sounds that she interpreted as we might interpret the speech of a friend, but not once came a single note that reflected the presence of Korak. But she knew that he would come. Nothing short of death itself could prevent her Korak from returning for her. What delayed him though?

When morning came again and the night had brought no succoring Korak, Meriem's faith and loyalty were still unshaken though misgivings began to assail her as to the safety of her friend. It seemed unbelievable that serious mishap could have overtaken her wonderful Korak who daily passed unscathed through all the terrors of the jungle. Yet morning came, the morning meal was eaten, the camp broken and the disreputable safari of the Swedes was on the move northward with still no sign of the rescue the girl momentarily expected.

All that day they marched, and the next and the next, nor did Korak even so much as show himself to the patient little waiter moving, silently and stately, beside her hard captors.

Malbihn remained scowling and angry. He replied to Jenssen's friendly advances in curt monosyllables. To Meriem he did not speak, but on several occasions she discovered him glaring at her from beneath half closed lids—greedily. The look sent a shudder through her. She hugged Geeka closer to her breast and doubly regretted the knife that they had taken from her when she was captured by Kovudoo.

It was on the fourth day that Meriem began definitely to give up hope. Something had happened to Korak. She knew it. He would never come now, and these men would take her far away. Presently they would kill her. She would never see her Korak again.

On this day the Swedes rested, for they had marched rapidly and their men were tired. Malbihn and Jenssen had gone from camp to hunt, taking different directions. They had been gone about an hour when the door of Meriem's tent was lifted and Malbihn entered. The look of a beast was on his face.

CHAPTER 14

With wide eyes fixed upon him, like a trapped creature horrified beneath the mesmeric gaze of a great serpent, the girl watched the approach of the man. Her hands were free, the Swedes having secured her with a length of ancient slave chain fastened at one end to an iron collar padlocked about her neck and at the other to a long stake driven deep into the ground.

Slowly Meriem shrank inch by inch toward the opposite end of the tent. Malbihn followed her. His hands were extended and his fingers half-opened—claw-like—to seize her. His lips were parted, and his breath came quickly, pantingly.

The girl recalled Jenssen's instructions to call him should Malbihn molest her; but Jenssen had gone into the jungle to hunt. Malbihn had chosen his time well. Yet she screamed, loud and shrill, once, twice, a third time, before Malbihn could leap across the tent and throttle her alarming cries with his brute fingers. Then she fought him, as any jungle she might fight, with tooth and nail. The man found her no easy prey. In that slender, young body, beneath the rounded curves and the fine, soft skin, lay the muscles of a young lioness. But Malbihn was no weakling. His character and appearance were brutal, nor did they belie his brawn. He was of giant stature and of giant strength. Slowly he forced the girl back upon the ground, striking her in the face when she hurt him badly either with teeth or nails. Meriem struck back, but she was growing weaker from the choking fingers at her throat.

Out in the jungle Jenssen had brought down two bucks. His hunting had not carried him far afield, nor was he prone to permit it to do so. He was suspicious of Malbihn. The very fact that his companion had refused to accompany him and elected instead to hunt alone in another direction would not, under ordinary circumstances, have seemed fraught with sinister suggestion; but Jenssen knew Malbihn well, and so, having secured meat, he turned immediately back toward camp, while his boys brought in his kill.

He had covered about half the return journey when a scream came faintly to his ears from the direction of camp. He halted to listen. It was repeated twice. Then silence. With a muttered curse Jenssen broke into a rapid run. He wondered if he would be too late. What a fool Malbihn was indeed to thus chance jeopardizing a fortune!

Further away from camp than Jenssen and upon the opposite side another heard Meriem's screams—a stranger who was not even aware of the proximity of white men other than himself—a hunter with a handful of sleek, black warriors. He, too, listened intently for a moment. That the voice was that of a woman in distress he could not doubt, and so he also hastened at a run in the direction of the affrighted voice; but he was much further away than Jenssen so that the latter reached the tent first. What the Swede found there roused no pity within his calloused heart, only anger against his fellow scoundrel. Meriem was still fighting off her attacker. Malbihn still was showering blows upon her. Jenssen, streaming foul curses upon his erstwhile friend, burst into the tent. Malbihn, interrupted, dropped his victim and turned to meet Jenssen's infuriated charge. He whipped a revolver from his hip. Jenssen, anticipating the lightning move of the other's hand, drew almost simultaneously, and both men fired at once. Jenssen was still moving toward Malbihn at the time, but at the flash of the explosion he stopped. His revolver dropped from nerveless fingers. For a moment he staggered drunkenly. Deliberately Malbihn put two more bullets into his friend's body at close range. Even in the midst of the excitement and her terror Meriem found herself wondering at the tenacity of life which the hit man displayed. His eyes were closed, his head dropped forward upon his breast, his hands hung limply before him. Yet still he stood there upon his feet, though he reeled horribly. It was not until the third bullet had found its mark within his body that he lunged forward upon his face. Then Malbihn approached him, and with an oath kicked him viciously. Then he returned once more to Meriem. Again he seized her, and at the same instant the flaps of the tent opened silently and a tall white man stood in the aperture. Neither Meriem or Malbihn saw the newcomer. The latter's back was toward him while his body hid the stranger from Meriem's eyes.

He crossed the tent quickly, stepping over Jenssen's body. The first intimation Malbihn had that he was not to carry out his design without further interruption was a heavy hand upon his shoulder. He wheeled to face an utter stranger—a tall, black-haired, gray-eyed stranger clad in khaki and pith helmet. Malbihn reached for his gun again, but another hand had been quicker than his and he saw the weapon tossed to the ground at the side of the tent—out of reach.

"What is the meaning of this?" the stranger addressed his question to Meriem in a tongue she did not understand. She shook her head and spoke in Arabic. Instantly the man changed his question to that language.

"These men are taking me away from Korak," explained the girl. "This one would have harmed me. The other, whom he had just killed, tried to stop him. They were both very bad men; but this one is the worse. If my Korak were here he would kill him. I suppose you are like them, so you will not kill him."

The stranger smiled. "He deserves killing?" he said. "There is no doubt of that. Once I should have killed him; but not now. I will see, though, that he does not bother you any more."

He was holding Malbihn in a grasp the giant Swede could not break, though he struggled to do so, and he was holding him as easily as Malbihn might have held a little child, yet Malbihn was a huge man, mightily thewed. The Swede began to rage and curse. He struck at his captor, only to be twisted about and held at arm's length. Then he shouted to his boys to come and kill the stranger. In response a dozen strange blacks entered the tent. They, too, were powerful, clean-limbed men, not at all like the mangy crew that followed the Swedes.

"We have had enough foolishness," said the stranger to Malbihn. "You deserve death, but I am not the law. I know now who you are. I have heard of you before. You and your friend here bear a most unsavory reputation. We do not want you in our country. I shall let you go this time; but should you ever return I shall take the law into my own hands. You understand?"

Malbihn blustered and threatened, finishing by applying a most uncomplimentary name to his captor. For this he received a shaking that rattled his teeth. Those who know say that the most painful punishment that can be inflicted upon an adult male, short of injuring him, is a good, old fashioned shaking. Malbihn received such a shaking.

"Now get out," said the stranger, "and next time you see me remember who I am," and he spoke a name in the Swede's ear—a name that more effectually subdued the scoundrel than many beatings—then he gave him a push that carried him bodily through the tent doorway to sprawl upon the turf beyond.

"Now," he said, turning toward Meriem, "who has the key to this thing about your neck?"

The girl pointed to Jenssen's body. "He carried it always," she said.

The stranger searched the clothing on the corpse until he came upon the key. A moment more Meriem was free.

"Will you let me go back to my Korak?" she asked.

"I will see that you are returned to your people," he replied. "Who are they and where is their village?"

He had been eyeing her strange, barbaric garmenture wonderingly. From her speech she was evidently an Arab girl; but he had never before seen one thus clothed.

"Who are your people? Who is Korak?" he asked again.

"Korak! Why Korak is an ape. I have no other people. Korak and I live in the jungle alone since A'ht went to be king of the apes." She had always thus pronounced Akut's name, for so it had sounded to her when first she came with Korak and the ape. "Korak could have been kind, but he would not."

A questioning expression entered the stranger's eyes. He looked at the girl closely.

"So Korak is an ape?" he said. "And what, pray, are you?"

"I am Meriem. I, also, am an ape."

"M-m," was the stranger's only oral comment upon this startling announcement; but what he thought might have been partially interpreted through the pitying light that entered his eyes. He approached the girl and started to lay his hand upon her forehead. She drew back with a savage little growl. A smile touched his lips.

"You need not fear me," he said. "I shall not harm you. I only wish to discover if you have fever—if you are entirely well. If you are we will set forth in search of Korak."

Meriem looked straight into the keen gray eyes. She must have found there an unquestionable assurance of the honorableness of their owner, for she permitted him to lay his palm upon her forehead and feel her pulse. Apparently she had no fever.

"How long have you been an ape?" asked the man.

"Since I was a little girl, many, many years ago, and Korak came and took me from my father who was beating me. Since then I have lived in the trees with Korak and A'ht."

"Where in the jungle lives Korak?" asked the stranger.

Meriem pointed with a sweep of her hand that took in, generously, half the continent of Africa. "Could you find your way back to him?"

"I do not know," she replied; "but he will find his way to me."

"Then I have a plan," said the stranger. "I live but a few marches from here. I shall take you home where my wife will look after you and care for you until we can find Korak or Korak finds us. If he could find you here he can find you at my village. Is it not so?"

Meriem thought that it was so; but she did not like the idea of not starting immediately back to meet Korak. On the other hand the man had no intention of permitting this poor, insane child to wander further amidst the dangers of the jungle. From whence she had come, or what she had undergone he could not guess, but that her Korak and their life among the apes was but a figment of a disordered mind he could not doubt. He knew the jungle well, and he knew that men have lived alone and naked among the savage beasts for years; but a frail and slender girl! No, it was not possible.

Together they went outside. Malbihn's boys were striking camp in preparation for a hasty departure. The stranger's blacks were conversing with them. Malbihn stood at a distance, angry and glowering. The stranger approached one of his own men.

"Find out where they got this girl," he commanded.

The Negro thus addressed questioned one of Malbihn's followers. Presently he returned to his master.

"They bought her from old Kovudoo," he said. "That is all that this fellow will tell me. He pretends that he knows nothing more, and I guess that he does not. These two white men were very bad men. They did many things that their boys knew not the meanings of. It would be well, Bwana, to kill the other."

"I wish that I might; but a new law is come into this part of the jungle. It is not as it was in the old days, Muviri," replied the master.

The stranger remained until Malbihn and his safari had disappeared into the jungle toward the north. Meriem, trustful now, stood at his side, Geeka clutched in one slim, brown hand. They talked together, the man wondering at the faltering Arabic of the girl, but attributing it finally to her defective mentality. Could he have known that years had elapsed since she had used it until she was taken by the Swedes he would not have wondered that she had half forgotten it. There was yet another reason why the language of The Sheik had thus readily eluded her; but of that reason she herself could not have guessed the truth any better than could the man.

He tried to persuade her to return with him to his "village" as he called it, or douar, in Arabic; but she was insistent upon searching immediately for Korak. As a last resort he determined to take her with him by force rather than sacrifice her life to the insane hallucination which haunted her; but, being a wise man, he determined to humor her first and then attempt to lead her as he would have her go. So when they took up their march it was in the direction of the south, though his own ranch lay almost due east.

By degrees he turned the direction of their way more and more eastward, and greatly was he pleased to note that the girl failed to discover that any change was being made. Little by little she became more trusting. At first she had had but her intuition to guide her belief that this big Tarmangani meant her no harm, but as the days passed and she saw that his kindness and consideration never faltered she came to compare him with Korak, and to be very fond of him; but never did her loyalty to her apeman flag.

On the fifth day they came suddenly upon a great plain and from the edge of the forest the girl saw in the distance fenced fields and many buildings. At the sight she drew back in astonishment.

"Where are we?" she asked, pointing.

"We could not find Korak," replied the man, "and as our way led near my douar I have brought you here to wait and rest with my wife until my men can find your ape, or he finds you. It is better thus, little one. You will be safer with us, and you will be happier."

"I am afraid, Bwana," said the girl. "In thy douar they will beat me as did The Sheik, my father. Let me go back into the jungle. There Korak will find me. He would not think to look for me in the douar of a white man."

"No one will beat you, child," replied the man. "I have not done so, have I? Well, here all belong to me. They will treat you well. Here no one is beaten. My wife will be very good to you, and at last Korak will come, for I shall send men to search for him."

The girl shook her head. "They could not bring him, for he would kill them, as all men have tried to kill him. I am afraid. Let me go, Bwana."

"You do not know the way to your own country. You would be lost. The leopards or the lions would get you the first night, and after all you would not find your Korak. It is better that you stay with us. Did I not save you from the bad man? Do you not owe me something for that? Well, then remain with us for a few weeks at least until we can determine what is best for you. You are only a little girl—it would be wicked to permit you to go alone into the jungle."

Meriem laughed. "The jungle," she said, "is my father and my mother. It has been kinder to me than have men. I am not afraid of the jungle. Nor am I afraid of the leopard or the lion. When my time comes I shall die. It may be that a leopard or a lion shall kill me, or it may be a tiny bug no bigger than the end of my littlest finger. When the lion leaps upon me, or the little bug stings me I shall be afraid—oh, then I shall be terribly afraid, I know; but life would be very miserable indeed were I to spend it in terror of the thing that has not yet happened. If it be the lion my terror shall be short of life; but if it be the little bug I may suffer for days before I die. And so I fear the lion least of all. He is great and noisy. I can hear him, or see him, or smell him in time to escape; but any moment I may place a hand or foot on the little bug, and never know that he is there until I feel his deadly sting. No, I do not fear the jungle. I love it. I should rather die than leave it forever; but your douar is close beside the jungle. You have been good to me. I will do as you wish, and remain here for a while to wait the coming of my Korak."

"Good!" said the man, and he led the way down toward the flower-covered bungalow behind which lay the barns and out-houses of a well-ordered African farm.

As they came nearer a dozen dogs ran barking toward them—gaunt wolf hounds, a huge great Dane, a nimble-footed collie and a number of yapping, quarrelsome fox terriers. At first their appearance was savage and unfriendly in the extreme; but once they recognized the foremost black warriors, and the white man behind them their attitude underwent a remarkable change. The collie and the fox terriers became frantic with delirious joy, and while the wolf hounds and the great Dane were not a whit less delighted at the return of their master their greetings were of a more dignified nature. Each in turn sniffed at Meriem who displayed not the slightest fear of any of them.

The wolf hounds bristled and growled at the scent of wild beasts that clung to her garment; but when she laid her hand upon their heads and her soft voice murmured caressingly they half-closed their eyes, lifting their upper lips in contented canine smiles. The man was watching them and he too smiled, for it was seldom that these savage brutes took thus kindly to strangers. It was as though in some subtle way the girl had breathed a message of kindred savagery to their savage hearts.

With her slim fingers grasping the collar of a wolf hound upon either side of her Meriem walked on toward the bungalow upon the porch of which a woman dressed in white waved a welcome to her returning lord. There was more fear in the girl's eyes now than there had been in the presence of strange men or savage beasts. She hesitated, turning an appealing glance toward the man.

"This is my wife," he said. "She will be glad to welcome you."

The woman came down the path to meet them. The man kissed her, and turning toward Meriem introduced them, speaking in the Arab tongue the girl understood.

"This is Meriem, my dear," he said, and he told the story of the jungle waif in so far as he knew it.

Meriem saw that the woman was beautiful. She saw that sweetness and goodness were stamped indelibly upon her countenance. She no longer feared her, and when her brief story had been narrated and the woman came and put her arms about her and kissed her and called her "poor little darling" something snapped in Meriem's little heart. She buried her face on the bosom of this new friend in whose voice was the mother tone that Meriem had not heard for so many years that she had forgotten its very existence. She buried her face on the kindly bosom and wept as she had not wept before in all her life—tears of relief and joy that she could not fathom.

And so came Meriem, the savage little Mangani, out of her beloved jungle into the midst of a home of culture and refinement. Already "Bwana" and "My Dear," as she first heard them called and continued to call them, were as father and mother to her. Once her savage fears allayed, she went to the opposite extreme of trustfulness and love. Now she was willing to wait here until they found Korak, or Korak found her. She did not give up that thought—Korak, her Korak always was first.

CHAPTER 15

And out in the jungle, far away, Korak, covered with wounds, stiff with clotted blood, burning with rage and sorrow, swung back upon the trail of the great baboons. He had not found them where he had last seen them, nor in any of their usual haunts; but he sought them along the well-marked spoor they had left behind them, and at last he overtook them. When first he came upon them they were moving slowly but steadily southward in one of those periodic migrations the reasons for which the baboon himself is best able to explain. At sight of the white warrior who came upon them from down wind the herd halted in response to the warning cry of the sentinel that had discovered him. There was much growling and muttering; much stiff-legged circling on the part of the bulls. The mothers, in nervous, high pitched tones, called their young to their sides, and with them moved to safety behind their lords and masters.

Korak called aloud to the king, who, at the familiar voice, advanced slowly, warily, and still stiff-legged. He must have the confirmatory evidence of his nose before venturing to rely too implicitly upon the testimony of his ears and eyes. Korak stood perfectly still. To have advanced then might have precipitated an immediate attack, or, as easily, a panic of flight. Wild beasts are creatures of nerves. It is a relatively simple thing to throw them into a species of hysteria which may induce either a mania for murder, or symptoms of apparent abject cowardice—it is a question, however, if a wild animal ever is actually a coward.

The king baboon approached Korak. He walked around him in an ever decreasing circle—growling, grunting, sniffing. Korak spoke to him.

"I am Korak," he said. "I opened the cage that held you. I saved you from the Tarmangani. I am Korak, The Killer. I am your friend."

"Huh," grunted the king. "Yes, you are Korak. My ears told me that you were Korak. My eyes told you that you were Korak. Now my nose tells me that you are Korak. My nose is never wrong. I am your friend. Come, we shall hunt together."

"Korak cannot hunt now," replied the ape-man. "The Gomangani have stolen Meriem. They have tied her in their village. They will not let her go. Korak, alone, was unable to set her free. Korak set you free. Now will you bring your people and set Korak's Meriem free?"

"The Gomangani have many sharp sticks which they throw. They pierce the bodies of my people. They kill us. The gomangani are bad people. They will kill us all if we enter their village."

"The Tarmangani have sticks that make a loud noise and kill at a great distance," replied Korak. "They had these when Korak set you free from their trap. If Korak had run away from them you would now be a prisoner among the Tarmangani."

The baboon scratched his head. In a rough circle about him and the ape-man squatted the bulls of his herd. They blinked their eyes, shouldered one another about for more advantageous positions, scratched in the rotting vegetation upon the chance of unearthing a toothsome worm, or sat listlessly eyeing their king and the strange Mangani, who called himself thus but who more closely resembled the hated Tarmangani. The king looked at some of the older of his subjects, as though inviting suggestion.

"We are too few," grunted one.

"There are the baboons of the hill country," suggested another. "They are as many as the leaves of the forest. They, too, hate the Gomangani. They love to fight. They are very savage. Let us ask them to accompany us. Then can we kill all the Gomangani in the jungle." He rose and growled horribly, bristling his stiff hair.

"That is the way to talk," cried The Killer, "but we do not need the baboons of the hill country. We are enough. It will take a long time to fetch them. Meriem may be dead and eaten before we could free her. Let us set out at once for the village of the Gomangani. If we travel very fast it will not take long to reach it. Then, all at the same time, we can charge into the village, growling and barking. The Gomangani will be very frightened and will run away. While they are gone we can seize Meriem and carry her off. We do not have to kill or be killed—all that Korak wishes is his Meriem."

"We are too few," croaked the old ape again.

"Yes, we are too few," echoed others.

Korak could not persuade them. They would help him, gladly; but they must do it in their own way and that meant enlisting the services of their kinsmen and allies of the hill country. So Korak was forced to give in. All he could do for the present was to urge them to haste, and at his suggestion the king baboon with a dozen of his mightiest bulls agreed to go to the hill country with Korak, leaving the balance of the herd behind.

Once enlisted in the adventure the baboons became quite enthusiastic about it. The delegation set off immediately. They traveled swiftly; but the ape-man found no difficulty in keeping up with them. They made a tremendous racket as they passed through the trees in an endeavor to suggest to enemies in their front that a great herd was approaching, for when the baboons travel in large numbers there is no jungle creature who cares to molest them. When the nature of the country required much travel upon the level, and the distance between trees was great, they moved silently, knowing that the lion and the leopard would not be fooled by noise when they could see plainly for themselves that only a handful of baboons were on the trail.

For two days the party raced through the savage country, passing out of the dense jungle into an open plain, and across this to timbered mountain slopes. Here Korak never before had been. It was a new country to him and the change from the monotony of the circumscribed view in the jungle was pleasing. But he had little desire to enjoy the beauties of nature at this time. Meriem, his Meriem was in danger. Until she was freed and returned to him he had little thought for aught else.

Once in the forest that clothed the mountain slopes the baboons advanced more slowly. Constantly they gave tongue to a plaintive note of calling. Then would follow silence while they listened. At last, faintly from the distance straight ahead came an answer.

The baboons continued to travel in the direction of the voices that floated through the forest to them in the intervals of their own silence. Thus, calling and listening, they came closer to their kinsmen, who, it was evident to Korak, were coming to meet them in great numbers; but when, at last, the baboons of the hill country came in view the ape-man was staggered at the reality that broke upon his vision.

What appeared a solid wall of huge baboons rose from the ground through the branches of the trees to the loftiest terrace to which they dared entrust their weight. Slowly they were approaching, voicing their weird, plaintive call, and behind them, as far as Korak's eyes could pierce the verdure, rose solid walls of their fellows treading close upon their heels. There were thousands of them. The ape-man could not but think of the fate of his little party should some untoward incident arouse even momentarily the rage of fear of a single one of all these thousands.

But nothing such befell. The two kings approached one another, as was their custom, with much sniffing and bristling. They satisfied themselves of each other's identity. Then each scratched the other's back. After

EDGAR RICE BURROUGHS

a moment they spoke together. Korak's friend explained the nature of their visit, and for the first time Korak showed himself. He had been hiding behind a bush. The excitement among the hill baboons was intense at sight of him. For a moment Korak feared that he should be torn to pieces; but his fear was for Meriem. Should he die there would be none to succor her.

The two kings, however, managed to quiet the multitude, and Korak was permitted to approach. Slowly the hill baboons came closer to him. They sniffed at him from every angle. When he spoke to them in their own tongue they were filled with wonder and delight. They talked to him and listened while he spoke. He told them of Meriem, and of their life in the jungle where they were the friends of all the ape folk from little Manu to Mangani, the great ape.

"The Gomangani, who are keeping Meriem from me, are no friends of yours," he said. "They kill you. The baboons of the low country are too few to go against them. They tell me that you are very many and very brave—that your numbers are as the numbers of the grasses upon the plains or the leaves within the forest, and that even Tantor, the elephant, fears you, so brave you are. They told me that you would be happy to accompany us to the village of the Gomangani and punish these bad people while I, Korak, The Killer, carry away my Meriem."

The king ape puffed out his chest and strutted about very stiff-legged indeed. So also did many of the other great bulls of his nation. They were pleased and flattered by the words of the strange Tarmangani, who called himself Mangani and spoke the language of the hairy progenitors of man.

"Yes," said one, "we of the hill country are mighty fighters. Tantor fears us. Numa fears us. Sheeta fears us. The Gomangani of the hill country are glad to pass us by in peace. I, for one, will come with you to the village of the Gomangani of the low places. I am the king's first he-child. Alone can I kill all the Gomangani of the low country," and he swelled his chest and strutted proudly back and forth, until the itching back of a comrade commanded his industrious attention.

"I am Goob," cried another. "My fighting fangs are long. They are sharp. They are strong. Into the soft flesh of many a Gomangani have they been buried. Alone I slew the sister of Sheeta. Goob will go to the low country with you and kill so many of the Gomangani that there will be none left to count the dead," and then he, too, strutted and pranced before the admiring eyes of the shes and the young.

Korak looked at the king, questioningly.

"Your bulls are very brave," he said; "but braver than any is the king."

Thus addressed, the shaggy bull, still in his prime—else he had been no longer king—growled ferociously. The forest echoed to his lusty challenges. The little baboons clutched fearfully at their mothers' hairy necks. The bulls, electrified, leaped high in air and took up the roaring challenge of their king. The din was terrific.

Korak came close to the king and shouted in his ear, "Come." Then he started off through the forest toward the plain that they must cross on their long journey back to the village of Kovudoo, the Gomangani. The king, still roaring and shrieking, wheeled and followed him. In their wake came the handful of low country baboons and the thousands of the hill clan—savage, wiry, dog-like creatures, athirst for blood.

And so they came, upon the second day, to the village of Kovudoo. It was mid-afternoon. The village was sunk in the quiet of the great equatorial sun-heat. The mighty herd traveled quietly now. Beneath the thousands of padded feet the forest gave forth no greater sound than might have been produced by the increased soughing of a stronger breeze through the leafy branches of the trees.

Korak and the two kings were in the lead. Close beside the village they halted until the stragglers had closed up. Now utter silence reigned. Korak, creeping stealthily, entered the tree that overhung the palisade. He glanced behind him. The pack were close upon his heels. The time had come. He had warned them continuously during the long march that no harm must befall the white she who lay a prisoner within the village. All others were their legitimate prey. Then, raising his face toward the sky, he gave voice to a single cry. It was the signal.

In response three thousand hairy bulls leaped screaming and barking into the village of the terrified blacks. Warriors poured from every hut. Mothers gathered their babies in their arms and fled toward the gates as they saw the horrid horde pouring into the village street. Kovudoo marshaled his fighting men about him and, leaping and yelling to arouse their courage, offered a bristling, spear tipped front to the charging horde.

Korak, as he had led the march, led the charge. The blacks were struck with horror and dismay at the sight of this white-skinned youth at the head of a pack of hideous baboons. For an instant they held their ground, hurling their spears once at the advancing multitude; but before they could fit arrows to their bows they wavered, gave, and turned in terrified rout. Into their ranks, upon their backs, sinking strong fangs into the muscles of their necks sprang the baboons and first among them, most ferocious, most blood-thirsty, most terrible was Korak, The Killer.

At the village gates, through which the blacks poured in panic, Korak left them to the tender mercies of his allies and turned himself eagerly toward the hut in which Meriem had been a prisoner. It was empty. One after another the filthy interiors revealed the same disheartening fact—Meriem was in none of them. That she had not been taken by the blacks in their flight from the village Korak knew for he had watched carefully for a glimpse of her among the fugitives.

To the mind of the ape-man, knowing as he did the proclivities of the savages, there was but a single explanation—Meriem had been killed and eaten. With the conviction that Meriem was dead there surged through Korak's brain a wave of blood red rage against those he believed to be her murderer. In the distance he could hear the snarling of the baboons mixed with the screams of their victims, and towards this he made his way. When he came upon them the baboons had commenced to tire of the sport of battle, and the blacks in a little knot were making a new stand, using their knob sticks effectively upon the few bulls who still persisted in attacking them.

Among these broke Korak from the branches of a tree above them—swift, relentless, terrible, he hurled himself upon the savage warriors of Kovudoo. Blind fury possessed him. Too, it protected him by its very ferocity. Like a wounded lioness he was here, there, everywhere, striking terrific blows with hard fists and with the precision and timeliness of the trained fighter. Again and again he buried his teeth in the flesh of a foeman. He was upon one and gone again to another before an effective blow could be dealt him. Yet, though great was the weight of his execution in determining the result of the combat, it was outweighed by the terror which he inspired in the simple, superstitious minds of his foeman. To them this white warrior, who consorted with the great apes and the fierce baboons, who growled and snarled and snapped like a beast, was not human. He was a demon of the forest—a fearsome god of evil whom they had offended, and who had come out of his lair deep in the jungle to punish them. And because of this belief there were many who offered but little defense, feeling as they did the futility of pitting their puny mortal strength against that of a deity.

Those who could fled, until at last there were no more to pay the penalty for a deed, which, while not beyond them, they were, nevertheless, not guilty of. Panting and bloody, Korak paused for want of further victims. The baboons gathered about him, sated themselves with blood and battle. They lolled upon the ground, fagged.

In the distance Kovudoo was gathering his scattered tribesmen, and taking account of injuries and losses. His people were panic stricken. Nothing could prevail upon them to remain longer in this country. They would not even return to the village for their belongings. Instead they insisted upon continuing their flight until they had put many miles between themselves and the stamping ground of the demon who had so bitterly attacked them. And thus it befell that Korak drove from their homes the only people who might have aided him in a search for Meriem, and cut off the only connecting link between him and her from whomsoever might come in search of him from the douar of the kindly Bwana who had befriended his little jungle sweetheart.

EDGAR RICE BURROUGHS

It was a sour and savage Korak who bade farewell to his baboon allies upon the following morning. They wished him to accompany him; but the ape-man had no heart for the society of any. Jungle life had encouraged taciturnity in him. His sorrow had deepened this to a sullen moroseness that could not brook even the savage companionship of the ill-natured baboons.

Brooding and despondent he took his solitary way into the deepest jungle. He moved along the ground when he knew that Numa was abroad and hungry. He took to the same trees that harbored Sheeta, the panther. He courted death in a hundred ways and a hundred forms. His mind was ever occupied with reminiscences of Meriem and the happy years that they had spent together. He realized now to the full what she had meant to him. The sweet face, the tanned, supple, little body, the bright smile that always had welcomed his return from the hunt haunted him continually.

Inaction soon threatened him with madness. He must be on the go. He must fill his days with labor and excitement that he might forget—that night might find him so exhausted that he should sleep in blessed unconsciousness of his misery until a new day had come.

Had he guessed that by any possibility Meriem might still live he would at least have had hope. His days could have been devoted to searching for her; but he implicitly believed that she was dead.

For a long year he led his solitary, roaming life. Occasionally he fell in with Akut and his tribe, hunting with them for a day or two; or he might travel to the hill country where the baboons had come to accept him as a matter of course; but most of all was he with Tantor, the elephant—the great gray battle ship of the jungle—the super-dreadnaught of his savage world.

The peaceful quiet of the monster bulls, the watchful solicitude of the mother cows, the awkward playfulness of the calves rested, interested, and amused Korak. The life of the huge beasts took his mind, temporarily from his own grief. He came to love them as he loved not even the great apes, and there was one gigantic tusker in particular of which he was very fond—the lord of the herd—a savage beast that was wont to charge a stranger upon the slightest provocation, or upon no provocation whatsoever. And to Korak this mountain of destruction was docile and affectionate as a lap dog.

He came when Korak called. He wound his trunk about the ape-man's body and lifted him to his broad neck in response to a gesture, and there would Korak lie at full length kicking his toes affectionately into the thick hide and brushing the flies from about the tender ears of his colossal chum with a leafy branch torn from a nearby tree by Tantor for the purpose.

And all the while Meriem was scarce a hundred miles away.

CHAPTER 16

To Meriem, in her new home, the days passed quickly. At first she was all anxiety to be off into the jungle searching for her Korak. Bwana, as she insisted upon calling her benefactor, dissuaded her from making the attempt at once by dispatching a head man with a party of blacks to Kovudoo's village with instructions to learn from the old savage how he came into possession of the white girl and as much of her antecedents as might be culled from the black chieftain. Bwana particularly charged his head man with the duty of questioning Kovudoo relative to the strange character whom the girl called Korak, and of searching for the ape-man if he found the slightest evidence upon which to ground a belief in the existence of such an individual. Bwana was more than fully convinced that Korak was a creature of the girl's disordered imagination. He believed that the terrors and hardships she had undergone during captivity among the blacks and her frightful experience with the two Swedes had unbalanced her mind but as the days passed and he became better acquainted with her and able to observe her under the ordinary conditions of the quiet of his African home he was forced to admit that her strange tale puzzled him not a little, for there was no other evidence whatever that Meriem was not in full possession of her normal faculties.

The white man's wife, whom Meriem had christened "My Dear" from having first heard her thus addressed by Bwana, took not only a deep interest in the little jungle waif because of her forlorn and friendless state,

407

but grew to love her as well for her sunny disposition and natural charm of temperament. And Meriem, similarly impressed by little attributes in the gentle, cultured woman, reciprocated the other's regard and affection.

And so the days flew by while Meriem waited the return of the head man and his party from the country of Kovudoo. They were short days, for into them were crowded many hours of insidious instruction of the unlettered child by the lonely woman. She commenced at once to teach the girl English without forcing it upon her as a task. She varied the instruction with lessons in sewing and deportment, nor once did she let Meriem guess that it was not all play. Nor was this difficult, since the girl was avid to learn. Then there were pretty dresses to be made to take the place of the single leopard skin and in this she found the child as responsive and enthusiastic as any civilized miss of her acquaintance.

A month passed before the head man returned—a month that had transformed the savage, half-naked little tarmangani into a daintily frocked girl of at least outward civilization. Meriem had progressed rapidly with the intricacies of the English language, for Bwana and My Dear had persistently refused to speak Arabic from the time they had decided that Meriem must learn English, which had been a day or two after her introduction into their home.

The report of the head man plunged Meriem into a period of despondency, for he had found the village of Kovudoo deserted nor, search as he would, could he discover a single native anywhere in the vicinity. For some time he had camped near the village, spending the days in a systematic search of the environs for traces of Meriem's Korak; but in this quest, too, had he failed. He had seen neither apes nor ape-man. Meriem at first insisted upon setting forth herself in search of Korak, but Bwana prevailed upon her to wait. He would go himself, he assured her, as soon as he could find the time, and at last Meriem consented to abide by his wishes; but it was months before she ceased to mourn almost hourly for her Korak.

My Dear grieved with the grieving girl and did her best to comfort and cheer her. She told her that if Korak lived he would find her; but all the time she believed that Korak had never existed beyond the child's dreams. She planned amusements to distract Meriem's attention from her sorrow, and she instituted a well-designed campaign to impress upon the child the desirability of civilized life and customs. Nor was this difficult, as she was soon to learn, for it rapidly became evident that beneath the uncouth savagery of the girl was a bed rock of innate refinement—a nicety of taste and predilection that quite equaled that of her instructor.

My Dear was delighted. She was lonely and childless, and so she lavished upon this little stranger all the mother love that would have gone to her own had she had one. The result was that by the end of the first year none might have guessed that Meriem ever had existed beyond the lap of culture and luxury.

She was sixteen now, though she easily might have passed for nineteen, and she was very good to look upon, with her black hair and her tanned skin and all the freshness and purity of health and innocence. Yet she still nursed her secret sorrow, though she no longer mentioned it to My Dear. Scarce an hour passed that did not bring its recollection of Korak, and its poignant yearning to see him again.

Meriem spoke English fluently now, and read and wrote it as well. One day My Dear spoke jokingly to her in French and to her surprise Meriem replied in the same tongue—slowly, it is true, and haltingly; but none the less in excellent French, such, though, as a little child might use. Thereafter they spoke a little French each day, and My Dear often marveled that the girl learned this language with a facility that was at times almost uncanny. At first Meriem had puckered her narrow, arched, little eye brows as though trying to force recollection of something all but forgotten which the new words suggested, and then, to her own astonishment as well as to that of her teacher she had used other French words than those in the lessons—used them properly and with a pronunciation that the English woman knew was more perfect than her own; but Meriem could neither read nor write what she spoke so well, and as My Dear considered a knowledge of correct English of the first importance, other than conversational French was postponed for a later day.

"You doubtless heard French spoken at times in your father's douar," suggested My Dear, as the most reasonable explanation.

Meriem shook her head.

"It may be," she said, "but I do not recall ever having seen a Frenchman in my father's company—he hated them and would have nothing whatever to do with them, and I am quite sure that I never heard any of these words before, yet at the same time I find them all familiar. I cannot understand it."

"Neither can I," agreed My Dear.

It was about this time that a runner brought a letter that, when she learned the contents, filled Meriem with excitement. Visitors were coming! A number of English ladies and gentlemen had accepted My Dear's invitation to spend a month of hunting and exploring with them. Meriem was all expectancy. What would these strangers be like? Would they be as nice to her as had Bwana and My Dear, or would they be like the other white folk she had known—cruel and relentless. My Dear assured her that they all were gentle folk and that she would find them kind, considerate and honorable.

To My Dear's surprise there was none of the shyness of the wild creature in Meriem's anticipation of the visit of strangers.

She looked forward to their coming with curiosity and with a certain pleasurable anticipation when once she was assured that they would not bite her. In fact she appeared no different than would any pretty young miss who had learned of the expected coming of company.

Korak's image was still often in her thoughts, but it aroused now a less well-defined sense of bereavement. A quiet sadness pervaded Meriem when she thought of him; but the poignant grief of her loss when it was young no longer goaded her to desperation. Yet she was still loyal to him. She still hoped that some day he would find her, nor did she doubt for a moment but that he was searching for her if he still lived. It was this last suggestion that caused her the greatest perturbation. Korak might be dead. It scarce seemed possible that one so well-equipped to meet the emergencies of jungle life should have succumbed so young; yet when she had last seen him he had been beset by a horde of armed warriors, and should he have returned to the village again, as she well knew he must have, he may have been killed. Even her Korak could not, single handed, slay an entire tribe.

At last the visitors arrived. There were three men and two women—the wives of the two older men. The youngest member of the party was Hon. Morison Baynes, a young man of considerable wealth who, having exhausted all the possibilities for pleasure offered by the capitals of Europe, had gladly seized upon this opportunity to turn to another continent for excitement and adventure.

He looked upon all things un-European as rather more than less impossible, still he was not at all averse to enjoying the novelty of unaccustomed places, and making the most of strangers indigenous thereto, however unspeakable they might have seemed to him at home. In manner he was suave and courteous to all—if possible a trifle more punctilious toward those he considered of meaner clay than toward the few he mentally admitted to equality.

Nature had favored him with a splendid physique and a handsome face, and also with sufficient good judgment to appreciate that while he might enjoy the contemplation of his superiority to the masses, there was little likelihood of the masses being equally entranced by the same cause. And so he easily maintained the reputation of being a most democratic and likeable fellow, and indeed he was likable. Just a shade of his egotism was occasionally apparent—never sufficient to become a burden to his associates. And this, briefly, was the Hon. Morison Baynes of luxurious European civilization. What would be the Hon. Morison Baynes of central Africa it were difficult to guess.

Meriem, at first, was shy and reserved in the presence of the strangers. Her benefactors had seen fit to ignore mention of her strange past, and so she passed as their ward whose antecedents not having been mentioned were not to be inquired into. The guests found her sweet and unassuming, laughing, vivacious and a never exhausted storehouse of quaint and interesting jungle lore.

She had ridden much during her year with Bwana and My Dear. She knew each favorite clump of concealing reeds along the river that the buffalo loved best. She knew a dozen places where lions laired, and every drinking hole in the drier country twenty-five miles back from the river. With unerring precision that was almost uncanny she could track the largest or the smallest beast to his hiding place. But the thing that baffled them all was her instant consciousness of the presence of carnivora that others, exerting their faculties to the utmost, could neither see nor hear.

The Hon. Morison Baynes found Meriem a most beautiful and charming companion. He was delighted with her from the first. Particularly so, it is possible, because he had not thought to find companionship of this sort upon the African estate of his London friends. They were together a great deal as they were the only unmarried couple in the little company. Meriem, entirely unaccustomed to the companionship of such as Baynes, was fascinated by him. His tales of the great, gay cities with which he was familiar filled her with admiration and with wonder. If the Hon. Morison always shone to advantage in these narratives Meriem saw in that fact but a most natural consequence to his presence upon the scene of his story—wherever Morison might be he must be a hero; so thought the girl.

With the actual presence and companionship of the young Englishman the image of Korak became less real. Where before it had been an actuality to her she now realized that Korak was but a memory. To that memory she still was loyal; but what weight has a memory in the presence of a fascinating reality?

Meriem had never accompanied the men upon a hunt since the arrival of the guests. She never had cared particularly for the sport of killing. The tracking she enjoyed; but the mere killing for the sake of killing she could not find pleasure in—little savage that she had been, and still, to some measure, was. When Bwana had gone forth to shoot for meat she had always been his enthusiastic companion; but with the coming of the London guests the hunting had deteriorated into mere killing. Slaughter the host would not permit; yet the purpose of the hunts were for heads and skins and not for food. So Meriem remained behind and spent her days either with My Dear upon the shaded verandah, or riding her favorite pony across the plains or to the forest edge. Here she would leave him untethered while she took to the trees for the moment's unalloyed pleasures of a return to the wild, free existence of her earlier childhood.

Then would come again visions of Korak, and, tired at last of leaping and swinging through the trees, she would stretch herself comfortably upon a branch and dream. And presently, as today, she found the features of Korak slowly dissolve and merge into those of another, and the figure of a tanned, half-naked tarmangani become a khaki clothed Englishman astride a hunting pony.

And while she dreamed there came to her ears from a distance, faintly, the terrified bleating of a kid. Meriem was instantly alert. You or I, even had we been able to hear the pitiful wail at so great distance, could not have interpreted it; but to Meriem it meant a species of terror that afflicts the ruminant when a carnivore is near and escape impossible.

It had been both a pleasure and a sport of Korak's to rob Numa of his prey whenever possible, and Meriem too had often enjoyed in the thrill of snatching some dainty morsel almost from the very jaws of the king of beasts. Now, at the sound of the kid's bleat, all the well remembered thrills recurred. Instantly she was all excitement to play again the game of hide and seek with death.

Quickly she loosened her riding skirt and tossed it aside—it was a heavy handicap to successful travel in the trees. Her boots and stockings followed the skirt, for the bare sole of the human foot does not slip upon dry or even wet bark as does the hard leather of a boot. She would have liked to discard her riding breeches also, but the motherly admonitions of My Dear had convinced Meriem that it was not good form to go naked through the world.

At her hip hung a hunting knife. Her rifle was still in its boot at her pony's withers. Her revolver she had not brought.

The kid was still bleating as Meriem started rapidly in its direction, which she knew was straight toward a certain water hole which had once been famous as a rendezvous for lions. Of late there had been no evidence of carnivora in the neighborhood of this drinking place; but Meriem was positive that the bleating of the kid was due to the presence of either lion or panther.

But she would soon know, for she was rapidly approaching the terrified animal. She wondered as she hastened onward that the sounds continued to come from the same point. Why did the kid not run away? And then she came in sight of the little animal and knew. The kid was tethered to a stake beside the waterhole.

Meriem paused in the branches of a near-by tree and scanned the surrounding clearing with quick, penetrating eyes. Where was the hunter? Bwana and his people did not hunt thus. Who could have tethered this poor little beast as a lure to Numa? Bwana never countenanced such acts in his country and his word was law among those who hunted within a radius of many miles of his estate.

Some wandering savages, doubtless, thought Meriem; but where were they? Not even her keen eyes could discover them. And where was Numa? Why had he not long since sprung upon this delicious and defenseless morsel? That he was close by was attested by the pitiful crying of the kid. Ah! Now she saw him. He was lying close in a clump of brush a few yards to her right. The kid was down wind from him and getting the full benefit of his terrorizing scent, which did not reach Meriem.

To circle to the opposite side of the clearing where the trees approached closer to the kid. To leap quickly to the little animal's side and cut the tether that held him would be the work of but a moment. In that moment Numa might charge, and then there would be scarce time to regain the safety of the trees, yet it might be done. Meriem had escaped from closer quarters than that many times before.

The doubt that gave her momentary pause was caused by fear of the unseen hunters more than by fear of Numa. If they were stranger blacks the spears that they held in readiness for Numa might as readily be loosed upon whomever dared release their bait as upon the prey they sought thus to trap. Again the kid struggled to be free. Again his piteous wail touched the tender heart strings of the girl. Tossing discretion aside, she commenced to circle the clearing. Only from Numa did she attempt to conceal her presence. At last she reached the opposite trees. An instant she paused to look toward the great lion, and at the same moment she saw the huge beast rise slowly to his full height. A low roar betokened that he was ready.

Meriem loosened her knife and leaped to the ground. A quick run brought her to the side of the kid. Numa saw her. He lashed his tail against his tawny sides. He roared terribly; but, for an instant, he remained where he stood—surprised into inaction, doubtless, by the strange apparition that had sprung so unexpectedly from the jungle.

Other eyes were upon Meriem, too—eyes in which were no less surprise than that reflected in the yellow-green orbs of the carnivore. A white man, hiding in a thorn boma, half rose as the young girl leaped into the clearing and dashed toward the kid. He saw Numa hesitate. He raised his rifle and covered the beast's breast. The girl reached the kid's side. Her knife flashed, and the little prisoner was free. With a parting bleat it dashed off into the jungle. Then the girl turned to retreat toward the safety of the tree from which she had dropped so suddenly and unexpectedly into the surprised view of the lion, the kid and the man.

As she turned the girl's face was turned toward the hunter. His eyes went wide as he saw her features. He gave a little gasp of surprise; but now the lion demanded all his attention—the baffled, angry beast was charging. His breast was still covered by the motionless rifle. The man could have fired and stopped the charge at once; but for some reason, since he had seen the girl's face, he hesitated. Could it be that he did not care to save her? Or, did he prefer, if possible, to remain unseen by her? It must have been the latter cause which kept the trigger finger of the steady hand from exerting the little pressure that would have brought the great beast to at least a temporary pause.

Like an eagle the man watched the race for life the girl was making. A second or two measured the time which the whole exciting event consumed from the moment that the lion broke into his charge. Nor once did the rifle sights fail to cover the broad breast of the tawny sire as the lion's course took him a little to the man's left. Once, at the very last moment, when escape seemed impossible, the hunter's finger tightened ever so little upon the trigger, but almost coincidentally the girl leaped for an over hanging branch and seized it. The lion leaped too; but the nimble Meriem had swung herself beyond his reach without a second or an inch to spare.

The man breathed a sigh of relief as he lowered his rifle. He saw the girl fling a grimace at the angry, roaring, maneater beneath her, and then, laughing, speed away into the forest. For an hour the lion remained about the water hole. A hundred times could the hunter have bagged his prey. Why did he fail to do so? Was he afraid that the shot might attract the girl and cause her to return?

At last Numa, still roaring angrily, strode majestically into the jungle. The hunter crawled from his boma, and half an hour later was entering a little camp snugly hidden in the forest. A handful of black followers greeted his return with sullen indifference. He was a great bearded man, a huge, yellow-bearded giant, when he entered his tent. Half an hour later he emerged smooth shaven.

His blacks looked at him in astonishment.

"Would you know me?" he asked.

"The hyena that bore you would not know you, Bwana," replied one.

The man aimed a heavy fist at the black's face; but long experience in dodging similar blows saved the presumptuous one.

CHAPTER 17

Meriem returned slowly toward the tree in which she had left her skirt, her shoes and her stockings. She was singing blithely; but her song came to a sudden stop when she came within sight of the tree, for there, disporting themselves with glee and pulling and hauling upon her belongings, were a number of baboons. When they saw her they showed no signs of terror. Instead they bared their fangs and growled at her. What was there to fear in a single she-Tarmangani? Nothing, absolutely nothing.

In the open plain beyond the forest the hunters were returning from the day's sport. They were widely separated, hoping to raise a wandering lion on the homeward journey across the plain. The Hon. Morison Baynes rode closest to the forest. As his eyes wandered back and forth across the undulating, shrub sprinkled ground they fell upon the form of a creature close beside the thick jungle where it terminated abruptly at the plain's edge.

He reined his mount in the direction of his discovery. It was yet too far away for his untrained eyes to recognize it; but as he came closer he saw that it was a horse, and was about to resume the original direction of his way when he thought that he discerned a saddle upon the beast's back. He rode a little closer. Yes, the animal was saddled. The Hon. Morison approached yet nearer, and as he did so his eyes expressed a pleasurable emotion of anticipation, for they had now recognized the pony as the special favorite of Meriem.

He galloped to the animal's side. Meriem must be within the wood. The man shuddered a little at the thought of an unprotected girl alone in the jungle that was still, to him, a fearful place of terrors and stealthily stalking death. He dismounted and left his horse beside Meriem's. On foot he entered the jungle. He knew that she was probably safe enough and he wished to surprise her by coming suddenly upon her.

He had gone but a short distance into the wood when he heard a great jabbering in a near-by tree. Coming closer he saw a band of baboons snarling over something. Looking intently he saw that one of them held a woman's riding skirt and that others had boots and stockings. His heart almost ceased to beat as he quite naturally placed the most direful explanation upon the scene. The baboons had killed Meriem and stripped this clothing from her body. Morison shuddered.

He was about to call aloud in the hope that after all the girl still lived when he saw her in a tree close beside that was occupied by the baboons, and now he saw that they were snarling and jabbering at her. To his amazement he saw the girl swing, ape-like, into the tree below the huge beasts. He saw her pause upon a branch a few feet from the nearest baboon. He was about to raise his rifle and put a bullet through the hideous creature that seemed about to leap upon her when he heard the girl speak. He almost dropped his rifle from surprise as a strange jabbering, identical with that of the apes, broke from Meriem's lips.

The baboons stopped their snarling and listened. It was quite evident that they were as much surprised as the Hon. Morison Baynes. Slowly and one by one they approached the girl. She gave not the slightest evidence of fear of them. They quite surrounded her now so that Baynes could not have fired without endangering the girl's life; but he no longer desired to fire. He was consumed with curiosity.

For several minutes the girl carried on what could be nothing less than a conversation with the baboons, and then with seeming alacrity every article of her apparel in their possession was handed over to her. The baboons still crowded eagerly about her as she donned them. They chattered to her and she chattered back. The Hon. Morison Baynes sat down at the foot of a tree and mopped his perspiring brow. Then he rose and made his way back to his mount.

When Meriem emerged from the forest a few minutes later she found him there, and he eyed her with wide eyes in which were both wonder and a sort of terror.

"I saw your horse here," he explained, "and thought that I would wait and ride home with you—you do not mind?"

"Of course not," she replied. "It will be lovely."

As they made their way stirrup to stirrup across the plain the Hon. Morison caught himself many times watching the girl's regular profile and wondering if his eyes had deceived him or if, in truth, he really had seen this lovely creature consorting with grotesque baboons and conversing with them as fluently as she conversed with him. The thing was uncanny—impossible; yet he had seen it with his own eyes.

And as he watched her another thought persisted in obtruding itself into his mind. She was most beautiful and very desirable; but what did he know of her? Was she not altogether impossible? Was the scene that he had but just witnessed not sufficient proof of her impossibility? A woman who climbed trees and conversed with the baboons of the jungle! It was quite horrible!

Again the Hon. Morison mopped his brow. Meriem glanced toward him.

"You are warm," she said. "Now that the sun is setting I find it quite cool. Why do you perspire now?"

He had not intended to let her know that he had seen her with the baboons; but quite suddenly, before he realized what he was saying, he had blurted it out.

"I perspire from emotion," he said. "I went into the jungle when I discovered your pony. I wanted to surprise you; but it was I who was surprised. I saw you in the trees with the baboons."

"Yes?" she said quite unemotionally, as though it was a matter of little moment that a young girl should be upon intimate terms with savage jungle beasts.

"It was horrible!" ejaculated the Hon. Morison.

"Horrible?" repeated Meriem, puckering her brows in bewilderment. "What was horrible about it? They are my friends. Is it horrible to talk with one's friends?"

"You were really talking with them, then?" cried the Hon. Morison. "You understood them and they understood you?"

"Certainly."

"But they are hideous creatures—degraded beasts of a lower order. How could you speak the language of beasts?"

"They are not hideous, and they are not degraded," replied Meriem. "Friends are never that. I lived among them for years before Bwana found me and brought me here. I scarce knew any other tongue than that of the mangani. Should I refuse to know them now simply because I happen, for the present, to live among humans?"

"For the present!" ejaculated the Hon. Morison. "You cannot mean that you expect to return to live among them? Come, come, what foolishness are we talking! The very idea! You are spoofing me, Miss Meriem. You have been kind to these baboons here and they know you and do not molest you; but that you once lived among them—no, that is preposterous."

"But I did, though," insisted the girl, seeing the real horror that the man felt in the presence of such an idea reflected in his tone and manner, and rather enjoying baiting him still further. "Yes, I lived, almost naked, among the great apes and the lesser apes. I dwelt among the branches of the trees. I pounced upon the smaller prey and devoured it—raw. With Korak and A'ht I hunted the antelope and the boar, and I sat upon a tree limb and made faces at Numa, the lion, and threw sticks at him and annoyed him until he roared so terribly in his rage that the earth shook.

"And Korak built me a lair high among the branches of a mighty tree. He brought me fruits and flesh. He fought for me and was kind to me—until I came to Bwana and My Dear I do not recall that any other than Korak was ever kind to me." There was a wistful note in the girl's voice now and she had forgotten that she was bantering the Hon. Morison. She was thinking of Korak. She had not thought of him a great deal of late.

For a time both were silently absorbed in their own reflections as they rode on toward the bungalow of their host. The girl was thinking of a god-like figure, a leopard skin half concealing his smooth, brown hide as he leaped nimbly through the trees to lay an offering of food before her on his return from a successful hunt. Behind him, shaggy and powerful, swung a huge anthropoid ape, while she, Meriem, laughing and shouting her welcome, swung upon a swaying limb before the entrance to her sylvan bower. It was a pretty picture as she recalled it. The other side seldom obtruded itself upon her memory—the long, black nights—the chill, terrible jungle nights—the cold and damp and discomfort of the rainy season—the hideous mouthings of the savage carnivora as they prowled through the Stygian darkness beneath—the constant menace of Sheeta, the panther, and Histah, the snake—the stinging insects—the loathesome vermin. For, in truth, all these had been outweighed by the happiness of the sunny days, the freedom of it all, and, most, the companionship of Korak.

The man's thoughts were rather jumbled. He had suddenly realized that he had come mighty near falling in love with this girl of whom he had known nothing up to the previous moment when she had voluntarily revealed a portion of her past to him. The more he thought upon the matter the more evident it became to him that he had given her his love—that he had been upon the verge of offering her his honorable name. He trembled a little at the narrowness of his escape. Yet, he still loved her. There was no objection to that according to the ethics of the Hon. Morison Baynes and his kind. She was a meaner clay than he. He could no more have taken her in marriage than he could have taken one of her baboon friends, nor would she, of course, expect such an offer from him. To have his love would be sufficient honor for her—his name he would, naturally, bestow upon one in his own elevated social sphere.

A girl who had consorted with apes, who, according to her own admission, had lived almost naked among them, could have no considerable sense of the finer qualities of virtue. The love that he would offer her, then, would, far from offending her, probably cover all that she might desire or expect.

The more the Hon. Morison Baynes thought upon the subject the more fully convinced he became that he was contemplating a most chivalrous and unselfish act. Europeans will better understand his point of view than Americans, poor, benighted provincials, who are denied a true appreciation of caste and of the fact that "the king can do no wrong." He did not even have to argue the point that she would be much happier amidst the luxuries of a London apartment, fortified as she would be by both his love and his bank account, than lawfully wed to such a one as her social position warranted. There was one question however, which he wished to have definitely answered before he committed himself even to the program he was considering.

"Who were Korak and A'ht?" he asked.

"A'ht was a Mangani," replied Meriem, "and Korak a Tarmangani."

"And what, pray, might a Mangani be, and a Tarmangani?"

The girl laughed.

"You are a Tarmangani," she replied. "The Mangani are covered with hair—you would call them apes."

"Then Korak was a white man?" he asked.

"Yes."

"And he was—ah—your—er—your—?" He paused, for he found it rather difficult to go on with that line of questioning while the girl's clear, beautiful eyes were looking straight into his.

"My what?" insisted Meriem, far too unsophisticated in her unspoiled innocence to guess what the Hon. Morison was driving at.

"Why—ah—your brother?" he stumbled.

"No, Korak was not my brother," she replied.

"Was he your husband, then?" he finally blurted.

Far from taking offense, Meriem broke into a merry laugh.

"My husband!" she cried. "Why how old do you think I am? I am too young to have a husband. I had never thought of such a thing. Korak was—why—," and now she hesitated, too, for she never before had attempted to analyse the relationship that existed between herself and Korak—"why, Korak was just Korak," and again she broke into a gay laugh as she realized the illuminating quality of her description.

Looking at her and listening to her the man beside her could not believe that depravity of any sort or degree entered into the girl's nature, yet he wanted to believe that she had not been virtuous, for otherwise his task was less a sinecure—the Hon. Morison was not entirely without conscience.

For several days the Hon. Morison made no appreciable progress toward the consummation of his scheme. Sometimes he almost abandoned it for he found himself time and again wondering how slight might be the provocation necessary to trick him into making a bona-fide offer of marriage to Meriem if he permitted himself to fall more deeply in love with her, and it was difficult to see her daily and not love her. There was a quality about her which, all unknown to the Hon. Morison, was making his task an extremely difficult one—it was that quality of innate goodness and cleanness which is a good girl's stoutest bulwark and protection—an impregnable barrier that only degeneracy has the effrontery to assail. The Hon. Morison Baynes would never be considered a degenerate.

He was sitting with Meriem upon the verandah one evening after the others had retired. Earlier they had been playing tennis—a game in which the Hon. Morison shone to advantage, as, in truth, he did in most all manly sports. He was telling Meriem stories of London and Paris, of balls and banquets, of the wonderful women and their wonderful gowns, of the pleasures and pastimes of the rich and powerful. The Hon. Morison was a past master in the art of insidious boasting. His egotism was never flagrant or tiresome—he was never crude in it, for crudeness was a plebeianism that the Hon. Morison studiously avoided, yet the impression derived by a listener to the Hon. Morison was one that was not at all calculated to detract from the glory of the house of Baynes, or from that of its representative.

Meriem was entranced. His tales were like fairy stories to this little jungle maid. The Hon. Morison loomed large and wonderful and magnificent in her mind's eye. He fascinated her, and when he drew closer to her after a short silence and took her hand she thrilled as one might thrill beneath the touch of a deity—a thrill of exaltation not unmixed with fear.

He bent his lips close to her ear.

"Meriem!" he whispered. "My little Meriem! May I hope to have the right to call you 'my little Meriem'?"

The girl turned wide eyes upward to his face; but it was in shadow. She trembled but she did not draw away. The man put an arm about her and drew her closer.

"I love you!" he whispered.

She did not reply. She did not know what to say. She knew nothing of love. She had never given it a thought; but she did know that it was very nice to be loved, whatever it meant. It was nice to have people kind to one. She had known so little of kindness or affection.

"Tell me," he said, "that you return my love."

His lips came steadily closer to hers. They had almost touched when a vision of Korak sprang like a miracle before her eyes. She saw Korak's face close to hers, she felt his lips hot against hers, and then for the first time in her life she guessed what love meant. She drew away, gently.

"I am not sure," she said, "that I love you. Let us wait. There is plenty of time. I am too young to marry yet, and I am not sure that I should be happy in London or Paris—they rather frighten me."

How easily and naturally she had connected his avowal of love with the idea of marriage! The Hon. Morison was perfectly sure that he had not mentioned marriage—he had been particularly careful not to do so. And then she was not sure that she loved him! That, too, came rather in the nature of a shock to his vanity. It seemed incredible that this little barbarian should have any doubts whatever as to the desirability of the Hon. Morison Baynes.

The first flush of passion cooled, the Hon. Morison was enabled to reason more logically. The start had been all wrong. It would be better now to wait and prepare her mind gradually for the only proposition which his exalted estate would permit him to offer her. He would go slow. He glanced down at the girl's profile. It was bathed in the silvery light of the great tropic moon. The Hon. Morison Baynes wondered if it were to be so easy a matter to "go slow." She was most alluring.

Meriem rose. The vision of Korak was still before her.

"Good night," she said. "It is almost too beautiful to leave," she waved her hand in a comprehensive gesture which took in the starry heavens, the great moon, the broad, silvered plain, and the dense shadows in the distance, that marked the jungle. "Oh, how I love it!"

"You would love London more," he said earnestly. "And London would love you. You would be a famous beauty in any capital of Europe. You would have the world at your feet, Meriem."

"Good night!" she repeated, and left him.

The Hon. Morison selected a cigarette from his crested case, lighted it, blew a thin line of blue smoke toward the moon, and smiled.

CHAPTER 18

Meriem and Bwana were sitting on the verandah together the following day when a horseman appeared in the distance riding across the plain toward the bungalow. Bwana shaded his eyes with his hand and gazed out toward the oncoming rider. He was puzzled. Strangers were few in Central Africa. Even the blacks for a distance of many miles in every direction were well known to him. No white man came within a hundred miles that word of his coming did not reach Bwana long before the stranger. His every move was reported to the big Bwana—just what animals he killed and how many of each species, how he killed them, too, for Bwana would not permit the use of prussic acid or strychnine; and how he treated his "boys."

Several European sportsmen had been turned back to the coast by the big Englishman's orders because of unwarranted cruelty to their black followers, and one, whose name had long been heralded in civilized communities as that of a great sportsman, was driven from Africa with orders never to return when Bwana found that his big bag of fourteen lions had been made by the diligent use of poisoned bait.

The result was that all good sportsmen and all the natives loved and respected him. His word was law where there had never been law before. There was scarce a head man from coast to coast who would not heed the big Bwana's commands in preference to those of the hunters who employed them, and so it was easy to turn back any undesirable stranger—Bwana had simply to threaten to order his boys to desert him.

But there was evidently one who had slipped into the country unheralded. Bwana could not imagine who the approaching horseman might be. After the manner of frontier hospitality the globe round he met the newcomer at the gate, welcoming him even before he had dismounted. He saw a tall, well knit man of thirty or over, blonde of hair and smooth shaven. There was a tantalizing familiarity about him that convinced Bwana that he should be able to call the visitor by name, yet he was unable to do so. The newcomer was evidently of Scandinavian origin—both his appearance and accent denoted that. His manner was rough but open. He made a good impression upon the Englishman, who was wont to accept strangers in this wild and savage country at their own valuation, asking no questions and assuming the best of them until they proved themselves undeserving of his friendship and hospitality.

"It is rather unusual that a white man comes unheralded," he said, as they walked together toward the field into which he had suggested that the traveler might turn his pony. "My friends, the natives, keep us rather well-posted."

"It is probably due to the fact that I came from the south," explained the stranger, "that you did not hear of my coming. I have seen no village for several marches."

"No, there are none to the south of us for many miles," replied Bwana. "Since Kovudoo deserted his country I rather doubt that one could find a native in that direction under two or three hundred miles."

Bwana was wondering how a lone white man could have made his way through the savage, unhospitable miles that lay toward the south. As though guessing what must be passing through the other's mind, the stranger vouchsafed an explanation.

"I came down from the north to do a little trading and hunting," he said, "and got way off the beaten track. My head man, who was the only member of the safari who had ever before been in the country, took sick and died. We could find no natives to guide us, and so I simply swung back straight north. We have been living on the fruits of our guns for over a month. Didn't have an idea there was a white man within a thousand miles of us when we camped last night by a water hole at the edge of the plain. This morning I started out to hunt and saw the smoke from your chimney, so I sent my gun bearer back to camp with the good news and rode straight over here myself. Of course I've heard of you—everybody who comes into Central Africa does—and I'd be mighty glad of permission to rest up and hunt around here for a couple of weeks."

"Certainly," replied Bwana. "Move your camp up close to the river below my boys' camp and make yourself at home."

They had reached the verandah now and Bwana was introducing the stranger to Meriem and My Dear, who had just come from the bungalow's interior.

"This is Mr. Hanson," he said, using the name the man had given him. "He is a trader who has lost his way in the jungle to the south."

My Dear and Meriem bowed their acknowledgments of the introduction. The man seemed rather ill at ease in their presence. His host attributed this to the fact that his guest was unaccustomed to the society of cultured women, and so found a pretext to quickly extricate him from his seemingly unpleasant position and lead him away to his study and the brandy and soda which were evidently much less embarrassing to Mr. Hanson.

When the two had left them Meriem turned toward My Dear.

"It is odd," she said, "but I could almost swear that I had known Mr. Hanson in the past. It is odd, but quite impossible," and she gave the matter no further thought.

Hanson did not accept Bwana's invitation to move his camp closer to the bungalow. He said his boys were inclined to be quarrelsome, and so were better off at a distance; and he, himself, was around but little, and then always avoided coming into contact with the ladies. A fact which naturally aroused only laughing comment on the rough trader's bashfulness. He accompanied the men on several hunting trips where they found him perfectly at home and well versed in all the finer points of big game hunting. Of an evening he often spent much time with the white foreman of the big farm, evidently finding in the society of this rougher man more common interests than the cultured guests of Bwana possessed for him. So it came that his was a familiar figure about the premises by night. He came and went as he saw fit, often wandering along in the great flower garden that was the especial pride and joy of My Dear and Meriem. The first time that he had been surprised there he apologized gruffly, explaining that he had always been fond of the good old blooms of northern Europe which My Dear had so successfully transplanted in African soil.

Was it, though, the ever beautiful blossoms of hollyhocks and phlox that drew him to the perfumed air of the garden, or that other infinitely more beautiful flower who wandered often among the blooms beneath the great moon—the black-haired, suntanned Meriem?

For three weeks Hanson had remained. During this time he said that his boys were resting and gaining strength after their terrible ordeals in the untracked jungle to the south; but he had not been as idle as he appeared to have been. He divided his small following into two parties, entrusting the leadership of each to men whom he believed that he could trust. To them he explained his plans and the rich reward that they would win from him if they carried his designs to a successful conclusion. One party he moved very slowly northward along the trail that connects with the great caravan routes entering the Sahara from the south. The other he ordered straight westward with orders to halt and go into permanent camp just beyond the great river which marks the natural boundary of the country that the big Bwana rightfully considers almost his own.

To his host he explained that he was moving his safari slowly toward the north—he said nothing of the party moving westward. Then, one day, he announced that half his boys had deserted, for a hunting party from the bungalow had come across his northerly camp and he feared that they might have noticed the reduced numbers of his following.

And thus matters stood when, one hot night, Meriem, unable to sleep, rose and wandered out into the garden. The Hon. Morison had been urging his suit once more that evening, and the girl's mind was in such a turmoil that she had been unable to sleep.

The wide heavens about her seemed to promise a greater freedom from doubt and questioning. Baynes had urged her to tell him that she loved him. A dozen times she thought that she might honestly give him the answer that he demanded. Korak fast was becoming but a memory. That he was dead she had come to believe, since otherwise he would have sought her out. She did not know that he had even better reason to believe her dead, and that it was because of that belief he had made no effort to find her after his raid upon the village of Kovudoo.

Behind a great flowering shrub Hanson lay gazing at the stars and waiting. He had lain thus and there many nights before. For what was he waiting, or for whom? He heard the girl approaching, and half raised himself to his elbow. A dozen paces away, the reins looped over a fence post, stood his pony.

Meriem, walking slowly, approached the bush behind which the waiter lay. Hanson drew a large bandanna handkerchief from his pocket and rose stealthily to his knees. A pony neighed down at the corrals. Far out across the plain a lion roared. Hanson changed his position until he squatted upon both feet, ready to come erect quickly.

Again the pony neighed—this time closer. There was the sound of his body brushing against shrubbery. Hanson heard and wondered how the animal had gotten from the corral, for it was evident that he was already in the garden. The man turned his head in the direction of the beast. What he saw sent him to the ground, huddled close beneath the shrubbery—a man was coming, leading two ponies.

Meriem heard now and stopped to look and listen. A moment later the Hon. Morison Baynes drew near, the two saddled mounts at his heels.

Meriem looked up at him in surprise. The Hon. Morison grinned sheepishly.

"I couldn't sleep," he explained, "and was going for a bit of a ride when I chanced to see you out here, and I thought you'd like to join me. Ripping good sport, you know, night riding. Come on."

Meriem laughed. The adventure appealed to her.

"All right," she said.

Hanson swore beneath his breath. The two led their horses from the garden to the gate and through it. There they discovered Hanson's mount.

"Why here's the trader's pony," remarked Baynes.

"He's probably down visiting with the foreman," said Meriem.

"Pretty late for him, isn't it?" remarked the Hon. Morison. "I'd hate to have to ride back through that jungle at night to his camp."

As though to give weight to his apprehensions the distant lion roared again. The Hon. Morison shivered and glanced at the girl to note the effect of the uncanny sound upon her. She appeared not to have noticed it.

A moment later the two had mounted and were moving slowly across the moon-bathed plain. The girl turned her pony's head straight toward the jungle. It was in the direction of the roaring of the hungry lion.

"Hadn't we better steer clear of that fellow?" suggested the Hon. Morison. "I guess you didn't hear him."

"Yes, I heard him," laughed Meriem. "Let's ride over and call on him."

The Hon. Morison laughed uneasily. He didn't care to appear at a disadvantage before this girl, nor did he care, either, to approach a hungry lion too closely at night. He carried his rifle in his saddle boot; but moonlight is an uncertain light to shoot by, nor ever had he faced a lion alone—even by day. The thought gave him a distinct nausea. The beast ceased his roaring now. They heard him no more and the Hon. Morison gained courage accordingly. They were riding down wind toward the jungle. The lion lay in a little swale to their right. He was old. For two nights he had not fed, for no longer was his charge as swift or his spring as mighty as in the days of his prime when he spread terror among the creatures of his wild domain. For two nights and days he had gone empty, and for long time before that he had fed only upon carrion. He was old; but he was yet a terrible engine of destruction.

At the edge of the forest the Hon. Morison drew rein. He had no desire to go further. Numa, silent upon his padded feet, crept into the jungle beyond them. The wind, now, was blowing gently between him and his intended prey. He had come a long way in search of man, for even in his youth he had tasted human flesh and while it was poor stuff by comparison with eland and zebra it was less difficult to kill. In Numa's estimation man was a slow-witted, slow-footed creature which commanded no respect unless accompanied by the acrid odor which spelled to the monarch's sensitive nostrils the great noise and the blinding flash of an express rifle.

He caught the dangerous scent tonight; but he was ravenous to madness. He would face a dozen rifles, if necessary, to fill his empty belly. He circled about into the forest that he might again be down wind from his victims, for should they get his scent he could not hope to overtake them. Numa was famished; but he was old and crafty.

Deep in the jungle another caught faintly the scent of man and of Numa both. He raised his head and sniffed. He cocked it upon one side and listened.

"Come on," said Meriem, "let's ride in a way—the forest is wonderful at night. It is open enough to permit us to ride."

The Hon. Morison hesitated. He shrank from revealing his fear in the presence of the girl. A braver man, sure of his own position, would have had the courage to have refused uselessly to expose the girl to danger. He would not have thought of himself at all; but the egotism of the Hon. Morison required that he think always of self first. He had planned the ride to get Meriem away from the bungalow. He wanted to talk to her alone and far enough away so should she take offense at his purposed suggestion he would have time in which to attempt to right himself in her eyes before they reached home. He had little doubt, of course, but that he should succeed; but it is to his credit that he did have some slight doubts.

"You needn't be afraid of the lion," said Meriem, noting his slight hesitancy. "There hasn't been a man eater around here for two years, Bwana says, and the game is so plentiful that there is no necessity to drive Numa to human flesh. Then, he has been so often hunted that he rather keeps out of man's way."

"Oh, I'm not afraid of lions," replied the Hon. Morison. "I was just thinking what a beastly uncomfortable place a forest is to ride in. What with the underbrush and the low branches and all that, you know, it's not exactly cut out for pleasure riding."

"Let's go a-foot then," suggested Meriem, and started to dismount.

"Oh, no," cried the Hon. Morison, aghast at this suggestion. "Let's ride," and he reined his pony into the dark shadows of the wood. Behind him came Meriem and in front, prowling ahead waiting a favorable opportunity, skulked Numa, the lion.

Out upon the plain a lone horseman muttered a low curse as he saw the two disappear from sight. It was Hanson. He had followed them from the bungalow. Their way led in the direction of his camp, so he had a ready and plausible excuse should they discover him; but they had not seen him for they had not turned their eyes behind.

Now he turned directly toward the spot at which they had entered the jungle. He no longer cared whether he was observed or not. There were two reasons for his indifference. The first was that he saw in Baynes' act a counterpart of his own planned abduction of the girl. In some way he might turn the thing to his own purposes. At least he would keep in touch with them and make sure that Baynes did not get her. His other reason was based on his knowledge of an event that had transpired at his camp the previous night—an event which he had not mentioned at the bungalow for fear of drawing undesired attention to his movements and bringing the blacks of the big Bwana into dangerous intercourse with his own boys. He had told at the bungalow that half his men had deserted. That story might be quickly disproved should his boys and Bwana's grow confidential.

The event that he had failed to mention and which now urged him hurriedly after the girl and her escort had occurred during his absence early the preceding evening. His men had been sitting around their camp fire, entirely encircled by a high, thorn boma, when, without the slightest warning, a huge lion had leaped amongst them and seized one of their number. It had been solely due to the loyalty and courage of his comrades that his life had been saved, and then only after a battle royal with the hunger-enraged beast had they been able to drive him off with burning brands, spears, and rifles.

From this Hanson knew that a man eater had wandered into the district or been developed by the aging of one of the many lions who ranged the plains and hills by night, or lay up in the cool wood by day. He had heard the roaring of a hungry lion not half an hour before, and there was little doubt in his mind but that the man eater was stalking Meriem and Baynes. He cursed the Englishman for a fool, and spurred rapidly after them.

Meriem and Baynes had drawn up in a small, natural clearing. A hundred yards beyond them Numa lay crouching in the underbrush, his yellow-green eyes fixed upon his prey, the tip of his sinuous tail jerking spasmodically. He was measuring the distance between him and them. He was wondering if he dared venture a charge, or should he wait yet a little longer in the hope that they might ride straight into his jaws. He was very hungry; but also was he very crafty. He could not chance losing his meat by a hasty and ill-considered rush. Had he waited the night before until the blacks slept he would not have been forced to go hungry for another twenty-four hours.

Behind him the other that had caught his scent and that of man together came to a sitting posture upon the branch of a tree in which he had reposed himself for slumber. Beneath him a lumbering gray hulk swayed to and fro in the darkness. The beast in the tree uttered a low guttural and dropped to the back of the gray mass. He whispered a word in one of the great ears and Tantor, the elephant, raised his trunk aloft, swinging it high and low to catch the scent that the word had warned him of. There was another whispered word—was it a command?—and the lumbering beast wheeled into an awkward, yet silent shuffle, in the direction of Numa, the lion, and the stranger Tarmangani his rider had scented.

Onward they went, the scent of the lion and his prey becoming stronger and stronger. Numa was becoming impatient. How much longer must he wait for his meat to come his way? He lashed his tail viciously now. He almost growled. All unconscious of their danger the man and the girl sat talking in the little clearing.

Their horses were pressed side by side. Baynes had found Meriem's hand and was pressing it as he poured words of love into her ear, and Meriem was listening.

"Come to London with me," urged the Hon. Morison. "I can gather a safari and we can be a whole day upon the way to the coast before they guess that we have gone."

"Why must we go that way?" asked the girl. "Bwana and My Dear would not object to our marriage."

"I cannot marry you just yet," explained the Hon. Morison, "there are some formalities to be attended to first—you do not understand. It will be all right. We will go to London. I cannot wait. If you love me you will come. What of the apes you lived with? Did they bother about marriage? They love as we love. Had you stayed among them you would have mated as they mate. It is the law of nature—no man-made law can abrogate the laws of God. What difference does it make if we love one another? What do we care for anyone in the world besides ourselves? I would give my life for you—will you give nothing for me?"

"You love me?" she said. "You will marry me when we have reached London?"

"I swear it," he cried.

"I will go with you," she whispered, "though I do not understand why it is necessary." She leaned toward him and he took her in his arms and bent to press his lips to hers.

At the same instant the head of a huge tusker poked through the trees that fringed the clearing. The Hon. Morison and Meriem, with eyes and ears for one another alone, did not see or hear; but Numa did. The man upon Tantor's broad head saw the girl in the man's arms. It was Korak; but in the trim figure of the neatly garbed girl he did not recognize his Meriem. He only saw a Tarmangani with his she. And then Numa charged.

With a frightful roar, fearful lest Tantor had come to frighten away his prey, the great beast leaped from his hiding place. The earth trembled to his mighty voice. The ponies stood for an instant transfixed with terror. The Hon. Morison Baynes went white and cold. The lion was charging toward them full in the brilliant light of the magnificent moon. The muscles of the Hon. Morison no longer obeyed his will—they flexed to the urge of a greater power—the power of Nature's first law. They drove his spurred heels deep into his pony's flanks, they bore the rein against the brute's neck that wheeled him with an impetuous drive toward the plain and safety.

The girl's pony, squealing in terror, reared and plunged upon the heels of his mate. The lion was close upon him. Only the girl was cool—the girl and the half-naked savage who bestrode the neck of his mighty mount and grinned at the exciting spectacle chance had staked for his enjoyment.

To Korak here were but two strange Tarmangani pursued by Numa, who was empty. It was Numa's right to prey; but one was a she. Korak felt an intuitive urge to rush to her protection. Why, he could not guess. All Tarmangani were enemies now. He had lived too long a beast to feel strongly the humanitarian impulses that were inherent in him—yet feel them he did, for the girl at least.

He urged Tantor forward. He raised his heavy spear and hurled it at the flying target of the lion's body. The girl's pony had reached the trees upon the opposite side of the clearing. Here he would become easy prey to the swiftly moving lion; but Numa, infuriated, preferred the woman upon his back. It was for her he leaped.

Korak gave an exclamation of astonishment and approval as Numa landed upon the pony's rump and at the same instant the girl swung free of her mount to the branches of a tree above her.

Korak's spear struck Numa in the shoulder, knocking him from his precarious hold upon the frantically plunging horse. Freed of the weight of both girl and lion the pony raced ahead toward safety. Numa tore and struck at the missile in his shoulder but could not dislodge it. Then he resumed the chase.

Korak guided Tantor into the seclusion of the jungle. He did not wish to be seen, nor had he.

Hanson had almost reached the wood when he heard the lion's terrific roars, and knew that the charge had come. An instant later the Hon. Morison broke upon his vision, racing like mad for safety. The man lay flat upon his pony's back hugging the animal's neck tightly with both arms and digging the spurs into his sides. An instant later the second pony appeared—riderless.

Hanson groaned as he guessed what had happened out of sight in the jungle. With an oath he spurred on in the hope of driving the lion from his prey—his rifle was ready in his hand. And then the lion came into view behind the girl's pony. Hanson could not understand. He knew that if Numa had succeeded in seizing the girl he would not have continued in pursuit of the others.

He drew in his own mount, took quick aim and fired. The lion stopped in his tracks, turned and bit at his side, then rolled over dead. Hanson rode on into the forest, calling aloud to the girl.

"Here I am," came a quick response from the foliage of the trees just ahead. "Did you hit him?"

"Yes," replied Hanson. "Where are you? You had a mighty narrow escape. It will teach you to keep out of the jungle at night."

Together they returned to the plain where they found the Hon. Morison riding slowly back toward them. He explained that his pony had bolted and that he had had hard work stopping him at all. Hanson grinned, for he recalled the pounding heels that he had seen driving sharp spurs into the flanks of Baynes' mount; but he said nothing of what he had seen. He took Meriem up behind him and the three rode in silence toward the bungalow.

CHAPTER 19

Behind them Korak emerged from the jungle and recovered his spear from Numa's side. He still was smiling. He had enjoyed the spectacle exceedingly. There was one thing that troubled him—the agility with which the she had clambered from her pony's back into the safety of the tree ABOVE her. That was more like mangani—more like his lost Meriem. He sighed. His lost Meriem! His little, dead Meriem! He wondered if this she stranger resembled his Meriem in other ways. A great longing to see her overwhelmed him. He looked after the three figures moving steadily across the plain. He wondered where might lie their destination. A desire to follow them came over him, but he only stood there watching until they had disappeared in the distance. The sight of the civilized girl and the dapper, khaki clad Englishman had aroused in Korak memories long dormant.

Once he had dreamed of returning to the world of such as these; but with the death of Meriem hope and ambition seemed to have deserted him. He cared now only to pass the remainder of his life in solitude, as far from man as possible. With a sigh he turned slowly back into the jungle.

Tantor, nervous by nature, had been far from reassured by close proximity to the three strange whites, and with the report of Hanson's rifle had turned and ambled away at his long, swinging shuffle. He was nowhere in sight when Korak returned to look for him. The ape-man, however, was little concerned by the absence of his friend. Tantor had a habit of wandering off unexpectedly. For a month they might not see one another, for Korak seldom took the trouble to follow the great pachyderm, nor did he upon this occasion. Instead he found a comfortable perch in a large tree and was soon asleep.

At the bungalow Bwana had met the returning adventurers on the verandah. In a moment of wakefulness he had heard the report of Hanson's rifle far out across the plain, and wondered what it might mean. Presently it had occurred to him that the man whom he considered in the light of a guest might have met with an accident on his way back to camp, so he had arisen and gone to his foreman's quarters where he had learned that Hanson had been there earlier in the evening but had departed several hours before. Returning from the foreman's quarters Bwana had noticed that the corral gate was open and further investigation revealed the fact that Meriem's pony was gone and also the one most often used by Baynes. Instantly Bwana assumed that the shot had been fired by Hon. Morison, and had again aroused his foreman and was making preparations to set forth in investigation when he had seen the party approaching across the plain.

Explanation on the part of the Englishman met a rather chilly reception from his host. Meriem was silent. She saw that Bwana was angry with her. It was the first time and she was heart broken.

"Go to your room, Meriem," he said; "and Baynes, if you will step into my study, I'd like to have a word with you in a moment."

He stepped toward Hanson as the others turned to obey him. There was something about Bwana even in his gentlest moods that commanded instant obedience.

"How did you happen to be with them, Hanson?" he asked.

"I'd been sitting in the garden," replied the trader, "after leaving Jervis' quarters. I have a habit of doing that as your lady probably knows. Tonight I fell asleep behind a bush, and was awakened by them two spooning. I couldn't hear what they said, but presently Baynes brings two ponies and they ride off. I didn't like to interfere for it wasn't any of my business, but I knew they hadn't ought to be ridin' about that time of night, leastways not the girl—it wasn't right and it wasn't safe. So I follows them and it's just as well I did. Baynes was gettin' away from the lion as fast as he could, leavin' the girl to take care of herself, when I got a lucky shot into the beast's shoulder that fixed him."

Hanson paused. Both men were silent for a time. Presently the trader coughed in an embarrassed manner as though there was something on his mind he felt in duty bound to say, but hated to.

"What is it, Hanson?" asked Bwana. "You were about to say something weren't you?"

"Well, you see it's like this," ventured Hanson. "Bein' around here evenings a good deal I've seen them two together a lot, and, beggin' your pardon, sir, but I don't think Mr. Baynes means the girl any good. I've overheard enough to make me think he's tryin' to get her to run off with him." Hanson, to fit his own ends, hit nearer the truth than he knew. He was afraid that Baynes would interfere with his own plans, and he had hit upon a scheme to both utilize the young Englishman and get rid of him at the same time.

"And I thought," continued the trader, "that inasmuch as I'm about due to move you might like to suggest to Mr. Baynes that he go with me. I'd be willin' to take him north to the caravan trails as a favor to you, sir."

Bwana stood in deep thought for a moment. Presently he looked up.

"Of course, Hanson, Mr. Baynes is my guest," he said, a grim twinkle in his eye. "Really I cannot accuse him of planning to run away with Meriem on the evidence that we have, and as he is my guest I should hate to be so discourteous as to ask him to leave; but, if I recall his words correctly, it seems to me that he has spoken of returning home, and I am sure that nothing would delight him more than going north with you—you say you start tomorrow? I think Mr. Baynes will accompany you. Drop over in the morning, if you please, and now good night, and thank you for keeping a watchful eye on Meriem."

Hanson hid a grin as he turned and sought his saddle. Bwana stepped from the verandah to his study, where he found the Hon. Morison pacing back and forth, evidently very ill at ease.

"Baynes," said Bwana, coming directly to the point, "Hanson is leaving for the north tomorrow. He has taken a great fancy to you, and just asked me to say to you that he'd be glad to have you accompany him. Good night, Baynes."

At Bwana's suggestion Meriem kept to her room the following morning until after the Hon. Morison Baynes had departed. Hanson had come for him early—in fact he had remained all night with the foreman, Jervis, that they might get an early start.

The farewell exchanges between the Hon. Morison and his host were of the most formal type, and when at last the guest rode away Bwana breathed a sigh of relief. It had been an unpleasant duty and he was glad that it was over; but he did not regret his action. He had not been blind to Baynes' infatuation for Meriem, and knowing the young man's pride in caste he had never for a moment believed that his guest would offer his name to this nameless Arab girl, for, extremely light in color though she was for a full blood Arab, Bwana believed her to be such.

He did not mention the subject again to Meriem, and in this he made a mistake, for the young girl, while realizing the debt of gratitude she owed Bwana and My Dear, was both proud and sensitive, so that Bwana's action in sending Baynes away and giving her no opportunity to explain or defend hurt and mortified her. Also it did much toward making a martyr of Baynes in her eyes and arousing in her breast a keen feeling of loyalty toward him.

What she had half-mistaken for love before, she now wholly mistook for love. Bwana and My Dear might have told her much of the social barriers that they only too well knew Baynes must feel existed between Meriem and himself, but they hesitated to wound her. It would have been better had they inflicted this lesser sorrow, and saved the child the misery that was to follow because of her ignorance.

As Hanson and Baynes rode toward the former's camp the Englishman maintained a morose silence. The other was attempting to formulate an opening that would lead naturally to the proposition he had in mind. He rode a neck behind his companion, grinning as he noted the sullen scowl upon the other's patrician face.

"Rather rough on you, wasn't he?" he ventured at last, jerking his head back in the direction of the bungalow as Baynes turned his eyes upon him at the remark. "He thinks a lot of the girl," continued Hanson, "and don't want nobody to marry her and take her away; but it looks to me as though he was doin' her more harm than good in sendin' you away. She ought to marry some time, and she couldn't do better than a fine young gentleman like you."

Baynes, who had at first felt inclined to take offense at the mention of his private affairs by this common fellow, was mollified by Hanson's final remark, and immediately commenced to see in him a man of fine discrimination.

"He's a darned bounder," grumbled the Hon. Morison; "but I'll get even with him. He may be the whole thing in Central Africa but I'm as big as he is in London, and he'll find it out when he comes home."

"If I was you," said Hanson, "I wouldn't let any man keep me from gettin' the girl I want. Between you and me I ain't got no use for him either, and if I can help you any way just call on me."

"It's mighty good of you, Hanson," replied Baynes, warming up a bit; "but what can a fellow do here in this God-forsaken hole?"

"I know what I'd do," said Hanson. "I'd take the girl along with me. If she loves you she'll go, all right."

"It can't be done," said Baynes. "He bosses this whole blooming country for miles around. He'd be sure to catch us."

"No, he wouldn't, not with me running things," said Hanson. "I've been trading and hunting here for ten years and I know as much about the country as he does. If you want to take the girl along I'll help you, and I'll guarantee that there won't nobody catch up with us before we reach the coast. I'll tell you what, you write her a note and I'll get it to her by my head man. Ask her to meet you to say goodbye—she won't refuse that. In the meantime we can be movin' camp a little further north all the time and you can make arrangements with her to be all ready on a certain night. Tell her I'll meet her then while you wait for us in camp. That'll be better for I know the country well and can cover it quicker than you. You can take care of the safari and be movin' along slow toward the north and the girl and I'll catch up to you."

"But suppose she won't come?" suggested Baynes.

"Then make another date for a last good-bye," said Hanson, "and instead of you I'll be there and I'll bring her along anyway. She'll have to come, and after it's all over she won't feel so bad about it—especially after livin' with you for two months while we're makin' the coast."

A shocked and angry protest rose to Baynes' lips; but he did not utter it, for almost simultaneously came the realization that this was practically the same thing he had been planning upon himself. It had sounded brutal and criminal from the lips of the rough trader; but nevertheless the young Englishman saw that with Hanson's help and his knowledge of African travel the possibilities of success would be much greater than as though the Hon. Morison were to attempt the thing single handed. And so he nodded a glum assent.

The balance of the long ride to Hanson's northerly camp was made in silence, for both men were occupied with their own thoughts, most of which were far from being either complimentary or loyal to the other. As they rode through the wood the sounds of their careless passage came to the ears of another jungle wayfarer. The Killer had determined to come back to the place where he had seen the white girl who took to the trees with the ability of long habitude. There was a compelling something in the recollection of her that drew him irresistibly toward her. He wished to see her by the light of day, to see her features, to see the color of her eyes and hair. It seemed to him that she must bear a strong resemblance to his lost Meriem, and yet he knew that the chances were that she did not. The fleeting glimpse that he had had of her in the moonlight as she swung from the back of her plunging pony into the branches of the tree above her had shown him a girl of about the same height as his Meriem; but of a more rounded and developed femininity.

Now he was moving lazily back in the direction of the spot where he had seen the girl when the sounds of the approaching horsemen came to his sharp ears. He moved stealthily through the branches until he came within sight of the riders. The younger man he instantly recognized as the same he had seen with his arms about the girl in the moonlit glade just the instant before Numa charged. The other he did not recognize though there was a familiarity about his carriage and figure that puzzled Korak.

The ape-man decided that to find the girl again he would but have to keep in touch with the young Englishman, and so he fell in behind the pair, following them to Hanson's camp. Here the Hon. Morison penned a brief note, which Hanson gave into the keeping of one of his boys who started off forthwith toward the south.

Korak remained in the vicinity of the camp, keeping a careful watch upon the Englishman. He had half expected to find the girl at the destination of the two riders and had been disappointed when no sign of her materialized about the camp.

Baynes was restless, pacing back and forth beneath the trees when he should have been resting against the forced marches of the coming flight. Hanson lay in his hammock and smoked. They spoke but little. Korak lay stretched upon a branch among the dense foliage above them. Thus passed the balance of the afternoon. Korak became hungry and thirsty. He doubted that either of the men would leave camp now before morning, so he withdrew, but toward the south, for there it seemed most likely the girl still was.

In the garden beside the bungalow Meriem wandered thoughtfully in the moonlight. She still smarted from Bwana's, to her, unjust treatment of the Hon. Morison Baynes. Nothing had been explained to her, for both Bwana and My Dear had wished to spare her the mortification and sorrow of the true explanation of Baynes' proposal. They knew, as Meriem did not, that the man had no intention of marrying her, else he would have come directly to Bwana, knowing full well that no objection would be interposed if Meriem really cared for him.

Meriem loved them both and was grateful to them for all that they had done for her; but deep in her little heart surged the savage love of liberty that her years of untrammeled freedom in the jungle had made part and parcel of her being. Now, for the first time since she had come to them, Meriem felt like a prisoner in the bungalow of Bwana and My Dear.

Like a caged tigress the girl paced the length of the enclosure. Once she paused near the outer fence, her head upon one side—listening. What was it she had heard? The pad of naked human feet just beyond the garden. She listened for a moment. The sound was not repeated. Then she resumed her restless walking. Down to the opposite end of the garden she passed, turned and retraced her steps toward the upper end. Upon the sward near the bushes that hid the fence, full in the glare of the moonlight, lay a white envelope that had not been there when she had turned almost upon the very spot a moment before.

Meriem stopped short in her tracks, listening again, and sniffing—more than ever the tigress; alert, ready. Beyond the bushes a naked black runner squatted, peering through the foliage. He saw her take a step closer to the letter. She had seen it. He rose quietly and following the shadows of the bushes that ran down to the corral was soon gone from sight.

Meriem's trained ears heard his every move. She made no attempt to seek closer knowledge of his identity. Already she had guessed that he was a messenger from the Hon. Morison. She stooped and picked up the envelope. Tearing it open she easily read the contents by the moon's brilliant light. It was, as she had guessed, from Baynes.

"I cannot go without seeing you again," it read. "Come to the clearing early tomorrow morning and say good-bye to me. Come alone."

There was a little more—words that made her heart beat faster and a happy flush mount her cheek.

CHAPTER 20

It was still dark when the Hon. Morison Baynes set forth for the trysting place. He insisted upon having a guide, saying that he was not sure that he could find his way back to the little clearing. As a matter of fact the thought of that lonely ride through the darkness before the sun rose had been too much for his courage, and he craved company. A black, therefore, preceded him on foot. Behind and above him came Korak, whom the noise in the camp had awakened.

It was nine o'clock before Baynes drew rein in the clearing. Meriem had not yet arrived. The black lay down to rest. Baynes lolled in his saddle. Korak stretched himself comfortably upon a lofty limb, where he could watch those beneath him without being seen.

An hour passed. Baynes gave evidence of nervousness. Korak had already guessed that the young Englishman had come here to meet another, nor was he at all in doubt as to the identity of that other. The Killer was perfectly satisfied that he was soon again to see the nimble she who had so forcefully reminded him of Meriem.

Presently the sound of an approaching horse came to Korak's ears. She was coming! She had almost reached the clearing before Baynes became aware of her presence, and then as he looked up, the foliage parted to the head and shoulders of her mount and Meriem rode into view. Baynes spurred to meet her. Korak looked searchingly down upon her, mentally anathematizing the broad-brimmed hat that hid her features from his eyes. She was abreast the Englishman now. Korak saw the man take both her hands and draw her close to his breast. He saw the man's face concealed for a moment beneath the same broad brim that hid the girl's. He could imagine their lips meeting, and a twinge of sorrow and sweet recollection combined to close his eyes for an instant in that involuntary muscular act with which we attempt to shut out from the mind's eye harrowing reflections.

When he looked again they had drawn apart and were conversing earnestly. Korak could see the man urging something. It was equally evident that the girl was holding back. There were many of her gestures, and the way in which she tossed her head up and to the right, tip-tilting her chin, that reminded Korak still more strongly of Meriem. And then the conversation was over and the man took the girl in his arms again to kiss her good-bye. She turned and rode toward the point from which she had come. The man sat on his horse watching her. At the edge of the jungle she turned to wave him a final farewell.

"Tonight!" she cried, throwing back her head as she called the words to him across the little distance which separated them—throwing back her head and revealing her face for the first time to the eyes of The Killer in the tree above. Korak started as though pierced through the heart with an arrow. He trembled and shook like a leaf. He closed his eyes, pressing his palms across them, and then he opened them again and looked but the girl was gone—only the waving foliage of the jungle's rim marked where she had disappeared. It was impossible! It could not be true! And yet, with his own eyes he had seen his Meriem—older a little, with figure more rounded by nearer maturity, and subtly changed in other ways; more beautiful than ever, yet still his little Meriem. Yes, he had seen the dead alive again; he had seen his Meriem in the flesh. She lived! She had not died! He had seen her—he had seen his *Meriem—in the arms of another man!* And that man sat below him now, within easy reach. Korak, The Killer, fondled his heavy spear. He played with the grass rope dangling from his gee-string. He stroked the hunting knife at his hip. And the man beneath him called to his drowsy guide, bent the rein to his pony's neck and moved off toward the north. Still sat Korak, The Killer, alone among the trees. Now his hands hung idly at his sides. His weapons and what he had intended were forgotten for the moment. Korak was thinking. He had noted that subtle change in Meriem. When last he had seen her she had been his little, half-naked Mangani—wild, savage, and uncouth. She had not seemed uncouth to him then; but now, in the change that had come over her, he knew that such she had been; yet no more uncouth than he, and he was still uncouth.

In her had taken place the change. In her he had just seen a sweet and lovely flower of refinement and civilization, and he shuddered as he recalled the fate that he himself had planned for her—to be the mate of an ape-man, his mate, in the savage jungle. Then he had seen no wrong in it, for he had loved her, and the way he had planned had been the way of the jungle which they two had chosen as their home; but now, after having seen the Meriem of civilized attire, he realized the hideousness of his once cherished plan, and he thanked God that chance and the blacks of Kovudoo had thwarted him.

Yet he still loved her, and jealousy seared his soul as he recalled the sight of her in the arms of the dapper young Englishman. What were his intentions toward her? Did he really love her? How could one not love her? And she loved him, of that Korak had had ample proof. Had she not loved him she would not have accepted his kisses. His Meriem loved another! For a long time he let that awful truth sink deep, and from it he tried to reason out his future plan of action. In his heart was a great desire to follow the man and slay him; but ever there rose in his consciousness the thought: She loves him. Could he slay the creature Meriem loved? Sadly he shook his head. No, he could not. Then came a partial decision to follow Meriem and speak with her. He half started, and then glanced down at his nakedness and was ashamed. He, the son of a British peer, had thus thrown away his life, had thus degraded himself to the level of a beast that he was ashamed to go to the woman he loved and lay his love at her feet. He was ashamed to go to the little Arab maid who had been his jungle playmate, for what had he to offer her?

For years circumstances had prevented a return to his father and mother, and at last pride had stepped in and expunged from his mind the last vestige of any intention to return. In a spirit of boyish adventure he had cast his lot with the jungle ape. The killing of the crook in the coast inn had filled his childish mind with terror of the law, and driven him deeper into the wilds. The rebuffs that he had met at the hands of men, both black and white, had had their effect upon his mind while yet it was in a formative state, and easily influenced.

He had come to believe that the hand of man was against him, and then he had found in Meriem the only human association he required or craved. When she had been snatched from him his sorrow had been so deep that the thought of ever mingling again with human beings grew still more unutterably distasteful. Finally and for all time, he thought, the die was cast. Of his own volition he had become a beast, a beast he had lived, a beast he would die.

Now that it was too late, he regretted it. For now Meriem, still living, had been revealed to him in a guise of progress and advancement that had carried her completely out of his life. Death itself could not have further removed her from him. In her new world she loved a man of her own kind. And Korak knew that it was right. She was not for him—not for the naked, savage ape. No, she was not for him; but he still was hers. If he could not have her and happiness, he would at least do all that lay in his power to assure happiness to her. He would follow the young Englishman. In the first place he would know that he meant Meriem no harm, and after that, though jealously wrenched his heart, he would watch over the man Meriem loved, for Meriem's sake; but God help that man if he thought to wrong her!

Slowly he aroused himself. He stood erect and stretched his great frame, the muscles of his arms gliding sinuously beneath his tanned skin as he bent his clenched fists behind his head. A movement on the ground beneath caught his eye. An antelope was entering the clearing. Immediately Korak became aware that he was empty—again he was a beast. For a moment love had lifted him to sublime heights of honor and renunciation.

The antelope was crossing the clearing. Korak dropped to the ground upon the opposite side of the tree, and so lightly that not even the sensitive ears of the antelope apprehended his presence. He uncoiled his grass rope—it was the latest addition to his armament, yet he was proficient with it. Often he traveled with nothing more than his knife and his rope—they were light and easy to carry. His spear and bow and arrows were cumbersome and he usually kept one or all of them hidden away in a private cache.

Now he held a single coil of the long rope in his right hand, and the balance in his left. The antelope was but a few paces from him. Silently Korak leaped from his hiding place swinging the rope free from the entangling shrubbery. The antelope sprang away almost instantly; but instantly, too, the coiled rope, with its sliding noose, flew through the air above him. With unerring precision it settled about the creature's neck. There was a quick wrist movement of the thrower, the noose tightened. The Killer braced himself with the rope across his hip, and as the antelope tautened the singing strands in a last frantic bound for liberty he was thrown over upon his back.

Then, instead of approaching the fallen animal as a roper of the western plains might do, Korak dragged his captive to himself, pulling him in hand over hand, and when he was within reach leaping upon him even as Sheeta the panther might have done, and burying his teeth in the animal's neck while he found its heart with the point of his hunting knife. Recoiling his rope, he cut a few generous strips from his kill and took to the trees again, where he ate in peace. Later he swung off in the direction of a nearby water hole, and then he slept.

In his mind, of course, was the suggestion of another meeting between Meriem and the young Englishman that had been borne to him by the girl's parting: "Tonight!"

He had not followed Meriem because he knew from the direction from which she had come and in which she returned that wheresoever she had found an asylum it lay out across the plains and not wishing to be discovered by the girl he had not cared to venture into the open after her. It would do as well to keep in touch with the young man, and that was precisely what he intended doing.

To you or me the possibility of locating the Hon. Morison in the jungle after having permitted him to get such a considerable start might have seemed remote; but to Korak it was not at all so. He guessed that the white man would return to his camp; but should he have done otherwise it would be a simple matter to The Killer to trail a mounted man accompanied by another on foot. Days might pass and still such a spoor would be sufficiently plain to lead Korak unfalteringly to its end; while a matter of a few hours only left it as clear to him as though the makers themselves were still in plain sight.

And so it came that a few minutes after the Hon. Morison Baynes entered the camp to be greeted by Hanson, Korak slipped noiselessly into a near-by tree. There he lay until late afternoon and still the young Englishman made no move to leave camp. Korak wondered if Meriem were coming there. A little later Hanson and one of his black boys rode out of camp. Korak merely noted the fact. He was not particularly interested in what any other member of the company than the young Englishman did.

Darkness came and still the young man remained. He ate his evening meal, afterward smoking numerous cigarettes. Presently he began to pace back and forth before his tent. He kept his boy busy replenishing the fire. A lion coughed and he went into his tent to reappear with an express rifle. Again he admonished the boy to throw more brush upon the fire. Korak saw that he was nervous and afraid, and his lip curled in a sneer of contempt.

Was this the creature who had supplanted him in the heart of his Meriem? Was this a man, who trembled when Numa coughed? How could such as he protect Meriem from the countless dangers of the jungle? Ah, but he would not have to. They would live in the safety of European civilization, where men in uniforms were hired to protect them. What need had a European of prowess to protect his mate? Again the sneer curled Korak's lip.

Hanson and his boy had ridden directly to the clearing. It was already dark when they arrived. Leaving the boy there Hanson rode to the edge of the plain, leading the boy's horse. There he waited. It was nine o'clock before he saw a solitary figure galloping toward him from the direction of the bungalow. A few moments later Meriem drew in her mount beside him. She was nervous and flushed. When she recognized Hanson she drew back, startled.

"Mr. Baynes' horse fell on him and sprained his ankle," Hanson hastened to explain. "He couldn't very well come so he sent me to meet you and bring you to camp."

The girl could not see in the darkness the gloating, triumphant expression on the speaker's face.

"We had better hurry," continued Hanson, "for we'll have to move along pretty fast if we don't want to be overtaken."

"Is he hurt badly?" asked Meriem.

"Only a little sprain," replied Hanson. "He can ride all right; but we both thought he'd better lie up tonight, and rest, for he'll have plenty hard riding in the next few weeks."

"Yes," agreed the girl.

Hanson swung his pony about and Meriem followed him. They rode north along the edge of the jungle for a mile and then turned straight into it toward the west. Meriem, following, payed little attention to directions. She did not know exactly where Hanson's camp lay and so she did not guess that he was not leading her toward it. All night they rode, straight toward the west. When morning came, Hanson permitted a short halt for breakfast, which he had provided in well-filled saddle bags before leaving his camp. Then they pushed on again, nor did they halt a second time until in the heat of the day he stopped and motioned the girl to dismount.

"We will sleep here for a time and let the ponies graze," he said.

"I had no idea the camp was so far away," said Meriem.

"I left orders that they were to move on at day break," explained the trader, "so that we could get a good start. I knew that you and I could easily overtake a laden safari. It may not be until tomorrow that we'll catch up with them."

But though they traveled part of the night and all the following day no sign of the safari appeared ahead of them. Meriem, an adept in jungle craft, knew that none had passed ahead of them for many days. Occasionally she saw indications of an old spoor, a very old spoor, of many men. For the most part they followed this well-marked trail along elephant paths and through park-like groves. It was an ideal trail for rapid traveling.

Meriem at last became suspicious. Gradually the attitude of the man at her side had begun to change. Often she surprised him devouring her with his eyes. Steadily the former sensation of previous acquaintanceship urged itself upon her. Somewhere, sometime before she had known this man. It was evident that he had not shaved for several days. A blonde stubble had commenced to cover his neck and cheeks and chin, and with it the assurance that he was no stranger continued to grow upon the girl.

It was not until the second day, however, that Meriem rebelled. She drew in her pony at last and voiced her doubts. Hanson assured her that the camp was but a few miles further on.

"We should have overtaken them yesterday," he said. "They must have marched much faster than I had believed possible."

"They have not marched here at all," said Meriem. "The spoor that we have been following is weeks old."

Hanson laughed.

"Oh, that's it, is it?" he cried. "Why didn't you say so before? I could have easily explained. We are not coming by the same route; but we'll pick up their trail sometime today, even if we don't overtake them."

Now, at last, Meriem knew the man was lying to her. What a fool he must be to think that anyone could believe such a ridiculous explanation? Who was so stupid as to believe that they could have expected to overtake another party, and he had certainly assured her that momentarily he expected to do so, when that party's route was not to meet theirs for several miles yet?

She kept her own counsel however, planning to escape at the first opportunity when she might have a sufficient start of her captor, as she now considered him, to give her some assurance of outdistancing him. She watched his face continually when she could without being observed. Tantalizingly the placing of his familiar features persisted in eluding her. Where had she known him? Under what conditions had they met before she had seen him about the farm of Bwana? She ran over in her mind all the few white men she ever had known. There were some who had come to her father's douar in the jungle. Few it is true, but there had been some. Ah, now she had it! She had seen him there! She almost seized upon his identity and then in an instant, it had slipped from her again.

It was mid afternoon when they suddenly broke out of the jungle upon the banks of a broad and placid river. Beyond, upon the opposite shore, Meriem described a camp surrounded by a high, thorn boma.

"Here we are at last," said Hanson. He drew his revolver and fired in the air. Instantly the camp across the river was astir. Black men ran down the river's bank. Hanson hailed them. But there was no sign of the Hon. Morison Baynes.

In accordance with their master's instructions the blacks manned a canoe and rowed across. Hanson placed Meriem in the little craft and entered it himself, leaving two boys to watch the horses, which the canoe was to return for and swim across to the camp side of the river.

Once in the camp Meriem asked for Baynes. For the moment her fears had been allayed by the sight of the camp, which she had come to look upon as more or less a myth. Hanson pointed toward the single tent that stood in the center of the enclosure.

"There," he said, and preceded her toward it. At the entrance he held the flap aside and motioned her within. Meriem entered and looked about. The tent was empty. She turned toward Hanson. There was a broad grin on his face.

"Where is Mr. Baynes?" she demanded.

"He ain't here," replied Hanson. "Leastwise I don't see him, do you? But I'm here, and I'm a damned sight better man than that thing ever was. You don't need him no more—you got me," and he laughed uproariously and reached for her.

Meriem struggled to free herself. Hanson encircled her arms and body in his powerful grip and bore her slowly backward toward the pile of blankets at the far end of the tent. His face was bent close to hers. His eyes were narrowed to two slits of heat and passion and desire. Meriem was looking full into his face as she fought for freedom when there came over her a sudden recollection of a similar scene in which she had been a participant and with it full recognition of her assailant. He was the Swede Malbihn who had attacked her once before, who had shot his companion who would have saved her, and from whom she had been rescued by Bwana. His smooth face had deceived her; but now with the growing beard and the similarity of conditions recognition came swift and sure.

But today there would be no Bwana to save her.

CHAPTER 21

The black boy whom Malbihn had left awaiting him in the clearing with instructions to remain until he returned sat crouched at the foot of a tree for an hour when he was suddenly startled by the coughing grunt of a lion behind him. With celerity born of the fear of death the boy clambered into the branches of the tree, and a moment later the king of beasts entered the clearing and approached the carcass of an antelope which, until now, the boy had not seen.

Until daylight the beast fed, while the black clung, sleepless, to his perch, wondering what had become of his master and the two ponies. He had been with Malbihn for a year, and so was fairly conversant with the character of the white. His knowledge presently led him to believe that he had been purposely abandoned. Like the balance of Malbihn's followers, this boy hated his master cordially—fear being the only bond that held him to the white man. His present uncomfortable predicament but added fuel to the fires of his hatred.

As the sun rose the lion withdrew into the jungle and the black descended from his tree and started upon his long journey back to camp. In his primitive brain revolved various fiendish plans for a revenge that he would not have the courage to put into effect when the test came and he stood face to face with one of the dominant race.

A mile from the clearing he came upon the spoor of two ponies crossing his path at right angles. A cunning look entered the black's eyes. He laughed uproariously and slapped his thighs.

Negroes are tireless gossipers, which, of course, is but a roundabout way of saying that they are human. Malbihn's boys had been no exception to the rule and as many of them had been with him at various times during the past ten years there was little about his acts and life in the African wilds that was not known directly or by hearsay to them all.

And so, knowing his master and many of his past deeds, knowing, too, a great deal about the plans of Malbihn and Baynes that had been overheard by himself, or other servants; and knowing well from the gossip of the head-men that half of Malbihn's party lay in camp by the great river far to the west, it was not difficult for the boy to put two and two together and arrive at four as the sum—the four being represented by a firm conviction that his master had deceived the other white man and taken the latter's woman to his western camp, leaving the other to suffer capture and punishment at the hands of the Big Bwana whom all feared. Again the boy bared his rows of big, white teeth and laughed aloud. Then he resumed his northward way, traveling at a dogged trot that ate up the miles with marvelous rapidity.

In the Swede's camp the Hon. Morison had spent an almost sleepless night of nervous apprehension and doubts and fears. Toward morning he had slept, utterly exhausted. It was the headman who awoke him shortly after sun rise to remind him that they must at once take up their northward journey. Baynes hung back. He wanted to wait for "Hanson" and Meriem. The headman urged upon him the danger that lay in loitering. The fellow knew his master's plans sufficiently well to understand that he had done something to arouse the ire of the Big Bwana and that it would fare ill with them all if they were overtaken in Big Bwana's country. At the suggestion Baynes took alarm.

What if the Big Bwana, as the head-man called him, had surprised "Hanson" in his nefarious work. Would he not guess the truth and possibly be already on the march to overtake and punish him? Baynes had heard much of his host's summary method of dealing out punishment to malefactors great and small who transgressed the laws or customs of his savage little world which lay beyond the outer ramparts of what men are pleased to call frontiers. In this savage world where there was no law the Big Bwana was law unto himself and all who dwelt about him. It was even rumored that he had extracted the death penalty from a white man who had maltreated a native girl.

Baynes shuddered at the recollection of this piece of gossip as he wondered what his host would exact of the man who had attempted to steal his young, white ward. The thought brought him to his feet.

"Yes," he said, nervously, "we must get away from here at once. Do you know the trail to the north?"

The head-man did, and he lost no time in getting the safari upon the march.

It was noon when a tired and sweat-covered runner overtook the trudging little column. The man was greeted with shouts of welcome from his fellows, to whom he imparted all that he knew and guessed of the actions of their master, so that the entire safari was aware of matters before Baynes, who marched close to the head of the column, was reached and acquainted with the facts and the imaginings of the black boy whom Malbihn had deserted in the clearing the night before.

When the Hon. Morison had listened to all that the boy had to say and realized that the trader had used him as a tool whereby he himself might get Meriem into his possession, his blood ran hot with rage and he trembled with apprehension for the girl's safety.

That another contemplated no worse a deed than he had contemplated in no way palliated the hideousness of the other's offense. At first it did not occur to him that he would have wronged Meriem no less than he believed "Hanson" contemplated wronging her. Now his rage was more the rage of a man beaten at his own game and robbed of the prize that he had thought already his.

"Do you know where your master has gone?" he asked the black.

"Yes, Bwana," replied the boy. "He has gone to the other camp beside the big afi that flows far toward the setting sun.

"Can you take me to him?" demanded Baynes.

The boy nodded affirmatively. Here he saw a method of revenging himself upon his hated Bwana and at the same time of escaping the wrath of the Big Bwana whom all were positive would first follow after the northerly safari.

"Can you and I, alone, reach his camp?" asked the Hon. Morison.

"Yes, Bwana," assured the black.

Baynes turned toward the head-man. He was conversant with "Hanson's" plans now. He understood why he had wished to move the northern camp as far as possible toward the northern boundary of the Big Bwana's country—it would give him far more time to make his escape toward the West Coast while the Big Bwana was chasing the northern contingent. Well, he would utilize the man's plans to his own end. He, too, must keep out of the clutches of his host.

"You may take the men north as fast as possible," he said to the head-man. "I shall return and attempt to lead the Big Bwana to the west."

The Negro assented with a grunt. He had no desire to follow this strange white man who was afraid at night; he had less to remain at the tender mercies of the Big Bwana's lusty warriors, between whom and his people there was long-standing blood feud; and he was more than delighted, into the bargain, for a legitimate excuse for deserting his much hated Swede master. He knew a way to the north and his own country that the white men did not know—a short cut across an arid plateau where lay water holes of which the white hunters and explorers that had passed from time to time the fringe of the dry country had never dreamed. He might even elude the Big Bwana should he follow them, and with this thought uppermost in his mind he gathered the remnants of Malbihn's safari into a semblance of order and moved off toward the north. And toward the southwest the black boy led the Hon. Morison Baynes into the jungles.

Korak had waited about the camp, watching the Hon. Morison until the safari had started north. Then, assured that the young Englishman was going in the wrong direction to meet Meriem he had abandoned him and returned slowly to the point where he had seen the girl, for whom his heart yearned, in the arms of another.

So great had been his happiness at seeing Meriem alive that, for the instant, no thought of jealousy had entered his mind. Later these thoughts had come—dark, bloody thoughts that would have made the flesh of the Hon. Morison creep could he have guessed that they were revolving in the brain of a savage creature creeping stealthily among the branches of the forest giant beneath which he waited the coming of "Hanson" and the girl.

And with passing of the hours had come subdued reflection in which he had weighed himself against the trimly clad English gentleman and—found that he was wanting. What had he to offer her by comparison with that which the other man might offer? What was his "mess of pottage" to the birthright that the other had preserved? How could he dare go, naked and unkempt, to that fair thing who had once been his jungle-fellow and propose the thing that had been in his mind when first the realization of his love had swept over him? He shuddered as he thought of the irreparable wrong that his love would have done the innocent child but for the chance that had snatched her from him before it was too late. Doubtless she knew now the horror that had been in his mind. Doubtless she hated and loathed him as he hated and loathed himself when he let his mind dwell upon it. He had lost her. No more surely had she been lost when he thought her dead than she was in reality now that he had seen her living—living in the guise of a refinement that had transfigured and sanctified her.

He had loved her before, now he worshipped her. He knew that he might never possess her now, but at least he might see her. From a distance he might look upon her. Perhaps he might serve her; but never must she guess that he had found her or that he lived.

He wondered if she ever thought of him—if the happy days that they had spent together never recurred to her mind. It seemed unbelievable that such could be the case, and yet, too, it seemed almost equally unbelievable that this beautiful girl was the same disheveled, half naked, little sprite who skipped nimbly among the branches of the trees as they ran and played in the lazy, happy days of the past. It could not be that her memory held more of the past than did her new appearance.

It was a sad Korak who ranged the jungle near the plain's edge waiting for the coming of his Meriem—the Meriem who never came.

But there came another—a tall, broad-shouldered man in khaki at the head of a swarthy crew of ebon warriors. The man's face was set in hard, stern lines and the marks of sorrow were writ deep about his mouth and eyes—so deep that the set expression of rage upon his features could not obliterate them.

Korak saw the man pass beneath him where he hid in the great tree that had harbored him before upon the edge of that fateful little clearing. He saw him come and he set rigid and frozen and suffering above him. He saw him search the ground with his keen eyes, and he only sat there watching with eyes that glazed from the intensity of his gaze. He saw him sign to his men that he had come upon that which he sought and he saw him pass out of sight toward the north, and still Korak sat like a graven image, with a heart that bled in dumb misery. An hour later Korak moved slowly away, back into the jungle toward the west. He went listlessly, with bent head and stooped shoulders, like an old man who bore upon his back the weight of a great sorrow.

Baynes, following his black guide, battled his way through the dense underbrush, riding stooped low over his horse's neck, or often he dismounted where the low branches swept too close to earth to permit him to remain in the saddle. The black was taking him the shortest way, which was no way at all for a horseman, and after the first day's march the young Englishman was forced to abandon his mount, and follow his nimble guide entirely on foot.

During the long hours of marching the Hon. Morison had much time to devote to thought, and as he pictured the probable fate of Meriem at the hands of the Swede his rage against the man became the greater. But presently there came to him a realization of the fact that his own base plans had led the girl into this terrible predicament, and that even had she escaped "Hanson" she would have found but little better deserts awaiting her with him.

There came too, the realization that Meriem was infinitely more precious to him than he had imagined. For the first time he commenced to compare her with other women of his acquaintance—women of birth and position—and almost to his surprise—he discovered that the young Arab girl suffered less than they by the comparison. And then from hating "Hanson" he came to look upon himself with hate and loathing—to see himself and his perfidious act in all their contemptible hideousness.

Thus, in the crucible of shame amidst the white heat of naked truths, the passion that the man had felt for the girl he had considered his social inferior was transmuted into love. And as he staggered on there burned within him beside his newborn love another great passion—the passion of hate urging him on to the consummation of revenge.

A creature of ease and luxury, he had never been subjected to the hardships and tortures which now were his constant companionship, yet, his clothing torn, his flesh scratched and bleeding, he urged the black to greater speed, though with every dozen steps he himself fell from exhaustion.

It was revenge which kept him going—that and a feeling that in his suffering he was partially expiating the great wrong he had done the girl he loved—for hope of saving her from the fate into which he had trapped her had never existed. "Too late! Too late!" was the dismal accompaniment of thought to which he marched. "Too late! Too late to save; but not too late to avenge!" That kept him up.

Only when it became too dark to see would he permit of a halt. A dozen times in the afternoon he had threatened the black with instant death when the tired guide insisted upon resting. The fellow was terrified. He could not understand the remarkable change that had so suddenly come over the white man who had been afraid in the dark the night before. He would have deserted this terrifying master had he had the opportunity; but Baynes guessed that some such thought might be in the other's mind, and so gave the fellow none. He kept close to him by day and slept touching him at night in the rude thorn boma they constructed as a slight protection against prowling carnivora.

That the Hon. Morison could sleep at all in the midst of the savage jungle was sufficient indication that he had changed considerably in the past twenty-four hours, and that he could lie close beside a none-too-fragrant black man spoke of possibilities for democracy within him yet all undreamed of.

Morning found him stiff and lame and sore, but none the less determined to push on in pursuit of "Hanson" as rapidly as possible. With his rifle he brought down a buck at a ford in a small stream shortly after they broke camp, breakfastless. Begrudgingly he permitted a halt while they cooked and ate, and then on again through the wilderness of trees and vines and underbrush.

And in the meantime Korak wandered slowly westward, coming upon the trail of Tantor, the elephant, whom he overtook browsing in the deep shade of the jungle. The ape-man, lonely and sorrowing, was glad of the companionship of his huge friend. Affectionately the sinuous trunk encircled him, and he was swung to the mighty back where so often before he had lolled and dreamed the long afternoon away.

Far to the north the Big Bwana and his black warriors clung tenaciously to the trail of the fleeing safari that was luring them further and further from the girl they sought to save, while back at the bungalow the woman who had loved Meriem as though she had been her own waited impatiently and in sorrow for the return of the rescuing party and the girl she was positive her invincible lord and master would bring back with him.

CHAPTER 22

As Meriem struggled with Malbihn, her hands pinioned to her sides by his brawny grip, hope died within her. She did not utter a sound for she knew that there was none to come to her assistance, and, too, the jungle training of her earlier life had taught her the futility of appeals for succor in the savage world of her up-bringing.

But as she fought to free herself one hand came in contact with the butt of Malbihn's revolver where it rested in the holster at his hip. Slowly he was dragging her toward the blankets, and slowly her fingers encircled the coveted prize and drew it from its resting place.

Then, as Malbihn stood at the edge of the disordered pile of blankets, Meriem suddenly ceased to draw away from him, and as quickly hurled her weight against him with the result that he was thrown backward, his feet stumbled against the bedding and he was hurled to his back. Instinctively his hands flew out to save himself and at the same instant Meriem leveled the revolver at his breast and pulled the trigger.

But the hammer fell futilely upon an empty shell, and Malbihn was again upon his feet clutching at her. For a moment she eluded him, and ran toward the entrance to the tent, but at the very doorway his heavy hand fell upon her shoulder and dragged her back. Wheeling upon him with the fury of a wounded lioness Meriem grasped the long revolver by the barrel, swung it high above her head and crashed it down full in Malbihn's face.

With an oath of pain and rage the man staggered backward, releasing his hold upon her and then sank unconscious to the ground. Without a backward look Meriem turned and fled into the open. Several of the blacks saw her and tried to intercept her flight, but the menace of the empty weapon kept them at a distance. And so she won beyond the encircling boma and disappeared into the jungle to the south.

Straight into the branches of a tree she went, true to the arboreal instincts of the little mangani she had been, and here she stripped off her riding skirt, her shoes and her stockings, for she knew that she had before her a journey and a flight which would not brook the burden of these garments. Her riding breeches and jacket would have to serve as protection from cold and thorns, nor would they hamper her over much; but a skirt and shoes were impossible among the trees.

She had not gone far before she commenced to realize how slight were her chances for survival without means of defense or a weapon to bring down meat. Why had she not thought to strip the cartridge belt from Malbihn's waist before she had left his tent! With cartridges for the revolver she might hope to bag small game, and to protect herself from all but the most ferocious of the enemies that would beset her way back to the beloved hearthstone of Bwana and My Dear.

With the thought came determination to return and obtain the coveted ammunition. She realized that she was taking great chances of recapture; but without means of defense and of obtaining meat she felt that she could never hope to reach safety. And so she turned her face back toward the camp from which she had but just escaped.

She thought Malbihn dead, so terrific a blow had she dealt him, and she hoped to find an opportunity after dark to enter the camp and search his tent for the cartridge belt; but scarcely had she found a hiding place in a great tree at the edge of the boma where she could watch without danger of being discovered, when she saw the Swede emerge from his tent, wiping blood from his face, and hurling a volley of oaths and questions at his terrified followers.

Shortly after the entire camp set forth in search of her and when Meriem was positive that all were gone she descended from her hiding place and ran quickly across the clearing to Malbihn's tent. A hasty survey of the interior revealed no ammunition; but in one corner was a box in which were packed the Swede's personal belongings that he had sent along by his headman to this westerly camp.

Meriem seized the receptacle as the possible container of extra ammunition. Quickly she loosed the cords that held the canvas covering about the box, and a moment later had raised the lid and was rummaging through the heterogeneous accumulation of odds and ends within. There were letters and papers and cuttings from old newspapers, and among other things the photograph of a little girl upon the back of which was pasted a cutting from a Paris daily—a cutting that she could not read, yellowed and dimmed by age and handling—but something about the photograph of the little girl which was also reproduced in the newspaper cutting held her attention. Where had she seen that picture before? And then, quite suddenly, it came to her that this was a picture of herself as she had been years and years before.

Where had it been taken? How had it come into the possession of this man? Why had it been reproduced in a newspaper? What was the story that the faded type told of it?

Meriem was baffled by the puzzle that her search for ammunition had revealed. She stood gazing at the faded photograph for a time and then bethought herself of the ammunition for which she had come. Turning again to the box she rummaged to the bottom and there in a corner she came upon a little box of cartridges. A single glance assured her that they were intended for the weapon she had thrust inside the band of her riding breeches, and slipping them into her pocket she turned once more for an examination of the baffling likeness of herself that she held in her hand.

As she stood thus in vain endeavor to fathom this inexplicable mystery the sound of voices broke upon her ears. Instantly she was all alert. They were coming closer! A second later she recognized the lurid profanity of the Swede. Malbihn, her persecutor, was returning! Meriem ran quickly to the opening of the tent and looked out. It was too late! She was fairly cornered! The white man and three of his black henchmen were coming straight across the clearing toward the tent. What was she to do? She slipped the photograph into her waist. Quickly she slipped a cartridge into each of the chambers of the revolver. Then she backed toward the end of the tent, keeping the entrance covered by her weapon. The man stopped outside, and Meriem could hear Malbihn profanely issuing instructions. He was a long time about it, and while he talked in his bellowing, brutish voice, the girl sought some avenue of escape. Stooping, she raised the bottom of the canvas and looked beneath and beyond. There was no one in sight upon that side. Throwing herself upon her stomach she wormed beneath the tent wall just as Malbihn, with a final word to his men, entered the tent.

Meriem heard him cross the floor, and then she rose and, stooping low, ran to a native hut directly behind. Once inside this she turned and glanced back. There was no one in sight. She had not been seen. And now from Malbihn's tent she heard a great cursing. The Swede had discovered the rifling of his box. He was shouting to his men, and as she heard them reply Meriem darted from the hut and ran toward the edge of the boma furthest from Malbihn's tent. Overhanging the boma at this point was a tree that had been too large, in the eyes of the rest-loving blacks, to cut down. So they had terminated the boma just short of it. Meriem was thankful for whatever circumstance had resulted in the leaving of that particular tree where it was, since it gave her the much-needed avenue of escape which she might not otherwise have had.

From her hiding place she saw Malbihn again enter the jungle, this time leaving a guard of three of his boys in the camp. He went toward the south, and after he had disappeared, Meriem skirted the outside of the enclosure and made her way to the river. Here lay the canoes that had been used in bringing the party from the opposite shore. They were unwieldy things for a lone girl to handle, but there was no other way and she must cross the river.

The landing place was in full view of the guard at the camp. To risk the crossing under their eyes would have meant undoubted capture. Her only hope lay in waiting until darkness had fallen, unless some fortuitous circumstance should arise before. For an hour she lay watching the guard, one of whom seemed always in a position where he would immediately discover her should she attempt to launch one of the canoes.

Presently Malbihn appeared, coming out of the jungle, hot and puffing. He ran immediately to the river where the canoes lay and counted them. It was evident that it had suddenly occurred to him that the girl must cross here if she wished to return to her protectors. The expression of relief on his face when he found that none of the canoes was gone was ample evidence of what was passing in his mind. He turned and spoke hurriedly to the head man who had followed him out of the jungle and with whom were several other blacks.

Following Malbihn's instructions they launched all the canoes but one. Malbihn called to the guards in the camp and a moment later the entire party had entered the boats and were paddling up stream.

Meriem watched them until a bend in the river directly above the camp hid them from her sight. They were gone! She was alone, and they had left a canoe in which lay a paddle! She could scarce believe the good fortune that had come to her. To delay now would be suicidal to her hopes. Quickly she ran from her hiding place and dropped to the ground. A dozen yards lay between her and the canoe.

Up stream, beyond the bend, Malbihn ordered his canoes in to shore. He landed with his head man and crossed the little point slowly in search of a spot where he might watch the canoe he had left at the landing place. He was smiling in anticipation of the almost certain success of his stratagem—sooner or later the girl would come back and attempt to cross the river in one of their canoes. It might be that the idea would not occur to her for some time. They might have to wait a day, or two days; but that she would come if she lived or was not captured by the men he had scouting the jungle for her Malbihn was sure. That she would come so soon, however, he had not guessed, and so when he topped the point and came again within sight of the river he saw that which drew an angry oath from his lips—his quarry already was half way across the river.

Turning, he ran rapidly back to his boats, the head man at his heels. Throwing themselves in, Malbihn urged his paddlers to their most powerful efforts. The canoes shot out into the stream and down with the current toward the fleeing quarry. She had almost completed the crossing when they came in sight of her. At the same instant she saw them, and redoubled her efforts to reach the opposite shore before they should overtake her. Two minutes' start of them was all Meriem cared for. Once in the trees she knew that she could outdistance and elude them. Her hopes were high—they could not overtake her now—she had had too good a start of them.

Malbihn, urging his men onward with a stream of hideous oaths and blows from his fists, realized that the girl was again slipping from his clutches. The leading canoe, in the bow of which he stood, was yet a hundred yards behind the fleeing Meriem when she ran the point of her craft beneath the overhanging trees on the shore of safety.

Malbihn screamed to her to halt. He seemed to have gone mad with rage at the realization that he could not overtake her, and then he threw his rifle to his shoulder, aimed carefully at the slim figure scrambling into the trees, and fired.

Malbihn was an excellent shot. His misses at so short a distance were practically non-existent, nor would he have missed this time but for an accident occurring at the very instant that his finger tightened upon the trigger—an accident to which Meriem owed her life—the providential presence of a water-logged tree trunk, one end of which was embedded in the mud of the river bottom and the other end of which floated just beneath the surface where the prow of Malbihn's canoe ran upon it as he fired. The slight deviation of the boat's direction was sufficient to throw the muzzle of the rifle out of aim. The bullet whizzed harmlessly by Meriem's head and an instant later she had disappeared into the foliage of the tree.

There was a smile on her lips as she dropped to the ground to cross a little clearing where once had stood a native village surrounded by its fields. The ruined huts still stood in crumbling decay. The rank vegetation of the jungle overgrew the cultivated ground. Small trees already had sprung up in what had been the village street; but desolation and loneliness hung like a pall above the scene. To Meriem, however, it presented but a place denuded of large trees which she must cross quickly to regain the jungle upon the opposite side before Malbihn should have landed.

The deserted huts were, to her, all the better because they were deserted—she did not see the keen eyes watching her from a dozen points, from tumbling doorways, from behind tottering granaries. In utter unconsciousness of impending danger she started up the village street because it offered the clearest pathway to the jungle.

A mile away toward the east, fighting his way through the jungle along the trail taken by Malbihn when he had brought Meriem to his camp, a man in torn khaki—filthy, haggard, unkempt—came to a sudden stop as the report of Malbihn's rifle resounded faintly through the tangled forest. The black man just ahead of him stopped, too.

"We are almost there, Bwana," he said. There was awe and respect in his tone and manner.

The white man nodded and motioned his ebon guide forward once more. It was the Hon. Morison Baynes—the fastidious—the exquisite. His face and hands were scratched and smeared with dried blood from the wounds he had come by in thorn and thicket. His clothes were tatters. But through the blood and the dirt and the rags a new Baynes shone forth—a handsomer Baynes than the dandy and the fop of yore.

In the heart and soul of every son of woman lies the germ of manhood and honor. Remorse for a scurvy act, and an honorable desire to right the wrong he had done the woman he now knew he really loved had excited these germs to rapid growth in Morison Baynes—and the metamorphosis had taken place.

Onward the two stumbled toward the point from which the single rifle shot had come. The black was unarmed—Baynes, fearing his loyalty had not dared trust him even to carry the rifle which the white man would have been glad to be relieved of many times upon the long march; but now that they were approaching their goal, and knowing as he did that hatred of Malbihn burned hot in the black man's brain, Baynes handed him the rifle, for he guessed that there would be fighting—he intended that there should, or he had come to avenge. Himself, an excellent revolver shot, would depend upon the smaller weapon at his side.

As the two forged ahead toward their goal they were startled by a volley of shots ahead of them. Then came a few scattering reports, some savage yells, and silence. Baynes was frantic in his endeavors to advance more rapidly, but there the jungle seemed a thousand times more tangled than before. A dozen times he tripped and fell. Twice the black followed a blind trail and they were forced to retrace their steps; but at last they came out into a little clearing near the big afi—a clearing that once held a thriving village, but lay somber and desolate in decay and ruin.

In the jungle vegetation that overgrew what had once been the main village street lay the body of a black man, pierced through the heart with a bullet, and still warm. Baynes and his companion looked about in all directions; but no sign of living being could they discover. They stood in silence listening intently.

What was that! Voices and the dip of paddles out upon the river?

Baynes ran across the dead village toward the fringe of jungle upon the river's brim. The black was at his side. Together they forced their way through the screening foliage until they could obtain a view of the river, and there, almost to the other shore, they saw Malbihn's canoes making rapidly for camp. The black recognized his companions immediately.

"How can we cross?" asked Baynes.

The black shook his head. There was no canoe and the crocodiles made it equivalent to suicide to enter the water in an attempt to swim across. Just then the fellow chanced to glance downward. Beneath him, wedged among the branches of a tree, lay the canoe in which Meriem had escaped. The Negro grasped Baynes' arm and pointed toward his find. The Hon. Morison could scarce repress a shout of exultation. Quickly the two slid down the drooping branches into the boat. The black seized the paddle and Baynes shoved them out from beneath the tree. A second later the canoe shot out upon the bosom of the river and headed toward the opposite shore and the camp of the Swede. Baynes squatted in the bow, straining his eyes after the men pulling the other canoes upon the bank across from him. He saw Malbihn step from the bow of the foremost of the little craft. He saw him turn and glance back across the river. He could see his start of surprise as his eyes fell upon the pursuing canoe, and called the attention of his followers to it.

Then he stood waiting, for there was but one canoe and two men—little danger to him and his followers in that. Malbihn was puzzled. Who was this white man? He did not recognize him though Baynes' canoe was now in mid stream and the features of both its occupants plainly discernible to those on shore. One of Malbihn's blacks it was who first recognized his fellow black in the person of Baynes' companion. Then Malbihn guessed who the white man must be, though he could scarce believe his own reasoning. It seemed beyond the pale of wildest conjecture to suppose that the Hon. Morison Baynes had followed him through the jungle with but a single companion—and yet it was true. Beneath the dirt and dishevelment he recognized him at last, and in the necessity of admitting that it was he, Malbihn was forced to recognize the incentive that had driven Baynes, the weakling and coward, through the savage jungle upon his trail.

The man had come to demand an accounting and to avenge. It seemed incredible, and yet there could be no other explanation. Malbihn shrugged. Well, others had sought Malbihn for similar reasons in the course of a long and checkered career. He fingered his rifle, and waited.

Now the canoe was within easy speaking distance of the shore.

"What do you want?" yelled Malbihn, raising his weapon threateningly.

The Hon. Morison Baynes leaped to his feet.

"You, damn you!" he shouted, whipping out his revolver and firing almost simultaneously with the Swede.

As the two reports rang out Malbihn dropped his rifle, clutched frantically at his breast, staggered, fell first to his knees and then lunged upon his face. Baynes stiffened. His head flew back spasmodically. For an instant he stood thus, and then crumpled very gently into the bottom of the boat.

The black paddler was at a loss as to what to do. If Malbihn really were dead he could continue on to join his fellows without fear; but should the Swede only be wounded he would be safer upon the far shore. Therefore he hesitated, holding the canoe in mid stream. He had come to have considerable respect for his new master and was not unmoved by his death. As he sat gazing at the crumpled body in the bow of the boat he saw it move. Very feebly the man essayed to turn over. He still lived. The black moved forward and lifted him to a sitting position. He was standing in front of him, his paddle in one hand, asking Baynes where he was hit when there was another shot from shore and the Negro pitched head long overboard, his paddle still clutched in his dead fingers—shot through the forehead.

Baynes turned weakly in the direction of the shore to see Malbihn drawn up upon his elbows levelling his rifle at him. The Englishman slid to the bottom of the canoe as a bullet whizzed above him. Malbihn, sore hit, took longer in aiming, nor was his aim as sure as formerly. With difficulty Baynes turned himself over on his belly and grasping his revolver in his right hand drew himself up until he could look over the edge of the canoe.

Malbihn saw him instantly and fired; but Baynes did not flinch or duck. With painstaking care he aimed at the target upon the shore from which he now was drifting with the current. His finger closed upon the trigger—there was a flash and a report, and Malbihn's giant frame jerked to the impact of another bullet.

But he was not yet dead. Again he aimed and fired, the bullet splintering the gunwale of the canoe close by Baynes' face. Baynes fired again as his canoe drifted further down stream and Malbihn answered from the shore where he lay in a pool of his own blood. And thus, doggedly, the two wounded men continued to carry on their weird duel until the winding African river had carried the Hon. Morison Baynes out of sight around a wooded point.

CHAPTER 23

Meriem had traversed half the length of the village street when a score of white-robed Negroes and half-castes leaped out upon her from the dark interiors of surrounding huts. She turned to flee, but heavy hands seized her, and when she turned at last to plead with them her eyes fell upon the face of a tall, grim, old man glaring down upon her from beneath the folds of his burnous.

At sight of him she staggered back in shocked and terrified surprise. It was The Sheik!

Instantly all the old fears and terrors of her childhood returned upon her. She stood trembling before this horrible old man, as a murderer before the judge about to pass sentence of death upon him. She knew that The Sheik recognized her. The years and the changed raiment had not altered her so much but what one who had known her features so well in childhood would know her now.

"So you have come back to your people, eh?" snarled The Sheik. "Come back begging for food and protection, eh?"

"Let me go," cried the girl. "I ask nothing of you, but that you let me go back to the Big Bwana."

"The Big Bwana?" almost screamed The Sheik, and then followed a stream of profane, Arabic invective against the white man whom all the transgressors of the jungle feared and hated. "You would go back to the Big Bwana, would you? So that is where you have been since you ran away from me, is it? And who comes now across the river after you—the Big Bwana?"

"The Swede whom you once chased away from your country when he and his companion conspired with Nbeeda to steal me from you," replied Meriem.

The Sheik's eyes blazed, and he called his men to approach the shore and hide among the bushes that they might ambush and annihilate Malbihn and his party; but Malbihn already had landed and crawling through the fringe of jungle was at that very moment looking with wide and incredulous eyes upon the scene being enacted in the street of the deserted village. He recognized The Sheik the moment his eyes fell upon him. There were two men in the world that Malbihn feared as he feared the devil. One was the Big Bwana and the other The Sheik. A single glance he took at that gaunt, familiar figure and then he turned tail and scurried back to his canoe calling his followers after him. And so it happened that the party was well out in the stream before The Sheik reached the shore, and after a volley and a few parting shots that were returned from the canoes the Arab called his men off and securing his prisoner set off toward the South.

One of the bullets from Malbihn's force had struck a black standing in the village street where he had been left with another to guard Meriem, and his companions had left him where he had fallen, after appropriating his apparel and belongings. His was the body that Baynes had discovered when he had entered the village.

The Sheik and his party had been marching southward along the river when one of them, dropping out of line to fetch water, had seen Meriem paddling desperately from the opposite shore. The fellow had called The Sheik's attention to the strange sight—a white woman alone in Central Africa and the old Arab had hidden his men in the deserted village to capture her when she landed, for thoughts of ransom were always in the mind of The Sheik. More than once before had glittering gold filtered through his fingers from a similar source. It was easy money and The Sheik had none too much easy money since the Big Bwana had so circumscribed the limits of his ancient domain that he dared not even steal ivory from natives within two hundred miles of the Big Bwana's douar. And when at last the woman had walked into the trap he had set for her and he had recognized her as the same little girl he had brutalized and mal-treated years before his gratification had been huge. Now he lost no time in establishing the old relations of father and daughter that had existed between them in the past. At the first opportunity he struck her a heavy blow across the face. He forced her to walk when he might have dismounted one of his men instead, or had her carried on a horse's rump. He seemed to revel in the discovery of new methods for torturing or humiliating her, and among all his followers she found no single one to offer her sympathy, or who dared defend her, even had they had the desire to do so.

A two days' march brought them at last to the familiar scenes of her childhood, and the first face upon which she set her eyes as she was driven through the gates into the strong stockade was that of the toothless, hideous Mabunu, her one time nurse. It was as though all the years that had intervened were but a dream. Had it not been for her clothing and the fact that she had grown in stature she might well have believed it so. All was there as she had left it—the new faces which supplanted some of the old were of the same bestial, degraded type. There were a few young Arabs who had joined The Sheik since she had been away. Otherwise all was the same—all but one. Geeka was not there, and she found herself missing Geeka as though the ivory-headed one had been a flesh and blood intimate and friend. She missed her ragged little confidante, into whose deaf ears she had been wont to pour her many miseries and her occasional joys—Geeka, of the splinter limbs and the ratskin torso—Geeka the disreputable—Geeka the beloved.

For a time the inhabitants of The Sheik's village who had not been upon the march with him amused themselves by inspecting the strangely clad white girl, whom some of them had known as a little child. Mabunu pretended great joy at her return, baring her toothless gums in a hideous grimace that was intended to be indicative of rejoicing. But Meriem could but shudder as she recalled the cruelties of this terrible old hag in the years gone by.

Among the Arabs who had come in her absence was a tall young fellow of twenty—a handsome, sinister looking youth—who stared at her in open admiration until The Sheik came and ordered him away, and Abdul Kamak went, scowling.

At last, their curiosity satisfied, Meriem was alone. As of old, she was permitted the freedom of the village, for the stockade was high and strong and the only gates were well-guarded by day and by night; but as of old she cared not for the companionship of the cruel Arabs and the degraded blacks who formed the following of The Sheik, and so, as had been her wont in the sad days of her childhood, she slunk down to an unfrequented corner of the enclosure where she had often played at house-keeping with her beloved Geeka beneath the spreading branches of the great tree that had overhung the palisade; but now the tree was gone, and Meriem guessed the reason. It was from this tree that Korak had descended and struck down The Sheik the day that he had rescued her from the life of misery and torture that had been her lot for so long that she could remember no other.

There were low bushes growing within the stockade, however, and in the shade of these Meriem sat down to think. A little glow of happiness warmed her heart as she recalled her first meeting with Korak and then the long years that he had cared for and protected her with the solicitude and purity of an elder brother. For months Korak had not so occupied her thoughts as he did today. He seemed closer and dearer now than ever he had before, and she wondered that her heart had drifted so far from loyalty to his memory. And then came the image of the Hon. Morison, the exquisite, and Meriem was troubled. Did she really love the flawless young Englishman? She thought of the glories of London, of which he had told her in such glowing language. She tried to picture herself admired and honored in the midst of the gayest society of the great capital. The pictures she drew were the pictures that the Hon. Morison had drawn for her. They were alluring pictures, but through them all the brawny, half-naked figure of the giant Adonis of the jungle persisted in obtruding itself.

Meriem pressed her hand above her heart as she stifled a sigh, and as she did so she felt the hard outlines of the photograph she had hidden there as she slunk from Malbihn's tent. Now she drew it forth and commenced to re-examine it more carefully than she had had time to do before. She was sure that the baby face was hers. She studied every detail of the picture. Half hidden in the lace of the dainty dress rested a chain and locket. Meriem puckered her brows. What tantalizing half-memories it awakened! Could this flower of evident civilization be the little Arab Meriem, daughter of The Sheik? It was impossible, and yet that locket? Meriem knew it. She could not refute the conviction of her memory. She had seen that locket before and it had been hers. What strange mystery lay buried in her past?

As she sat gazing at the picture she suddenly became aware that she was not alone—that someone was standing close behind her—some one who had approached her noiselessly. Guiltily she thrust the picture back into her waist. A hand fell upon her shoulder. She was sure that it was The Sheik and she awaited in dumb terror the blow that she knew would follow.

No blow came and she looked upward over her shoulder—into the eyes of Abdul Kamak, the young Arab.

"I saw," he said, "the picture that you have just hidden. It is you when you were a child—a very young child. May I see it again?"

Meriem drew away from him.

"I will give it back," he said. "I have heard of you and I know that you have no love for The Sheik, your father. Neither have I. I will not betray you. Let me see the picture."

Friendless among cruel enemies, Meriem clutched at the straw that Abdul Kamak held out to her. Perhaps in him she might find the friend she needed. Anyway he had seen the picture and if he was not a friend he could tell The Sheik about it and it would be taken away from her. So she might as well grant his request and hope that he had spoken fairly, and would deal fairly. She drew the photograph from its hiding place and handed it to him.

Abdul Kamak examined it carefully, comparing it, feature by feature with the girl sitting on the ground looking up into his face. Slowly he nodded his head.

"Yes," he said, "it is you, but where was it taken? How does it happen that The Sheik's daughter is clothed in the garments of the unbeliever?"

"I do not know," replied Meriem. "I never saw the picture until a couple of days ago, when I found it in the tent of the Swede, Malbihn."

Abdul Kamak raised his eyebrows. He turned the picture over and as his eyes fell upon the old newspaper cutting they went wide. He could read French, with difficulty, it is true; but he could read it. He had been to Paris. He had spent six months there with a troupe of his desert fellows, upon exhibition, and he had improved his time, learning many of the customs, some of the language, and most of the vices of his conquerors. Now he put his learning to use. Slowly, laboriously he read the yellowed cutting. His eyes were no longer wide. Instead they narrowed to two slits of cunning. When he had done he looked at the girl.

"You have read this?" he asked.

"It is French," she replied, "and I do not read French."

Abdul Kamak stood long in silence looking at the girl. She was very beautiful. He desired her, as had many other men who had seen her. At last he dropped to one knee beside her.

A wonderful idea had sprung to Abdul Kamak's mind. It was an idea that might be furthered if the girl were kept in ignorance of the contents of that newspaper cutting. It would certainly be doomed should she learn its contents.

"Meriem," he whispered, "never until today have my eyes beheld you, yet at once they told my heart that it must ever be your servant. You do not know me, but I ask that you trust me. I can help you. You hate The Sheik—so do I. Let me take you away from him. Come with me, and we will go back to the great desert where my father is a sheik mightier than is yours. Will you come?"

Meriem sat in silence. She hated to wound the only one who had offered her protection and friendship; but she did not want Abdul Kamak's love. Deceived by her silence the man seized her and strained her to him; but Meriem struggled to free herself.

"I do not love you," she cried. "Oh, please do not make me hate you. You are the only one who has shown kindness toward me, and I want to like you, but I cannot love you."

Abdul Kamak drew himself to his full height.

"You will learn to love me," he said, "for I shall take you whether you will or no. You hate The Sheik and so you will not tell him, for if you do I will tell him of the picture. I hate The Sheik, and—"

"You hate The Sheik?" came a grim voice from behind them.

Both turned to see The Sheik standing a few paces from them. Abdul still held the picture in his hand. Now he thrust it within his burnous.

"Yes," he said, "I hate the Sheik," and as he spoke he sprang toward the older man, felled him with a blow and dashed on across the village to the line where his horse was picketed, saddled and ready, for Abdul Kamak had been about to ride forth to hunt when he had seen the stranger girl alone by the bushes.

Leaping into the saddle Abdul Kamak dashed for the village gates. The Sheik, momentarily stunned by the blow that had felled him, now staggered to his feet, shouting lustily to his followers to stop the escaped Arab. A dozen blacks leaped forward to intercept the horseman, only to be ridden down or brushed aside by the muzzle of Abdul Kamak's long musket, which he lashed from side to side about him as he spurred on toward the gate. But here he must surely be intercepted. Already the two blacks stationed there were pushing the unwieldy portals to. Up flew the barrel of the fugitive's weapon. With reins flying loose and his horse at a mad gallop the son of the desert fired once—twice; and both the keepers of the gate dropped in their tracks. With a wild whoop of exultation, twirling his musket high above his head and turning in his saddle to laugh back into the faces of his pursuers Abdul Kamak dashed out of the village of The Sheik and was swallowed up by the jungle.

Foaming with rage The Sheik ordered immediate pursuit, and then strode rapidly back to where Meriem sat huddled by the bushes where he had left her.

"The picture!" he cried. "What picture did the dog speak of? Where is it? Give it to me at once!"

"He took it," replied Meriem, dully.

"What was it?" again demanded The Sheik, seizing the girl roughly by the hair and dragging her to her feet, where he shook her venomously. "What was it a picture of?"

"Of me," said Meriem, "when I was a little girl. I stole it from Malbihn, the Swede—it had printing on the back cut from an old newspaper."

The Sheik went white with rage.

"What said the printing?" he asked in a voice so low that she but barely caught his words.

"I do not know. It was in French and I cannot read French."

The Sheik seemed relieved. He almost smiled, nor did he again strike Meriem before he turned and strode away with the parting admonition that she speak never again to any other than Mabunu and himself. And along the caravan trail galloped Abdul Kamak toward the north.

As his canoe drifted out of sight and range of the wounded Swede the Hon. Morison sank weakly to its bottom where he lay for long hours in partial stupor.

It was night before he fully regained consciousness. And then he lay for a long time looking up at the stars and trying to recollect where he was, what accounted for the gently rocking motion of the thing upon which he lay, and why the position of the stars changed so rapidly and miraculously. For a while he thought he was dreaming, but when he would have moved to shake sleep from him the pain of his wound recalled to him the events that had led up to his present position. Then it was that he realized that he was floating down a great African river in a native canoe—alone, wounded, and lost.

Painfully he dragged himself to a sitting position. He noticed that the wound pained him less than he had imagined it would. He felt of it gingerly—it had ceased to bleed. Possibly it was but a flesh wound after all, and nothing serious. If it totally incapacitated him even for a few days it would mean death, for by that time he would be too weakened by hunger and pain to provide food for himself.

From his own troubles his mind turned to Meriem's. That she had been with the Swede at the time he had attempted to reach the fellow's camp he naturally believed; but he wondered what would become of her now. Even if Hanson died of his wounds would Meriem be any better off? She was in the power of equally villainous men—brutal savages of the lowest order. Baynes buried his face in his hands and rocked back and forth as the hideous picture of her fate burned itself into his consciousness. And it was he who had brought this fate upon her! His wicked desire had snatched a pure and innocent girl from the protection of those who loved her to hurl her into the clutches of the bestial Swede and his outcast following! And not until it had become too late had he realized the magnitude of the crime he himself had planned and contemplated. Not until it had become too late had he realized that greater than his desire, greater than his lust, greater than any passion he had ever felt before was the newborn love that burned within his breast for the girl he would have ruined.

The Hon. Morison Baynes did not fully realize the change that had taken place within him. Had one suggested that he ever had been aught than the soul of honor and chivalry he would have taken umbrage forthwith. He knew that he had done a vile thing when he had plotted to carry Meriem away to London, yet he excused it on the ground of his great passion for the girl having temporarily warped his moral standards by the intensity of its heat. But, as a matter of fact, a new Baynes had been born. Never again could this man be bent to dishonor by the intensity of a desire. His moral fiber had been strengthened by the mental suffering he had endured. His mind and his soul had been purged by sorrow and remorse.

His one thought now was to atone—win to Meriem's side and lay down his life, if necessary, in her protection. His eyes sought the length of the canoe in search of the paddle, for a determination had galvanized him to immediate action despite his weakness and his wound. But the paddle was gone. He turned his eyes toward the shore. Dimly through the darkness of a moonless night he saw the awful blackness of the jungle, yet it touched no responsive chord of terror within him now as it had done in the past. He did not even wonder that he was unafraid, for his mind was entirely occupied with thoughts of another's danger.

Drawing himself to his knees he leaned over the edge of the canoe and commenced to paddle vigorously with his open palm. Though it tired and hurt him he kept assiduously at his self imposed labor for hours. Little by little the drifting canoe moved nearer and nearer the shore. The Hon. Morison could hear a lion roaring directly opposite him and so close that he felt he must be almost to the shore. He drew his rifle closer to his side; but he did not cease to paddle.

After what seemed to the tired man an eternity of time he felt the brush of branches against the canoe and heard the swirl of the water about them. A moment later he reached out and clutched a leafy limb. Again the lion roared—very near it seemed now, and Baynes wondered if the brute could have been following along the shore waiting for him to land.

He tested the strength of the limb to which he clung. It seemed strong enough to support a dozen men. Then he reached down and lifted his rifle from the bottom of the canoe, slipping the sling over his shoulder. Again he tested the branch, and then reaching upward as far as he could for a safe hold he drew himself painfully and slowly upward until his feet swung clear of the canoe, which, released, floated silently from beneath him to be lost forever in the blackness of the dark shadows down stream.

He had burned his bridges behind him. He must either climb aloft or drop back into the river; but there had been no other way. He struggled to raise one leg over the limb, but found himself scarce equal to the effort, for he was very weak. For a time he hung there feeling his strength ebbing. He knew that he must gain the branch above at once or it would be too late.

443

Suddenly the lion roared almost in his ear. Baynes glanced up. He saw two spots of flame a short distance from and above him. The lion was standing on the bank of the river glaring at him, and—waiting for him. Well, thought the Hon. Morison, let him wait. Lions can't climb trees, and if I get into this one I shall be safe enough from him.

The young Englishman's feet hunt almost to the surface of the water—closer than he knew, for all was pitch dark below as above him. Presently he heard a slight commotion in the river beneath him and something banged against one of his feet, followed almost instantly by a sound that he felt he could not have mistaken—the click of great jaws snapping together.

"By George!" exclaimed the Hon. Morison, aloud. "The beggar nearly got me," and immediately he struggled again to climb higher and to comparative safety; but with that final effort he knew that it was futile. Hope that had survived persistently until now began to wane. He felt his tired, numbed fingers slipping from their hold—he was dropping back into the river—into the jaws of the frightful death that awaited him there.

And then he heard the leaves above him rustle to the movement of a creature among them. The branch to which he clung bent beneath an added weight—and no light weight, from the way it sagged; but still Baynes clung desperately—he would not give up voluntarily either to the death above or the death below.

He felt a soft, warm pad upon the fingers of one of his hands where they circled the branch to which he clung, and then something reached down out of the blackness above and dragged him up among the branches of the tree.

CHAPTER 24

Sometimes lolling upon Tantor's back, sometimes roaming the jungle in solitude, Korak made his way slowly toward the West and South. He made but a few miles a day, for he had a whole lifetime before him and no place in particular to go. Possibly he would have moved more rapidly but for the thought which continually haunted him that each mile he traversed carried him further and further away from Meriem—no longer his Meriem, as of yore, it is true! but still as dear to him as ever.

Thus he came upon the trail of The Sheik's band as it traveled down river from the point where The Sheik had captured Meriem to his own stockaded village. Korak pretty well knew who it was that had passed, for there were few in the great jungle with whom he was not familiar, though it had been years since he had come this far north. He had no particular business, however, with the old Sheik and so he did not propose following him—the further from men he could stay the better pleased he would be—he wished that he might never see a human face again. Men always brought him sorrow and misery.

The river suggested fishing and so he waddled upon its shores, catching fish after a fashion of his own devising and eating them raw. When night came he curled up in a great tree beside the stream—the one from which he had been fishing during the afternoon—and was soon asleep. Numa, roaring beneath him, awoke him. He was about to call out in anger to his noisy neighbor when something else caught his attention. He listened. Was there something in the tree beside himself? Yes, he heard the noise of something below him trying to clamber upward. Presently he heard the click of a crocodile's jaws in the waters beneath, and then, low but distinct: "By George! The beggar nearly got me." The voice was familiar.

Korak glanced downward toward the speaker. Outlined against the faint luminosity of the water he saw the figure of a man clinging to a lower branch of the tree. Silently and swiftly the ape-man clambered downward. He felt a hand beneath his foot. He reached down and clutched the figure beneath him and dragged it up among the branches. It struggled weakly and struck at him; but Korak paid no more attention than Tantor to an ant. He lugged his burden to the higher safety and greater comfort of a broad crotch, and there he propped it in a sitting position against the bole of the tree. Numa still was roaring beneath them, doubtless in anger that he had been robbed of his prey. Korak shouted down at him, calling him, in the language of the great apes, "Old green-eyed eater of carrion," "Brother of Dango," the hyena, and other choice appellations of jungle opprobrium.

The Hon. Morison Baynes, listening, felt assured that a gorilla had seized upon him. He felt for his revolver, and as he was drawing it stealthily from its holster a voice asked in perfectly good English, "Who are you?"

Baynes started so that he nearly fell from the branch.

"My God!" he exclaimed. "Are you a man?"

"What did you think I was?" asked Korak.

"A gorilla," replied Baynes, honestly.

Korak laughed.

"Who are you?" he repeated.

"I'm an Englishman by the name of Baynes; but who the devil are you?" asked the Hon. Morison.

"They call me The Killer," replied Korak, giving the English translation of the name that Akut had given him. And then after a pause during which the Hon. Morison attempted to pierce the darkness and catch a glimpse of the features of the strange being into whose hands he had fallen, "You are the same whom I saw kissing the girl at the edge of the great plain to the East, that time that the lion charged you?"

"Yes," replied Baynes.

"What are you doing here?"

"The girl was stolen—I am trying to rescue her."

"Stolen!" The word was shot out like a bullet from a gun. "Who stole her?"

"The Swede trader, Hanson," replied Baynes.

"Where is he?"

Baynes related to Korak all that had transpired since he had come upon Hanson's camp. Before he was done the first gray dawn had relieved the darkness. Korak made the Englishman comfortable in the tree. He filled his canteen from the river and fetched him fruits to eat. Then he bid him good-bye.

"I am going to the Swede's camp," he announced. "I will bring the girl back to you here."

"I shall go, too, then," insisted Baynes. "It is my right and my duty, for she was to have become my wife."

Korak winced. "You are wounded. You could not make the trip," he said. "I can go much faster alone."

"Go, then," replied Baynes; "but I shall follow. It is my right and duty."

"As you will," replied Korak, with a shrug. If the man wanted to be killed it was none of his affair. He wanted to kill him himself, but for Meriem's sake he would not. If she loved him then he must do what he could to preserve him, but he could not prevent his following him, more than to advise him against it, and this he did, earnestly.

And so Korak set out rapidly toward the North, and limping slowly and painfully along, soon far to the rear, came the tired and wounded Baynes. Korak had reached the river bank opposite Malbihn's camp before Baynes had covered two miles. Late in the afternoon the Englishman was still plodding wearily along, forced to stop often for rest when he heard the sound of the galloping feet of a horse behind him. Instinctively he drew into the concealing foliage of the underbrush and a moment later a white-robed Arab dashed by. Baynes did not hail the rider. He had heard of the nature of the Arabs who penetrate thus far to the South, and what he had heard had convinced him that a snake or a panther would as quickly befriend him as one of these villainous renegades from the Northland.

When Abdul Kamak had passed out of sight toward the North Baynes resumed his weary march. A half hour later he was again surprised by the unmistakable sound of galloping horses. This time there were many. Once more he sought a hiding place; but it chanced that he was crossing a clearing which offered little opportunity for concealment. He broke into a slow trot—the best that he could do in his weakened condition; but it did not suffice to carry him to safety and before he reached the opposite side of the clearing a band of white-robed horsemen dashed into view behind him.

At sight of him they shouted in Arabic, which, of course, he could not understand, and then they closed about him, threatening and angry. Their questions were unintelligible to him, and no more could they interpret his English. At last, evidently out of patience, the leader ordered two of his men to seize him, which they lost no time in doing. They disarmed him and ordered him to climb to the rump of one of the horses, and then the two who had been detailed to guard him turned and rode back toward the South, while the others continued their pursuit of Abdul Kamak.

As Korak came out upon the bank of the river across from which he could see the camp of Malbihn he was at a loss as to how he was to cross. He could see men moving about among the huts inside the boma—evidently Hanson was still there. Korak did not know the true identity of Meriem's abductor.

How was he to cross. Not even he would dare the perils of the river—almost certain death. For a moment he thought, then wheeled and sped away into the jungle, uttering a peculiar cry, shrill and piercing. Now and again he would halt to listen as though for an answer to his weird call, then on again, deeper and deeper into the wood.

At last his listening ears were rewarded by the sound they craved—the trumpeting of a bull elephant, and a few moments later Korak broke through the trees into the presence of Tantor, standing with upraised trunk, waving his great ears.

"Quick, Tantor!" shouted the ape-man, and the beast swung him to his head. "Hurry!" and the mighty pachyderm lumbered off through the jungle, guided by kicking of naked heels against the sides of his head.

Toward the northwest Korak guided his huge mount, until they came out upon the river a mile or more above the Swede's camp, at a point where Korak knew that there was an elephant ford. Never pausing the ape-man urged the beast into the river, and with trunk held high Tantor forged steadily toward the opposite bank. Once an unwary crocodile attacked him but the sinuous trunk dove beneath the surface and grasping the amphibian about the middle dragged it to light and hurled it a hundred feet down stream. And so, in safety, they made the opposite shore, Korak perched high and dry above the turgid flood.

Then back toward the South Tantor moved, steadily, relentlessly, and with a swinging gait which took no heed of any obstacle other than the larger jungle trees. At times Korak was forced to abandon the broad head and take to the trees above, so close the branches raked the back of the elephant; but at last they came to the edge of the clearing where lay the camp of the renegade Swede, nor even then did they hesitate or halt. The gate lay upon the east side of the camp, facing the river. Tantor and Korak approached from the north. There was no gate there; but what cared Tantor or Korak for gates.

At a word from the ape man and raising his tender trunk high above the thorns Tantor breasted the boma, walking through it as though it had not existed. A dozen blacks squatted before their huts looked up at the noise of his approach. With sudden howls of terror and amazement they leaped to their feet and fled for the open gates. Tantor would have pursued. He hated man, and he thought that Korak had come to hunt these; but the ape man held him back, guiding him toward a large, canvas tent that rose in the center of the clearing—there should be the girl and her abductor.

Malbihn lay in a hammock beneath canopy before his tent. His wounds were painful and he had lost much blood. He was very weak. He looked up in surprise as he heard the screams of his men and saw them running toward the gate. And then from around the corner of his tent loomed a huge bulk, and Tantor, the great tusker, towered above him. Malbihn's boy, feeling neither affection nor loyalty for his master, broke and ran at the first glimpse of the beast, and Malbihn was left alone and helpless.

The elephant stopped a couple of paces from the wounded man's hammock. Malbihn cowered, moaning. He was too weak to escape. He could only lie there with staring eyes gazing in horror into the blood rimmed, angry little orbs fixed upon him, and await his death.

Then, to his astonishment, a man slid to the ground from the elephant's back. Almost at once Malbihn recognized the strange figure as that of the creature who consorted with apes and baboons—the white warrior of the jungle who had freed the king baboon and led the whole angry horde of hairy devils upon him and Jenssen. Malbihn cowered still lower.

"Where is the girl?" demanded Korak, in English.

"What girl?" asked Malbihn. "There is no girl here—only the women of my boys. Is it one of them you want?"

"The white girl," replied Korak. "Do not lie to me—you lured her from her friends. You have her. Where is she?"

"It was not I," cried Malbihn. "It was an Englishman who hired me to steal her. He wished to take her to London with him. She was willing to go. His name is Baynes. Go to him, if you want to know where the girl is."

"I have just come from him," said Korak. "He sent me to you. The girl is not with him. Now stop your lying and tell me the truth. Where is she?" Korak took a threatening step toward the Swede.

Malbihn shrank from the anger in the other's face.

"I will tell you," he cried. "Do not harm me and I will tell you all that I know. I had the girl here; but it was Baynes who persuaded her to leave her friends—he had promised to marry her. He does not know who she is; but I do, and I know that there is a great reward for whoever takes her back to her people. It was the only reward I wanted. But she escaped and crossed the river in one of my canoes. I followed her, but The Sheik was there, God knows how, and he captured her and attacked me and drove me back. Then came Baynes, angry because he had lost the girl, and shot me. If you want her, go to The Sheik and ask him for her—she has passed as his daughter since childhood."

"She is not The Sheik's daughter?" asked Korak.

"She is not," replied Malbihn.

"Who is she then?" asked Korak.

Here Malbihn saw his chance. Possibly he could make use of his knowledge after all—it might even buy back his life for him. He was not so credulous as to believe that this savage ape-man would have any compunctions about slaying him.

"When you find her I will tell you," he said, "if you will promise to spare my life and divide the reward with me. If you kill me you will never know, for only The Sheik knows and he will never tell. The girl herself is ignorant of her origin."

"If you have told me the truth I will spare you," said Korak. "I shall go now to The Sheik's village and if the girl is not there I shall return and slay you. As for the other information you have, if the girl wants it when we have found her we will find a way to purchase it from you."

The look in the Killer's eyes and his emphasis of the word "purchase" were none too reassuring to Malbihn. Evidently, unless he found means to escape, this devil would have both his secret and his life before he was done with him. He wished he would be gone and take his evil-eyed companion away with him. The swaying bulk towering high above him, and the ugly little eyes of the elephant watching his every move made Malbihn nervous.

Korak stepped into the Swede's tent to assure himself that Meriem was not hid there. As he disappeared from view Tantor, his eyes still fixed upon Malbihn, took a step nearer the man. An elephant's eyesight is none too good; but the great tusker evidently had harbored suspicions of this yellow-bearded white man from the first. Now he advanced his snake-like trunk toward the Swede, who shrank still deeper into his hammock.

The sensitive member felt and smelled back and forth along the body of the terrified Malbihn. Tantor uttered a low, rumbling sound. His little eyes blazed. At last he had recognized the creature who had killed his mate long years before. Tantor, the elephant, never forgets and never forgives. Malbihn saw in the demoniacal visage above him the murderous purpose of the beast. He shrieked aloud to Korak. "Help! Help! The devil is going to kill me!"

Korak ran from the tent just in time to see the enraged elephant's trunk encircle the beast's victim, and then hammock, canopy and man were swung high over Tantor's head. Korak leaped before the animal, commanding him to put down his prey unharmed; but as well might he have ordered the eternal river to reverse its course. Tantor wheeled around like a cat, hurled Malbihn to the earth and kneeled upon him with the quickness of a cat. Then he gored the prostrate thing through and through with his mighty tusks, trumpeting and roaring in his rage, and at last, convinced that no slightest spark of life remained in the crushed and lacerated flesh, he lifted the shapeless clay that had been Sven Malbihn far aloft and hurled the bloody mass, still entangled in canopy and hammock, over the boma and out into the jungle.

Korak stood looking sorrowfully on at the tragedy he gladly would have averted. He had no love for the Swede, in fact only hatred; but he would have preserved the man for the sake of the secret he possessed. Now that secret was gone forever unless The Sheik could be made to divulge it; but in that possibility Korak placed little faith.

The ape-man, as unafraid of the mighty Tantor as though he had not just witnessed his shocking murder of a human being, signalled the beast to approach and lift him to its head, and Tantor came as he was bid, docile as a kitten, and hoisted The Killer tenderly aloft.

From the safety of their hiding places in the jungle Malbihn's boys had witnessed the killing of their master, and now, with wide, frightened eyes, they saw the strange white warrior, mounted upon the head of his ferocious charger, disappear into the jungle at the point from which he had emerged upon their terrified vision.

CHAPTER 25

The Sheik glowered at the prisoner which his two men brought back to him from the North. He had sent the party after Abdul Kamak, and he was wroth that instead of his erstwhile lieutenant they had sent back a wounded and useless Englishman. Why had they not dispatched him where they had found him? He was some penniless beggar of a trader who had wandered from his own district and became lost. He was worthless. The Sheik scowled terribly upon him.

"Who are you?" he asked in French.

"I am the Hon. Morison Baynes of London," replied his prisoner.

The title sounded promising, and at once the wily old robber had visions of ransom. His intentions, if not his attitude toward the prisoner underwent a change—he would investigate further.

"What were you doing poaching in my country?" growled he.

"I was not aware that you owned Africa," replied the Hon. Morison. "I was searching for a young woman who had been abducted from the home of a friend. The abductor wounded me and I drifted down river in a canoe—I was on my back to his camp when your men seized me."

"A young woman?" asked The Sheik. "Is that she?" and he pointed to his left over toward a clump of bushes near the stockade.

Baynes looked in the direction indicated and his eyes went wide, for there, sitting cross-legged upon the ground, her back toward them, was Meriem.

"Meriem!" he shouted, starting toward her; but one of his guards grasped his arm and jerked him back. The girl leaped to her feet and turned toward him as she heard her name.

"Morison!" she cried.

"Be still, and stay where you are," snapped The Sheik, and then to Baynes. "So you are the dog of a Christian who stole my daughter from me?"

"Your daughter?" ejaculated Baynes. "She is your daughter?"

"She is my daughter," growled the Arab, "and she is not for any unbeliever. You have earned death, Englishman, but if you can pay for your life I will give it to you."

Baynes' eyes were still wide at the unexpected sight of Meriem here in the camp of the Arab when he had thought her in Hanson's power. What had happened? How had she escaped the Swede? Had the Arab taken her by force from him, or had she escaped and come voluntarily back to the protection of the man who called her "daughter"? He would have given much for a word with her. If she was safe here he might only harm her by antagonizing the Arab in an attempt to take her away and return her to her English friends. No longer did the Hon. Morison harbor thoughts of luring the girl to London.

"Well?" asked The Sheik.

"Oh," exclaimed Baynes; "I beg your pardon—I was thinking of something else. Why yes, of course, glad to pay, I'm sure. How much do you think I'm worth?"

The Sheik named a sum that was rather less exorbitant than the Hon. Morison had anticipated. The latter nodded his head in token of his entire willingness to pay. He would have promised a sum far beyond his resources just as readily, for he had no intention of paying anything—his one reason for seeming to comply with The Sheik's demands was that the wait for the coming of the ransom money would give him the time and the opportunity to free Meriem if he found that she wished to be freed. The Arab's statement that he was her father naturally raised the question in the Hon. Morison's mind as to precisely what the girl's attitude toward escape might be. It seemed, of course, preposterous that this fair and beautiful young woman should prefer to remain in the filthy douar of an illiterate old Arab rather than return to the comforts, luxuries, and congenial associations of the hospitable African bungalow from which the Hon. Morison had tricked her. The man flushed at the thought of his duplicity which these recollections aroused—thoughts which were interrupted by The Sheik, who instructed the Hon. Morison to write a letter to the British consul at Algiers, dictating the exact phraseology of it with a fluency that indicated to his captive that this was not the first time the old rascal had had occasion to negotiate with English relatives for the ransom of a kinsman. Baynes demurred when he saw that the letter was addressed to the consul at Algiers, saying that it would require the better part of a year to get the money back to him; but The Sheik would not listen to Baynes' plan to send a messenger directly to the nearest coast town, and from there communicate with the nearest cable state, sending the Hon. Morison's request for funds straight to his own solicitors. No, The Sheik was cautious and wary. He knew his own plan had worked well in the past. In the other were too many untried elements. He was in no hurry for the money—he could wait a year, or two years if necessary; but it should not require over six months. He turned to one of the Arabs who had been standing behind him and gave the fellow instructions in relation to the prisoner.

Baynes could not understand the words, spoken in Arabic, but the jerk of the thumb toward him showed that he was the subject of conversation. The Arab addressed by The Sheik bowed to his master and beckoned Baynes to follow him. The Englishman looked toward The Sheik for confirmation. The latter nodded impatiently, and the Hon. Morison rose and followed his guide toward a native hut which lay close beside one of the outside goatskin tents. In the dark, stifling interior his guard led him, then stepped to the doorway and called to a couple of black boys squatting before their own huts. They came promptly and in accordance with the Arab's instructions bound Baynes' wrists and ankles securely. The Englishman objected strenuously; but as neither the blacks nor the Arab could understand a word he said his pleas were wasted. Having bound him they left the hut. The Hon. Morison lay for a long time contemplating the frightful future which awaited him during the long months which must intervene before his friends learned of his predicament and could get succor to him. Now he hoped that they would send the ransom—he would gladly pay all that he was worth to be out of this hole. At first it had been his intention to cable his solicitors to send no money but to communicate with the British West African authorities and have an expedition sent to his aid.

His patrician nose wrinkled in disgust as his nostrils were assailed by the awful stench of the hut. The nasty grasses upon which he lay exuded the effluvium of sweaty bodies, of decayed animal matter and of offal. But worse was yet to come. He had lain in the uncomfortable position in which they had thrown him but for a few minutes when he became distinctly conscious of an acute itching sensation upon his hands, his neck and scalp. He wriggled to a sitting posture horrified and disgusted. The itching rapidly extended to other parts of his body—it was torture, and his hands were bound securely at his back!

He tugged and pulled at his bonds until he was exhausted; but not entirely without hope, for he was sure that he was working enough slack out of the knot to eventually permit of his withdrawing one of his hands.

Night came. They brought him neither food nor drink. He wondered if they expected him to live on nothing for a year. The bites of the vermin grew less annoying though not less numerous. The Hon. Morison saw a ray of hope in this indication of future immunity through inoculation. He still worked weakly at his bonds, and then the rats came. If the vermin were disgusting the rats were terrifying. They scurried over his body, squealing and fighting. Finally one commenced to chew at one of his ears. With an oath, the Hon. Morison struggled to a sitting posture. The rats retreated. He worked his legs beneath him and came to his knees, and then, by superhuman effort, rose to his feet. There he stood, reeling drunkenly, dripping with cold sweat.

"God!" he muttered, "what have I done to deserve—" He paused. What had he done? He thought of the girl in another tent in that accursed village. He was getting his deserts. He set his jaws firmly with the realization. He would never complain again! At that moment he became aware of voices raised angrily in the goatskin tent close beside the hut in which he lay. One of them was a woman's. Could it be Meriem's? The language was probably Arabic—he could not understand a word of it; but the tones were hers.

He tried to think of some way of attracting her attention to his near presence. If she could remove his bonds they might escape together—if she wished to escape. That thought bothered him. He was not sure of her status in the village. If she were the petted child of the powerful Sheik then she would probably not care to escape. He must know, definitely.

At the bungalow he had often heard Meriem sing God Save the King, as My Dear accompanied her on the piano. Raising his voice he now hummed the tune. Immediately he heard Meriem's voice from the tent. She spoke rapidly.

"Good bye, Morison," she cried. "If God is good I shall be dead before morning, for if I still live I shall be worse than dead after tonight."

Then he heard an angry exclamation in a man's voice, followed by the sounds of a scuffle. Baynes went white with horror. He struggled frantically again with his bonds. They were giving. A moment later one hand was free. It was but the work of an instant then to loose the other. Stooping, he untied the rope from his ankles, then he straightened and started for the hut doorway bent on reaching Meriem's side. As he stepped out into the night the figure of a huge black rose and barred his progress.

When speed was required of him Korak depended upon no other muscles than his own, and so it was that the moment Tantor had landed him safely upon the same side of the river as lay the village of The Sheik, the ape-man deserted his bulky comrade and took to the trees in a rapid race toward the south and the spot where the Swede had told him Meriem might be. It was dark when he came to the palisade, strengthened considerably since the day that he had rescued Meriem from her pitiful life within its cruel confines. No longer did the giant tree spread its branches above the wooden rampart; but ordinary man-made defenses were scarce considered obstacles by Korak. Loosening the rope at his waist he tossed the noose over one of the sharpened posts that composed the palisade. A moment later his eyes were above the level of the obstacle taking in all within their range beyond. There was no one in sight close by, and Korak drew himself to the top and dropped lightly to the ground within the enclosure.

Then he commenced his stealthy search of the village. First toward the Arab tents he made his way, sniffing and listening. He passed behind them searching for some sign of Meriem. Not even the wild Arab curs heard his passage, so silently he went—a shadow passing through shadows. The odor of tobacco told him that the Arabs were smoking before their tents. The sound of laughter fell upon his ears, and then from the opposite side of the village came the notes of a once familiar tune: God Save the King. Korak halted in perplexity. Who might it be—the tones were those of a man. He recalled the young Englishman he had left on the river trail and who had disappeared before he returned. A moment later there came to him a woman's voice in reply—it was Meriem's, and The Killer, quickened into action, slunk rapidly in the direction of these two voices.

The evening meal over Meriem had gone to her pallet in the women's quarters of The Sheik's tent, a little corner screened off in the rear by a couple of priceless Persian rugs to form a partition. In these quarters she

EDGAR RICE BURROUGHS

had dwelt with Mabunu alone, for The Sheik had no wives. Nor were conditions altered now after the years of her absence—she and Mabunu were alone in the women's quarters.

Presently The Sheik came and parted the rugs. He glared through the dim light of the interior.

"Meriem!" he called. "Come hither."

The girl arose and came into the front of the tent. There the light of a fire illuminated the interior. She saw Ali ben Kadin, The Sheik's half brother, squatted upon a rug, smoking. The Sheik was standing. The Sheik and Ali ben Kadin had had the same father, but Ali ben Kadin's mother had been a slave—a West Coast Negress. Ali ben Kadin was old and hideous and almost black. His nose and part of one cheek were eaten away by disease. He looked up and grinned as Meriem entered.

The Sheik jerked his thumb toward Ali ben Kadin and addressed Meriem.

"I am getting old," he said, "I shall not live much longer. Therefore I have given you to Ali ben Kadin, my brother."

That was all. Ali ben Kadin rose and came toward her. Meriem shrank back, horrified. The man seized her wrist.

"Come!" he commanded, and dragged her from The Sheik's tent and to his own.

After they had gone The Sheik chuckled. "When I send her north in a few months," he soliloquized, "they will know the reward for slaying the son of the sister of Amor ben Khatour."

And in Ali ben Kadin's tent Meriem pleaded and threatened, but all to no avail. The hideous old halfcaste spoke soft words at first, but when Meriem loosed upon him the vials of her horror and loathing he became enraged, and rushing upon her seized her in his arms. Twice she tore away from him, and in one of the intervals during which she managed to elude him she heard Baynes' voice humming the tune that she knew was meant for her ears. At her reply Ali ben Kadin rushed upon her once again. This time he dragged her back into the rear apartment of his tent where three Negresses looked up in stolid indifference to the tragedy being enacted before them.

As the Hon. Morison saw his way blocked by the huge frame of the giant black his disappointment and rage filled him with a bestial fury that transformed him into a savage beast. With an oath he leaped upon the man before him, the momentum of his body hurling the black to the ground. There they fought, the black to draw his knife, the white to choke the life from the black.

Baynes' fingers shut off the cry for help that the other would have been glad to voice; but presently the Negro succeeded in drawing his weapon and an instant later Baynes felt the sharp steel in his shoulder. Again and again the weapon fell. The white man removed one hand from its choking grip upon the black throat. He felt around upon the ground beside him searching for some missile, and at last his fingers touched a stone and closed upon it. Raising it above his antagonist's head the Hon. Morison drove home a terrific blow. Instantly the black relaxed—stunned. Twice more Baynes struck him. Then he leaped to his feet and ran for the goat skin tent from which he had heard the voice of Meriem in distress.

But before him was another. Naked but for his leopard skin and his loin cloth, Korak, The Killer, slunk into the shadows at the back of Ali ben Kadin's tent. The half-caste had just dragged Meriem into the rear chamber as Korak's sharp knife slit a six foot opening in the tent wall, and Korak, tall and mighty, sprang through upon the astonished visions of the inmates.

Meriem saw and recognized him the instant that he entered the apartment. Her heart leaped in pride and joy at the sight of the noble figure for which it had hungered for so long.

"Korak!" she cried.

"Meriem!" He uttered the single word as he hurled himself upon the astonished Ali ben Kadin. The three Negresses leaped from their sleeping mats, screaming. Meriem tried to prevent them from escaping; but before she could succeed the terrified blacks had darted through the hole in the tent wall made by Korak's knife, and were gone screaming through the village.

451

The Killer's fingers closed once upon the throat of the hideous Ali. Once his knife plunged into the putrid heart—and Ali ben Kadin lay dead upon the floor of his tent. Korak turned toward Meriem and at the same moment a bloody and disheveled apparition leaped into the apartment.

"Morison!" cried the girl.

Korak turned and looked at the new comer. He had been about to take Meriem in his arms, forgetful of all that might have transpired since last he had seen her. Then the coming of the young Englishman recalled the scene he had witnessed in the little clearing, and a wave of misery swept over the ape man.

Already from without came the sounds of the alarm that the three Negresses had started. Men were running toward the tent of Ali ben Kadin. There was no time to be lost.

"Quick!" cried Korak, turning toward Baynes, who had scarce yet realized whether he was facing a friend or foe. "Take her to the palisade, following the rear of the tents. Here is my rope. With it you can scale the wall and make your escape."

"But you, Korak?" cried Meriem.

"I will remain," replied the ape-man. "I have business with The Sheik."

Meriem would have demurred, but The Killer seized them both by the shoulders and hustled them through the slit wall and out into the shadows beyond.

"Now run for it," he admonished, and turned to meet and hold those who were pouring into the tent from the front.

The ape-man fought well—fought as he had never fought before; but the odds were too great for victory, though he won that which he most craved—time for the Englishman to escape with Meriem. Then he was overwhelmed by numbers, and a few minutes later, bound and guarded, he was carried to The Sheik's tent.

The old men eyed him in silence for a long time. He was trying to fix in his own mind some form of torture that would gratify his rage and hatred toward this creature who twice had been the means of his losing possession of Meriem. The killing of Ali ben Kadin caused him little anger—always had he hated the hideous son of his father's hideous slave. The blow that this naked white warrior had once struck him added fuel to his rage. He could think of nothing adequate to the creature's offense.

And as he sat there looking upon Korak the silence was broken by the trumpeting of an elephant in the jungle beyond the palisade. A half smile touched Korak's lips. He turned his head a trifle in the direction from which the sound had come and then there broke from his lips, a low, weird call. One of the blacks guarding him struck him across the mouth with the haft of his spear; but none there knew the significance of his cry.

In the jungle Tantor cocked his ears as the sound of Korak's voice fell upon them. He approached the palisade and lifting his trunk above it, sniffed. Then he placed his head against the wooden logs and pushed; but the palisade was strong and only gave a little to the pressure.

In The Sheik's tent The Sheik rose at last, and, pointing toward the bound captive, turned to one of his lieutenants.

"Burn him," he commanded. "At once. The stake is set."

The guard pushed Korak from The Sheik's presence. They dragged him to the open space in the center of the village, where a high stake was set in the ground. It had not been intended for burnings, but offered a convenient place to tie up refractory slaves that they might be beaten—ofttimes until death relieved their agonies.

To this stake they bound Korak. Then they brought brush and piled about him, and The Sheik came and stood by that he might watch the agonies of his victim. But Korak did not wince even after they had fetched a brand and the flames had shot up among the dry tinder.

Once, then, he raised his voice in the low call that he had given in The Sheik's tent, and now, from beyond the palisade, came again the trumpeting of an elephant.

Old Tantor had been pushing at the palisade in vain. The sound of Korak's voice calling him, and the scent of man, his enemy, filled the great beast with rage and resentment against the dumb barrier that held him back. He wheeled and shuffled back a dozen paces, then he turned, lifted his trunk and gave voice to a mighty roaring, trumpet-call of anger, lowered his head and charged like a huge battering ram of flesh and bone and muscle straight for the mighty barrier.

The palisade sagged and splintered to the impact, and through the breach rushed the infuriated bull. Korak heard the sounds that the others heard, and he interpreted them as the others did not. The flames were creeping closer to him when one of the blacks, hearing a noise behind him turned to see the enormous bulk of Tantor lumbering toward them. The man screamed and fled, and then the bull elephant was among them tossing Negroes and Arabs to right and left as he tore through the flames he feared to the side of the comrade he loved.

The Sheik, calling orders to his followers, ran to his tent to get his rifle. Tantor wrapped his trunk about the body of Korak and the stake to which it was bound, and tore it from the ground. The flames were searing his sensitive hide—sensitive for all its thickness—so that in his frenzy to both rescue his friend and escape the hated fire he had all but crushed the life from the ape-man.

Lifting his burden high above his head the giant beast wheeled and raced for the breach that he had just made in the palisade. The Sheik, rifle in hand, rushed from his tent directly into the path of the maddened brute. He raised his weapon and fired once, the bullet missed its mark, and Tantor was upon him, crushing him beneath those gigantic feet as he raced over him as you and I might crush out the life of an ant that chanced to be in our pathway.

And then, bearing his burden carefully, Tantor, the elephant, entered the blackness of the jungle.

CHAPTER 26

Meriem, dazed by the unexpected sight of Korak whom she had long given up as dead, permitted herself to be led away by Baynes. Among the tents he guided her safely to the palisade, and there, following Korak's instructions, the Englishman pitched a noose over the top of one of the upright logs that formed the barrier. With difficulty he reached the top and then lowered his hand to assist Meriem to his side.

"Come!" he whispered. "We must hurry." And then, as though she had awakened from a sleep, Meriem came to herself. Back there, fighting her enemies, alone, was Korak—her Korak. Her place was by his side, fighting with him and for him. She glanced up at Baynes.

"Go!" she called. "Make your way back to Bwana and bring help. My place is here. You can do no good remaining. Get away while you can and bring the Big Bwana back with you."

Silently the Hon. Morison Baynes slid to the ground inside the palisade to Meriem's side.

"It was only for you that I left him," he said, nodding toward the tents they had just left. "I knew that he could hold them longer than I and give you a chance to escape that I might not be able to have given you. It was I though who should have remained. I heard you call him Korak and so I know now who he is. He befriended you. I would have wronged you. No—don't interrupt. I'm going to tell you the truth now and let you know just what a beast I have been. I planned to take you to London, as you know; but I did not plan to marry you. Yes, shrink from me—I deserve it. I deserve your contempt and loathing; but I didn't know then what love was. Since I have learned that I have learned something else—what a cad and what a coward I have been all my life. I looked down upon those whom I considered my social inferiors. I did not think you good enough to bear my name. Since Hanson tricked me and took you for himself I have been through hell; but it has made a man of me, though too late. Now I can come to you with an offer of honest love, which will realize the honor of having such as you share my name with me."

For a moment Meriem was silent, buried in thought. Her first question seemed irrelevant.

"How did you happen to be in this village?" she asked.

He told her all that had transpired since the black had told him of Hanson's duplicity.

"You say that you are a coward," she said, "and yet you have done all this to save me? The courage that it must have taken to tell me the things that you told me but a moment since, while courage of a different sort, proves that you are no moral coward, and the other proves that you are not a physical coward. I could not love a coward."

"You mean that you love me?" he gasped in astonishment, taking a step toward her as though to gather her into his arms; but she placed her hand against him and pushed him gently away, as much as to say, not yet. What she did mean she scarcely knew. She thought that she loved him, of that there can be no question; nor did she think that love for this young Englishman was disloyalty to Korak, for her love for Korak was undiminished—the love of a sister for an indulgent brother. As they stood there for the moment of their conversation the sounds of tumult in the village subsided.

"They have killed him," whispered Meriem.

The statement brought Baynes to a realization of the cause of their return.

"Wait here," he said. "I will go and see. If he is dead we can do him no good. If he lives I will do my best to free him."

"We will go together," replied Meriem. "Come!" And she led the way back toward the tent in which they last had seen Korak. As they went they were often forced to throw themselves to the ground in the shadow of a tent or hut, for people were passing hurriedly to and fro now—the whole village was aroused and moving about. The return to the tent of Ali ben Kadin took much longer than had their swift flight to the palisade. Cautiously they crept to the slit that Korak's knife had made in the rear wall. Meriem peered within—the rear apartment was empty. She crawled through the aperture, Baynes at her heels, and then silently crossed the space to the rugs that partitioned the tent into two rooms. Parting the hangings Meriem looked into the front room. It, too, was deserted. She crossed to the door of the tent and looked out. Then she gave a little gasp of horror. Baynes at her shoulder looked past her to the sight that had startled her, and he, too, exclaimed; but his was an oath of anger.

A hundred feet away they saw Korak bound to a stake—the brush piled about him already alight. The Englishman pushed Meriem to one side and started to run for the doomed man. What he could do in the face of scores of hostile blacks and Arabs he did not stop to consider. At the same instant Tantor broke through the palisade and charged the group. In the face of the maddened beast the crowd turned and fled, carrying Baynes backward with them. In a moment it was all over, and the elephant had disappeared with his prize; but pandemonium reigned throughout the village. Men, women and children ran helter skelter for safety. Curs fled, yelping. The horses and camels and donkeys, terrorized by the trumpeting of the pachyderm, kicked and pulled at their tethers. A dozen or more broke loose, and it was the galloping of these past him that brought a sudden idea into Baynes' head. He turned to search for Meriem only to find her at his elbow.

"The horses!" he cried. "If we can get a couple of them!"

Filled with the idea Meriem led him to the far end of the village.

"Loosen two of them," she said, "and lead them back into the shadows behind those huts. I know where there are saddles. I will bring them and the bridles," and before he could stop her she was gone.

Baynes quickly untied two of the restive animals and led them to the point designated by Meriem. Here he waited impatiently for what seemed an hour; but was, in reality, but a few minutes. Then he saw the girl approaching beneath the burden of two saddles. Quickly they placed these upon the horses. They could see by the light of the torture fire that still burned that the blacks and Arabs were recovering from their panic. Men were running about gathering in the loose stock, and two or three were already leading their captives back to the end of the village where Meriem and Baynes were busy with the trappings of their mounts.

Now the girl flung herself into the saddle.

"Hurry!" she whispered. "We shall have to run for it. Ride through the gap that Tantor made," and as she saw Baynes swing his leg over the back of his horse, she shook the reins free over her mount's neck. With a lunge, the nervous beast leaped forward. The shortest path led straight through the center of the village, and this Meriem took. Baynes was close behind her, their horses running at full speed.

So sudden and impetuous was their dash for escape that it carried them half-way across the village before the surprised inhabitants were aware of what was happening. Then an Arab recognized them, and, with a cry of alarm, raised his rifle and fired. The shot was a signal for a volley, and amid the rattle of musketry Meriem and Baynes leaped their flying mounts through the breach in the palisade and were gone up the well-worn trail toward the north.

And Korak?

Tantor carried him deep into the jungle, nor paused until no sound from the distant village reached his keen ears. Then he laid his burden gently down. Korak struggled to free himself from his bonds, but even his great strength was unable to cope with the many strands of hard-knotted cord that bound him. While he lay there, working and resting by turns, the elephant stood guard above him, nor was there jungle enemy with the hardihood to tempt the sudden death that lay in that mighty bulk.

Dawn came, and still Korak was no nearer freedom than before. He commenced to believe that he should die there of thirst and starvation with plenty all about him, for he knew that Tantor could not unloose the knots that held him.

And while he struggled through the night with his bonds, Baynes and Meriem were riding rapidly northward along the river. The girl had assured Baynes that Korak was safe in the jungle with Tantor. It had not occurred to her that the ape-man might not be able to burst his bonds. Baynes had been wounded by a shot from the rifle of one of the Arabs, and the girl wanted to get him back to Bwana's home, where he could be properly cared for.

"Then," she said, "I shall get Bwana to come with me and search for Korak. He must come and live with us."

All night they rode, and the day was still young when they came suddenly upon a party hurrying southward. It was Bwana himself and his sleek, black warriors. At sight of Baynes the big Englishman's brows contracted in a scowl; but he waited to hear Meriem's story before giving vent to the long anger in his breast. When she had finished he seemed to have forgotten Baynes. His thoughts were occupied with another subject.

"You say that you found Korak?" he asked. "You really saw him?"

"Yes," replied Meriem; "as plainly as I see you, and I want you to come with me, Bwana, and help me find him again."

"Did you see him?" He turned toward the Hon. Morison.

"Yes, sir," replied Baynes; "very plainly."

"What sort of appearing man is he?" continued Bwana. "About how old, should you say?"

"I should say he was an Englishman, about my own age," replied Baynes; "though he might be older. He is remarkably muscled, and exceedingly tanned."

"His eyes and hair, did you notice them?" Bwana spoke rapidly, almost excitedly. It was Meriem who answered him.

"Korak's hair is black and his eyes are gray," she said.

Bwana turned to his headman.

"Take Miss Meriem and Mr. Baynes home," he said. "I am going into the jungle."

"Let me go with you, Bwana," cried Meriem. "You are going to search for Korak. Let me go, too."

Bwana turned sadly but firmly upon the girl.

"Your place," he said, "is beside the man you love."

Then he motioned to his head-man to take his horse and commence the return journey to the farm. Meriem slowly mounted the tired Arab that had brought her from the village of The Sheik. A litter was rigged for the now feverish Baynes, and the little cavalcade was soon slowly winding off along the river trail.

Bwana stood watching them until they were out of sight. Not once had Meriem turned her eyes backward. She rode with bowed head and drooping shoulders. Bwana sighed. He loved the little Arab girl as he might have loved an own daughter. He realized that Baynes had redeemed himself, and so he could interpose no objections now if Meriem really loved the man; but, somehow, some way, Bwana could not convince himself that the Hon. Morison was worthy of his little Meriem. Slowly he turned toward a nearby tree. Leaping upward he caught a lower branch and drew himself up among the branches. His movements were cat-like and agile. High into the trees he made his way and there commenced to divest himself of his clothing. From the game bag slung across one shoulder he drew a long strip of doe-skin, a neatly coiled rope, and a wicked looking knife. The doe-skin, he fashioned into a loin cloth, the rope he looped over one shoulder, and the knife he thrust into the belt formed by his gee string.

When he stood erect, his head thrown back and his great chest expanded a grim smile touched his lips for a moment. His nostrils dilated as he sniffed the jungle odors. His gray eyes narrowed. He crouched and leaped to a lower limb and was away through the trees toward the southeast, bearing away from the river. He moved swiftly, stopping only occasionally to raise his voice in a weird and piercing scream, and to listen for a moment after for a reply.

He had traveled thus for several hours when, ahead of him and a little to his left, he heard, far off in the jungle, a faint response—the cry of a bull ape answering his cry. His nerves tingled and his eyes lighted as the sound fell upon his ears. Again he voiced his hideous call, and sped forward in the new direction.

Korak, finally becoming convinced that he must die if he remained where he was, waiting for the succor that could not come, spoke to Tantor in the strange tongue that the great beast understood. He commanded the elephant to lift him and carry him toward the northeast. There, recently, Korak had seen both white men and black. If he could come upon one of the latter it would be a simple matter to command Tantor to capture the fellow, and then Korak could get him to release him from the stake. It was worth trying at least—better than lying there in the jungle until he died. As Tantor bore him along through the forest Korak called aloud now and then in the hope of attracting Akut's band of anthropoids, whose wanderings often brought them into their neighborhood. Akut, he thought, might possibly be able to negotiate the knots—he had done so upon that other occasion when the Russian had bound Korak years before; and Akut, to the south of him, heard his calls faintly, and came. There was another who heard them, too.

After Bwana had left his party, sending them back toward the farm, Meriem had ridden for a short distance with bowed head. What thoughts passed through that active brain who may say? Presently she seemed to come to a decision. She called the headman to her side.

"I am going back with Bwana," she announced.

The black shook his head. "No!" he announced. "Bwana says I take you home. So I take you home."

"You refuse to let me go?" asked the girl.

The black nodded, and fell to the rear where he might better watch her. Meriem half smiled. Presently her horse passed beneath a low-hanging branch, and the black headman found himself gazing at the girl's empty saddle. He ran forward to the tree into which she had disappeared. He could see nothing of her. He called; but there was no response, unless it might have been a low, taunting laugh far to the right. He sent his men into the jungle to search for her; but they came back empty handed. After a while he resumed his march toward the farm, for Baynes, by this time, was delirious with fever.

Meriem raced straight back toward the point she imagined Tantor would make for—a point where she knew the elephants often gathered deep in the forest due east of The Sheik's village. She moved silently and swiftly. From her mind she had expunged all thoughts other than that she must reach Korak and bring him back with her. It was her place to do that. Then, too, had come the tantalizing fear that all might not be well with him. She upbraided herself for not thinking of that before—of letting her desire to get the wounded Morison back to the bungalow blind her to the possibilities of Korak's need for her. She had been traveling rapidly for several hours without rest when she heard ahead of her the familiar cry of a great ape calling to his kind.

She did not reply, only increased her speed until she almost flew. Now there came to her sensitive nostrils the scent of Tantor and she knew that she was on the right trail and close to him she sought. She did not call out because she wished to surprise him, and presently she did, breaking into sight of them as the great elephant shuffled ahead balancing the man and the heavy stake upon his head, holding them there with his upcurled trunk.

"Korak!" cried Meriem from the foliage above him.

Instantly the bull swung about, lowered his burden to the ground and, trumpeting savagely, prepared to defend his comrade. The ape-man, recognizing the girl's voice, felt a sudden lump in his throat.

"Meriem!" he called back to her.

Happily the girl clambered to the ground and ran forward to release Korak; but Tantor lowered his head ominously and trumpeted a warning.

"Go back! Go back!" cried Korak. "He will kill you."

Meriem paused. "Tantor!" she called to the huge brute. "Don't you remember me? I am little Meriem. I used to ride on your broad back;" but the bull only rumbled in his throat and shook his tusks in angry defiance. Then Korak tried to placate him. Tried to order him away, that the girl might approach and release him; but Tantor would not go. He saw in every human being other than Korak an enemy. He thought the girl bent upon harming his friend and he would take no chances. For an hour the girl and the man tried to find some means whereby they might circumvent the beast's ill directed guardianship, but all to no avail; Tantor stood his ground in grim determination to let no one approach Korak.

Presently the man hit upon a scheme. "Pretend to go away," he called to the girl. "Keep down wind from us so that Tantor won't get your scent, then follow us. After a while I'll have him put me down, and find some pretext for sending him away. While he is gone you can slip up and cut my bonds—have you a knife?"

"Yes, I have a knife," she replied. "I'll go now—I think we may be able to fool him; but don't be too sure—Tantor invented cunning."

Korak smiled, for he knew that the girl was right. Presently she had disappeared. The elephant listened, and raised his trunk to catch her scent. Korak commanded him to raise him to his head once more and proceed upon their way. After a moment's hesitation he did as he was bid. It was then that Korak heard the distant call of an ape.

"Akut!" he thought. "Good! Tantor knew Akut well. He would let him approach." Raising his voice Korak replied to the call of the ape; but he let Tantor move off with him through the jungle; it would do no harm to try the other plan. They had come to a clearing and plainly Korak smelled water. Here was a good place and a good excuse. He ordered Tantor to lay him down, and go and fetch him water in his trunk. The big beast deposited him upon the grass in the center of the clearing, then he stood with cocked ears and attentive trunk, searching for the slightest indication of danger—there seemed to be none and he moved away in the direction of the little brook that Korak knew was some two or three hundred yards away. The ape-man could scarce help smiling as he thought how cleverly he had tricked his friend; but well as he knew Tantor he little guessed the guile of his cunning brain. The animal ambled off across the clearing and disappeared in the jungle beyond in the direction of the stream; but scarce had his great bulk been screened by the dense foliage than he wheeled about and came cautiously back to the edge of the clearing where he could see without being seen. Tantor, by nature, is suspicious. Now he still feared the return of the she Tarmangani who had attempted to attack his Korak. He would just stand there for a moment and assure himself that all was well before he continued on toward the water. Ah! It was well that he did! There she was now dropping from the branches of a tree across the clearing and running swiftly toward the ape-man. Tantor waited. He would let her reach Korak before he charged—that would ensure that she had no chance of escape. His little eyes blazed savagely. His tail was elevated stiffly. He could scarce restrain a desire to trumpet forth his rage to the world.

Meriem was almost at Korak's side when Tantor saw the long knife in her hand, and then he broke forth from the jungle, bellowing horribly, and charged down upon the frail girl.

CHAPTER 27

Korak screamed commands to his huge protector, in an effort to halt him; but all to no avail. Meriem raced toward the bordering trees with all the speed that lay in her swift, little feet; but Tantor, for all his huge bulk, drove down upon her with the rapidity of an express train.

Korak lay where he could see the whole frightful tragedy. The cold sweat broke out upon his body. His heart seemed to have stopped its beating. Meriem might reach the trees before Tantor overtook her, but even her agility would not carry her beyond the reach of that relentless trunk—she would be dragged down and tossed. Korak could picture the whole frightful scene. Then Tantor would follow her up, goring the frail, little body with his relentless tusks, or trampling it into an unrecognizable mass beneath his ponderous feet.

He was almost upon her now. Korak wanted to close his eyes, but could not. His throat was dry and parched. Never in all his savage existence had he suffered such blighting terror—never before had he known what terror meant. A dozen more strides and the brute would seize her. What was that? Korak's eyes started from their sockets. A strange figure had leaped from the tree the shade of which Meriem already had reached—leaped beyond the girl straight into the path of the charging elephant. It was a naked white giant. Across his shoulder a coil of rope was looped. In the band of his gee string was a hunting knife. Otherwise he was unarmed. With naked hands he faced the maddening Tantor. A sharp command broke from the stranger's lips—the great beast halted in his tracks—and Meriem swung herself upward into the tree to safety. Korak breathed a sigh of relief not unmixed with wonder. He fastened his eyes upon the face of Meriem's deliverer and as recognition slowly filtered into his understanding they went wide in incredulity and surprise.

Tantor, still rumbling angrily, stood swaying to and fro close before the giant white man. Then the latter stepped straight beneath the upraised trunk and spoke a low word of command. The great beast ceased his muttering. The savage light died from his eyes, and as the stranger stepped forward toward Korak, Tantor trailed docilely at his heels.

Meriem was watching, too, and wondering. Suddenly the man turned toward her as though recollecting her presence after a moment of forgetfulness. "Come! Meriem," he called, and then she recognized him with a startled: "Bwana!" Quickly the girl dropped from the tree and ran to his side. Tantor cocked a questioning eye at the white giant, but receiving a warning word let Meriem approach. Together the two walked to where Korak lay, his eyes wide with wonder and filled with a pathetic appeal for forgiveness, and, mayhap, a glad thankfulness for the miracle that had brought these two of all others to his side.

"Jack!" cried the white giant, kneeling at the ape-man's side.

"Father!" came chokingly from The Killer's lips. "Thank God that it was you. No one else in all the jungle could have stopped Tantor."

Quickly the man cut the bonds that held Korak, and as the youth leaped to his feet and threw his arms about his father, the older man turned toward Meriem.

"I thought," he said, sternly, "that I told you to return to the farm."

Korak was looking at them wonderingly. In his heart was a great yearning to take the girl in his arms; but in time he remembered the other—the dapper young English gentleman—and that he was but a savage, uncouth ape-man.

Meriem looked up pleadingly into Bwana's eyes.

"You told me," she said, in a very small voice, "that my place was beside the man I loved," and she turned her eyes toward Korak all filled with the wonderful light that no other man had yet seen in them, and that none other ever would.

The Killer started toward her with outstretched arms; but suddenly he fell upon one knee before her, instead, and lifting her hand to his lips kissed it more reverently than he could have kissed the hand of his country's queen.

A rumble from Tantor brought the three, all jungle bred, to instant alertness. Tantor was looking toward the trees behind them, and as their eyes followed his gaze the head and shoulders of a great ape appeared amidst the foliage. For a moment the creature eyed them, and then from its throat rose a loud scream of recognition and of joy, and a moment later the beast had leaped to the ground, followed by a score of bulls like himself, and was waddling toward them, shouting in the primordial tongue of the anthropoid:

"Tarzan has returned! Tarzan, Lord of the Jungle!"

It was Akut, and instantly he commenced leaping and bounding about the trio, uttering hideous shrieks and mouthings that to any other human beings might have indicated the most ferocious rage; but these three knew that the king of the apes was doing homage to a king greater than himself. In his wake leaped his shaggy bulls, vying with one another as to which could spring the highest and which utter the most uncanny sounds.

Korak laid his hand affectionately upon his father's shoulder.

"There is but one Tarzan," he said. "There can never be another."

Two days later the three dropped from the trees on the edge of the plain across which they could see the smoke rising from the bungalow and the cook house chimneys. Tarzan of the Apes had regained his civilized clothing from the tree where he had hidden it, and as Korak refused to enter the presence of his mother in the savage half-raiment that he had worn so long and as Meriem would not leave him, for fear, as she explained, that he would change his mind and run off into the jungle again, the father went on ahead to the bungalow for horses and clothes.

My Dear met him at the gate, her eyes filled with questioning and sorrow, for she saw that Meriem was not with him.

"Where is she?" she asked, her voice trembling. "Muviri told me that she disobeyed your instructions and ran off into the jungle after you had left them. Oh, John, I cannot bear to lose her, too!" And Lady Greystoke broke down and wept, as she pillowed her head upon the broad breast where so often before she had found comfort in the great tragedies of her life.

Lord Greystoke raised her head and looked down into her eyes, his own smiling and filled with the light of happiness.

"What is it, John?" she cried. "You have good news—do not keep me waiting for it."

"I want to be quite sure that you can stand hearing the best news that ever came to either of us," he said.

"Joy never kills," she cried. "You have found—her?" She could not bring herself to hope for the impossible.

"Yes, Jane," he said, and his voice was husky with emotion; "I have found her, and—him!"

"Where is he? Where are they?" she demanded.

"Out there at the edge of the jungle. He wouldn't come to you in his savage leopard skin and his nakedness—he sent me to fetch him civilized clothing."

She clapped her hands in ecstasy, and turned to run toward the bungalow. "Wait!" she cried over her shoulder. "I have all his little suits—I have saved them all. I will bring one to you."

Tarzan laughed and called to her to stop.

"The only clothing on the place that will fit him," he said, "is mine—if it isn't too small for him—your little boy has grown, Jane."

She laughed, too; she felt like laughing at everything, or at nothing. The world was all love and happiness and joy once more—the world that had been shrouded in the gloom of her great sorrow for so many years. So great was her joy that for the moment she forgot the sad message that awaited Meriem. She called to Tarzan after he had ridden away to prepare her for it, but he did not hear and rode on without knowing himself what the event was to which his wife referred.

And so, an hour later, Korak, The Killer, rode home to his mother—the mother whose image had never faded in his boyish heart—and found in her arms and her eyes the love and forgiveness that he plead for.

And then the mother turned toward Meriem, an expression of pitying sorrow erasing the happiness from her eyes.

"My little girl," she said, "in the midst of our happiness a great sorrow awaits you—Mr. Baynes did not survive his wound."

The expression of sorrow in Meriem's eyes expressed only what she sincerely felt; but it was not the sorrow of a woman bereft of her best beloved.

"I am sorry," she said, quite simply. "He would have done me a great wrong; but he amply atoned before he died. Once I thought that I loved him. At first it was only fascination for a type that was new to me—then it was respect for a brave man who had the moral courage to admit a sin and the physical courage to face death to right the wrong he had committed. But it was not love. I did not know what love was until I knew that Korak lived," and she turned toward The Killer with a smile.

Lady Greystoke looked quickly up into the eyes of her son—the son who one day would be Lord Greystoke. No thought of the difference in the stations of the girl and her boy entered her mind. To her Meriem was fit for a king. She only wanted to know that Jack loved the little Arab waif. The look in his eyes answered the question in her heart, and she threw her arms about them both and kissed them each a dozen times.

"Now," she cried, "I shall really have a daughter!"

It was several weary marches to the nearest mission; but they only waited at the farm a few days for rest and preparation for the great event before setting out upon the journey, and after the marriage ceremony had been performed they kept on to the coast to take passage for England. Those days were the most wonderful of Meriem's life. She had not dreamed even vaguely of the marvels that civilization held in store for her. The great ocean and the commodious steamship filled her with awe. The noise, and bustle and confusion of the English railway station frightened her.

"If there was a good-sized tree at hand," she confided to Korak, "I know that I should run to the very top of it in terror of my life."

"And make faces and throw twigs at the engine?" he laughed back.

"Poor old Numa," sighed the girl. "What will he do without us?"

"Oh, there are others to tease him, my little Mangani," assured Korak.

The Greystoke town house quite took Meriem's breath away; but when strangers were about none might guess that she had not been to the manner born.

They had been home but a week when Lord Greystoke received a message from his friend of many years, D'Arnot.

It was in the form of a letter of introduction brought by one General Armand Jacot. Lord Greystoke recalled the name, as who familiar with modern French history would not, for Jacot was in reality the Prince de Cadrenet—that intense republican who refused to use, even by courtesy, a title that had belonged to his family for four hundred years.

"There is no place for princes in a republic," he was wont to say.

Lord Greystoke received the hawk-nosed, gray mustached soldier in his library, and after a dozen words the two men had formed a mutual esteem that was to endure through life.

"I have come to you," explained General Jacot, "because our dear Admiral tells me that there is no one in all the world who is more intimately acquainted with Central Africa than you.

"Let me tell you my story from the beginning. Many years ago my little daughter was stolen, presumably by Arabs, while I was serving with the Foreign Legion in Algeria. We did all that love and money and even government resources could do to discover her; but all to no avail. Her picture was published in the leading papers of every large city in the world, yet never did we find a man or woman who ever had seen her since the day she mysteriously disappeared.

"A week since there came to me in Paris a swarthy Arab, who called himself Abdul Kamak. He said that he had found my daughter and could lead me to her. I took him at once to Admiral d'Arnot, whom I knew had traveled some in Central Africa. The man's story led the Admiral to believe that the place where the white girl the Arab supposed to be my daughter was held in captivity was not far from your African estates, and he advised that I come at once and call upon you—that you would know if such a girl were in your neighborhood."

"What proof did the Arab bring that she was your daughter?" asked Lord Greystoke.

"None," replied the other. "That is why we thought best to consult you before organizing an expedition. The fellow had only an old photograph of her on the back of which was pasted a newspaper cutting describing her and offering a reward. We feared that having found this somewhere it had aroused his cupidity and led him to believe that in some way he could obtain the reward, possibly by foisting upon us a white girl on the chance that so many years had elapsed that we would not be able to recognize an imposter as such."

"Have you the photograph with you?" asked Lord Greystoke.

The General drew an envelope from his pocket, took a yellowed photograph from it and handed it to the Englishman.

Tears dimmed the old warrior's eyes as they fell again upon the pictured features of his lost daughter.

Lord Greystoke examined the photograph for a moment. A queer expression entered his eyes. He touched a bell at his elbow, and an instant later a footman entered.

"Ask my son's wife if she will be so good as to come to the library," he directed.

The two men sat in silence. General Jacot was too well bred to show in any way the chagrin and disappointment he felt in the summary manner in which Lord Greystoke had dismissed the subject of his call. As soon as the young lady had come and he had been presented he would make his departure. A moment later Meriem entered.

Lord Greystoke and General Jacot rose and faced her. The Englishman spoke no word of introduction—he wanted to mark the effect of the first sight of the girl's face on the Frenchman, for he had a theory—a heaven-born theory that had leaped into his mind the moment his eyes had rested on the baby face of Jeanne Jacot.

General Jacot took one look at Meriem, then he turned toward Lord Greystoke.

"How long have you known it?" he asked, a trifle accusingly.

"Since you showed me that photograph a moment ago," replied the Englishman.

"It is she," said Jacot, shaking with suppressed emotion; "but she does not recognize me—of course she could not." Then he turned to Meriem. "My child," he said, "I am your—"

But she interrupted him with a quick, glad cry, as she ran toward him with outstretched arms.

"I know you! I know you!" she cried. "Oh, now I remember," and the old man folded her in his arms.

Jack Clayton and his mother were summoned, and when the story had been told them they were only glad that little Meriem had found a father and a mother.

"And really you didn't marry an Arab waif after all," said Meriem. "Isn't it fine!"

"You are fine," replied The Killer. "I married my little Meriem, and I don't care, for my part, whether she is an Arab, or just a little Tarmangani."

"She is neither, my son," said General Armand Jacot. "She is a princess in her own right."

TARZAN AND THE JEWELS OF OPAR

BELGIAN AND ARAB

Lieutenant Albert Werper had only the prestige of the name he had dishonored to thank for his narrow escape from being cashiered. At first he had been humbly thankful, too, that they had sent him to this Godforsaken Congo post instead of court-martialing him, as he had so justly deserved; but now six months of the monotony, the frightful isolation and the loneliness had wrought a change. The young man brooded continually over his fate. His days were filled with morbid self-pity, which eventually engendered in his weak and vacillating mind a hatred for those who had sent him here—for the very men he had at first inwardly thanked for saving him from the ignominy of degradation.

He regretted the gay life of Brussels as he never had regretted the sins which had snatched him from that gayest of capitals, and as the days passed he came to center his resentment upon the representative in Congo land of the authority which had exiled him—his captain and immediate superior.

This officer was a cold, taciturn man, inspiring little love in those directly beneath him, yet respected and feared by the black soldiers of his little command.

Werper was accustomed to sit for hours glaring at his superior as the two sat upon the veranda of their common quarters, smoking their evening cigarets in a silence which neither seemed desirous of breaking. The senseless hatred of the lieutenant grew at last into a form of mania. The captain's natural taciturnity he distorted into a studied attempt to insult him because of his past shortcomings. He imagined that his superior held him in contempt, and so he chafed and fumed inwardly until one evening his madness became suddenly homicidal. He fingered the butt of the revolver at his hip, his eyes narrowed and his brows contracted. At last he spoke.

"You have insulted me for the last time!" he cried, springing to his feet. "I am an officer and a gentleman, and I shall put up with it no longer without an accounting from you, you pig."

The captain, an expression of surprise upon his features, turned toward his junior. He had seen men before with the jungle madness upon them—the madness of solitude and unrestrained brooding, and perhaps a touch of fever.

He rose and extended his hand to lay it upon the other's shoulder. Quiet words of counsel were upon his lips; but they were never spoken. Werper construed his superior's action into an attempt to close with him. His revolver was on a level with the captain's heart, and the latter had taken but a step when Werper pulled the trigger. Without a moan the man sank to the rough planking of the veranda, and as he fell the mists that had clouded Werper's brain lifted, so that he saw himself and the deed that he had done in the same light that those who must judge him would see them.

He heard excited exclamations from the quarters of the soldiers and he heard men running in his direction. They would seize him, and if they didn't kill him they would take him down the Congo to a point where a properly ordered military tribunal would do so just as effectively, though in a more regular manner.

Werper had no desire to die. Never before had he so yearned for life as in this moment that he had so effectively forfeited his right to live. The men were nearing him. What was he to do? He glanced about as though searching for the tangible form of a legitimate excuse for his crime; but he could find only the body of the man he had so causelessly shot down.

In despair, he turned and fled from the oncoming soldiery. Across the compound he ran, his revolver still clutched tightly in his hand. At the gates a sentry halted him. Werper did not pause to parley or to exert the influence of his commission—he merely raised his weapon and shot down the innocent black. A moment later the fugitive had torn open the gates and vanished into the blackness of the jungle, but not before he had transferred the rifle and ammunition belts of the dead sentry to his own person.

All that night Werper fled farther and farther into the heart of the wilderness. Now and again the voice of a lion brought him to a listening halt; but with cocked and ready rifle he pushed ahead again, more fearful of the human huntsmen in his rear than of the wild carnivora ahead.

Dawn came at last, but still the man plodded on. All sense of hunger and fatigue were lost in the terrors of contemplated capture. He could think only of escape. He dared not pause to rest or eat until there was no further danger from pursuit, and so he staggered on until at last he fell and could rise no more. How long he had fled he did not know, or try to know. When he could flee no longer the knowledge that he had reached his limit was hidden from him in the unconsciousness of utter exhaustion.

And thus it was that Achmet Zek, the Arab, found him. Achmet's followers were for running a spear through the body of their hereditary enemy; but Achmet would have it otherwise. First he would question the Belgian. It were easier to question a man first and kill him afterward, than kill him first and then question him.

So he had Lieutenant Albert Werper carried to his own tent, and there slaves administered wine and food in small quantities until at last the prisoner regained consciousness. As he opened his eyes he saw the faces of strange black men about him, and just outside the tent the figure of an Arab. Nowhere was the uniform of his soldiers to be seen.

The Arab turned and seeing the open eyes of the prisoner upon him, entered the tent.

"I am Achmet Zek," he announced. "Who are you, and what were you doing in my country? Where are your soldiers?"

Achmet Zek! Werper's eyes went wide, and his heart sank. He was in the clutches of the most notorious of cut-throats—a hater of all Europeans, especially those who wore the uniform of Belgium. For years the military forces of Belgian Congo had waged a fruitless war upon this man and his followers—a war in which quarter had never been asked nor expected by either side.

But presently in the very hatred of the man for Belgians, Werper saw a faint ray of hope for himself. He, too, was an outcast and an outlaw. So far, at least, they possessed a common interest, and Werper decided to play upon it for all that it might yield.

"I have heard of you," he replied, "and was searching for you. My people have turned against me. I hate them. Even now their soldiers are searching for me, to kill me. I knew that you would protect me from them, for you, too, hate them. In return I will take service with you. I am a trained soldier. I can fight, and your enemies are my enemies."

Achmet Zek eyed the European in silence. In his mind he revolved many thoughts, chief among which was that the unbeliever lied. Of course there was the chance that he did not lie, and if he told the truth then his proposition was one well worthy of consideration, since fighting men were never over plentiful—especially white men with the training and knowledge of military matters that a European officer must possess.

Achmet Zek scowled and Werper's heart sank; but Werper did not know Achmet Zek, who was quite apt to scowl where another would smile, and smile where another would scowl.

"And if you have lied to me," said Achmet Zek, "I will kill you at any time. What return, other than your life, do you expect for your services?"

"My keep only, at first," replied Werper. "Later, if I am worth more, we can easily reach an understanding." Werper's only desire at the moment was to preserve his life. And so the agreement was reached and Lieutenant Albert Werper became a member of the ivory and slave raiding band of the notorious Achmet Zek.

For months the renegade Belgian rode with the savage raider. He fought with a savage abandon, and a vicious cruelty fully equal to that of his fellow desperadoes. Achmet Zek watched his recruit with eagle eye, and with a growing satisfaction which finally found expression in a greater confidence in the man, and resulted in an increased independence of action for Werper.

Achmet Zek took the Belgian into his confidence to a great extent, and at last unfolded to him a pet scheme which the Arab had long fostered, but which he never had found an opportunity to effect. With the aid of a European, however, the thing might be easily accomplished. He sounded Werper.

"You have heard of the man men call Tarzan?" he asked.

Werper nodded. "I have heard of him; but I do not know him."

"But for him we might carry on our 'trading' in safety and with great profit," continued the Arab. "For years he has fought us, driving us from the richest part of the country, harassing us, and arming the natives that they may repel us when we come to 'trade.' He is very rich. If we could find some way to make him pay us many pieces of gold we should not only be avenged upon him; but repaid for much that he has prevented us from winning from the natives under his protection."

Werper withdrew a cigaret from a jeweled case and lighted it.

"And you have a plan to make him pay?" he asked.

"He has a wife," replied Achmet Zek, "whom men say is very beautiful. She would bring a great price farther north, if we found it too difficult to collect ransom money from this Tarzan."

Werper bent his head in thought. Achmet Zek stood awaiting his reply. What good remained in Albert Werper revolted at the thought of selling a white woman into the slavery and degradation of a Moslem harem. He looked up at Achmet Zek. He saw the Arab's eyes narrow, and he guessed that the other had sensed his antagonism to the plan. What would it mean to Werper to refuse? His life lay in the hands of this semi-barbarian, who esteemed the life of an unbeliever less highly than that of a dog. Werper loved life. What was this woman to him, anyway? She was a European, doubtless, a member of organized society. He was an outcast. The hand of every white man was against him. She was his natural enemy, and if he refused to lend himself to her undoing, Achmet Zek would have him killed.

"You hesitate," murmured the Arab.

"I was but weighing the chances of success," lied Werper, "and my reward. As a European I can gain admittance to their home and table. You have no other with you who could do so much. The risk will be great. I should be well paid, Achmet Zek."

A smile of relief passed over the raider's face.

"Well said, Werper," and Achmet Zek slapped his lieutenant upon the shoulder. "You should be well paid and you shall. Now let us sit together and plan how best the thing may be done," and the two men squatted upon a soft rug beneath the faded silks of Achmet's once gorgeous tent, and talked together in low voices well into the night. Both were tall and bearded, and the exposure to sun and wind had given an almost Arab hue to the European's complexion. In every detail of dress, too, he copied the fashions of his chief, so that outwardly he was as much an Arab as the other. It was late when he arose and retired to his own tent.

The following day Werper spent in overhauling his Belgian uniform, removing from it every vestige of evidence that might indicate its military purposes. From a heterogeneous collection of loot, Achmet Zek procured a pith helmet and a European saddle, and from his black slaves and followers a party of porters, askaris and tent boys to make up a modest safari for a big game hunter. At the head of this party Werper set out from camp.

ON THE ROAD TO OPAR

It was two weeks later that John Clayton, Lord Greystoke, riding in from a tour of inspection of his vast African estate, glimpsed the head of a column of men crossing the plain that lay between his bungalow and the forest to the north and west.

He reined in his horse and watched the little party as it emerged from a concealing swale. His keen eyes caught the reflection of the sun upon the white helmet of a mounted man, and with the conviction that a wandering European hunter was seeking his hospitality, he wheeled his mount and rode slowly forward to meet the newcomer.

A half hour later he was mounting the steps leading to the veranda of his bungalow, and introducing M. Jules Frecoult to Lady Greystoke.

"I was completely lost," M. Frecoult was explaining. "My head man had never before been in this part of the country and the guides who were to have accompanied me from the last village we passed knew even less of the country than we. They finally deserted us two days since. I am very fortunate indeed to have stumbled so providentially upon succor. I do not know what I should have done, had I not found you."

It was decided that Frecoult and his party should remain several days, or until they were thoroughly rested, when Lord Greystoke would furnish guides to lead them safely back into country with which Frecoult's head man was supposedly familiar.

In his guise of a French gentleman of leisure, Werper found little difficulty in deceiving his host and in ingratiating himself with both Tarzan and Jane Clayton; but the longer he remained the less hopeful he became of an easy accomplishment of his designs.

Lady Greystoke never rode alone at any great distance from the bungalow, and the savage loyalty of the ferocious Waziri warriors who formed a great part of Tarzan's followers seemed to preclude the possibility of a successful attempt at forcible abduction, or of the bribery of the Waziri themselves.

A week passed, and Werper was no nearer the fulfillment of his plan, in so far as he could judge, than upon the day of his arrival, but at that very moment something occurred which gave him renewed hope and set his mind upon an even greater reward than a woman's ransom.

A runner had arrived at the bungalow with the weekly mail, and Lord Greystoke had spent the afternoon in his study reading and answering letters. At dinner he seemed distraught, and early in the evening he excused himself and retired, Lady Greystoke following him very soon after. Werper, sitting upon the veranda, could hear their voices in earnest discussion, and having realized that something of unusual moment was afoot, he quietly rose from his chair, and keeping well in the shadow of the shrubbery growing profusely about the bungalow, made his silent way to a point beneath the window of the room in which his host and hostess slept.

Here he listened, and not without result, for almost the first words he overheard filled him with excitement. Lady Greystoke was speaking as Werper came within hearing.

"I always feared for the stability of the company," she was saying; "but it seems incredible that they should have failed for so enormous a sum—unless there has been some dishonest manipulation."

"That is what I suspect," replied Tarzan; "but whatever the cause, the fact remains that I have lost everything, and there is nothing for it but to return to Opar and get more."

"Oh, John," cried Lady Greystoke, and Werper could feel the shudder through her voice, "is there no other way? I cannot bear to think of you returning to that frightful city. I would rather live in poverty always than to have you risk the hideous dangers of Opar."

"You need have no fear," replied Tarzan, laughing. "I am pretty well able to take care of myself, and were I not, the Waziri who will accompany me will see that no harm befalls me."

"They ran away from Opar once, and left you to your fate," she reminded him.

"They will not do it again," he answered. "They were very much ashamed of themselves, and were coming back when I met them."

"But there must be some other way," insisted the woman.

"There is no other way half so easy to obtain another fortune, as to go to the treasure vaults of Opar and bring it away," he replied. "I shall be very careful, Jane, and the chances are that the inhabitants of Opar will never know that I have been there again and despoiled them of another portion of the treasure, the very existence of which they are as ignorant of as they would be of its value."

The finality in his tone seemed to assure Lady Greystoke that further argument was futile, and so she abandoned the subject.

Werper remained, listening, for a short time, and then, confident that he had overheard all that was necessary and fearing discovery, returned to the veranda, where he smoked numerous cigarets in rapid succession before retiring.

EDGAR RICE BURROUGHS

The following morning at breakfast, Werper announced his intention of making an early departure, and asked Tarzan's permission to hunt big game in the Waziri country on his way out—permission which Lord Greystoke readily granted.

The Belgian consumed two days in completing his preparations, but finally got away with his safari, accompanied by a single Waziri guide whom Lord Greystoke had loaned him. The party made but a single short march when Werper simulated illness, and announced his intention of remaining where he was until he had fully recovered. As they had gone but a short distance from the Greystoke bungalow, Werper dismissed the Waziri guide, telling the warrior that he would send for him when he was able to proceed. The Waziri gone, the Belgian summoned one of Achmet Zek's trusted blacks to his tent, and dispatched him to watch for the departure of Tarzan, returning immediately to advise Werper of the event and the direction taken by the Englishman.

The Belgian did not have long to wait, for the following day his emissary returned with word that Tarzan and a party of fifty Waziri warriors had set out toward the southeast early in the morning.

Werper called his head man to him, after writing a long letter to Achmet Zek. This letter he handed to the head man.

"Send a runner at once to Achmet Zek with this," he instructed the head man. "Remain here in camp awaiting further instructions from him or from me. If any come from the bungalow of the Englishman, tell them that I am very ill within my tent and can see no one. Now, give me six porters and six askaris—the strongest and bravest of the safari—and I will march after the Englishman and discover where his gold is hidden."

And so it was that as Tarzan, stripped to the loin cloth and armed after the primitive fashion he best loved, led his loyal Waziri toward the dead city of Opar, Werper, the renegade, haunted his trail through the long, hot days, and camped close behind him by night.

And as they marched, Achmet Zek rode with his entire following southward toward the Greystoke farm.

To Tarzan of the Apes the expedition was in the nature of a holiday outing. His civilization was at best but an outward veneer which he gladly peeled off with his uncomfortable European clothes whenever any reasonable pretext presented itself. It was a woman's love which kept Tarzan even to the semblance of civilization—a condition for which familiarity had bred contempt. He hated the shams and the hypocrisies of it and with the clear vision of an unspoiled mind he had penetrated to the rotten core of the heart of the thing—the cowardly greed for peace and ease and the safe-guarding of property rights. That the fine things of life—art, music and literature—had thriven upon such enervating ideals he strenuously denied, insisting, rather, that they had endured in spite of civilization.

"Show me the fat, opulent coward," he was wont to say, "who ever originated a beautiful ideal. In the clash of arms, in the battle for survival, amid hunger and death and danger, in the face of God as manifested in the display of Nature's most terrific forces, is born all that is finest and best in the human heart and mind."

And so Tarzan always came back to Nature in the spirit of a lover keeping a long deferred tryst after a period behind prison walls. His Waziri, at marrow, were more civilized than he. They cooked their meat before they ate it and they shunned many articles of food as unclean that Tarzan had eaten with gusto all his life and so insidious is the virus of hypocrisy that even the stalwart ape-man hesitated to give rein to his natural longings before them. He ate burnt flesh when he would have preferred it raw and unspoiled, and he brought down game with arrow or spear when he would far rather have leaped upon it from ambush and sunk his strong teeth in its jugular; but at last the call of the milk of the savage mother that had suckled him in infancy rose to an insistent demand—he craved the hot blood of a fresh kill and his muscles yearned to pit themselves against the savage jungle in the battle for existence that had been his sole birthright for the first twenty years of his life.

THE CALL OF THE JUNGLE

Moved by these vague yet all-powerful urgings the ape-man lay awake one night in the little thorn boma that protected, in a way, his party from the depredations of the great carnivora of the jungle. A single warrior stood sleepy guard beside the fire that yellow eyes out of the darkness beyond the camp made imperative. The moans and the coughing of the big cats mingled with the myriad noises of the lesser denizens of the jungle to fan the savage flame in the breast of this savage English lord. He tossed upon his bed of grasses, sleepless, for an hour and then he rose, noiseless as a wraith, and while the Waziri's back was turned, vaulted the boma wall in the face of the flaming eyes, swung silently into a great tree and was gone.

For a time in sheer exuberance of animal spirit he raced swiftly through the middle terrace, swinging perilously across wide spans from one jungle giant to the next, and then he clambered upward to the swaying, lesser boughs of the upper terrace where the moon shone full upon him and the air was stirred by little breezes and death lurked ready in each frail branch. Here he paused and raised his face to Goro, the moon. With uplifted arm he stood, the cry of the bull ape quivering upon his lips, yet he remained silent lest he arouse his faithful Waziri who were all too familiar with the hideous challenge of their master.

And then he went on more slowly and with greater stealth and caution, for now Tarzan of the Apes was seeking a kill. Down to the ground he came in the utter blackness of the close-set boles and the overhanging verdure of the jungle. He stooped from time to time and put his nose close to earth. He sought and found a wide game trail and at last his nostrils were rewarded with the scent of the fresh spoor of Bara, the deer. Tarzan's mouth watered and a low growl escaped his patrician lips. Sloughed from him was the last vestige of artificial caste—once again he was the primeval hunter—the first man—the highest caste type of the human race. Up wind he followed the elusive spoor with a sense of perception so transcending that of ordinary man as to be inconceivable to us. Through counter currents of the heavy stench of meat eaters he traced the trail of Bara; the sweet and cloying stink of Horta, the boar, could not drown his quarry's scent—the permeating, mellow musk of the deer's foot.

Presently the body scent of the deer told Tarzan that his prey was close at hand. It sent him into the trees again—into the lower terrace where he could watch the ground below and catch with ears and nose the first intimation of actual contact with his quarry. Nor was it long before the ape-man came upon Bara standing alert at the edge of a moon-bathed clearing. Noiselessly Tarzan crept through the trees until he was directly over the deer. In the ape-man's right hand was the long hunting knife of his father and in his heart the blood lust of the carnivore. Just for an instant he poised above the unsuspecting Bara and then he launched himself downward upon the sleek back. The impact of his weight carried the deer to its knees and before the animal could regain its feet the knife had found its heart. As Tarzan rose upon the body of his kill to scream forth his hideous victory cry into the face of the moon the wind carried to his nostrils something which froze him to statuesque immobility and silence. His savage eyes blazed into the direction from which the wind had borne down the warning to him and a moment later the grasses at one side of the clearing parted and Numa, the lion, strode majestically into view. His yellow-green eyes were fastened upon Tarzan as he halted just within the clearing and glared enviously at the successful hunter, for Numa had had no luck this night.

From the lips of the ape-man broke a rumbling growl of warning. Numa answered but he did not advance. Instead he stood waving his tail gently to and fro, and presently Tarzan squatted upon his kill and cut a generous portion from a hind quarter. Numa eyed him with growing resentment and rage as, between mouthfuls, the ape-man growled out his savage warnings. Now this particular lion had never before come in contact with Tarzan of the Apes and he was much mystified. Here was the appearance and the scent of a man-thing and Numa had tasted of human flesh and learned that though not the most palatable it was certainly by far the easiest to secure, yet there was that in the bestial growls of the strange creature which reminded him of formidable antagonists and gave him pause, while his hunger and the odor of the hot flesh of Bara goaded him almost to madness. Always Tarzan watched him, guessing what was passing in the little brain of the carnivore and well it was that he did watch him, for at last Numa could stand it no longer. His tail shot suddenly erect and at the same instant the wary ape-man, knowing all too well what the signal portended, grasped the remainder of the deer's hind quarter between his teeth and leaped into a nearby tree as Numa charged him with all the speed and a sufficient semblance of the weight of an express train.

Tarzan's retreat was no indication that he felt fear. Jungle life is ordered along different lines than ours and different standards prevail. Had Tarzan been famished he would, doubtless, have stood his ground and met the lion's charge. He had done the thing before upon more than one occasion, just as in the past he had charged lions himself; but tonight he was far from famished and in the hind quarter he had carried off with him was more raw flesh than he could eat; yet it was with no equanimity that he looked down upon Numa rending the flesh of Tarzan's kill. The presumption of this strange Numa must be punished! And forthwith Tarzan set out to make life miserable for the big cat. Close by were many trees bearing large, hard fruits and to one of these the ape-man swung with the agility of a squirrel. Then commenced a bombardment which brought forth earthshaking roars from Numa. One after another as rapidly as he could gather and hurl them, Tarzan pelted the hard fruit down upon the lion. It was impossible for the tawny cat to eat under that hail of missiles—he could but roar and growl and dodge and eventually he was driven away entirely from the carcass of Bara, the deer. He went roaring and resentful; but in the very center of the clearing his voice was suddenly hushed and Tarzan saw the great head lower and flatten out, the body crouch and the long tail quiver, as the beast slunk cautiously toward the trees upon the opposite side.

Immediately Tarzan was alert. He lifted his head and sniffed the slow, jungle breeze. What was it that had attracted Numa's attention and taken him soft-footed and silent away from the scene of his discomfiture? Just as the lion disappeared among the trees beyond the clearing Tarzan caught upon the down-coming wind the explanation of his new interest—the scent spoor of man was wafted strongly to the sensitive nostrils. Caching the remainder of the deer's hind quarter in the crotch of a tree the ape-man wiped his greasy palms upon his naked thighs and swung off in pursuit of Numa. A broad, well-beaten elephant path led into the forest from the clearing. Parallel to this slunk Numa, while above him Tarzan moved through the trees, the shadow of a wraith. The savage cat and the savage man saw Numa's quarry almost simultaneously, though both had known before it came within the vision of their eyes that it was a black man. Their sensitive nostrils had told them this much and Tarzan's had told him that the scent spoor was that of a stranger—old and a male, for race and sex and age each has its own distinctive scent. It was an old man that made his way alone through the gloomy jungle, a wrinkled, dried up, little old man hideously scarred and tattooed and strangely garbed, with the skin of a hyena about his shoulders and the dried head mounted upon his grey pate. Tarzan recognized the ear-marks of the witch-doctor and awaited Numa's charge with a feeling of pleasurable anticipation, for the ape-man had no love for witch-doctors; but in the instant that Numa did charge, the white man suddenly recalled that the lion had stolen his kill a few minutes before and that revenge is sweet.

The first intimation the black man had that he was in danger was the crash of twigs as Numa charged through the bushes into the game trail not twenty yards behind him. Then he turned to see a huge, black-maned lion racing toward him and even as he turned, Numa seized him. At the same instant the ape-man dropped from an overhanging limb full upon the lion's back and as he alighted he plunged his knife into the tawny side behind the left shoulder, tangled the fingers of his right hand in the long mane, buried his teeth in Numa's neck and wound his powerful legs about the beast's torso. With a roar of pain and rage, Numa reared up and fell backward upon the ape-man; but still the mighty man-thing clung to his hold and repeatedly the long knife plunged rapidly into his side. Over and over rolled Numa, the lion, clawing and biting at the air, roaring and growling horribly in savage attempt to reach the thing upon its back. More than once was Tarzan almost brushed from his hold. He was battered and bruised and covered with blood from Numa and dirt from the trail, yet not for an instant did he lessen the ferocity of his mad attack nor his grim hold upon the back of his antagonist. To have loosened for an instant his grip there, would have been to bring him within reach of those tearing talons or rending fangs, and have ended forever the grim career of this jungle-bred English lord. Where he had fallen beneath the spring of the lion the witch-doctor lay, torn and bleeding, unable to drag himself away and watched the terrific battle between these two lords of the jungle. His sunken eyes glittered and his wrinkled lips moved over toothless gums as he mumbled weird incantations to the demons of his cult.

For a time he felt no doubt as to the outcome—the strange white man must certainly succumb to terrible Simba—whoever heard of a lone man armed only with a knife slaying so mighty a beast! Yet presently the old black man's eyes went wider and he commenced to have his doubts and misgivings. What wonderful sort of creature was this that battled with Simba and held his own despite the mighty muscles of the king of beasts and slowly there dawned in those sunken eyes, gleaming so brightly from the scarred and wrinkled face, the light of a dawning recollection. Gropingly backward into the past reached the fingers of memory, until at last they seized upon a faint picture, faded and yellow with the passing years. It was the picture of a lithe, white-skinned youth swinging through the trees in company with a band of huge apes, and the old eyes blinked and a great fear came into them—the superstitious fear of one who believes in ghosts and spirits and demons.

And came the time once more when the witch-doctor no longer doubted the outcome of the duel, yet his first judgment was reversed, for now he knew that the jungle god would slay Simba and the old black was even more terrified of his own impending fate at the hands of the victor than he had been by the sure and sudden death which the triumphant lion would have meted out to him. He saw the lion weaken from loss of blood. He saw the mighty limbs tremble and stagger and at last he saw the beast sink down to rise no more. He saw the forest god or demon rise from the vanquished foe, and placing a foot upon the still quivering carcass, raise his face to the moon and bay out a hideous cry that froze the ebbing blood in the veins of the witch-doctor.

PROPHECY AND FULFILLMENT

Then Tarzan turned his attention to the man. He had not slain Numa to save the Negro—he had merely done it in revenge upon the lion; but now that he saw the old man lying helpless and dying before him something akin to pity touched his savage heart. In his youth he would have slain the witch-doctor without the slightest compunction; but civilization had had its softening effect upon him even as it does upon the nations and races which it touches, though it had not yet gone far enough with Tarzan to render him either cowardly or effeminate. He saw an old man suffering and dying, and he stooped and felt of his wounds and stanched the flow of blood.

"Who are you?" asked the old man in a trembling voice.

"I am Tarzan—Tarzan of the Apes," replied the ape-man and not without a greater touch of pride than he would have said, "I am John Clayton, Lord Greystoke."

The witch-doctor shook convulsively and closed his eyes. When he opened them again there was in them a resignation to whatever horrible fate awaited him at the hands of this feared demon of the woods. "Why do you not kill me?" he asked.

"Why should I kill you?" inquired Tarzan. "You have not harmed me, and anyway you are already dying. Numa, the lion, has killed you."

"You would not kill me?" Surprise and incredulity were in the tones of the quavering old voice.

"I would save you if I could," replied Tarzan, "but that cannot be done. Why did you think I would kill you?"

For a moment the old man was silent. When he spoke it was evidently after some little effort to muster his courage. "I knew you of old," he said, "when you ranged the jungle in the country of Mbonga, the chief. I was already a witch-doctor when you slew Kulonga and the others, and when you robbed our huts and our poison pot. At first I did not remember you; but at last I did—the white-skinned ape that lived with the hairy apes and made life miserable in the village of Mbonga, the chief—the forest god—the Munango-Keewati for whom we set food outside our gates and who came and ate it. Tell me before I die—are you man or devil?"

Tarzan laughed. "I am a man," he said.

The old fellow sighed and shook his head. "You have tried to save me from Simba," he said. "For that I shall reward you. I am a great witch-doctor. Listen to me, white man! I see bad days ahead of you. It is writ in my own blood which I have smeared upon my palm. A god greater even than you will rise up and strike you down. Turn back, Munango-Keewati! Turn back before it is too late. Danger lies ahead of you and danger lurks behind; but greater is the danger before. I see—" He paused and drew a long, gasping breath. Then he crumpled into a little, wrinkled heap and died. Tarzan wondered what else he had seen.

It was very late when the ape-man re-entered the boma and lay down among his black warriors. None had seen him go and none saw him return. He thought about the warning of the old witch-doctor before he fell asleep and he thought of it again after he awoke; but he did not turn back for he was unafraid, though had he known what lay in store for one he loved most in all the world he would have flown through the trees to her side and allowed the gold of Opar to remain forever hidden in its forgotten storehouse.

Behind him that morning another white man pondered something he had heard during the night and very nearly did he give up his project and turn back upon his trail. It was Werper, the murderer, who in the still of the night had heard far away upon the trail ahead of him a sound that had filled his cowardly soul with terror—a sound such as he never before had heard in all his life, nor dreamed that such a frightful thing could emanate from the lungs of a God-created creature. He had heard the victory cry of the bull ape as Tarzan had screamed it forth into the face of Goro, the moon, and he had trembled then and hidden his face; and now in the broad light of a new day he trembled again as he recalled it, and would have turned back from the nameless danger the echo of that frightful sound seemed to portend, had he not stood in even greater fear of Achmet Zek, his master.

And so Tarzan of the Apes forged steadily ahead toward Opar's ruined ramparts and behind him slunk Werper, jackal-like, and only God knew what lay in store for each.

At the edge of the desolate valley, overlooking the golden domes and minarets of Opar, Tarzan halted. By night he would go alone to the treasure vault, reconnoitering, for he had determined that caution should mark his every move upon this expedition.

With the coming of night he set forth, and Werper, who had scaled the cliffs alone behind the ape-man's party, and hidden through the day among the rough boulders of the mountain top, slunk stealthily after him. The boulder-strewn plain between the valley's edge and the mighty granite kopje, outside the city's walls, where lay the entrance to the passage-way leading to the treasure vault, gave the Belgian ample cover as he followed Tarzan toward Opar.

He saw the giant ape-man swing himself nimbly up the face of the great rock. Werper, clawing fearfully during the perilous ascent, sweating in terror, almost palsied by fear, but spurred on by avarice, following upward, until at last he stood upon the summit of the rocky hill.

Tarzan was nowhere in sight. For a time Werper hid behind one of the lesser boulders that were scattered over the top of the hill, but, seeing or hearing nothing of the Englishman, he crept from his place of concealment to undertake a systematic search of his surroundings, in the hope that he might discover the location of the treasure in ample time to make his escape before Tarzan returned, for it was the Belgian's desire merely to locate the gold, that, after Tarzan had departed, he might come in safety with his followers and carry away as much as he could transport.

He found the narrow cleft leading downward into the heart of the kopje along well-worn, granite steps. He advanced quite to the dark mouth of the tunnel into which the runway disappeared; but here he halted, fearing to enter, lest he meet Tarzan returning.

The ape-man, far ahead of him, groped his way along the rocky passage, until he came to the ancient wooden door. A moment later he stood within the treasure chamber, where, ages since, long-dead hands had ranged the lofty rows of precious ingots for the rulers of that great continent which now lies submerged beneath the waters of the Atlantic.

No sound broke the stillness of the subterranean vault. There was no evidence that another had discovered the forgotten wealth since last the ape-man had visited its hiding place.

Satisfied, Tarzan turned and retraced his steps toward the summit of the kopje. Werper, from the concealment of a jutting, granite shoulder, watched him pass up from the shadows of the stairway and advance toward the edge of the hill which faced the rim of the valley where the Waziri awaited the signal of their master. Then Werper, slipping stealthily from his hiding place, dropped into the somber darkness of the entrance and disappeared.

Tarzan, halting upon the kopje's edge, raised his voice in the thunderous roar of a lion. Twice, at regular intervals, he repeated the call, standing in attentive silence for several minutes after the echoes of the third call had died away. And then, from far across the valley, faintly, came an answering roar—once, twice, thrice. Basuli, the Waziri chieftain, had heard and replied.

Tarzan again made his way toward the treasure vault, knowing that in a few hours his blacks would be with him, ready to bear away another fortune in the strangely shaped, golden ingots of Opar. In the meantime he would carry as much of the precious metal to the summit of the kopje as he could.

Six trips he made in the five hours before Basuli reached the kopje, and at the end of that time he had transported forty-eight ingots to the edge of the great boulder, carrying upon each trip a load which might well have staggered two ordinary men, yet his giant frame showed no evidence of fatigue, as he helped to raise his ebon warriors to the hill top with the rope that had been brought for the purpose.

Six times he had returned to the treasure chamber, and six times Werper, the Belgian, had cowered in the black shadows at the far end of the long vault. Once again came the ape-man, and this time there came with him fifty fighting men, turning porters for love of the only creature in the world who might command of their fierce and haughty natures such menial service. Fifty-two more ingots passed out of the vaults, making the total of one hundred which Tarzan intended taking away with him.

As the last of the Waziri filed from the chamber, Tarzan turned back for a last glimpse of the fabulous wealth upon which his two inroads had made no appreciable impression. Before he extinguished the single candle he had brought with him for the purpose, and the flickering light of which had cast the first alleviating rays into the impenetrable darkness of the buried chamber, that it had known for the countless ages since it had lain forgotten of man, Tarzan's mind reverted to that first occasion upon which he had entered the treasure vault, coming upon it by chance as he fled from the pits beneath the temple, where he had been hidden by La, the High Priestess of the Sun Worshipers.

He recalled the scene within the temple when he had lain stretched upon the sacrificial altar, while La, with high-raised dagger, stood above him, and the rows of priests and priestesses awaited, in the ecstatic hysteria of fanaticism, the first gush of their victim's warm blood, that they might fill their golden goblets and drink to the glory of their Flaming God.

The brutal and bloody interruption by Tha, the mad priest, passed vividly before the ape-man's recollective eyes, the flight of the votaries before the insane blood lust of the hideous creature, the brutal attack upon La, and his own part of the grim tragedy when he had battled with the infuriated Oparian and left him dead at the feet of the priestess he would have profaned.

This and much more passed through Tarzan's memory as he stood gazing at the long tiers of dull-yellow metal. He wondered if La still ruled the temples of the ruined city whose crumbling walls rose upon the very foundations about him. Had she finally been forced into a union with one of her grotesque priests? It seemed a hideous fate, indeed, for one so beautiful. With a shake of his head, Tarzan stepped to the flickering candle, extinguished its feeble rays and turned toward the exit.

Behind him the spy waited for him to be gone. He had learned the secret for which he had come, and now he could return at his leisure to his waiting followers, bring them to the treasure vault and carry away all the gold that they could stagger under.

The Waziri had reached the outer end of the tunnel, and were winding upward toward the fresh air and the welcome starlight of the kopje's summit, before Tarzan shook off the detaining hand of reverie and started slowly after them.

Once again, and, he thought, for the last time, he closed the massive door of the treasure room. In the darkness behind him Werper rose and stretched his cramped muscles. He stretched forth a hand and lovingly caressed a golden ingot on the nearest tier. He raised it from its immemorial resting place and weighed it in his hands. He clutched it to his bosom in an ecstasy of avarice.

Tarzan dreamed of the happy homecoming which lay before him, of dear arms about his neck, and a soft cheek pressed to his; but there rose to dispel that dream the memory of the old witch-doctor and his warning.

And then, in the span of a few brief seconds, the hopes of both these men were shattered. The one forgot even his greed in the panic of terror—the other was plunged into total forgetfulness of the past by a jagged fragment of rock which gashed a deep cut upon his head.

THE ALTAR OF THE FLAMING GOD

It was at the moment that Tarzan turned from the closed door to pursue his way to the outer world. The thing came without warning. One instant all was quiet and stability—the next, and the world rocked, the tortured sides of the narrow passageway split and crumbled, great blocks of granite, dislodged from the ceiling, tumbled into the narrow way, choking it, and the walls bent inward upon the wreckage. Beneath the blow of a fragment of the roof, Tarzan staggered back against the door to the treasure room, his weight pushed it open and his body rolled inward upon the floor.

In the great apartment where the treasure lay less damage was wrought by the earthquake. A few ingots toppled from the higher tiers, a single piece of the rocky ceiling splintered off and crashed downward to the floor, and the walls cracked, though they did not collapse.

There was but the single shock, no other followed to complete the damage undertaken by the first. Werper, thrown to his length by the suddenness and violence of the disturbance, staggered to his feet when he found himself unhurt. Groping his way toward the far end of the chamber, he sought the candle which Tarzan had left stuck in its own wax upon the protruding end of an ingot.

By striking numerous matches the Belgian at last found what he sought, and when, a moment later, the sickly rays relieved the Stygian darkness about him, he breathed a nervous sigh of relief, for the impenetrable gloom had accentuated the terrors of his situation.

As they became accustomed to the light the man turned his eyes toward the door—his one thought now was of escape from this frightful tomb—and as he did so he saw the body of the naked giant lying stretched upon the floor just within the doorway. Werper drew back in sudden fear of detection; but a second glance convinced him that the Englishman was dead. From a great gash in the man's head a pool of blood had collected upon the concrete floor.

Quickly, the Belgian leaped over the prostrate form of his erstwhile host, and without a thought of succor for the man in whom, for aught he knew, life still remained, he bolted for the passageway and safety.

But his renewed hopes were soon dashed. Just beyond the doorway he found the passage completely clogged and choked by impenetrable masses of shattered rock. Once more he turned and re-entered the treasure vault. Taking the candle from its place he commenced a systematic search of the apartment, nor had he gone far before he discovered another door in the opposite end of the room, a door which gave upon creaking hinges to the weight of his body. Beyond the door lay another narrow passageway. Along this Werper made his way, ascending a flight of stone steps to another corridor twenty feet above the level of the first. The flickering candle lighted the way before him, and a moment later he was thankful for the possession of this crude and antiquated luminant, which, a few hours before he might have looked upon with contempt, for it showed him, just in time, a yawning pit, apparently terminating the tunnel he was traversing.

Before him was a circular shaft. He held the candle above it and peered downward. Below him, at a great distance, he saw the light reflected back from the surface of a pool of water. He had come upon a well. He raised the candle above his head and peered across the black void, and there upon the opposite side he saw the continuation of the tunnel; but how was he to span the gulf?

As he stood there measuring the distance to the opposite side and wondering if he dared venture so great a leap, there broke suddenly upon his startled ears a piercing scream which diminished gradually until it ended in a series of dismal moans. The voice seemed partly human, yet so hideous that it might well have emanated from the tortured throat of a lost soul, writhing in the fires of hell.

The Belgian shuddered and looked fearfully upward, for the scream had seemed to come from above him. As he looked he saw an opening far overhead, and a patch of sky pinked with brilliant stars.

His half-formed intention to call for help was expunged by the terrifying cry—where such a voice lived, no human creatures could dwell. He dared not reveal himself to whatever inhabitants dwelt in the place above him. He cursed himself for a fool that he had ever embarked upon such a mission. He wished himself safely back in the camp of Achmet Zek, and would almost have embraced an opportunity to give himself up to the military authorities of the Congo if by so doing he might be rescued from the frightful predicament in which he now was.

He listened fearfully, but the cry was not repeated, and at last spurred to desperate means, he gathered himself for the leap across the chasm. Going back twenty paces, he took a running start, and at the edge of the well, leaped upward and outward in an attempt to gain the opposite side.

In his hand he clutched the sputtering candle, and as he took the leap the rush of air extinguished it. In utter darkness he flew through space, clutching outward for a hold should his feet miss the invisible ledge.

He struck the edge of the door of the opposite terminus of the rocky tunnel with his knees, slipped backward, clutched desperately for a moment, and at last hung half within and half without the opening; but he was safe. For several minutes he dared not move; but clung, weak and sweating, where he lay. At last, cautiously, he drew himself well within the tunnel, and again he lay at full length upon the floor, fighting to regain control of his shattered nerves.

When his knees struck the edge of the tunnel he had dropped the candle. Presently, hoping against hope that it had fallen upon the floor of the passageway, rather than back into the depths of the well, he rose upon all fours and commenced a diligent search for the little tallow cylinder, which now seemed infinitely more precious to him than all the fabulous wealth of the hoarded ingots of Opar.

And when, at last, he found it, he clasped it to him and sank back sobbing and exhausted. For many minutes he lay trembling and broken; but finally he drew himself to a sitting posture, and taking a match from his pocket, lighted the stump of the candle which remained to him. With the light he found it easier to regain control of his nerves, and presently he was again making his way along the tunnel in search of an avenue of escape. The horrid cry that had come down to him from above through the ancient well-shaft still haunted him, so that he trembled in terror at even the sounds of his own cautious advance.

He had gone forward but a short distance, when, to his chagrin, a wall of masonry barred his farther progress, closing the tunnel completely from top to bottom and from side to side. What could it mean? Werper was an educated and intelligent man. His military training had taught him to use his mind for the purpose for which it was intended. A blind tunnel such as this was senseless. It must continue beyond the wall. Someone, at some time in the past, had had it blocked for an unknown purpose of his own. The man fell to examining the masonry by the light of his candle. To his delight he discovered that the thin blocks of hewn stone of which it was constructed were fitted in loosely without mortar or cement. He tugged upon one of them, and to his joy found that it was easily removable. One after another he pulled out the blocks until he had opened an aperture large enough to admit his body, then he crawled through into a large, low chamber. Across this another door barred his way; but this, too, gave before his efforts, for it was not barred. A long, dark corridor showed before him, but before he had followed it far, his candle burned down until it scorched his fingers. With an oath he dropped it to the floor, where it sputtered for a moment and went out.

Now he was in total darkness, and again terror rode heavily astride his neck. What further pitfalls and dangers lay ahead he could not guess; but that he was as far as ever from liberty he was quite willing to believe, so depressing is utter absence of light to one in unfamiliar surroundings.

Slowly he groped his way along, feeling with his hands upon the tunnel's walls, and cautiously with his feet ahead of him upon the floor before he could take a single forward step. How long he crept on thus he could not guess; but at last, feeling that the tunnel's length was interminable, and exhausted by his efforts, by terror, and loss of sleep, he determined to lie down and rest before proceeding farther.

When he awoke there was no change in the surrounding blackness. He might have slept a second or a day—he could not know; but that he had slept for some time was attested by the fact that he felt refreshed and hungry.

Again he commenced his groping advance; but this time he had gone but a short distance when he emerged into a room, which was lighted through an opening in the ceiling, from which a flight of concrete steps led downward to the floor of the chamber.

Above him, through the aperture, Werper could see sunlight glancing from massive columns, which were twined about by clinging vines. He listened; but he heard no sound other than the soughing of the wind through leafy branches, the hoarse cries of birds, and the chattering of monkeys.

Boldly he ascended the stairway, to find himself in a circular court. Just before him stood a stone altar, stained with rusty-brown discolorations. At the time Werper gave no thought to an explanation of these stains—later their origin became all too hideously apparent to him.

Beside the opening in the floor, just behind the altar, through which he had entered the court from the subterranean chamber below, the Belgian discovered several doors leading from the enclosure upon the level of the floor. Above, and circling the courtyard, was a series of open balconies. Monkeys scampered about the deserted ruins, and gaily plumaged birds flitted in and out among the columns and the galleries far above; but no sign of human presence was discernible. Werper felt relieved. He sighed, as though a great weight had been lifted from his shoulders. He took a step toward one of the exits, and then he halted, wide-eyed in astonishment and terror, for almost at the same instant a dozen doors opened in the courtyard wall and a horde of frightful men rushed in upon him.

They were the priests of the Flaming God of Opar—the same, shaggy, knotted, hideous little men who had dragged Jane Clayton to the sacrificial altar at this very spot years before. Their long arms, their short and crooked legs, their close-set, evil eyes, and their low, receding foreheads gave them a bestial appearance that sent a qualm of paralyzing fright through the shaken nerves of the Belgian.

With a scream he turned to flee back into the lesser terrors of the gloomy corridors and apartments from which he had just emerged, but the frightful men anticipated his intentions. They blocked the way; they seized him, and though he fell, groveling upon his knees before them, begging for his life, they bound him and hurled him to the floor of the inner temple.

The rest was but a repetition of what Tarzan and Jane Clayton had passed through. The priestesses came, and with them La, the High Priestess. Werper was raised and laid across the altar. Cold sweat exuded from his every pore as La raised the cruel, sacrificial knife above him. The death chant fell upon his tortured ears. His staring eyes wandered to the golden goblets from which the hideous votaries would soon quench their inhuman thirst in his own, warm life-blood.

He wished that he might be granted the brief respite of unconsciousness before the final plunge of the keen blade—and then there was a frightful roar that sounded almost in his ears. The High Priestess lowered her dagger. Her eyes went wide in horror. The priestesses, her votaresses, screamed and fled madly toward the exits. The priests roared out their rage and terror according to the temper of their courage. Werper strained his neck about to catch a sight of the cause of their panic, and when, at last he saw it, he too went cold in dread, for what his eyes beheld was the figure of a huge lion standing in the center of the temple, and already a single victim lay mangled beneath his cruel paws.

Again the lord of the wilderness roared, turning his baleful gaze upon the altar. La staggered forward, reeled, and fell across Werper in a swoon.

THE ARAB RAID

After their first terror had subsided subsequent to the shock of the earthquake, Basuli and his warriors hastened back into the passageway in search of Tarzan and two of their own number who were also missing.

They found the way blocked by jammed and distorted rock. For two days they labored to tear a way through to their imprisoned friends; but when, after Herculean efforts, they had unearthed but a few yards of the choked passage, and discovered the mangled remains of one of their fellows they were forced to the conclusion that Tarzan and the second Waziri also lay dead beneath the rock mass farther in, beyond human aid, and no longer susceptible of it.

Again and again as they labored they called aloud the names of their master and their comrade; but no answering call rewarded their listening ears. At last they gave up the search. Tearfully they cast a last look at the shattered tomb of their master, shouldered the heavy burden of gold that would at least furnish comfort, if not happiness, to their bereaved and beloved mistress, and made their mournful way back across the desolate valley of Opar, and downward through the forests beyond toward the distant bungalow.

And as they marched what sorry fate was already drawing down upon that peaceful, happy home!

From the north came Achmet Zek, riding to the summons of his lieutenant's letter. With him came his horde of renegade Arabs, outlawed marauders, these, and equally degraded blacks, garnered from the more debased and ignorant tribes of savage cannibals through whose countries the raider passed to and fro with perfect impunity.

Mugambi, the ebon Hercules, who had shared the dangers and vicissitudes of his beloved Bwana, from Jungle Island, almost to the headwaters of the Ugambi, was the first to note the bold approach of the sinister caravan.

He it was whom Tarzan had left in charge of the warriors who remained to guard Lady Greystoke, nor could a braver or more loyal guardian have been found in any clime or upon any soil. A giant in stature, a savage, fearless warrior, the huge black possessed also soul and judgment in proportion to his bulk and his ferocity.

Not once since his master had departed had he been beyond sight or sound of the bungalow, except when Lady Greystoke chose to canter across the broad plain, or relieve the monotony of her loneliness by a brief hunting excursion. On such occasions Mugambi, mounted upon a wiry Arab, had ridden close at her horse's heels.

The raiders were still a long way off when the warrior's keen eyes discovered them. For a time he stood scrutinizing the advancing party in silence, then he turned and ran rapidly in the direction of the native huts which lay a few hundred yards below the bungalow.

Here he called out to the lolling warriors. He issued orders rapidly. In compliance with them the men seized upon their weapons and their shields. Some ran to call in the workers from the fields and to warn the tenders of the flocks and herds. The majority followed Mugambi back toward the bungalow.

The dust of the raiders was still a long distance away. Mugambi could not know positively that it hid an enemy; but he had spent a lifetime of savage life in savage Africa, and he had seen parties before come thus unheralded. Sometimes they had come in peace and sometimes they had come in war—one could never tell. It was well to be prepared. Mugambi did not like the haste with which the strangers advanced.

The Greystoke bungalow was not well adapted for defense. No palisade surrounded it, for, situated as it was, in the heart of loyal Waziri, its master had anticipated no possibility of an attack in force by any enemy.

Heavy, wooden shutters there were to close the window apertures against hostile arrows, and these Mugambi was engaged in lowering when Lady Greystoke appeared upon the veranda.

"Why, Mugambi!" she exclaimed. "What has happened? Why are you lowering the shutters?"

Mugambi pointed out across the plain to where a white-robed force of mounted men was now distinctly visible.

"Arabs," he explained. "They come for no good purpose in the absence of the Great Bwana."

Beyond the neat lawn and the flowering shrubs, Jane Clayton saw the glistening bodies of her Waziri. The sun glanced from the tips of their metal-shod spears, picked out the gorgeous colors in the feathers of their war bonnets, and reflected the high-lights from the glossy skins of their broad shoulders and high cheek bones.

Jane Clayton surveyed them with unmixed feelings of pride and affection. What harm could befall her with such as these to protect her?

The raiders had halted now, a hundred yards out upon the plain. Mugambi had hastened down to join his warriors. He advanced a few yards before them and raising his voice hailed the strangers. Achmet Zek sat straight in his saddle before his henchmen.

"Arab!" cried Mugambi. "What do you here?"

"We come in peace," Achmet Zek called back.

"Then turn and go in peace," replied Mugambi. "We do not want you here. There can be no peace between Arab and Waziri."

Mugambi, although not born in Waziri, had been adopted into the tribe, which now contained no member more jealous of its traditions and its prowess than he.

Achmet Zek drew to one side of his horde, speaking to his men in a low voice. A moment later, without warning, a ragged volley was poured into the ranks of the Waziri. A couple of warriors fell, the others were for charging the attackers; but Mugambi was a cautious as well as a brave leader. He knew the futility of charging mounted men armed with muskets. He withdrew his force behind the shrubbery of the garden. Some he dispatched to various other parts of the grounds surrounding the bungalow. Half a dozen he sent to the bungalow itself with instructions to keep their mistress within doors, and to protect her with their lives.

Adopting the tactics of the desert fighters from which he had sprung, Achmet Zek led his followers at a gallop in a long, thin line, describing a great circle which drew closer and closer in toward the defenders.

At that part of the circle closest to the Waziri, a constant fusillade of shots was poured into the bushes behind which the black warriors had concealed themselves. The latter, on their part, loosed their slim shafts at the nearest of the enemy.

The Waziri, justly famed for their archery, found no cause to blush for their performance that day. Time and again some swarthy horseman threw hands above his head and toppled from his saddle, pierced by a deadly arrow; but the contest was uneven. The Arabs outnumbered the Waziri; their bullets penetrated the shrubbery and found marks that the Arab riflemen had not even seen; and then Achmet Zek circled inward a half mile above the bungalow, tore down a section of the fence, and led his marauders within the grounds.

Across the fields they charged at a mad run. Not again did they pause to lower fences, instead, they drove their wild mounts straight for them, clearing the obstacles as lightly as winged gulls.

Mugambi saw them coming, and, calling those of his warriors who remained, ran for the bungalow and the last stand. Upon the veranda Lady Greystoke stood, rifle in hand. More than a single raider had accounted to her steady nerves and cool aim for his outlawry; more than a single pony raced, riderless, in the wake of the charging horde.

Mugambi pushed his mistress back into the greater security of the interior, and with his depleted force prepared to make a last stand against the foe.

On came the Arabs, shouting and waving their long guns above their heads. Past the veranda they raced, pouring a deadly fire into the kneeling Waziri who discharged their volley of arrows from behind their long, oval shields—shields well adapted, perhaps, to stop a hostile arrow, or deflect a spear; but futile, quite, before the leaden missiles of the riflemen.

From beneath the half-raised shutters of the bungalow other bowmen did effective service in greater security, and after the first assault, Mugambi withdrew his entire force within the building.

Again and again the Arabs charged, at last forming a stationary circle about the little fortress, and outside the effective range of the defenders' arrows. From their new position they fired at will at the windows. One by one the Waziri fell. Fewer and fewer were the arrows that replied to the guns of the raiders, and at last Achmet Zek felt safe in ordering an assault.

Firing as they ran, the bloodthirsty horde raced for the veranda. A dozen of them fell to the arrows of the defenders; but the majority reached the door. Heavy gun butts fell upon it. The crash of splintered wood mingled with the report of a rifle as Jane Clayton fired through the panels upon the relentless foe.

Upon both sides of the door men fell; but at last the frail barrier gave to the vicious assaults of the maddened attackers; it crumpled inward and a dozen swarthy murderers leaped into the living-room. At the far end stood Jane Clayton surrounded by the remnant of her devoted guardians. The floor was covered by the bodies of those who already had given up their lives in her defense. In the forefront of her protectors stood the giant Mugambi. The Arabs raised their rifles to pour in the last volley that would effectually end all resistance; but Achmet Zek roared out a warning order that stayed their trigger fingers.

"Fire not upon the woman!" he cried. "Who harms her, dies. Take the woman alive!"

The Arabs rushed across the room; the Waziri met them with their heavy spears. Swords flashed, long-barreled pistols roared out their sullen death dooms. Mugambi launched his spear at the nearest of the enemy with a force that drove the heavy shaft completely through the Arab's body, then he seized a pistol from another, and grasping it by the barrel brained all who forced their way too near his mistress.

Emulating his example the few warriors who remained to him fought like demons; but one by one they fell, until only Mugambi remained to defend the life and honor of the ape-man's mate.

From across the room Achmet Zek watched the unequal struggle and urged on his minions. In his hands was a jeweled musket. Slowly he raised it to his shoulder, waiting until another move should place Mugambi at his mercy without endangering the lives of the woman or any of his own followers.

At last the moment came, and Achmet Zek pulled the trigger. Without a sound the brave Mugambi sank to the floor at the feet of Jane Clayton.

An instant later she was surrounded and disarmed. Without a word they dragged her from the bungalow. A giant Negro lifted her to the pommel of his saddle, and while the raiders searched the bungalow and outhouses for plunder he rode with her beyond the gates and waited the coming of his master.

Jane Clayton saw the raiders lead the horses from the corral, and drive the herds in from the fields. She saw her home plundered of all that represented intrinsic worth in the eyes of the Arabs, and then she saw the torch applied, and the flames lick up what remained.

And at last, when the raiders assembled after glutting their fury and their avarice, and rode away with her toward the north, she saw the smoke and the flames rising far into the heavens until the winding of the trail into the thick forests hid the sad view from her eyes.

As the flames ate their way into the living-room, reaching out forked tongues to lick up the bodies of the dead, one of that gruesome company whose bloody welterings had long since been stilled, moved again. It was a huge black who rolled over upon his side and opened blood-shot, suffering eyes. Mugambi, whom the Arabs had left for dead, still lived. The hot flames were almost upon him as he raised himself painfully upon his hands and knees and crawled slowly toward the doorway.

Again and again he sank weakly to the floor; but each time he rose again and continued his pitiful way toward safety. After what seemed to him an interminable time, during which the flames had become a veritable fiery furnace at the far side of the room, the great black managed to reach the veranda, roll down the steps, and crawl off into the cool safety of some nearby shrubbery.

All night he lay there, alternately unconscious and painfully sentient; and in the latter state watching with savage hatred the lurid flames which still rose from burning crib and hay cock. A prowling lion roared close at hand; but the giant black was unafraid. There was place for but a single thought in his savage mind—revenge! revenge! revenge!

THE JEWEL-ROOM OF OPAR

For some time Tarzan lay where he had fallen upon the floor of the treasure chamber beneath the ruined walls of Opar. He lay as one dead; but he was not dead. At length he stirred. His eyes opened upon the utter darkness of the room. He raised his hand to his head and brought it away sticky with clotted blood. He sniffed at his fingers, as a wild beast might sniff at the life-blood upon a wounded paw.

Slowly he rose to a sitting posture—listening. No sound reached to the buried depths of his sepulcher. He staggered to his feet, and groped his way about among the tiers of ingots. What was he? Where was he? His head ached; but otherwise he felt no ill effects from the blow that had felled him. The accident he did not recall, nor did he recall aught of what had led up to it.

He let his hands grope unfamiliarly over his limbs, his torso, and his head. He felt of the quiver at his back, the knife in his loin cloth. Something struggled for recognition within his brain. Ah! he had it. There was something missing. He crawled about upon the floor, feeling with his hands for the thing that instinct warned him was gone. At last he found it—the heavy war spear that in past years had formed so important a feature of his daily life, almost of his very existence, so inseparably had it been connected with his every action since the long-gone day that he had wrested his first spear from the body of a black victim of his savage training.

Tarzan was sure that there was another and more lovely world than that which was confined to the darkness of the four stone walls surrounding him. He continued his search and at last found the doorway leading inward beneath the city and the temple. This he followed, most incautiously. He came to the stone steps leading upward to the higher level. He ascended them and continued onward toward the well.

Nothing spurred his hurt memory to a recollection of past familiarity with his surroundings. He blundered on through the darkness as though he were traversing an open plain under the brilliance of a noonday sun, and suddenly there happened that which had to happen under the circumstances of his rash advance.

He reached the brink of the well, stepped outward into space, lunged forward, and shot downward into the inky depths below. Still clutching his spear, he struck the water, and sank beneath its surface, plumbing the depths.

The fall had not injured him, and when he rose to the surface, he shook the water from his eyes, and found that he could see. Daylight was filtering into the well from the orifice far above his head. It illumined the inner walls faintly. Tarzan gazed about him. On the level with the surface of the water he saw a large opening in the dark and slimy wall. He swam to it, and drew himself out upon the wet floor of a tunnel.

Along this he passed; but now he went warily, for Tarzan of the Apes was learning. The unexpected pit had taught him care in the traversing of dark passageways—he needed no second lesson.

For a long distance the passage went straight as an arrow. The floor was slippery, as though at times the rising waters of the well overflowed and flooded it. This, in itself, retarded Tarzan's pace, for it was with difficulty that he kept his footing.

The foot of a stairway ended the passage. Up this he made his way. It turned back and forth many times, leading, at last, into a small, circular chamber, the gloom of which was relieved by a faint light which found ingress through a tubular shaft several feet in diameter which rose from the center of the room's ceiling, upward to a distance of a hundred feet or more, where it terminated in a stone grating through which Tarzan could see a blue and sun-lit sky.

Curiosity prompted the ape-man to investigate his surroundings. Several metal-bound, copper-studded chests constituted the sole furniture of the round room. Tarzan let his hands run over these. He felt of the copper studs, he pulled upon the hinges, and at last, by chance, he raised the cover of one.

An exclamation of delight broke from his lips at sight of the pretty contents. Gleaming and glistening in the subdued light of the chamber, lay a great tray full of brilliant stones. Tarzan, reverted to the primitive by his accident, had no conception of the fabulous value of his find. To him they were but pretty pebbles. He plunged his hands into them and let the priceless gems filter through his fingers. He went to others of the chests, only to find still further stores of precious stones. Nearly all were cut, and from these he gathered a handful and filled the pouch which dangled at his side—the uncut stones he tossed back into the chests.

Unwittingly, the ape-man had stumbled upon the forgotten jewel-room of Opar. For ages it had lain buried beneath the temple of the Flaming God, midway of one of the many inky passages which the superstitious descendants of the ancient Sun Worshipers had either dared not or cared not to explore.

Tiring at last of this diversion, Tarzan took up his way along the corridor which led upward from the jewel-room by a steep incline. Winding and twisting, but always tending upward, the tunnel led him nearer and nearer to the surface, ending finally in a low-ceiled room, lighter than any that he had as yet discovered.

Above him an opening in the ceiling at the upper end of a flight of concrete steps revealed a brilliant sunlit scene. Tarzan viewed the vine-covered columns in mild wonderment. He puckered his brows in an attempt to recall some recollection of similar things. He was not sure of himself. There was a tantalizing suggestion always present in his mind that something was eluding him—that he should know many things which he did not know.

His earnest cogitation was rudely interrupted by a thunderous roar from the opening above him. Following the roar came the cries and screams of men and women. Tarzan grasped his spear more firmly and ascended the steps. A strange sight met his eyes as he emerged from the semi-darkness of the cellar to the brilliant light of the temple.

The creatures he saw before him he recognized for what they were—men and women, and a huge lion. The men and women were scuttling for the safety of the exits. The lion stood upon the body of one who had been less fortunate than the others. He was in the center of the temple. Directly before Tarzan, a woman stood beside a block of stone. Upon the top of the stone lay stretched a man, and as the ape-man watched the scene, he saw the lion glare terribly at the two who remained within the temple. Another thunderous roar broke from the savage throat, the woman screamed and swooned across the body of the man stretched prostrate upon the stone altar before her.

The lion advanced a few steps and crouched. The tip of his sinuous tail twitched nervously. He was upon the point of charging when his eyes were attracted toward the ape-man.

Werper, helpless upon the altar, saw the great carnivore preparing to leap upon him. He saw the sudden change in the beast's expression as his eyes wandered to something beyond the altar and out of the Belgian's view. He saw the formidable creature rise to a standing position. A figure darted past Werper. He saw a mighty arm upraised, and a stout spear shoot forward toward the lion, to bury itself in the broad chest.

He saw the lion snapping and tearing at the weapon's shaft, and he saw, wonder of wonders, the naked giant who had hurled the missile charging upon the great beast, only a long knife ready to meet those ferocious fangs and talons.

The lion reared up to meet this new enemy. The beast was growling frightfully, and then upon the startled ears of the Belgian, broke a similar savage growl from the lips of the man rushing upon the beast.

By a quick side step, Tarzan eluded the first swinging clutch of the lion's paws. Darting to the beast's side, he leaped upon the tawny back. His arms encircled the maned neck, his teeth sank deep into the brute's flesh. Roaring, leaping, rolling and struggling, the giant cat attempted to dislodge this savage enemy, and all the while one great, brown fist was driving a long keen blade repeatedly into the beast's side.

During the battle, La regained consciousness. Spellbound, she stood above her victim watching the spectacle. It seemed incredible that a human being could best the king of beasts in personal encounter and yet before her very eyes there was taking place just such an improbability.

At last Tarzan's knife found the great heart, and with a final, spasmodic struggle the lion rolled over upon the marble floor, dead. Leaping to his feet the conqueror placed a foot upon the carcass of his kill, raised his face toward the heavens, and gave voice to so hideous a cry that both La and Werper trembled as it reverberated through the temple.

Then the ape-man turned, and Werper recognized him as the man he had left for dead in the treasure room.

THE ESCAPE FROM OPAR

Werper was astounded. Could this creature be the same dignified Englishman who had entertained him so graciously in his luxurious African home? Could this wild beast, with blazing eyes, and bloody countenance, be at the same time a man? Could the horrid, victory cry he had but just heard have been formed in human throat?

Tarzan was eyeing the man and the woman, a puzzled expression in his eyes, but there was no faintest tinge of recognition. It was as though he had discovered some new species of living creature and was marveling at his find.

La was studying the ape-man's features. Slowly her large eyes opened very wide.

"Tarzan!" she exclaimed, and then, in the vernacular of the great apes which constant association with the anthropoids had rendered the common language of the Oparians: "You have come back to me! La has ignored the mandates of her religion, waiting, always waiting for Tarzan—for her Tarzan. She has taken no mate, for in all the world there was but one with whom La would mate. And now you have come back! Tell me, O Tarzan, that it is for me you have returned."

Werper listened to the unintelligible jargon. He looked from La to Tarzan. Would the latter understand this strange tongue? To the Belgian's surprise, the Englishman answered in a language evidently identical to hers.

"Tarzan," he repeated, musingly. "Tarzan. The name sounds familiar."

"It is your name—you are Tarzan," cried La.

"I am Tarzan?" The ape-man shrugged. "Well, it is a good name—I know no other, so I will keep it; but I do not know you. I did not come hither for you. Why I came, I do not know at all; neither do I know from whence I came. Can you tell me?"

La shook her head. "I never knew," she replied.

Tarzan turned toward Werper and put the same question to him; but in the language of the great apes. The Belgian shook his head.

"I do not understand that language," he said in French.

Without effort, and apparently without realizing that he made the change, Tarzan repeated his question in French. Werper suddenly came to a full realization of the magnitude of the injury of which Tarzan was a victim. The man had lost his memory—no longer could he recollect past events. The Belgian was upon the point of enlightening him, when it suddenly occurred to him that by keeping Tarzan in ignorance, for a time at least, of his true identity, it might be possible to turn the ape-man's misfortune to his own advantage.

"I cannot tell you from whence you came," he said; "but this I can tell you—if we do not get out of this horrible place we shall both be slain upon this bloody altar. The woman was about to plunge her knife into my heart when the lion interrupted the fiendish ritual. Come! Before they recover from their fright and reassemble, let us find a way out of their damnable temple."

Tarzan turned again toward La.

"Why," he asked, "would you have killed this man? Are you hungry?"

The High Priestess cried out in disgust.

"Did he attempt to kill you?" continued Tarzan.

The woman shook her head.

"Then why should you have wished to kill him?" Tarzan was determined to get to the bottom of the thing.

La raised her slender arm and pointed toward the sun.

"We were offering up his soul as a gift to the Flaming God," she said.

Tarzan looked puzzled. He was again an ape, and apes do not understand such matters as souls and Flaming Gods.

"Do you wish to die?" he asked Werper.

The Belgian assured him, with tears in his eyes, that he did not wish to die.

"Very well then, you shall not," said Tarzan. "Come! We will go. This *she* would kill you and keep me for herself. It is no place anyway for a Mangani. I should soon die, shut up behind these stone walls."

He turned toward La. "We are going now," he said.

The woman rushed forward and seized the ape-man's hands in hers.

"Do not leave me!" she cried. "Stay, and you shall be High Priest. La loves you. All Opar shall be yours. Slaves shall wait upon you. Stay, Tarzan of the Apes, and let love reward you."

The ape-man pushed the kneeling woman aside. "Tarzan does not desire you," he said, simply, and stepping to Werper's side he cut the Belgian's bonds and motioned him to follow.

Panting—her face convulsed with rage, La sprang to her feet.

"Stay, you shall!" she screamed. "La will have you—if she cannot have you alive, she will have you dead," and raising her face to the sun she gave voice to the same hideous shriek that Werper had heard once before and Tarzan many times.

In answer to her cry a babel of voices broke from the surrounding chambers and corridors.

"Come, Guardian Priests!" she cried. "The infidels have profaned the holiest of the holies. Come! Strike terror to their hearts; defend La and her altar; wash clean the temple with the blood of the polluters."

Tarzan understood, though Werper did not. The former glanced at the Belgian and saw that he was unarmed. Stepping quickly to La's side the ape-man seized her in his strong arms and though she fought with all the mad savagery of a demon, he soon disarmed her, handing her long, sacrificial knife to Werper.

"You will need this," he said, and then from each doorway a horde of the monstrous, little men of Opar streamed into the temple.

They were armed with bludgeons and knives, and fortified in their courage by fanatical hate and frenzy. Werper was terrified. Tarzan stood eyeing the foe in proud disdain. Slowly he advanced toward the exit he had chosen to utilize in making his way from the temple. A burly priest barred his way. Behind the first was a score of others. Tarzan swung his heavy spear, clublike, down upon the skull of the priest. The fellow collapsed, his head crushed.

Again and again the weapon fell as Tarzan made his way slowly toward the doorway. Werper pressed close behind, casting backward glances toward the shrieking, dancing mob menacing their rear. He held the sacrificial knife ready to strike whoever might come within its reach; but none came. For a time he wondered that they should so bravely battle with the giant ape-man, yet hesitate to rush upon him, who was relatively so weak. Had they done so he knew that he must have fallen at the first charge. Tarzan had reached the doorway over the corpses of all that had stood to dispute his way, before Werper guessed at the reason for his immunity. The priests feared the sacrificial knife! Willingly would they face death and welcome it if it came while they defended their High Priestess and her altar; but evidently there were deaths, and deaths. Some strange superstition must surround that polished blade, that no Oparian cared to chance a death thrust from it, yet gladly rushed to the slaughter of the ape-man's flaying spear.

Once outside the temple court, Werper communicated his discovery to Tarzan. The ape-man grinned, and let Werper go before him, brandishing the jeweled and holy weapon. Like leaves before a gale, the Oparians scattered in all directions and Tarzan and the Belgian found a clear passage through the corridors and chambers of the ancient temple.

The Belgian's eyes went wide as they passed through the room of the seven pillars of solid gold. With ill-concealed avarice he looked upon the age-old, golden tablets set in the walls of nearly every room and down the sides of many of the corridors. To the ape-man all this wealth appeared to mean nothing.

On the two went, chance leading them toward the broad avenue which lay between the stately piles of the half-ruined edifices and the inner wall of the city. Great apes jabbered at them and menaced them; but Tarzan answered them after their own kind, giving back taunt for taunt, insult for insult, challenge for challenge.

Werper saw a hairy bull swing down from a broken column and advance, stiff-legged and bristling, toward the naked giant. The yellow fangs were bared, angry snarls and barkings rumbled threateningly through the thick and hanging lips.

The Belgian watched his companion. To his horror, he saw the man stoop until his closed knuckles rested upon the ground as did those of the anthropoid. He saw him circle, stiff-legged about the circling ape. He heard the same bestial barkings and growlings issue from the human throat that were coming from the mouth of the brute. Had his eyes been closed he could not have known but that two giant apes were bridling for combat.

But there was no battle. It ended as the majority of such jungle encounters end—one of the boasters loses his nerve, and becomes suddenly interested in a blowing leaf, a beetle, or the lice upon his hairy stomach.

In this instance it was the anthropoid that retired in stiff dignity to inspect an unhappy caterpillar, which he presently devoured. For a moment Tarzan seemed inclined to pursue the argument. He swaggered truculently, stuck out his chest, roared and advanced closer to the bull. It was with difficulty that Werper finally persuaded him to leave well enough alone and continue his way from the ancient city of the Sun Worshipers.

The two searched for nearly an hour before they found the narrow exit through the inner wall. From there the well-worn trail led them beyond the outer fortification to the desolate valley of Opar.

Tarzan had no idea, in so far as Werper could discover, as to where he was or whence he came. He wandered aimlessly about, searching for food, which he discovered beneath small rocks, or hiding in the shade of the scant brush which dotted the ground.

The Belgian was horrified by the hideous menu of his companion. Beetles, rodents and caterpillars were devoured with seeming relish. Tarzan was indeed an ape again.

At last Werper succeeded in leading his companion toward the distant hills which mark the northwestern boundary of the valley, and together the two set out in the direction of the Greystoke bungalow.

What purpose prompted the Belgian in leading the victim of his treachery and greed back toward his former home it is difficult to guess, unless it was that without Tarzan there could be no ransom for Tarzan's wife.

That night they camped in the valley beyond the hills, and as they sat before a little fire where cooked a wild pig that had fallen to one of Tarzan's arrows, the latter sat lost in speculation. He seemed continually to be trying to grasp some mental image which as constantly eluded him.

At last he opened the leathern pouch which hung at his side. From it he poured into the palm of his hand a quantity of glittering gems. The firelight playing upon them conjured a multitude of scintillating rays, and as the wide eyes of the Belgian looked on in rapt fascination, the man's expression at last acknowledged a tangible purpose in courting the society of the ape-man.

THE THEFT OF THE JEWELS

For two days Werper sought for the party that had accompanied him from the camp to the barrier cliffs; but not until late in the afternoon of the second day did he find clew to its whereabouts, and then in such gruesome form that he was totally unnerved by the sight.

In an open glade he came upon the bodies of three of the blacks, terribly mutilated, nor did it require considerable deductive power to explain their murder. Of the little party only these three had not been slaves. The others, evidently tempted to hope for freedom from their cruel Arab master, had taken advantage of their separation from the main camp, to slay the three representatives of the hated power which held them in slavery, and vanish into the jungle.

Cold sweat exuded from Werper's forehead as he contemplated the fate which chance had permitted him to escape, for had he been present when the conspiracy bore fruit, he, too, must have been of the garnered.

Tarzan showed not the slightest surprise or interest in the discovery. Inherent in him was a calloused familiarity with violent death. The refinements of his recent civilization expunged by the force of the sad calamity which had befallen him, left only the primitive sensibilities which his childhood's training had imprinted indelibly upon the fabric of his mind.

The training of Kala, the examples and precepts of Kerchak, of Tublat, and of Terkoz now formed the basis of his every thought and action. He retained a mechanical knowledge of French and English speech. Werper had spoken to him in French, and Tarzan had replied in the same tongue without conscious realization that he had departed from the anthropoidal speech in which he had addressed La. Had Werper used English, the result would have been the same.

Again, that night, as the two sat before their camp fire, Tarzan played with his shining baubles. Werper asked him what they were and where he had found them. The ape-man replied that they were gay-colored stones, with which he purposed fashioning a necklace, and that he had found them far beneath the sacrificial court of the temple of the Flaming God.

Werper was relieved to find that Tarzan had no conception of the value of the gems. This would make it easier for the Belgian to obtain possession of them. Possibly the man would give them to him for the asking. Werper reached out his hand toward the little pile that Tarzan had arranged upon a piece of flat wood before him.

"Let me see them," said the Belgian.

Tarzan placed a large palm over his treasure. He bared his fighting fangs, and growled. Werper withdrew his hand more quickly than he had advanced it. Tarzan resumed his playing with the gems, and his conversation with Werper as though nothing unusual had occurred. He had but exhibited the beast's jealous protective instinct for a possession. When he killed he shared the meat with Werper; but had Werper ever, by accident, laid a hand upon Tarzan's share, he would have aroused the same savage, and resentful warning.

From that occurrence dated the beginning of a great fear in the breast of the Belgian for his savage companion. He had never understood the transformation that had been wrought in Tarzan by the blow upon his head, other than to attribute it to a form of amnesia. That Tarzan had once been, in truth, a savage, jungle beast, Werper had not known, and so, of course, he could not guess that the man had reverted to the state in which his childhood and young manhood had been spent.

Now Werper saw in the Englishman a dangerous maniac, whom the slightest untoward accident might turn upon him with rending fangs. Not for a moment did Werper attempt to delude himself into the belief that he could defend himself successfully against an attack by the ape-man. His one hope lay in eluding him, and making for the far distant camp of Achmet Zek as rapidly as he could; but armed only with the sacrificial knife, Werper shrank from attempting the journey through the jungle. Tarzan constituted a protection that was by no means despicable, even in the face of the larger carnivora, as Werper had reason to acknowledge from the evidence he had witnessed in the Oparian temple.

Too, Werper had his covetous soul set upon the pouch of gems, and so he was torn between the various emotions of avarice and fear. But avarice it was that burned most strongly in his breast, to the end that he dared the dangers and suffered the terrors of constant association with him he thought a mad man, rather than give up the hope of obtaining possession of the fortune which the contents of the little pouch represented.

Achmet Zek should know nothing of these—these would be for Werper alone, and so soon as he could encompass his design he would reach the coast and take passage for America, where he could conceal himself beneath the veil of a new identity and enjoy to some measure the fruits of his theft. He had it all planned out, did Lieutenant Albert Werper, living in anticipation the luxurious life of the idle rich. He even found himself regretting that America was so provincial, and that nowhere in the new world was a city that might compare with his beloved Brussels.

It was upon the third day of their progress from Opar that the keen ears of Tarzan caught the sound of men behind them. Werper heard nothing above the humming of the jungle insects, and the chattering life of the lesser monkeys and the birds.

For a time Tarzan stood in statuesque silence, listening, his sensitive nostrils dilating as he assayed each passing breeze. Then he withdrew Werper into the concealment of thick brush, and waited. Presently, along the game trail that Werper and Tarzan had been following, there came in sight a sleek, black warrior, alert and watchful.

In single file behind him, there followed, one after another, near fifty others, each burdened with two dull-yellow ingots lashed upon his back. Werper recognized the party immediately as that which had accompanied Tarzan on his journey to Opar. He glanced at the ape-man; but in the savage, watchful eyes he saw no recognition of Basuli and those other loyal Waziri.

When all had passed, Tarzan rose and emerged from concealment. He looked down the trail in the direction the party had gone. Then he turned to Werper.

"We will follow and slay them," he said.

"Why?" asked the Belgian.

"They are black," explained Tarzan. "It was a black who killed Kala. They are the enemies of the Manganis."

Werper did not relish the idea of engaging in a battle with Basuli and his fierce fighting men. And, again, he had welcomed the sight of them returning toward the Greystoke bungalow, for he had begun to have doubts as to his ability to retrace his steps to the Waziri country. Tarzan, he knew, had not the remotest idea of whither they were going. By keeping at a safe distance behind the laden warriors, they would have no difficulty in following them home. Once at the bungalow, Werper knew the way to the camp of Achmet Zek. There was still another reason why he did not wish to interfere with the Waziri—they were bearing the great burden of treasure in the direction he wished it borne. The farther they took it, the less the distance that he and Achmet Zek would have to transport it.

He argued with the ape-man therefore, against the latter's desire to exterminate the blacks, and at last he prevailed upon Tarzan to follow them in peace, saying that he was sure they would lead them out of the forest into a rich country, teeming with game.

It was many marches from Opar to the Waziri country; but at last came the hour when Tarzan and the Belgian, following the trail of the warriors, topped the last rise, and saw before them the broad Waziri plain, the winding river, and the distant forests to the north and west.

A mile or more ahead of them, the line of warriors was creeping like a giant caterpillar through the tall grasses of the plain. Beyond, grazing herds of zebra, hartebeest, and topi dotted the level landscape, while closer to the river a bull buffalo, his head and shoulders protruding from the reeds watched the advancing blacks for a moment, only to turn at last and disappear into the safety of his dank and gloomy retreat.

Tarzan looked out across the familiar vista with no faintest gleam of recognition in his eyes. He saw the game animals, and his mouth watered; but he did not look in the direction of his bungalow. Werper, however, did. A puzzled expression entered the Belgian's eyes. He shaded them with his palms and gazed long and earnestly toward the spot where the bungalow had stood. He could not credit the testimony of his eyes—there was no bungalow—no barns—no out-houses. The corrals, the hay stacks—all were gone. What could it mean?

And then, slowly there filtered into Werper's consciousness an explanation of the havoc that had been wrought in that peaceful valley since last his eyes had rested upon it—Achmet Zek had been there!

Basuli and his warriors had noted the devastation the moment they had come in sight of the farm. Now they hastened on toward it talking excitedly among themselves in animated speculation upon the cause and meaning of the catastrophe.

When, at last they crossed the trampled garden and stood before the charred ruins of their master's bungalow, their greatest fears became convictions in the light of the evidence about them.

Remnants of human dead, half devoured by prowling hyenas and others of the carnivora which infested the region, lay rotting upon the ground, and among the corpses remained sufficient remnants of their clothing and ornaments to make clear to Basuli the frightful story of the disaster that had befallen his master's house.

"The Arabs," he said, as his men clustered about him.

The Waziri gazed about in mute rage for several minutes. Everywhere they encountered only further evidence of the ruthlessness of the cruel enemy that had come during the Great Bwana's absence and laid waste his property.

"What did they with 'Lady'?" asked one of the blacks.

They had always called Lady Greystoke thus.

"The women they would have taken with them," said Basuli. "Our women and his."

A giant black raised his spear above his head, and gave voice to a savage cry of rage and hate. The others followed his example. Basuli silenced them with a gesture.

"This is no time for useless noises of the mouth," he said. "The Great Bwana has taught us that it is acts by which things are done, not words. Let us save our breath—we shall need it all to follow up the Arabs and slay them. If 'Lady' and our women live the greater the need of haste, and warriors cannot travel fast upon empty lungs."

From the shelter of the reeds along the river, Werper and Tarzan watched the blacks. They saw them dig a trench with their knives and fingers. They saw them lay their yellow burdens in it and scoop the overturned earth back over the tops of the ingots.

Tarzan seemed little interested, after Werper had assured him that that which they buried was not good to eat; but Werper was intensely interested. He would have given much had he had his own followers with him, that he might take away the treasure as soon as the blacks left, for he was sure that they would leave this scene of desolation and death as soon as possible.

The treasure buried, the blacks removed themselves a short distance up wind from the fetid corpses, where they made camp, that they might rest before setting out in pursuit of the Arabs. It was already dusk. Werper and Tarzan sat devouring some pieces of meat they had brought from their last camp. The Belgian was occupied with his plans for the immediate future. He was positive that the Waziri would pursue Achmet Zek, for he knew enough of savage warfare, and of the characteristics of the Arabs and their degraded followers to guess that they had carried the Waziri women off into slavery. This alone would assure immediate pursuit by so warlike a people as the Waziri.

Werper felt that he should find the means and the opportunity to push on ahead, that he might warn Achmet Zek of the coming of Basuli, and also of the location of the buried treasure. What the Arab would now do with Lady Greystoke, in view of the mental affliction of her husband, Werper neither knew nor cared. It was enough that the golden treasure buried upon the site of the burned bungalow was infinitely more valuable than any ransom that would have occurred even to the avaricious mind of the Arab, and if Werper could persuade the raider to share even a portion of it with him he would be well satisfied.

But by far the most important consideration, to Werper, at least, was the incalculably valuable treasure in the little leathern pouch at Tarzan's side. If he could but obtain possession of this! He must! He would!

His eyes wandered to the object of his greed. They measured Tarzan's giant frame, and rested upon the rounded muscles of his arms. It was hopeless. What could he, Werper, hope to accomplish, other than his own death, by an attempt to wrest the gems from their savage owner?

Disconsolate, Werper threw himself upon his side. His head was pillowed on one arm, the other rested across his face in such a way that his eyes were hidden from the ape-man, though one of them was fastened upon him from beneath the shadow of the Belgian's forearm. For a time he lay thus, glowering at Tarzan, and originating schemes for plundering him of his treasure—schemes that were discarded as futile as rapidly as they were born.

Tarzan presently let his own eyes rest upon Werper. The Belgian saw that he was being watched, and lay very still. After a few moments he simulated the regular breathing of deep slumber.

Tarzan had been thinking. He had seen the Waziri bury their belongings. Werper had told him that they were hiding them lest some one find them and take them away. This seemed to Tarzan a splendid plan for safeguarding valuables. Since Werper had evinced a desire to possess his glittering pebbles, Tarzan, with the suspicions of a savage, had guarded the baubles, of whose worth he was entirely ignorant, as zealously as though they spelled life or death to him.

For a long time the ape-man sat watching his companion. At last, convinced that he slept, Tarzan withdrew his hunting knife and commenced to dig a hole in the ground before him. With the blade he loosened up the earth, and with his hands he scooped it out until he had excavated a little cavity a few inches in diameter, and five or six inches in depth. Into this he placed the pouch of jewels. Werper almost forgot to breathe after the fashion of a sleeper as he saw what the ape-man was doing—he scarce repressed an ejaculation of satisfaction.

Tarzan become suddenly rigid as his keen ears noted the cessation of the regular inspirations and expirations of his companion. His narrowed eyes bored straight down upon the Belgian. Werper felt that he was lost—he must risk all on his ability to carry on the deception. He sighed, threw both arms outward, and turned over on his back mumbling as though in the throes of a bad dream. A moment later he resumed the regular breathing.

Now he could not watch Tarzan, but he was sure that the man sat for a long time looking at him. Then, faintly, Werper heard the other's hands scraping dirt, and later patting it down. He knew then that the jewels were buried.

It was an hour before Werper moved again, then he rolled over facing Tarzan and opened his eyes. The ape-man slept. By reaching out his hand Werper could touch the spot where the pouch was buried.

For a long time he lay watching and listening. He moved about, making more noise than necessary, yet Tarzan did not awaken. He drew the sacrificial knife from his belt, and plunged it into the ground. Tarzan did not move. Cautiously the Belgian pushed the blade downward through the loose earth above the pouch. He felt the point touch the soft, tough fabric of the leather. Then he pried down upon the handle. Slowly the little mound of loose earth rose and parted. An instant later a corner of the pouch came into view. Werper pulled it from its hiding place, and tucked it in his shirt. Then he refilled the hole and pressed the dirt carefully down as it had been before.

Greed had prompted him to an act, the discovery of which by his companion could lead only to the most frightful consequences for Werper. Already he could almost feel those strong, white fangs burying themselves in his neck. He shuddered. Far out across the plain a leopard screamed, and in the dense reeds behind him some great beast moved on padded feet.

Werper feared these prowlers of the night; but infinitely more he feared the just wrath of the human beast sleeping at his side. With utmost caution the Belgian arose. Tarzan did not move. Werper took a few steps toward the plain and the distant forest to the northwest, then he paused and fingered the hilt of the long knife in his belt. He turned and looked down upon the sleeper.

"Why not?" he mused. "Then I should be safe."

He returned and bent above the ape-man. Clutched tightly in his hand was the sacrificial knife of the High Priestess of the Flaming God!

ACHMET ZEK SEES THE JEWELS

Mugambi, weak and suffering, had dragged his painful way along the trail of the retreating raiders. He could move but slowly, resting often; but savage hatred and an equally savage desire for vengeance kept him to his task. As the days passed his wounds healed and his strength returned, until at last his giant frame had regained all of its former mighty powers. Now he went more rapidly; but the mounted Arabs had covered a great distance while the wounded black had been painfully crawling after them.

They had reached their fortified camp, and there Achmet Zek awaited the return of his lieutenant, Albert Werper. During the long, rough journey, Jane Clayton had suffered more in anticipation of her impending fate than from the hardships of the road.

Achmet Zek had not deigned to acquaint her with his intentions regarding her future. She prayed that she had been captured in the hope of ransom, for if such should prove the case, no great harm would befall her at the hands of the Arabs; but there was the chance, the horrid chance, that another fate awaited her. She had heard of many women, among whom were white women, who had been sold by outlaws such as Achmet Zek into the slavery of black harems, or taken farther north into the almost equally hideous existence of some Turkish seraglio.

Jane Clayton was of sterner stuff than that which bends in spineless terror before danger. Until hope proved futile she would not give it up; nor did she entertain thoughts of self-destruction only as a final escape from dishonor. So long as Tarzan lived there was every reason to expect succor. No man nor beast who roamed the savage continent could boast the cunning and the powers of her lord and master. To her, he was little short of omnipotent in his native world—this world of savage beasts and savage men. Tarzan would come, and she would be rescued and avenged, of that she was certain. She counted the days that must elapse before he would return from Opar and discover what had transpired during his absence. After that it would be but a short time before he had surrounded the Arab stronghold and punished the motley crew of wrongdoers who inhabited it.

That he could find her she had no slightest doubt. No spoor, however faint, could elude the keen vigilance of his senses. To him, the trail of the raiders would be as plain as the printed page of an open book to her.

And while she hoped, there came through the dark jungle another. Terrified by night and by day, came Albert Werper. A dozen times he had escaped the claws and fangs of the giant carnivora only by what seemed a miracle to him. Armed with nothing more than the knife he had brought with him from Opar, he had made his way through as savage a country as yet exists upon the face of the globe.

By night he had slept in trees. By day he had stumbled fearfully on, often taking refuge among the branches when sight or sound of some great cat warned him from danger. But at last he had come within sight of the palisade behind which were his fierce companions.

At almost the same time Mugambi came out of the jungle before the walled village. As he stood in the shadow of a great tree, reconnoitering, he saw a man, ragged and disheveled, emerge from the jungle almost at his elbow. Instantly he recognized the newcomer as he who had been a guest of his master before the latter had departed for Opar.

The black was upon the point of hailing the Belgian when something stayed him. He saw the white man walking confidently across the clearing toward the village gate. No sane man thus approached a village in this part of Africa unless he was sure of a friendly welcome. Mugambi waited. His suspicions were aroused.

He heard Werper halloo; he saw the gates swing open, and he witnessed the surprised and friendly welcome that was accorded the erstwhile guest of Lord and Lady Greystoke. A light broke upon the understanding of Mugambi. This white man had been a traitor and a spy. It was to him they owed the raid during the absence of the Great Bwana. To his hate for the Arabs, Mugambi added a still greater hate for the white spy.

Within the village Werper passed hurriedly toward the silken tent of Achmet Zek. The Arab arose as his lieutenant entered. His face showed surprise as he viewed the tattered apparel of the Belgian.

"What has happened?" he asked.

Werper narrated all, save the little matter of the pouch of gems which were now tightly strapped about his waist, beneath his clothing. The Arab's eyes narrowed greedily as his henchman described the treasure that the Waziri had buried beside the ruins of the Greystoke bungalow.

"It will be a simple matter now to return and get it," said Achmet Zek. "First we will await the coming of the rash Waziri, and after we have slain them we may take our time to the treasure—none will disturb it where it lies, for we shall leave none alive who knows of its existence.

"And the woman?" asked Werper.

"I shall sell her in the north," replied the raider. "It is the only way, now. She should bring a good price."

The Belgian nodded. He was thinking rapidly. If he could persuade Achmet Zek to send him in command of the party which took Lady Greystoke north it would give him the opportunity he craved to make his escape from his chief. He would forego a share of the gold, if he could but get away unscathed with the jewels.

He knew Achmet Zek well enough by this time to know that no member of his band ever was voluntarily released from the service of Achmet Zek. Most of the few who deserted were recaptured. More than once had Werper listened to their agonized screams as they were tortured before being put to death. The Belgian had no wish to take the slightest chance of recapture.

"Who will go north with the woman," he asked, "while we are returning for the gold that the Waziri buried by the bungalow of the Englishman?"

Achmet Zek thought for a moment. The buried gold was of much greater value than the price the woman would bring. It was necessary to rid himself of her as quickly as possible and it was also well to obtain the gold with the least possible delay. Of all his followers, the Belgian was the most logical lieutenant to intrust with the command of one of the parties. An Arab, as familiar with the trails and tribes as Achmet Zek himself, might collect the woman's price and make good his escape into the far north. Werper, on the other hand, could scarce make his escape alone through a country hostile to Europeans while the men he would send with the Belgian could be carefully selected with a view to preventing Werper from persuading any considerable portion of his command to accompany him should he contemplate desertion of his chief.

At last the Arab spoke: "It is not necessary that we both return for the gold. You shall go north with the woman, carrying a letter to a friend of mine who is always in touch with the best markets for such merchandise, while I return for the gold. We can meet again here when our business is concluded."

Werper could scarce disguise the joy with which he received this welcome decision. And that he did entirely disguise it from the keen and suspicious eyes of Achmet Zek is open to question. However, the decision reached, the Arab and his lieutenant discussed the details of their forthcoming ventures for a short time further, when Werper made his excuses and returned to his own tent for the comforts and luxury of a long-desired bath and shave.

Having bathed, the Belgian tied a small hand mirror to a cord sewn to the rear wall of his tent, placed a rude chair beside an equally rude table that stood beside the glass, and proceeded to remove the rough stubble from his face.

In the catalog of masculine pleasures there is scarce one which imparts a feeling of greater comfort and refreshment than follows a clean shave, and now, with weariness temporarily banished, Albert Werper sprawled in his rickety chair to enjoy a final cigaret before retiring. His thumbs, tucked in his belt in lazy support of the weight of his arms, touched the belt which held the jewel pouch about his waist. He tingled with excitement as he let his mind dwell upon the value of the treasure, which, unknown to all save himself, lay hidden beneath his clothing.

What would Achmet Zek say, if he knew? Werper grinned. How the old rascal's eyes would pop could he but have a glimpse of those scintillating beauties! Werper had never yet had an opportunity to feast his eyes for any great length of time upon them. He had not even counted them—only roughly had he guessed at their value.

He unfastened the belt and drew the pouch from its hiding place. He was alone. The balance of the camp, save the sentries, had retired—none would enter the Belgian's tent. He fingered the pouch, feeling out the shapes and sizes of the precious, little nodules within. He hefted the bag, first in one palm, then in the other, and at last he wheeled his chair slowly around before the table, and in the rays of his small lamp let the glittering gems roll out upon the rough wood.

The refulgent rays transformed the interior of the soiled and squalid canvas to the splendor of a palace in the eyes of the dreaming man. He saw the gilded halls of pleasure that would open their portals to the possessor of the wealth which lay scattered upon this stained and dented table top. He dreamed of joys and luxuries and power which always had been beyond his grasp, and as he dreamed his gaze lifted from the table, as the gaze of a dreamer will, to a far distant goal above the mean horizon of terrestrial commonplaceness.

Unseeing, his eyes rested upon the shaving mirror which still hung upon the tent wall above the table; but his sight was focused far beyond. And then a reflection moved within the polished surface of the tiny glass, the man's eyes shot back out of space to the mirror's face, and in it he saw reflected the grim visage of Achmet Zek, framed in the flaps of the tent doorway behind him.

Werper stifled a gasp of dismay. With rare self-possession he let his gaze drop, without appearing to have halted upon the mirror until it rested again upon the gems. Without haste, he replaced them in the pouch, tucked the latter into his shirt, selected a cigaret from his case, lighted it and rose. Yawning, and stretching his arms above his head, he turned slowly toward the opposite end of the tent. The face of Achmet Zek had disappeared from the opening.

To say that Albert Werper was terrified would be putting it mildly. He realized that he not only had sacrificed his treasure; but his life as well. Achmet Zek would never permit the wealth that he had discovered to slip through his fingers, nor would he forgive the duplicity of a lieutenant who had gained possession of such a treasure without offering to share it with his chief.

Slowly the Belgian prepared for bed. If he were being watched, he could not know; but if so the watcher saw no indication of the nervous excitement which the European strove to conceal. When ready for his blankets, the man crossed to the little table and extinguished the light.

It was two hours later that the flaps at the front of the tent separated silently and gave entrance to a dark-robed figure, which passed noiselessly from the darkness without to the darkness within. Cautiously the prowler crossed the interior. In one hand was a long knife. He came at last to the pile of blankets spread upon several rugs close to one of the tent walls.

Lightly, his fingers sought and found the bulk beneath the blankets—the bulk that should be Albert Werper. They traced out the figure of a man, and then an arm shot upward, poised for an instant and descended. Again and again it rose and fell, and each time the long blade of the knife buried itself in the thing beneath the blankets. But there was an initial lifelessness in the silent bulk that gave the assassin momentary wonder. Feverishly he threw back the coverlets, and searched with nervous hands for the pouch of jewels which he expected to find concealed upon his victim's body.

An instant later he rose with a curse upon his lips. It was Achmet Zek, and he cursed because he had discovered beneath the blankets of his lieutenant only a pile of discarded clothing arranged in the form and semblance of a sleeping man—Albert Werper had fled.

Out into the village ran the chief, calling in angry tones to the sleepy Arabs, who tumbled from their tents in answer to his voice. But though they searched the village again and again they found no trace of the Belgian. Foaming with anger, Achmet Zek called his followers to horse, and though the night was pitchy black they set out to scour the adjoining forest for their quarry.

As they galloped from the open gates, Mugambi, hiding in a nearby bush, slipped, unseen, within the palisade. A score of blacks crowded about the entrance to watch the searchers depart, and as the last of them passed out of the village the blacks seized the portals and drew them to, and Mugambi lent a hand in the work as though the best of his life had been spent among the raiders.

In the darkness he passed, unchallenged, as one of their number, and as they returned from the gates to their respective tents and huts, Mugambi melted into the shadows and disappeared.

For an hour he crept about in the rear of the various huts and tents in an effort to locate that in which his master's mate was imprisoned. One there was which he was reasonably assured contained her, for it was the only hut before the door of which a sentry had been posted. Mugambi was crouching in the shadow of this structure, just around the corner from the unsuspecting guard, when another approached to relieve his comrade.

"The prisoner is safe within?" asked the newcomer.

"She is," replied the other, "for none has passed this doorway since I came."

The new sentry squatted beside the door, while he whom he had relieved made his way to his own hut. Mugambi slunk closer to the corner of the building. In one powerful hand he gripped a heavy knob-stick. No sign of elation disturbed his phlegmatic calm, yet inwardly he was aroused to joy by the proof he had just heard that "Lady" really was within.

The sentry's back was toward the corner of the hut which hid the giant black. The fellow did not see the huge form which silently loomed behind him. The knob-stick swung upward in a curve, and downward again. There was the sound of a dull thud, the crushing of heavy bone, and the sentry slumped into a silent, inanimate lump of clay.

A moment later Mugambi was searching the interior of the hut. At first slowly, calling, "Lady!" in a low whisper, and finally with almost frantic haste, until the truth presently dawned upon him—the hut was empty!

TARZAN BECOMES A BEAST AGAIN

For a moment Werper had stood above the sleeping ape-man, his murderous knife poised for the fatal thrust; but fear stayed his hand. What if the first blow should fail to drive the point to his victim's heart? Werper shuddered in contemplation of the disastrous consequences to himself. Awakened, and even with a few moments of life remaining, the giant could literally tear his assailant to pieces should he choose, and the Belgian had no doubt but that Tarzan would so choose.

Again came the soft sound of padded footsteps in the reeds—closer this time. Werper abandoned his design. Before him stretched the wide plain and escape. The jewels were in his possession. To remain longer was to risk death at the hands of Tarzan, or the jaws of the hunter creeping ever nearer. Turning, he slunk away through the night, toward the distant forest.

Tarzan slept on. Where were those uncanny, guardian powers that had formerly rendered him immune from the dangers of surprise? Could this dull sleeper be the alert, sensitive Tarzan of old?

Perhaps the blow upon his head had numbed his senses, temporarily—who may say? Closer crept the stealthy creature through the reeds. The rustling curtain of vegetation parted a few paces from where the sleeper lay, and the massive head of a lion appeared. The beast surveyed the ape-man intently for a moment, then he crouched, his hind feet drawn well beneath him, his tail lashing from side to side.

It was the beating of the beast's tail against the reeds which awakened Tarzan. Jungle folk do not awaken slowly—instantly, full consciousness and full command of their every faculty returns to them from the depth of profound slumber.

Even as Tarzan opened his eyes he was upon his feet, his spear grasped firmly in his hand and ready for attack. Again was he Tarzan of the Apes, sentient, vigilant, ready.

No two lions have identical characteristics, nor does the same lion invariably act similarly under like circumstances. Whether it was surprise, fear or caution which prompted the lion crouching ready to spring upon the man, is immaterial—the fact remains that he did not carry out his original design, he did not spring at the man at all, but, instead, wheeled and sprang back into the reeds as Tarzan arose and confronted him.

The ape-man shrugged his broad shoulders and looked about for his companion. Werper was nowhere to be seen. At first Tarzan suspected that the man had been seized and dragged off by another lion, but upon examination of the ground he soon discovered that the Belgian had gone away alone out into the plain.

For a moment he was puzzled; but presently came to the conclusion that Werper had been frightened by the approach of the lion, and had sneaked off in terror. A sneer touched Tarzan's lips as he pondered the man's act—the desertion of a comrade in time of danger, and without warning. Well, if that was the sort of creature Werper was, Tarzan wished nothing more of him. He had gone, and for all the ape-man cared, he might remain away—Tarzan would not search for him.

A hundred yards from where he stood grew a large tree, alone upon the edge of the reedy jungle. Tarzan made his way to it, clambered into it, and finding a comfortable crotch among its branches, reposed himself for uninterrupted sleep until morning.

And when morning came Tarzan slept on long after the sun had risen. His mind, reverted to the primitive, was untroubled by any more serious obligations than those of providing sustenance, and safeguarding his life. Therefore, there was nothing to awaken for until danger threatened, or the pangs of hunger assailed. It was the latter which eventually aroused him.

Opening his eyes, he stretched his giant thews, yawned, rose and gazed about him through the leafy foliage of his retreat. Across the wasted meadowlands and fields of John Clayton, Lord Greystoke, Tarzan of the Apes looked, as a stranger, upon the moving figures of Basuli and his braves as they prepared their morning meal and made ready to set out upon the expedition which Basuli had planned after discovering the havoc and disaster which had befallen the estate of his dead master.

The ape-man eyed the blacks with curiosity. In the back of his brain loitered a fleeting sense of familiarity with all that he saw, yet he could not connect any of the various forms of life, animate and inanimate, which had fallen within the range of his vision since he had emerged from the darkness of the pits of Opar, with any particular event of the past.

Hazily he recalled a grim and hideous form, hairy, ferocious. A vague tenderness dominated his savage sentiments as this phantom memory struggled for recognition. His mind had reverted to his childhood days—it was the figure of the giant she-ape, Kala, that he saw; but only half recognized. He saw, too, other grotesque, manlike forms. They were of Terkoz, Tublat, Kerchak, and a smaller, less ferocious figure, that was Neeta, the little playmate of his boyhood.

Slowly, very slowly, as these visions of the past animated his lethargic memory, he came to recognize them. They took definite shape and form, adjusting themselves nicely to the various incidents of his life with which they had been intimately connected. His boyhood among the apes spread itself in a slow panorama before him, and as it unfolded it induced within him a mighty longing for the companionship of the shaggy, low-browed brutes of his past.

He watched the blacks scatter their cook fire and depart; but though the face of each of them had but recently been as familiar to him as his own, they awakened within him no recollections whatsoever.

When they had gone, he descended from the tree and sought food. Out upon the plain grazed numerous herds of wild ruminants. Toward a sleek, fat bunch of zebra he wormed his stealthy way. No intricate process of reasoning caused him to circle widely until he was down wind from his prey—he acted instinctively. He took advantage of every form of cover as he crawled upon all fours and often flat upon his stomach toward them.

A plump young mare and a fat stallion grazed nearest to him as he neared the herd. Again it was instinct which selected the former for his meat. A low bush grew but a few yards from the unsuspecting two. The ape-man reached its shelter. He gathered his spear firmly in his grasp. Cautiously he drew his feet beneath him. In a single swift move he rose and cast his heavy weapon at the mare's side. Nor did he wait to note the effect of his assault, but leaped cat-like after his spear, his hunting knife in his hand.

For an instant the two animals stood motionless. The tearing of the cruel barb into her side brought a sudden scream of pain and fright from the mare, and then they both wheeled and broke for safety; but Tarzan of the Apes, for a distance of a few yards, could equal the speed of even these, and the first stride of the mare found her overhauled, with a savage beast at her shoulder. She turned, biting and kicking at her foe. Her mate hesitated for an instant, as though about to rush to her assistance; but a backward glance revealed to him the flying heels of the balance of the herd, and with a snort and a shake of his head he wheeled and dashed away.

Clinging with one hand to the short mane of his quarry, Tarzan struck again and again with his knife at the unprotected heart. The result had, from the first, been inevitable. The mare fought bravely, but hopelessly, and presently sank to the earth, her heart pierced. The ape-man placed a foot upon her carcass and raised his voice in the victory call of the Mangani. In the distance, Basuli halted as the faint notes of the hideous scream broke upon his ears.

"The great apes," he said to his companion. "It has been long since I have heard them in the country of the Waziri. What could have brought them back?"

Tarzan grasped his kill and dragged it to the partial seclusion of the bush which had hidden his own near approach, and there he squatted upon it, cut a huge hunk of flesh from the loin and proceeded to satisfy his hunger with the warm and dripping meat.

Attracted by the shrill screams of the mare, a pair of hyenas slunk presently into view. They trotted to a point a few yards from the gorging ape-man, and halted. Tarzan looked up, bared his fighting fangs and growled. The hyenas returned the compliment, and withdrew a couple of paces. They made no move to attack; but continued to sit at a respectful distance until Tarzan had concluded his meal. After the ape-man had cut a few strips from the carcass to carry with him, he walked slowly off in the direction of the river to quench his thirst. His way lay directly toward the hyenas, nor did he alter his course because of them.

With all the lordly majesty of Numa, the lion, he strode straight toward the growling beasts. For a moment they held their ground, bristling and defiant; but only for a moment, and then slunk away to one side while the indifferent ape-man passed them on his lordly way. A moment later they were tearing at the remains of the zebra.

Back to the reeds went Tarzan, and through them toward the river. A herd of buffalo, startled by his approach, rose ready to charge or to fly. A great bull pawed the ground and bellowed as his bloodshot eyes discovered the intruder; but the ape-man passed across their front as though ignorant of their existence. The bull's bellowing lessened to a low rumbling, he turned and scraped a horde of flies from his side with his muzzle, cast a final glance at the ape-man and resumed his feeding. His numerous family either followed his example or stood gazing after Tarzan in mild-eyed curiosity, until the opposite reeds swallowed him from view.

At the river, Tarzan drank his fill and bathed. During the heat of the day he lay up under the shade of a tree near the ruins of his burned barns. His eyes wandered out across the plain toward the forest, and a longing for the pleasures of its mysterious depths possessed his thoughts for a considerable time. With the next sun he would cross the open and enter the forest! There was no hurry—there lay before him an endless vista of tomorrows with naught to fill them but the satisfying of the appetites and caprices of the moment.

TARZAN SUPER PACK

The ape-man's mind was untroubled by regret for the past, or aspiration for the future. He could lie at full length along a swaying branch, stretching his giant limbs, and luxuriating in the blessed peace of utter thoughtlessness, without an apprehension or a worry to sap his nervous energy and rob him of his peace of mind. Recalling only dimly any other existence, the ape-man was happy. Lord Greystoke had ceased to exist.

For several hours Tarzan lolled upon his swaying, leafy couch until once again hunger and thirst suggested an excursion. Stretching lazily he dropped to the ground and moved slowly toward the river. The game trail down which he walked had become by ages of use a deep, narrow trench, its walls topped on either side by impenetrable thicket and dense-growing trees closely interwoven with thick-stemmed creepers and lesser vines inextricably matted into two solid ramparts of vegetation. Tarzan had almost reached the point where the trail debouched upon the open river bottom when he saw a family of lions approaching along the path from the direction of the river. The ape-man counted seven—a male and two lionesses, full grown, and four young lions as large and quite as formidable as their parents. Tarzan halted, growling, and the lions paused, the great male in the lead baring his fangs and rumbling forth a warning roar. In his hand the ape-man held his heavy spear; but he had no intention of pitting his puny weapon against seven lions; yet he stood there growling and roaring and the lions did likewise. It was purely an exhibition of jungle bluff. Each was trying to frighten off the other. Neither wished to turn back and give way, nor did either at first desire to precipitate an encounter. The lions were fed sufficiently so as not to be goaded by pangs of hunger and as for Tarzan he seldom ate the meat of the carnivores; but a point of ethics was at stake and neither side wished to back down. So they stood there facing one another, making all sorts of hideous noises the while they hurled jungle invective back and forth. How long this bloodless duel would have persisted it is difficult to say, though eventually Tarzan would have been forced to yield to superior numbers.

There came, however, an interruption which put an end to the deadlock and it came from Tarzan's rear. He and the lions had been making so much noise that neither could hear anything above their concerted bedlam, and so it was that Tarzan did not hear the great bulk bearing down upon him from behind until an instant before it was upon him, and then he turned to see Buto, the rhinoceros, his little, pig eyes blazing, charging madly toward him and already so close that escape seemed impossible; yet so perfectly were mind and muscles coordinated in this unspoiled, primitive man that almost simultaneously with the sense perception of the threatened danger he wheeled and hurled his spear at Buto's chest. It was a heavy spear shod with iron, and behind it were the giant muscles of the ape-man, while coming to meet it was the enormous weight of Buto and the momentum of his rapid rush. All that happened in the instant that Tarzan turned to meet the charge of the irascible rhinoceros might take long to tell, and yet would have taxed the swiftest lens to record. As his spear left his hand the ape-man was looking down upon the mighty horn lowered to toss him, so close was Buto to him. The spear entered the rhinoceros' neck at its junction with the left shoulder and passed almost entirely through the beast's body, and at the instant that he launched it, Tarzan leaped straight into the air alighting upon Buto's back but escaping the mighty horn.

Then Buto espied the lions and bore madly down upon them while Tarzan of the Apes leaped nimbly into the tangled creepers at one side of the trail. The first lion met Buto's charge and was tossed high over the back of the maddened brute, torn and dying, and then the six remaining lions were upon the rhinoceros, rending and tearing the while they were being gored or trampled. From the safety of his perch Tarzan watched the royal battle with the keenest interest, for the more intelligent of the jungle folk are interested in such encounters. They are to them what the racetrack and the prize ring, the theater and the movies are to us. They see them often; but always they enjoy them for no two are precisely alike.

For a time it seemed to Tarzan that Buto, the rhinoceros, would prove victor in the gory battle. Already had he accounted for four of the seven lions and badly wounded the three remaining when in a momentary lull in the encounter he sank limply to his knees and rolled over upon his side. Tarzan's spear had done its work. It was the man-made weapon which killed the great beast that might easily have survived the assault

494

EDGAR RICE BURROUGHS

of seven mighty lions, for Tarzan's spear had pierced the great lungs, and Buto, with victory almost in sight, succumbed to internal hemorrhage.

Then Tarzan came down from his sanctuary and as the wounded lions, growling, dragged themselves away, the ape-man cut his spear from the body of Buto, hacked off a steak and vanished into the jungle. The episode was over. It had been all in the day's work—something which you and I might talk about for a lifetime Tarzan dismissed from his mind the moment that the scene passed from his sight.

LA SEEKS VENGEANCE

Swinging back through the jungle in a wide circle the ape-man came to the river at another point, drank and took to the trees again and while he hunted, all oblivious of his past and careless of his future, there came through the dark jungles and the open, parklike places and across the wide meadows, where grazed the countless herbivora of the mysterious continent, a weird and terrible caravan in search of him. There were fifty frightful men with hairy bodies and gnarled and crooked legs. They were armed with knives and great bludgeons and at their head marched an almost naked woman, beautiful beyond compare. It was La of Opar, High Priestess of the Flaming God, and fifty of her horrid priests searching for the purloiner of the sacred sacrificial knife.

Never before had La passed beyond the crumbling outer walls of Opar; but never before had need been so insistent. The sacred knife was gone! Handed down through countless ages it had come to her as a heritage and an insignia of her religious office and regal authority from some long-dead progenitor of lost and forgotten Atlantis. The loss of the crown jewels or the Great Seal of England could have brought no greater consternation to a British king than did the pilfering of the sacred knife bring to La, the Oparian, Queen and High Priestess of the degraded remnants of the oldest civilization upon earth. When Atlantis, with all her mighty cities and her cultivated fields and her great commerce and culture and riches sank into the sea long ages since, she took with her all but a handful of her colonists working the vast gold mines of Central Africa. From these and their degraded slaves and a later intermixture of the blood of the anthropoids sprung the gnarled men of Opar; but by some queer freak of fate, aided by natural selection, the old Atlantean strain had remained pure and undegraded in the females descended from a single princess of the royal house of Atlantis who had been in Opar at the time of the great catastrophe. Such was La.

Burning with white-hot anger was the High Priestess, her heart a seething, molten mass of hatred for Tarzan of the Apes. The zeal of the religious fanatic whose altar has been desecrated was triply enhanced by the rage of a woman scorned. Twice had she thrown her heart at the feet of the godlike ape-man and twice had she been repulsed. La knew that she was beautiful—and she was beautiful, not by the standards of prehistoric Atlantis alone, but by those of modern times was La physically a creature of perfection. Before Tarzan came that first time to Opar, La had never seen a human male other than the grotesque and knotted men of her clan. With one of these she must mate sooner or later that the direct line of high priestesses might not be broken, unless Fate should bring other men to Opar. Before Tarzan came upon his first visit, La had had no thought that such men as he existed, for she knew only her hideous little priests and the bulls of the tribe of great anthropoids that had dwelt from time immemorial in and about Opar, until they had come to be looked upon almost as equals by the Oparians. Among the legends of Opar were tales of godlike men of the olden time and of black men who had come more recently; but these latter had been enemies who killed and robbed. And, too, these legends always held forth the hope that some day that nameless continent from which their race had sprung, would rise once more out of the sea and with slaves at the long sweeps would send her carven, gold-picked galleys forth to succor the long-exiled colonists.

The coming of Tarzan had aroused within La's breast the wild hope that at last the fulfillment of this ancient prophecy was at hand; but more strongly still had it aroused the hot fires of love in a heart that never otherwise would have known the meaning of that all-consuming passion, for such a wondrous creature as La could never have felt love for any of the repulsive priests of Opar. Custom, duty and religious zeal might have commanded the union; but there could have been no love on La's part. She had grown to young womanhood a cold and heartless creature, daughter of a thousand other cold, heartless, beautiful women who had never known love. And so when love came to her it liberated all the pent passions of a thousand generations, transforming La into a pulsing, throbbing volcano of desire, and with desire thwarted this great force of love and gentleness and sacrifice was transmuted by its own fires into one of hatred and revenge.

It was in a state of mind superinduced by these conditions that La led forth her jabbering company to retrieve the sacred emblem of her high office and wreak vengeance upon the author of her wrongs. To Werper she gave little thought. The fact that the knife had been in his hand when it departed from Opar brought down no thoughts of vengeance upon his head. Of course, he should be slain when captured; but his death would give La no pleasure—she looked for that in the contemplated death agonies of Tarzan. He should be tortured. His should be a slow and frightful death. His punishment should be adequate to the immensity of his crime. He had wrested the sacred knife from La; he had lain sacreligious hands upon the High Priestess of the Flaming God; he had desecrated the altar and the temple. For these things he should die; but he had scorned the love of La, the woman, and for this he should die horribly with great anguish.

The march of La and her priests was not without its adventures. Unused were these to the ways of the jungle, since seldom did any venture forth from behind Opar's crumbling walls, yet their very numbers protected them and so they came without fatalities far along the trail of Tarzan and Werper. Three great apes accompanied them and to these was delegated the business of tracking the quarry, a feat beyond the senses of the Oparians. La commanded. She arranged the order of march, she selected the camps, she set the hour for halting and the hour for resuming and though she was inexperienced in such matters, her native intelligence was so far above that of the men or the apes that she did better than they could have done. She was a hard taskmaster, too, for she looked down with loathing and contempt upon the misshapen creatures amongst which cruel Fate had thrown her and to some extent vented upon them her dissatisfaction and her thwarted love. She made them build her a strong protection and shelter each night and keep a great fire burning before it from dusk to dawn. When she tired of walking they were forced to carry her upon an improvised litter, nor did one dare to question her authority or her right to such services. In fact they did not question either. To them she was a goddess and each loved her and each hoped that he would be chosen as her mate, so they slaved for her and bore the stinging lash of her displeasure and the habitually haughty disdain of her manner without a murmur.

For many days they marched, the apes following the trail easily and going a little distance ahead of the body of the caravan that they might warn the others of impending danger. It was during a noonday halt while all were lying resting after a tiresome march that one of the apes rose suddenly and sniffed the breeze. In a low guttural he cautioned the others to silence and a moment later was swinging quietly up wind into the jungle. La and the priests gathered silently together, the hideous little men fingering their knives and bludgeons, and awaited the return of the shaggy anthropoid.

Nor had they long to wait before they saw him emerge from a leafy thicket and approach them. Straight to La he came and in the language of the great apes which was also the language of decadent Opar he addressed her.

"The great Tarmangani lies asleep there," he said, pointing in the direction from which he had just come. "Come and we can kill him."

"Do not kill him," commanded La in cold tones. "Bring the great Tarmangani to me alive and unhurt. The vengeance is La's. Go; but make no sound!" and she waved her hands to include all her followers.

Cautiously the weird party crept through the jungle in the wake of the great ape until at last he halted them with a raised hand and pointed upward and a little ahead. There they saw the giant form of the ape-man stretched along a low bough and even in sleep one hand grasped a stout limb and one strong, brown leg reached out and overlapped another. At ease lay Tarzan of the Apes, sleeping heavily upon a full stomach and dreaming of Numa, the lion, and Horta, the boar, and other creatures of the jungle. No intimation of danger assailed the dormant faculties of the ape-man—he saw no crouching hairy figures upon the ground beneath him nor the three apes that swung quietly into the tree beside him.

The first intimation of danger that came to Tarzan was the impact of three bodies as the three apes leaped upon him and hurled him to the ground, where he alighted half stunned beneath their combined weight and was immediately set upon by the fifty hairy men or as many of them as could swarm upon his person. Instantly the ape-man became the center of a whirling, striking, biting maelstrom of horror. He fought nobly but the odds against him were too great. Slowly they overcame him though there was scarce one of them that did not feel the weight of his mighty fist or the rending of his fangs.

CONDEMNED TO TORTURE AND DEATH

La had followed her company and when she saw them clawing and biting at Tarzan, she raised her voice and cautioned them not to kill him. She saw that he was weakening and that soon the greater numbers would prevail over him, nor had she long to wait before the mighty jungle creature lay helpless and bound at her feet.

"Bring him to the place at which we stopped," she commanded and they carried Tarzan back to the little clearing and threw him down beneath a tree.

"Build me a shelter!" ordered La. "We shall stop here tonight and tomorrow in the face of the Flaming God, La will offer up the heart of this defiler of the temple. Where is the sacred knife? Who took it from him?"

But no one had seen it and each was positive in his assurance that the sacrificial weapon had not been upon Tarzan's person when they captured him. The ape-man looked upon the menacing creatures which surrounded him and snarled his defiance. He looked upon La and smiled. In the face of death he was unafraid.

"Where is the knife?" La asked him.

"I do not know," replied Tarzan. "The man took it with him when he slipped away during the night. Since you are so desirous for its return I would look for him and get it back for you, did you not hold me prisoner; but now that I am to die I cannot get it back. Of what good was your knife, anyway? You can make another. Did you follow us all this way for nothing more than a knife? Let me go and find him and I will bring it back to you."

La laughed a bitter laugh, for in her heart she knew that Tarzan's sin was greater than the purloining of the sacrificial knife of Opar; yet as she looked at him lying bound and helpless before her, tears rose to her eyes so that she had to turn away to hide them; but she remained inflexible in her determination to make him pay in frightful suffering and in eventual death for daring to spurn the love of La.

When the shelter was completed La had Tarzan transferred to it. "All night I shall torture him," she muttered to her priests, "and at the first streak of dawn you may prepare the flaming altar upon which his heart shall be offered up to the Flaming God. Gather wood well filled with pitch, lay it in the form and size of the altar at Opar in the center of the clearing that the Flaming God may look down upon our handiwork and be pleased."

During the balance of the day the priests of Opar were busy erecting an altar in the center of the clearing, and while they worked they chanted weird hymns in the ancient tongue of that lost continent that lies at the bottom of the Atlantic. They knew not the meanings of the words they mouthed; they but repeated the ritual that had been handed down from preceptor to neophyte since that long-gone day when the ancestors of the Piltdown man still swung by their tails in the humid jungles that are England now.

And in the shelter of the hut, La paced to and fro beside the stoic ape-man. Resigned to his fate was Tarzan. No hope of succor gleamed through the dead black of the death sentence hanging over him. He knew that his giant muscles could not part the many strands that bound his wrists and ankles, for he had strained often, but ineffectually for release. He had no hope of outside help and only enemies surrounded him within the camp, and yet he smiled at La as she paced nervously back and forth the length of the shelter.

And La? She fingered her knife and looked down upon her captive. She glared and muttered but she did not strike. "Tonight!" she thought. "Tonight, when it is dark I will torture him." She looked upon his perfect, godlike figure and upon his handsome, smiling face and then she steeled her heart again by thoughts of her love spurned; by religious thoughts that damned the infidel who had desecrated the holy of holies; who had taken from the blood-stained altar of Opar the offering to the Flaming God—and not once but thrice. Three times had Tarzan cheated the god of her fathers. At the thought La paused and knelt at his side. In her hand was a sharp knife. She placed its point against the ape-man's side and pressed upon the hilt; but Tarzan only smiled and shrugged his shoulders.

How beautiful he was! La bent low over him, looking into his eyes. How perfect was his figure. She compared it with those of the knurled and knotted men from whom she must choose a mate, and La shuddered at the thought. Dusk came and after dusk came night. A great fire blazed within the little thorn boma about the camp. The flames played upon the new altar erected in the center of the clearing, arousing in the mind of the High Priestess of the Flaming God a picture of the event of the coming dawn. She saw this giant and perfect form writhing amid the flames of the burning pyre. She saw those smiling lips, burned and blackened, falling away from the strong, white teeth. She saw the shock of black hair tousled upon Tarzan's well-shaped head disappear in a spurt of flame. She saw these and many other frightful pictures as she stood with closed eyes and clenched fists above the object of her hate—ah! was it hate that La of Opar felt?

The darkness of the jungle night had settled down upon the camp, relieved only by the fitful flarings of the fire that was kept up to warn off the man-eaters. Tarzan lay quietly in his bonds. He suffered from thirst and from the cutting of the tight strands about his wrists and ankles; but he made no complaint. A jungle beast was Tarzan with the stoicism of the beast and the intelligence of man. He knew that his doom was sealed—that no supplications would avail to temper the severity of his end and so he wasted no breath in pleadings; but waited patiently in the firm conviction that his sufferings could not endure forever.

In the darkness La stooped above him. In her hand was a sharp knife and in her mind the determination to initiate his torture without further delay. The knife was pressed against his side and La's face was close to his when a sudden burst of flame from new branches thrown upon the fire without, lighted up the interior of the shelter. Close beneath her lips La saw the perfect features of the forest god and into her woman's heart welled all the great love she had felt for Tarzan since first she had seen him, and all the accumulated passion of the years that she had dreamed of him.

Dagger in hand, La, the High Priestess, towered above the helpless creature that had dared to violate the sanctuary of her deity. There should be no torture—there should be instant death. No longer should the defiler of the temple pollute the sight of the lord god almighty. A single stroke of the heavy blade and then the corpse to the flaming pyre without. The knife arm stiffened ready for the downward plunge, and then La, the woman, collapsed weakly upon the body of the man she loved.

She ran her hands in mute caress over his naked flesh; she covered his forehead, his eyes, his lips with hot kisses; she covered him with her body as though to protect him from the hideous fate she had ordained for him, and in trembling, piteous tones she begged him for his love. For hours the frenzy of her passion possessed the burning hand-maiden of the Flaming God, until at last sleep overpowered her and she lapsed into unconsciousness beside the man she had sworn to torture and to slay. And Tarzan, untroubled by thoughts of the future, slept peacefully in La's embrace.

At the first hint of dawn the chanting of the priests of Opar brought Tarzan to wakefulness. Initiated in low and subdued tones, the sound soon rose in volume to the open diapason of barbaric blood lust. La stirred. Her perfect arm pressed Tarzan closer to her—a smile parted her lips and then she awoke, and slowly the smile faded and her eyes went wide in horror as the significance of the death chant impinged upon her understanding.

"Love me, Tarzan!" she cried. "Love me, and you shall be saved."

Tarzan's bonds hurt him. He was suffering the tortures of long-restricted circulation. With an angry growl he rolled over with his back toward La. That was her answer! The High Priestess leaped to her feet. A hot flush of shame mantled her cheek and then she went dead white and stepped to the shelter's entrance.

"Come, Priests of the Flaming God!" she cried, "and make ready the sacrifice."

The warped things advanced and entered the shelter. They laid hands upon Tarzan and bore him forth, and as they chanted they kept time with their crooked bodies, swaying to and fro to the rhythm of their song of blood and death. Behind them came La, swaying too; but not in unison with the chanted cadence. White and drawn was the face of the High Priestess—white and drawn with unrequited love and hideous terror of the moments to come. Yet stern in her resolve was La. The infidel should die! The scorner of her love should pay the price upon the fiery altar. She saw them lay the perfect body there upon the rough branches. She saw the High Priest, he to whom custom would unite her—bent, crooked, gnarled, stunted, hideous—advance with the flaming torch and stand awaiting her command to apply it to the faggots surrounding the sacrificial pyre. His hairy, bestial face was distorted in a yellow-fanged grin of anticipatory enjoyment. His hands were cupped to receive the life blood of the victim—the red nectar that at Opar would have filled the golden sacrificial goblets.

La approached with upraised knife, her face turned toward the rising sun and upon her lips a prayer to the burning deity of her people. The High Priest looked questioningly toward her—the brand was burning close to his hand and the faggots lay temptingly near. Tarzan closed his eyes and awaited the end. He knew that he would suffer, for he recalled the faint memories of past burns. He knew that he would suffer and die; but he did not flinch. Death is no great adventure to the jungle bred who walk hand-in-hand with the grim specter by day and lie down at his side by night through all the years of their lives. It is doubtful that the ape-man even speculated upon what came after death. As a matter of fact as his end approached, his mind was occupied by thoughts of the pretty pebbles he had lost, yet his every faculty still was open to what passed around him.

He felt La lean over him and he opened his eyes. He saw her white, drawn face and he saw tears blinding her eyes. "Tarzan, my Tarzan!" she moaned, "tell me that you love me—that you will return to Opar with me—and you shall live. Even in the face of the anger of my people I will save you. This last chance I give you. What is your answer?"

At the last moment the woman in La had triumphed over the High Priestess of a cruel cult. She saw upon the altar the only creature that ever had aroused the fires of love within her virgin breast; she saw the beast-faced fanatic who would one day be her mate, unless she found another less repulsive, standing with the burning torch ready to ignite the pyre; yet with all her mad passion for the ape-man she would give the word to apply the flame if Tarzan's final answer was unsatisfactory. With heaving bosom she leaned close above him. "Yes or no?" she whispered.

Through the jungle, out of the distance, came faintly a sound that brought a sudden light of hope to Tarzan's eyes. He raised his voice in a weird scream that sent La back from him a step or two. The impatient priest grumbled and switched the torch from one hand to the other at the same time holding it closer to the tinder at the base of the pyre.

"Your answer!" insisted La. "What is your answer to the love of La of Opar?"

Closer came the sound that had attracted Tarzan's attention and now the others heard it—the shrill trumpeting of an elephant. As La looked wide-eyed into Tarzan's face, there to read her fate for happiness or heartbreak, she saw an expression of concern shadow his features. Now, for the first time, she guessed the meaning of Tarzan's shrill scream—he had summoned Tantor, the elephant, to his rescue! La's brows contracted in a savage scowl. "You refuse La!" she cried. "Then die! The torch!" she commanded, turning toward the priest.

Tarzan looked up into her face. "Tantor is coming," he said. "I thought that he would rescue me; but I know now from his voice that he will slay me and you and all that fall in his path, searching out with the cunning of Sheeta, the panther, those who would hide from him, for Tantor is mad with the madness of love."

La knew only too well the insane ferocity of a bull elephant in MUST. She knew that Tarzan had not exaggerated. She knew that the devil in the cunning, cruel brain of the great beast might send it hither and thither hunting through the forest for those who escaped its first charge, or the beast might pass on without returning—no one might guess which.

"I cannot love you, La," said Tarzan in a low voice. "I do not know why, for you are very beautiful. I could not go back and live in Opar—I who have the whole broad jungle for my range. No, I cannot love you but I cannot see you die beneath the goring tusks of mad Tantor. Cut my bonds before it is too late. Already he is almost upon us. Cut them and I may yet save you."

A little spiral of curling smoke rose from one corner of the pyre—the flames licked upward, crackling. La stood there like a beautiful statue of despair gazing at Tarzan and at the spreading flames. In a moment they would reach out and grasp him. From the tangled forest came the sound of cracking limbs and crashing trunks—Tantor was coming down upon them, a huge Juggernaut of the jungle. The priests were becoming uneasy. They cast apprehensive glances in the direction of the approaching elephant and then back at La.

"Fly!" she commanded them and then she stooped and cut the bonds securing her prisoner's feet and hands. In an instant Tarzan was upon the ground. The priests screamed out their rage and disappointment. He with the torch took a menacing step toward La and the ape-man. "Traitor!" He shrieked at the woman. "For this you too shall die!" Raising his bludgeon he rushed upon the High Priestess; but Tarzan was there before her. Leaping in to close quarters the ape-man seized the upraised weapon and wrenched it from the hands of the frenzied fanatic and then the priest closed upon him with tooth and nail. Seizing the stocky, stunted body in his mighty hands Tarzan raised the creature high above his head, hurling him at his fellows who were now gathered ready to bear down upon their erstwhile captive. La stood proudly with ready knife behind the ape-man. No faint sign of fear marked her perfect brow—only haughty disdain for her priests and admiration for the man she loved so hopelessly filled her thoughts.

Suddenly upon this scene burst the mad bull—a huge tusker, his little eyes inflamed with insane rage. The priests stood for an instant paralyzed with terror; but Tarzan turned and gathering La in his arms raced for the nearest tree. Tantor bore down upon him trumpeting shrilly. La clung with both white arms about the ape-man's neck. She felt him leap into the air and marveled at his strength and his ability as, burdened with her weight, he swung nimbly into the lower branches of a large tree and quickly bore her upward beyond reach of the sinuous trunk of the pachyderm.

Momentarily baffled here, the huge elephant wheeled and bore down upon the hapless priests who had now scattered, terror-stricken, in every direction. The nearest he gored and threw high among the branches of a tree. One he seized in the coils of his trunk and broke upon a huge bole, dropping the mangled pulp to charge, trumpeting, after another. Two he trampled beneath his huge feet and by then the others had disappeared into the jungle. Now Tantor turned his attention once more to Tarzan for one of the symptoms of madness is a revulsion of affection—objects of sane love become the objects of insane hatred. Peculiar in the unwritten annals of the jungle was the proverbial love that had existed between the ape-man and the tribe of Tantor. No elephant in all the jungle would harm the Tarmangani—the white-ape; but with the madness of *must* upon him the great bull sought to destroy his long-time play-fellow.

Back to the tree where La and Tarzan perched came Tantor, the elephant. He reared up with his forefeet against the bole and reached high toward them with his long trunk; but Tarzan had foreseen this and clambered beyond the bull's longest reach. Failure but tended to further enrage the mad creature. He bellowed and trumpeted and screamed until the earth shook to the mighty volume of his noise. He put his head against the tree and pushed and the tree bent before his mighty strength; yet still it held.

The actions of Tarzan were peculiar in the extreme. Had Numa, or Sabor, or Sheeta, or any other beast of the jungle been seeking to destroy him, the ape-man would have danced about hurling missiles and invectives at his assailant. He would have insulted and taunted them, reviling in the jungle Billingsgate he knew so well; but now he sat silent out of Tantor's reach and upon his handsome face was an expression of deep sorrow and pity, for of all the jungle folk Tarzan loved Tantor the best. Could he have slain him he would not have thought of doing so. His one idea was to escape, for he knew that with the passing of the *must* Tantor would be sane again and that once more he might stretch at full length upon that mighty back and make foolish speech into those great, flapping ears.

Finding that the tree would not fall to his pushing, Tantor was but enraged the more. He looked up at the two perched high above him, his red-rimmed eyes blazing with insane hatred, and then he wound his trunk about the bole of the tree, spread his giant feet wide apart and tugged to uproot the jungle giant. A huge creature was Tantor, an enormous bull in the full prime of all his stupendous strength. Mightily he strove until presently, to Tarzan's consternation, the great tree gave slowly at the roots. The ground rose in little mounds and ridges about the base of the bole, the tree tilted—in another moment it would be uprooted and fall.

The ape-man whirled La to his back and just as the tree inclined slowly in its first movement out of the perpendicular, before the sudden rush of its final collapse, he swung to the branches of a lesser neighbor. It was a long and perilous leap. La closed her eyes and shuddered; but when she opened them again she found herself safe and Tarzan whirling onward through the forest. Behind them the uprooted tree crashed heavily to the ground, carrying with it the lesser trees in its path and then Tantor, realizing that his prey had escaped him, set up once more his hideous trumpeting and followed at a rapid charge upon their trail.

A PRIESTESS BUT YET A WOMAN

At first La closed her eyes and clung to Tarzan in terror, though she made no outcry; but presently she gained sufficient courage to look about her, to look down at the ground beneath and even to keep her eyes open during the wide, perilous swings from tree to tree, and then there came over her a sense of safety because of her confidence in the perfect physical creature in whose strength and nerve and agility her fate lay. Once she raised her eyes to the burning sun and murmured a prayer of thanks to her pagan god that she had not been permitted to destroy this godlike man, and her long lashes were wet with tears. A strange anomaly was La of Opar—a creature of circumstance torn by conflicting emotions. Now the cruel and bloodthirsty creature of a heartless god and again a melting woman filled with compassion and tenderness. Sometimes the incarnation of jealousy and revenge and sometimes a sobbing maiden, generous and forgiving; at once a virgin and a wanton; but always—a woman. Such was La.

She pressed her cheek close to Tarzan's shoulder. Slowly she turned her head until her hot lips were pressed against his flesh. She loved him and would gladly have died for him; yet within an hour she had been ready to plunge a knife into his heart and might again within the coming hour.

A hapless priest seeking shelter in the jungle chanced to show himself to enraged Tantor. The great beast turned to one side, bore down upon the crooked, little man, snuffed him out and then, diverted from his course, blundered away toward the south. In a few minutes even the noise of his trumpeting was lost in the distance.

Tarzan dropped to the ground and La slipped to her feet from his back. "Call your people together," said Tarzan.

"They will kill me," replied La.

"They will not kill you," contradicted the ape-man. "No one will kill you while Tarzan of the Apes is here. Call them and we will talk with them."

La raised her voice in a weird, flutelike call that carried far into the jungle on every side. From near and far came answering shouts in the barking tones of the Oparian priests: "We come! We come!" Again and again, La repeated her summons until singly and in pairs the greater portion of her following approached and halted a short distance away from the High Priestess and her savior. They came with scowling brows and threatening mien. When all had come Tarzan addressed them.

"Your La is safe," said the ape-man. "Had she slain me she would now herself be dead and many more of you; but she spared me that I might save her. Go your way with her back to Opar, and Tarzan will go his way into the jungle. Let there be peace always between Tarzan and La. What is your answer?"

The priests grumbled and shook their heads. They spoke together and La and Tarzan could see that they were not favorably inclined toward the proposition. They did not wish to take La back and they did wish to complete the sacrifice of Tarzan to the Flaming God. At last the ape-man became impatient.

"You will obey the commands of your queen," he said, "and go back to Opar with her or Tarzan of the Apes will call together the other creatures of the jungle and slay you all. La saved me that I might save you and her. I have served you better alive than I could have dead. If you are not all fools you will let me go my way in peace and you will return to Opar with La. I know not where the sacred knife is; but you can fashion another. Had I not taken it from La you would have slain me and now your god must be glad that I took it since I have saved his priestess from love-mad Tantor. Will you go back to Opar with La, promising that no harm shall befall her?"

The priests gathered together in a little knot arguing and discussing. They pounded upon their breasts with their fists; they raised their hands and eyes to their fiery god; they growled and barked among themselves until it became evident to Tarzan that one of their number was preventing the acceptance of his proposal. This was the High Priest whose heart was filled with jealous rage because La openly acknowledged her love for the stranger, when by the worldly customs of their cult she should have belonged to him. Seemingly there was to be no solution of the problem until another priest stepped forth and, raising his hand, addressed La.

"Cadj, the High Priest," he announced, "would sacrifice you both to the Flaming God; but all of us except Cadj would gladly return to Opar with our queen."

"You are many against one," spoke up Tarzan. "Why should you not have your will? Go your way with La to Opar and if Cadj interferes slay him."

The priests of Opar welcomed this suggestion with loud cries of approval. To them it appeared nothing short of divine inspiration. The influence of ages of unquestioning obedience to high priests had made it seem impossible to them to question his authority; but when they realized that they could force him to their will they were as happy as children with new toys.

They rushed forward and seized Cadj. They talked in loud menacing tones into his ear. They threatened him with bludgeon and knife until at last he acquiesced in their demands, though sullenly, and then Tarzan stepped close before Cadj.

"Priest," he said, "La goes back to her temple under the protection of her priests and the threat of Tarzan of the Apes that whoever harms her shall die. Tarzan will go again to Opar before the next rains and if harm has befallen La, woe betide Cadj, the High Priest."

Sullenly Cadj promised not to harm his queen.

"Protect her," cried Tarzan to the other Oparians. "Protect her so that when Tarzan comes again he will find La there to greet him."

"La will be there to greet thee," exclaimed the High Priestess, "and La will wait, longing, always longing, until you come again. Oh, tell me that you will come!"

"Who knows?" asked the ape-man as he swung quickly into the trees and raced off toward the east.

For a moment La stood looking after him, then her head drooped, a sigh escaped her lips and like an old woman she took up the march toward distant Opar.

EDGAR RICE BURROUGHS

Through the trees raced Tarzan of the Apes until the darkness of night had settled upon the jungle, then he lay down and slept, with no thought beyond the morrow and with even La but the shadow of a memory within his consciousness.

But a few marches to the north Lady Greystoke looked forward to the day when her mighty lord and master should discover the crime of Achmet Zek, and be speeding to rescue and avenge, and even as she pictured the coming of John Clayton, the object of her thoughts squatted almost naked, beside a fallen log, beneath which he was searching with grimy fingers for a chance beetle or a luscious grub.

Two days elapsed following the theft of the jewels before Tarzan gave them a thought. Then, as they chanced to enter his mind, he conceived a desire to play with them again, and, having nothing better to do than satisfy the first whim which possessed him, he rose and started across the plain from the forest in which he had spent the preceding day.

Though no mark showed where the gems had been buried, and though the spot resembled the balance of an unbroken stretch several miles in length, where the reeds terminated at the edge of the meadowland, yet the ape-man moved with unerring precision directly to the place where he had hid his treasure.

With his hunting knife he upturned the loose earth, beneath which the pouch should be; but, though he excavated to a greater distance than the depth of the original hole there was no sign of pouch or jewels. Tarzan's brow clouded as he discovered that he had been despoiled. Little or no reasoning was required to convince him of the identity of the guilty party, and with the same celerity that had marked his decision to unearth the jewels, he set out upon the trail of the thief.

Though the spoor was two days old, and practically obliterated in many places, Tarzan followed it with comparative ease. A white man could not have followed it twenty paces twelve hours after it had been made, a black man would have lost it within the first mile; but Tarzan of the Apes had been forced in childhood to develop senses that an ordinary mortal scarce ever uses.

We may note the garlic and whisky on the breath of a fellow strap hanger, or the cheap perfume emanating from the person of the wondrous lady sitting in front of us, and deplore the fact of our sensitive noses; but, as a matter of fact, we cannot smell at all, our olfactory organs are practically atrophied, by comparison with the development of the sense among the beasts of the wild.

Where a foot is placed an effluvium remains for a considerable time. It is beyond the range of our sensibilities; but to a creature of the lower orders, especially to the hunters and the hunted, as interesting and ofttimes more lucid than is the printed page to us.

Nor was Tarzan dependent alone upon his sense of smell. Vision and hearing had been brought to a marvelous state of development by the necessities of his early life, where survival itself depended almost daily upon the exercise of the keenest vigilance and the constant use of all his faculties.

And so he followed the old trail of the Belgian through the forest and toward the north; but because of the age of the trail he was constrained to a far from rapid progress. The man he followed was two days ahead of him when Tarzan took up the pursuit, and each day he gained upon the ape-man. The latter, however, felt not the slightest doubt as to the outcome. Some day he would overhaul his quarry—he could bide his time in peace until that day dawned. Doggedly he followed the faint spoor, pausing by day only to kill and eat, and at night only to sleep and refresh himself.

Occasionally he passed parties of savage warriors; but these he gave a wide berth, for he was hunting with a purpose that was not to be distracted by the minor accidents of the trail.

These parties were of the collecting hordes of the Waziri and their allies which Basuli had scattered his messengers broadcast to summon. They were marching to a common rendezvous in preparation for an assault upon the stronghold of Achmet Zek; but to Tarzan they were enemies—he retained no conscious memory of any friendship for the black men.

It was night when he halted outside the palisaded village of the Arab raider. Perched in the branches of a great tree he gazed down upon the life within the enclosure. To this place had the spoor led him. His quarry must be within; but how was he to find him among so many huts? Tarzan, although cognizant of his mighty powers, realized also his limitations. He knew that he could not successfully cope with great numbers in open battle. He must resort to the stealth and trickery of the wild beast, if he were to succeed.

Sitting in the safety of his tree, munching upon the leg bone of Horta, the boar, Tarzan waited a favorable opportunity to enter the village. For awhile he gnawed at the bulging, round ends of the large bone, splintering off small pieces between his strong jaws, and sucking at the delicious marrow within; but all the time he cast repeated glances into the village. He saw white-robed figures, and half-naked blacks; but not once did he see one who resembled the stealer of the gems.

Patiently he waited until the streets were deserted by all save the sentries at the gates, then he dropped lightly to the ground, circled to the opposite side of the village and approached the palisade.

At his side hung a long, rawhide rope—a natural and more dependable evolution from the grass rope of his childhood. Loosening this, he spread the noose upon the ground behind him, and with a quick movement of his wrist tossed the coils over one of the sharpened projections of the summit of the palisade.

Drawing the noose taut, he tested the solidity of its hold. Satisfied, the ape-man ran nimbly up the vertical wall, aided by the rope which he clutched in both hands. Once at the top it required but a moment to gather the dangling rope once more into its coils, make it fast again at his waist, take a quick glance downward within the palisade, and, assured that no one lurked directly beneath him, drop softly to the ground.

Now he was within the village. Before him stretched a series of tents and native huts. The business of exploring each of them would be fraught with danger; but danger was only a natural factor of each day's life—it never appalled Tarzan. The chances appealed to him—the chances of life and death, with his prowess and his faculties pitted against those of a worthy antagonist.

It was not necessary that he enter each habitation—through a door, a window or an open chink, his nose told him whether or not his prey lay within. For some time he found one disappointment following upon the heels of another in quick succession. No spoor of the Belgian was discernible. But at last he came to a tent where the smell of the thief was strong. Tarzan listened, his ear close to the canvas at the rear, but no sound came from within.

At last he cut one of the pin ropes, raised the bottom of the canvas, and intruded his head within the interior. All was quiet and dark. Tarzan crawled cautiously within—the scent of the Belgian was strong; but it was not live scent. Even before he had examined the interior minutely, Tarzan knew that no one was within it.

In one corner he found a pile of blankets and clothing scattered about; but no pouch of pretty pebbles. A careful examination of the balance of the tent revealed nothing more, at least nothing to indicate the presence of the jewels; but at the side where the blankets and clothing lay, the ape-man discovered that the tent wall had been loosened at the bottom, and presently he sensed that the Belgian had recently passed out of the tent by this avenue.

Tarzan was not long in following the way that his prey had fled. The spoor led always in the shadow and at the rear of the huts and tents of the village—it was quite evident to Tarzan that the Belgian had gone alone and secretly upon his mission. Evidently he feared the inhabitants of the village, or at least his work had been of such a nature that he dared not risk detection.

At the back of a native hut the spoor led through a small hole recently cut in the brush wall and into the dark interior beyond. Fearlessly, Tarzan followed the trail. On hands and knees, he crawled through the small aperture. Within the hut his nostrils were assailed by many odors; but clear and distinct among them was one that half aroused a latent memory of the past—it was the faint and delicate odor of a woman. With the cognizance of it there rose in the breast of the ape-man a strange uneasiness—the result of an irresistible force which he was destined to become acquainted with anew—the instinct which draws the male to his mate.

In the same hut was the scent spoor of the Belgian, too, and as both these assailed the nostrils of the ape-man, mingling one with the other, a jealous rage leaped and burned within him, though his memory held before the mirror of recollection no image of the she to which he had attached his desire.

Like the tent he had investigated, the hut, too, was empty, and after satisfying himself that his stolen pouch was secreted nowhere within, he left, as he had entered, by the hole in the rear wall.

Here he took up the spoor of the Belgian, followed it across the clearing, over the palisade, and out into the dark jungle beyond.

THE FLIGHT OF WERPER

After Werper had arranged the dummy in his bed, and sneaked out into the darkness of the village beneath the rear wall of his tent, he had gone directly to the hut in which Jane Clayton was held captive.

Before the doorway squatted a black sentry. Werper approached him boldly, spoke a few words in his ear, handed him a package of tobacco, and passed into the hut. The black grinned and winked as the European disappeared within the darkness of the interior.

The Belgian, being one of Achmet Zek's principal lieutenants, might naturally go where he wished within or without the village, and so the sentry had not questioned his right to enter the hut with the white, woman prisoner.

Within, Werper called in French and in a low whisper: "Lady Greystoke! It is I, M. Frecoult. Where are you?" But there was no response. Hastily the man felt around the interior, groping blindly through the darkness with outstretched hands. There was no one within!

Werper's astonishment surpassed words. He was on the point of stepping without to question the sentry, when his eyes, becoming accustomed to the dark, discovered a blotch of lesser blackness near the base of the rear wall of the hut. Examination revealed the fact that the blotch was an opening cut in the wall. It was large enough to permit the passage of his body, and assured as he was that Lady Greystoke had passed out through the aperture in an attempt to escape the village, he lost no time in availing himself of the same avenue; but neither did he lose time in a fruitless search for Jane Clayton.

His own life depended upon the chance of his eluding, or outdistancing Achmet Zek, when that worthy should have discovered that he had escaped. His original plan had contemplated connivance in the escape of Lady Greystoke for two very good and sufficient reasons. The first was that by saving her he would win the gratitude of the English, and thus lessen the chance of his extradition should his identity and his crime against his superior officer be charged against him.

The second reason was based upon the fact that only one direction of escape was safely open to him. He could not travel to the west because of the Belgian possessions which lay between him and the Atlantic. The south was closed to him by the feared presence of the savage ape-man he had robbed. To the north lay the friends and allies of Achmet Zek. Only toward the east, through British East Africa, lay reasonable assurance of freedom.

Accompanied by a titled Englishwoman whom he had rescued from a frightful fate, and his identity vouched for by her as that of a Frenchman by the name of Frecoult, he had looked forward, and not without reason, to the active assistance of the British from the moment that he came in contact with their first outpost.

But now that Lady Greystoke had disappeared, though he still looked toward the east for hope, his chances were lessened, and another, subsidiary design completely dashed. From the moment that he had first laid eyes upon Jane Clayton he had nursed within his breast a secret passion for the beautiful American wife of the English lord, and when Achmet Zek's discovery of the jewels had necessitated flight, the Belgian had dreamed, in his planning, of a future in which he might convince Lady Greystoke that her husband was dead, and by playing upon her gratitude win her for himself.

At that part of the village farthest from the gates, Werper discovered that two or three long poles, taken from a nearby pile which had been collected for the construction of huts, had been leaned against the top of the palisade, forming a precarious, though not impossible avenue of escape.

Rightly, he inferred that thus had Lady Greystoke found the means to scale the wall, nor did he lose even a moment in following her lead. Once in the jungle he struck out directly eastward.

A few miles south of him, Jane Clayton lay panting among the branches of a tree in which she had taken refuge from a prowling and hungry lioness.

Her escape from the village had been much easier than she had anticipated. The knife which she had used to cut her way through the brush wall of the hut to freedom she had found sticking in the wall of her prison, doubtless left there by accident when a former tenant had vacated the premises.

To cross the rear of the village, keeping always in the densest shadows, had required but a few moments, and the fortunate circumstance of the discovery of the hut poles lying so near the palisade had solved for her the problem of the passage of the high wall.

For an hour she had followed the old game trail toward the south, until there fell upon her trained hearing the stealthy padding of a stalking beast behind her. The nearest tree gave her instant sanctuary, for she was too wise in the ways of the jungle to chance her safety for a moment after discovering that she was being hunted.

Werper, with better success, traveled slowly onward until dawn, when, to his chagrin, he discovered a mounted Arab upon his trail. It was one of Achmet Zek's minions, many of whom were scattered in all directions through the forest, searching for the fugitive Belgian.

Jane Clayton's escape had not yet been discovered when Achmet Zek and his searchers set forth to overhaul Werper. The only man who had seen the Belgian after his departure from his tent was the black sentry before the doorway of Lady Greystoke's prison hut, and he had been silenced by the discovery of the dead body of the man who had relieved him, the sentry that Mugambi had dispatched.

The bribe taker naturally inferred that Werper had slain his fellow and dared not admit that he had permitted him to enter the hut, fearing as he did, the anger of Achmet Zek. So, as chance directed that he should be the one to discover the body of the sentry when the first alarm had been given following Achmet Zek's discovery that Werper had outwitted him, the crafty black had dragged the dead body to the interior of a nearby tent, and himself resumed his station before the doorway of the hut in which he still believed the woman to be.

With the discovery of the Arab close behind him, the Belgian hid in the foliage of a leafy bush. Here the trail ran straight for a considerable distance, and down the shady forest aisle, beneath the overarching branches of the trees, rode the white-robed figure of the pursuer.

Nearer and nearer he came. Werper crouched closer to the ground behind the leaves of his hiding place. Across the trail a vine moved. Werper's eyes instantly centered upon the spot. There was no wind to stir the foliage in the depths of the jungle. Again the vine moved. In the mind of the Belgian only the presence of a sinister and malevolent force could account for the phenomenon.

The man's eyes bored steadily into the screen of leaves upon the opposite side of the trail. Gradually a form took shape beyond them—a tawny form, grim and terrible, with yellow-green eyes glaring fearsomely across the narrow trail straight into his.

Werper could have screamed in fright, but up the trail was coming the messenger of another death, equally sure and no less terrible. He remained silent, almost paralyzed by fear. The Arab approached. Across the trail from Werper the lion crouched for the spring, when suddenly his attention was attracted toward the horseman.

The Belgian saw the massive head turn in the direction of the raider and his heart all but ceased its beating as he awaited the result of this interruption. At a walk the horseman approached. Would the nervous animal he rode take fright at the odor of the carnivore, and, bolting, leave Werper still to the mercies of the king of beasts?

But he seemed unmindful of the near presence of the great cat. On he came, his neck arched, champing at the bit between his teeth. The Belgian turned his eyes again toward the lion. The beast's whole attention now seemed riveted upon the horseman. They were abreast the lion now, and still the brute did not spring. Could he be but waiting for them to pass before returning his attention to the original prey? Werper shuddered and half rose. At the same instant the lion sprang from his place of concealment, full upon the mounted man. The horse, with a shrill neigh of terror, shrank sideways almost upon the Belgian, the lion dragged the helpless Arab from his saddle, and the horse leaped back into the trail and fled away toward the west.

But he did not flee alone. As the frightened beast had pressed in upon him, Werper had not been slow to note the quickly emptied saddle and the opportunity it presented. Scarcely had the lion dragged the Arab down from one side, than the Belgian, seizing the pommel of the saddle and the horse's mane, leaped upon the horse's back from the other.

A half hour later a naked giant, swinging easily through the lower branches of the trees, paused, and with raised head, and dilating nostrils sniffed the morning air. The smell of blood fell strong upon his senses, and mingled with it was the scent of Numa, the lion. The giant cocked his head upon one side and listened.

From a short distance up the trail came the unmistakable noises of the greedy feeding of a lion. The crunching of bones, the gulping of great pieces, the contented growling, all attested the nearness of the king at table.

Tarzan approached the spot, still keeping to the branches of the trees. He made no effort to conceal his approach, and presently he had evidence that Numa had heard him, from the ominous, rumbling warning that broke from a thicket beside the trail.

Halting upon a low branch just above the lion Tarzan looked down upon the grisly scene. Could this unrecognizable thing be the man he had been trailing? The ape-man wondered. From time to time he had descended to the trail and verified his judgment by the evidence of his scent that the Belgian had followed this game trail toward the east.

Now he proceeded beyond the lion and his feast, again descended and examined the ground with his nose. There was no scent spoor here of the man he had been trailing. Tarzan returned to the tree. With keen eyes he searched the ground about the mutilated corpse for a sign of the missing pouch of pretty pebbles; but naught could he see of it.

He scolded Numa and tried to drive the great beast away; but only angry growls rewarded his efforts. He tore small branches from a nearby limb and hurled them at his ancient enemy. Numa looked up with bared fangs, grinning hideously, but he did not rise from his kill.

Then Tarzan fitted an arrow to his bow, and drawing the slim shaft far back let drive with all the force of the tough wood that only he could bend. As the arrow sank deeply into his side, Numa leaped to his feet with a roar of mingled rage and pain. He leaped futilely at the grinning ape-man, tore at the protruding end of the shaft, and then, springing into the trail, paced back and forth beneath his tormentor. Again Tarzan loosed a swift bolt. This time the missile, aimed with care, lodged in the lion's spine. The great creature halted in its tracks, and lurched awkwardly forward upon its face, paralyzed.

Tarzan dropped to the trail, ran quickly to the beast's side, and drove his spear deep into the fierce heart, then after recovering his arrows turned his attention to the mutilated remains of the animal's prey in the nearby thicket.

The face was gone. The Arab garments aroused no doubt as to the man's identity, since he had trailed him into the Arab camp and out again, where he might easily have acquired the apparel. So sure was Tarzan that the body was that of he who had robbed him that he made no effort to verify his deductions by scent among the conglomerate odors of the great carnivore and the fresh blood of the victim.

He confined his attentions to a careful search for the pouch, but nowhere upon or about the corpse was any sign of the missing article or its contents. The ape-man was disappointed—possibly not so much because of the loss of the colored pebbles as with Numa for robbing him of the pleasures of revenge.

Wondering what could have become of his possessions, the ape-man turned slowly back along the trail in the direction from which he had come. In his mind he revolved a plan to enter and search the Arab camp, after darkness had again fallen. Taking to the trees, he moved directly south in search of prey, that he might satisfy his hunger before midday, and then lie up for the afternoon in some spot far from the camp, where he might sleep without fear of discovery until it came time to prosecute his design.

Scarcely had he quitted the trail when a tall, black warrior, moving at a dogged trot, passed toward the east. It was Mugambi, searching for his mistress. He continued along the trail, halting to examine the body of the dead lion. An expression of puzzlement crossed his features as he bent to search for the wounds which had caused the death of the jungle lord. Tarzan had removed his arrows, but to Mugambi the proof of death was as strong as though both the lighter missiles and the spear still protruded from the carcass.

The black looked furtively about him. The body was still warm, and from this fact he reasoned that the killer was close at hand, yet no sign of living man appeared. Mugambi shook his head, and continued along the trail, but with redoubled caution.

All day he traveled, stopping occasionally to call aloud the single word, "Lady," in the hope that at last she might hear and respond; but in the end his loyal devotion brought him to disaster.

From the northeast, for several months, Abdul Mourak, in command of a detachment of Abyssinian soldiers, had been assiduously searching for the Arab raider, Achmet Zek, who, six months previously, had affronted the majesty of Abdul Mourak's emperor by conducting a slave raid within the boundaries of Menelek's domain.

And now it happened that Abdul Mourak had halted for a short rest at noon upon this very day and along the same trail that Werper and Mugambi were following toward the east.

It was shortly after the soldiers had dismounted that the Belgian, unaware of their presence, rode his tired mount almost into their midst, before he had discovered them. Instantly he was surrounded, and a volley of questions hurled at him, as he was pulled from his horse and led toward the presence of the commander.

Falling back upon his European nationality, Werper assured Abdul Mourak that he was a Frenchman, hunting in Africa, and that he had been attacked by strangers, his safari killed or scattered, and himself escaping only by a miracle.

From a chance remark of the Abyssinian, Werper discovered the purpose of the expedition, and when he realized that these men were the enemies of Achmet Zek, he took heart, and immediately blamed his predicament upon the Arab.

Lest, however, he might again fall into the hands of the raider, he discouraged Abdul Mourak in the further prosecution of his pursuit, assuring the Abyssinian that Achmet Zek commanded a large and dangerous force, and also that he was marching rapidly toward the south.

Convinced that it would take a long time to overhaul the raider, and that the chances of engagement made the outcome extremely questionable, Mourak, none too unwillingly, abandoned his plan and gave the necessary orders for his command to pitch camp where they were, preparatory to taking up the return march toward Abyssinia the following morning.

It was late in the afternoon that the attention of the camp was attracted toward the west by the sound of a powerful voice calling a single word, repeated several times: "Lady! Lady! Lady!"

True to their instincts of precaution, a number of Abyssinians, acting under orders from Abdul Mourak, advanced stealthily through the jungle toward the author of the call.

A half hour later they returned, dragging Mugambi among them. The first person the big black's eyes fell upon as he was hustled into the presence of the Abyssinian officer, was M. Jules Frecoult, the Frenchman who had been the guest of his master and whom he last had seen entering the village of Achmet Zek under circumstances which pointed to his familiarity and friendship for the raiders.

Between the disasters that had befallen his master and his master's house, and the Frenchman, Mugambi saw a sinister relationship, which kept him from recalling to Werper's attention the identity which the latter evidently failed to recognize.

Pleading that he was but a harmless hunter from a tribe farther south, Mugambi begged to be allowed to go upon his way; but Abdul Mourak, admiring the warrior's splendid physique, decided to take him back to Adis Abeba and present him to Menelek. A few moments later Mugambi and Werper were marched away under guard, and the Belgian learned for the first time, that he too was a prisoner rather than a guest. In vain he protested against such treatment, until a strapping soldier struck him across the mouth and threatened to shoot him if he did not desist.

Mugambi took the matter less to heart, for he had not the slightest doubt but that during the course of the journey he would find ample opportunity to elude the vigilance of his guards and make good his escape. With this idea always uppermost in his mind, he courted the good opinion of the Abyssinians, asked them many questions about their emperor and their country, and evinced a growing desire to reach their destination, that he might enjoy all the good things which they assured him the city of Adis Abeba contained. Thus he disarmed their suspicions, and each day found a slight relaxation of their watchfulness over him.

By taking advantage of the fact that he and Werper always were kept together, Mugambi sought to learn what the other knew of the whereabouts of Tarzan, or the authorship of the raid upon the bungalow, as well as the fate of Lady Greystoke; but as he was confined to the accidents of conversation for this information, not daring to acquaint Werper with his true identity, and as Werper was equally anxious to conceal from the world his part in the destruction of his host's home and happiness, Mugambi learned nothing—at least in this way.

But there came a time when he learned a very surprising thing, by accident.

The party had camped early in the afternoon of a sultry day, upon the banks of a clear and beautiful stream. The bottom of the river was gravelly, there was no indication of crocodiles, those menaces to promiscuous bathing in the rivers of certain portions of the dark continent, and so the Abyssinians took advantage of the opportunity to perform long-deferred, and much needed, ablutions.

As Werper, who, with Mugambi, had been given permission to enter the water, removed his clothing, the black noted the care with which he unfastened something which circled his waist, and which he took off with his shirt, keeping the latter always around and concealing the object of his suspicious solicitude.

It was this very carefulness which attracted the black's attention to the thing, arousing a natural curiosity in the warrior's mind, and so it chanced that when the Belgian, in the nervousness of overcaution, fumbled the hidden article and dropped it, Mugambi saw it as it fell upon the ground, spilling a portion of its contents on the sward.

Now Mugambi had been to London with his master. He was not the unsophisticated savage that his apparel proclaimed him. He had mingled with the cosmopolitan hordes of the greatest city in the world; he had visited museums and inspected shop windows; and, besides, he was a shrewd and intelligent man.

The instant that the jewels of Opar rolled, scintillating, before his astonished eyes, he recognized them for what they were; but he recognized something else, too, that interested him far more deeply than the value of the stones. A thousand times he had seen the leathern pouch which dangled at his master's side, when Tarzan of the Apes had, in a spirit of play and adventure, elected to return for a few hours to the primitive manners and customs of his boyhood, and surrounded by his naked warriors hunt the lion and the leopard, the buffalo and the elephant after the manner he loved best.

Werper saw that Mugambi had seen the pouch and the stones. Hastily he gathered up the precious gems and returned them to their container, while Mugambi, assuming an air of indifference, strolled down to the river for his bath.

The following morning Abdul Mourak was enraged and chagrined to discover that this huge, black prisoner had escaped during the night, while Werper was terrified for the same reason, until his trembling fingers discovered the pouch still in its place beneath his shirt, and within it the hard outlines of its contents.

TARZAN AGAIN LEADS THE MANGANI

Achmet Zek with two of his followers had circled far to the south to intercept the flight of his deserting lieutenant, Werper. Others had spread out in various directions, so that a vast circle had been formed by them during the night, and now they were beating in toward the center.

Achmet and the two with him halted for a short rest just before noon. They squatted beneath the trees upon the southern edge of a clearing. The chief of the raiders was in ill humor. To have been outwitted by an unbeliever was bad enough; but to have, at the same time, lost the jewels upon which he had set his avaricious heart was altogether too much—Allah must, indeed be angry with his servant.

Well, he still had the woman. She would bring a fair price in the north, and there was, too, the buried treasure beside the ruins of the Englishman's house.

A slight noise in the jungle upon the opposite side of the clearing brought Achmet Zek to immediate and alert attention. He gathered his rifle in readiness for instant use, at the same time motioning his followers to silence and concealment. Crouching behind the bushes the three waited, their eyes fastened upon the far side of the open space.

Presently the foliage parted and a woman's face appeared, glancing fearfully from side to side. A moment later, evidently satisfied that no immediate danger lurked before her, she stepped out into the clearing in full view of the Arab.

Achmet Zek caught his breath with a muttered exclamation of incredulity and an imprecation. The woman was the prisoner he had thought safely guarded at his camp!

Apparently she was alone, but Achmet Zek waited that he might make sure of it before seizing her. Slowly Jane Clayton started across the clearing. Twice already since she had quitted the village of the raiders had she barely escaped the fangs of carnivora, and once she had almost stumbled into the path of one of the searchers. Though she was almost despairing of ever reaching safety she still was determined to fight on, until death or success terminated her endeavors.

As the Arabs watched her from the safety of their concealment, and Achmet Zek noted with satisfaction that she was walking directly into his clutches, another pair of eyes looked down upon the entire scene from the foliage of an adjacent tree.

Puzzled, troubled eyes they were, for all their gray and savage glint, for their owner was struggling with an intangible suggestion of the familiarity of the face and figure of the woman below him.

A sudden crashing of the bushes at the point from which Jane Clayton had emerged into the clearing brought her to a sudden stop and attracted the attention of the Arabs and the watcher in the tree to the same point.

The woman wheeled about to see what new danger menaced her from behind, and as she did so a great, anthropoid ape waddled into view. Behind him came another and another; but Lady Greystoke did not wait to learn how many more of the hideous creatures were so close upon her trail.

With a smothered scream she rushed toward the opposite jungle, and as she reached the bushes there, Achmet Zek and his two henchmen rose up and seized her. At the same instant a naked, brown giant dropped from the branches of a tree at the right of the clearing.

Turning toward the astonished apes he gave voice to a short volley of low gutturals, and without waiting to note the effect of his words upon them, wheeled and charged for the Arabs.

Achmet Zek was dragging Jane Clayton toward his tethered horse. His two men were hastily unfastening all three mounts. The woman, struggling to escape the Arab, turned and saw the ape-man running toward her. A glad light of hope illuminated her face.

"John!" she cried. "Thank God that you have come in time."

Behind Tarzan came the great apes, wondering, but obedient to his summons. The Arabs saw that they would not have time to mount and make their escape before the beasts and the man were upon them. Achmet Zek recognized the latter as the redoubtable enemy of such as he, and he saw, too, in the circumstance an opportunity to rid himself forever of the menace of the ape-man's presence.

Calling to his men to follow his example he raised his rifle and leveled it upon the charging giant. His followers, acting with no less alacrity than himself, fired almost simultaneously, and with the reports of the rifles, Tarzan of the Apes and two of his hairy henchmen pitched forward among the jungle grasses.

The noise of the rifle shots brought the balance of the apes to a wondering pause, and, taking advantage of their momentary distraction, Achmet Zek and his fellows leaped to their horses' backs and galloped away with the now hopeless and grief-stricken woman.

Back to the village they rode, and once again Lady Greystoke found herself incarcerated in the filthy, little hut from which she had thought to have escaped for good. But this time she was not only guarded by an additional sentry, but bound as well.

Singly and in twos the searchers who had ridden out with Achmet Zek upon the trail of the Belgian, returned empty handed. With the report of each the raider's rage and chagrin increased, until he was in such a transport of ferocious anger that none dared approach him. Threatening and cursing, Achmet Zek paced up and down the floor of his silken tent; but his temper served him naught—Werper was gone and with him the fortune in scintillating gems which had aroused the cupidity of his chief and placed the sentence of death upon the head of the lieutenant.

With the escape of the Arabs the great apes had turned their attention to their fallen comrades. One was dead, but another and the great white ape still breathed. The hairy monsters gathered about these two, grumbling and muttering after the fashion of their kind.

Tarzan was the first to regain consciousness. Sitting up, he looked about him. Blood was flowing from a wound in his shoulder. The shock had thrown him down and dazed him; but he was far from dead. Rising slowly to his feet he let his eyes wander toward the spot where last he had seen the she, who had aroused within his savage breast such strange emotions.

"Where is she?" he asked.

"The Tarmangani took her away," replied one of the apes. "Who are you who speak the language of the Mangani?"

"I am Tarzan," replied the ape-man; "mighty hunter, greatest of fighters. When I roar, the jungle is silent and trembles with terror. I am Tarzan of the Apes. I have been away; but now I have come back to my people."

"Yes," spoke up an old ape, "he is Tarzan. I know him. It is well that he has come back. Now we shall have good hunting."

The other apes came closer and sniffed at the ape-man. Tarzan stood very still, his fangs half bared, and his muscles tense and ready for action; but there was none there to question his right to be with them, and presently, the inspection satisfactorily concluded, the apes again returned their attention to the other survivor.

He too was but slightly wounded, a bullet, grazing his skull, having stunned him, so that when he regained consciousness he was apparently as fit as ever.

The apes told Tarzan that they had been traveling toward the east when the scent spoor of the she had attracted them and they had stalked her. Now they wished to continue upon their interrupted march; but Tarzan preferred to follow the Arabs and take the woman from them. After a considerable argument it was decided that they should first hunt toward the east for a few days and then return and search for the Arabs, and as time is of little moment to the ape folk, Tarzan acceded to their demands, he, himself, having reverted to a mental state but little superior to their own.

Another circumstance which decided him to postpone pursuit of the Arabs was the painfulness of his wound. It would be better to wait until that had healed before he pitted himself again against the guns of the Tarmangani.

And so, as Jane Clayton was pushed into her prison hut and her hands and feet securely bound, her natural protector roamed off toward the east in company with a score of hairy monsters, with whom he rubbed shoulders as familiarly as a few months before he had mingled with his immaculate fellow-members of one of London's most select and exclusive clubs.

But all the time there lurked in the back of his injured brain a troublesome conviction that he had no business where he was—that he should be, for some unaccountable reason, elsewhere and among another sort of creature. Also, there was the compelling urge to be upon the scent of the Arabs, undertaking the rescue of the woman who had appealed so strongly to his savage sentiments; though the thought-word which naturally occurred to him in the contemplation of the venture, was "capture," rather than "rescue."

To him she was as any other jungle she, and he had set his heart upon her as his mate. For an instant, as he had approached closer to her in the clearing where the Arabs had seized her, the subtle aroma which had first aroused his desires in the hut that had imprisoned her had fallen upon his nostrils, and told him that he had found the creature for whom he had developed so sudden and inexplicable a passion.

The matter of the pouch of jewels also occupied his thoughts to some extent, so that he found a double urge for his return to the camp of the raiders. He would obtain possession of both his pretty pebbles and the she. Then he would return to the great apes with his new mate and his baubles, and leading his hairy companions into a far wilderness beyond the ken of man, live out his life, hunting and battling among the lower orders after the only manner which he now recollected.

He spoke to his fellow-apes upon the matter, in an attempt to persuade them to accompany him; but all except Taglat and Chulk refused. The latter was young and strong, endowed with a greater intelligence than his fellows, and therefore the possessor of better developed powers of imagination. To him the expedition savored of adventure, and so appealed, strongly. With Taglat there was another incentive—a secret and sinister incentive, which, had Tarzan of the Apes had knowledge of it, would have sent him at the other's throat in jealous rage.

Taglat was no longer young; but he was still a formidable beast, mightily muscled, cruel, and, because of his greater experience, crafty and cunning. Too, he was of giant proportions, the very weight of his huge bulk serving ofttimes to discount in his favor the superior agility of a younger antagonist.

He was of a morose and sullen disposition that marked him even among his frowning fellows, where such characteristics are the rule rather than the exception, and, though Tarzan did not guess it, he hated the ape-man with a ferocity that he was able to hide only because the dominant spirit of the nobler creature had inspired within him a species of dread which was as powerful as it was inexplicable to him.

These two, then, were to be Tarzan's companions upon his return to the village of Achmet Zek. As they set off, the balance of the tribe vouchsafed them but a parting stare, and then resumed the serious business of feeding.

Tarzan found difficulty in keeping the minds of his fellows set upon the purpose of their adventure, for the mind of an ape lacks the power of long-sustained concentration. To set out upon a long journey, with a definite destination in view, is one thing, to remember that purpose and keep it uppermost in one's mind continually is quite another. There are so many things to distract one's attention along the way.

Chulk was, at first, for rushing rapidly ahead as though the village of the raiders lay but an hour's march before them instead of several days; but within a few minutes a fallen tree attracted his attention with its suggestion of rich and succulent forage beneath, and when Tarzan, missing him, returned in search, he found Chulk squatting beside the rotting bole, from beneath which he was assiduously engaged in digging out the grubs and beetles, whose kind form a considerable proportion of the diet of the apes.

EDGAR RICE BURROUGHS

Unless Tarzan desired to fight there was nothing to do but wait until Chulk had exhausted the storehouse, and this he did, only to discover that Taglat was now missing. After a considerable search, he found that worthy gentleman contemplating the sufferings of an injured rodent he had pounced upon. He would sit in apparent indifference, gazing in another direction, while the crippled creature, wriggled slowly and painfully away from him, and then, just as his victim felt assured of escape, he would reach out a giant palm and slam it down upon the fugitive. Again and again he repeated this operation, until, tiring of the sport, he ended the sufferings of his plaything by devouring it.

Such were the exasperating causes of delay which retarded Tarzan's return journey toward the village of Achmet Zek; but the ape-man was patient, for in his mind was a plan which necessitated the presence of Chulk and Taglat when he should have arrived at his destination.

It was not always an easy thing to maintain in the vacillating minds of the anthropoids a sustained interest in their venture. Chulk was wearying of the continued marching and the infrequency and short duration of the rests. He would gladly have abandoned this search for adventure had not Tarzan continually filled his mind with alluring pictures of the great stores of food which were to be found in the village of Tarmangani.

Taglat nursed his secret purpose to better advantage than might have been expected of an ape, yet there were times when he, too, would have abandoned the adventure had not Tarzan cajoled him on.

It was mid-afternoon of a sultry, tropical day when the keen senses of the three warned them of the proximity of the Arab camp. Stealthily they approached, keeping to the dense tangle of growing things which made concealment easy to their uncanny jungle craft.

First came the giant ape-man, his smooth, brown skin glistening with the sweat of exertion in the close, hot confines of the jungle. Behind him crept Chulk and Taglat, grotesque and shaggy caricatures of their godlike leader.

Silently they made their way to the edge of the clearing which surrounded the palisade, and here they clambered into the lower branches of a large tree overlooking the village occupied by the enemy, the better to spy upon his goings and comings.

A horseman, white burnoosed, rode out through the gateway of the village. Tarzan, whispering to Chulk and Taglat to remain where they were, swung, monkey-like, through the trees in the direction of the trail the Arab was riding. From one jungle giant to the next he sped with the rapidity of a squirrel and the silence of a ghost.

The Arab rode slowly onward, unconscious of the danger hovering in the trees behind him. The ape-man made a slight detour and increased his speed until he had reached a point upon the trail in advance of the horseman. Here he halted upon a leafy bough which overhung the narrow, jungle trail. On came the victim, humming a wild air of the great desert land of the north. Above him poised the savage brute that was today bent upon the destruction of a human life—the same creature who a few months before, had occupied his seat in the House of Lords at London, a respected and distinguished member of that august body.

The Arab passed beneath the overhanging bough, there was a slight rustling of the leaves above, the horse snorted and plunged as a brown-skinned creature dropped upon its rump. A pair of mighty arms encircled the Arab and he was dragged from his saddle to the trail.

Ten minutes later the ape-man, carrying the outer garments of an Arab bundled beneath an arm, rejoined his companions. He exhibited his trophies to them, explaining in low gutturals the details of his exploit. Chulk and Taglat fingered the fabrics, smelled of them, and, placing them to their ears, tried to listen to them.

Then Tarzan led them back through the jungle to the trail, where the three hid themselves and waited. Nor had they long to wait before two of Achmet Zek's blacks, clothed in habiliments similar to their master's, came down the trail on foot, returning to the camp.

One moment they were laughing and talking together—the next they lay stretched in death upon the trail, three mighty engines of destruction bending over them. Tarzan removed their outer garments as he had removed those of his first victim, and again retired with Chulk and Taglat to the greater seclusion of the tree they had first selected.

Here the ape-man arranged the garments upon his shaggy fellows and himself, until, at a distance, it might have appeared that three white-robed Arabs squatted silently among the branches of the forest.

Until dark they remained where they were, for from his point of vantage, Tarzan could view the enclosure within the palisade. He marked the position of the hut in which he had first discovered the scent spoor of the she he sought. He saw the two sentries standing before its doorway, and he located the habitation of Achmet Zek, where something told him he would most likely find the missing pouch and pebbles.

Chulk and Taglat were, at first, greatly interested in their wonderful raiment. They fingered the fabric, smelled of it, and regarded each other intently with every mark of satisfaction and pride. Chulk, a humorist in his way, stretched forth a long and hairy arm, and grasping the hood of Taglat's burnoose pulled it down over the latter's eyes, extinguishing him, snuffer-like, as it were.

The older ape, pessimistic by nature, recognized no such thing as humor. Creatures laid their paws upon him for but two things—to search for fleas and to attack. The pulling of the Tarmangani-scented thing about his head and eyes could not be for the performance of the former act; therefore it must be the latter. He was attacked! Chulk had attacked him.

With a snarl he was at the other's throat, not even waiting to lift the woolen veil which obscured his vision. Tarzan leaped upon the two, and swaying and toppling upon their insecure perch the three great beasts tussled and snapped at one another until the ape-man finally succeeded in separating the enraged anthropoids.

An apology is unknown to these savage progenitors of man, and explanation a laborious and usually futile process, Tarzan bridged the dangerous gulf by distracting their attention from their altercation to a consideration of their plans for the immediate future. Accustomed to frequent arguments in which more hair than blood is wasted, the apes speedily forget such trivial encounters, and presently Chulk and Taglat were again squatting in close proximity to each other and peaceful repose, awaiting the moment when the ape-man should lead them into the village of the Tarmangani.

It was long after darkness had fallen, that Tarzan led his companions from their hiding place in the tree to the ground and around the palisade to the far side of the village.

Gathering the skirts of his burnoose, beneath one arm, that his legs might have free action, the ape-man took a short running start, and scrambled to the top of the barrier. Fearing lest the apes should rend their garments to shreds in a similar attempt, he had directed them to wait below for him, and himself securely perched upon the summit of the palisade he unslung his spear and lowered one end of it to Chulk.

The ape seized it, and while Tarzan held tightly to the upper end, the anthropoid climbed quickly up the shaft until with one paw he grasped the top of the wall. To scramble then to Tarzan's side was the work of but an instant. In like manner Taglat was conducted to their sides, and a moment later the three dropped silently within the enclosure.

Tarzan led them first to the rear of the hut in which Jane Clayton was confined, where, through the roughly repaired aperture in the wall, he sought with his sensitive nostrils for proof that the she he had come for was within.

Chulk and Taglat, their hairy faces pressed close to that of the patrician, sniffed with him. Each caught the scent spoor of the woman within, and each reacted according to his temperament and his habits of thought.

It left Chulk indifferent. The she was for Tarzan—all that he desired was to bury his snout in the foodstuffs of the Tarmangani. He had come to eat his fill without labor—Tarzan had told him that that should be his reward, and he was satisfied.

But Taglat's wicked, bloodshot eyes, narrowed to the realization of the nearing fulfillment of his carefully nursed plan. It is true that sometimes during the several days that had elapsed since they had set out upon their expedition it had been difficult for Taglat to hold his idea uppermost in his mind, and on several occasions he had completely forgotten it, until Tarzan, by a chance word, had recalled it to him, but, for an ape, Taglat had done well.

Now, he licked his chops, and he made a sickening, sucking noise with his flabby lips as he drew in his breath.

Satisfied that the she was where he had hoped to find her, Tarzan led his apes toward the tent of Achmet Zek. A passing Arab and two slaves saw them, but the night was dark and the white burnooses hid the hairy limbs of the apes and the giant figure of their leader, so that the three, by squatting down as though in conversation, were passed by, unsuspected. To the rear of the tent they made their way. Within, Achmet Zek conversed with several of his lieutenants. Without, Tarzan listened.

THE DEADLY PERIL OF JANE CLAYTON

Lieutenant Albert Werper, terrified by contemplation of the fate which might await him at Adis Abeba, cast about for some scheme of escape, but after the black Mugambi had eluded their vigilance the Abyssinians redoubled their precautions to prevent Werper following the lead of the Negro.

For some time Werper entertained the idea of bribing Abdul Mourak with a portion of the contents of the pouch; but fearing that the man would demand all the gems as the price of liberty, the Belgian, influenced by avarice, sought another avenue from his dilemma.

It was then that there dawned upon him the possibility of the success of a different course which would still leave him in possession of the jewels, while at the same time satisfying the greed of the Abyssinian with the conviction that he had obtained all that Werper had to offer.

And so it was that a day or so after Mugambi had disappeared, Werper asked for an audience with Abdul Mourak. As the Belgian entered the presence of his captor the scowl upon the features of the latter boded ill for any hope which Werper might entertain, still he fortified himself by recalling the common weakness of mankind, which permits the most inflexible of natures to bend to the consuming desire for wealth.

Abdul Mourak eyed him, frowningly. "What do you want now?" he asked.

"My liberty," replied Werper.

The Abyssinian sneered. "And you disturbed me thus to tell me what any fool might know," he said.

"I can pay for it," said Werper.

Abdul Mourak laughed loudly. "Pay for it?" he cried. "What with—the rags that you have upon your back? Or, perhaps you are concealing beneath your coat a thousand pounds of ivory. Get out! You are a fool. Do not bother me again or I shall have you whipped."

But Werper persisted. His liberty and perhaps his life depended upon his success.

"Listen to me," he pleaded. "If I can give you as much gold as ten men may carry will you promise that I shall be conducted in safety to the nearest English commissioner?"

"As much gold as ten men may carry!" repeated Abdul Mourak. "You are crazy. Where have you so much gold as that?"

"I know where it is hid," said Werper. "Promise, and I will lead you to it—if ten loads is enough?"

Abdul Mourak had ceased to laugh. He was eyeing the Belgian intently. The fellow seemed sane enough—yet ten loads of gold! It was preposterous. The Abyssinian thought in silence for a moment.

"Well, and if I promise," he said. "How far is this gold?"

"A long week's march to the south," replied Werper.

"And if we do not find it where you say it is, do you realize what your punishment will be?"

"If it is not there I will forfeit my life," replied the Belgian. "I know it is there, for I saw it buried with my own eyes. And more—there are not only ten loads, but as many as fifty men may carry. It is all yours if you will promise to see me safely delivered into the protection of the English."

"You will stake your life against the finding of the gold?" asked Abdul.

Werper assented with a nod.

"Very well," said the Abyssinian, "I promise, and even if there be but five loads you shall have your freedom; but until the gold is in my possession you remain a prisoner."

"I am satisfied," said Werper. "Tomorrow we start?"

Abdul Mourak nodded, and the Belgian returned to his guards. The following day the Abyssinian soldiers were surprised to receive an order which turned their faces from the northeast to the south. And so it happened that upon the very night that Tarzan and the two apes entered the village of the raiders, the Abyssinians camped but a few miles to the east of the same spot.

While Werper dreamed of freedom and the unmolested enjoyment of the fortune in his stolen pouch, and Abdul Mourak lay awake in greedy contemplation of the fifty loads of gold which lay but a few days farther to the south of him, Achmet Zek gave orders to his lieutenants that they should prepare a force of fighting men and carriers to proceed to the ruins of the Englishman's DOUAR on the morrow and bring back the fabulous fortune which his renegade lieutenant had told him was buried there.

And as he delivered his instructions to those within, a silent listener crouched without his tent, waiting for the time when he might enter in safety and prosecute his search for the missing pouch and the pretty pebbles that had caught his fancy.

At last the swarthy companions of Achmet Zek quitted his tent, and the leader went with them to smoke a pipe with one of their number, leaving his own silken habitation unguarded. Scarcely had they left the interior when a knife blade was thrust through the fabric of the rear wall, some six feet above the ground, and a swift downward stroke opened an entrance to those who waited beyond.

Through the opening stepped the ape-man, and close behind him came the huge Chulk; but Taglat did not follow them. Instead he turned and slunk through the darkness toward the hut where the she who had arrested his brutish interest lay securely bound. Before the doorway the sentries sat upon their haunches, conversing in monotones. Within, the young woman lay upon a filthy sleeping mat, resigned, through utter hopelessness to whatever fate lay in store for her until the opportunity arrived which would permit her to free herself by the only means which now seemed even remotely possible—the hitherto detested act of self-destruction.

Creeping silently toward the sentries, a white-burnoosed figure approached the shadows at one end of the hut. The meager intellect of the creature denied it the advantage it might have taken of its disguise. Where it could have walked boldly to the very sides of the sentries, it chose rather to sneak upon them, unseen, from the rear.

It came to the corner of the hut and peered around. The sentries were but a few paces away; but the ape did not dare expose himself, even for an instant, to those feared and hated thunder-sticks which the Tarmangani knew so well how to use, if there were another and safer method of attack.

Taglat wished that there was a tree nearby from the over-hanging branches of which he might spring upon his unsuspecting prey; but, though there was no tree, the idea gave birth to a plan. The eaves of the hut were just above the heads of the sentries—from them he could leap upon the Tarmangani, unseen. A quick snap of those mighty jaws would dispose of one of them before the other realized that they were attacked, and the second would fall an easy prey to the strength, agility and ferocity of a second quick charge.

Taglat withdrew a few paces to the rear of the hut, gathered himself for the effort, ran quickly forward and leaped high into the air. He struck the roof directly above the rear wall of the hut, and the structure, reinforced by the wall beneath, held his enormous weight for an instant, then he moved forward a step, the roof sagged, the thatching parted and the great anthropoid shot through into the interior.

The sentries, hearing the crashing of the roof poles, leaped to their feet and rushed into the hut. Jane Clayton tried to roll aside as the great form lit upon the floor so close to her that one foot pinned her clothing to the ground.

The ape, feeling the movement beside him, reached down and gathered the girl in the hollow of one mighty arm. The burnoose covered the hairy body so that Jane Clayton believed that a human arm supported her, and from the extremity of hopelessness a great hope sprang into her breast that at last she was in the keeping of a rescuer.

The two sentries were now within the hut, but hesitating because of doubt as to the nature of the cause of the disturbance. Their eyes, not yet accustomed to the darkness of the interior, told them nothing, nor did they hear any sound, for the ape stood silently awaiting their attack.

Seeing that they stood without advancing, and realizing that, handicapped as he was by the weight of the she, he could put up but a poor battle, Taglat elected to risk a sudden break for liberty. Lowering his head, he charged straight for the two sentries who blocked the doorway. The impact of his mighty shoulders bowled them over upon their backs, and before they could scramble to their feet, the ape was gone, darting in the shadows of the huts toward the palisade at the far end of the village.

The speed and strength of her rescuer filled Jane Clayton with wonder. Could it be that Tarzan had survived the bullet of the Arab? Who else in all the jungle could bear the weight of a grown woman as lightly as he who held her? She spoke his name; but there was no response. Still she did not give up hope.

At the palisade the beast did not even hesitate. A single mighty leap carried it to the top, where it poised but for an instant before dropping to the ground upon the opposite side. Now the girl was almost positive that she was safe in the arms of her husband, and when the ape took to the trees and bore her swiftly into the jungle, as Tarzan had done at other times in the past, belief became conviction.

In a little moonlit glade, a mile or so from the camp of the raiders, her rescuer halted and dropped her to the ground. His roughness surprised her, but still she had no doubts. Again she called him by name, and at the same instant the ape, fretting under the restraints of the unaccustomed garments of the Tarmangani, tore the burnoose from him, revealing to the eyes of the horror-struck woman the hideous face and hairy form of a giant anthropoid.

With a piteous wail of terror, Jane Clayton swooned, while, from the concealment of a nearby bush, Numa, the lion, eyed the pair hungrily and licked his chops.

Tarzan, entering the tent of Achmet Zek, searched the interior thoroughly. He tore the bed to pieces and scattered the contents of box and bag about the floor. He investigated whatever his eyes discovered, nor did those keen organs overlook a single article within the habitation of the raider chief; but no pouch or pretty pebbles rewarded his thoroughness.

Satisfied at last that his belongings were not in the possession of Achmet Zek, unless they were on the person of the chief himself, Tarzan decided to secure the person of the she before further prosecuting his search for the pouch.

Motioning for Chulk to follow him, he passed out of the tent by the same way that he had entered it, and walking boldly through the village, made directly for the hut where Jane Clayton had been imprisoned.

He noted with surprise the absence of Taglat, whom he had expected to find awaiting him outside the tent of Achmet Zek; but, accustomed as he was to the unreliability of apes, he gave no serious attention to the present defection of his surly companion. So long as Taglat did not cause interference with his plans, Tarzan was indifferent to his absence.

As he approached the hut, the ape-man noticed that a crowd had collected about the entrance. He could see that the men who composed it were much excited, and fearing lest Chulk's disguise should prove inadequate to the concealment of his true identity in the face of so many observers, he commanded the ape to betake himself to the far end of the village, and there await him.

As Chulk waddled off, keeping to the shadows, Tarzan advanced boldly toward the excited group before the doorway of the hut. He mingled with the blacks and the Arabs in an endeavor to learn the cause of the commotion, in his interest forgetting that he alone of the assemblage carried a spear, a bow and arrows, and thus might become an object of suspicious attention.

Shouldering his way through the crowd he approached the doorway, and had almost reached it when one of the Arabs laid a hand upon his shoulder, crying: "Who is this?" at the same time snatching back the hood from the ape-man's face.

Tarzan of the Apes in all his savage life had never been accustomed to pause in argument with an antagonist. The primitive instinct of self-preservation acknowledges many arts and wiles; but argument is not one of them, nor did he now waste precious time in an attempt to convince the raiders that he was not a wolf in sheep's clothing. Instead he had his unmasker by the throat ere the man's words had scarce quitted his lips, and hurling him from side to side brushed away those who would have swarmed upon him.

Using the Arab as a weapon, Tarzan forced his way quickly to the doorway, and a moment later was within the hut. A hasty examination revealed the fact that it was empty, and his sense of smell discovered, too, the scent spoor of Taglat, the ape. Tarzan uttered a low, ominous growl. Those who were pressing forward at the doorway to seize him, fell back as the savage notes of the bestial challenge smote upon their ears. They looked at one another in surprise and consternation. A man had entered the hut alone, and yet with their own ears they had heard the voice of a wild beast within. What could it mean? Had a lion or a leopard sought sanctuary in the interior, unbeknown to the sentries?

Tarzan's quick eyes discovered the opening in the roof, through which Taglat had fallen. He guessed that the ape had either come or gone by way of the break, and while the Arabs hesitated without, he sprang, catlike, for the opening, grasped the top of the wall and clambered out upon the roof, dropping instantly to the ground at the rear of the hut.

When the Arabs finally mustered courage to enter the hut, after firing several volleys through the walls, they found the interior deserted. At the same time Tarzan, at the far end of the village, sought for Chulk; but the ape was nowhere to be found.

Robbed of his she, deserted by his companions, and as much in ignorance as ever as to the whereabouts of his pouch and pebbles, it was an angry Tarzan who climbed the palisade and vanished into the darkness of the jungle.

For the present he must give up the search for his pouch, since it would be paramount to self-destruction to enter the Arab camp now while all its inhabitants were aroused and upon the alert.

In his escape from the village, the ape-man had lost the spoor of the fleeing Taglat, and now he circled widely through the forest in an endeavor to again pick it up.

Chulk had remained at his post until the cries and shots of the Arabs had filled his simple soul with terror, for above all things the ape folk fear the thunder-sticks of the Tarmangani; then he had clambered nimbly over the palisade, tearing his burnoose in the effort, and fled into the depths of the jungle, grumbling and scolding as he went.

Tarzan, roaming the jungle in search of the trail of Taglat and the she, traveled swiftly. In a little moonlit glade ahead of him the great ape was bending over the prostrate form of the woman Tarzan sought. The beast was tearing at the bonds that confined her ankles and wrists, pulling and gnawing upon the cords.

The course the ape-man was taking would carry him but a short distance to the right of them, and though he could not have seen them the wind was bearing down from them to him, carrying their scent spoor strongly toward him.

A moment more and Jane Clayton's safety might have been assured, even though Numa, the lion, was already gathering himself in preparation for a charge; but Fate, already all too cruel, now outdid herself—the wind veered suddenly for a few moments, the scent spoor that would have led the ape-man to the girl's side was wafted in the opposite direction; Tarzan passed within fifty yards of the tragedy that was being enacted in the glade, and the opportunity was gone beyond recall.

EDGAR RICE BURROUGHS

THE FIGHT FOR THE TREASURE

It was morning before Tarzan could bring himself to a realization of the possibility of failure of his quest, and even then he would only admit that success was but delayed. He would eat and sleep, and then set forth again. The jungle was wide; but wide too were the experience and cunning of Tarzan. Taglat might travel far; but Tarzan would find him in the end, though he had to search every tree in the mighty forest.

Soliloquizing thus, the ape-man followed the spoor of Bara, the deer, the unfortunate upon which he had decided to satisfy his hunger. For half an hour the trail led the ape-man toward the east along a well-marked game path, when suddenly, to the stalker's astonishment, the quarry broke into sight, racing madly back along the narrow way straight toward the hunter.

Tarzan, who had been following along the trail, leaped so quickly to the concealing verdure at the side that the deer was still unaware of the presence of an enemy in this direction, and while the animal was still some distance away, the ape-man swung into the lower branches of the tree which overhung the trail. There he crouched, a savage beast of prey, awaiting the coming of its victim.

What had frightened the deer into so frantic a retreat, Tarzan did not know—Numa, the lion, perhaps, or Sheeta, the panther; but whatsoever it was mattered little to Tarzan of the Apes—he was ready and willing to defend his kill against any other denizen of the jungle. If he were unable to do it by means of physical prowess, he had at his command another and a greater power—his shrewd intelligence.

And so, on came the running deer, straight into the jaws of death. The ape-man turned so that his back was toward the approaching animal. He poised with bent knees upon the gently swaying limb above the trail, timing with keen ears the nearing hoof beats of frightened Bara.

In a moment the victim flashed beneath the limb and at the same instant the ape-man above sprang out and down upon its back. The weight of the man's body carried the deer to the ground. It stumbled forward once in a futile effort to rise, and then mighty muscles dragged its head far back, gave the neck a vicious wrench, and Bara was dead.

Quick had been the killing, and equally quick were the ape-man's subsequent actions, for who might know what manner of killer pursued Bara, or how close at hand he might be? Scarce had the neck of the victim snapped than the carcass was hanging over one of Tarzan's broad shoulders, and an instant later the ape-man was perched once more among the lower branches of a tree above the trail, his keen, gray eyes scanning the pathway down which the deer had fled.

Nor was it long before the cause of Bara's fright became evident to Tarzan, for presently came the unmistakable sounds of approaching horsemen. Dragging his kill after him the ape-man ascended to the middle terrace, and settling himself comfortably in the crotch of a tree where he could still view the trail beneath, cut a juicy steak from the deer's loin, and burying his strong, white teeth in the hot flesh proceeded to enjoy the fruits of his prowess and his cunning.

Nor did he neglect the trail beneath while he satisfied his hunger. His sharp eyes saw the muzzle of the leading horse as it came into view around a bend in the tortuous trail, and one by one they scrutinized the riders as they passed beneath him in single file.

Among them came one whom Tarzan recognized, but so schooled was the ape-man in the control of his emotions that no slightest change of expression, much less any hysterical demonstration that might have revealed his presence, betrayed the fact of his inward excitement.

Beneath him, as unconscious of his presence as were the Abyssinians before and behind him, rode Albert Werper, while the ape-man scrutinized the Belgian for some sign of the pouch which he had stolen.

As the Abyssinians rode toward the south, a giant figure hovered ever upon their trail—a huge, almost naked white man, who carried the bloody carcass of a deer upon his shoulders, for Tarzan knew that he might not have another opportunity to hunt for some time if he were to follow the Belgian.

To endeavor to snatch him from the midst of the armed horsemen, not even Tarzan would attempt other than in the last extremity, for the way of the wild is the way of caution and cunning, unless they be aroused to rashness by pain or anger.

So the Abyssinians and the Belgian marched southward and Tarzan of the Apes swung silently after them through the swaying branches of the middle terrace.

A two days' march brought them to a level plain beyond which lay mountains—a plain which Tarzan remembered and which aroused within him vague half memories and strange longings. Out upon the plain the horsemen rode, and at a safe distance behind them crept the ape-man, taking advantage of such cover as the ground afforded.

Beside a charred pile of timbers the Abyssinians halted, and Tarzan, sneaking close and concealing himself in nearby shrubbery, watched them in wonderment. He saw them digging up the earth, and he wondered if they had hidden meat there in the past and now had come for it. Then he recalled how he had buried his pretty pebbles, and the suggestion that had caused him to do it. They were digging for the things the blacks had buried here!

Presently he saw them uncover a dirty, yellow object, and he witnessed the joy of Werper and of Abdul Mourak as the grimy object was exposed to view. One by one they unearthed many similar pieces, all of the same uniform, dirty yellow, until a pile of them lay upon the ground, a pile which Abdul Mourak fondled and petted in an ecstasy of greed.

Something stirred in the ape-man's mind as he looked long upon the golden ingots. Where had he seen such before? What were they? Why did these Tarmangani covet them so greatly? To whom did they belong?

He recalled the black men who had buried them. The things must be theirs. Werper was stealing them as he had stolen Tarzan's pouch of pebbles. The ape-man's eyes blazed in anger. He would like to find the black men and lead them against these thieves. He wondered where their village might be.

As all these things ran through the active mind, a party of men moved out of the forest at the edge of the plain and advanced toward the ruins of the burned bungalow.

Abdul Mourak, always watchful, was the first to see them, but already they were halfway across the open. He called to his men to mount and hold themselves in readiness, for in the heart of Africa who may know whether a strange host be friend or foe?

Werper, swinging into his saddle, fastened his eyes upon the newcomers, then, white and trembling he turned toward Abdul Mourak.

"It is Achmet Zek and his raiders," he whispered. "They are come for the gold."

It must have been at about the same instant that Achmet Zek discovered the pile of yellow ingots and realized the actuality of what he had already feared since first his eyes had alighted upon the party beside the ruins of the Englishman's bungalow. Someone had forestalled him—another had come for the treasure ahead of him.

The Arab was crazed by rage. Recently everything had gone against him. He had lost the jewels, the Belgian, and for the second time he had lost the Englishwoman. Now some one had come to rob him of this treasure which he had thought as safe from disturbance here as though it never had been mined.

He cared not whom the thieves might be. They would not give up the gold without a battle, of that he was certain, and with a wild whoop and a command to his followers, Achmet Zek put spurs to his horse and dashed down upon the Abyssinians, and after him, waving their long guns above their heads, yelling and cursing, came his motley horde of cut-throat followers.

The men of Abdul Mourak met them with a volley which emptied a few saddles, and then the raiders were among them, and sword, pistol and musket, each was doing its most hideous and bloody work.

Achmet Zek, spying Werper at the first charge, bore down upon the Belgian, and the latter, terrified by contemplation of the fate he deserved, turned his horse's head and dashed madly away in an effort to escape. Shouting to a lieutenant to take command, and urging him upon pain of death to dispatch the Abyssinians and bring the gold back to his camp, Achmet Zek set off across the plain in pursuit of the Belgian, his wicked nature unable to forego the pleasures of revenge, even at the risk of sacrificing the treasure.

As the pursued and the pursuer raced madly toward the distant forest the battle behind them raged with bloody savageness. No quarter was asked or given by either the ferocious Abyssinians or the murderous cut-throats of Achmet Zek.

From the concealment of the shrubbery Tarzan watched the sanguinary conflict which so effectually surrounded him that he found no loop-hole through which he might escape to follow Werper and the Arab chief.

The Abyssinians were formed in a circle which included Tarzan's position, and around and into them galloped the yelling raiders, now darting away, now charging in to deliver thrusts and cuts with their curved swords.

Numerically the men of Achmet Zek were superior, and slowly but surely the soldiers of Menelek were being exterminated. To Tarzan the result was immaterial. He watched with but a single purpose—to escape the ring of blood-mad fighters and be away after the Belgian and his pouch.

When he had first discovered Werper upon the trail where he had slain Bara, he had thought that his eyes must be playing him false, so certain had he been that the thief had been slain and devoured by Numa; but after following the detachment for two days, with his keen eyes always upon the Belgian, he no longer doubted the identity of the man, though he was put to it to explain the identity of the mutilated corpse he had supposed was the man he sought.

As he crouched in hiding among the unkempt shrubbery which so short a while since had been the delight and pride of the wife he no longer recalled, an Arab and an Abyssinian wheeled their mounts close to his position as they slashed at each other with their swords.

Step by step the Arab beat back his adversary until the latter's horse all but trod upon the ape-man, and then a vicious cut clove the black warrior's skull, and the corpse toppled backward almost upon Tarzan.

As the Abyssinian tumbled from his saddle the possibility of escape which was represented by the riderless horse electrified the ape-man to instant action. Before the frightened beast could gather himself for flight a naked giant was astride his back. A strong hand had grasped his bridle rein, and the surprised Arab discovered a new foe in the saddle of him, whom he had slain.

But this enemy wielded no sword, and his spear and bow remained upon his back. The Arab, recovered from his first surprise, dashed in with raised sword to annihilate this presumptuous stranger. He aimed a mighty blow at the ape-man's head, a blow which swung harmlessly through thin air as Tarzan ducked from its path, and then the Arab felt the other's horse brushing his leg, a great arm shot out and encircled his waist, and before he could recover himself he was dragged from his saddle, and forming a shield for his antagonist was borne at a mad run straight through the encircling ranks of his fellows.

Just beyond them he was tossed aside upon the ground, and the last he saw of his strange foeman the latter was galloping off across the plain in the direction of the forest at its farther edge.

For another hour the battle raged nor did it cease until the last of the Abyssinians lay dead upon the ground, or had galloped off toward the north in flight. But a handful of men escaped, among them Abdul Mourak.

The victorious raiders collected about the pile of golden ingots which the Abyssinians had uncovered, and there awaited the return of their leader. Their exultation was slightly tempered by the glimpse they had had of the strange apparition of the naked white man galloping away upon the horse of one of their foemen and carrying a companion who was now among them expatiating upon the superhuman strength of the ape-man. None of them there but was familiar with the name and fame of Tarzan of the Apes, and the fact that they had recognized the white giant as the ferocious enemy of the wrongdoers of the jungle, added to their terror, for they had been assured that Tarzan was dead.

Naturally superstitious, they fully believed that they had seen the disembodied spirit of the dead man, and now they cast fearful glances about them in expectation of the ghost's early return to the scene of the ruin they had inflicted upon him during their recent raid upon his home, and discussed in affrighted whispers the probable nature of the vengeance which the spirit would inflict upon them should he return to find them in possession of his gold.

As they conversed their terror grew, while from the concealment of the reeds along the river below them a small party of naked, black warriors watched their every move. From the heights beyond the river these black men had heard the noise of the conflict, and creeping warily down to the stream had forded it and advanced through the reeds until they were in a position to watch every move of the combatants.

For a half hour the raiders awaited Achmet Zek's return, their fear of the earlier return of the ghost of Tarzan constantly undermining their loyalty to and fear of their chief. Finally one among them voiced the desires of all when he announced that he intended riding forth toward the forest in search of Achmet Zek. Instantly every man of them sprang to his mount.

"The gold will be safe here," cried one. "We have killed the Abyssinians and there are no others to carry it away. Let us ride in search of Achmet Zek!"

And a moment later, amidst a cloud of dust, the raiders were galloping madly across the plain, and out from the concealment of the reeds along the river, crept a party of black warriors toward the spot where the golden ingots of Opar lay piled on the ground.

Werper had still been in advance of Achmet Zek when he reached the forest; but the latter, better mounted, was gaining upon him. Riding with the reckless courage of desperation the Belgian urged his mount to greater speed even within the narrow confines of the winding, game trail that the beast was following.

Behind him he could hear the voice of Achmet Zek crying to him to halt; but Werper only dug the spurs deeper into the bleeding sides of his panting mount. Two hundred yards within the forest a broken branch lay across the trail. It was a small thing that a horse might ordinarily take in his natural stride without noticing its presence; but Werper's horse was jaded, his feet were heavy with weariness, and as the branch caught between his front legs he stumbled, was unable to recover himself, and went down, sprawling in the trail.

Werper, going over his head, rolled a few yards farther on, scrambled to his feet and ran back. Seizing the reins he tugged to drag the beast to his feet; but the animal would not or could not rise, and as the Belgian cursed and struck at him, Achmet Zek appeared in view.

Instantly the Belgian ceased his efforts with the dying animal at his feet, and seizing his rifle, dropped behind the horse and fired at the oncoming Arab.

His bullet, going low, struck Achmet Zek's horse in the breast, bringing him down a hundred yards from where Werper lay preparing to fire a second shot.

The Arab, who had gone down with his mount, was standing astride him, and seeing the Belgian's strategic position behind his fallen horse, lost no time in taking up a similar one behind his own.

And there the two lay, alternately firing at and cursing each other, while from behind the Arab, Tarzan of the Apes approached to the edge of the forest. Here he heard the occasional shots of the duelists, and choosing the safer and swifter avenue of the forest branches to the uncertain transportation afforded by a half-broken Abyssinian pony, took to the trees.

Keeping to one side of the trail, the ape-man came presently to a point where he could look down in comparative safety upon the fighters. First one and then the other would partially raise himself above his breastwork of horseflesh, fire his weapon and immediately drop flat behind his shelter, where he would reload and repeat the act a moment later.

Werper had but little ammunition, having been hastily armed by Abdul Mourak from the body of one of the first of the Abyssinians who had fallen in the fight about the pile of ingots, and now he realized that soon he would have used his last bullet, and be at the mercy of the Arab—a mercy with which he was well acquainted.

Facing both death and despoilment of his treasure, the Belgian cast about for some plan of escape, and the only one that appealed to him as containing even a remote possibility of success hinged upon the chance of bribing Achmet Zek.

Werper had fired all but a single cartridge, when, during a lull in the fighting, he called aloud to his opponent.

"Achmet Zek," he cried, "Allah alone knows which one of us may leave our bones to rot where he lies upon this trail today if we keep up our foolish battle. You wish the contents of the pouch I wear about my waist, and I wish my life and my liberty even more than I do the jewels. Let us each, then, take that which he most desires and go our separate ways in peace. I will lay the pouch upon the carcass of my horse, where you may see it, and you, in turn, will lay your gun upon your horse, with butt toward me. Then I will go away, leaving the pouch to you, and you will let me go in safety. I want only my life, and my freedom."

The Arab thought in silence for a moment. Then he spoke. His reply was influenced by the fact that he had expended his last shot.

"Go your way, then," he growled, "leaving the pouch in plain sight behind you. See, I lay my gun thus, with the butt toward you. Go."

Werper removed the pouch from about his waist. Sorrowfully and affectionately he let his fingers press the hard outlines of the contents. Ah, if he could extract a little handful of the precious stones! But Achmet Zek was standing now, his eagle eyes commanding a plain view of the Belgian and his every act.

Regretfully Werper laid the pouch, its contents undisturbed, upon the body of his horse, rose, and taking his rifle with him, backed slowly down the trail until a turn hid him from the view of the watchful Arab.

Even then Achmet Zek did not advance, fearful as he was of some such treachery as he himself might have been guilty of under like circumstances; nor were his suspicions groundless, for the Belgian, no sooner had he passed out of the range of the Arab's vision, halted behind the bole of a tree, where he still commanded an unobstructed view of his dead horse and the pouch, and raising his rifle covered the spot where the other's body must appear when he came forward to seize the treasure.

But Achmet Zek was no fool to expose himself to the blackened honor of a thief and a murderer. Taking his long gun with him, he left the trail, entering the rank and tangled vegetation which walled it, and crawling slowly forward on hands and knees he paralleled the trail; but never for an instant was his body exposed to the rifle of the hidden assassin.

Thus Achmet Zek advanced until he had come opposite the dead horse of his enemy. The pouch lay there in full view, while a short distance along the trail, Werper waited in growing impatience and nervousness, wondering why the Arab did not come to claim his reward.

Presently he saw the muzzle of a rifle appear suddenly and mysteriously a few inches above the pouch, and before he could realize the cunning trick that the Arab had played upon him the sight of the weapon was adroitly hooked into the rawhide thong which formed the carrying strap of the pouch, and the latter was drawn quickly from his view into the dense foliage at the trail's side.

Not for an instant had the raider exposed a square inch of his body, and Werper dared not fire his one remaining shot unless every chance of a successful hit was in his favor.

Chuckling to himself, Achmet Zek withdrew a few paces farther into the jungle, for he was as positive that Werper was waiting nearby for a chance to pot him as though his eyes had penetrated the jungle trees to the figure of the hiding Belgian, fingering his rifle behind the bole of the buttressed giant.

Werper did not dare advance—his cupidity would not permit him to depart, and so he stood there, his rifle ready in his hands, his eyes watching the trail before him with catlike intensity.

But there was another who had seen the pouch and recognized it, who did advance with Achmet Zek, hovering above him, as silent and as sure as death itself, and as the Arab, finding a little spot less overgrown with bushes than he had yet encountered, prepared to gloat his eyes upon the contents of the pouch, Tarzan paused directly above him, intent upon the same object.

Wetting his thin lips with his tongue, Achmet Zek loosened the tie strings which closed the mouth of the pouch, and cupping one claw-like hand poured forth a portion of the contents into his palm.

A single look he took at the stones lying in his hand. His eyes narrowed, a curse broke from his lips, and he hurled the small objects upon the ground, disdainfully. Quickly he emptied the balance of the contents until he had scanned each separate stone, and as he dumped them all upon the ground and stamped upon them his rage grew until the muscles of his face worked in demon-like fury, and his fingers clenched until his nails bit into the flesh.

Above, Tarzan watched in wonderment. He had been curious to discover what all the pow-wow about his pouch had meant. He wanted to see what the Arab would do after the other had gone away, leaving the pouch behind him, and, having satisfied his curiosity, he would then have pounced upon Achmet Zek and taken the pouch and his pretty pebbles away from him, for did they not belong to Tarzan?

He saw the Arab now throw aside the empty pouch, and grasping his long gun by the barrel, clublike, sneak stealthily through the jungle beside the trail along which Werper had gone.

As the man disappeared from his view, Tarzan dropped to the ground and commenced gathering up the spilled contents of the pouch, and the moment that he obtained his first near view of the scattered pebbles he understood the rage of the Arab, for instead of the glittering and scintillating gems which had first caught and held the attention of the ape-man, the pouch now contained but a collection of ordinary river pebbles.

JANE CLAYTON AND THE BEASTS OF THE JUNGLE

Mugambi, after his successful break for liberty, had fallen upon hard times. His way had led him through a country with which he was unfamiliar, a jungle country in which he could find no water, and but little food, so that after several days of wandering he found himself so reduced in strength that he could barely drag himself along.

It was with growing difficulty that he found the strength necessary to construct a shelter by night wherein he might be reasonably safe from the large carnivora, and by day he still further exhausted his strength in digging for edible roots, and searching for water.

A few stagnant pools at considerable distances apart saved him from death by thirst; but his was a pitiable state when finally he stumbled by accident upon a large river in a country where fruit was abundant, and small game which he might bag by means of a combination of stealth, cunning, and a crude knob-stick which he had fashioned from a fallen limb.

Realizing that he still had a long march ahead of him before he could reach even the outskirts of the Waziri country, Mugambi wisely decided to remain where he was until he had recuperated his strength and health. A few days' rest would accomplish wonders for him, he knew, and he could ill afford to sacrifice his chances for a safe return by setting forth handicapped by weakness.

And so it was that he constructed a substantial thorn boma, and rigged a thatched shelter within it, where he might sleep by night in security, and from which he sallied forth by day to hunt the flesh which alone could return to his giant thews their normal prowess.

One day, as he hunted, a pair of savage eyes discovered him from the concealment of the branches of a great tree beneath which the black warrior passed. Bloodshot, wicked eyes they were, set in a fierce and hairy face.

They watched Mugambi make his little kill of a small rodent, and they followed him as he returned to his hut, their owner moving quietly through the trees upon the trail of the Negro.

The creature was Chulk, and he looked down upon the unconscious man more in curiosity than in hate. The wearing of the Arab burnoose which Tarzan had placed upon his person had aroused in the mind of the anthropoid a desire for similar mimicry of the Tarmangani. The burnoose, though, had obstructed his movements and proven such a nuisance that the ape had long since torn it from him and thrown it away.

Now, however, he saw a Gomangani arrayed in less cumbersome apparel—a loin cloth, a few copper ornaments and a feather headdress. These were more in line with Chulk's desires than a flowing robe which was constantly getting between one's legs, and catching upon every limb and bush along the leafy trail.

Chulk eyed the pouch, which, suspended over Mugambi's shoulder, swung beside his black hip. This took his fancy, for it was ornamented with feathers and a fringe, and so the ape hung about Mugambi's boma, waiting an opportunity to seize either by stealth or might some object of the black's apparel.

Nor was it long before the opportunity came. Feeling safe within his thorny enclosure, Mugambi was wont to stretch himself in the shade of his shelter during the heat of the day, and sleep in peaceful security until the declining sun carried with it the enervating temperature of midday.

Watching from above, Chulk saw the black warrior stretched thus in the unconsciousness of sleep one sultry afternoon. Creeping out upon an overhanging branch the anthropoid dropped to the ground within the boma. He approached the sleeper upon padded feet which gave forth no sound, and with an uncanny woodcraft that rustled not a leaf or a grass blade.

Pausing beside the man, the ape bent over and examined his belongings. Great as was the strength of Chulk there lay in the back of his little brain a something which deterred him from arousing the man to combat—a sense that is inherent in all the lower orders, a strange fear of man, that rules even the most powerful of the jungle creatures at times.

To remove Mugambi's loin cloth without awakening him would be impossible, and the only detachable things were the knob-stick and the pouch, which had fallen from the black's shoulder as he rolled in sleep.

Seizing these two articles, as better than nothing at all, Chulk retreated with haste, and every indication of nervous terror, to the safety of the tree from which he had dropped, and, still haunted by that indefinable terror which the close proximity of man awakened in his breast, fled precipitately through the jungle. Aroused by attack, or supported by the presence of another of his kind, Chulk could have braved the presence of a score of human beings, but alone—ah, that was a different matter—alone, and unenraged.

It was some time after Mugambi awoke that he missed the pouch. Instantly he was all excitement. What could have become of it? It had been at his side when he lay down to sleep—of that he was certain, for had he not pushed it from beneath him when its bulging bulk, pressing against his ribs, caused him discomfort? Yes, it had been there when he lay down to sleep. How then had it vanished?

Mugambi's savage imagination was filled with visions of the spirits of departed friends and enemies, for only to the machinations of such as these could he attribute the disappearance of his pouch and knob-stick in the first excitement of the discovery of their loss; but later and more careful investigation, such as his woodcraft made possible, revealed indisputable evidence of a more material explanation than his excited fancy and superstition had at first led him to accept.

In the trampled turf beside him was the faint impress of huge, manlike feet. Mugambi raised his brows as the truth dawned upon him. Hastily leaving the boma he searched in all directions about the enclosure for some farther sign of the tell-tale spoor. He climbed trees and sought for evidence of the direction of the thief's flight; but the faint signs left by a wary ape who elects to travel through the trees eluded the woodcraft of Mugambi. Tarzan might have followed them; but no ordinary mortal could perceive them, or perceiving, translate.

The black, now strengthened and refreshed by his rest, felt ready to set out again for Waziri, and finding himself another knob-stick, turned his back upon the river and plunged into the mazes of the jungle.

As Taglat struggled with the bonds which secured the ankles and wrists of his captive, the great lion that eyed the two from behind a nearby clump of bushes wormed closer to his intended prey.

The ape's back was toward the lion. He did not see the broad head, fringed by its rough mane, protruding through the leafy wall. He could not know that the powerful hind paws were gathering close beneath the tawny belly preparatory to a sudden spring, and his first intimation of impending danger was the thunderous and triumphant roar which the charging lion could no longer suppress.

Scarce pausing for a backward glance, Taglat abandoned the unconscious woman and fled in the opposite direction from the horrid sound which had broken in so unexpected and terrifying a manner upon his startled ears; but the warning had come too late to save him, and the lion, in his second bound, alighted full upon the broad shoulders of the anthropoid.

As the great bull went down there was awakened in him to the full all the cunning, all the ferocity, all the physical prowess which obey the mightiest of the fundamental laws of nature, the law of self-preservation, and turning upon his back he closed with the carnivore in a death struggle so fearless and abandoned, that for a moment the great Numa himself may have trembled for the outcome.

Seizing the lion by the mane, Taglat buried his yellowed fangs deep in the monster's throat, growling hideously through the muffled gag of blood and hair. Mixed with the ape's voice the lion's roars of rage and pain reverberated through the jungle, till the lesser creatures of the wild, startled from their peaceful pursuits, scurried fearfully away.

Rolling over and over upon the turf the two battled with demoniac fury, until the colossal cat, by doubling his hind paws far up beneath his belly sank his talons deep into Taglat's chest, then, ripping downward with all his strength, Numa accomplished his design, and the disemboweled anthropoid, with a last spasmodic struggle, relaxed in limp and bloody dissolution beneath his titanic adversary.

Scrambling to his feet, Numa looked about quickly in all directions, as though seeking to detect the possible presence of other foes; but only the still and unconscious form of the girl, lying a few paces from him met his gaze, and with an angry growl he placed a forepaw upon the body of his kill and raising his head gave voice to his savage victory cry.

For another moment he stood with fierce eyes roving to and fro about the clearing. At last they halted for a second time upon the girl. A low growl rumbled from the lion's throat. His lower jaw rose and fell, and the slaver drooled and dripped upon the dead face of Taglat.

Like two yellow-green augurs, wide and unblinking, the terrible eyes remained fixed upon Jane Clayton. The erect and majestic pose of the great frame shrank suddenly into a sinister crouch as, slowly and gently as one who treads on eggs, the devil-faced cat crept forward toward the girl.

Beneficent Fate maintained her in happy unconsciousness of the dread presence sneaking stealthily upon her. She did not know when the lion paused at her side. She did not hear the sniffing of his nostrils as he smelled about her. She did not feel the heat of the fetid breath upon her face, nor the dripping of the saliva from the frightful jaws half opened so close above her.

Finally the lion lifted a forepaw and turned the body of the girl half over, then he stood again eyeing her as though still undetermined whether life was extinct or not. Some noise or odor from the nearby jungle attracted his attention for a moment. His eyes did not again return to Jane Clayton, and presently he left her, walked over to the remains of Taglat, and crouching down upon his kill with his back toward the girl, proceeded to devour the ape.

It was upon this scene that Jane Clayton at last opened her eyes. Inured to danger, she maintained her self-possession in the face of the startling surprise which her new-found consciousness revealed to her. She neither cried out nor moved a muscle, until she had taken in every detail of the scene which lay within the range of her vision.

She saw that the lion had killed the ape, and that he was devouring his prey less than fifty feet from where she lay; but what could she do? Her hands and feet were bound. She must wait then, in what patience she could command, until Numa had eaten and digested the ape, when, without doubt, he would return to feast upon her, unless, in the meantime, the dread hyenas should discover her, or some other of the numerous prowling carnivora of the jungle.

EDGAR RICE BURROUGHS

As she lay tormented by these frightful thoughts, she suddenly became conscious that the bonds at her wrists and ankles no longer hurt her, and then of the fact that her hands were separated, one lying upon either side of her, instead of both being confined at her back.

Wonderingly she moved a hand. What miracle had been performed? It was not bound! Stealthily and noiselessly she moved her other limbs, only to discover that she was free. She could not know how the thing had happened, that Taglat, gnawing upon them for sinister purposes of his own, had cut them through but an instant before Numa had frightened him from his victim.

For a moment Jane Clayton was overwhelmed with joy and thanksgiving; but only for a moment. What good was her new-found liberty in the face of the frightful beast crouching so close beside her? If she could have had this chance under different conditions, how happily she would have taken advantage of it; but now it was given to her when escape was practically impossible.

The nearest tree was a hundred feet away, the lion less than fifty. To rise and attempt to reach the safety of those tantalizing branches would be but to invite instant destruction, for Numa would doubtless be too jealous of this future meal to permit it to escape with ease. And yet, too, there was another possibility—a chance which hinged entirely upon the unknown temper of the great beast.

His belly already partially filled, he might watch with indifference the departure of the girl; yet could she afford to chance so improbable a contingency? She doubted it. Upon the other hand she was no more minded to allow this frail opportunity for life to entirely elude her without taking or attempting to take some advantage from it.

She watched the lion narrowly. He could not see her without turning his head more than halfway around. She would attempt a ruse. Silently she rolled over in the direction of the nearest tree, and away from the lion, until she lay again in the same position in which Numa had left her, but a few feet farther from him.

Here she lay breathless watching the lion; but the beast gave no indication that he had heard aught to arouse his suspicions. Again she rolled over, gaining a few more feet and again she lay in rigid contemplation of the beast's back.

During what seemed hours to her tense nerves, Jane Clayton continued these tactics, and still the lion fed on in apparent unconsciousness that his second prey was escaping him. Already the girl was but a few paces from the tree—a moment more and she would be close enough to chance springing to her feet, throwing caution aside and making a sudden, bold dash for safety. She was halfway over in her turn, her face away from the lion, when he suddenly turned his great head and fastened his eyes upon her. He saw her roll over upon her side away from him, and then her eyes were turned again toward him, and the cold sweat broke from the girl's every pore as she realized that with life almost within her grasp, death had found her out.

For a long time neither the girl nor the lion moved. The beast lay motionless, his head turned upon his shoulders and his glaring eyes fixed upon the rigid victim, now nearly fifty yards away. The girl stared back straight into those cruel orbs, daring not to move even a muscle.

The strain upon her nerves was becoming so unbearable that she could scarcely restrain a growing desire to scream, when Numa deliberately turned back to the business of feeding; but his back-layed ears attested a sinister regard for the actions of the girl behind him.

Realizing that she could not again turn without attracting his immediate and perhaps fatal attention, Jane Clayton resolved to risk all in one last attempt to reach the tree and clamber to the lower branches.

Gathering herself stealthily for the effort, she leaped suddenly to her feet, but almost simultaneously the lion sprang up, wheeled and with wide-distended jaws and terrific roars, charged swiftly down upon her.

Those who have spent lifetimes hunting the big game of Africa will tell you that scarcely any other creature in the world attains the speed of a charging lion. For the short distance that the great cat can maintain it, it resembles nothing more closely than the onrushing of a giant locomotive under full speed, and so, though the distance that Jane Clayton must cover was relatively small, the terrific speed of the lion rendered her hopes of escape almost negligible.

Yet fear can work wonders, and though the upward spring of the lion as he neared the tree into which she was scrambling brought his talons in contact with her boots she eluded his raking grasp, and as he hurtled against the bole of her sanctuary, the girl drew herself into the safety of the branches above his reach.

For some time the lion paced, growling and moaning, beneath the tree in which Jane Clayton crouched, panting and trembling. The girl was a prey to the nervous reaction from the frightful ordeal through which she had so recently passed, and in her overwrought state it seemed that never again should she dare descend to the ground among the fearsome dangers which infested the broad stretch of jungle that she knew must lie between herself and the nearest village of her faithful Waziri.

It was almost dark before the lion finally quit the clearing, and even had his place beside the remnants of the mangled ape not been immediately usurped by a pack of hyenas, Jane Clayton would scarcely have dared venture from her refuge in the face of impending night, and so she composed herself as best she could for the long and tiresome wait, until daylight might offer some means of escape from the dread vicinity in which she had witnessed such terrifying adventures.

Tired nature at last overcame even her fears, and she dropped into a deep slumber, cradled in a comparatively safe, though rather uncomfortable, position against the bole of the tree, and supported by two large branches which grew outward, almost horizontally, but a few inches apart.

The sun was high in the heavens when she at last awoke, and beneath her was no sign either of Numa or the hyenas. Only the clean-picked bones of the ape, scattered about the ground, attested the fact of what had transpired in this seemingly peaceful spot but a few hours before.

Both hunger and thirst assailed her now, and realizing that she must descend or die of starvation, she at last summoned courage to undertake the ordeal of continuing her journey through the jungle.

Descending from the tree, she set out in a southerly direction, toward the point where she believed the plains of Waziri lay, and though she knew that only ruin and desolation marked the spot where once her happy home had stood, she hoped that by coming to the broad plain she might eventually reach one of the numerous Waziri villages that were scattered over the surrounding country, or chance upon a roving band of these indefatigable huntsmen.

The day was half spent when there broke unexpectedly upon her startled ears the sound of a rifle shot not far ahead of her. As she paused to listen, this first shot was followed by another and another and another. What could it mean? The first explanation which sprung to her mind attributed the firing to an encounter between the Arab raiders and a party of Waziri; but as she did not know upon which side victory might rest, or whether she were behind friend or foe, she dared not advance nearer on the chance of revealing herself to an enemy.

After listening for several minutes she became convinced that no more than two or three rifles were engaged in the fight, since nothing approximating the sound of a volley reached her ears; but still she hesitated to approach, and at last, determining to take no chance, she climbed into the concealing foliage of a tree beside the trail she had been following and there fearfully awaited whatever might reveal itself.

As the firing became less rapid she caught the sound of men's voices, though she could distinguish no words, and at last the reports of the guns ceased, and she heard two men calling to each other in loud tones. Then there was a long silence which was finally broken by the stealthy padding of footfalls on the trail ahead of her, and in another moment a man appeared in view backing toward her, a rifle ready in his hands, and his eyes directed in careful watchfulness along the way that he had come.

Almost instantly Jane Clayton recognized the man as M. Jules Frecoult, who so recently had been a guest in her home. She was upon the point of calling to him in glad relief when she saw him leap quickly to one side and hide himself in the thick verdure at the trail's side. It was evident that he was being followed by an enemy, and so Jane Clayton kept silent, lest she distract Frecoult's attention, or guide his foe to his hiding place.

Scarcely had Frecoult hidden himself than the figure of a white-robed Arab crept silently along the trail in pursuit. From her hiding place, Jane Clayton could see both men plainly. She recognized Achmet Zek as the leader of the band of ruffians who had raided her home and made her a prisoner, and as she saw Frecoult, the supposed friend and ally, raise his gun and take careful aim at the Arab, her heart stood still and every power of her soul was directed upon a fervent prayer for the accuracy of his aim.

Achmet Zek paused in the middle of the trail. His keen eyes scanned every bush and tree within the radius of his vision. His tall figure presented a perfect target to the perfidious assassin. There was a sharp report, and a little puff of smoke arose from the bush that hid the Belgian, as Achmet Zek stumbled forward and pitched, face down, upon the trail.

As Werper stepped back into the trail, he was startled by the sound of a glad cry from above him, and as he wheeled about to discover the author of this unexpected interruption, he saw Jane Clayton drop lightly from a nearby tree and run forward with outstretched hands to congratulate him upon his victory.

JANE CLAYTON AGAIN A PRISONER

Though her clothes were torn and her hair disheveled, Albert Werper realized that he never before had looked upon such a vision of loveliness as that which Lady Greystoke presented in the relief and joy which she felt in coming so unexpectedly upon a friend and rescuer when hope had seemed so far away.

If the Belgian had entertained any doubts as to the woman's knowledge of his part in the perfidious attack upon her home and herself, it was quickly dissipated by the genuine friendliness of her greeting. She told him quickly of all that had befallen her since he had departed from her home, and as she spoke of the death of her husband her eyes were veiled by the tears which she could not repress.

"I am shocked," said Werper, in well-simulated sympathy; "but I am not surprised. That devil there," and he pointed toward the body of Achmet Zek, "has terrorized the entire country. Your Waziri are either exterminated, or have been driven out of their country, far to the south. The men of Achmet Zek occupy the plain about your former home—there is neither sanctuary nor escape in that direction. Our only hope lies in traveling northward as rapidly as we may, of coming to the camp of the raiders before the knowledge of Achmet Zek's death reaches those who were left there, and of obtaining, through some ruse, an escort toward the north.

"I think that the thing can be accomplished, for I was a guest of the raider's before I knew the nature of the man, and those at the camp are not aware that I turned against him when I discovered his villainy.

"Come! We will make all possible haste to reach the camp before those who accompanied Achmet Zek upon his last raid have found his body and carried the news of his death to the cut-throats who remained behind. It is our only hope, Lady Greystoke, and you must place your entire faith in me if I am to succeed. Wait for me here a moment while I take from the Arab's body the wallet that he stole from me," and Werper stepped quickly to the dead man's side, and, kneeling, sought with quick fingers the pouch of jewels. To his consternation, there was no sign of them in the garments of Achmet Zek. Rising, he walked back along the trail, searching for some trace of the missing pouch or its contents; but he found nothing, even though he searched carefully the vicinity of his dead horse, and for a few paces into the jungle on either side. Puzzled, disappointed and angry, he at last returned to the girl. "The wallet is gone," he explained, crisply, "and I dare not delay longer in search of it. We must reach the camp before the returning raiders."

Unsuspicious of the man's true character, Jane Clayton saw nothing peculiar in his plans, or in his specious explanation of his former friendship for the raider, and so she grasped with alacrity the seeming hope for safety which he proffered her, and turning about she set out with Albert Werper toward the hostile camp in which she so lately had been a prisoner.

It was late in the afternoon of the second day before they reached their destination, and as they paused upon the edge of the clearing before the gates of the walled village, Werper cautioned the girl to accede to whatever he might suggest by his conversation with the raiders.

"I shall tell them," he said, "that I apprehended you after you escaped from the camp, that I took you to Achmet Zek, and that as he was engaged in a stubborn battle with the Waziri, he directed me to return to camp with you, to obtain here a sufficient guard, and to ride north with you as rapidly as possible and dispose of you at the most advantageous terms to a certain slave broker whose name he gave me."

Again the girl was deceived by the apparent frankness of the Belgian. She realized that desperate situations required desperate handling, and though she trembled inwardly at the thought of again entering the vile and hideous village of the raiders she saw no better course than that which her companion had suggested.

Calling aloud to those who tended the gates, Werper, grasping Jane Clayton by the arm, walked boldly across the clearing. Those who opened the gates to him permitted their surprise to show clearly in their expressions. That the discredited and hunted lieutenant should be thus returning fearlessly of his own volition, seemed to disarm them quite as effectually as his manner toward Lady Greystoke had deceived her.

The sentries at the gate returned Werper's salutations, and viewed with astonishment the prisoner whom he brought into the village with him.

Immediately the Belgian sought the Arab who had been left in charge of the camp during Achmet Zek's absence, and again his boldness disarmed suspicion and won the acceptance of his false explanation of his return. The fact that he had brought back with him the woman prisoner who had escaped, added strength to his claims, and Mohammed Beyd soon found himself fraternizing good-naturedly with the very man whom he would have slain without compunction had he discovered him alone in the jungle a half hour before.

Jane Clayton was again confined to the prison hut she had formerly occupied, but as she realized that this was but a part of the deception which she and Frecoult were playing upon the credulous raiders, it was with quite a different sensation that she again entered the vile and filthy interior, from that which she had previously experienced, when hope was so far away.

Once more she was bound and sentries placed before the door of her prison; but before Werper left her he whispered words of cheer into her ear. Then he left, and made his way back to the tent of Mohammed Beyd. He had been wondering how long it would be before the raiders who had ridden out with Achmet Zek would return with the murdered body of their chief, and the more he thought upon the matter the greater his fears became, that without accomplices his plan would fail.

What, even, if he got away from the camp in safety before any returned with the true story of his guilt—of what value would this advantage be other than to protract for a few days his mental torture and his life? These hard riders, familiar with every trail and bypath, would get him long before he could hope to reach the coast.

As these thoughts passed through his mind he entered the tent where Mohammed Beyd sat cross-legged upon a rug, smoking. The Arab looked up as the European came into his presence.

"Greetings, O Brother!" he said.

"Greetings!" replied Werper.

For a while neither spoke further. The Arab was the first to break the silence.

"And my master, Achmet Zek, was well when last you saw him?" he asked.

"Never was he safer from the sins and dangers of mortality," replied the Belgian.

"It is well," said Mohammed Beyd, blowing a little puff of blue smoke straight out before him.

Again there was silence for several minutes.

"And if he were dead?" asked the Belgian, determined to lead up to the truth, and attempt to bribe Mohammed Beyd into his service.

The Arab's eyes narrowed and he leaned forward, his gaze boring straight into the eyes of the Belgian.

"I have been thinking much, Werper, since you returned so unexpectedly to the camp of the man whom you had deceived, and who sought you with death in his heart. I have been with Achmet Zek for many years—his own mother never knew him so well as I. He never forgives—much less would he again trust a man who had once betrayed him; that I know.

"I have thought much, as I said, and the result of my thinking has assured me that Achmet Zek is dead—for otherwise you would never have dared return to his camp, unless you be either a braver man or a bigger fool than I have imagined. And, if this evidence of my judgment is not sufficient, I have but just now received from your own lips even more confirmatory witness—for did you not say that Achmet Zek was never more safe from the sins and dangers of mortality?

"Achmet Zek is dead—you need not deny it. I was not his mother, or his mistress, so do not fear that my wailings shall disturb you. Tell me why you have come back here. Tell me what you want, and, Werper, if you still possess the jewels of which Achmet Zek told me, there is no reason why you and I should not ride north together and divide the ransom of the white woman and the contents of the pouch you wear about your person. Eh?"

The evil eyes narrowed, a vicious, thin-lipped smile tortured the villainous face, as Mohammed Beyd grinned knowingly into the face of the Belgian.

Werper was both relieved and disturbed by the Arab's attitude. The complacency with which he accepted the death of his chief lifted a considerable burden of apprehension from the shoulders of Achmet Zek's assassin; but his demand for a share of the jewels boded ill for Werper when Mohammed Beyd should have learned that the precious stones were no longer in the Belgian's possession.

To acknowledge that he had lost the jewels might be to arouse the wrath or suspicion of the Arab to such an extent as would jeopardize his new-found chances of escape. His one hope seemed, then, to lie in fostering Mohammed Beyd's belief that the jewels were still in his possession, and depend upon the accidents of the future to open an avenue of escape.

Could he contrive to tent with the Arab upon the march north, he might find opportunity in plenty to remove this menace to his life and liberty—it was worth trying, and, further, there seemed no other way out of his difficulty.

"Yes," he said, "Achmet Zek is dead. He fell in battle with a company of Abyssinian cavalry that held me captive. During the fighting I escaped; but I doubt if any of Achmet Zek's men live, and the gold they sought is in the possession of the Abyssinians. Even now they are doubtless marching on this camp, for they were sent by Menelek to punish Achmet Zek and his followers for a raid upon an Abyssinian village. There are many of them, and if we do not make haste to escape we shall all suffer the same fate as Achmet Zek."

Mohammed Beyd listened in silence. How much of the unbeliever's story he might safely believe he did not know; but as it afforded him an excuse for deserting the village and making for the north he was not inclined to cross-question the Belgian too minutely.

"And if I ride north with you," he asked, "half the jewels and half the ransom of the woman shall be mine?"

"Yes," replied Werper.

"Good," said Mohammed Beyd. "I go now to give the order for the breaking of camp early on the morrow," and he rose to leave the tent.

Werper laid a detaining hand upon his arm.

"Wait," he said, "let us determine how many shall accompany us. It is not well that we be burdened by the women and children, for then indeed we might be overtaken by the Abyssinians. It would be far better to select a small guard of your bravest men, and leave word behind that we are riding WEST. Then, when the Abyssinians come they will be put upon the wrong trail should they have it in their hearts to pursue us, and if they do not they will at least ride north with less rapidity than as though they thought that we were ahead of them."

"The serpent is less wise than thou, Werper," said Mohammed Beyd with a smile. "It shall be done as you say. Twenty men shall accompany us, and we shall ride *West*—when we leave the village."

"Good," cried the Belgian, and so it was arranged.

Early the next morning Jane Clayton, after an almost sleepless night, was aroused by the sound of voices outside her prison, and a moment later, M. Frecoult, and two Arabs entered. The latter unbound her ankles and lifted her to her feet. Then her wrists were loosed, she was given a handful of dry bread, and led out into the faint light of dawn.

She looked questioningly at Frecoult, and at a moment that the Arab's attention was attracted in another direction the man leaned toward her and whispered that all was working out as he had planned. Thus assured, the young woman felt a renewal of the hope which the long and miserable night of bondage had almost expunged.

Shortly after, she was lifted to the back of a horse, and surrounded by Arabs, was escorted through the gateway of the village and off into the jungle toward the west. Half an hour later the party turned north, and northerly was their direction for the balance of the march.

M. Frecoult spoke with her but seldom, and she understood that in carrying out his deception he must maintain the semblance of her captor, rather than protector, and so she suspected nothing though she saw the friendly relations which seemed to exist between the European and the Arab leader of the band.

If Werper succeeded in keeping himself from conversation with the young woman, he failed signally to expel her from his thoughts. A hundred times a day he found his eyes wandering in her direction and feasting themselves upon her charms of face and figure. Each hour his infatuation for her grew, until his desire to possess her gained almost the proportions of madness.

If either the girl or Mohammed Beyd could have guessed what passed in the mind of the man which each thought a friend and ally, the apparent harmony of the little company would have been rudely disturbed.

Werper had not succeeded in arranging to tent with Mohammed Beyd, and so he revolved many plans for the assassination of the Arab that would have been greatly simplified had he been permitted to share the other's nightly shelter.

Upon the second day out Mohammed Beyd reined his horse to the side of the animal on which the captive was mounted. It was, apparently, the first notice which the Arab had taken of the girl; but many times during these two days had his cunning eyes peered greedily from beneath the hood of his burnoose to gloat upon the beauties of the prisoner.

Nor was this hidden infatuation of any recent origin. He had conceived it when first the wife of the Englishman had fallen into the hands of Achmet Zek; but while that austere chieftain lived, Mohammed Beyd had not even dared hope for a realization of his imaginings.

Now, though, it was different—only a despised dog of a Christian stood between himself and possession of the girl. How easy it would be to slay the unbeliever, and take unto himself both the woman and the jewels! With the latter in his possession, the ransom which might be obtained for the captive would form no great inducement to her relinquishment in the face of the pleasures of sole ownership of her. Yes, he would kill Werper, retain all the jewels and keep the Englishwoman.

He turned his eyes upon her as she rode along at his side. How beautiful she was! His fingers opened and closed—skinny, brown talons itching to feel the soft flesh of the victim in their remorseless clutch.

"Do you know," he asked leaning toward her, "where this man would take you?"

Jane Clayton nodded affirmatively.

"And you are willing to become the plaything of a black sultan?"

The girl drew herself up to her full height, and turned her head away; but she did not reply. She feared lest her knowledge of the ruse that M. Frecoult was playing upon the Arab might cause her to betray herself through an insufficient display of terror and aversion.

"You can escape this fate," continued the Arab; "Mohammed Beyd will save you," and he reached out a brown hand and seized the fingers of her right hand in a grasp so sudden and so fierce that this brutal passion was revealed as clearly in the act as though his lips had confessed it in words. Jane Clayton wrenched herself from his grasp.

"You beast!" she cried. "Leave me or I shall call M. Frecoult."

Mohammed Beyd drew back with a scowl. His thin, upper lip curled upward, revealing his smooth, white teeth.

"M. Frecoult?" he jeered. "There is no such person. The man's name is Werper. He is a liar, a thief, and a murderer. He killed his captain in the Congo country and fled to the protection of Achmet Zek. He led Achmet Zek to the plunder of your home. He followed your husband, and planned to steal his gold from him. He has told me that you think him your protector, and he has played upon this to win your confidence that it might be easier to carry you north and sell you into some black sultan's harem. Mohammed Beyd is your only hope," and with this assertion to provide the captive with food for thought, the Arab spurred forward toward the head of the column.

Jane Clayton could not know how much of Mohammed Beyd's indictment might be true, or how much false; but at least it had the effect of dampening her hopes and causing her to review with suspicion every past act of the man upon whom she had been looking as her sole protector in the midst of a world of enemies and dangers.

On the march a separate tent had been provided for the captive, and at night it was pitched between those of Mohammed Beyd and Werper. A sentry was posted at the front and another at the back, and with these precautions it had not been thought necessary to confine the prisoner to bonds. The evening following her interview with Mohammed Beyd, Jane Clayton sat for some time at the opening of her tent watching the rough activities of the camp. She had eaten the meal that had been brought her by Mohammed Beyd's Negro slave—a meal of cassava cakes and a nondescript stew in which a new-killed monkey, a couple of squirrels and the remains of a zebra, slain the previous day, were impartially and unsavorily combined; but the one-time Baltimore belle had long since submerged in the stern battle for existence, an estheticism which formerly revolted at much slighter provocation.

As the girl's eyes wandered across the trampled jungle clearing, already squalid from the presence of man, she no longer apprehended either the nearer objects of the foreground, the uncouth men laughing or quarreling among themselves, or the jungle beyond, which circumscribed the extreme range of her material vision. Her gaze passed through all these, unseeing, to center itself upon a distant bungalow and scenes of happy security which brought to her eyes tears of mingled joy and sorrow. She saw a tall, broad-shouldered man riding in from distant fields; she saw herself waiting to greet him with an armful of fresh-cut roses from the bushes which flanked the little rustic gate before her. All this was gone, vanished into the past, wiped out by the torches and bullets and hatred of these hideous and degenerate men. With a stifled sob, and a little shudder, Jane Clayton turned back into her tent and sought the pile of unclean blankets which were her bed. Throwing herself face downward upon them she sobbed forth her misery until kindly sleep brought her, at least temporary, relief.

And while she slept a figure stole from the tent that stood to the right of hers. It approached the sentry before the doorway and whispered a few words in the man's ear. The latter nodded, and strode off through the darkness in the direction of his own blankets. The figure passed to the rear of Jane Clayton's tent and spoke again to the sentry there, and this man also left, following in the trail of the first.

Then he who had sent them away stole silently to the tent flap and untying the fastenings entered with the noiselessness of a disembodied spirit.

THE FLIGHT TO THE JUNGLE

Sleepless upon his blankets, Albert Werper let his evil mind dwell upon the charms of the woman in the nearby tent. He had noted Mohammed Beyd's sudden interest in the girl, and judging the man by his own standards, had guessed at the basis of the Arab's sudden change of attitude toward the prisoner.

And as he let his imaginings run riot they aroused within him a bestial jealousy of Mohammed Beyd, and a great fear that the other might encompass his base designs upon the defenseless girl. By a strange process of reasoning, Werper, whose designs were identical with the Arab's, pictured himself as Jane Clayton's protector, and presently convinced himself that the attentions which might seem hideous to her if proffered by Mohammed Beyd, would be welcomed from Albert Werper.

Her husband was dead, and Werper fancied that he could replace in the girl's heart the position which had been vacated by the act of the grim reaper. He could offer Jane Clayton marriage—a thing which Mohammed Beyd would not offer, and which the girl would spurn from him with as deep disgust as she would his unholy lust.

It was not long before the Belgian had succeeded in convincing himself that the captive not only had every reason for having conceived sentiments of love for him; but that she had by various feminine methods acknowledged her new-born affection.

And then a sudden resolution possessed him. He threw the blankets from him and rose to his feet. Pulling on his boots and buckling his cartridge belt and revolver about his hips he stepped to the flap of his tent and looked out. There was no sentry before the entrance to the prisoner's tent! What could it mean? Fate was indeed playing into his hands.

Stepping outside he passed to the rear of the girl's tent. There was no sentry there, either! And now, boldly, he walked to the entrance and stepped within.

Dimly the moonlight illumined the interior. Across the tent a figure bent above the blankets of a bed. There was a whispered word, and another figure rose from the blankets to a sitting position. Slowly Albert Werper's eyes were becoming accustomed to the half darkness of the tent. He saw that the figure leaning over the bed was that of a man, and he guessed at the truth of the nocturnal visitor's identity.

A sullen, jealous rage enveloped him. He took a step in the direction of the two. He heard a frightened cry break from the girl's lips as she recognized the features of the man above her, and he saw Mohammed Beyd seize her by the throat and bear her back upon the blankets.

Cheated passion cast a red blur before the eyes of the Belgian. No! The man should not have her. She was for him and him alone. He would not be robbed of his rights.

Quickly he ran across the tent and threw himself upon the back of Mohammed Beyd. The latter, though surprised by this sudden and unexpected attack, was not one to give up without a battle. The Belgian's fingers were feeling for his throat, but the Arab tore them away, and rising wheeled upon his adversary. As they faced each other Werper struck the Arab a heavy blow in the face, sending him staggering backward. If he had followed up his advantage he would have had Mohammed Beyd at his mercy in another moment; but instead he tugged at his revolver to draw it from its holster, and Fate ordained that at that particular moment the weapon should stick in its leather scabbard.

Before he could disengage it, Mohammed Beyd had recovered himself and was dashing upon him. Again Werper struck the other in the face, and the Arab returned the blow. Striking at each other and ceaselessly attempting to clinch, the two battled about the small interior of the tent, while the girl, wide-eyed in terror and astonishment, watched the duel in frozen silence.

Again and again Werper struggled to draw his weapon. Mohammed Beyd, anticipating no such opposition to his base desires, had come to the tent unarmed, except for a long knife which he now drew as he stood panting during the first brief rest of the encounter.

"Dog of a Christian," he whispered, "look upon this knife in the hands of Mohammed Beyd! Look well, unbeliever, for it is the last thing in life that you shall see or feel. With it Mohammed Beyd will cut out your black heart. If you have a God pray to him now—in a minute more you shall be dead," and with that he rushed viciously upon the Belgian, his knife raised high above his head.

Werper was still dragging futilely at his weapon. The Arab was almost upon him. In desperation the European waited until Mohammed Beyd was all but against him, then he threw himself to one side to the floor of the tent, leaving a leg extended in the path of the Arab.

The trick succeeded. Mohammed Beyd, carried on by the momentum of his charge, stumbled over the projecting obstacle and crashed to the ground. Instantly he was up again and wheeling to renew the battle; but Werper was on foot ahead of him, and now his revolver, loosened from its holster, flashed in his hand.

The Arab dove headfirst to grapple with him, there was a sharp report, a lurid gleam of flame in the darkness, and Mohammed Beyd rolled over and over upon the floor to come to a final rest beside the bed of the woman he had sought to dishonor.

Almost immediately following the report came the sound of excited voices in the camp without. Men were calling back and forth to one another asking the meaning of the shot. Werper could hear them running hither and thither, investigating.

Jane Clayton had risen to her feet as the Arab died, and now she came forward with outstretched hands toward Werper.

"How can I ever thank you, my friend?" she asked. "And to think that only today I had almost believed the infamous story which this beast told me of your perfidy and of your past. Forgive me, M. Frecoult. I might have known that a white man and a gentleman could be naught else than the protector of a woman of his own race amid the dangers of this savage land."

Werper's hands dropped limply at his sides. He stood looking at the girl; but he could find no words to reply to her. Her innocent arraignment of his true purposes was unanswerable.

Outside, the Arabs were searching for the author of the disturbing shot. The two sentries who had been relieved and sent to their blankets by Mohammed Beyd were the first to suggest going to the tent of the prisoner. It occurred to them that possibly the woman had successfully defended herself against their leader.

Werper heard the men approaching. To be apprehended as the slayer of Mohammed Beyd would be equivalent to a sentence of immediate death. The fierce and brutal raiders would tear to pieces a Christian who had dared spill the blood of their leader. He must find some excuse to delay the finding of Mohammed Beyd's dead body.

Returning his revolver to its holster, he walked quickly to the entrance of the tent. Parting the flaps he stepped out and confronted the men, who were rapidly approaching. Somehow he found within him the necessary bravado to force a smile to his lips, as he held up his hand to bar their farther progress.

"The woman resisted," he said, "and Mohammed Beyd was forced to shoot her. She is not dead—only slightly wounded. You may go back to your blankets. Mohammed Beyd and I will look after the prisoner;" then he turned and re-entered the tent, and the raiders, satisfied by this explanation, gladly returned to their broken slumbers.

As he again faced Jane Clayton, Werper found himself animated by quite different intentions than those which had lured him from his blankets but a few minutes before. The excitement of his encounter with Mohammed Beyd, as well as the dangers which he now faced at the hands of the raiders when morning must inevitably reveal the truth of what had occurred in the tent of the prisoner that night, had naturally cooled the hot passion which had dominated him when he entered the tent.

But another and stronger force was exerting itself in the girl's favor. However low a man may sink, honor and chivalry, has he ever possessed them, are never entirely eradicated from his character, and though Albert Werper had long since ceased to evidence the slightest claim to either the one or the other, the spontaneous acknowledgment of them which the girl's speech had presumed had reawakened them both within him.

For the first time he realized the almost hopeless and frightful position of the fair captive, and the depths of ignominy to which he had sunk, that had made it possible for him, a well-born, European gentleman, to have entertained even for a moment the part that he had taken in the ruin of her home, happiness, and herself.

Too much of baseness already lay at the threshold of his conscience for him ever to hope entirely to redeem himself; but in the first, sudden burst of contrition the man conceived an honest intention to undo, in so far as lay within his power, the evil that his criminal avarice had brought upon this sweet and unoffending woman.

As he stood apparently listening to the retreating footsteps—Jane Clayton approached him.

"What are we to do now?" she asked. "Morning will bring discovery of this," and she pointed to the still body of Mohammed Beyd. "They will kill you when they find him."

For a time Werper did not reply, then he turned suddenly toward the woman.

"I have a plan," he cried. "It will require nerve and courage on your part; but you have already shown that you possess both. Can you endure still more?"

"I can endure anything," she replied with a brave smile, "that may offer us even a slight chance for escape."

"You must simulate death," he explained, "while I carry you from the camp. I will explain to the sentries that Mohammed Beyd has ordered me to take your body into the jungle. This seemingly unnecessary act I shall explain upon the grounds that Mohammed Beyd had conceived a violent passion for you and that he so regretted the act by which he had become your slayer that he could not endure the silent reproach of your lifeless body."

The girl held up her hand to stop. A smile touched her lips.

"Are you quite mad?" she asked. "Do you imagine that the sentries will credit any such ridiculous tale?"

"You do not know them," he replied. "Beneath their rough exteriors, despite their calloused and criminal natures, there exists in each a well-defined strain of romantic emotionalism—you will find it among such as these throughout the world. It is romance which lures men to lead wild lives of outlawry and crime. The ruse will succeed—never fear."

Jane Clayton shrugged. "We can but try it—and then what?"

"I shall hide you in the jungle," continued the Belgian, "coming for you alone and with two horses in the morning."

"But how will you explain Mohammed Beyd's death?" she asked. "It will be discovered before ever you can escape the camp in the morning."

"I shall not explain it," replied Werper. "Mohammed Beyd shall explain it himself—we must leave that to him. Are you ready for the venture?"

"Yes."

"But wait, I must get you a weapon and ammunition," and Werper walked quickly from the tent.

Very shortly he returned with an extra revolver and ammunition belt strapped about his waist.

"Are you ready?" he asked.

"Quite ready," replied the girl.

"Then come and throw yourself limply across my left shoulder," and Werper knelt to receive her.

"There," he said, as he rose to his feet. "Now, let your arms, your legs and your head hang limply. Remember that you are dead."

A moment later the man walked out into the camp, the body of the woman across his shoulder.

A thorn boma had been thrown up about the camp, to discourage the bolder of the hungry carnivora. A couple of sentries paced to and fro in the light of a fire which they kept burning brightly. The nearer of these looked up in surprise as he saw Werper approaching.

"Who are you?" he cried. "What have you there?"

Werper raised the hood of his burnoose that the fellow might see his face.

"This is the body of the woman," he explained. "Mohammed Beyd has asked me to take it into the jungle, for he cannot bear to look upon the face of her whom he loved, and whom necessity compelled him to slay. He suffers greatly—he is inconsolable. It was with difficulty that I prevented him taking his own life."

Across the speaker's shoulder, limp and frightened, the girl waited for the Arab's reply. He would laugh at this preposterous story; of that she was sure. In an instant he would unmask the deception that M.

Frecoult was attempting to practice upon him, and they would both be lost. She tried to plan how best she might aid her would-be rescuer in the fight which must most certainly follow within a moment or two.

Then she heard the voice of the Arab as he replied to M. Frecoult.

"Are you going alone, or do you wish me to awaken someone to accompany you?" he asked, and his tone denoted not the least surprise that Mohammed Beyd had suddenly discovered such remarkably sensitive characteristics.

"I shall go alone," replied Werper, and he passed on and out through the narrow opening in the boma, by which the sentry stood.

A moment later he had entered among the boles of the trees with his burden, and when safely hidden from the sentry's view lowered the girl to her feet, with a low, "sh-sh," when she would have spoken.

Then he led her a little farther into the forest, halted beneath a large tree with spreading branches, buckled a cartridge belt and revolver about her waist, and assisted her to clamber into the lower branches.

"Tomorrow," he whispered, "as soon as I can elude them, I will return for you. Be brave, Lady Greystoke—we may yet escape."

"Thank you," she replied in a low tone. "You have been very kind, and very brave."

Werper did not reply, and the darkness of the night hid the scarlet flush of shame which swept upward across his face. Quickly he turned and made his way back to camp. The sentry, from his post, saw him enter his own tent; but he did not see him crawl under the canvas at the rear and sneak cautiously to the tent which the prisoner had occupied, where now lay the dead body of Mohammed Beyd.

Raising the lower edge of the rear wall, Werper crept within and approached the corpse. Without an instant's hesitation he seized the dead wrists and dragged the body upon its back to the point where he had just entered. On hands and knees he backed out as he had come in, drawing the corpse after him. Once outside the Belgian crept to the side of the tent and surveyed as much of the camp as lay within his vision—no one was watching.

Returning to the body, he lifted it to his shoulder, and risking all on a quick sally, ran swiftly across the narrow opening which separated the prisoner's tent from that of the dead man. Behind the silken wall he halted and lowered his burden to the ground, and there he remained motionless for several minutes, listening.

Satisfied, at last, that no one had seen him, he stooped and raised the bottom of the tent wall, backed in and dragged the thing that had been Mohammed Beyd after him. To the sleeping rugs of the dead raider he drew the corpse, then he fumbled about in the darkness until he had found Mohammed Beyd's revolver. With the weapon in his hand he returned to the side of the dead man, kneeled beside the bedding, and inserted his right hand with the weapon beneath the rugs, piled a number of thicknesses of the closely woven fabric over and about the revolver with his left hand. Then he pulled the trigger, and at the same time he coughed.

The muffled report could not have been heard above the sound of his cough by one directly outside the tent. Werper was satisfied. A grim smile touched his lips as he withdrew the weapon from the rugs and placed it carefully in the right hand of the dead man, fixing three of the fingers around the grip and the index finger inside the trigger guard.

A moment longer he tarried to rearrange the disordered rugs, and then he left as he had entered, fastening down the rear wall of the tent as it had been before he had raised it.

Going to the tent of the prisoner he removed there also the evidence that someone might have come or gone beneath the rear wall. Then he returned to his own tent, entered, fastened down the canvas, and crawled into his blankets.

The following morning he was awakened by the excited voice of Mohammed Beyd's slave calling to him at the entrance of his tent.

"Quick! Quick!" cried the black in a frightened tone. "Come! Mohammed Beyd is dead in his tent—dead by his own hand."

Werper sat up quickly in his blankets at the first alarm, a startled expression upon his countenance; but at the last words of the black a sigh of relief escaped his lips and a slight smile replaced the tense lines upon his face.

"I come," he called to the slave, and drawing on his boots, rose and went out of his tent.

Excited Arabs and blacks were running from all parts of the camp toward the silken tent of Mohammed Beyd, and when Werper entered he found a number of the raiders crowded about the corpse, now cold and stiff.

Shouldering his way among them, the Belgian halted beside the dead body of the raider. He looked down in silence for a moment upon the still face, then he wheeled upon the Arabs.

"Who has done this thing?" he cried. His tone was both menacing and accusing. "Who has murdered Mohammed Beyd?"

A sudden chorus of voices arose in tumultuous protest.

"Mohammed Beyd was not murdered," they cried. "He died by his own hand. This, and Allah, are our witnesses," and they pointed to a revolver in the dead man's hand.

For a time Werper pretended to be skeptical; but at last permitted himself to be convinced that Mohammed Beyd had indeed killed himself in remorse for the death of the white woman he had, all unknown to his followers, loved so devotedly.

Werper himself wrapped the blankets of the dead man about the corpse, taking care to fold inward the scorched and bullet-torn fabric that had muffled the report of the weapon he had fired the night before. Then six husky blacks carried the body out into the clearing where the camp stood, and deposited it in a shallow grave. As the loose earth fell upon the silent form beneath the tell-tale blankets, Albert Werper heaved another sigh of relief—his plan had worked out even better than he had dared hope.

With Achmet Zek and Mohammed Beyd both dead, the raiders were without a leader, and after a brief conference they decided to return into the north on visits to the various tribes to which they belonged, Werper, after learning the direction they intended taking, announced that for his part, he was going east to the coast, and as they knew of nothing he possessed which any of them coveted, they signified their willingness that he should go his way.

As they rode off, he sat his horse in the center of the clearing watching them disappear one by one into the jungle, and thanked his God that he had at last escaped their villainous clutches.

When he could no longer hear any sound of them, he turned to the right and rode into the forest toward the tree where he had hidden Lady Greystoke, and drawing rein beneath it, called up in a gay and hopeful voice a pleasant, "Good morning!"

There was no reply, and though his eyes searched the thick foliage above him, he could see no sign of the girl. Dismounting, he quickly climbed into the tree, where he could obtain a view of all its branches. The tree was empty—Jane Clayton had vanished during the silent watches of the jungle night.

TARZAN RECOVERS HIS REASON

As Tarzan let the pebbles from the recovered pouch run through his fingers, his thoughts returned to the pile of yellow ingots about which the Arabs and the Abyssinians had waged their relentless battle.

What was there in common between that pile of dirty metal and the beautiful, sparkling pebbles that had formerly been in his pouch? What was the metal? From whence had it come? What was that tantalizing half-conviction which seemed to demand the recognition of his memory that the yellow pile for which these men had fought and died had been intimately connected with his past—that it had been his?

EDGAR RICE BURROUGHS

What had been his past? He shook his head. Vaguely the memory of his apish childhood passed slowly in review—then came a strangely tangled mass of faces, figures and events which seemed to have no relation to Tarzan of the Apes, and yet which were, even in their fragmentary form, familiar.

Slowly and painfully, recollection was attempting to reassert itself, the hurt brain was mending, as the cause of its recent failure to function was being slowly absorbed or removed by the healing processes of perfect circulation.

The people who now passed before his mind's eye for the first time in weeks wore familiar faces; but yet he could neither place them in the niches they had once filled in his past life, nor call them by name. One was a fair she, and it was her face which most often moved through the tangled recollections of his convalescing brain. Who was she? What had she been to Tarzan of the Apes? He seemed to see her about the very spot upon which the pile of gold had been unearthed by the Abyssinians; but the surroundings were vastly different from those which now obtained.

There was a building—there were many buildings—and there were hedges, fences, and flowers. Tarzan puckered his brow in puzzled study of the wonderful problem. For an instant he seemed to grasp the whole of a true explanation, and then, just as success was within his grasp, the picture faded into a jungle scene where a naked, white youth danced in company with a band of hairy, primordial ape-things.

Tarzan shook his head and sighed. Why was it that he could not recollect? At least he was sure that in some way the pile of gold, the place where it lay, the subtle aroma of the elusive she he had been pursuing, the memory figure of the white woman, and he himself, were inextricably connected by the ties of a forgotten past.

If the woman belonged there, what better place to search or await her than the very spot which his broken recollections seemed to assign to her? It was worth trying. Tarzan slipped the thong of the empty pouch over his shoulder and started off through the trees in the direction of the plain.

At the outskirts of the forest he met the Arabs returning in search of Achmet Zek. Hiding, he let them pass, and then resumed his way toward the charred ruins of the home he had been almost upon the point of recalling to his memory.

His journey across the plain was interrupted by the discovery of a small herd of antelope in a little swale, where the cover and the wind were well combined to make stalking easy. A fat yearling rewarded a half hour of stealthy creeping and a sudden, savage rush, and it was late in the afternoon when the ape-man settled himself upon his haunches beside his kill to enjoy the fruits of his skill, his cunning, and his prowess.

His hunger satisfied, thirst next claimed his attention. The river lured him by the shortest path toward its refreshing waters, and when he had drunk, night already had fallen and he was some half mile or more down stream from the point where he had seen the pile of yellow ingots, and where he hoped to meet the memory woman, or find some clew to her whereabouts or her identity.

To the jungle bred, time is usually a matter of small moment, and haste, except when engendered by terror, by rage, or by hunger, is distasteful. Today was gone. Therefore tomorrow, of which there was an infinite procession, would answer admirably for Tarzan's further quest. And, besides, the ape-man was tired and would sleep.

A tree afforded him the safety, seclusion and comforts of a well-appointed bedchamber, and to the chorus of the hunters and the hunted of the wild river bank he soon dropped off into deep slumber.

Morning found him both hungry and thirsty again, and dropping from his tree he made his way to the drinking place at the river's edge. There he found Numa, the lion, ahead of him. The big fellow was lapping the water greedily, and at the approach of Tarzan along the trail in his rear, he raised his head, and turning his gaze backward across his maned shoulders glared at the intruder. A low growl of warning rumbled from his throat; but Tarzan, guessing that the beast had but just quitted his kill and was well filled, merely made a slight detour and continued to the river, where he stopped a few yards above the tawny cat, and dropping upon his hands and knees plunged his face into the cool water. For a moment the lion continued to eye the man; then he resumed his drinking, and man and beast quenched their thirst side by side each apparently oblivious of the other's presence.

Numa was the first to finish. Raising his head, he gazed across the river for a few minutes with that stony fixity of attention which is a characteristic of his kind. But for the ruffling of his black mane to the touch of the passing breeze he might have been wrought from golden bronze, so motionless, so statuesque his pose.

A deep sigh from the cavernous lungs dispelled the illusion. The mighty head swung slowly around until the yellow eyes rested upon the man. The bristled lip curved upward, exposing yellow fangs. Another warning growl vibrated the heavy jowls, and the king of beasts turned majestically about and paced slowly up the trail into the dense reeds.

Tarzan of the Apes drank on, but from the corners of his gray eyes he watched the great brute's every move until he had disappeared from view, and, after, his keen ears marked the movements of the carnivore.

A plunge in the river was followed by a scant breakfast of eggs which chance discovered to him, and then he set off up river toward the ruins of the bungalow where the golden ingots had marked the center of yesterday's battle.

And when he came upon the spot, great was his surprise and consternation, for the yellow metal had disappeared. The earth, trampled by the feet of horses and men, gave no clew. It was as though the ingots had evaporated into thin air.

The ape-man was at a loss to know where to turn or what next to do. There was no sign of any spoor which might denote that the she had been here. The metal was gone, and if there was any connection between the she and the metal it seemed useless to wait for her now that the latter had been removed elsewhere.

Everything seemed to elude him—the pretty pebbles, the yellow metal, the she, his memory. Tarzan was disgusted. He would go back into the jungle and look for Chulk, and so he turned his steps once more toward the forest. He moved rapidly, swinging across the plain in a long, easy trot, and at the edge of the forest, taking to the trees with the agility and speed of a small monkey.

His direction was aimless—he merely raced on and on through the jungle, the joy of unfettered action his principal urge, with the hope of stumbling upon some clew to Chulk or the she, a secondary incentive.

For two days he roamed about, killing, eating, drinking and sleeping wherever inclination and the means to indulge it occurred simultaneously. It was upon the morning of the third day that the scent spoor of horse and man were wafted faintly to his nostrils. Instantly he altered his course to glide silently through the branches in the direction from which the scent came.

It was not long before he came upon a solitary horseman riding toward the east. Instantly his eyes confirmed what his nose had previously suspected—the rider was he who had stolen his pretty pebbles. The light of rage flared suddenly in the gray eyes as the ape-man dropped lower among the branches until he moved almost directly above the unconscious Werper.

There was a quick leap, and the Belgian felt a heavy body hurtle onto the rump of his terror-stricken mount. The horse, snorting, leaped forward. Giant arms encircled the rider, and in the twinkling of an eye he was dragged from his saddle to find himself lying in the narrow trail with a naked, white giant kneeling upon his breast.

Recognition came to Werper with the first glance at his captor's face, and a pallor of fear overspread his features. Strong fingers were at his throat, fingers of steel. He tried to cry out, to plead for his life; but the cruel fingers denied him speech, as they were as surely denying him life.

"The pretty pebbles?" cried the man upon his breast. "What did you with the pretty pebbles—with Tarzan's pretty pebbles?"

The fingers relaxed to permit a reply. For some time Werper could only choke and cough—at last he regained the powers of speech.

"Achmet Zek, the Arab, stole them from me," he cried; "he made me give up the pouch and the pebbles."

"I saw all that," replied Tarzan; "but the pebbles in the pouch were not the pebbles of Tarzan—they were only such pebbles as fill the bottoms of the rivers, and the shelving banks beside them. Even the Arab would not have them, for he threw them away in anger when he had looked upon them. It is my pretty pebbles that I want—where are they?"

"I do not know, I do not know," cried Werper. "I gave them to Achmet Zek or he would have killed me. A few minutes later he followed me along the trail to slay me, although he had promised to molest me no further, and I shot and killed him; but the pouch was not upon his person and though I searched about the jungle for some time I could not find it."

"I found it, I tell you," growled Tarzan, "and I also found the pebbles which Achmet Zek had thrown away in disgust. They were not Tarzan's pebbles. You have hidden them! Tell me where they are or I will kill you," and the brown fingers of the ape-man closed a little tighter upon the throat of his victim.

Werper struggled to free himself. "My God, Lord Greystoke," he managed to scream, "would you commit murder for a handful of stones?"

The fingers at his throat relaxed, a puzzled, far-away expression softened the gray eyes.

"Lord Greystoke!" repeated the ape-man. "Lord Greystoke! Who is Lord Greystoke? Where have I heard that name before?"

"Why man, you are Lord Greystoke," cried the Belgian. "You were injured by a falling rock when the earthquake shattered the passage to the underground chamber to which you and your black Waziri had come to fetch golden ingots back to your bungalow. The blow shattered your memory. You are John Clayton, Lord Greystoke—don't you remember?"

"John Clayton, Lord Greystoke!" repeated Tarzan. Then for a moment he was silent. Presently his hand went falteringly to his forehead, an expression of wonderment filled his eyes—of wonderment and sudden understanding. The forgotten name had reawakened the returning memory that had been struggling to reassert itself. The ape-man relinquished his grasp upon the throat of the Belgian, and leaped to his feet.

"God!" he cried, and then, "Jane!" Suddenly he turned toward Werper. "My wife?" he asked. "What has become of her? The farm is in ruins. You know. You have had something to do with all this. You followed me to Opar, you stole the jewels which I thought but pretty pebbles. You are a crook! Do not try to tell me that you are not."

"He is worse than a crook," said a quiet voice close behind them.

Tarzan turned in astonishment to see a tall man in uniform standing in the trail a few paces from him. Back of the man were a number of black soldiers in the uniform of the Congo Free State.

"He is a murderer, Monsieur," continued the officer. "I have followed him for a long time to take him back to stand trial for the killing of his superior officer."

Werper was upon his feet now, gazing, white and trembling, at the fate which had overtaken him even in the fastness of the labyrinthine jungle. Instinctively he turned to flee; but Tarzan of the Apes reached out a strong hand and grasped him by the shoulder.

"Wait!" said the ape-man to his captive. "This gentleman wishes you, and so do I. When I am through with you, he may have you. Tell me what has become of my wife."

The Belgian officer eyed the almost naked, white giant with curiosity. He noted the strange contrast of primitive weapons and apparel, and the easy, fluent French which the man spoke. The former denoted the lowest, the latter the highest type of culture. He could not quite determine the social status of this strange creature; but he knew that he did not relish the easy assurance with which the fellow presumed to dictate when he might take possession of the prisoner.

"Pardon me," he said, stepping forward and placing his hand on Werper's other shoulder; "but this gentleman is my prisoner. He must come with me."

"When I am through with him," replied Tarzan, quietly.

The officer turned and beckoned to the soldiers standing in the trail behind him. A company of uniformed blacks stepped quickly forward and pushing past the three, surrounded the ape-man and his captive.

"Both the law and the power to enforce it are upon my side," announced the officer. "Let us have no trouble. If you have a grievance against this man you may return with me and enter your charge regularly before an authorized tribunal."

"Your legal rights are not above suspicion, my friend," replied Tarzan, "and your power to enforce your commands are only apparent—not real. You have presumed to enter British territory with an armed force. Where is your authority for this invasion? Where are the extradition papers which warrant the arrest of this man? And what assurance have you that I cannot bring an armed force about you that will prevent your return to the Congo Free State?"

The Belgian lost his temper. "I have no disposition to argue with a naked savage," he cried. "Unless you wish to be hurt you will not interfere with me. Take the prisoner, Sergeant!"

Werper raised his lips close to Tarzan's ear. "Keep me from them, and I can show you the very spot where I saw your wife last night," he whispered. "She cannot be far from here at this very minute."

The soldiers, following the signal from their sergeant, closed in to seize Werper. Tarzan grabbed the Belgian about the waist, and bearing him beneath his arm as he might have borne a sack of flour, leaped forward in an attempt to break through the cordon. His right fist caught the nearest soldier upon the jaw and sent him hurtling backward upon his fellows. Clubbed rifles were torn from the hands of those who barred his way, and right and left the black soldiers stumbled aside in the face of the ape-man's savage break for liberty.

So completely did the blacks surround the two that they dared not fire for fear of hitting one of their own number, and Tarzan was already through them and upon the point of dodging into the concealing mazes of the jungle when one who had sneaked upon him from behind struck him a heavy blow upon the head with a rifle.

In an instant the ape-man was down and a dozen black soldiers were upon his back. When he regained consciousness he found himself securely bound, as was Werper also. The Belgian officer, success having crowned his efforts, was in good humor, and inclined to chaff his prisoners about the ease with which they had been captured; but from Tarzan of the Apes he elicited no response. Werper, however, was voluble in his protests. He explained that Tarzan was an English lord; but the officer only laughed at the assertion, and advised his prisoner to save his breath for his defense in court.

As soon as Tarzan regained his senses and it was found that he was not seriously injured, the prisoners were hastened into line and the return march toward the Congo Free State boundary commenced.

Toward evening the column halted beside a stream, made camp and prepared the evening meal. From the thick foliage of the nearby jungle a pair of fierce eyes watched the activities of the uniformed blacks with silent intensity and curiosity. From beneath beetling brows the creature saw the boma constructed, the fires built, and the supper prepared.

Tarzan and Werper had been lying bound behind a small pile of knapsacks from the time that the company had halted; but with the preparation of the meal completed, their guard ordered them to rise and come forward to one of the fires where their hands would be unfettered that they might eat.

As the giant ape-man rose, a startled expression of recognition entered the eyes of the watcher in the jungle, and a low guttural broke from the savage lips. Instantly Tarzan was alert, but the answering growl died upon his lips, suppressed by the fear that it might arouse the suspicions of the soldiers.

Suddenly an inspiration came to him. He turned toward Werper.

"I am going to speak to you in a loud voice and in a tongue which you do not understand. Appear to listen intently to what I say, and occasionally mumble something as though replying in the same language—our escape may hinge upon the success of your efforts."

Werper nodded in assent and understanding, and immediately there broke from the lips of his companion a strange jargon which might have been compared with equal propriety to the barking and growling of a dog and the chattering of monkeys.

The nearer soldiers looked in surprise at the ape-man. Some of them laughed, while others drew away in evident superstitious fear. The officer approached the prisoners while Tarzan was still jabbering, and halted behind them, listening in perplexed interest. When Werper mumbled some ridiculous jargon in reply his curiosity broke bounds, and he stepped forward, demanding to know what language it was that they spoke.

Tarzan had gauged the measure of the man's culture from the nature and quality of his conversation during the march, and he rested the success of his reply upon the estimate he had made.

"Greek," he explained.

"Oh, I thought it was Greek," replied the officer; "but it has been so many years since I studied it that I was not sure. In future, however, I will thank you to speak in a language which I am more familiar with."

Werper turned his head to hide a grin, whispering to Tarzan: "It was Greek to him all right—and to me, too."

But one of the black soldiers mumbled in a low voice to a companion: "I have heard those sounds before—once at night when I was lost in the jungle, I heard the hairy men of the trees talking among themselves, and their words were like the words of this white man. I wish that we had not found him. He is not a man at all—he is a bad spirit, and we shall have bad luck if we do not let him go," and the fellow rolled his eyes fearfully toward the jungle.

His companion laughed nervously, and moved away, to repeat the conversation, with variations and exaggerations, to others of the black soldiery, so that it was not long before a frightful tale of black magic and sudden death was woven about the giant prisoner, and had gone the rounds of the camp.

And deep in the gloomy jungle amidst the darkening shadows of the falling night a hairy, manlike creature swung swiftly southward upon some secret mission of his own.

A NIGHT OF TERROR

To Jane Clayton, waiting in the tree where Werper had placed her, it seemed that the long night would never end, yet end it did at last, and within an hour of the coming of dawn her spirits leaped with renewed hope at sight of a solitary horseman approaching along the trail.

The flowing burnoose, with its loose hood, hid both the face and the figure of the rider; but that it was M. Frecoult the girl well knew, since he had been garbed as an Arab, and he alone might be expected to seek her hiding place.

That which she saw relieved the strain of the long night vigil; but there was much that she did not see. She did not see the black face beneath the white hood, nor the file of ebon horsemen beyond the trail's bend riding slowly in the wake of their leader. These things she did not see at first, and so she leaned downward toward the approaching rider, a cry of welcome forming in her throat.

At the first word the man looked up, reining in in surprise, and as she saw the black face of Abdul Mourak, the Abyssinian, she shrank back in terror among the branches; but it was too late. The man had seen her, and now he called to her to descend. At first she refused; but when a dozen black cavalrymen drew up behind their leader, and at Abdul Mourak's command one of them started to climb the tree after her she realized that resistance was futile, and came slowly down to stand upon the ground before this new captor and plead her cause in the name of justice and humanity.

Angered by recent defeat, and by the loss of the gold, the jewels, and his prisoners, Abdul Mourak was in no mood to be influenced by any appeal to those softer sentiments to which, as a matter of fact, he was almost a stranger even under the most favourable conditions.

He looked for degradation and possible death in punishment for his failures and his misfortunes when he should have returned to his native land and made his report to Menelek; but an acceptable gift might temper the wrath of the emperor, and surely this fair flower of another race should be gratefully received by the black ruler!

When Jane Clayton had concluded her appeal, Abdul Mourak replied briefly that he would promise her protection; but that he must take her to his emperor. The girl did not need ask him why, and once again hope died within her breast. Resignedly she permitted herself to be lifted to a seat behind one of the troopers, and again, under new masters, her journey was resumed toward what she now began to believe was her inevitable fate.

Abdul Mourak, bereft of his guides by the battle he had waged against the raiders, and himself unfamiliar with the country, had wandered far from the trail he should have followed, and as a result had made but little progress toward the north since the beginning of his flight. Today he was beating toward the west in the hope of coming upon a village where he might obtain guides; but night found him still as far from a realization of his hopes as had the rising sun.

It was a dispirited company which went into camp, waterless and hungry, in the dense jungle. Attracted by the horses, lions roared about the boma, and to their hideous din was added the shrill neighs of the terror-stricken beasts they hunted. There was little sleep for man or beast, and the sentries were doubled that there might be enough on duty both to guard against the sudden charge of an overbold, or overhungry lion, and to keep the fire blazing which was an even more effectual barrier against them than the thorny boma.

It was well past midnight, and as yet Jane Clayton, notwithstanding that she had passed a sleepless night the night before, had scarcely more than dozed. A sense of impending danger seemed to hang like a black pall over the camp. The veteran troopers of the black emperor were nervous and ill at ease. Abdul Mourak left his blankets a dozen times to pace restlessly back and forth between the tethered horses and the crackling fire. The girl could see his great frame silhouetted against the lurid glare of the flames, and she guessed from the quick, nervous movements of the man that he was afraid.

The roaring of the lions rose in sudden fury until the earth trembled to the hideous chorus. The horses shrilled their neighs of terror as they lay back upon their halter ropes in their mad endeavors to break loose. A trooper, braver than his fellows, leaped among the kicking, plunging, fear-maddened beasts in a futile attempt to quiet them. A lion, large, and fierce, and courageous, leaped almost to the boma, full in the bright light from the fire. A sentry raised his piece and fired, and the little leaden pellet unstoppered the vials of hell upon the terror-stricken camp.

The shot ploughed a deep and painful furrow in the lion's side, arousing all the bestial fury of the little brain; but abating not a whit the power and vigor of the great body.

Unwounded, the boma and the flames might have turned him back; but now the pain and the rage wiped caution from his mind, and with a loud, and angry roar he topped the barrier with an easy leap and was among the horses.

What had been pandemonium before became now an indescribable tumult of hideous sound. The stricken horse upon which the lion leaped shrieked out its terror and its agony. Several about it broke their tethers and plunged madly about the camp. Men leaped from their blankets and with guns ready ran toward the picket line, and then from the jungle beyond the boma a dozen lions, emboldened by the example of their fellow charged fearlessly upon the camp.

Singly and in twos and threes they leaped the boma, until the little enclosure was filled with cursing men and screaming horses battling for their lives with the green-eyed devils of the jungle.

With the charge of the first lion, Jane Clayton had scrambled to her feet, and now she stood horror-struck at the scene of savage slaughter that swirled and eddied about her. Once a bolting horse knocked her down, and a moment later a lion, leaping in pursuit of another terror-stricken animal, brushed her so closely that she was again thrown from her feet.

Amidst the cracking of the rifles and the growls of the carnivora rose the death screams of stricken men and horses as they were dragged down by the blood-mad cats. The leaping carnivora and the plunging horses, prevented any concerted action by the Abyssinians—it was every man for himself—and in the melee, the defenseless woman was either forgotten or ignored by her black captors. A score of times was her life menaced by charging lions, by plunging horses, or by the wildly fired bullets of the frightened troopers, yet there was no chance of escape, for now with the fiendish cunning of their kind, the tawny hunters commenced to circle about their prey, hemming them within a ring of mighty, yellow fangs, and sharp, long talons. Again and again an individual lion would dash suddenly among the frightened men and horses, and occasionally a horse, goaded to frenzy by pain or terror, succeeded in racing safely through the circling lions, leaping the boma, and escaping into the jungle; but for the men and the woman no such escape was possible.

A horse, struck by a stray bullet, fell beside Jane Clayton, a lion leaped across the expiring beast full upon the breast of a black trooper just beyond. The man clubbed his rifle and struck futilely at the broad head, and then he was down and the carnivore was standing above him.

Shrieking out his terror, the soldier clawed with puny fingers at the shaggy breast in vain endeavor to push away the grinning jaws. The lion lowered his head, the gaping fangs closed with a single sickening crunch upon the fear-distorted face, and turning strode back across the body of the dead horse dragging his limp and bloody burden with him.

Wide-eyed the girl stood watching. She saw the carnivore step upon the corpse, stumblingly, as the grisly thing swung between its forepaws, and her eyes remained fixed in fascination while the beast passed within a few paces of her.

The interference of the body seemed to enrage the lion. He shook the inanimate clay venomously. He growled and roared hideously at the dead, insensate thing, and then he dropped it and raised his head to look about in search of some living victim upon which to wreak his ill temper. His yellow eyes fastened themselves balefully upon the figure of the girl, the bristling lips raised, disclosing the grinning fangs. A terrific roar broke from the savage throat, and the great beast crouched to spring upon this new and helpless victim.

Quiet had fallen early upon the camp where Tarzan and Werper lay securely bound. Two nervous sentries paced their beats, their eyes rolling often toward the impenetrable shadows of the gloomy jungle. The others slept or tried to sleep—all but the ape-man. Silently and powerfully he strained at the bonds which fettered his wrists.

The muscles knotted beneath the smooth, brown skin of his arms and shoulders, the veins stood out upon his temples from the force of his exertions—a strand parted, another and another, and one hand was free. Then from the jungle came a low guttural, and the ape-man became suddenly a silent, rigid statue, with ears and nostrils straining to span the black void where his eyesight could not reach.

Again came the uncanny sound from the thick verdure beyond the camp. A sentry halted abruptly, straining his eyes into the gloom. The kinky wool upon his head stiffened and raised. He called to his comrade in a hoarse whisper.

"Did you hear it?" he asked.

The other came closer, trembling.

"Hear what?"

Again was the weird sound repeated, followed almost immediately by a similar and answering sound from the camp. The sentries drew close together, watching the black spot from which the voice seemed to come.

Trees overhung the boma at this point which was upon the opposite side of the camp from them. They dared not approach. Their terror even prevented them from arousing their fellows—they could only stand in frozen fear and watch for the fearsome apparition they momentarily expected to see leap from the jungle.

Nor had they long to wait. A dim, bulky form dropped lightly from the branches of a tree into the camp. At sight of it one of the sentries recovered command of his muscles and his voice. Screaming loudly to awaken the sleeping camp, he leaped toward the flickering watch fire and threw a mass of brush upon it.

The white officer and the black soldiers sprang from their blankets. The flames leaped high upon the rejuvenated fire, lighting the entire camp, and the awakened men shrank back in superstitious terror from the sight that met their frightened and astonished vision.

A dozen huge and hairy forms loomed large beneath the trees at the far side of the enclosure. The white giant, one hand freed, had struggled to his knees and was calling to the frightful, nocturnal visitors in a hideous medley of bestial gutturals, barkings and growlings.

Werper had managed to sit up. He, too, saw the savage faces of the approaching anthropoids and scarcely knew whether to be relieved or terror-stricken.

Growling, the great apes leaped forward toward Tarzan and Werper. Chulk led them. The Belgian officer called to his men to fire upon the intruders; but the Negroes held back, filled as they were with superstitious terror of the hairy treemen, and with the conviction that the white giant who could thus summon the beasts of the jungle to his aid was more than human.

Drawing his own weapon, the officer fired, and Tarzan fearing the effect of the noise upon his really timid friends called to them to hasten and fulfill his commands.

A couple of the apes turned and fled at the sound of the firearm; but Chulk and a half dozen others waddled rapidly forward, and, following the ape-man's directions, seized both him and Werper and bore them off toward the jungle.

By dint of threats, reproaches and profanity the Belgian officer succeeded in persuading his trembling command to fire a volley after the retreating apes. A ragged, straggling volley it was, but at least one of its bullets found a mark, for as the jungle closed about the hairy rescuers, Chulk, who bore Werper across one broad shoulder, staggered and fell.

In an instant he was up again; but the Belgian guessed from his unsteady gait that he was hard hit. He lagged far behind the others, and it was several minutes after they had halted at Tarzan's command before he came slowly up to them, reeling from side to side, and at last falling again beneath the weight of his burden and the shock of his wound.

As Chulk went down he dropped Werper, so that the latter fell face downward with the body of the ape lying half across him. In this position the Belgian felt something resting against his hands, which were still bound at his back—something that was not a part of the hairy body of the ape.

Mechanically the man's fingers felt of the object resting almost in their grasp—it was a soft pouch, filled with small, hard particles. Werper gasped in wonderment as recognition filtered through the incredulity of his mind. It was impossible, and yet—it was true!

Feverishly he strove to remove the pouch from the ape and transfer it to his own possession; but the restricted radius to which his bonds held his hands prevented this, though he did succeed in tucking the pouch with its precious contents inside the waist band of his trousers.

Tarzan, sitting at a short distance, was busy with the remaining knots of the cords which bound him. Presently he flung aside the last of them and rose to his feet. Approaching Werper he knelt beside him. For a moment he examined the ape.

"Quite dead," he announced. "It is too bad—he was a splendid creature," and then he turned to the work of liberating the Belgian.

He freed his hands first, and then commenced upon the knots at his ankles.

"I can do the rest," said the Belgian. "I have a small pocketknife which they overlooked when they searched me," and in this way he succeeded in ridding himself of the ape-man's attentions that he might find and open his little knife and cut the thong which fastened the pouch about Chulk's shoulder, and transfer it from his waist band to the breast of his shirt. Then he rose and approached Tarzan.

Once again had avarice claimed him. Forgotten were the good intentions which the confidence of Jane Clayton in his honor had awakened. What she had done, the little pouch had undone. How it had come upon the person of the great ape, Werper could not imagine, unless it had been that the anthropoid had witnessed his fight with Achmet Zek, seen the Arab with the pouch and taken it away from him; but that this pouch contained the jewels of Opar, Werper was positive, and that was all that interested him greatly.

"Now," said the ape-man, "keep your promise to me. Lead me to the spot where you last saw my wife."

It was slow work pushing through the jungle in the dead of night behind the slow-moving Belgian. The ape-man chafed at the delay, but the European could not swing through the trees as could his more agile and muscular companions, and so the speed of all was limited to that of the slowest.

The apes trailed out behind the two white men for a matter of a few miles; but presently their interest lagged, the foremost of them halted in a little glade and the others stopped at his side. There they sat peering from beneath their shaggy brows at the figures of the two men forging steadily ahead, until the latter disappeared in the leafy trail beyond the clearing. Then an ape sought a comfortable couch beneath a tree, and one by one the others followed his example, so that Werper and Tarzan continued their journey alone; nor was the latter either surprised or concerned.

The two had gone but a short distance beyond the glade where the apes had deserted them, when the roaring of distant lions fell upon their ears. The ape-man paid no attention to the familiar sounds until the crack of a rifle came faintly from the same direction, and when this was followed by the shrill neighing of horses, and an almost continuous fusillade of shots intermingled with increased and savage roaring of a large troop of lions, he became immediately concerned.

"Someone is having trouble over there," he said, turning toward Werper. "I'll have to go to them—they may be friends."

"Your wife might be among them," suggested the Belgian, for since he had again come into possession of the pouch he had become fearful and suspicious of the ape-man, and in his mind had constantly revolved many plans for eluding this giant Englishman, who was at once his savior and his captor.

At the suggestion Tarzan started as though struck with a whip.

"God!" he cried, "she might be, and the lions are attacking them—they are in the camp. I can tell from the screams of the horses—and there! that was the cry of a man in his death agonies. Stay here man—I will come back for you. I must go first to them," and swinging into a tree the lithe figure swung rapidly off into the night with the speed and silence of a disembodied spirit.

For a moment Werper stood where the ape-man had left him. Then a cunning smile crossed his lips. "Stay here?" he asked himself. "Stay here and wait until you return to find and take these jewels from me? Not I, my friend, not I," and turning abruptly eastward Albert Werper passed through the foliage of a hanging vine and out of the sight of his fellow-man—forever.

HOME

As Tarzan of the Apes hurtled through the trees the discordant sounds of the battle between the Abyssinians and the lions smote more and more distinctly upon his sensitive ears, redoubling his assurance that the plight of the human element of the conflict was critical indeed.

At last the glare of the camp fire shone plainly through the intervening trees, and a moment later the giant figure of the ape-man paused upon an overhanging bough to look down upon the bloody scene of carnage below.

His quick eye took in the whole scene with a single comprehending glance and stopped upon the figure of a woman standing facing a great lion across the carcass of a horse.

The carnivore was crouching to spring as Tarzan discovered the tragic tableau. Numa was almost beneath the branch upon which the ape-man stood, naked and unarmed. There was not even an instant's hesitation upon the part of the latter—it was as though he had not even paused in his swift progress through the trees, so lightning-like his survey and comprehension of the scene below him—so instantaneous his consequent action.

So hopeless had seemed her situation to her that Jane Clayton but stood in lethargic apathy awaiting the impact of the huge body that would hurl her to the ground—awaiting the momentary agony that cruel talons and grisly fangs may inflict before the coming of the merciful oblivion which would end her sorrow and her suffering.

What use to attempt escape? As well face the hideous end as to be dragged down from behind in futile flight. She did not even close her eyes to shut out the frightful aspect of that snarling face, and so it was that as she saw the lion preparing to charge she saw, too, a bronzed and mighty figure leap from an overhanging tree at the instant that Numa rose in his spring.

Wide went her eyes in wonder and incredulity, as she beheld this seeming apparition risen from the dead. The lion was forgotten—her own peril—everything save the wondrous miracle of this strange recrudescence. With parted lips, with palms tight pressed against her heaving bosom, the girl leaned forward, large-eyed, enthralled by the vision of her dead mate.

She saw the sinewy form leap to the shoulder of the lion, hurtling against the leaping beast like a huge, animate battering ram. She saw the carnivore brushed aside as he was almost upon her, and in the instant she realized that no substanceless wraith could thus turn the charge of a maddened lion with brute force greater than the brute's.

Tarzan, her Tarzan, lived! A cry of unspeakable gladness broke from her lips, only to die in terror as she saw the utter defenselessness of her mate, and realized that the lion had recovered himself and was turning upon Tarzan in mad lust for vengeance.

At the ape-man's feet lay the discarded rifle of the dead Abyssinian whose mutilated corpse sprawled where Numa had abandoned it. The quick glance which had swept the ground for some weapon of defense discovered it, and as the lion reared upon his hind legs to seize the rash man-thing who had dared interpose its puny strength between Numa and his prey, the heavy stock whirred through the air and splintered upon the broad forehead.

Not as an ordinary mortal might strike a blow did Tarzan of the Apes strike; but with the maddened frenzy of a wild beast backed by the steel thews which his wild, arboreal boyhood had bequeathed him. When the blow ended the splintered stock was driven through the splintered skull into the savage brain, and the heavy iron barrel was bent into a rude V.

In the instant that the lion sank, lifeless, to the ground, Jane Clayton threw herself into the eager arms of her husband. For a brief instant he strained her dear form to his breast, and then a glance about him awakened the ape-man to the dangers which still surrounded them.

Upon every hand the lions were still leaping upon new victims. Fear-maddened horses still menaced them with their erratic bolting from one side of the enclosure to the other. Bullets from the guns of the defenders who remained alive but added to the perils of their situation.

To remain was to court death. Tarzan seized Jane Clayton and lifted her to a broad shoulder. The blacks who had witnessed his advent looked on in amazement as they saw the naked giant leap easily into the branches of the tree from whence he had dropped so uncannily upon the scene, and vanish as he had come, bearing away their prisoner with him.

They were too well occupied in self-defense to attempt to halt him, nor could they have done so other than by the wasting of a precious bullet which might be needed the next instant to turn the charge of a savage foe.

And so, unmolested, Tarzan passed from the camp of the Abyssinians, from which the din of conflict followed him deep into the jungle until distance gradually obliterated it entirely.

Back to the spot where he had left Werper went the ape-man, joy in his heart now, where fear and sorrow had so recently reigned; and in his mind a determination to forgive the Belgian and aid him in making good his escape. But when he came to the place, Werper was gone, and though Tarzan called aloud many times he received no reply. Convinced that the man had purposely eluded him for reasons of his own, John

Clayton felt that he was under no obligations to expose his wife to further danger and discomfort in the prosecution of a more thorough search for the missing Belgian.

"He has acknowledged his guilt by his flight, Jane," he said. "We will let him go to lie in the bed that he has made for himself."

Straight as homing pigeons, the two made their way toward the ruin and desolation that had once been the center of their happy lives, and which was soon to be restored by the willing black hands of laughing laborers, made happy again by the return of the master and mistress whom they had mourned as dead.

Past the village of Achmet Zek their way led them, and there they found but the charred remains of the palisade and the native huts, still smoking, as mute evidence of the wrath and vengeance of a powerful enemy.

"The Waziri," commented Tarzan with a grim smile.

"God bless them!" cried Jane Clayton.

"They cannot be far ahead of us," said Tarzan, "Basuli and the others. The gold is gone and the jewels of Opar, Jane; but we have each other and the Waziri—and we have love and loyalty and friendship. And what are gold and jewels to these?"

"If only poor Mugambi lived," she replied, "and those other brave fellows who sacrificed their lives in vain endeavor to protect me!"

In the silence of mingled joy and sorrow they passed along through the familiar jungle, and as the afternoon was waning there came faintly to the ears of the ape-man the murmuring cadence of distant voices.

"We are nearing the Waziri, Jane," he said. "I can hear them ahead of us. They are going into camp for the night, I imagine."

A half hour later the two came upon a horde of ebon warriors which Basuli had collected for his war of vengeance upon the raiders. With them were the captured women of the tribe whom they had found in the village of Achmet Zek, and tall, even among the giant Waziri, loomed a familiar black form at the side of Basuli. It was Mugambi, whom Jane had thought dead amidst the charred ruins of the bungalow.

Ah, such a reunion! Long into the night the dancing and the singing and the laughter awoke the echoes of the somber wood. Again and again were the stories of their various adventures retold. Again and once again they fought their battles with savage beast and savage man, and dawn was already breaking when Basuli, for the fortieth time, narrated how he and a handful of his warriors had watched the battle for the golden ingots which the Abyssinians of Abdul Mourak had waged against the Arab raiders of Achmet Zek, and how, when the victors had ridden away they had sneaked out of the river reeds and stolen away with the precious ingots to hide them where no robber eye ever could discover them.

Pieced out from the fragments of their various experiences with the Belgian the truth concerning the malign activities of Albert Werper became apparent. Only Lady Greystoke found aught to praise in the conduct of the man, and it was difficult even for her to reconcile his many heinous acts with this one evidence of chivalry and honor.

"Deep in the soul of every man," said Tarzan, "must lurk the germ of righteousness. It was your own virtue, Jane, rather even than your helplessness which awakened for an instant the latent decency of this degraded man. In that one act he retrieved himself, and when he is called to face his Maker may it outweigh in the balance, all the sins he has committed."

And Jane Clayton breathed a fervent, "Amen!"

Months had passed. The labor of the Waziri and the gold of Opar had rebuilt and refurnished the wasted homestead of the Greystokes. Once more the simple life of the great African farm went on as it had before the coming of the Belgian and the Arab. Forgotten were the sorrows and dangers of yesterday.

For the first time in months Lord Greystoke felt that he might indulge in a holiday, and so a great hunt was organized that the faithful laborers might feast in celebration of the completion of their work.

In itself the hunt was a success, and ten days after its inauguration, a well-laden safari took up its return march toward the Waziri plain. Lord and Lady Greystoke with Basuli and Mugambi rode together at the head of the column, laughing and talking together in that easy familiarity which common interests and mutual respect breed between honest and intelligent men of any races.

Jane Clayton's horse shied suddenly at an object half hidden in the long grasses of an open space in the jungle. Tarzan's keen eyes sought quickly for an explanation of the animal's action.

"What have we here?" he cried, swinging from his saddle, and a moment later the four were grouped about a human skull and a little litter of whitened human bones.

Tarzan stooped and lifted a leathern pouch from the grisly relics of a man. The hard outlines of the contents brought an exclamation of surprise to his lips.

"The jewels of Opar!" he cried, holding the pouch aloft, "and," pointing to the bones at his feet, "all that remains of Werper, the Belgian."

Mugambi laughed. "Look within, Bwana," he cried, "and you will see what are the jewels of Opar—you will see what the Belgian gave his life for," and the black laughed aloud.

"Why do you laugh?" asked Tarzan.

"Because," replied Mugambi, "I filled the Belgian's pouch with river gravel before I escaped the camp of the Abyssinians whose prisoners we were. I left the Belgian only worthless stones, while I brought away with me the jewels he had stolen from you. That they were afterward stolen from me while I slept in the jungle is my shame and my disgrace; but at least the Belgian lost them—open his pouch and you will see."

Tarzan untied the thong which held the mouth of the leathern bag closed, and permitted the contents to trickle slowly forth into his open palm. Mugambi's eyes went wide at the sight, and the others uttered exclamations of surprise and incredulity, for from the rusty and weatherworn pouch ran a stream of brilliant, scintillating gems.

"The jewels of Opar!" cried Tarzan. "But how did Werper come by them again?"

None could answer, for both Chulk and Werper were dead, and no other knew.

"Poor devil!" said the ape-man, as he swung back into his saddle. "Even in death he has made restitution—let his sins lie with his bones."

JUNGLE TALES OF TARZAN

TARZAN'S FIRST LOVE

Teeka, stretched at luxurious ease in the shade of the tropical forest, presented, unquestionably, a most alluring picture of young, feminine loveliness. Or at least so thought Tarzan of the Apes, who squatted upon a low-swinging branch in a near-by tree and looked down upon her.

Just to have seen him there, lolling upon the swaying bough of the jungle-forest giant, his brown skin mottled by the brilliant equatorial sunlight which percolated through the leafy canopy of green above him, his clean-limbed body relaxed in graceful ease, his shapely head partly turned in contemplative absorption and his intelligent, gray eyes dreamily devouring the object of their devotion, you would have thought him the reincarnation of some demigod of old.

You would not have guessed that in infancy he had suckled at the breast of a hideous, hairy she-ape, nor that in all his conscious past since his parents had passed away in the little cabin by the landlocked harbor at the jungle's verge, he had known no other associates than the sullen bulls and the snarling cows of the tribe of Kerchak, the great ape.

Nor, could you have read the thoughts which passed through that active, healthy brain, the longings and desires and aspirations which the sight of Teeka inspired, would you have been any more inclined to give credence to the reality of the origin of the ape-man. For, from his thoughts alone, you could never have gleaned the truth—that he had been born to a gentle English lady or that his sire had been an English nobleman of time-honored lineage.

Lost to Tarzan of the Apes was the truth of his origin. That he was John Clayton, Lord Greystoke, with a seat in the House of Lords, he did not know, nor, knowing, would have understood.

Yes, Teeka was indeed beautiful!

Of course Kala had been beautiful—one's mother is always that—but Teeka was beautiful in a way all her own, an indescribable sort of way which Tarzan was just beginning to sense in a rather vague and hazy manner.

For years had Tarzan and Teeka been play-fellows, and Teeka still continued to be playful while the young bulls of her own age were rapidly becoming surly and morose. Tarzan, if he gave the matter much thought at all, probably reasoned that his growing attachment for the young female could be easily accounted for by the fact that of the former playmates she and he alone retained any desire to frolic as of old.

But today, as he sat gazing upon her, he found himself noting the beauties of Teeka's form and features—something he never had done before, since none of them had aught to do with Teeka's ability to race nimbly through the lower terraces of the forest in the primitive games of tag and hide-and-go-seek which Tarzan's fertile brain evolved. Tarzan scratched his head, running his fingers deep into the shock of black hair which framed his shapely, boyish face—he scratched his head and sighed. Teeka's new-found beauty became as suddenly his despair. He envied her the handsome coat of hair which covered her body. His own smooth, brown hide he hated with a hatred born of disgust and contempt. Years back he had harbored a hope that some day he, too, would be clothed in hair as were all his brothers and sisters; but of late he had been forced to abandon the delectable dream.

Then there were Teeka's great teeth, not so large as the males, of course, but still mighty, handsome things by comparison with Tarzan's feeble white ones. And her beetling brows, and broad, flat nose, and her mouth! Tarzan had often practiced making his mouth into a little round circle and then puffing out his cheeks while he winked his eyes rapidly; but he felt that he could never do it in the same cute and irresistible way in which Teeka did it.

And as he watched her that afternoon, and wondered, a young bull ape who had been lazily foraging for food beneath the damp, matted carpet of decaying vegetation at the roots of a near-by tree lumbered awkwardly in Teeka's direction. The other apes of the tribe of Kerchak moved listlessly about or lolled restfully in the midday heat of the equatorial jungle. From time to time one or another of them had passed close to Teeka, and Tarzan had been uninterested. Why was it then that his brows contracted and his muscles tensed as he saw Taug pause beside the young she and then squat down close to her?

Tarzan always had liked Taug. Since childhood they had romped together. Side by side they had squatted near the water, their quick, strong fingers ready to leap forth and seize Pisah, the fish, should that wary denizen of the cool depths dart surfaceward to the lure of the insects Tarzan tossed upon the face of the pool.

Together they had baited Tublat and teased Numa, the lion. Why, then, should Tarzan feel the rise of the short hairs at the nape of his neck merely because Taug sat close to Teeka?

It is true that Taug was no longer the frolicsome ape of yesterday. When his snarling-muscles bared his giant fangs no one could longer imagine that Taug was in as playful a mood as when he and Tarzan had rolled upon the turf in mimic battle. The Taug of today was a huge, sullen bull ape, somber and forbidding. Yet he and Tarzan never had quarreled.

For a few minutes the young ape-man watched Taug press closer to Teeka. He saw the rough caress of the huge paw as it stroked the sleek shoulder of the she, and then Tarzan of the Apes slipped catlike to the ground and approached the two.

As he came his upper lip curled into a snarl, exposing his fighting fangs, and a deep growl rumbled from his cavernous chest. Taug looked up, batting his blood-shot eyes. Teeka half raised herself and looked at Tarzan. Did she guess the cause of his perturbation? Who may say? At any rate, she was feminine, and so she reached up and scratched Taug behind one of his small, flat ears.

Tarzan saw, and in the instant that he saw, Teeka was no longer the little playmate of an hour ago; instead she was a wondrous thing—the most wondrous in the world—and a possession for which Tarzan would fight to the death against Taug or any other who dared question his right of proprietorship.

Stooped, his muscles rigid and one great shoulder turned toward the young bull, Tarzan of the Apes sidled nearer and nearer. His face was partly averted, but his keen gray eyes never left those of Taug, and as he came, his growls increased in depth and volume.

Taug rose upon his short legs, bristling. His fighting fangs were bared. He, too, sidled, stiff-legged, and growled.

"Teeka is Tarzan's," said the ape-man, in the low gutturals of the great anthropoids.

"Teeka is Taug's," replied the bull ape.

Thaka and Numgo and Gunto, disturbed by the growlings of the two young bulls, looked up half apathetic, half interested. They were sleepy, but they sensed a fight. It would break the monotony of the humdrum jungle life they led.

Coiled about his shoulders was Tarzan's long grass rope, in his hand was the hunting knife of the long-dead father he had never known. In Taug's little brain lay a great respect for the shiny bit of sharp metal which the ape-boy knew so well how to use. With it had he slain Tublat, his fierce foster father, and Bolgani, the gorilla. Taug knew these things, and so he came warily, circling about Tarzan in search of an opening. The latter, made cautious because of his lesser bulk and the inferiority of his natural armament, followed similar tactics.

For a time it seemed that the altercation would follow the way of the majority of such differences between members of the tribe and that one of them would finally lose interest and wander off to prosecute some other line of endeavor. Such might have been the end of it had the *Casus Belli* been other than it was; but Teeka was flattered at the attention that was being drawn to her and by the fact that these two young bulls were contemplating battle on her account. Such a thing never before had occurred in Teeka's brief life. She had seen other bulls battling for other and older shes, and in the depth of her wild little heart she had longed for the day when the jungle grasses would be reddened with the blood of mortal combat for her fair sake.

So now she squatted upon her haunches and insulted both her admirers impartially. She hurled taunts at them for their cowardice, and called them vile names, such as Histah, the snake, and Dango, the hyena. She threatened to call Mumga to chastise them with a stick—Mumga, who was so old that she could no longer climb and so toothless that she was forced to confine her diet almost exclusively to bananas and grub-worms.

The apes who were watching heard and laughed. Taug was infuriated. He made a sudden lunge for Tarzan, but the ape-boy leaped nimbly to one side, eluding him, and with the quickness of a cat wheeled and leaped back again to close quarters. His hunting knife was raised above his head as he came in, and he aimed a vicious blow at Taug's neck. The ape wheeled to dodge the weapon so that the keen blade struck him but a glancing blow upon the shoulder.

The spurt of red blood brought a shrill cry of delight from Teeka. Ah, but this was something worth while! She glanced about to see if others had witnessed this evidence of her popularity. Helen of Troy was never one whit more proud than was Teeka at that moment.

If Teeka had not been so absorbed in her own vaingloriousness she might have noted the rustling of leaves in the tree above her—a rustling which was not caused by any movement of the wind, since there was no wind. And had she looked up she might have seen a sleek body crouching almost directly over her and wicked yellow eyes glaring hungrily down upon her, but Teeka did not look up.

With his wound Taug had backed off growling horribly. Tarzan had followed him, screaming insults at him, and menacing him with his brandishing blade. Teeka moved from beneath the tree in an effort to keep close to the duelists.

The branch above Teeka bent and swayed a trifle with the movement of the body of the watcher stretched along it. Taug had halted now and was preparing to make a new stand. His lips were flecked with foam, and saliva drooled from his jowls. He stood with head lowered and arms outstretched, preparing for a sudden charge to close quarters. Could he but lay his mighty hands upon that soft, brown skin the battle would be his. Taug considered Tarzan's manner of fighting unfair. He would not close. Instead, he leaped nimbly just beyond the reach of Taug's muscular fingers.

The ape-boy had as yet never come to a real trial of strength with a bull ape, other than in play, and so he was not at all sure that it would be safe to put his muscles to the test in a life and death struggle. Not that he was afraid, for Tarzan knew nothing of fear. The instinct of self-preservation gave him caution—that was all. He took risks only when it seemed necessary, and then he would hesitate at nothing.

His own method of fighting seemed best fitted to his build and to his armament. His teeth, while strong and sharp, were, as weapons of offense, pitifully inadequate by comparison with the mighty fighting fangs of the anthropoids. By dancing about, just out of reach of an antagonist, Tarzan could do infinite injury with his long, sharp hunting knife, and at the same time escape many of the painful and dangerous wounds which would be sure to follow his falling into the clutches of a bull ape.

And so Taug charged and bellowed like a bull, and Tarzan of the Apes danced lightly to this side and that, hurling jungle billingsgate at his foe, the while he nicked him now and again with his knife.

There were lulls in the fighting when the two would stand panting for breath, facing each other, mustering their wits and their forces for a new onslaught. It was during a pause such as this that Taug chanced to let his eyes rove beyond his foeman. Instantly the entire aspect of the ape altered. Rage left his countenance to be supplanted by an expression of fear.

With a cry that every ape there recognized, Taug turned and fled. No need to question him—his warning proclaimed the near presence of their ancient enemy.

Tarzan started to seek safety, as did the other members of the tribe, and as he did so he heard a panther's scream mingled with the frightened cry of a she-ape. Taug heard, too; but he did not pause in his flight.

With the ape-boy, however, it was different. He looked back to see if any member of the tribe was close pressed by the beast of prey, and the sight that met his eyes filled them with an expression of horror.

Teeka it was who cried out in terror as she fled across a little clearing toward the trees upon the opposite side, for after her leaped Sheeta, the panther, in easy, graceful bounds. Sheeta appeared to be in no hurry.

His meat was assured, since even though the ape reached the trees ahead of him she could not climb beyond his clutches before he could be upon her.

Tarzan saw that Teeka must die. He cried to Taug and the other bulls to hasten to Teeka's assistance, and at the same time he ran toward the pursuing beast, taking down his rope as he came. Tarzan knew that once the great bulls were aroused none of the jungle, not even Numa, the lion, was anxious to measure fangs with them, and that if all those of the tribe who chanced to be present today would charge, Sheeta, the great cat, would doubtless turn tail and run for his life.

Taug heard, as did the others, but no one came to Tarzan's assistance or Teeka's rescue, and Sheeta was rapidly closing up the distance between himself and his prey.

The ape-boy, leaping after the panther, cried aloud to the beast in an effort to turn it from Teeka or otherwise distract its attention until the she-ape could gain the safety of the higher branches where Sheeta dared not go. He called the panther every opprobrious name that fell to his tongue. He dared him to stop and do battle with him; but Sheeta only loped on after the luscious titbit now almost within his reach.

Tarzan was not far behind and he was gaining, but the distance was so short that he scarce hoped to overhaul the carnivore before it had felled Teeka. In his right hand the boy swung his grass rope above his head as he ran. He hated to chance a miss, for the distance was much greater than he ever had cast before except in practice. It was the full length of his grass rope which separated him from Sheeta, and yet there was no other thing to do. He could not reach the brute's side before it overhauled Teeka. He must chance a throw.

And just as Teeka sprang for the lower limb of a great tree, and Sheeta rose behind her in a long, sinuous leap, the coils of the ape-boy's grass rope shot swiftly through the air, straightening into a long thin line as the open noose hovered for an instant above the savage head and the snarling jaws. Then it settled—clean and true about the tawny neck it settled, and Tarzan, with a quick twist of his rope-hand, drew the noose taut, bracing himself for the shock when Sheeta should have taken up the slack.

Just short of Teeka's glossy rump the cruel talons raked the air as the rope tightened and Sheeta was brought to a sudden stop—a stop that snapped the big beast over upon his back. Instantly Sheeta was up—with glaring eyes, and lashing tail, and gaping jaws, from which issued hideous cries of rage and disappointment.

He saw the ape-boy, the cause of his discomfiture, scarce forty feet before him, and Sheeta charged.

Teeka was safe now; Tarzan saw to that by a quick glance into the tree whose safety she had gained not an instant too soon, and Sheeta was charging. It was useless to risk his life in idle and unequal combat from which no good could come; but could he escape a battle with the enraged cat? And if he was forced to fight, what chance had he to survive? Tarzan was constrained to admit that his position was aught but a desirable one. The trees were too far to hope to reach in time to elude the cat. Tarzan could but stand facing that hideous charge. In his right hand he grasped his hunting knife—a puny, futile thing indeed by comparison with the great rows of mighty teeth which lined Sheeta's powerful jaws, and the sharp talons encased within his padded paws; yet the young Lord Greystoke faced it with the same courageous resignation with which some fearless ancestor went down to defeat and death on Senlac Hill by Hastings.

From safety points in the trees the great apes watched, screaming hatred at Sheeta and advice at Tarzan, for the progenitors of man have, naturally, many human traits. Teeka was frightened. She screamed at the bulls to hasten to Tarzan's assistance; but the bulls were otherwise engaged—principally in giving advice and making faces. Anyway, Tarzan was not a real Mangani, so why should they risk their lives in an effort to protect him?

And now Sheeta was almost upon the lithe, naked body, and—the body was not there. Quick as was the great cat, the ape-boy was quicker. He leaped to one side almost as the panther's talons were closing upon him, and as Sheeta went hurtling to the ground beyond, Tarzan was racing for the safety of the nearest tree.

The panther recovered himself almost immediately and, wheeling, tore after his prey, the ape-boy's rope dragging along the ground behind him. In doubling back after Tarzan, Sheeta had passed around a low bush.

It was a mere nothing in the path of any jungle creature of the size and weight of Sheeta—provided it had no trailing rope dangling behind. But Sheeta was handicapped by such a rope, and as he leaped once again after Tarzan of the Apes the rope encircled the small bush, became tangled in it and brought the panther to a sudden stop. An instant later Tarzan was safe among the higher branches of a small tree into which Sheeta could not follow him.

Here he perched, hurling twigs and epithets at the raging feline beneath him. The other members of the tribe now took up the bombardment, using such hard-shelled fruits and dead branches as came within their reach, until Sheeta, goaded to frenzy and snapping at the grass rope, finally succeeded in severing its strands. For a moment the panther stood glaring first at one of his tormentors and then at another, until, with a final scream of rage, he turned and slunk off into the tangled mazes of the jungle.

A half hour later the tribe was again upon the ground, feeding as though naught had occurred to interrupt the somber dullness of their lives. Tarzan had recovered the greater part of his rope and was busy fashioning a new noose, while Teeka squatted close behind him, in evident token that her choice was made.

Taug eyed them sullenly. Once when he came close, Teeka bared her fangs and growled at him, and Tarzan showed his canines in an ugly snarl; but Taug did not provoke a quarrel. He seemed to accept after the manner of his kind the decision of the she as an indication that he had been vanquished in his battle for her favors.

Later in the day, his rope repaired, Tarzan took to the trees in search of game. More than his fellows he required meat, and so, while they were satisfied with fruits and herbs and beetles, which could be discovered without much effort upon their part, Tarzan spent considerable time hunting the game animals whose flesh alone satisfied the cravings of his stomach and furnished sustenance and strength to the mighty thews which, day by day, were building beneath the soft, smooth texture of his brown hide.

Taug saw him depart, and then, quite casually, the big beast hunted closer and closer to Teeka in his search for food. At last he was within a few feet of her, and when he shot a covert glance at her he saw that she was appraising him and that there was no evidence of anger upon her face.

Taug expanded his great chest and rolled about on his short legs, making strange growlings in his throat. He raised his lips, baring his fangs. My, but what great, beautiful fangs he had! Teeka could not but notice them. She also let her eyes rest in admiration upon Taug's beetling brows and his short, powerful neck. What a beautiful creature he was indeed!

Taug, flattered by the unconcealed admiration in her eyes, strutted about, as proud and as vain as a peacock. Presently he began to inventory his assets, mentally, and shortly he found himself comparing them with those of his rival.

Taug grunted, for there was no comparison. How could one compare his beautiful coat with the smooth and naked hideousness of Tarzan's bare hide? Who could see beauty in the stingy nose of the Tarmangani after looking at Taug's broad nostrils? And Tarzan's eyes! Hideous things, showing white about them, and entirely unrimmed with red. Taug knew that his own blood-shot eyes were beautiful, for he had seen them reflected in the glassy surface of many a drinking pool.

The bull drew nearer to Teeka, finally squatting close against her. When Tarzan returned from his hunting a short time later it was to see Teeka contentedly scratching the back of his rival.

Tarzan was disgusted. Neither Taug nor Teeka saw him as he swung through the trees into the glade. He paused a moment, looking at them; then, with a sorrowful grimace, he turned and faded away into the labyrinth of leafy boughs and festooned moss out of which he had come.

Tarzan wished to be as far away from the cause of his heartache as he could. He was suffering the first pangs of blighted love, and he didn't quite know what was the matter with him. He thought that he was angry with Taug, and so he couldn't understand why it was that he had run away instead of rushing into mortal combat with the destroyer of his happiness.

He also thought that he was angry with Teeka, yet a vision of her many beauties persisted in haunting him, so that he could only see her in the light of love as the most desirable thing in the world.

The ape-boy craved affection. From babyhood until the time of her death, when the poisoned arrow of Kulonga had pierced her savage heart, Kala had represented to the English boy the sole object of love which he had known.

In her wild, fierce way Kala had loved her adopted son, and Tarzan had returned that love, though the outward demonstrations of it were no greater than might have been expected from any other beast of the jungle. It was not until he was bereft of her that the boy realized how deep had been his attachment for his mother, for as such he looked upon her.

In Teeka he had seen within the past few hours a substitute for Kala—someone to fight for and to hunt for—someone to caress; but now his dream was shattered. Something hurt within his breast. He placed his hand over his heart and wondered what had happened to him. Vaguely he attributed his pain to Teeka. The more he thought of Teeka as he had last seen her, caressing Taug, the more the thing within his breast hurt him.

Tarzan shook his head and growled; then on and on through the jungle he swung, and the farther he traveled and the more he thought upon his wrongs, the nearer he approached becoming an irreclaimable misogynist.

Two days later he was still hunting alone—very morose and very unhappy; but he was determined never to return to the tribe. He could not bear the thought of seeing Taug and Teeka always together. As he swung upon a great limb Numa, the lion, and Sabor, the lioness, passed beneath him, side by side, and Sabor leaned against the lion and bit playfully at his cheek. It was a half-caress. Tarzan sighed and hurled a nut at them.

Later he came upon several of Mbonga's black warriors. He was upon the point of dropping his noose about the neck of one of them, who was a little distance from his companions, when he became interested in the thing which occupied the savages. They were building a cage in the trail and covering it with leafy branches. When they had completed their work the structure was scarcely visible.

Tarzan wondered what the purpose of the thing might be, and why, when they had built it, they turned away and started back along the trail in the direction of their village.

It had been some time since Tarzan had visited the blacks and looked down from the shelter of the great trees which overhung their palisade upon the activities of his enemies, from among whom had come the slayer of Kala.

Although he hated them, Tarzan derived considerable entertainment in watching them at their daily life within the village, and especially at their dances, when the fires glared against their naked bodies as they leaped and turned and twisted in mimic warfare. It was rather in the hope of witnessing something of the kind that he now followed the warriors back toward their village, but in this he was disappointed, for there was no dance that night.

Instead, from the safe concealment of his tree, Tarzan saw little groups seated about tiny fires discussing the events of the day, and in the darker corners of the village he descried isolated couples talking and laughing together, and always one of each couple was a young man and the other a young woman.

Tarzan cocked his head upon one side and thought, and before he went to sleep that night, curled in the crotch of the great tree above the village, Teeka filled his mind, and afterward she filled his dreams—she and the young black men laughing and talking with the young black women.

Taug, hunting alone, had wandered some distance from the balance of the tribe. He was making his way slowly along an elephant path when he discovered that it was blocked with undergrowth. Now Taug, come into maturity, was an evil-natured brute of an exceeding short temper. When something thwarted him, his sole idea was to overcome it by brute strength and ferocity, and so now when he found his way blocked, he tore angrily into the leafy screen and an instant later found himself within a strange lair, his progress effectually blocked, notwithstanding his most violent efforts to forge ahead.

Biting and striking at the barrier, Taug finally worked himself into a frightful rage, but all to no avail; and at last he became convinced that he must turn back. But when he would have done so, what was his chagrin to discover that another barrier had dropped behind him while he fought to break down the one before him! Taug was trapped. Until exhaustion overcame him he fought frantically for his freedom; but all for naught.

In the morning a party of blacks set out from the village of Mbonga in the direction of the trap they had constructed the previous day, while among the branches of the trees above them hovered a naked young giant filled with the curiosity of the wild things. Manu, the monkey, chattered and scolded as Tarzan passed, and though he was not afraid of the familiar figure of the ape-boy, he hugged closer to him the little brown body of his life's companion. Tarzan laughed as he saw it; but the laugh was followed by a sudden clouding of his face and a deep sigh.

A little farther on, a gaily feathered bird strutted about before the admiring eyes of his somber-hued mate. It seemed to Tarzan that everything in the jungle was combining to remind him that he had lost Teeka; yet every day of his life he had seen these same things and thought nothing of them.

When the blacks reached the trap, Taug set up a great commotion. Seizing the bars of his prison, he shook them frantically, and all the while he roared and growled terrifically. The blacks were elated, for while they had not built their trap for this hairy tree man, they were delighted with their catch.

Tarzan pricked up his ears when he heard the voice of a great ape and, circling quickly until he was down wind from the trap, he sniffed at the air in search of the scent spoor of the prisoner. Nor was it long before there came to those delicate nostrils the familiar odor that told Tarzan the identity of the captive as unerringly as though he had looked upon Taug with his eyes. Yes, it was Taug, and he was alone.

Tarzan grinned as he approached to discover what the blacks would do to their prisoner. Doubtless they would slay him at once. Again Tarzan grinned. Now he could have Teeka for his own, with none to dispute his right to her. As he watched, he saw the black warriors strip the screen from about the cage, fasten ropes to it and drag it away along the trail in the direction of their village.

Tarzan watched until his rival passed out of sight, still beating upon the bars of his prison and growling out his anger and his threats. Then the ape-boy turned and swung rapidly off in search of the tribe, and Teeka.

Once, upon the journey, he surprised Sheeta and his family in a little overgrown clearing. The great cat lay stretched upon the ground, while his mate, one paw across her lord's savage face, licked at the soft white fur at his throat.

Tarzan increased his speed then until he fairly flew through the forest, nor was it long before he came upon the tribe. He saw them before they saw him, for of all the jungle creatures, none passed more quietly than Tarzan of the Apes. He saw Kamma and her mate feeding side by side, their hairy bodies rubbing against each other. And he saw Teeka feeding by herself. Not for long would she feed thus in loneliness, thought Tarzan, as with a bound he landed amongst them.

There was a startled rush and a chorus of angry and frightened snarls, for Tarzan had surprised them; but there was more, too, than mere nervous shock to account for the bristling neck hair which remained standing long after the apes had discovered the identity of the newcomer.

Tarzan noticed this as he had noticed it many times in the past—that always his sudden coming among them left them nervous and unstrung for a considerable time, and that they one and all found it necessary to satisfy themselves that he was indeed Tarzan by smelling about him a half dozen or more times before they calmed down.

Pushing through them, he made his way toward Teeka; but as he approached her the ape drew away.

"Teeka," he said, "it is Tarzan. You belong to Tarzan. I have come for you."

The ape drew closer, looking him over carefully. Finally she sniffed at him, as though to make assurance doubly sure.

"Where is Taug?" she asked.

"The Gomangani have him," replied Tarzan. "They will kill him."

In the eyes of the she, Tarzan saw a wistful expression and a troubled look of sorrow as he told her of Taug's fate; but she came quite close and snuggled against him, and Tarzan, Lord Greystoke, put his arm about her.

As he did so he noticed, with a start, the strange incongruity of that smooth, brown arm against the black and hairy coat of his lady-love. He recalled the paw of Sheeta's mate across Sheeta's face—no incongruity there. He thought of little Manu hugging his she, and how the one seemed to belong to the other. Even the proud male bird, with his gay plumage, bore a close resemblance to his quieter spouse, while Numa, but for his shaggy mane, was almost a counterpart of Sabor, the lioness. The males and the females differed, it was true; but not with such differences as existed between Tarzan and Teeka.

Tarzan was puzzled. There was something wrong. His arm dropped from the shoulder of Teeka. Very slowly he drew away from her. She looked at him with her head cocked upon one side. Tarzan rose to his full height and beat upon his breast with his fists. He raised his head toward the heavens and opened his mouth. From the depths of his lungs rose the fierce, weird challenge of the victorious bull ape. The tribe turned curiously to eye him. He had killed nothing, nor was there any antagonist to be goaded to madness by the savage scream. No, there was no excuse for it, and they turned back to their feeding, but with an eye upon the ape-man lest he be preparing to suddenly run amuck.

As they watched him they saw him swing into a near-by tree and disappear from sight. Then they forgot him, even Teeka.

Mbonga's black warriors, sweating beneath their strenuous task, and resting often, made slow progress toward their village. Always the savage beast in the primitive cage growled and roared when they moved him. He beat upon the bars and slavered at the mouth. His noise was hideous.

They had almost completed their journey and were making their final rest before forging ahead to gain the clearing in which lay their village. A few more minutes would have taken them out of the forest, and then, doubtless, the thing would not have happened which did happen.

A silent figure moved through the trees above them. Keen eyes inspected the cage and counted the number of warriors. An alert and daring brain figured upon the chances of success when a certain plan should be put to the test.

Tarzan watched the blacks lolling in the shade. They were exhausted. Already several of them slept. He crept closer, pausing just above them. Not a leaf rustled before his stealthy advance. He waited in the infinite patience of the beast of prey. Presently but two of the warriors remained awake, and one of these was dozing.

Tarzan of the Apes gathered himself, and as he did so the black who did not sleep arose and passed around to the rear of the cage. The ape-boy followed just above his head. Taug was eyeing the warrior and emitting low growls. Tarzan feared that the anthropoid would awaken the sleepers.

In a whisper which was inaudible to the ears of the Negro, Tarzan whispered Taug's name, cautioning the ape to silence, and Taug's growling ceased.

The black approached the rear of the cage and examined the fastenings of the door, and as he stood there the beast above him launched itself from the tree full upon his back. Steel fingers circled his throat, choking the cry which sprang to the lips of the terrified man. Strong teeth fastened themselves in his shoulder, and powerful legs wound themselves about his torso.

The black in a frenzy of terror tried to dislodge the silent thing which clung to him. He threw himself to the ground and rolled about; but still those mighty fingers closed more and more tightly their deadly grip.

The man's mouth gaped wide, his swollen tongue protruded, his eyes started from their sockets; but the relentless fingers only increased their pressure.

Taug was a silent witness of the struggle. In his fierce little brain he doubtless wondered what purpose prompted Tarzan to attack the black. Taug had not forgotten his recent battle with the ape-boy, nor the cause of it. Now he saw the form of the Gomangani suddenly go limp. There was a convulsive shiver and the man lay still.

Tarzan sprang from his prey and ran to the door of the cage. With nimble fingers he worked rapidly at the thongs which held the door in place. Taug could only watch—he could not help. Presently Tarzan pushed the thing up a couple of feet and Taug crawled out. The ape would have turned upon the sleeping blacks that he might wreak his pent vengeance; but Tarzan would not permit it.

Instead, the ape-boy dragged the body of the black within the cage and propped it against the side bars. Then he lowered the door and made fast the thongs as they had been before.

A happy smile lighted his features as he worked, for one of his principal diversions was the baiting of the blacks of Mbonga's village. He could imagine their terror when they awoke and found the dead body of their comrade fast in the cage where they had left the great ape safely secured but a few minutes before.

Tarzan and Taug took to the trees together, the shaggy coat of the fierce ape brushing the sleek skin of the English lordling as they passed through the primeval jungle side by side.

"Go back to Teeka," said Tarzan. "She is yours. Tarzan does not want her."

"Tarzan has found another she?" asked Taug.

The ape-boy shrugged.

"For the Gomangani there is another Gomangani," he said; "for Numa, the lion, there is Sabor, the lioness; for Sheeta there is a she of his own kind; for Bara, the deer; for Manu, the monkey; for all the beasts and the birds of jungle is there a mate. Only for Tarzan of the Apes is there none. Taug is an ape. Teeka is an ape. Go back to Teeka. Tarzan is a man. He will go alone."

THE CAPTURE OF TARZAN

The black warriors labored in the humid heat of the jungle's stifling shade. With war spears they loosened the thick, black loam and the deep layers of rotting vegetation. With heavy-nailed fingers they scooped away the disintegrated earth from the center of the age-old game trail. Often they ceased their labors to squat, resting and gossiping, with much laughter, at the edge of the pit they were digging.

Against the boles of near-by trees leaned their long, oval shields of thick buffalo hide, and the spears of those who were doing the scooping. Sweat glistened upon their smooth, ebon skins, beneath which rolled rounded muscles, supple in the perfection of nature's uncontaminated health.

A reed buck, stepping warily along the trail toward water, halted as a burst of laughter broke upon his startled ears. For a moment he stood statuesque but for his sensitively dilating nostrils; then he wheeled and fled noiselessly from the terrifying presence of man.

A hundred yards away, deep in the tangle of impenetrable jungle, Numa, the lion, raised his massive head. Numa had dined well until almost daybreak and it had required much noise to awaken him. Now he lifted his muzzle and sniffed the air, caught the acrid scent spoor of the reed buck and the heavy scent of man. But Numa was well filled. With a low, disgusted grunt he rose and slunk away.

Brilliantly plumaged birds with raucous voices darted from tree to tree. Little monkeys, chattering and scolding, swung through the swaying limbs above the black warriors. Yet they were alone, for the teeming jungle with all its myriad life, like the swarming streets of a great metropolis, is one of the loneliest spots in God's great universe.

But were they alone?

Above them, lightly balanced upon a leafy tree limb, a gray-eyed youth watched with eager intentness their every move. The fire of hate, restrained, smoldered beneath the lad's evident desire to know the purpose of the black men's labors. Such a one as these it was who had slain his beloved Kala. For them there could be naught but enmity, yet he liked well to watch them, avid as he was for greater knowledge of the ways of man.

He saw the pit grow in depth until a great hole yawned the width of the trail—a hole which was amply large enough to hold at one time all of the six excavators. Tarzan could not guess the purpose of so great a labor.

And when they cut long stakes, sharpened at their upper ends, and set them at intervals upright in the bottom of the pit, his wonderment but increased, nor was it satisfied with the placing of the light cross-poles over the pit, or the careful arrangement of leaves and earth which completely hid from view the work the black men had performed.

When they were done they surveyed their handiwork with evident satisfaction, and Tarzan surveyed it, too. Even to his practiced eye there remained scarce a vestige of evidence that the ancient game trail had been tampered with in any way.

So absorbed was the ape-man in speculation as to the purpose of the covered pit that he permitted the blacks to depart in the direction of their village without the usual baiting which had rendered him the terror of Mbonga's people and had afforded Tarzan both a vehicle of revenge and a source of inexhaustible delight.

Puzzle as he would, however, he could not solve the mystery of the concealed pit, for the ways of the blacks were still strange ways to Tarzan. They had entered his jungle but a short time before—the first of their kind to encroach upon the age-old supremacy of the beasts which laired there. To Numa, the lion, to Tantor, the elephant, to the great apes and the lesser apes, to each and all of the myriad creatures of this savage wild, the ways of man were new. They had much to learn of these black, hairless creatures that walked erect upon their hind paws—and they were learning it slowly, and always to their sorrow.

Shortly after the blacks had departed, Tarzan swung easily to the trail. Sniffing suspiciously, he circled the edge of the pit. Squatting upon his haunches, he scraped away a little earth to expose one of the cross-bars. He sniffed at this, touched it, cocked his head upon one side, and contemplated it gravely for several minutes. Then he carefully re-covered it, arranging the earth as neatly as had the blacks. This done, he swung himself back among the branches of the trees and moved off in search of his hairy fellows, the great apes of the tribe of Kerchak.

Once he crossed the trail of Numa, the lion, pausing for a moment to hurl a soft fruit at the snarling face of his enemy, and to taunt and insult him, calling him eater of carrion and brother of Dango, the hyena. Numa, his yellow-green eyes round and burning with concentrated hate, glared up at the dancing figure above him. Low growls vibrated his heavy jowls and his great rage transmitted to his sinuous tail a sharp, whiplike motion; but realizing from past experience the futility of long distance argument with the ape-man, he turned presently and struck off into the tangled vegetation which hid him from the view of his tormentor. With a final scream of jungle invective and an apelike grimace at his departing foe, Tarzan continued along his way.

Another mile and a shifting wind brought to his keen nostrils a familiar, pungent odor close at hand, and a moment later there loomed beneath him a huge, gray-black bulk forging steadily along the jungle trail. Tarzan seized and broke a small tree limb, and at the sudden cracking sound the ponderous figure halted. Great ears were thrown forward, and a long, supple trunk rose quickly to wave to and fro in search of the scent of an enemy, while two weak, little eyes peered suspiciously and futilely about in quest of the author of the noise which had disturbed his peaceful way.

Tarzan laughed aloud and came closer above the head of the pachyderm.

"Tantor! Tantor!" he cried. "Bara, the deer, is less fearful than you—you, Tantor, the elephant, greatest of the jungle folk with the strength of as many Numas as I have toes upon my feet and fingers upon my hands. Tantor, who can uproot great trees, trembles with fear at the sound of a broken twig."

A rumbling noise, which might have been either a sign of contempt or a sigh of relief, was Tantor's only reply as the uplifted trunk and ears came down and the beast's tail dropped to normal; but his eyes still roved about in search of Tarzan. He was not long kept in suspense, however, as to the whereabouts of the ape-man, for a second later the youth dropped lightly to the broad head of his old friend. Then stretching himself at full length, he drummed with his bare toes upon the thick hide, and as his fingers scratched the more tender surfaces beneath the great ears, he talked to Tantor of the gossip of the jungle as though the great beast understood every word that he said.

Much there was which Tarzan could make Tantor understand, and though the small talk of the wild was beyond the great, gray dreadnaught of the jungle, he stood with blinking eyes and gently swaying trunk as though drinking in every word of it with keenest appreciation. As a matter of fact it was the pleasant, friendly voice and caressing hands behind his ears which he enjoyed, and the close proximity of him whom he had often borne upon his back since Tarzan, as a little child, had once fearlessly approached the great bull, assuming upon the part of the pachyderm the same friendliness which filled his own heart.

In the years of their association Tarzan had discovered that he possessed an inexplicable power to govern and direct his mighty friend. At his bidding, Tantor would come from a great distance—as far as his keen ears could detect the shrill and piercing summons of the ape-man—and when Tarzan was squatted upon his head, Tantor would lumber through the jungle in any direction which his rider bade him go. It was the power of the man-mind over that of the brute and it was just as effective as though both fully understood its origin, though neither did.

For half an hour Tarzan sprawled there upon Tantor's back. Time had no meaning for either of them. Life, as they saw it, consisted principally in keeping their stomachs filled. To Tarzan this was a less arduous labor than to Tantor, for Tarzan's stomach was smaller, and being omnivorous, food was less difficult to obtain. If one sort did not come readily to hand, there were always many others to satisfy his hunger. He was less particular as to his diet than Tantor, who would eat only the bark of certain trees, and the wood of others, while a third appealed to him only through its leaves, and these, perhaps, just at certain seasons of the year.

Tantor must needs spend the better part of his life in filling his immense stomach against the needs of his mighty thews. It is thus with all the lower orders—their lives are so occupied either with searching for food or with the processes of digestion that they have little time for other considerations. Doubtless it is this handicap which has kept them from advancing as rapidly as man, who has more time to give to thought upon other matters.

However, these questions troubled Tarzan but little, and Tantor not at all. What the former knew was that he was happy in the companionship of the elephant. He did not know why. He did not know that because he was a human being— a normal, healthy human being—he craved some living thing upon which to lavish his affection. His childhood playmates among the apes of Kerchak were now great, sullen brutes. They felt nor inspired but little affection. The younger apes Tarzan still played with occasionally. In his savage way he loved them; but they were far from satisfying or restful companions. Tantor was a great mountain of calm, of poise, of stability. It was restful and satisfying to sprawl upon his rough pate and pour one's vague hopes and aspirations into the great ears which flapped ponderously to and fro in apparent understanding. Of all the jungle folk, Tantor commanded Tarzan's greatest love since Kala had been taken from him. Sometimes Tarzan wondered if Tantor reciprocated his affection. It was difficult to know.

It was the call of the stomach—the most compelling and insistent call which the jungle knows—that took Tarzan finally back to the trees and off in search of food, while Tantor continued his interrupted journey in the opposite direction.

For an hour the ape-man foraged. A lofty nest yielded its fresh, warm harvest. Fruits, berries, and tender plantain found a place upon his menu in the order that he happened upon them, for he did not seek such foods. Meat, meat, meat! It was always meat that Tarzan of the Apes hunted; but sometimes meat eluded him, as today.

And as he roamed the jungle his active mind busied itself not alone with his hunting, but with many other subjects. He had a habit of recalling often the events of the preceding days and hours. He lived over his visit with Tantor; he cogitated upon the digging blacks and the strange, covered pit they had left behind them. He wondered again and again what its purpose might be. He compared perceptions and arrived at judgments. He compared judgments, reaching conclusions—not always correct ones, it is true, but at least he used his brain for the purpose God intended it, which was the less difficult because he was not handicapped by the second-hand, and usually erroneous, judgment of others.

And as he puzzled over the covered pit, there loomed suddenly before his mental vision a huge, gray-black bulk which lumbered ponderously along a jungle trail. Instantly Tarzan tensed to the shock of a sudden fear. Decision and action usually occurred simultaneously in the life of the ape-man, and now he was away through the leafy branches ere the realization of the pit's purpose had scarce formed in his mind.

Swinging from swaying limb to swaying limb, he raced through the middle terraces where the trees grew close together. Again he dropped to the ground and sped, silently and light of foot, over the carpet of decaying vegetation, only to leap again into the trees where the tangled undergrowth precluded rapid advance upon the surface.

In his anxiety he cast discretion to the winds. The caution of the beast was lost in the loyalty of the man, and so it came that he entered a large clearing, denuded of trees, without a thought of what might lie there or upon the farther edge to dispute the way with him.

He was half way across when directly in his path and but a few yards away there rose from a clump of tall grasses a half dozen chattering birds. Instantly Tarzan turned aside, for he knew well enough what manner of creature the presence of these little sentinels proclaimed. Simultaneously Buto, the rhinoceros, scrambled to his short legs and charged furiously. Haphazard charges Buto, the rhinoceros. With his weak eyes he sees but poorly even at short distances, and whether his erratic rushes are due to the panic of fear as he attempts to escape, or to the irascible temper with which he is generally credited, it is difficult to determine. Nor is the matter of little moment to one whom Buto charges, for if he be caught and tossed, the chances are that naught will interest him thereafter.

And today it chanced that Buto bore down straight upon Tarzan, across the few yards of knee-deep grass which separated them. Accident started him in the direction of the ape-man, and then his weak eyes discerned the enemy, and with a series of snorts he charged straight for him. The little rhino birds fluttered and circled about their giant ward. Among the branches of the trees at the edge of the clearing, a score or more monkeys chattered and scolded as the loud snorts of the angry beast sent them scurrying affrightedly to the upper terraces. Tarzan alone appeared indifferent and serene.

Directly in the path of the charge he stood. There had been no time to seek safety in the trees beyond the clearing, nor had Tarzan any mind to delay his journey because of Buto. He had met the stupid beast before and held him in fine contempt.

And now Buto was upon him, the massive head lowered and the long, heavy horn inclined for the frightful work for which nature had designed it; but as he struck upward, his weapon raked only thin air, for the ape-man had sprung lightly aloft with a catlike leap that carried him above the threatening horn to the broad back of the rhinoceros. Another spring and he was on the ground behind the brute and racing like a deer for the trees.

Buto, angered and mystified by the strange disappearance of his prey, wheeled and charged frantically in another direction, which chanced to be not the direction of Tarzan's flight, and so the ape-man came in safety to the trees and continued on his swift way through the forest.

Some distance ahead of him Tantor moved steadily along the well-worn elephant trail, and ahead of Tantor a crouching, black warrior listened intently in the middle of the path. Presently he heard the sound for which he had been hoping— the cracking, snapping sound which heralded the approach of an elephant.

To his right and left in other parts of the jungle other warriors were watching. A low signal, passed from one to another, apprised the most distant that the quarry was afoot. Rapidly they converged toward the trail, taking positions in trees down wind from the point at which Tantor must pass them. Silently they waited and presently were rewarded by the sight of a mighty tusker carrying an amount of ivory in his long tusks that set their greedy hearts to palpitating.

No sooner had he passed their positions than the warriors clambered from their perches. No longer were they silent, but instead clapped their hands and shouted as they reached the ground. For an instant Tantor, the elephant, paused with upraised trunk and tail, with great ears up-pricked, and then he swung on along the trail at a rapid, shuffling pace—straight toward the covered pit with its sharpened stakes upstanding in the ground.

Behind him came the yelling warriors, urging him on in the rapid flight which would not permit a careful examination of the ground before him. Tantor, the elephant, who could have turned and scattered his adversaries with a single charge, fled like a frightened deer—fled toward a hideous, torturing death.

And behind them all came Tarzan of the Apes, racing through the jungle forest with the speed and agility of a squirrel, for he had heard the shouts of the warriors and had interpreted them correctly. Once he uttered a piercing call that reverberated through the jungle; but Tantor, in the panic of terror, either failed to hear, or hearing, dared not pause to heed.

Now the giant pachyderm was but a few yards from the hidden death lurking in his path, and the blacks, certain of success, were screaming and dancing in his wake, waving their war spears and celebrating in advance the acquisition of the splendid ivory carried by their prey and the surfeit of elephant meat which would be theirs this night.

So intent were they upon their gratulations that they entirely failed to note the silent passage of the man-beast above their heads, nor did Tantor, either, see or hear him, even though Tarzan called to him to stop.

A few more steps would precipitate Tantor upon the sharpened stakes; Tarzan fairly flew through the trees until he had come abreast of the fleeing animal and then had passed him. At the pit's verge the ape-man dropped to the ground in the center of the trail. Tantor was almost upon him before his weak eyes permitted him to recognize his old friend.

"Stop!" cried Tarzan, and the great beast halted to the upraised hand.

Tarzan turned and kicked aside some of the brush which hid the pit. Instantly Tantor saw and understood.

"Fight!" growled Tarzan. "They are coming behind you." But Tantor, the elephant, is a huge bunch of nerves, and now he was half panic-stricken by terror.

Before him yawned the pit, how far he did not know, but to right and left lay the primeval jungle untouched by man. With a squeal the great beast turned suddenly at right angles and burst his noisy way through the solid wall of matted vegetation that would have stopped any but him.

Tarzan, standing upon the edge of the pit, smiled as he watched Tantor's undignified flight. Soon the blacks would come. It was best that Tarzan of the Apes faded from the scene. He essayed a step from the pit's edge, and as he threw the weight of his body upon his left foot, the earth crumbled away. Tarzan made a single Herculean effort to throw himself forward, but it was too late. Backward and downward he went toward the sharpened stakes in the bottom of the pit.

When, a moment later, the blacks came they saw even from a distance that Tantor had eluded them, for the size of the hole in the pit covering was too small to have accommodated the huge bulk of an elephant. At first they thought that their prey had put one great foot through the top and then, warned, drawn back; but when they had come to the pit's verge and peered over, their eyes went wide in astonishment, for, quiet and still, at the bottom lay the naked figure of a white giant.

Some of them there had glimpsed this forest god before and they drew back in terror, awed by the presence which they had for some time believed to possess the miraculous powers of a demon; but others there were who pushed forward, thinking only of the capture of an enemy, and these leaped into the pit and lifted Tarzan out.

There was no scar upon his body. None of the sharpened stakes had pierced him—only a swollen spot at the base of the brain indicated the nature of his injury. In the falling backward his head had struck upon the side of one of the stakes, rendering him unconscious. The blacks were quick to discover this, and equally quick to bind their prisoner's arms and legs before he should regain consciousness, for they had learned to harbor a wholesome respect for this strange man-beast that consorted with the hairy tree folk.

EDGAR RICE BURROUGHS

They had carried him but a short distance toward their village when the ape-man's eyelids quivered and raised. He looked about him wonderingly for a moment, and then full consciousness returned and he realized the seriousness of his predicament. Accustomed almost from birth to relying solely upon his own resources, he did not cast about for outside aid now, but devoted his mind to a consideration of the possibilities for escape which lay within himself and his own powers.

He did not dare test the strength of his bonds while the blacks were carrying him, for fear they would become apprehensive and add to them. Presently his captors discovered that he was conscious, and as they had little stomach for carrying a heavy man through the jungle heat, they set him upon his feet and forced him forward among them, pricking him now and then with their spears, yet with every manifestation of the superstitious awe in which they held him.

When they discovered that their prodding brought no outward evidence of suffering, their awe increased, so that they soon desisted, half believing that this strange white giant was a supernatural being and so was immune from pain.

As they approached their village, they shouted aloud the victorious cries of successful warriors, so that by the time they reached the gate, dancing and waving their spears, a great crowd of men, women, and children were gathered there to greet them and hear the story of their adventure.

As the eyes of the villagers fell upon the prisoner, they went wild, and heavy jaws fell open in astonishment and incredulity. For months they had lived in perpetual terror of a weird, white demon whom but few had ever glimpsed and lived to describe. Warriors had disappeared from the paths almost within sight of the village and from the midst of their companions as mysteriously and completely as though they had been swallowed by the earth, and later, at night, their dead bodies had fallen, as from the heavens, into the village street.

This fearsome creature had appeared by night in the huts of the village, killed, and disappeared, leaving behind him in the huts with his dead, strange and terrifying evidences of an uncanny sense of humor.

But now he was in their power! No longer could he terrorize them. Slowly the realization of this dawned upon them. A woman, screaming, ran forward and struck the ape-man across the face. Another and another followed her example, until Tarzan of the Apes was surrounded by a fighting, clawing, yelling mob of natives.

And then Mbonga, the chief, came, and laying his spear heavily across the shoulders of his people, drove them from their prey.

"We will save him until night," he said.

Far out in the jungle Tantor, the elephant, his first panic of fear allayed, stood with up-pricked ears and undulating trunk. What was passing through the convolutions of his savage brain? Could he be searching for Tarzan? Could he recall and measure the service the ape-man had performed for him? Of that there can be no doubt. But did he feel gratitude? Would he have risked his own life to have saved Tarzan could he have known of the danger which confronted his friend? You will doubt it. Anyone at all familiar with elephants will doubt it. Englishmen who have hunted much with elephants in India will tell you that they never have heard of an instance in which one of these animals has gone to the aid of a man in danger, even though the man had often befriended it. And so it is to be doubted that Tantor would have attempted to overcome his instinctive fear of the black men in an effort to succor Tarzan.

The screams of the infuriated villagers came faintly to his sensitive ears, and he wheeled, as though in terror, contemplating flight; but something stayed him, and again he turned about, raised his trunk, and gave voice to a shrill cry.

Then he stood listening.

In the distant village where Mbonga had restored quiet and order, the voice of Tantor was scarcely audible to the blacks, but to the keen ears of Tarzan of the Apes it bore its message.

His captors were leading him to a hut where he might be confined and guarded against the coming of the nocturnal orgy that would mark his torture-laden death. He halted as he heard the notes of Tantor's call, and raising his head, gave vent to a terrifying scream that sent cold chills through the superstitious blacks and caused the warriors who guarded him to leap back even though their prisoner's arms were securely bound behind him.

With raised spears they encircled him as for a moment longer he stood listening. Faintly from the distance came another, an answering cry, and Tarzan of the Apes, satisfied, turned and quietly pursued his way toward the hut where he was to be imprisoned.

The afternoon wore on. From the surrounding village the ape-man heard the bustle of preparation for the feast. Through the doorway of the hut he saw the women laying the cooking fires and filling their earthen caldrons with water; but above it all his ears were bent across the jungle in eager listening for the coming of Tantor.

Even Tarzan but half believed that he would come. He knew Tantor even better than Tantor knew himself. He knew the timid heart which lay in the giant body. He knew the panic of terror which the scent of the Gomangani inspired within that savage breast, and as night drew on, hope died within his heart and in the stoic calm of the wild beast which he was, he resigned himself to meet the fate which awaited him.

All afternoon he had been working, working, working with the bonds that held his wrists. Very slowly they were giving. He might free his hands before they came to lead him out to be butchered, and if he did—Tarzan licked his lips in anticipation, and smiled a cold, grim smile. He could imagine the feel of soft flesh beneath his fingers and the sinking of his white teeth into the throats of his foemen. He would let them taste his wrath before they overpowered him!

At last they came—painted, befeathered warriors—even more hideous than nature had intended them. They came and pushed him into the open, where his appearance was greeted by wild shouts from the assembled villagers.

To the stake they led him, and as they pushed him roughly against it preparatory to binding him there securely for the dance of death that would presently encircle him, Tarzan tensed his mighty thews and with a single, powerful wrench parted the loosened thongs which had secured his hands. Like thought, for quickness, he leaped forward among the warriors nearest him. A blow sent one to earth, as, growling and snarling, the beast-man leaped upon the breast of another. His fangs were buried instantly in the jugular of his adversary and then a half hundred black men had leaped upon him and borne him to earth.

Striking, clawing, and snapping, the ape-man fought— fought as his foster people had taught him to fight—fought like a wild beast cornered. His strength, his agility, his courage, and his intelligence rendered him easily a match for half a dozen black men in a hand-to-hand struggle, but not even Tarzan of the Apes could hope to successfully cope with half a hundred.

Slowly they were overpowering him, though a score of them bled from ugly wounds, and two lay very still beneath the trampling feet, and the rolling bodies of the contestants.

Overpower him they might, but could they keep him overpowered while they bound him? A half hour of desperate endeavor convinced them that they could not, and so Mbonga, who, like all good rulers, had circled in the safety of the background, called to one to work his way in and spear the victim. Gradually, through the milling, battling men, the warrior approached the object of his quest.

He stood with poised spear above his head waiting for the instant that would expose a vulnerable part of the ape-man's body and still not endanger one of the blacks. Closer and closer he edged about, following the movements of the twisting, scuffling combatants. The growls of the ape-man sent cold chills up the warrior's spine, causing him to go carefully lest he miss at the first cast and lay himself open to an attack from those merciless teeth and mighty hands.

At last he found an opening. Higher he raised his spear, tensing his muscles, rolling beneath his glistening, ebon hide, and then from the jungle just beyond the palisade came a thunderous crashing. The spear-hand paused, the black cast a quick glance in the direction of the disturbance, as did the others of the blacks who were not occupied with the subjugation of the ape-man.

In the glare of the fires they saw a huge bulk topping the barrier. They saw the palisade belly and sway inward. They saw it burst as though built of straws, and an instant later Tantor, the elephant, thundered down upon them.

To right and left the blacks fled, screaming in terror. Some who hovered upon the verge of the strife with Tarzan heard and made good their escape, but a half dozen there were so wrapt in the blood-madness of battle that they failed to note the approach of the giant tusker.

Upon these Tantor charged, trumpeting furiously. Above them he stopped, his sensitive trunk weaving among them, and there, at the bottom, he found Tarzan, bloody, but still battling.

A warrior turned his eyes upward from the melee. Above him towered the gigantic bulk of the pachyderm, the little eyes flashing with the reflected light of the fires—wicked, frightful, terrifying. The warrior screamed, and as he screamed, the sinuous trunk encircled him, lifted him high above the ground, and hurled him far after the fleeing crowd.

Another and another Tantor wrenched from the body of the ape-man, throwing them to right and to left, where they lay either moaning or very quiet, as death came slowly or at once.

At a distance Mbonga rallied his warriors. His greedy eyes had noted the great ivory tusks of the bull. The first panic of terror relieved, he urged his men forward to attack with their heavy elephant spears; but as they came, Tantor swung Tarzan to his broad head, and, wheeling, lumbered off into the jungle through the great rent he had made in the palisade.

Elephant hunters may be right when they aver that this animal would not have rendered such service to a man, but to Tantor, Tarzan was not a man—he was but a fellow jungle beast.

And so it was that Tantor, the elephant, discharged an obligation to Tarzan of the Apes, cementing even more closely the friendship that had existed between them since Tarzan as a little, brown boy rode upon Tantor's huge back through the moonlit jungle beneath the equatorial stars.

THE FIGHT FOR THE BALU

Teeka had become a mother. Tarzan of the Apes was intensely interested, much more so, in fact, than Taug, the father. Tarzan was very fond of Teeka. Even the cares of prospective motherhood had not entirely quenched the fires of carefree youth, and Teeka had remained a good-natured playmate even at an age when other shes of the tribe of Kerchak had assumed the sullen dignity of maturity. She yet retained her childish delight in the primitive games of tag and hide-and-go-seek which Tarzan's fertile man-mind had evolved.

To play tag through the tree tops is an exciting and inspiring pastime. Tarzan delighted in it, but the bulls of his childhood had long since abandoned such childish practices. Teeka, though, had been keen for it always until shortly before the baby came; but with the advent of her first-born, even Teeka changed.

The evidence of the change surprised and hurt Tarzan immeasurably. One morning he saw Teeka squatted upon a low branch hugging something very close to her hairy breast— a wee something which squirmed and wriggled. Tarzan approached filled with the curiosity which is common to all creatures endowed with brains which have progressed beyond the microscopic stage.

Teeka rolled her eyes in his direction and strained the squirming mite still closer to her. Tarzan came nearer. Teeka drew away and bared her fangs. Tarzan was nonplussed. In all his experiences with Teeka, never before had she bared fangs at him other than in play; but today she did not look playful. Tarzan ran his brown fingers through his thick, black hair, cocked his head upon one side, and stared. Then he edged a bit nearer, craning his neck to have a better look at the thing which Teeka cuddled.

Again Teeka drew back her upper lip in a warning snarl. Tarzan reached forth a hand, cautiously, to touch the thing which Teeka held, and Teeka, with a hideous growl, turned suddenly upon him. Her teeth sank into the flesh of his forearm before the ape-man could snatch it away, and she pursued him for a short distance as he retreated incontinently through the trees; but Teeka, carrying her baby, could not overtake him. At a safe distance Tarzan stopped and turned to regard his erstwhile play-fellow in unconcealed astonishment. What had happened to so alter the gentle Teeka? She had so covered the thing in her arms that Tarzan had not yet been able to recognize it for what it was; but now, as she turned from the pursuit of him, he saw it. Through his pain and chagrin he smiled, for Tarzan had seen young ape mothers before. In a few days she would be less suspicious. Still Tarzan was hurt; it was not right that Teeka, of all others, should fear him. Why, not for the world would he harm her, or her balu, which is the ape word for baby.

And now, above the pain of his injured arm and the hurt to his pride, rose a still stronger desire to come close and inspect the new-born son of Taug. Possibly you will wonder that Tarzan of the Apes, mighty fighter that he was, should have fled before the irritable attack of a she, or that he should hesitate to return for the satisfaction of his curiosity when with ease he might have vanquished the weakened mother of the new-born cub; but you need not wonder. Were you an ape, you would know that only a bull in the throes of madness will turn upon a female other than to gently chastise her, with the occasional exception of the individual whom we find exemplified among our own kind, and who delights in beating up his better half because she happens to be smaller and weaker than he.

Tarzan again came toward the young mother—warily and with his line of retreat safely open. Again Teeka growled ferociously. Tarzan expostulated.

"Tarzan of the Apes will not harm Teeka's balu," he said. "Let me see it."

"Go away!" commanded Teeka. "Go away, or I will kill you."

"Let me see it," urged Tarzan.

"Go away," reiterated the she-ape. "Here comes Taug. He will make you go away. Taug will kill you. This is Taug's balu."

A savage growl close behind him apprised Tarzan of the nearness of Taug, and the fact that the bull had heard the warnings and threats of his mate and was coming to her succor.

Now Taug, as well as Teeka, had been Tarzan's play-fellow while the bull was still young enough to wish to play. Once Tarzan had saved Taug's life; but the memory of an ape is not overlong, nor would gratitude rise above the parental instinct. Tarzan and Taug had once measured strength, and Tarzan had been victorious. That fact Taug could be depended upon still to remember; but even so, he might readily face another defeat for his first-born—if he chanced to be in the proper mood.

From his hideous growls, which now rose in strength and volume, he seemed to be in quite the mood. Now Tarzan felt no fear of Taug, nor did the unwritten law of the jungle demand that he should flee from battle with any male, unless he cared to from purely personal reasons. But Tarzan liked Taug. He had no grudge against him, and his man-mind told him what the mind of an ape would never have deduced— that Taug's attitude in no sense indicated hatred. It was but the instinctive urge of the male to protect its offspring and its mate.

Tarzan had no desire to battle with Taug, nor did the blood of his English ancestors relish the thought of flight, yet when the bull charged, Tarzan leaped nimbly to one side, and thus encouraged, Taug wheeled and rushed again madly to the attack. Perhaps the memory of a past defeat at Tarzan's hands goaded him. Perhaps the fact that Teeka sat there watching him aroused a desire to vanquish the ape-man before her eyes, for in the breast of every jungle male lurks a vast egotism which finds expression in the performance of deeds of derring-do before an audience of the opposite sex.

At the ape-man's side swung his long grass rope—the play-thing of yesterday, the weapon of today—and as Taug charged the second time, Tarzan slipped the coils over his head and deftly shook out the sliding noose as he again nimbly eluded the ungainly beast. Before the ape could turn again, Tarzan had fled far aloft among the branches of the upper terrace.

Taug, now wrought to a frenzy of real rage, followed him. Teeka peered upward at them. It was difficult to say whether she was interested. Taug could not climb as rapidly as Tarzan, so the latter reached the high levels to which the heavy ape dared not follow before the former overtook him. There he halted and looked down upon his pursuer, making faces at him and calling him such choice names as occurred to the fertile man-brain. Then, when he had worked Taug to such a pitch of foaming rage that the great bull fairly danced upon the bending limb beneath him, Tarzan's hand shot suddenly outward, a widening noose dropped swiftly through the air, there was a quick jerk as it settled about Taug, falling to his knees, a jerk that tightened it securely about the hairy legs of the anthropoid.

Taug, slow of wit, realized too late the intention of his tormentor. He scrambled to escape, but the ape-man gave the rope a tremendous jerk that pulled Taug from his perch, and a moment later, growling hideously, the ape hung head downward thirty feet above the ground.

Tarzan secured the rope to a stout limb and descended to a point close to Taug.

"Taug," he said, "you are as stupid as Buto, the rhinoceros. Now you may hang here until you get a little sense in your thick head. You may hang here and watch while I go and talk with Teeka."

Taug blustered and threatened, but Tarzan only grinned at him as he dropped lightly to the lower levels. Here he again approached Teeka only to be again greeted with bared fangs and menacing growls. He sought to placate her; he urged his friendly intentions, and craned his neck to have a look at Teeka's balu; but the she-ape was not to be persuaded that he meant other than harm to her little one. Her motherhood was still so new that reason was yet subservient to instinct.

Realizing the futility of attempting to catch and chastise Tarzan, Teeka sought to escape him. She dropped to the ground and lumbered across the little clearing about which the apes of the tribe were disposed in rest or in the search of food, and presently Tarzan abandoned his attempts to persuade her to permit a close examination of the balu. The ape-man would have liked to handle the tiny thing. The very sight of it awakened in his breast a strange yearning. He wished to cuddle and fondle the grotesque little ape-thing. It was Teeka's balu and Tarzan had once lavished his young affections upon Teeka.

But now his attention was diverted by the voice of Taug. The threats that had filled the ape's mouth had turned to pleas. The tightening noose was stopping the circulation of the blood in his legs—he was beginning to suffer. Several apes sat near him highly interested in his predicament. They made uncomplimentary remarks about him, for each of them had felt the weight of Taug's mighty hands and the strength of his great jaws. They were enjoying revenge.

Teeka, seeing that Tarzan had turned back toward the trees, had halted in the center of the clearing, and there she sat hugging her balu and casting suspicious glances here and there. With the coming of the balu, Teeka's care-free world had suddenly become peopled with innumerable enemies. She saw an implacable foe in Tarzan, always heretofore her best friend. Even poor old Mumga, half blind and almost entirely toothless, searching patiently for grubworms beneath a fallen log, represented to her a malignant spirit thirsting for the blood of little balus.

And while Teeka guarded suspiciously against harm, where there was no harm, she failed to note two baleful, yellow-green eyes staring fixedly at her from behind a clump of bushes at the opposite side of the clearing.

Hollow from hunger, Sheeta, the panther, glared greedily at the tempting meat so close at hand, but the sight of the great bulls beyond gave him pause.

Ah, if the she-ape with her balu would but come just a trifle nearer! A quick spring and he would be upon them and away again with his meat before the bulls could prevent.

The tip of his tawny tail moved in spasmodic little jerks; his lower jaw hung low, exposing a red tongue and yellow fangs. But all this Teeka did not see, nor did any other of the apes who were feeding or resting about her. Nor did Tarzan or the apes in the trees.

Hearing the abuse which the bulls were pouring upon the helpless Taug, Tarzan clambered quickly among them. One was edging closer and leaning far out in an effort to reach the dangling ape. He had worked himself into quite a fury through recollection of the last occasion upon which Taug had mauled him, and now he was bent upon revenge. Once he had grasped the swinging ape, he would quickly have drawn him within reach of his jaws. Tarzan saw and was wroth. He loved a fair fight, but the thing which this ape contemplated revolted him. Already a hairy hand had clutched the helpless Taug when, with an angry growl of protest, Tarzan leaped to the branch at the attacking ape's side, and with a single mighty cuff, swept him from his perch.

Surprised and enraged, the bull clutched madly for support as he toppled sidewise, and then with an agile movement succeeded in projecting himself toward another limb a few feet below. Here he found a hand-hold, quickly righted himself, and as quickly clambered upward to be revenged upon Tarzan, but the ape-man was otherwise engaged and did not wish to be interrupted. He was explaining again to Taug the depths of the latter's abysmal ignorance, and pointing out how much greater and mightier was Tarzan of the Apes than Taug or any other ape.

In the end he would release Taug, but not until Taug was fully acquainted with his own inferiority. And then the maddened bull came from beneath, and instantly Tarzan was transformed from a good-natured, teasing youth into a snarling, savage beast. Along his scalp the hair bristled: his upper lip drew back that his fighting fangs might be uncovered and ready. He did not wait for the bull to reach him, for something in the appearance or the voice of the attacker aroused within the ape-man a feeling of belligerent antagonism that would not be denied. With a scream that carried no human note, Tarzan leaped straight at the throat of the attacker.

The impetuosity of this act and the weight and momentum of his body carried the bull backward, clutching and clawing for support, down through the leafy branches of the tree. For fifteen feet the two fell, Tarzan's teeth buried in the jugular of his opponent, when a stout branch stopped their descent. The bull struck full upon the small of his back across the limb, hung there for a moment with the ape-man still upon his breast, and then toppled over toward the ground.

Tarzan had felt the instantaneous relaxation of the body beneath him after the heavy impact with the tree limb, and as the other turned completely over and started again upon its fall toward the ground, he reached forth a hand and caught the branch in time to stay his own descent, while the ape dropped like a plummet to the foot of the tree.

Tarzan looked downward for a moment upon the still form of his late antagonist, then he rose to his full height, swelled his deep chest, smote upon it with his clenched fist and roared out the uncanny challenge of the victorious bull ape.

Even Sheeta, the panther, crouched for a spring at the edge of the little clearing, moved uneasily as the mighty voice sent its weird cry reverberating through the jungle. To right and left, nervously, glanced Sheeta, as though assuring himself that the way of escape lay ready at hand.

"I am Tarzan of the Apes," boasted the ape-man; "mighty hunter, mighty fighter! None in all the jungle so great as Tarzan."

Then he made his way back in the direction of Taug. Teeka had watched the happenings in the tree. She had even placed her precious balu upon the soft grasses and come a little nearer that she might better witness all that was passing in the branches above her. In her heart of hearts did she still esteem the smooth-skinned Tarzan? Did her savage breast swell with pride as she witnessed his victory over the ape? You will have to ask Teeka.

And Sheeta, the panther, saw that the she-ape had left her cub alone among the grasses. He moved his tail again, as though this closest approximation of lashing in which he dared indulge might stimulate his momentarily waned courage. The cry of the victorious ape-man still held his nerves beneath its spell. It would be several minutes before he again could bring himself to the point of charging into view of the giant anthropoids.

And as he regathered his forces, Tarzan reached Taug's side, and then clambering higher up to the point where the end of the grass rope was made fast, he unloosed it and lowered the ape slowly downward, swinging him in until the clutching hands fastened upon a limb.

Quickly Taug drew himself to a position of safety and shook off the noose. In his rage-maddened heart was no room for gratitude to the ape-man. He recalled only the fact that Tarzan had laid this painful indignity upon him. He would be revenged, but just at present his legs were so numb and his head so dizzy that he must postpone the gratification of his vengeance.

Tarzan was coiling his rope the while he lectured Taug on the futility of pitting his poor powers, physical and intellectual, against those of his betters. Teeka had come close beneath the tree and was peering upward. Sheeta was worming his way stealthily forward, his belly close to the ground. In another moment he would be clear of the underbrush and ready for the rapid charge and the quick retreat that would end the brief existence of Teeka's balu.

Then Tarzan chanced to look up and across the clearing. Instantly his attitude of good-natured bantering and pompous boastfulness dropped from him. Silently and swiftly he shot downward toward the ground. Teeka, seeing him coming, and thinking that he was after her or her balu, bristled and prepared to fight. But Tarzan sped by her, and as he went, her eyes followed him and she saw the cause of his sudden descent and his rapid charge across the clearing. There in full sight now was Sheeta, the panther, stalking slowly toward the tiny, wriggling balu which lay among the grasses many yards away.

Teeka gave voice to a shrill scream of terror and of warning as she dashed after the ape-man. Sheeta saw Tarzan coming. He saw the she-ape's cub before him, and he thought that this other was bent upon robbing him of his prey. With an angry growl, he charged.

Taug, warned by Teeka's cry, came lumbering down to her assistance. Several other bulls, growling and barking, closed in toward the clearing, but they were all much farther from the balu and the panther than was Tarzan of the Apes, so it was that Sheeta and the ape-man reached Teeka's little one almost simultaneously; and there they stood, one upon either side of it, baring their fangs and snarling at each other over the little creature.

Sheeta was afraid to seize the balu, for thus he would give the ape-man an opening for attack; and for the same reason Tarzan hesitated to snatch the panther's prey out of harm's way, for had he stooped to accomplish this, the great beast would have been upon him in an instant. Thus they stood while Teeka came across the clearing, going more slowly as she neared the panther, for even her mother love could scarce overcome her instinctive terror of this natural enemy of her kind.

Behind her came Taug, warily and with many pauses and much bluster, and still behind him came other bulls, snarling ferociously and uttering their uncanny challenges. Sheeta's yellow-green eyes glared terribly at Tarzan, and past Tarzan they shot brief glances at the apes of Kerchak advancing upon him. Discretion prompted him to turn and flee, but hunger and the close proximity of the tempting morsel in the grass before him urged him to remain. He reached forth a paw toward Teeka's balu, and as he did so, with a savage guttural, Tarzan of the Apes was upon him.

The panther reared to meet the ape-man's attack. He swung a frightful raking blow for Tarzan that would have wiped his face away had it landed, but it did not land, for Tarzan ducked beneath it and closed, his long knife ready in one strong hand—the knife of his dead father, of the father he never had known.

Instantly the balu was forgotten by Sheeta, the panther. He now thought only of tearing to ribbons with his powerful talons the flesh of his antagonist, of burying his long, yellow fangs in the soft, smooth hide of the ape-man, but Tarzan had fought before with clawed creatures of the jungle. Before now he had battled with fanged monsters, nor always had he come away unscathed. He knew the risk that he ran, but Tarzan of the Apes, inured to the sight of suffering and death, shrank from neither, for he feared neither.

The instant that he dodged beneath Sheeta's blow, he leaped to the beast's rear and then full upon the tawny back, burying his teeth in Sheeta's neck and the fingers of one hand in the fur at the throat, and with the other hand he drove his blade into Sheeta's side.

Over and over upon the grass rolled Sheeta, growling and screaming, clawing and biting, in a mad effort to dislodge his antagonist or get some portion of his body within range of teeth or talons.

As Tarzan leaped to close quarters with the panther, Teeka had run quickly in and snatched up her balu. Now she sat upon a high branch, safe out of harm's way, cuddling the little thing close to her hairy breast, the while her savage little eyes bored down upon the contestants in the clearing, and her ferocious voice urged Taug and the other bulls to leap into the melee.

Thus goaded the bulls came closer, redoubling their hideous clamor; but Sheeta was already sufficiently engaged— he did not even hear them. Once he succeeded in partially dislodging the ape-man from his back, so that Tarzan swung for an instant in front of those awful talons, and in the brief instant before he could regain his former hold, a raking blow from a hind paw laid open one leg from hip to knee.

It was the sight and smell of this blood, possibly, which wrought upon the encircling apes; but it was Taug who really was responsible for the thing they did.

Taug, but a moment before filled with rage toward Tarzan of the Apes, stood close to the battling pair, his red-rimmed, wicked little eyes glaring at them. What was passing in his savage brain? Did he gloat over the unenviable position of his recent tormentor? Did he long to see Sheeta's great fangs sink into the soft throat of the ape-man? Or did he realize the courageous unselfishness that had prompted Tarzan to rush to the rescue and imperil his life for Teeka's balu—for Taug's little balu? Is gratitude a possession of man only, or do the lower orders know it also?

With the spilling of Tarzan's blood, Taug answered these questions. With all the weight of his great body he leaped, hideously growling, upon Sheeta. His long fighting fangs buried themselves in the white throat. His powerful arms beat and clawed at the soft fur until it flew upward in the jungle breeze.

And with Taug's example before them the other bulls charged, burying Sheeta beneath rending fangs and filling all the forest with the wild din of their battle cries.

Ah! but it was a wondrous and inspiring sight—this battle of the primordial apes and the great, white ape-man with their ancestral foe, Sheeta, the panther.

In frenzied excitement, Teeka fairly danced upon the limb which swayed beneath her great weight as she urged on the males of her people, and Thaka, and Mumga, and Kamma, with the other shes of the tribe of Kerchak, added their shrill cries or fierce barkings to the pandemonium which now reigned within the jungle.

Bitten and biting, tearing and torn, Sheeta battled for his life; but the odds were against him. Even Numa, the lion, would have hesitated to have attacked an equal number of the great bulls of the tribe of Kerchak, and now, a half mile away, hearing the sounds of the terrific battle, the king of beasts rose uneasily from his midday slumber and slunk off farther into the jungle.

Presently Sheeta's torn and bloody body ceased its titanic struggles. It stiffened spasmodically, twitched and was still, yet the bulls continued to lacerate it until the beautiful coat was torn to shreds. At last they desisted from sheer physical weariness, and then from the tangle of bloody bodies rose a crimson giant, straight as an arrow.

He placed a foot upon the dead body of the panther, and lifting his blood-stained face to the blue of the equatorial heavens, gave voice to the horrid victory cry of the bull ape.

One by one his hairy fellows of the tribe of Kerchak followed his example. The shes came down from their perches of safety and struck and reviled the dead body of Sheeta. The young apes refought the battle in mimicry of their mighty elders.

Teeka was quite close to Tarzan. He turned and saw her with the balu hugged close to her hairy breast, and put out his hands to take the little one, expecting that Teeka would bare her fangs and spring upon him; but instead she placed the balu in his arms, and coming nearer, licked his frightful wounds.

And presently Taug, who had escaped with only a few scratches, came and squatted beside Tarzan and watched him as he played with the little balu, and at last he too leaned over and helped Teeka with the cleansing and the healing of the ape-man's hurts.

EDGAR RICE BURROUGHS

THE GOD OF TARZAN

Among the books of his dead father in the little cabin by the land-locked harbor, Tarzan of the Apes found many things to puzzle his young head. By much labor and through the medium of infinite patience as well, he had, without assistance, discovered the purpose of the little bugs which ran riot upon the printed pages. He had learned that in the many combinations in which he found them they spoke in a silent language, spoke in a strange tongue, spoke of wonderful things which a little ape-boy could not by any chance fully understand, arousing his curiosity, stimulating his imagination and filling his soul with a mighty longing for further knowledge.

A dictionary had proven itself a wonderful storehouse of information, when, after several years of tireless endeavor, he had solved the mystery of its purpose and the manner of its use. He had learned to make a species of game out of it, following up the spoor of a new thought through the mazes of the many definitions which each new word required him to consult. It was like following a quarry through the jungle— it was hunting, and Tarzan of the Apes was an indefatigable huntsman.

There were, of course, certain words which aroused his curiosity to a greater extent than others, words which, for one reason or another, excited his imagination. There was one, for example, the meaning of which was rather difficult to grasp. It was the word *God*. Tarzan first had been attracted to it by the fact that it was very short and that it commenced with a larger g-bug than those about it—a male g-bug it was to Tarzan, the lower-case letters being females. Another fact which attracted him to this word was the number of he-bugs which figured in its definition—Supreme Deity, Creator or Upholder of the Universe. This must be a very important word indeed, he would have to look into it, and he did, though it still baffled him after many months of thought and study.

However, Tarzan counted no time wasted which he devoted to these strange hunting expeditions into the game preserves of knowledge, for each word and each definition led on and on into strange places, into new worlds where, with increasing frequency, he met old, familiar faces. And always he added to his store of knowledge.

But of the meaning of *God* he was yet in doubt. Once he thought he had grasped it—that God was a mighty chieftain, king of all the Mangani. He was not quite sure, however, since that would mean that God was mightier than Tarzan— a point which Tarzan of the Apes, who acknowledged no equal in the jungle, was loath to concede.

But in all the books he had there was no picture of God, though he found much to confirm his belief that God was a great, an all-powerful individual. He saw pictures of places where God was worshiped; but never any sign of God. Finally he began to wonder if God were not of a different form than he, and at last he determined to set out in search of Him.

He commenced by questioning Mumga, who was very old and had seen many strange things in her long life; but Mumga, being an ape, had a faculty for recalling the trivial. That time when Gunto mistook a sting-bug for an edible beetle had made more impression upon Mumga than all the innumerable manifestations of the greatness of God which she had witnessed, and which, of course, she had not understood.

Numgo, overhearing Tarzan's questions, managed to wrest his attention long enough from the diversion of flea hunting to advance the theory that the power which made the lightning and the rain and the thunder came from Goro, the moon. He knew this, he said, because the Dum-Dum always was danced in the light of Goro. This reasoning, though entirely satisfactory to Numgo and Mumga, failed fully to convince Tarzan. However, it gave him a basis for further investigation along a new line. He would investigate the moon.

That night he clambered to the loftiest pinnacle of the tallest jungle giant. The moon was full, a great, glorious, equatorial moon. The ape-man, upright upon a slender, swaying limb, raised his bronzed face to the silver orb. Now that he had clambered to the highest point within his reach, he discovered, to his surprise, that Goro was as far away as when he viewed him from the ground. He thought that Goro was attempting to elude him.

"Come, Goro!" he cried, "Tarzan of the Apes will not harm you!" But still the moon held aloof.

"Tell me," he continued, "if you be the great king who sends Ara, the lightning; who makes the great noise and the mighty winds, and sends the waters down upon the jungle people when the days are dark and it is cold. Tell me, Goro, are you God?"

Of course he did not pronounce God as you or I would pronounce His name, for Tarzan knew naught of the spoken language of his English forbears; but he had a name of his own invention for each of the little bugs which constituted the alphabet. Unlike the apes he was not satisfied merely to have a mental picture of the things he knew, he must have a word descriptive of each. In reading he grasped a word in its entirety; but when he spoke the words he had learned from the books of his father, he pronounced each according to the names he had given the various little bugs which occurred in it, usually giving the gender prefix for each.

Thus it was an imposing word which Tarzan made of GOD. The masculine prefix of the apes is BU, the feminine MU; g Tarzan had named LA, o he pronounced TU, and d was MO. So the word God evolved itself into BULAMUTUMUMO, or, in English, he-g-she-o-she-d.

Similarly he had arrived at a strange and wonderful spelling of his own name. Tarzan is derived from the two ape words TAR and ZAN, meaning white skin. It was given him by his foster mother, Kala, the great she-ape. When Tarzan first put it into the written language of his own people he had not yet chanced upon either *White* or *Skin* in the dictionary; but in a primer he had seen the picture of a little white boy and so he wrote his name *bumude-mutomuro*, or he-boy.

To follow Tarzan's strange system of spelling would be laborious as well as futile, and so we shall in the future, as we have in the past, adhere to the more familiar forms of our grammar school copybooks. It would tire you to remember that *do* meant b, *tu* o, and *ro* y, and that to say he-boy you must prefix the ape masculine gender sound *bu* before the entire word and the feminine gender sound *Mu* before each of the lower-case letters which go to make up boy—it would tire you and it would bring me to the nineteenth hole several strokes under par.

And so Tarzan harangued the moon, and when Goro did not reply, Tarzan of the Apes waxed wroth. He swelled his giant chest and bared his fighting fangs, and hurled into the teeth of the dead satellite the challenge of the bull ape.

"You are not Bulamutumumo," he cried. "You are not king of the jungle folk. You are not so great as Tarzan, mighty fighter, mighty hunter. None there is so great as Tarzan. If there be a Bulamutumumo, Tarzan can kill him. Come down, Goro, great coward, and fight with Tarzan. Tarzan will kill you. I am Tarzan, the killer."

But the moon made no answer to the boasting of the ape-man, and when a cloud came and obscured her face, Tarzan thought that Goro was indeed afraid, and was hiding from him, so he came down out of the trees and awoke Numgo and told him how great was Tarzan—how he had frightened Goro out of the sky and made him tremble. Tarzan spoke of the moon as *he*, for all things large or awe inspiring are male to the ape folk.

Numgo was not much impressed; but he was very sleepy, so he told Tarzan to go away and leave his betters alone.

"But where shall I find God?" insisted Tarzan. "You are very old; if there is a God you must have seen Him. What does He look like? Where does He live?"

"I am God," replied Numgo. "Now sleep and disturb me no more."

Tarzan looked at Numgo steadily for several minutes, his shapely head sank just a trifle between his great shoulders, his square chin shot forward and his short upper lip drew back, exposing his white teeth. Then, with a low growl he leaped upon the ape and buried his fangs in the other's hairy shoulder, clutching the great neck in his mighty fingers. Twice he shook the old ape, then he released his tooth-hold.

"Are you God?" he demanded.

"No," wailed Numgo. "I am only a poor, old ape. Leave me alone. Go ask the Gomangani where God is. They are hairless like yourself and very wise, too. They should know."

Tarzan released Numgo and turned away. The suggestion that he consult the blacks appealed to him, and though his relations with the people of Mbonga, the chief, were the antithesis of friendly, he could at least spy upon his hated enemies and discover if they had intercourse with God.

So it was that Tarzan set forth through the trees toward the village of the blacks, all excitement at the prospect of discovering the Supreme Being, the Creator of all things. As he traveled he reviewed, mentally, his armament—the condition of his hunting knife, the number of his arrows, the newness of the gut which strung his bow—he hefted the war spear which had once been the pride of some black warrior of Mbonga's tribe.

If he met God, Tarzan would be prepared. One could never tell whether a grass rope, a war spear, or a poisoned arrow would be most efficacious against an unfamiliar foe. Tarzan of the Apes was quite content—if God wished to fight, the ape-man had no doubt as to the outcome of the struggle. There were many questions Tarzan wished to put to the Creator of the Universe and so he hoped that God would not prove a belligerent God; but his experience of life and the ways of living things had taught him that any creature with the means for offense and defense was quite likely to provoke attack if in the proper mood.

It was dark when Tarzan came to the village of Mbonga. As silently as the silent shadows of the night he sought his accustomed place among the branches of the great tree which overhung the palisade. Below him, in the village street, he saw men and women. The men were hideously painted—more hideously than usual. Among them moved a weird and grotesque figure, a tall figure that went upon the two legs of a man and yet had the head of a buffalo. A tail dangled to his ankles behind him, and in one hand he carried a zebra's tail while the other clutched a bunch of small arrows.

Tarzan was electrified. Could it be that chance had given him thus early an opportunity to look upon God? Surely this thing was neither man nor beast, so what could it be then other than the Creator of the Universe! The ape-man watched the every move of the strange creature. He saw the black men and women fall back at its approach as though they stood in terror of its mysterious powers.

Presently he discovered that the deity was speaking and that all listened in silence to his words. Tarzan was sure that none other than God could inspire such awe in the hearts of the Gomangani, or stop their mouths so effectually without recourse to arrows or spears. Tarzan had come to look with contempt upon the blacks, principally because of their garrulity. The small apes talked a great deal and ran away from an enemy. The big, old bulls of Kerchak talked but little and fought upon the slightest provocation. Numa, the lion, was not given to loquacity, yet of all the jungle folk there were few who fought more often than he.

Tarzan witnessed strange things that night, none of which he understood, and, perhaps because they were strange, he thought that they must have to do with the God he could not understand. He saw three youths receive their first war spears in a weird ceremony which the grotesque witch-doctor strove successfully to render uncanny and awesome.

Hugely interested, he watched the slashing of the three brown arms and the exchange of blood with Mbonga, the chief, in the rites of the ceremony of blood brotherhood. He saw the zebra's tail dipped into a caldron of water above which the witch-doctor had made magical passes the while he danced and leaped about it, and he saw the breasts and foreheads of each of the three novitiates sprinkled with the charmed liquid. Could the ape-man have known the purpose of this act, that it was intended to render the recipient invulnerable to the attacks of his enemies and fearless in the face of any danger, he would doubtless have leaped into the village street and appropriated the zebra's tail and a portion of the contents of the caldron.

But he did not know, and so he only wondered, not alone at what he saw but at the strange sensations which played up and down his naked spine, sensations induced, doubtless, by the same hypnotic influence which held the black spectators in tense awe upon the verge of a hysteric upheaval.

The longer Tarzan watched, the more convinced he became that his eyes were upon God, and with the conviction came determination to have word with the deity. With Tarzan of the Apes, to think was to act.

The people of Mbonga were keyed to the highest pitch of hysterical excitement. They needed little to release the accumulated pressure of static nerve force which the terrorizing mummery of the witch-doctor had induced.

A lion roared, suddenly and loud, close without the palisade. The blacks started nervously, dropping into utter silence as they listened for a repetition of that all-too-familiar and always terrorizing voice. Even the witch-doctor paused in the midst of an intricate step, remaining momentarily rigid and statuesque as he plumbed his cunning mind for a suggestion as how best he might take advantage of the condition of his audience and the timely interruption.

Already the evening had been vastly profitable to him. There would be three goats for the initiation of the three youths into full-fledged warriorship, and besides these he had received several gifts of grain and beads, together with a piece of copper wire from admiring and terrified members of his audience.

Numa's roar still reverberated along taut nerves when a woman's laugh, shrill and piercing, shattered the silence of the village. It was this moment that Tarzan chose to drop lightly from his tree into the village street. Fearless among his blood enemies he stood, taller by a full head than many of Mbonga's warriors, straight as their straightest arrow, muscled like Numa, the lion.

For a moment Tarzan stood looking straight at the witch-doctor. Every eye was upon him, yet no one had moved— a paralysis of terror held them, to be broken a moment later as the ape-man, with a toss of head, stepped straight toward the hideous figure beneath the buffalo head.

Then the nerves of the blacks could stand no more. For months the terror of the strange, white, jungle god had been upon them. Their arrows had been stolen from the very center of the village; their warriors had been silently slain upon the jungle trails and their dead bodies dropped mysteriously and by night into the village street as from the heavens above.

One or two there were who had glimpsed the strange figure of the new demon and it was from their oft-repeated descriptions that the entire village now recognized Tarzan as the author of many of their ills. Upon another occasion and by daylight, the warriors would doubtless have leaped to attack him, but at night, and this night of all others, when they were wrought to such a pitch of nervous dread by the uncanny artistry of their witch-doctor, they were helpless with terror. As one man they turned and fled, scattering for their huts, as Tarzan advanced. For a moment one and one only held his ground. It was the witch-doctor. More than half self-hypnotized into a belief in his own charlatanry he faced this new demon who threatened to undermine his ancient and lucrative profession.

"Are you God?" asked Tarzan.

The witch-doctor, having no idea of the meaning of the other's words, danced a few strange steps, leaped high in the air, turning completely around and alighting in a stooping posture with feet far outspread and head thrust out toward the ape-man. Thus he remained for an instant before he uttered a loud "Boo!" which was evidently intended to frighten Tarzan away; but in reality had no such effect.

Tarzan did not pause. He had set out to approach and examine God and nothing upon earth might now stay his feet. Seeing that his antics had no potency with the visitor, the witch-doctor tried some new medicine. Spitting upon the zebra's tail, which he still clutched in one hand, he made circles above it with the arrows in the other hand, meanwhile backing cautiously away from Tarzan and speaking confidentially to the bushy end of the tail.

This medicine must be short medicine, however, for the creature, god or demon, was steadily closing up the distance which had separated them. The circles therefore were few and rapid, and when they were completed, the witch-doctor struck an attitude which was intended to be awe inspiring and waving the zebra's tail before him, drew an imaginary line between himself and Tarzan.

"Beyond this line you cannot pass, for my medicine is strong medicine," he cried. "Stop, or you will fall dead as your foot touches this spot. My mother was a voodoo, my father was a snake; I live upon lions' hearts and the entrails of the panther; I eat young babies for breakfast and the demons of the jungle are my slaves. I am the most powerful witch-doctor in the world; I fear nothing, for I cannot die. I–" But he got no further; instead he turned and fled as Tarzan of the Apes crossed the magical dead line and still lived.

As the witch-doctor ran, Tarzan almost lost his temper. This was no way for God to act, at least not in accordance with the conception Tarzan had come to have of God.

"Come back!" he cried. "Come back, God, I will not harm you." But the witch-doctor was in full retreat by this time, stepping high as he leaped over cooking pots and the smoldering embers of small fires that had burned before the huts of villagers. Straight for his own hut ran the witch-doctor, terror-spurred to unwonted speed; but futile was his effort—the ape-man bore down upon him with the speed of Bara, the deer.

Just at the entrance to his hut the witch-doctor was overhauled. A heavy hand fell upon his shoulder to drag him back. It seized upon a portion of the buffalo hide, dragging the disguise from him. It was a naked black man that Tarzan saw dodge into the darkness of the hut's interior.

So this was what he had thought was God! Tarzan's lip curled in an angry snarl as he leaped into the hut after the terror-stricken witch-doctor. In the blackness within he found the man huddled at the far side and dragged him forth into the comparative lightness of the moonlit night.

The witch-doctor bit and scratched in an attempt to escape; but a few cuffs across the head brought him to a better realization of the futility of resistance. Beneath the moon Tarzan held the cringing figure upon its shaking feet.

"So you are God!" he cried. "If you be God, then Tarzan is greater than God," and so the ape-man thought. "I am Tarzan," he shouted into the ear of the black. "In all the jungle, or above it, or upon the running waters, or the sleeping waters, or upon the big water, or the little water, there is none so great as Tarzan. Tarzan is greater than the Mangani; he is greater than the Gomangani. With his own hands he has slain Numa, the lion, and Sheeta, the panther; there is none so great as Tarzan. Tarzan is greater than God. See!" and with a sudden wrench he twisted the black's neck until the fellow shrieked in pain and then slumped to the earth in a swoon.

Placing his foot upon the neck of the fallen witch-doctor, the ape-man raised his face to the moon and uttered the long, shrill scream of the victorious bull ape. Then he stooped and snatched the zebra's tail from the nerveless fingers of the unconscious man and without a backward glance retraced his footsteps across the village.

From several hut doorways frightened eyes watched him. Mbonga, the chief, was one of those who had seen what passed before the hut of the witch-doctor. Mbonga was greatly concerned. Wise old patriarch that he was, he never had more than half believed in witch-doctors, at least not since greater wisdom had come with age; but as a chief he was well convinced of the power of the witch-doctor as an arm of government, and often it was that Mbonga used the superstitious fears of his people to his own ends through the medium of the medicine-man.

Mbonga and the witch-doctor had worked together and divided the spoils, and now the "face" of the witch-doctor would be lost forever if any saw what Mbonga had seen; nor would this generation again have as much faith in any future witch-doctor.

Mbonga must do something to counteract the evil influence of the forest demon's victory over the witch-doctor. He raised his heavy spear and crept silently from his hut in the wake of the retreating ape-man. Down the village street walked Tarzan, as unconcerned and as deliberate as though only the friendly apes of Kerchak surrounded him instead of a village full of armed enemies.

Seeming only was the indifference of Tarzan, for alert and watchful was every well-trained sense. Mbonga, wily stalker of keen-eared jungle creatures, moved now in utter silence. Not even Bara, the deer, with his great ears could have guessed from any sound that Mbonga was near; but the black was not stalking Bara; he was stalking man, and so he sought only to avoid noise.

Closer and closer to the slowly moving ape-man he came. Now he raised his war spear, throwing his spear-hand far back above his right shoulder. Once and for all would Mbonga, the chief, rid himself and his people of the menace of this terrifying enemy. He would make no poor cast; he would take pains, and he would hurl his weapon with such great force as would finish the demon forever.

But Mbonga, sure as he thought himself, erred in his calculations. He might believe that he was stalking a man— he did not know, however, that it was a man with the delicate sense perception of the lower orders. Tarzan, when he had turned his back upon his enemies, had noted what Mbonga never would have thought of considering in the hunting of man—the wind. It was blowing in the same direction that Tarzan was proceeding, carrying to his delicate nostrils the odors which arose behind him. Thus it was that Tarzan knew that he was being followed, for even among the many stenches of an African village, the ape-man's uncanny faculty was equal to the task of differentiating one stench from another and locating with remarkable precision the source from whence it came.

He knew that a man was following him and coming closer, and his judgment warned him of the purpose of the stalker. When Mbonga, therefore, came within spear range of the ape-man, the latter suddenly wheeled upon him, so suddenly that the poised spear was shot a fraction of a second before Mbonga had intended. It went a trifle high and Tarzan stooped to let it pass over his head; then he sprang toward the chief. But Mbonga did not wait to receive him. Instead, he turned and fled for the dark doorway of the nearest hut, calling as he went for his warriors to fall upon the stranger and slay him.

Well indeed might Mbonga scream for help, for Tarzan, young and fleet-footed, covered the distance between them in great leaps, at the speed of a charging lion. He was growling, too, not at all unlike Numa himself. Mbonga heard and his blood ran cold. He could feel the wool stiffen upon his pate and a prickly chill run up his spine, as though Death had come and run his cold finger along Mbonga's back.

Others heard, too, and saw, from the darkness of their huts—bold warriors, hideously painted, grasping heavy war spears in nerveless fingers. Against Numa, the lion, they would have charged fearlessly. Against many times their own number of black warriors would they have raced to the protection of their chief; but this weird jungle demon filled them with terror. There was nothing human in the bestial growls that rumbled up from his deep chest; there was nothing human in the bared fangs, or the catlike leaps.

Mbonga's warriors were terrified—too terrified to leave the seeming security of their huts while they watched the beast-man spring full upon the back of their old chieftain.

Mbonga went down with a scream of terror. He was too frightened even to attempt to defend himself. He just lay beneath his antagonist in a paralysis of fear, screaming at the top of his lungs. Tarzan half rose and kneeled above the black. He turned Mbonga over and looked him in the face, exposing the man's throat, then he drew his long, keen knife, the knife that John Clayton, Lord Greystoke, had brought from England many years before. He raised it close above Mbonga's neck. The old black whimpered with terror. He pleaded for his life in a tongue which Tarzan could not understand.

For the first time the ape-man had a close view of the chief. He saw an old man, a very old man with scrawny neck and wrinkled face—a dried, parchment-like face which resembled some of the little monkeys Tarzan knew so well. He saw the terror in the man's eyes—never before had Tarzan seen such terror in the eyes of any animal, or such a piteous appeal for mercy upon the face of any creature.

Something stayed the ape-man's hand for an instant. He wondered why it was that he hesitated to make the kill; never before had he thus delayed. The old man seemed to wither and shrink to a bag of puny bones beneath his eyes. So weak and helpless and terror-stricken he appeared that the ape-man was filled with a great contempt; but another sensation also claimed him—something new to Tarzan of the Apes in relation to an enemy. It was pity—pity for a poor, frightened, old man.

Tarzan rose and turned away, leaving Mbonga, the chief, unharmed.

With head held high the ape-man walked through the village, swung himself into the branches of the tree which overhung the palisade and disappeared from the sight of the villagers.

All the way back to the stamping ground of the apes, Tarzan sought for an explanation of the strange power which had stayed his hand and prevented him from slaying Mbonga. It was as though someone greater than he had commanded him to spare the life of the old man. Tarzan could not understand, for he could conceive of nothing, or no one, with the authority to dictate to him what he should do, or what he should refrain from doing.

It was late when Tarzan sought a swaying couch among the trees beneath which slept the apes of Kerchak, and he was still absorbed in the solution of his strange problem when he fell asleep.

The sun was well up in the heavens when he awoke. The apes were astir in search of food. Tarzan watched them lazily from above as they scratched in the rotting loam for bugs and beetles and grubworms, or sought among the branches of the trees for eggs and young birds, or luscious caterpillars.

An orchid, dangling close beside his head, opened slowly, unfolding its delicate petals to the warmth and light of the sun which but recently had penetrated to its shady retreat. A thousand times had Tarzan of the Apes witnessed the beauteous miracle; but now it aroused a keener interest, for the ape-man was just commencing to ask himself questions about all the myriad wonders which heretofore he had but taken for granted.

What made the flower open? What made it grow from a tiny bud to a full-blown bloom? Why was it at all? Why was he? Where did Numa, the lion, come from? Who planted the first tree? How did Goro get way up into the darkness of the night sky to cast his welcome light upon the fearsome nocturnal jungle? And the sun! Did the sun merely happen there?

Why were all the peoples of the jungle not trees? Why were the trees not something else? Why was Tarzan different from Taug, and Taug different from Bara, the deer, and Bara different from Sheeta, the panther, and why was not Sheeta like Buto, the rhinoceros? Where and how, anyway, did they all come from—the trees, the flowers, the insects, the countless creatures of the jungle?

Quite unexpectedly an idea popped into Tarzan's head. In following out the many ramifications of the dictionary definition of *God* he had come upon the word *create*— "to cause to come into existence; to form out of nothing."

Tarzan almost had arrived at something tangible when a distant wail startled him from his preoccupation into sensibility of the present and the real. The wail came from the jungle at some little distance from Tarzan's swaying couch. It was the wail of a tiny balu. Tarzan recognized it at once as the voice of Gazan, Teeka's baby. They had called it Gazan because its soft, baby hair had been unusually red, and GAZAN in the language of the great apes, means red skin.

The wail was immediately followed by a real scream of terror from the small lungs. Tarzan was electrified into instant action. Like an arrow from a bow he shot through the trees in the direction of the sound. Ahead of him he heard the savage snarling of an adult she-ape. It was Teeka to the rescue. The danger must be very real. Tarzan could tell that by the note of rage mingled with fear in the voice of the she.

Running along bending limbs, swinging from one tree to another, the ape-man raced through the middle terraces toward the sounds which now had risen in volume to deafening proportions. From all directions the apes of Kerchak were hurrying in response to the appeal in the tones of the balu and its mother, and as they came, their roars reverberated through the forest.

But Tarzan, swifter than his heavy fellows, distanced them all. It was he who was first upon the scene. What he saw sent a cold chill through his giant frame, for the enemy was the most hated and loathed of all the jungle creatures.

Twined in a great tree was Histah, the snake—huge, ponderous, slimy—and in the folds of its deadly embrace was Teeka's little balu, Gazan. Nothing in the jungle inspired within the breast of Tarzan so near a semblance to fear as did the hideous Histah. The apes, too, loathed the terrifying reptile and feared him even more than they did Sheeta, the panther, or Numa, the lion. Of all their enemies there was none they gave a wider berth than they gave Histah, the snake.

Tarzan knew that Teeka was peculiarly fearful of this silent, repulsive foe, and as the scene broke upon his vision, it was the action of Teeka which filled him with the greatest wonder, for at the moment that he saw her, the she-ape leaped upon the glistening body of the snake, and as the mighty folds encircled her as well as her offspring, she made no effort to escape, but instead grasped the writhing body in a futile effort to tear it from her screaming balu.

Tarzan knew all too well how deep-rooted was Teeka's terror of Histah. He scarce could believe the testimony of his own eyes then, when they told him that she had voluntarily rushed into that deadly embrace. Nor was Teeka's innate dread of the monster much greater than Tarzan's own. Never, willingly, had he touched a snake. Why, he could not say, for he would admit fear of nothing; nor was it fear, but rather an inherent repulsion bequeathed to him by many generations of civilized ancestors, and back of them, perhaps, by countless myriads of such as Teeka, in the breasts of each of which had lurked the same nameless terror of the slimy reptile.

Yet Tarzan did not hesitate more than had Teeka, but leaped upon Histah with all the speed and impetuosity that he would have shown had he been springing upon Bara, the deer, to make a kill for food. Thus beset the snake writhed and twisted horribly; but not for an instant did it loose its hold upon any of its intended victims, for it had included the ape-man in its cold embrace the minute that he had fallen upon it.

Still clinging to the tree, the mighty reptile held the three as though they had been without weight, the while it sought to crush the life from them. Tarzan had drawn his knife and this he now plunged rapidly into the body of the enemy; but the encircling folds promised to sap his life before he had inflicted a death wound upon the snake. Yet on he fought, nor once did he seek to escape the horrid death that confronted him—his sole aim was to slay Histah and thus free Teeka and her balu.

The great, wide-gaping jaws of the snake turned and hovered above him. The elastic maw, which could accommodate a rabbit or a horned buck with equal facility, yawned for him; but Histah, in turning his attention upon the ape-man, brought his head within reach of Tarzan's blade. Instantly a brown hand leaped forth and seized the mottled neck, and another drove the heavy hunting knife to the hilt into the little brain.

Convulsively Histah shuddered and relaxed, tensed and relaxed again, whipping and striking with his great body; but no longer sentient or sensible. Histah was dead, but in his death throes he might easily dispatch a dozen apes or men.

Quickly Tarzan seized Teeka and dragged her from the loosened embrace, dropping her to the ground beneath, then he extricated the balu and tossed it to its mother. Still Histah whipped about, clinging to the ape-man; but after a dozen efforts Tarzan succeeded in wriggling free and leaping to the ground out of range of the mighty battering of the dying snake.

A circle of apes surrounded the scene of the battle; but the moment that Tarzan broke safely from the enemy they turned silently away to resume their interrupted feeding, and Teeka turned with them, apparently forgetful of all but her balu and the fact that when the interruption had occurred she just had discovered an ingeniously hidden nest containing three perfectly good eggs.

Tarzan, equally indifferent to a battle that was over, merely cast a parting glance at the still writhing body of Histah and wandered off toward the little pool which served to water the tribe at this point. Strangely, he did not give the victory cry over the vanquished Histah. Why, he could not have told you, other than that to him Histah was not an animal. He differed in some peculiar way from the other denizens of the jungle. Tarzan only knew that he hated him.

EDGAR RICE BURROUGHS

At the pool Tarzan drank his fill and lay stretched upon the soft grass beneath the shade of a tree. His mind reverted to the battle with Histah, the snake. It seemed strange to him that Teeka should have placed herself within the folds of the horrid monster. Why had she done it? Why, indeed, had he? Teeka did not belong to him, nor did Teeka's balu. They were both Taug's. Why then had he done this thing? Histah was not food for him when he was dead. There seemed to Tarzan, now that he gave the matter thought, no reason in the world why he should have done the thing he did, and presently it occurred to him that he had acted almost involuntarily, just as he had acted when he had released the old Gomangani the previous evening.

What made him do such things? Somebody more powerful than he must force him to act at times. "All-powerful," thought Tarzan. "The little bugs say that God is all-powerful. It must be that God made me do these things, for I never did them by myself. It was God who made Teeka rush upon Histah. Teeka would never go near Histah of her own volition. It was God who held my knife from the throat of the old Gomangani. God accomplishes strange things for he is 'all-powerful.' I cannot see Him; but I know that it must be God who does these things. No Mangani, no Gomangani, no Tarmangani could do them."

And the flowers—who made them grow? Ah, now it was all explained—the flowers, the trees, the moon, the sun, himself, every living creature in the jungle—they were all made by God out of nothing.

And what was God? What did God look like? Of that he had no conception; but he was sure that everything that was good came from God. His good act in refraining from slaying the poor, defenseless old Gomangani; Teeka's love that had hurled her into the embrace of death; his own loyalty to Teeka which had jeopardized his life that she might live. The flowers and the trees were good and beautiful. God had made them. He made the other creatures, too, that each might have food upon which to live. He had made Sheeta, the panther, with his beautiful coat; and Numa, the lion, with his noble head and his shaggy mane. He had made Bara, the deer, lovely and graceful.

Yes, Tarzan had found God, and he spent the whole day in attributing to Him all of the good and beautiful things of nature; but there was one thing which troubled him. He could not quite reconcile it to his conception of his new-found God.

Who made Histah, the snake?

TARZAN AND THE BLACK BOY

Tarzan of the Apes sat at the foot of a great tree braiding a new grass rope. Beside him lay the frayed remnants of the old one, torn and severed by the fangs and talons of Sheeta, the panther. Only half the original rope was there, the balance having been carried off by the angry cat as he bounded away through the jungle with the noose still about his savage neck and the loose end dragging among the underbrush.

Tarzan smiled as he recalled Sheeta's great rage, his frantic efforts to free himself from the entangling strands, his uncanny screams that were part hate, part anger, part terror. He smiled in retrospection at the discomfiture of his enemy, and in anticipation of another day as he added an extra strand to his new rope.

This would be the strongest, the heaviest rope that Tarzan of the Apes ever had fashioned. Visions of Numa, the lion, straining futilely in its embrace thrilled the ape-man. He was quite content, for his hands and his brain were busy. Content, too, were his fellows of the tribe of Kerchak, searching for food in the clearing and the surrounding trees about him. No perplexing thoughts of the future burdened their minds, and only occasionally, dimly arose recollections of the near past. They were stimulated to a species of brutal content by the delectable business of filling their bellies. Afterward they would sleep—it was their life, and they enjoyed it as we enjoy ours, you and I—as Tarzan enjoyed his. Possibly they enjoyed theirs more than we enjoy ours, for who shall say that the beasts of the jungle do not better fulfill the purposes for which they are created than does man with his many excursions into strange fields and his contraventions of the laws of nature? And what gives greater content and greater happiness than the fulfilling of a destiny?

As Tarzan worked, Gazan, Teeka's little balu, played about him while Teeka sought food upon the opposite side of the clearing. No more did Teeka, the mother, or Taug, the sullen sire, harbor suspicions of Tarzan's intentions toward their first-born. Had he not courted death to save their Gazan from the fangs and talons of Sheeta? Did he not fondle and cuddle the little one with even as great a show of affection as Teeka herself displayed? Their fears were allayed and Tarzan now found himself often in the role of nursemaid to a tiny anthropoid— an avocation which he found by no means irksome, since Gazan was a never-failing fount of surprises and entertainment.

Just now the apeling was developing those arboreal tendencies which were to stand him in such good stead during the years of his youth, when rapid flight into the upper terraces was of far more importance and value than his undeveloped muscles and untried fighting fangs. Backing off fifteen or twenty feet from the bole of the tree beneath the branches of which Tarzan worked upon his rope, Gazan scampered quickly forward, scrambling nimbly upward to the lower limbs. Here he would squat for a moment or two, quite proud of his achievement, then clamber to the ground again and repeat. Sometimes, quite often in fact, for he was an ape, his attention was distracted by other things, a beetle, a caterpillar, a tiny field mouse, and off he would go in pursuit; the caterpillars he always caught, and sometimes the beetles; but the field mice, never.

Now he discovered the tail of the rope upon which Tarzan was working. Grasping it in one small hand he bounced away, for all the world like an animated rubber ball, snatching it from the ape-man's hand and running off across the clearing. Tarzan leaped to his feet and was in pursuit in an instant, no trace of anger on his face or in his voice as he called to the roguish little balu to drop his rope.

Straight toward his mother raced Gazan, and after him came Tarzan. Teeka looked up from her feeding, and in the first instant that she realized that Gazan was fleeing and that another was in pursuit, she bared her fangs and bristled; but when she saw that the pursuer was Tarzan she turned back to the business that had been occupying her attention. At her very feet the ape-man overhauled the balu and, though the youngster squealed and fought when Tarzan seized him, Teeka only glanced casually in their direction. No longer did she fear harm to her first-born at the hands of the ape-man. Had he not saved Gazan on two occasions?

Rescuing his rope, Tarzan returned to his tree and resumed his labor; but thereafter it was necessary to watch carefully the playful balu, who was now possessed to steal it whenever he thought his great, smooth-skinned cousin was momentarily off his guard.

But even under this handicap Tarzan finally completed the rope, a long, pliant weapon, stronger than any he ever had made before. The discarded piece of his former one he gave to Gazan for a plaything, for Tarzan had it in his mind to instruct Teeka's balu after ideas of his own when the youngster should be old and strong enough to profit by his precepts. At present the little ape's innate aptitude for mimicry would be sufficient to familiarize him with Tarzan's ways and weapons, and so the ape-man swung off into the jungle, his new rope coiled over one shoulder, while little Gazan hopped about the clearing dragging the old one after him in childish glee.

As Tarzan traveled, dividing his quest for food with one for a sufficiently noble quarry whereupon to test his new weapon, his mind often was upon Gazan. The ape-man had realized a deep affection for Teeka's balu almost from the first, partly because the child belonged to Teeka, his first love, and partly for the little ape's own sake, and Tarzan's human longing for some sentient creature upon which to expend those natural affections of the soul which are inherent to all normal members of the GENUS HOMO. Tarzan envied Teeka. It was true that Gazan evidenced a considerable reciprocation of Tarzan's fondness for him, even preferring him to his own surly sire; but to Teeka the little one turned when in pain or terror, when tired or hungry. Then it was that Tarzan felt quite alone in the world and longed desperately for one who should turn first to him for succor and protection.

Taug had Teeka; Teeka had Gazan; and nearly every other bull and cow of the tribe of Kerchak had one or more to love and by whom to be loved. Of course Tarzan could scarcely formulate the thought in precisely this way—he only knew that he craved something which was denied him; something which seemed to be represented by those relations which existed between Teeka and her balu, and so he envied Teeka and longed for a balu of his own.

He saw Sheeta and his mate with their little family of three; and deeper inland toward the rocky hills, where one might lie up during the heat of the day, in the dense shade of a tangled thicket close under the cool face of an overhanging rock, Tarzan had found the lair of Numa, the lion, and of Sabor, the lioness. Here he had watched them with their little balus—playful creatures, spotted leopard-like. And he had seen the young fawn with Bara, the deer, and with Buto, the rhinoceros, its ungainly little one. Each of the creatures of the jungle had its own—except Tarzan. It made the ape-man sad to think upon this thing, sad and lonely; but presently the scent of game cleared his young mind of all other considerations, as catlike he crawled far out upon a bending limb above the game trail which led down to the ancient watering place of the wild things of this wild world.

How many thousands of times had this great, old limb bent to the savage form of some blood-thirsty hunter in the long years that it had spread its leafy branches above the deep-worn jungle path! Tarzan, the ape-man, Sheeta, the panther, and Histah, the snake, it knew well. They had worn smooth the bark upon its upper surface.

Today it was Horta, the boar, which came down toward the watcher in the old tree—Horta, the boar, whose formidable tusks and diabolical temper preserved him from all but the most ferocious or most famished of the largest carnivora.

But to Tarzan, meat was meat; naught that was edible or tasty might pass a hungry Tarzan unchallenged and unattacked. In hunger, as in battle, the ape-man out-savaged the dreariest denizens of the jungle. He knew neither fear nor mercy, except upon rare occasions when some strange, inexplicable force stayed his hand—a force inexplicable to him, perhaps, because of his ignorance of his own origin and of all the forces of humanitarianism and civilization that were his rightful heritage because of that origin.

So today, instead of staying his hand until a less formidable feast found its way toward him, Tarzan dropped his new noose about the neck of Horta, the boar. It was an excellent test for the untried strands. The angered boar bolted this way and that; but each time the new rope held him where Tarzan had made it fast about the stem of the tree above the branch from which he had cast it.

As Horta grunted and charged, slashing the sturdy jungle patriarch with his mighty tusks until the bark flew in every direction, Tarzan dropped to the ground behind him. In the ape-man's hand was the long, keen blade that had been his constant companion since that distant day upon which chance had directed its point into the body of Bolgani, the gorilla, and saved the torn and bleeding man-child from what else had been certain death.

Tarzan walked in toward Horta, who swung now to face his enemy. Mighty and muscled as was the young giant, it yet would have appeared but the maddest folly for him to face so formidable a creature as Horta, the boar, armed only with a slender hunting knife. So it would have seemed to one who knew Horta even slightly and Tarzan not at all.

For a moment Horta stood motionless facing the ape-man. His wicked, deep-set eyes flashed angrily. He shook his lowered head.

"Mud-eater!" jeered the ape-man. "Wallower in filth. Even your meat stinks, but it is juicy and makes Tarzan strong. Today I shall eat your heart, O Lord of the Great Tusks, that it shall keep savage that which pounds against my own ribs."

Horta, understanding nothing of what Tarzan said, was none the less enraged because of that. He saw only a naked man-thing, hairless and futile, pitting his puny fangs and soft muscles against his own indomitable savagery, and he charged.

Tarzan of the Apes waited until the upcut of a wicked tusk would have laid open his thigh, then he moved—just the least bit to one side; but so quickly that lightning was a sluggard by comparison, and as he moved, he stooped low and with all the great power of his right arm drove the long blade of his father's hunting knife straight into the heart of Horta, the boar. A quick leap carried him from the zone of the creature's death throes, and a moment later the hot and dripping heart of Horta was in his grasp.

His hunger satisfied, Tarzan did not seek a lying-up place for sleep, as was sometimes his way, but continued on through the jungle more in search of adventure than of food, for today he was restless. And so it came that he turned his footsteps toward the village of Mbonga, the black chief, whose people Tarzan had baited remorselessly since that day upon which Kulonga, the chief's son, had slain Kala.

A river winds close beside the village of the black men. Tarzan reached its side a little below the clearing where squat the thatched huts of the Negroes. The river life was ever fascinating to the ape-man. He found pleasure in watching the ungainly antics of Duro, the hippopotamus, and keen sport in tormenting the sluggish crocodile, Gimla, as he basked in the sun. Then, too, there were the shes and the balus of the black men of the Gomangani to frighten as they squatted by the river, the shes with their meager washing, the balus with their primitive toys.

This day he came upon a woman and her child farther down stream than usual. The former was searching for a species of shellfish which was to be found in the mud close to the river bank. She was a young black woman of about thirty. Her teeth were filed to sharp points, for her people ate the flesh of man. Her under lip was slit that it might support a rude pendant of copper which she had worn for so many years that the lip had been dragged downward to prodigious lengths, exposing the teeth and gums of her lower jaw. Her nose, too, was slit, and through the slit was a wooden skewer. Metal ornaments dangled from her ears, and upon her forehead and cheeks; upon her chin and the bridge of her nose were tattooings in colors that were mellowed now by age. She was naked except for a girdle of grasses about her waist. Altogether she was very beautiful in her own estimation and even in the estimation of the men of Mbonga's tribe, though she was of another people—a trophy of war seized in her maidenhood by one of Mbonga's fighting men.

Her child was a boy of ten, lithe, straight and, for a black, handsome. Tarzan looked upon the two from the concealing foliage of a near-by bush. He was about to leap forth before them with a terrifying scream, that he might enjoy the spectacle of their terror and their incontinent flight; but of a sudden a new whim seized him. Here was a balu fashioned as he himself was fashioned. Of course this one's skin was black; but what of it? Tarzan had never seen a white man. In so far as he knew, he was the sole representative of that strange form of life upon the earth. The black boy should make an excellent balu for Tarzan, since he had none of his own. He would tend him carefully, feed him well, protect him as only Tarzan of the Apes could protect his own, and teach him out of his half human, half bestial lore the secrets of the jungle from its rotting surface vegetation to the high tossed pinnacles of the forest's upper terraces.

*

Tarzan uncoiled his rope, and shook out the noose. The two before him, all ignorant of the near presence of that terrifying form, continued preoccupied in the search for shellfish, poking about in the mud with short sticks.

Tarzan stepped from the jungle behind them; his noose lay open upon the ground beside him. There was a quick movement of the right arm and the noose rose gracefully into the air, hovered an instant above the head of the unsuspecting youth, then settled. As it encompassed his body below the shoulders, Tarzan gave a quick jerk that tightened it about the boy's arms, pinioning them to his sides. A scream of terror broke from the lad's lips, and as his mother turned, affrighted at his cry, she saw him being dragged quickly toward a great white giant who stood just beneath the shade of a near-by tree, scarcely a dozen long paces from her.

With a savage cry of terror and rage, the woman leaped fearlessly toward the ape-man. In her mien Tarzan saw determination and courage which would shrink not even from death itself. She was very hideous and frightful even when her face was in repose; but convulsed by passion, her expression became terrifyingly fiendish. Even the ape-man drew back, but more in revulsion than fear—fear he knew not.

EDGAR RICE BURROUGHS

Biting and kicking was the black she's balu as Tarzan tucked him beneath his arm and vanished into the branches hanging low above him, just as the infuriated mother dashed forward to seize and do battle with him. And as he melted away into the depth of the jungle with his still struggling prize, he meditated upon the possibilities which might lie in the prowess of the Gomangani were the hes as formidable as the shes.

Once at a safe distance from the despoiled mother and out of earshot of her screams and menaces, Tarzan paused to inspect his prize, now so thoroughly terrorized that he had ceased his struggles and his outcries.

The frightened child rolled his eyes fearfully toward his captor, until the whites showed gleaming all about the irises.

"I am Tarzan," said the ape-man, in the vernacular of the anthropoids. "I will not harm you. You are to be Tarzan's balu. Tarzan will protect you. He will feed you. The best in the jungle shall be for Tarzan's balu, for Tarzan is a mighty hunter. None need you fear, not even Numa, the lion, for Tarzan is a mighty fighter. None so great as Tarzan, son of Kala. Do not fear."

But the child only whimpered and trembled, for he did not understand the tongue of the great apes, and the voice of Tarzan sounded to him like the barking and growling of a beast. Then, too, he had heard stories of this bad, white forest god. It was he who had slain Kulonga and others of the warriors of Mbonga, the chief. It was he who entered the village stealthily, by magic, in the darkness of the night, to steal arrows and poison, and frighten the women and the children and even the great warriors. Doubtless this wicked god fed upon little boys. Had his mother not said as much when he was naughty and she threatened to give him to the white god of the jungle if he were not good? Little black Tibo shook as with ague.

"Are you cold, Go-bu-balu?" asked Tarzan, using the simian equivalent of black he-baby in lieu of a better name. "The sun is hot; why do you shiver?"

Tibo could not understand; but he cried for his mamma and begged the great, white god to let him go, promising always to be a good boy thereafter if his plea were granted. Tarzan shook his head. Not a word could he understand. This would never do! He must teach Go-bu-balu a language which sounded like talk. It was quite certain to Tarzan that Go-bu-balu's speech was not talk at all. It sounded quite as senseless as the chattering of the silly birds. It would be best, thought the ape-man, quickly to get him among the tribe of Kerchak where he would hear the Mangani talking among themselves. Thus he would soon learn an intelligible form of speech.

Tarzan rose to his feet upon the swaying branch where he had halted far above the ground, and motioned to the child to follow him; but Tibo only clung tightly to the bole of the tree and wept. Being a boy, and a native African, he had, of course, climbed into trees many times before this; but the idea of racing off through the forest, leaping from one branch to another, as his captor, to his horror, had done when he had carried Tibo away from his mother, filled his childish heart with terror.

Tarzan sighed. His newly acquired balu had much indeed to learn. It was pitiful that a balu of his size and strength should be so backward. He tried to coax Tibo to follow him; but the child dared not, so Tarzan picked him up and carried him upon his back. Tibo no longer scratched or bit. Escape seemed impossible. Even now, were he set upon the ground, the chance was remote, he knew, that he could find his way back to the village of Mbonga, the chief. Even if he could, there were the lions and the leopards and the hyenas, any one of which, as Tibo was well aware, was particularly fond of the meat of little black boys.

So far the terrible white god of the jungle had offered him no harm. He could not expect even this much consideration from the frightful, green-eyed man-eaters. It would be the lesser of two evils, then, to let the white god carry him away without scratching and biting, as he had done at first.

As Tarzan swung rapidly through the trees, little Tibo closed his eyes in terror rather than look longer down into the frightful abysses beneath. Never before in all his life had Tibo been so frightened, yet as the white giant sped on with him through the forest there stole over the child an inexplicable sensation of security as he saw how true were the leaps of the ape-man, how unerring his grasp upon the swaying limbs which gave him hand-hold, and then, too, there was safety in the middle terraces of the forest, far above the reach of the dreaded lions.

And so Tarzan came to the clearing where the tribe fed, dropping among them with his new balu clinging tightly to his shoulders. He was fairly in the midst of them before Tibo spied a single one of the great hairy forms, or before the apes realized that Tarzan was not alone. When they saw the little Gomangani perched upon his back some of them came forward in curiosity with upcurled lips and snarling mien.

An hour before little Tibo would have said that he knew the uttermost depths of fear; but now, as he saw these fearsome beasts surrounding him, he realized that all that had gone before was as nothing by comparison. Why did the great white giant stand there so unconcernedly? Why did he not flee before these horrid, hairy, tree men fell upon them both and tore them to pieces? And then there came to Tibo a numbing recollection. It was none other than the story he had heard passed from mouth to mouth, fearfully, by the people of Mbonga, the chief, that this great white demon of the jungle was naught other than a hairless ape, for had not he been seen in company with these?

Tibo could only stare in wide-eyed horror at the approaching apes. He saw their beetling brows, their great fangs, their wicked eyes. He noted their mighty muscles rolling beneath their shaggy hides. Their every attitude and expression was a menace. Tarzan saw this, too. He drew Tibo around in front of him.

"This is Tarzan's Go-bu-balu," he said. "Do not harm him, or Tarzan will kill you," and he bared his own fangs in the teeth of the nearest ape.

"It is a Gomangani," replied the ape. "Let me kill it. It is a Gomangani. The Gomangani are our enemies. Let me kill it."

"Go away," snarled Tarzan. "I tell you, Gunto, it is Tarzan's balu. Go away or Tarzan will kill you," and the ape-man took a step toward the advancing ape.

The latter sidled off, quite stiff and haughty, after the manner of a dog which meets another and is too proud to fight and too fearful to turn his back and run.

Next came Teeka, prompted by curiosity. At her side skipped little Gazan. They were filled with wonder like the others; but Teeka did not bare her fangs. Tarzan saw this and motioned that she approach.

"Tarzan has a balu now," he said. "He and Teeka's balu can play together."

"It is a Gomangani, " replied Teeka. "It will kill my balu. Take it away, Tarzan."

Tarzan laughed. "It could not harm Pamba, the rat," he said. "It is but a little balu and very frightened. Let Gazan play with it."

Teeka still was fearful, for with all their mighty ferocity the great anthropoids are timid; but at last, assured by her great confidence in Tarzan, she pushed Gazan forward toward the little black boy. The small ape, guided by instinct, drew back toward its mother, baring its small fangs and screaming in mingled fear and rage.

Tibo, too, showed no signs of desiring a closer acquaintance with Gazan, so Tarzan gave up his efforts for the time.

During the week which followed, Tarzan found his time much occupied. His balu was a greater responsibility than he had counted upon. Not for a moment did he dare leave it, since of all the tribe, Teeka alone could have been depended upon to refrain from slaying the hapless black had it not been for Tarzan's constant watchfulness. When the ape-man hunted, he must carry Go-bu-balu about with him. It was irksome, and then the little black seemed so stupid and fearful to Tarzan. It was quite helpless against even the lesser of the jungle creatures. Tarzan wondered how it had survived at all. He tried to teach it, and found a ray of hope in the fact that Go-bu-balu had mastered a few words of the language of the anthropoids, and that he could now cling to a high-tossed branch without screaming in fear; but there was something about the child which worried Tarzan. He often had watched the blacks within their village. He had seen the children playing, and always there had been much laughter; but little Go-bu-balu never laughed. It was true that

Tarzan himself never laughed. Upon occasion he smiled, grimly, but to laughter he was a stranger. The black, however, should have laughed, reasoned the ape-man. It was the way of the Gomangani.

Also, he saw that the little fellow often refused food and was growing thinner day by day. At times he surprised the boy sobbing softly to himself. Tarzan tried to comfort him, even as fierce Kala had comforted Tarzan when the ape-man was a balu, but all to no avail. Go-bu-balu merely no longer feared Tarzan—that was all. He feared every other living thing within the jungle. He feared the jungle days with their long excursions through the dizzy tree tops. He feared the jungle nights with their swaying, perilous couches far above the ground, and the grunting and coughing of the great carnivora prowling beneath him.

Tarzan did not know what to do. His heritage of English blood rendered it a difficult thing even to consider a surrender of his project, though he was forced to admit to himself that his balu was not all that he had hoped. Though he was faithful to his self-imposed task, and even found that he had grown to like Go-bu-balu, he could not deceive himself into believing that he felt for it that fierce heat of passionate affection which Teeka revealed for Gazan, and which the black mother had shown for Go-bu-balu.

The little black boy from cringing terror at the sight of Tarzan passed by degrees into trustfulness and admiration. Only kindness had he ever received at the hands of the great white devil-god, yet he had seen with what ferocity his kindly captor could deal with others. He had seen him leap upon a certain he-ape which persisted in attempting to seize and slay Go-bu-balu. He had seen the strong, white teeth of the ape-man fastened in the neck of his adversary, and the mighty muscles tensed in battle. He had heard the savage, bestial snarls and roars of combat, and he had realized with a shudder that he could not differentiate between those of his guardian and those of the hairy ape.

He had seen Tarzan bring down a buck, just as Numa, the lion, might have done, leaping upon its back and fastening his fangs in the creature's neck. Tibo had shuddered at the sight, but he had thrilled, too, and for the first time there entered his dull, Negroid mind a vague desire to emulate his savage foster parent. But Tibo, the little black boy, lacked the divine spark which had permitted Tarzan, the white boy, to benefit by his training in the ways of the fierce jungle. In imagination he was wanting, and imagination is but another name for super-intelligence.

Imagination it is which builds bridges, and cities, and empires. The beasts know it not, the blacks only a little, while to one in a hundred thousand of earth's dominant race it is given as a gift from heaven that man may not perish from the earth.

While Tarzan pondered his problem concerning the future of his balu, Fate was arranging to take the matter out of his hands. Momaya, Tibo's mother, grief-stricken at the loss of her boy, had consulted the tribal witch-doctor, but to no avail. The medicine he made was not good medicine, for though Momaya paid him two goats for it, it did not bring back Tibo, nor even indicate where she might search for him with reasonable assurance of finding him. Momaya, being of a short temper and of another people, had little respect for the witch-doctor of her husband's tribe, and so, when he suggested that a further payment of two more fat goats would doubtless enable him to make stronger medicine, she promptly loosed her shrewish tongue upon him, and with such good effect that he was glad to take himself off with his zebra's tail and his pot of magic.

When he had gone and Momaya had succeeded in partially subduing her anger, she gave herself over to thought, as she so often had done since the abduction of her Tibo, in the hope that she finally might discover some feasible means of locating him, or at least assuring herself as to whether he were alive or dead.

It was known to the blacks that Tarzan did not eat the flesh of man, for he had slain more than one of their number, yet never tasted the flesh of any. Too, the bodies always had been found, sometimes dropping as though from the clouds to alight in the center of the village. As Tibo's body had not been found, Momaya argued that he still lived, but where?

Then it was that there came to her mind a recollection of Bukawai, the unclean, who dwelt in a cave in the hillside to the north, and who it was well known entertained devils in his evil lair. Few, if any, had the temerity to visit old Bukawai, firstly because of fear of his black magic and the two hyenas who dwelt with him and were commonly known to be devils masquerading, and secondly because of the loathsome disease which had caused Bukawai to be an outcast—a disease which was slowly eating away his face.

Now it was that Momaya reasoned shrewdly that if any might know the whereabouts of her Tibo, it would be Bukawai, who was in friendly intercourse with gods and demons, since a demon or a god it was who had stolen her baby; but even her great mother love was sorely taxed to find the courage to send her forth into the black jungle toward the distant hills and the uncanny abode of Bukawai, the unclean, and his devils.

Mother love, however, is one of the human passions which closely approximates to the dignity of an irresistible force. It drives the frail flesh of weak women to deeds of heroic measure. Momaya was neither frail nor weak, physically, but she was a woman, an ignorant, superstitious, African savage. She believed in devils, in black magic, and in witchcraft. To Momaya, the jungle was inhabited by far more terrifying things than lions and leopards—horrifying, nameless things which possessed the power of wreaking frightful harm under various innocent guises.

From one of the warriors of the village, whom she knew to have once stumbled upon the lair of Bukawai, the mother of Tibo learned how she might find it—near a spring of water which rose in a small rocky canon between two hills, the easternmost of which was easily recognizable because of a huge granite boulder which rested upon its summit. The westerly hill was lower than its companion, and was quite bare of vegetation except for a single mimosa tree which grew just a little below its summit.

These two hills, the man assured her, could be seen for some distance before she reached them, and together formed an excellent guide to her destination. He warned her, however, to abandon so foolish and dangerous an adventure, emphasizing what she already quite well knew, that if she escaped harm at the hands of Bukawai and his demons, the chances were that she would not be so fortunate with the great carnivora of the jungle through which she must pass going and returning.

The warrior even went to Momaya's husband, who, in turn, having little authority over the vixenish lady of his choice, went to Mbonga, the chief. The latter summoned Momaya, threatening her with the direst punishment should she venture forth upon so unholy an excursion. The old chief's interest in the matter was due solely to that age-old alliance which exists between church and state. The local witch-doctor, knowing his own medicine better than any other knew it, was jealous of all other pretenders to accomplishments in the black art. He long had heard of the power of Bukawai, and feared lest, should he succeed in recovering Momaya's lost child, much of the tribal patronage and consequent fees would be diverted to the unclean one. As Mbonga received, as chief, a certain proportion of the witch-doctor's fees and could expect nothing from Bukawai, his heart and soul were, quite naturally, wrapped up in the orthodox church.

But if Momaya could view with intrepid heart an excursion into the jungle and a visit to the fear-haunted abode of Bukawai, she was not likely to be deterred by threats of future punishment at the hands of old Mbonga, whom she secretly despised. Yet she appeared to accede to his injunctions, returning to her hut in silence.

She would have preferred starting upon her quest by day-light, but this was now out of the question, since she must carry food and a weapon of some sort—things which she never could pass out of the village with by day without being subjected to curious questioning that surely would come immediately to the ears of Mbonga.

So Momaya bided her time until night, and just before the gates of the village were closed, she slipped through into the darkness and the jungle. She was much frightened, but she set her face resolutely toward the north, and though she paused often to listen, breathlessly, for the huge cats which, here, were her greatest terror, she nevertheless continued her way staunchly for several hours, until a low moan a little to her right and behind her brought her to a sudden stop.

With palpitating heart the woman stood, scarce daring to breathe, and then, very faintly but unmistakable to her keen ears, came the stealthy crunching of twigs and grasses beneath padded feet.

EDGAR RICE BURROUGHS

All about Momaya grew the giant trees of the tropical jungle, festooned with hanging vines and mosses. She seized upon the nearest and started to clamber, apelike, to the branches above. As she did so, there was a sudden rush of a great body behind her, a menacing roar that caused the earth to tremble, and something crashed into the very creepers to which she was clinging—but below her.

Momaya drew herself to safety among the leafy branches and thanked the foresight which had prompted her to bring along the dried human ear which hung from a cord about her neck. She always had known that that ear was good medicine. It had been given her, when a girl, by the witch-doctor of her town tribe, and was nothing like the poor, weak medicine of Mbonga's witch-doctor.

All night Momaya clung to her perch, for although the lion sought other prey after a short time, she dared not descend into the darkness again, for fear she might encounter him or another of his kind; but at daylight she clambered down and resumed her way.

Tarzan of the Apes, finding that his balu never ceased to give evidence of terror in the presence of the apes of the tribe, and also that most of the adult apes were a constant menace to Go-bu-balu's life, so that Tarzan dared not leave him alone with them, took to hunting with the little black boy farther and farther from the stamping grounds of the anthropoids.

Little by little his absences from the tribe grew in length as he wandered farther away from them, until finally he found himself a greater distance to the north than he ever before had hunted, and with water and ample game and fruit, he felt not at all inclined to return to the tribe.

Little Go-bu-balu gave evidences of a greater interest in life, an interest which varied in direct proportion to the distance he was from the apes of Kerchak. He now trotted along behind Tarzan when the ape-man went upon the ground, and in the trees he even did his best to follow his mighty foster parent. The boy was still sad and lonely. His thin, little body had grown steadily thinner since he had come among the apes, for while, as a young cannibal, he was not overnice in the matter of diet, he found it not always to his taste to stomach the weird things which tickled the palates of epicures among the apes.

His large eyes were very large indeed now, his cheeks sunken, and every rib of his emaciated body plainly discernible to whomsoever should care to count them. Constant terror, perhaps, had had as much to do with his physical condition as had improper food. Tarzan noticed the change and was worried. He had hoped to see his balu wax sturdy and strong. His disappointment was great. In only one respect did Go-bu-balu seem to progress—he readily was mastering the language of the apes. Even now he and Tarzan could converse in a fairly satisfactory manner by supplementing the meager ape speech with signs; but for the most part, Go-bu-balu was silent other than to answer questions put to him. His great sorrow was yet too new and too poignant to be laid aside even momentarily. Always he pined for Momaya—shrewish, hideous, repulsive, perhaps, she would have been to you or me, but to Tibo she was mamma, the personification of that one great love which knows no selfishness and which does not consume itself in its own fires.

As the two hunted, or rather as Tarzan hunted and Go-bu-balu tagged along in his wake, the ape-man noticed many things and thought much. Once they came upon Sabor moaning in the tall grasses. About her romped and played two little balls of fur, but her eyes were for one which lay between her great forepaws and did not romp, one who never would romp again.

Tarzan read aright the anguish and the suffering of the huge mother cat. He had been minded to bait her. It was to do this that he had sneaked silently through the trees until he had come almost above her, but something held the ape-man as he saw the lioness grieving over her dead cub. With the acquisition of Go-bu-balu, Tarzan had come to realize the responsibilities and sorrows of parentage, without its joys. His heart went out to Sabor as it might not have done a few weeks before. As he watched her, there rose quite unbidden before him a vision of Momaya, the skewer through the septum of her nose, her pendulous under lip sagging beneath the weight which dragged it down. Tarzan saw not her unloveliness; he saw only the same anguish that was Sabor's, and he winced. That strange functioning of the mind which sometimes is called association of ideas snapped Teeka and Gazan before the ape-man's mental vision. What if one should come

589

and take Gazan from Teeka. Tarzan uttered a low and ominous growl as though Gazan were his own. Go-bu-balu glanced here and there apprehensively, thinking that Tarzan had espied an enemy. Sabor sprang suddenly to her feet, her yellow-green eyes blazing, her tail lashing as she cocked her ears, and raising her muzzle, sniffed the air for possible danger. The two little cubs, which had been playing, scampered quickly to her, and standing beneath her, peered out from between her forelegs, their big ears upstanding, their little heads cocked first upon one side and then upon the other.

With a shake of his black shock, Tarzan turned away and resumed his hunting in another direction; but all day there rose one after another, above the threshold of his objective mind, memory portraits of Sabor, of Momaya, and of Teeka—a lioness, a cannibal, and a she-ape, yet to the ape-man they were identical through motherhood.

It was noon of the third day when Momaya came within sight of the cave of Bukawai, the unclean. The old witch-doctor had rigged a framework of interlaced boughs to close the mouth of the cave from predatory beasts. This was now set to one side, and the black cavern beyond yawned mysterious and repellent. Momaya shivered as from a cold wind of the rainy season. No sign of life appeared about the cave, yet Momaya experienced that uncanny sensation as of unseen eyes regarding her malevolently. Again she shuddered. She tried to force her unwilling feet onward toward the cave, when from its depths issued an uncanny sound that was neither brute nor human, a weird sound that was akin to mirthless laughter.

With a stifled scream, Momaya turned and fled into the jungle. For a hundred yards she ran before she could control her terror, and then she paused, listening. Was all her labor, were all the terrors and dangers through which she had passed to go for naught? She tried to steel herself to return to the cave, but again fright overcame her.

Saddened, disheartened, she turned slowly upon the back trail toward the village of Mbonga. Her young shoulders now were drooped like those of an old woman who bears a great burden of many years with their accumulated pains and sorrows, and she walked with tired feet and a halting step. The spring of youth was gone from Momaya.

For another hundred yards she dragged her weary way, her brain half paralyzed from dumb terror and suffering, and then there came to her the memory of a little babe that suckled at her breast, and of a slim boy who romped, laughing, about her, and they were both Tibo—her Tibo!

Her shoulders straightened. She shook her savage head, and she turned about and walked boldly back to the mouth of the cave of Bukawai, the unclean—of Bukawai, the witch-doctor.

Again, from the interior of the cave came the hideous laughter that was not laughter. This time Momaya recognized it for what it was, the strange cry of a hyena. No more did she shudder, but she held her spear ready and called aloud to Bukawai to come out.

Instead of Bukawai came the repulsive head of a hyena. Momaya poked at it with her spear, and the ugly, sullen brute drew back with an angry growl. Again Momaya called Bukawai by name, and this time there came an answer in mumbling tones that were scarce more human than those of the beast.

"Who comes to Bukawai?" queried the voice.

"It is Momaya," replied the woman; "Momaya from the village of Mbonga, the chief.

"What do you want?"

"I want good medicine, better medicine than Mbonga's witch-doctor can make," replied Momaya. "The great, white, jungle god has stolen my Tibo, and I want medicine to bring him back, or to find where he is hidden that I may go and get him."

"Who is Tibo?" asked Bukawai.

Momaya told him.

"Bukawai's medicine is very strong," said the voice. "Five goats and a new sleeping mat are scarce enough in exchange for Bukawai's medicine."

"Two goats are enough," said Momaya, for the spirit of barter is strong in the breasts of the blacks.

EDGAR RICE BURROUGHS

The pleasure of haggling over the price was a sufficiently potent lure to draw Bukawai to the mouth of the cave. Momaya was sorry when she saw him that he had not remained within. There are some things too horrible, too hideous, too repulsive for description—Bukawai's face was of these. When Momaya saw him she understood why it was that he was almost inarticulate.

Beside him were two hyenas, which rumor had said were his only and constant companions. They made an excellent trio—the most repulsive of beasts with the most repulsive of humans.

"Five goats and a new sleeping mat," mumbled Bukawai.

"Two fat goats and a sleeping mat." Momaya raised her bid; but Bukawai was obdurate. He stuck for the five goats and the sleeping mat for a matter of half an hour, while the hyenas sniffed and growled and laughed hideously. Momaya was determined to give all that Bukawai asked if she could do no better, but haggling is second nature to black barterers, and in the end it partly repaid her, for a compromise finally was reached which included three fat goats, a new sleeping mat, and a piece of copper wire.

"Come back tonight," said Bukawai, "when the moon is two hours in the sky. Then will I make the strong medicine which shall bring Tibo back to you. Bring with you the three fat goats, the new sleeping mat, and the piece of copper wire the length of a large man's forearm."

"I cannot bring them," said Momaya. "You will have to come after them. When you have restored Tibo to me, you shall have them all at the village of Mbonga.

Bukawai shook his head.

"I will make no medicine," he said, "until I have the goats and the mat and the copper wire."

Momaya pleaded and threatened, but all to no avail. Finally, she turned away and started off through the jungle toward the village of Mbonga. How she could get three goats and a sleeping mat out of the village and through the jungle to the cave of Bukawai, she did not know, but that she would do it somehow she was quite positive—she would do it or die. Tibo must be restored to her.

Tarzan coming lazily through the jungle with little Go-bu-balu, caught the scent of Bara, the deer. Tarzan hungered for the flesh of Bara. Naught tickled his palate so greatly; but to stalk Bara with Go-bu-balu at his heels, was out of the question, so he hid the child in the crotch of a tree where the thick foliage screened him from view, and set off swiftly and silently upon the spoor of Bara.

Tibo alone was more terrified than Tibo even among the apes. Real and apparent dangers are less disconcerting than those which we imagine, and only the gods of his people knew how much Tibo imagined.

He had been but a short time in his hiding place when he heard something approaching through the jungle. He crouched closer to the limb upon which he lay and prayed that Tarzan would return quickly. His wide eyes searched the jungle in the direction of the moving creature.

What if it was a leopard that had caught his scent! It would be upon him in a minute. Hot tears flowed from the large eyes of little Tibo. The curtain of jungle foliage rustled close at hand. The thing was but a few paces from his tree! His eyes fairly popped from his black face as he watched for the appearance of the dread creature which presently would thrust a snarling countenance from between the vines and creepers.

And then the curtain parted and a woman stepped into full view. With a gasping cry, Tibo tumbled from his perch and raced toward her. Momaya suddenly started back and raised her spear, but a second later she cast it aside and caught the thin body in her strong arms.

Crushing it to her, she cried and laughed all at one and the same time, and hot tears of joy, mingled with the tears of Tibo, trickled down the crease between her naked breasts.

Disturbed by the noise so close at hand, there arose from his sleep in a near-by thicket Numa, the lion. He looked through the tangled underbrush and saw the black woman and her young. He licked his chops and measured the distance between them and himself. A short charge and a long leap would carry him upon them. He flicked the end of his tail and sighed.

A vagrant breeze, swirling suddenly in the wrong direction, carried the scent of Tarzan to the sensitive nostrils of Bara, the deer. There was a startled tensing of muscles and cocking of ears, a sudden dash, and

Tarzan's meat was gone. The ape-man angrily shook his head and turned back toward the spot where he had left Go-bu-balu. He came softly, as was his way. Before he reached the spot he heard strange sounds—the sound of a woman laughing and of a woman weeping, and the two which seemed to come from one throat were mingled with the convulsive sobbing of a child. Tarzan hastened, and when Tarzan hastened, only the birds and the wind went faster.

And as Tarzan approached the sounds, he heard another, a deep sigh. Momaya did not hear it, nor did Tibo; but the ears of Tarzan were as the ears of Bara, the deer. He heard the sigh, and he knew, so he unloosed the heavy spear which dangled at his back. Even as he sped through the branches of the trees, with the same ease that you or I might take out a pocket handkerchief as we strolled nonchalantly down a lazy country lane, Tarzan of the Apes took the spear from its thong that it might be ready against any emergency.

Numa, the lion, did not rush madly to attack. He reasoned again, and reason told him that already the prey was his, so he pushed his great bulk through the foliage and stood eyeing his meat with baleful, glaring eyes.

Momaya saw him and shrieked, drawing Tibo closer to her breast. To have found her child and to lose him, all in a moment! She raised her spear, throwing her hand far back of her shoulder. Numa roared and stepped slowly forward. Momaya cast her weapon. It grazed the tawny shoulder, inflicting a flesh wound which aroused all the terrific bestiality of the carnivore, and the lion charged.

Momaya tried to close her eyes, but could not. She saw the flashing swiftness of the huge, oncoming death, and then she saw something else. She saw a mighty, naked white man drop as from the heavens into the path of the charging lion. She saw the muscles of a great arm flash in the light of the equatorial sun as it filtered, dappling, through the foliage above. She saw a heavy hunting spear hurtle through the air to meet the lion in midleap.

Numa brought up upon his haunches, roaring terribly and striking at the spear which protruded from his breast. His great blows bent and twisted the weapon. Tarzan, crouching and with hunting knife in hand, circled warily about the frenzied cat. Momaya, wide-eyed, stood rooted to the spot, watching, fascinated.

In sudden fury Numa hurled himself toward the ape-man, but the wiry creature eluded the blundering charge, side-stepping quickly only to rush in upon his foe. Twice the hunting blade flashed in the air. Twice it fell upon the back of Numa, already weakening from the spear point so near his heart. The second stroke of the blade pierced far into the beast's spine, and with a last convulsive sweep of the fore-paws, in a vain attempt to reach his tormentor, Numa sprawled upon the ground, paralyzed and dying.

Bukawai, fearful lest he should lose any recompense, followed Momaya with the intention of persuading her to part with her ornaments of copper and iron against her return with the price of the medicine—to pay, as it were, for an option on his services as one pays a retaining fee to an attorney, for, like an attorney, Bukawai knew the value of his medicine and that it was well to collect as much as possible in advance.

The witch-doctor came upon the scene as Tarzan leaped to meet the lion's charge. He saw it all and marveled, guessing immediately that this must be the strange white demon concerning whom he had heard vague rumors before Momaya came to him.

Momaya, now that the lion was past harming her or hers, gazed with new terror upon Tarzan. It was he who had stolen her Tibo. Doubtless he would attempt to steal him again. Momaya hugged the boy close to her. She was determined to die this time rather than suffer Tibo to be taken from her again.

Tarzan eyed them in silence. The sight of the boy clinging, sobbing, to his mother aroused within his savage breast a melancholy loneliness. There was none thus to cling to Tarzan, who yearned so for the love of someone, of something.

At last Tibo looked up, because of the quiet that had fallen upon the jungle, and saw Tarzan. He did not shrink.

"Tarzan," he said, in the speech of the great apes of the tribe of Kerchak, "do not take me from Momaya, my mother. Do not take me again to the lair of the hairy, tree men, for I fear Taug and Gunto and the others. Let me stay with Momaya, O Tarzan, God of the Jungle! Let me stay with Momaya, my mother, and to the end of our days we will bless you and put food before the gates of the village of Mbonga that you may never hunger."

Tarzan sighed.

"Go," he said, "back to the village of Mbonga, and Tarzan will follow to see that no harm befalls you."

Tibo translated the words to his mother, and the two turned their backs upon the ape-man and started off toward home. In the heart of Momaya was a great fear and a great exultation, for never before had she walked with God, and never had she been so happy. She strained little Tibo to her, stroking his thin cheek. Tarzan saw and sighed again.

"For Teeka there is Teeka's balu," he soliloquized; "for Sabor there are balus, and for the she-Gomangani, and for Bara, and for Manu, and even for Pamba, the rat; but for Tarzan there can be none—neither a she nor a balu. Tarzan of the Apes is a man, and it must be that man walks alone."

Bukawai saw them go, and he mumbled through his rotting face, swearing a great oath that he would yet have the three fat goats, the new sleeping mat, and the bit of copper wire.

THE WITCH-DOCTOR SEEKS VENGEANCE

Lord Greystoke was hunting, or, to be more accurate, he was shooting pheasants at Chamston-Hedding. Lord Greystoke was immaculately and appropriately garbed—to the minutest detail he was vogue. To be sure, he was among the forward guns, not being considered a sporting shot, but what he lacked in skill he more than made up in appearance. At the end of the day he would, doubtless, have many birds to his credit, since he had two guns and a smart loader— many more birds than he could eat in a year, even had he been hungry, which he was not, having but just arisen from the breakfast table.

The beaters—there were twenty-three of them, in white smocks—had but just driven the birds into a patch of gorse, and were now circling to the opposite side that they might drive down toward the guns. Lord Greystoke was quite as excited as he ever permitted himself to become. There was an exhilaration in the sport that would not be denied. He felt his blood tingling through his veins as the beaters approached closer and closer to the birds. In a vague and stupid sort of way Lord Greystoke felt, as he always felt upon such occasions, that he was experiencing a sensation somewhat akin to a reversion to a prehistoric type—that the blood of an ancient forbear was coursing hot through him, a hairy, half-naked forbear who had lived by the hunt.

And far away in a matted equatorial jungle another Lord Greystoke, the real Lord Greystoke, hunted. By the standards which he knew, he, too, was vogue—utterly vogue, as was the primal ancestor before the first eviction. The day being sultry, the leopard skin had been left behind. The real Lord Greystoke had not two guns, to be sure, nor even one, neither did he have a smart loader; but he possessed something infinitely more efficacious than guns, or loaders, or even twenty-three beaters in white smocks—he possessed an appetite, an uncanny woodcraft, and muscles that were as steel springs.

Later that day, in England, a Lord Greystoke ate bountifully of things he had not killed, and he drank other things which were uncorked to the accompaniment of much noise. He patted his lips with snowy linen to remove the faint traces of his repast, quite ignorant of the fact that he was an impostor and that the rightful owner of his noble title was even then finishing his own dinner in far-off Africa. He was not using snowy linen, though. Instead he drew the back of a brown forearm and hand across his mouth and wiped his bloody fingers upon his thighs. Then he moved slowly through the jungle to the drinking place, where, upon all fours, he drank as drank his fellows, the other beasts of the jungle.

As he quenched his thirst, another denizen of the gloomy forest approached the stream along the path behind him. It was Numa, the lion, tawny of body and black of mane, scowling and sinister, rumbling out low, coughing roars. Tarzan of the Apes heard him long before he came within sight, but the ape-man went on with his drinking until he had had his fill; then he arose, slowly, with the easy grace of a creature of the wilds and all the quiet dignity that was his birthright.

Numa halted as he saw the man standing at the very spot where the king would drink. His jaws were parted, and his cruel eyes gleamed. He growled and advanced slowly. The man growled, too, backing slowly to one side, and watching, not the lion's face, but its tail. Should that commence to move from side to side in quick, nervous jerks, it would be well to be upon the alert, and should it rise suddenly erect, straight and stiff, then one might prepare to fight or flee; but it did neither, so Tarzan merely backed away and the lion came down and drank scarce fifty feet from where the man stood.

Tomorrow they might be at one another's throats, but today there existed one of those strange and inexplicable truces which so often are seen among the savage ones of the jungle. Before Numa had finished drinking, Tarzan had returned into the forest, and was swinging away in the direction of the village of Mbonga, the black chief.

It had been at least a moon since the ape-man had called upon the Gomangani. Not since he had restored little Tibo to his grief-stricken mother had the whim seized him to do so. The incident of the adopted balu was a closed one to Tarzan. He had sought to find something upon which to lavish such an affection as Teeka lavished upon her balu, but a short experience of the little black boy had made it quite plain to the ape-man that no such sentiment could exist between them.

The fact that he had for a time treated the little black as he might have treated a real balu of his own had in no way altered the vengeful sentiments with which he considered the murderers of Kala. The Gomangani were his deadly enemies, nor could they ever be aught else. Today he looked forward to some slight relief from the monotony of his existence in such excitement as he might derive from baiting the blacks.

It was not yet dark when he reached the village and took his place in the great tree overhanging the palisade. From beneath came a great wailing out of the depths of a near-by hut. The noise fell disagreeably upon Tarzan's ears—it jarred and grated. He did not like it, so he decided to go away for a while in the hopes that it might cease; but though he was gone for a couple of hours the wailing still continued when he returned.

With the intention of putting a violent termination to the annoying sound, Tarzan slipped silently from the tree into the shadows beneath. Creeping stealthily and keeping well in the cover of other huts, he approached that from which rose the sounds of lamentation. A fire burned brightly before the doorway as it did before other doorways in the village. A few females squatted about, occasionally adding their own mournful howlings to those of the master artist within.

The ape-man smiled a slow smile as he thought of the consternation which would follow the quick leap that would carry him among the females and into the full light of the fire. Then he would dart into the hut during the excitement, throttle the chief screamer, and be gone into the jungle before the blacks could gather their scattered nerves for an assault.

Many times had Tarzan behaved similarly in the village of Mbonga, the chief. His mysterious and unexpected appearances always filled the breasts of the poor, superstitious blacks with the panic of terror; never, it seemed, could they accustom themselves to the sight of him. It was this terror which lent to the adventures the spice of interest and amusement which the human mind of the ape-man craved. Merely to kill was not in itself sufficient. Accustomed to the sight of death, Tarzan found no great pleasure in it. Long since had he avenged the death of Kala, but in the accomplishment of it, he had learned the excitement and the pleasure to be derived from the baiting of the blacks. Of this he never tired.

It was just as he was about to spring forward with a savage roar that a figure appeared in the doorway of the hut. It was the figure of the wailer whom he had come to still, the figure of a young woman with a wooden skewer through the split septum of her nose, with a heavy metal ornament depending from her lower lip, which it had dragged down to hideous and repulsive deformity, with strange tattooing upon forehead, cheeks, and breasts, and a wonderful coiffure built up with mud and wire.

A sudden flare of the fire threw the grotesque figure into high relief, and Tarzan recognized her as Momaya, the mother of Tibo. The fire also threw out a fitful flame which carried to the shadows where

Tarzan lurked, picking out his light brown body from the surrounding darkness. Momaya saw him and knew him. With a cry, she leaped forward and Tarzan came to meet her. The other women, turning, saw him, too; but they did not come toward him. Instead they rose as one, shrieked as one, fled as one.

Momaya threw herself at Tarzan's feet, raising supplicating hands toward him and pouring forth from her mutilated lips a perfect cataract of words, not one of which the ape-man comprehended. For a moment he looked down upon the upturned, frightful face of the woman. He had come to slay, but that overwhelming torrent of speech filled him with consternation and with awe. He glanced about him apprehensively, then back at the woman. A revulsion of feeling seized him. He could not kill little Tibo's mother, nor could he stand and face this verbal geyser. With a quick gesture of impatience at the spoiling of his evening's entertainment, he wheeled and leaped away into the darkness. A moment later he was swinging through the black jungle night, the cries and lamentations of Momaya growing fainter in the distance.

It was with a sigh of relief that he finally reached a point from which he could no longer hear them, and finding a comfortable crotch high among the trees, composed himself for a night of dreamless slumber, while a prowling lion moaned and coughed beneath him, and in far-off England the other Lord Greystoke, with the assistance of a valet, disrobed and crawled between spotless sheets, swearing irritably as a cat meowed beneath his window.

As Tarzan followed the fresh spoor of Horta, the boar, the following morning, he came upon the tracks of two Gomangani, a large one and a small one. The ape-man, accustomed as he was to questioning closely all that fell to his perceptions, paused to read the story written in the soft mud of the game trail. You or I would have seen little of interest there, even if, by chance, we could have seen aught. Perhaps had one been there to point them out to us, we might have noted indentations in the mud, but there were countless indentations, one overlapping another into a confusion that would have been entirely meaningless to us. To Tarzan each told its own story. Tantor, the elephant, had passed that way as recently as three suns since. Numa had hunted here the night just gone, and Horta, the boar, had walked slowly along the trail within an hour; but what held Tarzan's attention was the spoor tale of the Gomangani. It told him that the day before an old man had gone toward the north in company with a little boy, and that with them had been two hyenas.

Tarzan scratched his head in puzzled incredulity. He could see by the overlapping of the footprints that the beasts had not been following the two, for sometimes one was ahead of them and one behind, and again both were in advance, or both were in the rear. It was very strange and quite inexplicable, especially where the spoor showed where the hyenas in the wider portions of the path had walked one on either side of the human pair, quite close to them. Then Tarzan read in the spoor of the smaller Gomangani a shrinking terror of the beast that brushed his side, but in that of the old man was no sign of fear.

At first Tarzan had been solely occupied by the remarkable juxtaposition of the spoor of Dango and Gomangani, but now his keen eyes caught something in the spoor of the little Gomangani which brought him to a sudden stop. It was as though, finding a letter in the road, you suddenly had discovered in it the familiar handwriting of a friend.

"Go-bu-balu!" exclaimed the ape-man, and at once memory flashed upon the screen of recollection the supplicating attitude of Momaya as she had hurled herself before him in the village of Mbonga the night before. Instantly all was explained—the wailing and lamentation, the pleading of the black mother, the sympathetic howling of the shes about the fire. Little Go-bu-balu had been stolen again, and this time by another than Tarzan. Doubtless the mother had thought that he was again in the power of Tarzan of the Apes, and she had been beseeching him to return her balu to her.

Yes, it was all quite plain now; but who could have stolen Go-bu-balu this time? Tarzan wondered, and he wondered, too, about the presence of Dango. He would investigate. The spoor was a day old and it ran toward the north. Tarzan set out to follow it. In places it was totally obliterated by the passage of many beasts, and where the way was rocky, even Tarzan of the Apes was almost baffled; but there was still the faint effluvium which clung to the human spoor, appreciable only to such highly trained perceptive powers as were Tarzan's.

It had all happened to little Tibo very suddenly and unexpectedly within the brief span of two suns. First had come Bukawai, the witch-doctor—Bukawai, the unclean—with the ragged bit of flesh which still clung to his rotting face. He had come alone and by day to the place at the river where Momaya went daily to wash her body and that of Tibo, her little boy. He had stepped out from behind a great bush quite close to Momaya, frightening little Tibo so that he ran screaming to his mother's protecting arms.

But Momaya, though startled, had wheeled to face the fearsome thing with all the savage ferocity of a she-tiger at bay. When she saw who it was, she breathed a sigh of partial relief, though she still clung tightly to Tibo.

"I have come," said Bukawai without preliminary, "for the three fat goats, the new sleeping mat, and the bit of copper wire as long as a tall man's arm."

"I have no goats for you," snapped Momaya, "nor a sleeping mat, nor any wire. Your medicine was never made. The white jungle god gave me back my Tibo. You had nothing to do with it."

"But I did," mumbled Bukawai through his fleshless jaws. "It was I who commanded the white jungle god to give back your Tibo."

Momaya laughed in his face. "Speaker of lies," she cried, "go back to your foul den and your hyenas. Go back and hide your stinking face in the belly of the mountain, lest the sun, seeing it, cover his face with a black cloud."

"I have come," reiterated Bukawai, "for the three fat goats, the new sleeping mat, and the bit of copper wire the length of a tall man's arm, which you were to pay me for the return of your Tibo."

"It was to be the length of a man's forearm," corrected Momaya, "but you shall have nothing, old thief. You would not make medicine until I had brought the payment in advance, and when I was returning to my village the great, white jungle god gave me back my Tibo—gave him to me out of the jaws of Numa. His medicine is true medicine— yours is the weak medicine of an old man with a hole in his face."

"I have come," repeated Bukawai patiently, "for the three fat—" But Momaya had not waited to hear more of what she already knew by heart. Clasping Tibo close to her side, she was hurrying away toward the palisaded village of Mbonga, the chief.

And the next day, when Momaya was working in the plantain field with others of the women of the tribe, and little Tibo had been playing at the edge of the jungle, casting a small spear in anticipation of the distant day when he should be a full-fledged warrior, Bukawai had come again.

Tibo had seen a squirrel scampering up the bole of a great tree. His childish mind had transformed it into the menacing figure of a hostile warrior. Little Tibo had raised his tiny spear, his heart filled with the savage blood lust of his race, as he pictured the night's orgy when he should dance about the corpse of his human kill as the women of his tribe prepared the meat for the feast to follow.

But when he cast the spear, he missed both squirrel and tree, losing his missile far among the tangled undergrowth of the jungle. However, it could be but a few steps within the forbidden labyrinth. The women were all about in the field. There were warriors on guard within easy hail, and so little Tibo boldly ventured into the dark place.

Just behind the screen of creepers and matted foliage lurked three horrid figures—an old, old man, black as the pit, with a face half eaten away by leprosy, his sharp-filed teeth, the teeth of a cannibal, showing yellow and repulsive through the great gaping hole where his mouth and nose had been. And beside him, equally hideous, stood two powerful hyenas—carrion-eaters consorting with carrion.

Tibo did not see them until, head down, he had forced his way through the thickly growing vines in search of his little spear, and then it was too late. As he looked up into the face of Bukawai, the old witch-doctor seized him, muffling his screams with a palm across his mouth. Tibo struggled futilely.

A moment later he was being hustled away through the dark and terrible jungle, the frightful old man still muffling his screams, and the two hideous hyenas pacing now on either side, now before, now behind, always prowling, always growling, snapping, snarling, or, worst of all, laughing hideously.

To little Tibo, who within his brief existence had passed through such experiences as are given to few to pass through in a lifetime, the northward journey was a nightmare of terror. He thought now of the time that he had been with the great, white jungle god, and he prayed with all his little soul that he might be back again with the white-skinned giant who consorted with the hairy tree men. Terror-stricken he had been then, but his surroundings had been nothing by comparison with those which he now endured.

The old man seldom addressed Tibo, though he kept up an almost continuous mumbling throughout the long day. Tibo caught repeated references to fat goats, sleeping mats, and pieces of copper wire. "Ten fat goats, ten fat goats," the old Negro would croon over and over again. By this little Tibo guessed that the price of his ransom had risen. Ten fat goats? Where would his mother get ten fat goats, or thin ones, either, for that matter, to buy back just a poor little boy? Mbonga would never let her have them, and Tibo knew that his father never had owned more than three goats at the same time in all his life. Ten fat goats! Tibo sniffled. The putrid old man would kill him and eat him, for the goats would never be forthcoming. Bukawai would throw his bones to the hyenas. The little black boy shuddered and became so weak that he almost fell in his tracks. Bukawai cuffed him on an ear and jerked him along.

After what seemed an eternity to Tibo, they arrived at the mouth of a cave between two rocky hills. The opening was low and narrow. A few saplings bound together with strips of rawhide closed it against stray beasts. Bukawai removed the primitive door and pushed Tibo within. The hyenas, snarling, rushed past him and were lost to view in the blackness of the interior. Bukawai replaced the saplings and seizing Tibo roughly by the arm, dragged him along a narrow, rocky passage. The floor was comparatively smooth, for the dirt which lay thick upon it had been trodden and tramped by many feet until few inequalities remained.

The passage was tortuous, and as it was very dark and the walls rough and rocky, Tibo was scratched and bruised from the many bumps he received. Bukawai walked as rapidly through the winding gallery as one would traverse a familiar lane by daylight. He knew every twist and turn as a mother knows the face of her child, and he seemed to be in a hurry. He jerked poor little Tibo possibly a trifle more ruthlessly than necessary even at the pace Bukawai set; but the old witch-doctor, an outcast from the society of man, diseased, shunned, hated, feared, was far from possessing an angelic temper. Nature had given him few of the kindlier characteristics of man, and these few Fate had eradicated entirely. Shrewd, cunning, cruel, vindictive, was Bukawai, the witch-doctor.

Frightful tales were whispered of the cruel tortures he inflicted upon his victims. Children were frightened into obedience by the threat of his name. Often had Tibo been thus frightened, and now he was reaping a grisly harvest of terror from the seeds his mother had innocently sown. The darkness, the presence of the dreaded witch-doctor, the pain of the contusions, with a haunting premonition of the future, and the fear of the hyenas combined to almost paralyze the child. He stumbled and reeled until Bukawai was dragging rather than leading him.

Presently Tibo saw a faint lightness ahead of them, and a moment later they emerged into a roughly circular chamber to which a little daylight filtered through a rift in the rocky ceiling. The hyenas were there ahead of them, waiting. As Bukawai entered with Tibo, the beasts slunk toward them, baring yellow fangs. They were hungry. Toward Tibo they came, and one snapped at his naked legs. Bukawai seized a stick from the floor of the chamber and struck a vicious blow at the beast, at the same time mumbling forth a volley of execrations. The hyena dodged and ran to the side of the chamber, where he stood growling. Bukawai took a step toward the creature, which bristled with rage at his approach. Fear and hatred shot from its evil eyes, but, fortunately for Bukawai, fear predominated.

Seeing that he was unnoticed, the second beast made a short, quick rush for Tibo. The child screamed and darted after the witch-doctor, who now turned his attention to the second hyena. This one he reached with his heavy stick, striking it repeatedly and driving it to the wall. There the two carrion-eaters commenced to circle the chamber while the human carrion, their master, now in a perfect frenzy of demoniacal rage, ran to and fro in an effort to intercept them, striking out with his cudgel and lashing them with his tongue, calling down upon them the curses of whatever gods and demons he could summon to memory, and describing in lurid figures the ignominy of their ancestors.

Several times one or the other of the beasts would turn to make a stand against the witch-doctor, and then Tibo would hold his breath in agonized terror, for never in his brief life had he seen such frightful hatred depicted upon the countenance of man or beast; but always fear overcame the rage of the savage creatures, so that they resumed their flight, snarling and bare-fanged, just at the moment that Tibo was certain they would spring at Bukawai's throat.

At last the witch-doctor tired of the futile chase. With a snarl quite as bestial as those of the beast, he turned toward Tibo. "I go to collect the ten fat goats, the new sleeping mat, and the two pieces of copper wire that your mother will pay for the medicine I shall make to bring you back to her," he said. "You will stay here. There," and he pointed toward the passage which they had followed to the chamber, "I will leave the hyenas. If you try to escape, they will eat you."

He cast aside the stick and called to the beasts. They came, snarling and slinking, their tails between their legs. Bukawai led them to the passage and drove them into it. Then he dragged a rude lattice into place before the opening after he, himself, had left the chamber. "This will keep them from you," he said. "If I do not get the ten fat goats and the other things, they shall at least have a few bones after I am through." And he left the boy to think over the meaning of his all-too-suggestive words.

When he was gone, Tibo threw himself upon the earth floor and broke into childish sobs of terror and loneliness. He knew that his mother had no ten fat goats to give and that when Bukawai returned, little Tibo would be killed and eaten. How long he lay there he did not know, but presently he was aroused by the growling of the hyenas. They had returned through the passage and were glaring at him from beyond the lattice. He could see their yellow eyes blazing through the darkness. They reared up and clawed at the barrier. Tibo shivered and withdrew to the opposite side of the chamber. He saw the lattice sag and sway to the attacks of the beasts. Momentarily he expected that it would fall inward, letting the creatures upon him.

Wearily the horror-ridden hours dragged their slow way. Night came, and for a time Tibo slept, but it seemed that the hungry beasts never slept. Always they stood just beyond the lattice growling their hideous growls or laughing their hideous laughs. Through the narrow rift in the rocky roof above him, Tibo could see a few stars, and once the moon crossed. At last daylight came again. Tibo was very hungry and thirsty, for he had not eaten since the morning before, and only once upon the long march had he been permitted to drink, but even hunger and thirst were almost forgotten in the terror of his position.

It was after daylight that the child discovered a second opening in the walls of the subterranean chamber, almost opposite that at which the hyenas still stood glaring hungrily at him. It was only a narrow slit in the rocky wall. It might lead in but a few feet, or it might lead to freedom! Tibo approached it and looked within. He could see nothing. He extended his arm into the blackness, but he dared not venture farther. Bukawai never would have left open a way of escape, Tibo reasoned, so this passage must lead either nowhere or to some still more hideous danger.

To the boy's fear of the actual dangers which menaced him—Bukawai and the two hyenas—his superstition added countless others quite too horrible even to name, for in the lives of the blacks, through the shadows of the jungle day and the black horrors of the jungle night, flit strange, fantastic shapes peopling the already hideously peopled forests with menacing figures, as though the lion and the leopard, the snake and the hyena, and the countless poisonous insects were not quite sufficient to strike terror to the hearts of the poor, simple creatures whose lot is cast in earth's most fearsome spot.

And so it was that little Tibo cringed not only from real menaces but from imaginary ones. He was afraid even to venture upon a road that might lead to escape, lest Bukawai had set to watch it some frightful demon of the jungle.

But the real menaces suddenly drove the imaginary ones from the boy's mind, for with the coming of daylight the half-famished hyenas renewed their efforts to break down the frail barrier which kept them from their prey. Rearing upon their hind feet they clawed and struck at the lattice. With wide eyes Tibo saw it sag and rock. Not for long, he knew, could it withstand the assaults of these two powerful and determined brutes. Already one corner had been forced past the rocky protuberance of the entrance way which had held it in place. A shaggy forearm protruded into the chamber. Tibo trembled as with ague, for he knew that the end was near.

Backing against the farther wall he stood flattened out as far from the beasts as he could get. He saw the lattice give still more. He saw a savage, snarling head forced past it, and grinning jaws snapping and gaping toward him. In another instant the pitiful fabric would fall inward, and the two would be upon him, rending his flesh from his bones, gnawing the bones themselves, fighting for possession of his entrails.

*

Bukawai came upon Momaya outside the palisade of Mbonga, the chief. At sight of him the woman drew back in revulsion, then she flew at him, tooth and nail; but Bukawai threatening her with a spear held her at a safe distance.

"Where is my baby?" she cried. "Where is my little Tibo?"

Bukawai opened his eyes in well-simulated amazement. "Your baby!" he exclaimed. "What should I know of him, other than that I rescued him from the white god of the jungle and have not yet received my pay. I come for the goats and the sleeping mat and the piece of copper wire the length of a tall man's arm from the shoulder to the tips of his fingers." "Offal of a hyena!" shrieked Momaya. "My child has been stolen, and you, rotting fragment of a man, have taken him. Return him to me or I shall tear your eyes from your head and feed your heart to the wild hogs."

Bukawai shrugged his shoulders. "What do I know about your child?" he asked. "I have not taken him. If he is stolen again, what should Bukawai know of the matter? Did Bukawai steal him before? No, the white jungle god stole him, and if he stole him once he would steal him again. It is nothing to me. I returned him to you before and I have come for my pay. If he is gone and you would have him returned, Bukawai will return him—for ten fat goats, a new sleeping mat and two pieces of copper wire the length of a tall man's arm from the shoulder to the tips of his fingers, and Bukawai will say nothing more about the goats and the sleeping mat and the copper wire which you were to pay for the first medicine."

"Ten fat goats!" screamed Momaya. "I could not pay you ten fat goats in as many years. Ten fat goats, indeed!"

"Ten fat goats," repeated Bukawai. "Ten fat goats, the new sleeping mat and two pieces of copper wire the length of—"

Momaya stopped him with an impatient gesture. "Wait! she cried. "I have no goats. You waste your breath. Stay here while I go to my man. He has but three goats, yet something may be done. Wait!"

Bukawai sat down beneath a tree. He felt quite content, for he knew that he should have either payment or revenge. He did not fear harm at the hands of these people of another tribe, although he well knew that they must fear and hate him. His leprosy alone would prevent their laying hands upon him, while his reputation as a witch-doctor rendered him doubly immune from attack. He was planning upon compelling them to drive the ten goats to the mouth of his cave when Momaya returned. With her were three warriors— Mbonga, the chief, Rabba Kega, the village witch-doctor, and Ibeto, Tibo's father. They were not pretty men even under ordinary circumstances, and now, with their faces marked by anger, they well might have inspired terror in the heart of anyone; but if Bukawai felt any fear, he did not betray it. Instead he greeted them with an insolent stare, intended to awe them, as they came and squatted in a semi-circle before him.

"Where is Ibeto's son?" asked Mbonga.

"How should I know?" returned Bukawai. "Doubtless the white devil-god has him. If I am paid I will make strong medicine and then we shall know where is Ibeto's son, and shall get him back again. It was my medicine which got him back the last time, for which I got no pay."

"I have my own witch-doctor to make medicine," replied Mbonga with dignity.

Bukawai sneered and rose to his feet. "Very well," he said, "let him make his medicine and see if he can bring Ibeto's son back." He took a few steps away from them, and then he turned angrily back. "His medicine will not bring the child back—that I know, and I also know that when you find him it will be too late for any medicine to bring him back, for he will be dead. This have I just found out, the ghost of my father's sister but now came to me and told me."

Now Mbonga and Rabba Kega might not take much stock in their own magic, and they might even be skeptical as to the magic of another; but there was always a chance of *something* being in it, especially if it were not their own. Was it not well known that old Bukawai had speech with the demons themselves and that two even lived with him in the forms of hyenas! Still they must not accede too hastily. There was the price to be considered, and Mbonga had no intention of parting lightly with ten goats to obtain the return of a single little boy who might die of smallpox long before he reached a warrior's estate.

"Wait," said Mbonga. "Let us see some of your magic, that we may know if it be good magic. Then we can talk about payment. Rabba Kega will make some magic, too. We will see who makes the best magic. Sit down, Bukawai."

"The payment will be ten goats—fat goats—a new sleeping mat and two pieces of copper wire the length of a tall man's arm from the shoulder to the ends of his fingers, and it will be made in advance, the goats being driven to my cave. Then will I make the medicine, and on the second day the boy will be returned to his mother. It cannot be done more quickly than that because it takes time to make such strong medicine."

"Make us some medicine now," said Mbonga. "Let us see what sort of medicine you make."

"Bring me fire," replied Bukawai, "and I will make you a little magic."

Momaya was dispatched for the fire, and while she was away Mbonga dickered with Bukawai about the price. Ten goats, he said, was a high price for an able-bodied warrior. He also called Bukawai's attention to the fact that he, Mbonga, was very poor, that his people were very poor, and that ten goats were at least eight too many, to say nothing of a new sleeping mat and the copper wire; but Bukawai was adamant. His medicine was very expensive and he would have to give at least five goats to the gods who helped him make it. They were still arguing when Momaya returned with the fire.

Bukawai placed a little on the ground before him, took a pinch of powder from a pouch at his side and sprinkled it on the embers. A cloud of smoke rose with a puff. Bukawai closed his eyes and rocked back and forth. Then he made a few passes in the air and pretended to swoon. Mbonga and the others were much impressed. Rabba Kega grew nervous. He saw his reputation waning. There was some fire left in the vessel which Momaya had brought. He seized the vessel, dropped a handful of dry leaves into it while no one was watching and then uttered a frightful scream which drew the attention of Bukawai's audience to him. It also brought Bukawai quite miraculously out of his swoon, but when the old witch-doctor saw the reason for the disturbance he quickly relapsed into unconsciousness before anyone discovered his *faux pas*.

Rabba Kega, seeing that he had the attention of Mbonga, Ibeto, and Momaya, blew suddenly into the vessel, with the result that the leaves commenced to smolder, and smoke issued from the mouth of the receptacle. Rabba Kega was careful to hold it so that none might see the dry leaves. Their eyes opened wide at this remarkable demonstration of the village witch-doctor's powers. The latter, greatly elated, let himself out. He shouted, jumped up and down, and made frightful grimaces; then he put his face close over the mouth of the vessel and appeared to be communing with the spirits within.

It was while he was thus engaged that Bukawai came out of his trance, his curiosity finally having gotten the better of him. No one was paying him the slightest attention. He blinked his one eye angrily, then he, too, let out a loud roar, and when he was sure that Mbonga had turned toward him, he stiffened rigidly and made spasmodic movements with his arms and legs.

"I see him!" he cried. "He is far away. The white devil-god did not get him. He is alone and in great danger; but," he added, "if the ten fat goats and the other things are paid to me quickly there is yet time to save him."

Rabba Kega had paused to listen. Mbonga looked toward him. The chief was in a quandary. He did not know which medicine was the better. "What does your magic tell you?" he asked of Rabba Kega.

"I, too, see him," screamed Rabba Kega; "but he is not where Bukawai says he is. He is dead at the bottom of the river."

At this Momaya commenced to howl loudly.

Tarzan had followed the spoor of the old man, the two hyenas, and the little black boy to the mouth of the cave in the rocky canon between the two hills. Here he paused a moment before the sapling barrier which Bukawai had set up, listening to the snarls and growls which came faintly from the far recesses of the cavern.

Presently, mingled with the beastly cries, there came faintly to the keen ears of the ape-man, the agonized moan of a child. No longer did Tarzan hesitate. Hurling the door aside, he sprang into the dark opening. Narrow and black was the corridor; but long use of his eyes in the Stygian blackness of the jungle nights had given to the ape-man something of the nocturnal visionary powers of the wild things with which he had consorted since babyhood.

He moved rapidly and yet with caution, for the place was dark, unfamiliar and winding. As he advanced, he heard more and more loudly the savage snarls of the two hyenas, mingled with the scraping and scratching of their paws upon wood. The moans of a child grew in volume, and Tarzan recognized in them the voice of the little black boy he once had sought to adopt as his balu.

There was no hysteria in the ape-man's advance. Too accustomed was he to the passing of life in the jungle to be greatly wrought even by the death of one whom he knew; but the lust for battle spurred him on. He was only a wild beast at heart and his wild beast's heart beat high in anticipation of conflict.

In the rocky chamber of the hill's center, little Tibo crouched low against the wall as far from the hunger-crazed beasts as he could drag himself. He saw the lattice giving to the frantic clawing of the hyenas. He knew that in a few minutes his little life would flicker out horribly beneath the rending, yellow fangs of these loathsome creatures.

Beneath the buffetings of the powerful bodies, the lattice sagged inward, until, with a crash it gave way, letting the carnivora in upon the boy. Tibo cast one affrighted glance toward them, then closed his eyes and buried his face in his arms, sobbing piteously.

For a moment the hyenas paused, caution and cowardice holding them from their prey. They stood thus glaring at the lad, then slowly, stealthily, crouching, they crept toward him. It was thus that Tarzan came upon them, bursting into the chamber swiftly and silently; but not so silently that the keen-eared beasts did not note his coming. With angry growls they turned from Tibo upon the ape-man, as, with a smile upon his lips, he ran toward them. For an instant one of the animals stood its ground; but the ape-man did not deign even to draw his hunting knife against despised Dango. Rushing in upon the brute he grasped it by the scruff of the neck, just as it attempted to dodge past him, and hurled it across the cavern after its fellow which already was slinking into the corridor, bent upon escape.

Then Tarzan picked Tibo from the floor, and when the child felt human hands upon him instead of the paws and fangs of the hyenas, he rolled his eyes upward in surprise and incredulity, and as they fell upon Tarzan, sobs of relief broke from the childish lips and his hands clutched at his deliverer as though the white devil-god was not the most feared of jungle creatures.

When Tarzan came to the cave mouth the hyenas were nowhere in sight, and after permitting Tibo to quench his thirst in the spring which rose near by, he lifted the boy to his shoulders and set off toward the jungle at a rapid trot, determined to still the annoying howlings of Momaya as quickly as possible, for he shrewdly had guessed that the absence of her balu was the cause of her lamentation.

"He is not dead at the bottom of the river," cried Bukawai. "What does this fellow know about making magic? Who is he, anyway, that he dare say Bukawai's magic is not good magic? Bukawai sees Momaya's son. He is far away and alone and in great danger. Hasten then with the ten fat goats, the—"

But he got no further. There was a sudden interruption from above, from the branches of the very tree beneath which they squatted, and as the five blacks looked up they almost swooned in fright as they saw the great, white devil-god looking down upon them; but before they could flee they saw another face, that of the lost little Tibo, and his face was laughing and very happy.

And then Tarzan dropped fearlessly among them, the boy still upon his back, and deposited him before his mother. Momaya, Ibeto, Rabba Kega, and Mbonga were all crowding around the lad trying to question him at the same time. Suddenly Momaya turned ferociously to fall upon Bukawai, for the boy had told her all that he had suffered at the hands of the cruel old man; but Bukawai was no longer there—he had required no recourse to black art to assure him that the vicinity of Momaya would be no healthful place for him after Tibo had told his story, and now he was running through the jungle as fast as his old legs would carry him toward the distant lair where he knew no black would dare pursue him.

Tarzan, too, had vanished, as he had a way of doing, to the mystification of the blacks. Then Momaya's eyes lighted upon Rabba Kega. The village witch-doctor saw something in those eyes of hers which boded no good to him, and backed away.

"So my Tibo is dead at the bottom of the river, is he?" the woman shrieked. "And he's far away and alone and in great danger, is he? Magic!" The scorn which Momaya crowded into that single word would have done credit to a Thespian of the first magnitude. "Magic, indeed!" she screamed. "Momaya will show you some magic of her own," and with that she seized upon a broken limb and struck Rabba Kega across the head. With a howl of pain, the man turned and fled, Momaya pursuing him and beating him across the shoulders, through the gateway and up the length of the village street, to the intense amusement of the warriors, the women, and the children who were so fortunate as to witness the spectacle, for one and all feared Rabba Kega, and to fear is to hate.

Thus it was that to his host of passive enemies, Tarzan of the Apes added that day two active foes, both of whom remained awake long into the night planning means of revenge upon the white devil-god who had brought them into ridicule and disrepute, but with their most malevolent schemings was mingled a vein of real fear and awe that would not down.

Young Lord Greystoke did not know that they planned against him, nor, knowing, would have cared. He slept as well that night as he did on any other night, and though there was no roof above him, and no doors to lock against intruders, he slept much better than his noble relative in England, who had eaten altogether too much lobster and drank too much wine at dinner that night.

THE END OF BUKAWAI

When Tarzan of the Apes was still but a boy he had learned, among other things, to fashion pliant ropes of fibrous jungle grass. Strong and tough were the ropes of Tarzan, the little Tarmangani. Tublat, his foster father, would have told you this much and more. Had you tempted him with a handful of fat caterpillars he even might have sufficiently unbended to narrate to you a few stories of the many indignities which Tarzan had heaped upon him by means of his hated rope; but then Tublat always worked himself into such a frightful rage when he devoted any considerable thought either to the rope or to Tarzan, that it might not have proved comfortable for you to have remained close enough to him to hear what he had to say.

So often had that snakelike noose settled unexpectedly over Tublat's head, so often had he been jerked ridiculously and painfully from his feet when he was least looking for such an occurrence, that there is little wonder he found scant space in his savage heart for love of his white-skinned foster child, or the inventions thereof. There had been other times, too, when Tublat had swung helplessly in midair, the noose tightening about his neck, death staring him in the face, and little Tarzan dancing upon a near-by limb, taunting him and making unseemly grimaces.

Then there had been another occasion in which the rope had figured prominently—an occasion, and the only one connected with the rope, which Tublat recalled with pleasure. Tarzan, as active in brain as he was in body, was always inventing new ways in which to play. It was through the medium of play that he learned much during his childhood. This day he learned something, and that he did not lose his life in the learning of it, was a matter of great surprise to Tarzan, and the fly in the ointment, to Tublat.

The man-child had, in throwing his noose at a playmate in a tree above him, caught a projecting branch instead. When he tried to shake it loose it but drew the tighter. Then Tarzan started to climb the rope to remove it from the branch. When he was part way up a frolicsome playmate seized that part of the rope which lay upon the ground and ran off with it as far as he could go. When Tarzan screamed at him to desist, the young ape released the rope a little and then drew it tight again. The result was to impart a swinging motion to Tarzan's body which the ape-boy suddenly realized was a new and pleasurable form of play. He urged the ape to continue until Tarzan was swinging to and fro as far as the short length of rope would permit, but the distance was not great enough, and, too, he was not far enough above the ground to give the necessary thrills which add so greatly to the pastimes of the young.

So he clambered to the branch where the noose was caught and after removing it carried the rope far aloft and out upon a long and powerful branch. Here he again made it fast, and taking the loose end in his hand, clambered quickly down among the branches as far as the rope would permit him to go; then he swung out upon the end of it, his lithe, young body turning and twisting—a human bob upon a pendulum of grass—thirty feet above the ground.

Ah, how delectable! This was indeed a new play of the first magnitude. Tarzan was entranced. Soon he discovered that by wriggling his body in just the right way at the proper time he could diminish or accelerate his oscillation, and, being a boy, he chose, naturally, to accelerate. Presently he was swinging far and wide, while below him, the apes of the tribe of Kerchak looked on in mild amaze.

Had it been you or I swinging there at the end of that grass rope, the thing which presently happened would not have happened, for we could not have hung on so long as to have made it possible; but Tarzan was quite as much at home swinging by his hands as he was standing upon his feet, or, at least, almost. At any rate he felt no fatigue long after the time that an ordinary mortal would have been numb with the strain of the physical exertion. And this was his undoing.

Tublat was watching him as were others of the tribe. Of all the creatures of the wild, there was none Tublat so cordially hated as he did this hideous, hairless, white-skinned, caricature of an ape. But for Tarzan's nimbleness, and the zealous watchfulness of savage Kala's mother love, Tublat would long since have rid himself of this stain upon his family escutcheon. So long had it been since Tarzan became a member of the tribe, that Tublat had forgotten the circumstances surrounding the entrance of the jungle waif into his family, with the result that he now imagined that Tarzan was his own offspring, adding greatly to his chagrin.

Wide and far swung Tarzan of the Apes, until at last, as he reached the highest point of the arc the rope, which rapidly had frayed on the rough bark of the tree limb, parted suddenly. The watching apes saw the smooth, brown body shoot outward, and down, plummet-like. Tublat leaped high in the air, emitting what in a human being would have been an exclamation of delight. This would be the end of Tarzan and most of Tublat's troubles. From now on he could lead his life in peace and security.

Tarzan fell quite forty feet, alighting on his back in a thick bush. Kala was the first to reach his side—ferocious, hideous, loving Kala. She had seen the life crushed from her own balu in just such a fall years before. Was she to lose this one too in the same way? Tarzan was lying quite still when she found him, embedded deeply in the bush. It took Kala several minutes to disentangle him and drag him forth; but he was not killed. He was not even badly injured. The bush had broken the force of the fall. A cut upon the back of his head showed where he had struck the tough stem of the shrub and explained his unconsciousness.

In a few minutes he was as active as ever. Tublat was furious. In his rage he snapped at a fellow-ape without first discovering the identity of his victim, and was badly mauled for his ill temper, having chosen to vent his spite upon a husky and belligerent young bull in the full prime of his vigor.

But Tarzan had learned something new. He had learned that continued friction would wear through the strands of his rope, though it was many years before this knowledge did more for him than merely to keep him from swinging too long at a time, or too far above the ground at the end of his rope.

The day came, however, when the very thing that had once all but killed him proved the means of saving his life.

He was no longer a child, but a mighty jungle male. There was none now to watch over him, solicitously, nor did he need such. Kala was dead. Dead, too, was Tublat, and though with Kala passed the one creature that ever really had loved him, there were still many who hated him after Tublat departed unto the arms of his fathers. It was not that he was more cruel or more savage than they that they hated him, for though he was both cruel and savage as were the beasts, his fellows, yet too was he often tender, which they never were. No, the thing which brought Tarzan most into disrepute with those who did not like him, was the possession and practice of a characteristic which they had not and could not understand— the human sense of humor. In Tarzan it was a trifle broad, perhaps, manifesting itself in rough and painful practical jokes upon his friends and cruel baiting of his enemies.

But to neither of these did he owe the enmity of Bukawai, the witch-doctor, who dwelt in the cave between the two hills far to the north of the village of Mbonga, the chief. Bukawai was jealous of Tarzan, and Bukawai it was who came near proving the undoing of the ape-man. For months Bukawai had nursed his hatred while revenge seemed remote indeed, since Tarzan of the Apes frequented another part of the jungle, miles away from the lair of Bukawai. Only once had the black witch-doctor seen the devil-god, as he was most often called among the blacks, and upon that occasion Tarzan had robbed him of a fat fee, at the same time putting the lie in the mouth of Bukawai, and making his medicine seem poor medicine. All this Bukawai never could forgive, though it seemed unlikely that the opportunity would come to be revenged.

Yet it did come, and quite unexpectedly. Tarzan was hunting far to the north. He had wandered away from the tribe, as he did more and more often as he approached maturity, to hunt alone for a few days. As a child he had enjoyed romping and playing with the young apes, his companions; but now these play-fellows of his had grown to surly, lowering bulls, or to touchy, suspicious mothers, jealously guarding helpless balus. So Tarzan found in his own man-mind a greater and a truer companionship than any or all of the apes of Kerchak could afford him.

This day, as Tarzan hunted, the sky slowly became overcast. Torn clouds, whipped to ragged streamers, fled low above the tree tops. They reminded Tarzan of frightened antelope fleeing the charge of a hungry lion. But though the light clouds raced so swiftly, the jungle was motionless. Not a leaf quivered and the silence was a great, dead weight— insupportable. Even the insects seemed stilled by apprehension of some frightful thing impending, and the larger things were soundless. Such a forest, such a jungle might have stood there in the beginning of that unthinkably far-gone age before God peopled the world with life, when there were no sounds because there were no ears to hear.

And over all lay a sickly, pallid ocher light through which the scourged clouds raced. Tarzan had seen all these conditions many times before, yet he never could escape a strange feeling at each recurrence of them. He knew no fear, but in the face of Nature's manifestations of her cruel, immeasurable powers, he felt very small—very small and very lonely.

Now he heard a low moaning, far away. "The lions seek their prey," he murmured to himself, looking up once again at the swift-flying clouds. The moaning rose to a great volume of sound. "They come!" said Tarzan of the Apes, and sought the shelter of a thickly foliaged tree. Quite suddenly the trees bent their tops simultaneously as though God had stretched a hand from the heavens and pressed His flat palm down upon the world. "They pass!" whispered Tarzan. "The lions pass." Then came a vivid flash of lightning, followed by deafening thunder. "The lions have sprung," cried Tarzan, "and now they roar above the bodies of their kills."

The trees were waving wildly in all directions now, a perfectly demoniacal wind threshed the jungle pitilessly. In the midst of it the rain came—not as it comes upon us of the northlands, but in a sudden, choking, blinding deluge. "The blood of the kill," thought Tarzan, huddling himself closer to the bole of the great tree beneath which he stood.

He was close to the edge of the jungle, and at a little distance he had seen two hills before the storm broke; but now he could see nothing. It amused him to look out into the beating rain, searching for the two hills and imagining that the torrents from above had washed them away, yet he knew that presently the rain would cease, the sun come out again and all be as it was before, except where a few branches had fallen and here and there some old and rotted patriarch had crashed back to enrich the soil upon which he had fatted for, maybe, centuries. All about him branches and leaves filled the air or fell to earth, torn away by the strength of the tornado and the weight of the water upon them. A gaunt corpse toppled and fell a few yards away; but Tarzan was protected from all these dangers by the wide-spreading branches of the sturdy young giant beneath which his jungle craft had guided him. Here there was but a single danger, and that a remote one. Yet it came. Without warning the tree above him was riven by lightning, and when the rain ceased and the sun came out Tarzan lay stretched as he had fallen, upon his face amidst the wreckage of the jungle giant that should have shielded him.

Bukawai came to the entrance of his cave after the rain and the storm had passed and looked out upon the scene. From his one eye Bukawai could see; but had he had a dozen eyes he could have found no beauty in the fresh sweetness of the revivified jungle, for to such things, in the chemistry of temperament, his brain failed to react; nor, even had he had a nose, which he had not for years, could he have found enjoyment or sweetness in the clean-washed air.

At either side of the leper stood his sole and constant companions, the two hyenas, sniffing the air. Presently one of them uttered a low growl and with flattened head started, sneaking and wary, toward the jungle. The other followed. Bukawai, his curiosity aroused, trailed after them, in his hand a heavy knob-stick.

The hyenas halted a few yards from the prostrate Tarzan, sniffing and growling. Then came Bukawai, and at first he could not believe the witness of his own eyes; but when he did and saw that it was indeed the devil-god his rage knew no bounds, for he thought him dead and himself cheated of the revenge he had so long dreamed upon.

The hyenas approached the ape-man with bared fangs. Bukawai, with an inarticulate scream, rushed upon them, striking cruel and heavy blows with his knob-stick, for there might still be life in the apparently lifeless form. The beasts, snapping and snarling, half turned upon their master and their tormentor, but long fear still held them from his putrid throat. They slunk away a few yards and squatted upon their haunches, hatred and baffled hunger gleaming from their savage eyes.

Bukawai stooped and placed his ear above the ape-man's heart. It still beat. As well as his sloughed features could register pleasure they did so; but it was not a pretty sight. At the ape-man's side lay his long, grass rope. Quickly Bukawai bound the limp arms behind his prisoner's back, then he raised him to one of his shoulders, for, though Bukawai was old and diseased, he was still a strong man. The hyenas fell in behind as the witch-doctor set off toward the cave, and through the long black corridors they followed as Bukawai bore his victim into the bowels of the hills. Through subterranean chambers, connected by winding passageways, Bukawai staggered with his load. At a sudden turning of the corridor, daylight flooded them and Bukawai stepped out into a small, circular basin in the hill, apparently the crater of an ancient volcano, one of those which never reached the dignity of a mountain and are little more than lava-rimmed pits closed to the earth's surface.

Steep walls rimmed the cavity. The only exit was through the passageway by which Bukawai had entered. A few stunted trees grew upon the rocky floor. A hundred feet above could be seen the ragged lips of this cold, dead mouth of hell.

Bukawai propped Tarzan against a tree and bound him there with his own grass rope, leaving his hands free but securing the knots in such a way that the ape-man could not reach them. The hyenas slunk to and fro, growling. Bukawai hated them and they hated him. He knew that they but waited for the time when he should be helpless, or when their hatred should rise to such a height as to submerge their cringing fear of him.

In his own heart was not a little fear of these repulsive creatures, and because of that fear, Bukawai always kept the beasts well fed, often hunting for them when their own forages for food failed, but ever was he cruel to them with the cruelty of a little brain, diseased, bestial, primitive.

He had had them since they were puppies. They had known no other life than that with him, and though they went abroad to hunt, always they returned. Of late Bukawai had come to believe that they returned not so much from habit as from a fiendish patience which would submit to every indignity and pain rather than forego the final vengeance, and Bukawai needed but little imagination to picture what that vengeance would be. Today he would see for himself what his end would be; but another should impersonate Bukawai.

When he had trussed Tarzan securely, Bukawai went back into the corridor, driving the hyenas ahead of him, and pulling across the opening a lattice of laced branches, which shut the pit from the cave during the night that Bukawai might sleep in security, for then the hyenas were penned in the crater that they might not sneak upon a sleeping Bukawai in the darkness.

Bukawai returned to the outer cave mouth, filled a vessel with water at the spring which rose in the little canon close at hand and returned toward the pit. The hyenas stood before the lattice looking hungrily toward Tarzan. They had been fed in this manner before.

With his water, the witch-doctor approached Tarzan and threw a portion of the contents of the vessel in the ape-man's face. There was fluttering of the eyelids, and at the second application Tarzan opened his eyes and looked about.

"Devil-god," cried Bukawai, "I am the great witch-doctor. My medicine is strong. Yours is weak. If it is not, why do you stay tied here like a goat that is bait for lions?"

Tarzan understood nothing the witch-doctor said, therefore he did not reply, but only stared straight at Bukawai with cold and level gaze. The hyenas crept up behind him. He heard them growl; but he did not even turn his head. He was a beast with a man's brain. The beast in him refused to show fear in the face of a death which the man-mind already admitted to be inevitable.

Bukawai, not yet ready to give his victim to the beasts, rushed upon the hyenas with his knob-stick. There was a short scrimmage in which the brutes came off second best, as they always did. Tarzan watched it. He saw and realized the hatred which existed between the two animals and the hideous semblance of a man.

With the hyenas subdued, Bukawai returned to the baiting of Tarzan; but finding that the ape-man understood nothing he said, the witch-doctor finally desisted. Then he withdrew into the corridor and pulled the latticework barrier across the opening. He went back into the cave and got a sleeping mat, which he brought to the opening, that he might lie down and watch the spectacle of his revenge in comfort.

The hyenas were sneaking furtively around the ape-man. Tarzan strained at his bonds for a moment, but soon realized that the rope he had braided to hold Numa, the lion, would hold him quite as successfully. He did not wish to die; but he could look death in the face now as he had many times before without a quaver.

As he pulled upon the rope he felt it rub against the small tree about which it was passed. Like a flash of the cinematograph upon the screen, a picture was flashed before his mind's eye from the storehouse of his memory. He saw a lithe, boyish figure swinging high above the ground at the end of a rope. He saw many apes watching from below, and then he saw the rope part and the boy hurtle downward toward the ground. Tarzan smiled. Immediately he commenced to draw the rope rapidly back and forth across the tree trunk.

EDGAR RICE BURROUGHS

The hyenas, gaining courage, came closer. They sniffed at his legs; but when he struck at them with his free arms they slunk off. He knew that with the growth of hunger they would attack. Coolly, methodically, without haste, Tarzan drew the rope back and forth against the rough trunk of the small tree.

In the entrance to the cavern Bukawai fell asleep. He thought it would be some time before the beasts gained sufficient courage or hunger to attack the captive. Their growls and the cries of the victim would awaken him. In the meantime he might as well rest, and he did.

Thus the day wore on, for the hyenas were not famished, and the rope with which Tarzan was bound was a stronger one than that of his boyhood, which had parted so quickly to the chafing of the rough tree bark. Yet, all the while hunger was growing upon the beasts and the strands of the grass rope were wearing thinner and thinner. Bukawai slept.

It was late afternoon before one of the beasts, irritated by the gnawing of appetite, made a quick, growling dash at the ape-man. The noise awoke Bukawai. He sat up quickly and watched what went on within the crater. He saw the hungry hyena charge the man, leaping for the unprotected throat. He saw Tarzan reach out and seize the growling animal, and then he saw the second beast spring for the devil-god's shoulder. There was a mighty heave of the great, smooth-skinned body. Rounded muscles shot into great, tensed piles beneath the brown hide—the ape-man surged forward with all his weight and all his great strength—the bonds parted, and the three were rolling upon the floor of the crater snarling, snapping, and rending.

Bukawai leaped to his feet. Could it be that the devil-god was to prevail against his servants? Impossible! The creature was unarmed, and he was down with two hyenas on top of him; but Bukawai did not know Tarzan.

The ape-man fastened his fingers upon the throat of one of the hyenas and rose to one knee, though the other beast tore at him frantically in an effort to pull him down. With a single hand Tarzan held the one, and with the other hand he reached forth and pulled toward him the second beast.

And then Bukawai, seeing the battle going against his forces, rushed forward from the cavern brandishing his knob-stick. Tarzan saw him coming, and rising now to both feet, a hyena in each hand, he hurled one of the foaming beasts straight at the witch-doctor's head. Down went the two in a snarling, biting heap. Tarzan tossed the second hyena across the crater, while the first gnawed at the rotting face of its master; but this did not suit the ape-man. With a kick he sent the beast howling after its companion, and springing to the side of the prostrate witch-doctor, dragged him to his feet.

Bukawai, still conscious, saw death, immediate and terrible, in the cold eyes of his captor, so he turned upon Tarzan with teeth and nails. The ape-man shuddered at the proximity of that raw face to his. The hyenas had had enough and disappeared through the small aperture leading into the cave. Tarzan had little difficulty in overpowering and binding Bukawai. Then he led him to the very tree to which he had been bound; but in binding Bukawai, Tarzan saw to it that escape after the same fashion that he had escaped would be out of the question; then he left him.

As he passed through the winding corridors and the subterranean apartments, Tarzan saw nothing of the hyenas.

"They will return," he said to himself.

In the crater between the towering walls Bukawai, cold with terror, trembled, trembled as with ague.

"They will return!" he cried, his voice rising to a fright-filled shriek.

And they did.

THE LION

Numa, the lion, crouched behind a thorn bush close beside the drinking pool where the river eddied just below the bend. There was a ford there and on either bank a well-worn trail, broadened far out at the river's brim, where, for countless centuries, the wild things of the jungle and of the plains beyond had come down to drink, the carnivora with bold and fearless majesty, the herbivora timorous, hesitating, fearful.

607

Numa, the lion, was hungry, he was very hungry, and so he was quite silent now. On his way to the drinking place he had moaned often and roared not a little; but as he neared the spot where he would lie in wait for Bara, the deer, or Horta, the boar, or some other of the many luscious-fleshed creatures who came hither to drink, he was silent. It was a grim, a terrible silence, shot through with yellow-green light of ferocious eyes, punctuated with undulating tremors of sinuous tail.

It was Pacco, the zebra, who came first, and Numa, the lion, could scarce restrain a roar of anger, for of all the plains people, none are more wary than Pacco, the zebra. Behind the black-striped stallion came a herd of thirty or forty of the plump and vicious little horselike beasts. As he neared the river, the leader paused often, cocking his ears and raising his muzzle to sniff the gentle breeze for the tell-tale scent spoor of the dread flesh-eaters.

Numa shifted uneasily, drawing his hind quarters far beneath his tawny body, gathering himself for the sudden charge and the savage assault. His eyes shot hungry fire. His great muscles quivered to the excitement of the moment.

Pacco came a little nearer, halted, snorted, and wheeled. There was a pattering of scurrying hoofs and the herd was gone; but Numa, the lion, moved not. He was familiar with the ways of Pacco, the zebra. He knew that he would return, though many times he might wheel and fly before he summoned the courage to lead his harem and his offspring to the water. There was the chance that Pacco might be frightened off entirely. Numa had seen this happen before, and so he became almost rigid lest he be the one to send them galloping, waterless, back to the plain.

Again and again came Pacco and his family, and again and again did they turn and flee; but each time they came closer to the river, until at last the plump stallion dipped his velvet muzzle daintily into the water. The others, stepping warily, approached their leader. Numa selected a sleek, fat filly and his flaming eyes burned greedily as they feasted upon her, for Numa, the lion, loves scarce anything better than the meat of Pacco, perhaps because Pacco is, of all the grass-eaters, the most difficult to catch.

Slowly the lion rose, and as he rose, a twig snapped beneath one of his great, padded paws. Like a shot from a rifle he charged upon the filly; but the snapped twig had been enough to startle the timorous quarry, so that they were in instant flight simultaneously with Numa's charge.

The stallion was last, and with a prodigious leap, the lion catapulted through the air to seize him; but the snapping twig had robbed Numa of his dinner, though his mighty talons raked the zebra's glossy rump, leaving four crimson bars across the beautiful coat.

It was an angry Numa that quitted the river and prowled, fierce, dangerous, and hungry, into the jungle. Far from particular now was his appetite. Even Dango, the hyena, would have seemed a tidbit to that ravenous maw. And in this temper it was that the lion came upon the tribe of Kerchak, the great ape.

One does not look for Numa, the lion, this late in the morning. He should be lying up asleep beside his last night's kill by now; but Numa had made no kill last night. He was still hunting, hungrier than ever.

The anthropoids were idling about the clearing, the first keen desire of the morning's hunger having been satisfied. Numa scented them long before he saw them. Ordinarily he would have turned away in search of other game, for even Numa respected the mighty muscles and the sharp fangs of the great bulls of the tribe of Kerchak, but today he kept on steadily toward them, his bristled snout wrinkled into a savage snarl.

Without an instant's hesitation, Numa charged the moment he reached a point from where the apes were visible to him. There were a dozen or more of the hairy, manlike creatures upon the ground in a little glade. In a tree at one side sat a brown-skinned youth. He saw Numa's swift charge; he saw the apes turn and flee, huge bulls trampling upon little balus; only a single she held her ground to meet the charge, a young she inspired by new motherhood to the great sacrifice that her balu might escape.

Tarzan leaped from his perch, screaming at the flying bulls beneath and at those who squatted in the safety of surrounding trees. Had the bulls stood their ground, Numa would not have carried through that charge unless goaded by great rage or the gnawing pangs of starvation. Even then he would not have come off unscathed.

If the bulls heard, they were too slow in responding, for Numa had seized the mother ape and dragged her into the jungle before the males had sufficiently collected their wits and their courage to rally in defense of their fellow. Tarzan's angry voice aroused similar anger in the breasts of the apes. Snarling and barking they followed Numa into the dense labyrinth of foliage wherein he sought to hide himself from them. The ape-man was in the lead, moving rapidly and yet with caution, depending even more upon his ears and nose than upon his eyes for information of the lion's whereabouts.

The spoor was easy to follow, for the dragged body of the victim left a plain trail, blood-spattered and scentful. Even such dull creatures as you or I might easily have followed it. To Tarzan and the apes of Kerchak it was as obvious as a cement sidewalk.

Tarzan knew that they were nearing the great cat even before he heard an angry growl of warning just ahead. Calling to the apes to follow his example, he swung into a tree and a moment later Numa was surrounded by a ring of growling beasts, well out of reach of his fangs and talons but within plain sight of him. The carnivore crouched with his fore-quarters upon the she-ape. Tarzan could see that the latter was already dead; but something within him made it seem quite necessary to rescue the useless body from the clutches of the enemy and to punish him.

He shrieked taunts and insults at Numa, and tearing dead branches from the tree in which he danced, hurled them at the lion. The apes followed his example. Numa roared out in rage and vexation. He was hungry, but under such conditions he could not feed.

The apes, if they had been left to themselves, would doubtless soon have left the lion to peaceful enjoyment of his feast, for was not the she dead? They could not restore her to life by throwing sticks at Numa, and they might even now be feeding in quiet themselves; but Tarzan was of a different mind. Numa must be punished and driven away. He must be taught that even though he killed a Mangani, he would not be permitted to feed upon his kill. The man-mind looked into the future, while the apes perceived only the immediate present. They would be content to escape today the menace of Numa, while Tarzan saw the necessity, and the means as well, of safeguarding the days to come.

So he urged the great anthropoids on until Numa was showered with missiles that kept his head dodging and his voice pealing forth its savage protest; but still he clung desperately to his kill.

The twigs and branches hurled at Numa, Tarzan soon realized, did not hurt him greatly even when they struck him, and did not injure him at all, so the ape-man looked about for more effective missiles, nor did he have to look long. An out-cropping of decomposed granite not far from Numa suggested ammunition of a much more painful nature. Calling to the apes to watch him, Tarzan slipped to the ground and gathered a handful of small fragments. He knew that when once they had seen him carry out his idea they would be much quicker to follow his lead than to obey his instructions, were he to command them to procure pieces of rock and hurl them at Numa, for Tarzan was not then king of the apes of the tribe of Kerchak. That came in later years. Now he was but a youth, though one who already had wrested for himself a place in the councils of the savage beasts among whom a strange fate had cast him. The sullen bulls of the older generation still hated him as beasts hate those of whom they are suspicious, whose scent characteristic is the scent characteristic of an alien order and, therefore, of an enemy order. The younger bulls, those who had grown up through childhood as his playmates, were as accustomed to Tarzan's scent as to that of any other member of the tribe. They felt no greater suspicion of him than of any other bull of their acquaintance; yet they did not love him, for they loved none outside the mating season, and the animosities aroused by other bulls during that season lasted well over until the next. They were a morose and peevish band at best, though here and there were those among them in whom germinated the primal seeds of humanity—reversions to type, these, doubtless; reversions to the ancient progenitor who took the first step out of ape-hood toward humanness, when he walked more often upon his hind feet and discovered other things for idle hands to do.

So now Tarzan led where he could not yet command. He had long since discovered the apish propensity for mimicry and learned to make use of it. Having filled his arms with fragments of rotted granite, he clambered again into a tree, and it pleased him to see that the apes had followed his example.

During the brief respite while they were gathering their ammunition, Numa had settled himself to feed; but scarce had he arranged himself and his kill when a sharp piece of rock hurled by the practiced hand of the ape-man struck him upon the cheek. His sudden roar of pain and rage was smothered by a volley from the apes, who had seen Tarzan's act. Numa shook his massive head and glared upward at his tormentors. For a half hour they pursued him with rocks and broken branches, and though he dragged his kill into densest thickets, yet they always found a way to reach him with their missiles, giving him no opportunity to feed, and driving him on and on.

The hairless ape-thing with the man scent was worst of all, for he had even the temerity to advance upon the ground to within a few yards of the Lord of the Jungle, that he might with greater accuracy and force hurl the sharp bits of granite and the heavy sticks at him. Time and again did Numa charge—sudden, vicious charges—but the lithe, active tormentor always managed to elude him and with such insolent ease that the lion forgot even his great hunger in the consuming passion of his rage, leaving his meat for considerable spaces of time in vain efforts to catch his enemy.

The apes and Tarzan pursued the great beast to a natural clearing, where Numa evidently determined to make a last stand, taking up his position in the center of the open space, which was far enough from any tree to render him practically immune from the rather erratic throwing of the apes, though Tarzan still found him with most persistent and aggravating frequency.

This, however, did not suit the ape-man, since Numa now suffered an occasional missile with no more than a snarl, while he settled himself to partake of his delayed feast. Tarzan scratched his head, pondering some more effective method of offense, for he had determined to prevent Numa from profiting in any way through his attack upon the tribe. The man-mind reasoned against the future, while the shaggy apes thought only of their present hatred of this ancestral enemy. Tarzan guessed that should Numa find it an easy thing to snatch a meal from the tribe of Kerchak, it would be but a short time before their existence would be one living nightmare of hideous watchfulness and dread. Numa must be taught that the killing of an ape brought immediate punishment and no rewards. It would take but a few lessons to insure the former safety of the tribe. This must be some old lion whose failing strength and agility had forced him to any prey that he could catch; but even a single lion, undisputed, could exterminate the tribe, or at least make its existence so precarious and so terrifying that life would no longer be a pleasant condition.

"Let him hunt among the Gomangani," thought Tarzan. "He will find them easier prey. I will teach ferocious Numa that he may not hunt the Mangani."

But how to wrest the body of his victim from the feeding lion was the first question to be solved. At last Tarzan hit upon a plan. To anyone but Tarzan of the Apes it might have seemed rather a risky plan, and perhaps it did even to him; but Tarzan rather liked things that contained a considerable element of danger. At any rate, I rather doubt that you or I would have chosen a similar plan for foiling an angry and a hungry lion.

Tarzan required assistance in the scheme he had hit upon and his assistant must be equally as brave and almost as active as he. The ape-man's eyes fell upon Taug, the playmate of his childhood, the rival in his first love and now, of all the bulls of the tribe, the only one that might be thought to hold in his savage brain any such feeling toward Tarzan as we describe among ourselves as friendship. At least, Tarzan knew, Taug was courageous, and he was young and agile and wonderfully muscled.

"Taug!" cried the ape-man. The great ape looked up from a dead limb he was attempting to tear from a lightning-blasted tree. "Go close to Numa and worry him," said Tarzan. "Worry him until he charges. Lead him away from the body of Mamka. Keep him away as long as you can."

Taug nodded. He was across the clearing from Tarzan. Wresting the limb at last from the tree he dropped to the ground and advanced toward Numa, growling and barking out his insults. The worried lion looked up and rose to his feet. His tail went stiffly erect and Taug turned in flight, for he knew that warming signal of the charge.

From behind the lion, Tarzan ran quickly toward the center of the clearing and the body of Mamka. Numa, all his eyes for Taug, did not see the ape-man. Instead he shot forward after the fleeing bull, who had turned in flight not an instant too soon, since he reached the nearest tree but a yard or two ahead of the pursuing demon. Like a cat the heavy anthropoid scampered up the bole of his sanctuary. Numa's talons missed him by little more than inches.

For a moment the lion paused beneath the tree, glaring up at the ape and roaring until the earth trembled, then he turned back again toward his kill, and as he did so, his tail shot once more to rigid erectness and he charged back even more ferociously than he had come, for what he saw was the naked man-thing running toward the farther trees with the bloody carcass of his prey across a giant shoulder.

The apes, watching the grim race from the safety of the trees, screamed taunts at Numa and warnings to Tarzan. The high sun, hot and brilliant, fell like a spotlight upon the actors in the little clearing, portraying them in glaring relief to the audience in the leafy shadows of the surrounding trees. The light-brown body of the naked youth, all but hidden by the shaggy carcass of the killed ape, the red blood streaking his smooth hide, his muscles rolling, velvety, beneath. Behind him the black-maned lion, head flattened, tail extended, racing, a jungle thoroughbred, across the sunlit clearing.

Ah, but this was life! With death at his heels, Tarzan thrilled with the joy of such living as this; but would he reach the trees ahead of the rampant death so close behind?

Gunto swung from a limb in a tree before him. Gunto was screaming warnings and advice.

"Catch me!" cried Tarzan, and with his heavy burden leaped straight for the big bull hanging there by his hind feet and one forepaw. And Gunto caught them—the big ape-man and the dead weight of the slain she-ape—caught them with one great, hairy paw and whirled them upward until Tarzan's fingers closed upon a near-by branch.

Beneath, Numa leaped; but Gunto, heavy and awkward as he may have appeared, was as quick as Manu, the monkey, so that the lion's talons but barely grazed him, scratching a bloody streak beneath one hairy arm.

Tarzan carried Mamka's corpse to a high crotch, where even Sheeta, the panther, could not get it. Numa paced angrily back and forth beneath the tree, roaring frightfully. He had been robbed of his kill and his revenge also. He was very savage indeed; but his despoilers were well out of his reach, and after hurling a few taunts and missiles at him they swung away through the trees, fiercely reviling him.

Tarzan thought much upon the little adventure of that day. He foresaw what might happen should the great carnivora of the jungle turn their serious attention upon the tribe of Kerchak, the great ape, but equally he thought upon the wild scramble of the apes for safety when Numa first charged among them. There is little humor in the jungle that is not grim and awful. The beasts have little or no conception of humor; but the young Englishman saw humor in many things which presented no humorous angle to his associates.

Since earliest childhood he had been a searcher after fun, much to the sorrow of his fellow-apes, and now he saw the humor of the frightened panic of the apes and the baffled rage of Numa even in this grim jungle adventure which had robbed Mamka of life, and jeopardized that of many members of the tribe.

It was but a few weeks later that Sheeta, the panther, made a sudden rush among the tribe and snatched a little balu from a tree where it had been hidden while its mother sought food. Sheeta got away with his small prize unmolested. Tarzan was very wroth. He spoke to the bulls of the ease with which Numa and Sheeta, in a single moon, had slain two members of the tribe.

"They will take us all for food," he cried. "We hunt as we will through the jungle, paying no heed to approaching enemies. Even Manu, the monkey, does not so. He keeps two or three always watching for enemies. Pacco, the zebra, and Wappi, the antelope, have those about the herd who keep watch while the others feed, while we, the great Mangani, let Numa, and Sabor, and Sheeta come when they will and carry us off to feed their balus.

"Gr-r-rmph," said Numgo.

"What are we to do?" asked Taug.

"We, too, should have two or three always watching for the approach of Numa, and Sabor, and Sheeta," replied Tarzan. "No others need we fear, except Histah, the snake, and if we watch for the others we will see Histah if he comes, though gliding ever so silently."

And so it was that the great apes of the tribe of Kerchak posted sentries thereafter, who watched upon three sides while the tribe hunted, scattered less than had been their wont.

But Tarzan went abroad alone, for Tarzan was a man-thing and sought amusement and adventure and such humor as the grim and terrible jungle offers to those who know it and do not fear it—a weird humor shot with blazing eyes and dappled with the crimson of lifeblood. While others sought only food and love, Tarzan of the Apes sought food and joy.

One day he hovered above the palisaded village of Mbonga, the chief, the jet cannibal of the jungle primeval. He saw, as he had seen many times before, the witch-doctor, Rabba Kega, decked out in the head and hide of Gorgo, the buffalo. It amused Tarzan to see a Gomangani parading as Gorgo; but it suggested nothing in particular to him until he chanced to see stretched against the side of Mbonga's hut the skin of a lion with the head still on. Then a broad grin widened the handsome face of the savage beast-youth.

Back into the jungle he went until chance, agility, strength, and cunning backed by his marvelous powers of perception, gave him an easy meal. If Tarzan felt that the world owed him a living he also realized that it was for him to collect it, nor was there ever a better collector than this son of an English lord, who knew even less of the ways of his forbears than he did of the forbears themselves, which was nothing.

It was quite dark when Tarzan returned to the village of Mbonga and took his now polished perch in the tree which overhangs the palisade upon one side of the walled enclosure. As there was nothing in particular to feast upon in the village there was little life in the single street, for only an orgy of flesh and native beer could draw out the people of Mbonga. Tonight they sat gossiping about their cooking fires, the older members of the tribe; or, if they were young, paired off in the shadows cast by the palm-thatched huts.

Tarzan dropped lightly into the village, and sneaking stealthily in the concealment of the denser shadows, approached the hut of the chief, Mbonga. Here he found that which he sought. There were warriors all about him; but they did not know that the feared devil-god slunk noiselessly so near them, nor did they see him possess himself of that which he coveted and depart from their village as noiselessly as he had come.

Later that night, as Tarzan curled himself for sleep, he lay for a long time looking up at the burning planets and the twinkling stars and at Goro the moon, and he smiled. He recalled how ludicrous the great bulls had appeared in their mad scramble for safety that day when Numa had charged among them and seized Mamka, and yet he knew them to be fierce and courageous. It was the sudden shock of surprise that always sent them into a panic; but of this Tarzan was not as yet fully aware. That was something he was to learn in the near future.

He fell asleep with a broad grin upon his face.

Manu, the monkey, awoke him in the morning by dropping discarded bean pods upon his upturned face from a branch a short distance above him. Tarzan looked up and smiled. He had been awakened thus before many times. He and Manu were fairly good friends, their friendship operating upon a reciprocal basis. Sometimes Manu would come running early in the morning to awaken Tarzan and tell him that Bara, the deer, was feeding close at hand, or that Horta, the boar, was asleep in a mudhole hard by, and in return

Tarzan broke open the shells of the harder nuts and fruits for Manu, or frightened away Histah, the snake, and Sheeta, the panther.

The sun had been up for some time, and the tribe had already wandered off in search of food. Manu indicated the direction they had taken with a wave of his hand and a few piping notes of his squeaky little voice.

"Come, Manu," said Tarzan, "and you will see that which shall make you dance for joy and squeal your wrinkled little head off. Come, follow Tarzan of the Apes."

With that he set off in the direction Manu had indicated and above him, chattering, scolding and squealing, skipped Manu, the monkey. Across Tarzan's shoulders was the thing he had stolen from the village of Mbonga, the chief, the evening before.

The tribe was feeding in the forest beside the clearing where Gunto, and Taug, and Tarzan had so harassed Numa and finally taken away from him the fruit of his kill. Some of them were in the clearing itself. In peace and content they fed, for were there not three sentries, each watching upon a different side of the herd? Tarzan had taught them this, and though he had been away for several days hunting alone, as he often did, or visiting at the cabin by the sea, they had not as yet forgotten his admonitions, and if they continued for a short time longer to post sentries, it would become a habit of their tribal life and thus be perpetuated indefinitely.

But Tarzan, who knew them better than they knew themselves, was confident that they had ceased to place the watchers about them the moment that he had left them, and now he planned not only to have a little fun at their expense but to teach them a lesson in preparedness, which, by the way, is even a more vital issue in the jungle than in civilized places. That you and I exist today must be due to the preparedness of some shaggy anthropoid of the Oligocene. Of course the apes of Kerchak were always prepared, after their own way—Tarzan had merely suggested a new and additional safeguard.

Gunto was posted today to the north of the clearing. He squatted in the fork of a tree from where he might view the jungle for quite a distance about him. It was he who first discovered the enemy. A rustling in the undergrowth attracted his attention, and a moment later he had a partial view of a shaggy mane and tawny yellow back. Just a glimpse it was through the matted foliage beneath him; but it brought from Gunto's leathern lungs a shrill "Kreeg-ah!" which is the ape for beware, or danger.

Instantly the tribe took up the cry until "Kreeg-ahs!" rang through the jungle about the clearing as apes swung quickly to places of safety among the lower branches of the trees and the great bulls hastened in the direction of Gunto.

And then into the clearing strode Numa, the lion— majestic and mighty, and from a deep chest issued the moan and the cough and the rumbling roar that set stiff hairs to bristling from shaggy craniums down the length of mighty spines.

Inside the clearing, Numa paused and on the instant there fell upon him from the trees near by a shower of broken rock and dead limbs torn from age-old trees. A dozen times he was hit, and then the apes ran down and gathered other rocks, pelting him unmercifully.

Numa turned to flee, but his way was barred by a fusilade of sharp-cornered missiles, and then, upon the edge of the clearing, great Taug met him with a huge fragment of rock as large as a man's head, and down went the Lord of the Jungle beneath the stunning blow.

With shrieks and roars and loud barkings the great apes of the tribe of Kerchak rushed upon the fallen lion. Sticks and stones and yellow fangs menaced the still form. In another moment, before he could regain consciousness, Numa would be battered and torn until only a bloody mass of broken bones and matted hair remained of what had once been the most dreaded of jungle creatures.

But even as the sticks and stones were raised above him and the great fangs bared to tear him, there descended like a plummet from the trees above a diminutive figure with long, white whiskers and a wrinkled face. Square upon the body of Numa it alighted and there it danced and screamed and shrieked out its challenge against the bulls of Kerchak.

For an instant they paused, paralyzed by the wonder of the thing. It was Manu, the monkey, Manu, the little coward, and here he was daring the ferocity of the great Mangani, hopping about upon the carcass of Numa, the lion, and crying out that they must not strike it again.

And when the bulls paused, Manu reached down and seized a tawny ear. With all his little might he tugged upon the heavy head until slowly it turned back, revealing the tousled, black head and clean-cut profile of Tarzan of the Apes.

Some of the older apes were for finishing what they had commenced; but Taug, sullen, mighty Taug, sprang quickly to the ape-man's side and straddling the unconscious form warned back those who would have struck his childhood playmate. And Teeka, his mate, came too, taking her place with bared fangs at Taug's side. others followed their example, until at last Tarzan was surrounded by a ring of hairy champions who would permit no enemy to approach him.

It was a surprised and chastened Tarzan who opened his eyes to consciousness a few minutes later. He looked about him at the surrounding apes and slowly there returned to him a realization of what had occurred.

Gradually a broad grin illuminated his features. His bruises were many and they hurt; but the good that had come from his adventure was worth all that it had cost. He had learned, for instance, that the apes of Kerchak had heeded his teaching, and he had learned that he had good friends among the sullen beasts whom he had thought without sentiment. He had discovered that Manu, the monkey—even little, cowardly Manu—had risked his life in his defense.

It made Tarzan very glad to know these things; but at the other lesson he had been taught he reddened. He had always been a joker, the only joker in the grim and terrible company; but now as he lay there half dead from his hurts, he almost swore a solemn oath forever to forego practical joking—almost; but not quite.

THE NIGHTMARE

The blacks of the village of Mbonga, the chief, were feasting, while above them in a large tree sat Tarzan of the Apes—grim, terrible, empty, and envious. Hunting had proved poor that day, for there are lean days as well as fat ones for even the greatest of the jungle hunters. Oftentimes Tarzan went empty for more than a full sun, and he had passed through entire moons during which he had been but barely able to stave off starvation; but such times were infrequent.

There once had been a period of sickness among the grass-eaters which had left the plains almost bare of game for several years, and again the great cats had increased so rapidly and so overrun the country that their prey, which was also Tarzan's, had been frightened off for a considerable time.

But for the most part Tarzan had fed well always. Today, though, he had gone empty, one misfortune following another as rapidly as he raised new quarry, so that now, as he sat perched in the tree above the feasting blacks, he experienced all the pangs of famine and his hatred for his lifelong enemies waxed strong in his breast. It was tantalizing, indeed, to sit there hungry while these Gomangani filled themselves so full of food that their stomachs seemed almost upon the point of bursting, and with elephant steaks at that!

It was true that Tarzan and Tantor were the best of friends, and that Tarzan never yet had tasted of the flesh of the elephant; but the Gomangani evidently had slain one, and as they were eating of the flesh of their kill, Tarzan was assailed by no doubts as to the ethics of his doing likewise, should he have the opportunity. Had he known that the elephant had died of sickness several days before the blacks discovered the carcass, he might not have been so keen to partake of the feast, for Tarzan of the Apes was no carrion-eater. Hunger, however, may blunt the most epicurean taste, and Tarzan was not exactly an epicure.

What he was at this moment was a very hungry wild beast whom caution was holding in leash, for the great cooking pot in the center of the village was surrounded by black warriors, through whom not even Tarzan of the Apes might hope to pass unharmed. It would be necessary, therefore, for the watcher to remain there hungry until the blacks had gorged themselves to stupor, and then, if they had left any scraps, to make the best meal he could from such; but to the impatient Tarzan it seemed that the greedy Gomangani would rather burst than leave the feast before the last morsel had been devoured. For a time they broke the monotony of eating by executing portions of a hunting dance, a maneuver which sufficiently stimulated digestion to permit them to fall to once more with renewed vigor; but with the consumption of appalling quantities of elephant meat and native beer they presently became too loggy for physical exertion of any sort, some reaching a stage where they no longer could rise from the ground, but lay conveniently close to the great cooking pot, stuffing themselves into unconsciousness.

It was well past midnight before Tarzan even could begin to see the end of the orgy. The blacks were now falling asleep rapidly; but a few still persisted. From before their condition Tarzan had no doubt but that he easily could enter the village and snatch a handful of meat from before their noses; but a handful was not what he wanted. Nothing less than a stomachful would allay the gnawing craving of that great emptiness. He must therefore have ample time to forage in peace.

At last but a single warrior remained true to his ideals— an old fellow whose once wrinkled belly was now as smooth and as tight as the head of a drum. With evidences of great discomfort, and even pain, he would crawl toward the pot and drag himself slowly to his knees, from which position he could reach into the receptacle and seize a piece of meat. Then he would roll over on his back with a loud groan and lie there while he slowly forced the food between his teeth and down into his gorged stomach.

It was evident to Tarzan that the old fellow would eat until he died, or until there was no more meat. The ape-man shook his head in disgust. What foul creatures were these Gomangani? Yet of all the jungle folk they alone resembled Tarzan closely in form. Tarzan was a man, and they, too, must be some manner of men, just as the little monkeys, and the great apes, and Bolgani, the gorilla, were quite evidently of one great family, though differing in size and appearance and customs. Tarzan was ashamed, for of all the beasts of the jungle, then, man was the most disgusting—man and Dango, the hyena. Only man and Dango ate until they swelled up like a dead rat. Tarzan had seen Dango eat his way into the carcass of a dead elephant and then continue to eat so much that he had been unable to get out of the hole through which he had entered. Now he could readily believe that man, given the opportunity, would do the same. Man, too, was the most unlovely of creatures—with his skinny legs and his big stomach, his filed teeth, and his thick, red lips. Man was disgusting. Tarzan's gaze was riveted upon the hideous old warrior wallowing in filth beneath him.

There! the thing was struggling to its knees to reach for another morsel of flesh. It groaned aloud in pain and yet it persisted in eating, eating, ever eating. Tarzan could endure it no longer—neither his hunger nor his disgust. Silently he slipped to the ground with the bole of the great tree between himself and the feaster.

The man was still kneeling, bent almost double in agony, before the cooking pot. His back was toward the ape-man. Swiftly and noiselessly Tarzan approached him. There was no sound as steel fingers closed about the black throat. The struggle was short, for the man was old and already half stupefied from the effects of the gorging and the beer.

Tarzan dropped the inert mass and scooped several large pieces of meat from the cooking pot—enough to satisfy even his great hunger—then he raised the body of the feaster and shoved it into the vessel. When the other blacks awoke they would have something to think about! Tarzan grinned. As he turned toward the tree with his meat, he picked up a vessel containing beer and raised it to his lips, but at the first taste he spat the stuff from his mouth and tossed the primitive tankard aside. He was quite sure that even Dango would draw the line at such filthy tasting drink as that, and his contempt for man increased with the conviction.

Tarzan swung off into the jungle some half mile or so before he paused to partake of his stolen food. He noticed that it gave forth a strange and unpleasant odor, but assumed that this was due to the fact that it had stood in a vessel of water above a fire. Tarzan was, of course, unaccustomed to cooked food. He did not like it; but he was very hungry and had eaten a considerable portion of his haul before it was really borne in upon him that the stuff was nauseating. It required far less than he had imagined it would to satisfy his appetite.

Throwing the balance to the ground he curled up in a convenient crotch and sought slumber; but slumber seemed difficult to woo. Ordinarily Tarzan of the Apes was asleep as quickly as a dog after it curls itself upon a hearthrug before a roaring blaze; but tonight he squirmed and twisted, for at the pit of his stomach was a peculiar feeling that resembled nothing more closely than an attempt upon the part of the fragments of elephant meat reposing there to come out into the night and search for their elephant; but Tarzan was adamant. He gritted his teeth and held them back. He was not to be robbed of his meal after waiting so long to obtain it.

He had succeeded in dozing when the roaring of a lion awoke him. He sat up to discover that it was broad daylight. Tarzan rubbed his eyes. Could it be that he had really slept? He did not feel particularly refreshed as he should have after a good sleep. A noise attracted his attention, and he looked down to see a lion standing at the foot of the tree gazing hungrily at him. Tarzan made a face at the king of beasts, whereat Numa, greatly to the ape-man's surprise, started to climb up into the branches toward him. Now, never before had Tarzan seen a lion climb a tree, yet, for some unaccountable reason, he was not greatly surprised that this particular lion should do so.

As the lion climbed slowly toward him, Tarzan sought higher branches; but to his chagrin, he discovered that it was with the utmost difficulty that he could climb at all. Again and again he slipped back, losing all that he had gained, while the lion kept steadily at his climbing, coming ever closer and closer to the ape-man. Tarzan could see the hungry light in the yellow-green eyes. He could see the slaver on the drooping jowls, and the great fangs agape to seize and destroy him. Clawing desperately, the ape-man at last succeeded in gaining a little upon his pursuer. He reached the more slender branches far aloft where he well knew no lion could follow; yet on and on came devil-faced Numa. It was incredible; but it was true. Yet what most amazed Tarzan was that though he realized the incredibility of it all, he at the same time accepted it as a matter of course, first that a lion should climb at all and second that he should enter the upper terraces where even Sheeta, the panther, dared not venture.

To the very top of a tall tree the ape-man clawed his awkward way and after him came Numa, the lion, moaning dismally. At last Tarzan stood balanced upon the very utmost pinnacle of a swaying branch, high above the forest. He could go no farther. Below him the lion came steadily upward, and Tarzan of the Apes realized that at last the end had come. He could not do battle upon a tiny branch with Numa, the lion, especially with such a Numa, to which swaying branches two hundred feet above the ground provided as substantial footing as the ground itself.

Nearer and nearer came the lion. Another moment and he could reach up with one great paw and drag the ape-man downward to those awful jaws. A whirring noise above his head caused Tarzan to glance apprehensively upward. A great bird was circling close above him. He never had seen so large a bird in all his life, yet he recognized it immediately, for had he not seen it hundreds of times in one of the books in the little cabin by the land-locked bay—the moss-grown cabin that with its contents was the sole heritage left by his dead and unknown father to the young Lord Greystoke?

In the picture-book the great bird was shown flying far above the ground with a small child in its talons while, beneath, a distracted mother stood with uplifted hands. The lion was already reaching forth a taloned paw to seize him when the bird swooped and buried no less formidable talons in Tarzan's back. The pain was numbing; but it was with a sense of relief that the ape-man felt himself snatched from the clutches of Numa.

With a great whirring of wings the bird rose rapidly until the forest lay far below. It made Tarzan sick and dizzy to look down upon it from so great a height, so he closed his eyes tight and held his breath. Higher and higher climbed the huge bird. Tarzan opened his eyes. The jungle was so far away that he could see only a dim, green blur below him, but just above and quite close was the sun. Tarzan reached out his hands and warmed them, for they were very cold. Then a sudden madness seized him. Where was the bird taking him?

Was he to submit thus passively to a feathered creature however enormous? Was he, Tarzan of the Apes, mighty fighter, to die without striking a blow in his own defense? Never!

He snatched the hunting blade from his gee-string and thrusting upward drove it once, twice, thrice into the breast above him. The mighty wings fluttered a few more times, spasmodically, the talons relaxed their hold, and Tarzan of the Apes fell hurtling downward toward the distant jungle.

It seemed to the ape-man that he fell for many minutes before he crashed through the leafy verdure of the tree tops. The smaller branches broke his fall, so that he came to rest for an instant upon the very branch upon which he had sought slumber the previous night. For an instant he toppled there in a frantic attempt to regain his equilibrium; but at last he rolled off, yet, clutching wildly, he succeeded in grasping the branch and hanging on.

Once more he opened his eyes, which he had closed during the fall. Again it was night. With all his old agility he clambered back to the crotch from which he had toppled. Below him a lion roared, and, looking downward, Tarzan could see the yellow-green eyes shining in the moonlight as they bored hungrily upward through the darkness of the jungle night toward him.

The ape-man gasped for breath. Cold sweat stood out from every pore, there was a great sickness at the pit of Tarzan's stomach. Tarzan of the Apes had dreamed his first dream.

For a long time he sat watching for Numa to climb into the tree after him, and listening for the sound of the great wings from above, for to Tarzan of the Apes his dream was a reality.

He could not believe what he had seen and yet, having seen even these incredible things, he could not disbelieve the evidence of his own perceptions. Never in all his life had Tarzan's senses deceived him badly, and so, naturally, he had great faith in them. Each perception which ever had been transmitted to Tarzan's brain had been, with varying accuracy, a true perception. He could not conceive of the possibility of apparently having passed through such a weird adventure in which there was no grain of truth. That a stomach, disordered by decayed elephant flesh, a lion roaring in the jungle, a picture-book, and sleep could have so truly portrayed all the clear-cut details of what he had seemingly experienced was quite beyond his knowledge; yet he knew that Numa could not climb a tree, he knew that there existed in the jungle no such bird as he had seen, and he knew, too, that he could not have fallen a tiny fraction of the distance he had hurtled downward, and lived.

To say the least, he was a very puzzled Tarzan as he tried to compose himself once more for slumber—a very puzzled and a very nauseated Tarzan.

As he thought deeply upon the strange occurrences of the night, he witnessed another remarkable happening. It was indeed quite preposterous, yet he saw it all with his own eyes—it was nothing less than Histah, the snake, wreathing his sinuous and slimy way up the bole of the tree below him—Histah, with the head of the old man Tarzan had shoved into the cooking pot—the head and the round, tight, black, distended stomach. As the old man's frightful face, with upturned eyes, set and glassy, came close to Tarzan, the jaws opened to seize him. The ape-man struck furiously at the hideous face, and as he struck the apparition disappeared.

Tarzan sat straight up upon his branch trembling in every limb, wide-eyed and panting. He looked all around him with his keen, jungle-trained eyes, but he saw naught of the old man with the body of Histah, the snake, but on his naked thigh the ape-man saw a caterpillar, dropped from a branch above him. With a grimace he flicked it off into the darkness beneath.

And so the night wore on, dream following dream, nightmare following nightmare, until the distracted ape-man started like a frightened deer at the rustling of the wind in the trees about him, or leaped to his feet as the uncanny laugh of a hyena burst suddenly upon a momentary jungle silence. But at last the tardy morning broke and a sick and feverish Tarzan wound sluggishly through the dank and gloomy mazes of the forest in search of water. His whole body seemed on fire, a great sickness surged upward to his throat. He saw a tangle of almost impenetrable thicket, and, like the wild beast he was, he crawled into it to die alone and unseen, safe from the attacks of predatory carnivora.

But he did not die. For a long time he wanted to; but presently nature and an outraged stomach relieved themselves in their own therapeutic manner, the ape-man broke into a violent perspiration and then fell into a normal and untroubled sleep which persisted well into the afternoon. When he awoke he found himself weak but no longer sick.

Once more he sought water, and after drinking deeply, took his way slowly toward the cabin by the sea. In times of loneliness and trouble it had long been his custom to seek there the quiet and restfulness which he could find nowhere else.

As he approached the cabin and raised the crude latch which his father had fashioned so many years before, two small, blood-shot eyes watched him from the concealing foliage of the jungle close by. From beneath shaggy, beetling brows they glared maliciously upon him, maliciously and with a keen curiosity; then Tarzan entered the cabin and closed the door after him. Here, with all the world shut out from him, he could dream without fear of interruption. He could curl up and look at the pictures in the strange things which were books, he could puzzle out the printed word he had learned to read without knowledge of the spoken language it represented, he could live in a wonderful world of which he had no knowledge beyond the covers of his beloved books. Numa and Sabor might prowl about close to him, the elements might rage in all their fury; but here at least, Tarzan might be entirely off his guard in a delightful relaxation which gave him all his faculties for the uninterrupted pursuit of this greatest of all his pleasures.

Today he turned to the picture of the huge bird which bore off the little Tarmangani in its talons. Tarzan puckered his brows as he examined the colored print. Yes, this was the very bird that had carried him off the day before, for to Tarzan the dream had been so great a reality that he still thought another day and a night had passed since he had lain down in the tree to sleep.

But the more he thought upon the matter the less positive he was as to the verity of the seeming adventure through which he had passed, yet where the real had ceased and the unreal commenced he was quite unable to determine. Had he really then been to the village of the blacks at all, had he killed the old Gomangani, had he eaten of the elephant meat, had he been sick? Tarzan scratched his tousled black head and wondered. It was all very strange, yet he knew that he never had seen Numa climb a tree, or Histah with the head and belly of an old black man whom Tarzan already had slain.

Finally, with a sigh he gave up trying to fathom the unfathomable, yet in his heart of hearts he knew that something had come into his life that he never before had experienced, another life which existed when he slept and the consciousness of which was carried over into his waking hours.

Then he commenced to wonder if some of these strange creatures which he met in his sleep might not slay him, for at such times Tarzan of the Apes seemed to be a different Tarzan, sluggish, helpless and timid—wishing to flee his enemies as fled Bara, the deer, most fearful of creatures.

Thus, with a dream, came the first faint tinge of a knowledge of fear, a knowledge which Tarzan, awake, had never experienced, and perhaps he was experiencing what his early forbears passed through and transmitted to posterity in the form of superstition first and religion later; for they, as Tarzan, had seen things at night which they could not explain by the daylight standards of sense perception or of reason, and so had built for themselves a weird explanation which included grotesque shapes, possessed of strange and uncanny powers, to whom they finally came to attribute all those inexplicable phenomena of nature which with each recurrence filled them with awe, with wonder, or with terror.

And as Tarzan concentrated his mind on the little bugs upon the printed page before him, the active recollection of the strange adventures presently merged into the text of that which he was reading—a story of Bolgani, the gorilla, in captivity. There was a more or less lifelike illustration of Bolgani in colors and in a cage, with many remarkable looking Tarmangani standing against a rail and peering curiously at the snarling brute. Tarzan wondered not a little, as he always did, at the odd and seemingly useless array of colored plumage which covered the bodies of the Tarmangani. It always caused him to grin a trifle when he looked at these strange creatures. He wondered if they so covered their bodies from shame of their hairlessness or because they thought the odd things they wore added any to the beauty of their appearance. Particularly was Tarzan amused by the grotesque headdresses of the pictured people. He wondered how some of the shes succeeded in balancing theirs in an upright position, and he came as near to laughing aloud as he ever had, as he contemplated the funny little round things upon the heads of the hes.

Slowly the ape-man picked out the meaning of the various combinations of letters on the printed page, and as he read, the little bugs, for as such he always thought of the letters, commenced to run about in a most confusing manner, blurring his vision and befuddling his thoughts. Twice he brushed the back of a hand smartly across his eyes; but only for a moment could he bring the bugs back to coherent and intelligible form. He had slept ill the night before and now he was exhausted from loss of sleep, from sickness, and from the slight fever he had had, so that it became more and more difficult to fix his attention, or to keep his eyes open.

Tarzan realized that he was falling asleep, and just as the realization was borne in upon him and he had decided to relinquish himself to an inclination which had assumed almost the proportions of a physical pain, he was aroused by the opening of the cabin door. Turning quickly toward the interruption Tarzan was amazed, for a moment, to see bulking large in the doorway the huge and hairy form of Bolgani, the gorilla.

Now there was scarcely a denizen of the great jungle with whom Tarzan would rather not have been cooped up inside the small cabin than Bolgani, the gorilla, yet he felt no fear, even though his quick eye noted that Bolgani was in the throes of that jungle madness which seizes upon so many of the fiercer males. Ordinarily the huge gorillas avoid conflict, hide themselves from the other jungle folk, and are generally the best of neighbors; but when they are attacked, or the madness seizes them, there is no jungle denizen so bold and fierce as to deliberately seek a quarrel with them.

But for Tarzan there was no escape. Bolgani was glowering at him from red-rimmed, wicked eyes. In a moment he would rush in and seize the ape-man. Tarzan reached for the hunting knife where he had lain it on the table beside him; but as his fingers did not immediately locate the weapon, he turned a quick glance in search of it. As he did so his eyes fell upon the book he had been looking at which still lay open at the picture of Bolgani. Tarzan found his knife, but he merely fingered it idly and grinned in the direction of the advancing gorilla.

Not again would he be fooled by empty things which came while he slept! In a moment, no doubt, Bolgani would turn into Pamba, the rat, with the head of Tantor, the elephant. Tarzan had seen enough of such strange happenings recently to have some idea as to what he might expect; but this time Bolgani did not alter his form as he came slowly toward the young ape-man.

Tarzan was a bit puzzled, too, that he felt no desire to rush frantically to some place of safety, as had been the sensation most conspicuous in the other of his new and remarkable adventures. He was just himself now, ready to fight, if necessary; but still sure that no flesh and blood gorilla stood before him.

The thing should be fading away into thin air by now, thought Tarzan, or changing into something else; yet it did not. Instead it loomed clear-cut and real as Bolgani himself, the magnificent dark coat glistening with life and health in a bar of sunlight which shot across the cabin through the high window behind the young Lord Greystoke. This was quite the most realistic of his sleep adventures, thought Tarzan, as he passively awaited the next amusing incident.

And then the gorilla charged. Two mighty, calloused hands seized upon the ape-man, great fangs were bared close to his face, a hideous growl burst from the cavernous throat and hot breath fanned Tarzan's cheek, and still he sat grinning at the apparition. Tarzan might be fooled once or twice, but not for so many times in succession! He knew that this Bolgani was no real Bolgani, for had he been he never could have gained entrance to the cabin, since only Tarzan knew how to operate the latch.

The gorilla seemed puzzled by the strange passivity of the hairless ape. He paused an instant with his jaws snarling close to the other's throat, then he seemed suddenly to come to some decision. Whirling the ape-man across a hairy shoulder, as easily as you or I might lift a babe in arms, Bolgani turned and dashed out into the open, racing toward the great trees.

Now, indeed, was Tarzan sure that this was a sleep adventure, and so grinned largely as the giant gorilla bore him, unresisting, away. Presently, reasoned Tarzan, he would awaken and find himself back in the cabin where he had fallen asleep. He glanced back at the thought and saw the cabin door standing wide open. This would never do! Always had he been careful to close and latch it against wild intruders. Manu, the monkey, would make sad havoc there among Tarzan's treasures should he have access to the interior for even a few minutes. The question which arose in Tarzan's mind was a baffling one. Where did sleep adventures end and reality commence? How was he to be sure that the cabin door was not really open? Everything about him appeared quite normal—there were none of the grotesque exaggerations of his former sleep adventures. It would be better then to be upon the safe side and make sure that the cabin door was closed—it would do no harm even if all that seemed to be happening were not happening at all.

Tarzan essayed to slip from Bolgani's shoulder; but the great beast only growled ominously and gripped him tighter. With a mighty effort the ape-man wrenched himself loose, and as he slid to the ground, the dream gorilla turned ferociously upon him, seized him once more and buried great fangs in a sleek, brown shoulder.

The grin of derision faded from Tarzan's lips as the pain and the hot blood aroused his fighting instincts. Asleep or awake, this thing was no longer a joke! Biting, tearing, and snarling, the two rolled over upon the ground. The gorilla now was frantic with insane rage. Again and again he loosed his hold upon the ape-man's shoulder in an attempt to seize the jugular; but Tarzan of the Apes had fought before with creatures who struck first for the vital vein, and each time he wriggled out of harm's way as he strove to get his fingers upon his adversary's throat. At last he succeeded—his great muscles tensed and knotted beneath his smooth hide as he forced with every ounce of his mighty strength to push the hairy torso from him. And as he choked Bolgani and strained him away, his other hand crept slowly upward between them until the point of the hunting knife rested over the savage heart—there was a quick movement of the steel-thewed wrist and the blade plunged to its goal.

Bolgani, the gorilla, voiced a single frightful shriek, tore himself loose from the grasp of the ape-man, rose to his feet, staggered a few steps and then plunged to earth. There were a few spasmodic movements of the limbs and the brute was still.

Tarzan of the Apes stood looking down upon his kill, and as he stood there he ran his fingers through his thick, black shock of hair. Presently he stooped and touched the dead body. Some of the red life-blood of the gorilla crimsoned his fingers. He raised them to his nose and sniffed. Then he shook his head and turned toward the cabin. The door was still open. He closed it and fastened the latch. Returning toward the body of his kill he again paused and scratched his head.

If this was a sleep adventure, what then was reality? How was he to know the one from the other? How much of all that had happened in his life had been real and how much unreal?

He placed a foot upon the prostrate form and raising his face to the heavens gave voice to the kill cry of the bull ape. Far in the distance a lion answered. It was very real and, yet, he did not know. Puzzled, he turned away into the jungle.

No, he did not know what was real and what was not; but there was one thing that he did know—never again would he eat of the flesh of Tantor, the elephant.

EDGAR RICE BURROUGHS

THE BATTLE FOR TEEKA

The day was perfect. A cool breeze tempered the heat of the equatorial sun. Peace had reigned within the tribe for weeks and no alien enemy had trespassed upon its preserves from without. To the ape-mind all this was sufficient evidence that the future would be identical with the immediate past—that Utopia would persist.

The sentinels, now from habit become a fixed tribal custom, either relaxed their vigilance or entirely deserted their posts, as the whim seized them. The tribe was far scattered in search of food. Thus may peace and prosperity undermine the safety of the most primitive community even as it does that of the most cultured.

Even the individuals became less watchful and alert, so that one might have thought Numa and Sabor and Sheeta entirely deleted from the scheme of things. The shes and the balus roamed unguarded through the sullen jungle, while the greedy males foraged far afield, and thus it was that Teeka and Gazan, her balu, hunted upon the extreme southern edge of the tribe with no great male near them.

Still farther south there moved through the forest a sinister figure—a huge bull ape, maddened by solitude and defeat. A week before he had contended for the kingship of a tribe far distant, and now battered, and still sore, he roamed the wilderness an outcast. Later he might return to his own tribe and submit to the will of the hairy brute he had attempted to dethrone; but for the time being he dared not do so, since he had sought not only the crown but the wives, as well, of his lord and master. It would require an entire moon at least to bring forgetfulness to him he had wronged, and so Toog wandered a strange jungle, grim, terrible, hate-filled.

It was in this mental state that Toog came unexpectedly upon a young she feeding alone in the jungle—a stranger she, lithe and strong and beautiful beyond compare. Toog caught his breath and slunk quickly to one side of the trail where the dense foliage of the tropical underbrush concealed him from Teeka while permitting him to feast his eyes upon her loveliness.

But not alone were they concerned with Teeka—they roved the surrounding jungle in search of the bulls and cows and balus of her tribe, though principally for the bulls. When one covets a she of an alien tribe one must take into consideration the great, fierce, hairy guardians who seldom wander far from their wards and who will fight a stranger to the death in protection of the mate or offspring of a fellow, precisely as they would fight for their own.

Toog could see no sign of any ape other than the strange she and a young balu playing near by. His wicked, blood-shot eyes half closed as they rested upon the charms of the former—as for the balu, one snap of those great jaws upon the back of its little neck would prevent it from raising any unnecessary alarm.

Toog was a fine, big male, resembling in many ways Teeka's mate, Taug. Each was in his prime, and each was wonderfully muscled, perfectly fanged and as horrifyingly ferocious as the most exacting and particular she could wish. Had Toog been of her own tribe, Teeka might as readily have yielded to him as to Taug when her mating time arrived; but now she was Taug's and no other male could claim her without first defeating Taug in personal combat. And even then Teeka retained some rights in the matter. If she did not favor a correspondent, she could enter the lists with her rightful mate and do her part toward discouraging his advances, a part, too, which would prove no mean assistance to her lord and master, for Teeka, even though her fangs were smaller than a male's, could use them to excellent effect.

Just now Teeka was occupied in a fascinating search for beetles, to the exclusion of all else. She did not realize how far she and Gazan had become separated from the balance of the tribe, nor were her defensive senses upon the alert as they should have been. Months of immunity from danger under the protecting watchfulness of the sentries, which Tarzan had taught the tribe to post, had lulled them all into a sense of peaceful security based on that fallacy which has wrecked many enlightened communities in the past and will continue to wreck others in the future—that because they have not been attacked they never will be.

Toog, having satisfied himself that only the she and her balu were in the immediate vicinity, crept stealthily forward. Teeka's back was toward him when he finally rushed upon her; but her senses were at last awakened to the presence of danger and she wheeled to face the strange bull just before he reached her. Toog halted a few paces from her. His anger had fled before the seductive feminine charms of the stranger. He made conciliatory noises—a species of clucking sound with his broad, flat lips—that were, too, not greatly dissimilar to that which might be produced in an osculatory solo.

But Teeka only bared her fangs and growled. Little Gazan started to run toward his mother, but she warned him away with a quick "Kreeg-ah!" telling him to run high into a tall tree. Evidently Teeka was not favorably impressed by her new suitor. Toog realized this and altered his methods accordingly. He swelled his giant chest, beat upon it with his calloused knuckles and swaggered to and fro before her.

"I am Toog," he boasted. "Look at my fighting fangs. Look at my great arms and my mighty legs. With one bite I can slay your biggest bull. Alone have I slain Sheeta. I am Toog. Toog wants you." Then he waited for the effect, nor did he have long to wait. Teeka turned with a swiftness which belied her great weight and bolted in the opposite direction. Toog, with an angry growl, leaped in pursuit; but the smaller, lighter female was too fleet for him. He chased her for a few yards and then, foaming and barking, he halted and beat upon the ground with his hard fists.

From the tree above him little Gazan looked down and witnessed the stranger bull's discomfiture. Being young, and thinking himself safe above the reach of the heavy male, Gazan screamed an ill-timed insult at their tormentor. Toog looked up. Teeka had halted at a little distance—she would not go far from her balu; that Toog quickly realized and as quickly determined to take advantage of. He saw that the tree in which the young ape squatted was isolated and that Gazan could not reach another without coming to earth. He would obtain the mother through her love for her young.

He swung himself into the lower branches of the tree. Little Gazan ceased to insult him; his expression of deviltry changed to one of apprehension, which was quickly followed by fear as Toog commenced to ascend toward him. Teeka screamed to Gazan to climb higher, and the little fellow scampered upward among the tiny branches which would not support the weight of the great bull; but nevertheless Toog kept on climbing. Teeka was not fearful. She knew that he could not ascend far enough to reach Gazan, so she sat at a little distance from the tree and applied jungle opprobrium to him. Being a female, she was a past master of the art.

But she did not know the malevolent cunning of Toog's little brain. She took it for granted that the bull would climb as high as he could toward Gazan and then, finding that he could not reach him, resume his pursuit of her, which she knew would prove equally fruitless. So sure was she of the safety of her balu and her own ability to take care of herself that she did not voice the cry for help which would soon have brought the other members of the tribe flocking to her side.

Toog slowly reached the limit to which he dared risk his great weight to the slender branches. Gazan was still fifteen feet above him. The bull braced himself and seized the main branch in his powerful hands, then he commenced shaking it vigorously. Teeka was appalled. Instantly she realized what the bull purposed. Gazan clung far out upon a swaying limb. At the first shake he lost his balance, though he did not quite fall, clinging still with his four hands; but Toog redoubled his efforts; the shaking produced a violent snapping of the limb to which the young ape clung. Teeka saw all too plainly what the outcome must be and forgetting her own danger in the depth of her mother love, rushed forward to ascend the tree and give battle to the fearsome creature that menaced the life of her little one.

But before ever she reached the bole, Toog had succeeded, by violent shaking of the branch, to loosen Gazan's hold. With a cry the little fellow plunged down through the foliage, clutching futilely for a new hold, and alighted with a sickening thud at his mother's feet, where he lay silent and motionless. Moaning, Teeka stooped to lift the still form in her arms; but at the same instant Toog was upon her.

Struggling and biting she fought to free herself; but the giant muscles of the great bull were too much for her lesser strength. Toog struck and choked her repeatedly until finally, half unconscious, she lapsed into quasi submission. Then the bull lifted her to his shoulder and turned back to the trail toward the south from whence he had come.

Upon the ground lay the quiet form of little Gazan. He did not moan. He did not move. The sun rose slowly toward meridian. A mangy thing, lifting its nose to scent the jungle breeze, crept through the underbrush. It was Dango, the hyena. Presently its ugly muzzle broke through some near-by foliage and its cruel eyes fastened upon Gazan.

Early that morning, Tarzan of the Apes had gone to the cabin by the sea, where he passed many an hour at such times as the tribe was ranging in the vicinity. On the floor lay the skeleton of a man—all that remained of the former Lord Greystoke—lay as it had fallen some twenty years before when Kerchak, the great ape, had thrown it, lifeless, there. Long since had the termites and the small rodents picked clean the sturdy English bones. For years Tarzan had seen it lying there, giving it no more attention than he gave the countless thousand bones that strewed his jungle haunts. On the bed another, smaller, skeleton reposed and the youth ignored it as he ignored the other. How could he know that the one had been his father, the other his mother? The little pile of bones in the rude cradle, fashioned with such loving care by the former Lord Greystoke, meant nothing to him— that one day that little skull was to help prove his right to a proud title was as far beyond his ken as the satellites of the suns of Orion. To Tarzan they were bones—just bones. He did not need them, for there was no meat left upon them, and they were not in his way, for he knew no necessity for a bed, and the skeleton upon the floor he easily could step over.

Today he was restless. He turned the pages first of one book and then of another. He glanced at pictures which he knew by heart, and tossed the books aside. He rummaged for the thousandth time in the cupboard. He took out a bag which contained several small, round pieces of metal. He had played with them many times in the years gone by; but always he replaced them carefully in the bag, and the bag in the cupboard, upon the very shelf where first he had discovered it. In strange ways did heredity manifest itself in the ape-man. Come of an orderly race, he himself was orderly without knowing why. The apes dropped things wherever their interest in them waned—in the tall grass or from the high-flung branches of the trees. What they dropped they sometimes found again, by accident; but not so the ways of Tarzan. For his few belongings he had a place and scrupulously he returned each thing to its proper place when he was done with it. The round pieces of metal in the little bag always interested him. Raised pictures were upon either side, the meaning of which he did not quite understand. The pieces were bright and shiny. It amused him to arrange them in various figures upon the table. Hundreds of times had he played thus. Today, while so engaged, he dropped a lovely yellow piece— an English sovereign—which rolled beneath the bed where lay all that was mortal of the once beautiful Lady Alice.

True to form, Tarzan at once dropped to his hands and knees and searched beneath the bed for the lost gold piece. Strange as it might appear, he had never before looked beneath the bed. He found the gold piece, and something else he found, too—a small wooden box with a loose cover. Bringing them both out he returned the sovereign to its bag and the bag to its shelf within the cupboard; then he investigated the box. It contained a quantity of cylindrical bits of metal, cone-shaped at one end and flat at the other, with a projecting rim. They were all quite green and dull, coated with years of verdigris.

Tarzan removed a handful of them from the box and examined them. He rubbed one upon another and discovered that the green came off, leaving a shiny surface for two-thirds of their length and a dull gray over the cone-shaped end. Finding a bit of wood he rubbed one of the cylinders rapidly and was rewarded by a lustrous sheen which pleased him.

At his side hung a pocket pouch taken from the body of one of the numerous black warriors he had slain. Into this pouch he put a handful of the new playthings, thinking to polish them at his leisure; then he replaced the box beneath the bed, and finding nothing more to amuse him, left the cabin and started back in the direction of the tribe.

Shortly before he reached them he heard a great commotion ahead of him—the loud screams of shes and balus, the savage, angry barking and growling of the great bulls. Instantly he increased his speed, for the "Kreeg-ahs" that came to his ears warned him that something was amiss with his fellows.

While Tarzan had been occupied with his own devices in the cabin of his dead sire, Taug, Teeka's mighty mate, had been hunting a mile to the north of the tribe. At last, his belly filled, he had turned lazily back toward the clearing where he had last seen the tribe and presently commenced passing its members scattered alone or in twos or threes. Nowhere did he see Teeka or Gazan, and soon he began inquiring of the other apes where they might be; but none had seen them recently.

Now the lower orders are not highly imaginative. They do not, as you and I, paint vivid mental pictures of things which might have occurred, and so Taug did not now apprehend that any misfortune had overtaken his mate and their off-spring— he merely knew that he wished to find Teeka that he might lie down in the shade and have her scratch his back while his breakfast digested; but though he called to her and searched for her and asked each whom he met, he could find no trace of Teeka, nor of Gazan either.

He was beginning to become peeved and had about made up his mind to chastise Teeka for wandering so far afield when he wanted her. He was moving south along a game trail, his calloused soles and knuckles giving forth no sound, when he came upon Dango at the opposite side of a small clearing. The eater of carrion did not see Taug, for all his eyes were for something which lay in the grass beneath a tree—something upon which he was sneaking with the cautious stealth of his breed.

Taug, always cautious himself, as it behooves one to be who fares up and down the jungle and desires to survive, swung noiselessly into a tree, where he could have a better view of the clearing. He did not fear Dango; but he wanted to see what it was that Dango stalked. In a way, possibly, he was actuated as much by curiosity as by caution.

And when Taug reached a place in the branches from which he could have an unobstructed view of the clearing he saw Dango already sniffing at something directly beneath him— something which Taug instantly recognized as the lifeless form of his little Gazan.

With a cry so frightful, so bestial, that it momentarily paralyzed the startled Dango, the great ape launched his mighty bulk upon the surprised hyena. With a cry and a snarl, Dango, crushed to earth, turned to tear at his assailant; but as effectively might a sparrow turn upon a hawk. Taug's great, gnarled fingers closed upon the hyena's throat and back, his jaws snapped once on the mangy neck, crushing the vertebrae, and then he hurled the dead body contemptuously aside.

Again he raised his voice in the call of the bull ape to its mate, but there was no reply; then he leaned down to sniff at the body of Gazan. In the breast of this savage, hideous beast there beat a heart which was moved, however slightly, by the same emotions of paternal love which affect us. Even had we no actual evidence of this, we must know it still, since only thus might be explained the survival of the human race in which the jealousy and selfishness of the bulls would, in the earliest stages of the race, have wiped out the young as rapidly as they were brought into the world had not God implanted in the savage bosom that paternal love which evidences itself most strongly in the protective instinct of the male.

In Taug the protective instinct was not alone highly developed; but affection for his offspring as well, for Taug was an unusually intelligent specimen of these great, manlike apes which the natives of the Gobi speak of in whispers; but which no white man ever had seen, or, if seeing, lived to tell of until Tarzan of the Apes came among them.

And so Taug felt sorrow as any other father might feel sorrow at the loss of a little child. To you little Gazan might have seemed a hideous and repulsive creature, but to Taug and Teeka he was as beautiful and as cute as is your little Mary or Johnnie or Elizabeth Ann to you, and he was their firstborn, their only balu, and a he—three things which might make a young ape the apple of any fond father's eye.

For a moment Taug sniffed at the quiet little form. With his muzzle and his tongue he smoothed and caressed the rumpled coat. From his savage lips broke a low moan; but quickly upon the heels of sorrow came the overmastering desire for revenge.

Leaping to his feet he screamed out a volley of "Kreegahs," punctuated from time to time by the blood-freezing cry of an angry, challenging bull—a rage-mad bull with the blood lust strong upon him.

Answering his cries came the cries of the tribe as they swung through the trees toward him. It was these that Tarzan heard on his return from his cabin, and in reply to them he raised his own voice and hurried forward with increased speed until he fairly flew through the middle terraces of the forest.

When at last he came upon the tribe he saw their members gathered about Taug and something which lay quietly upon the ground. Dropping among them, Tarzan approached the center of the group. Taug was stiff roaring out his challenges; but when he saw Tarzan he ceased and stooping picked up Gazan in his arms and held him out for Tarzan to see. Of all the bulls of the tribe, Taug held affection for Tarzan only. Tarzan he trusted and looked up to as one wiser and more cunning. To Tarzan he came now—to the playmate of his balu days, the companion of innumerable battles of his maturity.

When Tarzan saw the still form in Taug's arms, a low growl broke from his lips, for he too loved Teeka's little balu.

"Who did it?" he asked. "Where is Teeka?"

"I do not know," replied Taug. "I found him lying here with Dango about to feed upon him; but it was not Dango that did it—there are no fang marks upon him."

Tarzan came closer and placed an ear against Gazan's breast. "He is not dead," he said. "Maybe he will not die." He pressed through the crowd of apes and circled once about them, examining the ground step by step. Suddenly he stopped and placing his nose close to the earth sniffed. Then he sprang to his feet, giving a peculiar cry. Taug and the others pressed forward, for the sound told them that the hunter had found the spoor of his quarry.

"A stranger bull has been here," said Tarzan. "It was he that hurt Gazan. He has carried off Teeka."

Taug and the other bulls commenced to roar and threaten; but they did nothing. Had the stranger bull been within sight they would have torn him to pieces; but it did not occur to them to follow him.

"If the three bulls had been watching around the tribe this would not have happened," said Tarzan. "Such things will happen as long as you do not keep the three bulls watching for an enemy. The jungle is full of enemies, and yet you let your shes and your balus feed where they will, alone and unprotected. Tarzan goes now—he goes to find Teeka and bring her back to the tribe."

The idea appealed to the other bulls. "We will all go," they cried.

"No," said Tarzan, "you will not all go. We cannot take shes and balus when we go out to hunt and fight. You must remain to guard them or you will lose them all."

They scratched their heads. The wisdom of his advice was dawning upon them, but at first they had been carried away by the new idea—the idea of following up an enemy offender to wrest his prize from him and punish him. The community instinct was ingrained in their characters through ages of custom. They did not know why they had not thought to pursue and punish the offender—they could not know that it was because they had as yet not reached a mental plane which would permit them to work as individuals. In times of stress, the community instinct sent them huddling into a compact herd where the great bulls, by the weight of their combined strength and ferocity, could best protect them from an enemy. The idea of separating to do battle with a foe had not yet occurred to them—it was too foreign to custom, too inimical to community interests; but to Tarzan it was the first and most natural thought. His senses told him that there was but a single bull connected with the attack upon Teeka and Gazan. A single enemy did not require the entire tribe for his punishment. Two swift bulls could quickly overhaul him and rescue Teeka.

In the past no one ever had thought to go forth in search of the shes that were occasionally stolen from the tribe. If Numa, Sabor, Sheeta or a wandering bull ape from another tribe chanced to carry off a maid or a matron while no one was looking, that was the end of it—she was gone, that was all. The bereaved husband, if the victim chanced to have been mated, growled around for a day or two and then, if he were strong enough, took another mate within the tribe, and if not, wandered far into the jungle on the chance of stealing one from another community.

In the past Tarzan of the Apes had condoned this practice for the reason that he had had no interest in those who had been stolen; but Teeka had been his first love and Teeka's balu held a place in his heart such as a balu of his own would have held. Just once before had Tarzan wished to follow and revenge. That had been years before when Kulonga, the son of Mbonga, the chief, had slain Kala. Then, single-handed, Tarzan had pursued and avenged. Now, though to a lesser degree, he was moved by the same passion.

He turned toward Taug. "Leave Gazan with Mumga," he said. "She is old and her fangs are broken and she is no good; but she can take care of Gazan until we return with Teeka, and if Gazan is dead when we come back," he turned to address Mumga, "I will kill you, too."

"Where are we going?" asked Taug.

"We are going to get Teeka," replied the ape-man, "and kill the bull who has stolen her. Come!"

He turned again to the spoor of the stranger bull, which showed plainly to his trained senses, nor did he glance back to note if Taug followed. The latter laid Gazan in Mumga's arms with a parting: "If he dies Tarzan will kill you," and he followed after the brown-skinned figure that already was moving at a slow trot along the jungle trail.

No other bull of the tribe of Kerchak was so good a trailer as Tarzan, for his trained senses were aided by a high order of intelligence. His judgment told him the natural trail for a quarry to follow, so that he need but note the most apparent marks upon the way, and today the trail of Toog was as plain to him as type upon a printed page to you or me.

Following close behind the lithe figure of the ape-man came the huge and shaggy bull ape. No words passed between them. They moved as silently as two shadows among the myriad shadows of the forest. Alert as his eyes and ears, was Tarzan's patrician nose. The spoor was fresh, and now that they had passed from the range of the strong ape odor of the tribe he had little difficulty in following Toog and Teeka by scent alone. Teeka's familiar scent spoor told both Tarzan and Taug that they were upon her trail, and soon the scent of Toog became as familiar as the other.

They were progressing rapidly when suddenly dense clouds overcast the sun. Tarzan accelerated his pace. Now he fairly flew along the jungle trail, or, where Toog had taken to the trees, followed nimbly as a squirrel along the bending, undulating pathway of the foliage branches, swinging from tree to tree as Toog had swung before them; but more rapidly because they were not handicapped by a burden such as Toog's.

Tarzan felt that they must be almost upon the quarry, for the scent spoor was becoming stronger and stronger, when the jungle was suddenly shot by livid lightning, and a deafening roar of thunder reverberated through the heavens and the forest until the earth trembled and shook. Then came the rain—not as it comes to us of the temperate zones, but as a mighty avalanche of water—a deluge which spills tons instead of drops upon the bending forest giants and the terrified creatures which haunt their shade.

And the rain did what Tarzan knew that it would do— it wiped the spoor of the quarry from the face of the earth. For a half hour the torrents fell—then the sun burst forth, jeweling the forest with a million scintillant gems; but today the ape-man, usually alert to the changing wonders of the jungle, saw them not. Only the fact that the spoor of Teeka and her abductor was obliterated found lodgment in his thoughts.

Even among the branches of the trees there are well-worn trails, just as there are trails upon the surface of the ground; but in the trees they branch and cross more often, since the way is more open than among the dense undergrowth at the surface. Along one of these well-marked trails Tarzan and Taug continued after the rain had ceased, because the ape-man knew that this was the most logical path for the thief to follow; but when they came to a fork, they were at a loss. Here they halted, while Tarzan examined every branch and leaf which might have been touched by the fleeing ape.

He sniffed the bole of the tree, and with his keen eyes he sought to find upon the bark some sign of the way the quarry had taken. It was slow work and all the time, Tarzan knew, the bull of the alien tribe was forging steadily away from them—gaining precious minutes that might carry him to safety before they could catch up with him.

First along one fork he went, and then another, applying every test that his wonderful junglecraft was cognizant of; but again and again he was baffled, for the scent had been washed away by the heavy downpour, in every exposed place. For a half hour Tarzan and Taug searched, until at last, upon the bottom of a broad leaf, Tarzan's keen nose caught the faint trace of the scent spoor of Toog, where the leaf had brushed a hairy shoulder as the great ape passed through the foliage.

Once again the two took up the trail, but it was slow work now and there were many discouraging delays when the spoor seemed lost beyond recovery. To you or me there would have been no spoor, even before the coming of the rain, except, possibly, where Toog had come to earth and followed a game trail. In such places the imprint of a huge handlike foot and the knuckles of one great hand were sometimes plain enough for an ordinary mortal to read. Tarzan knew from these and other indications that the ape was yet carrying Teeka. The depth of the imprint of his feet indicated a much greater weight than that of any of the larger bulls, for they were made under the combined weight of Toog and Teeka, while the fact that the knuckles of but one hand touched the ground at any time showed that the other hand was occupied in some other business—the business of holding the prisoner to a hairy shoulder. Tarzan could follow, in sheltered places, the changing of the burden from one shoulder to another, as indicated by the deepening of the foot imprint upon the side of the load, and the changing of the knuckle imprints from one side of the trail to the other.

There were stretches along the surface paths where the ape had gone for considerable distances entirely erect upon his hind feet—walking as a man walks; but the same might have been true of any of the great anthropoids of the same species, for, unlike the chimpanzee and the gorilla, they walk without the aid of their hands quite as readily as with. It was such things, however, which helped to identify to Tarzan and to Taug the appearance of the abductor, and with his individual scent characteristic already indelibly impressed upon their memories, they were in a far better position to know him when they came upon him, even should he have disposed of Teeka before, than is a modern sleuth with his photographs and Bertillon measurements, equipped to recognize a fugitive from civilized justice.

But with all their high-strung and delicately attuned perceptive faculties the two bulls of the tribe of Kerchak were often sore pressed to follow the trail at all, and at best were so delayed that in the afternoon of the second day, they still had not overhauled the fugitive. The scent was now strong, for it had been made since the rain, and Tarzan knew that it would not be long before they came upon the thief and his loot. Above them, as they crept stealthily forward, chattered Manu, the monkey, and his thousand fellows; squawked and screamed the brazen-throated birds of plumage; buzzed and hummed the countless insects amid the rustling of the forest leaves, and, as they passed, a little gray-beard, squeaking and scolding upon a swaying branch, looked down and saw them. Instantly the scolding and squeaking ceased, and off tore the long-tailed mite as though Sheeta, the panther, had been endowed with wings and was in close pursuit of him. To all appearances he was only a very much frightened little monkey, fleeing for his life—there seemed nothing sinister about him.

And what of Teeka during all this time? Was she at last resigned to her fate and accompanying her new mate in the proper humility of a loving and tractable spouse? A single glance at the pair would have answered these questions to the utter satisfaction of the most captious. She was torn and bleeding from many wounds, inflicted by the sullen Toog in his vain efforts to subdue her to his will, and Toog too was disfigured and mutilated; but with stubborn ferocity, he still clung to his now useless prize.

On through the jungle he forced his way in the direction of the stamping ground of his tribe. He hoped that his king would have forgotten his treason; but if not he was still resigned to his fate—any fate would be better than suffering longer the sole companionship of this frightful she, and then, too, he wished to exhibit his captive to his fellows. Maybe he could wish her on the king—it is possible that such a thought urged him on.

At last they came upon two bulls feeding in a parklike grove—a beautiful grove dotted with huge boulders half embedded in the rich loam—mute monuments, possibly, to a forgotten age when mighty glaciers rolled their slow course where now a torrid sun beats down upon a tropic jungle.

The two bulls looked up, baring long fighting fangs, as Toog appeared in the distance. The latter recognized the two as friends. "It is Toog," he growled. "Toog has come back with a new she."

The apes waited his nearer approach. Teeka turned a snarling, fanged face toward them. She was not pretty to look upon, yet through the blood and hatred upon her countenance they realized that she was beautiful, and they envied Toog—alas! they did not know Teeka.

As they squatted looking at one another there raced through the trees toward them a long-tailed little monkey with gray whiskers. He was a very excited little monkey when he came to a halt upon the limb of a tree directly overhead. "Two strange bulls come," he cried. One is a Mangani, the other a hideous ape without hair upon his body. They follow the spoor of Toog. I saw them."

The four apes turned their eyes backward along the trail Toog had just come; then they looked at one another for a minute. "Come," said the larger of Toog's two friends, "we will wait for the strangers in the thick bushes beyond the clearing."

He turned and waddled away across the open place, the others following him. The little monkey danced about, all excitement. His chief diversion in life was to bring about bloody encounters between the larger denizens of the forest, that he might sit in the safety of the trees and witness the spectacles. He was a glutton for gore, was this little, whiskered, gray monkey, so long as it was the gore of others— a typical fight fan was the graybeard.

The apes hid themselves in the shrubbery beside the trail along which the two stranger bulls would pass. Teeka trembled with excitement. She had heard the words of Manu, and she knew that the hairless ape must be Tarzan, while the other was, doubtless, Taug. Never, in her wildest hopes, had she expected succor of this sort. Her one thought had been to escape and find her way back to the tribe of Kerchak; but even this had appeared to her practically impossible, so closely did Toog watch her.

As Taug and Tarzan reached the grove where Toog had come upon his friends, the ape scent became so strong that both knew the quarry was but a short distance ahead. And so they went even more cautiously, for they wished to come upon the thief from behind if they could and charge him before he was aware of their presence. That a little gray-whiskered monkey had forestalled them they did not know, nor that three pairs of savage eyes were already watching their every move and waiting for them to come within reach of itching paws and slavering jowls.

On they came across the grove, and as they entered the path leading into the dense jungle beyond, a sudden "Kreeg-ah!" shrilled out close before them—a "Kreeg-ah" in the familiar voice of Teeka. The small brains of Toog and his companions had not been able to foresee that Teeka might betray them, and now that she had, they went wild with rage. Toog struck the she a mighty blow that felled her, and then the three rushed forth to do battle with Tarzan and Taug. The little monkey danced upon his perch and screamed with delight.

And indeed he might well be delighted, for it was a lovely fight. There were no preliminaries, no formalities, no introductions— the five bulls merely charged and clinched. They rolled in the narrow trail and into the thick verdure beside it. They bit and clawed and scratched and struck, and all the while they kept up the most frightful chorus of growlings and barkings and roarings. In five minutes they were torn and bleeding, and the little graybeard leaped high, shrilling his primitive bravos; but always his attitude was "thumbs down." He wanted to see something killed. He did not care whether it were friend or foe. It was blood he wanted—blood and death.

Taug had been set upon by Toog and another of the apes, while Tarzan had the third—a huge brute with the strength of a buffalo. Never before had Tarzan's assailant beheld so strange a creature as this slippery, hairless bull with which he battled. Sweat and blood covered Tarzan's sleek, brown hide. Again and again he slipped from the clutches of the great bull, and all the while he struggled to free his hunting knife from the scabbard in which it had stuck.

At length he succeeded—a brown hand shot out and clutched a hairy throat, another flew upward clutching the sharp blade. Three swift, powerful strokes and the bull relaxed with a groan, falling limp beneath his antagonist. Instantly Tarzan broke from the clutches of the dying bull and sprang to Taug's assistance. Toog saw him coming and wheeled to meet him. In the impact of the charge, Tarzan's knife was wrenched from his hand and then Toog closed with him. Now was the battle even—two against two—while on the verge, Teeka, now recovered from the blow that had felled her, slunk waiting for an opportunity to aid. She saw Tarzan's knife and picked it up. She never had used it, but knew how Tarzan used it. Always had she been afraid of the thing which dealt death to the mightiest of the jungle people with the ease that Tantor's great tusks deal death to Tantor's enemies.

She saw Tarzan's pocket pouch torn from his side, and with the curiosity of an ape, that even danger and excitement cannot entirely dispel, she picked this up, too.

Now the bulls were standing—the clinches had been broken. Blood streamed down their sides—their faces were crimsoned with it. Little graybeard was so fascinated that at last he had even forgotten to scream and dance; but sat rigid with delight in the enjoyment of the spectacle.

Back across the grove Tarzan and Taug forced their adversaries. Teeka followed slowly. She scarce knew what to do. She was lame and sore and exhausted from the frightful ordeal through which she had passed, and she had the confidence of her sex in the prowess of her mate and the other bull of her tribe—they would not need the help of a she in their battle with these two strangers.

The roars and screams of the fighters reverberated through the jungle, awakening the echoes in the distant hills. From the throat of Tarzan's antagonist had come a score of "Kreeg-ahs!" and now from behind came the reply he had awaited. Into the grove, barking and growling, came a score of huge bull apes—the fighting men of Toog's tribe.

Teeka saw them first and screamed a warning to Tarzan and Taug. Then she fled past the fighters toward the opposite side of the clearing, fear for a moment claiming her. Nor can one censure her after the frightful ordeal from which she was still suffering.

Down upon them came the great apes. In a moment Tarzan and Taug would be torn to shreds that would later form the *Piece de Resistance* of the savage orgy of a Dum-Dum. Teeka turned to glance back. She saw the impending fate of her defenders and there sprung to life in her savage bosom the spark of martyrdom, that some common forbear had transmitted alike to Teeka, the wild ape, and the glorious women of a higher order who have invited death for their men. With a shrill scream she ran toward the battlers who were rolling in a great mass at the foot of one of the huge boulders which dotted the grove; but what could she do? The knife she held she could not use to advantage because of her lesser strength. She had seen Tarzan throw missiles, and she had learned this with many other things from her childhood playmate. She sought for something to throw and at last her fingers touched upon the hard objects in the pouch that had been torn from the ape-man. Tearing the receptacle open, she gathered a handful of shiny cylinders—heavy for their size, they seemed to her, and good missiles. With all her strength she hurled them at the apes battling in front of the granite boulder.

The result surprised Teeka quite as much as it did the apes. There was a loud explosion, which deafened the fighters, and a puff of acrid smoke. Never before had one there heard such a frightful noise. Screaming with terror, the stranger bulls leaped to their feet and fled back toward the stamping ground of their tribe, while Taug and Tarzan slowly gathered themselves together and arose, lame and bleeding, to their feet. They, too, would have fled had they not seen Teeka standing there before them, the knife and the pocket pouch in her hands.

"What was it?" asked Tarzan.

Teeka shook her head. "I hurled these at the stranger bulls," and she held forth another handful of the shiny metal cylinders with the dull gray, cone-shaped ends.

Tarzan looked at them and scratched his head.

"What are they?" asked Taug.

"I do not know," said Tarzan. "I found them."

The little monkey with the gray beard halted among the trees a mile away and huddled, terrified, against a branch. He did not know that the dead father of Tarzan of the Apes, reaching back out of the past across a span of twenty years, had saved his son's life.

Nor did Tarzan, Lord Greystoke, know it either.

A JUNGLE JOKE

Time seldom hung heavily upon Tarzan's hands. Even where there is sameness there cannot be monotony if most of the sameness consists in dodging death first in one form and then in another; or in inflicting death upon others. There is a spice to such an existence; but even this Tarzan of the Apes varied in activities of his own invention.

He was full grown now, with the grace of a Greek god and the thews of a bull, and, by all the tenets of apedom, should have been sullen, morose, and brooding; but he was not. His spirits seemed not to age at all—he was still a playful child, much to the discomfiture of his fellow-apes. They could not understand him or his ways, for with maturity they quickly forgot their youth and its pastimes.

Nor could Tarzan quite understand them. It seemed strange to him that a few moons since, he had roped Taug about an ankle and dragged him screaming through the tall jungle grasses, and then rolled and tumbled in good-natured mimic battle when the young ape had freed himself, and that today when he had come up behind the same Taug and pulled him over backward upon the turf, instead of the playful young ape, a great, snarling beast had whirled and leaped for his throat.

Easily Tarzan eluded the charge and quickly Taug's anger vanished, though it was not replaced with playfulness; yet the ape-man realized that Taug was not amused nor was he amusing. The big bull ape seemed to have lost whatever sense of humor he once may have possessed. With a grunt of disappointment, young Lord Greystoke turned to other fields of endeavor. A strand of black hair fell across one eye. He brushed it aside with the palm of a hand and a toss of his head. It suggested something to do, so he sought his quiver which lay cached in the hollow bole of a lightning-riven tree. Removing the arrows he turned the quiver upside down, emptying upon the ground the contents of its bottom— his few treasures. Among them was a flat bit of stone and a shell which he had picked up from the beach near his father's cabin.

With great care he rubbed the edge of the shell back and forth upon the flat stone until the soft edge was quite fine and sharp. He worked much as a barber does who hones a razor, and with every evidence of similar practice; but his proficiency was the result of years of painstaking effort. Unaided he had worked out a method of his own for putting an edge upon the shell—he even tested it with the ball of his thumb— and when it met with his approval he grasped a wisp of hair which fell across his eyes, grasped it between the thumb and first finger of his left hand and sawed upon it with the sharpened shell until it was severed. All around his head he went until his black shock was rudely bobbed with a ragged bang in front. For the appearance of it he cared nothing; but in the matter of safety and comfort it meant everything. A lock of hair falling in one's eyes at the wrong moment might mean all the difference between life and death, while straggly strands, hanging down one's back were most uncomfortable, especially when wet with dew or rain or perspiration.

As Tarzan labored at his tonsorial task, his active mind was busy with many things. He recalled his recent battle with Bolgani, the gorilla, the wounds of which were but just healed. He pondered the strange sleep adventures of his first dreams, and he smiled at the painful outcome of his last practical joke upon the tribe, when, dressed in the hide of Numa, the lion, he had come roaring upon them, only to be leaped upon and almost killed by the great bulls whom he had taught how to defend themselves from an attack of their ancient enemy.

His hair lopped off to his entire satisfaction, and seeing no possibility of pleasure in the company of the tribe, Tarzan swung leisurely into the trees and set off in the direction of his cabin; but when part way there his attention was attracted by a strong scent spoor coming from the north. It was the scent of the Gomangani.

Curiosity, that best-developed, common heritage of man and ape, always prompted Tarzan to investigate where the Gomangani were concerned. There was that about them which aroused his imagination. Possibly it was because of the diversity of their activities and interests. The apes lived to eat and sleep and propagate. The same was true of all the other denizens of the jungle, save the Gomangani.

These black fellows danced and sang, scratched around in the earth from which they had cleared the trees and underbrush; they watched things grow, and when they had ripened, they cut them down and put them in straw-thatched huts. They made bows and spears and arrows, poison, cooking pots, things of metal to wear around their arms and legs. If it hadn't been for their black faces, their hideously disfigured features, and the fact that one of them had slain Kala, Tarzan might have wished to be one of them. At least he sometimes thought so, but always at the thought there rose within him a strange revulsion of feeling, which he could not interpret or understand—he simply knew that he hated the Gomangani, and that he would rather be Histah, the snake, than one of these.

But their ways were interesting, and Tarzan never tired of spying upon them. and from them he learned much more than he realized, though always his principal thought was of some new way in which he could render their lives miserable. The baiting of the blacks was Tarzan's chief divertissement.

Tarzan realized now that the blacks were very near and that there were many of them, so he went silently and with great caution. Noiselessly he moved through the lush grasses of the open spaces, and where the forest was dense, swung from one swaying branch to another, or leaped lightly over tangled masses of fallen trees where there was no way through the lower terraces, and the ground was choked and impassable.

And so presently he came within sight of the black warriors of Mbonga, the chief. They were engaged in a pursuit with which Tarzan was more or less familiar, having watched them at it upon other occasions. They were placing and baiting a trap for Numa, the lion. In a cage upon wheels they were tying a kid, so fastening it that when Numa seized the unfortunate creature, the door of the cage would drop behind him, making him a prisoner.

These things the blacks had learned in their old home, before they escaped through the untracked jungle to their new village. Formerly they had dwelt in the Belgian Congo until the cruelties of their heartless oppressors had driven them to seek the safety of unexplored solitudes beyond the boundaries of Leopold's domain.

In their old life they often had trapped animals for the agents of European dealers, and had learned from them certain tricks, such as this one, which permitted them to capture even Numa without injuring him, and to transport him in safety and with comparative ease to their village.

No longer was there a white market for their savage wares; but there was still a sufficient incentive for the taking of Numa—alive. First was the necessity for ridding the jungle of man-eaters, and it was only after depredations by these grim and terrible scourges that a lion hunt was organized. Secondarily was the excuse for an orgy of celebration was the hunt successful, and the fact that such fetes were rendered doubly pleasurable by the presence of a live creature that might be put to death by torture.

Tarzan had witnessed these cruel rites in the past. Being himself more savage than the savage warriors of the Gomangani, he was not so shocked by the cruelty of them as he should have been, yet they did shock him. He could not understand the strange feeling of revulsion which possessed him at such times. He had no love for Numa, the lion, yet he bristled with rage when the blacks inflicted upon his enemy such indignities and cruelties as only the mind of the one creature molded in the image of God can conceive.

Upon two occasions he had freed Numa from the trap before the blacks had returned to discover the success or failure of their venture. He would do the same today—that he decided immediately he realized the nature of their intentions.

Leaving the trap in the center of a broad elephant trail near the drinking hole, the warriors turned back toward their village. On the morrow they would come again. Tarzan looked after them, upon his lips an unconscious sneer—the heritage of unguessed caste. He saw them file along the broad trail, beneath the overhanging verdure of leafy branch and looped and festooned creepers, brushing ebon shoulders against gorgeous blooms which inscrutable Nature has seen fit to lavish most profusely farthest from the eye of man.

As Tarzan watched, through narrowed lids, the last of the warriors disappear beyond a turn in the trail, his expression altered to the urge of a newborn thought. A slow, grim smile touched his lips. He looked down upon the frightened, bleating kid, advertising, in its fear and its innocence, its presence and its helplessness.

Dropping to the ground, Tarzan approached the trap and entered. Without disturbing the fiber cord, which was adjusted to drop the door at the proper time, he loosened the living bait, tucked it under an arm and stepped out of the cage.

With his hunting knife he quieted the frightened animal, severing its jugular; then he dragged it, bleeding, along the trail down to the drinking hole, the half smile persisting upon his ordinarily grave face. At the water's edge the ape-man stooped and with hunting knife and quick strong fingers deftly removed the dead kid's viscera. Scraping a hole in the mud, he buried these parts which he did not eat, and swinging the body to his shoulder took to the trees.

For a short distance he pursued his way in the wake of the black warriors, coming down presently to bury the meat of his kill where it would be safe from the depredations of Dango, the hyena, or the other meat-eating beasts and birds of the jungle. He was hungry. Had he been all beast he would have eaten; but his man-mind could entertain urges even more potent than those of the belly, and now he was concerned with an idea which kept a smile upon his lips and his eyes sparkling in anticipation. An idea, it was, which permitted him to forget that he was hungry.

The meat safely cached, Tarzan trotted along the elephant trail after the Gomangani. Two or three miles from the cage he overtook them and then he swung into the trees and followed above and behind them—waiting his chance.

Among the blacks was Rabba Kega, the witch-doctor. Tarzan hated them all; but Rabba Kega he especially hated. As the blacks filed along the winding path, Rabba Kega, being lazy, dropped behind. This Tarzan noted, and it filled him with satisfaction—his being radiated a grim and terrible content. Like an angel of death he hovered above the unsuspecting black.

Rabba Kega, knowing that the village was but a short distance ahead, sat down to rest. Rest well, O Rabba Kega! It is thy last opportunity.

Tarzan crept stealthily among the branches of the tree above the well-fed, self-satisfied witch-doctor. He made no noise that the dull ears of man could hear above the soughing of the gentle jungle breeze among the undulating foliage of the upper terraces, and when he came close above the black man he halted, well concealed by leafy branch and heavy creeper.

Rabba Kega sat with his back against the bole of a tree, facing Tarzan. The position was not such as the waiting beast of prey desired, and so, with the infinite patience of the wild hunter, the ape-man crouched motionless and silent as a graven image until the fruit should be ripe for the plucking. A poisonous insect buzzed angrily out of space. It loitered, circling, close to Tarzan's face. The ape-man saw and recognized it.

The virus of its sting spelled death for lesser things than he—for him it would mean days of anguish. He did not move. His glittering eyes remained fixed upon Rabba Kega after acknowledging the presence of the winged torture by a single glance. He heard and followed the movements of the insect with his keen ears, and then he felt it alight upon his forehead. No muscle twitched, for the muscles of such as he are the servants of the brain. Down across his face crept the horrid thing—over nose and lips and chin. Upon his throat it paused, and turning, retraced its steps. Tarzan watched Rabba Kega. Now not even his eyes moved. So motionless he crouched that only death might counterpart his movelessness. The insect crawled upward over the nut-brown cheek and stopped with its antennae brushing the lashes of his lower lid. You or I would have started back, closing our eyes and striking at the thing; but you and I are the slaves, not the masters of our nerves. Had the thing crawled upon the eyeball of the ape-man, it is believable that he could yet have remained wide-eyed and rigid; but it did not. For a moment it loitered there close to the lower lid, then it rose and buzzed away.

Down toward Rabba Kega it buzzed and the black man heard it, saw it, struck at it, and was stung upon the cheek before he killed it. Then he rose with a howl of pain and anger, and as he turned up the trail toward the village of Mbonga, the chief, his broad, black back was exposed to the silent thing waiting above him.

And as Rabba Kega turned, a lithe figure shot outward and downward from the tree above upon his broad shoulders. The impact of the springing creature carried Rabba Kega to the ground. He felt strong jaws close upon his neck, and when he tried to scream, steel fingers throttled his throat. The powerful black warrior struggled to free himself; but he was as a child in the grip of his adversary.

Presently Tarzan released his grip upon the other's throat; but each time that Rabba Kega essayed a scream, the cruel fingers choked him painfully. At last the warrior desisted. Then Tarzan half rose and kneeled upon his victim's back, and when Rabba Kega struggled to arise, the ape-man pushed his face down into the dirt of the trail. With a bit of the rope that had secured the kid, Tarzan made Rabba Kega's wrists secure behind his back, then he rose and jerked his prisoner to his feet, faced him back along the trail and pushed him on ahead.

Not until he came to his feet did Rabba Kega obtain a square look at his assailant. When he saw that it was the white devil-god his heart sank within him and his knees trembled; but as he walked along the trail ahead of his captor and was neither injured nor molested his spirits slowly rose, so that he took heart again. Possibly the devil-god did not intend to kill him after all. Had he not had little Tibo in his power for days without harming him, and had he not spared Momaya, Tibo's mother, when he easily might have slain her?

And then they came upon the cage which Rabba Kega, with the other black warriors of the village of Mbonga, the chief, had placed and baited for Numa. Rabba Kega saw that the bait was gone, though there was no lion within the cage, nor was the door dropped. He saw and he was filled with wonder not unmixed with apprehension. It entered his dull brain that in some way this combination of circumstances had a connection with his presence there as the prisoner of the white devil-god.

Nor was he wrong. Tarzan pushed him roughly into the cage, and in another moment Rabba Kega understood. Cold sweat broke from every pore of his body—he trembled as with ague—for the ape-man was binding him securely in the very spot the kid had previously occupied. The witch-doctor pleaded, first for his life, and then for a death less cruel; but he might as well have saved his pleas for Numa, since already they were directed toward a wild beast who understood no word of what he said.

But his constant jabbering not only annoyed Tarzan, who worked in silence, but suggested that later the black might raise his voice in cries for succor, so he stepped out of the cage, gathered a handful of grass and a small stick and returning, jammed the grass into Rabba Kega's mouth, laid the stick crosswise between his teeth and fastened it there with the thong from Rabba Kega's loin cloth. Now could the witch-doctor but roll his eyes and sweat. Thus Tarzan left him.

The ape-man went first to the spot where he had cached the body of the kid. Digging it up, he ascended into a tree and proceeded to satisfy his hunger. What remained he again buried; then he swung away through the trees to the water hole, and going to the spot where fresh, cold water bubbled from between two rocks, he drank deeply. The other beasts might wade in and drink stagnant water; but not Tarzan of the Apes. In such matters he was fastidious. From his hands he washed every trace of the repugnant scent of the Gomangani, and from his face the blood of the kid. Rising, he stretched himself not unlike some huge, lazy cat, climbed into a near-by tree and fell asleep.

When he awoke it was dark, though a faint luminosity still tinged the western heavens. A lion moaned and coughed as it strode through the jungle toward water. It was approaching the drinking hole. Tarzan grinned sleepily, changed his position and fell asleep again.

When the blacks of Mbonga, the chief, reached their village they discovered that Rabba Kega was not among them. When several hours had elapsed they decided that something had happened to him, and it was the hope of the majority of the tribe that whatever had happened to him might prove fatal. They did not love the witch-doctor. Love and fear seldom are playmates; but a warrior is a warrior, and so Mbonga organized a searching party. That his own grief was not unassuagable might have been gathered from the fact that he remained at home and went to sleep. The young warriors whom he sent out remained steadfast to their purpose for fully half an hour, when, unfortunately for Rabba Kega— upon so slight a thing may the fate of a man rest—a honey bird attracted the attention of the searchers and led them off for the delicious store it previously had marked down for betrayal, and Rabba Kega's doom was sealed.

When the searchers returned empty handed, Mbonga was wroth; but when he saw the great store of honey they brought with them his rage subsided. Already Tubuto, young, agile and evil-minded, with face hideously painted, was practicing the black art upon a sick infant in the fond hope of succeeding to the office and perquisites of Rabba Kega. Tonight the women of the old witch-doctor would moan and howl. Tomorrow he would be forgotten. Such is life, such is fame, such is power—in the center of the world's highest civilization, or in the depths of the black, primeval jungle. Always, everywhere, man is man, nor has he altered greatly beneath his veneer since he scurried into a hole between two rocks to escape the tyrannosaurus six million years ago.

The morning following the disappearance of Rabba Kega, the warriors set out with Mbonga, the chief, to examine the trap they had set for Numa. Long before they reached the cage, they heard the roaring of a great lion and guessed that they had made a successful bag, so it was with shouts of joy that they approached the spot where they should find their captive.

Yes! There he was, a great, magnificent specimen—a huge, black-maned lion. The warriors were frantic with delight. They leaped into the air and uttered savage cries—hoarse victory cries, and then they came closer, and the cries died upon their lips, and their eyes went wide so that the whites showed all around their irises, and their pendulous lower lips drooped with their drooping jaws. They drew back in terror at the sight within the cage—the mauled and mutilated corpse of what had, yesterday, been Rabba Kega, the witch-doctor.

The captured lion had been too angry and frightened to feed upon the body of his kill; but he had vented upon it much of his rage, until it was a frightful thing to behold.

From his perch in a near-by tree Tarzan of the Apes, Lord Greystoke, looked down upon the black warriors and grinned. Once again his self-pride in his ability as a practical joker asserted itself. It had lain dormant for some time following the painful mauling he had received that time he leaped among the apes of Kerchak clothed in the skin of Numa; but this joke was a decided success.

After a few moments of terror, the blacks came closer to the cage, rage taking the place of fear—rage and curiosity. How had Rabba Kega happened to be in the cage? Where was the kid? There was no sign nor remnant of the original bait. They looked closely and they saw, to their horror, that the corpse of their erstwhile fellow was bound with the very cord with which they had secured the kid. Who could have done this thing? They looked at one another.

EDGAR RICE BURROUGHS

Tubuto was the first to speak. He had come hopefully out with the expedition that morning. Somewhere he might find evidence of the death of Rabba Kega. Now he had found it, and he was the first to find an explanation.

"The white devil-god," he whispered. "It is the work of the white devil-god!"

No one contradicted Tubuto, for, indeed, who else could it have been but the great, hairless ape they all so feared? And so their hatred of Tarzan increased again with an increased fear of him. And Tarzan sat in his tree and hugged himself.

No one there felt sorrow because of the death of Rabba Kega; but each of the blacks experienced a personal fear of the ingenious mind which might discover for any of them a death equally horrible to that which the witch-doctor had suffered. It was a subdued and thoughtful company which dragged the captive lion along the broad elephant path back to the village of Mbonga, the chief.

And it was with a sigh of relief that they finally rolled it into the village and closed the gates behind them. Each had experienced the sensation of being spied upon from the moment they left the spot where the trap had been set, though none had seen or heard aught to give tangible food to his fears.

At the sight of the body within the cage with the lion, the women and children of the village set up a most frightful lamentation, working themselves into a joyous hysteria which far transcended the happy misery derived by their more civilized prototypes who make a business of dividing their time between the movies and the neighborhood funerals of friends and strangers—especially strangers.

From a tree overhanging the palisade, Tarzan watched all that passed within the village. He saw the frenzied women tantalizing the great lion with sticks and stones. The cruelty of the blacks toward a captive always induced in Tarzan a feeling of angry contempt for the Gomangani. Had he attempted to analyze this feeling he would have found it difficult, for during all his life he had been accustomed to sights of suffering and cruelty. He, himself, was cruel. All the beasts of the jungle were cruel; but the cruelty of the blacks was of a different order. It was the cruelty of wanton torture of the helpless, while the cruelty of Tarzan and the other beasts was the cruelty of necessity or of passion.

Perhaps, had he known it, he might have credited this feeling of repugnance at the sight of unnecessary suffering to heredity—to the germ of British love of fair play which had been bequeathed to him by his father and his mother; but, of course, he did not know, since he still believed that his mother had been Kala, the great ape.

And just in proportion as his anger rose against the Gomangani his savage sympathy went out to Numa, the lion, for, though Numa was his lifetime enemy, there was neither bitterness nor contempt in Tarzan's sentiments toward him. In the ape-man's mind, therefore, the determination formed to thwart the blacks and liberate the lion; but he must accomplish this in some way which would cause the Gomangani the greatest chagrin and discomfiture.

As he squatted there watching the proceeding beneath him, he saw the warriors seize upon the cage once more and drag it between two huts. Tarzan knew that it would remain there now until evening, and that the blacks were planning a feast and orgy in celebration of their capture. When he saw that two warriors were placed beside the cage, and that these drove off the women and children and young men who would have eventually tortured Numa to death, he knew that the lion would be safe until he was needed for the evening's entertainment, when he would be more cruelly and scientifically tortured for the edification of the entire tribe.

Now Tarzan preferred to bait the blacks in as theatric a manner as his fertile imagination could evolve. He had some half-formed conception of their superstitious fears and of their especial dread of night, and so he decided to wait until darkness fell and the blacks partially worked to hysteria by their dancing and religious rites before he took any steps toward the freeing of Numa. In the meantime, he hoped, an idea adequate to the possibilities of the various factors at hand would occur to him. Nor was it long before one did.

He had swung off through the jungle to search for food when the plan came to him. At first it made him smile a little and then look dubious, for he still retained a vivid memory of the dire results that had followed the carrying out of a very wonderful idea along almost identical lines, yet he did not abandon his intention, and a moment later, food temporarily forgotten, he was swinging through the middle terraces in rapid flight toward the stamping ground of the tribe of Kerchak, the great ape.

As was his wont, he alighted in the midst of the little band without announcing his approach save by a hideous scream just as he sprang from a branch above them. Fortunate are the apes of Kerchak that their kind is not subject to heart failure, for the methods of Tarzan subjected them to one severe shock after another, nor could they ever accustom themselves to the ape-man's peculiar style of humor.

Now, when they saw who it was they merely snarled and grumbled angrily for a moment and then resumed their feeding or their napping which he had interrupted, and he, having had his little joke, made his way to the hollow tree where he kept his treasures hid from the inquisitive eyes and fingers of his fellows and the mischievous little manus. Here he withdrew a closely rolled hide—the hide of Numa with the head on; a clever bit of primitive curing and mounting, which had once been the property of the witch-doctor, Rabba Kega, until Tarzan had stolen it from the village.

With this he made his way back through the jungle toward the village of the blacks, stopping to hunt and feed upon the way, and, in the afternoon, even napping for an hour, so that it was already dusk when he entered the great tree which overhung the palisade and gave him a view of the entire village. He saw that Numa was still alive and that the guards were even dozing beside the cage. A lion is no great novelty to a black man in the lion country, and the first keen edge of their desire to worry the brute having worn off, the villagers paid little or no attention to the great cat, preferring now to await the grand event of the night.

Nor was it long after dark before the festivities commenced. To the beating of tom-toms, a lone warrior, crouched half doubled, leaped into the firelight in the center of a great circle of other warriors, behind whom stood or squatted the women and the children. The dancer was painted and armed for the hunt and his movements and gestures suggested the search for the spoor of game. Bending low, sometimes resting for a moment on one knee, he searched the ground for signs of the quarry; again he poised, statuesque, listening. The warrior was young and lithe and graceful; he was full-muscled and arrow-straight. The firelight glistened upon his ebon body and brought out into bold relief the grotesque designs painted upon his face, breasts, and abdomen.

Presently he bent low to the earth, then leaped high in air. Every line of face and body showed that he had struck the scent. Immediately he leaped toward the circle of warriors about him, telling them of his find and summoning them to the hunt. It was all in pantomime; but so truly done that even Tarzan could follow it all to the least detail.

He saw the other warriors grasp their hunting spears and leap to their feet to join in the graceful, stealthy "stalking dance." It was very interesting; but Tarzan realized that if he was to carry his design to a successful conclusion he must act quickly. He had seen these dances before and knew that after the stalk would come the game at bay and then the kill, during which Numa would be surrounded by warriors, and unapproachable.

With the lion's skin under one arm the ape-man dropped to the ground in the dense shadows beneath the tree and then circled behind the huts until he came out directly in the rear of the cage, in which Numa paced nervously to and fro. The cage was now unguarded, the two warriors having left it to take their places among the other dancers.

Behind the cage Tarzan adjusted the lion's skin about him, just as he had upon that memorable occasion when the apes of Kerchak, failing to pierce his disguise, had all but slain him. Then, on hands and knees, he crept forward, emerged from between the two huts and stood a few paces back of the dusky audience, whose whole attention was centered upon the dancers before them.

Tarzan saw that the blacks had now worked themselves to a proper pitch of nervous excitement to be ripe for the lion. In a moment the ring of spectators would break at a point nearest the caged lion and the victim would be rolled into the center of the circle. It was for this moment that Tarzan waited.

At last it came. A signal was given by Mbonga, the chief, at which the women and children immediately in front of Tarzan rose and moved to one side, leaving a broad path opening toward the caged lion. At the same instant Tarzan gave voice to the low, couching roar of an angry lion and slunk slowly forward through the open lane toward the frenzied dancers.

A woman saw him first and screamed. Instantly there was a panic in the immediate vicinity of the ape-man. The strong light from the fire fell full upon the lion head and the blacks leaped to the conclusion, as Tarzan had known they would, that their captive had escaped his cage.

With another roar, Tarzan moved forward. The dancing warriors paused but an instant. They had been hunting a lion securely housed within a strong cage, and now that he was at liberty among them, an entirely different aspect was placed upon the matter. Their nerves were not attuned to this emergency. The women and children already had fled to the questionable safety of the nearest huts, and the warriors were not long in following their example, so that presently Tarzan was left in sole possession of the village street.

But not for long. Nor did he wish to be left thus long alone. It would not comport with his scheme. Presently a head peered forth from a near-by hut, and then another and another until a score or more of warriors were looking out upon him, waiting for his next move—waiting for the lion to charge or to attempt to escape from the village.

Their spears were ready in their hands against either a charge or a bolt for freedom, and then the lion rose erect upon its hind legs, the tawny skin dropped from it and there stood revealed before them in the firelight the straight young figure of the white devil-god.

For an instant the blacks were too astonished to act. They feared this apparition fully as much as they did Numa, yet they would gladly have slain the thing could they quickly enough have gathered together their wits; but fear and superstition and a natural mental density held them paralyzed while the ape-man stooped and gathered up the lion skin. They saw him turn then and walk back into the shadows at the far end of the village. Not until then did they gain courage to pursue him, and when they had come in force, with brandished spears and loud war cries, the quarry was gone.

Not an instant did Tarzan pause in the tree. Throwing the skin over a branch he leaped again into the village upon the opposite side of the great bole, and diving into the shadow of a hut, ran quickly to where lay the caged lion. Springing to the top of the cage he pulled upon the cord which raised the door, and a moment later a great lion in the prime of his strength and vigor leaped out into the village.

The warriors, returning from a futile search for Tarzan, saw him step into the firelight. Ah! there was the devil-god again, up to his old trick. Did he think he could twice fool the men of Mbonga, the chief, the same way in so short a time? They would show him! For long they had waited for such an opportunity to rid themselves forever of this fearsome jungle demon. As one they rushed forward with raised spears.

The women and the children came from the huts to witness the slaying of the devil-god. The lion turned blazing eyes upon them and then swung about toward the advancing warriors.

With shouts of savage joy and triumph they came toward him, menacing him with their spears. The devil-god was theirs!

And then, with a frightful roar, Numa, the lion, charged.

The men of Mbonga, the chief, met Numa with ready spears and screams of raillery. In a solid mass of muscled ebony they waited the coming of the devil-god; yet beneath their brave exteriors lurked a haunting fear that all might not be quite well with them—that this strange creature could yet prove invulnerable to their weapons and inflict upon them full punishment for their effrontery. The charging lion was all too lifelike—they saw that in the brief instant of the charge; but beneath the tawny hide they knew was hid the soft flesh of the white man, and how could that withstand the assault of many war spears?

In their forefront stood a huge young warrior in the full arrogance of his might and his youth. Afraid? Not he! He laughed as Numa bore down upon him; he laughed and couched his spear, setting the point for the broad breast. And then the lion was upon him. A great paw swept away the heavy war spear, splintering it as the hand of man might splinter a dry twig.

Down went the black, his skull crushed by another blow. And then the lion was in the midst of the warriors, clawing and tearing to right and left. Not for long did they stand their ground; but a dozen men were mauled before the others made good their escape from those frightful talons and gleaming fangs.

In terror the villagers fled hither and thither. No hut seemed a sufficiently secure asylum with Numa ranging within the palisade. From one to another fled the frightened blacks, while in the center of the village Numa stood glaring and growling above his kills.

At last a tribesman flung wide the gates of the village and sought safety amid the branches of the forest trees beyond. Like sheep his fellows followed him, until the lion and his dead remained alone in the village.

From the nearer trees the men of Mbonga saw the lion lower his great head and seize one of his victims by the shoulder and then with slow and stately tread move down the village street past the open gates and on into the jungle. They saw and shuddered, and from another tree Tarzan of the Apes saw and smiled.

A full hour elapsed after the lion had disappeared with his feast before the blacks ventured down from the trees and returned to their village. Wide eyes rolled from side to side, and naked flesh contracted more to the chill of fear than to the chill of the jungle night.

"It was he all the time," murmured one. "It was the devil-god."

"He changed himself from a lion to a man, and back again into a lion," whispered another.

"And he dragged Mweeza into the forest and is eating him," said a third, shuddering.

"We are no longer safe here," wailed a fourth. "Let us take our belongings and search for another village site far from the haunts of the wicked devil-god."

But with morning came renewed courage, so that the experiences of the preceding evening had little other effect than to increase their fear of Tarzan and strengthen their belief in his supernatural origin.

And thus waxed the fame and the power of the ape-man in the mysterious haunts of the savage jungle where he ranged, mightiest of beasts because of the man-mind which directed his giant muscles and his flawless courage.

TARZAN RESCUES THE MOON

The moon shone down out of a cloudless sky—a huge, swollen moon that seemed so close to earth that one might wonder that she did not brush the crooning tree tops. It was night, and Tarzan was abroad in the jungle—Tarzan, the ape-man; mighty fighter, mighty hunter. Why he swung through the dark shadows of the somber forest he could not have told you. It was not that he was hungry—he had fed well this day, and in a safe cache were the remains of his kill, ready against the coming of a new appetite. Perhaps it was the very joy of living that urged him from his arboreal couch to pit his muscles and his senses against the jungle night, and then, too, Tarzan always was goaded by an intense desire to know.

The jungle which is presided over by Kudu, the sun, is a very different jungle from that of Goro, the moon. The diurnal jungle has its own aspect—its own lights and shades, its own birds, its own blooms, its own beasts; its noises are the noises of the day. The lights and shades of the nocturnal jungle are as different as one might imagine the lights and shades of another world to differ from those of our world; its beasts, its blooms, and its birds are not those of the jungle of Kudu, the sun.

Because of these differences Tarzan loved to investigate the jungle by night. Not only was the life another life; but it was richer in numbers and in romance; it was richer in dangers, too, and to Tarzan of the Apes danger was the spice of life. And the noises of the jungle night—the roar of the lion, the scream of the leopard, the hideous laughter of Dango, the hyena, were music to the ears of the ape-man.

EDGAR RICE BURROUGHS

The soft padding of unseen feet, the rustling of leaves and grasses to the passage of fierce beasts, the sheen of opalesque eyes flaming through the dark, the million sounds which proclaimed the teeming life that one might hear and scent, though seldom see, constituted the appeal of the nocturnal jungle to Tarzan.

Tonight he had swung a wide circle—toward the east first and then toward the south, and now he was rounding back again into the north. His eyes, his ears and his keen nostrils were ever on the alert. Mingled with the sounds he knew, there were strange sounds—weird sounds which he never heard until after Kudu had sought his lair below the far edge of the big water-sounds which belonged to Goro, the moon—and to the mysterious period of Goro's supremacy. These sounds often caused Tarzan profound speculation. They baffled him because he thought that he knew his jungle so well that there could be nothing within it unfamiliar to him. Sometimes he thought that as colors and forms appeared to differ by night from their familiar daylight aspects, so sounds altered with the passage of Kudu and the coming of Goro, and these thoughts roused within his brain a vague conjecture that perhaps Goro and Kudu influenced these changes. And what more natural that eventually he came to attribute to the sun and the moon personalities as real as his own? The sun was a living creature and ruled the day. The moon, endowed with brains and miraculous powers, ruled the night.

Thus functioned the untrained man-mind groping through the dark night of ignorance for an explanation of the things he could not touch or smell or hear and of the great, unknown powers of nature which he could not see.

As Tarzan swung north again upon his wide circle the scent of the Gomangani came to his nostrils, mixed with the acrid odor of wood smoke. The ape-man moved quickly in the direction from which the scent was borne down to him upon the gentle night wind. Presently the ruddy sheen of a great fire filtered through the foliage to him ahead, and when Tarzan came to a halt in the trees near it, he saw a party of half a dozen black warriors huddled close to the blaze. It was evidently a hunting party from the village of Mbonga, the chief, caught out in the jungle after dark. In a rude circle about them they had constructed a thorn boma which, with the aid of the fire, they apparently hoped would discourage the advances of the larger carnivora.

That hope was not conviction was evidenced by the very palpable terror in which they crouched, wide-eyed and trembling, for already Numa and Sabor were moaning through the jungle toward them. There were other creatures, too, in the shadows beyond the firelight. Tarzan could see their yellow eyes flaming there. The blacks saw them and shivered. Then one arose and grasping a burning branch from the fire hurled it at the eyes, which immediately disappeared. The black sat down again. Tarzan watched and saw that it was several minutes before the eyes began to reappear in twos and fours.

Then came Numa, the lion, and Sabor, his mate. The other eyes scattered to right and left before the menacing growls of the great cats, and then the huge orbs of the man-eaters flamed alone out of the darkness. Some of the blacks threw themselves upon their faces and moaned; but he who before had hurled the burning branch now hurled another straight at the faces of the hungry lions, and they, too, disappeared as had the lesser lights before them. Tarzan was much interested. He saw a new reason for the nightly fires maintained by the blacks—a reason in addition to those connected with warmth and light and cooking. The beasts of the jungle feared fire, and so fire was, in a measure, a protection from them. Tarzan himself knew a certain awe of fire. Once he had, in investigating an abandoned fire in the village of the blacks, picked up a live coal. Since then he had maintained a respectful distance from such fires as he had seen. One experience had sufficed.

For a few minutes after the black hurled the firebrand no eyes appeared, though Tarzan could hear the soft padding of feet all about him. Then flashed once more the twin fire spots that marked the return of the lord of the jungle and a moment later, upon a slightly lower level, there appeared those of Sabor, his mate.

For some time they remained fixed and unwavering—a constellation of fierce stars in the jungle night—then the male lion advanced slowly toward the boma, where all but a single black still crouched in trembling terror. When this lone guardian saw that Numa was again approaching, he threw another firebrand, and, as before, Numa retreated and with him Sabor, the lioness; but not so far, this time, nor for so long. Almost instantly they turned and began circling the boma, their eyes turning constantly toward the firelight, while low, throaty growls evidenced their increasing displeasure. Beyond the lions glowed the flaming eyes of the lesser satellites, until the black jungle was shot all around the black men's camp with little spots of fire.

Again and again the black warrior hurled his puny brands at the two big cats; but Tarzan noticed that Numa paid little or no attention to them after the first few retreats. The ape-man knew by Numa's voice that the lion was hungry and surmised that he had made up his mind to feed upon a Gomangani; but would he dare a closer approach to the dreaded flames?

Even as the thought was passing in Tarzan's mind, Numa stopped his restless pacing and faced the boma. For a moment he stood motionless, except for the quick, nervous upcurving of his tail, then he walked deliberately forward, while Sabor moved restlessly to and fro where he had left her. The black man called to his comrades that the lion was coming, but they were too far gone in fear to do more than huddle closer together and moan more loudly than before.

Seizing a blazing branch the man cast it straight into the face of the lion. There was an angry roar, followed by a swift charge. With a single bound the savage beast cleared the boma wall as, with almost equal agility, the warrior cleared it upon the opposite side and, chancing the dangers lurking in the darkness, bolted for the nearest tree.

Numa was out of the boma almost as soon as he was inside it; but as he went back over the low thorn wall, he took a screaming negro with him. Dragging his victim along the ground he walked back toward Sabor, the lioness, who joined him, and the two continued into the blackness, their savage growls mingling with the piercing shrieks of the doomed and terrified man.

At a little distance from the blaze the lions halted, there ensued a short succession of unusually vicious growls and roars, during which the cries and moans of the black man ceased—forever.

Presently Numa reappeared in the firelight. He made a second trip into the boma and the former grisly tragedy was reenacted with another howling victim.

Tarzan rose and stretched lazily. The entertainment was beginning to bore him. He yawned and turned upon his way toward the clearing where the tribe would be sleeping in the encircling trees.

Yet even when he had found his familiar crotch and curled himself for slumber, he felt no desire to sleep. For a long time he lay awake thinking and dreaming. He looked up into the heavens and watched the moon and the stars. He wondered what they were and what power kept them from falling. His was an inquisitive mind. Always he had been full of questions concerning all that passed around him; but there never had been one to answer his questions. In childhood he had wanted to *know*, and, denied almost all knowledge, he still, in manhood, was filled with the great, unsatisfied curiosity of a child.

He was never quite content merely to perceive that things happened—he desired to know *why* they happened. He wanted to know what made things go. The secret of life interested him immensely. The miracle of death he could not quite fathom. Upon innumerable occasions he had investigated the internal mechanism of his kills, and once or twice he had opened the chest cavity of victims in time to see the heart still pumping.

He had learned from experience that a knife thrust through this organ brought immediate death nine times out of ten, while he might stab an antagonist innumerable times in other places without even disabling him. And so he had come to think of the heart, or, as he called it, "the red thing that breathes," as the seat and origin of life.

The brain and its functionings he did not comprehend at all. That his sense perceptions were transmitted to his brain and there translated, classified, and labeled was something quite beyond him. He thought that his fingers knew when they touched something, that his eyes knew when they saw, his ears when they heard, his nose when it scented.

He considered his throat, epidermis, and the hairs of his head as the three principal seats of emotion. When Kala had been slain a peculiar choking sensation had possessed his throat; contact with Histah, the snake, imparted an unpleasant sensation to the skin of his whole body; while the approach of an enemy made the hairs on his scalp stand erect.

Imagine, if you can, a child filled with the wonders of nature, bursting with queries and surrounded only by beasts of the jungle to whom his questionings were as strange as Sanskrit would have been. If he asked Gunto what made it rain, the big old ape would but gaze at him in dumb astonishment for an instant and then return to his interesting and edifying search for fleas; and when he questioned Mumga, who was very old and should have been very wise, but wasn't, as to the reason for the closing of certain flowers after Kudu had deserted the sky, and the opening of others during the night, he was surprised to discover that Mumga had never noticed these interesting facts, though she could tell to an inch just where the fattest grubworm should be hiding.

To Tarzan these things were wonders. They appealed to his intellect and to his imagination. He saw the flowers close and open; he saw certain blooms which turned their faces always toward the sun; he saw leaves which moved when there was no breeze; he saw vines crawl like living things up the boles and over the branches of great trees; and to Tarzan of the Apes the flowers and the vines and the trees were living creatures. He often talked to them, as he talked to Goro, the moon, and Kudu, the sun, and always was he disappointed that they did not reply. He asked them questions; but they could not answer, though he knew that the whispering of the leaves was the language of the leaves—they talked with one another.

The wind he attributed to the trees and grasses. He thought that they swayed themselves to and fro, creating the wind. In no other way could he account for this phenomenon. The rain he finally attributed to the stars, the moon, and the sun; but his hypothesis was entirely unlovely and unpoetical.

Tonight as Tarzan lay thinking, there sprang to his fertile imagination an explanation of the stars and the moon. He became quite excited about it. Taug was sleeping in a nearby crotch. Tarzan swung over beside him.

"Taug!" he cried. Instantly the great bull was awake and bristling, sensing danger from the nocturnal summons. "Look, Taug!" exclaimed Tarzan, pointing toward the stars. "See the eyes of Numa and Sabor, of Sheeta and Dango. They wait around Goro to leap in upon him for their kill. See the eyes and the nose and the mouth of Goro. And the light that shines upon his face is the light of the great fire he has built to frighten away Numa and Sabor and Dango and Sheeta.

"All about him are the eyes, Taug, you can see them! But they do not come very close to the fire—there are few eyes close to Goro. They fear the fire! It is the fire that saves Goro from Numa. Do you see them, Taug? Some night Numa will be very hungry and very angry—then he will leap over the thorn bushes which encircle Goro and we will have no more light after Kudu seeks his lair—the night will be black with the blackness that comes when Goro is lazy and sleeps late into the night, or when he wanders through the skies by day, forgetting the jungle and its people."

Taug looked stupidly at the heavens and then at Tarzan. A meteor fell, blazing a flaming way through the sky.

"Look!" cried Tarzan. "Goro has thrown a burning branch at Numa."

Taug grumbled. "Numa is down below," he said. "Numa does not hunt above the trees." But he looked curiously and a little fearfully at the bright stars above him, as though he saw them for the first time, and doubtless it was the first time that Taug ever had seen the stars, though they had been in the sky above him every night of his life. To Taug they were as the gorgeous jungle blooms—he could not eat them and so he ignored them.

Taug fidgeted and was nervous. For a long time he lay sleepless, watching the stars—the flaming eyes of the beasts of prey surrounding Goro, the moon—Goro, by whose light the apes danced to the beating of their earthen drums. If Goro should be eaten by Numa there could be no more Dum-Dums. Taug was overwhelmed by the thought. He glanced at Tarzan half fearfully. Why was his friend so different from the others of the tribe? No one else whom Taug ever had known had had such queer thoughts as Tarzan. The ape scratched his head and wondered, dimly, if Tarzan was a safe companion, and then he recalled slowly, and by a laborious mental process, that Tarzan had served him better than any other of the apes, even the strong and wise bulls of the tribe.

Tarzan it was who had freed him from the blacks at the very time that Taug had thought Tarzan wanted Teeka. It was Tarzan who had saved Taug's little balu from death. It was Tarzan who had conceived and carried out the plan to pursue Teeka's abductor and rescue the stolen one. Tarzan had fought and bled in Taug's service so many times that Taug, although only a brutal ape, had had impressed upon his mind a fierce loyalty which nothing now could swerve—his friendship for Tarzan had become a habit, a tradition almost, which would endure while Taug endured. He never showed any outward demonstration of affection—he growled at Tarzan as he growled at the other bulls who came too close while he was feeding—but he would have died for Tarzan. He knew it and Tarzan knew it; but of such things apes do not speak—their vocabulary, for the finer instincts, consisting more of actions than words. But now Taug was worried, and he fell asleep again still thinking of the strange words of his fellow.

The following day he thought of them again, and without any intention of disloyalty he mentioned to Gunto what Tarzan had suggested about the eyes surrounding Goro, and the possibility that sooner or later Numa would charge the moon and devour him. To the apes all large things in nature are male, and so Goro, being the largest creature in the heavens by night, was, to them, a bull.

Gunto bit a sliver from a horny finger and recalled the fact that Tarzan had once said that the trees talked to one another, and Gozan recounted having seen the ape-man dancing alone in the moonlight with Sheeta, the panther. They did not know that Tarzan had roped the savage beast and tied him to a tree before he came to earth and leaped about before the rearing cat, to tantalize him.

Others told of seeing Tarzan ride upon the back of Tantor, the elephant; of his bringing the black boy, Tibo, to the tribe, and of mysterious things with which he communed in the strange lair by the sea. They had never understood his books, and after he had shown them to one or two of the tribe and discovered that even the pictures carried no impression to their brains, he had desisted.

"Tarzan is not an ape," said Gunto. "He will bring Numa to eat us, as he is bringing him to eat Goro. We should kill him."

Immediately Taug bristled. Kill Tarzan! "First you will kill Taug," he said, and lumbered away to search for food.

But others joined the plotters. They thought of many things which Tarzan had done—things which apes did not do and could not understand. Again Gunto voiced the opinion that the Tarmangani, the white ape, should be slain, and the others, filled with terror about the stories they had heard, and thinking Tarzan was planning to slay Goro, greeted the proposal with growls of accord.

Among them was Teeka, listening with all her ears; but her voice was not raised in furtherance of the plan. Instead she bristled, showing her fangs, and afterward she went away in search of Tarzan; but she could not find him, as he was roaming far afield in search of meat. She found Taug, though, and told him what the others were planning, and the great bull stamped upon the ground and roared. His bloodshot eyes blazed with wrath, his upper lip curled up to expose his fighting fangs, and the hair upon his spine stood erect, and then a rodent scurried across the open and Taug sprang to seize it. In an instant he seemed to have forgotten his rage against the enemies of his friend; but such is the mind of an ape.

Several miles away Tarzan of the Apes lolled upon the broad head of Tantor, the elephant. He scratched beneath the great ears with the point of a sharp stick, and he talked to the huge pachyderm of everything which filled his black-thatched head. Little, or nothing, of what he said did Tantor understand; but Tantor is a good listener. Swaying from side to side he stood there enjoying the companionship of his friend, the friend he loved, and absorbing the delicious sensations of the scratching.

Numa, the lion, caught the scent of man, and warily stalked it until he came within sight of his prey upon the head of the mighty tusker; then he turned, growling and muttering, away in search of more propitious hunting grounds.

The elephant caught the scent of the lion, borne to him by an eddying breeze, and lifting his trunk trumpeted loudly. Tarzan stretched back luxuriously, lying supine at full length along the rough hide. Flies swarmed about his face; but with a leafy branch torn from a tree he lazily brushed them away.

"Tantor," he said, "it is good to be alive. It is good to lie in the cool shadows. It is good to look upon the green trees and the bright colors of the flowers—upon everything which Bulamutumumo has put here for us. He is very good to us, Tantor; He has given you tender leaves and bark, and rich grasses to eat; to me He has given Bara and Horta and Pisah, the fruits and the nuts and the roots. He provides for each the food that each likes best. All that He asks is that we be strong enough or cunning enough to go forth and take it. Yes, Tantor, it is good to live. I should hate to die."

Tantor made a little sound in his throat and curled his trunk upward that he might caress the ape-man's cheek with the finger at its tip.

"Tantor," said Tarzan presently, "turn and feed in the direction of the tribe of Kerchak, the great ape, that Tarzan may ride home upon your head without walking."

The tusker turned and moved slowly off along a broad, tree-arched trail, pausing occasionally to pluck a tender branch, or strip the edible bark from an adjacent tree. Tarzan sprawled face downward upon the beast's head and back, his legs hanging on either side, his head supported by his open palms, his elbows resting on the broad cranium. And thus they made their leisurely way toward the gathering place of the tribe.

Just before they arrived at the clearing from the north there reached it from the south another figure—that of a well-knit black warrior, who stepped cautiously through the jungle, every sense upon the alert against the many dangers which might lurk anywhere along the way. Yet he passed beneath the southernmost sentry that was posted in a great tree commanding the trail from the south. The ape permitted the Gomangani to pass unmolested, for he saw that he was alone; but the moment that the warrior had entered the clearing a loud "Kreeg-ah!" rang out from behind him, immediately followed by a chorus of replies from different directions, as the great bulls crashed through the trees in answer to the summons of their fellow.

The black man halted at the first cry and looked about him. He could see nothing, but he knew the voice of the hairy tree men whom he and his kind feared, not alone because of the strength and ferocity of the savage beings, but as well through a superstitious terror engendered by the manlike appearance of the apes.

But Bulabantu was no coward. He heard the apes all about him; he knew that escape was probably impossible, so he stood his ground, his spear ready in his hand and a war cry trembling on his lips. He would sell his life dearly, would Bulabantu, under-chief of the village of Mbonga, the chief.

Tarzan and Tantor were but a short distance away when the first cry of the sentry rang out through the quiet jungle. Like a flash the ape-man leaped from the elephant's back to a near-by tree and was swinging rapidly in the direction of the clearing before the echoes of the first "Kreeg-ah" had died away. When he arrived he saw a dozen bulls circling a single Gomangani. With a blood-curdling scream Tarzan sprang to the attack. He hated the blacks even more than did the apes, and here was an opportunity for a kill in the open. What had the Gomangani done? Had he slain one of the tribe?

Tarzan asked the nearest ape. No, the Gomangani had harmed none. Gozan, being on watch, had seen him coming through the forest and had warned the tribe—that was all. The ape-man pushed through the circle of bulls, none of which as yet had worked himself into sufficient frenzy for a charge, and came where he had a full and close view of the black. He recognized the man instantly. Only the night before he had seen him facing the eyes in the dark, while his fellows groveled in the dirt at his feet, too terrified even to defend themselves. Here was a brave man, and Tarzan had deep admiration for bravery. Even his hatred of the blacks was not so strong a passion as his love of courage. He would have joyed in battling with a black warrior at almost any time; but this one he did not wish to kill—he felt, vaguely, that the man had earned his life by his brave defense of it on the preceding night, nor did he fancy the odds that were pitted against the lone warrior.

He turned to the apes. "Go back to your feeding," he said, "and let this Gomangani go his way in peace. He has not harmed us, and last night I saw him fighting Numa and Sabor with fire, alone in the jungle. He is brave. Why should we kill one who is brave and who has not attacked us? Let him go."

The apes growled. They were displeased. "Kill the Gomangani!" cried one.

"Yes." roared another, "kill the Gomangani and the Tarmangani as well."

"Kill the white ape!" screamed Gozan, "he is no ape at all; but a Gomangani with his skin off."

"Kill Tarzan!" bellowed Gunto. "Kill! Kill! Kill!"

The bulls were now indeed working themselves into the frenzy of slaughter; but against Tarzan rather than the black man. A shaggy form charged through them, hurling those it came in contact with to one side as a strong man might scatter children. It was Taug—great, savage Taug.

"Who says 'kill Tarzan'?" he demanded. "Who kills Tarzan must kill Taug, too. Who can kill Taug? Taug will tear your insides from you and feed them to Dango."

"We can kill you all," replied Gunto. "There are many of us and few of you," and he was right. Tarzan knew that he was right. Taug knew it; but neither would admit such a possibility. It is not the way of bull apes.

"I am Tarzan," cried the ape-man. "I am Tarzan. Mighty hunter; mighty fighter. In all the jungle none so great as Tarzan."

Then, one by one, the opposing bulls recounted their virtues and their prowess. And all the time the combatants came closer and closer to one another. Thus do the bulls work themselves to the proper pitch before engaging in battle.

Gunto came, stiff-legged, close to Tarzan and sniffed at him, with bared fangs. Tarzan rumbled forth a low, menacing growl. They might repeat these tactics a dozen times; but sooner or later one bull would close with another and then the whole hideous pack would be tearing and rending at their prey.

Bulabantu, the black man, had stood wide-eyed in wonder from the moment he had seen Tarzan approaching through the apes. He had heard much of this devil-god who ran with the hairy tree people; but never before had he seen him in full daylight. He knew him well enough from the description of those who had seen him and from the glimpses he had had of the marauder upon several occasions when the ape-man had entered the village of Mbonga, the chief, by night, in the perpetration of one of his numerous ghastly jokes.

Bulabantu could not, of course, understand anything which passed between Tarzan and the apes; but he saw that the ape-man and one of the larger bulls were in argument with the others. He saw that these two were standing with their back toward him and between him and the balance of the tribe, and he guessed, though it seemed improbable, that they might be defending him. He knew that Tarzan had once spared the life of Mbonga, the chief, and that he had succored Tibo, and Tibo's mother, Momaya. So it was not impossible that he would help Bulabantu; but how he could accomplish it Bulabantu could not guess; nor as a matter of fact could Tarzan, for the odds against him were too great.

Gunto and the others were slowly forcing Tarzan and Taug back toward Bulabantu. The ape-man thought of his words with Tantor just a short time before: "Yes, Tantor, it is good to live. I should hate to die." And now he knew that he was about to die, for the temper of the great bulls was mounting rapidly against him. Always had many of them hated him, and all were suspicious of him. They knew he was different. Tarzan knew it too; but he was glad that he was—he was a *man*; that he had learned from his picture-books, and he was very proud of the distinction. Presently, though, he would be a dead man.

Gunto was preparing to charge. Tarzan knew the signs. He knew that the balance of the bulls would charge with Gunto. Then it would soon be over. Something moved among the verdure at the opposite side of the clearing. Tarzan saw it just as Gunto, with the terrifying cry of a challenging ape, sprang forward. Tarzan voiced a peculiar call and then crouched to meet the assault. Taug crouched, too, and Bulabantu, assured now that these two were fighting upon his side, couched his spear and sprang between them to receive the first charge of the enemy.

Simultaneously a huge bulk broke into the clearing from the jungle behind the charging bulls. The trumpeting of a mad tusker rose shrill above the cries of the anthropoids, as Tantor, the elephant, dashed swiftly across the clearing to the aid of his friend.

Gunto never closed upon the ape-man, nor did a fang enter flesh upon either side. The terrific reverberation of Tantor's challenge sent the bulls scurrying to the trees, jabbering and scolding. Taug raced off with them. Only Tarzan and Bulabantu remained. The latter stood his ground because he saw that the devil-god did not run, and because the black had the courage to face a certain and horrible death beside one who had quite evidently dared death for him.

But it was a surprised Gomangani who saw the mighty elephant come to a sudden halt in front of the ape-man and caress him with his long, sinuous trunk.

Tarzan turned toward the black man. "Go!" he said in the language of the apes, and pointed in the direction of the village of Mbonga. Bulabantu understood the gesture, if not the word, nor did he lose time in obeying. Tarzan stood watching him until he had disappeared. He knew that the apes would not follow. Then he said to the elephant: "Pick me up!" and the tusker swung him lightly to his head.

"Tarzan goes to his lair by the big water," shouted the ape-man to the apes in the trees. "All of you are more foolish than Manu, except Taug and Teeka. Taug and Teeka may come to see Tarzan; but the others must keep away. Tarzan is done with the tribe of Kerchak."

He prodded Tantor with a calloused toe and the big beast swung off across the clearing, the apes watching them until they were swallowed up by the jungle.

Before the night fell Taug killed Gunto, picking a quarrel with him over his attack upon Tarzan.

For a moon the tribe saw nothing of Tarzan of the Apes. Many of them probably never gave him a thought; but there were those who missed him more than Tarzan imagined. Taug and Teeka often wished that he was back, and Taug determined a dozen times to go and visit Tarzan in his seaside lair; but first one thing and then another interfered.

One night when Taug lay sleepless looking up at the starry heavens he recalled the strange things that Tarzan once had suggested to him—that the bright spots were the eyes of the meat-eaters waiting in the dark of the jungle sky to leap upon Goro, the moon, and devour him. The more he thought about this matter the more perturbed he became.

And then a strange thing happened. Even as Taug looked at Goro, he saw a portion of one edge disappear, precisely as though something was gnawing upon it. Larger and larger became the hole in the side of Goro. With a scream, Taug leaped to his feet. His frenzied "Kreeg-ahs!" brought the terrified tribe screaming and chattering toward him.

"Look!" cried Taug, pointing at the moon. "Look! It is as Tarzan said. Numa has sprung through the fires and is devouring Goro. You called Tarzan names and drove him from the tribe; now see how wise he was. Let one of you who hated Tarzan go to Goro's aid. See the eyes in the dark jungle all about Goro. He is in danger and none can help him—none except Tarzan. Soon Goro will be devoured by Numa and we shall have no more light after Kudu seeks his lair. How shall we dance the Dum-Dum without the light of Goro?"

The apes trembled and whimpered. Any manifestation of the powers of nature always filled them with terror, for they could not understand.

"Go and bring Tarzan," cried one, and then they all took up the cry of "Tarzan!" "Bring Tarzan!" "He will save Goro." But who was to travel the dark jungle by night to fetch him?

"I will go," volunteered Taug, and an instant later he was off through the Stygian gloom toward the little land-locked harbor by the sea.

And as the tribe waited they watched the slow devouring of the moon. Already Numa had eaten out a great semicircular piece. At that rate Goro would be entirely gone before Kudu came again. The apes trembled at the thought of perpetual darkness by night. They could not sleep. Restlessly they moved here and there among the branches of trees, watching Numa of the skies at his deadly feast, and listening for the coming of Taug with Tarzan.

Goro was nearly gone when the apes heard the sounds of the approach through the trees of the two they awaited, and presently Tarzan, followed by Taug, swung into a nearby tree.

The ape-man wasted no time in idle words. In his hand was his long bow and at his back hung a quiver full of arrows, poisoned arrows that he had stolen from the village of the blacks; just as he had stolen the bow. Up into a great tree he clambered, higher and higher until he stood swaying upon a small limb which bent low beneath his weight. Here he had a clear and unobstructed view of the heavens. He saw Goro and the inroads which the hungry Numa had made into his shining surface.

Raising his face to the moon, Tarzan shrilled forth his hideous challenge. Faintly and from afar came the roar of an answering lion. The apes shivered. Numa of the skies had answered Tarzan.

Then the ape-man fitted an arrow to his bow, and drawing the shaft far back, aimed its point at the heart of Numa where he lay in the heavens devouring Goro. There was a loud twang as the released bolt shot into the dark heavens. Again and again did Tarzan of the Apes launch his arrows at Numa, and all the while the apes of the tribe of Kerchak huddled together in terror.

At last came a cry from Taug. "Look! Look!" he screamed. "Numa is killed. Tarzan has killed Numa. See! Goro is emerging from the belly of Numa," and, sure enough, the moon was gradually emerging from whatever had devoured her, whether it was Numa, the lion, or the shadow of the earth; but were you to try to convince an ape of the tribe of Kerchak that it was aught but Numa who so nearly devoured Goro that night, or that another than Tarzan preserved the brilliant god of their savage and mysterious rites from a frightful death, you would have difficulty—and a fight on your hands.

And so Tarzan of the Apes came back to the tribe of Kerchak, and in his coming he took a long stride toward the kingship, which he ultimately won, for now the apes looked up to him as a superior being.

In all the tribe there was but one who was at all skeptical about the plausibility of Tarzan's remarkable rescue of Goro, and that one, strange as it may seem, was Tarzan of the Apes.

TARZAN THE UNTAMED

MURDER AND PILLAGE

Hauptmann Fritz Schneider trudged wearily through the somber aisles of the dark forest. Sweat rolled down his bullet head and stood upon his heavy jowls and bull neck. His lieutenant marched beside him while Underlieutenant von Goss brought up the rear, following with a handful of askaris the tired and all but exhausted porters whom the black soldiers, following the example of their white officer, encouraged with the sharp points of bayonets and the metal-shod butts of rifles.

There were no porters within reach of Hauptmann Schneider so he vented his Prussian spleen upon the askaris nearest at hand, yet with greater circumspection since these men bore loaded rifles--and the three white men were alone with them in the heart of Africa.

Ahead of the hauptmann marched half his company, behind him the other half—thus were the dangers of the savage jungle minimized for the German captain. At the forefront of the column staggered two naked savages fastened to each other by a neck chain. These were the native guides impressed into the service of Kultur and upon their poor, bruised bodies Kultur's brand was revealed in divers cruel wounds and bruises.

Thus even in darkest Africa was the light of German civilization commencing to reflect itself upon the undeserving natives just as at the same period, the fall of 1914, it was shedding its glorious effulgence upon benighted Belgium.

It is true that the guides had led the party astray; but this is the way of most African guides. Nor did it matter that ignorance rather than evil intent had been the cause of their failure. It was enough for Hauptmann Fritz Schneider to know that he was lost in the African wilderness and that he had at hand human beings less powerful than he who could be made to suffer by torture. That he did not kill them outright was partially due to a faint hope that they might eventually prove the means of extricating him from his difficulties and partially that so long as they lived they might still be made to suffer.

The poor creatures, hoping that chance might lead them at last upon the right trail, insisted that they knew the way and so led on through a dismal forest along a winding game trail trodden deep by the feet of countless generations of the savage denizens of the jungle.

Here Tantor, the elephant, took his long way from dust wallow to water. Here Buto, the rhinoceros, blundered blindly in his solitary majesty, while by night the great cats paced silently upon their padded feet beneath the dense canopy of overreaching trees toward the broad plain beyond, where they found their best hunting.

It was at the edge of this plain which came suddenly and unexpectedly before the eyes of the guides that their sad hearts beat with renewed hope. Here the hauptmann drew a deep sigh of relief, for after days of hopeless wandering through almost impenetrable jungle the broad vista of waving grasses dotted here and there with open park like woods and in the far distance the winding line of green shrubbery that denoted a river appeared to the European a veritable heaven.

The Hun smiled in his relief, passed a cheery word with his lieutenant, and then scanned the broad plain with his field glasses. Back and forth they swept across the rolling land until at last they came to rest upon a point near the center of the landscape and close to the green-fringed contours of the river.

"We are in luck," said Schneider to his companions. "Do you see it?"

The lieutenant, who was also gazing through his own glasses, finally brought them to rest upon the same spot that had held the attention of his superior.

"Yes," he said, "an English farm. It must be Greystoke's, for there is none other in this part of British East Africa. God is with us, Herr Captain."

"We have come upon the English schweinhund long before he can have learned that his country is at war with ours," replied Schneider. "Let him be the first to feel the iron hand of Germany."

"Let us hope that he is at home," said the lieutenant, "that we may take him with us when we report to Kraut at Nairobi. It will go well indeed with Herr Hauptmann Fritz Schneider if he brings in the famous Tarzan of the Apes as a prisoner of war."

648

Schneider smiled and puffed out his chest. "You are right, my friend," he said, "it will go well with both of us; but I shall have to travel far to catch General Kraut before he reaches Mombasa. These English pigs with their contemptible army will make good time to the Indian Ocean."

It was in a better frame of mind that the small force set out across the open country toward the trim and well-kept farm buildings of John Clayton, Lord Greystoke; but disappointment was to be their lot since neither Tarzan of the Apes nor his son was at home.

Lady Jane, ignorant of the fact that a state of war existed between Great Britain and Germany, welcomed the officers most hospitably and gave orders through her trusted Waziri to prepare a feast for the black soldiers of the enemy.

Far to the east, Tarzan of the Apes was traveling rapidly from Nairobi toward the farm. At Nairobi he had received news of the World War that had already started, and, anticipating an immediate invasion of British East Africa by the Germans, was hurrying homeward to fetch his wife to a place of greater security. With him were a score of his ebon warriors, but far too slow for the ape-man was the progress of these trained and hardened woodsmen.

When necessity demanded, Tarzan of the Apes sloughed the thin veneer of his civilization and with it the hampering apparel that was its badge. In a moment the polished English gentleman reverted to the naked ape man.

His mate was in danger. For the time, that single thought dominated. He did not think of her as Lady Jane Greystoke, but rather as the she he had won by the might of his steel thews, and that he must hold and protect by virtue of the same offensive armament.

It was no member of the House of Lords who swung swiftly and grimly through the tangled forest or trod with untiring muscles the wide stretches of open plain—it was a great he ape filled with a single purpose that excluded all thoughts of fatigue or danger.

Little Manu, the monkey, scolding and chattering in the upper terraces of the forest, saw him pass. Long had it been since he had thus beheld the great Tarmangani naked and alone hurtling through the jungle. Bearded and gray was Manu, the monkey, and to his dim old eyes came the fire of recollection of those days when Tarzan of the Apes had ruled supreme, Lord of the Jungle, over all the myriad life that trod the matted vegetation between the boles of the great trees, or flew or swung or climbed in the leafy fastness upward to the very apex of the loftiest terraces.

And Numa, the lion, lying up for the day close beside last night's successful kill, blinked his yellow-green eyes and twitched his tawny tail as he caught the scent spoor of his ancient enemy.

Nor was Tarzan senseless to the presence of Numa or Manu or any of the many jungle beasts he passed in his rapid flight towards the west. No particle had his shallow probing of English society dulled his marvelous sense faculties. His nose had picked out the presence of Numa, the lion, even before the majestic king of beasts was aware of his passing.

He had heard noisy little Manu, and even the soft rustling of the parting shrubbery where Sheeta passed before either of these alert animals sensed his presence.

But however keen the senses of the ape-man, however swift his progress through the wild country of his adoption, however mighty the muscles that bore him, he was still mortal. Time and space placed their inexorable limits upon him; nor was there another who realized this truth more keenly than Tarzan. He chafed and fretted that he could not travel with the swiftness of thought and that the long tedious miles stretching far ahead of him must require hours and hours of tireless effort upon his part before he would swing at last from the final bough of the fringing forest into the open plain and in sight of his goal.

Days it took, even though he lay up at night for but a few hours and left to chance the finding of meat directly on his trail. If Wappi, the antelope, or Horta, the boar, chanced in his way when he was hungry, he ate, pausing but long enough to make the kill and cut himself a steak.

TARZAN SUPER PACK

Then at last the long journey drew to its close and he was passing through the last stretch of heavy forest that bounded his estate upon the east, and then this was traversed and he stood upon the plain's edge looking out across his broad lands towards his home.

At the first glance his eyes narrowed and his muscles tensed. Even at that distance he could see that something was amiss. A thin spiral of smoke arose at the right of the bungalow where the barns had stood, but there were no barns there now, and from the bungalow chimney from which smoke should have arisen, there arose nothing.

Once again Tarzan of the Apes was speeding onward, this time even more swiftly than before, for he was goaded now by a nameless fear, more product of intuition than of reason. Even as the beasts, Tarzan of the Apes seemed to possess a sixth sense. Long before he reached the bungalow, he had almost pictured the scene that finally broke upon his view.

Silent and deserted was the vine-covered cottage. Smoldering embers marked the site of his great barns. Gone were the thatched huts of his sturdy retainers, empty the fields, the pastures, and corrals. Here and there vultures rose and circled above the carcasses of men and beasts.

It was with a feeling as nearly akin to terror as he ever had experienced that the ape-man finally forced himself to enter his home. The first sight that met his eyes set the red haze of hate and bloodlust across his vision, for there, crucified against the wall of the living-room, was Wasimbu, giant son of the faithful Muviro and for over a year the personal bodyguard of Lady Jane.

The overturned and shattered furniture of the room, the brown pools of dried blood upon the floor, and prints of bloody hands on walls and woodwork evidenced something of the frightfulness of the battle that had been waged within the narrow confines of the apartment. Across the baby grand piano lay the corpse of another black warrior, while before the door of Lady Jane's boudoir were the dead bodies of three more of the faithful Greystoke servants.

The door of this room was closed. With drooping shoulders and dull eyes Tarzan stood gazing dumbly at the insensate panel which hid from him what horrid secret he dared not even guess.

Slowly, with leaden feet, he moved toward the door. Gropingly his hand reached for the knob. Thus he stood for another long minute, and then with a sudden gesture he straightened his giant frame, threw back his mighty shoulders and, with fearless head held high, swung back the door and stepped across the threshold into the room which held for him the dearest memories and associations of his life. No change of expression crossed his grim and stern-set features as he strode across the room and stood beside the little couch and the inanimate form which lay face downward upon it; the still, silent thing that had pulsed with life and youth and love.

No tear dimmed the eye of the ape-man, but the God who made him alone could know the thoughts that passed through that still half-savage brain. For a long time he stood there just looking down upon the dead body, charred beyond recognition, and then he stooped and lifted it in his arms. As he turned the body over and saw how horribly death had been meted he plumbed, in that instant, the uttermost depths of grief and horror and hatred.

Nor did he require the evidence of the broken German rifle in the outer room, or the torn and blood-stained service cap upon the floor, to tell him who had been the perpetrators of this horrid and useless crime.

For a moment he had hoped against hope that the blackened corpse was not that of his mate, but when his eyes discovered and recognized the rings upon her fingers the last faint ray of hope forsook him.

In silence, in love, and in reverence he buried, in the little rose garden that had been Jane Clayton's pride and love, the poor, charred form and beside it the great black warriors who had given their lives so futilely in their mistress' protection.

At one side of the house Tarzan found other newly made graves and in these he sought final evidence of the identity of the real perpetrators of the atrocities that had been committed there in his absence.

Here he disinterred the bodies of a dozen German askaris and found upon their uniforms the insignia of the company and regiment to which they had belonged. This was enough for the ape-man. White officers had commanded these men, nor would it be a difficult task to discover who they were.

Returning to the rose garden, he stood among the Hun trampled blooms and bushes above the grave of his dead-with bowed head he stood there in a last mute farewell. As the sun sank slowly behind the towering forests of the west, he turned slowly away upon the still-distinct trail of Hauptmann Fritz Schneider and his blood-stained company.

His was the suffering of the dumb brute—mute; but though voiceless no less poignant. At first his vast sorrow numbed his other faculties of thought—his brain was overwhelmed by the calamity to such an extent that it reacted to but a single objective suggestion: She is dead! She is dead! She is dead! Again and again this phrase beat monotonously upon his brain—a dull, throbbing pain, yet mechanically his feet followed the trail of her slayer while, subconsciously, his every sense was upon the alert for the ever-present perils of the jungle.

Gradually the labor of his great grief brought forth another emotion so real, so tangible, that it seemed a companion walking at his side. It was Hate—and it brought to him a measure of solace and of comfort, for it was a sublime hate that ennobled him as it has ennobled countless thousands since-hatred for Germany and Germans. It centered about the slayer of his mate, of course; but it included everything German, animate or inanimate. As the thought took firm hold upon him he paused and raising his face to Goro, the moon, cursed with upraised hand the authors of the hideous crime that had been perpetrated in that once peaceful bungalow behind him; and he cursed their progenitors, their progeny, and all their kind the while he took silent oath to war upon them relentlessly until death overtook him.

There followed almost immediately a feeling of content, for, where before his future at best seemed but a void, now it was filled with possibilities the contemplation of which brought him, if not happiness, at least a surcease of absolute grief, for before him lay a great work that would occupy his time.

Stripped not only of all the outward symbols of civilization, Tarzan had also reverted morally and mentally to the status of the savage beast he had been reared. Never had his civilization been more than a veneer put on for the sake of her he loved because he thought it made her happier to see him thus. In reality he had always held the outward evidences of so-called culture in deep contempt. Civilization meant to Tarzan of the Apes a curtailment of freedom in all its aspects—freedom of action, freedom of thought, freedom of love, freedom of hate. Clothes he abhorred—uncomfortable, hideous, confining things that reminded him somehow of bonds securing him to the life he had seen the poor creatures of London and Paris living. Clothes were the emblems of that hypocrisy for which civilization stood—a pretense that the wearers were ashamed of what the clothes covered, of the human form made in the semblance of God. Tarzan knew how silly and pathetic the lower orders of animals appeared in the clothing of civilization, for he had seen several poor creatures thus appareled in various traveling shows in Europe, and he knew, too, how silly and pathetic man appears in them since the only men he had seen in the first twenty years of his life had been, like himself, naked savages. The ape-man had a keen admiration for a well-muscled, well-proportioned body, whether lion, or antelope, or man, and it had ever been beyond him to understand how clothes could be considered more beautiful than a clear, firm, healthy skin, or coat and trousers more graceful than the gentle curves of rounded muscles playing beneath a flexible hide.

In civilization Tarzan had found greed and selfishness and cruelty far beyond that which he had known in his familiar, savage jungle, and though civilization had given him his mate and several friends whom he loved and admired, he never had come to accept it as you and I who have known little or nothing else; so it was with a sense of relief that he now definitely abandoned it and all that it stood for, and went forth into the jungle once again stripped to his loin cloth and weapons.

The hunting knife of his father hung at his left hip, his bow and his quiver of arrows were slung across his shoulders, while around his chest over one shoulder and beneath the opposite arm was coiled the long grass rope without which Tarzan would have felt quite as naked as would you should you be suddenly thrust upon a busy highway clad only in a union suit. A heavy war spear which he sometimes carried in one hand and again slung by a thong about his neck so that it hung down his back completed his armament and his apparel. The diamond-studded locket with the pictures of his mother and father that he had worn always until he had given it as a token of his highest devotion to Jane Clayton before their marriage was missing. She always had worn it since, but it had not been upon her body when he found her slain in her boudoir, so that now his quest for vengeance included also a quest for the stolen trinket.

Toward midnight Tarzan commenced to feel the physical strain of his long hours of travel and to realize that even muscles such as his had their limitations. His pursuit of the murderers had not been characterized by excessive speed; but rather more in keeping with his mental attitude, which was marked by a dogged determination to require from the Germans more than an eye for an eye and more than a tooth for a tooth, the element of time entering but slightly into his calculations.

Inwardly as well as outwardly Tarzan had reverted to beast and in the lives of beasts, time, as a measurable aspect of duration, has no meaning. The beast is actively interested only in NOW, and as it is always NOW and always shall be, there is an eternity of time for the accomplishment of objects. The ape-man, naturally, had a slightly more comprehensive realization of the limitations of time; but, like the beasts, he moved with majestic deliberation when no emergency prompted him to swift action.

Having dedicated his life to vengeance, vengeance became his natural state and, therefore, no emergency, so he took his time in pursuit. That he had not rested earlier was due to the fact that he had felt no fatigue, his mind being occupied by thoughts of sorrow and revenge; but now he realized that he was tired, and so he sought a jungle giant that had harbored him upon more than a single other jungle night.

Dark clouds moving swiftly across the heavens now and again eclipsed the bright face of Goro, the moon, and forewarned the ape-man of impending storm. In the depth of the jungle the cloud shadows produced a thick blackness that might almost be felt—a blackness that to you and me might have proven terrifying with its accompaniment of rustling leaves and cracking twigs, and its even more suggestive intervals of utter silence in which the crudest of imaginations might have conjured crouching beasts of prey tensed for the fatal charge; but through it Tarzan passed unconcerned, yet always alert. Now he swung lightly to the lower terraces of the overarching trees when some subtle sense warned him that Numa lay upon a kill directly in his path, or again he sprang lightly to one side as Buto, the rhinoceros, lumbered toward him along the narrow, deep-worn trail, for the ape-man, ready to fight upon necessity's slightest pretext, avoided unnecessary quarrels.

When he swung himself at last into the tree he sought, the moon was obscured by a heavy cloud, and the tree tops were waving wildly in a steadily increasing wind whose soughing drowned the lesser noises of the jungle. Upward went Tarzan toward a sturdy crotch across which he long since had laid and secured a little platform of branches. It was very dark now, darker even than it had been before, for almost the entire sky was overcast by thick, black clouds.

Presently the man-beast paused, his sensitive nostrils dilating as he sniffed the air about him. Then, with the swiftness and agility of a cat, he leaped far outward upon a swaying branch, sprang upward through the darkness, caught another, swung himself upon it and then to one still higher. What could have so suddenly transformed his matter-of-fact ascent of the giant bole to the swift and wary action of his detour among the branches? You or I could have seen nothing—not even the little platform that an instant before had been just above him and which now was immediately below—but as he swung above it we should have heard an ominous growl; and then as the moon was momentarily uncovered, we should have seen both the platform, dimly, and a dark mass that lay stretched upon it—a dark mass that presently, as our eyes became accustomed to the lesser darkness, would take the form of Sheeta, the panther.

In answer to the cat's growl, a low and equally ferocious growl rumbled upward from the ape-man's deep chest—a growl of warning that told the panther he was trespassing upon the other's lair; but Sheeta was in no mood to be dispossessed. With upturned, snarling face he glared at the brown-skinned Tarmangani above him. Very slowly the ape-man moved inward along the branch until he was directly above the panther. In the man's hand was the hunting knife of his long-dead father—the weapon that had first given him his real ascendancy over the beasts of the jungle; but he hoped not to be forced to use it, knowing as he did that more jungle battles were settled by hideous growling than by actual combat, the law of bluff holding quite as good in the jungle as elsewhere—only in matters of love and food did the great beasts ordinarily close with fangs and talons.

Tarzan braced himself against the bole of the tree and leaned closer toward Sheeta.

"Stealer of balus!" he cried. The panther rose to a sitting position, his bared fangs but a few feet from the ape-man's taunting face. Tarzan growled hideously and struck at the cat's face with his knife. "I am Tarzan of the Apes," he roared. "This is Tarzan's lair. Go, or I will kill you."

Though he spoke in the language of the great apes of the jungle, it is doubtful that Sheeta understood the words, though he knew well enough that the hairless ape wished to frighten him from his well-chosen station past which edible creatures might be expected to wander sometime during the watches of the night.

Like lightning the cat reared and struck a vicious blow at his tormentor with great, bared talons that might well have torn away the ape-man's face had the blow landed; but it did not land—Tarzan was even quicker than Sheeta. As the panther came to all fours again upon the little platform, Tarzan un-slung his heavy spear and prodded at the snarling face, and as Sheeta warded off the blows, the two continued their horrid duet of blood-curdling roars and growls.

Goaded to frenzy the cat presently determined to come up after this disturber of his peace; but when he essayed to leap to the branch that held Tarzan he found the sharp spear point always in his face, and each time as he dropped back he was prodded viciously in some tender part; but at length, rage having conquered his better judgment, he leaped up the rough bole to the very branch upon which Tarzan stood. Now the two faced each other upon even footing and Sheeta saw a quick revenge and a supper all in one. The hairless ape-thing with the tiny fangs and the puny talons would be helpless before him.

The heavy limb bent beneath the weight of the two beasts as Sheeta crept cautiously out upon it and Tarzan backed slowly away, growling. The wind had risen to the proportions of a gale so that even the greatest giants of the forest swayed, groaning, to its force and the branch upon which the two faced each other rose and fell like the deck of a storm-tossed ship. Goro was now entirely obscured, but vivid flashes of lightning lit up the jungle at brief intervals, revealing the grim tableau of primitive passion upon the swaying limb.

Tarzan backed away, drawing Sheeta farther from the stem of the tree and out upon the tapering branch, where his footing became ever more precarious. The cat, infuriated by the pain of spear wounds, was overstepping the bounds of caution. Already he had reached a point where he could do little more than maintain a secure footing, and it was this moment that Tarzan chose to charge. With a roar that mingled with the booming thunder from above he leaped toward the panther, who could only claw futilely with one huge paw while he clung to the branch with the other; but the ape-man did not come within that parabola of destruction. Instead he leaped above menacing claws and snapping fangs, turning in mid-air and alighting upon Sheeta's back, and at the instant of impact his knife struck deep into the tawny side. Then Sheeta, impelled by pain and hate and rage and the first law of Nature, went mad. Screaming and clawing he attempted to turn upon the ape-thing clinging to his back. For an instant he toppled upon the now wildly gyrating limb, clutched frantically to save himself, and then plunged downward into the darkness with Tarzan still clinging to him. Crashing through splintering branches the two fell. Not for an instant did the ape-man consider relinquishing his death-hold upon his adversary. He had entered the lists in mortal combat and true to the primitive instincts of the wild—the unwritten law of the jungle—one or both must die before the battle ended.

Sheeta, catlike, alighted upon four out-sprawled feet, the weight of the ape-man crushing him to earth, the long knife again imbedded in his side. Once the panther struggled to rise; but only to sink to earth again. Tarzan felt the giant muscles relax beneath him. Sheeta was dead. Rising, the ape-man placed a foot upon the body of his vanquished foe, raised his face toward the thundering heavens, and as the lightning flashed and the torrential rain broke upon him, screamed forth the wild victory cry of the bull ape.

Having accomplished his aim and driven the enemy from his lair, Tarzan gathered an armful of large fronds and climbed to his dripping couch. Laying a few of the fronds upon the poles he lay down and covered himself against the rain with the others, and despite the wailing of the wind and the crashing of the thunder, immediately fell asleep.

THE LION'S CAVE

The rain lasted for twenty-four hours and much of the time it fell in torrents so that when it ceased, the trail he had been following was entirely obliterated. Cold and uncomfortable—it was a savage Tarzan who threaded the mazes of the soggy jungle. Manu, the monkey, shivering and chattering in the dank trees, scolded and fled at his approach. Even the panthers and the lions let the growling Tarmangani pass unmolested.

When the sun shone again upon the second day and a wide, open plain let the full heat of Kudu flood the chilled, brown body, Tarzan's spirits rose; but it was still a sullen, surly brute that moved steadily onward into the south where he hoped again to pick up the trail of the Germans. He was now in German East Africa and it was his intention to skirt the mountains west of Kilimanjaro, whose rugged peaks he was quite willing to give a wide berth, and then swing eastward along the south side of the range to the railway that led to Tanga, for his experience among men suggested that it was toward this railroad that German troops would be likely to converge.

Two days later, from the southern slopes of Kilimanjaro, he heard the boom of cannon far away to the east. The afternoon had been dull and cloudy and now as he was passing through a narrow gorge a few great drops of rain began to splatter upon his naked shoulders. Tarzan shook his head and growled his disapproval; then he cast his eyes about for shelter, for he had had quite enough of the cold and drenching. He wanted to hasten on in the direction of the booming noise, for he knew that there would be Germans fighting against the English. For an instant his bosom swelled with pride at the thought that he was English and then he shook his head again viciously. "No!" he muttered, "Tarzan of the Apes is not English, for the English are men and Tarzan is Tarmangani;" but he could not hide even from his sorrow or from his sullen hatred of mankind in general that his heart warmed at the thought it was Englishmen who fought the Germans. His regret was that the English were human and not great white apes as he again considered himself.

"Tomorrow," he thought, "I will travel that way and find the Germans," and then he set himself to the immediate task of discovering some shelter from the storm. Presently he espied the low and narrow entrance to what appeared to be a cave at the base of the cliffs which formed the northern side of the gorge. With drawn knife he approached the spot warily, for he knew that if it were a cave it was doubtless the lair of some other beast. Before the entrance lay many large fragments of rock of different sizes, similar to others scattered along the entire base of the cliff, and it was in Tarzan's mind that if he found the cave unoccupied he would barricade the door and insure himself a quiet and peaceful night's repose within the sheltered interior. Let the storm rage without-Tarzan would remain within until it ceased, comfortable and dry. A tiny rivulet of cold water trickled outward from the opening.

Close to the cave Tarzan kneeled and sniffed the ground. A low growl escaped him and his upper lip curved to expose his fighting fangs. "Numa!" he muttered; but he did not stop. Numa might not be at home—he would investigate. The entrance was so low that the ape-man was compelled to drop to all fours before he could poke his head within the aperture; but first he looked, listened, and sniffed in each direction at his rear—he would not be taken by surprise from that quarter.

His first glance within the cave revealed a narrow tunnel with daylight at its farther end. The interior of the tunnel was not so dark but that the ape-man could readily see that it was untenanted at present. Advancing cautiously he crawled toward the opposite end imbued with a full realization of what it would mean if Numa should suddenly enter the tunnel in front of him; but Numa did not appear and the ape-man emerged at length into the open and stood erect, finding himself in a rocky cleft whose precipitous walls rose almost sheer on every hand, the tunnel from the gorge passing through the cliff and forming a passageway from the outer world into a large pocket or gulch entirely enclosed by steep walls of rock. Except for the small passageway from the gorge, there was no other entrance to the gulch which was some hundred feet in length and about fifty in width and appeared to have been worn from the rocky cliff by the falling of water during long ages. A tiny stream from Kilimanjaro's eternal snow cap still trickled over the edge of the rocky wall at the upper end of the gulch, forming a little pool at the bottom of the cliff from which a small rivulet wound downward to the tunnel through which it passed to the gorge beyond. A single great tree flourished near the center of the gulch, while tufts of wiry grass were scattered here and there among the rocks of the gravelly floor.

The bones of many large animals lay about and among them were several human skulls. Tarzan raised his eyebrows. "A man-eater," he murmured, "and from appearances he has held sway here for a long time. Tonight Tarzan will take the lair of the man-eater and Numa may roar and grumble upon the outside."

The ape-man had advanced well into the gulch as he investigated his surroundings and now as he stood near the tree, satisfied that the tunnel would prove a dry and quiet retreat for the night, he turned to retrace his way to the outer end of the entrance that he might block it with boulders against Numa's return, but even with the thought there came something to his sensitive ears that froze him into statuesque immobility with eyes glued upon the tunnel's mouth. A moment later the head of a huge lion framed in a great black mane appeared in the opening. The yellow-green eyes glared, round and unblinking, straight at the trespassing Tarmangani, a low growl rumbled from the deep chest, and lips curled back to expose the mighty fangs.

"Brother of Dango!" shouted Tarzan, angered that Numa's return should have been so timed as to frustrate his plans for a comfortable night's repose. "I am Tarzan of the Apes, Lord of the Jungle. Tonight I lair here—go!"

But Numa did not go. Instead he rumbled forth a menacing roar and took a few steps in Tarzan's direction. The ape-man picked up a rock and hurled it at the snarling face. One can never be sure of a lion. This one might turn tail and run at the first intimation of attack—Tarzan had bluffed many in his time—but not now. The missile struck Numa full upon the snout—a tender part of a cat's anatomy—and instead of causing him to flee it transformed him into an infuriated engine of wrath and destruction.

Up went his tail, stiff and erect, and with a series of frightful roars he bore down upon the Tarmangani at the speed of an express train. Not an instant too soon did Tarzan reach the tree and swing himself into its branches and there he squatted, hurling insults at the king of beasts while Numa paced a circle beneath him, growling and roaring in rage.

It was raining now in earnest adding to the ape-man's discomfort and disappointment. He was very angry; but as only direct necessity had ever led him to close in mortal combat with a lion, knowing as he did that he had only luck and agility to pit against the frightful odds of muscle, weight, fangs, and talons, he did not now even consider descending and engaging in so unequal and useless a duel for the mere reward of a little added creature comfort. And so he sat perched in the tree while the rain fell steadily and the lion padded round and round beneath, casting a baleful eye upward after every few steps.

Tarzan scanned the precipitous walls for an avenue of escape. They would have baffled an ordinary man; but the ape-man, accustomed to climbing, saw several places where he might gain a foothold, precarious possibly; but enough to give him reasonable assurance of escape if Numa would but betake himself to the far end of the gulch for a moment. Numa, however, notwithstanding the rain, gave no evidence of quitting his post so that at last Tarzan really began to consider seriously if it might not be as well to take the chance of a battle with him rather than remain longer cold and wet and humiliated in the tree.

But even as he turned the matter over in his mind Numa turned suddenly and walked majestically toward the tunnel without even a backward glance. The instant that he disappeared, Tarzan dropped lightly to the ground upon the far side of the tree and was away at top speed for the cliff. The lion had no sooner entered the tunnel than he backed immediately out again and, pivoting like a flash, was off across the gulch in full charge after the flying ape-man; but Tarzan's lead was too great—if he could find finger or foothold upon the sheer wall he would be safe; but should he slip from the wet rocks his doom was already sealed as he would fall directly into Numa's clutches where even the Great Tarmangani would be helpless.

With the agility of a cat Tarzan ran up the cliff for thirty feet before he paused, and there finding a secure foothold, he stopped and looked down upon Numa who was leaping upward in a wild and futile attempt to scale the rocky wall to his prey. Fifteen or twenty feet from the ground the lion would scramble only to fall backward again defeated. Tarzan eyed him for a moment and then commenced a slow and cautious ascent toward the summit. Several times he had difficulty in finding holds but at last he drew himself over the edge, rose, picked up a bit of loose rock, hurled it at Numa and strode away.

Finding an easy descent to the gorge, he was about to pursue his journey in the direction of the still-booming guns when a sudden thought caused him to halt and a half-smile to play about his lips. Turning, he trotted quickly back to the outer opening of Numa's tunnel. Close beside it he listened for a moment and then rapidly began to gather large rocks and pile them within the entrance. He had almost closed the aperture when the lion appeared upon the inside—a very ferocious and angry lion that pawed and clawed at the rocks and uttered mighty roars that caused the earth to tremble; but roars did not frighten Tarzan of the Apes. At Kala's shaggy breast he had closed his infant eyes in sleep upon countless nights in years gone by to the savage chorus of similar roars. Scarcely a day or night of his jungle life—and practically all his life had been spent in the jungle—had he not heard the roaring of hungry lions, or angry lions, or love-sick lions. Such sounds affected Tarzan as the tooting of an automobile horn may affect you—if you are in front of the automobile it warns you out of the way, if you are not in front of it you scarcely notice it. Figuratively Tarzan was not in front of the automobile—Numa could not reach him and Tarzan knew it, so he continued deliberately to choke the entrance until there was no possibility of Numa's getting out again. When he was quite through he made a grimace at the hidden lion beyond the barrier and resumed his way toward the east. "A man-eater who will eat no more men," he soliloquized.

That night Tarzan lay up under an overhanging shelf of rock. The next morning he resumed his journey, stopping only long enough to make a kill and satisfy his hunger. The other beasts of the wild eat and lie up; but Tarzan never let his belly interfere with his plans. In this lay one of the greatest differences between the ape-man and his fellows of the jungles and forests. The firing ahead rose and fell during the day. He had noticed that it was highest at dawn and immediately after dusk and that during the night it almost ceased. In the middle of the afternoon of the second day he came upon troops moving up toward the front. They appeared to be raiding parties, for they drove goats and cows along with them and there were native porters laden with grain and other foodstuffs. He saw that these natives were all secured by neck chains and he also saw that the troops were composed of native soldiers in German uniforms. The officers were white men. No one saw Tarzan, yet he was here and there about and among them for two hours. He inspected the insignia upon their uniforms and saw that they were not the same as that which he had taken from one of the dead soldiers at the bungalow and then he passed on ahead of them, unseen in the dense bush. He had come upon Germans and had not killed them; but it was because the killing of Germans at large was not yet the prime motive of his existence—now it was to discover the individual who slew his mate.

After he had accounted for him he would take up the little matter of slaying ALL Germans who crossed his path, and he meant that many should cross it, for he would hunt them precisely as professional hunters hunt the man-eaters.

As he neared the front lines the troops became more numerous. There were motor trucks and ox teams and all the impedimenta of a small army and always there were wounded men walking or being carried toward the rear. He had crossed the railroad some distance back and judged that the wounded were being taken to it for transportation to a base hospital and possibly as far away as Tanga on the coast.

It was dusk when he reached a large camp hidden in the foothills of the Pare Mountains. As he was approaching from the rear he found it but lightly guarded and what sentinels there were, were not upon the alert, and so it was an easy thing for him to enter after darkness had fallen and prowl about listening at the backs of tents, searching for some clew to the slayer of his mate.

As he paused at the side of a tent before which sat a number of native soldiers he caught a few words spoken in native dialect that riveted his attention instantly: "The Waziri fought like devils; but we are greater fighters and we killed them all. When we were through the captain came and killed the woman. He stayed outside and yelled in a very loud voice until all the men were killed. Underlieutenant von Goss is braver—he came in and stood beside the door shouting at us, also in a very loud voice, and bade us nail one of the Waziri who was wounded to the wall, and then he laughed loudly because the man suffered. We all laughed. It was very funny."

Like a beast of prey, grim and terrible, Tarzan crouched in the shadows beside the tent. What thoughts passed through that savage mind? Who may say? No outward sign of passion was revealed by the expression of the handsome face; the cold, gray eyes denoted only intense watchfulness. Presently the soldier Tarzan had heard first rose and with a parting word turned away. He passed within ten feet of the ape-man and continued on toward the rear of the camp. Tarzan followed and in the shadows of a clump of bushes overtook his quarry. There was no sound as the man beast sprang upon the back of his prey and bore it to the ground for steel fingers closed simultaneously upon the soldier's throat, effectually stifling any outcry. By the neck Tarzan dragged his victim well into the concealment of the bushes.

"Make no sound," he cautioned in the man's own tribal dialect as he released his hold upon the other's throat.

The fellow gasped for breath, rolling frightened eyes upward to see what manner of creature it might be in whose power he was. In the darkness he saw only a naked brown body bending above him; but he still remembered the terrific strength of the mighty muscles that had closed upon his wind and dragged him into the bushes as though he had been but a little child. If any thought of resistance had crossed his mind he must have discarded it at once, as he made no move to escape.

"What is the name of the officer who killed the woman at the bungalow where you fought with the Waziri?" asked Tarzan.

"Hauptmann Schneider," replied the black when he could again command his voice.

"Where is he?" demanded the ape-man.

"He is here. It may be that he is at headquarters. Many of the officers go there in the evening to receive orders."

"Lead me there," commanded Tarzan, "and if I am discovered I will kill you immediately. Get up!"

The black rose and led the way by a roundabout route back through the camp. Several times they were forced to hide while soldiers passed; but at last they reached a great pile of baled hay from about the corner of which the black pointed out a two-story building in the distance.

"Headquarters," he said. "You can go no farther unseen. There are many soldiers about."

Tarzan realized that he could not proceed farther in company with the black. He turned and looked at the fellow for a moment as though pondering what disposition to make of him.

"You helped to crucify Wasimbu, the Waziri," he accused in a low yet none the less terrible tone.

The black trembled, his knees giving beneath him. "He ordered us to do it," he plead.

"Who ordered it done?" demanded Tarzan.

"Underlieutenant von Goss," replied the soldier. "He, too, is here."

"I shall find him," returned Tarzan, grimly. "You helped to crucify Wasimbu, the Waziri, and, while he suffered, you laughed."

The fellow reeled. It was as though in the accusation he read also his death sentence. With no other word Tarzan seized the man again by the neck. As before there was no outcry. The giant muscles tensed. The arms swung quickly upward and with them the body of the black soldier who had helped to crucify Wasimbu, the Waziri, described a circle in the air—once, twice, three times, and then it was flung aside and the ape-man turned in the direction of General Kraut's headquarters.

A single sentinel in the rear of the building barred the way. Tarzan crawled, belly to the ground, toward him, taking advantage of cover as only the jungle-bred beast of prey can do. When the sentinel's eyes were toward him, Tarzan hugged the ground, motionless as stone; when they were turned away, he moved swiftly forward. Presently he was within charging distance. He waited until the man had turned his back once more and then he rose and sped noiselessly down upon him. Again there was no sound as he carried the dead body with him toward the building.

The lower floor was lighted, the upper dark. Through the windows Tarzan saw a large front room and a smaller room in rear of it. In the former were many officers. Some moved about talking to one another, others sat at field tables writing. The windows were open and Tarzan could hear much of the conversation; but nothing that interested him. It was mostly about the German successes in Africa and conjectures as to when the German army in Europe would reach Paris. Some said the Kaiser was doubtlessly already there, and there was a great deal of damning Belgium.

In the smaller back room a large, red-faced man sat behind a table. Some other officers were also sitting a little in rear of him, while two stood at attention before the general, who was questioning them. As he talked, the general toyed with an oil lamp that stood upon the table before him. Presently there came a knock upon the door and an aide entered the room. He saluted and reported: "Fraulein Kircher has arrived, sir."

"Bid her enter," commanded the general, and then nodded to the two officers before him in sign of dismissal.

The Fraulein, entering, passed them at the door. The officers in the little room rose and saluted, the Fraulein acknowledging the courtesy with a bow and a slight smile. She was a very pretty girl. Even the rough, soiled riding habit and the caked dust upon her face could not conceal the fact, and she was young. She could not have been over nineteen.

She advanced to the table behind which the general stood and, taking a folded paper from an inside pocket of her coat, handed it to him.

"Be seated, Fraulein," he said, and another officer brought her a chair. No one spoke while the general read the contents of the paper.

Tarzan appraised the various people in the room. He wondered if one might not be Hauptmann Schneider, for two of them were captains. The girl he judged to be of the intelligence department—a spy. Her beauty held no appeal for him—without a glimmer of compunction he could have wrung that fair, young neck. She was German and that was enough; but he had other and more important work before him. He wanted Hauptmann Schneider.

Finally the general looked up from the paper.

"Good," he said to the girl, and then to one of his aides, "Send for Major Schneider."

Major Schneider! Tarzan felt the short hairs at the back of his neck rise. Already they had promoted the beast who had murdered his mate—doubtless they had promoted him for that very crime.

The aide left the room and the others fell into a general conversation from which it became apparent to Tarzan that the German East African forces greatly outnumbered the British and that the latter were suffering heavily. The ape-man stood so concealed in a clump of bushes that he could watch the interior of the room without being seen from within, while he was at the same time hidden from the view of anyone who might chance to pass along the post of the sentinel he had slain. Momentarily he was expecting a patrol or a relief to appear and discover that the sentinel was missing, when he knew an immediate and thorough search would be made.

Impatiently he awaited the coming of the man he sought and at last he was rewarded by the reappearance of the aide who had been dispatched to fetch him accompanied by an officer of medium size with fierce, upstanding mustaches. The newcomer strode to the table, halted and saluted, reporting. The general acknowledged the salute and turned toward the girl.

"Fraulein Kircher," he said, "allow me to present Major Schneider—"

Tarzan waited to hear no more. Placing a palm upon the sill of the window he vaulted into the room into the midst of an astounded company of the Kaiser's officers. With a stride he was at the table and with a sweep of his hand sent the lamp crashing into the fat belly of the general who, in his mad effort to escape cremation, fell over backward, chair and all, upon the floor. Two of the aides sprang for the ape-man who picked up the first and flung him in the face of the other. The girl had leaped from her chair and stood flattened against the wall. The other officers were calling aloud for the guard and for help. Tarzan's purpose centered upon but a single individual and him he never lost sight of. Freed from attack for an instant he seized Major Schneider, threw him over his shoulder and was out of the window so quickly that the astonished assemblage could scarce realize what had occurred.

A single glance showed him that the sentinel's post was still vacant and a moment later he and his burden were in the shadows of the hay dump. Major Schneider had made no outcry for the very excellent reason that his wind was shut off. Now Tarzan released his grasp enough to permit the man to breathe.

"If you make a sound you will be choked again," he said.

Cautiously and after infinite patience Tarzan passed the final outpost. Forcing his captive to walk before him he pushed on toward the west until, late into the night, he re-crossed the railway where he felt reasonably safe from discovery. The German had cursed and grumbled and threatened and asked questions; but his only reply was another prod from Tarzan's sharp war spear. The ape-man herded him along as he would have driven a hog with the difference that he would have had more respect and therefore more consideration for a hog.

Until now Tarzan had given little thought to the details of revenge. Now he pondered what form the punishment should take. Of only one thing was he certain—it must end in death. Like all brave men and courageous beasts Tarzan had little natural inclination to torture—none, in fact; but this case was unique in his experience. An inherent sense of justice called for an eye for an eye and his recent oath demanded even more. Yes, the creature must suffer even as he had caused Jane Clayton to suffer. Tarzan could not hope to make the man suffer as he had suffered, since physical pain may never approach the exquisiteness of mental torture.

All through the long night the ape-man goaded on the exhausted and now terrified Hun. The awful silence of his captor wrought upon the German's nerves. If he would only speak! Again and again Schneider tried to force or coax a word from him; but always the result was the same—continued silence and a vicious and painful prod from the spear point. Schneider was bleeding and sore. He was so exhausted that he staggered at every step, and often he fell only to be prodded to his feet again by that terrifying and remorseless spear.

It was not until morning that Tarzan reached a decision and it came to him then like an inspiration from above. A slow smile touched his lips and he immediately sought a place to lie up and rest—he wished his prisoner to be fit now for what lay in store for him. Ahead was a stream which Tarzan had crossed the day before. He knew the ford for a drinking place and a likely spot to make an easy kill. Cautioning the German to utter silence with a gesture the two approached the stream quietly. Down the game trail Tarzan saw some deer about to leave the water. He shoved Schneider into the brush at one side and, squatting next him, waited. The German watched the silent giant with puzzled, frightened eyes. In the new dawn he, for the first time, was able to obtain a good look at his captor, and, if he had been puzzled and frightened before, those sensations were nothing to what he experienced now.

Who and what could this almost naked, white savage be? He had heard him speak but once—when he had cautioned him to silence—and then in excellent German and the well-modulated tones of culture. He watched him now as the fascinated toad watches the snake that is about to devour it. He saw the graceful limbs and symmetrical body motionless as a marble statue as the creature crouched in the concealment of the leafy foliage. Not a muscle, not a nerve moved. He saw the deer coming slowly along the trail, down wind and unsuspecting. He saw a buck pass—an old buck—and then a young and plump one came opposite the giant in ambush, and Schneider's eyes went wide and a scream of terror almost broke from his lips as he saw the agile beast at his side spring straight for the throat of the young buck and heard from those human lips the hunting roar of a wild beast. Down went the buck and Tarzan and his captive had meat. The ape-man ate his raw, but he permitted the German to build a fire and cook his portion.

The two lay up until late in the afternoon and then took up the journey once again—a journey that was so frightful to Schneider because of his ignorance of its destination that he at times groveled at Tarzan's feet begging for an explanation and for mercy; but on and on in silence the ape-man went, prodding the failing Hun whenever the latter faltered.

It was noon of the third day before they reached their destination. After a steep climb and a short walk they halted at the edge of a precipitous cliff and Schneider looked down into a narrow gulch where a single tree grew beside a tiny rivulet and sparse grass broke from a rock-strewn soil. Tarzan motioned him over the edge; but the German drew back in terror. The Ape-man seized him and pushed him roughly toward the brink. "Descend," he said. It was the second time he had spoken in three days and perhaps his very silence, ominous in itself, had done more to arouse terror in the breast of the Boche than even the spear point, ever ready as it always was.

Schneider looked fearfully over the edge; but was about to essay the attempt when Tarzan halted him. "I am Lord Greystoke," he said. "It was my wife you murdered in the Waziri country. You will understand now why I came for you. Descend."

The German fell upon his knees. "I did not murder your wife," he cried. "Have mercy! I did not murder your wife. I do not know anything about—"

"Descend!" snapped Tarzan, raising the point of his spear. He knew that the man lied and was not surprised that he did. A man who would murder for no cause would lie for less. Schneider still hesitated and pled. The ape-man jabbed him with the spear and Schneider slid fearfully over the top and began the perilous descent. Tarzan accompanied and assisted him over the worst places until at last they were within a few feet of the bottom.

"Be quiet now," cautioned the ape-man. He pointed at the entrance to what appeared to be a cave at the far end of the gulch. "There is a hungry lion in there. If you can reach that tree before he discovers you, you will have several days longer in which to enjoy life and then—when you are too weak to cling longer to the branches of the tree Numa, the man-eater, will feed again for the last time." He pushed Schneider from his foothold to the ground below. "Now run," he said.

The German trembling in terror started for the tree. He had almost reached it when a horrid roar broke from the mouth of the cave and almost simultaneously a gaunt, hunger mad lion leaped into the daylight of the gulch. Schneider had but a few yards to cover; but the lion flew over the ground to circumvent him while Tarzan watched the race with a slight smile upon his lips.

Schneider won by a slender margin, and as Tarzan scaled the cliff to the summit, he heard behind him mingled with the roaring of the baffled cat, the gibbering of a human voice that was at the same time more bestial than the beast's.

Upon the brink of the cliff the ape-man turned and looked back into the gulch. High in the tree the German clung frantically to a branch across which his body lay. Beneath him was Numa—waiting.

The ape-man raised his face to Kudu, the sun, and from his mighty chest rose the savage victory cry of the bull ape.

EDGAR RICE BURROUGHS

IN THE GERMAN LINES

Tarzan was not yet fully revenged. There were many millions of Germans yet alive—enough to keep Tarzan pleasantly occupied the balance of his life, and yet not enough, should he kill them all, to recompense him for the great loss he had suffered—nor could the death of all those million Germans bring back his loved one.

While in the German camp in the Pare Mountains, which lie just east of the boundary line between German and British East Africa, Tarzan had overheard enough to suggest that the British were getting the worst of the fighting in Africa. At first he had given the matter but little thought, since, after the death of his wife, the one strong tie that had held him to civilization, he had renounced all mankind, considering himself no longer man, but ape.

After accounting for Schneider as satisfactorily as lay within his power he circled Kilimanjaro and hunted in the foothills to the north of that mightiest of mountains as he had discovered that in the neighborhood of the armies there was no hunting at all. Some pleasure he derived through conjuring mental pictures from time to time of the German he had left in the branches of the lone tree at the bottom of the high-walled gulch in which was penned the starving lion. He could imagine the man's mental anguish as he became weakened from hunger and maddened by thirst, knowing that sooner or later he must slip exhausted to the ground where waited the gaunt man-eater. Tarzan wondered if Schneider would have the courage to descend to the little rivulet for water should Numa leave the gulch and enter the cave, and then he pictured the mad race for the tree again when the lion charged out to seize his prey as he was certain to do, since the clumsy German could not descend to the rivulet without making at least some slight noise that would attract Numa's attention.

But even this pleasure palled, and more and more the ape-man found himself thinking of the English soldiers fighting against heavy odds and especially of the fact that it was Germans who were beating them. The thought made him lower his head and growl and it worried him not a little—a bit, perhaps, because he was finding it difficult to forget that he was an Englishman when he wanted only to be an ape. And at last the time came when he could not longer endure the thought of Germans killing Englishmen while he hunted in safety a bare march away.

His decision made, he set out in the direction of the German camp, no well-defined plan formulated; but with the general idea that once near the field of operations he might find an opportunity to harass the German command as he so well knew how to do. His way took him along the gorge close to the gulch in which he had left Schneider, and, yielding to a natural curiosity, he scaled the cliffs and made his way to the edge of the gulch. The tree was empty, nor was there sign of Numa, the lion. Picking up a rock he hurled it into the gulch, where it rolled to the very entrance to the cave. Instantly the lion appeared in the aperture; but such a different-looking lion from the great sleek brute that Tarzan had trapped there two weeks before. Now he was gaunt and emaciated, and when he walked he staggered.

"Where is the German?" shouted Tarzan. "Was he good eating, or only a bag of bones when he slipped and fell from the tree?"

Numa growled. "You look hungry, Numa," continued the ape-man. "You must have been very hungry to eat all the grass from your lair and even the bark from the tree as far up as you can reach. Would you like another German?" and smiling he turned away.

A few minutes later he came suddenly upon Bara, the deer, asleep beneath a tree, and as Tarzan was hungry he made a quick kill, and squatting beside his prey proceeded to eat his fill. As he was gnawing the last morsel from a bone his quick ears caught the padding of stealthy feet behind him, and turning he confronted Dango, the hyena, sneaking upon him. With a growl the ape-man picked up a fallen branch and hurled it at the skulking brute. "Go away, eater of carrion!" he cried; but Dango was hungry and being large and powerful he only snarled and circled slowly about as though watching for an opportunity to charge. Tarzan of the Apes knew Dango even better than Dango knew himself. He knew that the brute, made savage by hunger, was mustering its courage for an attack, that it was probably accustomed to man and therefore more or less fearless of him and so he un-slung his heavy spear and laid it ready at his side while he continued his meal, all the time keeping a watchful eye upon the hyena.

He felt no fear, for long familiarity with the dangers of his wild world had so accustomed him to them that he took whatever came as a part of each day's existence as you accept the homely though no less real dangers of the farm, the range, or the crowded metropolis. Being jungle bred he was ready to protect his kill from all comers within ordinary limitations of caution. Under favorable conditions Tarzan would face even Numa himself and, if forced to seek safety by flight, he could do so without any feeling of shame. There was no braver creature roamed those savage wilds and at the same time there was none more wise—the two factors that had permitted him to survive.

Dango might have charged sooner but for the savage growls of the ape-man—growls which, coming from human lips, raised a question and a fear in the hyena's heart. He had attacked women and children in the native fields and he had frightened their men about their fires at night; but he never had seen a man-thing who made this sound that reminded him more of Numa angry than of a man afraid.

When Tarzan had completed his repast he was about to rise and hurl a clean-picked bone at the beast before he went his way, leaving the remains of his kill to Dango; but a sudden thought stayed him and instead he picked up the carcass of the deer, threw it over his shoulder, and set off in the direction of the gulch. For a few yards Dango followed, growling, and then realizing that he was being robbed of even a taste of the luscious flesh he cast discretion to the winds and charged. Instantly, as though Nature had given him eyes in the back of his head, Tarzan sensed the impending danger and, dropping Bara to the ground, turned with raised spear. Far back went the brown, right hand and then forward, lightning-like, backed by the power of giant muscles and the weight of his brawn and bone. The spear, released at the right instant, drove straight for Dango, caught him in the neck where it joined the shoulders and passed through the body.

When he had withdrawn the shaft from the hyena Tarzan shouldered both carcasses and continued on toward the gulch. Below lay Numa beneath the shade of the lone tree and at the ape-man's call he staggered slowly to his feet, yet weak as he was, he still growled savagely, even essaying a roar at the sight of his enemy. Tarzan let the two bodies slide over the rim of the cliff. "Eat, Numa!" he cried. "It may be that I shall need you again." He saw the lion, quickened to new life at the sight of food, spring upon the body of the deer and then he left him rending and tearing the flesh as he bolted great pieces into his empty maw.

The following day Tarzan came within sight of the German lines. From a wooded spur of the hills he looked down upon the enemy's left flank and beyond to the British lines. His position gave him a bird's-eye view of the field of battle, and his keen eyesight picked out many details that would not have been apparent to a man whose every sense was not trained to the highest point of perfection as were the ape-man's. He noted machine-gun emplacements cunningly hidden from the view of the British and listening posts placed well out in No Man's Land.

As his interested gaze moved hither and thither from one point of interest to another he heard from a point upon the hillside below him, above the roar of cannon and the crack of rifle fire, a single rifle spit. Immediately his attention was centered upon the spot where he knew a sniper must be hid. Patiently he awaited the next shot that would tell him more surely the exact location of the rifleman, and when it came he moved down the steep hillside with the stealth and quietness of a panther. Apparently he took no cognizance of where he stepped, yet never a loose stone was disturbed nor a twig broken—it was as though his feet saw.

Presently, as he passed through a clump of bushes, he came to the edge of a low cliff and saw upon a ledge some fifteen feet below him a German soldier prone behind an embankment of loose rock and leafy boughs that hid him from the view of the British lines. The man must have been an excellent shot, for he was well back of the German lines, firing over the heads of his fellows. His high-powered rifle was equipped with telescope sights and he also carried binoculars which he was in the act of using as Tarzan discovered him, either to note the effect of his last shot or to discover a new target. Tarzan let his eye move quickly toward that part of the British line the German seemed to be scanning, his keen sight revealing many excellent targets for a rifle placed so high above the trenches.

The Hun, evidently satisfied with his observations, laid aside his binoculars and again took up his rifle, placed its butt in the hollow of his shoulder and took careful aim. At the same instant a brown body sprang outward from the cliff above him. There was no sound and it is doubtful that the German ever knew what manner of creature it was that alighted heavily upon his back, for at the instant of impact the sinewy fingers of the ape-man circled the hairy throat of the Boche. There was a moment of futile struggling followed by the sudden realization of dissolution—the sniper was dead.

Lying behind the rampart of rocks and boughs, Tarzan looked down upon the scene below. Near at hand were the trenches of the Germans. He could see officers and men moving about in them and almost in front of him a well-hidden machine gun was traversing No Man's Land in an oblique direction, striking the British at such an angle as to make it difficult for them to locate it.

Tarzan watched, toying idly with the rifle of the dead German. Presently he fell to examining the mechanism of the piece. He glanced again toward the German trenches and changed the adjustment of the sights, then he placed the rifle to his shoulder and took aim. Tarzan was an excellent shot. With his civilized friends he had hunted big game with the weapons of civilization and though he never had killed except for food or in self-defense he had amused himself firing at inanimate targets thrown into the air and had perfected himself in the use of firearms without realizing that he had done so. Now indeed would he hunt big game. A slow smile touched his lips as his finger closed gradually upon the trigger. The rifle spoke and a German machine gunner collapsed behind his weapon. In three minutes Tarzan picked off the crew of that gun. Then he spotted a German officer emerging from a dugout and the three men in the bay with him. Tarzan was careful to leave no one in the immediate vicinity to question how Germans could be shot in German trenches when they were entirely concealed from enemy view.

Again adjusting his sights he took a long-range shot at a distant machine-gun crew to his right. With calm deliberation he wiped them out to a man. Two guns were silenced. He saw men running through the trenches and he picked off several of them. By this time the Germans were aware that something was amiss—that an uncanny sniper had discovered a point of vantage from which this sector of the trenches was plainly visible to him. At first they sought to discover his location in No Man's Land; but when an officer looking over the parapet through a periscope was struck full in the back of the head with a rifle bullet which passed through his skull and fell to the bottom of the trench they realized that it was beyond the parados rather than the parapet that they should search.

One of the soldiers picked up the bullet that had killed his officer, and then it was that real excitement prevailed in that particular bay, for the bullet was obviously of German make. Hugging the parados, messengers carried the word in both directions and presently periscopes were leveled above the parados and keen eyes were searching out the traitor. It did not take them long to locate the position of the hidden sniper and then Tarzan saw a machine gun being trained upon him. Before it had gotten into action its crew lay dead about it; but there were other men to take their places, reluctantly perhaps; but driven on by their officers they were forced to it and at the same time two other machine guns were swung around toward the ape-man and put into operation.

Realizing that the game was about up Tarzan with a farewell shot laid aside the rifle and melted into the hills behind him. For many minutes he could hear the sputter of machinegun fire concentrated upon the spot he had just quit and smiled as he contemplated the waste of German ammunition.

"They have paid heavily for Wasimbu, the Waziri, whom they crucified, and for his slain fellows," he mused; "but for Jane they can never pay—no, not if I killed them all."

After dark that night he circled the flanks of both armies and passed through the British out-guards and into the British lines. No man saw him come. No man knew that he was there.

Headquarters of the Second Rhodesians occupied a sheltered position far enough back of the lines to be comparatively safe from enemy observation. Even lights were permitted, and Colonel Capell sat before a field table, on which was spread a military map, talking with several of his officers. A large tree spread above them, a lantern sputtered dimly upon the table, while a small fire burned upon the ground close at hand. The enemy had no planes and no other observers could have seen the lights from the German lines.

The officers were discussing the advantage in numbers possessed by the enemy and the inability of the British to more than hold their present position. They could not advance. Already they had sustained severe losses in every attack and had always been driven back by overwhelming numbers. There were hidden machine guns, too, that bothered the colonel considerably. It was evidenced by the fact that he often reverted to them during the conversation.

"Something silenced them for a while this afternoon," said one of the younger officers. "I was observing at the time and I couldn't make out what the fuss was about; but they seemed to be having a devil of a time in a section of trench on their left. At one time I could have sworn they were attacked in the rear—I reported it to you at the time, sir, you'll recall—for the blighters were pepperin' away at the side of that bluff behind them. I could see the dirt fly. I don't know what it could have been."

There was a slight rustling among the branches of the tree above them and simultaneously a lithe, brown body dropped in their midst. Hands moved quickly to the butts of pistols; but otherwise there was no movement among the officers. First they looked wonderingly at the almost naked white man standing there with the firelight playing upon rounded muscles, took in the primitive attire and the equally primitive armament and then all eyes turned toward the colonel.

"Who the devil are you, sir?" snapped that officer.

"Tarzan of the Apes," replied the newcomer.

"Oh, Greystoke!" cried a major, and stepped forward with outstretched hand.

"Preswick," acknowledged Tarzan as he took the proffered hand.

"I didn't recognize you at first," apologized the major. "The last time I saw you you were in London in evening dress. Quite a difference—'pon my word, man, you'll have to admit it."

Tarzan smiled and turned toward the colonel. "I overheard your conversation," he said. "I have just come from behind the German lines. Possibly I can help you."

The colonel looked questioningly toward Major Preswick who quickly rose to the occasion and presented the ape-man to his commanding officer and fellows. Briefly Tarzan told them what it was that brought him out alone in pursuit of the Germans.

"And now you have come to join us?" asked the colonel.

Tarzan shook his head. "Not regularly," he replied. "I must fight in my own way; but I can help you. Whenever I wish I can enter the German lines."

Capell smiled and shook his head. "It's not so easy as you think," he said; "I've lost two good officers in the last week trying it—and they were experienced men; none better in the Intelligence Department."

"Is it more difficult than entering the British lines?" asked Tarzan.

The colonel was about to reply when a new thought appeared to occur to him and he looked quizzically at the ape-man. "Who brought you here?" he asked. "Who passed you through our out-guards?"

"I have just come through the German lines and yours and passed through your camp," he replied. "Send word to ascertain if anyone saw me."

"But who accompanied you?" insisted Capell.

"I came alone," replied Tarzan and then, drawing himself to his full height, "You men of civilization, when you come into the jungle, are as dead among the quick. Manu, the monkey, is a sage by comparison. I marvel that you exist at all—only your numbers, your weapons, and your power of reasoning save you. Had I a few hundred great apes with your reasoning power I could drive the Germans into the ocean as quickly as the remnant of them could reach the coast. Fortunate it is for you that the dumb brutes cannot combine. Could they, Africa would remain forever free of men. But come, can I help you? Would you like to know where several machinegun emplacements are hidden?"

The colonel assured him that they would, and a moment later Tarzan had traced upon the map the location of three that had been bothering the English. "There is a weak spot here," he said, placing a finger upon the map. "It is held by blacks; but the machine guns out in front are manned by whites. If—wait! I have a plan. You can fill that trench with your own men and enfilade the trenches to its right with their own machine guns."

Colonel Capell smiled and shook his head. "It sounds very easy," he said.

"It *is* easy—for me," replied the ape-man. "I can empty that section of trench without a shot. I was raised in the jungle—I know the jungle folk—the Gomangani as well as the others. Look for me again on the second night," and he turned to leave.

"Wait," said the colonel. "I will send an officer to pass you through the lines."

Tarzan smiled and moved away. As he was leaving the little group about headquarters he passed a small figure wrapped in an officer's heavy overcoat. The collar was turned up and the visor of the military cap pulled well down over the eyes; but, as the ape-man passed, the light from the fire illuminated the features of the newcomer for an instant, revealing to Tarzan a vaguely familiar face. Some officer he had known in London, doubtless, he surmised, and went his way through the British camp and the British lines all unknown to the watchful sentinels of the out-guard.

Nearly all night he moved across Kilimanjaro's foothills, tracking by instinct an unknown way, for he guessed that what he sought would be found on some wooded slope higher up than he had come upon his other recent journeys in this, to him, little known country. Three hours before dawn his keen nostrils apprised him that somewhere in the vicinity he would find what he wanted, and so he climbed into a tall tree and settled himself for a few hours' sleep.

WHEN THE LION FED

Kudu, the sun, was well up in the heavens when Tarzan awoke. The ape-man stretched his giant limbs, ran his fingers through his thick hair, and swung lightly down to earth. Immediately he took up the trail he had come in search of, following it by scent down into a deep ravine. Cautiously he went now, for his nose told him that the quarry was close at hand, and presently from an overhanging bough he looked down upon Horta, the boar, and many of his kinsmen. Un-slinging his bow and selecting an arrow, Tarzan fitted the shaft and, drawing it far back, took careful aim at the largest of the great pigs. In the ape-man's teeth were other arrows, and no sooner had the first one sped, than he had fitted and shot another bolt. Instantly the pigs were in turmoil, not knowing from whence the danger threatened. They stood stupidly at first and then commenced milling around until six of their number lay dead or dying about them; then with a chorus of grunts and squeals they started off at a wild run, disappearing quickly in the dense underbrush.

Tarzan then descended from the tree, dispatched those that were not already dead and proceeded to skin the carcasses. As he worked, rapidly and with great skill, he neither hummed nor whistled as does the average man of civilization. It was in numerous little ways such as these that he differed from other men, due, probably, to his early jungle training. The beasts of the jungle that he had been reared among were playful to maturity but seldom thereafter. His fellow-apes, especially the bulls, became fierce and surly as they grew older. Life was a serious matter during lean seasons—one had to fight to secure one's share of food then, and the habit once formed became lifelong. Hunting for food was the life labor of the jungle bred, and a life labor is a thing not to be approached with levity nor prosecuted lightly. So all work found Tarzan serious, though he still retained what the other beasts lost as they grew older—a sense of humor, which he gave play to when the mood suited him. It was a grim humor and sometimes ghastly; but it satisfied Tarzan.

Then, too, were one to sing and whistle while working on the ground, concentration would be impossible. Tarzan possessed the ability to concentrate each of his five senses upon its particular business. Now he worked at skinning the six pigs and his eyes and his fingers worked as though there was naught else in all the world than these six carcasses; but his ears and his nose were as busily engaged elsewhere—the former ranging the forest all about and the latter assaying each passing zephyr. It was his nose that first discovered the approach of Sabor, the lioness, when the wind shifted for a moment.

As clearly as though he had seen her with his eyes, Tarzan knew that the lioness had caught the scent of the freshly killed pigs and immediately had moved down wind in their direction. He knew from the strength of the scent spoor and the rate of the wind about how far away she was and that she was approaching from behind him. He was finishing the last pig and he did not hurry. The five pelts lay close at hand-he had been careful to keep them thus together and near him—an ample tree waved its low branches above him.

He did not even turn his head for he knew she was not yet in sight; but he bent his ears just a bit more sharply for the first sound of her nearer approach. When the final skin had been removed he rose. Now he heard Sabor in the bushes to his rear, but not yet too close. Leisurely he gathered up the six pelts and one of the carcasses, and as the lioness appeared between the boles of two trees he swung upward into the branches above him. Here he hung the hides over a limb, seated himself comfortably upon another with his back against the bole of the tree, cut a hind quarter from the carcass he had carried with him and proceeded to satisfy his hunger. Sabor slunk, growling, from the brush, cast a wary eye upward toward the ape-man and then fell upon the nearest carcass.

Tarzan looked down upon her and grinned, recalling an argument he had once had with a famous big-game hunter who had declared that the king of beasts ate only what he himself had killed. Tarzan knew better for he had seen Numa and Sabor stoop even to carrion.

Having filled his belly, the ape-man fell to work upon the hides—all large and strong. First he cut strips from them about half an inch wide. When he had sufficient number of these strips he sewed two of the hides together, afterwards piercing holes every three or four inches around the edges. Running another strip through these holes gave him a large bag with a drawstring. In similar fashion he produced four other like bags, but smaller, from the four remaining hides and had several strips left over.

All this done he threw a large, juicy fruit at Sabor, cached the remainder of the pig in a crotch of the tree and swung off toward the southwest through the middle terraces of the forest, carrying his five bags with him. Straight he went to the rim of the gulch where he had imprisoned Numa, the lion. Very stealthily he approached the edge and peered over. Numa was not in sight. Tarzan sniffed and listened. He could hear nothing, yet he knew that Numa must be within the cave. He hoped that he slept—much depended upon Numa not discovering him.

Cautiously he lowered himself over the edge of the cliff, and with utter noiselessness commenced the descent toward the bottom of the gulch. He stopped often and turned his keen eyes and ears in the direction of the cave's mouth at the far end of the gulch, some hundred feet away. As he neared the foot of the cliff his danger increased greatly. If he could reach the bottom and cover half the distance to the tree that stood in the center of the gulch he would feel comparatively safe for then, even if Numa appeared, he felt that he could beat him either to the cliff or to the tree, but to scale the first thirty feet of the cliff rapidly enough to elude the leaping beast would require a running start of at least twenty feet as there were no very good hand- or footholds close to the bottom—he had had to run up the first twenty feet like a squirrel running up a tree that other time he had beaten an infuriated Numa to it. He had no desire to attempt it again unless the conditions were equally favorable at least, for he had escaped Numa's raking talons by only a matter of inches on the former occasion.

At last he stood upon the floor of the gulch. Silent as a disembodied spirit he advanced toward the tree. He was half way there and no sign of Numa. He reached the scarred bole from which the famished lion had devoured the bark and even torn pieces of the wood itself and yet Numa had not appeared. As he drew himself up to the lower branches he commenced to wonder if Numa were in the cave after all. Could it be possible that he had forced the barrier of rocks with which Tarzan had plugged the other end of the passage where it opened into the outer world of freedom? Or was Numa dead? The ape-man doubted the verity of the latter suggestion as he had fed the lion the entire carcasses of a deer and a hyena only a few days since—he could not have starved in so short a time, while the little rivulet running across the gulch furnished him with water a-plenty.

Tarzan started to descend and investigate the cavern when it occurred to him that it would save effort were he to lure Numa out instead. Acting upon the thought he uttered a low growl. Immediately he was rewarded by the sound of a movement within the cave and an instant later a wild-eyed, haggard lion rushed forth ready to face the devil himself were he edible. When Numa saw Tarzan, fat and sleek, perched in the tree he became suddenly the embodiment of frightful rage. His eyes and his nose told him that this was the creature responsible for his predicament and also that this creature was good to eat. Frantically the lion sought to scramble up the bole of the tree. Twice he leaped high enough to catch the lowest branches with his paws, but both times he fell backward to the earth. Each time he became more furious. His growls and roars were incessant and horrible and all the time Tarzan sat grinning down upon him, taunting him in jungle billingsgate for his inability to reach him and mentally exulting that always Numa was wasting his already waning strength.

Finally the ape-man rose and un-slung his rope. He arranged the coils carefully in his left hand and the noose in his right, and then he took a position with each foot on one of two branches that lay in about the same horizontal plane and with his back pressed firmly against the stem of the tree. There he stood hurling insults at Numa until the beast was again goaded into leaping upward at him, and as Numa rose the noose dropped quickly over his head and about his neck. A quick movement of Tarzan's rope hand tightened the coil and when Numa slipped backward to the ground only his hind feet touched, for the ape-man held him swinging by the neck.

Moving slowly outward upon the two branches Tarzan swung Numa out so that he could not reach the bole of the tree with his raking talons, then he made the rope fast after drawing the lion clear of the ground, dropped his five pigskin sacks to earth and leaped down himself. Numa was striking frantically at the grass rope with his fore claws. At any moment he might sever it and Tarzan must, therefore, work rapidly.

First he drew the larger bag over Numa's head and secured it about his neck with the draw string, then he managed, after considerable effort, during which he barely escaped being torn to ribbons by the mighty talons, to hog-tie Numa—drawing his four legs together and securing them in that position with the strips trimmed from the pigskins.

By this time the lion's efforts had almost ceased—it was evident that he was being rapidly strangled and as that did not at all suit the purpose of the Tarmangani the latter swung again into the tree, unfastened the rope from above and lowered the lion to the ground where he immediately followed it and loosed the noose about Numa's neck. Then he drew his hunting knife and cut two round holes in the front of the head bag opposite the lion's eyes for the double purpose of permitting him to see and giving him sufficient air to breathe.

This done Tarzan busied himself fitting the other bags, one over each of Numa's formidably armed paws. Those on the hind feet he secured not only by tightening the draw strings but also rigged garters that fastened tightly around the legs above the hocks. He secured the front-feet bags in place similarly above the great knees. Now, indeed, was Numa, the lion, reduced to the harmlessness of Bara, the deer.

By now Numa was showing signs of returning life. He gasped for breath and struggled; but the strips of pigskin that held his four legs together were numerous and tough. Tarzan watched and was sure that they would hold, yet Numa is mightily muscled and there was the chance, always, that he might struggle free of his bonds after which all would depend upon the efficacy of Tarzan's bags and draw strings.

After Numa had again breathed normally and was able to roar out his protests and his rage, his struggles increased to Titanic proportions for a short time; but as a lion's powers of endurance are in no way proportionate to his size and strength he soon tired and lay quietly. Amid renewed growling and another futile attempt to free himself, Numa was finally forced to submit to the further indignity of having a rope secured about his neck; but this time it was no noose that might tighten and strangle him; but a bowline knot, which does not tighten or slip under strain.

The other end of the rope Tarzan fastened to the stem of the tree, then he quickly cut the bonds securing Numa's legs and leaped aside as the beast sprang to his feet. For a moment the lion stood with legs far outspread, then he raised first one paw and then another, shaking them energetically in an effort to dislodge the strange footgear that Tarzan had fastened upon them. Finally he began to paw at the bag upon his head. The ape-man, standing with ready spear, watched Numa's efforts intently. Would the bags hold? He sincerely hoped so. Or would all his labor prove fruitless?

As the clinging things upon his feet and face resisted his every effort to dislodge them, Numa became frantic. He rolled upon the ground, fighting, biting, scratching, and roaring; he leaped to his feet and sprang into the air; he charged Tarzan, only to be brought to a sudden stop as the rope securing him to the tree tautened. Then Tarzan stepped in and rapped him smartly on the head with the shaft of his spear. Numa reared upon his hind feet and struck at the are-man and in return received a cuff on one ear that sent him reeling sideways. When he returned to the attack he was again sent sprawling. After the fourth effort it appeared to dawn upon the king of beasts that he had met his master, his head and tail dropped and when Tarzan advanced upon him he backed away, though still growling.

Leaving Numa tied to the tree Tarzan entered the tunnel and removed the barricade from the opposite end, after which he returned to the gulch and strode straight for the tree. Numa lay in his path and as Tarzan approached growled menacingly. The ape-man cuffed him aside and unfastened the rope from the tree. Then ensued a half-hour of stubbornly fought battle while Tarzan endeavored to drive Numa through the tunnel ahead of him and Numa persistently refused to be driven. At last, however, by dint of the unrestricted use of his spear point, the ape-man succeeded in forcing the lion to move ahead of him and eventually guided him into the passageway. Once inside, the problem became simpler since Tarzan followed closely in the rear with his sharp spear point, an unremitting incentive to forward movement on the part of the lion. If Numa hesitated he was prodded. If he backed up the result was extremely painful and so, being a wise lion who was learning rapidly, he decided to keep on going and at the end of the tunnel, emerging into the outer world, he sensed freedom, raised his head and tail and started off at a run.

Tarzan, still on his hands and knees just inside the entrance, was taken unaware with the result that he was sprawled forward upon his face and dragged a hundred yards across the rocky ground before Numa was brought to a stand. It was a scratched and angry Tarzan who scrambled to his feet. At first he was tempted to chastise Numa; but, as the ape-man seldom permitted his temper to guide him in any direction not countenanced by reason, he quickly abandoned the idea.

Having taught Numa the rudiments of being driven, he now urged him forward and there commenced as strange a journey as the unrecorded history of the jungle contains. The balance of that day was eventful both for Tarzan and for Numa. From open rebellion at first the lion passed through stages of stubborn resistance and grudging obedience to final surrender. He was a very tired, hungry, and thirsty lion when night overtook them; but there was to be no food for him that day or the next—Tarzan did not dare risk removing the head bag, though he did cut another hole which permitted Numa to quench his thirst shortly after dark. Then he tied him to a tree, sought food for himself, and stretched out among the branches above his captive for a few hours' sleep.

Early the following morning they resumed their journey, winding over the low foothills south of Kilimanjaro, toward the east. The beasts of the jungle who saw them took one look and fled. The scent spoor of Numa, alone, might have been enough to have provoked flight in many of the lesser animals, but the sight of this strange apparition that smelled like a lion, but looked like nothing they ever had seen before, being led through the jungles by a giant Tarmangani was too much for even the more formidable denizens of the wild.

EDGAR RICE BURROUGHS

Sabor, the lioness, recognizing from a distance the scent of her lord and master intermingled with that of a Tarmangani and the hide of Horta, the boar, trotted through the aisles of the forest to investigate. Tarzan and Numa heard her coming, for she voiced a plaintive and questioning whine as the baffling mixture of odors aroused her curiosity and her fears, for lions, however terrible they may appear, are often timid animals and Sabor, being of the gentler sex, was, naturally, habitually inquisitive as well.

Tarzan un-slung his spear for he knew that he might now easily have to fight to retain his prize. Numa halted and turned his outraged head in the direction of the coming she. He voiced a throaty growl that was almost a purr. Tarzan was upon the point of prodding him on again when Sabor broke into view, and behind her the ape-man saw that which gave him instant pause—four full-grown lions trailing the lioness.

To have goaded Numa then into active resistance might have brought the whole herd down upon him and so Tarzan waited to learn first what their attitude would be. He had no idea of relinquishing his lion without a battle; but knowing lions as he did, he knew that there was no assurance as to just what the newcomers would do.

The lioness was young and sleek, and the four males were in their prime—as handsome lions as he ever had seen. Three of the males were scantily maned but one, the foremost, carried a splendid, black mane that rippled in the breeze as he trotted majestically forward. The lioness halted a hundred feet from Tarzan, while the lions came on past her and stopped a few feet nearer. Their ears were upstanding and their eyes filled with curiosity. Tarzan could not even guess what they might do. The lion at his side faced them fully, standing silent now and watchful.

Suddenly the lioness gave vent to another little whine, at which Tarzan's lion voiced a terrific roar and leaped forward straight toward the beast of the black mane. The sight of this awesome creature with the strange face was too much for the lion toward which he leaped, dragging Tarzan after him, and with a growl the lion turned and fled, followed by his companions and the she.

Numa attempted to follow them; Tarzan held him in leash and when he turned upon him in rage, beat him unmercifully across the head with his spear. Shaking his head and growling, the lion at last moved off again in the direction they had been traveling; but it was an hour before he ceased to sulk. He was very hungry—half famished in fact—and consequently of an ugly temper, yet so thoroughly subdued by Tarzan's heroic methods of lion taming that he was presently pacing along at the ape-man's side like some huge St. Bernard.

It was dark when the two approached the British right, after a slight delay farther back because of a German patrol it had been necessary to elude. A short distance from the British line of out-guard sentinels Tarzan tied Numa to a tree and continued on alone. He evaded a sentinel, passed the out-guard and support, and by devious ways came again to Colonel Capell's headquarters, where he appeared before the officers gathered there as a disembodied spirit materializing out of thin air.

When they saw who it was that came thus unannounced they smiled and the colonel scratched his head in perplexity.

"Someone should be shot for this," he said. "I might just as well not establish an out-post if a man can filter through whenever he pleases."

Tarzan smiled. "Do not blame them," he said, "for I am not a man. I am Tarmangani. Any Mangani who wished to, could enter your camp almost at will; but if you have them for sentinels no one could enter without their knowledge."

"What are the Mangani?" asked the colonel. "Perhaps we might enlist a bunch of the beggars."

Tarzan shook his head. "They are the great apes," he explained; "my people; but you could not use them. They cannot concentrate long enough upon a single idea. If I told them of this they would be much interested for a short time-I might even hold the interest of a few long enough to get them here and explain their duties to them; but soon they would lose interest and when you needed them most they might be off in the forest searching for beetles instead of watching their posts. They have the minds of little children —that is why they remain what they are."

"You call them Mangani and yourself Tarmangani—what is the difference?" asked Major Preswick.

"Tar means white," replied Tarzan, "and Mangani, great ape. My name—the name they gave me in the tribe of Kerchak—means White-skin. When I was a little balu my skin, I presume, looked very white indeed against the beautiful, black coat of Kala, my foster mother and so they called me Tarzan, the Tarmangani. They call you, too, Tarmangani," he concluded, smiling.

Capell smiled. "It is no reproach, Greystoke," he said; "and, by Jove, it would be a mark of distinction if a fellow could act the part. And now how about your plan? Do you still think you can empty the trench opposite our sector?"

"Is it still held by Gomangani?" asked Tarzan.

"What are Gomangani?" inquired the colonel. "It is still held by native troops, if that is what you mean."

"Yes," replied the ape-man, "the Gomangani are the great black apes—the Negroes."

"What do you intend doing and what do you want us to do?" asked Capell.

Tarzan approached the table and placed a finger on the map. "Here is a listening post," he said; "they have a machine gun in it. A tunnel connects it with this trench at this point." His finger moved from place to place on the map as he talked. "Give me a bomb and when you hear it burst in this listening post let your men start across No Man's Land slowly. Presently they will hear a commotion in the enemy trench; but they need not hurry, and, whatever they do, have them come quietly. You might also warn them that I may be in the trench and that I do not care to be shot or bayoneted."

"And that is all?" queried Capell, after directing an officer to give Tarzan a hand grenade; "you will empty the trench alone?"

"Not exactly alone," replied Tarzan with a grim smile; "but I shall empty it, and, by the way, your men may come in through the tunnel from the listening post if you prefer. In about half an hour, Colonel," and he turned and left them.

As he passed through the camp there flashed suddenly upon the screen of recollection, conjured there by some reminder of his previous visit to headquarters, doubtless, the image of the officer he had passed as he quit the colonel that other time and simultaneously recognition of the face that had been revealed by the light from the fire. He shook his head dubiously. No, it could not be and yet the features of the young officer were identical with those of Fraulein Kircher, the German spy he had seen at German headquarters the night he took Major Schneider from under the nose of the Hun general and his staff.

Beyond the last line of sentinels Tarzan moved quickly in the direction of Numa, the lion. The beast was lying down as Tarzan approached, but he rose as the ape-man reached his side. A low whine escaped his muzzled lips. Tarzan smiled for he recognized in the new note almost a supplication—it was more like the whine of a hungry dog begging for food than the voice of the proud king of beasts.

"Soon you will kill—and feed," he murmured in the vernacular of the great apes.

He unfastened the rope from about the tree and, with Numa close at his side, slunk into No Man's Land. There was little rifle fire and only an occasional shell vouched for the presence of artillery behind the opposing lines. As the shells from both sides were falling well back of the trenches, they constituted no menace to Tarzan; but the noise of them and that of the rifle fire had a marked effect upon Numa who crouched, trembling, close to the Tarmangani as though seeking protection.

Cautiously the two beasts moved forward toward the listening post of the Germans. In one hand Tarzan carried the bomb the English had given him, in the other was the coiled rope attached to the lion. At last Tarzan could see the position a few yards ahead. His keen eyes picked out the head and shoulders of the sentinel on watch. The ape-man grasped the bomb firmly in his right hand. He measured the distance with his eye and gathered his feet beneath him, then in a single motion he rose and threw the missile, immediately flattening himself prone upon the ground.

Five seconds later there was a terrific explosion in the center of the listening post. Numa gave a nervous start and attempted to break away; but Tarzan held him and, leaping to his feet, ran forward, dragging Numa after him. At the edge of the post he saw below him but slight evidence that the position had been occupied at all, for only a few shreds of torn flesh remained. About the only thing that had not been demolished was a machine gun which had been protected by sand bags.

There was not an instant to lose. Already a relief might be crawling through the communication tunnel, for it must have been evident to the sentinels in the Hun trenches that the listening post had been demolished. Numa hesitated to follow Tarzan into the excavation; but the ape-man, who was in no mood to temporize, jerked him roughly to the bottom. Before them lay the mouth of the tunnel that led back from No Man's Land to the German trenches. Tarzan pushed Numa forward until his head was almost in the aperture, then as though it were an afterthought, he turned quickly and, taking the machine gun from the parapet, placed it in the bottom of the hole close at hand, after which he turned again to Numa, and with his knife quickly cut the garters that held the bags upon his front paws. Before the lion could know that a part of his formidable armament was again released for action, Tarzan had cut the rope from his neck and the head bag from his face, and grabbing the lion from the rear had thrust him partially into the mouth of the tunnel.

Then Numa balked, only to feel the sharp prick of Tarzan's knife point in his hind quarters. Goading him on the ape-man finally succeeded in getting the lion sufficiently far into the tunnel so that there was no chance of his escaping other than by going forward or deliberately backing into the sharp blade at his rear. Then Tarzan cut the bags from the great hind feet, placed his shoulder and his knife point against Numa's seat, dug his toes into the loose earth that had been broken up by the explosion of the bomb, and shoved.

Inch by inch at first Numa advanced. He was growling now and presently he commenced to roar. Suddenly he leaped forward and Tarzan knew that he had caught the scent of meat ahead. Dragging the machine gun beside him the ape-man followed quickly after the lion whose roars he could plainly hear ahead mingled with the unmistakable screams of frightened men. Once again a grim smile touched the lips of this man-beast.

"They murdered my Waziri," he muttered; "they crucified Wasimbu, son of Muviro."

When Tarzan reached the trench and emerged into it there was no one in sight in that particular bay, nor in the next, nor the next as he hurried forward in the direction of the German center; but in the fourth bay he saw a dozen men jammed in the angle of the traverse at the end while leaping upon them and rending with talons and fangs was Numa, a terrific incarnation of ferocity and ravenous hunger.

Whatever held the men at last gave way as they fought madly with one another in their efforts to escape this dread creature that from their infancy had filled them with terror, and again they were retreating. Some clambered over the parados and some even over the parapet preferring the dangers of No Man's Land to this other soul-searing menace.

As the British advanced slowly toward the German trenches, they first met terrified blacks who ran into their arms only too willing to surrender. That pandemonium had broken loose in the Hun trench was apparent to the Rhodesians not only from the appearance of the deserters, but from the sounds of screaming, cursing men which came clearly to their ears; but there was one that baffled them for it resembled nothing more closely than the infuriated growling of an angry lion.

And when at last they reached the trench, those farthest on the left of the advancing Britishers heard a machine gun sputter suddenly before them and saw a huge lion leap over the German parados with the body of a screaming Hun soldier between his jaws and vanish into the shadows of the night, while squatting upon a traverse to their left was Tarzan of the Apes with a machine gun before him with which he was raking the length of the German trenches.

The foremost Rhodesians saw something else—they saw a huge German officer emerge from a dugout just in rear of the ape-man. They saw him snatch up a discarded rifle with bayonet fixed and creep upon the apparently unconscious Tarzan. They ran forward, shouting warnings; but above the pandemonium of the trenches and the machine gun their voices could not reach him. The German leaped upon the parapet behind him—the fat hands raised the rifle butt aloft for the cowardly downward thrust into the naked back and then, as moves Ara, the lightning, moved Tarzan of the Apes.

It was no man who leaped forward upon that Boche officer, striking aside the sharp bayonet as one might strike aside a straw in a baby's hand—it was a wild beast and the roar of a wild beast was upon those savage lips, for as that strange sense that Tarzan owned in common with the other jungle-bred creatures of his wild domain warned him of the presence behind him and he had whirled to meet the attack, his eyes had seen the corps and regimental insignia upon the other's blouse—it was the same as that worn by the murderers of his wife and his people, by the despoilers of his home and his happiness.

It was a wild beast whose teeth fastened upon the shoulder of the Hun—it was a wild beast whose talons sought that fat neck. And then the boys of the Second Rhodesian Regiment saw that which will live forever in their memories. They saw the giant ape-man pick the heavy German from the ground and shake him as a terrier might shake a rat—as Sabor, the lioness, sometimes shakes her prey. They saw the eyes of the Hun bulge in horror as he vainly struck with his futile hands against the massive chest and head of his assailant. They saw Tarzan suddenly spin the man about and placing a knee in the middle of his back and an arm about his neck bend his shoulders slowly backward. The German's knees gave and he sank upon them, but still that irresistible force bent him further and further. He screamed in agony for a moment—then something snapped and Tarzan cast him aside, a limp and lifeless thing.

The Rhodesians started forward, a cheer upon their lips—a cheer that never was uttered—a cheer that froze in their throats, for at that moment Tarzan placed a foot upon the carcass of his kill and, raising his face to the heavens, gave voice to the weird and terrifying victory cry of the bull ape.

Underlieutenant von Goss was dead.

Without a backward glance at the awe-struck soldiers Tarzan leaped the trench and was gone.

THE GOLDEN LOCKET

The little British army in East Africa, after suffering severe reverses at the hands of a numerically much superior force, was at last coming into its own. The German offensive had been broken and the Huns were now slowly and doggedly retreating along the railway to Tanga. The break in the German lines had followed the clearing of a section of their left-flank trenches of native soldiers by Tarzan and Numa, the lion, upon that memorable night that the ape-man had loosed a famishing man-eater among the superstitious and terror-stricken blacks. The Second Rhodesian Regiment had immediately taken possession of the abandoned trench and from this position their flanking fire had raked contiguous sections of the German line, the diversion rendering possible a successful night attack on the part of the balance of the British forces.

Weeks had elapsed. The Germans were contesting stubbornly every mile of waterless, thorn-covered ground and clinging desperately to their positions along the railway. The officers of the Second Rhodesians had seen nothing more of Tarzan of the Apes since he had slain Underlieutenant von Goss and disappeared toward the very heart of the German position, and there were those among them who believed that he had been killed within the enemy lines.

"They may have killed him," assented Colonel Capell; "but I fancy they never captured the beggar alive."

Nor had they, nor killed him either. Tarzan had spent those intervening weeks pleasantly and profitably. He had amassed a considerable fund of knowledge concerning the disposition and strength of German troops, their methods of warfare, and the various ways in which a lone Tarmangani might annoy an army and lower its morale.

At present he was prompted by a specific desire. There was a certain German spy whom he wished to capture alive and take back to the British When he had made his first visit to German headquarters, he had seen a young woman deliver a paper to the German general, and later he had seen that same young woman within the British lines in the uniform of a British officer. The conclusions were obvious—she was a spy.

And so Tarzan haunted German headquarters upon many nights hoping to see her again or to pick up some clew as to her whereabouts, and at the same time he utilized many an artifice whereby he might bring terror to the hearts of the Germans. That he was successful was often demonstrated by the snatches of conversation he overheard as he prowled through the German camps. One night as he lay concealed in the bushes close beside a regimental headquarters he listened to the conversation of several Boche officers. One of the men reverted to the stories told by the native troops in connection with their rout by a lion several weeks before and the simultaneous appearance in their trenches of a naked, white giant whom they were perfectly assured was some demon of the jungle.

"The fellow must have been the same as he who leaped into the general's headquarters and carried off Schneider," asserted one. "I wonder how he happened to single out the poor major. They say the creature seemed interested in no one but Schneider. He had von Kelter in his grasp, and he might easily have taken the general himself; but he ignored them all except Schneider. Him he pursued about the room, seized and carried off into the night. Gott knows what his fate was."

"Captain Fritz Schneider has some sort of theory," said another. "He told me only a week or two ago that he thinks he knows why his brother was taken—that it was a case of mistaken identity. He was not so sure about it until von Goss was killed, apparently by the same creature, the night the lion entered the trenches. Von Goss was attached to Schneider's company. One of Schneider's men was found with his neck wrung the same night that the major was carried off and Schneider thinks that this devil is after him and his command —that it came for him that night and got his brother by mistake. He says Kraut told him that in presenting the major to Fraulein Kircher the former's name was no sooner spoken than this wild man leaped through the window and made for him."

Suddenly the little group became rigid—listening. "What was that?" snapped one, eyeing the bushes from which a smothered snarl had issued as Tarzan of the Apes realized that through his mistake the perpetrator of the horrid crime at his bungalow still lived—that the murderer of his wife went yet unpunished.

For a long minute the officers stood with tensed nerves, every eye riveted upon the bushes from whence the ominous sound had issued. Each recalled recent mysterious disappearances from the heart of camps as well as from lonely out-guards. Each thought of the silent dead he had seen, slain almost within sight of their fellows by some unseen creature. They thought of the marks upon dead throats-made by talons or by giant fingers, they could not tell which—and those upon shoulders and jugulars where powerful teeth had fastened and they waited with drawn pistols.

Once the bushes moved almost imperceptibly and an instant later one of the officers, without warning, fired into them; but Tarzan of the Apes was not there. In the interval between the moving of the bushes and the firing of the shot he had melted into the night. Ten minutes later he was hovering on the outskirts of that part of camp where were bivouacked for the night the black soldiers of a native company commanded by one Hauptmann Fritz Schneider. The men were stretched upon the ground without tents; but there were tents pitched for the officers. Toward these Tarzan crept. It was slow and perilous work, as the Germans were now upon the alert for the uncanny foe that crept into their camps to take his toll by night, yet the ape-man passed their sentinels, eluded the vigilance of the interior guard, and crept at last to the rear of the officers' line.

Here he flattened himself against the ground close behind the nearest tent and listened. From within came the regular breathing of a sleeping man—one only. Tarzan was satisfied. With his knife he cut the tie strings of the rear flap and entered. He made no noise. The shadow of a falling leaf, floating gently to earth upon a still day, could have been no more soundless. He moved to the side of the sleeping man and bent low over him. He could not know, of course, whether it was Schneider or another, as he had never seen Schneider; but he meant to know and to know even more. Gently he shook the man by the shoulder. The fellow turned heavily and grunted in a thick guttural.

"Silence!" admonished the ape-man in a low whisper. "Silence—I kill."

The Hun opened his eyes. In the dim light he saw a giant figure bending over him. Now a mighty hand grasped his shoulder and another closed lightly about his throat.

"Make no outcry," commanded Tarzan; "but answer in a whisper my questions. What is your name?"

"Luberg," replied the officer. He was trembling. The weird presence of this naked giant filled him with dread. He, too, recalled the men mysteriously murdered in the still watches of the night camps. "What do you want?"

"Where is Hauptmann Fritz Schneider?" asked Tarzan, "Which is his tent?"

"He is not here," replied Luberg. "He was sent to Wilhelmstal yesterday."

"I shall not kill you—now," said the ape-man. "First I shall go and learn if you have lied to me and if you have your death shall be the more terrible. Do you know how Major Schneider died?"

Luberg shook his head negatively.

"I do," continued Tarzan, "and it was not a nice way to die—even for an accursed German. Turn over with your face down and cover your eyes. Do not move or make any sound."

The man did as he was bid and the instant that his eyes were turned away, Tarzan slipped from the tent. An hour later he was outside the German camp and headed for the little hill town of Wilhelmstal, the summer seat of government of German East Africa.

Fraulein Bertha Kircher was lost. She was humiliated and angry—it was long before she would admit it, that she, who prided herself upon her woodcraft, was lost in this little patch of country between the Pangani and the Tanga railway. She knew that Wilhelmstal lay southeast of her about fifty miles; but, through a combination of untoward circumstances, she found herself unable to determine which was southeast.

In the first place she had set out from German headquarters on a well-marked road that was being traveled by troops and with every reason to believe that she would follow that road to Wilhelmstal. Later she had been warned from this road by word that a strong British patrol had come down the west bank of the Pangani, effected a crossing south of her, and was even then marching on the railway at Tonda.

After leaving the road she found herself in thick bush and as the sky was heavily overcast she presently had recourse to her compass and it was not until then that she discovered to her dismay that she did not have it with her. So sure was she of her woodcraft, however, that she continued on in the direction she thought west until she had covered sufficient distance to warrant her in feeling assured that, by now turning south, she could pass safely in rear of the British patrol.

Nor did she commence to feel any doubts until long after she had again turned toward the east well south, as she thought, of the patrol. It was late afternoon—she should long since have struck the road again south of Tonda; but she had found no road and now she began to feel real anxiety.

Her horse had traveled all day without food or water, night was approaching and with it a realization that she was hopelessly lost in a wild and trackless country notorious principally for its tsetse flies and savage beasts. It was maddening to know that she had absolutely no knowledge of the direction she was traveling—that she might be forging steadily further from the railway, deeper into the gloomy and forbidding country toward the Pangani; yet it was impossible to stop-she must go on.

Bertha Kircher was no coward, whatever else she may have been, but as night began to close down around her she could not shut out from her mind entirely contemplation of the terrors of the long hours ahead before the rising sun should dissipate the Stygian gloom—the horrid jungle night—that lures forth all the prowling, preying creatures of destruction.

She found, just before dark, an open meadow-like break in the almost interminable bush. There was a small clump of trees near the center and here she decided to camp. The grass was high and thick, affording feed for her horse and a bed for herself, and there was more than enough dead wood lying about the trees to furnish a good fire well through the night. Removing the saddle and bridle from her mount she placed them at the foot of a tree and then picketed the animal close by. Then she busied herself collecting firewood and by the time darkness had fallen she had a good fire and enough wood to last until morning.

From her saddlebags she took cold food and from her canteen a swallow of water. She could not afford more than a small swallow for she could not know how long a time it might be before she should find more. It filled her with sorrow that her poor horse must go waterless, for even German spies may have hearts and this one was very young and very feminine.

It was now dark. There was neither moon nor stars and the light from her fire only accentuated the blackness beyond. She could see the grass about her and the boles of the trees which stood out in brilliant relief against the solid background of impenetrable night, and beyond the firelight there was nothing.

The jungle seemed ominously quiet. Far away in the distance she heard faintly the boom of big guns; but she could not locate their direction. She strained her ears until her nerves were on the point of breaking; but she could not tell from whence the sound came. And it meant so much to her to know, for the battle-lines were north of her and if she could but locate the direction of the firing she would know which way to go in the morning.

In the morning! Would she live to see another morning? She squared her shoulders and shook herself together. Such thoughts must be banished—they would never do. Bravely she hummed an air as she arranged her saddle near the fire and pulled a quantity of long grass to make a comfortable seat over which she spread her saddle blanket. Then she un-strapped a heavy, military coat from the cantle of her saddle and donned it, for the air was already chill.

Seating herself where she could lean against the saddle she prepared to maintain a sleepless vigil throughout the night. For an hour the silence was broken only by the distant booming of the guns and the low noises of the feeding horse and then, from possibly a mile away, came the rumbling thunder of a lion's roar. The girl started and laid her hand upon the rifle at her side. A little shudder ran through her slight frame and she could feel the goose flesh rise upon her body.

Again and again was the awful sound repeated and each time she was certain that it came nearer. She could locate the direction of this sound although she could not that of the guns, for the origin of the former was much closer. The lion was up wind and so could not have caught her scent as yet, though he might be approaching to investigate the light of the fire which could doubtless be seen for a considerable distance.

For another fear-filled hour the girl sat straining her eyes and ears out into the black void beyond her little island of light. During all that time the lion did not roar again; but there was constantly the sensation that it was creeping upon her. Again and again she would start and turn to peer into the blackness beyond the trees behind her as her overwrought nerves conjured the stealthy fall of padded feet. She held the rifle across her knees at the ready now and she was trembling from head to foot.

Suddenly her horse raised his head and snorted, and with a little cry of terror the girl sprang to her feet. The animal turned and trotted back toward her until the picket rope brought him to a stand, and then he wheeled about and with ears up-pricked gazed out into the night; but the girl could neither see nor hear aught.

Still another hour of terror passed during which the horse often raised his head to peer long and searchingly into the dark. The girl replenished the fire from time to time. She found herself becoming very sleepy. Her heavy lids persisted in drooping; but she dared not sleep. Fearful lest she might be overcome by the drowsiness that was stealing through her she rose and walked briskly to and fro, then she threw some more wood on the fire, walked over and stroked her horse's muzzle and returned to her seat.

Leaning against the saddle she tried to occupy her mind with plans for the morrow; but she must have dozed. With a start she awoke. It was broad daylight. The hideous night with its indescribable terrors was gone.

She could scarce believe the testimony of her senses. She had slept for hours, the fire was out and yet she and the horse were safe and alive, nor was there sign of savage beast about. And, best of all, the sun was shining, pointing the straight road to the east. Hastily she ate a few mouthfuls of her precious rations, which with a swallow of water constituted her breakfast. Then she saddled her horse and mounted. Already she felt that she was as good as safe in Wilhelmstal.

Possibly, however, she might have revised her conclusions could she have seen the two pairs of eyes watching her every move intently from different points in the bush.

Light-hearted and unsuspecting, the girl rode across the clearing toward the bush while directly before her two yellow-green eyes glared round and terrible, a tawny tail twitched nervously and great, padded paws gathered beneath a sleek barrel for a mighty spring. The horse was almost at the edge of the bush when Numa, the lion, launched himself through the air. He struck the animal's right shoulder at the instant that it reared, terrified, to wheel in flight. The force of the impact hurled the horse backward to the ground and so quickly that the girl had no opportunity to extricate herself; but fell to the earth with her mount, her left leg pinned beneath its body.

Horror-stricken, she saw the king of beasts open his mighty jaws and seize the screaming creature by the back of its neck. The great jaws closed, there was an instant's struggle as Numa shook his prey. She could hear the vertebrae crack as the mighty fangs crunched through them, and then the muscles of her faithful friend relaxed in death.

Numa crouched upon his kill. His terrifying eyes riveted themselves upon the girl's face—she could feel his hot breath upon her cheek and the odor of the fetid vapor nauseated her. For what seemed an eternity to the girl the two lay staring at each other and then the lion uttered a menacing growl.

Never before had Bertha Kircher been so terrified—never before had she had such cause for terror. At her hip was a pistol—a formidable weapon with which to face a man; but a puny thing indeed with which to menace the great beast before her. She knew that at best it could but enrage him and yet she meant to sell her life dearly, for she felt that she must die. No human succor could have availed her even had it been there to offer itself. For a moment she tore her gaze from the hypnotic fascination of that awful face and breathed a last prayer to her God. She did not ask for aid, for she felt that she was beyond even divine succor—she only asked that the end might come quickly and with as little pain as possible.

No one can prophesy what a lion will do in any given emergency. This one glared and growled at the girl for a moment and then fell to feeding upon the dead horse. Fraulein Kircher wondered for an instant and then attempted to draw her leg cautiously from beneath the body of her mount; but she could not budge it. She increased the force of her efforts and Numa looked up from his feeding to growl again. The girl desisted. She hoped that he might satisfy his hunger and then depart to lie up, but she could not believe that he would leave her there alive. Doubtless he would drag the remains of his kill into the bush for hiding and, as there could be no doubt that he considered her part of his prey, he would certainly come back for her, or possibly drag her in first and kill her.

Again Numa fell to feeding. The girl's nerves were at the breaking point. She wondered that she had not fainted under the strain of terror and shock. She recalled that she often had wished she might see a lion, close to, make a kill and feed upon it. God! how realistically her wish had been granted.

Again she bethought herself of her pistol. As she had fallen, the holster had slipped around so that the weapon now lay beneath her. Very slowly she reached for it; but in so doing she was forced to raise her body from the ground. Instantly the lion was aroused. With the swiftness of a cat he reached across the carcass of the horse and placed a heavy, taloned paw upon her breast, crushing her back to earth, and all the time he growled and snarled horribly. His face was a picture of frightful rage incarnate. For a moment neither moved and then from behind her the girl heard a human voice uttering bestial sounds.

Numa suddenly looked up from the girl's face at the thing beyond her. His growls increased to roars as he drew back, ripping the front of the girl's waist almost from her body with his long talons, exposing her white bosom, which through some miracle of chance the great claws did not touch.

Tarzan of the Apes had witnessed the entire encounter from the moment that Numa had leaped upon his prey. For some time before, he had been watching the girl, and after the lion attacked her he had at first been minded to let Numa have his way with her. What was she but a hated German and a spy besides? He had seen her at General Kraut's headquarters, in conference with the German staff and again he had seen her within the British lines masquerading as a British officer. It was the latter thought that prompted him to interfere. Doubtless General Jan Smuts would be glad to meet and question her. She might be forced to divulge information of value to the British commander before Smuts had her shot.

Tarzan had recognized not only the girl, but the lion as well. All lions may look alike to you and me; but not so to their intimates of the jungle. Each has his individual characteristics of face and form and gait as well defined as those that differentiate members of the human family, and besides these the creatures of the jungle have a still more positive test-that of scent. Each of us, man or beast, has his own peculiar odor, and it is mostly by this that the beasts of the jungle, endowed with miraculous powers of scent, recognize individuals.

It is the final proof. You have seen it demonstrated a thousand times—a dog recognizes your voice and looks at you. He knows your face and figure. Good, there can be no doubt in his mind but that it is you; but is he satisfied? No, sir-he must come up and smell of you. All his other senses may be fallible, but not his sense of smell, and so he makes assurance positive by the final test.

Tarzan recognized Numa as he whom he had muzzled with the hide of Horta, the boar—as he whom he handled by a rope for two days and finally loosed in a German front-line trench, and he knew that Numa would recognize him—that he would remember the sharp spear that had goaded him into submission and obedience and Tarzan hoped that the lesson he had learned still remained with the lion.

Now he came forward calling to Numa in the language of the great apes—warning him away from the girl. It is open to question that Numa, the lion, understood him; but he did understand the menace of the heavy spear that the Tarmangani carried so ready in his brown, right hand, and so he drew back, growling, trying to decide in his little brain whether to charge or flee.

On came the ape-man with never a pause, straight for the lion. "Go away, Numa," he cried, "or Tarzan will tie you up again and lead you through the jungle without food. See Arad, my spear! Do you recall how his point stuck into you and how with his haft I beat you over the head? Go, Numa! I am Tarzan of the Apes!"

Numa wrinkled the skin of his face into great folds, until his eyes almost disappeared and he growled and roared and snarled and growled again, and when the spear point came at last quite close to him he struck at it viciously with his armed paw; but he drew back. Tarzan stepped over the dead horse and the girl lying behind him gazed in wide-eyed astonishment at the handsome figure driving an angry lion deliberately from its kill.

When Numa had retreated a few yards, the ape-man called back to the girl in perfect German, "Are you badly hurt?"

"I think not," she replied; "but I cannot extricate my foot from beneath my horse."

"Try again," commanded Tarzan. "I do not know how long I can hold Numa thus."

The girl struggled frantically; but at last she sank back upon an elbow.

"It is impossible," she called to him.

He backed slowly until he was again beside the horse, when he reached down and grasped the cinch, which was still intact. Then with one hand he raised the carcass from the ground. The girl freed herself and rose to her feet.

"You can walk?" asked Tarzan.

"Yes," she said; "my leg is numb; but it does not seem to be injured."

"Good," commented the ape-man. "Back slowly away behind me—make no sudden movements. I think he will not charge."

With utmost deliberation the two backed toward the bush. Numa stood for a moment, growling, then he followed them, slowly. Tarzan wondered if he would come beyond his kill or if he would stop there. If he followed them beyond, then they could look for a charge, and if Numa charged it was very likely that he would get one of them. When the lion reached the carcass of the horse Tarzan stopped and so did Numa, as Tarzan had thought that he would and the ape-man waited to see what the lion would do next. He eyed them for a moment, snarled angrily and then looked down at the tempting meat. Presently he crouched upon his kill and resumed feeding.

The girl breathed a deep sigh of relief as she and the ape-man resumed their slow retreat with only an occasional glance from the lion, and when at last they reached the bush and had turned and entered it, she felt a sudden giddiness overwhelm her so that she staggered and would have fallen had Tarzan not caught her. It was only a moment before she regained control of herself.

"I could not help it," she said, in half apology. "I was so close to death—such a horrible death—it unnerved me for an instant; but I am all right now. How can I ever thank you? It was so wonderful—you did not seem to fear the frightful creature in the least; yet he was afraid of you. Who are you?"

"He knows me," replied Tarzan, grimly—" that is why he fears me."

He was standing facing the girl now and for the first time he had a chance to look at her squarely and closely. She was very beautiful—that was undeniable; but Tarzan realized her beauty only in a subconscious way. It was superficial—it did not color her soul which must be black as sin. She was German—a German spy. He hated her and desired only to compass her destruction; but he would choose the manner so that it would work most grievously against the enemy cause.

He saw her naked breasts where Numa had torn her clothing from her and dangling there against the soft, white flesh he saw that which brought a sudden scowl of surprise and anger to his face—the diamond-studded, golden locket of his youth—the love token that had been stolen from the breast of his mate by Schneider, the Hun. The girl saw the scowl but did not interpret it correctly. Tarzan grasped her roughly by the arm.

"Where did you get this?" he demanded, as he tore the bauble from her.

The girl drew herself to her full height. "Take your hand from me," she demanded, but the ape-man paid no attention to her words, only seizing her more forcibly.

"Answer me!" he snapped. "Where did you get this?"

"What is it to you?" she countered.

"It is mine," he replied. "Tell me who gave it to you or I will throw you back to Numa."

"You would do that?" she asked.

"Why not?" he queried. "You are a spy and spies must die if they are caught."

"You were going to kill me, then?"

"I was going to take you to headquarters. They would dispose of you there; but Numa can do it quite as effectively. Which do you prefer?"

"Hauptmann Fritz Schneider gave it to me," she said.

"Headquarters it will be then," said Tarzan. "Come!" The girl moved at his side through the bush and all the time her mind worked quickly. They were moving east, which suited her, and as long as they continued to move east she was glad to have the protection of the great, white savage. She speculated much upon the fact that her pistol still swung at her hip. The man must be mad not to take it from her.

"What makes you think I am a spy?" she asked after a long silence.

"I saw you at German headquarters," he replied, "and then again inside the British lines."

She could not let him take her back to them. She must reach Wilhelmstal at once and she was determined to do so even if she must have recourse to her pistol. She cast a side glance at the tall figure. What a magnificent creature! But yet he was a brute who would kill her or have her killed if she did not slay him. And the locket! She must have that back—it must not fail to reach Wilhelmstal. Tarzan was now a foot or two ahead of her as the path was very narrow. Cautiously she drew her pistol. A single shot would suffice and he was so close that she could not miss. As she figured it all out her eyes rested on the brown skin with the graceful muscles rolling beneath it and the perfect limbs and head and the carriage that a proud king of old might have envied. A wave of revulsion for her contemplated act surged through her. No, she could not do it—yet, she must be free and she must regain possession of the locket. And then, almost blindly, she swung the weapon up and struck Tarzan heavily upon the back of the head with its butt. Like a felled ox he dropped in his tracks.

VENGEANCE AND MERCY

It was an hour later that Sheeta, the panther, hunting, chanced to glance upward into the blue sky where his attention was attracted by Ska, the vulture, circling slowly above the bush a mile away and downwind. For a long minute the yellow eyes stared intently at the gruesome bird. They saw Ska dive and rise again to continue his ominous circling and in these movements their woodcraft read that which, while obvious to Sheeta, would doubtless have meant nothing to you or me.

The hunting cat guessed that on the ground beneath Ska was some living thing of flesh—either a beast feeding upon its kill or a dying animal that Ska did not yet dare attack. In either event it might prove meat for Sheeta, and so the wary feline stalked by a circuitous route, upon soft, padded feet that gave forth no sound, until the circling aasvogel and his intended prey were upwind. Then, sniffing each vagrant zephyr, Sheeta, the panther, crept cautiously forward, nor had he advanced any considerable distance before his keen nostrils were rewarded with the scent of man—a Tarmangani.

Sheeta paused. He was not a hunter of men. He was young and in his prime; but always before he had avoided this hated presence. Of late he had become more accustomed to it with the passing of many soldiers through his ancient hunting ground, and as the soldiers had frightened away a great part of the game Sheeta had been wont to feed upon, the days had been lean, and Sheeta was hungry.

The circling Ska suggested that this Tarmangani might be helpless and upon the point of dying, else Ska would not have been interested in him, and so easy prey for Sheeta. With this thought in mind the cat resumed his stalking. Presently he pushed through the thick bush and his yellow-green eyes rested gloatingly upon the body of an almost naked Tarmangani lying face down in a narrow game trail.

Numa, sated, rose from the carcass of Bertha Kircher's horse and seized the partially devoured body by the neck and dragged it into the bush; then he started east toward the lair where he had left his mate. Being uncomfortably full he was inclined to be sleepy and far from belligerent. He moved slowly and majestically with no effort at silence or concealment. The king walked abroad, unafraid.

With an occasional regal glance to right or left he moved along a narrow game trail until at a turn he came to a sudden stop at what lay revealed before him—Sheeta, the panther, creeping stealthily upon the almost naked body of a Tarmangani lying face down in the deep dust of the pathway. Numa glared intently at the quiet body in the dust. Recognition came. It was his Tarmangani. A low growl of warning rumbled from his throat and Sheeta halted with one paw upon Tarzan's back and turned suddenly to eye the intruder.

What passed within those savage brains? Who may say? The panther seemed debating the wisdom of defending his find, for he growled horribly as though warning Numa away from the prey. And Numa? Was the idea of property rights dominating his thoughts? The Tarmangani was his, or he was the Tarmangani's. Had not the Great White Ape mastered and subdued him and, too, had he not fed him? Numa recalled the fear that he had felt of this man-thing and his cruel spear; but in savage brains fear is more likely to engender respect than hatred and so Numa found that he respected the creature who had subdued and mastered him. He saw Sheeta, upon whom he looked with contempt, daring to molest the master of the lion. Jealousy and greed alone might have been sufficient to prompt Numa to drive Sheeta away, even though the lion was not sufficiently hungry to devour the flesh that he thus wrested from the lesser cat; but then, too, there was in the little brain within the massive head a sense of loyalty, and perhaps this it was that sent Numa quickly forward, growling, toward the spitting Sheeta.

For a moment the latter stood his ground with arched back and snarling face, for all the world like a great, spotted tabby.

Numa had not felt like fighting; but the sight of Sheeta daring to dispute his rights kindled his ferocious brain to sudden fire. His rounded eyes glared with rage, his undulating tail snapped to stiff erectness as, with a frightful roar, he charged this presuming vassal.

It came so suddenly and from so short a distance that Sheeta had no chance to turn and flee the rush, and so he met it with raking talons and snapping jaws; but the odds were all against him. To the larger fangs and the more powerful jaws of his adversary were added huge talons and the preponderance of the lion's great weight. At the first clash Sheeta was crushed and, though he deliberately fell upon his back and drew up his powerful hind legs beneath Numa with the intention of disemboweling him, the lion forestalled him and at the same time closed his awful jaws upon Sheeta's throat.

It was soon over. Numa rose, shaking himself, and stood above the torn and mutilated body of his foe. His own sleek coat was cut and the red blood trickled down his flank; though it was but a minor injury, it angered him. He glared down at the dead panther and then, in a fit of rage, he seized and mauled the body only to drop it in a moment, lower his head, voice a single terrific roar, and turn toward the ape-man.

Approaching the still form he sniffed it over from head to foot. Then he placed a huge paw upon it and turned it over with its face up. Again he smelled about the body and at last with his rough tongue licked Tarzan's face. It was then that Tarzan opened his eyes.

Above him towered the huge lion, its hot breath upon his face, its rough tongue upon his cheek. The ape-man had often been close to death; but never before so close as this, he thought, for he was convinced that death was but a matter of seconds. His brain was still numb from the effects of the blow that had felled him, and so he did not, for a moment, recognize the lion that stood over him as the one he had so recently encountered.

Presently, however, recognition dawned upon him and with it a realization of the astounding fact that Numa did not seem bent on devouring him—at least not immediately. His position was a delicate one. The lion stood astraddle Tarzan with his front paws. The ape-man could not rise, therefore, without pushing the lion away and whether Numa would tolerate being pushed was an open question. Too, the beast might consider him already dead and any movement that indicated the contrary was true would, in all likelihood, arouse the killing instinct of the man-eater.

But Tarzan was tiring of the situation. He was in no mood to lie there forever, especially when he contemplated the fact that the girl spy who had tried to brain him was undoubtedly escaping as rapidly as possible.

Numa was looking right into his eyes now evidently aware that he was alive. Presently the lion cocked his head on one side and whined. Tarzan knew the note, and he knew that it spelled neither rage nor hunger, and then he risked all on a single throw, encouraged by that low whine.

"Move, Numa!" he commanded and placing a palm against the tawny shoulder he pushed the lion aside. Then he rose and with a hand on his hunting knife awaited that which might follow. It was then that his eyes fell for the first time on the torn body of Sheeta. He looked from the dead cat to the live one and saw the marks of conflict upon the latter, too, and in an instant realized something of what had happened—Numa had saved him from the panther!

It seemed incredible and yet the evidence pointed clearly to the fact. He turned toward the lion and without fear approached and examined his wounds which he found superficial, and as Tarzan knelt beside him Numa rubbed an itching ear against the naked, brown shoulder. Then the ape-man stroked the great head, picked up his spear, and looked about for the trail of the girl. This he soon found leading toward the east, and as he set out upon it something prompted him to feel for the locket he had hung about his neck. It was gone!

No trace of anger was apparent upon the ape-man's face unless it was a slight tightening of the jaws; but he put his hand ruefully to the back of his head where a bump marked the place where the girl had struck him and a moment later a half-smile played across his lips. He could not help but admit that she had tricked him neatly, and that it must have taken nerve to do the thing she did and to set out armed only with a pistol through the trackless waste that lay between them and the railway and beyond into the hills where Wilhelmstal lies.

Tarzan admired courage. He was big enough to admit it and admire it even in a German spy, but he saw that in this case it only added to her resourcefulness and made her all the more dangerous and the necessity for putting her out of the way paramount. He hoped to overtake her before she reached Wilhelmstal and so he set out at the swinging trot that he could hold for hours at a stretch without apparent fatigue.

That the girl could hope to reach the town on foot in less than two days seemed improbable, for it was a good thirty miles and part of it hilly. Even as the thought crossed his mind he heard the whistle of a locomotive to the east and knew that the railway was in operation again after a shutdown of several days. If the train was going south the girl would signal it if she had reached the right of way. His keen ears caught the whining of brake shoes on wheels and a few minutes later the signal blast for brakes off. The train had stopped and started again and, as it gained headway and greater distance, Tarzan could tell from the direction of the sound that it was moving south.

The ape-man followed the trail to the railway where it ended abruptly on the west side of the track, showing that the girl had boarded the train, just as he thought. There was nothing now but to follow on to Wilhelmstal, where he hoped to find Captain Fritz Schneider, as well as the girl, and to recover his diamond-studded locket.

It was dark when Tarzan reached the little hill town of Wilhelmstal. He loitered on the outskirts, getting his bearings and trying to determine how an almost naked white man might explore the village without arousing suspicion. There were many soldiers about and the town was under guard, for he could see a lone sentinel walking his post scarce a hundred yards from him. To elude this one would not be difficult; but to enter the village and search it would be practically impossible, garbed, or un-garbed, as he was.

Creeping forward, taking advantage of every cover, lying flat and motionless when the sentry's face was toward him, the ape-man at last reached the sheltering shadows of an outhouse just inside the lines. From there he moved stealthily from building to building until at last he was discovered by a large dog in the rear of one of the bungalows. The brute came slowly toward him, growling. Tarzan stood motionless beside a tree. He could see a light in the bungalow and uniformed men moving about and he hoped that the dog would not bark. He did not; but he growled more savagely and, just at the moment that the rear door of the bungalow opened and a man stepped out, the animal charged.

He was a large dog, as large as Dango, the hyena, and he charged with all the vicious impetuosity of Numa, the lion. As he came Tarzan knelt and the dog shot through the air for his throat; but he was dealing with no man now and he found his quickness more than matched by the quickness of the Tarmangani. His teeth never reached the soft flesh—strong fingers, fingers of steel, seized his neck. He voiced a single startled yelp and clawed at the naked breast before him with his talons; but he was powerless. The mighty fingers closed upon his throat; the man rose, snapped the clawing body once, and cast it aside. At the same time a voice from the open bungalow door called: "Simba!"

There was no response. Repeating the call the man descended the steps and advanced toward the tree. In the light from the doorway Tarzan could see that he was a tall, broad-shouldered man in the uniform of a German officer. The ape-man withdrew into the shadow of the tree's stem. The man came closer, still calling the dog—he did not see the savage beast, crouching now in the shadow, awaiting him. When he had approached within ten feet of the Tarmangani, Tarzan leaped upon him—as Sabor springs to the kill, so sprang the ape-man. The momentum and weight of his body hurled the German to the ground, powerful fingers prevented an outcry and, though the officer struggled, he had no chance and a moment later lay dead beside the body of the dog.

As Tarzan stood for a moment looking down upon his kill and regretting that he could not risk voicing his beloved victory cry, the sight of the uniform suggested a means whereby he might pass to and fro through

Wilhelmstal with the minimum chance of detection. Ten minutes later a tall, broad-shouldered officer stepped from the yard of the bungalow leaving behind him the corpses of a dog and a naked man.

He walked boldly along the little street and those who passed him could not guess that beneath Imperial Germany's uniform beat a savage heart that pulsed with implacable hatred for the Hun. Tarzan's first concern was to locate the hotel, for here he guessed he would find the girl, and where the girl was doubtless would be Hauptmann Fritz Schneider, who was either her confederate, her sweetheart, or both, and there, too, would be Tarzan's precious locket.

He found the hotel at last, a low, two-storied building with a veranda. There were lights on both floors and people, mostly officers, could be seen within. The ape-man considered entering and inquiring for those he sought; but his better judgment finally prompted him to reconnoiter first. Passing around the building he looked into all the lighted rooms on the first floor and, seeing neither of those for whom he had come, he swung lightly to the roof of the veranda and continued his investigations through windows of the second story.

At one corner of the hotel in a rear room the blinds were drawn; but he heard voices within and once he saw a figure silhouetted momentarily against the blind. It appeared to be the figure of a woman; but it was gone so quickly that he could not be sure. Tarzan crept close to the window and listened. Yes, there was a woman there and a man—he heard distinctly the tones of their voices although he could overhear no words, as they seemed to be whispering.

The adjoining room was dark. Tarzan tried the window and found it unlatched. All was quiet within. He raised the sash and listened again—still silence. Placing a leg over the sill he slipped within and hurriedly glanced about. The room was vacant. Crossing to the door he opened it and looked out into the hall. There was no one there, either, and he stepped out and approached the door of the adjoining room where the man and woman were.

Pressing close to the door he listened. Now he distinguished words, for the two had raised their voices as though in argument. The woman was speaking.

"I have brought the locket," she said, "as was agreed upon between you and General Kraut, as my identification. I carry no other credentials. This was to be enough. You have nothing to do but give me the papers and let me go."

The man replied in so low a tone that Tarzan could not catch the words and then the woman spoke again—a note of scorn and perhaps a little of fear in her voice.

"You would not dare, Hauptmann Schneider," she said, and then: "Do not touch me! Take your hands from me!"

It was then that Tarzan of the Apes opened the door and stepped into the room. What he saw was a huge, bull-necked German officer with one arm about the waist of Fraulein Bertha Kircher and a hand upon her forehead pushing her head back as he tried to kiss her on the mouth. The girl was struggling against the great brute; but her efforts were futile. Slowly the man's lips were coming closer to hers and slowly, step by step, she was being carried backward.

Schneider heard the noise of the opening and closing door behind him and turned. At sight of this strange officer he dropped the girl and straightened up.

"What is the meaning of this intrusion, Lieutenant?" he demanded, noting the other's epaulettes. "Leave the room at once."

Tarzan made no articulate reply; but the two there with him heard a low growl break from those firm lips—a growl that sent a shudder through the frame of the girl and brought a pallor to the red face of the Hun and his hand to his pistol but even as he drew his weapon it was wrested from him and hurled through the blind and window to the yard beyond. Then Tarzan backed against the door and slowly removed the uniform coat.

"You are Hauptmann Schneider," he said to the German.

"What of it?" growled the latter.

"I am Tarzan of the Apes," replied the ape-man. "Now you know why I intrude."

The two before him saw that he was naked beneath the coat which he threw upon the floor and then he slipped quickly from the trousers and stood there clothed only in his loin cloth. The girl had recognized him by this time, too.

"Take your hand off that pistol," Tarzan admonished her. Her hand dropped at her side. "Now come here!"

She approached and Tarzan removed the weapon and hurled it after the other. At the mention of his name Tarzan had noted the sickly pallor that overspread the features of the Hun. At last he had found the right man. At last his mate would be partially avenged—never could she be entirely avenged. Life was too short and there were too many Germans.

"What do you want of me?" demanded Schneider.

"You are going to pay the price for the thing you did at the little bungalow in the Waziri country," replied the ape-man.

Schneider commenced to bluster and threaten. Tarzan turned the key in the lock of the door and hurled the former through the window after the pistols. Then he turned to the girl. "Keep out of the way," he said in a low voice. "Tarzan of the Apes is going to kill."

The Hun ceased blustering and began to plead. "I have a wife and children at home," he cried. "I have done nothing," I–"

"You are going to die as befits your kind," said Tarzan, "with blood on your hands and a lie on your lips." He started across the room toward the burly Hauptmann. Schneider was a large and powerful man—about the height of the ape-man but much heavier. He saw that neither threats nor pleas would avail him and so he prepared to fight as a cornered rat fights for its life with all the maniacal rage, cunning, and ferocity that the first law of nature imparts to many beasts.

Lowering his bull head he charged for the ape-man and in the center of the floor the two clinched. There they stood locked and swaying for a moment until Tarzan succeeded in forcing his antagonist backward over a table which crashed to the floor, splintered by the weight of the two heavy bodies.

The girl stood watching the battle with wide eyes. She saw the two men rolling hither and thither across the floor and she heard with horror the low growls that came from the lips of the naked giant. Schneider was trying to reach his foe's throat with his fingers while, horror of horrors, Bertha Kircher could see that the other was searching for the German's jugular with his teeth!

Schneider seemed to realize this too, for he redoubled his efforts to escape and finally succeeded in rolling over on top of the ape-man and breaking away. Leaping to his feet he ran for the window; but the ape-man was too quick for him and before he could leap through the sash a heavy hand fell upon his shoulder and he was jerked back and hurled across the room to the opposite wall. There Tarzan followed him, and once again they locked, dealing each other terrific blows, until Schneider in a piercing voice screamed, "Kamerad! Kamerad!"

Tarzan grasped the man by the throat and drew his hunting knife. Schneider's back was against the wall so that though his knees wobbled he was held erect by the ape-man. Tarzan brought the sharp point to the lower part of the German's abdomen.

"Thus you slew my mate," he hissed in a terrible voice. "Thus shall you die!"

The girl staggered forward. "Oh, God, no!" she cried. "Not that. You are too brave—you cannot be such a beast as that!"

Tarzan turned at her. "No," he said, "you are right, I cannot do it—I am no German," and he raised the point of his blade and sunk it deep into the putrid heart of Hauptmann Fritz Schneider, putting a bloody period to the Hun's last gasping cry: "I did not do it! She is not–"

Then Tarzan turned toward the girl and held out his hand. "Give me my locket," he said.

She pointed toward the dead officer. "He has it." Tarzan searched him and found the trinket. "Now you may give me the papers," he said to the girl, and without a word she handed him a folded document.

For a long time he stood looking at her before ho spoke again.

"I came for you, too," he said. "It would be difficult to take you back from here and so I was going to kill you, as I have sworn to kill all your kind; but you were right when you said that I was not such a beast as that slayer of women. I could not slay him as he slew mine, nor can I slay you, who are a woman."

He crossed to the window, raised the sash and an instant later he had stepped out and disappeared into the night. And then Fraulein Bertha Kircher stepped quickly to the corpse upon the floor, slipped her hand inside the blouse and drew forth a little sheaf of papers which she tucked into her waist before she went to the window and called for help.

WHEN BLOOD TOLD

Tarzan of the Apes was disgusted. He had had the German spy, Bertha Kircher, in his power and had left her unscathed. It is true that he had slain Hauptmann Fritz Schneider, that Underlieutenant von Goss had died at his hands, and that he had otherwise wreaked vengeance upon the men of the German company who had murdered, pillaged, and raped at Tarzan's bungalow in the Waziri country. There was still another officer to be accounted for, but him he could not find. It was Lieutenant Obergatz he still sought, though vainly, for at last he learned that the man had been sent upon some special mission, whether in Africa or back to Europe Tarzan's informant either did not know or would not divulge.

But the fact that he had permitted sentiment to stay his hand when he might so easily have put Bertha Kircher out of the way in the hotel at Wilhelmstal that night rankled in the ape-man's bosom. He was shamed by his weakness, and when he had handed the paper she had given him to the British chief of staff, even though the information it contained permitted the British to frustrate a German flank attack, he was still much dissatisfied with himself. And possibly the root of this dissatisfaction lay in the fact that he realized that were he again to have the same opportunity he would still find it as impossible to slay a woman as it had been in Wilhelmstal that night.

Tarzan blamed this weakness, as he considered it, upon his association with the effeminizing influences of civilization, for in the bottom of his savage heart he held in contempt both civilization and its representatives—the men and women of the civilized countries of the world. Always was he comparing their weaknesses, their vices, their hypocrisies, and their little vanities with the open, primitive ways of his ferocious jungle mates, and all the while there battled in that same big heart with these forces another mighty force—Tarzan's love and loyalty for his friends of the civilized world.

The ape-man, reared as he had been by savage beasts amid savage beasts, was slow to make friends. Acquaintances he numbered by the hundreds; but of friends he had few. These few he would have died for as, doubtless, they would have died for him; but there were none of these fighting with the British forces in East Africa, and so, sickened and disgusted by the sight of man waging his cruel and inhuman warfare, Tarzan determined to heed the insistent call of the remote jungle of his youth, for the Germans were now on the run and the war in East Africa was so nearly over that he realized that his further services would be of negligible value.

Never regularly sworn into the service of the King, he was under no obligation to remain now that the moral obligation had been removed, and so it was that he disappeared from the British camp as mysteriously as he had appeared a few months before.

More than once had Tarzan reverted to the primitive only to return again to civilization through love for his mate; but now that she was gone he felt that this time he had definitely departed forever from the haunts of man, and that he should live and die a beast among beasts even as he had been from infancy to maturity.

Between him and destination lay a trackless wilderness of untouched primeval savagery where, doubtless in many spots, his would be the first human foot to touch the virgin turf. Nor did this prospect dismay the

Tarmangani—rather was it an urge and an inducement, for rich in his veins flowed that noble strain of blood that has made most of the earth's surface habitable for man.

The question of food and water that would have risen paramount in the mind of an ordinary man contemplating such an excursion gave Tarzan little concern. The wilderness was his natural habitat and woodcraft as inherent to him as breathing. Like other jungle animals he could scent water from a great distance and, where you or I might die of thirst, the ape-man would unerringly select the exact spot at which to dig and find water.

For several days Tarzan traversed a country rich in game and watercourses. He moved slowly, hunting and fishing, or again fraternizing or quarreling with the other savage denizens of the jungle. Now it was little Manu, the monkey, who chattered and scolded at the mighty Tarmangani and in the next breath warned him that Histah, the snake, lay coiled in the long grass just ahead. Of Manu Tarzan inquired concerning the great apes—the Mangani—and was told that few inhabited this part of the jungle, and that even these were hunting farther to the north this season of the year.

"But there is Bolgani," said Manu. "Would you like to see Bolgani?"

Manu's tone was sneering, and Tarzan knew that it was because little Manu thought all creatures feared mighty Bolgani, the gorilla. Tarzan arched his great chest and struck it with a clinched fist. "I am Tarzan," he cried. "While Tarzan was yet a balu he slew a Bolgani. Tarzan seeks the Mangani, who are his brothers, but Bolgani he does not seek, so let Bolgani keep from the path of Tarzan."

Little Manu, the monkey, was much impressed, for the way of the jungle is to boast and to believe. It was then that he condescended to tell Tarzan more of the Mangani.

"They go there and there and there," he said, making a wide sweep with a brown hand first toward the north, then west, and then south again. "For there," and he pointed due west, "is much hunting; but between lies a great place where there is no food and no water, so they must go that way," and again he swung his hand through the half-circle that explained to Tarzan the great detour the apes made to come to their hunting ground to the west.

That was all right for the Mangani, who are lazy and do not care to move rapidly; but for Tarzan the straight road would be the best. He would cross the dry country and come to the good hunting in a third of the time that it would take to go far to the north and circle back again. And so it was that he continued on toward the west, and crossing a range of low mountains came in sight of a broad plateau, rock strewn and desolate. Far in the distance he saw another range of mountains beyond which he felt must lie the hunting ground of the Mangani. There he would join them and remain for a while before continuing on toward the coast and the little cabin that his father had built beside the land-locked harbor at the jungle's edge.

Tarzan was full of plans. He would rebuild and enlarge the cabin of his birth, constructing storage houses where he would make the apes lay away food when it was plenty against the times that were lean—a thing no ape ever had dreamed of doing. And the tribe would remain always in the locality and he would be king again as he had in the past. He would try to teach them some of the better things that he had learned from man, yet knowing the ape-mind as only Tarzan could, he feared that his labors would be for naught.

The ape-man found the country he was crossing rough in the extreme, the roughest he ever had encountered. The plateau was cut by frequent canyons the passage of which often entailed hours of wearing effort. The vegetation was sparse and of a faded brown color that lent to the whole landscape a most depressing aspect. Great rocks were strewn in every direction as far as the eye could see, lying partially embedded in an impalpable dust that rose in clouds about him at every step. The sun beat down mercilessly out of a cloudless sky.

For a day Tarzan toiled across this now hateful land and at the going down of the sun the distant mountains to the west seemed no nearer than at morn. Never a sign of living thing had the ape-man seen, other than Ska, that bird of ill omen, that had followed him tirelessly since he had entered this parched waste.

No littlest beetle that he might eat had given evidence that life of any sort existed here, and it was a hungry and thirsty Tarzan who lay down to rest in the evening. He decided now to push on during the cool of the night, for he realized that even mighty Tarzan had his limitations and that where there was no food one could not eat and where there was no water the greatest woodcraft in the world could find none. It was a totally new experience to Tarzan to find so barren and terrible a country in his beloved Africa. Even the Sahara had its oases; but this frightful world gave no indication of containing a square foot of hospitable ground.

However, he had no misgivings but that he would fare forth into the wonder country of which little Manu had told him, though it was certain that he would do it with a dry skin and an empty belly. And so he fought on until daylight, when he again felt the need of rest. He was at the edge of another of those terrible canyons, the eighth he had crossed, whose precipitous sides would have taxed to the uttermost the strength of an untired man well fortified by food and water, and for the first time, as he looked down into the abyss and then at the opposite side that he must scale, misgivings began to assail his mind.

He did not fear death—with the memory of his murdered mate still fresh in his mind he almost courted it, yet strong within him was that primal instinct of self-preservation—the battling force of life that would keep him an active contender against the Great Reaper until, fighting to the very last, he should be overcome by a superior power.

A shadow swung slowly across the ground beside him, and looking up, the ape-man saw Ska, the vulture, wheeling a wide circle above him. The grim and persistent harbinger of evil aroused the man to renewed determination. He arose and approached the edge of the canyon, and then, wheeling, with his face turned upward toward the circling bird of prey, he bellowed forth the challenge of the bull ape.

"I am Tarzan," he shouted, "Lord of the Jungle. Tarzan of the Apes is not for Ska, eater of carrion. Go back to the lair of Dango and feed off the leavings of the hyenas, for Tarzan will leave no bones for Ska to pick in this empty wilderness of death."

But before he reached the bottom of the canyon he again was forced to the realization that his great strength was waning, and when he dropped exhausted at the foot of the cliff and saw before him the opposite wall that must be scaled, he bared his fighting fangs and growled. For an hour he lay resting in the cool shade at the foot of the cliff. All about him reigned utter silence—the silence of the tomb. No fluttering birds, no humming insects, no scurrying reptiles relieved the deathlike stillness. This indeed was the valley of death. He felt the depressing influence of the horrible place setting down upon him; but he staggered to his feet, shaking himself like a great lion, for was he not still Tarzan, mighty Tarzan of the Apes? Yes, and Tarzan the mighty he would be until the last throb of that savage heart!

As he crossed the floor of the canyon he saw something lying close to the base of the side wall he was approaching-something that stood out in startling contrast to all the surroundings and yet seemed so much a part and parcel of the somber scene as to suggest an actor amid the settings of a well-appointed stage, and, as though to carry out the allegory, the pitiless rays of flaming Kudu topped the eastern cliff, picking out the thing lying at the foot of the western wall like a giant spotlight.

And as Tarzan came nearer he saw the bleached skull and bones of a human being about which were remnants of clothing and articles of equipment that, as he examined them, filled the ape-man with curiosity to such an extent that for a time he forgot his own predicament in contemplation of the remarkable story suggested by these mute evidences of a tragedy of a time long past.

The bones were in a fair state of preservation and indicated by their intactness that the flesh had probably been picked from them by vultures as none was broken; but the pieces of equipment bore out the suggestion of their great age. In this protected spot where there were no frosts and evidently but little rainfall, the bones might have lain for ages without disintegrating, for there were here no other forces to scatter or disturb them.

Near the skeleton lay a helmet of hammered brass and a corroded breastplate of steel while at one side was a long, straight sword in its scabbard and an ancient harquebus. The bones were those of a large man—a man of wondrous strength and vitality Tarzan knew he must have been to have penetrated thus far through the dangers of Africa with such a ponderous yet at the same time futile armament.

The ape-man felt a sense of deep admiration for this nameless adventurer of a bygone day. What a brute of a man he must have been and what a glorious tale of battle and kaleidoscopic vicissitudes of fortune must once have been locked within that whitened skull! Tarzan stooped to examine the shreds of clothing that still lay about the bones. Every particle of leather had disappeared, doubtless eaten by Ska. No boots remained, if the man had worn boots, but there were several buckles scattered about suggesting that a great part of his trappings had been of leather, while just beneath the bones of one hand lay a metal cylinder about eight inches long and two inches in diameter. As Tarzan picked it up he saw that it had been heavily lacquered and had withstood the slight ravages of time so well as to be in as perfect a state of preservation today as it had been when its owner dropped into his last, long sleep perhaps centuries ago.

As he examined it he discovered that one end was closed with a friction cover which a little twisting force soon loosened and removed, revealing within a roll of parchment which the ape-man removed and opened, disclosing a number of age-yellowed sheets closely written upon in a fine hand in a language which he guessed to be Spanish but which he could not decipher. Upon the last sheet was a roughly drawn map with numerous reference points marked upon it, all unintelligible to Tarzan, who, after a brief examination of the papers, returned them to their metal case, replaced the top and was about to toss the little cylinder to the ground beside the mute remains of its former possessor when some whim of curiosity unsatisfied prompted him to slip it into the quiver with his arrows, though as he did so it was with the grim thought that possibly centuries hence it might again come to the sight of man beside his own bleached bones.

And then, with a parting glance at the ancient skeleton, he turned to the task of ascending the western wall of the canyon. Slowly and with many rests he dragged his weakening body upwards. Again and again he slipped back from sheer exhaustion and would have fallen to the floor of the canyon but for merest chance. How long it took him to scale that frightful wall he could not have told, and when at last he dragged himself over the top it was to lie weak and gasping, too spent to rise or even to move a few inches farther from the perilous edge of the chasm.

At last he arose, very slowly and with evident effort gaining his knees first and then staggering to his feet, yet his indomitable will was evidenced by a sudden straightening of his shoulders and a determined shake of his head as he lurched forward on unsteady legs to take up his valiant fight for survival. Ahead he scanned the rough landscape for sign of another canyon which he knew would spell inevitable doom. The western hills rose closer now though weirdly unreal as they seemed to dance in the sunlight as though mocking him with their nearness at the moment that exhaustion was about to render them forever unattainable.

Beyond them he knew must be the fertile hunting grounds of which Manu had told. Even if no canyon intervened, his chances of surmounting even low hills seemed remote should he have the fortune to reach their base; but with another canyon hope was dead. Above them Ska still circled, and it seemed to the ape-man that the ill-omened bird hovered ever lower and lower as though reading in that failing gait the nearing of the end, and through cracked lips Tarzan growled out his defiance.

Mile after mile Tarzan of the Apes put slowly behind him, borne up by sheer force of will where a lesser man would have lain down to die and rest forever tired muscles whose every move was an agony of effort; but at last his progress became practically mechanical—he staggered on with a dazed mind that reacted numbly to a single urge—on, on, on! The hills were now but a dim, ill-defined blur ahead. Sometimes he forgot that they were hills, and again he wondered vaguely why he must go on forever through all this torture endeavoring to overtake them—the fleeing, elusive hills. Presently he began to hate them and there formed within his half-delirious brain the hallucination that the hills were German hills, that they had slain someone dear to him, whom he could never quite recall, and that he was pursuing to slay them.

This idea, growing, appeared to give him strength—a new and revivifying purpose—so that for a time he no longer staggered; but went forward steadily with head erect. Once he stumbled and fell, and when he tried to rise he found that he could not—that his strength was so far gone that he could only crawl forward on his hands and knees for a few yards and then sink down again to rest.

It was during one of these frequent periods of utter exhaustion that he heard the flap of dismal wings close above him. With his remaining strength he turned himself over on his back to see Ska wheel quickly upward. With the sight Tarzan's mind cleared for a while.

"Is the end so near as that?" he thought. "Does Ska know that I am so near gone that he dares come down and perch upon my carcass?" And even then a grim smile touched those swollen lips as into the savage mind came a sudden thought-the cunning of the wild beast at bay. Closing his eyes he threw a forearm across them to protect them from Ska's powerful beak and then he lay very still and waited.

It was restful lying there, for the sun was now obscured by clouds and Tarzan was very tired. He feared that he might sleep and something told him that if he did he would never awaken, and so he concentrated all his remaining powers upon the one thought of remaining awake. Not a muscle moved-to Ska, circling above, it became evident that the end had come—that at last he should be rewarded for his long vigil

Circling slowly he dropped closer and closer to the dying man. Why did not Tarzan move? Had he indeed been overcome by the sleep of exhaustion, or was Ska right—had death at last claimed that mighty body? Was that great, savage heart stilled forever? It is unthinkable.

Ska, filled with suspicions, circled warily. Twice he almost alighted upon the great, naked breast only to wheel suddenly away; but the third time his talons touched the brown skin. It was as though the contact closed an electric circuit that instantaneously vitalized the quiet clod that had lain motionless so long. A brown hand swept downward from the brown forehead and before Ska could raise a wing in flight he was in the clutches of his intended victim.

Ska fought, but he was no match for even a dying Tarzan, and a moment later the ape-man's teeth closed upon the carrion-eater. The flesh was coarse and tough and gave off an unpleasant odor and a worse taste; but it was food and the blood was drink and Tarzan only an ape at heart and a dying ape into the bargain—dying of starvation and thirst.

Even mentally weakened as he was the ape-man was still master of his appetite and so he ate but sparingly, saving the rest, and then, feeling that he now could do so safely, he turned upon his side and slept.

Rain, beating heavily upon his body, awakened him and sitting up he cupped his hands and caught the precious drops which he transferred to his parched throat. Only a little he got at a time; but that was best. The few mouthfuls of Ska that he had eaten, together with the blood and rain water and the sleep had refreshed him greatly and put new strength into his tired muscles.

Now he could see the hills again and they were close and, though there was no sun, the world looked bright and cheerful, for Tarzan knew that he was saved. The bird that would have devoured him, and the providential rain, had saved him at the very moment that death seemed inevitable.

Again partaking of a few mouthfuls of the unsavory flesh of Ska, the vulture, the ape-man arose with something of his old force and set out with steady gait toward the hills of promise rising alluringly ahead. Darkness fell before he reached them; but he kept on until he felt the steeply rising ground that proclaimed his arrival at the base of the hills proper, and then he lay down and waited until morning should reveal the easiest passage to the land beyond. The rain had ceased, but the sky still was overcast so that even his keen eyes could not penetrate the darkness farther than a few feet. And there he slept, after eating again of what remained of Ska, until the morning sun awakened him with a new sense of strength and well-being.

And so at last he came through the hills out of the valley of death into a land of park-like beauty, rich in game. Below him lay a deep valley through the center of which dense jungle vegetation marked the course of a river beyond which a primeval forest extended for miles to terminate at last at the foot of lofty, snow-capped mountains. It was a land that Tarzan never had looked upon before, nor was it likely that the foot of another white man ever had touched it unless, possibly, in some long-gone day the adventurer whose skeleton he had found bleaching in the canyon had traversed it.

EDGAR RICE BURROUGHS

TARZAN AND THE GREAT APES

Three days the ape-man spent in resting and recuperating, eating fruits and nuts and the smaller animals that were most easily bagged, and upon the fourth he set out to explore the valley and search for the great apes. Time was a negligible factor in the equation of life—it was all the same to Tarzan if he reached the west coast in a month or a year or three years. All time was his and all Africa. His was absolute freedom—the last tie that had bound him to civilization and custom had been severed. He was alone but he was not exactly lonely. The greater part of his life had been spent thus, and though there was no other of his kind, he was at all times surrounded by the jungle peoples for whom familiarity had bred no contempt within his breast. The least of them interested him, and, too, there were those with whom he always made friends easily, and there were his hereditary enemies whose presence gave a spice to life that might otherwise have become humdrum and monotonous.

And so it was that on the fourth day he set out to explore the valley and search for his fellow-apes. He had proceeded southward for a short distance when his nostrils were assailed by the scent of man, of Gomangani, the black man. There were many of them, and mixed with their scent was another-that of a she Tarmangani.

Swinging through the trees Tarzan approached the authors of these disturbing scents. He came warily from the flank, but paying no attention to the wind, for he knew that man with his dull senses could apprehend him only through his eyes or ears and then only when comparatively close. Had he been stalking Numa or Sheeta he would have circled about until his quarry was upwind from him, thus taking practically all the advantage up to the very moment that he came within sight or hearing; but in the stalking of the dull clod, man, he approached with almost contemptuous indifference, so that all the jungle about him knew that he was passing—all but the men he stalked.

From the dense foliage of a great tree he watched them pass—a disreputable mob of blacks, some garbed in the uniform of German East African native troops, others wearing a single garment of the same uniform, while many had reverted to the simple dress of their forbears—approximating nudity. There were many black women with them, laughing and talking as they kept pace with the men, all of whom were armed with German rifles and equipped with German belts and ammunition.

There were no white officers there, but it was none the less apparent to Tarzan that these men were from some German native command, and he guessed that they had slain their officers and taken to the jungle with their women, or had stolen some from native villages through which they must have passed. It was evident that they were putting as much ground between themselves and the coast as possible and doubtless were seeking some impenetrable fastness of the vast interior where they might inaugurate a reign of terror among the primitively armed inhabitants and by raiding, looting, and rape grow rich in goods and women at the expense of the district upon which they settled themselves.

Between two of the black women marched a slender white girl. She was hatless and with torn and disheveled clothing that had evidently once been a trim riding habit. Her coat was gone and her waist half torn from her body. Occasionally and without apparent provocation one or the other of the Negresses struck or pushed her roughly. Tarzan watched through half-closed eyes. His first impulse was to leap among them and bear the girl from their cruel clutches. He had recognized her immediately and it was because of this fact that he hesitated.

What was it to Tarzan of the Apes what fate befell this enemy spy? He had been unable to kill her himself because of an inherent weakness that would not permit him to lay hands upon a woman, all of which of course had no bearing upon what others might do to her. That her fate would now be infinitely more horrible than the quick and painless death that the ape-man would have meted to her only interested Tarzan to the extent that the more frightful the end of a German the more in keeping it would be with what they all deserved.

And so he let the blacks pass with Fraulein Bertha Kircher in their midst, or at least until the last straggling warrior suggested to his mind the pleasures of black-baiting—an amusement and a sport in which he had

689

grown ever more proficient since that long-gone day when Kulonga, the son of Mbonga, the chief, had cast his unfortunate spear at Kala, the ape-man's foster mother.

The last man, who must have stopped for some purpose, was fully a quarter of a mile in rear of the party. He was hurrying to catch up when Tarzan saw him, and as he passed beneath the tree in which the ape-man perched above the trail, a silent noose dropped deftly about his neck. The main body still was in plain sight, and as the frightened man voiced a piercing shriek of terror, they looked back to see his body rise as though by magic straight into the air and disappear amidst the leafy foliage above.

For a moment the blacks stood paralyzed by astonishment and fear; but presently the burly sergeant, Usanga, who led them, started back along the trail at a run, calling to the others to follow him. Loading their guns as they came the blacks ran to succor their fellow, and at Usanga's command they spread into a thin line that presently entirely surrounded the tree into which their comrade had vanished.

Usanga called but received no reply; then he advanced slowly with rifle at the ready, peering up into the tree. He could see no one—nothing. The circle closed in until fifty blacks were searching among the branches with their keen eyes. What had become of their fellow? They had seen him rise into the tree and since then many eyes had been fastened upon the spot, yet there was no sign of him. One, more venturesome than his fellows, volunteered to climb into the tree and investigate. He was gone but a minute or two and when he dropped to earth again he swore that there was no sign of a creature there.

Perplexed, and by this time a bit awed, the blacks drew slowly away from the spot and with many backward glances and less laughing continued upon their journey until, when about a mile beyond the spot at which their fellow had disappeared, those in the lead saw him peering from behind a tree at one side of the trail just in front of them. With shouts to their companions that he had been found they ran forwards; but those who were first to reach the tree stopped suddenly and shrank back, their eyes rolling fearfully first in one direction and then in another as though they expected some nameless horror to leap out upon them.

Nor was their terror without foundation. Impaled upon the end of a broken branch the head of their companion was propped behind the tree so that it appeared to be looking out at them from the opposite side of the bole.

It was then that many wished to turn back, arguing that they had offended some demon of the wood upon whose preserve they had trespassed; but Usanga refused to listen to them, assuring them that inevitable torture and death awaited them should they return and fall again into the hands of their cruel German masters. At last his reasoning prevailed to the end that a much-subdued and terrified band moved in a compact mass, like a drove of sheep, forward through the valley and there were no stragglers.

It is a happy characteristic of the Negro race, which they hold in common with little children, that their spirits seldom remain depressed for a considerable length of time after the immediate cause of depression is removed, and so it was that in half an hour Usanga's band was again beginning to take on to some extent its former appearance of carefree lightheartedness. Thus were the heavy clouds of fear slowly dissipating when a turn in the trail brought them suddenly upon the headless body of their erstwhile companion lying directly in their path, and they were again plunged into the depth of fear and gloomy forebodings.

So utterly inexplicable and uncanny had the entire occurrence been that there was not a one of them who could find a ray of comfort penetrating the dead blackness of its ominous portent. What had happened to one of their number each conceived as being a wholly possible fate for himself—in fact quite his probable fate. If such a thing could happen in broad daylight what frightful thing might not fall to their lot when night had enshrouded them in her mantle of darkness. They trembled in anticipation.

The white girl in their midst was no less mystified than they; but far less moved, since sudden death was the most merciful fate to which she might now look forward. So far she had been subjected to nothing worse than the petty cruelties of the women, while, on the other hand, it had alone been the presence of the women that had saved her from worse treatment at the hands of some of the men—notably the brutal, black sergeant, Usanga. His own woman was of the party—a veritable giantess, a virago of the first magnitude—and

690

she was evidently the only thing in the world of which Usanga stood in awe. Even though she was particularly cruel to the young woman, the latter believed that she was her sole protection from the degraded black tyrant.

Late in the afternoon the band came upon a small palisaded village of thatched huts set in a clearing in the jungle close beside a placid river. At their approach the villagers came pouring out, and Usanga advanced with two of his warriors to palaver with the chief. The experiences of the day had so shaken the nerves of the black sergeant that he was ready to treat with these people rather than take their village by force of arms, as would ordinarily have been his preference; but now a vague conviction influenced him that there watched over this part of the jungle a powerful demon who wielded miraculous power for evil against those who offended him. First Usanga would learn how these villagers stood with this savage god and if they had his good will Usanga would be most careful to treat them with kindness and respect.

At the palaver it developed that the village chief had food, goats, and fowl which he would be glad to dispose of for a proper consideration; but as the consideration would have meant parting with precious rifles and ammunition, or the very clothing from their backs, Usanga began to see that after all it might be forced upon him to wage war to obtain food.

A happy solution was arrived at by a suggestion of one of his men—that the soldiers go forth the following day and hunt for the villagers, bringing them in so much fresh meat in return for their hospitality. This the chief agreed to, stipulating the kind and quantity of game to be paid in return for flour, goats, and fowl, and a certain number of huts that were to be turned over to the visitors. The details having been settled after an hour or more of that bickering argument of which the native African is so fond, the newcomers entered the village where they were assigned to huts.

Bertha Kircher found herself alone in a small hut to the palisade at the far end of the village street, and though she was neither bound nor guarded, she was assured by Usanga that she could not escape the village without running into almost certain death in the jungle, which the villagers assured them was infested by lions of great size and ferocity. "Be good to Usanga," he concluded, "and no harm will befall you. I will come again to see you after the others are asleep. Let us be friends."

As the brute left her the girl's frame was racked by a convulsive shudder as she sank to the floor of the hut and covered her face with her hands. She realized now why the women had not been left to guard her. It was the work of the cunning Usanga, but would not his woman suspect something of his intentions? She was no fool and, further, being imbued with insane jealousy she was ever looking for some overt act upon the part of her ebon lord. Bertha Kircher felt that only she might save her and that she would save her if word could be but gotten to her. But how?

Left alone and away from the eyes of her captors for the first time since the previous night, the girl immediately took advantage of the opportunity to assure herself that the papers she had taken from the body of Hauptmann Fritz Schneider were still safely sewn inside one of her undergarments.

Alas! Of what value could they now ever be to her beloved country? But habit and loyalty were so strong within her that she still clung to the determined hope of eventually delivering the little packet to her chief.

The natives seemed to have forgotten her existence—no one came near the hut, not even to bring her food. She could hear them at the other end of the village laughing and yelling and knew that they were celebrating with food and native beer—knowledge which only increased her apprehension. To be prisoner in a native village in the very heart of an unexplored region of Central Africa—the only white woman among a band of drunken Negroes! The very thought appalled her. Yet there was a slight promise in the fact that she had so far been unmolested—the promise that they might, indeed, have forgotten her and that soon they might become so hopelessly drunk as to be harmless.

Darkness had fallen and still no one came. The girl wondered if she dared venture forth in search of Naratu, Usanga's woman, for Usanga might not forget that he had promised to return. No one was near as she stepped out of the hut and made her way toward the part of the village where the revelers were making merry about a fire. As she approached she saw the villagers and their guests squatting in a large circle about the blaze before which a half-dozen naked warriors leaped and bent and stamped in some grotesque dance. Pots of food and gourds of drink were being passed about among the audience. Dirty hands were plunged into the food pots and the captured portions devoured so greedily that one might have thought the entire community had been upon the point of starvation. The gourds they held to their lips until the beer ran down their chins and the vessels were wrested from them by greedy neighbors. The drink had now begun to take noticeable effect upon most of them, with the result that they were beginning to give themselves up to utter and licentious abandon.

As the girl came nearer, keeping in the shadow of the huts, looking for Naratu she was suddenly discovered by one upon the edge of the crowd—a huge woman, who rose, shrieking, and came toward her. From her aspect the white girl thought that the woman meant literally to tear her to pieces. So utterly wanton and uncalled-for was the attack that it found the girl entirely unprepared, and what would have happened had not a warrior interfered may only be guessed. And then Usanga, noting the interruption, came lurching forward to question her.

"What do you want," he cried, "food and drink? Come with me!" and he threw an arm about her and dragged her toward the circle.

"No!" she cried, "I want Naratu. Where is Naratu?"

This seemed to sober the black for a moment as though he had temporarily forgotten his better half. He cast quick, fearful glances about, and then, evidently assured that Naratu had noticed nothing, he ordered the warrior who was still holding the infuriated black woman from the white girl to take the latter back to her hut and to remain there on guard over her.

First appropriating a gourd of beer for himself the warrior motioned the girl to precede him, and thus guarded she returned to her hut, the fellow squatting down just outside the doorway, where he confined his attentions for some time to the gourd.

Bertha Kircher sat down at the far side of the hut awaiting she knew not what impending fate. She could not sleep so filled was her mind with wild schemes of escape though each new one must always be discarded as impractical. Half an hour after the warrior had returned her to her prison he rose and entered the hut, where he tried to engage in conversation with her. Groping across the interior he leaned his short spear against the wall and sat down beside her, and as he talked he edged closer and closer until at last he could reach out and touch her. Shrinking, she drew away.

"Do not touch me!" she cried. "I will tell Usanga if you do not leave me alone, and you know what he will do to you."

The man only laughed drunkenly, and, reaching out his hand, grabbed her arm and dragged her toward him. She fought and cried aloud for Usanga and at the same instant the entrance to the hut was darkened by the form of a man.

"What is the matter?" shouted the newcomer in the deep tones that the girl recognized as belonging to the black sergeant. He had come, but would she be any better off? She knew that she would not unless she could play upon Usanga's fear of his woman.

When Usanga found what had happened he kicked the warrior out of the hut and bade him begone, and when the fellow had disappeared, muttering and grumbling, the sergeant approached the white girl. He was very drunk, so drunk that several times she succeeded in eluding him and twice she pushed him so violently away that he stumbled and fell.

Finally he became enraged and rushing upon her, seized her in his long, apelike arms. Striking at his face with clenched fists she tried to protect herself and drive him away. She threatened him with the wrath of Naratu, and at that he changed his tactics and began to plead, and as he argued with her, promising her safety and eventual freedom, the warrior he had kicked out of the hut made his staggering way to the hut occupied by Naratu.

Usanga finding that pleas and promises were as unavailing as threats, at last lost both his patience and his head, seizing the girl roughly, and simultaneously there burst into the hut a raging demon of jealousy. Naratu had come. Kicking, scratching, striking, biting, she routed the terrified Usanga in short order, and so obsessed was she by her desire to inflict punishment upon her unfaithful lord and master that she quite forgot the object of his infatuation.

Bertha Kircher heard her screaming down the village street at Usanga's heels and trembled at the thought of what lay in store for her at the hands of these two, for she knew that tomorrow at the latest Naratu would take out upon her the full measure of her jealous hatred after she had spent her first wrath upon Usanga.

The two had departed but a few minutes when the warrior guard returned. He looked into the hut and then entered. "No one will stop me now, white woman," he growled as he stepped quickly across the hut toward her.

Tarzan of the Apes, feasting well upon a juicy haunch from Bara, the deer, was vaguely conscious of a troubled mind. He should have been at peace with himself and all the world, for was he not in his native element surrounded by game in plenty and rapidly filling his belly with the flesh he loved best? But Tarzan of the Apes was haunted by the picture of a slight, young girl being shoved and struck by brutal Negresses, and in imagination could see her now camped in this savage country a prisoner among degraded blacks.

Why was it so difficult to remember that she was only a hated German and a spy? Why would the fact that she was a woman and white always obtrude itself upon his consciousness? He hated her as he hated all her kind, and the fate that was sure to be hers was no more terrible than she in common with all her people deserved. The matter was settled and Tarzan composed himself to think of other things, yet the picture would not die—it rose in all its details and annoyed him. He began to wonder what they were doing to her and where they were taking her. He was very much ashamed of himself as he had been after the episode in Wilhelmstal when his weakness had permitted him to spare this spy's life. Was he to be thus weak again? No!

Night came and he settled himself in an ample tree to rest until morning; but sleep would not come. Instead came the vision of a white girl being beaten by black women, and again of the same girl at the mercy of the warriors somewhere in that dark and forbidding jungle.

With a growl of anger and self-contempt Tarzan arose, shook himself, and swung from his tree to that adjoining, and thus, through the lower terraces, he followed the trail that Usanga's party had taken earlier in the afternoon. He had little difficulty as the band had followed a well-beaten path and when toward midnight the stench of a native village assailed his delicate nostrils he guessed that his goal was near and that presently he should find her whom he sought.

Prowling stealthily as prowls Numa, the lion, stalking a wary prey, Tarzan moved noiselessly about the palisade, listening and sniffing. At the rear of the village he discovered a tree whose branches extended over the top of the palisade and a moment later he had dropped quietly into the village.

From hut to hut he went searching with keen ears and nostrils some confirming evidence of the presence of the girl, and at last, faint and almost obliterated by the odor of the Gomangani, he found it hanging like a delicate vapor about a small hut. The village was quiet now, for the last of the beer and the food had been disposed of and the blacks lay in their huts overcome by stupor, yet Tarzan made no noise that even a sober man keenly alert might have heard.

He passed around to the entrance of the hut and listened. From within came no sound, not even the low breathing of one awake; yet he was sure that the girl had been here and perhaps was even now, and so he entered, slipping in as silently as a disembodied spirit. For a moment he stood motionless just within the entranceway, listening. No, there was no one here, of that he was sure, but he would investigate. As his eyes became accustomed to the greater darkness within the hut an object began to take form that presently outlined itself in a human form supine upon the floor.

Tarzan stepped closer and leaned over to examine it—it was the dead body of a naked warrior from whose chest protruded a short spear. Then he searched carefully every square foot of the remaining floor space and at last returned to the body again where he stooped and smelled of the haft of the weapon that had slain the black. A slow smile touched his lips—that and a slight movement of his head betokened that he understood.

A rapid search of the balance of the village assured him that the girl had escaped and a feeling of relief came over him that no harm had befallen her. That her life was equally in jeopardy in the savage jungle to which she must have flown did not impress him as it would have you or me, since to Tarzan the jungle was not a dangerous place—he considered one safer there than in Paris or London by night.

He had entered the trees again and was outside the palisade when there came faintly to his ears from far beyond the village an old, familiar sound. Balancing lightly upon a swaying branch he stood, a graceful statue of a forest god, listening intently. For a minute he stood thus and then there broke from his lips the long, weird cry of ape calling to ape and he was away through the jungle toward the sound of the booming drum of the anthropoids leaving behind him an awakened and terrified village of cringing blacks, who would forever after connect that eerie cry with the disappearance of their white prisoner and the death of their fellow-warrior.

Bertha Kircher, hurrying through the jungle along a well-beaten game trail, thought only of putting as much distance as possible between herself and the village before daylight could permit pursuit of her. Whither she was going she did not know, nor was it a matter of great moment since death must be her lot sooner or later.

Fortune favored her that night, for she passed unscathed through as savage and lion-ridden an area as there is in all Africa—a natural hunting ground which the white man has not yet discovered, where deer and antelope and zebra, giraffe and elephant, buffalo, rhinoceros, and the other herbivorous animals of central Africa abound unmolested by none but their natural enemies, the great cats, which, lured here by easy prey and immunity from the rifles of big-game hunters, swarm the district.

She had fled for an hour or two, perhaps, when her attention was arrested by the sound of animals moving about, muttering and growling close ahead. Assured that she had covered a sufficient distance to insure her a good start in the morning before the blacks could take to her trail, and fearful of what the creatures might be, she climbed into a large tree with the intention of spending the balance of the night there.

She had no sooner reached a safe and comfortable branch when she discovered that the tree stood upon the edge of a small clearing that had been hidden from her by the heavy undergrowth upon the ground below, and simultaneously she discovered the identity of the beasts she had heard.

In the center of the clearing below her, clearly visible in the bright moonlight, she saw fully twenty huge, manlike apes—great, shaggy fellows who went upon their hind feet with only slight assistance from the knuckles of their hands. The moonlight glanced from their glossy coats, the numerous gray-tipped hairs imparting a sheen that made the hideous creatures almost magnificent in their appearance.

The girl had watched them but a minute or two when the little band was joined by others, coming singly and in groups until there were fully fifty of the great brutes gathered there in the moonlight. Among them were young apes and several little ones clinging tightly to their mothers' shaggy shoulders. Presently the group parted to form a circle about what appeared to be a small, flat-topped mound of earth in the center of the clearing. Squatting close about this mound were three old females armed with short, heavy clubs with which they presently began to pound upon the flat top of the earth mound which gave forth a dull, booming sound, and almost immediately the other apes commenced to move about restlessly, weaving in and out aimlessly until they carried the impression of a moving mass of great, black maggots.

The beating of the drum was in a slow, ponderous cadence, at first without time but presently settling into a heavy rhythm to which the apes kept time with measured tread and swaying bodies. Slowly the mass separated into two rings, the outer of which was composed of shes and the very young, the inner of mature bulls. The former ceased to move and squatted upon their haunches, while the bulls now moved slowly about in a circle the center of which was the drum and all now in the same direction.

It was then that there came faintly to the ears of the girl from the direction of the village she had recently quitted a weird and high-pitched cry. The effect upon the apes was electrical—they stopped their movements and stood in attitudes of intent listening for a moment, and then one fellow, huger than his companions, raised his face to the heavens and in a voice that sent the cold shudders through the girl's slight frame answered the far-off cry.

Once again the beaters took up their drumming and the slow dance went on. There was a certain fascination in the savage ceremony that held the girl spellbound, and as there seemed little likelihood of her being discovered, she felt that she might as well remain the balance of the night in her tree and resume her flight by the comparatively greater safety of daylight.

Assuring herself that her packet of papers was safe she sought as comfortable a position as possible among the branches, and settled herself to watch the weird proceedings in the clearing below her.

A half-hour passed, during which the cadence of the drum increased gradually. Now the great bull that had replied to the distant call leaped from the inner circle to dance alone between the drummers and the other bulls. He leaped and crouched and leaped again, now growling and barking, again stopping to raise his hideous face to Goro, the moon, and, beating upon his shaggy breast, uttered a piercing scream-the challenge of the bull ape, had the girl but known it.

He stood thus in the full glare of the great moon, motionless after screaming forth his weird challenge, in the setting of the primeval jungle and the circling apes a picture of primitive savagery and power—a mightily muscled Hercules out of the dawn of life—when from close behind her the girl heard an answering scream, and an instant later saw an almost naked white man drop from a near-by tree into the clearing.

Instantly the apes became a roaring, snarling pack of angry beasts. Bertha Kircher held her breath. What maniac was this who dared approach these frightful creatures in their own haunts, alone against fifty? She saw the brown-skinned figure bathed in moonlight walk straight toward the snarling pack. She saw the symmetry and the beauty of that perfect body—its grace, its strength, its wondrous proportioning, and then she recognized him. It was the same creature whom she had seen carry Major Schneider from General Kraut's headquarters, the same who had rescued her from Numa, the lion; the same whom she had struck down with the butt of her pistol and escaped when he would have returned her to her enemies, the same who had slain Hauptmann Fritz Schneider and spared her life that night in Wilhelmstal.

Fear-filled and fascinated she watched him as he neared the apes. She heard sounds issue from his throat—sounds identical with those uttered by the apes—and though she could scarce believe the testimony of her own ears, she knew that this godlike creature was conversing with the brutes in their own tongue.

Tarzan halted just before he reached the shes of the outer circle. "I am Tarzan of the Apes!" he cried. "You do not know me because I am of another tribe, but Tarzan comes in peace or he comes to fight—which shall it be? Tarzan will talk with your king," and so saying he pushed straight forward through the shes and the young who now gave way before him, making a narrow lane through which he passed toward the inner circle.

Shes and balus growled and bristled as he passed closer, but none hindered him and thus he came to the inner circle of bulls. Here bared fangs menaced him and growling faces hideously contorted. "I am Tarzan," he repeated. "Tarzan comes to dance the Dum-Dum with his brothers. Where is your king?" Again he pressed forward and the girl in the tree clapped her palms to her cheeks as she watched, wide-eyed, this madman going to a frightful death. In another instant they would be upon him, rending and tearing until that perfect form had been ripped to shreds; but again the ring parted, and though the apes roared and menaced him they did not attack, and at last he stood in the inner circle close to the drum and faced the great king ape.

Again he spoke. "I am Tarzan of the Apes," he cried. "Tarzan comes to live with his brothers. He will come in peace and live in peace or he will kill; but he has come and he will stay. Which—shall Tarzan dance the Dum-Dum in peace with his brothers, or shall Tarzan kill first?"

"I am Go-lat, King of the Apes," screamed the great bull. "I kill! I kill! I kill!" and with a sullen roar he charged the Tarmangani.

The ape-man, as the girl watched him, seemed entirely unprepared for the charge and she looked to see him borne down and slain at the first rush. The great bull was almost upon him with huge hands outstretched to seize him before Tarzan made a move, but when he did move his quickness would have put Ara, the lightning, to shame. As darts forward the head of Histah, the snake, so darted forward the left hand of the man-beast as he seized the left wrist of his antagonist. A quick turn and the bull's right arm was locked beneath the right arm of his foe in a jujutsu hold that Tarzan had learned among civilized men—a hold with which he might easily break the great bones, a hold that left the ape helpless.

"I am Tarzan of the Apes!" screamed the ape-man. "Shall Tarzan dance in peace or shall Tarzan kill?"

"I kill! I kill! I kill!" shrieked Go-lat.

With the quickness of a cat Tarzan swung the king ape over one hip and sent him sprawling to the ground. "I am Tarzan, King of all the Apes!" he shouted. "Shall it be peace?"

Go-lat, infuriated, leaped to his feet and charged again, shouting his war cry: "I kill! I kill! I kill!" and again Tarzan met him with a sudden hold that the stupid bull, being ignorant of, could not possibly avert—a hold and a throw that brought a scream of delight from the interested audience and suddenly filled the girl with doubts as to the man's madness—evidently he was quite safe among the apes, for she saw him swing Go-lat to his back and then catapult him over his shoulder. The king ape fell upon his head and lay very still.

"I am Tarzan of the Apes!" cried the ape-man. "I come to dance the Dum-Dum with my brothers," and he made a motion to the drummers, who immediately took up the cadence of the dance where they had dropped it to watch their king slay the foolish Tarmangani.

It was then that Go-lat raised his head and slowly crawled to his feet. Tarzan approached him. "I am Tarzan of the Apes," he cried. "Shall Tarzan dance the Dum-Dum with his brothers now, or shall he kill first?"

Go-lat raised his bloodshot eyes to the face of the Tarmangani. "Kagoda!" he cried "Tarzan of the Apes will dance the Dum-Dum with his brothers and Go-lat will dance with him!"

And then the girl in the tree saw the savage man leaping, bending, and stamping with the savage apes in the ancient rite of the Dum-Dum. His roars and growls were more beastly than the beasts. His handsome face was distorted with savage ferocity. He beat upon his great breast and screamed forth his challenge as his smooth, brown hide brushed the shaggy coats of his fellows. It was weird; it was wonderful; and in its primitive savagery it was not without beauty—the strange scene she looked upon, such a scene as no other human being, probably, ever had witnessed—and yet, withal, it was horrible.

As she gazed, spell-bound, a stealthy movement in the tree behind her caused her to turn her head, and there, back of her, blazing in the reflected moonlight, shone two great, yellow-green eyes. Sheeta, the panther, had found her out.

The beast was so close that it might have reached out and touched her with a great, taloned paw. There was no time to think, no time to weigh chances or to choose alternatives. Terror-inspired impulse was her guide as, with a loud scream, she leaped from the tree into the clearing.

Instantly the apes, now maddened by the effects of the dancing and the moonlight, turned to note the cause of the interruption. They saw this she Tarmangani, helpless and alone and they started for her. Sheeta, the panther, knowing that not even Numa, the lion, unless maddened by starvation, dares meddle with the great apes at their Dum-Dum, had silently vanished into the night, seeking his supper elsewhere.

Tarzan, turning with the other apes toward the cause of the interruption, saw the girl, recognized her and also her peril. Here again might she die at the hands of others; but why consider it! He knew that he could not permit it, and though the acknowledgment shamed him, it had to be admitted.

The leading shes were almost upon the girl when Tarzan leaped among them, and with heavy blows scattered them to right and left; and then as the bulls came to share in the kill they thought this new ape-thing was about to make that he might steal all the flesh for himself, they found him facing them with an arm thrown about the creature as though to protect her.

"This is Tarzan's she," he said. "Do not harm her." It was the only way he could make them understand that they must not slay her. He was glad that she could not interpret the words. It was humiliating enough to make such a statement to wild apes about this hated enemy.

So once again Tarzan of the Apes was forced to protect a Hun. Growling, he muttered to himself in extenuation:

"She is a woman and I am not a German, so it could not be otherwise!"

DROPPED FROM THE SKY

Lieutenant Harold Percy Smith-Oldwick, Royal Air Service, was on reconnaissance. A report, or it would be better to say a rumor, had come to the British headquarters in German East Africa that the enemy had landed in force on the west coast and was marching across the dark continent to reinforce their colonial troops. In fact the new army was supposed to be no more than ten or twelve days' march to the west. Of course the thing was ridiculous—preposterous—but preposterous things often happen in war; and anyway no good general permits the least rumor of enemy activity to go uninvestigated.

Therefore Lieutenant Harold Percy Smith-Oldwick flew low toward the west, searching with keen eyes for signs of a Hun army. Vast forests unrolled beneath him in which a German army corps might have lain concealed, so dense was the overhanging foliage of the great trees. Mountain, meadowland, and desert passed in lovely panorama; but never a sight of man had the young lieutenant.

Always hoping that he might discover some sign of their passage—a discarded lorry, a broken limber, or an old camp site—he continued farther and farther into the west until well into the afternoon. Above a tree-dotted plain through the center of which flowed a winding river he determined to turn about and start for camp. It would take straight flying at top speed to cover the distance before dark; but as he had ample gasoline and a trustworthy machine there was no doubt in his mind but that he could accomplish his aim. It was then that his engine stalled.

He was too low to do anything but land, and that immediately, while he had the more open country accessible, for directly east of him was a vast forest into which a stalled engine could only have plunged him to certain injury and probable death; and so he came down in the meadowland near the winding river and there started to tinker with his motor.

As he worked he hummed a tune, some music-hall air that had been popular in London the year before, so that one might have thought him working in the security of an English flying field surrounded by innumerable comrades rather than alone in the heart of an unexplored African wilderness. It was typical of the man that he should be wholly indifferent to his surroundings, although his looks entirely belied any assumption that he was of particularly heroic strain.

Lieutenant Harold Percy Smith-Oldwick was fair-hatred, blue-eyed, and slender, with a rosy, boyish face that might have been molded more by an environment of luxury, indolence, and ease than the more strenuous exigencies of life's sterner requirements.

And not only was the young lieutenant outwardly careless of the immediate future and of his surroundings, but actually so. That the district might be infested by countless enemies seemed not to have occurred to him in the remotest degree. He bent assiduously to the work of correcting the adjustment that had caused his motor to stall without so much as an upward glance at the surrounding country. The forest to the east of him, and the more distant jungle that bordered the winding river, might have harbored an army of bloodthirsty savages, but neither could elicit even a passing show of interest on the part of Lieutenant Smith-Oldwick

And even had he looked, it is doubtful if he would have seen the score of figures crouching in the concealment of the undergrowth at the forest's edge. There are those who are reputed to be endowed with that which is sometimes, for want of a better appellation, known as the sixth sense—a species of intuition which apprises them of the presence of an unseen danger. The concentrated gaze of a hidden observer provokes a warning sensation of nervous unrest in such as these, but though twenty pairs of savage eyes were gazing fixedly at Lieutenant Harold Percy Smith-Oldwick, the fact aroused no responsive sensation of impending danger in his placid breast. He hummed peacefully and, his adjustment completed, tried out his motor for a minute or two, then shut it off and descended to the ground with the intention of stretching his legs and taking a smoke before continuing his return flight to camp. Now for the first time he took note of his surroundings, to be immediately impressed by both the wildness and the beauty of the scene. In some respects the tree-dotted meadowland reminded him of a park-like English forest, and that wild beasts and savage men could ever be a part of so quiet a scene seemed the remotest of contingencies.

Some gorgeous blooms upon a flowering shrub at a little distance from his machine caught the attention of his aesthetic eye, and as he puffed upon his cigarette, he walked over to examine the flowers more closely. As he bent above them he was probably some hundred yards from his plane and it was at this instant that Numabo, chief of the Wamabo, chose to leap from his ambush and lead his warriors in a sudden rush upon the white man.

The young Englishman's first intimation of danger was a chorus of savage yells from the forest behind him. Turning, he saw a score of naked, black warriors advancing rapidly toward him. They moved in a compact mass and as they approached more closely their rate of speed noticeably diminished. Lieutenant Smith-Oldwick realized in a quick glance that the direction of their approach and their proximity had cut off all chances of retreating to his plane, and he also understood that their attitude was entirely warlike and menacing. He saw that they were armed with spears and with bows and arrows, and he felt quite confident that notwithstanding the fact that he was armed with a pistol they could overcome him with the first rush. What he did not know about their tactics was that at any show of resistance they would fall back, which is the nature of the native Negroes, but that after numerous advances and retreats, during which they would work themselves into a frenzy of rage by much shrieking, leaping, and dancing, they would eventually come to the point of a determined and final assault.

Numabo was in the forefront, a fact which taken in connection with his considerably greater size and more warlike appearance, indicated him as the natural target and it was at Numabo that the Englishman aimed his first shot. Unfortunately for him it missed its target, as the killing of the chief might have permanently dispersed the others. The bullet passed Numabo to lodge in the breast of a warrior behind him and as the fellow lunged forward with a scream the others turned and retreated, but to the lieutenant's chagrin they ran in the direction of the plane instead of back toward the forest so that he was still cut off from reaching his machine.

Presently they stopped and faced him again. They were talking loudly and gesticulating, and after a moment one of them leaped into the air, brandishing his spear and uttering savage war cries, which soon had their effect upon his fellows so that it was not long ere all of them were taking part in the wild show of savagery, which would bolster their waning courage and presently spur them on to another attack.

The second charge brought them closer to the Englishman, and though he dropped another with his pistol, it was not before two or three spears had been launched at him. He now had five shots remaining and there were still eighteen warriors to be accounted for, so that unless he could frighten them off, it was evident that his fate was sealed.

That they must pay the price of one life for every attempt to take his had its effect upon them and they were longer now in initiating a new rush and when they did so it was more skillfully ordered than those that had preceded it, for they scattered into three bands which, partially surrounding him, came simultaneously toward him from different directions, and though he emptied his pistol with good effect, they reached him at last. They seemed to know that his ammunition was exhausted, for they circled close about him now with the evident intention of taking him alive, since they might easily have riddled him with their sharp spears with perfect safety to themselves.

For two or three minutes they circled about him until, at a word from Numabo, they closed in simultaneously, and though the slender young lieutenant struck out to right and left, he was soon overwhelmed by superior numbers and beaten down by the hafts of spears in brawny hands.

He was all but unconscious when they finally dragged him to his feet, and after securing his hands behind his back, pushed him roughly along ahead of them toward the jungle.

As the guard prodded him along the narrow trail, Lieutenant Smith-Oldwick could not but wonder why they had wished to take him alive. He knew that he was too far inland for his uniform to have any significance to this native tribe to whom no inkling of the World War probably ever had come, and he could only assume that he had fallen into the hands of the warriors of some savage potentate upon whose royal caprice his fate would hinge.

They had marched for perhaps half an hour when the Englishman saw ahead of them, in a little clearing upon the bank of the river, the thatched roofs of native huts showing above a crude but strong palisade; and presently he was ushered into a village street where he was immediately surrounded by a throng of women and children and warriors. Here he was soon the center of an excited mob whose intent seemed to be to dispatch him as quickly as possible. The women were more venomous than the men, striking and scratching him whenever they could reach him, until at last Numabo, the chief, was obliged to interfere to save his prisoner for whatever purpose he was destined.

As the warriors pushed the crowd back, opening a space through which the white man was led toward a hut, Lieutenant Smith-Oldwick saw coming from the opposite end of the village a number of Negroes wearing odds and ends of German uniforms. He was not a little surprised at this, and his first thought was that he had at last come in contact with some portion of the army which was rumored to be crossing from the west coast and for signs of which he had been searching.

A rueful smile touched his lips as he contemplated the unhappy circumstances which surrounded the accession of this knowledge for though he was far from being without hope, he realized that only by the merest chance could he escape these people and regain his machine.

Among the partially uniformed blacks was a huge fellow in the tunic of a sergeant and as this man's eyes fell upon the British officer, a loud cry of exultation broke from his lips, and immediately his followers took up the cry and pressed forward to bait the prisoner.

"Where did you get the Englishman?" asked Usanga, the black sergeant, of the chief Numabo. "Are there many more with him?"

"He came down from the sky," replied the native chief "in a strange thing which flies like a bird and which frightened us very much at first; but we watched for a long time and saw that it did not seem to be alive, and when this white man left it we attacked him and though he killed some of my warriors, we took him, for we Wamabos are brave men and great warriors."

Usanga's eyes went wide. "He flew here through the sky?" he asked.

"Yes," said Numabo. "In a great thing which resembled a bird he flew down out of the sky. The thing is still there where it came down close to the four trees near the second bend in the river. We left it there because, not knowing what it was, we were afraid to touch it and it is still there if it has not flown away again."

"It cannot fly," said Usanga, "without this man in it. It is a terrible thing which filled the hearts of our soldiers with terror, for it flew over our camps at night and dropped bombs upon us. It is well that you captured this white man, Numabo, for with his great bird he would have flown over your village tonight and killed all your people. These Englishman are very wicked white men."

"He will fly no more," said Numabo "It is not intended that a man should fly through the air; only wicked demons do such things as that and Numabo, the chief, will see that this white man does not do it again," and with the words he pushed the young officer roughly toward a hut in the center of the village, where he was left under guard of two stalwart warriors.

For an hour or more the prisoner was left to his own devices, which consisted in vain and unremitting attempts to loosen the strands which fettered his wrists, and then he was interrupted by the appearance of the black sergeant Usanga, who entered his hut and approached him.

"What are they going to do with me?" asked the Englishman. "My country is not at war with these people. You speak their language. Tell them that I am not an enemy, that my people are the friends of the black people and that they must let me go in peace."

Usanga laughed. "They do not know an Englishman from a German," he replied. "It is nothing to them what you are, except that you are a white man and an enemy."

"Then why did they take me alive?" asked the lieutenant.

"Come," said Usanga and he led the Englishman to the doorway of the hut. "Look," he said, and pointed a black forefinger toward the end of the village street where a wider space between the huts left a sort of plaza.

Here Lieutenant Harold Percy Smith-Oldwick saw a number of Negresses engaged in laying fagots around a stake and in preparing fires beneath a number of large cooking vessels. The sinister suggestion was only too obvious.

Usanga was eyeing the white man closely, but if he expected to be rewarded by any signs of fear, he was doomed to disappointment and the young lieutenant merely turned toward him with a shrug: "Really now, do you beggars intend eating me?"

"Not my people," replied Usanga. "We do not eat human flesh, but the Wamabos do. It is they who will eat you, but we will kill you for the feast, Englishman."

The Englishman remained standing in the doorway of the hut, an interested spectator of the preparations for the coming orgy that was so horribly to terminate his earthly existence. It can hardly be assumed that he felt no fear; yet, if he did, he hid it perfectly beneath an imperturbable mask of coolness. Even the brutal Usanga must have been impressed by the bravery of his victim since, though he had come to abuse and possibly to torture the helpless prisoner, he now did neither, contenting himself merely with berating whites as a race and Englishmen especially, because of the terror the British aviators had caused Germany's native troops in East Africa.

"No more," he concluded, "will your great bird fly over our people dropping death among them from the skies—Usanga will see to that," and he walked abruptly away toward a group of his own fighting men who were congregated near the stake where they were laughing and joking with the women.

A few minutes later the Englishman saw them pass out of the village gate, and once again his thoughts reverted to various futile plans for escape.

Several miles north of the village on a little rise of ground close to the river where the jungle, halting at the base of a knoll, had left a few acres of grassy land sparsely wooded, a man and a girl were busily engaged in constructing a small boma, in the center of which a thatched hut already had been erected.

They worked almost in silence with only an occasional word of direction or interrogation between them.

Except for a loin cloth, the man was naked, his smooth skin tanned to a deep brown by the action of sun and wind. He moved with the graceful ease of a jungle cat and when he lifted heavy weights, the action seemed as effortless as the raising of empty hands.

When he was not looking at her, and it was seldom that he did, the girl found her eyes wandering toward him, and at such times there was always a puzzled expression upon her face as though she found in him an enigma which she could not solve. As a matter of fact, her feelings toward him were not un-tinged with awe, since in the brief period of their association she had discovered in this handsome, godlike giant the attributes of the superman and the savage beast closely intermingled. At first she had felt only that unreasoning feminine terror which her unhappy position naturally induced.

To be alone in the heart of an unexplored wilderness of Central Africa with a savage wild man was in itself sufficiently appalling, but to feel also that this man was a blood enemy, that he hated her and her kind and that in addition thereto he owed her a personal grudge for an attack she had made upon him in the past, left no loophole for any hope that he might accord her even the minutest measure of consideration.

She had seen him first months since when he had entered the headquarters of the German high command in East Africa and carried off the luckless Major Schneider, of whose fate no hint had ever reached the German officers; and she had seen him again upon that occasion when he had rescued her from the clutches of the lion and, after explaining to her that he had recognized her in the British camp, had made her prisoner. It was then that she had struck him down with the butt of her pistol and escaped. That he might seek no personal revenge for her act had been evidenced in Wilhelmstal the night that he had killed Hauptmann Fritz Schneider and left without molesting her.

No, she could not fathom him. He hated her and at the same time he had protected her as had been evidenced again when he had kept the great apes from tearing her to pieces after she had escaped from the Wamabo village to which Usanga, the black sergeant, had brought her a captive; but why was he saving her? For what sinister purpose could this savage enemy be protecting her from the other denizens of his cruel jungle? She tried to put from her mind the probable fate which awaited her, yet it persisted in obtruding itself upon her thoughts, though always she was forced to admit that there was nothing in the demeanor of the man to indicate that her fears were well grounded. She judged him perhaps by the standards other men had taught her and because she looked upon him as a savage creature, she felt that she could not expect more of chivalry from him than was to be found in the breasts of the civilized men of her acquaintance.

Fraulein Bertha Kircher was by nature a companionable and cheerful character. She was not given to morbid forebodings, and above all things she craved the society of her kind and that interchange of thought which is one of the marked distinctions between man and the lower animals. Tarzan, on the other hand, was sufficient unto himself. Long years of semi-solitude among creatures whose powers of oral expression are extremely limited had thrown him almost entirely upon his own resources for entertainment.

His active mind was never idle, but because his jungle mates could neither follow nor grasp the vivid train of imaginings that his man-mind wrought, he had long since learned to keep them to himself; and so now he found no need for confiding them in others. This fact, linked with that of his dislike for the girl, was sufficient to seal his lips for other than necessary conversation, and so they worked on together in comparative silence. Bertha Kircher, however, was nothing if not feminine and she soon found that having someone to talk to who would not talk was extremely irksome. Her fear of the man was gradually departing, and she was full of a thousand unsatisfied curiosities as to his plans for the future in so far as they related to her, as well as more personal questions regarding himself, since she could not but wonder as to his antecedents and his strange and solitary life in the jungle, as well as his friendly intercourse with the savage apes among which she had found him.

With the waning of her fears she became sufficiently emboldened to question him, and so she asked him what he intended doing after the hut and boma were completed.

"I am going to the west coast where I was born," replied Tarzan. "I do not know when. I have all my life before me and in the jungle there is no reason for haste. We are not forever running as fast as we can from one place to another as are you of the outer world. When I have been here long enough I will go on toward the west, but first I must see that you have a safe place in which to sleep, and that you have learned how to provide yourself with necessaries. That will take time."

"You are going to leave me here alone?" cried the girl; her tones marked the fear which the prospect induced. "You are going to leave me here alone in this terrible jungle, a prey to wild beasts and savage men, hundreds of miles from a white settlement and in a country which gives every evidence of never having been touched by the foot of civilized men?"

"Why not?" asked Tarzan. "I did not bring you here. Would one of your men accord any better treatment to an enemy woman?"

"Yes," she exclaimed. "They certainly would. No man of my race would leave a defenseless white woman alone in this horrible place."

Tarzan shrugged his broad shoulders. The conversation seemed profitless and it was further distasteful to him for the reason that it was carried on in German, a tongue which he detested as much as he did the people who spoke it. He wished that the girl spoke English and then it occurred to him that as he had seen her in disguise in the British camp carrying on her nefarious work as a German spy, she probably did speak English and so he asked her.

"Of course I speak English," she exclaimed, "but I did not know that you did."

Tarzan looked his wonderment but made no comment. He only wondered why the girl should have any doubts as to the ability of an Englishman to speak English, and then suddenly it occurred to him that she probably looked upon him merely as a beast of the jungle who by accident had learned to speak German through frequenting the district which Germany had colonized. It was there only that she had seen him and so she might not know that he was an Englishman by birth, and that he had had a home in British East Africa. It was as well, he thought, that she knew little of him, as the less she knew the more he might learn from her as to her activities in behalf of the Germans and of the German spy system of which she was a representative; and so it occurred to him to let her continue to think that he was only what he appeared to be—a savage denizen of his savage jungle, a man of no race and no country, hating all white men impartially; and this in truth, was what she did think of him. It explained perfectly his attacks upon Major Schneider and the Major's brother, Hauptmann Fritz.

Again they worked on in silence upon the boma which was now nearly completed, the girl helping the man to the best of her small ability. Tarzan could not but note with grudging approval the spirit of helpfulness she manifested in the oft-times painful labor of gathering and arranging the thorn bushes which constituted the temporary protection against roaming carnivores. Her hands and arms gave bloody token of the sharpness of the numerous points that had lacerated her soft flesh, and even though she were an enemy Tarzan could not but feel compunction that he had permitted her to do this work, and at last he bade her stop.

"Why?" she asked. "It is no more painful to me than it must be to you, and, as it is solely for my protection that you are building this boma, there is no reason why I should not do my share."

"You are a woman," replied Tarzan. "This is not a woman's work. If you wish to do something, take those gourds I brought this morning and fill them with water at the river. You may need it while I am away."

"While you are away—" she said. "You are going away?"

"When the boma is built I am going out after meat," he replied. "Tomorrow I will go again and take you and show you how you may make your own kills after I am gone."

Without a word she took the gourds and walked toward the river. As she filled them, her mind was occupied with painful forebodings of the future. She knew that Tarzan had passed a death sentence upon her, and that the moment that he left her, her doom was sealed, for it could be but a question of time—a very short time—before the grim jungle would claim her, for how could a lone woman hope successfully to combat the savage forces of destruction which constituted so large a part of existence in the jungle?

So occupied was she with the gloomy prophecies that she had neither ears nor eyes for what went on about her. Mechanically she filled the gourds and, taking them up, turned slowly to retrace her steps to the boma only to voice immediately a half-stifled scream and shrank back from the menacing figure looming before her and blocking her way to the hut.

Go-lat, the king ape, hunting a little apart from his tribe, had seen the woman go to the river for water, and it was he who confronted her when she turned back with her filled gourds. Go-lat was not a pretty creature when judged by standards of civilized humanity, though the shes of his tribe and even Go-lat himself, considered his glossy black coat shot with silver, his huge arms dangling to his knees, his bullet head sunk between his mighty shoulders, marks of great personal beauty. His wicked, bloodshot eyes and broad nose, his ample mouth and great fighting fangs only enhanced the claim of this Adonis of the forest upon the affections of his shes.

Doubtless in the little, savage brain there was a well-formed conviction that this strange she belonging to the Tarmangani must look with admiration upon so handsome a creature as Go-lat, for there could be no doubt in the mind of any that his beauty entirely eclipsed such as the hairless white ape might lay claim to.

But Bertha Kircher saw only a hideous beast, a fierce and terrible caricature of man. Could Go-lat have known what passed through her mind, he must have been terribly chagrined, though the chances are that he would have attributed it to a lack of discernment on her part. Tarzan heard the girl's cry and looking up saw at a glance the cause of her terror. Leaping lightly over the boma, he ran swiftly toward her as Go-lat lumbered closer to the girl the while he voiced his emotions in low gutturals which, while in reality the most amicable of advances, sounded to the girl like the growling of an enraged beast. As Tarzan drew nearer he called aloud to the ape and the girl heard from the human lips the same sounds that had fallen from those of the anthropoid.

"I will not harm your she," Go-lat called to Tarzan.

"I know it," replied the ape-man, "but she does not. She is like Numa and Sheeta, who do not understand our talk. She thinks you come to harm her."

By this time Tarzan was beside the girl. "He will not harm you," he said to her. "You need not be afraid. This ape has learned his lesson. He has learned that Tarzan is lord of the jungle. He will not harm that which is Tarzan's."

The girl cast a quick glance at the man's face. It was evident to her that the words he had spoken meant nothing to him and that the assumed proprietorship over her was, like the boma, only another means for her protection.

"But I am afraid of him," she said.

"You must not show your fear. You will be often surrounded by these apes. At such times you will be safest. Before I leave you I will give you the means of protecting yourself against them should one of them chance to turn upon you. If I were you I would seek their society. Few are the animals of the jungle that dare attack the great apes when there are several of them together. If you let them know that you are afraid of them, they will take advantage of it and your life will be constantly menaced. The shes especially would attack you. I will let them know that you have the means of protecting yourself and of killing them. If necessary, I will show you how and then they will respect and fear you."

"I will try," said the girl, "but I am afraid that it will be difficult. He is the most frightful creature I ever have seen." Tarzan smiled. "Doubtless he thinks the same of you," he said.

By this time other apes had entered the clearing and they were now the center of a considerable group, among which were several bulls, some young shes, and some older ones with their little balus clinging to their backs or frolicking around at their feet. Though they had seen the girl the night of the Dum-Dum when Sheeta had forced her to leap from her concealment into the arena where the apes were dancing, they still evinced a great curiosity regarding her. Some of the shes came very close and plucked at her garments, commenting upon them to one another in their strange tongue. The girl, by the exercise of all the will power she could command, succeeded in passing through the ordeal without evincing any of the terror and revulsion that she felt. Tarzan watched her closely, a half-smile upon his face. He was not so far removed from recent contact with civilized people that he could not realize the torture that she was undergoing, but he felt no pity for this woman of a cruel enemy who doubtless deserved the worst suffering that could be meted to her. Yet, notwithstanding his sentiments toward her, he was forced to admire her fine display of courage. Suddenly he turned to the apes.

"Tarzan goes to hunt for himself and his she," he said. "The she will remain there," and he pointed toward the hut. "See that no member of the tribe harms her. Do you understand?"

The apes nodded. "We will not harm her," said Go-lat.

"No," said Tarzan. "You will not. For if you do, Tarzan will kill you," and then turning to the girl, "Come," he said, "I am going to hunt now. You had better remain at the hut. The apes have promised not to harm you. I will leave my spear with you. It will be the best weapon you could have in case you should need to protect yourself, but I doubt if you will be in any danger for the short time that I am away."

He walked with her as far as the boma and when she had entered he closed the gap with thorn bushes and turned away toward the forest. She watched him moving across the clearing, noting the easy, catlike tread and the grace of every movement that harmonized so well with the symmetry and perfection of his figure. At the forest's edge she saw him swing lightly into a tree and disappear from view, and then, being a woman, she entered the hut and, throwing herself upon the ground, burst into tears.

IN THE HANDS OF SAVAGES

Tarzan sought Bara, the deer, or Horta, the boar, for of all the jungle animals he doubted if any would prove more palatable to the white woman, but though his keen nostrils were ever on the alert, he traveled far without being rewarded with even the faintest scent spoor of the game he sought. Keeping close to the river where he hoped to find Bara or Horta approaching or leaving a drinking place he came at last upon the strong odor of the Wamabo village and being ever ready to pay his hereditary enemies, the Gomangani, an undesired visit, he swung into a detour and came up in the rear of the village. From a tree which overhung the palisade he looked down into the street where he saw the preparations going on which his experience told him indicated the approach of one of those frightful feasts the piece de resistance of which is human flesh.

One of Tarzan's chief divertisements was the baiting of the blacks. He realized more keen enjoyment through annoying and terrifying them than from any other source of amusement the grim jungle offered. To rob them of their feast in some way that would strike terror to their hearts would give him the keenest of pleasure, and so he searched the village with his eyes for some indication of the whereabouts of the prisoner. His view was circumscribed by the dense foliage of the tree in which he sat, and, so that he might obtain a better view, he climbed further aloft and moved cautiously out upon a slender branch.

Tarzan of the Apes possessed a woodcraft scarcely short of the marvelous but even Tarzan's wondrous senses were not infallible. The branch upon which he made his way outward from the bole was no smaller than many that had borne his weight upon countless other occasions. Outwardly it appeared strong and healthy and was in full foliage, nor could Tarzan know that close to the stem a burrowing insect had eaten away half the heart of the solid wood beneath the bark.

And so when he reached a point far out upon the limb, it snapped close to the bole of the tree without warning. Below him were no larger branches that he might clutch and as he lunged downward his foot caught in a looped creeper so that he turned completely over and alighted on the flat of his back in the center of the village street.

At the sound of the breaking limb and the crashing body falling through the branches the startled blacks scurried to their huts for weapons, and when the braver of them emerged, they saw the still form of an almost naked white man lying where he had fallen. Emboldened by the fact that he did not move they approached more closely, and when their eyes discovered no signs of others of his kind in the tree, they rushed forward until a dozen warriors stood about him with ready spears. At first they thought that the falling had killed him, but upon closer examination they discovered that the man was only stunned. One of the warriors was for thrusting a spear through his heart, but Numabo, the chief, would not permit it.

"Bind him," he said. "We will feed well tonight."

And so they bound his hands and feet with thongs of gut and carried him into the hut where Lieutenant Harold Percy Smith-Oldwick awaited his fate. The Englishman had also been bound hand and foot by this time for fear that at the last moment he might escape and rob them of their feast. A great crowd of natives were gathered about the hut attempting to get a glimpse of the new prisoner, but Numabo doubled the guard before the entrance for fear that some of his people, in the exuberance of their savage joy, might rob the others of the pleasures of the death dance which would precede the killing of the victims.

The young Englishman had heard the sound of Tarzan's body crashing through the tree to the ground and the commotion in the village which immediately followed, and now, as he stood with his back against the wall of the hut, he looked upon the fellow-prisoner that the blacks carried in and laid upon the floor with mixed feelings of surprise and compassion. He realized that he never had seen a more perfect specimen of manhood than that of the unconscious figure before him, and he wondered to what sad circumstances the man owed his capture. It was evident that the new prisoner was himself as much a savage as his captors if apparel and weapons were any criterion by which to judge; yet it was also equally evident that he was a white man and from his well-shaped head and clean-cut features that he was not one of those unhappy halfwits who so often revert to savagery even in the heart of civilized communities.

As he watched the man, he presently noticed that his eyelids were moving. Slowly they opened and a pair of gray eyes looked blankly about. With returning consciousness the eyes assumed their natural expression of keen intelligence, and a moment later, with an effort, the prisoner rolled over upon his side and drew himself to a sitting position. He was facing the Englishman, and as his eyes took in the bound ankles and the arms drawn tightly behind the other's back, a slow smile lighted his features.

"They will fill their bellies tonight," he said.

The Englishman grinned. "From the fuss they made," he said, "the beggars must be awfully hungry. They like to have eaten me alive when they brought me in. How did they get you?"

Tarzan shrugged his head ruefully. "It was my own fault," he replied. "I deserve to be eaten. I crawled out upon a branch that would not bear my weight and when it broke, instead of alighting on my feet, I caught my foot in a trailer and came down on my head. Otherwise they would not have taken me—alive."

"Is there no escape?" asked the Englishman.

"I have escaped them before," replied Tarzan, "and I have seen others escape them. I have seen a man taken away from the stake after a dozen spear thrusts had pierced his body and the fire had been lighted about his feet."

Lieutenant Smith-Oldwick shuddered. "God!" he exclaimed, "I hope I don't have to face that. I believe I could stand anything but the thought of the fire. I should hate like the devil to go into a funk before the devils at the last moment."

"Don't worry," said Tarzan. "It doesn't last long and you won't funk. It is really not half as bad as it sounds. There is only a brief period of pain before you lose consciousness. I have seen it many times before. It is as good a way to go as another. We must die sometime. What difference whether it be tonight, tomorrow night, or a year hence, just so that we have lived—and I have lived!"

"Your philosophy may be all right, old top," said the young lieutenant, "but I can't say that it is exactly satisfying."

Tarzan laughed. "Roll over here," he said, "where I can get at your bonds with my teeth." The Englishman did as he was bid and presently Tarzan was working at the thongs with his strong white teeth. He felt them giving slowly beneath his efforts. In another moment they would part, and then it would be a comparatively simple thing for the Englishman to remove the remaining bonds from Tarzan and himself.

It was then that one of the guards entered the hut. In an instant he saw what the new prisoner was doing and raising his spear, struck the ape-man a vicious blow across the head with its shaft. Then he called in the other guards and together they fell upon the luckless men, kicking and beating them unmercifully, after which they bound the Englishman more securely than before and tied both men fast on opposite sides of the hut. When they had gone Tarzan looked across at his companion in misery.

"While there is life," he said, "there is hope," but he grinned as he voiced the ancient truism.

Lieutenant Harold Percy Smith-Oldwick returned the other's smile. "I fancy," he said, "that we are getting short on both. It must be close to supper time now."

Zu-tag hunted alone far from the balance of the tribe of Go-lat, the great ape. Zu-tag (Big-neck) was a young bull but recently arrived at maturity. He was large, powerful, and ferocious and at the same time far above the average of his kind in intelligence as was denoted by a fuller and less receding forehead. Already Go-lat saw in this young ape a possible contender for the laurels of his kingship and consequently the old bull looked upon Zu-tag with jealousy and disfavor. It was for this reason, possibly, as much as another that Zu-tag hunted so often alone; but it was his utter fearlessness that permitted him to wander far afield away from the protection which numbers gave the great apes. One of the results of this habit was a greatly increased resourcefulness which found him constantly growing in intelligence and powers of observation.

Today he had been hunting toward the south and was returning along the river upon a path he often followed because it led by the village of the Gomangani whose strange and almost apelike actions and peculiar manners of living had aroused his interest and curiosity. As he had done upon other occasions he took up his position in a tree from which he could overlook the interior of the village and watch the blacks at their vocations in the street below.

Zu-tag had scarcely more than established himself in his tree when, with the blacks, he was startled by the crashing of Tarzan's body from the branches of another jungle giant to the ground within the palisade. He saw the Negroes gather about the prostrate form and later carry it into the hut; and once he rose to his full height upon the limb where he had been squatting and raised his face to the heavens to scream out a savage protest and a challenge, for he had recognized in the brown-skinned Tarmangani the strange white ape who had come among them a night or two before in the midst of their Dum-Dum, and who by so easily mastering the greatest among them, had won the savage respect and admiration of this fierce young bull.

But Zu-tag's ferocity was tempered by a certain native cunning and caution. Before he had voiced his protest there formed in his mind the thought that he would like to save this wonderful white ape from the common enemy, the Gomangani, and so he screamed forth no challenge, wisely determined that more could be accomplished by secrecy and stealth than by force of muscle and fang.

At first he thought to enter the village alone and carry off the Tarmangani; but when he saw how numerous were the warriors and that several sat directly before the entrance to the lair into which the prisoner had been carried, it occurred to him that this was work for many rather than one, and so, as silently as he had come, he slipped away though the foliage toward the north.

The tribe was still loitering about the clearing where stood the hut that Tarzan and Bertha Kircher had built. Some were idly searching for food just within the forest's edge, while others squatted beneath the shade of trees within the clearing.

The girl had emerged from the hut, her tears dried and was gazing anxiously toward the south into the jungle where Tarzan had disappeared. Occasionally she cast suspicious glances in the direction of the huge shaggy anthropoids about her. How easy it would be for one of those great beasts to enter the boma and slay her. How helpless she was, even with the spear that the white man had left her, she realized as she noted for the thousandth time the massive shoulders, the bull necks, and the great muscles gliding so easily beneath the glossy coats. Never, she thought, had she seen such personifications of brute power as were represented by these mighty bulls. Those huge hands would snap her futile spear as she might snap a match in two, while their lightest blow could crush her into insensibility and death.

It was while she was occupied with these depressing thoughts that there dropped suddenly into the clearing from the trees upon the south the figure of a mighty young bull. At that time all of the apes looked much alike to Bertha Kircher, nor was it until some time later that she realized that each differed from the others in individual characteristics of face and figure as do individuals of the human races. Yet even then she could not help but note the wondrous strength and agility of this great beast, and as he approached she even found herself admiring the sheen of his heavy, black, silvershot coat.

It was evident that the newcomer was filled with suppressed excitement. His demeanor and bearing proclaimed this even from afar, nor was the girl the only one to note it. For as they saw him coming many of the apes arose and advanced to meet him, bristling and growling as is their way. Go-lat was among these latter, and he advanced stiffly with the hairs upon his neck and down his spine erect, uttering low growls and baring his fighting fangs, for who might say whether Zu-tag came in peace or otherwise? The old king had seen other young apes come thus in his day filled with a sudden resolution to wrest the kingship from their chief. He had seen bulls about to run amuck burst thus suddenly from the jungle upon the members of the tribe, and so Go-lat took no chances.

Had Zu-tag come indolently, feeding as he came, he might have entered the tribe without arousing notice or suspicion, but when one comes thus precipitately, evidently bursting with some emotion out of the ordinary, let all apes beware. There was a certain amount of preliminary circling, growling, and sniffing, stiff-legged and stiff-haired, before each side discovered that the other had no intention of initiating an attack and then Zu-tag told Go-lat what he had seen among the lairs of the Gomangani.

Go-lat grunted in disgust and turned away. "Let the white ape take care of himself," he said.

"He is a great ape," said Zu-tag. "He came to live in peace with the tribe of Go-lat. Let us save him from the Gomangani."

Go-lat grunted again and continued to move away.

"Zu-tag will go alone and get him," cried the young ape, "if Go-lat is afraid of the Gomangani."

The king ape wheeled in anger, growling loudly and beating upon his breast. "Go-lat is not afraid," he screamed, "but he will not go, for the white ape is not of his tribe. Go yourself and take the Tarmangani's she with you if you wish so much to save the white ape."

"Zu-tag will go," replied the younger bull, "and he will take the Tarmangani's she and all the bulls of Go-lat who are not cowards," and so saying he cast his eyes inquiringly about at the other apes. "Who will go with Zu-tag to fight the Gomangani and bring away our brother," he demanded.

Eight young bulls in the full prime of their vigor pressed forward to Zu-tag's side, but the old bulls with the conservatism and caution of many years upon their gray shoulders, shook their heads and waddled away after Go-lat.

"Good," cried Zu-tag. "We want no old shes to go with us to fight the Gomangani for that is work for the fighters of the tribe."

The old bulls paid no attention to his boastful words, but the eight who had volunteered to accompany him were filled with self-pride so that they stood around vaingloriously beating upon their breasts, baring their fangs and screaming their hideous challenge until the jungle reverberated to the horrid sound.

All this time Bertha Kircher was a wide-eyed and terrified spectator to what, as she thought, could end only in a terrific battle between these frightful beasts, and when Zu-tag and his followers began screaming forth their fearsome challenge, the girl found herself trembling in terror, for of all the sounds of the jungle there is none more awe inspiring than that of the great bull ape when he issues his challenge or shrieks forth his victory cry.

If she had been terrified before she was almost paralyzed with fear now as she saw Zu-tag and his apes turn toward the boma and approach her. With the agility of a cat Zu-tag leaped completely over the protecting wall and stood before her. Valiantly she held her spear before her, pointing it at his breast. He commenced to jabber and gesticulate, and even with her scant acquaintance with the ways of the anthropoids, she realized that he was not menacing her, for there was little or no baring of fighting fangs and his whole expression and attitude was of one attempting to explain a knotty problem or plead a worthy cause. At last he became evidently impatient, for with a sweep of one great paw he struck the spear from her hand and coming close, seized her by the arm, but not roughly. She shrank away in terror and yet some sense within her seemed to be trying to assure her that she was in no danger from this great beast. Zu-tag jabbered loudly, ever and again pointing into the jungle toward the south and moving toward the boma, pulling the girl with him. He seemed almost frantic in his efforts to explain something to her. He pointed toward the boma, herself, and then to the forest, and then, at last, as though by a sudden inspiration, he reached down and, seizing the spear, repeatedly touched it with his forefinger and again pointed toward the south. Suddenly it dawned upon the girl that what the ape was trying to explain to her was related in some way to the white man whose property they thought she was. Possibly her grim protector was in trouble and with this thought firmly established, she no longer held back, but started forward as though to accompany the young bull. At the point in the boma where Tarzan had blocked the entrance, she started to pull away the thorn bushes, and, when Zu-tag saw what she was doing, he fell to and assisted her so that presently they had an opening through the boma through which she passed with the great ape.

Immediately Zu-tag and his eight apes started off rapidly toward the jungle, so rapidly that Bertha Kircher would have had to run at top speed to keep up with them. This she realized she could not do, and so she was forced to lag behind, much to the chagrin of Zu-tag, who constantly kept running back and urging her to greater speed. Once he took her by the arm and tried to draw her along. Her protests were of no avail since the beast could not know that they were protests, nor did he desist until she caught her foot in some tangled grass and fell to the ground. Then indeed was Zu-tag furious and growled hideously. His apes were waiting at the edge of the forest for him to lead them. He suddenly realized that this poor weak she could not keep up with them and that if they traveled at her slow rate they might be too late to render assistance to the Tarmangani, and so without more ado, the giant anthropoid picked Bertha Kircher bodily from the ground and swung her to his back. Her arms were about his neck and in this position he seized her wrists in one great paw so that she could not fall off and started at a rapid rate to join his companions.

Dressed as she was in riding breeches with no entangling skirts to hinder or catch upon passing shrubbery, she soon found that she could cling tightly to the back of the mighty bull and when a moment later he took to the lower branches of the trees, she closed her eyes and clung to him in terror lest she be precipitated to the ground below.

That journey through the primeval forest with the nine great apes will live in the memory of Bertha Kircher for the balance of her life, as clearly delineated as at the moment of its enactment.

The first overwhelming wave of fear having passed, she was at last able to open her eyes and view her surroundings with increased interest and presently the sensation of terror slowly left her to be replaced by one of comparative security when she saw the ease and surety with which these great beasts traveled through the trees; and later her admiration for the young bull increased as it became evident that even burdened with her additional weight, he moved more rapidly and with no greater signs of fatigue than his unburdened fellows.

Not once did Zu-tag pause until he came to a stop among the branches of a tree no great distance from the native village. They could hear the noises of the life within the palisade, the laughing and shouting of the Negroes, and the barking of dogs, and through the foliage the girl caught glimpses of the village from which she had so recently escaped. She shuddered to think of the possibility of having to return to it and of possible recapture, and she wondered why Zu-tag had brought her here.

Now the apes advanced slowly once more and with great caution, moving as noiselessly through the trees as the squirrels themselves until they had reached a point where they could easily overlook the palisade and the village street below.

Zu-tag squatted upon a great branch close to the bole of the tree and by loosening the girl's arms from about his neck, indicated that she was to find a footing for herself and when she had done so, he turned toward her and pointed repeatedly at the open doorway of a hut upon the opposite side of the street below them. By various gestures he seemed to be trying to explain something to her and at last she caught at the germ of his idea—that her white man was a prisoner there.

Beneath them was the roof of a hut onto which she saw that she could easily drop, but what she could do after she had entered the village was beyond her.

Darkness was already falling and the fires beneath the cooking pots had been lighted. The girl saw the stake in the village street and the piles of fagots about it and in terror she suddenly realized the portent of these grisly preparations. Oh, if she but only had some sort of a weapon that might give her even a faint hope, some slight advantage against the blacks. Then she would not hesitate to venture into the village in an attempt to save the man who had upon three different occasions saved her. She knew that he hated her and yet strong within her breast burned the sense of her obligation to him. She could not fathom him. Never in her life had she seen a man at once so paradoxical and dependable. In many of his ways he was more savage than the beasts with which he associated and yet, on the other hand, he was as chivalrous as a knight of old. For several days she had been lost with him in the jungle absolutely at his mercy, yet she had come to trust so implicitly in his honor that any fear she had had of him was rapidly disappearing.

On the other hand, that he might be hideously cruel was evidenced to her by the fact that he was planning to leave her alone in the midst of the frightful dangers which menaced her by night and by day.

Zu-tag was evidently waiting for darkness to fall before carrying out whatever plans had matured in his savage little brain, for he and his fellows sat quietly in the tree about her, watching the preparations of the blacks. Presently it became apparent that some altercation had arisen among the Negroes, for a score or more of them were gathered around one who appeared to be their chief, and all were talking and gesticulating heatedly. The argument lasted for some five or ten minutes when suddenly the little knot broke and two warriors ran to the opposite side of the village from whence they presently returned with a large stake which they soon set up beside the one already in place. The girl wondered what the purpose of the second stake might be, nor did she have long to wait for an explanation.

It was quite dark by this time, the village being lighted by the fitful glare of many fires, and now she saw a number of warriors approach and enter the hut Zu-tag had been watching. A moment later they reappeared, dragging between them two captives, one of whom the girl immediately recognized as her protector and the other as an Englishman in the uniform of an aviator. This, then, was the reason for the two stakes.

Arising quickly she placed a hand upon Zu-tag's shoulder and pointed down into the village. "Come," she said, as if she had been talking to one of her own kind, and with the word she swung lightly to the roof of the hut below. From there to the ground was but a short drop and a moment later she was circling the hut upon the side farthest from the fires, keeping in the dense shadows where there was little likelihood of being discovered. She turned once to see that Zu-tag was directly behind her and could see his huge bulk looming up in the dark, while beyond was another one of his eight. Doubtless they had all followed her and this fact gave her a greater sense of security and hope than she had before experienced.

Pausing beside the hut next to the street, she peered cautiously about the corner. A few inches from her was the open doorway of the structure, and beyond, farther down the village street, the blacks were congregating about the prisoners, who were already being bound to the stakes. All eyes were centered upon the victims, and there was only the remotest chance that she and her companions would be discovered until they were close upon the blacks. She wished, however, that she might have some sort of a weapon with which to lead the attack, for she could not know, of course, for a certainty whether the great apes would follow her or not. Hoping that she might find something within the hut, she slipped quickly around the corner and into the doorway and after her, one by one, came the nine bulls. Searching quickly about the interior, she presently discovered a spear, and, armed with this, she again approached the entrance.

Tarzan of the Apes and Lieutenant Harold Percy SmithOldwick were bound securely to their respective stakes. Neither had spoken for some time. The Englishman turned his head so that he could see his companion in misery. Tarzan stood straight against his stake. His face was entirely expressionless in so far as either fear or anger were concerned. His countenance portrayed bored indifference though both men knew that they were about to be tortured.

"Good-bye, old top," whispered the young lieutenant.

Tarzan turned his eyes in the direction of the other and smiled. "Good-bye," he said. "If you want to get it over in a hurry, inhale the smoke and flames as rapidly as you can."

"Thanks," replied the aviator and though he made a wry face, he drew himself up very straight and squared his shoulders.

The women and children had seated themselves in a wide circle about the victims while the warriors, hideously painted, were forming slowly to commence the dance of death. Again Tarzan turned to his companion. "If you'd like to spoil their fun," he said, "don't make any fuss no matter how much you suffer. If you can carry on to the end without changing the expression upon your face or uttering a single word, you will deprive them of all the pleasures of this part of the entertainment. Good-bye again and good luck."

The young Englishman made no reply but it was evident from the set of his jaws that the Negroes would get little enjoyment out of him.

The warriors were circling now. Presently Numabo would draw first blood with his sharp spear which would be the signal for the beginning of the torture after a little of which the fagots would be lighted around the feet of the victims.

Closer and closer danced the hideous chief, his yellow, sharp-filed teeth showing in the firelight between his thick, red lips. Now bending double, now stamping furiously upon the ground, now leaping into the air, he danced step by step in the narrowing circle that would presently bring him within spear reach of the intended feast.

At last the spear reached out and touched the ape-man on the breast and when it came away, a little trickle of blood ran down the smooth, brown hide and almost simultaneously there broke from the outer periphery of the expectant audience a woman's shriek which seemed a signal for a series of hideous screamings, growlings and barkings, and a great commotion upon that side of the circle. The victims could not see the cause of the disturbance, but Tarzan did not have to see, for he knew by the voices of the apes the identity of the disturbers. He only wondered what had brought them and what the purpose of the attack, for he could not believe that they had come to rescue him.

Numabo and his warriors broke quickly from the circle of their dance to see pushing toward them through the ranks of their screaming and terrified people the very white girl who had escaped them a few nights before, and at her back what appeared to their surprised eyes a veritable horde of the huge and hairy forest men upon whom they looked with considerable fear and awe.

Striking to right and left with his heavy fists, tearing with his great fangs, came Zu-tag, the young bull, while at his heels, emulating his example, surged his hideous apes. Quickly they came through the old men and the women and children, for straight toward Numabo and his warriors the girl led them. It was then that they came within range of Tarzan's vision and he saw with unmixed surprise who it was that led the apes to his rescue.

To Zu-tag he shouted: "Go for the big bulls while the she unbinds me," and to Bertha Kircher: "Quick! Cut these bonds. The apes will take care of the blacks."

Turning from her advance the girl ran to his side. She had no knife and the bonds were tied tightly but she worked quickly and cooly and as Zu-tag and his apes closed with the warriors, she succeeded in loosening Tarzan's bonds sufficiently to permit him to extricate his own hands so that in another minute he had freed himself.

"Now unbind the Englishman," he cried, and, leaping forward, ran to join Zu-tag and his fellows in their battle against the blacks. Numabo and his warriors, realizing now the relatively small numbers of the apes against them, had made a determined stand and with spears and other weapons were endeavoring to overcome the invaders. Three of the apes were already down, killed or mortally wounded, when Tarzan, realizing that the battle must eventually go against the apes unless some means could be found to break the morale of the Negroes, cast about him for some means of bringing about the desired end. And suddenly his eye lighted upon a number of weapons which he knew would accomplish the result. A grim smile touched his lips as he snatched a vessel of boiling water from one of the fires and hurled it full in the faces of the warriors. Screaming with terror and pain they fell back though Numabo urged them to rush forward.

Scarcely had the first cauldron of boiling water spilled its contents upon them ere Tarzan deluged them with a second, nor was there any third needed to send them shrieking in every direction to the security of their huts.

By the time Tarzan had recovered his own weapons the girl had released the young Englishman, and, with the six remaining apes, the three Europeans moved slowly toward the village gate, the aviator arming himself with a spear discarded by one of the scalded warriors, as they eagerly advanced toward the outer darkness.

Numabo was unable to rally the now thoroughly terrified and painfully burned warriors so that rescued and rescuers passed out of the village into the blackness of the jungle without further interference.

Tarzan strode through the jungle in silence. Beside him walked Zu-tag, the great ape, and behind them strung the surviving anthropoids followed by Fraulein Bertha Kircher and Lieutenant Harold Percy Smith-Oldwick, the latter a thoroughly astonished and mystified Englishman.

In all his life Tarzan of the Apes had been obliged to acknowledge but few obligations. He won his way through his savage world by the might of his own muscle, the superior keenness of his five senses and his God-given power to reason. Tonight the greatest of all obligations had been placed upon him—his life had been saved by another and Tarzan shook his head and growled, for it had been saved by one whom he hated above all others.

FINDING THE AIRPLANE

Tarzan of the Apes, returning from a successful hunt, with the body of Bara, the deer, across one sleek, brown shoulder, paused in the branches of a great tree at the edge of a clearing and gazed ruefully at two figures walking from the river to the boma-encircled hut a short distance away.

The ape-man shook his tousled head and sighed. His eyes wandered toward the west and his thoughts to the far-away cabin by the land-locked harbor of the great water that washed the beach of his boyhood home—to the cabin of his long-dead father to which the memories and treasures of a happy childhood lured him. Since the loss of his mate, a great longing had possessed him to return to the haunts of his youth—to the untracked jungle wilderness where he had lived the life he loved best long before man had invaded the precincts of his wild stamping grounds. There he hoped in a renewal of the old life under the old conditions to win surcease from sorrow and perhaps some measure of forgetfulness.

But the little cabin and the land-locked harbor were many long, weary marches away, and he was handicapped by the duty which he felt he owed to the two figures walking in the clearing before him. One was a young man in a worn and ragged uniform of the British Royal Air Forces, the other, a young woman in the even more disreputable remnants of what once had been trim riding togs.

A freak of fate had thrown these three radically different types together. One was a savage, almost naked beast-man, one an English army officer, and the woman, she whom the ape-man knew and hated as a German spy.

How he was to get rid of them Tarzan could not imagine unless he accompanied them upon the weary march back to the east coast, a march that would necessitate his once more retracing the long, weary way he already had covered towards his goal, yet what else could be done? These two had neither the strength, endurance, nor jungle-craft to accompany him through the unknown country to the west, nor did he wish them with him. The man he might have tolerated, but he could not even consider the presence of the girl in the far-off cabin, which had in a way become sacred to him through its memories, without a growl or anger rising to his lips. There remained, then, but the one way, since he could not desert them. He must move by slow and irksome marches back to the east coast, or at least to the first white settlement in that direction.

He had, it is true, contemplated leaving the girl to her fate but that was before she had been instrumental in saving him from torture and death at the hands of the black Wamabos. He chafed under the obligation she had put upon him, but no less did he acknowledge it and as he watched the two, the rueful expression upon his face was lightened by a smile as he thought of the helplessness of them. What a puny thing, indeed, was man! How ill equipped to combat the savage forces of nature and of nature's jungle. Why, even the tiny balu of the tribe of Go-lat, the great ape, was better fitted to survive than these, for a balu could at least escape the numerous creatures that menaced its existence, while with the possible exception of Kota, the tortoise, none moved so slowly as did helpless and feeble man.

Without him these two doubtless would starve in the midst of plenty, should they by some miracle escape the other forces of destruction which constantly threatened them. That morning Tarzan had brought them fruit, nuts, and plantain, and now he was bringing them the flesh of his kill, while the best that they might do was to fetch water from the river. Even now, as they walked across the clearing toward the boma, they were in utter ignorance of the presence of Tarzan near them. They did not know that his sharp eyes were watching them, nor that other eyes less friendly were glaring at them from a clump of bushes close beside the boma entrance. They did not know these things, but Tarzan did. No more than they could he see the creature crouching in the concealment of the foliage, yet he knew that it was there and what it was and what its intentions, precisely as well as though it had been lying in the open.

A slight movement of the leaves at the top of a single stem had apprised him of the presence of a creature there, for the movement was not that imparted by the wind. It came from pressure at the bottom of the stem which communicates a different movement to the leaves than does the wind passing among them, as anyone who has lived his lifetime in the jungle well knows, and the same wind that passed through the foliage of the bush brought to the ape-man's sensitive nostrils indisputable evidence of the fact that Sheeta, the panther, waited there for the two returning from the river.

They had covered half the distance to the boma entrance when Tarzan called to them to stop. They looked in surprise in the direction from which his voice had come to see him drop lightly to the ground and advance toward them.

"Come slowly toward me," he called to them. "Do not run for if you run Sheeta will charge."

They did as he bid, their faces filled with questioning wonderment.

"What do you mean?" asked the young Englishman. "Who is Sheeta?" but for answer the ape-man suddenly hurled the carcass of Bara, the deer, to the ground and leaped quickly toward them, his eyes upon something in their rear; and then it was that the two turned and learned the identity of Sheeta, for behind them was a devil-faced cat charging rapidly toward them.

Sheeta with rising anger and suspicion had seen the ape-man leap from the tree and approach the quarry. His life's experiences backed by instinct told him that the Tarmangani was about to rob him of his prey and as Sheeta was hungry, he had no intention of being thus easily deprived of the flesh he already considered his own.

The girl stifled an involuntary scream as she saw the proximity of the fanged fury bearing down upon them. She shrank close to the man and clung to him and all unarmed and defenseless as he was, the Englishman pushed her behind him and shielding her with his body, stood squarely in the face of the panther's charge. Tarzan noted the act, and though accustomed as he was to acts of courage, he experienced a thrill from the hopeless and futile bravery of the man.

The charging panther moved rapidly, and the distance which separated the bush in which he had concealed himself from the objects of his desire was not great. In the time that one might understandingly read a dozen words the strong-limbed cat could have covered the entire distance and made his kill, yet if Sheeta was quick, quick too was Tarzan. The English lieutenant saw the ape-man flash by him like the wind. He saw the great cat veer in his charge as though to elude the naked savage rushing to meet him, as it was evidently Sheeta's intention to make good his kill before attempting to protect it from Tarzan.

Lieutenant Smith-Oldwick saw these things and then with increasing wonder he saw the ape-man swerve, too, and leap for the spotted cat as a football player leaps for a runner. He saw the strong, brown arms encircling the body of the carnivore, the left arm in front of the beast's left shoulder and the right arm behind his right foreleg, and with the impact the two together rolling over and over upon the turf. He heard the snarls and growls of bestial combat, and it was with a feeling of no little horror that he realized that the sounds coming from the human throat of the battling man could scarce be distinguished from those of the panther.

The first momentary shock of terror over, the girl released her grasp upon the Englishman's arm. "Cannot we do something?" she asked. "Cannot we help him before the beast kills him?"

The Englishman looked upon the ground for some missile with which to attack the panther and then the girl uttered an exclamation and started at a run toward the hut. "Wait there," she called over her shoulder. "I will fetch the spear that he left me."

Smith-Oldwick saw the raking talons of the panther searching for the flesh of the man and the man on his part straining every muscle and using every artifice to keep his body out of range of them. The muscles of his arms knotted under the brown hide. The veins stood out upon his neck and forehead as with ever-increasing power he strove to crush the life from the great cat. The ape-man's teeth were fastened in the back of Sheeta's neck and now he succeeded in encircling the beast's torso with his legs which he crossed and locked beneath the cat's belly. Leaping and snarling, Sheeta sought to dislodge the ape-man's hold upon him. He hurled himself upon the ground and rolled over and over. He reared upon his hind legs and threw himself backwards but always the savage creature upon his back clung tenaciously to him, and always the mighty brown arms crushed tighter and tighter about his chest.

And then the girl, panting from her quick run, returned with the short spear Tarzan had left her as her sole weapon of protection. She did not wait to hand it to the Englishman who ran forward to receive it, but brushed past him and leaped into close quarters beside the growling, tumbling mass of yellow fur and smooth brown hide. Several times she attempted to press the point home into the cat's body, but on both occasions the fear of endangering the ape-man caused her to desist, but at last the two lay motionless for a moment as the carnivore sought a moment's rest from the strenuous exertions of battle, and then it was that Bertha Kircher pressed the point of the spear to the tawny side and drove it deep into the savage heart.

Tarzan rose from the dead body of Sheeta and shook himself after the manner of beasts that are entirely clothed with hair. Like many other of his traits and mannerisms this was the result of environment rather than heredity or reversion, and even though he was outwardly a man, the Englishman and the girl were both impressed with the naturalness of the act. It was as though Numa, emerging from a fight, had shaken himself to straighten his rumpled mane and coat, and yet, too, there was something uncanny about it as there had been when the savage growls and hideous snarls issued from those clean-cut lips.

Tarzan looked at the girl, a quizzical expression upon his face. Again had she placed him under obligations to her, and Tarzan of the Apes did not wish to be obligated to a German spy; yet in his honest heart he could not but admit a certain admiration for her courage, a trait which always greatly impressed the ape-man, he himself the personification of courage.

"Here is the kill," he said, picking the carcass of Bara from the ground. "You will want to cook your portion, I presume, but Tarzan does not spoil his meat with fire."

They followed him to the boma where he cut several pieces of meat from the carcass for them, retaining a joint for himself. The young lieutenant prepared a fire, and the girl presided over the primitive culinary rights of their simple meal. As she worked some little way apart from them, the lieutenant and the ape-man watched her.

"She is wonderful. Is she not?" murmured Smith-Oldwick.

"She is a German and a spy," replied Tarzan.

The Englishman turned quickly upon him. "What do you mean?" he cried.

"I mean what I say," replied the ape-man. "She is a German and a spy."

"I do not believe it!" exclaimed the aviator.

"You do not have to," Tarzan assured him. "It is nothing to me what you believe. I saw her in conference with the Boche general and his staff at the camp near Taveta. They all knew her and called her by name and she handed him a paper. The next time I saw her she was inside the British lines in disguise, and again I saw her bearing word to a German officer at Wilhelmstal. She is a German and a spy, but she is a woman and therefore I cannot destroy her."

"You really believe that what you say is true?" asked the young lieutenant. "My God! I cannot believe it. She is so sweet and brave and good."

The ape-man shrugged his shoulders. "She is brave," he said, "but even Pamba, the rat, must have some good quality, but she is what I have told you and therefore I hate her and you should hate her."

Lieutenant Harold Percy Smith-Oldwick buried his face in his hands. "God forgive me," he said at last. "I cannot hate her."

The ape-man cast a contemptuous look at his companion and arose. "Tarzan goes again to hunt," he said. "You have enough food for two days. By that time he will return."

The two watched him until he had disappeared in the foliage of the trees at the further side of the clearing.

When he had gone the girl felt a vague sense of apprehension that she never experienced when Tarzan was present. The invisible menaces lurking in the grim jungle seemed more real and much more imminent now that the ape-man was no longer near. While he had been there talking with them, the little thatched hut and its surrounding thorn boma had seemed as safe a place as the world might afford. She wished that he had remained—two days seemed an eternity in contemplation-two days of constant fear, two days, every moment of which would be fraught with danger. She turned toward her companion.

"I wish that he had remained," she said. "I always feel so much safer when he is near. He is very grim and very terrible, and yet I feel safer with him than with any man I ever have known. He seems to dislike me and yet I know that he would let no harm befall me. I cannot understand him."

"Neither do I understand him," replied the Englishman; "but I know this much—our presence here is interfering with his plans. He would like to be rid of us, and I half imagine that he rather hopes to find when he returns that we have succumbed to one of the dangers which must always confront us in this savage land.

"I think that we should try to return to the white settlements. This man does not want us here, nor is it reasonable to assume that we could long survive in such a savage wilderness. I have traveled and hunted in several parts of Africa, but never have I seen or heard of any single locality so overrun with savage beasts and dangerous natives. If we set out for the east coast at once we would be in but little more danger than we are here, and if we could survive a day's march, I believe that we will find the means of reaching the coast in a few hours, for my plane must still be in the same place that I landed just before the blacks captured me. Of course there is no one here who could operate it nor is there any reason why they should have destroyed it. As a matter of fact, the natives would be so fearful and suspicious of so strange and incomprehensible a thing that the chances are they would not dare approach it. Yes, it must be where I left it and all ready to carry us safely to the settlements."

"But we cannot leave," said the girl, "until he returns. We could not go away like that without thanking him or bidding him farewell. We are under too great obligations to him."

The man looked at her in silence for a moment. He wondered if she knew how Tarzan felt toward her and then he himself began to speculate upon the truth of the ape-man's charges. The longer he looked at the girl, the less easy was it to entertain the thought that she was an enemy spy. He was upon the point of asking her point-blank but he could not bring himself to do so, finally determining to wait until time and longer acquaintance should reveal the truth or falsity of the accusation.

"I believe," he said as though there had been no pause in their conversation, "that the man would be more than glad to find us gone when he returns. It is not necessary to jeopardize our lives for two more days in order that we may thank him, however much we may appreciate his services to us. You have more than balanced your obligations to him and from what he told me I feel that you especially should not remain here longer."

The girl looked up at him in astonishment. "What do you mean?" she asked.

"I do not like to tell," said the Englishman, digging nervously at the turf with the point of a stick, "but you have my word that he would rather you were not here."

"Tell me what he said," she insisted, "I have a right to know."

Lieutenant Smith-Oldwick squared his shoulders and raised his eyes to those of the girl. "He said that he hated you," he blurted. "He has only aided you at all from a sense of duty because you are a woman."

The girl paled and then flushed. "I will be ready to go," she said, "in just a moment. We had better take some of this meat with us. There is no telling when we will be able to get more."

And so the two set out down the river toward the south. The man carried the short spear that Tarzan had left with the girl, while she was entirely unarmed except for a stick she had picked up from among those left after the building of the hut. Before departing she had insisted that the man leave a note for Tarzan thanking him for his care of them and bidding him goodbye. This they left pinned to the inside wall of the hut with a little sliver of wood.

It was necessary that they be constantly on the alert since they never knew what might confront them at the next turn of the winding jungle trail or what might lie concealed in the tangled bushes at either side. There was also the ever-present danger of meeting some of Numabo's black warriors and as the village lay directly in their line of march, there was the necessity for making a wide detour before they reached it in order to pass around it without being discovered.

"I am not so much afraid of the native blacks," said the girl, "as I am of Usanga and his people. He and his men were all attached to a German native regiment. They brought me along with them when they deserted, either with the intention of holding me ransom or selling me into the harem of one of the black sultans of the north. Usanga is much more to be feared than Numabo for he has had the advantage of European military training and is armed with more or less modern weapons and ammunition."

"It is lucky for me," remarked the Englishman, "that it was the ignorant Numabo who discovered and captured me rather than the worldly wise Usanga. He would have felt less fear of the giant flying machine and would have known only too well how to wreck it."

"Let us pray that the black sergeant has not discovered it," said the girl.

They made their way to a point which they guessed was about a mile above the village, then they turned into the trackless tangle of undergrowth to the east. So dense was the verdure at many points that it was with the utmost difficulty they wormed their way through, sometimes on hands and knees and again by clambering over numerous fallen tree trunks. Interwoven with dead limbs and living branches were the tough and ropelike creepers which formed a tangled network across their path.

South of them in an open meadowland a number of black warriors were gathered about an object which elicited much wondering comment. The blacks were clothed in fragments of what had once been uniforms of a native German command. They were a most unlovely band and chief among them in authority and repulsiveness was the black sergeant Usanga. The object of their interest was a British aeroplane.

Immediately after the Englishman had been brought to Numabo's village Usanga had gone out in search of the plane, prompted partially by curiosity and partially by an intention to destroy it, but when he had found it, some new thought had deterred him from carrying out his design. The thing represented considerable value as he well knew and it had occurred to him that in some way he might turn his prize to profit. Every day he had returned to it, and while at first it had filled him with considerable awe, he eventually came to look upon it with the accustomed eye of a proprietor, so that he now clambered into the fuselage and even advanced so far as to wish that he might learn to operate it.

What a feat it would be indeed to fly like a bird far above the highest tree top! How it would fill his less favored companions with awe and admiration! If Usanga could but fly, so great would be the respect of all the tribesmen throughout the scattered villages of the great interior, they would look upon him as little less than a god.

Usanga rubbed his palms together and smacked his thick lips. Then indeed, would he be very rich, for all the villages would pay tribute to him and he could even have as many as a dozen wives. With that thought, however, came a mental picture of Naratu, the black termagant, who ruled him with an iron hand. Usanga made a wry face and tried to forget the extra dozen wives, but the lure of the idea remained and appealed so strongly to him that he presently found himself reasoning most logically that a god would not be much of a god with less than twenty-four wives.

He fingered the instruments and the control, half hoping and half fearing that he would alight upon the combination that would put the machine in flight. Often had he watched the British air-men soaring above the German lines and it looked so simple he was quite sure that he could do it himself if there was somebody who could but once show him how. There was, of course, always the hope that the white man who came in the machine and who had escaped from Numabo's village might fall into Usanga's hands and then indeed would he be able to learn how to fly. It was in this hope that Usanga spent so much time in the vicinity of the plane, reasoning as he did that eventually the white man would return in search of it.

And at last he was rewarded, for upon this very day after he had quit the machine and entered the jungle with his warriors, he heard voices to the north and when he and his men had hidden in the dense foliage upon either side of the trail, Usanga was presently filled with elation by the appearance of the British officer and the white girl whom the black sergeant had coveted and who had escaped him.

The Negro could scarce restrain a shout of elation, for he had not hoped that fate would be so kind as to throw these two whom he most desired into his power at the same time.

As the two came down the trail all unconscious of impending danger, the man was explaining that they must be very close to the point at which the plane had landed. Their entire attention was centered on the trail directly ahead of them, as they momentarily expected it to break into the meadowland where they were sure they would see the plane that would spell life and liberty for them.

The trail was broad, and they were walking side by side so that at a sharp turn the park-like clearing was revealed to them simultaneously with the outlines of the machine they sought.

Exclamations of relief and delight broke from their lips, and at the same instant Usanga and his black warriors rose from the bushes all about them.

THE BLACK FLIER

The girl was almost crushed by terror and disappointment. To have been thus close to safety and then to have all hope snatched away by a cruel stroke of fate seemed unendurable. The man was disappointed, too, but more was he angry. He noted the remnants of the uniforms upon the blacks and immediately he demanded to know where were their officers.

"They cannot understand you," said the girl and so in the bastard tongue that is the medium of communication between the Germans and the blacks of their colony, she repeated the white man's question.

Usanga grinned. "You know where they are, white woman," he replied. "They are dead, and if this white man does not do as I tell him, he, too, will be dead."

"What do you want of him?" asked the girl.

"I want him to teach me how to fly like a bird," replied Usanga.

Bertha Kircher looked her astonishment, but repeated the demand to the lieutenant.

The Englishman meditated for a moment. "He wants to learn to fly, does he?" he repeated. "Ask him if he will give us our freedom if I teach him to fly."

The girl put the question to Usanga, who, degraded, cunning, and entirely unprincipled, was always perfectly willing to promise anything whether he had any intentions of fulfilling his promises or not, and so immediately assented to the proposition.

716

"Let the white man teach me to fly," he said, "and I will take you back close to the settlements of your people, but in return for this I shall keep the great bird," and he waved a black hand in the direction of the aeroplane.

When Bertha Kircher had repeated Usanga's proposition to the aviator, the latter shrugged his shoulders and with a wry face finally agreed. "I fancy there is no other way out of it," he said. "In any event the plane is lost to the British government. If I refuse the black scoundrel's request, there is no doubt but what he will make short work of me with the result that the machine will lie here until it rots. If I accept his offer it will at least be the means of assuring your safe return to civilization and that" he added, "is worth more to me than all the planes in the British Air Service."

The girl cast a quick glance at him. These were the first words he had addressed to her that might indicate that his sentiments toward her were more than those of a companion in distress. She regretted that he had spoken as he had and he, too, regretted it almost instantly as he saw the shadow cross her face and realized that he had unwittingly added to the difficulties of her already almost unbearable situation.

"Forgive me," he said quickly. "Please forget what that remark implied. I promise you that I will not offend again, if it does offend you, until after we are both safely out of this mess."

She smiled and thanked him, but the thing had been said and could never be unsaid, and Bertha Kircher knew even more surely than as though he had fallen upon his knees and protested undying devotion that the young English officer loved her.

Usanga was for taking his first lesson in aviation immediately. The Englishman attempted to dissuade him, but immediately the black became threatening and abusive, since, like all those who are ignorant, he was suspicious that the intentions of others were always ulterior unless they perfectly coincided with his wishes.

"All right, old top," muttered the Englishman, "I will give you the lesson of your life," and then turning to the girl: "Persuade him to let you accompany us. I shall be afraid to leave you here with these devilish scoundrels." But when she put the suggestion to Usanga the black immediately suspected some plan to thwart him—possibly to carry him against his will back to the German masters he had traitorously deserted, and glowering at her savagely, he obstinately refused to entertain the suggestion.

"The white woman will remain here with my people," he said. "They will not harm her unless you fail to bring me back safely."

"Tell him," said the Englishman, "that if you are not standing in plain sight in this meadow when I return, I will not land, but will carry Usanga back to the British camp and have him hanged."

Usanga promised that the girl would be in evidence upon their return, and took immediate steps to impress upon his warriors that under penalty of death they must not harm her. Then, followed by the other members of his party, he crossed the clearing toward the plane with the Englishman. Once seated within what he already considered his new possession, the black's courage began to wane and when the motor was started and the great propeller commenced to whir, he screamed to the Englishman to stop the thing and permit him to alight, but the aviator could neither hear nor understand the black above the noise of the propeller and exhaust. By this time the plane was moving along the ground and even then Usanga was upon the verge of leaping out, and would have done so had he been able to unfasten the strap from about his waist. Then the plane rose from the ground and in a moment soared gracefully in a wide circle until it topped the trees. The black sergeant was in a veritable collapse of terror. He saw the earth dropping rapidly from beneath him. He saw the trees and river and at a distance the little clearing with the thatched huts of Numabo's village. He tried hard not to think of the results of a sudden fall to the rapidly receding ground below. He attempted to concentrate his mind upon the twenty-four wives which this great bird most assuredly would permit him to command. Higher and higher rose the plane, swinging in a wide circle above the forest, river, and meadowland and presently, much to his surprise, Usanga discovered that his terror was rapidly waning, so that it was not long before there was forced upon him a consciousness of utter security, and then it was that he began to take notice of the manner in which the white man guided and manipulated the plane.

After half an hour of skillful maneuvering, the Englishman rose rapidly to a considerable altitude, and then, suddenly, without warning, he looped and flew with the plane inverted for a few seconds.

"I said I'd give this beggar the lesson of his life," he murmured as he heard, even above the whir of the propeller, the shriek of the terrified Negro. A moment later Smith-Oldwick had righted the machine and was dropping rapidly toward the earth. He circled slowly a few times above the meadow until he had assured himself that Bertha Kircher was there and apparently unharmed, then he dropped gently to the ground so that the machine came to a stop a short distance from where the girl and the warriors awaited them.

It was a trembling and ashen-hued Usanga who tumbled out of the fuselage, for his nerves were still on edge as a result of the harrowing experience of the loop, yet with terra firma once more under foot, he quickly regained his composure. Strutting about with great show and braggadocio, he strove to impress his followers with the mere nothingness of so trivial a feat as flying birdlike thousands of yards above the jungle, though it was long until he had thoroughly convinced himself by the force of autosuggestion that he had enjoyed every instant of the flight and was already far advanced in the art of aviation.

So jealous was the black of his new-found toy that he would not return to the village of Numabo, but insisted on making camp close beside the plane, lest in some inconceivable fashion it should be stolen from him. For two days they camped there, and constantly during daylight hours Usanga compelled the Englishman to instruct him in the art of flying.

Smith-Oldwick, in recalling the long months of arduous training he had undergone himself before he had been considered sufficiently adept to be considered a finished flier, smiled at the conceit of the ignorant African who was already demanding that he be permitted to make a flight alone.

"If it was not for losing the machine," the Englishman explained to the girl, "I'd let the bounder take it up and break his fool neck as he would do inside of two minutes."

However, he finally persuaded Usanga to bide his time for a few more days of instruction, but in the suspicious mind of the Negro there was a growing conviction that the white man's advice was prompted by some ulterior motive; that it was in the hope of escaping with the machine himself by night that he refused to admit that Usanga was entirely capable of handling it alone and therefore in no further need of help or instruction, and so in the mind of the black there formed a determination to outwit the white man. The lure of the twenty-four seductive wives proved in itself a sufficient incentive and there, too, was added his desire for the white girl whom he had long since determined to possess.

It was with these thoughts in mind that Usanga lay down to sleep in the evening of the second day. Constantly, however, the thought of Naratu and her temper arose to take the keen edge from his pleasant imaginings. If he could but rid himself of her! The thought having taken form persisted, but always it was more than outweighed by the fact that the black sergeant was actually afraid of his woman, so much afraid of her in fact that he would not have dared to attempt to put her out of the way unless he could do so secretly while she slept. However, as one plan after another was conjured by the strength of his desires, he at last hit upon one which came to him almost with the force of a blow and brought him sitting upright among his sleeping companions.

When morning dawned Usanga could scarce wait for an opportunity to put his scheme into execution, and the moment that he had eaten, he called several of his warriors aside and talked with them for some moments.

The Englishman, who usually kept an eye upon his black captor, saw now that the latter was explaining something in detail to his warriors, and from his gestures and his manner it was apparent that he was persuading them to some new plan as well as giving them instructions as to what they were to do. Several times, too, he saw the eyes of the Negroes turned upon him and once they flashed simultaneously toward the white girl.

Everything about the occurrence, which in itself seemed trivial enough, aroused in the mind of the Englishman a well-defined apprehension that something was afoot that boded ill for him and for the girl. He could not free himself of the idea and so he kept a still closer watch over the black although, as he was forced to admit to himself, he was quite powerless to avert any fate that lay in store for them. Even the spear that he had had when captured had been taken away from him, so that now he was unarmed and absolutely at the mercy of the black sergeant and his followers.

Lieutenant Harold Percy Smith-Oldwick did not have long to wait before discovering something of Usanga's plan, for almost immediately after the sergeant finished giving his instructions, a number of warriors approached the Englishman, while three went directly to the girl.

Without a word of explanation the warriors seized the young officer and threw him to the ground upon his face. For a moment he struggled to free himself and succeeded in landing a few heavy blows among his assailants, but he was too greatly outnumbered to hope to more than delay them in the accomplishment of their object which he soon discovered was to bind him securely hand and foot. When they had finally secured him to their satisfaction, they rolled him over on his side and then it was he saw Bertha Kircher had been similarly trussed.

Smith-Oldwick lay in such a position that he could see nearly the entire expanse of meadow and the aeroplane a short distance away. Usanga was talking to the girl who was shaking her head in vehement negatives.

"What is he saying?" called the Englishman.

"He is going to take me away in the plane," the girl called back. "He is going to take me farther inland to another country where he says that he will be king and I am to be one of his wives," and then to the Englishman's surprise she turned a smiling face toward him, "but there is no danger," she continued, "for we shall both be dead within a few minutes—just give him time enough to get the machine under way, and if he can rise a hundred feet from the ground I shall never need fear him more."

"God!" cried the man. "Is there no way that you can dissuade him? Promise him anything. Anything that you want. I have money, more money than that poor fool could imagine there was in the whole world. With it he can buy anything that money will purchase, fine clothes and food and women, all the women he wants. Tell him this and tell him that if he will spare you I give him my word that I will fetch it all to him."

The girl shook her head. "It is useless," she said. "He would not understand and if he did understand, he would not trust you. The blacks are so unprincipled themselves that they can imagine no such thing as principle or honor in others, and especially do these blacks distrust an Englishman whom the Germans have taught them to believe are the most treacherous and degraded of people. No, it is better thus. I am sorry that you cannot go with us, for if he goes high enough my death will be much easier than that which probably awaits you."

Usanga had been continually interrupting their brief conversation in an attempt to compel the girl to translate it to him, for he feared that they were concocting some plan to thwart him, and to quiet and appease him, she told him that the Englishman was merely bidding her farewell and wishing her good luck. Suddenly she turned to the black. "Will you do something for me?" she asked. "If I go willingly with you?"

"What is it you want?" he inquired.

"Tell your men to free the white man after we are gone. He can never catch us. That is all I ask of you. If you will grant him his freedom and his life, I will go willingly with you.

"You will go with me anyway," growled Usanga. "It is nothing to me whether you go willingly or not. I am going to be a great king and you will do whatever I tell you to do."

He had in mind that he would start properly with this woman. There should be no repetition of his harrowing experience with Naratu. This wife and the twenty-four others should be carefully selected and well trained. Hereafter Usanga would be master in his own house.

Bertha Kircher saw that it was useless to appeal to the brute and so she held her peace though she was filled with sorrow in contemplating the fate that awaited the young officer, scarce more than a boy, who had impulsively revealed his love for her.

At Usanga's order one of the blacks lifted her from the ground and carried her to the machine, and after Usanga had clambered aboard, they lifted her up and he reached down and drew her into the fuselage where he removed the thongs from her wrists and strapped her into her seat and then took his own directly ahead of her.

The girl turned her eyes toward the Englishman. She was very pale but her lips smiled bravely.

"Good-bye!" she cried.

"Good-bye, and God bless you!" he called back—his voice the least bit husky—and then: "The thing I wanted to say-may I say it now, we are so very near the end?"

Her lips moved but whether they voiced consent or refusal he did not know, for the words were drowned in the whir of the propeller.

The black had learned his lesson sufficiently well so that the motor was started without bungling and the machine was soon under way across the meadowland. A groan escaped the lips of the distracted Englishman as he watched the woman he loved being carried to almost certain death. He saw the plane tilt and the machine rise from the ground. It was a good take-off—as good as Lieutenant Harold Percy Smith-Oldwick could make himself but he realized that it was only so by chance. At any instant the machine might plunge to earth and even if, by some miracle of chance, the black could succeed in rising above the tree tops and make a successful flight, there was not one chance in one hundred thousand that he could ever land again without killing his fair captive and himself.

But what was that? His heart stood still.

USANGA'S REWARD

For two days Tarzan of the Apes had been hunting leisurely to the north, and swinging in a wide circle, he had returned to within a short distance of the clearing where he had left Bertha Kircher and the young lieutenant. He had spent the night in a large tree that overhung the river only a short distance from the clearing, and now in the early morning hours he was crouching at the water's edge waiting for an opportunity to capture Pisah, the fish, thinking that he would take it back with him to the hut where the girl could cook it for herself and her companion.

Motionless as a bronze statue was the wily ape-man, for well he knew how wary is Pisah, the fish. The slightest movement would frighten him away and only by infinite patience might he be captured at all. Tarzan depended upon his own quickness and the suddenness of his attack, for he had no bait or hook. His knowledge of the ways of the denizens of the water told him where to wait for Pisah. It might be a minute or it might be an hour before the fish would swim into the little pool above which he crouched, but sooner or later one would come. That the ape-man knew, so with the patience of the beast of prey he waited for his quarry.

At last there was a glint of shiny scales. Pisah was coming. In a moment he would be within reach and then with the swiftness of light two strong, brown hands would plunge into the pool and seize him, but, just at the moment that the fish was about to come within reach, there was a great crashing in the underbrush behind the ape-man. Instantly Pisah was gone and Tarzan, growling, had wheeled about to face whatever creature might be menacing him. The moment that he turned he saw that the author of the disturbance was Zu-tag.

"What does Zu-tag want?" asked the ape-man.

"Zu-tag comes to the water to drink," replied the ape.

"Where is the tribe?" asked Tarzan.

"They are hunting for pisangs and scimatines farther back in the forest," replied Zu-tag.

"And the Tarmangani she and bull—" asked Tarzan, "are they safe?"

"They have gone away," replied Zu-tag. "Kudu has come out of his lair twice since they left."

"Did the tribe chase them away?" asked Tarzan.

"No," replied the ape. "We did not see them go. We do not know why they left."

Tarzan swung quickly through the trees toward the clearing. The hut and boma were as he had left them, but there was no sign of either the man or the woman. Crossing the clearing, he entered the boma and then the hut. Both were empty, and his trained nostrils told him that they had been gone for at least two days. As he was about to leave the hut he saw a paper pinned upon the wall with a sliver of wood and taking it down, he read:

After what you told me about Miss Kircher, and knowing that you dislike her, I feel that it is not fair to her and to you that we should impose longer upon you. I know that our presence is keeping you from continuing your journey to the west coast, and so I have decided that it is better for us to try and reach the white settlements immediately without imposing further upon you. We both thank you for your kindness and protection. If there was any way that I might repay the obligation I feel, I should be only too glad to do so.

It was signed by Lieutenant Harold Percy Smith-Oldwick.

Tarzan shrugged his shoulders, crumpled the note in his hand and tossed it aside. He felt a certain sense of relief from responsibility and was glad that they had taken the matter out of his hands. They were gone and would forget, but somehow he could not forget. He walked out across the boma and into the clearing. He felt uneasy and restless. Once he started toward the north in response to a sudden determination to continue his way to the west coast. He would follow the winding river toward the north a few miles where its course turned to the west and then on toward its source across a wooded plateau and up into the foothills and the mountains. Upon the other side of the range he would search for a stream running downward toward the west coast, and thus following the rivers he would be sure of game and water in plenty.

But he did not go far. A dozen steps, perhaps, and he came to a sudden stop. "He is an Englishman," he muttered, "and the other is a woman. They can never reach the settlements without my help. I could not kill her with my own hands when I tried, and if I let them go on alone, I will have killed her just as surely as though I had run my knife into her heart. No," and again he shook his head. "Tarzan of the Apes is a fool and a weak, old woman," and he turned back toward the south.

Manu, the monkey, had seen the two Tarmangani pass two days before. Chattering and scolding, he told Tarzan all about it. They had gone in the direction of the village of the Gomangani, that much had Manu seen with his own eyes, so the ape-man swung on through the jungle in a southerly direction and though with no concentrated effort to follow the spoor of those he trailed, he passed numerous evidences that they had gone this way—faint suggestions of their scent spoor clung lightly to leaf or branch or bole that one or the other had touched, or in the earth of the trail their feet had trod, and where the way wound through the gloomy depth of dank forest, the impress of their shoes still showed occasionally in the damp mass of decaying vegetation that floored the way.

An inexplicable urge spurred Tarzan to increasing, speed. The same still, small voice that chided him for having neglected them seemed constantly whispering that they were in dire need of him now. Tarzan's conscience was troubling him, which accounted for the fact that he compared himself to a weak, old woman, for the ape-man, reared in savagery and inured to hardships and cruelty, disliked to admit any of the gentler traits that in reality were his birthright.

The trail made a detour to the east of the village of the Wamabos, and then returned to the wide elephant path nearer to the river, where it continued in a southerly direction for several miles. At last there came to the ears of the ape-man a peculiar whirring, throbbing sound. For an instant he paused, listening intently, "An aeroplane!" he muttered, and hastened forward at greatly increased speed.

When Tarzan of the Apes finally reached the edge of the meadowland where Smith-Oldwick's plane had landed, he took in the entire scene in one quick glance and grasped the situation, although he could scarce give credence to the things he saw. Bound and helpless, the English officer lay upon the ground at one side of the meadow, while around him stood a number of the black deserters from the German command. Tarzan had seen these men before and knew who they were. Coming toward him down the meadow was an aeroplane piloted by the black Usanga and in the seat behind the pilot was the white girl, Bertha Kircher. How it befell that the ignorant savage could operate the plane, Tarzan could not guess nor had he time in which to speculate upon the subject. His knowledge of Usanga, together with the position of the white man, told him that the black sergeant was attempting to carry off the white girl. Why he should be doing this when he had her in his power and had also captured and secured the only creature in the jungle who might wish to defend her in so far as the black could know, Tarzan could not guess, for he knew nothing of Usanga's twenty-four dream wives nor of the black's fear of the horrid temper of Naratu, his present mate. He did not know, then, that Usanga had determined to fly away with the white girl never to return, and to put so great a distance between himself and Naratu that the latter never could find him again; but it was this very thing that was in the black's mind although not even his own warriors guessed it. He had told them that he would take the captive to a sultan of the north and there obtain a great price for her and that when he returned they should have some of the spoils.

These things Tarzan did not know. All he knew was what he saw—a Negro attempting to fly away with a white girl. Already the machine was slowly leaving the ground. In a moment more it would rise swiftly out of reach. At first Tarzan thought of fitting an arrow to his bow and slaying Usanga, but as quickly he abandoned the idea because he knew that the moment the pilot was slain the machine, running wild, would dash the girl to death among the trees.

There was but one way in which he might hope to succor her—a way which if it failed must send him to instant death and yet he did not hesitate in an attempt to put it into execution.

Usanga did not see him, being too intent upon the unaccustomed duties of a pilot, but the blacks across the meadow saw him and they ran forward with loud and savage cries and menacing rifles to intercept him. They saw a giant white man leap from the branches of a tree to the turf and race rapidly toward the plane. They saw him take a long grass rope from about his shoulders as he ran. They saw the noose swinging in an undulating circle above his head. They saw the white girl in the machine glance down and discover him.

Twenty feet above the running ape-man soared the huge plane. The open noose shot up to meet it, and the girl, half guessing the ape-man's intentions, reached out and caught the noose and, bracing herself, clung tightly to it with both hands. Simultaneously Tarzan was dragged from his feet and the plane lurched sideways in response to the new strain. Usanga clutched wildly at the control and the machine shot upward at a steep angle. Dangling at the end of the rope the ape-man swung pendulum-like in space. The Englishman, lying bound upon the ground, had been a witness of all these happenings. His heart stood still as he saw Tarzan's body hurtling through the air toward the tree tops among which it seemed he must inevitably crash; but the plane was rising rapidly, so that the beast-man cleared the top-most branches. Then slowly, hand over hand, he climbed toward the fuselage. The girl, clinging desperately to the noose, strained every muscle to hold the great weight dangling at the lower end of the rope.

Usanga, all unconscious of what was going on behind him, drove the plane higher and higher into the air.

Tarzan glanced downward. Below him the tree tops and the river passed rapidly to the rear and only a slender grass rope and the muscles of a frail girl stood between him and the death yawning there thousands of feet below.

It seemed to Bertha Kircher that the fingers of her hands were dead. The numbness was running up her arms to her elbows. How much longer she could cling to the straining strands she could not guess. It seemed to her that those lifeless fingers must relax at any instant and then, when she had about given up hope, she saw a strong brown hand reach up and grasp the side of the fuselage. Instantly the weight upon the rope was removed and a moment later Tarzan of the Apes raised his body above the side and threw a leg over the edge. He glanced forward at Usanga and then, placing his mouth close to the girl's ear he cried: "Have you ever piloted a plane?" The girl nodded a quick affirmative.

"Have you the courage to climb up there beside the black and seize the control while I take care of him?"

The girl looked toward Usanga and shuddered. "Yes," she replied, "but my feet are bound."

Tarzan drew his hunting knife from its sheath and reaching down, severed the thongs that bound her ankles. Then the girl unsnapped the strap that held her to her seat. With one hand Tarzan grasped the girl's arm and steadied her as the two crawled slowly across the few feet which intervened between the two seats. A single slight tip of the plane would have cast them both into eternity. Tarzan realized that only through a miracle of chance could they reach Usanga and effect the change in pilots and yet he knew that that chance must be taken, for in the brief moments since he had first seen the plane, he had realized that the black was almost without experience as a pilot and that death surely awaited them in any event should the black sergeant remain at the control.

The first intimation Usanga had that all was not well with him was when the girl slipped suddenly to his side and grasped the control and at the same instant steel-like fingers seized his throat. A brown hand shot down with a keen blade and severed the strap about his waist and giant muscles lifted him bodily from his seat. Usanga clawed the air and shrieked but he was helpless as a babe. Far below the watchers in the meadow could see the aeroplane careening in the sky, for with the change of control it had taken a sudden dive. They saw it right itself and, turning in a short circle, return in their direction, but it was so far above them and the light of the sun so strong that they could see nothing of what was going on within the fuselage; but presently Lieutenant Smith-Oldwick gave a gasp of dismay as he saw a human body plunge downward from the plane. Turning and twisting in mid-air it fell with ever-increasing velocity and the Englishman held his breath as the thing hurtled toward them.

With a muffled thud it flattened upon the turf near the center of the meadow, and when at last the Englishman could gain the courage to again turn his eyes upon it, he breathed a fervent prayer of thanks, for the shapeless mass that lay upon the blood-stained turf was covered with an ebon hide. Usanga had reaped his reward.

Again and again the plane circled above the meadow. The blacks, at first dismayed at the death of their leader, were now worked to a frenzy of rage and a determination to be avenged. The girl and the ape-man saw them gather in a knot about the body of their fallen chief. They saw as they circled above the meadow the black fists shaken at them, and the rifles brandishing a menace toward them. Tarzan still clung to the fuselage directly behind the pilot's seat. His face was close beside Bertha Kircher's, and at the top of his voice, above the noise of propeller, engine and exhaust, he screamed a few words of instruction into her ear.

As the girl grasped the significance of his words she paled, but her lips set in a hard line and her eyes shone with a sudden fire of determination as she dropped the plane to within a few feet of the ground and at the opposite end of the meadow from the blacks and then at full speed bore down upon the savages. So quickly the plane came that Usanga's men had no time to escape it after they realized its menace. It touched the ground just as it struck among them and mowed through them, a veritable juggernaut of destruction. When it came to rest at the edge of the forest the ape-man leaped quickly to the ground and ran toward the young lieutenant, and as he went he glanced at the spot where the warriors had stood, ready to defend himself if necessary, but there was none there to oppose him. Dead and dying they lay strewn for fifty feet along the turf.

By the time Tarzan had freed the Englishman the girl joined them. She tried to voice her thanks to the ape-man but he silenced her with a gesture.

"You saved yourself," he insisted, "for had you been unable to pilot the plane, I could not have helped you, and now," he said, "you two have the means of returning to the settlements. The day is still young. You can easily cover the distance in a few hours if you have sufficient petrol." He looked inquiringly toward the aviator.

Smith-Oldwick nodded his head affirmatively. "I have plenty," he replied.

"Then go at once," said the ape-man. "Neither of you belong in the jungle." A slight smile touched his lips as he spoke.

The girl and the Englishman smiled too. "This jungle is no place for us at least," said Smith-Oldwick, "and it is no place for any other white man. Why don't you come back to civilization with us?"

Tarzan shook his head. "I prefer the jungle," he said.

The aviator dug his toe into the ground and still looking down, blurted something which he evidently hated to say. "If it is a matter of living, old top," he said, "er—money, er—you know—"

Tarzan laughed. "No," he said. "I know what you are trying to say. It is not that. I was born in the jungle. I have lived all my life in the jungle, and I shall die in the jungle. I do not wish to live or die elsewhere."

The others shook their heads. They could not understand him.

"Go," said the ape-man. "The quicker you go, the quicker you will reach safety."

They walked to the plane together. Smith-Oldwick pressed the ape-man's hand and clambered into the pilot's seat. "Good-bye," said the girl as she extended her hand to Tarzan. "Before I go won't you tell me you don't hate me any more?" Tarzan's face clouded. Without a word he picked her up and lifted her to her place behind the Englishman. An expression of pain crossed Bertha Kircher's face. The motor started and a moment later the two were being borne rapidly toward the east.

In the center of the meadow stood the ape-man watching them. "It is too bad that she is a German and a spy," he said, "for she is very hard to hate."

THE BLACK LION

Numa, the lion, was hungry. He had come out of the desert country to the east into a land of plenty but though he was young and strong, the wary grass-eaters had managed to elude his mighty talons each time he had thought to make a kill.

Numa, the lion, was hungry and very savage. For two days he had not eaten and now he hunted in the ugliest of humors. No more did Numa roar forth a rumbling challenge to the world but rather he moved silent and grim, stepping softly that no cracking twig might betray his presence to the keen-eared quarry he sought.

Fresh was the spoor of Bara, the deer, that Numa picked up in the well-beaten game trail he was following. No hour had passed since Bara had come this way; the time could be measured in minutes and so the great lion redoubled the cautiousness of his advance as he crept stealthily in pursuit of his quarry.

A light wind was moving through the jungle aisles, and it wafted down now to the nostrils of the eager carnivore the strong scent spoor of the deer, exciting his already avid appetite to a point where it became a gnawing pain. Yet Numa did not permit himself to be carried away by his desires into any premature charge such as had recently lost him the juicy meat of Pacco, the zebra. Increasing his gait but slightly he followed the tortuous windings of the trail until suddenly just before him, where the trail wound about the bole of a huge tree, he saw a young buck moving slowly ahead of him.

Numa judged the distance with his keen eyes, glowing now like two terrible spots of yellow fire in his wrinkled, snarling face. He could do it—this time he was sure. One terrific roar that would paralyze the poor creature ahead of him into momentary inaction, and a simultaneous charge of lightning-like rapidity and Numa, the lion, would feed. The sinuous tail, undulating slowly at its tufted extremity, whipped suddenly erect. It was the signal for the charge and the vocal organs were shaped for the thunderous roar when, as lightning out of a clear sky, Sheeta, the panther, leaped suddenly into the trail between Numa and the deer.

A blundering charge made Sheeta, for with the first crash of his spotted body through the foliage verging the trail, Bara gave a single startled backward glance and was gone.

The roar that was intended to paralyze the deer broke horribly from the deep throat of the great cat—an angry roar of rage against the meddling Sheeta who had robbed him of his kill, and the charge that was intended for Bara was launched against the panther; but here too Numa was doomed to disappointment, for with the first notes of his fearsome roar Sheeta, considering well the better part of valor, leaped into a near-by tree.

A half-hour later it was a thoroughly furious Numa who came unexpectedly upon the scent of man. Heretofore the lord of the jungle had disdained the unpalatable flesh of the despised man-thing. Such meat was only for the old, the toothless, and the decrepit who no longer could make their kills among the fleet-footed grass-eaters. Bara, the deer, Horta, the boar, and, best and wariest, Pacco, the zebra, were for the young, the strong, and the agile, but Numa was hungry-hungrier than he ever had been in the five short years of his life.

What if he was a young, powerful, cunning, and ferocious beast? In the face of hunger, the great leveler, he was as the old, the toothless, and the decrepit. His belly cried aloud in anguish and his jowls slavered for flesh. Zebra or deer or man, what mattered it so that it was warm flesh, red with the hot juices of life? Even Dango, the hyena, eater of offal, would, at the moment, have seemed a tidbit to Numa.

The great lion knew the habits and frailties of man, though he never before had hunted man for food. He knew the despised Gomangani as the slowest, the most stupid, and the most defenseless of creatures. No woodcraft, no cunning, no stealth was necessary in the hunting of man, nor had Numa any stomach for either delay or silence.

His rage had become an almost equally consuming passion with his hunger, so that now, as his delicate nostrils apprised him of the recent passage of man, he lowered his head and rumbled forth a thunderous roar, and at a swift walk, careless of the noise he made, set forth upon the trail of his intended quarry.

Majestic and terrible, regally careless of his surroundings, the king of beasts strode down the beaten trail. The natural caution that is inherent to all creatures of the wild had deserted him. What had he, lord of the jungle, to fear and, with only man to hunt, what need of caution? And so he did not see or scent what a more wary Numa might readily have discovered until, with the cracking of twigs and a tumbling of earth, he was precipitated into a cunningly devised pit that the wily Wamabos had excavated for just this purpose in the center of the game trail.

Tarzan of the Apes stood in the center of the clearing watching the plane shrinking to diminutive toy-like proportions in the eastern sky. He had breathed a sigh of relief as he saw it rise safely with the British flier and Fraulein Bertha Kircher. For weeks he had felt the hampering responsibility of their welfare in this savage wilderness where their utter helplessness would have rendered them easy prey for the savage carnivores or the cruel Wamabos. Tarzan of the Apes loved unfettered freedom, and now that these two were safely off his hands, he felt that he could continue upon his journey toward the west coast and the long-untenanted cabin of his dead father.

And yet, as he stood there watching the tiny speck in the east, another sigh heaved his broad chest, nor was it a sigh of relief, but rather a sensation which Tarzan had never expected to feel again and which he now disliked to admit even to himself. It could not be possible that he, the jungle bred, who had renounced forever the society of man to return to his beloved beasts of the wilds, could be feeling anything akin to regret at the departure of these two, or any slightest loneliness now that they were gone. Lieutenant Harold Percy Smith-Oldwick Tarzan had liked, but the woman whom he had known as a German spy he had hated, though he never had found it in his heart to slay her as he had sworn to slay all Huns. He had attributed this weakness to the fact that she was a woman, although he had been rather troubled by the apparent inconsistency of his hatred for her and his repeated protection of her when danger threatened.

With an irritable toss of his head he wheeled suddenly toward the west as though by turning his back upon the fast disappearing plane he might expunge thoughts of its passengers from his memory. At the edge of the clearing he paused; a giant tree loomed directly ahead of him and, as though actuated by sudden and irresistible impulse, he leaped into the branches and swung himself with apelike agility to the topmost limbs that would sustain his weight. There, balancing lightly upon a swaying bough, he sought in the direction of the eastern horizon for the tiny speck that would be the British plane bearing away from him the last of his own race and kind that he expected ever again to see.

At last his keen eyes picked up the ship flying at a considerable altitude far in the east. For a few seconds he watched it speeding evenly eastward, when, to his horror, he saw the speck dive suddenly downward. The fall seemed interminable to the watcher and he realized how great must have been the altitude of the plane before the drop commenced. Just before it disappeared from sight its downward momentum appeared to abate suddenly, but it was still moving rapidly at a steep angle when it finally disappeared from view behind the far hills.

For half a minute the ape-man stood noting distant landmarks that he judged might be in the vicinity of the fallen plane, for no sooner had he realized that these people were again in trouble than his inherent sense of duty to his own kind impelled him once more to forego his plans and seek to aid them.

The ape-man feared from what he judged of the location of the machine that it had fallen among the almost impassable gorges of the arid country just beyond the fertile basin that was bounded by the hills to the east of him. He had crossed that parched and desolate country of the dead himself and he knew from his own experience and the narrow escape he had had from succumbing to its relentless cruelty no lesser man could hope to win his way to safety from any considerable distance within its borders. Vividly he recalled the bleached bones of the long-dead warrior in the bottom of the precipitous gorge that had all but proved a trap for him as well. He saw the helmet of hammered brass and the corroded breastplate of steel and the long straight sword in its scabbard and the ancient harquebus—mute testimonials to the mighty physique and the warlike spirit of him who had somehow won, thus illy caparisoned and pitifully armed, to the center of savage, ancient Africa; and he saw the slender English youth and the slight figure of the girl cast into the same fateful trap from which this giant of old had been unable to escape—cast there wounded and broken perhaps, if not killed.

His judgment told him that the latter possibility was probably the fact, and yet there was a chance that they might have landed without fatal injuries, and so upon this slim chance he started out upon what he knew would be an arduous journey, fraught with many hardships and unspeakable peril, that he might attempt to save them if they still lived.

He had covered a mile perhaps when his quick ears caught the sound of rapid movement along the game trail ahead of him. The sound, increasing in volume, proclaimed the fact that whatever caused it was moving in his direction and moving rapidly. Nor was it long before his trained senses convinced him that the footfalls were those of Bara, the deer, in rapid flight. Inextricably confused in Tarzan's character were the attributes of man and of beasts. Long experience had taught him that he fights best or travels fastest who is best nourished, and so, with few exceptions, Tarzan could delay his most urgent business to take advantage of an opportunity to kill and feed. This perhaps was the predominant beast trait in him. The transformation from an English gentleman, impelled by the most humanitarian motives, to that of a wild beast crouching in the concealment of a dense bush ready to spring upon its approaching prey, was instantaneous.

And so, when Bara came, escaping the clutches of Numa and Sheeta, his terror and his haste precluded the possibility of his sensing that other equally formidable foe lying in ambush for him. Abreast of the ape-man came the deer; a light-brown body shot from the concealing verdure of the bush, strong arms encircled the sleek neck of the young buck and powerful teeth fastened themselves in the soft flesh. Together the two rolled over in the trail and a moment later the ape-man rose, and, with one foot upon the carcass of his kill, raised his voice in the victory cry of the bull ape.

Like an answering challenge came suddenly to the ears of the ape-man the thunderous roar of a lion, a hideous angry roar in which Tarzan thought that he discerned a note of surprise and terror. In the breast of the wild things of the jungle, as in the breasts of their more enlightened brothers and sisters of the human race, the characteristic of curiosity is well developed. Nor was Tarzan far from innocent of it. The peculiar note in the roar of his hereditary enemy aroused a desire to investigate, and so, throwing the carcass of Bara, the deer, across his shoulder, the ape-man took to the lower terraces of the forest and moved quickly in the direction from which the sound had come, which was in line with the trail he had set out upon.

As the distance lessened, the sounds increased in volume, which indicated that he was approaching a very angry lion and presently, where a jungle giant overspread the broad game trail that countless thousands of hoofed and padded feet had worn and trampled into a deep furrow during perhaps countless ages, he saw beneath him the lion pit of the Wamabos and in it, leaping futilely for freedom such a lion as even Tarzan of the Apes never before had beheld. A mighty beast it was that glared up at the ape-man—large, powerful and young, with a huge black mane and a coat so much darker than any Tarzan ever had seen that in the depths of the pit it looked almost black—a black lion!

Tarzan who had been upon the point of taunting and reviling his captive foe was suddenly turned to open admiration for the beauty of the splendid beast. What a creature! How by comparison the ordinary forest lion was dwarfed into insignificance! Here indeed was one worthy to be called king of beasts. With his first sight of the great cat the ape-man knew that he had heard no note of terror in that initial roar; surprise doubtless, but the vocal chords of that mighty throat never had reacted to fear.

With growing admiration came a feeling of quick pity for the hapless situation of the great brute rendered futile and helpless by the wiles of the Gomangani. Enemy though the beast was, he was less an enemy to the ape-man than those blacks who had trapped him, for though Tarzan of the Apes claimed many fast and loyal friends among certain tribes of African natives, there were others of degraded character and bestial habits that he looked upon with utter loathing, and of such were the human flesh-eaters of Numabo the chief. For a moment Numa, the lion, glared ferociously at the naked man-thing upon the tree limb above him. Steadily those yellow-green eyes bored into the clear eyes of the ape-man, and then the sensitive nostrils caught the scent of the fresh blood of Bara and the eyes moved to the carcass lying across the brown shoulder, and there came from the cavernous depths of the savage throat a low whine.

Tarzan of the Apes smiled. As unmistakably as though a human voice had spoken, the lion had said to him "I am hungry, even more than hungry. I am starving," and the ape-man looked down upon the lion beneath him and smiled, a slow quizzical smile, and then he shifted the carcass from his shoulder to the branch before him and, drawing the long blade that had been his father's, deftly cut off a hind quarter and, wiping the bloody blade upon Bara's smooth coat, he returned it to its scabbard. Numa, with watering jaws, looked up at the tempting meat and whined again and the ape-man smiled down upon him his slow smile and, raising the hind quarter in his strong brown hands buried his teeth in the tender, juicy flesh.

For the third time Numa, the lion, uttered that low pleading whine and then, with a rueful and disgusted shake of his head, Tarzan of the Apes raised the balance of the carcass of Bara, the deer, and hurled it to the famished beast below.

"Old woman," muttered the ape-man. "Tarzan has become a weak old woman. Presently he would shed tears because he has killed Bara, the deer. He cannot see Numa, his enemy, go hungry, because Tarzan's heart is turning to water by contact with the soft, weak creatures of civilization." But yet he smiled, nor was he sorry that he had given way to the dictates of a kindly impulse.

As Tarzan tore the flesh from that portion of the kill he had retained for himself his eyes were taking in each detail of the scene below. He saw the avidity with which Numa devoured the carcass; he noted with growing admiration the finer points of the beast, and also the cunning construction of the trap. The ordinary lion pit with which Tarzan was familiar had stakes imbedded in the bottom, upon whose sharpened points the hapless lion would be impaled, but this pit was not so made. Here the short stakes were set at intervals of about a foot around the walls near the top, their sharpened points inclining downward so that the lion had fallen unhurt into the trap but could not leap out because each time he essayed it his head came in contact with the sharp end of a stake above him.

Evidently, then, the purpose of the Wamabos was to capture a lion alive. As this tribe had no contact whatsoever with white men in so far as Tarzan knew, their motive was doubtless due to a desire to torture the beast to death that they might enjoy to the utmost his dying agonies.

TARZAN SUPER PACK

Having fed the lion, it presently occurred to Tarzan that his act would be futile were he to leave the beast to the mercies of the blacks, and then too it occurred to him that he could derive more pleasure through causing the blacks discomfiture than by leaving Numa to his fate. But how was he to release him? By removing two stakes there would be left plenty of room for the lion to leap from the pit, which was not of any great depth. However, what assurance had Tarzan that Numa would not leap out instantly the way to freedom was open, and before the ape-man could gain the safety of the trees? Regardless of the fact that Tarzan felt no such fear of the lion as you and I might experience under like circumstances, he yet was imbued with the sense of caution that is necessary to all creatures of the wild if they are to survive. Should necessity require, Tarzan could face Numa in battle, although he was not so egotistical as to think that he could best a full-grown lion in mortal combat other than through accident or the utilization of the cunning of his superior man-mind. To lay himself liable to death futilely, he would have considered as reprehensible as to have shunned danger in time of necessity; but when Tarzan elected to do a thing he usually found the means to accomplish it.

He had now fully determined to liberate Numa, and having so determined, he would accomplish it even though it entailed considerable personal risk. He knew that the lion would be occupied with his feeding for some time, but he also knew that while feeding he would be doubly resentful of any fancied interference. Therefore Tarzan must work with caution.

Coming to the ground at the side of the pit, he examined the stakes and as he did so was rather surprised to note that Numa gave no evidence of anger at his approach. Once he turned a searching gaze upon the ape-man for a moment and then returned to the flesh of Bara. Tarzan felt of the stakes and tested them with his weight. He pulled upon them with the muscles of his strong arms, presently discovering that by working them back and forth he could loosen them: and then a new plan was suggested to him so that he fell to work excavating with his knife at a point above where one of the stakes was imbedded. The loam was soft and easily removed, and it was not long until Tarzan had exposed that part of one of the stakes which was imbedded in the wall of the pit to almost its entire length, leaving only enough imbedded to prevent the stake from falling into the excavation. Then he turned his attention to an adjoining stake and soon had it similarly exposed, after which he threw the noose of his grass rope over the two and swung quickly to the branch of the tree above. Here he gathered in the slack of the rope and, bracing himself against the bole of the tree, pulled steadily upward. Slowly the stakes rose from the trench in which they were imbedded and with them rose Numa's suspicion and growling.

Was this some new encroachment upon his rights and his liberties? He was puzzled and, like all lions, being short of temper, he was irritated. He had not minded it when the Tarmangani squatted upon the verge of the pit and looked down upon him, for had not this Tarmangani fed him? But now something else was afoot and the suspicion of the wild beast was aroused. As he watched, however, Numa saw the stakes rise slowly to an erect position, tumble against each other and then fall backwards out of his sight upon the surface of the ground above. Instantly the lion grasped the possibilities of the situation, and, too, perhaps he sensed the fact that the man-thing had deliberately opened a way for his escape. Seizing the remains of Bara in his great jaws, Numa, the lion, leaped agilely from the pit of the Wamabos and Tarzan of the Apes melted into the jungles to the east.

On the surface of the ground or through the swaying branches of the trees the spoor of man or beast was an open book to the ape-man, but even his acute senses were baffled by the spoorless trail of the airship. Of what good were eyes, or ears, or the sense of smell in following a thing whose path had lain through the shifting air thousands of feet above the tree tops? Only upon his sense of direction could Tarzan depend in his search for the fallen plane. He could not even judge accurately as to the distance it might lie from him, and he knew that from the moment that it disappeared beyond the hills it might have traveled a considerable distance at right angles to its original course before it crashed to earth. If its occupants were killed or badly injured the ape-man might search futilely in their immediate vicinity for some time before finding them.

There was but one thing to do and that was to travel to a point as close as possible to where he judged the plane had landed, and then to follow in ever-widening circles until he picked up their scent spoor. And this he did.

Before he left the valley of plenty he made several kills and carried the choicest cuts of meat with him, leaving all the dead weight of bones behind. The dense vegetation of the jungle terminated at the foot of the western slope, growing less and less abundant as he neared the summit beyond which was a sparse growth of sickly scrub and sunburned grasses, with here and there a gnarled and hardy tree that had withstood the vicissitudes of an almost waterless existence.

From the summit of the hills Tarzan's keen eyes searched the arid landscape before him. In the distance he discerned the ragged tortuous lines that marked the winding course of the hideous gorges which scored the broad plain at intervals—the terrible gorges that had so nearly claimed his life in punishment for his temerity in attempting to invade the sanctity of their ancient solitude.

For two days Tarzan sought futilely for some clew to the whereabouts of the machine or its occupants. He cached portions of his kills at different points, building cairns of rock to mark their locations. He crossed the first deep gorge and circled far beyond it. Occasionally he stopped and called aloud, listening for some response but only silence rewarded him-a sinister silence that his cries only accentuated.

Late in the evening of the second day he came to the well-remembered gorge in which lay the clean-picked bones of the ancient adventurer, and here, for the first time, Ska, the vulture, picked up his trail. "Not this time, Ska," cried the ape-man in a taunting voice, "for now indeed is Tarzan Tarzan. Before, you stalked the grim skeleton of a Tarmangani and even then you lost. Waste not your time upon Tarzan of the Apes in the full of his strength." But still Ska, the vulture, circled and soared above him, and the ape-man, notwithstanding his boasts, felt a shudder of apprehension. Through his brain ran a persistent and doleful chant to which he involuntarily set two words, repeated over and over again in horrible monotony: "Ska knows! Ska knows!" until, shaking himself in anger, he picked up a rock and hurled it at the grim scavenger.

Lowering himself over the precipitous side of the gorge Tarzan half clambered and half slid to the sandy floor beneath. He had come upon the rift at almost the exact spot at which he had clambered from it weeks before, and there he saw, just as he had left it, just, doubtless, as it had lain for centuries, the mighty skeleton and its mighty armor.

As he stood looking down upon this grim reminder that another man of might had succumbed to the cruel powers of the desert, he was brought to startled attention by the report of a firearm, the sound of which came from the depths of the gorge to the south of him, and reverberated along the steep walls of the narrow rift.

MYSTERIOUS FOOTPRINTS

As the British plane piloted by Lieutenant Harold Percy Smith-Oldwick rose above the jungle wilderness where Bertha Kircher's life had so often been upon the point of extinction, and sped toward the east, the girl felt a sudden contraction of the muscles of her throat. She tried very hard to swallow something that was not there. It seemed strange to her that she should feel regret in leaving behind her such hideous perils, and yet it was plain to her that such was the fact, for she was also leaving behind something beside the dangers that had menaced her—a unique figure that had entered her life, and for which she felt an unaccountable attraction.

Before her in the pilot's seat sat an English officer and gentleman whom, she knew, loved her, and yet she dared to feel regret in his company at leaving the stamping ground of a wild beast!

Lieutenant Smith-Oldwick, on his part, was in the seventh heaven of elation. He was in possession again of his beloved ship, he was flying swiftly in the direction of his comrades and his duty, and with him was the woman he loved. The fly in the ointment, however, was the accusation Tarzan had made against this woman. He had said that she was a German, and a spy, and from the heights of bliss the English officer was occasionally plunged to the depths of despair in contemplation of the inevitable, were the ape-man's charges to prove true. He found himself torn between sentiments of love and honor. On the one hand he could not surrender the woman he loved to the certain fate that must be meted out to her if she were in truth an enemy spy, while on the other it would be equally impossible for him as an Englishman and an officer to give her aid or protection.

The young man contented himself therefore with repeated mental denials of her guilt. He tried to convince himself that Tarzan was mistaken, and when he conjured upon the screen of recollection the face of the girl behind him, he was doubly reassured that those lines of sweet femininity and character, those clear and honest eyes, could not belong to one of the hated alien race.

And so they sped toward the east, each wrapped in his own thoughts. Below them they saw the dense vegetation of the jungle give place to the scantier growth upon the hillside, and then before them there spread the wide expanse of arid wastelands marked by the deep scarring of the narrow gorges that long-gone rivers had cut there in some forgotten age.

Shortly after they passed the summit of the ridge which formed the boundary between the desert and the fertile country, Ska, the vulture, winging his way at a high altitude toward his aerie, caught sight of a strange new bird of gigantic proportions encroaching upon the preserves of his aerial domain. Whether with intent to give battle to the interloper or merely impelled by curiosity, Ska rose suddenly upward to meet the plane. Doubtless he misjudged the speed of the newcomer, but be that as it may, the tip of the propeller blade touched him and simultaneously many things happened. The lifeless body of Ska, torn and bleeding, dropped plummet-like toward the ground; a bit of splintered spruce drove backward to strike the pilot on the forehead; the plane shuddered and trembled and as Lieutenant Harold Percy Smith-Oldwick sank forward in momentary unconsciousness the ship dived headlong toward the earth.

Only for an instant was the pilot unconscious, but that instant almost proved their undoing. When he awoke to a realization of their peril it was also to discover that his motor had stalled. The plane had attained frightful momentum, and the ground seemed too close for him to hope to flatten out in time to make a safe landing. Directly beneath him was a deep rift in the plateau, a narrow gorge, the bottom of which appeared comparatively level and sand covered.

In the brief instant in which he must reach a decision, the safest plan seemed to attempt a landing in the gorge, and this he did, but not without considerable damage to the plane and a severe shaking-up for himself and his passenger.

Fortunately neither of them was injured but their condition seemed indeed a hopeless one. It was a grave question as to whether the man could repair his plane and continue the journey, and it seemed equally questionable as to their ability either to proceed on foot to the coast or retrace their way to the country they had just left. The man was confident that they could not hope to cross the desert country to the east in the face of thirst and hunger, while behind them in the valley of plenty lay almost equal danger in the form of carnivores and the warlike natives.

After the plane came to its sudden and disastrous stop, Smith-Oldwick turned quickly to see what the effect of the accident had been on the girl. He found her pale but smiling, and for several seconds the two sat looking at each other in silence.

"This is the end?" the girl asked.

The Englishman shook his head. "It is the end of the first leg, anyway," he replied.

"But you can't hope to make repairs here," she said dubiously.

"No," he said, "not if they amount to anything, but I may be able to patch it up. I will have to look her over a bit first. Let us hope there is nothing serious. It's a long, long way to the Tanga railway."

"We would not get far," said the girl, a slight note of hopelessness in her tone. "Entirely unarmed as we are, it would be little less than a miracle if we covered even a small fraction of the distance."

"But we are not unarmed," replied the man. "I have an extra pistol here, that the beggars didn't discover," and, removing the cover of a compartment, he drew forth an automatic.

Bertha Kircher leaned back in her seat and laughed aloud, a mirthless, half-hysterical laugh. "That popgun!" she exclaimed. "What earthly good would it do other than to infuriate any beast of prey you might happen to hit with it?"

Smith-Oldwick looked rather crestfallen. "But it is a weapon," he said. "You will have to admit that, and certainly I could kill a man with it."

"You could if you happened to hit him," said the girl, "or the thing didn't jam. Really, I haven't much faith in an automatic. I have used them myself."

"Oh, of course," he said ironically, "an express rifle would be better, for who knows but we might meet an elephant here in the desert."

The girl saw that he was hurt, and she was sorry, for she realized that there was nothing he would not do in her service or protection, and that it was through no fault of his that he was so illy armed. Doubtless, too, he realized as well as she the futility of his weapon, and that he had only called attention to it in the hope of reassuring her and lessening her anxiety.

"Forgive me," she said. "I did not mean to be nasty, but this accident is the proverbial last straw. It seems to me that I have borne all that I can. Though I was willing to give my life in the service of my country, I did not imagine that my death agonies would be so long drawn out, for I realize now that I have been dying for many weeks."

"What do you mean!" he exclaimed; "what do you mean by that! You are not dying. There is nothing the matter with you."

"Oh, not that," she said, "I did not mean that. What I mean is that at the moment the black sergeant, Usanga, and his renegade German native troops captured me and brought me inland, my death warrant was signed. Sometimes I have imagined that a reprieve has been granted. Sometimes I have hoped that I might be upon the verge of winning a full pardon, but really in the depths of my heart I have known that I should never live to regain civilization. I have done my bit for my country, and though it was not much I can at least go with the realization that it was the best I was able to offer. All that I can hope for now, all that I ask for, is a speedy fulfillment of the death sentence. I do not wish to linger any more to face constant terror and apprehension. Even physical torture would be preferable to what I have passed through. I have no doubt that you consider me a brave woman, but really my terror has been boundless. The cries of the carnivores at night fill me with a dread so tangible that I am in actual pain. I feel the rending talons in my flesh and the cruel fangs munching upon my bones—it is as real to me as though I were actually enduring the horrors of such a death. I doubt if you can understand it—men are so different."

"Yes," he said, "I think I can understand it, and because I understand I can appreciate more than you imagine the heroism you have shown in your endurance of all that you have passed through. There can be no bravery where there is no fear. A child might walk into a lion's den, but it would take a very brave man to go to its rescue."

"Thank you," she said, "but I am not brave at all, and now I am very much ashamed of my thoughtlessness for your own feelings. I will try and take a new grip upon myself and we will both hope for the best. I will help you all I can if you will tell me what I may do."

"The first thing," he replied, "is to find out just how serious our damage is, and then to see what we can do in the way of repairs."

For two days Smith-Oldwick worked upon the damaged plane—worked in the face of the fact that from the first he realized the case was hopeless. And at last he told her.

'I knew it," she said, "but I believe that I felt much as you must have; that however futile our efforts here might be, it would be infinitely as fatal to attempt to retrace our way to the jungle we just left or to go on toward the coast. You know and I know that we could not reach the Tanga railway on foot. We should die of thirst and starvation before we had covered half the distance, and if we return to the jungle, even were we able to reach it, it would be but to court an equally certain, though different, fate."

"So we might as well sit here and wait for death as to uselessly waste our energies in what we know would be a futile attempt at escape?" he asked.

"No," she replied, "I shall never give up like that. What I meant was that it was useless to attempt to reach either of the places where we know that there is food and water in abundance, so we must strike out in a new direction. Somewhere there may be water in this wilderness and if there is, the best chance of our finding it would be to follow this gorge downward. We have enough food and water left, if we are careful of it, for a couple of days and in that time we might stumble upon a spring or possibly even reach the fertile country which I know lies to the south. When Usanga brought me to the Wamabo country from the coast he took a southerly route along which there was usually water and game in plenty. It was not until we neared our destination that the country became overrun with carnivores. So there is hope if we can reach the fertile country south of us that we can manage to pull through to the coast."

The man shook his head dubiously. "We can try it," he said. "Personally, I do not fancy sitting here waiting for death."

Smith-Oldwick was leaning against the ship, his dejected gaze directed upon the ground at his feet. The girl was looking south down the gorge in the direction of their one slender chance of life. Suddenly she touched him on the arm.

"Look," she whispered.

The man raised his eyes quickly in the direction of her gaze to see the massive head of a great lion who was regarding them from beyond a rocky projection at the first turning of the gorge.

"Phew!" he exclaimed, "the beggars are everywhere."

"They do not go far from water do they," asked the girl hopefully.

"I should imagine not," he replied; "a lion is not particularly strong on endurance."

"Then he is a harbinger of hope," she exclaimed.

The man laughed. "Cute little harbinger of hope!" he said. "Reminds me of Cock Robin heralding spring."

The girl cast a quick glance at him. "Don't be silly, and I don't care if you do laugh. He fills me with hope."

"It is probably mutual," replied Smith-Oldwick, "as we doubtless fill him with hope."

The lion evidently having satisfied himself as to the nature of the creatures before him advanced slowly now in their direction.

"Come," said the man, 'let's climb aboard," and he helped the girl over the side of the ship.

"Can't he get in here?" she asked.

"I think he can," said the man.

"You are reassuring," she returned.

"I don't feel so." He drew his pistol.

"For heaven's sake," she cried, "don't shoot at him with that thing. You might hit him."

"I don't intend to shoot at him but I might succeed in frightening him away if he attempts to reach us here. Haven't you ever seen a trainer work with lions? He carries a silly little pop-gun loaded with blank cartridges. With that and a kitchen chair he subdues the most ferocious of beasts."

"But you haven't a kitchen chair," she reminded him.

"No," he said, "Government is always muddling things. I have always maintained that airplanes should be equipped with kitchen chairs."

Bertha Kircher laughed as evenly and with as little hysteria as though she were moved by the small talk of an afternoon tea.

Numa, the lion, came steadily toward them; his attitude seemed more that of curiosity than of belligerency. Close to the side of the ship he stopped and stood gazing up at them.

"Magnificent, isn't he?" exclaimed the man.

"I never saw a more beautiful creature," she replied, "nor one with such a dark coat. Why, he is almost black."

EDGAR RICE BURROUGHS

The sound of their voices seemed not to please the lord of the jungle, for he suddenly wrinkled his great face into deep furrows as he bared his fangs beneath snarling lips and gave vent to an angry growl. Almost simultaneously he crouched for a spring and immediately Smith-Oldwick discharged his pistol into the ground in front of the lion. The effect of the noise upon Numa seemed but to enrage him further, and with a horrid roar he sprang for the author of the new and disquieting sound that had outraged his ears.

Simultaneously Lieutenant Harold Percy Smith-Oldwick vaulted nimbly out of the cockpit on the opposite side of his plane, calling to the girl to follow his example. The girl, realizing the futility of leaping to the ground, chose the remaining alternative and clambered to the top of the upper plane.

Numa, unaccustomed to the idiosyncrasies of construction of an airship and having gained the forward cockpit, watched the girl clamber out of his reach without at first endeavoring to prevent her. Having taken possession of the plane his anger seemed suddenly to leave him and he made no immediate move toward following Smith-Oldwick. The girl, realizing the comparative safety of her position, had crawled to the outer edge of the wing and was calling to the man to try and reach the opposite end of the upper plane.

It was this scene upon which Tarzan of the Apes looked as he rounded the bend of the gorge above the plane after the pistol shot had attracted his attention. The girl was so intent upon watching the efforts of the Englishman to reach a place of safety, and the latter was so busily occupied in attempting to do so that neither at once noticed the silent approach of the ape-man.

It was Numa who first noticed the intruder. The lion immediately evinced his displeasure by directing toward him a snarling countenance and a series of warning growls. His action called the attention of the two upon the upper plane to the newcomer, eliciting a stifled "Thank God!" from the girl, even though she could scarce credit the evidence of her own eyes that it was indeed the savage man, whose presence always assured her safety, who had come so providentially in the nick of time.

Almost immediately both were horrified to see Numa leap from the cockpit and advance upon Tarzan. The ape-man, carrying his stout spear in readiness, moved deliberately onward to meet the carnivore, which he had recognized as the lion of the Wamabos' pit. He knew from the manner of Numa's approach what neither Bertha Kircher nor Smith-Oldwick knew—that there was more of curiosity than belligerency in it, and he wondered if in that great head there might not be a semblance of gratitude for the kindness that Tarzan had done him.

There was no question in Tarzan's mind but that Numa recognized him, for he knew his fellows of the jungle well enough to know that while they oft-times forgot certain sensations more quickly than man there are others which remain in their memories for years. A well-defined scent spoor might never be forgotten by a beast if it had first been sensed under unusual circumstances, and so Tarzan was confident that Numa's nose had already reminded him of all the circumstances of their brief connection.

Love of the sporting chance is inherent in the Anglo-Saxon race and it was not now Tarzan of the Apes but rather John Clayton, Lord Greystoke, who smilingly welcomed the sporting chance which he must take to discover how far-reaching was Numa's gratitude.

Smith-Oldwick and the girl saw the two nearing each other. The former swore softly beneath his breath while he nervously fingered the pitiful weapon at his hip. The girl pressed her open palms to her cheeks as she leaned forward in stony-eyed, horror-stricken silence. While she had every confidence in the prowess of the godlike creature who thus dared brazenly to face the king of beasts, she had no false conception of what must certainly happen when they met. She had seen Tarzan battle with Sheeta, the panther, and she had realized then that powerful as the man was, it was only agility, cunning, and chance that placed him upon anywhere near an equal footing with his savage adversary, and that of the three factors upon his side chance was the greatest.

She saw the man and the lion stop simultaneously, not more than a yard apart. She saw the beast's tail whipping from side to side and she could hear his deep-throated growls rumbling from his cavernous breast, but she could read correctly neither the movement of the lashing tail nor the notes of the growl.

To her they seemed to indicate nothing but bestial rage while to Tarzan of the Apes they were conciliatory and reassuring in the extreme. And then she saw Numa move forward again until his nose touched the man's naked leg and she closed her eyes and covered them with her palms. For what seemed an eternity she waited for the horrid sound of the conflict which she knew must come, but all she heard was an explosive sigh of relief from Smith-Oldwick and a half-hysterical "By Jove! Just fancy it!"

She looked up to see the great lion rubbing his shaggy head against the man's hip, and Tarzan's free hand entangled in the black mane as he scratched Numa, the lion, behind a back-laid ear.

Strange friendships are often formed between the lower animals of different species, but less often between man and the savage felidae, because of the former's inherent fear of the great cats. And so after all, therefore, the friendship so suddenly developed between the savage lion and the savage man was not inexplicable.

As Tarzan approached the plane Numa walked at his side, and when Tarzan stopped and looked up at the girl and the man Numa stopped also.

"I had about given up hope of finding you," said the ape-man, "and it is evident that I found you just in time."

"But how did you know we were in trouble?" asked the English officer.

"I saw your plane fall," replied Tarzan. "I was watching you from a tree beside the clearing where you took off. I didn't have much to locate you by other than the general direction, but it seems that you volplaned a considerable distance toward the south after you disappeared from my view behind the hills. I have been looking for you further toward the north. I was just about to turn back when I heard your pistol shot. Is your ship beyond repair?"

"Yes," replied Smith-Oldwick, "it is hopeless."

"What are your plans, then? What do you wish to do?" Tarzan directed his question to the girl.

"We want to reach the coast," she said, "but it seems impossible now."

"I should have thought so a little while ago," replied the ape-man, "but if Numa is here there must be water within a reasonable distance. I ran across this lion two days ago in the Wamabo country. I liberated him from one of their pits. To have reached this spot he must have come by some trail unknown to me—at least I crossed no game trail and no spoor of any animal after I came over the hills out of the fertile country. From which direction did he come upon you?"

"It was from the south," replied the girl. "We thought, too, that there must be water in that direction."

"Let's find out then," said Tarzan.

"But how about the lion?" asked Smith-Oldwick.

"That we will have to discover," replied the ape-man, "and we can only do so if you will come down from your perch."

The officer shrugged his shoulders. The girl turned her gaze upon him to note the effect of Tarzan's proposal. The Englishman grew suddenly very white, but there was a smile upon his lips as without a word he slipped over the edge of the plane and clambered to the ground behind Tarzan.

Bertha Kircher realized that the man was afraid nor did she blame him, and she also realized the remarkable courage that he had shown in thus facing a danger that was very real to him.

Numa standing close to Tarzan's side raised his head and glared at the young Englishman, growled once, and looked up at the ape-man. Tarzan retained a hold upon the beast's mane and spoke to him in the language of the great apes. To the girl and Smith-Oldwick the growling gutturals falling from human lips sounded uncanny in the extreme, but whether Numa understood them or not they appeared to have the desired effect upon him, as he ceased growling, and as Tarzan walked to Smith-Oldwick's side Numa accompanied him, nor did he offer to molest the officer.

"What did you say to him?" asked the girl.

Tarzan smiled. "I told him," he replied, "that I am Tarzan of the Apes, mighty hunter, killer of beasts, lord of the jungle, and that you are my friends. I have never been sure that all of the other beasts understand the language of the Mangani. I know that Manu, the monkey, speaks nearly the same tongue and I am sure that Tantor, the elephant, understands all that I say to him. We of the jungle are great boasters. In our speech, in our carriage, in every detail of our demeanor we must impress others with our physical power and our ferocity. That is why we growl at our enemies. We are telling them to beware or we shall fall upon them and tear them to pieces. Perhaps Numa does not understand the words that I use but I believe that my tones and my manner carry the impression that I wish them to convey. Now you may come down and be introduced."

It required all the courage that Bertha Kircher possessed to lower herself to the ground within reach of the talons and fangs of this untamed forest beast, but she did it. Nor did Numa do more than bare his teeth and growl a little as she came close to the ape-man.

"I think you are safe from him as long as I am present," said the ape-man. "The best thing to do is simply to ignore him. Make no advances, but be sure to give no indication of fear and, if possible always keep me between you and him. He will go away presently I am sure and the chances are that we shall not see him again."

At Tarzan's suggestion Smith-Oldwick removed the remaining water and provisions from the plane and, distributing the burden among them, they set off toward the south. Numa did not follow them, but stood by the plane watching until they finally disappeared from view around a bend in the gorge.

Tarzan had picked up Numa's trail with the intention of following it southward in the belief that it would lead to water. In the sand that floored the bottom of the gorge tracks were plain and easily followed. At first only the fresh tracks of Numa were visible, but later in the day the ape-man discovered the older tracks of other lions and just before dark he stopped suddenly in evident surprise. His two companions looked at him questioningly, and in answer to their implied interrogations he pointed at the ground directly in front of him.

"Look at those," he exclaimed.

At first neither Smith-Oldwick nor the girl saw anything but a confusion of intermingled prints of padded feet in the sand, but presently the girl discovered what Tarzan had seen, and an exclamation of surprise broke from her lips.

"The imprint of human feet!" she cried.

Tarzan nodded.

"But there are no toes," the girl pointed out.

"The feet were shod with a soft sandal," explained Tarzan.

"Then there must be a native village somewhere in the vicinity," said Smith-Oldwick.

"Yes," replied the ape-man, "but not the sort of natives which we would expect to find here in this part of Africa where others all go unshod with the exception of a few of Usanga's renegade German native troops who wear German army shoes. I don't know that you can notice it, but it is evident to me that the foot inside the sandal that made these imprints were not the foot of a Negro. If you will examine them carefully you will notice that the impression of the heel and ball of the foot are well marked even through the sole of the sandal. The weight comes more nearly in the center of a Negro's footprint.

"Then you think these were made by a white person?"

"It looks that way," replied Tarzan, and suddenly, to the surprise of both the girl and Smith-Oldwick, he dropped to his hands and knees and sniffed at the tracks—again a beast utilizing the senses and woodcraft of a beast. Over an area of several square yards his keen nostrils sought the identity of the makers of the tracks. At length he rose to his feet.

"It is not the spoor of the Gomangani," he said, "nor is it exactly like that of white men. There were three who came this way. They were men, but of what race I do not know."

There was no apparent change in the nature of the gorge except that it had steadily grown deeper as they followed it downward until now the rocky and precipitous sides rose far above them. At different points natural caves, which appeared to have been eroded by the action of water in some forgotten age, pitted the side walls at various heights. Near them was such a cavity at the ground's level—an arched cavern floored with white sand. Tarzan indicated it with a gesture of his hand.

"We will lair here tonight," he said, and then with one of his rare, slow smiles: "We will CAMP here tonight."

Having eaten their meager supper Tarzan bade the girl enter the cavern.

"You will sleep inside," he said. "The lieutenant and I will lie outside at the entrance."

THE NIGHT ATTACK

As the girl turned to bid them good night, she thought that she saw a shadowy form moving in the darkness beyond them, and almost simultaneously she was sure that she heard the sounds of stealthy movement in the same direction.

"What is that?" she whispered. "There is something out there in the darkness."

"Yes," replied Tarzan, "it is a lion. It has been there for some time. Hadn't you noticed it before?"

"Oh!" cried the girl, breathing a sigh of relief, "is it our lion?"

"No," said Tarzan, "it is not our lion; it is another lion and he is hunting."

"He is stalking us?" asked the girl.

"He is," replied the ape-man. Smith-Oldwick fingered the grip of his pistol.

Tarzan saw the involuntary movement and shook his head.

"Leave that thing where it is, Lieutenant," he said.

The officer laughed nervously. "I couldn't help it, you know, old man," he said; "instinct of self-preservation and all that."

"It would prove an instinct of self-destruction," said Tarzan. "There are at least three hunting lions out there watching us. If we had a fire or the moon were up you would see their eyes plainly. Presently they may come after us but the chances are that they will not. If you are very anxious that they should, fire your pistol and hit one of them."

"What if they do charge?" asked the girl; "there is no means of escape."

"Why, we should have to fight them," replied Tarzan.

"What chance would we three have against them?" asked the girl.

The ape-man shrugged his shoulders. "One must die sometime," he said. "To you doubtless it may seem terrible—such a death; but Tarzan of the Apes has always expected to go out in some such way. Few of us die of old age in the jungle, nor should I care to die thus. Some day Numa will get me, or Sheeta, or a black warrior. These or some of the others. What difference does it make which it is, or whether it comes tonight or next year or in ten years? After it is over it will be all the same."

The girl shuddered. "Yes," she said in a dull, hopeless voice, "after it is over it will be all the same."

Then she went into the cavern and lay down upon the sand. Smith-Oldwick sat in the entrance and leaned against the cliff. Tarzan squatted on the opposite side.

"May I smoke?" questioned the officer of Tarzan. "I have been hoarding a few cigarettes and if it won't attract those bouncers out there I would like to have one last smoke before I cash in. Will you join me?" and he proffered the ape-man a cigarette.

"No, thanks," said Tarzan, "but it will be all right if you smoke. No wild animal is particularly fond of the fumes of tobacco so it certainly won't entice them any closer."

Smith-Oldwick lighted his cigarette and sat puffing slowly upon it. He had proffered one to the girl but she had refused, and thus they sat in silence for some time, the silence of the night ruffled occasionally by the faint crunching of padded feet upon the soft sands of the gorge's floor.

It was Smith-Oldwick who broke the silence. "Aren't they unusually quiet for lions?" he asked.

"No," replied the ape-man; "the lion that goes roaring around the jungle does not do it to attract prey. They are very quiet when they are stalking their quarry."

"I wish they would roar," said the officer. "I wish they would do anything, even charge. Just knowing that they are there and occasionally seeing something like a shadow in the darkness and the faint sounds that come to us from them are getting on my nerves. But I hope," he said, "that all three don't charge at once."

"Three?" said Tarzan. "There are seven of them out there now."

"Good Lord! exclaimed Smith-Oldwick.

"Couldn't we build a fire," asked the girl, "and frighten them away?"

"I don't know that it would do any good," said Tarzan, "as I have an idea that these lions are a little different from any that we are familiar with and possibly for the same reason which at first puzzled me a little—I refer to the apparent docility in the presence of a man of the lion who was with us today. A man is out there now with those lions."

"It is impossible!" exclaimed Smith-Oldwick. "They would tear him to pieces."

"What makes you think there is a man there?" asked the girl.

Tarzan smiled and shook his head. "I am afraid you would not understand," he replied. "It is difficult for us to understand anything that is beyond our own powers."

"What do you mean by that?" asked the officer.

"Well," said Tarzan, "if you had been born without eyes you could not understand sense impressions that the eyes of others transmit to their brains, and as you have both been born without any sense of smell I am afraid you cannot understand how I can know that there is a man there."

"You mean that you scent a man?" asked the girl.

Tarzan nodded affirmatively.

"And in the same way you know the number of lions?" asked the man.

"Yes," said Tarzan. "No two lions look alike, no two have the same scent."

The young Englishman shook his head. "No," he said, "I cannot understand."

"I doubt if the lions or the man are here necessarily for the purpose of harming us," said Tarzan, "because there has been nothing to prevent their doing so long before had they wished to. I have a theory, but it is utterly preposterous."

"What is it?" asked the girl.

"I think they are here," replied Tarzan, "to prevent us from going some place that they do not wish us to go; in other words we are under surveillance, and possibly as long as we don't go where we are not wanted we shall not be bothered."

"But how are we to know where they don't want us to go?" asked Smith-Oldwick.

"We can't know," replied Tarzan, "and the chances are that the very place we are seeking is the place they don't wish us to trespass on."

"You mean the water?" asked the girl.

"Yes," replied Tarzan.

For some time they sat in silence which was broken only by an occasional sound of movement from the outer darkness. It must have been an hour later that the ape-man rose quietly and drew his long blade from its sheath. Smith-Oldwick was dozing against the rocky wall of the cavern entrance, while the girl, exhausted by the excitement and fatigue of the day, had fallen into deep slumber. An instant after Tarzan arose, Smith-Oldwick and the girl were aroused by a volley of thunderous roars and the noise of many padded feet rushing toward them.

Tarzan of the Apes stood directly before the entrance to the cavern, his knife in his hand, awaiting the charge. The ape-man had not expected any such concerted action as he now realized had been taken by those watching them. He had known for some time that other men had joined those who were with the lions earlier in the evening, and when he arose to his feet it was because he knew that the lions and the men were moving cautiously closer to him and his party. He might easily have eluded them, for he had seen that the face of the cliff rising above the mouth of the cavern might be scaled by as good a climber as himself. It might have been wiser had he tried to escape, for he knew that in the face of such odds even he was helpless, but he stood his ground though I doubt if he could have told why.

He owed nothing either of duty or friendship to the girl sleeping in the cavern, nor could he longer be of any protection to her or her companion. Yet something held him there in futile self-sacrifice.

The great Tarmangani had not even the satisfaction of striking a blow in self-defense. A veritable avalanche of savage beasts rolled over him and threw him heavily to the ground. In falling his head struck the rocky surface of the cliff, stunning him.

It was daylight when he regained consciousness. The first dim impression borne to his awakening mind was a confusion of savage sounds which gradually resolved themselves into the growling of lions, and then, little by little, there came back to him the recollections of what had preceded the blow that had felled him.

Strong in his nostrils was the scent of Numa, the lion, and against one naked leg he could feel the coat of some animal. Slowly Tarzan opened his eyes. He was lying on his side and as he looked down his body, he saw that a great lion stood straddling him—a great lion who growled hideously at something which Tarzan could not see.

With the full return of his senses Tarzan's nose told him that the beast above him was Numa of the Wamabo pit.

Thus reassured, the ape-man spoke to the lion and at the same time made a motion as though he would arise. Immediately Numa stepped from above him. As Tarzan raised his head, he saw that he still lay where he had fallen before the opening of the cliff where the girl had been sleeping and that Numa, backed against the cliffside, was apparently defending him from two other lions who paced to and fro a short distance from their intended victim.

And then Tarzan turned his eyes into the cave and saw that the girl and Smith-Oldwick were gone.

His efforts had been for naught. With an angry toss of his head, the ape-man turned upon the two lions who had continued to pace back and forth a few yards from him. Numa of the lion pit turned a friendly glance in Tarzan's direction, rubbed his head against the ape-man's side, and then directed his snarling countenance toward the two hunters.

"I think," said Tarzan to Numa, "that you and I together can make these beasts very unhappy." He spoke in English, which, of course, Numa did not understand at all, but there must have been something reassuring in the tone, for Numa whined pleadingly and moved impatiently to and fro parallel with their antagonists.

"Come," said Tarzan suddenly and grasping the lion's mane with his left hand he moved toward the other lions, his companion pacing at his side. As the two advanced the others drew slowly back and, finally separating, moved off to either side. Tarzan and Numa passed between them but neither the great black-maned lion nor the man failed to keep an eye upon the beast nearer him so that they were not caught unawares when, as though at some preconcerted signal, the two cats charged simultaneously from opposite directions.

The ape-man met the charge of his antagonist after the same fashion of fighting that he had been accustomed to employing in previous encounters with Numa and Sheeta. To have attempted to meet the full shock of a lion's charge would have been suicidal even for the giant Tarmangani. Instead he resorted to methods of agility and cunning, for quick as are the great cats, even quicker is Tarzan of the Apes.

With outspread, raking talons and bared fangs Numa sprang for the naked chest of the ape-man. Throwing up his left arm as a boxer might ward off a blow, Tarzan struck upward beneath the left forearm of the lion, at the same time rushing in with his shoulder beneath the animal's body and simultaneously drove his blade into the tawny hide behind the shoulder. With a roar of pain Numa wheeled again, the personification of bestial rage. Now indeed would he exterminate this presumptuous man-thing who dared even to think that he could thwart the king of beasts in his desires. But as he wheeled, his intended quarry wheeled with him, brown fingers locked in the heavy mane on the powerful neck and again the blade struck deep into the lion's side.

Then it was that Numa went mad with hate and pain and at the same instant the ape-man leaped full upon his back. Easily before had Tarzan locked his legs beneath the belly of a lion while he clung to its long mane and stabbed it until his point reached its heart. So easy it had seemed before that he experienced a sharp feeling of resentment that he was unable to do so now, for the quick movements of the lion prevented him, and presently, to his dismay, as the lion leaped and threw him about, the ape-man realized that he was swinging inevitably beneath those frightful talons.

With a final effort he threw himself from Numa's back and sought, by his quickness, to elude the frenzied beast for the fraction of an instant that would permit him to regain his feet and meet the animal again upon a more even footing. But this time Numa was too quick for him and he was but partially up when a great paw struck him on the side of the head and bowled him over.

As he fell he saw a black streak shoot above him and another lion close upon his antagonist. Rolling from beneath the two battling lions Tarzan regained his feet, though he was half dazed and staggering from the impact of the terrible blow he had received. Behind him he saw a lifeless lion lying torn and bleeding upon the sand, and before him Numa of the pit was savagely mauling the second lion.

He of the black coat tremendously outclassed his adversary in point of size and strength as well as in ferocity. The battling beasts made a few feints and passes at each other before the larger succeeded in fastening his fangs in the other's throat, and then, as a cat shakes a mouse, the larger lion shook the lesser, and when his dying foe sought to roll beneath and rake his conqueror with his hind claws, the other met him halfway at his own game, and as the great talons buried themselves in the lower part of the other's chest and then were raked downward with all the terrific strength of the mighty hind legs, the battle was ended.

As Numa rose from his second victim and shook himself, Tarzan could not but again note the wondrous proportions and symmetry of the beast. The lions they had bested were splendid specimens themselves and in their coats Tarzan noted a suggestion of the black which was such a strongly marked characteristic of Numa of the pit. Their manes were just a trifle darker than an ordinary black-maned lion but the tawny shade on the balance of their coats predominated. However, the ape-man realized that they were a distinct species from any he had seen as though they had sprung originally from a cross between the forest lion of his acquaintance and a breed of which Numa of the pit might be typical.

The immediate obstruction in his way having been removed, Tarzan was for setting out in search of the spoor of the girl and Smith-Oldwick, that he might discover their fate. He suddenly found himself tremendously hungry and as he circled about over the sandy bottom searching among the tangled network of innumerable tracks for those of his proteges, there broke from his lips involuntarily the whine of a hungry beast. Immediately Numa of the pit pricked up his ears and, regarding the ape-man steadily for a moment, he answered the call of hunger and started briskly off toward the south, stopping occasionally to see if Tarzan was following.

The ape-man realized that the beast was leading him to food, and so he followed and as he followed his keen eyes and sensitive nostrils sought for some indication of the direction taken by the man and the girl. Presently out of the mass of lion tracks, Tarzan picked up those of many sandaled feet and the scent spoor of the members of the strange race such as had been with the lions the night before, and then faintly he caught the scent spoor of the girl and a little later that of Smith-Oldwick. Presently the tracks thinned and here those of the girl and the Englishman became well marked.

They had been walking side by side and there had been men and lions to the right and left of them, and men and lions in front and behind. The ape-man was puzzled by the possibilities suggested by the tracks, but in the light of any previous experience he could not explain satisfactorily to himself what his perceptions indicated.

There was little change in the formation of the gorge; it still wound its erratic course between precipitous cliffs. In places it widened out and again it became very narrow and always deeper the further south they traveled. Presently the bottom of the gorge began to slope more rapidly. Here and there were indications of ancient rapids and waterfalls. The trail became more difficult but was well marked and showed indications of great antiquity, and, in places, the handiwork of man. They had proceeded for a half or three-quarters of a mile when, at a turning of the gorge, Tarzan saw before him a narrow valley cut deep into the living rock of the earth's crust, with lofty mountain ranges bounding it upon the south. How far it extended east and west he could not see, but apparently it was no more than three or four miles across from north to south.

That it was a well-watered valley was indicated by the wealth of vegetation that carpeted its floor from the rocky cliffs upon the north to the mountains on the south.

Over the edge of the cliffs from which the ape-man viewed the valley a trail had been hewn that led downward to the base. Preceded by the lion Tarzan descended into the valley, which, at this point, was forested with large trees. Before him the trail wound onward toward the center of the valley. Raucous-voiced birds of brilliant plumage screamed among the branches while innumerable monkeys chattered and scolded above him.

The forest teemed with life, and yet there was borne in upon the ape-man a sense of unutterable loneliness, a sensation that he never before had felt in his beloved jungles. There was unreality in everything about him—in the valley itself, lying hidden and forgotten in what was supposed to be an arid waste. The birds and the monkeys, while similar in type to many with which he was familiar, were identical with none, nor was the vegetation without its idiosyncrasies. It was as though he had been suddenly transported to another world and he felt a strange restlessness that might easily have been a premonition of danger.

Fruits were growing among the trees and some of these he saw that Manu, the monkey, ate. Being hungry he swung to the lower branches and, amidst a great chattering of the monkeys, proceeded to eat such of the fruit as he saw the monkeys ate in safety. When he had partially satisfied his hunger, for meat alone could fully do so, he looked about him for Numa of the pit to discover that the lion had gone.

THE WALLED CITY

Dropping to the ground once more he picked up the trail of the girl and her captors, which he followed easily along what appeared to be a well-beaten trail. It was not long before he came to a small stream, where he quenched his thirst, and thereafter he saw that the trail followed in the general direction of the stream, which ran southwesterly. Here and there were cross trails and others which joined the main avenue, and always upon each of them were the tracks and scent of the great cats, of Numa, the lion, and Sheeta, the panther.

With the exception of a few small rodents there appeared to be no other wild life on the surface of the valley. There was no indication of Bara, the deer, or Horta, the boar, or of Gorgo, the buffalo, Buto, Tantor, or Duro. Histah, the snake, was there. He saw him in the trees in greater numbers than he ever had seen Histah before; and once beside a reedy pool he caught a scent that could have belonged to none other than Gimla the crocodile, but upon none of these did the Tarmangani care to feed.

And so, as he craved meat, he turned his attention to the birds above him. His assailants of the night before had not disarmed him. Either in the darkness and the rush of the charging lions the human foe had overlooked him or else they had considered him dead; but whatever the reason he still retained his weapons—his spear and his long knife, his bow and arrows, and his grass rope.

Fitting a shaft to his bow Tarzan awaited an opportunity to bring down one of the larger birds, and when the opportunity finally presented itself he drove the arrow straight to its mark. As the gaily plumaged creature fluttered to earth its companions and the little monkeys set up a most terrific chorus of wails and screaming protests. The whole forest became suddenly a babel of hoarse screams and shrill shrieks.

Tarzan would not have been surprised had one or two birds in the immediate vicinity given voice to terror as they fled, but that the whole life of the jungle should set up so weird a protest filled him with disgust. It was an angry face that he turned up toward the monkeys and the birds as there suddenly stirred within him a savage inclination to voice his displeasure and his answer to what he considered their challenge. And so it was that there broke upon this jungle for the first time Tarzan's hideous scream of victory and challenge.

The effect upon the creatures above him was instantaneous. Where before the air had trembled to the din of their voices, now utter silence reigned and a moment later the ape-man was alone with his puny kill.

The silence following so closely the previous tumult carried a sinister impression to the ape-man, which still further aroused his anger. Picking the bird from where it had fallen he withdrew his arrow from the body and returned it to his quiver. Then with his knife he quickly and deftly removed the skin and feathers together. He ate angrily, growling as though actually menaced by a near-by foe, and perhaps, too, his growls were partially induced by the fact that he did not care for the flesh of birds. Better this, however, than nothing and from what his senses had told him there was no flesh in the vicinity such as he was accustomed to and cared most for. How he would have enjoyed a juicy haunch from Pacco, the zebra, or a steak from the loin of Gorgo, the buffalo! The very thought made his mouth water and increased his resentment against this unnatural forest that harbored no such delicious quarry.

He had but partially consumed his kill when he suddenly became aware of a movement in the brush at no great distance from him and downwind, and a moment later his nostrils picked up the scent of Numa from the opposite direction, and then upon either side he caught the fall of padded feet and the brushing of bodies against leafy branches. The ape-man smiled. What stupid creature did they think him, to be surprised by such clumsy stalkers? Gradually the sounds and scents indicated that lions were moving upon him from all directions, that he was in the center of a steadily converging circle of beasts. Evidently they were so sure of their prey that they were making no effort toward stealth, for he heard twigs crack beneath their feet, and the brushing of their bodies against the vegetation through which they forced their way.

He wondered what could have brought them. It seemed unreasonable to believe that the cries of the birds and the monkeys should have summoned them, and yet, if not, it was indeed a remarkable coincidence. His judgment told him that the death of a single bird in this forest which teemed with birds could scarce be of sufficient moment to warrant that which followed. Yet even in the face of reason and past experience he found that the whole affair perplexed him.

He stood in the center of the trail awaiting the coming of the lions and wondering what would be the method of their attack or if they would indeed attack. Presently a maned lion came into view along the trail below him. At sight of him the lion halted. The beast was similar to those that had attacked him earlier in the day, a trifle larger and a trifle darker than the lions of his native jungles, but neither so large nor so black as Numa of the pit.

Presently he distinguished the outlines of other lions in the surrounding brush and among the trees. Each of them halted as it came within sight of the ape-man and there they stood regarding him in silence. Tarzan wondered how long it would be before they charged and while he waited he resumed his feeding, though with every sense constantly alert.

One by one the lions lay down, but always their faces were toward him and their eyes upon him. There had been no growling and no roaring—just the quiet drawing of the silent circle about him. It was all so entirely foreign to anything that Tarzan ever before had seen lions do that it irritated him so that presently, having finished his repast, he fell to making insulting remarks to first one and then another of the lions, after the habit he had learned from the apes of his childhood.

"Dango, eater of carrion," he called them, and he compared them most unfavorably with Histah, the snake, the most loathed and repulsive creature of the jungle. Finally he threw handfuls of earth at them and bits of broken twigs, and then the lions growled and bared their fangs, but none of them advanced.

"Cowards," Tarzan taunted them. "Numa with a heart of Bara, the deer." He told them who he was, and after the manner of the jungle folk he boasted as to the horrible things he would do to them, but the lions only lay and watched him.

It must have been a half hour after their coming that Tarzan caught in the distance along the trail the sound of footsteps approaching. They were the footsteps of a creature who walked upon two legs, and though Tarzan could catch no scent spoor from that direction he knew that a man was approaching. Nor had he long to wait before his judgment was confirmed by the appearance of a man who halted in the trail directly behind the first lion that Tarzan had seen.

At sight of the newcomer the ape-man realized that here was one similar to those who had given off the unfamiliar scent spoor that he had detected the previous night, and he saw that not only in the matter of scent did the man differ from other human beings with whom Tarzan was familiar.

The fellow was strongly built with skin of a leathery appearance, like parchment yellowed with age. His hair, which was coal black and three or four inches in length, grew out stiffly at right angles to his scalp. His eyes were close set and the irises densely black and very small, so that the white of the eyeball showed around them. The man's face was smooth except for a few straggly hairs on his chin and upper lip. The nose was aquiline and fine, but the hair grew so far down on the forehead as to suggest a very low and brutal type. The upper lip was short and fine while the lower lip was rather heavy and inclined to be pendulous, the chin being equally weak. Altogether the face carried the suggestion of a once strong and handsome countenance entirely altered by physical violence or by degraded habits and thoughts. The man's arms were long, though not abnormally so, while his legs were short, though straight.

He was clothed in tight-fitting nether garments and a loose, sleeveless tunic that fell just below his hips, while his feet were shod in soft-soled sandals, the wrappings of which extended halfway to his knees, closely resembling a modern spiral military legging. He carried a short, heavy spear, and at his side swung a weapon that at first so astonished the ape-man that he could scarcely believe the evidence of his senses—a heavy saber in a leather-covered scabbard. The man's tunic appeared to have been fabricated upon a loom—it was certainly not made of skins, while the garments that covered his legs were quite as evidently made from the hides of rodents.

Tarzan noted the utter unconcern with which the man approached the lions, and the equal indifference of Numa to him. The fellow paused for a moment as though appraising the ape-man and then pushed on past the lions, brushing against the tawny hide as he passed him in the trail.

About twenty feet from Tarzan the man stopped, addressing the former in a strange jargon, no syllable of which was intelligible to the Tarmangani. His gestures indicated numerous references to the lions surrounding them, and once he touched his spear with the forefinger of his left hand and twice he struck the saber at his hip.

While he spoke Tarzan studied the fellow closely, with the result that there fastened itself upon his mind a strange conviction—that the man who addressed him was what might only be described as a rational maniac. As the thought came to the ape-man he could not but smile, so paradoxical the description seemed. Yet a closer study of the man's features, carriage, and the contour of his head carried almost incontrovertibly the assurance that he was insane, while the tones of his voice and his gestures resembled those of a sane and intelligent mortal.

Presently the man had concluded his speech and appeared to be waiting questioningly Tarzan's reply. The ape-man spoke to the other first in the language of the great apes, but he soon saw that the words carried no conviction to his listener. Then with equal futility he tried several native dialects but to none of these did the man respond.

By this time Tarzan began to lose patience. He had wasted sufficient time by the road, and as he had never depended much upon speech in the accomplishment of his ends, he now raised his spear and advanced toward the other. This, evidently, was a language common to both, for instantly the fellow raised his own weapon and at the same time a low call broke from his lips, a call which instantly brought to action every lion in the hitherto silent circle. A volley of roars shattered the silence of the forest and simultaneously lions sprang into view upon all sides as they closed in rapidly upon their quarry. The man who had called them stepped back, his teeth bared in a mirthless grin.

It was then that Tarzan first noticed that the fellow's upper canines were unusually long and exceedingly sharp. It was just a flashing glimpse he got of them as he leaped agilely from the ground and, to the consternation of both the lions and their master, disappeared in the foliage of the lower terrace, flinging back over his shoulder as he swung rapidly away: "I am Tarzan of the Apes; mighty hunter; mighty fighter! None in the jungle more powerful, none more cunning than Tarzan!"

A short distance beyond the point at which they had surrounded him, Tarzan came to the trail again and sought for the spoor of Bertha Kircher and Lieutenant Smith-Oldwick. He found them quickly and continued upon his search for the two. The spoor lay directly along the trail for another half-mile when the way suddenly debouched from the forest into open land and there broke upon the astonished view of the ape-man the domes and minarets of a walled city.

Directly before him in the wall nearest him Tarzan saw a low-arched gateway to which a well-beaten trail led from that which he had been following. In the open space between the forest and the city walls, quantities of garden stuff was growing, while before him at his feet, in an open man-made ditch, ran a stream of water! The plants in the garden were laid out in well-spaced, symmetrical rows and appeared to have been given excellent attention and cultivation. Tiny streams were trickling between the rows from the main ditch before him and at some distance to his right he could see people at work among the plants.

The city wall appeared to be about thirty feet in height, its plastered expanse unbroken except by occasional embrasures. Beyond the wall rose the domes of several structures and numerous minarets dotted the sky line of the city. The largest and central dome appeared to be gilded, while others were red, or blue, or yellow. The architecture of the wall itself was of uncompromising simplicity. It was of a cream shade and appeared to be plastered and painted. At its base was a line of well-tended shrubs and at some distance towards its eastern extremity it was vine covered to the top.

As he stood in the shadow of the trail, his keen eyes taking in every detail of the picture before him, he became aware of the approach of a party in his rear and there was borne to him the scent of the man and the lions whom he had so readily escaped. Taking to the trees Tarzan moved a short distance to the west and, finding a comfortable crotch at the edge of the forest where he could watch the trail leading through the gardens to the city gate, he awaited the return of his would-be captors. And soon they came—the strange man followed by the pack of great lions. Like dogs they moved along behind him down the trail among the gardens to the gate.

Here the man struck upon the panels of the door with the butt of his spear, and when it opened in response to his signal he passed in with his lions. Beyond the open door Tarzan, from his distant perch, caught but a fleeting glimpse of life within the city, just enough to indicate that there were other human creatures who abode there, and then the door closed.

Through that door he knew that the girl and the man whom he sought to succor had been taken into the city. What fate lay in store for them or whether already it had been meted out to them he could not even guess, nor where, within that forbidding wall, they were incarcerated he could not know. But of one thing he was assured: that if he were to aid them he could not do it from outside the wall. He must gain entrance to the city first, nor did he doubt, that once within, his keen senses would eventually reveal the whereabouts of those whom he sought.

The low sun was casting long shadows across the gardens when Tarzan saw the workers returning from the eastern field. A man came first, and as he came he lowered little gates along the large ditch of running water, shutting off the streams that had run between the rows of growing plants; and behind him came other men carrying burdens of fresh vegetables in great woven baskets upon their shoulders. Tarzan had not realized that there had been so many men working in the field, but now as he sat there at the close of the day he saw a procession filing in from the east, bearing the tools and the produce back into the city.

And then, to gain a better view, the ape-man ascended to the topmost branches of a tall tree where he overlooked the nearer wall. From this point of vantage he saw that the city was long and narrow, and that while the outer walls formed a perfect rectangle, the streets within were winding. Toward the center of the city there appeared to be a low, white building around which the larger edifices of the city had been built, and here, in the fast-waning light, Tarzan thought that between two buildings he caught the glint of water, but of that he was not sure. His experience of the centers of civilization naturally inclined him to believe that this central area was a plaza about which the larger buildings were grouped and that there would be the most logical place to search first for Bertha Kircher and her companion.

And then the sun went down and darkness quickly enveloped the city—a darkness that was accentuated for the ape-man rather than relieved by the artificial lights which immediately appeared in many of the windows visible to him.

Tarzan had noticed that the roofs of most of the buildings were flat, the few exceptions being those of what he imagined to be the more pretentious public structures. How this city had come to exist in this forgotten part of unexplored Africa the ape-man could not conceive. Better than another, he realized something of the unsolved secrets of the Great Dark Continent, enormous areas of which have as yet been untouched by the foot of civilized man. Yet he could scarce believe that a city of this size and apparently thus well constructed could have existed for the generations that it must have been there, without intercourse with the outer world. Even though it was surrounded by a trackless desert waste, as he knew it to be, he could not conceive that generation after generation of men could be born and die there without attempting to solve the mysteries of the world beyond the confines of their little valley.

And yet, here was the city surrounded by tilled land and filled with people!

With the coming of night there arose throughout the jungle the cries of the great cats, the voice of Numa blended with that of Sheeta, and the thunderous roars of the great males reverberated through the forest until the earth trembled, and from within the city came the answering roars of other lions.

A simple plan for gaining entrance to the city had occurred to Tarzan, and now that darkness had fallen he set about to put it into effect. Its success hinged entirely upon the strength of the vines he had seen surmounting the wall toward the east. In this direction he made his way, while from out of the forest about him the cries of the flesh-eaters increased in volume and ferocity. A quarter of a mile intervened between the forest and the city wall—a quarter of a mile of cultivated land unrelieved by a single tree. Tarzan of the Apes realized his limitations and so he knew that it would undoubtedly spell death for him to be caught in the open space by one of the great black lions of the forest if, as he had already surmised, Numa of the pit was a specimen of the forest lion of the valley.

He must, therefore, depend entirely upon his cunning and his speed, and upon the chance that the vine would sustain his weight.

He moved through the middle terrace, where the way is always easiest, until he reached a point opposite the vine-clad portion of the wall, and there he waited, listening and scenting, until he might assure himself that there was no Numa within his immediate vicinity, or, at least, none that sought him. And when he was quite sure that there was no lion close by in the forest, and none in the clearing between himself and the wall, he dropped lightly to the ground and moved stealthily out into the open.

The rising moon, just topping the eastern cliffs, cast its bright rays upon the long stretch of open garden beneath the wall. And, too, it picked out in clear relief for any curious eyes that chanced to be cast in that direction, the figure of the giant ape-man moving across the clearing. It was only chance, of course, that a great lion hunting at the edge of the forest saw the figure of the man halfway between the forest and the wall. Suddenly there broke upon Tarzan's ears a menacing sound. It was not the roar of a hungry lion, but the roar of a lion in rage, and, as he glanced back in the direction from which the sound came, he saw a huge beast moving out from the shadow of the forest toward him.

Even in the moonlight and at a distance Tarzan saw that the lion was huge; that it was indeed another of the black-maned monsters similar to Numa of the pit. For an instant he was impelled to turn and fight, but at the same time the thought of the helpless girl imprisoned in the city flashed through his brain and, without an instant's hesitation, Tarzan of the Apes wheeled and ran for the wall. Then it was that Numa charged.

Numa, the lion, can run swiftly for a short distance, but he lacks endurance. For the period of an ordinary charge he can cover the ground with greater rapidity possibly than any other creature in the world. Tarzan, on the other hand, could run at great speed for long distances, though never as rapidly as Numa when the latter charged.

The question of his fate, then, rested upon whether, with his start he could elude Numa for a few seconds; and, if so, if the lion would then have sufficient stamina remaining to pursue him at a reduced gait for the balance of the distance to the wall.

Never before, perhaps, was staged a more thrilling race, and yet it was run with only the moon and stars to see. Alone and in silence the two beasts sped across the moonlit clearing. Numa gained with appalling rapidity upon the fleeing man, yet at every bound Tarzan was nearer to the vine-clad wall. Once the ape-man glanced back. Numa was so close upon him that it seemed inevitable that at the next bound he should drag him down; so close was he that the ape-man drew his knife as he ran, that he might at least give a good account of himself in the last moments of his life.

But Numa had reached the limit of his speed and endurance. Gradually he dropped behind but he did not give up the pursuit, and now Tarzan realized how much hinged upon the strength of the untested vines.

If, at the inception of the race, only Goro and the stars had looked down upon the contestants, such was not the case at its finish, since from an embrasure near the summit of the wall two close-set black eyes peered down upon the two. Tarzan was a dozen yards ahead of Numa when he reached the wall. There was no time to stop and institute a search for sturdy stems and safe handholds. His fate was in the hands of chance and with the realization he gave a final spurt and running catlike up the side of the wall among the vines, sought with his hands for something that would sustain his weight. Below him Numa leaped also.

AMONG THE MANIACS

As the lions swarmed over her protectors, Bertha Kircher shrank back in the cave in a momentary paralysis of fright super-induced, perhaps, by the long days of terrific nerve strain which she had undergone.

Mingled with the roars of the lions had been the voices of men, and presently out of the confusion and turmoil she felt the near presence of a human being, and then hands reached forth and seized her. It was dark and she could see but little, nor any sign of the English officer or the ape-man. The man who seized her kept the lions from her with what appeared to be a stout spear, the haft of which he used to beat off the beasts. The fellow dragged her from the cavern the while he shouted what appeared to be commands and warnings to the lions.

Once out upon the light sands of the bottom of the gorge objects became more distinguishable, and then she saw that there were other men in the party and that two half led and half carried the stumbling figure of a third, whom she guessed must be Smith-Oldwick.

For a time the lions made frenzied efforts to reach the two captives but always the men with them succeeded in beating them off. The fellows seemed utterly unafraid of the great beasts leaping and snarling about them, handling them much the same as one might handle a pack of obstreperous dogs. Along the bed of the old watercourse that once ran through the gorge they made their way, and as the first faint lightening of the eastern horizon presaged the coming dawn, they paused for a moment upon the edge of a declivity, which appeared to the girl in the strange light of the waning night as a vast, bottomless pit; but, as their captors resumed their way and the light of the new day became stronger, she saw that they were moving downward toward a dense forest.

Once beneath the over-arching trees all was again Cimmerian darkness, nor was the gloom relieved until the sun finally arose beyond the eastern cliffs, when she saw that they were following what appeared to be a broad and well-beaten game trail through a forest of great trees. The ground was unusually dry for an African forest and the underbrush, while heavily foliaged, was not nearly so rank and impenetrable as that which she had been accustomed to find in similar woods. It was as though the trees and the bushes grew in a waterless country, nor was there the musty odor of decaying vegetation or the myriads of tiny insects such as are bred in damp places.

As they proceeded and the sun rose higher, the voices of the arboreal jungle life rose in discordant notes and loud chattering about them. Innumerable monkeys scolded and screamed in the branches overhead, while harsh-voiced birds of brilliant plumage darted hither and thither. She noticed presently that their captors often cast apprehensive glances in the direction of the birds and on numerous occasions seemed to be addressing the winged denizens of the forest.

One incident made a marked impression on her. The man who immediately preceded her was a fellow of powerful build, yet, when a brilliantly colored parrot swooped downward toward him, he dropped upon his knees and covering his face with his arms bent forward until his head touched the ground. Some of the others looked at him and laughed nervously. Presently the man glanced upward and seeing that the bird had gone, rose to his feet and continued along the trail.

It was at this brief halt that Smith-Oldwick was brought to her side by the men who had been supporting him. He had been rather badly mauled by one of the lions; but was now able to walk alone, though he was extremely weak from shock and loss of blood.

"Pretty mess, what?" he remarked with a wry smile, indicating his bloody and disheveled state.

"It is terrible," said the girl. "I hope you are not suffering."

"Not as much as I should have expected," he replied, "but I feel as weak as a fool. What sort of creatures are these beggars, anyway?"

"I don't know," she replied, "there is something terribly uncanny about their appearance."

The man regarded one of their captors closely for a moment and then, turning to the girl asked, "Did you ever visit a madhouse?"

She looked up at him in quick understanding and with a horrified expression in her eyes. "That's it!" she cried.

"They have all the earmarks," he said. "Whites of the eyes showing all around the irises, hair growing stiffly erect from the scalp and low down upon the forehead—even their mannerisms and their carriage are those of maniacs."

The girl shuddered.

"Another thing about them," continued the Englishman, "that doesn't appear normal is that they are afraid of parrots and utterly fearless of lions."

"Yes," said the girl; "and did you notice that the birds seem utterly fearless of them—really seem to hold them in contempt? Have you any idea what language they speak?"

'No," said the man, "I have been trying to figure that out. It's not like any of the few native dialects of which I have any knowledge."

"It doesn't sound at all like the native language," said the girl, "but there is something familiar about it. You know, every now and then I feel that I am just on the verge of understanding what they are saying, or at least that somewhere I have heard their tongue before, but final recognition always eludes me."

"I doubt if you ever heard their language spoken," said the man. "These people must have lived in this out-of-the-way valley for ages and even if they had retained the original language of their ancestors without change, which is doubtful, it must be some tongue that is no longer spoken in the outer world."

At one point where a stream of water crossed the trail the party halted while the lions and the men drank. They motioned to their captors to drink too, and as Bertha Kircher and Smith-Oldwick, lying prone upon the ground drank from the clear, cool water of the rivulet, they were suddenly startled by the thunderous roar of a lion a short distance ahead of them. Instantly the lions with them set up a hideous response, moving restlessly to and fro with their eyes always either turned in the direction from which the roar had come or toward their masters, against whom the tawny beasts slunk. The men loosened the sabers in their scabbards, the weapons that had aroused Smith-Oldwick's curiosity as they had Tarzan's, and grasped their spears more firmly.

Evidently there were lions and lions, and while they evinced no fear of the beasts which accompanied them, it was quite evident that the voice of the newcomer had an entirely different effect upon them, although the men seemed less terrified than the lions. Neither, however, showed any indication of an inclination to flee; on the contrary the entire party advanced along the trail in the direction of the menacing roars, and presently there appeared in the center of the path a black lion of gigantic proportions. To Smith-Oldwick and the girl he appeared to be the same lion that they had encountered at the plane and from which Tarzan had rescued them. But it was not Numa of the pit, although he resembled him closely.

The black beast stood directly in the center of the trail lashing his tail and growling menacingly at the advancing party. The men urged on their own beasts, who growled and whined but hesitated to charge. Evidently becoming impatient, and in full consciousness of his might the intruder raised his tail stiffly erect and shot forward. Several of the defending lions made a half-hearted attempt to obstruct his passage, but they might as well have placed themselves in the path of an express train, as hurling them aside the great beast leaped straight for one of the men. A dozen spears were launched at him and a dozen sabers leaped from their scabbards; gleaming, razor-edged weapons they were, but for the instant rendered futile by the terrific speed of the charging beast.

Two of the spears entering his body but served to further enrage him as, with demoniacal roars, he sprang upon the hapless man he had singled out for his prey. Scarcely pausing in his charge he seized the fellow by the shoulder and, turning quickly at right angles, leaped into the concealing foliage that flanked the trail, and was gone, bearing his victim with him.

So quickly had the whole occurrence transpired that the formation of the little party was scarcely altered. There had been no opportunity for flight, even if it had been contemplated; and now that the lion was gone with his prey the men made no move to pursue him. They paused only long enough to recall the two or three of their lions that had scattered and then resumed the march along the trail.

"Might be an everyday occurrence from all the effect it has on them," remarked Smith-Oldwick to the girl.

"Yes," she said. "They seem to be neither surprised nor disconcerted, and evidently they are quite sure that the lion, having got what he came for, will not molest them further."

"I had thought," said the Englishman, "that the lions of the Wamabo country were about the most ferocious in existence, but they are regular tabby cats by comparison with these big black fellows. Did you ever see anything more utterly fearless or more terribly irresistible than that charge?"

For a while, as they walked side by side, their thoughts and conversation centered upon this latest experience, until the trail emerging from the forest opened to their view a walled city and an area of cultivated land. Neither could suppress an exclamation of surprise.

"Why, that wall is a regular engineering job," exclaimed Smith-Oldwick

"And look at the domes and minarets of the city beyond," cried the girl. "There must be a civilized people beyond that wall. Possibly we are fortunate to have fallen into their hands."

Smith-Oldwick shrugged his shoulders. "I hope so," he said, "though I am not at all sure about people who travel about with lions and are afraid of parrots. There must be something wrong with them."

The party followed the trail across the field to an arched gateway which opened at the summons of one of their captors, who beat upon the heavy wooden panels with his spear. Beyond, the gate opened into a narrow street which seemed but a continuation of the jungle trail leading from the forest. Buildings on either hand adjoined the wall and fronted the narrow, winding street, which was only visible for a short distance ahead.

The houses were practically all two-storied structures, the upper stories flush with the street while the walls of the first story were set back some ten feet, a series of simple columns and arches supporting the front of the second story and forming an arcade on either side of the narrow thoroughfare.

The pathway in the center of the street was unpaved, but the floors of the arcades were cut stone of various shapes and sizes but all carefully fitted and laid without mortar. These floors gave evidence of great antiquity, there being a distinct depression down the center as though the stone had been worn away by the passage of countless sandaled feet during the ages that it had lain there.

There were few people astir at this early hour, and these were of the same type as their captors. At first those whom they saw were only men, but as they went deeper into the city they came upon a few naked children playing in the soft dust of the roadway. Many they passed showed the greatest surprise and curiosity in the prisoners, and often made inquiries of the guards, which the two assumed must have been in relation to themselves, while others appeared not to notice them at all.

"I wish we could understand their bally language," exclaimed Smith-Oldwick.

"Yes," said the girl, "I would like to ask them what they are going to do with us."

"That would be interesting," said the man. "I have been doing considerable wondering along that line myself."

"I don't like the way their canine teeth are filed," said the girl. "It's too suggestive of some of the cannibals I have seen."

"You don't really believe they are cannibals, do you?" asked the man. "You don't think white people are ever cannibals, do you?"

"Are these people white?" asked the girl.

"They're not Negroes, that's certain," rejoined the man. "Their skin is yellow, but yet it doesn't resemble the Chinese exactly, nor are any of their features Chinese."

It was at this juncture that they caught their first glimpse of a native woman. She was similar in most respects to the men though her stature was smaller and her figure more symmetrical. Her face was more repulsive than that of the men, possibly because of the fact that she was a woman, which rather accentuated the idiosyncrasies of eyes, pendulous lip, pointed tusks and stiff, low-growing hair. The latter was longer than that of the men and much heavier. It hung about her shoulders and was confined by a colored bit of some lacy fabric. Her single garment appeared to be nothing more than a filmy scarf which was wound tightly around her body from below her naked breasts, being caught up some way at the bottom near her ankles. Bits of shiny metal resembling gold, ornamented both the headdress and the skirt. Otherwise the woman was entirely without jewelry. Her bare arms were slender and shapely and her hands and feet well proportioned and symmetrical.

She came close to the party as they passed her, jabbering to the guards who paid no attention to her. The prisoners had an opportunity to observe her closely as she followed at their side for a short distance.

"The figure of a houri," remarked Smith-Oldwick, "with the face of an imbecile."

The street they followed was intersected at irregular intervals by crossroads which, as they glanced down them, proved to be equally as tortuous as that through which they were being conducted. The houses varied but little in design. Occasionally there were bits of color, or some attempt at other architectural ornamentation. Through open windows and doors they could see that the walls of the houses were very thick and that all apertures were quite small, as though the people had built against extreme heat, which they realized must have been necessary in this valley buried deep in an African desert.

Ahead they occasionally caught glimpses of larger structures, and as they approached them, came upon what was evidently a part of the business section of the city. There were numerous small shops and bazaars interspersed among the residences, and over the doors of these were signs painted in characters strongly suggesting Greek origin and yet it was not Greek as both the Englishman and the girl knew.

Smith-Oldwick was by this time beginning to feel more acutely the pain of his wounds and the consequent weakness that was greatly aggravated by loss of blood. He staggered now occasionally and the girl, seeing his plight, offered him her arm.

"No," he expostulated, "you have passed through too much yourself to have any extra burden imposed upon you." But though he made a valiant effort to keep up with their captors he occasionally lagged, and upon one such occasion the guards for the first time showed any disposition toward brutality.

It was a big fellow who walked at Smith-Oldwick's left. Several times he took hold of the Englishman's arm and pushed him forward not ungently, but when the captive lagged again and again the fellow suddenly, and certainly with no just provocation, flew into a perfect frenzy of rage. He leaped upon the wounded man, striking him viciously with his fists and, bearing him to the ground, grasped his throat in his left hand while with his right he drew his long sharp saber. Screaming terribly he waved the blade above his head.

The others stopped and turned to look upon the encounter with no particular show of interest. It was as though one of the party had paused to readjust a sandal and the others merely waited until he was ready to march on again.

But if their captors were indifferent, Bertha Kircher was not. The close-set blazing eyes, the snarling fanged face, and the frightful screams filled her with horror, while the brutal and wanton attack upon the wounded man aroused within her the spirit of protection for the weak that is inherent in all women. Forgetful of everything other than that a weak and defenseless man was being brutally murdered before her eyes, the girl cast aside discretion and, rushing to Smith-Oldwick's assistance, seized the uplifted sword arm of the shrieking creature upon the prostrate Englishman.

Clinging desperately to the fellow she surged backward with all her weight and strength with the result that she overbalanced him and sent him sprawling to the pavement upon his back. In his efforts to save himself he relaxed his grasp upon the grip of his saber which had no sooner fallen to the ground than it was seized upon by the girl. Standing erect beside the prostrate form of the English officer Bertha Kircher, the razor-edged weapon grasped firmly in her hand, faced their captors.

She was a brave figure; even her soiled and torn riding togs and disheveled hair detracted nothing from her appearance. The creature she had felled scrambled quickly to his feet and in the instant his whole demeanor changed. From demoniacal rage he became suddenly convulsed with hysterical laughter although it was a question in the girl's mind as to which was the more terrifying. His companions stood looking on with vacuous grins upon their countenances, while he from whom the girl had wrested the weapon leaped up and down shrieking with laughter. If Bertha Kircher had needed further evidence to assure her that they were in the hands of a mentally deranged people the man's present actions would have been sufficient to convince her. The sudden uncontrolled rage and now the equally uncontrolled and mirthless laughter but emphasized the facial attributes of idiocy.

Suddenly realizing how helpless she was in the event any one of the men should seek to overpower her, and moved by a sudden revulsion of feeling that brought on almost a nausea of disgust, the girl hurled the weapon upon the ground at the feet of the laughing maniac and, turning, kneeled beside the Englishman.

"It was wonderful of you," he said, "but you shouldn't have done it. Don't antagonize them: I believe that they are all mad and you know they say that one should always humor a madman."

She shook her head. "I couldn't see him kill you," she said.

A sudden light sprang to the man's eyes as he reached out a hand and grasped the girl's fingers. "Do you care a little now?" he asked. "Can't you tell me that you do—just a bit?"

She did not withdraw her hand from his but she shook her head sadly. "Please don't," she said. "I am sorry that I can only like you very much."

The light died from his eyes and his fingers relaxed their grasp on hers. "Please forgive me," he murmured. "I intended waiting until we got out of this mess and you were safe among your own people. It must have been the shock or something like that, and seeing you defending me as you did. Anyway, I couldn't help it and really it doesn't make much difference what I say now, does it?"

"What do you mean?" she asked quickly.

He shrugged and smiled ruefully. "I will never leave this city alive," he said. "I wouldn't mention it except that I realize that you must know it as well as I. I was pretty badly torn up by the lion and this fellow here has about finished me. There might be some hope if we were among civilized people, but here with these frightful creatures what care could we get even if they were friendly?"

Bertha Kircher knew that he spoke the truth, and yet she could not bring herself to an admission that Smith-Oldwick would die. She was very fond of him, in fact her great regret was that she did not love him, but she knew that she did not.

It seemed to her that it could be such an easy thing for any girl to love Lieutenant Harold Percy Smith-Oldwick—an English officer and a gentleman, the scion of an old family and himself a man of ample means, young, good-looking and affable. What more could a girl ask for than to have such a man love her and that she possessed Smith-Oldwick's love there was no doubt in Bertha Kircher's mind.

She sighed, and then, laying her hand impulsively on his forehead, she whispered, "Do not give up hope, though. Try to live for my sake and for your sake I will try to love you."

It was as though new life had suddenly been injected into the man's veins. His face lightened instantly and with strength that he himself did not know he possessed he rose slowly to his feet, albeit somewhat unsteadily. The girl helped him and supported him after he had arisen.

For the moment they had been entirely unconscious of their surroundings and now as she looked at their captors she saw that they had fallen again into their almost habitual manner of stolid indifference, and at a gesture from one of them the march was resumed as though no untoward incident had occurred.

Bertha Kircher experienced a sudden reaction from the momentary exaltation of her recent promise to the Englishman. She knew that she had spoken more for him than for herself but now that it was over she realized, as she had realized the moment before she had spoken, that it was unlikely she would ever care for him the way he wished. But what had she promised? Only that she would try to love him. "And now?" she asked herself.

She realized that there might be little hope of their ever returning to civilization. Even if these people should prove friendly and willing to let them depart in peace, how were they to find their way back to the coast? With Tarzan dead, as she fully believed him after having seen his body lying lifeless at the mouth of the cave when she had been dragged forth by her captor, there seemed no power at their command which could guide them safely.

The two had scarcely mentioned the ape-man since their capture, for each realized fully what his loss meant to them. They had compared notes relative to those few exciting moments of the final attack and capture and had found that they agreed perfectly upon all that had occurred. Smith-Oldwick had even seen the lion leap upon Tarzan at the instant that the former was awakened by the roars of the charging beasts, and though the night had been dark, he had been able to see that the body of the savage ape-man had never moved from the instant that it had come down beneath the beast.

And so, if at other times within the past few weeks Bertha Kircher had felt that her situation was particularly hopeless, she was now ready to admit that hope was absolutely extinct.

The streets were beginning to fill with the strange men and women of this strange city. Sometimes individuals would notice them and seem to take a great interest in them, and again others would pass with vacant stares, seemingly unconscious of their immediate surroundings and paying no attention whatsoever to the prisoners. Once they heard hideous screams up a side street, and looking they saw a man in the throes of a demoniacal outburst of rage, similar to that which they had witnessed in the recent attack upon Smith-Oldwick. This creature was venting his insane rage upon a child which he repeatedly struck and bit, pausing only long enough to shriek at frequent intervals. Finally, just before they passed out of sight the creature raised the limp body of the child high above his head and cast it down with all his strength upon the pavement, and then, wheeling and screaming madly at the top of his lungs, he dashed headlong up the winding street.

Two women and several men had stood looking on at the cruel attack. They were at too great a distance for the Europeans to know whether their facial expressions portrayed pity or rage, but be that as it may, none offered to interfere.

A few yards farther on a hideous hag leaned from a second story window where she laughed and jibbered and made horrid grimaces at all who passed her. Others went their ways apparently attending to whatever duties called them, as soberly as the inhabitants of any civilized community.

"God," muttered Smith-Oldwick, "what an awful place!"

The girl turned suddenly toward him. "You still have your pistol?" she asked him.

"Yes," he replied. "I tucked it inside my shirt. They did not search me and it was too dark for them to see whether I carried any weapons or not. So I hid it in the hope that I might get through with it."

She moved closer to him and took hold of his hand. "Save one cartridge for me, please?" she begged.

Smith-Oldwick looked down at her and blinked his eyes very rapidly. An unfamiliar and disconcerting moisture had come into them. He had realized, of course, how bad a plight was theirs but somehow it had seemed to affect him only: it did not seem possible that anyone could harm this sweet and beautiful girl.

And that she should have to be destroyed—destroyed by him! It was too hideous: it was unbelievable, unthinkable! If he had been filled with apprehension before, he was doubly perturbed now.

"I don't believe I could do it, Bertha," he said.

"Not even to save me from something worse?" she asked.

He shook his head dismally. "I could never do it," he replied.

The street that they were following suddenly opened upon a wide avenue, and before them spread a broad and beautiful lagoon, the quiet surface of which mirrored the clear cerulean of the sky. Here the aspect of all their surroundings changed. The buildings were higher and much more pretentious in design and ornamentation. The street itself was paved in mosaics of barbaric but stunningly beautiful design. In the ornamentation of the buildings there was considerable color and a great deal of what appeared to be gold leaf. In all the decorations there was utilized in various ways the conventional figure of the parrot, and, to a lesser extent, that of the lion and the monkey.

Their captors led them along the pavement beside the lagoon for a short distance and then through an arched doorway into one of the buildings facing the avenue. Here, directly within the entrance was a large room furnished with massive benches and tables, many of which were elaborately hand carved with the figures of the inevitable parrot, the lion, or the monkey, the parrot always predominating.

Behind one of the tables sat a man who differed in no way that the captives could discover from those who accompanied them. Before this person the party halted, and one of the men who had brought them made what seemed to be an oral report. Whether they were before a judge, a military officer, or a civil dignitary they could not know, but evidently he was a man of authority, for, after listening to whatever recital was being made to him the while he closely scrutinized the two captives, he made a single futile attempt to converse with them and then issued some curt orders to him who had made the report.

Almost immediately two of the men approached Bertha Kircher and signaled her to accompany them. Smith-Oldwick started to follow her but was intercepted by one of their guards. The girl stopped then and turned back, at the same time looking at the man at the table and making signs with her hands, indicating, as best she could, that she wished Smith-Oldwick to remain with her, but the fellow only shook his head negatively and motioned to the guards to remove her. The Englishman again attempted to follow but was restrained. He was too weak and helpless even to make an attempt to enforce his wishes. He thought of the pistol inside his shirt and then of the futility of attempting to overcome an entire city with the few rounds of ammunition left to him.

So far, with the single exception of the attack made upon him, they had no reason to believe that they might not receive fair treatment from their captors, and so he reasoned that it might be wiser to avoid antagonizing them until such a time as he became thoroughly convinced that their intentions were entirely hostile. He saw the girl led from the building and just before she disappeared from his view she turned and waved her hand to him:

"Good luck!" she cried, and was gone.

The lions that had entered the building with the party had, during their examination by the man at the table, been driven from the apartment through a doorway behind him. Toward this same doorway two of the men now led Smith-Oldwick. He found himself in a long corridor from the sides of which other doorways opened, presumably into other apartments of the building. At the far end of the corridor he saw a heavy grating beyond which appeared an open courtyard. Into this courtyard the prisoner was conducted, and as he entered it with the two guards he found himself in an opening which was bounded by the inner walls of the building. It was in the nature of a garden in which a number of trees and flowering shrubs grew. Beneath several of the trees were benches and there was a bench along the south wall, but what aroused his most immediate attention was the fact that the lions who had assisted in their capture and who had accompanied them upon the return to the city, lay sprawled about upon the ground or wandered restlessly to and fro.

Just inside the gate his guard halted. The two men exchanged a few words and then turned and reentered the corridor. The Englishman was horror-stricken as the full realization of his terrible plight forced itself upon his tired brain. He turned and seized the grating in an attempt to open it and gain the safety of the corridor, but he found it securely locked against his every effort, and then he called aloud to the retreating figure of the men within. The only reply he received was a high-pitched, mirthless laugh, and then the two passed through the doorway at the far end of the corridor and he was alone with the lions.

THE QUEEN'S STORY

In the meantime Bertha Kircher was conducted the length of the plaza toward the largest and most pretentious of the buildings surrounding it. This edifice covered the entire width of one end of the plaza. It was several stories in height, the main entrance being approached by a wide flight of stone steps, the bottom of which was guarded by enormous stone lions, while at the top there were two pedestals flanking the entrance and of the same height, upon each of which was the stone image of a large parrot. As the girl neared these latter images she saw that the capital of each column was hewn into the semblance of a human skull upon which the parrots perched. Above the arched doorway and upon the walls of the building were the figures of other parrots, of lions, and of monkeys. Some of these were carved in bas-relief; others were delineated in mosaics, while still others appeared to have been painted upon the surface of the wall.

The colorings of the last were apparently much subdued by age with the result that the general effect was soft and beautiful. The sculpturing and mosaic work were both finely executed, giving evidence of a high degree of artistic skill. Unlike the first building into which she had been conducted, the entrance to which had been doorless, massive doors closed the entrance which she now approached. In the niches formed by the columns which supported the door's arch, and about the base of the pedestals of the stone parrots, as well as in various other places on the broad stairway, lolled some score of armed men. The tunics of these were all of a vivid yellow and upon the breast and back of each was embroidered the figure of a parrot.

As she was conducted up the stairway one of these yellow-coated warriors approached and halted her guides at the top of the steps. Here they exchanged a few words and while they were talking the girl noticed that he who had halted them, as well as those whom she could see of his companions, appeared to be, if possible, of a lower mentality than her original captors.

Their coarse, bristling hair grew so low upon their foreheads as, in some instances, to almost join their eyebrows, while the irises were smaller, exposing more of the white of the eyeball.

After a short parley the man in charge of the doorway, for such he seemed to be, turned and struck upon one of the panels with the butt of his spear, at the same time calling to several of his companions, who rose and came forward at his command. Soon the great doors commenced slowly to swing creakingly open, and presently, as they separated, the girl saw behind them the motive force which operated the massive doors—to each door a half-dozen naked Negroes.

At the doorway her two guards were turned back and their places taken by a half dozen of the yellow-coated soldiery. These conducted her through the doorway which the blacks, pulling upon heavy chains, closed behind them. And as the girl watched them she noted with horror that the poor creatures were chained by the neck to the doors.

Before her led a broad hallway in the center of which was a little pool of clear water. Here again in floor and walls was repeated in new and ever-changing combinations and designs, the parrots, the monkeys, and the lions, but now many of the figures were of what the girl was convinced must be gold. The walls of the corridor consisted of a series of open archways through which, upon either side, other spacious apartments were visible. The hallway was entirely unfurnished, but the rooms on either side contained benches and tables. Glimpses of some of the walls revealed the fact that they were covered with hangings of some colored fabric, while upon the floors were thick rugs of barbaric design and the skins of black lions and beautifully marked leopards.

The room directly to the right of the entrance was filled with men wearing the yellow tunics of her new guard while the walls were hung with numerous spears and sabers. At the far end of the corridor a low flight of steps led to another closed doorway. Here the guard was again halted. One of the guards at this doorway, after receiving the report of one of those who accompanied her, passed through the door, leaving them standing outside. It was fully fifteen minutes before he returned, when the guard was again changed and the girl conducted into the chamber beyond.

Through three other chambers and past three more massive doors, at each of which her guard was changed, the girl was conducted before she was ushered into a comparatively small room, back and forth across the floor of which paced a man in a scarlet tunic, upon the front and back of which was embroidered an enormous parrot and upon whose head was a barbaric headdress surmounted by a stuffed parrot.

The walls of this room were entirely hidden by hangings upon which hundreds, even thousands, of parrots were embroidered. Inlaid in the floor were golden parrots, while, as thickly as they could be painted, upon the ceiling were brilliant-hued parrots with wings outspread as though in the act of flying.

The man himself was larger of stature than any she had yet seen within the city. His parchment-like skin was wrinkled with age and he was much fatter than any other of his kind that she had seen. His bared arms, however, gave evidence of great strength and his gait was not that of an old man. His facial expression denoted almost utter imbecility and he was quite the most repulsive creature that ever Bertha Kircher had looked upon.

For several minutes after she was conducted into his presence he appeared not to be aware that she was there but continued his restless pacing to and fro. Suddenly, without the slightest warning, and while he was at the far end of the room from her with his back toward her, he wheeled and rushed madly at her. Involuntarily the girl shrank back, extending her open palms toward the frightful creature as though to hold him aloof but a man upon either side of her, the two who had conducted her into the apartment, seized and held her.

Although he rushed violently toward her the man stopped without touching her. For a moment his horrid white-rimmed eyes glared searchingly into her face, immediately following which he burst into maniacal laughter. For two or three minutes the creature gave himself over to merriment and then, stopping as suddenly as he had commenced to laugh, he fell to examining the prisoner. He felt of her hair, her skin, the texture of the garment she wore and by means of signs made her understand she was to open her mouth. In the latter he seemed much interested, calling the attention of one of the guards to her canine teeth and then baring his own sharp fangs for the prisoner to see.

Presently he resumed pacing to and fro across the floor, and it was fully fifteen minutes before he again noticed the prisoner, and then it was to issue a curt order to her guards, who immediately conducted her from the apartment.

The guards now led the girl through a series of corridors and apartments to a narrow stone stairway which led to the floor above, finally stopping before a small door where stood a naked Negro armed with a spear. At a word from one of her guards the Negro opened the door and the party passed into a low-ceiled apartment, the windows of which immediately caught the girl's attention through the fact that they were heavily barred. The room was furnished similarly to those that she had seen in other parts of the building, the same carved tables and benches, the rugs upon the floor, the decorations upon the walls, although in every respect it was simpler than anything she had seen on the floor below. In one corner was a low couch covered with a rug similar to those on the floor except that it was of a lighter texture, and upon this sat a woman.

As Bertha Kircher's eyes alighted upon the occupant of the room the girl gave a little gasp of astonishment, for she recognized immediately that here was a creature more nearly of her own kind than any she had seen within the city's walls. An old woman it was who looked at her through faded blue eyes, sunken deep in a wrinkled and toothless face. But the eyes were those of a sane and intelligent creature, and the wrinkled face was the face of a white woman.

At sight of the girl the woman rose and came forward, her gait so feeble and unsteady that she was forced to support herself with a long staff which she grasped in both her hands. One of the guards spoke a few words to her and then the men turned and left the apartment. The girl stood just within the door waiting in silence for what might next befall her.

The old woman crossed the room and stopped before her, raising her weak and watery eyes to the fresh young face of the newcomer. Then she scanned her from head to foot and once again the old eyes returned to the girl's face. Bertha Kircher on her part was not less frank in her survey of the little old woman. It was the latter who spoke first. In a thin, cracked voice she spoke, hesitatingly, falteringly, as though she were using unfamiliar words and speaking a strange tongue.

"You are from the outer world?" she asked in English. "God grant that you may speak and understand this tongue."

"English?" the girl exclaimed, "Yes, of course, I speak English."

"Thank God!" cried the little old woman. "I did not know whether I myself might speak it so that another could understand. For sixty years I have spoken only their accursed gibberish. For sixty years I have not heard a word in my native language. Poor creature! Poor creature!" she mumbled. "What accursed misfortune threw you into their hands?"

"You are an English woman?" asked Bertha Kircher. "Did I understand you aright that you are an English woman and have been here for sixty years?"

The old woman nodded her head affirmatively. "For sixty years I have never been outside of this palace. Come," she said, stretching forth a bony hand. "I am very old and cannot stand long. Come and sit with me on my couch."

The girl took the proffered hand and assisted the old lady back to the opposite side of the room and when she was seated the girl sat down beside her.

"Poor child! Poor child!" moaned the old woman. "Far better to have died than to have let them bring you here. At first I might have destroyed myself but there was always the hope that someone would come who would take me away, but none ever comes. Tell me how they got you."

Very briefly the girl narrated the principal incidents which led up to her capture by some of the creatures of the city.

"Then there is a man with you in the city?" asked the old woman.

"Yes," said the girl, "but I do not know where he is nor what are their intentions in regard to him. In fact, I do not know what their intentions toward me are."

"No one might even guess," said the old woman. "They do not know themselves from one minute to the next what their intentions are, but I think you can rest assured, my poor child, that you will never see your friend again."

"But they haven't slain you," the girl reminded her, "and you have been their prisoner, you say, for sixty years."

"No," replied her companion, "they have not killed me, nor will they kill you, though God knows before you have lived long in this horrible place you will beg them to kill you."

"Who are they—" asked Bertha Kircher, "what kind of people? They differ from any that I ever have seen. And tell me, too, how you came here."

"It was long ago," said the old woman, rocking back and forth on the couch. "It was long ago. Oh, how long it was! I was only twenty then. Think of it, child! Look at me. I have no mirror other than my bath, I cannot see what I look like for my eyes are old, but with my fingers I can feel my old and wrinkled face, my sunken eyes, and these flabby lips drawn in over toothless gums. I am old and bent and hideous, but then I was young and they said that I was beautiful. No, I will not be a hypocrite; I was beautiful. My glass told me that.

"My father was a missionary in the interior and one day there came a band of Arabian slave raiders. They took the men and women of the little native village where my father labored, and they took me, too. They did not know much about our part of the country so they were compelled to rely upon the men of our village whom they had captured to guide them. They told me that they never before had been so far south and that they had heard there was a country rich in ivory and slaves west of us. They wanted to go there and from there they would take us north, where I was to be sold into the harem of some black sultan.

"They often discussed the price I would bring, and that that price might not lessen, they guarded me jealously from one another so the journeys were made as little fatiguing for me as possible. I was given the best food at their command and I was not harmed.

"But after a short time, when we had reached the confines of the country with which the men of our village were familiar and had entered upon a desolate and arid desert waste, the Arabs realized at last that we were lost. But they still kept on, ever toward the west, crossing hideous gorges and marching across the face of a burning land beneath the pitiless sun. The poor slaves they had captured were, of course, compelled to carry all the camp equipage and loot and thus heavily burdened, half starved and without water, they soon commenced to die like flies.

"We had not been in the desert land long before the Arabs were forced to kill their horses for food, and when we reached the first gorge, across which it would have been impossible to transport the animals, the balance of them were slaughtered and the meat loaded upon the poor staggering blacks who still survived.

"Thus we continued for two more days and now all but a handful of blacks were dead, and the Arabs themselves had commenced to succumb to hunger and thirst and the intense heat of the desert. As far as the eye could reach back toward the land of plenty from whence we had come, our route was marked by circling vultures in the sky and by the bodies of the dead who lay down in the trackless waste for the last time. The ivory had been abandoned tusk by tusk as the blacks gave out, and along the trail of death was strewn the camp equipage and the horse trappings of a hundred men.

"For some reason the Arab chief favored me to the last, possibly with the idea that of all his other treasures I could be most easily transported, for I was young and strong and after the horses were killed I had walked and kept up with the best of the men. We English, you know, are great walkers, while these Arabians had never walked since they were old enough to ride a horse.

"I cannot tell you how much longer we kept on but at last, with our strength almost gone, a handful of us reached the bottom of a deep gorge. To scale the opposite side was out of the question and so we kept on down along the sands of what must have been the bed of an ancient river, until finally we came to a point where we looked out upon what appeared to be a beautiful valley in which we felt assured that we would find game in plenty.

"By then there were only two of us left—the chief and myself. I do not need to tell you what the valley was, for you found it in much the same way as I did. So quickly were we captured that it seemed they must have been waiting for us, and I learned later that such was the case, just as they were waiting for you.

"As you came through the forest you must have seen the monkeys and parrots and since you have entered the palace, how constantly these animals, and the lions, are used in the decorations. At home we were all familiar with talking parrots who repeated the things that they were taught to say, but these parrots are different in that they all talk in the same language that the people of the city use, and they say that the monkeys talk to the parrots and the parrots fly to the city and tell the people what the monkeys say. And, although it is hard to believe, I have learned that this is so, for I have lived here among them for sixty years in the palace of their king.

"They brought me, as they brought you, directly to the palace. The Arabian chief was taken elsewhere. I never knew what became of him. Ago XXV was king then. I have seen many kings since that day. He was a terrible man; but then, they are all terrible."

"What is the matter with them?" asked the girl.

"They are a race of maniacs," replied the old woman. "Had you not guessed it? Among them are excellent craftsmen and good farmers and a certain amount of law and order, such as it is.

"They reverence all birds, but the parrot is their chief deity. There is one who is held here in the palace in a very beautiful apartment. He is their god of gods. He is a very old bird. If what Ago told me when I came is true, he must be nearly three hundred years old by now. Their religious rites are revolting in the extreme, and I believe that it may be the practice of these rites through ages that has brought the race to its present condition of imbecility.

"And yet, as I said, they are not without some redeeming qualities. If legend may be credited, their forebears—a little handful of men and women who came from somewhere out of the north and became lost in the wilderness of central Africa—found here only a barren desert valley. To my own knowledge rain seldom, if ever, falls here, and yet you have seen a great forest and luxuriant vegetation outside of the city as well as within. This miracle is accomplished by the utilization of natural springs which their ancestors developed, and upon which they have improved to such an extent that the entire valley receives an adequate amount of moisture at all times.

"Ago told me that many generations before his time the forest was irrigated by changing the course of the streams which carried the spring water to the city but that when the trees had sent their roots down to the natural moisture of the soil and required no further irrigation, the course of the stream was changed and other trees were planted. And so the forest grew until today it covers almost the entire floor of the valley except for the open space where the city stands. I do not know that this is true. It may be that the forest has always been here, but it is one of their legends and it is borne out by the fact that there is not sufficient rainfall here to support vegetation.

"They are peculiar people in many respects, not only in their form of worship and religious rites but also in that they breed lions as other people breed cattle. You have seen how they use some of these lions but the majority of them they fatten and eat. At first, I imagine, they ate lion meat as a part of their religious ceremony but after many generations they came to crave it so that now it is practically the only flesh they eat. They would, of course, rather die than eat the flesh of a bird, nor will they eat monkey's meat, while the herbivorous animals they raise only for milk, hides, and flesh for the lions. Upon the south side of the city are the corrals and pastures where the herbivorous animals are raised. Boar, deer, and antelope are used principally for the lions, while goats are kept for milk for the human inhabitants of the city."

"And you have lived here all these years," exclaimed the girl, "without ever seeing one of your own kind?" The old woman nodded affirmatively.

"For sixty years you have lived here," continued Bertha Kircher, "and they have not harmed you!"

"I did not say they had not harmed me," said the old woman, "they did not kill me, that is all."

"What"—the girl hesitated—" what," she continued at last, "was your position among them? Pardon me," she added quickly, "I think I know but I should like to hear from your own lips, for whatever your position was, mine will doubtless be the same."

The old woman nodded. "Yes," she said, "doubtless; if they can keep you away from the women."

"What do you mean?" asked the girl.

"For sixty years I have never been allowed near a woman. They would kill me, even now, if they could reach me. The men are frightful, God knows they are frightful! But heaven keep you from the women!"

"You mean," asked the girl, "that the men will not harm me?"

"Ago XXV made me his queen," said the old woman. "But he had many other queens, nor were they all human. He was not murdered for ten years after I came here. Then the next king took me, and so it has been always. I am the oldest queen now. Very few of their women live to a great age. Not only are they constantly liable to assassination but, owing to their subnormal mentalities, they are subject to periods of depression during which they are very likely to destroy themselves."

She turned suddenly and pointed to the barred windows. "You see this room," she said, "with the black eunuch outside? Wherever you see these you will know that there are women, for with very few exceptions they are never allowed out of captivity. They are considered and really are more violent than the men."

For several minutes the two sat in silence, and then the younger woman turned to the older.

"Is there no way to escape?" she asked.

The old woman pointed again to the barred windows and then to the door, saying: "And there is the armed eunuch. And if you should pass him, how could you reach the street? And if you reached the street, how could you pass through the city to the outer wall? And even if, by some miracle, you should gain the outer wall, and, by another miracle, you should be permitted to pass through the gate, could you ever hope to traverse the forest where the great black lions roam and feed upon men? No!" she exclaimed, answering her own question, "there is no escape, for after one had escaped from the palace and the city and the forest it would be but to invite death in the frightful desert land beyond.

"In sixty years you are the first to find this buried city. In a thousand no denizen of this valley has ever left it, and within the memory of man, or even in their legends, none had found them prior to my coming other than a single warlike giant, the story of whom has been handed down from father to son.

"I think from the description that he must have been a Spaniard, a giant of a man in buckler and helmet, who fought his way through the terrible forest to the city gate, who fell upon those who were sent out to capture him and slew them with his mighty sword. And when he had eaten of the vegetables from the gardens, and the fruit from the trees and drank of the water from the stream, he turned about and fought his way back through the forest to the mouth of the gorge. But though he escaped the city and the forest he did not escape the desert. For a legend runs that the king, fearful that he would bring others to attack them, sent a party after him to slay him.

"For three weeks they did not find him, for they went in the wrong direction, but at last they came upon his bones picked clean by the vultures, lying a day's march up the same gorge through which you and I entered the valley. I do not know," continued the old woman, "that this is true. It is just one of their many legends."

"Yes," said the girl, "it is true. I am sure it is true, for I have seen the skeleton and the corroded armor of this great giant."

At this juncture the door was thrown open without ceremony and a Negro entered bearing two flat vessels in which were several smaller ones. These he set down on one of the tables near the women, and, without a word, turned and left. With the entrance of the man with the vessels, a delightful odor of cooked food had aroused the realization in the girl's mind that she was very hungry, and at a word from the old woman she walked to the table to examine the viands. The larger vessels which contained the smaller ones were of pottery while those within them were quite evidently of hammered gold. To her intense surprise she found lying between the smaller vessels a spoon and a fork, which, while of quaint design, were quite as serviceable as any she had seen in more civilized communities. The tines of the fork were quite evidently of iron or steel, the girl did not know which, while the handle and the spoon were of the same material as the smaller vessels.

There was a highly seasoned stew with meat and vegetables, a dish of fresh fruit, and a bowl of milk beside which was a little jug containing something which resembled marmalade. So ravenous was she that she did not even wait for her companion to reach the table, and as she ate she could have sworn that never before had she tasted more palatable food. The old woman came slowly and sat down on one of the benches opposite her.

As she removed the smaller vessels from the larger and arranged them before her on the table a crooked smile twisted her lips as she watched the younger woman eat.

"Hunger is a great leveler," she said with a laugh.

"What do you mean?" asked the girl.

"I venture to say that a few weeks ago you would have been nauseated at the idea of eating cat."

"Cat?" exclaimed the girl.

"Yes," said the old woman. "What is the difference—a lion is a cat."

"You mean I am eating lion now?"

"Yes," said the old woman, "and as they prepare it, it is very palatable. You will grow very fond of it."

Bertha Kircher smiled a trifle dubiously. "I could not tell it," she said, "from lamb or veal."

"No," said the woman, "it tastes as good to me. But these lions are very carefully kept and very carefully fed and their flesh is so seasoned and prepared that it might be anything so far as taste is concerned."

And so Bertha Kircher broke her long fast upon strange fruits, lion meat, and goat's milk.

Scarcely had she finished when again the door opened and there entered a yellow-coated soldier. He spoke to the old woman.

"The king," she said, "has commanded that you be prepared and brought to him. You are to share these apartments with me. The king knows that I am not like his other women. He never would have dared to put you with them. Herog XVI has occasional lucid intervals. You must have been brought to him during one of these. Like the rest of them he thinks that he alone of all the community is sane, but more than once I have thought that the various men with whom I have come in contact here, including the kings themselves, looked upon me as, at least, less mad than the others. Yet how I have retained my senses all these years is beyond me."

"What do you mean by prepare?" asked Bertha Kircher. "You said that the king had commanded I be prepared and brought to him."

"You will be bathed and furnished with a robe similar to that which I wear."

"Is there no escape?" asked the girl. "Is there no way even in which I can kill myself?"

The woman handed her the fork. "This is the only way," she said, "and you will notice that the tines are very short and blunt."

The girl shuddered and the old woman laid a hand gently upon her shoulder. "He may only look at you and send you away," she said. "Ago XXV sent for me once, tried to talk with me, discovered that I could not understand him and that he could not understand me, ordered that I be taught the language of his people, and then apparently forgot me for a year. Sometimes I do not see the king for a long period. There was one king who ruled for five years whom I never saw. There is always hope; even I whose very memory has doubtless been forgotten beyond these palace walls still hope, though none knows better how futilely."

The old woman led Bertha Kircher to an adjoining apartment in the floor of which was a pool of water. Here the girl bathed and afterward her companion brought her one of the clinging garments of the native women and adjusted it about her figure. The material of the robe was of a gauzy fabric which accentuated the rounded beauty of the girlish form.

"There," said the old woman, as she gave a final pat to one of the folds of the garment, "you are a queen indeed!"

The girl looked down at her naked breasts and but half-concealed limbs in horror. "They are going to lead me into the presence of men in this half-nude condition!" she exclaimed.

The old woman smiled her crooked smile. "It is nothing," she said. "You will become accustomed to it as did I who was brought up in the home of a minister of the gospel, where it was considered little short of a crime for a woman to expose her stockinged ankle. By comparison with what you will doubtless see and the things that you may be called upon to undergo, this is but a trifle."

For what seemed hours to the distraught girl she paced the floor of her apartment, awaiting the final summons to the presence of the mad king. Darkness had fallen and the oil flares within the palace had been lighted long before two messengers appeared with instructions that Herog demanded her immediate presence and that the old woman, whom they called Xanila, was to accompany her. The girl felt some slight relief when she discovered that she was to have at least one friend with her, however powerless to assist her the old woman might be.

The messengers conducted the two to a small apartment on the floor below. Xanila explained that this was one of the anterooms off the main throneroom in which the king was accustomed to hold court with his entire retinue. A number of yellow-tunicked warriors sat about upon the benches within the room. For the most part their eyes were bent upon the floor and their attitudes that of moody dejection. As the two women entered several glanced indifferently at them, but for the most part no attention was paid to them.

While they were waiting in the anteroom there entered from another apartment a young man uniformed similarly to the others with the exception that upon his head was a fillet of gold, in the front of which a single parrot feather rose erectly above his forehead. As he entered, the other soldiers in the room rose to their feet.

"That is Metak, one of the king's sons," Xanila whispered to the girl.

The prince was crossing the room toward the audience chamber when his glance happened to fall upon Bertha Kircher. He halted in his tracks and stood looking at her for a full minute without speaking. The girl, embarrassed by his bold stare and her scant attire, flushed and, dropping her gaze to the floor, turned away. Metak suddenly commenced to tremble from head to foot and then, without warning other than a loud, hoarse scream he sprang forward and seized the girl in his arms.

Instantly pandemonium ensued. The two messengers who had been charged with the duty of conducting the girl to the king's presence danced, shrieking, about the prince, waving their arms and gesticulating wildly as though they would force him to relinquish her, the while they dared not lay hands upon royalty. The other guardsmen, as though suffering in sympathy the madness of their prince, ran forward screaming and brandishing their sabers.

The girl fought to release herself from the horrid embrace of the maniac, but with his left arm about her he held her as easily as though she had been but a babe, while with his free hand he drew his saber and struck viciously at those nearest him.

One of the messengers was the first to feel the keen edge of Metak's blade. With a single fierce cut the prince drove through the fellow's collar bone and downward to the center of his chest. With a shrill shriek that rose above the screaming of the other guardsmen the man dropped to the floor, and as the blood gushed from the frightful wound he struggled to rise once more to his feet and then sank back again and died in a great pool of his own blood.

In the meantime Metak, still clinging desperately to the girl, had backed toward the opposite door. At the sight of the blood two of the guardsmen, as though suddenly aroused to maniacal frenzy, dropped their sabers to the floor and fell upon each other with nails and teeth, while some sought to reach the prince and some to defend him. In a corner of the room sat one of the guardsmen laughing uproariously and just as Metak succeeded in reaching the door and taking the girl through, she thought that she saw another of the men spring upon the corpse of the dead messenger and bury his teeth in its flesh.

During the orgy of madness Xanila had kept closely at the girl's side but at the door of the room Metak had seen her and, wheeling suddenly, cut viciously at her. Fortunately for Xanila she was halfway through the door at the time, so that Metak's blade but dented itself upon the stone arch of the portal, and then Xanila, guided doubtless by the wisdom of sixty years of similar experiences, fled down the corridor as fast as her old and tottering legs would carry her.

Metak, once outside the door, returned his saber to its scabbard and lifting the girl bodily from the ground carried her off in the opposite direction from that taken by Xanila.

CAME TARZAN

Just before dark that evening, an almost exhausted flier entered the headquarters of Colonel Capell of the Second Rhodesians and saluted.

"Well, Thompson," asked the superior, "what luck? The others have all returned. Never saw a thing of Oldwick or his plane. I guess we shall have to give it up unless you were more successful."

"I was," replied the young officer. "I found the plane."

"No!" ejaculated Colonel Capell. "Where was it? Any sign of Oldwick?"

"It is in the rottenest hole in the ground you ever saw, quite a bit inland. Narrow gorge. Saw the plane all right but can't reach it. There was a regular devil of a lion wandering around it. I landed near the edge of the cliff and was going to climb down and take a look at the plane. But this fellow hung around for an hour or more and I finally had to give it up."

"Do you think the lions got Oldwick?" asked the colonel.

"I doubt it," replied Lieutenant Thompson, "from the fact that there was no indication that the lion had fed anywhere about the plane. I arose after I found it was impossible to get down around the plane and reconnoitered up and down the gorge. Several miles to the south I found a small, wooded valley in the center of which—please don't think me crazy, sir—is a regular city—streets, buildings, a central plaza with a lagoon, good-sized buildings with domes and minarets and all that sort of stuff."

The elder officer looked at the younger compassionately. "You're all wrought up, Thompson," he said. "Go and take a good sleep. You have been on this job now for a long while and it must have gotten on your nerves."

The young man shook his head a bit irritably. "Pardon me, sir," he said, "but I am telling you the truth. I am not mistaken. I circled over the place several times. It may be that Oldwick has found his way there—or has been captured by these people."

"Were there people in the city?" asked the colonel.

"Yes, I saw them in the streets."

"Do you think cavalry could reach the valley?" asked the colonel.

"No," replied Thompson, "the country is all cut up with these deep gorges. Even infantry would have a devil of a time of it, and there is absolutely no water that I could discover for at least a two days' march."

It was at this juncture that a big Vauxhall drew up in front of the headquarters of the Second Rhodesians and a moment later General Smuts alighted and entered. Colonel Capell arose from his chair and saluted his superior, and the young lieutenant saluted and stood at attention.

"I was passing," said the general, "and I thought I would stop for a chat. By the way, how is the search for Lieutenant Smith-Oldwick progressing? I see Thompson here and I believe he was one of those detailed to the search."

"Yes," said Capell, "he was. He is the last to come in. He found the lieutenant's ship," and then he repeated what Lieutenant Thompson had reported to him. The general sat down at the table with Colonel Capell, and together the two officers, with the assistance of the flier, marked the approximate location of the city which Thompson had reported he'd discovered.

"It's a mighty rough country," remarked Smuts, "but we can't leave a stone unturned until we have exhausted every resource to find that boy. We will send out a small force; a small one will be more likely to succeed than a large one. About one company, Colonel, or say two, with sufficient motor lorries for transport of rations and water. Put a good man in command and let him establish a base as far to the west as the motors can travel. You can leave one company there and send the other forward. I am inclined to believe you can establish your base within a day's march of the city and if such is the case the force you send ahead should have no trouble on the score of lack of water as there certainly must be water in the valley where the city lies. Detail a couple of planes for reconnaissance and messenger service so that the base can keep in touch at all times with the advance party. When can your force move out?"

"We can load the lorries tonight," replied Capell, "and march about one o'clock tomorrow morning."

"Good," said the general, "keep me advised," and returning the others' salutes he departed.

As Tarzan leaped for the vines he realized that the lion was close upon him and that his life depended upon the strength of the creepers clinging to the city walls; but to his intense relief he found the stems as large around as a man's arm, and the tendrils which had fastened themselves to the wall so firmly fixed, that his weight upon the stem appeared to have no appreciable effect upon them.

He heard Numa's baffled roar as the lion slipped downward clawing futilely at the leafy creepers, and then with the agility of the apes who had reared him, Tarzan bounded nimbly aloft to the summit of the wall.

A few feet below him was the flat roof of the adjoining building and as he dropped to it his back was toward the niche from which an embrasure looked out upon the gardens and the forest beyond, so that he did not see the figure crouching there in the dark shadow. But if he did not see he was not long in ignorance of the fact that he was not alone, for scarcely had his feet touched the roof when a heavy body leaped upon him from behind and brawny arms encircled him about the waist.

Taken at a disadvantage and lifted from his feet, the ape-man was, for the time being, helpless. Whatever the creature was that had seized him, it apparently had a well-defined purpose in mind, for it walked directly toward the edge of the roof so that it was soon apparent to Tarzan that he was to be hurled to the pavement below—a most efficacious manner of disposing of an intruder. That he would be either maimed or killed the ape-man was confident; but he had no intention of permitting his assailant to carry out the plan.

Tarzan's arms and legs were free but he was in such a disadvantageous position that he could not use them to any good effect. His only hope lay in throwing the creature off its balance, and to this end Tarzan straightened his body and leaned as far back against his captor as he could, and then suddenly lunged forward. The result was as satisfactory as he could possibly have hoped. The great weight of the ape-man thrown suddenly out from an erect position caused the other also to lunge violently forward with the result that to save himself he involuntarily released his grasp. Catlike in his movements, the ape-man had no sooner touched the roof than he was upon his feet again, facing his adversary, a man almost as large as himself and armed with a saber which he now whipped from its scabbard. Tarzan, however, had no mind to allow the use of this formidable weapon and so he dove for the other's legs beneath the vicious cut that was directed at him from the side, and as a football player tackles an opposing runner, Tarzan tackled his antagonist, carrying him backward several yards and throwing him heavily to the roof upon his back.

No sooner had the man touched the roof than the ape-man was upon his chest, one brawny hand sought and found the sword wrist and the other the throat of the yellow-tunicked guardsman. Until then the fellow had fought in silence but just as Tarzan's fingers touched his throat he emitted a single piercing shriek that the brown fingers cut off almost instantly. The fellow struggled to escape the clutch of the naked creature upon his breast but equally as well might he have fought to escape the talons of Numa, the lion.

Gradually his struggles lessened, his pin-point eyes popped from their sockets, rolling horribly upward, while from his foam-flecked lips his swollen tongue protruded. As his struggles ceased Tarzan arose, and placing a foot upon the carcass of his kill, was upon the point of screaming forth his victory cry when the thought that the work before him required the utmost caution sealed his lips.

Walking to the edge of the roof he looked down into the narrow, winding street below. At intervals, apparently at each street intersection, an oil flare sputtered dimly from brackets set in the walls a trifle higher than a man's head. For the most part the winding alleys were in dense shadow and even in the immediate vicinity of the flares the illumination was far from brilliant. In the restricted area of his vision he could see that there were still a few of the strange inhabitants moving about the narrow thoroughfares.

To prosecute his search for the young officer and the girl he must be able to move about the city as freely as possible, but to pass beneath one of the corner flares, naked as he was except for a loin cloth, and in every other respect markedly different from the inhabitants of the city, would be but to court almost immediate discovery. As these thoughts flashed through his mind and he cast about for some feasible plan of action, his eyes fell upon the corpse upon the roof near him, and immediately there occurred to him the possibility of disguising himself in the raiment of his conquered adversary.

It required but a few moments for the ape-man to clothe himself in the tights, sandals, and parrot emblazoned yellow tunic of the dead soldier. Around his waist he buckled the saber belt but beneath the tunic he retained the hunting knife of his dead father. His other weapons he could not lightly discard, and so, in the hope that he might eventually recover them, he carried them to the edge of the wall and dropped them among the foliage at its base. At the last moment he found it difficult to part with his rope, which, with his knife, was his most accustomed weapon, and one which he had used for the greatest length of time. He found that by removing the saber belt he could wind the rope about his waist beneath his tunic, and then replacing the belt still retain it entirely concealed from chance observation.

At last, satisfactorily disguised, and with even his shock of black hair adding to the verisimilitude of his likeness to the natives of the city, he sought for some means of reaching the street below. While he might have risked a drop from the eaves of the roof he feared to do so lest he attract the attention of passers-by, and probable discovery. The roofs of the buildings varied in height but as the ceilings were all low he found that he could easily travel along the roof tops and this he did for some little distance, until he suddenly discovered just ahead of him several figures reclining upon the roof of a near-by building.

He had noticed openings in each roof, evidently giving ingress to the apartments below, and now, his advance cut off by those ahead of him, he decided to risk the chance of reaching the street through the interior of one of the buildings. Approaching one of the openings he leaned over the black hole and, listened for sounds of life in the apartment below. Neither his ears nor his nose registered evidence of the presence of any living creature in the immediate vicinity, and so without further hesitation the ape-man lowered his body through the aperture and was about to drop when his foot came in contact with the rung of a ladder, which he immediately took advantage of to descend to the floor of the room below.

Here, all was almost total darkness until his eyes became accustomed to the interior, the darkness of which was slightly alleviated by the reflected light from a distant street flare which shone intermittently through the narrow windows fronting the thoroughfare. Finally, assured that the apartment was unoccupied, Tarzan sought for a stairway to the ground floor. This he found in a dark hallway upon which the room opened—a flight of narrow stone steps leading downward toward the street. Chance favored him so that he reached the shadows of the arcade without encountering any of the inmates of the house.

Once on the street he was not at a loss as to the direction in which he wished to go, for he had tracked the two Europeans practically to the gate, which he felt assured must have given them entry to the city. His keen sense of direction and location made it possible for him to judge with considerable accuracy the point within the city where he might hope to pick up the spoor of those whom he sought.

The first need, however, was to discover a street paralleling the northern wall along which he could make his way in the direction of the gate he had seen from the forest. Realizing that his greatest hope of success lay in the boldness of his operations he moved off in the direction of the nearest street flare without making any other attempt at concealment than keeping in the shadows of the arcade, which he judged would draw no particular attention to him in that he saw other pedestrians doing likewise. The few he passed gave him no heed, and he had almost reached the nearest intersection when he saw several men wearing yellow tunics identical to that which he had taken from his prisoner.

They were coming directly toward him and the ape-man saw that should he continue on he would meet them directly at the intersection of the two streets in the full light of the flare. His first inclination was to go steadily on, for personally he had no objection to chancing a scrimmage with them; but a sudden recollection of the girl, possibly a helpless prisoner in the hands of these people, caused him to seek some other and less hazardous plan of action.

He had almost emerged from the shadow of the arcade into the full light of the flare and the approaching men were but a few yards from him, when he suddenly kneeled and pretended to adjust the wrappings of his sandals—wrappings, which, by the way, he was not at all sure that he had adjusted as their makers had intended them to be adjusted. He was still kneeling when the soldiers came abreast of him. Like the others he had passed they paid no attention to him and the moment they were behind him he continued upon his way, turning to the right at the intersection of the two streets.

The street he now took was, at this point, so extremely winding that, for the most part, it received no benefit from the flares at either corner, so that he was forced practically to grope his way in the dense shadows of the arcade. The street became a little straighter just before he reached the next flare, and as he came within sight of it he saw silhouetted against a patch of light the figure of a lion. The beast was coming slowly down the street in Tarzan's direction.

A woman crossed the way directly in front of it and the lion paid no attention to her, nor she to the lion. An instant later a little child ran after the woman and so close did he run before the lion that the beast was forced to turn out of its way a step to avoid colliding with the little one. The ape-man grinned and crossed quickly to the opposite side of the street, for his delicate senses indicated that at this point the breeze stirring through the city streets and deflected by the opposite wall would now blow from the lion toward him as the beast passed, whereas if he remained upon the side of the street upon which he had been walking when he discovered the carnivore, his scent would have been borne to the nostrils of the animal, and Tarzan was sufficiently jungle-wise to realize that while he might deceive the eyes of man and beast he could not so easily disguise from the nostrils of one of the great cats that he was a creature of a different species from the inhabitants of the city, the only human beings, possibly, that Numa was familiar with. In him the cat would recognize a stranger, and, therefore, an enemy, and Tarzan had no desire to be delayed by an encounter with a savage lion. His ruse worked successfully, the lion passing him with not more than a side glance in his direction.

He had proceeded for some little distance and had about reached a point where he judged he would find the street which led up from the city gate when, at an intersection of two streets, his nostrils caught the scent spoor of the girl. Out of a maze of other scent spoors the ape-man picked the familiar odor of the girl and, a second later, that of Smith-Oldwick. He had been forced to accomplish it, however, by bending very low at each street intersection in repeated attention to his sandal wrappings, bringing his nostrils as close to the pavement as possible.

As he advanced along the street through which the two had been conducted earlier in the day he noted, as had they, the change in the type of buildings as he passed from a residence district into that portion occupied by shops and bazaars. Here the number of flares was increased so that they appeared not only at street intersections but midway between as well, and there were many more people abroad. The shops were open and lighted, for with the setting of the sun the intense heat of the day had given place to a pleasant coolness. Here also the number of lions, roaming loose through the thoroughfares, increased, and also for the first time Tarzan noted the idiosyncrasies of the people.

Once he was nearly upset by a naked man running rapidly through the street screaming at the top of his voice. And again he nearly stumbled over a woman who was making her way in the shadows of one of the arcades upon all fours. At first the ape-man thought she was hunting for something she had dropped, but as he drew to one side to watch her, he saw that she was doing nothing of the kind—that she had merely elected to walk upon her hands and knees rather than erect upon her feet. In another block he saw two creatures struggling upon the roof of an adjacent building until finally one of them, wrenching himself free from the grasp of the other, gave his adversary a mighty push which hurled him to the pavement below, where he lay motionless upon the dusty road. For an instant a wild shriek re-echoed through the city from the lungs of the victor and then, without an instant's hesitation, the fellow leaped headfirst to the street beside the body of his victim. A lion moved out from the dense shadows of a doorway and approached the two bloody and lifeless things before him. Tarzan wondered what effect the odor of blood would have upon the beast and was surprised to see that the animal only sniffed at the corpses and the hot red blood and then lay down beside the two dead men.

He had passed the lion but a short distance when his attention was called to the figure of a man lowering himself laboriously from the roof of a building upon the east side of the thoroughfare. Tarzan's curiosity was aroused.

IN THE ALCOVE

As Smith-Oldwick realized that he was alone and practically defenseless in an enclosure filled with great lions he was, in his weakened condition, almost in a state verging upon hysterical terror. Clinging to the grating for support he dared not turn his head in the direction of the beasts behind him. He felt his knees giving weakly beneath him. Something within his head spun rapidly around. He became very dizzy and nauseated and then suddenly all went black before his eyes as his limp body collapsed at the foot of the grating.

How long he lay there unconscious he never knew; but as reason slowly reasserted itself in his semi-conscious state he was aware that he lay in a cool bed upon the whitest of linen in a bright and cheery room, and that upon one side close to him was an open window, the delicate hangings of which were fluttering in a soft summer breeze which blew in from a sun-kissed orchard of ripening fruit which he could see without—an old orchard in which soft, green grass grew between the laden trees, and where the sun filtered through the foliage; and upon the dappled greensward a little child was playing with a frolicsome puppy.

"God," thought the man, "what a horrible nightmare I have passed through!" and then he felt a hand stroking his brow and cheek—a cool and gentle hand that smoothed away his troubled recollections. For a long minute Smith-Oldwick lay in utter peace and content until gradually there was forced upon his sensibilities the fact that the hand had become rough, and that it was no longer cool but hot and moist; and suddenly he opened his eyes and looked up into the face of a huge lion.

Lieutenant Harold Percy Smith-Oldwick was not only an English gentleman and an officer in name, he was also what these implied—a brave man; but when he realized that the sweet picture he had looked upon was but the figment of a dream, and that in reality he still lay where he had fallen at the foot of the grating with a lion standing over him licking his face, the tears sprang to his eyes and ran down his cheeks. Never, he thought, had an unkind fate played so cruel a joke upon a human being.

For some time he lay feigning death while the lion, having ceased to lick him, sniffed about his body. There are some things than which death is to be preferred; and there came at last to the Englishman the realization that it would be better to die swiftly than to lie in this horrible predicament until his mind broke beneath the strain and he went mad.

And so, deliberately and without haste, he rose, clinging to the grating for support. At his first move the lion growled, but after that he paid no further attention to the man, and when at last Smith-Oldwick had regained his feet the lion moved indifferently away. Then it was that the man turned and looked about the enclosure.

Sprawled beneath the shade of the trees and lying upon the long bench beside the south wall the great beasts rested, with the exception of two or three who moved restlessly about. It was these that the man feared and yet when two more of them had passed him by he began to feel reassured, recalling the fact that they were accustomed to the presence of man.

And yet he dared not move from the grating. As the man examined his surroundings he noted that the branches of one of the trees near the further wall spread close beneath an open window. If he could reach that tree and had strength to do so, he could easily climb out upon the branch and escape, at least, from the enclosure of the lions. But in order to reach the tree he must pass the full length of the enclosure, and at the very bole of the tree itself two lions lay sprawled out in slumber.

For half an hour the man stood gazing longingly at this seeming avenue of escape, and at last, with a muttered oath, he straightened up and throwing back his shoulders in a gesture of defiance, he walked slowly and deliberately down the center of the courtyard. One of the prowling lions turned from the side wall and moved toward the center directly in the man's path, but Smith-Oldwick was committed to what he considered his one chance, for even temporary safety, and so he kept on, ignoring the presence of the beast. The lion slouched to his side and sniffed him and then, growling, he bared his teeth.

Smith-Oldwick drew the pistol from his shirt. "If he has made up his mind to kill me," he thought. "I can't see that it will make any difference in the long run whether I infuriate him or not. The beggar can't kill me any deader in one mood than another."

But with the man's movement in withdrawing the weapon from his shirt the lion's attitude suddenly altered and though he still growled he turned and sprang away, and then at last the Englishman stood almost at the foot of the tree that was his goal, and between him and safety sprawled a sleeping lion.

Above him was a limb that ordinarily he could have leaped for and reached with ease; but weak from his wounds and loss of blood he doubted his ability to do so now. There was even a question as to whether he would be able to ascend the tree at all. There was just one chance: the lowest branch left the bole within easy reach of a man standing on the ground close to the tree's stem, but to reach a position where the branch would be accessible he must step over the body of a lion. Taking a deep breath he placed one foot between the sprawled legs of the beast and gingerly raised the other to plant it upon the opposite side of the tawny body. "What," he thought, "if the beggar should happen to wake now?" The suggestion sent a shudder through his frame but he did not hesitate or withdraw his foot. Gingerly he planted it beyond the lion, threw his weight forward upon it and cautiously brought his other foot to the side of the first. He had passed and the lion had not awakened.

Smith-Oldwick was weak from loss of blood and the hardships he had undergone, but the realization of his situation impelled him to a show of agility and energy which he probably could scarcely have equaled when in possession of his normal strength. With his life depending upon the success of his efforts, he swung himself quickly to the lower branches of the tree and scrambled upward out of reach of possible harm from the lions below—though the sudden movement in the branches above them awakened both the sleeping beasts. The animals raised their heads and looked questioningly up for a moment and then lay back again to resume their broken slumber.

So easily had the Englishman succeeded thus far that he suddenly began to question as to whether he had at any time been in real danger. The lions, as he knew, were accustomed to the presence of men, but yet they were still lions and he was free to admit that he breathed more easily now that he was safe above their clutches.

Before him lay the open window he had seen from the ground. He was now on a level with it and could see an apparently unoccupied chamber beyond, and toward this he made his way along a stout branch that swung beneath the opening. It was not a difficult feat to reach the window, and a moment later he drew himself over the sill and dropped into the room.

He found himself in a rather spacious apartment, the floor of which was covered with rugs of barbaric design, while the few pieces of furniture were of a similar type to that which he had seen in the room on the first floor into which he and Bertha Kircher had been ushered at the conclusion of their journey. At one end of the room was what appeared to be a curtained alcove, the heavy hangings of which completely hid the interior. In the wall opposite the window and near the alcove was a closed door, apparently the only exit from the room.

He could see, in the waning light without, that the close of the day was fast approaching, and he hesitated while he deliberated the advisability of waiting until darkness had fallen, or of immediately searching for some means of escape from the building and the city. He at last decided that it would do no harm to investigate beyond the room, that he might have some idea as how best to plan his escape after dark. To this end he crossed the room toward the door but he had taken only a few steps when the hangings before the alcove separated and the figure of a woman appeared in the opening.

She was young and beautifully formed; the single drapery wound around her body from below her breasts left no detail of her symmetrical proportions unrevealed, but her face was the face of an imbecile. At sight of her Smith-Oldwick halted, momentarily expecting that his presence would elicit screams for help from her. On the contrary she came toward him smiling, and when she was close her slender, shapely fingers touched the sleeve of his torn blouse as a curious child might handle a new toy, and still with the same smile she examined him from head to foot, taking in, in childish wonderment, every detail of his apparel.

Presently she spoke to him in a soft, well-modulated voice which contrasted sharply with her facial appearance. The voice and the girlish figure harmonized perfectly and seemed to belong to each other, while the head and face were those of another creature. Smith-Oldwick could understand no word of what she said, but nevertheless he spoke to her in his own cultured tone, the effect of which upon her was evidently most gratifying, for before he realized her intentions or could prevent her she had thrown both arms about his neck and was kissing him with the utmost abandon.

The man tried to free himself from her rather surprising attentions, but she only clung more tightly to him, and suddenly, as he recalled that he had always heard that one must humor the mentally deficient, and at the same time seeing in her a possible agency of escape, he closed his eyes and returned her embraces.

It was at this juncture that the door opened and a man entered. With the sound from the first movement of the latch, Smith-Oldwick opened his eyes, but though he endeavored to disengage himself from the girl he realized that the newcomer had seen their rather compromising position. The girl, whose back was toward the door, seemed at first not to realize that someone had entered, but when she did she turned quickly and as her eyes fell upon the man whose terrible face was now distorted with an expression of hideous rage she turned, screaming, and fled toward the alcove. The Englishman, flushed and embarrassed, stood where she had left him. With the sudden realization of the futility of attempting an explanation, came that of the menacing appearance of the man, whom he now recognized as the official who had received them in the room below. The fellow's face, livid with insane rage and, possibly, jealousy, was twitching violently, accentuating the maniacal expression that it habitually wore.

For a moment he seemed paralyzed by anger, and then with a loud shriek that rose into an uncanny wail, he drew his curved saber and sprang toward the Englishman. To Smith-Oldwick there seemed no possible hope of escaping the keen-edged weapon in the hands of the infuriated man, and though he felt assured that it would draw down upon him an equally sudden and possibly more terrible death, he did the only thing that remained for him to do—drew his pistol and fired straight for the heart of the oncoming man. Without even so much as a groan the fellow lunged forward upon the floor at Smith-Oldwick's feet—killed instantly with a bullet through the heart. For several seconds the silence of the tomb reigned in the apartment.

The Englishman, standing over the prostrate figure of the dead man, watched the door with drawn weapon, expecting momentarily to hear the rush of feet of those whom he was sure would immediately investigate the report of the pistol. But no sounds came from below to indicate that anyone there had heard the explosion, and presently the man's attention was distracted from the door to the alcove, between the hangings of which the face of the girl appeared. The eyes were widely dilated and the lower jaw dropped in an expression of surprise and awe.

The girl's gaze was riveted upon the figure upon the floor, and presently she crept stealthily into the room and tiptoed toward the corpse. She appeared as though constantly poised for flight, and when she had come to within two or three feet of the body she stopped and, looking up at Smith-Oldwick, voiced some interrogation which he could not, of course, understand. Then she came close to the side of the dead man and kneeling upon the floor felt gingerly of the body.

Presently she shook the corpse by the shoulder, and then with a show of strength which her tenderly girlish form belied, she turned the body over on its back. If she had been in doubt before, one glance at the hideous features set in death must have convinced her that life was extinct, and with the realization there broke from her lips peal after peal of mad, maniacal laughter as with her little hands she beat upon the upturned face and breast of the dead man. It was a gruesome sight from which the Englishman involuntarily drew back-a gruesome, disgusting sight such as, he realized, might never be witnessed outside a madhouse or this frightful city.

In the midst of her frenzied rejoicing at the death of the man, and Smith-Oldwick could attribute her actions to no other cause, she suddenly desisted from her futile attacks upon the insensate flesh and, leaping to her feet, ran quickly to the door, where she shot a wooden bolt into its socket, thus securing them from interference from without. Then she returned to the center of the room and spoke rapidly to the Englishman, gesturing occasionally toward the body of the slain man. When he could not understand, she presently became provoked and in a sudden hysteria of madness she rushed forward as though to strike the Englishman. Smith-Oldwick dropped back a few steps and leveled his pistol upon her. Mad though she must have been, she evidently was not so mad but what she had connected the loud report, the diminutive weapon, and the sudden death of the man in whose house she dwelt, for she instantly desisted and quite as suddenly as it had come upon her, her homicidal mood departed.

Again the vacuous, imbecile smile took possession of her features, and her voice, dropping its harshness, resumed the soft, well-modulated tones with which she had first addressed him. Now she attempted by signs to indicate her wishes, and motioning Smith-Oldwick to follow her she went to the hangings and opening them disclosed the alcove. It was rather more than an alcove, being a fair-sized room heavy with rugs and hangings and soft, pillowed couches. Turning at the entrance she pointed to the corpse upon the floor of the outer room, and then crossing the alcove she raised some draperies which covered a couch and fell to the floor upon all sides, disclosing an opening beneath the furniture.

To this opening she pointed and then again to the corpse, indicating plainly to the Englishman that it was her desire that the body be hidden here. But if he had been in doubt, she essayed to dispel it by grasping his sleeve and urging him in the direction of the body which the two of them then lifted and half carried and half dragged into the alcove. At first they encountered some difficulty when they endeavored to force the body of the man into the small space she had selected for it, but eventually they succeeded in doing so. Smith-Oldwick was again impressed by the fiendish brutality of the girl. In the center of the room lay a blood-stained rug which the girl quickly gathered up and draped over a piece of furniture in such a way that the stain was hidden. By rearranging the other rugs and by bringing one from the alcove she restored the room to order so no outward indication of the tragedy so recently enacted there was apparent.

These things attended to, and the hangings draped once more about the couch that they might hide the gruesome thing beneath, the girl once more threw her arms about the Englishman's neck and dragged him toward the soft and luxurious pillows above the dead man. Acutely conscious of the horror of his position, filled with loathing, disgust, and an outraged sense of decency, Smith-Oldwick was also acutely alive to the demands of self-preservation. He felt that he was warranted in buying his life at almost any price; but there was a point at which his finer nature rebelled.

It was at this juncture that a loud knock sounded upon the door of the outer room. Springing from the couch, the girl seized the man by the arm and dragged him after her to the wall close by the head of the couch. Here she drew back one of the hangings, revealing a little niche behind, into which she shoved the Englishman and dropped the hangings before him, effectually hiding him from observation from the rooms beyond.

He heard her cross the alcove to the door of the outer room, and heard the bolt withdrawn followed by the voice of a man mingled with that of the girl. The tones of both seemed rational so that he might have been listening to an ordinary conversation in some foreign tongue. Yet with the gruesome experiences of the day behind him, he could not but momentarily expect some insane outbreak from beyond the hangings.

He was aware from the sounds that the two had entered the alcove, and, prompted by a desire to know what manner of man he might next have to contend with, he slightly parted the heavy folds that hid the two from his view and looking out saw them sitting on the couch with their arms about each other, the girl with the same expressionless smile upon her face that she had vouchsafed him. He found he could so arrange the hangings that a very narrow slit between two of them permitted him to watch the actions of those in the alcove without revealing himself or increasing his liability of detection.

He saw the girl lavishing her kisses upon the newcomer, a much younger man than he whom Smith-Oldwick had dispatched. Presently the girl disengaged herself from the embrace of her lover as though struck by a sudden memory. Her brows puckered as in labored thought and then with a startled expression, she threw a glance backward toward the hidden niche where the Englishman stood, after which she whispered rapidly to her companion, occasionally jerking her head in the direction of the niche and on several occasions making a move with one hand and forefinger, which Smith-Oldwick could not mistake as other than an attempt to describe his pistol and its use.

It was evident then to him that she was betraying him, and without further loss of time he turned his back toward the hangings and commenced a rapid examination of his hiding place. In the alcove the man and the girl whispered, and then cautiously and with great stealth, the man rose and drew his curved saber. On tiptoe he approached the hangings, the girl creeping at his side. Neither spoke now, nor was there any sound in the room as the girl sprang forward and with outstretched arm and pointing finger indicated a point upon the curtain at the height of a man's breast. Then she stepped to one side, and her companion, raising his blade to a horizontal position, lunged suddenly forward and with the full weight of his body and his right arm, drove the sharp point through the hangings and into the niche behind for its full length.

Bertha Kircher, finding her struggles futile and realizing that she must conserve her strength for some chance opportunity of escape, desisted from her efforts to break from the grasp of Prince Metak as the fellow fled with her through the dimly lighted corridors of the palace. Through many chambers the prince fled, bearing his prize. It was evident to the girl that, though her captor was the king's son, he was not above capture and punishment for his deeds, as otherwise he would not have shown such evident anxiety to escape with her, as well as from the results of his act.

From the fact that he was constantly turning affrighted eyes behind them, and glancing suspiciously into every nook and corner that they passed, she guessed that the prince's punishment might be both speedy and terrible were he caught.

EDGAR RICE BURROUGHS

She knew from their route that they must have doubled back several times although she had quite lost all sense of direction; but she did not know that the prince was as equally confused as she, and that really he was running in an aimless, erratic manner, hoping that he might stumble eventually upon a place of refuge.

Nor is it to be wondered at that this offspring of maniacs should have difficulty in orienting himself in the winding mazes of a palace designed by maniacs for a maniac king. Now a corridor turned gradually and almost imperceptibly in a new direction, again one doubled back upon and crossed itself; here the floor rose gradually to the level of another story, or again there might be a spiral stairway down which the mad prince rushed dizzily with his burden. Upon what floor they were or in what part of the palace even Metak had no idea until, halting abruptly at a closed door, he pushed it open to step into a brilliantly lighted chamber filled with warriors, at one end of which sat the king upon a great throne; beside this, to the girl's surprise, she saw another throne where was seated a huge lioness, recalling to her the words of Xanila which, at the time, had made no impression on her: "But he had many other queens, nor were they all human."

At sight of Metak and the girl, the king rose from his throne and started across the chamber, all semblance of royalty vanishing in the maniac's uncontrollable passion. And as he came he shrieked orders and commands at the top of his voice. No sooner had Metak so unwarily opened the door to this hornets' nest than he immediately withdrew and, turning, fled again in a new direction. But now a hundred men were close upon his heels, laughing, shrieking, and possibly cursing. He dodged hither and thither, distancing them for several minutes until, at the bottom of a long runway that inclined steeply downward from a higher level, he burst into a subterranean apartment lighted by many flares.

In the center of the room was a pool of considerable size, the level of the water being but a few inches below the floor. Those behind the fleeing prince and his captive entered the chamber in time to see Metak leap into the water with the girl and disappear beneath the surface taking his captive with him, nor, though they waited excitedly around the rim of the pool, did either of the two again emerge.

When Smith-Oldwick turned to investigate his hiding place, his hands, groping upon the rear wall, immediately came in contact with the wooden panels of a door and a bolt such as that which secured the door of the outer room. Cautiously and silently drawing the wooden bar he pushed gently against the panel to find that the door swung easily and noiselessly outward into utter darkness. Moving carefully and feeling forward for each step he passed out of the niche, closing the door behind him.

Peeling about, he discovered that he was in a narrow corridor which he followed cautiously for a few yards to be brought up suddenly by what appeared to be a ladder across the passageway. He felt of the obstruction carefully with his hands until he was assured that it was indeed a ladder and that a solid wall was just beyond it, ending the corridor. Therefore, as he could not go forward and as the ladder ended at the floor upon which he stood, and as he did not care to retrace his steps, there was no alternative but to climb upward, and this he did, his pistol ready in a side pocket of his blouse.

He had ascended but two or three rungs when his head came suddenly and painfully in contact with a hard surface above him. Groping about with one hand over his head he discovered that the obstacle seemed to be the covering to a trap door in the ceiling which, with a little effort, he succeeded in raising a couple of inches, revealing through the cracks the stars of a clear African night.

With a sigh of relief, but with unabated caution, he gently slid the trapdoor to one side far enough to permit him to raise his eyes above the level of the roof. A quick glance assured him that there was none near enough to observe his movements, nor, in fact, as far as he could see, was anyone in sight.

Drawing himself quickly through the aperture he replaced the cover and endeavored to regain his bearings. Directly to the south of him the low roof he stood upon adjoined a much loftier portion of the building, which rose several stories above his head. A few yards to the west he could see the flickering light of the flares of a winding street, and toward this he made his way.

From the edge of the roof he looked down upon the night life of the mad city. He saw men and women and children and lions, and of all that he saw it was quite evident to him that only the lions were sane. With the aid of the stars he easily picked out the points of the compass, and following carefully in his memory the steps that had led him into the city and to the roof upon which he now stood, he knew that the thoroughfare upon which he looked was the same along which he and Bertha Kircher had been led as prisoners earlier in the day.

If he could reach this he might be able to pass undetected in the shadows of the arcade to the city gate. He had already given up as futile the thought of seeking out the girl and attempting to succor her, for he knew that alone and with the few remaining rounds of ammunition he possessed, he could do nothing against this city-full of armed men. That he could live to cross the lion-infested forest beyond the city was doubtful, and having, by some miracle, won to the desert beyond, his fate would be certainly sealed; but yet he was consumed with but one desire—to leave behind him as far as possible this horrid city of maniacs.

He saw that the roofs rose to the same level as that upon which he stood unbroken to the north to the next street intersection. Directly below him was a flare. To reach the pavement in safety it was necessary that he find as dark a portion of the avenue as possible. And so he sought along the edge of the roofs for a place where he might descend in comparative concealment.

He had proceeded some little way beyond a point where the street curved abruptly to the east before he discovered a location sufficiently to his liking. But even here he was compelled to wait a considerable time for a satisfactory moment for his descent, which he had decided to make down one of the pillars of the arcade. Each time he prepared to lower himself over the edge of the roofs, footsteps approaching in one direction or another deterred him until at last he had almost come to the conclusion that he would have to wait for the entire city to sleep before continuing his flight.

But finally came a moment which he felt propitious and though with inward qualms, it was with outward calm that he commenced the descent to the street below.

When at last he stood beneath the arcade he was congratulating himself upon the success that had attended his efforts up to this point when, at a slight sound behind him, he turned to see a tall figure in the yellow tunic of a warrior confronting him.

OUT OF THE NICHE

Numa, the lion, growled futilely in baffled rage as he slipped back to the ground at the foot of the wall after his unsuccessful attempt to drag down the fleeing ape-man. He poised to make a second effort to follow his escaping quarry when his nose picked up a hitherto unnoticed quality in the scent spoor of his intended prey. Sniffing at the ground that Tarzan's feet had barely touched, Numa's growl changed to a low whine, for he had recognized the scent spoor of the man-thing that had rescued him from the pit of the Wamabos.

What thoughts passed through that massive head? Who may say? But now there was no indication of baffled rage as the great lion turned and moved majestically eastward along the wall. At the eastern end of the city he turned toward the south, continuing his way to the south side of the wall along which were the pens and corrals where the herbivorous flocks were fattened for the herds of domesticated lions within the city. The great black lions of the forest fed with almost equal impartiality upon the flesh of the grass-eaters and man. Like Numa of the pit they occasionally made excursions across the desert to the fertile valley of the Wamabos, but principally they took their toll of meat from the herds of the walled city of Herog, the mad king, or seized upon some of his luckless subjects.

Numa of the pit was in some respect an exception to the rule which guided his fellows of the forest in that as a cub he had been trapped and carried into the city, where he was kept for breeding purposes, only to escape in his second year. They had tried to teach him in the city of maniacs that he must not eat the flesh of man, and the result of their schooling was that only when aroused to anger or upon that one occasion that he had been impelled by the pangs of hunger, did he ever attack man.

The animal corrals of the maniacs are protected by an outer wall or palisade of upright logs, the lower ends of which are imbedded in the ground, the logs themselves being placed as close together as possible and further reinforced and bound together by withes. At intervals there are gates through which the flocks are turned on to the grazing land south of the city during the daytime. It is at such times that the black lions of the forest take their greatest toll from the herds, and it is infrequent that a lion attempts to enter the corrals at night. But Numa of the pit, having scented the spoor of his benefactor, was minded again to pass into the walled city, and with that idea in his cunning brain he crept stealthily along the outer side of the palisade, testing each gateway with a padded foot until at last he discovered one which seemed insecurely fastened. Lowering his great head he pressed against the gate, surging forward with all the weight of his huge body and the strength of his giant sinews—one mighty effort and Numa was within the corral.

The enclosure contained a herd of goats which immediately upon the advent of the carnivore started a mad stampede to the opposite end of the corral which was bounded by the south wall of the city. Numa had been within such a corral as this before, so that he knew that somewhere in the wall was a small door through which the goatherd might pass from the city to his flock; toward this door he made his way, whether by plan or accident it is difficult to say, though in the light of ensuing events it seems possible that the former was the case.

To reach the gate he must pass directly through the herd which had huddled affrightedly close to the opening so that once again there was a furious rush of hoofs as Numa strode quickly to the side of the portal. If Numa had planned, he had planned well, for scarcely had he reached his position when the door opened and a herder's head was projected into the enclosure, the fellow evidently seeking an explanation of the disturbance among his flock. Possibly he discovered the cause of the commotion, but it is doubtful, for it was dark and the great, taloned paw that reached up and struck downward a mighty blow that almost severed his head from his body, moved so quickly and silently that the man was dead within a fraction of a second from the moment that he opened the door, and then Numa, knowing now his way, passed through the wall into the dimly lighted streets of the city beyond.

Smith-Oldwick's first thought when he was accosted by the figure in the yellow tunic of a soldier was to shoot the man dead and trust to his legs and the dimly lighted, winding streets to permit his escape, for he knew that to be accosted was equivalent to recapture since no inhabitant of this weird city but would recognize him as an alien. It would be a simple thing to shoot the man from the pocket where the pistol lay without drawing the weapon, and with this purpose in mind the Englishman slipped his hands into the side pocket of his blouse, but simultaneously with this action his wrist was seized in a powerful grasp and a low voice whispered in English: "Lieutenant, it is I, Tarzan of the Apes."

The relief from the nervous strain under which he had been laboring for so long, left Smith-Oldwick suddenly as weak as a babe, so that he was forced to grasp the ape-man's arm for support—and when he found his voice all he could do was to repeat: "You? You? I thought you were dead!"

"No, not dead," replied Tarzan, "and I see that you are not either. But how about the girl?"

"I haven't seen her," replied the Englishman, "since we were brought here. We were taken into a building on the plaza close by and there we were separated. She was led away by guards and I was put into a den of lions. I haven't seen her since."

"How did you escape?" asked the ape-man.

"The lions didn't seem to pay much attention to me and I climbed out of the place by way of a tree and through a window into a room on the second floor. Had a little scrimmage there with a fellow and was hidden by one of their women in a hole in the wall. The loony thing then betrayed me to another bounder who happened in, but I found a way out and up onto the roof where I have been for quite some time now waiting for a chance to get down into the street without being seen. That's all I know, but I haven't the slightest idea in the world where to look for Miss Kircher."

"Where were you going now?" asked Tarzan.

Smith-Oldwick hesitated. "I—well, I couldn't do anything here alone and I was going to try to get out of the city and in some way reach the British forces east and bring help."

"You couldn't do it," said Tarzan. "Even if you got through the forest alive you could never cross the desert country without food or water."

"What shall we do, then?" asked the Englishman.

"We will see if we can find the girl," replied the ape-man, and then, as though he had forgotten the presence of the Englishman and was arguing to convince himself, "She may be a German and a spy, but she is a woman—a white woman—I can't leave her here."

"But how are we going to find her?" asked the Englishman.

"I have followed her this far," replied Tarzan, "and unless I am greatly mistaken I can follow her still farther."

"But I cannot accompany you in these clothes without exposing us both to detection and arrest," argued Smith-Oldwick.

"We will get you other clothes, then," said Tarzan.

"How?" asked the Englishman.

"Go back to the roof beside the city wall where I entered," replied the ape-man with a grim smile, "and ask the naked dead man there how I got my disguise."

Smith-Oldwick looked quickly up at his companion. "I have it," he exclaimed. "I know where there is a fellow who doesn't need his clothes anymore, and if we can get back on this roof I think we can find him and get his apparel without much resistance. Only a girl and a young fellow whom we could easily surprise and overcome."

"What do you mean?" asked Tarzan. "How do you know that the man doesn't need his clothes any more."

"I know he doesn't need them," replied the Englishman, "because I killed him."

"Oh!" exclaimed the ape-man, "I see. I guess it might be easier that way than to tackle one of these fellows in the street where there is more chance of our being interrupted."

"But how are we going to reach the roof again, after all?" queried Smith-Oldwick.

"The same way you came down," replied Tarzan. "This roof is low and there is a little ledge formed by the capital of each column; I noticed that when you descended. Some of the buildings wouldn't have been so easy to negotiate."

Smith-Oldwick looked up toward the eaves of the low roof. "It's not very high," he said, "but I am afraid I can't make it. I'll try—I've been pretty weak since a lion mauled me and the guards beat me up, and too, I haven't eaten since yesterday."

Tarzan thought a moment. "You've got to go with me," he said at last. "I can't leave you here. The only chance you have of escape is through me and I can't go with you now until we have found the girl."

"I want to go with you," replied Smith-Oldwick. "I'm not much good now but at that two of us may be better than one."

"All right," said Tarzan, "come on," and before the Englishman realized what the other contemplated Tarzan had picked him up and thrown him across his shoulder. "Now, hang on," whispered the ape-man, and with a short run he clambered apelike up the front of the low arcade. So quickly and easily was it done that the Englishman scarcely had time to realize what was happening before he was deposited safely upon the roof.

"There," remarked Tarzan. "Now, lead me to the place you speak of."

Smith-Oldwick had no difficulty in locating the trap in the roof through which he had escaped. Removing the cover the ape-man bent low, listening and sniffing. "Come," he said after a moment's investigation and lowered himself to the floor beneath. Smith-Oldwick followed him, and together the two crept through the darkness toward the door in the back wall of the niche in which the Englishman had been hidden by the girl. They found the door ajar and opening it Tarzan saw a streak of light showing through the hangings that separated it from the alcove.

Placing his eye close to the aperture he saw the girl and the young man of which the Englishman had spoken seated on opposite sides of a low table upon which food was spread. Serving them was a giant Negro and it was he whom the ape-man watched most closely. Familiar with the tribal idiosyncrasies of a great number of African tribes over a considerable proportion of the Dark Continent, the Tarmangani at last felt reasonably assured that he knew from what part of Africa this slave had come, and the dialect of his people. There was, however, the chance that the fellow had been captured in childhood and that through long years of non-use his native language had become lost to him, but then there always had been an element of chance connected with nearly every event of Tarzan's life, so he waited patiently until in the performance of his duties the black man approached a little table which stood near the niche in which Tarzan and the Englishman hid.

As the slave bent over some dish which stood upon the table his ear was not far from the aperture through which Tarzan looked. Apparently from a solid wall, for the Negro had no knowledge of the existence of the niche, came to him in the tongue of his own people, the whispered words: "If you would return to the land of the Wamabo say nothing, but do as I bid you."

The black rolled terrified eyes toward the hangings at his side. The ape-man could see him tremble and for a moment was fearful that in his terror he would betray them. "Fear not," he whispered, "we are your friends."

At last the Negro spoke in a low whisper, scarcely audible even to the keen ears of the ape-man. "What," he asked, "can poor Otobu do for the god who speaks to him out of the solid wall?"

"This," replied Tarzan. "Two of us are coming into this room. Help us prevent this man and woman from escaping or raising an outcry that will bring others to their aid."

"I will help you," replied the Negro, "to keep them within this room, but do not fear that their outcries will bring others. These walls are built so that no sound may pass through, and even if it did what difference would it make in this village which is constantly filled with the screams of its mad people. Do not fear their cries. No one will notice them. I go to do your bidding."

Tarzan saw the black cross the room to the table upon which he placed another dish of food before the feasters. Then he stepped to a place behind the man and as he did so raised his eyes to the point in the wall from which the ape-man's voice had come to him, as much as to say, "Master, I am ready."

Without more delay Tarzan threw aside the hangings and stepped into the room. As he did so the young man rose from the table to be instantly seized from behind by the black slave. The girl, whose back was toward the ape-man and his companion, was not at first aware of their presence but saw only the attack of the slave upon her lover, and with a loud scream she leaped forward to assist the latter. Tarzan sprang to her side and laid a heavy hand upon her arm before she could interfere with Otobu's attentions to the young man. At first, as she turned toward the ape-man, her face reflected only mad rage, but almost instantly this changed into the vapid smile with which Smith-Oldwick was already familiar and her slim fingers commenced their soft appraisement of the newcomer.

Almost immediately she discovered Smith-Oldwick but there was neither surprise nor anger upon her countenance. Evidently the poor mad creature knew but two principal moods, from one to the other of which she changed with lightning-like rapidity.

"Watch her a moment," said Tarzan to the Englishman, "while I disarm that fellow," and stepping to the side of the young man whom Otobu was having difficulty in subduing Tarzan relieved him of his saber. "Tell them," he said to the Negro, "if you speak their language, that we will not harm them if they leave us alone and let us depart in peace."

The black had been looking at Tarzan with wide eyes, evidently not comprehending how this god could appear in so material a form, and with the voice of a white bwana and the uniform of a warrior of this city to which he quite evidently did not belong. But nevertheless his first confidence in the voice that offered him freedom was not lessened and he did as Tarzan bid him.

"They want to know what you want," said Otobu, after he had spoken to the man and the girl.

"Tell them that we want food for one thing," said Tarzan, "and something else that we know where to find in this room. Take the man's spear, Otobu; I see it leaning against the wall in the corner of the room. And you, Lieutenant, take his saber," and then again to Otobu, "I will watch the man while you go and bring forth that which is beneath the couch over against this wall," and Tarzan indicated the location of the piece of furniture.

Otobu, trained to obey, did as he was bid. The eyes of the man and the girl followed him, and as he drew back the hangings and dragged forth the corpse of the man Smith-Oldwick had slain, the girl's lover voiced a loud scream and attempted to leap forward to the side of the corpse. Tarzan, however, seized him and then the fellow turned upon him with teeth and nails. It was with no little difficulty that Tarzan finally subdued the man, and while Otobu was removing the outer clothing from the corpse, Tarzan asked the black to question the young man as to his evident excitement at the sight of the body.

"I can tell you Bwana," replied Otobu. "This man was his father."

"What is he saying to the girl?" asked Tarzan.

"He is asking her if she knew that the body of his father was under the couch. And she is saying that she did not know it."

Tarzan repeated the conversation to Smith-Oldwick, who smiled. "If the chap could have seen her removing all evidence of the crime and arranging the hangings of the couch so that the body was concealed after she had helped me drag it across the room, he wouldn't have very much doubt as to her knowledge of the affair. The rug you see draped over the bench in the corner was arranged to hide the blood stain—in some ways they are not so loony after all."

The black man had now removed the outer garments from the dead man, and Smith-Oldwick was hastily drawing them on over his own clothing. "And now," said Tarzan, "we will sit down and eat. One accomplishes little on an empty stomach." As they ate the ape-man attempted to carry on a conversation with the two natives through Otobu. He learned that they were in the palace which had belonged to the dead man lying upon the floor beside them. He had held an official position of some nature, and he and his family were of the ruling class but were not members of the court.

When Tarzan questioned them about Bertha Kircher, the young man said that she had been taken to the king's palace; and when asked why replied: "For the king, of course."

During the conversation both the man and the girl appeared quite rational, even asking some questions as to the country from which their uninvited guests had come, and evidencing much surprise when informed that there was anything but waterless wastes beyond their own valley.

When Otobu asked the man, at Tarzan's suggestion, if he was familiar with the interior of the king's palace, he replied that he was; that he was a friend of Prince Metak, one of the king's sons, and that he often visited the palace and that Metak also came here to his father's palace frequently. As Tarzan ate he racked his brain for some plan whereby he might utilize the knowledge of the young man to gain entrance to the palace, but he had arrived at nothing which he considered feasible when there came a loud knocking upon the door of the outer room.

For a moment no one spoke and then the young man raised his voice and cried aloud to those without. Immediately Otobu sprang for the fellow and attempted to smother his words by clapping a palm over his mouth.

"What is he saying?" asked Tarzan.

"He is telling them to break down the door and rescue him and the girl from two strangers who entered and made them prisoners. If they enter they will kill us all."

"Tell him," said Tarzan, "to hold his peace or I will slay him."

Otobu did as he was instructed and the young maniac lapsed into scowling silence. Tarzan crossed the alcove and entered the outer room to note the effect of the assaults upon the door. Smith-Oldwick followed him a few steps, leaving Otobu to guard the two prisoners. The ape-man saw that the door could not long withstand the heavy blows being dealt the panels from without. "I wanted to use that fellow in the other room," he said to Smith-Oldwick, "but I am afraid we will have to get out of here the way we came. We can't accomplish anything by waiting here and meeting these fellows. From the noise out there there must be a dozen of them. Come," he said, "you go first and I will follow."

As the two turned back from the alcove they witnessed an entirely different scene from that upon which they had turned their backs but a moment or two before. Stretched on the floor and apparently lifeless lay the body of the black slave, while the two prisoners had vanished completely.

THE FLIGHT FROM XUJA

As Metak bore Bertha Kircher toward the edge of the pool, the girl at first had no conception of the deed he contemplated but when, as they approached the edge, he did not lessen his speed she guessed the frightful truth. As he leaped head foremost with her into the water, she closed her eyes and breathed a silent prayer, for she was confident that the maniac had no other purpose than to drown himself and her. And yet, so potent is the first law of nature that even in the face of certain death, as she surely believed herself, she clung tenaciously to life, and while she struggled to free herself from the powerful clutches of the madman, she held her breath against the final moment when the asphyxiating waters must inevitably flood her lungs.

Through the frightful ordeal she maintained absolute control of her senses so that, after the first plunge, she was aware that the man was swimming with her beneath the surface. He took perhaps not more than a dozen strokes directly toward the end wall of the pool and then he arose; and once again she knew that her head was above the surface. She opened her eyes to see that they were in a corridor dimly lighted by gratings set in its roof—a winding corridor, water filled from wall to wall.

Along this the man was swimming with easy powerful strokes, at the same time holding her chin above the water. For ten minutes he swam thus without stopping and the girl heard him speak to her, though she could not understand what he said, as he evidently immediately realized, for, half floating, he shifted his hold upon her so that he could touch her nose and mouth with the fingers of one hand. She grasped what he meant and immediately took a deep breath, whereat he dove quickly beneath the surface pulling her down with him and again for a dozen strokes or more he swam thus wholly submerged.

When they again came to the surface, Bertha Kircher saw that they were in a large lagoon and that the bright stars were shining high above them, while on either hand domed and minareted buildings were silhouetted sharply against the starlit sky. Metak swam swiftly to the north side of the lagoon where, by means of a ladder, the two climbed out upon the embankment. There were others in the plaza but they paid but little if any attention to the two bedraggled figures. As Metak walked quickly across the pavement with the girl at his side, Bertha Kircher could only guess at the man's intentions. She could see no way in which to escape and so she went docilely with him, hoping against hope that some fortuitous circumstance might eventually arise that would give her the coveted chance for freedom and life.

Metak led her toward a building which, as she entered, she recognized as the same to which she and Lieutenant Smith-Oldwick had been led when they were brought into the city. There was no man sitting behind the carved desk now, but about the room were a dozen or more warriors in the tunics of the house to which they were attached, in this case white with a small lion in the form of a crest or badge upon the breast and back of each.

As Metak entered and the men recognized him they arose, and in answer to a query he put, they pointed to an arched doorway at the rear of the room. Toward this Metak led the girl, and then, as though filled with a sudden suspicion, his eyes narrowed cunningly and turning toward the soldiery he issued an order which resulted in their all preceding him through the small doorway and up a flight of stairs a short distance beyond.

The stairway and the corridor above were lighted by small flares which revealed several doors in the walls of the upper passageway. To one of these the men led the prince. Bertha Kircher saw them knock upon the door and heard a voice reply faintly through the thick door to the summons. The effect upon those about her was electrical. Instantly excitement reigned, and in response to orders from the king's son the soldiers commenced to beat heavily upon the door, to throw their bodies against it and to attempt to hew away the panels with their sabers. The girl wondered at the cause of the evident excitement of her captors.

She saw the door giving to each renewed assault, but what she did not see just before it crashed inward was the figures of the two men who alone, in all the world, might have saved her, pass between the heavy hangings in an adjoining alcove and disappear into a dark corridor.

As the door gave and the warriors rushed into the apartment followed by the prince, the latter became immediately filled with baffled rage, for the rooms were deserted except for the dead body of the owner of the palace, and the still form of the black slave, Otobu, where they lay stretched upon the floor of the alcove.

The prince rushed to the windows and looked out, but as the suite overlooked the barred den of lions from which, the prince thought, there could be no escape, his puzzlement was only increased. Though he searched about the room for some clue to the whereabouts of its former occupants he did not discover the niche behind the hangings. With the fickleness of insanity he quickly tired of the search, and, turning to the soldiers who had accompanied him from the floor below, dismissed them.

After setting up the broken door as best they could, the men left the apartment and when they were again alone Metak turned toward the girl. As he approached her, his face distorted by a hideous leer, his features worked rapidly in spasmodic twitches. The girl, who was standing at the entrance of the alcove, shrank back, her horror reflected in her face. Step by step she backed across the room, while the crouching maniac crept stealthily after her with claw-like fingers poised in anticipation of the moment they should leap forth and seize her.

As she passed the body of the Negro, her foot touched some obstacle at her side, and glancing down she saw the spear with which Otobu had been supposed to hold the prisoners. Instantly she leaned forward and snatched it from the floor with its sharp point directed at the body of the madman. The effect upon Metak was electrical. From stealthy silence he broke into harsh peals of laughter, and drawing his saber danced to and fro before the girl, but whichever way he went the point of the spear still threatened him.

Gradually the girl noticed a change in the tone of the creature's screams that was also reflected in the changing expression upon his hideous countenance. His hysterical laughter was slowly changing into cries of rage while the silly leer upon his face was supplanted by a ferocious scowl and up-curled lips, which revealed the sharpened fangs beneath.

He now ran rapidly in almost to the spear's point, only to jump away, run a few steps to one side and again attempt to make an entrance, the while he slashed and hewed at the spear with such violence that it was with difficulty the girl maintained her guard, and all the time was forced to give ground step by step. She had reached the point where she was standing squarely against the couch at the side of the room when, with an incredibly swift movement, Metak stooped and grasping a low stool hurled it directly at her head.

She raised the spear to fend off the heavy missile, but she was not entirely successful, and the impact of the blow carried her backward upon the couch, and instantly Metak was upon her.

Tarzan and Smith-Oldwick gave little thought as to what had become of the other two occupants of the room. They were gone, and so far as these two were concerned they might never return. Tarzan's one desire was to reach the street again, where, now that both of them were in some sort of disguise, they should be able to proceed with comparative safety to the palace and continue their search for the girl.

Smith-Oldwick preceded Tarzan along the corridor and as they reached the ladder he climbed aloft to remove the trap. He worked for a moment and then, turning, addressed Tarzan.

"Did we replace the cover on this trap when we came down? I don't recall that we did."

"No," said Tarzan, "it was left open."

"So I thought," said Smith-Oldwick, "but it's closed now and locked. I cannot move it. Possibly you can," and he descended the ladder.

Even Tarzan's immense strength, however, had no effect other than to break one of the rungs of the ladder against which he was pushing, nearly precipitating him to the floor below. After the rung broke he rested for a moment before renewing his efforts, and as he stood with his head near the cover of the trap, he distinctly heard voices on the roof above him.

Dropping down to Oldwick's side he told him what he had heard. "We had better find some other way out," he said, and the two started to retrace their steps toward the alcove. Tarzan was again in the lead, and as he opened the door in the back of the niche, he was suddenly startled to hear, in tones of terror and in a woman's voice, the words: "O God, be merciful" from just beyond the hangings.

Here was no time for cautious investigation and, not even waiting to find the aperture and part the hangings, but with one sweep of a brawny hand dragging them from their support, the ape-man leaped from the niche into the alcove.

At the sound of his entry the maniac looked up, and as he saw at first only a man in the uniform of his father's soldiers, he shrieked forth an angry order, but at the second glance, which revealed the face of the newcomer, the madman leaped from the prostrate form of his victim and, apparently forgetful of the saber which he had dropped upon the floor beside the couch as he leaped to grapple with the girl, closed with bare hands upon his antagonist, his sharp-filed teeth searching for the other's throat.

Metak, the son of Herog, was no weakling. Powerful by nature and rendered still more so in the throes of one of his maniacal fits of fury he was no mean antagonist, even for the mighty ape-man, and to this a distinct advantage for him was added by the fact that almost at the outset of their battle Tarzan, in stepping backward, struck his heel against the corpse of the man whom Smith-Oldwick had killed, and fell heavily backward to the floor with Metak upon his breast.

With the quickness of a cat the maniac made an attempt to fasten his teeth in Tarzan's jugular, but a quick movement of the latter resulted in his finding a hold only upon the Tarmangani's shoulder. Here he clung while his fingers sought Tarzan's throat, and it was then that the ape-man, realizing the possibility of defeat, called to Smith-Oldwick to take the girl and seek to escape.

The Englishman looked questioningly at Bertha Kircher, who had now risen from the couch, shaking and trembling. She saw the question in his eyes and with an effort she drew herself to her full height. "No," she cried, "if he dies here I shall die with him. Go if you wish to. You can do nothing here, but I—I cannot go."

Tarzan had now regained his feet, but the maniac still clung to him tenaciously. The girl turned suddenly to Smith-Oldwick. "Your pistol!" she cried. "Why don't you shoot him?"

The man drew the weapon from his pocket and approached the two antagonists, but by this time they were moving so rapidly that there was no opportunity for shooting one without the danger of hitting the other. At the same time Bertha Kircher circled about them with the prince's saber, but neither could she find an opening. Again and again the two men fell to the floor, until presently Tarzan found a hold upon the other's throat, against which contingency Metak had been constantly battling, and slowly, as the giant fingers closed, the other's mad eyes protruded from his livid face, his jaws gaped and released their hold upon Tarzan's shoulder, and then in a sudden excess of disgust and rage the ape-man lifted the body of the prince high above his head and with all the strength of his great arms hurled it across the room and through the window where it fell with a sickening thud into the pit of lions beneath.

As Tarzan turned again toward his companions, the girl was standing with the saber still in her hand and an expression upon her face that he never had seen there before. Her eyes were wide and misty with unshed tears, while her sensitive lips trembled as though she were upon the point of giving way to some pent emotion which her rapidly rising and falling bosom plainly indicated she was fighting to control.

"If we are going to get out of here," said the ape-man, "we can't lose any time. We are together at last and nothing can be gained by delay. The question now is the safest way. The couple who escaped us evidently departed through the passageway to the roof and secured the trap against us so that we are cut off in that direction. What chance have we below? You came that way," and he turned toward the girl.

"At the foot of the stairs," she said, "is a room full of armed men. I doubt if we could pass that way."

It was then that Otobu raised himself to a sitting posture. "So you are not dead after all," exclaimed the ape-man. "Come, how badly are you hurt?"

The Negro rose gingerly to his feet, moved his arms and legs and felt of his head.

"Otobu does not seem to be hurt at all, Bwana," he replied, "only for a great ache in his head."

"Good," said the ape-man. "You want to return to the Wamabo country?"

"Yes, Bwana."

"Then lead us from the city by the safest way."

"There is no safe way," replied the black, "and even if we reach the gates we shall have to fight. I can lead you from this building to a side street with little danger of meeting anyone on the way. Beyond that we must take our chance of discovery. You are all dressed as are the people of this wicked city so perhaps we may pass unnoticed, but at the gate it will be a different matter, for none is permitted to leave the city at night."

"Very well," replied the ape-man, "let us be on our way."

Otobu led them through the broken door of the outer room, and part way down the corridor he turned into another apartment at the right. This they crossed to a passageway beyond, and, finally, traversing several rooms and corridors, he led them down a flight of steps to a door which opened directly upon a side street in rear of the palace.

Two men, a woman, and a black slave were not so extraordinary a sight upon the streets of the city as to arouse comment. When passing beneath the flares the three Europeans were careful to choose a moment when no chance pedestrian might happen to get a view of their features, but in the shadow of the arcades there seemed little danger of detection. They had covered a good portion of the distance to the gate without mishap when there came to their ears from the central portion of the city sounds of a great commotion.

"What does that mean?" Tarzan asked of Otobu, who was now trembling violently.

"Master," he replied, "they have discovered that which has happened in the palace of Veza, mayor of the city. His son and the girl escaped and summoned soldiers who have now doubtless discovered the body of Veza."

"I wonder," said Tarzan, "if they have discovered the party I threw through the window."

Bertha Kircher, who understood enough of the dialect to follow their conversation, asked Tarzan if he knew that the man he had thrown from the window was the king's son. The ape-man laughed. "No," he said, "I did not. That rather complicates matters—at least if they have found him."

Suddenly there broke above the turmoil behind them the clear strains of a bugle. Otobu increased his pace. "Hurry, Master," he cried, "it is worse than I had thought."

"What do you mean?" asked Tarzan.

"For some reason the king's guard and the king's lions are being called out. I fear, O Bwana, that we cannot escape them. But why they should be called out for us I do not know."

But if Otobu did not know, Tarzan at least guessed that they had found the body of the king's son. Once again the notes of the bugle rose high and clear upon the night air. "Calling more lions?" asked Tarzan.

"No, Master," replied Otobu. "It is the parrots they are calling."

They moved on rapidly in silence for a few minutes when their attention was attracted by the flapping of the wings of a bird above them. They looked up to discover a parrot circling about over their heads.

"Here are the parrots, Otobu," said Tarzan with a grin. "Do they expect to kill us with parrots?"

The Negro moaned as the bird darted suddenly ahead of them toward the city wall. "Now indeed are we lost, Master," cried the black. "The bird that found us has flown to the gate to warn the guard."

"Come, Otobu, what are you talking about?" exclaimed Tarzan irritably. "Have you lived among these lunatics so long that you are yourself mad?"

"No, Master," replied Otobu. "I am not mad. You do not know them. These terrible birds are like human beings without hearts or souls. They speak the language of the people of this city of Xuja. They are demons, Master, and when in sufficient numbers they might even attack and kill us."

"How far are we from the gate?" asked Tarzan.

"We are not very far," replied the Negro. "Beyond this next turn we will see it a few paces ahead of us. But the bird has reached it before us and by now they are summoning the guard," the truth of which statement was almost immediately indicated by sounds of many voices raised evidently in commands just ahead of them, while from behind came increased evidence of approaching pursuit—loud screams and the roars of lions.

A few steps ahead a narrow alley opened from the east into the thoroughfare they were following and as they approached it there emerged from its dark shadows the figure of a mighty lion. Otobu halted in his tracks and shrank back against Tarzan. "Look, Master," he whimpered, "a great black lion of the forest!"

Tarzan drew the saber which still hung at his side. "We cannot go back," he said. "Lions, parrots, or men, it must be all the same," and he moved steadily forward in the direction of the gate. What wind was stirring in the city street moved from Tarzan toward the lion and when the ape-man had approached to within a few yards of the beast, who had stood silently eyeing them up to this time, instead of the expected roar, a whine broke from the beast's throat. The ape-man was conscious of a very decided feeling of relief. "It's Numa of the pit," he called back to his companions, and to Otobu, "Do not fear, this lion will not harm us."

Numa moved forward to the ape-man's side and then turning, paced beside him along the narrow street. At the next turn they came in sight of the gate, where, beneath several flares, they saw a group of at least twenty warriors prepared to seize them, while from the opposite direction the roars of the pursuing lions sounded close upon them, mingling with the screams of numerous parrots which now circled about their heads. Tarzan halted and turned to the young aviator. "How many rounds of ammunition have you left?" he asked.

"I have seven in the pistol," replied Smith-Oldwick, "and perhaps a dozen more cartridges in my blouse pocket."

"I'm going to rush them," said Tarzan. "Otobu, you stay at the side of the woman. Oldwick, you and I will go ahead, you upon my left. I think we need not try to tell Numa what to do," for even then the great lion was baring his fangs and growling ferociously at the guardsmen, who appeared uneasy in the face of this creature which, above all others, they feared.

"As we advance, Oldwick," said the ape-man, "fire one shot. It may frighten them, and after that fire only when necessary. All ready? Let's go!" and he moved forward toward the gate. At the same time, Smith-Oldwick discharged his weapon and a yellow-coated warrior screamed and crumpled forward upon his face. For a minute the others showed symptoms of panic but one, who seemed to be an officer, rallied them. "Now," said Tarzan, "all together!" and he started at a run for the gate. Simultaneously the lion, evidently scenting the purpose of the Tarmangani, broke into a full charge toward the guard.

Shaken by the report of the unfamiliar weapon, the ranks of the guardsmen broke before the furious assault of the great beast. The officer screamed forth a volley of commands in a mad fury of uncontrolled rage but the guardsmen, obeying the first law of nature as well as actuated by their inherent fear of the black denizen of the forest scattered to right and left to elude the monster. With ferocious growls Numa wheeled to the right, and with raking talons struck right and left among a little handful of terrified guardsmen who were endeavoring to elude him, and then Tarzan and Smith-Oldwick closed with the others.

For a moment their most formidable antagonist was the officer in command. He wielded his curved saber as only an adept might as he faced Tarzan, to whom the similar weapon in his own hand was most unfamiliar. Smith-Oldwick could not fire for fear of hitting the ape-man when suddenly to his dismay he saw Tarzan's weapon fly from his grasp as the Xujan warrior neatly disarmed his opponent. With a scream the fellow raised his saber for the final cut that would terminate the earthly career of Tarzan of the Apes when, to the astonishment of both the ape-man and Smith-Oldwick, the fellow stiffened rigidly, his weapon dropped from the nerveless fingers of his upraised hand, his mad eyes rolled upward and foam flecked his bared lip. Gasping as though in the throes of strangulation the fellow pitched forward at Tarzan's feet.

Tarzan stooped and picked up the dead man's weapon, a smile upon his face as he turned and glanced toward the young Englishman.

"The fellow is an epileptic," said Smith-Oldwick. "I suppose many of them are. Their nervous condition is not without its good points—a normal man would have gotten you."

The other guardsmen seemed utterly demoralized at the loss of their leader. They were huddled upon the opposite side of the street at the left of the gate, screaming at the tops of their voices and looking in the direction from which sounds of reinforcements were coming, as though urging on the men and lions that were already too close for the comfort of the fugitives. Six guardsmen still stood with their backs against the gate, their weapons flashing in the light of the flares and their parchment-like faces distorted in horrid grimaces of rage and terror.

Numa had pursued two fleeing warriors down the street which paralleled the wall for a short distance at this point. The ape-man turned to Smith-Oldwick. "You will have to use your pistol now," he said, "and we must get by these fellows at once;" and as the young Englishman fired, Tarzan rushed in to close quarters as though he had not already discovered that with the saber he was no match for these trained swordsmen. Two men fell to Smith-Oldwick's first two shots and then he missed, while the four remaining divided, two leaping for the aviator and two for Tarzan.

The ape-man rushed in in an effort to close with one of his antagonists where the other's saber would be comparatively useless. Smith-Oldwick dropped one of his assailants with a bullet through the chest and pulled his trigger on the second, only to have the hammer fall futilely upon an empty chamber. The cartridges in his weapon were exhausted and the warrior with his razor-edged, gleaming saber was upon him.

Tarzan raised his own weapon but once and that to divert a vicious cut for his head. Then he was upon one of his assailants and before the fellow could regain his equilibrium and leap back after delivering his cut, the ape-man had seized him by the neck and crotch. Tarzan's other antagonist was edging around to one side where he might use his weapon, and as he raised the blade to strike at the back of the Tarmangani's neck, the latter swung the body of his comrade upward so that it received the full force of the blow. The blade sank deep into the body of the warrior, eliciting a single frightful scream, and then Tarzan hurled the dying man in the face of his final adversary.

Smith-Oldwick, hard pressed and now utterly defenseless, had given up all hope in the instant that he realized his weapon was empty, when, from his left, a living bolt of black-maned ferocity shot past him to the breast of his opponent. Down went the Xujan, his face bitten away by one snap of the powerful jaws of Numa of the pit.

In the few seconds that had been required for the consummation of these rapidly ensuing events, Otobu had dragged Bertha Kircher to the gate which he had unbarred and thrown open, and with the vanquishing of the last of the active guardsmen, the party passed out of the maniac city of Xuja into the outer darkness beyond. At the same moment a half dozen lions rounded the last turn in the road leading back toward the plaza, and at sight of them Numa of the pit wheeled and charged. For a moment the lions of the city stood their ground, but only for a moment, and then before the black beast was upon them, they turned and fled, while Tarzan and his party moved rapidly toward the blackness of the forest beyond the garden.

"Will they follow us out of the city?" Tarzan asked Otobu.

"Not at night," replied the black. "I have been a slave here for five years but never have I known these people to leave the city by night. If they go beyond the forest in the daytime they usually wait until the dawn of another day before they return, as they fear to pass through the country of the black lions after dark. No, I think, Master, that they will not follow us tonight, but tomorrow they will come, and, O Bwana, then will they surely get us, or those that are left of us, for at least one among us must be the toll of the black lions as we pass through their forest."

As they crossed the garden, Smith-Oldwick refilled the magazine of his pistol and inserted a cartridge in the chamber. The girl moved silently at Tarzan's left, between him and the aviator. Suddenly the ape-man stopped and turned toward the city, his mighty frame, clothed in the yellow tunic of Herog's soldiery, plainly visible to the others beneath the light of the stars. They saw him raise his head and they heard break from his lips the plaintive note of a lion calling to his fellows. Smith-Oldwick felt a distinct shudder pass through his frame, while Otobu, rolling the whites of his eyes in terrified surprise, sank tremblingly to his knees. But the girl thrilled and she felt her heart beat in a strange exultation, and then she drew nearer to the beast-man until her shoulder touched his arm. The act was involuntary and for a moment she scarce realized what she had done, and then she stepped silently back, thankful that the light of the stars was not sufficient to reveal to the eyes of her companions the flush which she felt mantling her cheek. Yet she was not ashamed of the impulse that had prompted her, but rather of the act itself which she knew, had Tarzan noticed it, would have been repulsive to him.

From the open gate of the city of maniacs came the answering cry of a lion. The little group waited where they stood until presently they saw the majestic proportions of the black lion as he approached them along the trail. When he had rejoined them Tarzan fastened the fingers of one hand in the black mane and started on once more toward the forest. Behind them, from the city, rose a bedlam of horrid sounds, the roaring of lions mingling with the raucous voices of the screaming parrots and the mad shrieks of the maniacs. As they entered the Stygian darkness of the forest the girl once again involuntarily shrank closer to the ape-man, and this time Tarzan was aware of the contact.

Himself without fear, he yet instinctively appreciated how terrified the girl must be. Actuated by a sudden kindly impulse he found her hand and took it in his own and thus they continued upon their way, groping through the blackness of the trail. Twice they were approached by forest lions, but upon both occasions the deep growls of Numa of the pit drove off their assailants. Several times they were compelled to rest, for Smith-Oldwick was constantly upon the verge of exhaustion, and toward morning Tarzan was forced to carry him on the steep ascent from the bed of the valley.

THE TOMMIES

Daylight overtook them after they had entered the gorge, but, tired as they all were with the exception of Tarzan, they realized that they must keep on at all costs until they found a spot where they might ascend the precipitous side of the gorge to the floor of the plateau above. Tarzan and Otobu were both equally confident that the Xujans would not follow them beyond the gorge, but though they scanned every inch of the frowning cliffs upon either hand noon came and there was still no indication of any avenue of escape to right or left. There were places where the ape-man alone might have negotiated the ascent but none where the others could hope successfully to reach the plateau, nor where Tarzan, powerful and agile as he was, could have ventured safely to carry them aloft.

For half a day the ape-man had been either carrying or supporting Smith-Oldwick and now, to his chagrin, he saw that the girl was faltering. He had realized well how much she had undergone and how greatly the hardships and dangers and the fatigue of the past weeks must have told upon her vitality. He saw how bravely she attempted to keep up, yet how often she stumbled and staggered as she labored through the sand and gravel of the gorge. Nor could he help but admire her fortitude and the uncomplaining effort she was making to push on.

The Englishman must have noticed her condition too, for some time after noon, he stopped suddenly and sat down in the sand. "It's no use," he said to Tarzan. "I can go no farther. Miss Kircher is rapidly weakening. You will have to go on without me."

"No," said the girl, "we cannot do that. We have all been through so much together and the chances of our escape are still so remote that whatever comes, let us remain together, unless," and she looked up at Tarzan, "you, who have done so much for us to whom you are under no obligations, will go on without us.

I for one wish that you would. It must be as evident to you as it is to me that you cannot save us, for though you succeeded in dragging us from the path of our pursuers, even your great strength and endurance could never take one of us across the desert waste which lies between here and the nearest fertile country."

The ape-man returned her serious look with a smile. "You are not dead," he said to her, "nor is the lieutenant, nor Otobu, nor myself. One is either dead or alive, and until we are dead we should plan only upon continuing to live. Because we remain here and rest is no indication that we shall die here. I cannot carry you both to the country of the Wamabos, which is the nearest spot at which we may expect to find game and water, but we shall not give up on that account. So far we have found a way. Let us take things as they come. Let us rest now because you and Lieutenant Smith-Oldwick need the rest, and when you are stronger we will go on again."

"But the Xujans—?" she asked, "may they not follow us here?"

"Yes," he said, "they probably will. But we need not be concerned with them until they come."

"I wish," said the girl, "that I possessed your philosophy but I am afraid it is beyond me."

"You were not born and reared in the jungle by wild beasts and among wild beasts, or you would possess, as I do, the fatalism of the jungle."

And so they moved to the side of the gorge beneath the shade of an overhanging rock and lay down in the hot sand to rest. Numa wandered restlessly to and fro and finally, after sprawling for a moment close beside the ape-man, rose and moved off up the gorge to be lost to view a moment later beyond the nearest turn.

For an hour the little party rested and then Tarzan suddenly rose and, motioning the others to silence, listened. For a minute he stood motionless, his keen ears acutely receptive to sounds so faint and distant that none of the other three could detect the slightest break in the utter and deathlike quiet of the gorge. Finally the ape-man relaxed and turned toward them. "What is it?" asked the girl.

"They are coming," he replied. "They are yet some distance away, though not far, for the sandaled feet of the men and the pads of the lions make little noise upon the soft sands."

"What shall we do—try to go on?" asked Smith-Oldwick. "I believe I could make a go of it now for a short way. I am much rested. How about you Miss Kircher?"

"Oh, yes," she said, "I am much stronger. Yes, surely I can go on."

Tarzan knew that neither of them quite spoke the truth, that people do not recover so quickly from utter exhaustion, but he saw no other way and there was always the hope that just beyond the next turn would be a way out of the gorge.

"You help the lieutenant, Otobu," he said, turning to the black, "and I will carry Miss Kircher," and though the girl objected, saying that he must not waste his strength, he lifted her lightly in his arms and moved off up the canyon, followed by Otobu and the Englishman. They had gone no great distance when the others of the party became aware of the sounds of pursuit, for now the lions were whining as though the fresh scent spoor of their quarry had reached their nostrils.

"I wish that your Numa would return," said the girl.

"Yes," said Tarzan, "but we shall have to do the best we can without him. I should like to find some place where we can barricade ourselves against attack from all sides. Possibly then we might hold them off. Smith-Oldwick is a good shot and if there are not too many men he might be able to dispose of them provided they can only come at him one at a time. The lions don't bother me so much. Sometimes they are stupid animals, and I am sure that these that pursue us, and who are so dependent upon the masters that have raised and trained them, will be easily handled after the warriors are disposed of."

"You think there is some hope, then?" she asked.

"We are still alive," was his only answer.

"There," he said presently, "I thought I recalled this very spot." He pointed toward a fragment that had evidently fallen from the summit of the cliff and which now lay imbedded in the sand a few feet from the base. It was a jagged fragment of rock which rose some ten feet above the surface of the sand, leaving a narrow aperture between it and the cliff behind. Toward this they directed their steps and when finally they reached their goal they found a space about two feet wide and ten feet long between the rock and the cliff. To be sure it was open at both ends but at least they could not be attacked upon all sides at once.

They had scarcely concealed themselves before Tarzan's quick ears caught a sound upon the face of the cliff above them, and looking up he saw a diminutive monkey perched upon a slight projection—an ugly-faced little monkey who looked down upon them for a moment and then scampered away toward the south in the direction from which their pursuers were coming. Otobu had seen the monkey too. "He will tell the parrots," said the black, "and the parrots will tell the madmen."

"It is all the same," replied Tarzan; "the lions would have found us here. We could not hope to hide from them."

He placed Smith-Oldwick, with his pistol, at the north opening of their haven and told Otobu to stand with his spear at the Englishman's shoulder, while he himself prepared to guard the southern approach. Between them he had the girl lie down in the sand. "You will be safe there in the event that they use their spears," he said.

The minutes that dragged by seemed veritable eternities to Bertha Kircher and then at last, and almost with relief, she knew that the pursuers were upon them. She heard the angry roaring of the lions and the cries of the madmen. For several minutes the men seemed to be investigating the stronghold which their quarry had discovered. She could hear them both to the north and south and then from where she lay she saw a lion charging for the ape-man before her. She saw the giant arm swing back with the curved saber and she saw it fall with terrific velocity and meet the lion as he rose to grapple with the man, cleaving his skull as cleanly as a butcher opens up a sheep.

Then she heard footsteps running rapidly toward Smith-Oldwick and, as his pistol spoke, there was a scream and the sound of a falling body. Evidently disheartened by the failure of their first attempt the assaulters drew off, but only for a short time. Again they came, this time a man opposing Tarzan and a lion seeking to overcome Smith-Oldwick. Tarzan had cautioned the young Englishman not to waste his cartridges upon the lions and it was Otobu with the Xujan spear who met the beast, which was not subdued until both he and Smith-Oldwick had been mauled, and the latter had succeeded in running the point of the saber the girl had carried, into the beast's heart. The man who opposed Tarzan inadvertently came too close in an attempt to cut at the ape-man's head, with the result that an instant later his corpse lay with the neck broken upon the body of the lion.

Once again the enemy withdrew, but again only for a short time, and now they came in full force, the lions and the men, possibly a half dozen of each, the men casting their spears and the lions waiting just behind, evidently for the signal to charge.

"Is this the end?" asked the girl.

"No," cried the ape-man, "for we still live!"

The words had scarcely passed his lips when the remaining warriors, rushing in, cast their spears simultaneously from both sides. In attempting to shield the girl, Tarzan received one of the shafts in the shoulder, and so heavily had the weapon been hurled that it bore him backward to the ground. Smith-Oldwick fired his pistol twice when he too was struck down, the weapon entering his right leg midway between hip and knee. Only Otobu remained to face the enemy, for the Englishman, already weak from his wounds and from the latest mauling he had received at the claws of the lion, had lost consciousness as he sank to the ground with this new hurt.

As he fell his pistol dropped from his fingers, and the girl, seeing, snatched it up. As Tarzan struggled to rise, one of the warriors leaped full upon his breast and bore him back as, with fiendish shrieks, he raised the point of his saber above the other's heart. Before he could drive it home the girl leveled Smith-Oldwick's pistol and fired point-blank at the fiend's face.

Simultaneously there broke upon the astonished ears of both attackers and attacked a volley of shots from the gorge. With the sweetness of the voice of an angel from heaven the Europeans heard the sharp-barked commands of an English noncom. Even above the roars of the lions and the screams of the maniacs, those beloved tones reached the ears of Tarzan and the girl at the very moment that even the ape-man had given up the last vestige of hope.

Rolling the body of the warrior to one side Tarzan struggled to his feet, the spear still protruding from his shoulder. The girl rose too, and as Tarzan wrenched the weapon from his flesh and stepped out from behind the concealment of their refuge, she followed at his side. The skirmish that had resulted in their rescue was soon over. Most of the lions escaped but all of the pursuing Xujans had been slain. As Tarzan and the girl came into full view of the group, a British Tommy leveled his rifle at the ape-man. Seeing the fellow's actions and realizing instantly the natural error that Tarzan's yellow tunic had occasioned the girl sprang between him and the soldier. "Don't shoot," she cried to the latter, "we are both friends."

"Hold up your hands, you, then," he commanded Tarzan. "I ain't taking no chances with any duffer with a yellow shirt."

At this juncture the British sergeant who had been in command of the advance guard approached and when Tarzan and the girl spoke to him in English, explaining their disguises, he accepted their word, since they were evidently not of the same race as the creatures which lay dead about them. Ten minutes later the main body of the expedition came into view. Smith-Oldwick's wounds were dressed, as well as were those of the ape-man, and in half an hour they were on their way to the camp of their rescuers.

That night it was arranged that the following day Smith-Oldwick and Bertha Kircher should be transported to British headquarters near the coast by aeroplane, the two planes attached to the expeditionary force being requisitioned for the purpose. Tarzan and Otobu declined the offers of the British captain to accompany his force overland on the return march as Tarzan explained that his country lay to the west, as did Otobu's, and that they would travel together as far as the country of the Wamabos.

"You are not going back with us, then?" asked the girl.

"No," replied the ape-man. "My home is upon the west coast. I will continue my journey in that direction."

She cast appealing eyes toward him. "You will go back into that terrible jungle?" she asked. "We shall never see you again?"

He looked at her a moment in silence. "Never," he said, and without another word turned and walked away.

In the morning Colonel Capell came from the base camp in one of the planes that was to carry Smith-Oldwick and the girl to the east. Tarzan was standing some distance away as the ship landed and the officer descended to the ground. He saw the colonel greet his junior in command of the advance detachment, and then he saw him turn toward Bertha Kircher who was standing a few paces behind the captain. Tarzan wondered how the German spy felt in this situation, especially when she must know that there was one there who knew her real status. He saw Colonel Capell walk toward her with outstretched hands and smiling face and, although he could not hear the words of his greeting, he saw that it was friendly and cordial to a degree.

Tarzan turned away scowling, and if any had been close by they might have heard a low growl rumble from his chest. He knew that his country was at war with Germany and that not only his duty to the land of his fathers, but also his personal grievance against the enemy people and his hatred of them, demanded that he expose the girl's perfidy, and yet he hesitated, and because he hesitated he growled—not at the German spy but at himself for his weakness.

He did not see her again before she entered a plane and was borne away toward the east. He bid farewell to Smith-Oldwick and received again the oft-repeated thanks of the young Englishman. And then he saw him too borne aloft in the high circling plane and watched until the ship became a speck far above the eastern horizon to disappear at last high in air.

The Tommies, their packs and accouterments slung, were waiting the summons to continue their return march. Colonel Capell had, through a desire to personally observe the stretch of country between the camp of the advance detachment and the base, decided to march back his troops. Now that all was in readiness for departure he turned to Tarzan. "I wish you would come back with us, Greystoke," he said, "and if my appeal carries no inducement possibly that of Smith-Oldwick 'and the young lady who just left us may. They asked me to urge you to return to civilization."

"No;" said Tarzan, "I shall go my own way. Miss Kircher and Lieutenant Smith-Oldwick were only prompted by a sense of gratitude in considering my welfare."

"Miss Kircher?" exclaimed Capell and then he laughed, "You know her then as Bertha Kircher, the German spy?"

Tarzan looked at the other a moment in silence. It was beyond him to conceive that a British officer should thus laconically speak of an enemy spy whom he had had within his power and permitted to escape. "Yes," he replied, "I knew that she was Bertha Kircher, the German spy?"

"Is that all you knew?" asked Capell.

"That is all," said the ape-man.

"She is the Honorable Patricia Canby," said Capell, "one of the most valuable members of the British Intelligence Service attached to the East African forces. Her father and I served in India together and I have known her ever since she was born.

"Why, here's a packet of papers she took from a German officer and has been carrying it through all her vicissitudes-single-minded in the performance of her duty. Look! I haven't yet had time to examine them but as you see here is a military sketch map, a bundle of reports, and the diary of one Hauptmann Fritz Schneider."

"The diary of Hauptmann Fritz Schneider!" repeated Tarzan in a constrained voice. "May I see it, Capell? He is the man who murdered Lady Greystoke."

The Englishman handed the little volume over to the other without a word. Tarzan ran through the pages quickly looking for a certain date—the date that the horror had been committed—and when he found it he read rapidly. Suddenly a gasp of incredulity burst from his lips. Capell looked at him questioningly.

"God!" exclaimed the ape-man. "Can this be true? Listen!" and he read an excerpt from the closely written page:

"'Played a little joke on the English pig. When he comes home he will find the burned body of his wife in her boudoir-but he will only think it is his wife. Had von Goss substitute the body of a dead Negress and char it after putting Lady Greystoke's rings on it—Lady G will be of more value to the High Command alive than dead.'"

"She lives!" cried Tarzan.

"Thank God!" exclaimed Capell. "And now?"

"I will return with you, of course. How terribly I have wronged Miss Canby, but how could I know? I even told Smith-Oldwick, who loves her, that she was a German spy.

"Not only must I return to find my wife but I must right this wrong."

"Don't worry about that," said Capell, "she must have convinced him that she is no enemy spy, for just before they left this morning he told me she had promised to marry him."

TARZAN THE TERRIBLE

THE PITHECANTHROPUS

Silent as the shadows through which he moved, the great beast slunk through the midnight jungle, his yellow-green eyes round and staring, his sinewy tail undulating behind him, his head lowered and flattened, and every muscle vibrant to the thrill of the hunt. The jungle moon dappled an occasional clearing which the great cat was always careful to avoid. Though he moved through thick verdure across a carpet of innumerable twigs, broken branches, and leaves, his passing gave forth no sound that might have been apprehended by dull human ears.

Apparently less cautious was the hunted thing moving even as silently as the lion a hundred paces ahead of the tawny carnivore, for instead of skirting the moon-splashed natural clearings it passed directly across them, and by the tortuous record of its spoor it might indeed be guessed that it sought these avenues of least resistance, as well it might, since, unlike its grim stalker, it walked erect upon two feet—it walked upon two feet and was hairless except for a black thatch upon its head; its arms were well shaped and muscular; its hands powerful and slender with long tapering fingers and thumbs reaching almost to the first joint of the index fingers. Its legs too were shapely but its feet departed from the standards of all races of men, except possibly a few of the lowest races, in that the great toes protruded at right angles from the foot.

Pausing momentarily in the full light of the gorgeous African moon the creature turned an attentive ear to the rear and then, his head lifted, his features might readily have been discerned in the moonlight. They were strong, clean cut, and regular—features that would have attracted attention for their masculine beauty in any of the great capitals of the world. But was this thing a man? It would have been hard for a watcher in the trees to have decided as the lion's prey resumed its way across the silver tapestry that Luna had laid upon the floor of the dismal jungle, for from beneath the loin cloth of black fur that girdled its thighs there depended a long hairless, white tail.

In one hand the creature carried a stout club, and suspended at its left side from a shoulder belt was a short, sheathed knife, while a cross belt supported a pouch at its right hip. Confining these straps to the body and also apparently supporting the loin cloth was a broad girdle which glittered in the moonlight as though encrusted with virgin gold, and was clasped in the center of the belly with a huge buckle of ornate design that scintillated as with precious stones.

Closer and closer crept Numa, the lion, to his intended victim, and that the latter was not entirely unaware of his danger was evidenced by the increasing frequency with which he turned his ear and his sharp black eyes in the direction of the cat upon his trail. He did not greatly increase his speed, a long swinging walk where the open places permitted, but he loosened the knife in its scabbard and at all times kept his club in readiness for instant action.

Forging at last through a narrow strip of dense jungle vegetation the man-thing broke through into an almost treeless area of considerable extent. For an instant he hesitated, glancing quickly behind him and then up at the security of the branches of the great trees waving overhead, but some greater urge than fear or caution influenced his decision apparently, for he moved off again across the little plain leaving the safety of the trees behind him. At greater or less intervals leafy sanctuaries dotted the grassy expanse ahead of him and the route he took, leading from one to another, indicated that he had not entirely cast discretion to the winds. But after the second tree had been left behind the distance to the next was considerable, and it was then that Numa walked from the concealing cover of the jungle and, seeing his quarry apparently helpless before him, raised his tail stiffly erect and charged.

Two months—two long, weary months filled with hunger, with thirst, with hardships, with disappointment, and, greater than all, with gnawing pain—had passed since Tarzan of the Apes learned from the diary of the dead German captain that his wife still lived. A brief investigation in which he was enthusiastically aided by the Intelligence Department of the British East African Expedition revealed the fact that an attempt had been made to keep Lady Jane in hiding in the interior, for reasons of which only the German High Command might be cognizant.

787

In charge of Lieutenant Obergatz and a detachment of native German troops she had been sent across the border into the Congo Free State.

Starting out alone in search of her, Tarzan had succeeded in finding the village in which she had been incarcerated only to learn that she had escaped months before, and that the German officer had disappeared at the same time. From there on the stories of the chiefs and the warriors whom he quizzed, were vague and often contradictory. Even the direction that the fugitives had taken Tarzan could only guess at by piecing together bits of fragmentary evidence gleaned from various sources.

Sinister conjectures were forced upon him by various observations which he made in the village. One was incontrovertible proof that these people were man-eaters; the other, the presence in the village of various articles of native German uniforms and equipment. At great risk and in the face of surly objection on the part of the chief, the ape-man made a careful inspection of every hut in the village from which at least a little ray of hope resulted from the fact that he found no article that might have belonged to his wife.

Leaving the village he had made his way toward the southwest, crossing, after the most appalling hardships, a vast waterless steppe covered for the most part with dense thorn, coming at last into a district that had probably never been previously entered by any white man and which was known only in the legends of the tribes whose country bordered it. Here were precipitous mountains, well-watered plateaus, wide plains, and vast swampy morasses, but neither the plains, nor the plateaus, nor the mountains were accessible to him until after weeks of arduous effort he succeeded in finding a spot where he might cross the morasses—a hideous stretch infested by venomous snakes and other larger dangerous reptiles. On several occasions he glimpsed at distances or by night what might have been titanic reptilian monsters, but as there were hippopotami, rhinoceri, and elephants in great numbers in and about the marsh he was never positive that the forms he saw were not of these.

When at last he stood upon firm ground after crossing the morasses he realized why it was that for perhaps countless ages this territory had defied the courage and hardihood of the heroic races of the outer world that had, after innumerable reverses and unbelievable suffering penetrated to practically every other region, from pole to pole.

From the abundance and diversity of the game it might have appeared that every known species of bird and beast and reptile had sought here a refuge wherein they might take their last stand against the encroaching multitudes of men that had steadily spread themselves over the surface of the earth, wresting the hunting grounds from the lower orders, from the moment that the first ape shed his hair and ceased to walk upon his knuckles. Even the species with which Tarzan was familiar showed here either the results of a divergent line of evolution or an unaltered form that had been transmitted without variation for countless ages.

Too, there were many hybrid strains, not the least interesting of which to Tarzan was a yellow and black striped lion. Smaller than the species with which Tarzan was familiar, but still a most formidable beast, since it possessed in addition to sharp saber-like canines the disposition of a devil. To Tarzan it presented evidence that tigers had once roamed the jungles of Africa, possibly giant saber-tooths of another epoch, and these apparently had crossed with lions with the resultant terrors that he occasionally encountered at the present day.

The true lions of this new, Old World differed but little from those with which he was familiar; in size and conformation they were almost identical, but instead of shedding the leopard spots of cubhood, they retained them through life as definitely marked as those of the leopard.

Two months of effort had revealed no slightest evidence that she he sought had entered this beautiful yet forbidding land. His investigation, however, of the cannibal village and his questioning of other tribes in the neighborhood had convinced him that if Lady Jane still lived it must be in this direction that he seek her, since by a process of elimination he had reduced the direction of her flight to only this possibility. How she had crossed the morass he could not guess and yet something within seemed to urge upon him belief that she had crossed it, and that if she still lived it was here that she must be sought. But this unknown, untraversed wild was of vast extent; grim, forbidding mountains blocked his way, torrents tumbling from rocky fastnesses impeded his progress, and at every turn he was forced to match wits and muscles with the great carnivora that he might procure sustenance.

Time and again Tarzan and Numa stalked the same quarry and now one, now the other bore off the prize. Seldom however did the ape-man go hungry for the country was rich in game animals and birds and fish, in fruit and the countless other forms of vegetable life upon which the jungle-bred man may subsist.

Tarzan often wondered why in so rich a country he found no evidences of man and had at last come to the conclusion that the parched, thorn-covered steppe and the hideous morasses had formed a sufficient barrier to protect this country effectively from the inroads of mankind.

After days of searching he had succeeded finally in discovering a pass through the mountains and, coming down upon the opposite side, had found himself in a country practically identical with that which he had left. The hunting was good and at a water hole in the mouth of a canon where it debouched upon a tree-covered plain Bara, the deer, fell an easy victim to the ape-man's cunning.

It was just at dusk. The voices of great four-footed hunters rose now and again from various directions, and as the canon afforded among its trees no comfortable retreat the ape-man shouldered the carcass of the deer and started downward onto the plain. At its opposite side rose lofty trees—a great forest which suggested to his practiced eye a mighty jungle. Toward this the ape-man bent his step, but when midway of the plain he discovered standing alone such a tree as best suited him for a night's abode, swung lightly to its branches and, presently, a comfortable resting place.

Here he ate the flesh of Bara and when satisfied carried the balance of the carcass to the opposite side of the tree where he deposited it far above the ground in a secure place. Returning to his crotch he settled himself for sleep and in another moment the roars of the lions and the howlings of the lesser cats fell upon deaf ears.

The usual noises of the jungle composed rather than disturbed the ape-man but an unusual sound, however imperceptible to the awakened ear of civilized man, seldom failed to impinge upon the consciousness of Tarzan, however deep his slumber, and so it was that when the moon was high a sudden rush of feet across the grassy carpet in the vicinity of his tree brought him to alert and ready activity. Tarzan does not awaken as you and I with the weight of slumber still upon his eyes and brain, for did the creatures of the wild awaken thus, their awakenings would be few. As his eyes snapped open, clear and bright, so, clear and bright upon the nerve centers of his brain, were registered the various perceptions of all his senses.

Almost beneath him, racing toward his tree was what at first glance appeared to be an almost naked white man, yet even at the first instant of discovery the long, white tail projecting rearward did not escape the ape-man. Behind the fleeing figure, escaping, came Numa, the lion, in full charge. Voiceless the prey, voiceless the killer; as two spirits in a dead world the two moved in silent swiftness toward the culminating tragedy of this grim race.

Even as his eyes opened and took in the scene beneath him—even in that brief instant of perception, followed reason, judgment, and decision, so rapidly one upon the heels of the other that almost simultaneously the ape-man was in mid-air, for he had seen a white-skinned creature cast in a mold similar to his own, pursued by Tarzan's hereditary enemy. So close was the lion to the fleeing man-thing that Tarzan had no time carefully to choose the method of his attack. As a diver leaps from the springboard headforemost into the waters beneath, so Tarzan of the Apes dove straight for Numa, the lion; naked in his right hand the blade of his father that so many times before had tasted the blood of lions.

A raking talon caught Tarzan on the side, inflicting a long, deep wound and then the ape-man was on Numa's back and the blade was sinking again and again into the savage side. Nor was the man-thing either longer fleeing, or idle. He too, creature of the wild, had sensed on the instant the truth of the miracle of his saving, and turning in his tracks, had leaped forward with raised bludgeon to Tarzan's assistance and Numa's undoing. A single terrific blow upon the flattened skull of the beast laid him insensible and then as Tarzan's knife found the wild heart a few convulsive shudders and a sudden relaxation marked the passing of the carnivore.

Leaping to his feet the ape-man placed his foot upon the carcass of his kill and, raising his face to Goro, the moon, voiced the savage victory cry that had so often awakened the echoes of his native jungle.

As the hideous scream burst from the ape-man's lips the man-thing stepped quickly back as in sudden awe, but when Tarzan returned his hunting knife to its sheath and turned toward him the other saw in the quiet dignity of his demeanor no cause for apprehension.

For a moment the two stood appraising each other, and then the man-thing spoke. Tarzan realized that the creature before him was uttering articulate sounds which expressed in speech, though in a language with which Tarzan was unfamiliar, the thoughts of a man possessing to a greater or less extent the same powers of reason that he possessed. In other words, that though the creature before him had the tail and thumbs and great toes of a monkey, it was, in all other respects, quite evidently a man.

The blood, which was now flowing down Tarzan's side, caught the creature's attention. From the pocket-pouch at his side he took a small bag and approaching Tarzan indicated by signs that he wished the ape-man to lie down that he might treat the wound, whereupon, spreading the edges of the cut apart, he sprinkled the raw flesh with powder from the little bag. The pain of the wound was as nothing to the exquisite torture of the remedy but, accustomed to physical suffering, the ape-man withstood it stoically and in a few moments not only had the bleeding ceased but the pain as well.

In reply to the soft and far from unpleasant modulations of the other's voice, Tarzan spoke in various tribal dialects of the interior as well as in the language of the great apes, but it was evident that the man understood none of these. Seeing that they could not make each other understood, the pithecanthropus advanced toward Tarzan and placing his left hand over his own heart laid the palm of his right hand over the heart of the ape-man. To the latter the action appeared as a form of friendly greeting and, being versed in the ways of uncivilized races, he responded in kind as he realized it was doubtless intended that he should. His action seemed to satisfy and please his new-found acquaintance, who immediately fell to talking again and finally, with his head tipped back, sniffed the air in the direction of the tree above them and then suddenly pointing toward the carcass of Bara, the deer, he touched his stomach in a sign language which even the densest might interpret. With a wave of his hand Tarzan invited his guest to partake of the remains of his savage repast, and the other, leaping nimbly as a little monkey to the lower branches of the tree, made his way quickly to the flesh, assisted always by his long, strong sinuous tail.

The pithecanthropus ate in silence, cutting small strips from the deer's loin with his keen knife. From his crotch in the tree Tarzan watched his companion, noting the preponderance of human attributes which were doubtless accentuated by the paradoxical thumbs, great toes, and tail.

He wondered if this creature was representative of some strange race or if, what seemed more likely, but an atavism. Either supposition would have seemed preposterous enough did he not have before him the evidence of the creature's existence. There he was, however, a tailed man with distinctly arboreal hands and feet. His trappings, gold encrusted and jewel studded, could have been wrought only by skilled artisans; but whether they were the work of this individual or of others like him, or of an entirely different race, Tarzan could not, of course, determine.

His meal finished, the guest wiped his fingers and lips with leaves broken from a nearby branch, looked up at Tarzan with a pleasant smile that revealed a row of strong white teeth, the canines of which were no longer than Tarzan's own, spoke a few words which Tarzan judged were a polite expression of thanks and then sought a comfortable place in the tree for the night.

The earth was shadowed in the darkness which precedes the dawn when Tarzan was awakened by a violent shaking of the tree in which he had found shelter. As he opened his eyes he saw that his companion was also astir, and glancing around quickly to apprehend the cause of the disturbance, the ape-man was astounded at the sight which met his eyes.

The dim shadow of a colossal form reared close beside the tree and he saw that it was the scraping of the giant body against the branches that had awakened him. That such a tremendous creature could have approached so closely without disturbing him filled Tarzan with both wonderment and chagrin. In the gloom the ape-man at first conceived the intruder to be an elephant; yet, if so, one of greater proportions than any he had ever before seen, but as the dim outlines became less indistinct he saw on a line with his eyes and twenty feet above the ground the dim silhouette of a grotesquely serrated back that gave the impression of a creature whose each and every spinal vertebra grew a thick, heavy horn. Only a portion of the back was visible to the ape-man, the rest of the body being lost in the dense shadows beneath the tree, from whence there now arose the sound of giant jaws powerfully crunching flesh and bones. From the odors that rose to the ape-man's sensitive nostrils he presently realized that beneath him was some huge reptile feeding upon the carcass of the lion that had been slain there earlier in the night.

As Tarzan's eyes, straining with curiosity, bored futilely into the dark shadows he felt a light touch upon his shoulder, and, turning, saw that his companion was attempting to attract his attention. The creature, pressing a forefinger to his own lips as to enjoin silence, attempted by pulling on Tarzan's arm to indicate that they should leave at once.

Realizing that he was in a strange country, evidently infested by creatures of titanic size, with the habits and powers of which he was entirely unfamiliar, the ape-man permitted himself to be drawn away. With the utmost caution the pithecanthropus descended the tree upon the opposite side from the great nocturnal prowler, and, closely followed by Tarzan, moved silently away through the night across the plain.

The ape-man was rather loath thus to relinquish an opportunity to inspect a creature which he realized was probably entirely different from anything in his past experience; yet he was wise enough to know when discretion was the better part of valor and now, as in the past, he yielded to that law which dominates the kindred of the wild, preventing them from courting danger uselessly, whose lives are sufficiently filled with danger in their ordinary routine of feeding and mating.

As the rising sun dispelled the shadows of the night, Tarzan found himself again upon the verge of a great forest into which his guide plunged, taking nimbly to the branches of the trees through which he made his way with the celerity of long habitude and hereditary instinct, but though aided by a prehensile tail, fingers, and toes, the man-thing moved through the forest with no greater ease or surety than did the giant ape-man.

It was during this journey that Tarzan recalled the wound in his side inflicted upon him the previous night by the raking talons of Numa, the lion, and examining it was surprised to discover that not only was it painless but along its edges were no indications of inflammation, the results doubtless of the antiseptic powder his strange companion had sprinkled upon it.

They had proceeded for a mile or two when Tarzan's companion came to earth upon a grassy slope beneath a great tree whose branches overhung a clear brook. Here they drank and Tarzan discovered the water to be not only deliciously pure and fresh but of an icy temperature that indicated its rapid descent from the lofty mountains of its origin.

Casting aside his loin cloth and weapons Tarzan entered the little pool beneath the tree and after a moment emerged, greatly refreshed and filled with a keen desire to breakfast. As he came out of the pool he noticed his companion examining him with a puzzled expression upon his face. Taking the ape-man by the shoulder he turned him around so that Tarzan's back was toward him and then, touching the end of Tarzan's spine with his forefinger, he curled his own tail up over his shoulder and, wheeling the ape-man about again, pointed first at Tarzan and then at his own caudal appendage, a look of puzzlement upon his face, the while he jabbered excitedly in his strange tongue.

The ape-man realized that probably for the first time his companion had discovered that he was tailless by nature rather than by accident, and so he called attention to his own great toes and thumbs to further impress upon the creature that they were of different species.

The fellow shook his head dubiously as though entirely unable to comprehend why Tarzan should differ so from him but at last, apparently giving the problem up with a shrug, he laid aside his own harness, skin, and weapons and entered the pool.

His ablutions completed and his meager apparel redonned he seated himself at the foot of the tree and motioning Tarzan to a place beside him, opened the pouch that hung at his right side taking from it strips of dried flesh and a couple of handfuls of thin-shelled nuts with which Tarzan was unfamiliar. Seeing the other break them with his teeth and eat the kernel, Tarzan followed the example thus set him, discovering the meat to be rich and well flavored. The dried flesh also was far from unpalatable, though it had evidently been jerked without salt, a commodity which Tarzan imagined might be rather difficult to obtain in this locality.

As they ate Tarzan's companion pointed to the nuts, the dried meat, and various other nearby objects, in each instance repeating what Tarzan readily discovered must be the names of these things in the creature's native language. The ape-man could but smile at this evident desire upon the part of his new-found acquaintance to impart to him instructions that eventually might lead to an exchange of thoughts between them. Having already mastered several languages and a multitude of dialects the ape-man felt that he could readily assimilate another even though this appeared one entirely unrelated to any with which he was familiar.

So occupied were they with their breakfast and the lesson that neither was aware of the beady eyes glittering down upon them from above; nor was Tarzan cognizant of any impending danger until the instant that a huge, hairy body leaped full upon his companion from the branches above them.

"TO THE DEATH!"

In the moment of discovery Tarzan saw that the creature was almost a counterpart of his companion in size and conformation, with the exception that his body was entirely clothed with a coat of shaggy black hair which almost concealed his features, while his harness and weapons were similar to those of the creature he had attacked. Ere Tarzan could prevent the creature had struck the ape-man's companion a blow upon the head with his knotted club that felled him, unconscious, to the earth; but before he could inflict further injury upon his defenseless prey the ape-man had closed with him.

Instantly Tarzan realized that he was locked with a creature of almost superhuman strength. The sinewy fingers of a powerful hand sought his throat while the other lifted the bludgeon above his head. But if the strength of the hairy attacker was great, great too was that of his smooth-skinned antagonist. Swinging a single terrific blow with clenched fist to the point of the other's chin, Tarzan momentarily staggered his assailant and then his own fingers closed upon the shaggy throat, as with the other hand he seized the wrist of the arm that swung the club. With equal celerity he shot his right leg behind the shaggy brute and throwing his weight forward hurled the thing over his hip heavily to the ground, at the same time precipitating his own body upon the other's chest.

With the shock of the impact the club fell from the brute's hand and Tarzan's hold was wrenched from its throat. Instantly the two were locked in a deathlike embrace. Though the creature bit at Tarzan the latter was quickly aware that this was not a particularly formidable method of offense or defense, since its canines were scarcely more developed than his own. The thing that he had principally to guard against was the sinuous tail which sought steadily to wrap itself about his throat and against which experience had afforded him no defense.

Struggling and snarling the two rolled growling about the sward at the foot of the tree, first one on top and then the other but each more occupied at present in defending his throat from the other's choking grasp than in aggressive, offensive tactics. But presently the ape-man saw his opportunity and as they rolled about he forced the creature closer and closer to the pool, upon the banks of which the battle was progressing. At last they lay upon the very verge of the water and now it remained for Tarzan to precipitate them both beneath the surface but in such a way that he might remain on top.

At the same instant there came within range of Tarzan's vision, just behind the prostrate form of his companion, the crouching, devil-faced figure of the striped saber-tooth hybrid, eyeing him with snarling, malevolent face.

Almost simultaneously Tarzan's shaggy antagonist discovered the menacing figure of the great cat. Immediately he ceased his belligerent activities against Tarzan and, jabbering and chattering to the ape-man, he tried to disengage himself from Tarzan's hold but in such a way that indicated that as far as he was concerned their battle was over. Appreciating the danger to his unconscious companion and being anxious to protect him from the saber-tooth the ape-man relinquished his hold upon his adversary and together the two rose to their feet.

Drawing his knife Tarzan moved slowly toward the body of his companion, expecting that his recent antagonist would grasp the opportunity for escape. To his surprise, however, the beast, after regaining its club, advanced at his side.

The great cat, flattened upon its belly, remained motionless except for twitching tail and snarling lips where it lay perhaps fifty feet beyond the body of the pithecanthropus. As Tarzan stepped over the body of the latter he saw the eyelids quiver and open, and in his heart he felt a strange sense of relief that the creature was not dead and a realization that without his suspecting it there had arisen within his savage bosom a bond of attachment for this strange new friend.

Tarzan continued to approach the saber-tooth, nor did the shaggy beast at his right lag behind. Closer and closer they came until at a distance of about twenty feet the hybrid charged. Its rush was directed toward the shaggy manlike ape who halted in his tracks with upraised bludgeon to meet the assault. Tarzan, on the contrary, leaped forward and with a celerity second not even to that of the swift-moving cat, he threw himself headlong upon him as might a Rugby tackler on an American gridiron. His right arm circled the beast's neck in front of the right shoulder, his left behind the left foreleg, and so great was the force of the impact that the two rolled over and over several times upon the ground, the cat screaming and clawing to liberate itself that it might turn upon its attacker, the man clinging desperately to his hold.

Seemingly the attack was one of mad, senseless ferocity unguided by either reason or skill. Nothing, however, could have been farther from the truth than such an assumption since every muscle in the ape-man's giant frame obeyed the dictates of the cunning mind that long experience had trained to meet every exigency of such an encounter. The long, powerful legs, though seemingly inextricably entangled with the hind feet of the clawing cat, ever as by a miracle, escaped the raking talons and yet at just the proper instant in the midst of all the rolling and tossing they were where they should be to carry out the ape-man's plan of offense. So that on the instant that the cat believed it had won the mastery of its antagonist it was jerked suddenly upward as the ape-man rose to his feet, holding the striped back close against his body as he rose and forcing it backward until it could but claw the air helplessly.

Instantly the shaggy black rushed in with drawn knife which it buried in the beast's heart. For a few moments Tarzan retained his hold but when the body had relaxed in final dissolution he pushed it from him and the two who had formerly been locked in mortal combat stood facing each other across the body of the common foe.

Tarzan waited, ready either for peace or war. Presently two shaggy black hands were raised; the left was laid upon its own heart and the right extended until the palm touched Tarzan's breast. It was the same form of friendly salutation with which the pithecanthropus had sealed his alliance with the ape-man and Tarzan, glad of every ally he could win in this strange and savage world, quickly accepted the proffered friendship.

At the conclusion of the brief ceremony Tarzan, glancing in the direction of the hairless pithecanthropus, discovered that the latter had recovered consciousness and was sitting erect watching them intently. He now rose slowly and at the same time the shaggy black turned in his direction and addressed him in what evidently was their common language. The hairless one replied and the two approached each other slowly. Tarzan watched interestedly the outcome of their meeting. They halted a few paces apart, first one and then the other speaking rapidly but without apparent excitement, each occasionally glancing or nodding toward Tarzan, indicating that he was to some extent the subject of their conversation.

Presently they advanced again until they met, whereupon was repeated the brief ceremony of alliance which had previously marked the cessation of hostilities between Tarzan and the black. They then advanced toward the ape-man addressing him earnestly as though endeavoring to convey to him some important information. Presently, however, they gave it up as an unprofitable job and, resorting to sign language, conveyed to Tarzan that they were proceeding upon their way together and were urging him to accompany them.

As the direction they indicated was a route which Tarzan had not previously traversed he was extremely willing to accede to their request, as he had determined thoroughly to explore this unknown land before definitely abandoning search for Lady Jane therein.

For several days their way led through the foothills parallel to the lofty range towering above. Often were they menaced by the savage denizens of this remote fastness, and occasionally Tarzan glimpsed weird forms of gigantic proportions amidst the shadows of the nights.

On the third day they came upon a large natural cave in the face of a low cliff at the foot of which tumbled one of the numerous mountain brooks that watered the plain below and fed the morasses in the lowlands at the country's edge. Here the three took up their temporary abode where Tarzan's instruction in the language of his companions progressed more rapidly than while on the march.

The cave gave evidence of having harbored other manlike forms in the past. Remnants of a crude, rock fireplace remained and the walls and ceiling were blackened with the smoke of many fires. Scratched in the soot, and sometimes deeply into the rock beneath, were strange hieroglyphics and the outlines of beasts and birds and reptiles, some of the latter of weird form suggesting the extinct creatures of Jurassic times. Some of the more recently made hieroglyphics Tarzan's companions read with interest and commented upon, and then with the points of their knives they too added to the possibly age-old record of the blackened walls.

Tarzan's curiosity was aroused, but the only explanation at which he could arrive was that he was looking upon possibly the world's most primitive hotel register. At least it gave him a further insight into the development of the strange creatures with which Fate had thrown him. Here were men with the tails of monkeys, one of them as hair covered as any fur-bearing brute of the lower orders, and yet it was evident that they possessed not only a spoken, but a written language. The former he was slowly mastering and at this new evidence of unlooked-for civilization in creatures possessing so many of the physical attributes of beasts, Tarzan's curiosity was still further piqued and his desire quickly to master their tongue strengthened, with the result that he fell to with even greater assiduity to the task he had set himself. Already he knew the names of his companions and the common names of the fauna and flora with which they had most often come in contact.

Ta-den, he of the hairless, white skin, having assumed the role of tutor, prosecuted his task with a singleness of purpose that was reflected in his pupil's rapid mastery of Ta-den's mother tongue. Om-at, the hairy black, also seemed to feel that there rested upon his broad shoulders a portion of the burden of responsibility for Tarzan's education, with the result that either one or the other of them was almost constantly coaching the ape-man during his waking hours. The result was only what might have been expected—a rapid assimilation of the teachings to the end that before any of them realized it, communication by word of mouth became an accomplished fact.

Tarzan explained to his companions the purpose of his mission but neither could give him any slightest thread of hope to weave into the fabric of his longing. Never had there been in their country a woman such as he described, nor any tailless man other than himself that they ever had seen.

"I have been gone from A-lur while Bu, the moon, has eaten seven times," said Ta-den. "Many things may happen in seven times twenty-eight days; but I doubt that your woman could have entered our country across the terrible morasses which even you found an almost insurmountable obstacle, and if she had, could she have survived the perils that you already have encountered beside those of which you have yet to learn? Not even our own women venture into the savage lands beyond the cities."

"'A-lur,' Light-city, City of Light," mused Tarzan, translating the word into his own tongue. "And where is A-lur?" he asked. "Is it your city, Ta-den, and Om-at's?"

"It is mine," replied the hairless one; "but not Om-at's. The Waz-don have no cities—they live in the trees of the forests and the caves of the hills—is it not so, black man?" he concluded, turning toward the hairy giant beside him.

"Yes," replied Om-at, "We Waz-don are free—only the Hodon imprison themselves in cities. I would not be a white man!"

Tarzan smiled. Even here was the racial distinction between white man and black man—Ho-don and Waz-don. Not even the fact that they appeared to be equals in the matter of intelligence made any difference—one was white and one was black, and it was easy to see that the white considered himself superior to the other—one could see it in his quiet smile.

"Where is A-lur?" Tarzan asked again. "You are returning to it?"

"It is beyond the mountains," replied Ta-den. "I do not return to it—not yet. Not until Ko-tan is no more."

"Ko-tan?" queried Tarzan.

"Ko-tan is king," explained the pithecanthropus. "He rules this land. I was one of his warriors. I lived in the palace of Ko-tan and there I met O-lo-a, his daughter. We loved, Likestar-light, and I; but Ko-tan would have none of me. He sent me away to fight with the men of the village of Dak-at, who had refused to pay his tribute to the king, thinking that I would be killed, for Dak-at is famous for his many fine warriors. And I was not killed. Instead I returned victorious with the tribute and with Dak-at himself my prisoner; but Ko-tan was not pleased because he saw that O-lo-a loved me even more than before, her love being strengthened and fortified by pride in my achievement.

"Powerful is my father, Ja-don, the Lion-man, chief of the largest village outside of A-lur. Him Ko-tan hesitated to affront and so he could not but praise me for my success, though he did it with half a smile. But you do not understand! It is what we call a smile that moves only the muscles of the face and affects not the light of the eyes—it means hypocrisy and duplicity. I must be praised and rewarded. What better than that he reward me with the hand of O-lo-a, his daughter? But no, he saves O-lo-a for Bu-lot, son of Mo-sar, the chief whose great-grandfather was king and who thinks that he should be king. Thus would Ko-tan appease the wrath of Mo-sar and win the friendship of those who think with Mo-sar that Mo-sar should be king.

"But what reward shall repay the faithful Ta-den? Greatly do we honor our priests. Within the temples even the chiefs and the king himself bow down to them. No greater honor could Ko-tan confer upon a subject—who wished to be a priest, but I did not so wish. Priests other than the high priest must become eunuchs for they may never marry.

"It was O-lo-a herself who brought word to me that her father had given the commands that would set in motion the machinery of the temple. A messenger was on his way in search of me to summon me to Ko-tan's presence. To have refused the priesthood once it was offered me by the king would have been to have affronted the temple and the gods—that would have meant death; but if I did not appear before Ko-tan I would not have to refuse anything. O-lo-a and I decided that I must not appear. It was better to fly, carrying in my bosom a shred of hope, than to remain and, with my priesthood, abandon hope forever.

"Beneath the shadows of the great trees that grow within the palace grounds I pressed her to me for, perhaps, the last time and then, lest by ill-fate I meet the messenger, I scaled the great wall that guards the palace and passed through the darkened city. My name and rank carried me beyond the city gate. Since then I have wandered far from the haunts of the Ho-don but strong within me is the urge to return if even but to look from without her walls upon the city that holds her most dear to me and again to visit the village of my birth, to see again my father and my mother."

"But the risk is too great?" asked Tarzan.

"It is great, but not too great," replied Ta-den. "I shall go."

"And I shall go with you, if I may," said the ape-man, "for I must see this City of Light, this A-lur of yours, and search there for my lost mate even though you believe that there is little chance that I find her. And you, Om-at, do you come with us?"

"Why not?" asked the hairy one. "The lairs of my tribe lie in the crags above A-lur and though Es-sat, our chief, drove me out I should like to return again, for there is a she there upon whom I should be glad to look once more and who would be glad to look upon me. Yes, I will go with you. Es-sat feared that I might become chief and who knows but that Es-sat was right. But Pan-at-lee! it is she I seek first even before a chieftainship."

"We three, then, shall travel together," said Tarzan.

"And fight together," added Ta-den; "the three as one," and as he spoke he drew his knife and held it above his head.

"The three as one," repeated Om-at, drawing his weapon and duplicating Ta-den's act. "It is spoken!"

"The three as one!" cried Tarzan of the Apes. "To the death!" and his blade flashed in the sunlight.

"Let us go, then," said Om-at; "my knife is dry and cries aloud for the blood of Es-sat."

The trail over which Ta-den and Om-at led and which scarcely could be dignified even by the name of trail was suited more to mountain sheep, monkeys, or birds than to man; but the three that followed it were trained to ways which no ordinary man might essay. Now, upon the lower slopes, it led through dense forests where the ground was so matted with fallen trees and over-rioting vines and brush that the way held always to the swaying branches high above the tangle; again it skirted yawning gorges whose slippery-faced rocks gave but momentary foothold even to the bare feet that lightly touched them as the three leaped chamois-like from one precarious foothold to the next. Dizzy and terrifying was the way that Om-at chose across the summit as he led them around the shoulder of a towering crag that rose a sheer two thousand feet of perpendicular rock above a tumbling river. And when at last they stood upon comparatively level ground again Om-at turned and looked at them both intently and especially at Tarzan of the Apes.

"You will both do," he said. "You are fit companions for Om-at, the Waz-don."

"What do you mean?" asked Tarzan.

"I brought you this way," replied the black, "to learn if either lacked the courage to follow where Om-at led. It is here that the young warriors of Es-sat come to prove their courage. And yet, though we are born and raised upon cliff sides, it is considered no disgrace to admit that Pastar-ul-ved, the Father of Mountains, has defeated us, for of those who try it only a few succeed—the bones of the others lie at the feet of Pastar-ul-ved."

Ta-den laughed. "I would not care to come this way often," he said.

"No," replied Om-at; "but it has shortened our journey by at least a full day. So much the sooner shall Tarzan look upon the Valley of Jad-ben-Otho. Come!" and he led the way upward along the shoulder of Pastar-ul-ved until there lay spread below them a scene of mystery and of beauty—a green valley girt by towering cliffs of marble whiteness—a green valley dotted by deep blue lakes and crossed by the blue trail of a winding river. In the center a city of the whiteness of the marble cliffs—a city which even at so great a distance evidenced a strange, yet artistic architecture. Outside the city there were visible about the valley isolated groups of buildings—sometimes one, again two and three and four in a cluster—but always of the same glaring whiteness, and always in some fantastic form.

About the valley the cliffs were occasionally cleft by deep gorges, verdure filled, giving the appearance of green rivers rioting downward toward a central sea of green.

"Jad Pele ul Jad-ben-Otho," murmured Tarzan in the tongue of the pithecanthropi; "The Valley of the Great God—it is beautiful!"

"Here, in A-lur, lives Ko-tan, the king, ruler over all Pal-ul-don," said Ta-den.

"And here in these gorges live the Waz-don," exclaimed Om-at, "who do not acknowledge that Ko-tan is the ruler over all the Land-of-man."

Ta-den smiled and shrugged. "We will not quarrel, you and I," he said to Om-at, "over that which all the ages have not proved sufficient time in which to reconcile the Ho-don and Waz-don; but let me whisper to you a secret, Om-at. The Ho-don live together in greater or less peace under one ruler so that when danger threatens them they face the enemy with many warriors, for every fighting Ho-don of Pal-ul-don is there. But you Waz-don, how is it with you? You have a dozen kings who fight not only with the Ho-don but with one another. When one of your tribes goes forth upon the fighting trail, even against the Ho-don, it must leave behind sufficient warriors to protect its women and its children from the neighbors upon either hand. When we want eunuchs for the temples or servants for the fields or the homes we march forth in great numbers upon one of your villages. You cannot even flee, for upon either side of you are enemies and though you fight bravely we come back with those who will presently be eunuchs in the temples and servants in our fields and homes. So long as the Waz-don are thus foolish the Ho-don will dominate and their king will be king of Pal-ul-don."

"Perhaps you are right," admitted Om-at. "It is because our neighbors are fools, each thinking that his tribe is the greatest and should rule among the Waz-don. They will not admit that the warriors of my tribe are the bravest and our shes the most beautiful."

Ta-den grinned. "Each of the others presents precisely the same arguments that you present, Om-at," he said, "which, my friend, is the strongest bulwark of defense possessed by the Ho-don."

"Come!" exclaimed Tarzan; "such discussions often lead to quarrels and we three must have no quarrels. I, of course, am interested in learning what I can of the political and economic conditions of your land; I should like to know something of your religion; but not at the expense of bitterness between my only friends in Pal-ul-don. Possibly, however, you hold to the same god?"

"There indeed we do differ," cried Om-at, somewhat bitterly and with a trace of excitement in his voice.

"Differ!" almost shouted Ta-den; "and why should we not differ? Who could agree with the preposterous——"

"Stop!" cried Tarzan. "Now, indeed, have I stirred up a hornets' nest. Let us speak no more of matters political or religious."

"That is wiser," agreed Om-at; "but I might mention, for your information, that the one and only god has a long tail."

"It is sacrilege," cried Ta-den, laying his hand upon his knife; "Jad-ben-Otho has no tail!"

"Stop!" shrieked Om-at, springing forward; but instantly Tarzan interposed himself between them.

"Enough!" he snapped. "Let us be true to our oaths of friendship that we may be honorable in the sight of God in whatever form we conceive Him."

"You are right, Tailless One," said Ta-den. "Come, Om-at, let us look after our friendship and ourselves, secure in the conviction that Jad-ben-Otho is sufficiently powerful to look after himself."

"Done!" agreed Om-at, "but—"

"No 'buts,' Om-at," admonished Tarzan.

The shaggy black shrugged his shoulders and smiled. "Shall we make our way down toward the valley?" he asked. "The gorge below us is uninhabited; that to the left contains the caves of my people. I would see Pan-at-lee once more. Ta-den would visit his father in the valley below and Tarzan seeks entrance to A-lur in search of the mate that would be better dead than in the clutches of the Ho-don priests of Jad-ben-Otho. How shall we proceed?"

"Let us remain together as long as possible," urged Ta-den. "You, Om-at, must seek Pan-at-lee by night and by stealth, for three, even we three, may not hope to overcome Es-sat and all his warriors. At any time may we go to the village where my father is chief, for Ja-don always will welcome the friends of his son. But for Tarzan to enter A-lur is another matter, though there is a way and he has the courage to put it to the test—listen, come close for Jad-ben-Otho has keen ears and this he must not hear," and with his lips close to the ears of his companions Ta-den, the Tall-tree, son of Ja-don, the Lion-man, unfolded his daring plan.

And at the same moment, a hundred miles away, a lithe figure, naked but for a loin cloth and weapons, moved silently across a thorn-covered, waterless steppe, searching always along the ground before him with keen eyes and sensitive nostrils.

PAN-AT-LEE

Night had fallen upon unchartered Pal-ul-don. A slender moon, low in the west, bathed the white faces of the chalk cliffs presented to her, in a mellow, unearthly glow. Black were the shadows in Kor-ul-ja, Gorge-of-lions, where dwelt the tribe of the same name under Es-sat, their chief. From an aperture near the summit of the lofty escarpment a hairy figure emerged—the head and shoulders first—and fierce eyes scanned the cliff side in every direction.

It was Es-sat, the chief. To right and left and below he looked as though to assure himself that he was unobserved, but no other figure moved upon the cliff face, nor did another hairy body protrude from any of the numerous cave mouths from the high-flung abode of the chief to the habitations of the more lowly members of the tribe nearer the cliff's base. Then he moved outward upon the sheer face of the white chalk wall. In the half-light of the baby moon it appeared that the heavy, shaggy black figure moved across the face of the perpendicular wall in some miraculous manner, but closer examination would have revealed stout pegs, as large around as a man's wrist protruding from holes in the cliff into which they were driven. Es-sat's four handlike members and his long, sinuous tail permitted him to move with consummate ease whither he chose—a gigantic rat upon a mighty wall. As he progressed upon his way he avoided the cave mouths, passing either above or below those that lay in his path.

The outward appearance of these caves was similar. An opening from eight to as much as twenty feet long by eight high and four to six feet deep was cut into the chalklike rock of the cliff, in the back of this large opening, which formed what might be described as the front veranda of the home, was an opening about three feet wide and six feet high, evidently forming the doorway to the interior apartment or apartments. On either side of this doorway were smaller openings which it were easy to assume were windows through which light and air might find their way to the inhabitants. Similar windows were also dotted over the cliff face between the entrance porches, suggesting that the entire face of the cliff was honeycombed with apartments. From many of these smaller apertures small streams of water trickled down the escarpment, and the walls above others was blackened as by smoke. Where the water ran the wall was eroded to a depth of from a few inches to as much as a foot, suggesting that some of the tiny streams had been trickling downward to the green carpet of vegetation below for ages.

In this primeval setting the great pithecanthropus aroused no jarring discord for he was as much a part of it as the trees that grew upon the summit of the cliff or those that hid their feet among the dank ferns in the bottom of the gorge.

Now he paused before an entrance-way and listened and then, noiselessly as the moonlight upon the trickling waters, he merged with the shadows of the outer porch. At the doorway leading into the interior he paused again, listening, and then quietly pushing aside the heavy skin that covered the aperture he passed within a large chamber hewn from the living rock. From the far end, through another doorway, shone a light, dimly. Toward this he crept with utmost stealth, his naked feet giving forth no sound. The knotted club that had been hanging at his back from a thong about his neck he now removed and carried in his left hand.

Beyond the second doorway was a corridor running parallel with the cliff face. In this corridor were three more doorways, one at each end and a third almost opposite that in which Es-sat stood. The light was coming from an apartment at the end of the corridor at his left. A sputtering flame rose and fell in a small stone receptacle that stood upon a table or bench of the same material, a monolithic bench fashioned at the time the room was excavated, rising massively from the floor, of which it was a part.

In one corner of the room beyond the table had been left a dais of stone about four feet wide and eight feet long. Upon this were piled a foot or so of softly tanned pelts from which the fur had not been removed. Upon the edge of this dais sat a young female Waz-don. In one hand she held a thin piece of metal, apparently of hammered gold, with serrated edges, and in the other a short, stiff brush. With these she was occupied in going over her smooth, glossy coat which bore a remarkable resemblance to plucked sealskin. Her loin cloth of yellow and black striped jato-skin lay on the couch beside her with the circular breastplates of beaten gold, revealing the symmetrical lines of her nude figure in all its beauty and harmony of contour, for even though the creature was jet black and entirely covered with hair yet she was undeniably beautiful.

That she was beautiful in the eyes of Es-sat, the chief, was evidenced by the gloating expression upon his fierce countenance and the increased rapidity of his breathing. Moving quickly forward he entered the room and as he did so the young she looked up. Instantly her eyes filled with terror and as quickly she seized the loin cloth and with a few deft movements adjusted it about her. As she gathered up her breastplates Es-sat rounded the table and moved quickly toward her.

"What do you want?" she whispered, though she knew full well.

"Pan-at-lee," he said, "your chief has come for you."

"It was for this that you sent away my father and my brothers to spy upon the Kor-ul-lul? I will not have you. Leave the cave of my ancestors!"

Es-sat smiled. It was the smile of a strong and wicked man who knows his power—not a pleasant smile at all. "I will leave, Pan-at-lee," he said; "but you shall go with me—to the cave of Es-sat, the chief, to be the envied of the shes of Kor-ul-ja. Come!"

"Never!" cried Pan-at-lee. "I hate you. Sooner would I mate with a Ho-don than with you, beater of women, murderer of babes."

A frightful scowl distorted the features of the chief. "She-jato!" he cried. "I will tame you! I will break you! Es-sat, the chief, takes what he will and who dares question his right, or combat his least purpose, will first serve that purpose and then be broken as I break this," and he picked a stone platter from the table and broke it in his powerful hands. "You might have been first and most favored in the cave of the ancestors of Es-sat; but now shall you be last and least and when I am done with you you shall belong to all of the men of Es-sat's cave. Thus for those who spurn the love of their chief!"

He advanced quickly to seize her and as he laid a rough hand upon her she struck him heavily upon the side of his head with her golden breastplates. Without a sound Es-sat, the chief, sank to the floor of the apartment. For a moment Pan-at-lee bent over him, her improvised weapon raised to strike again should he show signs of returning consciousness, her glossy breasts rising and falling with her quickened breathing. Suddenly she stooped and removed Es-sat's knife with its scabbard and shoulder belt. Slipping it over her own shoulder she quickly adjusted her breastplates and keeping a watchful glance upon the figure of the fallen chief, backed from the room.

In a niche in the outer room, just beside the doorway leading to the balcony, were neatly piled a number of rounded pegs from eighteen to twenty inches in length. Selecting five of these she made them into a little bundle about which she twined the lower extremity of her sinuous tail and thus carrying them made her way to the outer edge of the balcony. Assuring herself that there was none about to see, or hinder her, she took quickly to the pegs already set in the face of the cliff and with the celerity of a monkey clambered swiftly aloft to the highest row of pegs which she followed in the direction of the lower end of the gorge for a matter of some hundred yards. Here, above her head, were a series of small round holes placed one above another in three parallel rows. Clinging only with her toes she removed two of the pegs from the bundle carried in her tail and taking one in either hand she inserted them in two opposite holes of the outer rows as far above her as she could reach. Hanging by these new holds she now took one of the three remaining pegs in each of her feet, leaving the fifth grasped securely in her tail. Reaching above her with this member she inserted the fifth peg in one of the holes of the center row and then, alternately hanging by her tail, her feet, or her hands, she moved the pegs upward to new holes, thus carrying her stairway with her as she ascended.

At the summit of the cliff a gnarled tree exposed its time-worn roots above the topmost holes forming the last step from the sheer face of the precipice to level footing. This was the last avenue of escape for members of the tribe hard pressed by enemies from below. There were three such emergency exits from the village and it were death to use them in other than an emergency. This Pan-at-lee well knew; but she knew, too, that it were worse than death to remain where the angered Es-sat might lay hands upon her.

When she had gained the summit, the girl moved quickly through the darkness in the direction of the next gorge which cut the mountain-side a mile beyond Kor-ul-ja. It was the Gorge-of-water, Kor-ul-lul, to which her father and two brothers had been sent by Es-sat ostensibly to spy upon the neighboring tribe. There was a chance, a slender chance, that she might find them; if not there was the deserted Kor-ul-gryf several miles beyond, where she might hide indefinitely from man if she could elude the frightful monster from which the gorge derived its name and whose presence there had rendered its caves uninhabitable for generations.

Pan-at-lee crept stealthily along the rim of the Kor-ul-lul. Just where her father and brothers would watch she did not know. Sometimes their spies remained upon the rim, sometimes they watched from the gorge's bottom. Pan-at-lee was at a loss to know what to do or where to go. She felt very small and helpless alone in the vast darkness of the night. Strange noises fell upon her ears. They came from the lonely reaches of the towering mountains above her, from far away in the invisible valley and from the nearer foothills and once, in the distance, she heard what she thought was the bellow of a bull gryf. It came from the direction of the Kor-ul-gryf. She shuddered.

Presently there came to her keen ears another sound. Something approached her along the rim of the gorge. It was coming from above. She halted, listening. Perhaps it was her father, or a brother. It was coming closer. She strained her eyes through the darkness. She did not move—she scarcely breathed. And then, of a sudden, quite close it seemed, there blazed through the black night two yellow-green spots of fire.

Pan-at-lee was brave, but as always with the primitive, the darkness held infinite terrors for her. Not alone the terrors of the known but more frightful ones as well—those of the unknown. She had passed through much this night and her nerves were keyed to the highest pitch—raw, taut nerves, they were, ready to react in an exaggerated form to the slightest shock.

But this was no slight shock. To hope for a father and a brother and to see death instead glaring out of the darkness! Yes, Pan-at-lee was brave, but she was not of iron. With a shriek that reverberated among the hills she turned and fled along the rim of Kor-ul-lul and behind her, swiftly, came the devil-eyed lion of the mountains of Pal-ul-don.

Pan-at-lee was lost. Death was inevitable. Of this there could be no doubt, but to die beneath the rending fangs of the carnivore, congenital terror of her kind—it was unthinkable. But there was an alternative. The lion was almost upon her—another instant and he would seize her. Pan-at-lee turned sharply to her left. Just a few steps she took in the new direction before she disappeared over the rim of Kor-ul-lul. The baffled lion, planting all four feet, barely stopped upon the verge of the abyss. Glaring down into the black shadows beneath he mounted an angry roar.

Through the darkness at the bottom of Kor-ul-ja, Om-at led the way toward the caves of his people. Behind him came Tarzan and Ta-den. Presently they halted beneath a great tree that grew close to the cliff.

"First," whispered Om-at, "I will go to the cave of Pan-at-lee. Then will I seek the cave of my ancestors to have speech with my own blood. It will not take long. Wait here—I shall return soon. Afterward shall we go together to Ta-den's people."

He moved silently toward the foot of the cliff up which Tarzan could presently see him ascending like a great fly on a wall. In the dim light the ape-man could not see the pegs set in the face of the cliff. Om-at moved warily. In the lower tier of caves there should be a sentry. His knowledge of his people and their customs told him, however, that in all probability the sentry was asleep. In this he was not mistaken, yet he did not in any way abate his wariness. Smoothly and swiftly he ascended toward the cave of Pan-at-lee while from below Tarzan and Ta-den watched him.

"How does he do it?" asked Tarzan. "I can see no foothold upon that vertical surface and yet he appears to be climbing with the utmost ease."

Ta-den explained the stairway of pegs. "You could ascend easily," he said, "although a tail would be of great assistance."

They watched until Om-at was about to enter the cave of Pan-at-lee without seeing any indication that he had been observed and then, simultaneously, both saw a head appear in the mouth of one of the lower caves. It was quickly evident that its owner had discovered Om-at for immediately he started upward in pursuit. Without a word Tarzan and Ta-den sprang forward toward the foot of the cliff. The pithecanthropus was the first to reach it and the ape-man saw him spring upward for a handhold on the lowest peg above him. Now Tarzan saw other pegs roughly paralleling each other in zigzag rows up the cliff face. He sprang and caught one of these, pulled himself upward by one hand until he could reach a second with his other hand; and when he had ascended far enough to use his feet, discovered that he could make rapid progress. Ta-den was outstripping him, however, for these precarious ladders were no novelty to him and, further, he had an advantage in possessing a tail.

Nevertheless, the ape-man gave a good account of himself, being presently urged to redoubled efforts by the fact that the Waz-don above Ta-den glanced down and discovered his pursuers just before the Ho-don overtook him. Instantly a wild cry shattered the silence of the gorge—a cry that was immediately answered by hundreds of savage throats as warrior after warrior emerged from the entrance to his cave.

The creature who had raised the alarm had now reached the recess before Pan-at-lee's cave and here he halted and turned to give battle to Ta-den. Unslinging his club which had hung down his back from a thong about his neck he stood upon the level floor of the entrance-way effectually blocking Ta-den's ascent. From all directions the warriors of Kor-ul-ja were swarming toward the interlopers. Tarzan, who had reached a point on the same level with Ta-den but a little to the latter's left, saw that nothing short of a miracle could save them. Just at the ape-man's left was the entrance to a cave that either was deserted or whose occupants had not as yet been aroused, for the level recess remained unoccupied. Resourceful was the alert mind of Tarzan of the Apes and quick to respond were the trained muscles. In the time that you or I might give to debating an action he would accomplish it and now, though only seconds separated his nearest antagonist from him, in the brief span of time at his disposal he had stepped into the recess, unslung his long rope and leaning far out shot the sinuous noose, with the precision of long habitude, toward the menacing figure wielding its heavy club above Ta-den. There was a momentary pause of the rope-hand as the noose sped toward its goal, a quick movement of the right wrist that closed it upon its victim as it settled over his head and then a surging tug as, seizing the rope in both hands, Tarzan threw back upon it all the weight of his great frame.

Voicing a terrified shriek, the Waz-don lunged headforemost from the recess above Ta-den. Tarzan braced himself for the coming shock when the creature's body should have fallen the full length of the rope and as it did there was a snap of the vertebrae that rose sickeningly in the momentary silence that had followed the doomed man's departing scream. Unshaken by the stress of the suddenly arrested weight at the end of the rope, Tarzan quickly pulled the body to his side that he might remove the noose from about its neck, for he could not afford to lose so priceless a weapon.

During the several seconds that had elapsed since he cast the rope the Waz-don warriors had remained inert as though paralyzed by wonder or by terror. Now, again, one of them found his voice and his head and straightway, shrieking invectives at the strange intruder, started upward for the ape-man, urging his fellows to attack. This man was the closest to Tarzan. But for him the ape-man could easily have reached Ta-den's side as the latter was urging him to do. Tarzan raised the body of the dead Waz-don above his head, held it poised there for a moment as with face raised to the heavens he screamed forth the horrid challenge of the bull apes of the tribe of Kerchak, and with all the strength of his giant sinews he hurled the corpse heavily upon the ascending warrior. So great was the force of the impact that not only was the Waz-don torn from his hold but two of the pegs to which he clung were broken short in their sockets.

As the two bodies, the living and the dead, hurtled downward toward the foot of the cliff a great cry arose from the Waz-don. "Jad-guru-don! Jad-guru-don!" they screamed, and then: "Kill him! Kill him!"

And now Tarzan stood in the recess beside Ta-den. Jad-guru-don!" repeated the latter, smiling—"The terrible man! Tarzan the Terrible! They may kill you, but they will never forget you."

"They shall not ki—What have we here?" Tarzan's statement as to what "they" should not do was interrupted by a sudden ejaculation as two figures, locked in deathlike embrace, stumbled through the doorway of the cave to the outer porch. One was Om-at, the other a creature of his own kind but with a rough coat, the hairs of which seemed to grow straight outward from the skin, stiffly, unlike Om-at's sleek covering. The two were quite evidently well matched and equally evident was the fact that each was bent upon murder. They fought almost in silence except for an occasional low growl as one or the other acknowledged thus some new hurt.

Tarzan, following a natural impulse to aid his ally, leaped forward to enter the dispute only to be checked by a grunted admonition from Om-at. "Back!" he said. "This fight is mine, alone."

The ape-man understood and stepped aside.

"It is a gund-bar," explained Ta-den, "a chief-battle. This fellow must be Es-sat, the chief. If Om-at kills him without assistance Om-at may become chief."

Tarzan smiled. It was the law of his own jungle—the law of the tribe of Kerchak, the bull ape—the ancient law of primitive man that needed but the refining influences of civilization to introduce the hired dagger and the poison cup. Then his attention was drawn to the outer edge of the vestibule. Above it appeared the shaggy face of one of Es-sat's warriors. Tarzan sprang to intercept the man; but Ta-den was there ahead of him. "Back!" cried the Ho-don to the newcomer. "It is gund-bar." The fellow looked scrutinizingly at the two fighters, then turned his face downward toward his fellows. "Back!" he cried, "it is gund-bar between Es-sat and Om-at." Then he looked back at Ta-den and Tarzan. "Who are you?" he asked.

"We are Om-at's friends," replied Ta-den.

The fellow nodded. "We will attend to you later," he said and disappeared below the edge of the recess.

The battle upon the ledge continued with unabated ferocity, Tarzan and Ta-den having difficulty in keeping out of the way of the contestants who tore and beat at each other with hands and feet and lashing tails. Es-sat was unarmed—Pan-at-lee had seen to that—but at Om-at's side swung a sheathed knife which he made no effort to draw. That would have been contrary to their savage and primitive code for the chief-battle must be fought with nature's weapons.

Sometimes they separated for an instant only to rush upon each other again with all the ferocity and nearly the strength of mad bulls. Presently one of them tripped the other but in that viselike embrace one could not fall alone—Es-sat dragged Om-at with him, toppling upon the brink of the niche. Even Tarzan held his breath. There they surged to and fro perilously for a moment and then the inevitable happened—the two, locked in murderous embrace, rolled over the edge and disappeared from the ape-man's view.

Tarzan voiced a suppressed sigh for he had liked Om-at and then, with Ta-den, approached the edge and looked over. Far below, in the dim light of the coming dawn, two inert forms should be lying stark in death; but, to Tarzan's amazement, such was far from the sight that met his eyes. Instead, there were the two figures still vibrant with life and still battling only a few feet below him. Clinging always to the pegs with two holds—a hand and a foot, or a foot and a tail, they seemed as much at home upon the perpendicular wall as upon the level surface of the vestibule; but now their tactics were slightly altered, for each seemed particularly bent upon dislodging his antagonist from his holds and precipitating him to certain death below. It was soon evident that Om-at, younger and with greater powers of endurance than Es-sat, was gaining an advantage. Now was the chief almost wholly on the defensive. Holding him by the cross belt with one mighty hand Om-at was forcing his foeman straight out from the cliff, and with the other hand and one foot was rapidly breaking first one of Es-sat's holds and then another, alternating his efforts, or rather punctuating them, with vicious blows to the pit of his adversary's stomach. Rapidly was Es-sat weakening and with the knowledge of impending death there came, as there comes to every coward and bully under similar circumstances, a crumbling of the veneer of bravado which had long masqueraded as courage and with it crumbled his code of ethics. Now was Es-sat no longer chief of Kor-ul-ja—instead he was a whimpering craven battling for life. Clutching at Om-at, clutching at the nearest pegs he sought any support that would save him from that awful fall, and as he strove to push aside the hand of death, whose cold fingers he already felt upon his heart, his tail sought Om-at's side and the handle of the knife that hung there.

Tarzan saw and even as Es-sat drew the blade from its sheath he dropped catlike to the pegs beside the battling men. Es-sat's tail had drawn back for the cowardly fatal thrust. Now many others saw the perfidious act and a great cry of rage and disgust arose from savage throats; but as the blade sped toward its goal, the ape-man seized the hairy member that wielded it, and at the same instant Om-at thrust the body of Es-sat from him with such force that its weakened holds were broken and it hurtled downward, a brief meteor of screaming fear, to death.

TARZAN-JAD-GURU

As Tarzan and Om-at clambered back to the vestibule of Pan-at-lee's cave and took their stand beside Ta-den in readiness for whatever eventuality might follow the death of Es-sat, the sun that topped the eastern hills touched also the figure of a sleeper upon a distant, thorn-covered steppe awakening him to another day of tireless tracking along a faint and rapidly disappearing spoor.

For a time silence reigned in the Kor-ul-ja. The tribesmen waited, looking now down upon the dead thing that had been their chief, now at one another, and now at Om-at and the two who stood upon his either side. Presently Om-at spoke. "I am Om-at," he cried. "Who will say that Om-at is not gund of Kor-ul-ja?"

He waited for a taker of his challenge. One or two of the larger young bucks fidgeted restlessly and eyed him; but there was no reply.

"Then Om-at is gund," he said with finality. "Now tell me, where are Pan-at-lee, her father, and her brothers?"

An old warrior spoke. "Pan-at-lee should be in her cave. Who should know that better than you who are there now? Her father and her brothers were sent to watch Kor-ul-lul; but neither of these questions arouse any tumult in our breasts. There is one that does: Can Om-at be chief of Kor-ul-ja and yet stand at bay against his own people with a Ho-don and that terrible man at his side—that terrible man who has no tail? Hand the strangers over to your people to be slain as is the way of the Waz-don and then may Om-at be gund."

Neither Tarzan nor Ta-den spoke then, they but stood watching Om-at and waiting for his decision, the ghost of a smile upon the lips of the ape-man. Ta-den, at least, knew that the old warrior had spoken the truth—the Waz-don entertain no strangers and take no prisoners of an alien race.

Then spoke Om-at. "Always there is change," he said. "Even the old hills of Pal-ul-don appear never twice alike—the brilliant sun, a passing cloud, the moon, a mist, the changing seasons, the sharp clearness following a storm; these things bring each a new change in our hills. From birth to death, day by day, there is constant change in each of us. Change, then, is one of Jad-ben-Otho's laws.

"And now I, Om-at, your gund, bring another change. Strangers who are brave men and good friends shall no longer be slain by the Waz-don of Kor-ul-ja!"

There were growls and murmurings and a restless moving among the warriors as each eyed the others to see who would take the initiative against Om-at, the iconoclast.

"Cease your mutterings," admonished the new gund. "I am your chief. My word is your law. You had no part in making me chief. Some of you helped Es-sat to drive me from the cave of my ancestors; the rest of you permitted it. I owe you nothing. Only these two, whom you would have me kill, were loyal to me. I am gund and if there be any who doubts it let him speak—he cannot die younger."

Tarzan was pleased. Here was a man after his own heart. He admired the fearlessness of Om-at's challenge and he was a sufficiently good judge of men to know that he had listened to no idle bluff—Om-at would back up his words to the death, if necessary, and the chances were that he would not be the one to die. Evidently the majority of the Kor-ul-jaians entertained the same conviction.

"I will make you a good gund," said Om-at, seeing that no one appeared inclined to dispute his rights. "Your wives and daughters will be safe—they were not safe while Es-sat ruled. Go now to your crops and your hunting. I leave to search for Pan-at-lee. Ab-on will be gund while I am away—look to him for guidance and to me for an accounting when I return—and may Jad-ben-Otho smile upon you."

He turned toward Tarzan and the Ho-don. "And you, my friends," he said, "are free to go among my people; the cave of my ancestors is yours, do what you will."

"I," said Tarzan, "will go with Om-at to search for Pan-at-lee."

"And I," said Ta-den.

Om-at smiled. "Good!" he exclaimed. "And when we have found her we shall go together upon Tarzan's business and Ta-den's. Where first shall we search?" He turned toward his warriors. "Who knows where she may be?"

None knew other than that Pan-at-lee had gone to her cave with the others the previous evening—there was no clew, no suggestion as to her whereabouts.

"Show me where she sleeps," said Tarzan; "let me see something that belongs to her—an article of her apparel—then, doubtless, I can help you."

Two young warriors climbed closer to the ledge upon which Om-at stood. They were In-sad and O-dan. It was the latter who spoke.

"Gund of Kor-ul-ja," he said, "we would go with you to search for Pan-at-lee."

It was the first acknowledgment of Om-at's chieftainship and immediately following it the tenseness that had prevailed seemed to relax—the warriors spoke aloud instead of in whispers, and the women appeared from the mouths of caves as with the passing of a sudden storm. In-sad and O-dan had taken the lead and now all seemed glad to follow. Some came to talk with Om-at and to look more closely at Tarzan; others, heads of caves, gathered their hunters and discussed the business of the day. The women and children prepared to descend to the fields with the youths and the old men, whose duty it was to guard them.

"O-dan and In-sad shall go with us," announced Om-at, "we shall not need more. Tarzan, come with me and I shall show you where Pan-at-lee sleeps, though why you should wish to know I cannot guess—she is not there. I have looked for myself."

The two entered the cave where Om-at led the way to the apartment in which Es-sat had surprised Pan-at-lee the previous night.

"All here are hers," said Om-at, "except the war club lying on the floor—that was Es-sat's."

The ape-man moved silently about the apartment, the quivering of his sensitive nostrils scarcely apparent to his companion who only wondered what good purpose could be served here and chafed at the delay.

"Come!" said the ape-man, presently, and led the way toward the outer recess.

Here their three companions were awaiting them. Tarzan passed to the left side of the niche and examined the pegs that lay within reach. He looked at them but it was not his eyes that were examining them. Keener than his keen eyes was that marvelously trained sense of scent that had first been developed in him during infancy under the tutorage of his foster mother, Kala, the she-ape, and further sharpened in the grim jungles by that master teacher—the instinct of self-preservation.

From the left side of the niche he turned to the right. Om-at was becoming impatient.

"Let us be off," he said. "We must search for Pan-at-lee if we would ever find her."

"Where shall we search?" asked Tarzan.

Om-at scratched his head. "Where?" he repeated. "Why all Pal-ul-don, if necessary."

"A large job," said Tarzan. "Come," he added, "she went this way," and he took to the pegs that led aloft toward the summit of the cliff. Here he followed the scent easily since none had passed that way since Pan-at-lee had fled. At the point at which she had left the permanent pegs and resorted to those carried with her Tarzan came to an abrupt halt. "She went this way to the summit," he called back to Om-at who was directly behind him; "but there are no pegs here."

"I do not know how you know that she went this way," said Om-at; "but we will get pegs. In-sad, return and fetch climbing pegs for five."

The young warrior was soon back and the pegs distributed. Om-at handed five to Tarzan and explained their use. The ape-man returned one. "I need but four," he said.

Om-at smiled. "What a wonderful creature you would be if you were not deformed," he said, glancing with pride at his own strong tail.

"I admit that I am handicapped," replied Tarzan. "You others go ahead and leave the pegs in place for me. I am afraid that otherwise it will be slow work as I cannot hold the pegs in my toes as you do."

"All right," agreed Om-at; "Ta-den, In-sad, and I will go first, you follow and O-dan bring up the rear and collect the pegs—we cannot leave them here for our enemies."

"Can't your enemies bring their own pegs?" asked Tarzan.

"Yes; but it delays them and makes easier our defense and—they do not know which of all the holes you see are deep enough for pegs—the others are made to confuse our enemies and are too shallow to hold a peg."

At the top of the cliff beside the gnarled tree Tarzan again took up the trail. Here the scent was fully as strong as upon the pegs and the ape-man moved rapidly across the ridge in the direction of the Kor-ul-lul.

Presently he paused and turned toward Om-at. "Here she moved swiftly, running at top speed, and, Om-at, she was pursued by a lion."

"You can read that in the grass?" asked O-dan as the others gathered about the ape-man.

Tarzan nodded. "I do not think the lion got her," he added; "but that we shall determine quickly. No, he did not get her—look!" and he pointed toward the southwest, down the ridge.

Following the direction indicated by his finger, the others presently detected a movement in some bushes a couple of hundred yards away.

"What is it?" asked Om-at. "It is she?" and he started toward the spot.

"Wait," advised Tarzan. "It is the lion which pursued her."

"You can see him?" asked Ta-den.

"No, I can smell him."

The others looked their astonishment and incredulity; but of the fact that it was indeed a lion they were not left long in doubt. Presently the bushes parted and the creature stepped out in full view, facing them. It was a magnificent beast, large and beautifully maned, with the brilliant leopard spots of its kind well marked and symmetrical. For a moment it eyed them and then, still chafing at the loss of its prey earlier in the morning, it charged.

The Pal-ul-donians unslung their clubs and stood waiting the onrushing beast. Tarzan of the Apes drew his hunting knife and crouched in the path of the fanged fury. It was almost upon him when it swerved to the right and leaped for Om-at only to be sent to earth with a staggering blow upon the head. Almost instantly it was up and though the men rushed fearlessly in, it managed to sweep aside their weapons with its mighty paws. A single blow wrenched O-dan's club from his hand and sent it hurtling against Ta-den, knocking him from his feet. Taking advantage of its opportunity the lion rose to throw itself upon O-dan and at the same instant Tarzan flung himself upon its back. Strong, white teeth buried themselves in the spotted neck, mighty arms encircled the savage throat and the sinewy legs of the ape-man locked themselves about the gaunt belly.

The others, powerless to aid, stood breathlessly about as the great lion lunged hither and thither, clawing and biting fearfully and futilely at the savage creature that had fastened itself upon him. Over and over they rolled and now the onlookers saw a brown hand raised above the lion's side—a brown hand grasping a keen blade. They saw it fall and rise and fall again—each time with terrific force and in its wake they saw a crimson stream trickling down ja's gorgeous coat.

Now from the lion's throat rose hideous screams of hate and rage and pain as he redoubled his efforts to dislodge and punish his tormentor; but always the tousled black head remained half buried in the dark brown mane and the mighty arm rose and fell to plunge the knife again and again into the dying beast.

The Pal-ul-donians stood in mute wonder and admiration. Brave men and mighty hunters they were and as such the first to accord honor to a mightier.

"And you would have had me slay him!" cried Om-at, glancing at In-sad and O-dan.

"Jad-ben-Otho reward you that you did not," breathed In-sad.

And now the lion lunged suddenly to earth and with a few spasmodic quiverings lay still. The ape-man rose and shook himself, even as might ja, the leopard-coated lion of Pal-ul-don, had he been the one to survive.

O-dan advanced quickly toward Tarzan. Placing a palm upon his own breast and the other on Tarzan's, "Tarzan the Terrible," he said, "I ask no greater honor than your friendship."

"And I no more than the friendship of Om-at's friends," replied the ape-man simply, returning the other's salute.

"Do you think," asked Om-at, coming close to Tarzan and laying a hand upon the other's shoulder, "that he got her?"

"No, my friend; it was a hungry lion that charged us."

"You seem to know much of lions," said In-sad.

"Had I a brother I could not know him better," replied Tarzan.

"Then where can she be?" continued Om-at.

"We can but follow while the spoor is fresh," answered the ape-man and again taking up his interrupted tracking he led them down the ridge and at a sharp turning of the trail to the left brought them to the verge of the cliff that dropped into the Kor-ul-lul. For a moment Tarzan examined the ground to the right and to the left, then he stood erect and looking at Om-at pointed into the gorge.

For a moment the Waz-don gazed down into the green rift at the bottom of which a tumultuous river tumbled downward along its rocky bed, then he closed his eyes as to a sudden spasm of pain and turned away.

"You—mean—she jumped?" he asked.

"To escape the lion," replied Tarzan. "He was right behind her—look, you can see where his four paws left their impress in the turf as he checked his charge upon the very verge of the abyss."

"Is there any chance—" commenced Om-at, to be suddenly silenced by a warning gesture from Tarzan.

"Down!" whispered the ape-man, "many men are coming. They are running—from down the ridge." He flattened himself upon his belly in the grass, the others following his example.

For some minutes they waited thus and then the others, too, heard the sound of running feet and now a hoarse shout followed by many more.

"It is the war cry of the Kor-ul-lul," whispered Om-at—" the hunting cry of men who hunt men. Presently shall we see them and if Jad-ben-Otho is pleased with us they shall not too greatly outnumber us."

"They are many," said Tarzan, "forty or fifty, I should say; but how many are the pursued and how many the pursuers we cannot even guess, except that the latter must greatly outnumber the former, else these would not run so fast."

"Here they come," said Ta-den.

"It is An-un, father of Pan-at-lee, and his two sons," exclaimed O-dan. "They will pass without seeing us if we do not hurry," he added looking at Om-at, the chief, for a sign.

"Come!" cried the latter, springing to his feet and running rapidly to intercept the three fugitives. The others followed him.

"Five friends!" shouted Om-at as An-un and his sons discovered them.

"Adenen yo!" echoed O-dan and In-sad.

The fugitives scarcely paused as these unexpected reinforcements joined them but they eyed Ta-den and Tarzan with puzzled glances.

"The Kor-ul-lul are many," shouted An-un. "Would that we might pause and fight; but first we must warn Es-sat and our people."

"Yes," said Om-at, "we must warn our people."

"Es-sat is dead," said In-sad.

"Who is chief?" asked one of An-un's sons.

"Om-at," replied O-dan.

"It is well," cried An-un. "Pan-at-lee said that you would come back and slay Es-sat."

Now the enemy broke into sight behind them.

"Come!" cried Tarzan," let us turn and charge them, raising a great cry. They pursued but three and when they see eight charging upon them they will think that many men have come to do battle. They will believe that there are more even than they see and then one who is swift will have time to reach the gorge and warn your people."

"It is well," said Om-at. "Id-an, you are swift—carry word to the warriors of Kor-ul-ja that we fight the Kor-ul-lul upon the ridge and that Ab-on shall send a hundred men."

Id-an, the son of An-un, sped swiftly toward the cliff-dwellings of the Kor-ul-ja while the others charged the oncoming Kor-ul-lul, the war cries of the two tribes rising and falling in a certain grim harmony. The leaders of the Kor-ul-lul paused at sight of the reinforcements, waiting apparently for those behind to catch up with them and, possibly, also to learn how great a force confronted them. The leaders, swifter runners than their fellows, perhaps, were far in advance while the balance of their number had not yet emerged from the brush; and now as Om-at and his companions fell upon them with a ferocity born of necessity they fell back, so that when their companions at last came in sight of them they appeared to be in full rout. The natural result was that the others turned and fled.

Encouraged by this first success Om-at followed them into the brush, his little company charging valiantly upon his either side, and loud and terrifying were the savage yells with which they pursued the fleeing enemy. The brush, while not growing so closely together as to impede progress, was of such height as to hide the members of the party from one another when they became separated by even a few yards. The result was that Tarzan, always swift and always keen for battle, was soon pursuing the enemy far in the lead of the others—a lack of prudence which was to prove his undoing.

The warriors of Kor-ul-lul, doubtless as valorous as their foemen, retreated only to a more strategic position in the brush, nor were they long in guessing that the number of their pursuers was fewer than their own. They made a stand then where the brush was densest—an ambush it was, and into this ran Tarzan of the Apes. They tricked him neatly. Yes, sad as is the narration of it, they tricked the wily jungle lord. But then they were fighting on their own ground, every foot of which they knew as you know your front parlor, and they were following their own tactics, of which Tarzan knew nothing.

A single black warrior appeared to Tarzan a laggard in the rear of the retreating enemy and thus retreating he lured Tarzan on. At last he turned at bay confronting the ape-man with bludgeon and drawn knife and as Tarzan charged him a score of burly Waz-don leaped from the surrounding brush. Instantly, but too late, the giant Tarmangani realized his peril. There flashed before him a vision of his lost mate and a great and sickening regret surged through him with the realization that if she still lived she might no longer hope, for though she might never know of the passing of her lord the fact of it must inevitably seal her doom.

And consequent to this thought there enveloped him a blind frenzy of hatred for these creatures who dared thwart his purpose and menace the welfare of his wife. With a savage growl he threw himself upon the warrior before him twisting the heavy club from the creature's hand as if he had been a little child, and with his left fist backed by the weight and sinew of his giant frame, he crashed a shattering blow to the center of the Waz-don's face—a blow that crushed the bones and dropped the fellow in his tracks. Then he swung upon the others with their fallen comrade's bludgeon striking to right and left mighty, unmerciful blows that drove down their own weapons until that wielded by the ape-man was splintered and shattered. On either hand they fell before his cudgel; so rapid the delivery of his blows, so catlike his recovery that in the first few moments of the battle he seemed invulnerable to their attack; but it could not last—he was outnumbered twenty to one and his undoing came from a thrown club. It struck him upon the back of the head. For a moment he stood swaying and then like a great pine beneath the woodsman's ax he crashed to earth.

Others of the Kor-ul-lul had rushed to engage the balance of Om-at's party. They could be heard fighting at a short distance and it was evident that the Kor-ul-ja were falling slowly back and as they fell Om-at called to the missing one: "Tarzan the Terrible! Tarzan the Terrible!"

"Jad-guru, indeed," repeated one of the Kor-ul-lul rising from where Tarzan had dropped him. "Tarzan-jad-guru! He was worse than that."

IN THE KOR-UL-GRYF

As Tarzan fell among his enemies a man halted many miles away upon the outer verge of the morass that encircles Pal-ul-don. Naked he was except for a loin cloth and three belts of cartridges, two of which passed over his shoulders, crossing upon his chest and back, while the third encircled his waist. Slung to his back by its leathern sling-strap was an Enfield, and he carried too a long knife, a bow and a quiver of arrows. He had come far, through wild and savage lands, menaced by fierce beasts and fiercer men, yet intact to the last cartridge was the ammunition that had filled his belts the day that he set out.

The bow and the arrows and the long knife had brought him thus far safely, yet often in the face of great risks that could have been minimized by a single shot from the well-kept rifle at his back. What purpose might he have for conserving this precious ammunition? in risking his life to bring the last bright shining missile to his unknown goal? For what, for whom were these death-dealing bits of metal preserved? In all the world only he knew.

When Pan-at-lee stepped over the edge of the cliff above Kor-ul-lul she expected to be dashed to instant death upon the rocks below; but she had chosen this in preference to the rending fangs of ja. Instead, chance had ordained that she make the frightful plunge at a point where the tumbling river swung close beneath the overhanging cliff to eddy for a slow moment in a deep pool before plunging madly downward again in a cataract of boiling foam, and water thundering against rocks.

Into this icy pool the girl shot, and down and down beneath the watery surface until, half choked, yet fighting bravely, she battled her way once more to air. Swimming strongly she made the opposite shore and there dragged herself out upon the bank to lie panting and spent until the approaching dawn warned her to seek concealment, for she was in the country of her people's enemies.

Rising, she moved into the concealment of the rank vegetation that grows so riotously in the well-watered kors of Pal-ul-don.

Hidden amidst the plant life from the sight of any who might chance to pass along the well-beaten trail that skirted the river Pan-at-lee sought rest and food, the latter growing in abundance all about her in the form of fruits and berries and succulent tubers which she scooped from the earth with the knife of the dead Es-sat.

Ah! if she had but known that he was dead! What trials and risks and terrors she might have been saved; but she thought that he still lived and so she dared not return to Kor-ul-ja. At least not yet while his rage was at white heat. Later, perhaps, her father and brothers returned to their cave, she might risk it; but not now—not now. Nor could she for long remain here in the neighborhood of the hostile Kor-ul-lul and somewhere she must find safety from beasts before the night set in.

As she sat upon the bole of a fallen tree seeking some solution of the problem of existence that confronted her, there broke upon her ears from up the gorge the voices of shouting men—a sound that she recognized all too well. It was the war cry of the Kor-ul-lul. Closer and closer it approached her hiding place. Then, through the veil of foliage she caught glimpses of three figures fleeing along the trail, and behind them the shouting of the pursuers rose louder and louder as they neared her. Again she caught sight of the fugitives crossing the river below the cataract and again they were lost to sight. And now the pursuers came into view—shouting Kor-ul-lul warriors, fierce and implacable. Forty, perhaps fifty of them. She waited breathless; but they did not swerve from the trail and passed her, unguessing that an enemy she lay hid within a few yards of them.

Once again she caught sight of the pursued—three Waz-don warriors clambering the cliff face at a point where portions of the summit had fallen away presenting a steep slope that might be ascended by such as these. Suddenly her attention was riveted upon the three. Could it be? O Jad-ben-Otho! had she but known a moment before. When they passed she might have joined them, for they were her father and two brothers. Now it was too late. With bated breath and tense muscles she watched the race. Would they reach the summit? Would the Kor-ul-lul overhaul them? They climbed well, but, oh, so slowly. Now one lost his footing in the loose shale and slipped back! The Kor-ul-lul were ascending—one hurled his club at the nearest fugitive. The Great God was pleased with the brother of Pan-at-lee, for he caused the club to fall short of its target, and to fall, rolling and bounding, back upon its owner carrying him from his feet and precipitating him to the bottom of the gorge.

Standing now, her hands pressed tight above her golden breastplates, Pan-at-lee watched the race for life. Now one, her older brother, reached the summit and clinging there to something that she could not see he lowered his body and his long tail to the father beneath him. The latter, seizing this support, extended his own tail to the son below—the one who had slipped back—and thus, upon a living ladder of their own making, the three reached the summit and disappeared from view before the Kor-ul-lul overtook them. But the latter did not abandon the chase. On they went until they too had disappeared from sight and only a faint shouting came down to Pan-at-lee to tell her that the pursuit continued.

The girl knew that she must move on. At any moment now might come a hunting party, combing the gorge for the smaller animals that fed or bedded there.

Behind her were Es-sat and the returning party of Kor-ul-lul that had pursued her kin; before her, across the next ridge, was the Kor-ul-gryf, the lair of the terrifying monsters that brought the chill of fear to every inhabitant of Pal-ul-don; below her, in the valley, was the country of the Ho-don, where she could look for only slavery, or death; here were the Kor-ul-lul, the ancient enemies of her people and everywhere were the wild beasts that eat the flesh of man.

For but a moment she debated and then turning her face toward the southeast she set out across the gorge of water toward the Kor-ul-gryf—at least there were no men there. As it is now, so it was in the beginning, back to the primitive progenitor of man which is typified by Pan-at-lee and her kind today, of all the hunters that woman fears, man is the most relentless, the most terrible. To the dangers of man she preferred the dangers of the gryf.

Moving cautiously she reached the foot of the cliff at the far side of Kor-ul-lul and here, toward noon, she found a comparatively easy ascent. Crossing the ridge she stood at last upon the brink of Kor-ul-gryf—the horror place of the folklore of her race. Dank and mysterious grew the vegetation below; giant trees waved their plumed tops almost level with the summit of the cliff; and over all brooded an ominous silence.

Pan-at-lee lay upon her belly and stretching over the edge scanned the cliff face below her. She could see caves there and the stone pegs which the ancients had fashioned so laboriously by hand. She had heard of these in the firelight tales of her childhood and of how the gryfs had come from the morasses across the mountains and of how at last the people had fled after many had been seized and devoured by the hideous creatures, leaving their caves untenanted for no man living knew how long. Some said that Jad-ben-Otho, who has lived forever, was still a little boy. Pan-at-lee shuddered; but there were caves and in them she would be safe even from the gryfs.

She found a place where the stone pegs reached to the very summit of the cliff, left there no doubt in the final exodus of the tribe when there was no longer need of safeguarding the deserted caves against invasion. Pan-at-lee clambered slowly down toward the uppermost cave. She found the recess in front of the doorway almost identical with those of her own tribe. The floor of it, though, was littered with twigs and old nests and the droppings of birds, until it was half choked. She moved along to another recess and still another, but all were alike in the accumulated filth. Evidently there was no need in looking further. This one seemed large and commodious. With her knife she fell to work cleaning away the debris by the simple expedient of pushing it over the edge, and always her eyes turned constantly toward the silent gorge where lurked the fearsome creatures of Pal-ul-don. And other eyes there were, eyes she did not see, but that saw her and watched her every move—fierce eyes, greedy eyes, cunning and cruel. They watched her, and a red tongue licked flabby, pendulous lips. They watched her, and a half-human brain laboriously evolved a brutish design.

As in her own Kor-ul-ja, the natural springs in the cliff had been developed by the long-dead builders of the caves so that fresh, pure water trickled now, as it had for ages, within easy access to the cave entrances. Her only difficulty would be in procuring food and for that she must take the risk at least once in two days, for she was sure that she could find fruits and tubers and perhaps small animals, birds, and eggs near the foot of the cliff, the last two, possibly, in the caves themselves. Thus might she live on here indefinitely. She felt now a certain sense of security imparted doubtless by the impregnability of her high-flung sanctuary that she knew to be safe from all the more dangerous beasts, and this one from men, too, since it lay in the abjured Kor-ul-gryf.

Now she determined to inspect the interior of her new home. The sun still in the south, lighted the interior of the first apartment. It was similar to those of her experience—the same beasts and men were depicted in the same crude fashion in the carvings on the walls—evidently there had been little progress in the race of Waz-don during the generations that had come and departed since Kor-ul-gryf had been abandoned by men. Of course Pan-at-lee thought no such thoughts, for evolution and progress existed not for her, or her kind. Things were as they had always been and would always be as they were.

That these strange creatures have existed thus for incalculable ages it can scarce be doubted, so marked are the indications of antiquity about their dwellings—deep furrows worn by naked feet in living rock; the hollow in the jamb of a stone doorway where many arms have touched in passing; the endless carvings that cover, ofttimes, the entire face of a great cliff and all the walls and ceilings of every cave and each carving wrought by a different hand, for each is the coat of arms, one might say, of the adult male who traced it.

And so Pan-at-lee found this ancient cave homelike and familiar. There was less litter within than she had found without and what there was was mostly an accumulation of dust. Beside the doorway was the niche in which wood and tinder were kept, but there remained nothing now other than mere dust. She had however saved a little pile of twigs from the debris on the porch. In a short time she had made a light by firing a bundle of twigs and lighting others from this fire she explored some of the inner rooms. Nor here did she find aught that was new or strange nor any relic of the departed owners other than a few broken stone dishes. She had been looking for something soft to sleep upon, but was doomed to disappointment as the former owners had evidently made a leisurely departure, carrying all their belongings with them. Below, in the gorge were leaves and grasses and fragrant branches, but Pan-at-lee felt no stomach for descending into that horrid abyss for the gratification of mere creature comfort—only the necessity for food would drive her there.

And so, as the shadows lengthened and night approached she prepared to make as comfortable a bed as she could by gathering the dust of ages into a little pile and spreading it between her soft body and the hard floor—at best it was only better than nothing. But Pan-at-lee was very tired. She had not slept since two nights before and in the interval she had experienced many dangers and hardships. What wonder then that despite the hard bed, she was asleep almost immediately she had composed herself for rest.

She slept and the moon rose, casting its silver light upon the cliff's white face and lessening the gloom of the dark forest and the dismal gorge. In the distance a lion roared. There was a long silence. From the upper reaches of the gorge came a deep bellow. There was a movement in the trees at the cliff's foot. Again the bellow, low and ominous. It was answered from below the deserted village. Something dropped from the foliage of a tree directly below the cave in which Pan-at-lee slept—it dropped to the ground among the dense shadows. Now it moved, cautiously. It moved toward the foot of the cliff, taking form and shape in the moonlight. It moved like the creature of a bad dream—slowly, sluggishly. It might have been a huge sloth—it might have been a man, with so grotesque a brush does the moon paint—master cubist.

Slowly it moved up the face of the cliff—like a great grubworm it moved, but now the moon-brush touched it again and it had hands and feet and with them it clung to the stone pegs and raised itself laboriously aloft toward the cave where Pan-at-lee slept. From the lower reaches of the gorge came again the sound of bellowing, and it was answered from above the village.

Tarzan of the Apes opened his eyes. He was conscious of a pain in his head, and at first that was about all. A moment later grotesque shadows, rising and falling, focused his arousing perceptions. Presently he saw that he was in a cave. A dozen Waz-don warriors squatted about, talking. A rude stone cresset containing burning oil lighted the interior and as the flame rose and fell the exaggerated shadows of the warriors danced upon the walls behind them.

"We brought him to you alive, Gund," he heard one of them saying, "because never before was Ho-don like him seen. He has no tail—he was born without one, for there is no scar to mark where a tail had been cut off. The thumbs upon his hands and feet are unlike those of the races of Pal-ul-don. He is more powerful than many men put together and he attacks with the fearlessness of ja. We brought him alive, that you might see him before he is slain."

The chief rose and approached the ape-man, who closed his eyes and feigned unconsciousness. He felt hairy hands upon him as he was turned over, none too gently. The gund examined him from head to foot, making comments, especially upon the shape and size of his thumbs and great toes.

"With these and with no tail," he said, "it cannot climb."

"No," agreed one of the warriors, "it would surely fall even from the cliff pegs."

"I have never seen a thing like it," said the chief. "It is neither Waz-don nor Ho-don. I wonder from whence it came and what it is called."

"The Kor-ul-ja shouted aloud, 'Tarzan-jad-guru!' and we thought that they might be calling this one," said a warrior. "Shall we kill it now?"

"No," replied the chief, "we will wait until it's life returns into its head that I may question it. Remain here, In-tan, and watch it. When it can again hear and speak call me."

He turned and departed from the cave, the others, except In-tan, following him. As they moved past him and out of the chamber Tarzan caught snatches of their conversation which indicated that the Kor-ul-ja reinforcements had fallen upon their little party in great numbers and driven them away. Evidently the swift feet of Id-an had saved the day for the warriors of Om-at. The ape-man smiled, then he partially opened an eye and cast it upon In-tan. The warrior stood at the entrance to the cave looking out—his back was toward his prisoner. Tarzan tested the bonds that secured his wrists. They seemed none too stout and they had tied his hands in front of him! Evidence indeed that the Waz-don took few prisoners—if any.

Cautiously he raised his wrists until he could examine the thongs that confined them. A grim smile lighted his features. Instantly he was at work upon the bonds with his strong teeth, but ever a wary eye was upon In-tan, the warrior of Kor-ul-lul. The last knot had been loosened and Tarzan's hands were free when In-tan turned to cast an appraising eye upon his ward. He saw that the prisoner's position was changed—he no longer lay upon his back as they had left him, but upon his side and his hands were drawn up against his face. In-tan came closer and bent down. The bonds seemed very loose upon the prisoner's wrists. He extended his hand to examine them with his fingers and instantly the two hands leaped from their bonds—one to seize his own wrist, the other his throat. So unexpected the catlike attack that In-tan had not even time to cry out before steel fingers silenced him. The creature pulled him suddenly forward so that he lost his balance and rolled over upon the prisoner and to the floor beyond to stop with Tarzan upon his breast. In-tan struggled to release himself—struggled to draw his knife; but Tarzan found it before him. The Waz-don's tail leaped to the other's throat, encircling it—he too could choke; but his own knife, in the hands of his antagonist, severed the beloved member close to its root.

The Waz-don's struggles became weaker—a film was obscuring his vision. He knew that he was dying and he was right. A moment later he was dead. Tarzan rose to his feet and placed one foot upon the breast of his dead foe. How the urge seized him to roar forth the victory cry of his kind! But he dared not. He discovered that they had not removed his rope from his shoulders and that they had replaced his knife in its sheath. It had been in his hand when he was felled. Strange creatures! He did not know that they held a superstitious fear of the weapons of a dead enemy, believing that if buried without them he would forever haunt his slayers in search of them and that when he found them he would kill the man who killed him. Against the wall leaned his bow and quiver of arrows.

Tarzan stepped toward the doorway of the cave and looked out. Night had just fallen. He could hear voices from the nearer caves and there floated to his nostrils the odor of cooking food. He looked down and experienced a sensation of relief. The cave in which he had been held was in the lowest tier—scarce thirty feet from the base of the cliff. He was about to chance an immediate descent when there occurred to him a thought that brought a grin to his savage lips—a thought that was born of the name the Waz-don had given him Tarzan-jad-guru—Tarzan the Terrible—and a recollection of the days when he had delighted in baiting the blacks of the distant jungle of his birth. He turned back into the cave where lay the dead body of In-tan. With his knife he severed the warrior's head and carrying it to the outer edge of the recess tossed it to the ground below, then he dropped swiftly and silently down the ladder of pegs in a way that would have surprised the Kor-ul-lul who had been so sure that he could not climb.

At the bottom he picked up the head of In-tan and disappeared among the shadows of the trees carrying the grisly trophy by its shock of shaggy hair. Horrible? But you are judging a wild beast by the standards of civilization. You may teach a lion tricks, but he is still a lion. Tarzan looked well in a Tuxedo, but he was still a Tarmangani and beneath his pleated shirt beat a wild and savage heart.

Nor was his madness lacking in method. He knew that the hearts of the Kor-ul-lul would be filled with rage when they discovered the thing that he had done and he knew too, that mixed with the rage would be a leaven of fear and it was fear of him that had made Tarzan master of many jungles—one does not win the respect of the killers with bonbons.

Below the village Tarzan returned to the foot of the cliff searching for a point where he could make the ascent to the ridge and thus back to the village of Om-at, the Kor-ul-ja. He came at last to a place where the river ran so close to the rocky wall that he was forced to swim it in search of a trail upon the opposite side and here it was that his keen nostrils detected a familiar spoor. It was the scent of Pan-at-lee at the spot where she had emerged from the pool and taken to the safety of the jungle.

Immediately the ape-man's plans were changed. Pan-at-lee lived, or at least she had lived after the leap from the cliff's summit. He had started in search of her for Om-at, his friend, and for Om-at he would continue upon the trail he had picked up thus fortuitously by accident. It led him into the jungle and across the gorge and then to the point at which Pan-at-lee had commenced the ascent of the opposite cliffs. Here Tarzan abandoned the head of In-tan, tying it to the lower branch of a tree, for he knew that it would handicap him in his ascent of the steep escarpment. Apelike he ascended, following easily the scent spoor of Pan-at-lee. Over the summit and across the ridge the trail lay, plain as a printed page to the delicate senses of the jungle-bred tracker.

Tarzan knew naught of the Kor-ul-gryf. He had seen, dimly in the shadows of the night, strange, monstrous forms and Ta-den and Om-at had spoken of great creatures that all men feared; but always, everywhere, by night and by day, there were dangers. From infancy death had stalked, grim and terrible, at his heels. He knew little of any other existence. To cope with danger was his life and he lived his life as simply and as naturally as you live yours amidst the dangers of the crowded city streets. The black man who goes abroad in the jungle by night is afraid, for he has spent his life since infancy surrounded by numbers of his own kind and safeguarded, especially at night, by such crude means as lie within his powers. But Tarzan had lived as the lion lives and the panther and the elephant and the ape—a true jungle creature dependent solely upon his prowess and his wits, playing a lone hand against creation. Therefore he was surprised at nothing and feared nothing and so he walked through the strange night as undisturbed and unapprehensive as the farmer to the cow lot in the darkness before the dawn.

Once more Pan-at-lee's trail ended at the verge of a cliff; but this time there was no indication that she had leaped over the edge and a moment's search revealed to Tarzan the stone pegs upon which she had made her descent. As he lay upon his belly leaning over the top of the cliff examining the pegs his attention was suddenly attracted by something at the foot of the cliff. He could not distinguish its identity, but he saw that it moved and presently that it was ascending slowly, apparently by means of pegs similar to those directly below him. He watched it intently as it rose higher and higher until he was able to distinguish its form more clearly, with the result that he became convinced that it more nearly resembled some form of great ape than a lower order. It had a tail, though, and in other respects it did not seem a true ape.

Slowly it ascended to the upper tier of caves, into one of which it disappeared. Then Tarzan took up again the trail of Pan-at-lee. He followed it down the stone pegs to the nearest cave and then further along the upper tier. The ape-man raised his eyebrows when he saw the direction in which it led, and quickened his pace. He had almost reached the third cave when the echoes of Kor-ul-gryf were awakened by a shrill scream of terror.

THE TOR-O-DON

Pan-at-lee slept—the troubled sleep, of physical and nervous exhaustion, filled with weird dreamings. She dreamed that she slept beneath a great tree in the bottom of the Kor-ul-gryf and that one of the fearsome beasts was creeping upon her but she could not open her eyes nor move. She tried to scream but no sound issued from her lips. She felt the thing touch her throat, her breast, her arm, and there it closed and seemed to be dragging her toward it. With a super-human effort of will she opened her eyes. In the instant she knew that she was dreaming and that quickly the hallucination of the dream would fade—it had happened to her many times before. But it persisted. In the dim light that filtered into the dark chamber she saw a form beside her, she felt hairy fingers upon her and a hairy breast against which she was being drawn. Jad-ben-Otho! this was no dream. And then she screamed and tried to fight the thing from her; but her scream was answered by a low growl and another hairy hand seized her by the hair of the head. The beast rose now upon its hind legs and dragged her from the cave to the moonlit recess without and at the same instant she saw the figure of what she took to be a Ho-don rise above the outer edge of the niche.

The beast that held her saw it too and growled ominously but it did not relinquish its hold upon her hair. It crouched as though waiting an attack, and it increased the volume and frequency of its growls until the horrid sounds reverberated through the gorge, drowning even the deep bellowings of the beasts below, whose mighty thunderings had broken out anew with the sudden commotion from the high-flung cave. The beast that held her crouched and the creature that faced it crouched also, and growled—as hideously as the other. Pan-at-lee trembled. This was no Ho-don and though she feared the Ho-don she feared this thing more, with its catlike crouch and its beastly growls. She was lost—that Pan-at-lee knew. The two things might fight for her, but whichever won she was lost. Perhaps, during the battle, if it came to that, she might find the opportunity to throw herself over into the Kor-ul-gryf.

The thing that held her she had recognized now as a Tor-o-don, but the other thing she could not place, though in the moonlight she could see it very distinctly. It had no tail. She could see its hands and its feet, and they were not the hands and feet of the races of Pal-ul-don. It was slowly closing upon the Tor-o-don and in one hand it held a gleaming knife. Now it spoke and to Pan-at-lee's terror was added an equal weight of consternation.

"When it leaves go of you," it said, "as it will presently to defend itself, run quickly behind me, Pan-at-lee, and go to the cave nearest the pegs you descended from the cliff top. Watch from there. If I am defeated you will have time to escape this slow thing; if I am not I will come to you there. I am Om-at's friend and yours."

The last words took the keen edge from Pan-at-lee's terror; but she did not understand. How did this strange creature know her name? How did it know that she had descended the pegs by a certain cave? It must, then, have been here when she came. Pan-at-lee was puzzled.

"Who are you?" she asked, "and from whence do you come?"

"I am Tarzan," he replied, "and just now I came from Om-at, of Kor-ul-ja, in search of you."

Om-at, gund of Kor-ul-ja! What wild talk was this? She would have questioned him further, but now he was approaching the Tor-o-don and the latter was screaming and growling so loudly as to drown the sound of her voice. And then it did what the strange creature had said that it would do—it released its hold upon her hair as it prepared to charge. Charge it did and in those close quarters there was no room to fence for openings. Instantly the two beasts locked in deadly embrace, each seeking the other's throat. Pan-at-lee watched, taking no advantage of the opportunity to escape which their preoccupation gave her. She watched and waited, for into her savage little brain had come the resolve to pin her faith to this strange creature who had unlocked her heart with those four words—"I am O—" m-at's friend!" And so she waited, with drawn knife, the opportunity to do her bit in the vanquishing of the Tor-o-don. That the newcomer could do it unaided she well knew to be beyond the realms of possibility, for she knew well the prowess of the beastlike man with whom it fought. There were not many of them in Pal-ul-don, but what few there were a terror to the women of the Waz-don and the Ho-don, for the old Tor-o-don bulls roamed the mountains and the valleys of Pal-ul-don between rutting seasons and woe betide the women who fell in their paths.

With his tail the Tor-o-don sought one of Tarzan's ankles, and finding it, tripped him. The two fell heavily, but so agile was the ape-man and so quick his powerful muscles that even in falling he twisted the beast beneath him, so that Tarzan fell on top and now the tail that had tripped him sought his throat as had the tail of In-tan, the Kor-ul-lul. In the effort of turning his antagonist's body during the fall Tarzan had had to relinquish his knife that he might seize the shaggy body with both hands and now the weapon lay out of reach at the very edge of the recess. Both hands were occupied for the moment in fending off the clutching fingers that sought to seize him and drag his throat within reach of his foe's formidable fangs and now the tail was seeking its deadly hold with a formidable persistence that would not be denied.

Pan-at-lee hovered about, breathless, her dagger ready, but there was no opening that did not also endanger Tarzan, so constantly were the two duelists changing their positions. Tarzan felt the tail slowly but surely insinuating itself about his neck though he had drawn his head down between the muscles of his shoulders in an effort to protect this vulnerable part. The battle seemed to be going against him for the giant beast against which he strove would have been a fair match in weight and strength for Bolgani, the gorilla. And knowing this he suddenly exerted a single super-human effort, thrust far apart the giant hands and with the swiftness of a striking snake buried his fangs in the jugular of the Tor-o-don. At the same instant the creature's tail coiled about his own throat and then commenced a battle royal of turning and twisting bodies as each sought to dislodge the fatal hold of the other, but the acts of the ape-man were guided by a human brain and thus it was that the rolling bodies rolled in the direction that Tarzan wished—toward the edge of the recess.

The choking tail had shut the air from his lungs, he knew that his gasping lips were parted and his tongue protruding; and now his brain reeled and his sight grew dim; but not before he reached his goal and a quick hand shot out to seize the knife that now lay within reach as the two bodies tottered perilously upon the brink of the chasm.

With all his remaining strength the ape-man drove home the blade—once, twice, thrice, and then all went black before him as he felt himself, still in the clutches of the Tor-o-don, topple from the recess.

Fortunate it was for Tarzan that Pan-at-lee had not obeyed his injunction to make good her escape while he engaged the Tor-o-don, for it was to this fact that he owed his life. Close beside the struggling forms during the brief moments of the terrific climax she had realized every detail of the danger to Tarzan with which the emergency was fraught and as she saw the two rolling over the outer edge of the niche she seized the ape-man by an ankle at the same time throwing herself prone upon the rocky floor. The muscles of the Tor-o-don relaxed in death with the last thrust of Tarzan's knife and with its hold upon the ape-man released it shot from sight into the gorge below.

It was with infinite difficulty that Pan-at-lee retained her hold upon the ankle of her protector, but she did so and then, slowly, she sought to drag the dead weight back to the safety of the niche. This, however, was beyond her strength and she could but hold on tightly, hoping that some plan would suggest itself before her powers of endurance failed. She wondered if, after all, the creature was already dead, but that she could not bring herself to believe—and if not dead how long it would be before he regained consciousness. If he did not regain it soon he never would regain it, that she knew, for she felt her fingers numbing to the strain upon them and slipping, slowly, slowly, from their hold. It was then that Tarzan regained consciousness. He could not know what power upheld him, but he felt that whatever it was it was slowly releasing its hold upon his ankle. Within easy reach of his hands were two pegs and these he seized upon just as Pan-at-lee's fingers slipped from their hold.

As it was he came near to being precipitated into the gorge—only his great strength saved him. He was upright now and his feet found other pegs. His first thought was of his foe. Where was he? Waiting above there to finish him? Tarzan looked up just as the frightened face of Pan-at-lee appeared over the threshold of the recess.

"You live?" she cried.

"Yes," replied Tarzan. "Where is the shaggy one?"

Pan-at-lee pointed downward. "There," she said, "dead."

"Good!" exclaimed the ape-man, clambering to her side. "You are unharmed?" he asked.

"You came just in time," replied Pan-at-lee; "but who are you and how did you know that I was here and what do you know of Om-at and where did you come from and what did you mean by calling Om-at, gund?"

"Wait, wait," cried Tarzan; "one at a time. My, but you are all alike—the shes of the tribe of Kerchak, the ladies of England, and their sisters of Pal-ul-don. Have patience and I will try to tell you all that you wish to know. Four of us set out with Om-at from Kor-ul-ja to search for you. We were attacked by the Kor-ul-lul and separated. I was taken prisoner, but escaped. Again I stumbled upon your trail and followed it, reaching the summit of this cliff just as the hairy one was climbing up after you. I was coming to investigate when I heard your scream—the rest you know."

"But you called Om-at, gund of Kor-ul-ja," she insisted. "Es-sat is gund."

"Es-sat is dead," explained the ape-man. "Om-at slew him and now Om-at is gund. Om-at came back seeking you. He found Es-sat in your cave and killed him."

"Yes," said the girl, "Es-sat came to my cave and I struck him down with my golden breastplates and escaped."

"And a lion pursued you," continued Tarzan, "and you leaped from the cliff into Kor-ul-lul, but why you were not killed is beyond me."

"Is there anything beyond you?" exclaimed Pan-at-lee. "How could you know that a lion pursued me and that I leaped from the cliff and not know that it was the pool of deep water below that saved me?"

"I would have known that, too, had not the Kor-ul-lul come then and prevented me continuing upon your trail. But now I would ask you a question—by what name do you call the thing with which I just fought?"

"It was a Tor-o-don," she replied. "I have seen but one before. They are terrible creatures with the cunning of man and the ferocity of a beast. Great indeed must be the warrior who slays one single-handed." She gazed at him in open admiration.

"And now," said Tarzan, "you must sleep, for tomorrow we shall return to Kor-ul-ja and Om-at, and I doubt that you have had much rest these two nights."

Pan-at-lee, lulled by a feeling of security, slept peacefully into the morning while Tarzan stretched himself upon the hard floor of the recess just outside her cave.

The sun was high in the heavens when he awoke; for two hours it had looked down upon another heroic figure miles away—the figure of a godlike man fighting his way through the hideous morass that lies like a filthy moat defending Pal-ul-don from the creatures of the outer world. Now waist deep in the sucking ooze, now menaced by loathsome reptiles, the man advanced only by virtue of Herculean efforts gaining laboriously by inches along the devious way that he was forced to choose in selecting the least precarious footing. Near the center of the morass was open water—slimy, green-hued water. He reached it at last after more than two hours of such effort as would have left an ordinary man spent and dying in the sticky mud, yet he was less than halfway across the marsh. Greasy with slime and mud was his smooth, brown hide, and greasy with slime and mud was his beloved Enfield that had shone so brightly in the first rays of the rising sun.

He paused a moment upon the edge of the open water and then throwing himself forward struck out to swim across. He swam with long, easy, powerful strokes calculated less for speed than for endurance, for his was, primarily, a test of the latter, since beyond the open water was another two hours or more of gruelling effort between it and solid ground. He was, perhaps, halfway across and congratulating himself upon the ease of the achievement of this portion of his task when there arose from the depths directly in his path a hideous reptile, which, with wide-distended jaws, bore down upon him, hissing shrilly.

Tarzan arose and stretched, expanded his great chest and drank in deep draughts of the fresh morning air. His clear eyes scanned the wondrous beauties of the landscape spread out before them. Directly below lay Kor-ul-gryf, a dense, somber green of gently moving tree tops. To Tarzan it was neither grim, nor forbidding—it was jungle, beloved jungle. To his right there spread a panorama of the lower reaches of the Valley of Jad-ben-Otho, with its winding streams and its blue lakes. Gleaming whitely in the sunlight were scattered groups of dwellings—the feudal strongholds of the lesser chiefs of the Ho-don. A-lur, the City of Light, he could not see as it was hidden by the shoulder of the cliff in which the deserted village lay.

For a moment Tarzan gave himself over to that spiritual enjoyment of beauty that only the man-mind may attain and then Nature asserted herself and the belly of the beast called aloud that it was hungry. Again Tarzan looked down at Kor-ul-gryf. There was the jungle! Grew there a jungle that would not feed Tarzan? The ape-man smiled and commenced the descent to the gorge. Was there danger there? Of course. Who knew it better than Tarzan? In all jungles lies death, for life and death go hand in hand and where life teems death reaps his fullest harvest. Never had Tarzan met a creature of the jungle with which he could not cope—sometimes by virtue of brute strength alone, again by a combination of brute strength and the cunning of the man-mind; but Tarzan had never met a gryf.

He had heard the bellowings in the gorge the night before after he had lain down to sleep and he had meant to ask Pan-at-lee this morning what manner of beast so disturbed the slumbers of its betters. He reached the foot of the cliff and strode into the jungle and here he halted, his keen eyes and ears watchful and alert, his sensitive nostrils searching each shifting air current for the scent spoor of game. Again he advanced deeper into the wood, his light step giving forth no sound, his bow and arrows in readiness. A light morning breeze was blowing from up the gorge and in this direction he bent his steps. Many odors impinged upon his organs of scent. Some of these he classified without effort, but others were strange—the odors of beasts and of birds, of trees and shrubs and flowers with which he was unfamiliar. He sensed faintly the reptilian odor that he had learned to connect with the strange, nocturnal forms that had loomed dim and bulky on several occasions since his introduction to Pal-ul-don.

And then, suddenly he caught plainly the strong, sweet odor of Bara, the deer. Were the belly vocal, Tarzan's would have given a little cry of joy, for it loved the flesh of Bara. The ape-man moved rapidly, but cautiously forward. The prey was not far distant and as the hunter approached it, he took silently to the trees and still in his nostrils was the faint reptilian odor that spoke of a great creature which he had never yet seen except as a denser shadow among the dense shadows of the night; but the odor was of such a faintness as suggests to the jungle bred the distance of absolute safety.

And now, moving noiselessly, Tarzan came within sight of Bara drinking at a pool where the stream that waters Kor-ul-gryf crosses an open place in the jungle. The deer was too far from the nearest tree to risk a charge, so the ape-man must depend upon the accuracy and force of his first arrow, which must drop the deer in its tracks or forfeit both deer and shaft. Far back came the right hand and the bow, that you or I might not move, bent easily beneath the muscles of the forest god. There was a singing twang and Bara, leaping high in air, collapsed upon the ground, an arrow through his heart. Tarzan dropped to earth and ran to his kill, lest the animal might even yet rise and escape; but Bara was safely dead. As Tarzan stooped to lift it to his shoulder there fell upon his ears a thunderous bellow that seemed almost at his right elbow, and as his eyes shot in the direction of the sound, there broke upon his vision such a creature as paleontologists have dreamed as having possibly existed in the dimmest vistas of Earth's infancy—a gigantic creature, vibrant with mad rage, that charged, bellowing, upon him.

When Pan-at-lee awoke she looked out upon the niche in search of Tarzan. He was not there. She sprang to her feet and rushed out, looking down into Kor-ul-gryf guessing that he had gone down in search of food and there she caught a glimpse of him disappearing into the forest. For an instant she was panic-stricken. She knew that he was a stranger in Pal-ul-don and that, so, he might not realize the dangers that lay in that gorge of terror. Why did she not call to him to return? You or I might have done so, but no Pal-ul-don, for they know the ways of the gryf—they know the weak eyes and the keen ears, and that at the sound of a human voice they come. To have called to Tarzan, then, would but have been to invite disaster and so she did not call. Instead, afraid though she was, she descended into the gorge for the purpose of overhauling Tarzan and warning him in whispers of his danger. It was a brave act, since it was performed in the face of countless ages of inherited fear of the creatures that she might be called upon to face. Men have been decorated for less.

Pan-at-lee, descended from a long line of hunters, assumed that Tarzan would move up wind and in this direction she sought his tracks, which she soon found well marked, since he had made no effort to conceal them. She moved rapidly until she reached the point at which Tarzan had taken to the trees. Of course she knew what had happened; since her own people were semi-arboreal; but she could not track him through the trees, having no such well-developed sense of scent as he.

She could but hope that he had continued on up wind and in this direction she moved, her heart pounding in terror against her ribs, her eyes glancing first in one direction and then another. She had reached the edge of a clearing when two things happened—she caught sight of Tarzan bending over a dead deer and at the same instant a deafening roar sounded almost beside her. It terrified her beyond description, but it brought no paralysis of fear. Instead it galvanized her into instant action with the result that Pan-at-lee swarmed up the nearest tree to the very loftiest branch that would sustain her weight. Then she looked down.

The thing that Tarzan saw charging him when the warning bellow attracted his surprised eyes loomed terrifically monstrous before him—monstrous and awe-inspiring; but it did not terrify Tarzan, it only angered him, for he saw that it was beyond even his powers to combat and that meant that it might cause him to lose his kill, and Tarzan was hungry. There was but a single alternative to remaining for annihilation and that was flight—swift and immediate. And Tarzan fled, but he carried the carcass of Bara, the deer, with him. He had not more than a dozen paces start, but on the other hand the nearest tree was almost as close. His greatest danger lay, he imagined, in the great, towering height of the creature pursuing him, for even though he reached the tree he would have to climb high in an incredibly short time as, unless appearances were deceiving, the thing could reach up and pluck him down from any branch under thirty feet above the ground, and possibly from those up to fifty feet, if it reared up on its hind legs.

But Tarzan was no sluggard and though the gryf was incredibly fast despite its great bulk, it was no match for Tarzan, and when it comes to climbing, the little monkeys gaze with envy upon the feats of the ape-man. And so it was that the bellowing gryf came to a baffled stop at the foot of the tree and even though he reared up and sought to seize his prey among the branches, as Tarzan had guessed he might, he failed in this also. And then, well out of reach, Tarzan came to a stop and there, just above him, he saw Pan-at-lee sitting, wide-eyed and trembling.

"How came you here?" he asked.

She told him. "You came to warn me!" he said. "It was very brave and unselfish of you. I am chagrined that I should have been thus surprised. The creature was up wind from me and yet I did not sense its near presence until it charged. I cannot understand it."

"It is not strange," said Pan-at-lee. "That is one of the peculiarities of the gryf—it is said that man never knows of its presence until it is upon him—so silently does it move despite its great size."

"But I should have smelled it," cried Tarzan, disgustedly.

"Smelled it!" ejaculated Pan-at-lee. "Smelled it?"

"Certainly. How do you suppose I found this deer so quickly? And I sensed the gryf, too, but faintly as at a great distance." Tarzan suddenly ceased speaking and looked down at the bellowing creature below them—his nostrils quivered as though searching for a scent. "Ah!" he exclaimed. "I have it!"

"What?" asked Pan-at-lee.

"I was deceived because the creature gives off practically no odor," explained the ape-man. "What I smelled was the faint aroma that doubtless permeates the entire jungle because of the long presence of many of the creatures—it is the sort of odor that would remain for a long time, faint as it is.

"Pan-at-lee, did you ever hear of a triceratops? No? Well this thing that you call a gryf is a triceratops and it has been extinct for hundreds of thousands of years. I have seen its skeleton in the museum in London and a figure of one restored. I always thought that the scientists who did such work depended principally upon an overwrought imagination, but I see that I was wrong. This living thing is not an exact counterpart of the restoration that I saw; but it is so similar as to be easily recognizable, and then, too, we must remember that during the ages that have elapsed since the paleontologist's specimen lived many changes might have been wrought by evolution in the living line that has quite evidently persisted in Pal-ul-don."

"Triceratops, London, paleo—I don't know what you are talking about," cried Pan-at-lee.

Tarzan smiled and threw a piece of dead wood at the face of the angry creature below them. Instantly the great bony hood over the neck was erected and a mad bellow rolled upward from the gigantic body. Full twenty feet at the shoulder the thing stood, a dirty slate-blue in color except for its yellow face with the blue bands encircling the eyes, the red hood with the yellow lining and the yellow belly. The three parallel lines of bony protuberances down the back gave a further touch of color to the body, those following the line of the spine being red, while those on either side are yellow. The five- and three-toed hoofs of the ancient horned dinosaurs had become talons in the gryf, but the three horns, two large ones above the eyes and a median horn on the nose, had persisted through all the ages. Weird and terrible as was its appearance Tarzan could not but admire the mighty creature looming big below him, its seventy-five feet of length majestically typifying those things which all his life the ape-man had admired—courage and strength. In that massive tail alone was the strength of an elephant.

The wicked little eyes looked up at him and the horny beak opened to disclose a full set of powerful teeth.

"Herbivorous!" murmured the ape-man. "Your ancestors may have been, but not you," and then to Pan-at-lee: "Let us go now. At the cave we will have deer meat and then—back to Kor-ul-ja and Om-at."

The girl shuddered. "Go?" she repeated. "We will never go from here."

"Why not?" asked Tarzan.

For answer she but pointed to the gryf.

"Nonsense!" exclaimed the man. "It cannot climb. We can reach the cliff through the trees and be back in the cave before it knows what has become of us."

"You do not know the gryf," replied Pan-at-lee gloomily.

"Wherever we go it will follow and always it will be ready at the foot of each tree when we would descend. It will never give us up."

"We can live in the trees for a long time if necessary," replied Tarzan, "and sometime the thing will leave."

The girl shook her head. "Never," she said, "and then there are the Tor-o-don. They will come and kill us and after eating a little will throw the balance to the gryf—the gryf and Tor-o-don are friends, because the Tor-o-don shares his food with the gryf."

"You may be right," said Tarzan; "but even so I don't intend waiting here for someone to come along and eat part of me and then feed the balance to that beast below. If I don't get out of this place whole it won't be my fault. Come along now and we'll make a try at it," and so saying he moved off through the tree tops with Pan-at-lee close behind. Below them, on the ground, moved the horned dinosaur and when they reached the edge of the forest where there lay fifty yards of open ground to cross to the foot of the cliff he was there with them, at the bottom of the tree, waiting.

Tarzan looked ruefully down and scratched his head.

JUNGLE CRAFT

Presently he looked up and at Pan-at-lee. "Can you cross the gorge through the trees very rapidly?" he questioned.

"Alone?" she asked.

"No," replied Tarzan.

"I can follow wherever you can lead," she said then.

"Across and back again?"

"Yes."

"Then come, and do exactly as I bid." He started back again through the trees, swiftly, swinging monkey-like from limb to limb, following a zigzag course that he tried to select with an eye for the difficulties of the trail beneath. Where the underbrush was heaviest, where fallen trees blocked the way, he led the footsteps of the creature below them; but all to no avail. When they reached the opposite side of the gorge the gryf was with them.

"Back again," said Tarzan, and, turning, the two retraced their high-flung way through the upper terraces of the ancient forest of Kor-ul-gryf. But the result was the same—no, not quite; it was worse, for another gryf had joined the first and now two waited beneath the tree in which they stopped.

The cliff looming high above them with its innumerable cave mouths seemed to beckon and to taunt them. It was so near, yet eternity yawned between. The body of the Tor-o-don lay at the cliff's foot where it had fallen. It was in plain view of the two in the tree. One of the gryfs walked over and sniffed about it, but did not offer to devour it. Tarzan had examined it casually as he had passed earlier in the morning. He guessed that it represented either a very high order of ape or a very low order of man—something akin to the Java man, perhaps; a truer example of the pithecanthropi than either the Ho-don or the Waz-don; possibly the precursor of them both. As his eyes wandered idly over the scene below his active brain was working out the details of the plan that he had made to permit Pan-at-lee's escape from the gorge. His thoughts were interrupted by a strange cry from above them in the gorge.

"Whee-oo! Whee-oo!" it sounded, coming closer.

The gryfs below raised their heads and looked in the direction of the interruption. One of them made a low, rumbling sound in its throat. It was not a bellow and it did not indicate anger. Immediately the "Whee-oo!" responded. The gryfs repeated the rumbling and at intervals the "Whee-oo!" was repeated, coming ever closer.

Tarzan looked at Pan-at-lee. "What is it?" he asked.

"I do not know," she replied. "Perhaps a strange bird, or another horrid beast that dwells in this frightful place."

"Ah," exclaimed Tarzan; "there it is. Look!"

Pan-at-lee voiced a cry of despair. "A Tor-o-don!"

The creature, walking erect and carrying a stick in one hand, advanced at a slow, lumbering gait. It walked directly toward the gryfs who moved aside, as though afraid. Tarzan watched intently. The Tor-o-don was now quite close to one of the triceratops. It swung its head and snapped at him viciously. Instantly the Tor-o-don sprang in and commenced to belabor the huge beast across the face with his stick. To the ape-man's amazement the gryf, that might have annihilated the comparatively puny Tor-o-don instantly in any of a dozen ways, cringed like a whipped cur.

"Whee-oo! Whee-oo!" shouted the Tor-o-don and the gryf came slowly toward him. A whack on the median horn brought it to a stop. Then the Tor-o-don walked around behind it, clambered up its tail and seated himself astraddle of the huge back. "Whee-oo!" he shouted and prodded the beast with a sharp point of his stick. The gryf commenced to move off.

So rapt had Tarzan been in the scene below him that he had given no thought to escape, for he realized that for him and Pan-at-lee time had in these brief moments turned back countless ages to spread before their eyes a page of the dim and distant past. They two had looked upon the first man and his primitive beasts of burden.

And now the ridden gryf halted and looked up at them, bellowing. It was sufficient. The creature had warned its master of their presence. Instantly the Tor-o-don urged the beast close beneath the tree which held them, at the same time leaping to his feet upon the horny back. Tarzan saw the bestial face, the great fangs, the mighty muscles. From the loins of such had sprung the human race—and only from such could it have sprung, for only such as this might have survived the horrid dangers of the age that was theirs.

The Tor-o-don beat upon his breast and growled horribly—hideous, uncouth, beastly. Tarzan rose to his full height upon a swaying branch—straight and beautiful as a demigod—unspoiled by the taint of civilization—a perfect specimen of what the human race might have been had the laws of man not interfered with the laws of nature.

The Present fitted an arrow to his bow and drew the shaft far back. The Past basing its claims upon brute strength sought to reach the other and drag him down; but the loosed arrow sank deep into the savage heart and the Past sank back into the oblivion that had claimed his kind.

"Tarzan-jad-guru!" murmured Pan-at-lee, unknowingly giving him out of the fullness of her admiration the same title that the warriors of her tribe had bestowed upon him.

The ape-man turned to her. "Pan-at-lee," he said, "these beasts may keep us treed here indefinitely. I doubt if we can escape together, but I have a plan. You remain here, hiding yourself in the foliage, while I start back across the gorge in sight of them and yelling to attract their attention. Unless they have more brains than I suspect they will follow me. When they are gone you make for the cliff. Wait for me in the cave not longer than today. If I do not come by tomorrow's sun you will have to start back for Kor-ul-ja alone. Here is a joint of deer meat for you." He had severed one of the deer's hind legs and this he passed up to her.

"I cannot desert you," she said simply; "it is not the way of my people to desert a friend and ally. Om-at would never forgive me."

"Tell Om-at that I commanded you to go," replied Tarzan.

"It is a command?" she asked.

"It is! Good-bye, Pan-at-lee. Hasten back to Om-at—you are a fitting mate for the chief of Kor-ul-ja." He moved off slowly through the trees.

"Good-bye, Tarzan-jad-guru!" she called after him. "Fortunate are my Om-at and his Pan-at-lee in owning such a friend."

Tarzan, shouting aloud, continued upon his way and the great gryfs, lured by his voice, followed beneath. His ruse was evidently proving successful and he was filled with elation as he led the bellowing beasts farther and farther from Pan-at-lee. He hoped that she would take advantage of the opportunity afforded her for escape, yet at the same time he was filled with concern as to her ability to survive the dangers which lay between Kor-ul-gryf and Kor-ul-ja. There were lions and Tor-o-dons and the unfriendly tribe of Kor-ul-lul to hinder her progress, though the distance in itself to the cliffs of her people was not great.

He realized her bravery and understood the resourcefulness that she must share in common with all primitive people who, day by day, must contend face to face with nature's law of the survival of the fittest, unaided by any of the numerous artificial protections that civilization has thrown around its brood of weaklings.

Several times during this crossing of the gorge Tarzan endeavored to outwit his keen pursuers, but all to no avail. Double as he would he could not throw them off his track and ever as he changed his course they changed theirs to conform. Along the verge of the forest upon the southeastern side of the gorge he sought some point at which the trees touched some negotiable portion of the cliff, but though he traveled far both up and down the gorge he discovered no such easy avenue of escape. The ape-man finally commenced to entertain an idea of the hopelessness of his case and to realize to the full why the Kor-ul-gryf had been religiously abjured by the races of Pal-ul-don for all these many ages.

Night was falling and though since early morning he had sought diligently a way out of this cul-de-sac he was no nearer to liberty than at the moment the first bellowing gryf had charged him as he stooped over the carcass of his kill: but with the falling of night came renewed hope for, in common with the great cats, Tarzan was, to a greater or lesser extent, a nocturnal beast. It is true he could not see by night as well as they, but that lack was largely recompensed for by the keenness of his scent and the highly developed sensitiveness of his other organs of perception. As the blind follow and interpret their Braille characters with deft fingers, so Tarzan reads the book of the jungle with feet and hands and eyes and ears and nose; each contributing its share to the quick and accurate translation of the text.

But again he was doomed to be thwarted by one vital weakness—he did not know the gryf, and before the night was over he wondered if the things never slept, for wheresoever he moved they moved also, and always they barred his road to liberty. Finally, just before dawn, he relinquished his immediate effort and sought rest in a friendly tree crotch in the safety of the middle terrace.

Once again was the sun high when Tarzan awoke, rested and refreshed. Keen to the necessities of the moment he made no effort to locate his jailers lest in the act he might apprise them of his movements. Instead he sought cautiously and silently to melt away among the foliage of the trees. His first move, however, was heralded by a deep bellow from below.

Among the numerous refinements of civilization that Tarzan had failed to acquire was that of profanity, and possibly it is to be regretted since there are circumstances under which it is at least a relief to pent emotion. And it may be that in effect Tarzan resorted to profanity if there can be physical as well as vocal swearing, since immediately the bellow announced that his hopes had been again frustrated, he turned quickly and seeing the hideous face of the gryf below him seized a large fruit from a nearby branch and hurled it viciously at the horned snout. The missile struck full between the creature's eyes, resulting in a reaction that surprised the ape-man; it did not arouse the beast to a show of revengeful rage as Tarzan had expected and hoped; instead the creature gave a single vicious side snap at the fruit as it bounded from his skull and then turned sulkily away, walking off a few steps.

There was that in the act that recalled immediately to Tarzan's mind similar action on the preceding day when the Tor-o-don had struck one of the creatures across the face with his staff, and instantly there sprung to the cunning and courageous brain a plan of escape from his predicament that might have blanched the cheek of the most heroic.

The gambling instinct is not strong among creatures of the wild; the chances of their daily life are sufficient stimuli for the beneficial excitement of their nerve centers. It has remained for civilized man, protected in a measure from the natural dangers of existence, to invent artificial stimulants in the form of cards and dice and roulette wheels. Yet when necessity bids there are no greater gamblers than the savage denizens of the jungle, the forest, and the hills, for as lightly as you roll the ivory cubes upon the green cloth they will gamble with death—their own lives the stake.

And so Tarzan would gamble now, pitting the seemingly wild deductions of his shrewd brain against all the proofs of the bestial ferocity of his antagonists that his experience of them had adduced—against all the age-old folklore and legend that had been handed down for countless generations and passed on to him through the lips of Pan-at-lee.

Yet as he worked in preparation for the greatest play that man can make in the game of life, he smiled; nor was there any indication of haste or excitement or nervousness in his demeanor.

First he selected a long, straight branch about two inches in diameter at its base. This he cut from the tree with his knife, removed the smaller branches and twigs until he had fashioned a pole about ten feet in length. This he sharpened at the smaller end. The staff finished to his satisfaction he looked down upon the triceratops.

"Whee-oo!" he cried.

Instantly the beasts raised their heads and looked at him. From the throat of one of them came faintly a low rumbling sound.

"Whee-oo!" repeated Tarzan and hurled the balance of the carcass of the deer to them.

Instantly the gryfs fell upon it with much bellowing, one of them attempting to seize it and keep it from the other: but finally the second obtained a hold and an instant later it had been torn asunder and greedily devoured. Once again they looked up at the ape-man and this time they saw him descending to the ground.

One of them started toward him. Again Tarzan repeated the weird cry of the Tor-o-don. The gryf halted in his track, apparently puzzled, while Tarzan slipped lightly to the earth and advanced toward the nearer beast, his staff raised menacingly and the call of the first-man upon his lips.

Would the cry be answered by the low rumbling of the beast of burden or the horrid bellow of the man-eater? Upon the answer to this question hung the fate of the ape-man.

Pan-at-lee was listening intently to the sounds of the departing gryfs as Tarzan led them cunningly from her, and when she was sure that they were far enough away to insure her safe retreat she dropped swiftly from the branches to the ground and sped like a frightened deer across the open space to the foot of the cliff, stepped over the body of the Tor-o-don who had attacked her the night before and was soon climbing rapidly up the ancient stone pegs of the deserted cliff village. In the mouth of the cave near that which she had occupied she kindled a fire and cooked the haunch of venison that Tarzan had left her, and from one of the trickling streams that ran down the face of the escarpment she obtained water to satisfy her thirst.

All day she waited, hearing in the distance, and sometimes close at hand, the bellowing of the gryfs which pursued the strange creature that had dropped so miraculously into her life. For him she felt the same keen, almost fanatical loyalty that many another had experienced for Tarzan of the Apes. Beast and human, he had held them to him with bonds that were stronger than steel—those of them that were clean and courageous, and the weak and the helpless; but never could Tarzan claim among his admirers the coward, the ingrate or the scoundrel; from such, both man and beast, he had won fear and hatred.

To Pan-at-lee he was all that was brave and noble and heroic and, too, he was Om-at's friend—the friend of the man she loved. For any one of these reasons Pan-at-lee would have died for Tarzan, for such is the loyalty of the simple-minded children of nature. It has remained for civilization to teach us to weigh the relative rewards of loyalty and its antithesis. The loyalty of the primitive is spontaneous, unreasoning, unselfish and such was the loyalty of Pan-at-lee for the Tarmangani.

And so it was that she waited that day and night, hoping that he would return that she might accompany him back to Om-at, for her experience had taught her that in the face of danger two have a better chance than one. But Tarzan-jad-guru had not come, and so upon the following morning Pan-at-lee set out upon her return to Kor-ul-ja.

She knew the dangers and yet she faced them with the stolid indifference of her race. When they directly confronted and menaced her would be time enough to experience fear or excitement or confidence. In the meantime it was unnecessary to waste nerve energy by anticipating them. She moved therefore through her savage land with no greater show of concern than might mark your sauntering to a corner drug-store for a sundae. But this is your life and that is Pan-at-lee's and even now as you read this Pan-at-lee may be sitting upon the edge of the recess of Om-at's cave while the ja and jato roar from the gorge below and from the ridge above, and the Kor-ul-lul threaten upon the south and the Ho-don from the Valley of Jad-ben-Otho far below, for Pan-at-lee still lives and preens her silky coat of jet beneath the tropical moonlight of Pal-ul-don.

But she was not to reach Kor-ul-ja this day, nor the next, nor for many days after though the danger that threatened her was neither Waz-don enemy nor savage beast.

She came without misadventure to the Kor-ul-lul and after descending its rocky southern wall without catching the slightest glimpse of the hereditary enemies of her people, she experienced a renewal of confidence that was little short of practical assurance that she would successfully terminate her venture and be restored once more to her own people and the lover she had not seen for so many long and weary moons.

She was almost across the gorge now and moving with an extreme caution abated no wit by her confidence, for wariness is an instinctive trait of the primitive, something which cannot be laid aside even momentarily if one would survive. And so she came to the trail that follows the windings of Kor-ul-lul from its uppermost reaches down into the broad and fertile Valley of Jad-ben-Otho.

And as she stepped into the trail there arose on either side of her from out of the bushes that border the path, as though materialized from thin air, a score of tall, white warriors of the Ho-don. Like a frightened deer Pan-at-lee cast a single startled look at these menacers of her freedom and leaped quickly toward the bushes in an effort to escape; but the warriors were too close at hand. They closed upon her from every side and then, drawing her knife she turned at bay, metamorphosed by the fires of fear and hate from a startled deer to a raging tiger-cat. They did not try to kill her, but only to subdue and capture her; and so it was that more than a single Ho-don warrior felt the keen edge of her blade in his flesh before they had succeeded in overpowering her by numbers. And still she fought and scratched and bit after they had taken the knife from her until it was necessary to tie her hands and fasten a piece of wood between her teeth by means of thongs passed behind her head.

At first she refused to walk when they started off in the direction of the valley but after two of them had seized her by the hair and dragged her for a number of yards she thought better of her original decision and came along with them, though still as defiant as her bound wrists and gagged mouth would permit.

Near the entrance to Kor-ul-lul they came upon another body of their warriors with which were several Waz-don prisoners from the tribe of Kor-ul-lul. It was a raiding party come up from a Ho-don city of the valley after slaves. This Pan-at-lee knew for the occurrence was by no means unusual. During her lifetime the tribe to which she belonged had been sufficiently fortunate, or powerful, to withstand successfully the majority of such raids made upon them, but yet Pan-at-lee had known of friends and relatives who had been carried into slavery by the Ho-don and she knew, too, another thing which gave her hope, as doubtless it did to each of the other captives—that occasionally the prisoners escaped from the cities of the hairless whites.

After they had joined the other party the entire band set forth into the valley and presently, from the conversation of her captors, Pan-at-lee knew that she was headed for A-lur, the City of Light; while in the cave of his ancestors, Om-at, chief of the Kor-ul-ja, bemoaned the loss of both his friend and she that was to have been his mate.

A-LUR

As the hissing reptile bore down upon the stranger swimming in the open water near the center of the morass on the frontier of Pal-ul-don it seemed to the man that this indeed must be the futile termination of an arduous and danger-filled journey. It seemed, too, equally futile to pit his puny knife against this frightful creature. Had he been attacked on land it is possible that he might as a last resort have used his Enfield, though he had come thus far through all these weary, danger-ridden miles without recourse to it, though again and again had his life hung in the balance in the face of the savage denizens of forest, jungle, and steppe. For whatever it may have been for which he was preserving his precious ammunition he evidently held it more sacred even than his life, for as yet he had not used a single round and now the decision was not required of him, since it would have been impossible for him to have unslung his Enfield, loaded and fired with the necessary celerity while swimming.

Though his chance for survival seemed slender, and hope at its lowest ebb, he was not minded therefore to give up without a struggle. Instead he drew his blade and awaited the oncoming reptile. The creature was like no living thing he ever before had seen although possibly it resembled a crocodile in some respects more than it did anything with which he was familiar.

As this frightful survivor of some extinct progenitor charged upon him with distended jaws there came to the man quickly a full consciousness of the futility of endeavoring to stay the mad rush or pierce the armor-coated hide with his little knife. The thing was almost upon him now and whatever form of defense he chose must be made quickly. There seemed but a single alternative to instant death, and this he took at almost the instant the great reptile towered directly above him.

With the celerity of a seal he dove headforemost beneath the oncoming body and at the same instant, turning upon his back, he plunged his blade into the soft, cold surface of the slimy belly as the momentum of the hurtling reptile carried it swiftly over him; and then with powerful strokes he swam on beneath the surface for a dozen yards before he rose. A glance showed him the stricken monster plunging madly in pain and rage upon the surface of the water behind him. That it was writhing in its death agonies was evidenced by the fact that it made no effort to pursue him, and so, to the accompaniment of the shrill screaming of the dying monster, the man won at last to the farther edge of the open water to take up once more the almost superhuman effort of crossing the last stretch of clinging mud which separated him from the solid ground of Pal-ul-don.

A good two hours it took him to drag his now weary body through the clinging, stinking muck, but at last, mud covered and spent, he dragged himself out upon the soft grasses of the bank. A hundred yards away a stream, winding its way down from the distant mountains, emptied into the morass, and, after a short rest, he made his way to this and seeking a quiet pool, bathed himself and washed the mud and slime from his weapons, accouterments, and loin cloth. Another hour was spent beneath the rays of the hot sun in wiping, polishing, and oiling his Enfield though the means at hand for drying it consisted principally of dry grasses. It was afternoon before he had satisfied himself that his precious weapon was safe from any harm by dirt, or dampness, and then he arose and took up the search for the spoor he had followed to the opposite side of the swamp.

Would he find again the trail that had led into the opposite side of the morass, to be lost there, even to his trained senses? If he found it not again upon this side of the almost impassable barrier he might assume that his long journey had ended in failure. And so he sought up and down the verge of the stagnant water for traces of an old spoor that would have been invisible to your eyes or mine, even had we followed directly in the tracks of its maker.

As Tarzan advanced upon the gryfs he imitated as closely as he could recall them the methods and mannerisms of the Tor-o-don, but up to the instant that he stood close beside one of the huge creatures he realized that his fate still hung in the balance, for the thing gave forth no sign, either menacing or otherwise. It only stood there, watching him out of its cold, reptilian eyes and then Tarzan raised his staff and with a menacing "Whee-oo!" struck the gryf a vicious blow across the face.

The creature made a sudden side snap in his direction, a snap that did not reach him, and then turned sullenly away, precisely as it had when the Tor-o-don commanded it. Walking around to its rear as he had seen the shaggy first-man do, Tarzan ran up the broad tail and seated himself upon the creature's back, and then again imitating the acts of the Tor-o-don he prodded it with the sharpened point of his staff, and thus goading it forward and guiding it with blows, first upon one side and then upon the other, he started it down the gorge in the direction of the valley.

At first it had been in his mind only to determine if he could successfully assert any authority over the great monsters, realizing that in this possibility lay his only hope of immediate escape from his jailers. But once seated upon the back of his titanic mount the ape-man experienced the sensation of a new thrill that recalled to him the day in his boyhood that he had first clambered to the broad head of Tantor, the elephant, and this, together with the sense of mastery that was always meat and drink to the lord of the jungle, decided him to put his newly acquired power to some utilitarian purpose.

Pan-at-lee he judged must either have already reached safety or met with death. At least, no longer could he be of service to her, while below Kor-ul-gryf, in the soft green valley, lay A-lur, the City of Light, which, since he had gazed upon it from the shoulder of Pastar-ul-ved, had been his ambition and his goal.

Whether or not its gleaming walls held the secret of his lost mate he could not even guess but if she lived at all within the precincts of Pal-ul-don it must be among the Ho-don, since the hairy black men of this forgotten world took no prisoners. And so to A-lur he would go, and how more effectively than upon the back of this grim and terrible creature that the races of Pal-ul-don held in such awe?

A little mountain stream tumbles down from Kor-ul-gryf to be joined in the foothills with that which empties the waters of Kor-ul-lul into the valley, forming a small river which runs southwest, eventually entering the valley's largest lake at the City of A-lur, through the center of which the stream passes. An ancient trail, well marked by countless generations of naked feet of man and beast, leads down toward A-lur beside the river, and along this Tarzan guided the gryf. Once clear of the forest which ran below the mouth of the gorge, Tarzan caught occasional glimpses of the city gleaming in the distance far below him.

The country through which he passed was resplendent with the riotous beauties of tropical verdure. Thick, lush grasses grew waist high upon either side of the trail and the way was broken now and again by patches of open park-like forest, or perhaps a little patch of dense jungle where the trees overarched the way and trailing creepers depended in graceful loops from branch to branch.

At times the ape-man had difficulty in commanding obedience upon the part of his unruly beast, but always in the end its fear of the relatively puny goad urged it on to obedience. Late in the afternoon as they approached the confluence of the stream they were skirting and another which appeared to come from the direction of Kor-ul-ja the ape-man, emerging from one of the jungle patches, discovered a considerable party of Ho-don upon the opposite bank. Simultaneously they saw him and the mighty creature he bestrode. For a moment they stood in wide-eyed amazement and then, in answer to the command of their leader, they turned and bolted for the shelter of the nearby wood.

The ape-man had but a brief glimpse of them but it was sufficient indication that there were Waz-don with them, doubtless prisoners taken in one of the raids upon the Waz-don villages of which Ta-den and Om-at had told him.

At the sound of their voices the gryf had bellowed terrifically and started in pursuit even though a river intervened, but by dint of much prodding and beating, Tarzan had succeeded in heading the animal back into the path though thereafter for a long time it was sullen and more intractable than ever.

As the sun dropped nearer the summit of the western hills Tarzan became aware that his plan to enter A-lur upon the back of a gryf was likely doomed to failure, since the stubbornness of the great beast was increasing momentarily, doubtless due to the fact that its huge belly was crying out for food. The ape-man wondered if the Tor-o-dons had any means of picketing their beasts for the night, but as he did not know and as no plan suggested itself, he determined that he should have to trust to the chance of finding it again in the morning.

There now arose in his mind a question as to what would be their relationship when Tarzan had dismounted. Would it again revert to that of hunter and quarry or would fear of the goad continue to hold its supremacy over the natural instinct of the hunting flesh-eater? Tarzan wondered but as he could not remain upon the gryf forever, and as he preferred dismounting and putting the matter to a final test while it was still light, he decided to act at once.

How to stop the creature he did not know, as up to this time his sole desire had been to urge it forward. By experimenting with his staff, however, he found that he could bring it to a halt by reaching forward and striking the thing upon its beaklike snout. Close by grew a number of leafy trees, in any one of which the ape-man could have found sanctuary, but it had occurred to him that should he immediately take to the trees it might suggest to the mind of the gryf that the creature that had been commanding him all day feared him, with the result that Tarzan would once again be held a prisoner by the triceratops.

And so, when the gryf halted, Tarzan slid to the ground, struck the creature a careless blow across the flank as though in dismissal and walked indifferently away. From the throat of the beast came a low rumbling sound and without even a glance at Tarzan it turned and entered the river where it stood drinking for a long time.

Convinced that the gryf no longer constituted a menace to him the ape-man, spurred on himself by the gnawing of hunger, unslung his bow and selecting a handful of arrows set forth cautiously in search of food, evidence of the near presence of which was being borne up to him by a breeze from down river.

Ten minutes later he had made his kill, again one of the Pal-ul-don specimens of antelope, all species of which Tarzan had known since childhood as Bara, the deer, since in the little primer that had been the basis of his education the picture of a deer had been the nearest approach to the likeness of the antelope, from the giant eland to the smaller bushbuck of the hunting grounds of his youth.

Cutting off a haunch he cached it in a nearby tree, and throwing the balance of the carcass across his shoulder trotted back toward the spot at which he had left the gryf. The great beast was just emerging from the river when Tarzan, seeing it, issued the weird cry of the Tor-o-don. The creature looked in the direction of the sound voicing at the same time the low rumble with which it answered the call of its master. Twice Tarzan repeated his cry before the beast moved slowly toward him, and when it had come within a few paces he tossed the carcass of the deer to it, upon which it fell with greedy jaws.

"If anything will keep it within call," mused the ape-man as he returned to the tree in which he had cached his own portion of his kill, "it is the knowledge that I will feed it." But as he finished his repast and settled himself comfortably for the night high among the swaying branches of his eyrie he had little confidence that he would ride into A-lur the following day upon his prehistoric steed.

When Tarzan awoke early the following morning he dropped lightly to the ground and made his way to the stream. Removing his weapons and loin cloth he entered the cold waters of the little pool, and after his refreshing bath returned to the tree to breakfast upon another portion of Bara, the deer, adding to his repast some fruits and berries which grew in abundance nearby.

His meal over he sought the ground again and raising his voice in the weird cry that he had learned, he called aloud on the chance of attracting the gryf, but though he waited for some time and continued calling there was no response, and he was finally forced to the conclusion that he had seen the last of his great mount of the preceding day.

And so he set his face toward A-lur, pinning his faith upon his knowledge of the Ho-don tongue, his great strength and his native wit.

Refreshed by food and rest, the journey toward A-lur, made in the cool of the morning along the bank of the joyous river, he found delightful in the extreme. Differentiating him from his fellows of the savage jungle were many characteristics other than those physical and mental. Not the least of these were in a measure spiritual, and one that had doubtless been as strong as another in influencing Tarzan's love of the jungle had been his appreciation of the beauties of nature. The apes cared more for a grubworm in a rotten log than for all the majestic grandeur of the forest giants waving above them. The only beauties that Numa acknowledged were those of his own person as he paraded them before the admiring eyes of his mate, but in all the manifestations of the creative power of nature of which Tarzan was cognizant he appreciated the beauties.

As Tarzan neared the city his interest became centered upon the architecture of the outlying buildings which were hewn from the chalklike limestone of what had once been a group of low hills, similar to the many grass-covered hillocks that dotted the valley in every direction. Ta-den's explanation of the Ho-don methods of house construction accounted for the ofttimes remarkable shapes and proportions of the buildings which, during the ages that must have been required for their construction, had been hewn from the limestone hills, the exteriors chiseled to such architectural forms as appealed to the eyes of the builders while at the same time following roughly the original outlines of the hills in an evident desire to economize both labor and space. The excavation of the apartments within had been similarly governed by necessity.

As he came nearer Tarzan saw that the waste material from these building operations had been utilized in the construction of outer walls about each building or group of buildings resulting from a single hillock, and later he was to learn that it had also been used for the filling of inequalities between the hills and the forming of paved streets throughout the city, the result, possibly, more of the adoption of an easy method of disposing of the quantities of broken limestone than by any real necessity for pavements.

There were people moving about within the city and upon the narrow ledges and terraces that broke the lines of the buildings and which seemed to be a peculiarity of Ho-don architecture, a concession, no doubt, to some inherent instinct that might be traced back to their early cliff-dwelling progenitors.

Tarzan was not surprised that at a short distance he aroused no suspicion or curiosity in the minds of those who saw him, since, until closer scrutiny was possible, there was little to distinguish him from a native either in his general conformation or his color. He had, of course, formulated a plan of action and, having decided, he did not hesitate in the carrying out his plan.

With the same assurance that you might venture upon the main street of a neighboring city Tarzan strode into the Ho-don city of A-lur. The first person to detect his spuriousness was a little child playing in the arched gateway of one of the walled buildings. "No tail! no tail!" it shouted, throwing a stone at him, and then it suddenly grew dumb and its eyes wide as it sensed that this creature was something other than a mere Ho-don warrior who had lost his tail. With a gasp the child turned and fled screaming into the courtyard of its home.

Tarzan continued on his way, fully realizing that the moment was imminent when the fate of his plan would be decided. Nor had he long to wait since at the next turning of the winding street he came face to face with a Ho-don warrior. He saw the sudden surprise in the latter's eyes, followed instantly by one of suspicion, but before the fellow could speak Tarzan addressed him.

"I am a stranger from another land," he said; "I would speak with Ko-tan, your king."

The fellow stepped back, laying his hand upon his knife. "There are no strangers that come to the gates of A-lur," he said, "other than as enemies or slaves."

"I come neither as a slave nor an enemy," replied Tarzan. "I come directly from Jad-ben-Otho. Look!" and he held out his hands that the Ho-don might see how greatly they differed from his own, and then wheeled about that the other might see that he was tailless, for it was upon this fact that his plan had been based, due to his recollection of the quarrel between Ta-den and Om-at, in which the Waz-don had claimed that Jad-ben-Otho had a long tail while the Ho-don had been equally willing to fight for his faith in the taillessness of his god.

The warrior's eyes widened and an expression of awe crept into them, though it was still tinged with suspicion. "Jad-ben-Otho!" he murmured, and then, "It is true that you are neither Ho-don nor Waz-don, and it is also true that Jad-ben-Otho has no tail. Come," he said, "I will take you to Ko-tan, for this is a matter in which no common warrior may interfere. Follow me," and still clutching the handle of his knife and keeping a wary side glance upon the ape-man he led the way through A-lur.

The city covered a large area. Sometimes there was a considerable distance between groups of buildings, and again they were quite close together. There were numerous imposing groups, evidently hewn from the larger hills, often rising to a height of a hundred feet or more. As they advanced they met numerous warriors and women, all of whom showed great curiosity in the stranger, but there was no attempt to menace him when it was found that he was being conducted to the palace of the king.

They came at last to a great pile that sprawled over a considerable area, its western front facing upon a large blue lake and evidently hewn from what had once been a natural cliff. This group of buildings was surrounded by a wall of considerably greater height than any that Tarzan had before seen. His guide led him to a gateway before which waited a dozen or more warriors who had risen to their feet and formed a barrier across the entrance-way as Tarzan and his party appeared around the corner of the palace wall, for by this time he had accumulated such a following of the curious as presented to the guards the appearance of a formidable mob.

The guide's story told, Tarzan was conducted into the courtyard where he was held while one of the warriors entered the palace, evidently with the intention of notifying Ko-tan. Fifteen minutes later a large warrior appeared, followed by several others, all of whom examined Tarzan with every sign of curiosity as they approached.

The leader of the party halted before the ape-man. "Who are you?" he asked, "and what do you want of Ko-tan, the king?"

"I am a friend," replied the ape-man, "and I have come from the country of Jad-ben-Otho to visit Ko-tan of Pal-ul-don."

The warrior and his followers seemed impressed. Tarzan could see the latter whispering among themselves.

"How come you here," asked the spokesman, "and what do you want of Ko-tan?"

Tarzan drew himself to his full height. "Enough!" he cried. "Must the messenger of Jad-ben-Otho be subjected to the treatment that might be accorded to a wandering Waz-don? Take me to the king at once lest the wrath of Jad-ben-Otho fall upon you."

There was some question in the mind of the ape-man as to how far he might carry his unwarranted show of assurance, and he waited therefore with amused interest the result of his demand. He did not, however, have long to wait for almost immediately the attitude of his questioner changed. He whitened, cast an

EDGAR RICE BURROUGHS

apprehensive glance toward the eastern sky and then extended his right palm toward Tarzan, placing his left over his own heart in the sign of amity that was common among the peoples of Pal-ul-don.

Tarzan stepped quickly back as though from a profaning hand, a feigned expression of horror and disgust upon his face.

"Stop!" he cried, "who would dare touch the sacred person of the messenger of Jad-ben-Otho? Only as a special mark of favor from Jad-ben-Otho may even Ko-tan himself receive this honor from me. Hasten! Already now have I waited too long! What manner of reception the Ho-don of A-lur would extend to the son of my father!"

At first Tarzan had been inclined to adopt the role of Jad-ben-Otho himself but it occurred to him that it might prove embarrassing and considerable of a bore to be compelled constantly to portray the character of a god, but with the growing success of his scheme it had suddenly occurred to him that the authority of the son of Jad-ben-Otho would be far greater than that of an ordinary messenger of a god, while at the same time giving him some leeway in the matter of his acts and demeanor, the ape-man reasoning that a young god would not be held so strictly accountable in the matter of his dignity and bearing as an older and greater god.

This time the effect of his words was immediately and painfully noticeable upon all those near him. With one accord they shrank back, the spokesman almost collapsing in evident terror. His apologies, when finally the paralysis of his fear would permit him to voice them, were so abject that the ape-man could scarce repress a smile of amused contempt.

"Have mercy, O Dor-ul-Otho," he pleaded, "on poor old Dak-lot. Precede me and I will show you to where Ko-tan, the king, awaits you, trembling. Aside, snakes and vermin," he cried pushing his warriors to right and left for the purpose of forming an avenue for Tarzan.

"Come!" cried the ape-man peremptorily, "lead the way, and let these others follow."

The now thoroughly frightened Dak-lot did as he was bid, and Tarzan of the Apes was ushered into the palace of Kotan, King of Pal-ul-don.

BLOOD-STAINED ALTARS

The entrance through which he caught his first glimpse of the interior was rather beautifully carved in geometric designs, and within the walls were similarly treated, though as he proceeded from one apartment to another he found also the figures of animals, birds, and men taking their places among the more formal figures of the mural decorator's art. Stone vessels were much in evidence as well as ornaments of gold and the skins of many animals, but nowhere did he see an indication of any woven fabric, indicating that in that respect at least the Ho-don were still low in the scale of evolution, and yet the proportions and symmetry of the corridors and apartments bespoke a degree of civilization.

The way led through several apartments and long corridors, up at least three flights of stone stairs and finally out upon a ledge upon the western side of the building overlooking the blue lake. Along this ledge, or arcade, his guide led him for a hundred yards, to stop at last before a wide entrance-way leading into another apartment of the palace.

Here Tarzan beheld a considerable concourse of warriors in an enormous apartment, the domed ceiling of which was fully fifty feet above the floor. Almost filling the chamber was a great pyramid ascending in broad steps well up under the dome in which were a number of round apertures which let in the light. The steps of the pyramid were occupied by warriors to the very pinnacle, upon which sat a large, imposing figure of a man whose golden trappings shone brightly in the light of the afternoon sun, a shaft of which poured through one of the tiny apertures of the dome.

"Ko-tan!" cried Dak-lot, addressing the resplendent figure at the pinnacle of the pyramid. "Ko-tan and warriors of Pal-ul-don! Behold the honor that Jad-ben-Otho has done you in sending as his messenger his own son," and Dak-lot, stepping aside, indicated Tarzan with a dramatic sweep of his hand.

Ko-tan rose to his feet and every warrior within sight craned his neck to have a better view of the newcomer. Those upon the opposite side of the pyramid crowded to the front as the words of the old warrior reached them. Skeptical were the expressions on most of the faces; but theirs was a skepticism marked with caution. No matter which way fortune jumped they wished to be upon the right side of the fence. For a moment all eyes were centered upon Tarzan and then gradually they drifted to Ko-tan, for from his attitude would they receive the cue that would determine theirs. But Ko-tan was evidently in the same quandary as they—the very attitude of his body indicated it—it was one of indecision and of doubt.

The ape-man stood erect, his arms folded upon his broad breast, an expression of haughty disdain upon his handsome face; but to Dak-lot there seemed to be indications also of growing anger. The situation was becoming strained. Dak-lot fidgeted, casting apprehensive glances at Tarzan and appealing ones at Ko-tan. The silence of the tomb wrapped the great chamber of the throneroom of Pal-ul-don.

At last Ko-tan spoke. "Who says that he is Dor-ul-Otho?" he asked, casting a terrible look at Dak-lot.

"He does!" almost shouted that terrified noble.

"And so it must be true?" queried Ko-tan.

Could it be that there was a trace of irony in the chief's tone? Otho forbid! Dak-lot cast a side glance at Tarzan—a glance that he intended should carry the assurance of his own faith; but that succeeded only in impressing the ape-man with the other's pitiable terror.

"O Ko-tan!" pleaded Dak-lot, "your own eyes must convince you that indeed he is the son of Otho. Behold his godlike figure, his hands, and his feet, that are not as ours, and that he is entirely tailless as is his mighty father."

Ko-tan appeared to be perceiving these facts for the first time and there was an indication that his skepticism was faltering. At that moment a young warrior who had pushed his way forward from the opposite side of the pyramid to where he could obtain a good look at Tarzan raised his voice.

"Ko-tan," he cried, "it must be even as Dak-lot says, for I am sure now that I have seen Dor-ul-Otho before. Yesterday as we were returning with the Kor-ul-lul prisoners we beheld him seated upon the back of a great gryf. We hid in the woods before he came too near, but I saw enough to make sure that he who rode upon the great beast was none other than the messenger who stands here now."

This evidence seemed to be quite enough to convince the majority of the warriors that they indeed stood in the presence of deity—their faces showed it only too plainly, and a sudden modesty that caused them to shrink behind their neighbors. As their neighbors were attempting to do the same thing, the result was a sudden melting away of those who stood nearest the ape-man, until the steps of the pyramid directly before him lay vacant to the very apex and to Ko-tan. The latter, possibly influenced as much by the fearful attitude of his followers as by the evidence adduced, now altered his tone and his manner in such a degree as might comport with the requirements if the stranger was indeed the Dor-ul-Otho while leaving his dignity a loophole of escape should it appear that he had entertained an impostor.

"If indeed you are the Dor-ul-Otho," he said, addressing Tarzan, "you will know that our doubts were but natural since we have received no sign from Jad-ben-Otho that he intended honoring us so greatly, nor how could we know, even, that the Great God had a son? If you are he, all Pal-ul-don rejoices to honor you; if you are not he, swift and terrible shall be the punishment of your temerity. I, Ko-tan, King of Pal-ul-don, have spoken."

"And spoken well, as a king should speak," said Tarzan, breaking his long silence, "who fears and honors the god of his people. It is well that you insist that I indeed be the Dor-ul-Otho before you accord me the homage that is my due. Jad-ben-Otho charged me specially to ascertain if you were fit to rule his people. My first experience of you indicates that Jad-ben-Otho chose well when he breathed the spirit of a king into the babe at your mother's breast."

The effect of this statement, made so casually, was marked in the expressions and excited whispers of the now awe-struck assemblage. At last they knew how kings were made! It was decided by Jad-ben-Otho while the candidate was still a suckling babe! Wonderful! A miracle! and this divine creature in whose presence they stood knew all about it. Doubtless he even discussed such matters with their god daily. If there had been an atheist among them before, or an agnostic, there was none now, for had they not looked with their own eyes upon the son of god?

"It is well then," continued the ape-man, "that you should assure yourself that I am no impostor. Come closer that you may see that I am not as are men. Furthermore it is not meet that you stand upon a higher level than the son of your god." There was a sudden scramble to reach the floor of the throne-room, nor was Ko-tan far behind his warriors, though he managed to maintain a certain majestic dignity as he descended the broad stairs that countless naked feet had polished to a gleaming smoothness through the ages. "And now," said Tarzan as the king stood before him, "you can have no doubt that I am not of the same race as you. Your priests have told you that Jad-ben-Otho is tailless. Tailless, therefore, must be the race of gods that spring from his loins. But enough of such proofs as these! You know the power of Jad-ben-Otho; how his lightnings gleaming out of the sky carry death as he wills it; how the rains come at his bidding, and the fruits and the berries and the grains, the grasses, the trees and the flowers spring to life at his divine direction; you have witnessed birth and death, and those who honor their god honor him because he controls these things. How would it fare then with an impostor who claimed to be the son of this all-powerful god? This then is all the proof that you require, for as he would strike you down should you deny me, so would he strike down one who wrongfully claimed kinship with him."

This line of argument being unanswerable must needs be convincing. There could be no questioning of this creature's statements without the tacit admission of lack of faith in the omnipotence of Jad-ben-Otho. Ko-tan was satisfied that he was entertaining deity, but as to just what form his entertainment should take he was rather at a loss to know. His conception of god had been rather a vague and hazy affair, though in common with all primitive people his god was a personal one as were his devils and demons. The pleasures of Jad-ben-Otho he had assumed to be the excesses which he himself enjoyed, but devoid of any unpleasant reaction. It therefore occurred to him that the Dor-ul-Otho would be greatly entertained by eating—eating large quantities of everything that Ko-tan liked best and that he had found most injurious; and there was also a drink that the women of the Ho-don made by allowing corn to soak in the juices of succulent fruits, to which they had added certain other ingredients best known to themselves. Ko-tan knew by experience that a single draught of this potent liquor would bring happiness and surcease from worry, while several would cause even a king to do things and enjoy things that he would never even think of doing or enjoying while not under the magical influence of the potion, but unfortunately the next morning brought suffering in direct ratio to the joy of the preceding day. A god, Ko-tan reasoned, could experience all the pleasure without the headache, but for the immediate present he must think of the necessary dignities and honors to be accorded his immortal guest.

No foot other than a king's had touched the surface of the apex of the pyramid in the throneroom at A-lur during all the forgotten ages through which the kings of Pal-ul-don had ruled from its high eminence. So what higher honor could Ko-tan offer than to give place beside him to the Dor-ul-Otho? And so he invited Tarzan to ascend the pyramid and take his place upon the stone bench that topped it. As they reached the step below the sacred pinnacle Ko-tan continued as though to mount to his throne, but Tarzan laid a detaining hand upon his arm.

"None may sit upon a level with the gods," he admonished, stepping confidently up and seating himself upon the throne. The abashed Ko-tan showed his embarrassment, an embarrassment he feared to voice lest he incur the wrath of the king of kings.

"But," added Tarzan, "a god may honor his faithful servant by inviting him to a place at his side. Come, Ko-tan; thus would I honor you in the name of Jad-ben-Otho."

The ape-man's policy had for its basis an attempt not only to arouse the fearful respect of Ko-tan but to do it without making of him an enemy at heart, for he did not know how strong a hold the religion of the

Ho-don had upon them, for since the time that he had prevented Ta-den and Om-at from quarreling over a religious difference the subject had been utterly taboo among them. He was therefore quick to note the evident though wordless resentment of Ko-tan at the suggestion that he entirely relinquish his throne to his guest. On the whole, however, the effect had been satisfactory as he could see from the renewed evidence of awe upon the faces of the warriors.

At Tarzan's direction the business of the court continued where it had been interrupted by his advent. It consisted principally in the settling of disputes between warriors. There was present one who stood upon the step just below the throne and which Tarzan was to learn was the place reserved for the higher chiefs of the allied tribes which made up Ko-tan's kingdom. The one who attracted Tarzan's attention was a stalwart warrior of powerful physique and massive, lion-like features. He was addressing Ko-tan on a question that is as old as government and that will continue in unabated importance until man ceases to exist. It had to do with a boundary dispute with one of his neighbors.

The matter itself held little or no interest for Tarzan, but he was impressed by the appearance of the speaker and when Ko-tan addressed him as Ja-don the ape-man's interest was permanently crystallized, for Ja-don was the father of Ta-den. That the knowledge would benefit him in any way seemed rather a remote possibility since he could not reveal to Ja-don his friendly relations with his son without admitting the falsity of his claims to godship.

When the affairs of the audience were concluded Ko-tan suggested that the son of Jad-ben-Otho might wish to visit the temple in which were performed the religious rites coincident to the worship of the Great God. And so the ape-man was conducted by the king himself, followed by the warriors of his court, through the corridors of the palace toward the northern end of the group of buildings within the royal enclosure.

The temple itself was really a part of the palace and similar in architecture. There were several ceremonial places of varying sizes, the purposes of which Tarzan could only conjecture. Each had an altar in the west end and another in the east and were oval in shape, their longest diameter lying due east and west. Each was excavated from the summit of a small hillock and all were without roofs. The western altars invariably were a single block of stone the top of which was hollowed into an oblong basin. Those at the eastern ends were similar blocks of stone with flat tops and these latter, unlike those at the opposite ends of the ovals were invariably stained or painted a reddish brown, nor did Tarzan need to examine them closely to be assured of what his keen nostrils already had told him—that the brown stains were dried and drying human blood.

Below these temple courts were corridors and apartments reaching far into the bowels of the hills, dim, gloomy passages that Tarzan glimpsed as he was led from place to place on his tour of inspection of the temple. A messenger had been dispatched by Ko-tan to announce the coming visit of the son of Jad-ben-Otho with the result that they were accompanied through the temple by a considerable procession of priests whose distinguishing mark of profession seemed to consist in grotesque headdresses; sometimes hideous faces carved from wood and entirely concealing the countenances of their wearers, or again, the head of a wild beast cunningly fitted over the head of a man. The high priest alone wore no such head-dress. He was an old man with close-set, cunning eyes and a cruel, thin-lipped mouth.

At first sight of him Tarzan realized that here lay the greatest danger to his ruse, for he saw at a glance that the man was antagonistic toward him and his pretensions, and he knew too that doubtless of all the people of Pal-ul-don the high priest was most likely to harbor the truest estimate of Jad-ben-Otho, and, therefore, would look with suspicion on one who claimed to be the son of a fabulous god.

No matter what suspicion lurked within his crafty mind, Lu-don, the high priest of A-lur, did not openly question Tarzan's right to the title of Dor-ul-Otho, and it may be that he was restrained by the same doubts which had originally restrained Ko-tan and his warriors—the doubt that is at the bottom of the minds of all blasphemers even and which is based upon the fear that after all there may be a god. So, for the time being at least Lu-don played safe. Yet Tarzan knew as well as though the man had spoken aloud his inmost thoughts that it was in the heart of the high priest to tear the veil from his imposture.

At the entrance to the temple Ko-tan had relinquished the guidance of the guest to Lu-don and now the latter led Tarzan through those portions of the temple that he wished him to see. He showed him the great room where the votive offerings were kept, gifts from the barbaric chiefs of Pal-ul-don and from their followers. These things ranged in value from presents of dried fruits to massive vessels of beaten gold, so that in the great main storeroom and its connecting chambers and corridors was an accumulation of wealth that amazed even the eyes of the owner of the secret of the treasure vaults of Opar.

Moving to and fro throughout the temple were sleek black Waz-don slaves, fruits of the Ho-don raids upon the villages of their less civilized neighbors. As they passed the barred entrance to a dim corridor, Tarzan saw within a great company of pithecanthropi of all ages and of both sexes, Ho-don as well as Waz-don, the majority of them squatted upon the stone floor in attitudes of utter dejection while some paced back and forth, their features stamped with the despair of utter hopelessness.

"And who are these who lie here thus unhappily?" he asked of Lu-don. It was the first question that he had put to the high priest since entering the temple, and instantly he regretted that he had asked it, for Lu-don turned upon him a face upon which the expression of suspicion was but thinly veiled.

"Who should know better than the son of Jad-ben-Otho?" he retorted.

"The questions of Dor-ul-Otho are not with impunity answered with other questions," said the ape-man quietly, "and it may interest Lu-don, the high priest, to know that the blood of a false priest upon the altar of his temple is not displeasing in the eyes of Jad-ben-Otho."

Lu-don paled as he answered Tarzan's question. "They are the offerings whose blood must refresh the eastern altars as the sun returns to your father at the day's end."

"And who told you," asked Tarzan, "that Jad-ben-Otho was pleased that his people were slain upon his altars? What if you were mistaken?"

"Then countless thousands have died in vain," replied Lu-don.

Ko-tan and the surrounding warriors and priests were listening attentively to the dialogue. Some of the poor victims behind the barred gateway had heard and rising, pressed close to the barrier through which one was conducted just before sunset each day, never to return.

"Liberate them!" cried Tarzan with a wave of his hand toward the imprisoned victims of a cruel superstition, "for I can tell you in the name of Jad-ben-Otho that you are mistaken."

THE FORBIDDEN GARDEN

Lu-don paled. "It is sacrilege," he cried; "for countless ages have the priests of the Great God offered each night a life to the spirit of Jad-ben-Otho as it returned below the western horizon to its master, and never has the Great God given sign that he was displeased."

"Stop!" commanded Tarzan. "It is the blindness of the priesthood that has failed to read the messages of their god. Your warriors die beneath the knives and clubs of the Wazdon; your hunters are taken by ja and jato; no day goes by but witnesses the deaths of few or many in the villages of the Ho-don, and one death each day of those that die are the toll which Jad-ben-Otho has exacted for the lives you take upon the eastern altar. What greater sign of his displeasure could you require, O stupid priest?"

Lu-don was silent. There was raging within him a great conflict between his fear that this indeed might be the son of god and his hope that it was not, but at last his fear won and he bowed his head. "The son of Jad-ben-Otho has spoken," he said, and turning to one of the lesser priests: "Remove the bars and return these people from whence they came."

He thus addressed did as he was bid and as the bars came down the prisoners, now all fully aware of the miracle that had saved them, crowded forward and throwing themselves upon their knees before Tarzan raised their voices in thanksgiving.

Ko-tan was almost as staggered as the high priest by this ruthless overturning of an age-old religious rite. "But what," he cried, "may we do that will be pleasing in the eyes of Jad-ben-Otho?" turning a look of puzzled apprehension toward the ape-man.

"If you seek to please your god," he replied, "place upon your altars such gifts of food and apparel as are most welcome in the city of your people. These things will Jad-ben-Otho bless, when you may distribute them among those of the city who need them most. With such things are your storerooms filled as I have seen with mine own eyes, and other gifts will be brought when the priests tell the people that in this way they find favor before their god," and Tarzan turned and signified that he would leave the temple.

As they were leaving the precincts devoted to the worship of their deity, the ape-man noticed a small but rather ornate building that stood entirely detached from the others as though it had been cut from a little pinnacle of limestone which had stood out from its fellows. As his interested glance passed over it he noticed that its door and windows were barred.

"To what purpose is that building dedicated?" he asked of Lu-don. "Who do you keep imprisoned there?"

"It is nothing," replied the high priest nervously, "there is no one there. The place is vacant. Once it was used but not now for many years," and he moved on toward the gateway which led back into the palace. Here he and the priests halted while Tarzan with Ko-tan and his warriors passed out from the sacred precincts of the temple grounds.

The one question which Tarzan would have asked he had feared to ask for he knew that in the hearts of many lay a suspicion as to his genuineness, but he determined that before he slept he would put the question to Ko-tan, either directly or indirectly—as to whether there was, or had been recently within the city of A-lur a female of the same race as his.

As their evening meal was being served to them in the banquet hall of Ko-tan's palace by a part of the army of black slaves upon whose shoulders fell the burden of all the heavy and menial tasks of the city, Tarzan noticed that there came to the eyes of one of the slaves what was apparently an expression of startled recognition, as he looked upon the ape-man for the first time in the banquet hall of Ko-tan. And again later he saw the fellow whisper to another slave and nod his head in his direction. The ape-man did not recall ever having seen this Waz-don before and he was at a loss to account for an explanation of the fellow's interest in him, and presently the incident was all but forgotten.

Ko-tan was surprised and inwardly disgusted to discover that his godly guest had no desire to gorge himself upon rich foods and that he would not even so much as taste the villainous brew of the Ho-don. To Tarzan the banquet was a dismal and tiresome affair, since so great was the interest of the guests in gorging themselves with food and drink that they had no time for conversation, the only vocal sounds being confined to a continuous grunting which, together with their table manners reminded Tarzan of a visit he had once made to the famous Berkshire herd of His Grace, the Duke of Westminster at Woodhouse, Chester.

One by one the diners succumbed to the stupefying effects of the liquor with the result that the grunting gave place to snores, so presently Tarzan and the slaves were the only conscious creatures in the banquet hall.

Rising, the ape-man turned to a tall black who stood behind him. "I would sleep," he said, "show me to my apartment."

As the fellow conducted him from the chamber the slave who had shown surprise earlier in the evening at sight of him, spoke again at length to one of his fellows. The latter cast a half-frightened look in the direction of the departing ape-man. "If you are right," he said, "they should reward us with our liberty, but if you are wrong, O Jad-ben-Otho, what will be our fate?"

"But I am not wrong!" cried the other.

"Then there is but one to tell this to, for I have heard that he looked sour when this Dor-ul-Otho was brought to the temple and that while the so-called son of Jad-ben-Otho was there he gave this one every cause to fear and hate him. I mean Lu-don, the high priest."

"You know him?" asked the other slave.

"I have worked in the temple," replied his companion.

"Then go to him at once and tell him, but be sure to exact the promise of our freedom for the proof."

And so a black Waz-don came to the temple gate and asked to see Lu-don, the high priest, on a matter of great importance, and though the hour was late Lu-don saw him, and when he had heard his story he promised him and his friend not only their freedom but many gifts if they could prove the correctness of their claims.

And as the slave talked with the high priest in the temple at A-lur the figure of a man groped its way around the shoulder of Pastar-ul-ved and the moonlight glistened from the shiny barrel of an Enfield that was strapped to the naked back, and brass cartridges shed tiny rays of reflected light from their polished cases where they hung in the bandoliers across the broad brown shoulders and the lean waist.

Tarzan's guide conducted him to a chamber overlooking the blue lake where he found a bed similar to that which he had seen in the villages of the Waz-don, merely a raised dais of stone upon which was piled great quantities of furry pelts. And so he lay down to sleep, the question that he most wished to put still unasked and unanswered.

With the coming of a new day he was awake and wandering about the palace and the palace grounds before there was sign of any of the inmates of the palace other than slaves, or at least he saw no others at first, though presently he stumbled upon an enclosure which lay almost within the center of the palace grounds surrounded by a wall that piqued the ape-man's curiosity, since he had determined to investigate as fully as possible every part of the palace and its environs.

This place, whatever it might be, was apparently without doors or windows but that it was at least partially roofless was evidenced by the sight of the waving branches of a tree which spread above the top of the wall near him. Finding no other method of access, the ape-man uncoiled his rope and throwing it over the branch of the tree where it projected beyond the wall, was soon climbing with the ease of a monkey to the summit.

There he found that the wall surrounded an enclosed garden in which grew trees and shrubs and flowers in riotous profusion. Without waiting to ascertain whether the garden was empty or contained Ho-don, Waz-don, or wild beasts, Tarzan dropped lightly to the sward on the inside and without further loss of time commenced a systematic investigation of the enclosure.

His curiosity was aroused by the very evident fact that the place was not for general use, even by those who had free access to other parts of the palace grounds and so there was added to its natural beauties an absence of mortals which rendered its exploration all the more alluring to Tarzan since it suggested that in such a place might he hope to come upon the object of his long and difficult search.

In the garden were tiny artificial streams and little pools of water, flanked by flowering bushes, as though it all had been designed by the cunning hand of some master gardener, so faithfully did it carry out the beauties and contours of nature upon a miniature scale.

The interior surface of the wall was fashioned to represent the white cliffs of Pal-ul-don, broken occasionally by small replicas of the verdure-filled gorges of the original.

Filled with admiration and thoroughly enjoying each new surprise which the scene offered, Tarzan moved slowly around the garden, and as always he moved silently. Passing through a miniature forest he came presently upon a tiny area of flowerstudded sward and at the same time beheld before him the first Ho-don female he had seen since entering the palace. A young and beautiful woman stood in the center of the little open space, stroking the head of a bird which she held against her golden breastplate with one hand. Her profile was presented to the ape-man and he saw that by the standards of any land she would have been accounted more than lovely.

Seated in the grass at her feet, with her back toward him, was a female Waz-don slave. Seeing that she he sought was not there and apprehensive that an alarm be raised were he discovered by the two women, Tarzan moved back to hide himself in the foliage, but before he had succeeded the Ho-don girl turned quickly toward him as though apprised of his presence by that unnamed sense, the manifestations of which are more or less familiar to us all.

At sight of him her eyes registered only her surprise though there was no expression of terror reflected in them, nor did she scream or even raise her well-modulated voice as she addressed him.

"Who are you," she asked, "who enters thus boldly the Forbidden Garden?"

At sound of her mistress' voice the slave maiden turned quickly, rising to her feet. "Tarzan-jad-guru!" she exclaimed in tones of mingled astonishment and relief.

"You know him?" cried her mistress turning toward the slave and affording Tarzan an opportunity to raise a cautioning finger to his lips lest Pan-at-lee further betray him, for it was Pan-at-lee indeed who stood before him, no less a source of surprise to him than had his presence been to her.

Thus questioned by her mistress and simultaneously admonished to silence by Tarzan, Pan-at-lee was momentarily silenced and then haltingly she groped for a way to extricate herself from her dilemma. "I thought—" she faltered, "but no, I am mistaken—I thought that he was one whom I had seen before near the Kor-ul-gryf."

The Ho-don looked first at one and then at the other an expression of doubt and questioning in her eyes. "But you have not answered me," she continued presently; "who are you?"

"You have not heard then," asked Tarzan, "of the visitor who arrived at your king's court yesterday?"

"You mean," she exclaimed, "that you are the Dor-ul-Otho?" And now the erstwhile doubting eyes reflected naught but awe.

"I am he," replied Tarzan; "and you?"

"I am O-lo-a, daughter of Ko-tan, the king," she replied.

So this was O-lo-a, for love of whom Ta-den had chosen exile rather than priesthood. Tarzan had approached more closely the dainty barbarian princess. "Daughter of Ko-tan," he said, "Jad-ben-Otho is pleased with you and as a mark of his favor he has preserved for you through many dangers him whom you love."

"I do not understand," replied the girl but the flush that mounted to her cheek belied her words. "Bu-lat is a guest in the palace of Ko-tan, my father. I do not know that he has faced any danger. It is to Bu-lat that I am betrothed."

"But it is not Bu-lat whom you love," said Tarzan.

Again the flush and the girl half turned her face away. "Have I then displeased the Great God?" she asked.

"No," replied Tarzan; "as I told you he is well satisfied and for your sake he has saved Ta-den for you."

"Jad-ben-Otho knows all," whispered the girl, "and his son shares his great knowledge."

"No," Tarzan hastened to correct her lest a reputation for omniscience might prove embarrassing. "I know only what Jad-ben-Otho wishes me to know."

"But tell me," she said, "I shall be reunited with Ta-den? Surely the son of god can read the future."

The ape-man was glad that he had left himself an avenue of escape. "I know nothing of the future," he replied, "other than what Jad-ben-Otho tells me. But I think you need have no fear for the future if you remain faithful to Ta-den and Ta-den's friends."

"You have seen him?" asked O-lo-a. "Tell me, where is he?"

"Yes," replied Tarzan, "I have seen him. He was with Om-at, the gund of Kor-ul-ja."

"A prisoner of the Waz-don?" interrupted the girl.

"Not a prisoner but an honored guest," replied the ape-man.

"Wait," he exclaimed, raising his face toward the heavens; "do not speak. I am receiving a message from Jad-ben-Otho, my father."

The two women dropped to their knees, covering their faces with their hands, stricken with awe at the thought of the awful nearness of the Great God. Presently Tarzan touched O-lo-a on the shoulder.

"Rise," he said. "Jad-ben-Otho has spoken. He has told me that this slave girl is from the tribe of Kor-ul-ja, where Ta-den is, and that she is betrothed to Om-at, their chief. Her name is Pan-at-lee."

O-lo-a turned questioningly toward Pan-at-lee. The latter nodded, her simple mind unable to determine whether or not she and her mistress were the victims of a colossal hoax. "It is even as he says," she whispered.

O-lo-a fell upon her knees and touched her forehead to Tarzan's feet. "Great is the honor that Jad-ben-Otho has done his poor servant," she cried. "Carry to him my poor thanks for the happiness that he has brought to O-lo-a."

"It would please my father," said Tarzan, "if you were to cause Pan-at-lee to be returned in safety to the village of her people."

"What cares Jad-ben-Otho for such as she?" asked O-lo-a, a slight trace of hauteur in her tone.

"There is but one god," replied Tarzan, "and he is the god of the Waz-don as well as of the Ho-don; of the birds and the beasts and the flowers and of everything that grows upon the earth or beneath the waters. If Pan-at-lee does right she is greater in the eyes of Jad-ben-Otho than would be the daughter of Ko-tan should she do wrong."

It was evident that O-lo-a did not quite understand this interpretation of divine favor, so contrary was it to the teachings of the priesthood of her people. In one respect only did Tarzan's teachings coincide with her belief—that there was but one god. For the rest she had always been taught that he was solely the god of the Ho-don in every sense, other than that other creatures were created by Jad-ben-Otho to serve some useful purpose for the benefit of the Ho-don race. And now to be told by the son of god that she stood no higher in divine esteem than the black handmaiden at her side was indeed a shock to her pride, her vanity, and her faith. But who could question the word of Dor-ul-Otho, especially when she had with her own eyes seen him in actual communion with god in heaven?

"The will of Jad-ben-Otho be done," said O-lo-a meekly, "if it lies within my power. But it would be best, O Dor-ul-Otho, to communicate your father's wish directly to the king."

"Then keep her with you," said Tarzan, "and see that no harm befalls her."

O-lo-a looked ruefully at Pan-at-lee. "She was brought to me but yesterday," she said, "and never have I had slave woman who pleased me better. I shall hate to part with her."

"But there are others," said Tarzan.

"Yes," replied O-lo-a, "there are others, but there is only one Pan-at-lee."

"Many slaves are brought to the city?" asked Tarzan.

"Yes," she replied.

"And many strangers come from other lands?" he asked.

She shook her head negatively. "Only the Ho-don from the other side of the Valley of Jad-ben-Otho," she replied, "and they are not strangers."

"Am I then the first stranger to enter the gates of A-lur?" he asked.

"Can it be," she parried, "that the son of Jad-ben-Otho need question a poor ignorant mortal like O-lo-a?"

"As I told you before," replied Tarzan, "Jad-ben-Otho alone is all-knowing."

"Then if he wished you to know this thing," retorted O-lo-a quickly, "you would know it."

Inwardly the ape-man smiled that this little heathen's astuteness should beat him at his own game, yet in a measure her evasion of the question might be an answer to it. "There have been other strangers here then recently?" he persisted.

"I cannot tell you what I do not know," she replied. "Always is the palace of Ko-tan filled with rumors, but how much fact and how much fancy how may a woman of the palace know?"

"There has been such a rumor then?" he asked.

"It was only rumor that reached the Forbidden Garden," she replied.

"It described, perhaps, a woman of another race?" As he put the question and awaited her answer he thought that his heart ceased to beat, so grave to him was the issue at stake.

The girl hesitated before replying, and then. "No," she said, "I cannot speak of this thing, for if it be of sufficient importance to elicit the interest of the gods then indeed would I be subject to the wrath of my father should I discuss it."

"In the name of Jad-ben-Otho I command you to speak," said Tarzan. "In the name of Jad-ben-Otho in whose hands lies the fate of Ta-den!"

The girl paled. "Have mercy!" she cried, "and for the sake of Ta-den I will tell you all that I know."

"Tell what?" demanded a stern voice from the shrubbery behind them. The three turned to see the figure of Ko-tan emerging from the foliage. An angry scowl distorted his kingly features but at sight of Tarzan it gave place to an expression of surprise not unmixed with fear. "Dor-ul-Otho!" he exclaimed, "I did not know that it was you," and then, raising his head and squaring his shoulders he said, "but there are places where even the son of the Great God may not walk and this, the Forbidden Garden of Ko-tan, is one."

It was a challenge but despite the king's bold front there was a note of apology in it, indicating that in his superstitious mind there flourished the inherent fear of man for his Maker. "Come, Dor-ul-Otho," he continued, "I do not know all this foolish child has said to you but whatever you would know Ko-tan, the king, will tell you. O-lo-a, go to your quarters immediately," and he pointed with stern finger toward the opposite end of the garden.

The princess, followed by Pan-at-lee, turned at once and left them.

"We will go this way," said Ko-tan and preceding, led Tarzan in another direction. Close to that part of the wall which they approached Tarzan perceived a grotto in the miniature cliff into the interior of which Ko-tan led him, and down a rocky stairway to a gloomy corridor the opposite end of which opened into the palace proper. Two armed warriors stood at this entrance to the Forbidden Garden, evidencing how jealously were the sacred precincts of the place guarded.

In silence Ko-tan led the way back to his own quarters in the palace. A large chamber just outside the room toward which Ko-tan was leading his guest was filled with chiefs and warriors awaiting the pleasure of their ruler. As the two entered, an aisle was formed for them the length of the chamber, down which they passed in silence.

Close to the farther door and half hidden by the warriors who stood before him was Lu-don, the high priest. Tarzan glimpsed him but briefly but in that short period he was aware of a cunning and malevolent expression upon the cruel countenance that he was subconsciously aware boded him no good, and then with Ko-tan he passed into the adjoining room and the hangings dropped.

At the same moment the hideous headdress of an under priest appeared in the entrance of the outer chamber. Its owner, pausing for a moment, glanced quickly around the interior and then having located him whom he sought moved rapidly in the direction of Lu-don. There was a whispered conversation which was terminated by the high priest.

"Return immediately to the quarters of the princess," he said, "and see that the slave is sent to me at the temple at once." The under priest turned and departed upon his mission while Lu-don also left the apartment and directed his footsteps toward the sacred enclosure over which he ruled.

A half-hour later a warrior was ushered into the presence of Ko-tan. "Lu-don, the high priest, desires the presence of Ko-tan, the king, in the temple," he announced, "and it is his wish that he come alone."

Ko-tan nodded to indicate that he accepted the command which even the king must obey. "I will return presently, Dor-ul-Otho," he said to Tarzan, "and in the meantime my warriors and my slaves are yours to command."

THE SENTENCE OF DEATH

But it was an hour before the king re-entered the apartment and in the meantime the ape-man had occupied himself in examining the carvings upon the walls and the numerous specimens of the handicraft of Pal-ul-donian artisans which combined to impart an atmosphere of richness and luxury to the apartment.

The limestone of the country, close-grained and of marble whiteness yet worked with comparative ease with crude implements, had been wrought by cunning craftsmen into bowls and urns and vases of considerable grace and beauty. Into the carved designs of many of these virgin gold had been hammered, presenting the effect of a rich and magnificent cloisonne. A barbarian himself the art of barbarians had always appealed to the ape-man to whom they represented a natural expression of man's love of the beautiful to even a greater extent than the studied and artificial efforts of civilization. Here was the real art of old masters, the other the cheap imitation of the chromo.

It was while he was thus pleasurably engaged that Ko-tan returned. As Tarzan, attracted by the movement of the hangings through which the king entered, turned and faced him he was almost shocked by the remarkable alteration of the king's appearance. His face was livid; his hands trembled as with palsy, and his eyes were wide as with fright. His appearance was one apparently of a combination of consuming anger and withering fear. Tarzan looked at him questioningly.

"You have had bad news, Ko-tan?" he asked.

The king mumbled an unintelligible reply. Behind there thronged into the apartment so great a number of warriors that they choked the entrance-way. The king looked apprehensively to right and left. He cast terrified glances at the ape-man and then raising his face and turning his eyes upward he cried: "Jad-ben-Otho be my witness that I do not this thing of my own accord." There was a moment's silence which was again broken by Ko-tan. "Seize him," he cried to the warriors about him, "for Lu-don, the high priest, swears that he is an impostor."

To have offered armed resistance to this great concourse of warriors in the very heart of the palace of their king would have been worse than fatal. Already Tarzan had come far by his wits and now that within a few hours he had had his hopes and his suspicions partially verified by the vague admissions of O-lo-a he was impressed with the necessity of inviting no mortal risk that he could avoid.

"Stop!" he cried, raising his palm against them. "What is the meaning of this?"

"Lu-don claims he has proof that you are not the son of Jad-ben-Otho," replied Ko-tan. "He demands that you be brought to the throneroom to face your accusers. If you are what you claim to be none knows better than you that you need have no fear in acquiescing to his demands, but remember always that in such matters the high priest commands the king and that I am only the bearer of these commands, not their author."

Tarzan saw that Ko-tan was not entirely convinced of his duplicity as was evidenced by his palpable design to play safe.

"Let not your warriors seize me," he said to Ko-tan, "lest Jad-ben-Otho, mistaking their intention, strike them dead." The effect of his words was immediate upon the men in the front rank of those who faced him, each seeming suddenly to acquire a new modesty that compelled him to self-effacement behind those directly in his rear—a modesty that became rapidly contagious.

The ape-man smiled. "Fear not," he said, "I will go willingly to the audience chamber to face the blasphemers who accuse me."

Arrived at the great throneroom a new complication arose. Ko-tan would not acknowledge the right of Lu-don to occupy the apex of the pyramid and Lu-don would not consent to occupying an inferior position while Tarzan, to remain consistent with his high claims, insisted that no one should stand above him, but only to the ape-man was the humor of the situation apparent.

To relieve the situation Ja-don suggested that all three of them occupy the throne, but this suggestion was repudiated by Ko-tan who argued that no mortal other than a king of Pal-ul-don had ever sat upon the high eminence, and that furthermore there was not room for three there.

"But who," said Tarzan, "is my accuser and who is my judge?"

"Lu-don is your accuser," explained Ko-tan.

"And Lu-don is your judge," cried the high priest.

"I am to be judged by him who accuses me then," said Tarzan. "It were better to dispense then with any formalities and ask Lu-don to sentence me." His tone was ironical and his sneering face, looking straight into that of the high priest, but caused the latter's hatred to rise to still greater proportions.

It was evident that Ko-tan and his warriors saw the justice of Tarzan's implied objection to this unfair method of dispensing justice. "Only Ko-tan can judge in the throneroom of his palace," said Ja-don, "let him hear Lu-don's charges and the testimony of his witnesses, and then let Ko-tan's judgment be final."

Ko-tan, however, was not particularly enthusiastic over the prospect of sitting in trial upon one who might after all very possibly be the son of his god, and so he temporized, seeking for an avenue of escape. "It is purely a religious matter," he said, "and it is traditional that the kings of Pal-ul-don interfere not in questions of the church."

"Then let the trial be held in the temple," cried one of the chiefs, for the warriors were as anxious as their king to be relieved of all responsibility in the matter. This suggestion was more than satisfactory to the high priest who inwardly condemned himself for not having thought of it before.

"It is true," he said, "this man's sin is against the temple. Let him be dragged thither then for trial."

"The son of Jad-ben-Otho will be dragged nowhere," cried Tarzan. "But when this trial is over it is possible that the corpse of Lu-don, the high priest, will be dragged from the temple of the god he would desecrate. Think well, then, Lu-don before you commit this folly."

His words, intended to frighten the high priest from his position failed utterly in consummating their purpose. Lu-don showed no terror at the suggestion the ape-man's words implied.

"Here is one," thought Tarzan, "who, knowing more of his religion than any of his fellows, realizes fully the falsity of my claims as he does the falsity of the faith he preaches."

He realized, however, that his only hope lay in seeming indifference to the charges. Ko-tan and the warriors were still under the spell of their belief in him and upon this fact must he depend in the final act of the drama that Lu-don was staging for his rescue from the jealous priest whom he knew had already passed sentence upon him in his own heart.

With a shrug he descended the steps of the pyramid. "It matters not to Dor-ul-Otho," he said, "where Lu-don enrages his god, for Jad-ben-Otho can reach as easily into the chambers of the temple as into the throneroom of Ko-tan."

Immeasurably relieved by this easy solution of their problem the king and the warriors thronged from the throneroom toward the temple grounds, their faith in Tarzan increased by his apparent indifference to the charges against him. Lu-don led them to the largest of the altar courts.

Taking his place behind the western altar he motioned Ko-tan to a place upon the platform at the left hand of the altar and directed Tarzan to a similar place at the right.

As Tarzan ascended the platform his eyes narrowed angrily at the sight which met them. The basin hollowed in the top of the altar was filled with water in which floated the naked corpse of a new-born babe. "What means this?" he cried angrily, turning upon Lu-don.

The latter smiled malevolently. "That you do not know," he replied, "is but added evidence of the falsity of your claim. He who poses as the son of god did not know that as the last rays of the setting sun flood the eastern altar of the temple the lifeblood of an adult reddens the white stone for the edification of Jad-ben-Otho, and that when the sun rises again from the body of its maker it looks first upon this western altar and rejoices in the death of a new-born babe each day, the ghost of which accompanies it across the heavens by day as the ghost of the adult returns with it to Jad-ben-Otho at night.

"Even the little children of the Ho-don know these things, while he who claims to be the son of Jad-ben-Otho knows them not; and if this proof be not enough, there is more. Come, Waz-don," he cried, pointing to a tall slave who stood with a group of other blacks and priests on the temple floor at the left of the altar.

The fellow came forward fearfully. "Tell us what you know of this creature," cried Lu-don, pointing to Tarzan.

"I have seen him before," said the Waz-don. "I am of the tribe of Kor-ul-lul, and one day recently a party of which I was one encountered a few of the warriors of the Kor-ul-ja upon the ridge which separates our villages. Among the enemy was this strange creature whom they called Tarzan-jad-guru; and terrible indeed was he for he fought with the strength of many men so that it required twenty of us to subdue him. But he did not fight as a god fights, and when a club struck him upon the head he sank unconscious as might an ordinary mortal.

"We carried him with us to our village as a prisoner but he escaped after cutting off the head of the warrior we left to guard him and carrying it down into the gorge and tying it to the branch of a tree upon the opposite side."

"The word of a slave against that of a god!" cried Ja-don, who had shown previously a friendly interest in the pseudo godling.

"It is only a step in the progress toward truth," interjected Lu-don. "Possibly the evidence of the only princess of the house of Ko-tan will have greater weight with the great chief from the north, though the father of a son who fled the holy offer of the priesthood may not receive with willing ears any testimony against another blasphemer."

Ja-don's hand leaped to his knife, but the warriors next him laid detaining fingers upon his arms. "You are in the temple of Jad-ben-Otho, Ja-don," they cautioned and the great chief was forced to swallow Lu-don's affront though it left in his heart bitter hatred of the high priest.

And now Ko-tan turned toward Lu-don. "What knoweth my daughter of this matter?" he asked. "You would not bring a princess of my house to testify thus publicly?"

"No," replied Lu-don, "not in person, but I have here one who will testify for her." He beckoned to an under priest. "Fetch the slave of the princess," he said.

His grotesque headdress adding a touch of the hideous to the scene, the priest stepped forward dragging the reluctant Pan-at-lee by the wrist.

"The Princess O-lo-a was alone in the Forbidden Garden with but this one slave," explained the priest, "when there suddenly appeared from the foliage nearby this creature who claims to be the Dor-ul-Otho. When the slave saw him the princess says that she cried aloud in startled recognition and called the creature by name—Tarzan-jad-guru—the same name that the slave from Kor-ul-lul gave him. This woman is not from Kor-ul-lul but from Kor-ul-ja, the very tribe with which the Kor-ul-lul says the creature was associating when he first saw him. And further the princess said that when this woman, whose name is Pan-at-lee, was brought to her yesterday she told a strange story of having been rescued from a Tor-o-don in the Kor-ul-gryf by a creature such as this, whom she spoke of then as Tarzan-jad-guru; and of how the two were pursued in the bottom of the gorge by two monster gryfs, and of how the man led them away while Pan-at-lee escaped, only to be taken prisoner in the Kor-ul-lul as she was seeking to return to her own tribe."

"Is it not plain now," cried Lu-don, "that this creature is no god. Did he tell you that he was the son of god?" he almost shouted, turning suddenly upon Pan-at-lee.

The girl shrank back terrified. "Answer me, slave!" cried the high priest.

"He seemed more than mortal," parried Pan-at-lee.

"Did he tell you that he was the son of god? Answer my question," insisted Lu-don.

"No," she admitted in a low voice, casting an appealing look of forgiveness at Tarzan who returned a smile of encouragement and friendship.

"That is no proof that he is not the son of god," cried Ja-don. "Dost think Jad-ben-Otho goes about crying 'I am god! I am god!' Hast ever heard him Lu-don? No, you have not. Why should his son do that which the father does not do?"

"Enough," cried Lu-don. "The evidence is clear. The creature is an impostor and I, the head priest of Jad-ben-Otho in the city of A-lur, do condemn him to die." There was a moment's silence during which Lu-don evidently paused for the dramatic effect of his climax. "And if I am wrong may Jad-ben-Otho pierce my heart with his lightnings as I stand here before you all."

The lapping of the wavelets of the lake against the foot of the palace wall was distinctly audible in the utter and almost breathless silence which ensued. Lu-don stood with his face turned toward the heavens and his arms outstretched in the attitude of one who bares his breast to the dagger of an executioner. The warriors and the priests and the slaves gathered in the sacred court awaited the consuming vengeance of their god.

It was Tarzan who broke the silence. "Your god ignores you Lu-don," he taunted, with a sneer that he meant to still further anger the high priest, "he ignores you and I can prove it before the eyes of your priests and your people."

"Prove it, blasphemer! How can you prove it?"

"You have called me a blasphemer," replied Tarzan, "you have proved to your own satisfaction that I am an impostor, that I, an ordinary mortal, have posed as the son of god. Demand then that Jad-ben-Otho uphold his godship and the dignity of his priesthood by directing his consuming fires through my own bosom."

Again there ensued a brief silence while the onlookers waited for Lu-don to thus consummate the destruction of this presumptuous impostor.

"You dare not," taunted Tarzan, "for you know that I would be struck dead no quicker than were you."

"You lie," cried Lu-don, "and I would do it had I not but just received a message from Jad-ben-Otho directing that your fate be different."

A chorus of admiring and reverential "Ahs" arose from the priesthood. Ko-tan and his warriors were in a state of mental confusion. Secretly they hated and feared Lu-don, but so ingrained was their sense of reverence for the office of the high priest that none dared raise a voice against him.

None? Well, there was Ja-don, fearless old Lion-man of the north. "The proposition was a fair one," he cried. "Invoke the lightnings of Jad-ben-Otho upon this man if you would ever convince us of his guilt."

"Enough of this," snapped Lu-don. "Since when was Ja-don created high priest? Seize the prisoner," he cried to the priests and warriors, "and on the morrow he shall die in the manner that Jad-ben-Otho has willed."

There was no immediate movement on the part of any of the warriors to obey the high priest's command, but the lesser priests on the other hand, imbued with the courage of fanaticism leaped eagerly forward like a flock of hideous harpies to seize upon their prey.

The game was up. That Tarzan knew. No longer could cunning and diplomacy usurp the functions of the weapons of defense he best loved. And so the first hideous priest who leaped to the platform was confronted by no suave ambassador from heaven, but rather a grim and ferocious beast whose temper savored more of hell.

The altar stood close to the western wall of the enclosure. There was just room between the two for the high priest to stand during the performance of the sacrificial ceremonies and only Lu-don stood there now behind Tarzan, while before him were perhaps two hundred warriors and priests.

The presumptuous one who would have had the glory of first laying arresting hands upon the blasphemous impersonator rushed forward with outstretched hand to seize the ape-man. Instead it was he who was seized; seized by steel fingers that snapped him up as though he had been a dummy of straw, grasped him by one leg and the harness at his back and raised him with giant arms high above the altar. Close at his heels were others ready to seize the ape-man and drag him down, and beyond the altar was Lu-don with drawn knife advancing toward him.

There was no instant to waste, nor was it the way of the ape-man to fritter away precious moments in the uncertainty of belated decision. Before Lu-don or any other could guess what was in the mind of the condemned, Tarzan with all the force of his great muscles dashed the screaming hierophant in the face of the high priest, and, as though the two actions were one, so quickly did he move, he had leaped to the top of the altar and from there to a handhold upon the summit of the temple wall. As he gained a footing there he turned and looked down upon those beneath. For a moment he stood in silence and then he spoke.

"Who dare believe," he cried, "that Jad-ben-Otho would forsake his son?" and then he dropped from their sight upon the other side.

There were two at least left within the enclosure whose hearts leaped with involuntary elation at the success of the ape-man's maneuver, and one of them smiled openly. This was Ja-don, and the other, Pan-at-lee.

The brains of the priest that Tarzan had thrown at the head of Lu-don had been dashed out against the temple wall while the high priest himself had escaped with only a few bruises, sustained in his fall to the hard pavement. Quickly scrambling to his feet he looked around in fear, in terror and finally in bewilderment, for he had not been a witness to the ape-man's escape. "Seize him," he cried; "seize the blasphemer," and he continued to look around in search of his victim with such a ridiculous expression of bewilderment that more than a single warrior was compelled to hide his smiles beneath his palm.

The priests were rushing around wildly, exhorting the warriors to pursue the fugitive but these awaited now stolidly the command of their king or high priest. Ko-tan, more or less secretly pleased by the discomfiture of Lu-don, waited for that worthy to give the necessary directions which he presently did when one of his acolytes excitedly explained to him the manner of Tarzan's escape.

Instantly the necessary orders were issued and priests and warriors sought the temple exit in pursuit of the ape-man. His departing words, hurled at them from the summit of the temple wall, had had little effect in impressing the majority that his claims had not been disproven by Lu-don, but in the hearts of the warriors was admiration for a brave man and in many the same unholy gratification that had risen in that of their ruler at the discomfiture of Lu-don.

A careful search of the temple grounds revealed no trace of the quarry. The secret recesses of the subterranean chambers, familiar only to the priesthood, were examined by these while the warriors scattered through the palace and the palace grounds without the temple. Swift runners were dispatched to the city to arouse the people there that all might be upon the lookout for Tarzan the Terrible. The story of his imposture and of his escape, and the tales that the Waz-don slaves had brought into the city concerning him were soon spread throughout A-lur, nor did they lose aught in the spreading, so that before an hour had passed the women and children were hiding behind barred doorways while the warriors crept apprehensively through the streets expecting momentarily to be pounced upon by a ferocious demon who, bare-handed, did victorious battle with huge gryfs and whose lightest pastime consisted in tearing strong men limb from limb.

THE GIANT STRANGER

And while the warriors and the priests of A-lur searched the temple and the palace and the city for the vanished ape-man there entered the head of Kor-ul-ja down the precipitous trail from the mountains, a naked stranger bearing an Enfield upon his back. Silently he moved downward toward the bottom of the gorge and there where the ancient trail unfolded more levelly before him he swung along with easy strides, though always with the utmost alertness against possible dangers. A gentle breeze came down from the mountains behind him so that only his ears and his eyes were of value in detecting the presence of danger ahead. Generally the trail followed along the banks of the winding brooklet at the bottom of the gorge, but in some places where the waters tumbled over a precipitous ledge the trail made a detour along the side of the gorge, and again it wound in and out among rocky outcroppings, and presently where it rounded sharply the projecting shoulder of a cliff the stranger came suddenly face to face with one who was ascending the gorge.

Separated by a hundred paces the two halted simultaneously. Before him the stranger saw a tall white warrior, naked but for a loin cloth, cross belts, and a girdle. The man was armed with a heavy, knotted club and a short knife, the latter hanging in its sheath at his left hip from the end of one of his cross belts, the opposite belt supporting a leathern pouch at his right side. It was Ta-den hunting alone in the gorge of his friend, the chief of Kor-ul-ja. He contemplated the stranger with surprise but no wonder, since he recognized in him a member of the race with which his experience of Tarzan the Terrible had made him familiar and also, thanks to his friendship for the ape-man, he looked upon the newcomer without hostility.

The latter was the first to make outward sign of his intentions, raising his palm toward Ta-den in that gesture which has been a symbol of peace from pole to pole since man ceased to walk upon his knuckles. Simultaneously he advanced a few paces and halted.

Ta-den, assuming that one so like Tarzan the Terrible must be a fellow-tribesman of his lost friend, was more than glad to accept this overture of peace, the sign of which he returned in kind as he ascended the trail to where the other stood. "Who are you?" he asked, but the newcomer only shook his head to indicate that he did not understand.

By signs he tried to carry to the Ho-don the fact that he was following a trail that had led him over a period of many days from some place beyond the mountains and Ta-den was convinced that the newcomer sought Tarzan-jad-guru. He wished, however, that he might discover whether as friend or foe.

The stranger perceived the Ho-don's prehensile thumbs and great toes and his long tail with an astonishment which he sought to conceal, but greater than all was the sense of relief that the first inhabitant of this strange country whom he had met had proven friendly, so greatly would he have been handicapped by the necessity for forcing his way through a hostile land.

Ta-den, who had been hunting for some of the smaller mammals, the meat of which is especially relished by the Ho-don, forgot his intended sport in the greater interest of his new discovery. He would take the stranger to Om-at and possibly together the two would find some way of discovering the true intentions of the newcomer. And so again through signs he apprised the other that he would accompany him and together they descended toward the cliffs of Om-at's people.

As they approached these they came upon the women and children working under guard of the old men and the youths—gathering the wild fruits and herbs which constitute a part of their diet, as well as tending the small acres of growing crops which they cultivate. The fields lay in small level patches that had been cleared of trees and brush. Their farm implements consisted of metal-shod poles which bore a closer resemblance to spears than to tools of peaceful agriculture. Supplementing these were others with flattened blades that were neither hoes nor spades, but instead possessed the appearance of an unhappy attempt to combine the two implements in one.

At first sight of these people the stranger halted and unslung his bow for these creatures were black as night, their bodies entirely covered with hair. But Ta-den, interpreting the doubt in the other's mind, reassured him with a gesture and a smile. The Waz-don, however, gathered around excitedly jabbering questions in a language which the stranger discovered his guide understood though it was entirely unintelligible to the former. They made no attempt to molest him and he was now sure that he had fallen among a peaceful and friendly people.

It was but a short distance now to the caves and when they reached these Ta-den led the way aloft upon the wooden pegs, assured that this creature whom he had discovered would have no more difficulty in following him than had Tarzan the Terrible. Nor was he mistaken for the other mounted with ease until presently the two stood within the recess before the cave of Om-at, the chief.

The latter was not there and it was mid-afternoon before he returned, but in the meantime many warriors came to look upon the visitor and in each instance the latter was more thoroughly impressed with the friendly and peaceable spirit of his hosts, little guessing that he was being entertained by a ferocious and warlike tribe who never before the coming of Ta-den and Tarzan had suffered a stranger among them.

At last Om-at returned and the guest sensed intuitively that he was in the presence of a great man among these people, possibly a chief or king, for not only did the attitude of the other black warriors indicate this but it was written also in the mien and bearing of the splendid creature who stood looking at him while

Ta-den explained the circumstances of their meeting. "And I believe, Om-at," concluded the Ho-don, "that he seeks Tarzan the Terrible."

At the sound of that name, the first intelligible word that had fallen upon the ears of the stranger since he had come among them, his face lightened. "Tarzan!" he cried, "Tarzan of the Apes!" and by signs he tried to tell them that it was he whom he sought.

They understood, and also they guessed from the expression of his face that he sought Tarzan from motives of affection rather than the reverse, but of this Om-at wished to make sure. He pointed to the stranger's knife, and repeating Tarzan's name, seized Ta-den and pretended to stab him, immediately turning questioningly toward the stranger.

The latter shook his head vehemently and then first placing a hand above his heart he raised his palm in the symbol of peace.

"He is a friend of Tarzan-jad-guru," exclaimed Ta-den.

"Either a friend or a great liar," replied Om-at.

"Tarzan," continued the stranger, "you know him? He lives? O God, if I could only speak your language." And again reverting to sign language he sought to ascertain where Tarzan was. He would pronounce the name and point in different directions, in the cave, down into the gorge, back toward the mountains, or out upon the valley below, and each time he would raise his brows questioningly and voice the universal "eh?" of interrogation which they could not fail to understand. But always Om-at shook his head and spread his palms in a gesture which indicated that while he understood the question he was ignorant as to the whereabouts of the ape-man, and then the black chief attempted as best he might to explain to the stranger what he knew of the whereabouts of Tarzan.

He called the newcomer Jar-don, which in the language of Pal-ul-don means "stranger," and he pointed to the sun and said as. This he repeated several times and then he held up one hand with the fingers outspread and touching them one by one, including the thumb, repeated the word adenen until the stranger understood that he meant five. Again he pointed to the sun and describing an arc with his forefinger starting at the eastern horizon and terminating at the western, he repeated again the words as adenen. It was plain to the stranger that the words meant that the sun had crossed the heavens five times. In other words, five days had passed. Om-at then pointed to the cave where they stood, pronouncing Tarzan's name and imitating a walking man with the first and second fingers of his right hand upon the floor of the recess, sought to show that Tarzan had walked out of the cave and climbed upward on the pegs five days before, but this was as far as the sign language would permit him to go.

This far the stranger followed him and, indicating that he understood he pointed to himself and then indicating the pegs leading above announced that he would follow Tarzan.

"Let us go with him," said Om-at, "for as yet we have not punished the Kor-ul-lul for killing our friend and ally."

"Persuade him to wait until morning," said Ta-den, "that you may take with you many warriors and make a great raid upon the Kor-ul-lul, and this time, Om-at, do not kill your prisoners. Take as many as you can alive and from some of them we may learn the fate of Tarzan-jad-guru."

"Great is the wisdom of the Ho-don," replied Om-at. "It shall be as you say, and having made prisoners of all the Kor-ul-lul we shall make them tell us what we wish to know. And then we shall march them to the rim of Kor-ul-gryf and push them over the edge of the cliff."

Ta-den smiled. He knew that they would not take prisoner all the Kor-ul-lul warriors—that they would be fortunate if they took one and it was also possible that they might even be driven back in defeat, but he knew too that Om-at would not hesitate to carry out his threat if he had the opportunity, so implacable was the hatred of these neighbors for each other.

It was not difficult to explain Om-at's plan to the stranger or to win his consent since he was aware, when the great black had made it plain that they would be accompanied by many warriors, that their venture would probably lead them into a hostile country and every safeguard that he could employ he was glad to avail himself of, since the furtherance of his quest was the paramount issue.

He slept that night upon a pile of furs in one of the compartments of Om-at's ancestral cave, and early the next day following the morning meal they sallied forth, a hundred savage warriors swarming up the face of the sheer cliff and out upon the summit of the ridge, the main body preceded by two warriors whose duties coincided with those of the point of modern military maneuvers, safeguarding the column against the danger of too sudden contact with the enemy.

Across the ridge they went and down into the Kor-ul-lul and there almost immediately they came upon a lone and unarmed Waz-don who was making his way fearfully up the gorge toward the village of his tribe. Him they took prisoner which, strangely, only added to his terror since from the moment that he had seen them and realized that escape was impossible, he had expected to be slain immediately.

"Take him back to Kor-ul-ja," said Om-at, to one of his warriors, "and hold him there unharmed until I return."

And so the puzzled Kor-ul-lul was led away while the savage company moved stealthily from tree to tree in its closer advance upon the village. Fortune smiled upon Om-at in that it gave him quickly what he sought—a battle royal, for they had not yet come in sight of the caves of the Kor-ul-lul when they encountered a considerable band of warriors headed down the gorge upon some expedition.

Like shadows the Kor-ul-ja melted into the concealment of the foliage upon either side of the trail. Ignorant of impending danger, safe in the knowledge that they trod their own domain where each rock and stone was as familiar as the features of their mates, the Kor-ul-lul walked innocently into the ambush. Suddenly the quiet of that seeming peace was shattered by a savage cry and a hurled club felled a Kor-ul-lul.

The cry was a signal for a savage chorus from a hundred Kor-ul-ja throats with which were soon mingled the war cries of their enemies. The air was filled with flying clubs and then as the two forces mingled, the battle resolved itself into a number of individual encounters as each warrior singled out a foe and closed upon him. Knives gleamed and flashed in the mottling sunlight that filtered through the foliage of the trees above. Sleek black coats were streaked with crimson stains.

In the thick of the fight the smooth brown skin of the stranger mingled with the black bodies of friend and foe. Only his keen eyes and his quick wit had shown him how to differentiate between Kor-ul-lul and Kor-ul-ja since with the single exception of apparel they were identical, but at the first rush of the enemy he had noticed that their loin cloths were not of the leopard-matted hides such as were worn by his allies.

Om-at, after dispatching his first antagonist, glanced at Jar-don. "He fights with the ferocity of jato," mused the chief. "Powerful indeed must be the tribe from which he and Tarzan-jad-guru come," and then his whole attention was occupied by a new assailant.

The fighters surged to and fro through the forest until those who survived were spent with exhaustion. All but the stranger who seemed not to know the sense of fatigue. He fought on when each new antagonist would have gladly quit, and when there were no more Kor-ul-lul who were not engaged, he leaped upon those who stood pantingly facing the exhausted Kor-ul-ja.

And always he carried upon his back the peculiar thing which Om-at had thought was some manner of strange weapon but the purpose of which he could not now account for in view of the fact that Jar-don never used it, and that for the most part it seemed but a nuisance and needless encumbrance since it banged and smashed against its owner as he leaped, catlike, hither and thither in the course of his victorious duels. The bow and arrows he had tossed aside at the beginning of the fight but the Enfield he would not discard, for where he went he meant that it should go until its mission had been fulfilled.

Presently the Kor-ul-ja, seemingly shamed by the example of Jar-don closed once more with the enemy, but the latter, moved no doubt to terror by the presence of the stranger, a tireless demon who appeared invulnerable to their attacks, lost heart and sought to flee. And then it was that at Om-at's command his warriors surrounded a half-dozen of the most exhausted and made them prisoners.

It was a tired, bloody, and elated company that returned victorious to the Kor-ul-ja. Twenty of their number were carried back and six of these were dead men. It was the most glorious and successful raid that the Kor-ul-ja had made upon the Kor-ul-lul in the memory of man, and it marked Om-at as the greatest of chiefs, but that fierce warrior knew that advantage had lain upon his side largely because of the presence of his strange ally. Nor did he hesitate to give credit where credit belonged, with the result that Jar-don and his exploits were upon the tongue of every member of the tribe of Kor-ul-ja and great was the fame of the race that could produce two such as he and Tarzan-jad-guru.

And in the gorge of Kor-ul-lul beyond the ridge the survivors spoke in bated breath of this second demon that had joined forces with their ancient enemy.

Returned to his cave Om-at caused the Kor-ul-lul prisoners to be brought into his presence singly, and each he questioned as to the fate of Tarzan. Without exception they told him the same story—that Tarzan had been taken prisoner by them five days before but that he had slain the warrior left to guard him and escaped, carrying the head of the unfortunate sentry to the opposite side of Kor-ul-lul where he had left it suspended by its hair from the branch of a tree. But what had become of him after, they did not know; not one of them, until the last prisoner was examined, he whom they had taken first—the unarmed Kor-ul-lul making his way from the direction of the Valley of Jad-ben-Otho toward the caves of his people.

This one, when he discovered the purpose of their questioning, bartered with them for the lives and liberty of himself and his fellows. "I can tell you much of this terrible man of whom you ask, Kor-ul-ja," he said. "I saw him yesterday and I know where he is, and if you will promise to let me and my fellows return in safety to the caves of our ancestors I will tell you all, and truthfully, that which I know."

"You will tell us anyway," replied Om-at, "or we shall kill you."

"You will kill me anyway," retorted the prisoner, "unless you make me this promise; so if I am to be killed the thing I know shall go with me."

"He is right, Om-at," said Ta-den, "promise him that they shall have their liberty."

"Very well," said Om-at. "Speak Kor-ul-lul, and when you have told me all, you and your fellows may return unharmed to your tribe."

"It was thus," commenced the prisoner. "Three days since I was hunting with a party of my fellows near the mouth of Kor-ul-lul not far from where you captured me this morning, when we were surprised and set upon by a large number of Ho-don who took us prisoners and carried us to A-lur where a few were chosen to be slaves and the rest were cast into a chamber beneath the temple where are held for sacrifice the victims that are offered by the Ho-don to Jad-ben-Otho upon the sacrificial altars of the temple at A-lur.

"It seemed then that indeed was my fate sealed and that lucky were those who had been selected for slaves among the Ho-don, for they at least might hope to escape—those in the chamber with me must be without hope.

"But yesterday a strange thing happened. There came to the temple, accompanied by all the priests and by the king and many of his warriors, one whom all did great reverence, and when he came to the barred gateway leading to the chamber in which we wretched ones awaited our fate, I saw to my surprise that it was none other than that terrible man who had so recently been a prisoner in the village of Kor-ul-lul—he whom you call Tarzan-jad-guru but whom they addressed as Dor-ul-Otho. And he looked upon us and questioned the high priest and when he was told of the purpose for which we were imprisoned there he grew angry and cried that it was not the will of Jad-ben-Otho that his people be thus sacrificed, and he commanded the high priest to liberate us, and this was done.

"The Ho-don prisoners were permitted to return to their homes and we were led beyond the City of A-lur and set upon our way toward Kor-ul-lul. There were three of us, but many are the dangers that lie between A-lur and Kor-ul-lul and we were only three and unarmed. Therefore none of us reached the village of our people and only one of us lives. I have spoken."

"That is all you know concerning Tarzan-jad-guru?" asked Om-at.

"That is all I know," replied the prisoner, "other than that he whom they call Lu-don, the high priest at A-lur, was very angry, and that one of the two priests who guided us out of the city said to the other that the stranger was not Dor-ul-Otho at all; that Lu-don had said so and that he had also said that he would expose him and that he should be punished with death for his presumption. That is all they said within my hearing.

"And now, chief of Kor-ul-ja, let us depart."

Om-at nodded. "Go your way," he said, "and Ab-on, send warriors to guard them until they are safely within the Kor-ul-lul.

"Jar-don," he said beckoning to the stranger, "come with me," and rising he led the way toward the summit of the cliff, and when they stood upon the ridge Om-at pointed down into the valley toward the City of A-lur gleaming in the light of the western sun.

"There is Tarzan-jad-guru," he said, and Jar-don understood.

THE MASQUERADER

As Tarzan dropped to the ground beyond the temple wall there was in his mind no intention to escape from the City of A-lur until he had satisfied himself that his mate was not a prisoner there, but how, in this strange city in which every man's hand must be now against him, he was to live and prosecute his search was far from clear to him.

There was only one place of which he knew that he might find even temporary sanctuary and that was the Forbidden Garden of the king. There was thick shrubbery in which a man might hide, and water and fruits. A cunning jungle creature, if he could reach the spot unsuspected, might remain concealed there for a considerable time, but how he was to traverse the distance between the temple grounds and the garden unseen was a question the seriousness of which he fully appreciated.

"Mighty is Tarzan," he soliloquized, "in his native jungle, but in the cities of man he is little better than they."

Depending upon his keen observation and sense of location he felt safe in assuming that he could reach the palace grounds by means of the subterranean corridors and chambers of the temple through which he had been conducted the day before, nor any slightest detail of which had escaped his keen eyes. That would be better, he reasoned, than crossing the open grounds above where his pursuers would naturally immediately follow him from the temple and quickly discover him.

And so a dozen paces from the temple wall he disappeared from sight of any chance observer above, down one of the stone stairways that led to the apartments beneath. The way that he had been conducted the previous day had followed the windings and turnings of numerous corridors and apartments, but Tarzan, sure of himself in such matters, retraced the route accurately without hesitation.

He had little fear of immediate apprehension here since he believed that all the priests of the temple had assembled in the court above to witness his trial and his humiliation and his death, and with this idea firmly implanted in his mind he rounded the turn of the corridor and came face to face with an under priest, his grotesque headdress concealing whatever emotion the sight of Tarzan may have aroused.

However, Tarzan had one advantage over the masked votary of Jad-ben-Otho in that the moment he saw the priest he knew his intention concerning him, and therefore was not compelled to delay action. And so it was that before the priest could determine on any suitable line of conduct in the premises a long, keen knife had been slipped into his heart.

As the body lunged toward the floor Tarzan caught it and snatched the headdress from its shoulders, for the first sight of the creature had suggested to his ever-alert mind a bold scheme for deceiving his enemies.

The headdress saved from such possible damage as it must have sustained had it fallen to the floor with the body of its owner, Tarzan relinquished his hold upon the corpse, set the headdress carefully upon the floor and stooping down severed the tail of the Ho-don close to its root. Near by at his right was a small chamber from which the priest had evidently just emerged and into this Tarzan dragged the corpse, the headdress, and the tail.

Quickly cutting a thin strip of hide from the loin cloth of the priest, Tarzan tied it securely about the upper end of the severed member and then tucking the tail under his loin cloth behind him, secured it in place as best he could. Then he fitted the headdress over his shoulders and stepped from the apartment, to all appearances a priest of the temple of Jad-ben-Otho unless one examined too closely his thumbs and his great toes.

He had noticed that among both the Ho-don and the Waz-don it was not at all unusual that the end of the tail be carried in one hand, and so he caught his own tail up thus lest the lifeless appearance of it dragging along behind him should arouse suspicion.

Passing along the corridor and through the various chambers he emerged at last into the palace grounds beyond the temple. The pursuit had not yet reached this point though he was conscious of a commotion not far behind him. He met now both warriors and slaves but none gave him more than a passing glance, a priest being too common a sight about the palace.

And so, passing the guards unchallenged, he came at last to the inner entrance to the Forbidden Garden and there he paused and scanned quickly that portion of the beautiful spot that lay before his eyes. To his relief it seemed unoccupied and congratulating himself upon the ease with which he had so far outwitted the high powers of A-lur he moved rapidly to the opposite end of the enclosure. Here he found a patch of flowering shrubbery that might safely have concealed a dozen men.

Crawling well within he removed the uncomfortable headdress and sat down to await whatever eventualities fate might have in store for him the while he formulated plans for the future. The one night that he had spent in A-lur had kept him up to a late hour, apprising him of the fact that while there were few abroad in the temple grounds at night, there were yet enough to make it possible for him to fare forth under cover of his disguise without attracting the unpleasant attention of the guards, and, too, he had noticed that the priesthood constituted a privileged class that seemed to come and go at will and unchallenged throughout the palace as well as the temple. Altogether then, he decided, night furnished the most propitious hours for his investigation—by day he could lie up in the shrubbery of the Forbidden Garden, reasonably free from detection. From beyond the garden he heard the voices of men calling to one another both far and near, and he guessed that diligent was the search that was being prosecuted for him.

The idle moments afforded him an opportunity to evolve a more satisfactory scheme for attaching his stolen caudal appendage. He arranged it in such a way that it might be quickly assumed or discarded, and this done he fell to examining the weird mask that had so effectively hidden his features.

The thing had been very cunningly wrought from a single block of wood, very probably a section of a tree, upon which the features had been carved and afterward the interior hollowed out until only a comparatively thin shell remained. Two-semicircular notches had been rounded out from opposite sides of the lower edge. These fitted snugly over his shoulders, aprons of wood extending downward a few inches upon his chest and back. From these aprons hung long tassels or switches of hair tapering from the outer edges toward the center which reached below the bottom of his torso. It required but the most cursory examination to indicate to the ape-man that these ornaments consisted of human scalps, taken, doubtless, from the heads of the sacrifices upon the eastern altars. The headdress itself had been carved to depict in formal design a hideous face that suggested both man and gryf. There were the three white horns, the yellow face with the blue bands encircling the eyes and the red hood which took the form of the posterior and anterior aprons.

As Tarzan sat within the concealing foliage of the shrubbery meditating upon the hideous priest-mask which he held in his hands he became aware that he was not alone in the garden. He sensed another presence and presently his trained ears detected the slow approach of naked feet across the sward. At first he suspected that it might be one stealthily searching the Forbidden Garden for him but a little later the figure came within the limited area of his vision which was circumscribed by stems and foliage and flowers.

He saw then that it was the princess O-lo-a and that she was alone and walking with bowed head as though in meditation—sorrowful meditation for there were traces of tears upon her lids.

Shortly after his ears warned him that others had entered the garden—men they were and their footsteps proclaimed that they walked neither slowly nor meditatively. They came directly toward the princess and when Tarzan could see them he discovered that both were priests.

"O-lo-a, Princess of Pal-ul-don," said one, addressing her, "the stranger who told us that he was the son of Jad-ben-Otho has but just fled from the wrath of Lu-don, the high priest, who exposed him and all his wicked blasphemy. The temple, and the palace, and the city are being searched and we have been sent to search the Forbidden Garden, since Ko-tan, the king, said that only this morning he found him here, though how he passed the guards he could not guess."

"He is not here," said O-lo-a. "I have been in the garden for some time and have seen nor heard no other than myself. However, search it if you will."

"No," said the priest who had before spoken, "it is not necessary since he could not have entered without your knowledge and the connivance of the guards, and even had he, the priest who preceded us must have seen him."

"What priest?" asked O-lo-a.

"One passed the guards shortly before us," explained the man.

"I did not see him," said O-lo-a.

"Doubtless he left by another exit," remarked the second priest.

"Yes, doubtless," acquiesced O-lo-a, "but it is strange that I did not see him." The two priests made their obeisance and turned to depart.

"Stupid as Buto, the rhinoceros," soliloquized Tarzan, who considered Buto a very stupid creature indeed. "It should be easy to outwit such as these."

The priests had scarce departed when there came the sound of feet running rapidly across the garden in the direction of the princess to an accompaniment of rapid breathing as of one almost spent, either from fatigue or excitement.

"Pan-at-lee," exclaimed O-lo-a, "what has happened? You look as terrified as the doe for which you were named!"

"O Princess of Pal-ul-don," cried Pan-at-lee, "they would have killed him in the temple. They would have killed the wondrous stranger who claimed to be the Dor-ul-Otho."

"But he escaped," said O-lo-a. "You were there. Tell me about it."

"The head priest would have had him seized and slain, but when they rushed upon him he hurled one in the face of Lu-don with the same ease that you might cast your breastplates at me, and then he leaped upon the altar and from there to the top of the temple wall and disappeared below. They are searching for him, but, O Princess, I pray that they do not find him."

"And why do you pray that?" asked O-lo-a. "Has not one who has so blasphemed earned death?"

"Ah, but you do not know him," replied Pan-at-lee.

"And you do, then?" retorted O-lo-a quickly. "This morning you betrayed yourself and then attempted to deceive me. The slaves of O-lo-a do not such things with impunity. He is then the same Tarzan-jad-guru of whom you told me? Speak woman and speak only the truth."

Pan-at-lee drew herself up very erect, her little chin held high, for was not she too among her own people already as good as a princess? "Pan-at-lee, the Kor-ul-ja does not lie," she said, "to protect herself."

"Then tell me what you know of this Tarzan-jad-guru," insisted O-lo-a.

"I know that he is a wondrous man and very brave," said Pan-at-lee, "and that he saved me from the Tor-o-don and the gryf as I told you, and that he is indeed the same who came into the garden this morning; and even now I do not know that he is not the son of Jad-ben-Otho for his courage and his strength are more than those of mortal man, as are also his kindness and his honor: for when he might have harmed me he protected me, and when he might have saved himself he thought only of me. And all this he did because of his friendship for Om-at, who is gund of Kor-ul-ja and with whom I should have mated had the Ho-don not captured me."

"He was indeed a wonderful man to look upon," mused O-lo-a, "and he was not as are other men, not alone in the conformation of his hands and feet or the fact that he was tailless, but there was that about him which made him seem different in ways more important than these."

"And," supplemented Pan-at-lee, her savage little heart loyal to the man who had befriended her and hoping to win for him the consideration of the princess even though it might not avail him; "and," she said, "did he not know all about Ta-den and even his whereabouts. Tell me, O Princess, could mortal know such things as these?"

"Perhaps he saw Ta-den," suggested O-lo-a.

"But how would he know that you loved Ta-den," parried Pan-at-lee. "I tell you, my Princess, that if he is not a god he is at least more than Ho-don or Waz-don. He followed me from the cave of Es-sat in Kor-ul-ja across Kor-ul-lul and two wide ridges to the very cave in Kor-ul-gryf where I hid, though many hours had passed since I had come that way and my bare feet left no impress upon the ground. What mortal man could do such things as these? And where in all Pal-ul-don would virgin maid find friend and protector in a strange male other than he?"

"Perhaps Lu-don may be mistaken—perhaps he is a god," said O-lo-a, influenced by her slave's enthusiastic championing of the stranger.

"But whether god or man he is too wonderful to die," cried Pan-at-lee. "Would that I might save him. If he lived he might even find a way to give you your Ta-den, Princess."

"Ah, if he only could," sighed O-lo-a, "but alas it is too late for tomorrow I am to be given to Bu-lot."

"He who came to your quarters yesterday with your father?" asked Pan-at-lee.

"Yes; the one with the awful round face and the big belly," exclaimed the Princess disgustedly. "He is so lazy he will neither hunt nor fight. To eat and to drink is all that Bu-lot is fit for, and he thinks of naught else except these things and his slave women. But come, Pan-at-lee, gather for me some of these beautiful blossoms. I would have them spread around my couch tonight that I may carry away with me in the morning the memory of the fragrance that I love best and which I know that I shall not find in the village of Mo-sar, the father of Bu-lot. I will help you, Pan-at-lee, and we will gather armfuls of them, for I love to gather them, as I love nothing else—they were Ta-den's favorite flowers."

The two approached the flowering shrubbery where Tarzan hid, but as the blooms grew plentifully upon every bush the ape-man guessed there would be no necessity for them to enter the patch far enough to discover him. With little exclamations of pleasure as they found particularly large or perfect blooms the two moved from place to place upon the outskirts of Tarzan's retreat.

"Oh, look, Pan-at-lee," cried O-lo-a presently; "there is the king of them all. Never did I see so wonderful a flower—No! I will get it myself—it is so large and wonderful no other hand shall touch it," and the princess wound in among the bushes toward the point where the great flower bloomed upon a bush above the ape-man's head.

So sudden and unexpected her approach that there was no opportunity to escape and Tarzan sat silently trusting that fate might be kind to him and lead Ko-tan's daughter away before her eyes dropped from the high-growing bloom to him. But as the girl cut the long stem with her knife she looked down straight into the smiling face of Tarzan-jad-guru.

With a stifled scream she drew back and the ape-man rose and faced her.

"Have no fear, Princess," he assured her. "It is the friend of Ta-den who salutes you," raising her fingers to his lips.

Pan-at-lee came now excitedly forward. "O Jad-ben-Otho, it is he!"

"And now that you have found me," queried Tarzan, "will you give me up to Lu-don, the high priest?"

Pan-at-lee threw herself upon her knees at O-lo-a's feet. "Princess! Princess!" she beseeched, "do not discover him to his enemies."

"But Ko-tan, my father," whispered O-lo-a fearfully, "if he knew of my perfidy his rage would be beyond naming. Even though I am a princess Lu-don might demand that I be sacrificed to appease the wrath of Jad-ben-Otho, and between the two of them I should be lost."

"But they need never know," cried Pan-at-lee, "that you have seen him unless you tell them yourself for as Jad-ben-Otho is my witness I will never betray you."

"Oh, tell me, stranger," implored O-lo-a, "are you indeed a god?"

"Jad-ben-Otho is not more so," replied Tarzan truthfully.

"But why do you seek to escape then from the hands of mortals if you are a god?" she asked.

"When gods mingle with mortals," replied Tarzan, "they are no less vulnerable than mortals. Even Jad-ben-Otho, should he appear before you in the flesh, might be slain."

"You have seen Ta-den and spoken with him?" she asked with apparent irrelevancy.

"Yes, I have seen him and spoken with him," replied the ape-man. "For the duration of a moon I was with him constantly."

"And—" she hesitated—"he—" she cast her eyes toward the ground and a flush mantled her cheek—"he still loves me?" and Tarzan knew that she had been won over.

"Yes," he said, "Ta-den speaks only of O-lo-a and he waits and hopes for the day when he can claim her."

"But tomorrow they give me to Bu-lot," she said sadly.

"May it be always tomorrow," replied Tarzan, "for tomorrow never comes."

"Ah, but this unhappiness will come, and for all the tomorrows of my life I must pine in misery for the Ta-den who will never be mine."

"But for Lu-don I might have helped you," said the ape-man. "And who knows that I may not help you yet?"

"Ah, if you only could, Dor-ul-Otho," cried the girl, "and I know that you would if it were possible for Pan-at-lee has told me how brave you are, and at the same time how kind."

"Only Jad-ben-Otho knows what the future may bring," said Tarzan. "And now you two go your way lest someone should discover you and become suspicious."

"We will go," said O-lo-a, "but Pan-at-lee will return with food. I hope that you escape and that Jad-ben-Otho is pleased with what I have done." She turned and walked away and Pan-at-lee followed while the ape-man again resumed his hiding.

At dusk Pan-at-lee came with food and having her alone Tarzan put the question that he had been anxious to put since his conversation earlier in the day with O-lo-a.

"Tell me," he said, "what you know of the rumors of which O-lo-a spoke of the mysterious stranger which is supposed to be hidden in A-lur. Have you too heard of this during the short time that you have been here?"

"Yes," said Pan-at-lee, "I have heard it spoken of among the other slaves. It is something of which all whisper among themselves but of which none dares to speak aloud. They say that there is a strange she hidden in the temple and that Lu-don wants her for a priestess and that Ko-tan wants her for a wife and that neither as yet dares take her for fear of the other."

"Do you know where she is hidden in the temple?" asked Tarzan.

"No," said Pan-at-lee. "How should I know? I do not even know that it is more than a story and I but tell you that which I have heard others say."

"There was only one," asked Tarzan, "whom they spoke of?"

"No, they speak of another who came with her but none seems to know what became of this one."

Tarzan nodded. "Thank you Pan-at-lee," he said. "You may have helped me more than either of us guess."

"I hope that I have helped you," said the girl as she turned back toward the palace.

"And I hope so too," exclaimed Tarzan emphatically.

EDGAR RICE BURROUGHS

THE TEMPLE OF THE GRYF

When night had fallen Tarzan donned the mask and the dead tail of the priest he had slain in the vaults beneath the temple. He judged that it would not do to attempt again to pass the guard, especially so late at night as it would be likely to arouse comment and suspicion, and so he swung into the tree that overhung the garden wall and from its branches dropped to the ground beyond.

Avoiding too grave risk of apprehension the ape-man passed through the grounds to the court of the palace, approaching the temple from the side opposite to that at which he had left it at the time of his escape. He came thus it is true through a portion of the grounds with which he was unfamiliar but he preferred this to the danger of following the beaten track between the palace apartments and those of the temple. Having a definite goal in mind and endowed as he was with an almost miraculous sense of location he moved with great assurance through the shadows of the temple yard.

Taking advantage of the denser shadows close to the walls and of what shrubs and trees there were he came without mishap at last to the ornate building concerning the purpose of which he had asked Lu-don only to be put off with the assertion that it was forgotten—nothing strange in itself but given possible importance by the apparent hesitancy of the priest to discuss its use and the impression the ape-man had gained at the time that Lu-don lied.

And now he stood at last alone before the structure which was three stories in height and detached from all the other temple buildings. It had a single barred entrance which was carved from the living rock in representation of the head of a gryf, whose wide-open mouth constituted the doorway. The head, hood, and front paws of the creature were depicted as though it lay crouching with its lower jaw on the ground between its outspread paws. Small oval windows, which were likewise barred, flanked the doorway.

Seeing that the coast was clear, Tarzan stepped into the darkened entrance where he tried the bars only to discover that they were ingeniously locked in place by some device with which he was unfamiliar and that they also were probably too strong to be broken even if he could have risked the noise which would have resulted. Nothing was visible within the darkened interior and so, momentarily baffled, he sought the windows. Here also the bars refused to yield up their secret, but again Tarzan was not dismayed since he had counted upon nothing different.

If the bars would not yield to his cunning they would yield to his giant strength if there proved no other means of ingress, but first he would assure himself that this latter was the case. Moving entirely around the building he examined it carefully. There were other windows but they were similarly barred. He stopped often to look and listen but he saw no one and the sounds that he heard were too far away to cause him any apprehension.

He glanced above him at the wall of the building. Like so many of the other walls of the city, palace, and temple, it was ornately carved and there were too the peculiar ledges that ran sometimes in a horizontal plane and again were tilted at an angle, giving ofttimes an impression of irregularity and even crookedness to the buildings. It was not a difficult wall to climb, at least not difficult for the ape-man.

But he found the bulky and awkward headdress a considerable handicap and so he laid it aside upon the ground at the foot of the wall. Nimbly he ascended to find the windows of the second floor not only barred but curtained within. He did not delay long at the second floor since he had in mind an idea that he would find the easiest entrance through the roof which he had noticed was roughly dome shaped like the throneroom of Ko-tan. Here there were apertures. He had seen them from the ground, and if the construction of the interior resembled even slightly that of the throneroom, bars would not be necessary upon these apertures, since no one could reach them from the floor of the room.

There was but a single question: would they be large enough to admit the broad shoulders of the ape-man.

He paused again at the third floor, and here, in spite of the hangings, he saw that the interior was lighted and simultaneously there came to his nostrils from within a scent that stripped from him temporarily any remnant of civilization that might have remained and left him a fierce and terrible bull of the jungles of

853

Kerchak. So sudden and complete was the metamorphosis that there almost broke from the savage lips the hideous challenge of his kind, but the cunning brute-mind saved him this blunder.

And now he heard voices within—the voice of Lu-don he could have sworn, demanding. And haughty and disdainful came the answering words though utter hopelessness spoke in the tones of this other voice which brought Tarzan to the pinnacle of frenzy.

The dome with its possible apertures was forgotten. Every consideration of stealth and quiet was cast aside as the ape-man drew back his mighty fist and struck a single terrific blow upon the bars of the small window before him, a blow that sent the bars and the casing that held them clattering to the floor of the apartment within.

Instantly Tarzan dove headforemost through the aperture carrying the hangings of antelope hide with him to the floor below. Leaping to his feet he tore the entangling pelt from about his head only to find himself in utter darkness and in silence. He called aloud a name that had not passed his lips for many weary months. "Jane, Jane," he cried, "where are you?" But there was only silence in reply.

Again and again he called, groping with outstretched hands through the Stygian blackness of the room, his nostrils assailed and his brain tantalized by the delicate effluvia that had first assured him that his mate had been within this very room. And he had heard her dear voice combatting the base demands of the vile priest. Ah, if he had but acted with greater caution! If he had but continued to move with quiet and stealth he might even at this moment be holding her in his arms while the body of Lu-don, beneath his foot, spoke eloquently of vengeance achieved. But there was no time now for idle self-reproaches.

He stumbled blindly forward, groping for he knew not what till suddenly the floor beneath him tilted and he shot downward into a darkness even more utter than that above. He felt his body strike a smooth surface and he realized that he was hurtling downward as through a polished chute while from above there came the mocking tones of a taunting laugh and the voice of Lu-don screamed after him: "Return to thy father, O Dor-ul-Otho!"

The ape-man came to a sudden and painful stop upon a rocky floor. Directly before him was an oval window crossed by many bars, and beyond he saw the moonlight playing on the waters of the blue lake below. Simultaneously he was conscious of a familiar odor in the air of the chamber, which a quick glance revealed in the semidarkness as of considerable proportion.

It was the faint, but unmistakable odor of the gryf, and now Tarzan stood silently listening. At first he detected no sounds other than those of the city that came to him through the window overlooking the lake; but presently, faintly, as though from a distance he heard the shuffling of padded feet along a stone pavement, and as he listened he was aware that the sound approached.

Nearer and nearer it came, and now even the breathing of the beast was audible. Evidently attracted by the noise of his descent into its cavernous retreat it was approaching to investigate. He could not see it but he knew that it was not far distant, and then, deafeningly there reverberated through those gloomy corridors the mad bellow of the gryf.

Aware of the poor eyesight of the beast, and his own eyes now grown accustomed to the darkness of the cavern, the ape-man sought to elude the infuriated charge which he well knew no living creature could withstand. Neither did he dare risk the chance of experimenting upon this strange gryf with the tactics of the Tor-o-don that he had found so efficacious upon that other occasion when his life and liberty had been the stakes for which he cast. In many respects the conditions were dissimilar. Before, in broad daylight, he had been able to approach the gryf under normal conditions in its natural state, and the gryf itself was one that he had seen subjected to the authority of man, or at least of a manlike creature; but here he was confronted by an imprisoned beast in the full swing of a furious charge and he had every reason to suspect that this gryf might never have felt the restraining influence of authority, confined as it was in this gloomy pit to serve likely but the single purpose that Tarzan had already seen so graphically portrayed in his own experience of the past few moments.

To elude the creature, then, upon the possibility of discovering some loophole of escape from his predicament seemed to the ape-man the wisest course to pursue. Too much was at stake to risk an encounter that might be avoided—an encounter the outcome of which there was every reason to apprehend would seal the fate of the mate that he had just found, only to lose again so harrowingly. Yet high as his disappointment and chagrin ran, hopeless as his present estate now appeared, there tingled in the veins of the savage lord a warm glow of thanksgiving and elation. She lived! After all these weary months of hopelessness and fear he had found her. She lived!

To the opposite side of the chamber, silently as the wraith of a disembodied soul, the swift jungle creature moved from the path of the charging Titan that, guided solely in the semi-darkness by its keen ears, bore down upon the spot toward which Tarzan's noisy entrance into its lair had attracted it. Along the further wall the ape-man hurried. Before him now appeared the black opening of the corridor from which the beast had emerged into the larger chamber. Without hesitation Tarzan plunged into it. Even here his eyes, long accustomed to darkness that would have seemed total to you or to me, saw dimly the floor and the walls within a radius of a few feet—enough at least to prevent him plunging into any unguessed abyss, or dashing himself upon solid rock at a sudden turning.

The corridor was both wide and lofty, which indeed it must be to accommodate the colossal proportions of the creature whose habitat it was, and so Tarzan encountered no difficulty in moving with reasonable speed along its winding trail. He was aware as he proceeded that the trend of the passage was downward, though not steeply, but it seemed interminable and he wondered to what distant subterranean lair it might lead. There was a feeling that perhaps after all he might better have remained in the larger chamber and risked all on the chance of subduing the gryf where there was at least sufficient room and light to lend to the experiment some slight chance of success. To be overtaken here in the narrow confines of the black corridor where he was assured the gryf could not see him at all would spell almost certain death and now he heard the thing approaching from behind. Its thunderous bellows fairly shook the cliff from which the cavernous chambers were excavated. To halt and meet this monstrous incarnation of fury with a futile whee-oo! seemed to Tarzan the height of insanity and so he continued along the corridor, increasing his pace as he realized that the gryf was overhauling him.

Presently the darkness lessened and at the final turning of the passage he saw before him an area of moonlight. With renewed hope he sprang rapidly forward and emerged from the mouth of the corridor to find himself in a large circular enclosure the towering white walls of which rose high upon every side—smooth perpendicular walls upon the sheer face of which was no slightest foothold. To his left lay a pool of water, one side of which lapped the foot of the wall at this point. It was, doubtless, the wallow and the drinking pool of the gryf.

And now the creature emerged from the corridor and Tarzan retreated to the edge of the pool to make his last stand. There was no staff with which to enforce the authority of his voice, but yet he made his stand for there seemed naught else to do. Just beyond the entrance to the corridor the gryf paused, turning its weak eyes in all directions as though searching for its prey. This then seemed the psychological moment for his attempt and raising his voice in peremptory command the ape-man voiced the weird whee-oo! of the Tor-o-don. Its effect upon the gryf was instantaneous and complete—with a terrific bellow it lowered its three horns and dashed madly in the direction of the sound.

To right nor to left was any avenue of escape, for behind him lay the placid waters of the pool, while down upon him from before thundered annihilation. The mighty body seemed already to tower above him as the ape-man turned and dove into the dark waters.

Dead in her breast lay hope. Battling for life during harrowing months of imprisonment and danger and hardship it had fitfully flickered and flamed only to sink after each renewal to smaller proportions than before and now it had died out entirely leaving only cold, charred embers that Jane Clayton knew would never again be rekindled. Hope was dead as she faced Lu-don, the high priest, in her prison quarters in the

Temple of the Gryf at A-lur. Both time and hardship had failed to leave their impress upon her physical beauty—the contours of her perfect form, the glory of her radiant loveliness had defied them, yet to these very attributes she owed the danger which now confronted her, for Lu-don desired her. From the lesser priests she had been safe, but from Lu-don, she was not safe, for Lu-don was not as they, since the high priestship of Pal-ul-don may descend from father to son.

Ko-tan, the king, had wanted her and all that had so far saved her from either was the fear of each for the other, but at last Lu-don had cast aside discretion and had come in the silent watches of the night to claim her. Haughtily had she repulsed him, seeking ever to gain time, though what time might bring her of relief or renewed hope she could not even remotely conjecture. A leer of lust and greed shone hungrily upon his cruel countenance as he advanced across the room to seize her. She did not shrink nor cower, but stood there very erect, her chin up, her level gaze freighted with the loathing and contempt she felt for him. He read her expression and while it angered him, it but increased his desire for possession. Here indeed was a queen, perhaps a goddess; fit mate for the high priest.

"You shall not!" she said as he would have touched her. "One of us shall die before ever your purpose is accomplished."

He was close beside her now. His laugh grated upon her ears. "Love does not kill," he replied mockingly.

He reached for her arm and at the same instant something clashed against the bars of one of the windows, crashing them inward to the floor, to be followed almost simultaneously by a human figure which dove headforemost into the room, its head enveloped in the skin window hangings which it carried with it in its impetuous entry.

Jane Clayton saw surprise and something of terror too leap to the countenance of the high priest and then she saw him spring forward and jerk upon a leather thong that depended from the ceiling of the apartment. Instantly there dropped from above a cunningly contrived partition that fell between them and the intruder, effectively barring him from them and at the same time leaving him to grope upon its opposite side in darkness, since the only cresset the room contained was upon their side of the partition.

Faintly from beyond the wall Jane heard a voice calling, but whose it was and what the words she could not distinguish. Then she saw Lu-don jerk upon another thong and wait in evident expectancy of some consequent happening. He did not have long to wait. She saw the thong move suddenly as though jerked from above and then Lu-don smiled and with another signal put in motion whatever machinery it was that raised the partition again to its place in the ceiling.

Advancing into that portion of the room that the partition had shut off from them, the high priest knelt upon the floor, and down tilting a section of it, revealed the dark mouth of a shaft leading below. Laughing loudly he shouted into the hole: "Return to thy father, O Dor-ul-Otho!"

Making fast the catch that prevented the trapdoor from opening beneath the feet of the unwary until such time as Lu-don chose the high priest rose again to his feet.

"Now, Beautiful One!" he cried, and then, "Ja-don! what do you here?"

Jane Clayton turned to follow the direction of Lu-don's eyes and there she saw framed in the entrance-way to the apartment the mighty figure of a warrior, upon whose massive features sat an expression of stern and uncompromising authority.

"I come from Ko-tan, the king," replied Ja-don, "to remove the beautiful stranger to the Forbidden Garden."

"The king defies me, the high priest of Jad-ben-Otho?" cried Lu-don.

"It is the king's command—I have spoken," snapped Ja-don, in whose manner was no sign of either fear or respect for the priest.

Lu-don well knew why the king had chosen this messenger whose heresy was notorious, but whose power had as yet protected him from the machinations of the priest. Lu-don cast a surreptitious glance at the thongs hanging from the ceiling. Why not? If he could but maneuver to entice Ja-don to the opposite side of the chamber!

"Come," he said in a conciliatory tone, "let us discuss the matter," and moved toward the spot where he would have Ja-don follow him.

"There is nothing to discuss," replied Ja-don, yet he followed the priest, fearing treachery.

Jane watched them. In the face and figure of the warrior she found reflected those admirable traits of courage and honor that the profession of arms best develops. In the hypocritical priest there was no redeeming quality. Of the two then she might best choose the warrior. With him there was a chance—with Lu-don, none. Even the very process of exchange from one prison to another might offer some possibility of escape. She weighed all these things and decided, for Lu-don's quick glance at the thongs had not gone unnoticed nor uninterpreted by her.

"Warrior," she said, addressing Ja-don, "if you would live enter not that portion of the room."

Lu-don cast an angry glance upon her. "Silence, slave!" he cried.

"And where lies the danger?" Ja-don asked of Jane, ignoring Lu-don.

The woman pointed to the thongs. "Look," she said, and before the high priest could prevent she had seized that which controlled the partition which shot downward separating Lu-don from the warrior and herself.

Ja-don looked inquiringly at her. "He would have tricked me neatly but for you," he said; "kept me imprisoned there while he secreted you elsewhere in the mazes of his temple."

"He would have done more than that," replied Jane, as she pulled upon the other thong. "This releases the fastenings of a trapdoor in the floor beyond the partition. When you stepped on that you would have been precipitated into a pit beneath the temple. Lu-don has threatened me with this fate often. I do not know that he speaks the truth, but he says that a demon of the temple is imprisoned there—a huge gryf."

"There is a gryf within the temple," said Ja-don. "What with it and the sacrifices, the priests keep us busy supplying them with prisoners, though the victims are sometimes those for whom Lu-don has conceived hatred among our own people. He has had his eyes upon me for a long time. This would have been his chance but for you. Tell me, woman, why you warned me. Are we not all equally your jailers and your enemies?"

"None could be more horrible than Lu-don," she replied; "and you have the appearance of a brave and honorable warrior. I could not hope, for hope has died and yet there is the possibility that among so many fighting men, even though they be of another race than mine, there is one who would accord honorable treatment to a stranger within his gates—even though she be a woman."

Ja-don looked at her for a long minute. "Ko-tan would make you his queen," he said. "That he told me himself and surely that were honorable treatment from one who might make you a slave."

"Why, then, would he make me queen?" she asked.

Ja-don came closer as though in fear his words might be overheard. "He believes, although he did not tell me so in fact, that you are of the race of gods. And why not? Jad-ben-Otho is tailless, therefore it is not strange that Ko-tan should suspect that only the gods are thus. His queen is dead leaving only a single daughter. He craves a son and what more desirable than that he should found a line of rulers for Pal-ul-don descended from the gods?"

"But I am already wed," cried Jane. "I cannot wed another. I do not want him or his throne."

"Ko-tan is king," replied Ja-don simply as though that explained and simplified everything.

"You will not save me then?" she asked.

"If you were in Ja-lur," he replied, "I might protect you, even against the king."

"What and where is Ja-lur?" she asked, grasping at any straw.

"It is the city where I rule," he answered. "I am chief there and of all the valley beyond."

"Where is it?" she insisted, and "is it far?"

"No," he replied, smiling, "it is not far, but do not think of that—you could never reach it. There are too many to pursue and capture you. If you wish to know, however, it lies up the river that empties into Jad-ben-lul whose waters kiss the walls of A-lur—up the western fork it lies with water upon three sides. Impregnable city of Pal-ul-don—alone of all the cities it has never been entered by a foeman since it was built there while Jad-ben-Otho was a boy."

"And there I would be safe?" she asked.

"Perhaps," he replied.

Ah, dead Hope; upon what slender provocation would you seek to glow again! She sighed and shook her head, realizing the inutility of Hope—yet the tempting bait dangled before her mind's eye—Ja-lur!

"You are wise," commented Ja-don interpreting her sigh. "Come now, we will go to the quarters of the princess beside the Forbidden Garden. There you will remain with O-lo-a, the king's daughter. It will be better than this prison you have occupied."

"And Ko-tan?" she asked, a shudder passing through her slender frame.

"There are ceremonies," explained Ja-don, "that may occupy several days before you become queen, and one of them may be difficult of arrangement." He laughed, then.

"What?" she asked.

"Only the high priest may perform the marriage ceremony for a king," he explained.

"Delay!" she murmured; "blessed delay!" Tenacious indeed of life is Hope even though it be reduced to cold and lifeless char—a veritable phoenix.

"THE KING IS DEAD!"

As they conversed Ja-don had led her down the stone stairway that leads from the upper floors of the Temple of the Gryf to the chambers and the corridors that honeycomb the rocky hills from which the temple and the palace are hewn and now they passed from one to the other through a doorway upon one side of which two priests stood guard and upon the other two warriors. The former would have halted Ja-don when they saw who it was that accompanied him for well known throughout the temple was the quarrel between king and high priest for possession of this beautiful stranger.

"Only by order of Lu-don may she pass," said one, placing himself directly in front of Jane Clayton, barring her progress. Through the hollow eyes of the hideous mask the woman could see those of the priest beneath gleaming with the fires of fanaticism. Ja-don placed an arm about her shoulders and laid his hand upon his knife.

"She passes by order of Ko-tan, the king," he said, "and by virtue of the fact that Ja-don, the chief, is her guide. Stand aside!"

The two warriors upon the palace side pressed forward. "We are here, gund of Ja-lur," said one, addressing Ja-don, "to receive and obey your commands."

The second priest now interposed. "Let them pass," he admonished his companion. "We have received no direct commands from Lu-don to the contrary and it is a law of the temple and the palace that chiefs and priests may come and go without interference."

"But I know Lu-don's wishes," insisted the other.

"He told you then that Ja-don must not pass with the stranger?"

"No—but—"

"Then let them pass, for they are three to two and will pass anyway—we have done our best."

Grumbling, the priest stepped aside. "Lu-don will exact an accounting," he cried angrily.

Ja-don turned upon him. "And get it when and where he will," he snapped.

They came at last to the quarters of the Princess O-lo-a where, in the main entrance-way, loitered a small guard of palace warriors and several stalwart black eunuchs belonging to the princess, or her women. To one of the latter Ja-don relinquished his charge.

"Take her to the princess," he commanded, "and see that she does not escape."

Through a number of corridors and apartments lighted by stone cressets the eunuch led Lady Greystoke halting at last before a doorway concealed by hangings of jato skin, where the guide beat with his staff upon the wall beside the door.

"O-lo-a, Princess of Pal-ul-don," he called, "here is the stranger woman, the prisoner from the temple."

"Bid her enter," Jane heard a sweet voice from within command.

The eunuch drew aside the hangings and Lady Greystoke stepped within. Before her was a low-ceiled room of moderate size. In each of the four corners a kneeling figure of stone seemed to be bearing its portion of the weight of the ceiling upon its shoulders. These figures were evidently intended to represent Waz-don slaves and were not without bold artistic beauty. The ceiling itself was slightly arched to a central dome which was pierced to admit light by day, and air. Upon one side of the room were many windows, the other three walls being blank except for a doorway in each. The princess lay upon a pile of furs which were arranged over a low stone dais in one corner of the apartment and was alone except for a single Waz-don slave girl who sat upon the edge of the dais near her feet.

As Jane entered O-lo-a beckoned her to approach and when she stood beside the couch the girl half rose upon an elbow and surveyed her critically.

"How beautiful you are," she said simply.

Jane smiled, sadly; for she had found that beauty may be a curse.

"That is indeed a compliment," she replied quickly, "from one so radiant as the Princess O-lo-a."

"Ah!" exclaimed the princess delightedly; "you speak my language! I was told that you were of another race and from some far land of which we of Pal-ul-don have never heard."

"Lu-don saw to it that the priests instructed me," explained Jane; "but I am from a far country, Princess; one to which I long to return—and I am very unhappy."

"But Ko-tan, my father, would make you his queen," cried the girl; "that should make you very happy."

"But it does not," replied the prisoner; "I love another to whom I am already wed. Ah, Princess, if you had known what it was to love and to be forced into marriage with another you would sympathize with me."

The Princess O-lo-a was silent for a long moment. "I know," she said at last, "and I am very sorry for you; but if the king's daughter cannot save herself from such a fate who may save a slave woman? for such in fact you are."

The drinking in the great banquet hall of the palace of Ko-tan, king of Pal-ul-don had commenced earlier this night than was usual, for the king was celebrating the morrow's betrothal of his only daughter to Bu-lot, son of Mo-sar, the chief, whose great-grandfather had been king of Pal-ul-don and who thought that he should be king, and Mo-sar was drunk and so was Bu-lot, his son. For that matter nearly all of the warriors, including the king himself, were drunk. In the heart of Ko-tan was no love either for Mo-sar, or Bu-lot, nor did either of these love the king. Ko-tan was giving his daughter to Bu-lot in the hope that the alliance would prevent Mo-sar from insisting upon his claims to the throne, for, next to Ja-don, Mo-sar was the most powerful of the chiefs and while Ko-tan looked with fear upon Ja-don, too, he had no fear that the old Lion-man would attempt to seize the throne, though which way he would throw his influence and his warriors in the event that Mo-sar declare war upon Ko-tan, the king could not guess.

Primitive people who are also warlike are seldom inclined toward either tact or diplomacy even when sober; but drunk they know not the words, if aroused. It was really Bu-lot who started it.

"This," he said, "I drink to O-lo-a," and he emptied his tankard at a single gulp. "And this," seizing a full one from a neighbor, "to her son and mine who will bring back the throne of Pal-ul-don to its rightful owners!"

"The king is not yet dead!" cried Ko-tan, rising to his feet; "nor is Bu-lot yet married to his daughter—and there is yet time to save Pal-ul-don from the spawn of the rabbit breed."

The king's angry tone and his insulting reference to Bu-lot's well-known cowardice brought a sudden, sobering silence upon the roistering company. Every eye turned upon Bu-lot and Mo-sar, who sat together directly opposite the king. The first was very drunk though suddenly he seemed quite sober. He was so drunk that for an instant he forgot to be a coward, since his reasoning powers were so effectually paralyzed by the fumes of liquor that he could not intelligently weigh the consequences of his acts. It is reasonably conceivable that a drunk and angry rabbit might commit a rash deed. Upon no other hypothesis is the thing that Bu-lot now did explicable. He rose suddenly from the seat to which he had sunk after delivering his toast and seizing the knife from the sheath of the warrior upon his right hurled it with terrific force at Ko-tan. Skilled in the art of throwing both their knives and their clubs are the warriors of Pal-ul-don and at this short distance and coming as it did without warning there was no defense and but one possible result—Ko-tan, the king, lunged forward across the table, the blade buried in his heart.

A brief silence followed the assassin's cowardly act. White with terror, now, Bu-lot fell slowly back toward the doorway at his rear, when suddenly angry warriors leaped with drawn knives to prevent his escape and to avenge their king. But Mo-sar now took his stand beside his son.

"Ko-tan is dead!" he cried. "Mo-sar is king! Let the loyal warriors of Pal-ul-don protect their ruler!"

Mo-sar commanded a goodly following and these quickly surrounded him and Bu-lot, but there were many knives against them and now Ja-don pressed forward through those who confronted the pretender.

"Take them both!" he shouted. "The warriors of Pal-ul-don will choose their own king after the assassin of Ko-tan has paid the penalty of his treachery."

Directed now by a leader whom they both respected and admired those who had been loyal to Ko-tan rushed forward upon the faction that had surrounded Mo-sar. Fierce and terrible was the fighting, devoid, apparently, of all else than the ferocious lust to kill and while it was at its height Mo-sar and Bu-lot slipped unnoticed from the banquet hall.

To that part of the palace assigned to them during their visit to A-lur they hastened. Here were their servants and the lesser warriors of their party who had not been bidden to the feast of Ko-tan. These were directed quickly to gather together their belongings for immediate departure. When all was ready, and it did not take long, since the warriors of Pal-ul-don require but little impedimenta on the march, they moved toward the palace gate.

Suddenly Mo-sar approached his son. "The princess," he whispered. "We must not leave the city without her—she is half the battle for the throne."

Bu-lot, now entirely sober, demurred. He had had enough of fighting and of risk. "Let us get out of A-lur quickly," he urged, "or we shall have the whole city upon us. She would not come without a struggle and that would delay us too long."

"There is plenty of time," insisted Mo-sar. "They are still fighting in the pal-e-don-so. It will be long before they miss us and, with Ko-tan dead, long before any will think to look to the safety of the princess. Our time is now—it was made for us by Jad-ben-Otho. Come!"

Reluctantly Bu-lot followed his father, who first instructed the warriors to await them just inside the gateway of the palace. Rapidly the two approached the quarters of the princess. Within the entrance-way only a handful of warriors were on guard. The eunuchs had retired.

"There is fighting in the pal-e-don-so," Mo-sar announced in feigned excitement as they entered the presence of the guards. "The king desires you to come at once and has sent us to guard the apartments of the princess. Make haste!" he commanded as the men hesitated.

The warriors knew him and that on the morrow the princess was to be betrothed to Bu-lot, his son. If there was trouble what more natural than that Mo-sar and Bu-lot should be intrusted with the safety of the princess. And then, too, was not Mo-sar a powerful chief to whose orders disobedience might prove a dangerous thing? They were but common fighting men disciplined in the rough school of tribal warfare, but they had learned to obey a superior and so they departed for the banquet hall—the place-where-men-eat.

Barely waiting until they had disappeared Mo-sar crossed to the hangings at the opposite end of the entrance-hall and followed by Bu-lot made his way toward the sleeping apartment of O-lo-a and a moment later, without warning, the two men burst in upon the three occupants of the room. At sight of them O-lo-a sprang to her feet.

"What is the meaning of this?" she demanded angrily.

Mo-sar advanced and halted before her. Into his cunning mind had entered a plan to trick her. If it succeeded it would prove easier than taking her by force, and then his eyes fell upon Jane Clayton and he almost gasped in astonishment and admiration, but he caught himself and returned to the business of the moment.

"O-lo-a," he cried, "when you know the urgency of our mission you will forgive us. We have sad news for you. There has been an uprising in the palace and Ko-tan, the king, has been slain. The rebels are drunk with liquor and now on their way here. We must get you out of A-lur at once—there is not a moment to lose. Come, and quickly!"

"My father dead?" cried O-lo-a, and suddenly her eyes went wide. "Then my place is here with my people," she cried. "If Ko-tan is dead I am queen until the warriors choose a new ruler—that is the law of Pal-ul-don. And if I am queen none can make me wed whom I do not wish to wed—and Jad-ben-Otho knows I never wished to wed thy cowardly son. Go!" She pointed a slim forefinger imperiously toward the doorway.

Mo-sar saw that neither trickery nor persuasion would avail now and every precious minute counted. He looked again at the beautiful woman who stood beside O-lo-a. He had never before seen her but he well knew from palace gossip that she could be no other than the godlike stranger whom Ko-tan had planned to make his queen.

"Bu-lot," he cried to his son, "take you your own woman and I will take—mine!" and with that he sprang suddenly forward and seizing Jane about the waist lifted her in his arms, so that before O-lo-a or Pan-at-lee might even guess his purpose he had disappeared through the hangings near the foot of the dais and was gone with the stranger woman struggling and fighting in his grasp.

And then Bu-lot sought to seize O-lo-a, but O-lo-a had her Pan-at-lee—fierce little tiger-girl of the savage Kor-ul-ja—Pan-at-lee whose name belied her—and Bu-lot found that with the two of them his hands were full. When he would have lifted O-lo-a and borne her away Pan-at-lee seized him around the legs and strove to drag him down. Viciously he kicked her, but she would not desist, and finally, realizing that he might not only lose his princess but be so delayed as to invite capture if he did not rid himself of this clawing, scratching she-jato, he hurled O-lo-a to the floor and seizing Pan-at-lee by the hair drew his knife and—

The curtains behind him suddenly parted. In two swift bounds a lithe figure crossed the room and before ever the knife of Bu-lot reached its goal his wrist was seized from behind and a terrific blow crashing to the base of his brain dropped him, lifeless, to the floor. Bu-lot, coward, traitor, and assassin, died without knowing who struck him down.

As Tarzan of the Apes leaped into the pool in the gryf pit of the temple at A-lur one might have accounted for his act on the hypothesis that it was the last blind urge of self-preservation to delay, even for a moment, the inevitable tragedy in which each some day must play the leading role upon his little stage; but no—those cool, gray eyes had caught the sole possibility for escape that the surroundings and the circumstances offered—a tiny, moonlit patch of water glimmering through a small aperture in the cliff at the surface of the pool upon its farther side. With swift, bold strokes he swam for speed alone knowing that the water would in no way deter his pursuer. Nor did it. Tarzan heard the great splash as the huge creature plunged into the pool behind him; he heard the churning waters as it forged rapidly onward in his wake. He was nearing the opening—would it be large enough to permit the passage of his body? That portion of it which showed above the surface of the water most certainly would not. His life, then, depended upon how much of the aperture was submerged. And now it was directly before him and the gryf directly behind. There was no alternative—there was no other hope. The ape-man threw all the resources of his great strength into the last few strokes, extended his hands before him as a cutwater, submerged to the water's level and shot forward toward the hole.

Frothing with rage was the baffled Lu-don as he realized how neatly the stranger she had turned his own tables upon him. He could of course escape the Temple of the Gryf in which her quick wit had temporarily imprisoned him; but during the delay, however brief, Ja-don would find time to steal her from the temple and deliver her to Ko-tan. But he would have her yet—that the high priest swore in the names of Jad-ben-Otho and all the demons of his faith. He hated Ko-tan. Secretly he had espoused the cause of Mo-sar, in whom he would have a willing tool. Perhaps, then, this would give him the opportunity he had long awaited—a pretext for inciting the revolt that would dethrone Ko-tan and place Mo-sar in power—with Lu-don the real ruler of Pal-ul-don. He licked his thin lips as he sought the window through which Tarzan had entered and now Lu-don's only avenue of escape. Cautiously he made his way across the floor, feeling before him with his hands, and when they discovered that the trap was set for him an ugly snarl broke from the priest's lips. "The she-devil!" he muttered; "but she shall pay, she shall pay—ah, Jad-ben-Otho; how she shall pay for the trick she has played upon Lu-don!"

He crawled through the window and climbed easily downward to the ground. Should he pursue Ja-don and the woman, chancing an encounter with the fierce chief, or bide his time until treachery and intrigue should accomplish his design? He chose the latter solution, as might have been expected of such as he.

Going to his quarters he summoned several of his priests—those who were most in his confidence and who shared his ambitions for absolute power of the temple over the palace—all men who hated Ko-tan.

"The time has come," he told them, "when the authority of the temple must be placed definitely above that of the palace. Ko-tan must make way for Mo-sar, for Ko-tan has defied your high priest. Go then, Pan-sat, and summon Mo-sar secretly to the temple, and you others go to the city and prepare the faithful warriors that they may be in readiness when the time comes."

For another hour they discussed the details of the coup d'etat that was to overthrow the government of Pal-ul-don. One knew a slave who, as the signal sounded from the temple gong, would thrust a knife into the heart of Ko-tan, for the price of liberty. Another held personal knowledge of an officer of the palace that he could use to compel the latter to admit a number of Lu-don's warriors to various parts of the palace. With Mo-sar as the cat's paw, the plan seemed scarce possible of failure and so they separated, going upon their immediate errands to palace and to city.

As Pan-sat entered the palace grounds he was aware of a sudden commotion in the direction of the pal-e-don-so and a few minutes later Lu-don was surprised to see him return to the apartments of the high priest, breathless and excited.

"What now, Pan-sat?" cried Lu-don. "Are you pursued by demons?"

"O master, our time has come and gone while we sat here planning. Ko-tan is already dead and Mo-sar fled. His friends are fighting with the warriors of the palace but they have no head, while Ja-don leads the others. I could learn but little from frightened slaves who had fled at the outburst of the quarrel. One told me that Bu-lot had slain the king and that he had seen Mo-sar and the assassin hurrying from the palace."

"Ja-don," muttered the high priest. "The fools will make him king if we do not act and act quickly. Get into the city, Pan-sat—let your feet fly and raise the cry that Ja-don has killed the king and is seeking to wrest the throne from O-lo-a. Spread the word as you know best how to spread it that Ja-don has threatened to destroy the priests and hurl the altars of the temple into Jad-ben-lul. Rouse the warriors of the city and urge them to attack at once. Lead them into the temple by the secret way that only the priests know and from here we may spew them out upon the palace before they learn the truth. Go, Pan-sat, immediately—delay not an instant."

"But stay," he called as the under priest turned to leave the apartment; "saw or heard you anything of the strange white woman that Ja-don stole from the Temple of the Gryf where we have had her imprisoned?"

"Only that Ja-don took her into the palace where he threatened the priests with violence if they did not permit him to pass," replied Pan-sat. "This they told me, but where within the palace she is hidden I know not."

"Ko-tan ordered her to the Forbidden Garden," said Lu-don, "doubtless we shall find her there. And now, Pan-sat, be upon your errand."

In a corridor by Lu-don's chamber a hideously masked priest leaned close to the curtained aperture that led within. Were he listening he must have heard all that passed between Pan-sat and the high priest, and that he had listened was evidenced by his hasty withdrawal to the shadows of a nearby passage as the lesser priest moved across the chamber toward the doorway. Pan-sat went his way in ignorance of the near presence that he almost brushed against as he hurried toward the secret passage that leads from the temple of Jad-ben-Otho, far beneath the palace, to the city beyond, nor did he sense the silent creature following in his footsteps.

THE SECRET WAY

It was a baffled gryf that bellowed in angry rage as Tarzan's sleek brown body cutting the moonlit waters shot through the aperture in the wall of the gryf pool and out into the lake beyond. The ape-man smiled as he thought of the comparative ease with which he had defeated the purpose of the high priest but his face clouded again at the ensuing remembrance of the grave danger that threatened his mate. His sole object now must be to return as quickly as he might to the chamber where he had last seen her on the third floor of the Temple of the Gryf, but how he was to find his way again into the temple grounds was a question not easy of solution.

In the moonlight he could see the sheer cliff rising from the water for a great distance along the shore—far beyond the precincts of the temple and the palace—towering high above him, a seemingly impregnable barrier against his return. Swimming close in, he skirted the wall searching diligently for some foothold, however slight, upon its smooth, forbidding surface. Above him and quite out of reach were numerous apertures, but there were no means at hand by which he could reach them. Presently, however, his hopes were raised by the sight of an opening level with the surface of the water. It lay just ahead and a few strokes brought him to it—cautious strokes that brought forth no sound from the yielding waters. At the nearer side of the opening he stopped and reconnoitered. There was no one in sight. Carefully he raised his body to the threshold of the entrance-way, his smooth brown hide glistening in the moonlight as it shed the water in tiny sparkling rivulets.

Before him stretched a gloomy corridor, unlighted save for the faint illumination of the diffused moonlight that penetrated it for but a short distance from the opening. Moving as rapidly as reasonable caution warranted, Tarzan followed the corridor into the bowels of the cave. There was an abrupt turn and then a flight of steps at the top of which lay another corridor running parallel with the face of the cliff. This passage was dimly lighted by flickering cressets set in niches in the walls at considerable distances apart. A quick survey showed the ape-man numerous openings upon each side of the corridor and his quick ears caught sounds that indicated that there were other beings not far distant—priests, he concluded, in some of the apartments letting upon the passageway.

To pass undetected through this hive of enemies appeared quite beyond the range of possibility. He must again seek disguise and knowing from experience how best to secure such he crept stealthily along the corridor toward the nearest doorway. Like Numa, the lion, stalking a wary prey he crept with quivering nostrils to the hangings that shut off his view from the interior of the apartment beyond. A moment later his head disappeared within; then his shoulders, and his lithe body, and the hangings dropped quietly into place again. A moment later there filtered to the vacant corridor without a brief, gasping gurgle and again silence. A minute passed; a second, and a third, and then the hangings were thrust aside and a grimly masked priest of the temple of Jad-ben-Otho strode into the passageway.

With bold steps he moved along and was about to turn into a diverging gallery when his attention was aroused by voices coming from a room upon his left. Instantly the figure halted and crossing the corridor stood with an ear close to the skins that concealed the occupants of the room from him, and him from them. Presently he leaped back into the concealing shadows of the diverging gallery and immediately thereafter the hangings by which he had been listening parted and a priest emerged to turn quickly down the main corridor. The eavesdropper waited until the other had gained a little distance and then stepping from his place of concealment followed silently behind.

The way led along the corridor which ran parallel with the face of the cliff for some little distance and then Pan-sat, taking a cresset from one of the wall niches, turned abruptly into a small apartment at his left. The tracker followed cautiously in time to see the rays of the flickering light dimly visible from an aperture in the floor before him. Here he found a series of steps, similar to those used by the Waz-don in scaling the cliff to their caves, leading to a lower level.

First satisfying himself that his guide was continuing upon his way unsuspecting, the other descended after him and continued his stealthy stalking. The passageway was now both narrow and low, giving but bare headroom to a tall man, and it was broken often by flights of steps leading always downward. The steps in each unit seldom numbered more than six and sometimes there was only one or two but in the aggregate the tracker imagined that they had descended between fifty and seventy-five feet from the level of the upper corridor when the passageway terminated in a small apartment at one side of which was a little pile of rubble.

Setting his cresset upon the ground, Pan-sat commenced hurriedly to toss the bits of broken stone aside, presently revealing a small aperture at the base of the wall upon the opposite side of which there appeared to be a further accumulation of rubble. This he also removed until he had a hole of sufficient size to permit the passage of his body, and leaving the cresset still burning upon the floor the priest crawled through the opening he had made and disappeared from the sight of the watcher hiding in the shadows of the narrow passageway behind him.

No sooner, however, was he safely gone than the other followed, finding himself, after passing through the hole, on a little ledge about halfway between the surface of the lake and the top of the cliff above. The ledge inclined steeply upward, ending at the rear of a building which stood upon the edge of the cliff and which the second priest entered just in time to see Pan-sat pass out into the city beyond.

As the latter turned a nearby corner the other emerged from the doorway and quickly surveyed his surroundings. He was satisfied the priest who had led him hither had served his purpose in so far as the tracker was concerned. Above him, and perhaps a hundred yards away, the white walls of the palace gleamed against the northern sky. The time that it had taken him to acquire definite knowledge concerning the secret passageway between the temple and the city he did not count as lost, though he begrudged every instant that kept him from the prosecution of his main objective. It had seemed to him, however, necessary to the success of a bold plan that he had formulated upon overhearing the conversation between Lu-don and Pan-sat as he stood without the hangings of the apartment of the high priest.

Alone against a nation of suspicious and half-savage enemies he could scarce hope for a successful outcome to the one great issue upon which hung the life and happiness of the creature he loved best. For her sake he must win allies and it was for this purpose that he had sacrificed these precious moments, but now he lost no further time in seeking to regain entrance to the palace grounds that he might search out whatever new prison they had found in which to incarcerate his lost love.

He found no difficulty in passing the guards at the entrance to the palace for, as he had guessed, his priestly disguise disarmed all suspicion. As he approached the warriors he kept his hands behind him and trusted to fate that the sickly light of the single torch which stood beside the doorway would not reveal his un-Pal-ul-donian feet. As a matter of fact so accustomed were they to the comings and goings of the priesthood that they paid scant attention to him and he passed on into the palace grounds without even a moment's delay.

His goal now was the Forbidden Garden and this he had little difficulty in reaching though he elected to enter it over the wall rather than to chance arousing any suspicion on the part of the guards at the inner entrance, since he could imagine no reason why a priest should seek entrance there thus late at night.

He found the garden deserted, nor any sign of her he sought. That she had been brought hither he had learned from the conversation he had overheard between Lu-don and Pan-sat, and he was sure that there had been no time or opportunity for the high priest to remove her from the palace grounds. The garden he knew to be devoted exclusively to the uses of the princess and her women and it was only reasonable to assume therefore that if Jane had been brought to the garden it could only have been upon an order from Ko-tan. This being the case the natural assumption would follow that he would find her in some other portion of O-lo-a's quarters.

Just where these lay he could only conjecture, but it seemed reasonable to believe that they must be adjacent to the garden, so once more he scaled the wall and passing around its end directed his steps toward an entrance-way which he judged must lead to that portion of the palace nearest the Forbidden Garden.

To his surprise he found the place unguarded and then there fell upon his ear from an interior apartment the sound of voices raised in anger and excitement. Guided by the sound he quickly traversed several corridors and chambers until he stood before the hangings which separated him from the chamber from which issued the sounds of altercation. Raising the skins slightly he looked within. There were two women battling with a Ho-don warrior. One was the daughter of Ko-tan and the other Pan-at-lee, the Kor-ul-ja.

At the moment that Tarzan lifted the hangings, the warrior threw O-lo-a viciously to the ground and seizing Pan-at-lee by the hair drew his knife and raised it above her head. Casting the encumbering headdress of the dead priest from his shoulders the ape-man leaped across the intervening space and seizing the brute from behind struck him a single terrible blow.

As the man fell forward dead, the two women recognized Tarzan simultaneously. Pan-at-lee fell upon her knees and would have bowed her head upon his feet had he not, with an impatient gesture, commanded her to rise. He had no time to listen to their protestations of gratitude or answer the numerous questions which he knew would soon be flowing from those two feminine tongues.

"Tell me," he cried, "where is the woman of my own race whom Ja-don brought here from the temple?"

"She is but this moment gone," cried O-lo-a. "Mo-sar, the father of this thing here," and she indicated the body of Bu-lot with a scornful finger, "seized her and carried her away."

"Which way?" he cried. "Tell me quickly, in what direction he took her."

"That way," cried Pan-at-lee, pointing to the doorway through which Mo-sar had passed. "They would have taken the princess and the stranger woman to Tu-lur, Mo-sar's city by the Dark Lake."

"I go to find her," he said to Pan-at-lee, "she is my mate. And if I survive I shall find means to liberate you too and return you to Om-at."

Before the girl could reply he had disappeared behind the hangings of the door near the foot of the dais. The corridor through which he ran was illy lighted and like nearly all its kind in the Ho-don city wound in and out and up and down, but at last it terminated at a sudden turn which brought him into a courtyard filled with warriors, a portion of the palace guard that had just been summoned by one of the lesser palace chiefs to join the warriors of Ko-tan in the battle that was raging in the banquet hall.

At sight of Tarzan, who in his haste had forgotten to recover his disguising headdress, a great shout arose. "Blasphemer!" "Defiler of the temple!" burst hoarsely from savage throats, and mingling with these were a few who cried, "Dor-ul-Otho!" evidencing the fact that there were among them still some who clung to their belief in his divinity.

To cross the courtyard armed only with a knife, in the face of this great throng of savage fighting men seemed even to the giant ape-man a thing impossible of achievement. He must use his wits now and quickly too, for they were closing upon him. He might have turned and fled back through the corridor but flight now even in the face of dire necessity would but delay him in his pursuit of Mo-sar and his mate.

"Stop!" he cried, raising his palm against them. "I am the Dor-ul-Otho and I come to you with a word from Ja-don, who it is my father's will shall be your king now that Ko-tan is slain. Lu-don, the high priest, has planned to seize the palace and destroy the loyal warriors that Mo-sar may be made king—Mo-sar who will be the tool and creature of Lu-don. Follow me. There is no time to lose if you would prevent the traitors whom Lu-don has organized in the city from entering the palace by a secret way and overpowering Ja-don and the faithful band within."

For a moment they hesitated. At last one spoke. "What guarantee have we," he demanded, "that it is not you who would betray us and by leading us now away from the fighting in the banquet hall cause those who fight at Ja-don's side to be defeated?"

"My life will be your guarantee," replied Tarzan. "If you find that I have not spoken the truth you are sufficient in numbers to execute whatever penalty you choose. But come, there is not time to lose. Already are the lesser priests gathering their warriors in the city below," and without waiting for any further parley he strode directly toward them in the direction of the gate upon the opposite side of the courtyard which led toward the principal entrance to the palace ground.

Slower in wit than he, they were swept away by his greater initiative and that compelling power which is inherent to all natural leaders. And so they followed him, the giant ape-man with a dead tail dragging the ground behind him—a demi-god where another would have been ridiculous. Out into the city he led them and down toward the unpretentious building that hid Lu-don's secret passageway from the city to the temple, and as they rounded the last turn they saw before them a gathering of warriors which was being rapidly augmented from all directions as the traitors of A-lur mobilized at the call of the priesthood.

"You spoke the truth, stranger," said the chief who marched at Tarzan's side, "for there are the warriors with the priests among them, even as you told us."

"And now," replied the ape-man, "that I have fulfilled my promise I will go my way after Mo-sar, who has done me a great wrong. Tell Ja-don that Jad-ben-Otho is upon his side, nor do you forget to tell him also that it was the Dor-ul-Otho who thwarted Lu-don's plan to seize the palace."

"I will not forget," replied the chief. "Go your way. We are enough to overpower the traitors."

"Tell me," asked Tarzan, "how I may know this city of Tu-lur?"

"It lies upon the south shore of the second lake below A-lur," replied the chief, "the lake that is called Jad-in-lul."

They were now approaching the band of traitors, who evidently thought that this was another contingent of their own party since they made no effort either toward defense or retreat. Suddenly the chief raised his voice in a savage war cry that was immediately taken up by his followers, and simultaneously, as though the cry were a command, the entire party broke into a mad charge upon the surprised rebels.

Satisfied with the outcome of his suddenly conceived plan and sure that it would work to the disadvantage of Lu-don, Tarzan turned into a side street and pointed his steps toward the outskirts of the city in search of the trail that led southward toward Tu-lur.

BY JAD-BAL-LUL

As Mo-sar carried Jane Clayton from the palace of Ko-tan, the king, the woman struggled incessantly to regain her freedom. He tried to compel her to walk, but despite his threats and his abuse she would not voluntarily take a single step in the direction in which he wished her to go. Instead she threw herself to the ground each time he sought to place her upon her feet, and so of necessity he was compelled to carry her though at last he tied her hands and gagged her to save himself from further lacerations, for the beauty and slenderness of the woman belied her strength and courage. When he came at last to where his men had gathered he was glad indeed to turn her over to a couple of stalwart warriors, but these too were forced to carry her since Mo-sar's fear of the vengeance of Ko-tan's retainers would brook no delays.

And thus they came down out of the hills from which A-lur is carved, to the meadows that skirt the lower end of Jad-ben-lul, with Jane Clayton carried between two of Mo-sar's men. At the edge of the lake lay a fleet of strong canoes, hollowed from the trunks of trees, their bows and sterns carved in the semblance of grotesque beasts or birds and vividly colored by some master in that primitive school of art, which fortunately is not without its devotees today.

Into the stern of one of these canoes the warriors tossed their captive at a sign from Mo-sar, who came and stood beside her as the warriors were finding their places in the canoes and selecting their paddles.

"Come, Beautiful One," he said, "let us be friends and you shall not be harmed. You will find Mo-sar a kind master if you do his bidding," and thinking to make a good impression on her he removed the gag from her mouth and the thongs from her wrists, knowing well that she could not escape surrounded as she was by his warriors, and presently, when they were out on the lake, she would be as safely imprisoned as though he held her behind bars.

And so the fleet moved off to the accompaniment of the gentle splashing of a hundred paddles, to follow the windings of the rivers and lakes through which the waters of the Valley of Jad-ben-Otho empty into the great morass to the south. The warriors, resting upon one knee, faced the bow and in the last canoe Mo-sar tiring of his fruitless attempts to win responses from his sullen captive, squatted in the bottom of the canoe with his back toward her and resting his head upon the gunwale sought sleep.

Thus they moved in silence between the verdure-clad banks of the little river through which the waters of Jad-ben-lul emptied—now in the moonlight, now in dense shadow where great trees overhung the stream, and at last out upon the waters of another lake, the black shores of which seemed far away under the weird influence of a moonlight night.

Jane Clayton sat alert in the stern of the last canoe. For months she had been under constant surveillance, the prisoner first of one ruthless race and now the prisoner of another. Since the long-gone day that Hauptmann Fritz Schneider and his band of native German troops had treacherously wrought the Kaiser's work of rapine and destruction on the Greystoke bungalow and carried her away to captivity she had not drawn a free breath. That she had survived unharmed the countless dangers through which she had passed she attributed solely to the beneficence of a kind and watchful Providence.

At first she had been held on the orders of the German High Command with a view of her ultimate value as a hostage and during these months she had been subjected to neither hardship nor oppression, but when the Germans had become hard pressed toward the close of their unsuccessful campaign in East Africa it had been determined to take her further into the interior and now there was an element of revenge in their motives, since it must have been apparent that she could no longer be of any possible military value.

Bitter indeed were the Germans against that half-savage mate of hers who had cunningly annoyed and harassed them with a fiendishness of persistence and ingenuity that had resulted in a noticeable loss in morale in the sector he had chosen for his operations. They had to charge against him the lives of certain officers that he had deliberately taken with his own hands, and one entire section of trench that had made possible a disastrous turning movement by the British. Tarzan had out-generaled them at every point. He had met cunning with cunning and cruelty with cruelties until they feared and loathed his very name. The cunning trick that they had played upon him in destroying his home, murdering his retainers, and covering the abduction of his wife in such a way as to lead him to believe that she had been killed, they had regretted a thousand times, for a thousandfold had they paid the price for their senseless ruthlessness, and now, unable to wreak their vengeance directly upon him, they had conceived the idea of inflicting further suffering upon his mate.

In sending her into the interior to avoid the path of the victorious British, they had chosen as her escort Lieutenant Erich Obergatz who had been second in command of Schneider's company, and who alone of its officers had escaped the consuming vengeance of the ape-man. For a long time Obergatz had held her in a native village, the chief of which was still under the domination of his fear of the ruthless German oppressors. While here only hardships and discomforts assailed her, Obergatz himself being held in leash by the orders of his distant superior but as time went on the life in the village grew to be a veritable hell of cruelties and oppressions practiced by the arrogant Prussian upon the villagers and the members of his native command—for time hung heavily upon the hands of the lieutenant and with idleness combining with the personal discomforts he was compelled to endure, his none too agreeable temper found an outlet first in petty interference with the chiefs and later in the practice of absolute cruelties upon them.

What the self-sufficient German could not see was plain to Jane Clayton—that the sympaties of Obergatz' native soldiers lay with the villagers and that all were so heartily sickened by his abuse that it needed now but the slightest spark to detonate the mine of revenge and hatred that the pig-headed Hun had been assiduously fabricating beneath his own person.

And at last it came, but from an unexpected source in the form of a German native deserter from the theater of war. Footsore, weary, and spent, he dragged himself into the village late one afternoon, and before Obergatz was even aware of his presence the whole village knew that the power of Germany in Africa was at an end. It did not take long for the lieutenant's native soldiers to realize that the authority that held them in service no longer existed and that with it had gone the power to pay them their miserable wage. Or at least, so they reasoned. To them Obergatz no longer represented aught else than a powerless and hated foreigner, and short indeed would have been his shrift had not a native woman who had conceived a doglike affection for Jane Clayton hurried to her with word of the murderous plan, for the fate of the innocent white woman lay in the balance beside that of the guilty Teuton.

"Already they are quarreling as to which one shall possess you," she told Jane.

"When will they come for us?" asked Jane. "Did you hear them say?"

"Tonight," replied the woman, "for even now that he has none to fight for him they still fear the white man. And so they will come at night and kill him while he sleeps."

Jane thanked the woman and sent her away lest the suspicion of her fellows be aroused against her when they discovered that the two whites had learned of their intentions. The woman went at once to the hut occupied by Obergatz. She had never gone there before and the German looked up in surprise as he saw who his visitor was.

Briefly she told him what she had heard. At first he was inclined to bluster arrogantly, with a great display of bravado but she silenced him peremptorily.

"Such talk is useless," she said shortly. "You have brought upon yourself the just hatred of these people. Regardless of the truth or falsity of the report which has been brought to them, they believe in it and there is nothing now between you and your Maker other than flight. We shall both be dead before morning if we are unable to escape from the village unseen. If you go to them now with your silly protestations of authority you will be dead a little sooner, that is all."

"You think it is as bad as that?" he said, a noticeable alteration in his tone and manner.

"It is precisely as I have told you," she replied. "They will come tonight and kill you while you sleep. Find me pistols and a rifle and ammunition and we will pretend that we go into the jungle to hunt. That you have done often. Perhaps it will arouse suspicion that I accompany you but that we must chance. And be sure my dear Herr Lieutenant to bluster and curse and abuse your servants unless they note a change in your manner and realizing your fear know that you suspect their intention. If all goes well then we can go out into the jungle to hunt and we need not return.

"But first and now you must swear never to harm me, or otherwise it would be better that I called the chief and turned you over to him and then put a bullet into my own head, for unless you swear as I have asked I were no better alone in the jungle with you than here at the mercies of these degraded blacks."

"I swear," he replied solemnly, "in the names of my God and my Kaiser that no harm shall befall you at my hands, Lady Greystoke."

"Very well," she said, "we will make this pact to assist each other to return to civilization, but let it be understood that there is and never can be any semblance even of respect for you upon my part. I am drowning and you are the straw. Carry that always in your mind, German."

If Obergatz had held any doubt as to the sincerity of her word it would have been wholly dissipated by the scathing contempt of her tone. And so Obergatz, without further parley, got pistols and an extra rifle for Jane, as well as bandoleers of cartridges. In his usual arrogant and disagreeable manner he called his servants, telling them that he and the white kali were going out into the brush to hunt. The beaters would go north as far as the little hill and then circle back to the east and in toward the village. The gun carriers he directed to take the extra pieces and precede himself and Jane slowly toward the east, waiting for them at the ford about half a mile distant. The blacks responded with greater alacrity than usual and it was noticeable to both Jane and Obergatz that they left the village whispering and laughing.

"The swine think it is a great joke," growled Obergatz, "that the afternoon before I die I go out and hunt meat for them."

As soon as the gun bearers disappeared in the jungle beyond the village the two Europeans followed along the same trail, nor was there any attempt upon the part of Obergatz' native soldiers, or the warriors of the chief to detain them, for they too doubtless were more than willing that the whites should bring them in one more mess of meat before they killed them.

A quarter of a mile from the village, Obergatz turned toward the south from the trail that led to the ford and hurrying onward the two put as great a distance as possible between them and the village before night fell. They knew from the habits of their erstwhile hosts that there was little danger of pursuit by night since the villagers held Numa, the lion, in too great respect to venture needlessly beyond their stockade during the hours that the king of beasts was prone to choose for hunting.

And thus began a seemingly endless sequence of frightful days and horror-laden nights as the two fought their way toward the south in the face of almost inconceivable hardships, privations, and dangers. The east coast was nearer but Obergatz positively refused to chance throwing himself into the hands of the British by returning to the territory which they now controlled, insisting instead upon attempting to make his way through an unknown wilderness to South Africa where, among the Boers, he was convinced he would find willing sympathizers who would find some way to return him in safety to Germany, and the woman was perforce compelled to accompany him.

And so they had crossed the great thorny, waterless steppe and come at last to the edge of the morass before Pal-ul-don. They had reached this point just before the rainy season when the waters of the morass were at their lowest ebb. At this time a hard crust is baked upon the dried surface of the marsh and there is only the open water at the center to materially impede progress. It is a condition that exists perhaps not more than a few weeks, or even days at the termination of long periods of drought, and so the two crossed the otherwise almost impassable barrier without realizing its latent terrors. Even the open water in the center chanced to be deserted at the time by its frightful denizens which the drought and the receding waters had driven southward toward the mouth of Pal-ul-don's largest river which carries the waters out of the Valley of Jad-ben-Otho.

Their wanderings carried them across the mountains and into the Valley of Jad-ben-Otho at the source of one of the larger streams which bears the mountain waters down into the valley to empty them into the main river just below The Great Lake on whose northern shore lies A-lur. As they had come down out of the mountains they had been surprised by a party of Ho-don hunters. Obergatz had escaped while Jane had been taken prisoner and brought to A-lur. She had neither seen nor heard aught of the German since that time and she did not know whether he had perished in this strange land, or succeeded in successfully eluding its savage denizens and making his way at last into South Africa.

For her part, she had been incarcerated alternately in the palace and the temple as either Ko-tan or Lu-don succeeded in wresting her temporarily from the other by various strokes of cunning and intrigue. And now at last she was in the power of a new captor, one whom she knew from the gossip of the temple and the palace to be cruel and degraded. And she was in the stern of the last canoe, and every enemy back was toward her, while almost at her feet Mo-sar's loud snores gave ample evidence of his unconsciousness to his immediate surroundings.

The dark shore loomed closer to the south as Jane Clayton, Lady Greystoke, slid quietly over the stern of the canoe into the chill waters of the lake. She scarcely moved other than to keep her nostrils above the surface while the canoe was yet discernible in the last rays of the declining moon. Then she struck out toward the southern shore.

Alone, unarmed, all but naked, in a country overrun by savage beasts and hostile men, she yet felt for the first time in many months a sensation of elation and relief. She was free! What if the next moment brought death, she knew again, at least a brief instant of absolute freedom. Her blood tingled to the almost forgotten sensation and it was with difficulty that she restrained a glad triumphant cry as she clambered from the quiet waters and stood upon the silent beach.

Before her loomed a forest, darkly, and from its depths came those nameless sounds that are a part of the night life of the jungle—the rustling of leaves in the wind, the rubbing together of contiguous branches, the scurrying of a rodent, all magnified by the darkness to sinister and awe-inspiring proportions; the hoot of an owl, the distant scream of a great cat, the barking of wild dogs, attested the presence of the myriad life she could not see—the savage life, the free life of which she was now a part. And then there came to her, possibly for the first time since the giant ape-man had come into her life, a fuller realization of what the jungle meant to him, for though alone and unprotected from its hideous dangers she yet felt its lure upon her and an exaltation that she had not dared hope to feel again.

Ah, if that mighty mate of hers were but by her side! What utter joy and bliss would be hers! She longed for no more than this. The parade of cities, the comforts and luxuries of civilization held forth no allure half as insistent as the glorious freedom of the jungle.

A lion moaned in the blackness to her right, eliciting delicious thrills that crept along her spine. The hair at the back of her head seemed to stand erect—yet she was unafraid. The muscles bequeathed her by some primordial ancestor reacted instinctively to the presence of an ancient enemy—that was all. The woman moved slowly and deliberately toward the wood. Again the lion moaned; this time nearer. She sought a low-hanging branch and finding it swung easily into the friendly shelter of the tree. The long and perilous journey with Obergatz had trained her muscles and her nerves to such unaccustomed habits. She found a safe resting place such as Tarzan had taught her was best and there she curled herself, thirty feet above the ground, for a night's rest. She was cold and uncomfortable and yet she slept, for her heart was warm with renewed hope and her tired brain had found temporary surcease from worry.

She slept until the heat of the sun, high in the heavens, awakened her. She was rested and now her body was well as her heart was warm. A sensation of ease and comfort and happiness pervaded her being. She rose upon her gently swaying couch and stretched luxuriously, her naked limbs and lithe body mottled by the sunlight filtering through the foliage above combined with the lazy gesture to impart to her appearance something of the leopard. With careful eye she scrutinized the ground below and with attentive ear she listened for any warning sound that might suggest the near presence of enemies, either man or beast. Satisfied at last that there was nothing close of which she need have fear she clambered to the ground. She wished to bathe but the lake was too exposed and just a bit too far from the safety of the trees for her to risk it until she became more familiar with her surroundings. She wandered aimlessly through the forest searching for food which she found in abundance. She ate and rested, for she had no objective as yet. Her freedom was too new to be spoiled by plannings for the future. The haunts of civilized man seemed to her now as vague and unattainable as the half-forgotten substance of a dream. If she could but live on here in peace, waiting, waiting for—him. It was the old hope revived. She knew that he would come some day, if he lived. She had always known that, though recently she had believed that he would come too late. If he lived!

Yes, he would come if he lived, and if he did not live she were as well off here as elsewhere, for then nothing mattered, only to wait for the end as patiently as might be.

Her wanderings brought her to a crystal brook and there she drank and bathed beneath an overhanging tree that offered her quick asylum in the event of danger. It was a quiet and beautiful spot and she loved it from the first. The bottom of the brook was paved with pretty stones and bits of glassy obsidian. As she gathered a handful of the pebbles and held them up to look at them she noticed that one of her fingers was bleeding from a clean, straight cut. She fell to searching for the cause and presently discovered it in one of the fragments of volcanic glass which revealed an edge that was almost razor-like. Jane Clayton was elated. Here, God-given to her hands, was the first beginning with which she might eventually arrive at both weapons and tools—a cutting edge. Everything was possible to him who possessed it—nothing without.

She sought until she had collected many of the precious bits of stone—until the pouch that hung at her right side was almost filled. Then she climbed into the great tree to examine them at leisure. There were some that looked like knife blades, and some that could easily be fashioned into spear heads, and many smaller ones that nature seemed to have intended for the tips of savage arrows.

The spear she would essay first—that would be easiest. There was a hollow in the bole of the tree in a great crotch high above the ground. Here she cached all of her treasure except a single knifelike sliver. With this she descended to the ground and searching out a slender sapling that grew arrow-straight she hacked and sawed until she could break it off without splitting the wood. It was just the right diameter for the shaft of a spear—a hunting spear such as her beloved Waziri had liked best. How often had she watched them fashioning them, and they had taught her how to use them, too—them and the heavy war spears—laughing and clapping their hands as her proficiency increased.

She knew the arborescent grasses that yielded the longest and toughest fibers and these she sought and carried to her tree with the spear shaft that was to be. Clambering to her crotch she bent to her work, humming softly a little tune. She caught herself and smiled—it was the first time in all these bitter months that song had passed her lips or such a smile.

"I feel," she sighed, "I almost feel that John is near—my John—my Tarzan!"

She cut the spear shaft to the proper length and removed the twigs and branches and the bark, whittling and scraping at the nubs until the surface was all smooth and straight. Then she split one end and inserted a spear point, shaping the wood until it fitted perfectly. This done she laid the shaft aside and fell to splitting the thick grass stems and pounding and twisting them until she had separated and partially cleaned the fibers. These she took down to the brook and washed and brought back again and wound tightly around the cleft end of the shaft, which she had notched to receive them, and the upper part of the spear head which she had also notched slightly with a bit of stone. It was a crude spear but the best that she could attain in so short a time. Later, she promised herself, she should have others—many of them—and they would be spears of which even the greatest of the Waziri spear-men might be proud.

THE LION PIT OF TU-LUR

Though Tarzan searched the outskirts of the city until nearly dawn he discovered nowhere the spoor of his mate. The breeze coming down from the mountains brought to his nostrils a diversity of scents but there was not among them the slightest suggestion of her whom he sought. The natural deduction was therefore that she had been taken in some other direction. In his search he had many times crossed the fresh tracks of many men leading toward the lake and these he concluded had probably been made by Jane Clayton's abductors. It had only been to minimize the chance of error by the process of elimination that he had carefully reconnoitered every other avenue leading from A-lur toward the southeast where lay Mo-sar's city of Tu-lur, and now he followed the trail to the shores of Jad-ben-lul where the party had embarked upon the quiet waters in their sturdy canoes.

He found many other craft of the same description moored along the shore and one of these he commandeered for the purpose of pursuit. It was daylight when he passed through the lake which lies next below Jad-ben-lul and paddling strongly passed within sight of the very tree in which his lost mate lay sleeping.

Had the gentle wind that caressed the bosom of the lake been blowing from a southerly direction the giant ape-man and Jane Clayton would have been reunited then, but an unkind fate had willed otherwise and the opportunity passed with the passing of his canoe which presently his powerful strokes carried out of sight into the stream at the lower end of the lake.

Following the winding river which bore a considerable distance to the north before doubling back to empty into the Jad-in-lul, the ape-man missed a portage that would have saved him hours of paddling.

It was at the upper end of this portage where Mo-sar and his warriors had debarked that the chief discovered the absence of his captive. As Mo-sar had been asleep since shortly after their departure from A-lur, and as none of the warriors recalled when she had last been seen, it was impossible to conjecture with any degree of accuracy the place where she had escaped. The consensus of opinion was, however, that it had been in the narrow river connecting Jad-ben-lul with the lake next below it, which is called Jad-bal-lul, which freely translated means the lake of gold. Mo-sar had been very wroth and having himself been the only one at fault he naturally sought with great diligence to fix the blame upon another.

He would have returned in search of her had he not feared to meet a pursuing company dispatched either by Ja-don or the high priest, both of whom, he knew, had just grievances against him. He would not even spare a boatload of his warriors from his own protection to return in quest of the fugitive but hastened onward with as little delay as possible across the portage and out upon the waters of Jad-in-lul.

The morning sun was just touching the white domes of Tu-lur when Mo-sar's paddlers brought their canoes against the shore at the city's edge. Safe once more behind his own walls and protected by many warriors, the courage of the chief returned sufficiently at least to permit him to dispatch three canoes in search of Jane Clayton, and also to go as far as A-lur if possible to learn what had delayed Bu-lot, whose failure to reach the canoes with the balance of the party at the time of the flight from the northern city had in no way delayed Mo-sar's departure, his own safety being of far greater moment than that of his son.

As the three canoes reached the portage on their return journey the warriors who were dragging them from the water were suddenly startled by the appearance of two priests, carrying a light canoe in the direction of Jad-in-lul. At first they thought them the advance guard of a larger force of Lu-don's followers, although the correctness of such a theory was belied by their knowledge that priests never accepted the risks or perils of a warrior's vocation, nor even fought until driven into a corner and forced to do so. Secretly the warriors of Pal-ul-don held the emasculated priesthood in contempt and so instead of immediately taking up the offensive as they would have had the two men been warriors from A-lur instead of priests, they waited to question them.

At sight of the warriors the priests made the sign of peace and upon being asked if they were alone they answered in the affirmative.

The leader of Mo-sar's warriors permitted them to approach. "What do you here," he asked, "in the country of Mo-sar, so far from your own city?"

"We carry a message from Lu-don, the high priest, to Mo-sar," explained one.

"Is it a message of peace or of war?" asked the warrior.

"It is an offer of peace," replied the priest.

"And Lu-don is sending no warriors behind you?" queried the fighting man.

"We are alone," the priest assured him. "None in A-lur save Lu-don knows that we have come upon this errand."

"Then go your way," said the warrior.

"Who is that?" asked one of the priests suddenly, pointing toward the upper end of the lake at the point where the river from Jad-bal-lul entered it.

All eyes turned in the direction that he had indicated to see a lone warrior paddling rapidly into Jad-in-lul, the prow of his canoe pointing toward Tu-lur. The warriors and the priests drew into the concealment of the bushes on either side of the portage.

"It is the terrible man who called himself the Dor-ul-Otho," whispered one of the priests. "I would know that figure among a great multitude as far as I could see it."

"You are right, priest," cried one of the warriors who had seen Tarzan the day that he had first entered Ko-tan's palace. "It is indeed he who has been rightly called Tarzan-jad-guru."

"Hasten priests," cried the leader of the party. "You are two paddles in a light canoe. Easily can you reach Tu-lur ahead of him and warn Mo-sar of his coming, for he has but only entered the lake."

For a moment the priests demurred for they had no stomach for an encounter with this terrible man, but the warrior insisted and even went so far as to threaten them. Their canoe was taken from them and pushed into the lake and they were all but lifted bodily from their feet and put aboard it. Still protesting they were shoved out upon the water where they were immediately in full view of the lone paddler above them. Now there was no alternative. The city of Tu-lur offered the only safety and bending to their paddles the two priests sent their craft swiftly in the direction of the city.

The warriors withdrew again to the concealment of the foliage. If Tarzan had seen them and should come hither to investigate there were thirty of them against one and naturally they had no fear of the outcome, but they did not consider it necessary to go out upon the lake to meet him since they had been sent to look for the escaped prisoner and not to intercept the strange warrior, the stories of whose ferocity and prowess doubtless helped them to arrive at their decision to provoke no uncalled-for quarrel with him.

If he had seen them he gave no sign, but continued paddling steadily and strongly toward the city, nor did he increase his speed as the two priests shot out in full view. The moment the priests' canoe touched the shore by the city its occupants leaped out and hurried swiftly toward the palace gate, casting affrighted glances behind them. They sought immediate audience with Mo-sar, after warning the warriors on guard that Tarzan was approaching.

They were conducted at once to the chief, whose court was a smaller replica of that of the king of A-lur. "We come from Lu-don, the high priest," explained the spokesman. "He wishes the friendship of Mo-sar, who has always been his friend. Ja-don is gathering warriors to make himself king. Throughout the villages of the Ho-don are thousands who will obey the commands of Lu-don, the high priest. Only with Lu-don's assistance can Mo-sar become king, and the message from Lu-don is that if Mo-sar would retain the friendship of Lu-don he must return immediately the woman he took from the quarters of the Princess O-lo-a."

At this juncture a warrior entered. His excitement was evident. "The Dor-ul-Otho has come to Tu-lur and demands to see Mo-sar at once," he said.

"The Dor-ul-Otho!" exclaimed Mo-sar.

"That is the message he sent," replied the warrior, "and indeed he is not as are the people of Pal-ul-don. He is, we think, the same of whom the warriors that returned from A-lur today told us and whom some call Tarzan-jad-guru and some Dor-ul-Otho. But indeed only the son of god would dare come thus alone to a strange city, so it must be that he speaks the truth."

Mo-sar, his heart filled with terror and indecision, turned questioningly toward the priests.

"Receive him graciously, Mo-sar," counseled he who had spoken before, his advice prompted by the petty shrewdness of his defective brain which, under the added influence of Lu-don's tutorage leaned always toward duplicity. "Receive him graciously and when he is quite convinced of your friendship he will be off his guard, and then you may do with him as you will. But if possible, Mo-sar, and you would win the undying gratitude of Lu-don, the high-priest, save him alive for my master."

Mo-sar nodded understandingly and turning to the warrior commanded that he conduct the visitor to him.

"We must not be seen by the creature," said one of the priests. "Give us your answer to Lu-don, Mo-sar, and we will go our way."

"Tell Lu-don," replied the chief, "that the woman would have been lost to him entirely had it not been for me. I sought to bring her to Tu-lur that I might save her for him from the clutches of Ja-don, but during the night she escaped. Tell Lu-don that I have sent thirty warriors to search for her. It is strange you did not see them as you came."

"We did," replied the priests, "but they told us nothing of the purpose of their journey."

"It is as I have told you," said Mo-sar, "and if they find her, assure your master that she will be kept unharmed in Tu-lur for him. Also tell him that I will send my warriors to join with his against Ja-don whenever he sends word that he wants them. Now go, for Tarzan-jad-guru will soon be here."

He signaled to a slave. "Lead the priests to the temple," he commanded, "and ask the high priest of Tu-lur to see that they are fed and permitted to return to A-lur when they will."

The two priests were conducted from the apartment by the slave through a doorway other than that at which they had entered, and a moment later Tarzan-jad-guru strode into the presence of Mo-sar, ahead of the warrior whose duty it had been to conduct and announce him. The ape-man made no sign of greeting or of peace but strode directly toward the chief who, only by the exertion of his utmost powers of will, hid the terror that was in his heart at sight of the giant figure and the scowling face.

"I am the Dor-ul-Otho," said the ape-man in level tones that carried to the mind of Mo-sar a suggestion of cold steel; "I am Dor-ul-Otho, and I come to Tu-lur for the woman you stole from the apartments of O-lo-a, the princess."

The very boldness of Tarzan's entry into this hostile city had had the effect of giving him a great moral advantage over Mo-sar and the savage warriors who stood upon either side of the chief. Truly it seemed to them that no other than the son of Jad-ben-Otho would dare so heroic an act. Would any mortal warrior act thus boldly, and alone enter the presence of a powerful chief and, in the midst of a score of warriors, arrogantly demand an accounting? No, it was beyond reason. Mo-sar was faltering in his decision to betray the stranger by seeming friendliness. He even paled to a sudden thought—Jad-ben-Otho knew everything, even our inmost thoughts. Was it not therefore possible that this creature, if after all it should prove true that he was the Dor-ul-Otho, might even now be reading the wicked design that the priests had implanted in the brain of Mo-sar and which he had entertained so favorably? The chief squirmed and fidgeted upon the bench of hewn rock that was his throne.

"Quick," snapped the ape-man, "Where is she?"

"She is not here," cried Mo-sar.

"You lie," replied Tarzan.

"As Jad-ben-Otho is my witness, she is not in Tu-lur," insisted the chief. "You may search the palace and the temple and the entire city but you will not find her, for she is not here."

"Where is she, then?" demanded the ape-man. "You took her from the palace at A-lur. If she is not here, where is she? Tell me not that harm has befallen her," and he took a sudden threatening step toward Mo-sar, that sent the chief shrinking back in terror.

"Wait," he cried, "if you are indeed the Dor-ul-Otho you will know that I speak the truth. I took her from the palace of Ko-tan to save her for Lu-don, the high priest, lest with Ko-tan dead Ja-don seize her. But during the night she escaped from me between here and A-lur, and I have but just sent three canoes full-manned in search of her."

Something in the chief's tone and manner assured the ape-man that he spoke in part the truth, and that once again he had braved incalculable dangers and suffered loss of time futilely.

"What wanted the priests of Lu-don that preceded me here?" demanded Tarzan chancing a shrewd guess that the two he had seen paddling so frantically to avoid a meeting with him had indeed come from the high priest at A-lur.

"They came upon an errand similar to yours," replied Mo-sar; "to demand the return of the woman whom Lu-don thought I had stolen from him, thus wronging me as deeply, O Dor-ul-Otho, as have you."

"I would question the priests," said Tarzan. "Bring them hither." His peremptory and arrogant manner left Mo-sar in doubt as to whether to be more incensed, or terrified, but ever as is the way with such as he, he concluded that the first consideration was his own safety. If he could transfer the attention and the wrath of this terrible man from himself to Lu-don's priests it would more than satisfy him and if they should conspire to harm him, then Mo-sar would be safe in the eyes of Jad-ben-Otho if it finally developed that the stranger was in reality the son of god. He felt uncomfortable in Tarzan's presence and this fact rather accentuated his doubt, for thus indeed would mortal feel in the presence of a god. Now he saw a way to escape, at least temporarily.

"I will fetch them myself, Dor-ul-Otho," he said, and turning, left the apartment. His hurried steps brought him quickly to the temple, for the palace grounds of Tu-lur, which also included the temple as in all of the Ho-don cities, covered a much smaller area than those of the larger city of A-lur. He found Lu-don's messengers with the high priest of his own temple and quickly transmitted to them the commands of the ape-man.

"What do you intend to do with him?" asked one of the priests.

"I have no quarrel with him," replied Mo-sar. "He came in peace and he may depart in peace, for who knows but that he is indeed the Dor-ul-Otho?"

"We know that he is not," replied Lu-don's emissary. "We have every proof that he is only mortal, a strange creature from another country. Already has Lu-don offered his life to Jad-ben-Otho if he is wrong in his belief that this creature is not the son of god. If the high priest of A-lur, who is the highest priest of all the high priests of Pal-ul-don is thus so sure that the creature in an impostor as to stake his life upon his judgment then who are we to give credence to the claims of this stranger? No, Mo-sar, you need not fear him. He is only a warrior who may be overcome with the same weapons that subdue your own fighting men. Were it not for Lu-don's command that he be taken alive I would urge you to set your warriors upon him and slay him, but the commands of Lu-don are the commands of Jad-ben-Otho himself, and those we may not disobey."

But still the remnant of a doubt stirred within the cowardly breast of Mo-sar, urging him to let another take the initiative against the stranger.

"He is yours then," he replied, "to do with as you will. I have no quarrel with him. What you may command shall be the command of Lu-don, the high priest, and further than that I shall have nothing to do in the matter."

The priests turned to him who guided the destinies of the temple at Tu-lur. "Have you no plan?" they asked. "High indeed will he stand in the counsels of Lu-don and in the eyes of Jad-ben-Otho who finds the means to capture this impostor alive."

"There is the lion pit," whispered the high priest. "It is now vacant and what will hold ja and jato will hold this stranger if he is not the Dor-ul-Otho."

"It will hold him," said Mo-sar; "doubtless too it would hold a gryf, but first you would have to get the gryf into it."

The priests pondered this bit of wisdom thoughtfully and then one of those from A-lur spoke. "It should not be difficult," he said, "if we use the wits that Jad-ben-Otho gave us instead of the worldly muscles which were handed down to us from our fathers and our mothers and which have not even the power possessed by those of the beasts that run about on four feet."

"Lu-don matched his wits with the stranger and lost," suggested Mo-sar. "But this is your own affair. Carry it out as you see best."

"At A-lur, Ko-tan made much of this Dor-ul-Otho and the priests conducted him through the temple. It would arouse in his mind no suspicion were you to do the same, and let the high priest of Tu-lur invite him to the temple and gathering all the priests make a great show of belief in his kinship to Jad-ben-Otho. And what more natural then than that the high priest should wish to show him through the temple as did Lu-don at A-lur when Ko-tan commanded it, and if by chance he should be led through the lion pit it would be a simple matter for those who bear the torches to extinguish them suddenly and before the stranger was aware of what had happened, the stone gates could be dropped, thus safely securing him."

"But there are windows in the pit that let in light," interposed the high priest, "and even though the torches were extinguished he could still see and might escape before the stone door could be lowered."

"Send one who will cover the windows tightly with hides," said the priest from A-lur.

"The plan is a good one," said Mo-sar, seeing an opportunity for entirely eliminating himself from any suspicion of complicity, "for it will require the presence of no warriors, and thus with only priests about him his mind will entertain no suspicion of harm."

They were interrupted at this point by a messenger from the palace who brought word that the Dor-ul-Otho was becoming impatient and if the priests from A-lur were not brought to him at once he would come himself to the temple and get them. Mo-sar shook his head. He could not conceive of such brazen courage in mortal breast and glad he was that the plan evolved for Tarzan's undoing did not necessitate his active participation.

And so, while Mo-sar left for a secret corner of the palace by a roundabout way, three priests were dispatched to Tarzan and with whining words that did not entirely deceive him, they acknowledged his kinship to Jad-ben-Otho and begged him in the name of the high priest to honor the temple with a visit, when the priests from A-lur would be brought to him and would answer any questions that he put to them.

Confident that a continuation of his bravado would best serve his purpose, and also that if suspicion against him should crystallize into conviction on the part of Mo-sar and his followers that he would be no worse off in the temple than in the palace, the ape-man haughtily accepted the invitation of the high priest.

And so he came into the temple and was received in a manner befitting his high claims. He questioned the two priests of A-lur from whom he obtained only a repetition of the story that Mo-sar had told him, and then the high priest invited him to inspect the temple.

They took him first to the altar court, of which there was only one in Tu-lur. It was almost identical in every respect with those at A-lur. There was a bloody altar at the east end and the drowning basin at the west, and the grizzly fringes upon the headdresses of the priests attested the fact that the eastern altar was an active force in the rites of the temple. Through the chambers and corridors beneath they led him, and finally, with torch bearers to light their steps, into a damp and gloomy labyrinth at a low level and here in a large chamber, the air of which was still heavy with the odor of lions, the crafty priests of Tu-lur encompassed their shrewd design.

The torches were suddenly extinguished. There was a hurried confusion of bare feet moving rapidly across the stone floor. There was a loud crash as of a heavy weight of stone falling upon stone, and then surrounding the ape-man naught but the darkness and the silence of the tomb.

DIANA OF THE JUNGLE

Jane had made her first kill and she was very proud of it. It was not a very formidable animal—only a hare; but it marked an epoch in her existence. Just as in the dim past the first hunter had shaped the destinies of mankind so it seemed that this event might shape hers in some new mold. No longer was she dependent upon the wild fruits and vegetables for sustenance. Now she might command meat, the giver of the strength and endurance she would require successfully to cope with the necessities of her primitive existence.

The next step was fire. She might learn to eat raw flesh as had her lord and master; but she shrank from that. The thought even was repulsive. She had, however, a plan for fire. She had given the matter thought, but had been too busy to put it into execution so long as fire could be of no immediate use to her. Now it was different—she had something to cook and her mouth watered for the flesh of her kill. She would grill it above glowing embers. Jane hastened to her tree. Among the treasures she had gathered in the bed of the stream were several pieces of volcanic glass, clear as crystal. She sought until she had found the one in mind, which was convex. Then she hurried to the ground and gathered a little pile of powdered bark that was very dry, and some dead leaves and grasses that had lain long in the hot sun. Near at hand she arranged a supply of dead twigs and branches—small and large.

Vibrant with suppressed excitement she held the bit of glass above the tinder, moving it slowly until she had focused the sun's rays upon a tiny spot. She waited breathlessly. How slow it was! Were her high hopes to be dashed in spite of all her clever planning? No! A thin thread of smoke rose gracefully into the quiet air. Presently the tinder glowed and broke suddenly into flame. Jane clasped her hands beneath her chin with a little gurgling exclamation of delight. She had achieved fire!

She piled on twigs and then larger branches and at last dragged a small log to the flames and pushed an end of it into the fire which was crackling merrily. It was the sweetest sound that she had heard for many a month. But she could not wait for the mass of embers that would be required to cook her hare. As quickly as might be she skinned and cleaned her kill, burying the hide and entrails. That she had learned from Tarzan. It served two purposes. One was the necessity for keeping a sanitary camp and the other the obliteration of the scent that most quickly attracts the man-eaters.

Then she ran a stick through the carcass and held it above the flames. By turning it often she prevented burning and at the same time permitted the meat to cook thoroughly all the way through. When it was done she scampered high into the safety of her tree to enjoy her meal in quiet and peace. Never, thought Lady Greystoke, had aught more delicious passed her lips. She patted her spear affectionately. It had brought her this toothsome dainty and with it a feeling of greater confidence and safety than she had enjoyed since that frightful day that she and Obergatz had spent their last cartridge. She would never forget that day—it had seemed one hideous succession of frightful beast after frightful beast. They had not been long in this strange country, yet they thought that they were hardened to dangers, for daily they had had encounters with ferocious creatures; but this day—she shuddered when she thought of it. And with her last cartridge she had killed a black and yellow striped lion-thing with great saber teeth just as it was about to spring upon Obergatz who had futilely emptied his rifle into it—the last shot—his final cartridge. For another day they had carried the now useless rifles; but at last they had discarded them and thrown away the cumbersome bandoleers, as well. How they had managed to survive during the ensuing week she could never quite understand, and then the Ho-don had come upon them and captured her. Obergatz had escaped—she was living it all over again. Doubtless he was dead unless he had been able to reach this side of the valley which was quite evidently less overrun with savage beasts.

Jane's days were very full ones now, and the daylight hours seemed all too short in which to accomplish the many things she had determined upon, since she had concluded that this spot presented as ideal a place as she could find to live until she could fashion the weapons she considered necessary for the obtaining of meat and for self-defense.

She felt that she must have, in addition to a good spear, a knife, and bow and arrows. Possibly when these had been achieved she might seriously consider an attempt to fight her way to one of civilization's nearest outposts. In the meantime it was necessary to construct some sort of protective shelter in which she might feel a greater sense of security by night, for she knew that there was a possibility that any night she might receive a visit from a prowling panther, although she had as yet seen none upon this side of the valley. Aside from this danger she felt comparatively safe in her aerial retreat.

The cutting of the long poles for her home occupied all of the daylight hours that were not engaged in the search for food. These poles she carried high into her tree and with them constructed a flooring across two stout branches binding the poles together and also to the branches with fibers from the tough arboraceous grasses that grew in profusion near the stream. Similarly she built walls and a roof, the latter thatched with many layers of great leaves. The fashioning of the barred windows and the door were matters of great importance and consuming interest. The windows, there were two of them, were large and the bars permanently fixed; but the door was small, the opening just large enough to permit her to pass through easily on hands and knees, which made it easier to barricade. She lost count of the days that the house cost her; but time was a cheap commodity—she had more of it than of anything else. It meant so little to her that she had not even any desire to keep account of it. How long since she and Obergatz had fled from the wrath of the Negro villagers she did not know and she could only roughly guess at the seasons. She worked hard for two reasons; one was to hasten the completion of her little place of refuge, and the other a desire for such physical exhaustion at night that she would sleep through those dreaded hours to a new day. As a matter of fact the house was finished in less than a week—that is, it was made as safe as it ever would be, though regardless of how long she might occupy it she would keep on adding touches and refinements here and there.

Her daily life was filled with her house building and her hunting, to which was added an occasional spice of excitement contributed by roving lions. To the woodcraft that she had learned from Tarzan, that master of the art, was added a considerable store of practical experience derived from her own past adventures in the jungle and the long months with Obergatz, nor was any day now lacking in some added store of useful knowledge. To these facts was attributable her apparent immunity from harm, since they told her when ja was approaching before he crept close enough for a successful charge and, too, they kept her close to those never-failing havens of retreat—the trees.

The nights, filled with their weird noises, were lonely and depressing. Only her ability to sleep quickly and soundly made them endurable. The first night that she spent in her completed house behind barred windows and barricaded door was one of almost undiluted peace and happiness. The night noises seemed far removed and impersonal and the soughing of the wind in the trees was gently soothing. Before, it had carried a mournful note and was sinister in that it might hide the approach of some real danger. That night she slept indeed.

She went further afield now in search of food. So far nothing but rodents had fallen to her spear—her ambition was an antelope, since beside the flesh it would give her, and the gut for her bow, the hide would prove invaluable during the colder weather that she knew would accompany the rainy season. She had caught glimpses of these wary animals and was sure that they always crossed the stream at a certain spot above her camp. It was to this place that she went to hunt them. With the stealth and cunning of a panther she crept through the forest, circling about to get up wind from the ford, pausing often to look and listen for aught that might menace her—herself the personification of a hunted deer. Now she moved silently down upon the chosen spot. What luck! A beautiful buck stood drinking in the stream. The woman wormed her way closer. Now she lay upon her belly behind a small bush within throwing distance of the quarry. She must rise to her full height and throw her spear almost in the same instant and she must throw it with great force and perfect accuracy. She thrilled with the excitement of the minute, yet cool and steady were her swift muscles as she rose and cast her missile. Scarce by the width of a finger did the point strike from the spot at which it had been directed. The buck leaped high, landed upon the bank of the stream, and fell dead. Jane Clayton sprang quickly forward toward her kill.

"Bravo!" A man's voice spoke in English from the shrubbery upon the opposite side of the stream. Jane Clayton halted in her tracks—stunned, almost, by surprise. And then a strange, unkempt figure of a man stepped into view. At first she did not recognize him, but when she did, instinctively she stepped back.

"Lieutenant Obergatz!" she cried. "Can it be you?"

"It can. It is," replied the German. "I am a strange sight, no doubt; but still it is I, Erich Obergatz. And you? You have changed too, is it not?"

He was looking at her naked limbs and her golden breastplates, the loin cloth of jato-hide, the harness and ornaments that constitute the apparel of a Ho-don woman—the things that Lu-don had dressed her in as his passion for her grew. Not Ko-tan's daughter, even, had finer trappings.

"But why are you here?" Jane insisted. "I had thought you safely among civilized men by this time, if you still lived."

"Gott!" he exclaimed. "I do not know why I continue to live. I have prayed to die and yet I cling to life. There is no hope. We are doomed to remain in this horrible land until we die. The bog! The frightful bog! I have searched its shores for a place to cross until I have entirely circled the hideous country. Easily enough we entered; but the rains have come since and now no living man could pass that slough of slimy mud and hungry reptiles. Have I not tried it! And the beasts that roam this accursed land. They hunt me by day and by night."

"But how have you escaped them?" she asked.

"I do not know," he replied gloomily. "I have fled and fled and fled. I have remained hungry and thirsty in tree tops for days at a time. I have fashioned weapons—clubs and spears—and I have learned to use them. I have slain a lion with my club. So even will a cornered rat fight. And we are no better than rats in this land of stupendous dangers, you and I. But tell me about yourself. If it is surprising that I live, how much more so that you still survive."

Briefly she told him and all the while she was wondering what she might do to rid herself of him. She could not conceive of a prolonged existence with him as her sole companion. Better, a thousand times better, to be alone. Never had her hatred and contempt for him lessened through the long weeks and months of their constant companionship, and now that he could be of no service in returning her to civilization, she shrank from the thought of seeing him daily. And, too, she feared him. Never had she trusted him; but now there was a strange light in his eye that had not been there when last she saw him. She could not interpret it—all she knew was that it gave her a feeling of apprehension—a nameless dread.

"You lived long then in the city of A-lur?" he said, speaking in the language of Pal-ul-don.

"You have learned this tongue?" she asked. "How?"

"I fell in with a band of half-breeds," he replied, "members of a proscribed race that dwells in the rock-bound gut through which the principal river of the valley empties into the morass. They are called Waz-ho-don and their village is partly made up of cave dwellings and partly of houses carved from the soft rock at the foot of the cliff. They are very ignorant and superstitious and when they first saw me and realized that I had no tail and that my hands and feet were not like theirs they were afraid of me. They thought that I was either god or demon. Being in a position where I could neither escape them nor defend myself, I made a bold front and succeeded in impressing them to such an extent that they conducted me to their city, which they call Bu-lur, and there they fed me and treated me with kindness. As I learned their language I sought to impress them more and more with the idea that I was a god, and I succeeded, too, until an old fellow who was something of a priest among them, or medicine-man, became jealous of my growing power. That was the beginning of the end and came near to being the end in fact. He told them that if I was a god I would not bleed if a knife was stuck into me—if I did bleed it would prove conclusively that I was not a god. Without my knowledge he arranged to stage the ordeal before the whole village upon a certain night—it was upon one of those numerous occasions when they eat and drink to Jad-ben-Otho, their pagan deity. Under the influence of their vile liquor they would be ripe for any bloodthirsty scheme the medicine-man might evolve. One of the women told me about the plan—not with any intent to warn me of danger, but prompted merely by feminine curiosity as to whether or not I would bleed if stuck with a dagger. She could not wait, it seemed, for the orderly procedure of the ordeal—she wanted to know at once, and when I caught her trying to slip a knife into my side and questioned her she explained the whole thing with the utmost naivete. The warriors already had commenced drinking—it would have been futile to make any sort of appeal either to their intellects or their superstitions. There was but one alternative to death and that was flight. I told the woman that I was very much outraged and offended at this reflection upon my godhood and that as a mark of my disfavor I should abandon them to their fate.

"'I shall return to heaven at once!' I exclaimed.

"She wanted to hang around and see me go, but I told her that her eyes would be blasted by the fire surrounding my departure and that she must leave at once and not return to the spot for at least an hour. I also impressed upon her the fact that should any other approach this part of the village within that time not only they, but she as well, would burst into flames and be consumed.

"She was very much impressed and lost no time in leaving, calling back as she departed that if I were indeed gone in an hour she and all the village would know that I was no less than Jad-ben-Otho himself, and so they must thank me, for I can assure you that I was gone in much less than an hour, nor have I ventured close to the neighborhood of the city of Bu-lur since," and he fell to laughing in harsh, cackling notes that sent a shiver through the woman's frame.

As Obergatz talked Jane had recovered her spear from the carcass of the antelope and commenced busying herself with the removal of the hide. The man made no attempt to assist her, but stood by talking and watching her, the while he continually ran his filthy fingers through his matted hair and beard. His face and body were caked with dirt and he was naked except for a torn greasy hide about his loins. His weapons consisted of a club and knife of Waz-don pattern, that he had stolen from the city of Bu-lur; but what more greatly concerned the woman than his filth or his armament were his cackling laughter and the strange expression in his eyes.

She went on with her work, however, removing those parts of the buck she wanted, taking only as much meat as she might consume before it spoiled, as she was not sufficiently a true jungle creature to relish it beyond that stage, and then she straightened up and faced the man.

"Lieutenant Obergatz," she said, "by a chance of accident we have met again. Certainly you would not have sought the meeting any more than I. We have nothing in common other than those sentiments which may have been engendered by my natural dislike and suspicion of you, one of the authors of all the misery and sorrow that I have endured for endless months. This little corner of the world is mine by right of discovery and occupation. Go away and leave me to enjoy here what peace I may. It is the least that you can do to amend the wrong that you have done me and mine."

The man stared at her through his fishy eyes for a moment in silence, then there broke from his lips a peal of mirthless, uncanny laughter.

"Go away! Leave you alone!" he cried. "I have found you. We are going to be good friends. There is no one else in the world but us. No one will ever know what we do or what becomes of us and now you ask me to go away and live alone in this hellish solitude." Again he laughed, though neither the muscles of his eyes or his mouth reflected any mirth—it was just a hollow sound that imitated laughter.

"Remember your promise," she said.

"Promise! Promise! What are promises? They are made to be broken—we taught the world that at Liege and Louvain. No, no! I will not go away. I shall stay and protect you."

"I do not need your protection," she insisted. "You have already seen that I can use a spear."

"Yes," he said; "but it would not be right to leave you here alone—you are but a woman. No, no; I am an officer of the Kaiser and I cannot abandon you."

Once more he laughed. "We could be very happy here together," he added.

The woman could not repress a shudder, nor, in fact, did she attempt to hide her aversion.

"You do not like me?" he asked. "Ah, well; it is too sad. But some day you will love me," and again the hideous laughter.

The woman had wrapped the pieces of the buck in the hide and this she now raised and threw across her shoulder. In her other hand she held her spear and faced the German.

"Go!" she commanded. "We have wasted enough words. This is my country and I shall defend it. If I see you about again I shall kill you. Do you understand?"

An expression of rage contorted Obergatz' features. He raised his club and started toward her.

"Stop!" she commanded, throwing her spear-hand backward for a cast. "You saw me kill this buck and you have said truthfully that no one will ever know what we do here. Put these two facts together, German, and draw your own conclusions before you take another step in my direction."

The man halted and his club-hand dropped to his side. "Come," he begged in what he intended as a conciliatory tone. "Let us be friends, Lady Greystoke. We can be of great assistance to each other and I promise not to harm you."

"Remember Liege and Louvain," she reminded him with a sneer. "I am going now—be sure that you do not follow me. As far as you can walk in a day from this spot in any direction you may consider the limits of my domain. If ever again I see you within these limits I shall kill you."

There could be no question that she meant what she said and the man seemed convinced for he but stood sullenly eyeing her as she backed from sight beyond a turn in the game trail that crossed the ford where they had met, and disappeared in the forest.

SILENTLY IN THE NIGHT

In A-lur the fortunes of the city had been tossed from hand to hand. The party of Ko-tan's loyal warriors that Tarzan had led to the rendezvous at the entrance to the secret passage below the palace gates had met with disaster. Their first rush had been met with soft words from the priests. They had been exhorted to defend the faith of their fathers from blasphemers. Ja-don was painted to them as a defiler of temples, and the wrath of Jad-ben-Otho was prophesied for those who embraced his cause. The priests insisted that Lu-don's only wish was to prevent the seizure of the throne by Ja-don until a new king could be chosen according to the laws of the Ho-don.

The result was that many of the palace warriors joined their fellows of the city, and when the priests saw that those whom they could influence outnumbered those who remained loyal to the palace, they caused the former to fall upon the latter with the result that many were killed and only a handful succeeded in reaching the safety of the palace gates, which they quickly barred.

The priests led their own forces through the secret passageway into the temple, while some of the loyal ones sought out Ja-don and told him all that had happened. The fight in the banquet hall had spread over a considerable portion of the palace grounds and had at last resulted in the temporary defeat of those who had opposed Ja-don. This force, counseled by under priests sent for the purpose by Lu-don, had withdrawn within the temple grounds so that now the issue was plainly marked as between Ja-don on the one side and Lu-don on the other.

The former had been told of all that had occurred in the apartments of O-lo-a to whose safety he had attended at the first opportunity and he had also learned of Tarzan's part in leading his men to the gathering of Lu-don's warriors.

These things had naturally increased the old warrior's former inclinations of friendliness toward the ape-man, and now he regretted that the other had departed from the city.

The testimony of O-lo-a and Pan-at-lee was such as to strengthen whatever belief in the godliness of the stranger Ja-don and others of the warriors had previously entertained, until presently there appeared a strong tendency upon the part of this palace faction to make the Dor-ul-otho an issue of their original quarrel with Lu-don. Whether this occurred as the natural sequence to repeated narrations of the ape-man's exploits, which lost nothing by repetition, in conjunction with Lu-don's enmity toward him, or whether it was the shrewd design of some wily old warrior such as Ja-don, who realized the value of adding a religious cause to their temporal one, it were difficult to determine; but the fact remained that Ja-don's followers developed bitter hatred for the followers of Lu-don because of the high priest's antagonism to Tarzan.

Unfortunately however Tarzan was not there to inspire the followers of Ja-don with the holy zeal that might have quickly settled the dispute in the old chieftain's favor. Instead, he was miles away and because their repeated prayers for his presence were unanswered, the weaker spirits among them commenced to suspect that their cause did not have divine favor. There was also another and a potent cause for defection from the ranks of Ja-don. It emanated from the city where the friends and relatives of the palace warriors, who were largely also the friends and relatives of Lu-don's forces, found the means, urged on by the priesthood, to circulate throughout the palace pernicious propaganda aimed at Ja-don's cause.

The result was that Lu-don's power increased while that of Ja-don waned. Then followed a sortie from the temple which resulted in the defeat of the palace forces, and though they were able to withdraw in decent order withdraw they did, leaving the palace to Lu-don, who was now virtually ruler of Pal-ul-don.

Ja-don, taking with him the princess, her women, and their slaves, including Pan-at-lee, as well as the women and children of his faithful followers, retreated not only from the palace but from the city of A-lur as well and fell back upon his own city of Ja-lur. Here he remained, recruiting his forces from the surrounding villages of the north which, being far removed from the influence of the priesthood of A-lur, were enthusiastic partisans in any cause that the old chieftain espoused, since for years he had been revered as their friend and protector.

And while these events were transpiring in the north, Tarzan-jad-guru lay in the lion pit at Tu-lur while messengers passed back and forth between Mo-sar and Lu-don as the two dickered for the throne of Pal-ul-don. Mo-sar was cunning enough to guess that should an open breach occur between himself and the high priest he might use his prisoner to his own advantage, for he had heard whisperings among even his own people that suggested that there were those who were more than a trifle inclined to belief in the divinity of the stranger and that he might indeed be the Dor-ul-Otho. Lu-don wanted Tarzan himself. He wanted to sacrifice him upon the eastern altar with his own hands before a multitude of people, since he was not without evidence that his own standing and authority had been lessened by the claims of the bold and heroic figure of the stranger.

The method that the high priest of Tu-lur had employed to trap Tarzan had left the ape-man in possession of his weapons though there seemed little likelihood of their being of any service to him. He also had his pouch, in which were the various odds and ends which are the natural accumulation of all receptacles from a gold meshbag to an attic. There were bits of obsidian and choice feathers for arrows, some pieces of flint and a couple of steel, an old knife, a heavy bone needle, and strips of dried gut. Nothing very useful to you or me, perhaps; but nothing useless to the savage life of the ape-man.

When Tarzan realized the trick that had been so neatly played upon him he had awaited expectantly the coming of the lion, for though the scent of ja was old he was sure that sooner or later they would let one of the beasts in upon him. His first consideration was a thorough exploration of his prison. He had noticed the hide-covered windows and these he immediately uncovered, letting in the light, and revealing the fact that though the chamber was far below the level of the temple courts it was yet many feet above the base of the hill from which the temple was hewn. The windows were so closely barred that he could not see over the edge of the thick wall in which they were cut to determine what lay close in below him. At a little distance were the blue waters of Jad-in-lul and beyond, the verdure-clad farther shore, and beyond that the mountains. It was a beautiful picture upon which he looked—a picture of peace and harmony and quiet. Nor anywhere a slightest suggestion of the savage men and beasts that claimed this lovely landscape as their own. What a paradise! And some day civilized man would come and—spoil it! Ruthless axes would raze that age-old wood; black, sticky smoke would rise from ugly chimneys against that azure sky; grimy little boats with wheels behind or upon either side would churn the mud from the bottom of Jad-in-lul, turning its blue waters to a dirty brown; hideous piers would project into the lake from squalid buildings of corrugated iron, doubtless, for of such are the pioneer cities of the world.

But would civilized man come? Tarzan hoped not. For countless generations civilization had ramped about the globe; it had dispatched its emissaries to the North Pole and the South; it had circled Pal-ul-don once, perhaps many times, but it had never touched her. God grant that it never would. Perhaps He was saving this

EDGAR RICE BURROUGHS

little spot to be always just as He had made it, for the scratching of the Ho-don and the Waz-don upon His rocks had not altered the fair face of Nature.

Through the windows came sufficient light to reveal the whole interior to Tarzan. The room was fairly large and there was a door at each end—a large door for men and a smaller one for lions. Both were closed with heavy masses of stone that had been lowered in grooves running to the floor. The two windows were small and closely barred with the first iron that Tarzan had seen in Pal-ul-don. The bars were let into holes in the casing, and the whole so strongly and neatly contrived that escape seemed impossible. Yet within a few minutes of his incarceration Tarzan had commenced to undertake his escape. The old knife in his pouch was brought into requisition and slowly the ape-man began to scrape and chip away the stone from about the bars of one of the windows. It was slow work but Tarzan had the patience of absolute health.

Each day food and water were brought him and slipped quickly beneath the smaller door which was raised just sufficiently to allow the stone receptacles to pass in. The prisoner began to believe that he was being preserved for something beside lions. However that was immaterial. If they would but hold off for a few more days they might select what fate they would—he would not be there when they arrived to announce it.

And then one day came Pan-sat, Lu-don's chief tool, to the city of Tu-lur. He came ostensibly with a fair message for Mo-sar from the high priest at A-lur. Lu-don had decided that Mo-sar should be king and he invited Mo-sar to come at once to A-lur and then Pan-sat, having delivered the message, asked that he might go to the temple of Tu-lur and pray, and there he sought the high priest of Tu-lur to whom was the true message that Lu-don had sent. The two were closeted alone in a little chamber and Pan-sat whispered into the ear of the high priest.

"Mo-sar wishes to be king," he said, "and Lu-don wishes to be king. Mo-sar wishes to retain the stranger who claims to be the Dor-ul-Otho and Lu-don wishes to kill him, and now," he leaned even closer to the ear of the high priest of Tu-lur, "if you would be high priest at A-lur it is within your power."

Pan-sat ceased speaking and waited for the other's reply. The high priest was visibly affected. To be high priest at A-lur! That was almost as good as being king of all Pal-ul-don, for great were the powers of him who conducted the sacrifices upon the altars of A-lur.

"How?" whispered the high priest. "How may I become high priest at A-lur?"

Again Pan-sat leaned close: "By killing the one and bringing the other to A-lur," replied he. Then he rose and departed knowing chat the other had swallowed the bait and could be depended upon to do whatever was required to win him the great prize.

Nor was Pan-sat mistaken other than in one trivial consideration. This high priest would indeed commit murder and treason to attain the high office at A-lur; but he had misunderstood which of his victims was to be killed and which to be delivered to Lu-don. Pan-sat, knowing himself all the details of the plannings of Lu-don, had made the quite natural error of assuming that the ocher was perfectly aware that only by publicly sacrificing the false Dor-ul-Otho could the high priest at A-lur bolster his waning power and that the assassination of Mo-sar, the pretender, would remove from Lu-don's camp the only obstacle to his combining the offices of high priest and king. The high priest at Tu-lur thought that he had been commissioned to kill Tarzan and bring Mo-sar to A-lur. He also thought that when he had done these things he would be made high priest at A-lur; but he did not know that already the priest had been selected who was to murder him within the hour that he arrived at A-lur, nor did he know that a secret grave had been prepared for him in the floor of a subterranean chamber in the very temple he dreamed of controlling.

And so when he should have been arranging the assassination of his chief he was leading a dozen heavily bribed warriors through the dark corridors beneath the temple to slay Tarzan in the lion pit. Night had fallen. A single torch guided the footsteps of the murderers as they crept stealthily upon their evil way, for they knew that they were doing the thing that their chief did not want done and their guilty consciences warned them to stealth.

In the dark of his cell the ape-man worked at his seemingly endless chipping and scraping. His keen ears detected the coming of footsteps along the corridor without—footsteps that approached the larger door. Always before had they come to the smaller door—the footsteps of a single slave who brought his food. This time there were many more than one and their coming at this time of night carried a sinister suggestion. Tarzan continued to work at his scraping and chipping. He heard them stop beyond the door. All was silence broken only by the scrape, scrape, scrape of the ape-man's tireless blade.

Those without heard it and listening sought to explain it. They whispered in low tones making their plans. Two would raise the door quickly and the others would rush in and hurl their clubs at the prisoner. They would take no chances, for the stories that had circulated in A-lur had been brought to Tu-lur—stories of the great strength and wonderful prowess of Tarzan-jad-guru that caused the sweat to stand upon the brows of the warriors, though it was cool in the damp corridor and they were twelve to one.

And then the high priest gave the signal—the door shot upward and ten warriors leaped into the chamber with poised clubs. Three of the heavy weapons flew across the room toward a darker shadow that lay in the shadow of the opposite wall, then the flare of the torch in the priest's hand lighted the interior and they saw that the thing at which they had flung their clubs was a pile of skins torn from the windows and that except for themselves the chamber was vacant.

One of them hastened to a window. All but a single bar was gone and to this was tied one end of a braided rope fashioned from strips cut from the leather window hangings.

To the ordinary dangers of Jane Clayton's existence was now added the menace of Obergatz' knowledge of her whereabouts. The lion and the panther had given her less cause for anxiety than did the return of the unscrupulous Hun, whom she had always distrusted and feared, and whose repulsiveness was now immeasurably augmented by his unkempt and filthy appearance, his strange and mirthless laughter, and his unnatural demeanor. She feared him now with a new fear as though he had suddenly become the personification of some nameless horror. The wholesome, outdoor life that she had been leading had strengthened and rebuilt her nervous system yet it seemed to her as she thought of him that if this man should ever touch her she should scream, and, possibly, even faint. Again and again during the day following their unexpected meeting the woman reproached herself for not having killed him as she would ja or jato or any other predatory beast that menaced her existence or her safety. There was no attempt at self-justification for these sinister reflections—they needed no justification. The standards by which the acts of such as you or I may be judged could not apply to hers. We have recourse to the protection of friends and relatives and the civil soldiery that upholds the majesty of the law and which may be invoked to protect the righteous weak against the unrighteous strong; but Jane Clayton comprised within herself not only the righteous weak but all the various agencies for the protection of the weak. To her, then, Lieutenant Erich Obergatz presented no different problem than did ja, the lion, other than that she considered the former the more dangerous animal. And so she determined that should he ignore her warning there would be no temporizing upon the occasion of their next meeting—the same swift spear that would meet ja's advances would meet his.

That night her snug little nest perched high in the great tree seemed less the sanctuary that it had before. What might resist the sanguinary intentions of a prowling panther would prove no great barrier to man, and influenced by this thought she slept less well than before. The slightest noise that broke the monotonous hum of the nocturnal jungle startled her into alert wakefulness to lie with straining ears in an attempt to classify the origin of the disturbance, and once she was awakened thus by a sound that seemed to come from something moving in her own tree. She listened intently—scarce breathing. Yes, there it was again. A scuffing of something soft against the hard bark of the tree. The woman reached out in the darkness and grasped her spear. Now she felt a slight sagging of one of the limbs that supported her shelter as though the thing, whatever it was, was slowly raising its weight to the branch. It came nearer. Now she thought that she could detect its breathing. It was at the door. She could hear it fumbling with the frail barrier. What could it be?

It made no sound by which she might identify it. She raised herself upon her hands and knees and crept stealthily the little distance to the doorway, her spear clutched tightly in her hand. Whatever the thing was, it was evidently attempting to gain entrance without awakening her. It was just beyond the pitiful little contraption of slender boughs that she had bound together with grasses and called a door—only a few inches lay between the thing and her. Rising to her knees she reached out with her left hand and felt until she found a place where a crooked branch had left an opening a couple of inches wide near the center of the barrier. Into this she inserted the point of her spear. The thing must have heard her move within for suddenly it abandoned its efforts for stealth and tore angrily at the obstacle. At the same moment Jane thrust her spear forward with all her strength. She felt it enter flesh. There was a scream and a curse from without, followed by the crashing of a body through limbs and foliage. Her spear was almost dragged from her grasp, but she held to it until it broke free from the thing it had pierced.

It was Obergatz; the curse had told her that. From below came no further sound. Had she, then, killed him? She prayed so—with all her heart she prayed it. To be freed from the menace of this loathsome creature were relief indeed. During all the balance of the night she lay there awake, listening. Below her, she imagined, she could see the dead man with his hideous face bathed in the cold light of the moon—lying there upon his back staring up at her.

She prayed that ja might come and drag it away, but all during the remainder of the night she heard never another sound above the drowsy hum of the jungle. She was glad that he was dead, but she dreaded the gruesome ordeal that awaited her on the morrow, for she must bury the thing that had been Erich Obergatz and live on there above the shallow grave of the man she had slain.

She reproached herself for her weakness, repeating over and over that she had killed in self-defense, that her act was justified; but she was still a woman of today, and strong upon her were the iron mandates of the social order from which she had sprung, its interdictions and its superstitions.

At last came the tardy dawn. Slowly the sun topped the distant mountains beyond Jad-in-lul. And yet she hesitated to loosen the fastenings of her door and look out upon the thing below. But it must be done. She steeled herself and untied the rawhide thong that secured the barrier. She looked down and only the grass and the flowers looked up at her. She came from her shelter and examined the ground upon the opposite side of the tree—there was no dead man there, nor anywhere as far as she could see. Slowly she descended, keeping a wary eye and an alert ear ready for the first intimation of danger.

At the foot of the tree was a pool of blood and a little trail of crimson drops upon the grass, leading away parallel with the shore of Jad-ben-lul. Then she had not slain him! She was vaguely aware of a peculiar, double sensation of relief and regret. Now she would be always in doubt. He might return; but at least she would not have to live above his grave.

She thought some of following the bloody spoor on the chance that he might have crawled away to die later, but she gave up the idea for fear that she might find him dead nearby, or, worse yet badly wounded. What then could she do? She could not finish him with her spear—no, she knew that she could not do that, nor could she bring him back and nurse him, nor could she leave him there to die of hunger or of thirst, or to become the prey of some prowling beast. It were better then not to search for him for fear that she might find him.

That day was one of nervous starting to every sudden sound. The day before she would have said that her nerves were of iron; but not today. She knew now the shock that she had suffered and that this was the reaction. Tomorrow it might be different, but something told her that never again would her little shelter and the patch of forest and jungle that she called her own be the same. There would hang over them always the menace of this man. No longer would she pass restful nights of deep slumber. The peace of her little world was shattered forever.

That night she made her door doubly secure with additional thongs of rawhide cut from the pelt of the buck she had slain the day that she met Obergatz. She was very tired for she had lost much sleep the night before; but for a long time she lay with wide-open eyes staring into the darkness. What saw she there? Visions that brought tears to those brave and beautiful eyes—visions of a rambling bungalow that had been home to her and that was no more, destroyed by the same cruel force that haunted her even now in this remote, uncharted corner of the earth; visions of a strong man whose protecting arm would never press her close again; visions of a tall, straight son who looked at her adoringly out of brave, smiling eyes that were like his father's. Always the vision of the crude simple bungalow rather than of the stately halls that had been as much a part of her life as the other. But he had loved the bungalow and the broad, free acres best and so she had come to love them best, too.

At last she slept, the sleep of utter exhaustion. How long it lasted she did not know; but suddenly she was wide awake and once again she heard the scuffing of a body against the bark of her tree and again the limb bent to a heavy weight. He had returned! She went cold, trembling as with ague. Was it he, or, O God! had she killed him then and was this—? She tried to drive the horrid thought from her mind, for this way, she knew, lay madness.

And once again she crept to the door, for the thing was outside just as it had been last night. Her hands trembled as she placed the point of her weapon to the opening. She wondered if it would scream as it fell.

THE MANIAC

The last bar that would make the opening large enough to permit his body to pass had been removed as Tarzan heard the warriors whispering beyond the stone door of his prison. Long since had the rope of hide been braided. To secure one end to the remaining bar that he had left for this purpose was the work of but a moment, and while the warriors whispered without, the brown body of the ape-man slipped through the small aperture and disappeared below the sill.

Tarzan's escape from the cell left him still within the walled area that comprised the palace and temple grounds and buildings. He had reconnoitered as best he might from the window after he had removed enough bars to permit him to pass his head through the opening, so that he knew what lay immediately before him—a winding and usually deserted alleyway leading in the direction of the outer gate that opened from the palace grounds into the city.

The darkness would facilitate his escape. He might even pass out of the palace and the city without detection. If he could elude the guard at the palace gate the rest would be easy. He strode along confidently, exhibiting no fear of detection, for he reasoned that thus would he disarm suspicion. In the darkness he easily could pass for a Ho-don and in truth, though he passed several after leaving the deserted alley, no one accosted or detained him, and thus he came at last to the guard of a half-dozen warriors before the palace gate. These he attempted to pass in the same unconcerned fashion and he might have succeeded had it not been for one who came running rapidly from the direction of the temple shouting: "Let no one pass the gates! The prisoner has escaped from the pal-ul-ja!"

Instantly a warrior barred his way and simultaneously the fellow recognized him. "Xot tor!" he exclaimed: "Here he is now. Fall upon him! Fall upon him! Back! Back before I kill you."

The others came forward. It cannot be said that they rushed forward. If it was their wish to fall upon him there was a noticeable lack of enthusiasm other than that which directed their efforts to persuade someone else to fall upon him. His fame as a fighter had been too long a topic of conversation for the good of the morale of Mo-sar's warriors. It were safer to stand at a distance and hurl their clubs and this they did, but the ape-man had learned something of the use of this weapon since he had arrived in Pal-ul-don. And as he learned great had grown his respect for this most primitive of arms. He had come to realize that the black savages he had known had never appreciated the possibilities of their knob sticks, nor had he, and he had discovered, too, why the Pal-ul-donians had turned their ancient spears into plowshares and pinned their faith to the heavy-ended club alone. In deadly execution it was far more effective than a spear and it answered, too, every purpose of a shield, combining the two in one and thus reducing the burden of the warrior. Thrown as they throw it, after the manner of the hammer-throwers of the Olympian games, an ordinary shield would prove more a weakness than a strength while one that would be strong enough to prove a protection would be too heavy to carry. Only another club, deftly wielded to deflect the course of an enemy missile, is in any way effective against these formidable weapons and, too, the war club of Pal-ul-don can be thrown with accuracy a far greater distance than any spear.

And now was put to the test that which Tarzan had learned from Om-at and Ta-den. His eyes and his muscles trained by a lifetime of necessity moved with the rapidity of light and his brain functioned with an uncanny celerity that suggested nothing less than prescience, and these things more than compensated for his lack of experience with the war club he handled so dexterously. Weapon after weapon he warded off and always he moved with a single idea in mind—to place himself within reach of one of his antagonists. But they were wary for they feared this strange creature to whom the superstitious fears of many of them attributed the miraculous powers of deity. They managed to keep between Tarzan and the gateway and all the time they bawled lustily for reinforcements. Should these come before he had made his escape the ape-man realized that the odds against him would be unsurmountable, and so he redoubled his efforts to carry out his design.

Following their usual tactics two or three of the warriors were always circling behind him collecting the thrown clubs when Tarzan's attention was directed elsewhere. He himself retrieved several of them which he hurled with such deadly effect as to dispose of two of his antagonists, but now he heard the approach of hurrying warriors, the patter of their bare feet upon the stone pavement and then the savage cries which were to bolster the courage of their fellows and fill the enemy with fear.

There was no time to lose. Tarzan held a club in either hand and, swinging one he hurled it at a warrior before him and as the man dodged he rushed in and seized him, at the same time casting his second club at another of his opponents. The Ho-don with whom he grappled reached instantly for his knife but the ape-man grasped his wrist. There was a sudden twist, the snapping of a bone and an agonized scream, then the warrior was lifted bodily from his feet and held as a shield between his fellows and the fugitive as the latter backed through the gateway. Beside Tarzan stood the single torch that lighted the entrance to the palace grounds. The warriors were advancing to the succor of their fellow when the ape-man raised his captive high above his head and flung him full in the face of the foremost attacker. The fellow went down and two directly behind him sprawled headlong over their companion as the ape-man seized the torch and cast it back into the palace grounds to be extinguished as it struck the bodies of those who led the charging reinforcements.

In the ensuing darkness Tarzan disappeared in the streets of Tu-lur beyond the palace gate. For a time he was aware of sounds of pursuit but the fact that they trailed away and died in the direction of Jad-in-lul informed him that they were searching in the wrong direction, for he had turned south out of Tu-lur purposely to throw them off his track. Beyond the outskirts of the city he turned directly toward the northwest, in which direction lay A-lur.

In his path he knew lay Jad-bal-lul, the shore of which he was compelled to skirt, and there would be a river to cross at the lower end of the great lake upon the shores of which lay A-lur. What other obstacles lay in his way he did not know but he believed that he could make better time on foot than by attempting to steal a canoe and force his way up stream with a single paddle. It was his intention to put as much distance as possible between himself and Tu-lur before he slept for he was sure that Mo-sar would not lightly accept his loss, but that with the coming of day, or possibly even before, he would dispatch warriors in search of him.

A mile or two from the city he entered a forest and here at last he felt such a measure of safety as he never knew in open spaces or in cities. The forest and the jungle were his birthright. No creature that went upon the ground upon four feet, or climbed among the trees, or crawled upon its belly had any advantage over the ape-man in his native heath. As myrrh and frankincense were the dank odors of rotting vegetation in the nostrils of the great Tarmangani. He squared his broad shoulders and lifting his head filled his lungs with the air that he loved best. The heavy fragrance of tropical blooms, the commingled odors of the myriad-scented life of the jungle went to his head with a pleasurable intoxication far more potent than aught contained in the oldest vintages of civilization.

He took to the trees now, not from necessity but from pure love of the wild freedom that had been denied him so long. Though it was dark and the forest strange yet he moved with a surety and ease that bespoke more a strange uncanny sense than wondrous skill. He heard ja moaning somewhere ahead and an owl hooted mournfully to the right of him—long familiar sounds that imparted to him no sense of loneliness as they might to you or to me, but on the contrary one of companionship for they betokened the presence of his fellows of the jungle, and whether friend or foe it was all the same to the ape-man.

He came at last to a little stream at a spot where the trees did not meet above it so he was forced to descend to the ground and wade through the water and upon the opposite shore he stopped as though suddenly his godlike figure had been transmuted from flesh to marble. Only his dilating nostrils bespoke his pulsing vitality. For a long moment he stood there thus and then swiftly, but with a caution and silence that were inherent in him he moved forward again, but now his whole attitude bespoke a new urge. There was a definite and masterful purpose in every movement of those steel muscles rolling softly beneath the smooth brown hide. He moved now toward a certain goal that quite evidently filled him with far greater enthusiasm than had the possible event of his return to A-lur.

And so he came at last to the foot of a great tree and there he stopped and looked up above him among the foliage where the dim outlines of a roughly rectangular bulk loomed darkly. There was a choking sensation in Tarzan's throat as he raised himself gently into the branches. It was as though his heart were swelling either to a great happiness or a great fear.

Before the rude shelter built among the branches he paused listening. From within there came to his sensitive nostrils the same delicate aroma that had arrested his eager attention at the little stream a mile away. He crouched upon the branch close to the little door.

"Jane," he called, "heart of my heart, it is I."

The only answer from within was as the sudden indrawing of a breath that was half gasp and half sigh, and the sound of a body falling to the floor. Hurriedly Tarzan sought to release the thongs which held the door but they were fastened from the inside, and at last, impatient with further delay, he seized the frail barrier in one giant hand and with a single effort tore it completely away. And then he entered to find the seemingly lifeless body of his mate stretched upon the floor.

He gathered her in his arms; her heart beat; she still breathed, and presently he realized that she had but swooned.

When Jane Clayton regained consciousness it was to find herself held tightly in two strong arms, her head pillowed upon the broad shoulder where so often before her fears had been soothed and her sorrows comforted. At first she was not sure but that it was all a dream. Timidly her hand stole to his cheek.

"John," she murmured, "tell me, is it really you?"

In reply he drew her more closely to him. "It is I," he replied. "But there is something in my throat," he said haltingly, "that makes it hard for me to speak."

She smiled and snuggled closer to him. "God has been good to us, Tarzan of the Apes," she said.

For some time neither spoke. It was enough that they were reunited and that each knew that the other was alive and safe. But at last they found their voices and when the sun rose they were still talking, so much had each to tell the other; so many questions there were to be asked and answered.

"And Jack," she asked, "where is he?"

"I do not know," replied Tarzan. "The last I heard of him he was on the Argonne Front."

"Ah, then our happiness is not quite complete," she said, a little note of sadness creeping into her voice.

"No," he replied, "but the same is true in countless other English homes today, and pride is learning to take the place of happiness in these."

She shook her head, "I want my boy," she said.

"And I too," replied Tarzan, "and we may have him yet. He was safe and unwounded the last word I had. And now," he said, "we must plan upon our return. Would you like to rebuild the bungalow and gather together the remnants of our Waziri or would you rather return to London?"

"Only to find Jack," she said. "I dream always of the bungalow and never of the city, but John, we can only dream, for Obergatz told me that he had circled this whole country and found no place where he might cross the morass."

"I am not Obergatz," Tarzan reminded her, smiling. "We will rest today and tomorrow we will set out toward the north. It is a savage country, but we have crossed it once and we can cross it again."

And so, upon the following morning, the Tarmangani and his mate went forth upon their journey across the Valley of Jad-ben-Otho, and ahead of them were fierce men and savage beasts, and the lofty mountains of Pal-ul-don; and beyond the mountains the reptiles and the morass, and beyond that the arid, thorn-covered steppe, and other savage beasts and men and weary, hostile miles of untracked wilderness between them and the charred ruins of their home.

Lieutenant Erich Obergatz crawled through the grass upon all fours, leaving a trail of blood behind him after Jane's spear had sent him crashing to the ground beneath her tree. He made no sound after the one piercing scream that had acknowledged the severity of his wound. He was quiet because of a great fear that had crept into his warped brain that the devil woman would pursue and slay him. And so he crawled away like some filthy beast of prey, seeking a thicket where he might lie down and hide.

He thought that he was going to die, but he did not, and with the coming of the new day he discovered that his wound was superficial. The rough obsidian-shod spear had entered the muscles of his side beneath his right arm inflicting a painful, but not a fatal wound. With the realization of this fact came a renewed desire to put as much distance as possible between himself and Jane Clayton. And so he moved on, still going upon all fours because of a persistent hallucination that in this way he might escape observation. Yet though he fled his mind still revolved muddily about a central desire—while he fled from her he still planned to pursue her, and to his lust of possession was added a desire for revenge. She should pay for the suffering she had inflicted upon him. She should pay for rebuffing him, but for some reason which he did not try to explain to himself he would crawl away and hide. He would come back though. He would come back and when he had finished with her, he would take that smooth throat in his two hands and crush the life from her.

He kept repeating this over and over to himself and then he fell to laughing out loud, the cackling, hideous laughter that had terrified Jane. Presently he realized his knees were bleeding and that they hurt him. He looked cautiously behind. No one was in sight. He listened. He could hear no indications of pursuit and so he rose to his feet and continued upon his way a sorry sight—covered with filth and blood, his beard and hair tangled and matted and filled with burrs and dried mud and unspeakable filth. He kept no track of time. He ate fruits and berries and tubers that he dug from the earth with his fingers. He followed the shore of the lake and the river that he might be near water, and when ja roared or moaned he climbed a tree and hid there, shivering.

And so after a time he came up the southern shore of Jad-ben-lul until a wide river stopped his progress. Across the blue water a white city glimmered in the sun. He looked at it for a long time, blinking his eyes like an owl. Slowly a recollection forced itself through his tangled brain. This was A-lur, the City of Light. The association of ideas recalled Bu-lur and the Waz-ho-don. They had called him Jad-ben-Otho. He commenced to laugh aloud and stood up very straight and strode back and forth along the shore. "I am Jad-ben-Otho," he cried, "I am the Great God. In A-lur is my temple and my high priests. What is Jad-ben-Otho doing here alone in the jungle?"

He stepped out into the water and raising his voice shrieked loudly across toward A-lur. "I am Jad-ben-Otho!" he screamed. "Come hither slaves and take your god to his temple." But the distance was great and they did not hear him and no one came, and the feeble mind was distracted by other things—a bird flying in the air, a school of minnows swimming around his feet. He lunged at them trying to catch them, and falling upon his hands and knees he crawled through the water grasping futilely at the elusive fish.

Presently it occurred to him that he was a sea lion and he forgot the fish and lay down and tried to swim by wriggling his feet in the water as though they were a tail. The hardships, the privations, the terrors, and for the past few weeks the lack of proper nourishment had reduced Erich Obergatz to little more than a gibbering idiot.

A water snake swam out upon the surface of the lake and the man pursued it, crawling upon his hands and knees. The snake swam toward the shore just within the mouth of the river where tall reeds grew thickly and Obergatz followed, making grunting noises like a pig. He lost the snake within the reeds but he came upon something else—a canoe hidden there close to the bank. He examined it with cackling laughter. There were two paddles within it which he took and threw out into the current of the river. He watched them for a while and then he sat down beside the canoe and commenced to splash his hands up and down upon the water. He liked to hear the noise and see the little splashes of spray. He rubbed his left forearm with his right palm and the dirt came off and left a white spot that drew his attention. He rubbed again upon the now thoroughly soaked blood and grime that covered his body. He was not attempting to wash himself; he was merely amused by the strange results. "I am turning white," he cried. His glance wandered from his body now that the grime and blood were all removed and caught again the white city shimmering beneath the hot sun.

"A-lur—City of Light!" he shrieked and that reminded him again of Tu-lur and by the same process of associated ideas that had before suggested it, he recalled that the Waz-ho-don had thought him Jad-ben-Otho.

"I am Jad-ben-Otho!" he screamed and then his eyes fell again upon the canoe. A new idea came and persisted. He looked down at himself, examining his body, and seeing the filthy loin cloth, now water soaked and more bedraggled than before, he tore it from him and flung it into the lake. "Gods do not wear dirty rags," he said aloud. "They do not wear anything but wreaths and garlands of flowers and I am a god—I am Jad-ben-Otho—and I go in state to my sacred city of A-lur."

He ran his fingers through his matted hair and beard. The water had softened the burrs but had not removed them. The man shook his head. His hair and beard failed to harmonize with his other godly attributes. He was commencing to think more clearly now, for the great idea had taken hold of his scattered wits and concentrated them upon a single purpose, but he was still a maniac. The only difference being that he was now a maniac with a fixed intent. He went out on the shore and gathered flowers and ferns and wove them in his beard and hair—blazing blooms of different colors—green ferns that trailed about his ears or rose bravely upward like the plumes in a lady's hat.

When he was satisfied that his appearance would impress the most casual observer with his evident deity he returned to the canoe, pushed it from shore and jumped in. The impetus carried it into the river's current and the current bore it out upon the lake. The naked man stood erect in the center of the little craft, his arms folded upon his chest. He screamed aloud his message to the city: "I am Jad-ben-Otho! Let the high priest and the under priests attend upon me!"

As the current of the river was dissipated by the waters of the lake the wind caught him and his craft and carried them bravely forward. Sometimes he drifted with his back toward A-lur and sometimes with his face toward it, and at intervals he shrieked his message and his commands. He was still in the middle of the lake when someone discovered him from the palace wall, and as he drew nearer, a crowd of warriors and women and children were congregated there watching him and along the temple walls were many priests and among them Lu-don, the high priest. When the boat had drifted close enough for them to distinguish the bizarre figure standing in it and for them to catch the meaning of his words Lu-don's cunning eyes narrowed. The high priest had learned of the escape of Tarzan and he feared that should he join Ja-don's forces, as seemed likely, he would attract many recruits who might still believe in him, and the Dor-ul-Otho, even if a false one, upon the side of the enemy might easily work havoc with Lu-don's plans.

The man was drifting close in. His canoe would soon be caught in the current that ran close to shore here and carried toward the river that emptied the waters of Jad-ben-lul into Jad-bal-lul. The under priests were looking toward Lu-don for instructions.

"Fetch him hither!" he commanded. "If he is Jad-ben-Otho I shall know him."

The priests hurried to the palace grounds and summoned warriors. "Go, bring the stranger to Lu-don. If he is Jad-ben-Otho we shall know him."

And so Lieutenant Erich Obergatz was brought before the high priest at A-lur. Lu-don looked closely at the naked man with the fantastic headdress.

"Where did you come from?" he asked.

"I am Jad-ben-Otho," cried the German. "I came from heaven. Where is my high priest?"

"I am the high priest," replied Lu-don.

Obergatz clapped his hands. "Have my feet bathed and food brought to me," he commanded.

Lu-don's eyes narrowed to mere slits of crafty cunning. He bowed low until his forehead touched the feet of the stranger. Before the eyes of many priests, and warriors from the palace he did it.

"Ho, slaves," he cried, rising; "fetch water and food for the Great God," and thus the high priest acknowledged before his people the godhood of Lieutenant Erich Obergatz, nor was it long before the story ran like wildfire through the palace and out into the city and beyond that to the lesser villages all the way from A-lur to Tu-lur.

The real god had come—Jad-ben-Otho himself, and he had espoused the cause of Lu-don, the high priest. Mo-sar lost no time in placing himself at the disposal of Lu-don, nor did he mention aught about his claims to the throne. It was Mo-sar's opinion that he might consider himself fortunate were he allowed to remain in peaceful occupation of his chieftainship at Tu-lur, nor was Mo-sar wrong in his deductions.

But Lu-don could still use him and so he let him live and sent word to him to come to A-lur with all his warriors, for it was rumored that Ja-don was raising a great army in the north and might soon march upon the City of Light.

Obergatz thoroughly enjoyed being a god. Plenty of food and peace of mind and rest partially brought back to him the reason that had been so rapidly slipping from him; but in one respect he was madder than ever, since now no power on earth would ever be able to convince him that he was not a god. Slaves were put at his disposal and these he ordered about in godly fashion. The same portion of his naturally cruel mind met upon common ground the mind of Lu-don, so that the two seemed always in accord. The high priest saw in the stranger a mighty force wherewith to hold forever his power over all Pal-ul-don and thus the future of Obergatz was assured so long as he cared to play god to Lu-don's high priest.

A throne was erected in the main temple court before the eastern altar where Jad-ben-Otho might sit in person and behold the sacrifices that were offered up to him there each day at sunset. So much did the cruel, half-crazed mind enjoy these spectacles that at times he even insisted upon wielding the sacrificial knife himself and upon such occasions the priests and the people fell upon their faces in awe of the dread deity.

If Obergatz taught them not to love their god more he taught them to fear him as they never had before, so that the name of Jad-ben-Otho was whispered in the city and little children were frightened into obedience by the mere mention of it. Lu-don, through his priests and slaves, circulated the information that Jad-ben-Otho had commanded all his faithful followers to flock to the standard of the high priest at A-lur and that all others were cursed, especially Ja-don and the base impostor who had posed as the Dor-ul-Otho. The curse was to take the form of early death following terrible suffering, and Lu-don caused it to be published abroad that the name of any warrior who complained of a pain should be brought to him, for such might be deemed to be under suspicion, since the first effects of the curse would result in slight pains attacking the unholy. He counseled those who felt pains to look carefully to their loyalty. The result was remarkable and immediate—half a nation without a pain, and recruits pouring into A-lur to offer their services to Lu-don while secretly hoping that the little pains they had felt in arm or leg or belly would not recur in aggravated form.

A JOURNEY ON A GRYF

Tarzan and Jane skirted the shore of Jad-bal-lul and crossed the river at the head of the lake. They moved in leisurely fashion with an eye to comfort and safety, for the ape-man, now that he had found his mate, was determined to court no chance that might again separate them, or delay or prevent their escape from Pal-ul-don. How they were to recross the morass was a matter of little concern to him as yet—it would be time enough to consider that matter when it became of more immediate moment. Their hours were filled with the happiness and content of reunion after long separation; they had much to talk of, for each had passed through many trials and vicissitudes and strange adventures, and no important hour might go unaccounted for since last they met.

It was Tarzan's intention to choose a way above A-lur and the scattered Ho-don villages below it, passing about midway between them and the mountains, thus avoiding, in so far as possible, both the Ho-don and Waz-don, for in this area lay the neutral territory that was uninhabited by either. Thus he would travel northwest until opposite the Kor-ul-ja where he planned to stop to pay his respects to Om-at and give the gund word of Pan-at-lee, and a plan Tarzan had for insuring her safe return to her people. It was upon the third day of their journey and they had almost reached the river that passes through A-lur when Jane suddenly clutched Tarzan's arm and pointed ahead toward the edge of a forest that they were approaching. Beneath the shadows of the trees loomed a great bulk that the ape-man instantly recognized.

"What is it?" whispered Jane.

"A gryf," replied the ape-man, "and we have met him in the worst place that we could possibly have found. There is not a large tree within a quarter of a mile, other than those among which he stands. Come, we shall have to go back, Jane; I cannot risk it with you along. The best we can do is to pray that he does not discover us."

"And if he does?"

"Then I shall have to risk it."

"Risk what?"

"The chance that I can subdue him as I subdued one of his fellows," replied Tarzan. "I told you—you recall?"

"Yes, but I did not picture so huge a creature. Why, John, he is as big as a battleship."

The ape-man laughed. "Not quite, though I'll admit he looks quite as formidable as one when he charges." They were moving away slowly so as not to attract the attention of the beast.

"I believe we're going to make it," whispered the woman, her voice tense with suppressed excitement. A low rumble rolled like distant thunder from the wood. Tarzan shook his head.

"'The big show is about to commence in the main tent,'" he quoted, grinning. He caught the woman suddenly to his breast and kissed her. "One can never tell, Jane," he said. "We'll do our best—that is all we can do. Give me your spear, and—don't run. The only hope we have lies in that little brain more than in us. If I can control it—well, let us see."

The beast had emerged from the forest and was looking about through his weak eyes, evidently in search of them. Tarzan raised his voice in the weird notes of the Tor-o-don's cry, "Whee-oo! Whee-oo! Whee-oo!" For a moment the great beast stood motionless, his attention riveted by the call. The ape-man advanced straight toward him, Jane Clayton at his elbow. "Whee-oo!" he cried again peremptorily. A low rumble rolled from the gryf's cavernous chest in answer to the call, and the beast moved slowly toward them.

"Fine!" exclaimed Tarzan. "The odds are in our favor now. You can keep your nerve?—but I do not need to ask."

"I know no fear when I am with Tarzan of the Apes," she replied softly, and he felt the pressure of her soft fingers on his arm.

And thus the two approached the giant monster of a forgotten epoch until they stood close in the shadow of a mighty shoulder. "Whee-oo!" shouted Tarzan and struck the hideous snout with the shaft of the spear. The vicious side snap that did not reach its mark—that evidently was not intended to reach its mark—was the hoped-for answer.

"Come," said Tarzan, and taking Jane by the hand he led her around behind the monster and up the broad tail to the great, horned back. "Now will we ride in the state that our forebears knew, before which the pomp of modern kings pales into cheap and tawdry insignificance. How would you like to canter through Hyde Park on a mount like this?"

"I am afraid the Bobbies would be shocked by our riding habits, John," she cried, laughingly.

Tarzan guided the gryf in the direction that they wished to go. Steep embankments and rivers proved no slightest obstacle to the ponderous creature.

"A prehistoric tank, this," Jane assured him, and laughing and talking they continued on their way. Once they came unexpectedly upon a dozen Ho-don warriors as the gryf emerged suddenly into a small clearing. The fellows were lying about in the shade of a single tree that grew alone. When they saw the beast they leaped to their feet in consternation and at their shouts the gryf issued his hideous, challenging bellow and charged them. The warriors fled in all directions while Tarzan belabored the beast across the snout with his spear in an effort to control him, and at last he succeeded, just as the gryf was almost upon one poor devil that it seemed to have singled out for its special prey. With an angry grunt the gryf stopped and the man, with a single backward glance that showed a face white with terror, disappeared in the jungle he had been seeking to reach.

The ape-man was elated. He had doubted that he could control the beast should it take it into its head to charge a victim and had intended abandoning it before they reached the Kor-ul-ja. Now he altered his plans—they would ride to the very village of Om-at upon the gryf, and the Kor-ul-ja would have food for conversation for many generations to come. Nor was it the theatric instinct of the ape-man alone that gave favor to this plan. The element of Jane's safety entered into the matter for he knew that she would be safe from man and beast alike so long as she rode upon the back of Pal-ul-don's most formidable creature.

As they proceeded slowly in the direction of the Kor-ul-ja, for the natural gait of the gryf is far from rapid, a handful of terrified warriors came panting into A-lur, spreading a weird story of the Dor-ul-Otho, only none dared call him the Dor-ul-Otho aloud. Instead they spoke of him as Tarzan-jad-guru and they told of meeting him mounted upon a mighty gryf beside the beautiful stranger woman whom Ko-tan would have made queen of Pal-ul-don. This story was brought to Lu-don who caused the warriors to be hailed to his presence, when he questioned them closely until finally he was convinced that they spoke the truth and when they had told him the direction in which the two were traveling, Lu-don guessed that they were on their way to Ja-lur to join Ja-don, a contingency that he felt must be prevented at any cost. As was his wont in the stress of emergency, he called Pan-sat into consultation and for long the two sat in close conference. When they arose a plan had been developed. Pan-sat went immediately to his own quarters where he removed the headdress and trappings of a priest to don in their stead the harness and weapons of a warrior. Then he returned to Lu-don.

"Good!" cried the latter, when he saw him. "Not even your fellow-priests or the slaves that wait upon you daily would know you now. Lose no time, Pan-sat, for all depends upon the speed with which you strike and—remember! Kill the man if you can; but in any event bring the woman to me here, alive. You understand?"

"Yes, master," replied the priest, and so it was that a lone warrior set out from A-lur and made his way northwest in the direction of Ja-lur.

The gorge next above Kor-ul-ja is uninhabited and here the wily Ja-don had chosen to mobilize his army for its descent upon A-lur. Two considerations influenced him—one being the fact that could he keep his plans a secret from the enemy he would have the advantage of delivering a surprise attack upon the forces of Lu-don from a direction that they would not expect attack, and in the meantime he would be able to keep his men from the gossip of the cities where strange tales were already circulating relative to the coming of Jad-ben-Otho in person to aid the high priest in his war against Ja-don. It took stout hearts and loyal ones to ignore the implied threats of divine vengeance that these tales suggested. Already there had been desertions and the cause of Ja-don seemed tottering to destruction.

Such was the state of affairs when a sentry posted on the knoll in the mouth of the gorge sent word that he had observed in the valley below what appeared at a distance to be nothing less than two people mounted upon the back of a gryf. He said that he had caught glimpses of them, as they passed open spaces, and they seemed to be traveling up the river in the direction of the Kor-ul-ja.

At first Ja-don was inclined to doubt the veracity of his informant; but, like all good generals, he could not permit even palpably false information to go uninvestigated and so he determined to visit the knoll himself and learn precisely what it was that the sentry had observed through the distorting spectacles of fear. He had scarce taken his place beside the man ere the fellow touched his arm and pointed. "They are closer now," he whispered, "you can see them plainly." And sure enough, not a quarter of a mile away Ja-don saw that which in his long experience in Pal-ul-don he had never before seen—two humans riding upon the broad back of a gryf.

At first he could scarce credit even this testimony of his own eyes, but soon he realized that the creatures below could be naught else than they appeared, and then he recognized the man and rose to his feet with a loud cry.

"It is he!" he shouted to those about him. "It is the Dor-ul-Otho himself."

The gryf and his riders heard the shout though not the words. The former bellowed terrifically and started in the direction of the knoll, and Ja-don, followed by a few of his more intrepid warriors, ran to meet him. Tarzan, loath to enter an unnecessary quarrel, tried to turn the animal, but as the beast was far from tractable it always took a few minutes to force the will of its master upon it; and so the two parties were quite close before the ape-man succeeded in stopping the mad charge of his furious mount.

Ja-don and his warriors, however, had come to the realization that this bellowing creature was bearing down upon them with evil intent and they had assumed the better part of valor and taken to trees, accordingly. It was beneath these trees that Tarzan finally stopped the gryf. Ja-don called down to him.

"We are friends," he cried. "I am Ja-don, Chief of Ja-lur. I and my warriors lay our foreheads upon the feet of Dor-ul-Otho and pray that he will aid us in our righteous fight with Lu-don, the high priest."

"You have not defeated him yet?" asked Tarzan. "Why I thought you would be king of Pal-ul-don long before this."

"No," replied Ja-don. "The people fear the high priest and now that he has in the temple one whom he claims to be Jad-ben-Otho many of my warriors are afraid. If they but knew that the Dor-ul-Otho had returned and that he had blessed the cause of Ja-don I am sure that victory would be ours."

Tarzan thought for a long minute and then he spoke. "Ja-don," he said, "was one of the few who believed in me and who wished to accord me fair treatment. I have a debt to pay to Ja-don and an account to settle with Lu-don, not alone on my own behalf, but principally upon that of my mate. I will go with you Ja-don to mete to Lu-don the punishment he deserves. Tell me, chief, how may the Dor-ul-Otho best serve his father's people?"

"By coming with me to Ja-lur and the villages between," replied Ja-don quickly, "that the people may see that it is indeed the Dor-ul-Otho and that he smiles upon the cause of Ja-don."

"You think that they will believe in me more now than before?" asked the ape-man.

"Who will dare doubt that he who rides upon the great gryf is less than a god?" returned the old chief.

"And if I go with you to the battle at A-lur," asked Tarzan, "can you assure the safety of my mate while I am gone from her?"

"She shall remain in Ja-lur with the Princess O-lo-a and my own women," replied Ja-don. "There she will be safe for there I shall leave trusted warriors to protect them. Say that you will come, O Dor-ul-Otho, and my cup of happiness will be full, for even now Ta-den, my son, marches toward A-lur with a force from the northwest and if we can attack, with the Dor-ul-Otho at our head, from the northeast our arms should be victorious."

"It shall be as you wish, Ja-don," replied the ape-man; "but first you must have meat fetched for my gryf."

"There are many carcasses in the camp above," replied Ja-don, "for my men have little else to do than hunt."

"Good," exclaimed Tarzan. "Have them brought at once."

And when the meat was brought and laid at a distance the ape-man slipped from the back of his fierce charger and fed him with his own hand. "See that there is always plenty of flesh for him," he said to Ja-don, for he guessed that his mastery might be short-lived should the vicious beast become over-hungry.

It was morning before they could leave for Ja-lur, but Tarzan found the gryf lying where he had left him the night before beside the carcasses of two antelope and a lion; but now there was nothing but the gryf.

"The paleontologists say that he was herbivorous," said Tarzan as he and Jane approached the beast.

The journey to Ja-lur was made through the scattered villages where Ja-don hoped to arouse a keener enthusiasm for his cause. A party of warriors preceded Tarzan that the people might properly be prepared, not only for the sight of the gryf but to receive the Dor-ul-Otho as became his high station. The results were all that Ja-don could have hoped and in no village through which they passed was there one who doubted the deity of the ape-man.

As they approached Ja-lur a strange warrior joined them, one whom none of Ja-don's following knew. He said he came from one of the villages to the south and that he had been treated unfairly by one of Lu-don's chiefs. For this reason he had deserted the cause of the high priest and come north in the hope of finding a home in Ja-lur. As every addition to his forces was welcome to the old chief he permitted the stranger to accompany them, and so he came into Ja-lur with them.

There arose now the question as to what was to be done with the gryf while they remained in the city. It was with difficulty that Tarzan had prevented the savage beast from attacking all who came near it when they had first entered the camp of Ja-don in the uninhabited gorge next to the Kor-ul-ja, but during the march to Ja-lur the creature had seemed to become accustomed to the presence of the Ho-don. The latter, however, gave him no cause for annoyance since they kept as far from him as possible and when he passed through the streets of the city he was viewed from the safety of lofty windows and roofs. However tractable he appeared to have become there would have been no enthusiastic seconding of a suggestion to turn him loose within the city. It was finally suggested that he be turned into a walled enclosure within the palace grounds and this was done, Tarzan driving him in after Jane had dismounted. More meat was thrown to him and he was left to his own devices, the awe-struck inhabitants of the palace not even venturing to climb upon the walls to look at him.

Ja-don led Tarzan and Jane to the quarters of the Princess O-lo-a who, the moment that she beheld the ape-man, threw herself to the ground and touched her forehead to his feet. Pan-at-lee was there with her and she too seemed happy to see Tarzan-jad-guru again. When they found that Jane was his mate they looked with almost equal awe upon her, since even the most skeptical of the warriors of Ja-don were now convinced that they were entertaining a god and a goddess within the city of Ja-lur, and that with the assistance of the power of these two, the cause of Ja-don would soon be victorious and the old Lion-man set upon the throne of Pal-ul-don.

From O-lo-a Tarzan learned that Ta-den had returned and that they were to be united in marriage with the weird rites of their religion and in accordance with the custom of their people as soon as Ta-den came home from the battle that was to be fought at A-lur.

The recruits were now gathering at the city and it was decided that the next day Ja-don and Tarzan would return to the main body in the hidden camp and immediately under cover of night the attack should be made in force upon Lu-don's forces at A-lur. Word of this was sent to Ta-den where he awaited with his warriors upon the north side of Jad-ben-lul, only a few miles from A-lur.

In the carrying out of these plans it was necessary to leave Jane behind in Ja-don's palace at Ja-lur, but O-lo-a and her women were with her and there were many warriors to guard them, so Tarzan bid his mate good-bye with no feelings of apprehension as to her safety, and again seated upon the gryf made his way out of the city with Ja-don and his warriors.

At the mouth of the gorge the ape-man abandoned his huge mount since it had served its purpose and could be of no further value to him in their attack upon A-lur, which was to be made just before dawn the following day when, as he could not have been seen by the enemy, the effect of his entry to the city upon the gryf would have been totally lost. A couple of sharp blows with the spear sent the big animal rumbling and growling in the direction of the Kor-ul-gryf nor was the ape-man sorry to see it depart since he had never known at what instant its short temper and insatiable appetite for flesh might turn it upon some of his companions.

Immediately upon their arrival at the gorge the march on A-lur was commenced.

TAKEN ALIVE

As night fell a warrior from the palace of Ja-lur slipped into the temple grounds. He made his way to where the lesser priests were quartered. His presence aroused no suspicion as it was not unusual for warriors to have business within the temple. He came at last to a chamber where several priests were congregated after the evening meal. The rites and ceremonies of the sacrifice had been concluded and there was nothing more of a religious nature to make call upon their time until the rites at sunrise.

Now the warrior knew, as in fact nearly all Pal-ul-don knew, that there was no strong bond between the temple and the palace at Ja-lur and that Ja-don only suffered the presence of the priests and permitted their cruel and abhorrent acts because of the fact that these things had been the custom of the Ho-don of Pal-ul-don for countless ages, and rash indeed must have been the man who would have attempted to interfere with the priests or their ceremonies. That Ja-don never entered the temple was well known, and that his high priest never entered the palace, but the people came to the temple with their votive offerings and the sacrifices were made night and morning as in every other temple in Pal-ul-don.

The warriors knew these things, knew them better perhaps than a simple warrior should have known them. And so it was here in the temple that he looked for the aid that he sought in the carrying out of whatever design he had.

As he entered the apartment where the priests were he greeted them after the manner which was customary in Pal-ul-don, but at the same time he made a sign with his finger that might have attracted little attention or scarcely been noticed at all by one who knew not its meaning. That there were those within the room who noticed it and interpreted it was quickly apparent, through the fact that two of the priests rose and came close to him as he stood just within the doorway and each of them, as he came, returned the signal that the warrior had made.

The three talked for but a moment and then the warrior turned and left the apartment. A little later one of the priests who had talked with him left also and shortly after that the other.

In the corridor they found the warrior waiting, and led him to a little chamber which opened upon a smaller corridor just beyond where it joined the larger. Here the three remained in whispered conversation for some little time and then the warrior returned to the palace and the two priests to their quarters.

The apartments of the women of the palace at Ja-lur are all upon the same side of a long, straight corridor. Each has a single door leading into the corridor and at the opposite end several windows overlooking a garden. It was in one of these rooms that Jane slept alone. At each end of the corridor was a sentinel, the main body of the guard being stationed in a room near the outer entrance to the women's quarters.

The palace slept for they kept early hours there where Ja-don ruled. The pal-e-don-so of the great chieftain of the north knew no such wild orgies as had resounded through the palace of the king at A-lur. Ja-lur was a quiet city by comparison with the capital, yet there was always a guard kept at every entrance to the chambers of Ja-don and his immediate family as well as at the gate leading into the temple and that which opened upon the city.

These guards, however, were small, consisting usually of not more than five or six warriors, one of whom remained awake while the others slept. Such were the conditions then when two warriors presented themselves, one at either end of the corridor, to the sentries who watched over the safety of Jane Clayton and the Princess O-lo-a, and each of the newcomers repeated to the sentinels the stereotyped words which announced that they were relieved and these others sent to watch in their stead. Never is a warrior loath to be relieved of sentry duty. Where, under different circumstances he might ask numerous questions he is now too well satisfied to escape the monotonies of that universally hated duty. And so these two men accepted their relief without question and hastened away to their pallets.

And then a third warrior entered the corridor and all of the newcomers came together before the door of the ape-man's slumbering mate. And one was the strange warrior who had met Ja-don and Tarzan outside the city of Ja-lur as they had approached it the previous day; and he was the same warrior who had entered the temple a short hour before, but the faces of his fellows were unfamiliar, even to one another, since it is seldom that a priest removes his hideous headdress in the presence even of his associates.

Silently they lifted the hangings that hid the interior of the room from the view of those who passed through the corridor, and stealthily slunk within. Upon a pile of furs in a far corner lay the sleeping form of Lady Greystoke. The bare feet of the intruders gave forth no sound as they crossed the stone floor toward her. A ray of moonlight entering through a window near her couch shone full upon her, revealing the beautiful contours of an arm and shoulder in cameo-distinctness against the dark furry pelt beneath which she slept, and the perfect profile that was turned toward the skulking three.

But neither the beauty nor the helplessness of the sleeper aroused such sentiments of passion or pity as might stir in the breasts of normal men. To the three priests she was but a lump of clay, nor could they conceive aught of that passion which had aroused men to intrigue and to murder for possession of this beautiful American girl, and which even now was influencing the destiny of undiscovered Pal-ul-don.

Upon the floor of the chamber were numerous pelts and as the leader of the trio came close to the sleeping woman he stooped and gathered up one of the smaller of these. Standing close to her head he held the rug outspread above her face. "Now," he whispered and simultaneously he threw the rug over the woman's head and his two fellows leaped upon her, seizing her arms and pinioning her body while their leader stifled her cries with the furry pelt. Quickly and silently they bound her wrists and gagged her and during the brief time that their work required there was no sound that might have been heard by occupants of the adjoining apartments.

Jerking her roughly to her feet they forced her toward a window but she refused to walk, throwing herself instead upon the floor. They were very angry and would have resorted to cruelties to compel her obedience but dared not, since the wrath of Lu-don might fall heavily upon whoever mutilated his fair prize.

And so they were forced to lift and carry her bodily. Nor was the task any sinecure since the captive kicked and struggled as best she might, making their labor as arduous as possible. But finally they succeeded in getting her through the window and into the garden beyond where one of the two priests from the Ja-lur temple directed their steps toward a small barred gateway in the south wall of the enclosure.

Immediately beyond this a flight of stone stairs led downward toward the river and at the foot of the stairs were moored several canoes. Pan-sat had indeed been fortunate in enlisting aid from those who knew the temple and the palace so well, or otherwise he might never have escaped from Ja-lur with his captive. Placing the woman in the bottom of a light canoe Pan-sat entered it and took up the paddle. His companions unfastened the moorings and shoved the little craft out into the current of the stream. Their traitorous work completed they turned and retraced their steps toward the temple, while Pan-sat, paddling strongly with the current, moved rapidly down the river that would carry him to the Jad-ben-lul and A-lur.

The moon had set and the eastern horizon still gave no hint of approaching day as a long file of warriors wound stealthily through the darkness into the city of A-lur. Their plans were all laid and there seemed no likelihood of their miscarriage. A messenger had been dispatched to Ta-den whose forces lay northwest of the city. Tarzan, with a small contingent, was to enter the temple through the secret passageway, the location of which he alone knew, while Ja-don, with the greater proportion of the warriors, was to attack the palace gates.

The ape-man, leading his little band, moved stealthily through the winding alleys of A-lur, arriving undetected at the building which hid the entrance to the secret passageway. This spot being best protected by the fact that its existence was unknown to others than the priests, was unguarded. To facilitate the passage of his little company through the narrow winding, uneven tunnel, Tarzan lighted a torch which had been brought for the purpose and preceding his warriors led the way toward the temple.

That he could accomplish much once he reached the inner chambers of the temple with his little band of picked warriors the ape-man was confident since an attack at this point would bring confusion and consternation to the easily overpowered priests, and permit Tarzan to attack the palace forces in the rear at the same time that Ja-don engaged them at the palace gates, while Ta-den and his forces swarmed the northern walls. Great value had been placed by Ja-don on the moral effect of the Dor-ul-Otho's mysterious appearance in the heart of the temple and he had urged Tarzan to take every advantage of the old chieftain's belief that many of Lu-don's warriors still wavered in their allegiance between the high priest and the Dor-ul-Otho, being held to the former more by the fear which he engendered in the breasts of all his followers than by any love or loyalty they might feel toward him.

There is a Pal-ul-donian proverb setting forth a truth similar to that contained in the old Scotch adage that "The best laid schemes o' mice and men gang aft a-gley." Freely translated it might read, "He who follows the right trail sometimes reaches the wrong destination," and such apparently was the fate that lay in the footsteps of the great chieftain of the north and his godlike ally.

Tarzan, more familiar with the windings of the corridors than his fellows and having the advantage of the full light of the torch, which at best was but a dim and flickering affair, was some distance ahead of the others, and in his keen anxiety to close with the enemy he gave too little thought to those who were to support him. Nor is this strange, since from childhood the ape-man had been accustomed to fight the battles of life single-handed so that it had become habitual for him to depend solely upon his own cunning and prowess.

And so it was that he came into the upper corridor from which opened the chambers of Lu-don and the lesser priests far in advance of his warriors, and as he turned into this corridor with its dim cressets flickering somberly, he saw another enter it from a corridor before him—a warrior half carrying, half dragging the figure of a woman. Instantly Tarzan recognized the gagged and fettered captive whom he had thought safe in the palace of Ja-don at Ja-lur.

The warrior with the woman had seen Tarzan at the same instant that the latter had discovered him. He heard the low beastlike growl that broke from the ape-man's lips as he sprang forward to wrest his mate from her captor and wreak upon him the vengeance that was in the Tarmangani's savage heart. Across the corridor from Pan-sat was the entrance to a smaller chamber. Into this he leaped carrying the woman with him.

Close behind came Tarzan of the Apes. He had cast aside his torch and drawn the long knife that had been his father's. With the impetuosity of a charging bull he rushed into the chamber in pursuit of Pan-sat to find himself, when the hangings dropped behind him, in utter darkness. Almost immediately there was a crash of stone on stone before him followed a moment later by a similar crash behind. No other evidence was necessary to announce to the ape-man that he was again a prisoner in Lu-don's temple.

He stood perfectly still where he had halted at the first sound of the descending stone door. Not again would he easily be precipitated to the gryf pit, or some similar danger, as had occurred when Lu-don had trapped him in the Temple of the Gryf. As he stood there his eyes slowly grew accustomed to the darkness and he became aware that a dim light was entering the chamber through some opening, though it was several minutes before he discovered its source. In the roof of the chamber he finally discerned a small aperture, possibly three feet in diameter and it was through this that what was really only a lesser darkness rather than a light was penetrating its Stygian blackness of the chamber in which he was imprisoned.

Since the doors had fallen he had heard no sound though his keen ears were constantly strained in an effort to discover a clue to the direction taken by the abductor of his mate. Presently he could discern the outlines of his prison cell. It was a small room, not over fifteen feet across. On hands and knees, with the utmost caution, he examined the entire area of the floor. In the exact center, directly beneath the opening in the roof, was a trap, but otherwise the floor was solid. With this knowledge it was only necessary to avoid this spot in so far as the floor was concerned. The walls next received his attention. There were only two openings. One the doorway through which he had entered, and upon the opposite side that through which the warrior had borne Jane Clayton. These were both closed by the slabs of stone which the fleeing warrior had released as he departed.

Lu-don, the high priest, licked his thin lips and rubbed his bony white hands together in gratification as Pan-sat bore Jane Clayton into his presence and laid her on the floor of the chamber before him.

"Good, Pan-sat!" he exclaimed. "You shall be well rewarded for this service. Now, if we but had the false Dor-ul-Otho in our power all Pal-ul-don would be at our feet."

"Master, I have him!" cried Pan-sat.

"What!" exclaimed Lu-don, "you have Tarzan-jad-guru? You have slain him perhaps. Tell me, my wonderful Pan-sat, tell me quickly. My breast is bursting with a desire to know."

"I have taken him alive, Lu-don, my master," replied Pan-sat. "He is in the little chamber that the ancients built to trap those who were too powerful to take alive in personal encounter."

"You have done well, Pan-sat, I—"

A frightened priest burst into the apartment. "Quick, master, quick," he cried, "the corridors are filled with the warriors of Ja-don."

"You are mad," cried the high priest. "My warriors hold the palace and the temple."

"I speak the truth, master," replied the priest, "there are warriors in the corridor approaching this very chamber, and they come from the direction of the secret passage which leads hither from the city."

"It may be even as he says," exclaimed Pan-sat. "It was from that direction that Tarzan-jad-guru was coming when I discovered and trapped him. He was leading his warriors to the very holy of holies."

Lu-don ran quickly to the doorway and looked out into the corridor. At a glance he saw that the fears of the frightened priest were well founded. A dozen warriors were moving along the corridor toward him but they seemed confused and far from sure of themselves. The high priest guessed that deprived of the leadership of Tarzan they were little better than lost in the unknown mazes of the subterranean precincts of the temple.

Stepping back into the apartment he seized a leathern thong that depended from the ceiling. He pulled upon it sharply and through the temple boomed the deep tones of a metal gong. Five times the clanging notes rang through the corridors, then he turned toward the two priests. "Bring the woman and follow me," he directed.

Crossing the chamber he passed through a small doorway, the others lifting Jane Clayton from the floor and following him. Through a narrow corridor and up a flight of steps they went, turning to right and left and doubling back through a maze of winding passageways which terminated in a spiral staircase that gave forth at the surface of the ground within the largest of the inner altar courts close beside the eastern altar.

From all directions now, in the corridors below and the grounds above, came the sound of hurrying footsteps. The five strokes of the great gong had summoned the faithful to the defense of Lu-don in his private chambers. The priests who knew the way led the less familiar warriors to the spot and presently those who had accompanied Tarzan found themselves not only leaderless but facing a vastly superior force. They were brave men but under the circumstances they were helpless and so they fell back the way they had come, and when they reached the narrow confines of the smaller passageway their safety was assured since only one foeman could attack them at a time. But their plans were frustrated and possibly also their entire cause lost, so heavily had Ja-don banked upon the success of their venture.

With the clanging of the temple gong Ja-don assumed that Tarzan and his party had struck their initial blow and so he launched his attack upon the palace gate. To the ears of Lu-don in the inner temple court came the savage war cries that announced the beginning of the battle. Leaving Pan-sat and the other priest to guard the woman he hastened toward the palace personally to direct his force and as he passed through the temple grounds he dispatched a messenger to learn the outcome of the fight in the corridors below, and other messengers to spread the news among his followers that the false Dor-ul-Otho was a prisoner in the temple.

As the din of battle rose above A-lur, Lieutenant Erich Obergatz turned upon his bed of soft hides and sat up. He rubbed his eyes and looked about him. It was still dark without.

"I am Jad-ben-Otho," he cried, "who dares disturb my slumber?"

A slave squatting upon the floor at the foot of his couch shuddered and touched her forehead to the floor. "It must be that the enemy have come, O Jad-ben-Otho." She spoke soothingly for she had reason to know the terrors of the mad frenzy into which trivial things sometimes threw the Great God.

A priest burst suddenly through the hangings of the doorway and falling upon his hands and knees rubbed his forehead against the stone flagging. "O Jad-ben-Otho," he cried, "the warriors of Ja-don have attacked the palace and the temple. Even now they are fighting in the corridors near the quarters of Lu-don, and the high priest begs that you come to the palace and encourage your faithful warriors by your presence."

Obergatz sprang to his feet. "I am Jad-ben-Otho," he screamed. "With lightning I will blast the blasphemers who dare attack the holy city of A-lur."

For a moment he rushed aimlessly and madly about the room, while the priest and the slave remained upon hands and knees with their foreheads against the floor.

"Come," cried Obergatz, planting a vicious kick in the side of the slave girl. "Come! Would you wait here all day while the forces of darkness overwhelm the City of Light?"

Thoroughly frightened as were all those who were forced to serve the Great God, the two arose and followed Obergatz towards the palace.

Above the shouting of the warriors rose constantly the cries of the temple priests: "Jad-ben-Otho is here and the false Dor-ul-Otho is a prisoner in the temple." The persistent cries reached even to the ears of the enemy as it was intended that they should.

THE MESSENGER OF DEATH

The sun rose to see the forces of Ja-don still held at the palace gate. The old warrior had seized the tall structure that stood just beyond the palace and at the summit of this he kept a warrior stationed to look toward the northern wall of the palace where Ta-den was to make his attack; but as the minutes wore into hours no sign of the other force appeared, and now in the full light of the new sun upon the roof of one of the palace buildings appeared Lu-don, the high priest, Mo-sar, the pretender, and the strange, naked figure of a man, into whose long hair and beard were woven fresh ferns and flowers. Behind them were banked a score of lesser priests who chanted in unison: "This is Jad-ben-Otho. Lay down your arms and surrender." This they repeated again and again, alternating it with the cry: "The false Dor-ul-Otho is a prisoner."

In one of those lulls which are common in battles between forces armed with weapons that require great physical effort in their use, a voice suddenly arose from among the followers of Ja-don: "Show us the Dor-ul-Otho. We do not believe you!"

"Wait," cried Lu-don. "If I do not produce him before the sun has moved his own width, the gates of the palace shall be opened to you and my warriors will lay down their arms."

He turned to one of his priests and issued brief instructions.

The ape-man paced the confines of his narrow cell. Bitterly he reproached himself for the stupidity which had led him into this trap, and yet was it stupidity? What else might he have done other than rush to the succor of his mate? He wondered how they had stolen her from Ja-lur, and then suddenly there flashed to his mind the features of the warrior whom he had just seen with her. They were strangely familiar. He racked his brain to recall where he had seen the man before and then it came to him. He was the strange warrior who had joined Ja-don's forces outside of Ja-lur the day that Tarzan had ridden upon the great gryf from the uninhabited gorge next to the Kor-ul-ja down to the capital city of the chieftain of the north. But who could the man be? Tarzan knew that never before that other day had he seen him.

Presently he heard the clanging of a gong from the corridor without and very faintly the rush of feet, and shouts. He guessed that his warriors had been discovered and a fight was in progress. He fretted and chafed at the chance that had denied him participation in it.

Again and again he tried the doors of his prison and the trap in the center of the floor, but none would give to his utmost endeavors. He strained his eyes toward the aperture above but he could see nothing, and then he continued his futile pacing to and fro like a caged lion behind its bars.

The minutes dragged slowly into hours. Faintly sounds came to him as of shouting men at a great distance. The battle was in progress. He wondered if Ja-don would be victorious and should he be, would his friends ever discover him in this hidden chamber in the bowels of the hill? He doubted it.

And now as he looked again toward the aperture in the roof there appeared to be something depending through its center. He came closer and strained his eyes to see. Yes, there was something there. It appeared to be a rope. Tarzan wondered if it had been there all the time. It must have, he reasoned, since he had heard no sound from above and it was so dark within the chamber that he might easily have overlooked it.

He raised his hand toward it. The end of it was just within his reach. He bore his weight upon it to see if it would hold him. Then he released it and backed away, still watching it, as you have seen an animal do after investigating some unfamiliar object, one of the little traits that differentiated Tarzan from other men, accentuating his similarity to the savage beasts of his native jungle. Again and again he touched and tested the braided leather rope, and always he listened for any warning sound from above.

He was very careful not to step upon the trap at any time and when finally he bore all his weight upon the rope and took his feet from the floor he spread them wide apart so that if he fell he would fall astride the trap. The rope held him. There was no sound from above, nor any from the trap below.

Slowly and cautiously he drew himself upward, hand over hand. Nearer and nearer the roof he came. In a moment his eyes would be above the level of the floor above. Already his extended arms projected into the upper chamber and then something closed suddenly upon both his forearms, pinioning them tightly and leaving him hanging in mid-air unable to advance or retreat.

Immediately a light appeared in the room above him and presently he saw the hideous mask of a priest peering down upon him. In the priest's hands were leathern thongs and these he tied about Tarzan's wrists and forearms until they were completely bound together from his elbows almost to his fingers. Behind this priest Tarzan presently saw others and soon several lay hold of him and pulled him up through the hole.

Almost instantly his eyes were above the level of the floor he understood how they had trapped him. Two nooses had lain encircling the aperture into the cell below. A priest had waited at the end of each of these ropes and at opposite sides of the chamber. When he had climbed to a sufficient height upon the rope that had dangled into his prison below and his arms were well within the encircling snares the two priests had pulled quickly upon their ropes and he had been made an easy captive without any opportunity of defending himself or inflicting injury upon his captors.

And now they bound his legs from his ankles to his knees and picking him up carried him from the chamber. No word did they speak to him as they bore him upward to the temple yard.

The din of battle had risen again as Ja-don had urged his forces to renewed efforts. Ta-den had not arrived and the forces of the old chieftain were revealing in their lessened efforts their increasing demoralization, and then it was that the priests carried Tarzan-jad-guru to the roof of the palace and exhibited him in the sight of the warriors of both factions.

"Here is the false Dor-ul-Otho," screamed Lu-don.

Obergatz, his shattered mentality having never grasped fully the meaning of much that was going on about him, cast a casual glance at the bound and helpless prisoner, and as his eyes fell upon the noble features of the ape-man, they went wide in astonishment and fright, and his pasty countenance turned a sickly blue. Once before had he seen Tarzan of the Apes, but many times had he dreamed that he had seen him and always was the giant ape-man avenging the wrongs that had been committed upon him and his by the ruthless hands of the three German officers who had led their native troops in the ravishing of Tarzan's peaceful home. Hauptmann Fritz Schneider had paid the penalty of his needless cruelties; Unter-lieutenant von Goss, too, had paid; and now Obergatz, the last of the three, stood face to face with the Nemesis that had trailed him through his dreams for long, weary months. That he was bound and helpless lessened not the German's terror—he seemed not to realize that the man could not harm him. He but stood cringing and jibbering and Lu-don saw and was filled with apprehension that others might see and seeing realize that this bewhiskered idiot was no god—that of the two Tarzan-jad-guru was the more godly figure. Already the high priest noted that some of the palace warriors standing near were whispering together and pointing. He stepped closer to Obergatz. "You are Jad-ben-Otho," he whispered, "denounce him!"

The German shook himself. His mind cleared of all but his great terror and the words of the high priest gave him the clue to safety.

"I am Jad-ben-Otho!" he screamed.

Tarzan looked him straight in the eye. "You are Lieutenant Obergatz of the German Army," he said in excellent German. "You are the last of the three I have sought so long and in your putrid heart you know that God has not brought us together at last for nothing."

The mind of Lieutenant Obergatz was functioning clearly and rapidly at last. He too saw the questioning looks upon the faces of some of those around them. He saw the opposing warriors of both cities standing by the gate inactive, every eye turned upon him, and the trussed figure of the ape-man. He realized that indecision now meant ruin, and ruin, death. He raised his voice in the sharp barking tones of a Prussian officer, so unlike his former maniacal screaming as to quickly arouse the attention of every ear and to cause an expression of puzzlement to cross the crafty face of Lu-don.

"I am Jad-ben-Otho," snapped Obergatz. "This creature is no son of mine. As a lesson to all blasphemers he shall die upon the altar at the hand of the god he has profaned. Take him from my sight, and when the sun stands at zenith let the faithful congregate in the temple court and witness the wrath of this divine hand," and he held aloft his right palm.

Those who had brought Tarzan took him away then as Obergatz had directed, and the German turned once more to the warriors by the gate. "Throw down your arms, warriors of Ja-don," he cried, "lest I call down my lightnings to blast you where you stand. Those who do as I bid shall be forgiven. Come! Throw down your arms."

EDGAR RICE BURROUGHS

The warriors of Ja-don moved uneasily, casting looks of appeal at their leader and of apprehension toward the figures upon the palace roof. Ja-don sprang forward among his men. "Let the cowards and knaves throw down their arms and enter the palace," he cried, "but never will Ja-don and the warriors of Ja-lur touch their foreheads to the feet of Lu-don and his false god. Make your decision now," he cried to his followers.

A few threw down their arms and with sheepish looks passed through the gateway into the palace, and with the example of these to bolster their courage others joined in the desertion from the old chieftain of the north, but staunch and true around him stood the majority of his warriors and when the last weakling had left their ranks Ja-don voiced the savage cry with which he led his followers to the attack, and once again the battle raged about the palace gate.

At times Ja-don's forces pushed the defenders far into the palace ground and then the wave of combat would recede and pass out into the city again. And still Ta-den and the reinforcements did not come. It was drawing close to noon. Lu-don had mustered every available man that was not actually needed for the defense of the gate within the temple, and these he sent, under the leadership of Pan-sat, out into the city through the secret passageway and there they fell upon Ja-don's forces from the rear while those at the gate hammered them in front.

Attacked on two sides by a vastly superior force the result was inevitable and finally the last remnant of Ja-don's little army capitulated and the old chief was taken a prisoner before Lu-don. "Take him to the temple court," cried the high priest. "He shall witness the death of his accomplice and perhaps Jad-ben-Otho shall pass a similar sentence upon him as well."

The inner temple court was packed with humanity. At either end of the western altar stood Tarzan and his mate, bound and helpless. The sounds of battle had ceased and presently the ape-man saw Ja-don being led into the inner court, his wrists bound tightly together before him. Tarzan turned his eyes toward Jane and nodded in the direction of Ja-don. "This looks like the end," he said quietly. "He was our last and only hope."

"We have at least found each other, John," she replied, "and our last days have been spent together. My only prayer now is that if they take you they do not leave me."

Tarzan made no reply for in his heart was the same bitter thought that her own contained—not the fear that they would kill him but the fear that they would not kill her. The ape-man strained at his bonds but they were too many and too strong. A priest near him saw and with a jeering laugh struck the defenseless ape-man in the face.

"The brute!" cried Jane Clayton.

Tarzan smiled. "I have been struck thus before, Jane," he said, "and always has the striker died."

"You still have hope?" she asked.

"I am still alive," he said as though that were sufficient answer. She was a woman and she did not have the courage of this man who knew no fear. In her heart of hearts she knew that he would die upon the altar at high noon for he had told her, after he had been brought to the inner court, of the sentence of death that Obergatz had pronounced upon him, and she knew too that Tarzan knew that he would die, but that he was too courageous to admit it even to himself.

As she looked upon him standing there so straight and wonderful and brave among his savage captors her heart cried out against the cruelty of the fate that had overtaken him. It seemed a gross and hideous wrong that that wonderful creature, now so quick with exuberant life and strength and purpose should be presently naught but a bleeding lump of clay—and all so uselessly and wantonly. Gladly would she have offered her life for his but she knew that it was a waste of words since their captors would work upon them whatever it was their will to do—for him, death; for her—she shuddered at the thought.

And now came Lu-don and the naked Obergatz, and the high priest led the German to his place behind the altar, himself standing upon the other's left. Lu-don whispered a word to Obergatz, at the same time nodding in the direction of Ja-don. The Hun cast a scowling look upon the old warrior.

"And after the false god," he cried, "the false prophet," and he pointed an accusing finger at Ja-don. Then his eyes wandered to the form of Jane Clayton.

"And the woman, too?" asked Lu-don.

"The case of the woman I will attend to later," replied Obergatz. "I will talk with her tonight after she has had a chance to meditate upon the consequences of arousing the wrath of Jad-ben-Otho."

He cast his eyes upward at the sun. "The time approaches," he said to Lu-don. "Prepare the sacrifice."

Lu-don nodded to the priests who were gathered about Tarzan. They seized the ape-man and lifted him bodily to the altar where they laid him upon his back with his head at the south end of the monolith, but a few feet from where Jane Clayton stood. Impulsively and before they could restrain her the woman rushed forward and bending quickly kissed her mate upon the forehead. "Good-bye, John," she whispered.

"Good-bye," he answered, smiling.

The priests seized her and dragged her away. Lu-don handed the sacrificial knife to Obergatz. "I am the Great God," cried the German, "thus falleth the divine wrath upon all my enemies!" He looked up at the sun and then raised the knife high above his head.

"Thus die the blasphemers of God!" he screamed, and at the same instant a sharp staccato note rang out above the silent, spell-bound multitude. There was a screaming whistle in the air and Jad-ben-Otho crumpled forward across the body of his intended victim. Again the same alarming noise and Lu-don fell, a third and Mo-sar crumpled to the ground. And now the warriors and the people, locating the direction of this new and unknown sound turned toward the western end of the court.

Upon the summit of the temple wall they saw two figures—a Ho-don warrior and beside him an almost naked creature of the race of Tarzan-jad-guru, across his shoulders and about his hips were strange broad belts studded with beautiful cylinders that glinted in the mid-day sun, and in his hands a shining thing of wood and metal from the end of which rose a thin wreath of blue-gray smoke.

And then the voice of the Ho-don warrior rang clear upon the ears of the silent throng. "Thus speaks the true Jad-ben-Otho," he cried, "through this his Messenger of Death. Cut the bonds of the prisoners. Cut the bonds of the Dor-ul-Otho and of Ja-don, King of Pal-ul-don, and of the woman who is the mate of the son of god."

Pan-sat, filled with the frenzy of fanaticism saw the power and the glory of the regime he had served crumpled and gone. To one and only one did he attribute the blame for the disaster that had but just overwhelmed him. It was the creature who lay upon the sacrificial altar who had brought Lu-don to his death and toppled the dreams of power that day by day had been growing in the brain of the under priest.

The sacrificial knife lay upon the altar where it had fallen from the dead fingers of Obergatz. Pan-sat crept closer and then with a sudden lunge he reached forth to seize the handle of the blade, and even as his clutching fingers were poised above it, the strange thing in the hands of the strange creature upon the temple wall cried out its crashing word of doom and Pan-sat the under priest, screaming, fell back upon the dead body of his master.

"Seize all the priests," cried Ta-den to the warriors, "and let none hesitate lest Jad-ben-Otho's messenger send forth still other bolts of lightning."

The warriors and the people had now witnessed such an exhibition of divine power as might have convinced an even less superstitious and more enlightened people, and since many of them had but lately wavered between the Jad-ben-Otho of Lu-don and the Dor-ul-Otho of Ja-don it was not difficult for them to swing quickly back to the latter, especially in view of the unanswerable argument in the hands of him whom Ta-den had described as the Messenger of the Great God.

And so the warriors sprang forward now with alacrity and surrounded the priests, and when they looked again at the western wall of the temple court they saw pouring over it a great force of warriors. And the thing that startled and appalled them was the fact that many of these were black and hairy Waz-don.

At their head came the stranger with the shiny weapon and on his right was Ta-den, the Ho-don, and on his left Om-at, the black gund of Kor-ul-ja.

A warrior near the altar had seized the sacrificial knife and cut Tarzan's bonds and also those of Ja-don and Jane Clayton, and now the three stood together beside the altar and as the newcomers from the western end of the temple court pushed their way toward them the eyes of the woman went wide in mingled astonishment, incredulity, and hope. And the stranger, slinging his weapon across his back by a leather strap, rushed forward and took her in his arms.

"Jack!" she cried, sobbing on his shoulder. "Jack, my son!"

And Tarzan of the Apes came then and put his arms around them both, and the King of Pal-ul-don and the warriors and the people kneeled in the temple court and placed their foreheads to the ground before the altar where the three stood.

HOME

Within an hour of the fall of Lu-don and Mo-sar, the chiefs and principal warriors of Pal-ul-don gathered in the great throneroom of the palace at A-lur upon the steps of the lofty pyramid and placing Ja-don at the apex proclaimed him king. Upon one side of the old chieftain stood Tarzan of the Apes, and upon the other Korak, the Killer, worthy son of the mighty ape-man.

And when the brief ceremony was over and the warriors with upraised clubs had sworn fealty to their new ruler, Ja-don dispatched a trusted company to fetch O-lo-a and Pan-at-lee and the women of his own household from Ja-lur.

And then the warriors discussed the future of Pal-ul-don and the question arose as to the administration of the temples and the fate of the priests, who practically without exception had been disloyal to the government of the king, seeking always only their own power and comfort and aggrandizement. And then it was that Ja-don turned to Tarzan. "Let the Dor-ul-Otho transmit to his people the wishes of his father," he said.

"Your problem is a simple one," said the ape-man, "if you but wish to do that which shall be pleasing in the eyes of God. Your priests, to increase their power, have taught you that Jad-ben-Otho is a cruel god, that his eyes love to dwell upon blood and upon suffering. But the falsity of their teachings has been demonstrated to you today in the utter defeat of the priesthood.

"Take then the temples from the men and give them instead to the women that they may be administered in kindness and charity and love. Wash the blood from your eastern altar and drain forever the water from the western.

"Once I gave Lu-don the opportunity to do these things but he ignored my commands, and again is the corridor of sacrifice filled with its victims. Liberate these from every temple in Pal-ul-don. Bring offerings of such gifts as your people like and place them upon the altars of your god. And there he will bless them and the priestesses of Jad-ben-Otho can distribute them among those who need them most."

As he ceased speaking a murmur of evident approval ran through the throng. Long had they been weary of the avarice and cruelty of the priests and now that authority had come from a high source with a feasible plan for ridding themselves of the old religious order without necessitating any change in the faith of the people they welcomed it.

"And the priests," cried one. "We shall put them to death upon their own altars if it pleases the Dor-ul-Otho to give the word."

"No," cried Tarzan. "Let no more blood be spilled. Give them their freedom and the right to take up such occupations as they choose."

That night a great feast was spread in the pal-e-don-so and for the first time in the history of ancient Pal-ul-don black warriors sat in peace and friendship with white. And a pact was sealed between Ja-don and Om-at that would ever make his tribe and the Ho-don allies and friends.

It was here that Tarzan learned the cause of Ta-den's failure to attack at the stipulated time. A messenger had come from Ja-don carrying instructions to delay the attack until noon, nor had they discovered until almost too late that the messenger was a disguised priest of Lu-don. And they had put him to death and scaled the walls and come to the inner temple court with not a moment to spare.

The following day O-lo-a and Pan-at-lee and the women of Ja-don's family arrived at the palace at A-lur and in the great throneroom Ta-den and O-lo-a were wed, and Om-at and Pan-at-lee.

For a week Tarzan and Jane and Korak remained the guests of Ja-don, as did Om-at and his black warriors. And then the ape-man announced that he would depart from Pal-ul-don. Hazy in the minds of their hosts was the location of heaven and equally so the means by which the gods traveled between their celestial homes and the haunts of men and so no questionings arose when it was found that the Dor-ul-Otho with his mate and son would travel overland across the mountains and out of Pal-ul-don toward the north.

They went by way of the Kor-ul-ja accompanied by the warriors of that tribe and a great contingent of Ho-don warriors under Ta-den. The king and many warriors and a multitude of people accompanied them beyond the limits of A-lur and after they had bid them good-bye and Tarzan had invoked the blessings of God upon them the three Europeans saw their simple, loyal friends prostrate in the dust behind them until the cavalcade had wound out of the city and disappeared among the trees of the nearby forest.

They rested for a day among the Kor-ul-ja while Jane investigated the ancient caves of these strange people and then they moved on, avoiding the rugged shoulder of Pastar-ul-ved and winding down the opposite slope toward the great morass. They moved in comfort and in safety, surrounded by their escort of Ho-don and Waz-don.

In the minds of many there was doubtless a question as to how the three would cross the great morass but least of all was Tarzan worried by the problem. In the course of his life he had been confronted by many obstacles only to learn that he who will may always pass. In his mind lurked an easy solution of the passage but it was one which depended wholly upon chance.

It was the morning of the last day that, as they were breaking camp to take up the march, a deep bellow thundered from a nearby grove. The ape-man smiled. The chance had come. Fittingly then would the Dor-ul-Otho and his mate and their son depart from unmapped Pal-ul-don.

He still carried the spear that Jane had made, which he had prized so highly because it was her handiwork that he had caused a search to be made for it through the temple in A-lur after his release, and it had been found and brought to him. He had told her laughingly that it should have the place of honor above their hearth as the ancient flintlock of her Puritan grandsire had held a similar place of honor above the fireplace of Professor Porter, her father.

At the sound of the bellowing the Ho-don warriors, some of whom had accompanied Tarzan from Ja-don's camp to Ja-lur, looked questioningly at the ape-man while Om-at's Waz-don looked for trees, since the gryf was the one creature of Pal-ul-don which might not be safely encountered even by a great multitude of warriors. Its tough, armored hide was impregnable to their knife thrusts while their thrown clubs rattled from it as futilely as if hurled at the rocky shoulder of Pastar-ul-ved.

"Wait," said the ape-man, and with his spear in hand he advanced toward the gryf, voicing the weird cry of the Tor-o-don. The bellowing ceased and turned to low rumblings and presently the huge beast appeared. What followed was but a repetition of the ape-man's previous experience with these huge and ferocious creatures.

And so it was that Jane and Korak and Tarzan rode through the morass that hems Pa-ul-don, upon the back of a prehistoric triceratops while the lesser reptiles of the swamp fled hissing in terror. Upon the opposite shore they turned and called back their farewells to Ta-den and Om-at and the brave warriors they had learned to admire and respect. And then Tarzan urged their titanic mount onward toward the north, abandoning him only when he was assured that the Waz-don and the Ho-don had had time to reach a point of comparative safety among the craggy ravines of the foothills.

Turning the beast's head again toward Pal-ul-don the three dismounted and a sharp blow upon the thick hide sent the creature lumbering majestically back in the direction of its native haunts. For a time they stood looking back upon the land they had just quit—the land of Tor-o-don and gryf; of ja and jato; of Waz-don and Ho-don; a primitive land of terror and sudden death and peace and beauty; a land that they all had learned to love.

And then they turned once more toward the north and with light hearts and brave hearts took up their long journey toward the land that is best of all—home.

TARZAN AND THE GOLDEN LION

THE GOLDEN LION

Sabor, the lioness, suckled her young—a single fuzzy ball, spotted like Sheeta, the leopard. She lay in the warm sunshine before the rocky cavern that was her lair, stretched out upon her side with half closed eyes, yet Sabor was alert. There had been three of these little, fuzzy balls at first—two daughters and a son—and Sabor and Numa, their sire, had been proud of them; proud and happy. But kills had not been plentiful, and Sabor, undernourished, had been unable to produce sufficient milk to nourish properly three lusty cubs, and then a cold rain had come, and the little ones had sickened. Only the strongest survived—the two daughters had died. Sabor had mourned, pacing to and fro beside the pitiful bits of bedraggled fur, whining and moaning. Now and again she would nose them with her muzzle as though she would awaken them from the long sleep that knows no waking. At last, however, she abandoned her efforts, and now her whole savage heart was filled with concern for the little male cub that remained to her. That was why Sabor was more alert than usual.

Numa, the lion, was away. Two nights before he had made a kill and dragged it to their lair and last night he had fared forth again, but he had not returned. Sabor was thinking, as she half dozed, of Wappi, the plump antelope, that her splendid mate might this very minute be dragging through the tangled jungle to her. Or perhaps it would be Pacco, the zebra, whose flesh was the best beloved of her kind—juicy, succulent Pacco. Sabor's mouth watered.

Ah, what was that? The shadow of a sound had come to those keen ears. She raised her head, cocking it first upon one side and then the other, as with up-pricked ears she sought to catch the faintest repetition of that which had disturbed her. Her nose sniffed the air. There was but the suggestion of a breeze, but what there was moved toward her from the direction of the sound she had heard, and which she still heard in a slightly increasing volume that told her that whatever was making it was approaching her. As it drew closer the beast's nervousness increased and she rolled over on her belly, shutting off the milk supply from the cub, which vented its disapproval in miniature growls until a low, querulous whine from the lioness silenced him, then he stood at her side, looking first at her and then in the direction toward which she looked, cocking his little head first on one side and then on the other.

Evidently there was a disturbing quality in the sound that Sabor heard—something that inspired a certain restlessness, if not actual apprehension—though she could not be sure as yet that it boded ill. It might be her great lord returning, but it did not sound like the movement of a lion, certainly not like a lion dragging a heavy kill. She glanced at her cub, breathing as she did so a plaintive whine. There was always the fear that some danger menaced him—this last of her little family—but she, Sabor the lioness, was there to defend him.

Presently the breeze brought to her nostrils the scent spoor of the thing that moved toward her through the jungle. Instantly the troubled mother-face was metamorphosed into a bare-fanged, glittering-eyed mask of savage rage, for the scent that had come up to her through the jungle was the hated man-scent. She rose to her feet, her head flattened, her sinuous tail twitching nervously. Through that strange medium by which animals communicate with one another she cautioned her cub to lie down and remain where he was until she returned, then she moved rapidly and silently to meet the intruder.

The cub had heard what its mother heard and now he caught the smell of man—an unfamiliar smell that had never impinged upon his nostrils before, yet a smell that he knew at once for that of an enemy—a smell that brought a reaction as typical as that which marked the attitude of the grown lioness, bringing the hairs along his little spine erect and baring his tiny fangs. As the adult moved quickly and stealthily into the underbrush the small cub, ignoring her injunction, followed after her, his hind quarters wobbling from side to side, after the manner of the very young of his kind, the ridiculous gait comporting ill with the dignified bearing of his fore quarters; but the lioness, intent upon that which lay before her, did not know that he followed her.

There was dense jungle before the two for a hundred yards, but through it the lions had worn a tunnel-like path to their lair; and then there was a small clearing through which ran a well-worn jungle trail, out of the jungle at one end of the clearing and into the jungle again at the other. As Sabor reached the clearing she saw the object of her fear and hatred well within it. What if the man-thing were not hunting her or hers? What if he even dreamed not of their presence? These facts were as nothing to Sabor, the lioness, today. Ordinarily she would have let him pass unmolested, so long as he did not come close enough to threaten the safety of her cub; or, cubless, she would have slunk away at the first intimation of his approach. But today the lioness was nervous and fearful—fearful because of the single cub that remained to her—her maternal instincts centered threefold, perhaps, upon this lone and triply loved survivor—and so she did not wait for the man to threaten the safety of her little one; but instead she moved to meet him and to stop him. From the soft mother she had become a terrifying creature of destruction, her brain obsessed by a single thought—to kill.

She did not hesitate an instant at the edge of the clearing, nor did she give the slightest warning. The first intimation that the black warrior had that there was a lion within twenty miles of him, was the terrifying apparition of this devil-faced cat charging across the clearing toward him with the speed of an arrow. The black was not searching for lions. Had he known that there was one near he would have given it a wide berth. He would have fled now had there been anywhere to flee. The nearest tree was farther from him than was the lioness. She could overhaul him before he would have covered a quarter of the distance. There was no hope and there was only one thing to do. The beast was almost upon him and behind her he saw a tiny cub. The man bore a heavy spear. He carried it far back with his right hand and hurled it at the very instant that Sabor rose to seize him. The spear passed through the savage heart and almost simultaneously the giant jaws closed upon the face and skull of the warrior. The momentum of the lioness carried the two heavily to the ground, dead except for a few spasmodic twitchings of their muscles.

The orphaned cub stopped twenty feet away and surveyed the first great catastrophe of his life with questioning eyes. He wanted to approach his dam but a natural fear of the man-scent held him away. Presently he commenced to whine in a tone that always brought his mother to him hurriedly; but this time she did not come—she did not even rise and look toward him. He was puzzled—he could not understand it. He continued to cry, feeling all the while more sad and more lonely. Gradually he crept closer to his mother. He saw that the strange creature she had killed did not move and after a while he felt less terror of it, so that at last he found the courage to come quite close to his mother and sniff at her. He still whined to her, but she did not answer. It dawned on him at last that there was something wrong—that his great, beautiful mother was not as she had been—a change had come over her; yet still he clung to her, crying much until at last he fell asleep, cuddled close to her dead body.

It was thus that Tarzan found him—Tarzan and Jane, his wife, and their son, Korak the Killer, returning from the mysterious land of Pal-ul-don from which the two men had rescued Jane Clayton. At the sound of their approach the cub opened his eyes and rising, flattened his ears and snarled at them, backing close against his dead mother. At sight of him the ape-man smiled.

"Plucky little devil," he commented, taking in the story of the tragedy at a single glance. He approached the spitting cub, expecting it to turn and run away; but it did nothing of the sort. Instead it snarled more ferociously and struck at his extended hand as he stooped and reached for it.

"What a brave little fellow," cried Jane. "Poor little orphan!"

"He's going to make a great lion, or he would have if his dam had lived," said Korak. "Look at that back—as straight and strong as a spear. Too bad the rascal has got to die."

"He doesn't have to die," returned Tarzan.

"There's not much chance for him—he'll need milk for a couple of months more, and who's going to get it for him?"

"I am," replied Tarzan.

"You're going to adopt him?"

Tarzan nodded.

Korak and Jane laughed. "That'll be fine," commented the former.

"Lord Greystoke, foster mother to the son of Numa," laughed Jane.

Tarzan smiled with them, but he did not cease his attentions toward the cub. Reaching out suddenly he caught the little lion by the scruff of its neck and then stroking it gently he talked to it in a low, crooning tone. I do not know what he said; but perhaps the cub did, for presently it ceased its struggles and no longer sought to scratch or bite the caressing hand. After that he picked it up and held it against his breast. It did not seem afraid now, nor did it even bare its fangs against this close proximity to the erstwhile hated man-scent.

"How do you do it?" exclaimed Jane Clayton.

Tarzan shrugged his broad shoulders. "Your kind are not afraid of you—these are really my kind, try to civilize me as you will, and perhaps that is why they are not afraid of me when I give them the signs of friendship. Even this little rascal seems to know it, doesn't he?"

"I can never understand it," commented Korak. "I think I am rather familiar with African animals, yet I haven't the power over them or the understanding that you have. Why is it?"

"There is but one Tarzan," said Lady Greystoke, smiling at her son teasingly, and yet her tone was not without a note of pride.

"Remember that I was born among beasts and, raised by beasts," Tarzan reminded him. "Perhaps after all my father was an ape—you know Kala always insisted that he was."

"John! How can you?" exclaimed Jane. "You know perfectly well who your father and mother were."

Tarzan looked solemnly at his son and closed, one eye. "Your mother never can learn to appreciate the fine qualities of the anthropoids. One might almost think that she objected to the suggestion that she had mated with one of them."

"John Clayton, I shall never speak to you again if you don't stop saying such hideous things. I am ashamed of you. It is bad enough that you are an unregenerate wild-man, without trying to suggest that you may be an ape into the bargain."

*

The long journey from Pal-ul-don was almost completed—inside the week they should be again at the site of their former home. Whether anything now remained of the ruins the Germans had left was problematical. The barns and outhouses had all been burned and the interior of the bungalow partially wrecked. Those of the Waziri, the faithful native retainers of the Greystokes, who had not been killed by Hauptman Fritz Schneider's soldiers, had rallied to the beat of the war-drum and gone to place themselves at the disposal of the English in whatever capacity they might be found useful to the great cause of humanity. This much Tarzan had known before he set out in search of Lady Jane; but how many of his warlike Waziri had survived the war and what further had befallen his vast estates he did not know. Wandering tribes of natives, or raiding bands of Arab slavers might have completed the demolition inaugurated by the Hun, and it was likely, too, that the jungle had swept up and reclaimed its own, covering his clearings and burying amidst its riot of lush verdure every sign of man's brief trespass upon its world-old preserves.

Following the adoption of the tiny Numa, Tarzan was compelled to an immediate consideration of the needs of his protégé in planning his marches and his halts, for the cub must have sustenance and that sustenance could be naught but milk. Lion's milk was out of the question, but fortunately they were now in a comparatively well peopled country where villages were not infrequent and where the great Lord of the Jungle was known, feared, and respected, and so it was that upon the afternoon of the day he had found the young lion Tarzan approached a village for the purpose of obtaining milk for the cub.

At first the natives appeared sullen and indifferent, looking with contempt upon whites who traveled without a large safari—with contempt and without fear. With no safari these strangers could carry no presents for them, nor anything wherewith to repay for the food they would doubtless desire, and with no askari they could not demand food, or rather they could not enforce an order, nor could they protect themselves should it seem worth while to molest them. Sullen and indifferent the natives seemed, yet they were scarce unconcerned, their curiosity being aroused by the unusual apparel and ornamentation of these whites. They saw them almost as naked as themselves and armed similarly except that one, the younger man, carried a rifle. All three wore the trappings of Pal-ul-don, primitive and barbaric, and entirely strange to the eyes of the simple blacks.

"Where is your chief?" asked Tarzan as he strode into the village amongst the women, the children, and the yapping dogs.

A few dozing warriors rose from the shadows of the huts where they had been lying and approached the newcomers.

"The chief sleeps," replied one. "Who are you to awaken him? What do you want?"

"I wish to speak to your chief. Go and fetch him!"

The warrior looked at him in wide-eyed amaze, and then broke into a loud laugh.

"The chief must be brought to him," he cried, addressing his fellows, and then, laughing loudly, he slapped his thigh and nudged those nearest him with his elbows.

"Tell him," continued the ape-man, "that Tarzan would speak with him."

Instantly the attitude of his auditors underwent a remarkable transformation—they fell back from him and they ceased laughing—their eyes very wide and round. He who had laughed loudest became suddenly solemn. "Bring mats," he cried, "for Tarzan and his people to sit upon, while I fetch Umanga the chief," and off he ran as fast as he could as though glad of the excuse to escape the presence of the mighty one he feared he had offended.

It made no difference now that they had no safari, no askari, nor any presents. The villagers were vying with one another to do them honor. Even before the chief came many had already brought presents of food and ornaments. Presently Umanga appeared. He was an old man who had been a chief even before Tarzan of the Apes was born. His manner was patriarchal and dignified and he greeted his guest as one great man might greet another, yet he was undeniably pleased that the Lord of the Jungle had honored his village with a visit.

When Tarzan explained his wishes and exhibited the lion cub Umanga assured him that there would be milk a-plenty so long as Tarzan honored them with his presence—warm milk, fresh from the chief's own goats. As they palavered the ape-man's keen eyes took in every detail of the village and its people, and presently they alighted upon a large bitch among the numerous curs that overran the huts and the street. Her udder was swollen with milk and the sight of it suggested a plan to Tarzan. He jerked a thumb in the direction of the animal. "I would buy her," he said to Umanga.

"She is yours, Bwana, without payment," replied the chief. "She whelped two days since and last night her pups were all stolen from her nest, doubtless by a great snake; but if you will accept them I will give you instead as many younger and fatter dogs as you wish, for I am sure that this one would prove poor eating."

"I do not wish to eat her," replied Tarzan. "I will take her along with me to furnish milk for the cub. Have her brought to me."

Some boys then caught the animal and tying a thong about its neck dragged it to the ape-man. Like the lion, the dog was at first afraid, for the scent of the Tarmangani was not as the scent of the blacks, and it snarled and snapped at its new master; but at length he won the animal's confidence so that it lay quietly beside him while he stroked its head. To get the lion close to it was, however, another matter, for here both were terrified by the enemy scent of the other—the lion snarling and spitting and the dog bare-fanged and growling. It required patience—infinite patience—but at last the thing was an accomplished fact and the cur bitch suckled the son of Numa. Hunger had succeeded in overcoming the natural suspicion of the lion, while the firm yet kindly attitude of the ape-man had won the confidence of the canine, which had been accustomed through life to more of cuffs and kicks than kindness.

That night Tarzan had the dog tied in the hut he occupied, and twice before morning he made her lie while the cub fed. The next day they took leave of Umanga and his people and with the dog still upon a leash trotting beside them they set off once more toward home, the young lion cuddled in the hollow of one of Tarzan's arms or carried in a sack slung across his shoulder.

They named the lion Jad-bal-ja, which in the language of the pithecanthropi of Pal-ul-don, means the Golden Lion, because of his color. Every day he became more accustomed to them and to his foster mother, who finally came to accept him as flesh of her flesh. The bitch they called Za, meaning girl. The second day they removed her leash and she followed them willingly through the jungle, nor ever after did she seek to leave them, nor was happy unless she was near one of the three.

As the moment approached when the trail should break from the jungle onto the edge of the rolling plain where their home had been, the three were filled with suppressed excitement, though none uttered a syllable of the hope and fear that was in the heart of each. What would they find? What could they find other than the same tangled mass of vegetation that the ape-man had cleared away to build his home when first he had come there with his bride?

At last they stepped from the concealing verdure of the forest to look out across the plain where, in the distance, the outlines of the bungalow had once been clearly discernible nestled amidst the trees and shrubs that had been retained or imported to beautify the grounds.

"Look!" cried Lady Jane. "It is there—it is still there!"

"But what are those other things to the left, beyond it?" asked Korak.

"They are the huts of natives," replied Tarzan.

"The fields are being cultivated!" exclaimed the woman.

"And some of the outbuildings have been rebuilt," said Tarzan. "It can mean but one thing—the Waziri have come back from the war—my faithful Waziri. They have restored what the Hun destroyed and are watching over our home until we return."

THE TRAINING OF JAD-BAL-JA

And so Tarzan of the Apes, and Jane Clayton, and Korak came home after a long absence and with them came Jad-bal-ja, the golden lion, and Za, the bitch. Among the first to meet them and to welcome them home was old Muviro, father of Wasimbu, who had given his life in defense of the home and wife of the ape-man.

"Ah, Bwana," cried the faithful black, "my old eyes are made young again by the sight of you. It has been long that you have been gone, but though many doubted that you would return, old Muviro knew that the great world held nothing that might overcome his master. And so he knew, too, that his master would return to the home of his love and the land where his faithful Waziri awaited him; but that she, whom we have mourned as dead, should have returned is beyond belief, and great shall be the rejoicing in the huts of the Waziri tonight. And the earth shall tremble to the dancing feet of the warriors and the heavens ring with the glad cries of their women, since the three they love most on earth have come back to them."

And in truth, great indeed was the rejoicing in the huts of the Waziri. And not for one night alone, but for many nights did the dancing and the rejoicing continue until Tarzan was compelled to put a stop to the festivities that he and his family might gain a few hours of unbroken slumber. The ape-man found that not only had his faithful Waziri, under the equally faithful guidance of his English foreman, Jervis, completely rehabilitated his stables, corrals, and outbuildings as well as the native huts, but had restored the interior of the bungalow, so that in all outward appearances the place was precisely as it had been before the raid of the Germans.

Jervis was at Nairobi on the business of the estate, and it was some days after their arrival that he returned to the ranch. His surprise and happiness were no less genuine than those of the Waziri. With the chief and warriors he sat for hours at the feet of the Big Bwana, listening to an account of the strange land of Pal-ul-don and the adventures that had befallen the three during Lady Greystoke's captivity there, and with the Waziri he marveled at the queer pets the ape-man had brought back with him. That Tarzan might have fancied a mongrel native cur was strange enough, but that he should have adopted a cub of his hereditary enemies, Numa and Sabor, seemed beyond all belief. And equally surprising to them all was the manner of Tarzan's education of the cub.

The golden lion and his foster mother occupied a corner of the ape-man's bedroom, and many was the hour each day that he spent in training and educating the little spotted, yellow ball—all playfulness and affection now, but one day to grow into a great, savage beast of prey.

As the days passed and the golden lion grew, Tarzan taught it many tricks—to fetch and carry, to lie motionless in hiding at his almost inaudible word of command, to move from point to point as he indicated, to hunt for hidden things by scent and to retrieve them, and when meat was added to its diet he fed it always in a way that brought grim smiles to the savage lips of the Waziri warriors, for Tarzan had built for him a dummy in the semblance of a man and the meat that the lion was to eat was fastened always at the throat of the dummy. Never did the manner of feeding vary. At a word from the ape-man the golden lion would crouch, belly to the ground, and then Tarzan would point at the dummy and whisper the single word "kill." However hungry he might be, the lion learned never to move toward his meat until that single word had been uttered by its master; and then with a rush and a savage growl it drove straight for the flesh. While it was little it had difficulty at first in clambering up the dummy to the savory morsel fastened at the figure's throat, but as it grew older and larger it gained the objective more easily, and finally a single leap would carry it to its goal and down would go the dummy upon its back with the young lion tearing at its throat.

There was one lesson that, of all the others, was most difficult to learn and it is doubtful that any other than Tarzan of the Apes, reared by beasts, among beasts, could have overcome the savage blood-lust of the carnivore and rendered his natural instinct subservient to the will of his master. It took weeks and months of patient endeavor to accomplish this single item of the lion's education, which consisted in teaching him that at the word "fetch" he must find any indicated object and return with it to his master, even the dummy with raw meat tied at its throat, and that he must not touch the meat nor harm the dummy nor any other article that he was fetching, but place them carefully at the ape-man's feet. Afterward he learned always to be sure of his reward, which usually consisted in a double portion of the meat that he loved best.

Lady Greystoke and Korak were often interested spectators of the education of the golden lion, though the former expressed mystification as to the purpose of such elaborate training of the young cub and some misgivings as to the wisdom of the ape-man's program.

"What in the world can you do with such a brute after he is grown?" she asked. "He bids fair to be a mighty Numa. Being accustomed to men he will be utterly fearless of them, and having fed always at the throat of a dummy he will look there at the throat of living men for his food hereafter."

"He will feed only upon what I tell him to feed," replied the ape-man.

"But you do not expect him to feed always upon men?" she interrogated, laughingly.

"He will never feed upon men."

"But how can you prevent it, having taught him from cubhood always to feed upon men?"

"I am afraid, Jane, that you under-estimate the intelligence of a lion, or else I very much over-estimate it. If your theory is correct the hardest part of my work is yet before me, but if I am right it is practically complete now. However, we will experiment a bit and see which is right. We shall take Jad-bal-ja out upon the plain with us this afternoon. Game is plentiful and we shall have no difficulty in ascertaining just how much control I have over young Numa after all."

"I'll wager a hundred pounds," said Korak, laughing, "that he does just what he jolly well pleases after he gets a taste of live blood."

"You're on, my son," said the ape-man. "I think I am going to show you and your mother this afternoon what you or anyone else never dreamed could be accomplished."

EDGAR RICE BURROUGHS

"Lord Greystoke, the world's premier animal trainer!" cried Lady Greystoke, and Tarzan joined them in their laughter.

"It is not animal training," said the ape-man. "The plan upon which I work would be impossible to anyone but Tarzan of the Apes. Let us take a hypothetical case to illustrate what I mean. There comes to you some creature whom you hate, whom by instinct and heredity you consider a deadly enemy. You are afraid of him. You understand no word that he speaks. Finally, by means sometimes brutal he impresses upon your mind his wishes. You may do the thing he wants, but do you do it with a spirit of unselfish loyalty? You do not—you do it under compulsion, hating the creature that forces his will upon you. At any moment that you felt it was in your power to do so, you would disobey him. You would even go further—you would turn upon him and destroy him. On the other hand, there comes to you one with whom you are familiar; he is a friend, a protector. He understands and speaks the language that you understand and speak. He has fed you, he has gained your confidence by kindness and protection, he asks you to do something for him. Do you refuse? No, you obey willingly. It is thus that the golden lion will obey me."

"As long as it suits his purpose to do so," commented Korak.

"Let me go a step farther then," said the ape-man. "Suppose that this creature, whom you love and obey, has the power to punish, even to kill you, if it is necessary so to do to enforce his commands. How then about your obedience?"

"We'll see," said Korak, "how easily the golden lion will make one hundred pounds for me."

That afternoon they set out across the plain, Jad-bal-ja following Tarzan's horse's heels. They dismounted at a little clump of trees some distance from the bungalow and from there proceeded onward warily toward a swale in which antelopes were usually to be found, moving up which they came cautiously to the heavy brush that bordered the swale upon their side. There was Tarzan, Jane, and Korak, and close beside Tarzan the golden lion—four jungle hunters—and of the four Jad-bal-ja, the lion, was the least accomplished. Stealthily they crawled through the brush, scarce a leaf rustling to their passage, until at last they looked down into the swale upon a small herd of antelope grazing peacefully below. Closest to them was an old buck, and him Tarzan pointed out in some mysterious manner to Jad-bal-ja.

"Fetch him," he whispered, and the golden lion rumbled a scarce audible acknowledgment of the command.

Stealthily he worked his way through the brush. The antelopes fed on, unsuspecting. The distance separating the lion from his prey was over great for a successful charge, and so Jad-bal-ja waited, hiding in the brush, until the antelope should either graze closer to him or turn its back toward him. No sound came from the four watching the grazing herbivora, nor did the latter give any indication of a suspicion of the nearness of danger. The old buck moved slowly closer to Jad-bal-ja. Almost imperceptibly the lion was gathering for the charge. The only noticeable movement was the twitching of his tail's tip, and then, as lightning from the sky, as an arrow from a bow, he shot from immobility to tremendous speed in an instant. He was almost upon the buck before the latter realized the proximity of danger, and then it was too late, for scarcely had the antelope wheeled than the lion rose upon its hind legs and seized it, while the balance of the herd broke into precipitate flight.

"Now," said Korak, "we shall see."

"He will bring the antelope to me," said Tarzan confidently.

The golden lion hesitated a moment, growling over the carcass of his kill. Then he seized it by the back and with his head turned to one side dragged it along the ground beside him, as he made his way slowly back toward Tarzan. Through the brush he dragged the slain antelope until he had dropped it at the feet of his master, where he stood, looking up at the face of the ape-man with an expression that could not have been construed into aught but pride in his achievement and a plea for commendation.

Tarzan stroked his head and spoke to him in a low voice, praising him, and then, drawing his hunting knife, he cut the jugular of the antelope and let the blood from the carcass. Jane and Korak stood close,

TARZAN SUPER PACK

watching Jad-bal-ja—what would the lion do with the smell of fresh, hot blood in his nostrils? He sniffed at it and growled, and with bared fangs he eyed the three wickedly. The ape-man pushed him away with his open palm and the lion growled again angrily and snapped at him.

Quick is Numa, quick is Bara, the deer, but Tarzan of the Apes is lightning. So swiftly did he strike, and so heavily, that Jad-bal-ja was falling on his back almost in the very instant that he had growled at his master. Swiftly he came to his feet again and the two stood facing one another.

"Down!" commanded the ape-man. "Lie down, Jad-bal-ja!" His voice was low and firm. The lion hesitated but for an instant, and then lay down as Tarzan of the Apes had taught him to do at the word of command. Tarzan turned and lifted the carcass of the antelope to his shoulder.

"Come," he said to Jad-bal-ja. "Heel!" and without another glance at the carnivore he moved off toward the horses.

"I might have known it," said Korak, with a laugh, "and saved my hundred pounds."

"Of course you might have known it," said his mother.

A MEETING OF MYSTERY

A rather attractive-looking, though overdressed, young woman was dining in a second-rate chop-house in London. She was noticeable, not so much for her fine figure and coarsely beautiful face as for the size and appearance of her companion, a large, well-proportioned man in the mid-twenties, with such a tremendous beard that it gave him the appearance of hiding in ambush. He stood fully three inches over six feet. His shoulders were broad, his chest deep, and his hips narrow. His physique, his carriage, everything about him, suggested indubitably the trained athlete.

The two were in close conversation, a conversation that occasionally gave every evidence of bordering upon heated argument.

"I tell you," said the man, "that I do not see what we need of the others. Why should they share with us—why divide into six portions that which you and I might have alone?"

"It takes money to carry the plan through," she replied, "and neither you nor I have any money. *They* have it and they will back us with it—me for my knowledge and you for your appearance and your strength. They searched for you, Esteban, for two years, and, now that they have found you, I should not care to be in your shoes if you betrayed them. They would just as soon slit your throat as not, Esteban, if they no more than thought they couldn't use you, now that you have all the details of their plan. But if you should try to take all the profit from them—" She paused, shrugging her shoulders. "No, my dear, I love life too well to join you in any such conspiracy as that."

"But I tell you, Flora, we ought to get more out of it than they want to give. You furnish all the knowledge and I take all the risk—why shouldn't we have more than a sixth apiece?"

"Talk to them yourself, then, Esteban," said the girl, with a shrug, "but if you will take my advice you will be satisfied with what you are offered. Not only have I the information, without which they can do nothing, but I found you into the bargain, yet I do not ask it all—I shall be perfectly satisfied with one-sixth, and I can assure you that if you do not muddle the thing, one-sixth of what you bring out will be enough for any one of us for the rest of his natural life."

The man did not seem convinced, and the young woman had a feeling that he would bear watching. Really, she knew very little about him, and had seen him in person only a few times since her first discovery of him some two months before, upon the screen of a London cinema house in a spectacular feature in which he had played the rôle of a Roman soldier of the Pretorian Guard.

Here his heroic size and perfect physique had alone entitled him to consideration, for his part was a minor one, and doubtless of all the thousands who saw him upon the silver sheet Flora Hawkes was the only one who took more than a passing interest in him, and her interest was aroused, not by his histrionic ability, but rather because for some two years she and her confederates had been searching for such a type as Esteban

Miranda so admirably represented. To find him in the flesh bade fair to prove difficult of accomplishment, but after a month of seemingly fruitless searching she finally discovered him among a score of extra men at the studio of one of London's lesser producing companies. She needed no other credentials than her good looks to form his acquaintance, and while that was ripening into intimacy she made no mention to him of the real purpose of her association with him.

That he was a Spaniard and apparently of good family was evident to her, and that he was unscrupulous was to be guessed by the celerity with which he agreed to take part in the shady transaction that had been conceived in the mind of Flora Hawkes, and the details of which had been perfected by her and her four confederates. So, therefore, knowing that he was unscrupulous, she was aware that every precaution must be taken to prevent him taking advantage of the knowledge of their plan that he must one day have in detail, the key to which she, up to the present moment, had kept entirely to herself, not even confiding it to any one of her four other confederates.

They sat for a moment in silence, toying with the empty glasses from which they had been drinking. Presently she looked up to find his gaze fixed upon her and an expression in his eyes that even a less sophisticated woman than Flora Hawkes might readily have interpreted.

"You can make me do anything you want, Flora," he said, "for when I am with you I forget the gold, and think only of that other reward which you continually deny me, but which one day I shall win."

"Love and business do not mix well," replied the girl. "Wait until you have succeeded in this work, Esteban, and then we may talk of love."

"You do not love me," he whispered, hoarsely. "I know—I have seen—that each of the others loves you. That is why I could hate them. And if I thought that you loved one of them, I could cut his heart out. Sometimes I have thought that you did—first one of them and then another. You are too familiar with them, Flora. I have seen John Peebles squeeze your hand when he thought no one was looking, and when you dance with Dick Throck he holds you too close and you dance cheek to cheek. I tell you I do not like it, Flora, and one of these days I shall forget all about the gold and think only of you, and then something will happen and there will not be so many to divide the ingots that I shall bring back from Africa. And Bluber and Kraski are almost as bad; perhaps Kraski is the worst of all, for he is a good-looking devil and I do not like the way in which you cast sheep's eyes at him."

The fire of growing anger was leaping to the girl's eyes. With an angry gesture she silenced him.

"What business is it of yours, Señor Miranda, who I choose for my friends, or how I treat them or how they treat me? I will have you understand that I have known these men for years, while I have known you for but a few weeks, and if any has a right to dictate my behavior, which, thank God, none has, it would be one of them rather than you."

His eyes blazed angrily.

"It is as I thought!" he cried. "You love one of them." He half rose from the table and leaned across it toward her, menacingly. "Just let me find out which one it is and I will cut him into pieces!"

He ran his fingers through his long, black hair until it stood up on end like the mane of an angry lion. His eyes were blazing with a light that sent a chill of dread through the girl's heart. He appeared a man temporarily bereft of reason—if he were not a maniac he most certainly looked one, and the girl was afraid and realized that she must placate him.

"Come, come, Esteban," she whispered softly, "there is no need for working yourself into a towering rage over nothing. I have not said that I loved one of these, nor have I said that I do not love you, but I am not used to being wooed in such fashion. Perhaps your Spanish señoritas like it, but I am an English girl and if you love me treat me as an English lover would treat me."

"You have not said that you loved one of these others—no, but on the other hand you have not said that you do not love one of them—tell me, Flora, which one of them is it that you love?"

His eyes were still blazing, and his great frame trembling with suppressed passion.

"I do not love any of them, Esteban," she replied, "nor, as yet, do I love you. But I could, Esteban, that much I will tell you. I could love you, Esteban, as I could never love another, but I shall not permit myself to do so until after you have returned and we are free to live where and how we like. Then, maybe—but, even so, I do not promise."

"You had better promise," he said, sullenly, though evidently somewhat mollified. "You had better promise, Flora, for I care nothing for the gold if I may not have you also."

"Hush," she cautioned, "here they come now, and it is about time; they are fully a half-hour late."

The man turned his eyes in the direction of her gaze, and the two sat watching the approach of four men who had just entered the chop-house. Two of them were evidently Englishmen—big, meaty fellows of the middle class, who looked what they really were, former pugilists; the third, Adolph Bluber, was a short, fat German, with a round, red face and a bull neck; the other, the youngest of the four, was by far the best looking. His smooth face, clear complexion, and large dark eyes might of themselves have proven sufficient grounds for Miranda's jealousy, but supplementing these were a mop of wavy, brown hair, the figure of a Greek god and the grace of a Russian dancer, which, in truth, was what Carl Kraski was when he chose to be other than a rogue.

The girl greeted the four pleasantly, while the Spaniard vouchsafed them but a single, surly nod, as they found chairs and seated themselves at the table.

"Hale!" cried Peebles, pounding the table to attract the attention of a waiter, "let us 'ave hale."

The suggestion met with unanimous approval, and as they waited for their drink they spoke casually of unimportant things; the heat, the circumstance that had delayed them, the trivial occurrences since they had last met; throughout which Esteban sat in sullen silence, but after the waiter had returned and they drank to Flora, with which ceremony it had long been their custom to signalize each gathering, they got down to business.

"Now," cried Peebles, pounding the table with his meaty fist, "'ere we are, and that's that! We 'ave everything, Flora—the plans, the money, Señor Miranda—and are jolly well ready, old dear, for your part of it."

"How much money have you?" asked Flora. "It is going to take a lot of money, and there is no use starting unless you have plenty to carry on with."

Peebles turned to Bluber. "There," he said, pointing a pudgy finger at him, "is the bloomin' treasurer. 'E can tell you 'ow much we 'ave, the fat rascal of a Dutchman."

Bluber smiled an oily smile and rubbed his fat palms together. "Vell," he said, "how much you t'ink, Miss Flora, ve should have?"

"Not less than two thousand pounds to be on the safe side," she replied quickly.

"Oi! Oi!" exclaimed Bluber. "But dot is a lot of money—two t'ousand pounds. Oi! Oi!"

The girl made a gesture of disgust. "I told you in the first place that I wouldn't have anything to do with a bunch of cheap screws, and that until you had enough money to carry the thing out properly I would not give you the maps and directions, without which you cannot hope to reach the vaults, where there is stored enough gold to buy this whole, tight, little island if half that what I have heard them say about it is true. You can go along and spend your own money, but you've got to show me that you have at least two thousand pounds to spend before I give up the information that will make you the richest men in the world."

"The blighter's got the money," growled Throck. "Blime if I know what he's beefin' about."

"He can't help it," growled the Russian, "it's a racial characteristic; Bluber would try to jew down the marriage license clerk if he were going to get married."

"Oh, vell," sighed Bluber, "for vy should we spend more money than is necessary? If ve can do it for vone t'ousand pounds so much the better."

EDGAR RICE BURROUGHS

"Certainly," snapped the girl, "and if it don't take but one thousand, that is all that you will have to spend, but you've got to have the two thousand in case of emergencies, and from what I have seen of that country you are likely to run up against more emergencies than anything else.

"*Oi! Oi!*" cried Bluber.

"'E's got the money all right," said Peebles, "now let's get busy."

"He may have it, but I want to see it first," replied the girl.

"Vat you t'ink; I carry all dot money around in my pocket?" cried Bluber.

"Can't you take our word for it?" grumbled Throck.

"You're a nice bunch of crooks to ask me that," she replied, laughing in the face of the burly ruffians. "I'll take Carl's word for it, though; if he tells me that you have it, and that it is in such shape that it can, and will, be used to pay all the necessary expenses of our expedition, I will believe him."

Peebles and Throck scowled angrily, and Miranda's eyes closed to two narrow, nasty slits, as he directed his gaze upon the Russian. Bluber, on the contrary, was affected not at all; the more he was insulted, the better, apparently, he liked it. Toward one who treated him with consideration or respect he would have become arrogant, while he fawned upon the hand that struck him. Kraski, alone, smiled a self-satisfied smile that set the blood of the Spaniard boiling.

"Bluber has the money, Flora," he said; "each of us has contributed his share. We'll make Bluber treasurer, because we know that he will squeeze the last farthing until it shrieks before he will let it escape him. It is our plan now to set out from London in pairs."

He drew a map from his pocket, and unfolding it, spread it out upon the table before them. With his finger he indicated a point marked X. "Here we will meet and here we will equip our expedition. Bluber and Miranda will go first; then Peebles and Throck. By the time that you and I arrive everything will be in shape for moving immediately into the interior, where we shall establish a permanent camp, off the beaten track and as near our objective as possible. Miranda will disport himself behind his whiskers until he is ready to set out upon the final stage of his long journey. I understand that he is well schooled in the part that he is to play and that he can depict the character to perfection. As he will have only ignorant natives and wild beasts to deceive it should not tax his histrionic ability too greatly." There was a veiled note of sarcasm in the soft, drawling tone that caused the black eyes of the Spaniard to gleam wickedly.

"Do I understand," asked Miranda, his soft tone belying his angry scowl, "that you and Miss Hawkes travel alone to X?"

"You do, unless your understanding is poor," replied the Russian.

The Spaniard half rose from the table and leaned across it menacingly toward Kraski. The girl, who was sitting next to him, seized his coat.

"None of that!" she said, dragging him back into his chair. "There has been too much of it among you already, and if there is any more I shall cut you all and seek more congenial companions for my expedition."

"Yes, cut it out; 'ere we are, and that's that!" exclaimed Peebles belligerently.

"John's right," rumbled Throck, in his deep bass, "and I'm here to back him up. Flora's right, and I'm here to back her up. And if there is any more of it, blime if I don't bash a couple of you pretty 'uns," and he looked first at Miranda and then at Kraski.

"Now," soothed Bluber, "let's all shake hands and be good friends."

"Right-o," cried Peebles, "that's the talk. Give 'im your 'and, Esteban. Come, Carl, bury the 'atchet. We can't start in on this thing with no hanimosities, and 'ere we are, and that's that."

The Russian, feeling secure in his position with Flora, and therefore in a magnanimous mood, extended his hand across the table toward the Spaniard. For a moment Esteban hesitated.

"Come, man, shake!" growled Throck, "or you can go back to your job as an extra man, blime, and we'll find someone else to do your work and divvy the swag with."

Suddenly the dark countenance of the Spaniard was lighted by a pleasant smile. He extended his hand quickly and clasped Kraski's. "Forgive me," he said, "I am hot-tempered, but I mean nothing. Miss Hawkes is right, we must all be friends, and here's my hand on it, Kraski, as far as I am concerned."

"Good," said Kraski, "and I am sorry if I offended you;" but he forgot that the other was an actor, and if he could have seen into the depths of that dark soul he would have shuddered.

"Und now, dot ve are all good friends," said Bluber, rubbing his hands together unctuously, "vy not arrange for vhen ve shall commence starting to finish up everyt'ings? Miss Flora, she gives me the map und der directions und we start commencing immediately."

"Loan me a pencil, Carl," said the girl, and when the man had handed her one she searched out a spot upon the map some distance into the interior from X, where she drew a tiny circle. "This is O," she said. "When we all reach here you shall have the final directions and not before."

Bluber threw up his hands. "Oi! Miss Flora, vhat you t'ink, ve spend two t'ousand pounds to buy a pig in a poke? Oi! Oi! you vouldn't ask us to do dot? Ve must see everyt'ing, ve must know everyt'ing, before ve spend vun farthing."

"Yes, and 'ere we are, and that's that!" roared John Peebles, striking the table with his fist.

The girl rose leisurely from her seat. "Oh, very well," she said with a shrug. "If you feel that way about it we might as well call it all off."

"Oh, vait, vait, Miss Flora," cried Bluber, rising hurriedly. "Don't be ogcited. But can't you see vere ve are? Two t'ousand pounds is a lot of money, and ve are good business men. Ve shouldn't be spending it all vit'out getting not'ings for it."

"I am not asking you to spend it and get nothing for it," replied the girl, tartly; "but if anyone has got to trust anyone else in this outfit, it is you who are going to trust me. If I give you all the information I have, there is nothing in the world that could prevent you from going ahead and leaving me out in the cold, and I don't intend that that shall happen."

"But we are not gonoffs, Miss Flora," insisted the Jew. "Ve vould not t'ink for vun minute of cheating you."

"You're not angels, either, Bluber, any of you," retorted the girl. "If you want to go ahead with this you've got to do it in my way, and I am going to be there at the finish to see that I get what is coming to me. You've taken my word for it, up to the present time, that I had the dope, and now you've got to take it the rest of the way or all bets are off. What good would it do me to go over into a bally jungle and suffer all the hardships that we are bound to suffer, dragging you along with me, if I were not going to be able to deliver the goods when I got there? And I am not such a softy as to think I could get away with it with a bunch of bandits like you if I tried to put anything of that kind over on you. And as long as I do play straight I feel perfectly safe, for I know that either Esteban or Carl will look after me, and I don't know but what the rest of you would, too. Is it a go or isn't it?"

"Vell, John, vot do you und Dick t'ink?" asked Bluber, addressing the two ex-prize-fighters. "Carl, I know he vill t'ink v'hatever Flora t'inks. Hey? V'at?"

"Blime," said Throck, "I never was much of a hand at trusting nobody unless I had to, but it looks now as though we had to trust Flora."

"Same 'ere," said John Peebles. "If you try any funny work, Flora—" He made a significant movement with his finger across his throat.

"I understand, John," said the girl with a smile, "and I know that you would do it as quickly for two pounds as you would for two thousand. But you are all agreed, then, to carry on according to my plans? You too, Carl?"

The Russian nodded. "Whatever the rest say goes with me," he remarked.

And so the gentle little coterie discussed their plans in so far as they could—each minutest detail that would be necessary to place them all at the O which the girl had drawn upon the map.

EDGAR RICE BURROUGHS

WHAT THE FOOTPRINTS TOLD

When Jad-bal-ja, the golden lion, was two years old, he was as magnificent a specimen of his kind as the Greystokes had ever looked upon. In size he was far above the average of that attained by mature males; in conformation he was superb, his noble head and his great black mane giving him the appearance of a full-grown male, while in intelligence he far outranked his savage brothers of the forest.

Jad-bal-ja was a never-ending source of pride and delight to the ape-man who had trained him so carefully, and nourished him cunningly for the purpose of developing to the full all the latent powers within him. The lion no longer slept at the foot of his master's bed, but occupied a strong cage that Tarzan had had constructed for him at the rear of the bungalow, for who knew better than the ape-man that a lion, wherever he may be or however he may have been raised, is yet a lion—a savage flesh-eater. For the first year he had roamed at will about the house and grounds; after that he went abroad only in the company of Tarzan. Often the two roamed the plain and the jungle hunting together. In a way the lion was almost equally as familiar with Jane and Korak, and neither of them feared or mistrusted him, but toward Tarzan of the Apes did he show the greatest affection. The blacks of Tarzan's household he tolerated, nor did he ever offer to molest any of the domestic animals or fowl, after Tarzan had impressed upon him in his early cubhood that appropriate punishment followed immediately upon any predatory excursion into the corrals or henhouses. The fact that he was never permitted to become ravenously hungry was doubtless the deciding factor in safeguarding the live stock of the farm.

The man and the beast seemed to understand one another perfectly. It is doubtful that the lion understood all that Tarzan said to him, but be that as it may the ease with which he communicated his wishes to the lion bordered upon the uncanny. The obedience that a combination of sternness and affection had elicited from the cub had become largely habit in the grown lion. At Tarzan's command he would go to great distances and bring back antelope or zebra, laying his kill at his master's feet without offering to taste the flesh himself, and he had even retrieved living animals without harming them. Such, then, was the golden lion that roamed the primeval forest with his godlike master.

It was at about this time that there commenced to drift in to the ape-man rumors of a predatory band to the west and south of his estate; ugly stories of ivory-raiding, slave-running and torture, such as had not disturbed the quiet of the ape-man's savage jungle since the days of Sheik Amor Ben Khatour, and there came other tales, too, that caused Tarzan of the Apes to pucker his brows in puzzlement and thought, and then a month elapsed during which Tarzan heard no more of the rumors from the west.

*

The war had reduced the resources of the Greystokes to but a meager income. They had given practically all to the cause of the Allies, and now what little had remained to them had been all but exhausted in the rehabilitation of Tarzan's African estate.

"It looks very much, Jane," he said to his wife one night, "as though another trip to Opar were on the books."

"I dread to think of it. I do not want you to go," she said. "You have come away from that awful city twice, but barely with your life. The third time you may not be so fortunate. We have enough, John, to permit us to live here in comfort and in happiness. Why jeopardize those two things which are greater than all wealth in another attempt to raid the treasure vaults?"

"There is no danger, Jane," he assured her. "The last time Werper dogged my footsteps, and between him and the earthquake I was nearly done for. But there is no chance of any such combination of circumstances thwarting me again."

"You will not go alone, John?" she asked. "You will take Korak with you?"

"No," he said, "I shall not take him. He must remain here with you, for really my long absences are more dangerous to you than to me. I shall take fifty of the Waziri, as porters, to carry the gold, and thus we should be able to bring out enough to last us for a long time."

"And Jad-bal-ja," she asked, "shall you take him?"

"No, he had better remain here; Korak can look after him and take him out for a hunt occasionally. I am going to travel light and fast and it would be too hard a trip for him—lions don't care to move around much in the hot sun, and as we shall travel mostly by day I doubt if Jad-bal-ja would last long."

And so it befell that Tarzan of the Apes set out once more upon the long trail that leads to Opar. Behind him marched fifty giant Waziri, the pick of the warlike tribe that had adopted Tarzan as its Chief. Upon the veranda of the bungalow stood Jane and Korak waving their adieux, while from the rear of the building there came to the ape-man's ears the rumbling roar of Jad-bal-ja, the golden lion. And as they marched away the voice of Numa accompanied them out upon the rolling plain, until at last it trailed off to nothingness in the distance.

His speed determined by that of the slowest of the blacks, Tarzan made but comparatively rapid progress. Opar lay a good twenty-five days' trek from the farm for men traveling light, as were these, but upon the return journey, laden as they would be with the ingots of gold, their progress would be slower. And because of this the ape-man had allotted two months for the venture. His safari, consisting of seasoned warriors only, permitted of really rapid progress. They carried no supplies, for they were all hunters and were moving through a country in which game was abundant—no need then for burdening themselves with the cumbersome impedimenta of white huntsmen.

A thorn boma and a few leaves furnished their shelter for the night, while spears and arrows and the powers of their great white chief insured that their bellies would never go empty. With the picked men that he had brought with him Tarzan expected to make the trip to Opar in twenty-one days, though had he been traveling alone he would have moved two or three times as fast, since, when Tarzan elected to travel with speed, he fairly flew through the jungle, equally at home in it by day or by night and practically tireless.

It was a mid-afternoon the third week of the march that Tarzan, ranging far ahead of his blacks in search of game, came suddenly upon the carcass of Bara, the deer, a feathered arrow protruding from its flank. It was evident that Bara had been wounded at some little distance from where it had lain down to die, for the location of the missile indicated that the wound could not have caused immediate death. But what particularly caught the attention of the ape-man, even before he had come close enough to make a minute examination, was the design of the arrow, and immediately he withdrew it from the body of the deer he knew it for what it was, and was filled with such wonderment as might come to you or to me were we to see a native Swazi headdress upon Broadway or the Strand, for the arrow was precisely such as one may purchase in most any sporting-goods house in any large city of the world—such an arrow as is sold and used for archery practice in the parks and suburbs. Nothing could have been more incongruous than this silly toy in the heart of savage Africa, and yet that it had done its work effectively was evident by the dead body of Bara, though the ape-man guessed that the shaft had been sped by no practiced, savage hand.

Tarzan's curiosity was aroused and also his inherent jungle caution. One must know his jungle well to survive long the jungle, and if one would know it well he must let no unusual occurrence or circumstance go unexplained. And so it was that Tarzan set out upon the back track of Bara for the purpose of ascertaining, if possible, the nature of Bara's slayer. The bloody spoor was easily followed and the ape-man wondered why it was that the hunter had not tracked and overtaken his quarry, which had evidently been dead since the previous day. He found that Bara had traveled far, and the sun was already low in the west before Tarzan came upon the first indications of the slayer of the animal. These were in the nature of footprints that filled him with quite as much surprise as had the arrow. He examined them carefully, and, stooping low, even sniffed at them with his sensitive nostrils. Improbable, nay impossible though it seemed, the naked footprints were those of a *white man*—a large man, probably as large as Tarzan himself. As the foster-son of Kala stood gazing upon the spoor of the mysterious stranger he ran the fingers of one hand through his thick, black hair in a characteristic gesture indicative of deep puzzlement.

EDGAR RICE BURROUGHS

What naked white man could there be in Tarzan's jungle who slew Tarzan's game with the pretty arrow of an archery club? It was incredible that there should be such a one, and yet there recurred to the ape-man's mind the vague rumors that he had heard weeks before. Determined to solve the mystery he set out now upon the trail of the stranger—an erratic trail which wound about through the jungle, apparently aimlessly, prompted, Tarzan guessed, by the ignorance of an inexperienced hunter. But night fell before he had arrived at a solution of the riddle, and it was pitch dark as the ape-man turned his steps toward camp.

He knew that his Waziri would be expecting meat and it was not Tarzan's intention to disappoint them, though he then discovered that he was not the only carnivore hunting the district that night. The coughing grunt of a lion close by apprised him of it first, and then, from the distance, the deep roar of another. But of what moment was it to the ape-man that others hunted? It would not be the first time that he had pitted his cunning, his strength, and his agility against the other hunters of his savage world—both man and beast.

And so it was that Tarzan made his kill at last, snatching it almost from under the nose of a disappointed and infuriated lion—a fat antelope that the latter had marked as his own. Throwing his kill to his shoulder almost in the path of the charging Numa, the ape-man swung lightly to the lower terraces and with a taunting laugh for the infuriated cat, vanished noiselessly into the night.

He found the camp and his hungry Waziri without trouble, and so great was their faith in him that they not for a moment doubted but that he would return with meat for them.

Early the following morning Tarzan set out again toward Opar, and directing his Waziri to continue the march in the most direct way, he left them that he might pursue further his investigations of the mysterious presence in his jungle that the arrow and the footsteps had apprised him of. Coming again to the spot at which darkness had forced him to abandon his investigations, he took up the spoor of the stranger. Nor had he followed it far before he came upon further evidence of the presence of this new and malign personality—stretched before him in the trail was the body of a giant ape, one of the tribe of great anthropoids among whom Tarzan had been raised. Protruding from the hairy abdomen of the Mangani was another of the machine-made arrows of civilization. The ape-man's eyes narrowed and a scowl darkened his brow. Who was this who dared invade his sacred preserves and slaughter thus ruthlessly Tarzan's people?

A low growl rumbled in the throat of the ape-man. Sloughed with the habiliments of civilization was the thin veneer of civilization that Tarzan wore among white men. No English lord was this who looked upon the corpse of his hairy cousin, but another jungle beast in whose breast raged the unquenchable fire of suspicion and hatred for the man-thing that is the heritage of the jungle-bred. A beast of prey viewed the bloody work of ruthless man. Nor was there in the consciousness of Tarzan any acknowledgment of his blood relationship to the killer.

Realizing that the trail had been made upon the second day before, Tarzan hastened on in pursuit of the slayer. There was no doubt in his mind but that plain murder had been committed, for he was sufficiently familiar with the traits of the Mangani to know that none of them would provoke assault unless driven to it.

Tarzan was traveling up wind, and some half-hour after he had discovered the body of the ape his keen nostrils caught the scent spoor of others of its kind. Knowing the timidity of these fierce denizens of the jungle he moved forward now with great wariness, lest, warned of his approach, they take flight before they were aware of his identity. He did not see them often, yet he knew that there were always those among them who recalled him, and that through these he could always establish amicable relations with the balance of the tribe.

Owing to the denseness of the undergrowth Tarzan chose the middle terraces for his advance, and here, swinging freely and swiftly among the leafy boughs, he came presently upon the giant anthropoids. There were about twenty of them in the band, and they were engaged, in a little natural clearing, in their never-ending search for caterpillars and beetles, which formed important items in the diet of the Mangani.

A faint smile overspread the ape-man's face as he paused upon a great branch, himself hidden by the leafy foliage about him, and watched the little band below him. Every action, every movement of the great apes, recalled vividly to Tarzan's mind the long years of his childhood, when, protected by the fierce mother-love of Kala, the she-ape, he had ranged the jungle with the tribe of Kerchak. In the romping young, he saw again Neeta and his other childhood playmates and in the adults all the great, savage brutes he had feared in youth and conquered in manhood. The ways of man may change but the ways of the ape are the same, yesterday, today and forever.

He watched them in silence for some minutes. How glad they would be to see him when they discovered his identity! For Tarzan of the Apes was known the length and the breadth of the great jungle as the friend and protector of the Mangani. At first they would growl at him and threaten him, for they would not depend solely on either their eyes or their ears for confirmation of his identity. Not until he had entered the clearing, and bristling bulls with bared fighting fangs had circled him stiffly until they had come close enough for their nostrils to verify the evidence of their eyes and ears, would they finally accept him. Then doubtless there would be great excitement for a few minutes, until, following the instincts of the ape mind, their attention was weaned from him by a blowing leaf, a caterpillar, or a bird's egg, and then they would move about their business, taking no further notice of him more than of any other member of the tribe. But this would not come until after each individual had smelled of him, and perhaps, pawed his flesh with calloused hands.

Now it was that Tarzan made a friendly sound of greeting, and as the apes looked up stepped from his concealment into plain view of them. "I am Tarzan of the Apes," he said, "mighty fighter, friend of the Mangani. Tarzan comes in friendship to his people," and with these words he dropped lightly to the lush grass of the clearing.

Instantly pandemonium reigned. Screaming warnings, the shes raced with the young for the opposite side of the clearing, while the bulls, bristling and growling, faced the intruder.

"Come," cried Tarzan, "do you not know me? I am Tarzan of the Apes, friend of the Mangani, son of Kala, and king of the tribe of Kerchak."

"We know you," growled one of the old bulls; "yesterday we saw you when you killed Gobu. Go away or we shall kill you."

"I did not kill Gobu," replied the ape-man. "I found his dead body yesterday and I was following the spoor of his slayer, when I came upon you."

"We saw you," repeated the old bull; "go away or we shall kill you. You are no longer the friend of the Mangani."

The ape-man stood with brows contracted in thought. It was evident that these apes really believed that they had seen him kill their fellow. What was the explanation? How could it be accounted for? Did the naked footprints of the great white man whom he had been following mean more, then, than he had guessed? Tarzan wondered. He raised his eyes and again addressed the bulls.

"It was not I who killed Gobu," he insisted. "Many of you have known me all your lives. You know that only in fair fight, as one bull fights another, have I ever killed a Mangani. You know that, of all the jungle people, the Mangani are my best friends, and that Tarzan of the Apes is the best friend the Mangani have. How, then, could I slay one of my own people?"

"We only know," replied the old bull, "that we saw you kill Gobu. With our own eyes we saw you kill him. Go away quickly, therefore, or we shall kill you. Mighty fighter is Tarzan of the Apes, but mightier even than he are all the great bulls of Pagth. I am Pagth, king of the tribe of Pagth. Go away before we kill you."

Tarzan tried to reason with them but they would not listen, so confident were they that it was he who had slain their fellow, the bull Gobu. Finally, rather than chance a quarrel in which some of them must inevitably be killed, he turned sorrowfully away. But more than ever, now, was he determined to seek out the slayer of Gobu that he might demand an accounting of one who dared thus invade his life-long domain.

Tarzan trailed the spoor until it mingled with the tracks of many men—barefooted blacks, mostly, but among them the footprints of booted white men, and once he saw the footprints of a woman or a child, which, he could not tell. The trail led apparently toward the rocky hills which protected the barren valley of Opar.

Forgetful now of his original mission and imbued only with a savage desire to wrest from the interlopers a full accounting for their presence in the jungle, and to mete out to the slayer of Gobu his just deserts, Tarzan forged ahead upon the now broad and well-marked trail of the considerable party which could not now be much more than a half-day's march ahead of him, which meant that they were doubtless now already upon the rim of the valley of Opar, if this was their ultimate destination. And what other they could have in view Tarzan could not imagine.

He had always kept closely to himself the location of Opar. In so far as he knew no white person other than Jane, and their son, Korak, knew of the location of the forgotten city of the ancient Atlantians. Yet what else could have drawn these white men, with so large a party, into the savage, unexplored wilderness which hemmed Opar upon all sides?

Such were the thoughts that occupied Tarzan's mind as he followed swiftly the trail that led toward Opar. Darkness fell, but so fresh was the spoor that the ape-man could follow it by scent even when he could not see the imprints upon the ground, and presently, in the distance, he saw the light of a camp ahead of him.

THE FATAL DROPS

at home, the life in the bungalow and at the farm followed its usual routine as it had before the departure of Tarzan. Korak, sometimes on foot and sometimes on horseback, followed the activities of the farm hands and the herders, sometimes alone, but more often in company with the white foreman, Jervis, and often, especially when they rode, Jane accompanied them.

The golden lion Korak exercised upon a leash, since he was not at all confident of his powers of control over the beast, and feared lest, in the absence of his master, Jad-bal-ja might take to the forest and revert to his natural savage state. Such a lion, abroad in the jungle, would be a distinct menace to human life, for Jad-bal-ja, reared among men, lacked that natural timidity of men that is so marked a trait of all wild beasts. Trained as he had been to make his kill at the throat of a human effigy, it required no considerable powers of imagination upon the part of Korak to visualize what might occur should the golden lion, loosed from all restraint, be thrown upon his own resources in the surrounding jungle.

It was during the first week of Tarzan's absence that a runner from Nairobi brought a cable message to Lady Greystoke, announcing the serious illness of her father in London. Mother and son discussed the situation. It would be five or six weeks before Tarzan could return, even if they sent a runner after him, and, were Jane to await him, there would be little likelihood of her reaching her father in time. Even should she depart at once, there seemed only a faint hope that she would arrive early enough to see him alive. It was decided, therefore, that she should set out immediately, Korak accompanying her as far as Nairobi, and then returning to the ranch and resuming its general supervision until his father's return.

It is a long trek from the Greystoke estate to Nairobi, and Korak had not yet returned when, about three weeks after Tarzan's departure, a black, whose duty it was to feed and care for Jad-bal-ja, carelessly left the door of the cage unfastened while he was cleaning it. The golden lion paced back and forth while the black wielded his broom within the cage. They were old friends, and the Waziri felt no fear of the great lion, with the result that his back was as often turned to him as not. The black was working in the far corner of the cage when Jad-bal-ja paused a moment at the door at the opposite end. The beast saw that the gate hung slightly ajar upon its hinges. Silently he raised a great padded paw and inserted it in the opening—a slight pull and the gate swung in. Instantly the golden lion inserted his snout in the widened aperture, and as he swung the barrier aside the horrified black looked up to see his charge drop softly to the ground outside.

"Stop, Jad-bal-ja! Stop!" screamed the frightened black, leaping after him. But the golden lion only increased his pace, and leaping the fence, loped off in the direction of the forest.

The black pursued him with brandishing broom, emitting loud yells that brought the inmates of the Waziri huts into the open, where they joined their fellow in pursuit of the lion. Across the rolling plains they followed him, but as well have sought to snare the elusive will-o'-the-wisp as this swift and wary fugitive, who heeded neither their blandishments nor their threats. And so it was that they saw the golden lion disappear into the primeval forest and, though they searched diligently until almost dark, they were forced at length to give up their quest and return crestfallen to the farm.

"Ah," cried the unhappy black, who had been responsible for the escape of Jad-bal-ja, "what will the Big Bwana say to me, what will he do to me when he finds that I have permitted the golden lion to get away!"

"You will be banished from the bungalow for a long time, Keewazi," old Muviro assured him. "And doubtless you will be sent to the grazing ground far to the east to guard the herd there, where you will have plenty of lions for company, though they will not be as friendly as was Jad-bal-ja. It is not half what you deserve, and were the heart of the Big Bwana not filled with love for his black children—were he like other white Bwanas old Muviro has seen—you would be lashed until you could not stand, perhaps until you died."

"I am a man," replied Keewazi. "I am a warrior and a Waziri. Whatever punishment the Big Bwana inflicts I will accept as a man should."

It was that same night that Tarzan approached the camp-fires of the strange party he had been tracking. Unseen by them, he halted in the foliage of a tree directly in the center of their camp, which was surrounded by an enormous thorn boma, and brilliantly lighted by numerous fires which blacks were diligently feeding with branches from an enormous pile of firewood that they had evidently gathered earlier in the day for this purpose. Near the center of the camp were several tents, and before one, in the light of a fire, sat four white men. Two of them were great, bull-necked, red-faced fellows, apparently Englishmen of the lower class, the third appeared to be a short, fat, German Jew, while the fourth was a tall, slender, handsome fellow, with dark, wavy brown hair and regular features. He and the German were most meticulously garbed for Central African traveling, after the highly idealized standard of motion pictures, in fact either one of them might have stepped directly from a screening of the latest jungle thriller. The young man was evidently not of English descent and Tarzan mentally cataloged him, almost immediately, as a Slav. Shortly after Tarzan's arrival this one arose and entered one of the nearby tents, from which Tarzan immediately heard the sound of voices in low conversation. He could not distinguish the words, but the tones of one seemed quite distinctly feminine. The three remaining at the fire were carrying on a desultory conversation, when suddenly from near at hand beyond the boma wall, a lion's roar broke the silence of the jungle.

With a startled shriek the Jew leaped to his feet, so suddenly that he cleared the ground a good foot, and then, stepping backward, he lost his balance, tripped over his camp-stool, and sprawled upon his back.

"My Gord, Adolph!" roared one of his companions. "If you do that again, damn me if I don't break your neck. 'Ere we are, and that's that."

"Blime if 'e aint worse'n a bloomin' lion," growled the other.

The Jew crawled to his feet. "Mein Gott!" he cried, his voice quavering, "I t'ought sure he vas coming over the fence. S'elp me if I ever get out of diss, neffer again—not for all der gold in Africa vould I go t'rough vat I haf been t'rough dese past t'ree mont's. Oi! Oi! ven I t'ink of it, Oi! Oi! Lions, und leopards, und rhinoceroses und hippopotamuses, Oi! Oi!"

His companions laughed. "Dick and I tells you right along from the beginning that you 'adn't oughter come into the interior," said one of them.

"But for vy I buy all dese clo's?" wailed the German. "Mein Gott, dis suit, it stands me tventy guineas, vot I stand in. Ach, had I know somet'ing, vun guinea vould have bought me my whole wardrobe—tventy guineas for dis und no vun to see it but niggers und lions."

"And you look like 'ell in it, besides," commented one of his friends.

"Und look at it, it's all dirty and torn. How should I know it I spoil dis suit? Mit mine own eyes I see it at der Princess Teayter, how der hero spend t'ree mont's in Africa hunting lions und killing cannibals, und ven he comes ouid he hasn't even got a grease spot on his pants—how should I know it Africa was so dirty und full of thorns?"

It was at this point that Tarzan of the Apes elected to drop quietly into the circle of firelight before them. The two Englishmen leaped to their feet, quite evidently startled, and the Jew turned and took a half step as though in flight, but immediately his eyes rested upon the ape-man he halted, a look of relief supplanting that of terror which had overspread his countenance, as Tarzan had dropped upon them apparently from the heavens.

"Mein Gott, Esteban," shrilled the German, "vy you come back so soon, and for vy you come back like dot, sudden—don't you suppose ve got nerves?"

Tarzan was angry, angry at these raw intruders, who dared enter without his permission, the wide domain in which he kept peace and order. When Tarzan was angry there flamed upon his forehead the scar that Bolgani, the gorilla, had placed there upon that long-gone day when the boy Tarzan had met the great beast in mortal combat, and first learned the true value of his father's hunting knife—the knife that had placed him, the comparatively weak little Tarmangani, upon an even footing with the great beasts of the jungle.

His gray eyes were narrowed, his voice came cold and level as he addressed them. "Who are you," he demanded, "who dare thus invade the country of the Waziri, the land of Tarzan, without permission from the Lord of the Jungle?"

"Where do you get that stuff, Esteban," demanded one of the Englishmen, "and wat in 'ell are you doin' back 'ere alone and so soon? Where are your porters, where is the bloomin' gold?"

The ape-man eyed the speaker in silence for a moment. "I am Tarzan of the Apes," he said. "I do not know what you are talking about. I only, know that I come in search of him who slew Gobu, the great ape; him who slew Bara, the deer, without my permission."

"Oh, 'ell," exploded the other Englishman, "stow the guff, Esteban—if you're tryin' for to be funny we don't see the joke, 'ere we are, and that's that."

Inside the tent, which the fourth white man had entered while Tarzan was watching the camp from his hiding place in the tree above, a woman, evidently suddenly stirred by terror, touched the arm of her companion frantically, and pointed toward the tall, almost naked figure of the ape-man as he stood revealed in the full light of the beast fires. "God, Carl," she whispered, in trembling tones, "look!"

"What's wrong, Flora?" inquired her companion. "I see only Esteban."

"It is not Esteban," hissed the girl. "It is Lord Greystoke himself—it is Tarzan of the Apes!"

"You are mad, Flora," replied the man, "it cannot be he."

"It is he, though," she insisted. "Do you suppose that I do not know him? Did I not work in his town house for years? Did I not see him nearly every day? Do you suppose that I do not know Tarzan of the Apes? Look at that red scar flaming on his forehead—I have heard the story of that scar and I have seen it burn scarlet when he was aroused to anger. It is scarlet now, and Tarzan of the Apes is angry."

"Well, suppose it is Tarzan of the Apes, what can he do?"

"You do not know him," replied the girl. "You do not guess the tremendous power he wields here—the power of life and death over man and beast. If he knew our mission here not one of us would ever reach the coast alive. The very fact that he is here now makes me believe that he may have discovered our purpose, and if he has, God help us—unless—unless——"

"Unless what?" demanded the man.

The girl was silent in thought for a moment. "There is only one way," she said finally. "We dare not kill him. His savage blacks would learn of it, and no power on earth could save us then. There is a way, though, if we act quickly." She turned and searched for a moment in one of her bags, and presently she handed the man a small bottle, containing liquid. "Go out and talk to him," she said, "make friends with him. Lie to him. Tell him anything. Promise anything. But get on friendly enough terms with him so that you can offer him coffee. He does not drink wine or anything with alcohol in it, but I know that he likes coffee. I have often served it to him in his room late at night upon his return from the theater or a ball. Get him to drink coffee and then you will know what to do with this." And she indicated the bottle which the man still held in his hand.

Kraski nodded. "I understand," he said, and, turning, left the tent.

He had taken but a step when the girl recalled him. "Do not let him see me. Do not let him guess that I am here or that you know me."

The man nodded and left her. Approaching the tense figures before the fire he greeted Tarzan with a pleasant smile and a cheery word.

"Welcome," he said, "we are always glad to see a stranger in our camp. Sit down. Hand the gentleman a stool, John," he said to Peebles.

The ape-man eyed Kraski as he had eyed the others. There was no answering friendly light in his eyes responding to the Russian's greeting.

"I have been trying to find out what your party is doing here," he said sharply to the Russian, "but they still insist that I am someone whom I am not. They are either fools or knaves, and I intend to find out which, and deal with them accordingly."

"Come, come," cried Kraski, soothingly. "There must be some mistake, I am sure. But tell me, who are you?"

"I am Tarzan of the Apes," replied the ape-man. "No hunters enter this part of Africa without my permission. That fact is so well known that there is no chance of your having passed the coast without having been so advised. I seek an explanation, and that quickly."

"Ah, you are Tarzan of the Apes," exclaimed Kraski. "Fortunate indeed are we, for now may we be set straight upon our way, and escape from our frightful dilemma is assured. We are lost, sir, inextricably lost, due to the ignorance or knavery of our guide, who deserted us several weeks ago. Surely we knew of you; who does not know of Tarzan of the Apes? But it was not our intention to cross the boundaries of your territory. We were searching farther south for specimens of the fauna of the district, which our good friend and employer, here, Mr. Adolph Bluber, is collecting at great expense for presentation to a museum in his home city in America. Now I am sure that you can tell us where we are and direct us upon our proper course."

Peebles, Throck, and Bluber stood fascinated by Kraski's glib lies, but it was the German Jew who first rose to the occasion. Too thick were the skulls of the English pugs to grasp quickly the clever ruse of the Russian.

"Vy yes," said the oily Bluber, rubbing his palms together, "dot iss it, yust vot I vas going to tell you."

Tarzan turned sharply upon him. "Then what was all this talk about Esteban?" he asked. "Was it not by that name that these others addressed me?"

"Ah," cried Bluber, "John will haf his leetle joke. He iss ignorant of Africa; he has neffer been here before. He t'ought perhaps dat you vere a native. John he calls all der natives Esteban, und he has great jokes by himself mit dem, because he knows dey cannot onderstand vot he says. Hey John, iss it not so, vot it iss I say?" But the shrewd Bluber did not wait for John to reply. "You see," he went on, "ve are lost, und you take us ouid mit dis jungle, ve pay you anyt'ing—you name your own price."

The ape-man only half believed him, yet he was somewhat mollified by their evidently friendly intentions. Perhaps after all they were telling him a half-truth and had, really, wandered into his territory unwittingly. That, however, he would find out definitely from their native carriers, from whom his own Waziri would wean the truth. But the matter of his having been mistaken for Esteban still piqued his curiosity, also he was still desirous of learning the identity of the slayer of Gobu, the great ape.

"Please sit down," urged Kraski. "We were about to have coffee and we should be delighted to have you join us. We meant no wrong in coming here, and I can assure you that we will gladly and willingly make full amends to you, or to whomever else we may have unintentionally wronged."

To take coffee with these men would do no harm. Perhaps he had wronged them, but however that might be a cup of their coffee would place no great obligation upon him. Flora had been right in her assertion that if Tarzan of the Apes had any weakness whatsoever it was for an occasional cup of black coffee late at night. He did not accept the proffered camp-stool, but squatted, ape-fashion, before them, the flickering light of the beast fires playing upon his bronzed hide and bringing into relief the gracefully contoured muscles of his godlike frame. Not as the muscles of the blacksmith or the professional strong man were the muscles of Tarzan of the Apes, but rather those of Mercury or Apollo, so symmetrically balanced were their proportions, suggesting only the great strength that lay in them. Trained to speed and agility were they as well as to strength, and thus, clothing as they did his giant frame, they imparted to him the appearance of a demi-god.

Throck, Peebles, and Bluber sat watching him in spellbound fascination, while Kraski walked over to the cook fire to arrange for the coffee. The two Englishmen were as yet only half awakened to the fact that they had mistaken this newcomer for another, and as it was, Peebles still scratched his head and grumbled to himself in inarticulate half-denial of Kraski's assumption of the new identity of Tarzan. Bluber was inwardly terror-stricken. His keener intelligence had quickly grasped the truth of Kraski's recognition of the man for what he was rather than for what Peebles and Throck thought him to be, and, as Bluber knew nothing of Flora's plan, he was in quite a state of funk as he tried to visualize the outcome of Tarzan's discovery of them at the very threshold of Opar. He did not realize, as did Flora, that their very lives were in danger—that it was Tarzan of the Apes, a beast of the jungle, with whom they had to deal, and not John Clayton, Lord Greystoke, an English peer. Rather was Bluber considering the two thousand pounds that they stood to lose through this deplorable termination of their expedition, for he was sufficiently familiar with the reputation of the ape-man to know that they would never be permitted to take with them the gold that Esteban was very likely, at this moment, pilfering from the vaults of Opar. Really Bluber was almost upon the verge of tears when Kraski returned with the coffee, which he brought himself.

From the dark shadows of the tent's interior Flora Hawkes looked nervously out upon the scene before her. She was terrified at the possibility of discovery by her former employer, for she had been a maid in the Greystokes' London town house as well as at the African bungalow and knew that Lord Greystoke would recognize her instantly should he chance to see her. She entertained for him, now, in his jungle haunts, a fear that was possibly greater than Tarzan's true character warranted, but none the less real was it to the girl whose guilty conscience conjured all sorts of possible punishments for her disloyalty to those who had always treated her with uniform kindliness and consideration.

Constant dreaming of the fabulous wealth of the treasure vaults of Opar, concerning which she had heard so much in detail from the conversations of the Greystokes, had aroused within her naturally crafty and unscrupulous mind a desire for possession, and in consequence thereof she had slowly visualized a scheme whereby she might loot the treasure vaults of a sufficient number of the golden ingots to make her independently wealthy for life. The entire plan had been hers. She had at first interested Kraski, who had in turn enlisted the coöperation of the two Englishmen and Bluber, and these four had raised the necessary money to defray the cost of the expedition. It had been Flora who had searched for a type of man who might successfully impersonate Tarzan in his own jungle, and she had found Esteban Miranda, a handsome, powerful, and unscrupulous Spaniard, whose histrionic ability aided by the art of make-up, of which he was a past master, permitted him to almost faultlessly impersonate the character they desired him to portray, in so far, as least, as outward appearances were concerned.

The Spaniard was not only powerful and active, but physically courageous as well, and since he had shaved his beard and donned the jungle habiliments of a Tarzan, he had lost no opportunity for emulating the ape-man in every way that lay within his ability. Of jungle craft he had none of course, and personal combats with the more savage jungle beasts caution prompted him to eschew, but he hunted the lesser game with spear and with arrow and practiced continually with the grass rope that was a part of his make-up.

And now Flora Hawkes saw all her well-laid plans upon the verge of destruction. She trembled as she watched the men before the fire, for her fear of Tarzan was very real, and then she became tense with nervous anticipation as she saw Kraski approaching the group with the coffee pot in one hand and cups in the other. Kraski set the pot and the cups upon the ground a little in the rear of Tarzan, and, as he filled the latter, she saw him pour a portion of the contents of the bottle she had given him into one of the cups. A cold sweat broke out upon her forehead as Kraski lifted this cup and offered it to the ape-man. Would he take it? Would he suspect? If he did suspect what horrible punishment would be meted to them all for their temerity? She saw Kraski hand another cup to Peebles, Throck, and Bluber, then return to the circle with the last one for himself. As the Russian raised it before his face and bowed politely to the ape-man, she saw the five men drink. The reaction which ensued left her weak and spent. Turning, she collapsed upon her cot, and lay there trembling, her face buried in her arm. And, outside, Tarzan of the Apes drained his cup to the last drop.

DEATH STEALS BEHIND

During the afternoon of the day that Tarzan discovered the camp of the conspirators, a watcher upon the crumbling outer wall of the ruined city of Opar descried a party of men moving downward into the valley from the summit of the encircling cliff. Tarzan, Jane Clayton, and their black Waziri were the only strangers that the denizens of Opar had ever seen within their valley during the lifetime of the oldest among them, and only in half-forgotten legends of a by-gone past was there any suggestion that strangers other than these had ever visited Opar. Yet from time immemorial a guard had always remained upon the summit of the outer wall. Now a single knurled and crippled man-like creature was all that recalled the numerous, lithe warriors of lost Atlantis. For down through the long ages the race had deteriorated and finally, through occasional mating with the great apes, the men had become the beast-like things of modern Opar. Strange and inexplicable had been the providence of nature that had confined this deterioration almost solely to the males, leaving the females straight, well-formed, often of comely and even beautiful features, a condition that might be largely attributable to the fact that female infants possessing ape-like characteristics were immediately destroyed, while, on the other hand, boy babies who possessed purely human attributes were also done away with.

Typical indeed of the male inhabitants of Opar was the lone watcher upon the outer city wall, a short, stocky man with matted hair and beard, his tangled locks growing low upon a low, receding forehead; small, close-set eyes and fang-like teeth bore evidence of his simian ancestry, as did his short, crooked legs and long, muscular ape-like arms, all scantily hair-covered as was his torso.

As his wicked, blood-rimmed eyes watched the progress of the party across the valley toward Opar, evidences of his growing excitement were manifested in the increased rapidity of his breathing, and low, almost inaudible growls that issued from his throat. The strangers were too far distant to be recognizable only as human beings, and their number to be roughly approximated as between two and three score. Having assured himself of these two facts the watcher descended from the outer wall, crossed the space between it and the inner wall, through which he passed, and at a rapid trot crossed the broad avenue beyond and disappeared within the crumbling but still magnificent temple beyond.

Cadj, the High Priest of Opar, squatted beneath the shade of the giant trees which now overgrew what had once been one of the gardens of the ancient temple. With him were a dozen members of the lesser priesthood, the intimate cronies of the High Priest, who were startled by the sudden advent of one of the inferior members of the clan of Opar. The fellow hurried breathlessly to Cadj.

"Cadj," he cried, "strange men descend upon Opar! From the northwest they have come into the valley from beyond the barrier cliffs—fifty of them at least, perhaps half again that number. I saw them as I watched from the summit of the outer wall, but further than they are men I cannot say, for they are still a great distance away. Not since the great Tarmangani came among us last have there been strangers within Opar."

"It has been many moons since the great Tarmangani who called himself Tarzan of the Apes was among us," said Cadj. "He promised us to return before the rain to see that no harm had befallen La, but he did not come back and La has always insisted that he is dead. Have you told any other of what you have seen?" he demanded, turning suddenly upon the messenger.

"No," replied the latter.

"Good!" exclaimed Cadj. "Come, we will all go to the outer wall and see who it is who dares enter forbidden Opar, and let no one breathe a word of what Blagh has told us until I give permission."

"The word of Cadj is law until La speaks," murmured one of the priests.

Cadj turned a scowling face upon the speaker. "I am High Priest of Opar," he growled. "Who dares disobey me?"

"But La is High Priestess," said one, "and the High Priestess is the queen of Opar."

"But the High Priest can offer whom he will as sacrifice in the Chamber of the Dead or to the Flaming God," Cadj reminded the other meaningly.

"We shall keep silence, Cadj," replied the priest, cringing.

"Good!" growled the High Priest and led the way from the garden through the corridors of the temple back toward the outer wall of Opar. From here they watched the approaching party that was in plain view of them, far out across the valley. The watchers conversed in low gutturals in the language of the great apes, interspersed with which were occasional words and phrases of a strange tongue that were doubtless corrupted forms of the ancient language of Atlantis handed down through countless generations from their human progenitors—that now extinct race whose cities and civilization lie buried deep beneath the tossing waves of the Atlantic, and whose adventurous spirit had, in remote ages, caused them to penetrate into the heart of Africa in search of gold and to build there, in duplication of their far home cities, the magnificent city of Opar.

As Cadj and his followers watched from beneath shaggy brows the strangers plodding laboriously beneath the now declining equatorial sun across the rocky, barren valley, a gray little monkey eyed them from amidst the foliage of one of the giant trees that had forced its way through the pavement of the ancient avenue behind them. A solemn, sad-faced little monkey it was, but like all his kind overcome by curiosity, and finally to such an extent that his fear of the fierce males of Opar was so considerably overcome that he at last swung lightly from the tree to the pavement, made his way through the inner wall and up the inside of the outer wall to a position in their rear where he could hide behind one of the massive granite blocks of the crumbling wall in comparative safety from detection, the while he might overhear the conversation of the Oparians, all of which that was carried on in the language of the great apes he could understand perfectly.

The afternoon was drawing to a close before the slowly moving company approaching Opar was close enough for individuals to be recognizable in any way, and then presently one of the younger priests exclaimed excitedly:

"It is he, Cadj. It is the great Tarmangani who calls himself Tarzan of the Apes. I can see him plainly; the others are all black men. He is urging them on, prodding them with his spear. They act as though they were afraid and very tired, but he is forcing them forward."

"You are sure," demanded Cadj, "you are sure that it is Tarzan of the Apes?"

"I am positive," replied the speaker, and then another of the priests joined his assurances to that of his fellow. At last they were close enough so that Cadj himself, whose eyesight was not as good as that of the younger members of the company, realized that it was indeed Tarzan of the Apes who was returning to Opar. The High Priest scowled angrily in thought. Suddenly he turned upon the others.

"He must not come," he cried; "he must not enter Opar. Hasten and fetch a hundred fighting men. We will meet them as they come through the outer wall and slay them one by one."

"But La," cried he who had aroused Cadj's anger in the garden, "I distinctly recall that La offered the friendship of Opar to Tarzan of the Apes upon that time, many moons ago, that he saved her from the tusks of infuriated Tantor."

"Silence," growled Cadj, "he shall not enter; we shall slay them all, though we need not know their identity until it is too late. Do you understand? And know, too, that whosoever attempts to thwart my purpose shall die—and he die not as a sacrifice, he shall die at my hands, but die he shall. You hear me?" And he pointed an unclean finger at the trembling priest.

Manu, the monkey, hearing all this, was almost bursting with excitement. He knew Tarzan of the Apes—as all the migratory monkeys the length and breadth of Africa knew him—he knew him for a friend and protector. To Manu the males of Opar were neither beast, nor man, nor friend. He knew them as cruel and surly creatures who ate the flesh of his kind, and he hated them accordingly. He was therefore greatly exercised at the plot that he had heard discussed which was aimed at the life of the great Tarmangani. He scratched his little gray head, and the root of his tail, and his belly, as he attempted to mentally digest what he had heard, and bring forth from the dim recesses of his little brain a plan to foil the priests and save Tarzan of the Apes. He made grotesque grimaces that were aimed at the unsuspecting Cadj and his followers, but which failed to perturb them, possibly because a huge granite block hid the little monkey from them. This was quite the most momentous thing that had occurred in the life of Manu. He wanted to jump up and down and dance and screech and jabber—to scold and threaten the hated Oparians, but something told him that nothing would be gained by this, other than, perhaps, to launch in his direction a shower of granite missiles, which the priests knew only too well how to throw with accuracy. Now Manu is not a deep thinker, but upon this occasion he quite outdid himself, and managed to concentrate his mind upon the thing at hand rather than permit its being distracted by each falling leaf or buzzing insect. He even permitted a succulent caterpillar to crawl within his reach and out again with impunity.

Just before darkness fell, Cadj saw a little gray monkey disappear over the summit of the outer wall fifty paces from where he crouched with his fellows, waiting for the coming of the fighting men. But so numerous were the monkeys about the ruins of Opar that the occurrence left Cadj's mind almost as quickly as the monkey disappeared from his view, and in the gathering gloom he did not see the little gray figure scampering off across the valley toward the band of intruders who now appeared to have stopped to rest at the foot of a large kopje that stood alone out in the valley, about a mile from the city.

Little Manu was very much afraid out there alone in the growing dusk, and he scampered very fast with his tail bowed up and out behind him. All the time he cast affrighted glances to the right and left. The moment he reached the kopje he scampered up its face as fast as he could. It was really a huge, precipitous granite rock with almost perpendicular sides, but sufficiently weather-worn to make its ascent easy to little Manu. He paused a moment at the summit to get his breath and still the beatings of his frightened little heart, and then he made his way around to a point where he could look down upon the party beneath.

There, indeed, was the great Tarmangani Tarzan, and with him were some fifty Gomangani. The latter were splicing together a number of long, straight poles, which they had laid upon the ground in two parallel lines. Across these two, at intervals of a foot or more, they were lashing smaller straight branches about eighteen inches in length, the whole forming a crude but substantial ladder. The purpose of all this Manu, of course, did not understand, nor did he know that it had been evolved from the fertile brain of Flora Hawkes as a means of scaling the precipitous kopje, at the summit of which lay the outer entrance to the treasure vaults of Opar. Nor did Manu know that the party had no intention of entering the city of Opar and were therefore in no danger of becoming victims of Cadj's hidden assassins. To him, the danger to Tarzan of the Apes was very real, and so, having regained his breath, he lost no time in delivering his warning to the friend of his people.

"Tarzan," he cried, in the language that was common to both.

The white man and the blacks looked up at the sound of his chattering voice.

"It is Manu, Tarzan," continued the little monkey, "who has come to tell you not to go to Opar. Cadj and his people await within the outer wall to slay you."

The blacks, having discovered that the author of the disturbance was nothing but a little gray monkey, returned immediately to their work, while the white man similarly ignored his words of warning. Manu was not surprised at the lack of interest displayed by the blacks, for he knew that they did not understand his language, but he could not comprehend why Tarzan failed to pay any attention whatsoever to him. Again and again he called Tarzan by name. Again and again he shrieked his warning to the ape-man, but without eliciting any reply or any information that the great Tarmangani had either heard or understood him. Manu was mystified. What had occurred to render Tarzan of the Apes so indifferent to the warnings of his old friend?

At last the little monkey gave it up and looked longingly back in the direction of the trees within the walled city of Opar. It was now very dark and he trembled at the thought of recrossing the valley, where he knew enemies might prowl by night. He scratched his head and he hugged his knees, then sat there whimpering, a very forlorn and unhappy little ball of a monkey. But however uncomfortable he was upon the high kopje, he was comparatively safe, and so he decided to remain there during the night rather than venture the terrifying return trip through the darkness. Thus it was that he saw the ladder completed and erected against the side of the kopje; and when the moon rose at last and lighted the scene, he saw Tarzan of the Apes urging his men to mount the ladder. He had never seen Tarzan thus rough and cruel with the blacks who accompanied him. Manu knew how ferocious the great Tarmangani could be with an enemy, whether man or beast, but he had never seen him accord such treatment to the blacks who were his friends.

One by one and with evident reluctance the blacks ascended the ladder, continually urged forward to greater speed by the sharp spear of the white man; when they had all ascended Tarzan followed, and Manu saw them disappear apparently into the heart of the great rock.

It was only a short time later that they commenced to reappear, and now each was burdened by two heavy objects which appeared to Manu to be very similar to some of the smaller stone blocks that had been used in the construction of the buildings in Opar. He saw them take the blocks to the edge of the kopje and cast them over to the ground beneath, and when the last of the blacks had emerged with his load and cast it to the valley below, one by one the party descended the ladder to the foot of the kopje. But this time Tarzan of the Apes went first. Then they lowered the ladder and took it apart and laid its pieces close to the foot of the cliff, after which they took up the blocks which they had brought from the heart of the kopje, and following Tarzan, who set out in the lead, they commenced to retrace their steps toward the rim of the valley.

Manu would have been very much mystified had he been a man, but being only a monkey he saw only what he saw without attempting to reason very much about it. He knew that the ways of men were peculiar, and oftentimes unaccountable. For example, the Gomangani who could not travel through the jungle and the forest with the ease of any other of the animals which frequented them, added to their difficulties by loading themselves down with additional weights in the form of metal anklets and armlets, with necklaces and girdles, and with skins of animals, which did nothing more than impede their progress and render life much more complicated than that which the untrammeled beasts enjoyed. Manu, whenever he gave the matter a thought, congratulated himself that he was not a man—he pitied the foolish, unreasonable creatures.

*

Manu must have slept. He thought that he had only closed his eyes a moment, but when he opened them the rosy light of dawn had overspread the desolate valley. Just disappearing over the cliffs to the northeast he could see the last of Tarzan's party commencing the descent of the barrier, then Manu turned his face toward Opar and prepared to descend from the kopje, and scamper back to the safety of his trees within the walls of Opar. But first he would reconnoiter—Sheeta, the panther, might be still abroad, and so he scampered around the edge of the kopje to a point where he could see the entire valley floor between himself and Opar. And there it was that he saw again that which filled him with greatest excitement. For, debouching from the ruined outer wall of Opar was a large company of Opar's frightful men—fully a hundred of them Manu could have counted had Manu been able to count.

They seemed to be coming toward the kopje, and he sat and watched them as they approached, deciding to defer his return to the city until after the path was cleared of hated Oparians. It occurred to him that they were coming after him, for the egotism of the lower animals is inordinate. Because he was a monkey, the idea did not seem at all ridiculous and so he hid behind a jutting rock, with only one little, bright eye exposed to the enemy. He saw them come closer and he grew very much excited, though he was not at all afraid, for he knew that if they ascended one side of the kopje he could descend the other and be half-way to Opar before they could possibly locate him again.

On and on they came, but they did not stop at the kopje—as a matter of fact they did not come very close to it, but continued on beyond it. Then it was that the truth of the matter flashed into the little brain of the monkey—Cadj and his people were pursuing Tarzan of the Apes to slay him. If Manu had been offended by Tarzan's indifference to him upon the night before, he had evidently forgotten it, for now he was quite as excited about the danger which he saw menace the ape-man as he had been upon the afternoon previous. At first he thought of running ahead, and again warning Tarzan, but he feared to venture so far from the trees of Opar, even if the thought of having to pass the hated Oparians had not been sufficient to deter him from carrying out this plan. For a few minutes he sat watching them, until they had all passed the kopje, and then it became quite clear to him that they were heading directly for the spot at which the last of Tarzan's party had disappeared from the valley—there could be no doubt that they were in pursuit of the ape-man.

Manu scanned the valley once more toward Opar. There was nothing in sight to deter him from an attempted return, and so, with the agility of his kind, he scampered down the vertical face of the kopje and was off at great speed toward the city's wall. Just when he formulated the plan that he eventually followed it is difficult to say. Perhaps he thought it all out as he sat upon the kopje, watching Cadj and his people upon the trail of the ape-man, or perhaps it occurred to him while he was scampering across the barren waste toward Opar. It may just have popped into his mind from a clear sky after he had regained the leafy sanctuary of his own trees. Be that, however as it may, the fact remains, that as La, High Priestess and princess of Opar, in company with several of her priestesses, was bathing in a pool in one of the temple gardens, she was startled by the screaming of a monkey, swinging frantically by his tail from the branch of a great tree which overspread the pool—it was a little gray monkey with a face so wise and serious that one might easily have imagined that the fate of nations lay constantly upon the shoulders of its owner.

"La, La," it screamed, "they have gone to kill Tarzan. They have gone to kill Tarzan."

At the sound of that name La was instantly all attention. Standing waist deep in the pool she looked up at the little monkey questioningly. "What do you mean, Manu?" she asked. "It has been many moons since Tarzan was at Opar. He is not here now. What are you talking about?"

"I saw him," screamed Manu, "I saw him last night with many Gomangani. He came to the great rock that lies in the valley before Opar; with all his men he climbed to the top of it, went into the heart of it, and came out with stones which they threw down into the valley. Afterward they descended from the rock, and picked up the stones again and left the valley—there," and Manu pointed toward the northeast with one of his hairy little fingers.

"How do you know it was Tarzan of the Apes?" asked La.

"Does Manu not know his cousin and his friend?" demanded the monkey. "With my eyes I saw him—it was Tarzan of the Apes."

La of Opar puckered her brows in thought. Deep in her heart smoldered the fires of her great love for Tarzan. Fires that had been quenched by the necessity that had compelled her marriage with Cadj since last she had seen the ape-man. For it is written among the laws of Opar that the High Priestess of the Flaming God must take a mate within a certain number of years after her consecration. For many moons had La longed to make Tarzan that mate. The ape-man had not loved her, and finally she had come to a realization that he could never love her. Afterward she had bowed to the frightful fate that had placed her in the arms of Cadj.

As month after month had passed and Tarzan had not returned to Opar, as he had promised he would do, to see that no harm befell La, she had come to accept the opinion of Cadj that the ape-man was dead, and though she hated the repulsive Cadj none the less, her love for Tarzan had gradually become little more than a sorrowful memory. Now to learn that he was alive and had been so near was like re-opening an old wound. At first she comprehended little else than that Tarzan had been close to Opar, but presently the cries of Manu aroused her to a realization that the ape-man was in danger—just what the danger was, she did not know.

"Who has gone to kill Tarzan of the Apes?" she demanded suddenly.

"Cadj, Cadj!" shrieked Manu. "He has gone with many, many men, and is following upon the spoor of Tarzan."

La sprang quickly from the pool, seized her girdle and ornaments from her attendant and adjusting them hurriedly, sped through the garden and into the temple.

"YOU MUST SACRIFICE HIM"

Warily Cadj and his hundred frightful followers, armed with their bludgeons and knives, crept stealthily down the face of the barrier into the valley below, upon the trail of the white man and his black companions. They made no haste, for they had noted from the summit of Opar's outer wall, that the party they were pursuing moved very slowly, though why, they did not know, for they had been at too great a distance to see the burden that each of the blacks carried. Nor was it Cadj's desire to overtake his quarry by daylight, his plans contemplating a stealthy night attack, the suddenness of which, together with the great number of his followers, might easily confuse and overwhelm a sleeping camp.

The spoor they followed was well marked. There could be no mistaking it, and they moved slowly down the now gentle declivity, toward the bottom of the valley. It was close to noon that they were brought to a sudden halt by the discovery of a thorn boma recently constructed in a small clearing just ahead of them. From the center of the boma arose the thin smoke of a dying fire. Here, then, was the camp of the ape-man.

Cadj drew his followers into the concealment of the thick bushes that bordered the trail, and from there he sent ahead a single man to reconnoiter. It was but a few moments later that the latter returned to say that the camp was deserted, and once again Cadj moved forward with his men. Entering the boma they examined it in an effort to estimate the size of the party that accompanied Tarzan. As they were thus occupied Cadj saw something lying half concealed by bushes at the far end of the boma. Very warily he approached it, for there was that about it which not only aroused his curiosity but prompted him to caution, for it resembled indistinctly the figure of a man, lying huddled upon the ground.

With ready bludgeons a dozen of them approached the thing that had aroused Cadj's curiosity, and when they had come close to it they saw lying before them the lifeless figure of Tarzan of the Apes.

"The Flaming God has reached forth to avenge his desecrated altar," cried the High Priest, his eyes glowing with the maniacal fires of fanaticism. But another priest, more practical, perhaps, or at least more cautious, knelt beside the figure of the ape-man and placed his ear against the latter's heart.

"He is not dead," he whispered; "perhaps he only sleeps."

"Seize him, then, quickly," cried Cadj, and an instant later Tarzan's body was covered by the hairy forms of as many of the frightful men as could pile upon him. He offered no resistance—he did not even open his eyes, and presently his arms were securely bound behind him.

"Drag him forth where the eye of the Flaming God may rest upon him," cried Cadj. They dragged Tarzan out into the center of the boma into the full light of the sun, and Cadj, the High Priest, drawing his knife from his loin cloth, raised it above his head and stood over the prostrate form of his intended victim. Cadj's followers formed a rough circle about the ape-man and some of them pressed close behind their leader. They appeared uneasy, looking alternately at Tarzan and their High Priest, and then casting furtive glances at the sun, riding high in a cloud-mottled sky. But whatever the thoughts that troubled their half-savage brains, there was only one who dared voice his, and he was the same priest who, upon the preceding day, had questioned Cadj's proposal to slay the ape-man.

"Cadj," he said now, "who are you to offer up a sacrifice to the Flaming God? It is the privilege alone of La, our High Priestess and our queen, and indeed will she be angry when she learns what you have done."

"Silence, Dooth!" cried Cadj; "I, Cadj, am the High Priest of Opar. I, Cadj, am the mate of La, the queen. My word, too, is law in Opar. And you would remain a priest, and you would remain alive, keep silence."

"Your word is not law," replied Booth, angrily, "and if you anger La, the High Priestess, or if you anger the Flaming God, you may be punished as another. If you make this sacrifice both will be angry."

"Enough," cried Cadj; "the Flaming God has spoken to me and has demanded that I offer up as sacrifice this defiler of his temple."

He knelt beside the ape-man and touched his breast above the heart with the point of his sharp blade, and then he raised the weapon high above him, preparatory to the fatal plunge into the living heart. At that instant a cloud passed before the face of the sun and a shadow rested upon them. A murmur rose from the surrounding priests.

"Look," cried Dooth, "the Flaming God is angry. He has hidden his face from the people of Opar."

Cadj paused. He cast a half-defiant, half-frightened look at the cloud obscuring the face or the sun. Then he rose slowly to his feet, and extending his arms upward toward the hidden god of day, he remained for a moment silent in apparently attentive and listening attitude. Then, suddenly, he turned upon his followers.

"Priests of Opar," he cried, "the Flaming God has spoken to his High Priest, Cadj. He is not angered. He but wishes to speak to me alone, and he directs that you go away into the jungle and wait until he has come and spoken to Cadj, after which I shall call you to return. Go!"

For the most part they seemed to accept the word of Cadj as law, but Dooth and a few others, doubtless prompted by a certain skepticism, hesitated.

"Be gone!" commanded Cadj. And so powerful is the habit of obedience that the doubters finally turned away and melted into the jungle with the others. A crafty smile lighted the cruel face of the High Priest as the last of them disappeared from sight, and then he once again turned his attention to the ape-man. That, deep within his breast however, lurked an inherent fear of his deity, was evidenced by the fact that he turned questioning glances toward the sky. He had determined to slay the ape-man while Dooth and the others were absent, yet the fear of his god restrained his hand until the light of his deity should shine forth upon him once more and assure him that the thing he contemplated might meet with favor.

It was a large cloud that overcast the sun, and while Cadj waited his nervousness increased. Six times he raised his knife for the fatal blow, yet in each instance his superstition prevented the consummation of the act. Five, ten, fifteen minutes passed, and still the sun remained obscured. But now at last Cadj could see that it was nearing the edge of the cloud, and once again he took his position kneeling beside the ape-man with his blade ready for the moment that the sunlight should flood again, for the last time, the living Tarzan. He saw it sweeping slowly across the boma toward him, and as it came a look of demoniacal hatred shone in his close-set, wicked eyes. Another instant and the Flaming God would have set the seal of his approval upon the sacrifice. Cadj trembled in anticipation. He raised the knife a trifle higher, his muscles tensed for the downward plunge, and then the silence of the jungle was broken by a woman's voice, raised almost to a scream.

"Cadj!" came the single word, but with all the suddenness and all the surprising effect of lightning from a clear sky.

His knife still poised on high, the High Priest turned in the direction of the interruption to see at the clearing's edge the figure of La, the High Priestess, and behind her Dooth and a score of the lesser priests.

"What means this, Cadj?" demanded La, angrily, approaching rapidly toward him across the clearing. Sullenly the High Priest rose.

"The Flaming God demanded the life of this unbeliever," he cried.

"Speaker of lies," retorted La, "the Flaming God communicates with men through the lips of his High Priestess only. Too often already have you attempted to thwart the will of your queen. Know, then, Cadj, that the power of life and death which your queen holds is as potent over you as another. During the long ages that Opar has endured, our legends tell us that more than one High Priest has been offered upon the altar to the Flaming God. And it is not unlikely that yet another may go the way of the presumptuous. Curb, therefore, your vanity and your lust for power, lest they prove your undoing."

Cadj sheathed his knife and turned sullenly away, casting a venomous look at Dooth, to whom he evidently attributed his undoing. That he was temporarily abashed by the presence of his queen was evident, but to those who knew Cadj there was little doubt that he still harbored his intention to despatch the ape-man, and if the opportunity ever presented itself that he would do so, for Cadj had a strong following among the people and priests of Opar. There were many who doubted that La would ever dare to incur the displeasure and anger of so important a portion of her followers as to cause the death or degradation of their high priest, who occupied his office by virtue of laws and customs so old that their origin had been long lost in antiquity.

For years she had found first one excuse and then another to delay the ceremonies that would unite her in marriage to the High Priest. She had further aroused the antagonism of her people by palpable proofs of her infatuation for the ape-man, and even though at last she had been compelled to mate with Cadj, she had made no effort whatsoever to conceal her hatred and loathing for the man. How much further she could go with impunity was a question that often troubled those whose position in Opar depended upon her favor, and, knowing all these conditions as he did, it was not strange that Cadj should entertain treasonable thoughts toward his queen. Leagued with him in his treachery was Oah, a priestess who aspired to the power and offices of La. If La could be done away with, then Cadj had the influence to see that Oah became High Priestess. He also had Oah's promise to mate with him and permit him to rule as king, but as yet both were bound by the superstitious fear of their flaming deity, and because of this fact was the life of La temporarily made safe. It required, however, but the slightest spark to ignite the flames of treason that were smoldering about her.

So far, she was well within her rights in forbidding the sacrifice of Tarzan by the High Priest. But her fate, her very life, perhaps, depended upon her future treatment of the prisoner. Should she spare him, should she evidence in any way a return of the great love she had once almost publicly avowed for him, it was likely that her doom would be sealed. It was even questionable whether or not she might with impunity spare his life and set him at liberty.

Cadj and the others watched her closely now as she crossed to the side of Tarzan. Standing there silently for several moments she looked down upon him.

"He is already dead?" she asked.

"He was not dead when Cadj sent us away," volunteered Dooth. "If he is dead now it is because Cadj killed him while we were away."

"I did not kill him," said Cadj. "That remains, as La, our queen, has told you, for her to do. The eye of the Flaming God looks down upon you, High Priestess of Opar. The knife is at your hip, the sacrifice lies before you."

La ignored the man's words and turned toward Dooth. "If he still lives," she said, "construct a litter and bear him back to Opar."

Thus, once more, came Tarzan of the Apes into the ancient colonial city of the Atlantians. The effects of the narcotic that Kraski had administered to him did not wear off for many hours. It was night when he opened his eyes, and for a moment he was bewildered by the darkness and the silence that surrounded him. All that he could scent at first was that he lay upon a pile of furs and that he was uninjured; for he felt no pain. Slowly there broke through the fog of his drugged brain recollection of the last moment before unconsciousness had overcome him, and presently he realized the trick that had been played upon him. For how long he had been unconscious and where he then was he could not imagine. Slowly he arose to his feet, finding that except for a slight dizziness he was quite himself. Cautiously he felt around in the darkness, moving with care, a hand outstretched, and always feeling carefully with his feet for a secure footing. Almost immediately a stone wall stopped his progress, and this he followed around four sides of what he soon realized was a small room in which there were but two openings, a door upon each of the opposite sides. Only his senses of touch and smell were of value to him here. These told him only at first that he was imprisoned in a subterranean chamber, but as the effects of the narcotic diminished, the keenness of the latter returned, and with its return there was borne in upon Tarzan's brain an insistent impression of familiarity in certain fragrant odors that impinged upon his olfactory organs—a haunting suggestion that he had known them before under similar circumstances. Presently from above, through earth and masonry, came the shadow of an uncanny scream—just the faintest suggestion of it reached the keen ears of the ape-man, but it was sufficient to flood his mind with vivid recollections, and, by association of ideas, to fix the identity of the familiar odors about him. He knew at last that he was in the dark pit beneath Opar.

Above him, in her chamber in the temple, La, the High Priestess, tossed upon a sleepless couch. She knew all too well the temper of her people and the treachery of the High Priest, Cadj. She knew the religious fanaticism which prompted the ofttime maniacal actions of her bestial and ignorant followers, and she guessed truly that Cadj would inflame them against her should she fail this time in sacrificing the ape-man to the Flaming God. And it was the effort to find an escape from her dilemma that left her sleepless, for it was not in the heart of La to sacrifice Tarzan of the Apes. High Priestess of a horrid cult, though she was, and queen of a race of half-beasts, yet she was a woman, too, a woman who had loved but once and given that love to the godlike ape-man who was again within her power. Twice before had he escaped her sacrificial knife; in the final instance love had at last triumphed over jealousy and fanaticism, and La, the woman, had realized that never again could she place in jeopardy the life of the man she loved, however hopeless she knew that love to be.

Tonight she was faced with a problem that she felt almost beyond her powers of solution. The fact that she was mated with Cadj removed the last vestige of hope that she had ever had of becoming the wife of the ape-man. Yet she was no less determined to save Tarzan if it were possible. Twice had he saved her life, once from a mad priest, and once from Tantor in must. Then, too, she had given her word that when Tarzan came again to Opar he came in friendship and would be received in friendship. But the influence of Cadj was great, and she knew that that influence had been directed unremittingly against the ape-man—she had seen it in the attitude of her followers from the very moment that they had placed Tarzan upon a litter to bear him back to Opar—she had seen it in the evil glances that had been cast at her. Sooner or later they would dare denounce her—all that they needed was some slight, new excuse, that, she knew, they eagerly awaited in her forthcoming attitude toward Tarzan. It was well after midnight when there came to her one of the priestesses who remained always upon guard outside her chamber door.

"Dooth would speak with you," whispered the hand-maiden.

"It is late," replied La, "and men are not permitted in this part of the temple. How came he here, and why?"

"He says that he comes in the service of La, who is in great danger," replied the girl.

"Fetch him here then," said La, "and as you value your life see that you tell no one."

"I shall be as voiceless as the stones of the altar," replied the girl, as she turned and left the chamber.

A moment later she returned, bringing Dooth, who halted a few feet from the High Priestess and saluted her. La signaled to the girl who had brought him, to depart, and then she turned questioningly to the man.

"Speak, Dooth!" she commanded.

"We all know," he said, "of La's love for the strange ape-man, and it is not for me, a lesser priest, to question the thoughts or acts of my High Priestess. It is only for me to serve, as those would do better to serve who now plot against you."

"What do you mean, Dooth? Who plots against me?"

"Even at this minute are Cadj and Oah and several of the priests and priestesses carrying out a plan for your undoing. They are setting spies to watch you, knowing that you would liberate the ape-man, because there will come to you one who will tell you that to permit him to escape will be the easiest solution of your problem. This one will be sent by Cadj, and then those who watch you will report to the people and to the priests that they have seen you lead the sacrifice to liberty. But even that will avail you nothing, for Cadj and Oah and the others have placed upon the trail from Opar many men in hiding, who will fall upon the ape-man and slay him before the Flaming God has descended twice into the western forest. In but one way only may you save yourself, La of Opar."

"And what is that way?" she asked.

"You must, with your own hands, upon the altar of our temple, sacrifice the ape-man to the Flaming God."

MYSTERY OF THE PAST

La had breakfasted the following morning, and had sent Dooth with food for Tarzan, when there came to her a young priestess, who was the sister of Oah. Even before the girl had spoken La knew that she was an emissary from Cadj, and that the treachery of which Dooth had warned her was already under way. The girl was ill at ease and quite evidently frightened, for she was young and held in high revere the queen whom she had good reason to know was all-powerful, and who might even inflict death upon her if she so wished. La, who had already determined upon a plan of action that she knew would be most embarrassing to Cadj and his conspirators, waited in silence for the girl to speak. But it was some time before the girl could muster up her courage or find a proper opening. Instead, she spoke of many things that had no bearing whatsoever upon her subject, and La, the High Priestess, was amused at her discomfiture.

"It is not often," said La, "that the sister of Oah comes to the apartments of her queen unless she is bidden. I am glad to see that she at last realizes the service that she owes to the High Priestess of the Flaming God."

"I come," said the girl, at last, speaking almost as one who has learned a part, "to tell you that I have overheard that which may be of interest to you, and which I am sure that you will be glad to hear."

"Yes?" interrogated La, raising her arched eyebrows.

"I overheard Cadj speaking with the lesser priests," the girl continued, "and I distinctly heard him say that he would be glad if the ape-man escaped, as that would relieve you, and Cadj as well, of much embarrassment. I thought that La, the queen, would be glad to know this, for it is known by all of us that La has promised friendship to the ape-man, and therefore does not wish to sacrifice him upon the altar of the Flaming God."

"My duty is plain to me," replied La, in a haughty voice, "and I do not need Cadj nor any hand-maiden to interpret it to me. I also know the prerogatives of a High Priestess, and that the right of sacrifice is one of them. For this reason I prevented Cadj from sacrificing the stranger. No other hand than mine may offer his heart's blood to the Flaming God, and upon the third day he shall die beneath my knife upon the altar of our temple."

The effect of these words upon the girl were precisely what La had anticipated. She saw disappointment and chagrin written upon the face of Cadj's messenger, who now had no answer, for her instructions had not foreseen this attitude upon the part of La. Presently the girl found some lame pretext upon which to withdraw, and when she had left the presence of the High Priestess, La could scarcely restrain a smile. She had no intention of sacrificing Tarzan, but this, of course, the sister of Oah did not know. So she returned to Cadj and repeated as nearly as she could recall it, all that La had said to her. The High Priest was much chagrined, for his plan had been now, not so much to encompass the destruction of Tarzan as to lead La into the commission of an act that would bring upon her the wrath of the priests and people of Opar, who, properly instigated, would demand her life in expiation. Oah, who was present when her sister returned, bit her lips, for great was her disappointment. Never before had she seen so close at hand the longed-for possibility of becoming High Priestess. For several minutes she paced to and fro in deep thought, and then, suddenly, she halted before Cadj.

"La loves this ape-man," she said, "and even though she may sacrifice him, it is only because of fear of her people. She loves him still—loves him better, Cadj, than she has ever loved you. The ape-man knows it, and trusts her, and because he knows it there is a way. Listen, Cadj, to Oah. We will send one to the ape-man who shall tell him that she comes from La, and that La has instructed her to lead him out of Opar and set him free. This one shall lead him into our ambush and when he is killed we shall go, many of us, before La, and accuse her of treachery. The one who led the ape-man from Opar shall say that La ordered her to do it, and the priests and the people will be very angry, and then you shall demand the life of La. It will be very easy and we shall be rid of both of them."

"Good!" exclaimed Cadj. "We shall do this thing at dawn upon the morrow, and before the Flaming God goes to his rest at night he shall look upon a new High Priestess in Opar."

That night Tarzan was aroused from his sleep by a sound at one of the doors of his prison cell. He heard the bolt slipped back and the door creak slowly open upon its ancient hinges. In the inky darkness he could discern no presence, but he heard the stealthy movement of sandaled feet upon the concrete floor, and then, out of the darkness, his name was whispered, in a woman's voice.

"I am here," he replied. "Who are you and what do you want of Tarzan of the Apes?"

"Your life is in danger," replied the voice. "Come, follow me."

"Who sent you?" demanded the ape-man, his sensitive nostrils searching for a clue to the identity of the nocturnal visitor, but so heavily was the air laden with the pungent odor of some heavy perfume with which the body of the woman seemed to have been anointed, that there was no distinguishing clue by which he might judge as to whether she was one of the priestesses he had known upon the occasion of his former visits to Opar, or an entire stranger to him.

"La sent me," she said, "to lead you from the pits of Opar to the freedom of the outside world beyond the city's walls." Groping in the darkness she finally found him. "Here are your weapons," she said, handing them to him, and then she took his hand, turned and led him from the dungeon, through a long, winding, and equally black corridor, down flights of age-old concrete steps, through passages and corridors, opening and closing door after door that creaked and groaned upon rusty hinges. How far they traveled thus, and in what direction, Tarzan could not guess. He had gleaned enough from Dooth, when the latter brought him his food, to believe that in La he had a friend who would aid him, for Dooth had told him that she had saved him from Cadj when the latter had discovered him unconscious in the deserted boma of the Europeans who had drugged and left him. And so, the woman having said that she came from La, Tarzan followed her willingly. He could not but recall Jane's prophecy of the evils that he might expect to befall him should he persist in undertaking this third trip to Opar, and he wondered if, after all, his wife was right, that he should never again escape from the toils of the fanatical priests of the Flaming God. He had not, of course, expected to enter Opar, but there seemed to hang over the accursed city a guardian demon that threatened the life of whosoever dared approach the forbidden spot or wrest from the forgotten treasure vaults a portion of their great hoard.

For more than an hour his guide led him through the Stygian darkness of underground passages, until, ascending a flight of steps they emerged into the center of a clump of bushes, through which the pale light of the moon was barely discernible. The fresh air, however, told him that they had reached the surface of the ground, and now the woman, who had not spoken a word since she had led him from his cell, continued on in silence, following a devious trail that wound hither and thither in an erratic fashion through a heavy forest choked with undergrowth, and always upward.

From the location of the stars and moon, and from the upward trend of the trail, Tarzan knew that he was being led into the mountains that lie behind Opar—a place he had never thought of visiting, since the country appeared rough and uninviting, and not likely to harbor game such as Tarzan cared most to hunt. He was already surprised by the nature of the vegetation, for he had thought the hills barren except for stunted trees and scraggy bush. As they continued upon their way, climbing ever upward, the moon rose higher in the heavens, until its soft light revealed more clearly to the keen eyes of the ape-man the topography of the country they were traversing, and then it was that he saw they were ascending a narrow, thickly wooded gorge, and he understood why the heavy vegetation had been invisible from the plain before Opar. Himself naturally uncommunicative, the woman's silence made no particular impression upon Tarzan. Had he had anything to say he should have said it, and likewise he assumed that there was no necessity for her speaking unless there was some good reason for speaking, for those who travel far and fast have no breath to waste upon conversation.

The eastern stars were fading at the first hint of coming dawn when the two scrambled up a precipitous bank that formed the upper end of the ravine, and came out upon comparatively level ground. As they advanced the sky lightened, and presently the woman halted at the edge of a declivity, and as the day broke Tarzan saw below him a wooded basin in the heart of the mountain, and, showing through the trees at what appeared to be some two or three miles distant, the outlines of a building that glistened and sparkled and scintillated in the light of the new sun. Then he turned and looked at his companion, and surprise and consternation were writ upon his face, for standing before him was La, the High Priestess of Opar.

"You?" he exclaimed. "Now indeed will Cadj have the excuse that Dooth said he sought to put you out of the way."

"He will never have the opportunity to put me out of the way," replied La, "for I shall never return to Opar."

"Never return to Opar!" he exclaimed, "then where are you going? Where can you go?"

"I am going with you," she replied. "I do not ask that you love me. I only ask that you take me away from Opar and from the enemies who would slay me. There was no other way. Manu, the monkey, overheard them plotting, and he came to me and told me all that they would do. Whether I saved you or sacrificed you, it had all been the same with me. They were determined to do away with me, that Oah might be High Priestess and Cadj king of Opar. But I should not have sacrificed you, Tarzan, under any circumstances, and this, then, seemed the only way in which we might both be saved. We could not go to the north or the west across the plain of Opar for there Cadj has placed warriors in ambush to waylay you, and though you be Tarzan and a mighty fighter, they would overwhelm you by their very numbers and slay you."

"But where are you leading me?" asked Tarzan.

"I have chosen the lesser of two evils; in this direction lies an unknown country, filled for us Oparians with legends of grim monsters and strange people. Never has an Oparian ventured here and returned again to Opar. But if there lives in all the world a creature who could win through this unknown valley, it be you, Tarzan of the Apes."

"But if you know nothing of this country, or its inhabitants," demanded Tarzan, "how is it that you so well know the trail that leads to it?"

"We well know the trail to the summit, but that is as far as I have ever been before. The great apes and the lions use this trail when they come down into Opar. The lions, of course, cannot tell us where it leads, and the great apes will not, for usually we are at war with them. Along this trail they come down into Opar to steal our people, and upon this trail we await to capture them, for often we offer a great ape in sacrifice to the Flaming God, or rather that was our former custom, but for many years they have been too wary for us, the toll being upon the other side, though we do not know for what purpose they steal our people, unless it be that they eat them. They are a very powerful race, standing higher than Bolgani, the gorilla, and infinitely more cunning, for, as there is ape blood in our veins, so is there human blood in the veins of these great apes that dwell in the valley above Opar."

"Why is it, La, that we must pass through this valley in order to escape from Opar? There must be some other way."

"There is no other way, Tarzan of the Apes," she replied. "The avenues across the valley are guarded by Cadj's people. Our only chance of escape lies in this direction, and I have brought you along the only trail that pierces the precipitous cliffs that guard Opar upon the south. Across or around this valley we must go in an attempt to find an avenue across the mountain and down upon the other side."

The ape-man stood gazing down into the wooded basin below them, his mind occupied with the problems of the moment. Had he been alone he would not have come this way, for he was sufficiently confident of his own prowess to believe that he might easily have crossed the valley of Opar in comparative safety, regardless of Cadj's plans to the contrary. But he was not alone. He had now to think of La, and he realized that in her efforts to save him she had placed him under a moral obligation which he might not disregard.

To skirt the basin, keeping as far as possible from the building, which he could see in the distance, seemed the wisest course to pursue, since, of course, his sole purpose was to find a way across the mountain and out of this inhospitable country. But the glimpses he caught of the edifice, half concealed as it was amid the foliage of great trees, piqued his curiosity to such an extent that he felt an almost irresistible urge to investigate. He did not believe that the basin was inhabited by other than wild beasts, and he attributed the building which he saw to the handiwork of an extinct or departed people, either contemporaneous with the ancient Atlantians who had built Opar or, perhaps, built by the original Oparians themselves, but now forgotten by their descendants. The glimpses which he caught of the building suggested such size and magnificence as might belong to a palace.

The ape-man knew no fear, though he possessed to a reasonable extent that caution which is inherent in all wild beasts. He would not have hesitated to pit his cunning and his prowess against the lower orders, however ferocious they might be, for, unlike man, they could not band together to his undoing. But should men elect to hunt him in numbers he knew that a real danger would confront him, and that, in the face of their combined strength and intelligence, his own might not avail him. There was little likelihood, however, he reasoned, that the basin was inhabited by human beings. Doubtless closer investigation of the building he saw would reveal that it was but a deserted ruin, and that the most formidable foes he would encounter would be the great apes and the lions. Of neither of these had he any fear; with the former it was even reasonable to imagine that he might establish amicable relations. Believing as he did that he must look for egress from the basin upon its opposite side, it was only natural that he should wish to choose the most direct route across the basin. Therefore his inclinations to explore the valley were seconded by considerations of speed and expediency.

"Come," he said to La, and started down the declivity which led into the basin in the direction of the building ahead of them.

"You are not going that way?" she cried in astonishment.

"Why not?" he said. "It is the shortest way across the valley, and in so far as I can judge our trail over the mountains is more likely to lie in that direction than elsewhere."

"But I am afraid," she said. "The Flaming God alone knows what hideous dangers lurk in the depths of that forest below us."

"Only Numa and the Mangani," he said. "Of these we need have no fear."

"You fear nothing," she said, "but I am only a woman."

"We can die but once," replied Tarzan, "and that once we must die. To be always fearing, then, would not avert it, and would make life miserable. We shall go the short way, then, and perhaps we shall see enough to make the risk well worth while."

They followed a well-worn trail downward among the brush, the trees increasing in both size and number as they approached the floor of the basin, until at last they were walking beneath the foliage of a great forest. What wind there was at their back, and the ape-man, though he moved at a swinging walk, was constantly on the alert. Upon the hard-packed earth of the trail there were few signs to indicate the nature of the animals that had passed to and fro, but here and there the spoor of a lion was in evidence. Several times Tarzan stopped and listened, often he raised his head and his sensitive nostrils dilated as he sought for whatever the surrounding air might hold for him.

"I think there are men in this valley," he said presently. "For some time I have been almost positive that we are being watched. But whoever is stalking us is clever beyond words, for it is only the barest suggestion of another presence that I can scent."

La looked about apprehensively and drew close to his side. "I see no one," she said, in a low voice.

"Nor I," he replied. "Nor can I catch any well-defined scent spoor, yet I am positive that someone is following us. Someone or something that trails by scent, and is clever enough to keep its scent from us. It is more than likely that, whatever it is, it is passing through the trees, at a sufficient height to keep its scent spoor always above us. The air is right for that, and even if he were up wind from us we might not catch his scent at all. Wait here, I will make sure," and he swung lightly into the branches of a nearby tree and swarmed upward with the agility of Manu, the monkey. A moment later he descended to the girl's side.

"I was right," he said, "there is someone, or something, not far off. But whether it is man or Mangani I cannot say, for the odor is a strange one to me, suggesting neither, yet both. But two can play at that game. Come!" And he swung the girl to his shoulder and a moment later had carried her high into the trees. "Unless he is close enough to watch us, which I doubt," he said, "our spoor will be carried over his head and it will be some time before he can pick it up again, unless he is wise enough to rise to a higher level."

La marveled at the strength of the ape-man as he carried her easily from tree to tree, and at the speed with which he traversed the swaying, leafy trail. For half an hour he continued onward, and then quite suddenly he stopped, poised high upon a swaying bough.

"Look!" he said, pointing ahead and below them. Looking in the direction that he indicated the girl saw through the leafy foliage a small, heavily stockaded compound, in which were some dozen huts that immediately riveted her surprised attention, nor no less was the ape-man's curiosity piqued by what he glimpsed vaguely through the foliage. Huts they evidently were, but they seemed to be moving to and fro in the air, some moving gently backward and forward, while others jumped up and down in more or less violent agitation. Tarzan swung to a nearer tree and descended to a sturdy branch, to which he lowered La from his shoulder. Then he crept forward stealthily, the girl following, for she was, in common with the other Oparians, slightly arboreal. Presently they reached a point where they could see plainly the village below them, and immediately the seeming mystery of the dancing huts was explained.

They were of the bee-hive type, common to many African tribes, and were about seven feet in diameter by six or seven in height, but instead of resting on the ground, each hut was suspended by a heavy hawser-like grass rope to a branch of one of the several giant trees that grew within the stockade. From the center of the bottom of each hut trailed another lighter rope. From his position above them Tarzan saw no openings in any of the huts large enough to admit the body of a man, though there were several openings four or five inches in diameter in the sides of each hut about three feet above the floor. Upon the ground, inside the compound, were several of the inhabitants of the village, if the little collection of swinging houses could be dignified by such a name. Nor were the people any less strange to Tarzan than their peculiar domiciles. That they were negroes was evident, but of a type entirely unfamiliar to the ape-man. All were naked, and without any ornamentation whatsoever other than a few daubs of color, placed apparently at random upon their bodies. They were tall, and very muscular appearing, though their legs seemed much too short and their arms too long for perfect symmetry, while their faces were almost bestial in contour, their jaws being exaggeratedly prognathous while above their beetling brows there was no forehead, the skull running back in an almost horizontal plane to a point.

As Tarzan stood looking at them he saw another descend one of the ropes that dangled from the bottom of a hut, and immediately he understood the purpose of the ropes and the location of the entrances to the dwellings. The creatures squatting about upon their haunches were engaged in feeding. Several had bones from which they were tearing the uncooked flesh with their great teeth, while others ate fruit and tubers. There were individuals of both sexes and of various ages, from childhood to maturity, but there was none that seemed very old. They were practically hairless, except for scraggy, reddish brown locks upon their heads. They spoke but seldom and then in tones which resembled the growling of beasts, nor once, while Tarzan watched them, did he see one laugh or even smile, which, of all their traits, rendered them most unlike the average native of Africa. Though Tarzan's eyes searched the compound carefully he saw no indication of cooking utensils or of any fire. Upon the ground about them lay their weapons, short javelin-like spears and a sort of battle-ax with a sharpened, metal blade. Tarzan of the Apes was glad that he had come this way, for it had permitted him to see such a type of native as he had not dreamed existed—a type so low that it bordered closely upon the brute. Even the Waz-dons and Ho-dons of Pal-ul-don were far advanced in the scale of evolution compared to these.

As he looked at them he could not but wonder that they were sufficiently intelligent to manufacture the weapons they possessed, which he could see, even at a distance, were of fine workmanship and design. Their huts, too, seemed well and ingeniously made, while the stockade which surrounded the little compound was tall, strong, and well-built, evidently for the purpose of safeguarding them against the lions which infested the basin.

As Tarzan and La watched these people they became presently aware of the approach of some creature from their left, and a moment later they saw a man similar to those of the compound swing from a tree that overhung the stockade and drop within. The others acknowledged his coming with scarce more than indifferent glances. He came forward and, squatting among them, appeared to be telling them of something, and though Tarzan could not hear his words he judged from his gestures and the sign language which he used to supplement his meager speech, that he was telling his fellows of the strange creatures he had seen in the forest a short time before, and the ape-man immediately judged that this was the same whom he had been aware was following them and whom he had successfully put off the scent. The narration evidently excited them, for some of them arose, and leaping up and down with bent knees, slapped their arms against their sides grotesquely. The expressions upon their faces scarcely changed, however, and after a moment each squatted down again as he had been before.

It was while they were thus engaged that there echoed through the forest a loud scream that awakened in the mind of the ape-man many savage memories.

"Bolgani," he whispered to La.

"It is one of the great apes," she said, and shuddered.

Presently they saw him, swinging down the jungle trail toward the compound. A huge gorilla, but such a gorilla as Tarzan of the Apes had never looked on before. Of almost gigantic stature, the creature was walking erect with the stride of a man, not ever once touching his knuckles to the ground. His head and face were almost those of a gorilla, and yet there was a difference, as Tarzan could note as the creature came nearer—it was Bolgani, with the soul and brain of a man—nor was this all that rendered the creature startling and unique. Stranger perhaps than aught else was the fact that it wore ornaments—and such ornaments! Gold and diamonds sparkled against its shaggy coat, above its elbows were numerous armlets and there were anklets upon its legs, while from a girdle about its middle there depended before and behind a long narrow strip that almost touched the ground and which seemed to be entirely constructed of golden spangles set with small diamonds. Never before had John Clayton, Lord Greystoke, seen such a display of barbaric finery, nor even amidst the jewels of Opar such a wealth of priceless stones.

Immediately after the hideous scream had first broken the comparative silence of the forest, Tarzan had noticed its effects upon the inmates of the compound. Instantly they had arisen to their feet. The women and children scurried behind the boles of the trees or clambered up the ropes into their swinging cages, while some of the men advanced to what Tarzan now saw was the gate of the compound. Outside this gate the gorilla halted and again raised his voice, but this time in speech rather than his hideous scream.

THE SHAFT OF DEATH

As the huge, man-like gorilla entered the compound the warriors closed the gate, and fell back respectfully as he advanced to the center of the village where he stood for a moment, looking about.

"Where are the shes and the balus?" he asked, tersely. "Call them."

The women and the children must have heard the command, but they did not emerge from their hiding places. The warriors moved about uneasily, evidently torn by the conflicting emotions of fear of the creature who had issued the order, and reluctance to fulfil his commands.

"Call them," he repeated, "or go and fetch them." But at last one of the warriors mustered the courage to address him.

"This village has already furnished one woman within the moon," he said. "It is the turn of another village."

"Silence!" roared the gorilla-man, advancing threateningly toward him. "You are a rash Gomangani to threaten the will of a Bolgani—I speak with the voice of Numa, the Emperor; obey or die."

Trembling, the black turned and called the women and children, but none responded to his summons. The Bolgani gestured impatiently.

"Go and fetch them," he demanded. And the blacks, cringing, moved sullenly across the compound toward the hiding places of their women and children. Presently they returned, dragging them with them, by the arms sometimes, but usually by the hair. Although they had seemed loath to give them up, they showed no gentleness toward them, nor any indication of affection. Their attitude toward them, however, was presently explained to Tarzan by the next words of the warrior who had spoken previously.

"Great Bolgani," he said, addressing the gorilla-man, "if Numa takes always from this village, there will soon be not enough women for the warriors here, and there will be too few children, and in a little time there will be none of us left."

"What of that?" growled the gorilla-man. "There are already too many Gomangani in the world. For what other purpose were you created than to serve Numa, the Emperor, and his chosen people, the Bolgani?" As he spoke he was examining the women and children, pinching their flesh and pounding upon their chests and backs. Presently he returned to a comparatively young woman, straddling whose hip was a small child.

"This one will do," he said, snatching the child from its mother and hurling it roughly across the compound, where it lay against the face of the palisade, moaning pitifully, and perchance broken and dying. The poor, stupid mother, apparently more beast than human, stood for a moment trembling in dumb anguish, and then she started to rush forward to her child. But the gorilla-man seized her with one of his great hands and hurled her to the ground. Simultaneously there arose from the silent foliage above them the fierce and terrible scream of the challenging bull ape. In terror the simple blacks cast affrighted glances upward, while the gorilla-man raised his hideous face in snarling anger toward the author of the bestial cry.

Swaying upon a leafy bough they beheld such a creature as none of them had ever looked upon before—a white man, a Tarmangani, with hide as hairless as the body of Histah, the snake. In the instant that they looked they saw the spear hand of the stranger drive forward, and the shaft, speeding with the swiftness of thought, bury itself in the breast of the Bolgani. With a single scream of rage and pain, the gorilla-man crumbled to the earth, where he struggled spasmodically for a moment and then lay still, in death.

The ape-man held no great love for the Gomangani as a race, but inherent in his English brain and heart was the spirit of fair play, which prompted him to spontaneous espousal of the cause of the weak. On the other hand Bolgani was his hereditary enemy. His first battle had been with Bolgani, and his first kill.

The poor blacks were still standing in stupefied wonderment when he dropped from the tree to the ground among them. They stepped back in terror, and simultaneously they raised their spears menacingly against him.

"I am a friend," he said. "I am Tarzan of the Apes. Lower your spears." And then he turned and withdrew his own weapon from the carcass of Bolgani. "Who is this creature, that may come into your village and slay your balus and steal your shes? Who is he, that you dare not drive your spears through him?"

"He is one of the great Bolgani," said the warrior, who seemed to be spokesman, and the leader in the village. "He is one of the chosen people of Numa, the Emperor, and when Numa learns that he has been killed in our village, we shall all die for what you have done."

"Who is Numa?" demanded the ape-man, to whom Numa, in the language of the great apes, meant only lion.

"Numa is the Emperor," replied the black, "who lives with the Bolgani in the Palace of Diamonds."

He did not express himself in just these words, for the meager language of the great apes, even though amplified by the higher intelligence and greater development of the Oparians, is still primitive in the extreme. What he had really said was more nearly "Numa, the king of kings, who lives in the king's hut of glittering stones," which carried to the ape-man's mind the faithful impression of the fact. Numa, evidently, was the name adopted by the king of the Bolgani, and the title emperor, indicated merely his preeminence among the chiefs.

The instant that Bolgani had fallen the bereaved mother rushed forward and gathered her injured infant into her arms. She squatted now against the palisade, cuddling it to her breast, and crooning softly to pacify its cries, which Tarzan suddenly discovered were more the result of fright than injury. At first the mother had been frightened when he had attempted to examine the child, drawing away and baring her fighting fangs, much after the manner of a wild beast. But presently there had seemed to come to her dull brain a realization that this creature had saved her from Bolgani, that he had permitted her to recover her infant and that he was making no effort to harm either of them. Convinced at last that the child was only bruised, Tarzan turned again toward the warriors, who were talking together in an excited little group a few paces away. As they saw him advancing, they spread into a semi-circle and stood facing him.

"The Bolgani will send and slay us all," they said, "when they learn what has happened in our village, unless we can take to them the creature that cast the spear. Therefore, Tarmangani, you shall go with us to the Palace of Diamonds, and there we shall give you over to the Bolgani and perhaps Numa will forgive us."

The ape-man smiled. What kind of creature did the simple blacks think him, to believe that he would permit himself to be easily led into the avenging hands of Numa, the Emperor of the Bolgani. Although he was fully aware of the risk that he had taken in entering the village, he knew too that because he was Tarzan of the Apes there was a greater chance that he would be able to escape than that they could hold him. He had faced savage spearmen before and knew precisely what to expect in the event of hostilities. He preferred, however, to make peace with these people, for it had been in his mind to find some means of questioning them the moment that he had discovered their village hidden away in this wild forest.

"Wait," he said, therefore. "Would you betray a friend who enters your village to protect you from an enemy?"

"We will not slay you, Tarmangani. We will take you to the Bolgani for Numa, the Emperor."

"But that would amount to the same thing," returned Tarzan, "for you well know that Numa, the Emperor, will have me slain."

"That we cannot help," replied the spokesman. "If we could save you we would, but when the Bolgani discover what has happened in our village, it is we who must suffer, unless, perhaps, they are satisfied to punish you instead."

"But why need they know that the Bolgani has been slain in your village?" asked Tarzan.

"Will they not see his body next time they come?" asked the spokesman.

"Not if you remove his body," replied Tarzan.

The blacks scratched their heads. Into their dull, ignorant minds had crept no such suggestion of a solution of their problem. What the stranger said was true. None but they and he knew that Bolgani had been slain within their palisade. To remove the body, then, would be to remove all suspicion from their village. But where were they to take it? They put the question to Tarzan.

"I will dispose of him for you," replied the Tarmangani. "Answer my questions truthfully and I will promise to take him away and dispose of him in such a manner that no one will know how he died, or where."

"What are your questions?" asked the spokesman.

"I am a stranger in your country. I am lost here," replied the ape-man. "And I would find a way out of the valley in that direction." And he pointed toward the southeast.

The black shook his head. "There may be a way out of the valley in that direction," he said, "but what lies beyond no man knows, nor do I know whether there be a way out or whether there be anything beyond. It is said that all is fire beyond the mountain, and no one dares to go and see. As for myself, I have never been far from my village—at most only a day's march to hunt for game for the Bolgani, and to gather fruit and nuts and plantains for them. If there is a way out I do not know, nor would any man dare take it if there were."

"Does no one ever leave the valley?" asked Tarzan.

"I know not what others do," replied the spokesman, "but those of this village never leave the valley."

"What lies in that direction?" asked Tarzan, pointing toward Opar.

"I do not know," replied the black, "only that sometimes the Bolgani come from that way, bringing with them strange creatures; little men with white skins and much hair, with short, crooked legs and long arms, and sometimes white shes, who do not look at all like the strange little Tarmangani. But where they get them I do not know, nor do they ever tell us. Are these all the questions that you wish to ask?"

"Yes, that is all," replied Tarzan, seeing that he could gain no information whatsoever from these ignorant villagers. Realizing that he must find his own way out of the valley, and knowing that he could do so much more quickly and safely if he was alone, he decided to sound the blacks in relation to a plan that had entered his mind.

"If I take the Bolgani away, so that the others will not know that he was slain in your village, will you treat me as a friend?" he asked.

"Yes," replied the spokesman.

"Then," said Tarzan, "will you keep here for me my white she until I return again to your village? You can hide her in one of your huts if a Bolgani comes, and no one need ever know that she is among you. What do you say?"

The blacks looked around. "We do not see her," said the spokesman. "Where is she?"

"If you will promise to protect her and hide her, I will bring her here," replied the ape-man.

"I will not harm her," said the head man, "but I do not know about the others."

Tarzan turned toward the others who were clustered about, listening. "I am going to bring my mate into your village," he said, "and you are going to hide her, and feed her, and protect her until I return. I shall take away the body of Bolgani, so that no suspicion shall fall upon you, and when I come back I shall expect to find my mate safe and unharmed."

He had thought it best to describe La as his mate, since thus they might understand that she was under his protection, and if they felt either gratitude or fear toward him, La would be safer. Raising his face toward the tree where she was hidden, he called to La to descend, and a moment later she clambered down to the lower branches of one of the trees in the compound and dropped into Tarzan's arms.

"This is she," he said to the assembled blacks, "guard her well and hide her from the Bolgani. If, upon my return, I find that any harm has befallen her, I shall take word to the Bolgani that it was you who did this," and he pointed to the corpse of the gorilla-man.

La turned appealingly toward him, fear showing in her eyes. "You are not going to leave me here?" she asked.

"Temporarily only," replied Tarzan. "These poor people are afraid that if the death of this creature is traced to their village they shall all suffer the wrath of his fellows, and so I have promised that I will remove the evidence in such a way as to direct suspicion elsewhere. If they are sufficiently high in the scale of evolution to harbor sentiments of gratitude, which I doubt, they will feel obligated to me for having slain this beast, as well as for preventing suspicion falling upon them. For these reasons they should protect you, but to make assurance doubly sure I have appealed also to their fear of the Bolgani—a characteristic which I know they possess. I am sure that you will be as safe here as with me until I return, otherwise I would not leave you. But alone I can travel much faster, and while I am gone I intend to find a way out of this valley, then I shall return for you and together we may make our escape easily, or at least with greater assurance of success than were we to blunder slowly about together."

"You will come back?" she asked, a note of fear, longing, and appeal in her voice.

"I will come back," he replied, and then turning to the blacks: "Clear out one of these huts for my mate, and see that she is not molested, and that she is furnished with food and water. And remember what I said, upon her safety your lives depend."

Stooping, Tarzan lifted the dead gorilla-man to his shoulder, and the simple blacks marveled at his prowess. Of great physical strength themselves, there was not one of them but would have staggered under the weight of Bolgani, yet this strange Tarmangani walked easily beneath his burden, and when they had opened the gate in the palisade he trotted down the jungle trail as though he carried nothing but his own frame. A moment later he disappeared at a turn and was swallowed by the forest.

La turned to the blacks: "Prepare my hut," she said, for she was very tired and longed to rest. They eyed her askance and whispered among themselves. It was evident to her that there was a difference of opinion among them, and presently from snatches of conversation which she overheard she realized that while some of the blacks were in favor of obeying Tarzan's injunctions implicitly, there were others who objected strenuously and who wished to rid their village of her, lest she be discovered there by the Bolgani, and the villagers be punished accordingly.

"It would be better," she heard one of the blacks say, "to turn her over to the Bolgani at once and tell them that we saw her mate slay the messenger of Numa. We will say that we tried to capture the Tarmangani but that he escaped, and that we were only able to seize his mate. Thus will we win the favor of Numa, and perhaps then he will not take so many of our women and children."

"But the Tarmangani is great," replied one of the others. "He is more powerful even than Bolgani. He would make a terrible enemy, and, as the chances are that the Bolgani would not believe us we should then have not only them but the Tarmangani to fear."

"You are right," cried La, "the Tarmangani is great. Far better will it be for you to have him for friend than enemy. Single-handed he grapples with Numa, the lion, and slays him. You saw with what ease he lifted the body of the mighty Bolgani to his shoulder. You saw him trot lightly down the jungle trail beneath his burden. With equal ease will he carry the corpse through the trees of the forest, far above the ground. In all the world there is no other like him, no other like Tarzan of the Apes. If you are wise, Gomangani, you will have Tarzan for a friend."

The blacks listened to her, their dull faces revealing nothing of what was passing in their stupid brains. For a few moments they stood thus in silence, the hulking, ignorant blacks upon one side, the slender, beautiful white woman upon the other. Then La spoke.

"Go," she cried imperiously, "and prepare my hut." It was the High Priestess of the Flaming God; La, the queen of Opar, addressing slaves. Her regal mien, her commanding tones, wrought an instant change in the villagers, and La knew then that Tarzan was right in his assumption that they could be moved only through fear, for now they turned quickly, cowering like whipped dogs, and hastened to a nearby hut, which they quickly prepared for her, fetching fresh leaves and grasses for its floor, and fruit and nuts and plantains for her meal.

When all was ready, La clambered up the rope and through the circular opening in the floor of the hanging hut, which she found large and airy, and now reasonably clean. She drew the rope up after her and threw herself upon the soft bed they had prepared for her, and soon the gentle swaying of the swinging hut, the soft murmur of the leaves above her, the voices of the birds and insects combined with her own physical exhaustion to lull her into deep slumber.

MAD TREACHERY

To the northwest of the valley of Opar the smoke rose from the cook fires of a camp in which some hundred blacks and six whites were eating their evening meal. The negroes squatted sullen and morose, mumbling together in low tones over their meager fare, the whites, scowling and apprehensive, kept their firearms close at hand. One of them, a girl, and the only member of her sex in the party, was addressing her fellows:

"We have Adolph's stinginess and Esteban's braggadocio to thank for the condition in which we are," she said.

The fat Bluber shrugged his shoulder, the big Spaniard scowled.

"For vy," asked Adolph, "am I to blame?"

"You were too stingy to employ enough carriers. I told you at the time that we ought to have had two hundred blacks in our party, but you wanted to save a little money, and now what is the result? Fifty men carrying eighty pounds of gold apiece and the other carriers are overburdened with camp equipment, while there are scarce enough left for askari to guard us properly. We have to drive them like beasts to make any progress and to keep them from throwing away their loads, and they are fagged out and angry. They don't require much of an excuse to kill us all on the spot. On top of all this they are underfed. If we could keep their bellies filled we could probably keep them happy and reasonably contented, but I have learned enough about natives to know that if they are hungry they are neither happy nor contented, even in idleness. If Esteban had not bragged so much about his prowess as a hunter we should have brought enough provisions to last us through, but now, though we are barely started upon our return journey, we are upon less than half rations."

"I can't kill game when there isn't any game," growled the Spaniard.

"There is plenty of game," said Kraski, the Russian. "We see the tracks of it every day."

The Spaniard eyed him venomously. "If there is so much game," he said, "go out and get it yourself."

"I never claimed to be a hunter," replied Kraski, "though I could go out with a sling shot and a pea shooter and do as well as you have."

The Spaniard leaped to his feet menacingly, and instantly the Russian covered him with a heavy service revolver.

"Cut that business," cried the girl, sharply, leaping between them.

"Let the blighters fight," growled John Peebles. "If one of 'em kills the hother there'll be fewer to split the swag, and 'ere we are 'n that's that."

"For vy should ve quarrel?" demanded Bluber. "Dere is enough for all—over forty-tree t'ousand pounds apiece. Ven you get mad at me you call me a dirty Jew und say dat I am stingy, but Mein Gott! you Christians are vorser. You vould kill vun of your friends to get more money. Oi! Oi! tank Gott dat I am not a Christian."

"Shut up," growled Throck, "or we'll have forty-three thousand pounds more to divide."

Bluber eyed the big Englishman fearfully. "Come, come, Dick," he oozed, in his oiliest tones, "you vouldn't get mad at a leedle choke vould you, und me your best friend?"

"I'm sick of all this grousin'," said Throck. "I h'ain't no high-brow, I h'ain't nothin' but a pug. But I got sense enough to know that Flora's the only one in the bloomin' bunch whose brains wouldn't rattle around in a peanut shell. John, Bluber, Kraski and me, we're here because we could raise the money to carry out Flora's plan. The dago there"—and he indicated Esteban—"because his face and his figure filled the bill. There don't any of us need no brains for this work, and there ain't any of us got any more brains than we need. Flora's the brains of this outfit, and the sooner everyone understands that and takes orders from her, the better off we'll all be. She's been to Africa with this Lord Greystoke feller before—you wuz his wife's maid, wasn't you, Flora? And she knows somethin' about the country and the natives and the animals, and there don't none of us know nuttin'."

"Throck is right," said Kraski, quickly, "we've been muddling long enough. We haven't had a boss, and the thing to do is to make Flora boss from now on. If anyone can get us out of this, she can, and from the way those fellows over there are acting," and he nodded toward the blacks, "we'll be lucky if we ever get out with our skins, let alone taking any of the gold with us."

"Oi! Oi! You don't mean to leave the gold?" almost shrieked Bluber.

"I mean that we do whatever Flora thinks best," replied Kraski. "If she says to leave the gold, we'll leave it."

"That we do," seconded Throck.

"I'm for it," said Peebles. "Whatever Flora says goes."

The Spaniard nodded his assent sullenly.

"The rest of us are all for it, Bluber. How about you?" asked Kraski.

"O vell—sure—if you say so," said Bluber, "und as John says 'und here ve ain't und vat's dat.'?"

"And now, Flora," said Peebles, "you're the big 'un. What you say goes. What'll we do next?"

"Very well," said the girl; "we shall camp here until these men are rested, and early tomorrow we'll start out intelligently and systematically, and get meat for them. With their help we can do it. When they are rested and well fed we will start on again for the coast, moving very slowly, so as not to tire them too much. This is my first plan, but it all hinges upon our ability to get meat. If we do not find it I shall bury the gold here, and we will do our best to reach the coast as quickly as possible. There we shall recruit new porters—twice as many as we have now—and purchase enough provisions to carry us in and out again. As we come back in, we will cache provisions at every camping place for our return trip, thus saving the necessity of carrying heavy loads all the way in and out again. In this way we can come out light, with twice as many porters as we actually need. And by working them in shifts we will travel much faster and there will be no grumbling. These are my two plans. I am not asking you what you think of them, because I do not care. You have made me chief, and I am going to run this from now on as I think best."

"Bully for you," roared Peebles; "that's the kind of talk I likes to hear."

"Tell the head man I want to see him, Carl," said the girl, turning to Kraski, and a moment later the Russian returned with a burly negro.

"Owaza," said the girl, as the black halted before her, "we are short of food and the men are burdened with loads twice as heavy as they should carry. Tell them that we shall wait here until they are rested and that tomorrow we shall all go out and hunt for meat. You will send your boys out under three good men, and they will act as beaters and drive the game in to us. In this way we should get plenty of meat, and when the men are rested and well fed we will move on slowly. Where game is plentiful we will hunt and rest. Tell them that if they do this and we reach the coast in safety and with all our loads, I shall pay them twice what they agreed to come for."

"Oi! Oi!" spluttered Bluber, "twice vat dey agreed to come for! Oh, Flora, vy not offer dem ten per cent? Dot vould be fine interest on their money."

"Shut up, you fool," snapped Kraski, and Bluber subsided, though he rocked back and forth, shaking his head in disapproval.

The black, who had presented himself for the interview with sullen and scowling demeanor, brightened visibly now. "I will tell them," he said, "and I think that you will have no more trouble."

"Good," said Flora, "go and tell them now," and the black turned and left.

"There," said the girl, with a sigh of relief, "I believe that we can see light ahead at last."

"Tvice vat ve promised to pay them!" bawled Bluber, "Oi! Oi!"

Early the following morning they prepared to set out upon the hunt. The blacks were now smiling and happy in anticipation of plenty of meat, and as they tramped off into the jungle they were singing gayly. Flora had divided them into three parties, each under a head man, with explicit directions for the position each party was to take in the line of beaters. Others had been detailed to the whites as gun-bearers, while a small party of the askari were left behind to guard the camp. The whites, with the exception of Esteban, were armed with rifles. He alone seemed inclined to question Flora's authority, insisting that he preferred to hunt with spear and arrows in keeping with the part he was playing. The fact that, though he had hunted assiduously for weeks, yet had never brought in a single kill, was not sufficient to dampen his egotism. So genuinely had he entered his part that he really thought he was Tarzan of the Apes, and with such fidelity had he equipped himself in every detail, and such a master of the art of make-up was he, that, in conjunction with his splendid figure and his handsome face that were almost a counterpart of Tarzan's, it was scarcely to be wondered at that he almost fooled himself as successfully as he had fooled others, for there were men among the carriers who had known the great ape-man, and even these were deceived, though they wondered at the change in him, since in little things he did not deport himself as Tarzan, and in the matter of kills he was disappointing.

Flora Hawkes, who was endowed with more than a fair share of intelligence, realized that it would not be well to cross any of her companions unnecessarily, and so she permitted Esteban to hunt that morning in his own way, though some of the others grumbled a little at her decision.

"What is the difference?" she asked them, after the Spaniard had set out alone. "The chances are that he could use a rifle no better than he uses his spear and arrows. Carl and Dick are really the only shots among us, and it is upon them we depend principally for the success of our hunt today. Esteban's egotism has been so badly bumped that it is possible that he will go to the last extremity to make a kill today—let us hope that he is successful."

"I hope he breaks his fool neck," said Kraski. "He has served our purpose and we would be better off if we were rid of him."

The girl shook her head negatively. "No," she said, "we must not think or speak of anything of that kind. We went into this thing together, let us stick together until the end. If you are wishing that one of us is dead, how do you know that others are not wishing that you were dead?"

"I haven't any doubt but that Miranda wishes I were dead," replied Kraski. "I never go to bed at night without thinking that the damned greaser may try to stick a knife into me before morning. And it don't make me feel any kinder toward him to hear you defending him, Flora. You've been a bit soft on him from the start."

"If I have, it's none of your business," retorted the girl.

And so they started out upon their hunt, the Russian scowling and angry, harboring thoughts of vengeance or worse against Esteban, and Esteban, hunting through the jungle, was occupied with his hatred and his jealousy. His dark mind was open to every chance suggestion of a means for putting the other men of the party out of the way, and taking the woman and the gold for himself. He hated them all; in each he saw a possible rival for the affections of Flora, and in the death of each he saw not only one less suitor for the girl's affections, but forty-three thousand additional pounds to be divided among fewer people. His mind was thus occupied to the exclusion of the business of hunting, which should have occupied him solely, when he came through a patch of heavy underbrush, and stepped into the glaring sunlight of a large clearing, face to face with a party of some fifty magnificent ebon warriors. For just an instant Esteban stood frozen in a paralysis of terror, forgetting momentarily the part he was playing—thinking of himself only as a lone white man in the heart of savage Africa facing a large band of warlike natives—cannibals, perhaps. It was that moment of utter silence and inaction that saved him, for, as he stood thus before them, the Waziri saw in the silent, majestic figure their beloved lord in a characteristic pose.

"O Bwana, Bwana," cried one of the warriors, rushing forward, "it is indeed you, Tarzan of the Apes, Lord of the Jungle, whom we had given up as lost. We, your faithful Waziri, have been searching for you, and even now we were about to dare the dangers of Opar, fearing that you might have ventured there without us and had been captured."

The black, who had at one time accompanied Tarzan to London as a body servant, spoke broken English, an accomplishment of which he was inordinately proud, losing no opportunity to air his attainment before his less fortunate fellows. The fact that it had been he whom fate had chosen to act as spokesman was indeed a fortunate circumstance to Miranda. Although the latter had applied himself assiduously to mastering the dialect of the west coast carriers, he would have been hard put to it to carry on a conversation with one of them, while he understood nothing of the Waziri tongue. Flora had schooled him carefully and well in the lore of Tarzan, so that he realized now that he was in the presence of a band of the ape-man's faithful Waziri. Never before had he seen such magnificent blacks—clean-cut, powerful men, with intelligent faces and well molded features, appearing as much higher in the scale of evolution as were the west coast blacks above the apes. Lucky indeed was Esteban Miranda that he was quick witted and a consummate actor. Otherwise must he have betrayed his terror and his chagrin upon learning that this band of Tarzan's fierce and faithful followers was in this part of the country. For a moment longer he stood in silence before them, gathering his wits, and then he spoke, realizing that his very life depended upon his plausibility. And as he thought a great light broke upon the shrewd brain of the unscrupulous Spaniard.

"Since I last saw you," he said, "I discovered that a party of white men had entered the country for the purpose of robbing the treasure vaults of Opar. I followed them until I found their camp, and then I came in search of you, for there are many of them and they have many ingots of gold, for they have already been to Opar. Follow me, and we will raid their camp and take the gold from them. Come!" and he turned back toward the camp that he had just quitted.

As they made their way along the jungle trail, Usula, the Waziri who had spoken English to him, walked at Esteban's side. Behind them the Spaniard could hear the other warriors speaking in their native tongue, no word of which he understood, and it occurred to him that his position would be most embarrassing should he be addressed in the Waziri language, which, of course, Tarzan must have understood perfectly. As he listened to the chatter of Usula his mind was working rapidly, and presently, as though it were an inspiration, there recurred to him the memory of an accident that had befallen Tarzan, which had been narrated to him by Flora—the story of the injury he had received in the treasure vaults of Opar upon the occasion that he had lost his memory because of a blow upon the head. Esteban wondered if he had committed himself too deeply at first to attribute to amnesia any shortcomings in the portrayal of the rôle he was acting. At its worst, however, it seemed to him the best that he could do. He turned suddenly upon Usula.

"Do you remember," he asked, "the accident that befell me in the treasure vaults of Opar, depriving me of my memory?"

"Yes, Bwana, I remember it well," replied the black.

"A similar accident has befallen me," said Esteban. "A great tree fell in my path, and in falling a branch struck me upon the head. It has not caused me to lose my memory entirely, but since then it is with difficulty that I recall many things, and there are others which I must have forgotten entirely, for I do not know your name, nor do I understand the words that my other Waziri are speaking about me."

Usula looked at him compassionately. "Ah, Bwana, sad indeed is the heart of Usula to hear that this accident has befallen you. Doubtless it will soon pass away as did the other, and in the meantime I, Usula, will be your memory for you."

"Good," said Esteban, "tell the others that they may understand, and tell them also that I have lost the memory of other things besides. I could not now find my way home without you, and my other senses are dull as well. But as you say, Usula, it will soon pass off, and I shall be myself again."

"Your faithful Waziri will rejoice indeed with the coming of that moment," said Usula.

As they approached the camp, Miranda cautioned Usula to warn his followers to silence, and presently he halted them at the outskirts of the clearing where they could attain a view of the boma and the tents, guarding which was a little band of a half-dozen askari.

"When they see our greater numbers they will make no resistance," said Esteban. "Let us surround the camp, therefore, and at a signal from me we will advance together, when you shall address them, saying that Tarzan of the Apes comes with his Waziri for the gold they have stolen, but that he will spare them if they will leave the country at once and never return."

Had it fulfilled his purpose as well, the Spaniard would have willingly ordered his Waziri to fall upon the men guarding the camp and destroy them all, but to his cunning brain had been born a cleverer scheme. He wanted these men to see him with the Waziri and to live to tell the others that they had seen him, and to repeat to Flora and her followers the thing that Esteban had in his mind to tell one of the askari, while the Waziri were gathering up the gold ingots from the camp.

In directing Usula to station his men about the camp, Esteban had him warn them that they were not to show themselves until he had crept out into the clearing and attracted the attention of the askari on guard. Fifteen minutes, perhaps, were consumed in stationing his men, and then Usula returned to Esteban to report that all was ready.

"When I raise my hand then you will know that they have recognized me and that you are to advance," Esteban cautioned him, and stepped forward slowly into the clearing. One of the askari saw him and recognized him as Esteban. The Spaniard took a few steps closer to the boma and then halted.

"I am Tarzan of the Apes," he said; "your camp is entirely surrounded by my warriors. Make no move against us and we shall not hurt you."

He waved his hand. Fifty stalwart Waziri stepped into view from the concealing verdure of the surrounding jungle. The askari eyed them in ill-concealed terror, fingering their rifles nervously.

"Do not shoot," cautioned Esteban, "or we shall slay you all." He approached more closely and his Waziri closed in about him, entirely surrounding the boma.

"Speak to them, Usula," said Esteban. The black stepped forward.

"We are the Waziri," he cried, "and this is Tarzan of the Apes, Lord of the Jungle, our master. We have come to recover the gold of Tarzan that you have stolen from the treasure vaults of Opar. This time we shall spare you on condition that you leave the country and never return. Tell this word to your masters; tell them that Tarzan watches, and that his Waziri watch with him. Lay down your rifles."

The askari, glad to escape so easily, complied with the demands of Usula, and a moment later the Waziri had entered the boma, and at Esteban's direction were gathering up the golden ingots. As they worked, Esteban approached one of the askari, whom he knew spoke broken English.

"Tell your master," he said, "to give thanks for the mercy of Tarzan who has exacted a toll of but one life for this invasion of his country and theft of his treasure. The creature who presumes to pose as Tarzan I have slain, and his body I shall take away with me and feed to the lions. Tell them that Tarzan forgives even their attempt to poison him upon the occasion that he visited their camp, but only upon the condition that they never return to Africa, and that they divulge the secret of Opar to no others. Tarzan watches and his Waziri watch, and no man may enter Africa without Tarzan's knowledge. Even before they left London I knew that they were coming. Tell them that."

It took but a few minutes for the Waziri to gather up the golden ingots, and before the askari had recovered from the surprise of their appearance, they had gone again into the jungle, with Tarzan, their master.

It was late in the afternoon before Flora and the four white men returned from their hunt, surrounded by happy, laughing blacks, bearing the fruits of a successful chase.

"Now that you are in charge, Flora," Kraski was saying, "fortune is smiling upon us indeed. We have enough meat here for several days, and with plenty of meat in their bellies they ought to make good progress."

"I vill say it myself dot t'ings look brighter," said Bluber.

"Blime, they do that," said Throck. "I'm tellin' yu Flora's a bright one."

"What the devil is this?" demanded Peebles, "what's wrong with them beggars." And he pointed toward the boma which was now in sight, and from which the askari were issuing at a run, jabbering excitedly as they raced toward them.

"Tarzan of the Apes has been here," they cried excitedly. "He has been here with all his Waziri—a thousand great warriors—and though we fought, they overcame us, and taking the gold they went away. Tarzan of the Apes spoke strange words to me before they left. He said that he had killed one of your number who had dared to call himself Tarzan of the Apes. We do not understand it. He went away alone to hunt when you went in the morning, and he came back shortly with a thousand warriors, and he took all the gold and he threatened to kill us and you if you ever return to this country again."

"Vot, vot?" cried Bluber, "der gold iss gone? Oi! Oi!" And then they all commenced to ask questions at once until Flora silenced them.

"Come," she said to the leader of the askari, "we will return to the boma and then you shall tell me slowly and carefully all that has happened since we left."

She listened intently to his narrative, and then questioned him carefully upon various points several times. At last she dismissed him. Then she turned to her confederates.

"It is all clear to me," she said. "Tarzan recovered from the effects of the drug we administered. Then he followed us with his Waziri, caught Esteban and killed him and, finding the camp, has taken the gold away. We shall be fortunate indeed if we escape from Africa with our lives."

"Oi! Oi!" almost shrieked Bluber, "der dirty crook. He steals all our gold, und ve lose our two t'ousand pounds into the bargain. Oi! Oi!"

"Shut up, you dirty Jew," growled Throck. "If it hadn't a' been for you and the dago this 'ere thing would never a 'appened. With 'im abraggin' about 'is 'unting and not bein' able to kill anything, and you a-squeezin' every bloomin' hapenny, we're in a rotten mess—that we are. This 'ere Tarzan bounder he bumped off Esteban, which is the best work what 'e ever done. Too bloody bad you weren't 'ere to get it too, and what I got a good mind to do is to slit your throat meself."

"Stow the guff, Dick," roared Peebles; "it wasn't nobody's fault, as far as I can see. Instead of talkin' what we oughter do is to go after this 'ere Tarzan feller and take the bloomin' gold away from 'im."

Flora Hawkes laughed. "We haven't a chance in the world," she said. "I know this Tarzan bloke. If he was all alone we wouldn't be a match for him, but he's got a bunch of his Waziri with him, and there are no finer warriors in Africa than they. And they'd fight for him to the last man. You just tell Owaza that you're thinking of going after Tarzan of the Apes and his Waziri to take the gold away from them, and see how long it'd be before we wouldn't have a single nigger with us. The very name of Tarzan scares these west coast blacks out of a year's growth. They would sooner face the devil. No, sir, we've lost, and all we can do is to get out of the country, and thank our lucky stars if we manage to get out alive. The ape-man will watch us. I should not be surprised if he were watching us this minute." Her companions looked around apprehensively at this, casting nervous glances toward the jungle. "And he'd never let us get back to Opar for another load, even if we could prevail upon our blacks to return there."

"Two t'ousand pounds, two t'ousand pounds!" wailed Bluber. "Und all dis suit, vot it cost me twenty guineas vot I can't vear it again in England unless I go to a fancy dress ball, vich I never do."

Kraski had not spoken, but had sat with eyes upon the ground, listening to the others. Now he raised his head. "We have lost our gold," he said, "and before we get back to England we stand to spend the balance of our two thousand pounds—in other words our expedition is a total loss. The rest of you may be satisfied to go back broke, but I am not. There are other things in Africa besides the gold of Opar, and when we leave the country there is no reason why we shouldn't take something with us that will repay us for our time and investment."

"What do you mean?" asked Peebles.

"I have spent a lot of time talking with Owaza," replied Kraski, "trying to learn their crazy language, and I have come to find out a lot about the old villain. He's as crooked as they make 'em, and if he were to be hanged for all his murders, he'd have to have more lives than a cat, but notwithstanding all that, he's a shrewd old fellow, and I've learned a lot more from him than just his monkey talk—I have learned enough, in fact, so that I feel safe in saying that if we stick together we can go out of Africa with a pretty good sized stake. Personally, I haven't given up the gold of Opar yet. What we've lost, we've lost, but there's plenty left where that came from, and some day, after this blows over, I'm coming back to get my share."

"But how about this other thing?" asked Flora. "How can Owaza help us?"

"There's a little bunch of Arabs down here," explained Kraski, "stealing slaves and ivory. Owaza knows where they are working and where their main camp is. There are only a few of them, and their blacks are nearly all slaves who would turn on them in a minute. Now the idea is this: we have a big enough party to overpower them and take their ivory away from them if we can get their slaves to take our side. We don't want the slaves; we couldn't do anything with them if we had them, so we can promise them their freedom for their help, and give Owaza and his gang a share in the ivory."

"How do you know Owaza will help us?" asked Flora.

"The idea is his; that's the reason I know," replied Kraski.

"It sounds good to me," said Peebles; "I ain't fer goin' 'ome empty 'anded." And in turn the others signified their approval of the scheme.

STRANGE INCENSE BURNS

As Tarzan carried the dead Bolgani from the village of the Gomangani, he set his steps in the direction of the building he had seen from the rim of the valley, the curiosity of the man overcoming the natural caution of the beast. He was traveling up wind and the odors wafted down to his nostrils told him that he was approaching the habitat of the Bolgani. Intermingled with the scent spoor of the gorilla-men was that of Gomangani and the odor of cooked food, and the suggestion of a heavily sweet scent, which the ape-man could connect only with burning incense, though it seemed impossible that such a fragrance could emanate from the dwellings of the Bolgani. Perhaps it came from the great edifice he had seen—a building which must have been constructed by human beings, and in which human beings might still dwell, though never among the multitudinous odors that assailed his nostrils did he once catch the faintest suggestion of the man scent of whites.

When he perceived from the increasing strength of their odor, that he was approaching close to the Bolgani, Tarzan took to the trees with his burden, that he might thus stand a better chance of avoiding discovery, and presently, through the foliage ahead, he saw a lofty wall, and, beyond, the outlines of the weird architecture of a strange and mysterious pile—outlines that suggested a building of another world, so unearthly were they, and from beyond the wall came the odor of the Bolgani and the fragrance of the incense, intermingled with the scent spoor of Numa, the lion. The jungle was cleared away for fifty feet outside the wall surrounding the building, so that there was no tree overhanging the wall, but Tarzan approached as closely as he could, while still remaining reasonably well concealed by the foliage. He had chosen a point at a sufficient height above the ground to permit him to see over the top of the wall.

The building within the enclosure was of great size, its different parts appearing to have been constructed at various periods, and each with utter disregard to uniformity, resulting in a conglomeration of connecting buildings and towers, no two of which were alike, though the whole presented a rather pleasing, if somewhat bizarre appearance. The building stood upon an artificial elevation about ten feet high, surrounded by a retaining wall of granite, a wide staircase leading to the ground level below. About the building were shrubbery and trees, some of the latter appearing to be of great antiquity, while one enormous tower was almost entirely covered by ivy. By far the most remarkable feature of the building, however, lay in its rich and barbaric ornamentation. Set into the polished granite of which it was composed was an intricate mosaic of gold and diamonds; glittering stones in countless thousands scintillated from façades, minarets, domes, and towers.

The enclosure, which comprised some fifteen or twenty acres, was occupied for the most part by the building. The terrace upon which it stood was devoted to walks, flowers, shrubs, and ornamental trees, while that part of the area below, which was within the range of Tarzan's vision, seemed to be given over to the raising of garden truck. In the garden and upon the terrace were naked blacks, such as he had seen in the village where he had left La. There were both men and women, and these were occupied with the care of growing things within the enclosure. Among them were several of the gorilla-like creatures such as Tarzan had slain in the village, but these performed no labor, devoting themselves, rather, it seemed, to directing the work of the blacks, toward whom their manner was haughty and domineering, sometimes even brutal. These gorilla-men were trapped in rich ornaments, similar to those upon the body which now rested in a crotch of the tree behind the ape-man.

As Tarzan watched with interest the scene below him, two Bolgani emerged from the main entrance, a huge portal, some thirty feet in width, and perhaps fifteen feet high. The two wore head-bands, supporting tall, white feathers. As they emerged they took post on either side of the entrance, and cupping their hands before their mouths gave voice to a series of shrill cries that bore a marked resemblance to trumpet calls. Immediately the blacks ceased work and hastened to the foot of the stairs descending from the terrace to the garden. Here they formed lines on either side of the stairway, and similarly the Bolgani formed two lines upon the terrace from the main portal to the stairway, forming a living aisle from one to the other. Presently from the interior of the building came other trumpet-like calls, and a moment later Tarzan saw the head of a procession emerging. First came four Bolgani abreast, each bedecked with an ornate feather headdress, and each carrying a huge bludgeon erect before him. Behind these came two trumpeters, and twenty feet behind the trumpeters paced a huge, black-maned lion, held in leash by four sturdy blacks, two upon either side, holding what appeared to be golden chains that ran to a scintillant diamond collar about the beast's neck. Behind the lion marched twenty more Bolgani, four abreast. These carried spears, but whether they were for the purpose of protecting the lion from the people or the people from the lion Tarzan was at a loss to know.

The attitude of the Bolgani lining either side of the way between the portal and the stairway indicated extreme deference, for they bent their bodies from their waists in a profound bow while Numa was passing between their lines. When the beast reached the top of the stairway the procession halted, and immediately the Gomangani ranged below prostrated themselves and placed their foreheads on the ground. Numa, who was evidently an old lion, stood with lordly mien surveying the prostrate humans before him. His evil eyes glared glassily, the while he bared his tusks in a savage grimace, and from his deep lungs rumbled forth an ominous roar, at the sound of which the Gomangani trembled in unfeigned terror. The ape-man knit his brows in thought. Never before had he been called upon to witness so remarkable a scene of the abasement of man before a beast. Presently the procession continued upon its way descending the staircase and turning to the right along a path through the garden, and when it had passed them the Gomangani and the Bolgani arose and resumed their interrupted duties.

Tarzan remained in his concealment watching them, trying to discover some explanation for the strange, paradoxical conditions that he had witnessed. The lion, with his retinue, had turned the far corner of the palace and disappeared from sight. What was he to these people, to these strange creatures? What did he represent? Why this topsy-turvy arrangement of species? Here man ranked lower than the half-beast, and above all, from the deference that had been accorded him, stood a true beast—a savage carnivore.

He had been occupied with his thoughts and his observations for some fifteen minutes following the disappearance of Numa around the eastern end of the palace, when his attention was attracted to the opposite end of the structure by the sound of other shrill trumpet calls. Turning his eyes in that direction, he saw the procession emerging again into view, and proceeding toward the staircase down which they had entered the garden. Immediately the notes of the shrill call sounded upon their ears the Gomangani and the Bolgani resumed their original positions from below the foot of the staircase to the entrance to the palace, and once again was homage paid to Numa as he made his triumphal entry into the building.

Tarzan of the Apes ran his fingers through his mass of tousled hair, but finally he was forced to shake his head in defeat—he could find no explanation whatsoever for all that he had witnessed. His curiosity, however, was so keenly piqued that he determined to investigate the palace and surrounding grounds further before continuing on his way in search of a trail out of the valley.

Leaving the body of Bolgani where he had cached it, he started slowly to circle the building that he might examine it from all sides from the concealing foliage of the surrounding forest. He found the architecture equally unique upon all sides, and that the garden extended entirely around the building, though a portion upon the south side of the palace was given over to corrals and pens in which were kept numerous goats and a considerable flock of chickens. Upon this side, also, were several hundred swinging, beehive huts, such as he had seen in the native village of the Gomangani. These he took to be the quarters of the black slaves, who performed all the arduous and menial labor connected with the palace.

The lofty granite wall which surrounded the entire enclosure was pierced by but a single gate which opened opposite the east end of the palace. This gate was large and of massive construction, appearing to have been built to withstand the assault of numerous and well-armed forces. So strong did it appear that the ape-man could not but harbor the opinion that it had been constructed to protect the interior against forces equipped with heavy battering rams. That such a force had ever existed within the vicinity in historic times seemed most unlikely, and Tarzan conjectured, therefore, that the wall and the gate were of almost unthinkable antiquity, dating, doubtless, from the forgotten age of the Atlantians, and constructed, perhaps, to protect the builders of the Palace of Diamonds from the well-armed forces that had come from Atlantis to work the gold mines of Opar and to colonize central Africa.

While the wall, the gate, and the palace itself, suggested in many ways almost unbelievable age, yet they were in such an excellent state of repair that it was evident that they were still inhabited by rational and intelligent creatures; while upon the south side Tarzan had seen a new tower in process of construction, where a number of blacks working under the direction of Bolgani were cutting and shaping granite blocks and putting them in place.

Tarzan had halted in a tree near the east gate to watch the life passing in and out of the palace grounds beneath the ancient portal, and as he watched, a long cavalcade of powerful Gomangani emerged from the forest and entered the enclosure. Swung in hides between two poles, this party was carrying rough-hewn blocks of granite, four men to a block. Two or three Bolgani accompanied the long line of carriers, which was preceded and followed by a detachment of black warriors, armed with battle-axes and spears. The demeanor and attitude of the black porters, as well as of the Bolgani, suggested to the ape-man nothing more nor less than a caravan of donkeys, plodding their stupid way at the behest of their drivers. If one lagged he was prodded with the point of a spear or struck with its haft. There was no greater brutality shown than in the ordinary handling of beasts of burden the world around, nor in the demeanor of the blacks was there any more indication of objection or revolt than you see depicted upon the faces of a long line of burden-bearing mules; to all intents and purposes they were dumb, driven cattle. Slowly they filed through the gateway and disappeared from sight.

A few moments later another party came out of the forest and passed into the palace grounds. This consisted of fully fifty armed Bolgani and twice as many black warriors with spears and axes. Entirely surrounded by these armed creatures were four brawny porters, carrying a small litter, upon which was fastened an ornate chest about two feet wide by four feet long, with a depth of approximately two feet. The chest itself was of some dark, weather-worn wood, and was reinforced by bands and corners of what appeared to be virgin gold in which were set many diamonds. What the chest contained Tarzan could not, of course, conceive, but that it was considered of great value was evidenced by the precautions for safety with which it had been surrounded. The chest was borne directly into the huge, ivy-covered tower at the northeast corner of the palace, the entrance to which, Tarzan now first observed, was secured by doors as large and heavy as the east gate itself.

At the first opportunity that he could seize to accomplish it undiscovered, Tarzan swung across the jungle trail and continued through the trees to that one in which he had left the body of the Bolgani. Throwing this across his shoulder he returned to a point close above the trail near the east gate, and seizing upon a moment when there was a lull in the traffic he hurled the body as close to the portal as possible.

"Now," thought the ape-man, "let them guess who slew their fellow if they can."

Making his way toward the southeast, Tarzan approached the mountains which lie back of the Valley of the Palace of Diamonds. He had often to make detours to avoid native villages and to keep out of sight of the numerous parties of Bolgani that seemed to be moving in all directions through the forest. Late in the afternoon he came out of the hills into full view of the mountains beyond—rough, granite hills they were, whose precipitous peaks arose far above the timber line. Directly before him a well-marked trail led into a canyon, which he could see wound far upward toward the summit. This, then, would be as good a place to commence his investigations as another. And so, seeing that the coast was clear, the ape-man descended from the trees, and taking advantage of the underbrush bordering the trail, made his way silently, yet swiftly, into the hills. For the most part he was compelled to worm his way through thickets, for the trail was in constant use by Gomangani and Bolgani, parties passing up it empty-handed and, returning, bearing blocks of granite. As he advanced more deeply into the hills the heavy underbrush gave way to a lighter growth of scrub, through which he could pass with far greater ease though with considerable more risk of discovery. However, the instinct of the beast that dominated Tarzan's jungle craft permitted him to find cover where another would have been in full view of every enemy. Half way up the mountain the trail passed through a narrow gorge, not more than twenty feet wide and eroded from solid granite cliffs. Here there was no concealment whatsoever, and the ape-man realized that to enter it would mean almost immediate discovery. Glancing about, he saw that by making a slight detour he could reach the summit of the gorge, where, amid tumbled, granite boulders and stunted trees and shrubs, he knew that he could find sufficient concealment, and perhaps a plainer view of the trail beyond.

Nor was he mistaken, for, when he had reached a vantage point far above the trail, he saw ahead an open pocket in the mountain, the cliffs surrounding which were honeycombed with numerous openings, which, it seemed to Tarzan, could be naught else than the mouths of tunnels. Rough wooden ladders reached to some of them, closer to the base of the cliffs, while from others knotted ropes dangled to the ground below. Out of these tunnels emerged men carrying little sacks of earth, which they dumped in a common pile beside a rivulet which ran through the gorge. Here other blacks, supervised by Bolgani, were engaged in washing the dirt, but what they hoped to find or what they did find, Tarzan could not guess.

Along one side of the rocky basin many other blacks were engaged in quarrying the granite from the cliffs, which had been cut away through similar operations into a series of terraces running from the floor of the basin to the summit of the cliff. Here naked blacks toiled with primitive tools under the supervision of savage Bolgani. The activities of the quarrymen were obvious enough, but what the others were bringing from the mouths of the tunnels Tarzan could not be positive, though the natural assumption was that it was gold. Where, then, did they obtain their diamonds? Certainly not from these solid granite cliffs.

A few minutes' observation convinced Tarzan that the trail he had followed from the forest ended in this little cul-de-sac, and so he sought a way upward and around it, in search of a pass across the range.

The balance of that day and nearly all the next he devoted to his efforts in this direction, only in the end to be forced to admit that there was no egress from the valley upon this side. To points far above the timber line he made his way, but there, always, he came face to face with sheer, perpendicular cliffs of granite towering high above him, upon the face of which not even the ape-man could find foothold. Along the southern and eastern sides of the basin he carried his investigation, but with similar disappointing results, and then at last he turned his steps back toward the forest with the intention of seeking a way out through the valley of Opar with La, after darkness had fallen.

The sun had just risen when Tarzan arrived at the native village in which he had left La, and no sooner did his eyes rest upon it than he became apprehensive that something was amiss, for, not only was the gate wide open but there was no sign of life within the palisade, nor was there any movement of the swinging huts that would indicate that they were occupied. Always wary of ambush, Tarzan reconnoitered carefully before descending into the village. To his trained observation it became evident that the village had been deserted for at least twenty-four hours. Running to the hut in which La had been hidden he hastily ascended the rope and examined the interior—it was vacant, nor was there any sign of the High Priestess. Descending to the ground, the ape-man started to make a thorough investigation of the village in search of clews to the fate of its inhabitants and of La. He had examined the interiors of several huts when his keen eyes noted a slight movement of one of the swinging, cage-like habitations some distance from him. Quickly he crossed the intervening space, and as he approached the hut he saw that no rope trailed from its doorway. Halting beneath, Tarzan raised his face to the aperture, through which nothing but the roof of the hut was visible.

"Gomangani," he cried, "it is I, Tarzan of the Apes. Come to the opening and tell me what has become of your fellows and of my mate, whom I left here under the protection of your warriors."

There was no answer, and again Tarzan called, for he was positive that someone was hiding in the hut.

"Come down," he called again, "or I will come up after you."

Still there was no reply. A grim smile touched the ape-man's lips as he drew his hunting knife from its sheath and placed it between his teeth, and then, with a cat-like spring, leaped for the opening, and catching its sides, drew his body up into the interior of the hut.

If he had expected opposition, he met with none, nor in the dimly lighted interior could he at first distinguish any presence, though, when his eyes became accustomed to the semi-darkness, he descried a bundle of leaves and grasses lying against the opposite wall of the structure. Crossing to these he tore them aside revealing the huddled form of a terrified woman. Seizing her by a shoulder he drew her to a sitting position.

"What has happened?" he demanded. "Where are the villagers? Where is my mate?"

"Do not kill me! Do not kill me!" she cried. "It was not I. It was not my fault."

"I do not intend to kill you," replied Tarzan. "Tell me the truth and you shall be safe."

"The Bolgani have taken them away," cried the woman. "They came when the sun was low upon the day that you arrived, and they were very angry, for they had found the body of their fellow outside the gate of the Palace of Diamonds. They knew that he had come here to our village, and no one had seen him alive since he had departed from the palace. They came, then, and threatened and tortured our people, until at last the warriors told them all. I hid. I do not know why they did not find me. But at last they went away, taking all the others with them; taking your mate, too. They will never come back."

"You think that the Bolgani will kill them?" asked Tarzan.

"Yes," she replied, "they kill all who displease them."

Alone, now, and relieved of the responsibility of La, Tarzan might easily make his way by night through the valley of Opar and to safety beyond the barrier. But perhaps such a thought never entered his head. Gratitude and loyalty were marked characteristics of the ape-man. La had saved him from the fanaticism and intrigue of her people. She had saved him at a cost of all that was most dear to her, power and position, peace and safety. She had jeopardized her life for him, and become an exile from her own country. The mere fact then that the Bolgani had taken her with the possible intention of slaying her, was not sufficient for the ape-man. He must know whether or not she lived, and if she lived he must devote his every energy to winning her release and her eventual escape from the dangers of this valley.

Tarzan spent the day reconnoitering outside the palace grounds, seeking an opportunity of gaining entrance without detection, but this he found impossible inasmuch as there was never a moment that there were not Gomangani or Bolgani in the outer garden. But with the approach of darkness the great east gate was closed, and the inmates of the huts and palace withdrew within their walls, leaving not even a single sentinel without—a fact that indicated clearly that the Bolgani had no reason to apprehend an attack. The subjugation of the Gomangani, then, was apparently complete, and so the towering wall surrounding their palace, which was more than sufficient to protect them from the inroads of lions, was but the reminder of an ancient day when a once-powerful, but now vanished, enemy threatened their peace and safety.

When darkness had finally settled Tarzan approached the gate, and throwing the noose of his grass rope over one of the carved lions that capped the gate posts, ascended quickly to the summit of the wall, from where he dropped lightly into the garden below. To insure an avenue for quick escape in the event that he found La, he unlatched the heavy gates and swung them open. Then he crept stealthily toward the ivy-covered east tower, which he had chosen after a day of investigation as offering easiest ingress to the palace. The success of his plan hinged largely upon the age and strength of the ivy which grew almost to the summit of the tower, and, to his immense relief, he found that it would easily support his weight.

Far above the ground, near the summit of the tower, he had seen from the trees surrounding the palace an open window, which, unlike the balance of those in this part of the palace, was without bars. Dim lights shone from several of the tower windows, as from those of other parts of the palace. Avoiding these lighted apertures, Tarzan ascended quickly, though carefully, toward the unbarred window above, and as he reached it and cautiously raised his eyes above the level of the sill, he was delighted to find that it opened into an unlighted chamber, the interior of which, however, was so shrouded in darkness that he could discern nothing within. Drawing himself carefully to the level of the sill he crept quietly into the apartment beyond. Groping through the blackness, he cautiously made the rounds of the room, which he found to contain a carved bedstead of peculiar design, a table, and a couple of benches. Upon the bedstead were stuffs of woven material, thrown over the softly tanned pelts of antelopes and leopards.

Opposite the window through which he had entered was a closed door. This he opened slowly and silently, until, through a tiny aperture he could look out upon a dimly lighted corridor or circular hallway, in the center of which was an opening about four feet in diameter, passing through which and disappearing beyond a similar opening in the ceiling directly above was a straight pole with short crosspieces fastened to it at intervals of about a foot—quite evidently the primitive staircase which gave communication between the various floors of the tower. Three upright columns, set at equal intervals about the circumference of the circular opening in the center of the floor helped to support the ceiling above. Around the outside of this circular hallway there were other doors, similar to that opening into the apartment in which he was.

Hearing no noise and seeing no evidence of another than himself, Tarzan opened the door and stepped into the hallway. His nostrils were now assailed strongly by the same heavy fragrance of incense that had first greeted him upon his approach to the palace several days before. In the interior of the tower, however, it was much more powerful, practically obliterating all other odors, and placing upon the ape-man an almost prohibitive handicap in his search for La. In fact as he viewed the doors upon this single stage of the tower, he was filled with consternation at the prospect of the well-nigh impossible task that confronted him. To search this great tower alone, without any assistance whatever from his keen sense of scent, seemed impossible of accomplishment, if he were to take even the most ordinary precautions against detection.

The ape-man's self-confidence was in no measure blundering egotism. Knowing his limitations, he knew that he would have little or no chance against even a few Bolgani were he to be discovered within their palace, where all was familiar to them and strange to him. Behind him was the open window, and the silent jungle night, and freedom. Ahead danger, predestined failure; and, quite likely, death. Which should he choose? For a moment he stood in silent thought, and then, raising his head and squaring his great shoulders, he shook his black locks defiantly and stepped boldly toward the nearest door. Room after room he had investigated until he had made the entire circle of the landing, but in so far as La or any clew to her were concerned his search was fruitless. He found quaint furniture and rugs and tapestries, and ornaments of gold and diamonds, and in one dimly lighted chamber he came upon a sleeping Bolgani, but so silent were the movements of the ape-man that the sleeper slept on undisturbed, even though Tarzan passed entirely around his bed, which was set in the center of the chamber, and investigated a curtained alcove beyond.

Having completed the rounds of this floor, Tarzan determined to work upward first and then, returning, investigate the lower stages later. Pursuant to this plan, therefore, he ascended the strange stairway. Three landings he passed before he reached the upper floor of the tower. Circling each floor was a ring of doors, all of which were closed, while dimly lighting each landing were feebly burning cressets—shallow, golden bowls—containing what appeared to be tallow, in which floated a tow-like wick.

Upon the upper landing there were but three doors, all of which were closed. The ceiling of this hallway was the dome-like roof of the tower, in the center of which was another circular opening, through which the stairway protruded into the darkness of the night above.

As Tarzan opened the door nearest him it creaked upon its hinges, giving forth the first audible sound that had resulted from his investigations up to this point. The interior of the apartment before him was unlighted, and as Tarzan stood there in the entrance in statuesque silence for a few seconds following the creaking of the hinge, he was suddenly aware of movement—of the faintest shadow of a sound—behind him. Wheeling quickly he saw the figure of a man standing in an open doorway upon the opposite side of the landing.

THE GOLDEN INGOTS

Esteban Miranda had played the rôle of Tarzan of the Apes with the Waziri as his audience for less than twenty-four hours when he began to realize that, even with the lee-way that his supposedly injured brain gave him, it was going to be a very difficult thing to carry on the deception indefinitely. In the first place Usula did not seem at all pleased at the idea of merely taking the gold away from the intruders and then running from them. Nor did his fellow warriors seem any more enthusiastic over the plan than he. As a matter of fact they could not conceive that any number of bumps upon the head could render their Tarzan of the Apes a coward, and to run away from these west coast blacks and a handful of inexperienced whites seemed nothing less than cowardly.

Following all this, there had occurred in the afternoon that which finally decided the Spaniard that he was building for himself anything other than a bed of roses, and that the sooner he found an excuse for quitting the company of the Waziri the greater would be his life expectancy.

They were passing through rather open jungle at the time. The brush was not particularly heavy and the trees were at considerable distances apart, when suddenly, without warning, a rhinoceros charged them. To the consternation of the Waziri, Tarzan of the Apes turned and fled for the nearest tree the instant his eyes alighted upon charging Buto. In his haste Esteban tripped and fell, and when at last he reached the tree instead of leaping agilely into the lower branches, he attempted to shin up the huge bole as a schoolboy shins up a telegraph pole, only to slip and fall back again to the ground.

In the meantime Buto, who charges either by scent or hearing, rather than by eyesight, his powers of which are extremely poor, had been distracted from his original direction by one of the Waziri, and after missing the fellow had gone blundering on to disappear in the underbrush beyond.

When Esteban finally arose and discovered that the rhinoceros was gone, he saw surrounding him a semi-circle of huge blacks, upon whose faces were written expressions of pity and sorrow, not unmingled, in some instances, with a tinge of contempt. The Spaniard saw that he had been terrified into a practically irreparable blunder, yet he seized despairingly upon the only excuse he could conjure up.

"My poor head," he cried, pressing both palms to his temples.

"The blow was upon your head, Bwana," said Usula, "and your faithful Waziri thought that it was the heart of their master that knew no fear."

Esteban made no reply, and in silence they resumed their march. In silence they continued until they made camp before dark upon the bank of the river just above a waterfall. During the afternoon Esteban had evolved a plan of escape from his dilemma, and no sooner had he made camp than he ordered the Waziri to bury the treasure.

"We shall leave it here," he said, "and tomorrow we shall set forth in search of the thieves, for I have decided to punish them. They must be taught that they may not come into the jungle of Tarzan with impunity. It was only the injury to my head that prevented me from slaying them immediately I discovered their perfidy."

This attitude pleased the Waziri better. They commenced to see a ray of hope. Once again was Tarzan of the Apes becoming Tarzan. And so it was that with lighter hearts and a new cheerfulness they set forth the next morning in search of the camp of the Englishmen, and by shrewd guessing on Usula's part they cut across the jungle to intercept the probable line of march of the Europeans to such advantage that they came upon them just as they were making camp that night. Long before they reached them they smelled the smoke of their fires and heard the songs and chatter of the west coast carriers.

Then it was that Esteban gathered the Waziri about him. "My children," he said, addressing Usula in English, "these strangers have come here to wrong Tarzan. To Tarzan, then, belongs the vengeance. Go, therefore, and leave me to punish my enemies alone and in my own way. Return home, leave the gold where it is, for it will be a long time before I shall need it."

The Waziri were disappointed, for this new plan did not at all accord with their desires, which contemplated a cheerful massacre of the west coast blacks. But as yet the man before them was Tarzan, their big Bwana, to whom they had never failed in implicit obedience. For a few moments following Esteban's declaration of his intention, they stood in silence shifting uneasily, and then at last they commenced to speak to one another in Waziri. What they said the Spaniard did not know, but evidently they were urging something upon Usula, who presently turned toward him.

"Oh, Bwana," cried the black. "How can we return home to the Lady Jane and tell her that we left you injured and alone to face the rifles of the white men and their askari? Do not ask us to do it, Bwana. If you were yourself we should not fear for your safety, but since the injury to your head you have not been the same, and we fear to leave you alone in the jungle. Let us, then, your faithful Waziri, punish these people, after which we will take you home in safety, where you may be cured of the evils that have fallen upon you."

The Spaniard laughed. "I am entirely recovered," he said, "and I am in no more danger alone than I would be with you," which he knew, even better than they, was but a mild statement of the facts. "You will obey my wishes," he continued sternly. "Go back at once the way that we have come. After you have gone at least two miles you may make camp for the night, and in the morning start out again for home. Make no noise, I do not want them to know that I am here. Do not worry about me. I am all right, and I shall probably overtake you before you reach home. Go!"

Sorrowfully the Waziri turned back upon the trail they had just covered and a moment later the last of them disappeared from the sight of the Spaniard.

With a sigh of relief Esteban Miranda turned toward the camp of his own people. Fearing that to surprise them suddenly might invite a volley of shots from the askari he whistled, and then called aloud as he approached.

"It is Tarzan!" cried the first of the blacks who saw him. "Now indeed shall we all be killed."

Esteban saw the growing excitement among the carriers and askari—he saw the latter seize their rifles and that they were fingering the triggers nervously.

"It is I, Esteban Miranda," he called aloud. "Flora! Flora, tell those fools to lay aside their rifles."

The whites, too, were standing watching him, and at the sound of his voice Flora turned toward the blacks. "It is all right," she said, "that is not Tarzan. Lay aside your rifles."

Esteban entered the camp, smiling. "Here I am," he said.

"We thought that you were dead," said Kraski. "Some of these fellows said that Tarzan said that he had killed you."

"He captured me," said Esteban, "but as you see he did not kill me. I thought that he was going to, but he did not, and finally he turned me loose in the jungle. He may have thought that I could not survive and that he would accomplish his end just as surely without having my blood upon his hands."

"'E must have knowed you," said Peebles. "You'd die, all right, if you were left alone very long in the jungle—you'd starve to death."

Esteban made no reply to the sally but turned toward Flora. "Are you not glad to see me, Flora?" he asked.

The girl shrugged her shoulders. "What is the difference?" she asked. "Our expedition is a failure. Some of them think you were largely to blame." She nodded her head in the general direction of the other whites.

The Spaniard scowled. None of them cared very much to see him. He did not care about the others, but he had hoped that Flora would show some enthusiasm about his return. Well, if she had known what he had in his mind, she might have been happier to see him, and only too glad to show some kind of affection. But she did not know. She did not know that Esteban Miranda had hidden the golden ingots where he might go another day and get them. It had been his intention to persuade her to desert the others, and then, later, the two would return and recover the treasure, but now he was piqued and offended—none of them should have a shilling of it—he would wait until they left Africa and then he would return and take it all for himself. The only fly in the ointment was the thought that the Waziri knew the location of the treasure, and that, sooner or later, they would return with Tarzan and get it. This weak spot in his calculations must be strengthened, and to strengthen it he must have assistance which would mean sharing his secret with another, but whom?

Outwardly oblivious of the sullen glances of his companions he took his place among them. It was evident to him that they were far from being glad to see him, but just why he did not know, for he had not heard of the plan that Kraski and Owaza had hatched to steal the loot of the ivory raiders, and that their main objection to his presence was the fear that they would be compelled to share the loot with him. It was Kraski who first voiced the thought that was in the minds of all but Esteban.

"Miranda," he said, "it is the consensus of opinion that you and Bluber are largely responsible for the failure of our venture. We are not finding fault. I just mention it as a fact. But since you have been away we have struck upon a plan to take something out of Africa that will partially recompense us for the loss of the gold. We have worked the thing all out carefully and made our plans. We don't need you to carry them out. We have no objection to your coming along with us, if you want to, for company, but we want to have it understood from the beginning that you are not to share in anything that we get out of this."

The Spaniard smiled and waved a gesture of unconcern. "It is perfectly all right," he said. "I shall ask for nothing. I would not wish to take anything from any of you." And he grinned inwardly as he thought of the more than quarter of a million pounds in gold which he would one day take out of Africa for himself, alone.

At this unexpected attitude of acquiescence upon Esteban's part the others were greatly relieved, and immediately the entire atmosphere of constraint was removed.

"You're a good fellow, Esteban," said Peebles. "I've been sayin' right along that you'd want to do the right thing, and I want to say that I'm mighty glad to see you back here safe an' sound. I felt terrible when I 'eard you was croaked, that I did."

"Yes," said Bluber, "John he feel so bad he cry himself to sleep every night, ain't it, John?"

"Don't try to start nothin', Bluber," growled Peebles, glaring at the Jew.

"I vasn't commencing to start nodding," replied Adolph, seeing that the big Englishman was angry; "of course ve vere all sorry dat ve t'ought Esteban was killed und ve is all glad dot he is back."

"And that he don't want any of the swag," added Throck.

"Don't worry," said Esteban, "If I get back to London I'll be happy enough—I've had enough of Africa to last me all the rest of my life."

Before he could get to sleep that night, the Spaniard spent a wakeful hour or two trying to evolve a plan whereby he might secure the gold absolutely to himself, without fear of its being removed by the Waziri later. He knew that he could easily find the spot where he had buried it and remove it to another close by, provided that he could return immediately over the trail along which Usula had led them that day, and he could do this alone, insuring that no one but himself would know the new location of the hiding place of the gold, but he was equally positive that he could never again return later from the coast and find where he had hidden it. This meant that he must share his secret with another—one familiar with the country who could find the spot again at any time and from any direction. But who was there whom he might trust! In his mind he went carefully over the entire personnel of their safari, and continually his mind reverted to a single individual—Owaza. He had no confidence in the wily old scoundrel's integrity, but there was no other who suited his purpose as well, and finally he was forced to the conclusion that he must share his secret with this black, and depend upon avarice rather than honor for his protection. He could repay the fellow well—make him rich beyond his wildest dreams, and this the Spaniard could well afford to do in view of the tremendous fortune at stake. And so he fell asleep dreaming of what gold, to the value of over a quarter of a million pounds sterling, would accomplish in the gay capitals of the world.

The following morning while they were breakfasting Esteban mentioned casually that he had passed a large herd of antelope not far from their camp the previous day, and suggested that he take four or five men and do a little hunting, joining the balance of the party at camp that night. No one raised any objection, possibly for the reason that they assumed that the more he hunted and the further from the safari he went the greater the chances of his being killed, a contingency that none of them would have regretted, since at heart they had neither liking nor trust for him.

"I will take Owaza," he said. "He is the cleverest hunter of them all, and five or six men of his choosing." But later, when he approached Owaza, the black interposed objections to the hunt.

"We have plenty of meat for two days," he said. "Let us go on as fast as we can, away from the land of the Waziri and Tarzan. I can find plenty of game anywhere between here and the coast. March for two days, and then I will hunt with you."

"Listen," said Esteban, in a whisper. "It is more than antelope that I would hunt. I cannot tell you here in camp, but when we have left the others I will explain. It will pay you better to come with me today than all the ivory you can hope to get from the raiders." Owaza cocked an attentive ear and scratched his woolly head.

"It is a good day to hunt, Bwana," he said. "I will come with you and bring five boys."

After Owaza had planned the march for the main party and arranged for the camping place for the night, so that he and the Spaniard could find them again, the hunting party set out upon the trail that Usula had followed from the buried treasure the preceding day. They had not gone far before Owaza discovered the fresh spoor of the Waziri.

"Many men passed here late yesterday," he said to Esteban, eyeing the Spaniard quizzically.

"I saw nothing of them," replied the latter. "They must have come this way after I passed."

"They came almost to our camp, and then they turned about and went away again," said Owaza. "Listen, Bwana, I carry a rifle and you shall march ahead of me. If these tracks were made by your people, and you are leading me into ambush, you shall be the first to die."

"Listen, Owaza," said Esteban, "we are far enough from camp now so that I may tell you all. These tracks were made by the Waziri of Tarzan of the Apes, who buried the gold for me a day's march from here. I have sent them home, and I wish you to go back with me and move the gold to another hiding place. After these others have gotten their ivory and returned to England, you and I will come back and get the gold, and then, indeed, shall you be well rewarded."

"Who are you, then?" asked Owaza. "Often have I doubted that you are Tarzan of the Apes. The day that we left the camp outside of Opar one of my men told me that you had been poisoned by your own people and left in the camp. He said that he saw it with his own eyes—your body lying hidden behind some bushes—and yet you were with us upon the march that day. I thought that he lied to me, but I saw the consternation in his face when he saw you, and so I have often wondered if there were two Tarzans of the Apes."

"I am not Tarzan of the Apes," said Esteban. "It was Tarzan of the Apes who was poisoned in our camp by the others. But they only gave him something that would put him to sleep for a long time, possibly with the hope that he would be killed by wild animals before he awoke. Whether or not he still lives we do not know. Therefore you have nothing to fear from the Waziri or Tarzan on my account, Owaza, for I want to keep out of their way even more than you."

The black nodded. "Perhaps you speak the truth," he said, but still he walked behind, with his rifle always ready in his hand.

They went warily, for fear of overtaking the Waziri, but shortly after passing the spot where the latter had camped they saw that they had taken another route and that there was now no danger of coming in contact with them.

When they had reached a point within about a mile of the spot where the gold had been buried, Esteban told Owaza to have his boys remain there while they went ahead alone to effect the transfer of the ingots.

"The fewer who know of this," he said to the black, "the safer we shall be."

"The Bwana speaks words of wisdom," replied the wily black.

Esteban found the spot near the waterfall without difficulty, and upon questioning Owaza he discovered that the latter knew the location perfectly, and would have no difficulty in coming directly to it again from the coast. They transferred the gold but a short distance, concealing it in a heavy thicket near the edge of the river, knowing that it would be as safe from discovery there as though they had transported it a hundred miles, for the chances were extremely slight that the Waziri or anyone else who should learn of its original hiding place would imagine that anyone would go to the trouble of removing it but a matter of a hundred yards.

When they had finished Owaza looked at the sun.

"We will never reach camp tonight," he said, "and we will have to travel fast to overtake them even tomorrow."

"I did not expect to," replied Esteban, "but I could not tell them that. If we never find them again I shall be satisfied." Owaza grinned. In his crafty mind an idea was formed.

"Why," he thought, "risk death in a battle with the Arab ivory raiders on the chance of securing a few tusks, when all this gold awaits only transportation to the coast to be ours?"

A STRANGE, FLAT TOWER

Tarzan, turning, discovered the man standing behind him on the top level of the ivy-covered east tower of the Palace of Diamonds. His knife leaped from its sheath at the touch of his quick fingers. But almost simultaneously his hand dropped to his side, and he stood contemplating the other, with an expression of incredulity upon his face that but reflected a similar emotion registered upon the countenance of the stranger. For what Tarzan saw was no Bolgani, nor a Gomangani, but a white man, bald and old and shriveled, with a long, white beard—a white man, naked but for barbaric ornaments of gold spangles and diamonds.

"God!" exclaimed the strange apparition.

Tarzan eyed the other quizzically. That single English word opened up such tremendous possibilities for conjecture as baffled the mind of the ape-man.

"What are you? Who are you?" continued the old man, but this time in the dialect of the great apes.

"You used an English word a moment ago," said Tarzan. "Do you speak that language?" Tarzan himself spoke in English.

"Ah, dear God!" cried the old man, "that I should have lived to hear that sweet tongue again." And he, too, now spoke in English, halting English, as might one who was long unaccustomed to voicing the language.

"Who are you?" asked Tarzan, "and what are you doing here?"

"It is the same question that I asked you," replied the old man. "Do not be afraid to answer me. You are evidently an Englishman, and you have nothing to fear from me."

"I am here after a woman, captured by the Bolgani," replied Tarzan.

The other nodded. "Yes," he said, "I know. She is here."

"Is she safe?" asked Tarzan.

"She has not been harmed. She will be safe until tomorrow or the next day," replied the old man. "But who are you, and how did you find your way here from the outer world?"

"I am Tarzan of the Apes," replied the ape-man. "I came into this valley looking for a way out of the valley of Opar where the life of my companion was in danger. And you?"

"I am an old man," replied the other, "and I have been here ever since I was a boy. I was a stowaway on the ship that brought Stanley to Africa after the establishment of the station on Stanley Pool, and I came into the interior with him. I went out from camp to hunt, alone, one day. I lost my way and later was captured by unfriendly natives. They took me farther into the interior to their village from which I finally escaped, but so utterly confused and lost that I had no idea what direction to take to find a trail to the coast. I wandered thus for months, until finally, upon an accursed day I found an entrance to this valley. I do not know why they did not put me to death at once, but they did not, and later they discovered that my knowledge could be turned to advantage to them. Since then I have helped them in their quarrying and mining and in their diamond cutting. I have given them iron drills with hardened points and drills tipped with diamonds. Now I am practically one of them, but always in my heart has been the hope that some day I might escape from the valley—a hopeless hope, though, I may assure you."

"There is no way out?" asked Tarzan.

"There is a way, but it is always guarded."

"Where is it?" queried Tarzan.

"It is a continuation of one of the mine tunnels, passing entirely through the mountain to the valley beyond. The mines have been worked by the ancestors of this race for an almost incalculable length of time. The mountains are honeycombed with their shafts and tunnels. Back of the gold-bearing quartz lies an enormous deposit of altered peridotite, which contains diamonds, in the search for which it evidently became necessary to extend one of the shafts to the opposite side of the mountain, possibly for purposes of ventilation. This tunnel and the trail leading down into Opar are the only means of ingress to the valley. From time immemorial they have kept the tunnel guarded, more particularly, I imagine, to prevent the escape of slaves than to thwart the inroads of an enemy, since they believe that there is no fear of the latter emergency. The trail to Opar they do not guard, because they no longer fear the Oparians, and know quite well that none of their Gomangani slaves would dare enter the valley of the sunworshipers. For the same reason, then, that the slaves cannot escape, we, too, must remain prisoners here forever."

"How is the tunnel guarded?" asked Tarzan.

"Two Bolgani and a dozen or more Gomangani warriors are always upon duty there," replied the old man.

"The Gomangani would like to escape?"

"They have tried it many times in the past, I am told," replied the old man, "though never since I have lived here, and always they were caught and tortured. And all their race was punished and worked the harder because of these attempts upon the part of a few."

"They are numerous—the Gomangani?"

"There are probably five thousand of them in the valley," replied the old man.

"And how many Bolgani?" the ape-man asked.

"Between ten and eleven hundred."

"Five to one," murmured Tarzan, "and yet they are afraid to attempt to escape."

"But you must remember," said the old man, "that the Bolgani are the dominant and intelligent race—the others are intellectually little above the beasts of the forest."

"Yet they are men," Tarzan reminded him.

"In figure only," replied the old man. "They cannot band together as men do. They have not as yet reached the community plane of evolution. It is true that families reside in a single village, but that idea, together with their weapons, was given to them by the Bolgani that they might not be entirely exterminated by the lions and panthers. Formerly, I am told, each individual Gomangani, when he became old enough to hunt for himself, constructed a hut apart from others and took up his solitary life, there being at that time no slightest semblance of family life. Then the Bolgani taught them how to build palisaded villages and compelled the men and women to remain in them and rear their children to maturity, after which the children were required to remain in the village, so that now some of the communities can claim as many as forty or fifty people. But the death rate is high among them, and they cannot multiply as rapidly as people living under normal conditions of peace and security. The brutalities of the Bolgani kill many; the carnivora take a considerable toll."

"Five to one, and still they remain in slavery—what cowards they must be," said the ape-man.

"On the contrary, they are far from cowardly," replied the old man. "They will face a lion with the utmost bravery. But for so many ages have they been subservient to the will of the Bolgani, that it has become a fixed habit in them—as the fear of God is inherent in us, so is the fear of the Bolgani inherent in the minds of the Gomangani from birth."

"It is interesting," said Tarzan. "But tell me now where the woman is of whom I have come in search."

"She is your mate?" asked the old man.

"No," replied Tarzan. "I told the Gomangani that she was, so that they would protect her. She is La, queen of Opar, High Priestess of the Flaming God."

The old man looked his incredulity. "Impossible!" he cried. "It cannot be that the queen of Opar has risked her life by coming to the home of her hereditary enemies."

"She was forced to it," replied Tarzan, "her life being threatened by a part of her people because she had refused to sacrifice me to their god."

"If the Bolgani knew this there would be great rejoicing," replied the old man.

"Tell me where she is," demanded Tarzan. "She preserved me from her people, and I must save her from whatever fate the Bolgani contemplate for her."

"It is hopeless," said the old man. "I can tell you where she is, but you cannot rescue her."

"I can try," replied the ape-man.

"But you will fail and die."

"If what you tell me is true, that there is absolutely no chance of my escaping from the valley, I might as well die," replied the ape-man. "However, I do not agree with you."

The old man shrugged. "You do not know the Bolgani," he said.

"Tell me where the woman is," said Tarzan.

"Look," replied the old man, motioning Tarzan to follow him into his apartment, and approaching a window which faced toward the west, he pointed towards a strange flat tower which rose above the roof of the main building near the west end of the palace. "She is probably somewhere in the interior of that tower," said the old man to Tarzan, "but as far as you are concerned, she might as well be at the north pole."

Tarzan stood in silence for a moment, his keen eyes taking in every salient detail of the prospect before him. He saw the strange, flat-topped tower, which it seemed to him might be reached from the roof of the main building. He saw, too, branches of the ancient trees that sometimes topped the roof itself, and except for the dim light shining through some of the palace windows he saw no signs of life. He turned suddenly upon the old man.

"I do not know you," he said, "but I believe that I may trust you, since after all blood ties are strong, and we are the only men of our race in this valley. You might gain something in favor by betraying me, but I cannot believe that you will do it."

"Do not fear," said the old man, "I hate them. If I could help you I would, but I know that there is no hope of success for whatever plan you may have in mind—the woman will never be rescued; you will never leave the Valley of the Palace of Diamonds—you will never leave the palace itself unless the Bolgani wish it."

The ape-man grinned. "You have been here so long," he said, "that you are beginning to assume the attitude of mind that keeps the Gomangani in perpetual slavery. If you want to escape, come with me. We may not succeed, but at least you will have a better chance if you try than as if you remained forever in this tower."

The old man shook his head. "No," he said, "it is hopeless. If escape had been possible I should have been away from here long ago."

"Good-bye then," said Tarzan, and swinging out of the window he clambered toward the roof below, along the stout stem of the old ivy.

The old man watched him for a moment until he saw him make his way carefully across the roof toward the flat-topped tower where he hoped to find and liberate La. Then the old fellow turned and hurried rapidly down the crude stairway that rose ladder-like to the center of the tower.

Tarzan made his way across the uneven roof of the main building, clambering up the sides of its higher elevations and dropping again to its lower levels as he covered a considerable distance between the east tower and that flat-topped structure of peculiar design in which La was supposed to be incarcerated. His progress was slow, for he moved with the caution of a beast of prey, stopping often in dense shadows to listen.

When at last he reached the tower, he found that it had many openings letting upon the roof—openings which were closed only with hangings of the heavy tapestried stuff which he had seen in the tower. Drawing one of these slightly aside he looked within upon a large chamber, bare of furnishings, from the center of which there protruded through a circular aperture the top of a stairway similar to that he had ascended in the east tower. There was no one in sight within the chamber, and Tarzan crossed immediately to the stairway. Peering cautiously into the opening Tarzan saw that the stairway descended for a great distance, passing many floors. How far it went he could not judge, except it seemed likely that it pierced subterranean chambers beneath the palace. Sounds of life came up to him through the shaft, and odors, too, but the latter largely nullified, in so far as the scent impressions which they offered Tarzan were concerned, by the heavy incense which pervaded the entire palace.

It was this perfume that was to prove the ape-man's undoing, for otherwise his keen nostrils would have detected the scent of a near-by Gomangani. The fellow lay behind one of the hangings at an aperture in the tower wall. He had been lying in such a position that he had seen Tarzan enter the chamber, and he was watching him now as the ape-man stood looking down the shaft of the stairway. The eyes of the black had at first gone wide in terror at sight of this strange apparition, the like of which he had never seen before. Had the creature been of sufficient intelligence to harbor superstition, he would have thought Tarzan a god descended from above. But being of too low an order to possess any imagination whatsoever, he merely knew that he saw a strange creature, and that all strange creatures must be enemies, he was convinced. His duty was to apprise his masters of this presence in the palace, but he did not dare to move until the apparition had reached a sufficient distance from him to insure that the movements of the Gomangani would not be noticed by the intruder—he did not care to call attention to himself, for he had found that the more one effaced oneself in the presence of the Bolgani, the less one was likely to suffer. For a long time the stranger peered down the shaft of the stairway, and for a long time the Gomangani lay quietly watching him. But at last the former descended the stairs and passed out of sight of the watcher, who immediately leaped to his feet and scurried away across the roof of the palace toward a large tower arising at its western end.

As Tarzan descended the ladder the fumes of the incense became more and more annoying. Where otherwise he might have investigated quickly by scent he was now compelled to listen for every sound, and in many cases to investigate the chambers opening upon the central corridor by entering them. Where the doors were locked, he lay flat and listened close to the aperture at their base. On several occasions he risked calling La by name, but in no case did he receive any reply.

He had investigated four landings and was descending to the fifth when he saw standing in one of the doorways upon this level an evidently much excited and possibly terrified black. The fellow was of giant proportions and entirely unarmed. He stood looking at the ape-man with wide eyes as the latter jumped lightly from the stairway and stood facing him upon the same level.

"What do you want?" finally stammered the black. "Are you looking for the white she, your mate, whom the Bolgani took?"

"Yes," replied Tarzan. "What do you know of her?"

"I know where she is hidden," replied the black, "and if you will follow me I will lead you to her."

"Why do you offer to do this for me?" asked Tarzan, immediately suspicious. "Why is it that you do not go at once to your masters and tell them that I am here that they may send men to capture me?"

"I do not know the reason that I was sent to tell you this," replied the black. "The Bolgani sent me. I did not wish to come for I was afraid."

"Where did they tell you to lead me?" asked Tarzan.

"I am to lead you into a chamber, the door of which will be immediately bolted upon us. You will then be a prisoner."

"And you?" inquired Tarzan.

"I, too, shall be a prisoner with you. The Bolgani do not care what becomes of me. Perhaps you will kill me, but they do not care."

"If you lead me into a trap I shall kill you," replied Tarzan. "But if you lead me to the woman perhaps we shall all escape. You would like to escape, would you not?"

"I should like to escape, but I cannot."

"Have you ever tried?"

"No, I have not. Why should I try to do something that cannot be done?"

"If you lead me into the trap I shall surely kill you. If you lead me to the woman, you at least have the chance that I do to live. Which will you do?"

The black scratched his head in thought, the idea slowly filtering through his stupid mind. At last he spoke.

"You are very wise," he said. "I will lead you to the woman."

"Go ahead, then," said Tarzan, "and I will follow you."

The black descended to the next level and opening the door entered a long, straight corridor. As the ape-man followed his guide he had leisure to reflect upon the means through which the Bolgani had learned of his presence in the tower, and the only conclusion he could arrive at was that the old man had betrayed him, since in so far as Tarzan was aware he alone knew that the ape-man was in the palace. The corridor along which the black was leading him was very dark, receiving a dim and inadequate illumination from the dimly lighted corridor they had just left, the door into which remained open behind them. Presently the black stopped, before a closed door.

"The woman is in there," said the black, pointing to the door.

"She is alone?" asked Tarzan.

"No," replied the black. "Look," and he opened the door, revealing a heavy hanging, which he gently separated, revealing to Tarzan the interior of the chamber beyond.

Seizing the black by the wrist, that he might not escape, Tarzan stepped forward and put his eyes to the aperture. Before him lay a large chamber, at one end of which was a raised dais, the base of which was of a dark, ornately carved wood. The central figure upon this dais was a huge, black-maned lion—the same that Tarzan had seen escorted through the gardens of the palace. His golden chains were now fastened to rings in the floor, while the four blacks stood in statuesque rigidity, two upon either side of the beast. Upon golden thrones behind the lion sat three magnificently ornamented Bolgani. At the foot of the steps leading to the stair stood La, between two Gomangani guards. Upon either side of a central aisle were carved benches facing the dais, and occupying the front section of these were some fifty Bolgani, among whom Tarzan almost immediately espied the little, old man that he had met in the tower, the sight of whom instantly crystallized the ape-man's conviction of the source of his betrayal.

The chamber was lighted by hundreds of cressets, burning a substance which gave forth both light and the heavy incense that had assailed Tarzan's nostrils since first he entered the domain of the Bolgani. The long, cathedralesque windows upon one side of the apartment were thrown wide, admitting the soft air of the jungle summer night. Through them Tarzan could see the palace grounds and that this chamber was upon the same level as the terrace upon which the palace stood. Beyond those windows was an open gate-way to the jungle and freedom, but interposed between him and the windows were fifty armed gorilla-men. Perhaps, then, strategy would be a better weapon than force with which to carve his way to freedom with La. Yet to the forefront of his mind was evidently a belief in the probability that in the end it would be force rather than strategy upon which he must depend. He turned to the black at his side.

"Would the Gomangani guarding the lion like to escape from the Bolgani?" he asked.

"The Gomangani would all escape if they could," replied the black.

"If it is necessary for me to enter the room, then," said Tarzan to the black, "will you accompany me and tell the other Gomangani that if they will fight for me I will take them out of the valley?"

"I will tell them, but they will not believe," replied the black.

"Tell them that they will die if they do not help me, then," said Tarzan.

"I will tell them."

As Tarzan turned his attention again to the chamber before him he saw that the Bolgani occupying the central golden throne was speaking.

"Nobles of Numa, King of Beasts, Emperor of All Created Things," he said in deep, growling tones, "Numa has heard the words that this she has spoken, and it is the will of Numa that she die. The Great Emperor is hungry. He, himself, will devour her here in the presence of his Nobles and the Imperial Council of Three. It is the will of Numa."

A growl of approval arose from the beast-like audience, while the great lion bared his hideous fangs and roared until the palace trembled, his wicked, yellow-green eyes fixed terribly upon the woman before him, evidencing the fact that these ceremonies were of sufficient frequency to have accustomed the lion to what he might expect as the logical termination of them.

"Day after tomorrow," continued the speaker, "the mate of this creature, who is by this time safely imprisoned in the Tower of the Emperors, will be brought before Numa for judgment. Slaves," he cried suddenly in a loud voice, rising to his feet and glaring at the guards holding La, "drag the woman to your emperor."

Instantly the lion became frantic, lashing its tail and straining at its stout chains, roaring and snarling as it reared upon its hind feet and sought to leap upon La, who was now being forcibly conducted up the steps of the dais toward the bejeweled man-eater so impatiently awaiting her.

She did not cry out in terror, but she sought to twist herself free from the detaining hands of the powerful Gomangani—all futilely, however.

They had reached the last step, and were about to push La into the claws of the lion, when they were arrested by a loud cry from one side of the chamber—a cry that halted the Gomangani and brought the assembled Bolgani to their feet in astonishment and anger, for the sight that met their eyes was well qualified to arouse the latter within them. Leaping into the room with raised spear was the almost naked white man of whom they had heard, but whom none of them had as yet seen. And so quick was he that in the very instant of entry—even before they could rise to their feet—he had launched his spear.

THE CHAMBER OF HORRORS

A black-maned lion moved through the jungle night. With majestic unconcern for all other created things he took his lordly way through the primeval forest. He was not hunting, for he made no efforts toward stealth, nor, on the other hand, did he utter any vocal sound. He moved swiftly, though sometimes stopping with uplifted nose to scent the air and to listen. And thus at last he came to a high wall, along the face of which he sniffed, until the wall was broken by a half-opened gateway, through which he passed into the enclosure.

Before him loomed a great building, and presently as he stood watching it and listening, there broke from the interior the thunderous roar of an angry lion.

He of the black mane cocked his head upon one side and moved stealthily forward.

At the very instant that La was about to be thrust into the clutches of Numa, Tarzan of the Apes leaped into the apartment with a loud cry that brought to momentary pause the Gomangani that were dragging her to her doom, and in that brief instant of respite which the ape-man knew would follow his interruption the swift spear was launched. To the rage and consternation of the Bolgani they saw it bury itself in the heart of their Emperor—the great, black-maned lion.

At Tarzan's side stood the Gomangani whom he had terrified into service, and as Tarzan rushed forward toward La the black accompanied him, crying to his fellows that if they would help this stranger they might be free and escape from the Bolgani forever.

"You have permitted the great Emperor to be slain," he cried to the poor Gomangani who guarded Numa. "For this the Bolgani will kill you. Help to save the strange Tarmangani and his mate and you have at least a chance for life and freedom. And you," he added, addressing the two who had been guarding La, "they will hold you responsible also—your only hope lies with us."

Tarzan had reached La's side and was dragging her up the steps of the dais where he hoped that he might make a momentary stand against the fifty Bolgani who were now rushing forward from their seats toward him.

"Slay the three who sit upon the dais," cried Tarzan to the Gomangani, who were now evidently hesitating as to which side they would cast their lot with. "Slay them if you wish your freedom! Slay them if you wish to live!"

The authoritative tones of his voice, the magnetic appeal of his personality, his natural leadership won them to him for the brief instant that was necessary to turn them upon the hated authority that the three Bolgani upon the dais represented, and as they drove their spears into the shaggy black bodies of their masters they became then and forever the creatures of Tarzan of the Apes, for there could be no future hope for them in the land of the Bolgani.

With one arm around La's waist the ape-man carried her to the summit of the dais, where he seized his spear and drew it from the body of the dead lion. Then, turning about, and facing the advancing Bolgani, he placed one foot upon the carcass of his kill and raised his voice in the terrifying victory cry of the apes of Kerchak.

Before him the Bolgani paused, behind him the Gomangani quailed in terror.

"Stop!" cried Tarzan, raising a palm toward the Bolgani. "Listen! I am Tarzan of the Apes. I sought no quarrel with your people. I but look for a passage through your country to my own. Let me go my way in peace with this woman, taking these Gomangani with me."

For answer a chorus of savage growls arose from the Bolgani as they started forward again toward the dais. From their ranks there suddenly leaped the old man of the east tower, who ran swiftly toward Tarzan.

"Ah, traitor," cried the ape-man, "you would be the first, then, to taste the wrath of Tarzan?" He spoke in English and the old man replied ill the same tongue.

"Traitor?" he exclaimed in surprise.

"Yes, traitor," thundered Tarzan. "Did you not hurry here to tell the Bolgani that I was in the palace, that they might send the Gomangani to lure me to a trap?"

"I did nothing of the kind," replied the other. "I came here to place myself near the white woman, with the thought that I might be of service to her or you if I were needed. I come now, Englishman, to stand at your side and die at your side, for die you shall, as sure as there is a God in heaven. Nothing can save you now from the wrath of the Bolgani whose Emperor you have killed."

"Come, then," cried Tarzan, "and prove your loyalty. It were better to die now than to live in slavery forever."

The six Gomangani had ranged themselves, three upon either side of Tarzan and La, while the seventh, who had entered the chamber with Tarzan unarmed, was taking weapons from the body of one of the three Bolgani who had been slain upon the dais.

Before this array of force so new to them, the Bolgani paused at the foot of the steps leading to the dais. But only for a moment they paused, for there were but nine against fifty, and as they surged up the steps, Tarzan and his Gomangani met them with battle-ax, and spear, and bludgeon. For a moment they pressed them back, but the numbers against them were too great, and once again a wave swept up that seemed likely to overwhelm them, when there broke upon the ears of the contestants a frightful roar, which, coming from almost at their sides, brought a sudden, momentary cessation of the battle.

Turning their eyes in the direction of the sound they saw a huge, black-maned lion standing upon the floor of the apartment, just within one of the windows. For an instant he stood like a statue of golden bronze, and then again the building trembled to the reverberations of his mighty roar.

Towering above them all Tarzan of the Apes looked down from the dais upon the great beast below him, and then in quick elation he raised his voice above the growlings of the Bolgani.

"Jad-bal-ja," he cried, and pointing toward the Bolgani, "Kill! Kill!"

Scarcely had the words been uttered ere the huge monster, a veritable devil incarnate, was upon the hairy gorilla-men. And simultaneously there occurred to the mind of the ape-man a daring plan of salvation for himself and the others who were dependent upon him.

"Quick," he cried to the Gomangani, "fall upon the Bolgani. Here at last is the true Numa, King of Beasts, and ruler of all creation. He slays his enemies but he will protect Tarzan of the Apes and the Gomangani, who are his friends."

Seeing their hated masters falling back before the terrific onslaughts of the lion, the Gomangani rushed in with battle-axes and clubs, while Tarzan, casting aside his spear, took his place among them with drawn knife, and, keeping close to Jad-bal-ja, directed the lion from one victim to another, lest he fall by mistake upon the Gomangani or the little, old, white man, or even La, herself. Twenty of the Bolgani lay dead upon the floor before the balance managed to escape from the chamber, and then Tarzan, turning to Jad-bal-ja, called him to heel.

"Go!" he said, turning toward the Gomangani, "and drag the body of the false Numa from the dais. Remove it from the room, for the true Emperor has come to claim his throne."

The old man and La were eyeing Tarzan and the lion in amazement.

"Who are you," asked the former, "that you can work such miracles with a savage beast of the jungle? Who are you, and what do you intend to do?"

"Wait and see," said Tarzan with a grim smile. "I think that we shall all be safe now, and that the Gomangani may live in comfort for a long time hereafter."

When the blacks had removed the carcass of the lion from the dais and thrown it from one of the windows of the chamber, Tarzan sent Jad-bal-ja to sit in the place upon the dais that had formerly been occupied by the lion, Numa.

"There," he said, turning to the Gomangani, "you see the true Emperor, who does not have to be chained to his throne. Three of you will go to the huts of your people behind the palace and summon them to the throne room, that they, too, may see what has transpired. Hurry, that we may have many warriors here before the Bolgani return in force."

Filled with an excitement which almost shook their dull minds into a semblance of intelligence three of the Gomangani hastened to do Tarzan's bidding, while the others stood gazing at Tarzan with expressions of such awe that might only be engendered by the sight of deity. La came then and stood beside Tarzan, looking up into his face with eyes that reflected a reverence fully as deep as that held by the blacks.

"I have not thanked you, Tarzan of the Apes," she said, "for what you have risked and done for me. I know that you must have come here in search of me, to save me from these creatures, and I know that it was not love that impelled you to this heroic and well-nigh hopeless act. That you have succeeded thus far is little short of miraculous, but I, in the legends of whose people are recounted the exploits of the Bolgani, know that there can be no hope of eventual escape for us all, and so I beseech that you go at once and make good your escape alone, if possible, for you alone of us have any possible chance of escape."

"I do not agree with you that we have no chance to escape, La," replied the ape-man. "It seems to me that now we not only have every reason to believe that we are practically assured of escape, but that we may insure also to these poor Gomangani freedom from slavery and from the tyranny of the Bolgani. But this is not all. With this I shall not be satisfied. Not only must these people who show no hospitality to strangers be punished, but your own disloyal priests as well. To this latter end I intend to march out of the Valley of the Palace of Diamonds, down upon the city of Opar with a force of Gomangani sufficient to compel Cadj to relinquish the power he has usurped and replace you upon the throne of Opar. Nothing less than this shall satisfy me, and nothing less than this shall I accomplish before I leave."

"You are a brave man," said the old man, "and you have succeeded beyond what I thought could be possible, but La is right, you do not know the ferocity or the resources of the Bolgani, or the power which they wield over the Gomangani. Could you raise from the stupid minds of the blacks the incubus of fear that rests so heavily upon them you might win over a sufficient number to make good your escape from the valley, but that, I fear, is beyond even you. Our only hope, therefore, is to escape from the palace while they are momentarily disorganized, and trust to fleetness and to luck to carry us beyond the limits of the valley before we are apprehended."

"See," cried La, pointing; "even now it is too late—they return."

Tarzan looked in the direction that she indicated and saw through the open doorway at the far end of the chamber a large number of gorilla-men approaching. His eyes moved swiftly to the windows in the other wall. "But wait," he said, "behold another factor in the equation!"

The others looked toward the windows which opened upon the terrace, and they saw beyond them what appeared to be a crowd of several hundred blacks running rapidly toward the windows. The other blacks upon the dais cried out excitedly: "They come! They come! We shall be free, and no longer shall the Bolgani be able to make us work until we drop from exhaustion, or beat us, or torture us, or feed us to Numa."

As the first of the Bolgani reached the doorway leading into the chamber, the Gomangani commenced to pour through the several windows in the opposite wall. They were led by the three who had been sent to fetch them, and to such good effect had these carried their message that the blacks already seemed like a new people, so transfigured were they by the thought of immediate freedom. At sight of them the leader of the Bolgani cried aloud for them to seize the intruders upon the dais, but his answer was a spear hurled by the nearest black, and as he lunged forward, dead, the battle was on.

The Bolgani in the palace greatly outnumbered the blacks, but the latter had the advantage of holding the interior of the throne room in sufficient numbers to prevent the entry of many Bolgani simultaneously. Tarzan, immediately he recognized the temper of the blacks, called Jad-bal-ja to follow him, and, descending from the dais, he took command of the Gomangani. At each opening he placed sufficient men to guard it, and at the center of the room he held the balance in reserve. Then he called the old man into consultation.

"The gate in the east wall is open," he said. "I left it so when I entered. Would it be possible for twenty or thirty blacks to reach it in safety and, entering the forest, carry word to the villagers of what is transpiring here in the palace, and prevail upon them to send all of their warriors immediately to complete the work of emancipation that we have begun?"

"It is an excellent plan," replied the old man. "The Bolgani are not upon that side of the palace between us and the gate, and if it may ever be accomplished, now is the time. I will pick your men for you. They must be head-men, whose words will carry some weight with the villagers outside the palace walls."

"Good!" exclaimed Tarzan. "Select them immediately; tell them what we want and urge upon them the necessity for haste."

One by one the old man chose thirty warriors, whose duty he carefully explained to each. They were delighted with the plan and assured Tarzan that in less than an hour the first of the reinforcements would come.

"As you leave the enclosure," said the ape-man, "destroy the lock if you can, so that the Bolgani may not lock it again and bar out our reinforcements. Carry also the word that the first who come are to remain outside the wall until a sufficient number have arrived to make entry into the palace grounds reasonably safe—at least as many as are within this room now."

The blacks signified their understanding, and a moment later passed out of the room through one of the windows and disappeared into the darkness of the night beyond.

Shortly after the blacks had left the Bolgani made a determined rush upon the Gomangani guarding the main entrance to the throne room, with the result that a score or more of the gorilla-men succeeded in cutting their way into the room. At this first indication of reversal the blacks showed signs of faltering, the fear of the Bolgani that was inherent in them showing in their wavering attitude and seeming reluctance to force a counter attack. As Tarzan leaped forward to assist in checking the rush of the Bolgani into the throne room he called to Jad-bal-ja, and as the great lion leaped from the dais the ape-man, pointing to the nearest Bolgani, cried: "Kill! Kill!"

Straight for the throat of the nearest leaped Jad-bal-ja. The great jaws closed upon the snarling face of the frightened gorilla-man but once, and then, at the command of his master the golden lion dropped the carcass after a single shake and leaped upon another. Three had died thus in quick succession when the balance of the Bolgani turned to flee this chamber of horrors; but the Gomangani, their confidence restored by the ease with which this fierce ally brought death and terror to the tyrants, interposed themselves between the Bolgani and the doorway, shutting off their retreat.

"Hold them! Hold them!" cried Tarzan. "Do not kill them!" And then to the Bolgani: "Surrender and you will not be harmed!"

Jad-bal-ja clung close to the side of his master, glaring and growling at the Bolgani, and casting an occasional beseeching look at the ape-man which said plainer than words, "Send me among them."

Fifteen of the Bolgani who had entered the room survived. For a moment they hesitated, and then one of them threw his weapons upon the floor. Immediately the others followed suit.

Tarzan turned toward Jad-bal-ja. "Back!" he said, pointing toward the dais, and as the lion wheeled and slunk away toward the platform, Tarzan turned again toward the Bolgani.

"Let one of your number go," he said, "and announce to your fellows that I demand their immediate surrender."

The Bolgani whispered among themselves for a few moments and finally one of them announced that he would go and see the others. After he had left the room the old man approached Tarzan.

"They will never surrender," he said. "Look out for treachery."

"It is all right," said Tarzan. "I am expecting that, but I am gaining time, and that is what we need most. If there were a place near where I might confine these others I should feel better, for it would cut down our antagonists by at least that many."

"There is a room there," said the old man, pointing toward one of the doorways in the throne room, "where you can confine them—there are many such rooms in the Tower of the Emperors."

"Good," said Tarzan, and a moment later, following his instructions the Bolgani were safely locked in a room adjoining the throne room. In the corridors without they could hear the main body of the gorilla-men in argument. It was evident that they were discussing the message sent to them by Tarzan. Fifteen minutes passed, and finally thirty, with no word from the Bolgani and no resumption of hostilities, and then there came to the main entrance of the throne room the fellow whom Tarzan had despatched with his demand for surrender.

"Well," asked the ape-man, "what is their answer?"

"They will not surrender," replied the Bolgani, "but they will permit you to leave the valley provided that you will release those whom you have taken prisoner and harm no others."

The ape-man shook his head. "That will not do," he replied. "I hold the power to crush the Bolgani of the Valley of Diamonds. Look," and he pointed toward Jad-bal-ja, "here is the true Numa. The creature you had upon your throne was but a wild beast, but this is Numa, King of Beasts, Emperor of All Created Things. Look at him. Must he be held in leash by golden chains like some prisoner or slave? No! He is indeed an Emperor. But there is one yet greater than he, one from whom he takes commands. And that one is I, Tarzan of the Apes. Anger me and you shall feel not only the wrath of Numa, but the wrath of Tarzan, as well. The Gomangani are my people, the Bolgani shall be my slaves. Go and tell your fellows that, and that if they would live at all they had best come soon and sue for mercy. Go!"

When the messenger had again departed Tarzan looked at the old man, who was eyeing him with an expression which might have denoted either awe or reverence, were it not for the vaguest hint of a twinkle in the corners of the eyes. The ape-man breathed a deep sigh of relief. "That will give us at least another half hour," he said.

"We shall need it, and more, too," replied the old man, "though, at that, you have accomplished more than I had thought possible, for at least you have put a doubt in the minds of the Bolgani, who never before have had cause to question their own power."

Presently from the outer corridors the sounds of argument and discussion gave place to that of movement among the Bolgani. A company, comprising some fifty of the gorilla-men, took post directly outside the main entrance of the throne room where they stood in silence, their weapons ready, as though for the purpose of disputing any effort upon the part of the inmates of the room to escape. Beyond them the balance of the gorilla-men could be seen moving away and disappearing through doorways and corridors leading from the main hallway of the palace. The Gomangani, together with La and the old man, watched impatiently for the coming of the black reinforcements, while Tarzan sat upon the edge of the dais half-reclining, with an arm about the neck of Jad-bal-ja.

"They are up to something," said the old man. "We must watch carefully against a surprise. If the blacks would but come now, while the doorway is held by only fifty, we should overcome them easily, and have, I do verily believe, some slight chance of escaping from the palace grounds."

"Your long residence here," said Tarzan, "has filled you with the same senseless fear of the Bolgani that the Gomangani hold. From the attitude of mind which you hold toward them one would think them some manner of supermen—they are only beasts, my friend, and if we remain loyal to our cause we shall overcome them."

"Beasts they may be," replied the old man, "but they are beasts with the brains of men—their cunning and their cruelty are diabolical."

A long silence ensued, broken only by the nervous whisperings of the Gomangani, whose morale, it was evident, was slowly disintegrating under the nervous strain of the enforced wait, and the failure of their fellows of the forest to come quickly to their aid. To this was added the demoralizing effect of speculation upon what the Bolgani were planning or what plan they already were putting into effect. The very silence of the gorilla-men was more terrible than the din of actual assault. La was the first of the whites to break the silence.

"If thirty of the Gomangani could leave the palace so easily, why might not we leave also?" she asked.

"There were two reasons," replied Tarzan. "One was that should we have left simultaneously the Bolgani, greatly outnumbering us as they did, could have harassed us and detained us for a sufficient length of time to have permitted their messengers to reach the villagers ahead of us, with the result that in a short time we should have been surrounded by thousands of hostile warriors. The second reason is that I desire to punish the creatures, so that in future a stranger may be safe in the Valley of the Palace of Diamonds." He paused. "And now I shall give you a third reason why we may not seek to escape at this moment." He pointed toward the windows overlooking the terrace. "Look," he said, "the terrace and the gardens are filled with Bolgani. Whatever their plan I think its success depends upon our attempt to escape from this room through the windows, for, unless I am mistaken, the Bolgani upon the terrace and in the gardens are making an attempt to hide themselves from us."

The old man walked to a part of the room from which he could see the greater part of the terrace and gardens upon which the windows of the throne room looked.

"You are right," he said when he returned to the ape-man's side; "the Bolgani are all massed outside these windows with the exception of those who guard the entrance, and possibly some others at the doorways at other portions of the throne room. That, however, we must determine." He walked quickly to the opposite side of the chamber and drew back the hangings before one of the apertures, disclosing beyond a small band of Bolgani. They stood there motionless, not making any effort to seize or harm him. To another exit, and another, he went, and beyond each discovered to the occupants of the chamber the same silent gorilla guardians. He made the circle of the room, passing over the dais behind the three thrones, and then he came back to Tarzan and La.

"It is as I suspected," he said, "we are entirely surrounded. Unless help comes soon we are lost."

"But their force is divided," Tarzan reminded him.

"Even so, it is sufficient to account for us," replied the old man.

"Perhaps you are right," said Tarzan, "but at least we shall have a bully fight."

"What is that!" exclaimed La, and simultaneously, attracted by the same noise, the inmates of the throne room raised their eyes to the ceiling above them, where they saw that traps had been lifted from a dozen openings, revealing the scowling faces of several score of gorilla-men.

"What are they up to now!" exclaimed Tarzan, and as though in answer to the query the Bolgani above began hurling bundles of burning, oil-soaked rags, tied in goat skins, into the throne room, which immediately commenced to fill it with a thick, suffocating smoke, accompanied by the stench of burning hide and hair.

THE MAP OF BLOOD

After Esteban and Owaza had buried the gold they returned to the spot where they had left their five boys, and proceeding with them to the river made camp for the night. Here they discussed their plans, deciding to abandon the balance of the party to reach the coast as best they might, while they returned to another section of the coast where they could recruit sufficient porters to carry out the gold.

"Instead of going way back to the coast for porters," asked Esteban, "why could we not just as well recruit them from the nearest village?"

"Such men would not go with us way to the coast," replied Owaza. "They are not porters. At best they would but carry our gold to the next village."

"Why not that, then?" inquired the Spaniard. "And at the next village we could employ porters to carry us on still farther, until we could employ other men to continue on with us."

Owaza shook his head. "It is a good plan, Bwana, but we cannot do it, because we have nothing with which to pay our porters."

Esteban scratched his head. "You are right," he said, "but it would save us that damnable trip to the coast and return." They sat for some moments in silence, thinking. "I have it!" at last exclaimed the Spaniard. "Even if we had the porters now we could not go directly to the coast for fear of meeting Flora Hawkes's party—we must let them get out of Africa before we take the gold to the coast. Two months will be none too long to wait, for they are going to have a devil of a time getting to the coast at all with that bunch of mutinous porters. While we are waiting, therefore, let us take one of the ingots of gold to the nearest point at which we can dispose of it for trade goods. Then we can return and hire porters to carry it from village to village."

"The Bwana speaks words of wisdom," replied Owaza. "It is not as far to the nearest trading post as it is back to the coast, and thus we shall not only save time, but also many long, hard marches."

"In the morning, then, we shall return and unearth one of the ingots, but we must be sure that none of your men accompanies us, for no one must know until it is absolutely necessary where the gold is buried. When we return for it, of course, then others must know, too, but inasmuch as we shall be with it constantly thereafter there will be little danger of its being taken from us."

And so upon the following morning the Spaniard and Owaza returned to the buried treasure, where they unearthed a single ingot.

Before he left the spot the Spaniard drew upon the inner surface of the leopard skin that he wore across his shoulder an accurate map of the location of the treasure, making the drawing with a sharpened stick, dipped in the blood of a small rodent he had killed for the purpose. From Owaza he obtained the native names of the river and of such landmarks as were visible from the spot at which the treasure was buried, together with as explicit directions as possible for reaching the place from the coast. This information, too, he wrote below the map, and when he had finished he felt much relieved from the fear that should aught befall Owaza he might never be able to locate the gold.

*

When Jane Clayton reached the coast to take passage for London she found awaiting her a wire stating that her father was entirely out of danger, and that there was no necessity for her coming to him. She, therefore, after a few days of rest, turned her face again toward home, and commenced to retrace the steps of the long, hot, weary journey that she had just completed. When, finally, she arrived at the bungalow she learned, to her consternation, that Tarzan of the Apes had not yet returned from his expedition to the city of Opar after the gold from the treasure vaults. She found Korak, evidently much exercised, but unwilling to voice a doubt as to the ability of his father to care for himself. She learned of the escape of the golden lion with regret, for she knew that Tarzan had become much attached to the noble beast.

It was the second day after her return that the Waziri who had accompanied Tarzan returned without him. Then, indeed, was her heart filled with fear for her lord and master. She questioned the men carefully, and when she learned from them that Tarzan had suffered another accident that had again affected his memory, she immediately announced that she would set out on the following day in search of him, commanding the Waziri who had just returned to accompany her.

Korak attempted to dissuade her, but failing in that insisted upon accompanying her.

"We must not all be away at once," she said. "You remain here, my son. If I fail I shall return and let you go."

"I cannot let you go alone, Mother," replied Korak.

"I am not alone when the Waziri are with me," she laughed. "And you know perfectly well, boy, that I am as safe anywhere in the heart of Africa with them as I am here at the ranch."

"Yes, yes, I suppose so," he replied, "but I wish I might go, or that Meriem were here."

"Yes, I, too, wish that Meriem were here," replied Lady Greystoke. "However, do not worry. You know that my jungle-craft, while not equal to that of Tarzan or Korak, is by no means a poor asset, and that, surrounded by the loyalty and bravery of the Waziri, I shall be safe."

"I suppose you are right," replied Korak, "but I do not like to see you go without me."

And so, notwithstanding his objections, Jane Clayton set out the next morning with fifty Waziri warriors in search of her savage mate.

*

When Esteban and Owaza had not returned to camp as they had promised, the other members of the party were at first inclined to anger, which was later replaced by concern, not so much for the safety of the Spaniard but for fear that Owaza might have met with an accident and would not return to take them in safety to the coast, for of all the blacks he alone seemed competent to handle the surly and mutinous carriers. The negroes scouted the idea that Owaza had become lost and were more inclined to the opinion that he and Esteban had deliberately deserted them. Luvini, who acted as head-man in Owaza's absence, had a theory of his own.

"Owaza and the Bwana have gone after the ivory raiders alone. By trickery they may accomplish as much as we could have accomplished by force, and there will only be two among whom to divide the ivory."

"But how may two men overcome a band of raiders?" inquired Flora, skeptically.

"You do not know Owaza," answered Luvini. "If he can gain the ears of their slaves he will win them over, and when the Arabs see that he who accompanies Owaza and who fights at the head of the mutinous slaves is Tarzan of the Apes, they will flee in terror."

"I believe he is right," muttered Kraski, "it sounds just like the Spaniard," and then suddenly he turned upon Luvini. "Can you lead us to the raiders' camp?" he demanded.

"Yes," replied the negro.

"Good," exclaimed Kraski; "and now, Flora, what do you think of this plan? Let us send a swift runner to the raiders, warning them against Owaza and the Spaniard, and telling them that the latter is not Tarzan of the Apes, but an impostor. We can ask them to capture and hold the two until we come, and after we arrive we can make such further plans as the circumstances permit. Very possibly we can carry out our original design after we have once entered their camp as friends."

"Yes, that sounds good," replied Flora, "and it is certainly crooked enough—just like you, yourself."

The Russian blushed. "'Birds of a feather'—" he quoted.

The girl shrugged her shoulders indifferently, but Bluber, who, with Peebles and Throck, had been silent listeners to the conversation, blustered.

"Vot do you mean birds vit fedders?" he demanded. "Who vas a crook? I tell you, Mister Carl Kraski, I am an honest man, dot is von t'ing dot no man don't say about Adolph Bluber, he is a crook."

"O shut up," snapped Kraski, "if there's anything in it you'll be for it—if there's no risk. These fellows stole the ivory themselves, and killed a lot of people, probably, to do it. In addition they have taken slaves, which we will free."

"O vell," said Bluber, "if it is fair und eqvitable, vy, all right, but just remember, Mister Kraski, dot I am an honest man."

"Blime!" exclaimed Throck, "we're all honest; I've never seen such a downy bunch of parsons in all me life."

"Sure we're honest," roared John Peebles, "and anyone 'at says we ain't gets 'is bally 'ead knocked off, and 'ere we are, 'n that's that."

The girl smiled wearily. "You can always tell honest men," she said. "They go around telling the world how honest they are. But never mind that; the thing now is to decide whether we want to follow Kraski's suggestion or not. It's something we've got all pretty well to agree upon before we undertake it. There are five of us. Let's leave it to a vote. Do we, or don't we?"

"Will the men accompany us?" asked Kraski, turning to Luvini.

"If they are promised a share of the ivory they will," replied the black.

"How many are in favor of Carl's plan?" asked Flora.

They were unanimously for it, and so it was decided that they would undertake the venture, and a half hour later a runner was despatched on the trail to the raiders' camp with a message for the raider chief. Shortly after, the party broke camp and took up its march in the same direction.

A week later, when they reached the camp of the raiders they found that their messenger had arrived safely and that they were expected. Esteban and Owaza had not put in an appearance nor had anything been seen or heard of them in the vicinity. The result was that the Arabs were inclined to be suspicious and surly, fearing that the message: brought to them had been but a ruse to permit this considerable body of whites and armed blacks to enter their stockade in safety.

Jane Clayton and her Waziri moving rapidly, picked up the spoor of Flora Hawkes's safari at the camp where the Waziri had last seen Esteban, whom they still thought to have been Tarzan of the Apes. Following the plainly marked trail, and moving much more rapidly than the Hawkes safari, Jane and the Waziri made camp within a mile of the ivory raiders only about a week after the Hawkes party had arrived and where they still remained, waiting either for the coming of Owaza and Esteban, or for a propitious moment in which they could launch their traitorous assault upon the Arabs. In the meantime, Luvini and some of the other blacks had succeeded in secretly spreading the propaganda of revolt among the slaves of the Arabs. Though he reported his progress daily to Flora Hawkes, he did not report the steady growth and development of a little private plan of his own, which contemplated, in addition to the revolt of the slaves, and the slaying of the Arabs, the murder of all the whites in the camp, with the exception of Flora Hawkes, whom Luvini wished to preserve either for himself or for sale to some black sultan of the north. It was Luvini's shrewd plan to first slay the Arabs, with the assistance of the whites, and then to fall upon the whites and slay them, after their body servants had stolen their weapons from them.

That Luvini would have been able to carry out his plan with ease there is little doubt, had it not been for the loyalty and affection of a young black boy attached to Flora Hawkes for her personal service.

The young white woman, notwithstanding the length to which she would go in the satisfaction of her greed and avarice, was a kind and indulgent mistress. The kindnesses she had shown this ignorant little black boy were presently to return her dividends far beyond her investment.

Luvini had been to her upon a certain afternoon to advise her that all was ready, and that the revolt of the slaves and the murder of the Arabs should take place that evening, immediately after dark. The cupidity of the whites had long been aroused by the store of ivory possessed by the raiders, with the result that all were more than eager for the final step in the conspiracy that would put them in possession of considerable wealth.

It was just before the evening meal that the little negro boy crept into Flora Hawkes's tent. He was very wide-eyed, and terribly frightened.

"What is the matter?" she demanded.

"S-sh!" he cautioned. "Do not let them hear you speak to me, but put your ear close to me while I tell you in a low voice what Luvini is planning."

The girl bent her head close to the lips of the little black. "You have been kind to me," he whispered, "and now that Luvini would harm you I have come to tell you."

"What do you mean?" exclaimed Flora, in a low voice.

"I mean that Luvini, after the Arabs are killed, has given orders that the black boys kill all the white men and take you prisoner. He intends to either keep you for himself or to sell you in the north for a great sum of money."

"But how do you know all this?" demanded the girl.

"All the blacks in camp know it," replied the boy. "I was to have stolen your rifle and your pistol, as each of the boys will steal the weapons of his white master."

The girl sprang to her feet. "I'll teach that nigger a lesson," she cried, seizing her pistol and striding toward the flap of the tent.

The boy seized her about the knees and held her. "No! no!" he cried. "Do not do it. Do not say anything. It will only mean that they will kill the white men sooner and take you prisoner just the same. Every black boy in the camp is against you. Luvini has promised that the ivory shall be divided equally among them all. They are ready now, and if you should threaten Luvini, or if in any other way they should learn that you were aware of the plot, they would fall upon you immediately."

"What do you expect me to do then?" she asked.

"There is but one hope, and that is in flight. You and the white men must escape into the jungle. Not even I may accompany you."

The girl stood looking at the little boy in silence for a moment, and then finally she said, "Very well, I will do as you say. You have saved my life. Perhaps I may never be able to repay you, and perhaps, again, I may. Go, now, before suspicion alights upon you."

The black withdrew from the tent, crawling beneath the back wall to avoid being seen by any of his fellows who were in the center of the camp from which the front of the tent was in plain view. Immediately he was gone Flora walked casually into the open and went to Kraski's tent, which the Russian occupied in common with Bluber. She found the two men and in low whispers apprised them of what the black had told her. Kraski then called Peebles and Throck, it being decided that they should give no outward sign of holding any suspicion that aught was wrong. The Englishmen were for jumping in upon the blacks and annihilating them, but Flora Hawkes dissuaded them from any such rash act by pointing out how greatly they were outnumbered by the natives, and how hopeless it would be to attempt to overpower them.

Bluber, with his usual cunning and shrewdness which inclined always to double dealing where there was the slightest possibility for it, suggested that they secretly advise the Arabs of what they had learned, and joining forces with them take up as strong a position in the camp as possible and commence to fire into the blacks without waiting for their attack.

Again Flora Hawkes vetoed the suggestion. "It will not do," she said, "for the Arabs are at heart as much our enemies as the blacks. If we were successful in subduing the niggers it would be but a question of minutes before the Arabs knew every detail of the plot that we had laid against them, after which our lives would not be worth that," and she snapped her fingers.

"I guess Flora is right, as usual," growled Peebles, "but what in 'ell are we goin' to do wanderin' around in this 'ere jungle without no niggers to hunt for us, or cook for us, or carry things for us, or find our way for us, that's wot I'd like to know, and 'ere we are, 'n that's that."

"No, I guess there ain't nothin' else to do," said Throck; "but blime if I likes to run away, says I, leastwise not for no dirty niggers."

There came then to the ears of the whites, rumbling from the far distance in the jungle, the roar of a lion.

"*Oi! Oi!*" cried Bluber. "Ve go out all alone in dot jungle? *Mein Gott!* I just as soon stay here und get killed like a vite man."

"They won't kill you like a white man," said Kraski. "They'll torture you if you stay."

Bluber wrung his hands, and the sweat of fear rolled down his oily face. "*Oi!* vy did I done it? vy did I done it?" he wailed. "Vy didn't I stay home in London vere I belong?"

"Shut up!" snapped Flora. "Don't you know that if you do anything to arouse the suspicion of these fellows they will be on us at once? There is only one thing for us to do and that is to wait until they precipitate the attack upon the Arabs. We will still have our weapons, for they do not plan to steal them from us until after the Arabs are killed. In the confusion of the fight, we must make our escape into the jungle, and after that—God knows—and God help us."

"Yes," blubbered Bluber, who was in a blue funk, "Gott help us!"

A moment later Luvini came to them. "All is ready, Bwanas," he said. "As soon as the evening meal has been eaten, be in readiness. You will hear a shot, that will be the signal. Then open fire upon the Arabs."

"Good," said Kraski; "we have just been talking about it and we have decided that we will take our stand near the gate to prevent their escape."

"It is well," said Luvini, "but you must remain here." He was addressing Flora. "It would not be safe for you to be where there is to be fighting. Remain here in your tent, and we will confine the fighting to the other side of the village and possibly to the gate, if any of them makes a break for escape."

"All right," said Flora, "I will remain here where it is safe."

Satisfied that things could not have worked into his hands to better advantage the black left them, and presently the entire camp was occupied with the evening meal. There was an atmosphere of restraint, and high, nervous tension throughout the entire camp that must have been noticeable, even to the Arabs, though they, alone of the entire company, were ignorant as to its cause. Bluber was so terrified that he could not eat, but sat white and trembling with his eyes roving wildly about the camp—first to the blacks, then to the Arabs, and then to the gate, the distance to which he must have measured a hundred times as he sat there waiting for the shot that was to be the signal for the massacre that was to send him out into the jungle to be, he surely thought, the immediate prey of the first hunting lion that passed.

Peebles and Throck ate their meal stolidly, much to Bluber's disgust. Kraski, being of a highly nervous temperament, ate but little, but he showed no signs of fear. Nor did Flora Hawkes, though at heart she realized the hopelessness of their situation.

Darkness had fallen. Some of the blacks and Arabs were still eating, when suddenly the silence was shattered by the sharp staccato report of a rifle. An Arab sank silently to the earth. Kraski rose and grasped Flora by the arm. "Come!" he cried.

Followed by Peebles and Throck, and preceded by Bluber, to whose feet fright had lent wings, they hurried toward the gate of the palisade.

By now the air was filled with the hoarse cries of fighting men and the report of rifles. The Arabs, who had numbered but about a dozen, were putting up a game fight, and being far better marksmen than the blacks, the issue of the battle was still in doubt when Kraski opened the gate and the five whites fled into the darkness of the jungle.

The outcome of the fight within the camp could not have been other than it was, for so greatly did the blacks outnumber the Arabs, that eventually, notwithstanding their poor marksmanship, they succeeded in shooting down the last of the nomads of the north. Then it was that Luvini turned his attention to the other whites only to discover that they had fled the village. The black realized two things instantly. One was that someone had betrayed him, and the other, that the whites could not have gone far in the short time since they had left the camp.

Calling his warriors about him he explained to them what had happened, and impressing upon them that the whites, if permitted to escape, would eventually return with reinforcements to punish the blacks, he aroused his followers, who now numbered over two hundred warriors, to the necessity of setting out immediately upon the trail of the fugitives and overtaking them before they could carry word even to a neighboring village, the nearest of which was not more than a day's march distant.

THE DIAMOND HOARD

As the primitive smoke bombs filled the throne room of the Tower of the Emperors with their suffocating fumes, the Gomangani clustered about Tarzan begging him to save them, for they, too, had seen the massed Bolgani before every entrance and the great body of them that awaited in the gardens and upon the terrace without.

"Wait a minute," said Tarzan, "until the smoke is thick enough to hide our movements from the Bolgani, and then we will rush the windows overlooking the terrace, for they are nearer the east gate than any other exit, and thus some of us will have a better chance for escape."

"I have a better plan," said the old man. "When the smoke conceals us, follow me. There is one exit that is unguarded, probably because they do not dream that we would use it. When I passed over the dais behind the throne I took occasion to note that there were no Bolgani guarding it."

"Where does it lead?" asked Tarzan.

"Into the basement of the Tower of Diamonds—the tower in which I discovered you. That portion of the palace is nearest to the east gate, and if we can reach it before they suspect our purpose there will be little doubt that we can reach the forest at least."

"Splendid!" ejaculated the ape-man. "It will not be long now before the smoke hides us from the Bolgani."

In fact it was so thick by this time that the occupants of the throne room were finding difficulty in breathing. Many of them were coughing and choking and the eyes of all were watering from the effects of the acrid smoke. And yet they were not entirely hidden from the observation of the watchers all about them.

"I don't know how much more of this we can stand," said Tarzan. "I have about all I care for, now."

"It is thickening up a bit," said the old man. "Just a moment more and I think we can make it unseen."

"I can stand it no longer," cried La. "I am suffocating and I am half-blinded."

"Very well," said the old man; "I doubt if they can see us now. It is pretty thick. Come, follow me;" and he led the way up the steps of the dais and through an aperture behind the thrones—a small opening hidden by hangings. The old man went first, and then La, followed by Tarzan and Jad-bal-ja, who had about reached the limit of his endurance and patience, so that it had been with difficulty that Tarzan had restrained him, and who now was voicing his anger in deep growls which might have apprised the Bolgani of their avenue of escape. Behind Tarzan and the lion crowded the coughing Gomangani; but because Jad-bal-ja was just in front of them they did not crowd as closely upon the party ahead of them as they probably would have done otherwise.

The aperture opened into a dark corridor which led down a flight of rough steps to a lower level, and then straight through utter darkness for the rather considerable distance which separated the Tower of Diamonds from the Tower of the Emperors. So great was their relief at escaping the dense smoke of the throne room that none of the party minded the darkness of the corridor, but followed patiently the lead of the old man who had explained that the first stairs down which they had passed were the only obstacles to be encountered in the tunnel.

At the corridor's end the old man halted before a heavy door, which after considerable difficulty he managed to open.

"Wait a moment," he said, "until I find a cresset and make a light."

They heard him moving about beyond the doorway for a moment and then a dim light flared, and presently the wick in a cresset flickered. In the dim rays Tarzan saw before them a large rectangular chamber, the great size of which was only partially suggested in the wavering light of the cresset.

"Get them all in," said the old man, "and close the door;" and when that had been done he called to Tarzan. "Come!" he said. "Before we leave this chamber I want to show you such a sight as no other human eyes have ever rested upon."

He led him to the far side of the chamber where, in the light of the cresset, Tarzan saw tier after tier of shelves, upon which were stacked small sacks made of skins. The old man set the cresset upon one of the shelves and taking a sack opened it and spilled a portion of the contents into the palm of his hand. "Diamonds," he said. "Each of these packages weighs five pounds and each contains diamonds. They have been accumulating them for countless ages, for they mine far more than they can use themselves. In their legends is the belief that some day the Atlantians will return and they can sell the diamonds to them. And so they continue to mine them and store them as though there was a constant and ready market for them. Here, take one of the bags with you," he said. He handed one to Tarzan and another to La.

"I do not believe that we shall ever leave the valley alive, but we might;" and he took a third bag for himself.

From the diamond vault the old man led them up a primitive ladder to the floor above, and quickly to the main entrance of the Tower. Only two heavy doors, bolted upon the inside, now lay between them and the terrace, a short distance beyond which the east gate swung open. The old man was about to open the doors when Tarzan stopped him.

"Wait a moment," he said, "until the rest of the Gomangani come. It takes them some time to ascend the ladder. When they are all here behind us, swing the doors open, and you and La, with this ten or a dozen Gomangani that are immediately around us, make a break for the gate. The rest of us will bring up the rear and hold the Bolgani off in case they attack us. Get ready," he added a moment later, "I think they are all up."

Carefully Tarzan explained to the Gomangani the plan he had in mind, and then, turning to the old man, he commanded "Now!" The bolt slipped, the doors swung open, and simultaneously the entire party started at a run toward the east gate.

The Bolgani, who were still massed about the throne room, were not aware that their victims had eluded them until Tarzan, bringing up the rear with Jad-bal-ja was passing through the east gate. Then the Bolgani discovered him, and immediately set up a hue and cry that brought several hundred of them on a mad run in pursuit.

"Here they come," cried Tarzan to the others, "make a run of it—straight down the valley toward Opar, La."

"And you?" demanded the young woman.

"I shall remain a moment with the Gomangani, and attempt to punish these fellows."

La stopped in her tracks. "I shall not go a step without you, Tarzan of the Apes," she said. "Too great already are the risks you have taken for me. No; I shall not go without you."

The ape-man shrugged. "As you will," he said. "Here they come."

With great difficulty he rallied a portion of the Gomangani who, once through the gate, seemed imbued but with a single purpose, and that to put as much distance between the Palace of Diamonds and themselves as possible. Perhaps fifty warriors rallied to his call, and with these he stood in the gateway toward which several hundred Bolgani were now charging.

The old man came and touched Tarzan on the arm. "You had better fly," he said. "The Gomangani will break and run at the first assault."

"We will gain nothing by flying," said Tarzan, "for we should only lose what we have gained with the Gomangani, and then we should have the whole valley about us like hornets."

He had scarcely finished speaking when one of the Gomangani cried: "Look! Look! They come;" and pointed along the trail into the forest.

"And just in time, too," remarked Tarzan, as he saw the first of a swarm of Gomangani pouring out of the forest toward the east gate. "Come!" he cried to the advancing blacks, "the Bolgani are upon us. Come, and avenge your wrongs!" Then he turned, and calling to the blacks around him, leaped forward to meet the onrushing gorilla-men. Behind them wave after wave of Gomangani rolled through the east gate of the Palace of Diamonds, carrying everything before them to break at last like surf upon the wavering wall of Bolgani that was being relentlessly hurled back against the palace walls.

The shouting and the fighting and the blood worked Jad-bal-ja into such a frenzy of excitement that Tarzan with difficulty restrained him from springing upon friend and foe alike, with the result that it required so much of the ape-man's time to hold in leash his ferocious ally that he was able to take but little part in the battle, yet he saw that it was going his way, and that, but for the occurrence of some untoward event, the complete defeat of the Bolgani was assured.

Nor were his deductions erroneous. So frantic were the Gomangani with the blood-lust of revenge and so enthused by the first fruits of victory, that they went fully as mad as Jad-bal-ja himself. They neither gave nor asked quarter, and the fighting ended only when they could find no more Bolgani to slay.

The fighting over, Tarzan, with La and the old man, returned to the throne room, from which the fumes of the smoke bombs had now disappeared. To them they summoned the head-man of each village, and when they had assembled before the dais, above which stood the three whites, with the great, black-maned lion Jad-bal-ja, Tarzan addressed them.

"Gomangani of the Valley of the Palace of Diamonds," he said, "you have this night won your freedom from the tyrannical masters that have oppressed you since far beyond the time the oldest of you may remember. For so many countless ages have you been oppressed that there has never developed among you a leader capable of ruling you wisely and justly. Therefore you must select a ruler from another race than your own."

"You! You!" cried voice after voice as the head-men clamored to make Tarzan of the Apes their king.

"No," cried the ape-man, holding up his hand for silence, "but there is one here who has lived long among you, and who knows your habits and your customs, your hopes and your needs better than any other. If he will stay with you and rule you he will, I am sure, make you a good king," and Tarzan pointed to the old man.

The old man looked at Tarzan in bewilderment. "But I want to go away from here," he said; "I want to get back into the world of civilization, from which I have been buried all these years."

"You do not know what you are talking about," replied the ape-man. "You have been gone very long. You will find no friends left back there from whence you came. You will find deceit, and hypocrisy, and greed, and avarice, and cruelty. You will find that no one will be interested in you and that you will be interested in no one there. I, Tarzan of the Apes, have left my jungle and gone to the cities built by men, but always I have been disgusted and been glad to return to my jungle—to the noble beasts that are honest in their loves and in their hates—to the freedom and genuineness of nature.

"If you return you will be disappointed, and you will realize that you have thrown away an opportunity of accomplishing a work well worth your while. These poor creatures need you. I cannot remain to guide them out of darkness, but you may, and you may so mold them that they will be an industrious, virtuous, and kindly people, not untrained, however, in the arts of warfare, for when we have that which is good, there will always be those who are envious and who, if they are more powerful than we, will attempt to come and take what we have by force. Therefore, you must train your people to protect their country and their rights, and to protect them they must have the ability and the knowledge to fight successfully, and the weapons wherewith to wage their wars."

"You speak the truth, Tarzan of the Apes," replied the old man. "There is nothing for me in that other world, so, if the Gomangani wish me to be their chief I will remain here."

The head-men, when he questioned them, assured Tarzan that if they could not have him for chief they would be very glad to have the old man, whom they all knew, either by sight or reputation, as one who had never perpetrated any cruelties upon the Gomangani.

The few surviving Bolgani who had taken refuge in various parts of the palace were sought out and brought to the throne room. Here they were given the option of remaining in the valley as slaves, or leaving the country entirely. The Gomangani would have fallen upon them and slain them, but that their new king would not permit.

"But where shall we go if we leave the Valley of the Palace of Diamonds?" asked one of the Bolgani. "Beyond the city of Opar we know not what exists, and in Opar may we find only enemies."

Tarzan sat eyeing them quizzically, and in silence. For a long time he did not speak, while several of the Gomangani head-men, and others of the Bolgani, made suggestions for the future of the gorilla-men. Finally the ape-man arose and nodded toward the Bolgani.

"There are about a hundred of you," he said. "You are powerful creatures and should be ferocious fighters. Beside me sits La, the High Priestess and queen of Opar. A wicked priest, usurping her power, has driven her from her throne, but tomorrow we march upon Opar with the bravest Gomangani of the Valley of the Palace of Diamonds, and there we punish Cadj, the High Priest, who has proven a traitor to his queen; and La, once more, ascends the throne of Opar. But where the seeds of treason have once been broadcast the plant may spring up at any time and where least expected. It will be long, therefore, before La of Opar may have full confidence in the loyalty of her people—a fact which offers you an opportunity and a country. Accompany us, therefore, to Opar, and fight with us to replace La upon her throne, and then, when the fighting is over, remain there as La's bodyguard to protect her, not only from enemies without, but from enemies within."

The Bolgani discussed the matter for several minutes, and then one of them came to Tarzan. "We will do as you suggest," he said.

"And you will be loyal to La?" asked the ape-man.

"A Bolgani is never a traitor," replied the gorilla-man.

"Good!" exclaimed Tarzan, "and you, La, are you satisfied with this arrangement?"

"I accept them in my service," replied she.

Early the next morning Tarzan and La set out with three thousand Gomangani and a hundred Bolgani to punish the traitorous Cadj. There was little or no attempt at strategy or deception. They simply marched down through the Valley of the Palace of Diamonds, descended the rocky ravine into the valley of Opar, and made straight for the rear of the palace of La.

A little gray monkey, sitting among the vines and creepers upon the top of the temple walls, saw them coming. He cocked his head, first upon one side and then upon the other, and became so interested and excited that for a moment he forgot to scratch his belly—an occupation he had been assiduously pursuing for some time. The closer the column approached the more excited became Manu, the monkey, and when he realized vaguely the great numbers of the Gomangani he was fairly beside himself, but the last straw that sent him scampering madly back to the palace of Opar was the sight of the Bolgani—the ogres of his little world.

Cadj was in the courtyard of the inner temple, where at sunrise he had performed a sacrifice to the Flaming God. With Cadj were a number of the lesser priests, and Oah and her priestesses. That there was dissension among them was evident by the scowling faces fully as much as by the words which Oah directed at Cadj.

"Once again have you gone too far, Cadj," she cried bitterly. "Only may the High Priestess of the Flaming God perform the act of sacrifice. Yet again and again do you persist in defiling the sacred knife with your unworthy hand."

"Silence, woman," growled the High Priest. "I am Cadj, King of Opar, High Priest of the Flaming God. You are what you are only because of the favor of Cadj. Try not my patience too far or you shall indeed know the feel of the sacred knife." There could be no mistaking the sinister menace in his words. Several of those about him could ill conceal the shocked surprise they felt at his sacrilegious attitude toward their High Priestess. However little they thought of Oah, the fact remained that she had been elevated to the highest place among them, and those that believed that La was dead, as Cadj had taken great pains to lead them all to believe, gave in full to Oah the reverence which her high office entitled her to.

"Have a care, Cadj," warned one of the older priests. "There is a limit beyond which not even you may pass."

"You dare threaten me?" cried Cadj, the maniacal fury of fanaticism gleaming in his eyes. "You dare threaten me, Cadj, the High Priest of the Flaming God?" And as he spoke he leaped toward the offending man, the sacrificial knife raised menacingly above his head, and just at that moment a little gray monkey came chattering and screaming through an embrasure in the wall overlooking the court of the temple.

"The Bolgani! The Bolgani!" he shrieked. "They come! They come!"

Cadj stopped and wheeled toward Manu, the hand that held the knife dropping at his side. "You saw them, Manu?" he asked. "You are speaking the truth? If this is another of your tricks you will not live to play another joke upon Cadj."

"I speak the truth," chattered the little monkey. "I saw them with my own eyes."

"How many of them are there?" asked Cadj. "And how near to Opar have they come?"

"They are as many as the leaves upon the trees," replied Manu, "and they are already close to the temple wall—the Bolgani and the Gomangani, they come as the grasses that grow in the ravines where it is cool and damp."

Cadj turned and raised his face toward the sun, and throwing back his head gave voice to a long-drawn scream that ended in a piercing shriek. Three times he voiced the hideous cry, and then with a command to the others in the court to follow him he started at a brisk trot toward the palace proper. As Cadj directed his steps toward the ancient avenue, upon which the palace of Opar faced, there issued from every corridor and doorway groups of the knurled and hairy men of Opar, armed with their heavy bludgeons and their knives. Screaming and chattering in the trees above them were a score or more of little gray monkeys.

"Not here," they cried, "not here," and pointed toward the south side of the city.

Like an undisciplined mob the horde of priests and warriors reentered the palace at Cadj's heels, and retraced their steps toward the opposite side of the edifice. Here they scrambled to the summit of the lofty wall which guards the palace, just as Tarzan's forces came to a halt outside.

"Rocks! Rocks!" screamed Cadj, and in answer to his commands the women in the courtyard below commenced to gather the loose fragments of stone that had crumbled from the wall and from the palace, and to toss them up to the warriors above.

"Go away!" screamed Cadj to the army outside his gates. "Go away! I am Cadj, High Priest of the Flaming God, and this is his temple. Defile not the temple of the Flaming God or you shall know his wrath."

Tarzan stepped forward a little ahead of the others, and raised his hand for silence.

"La, your High Priestess and your queen, is here," he cried to the Oparians upon the wall. "Cadj is a traitor and an impostor. Open your gates and receive your queen. Give up the traitors to justice, and no harm will befall you; but refuse La entry to her city and we shall take by force and with bloodshed that which belongs to La rightfully."

As he ceased speaking La stepped to his side that all her people might see her, and immediately there were scattering cries for La and a voice or two raised against Cadj. Evidently realizing that it would not take much to turn the scale against him, Cadj shrieked to his men to attack, and simultaneously launched a stone at Tarzan. Only the wondrous agility that he possessed saved the ape-man, and the missile passed by, and striking a Gomangani over the heart, felled him. Instantly a shower of missiles fell upon them, and then

Tarzan called to his followers to charge. Roaring and growling, the Bolgani and the Gomangani leaped forward to the attack. Cat-like they ran up the rough wall in the face of the menacing bludgeons above. Tarzan, who had chosen Cadj as his objective, was among the first to reach the summit. A hairy, crooked warrior struck at him with a bludgeon, and hanging to the summit of the wall with one hand, Tarzan caught the weapon in the other and wrested it from his assailant. At the same time he saw Cadj turn and disappear into the courtyard beyond. Then Tarzan drew himself to the top where he was immediately engaged by two other warriors of Opar. With the weapon he had wrested from their fellow he knocked them to right and left, so great an advantage his great height and strength gave him over them, and then, remembering only that Cadj, who was the ringleader of the revolt against La, must not be permitted to escape Tarzan leaped to the pavement below just as the High Priest disappeared through an archway at the opposite end of the courtyard.

Some priests and priestesses sought to impede his progress. Seizing one of the former by the ankles he swung the body in circles about him, clearing his own pathway as he ran for the opposite end of the courtyard, and there he halted and wheeled and putting all the strength of his great muscles into the effort, he swung the body of the priest once more and hurled it back into the faces of his pursuers.

Without waiting to note the effect of his act he turned again and continued in pursuit of Cadj. The fellow kept always just ahead of him, because Cadj knew his way through the labyrinthian mazes of the palace and temple and courtyards better than Tarzan. That the trail was leading toward the inner courts of the temple Tarzan was convinced. There Cadj would find easy ingress to the pits beneath the palace and a hiding place from which it would be difficult to dislodge him, so numerous and winding were the dark subterranean tunnels. And so Tarzan put forth every effort to reach the sacrificial court in time to prevent Cadj from gaining the comparative safety of the underground passages; but as he finally leaped through the doorway into the court, a noose, cunningly laid, closed about one of his ankles and he was hurled heavily to the ground. Almost instantly a number of the crooked little men of Opar leaped upon him, where he lay, half-stunned by the fall, and before he had fully regained his faculties they had trussed him securely.

Only about half conscious, he felt them raise him from the ground and carry him, and presently he was deposited upon a cold stone surface. Then it was that full consciousness returned to him, and he realized that he lay outstretched once more upon the sacrificial altar of the inner court of the Temple of the Flaming God and above him stood Cadj, the High Priest, his cruel face contorted in a grimace of hate and the anticipation of revenge long deferred.

"At last!" gloated the creature of hate. "This time, Tarzan of the Apes, you shall know the fury not of the Flaming God, but of Cadj, the man; nor shall there be any wait nor any interference."

He swung the sacrificial knife high above his head. Beyond the point of the knife Tarzan of the Apes saw the summit of the courtyard wall, and just surmounting it the head and shoulders of a mighty, black-maned lion.

"Jad-bal-ja!" he cried. "Kill! Kill!"

Cadj hesitated, his knife poised on high. He saw the direction of the ape-man's eyes and followed them, and in that instant the golden lion leaped to the pavement, and with two mighty bounds was upon the High Priest of Opar. The knife clattered to the floor and the great jaws closed upon the horrid face.

The lesser priests who had seized Tarzan, and who had remained to witness his death at the hands of Cadj, had fled screaming from the court the instant that the golden lion had leaped upon their master, and now Tarzan and Jad-bal-ja and the corpse of Cadj were the sole occupants of the sacrificial courtyard of the temple.

"Come, Jad-bal-ja," commanded Tarzan; "let no one harm Tarzan of the Apes."

An hour later the victorious forces of La were overrunning the ancient palace and temples of Opar. The priests and warriors who had not been killed had quickly surrendered and acknowledged La as their queen and High Priestess, and now at La's command the city was being searched for Tarzan and Cadj. It was thus that La, herself, leading a searching party, entered the sacrificial courtyard.

The sight that met her eyes brought her to a sudden halt, for there, bound upon the altar, lay Tarzan of the Apes, and standing above him, his snarling face and gleaming eyes glaring directly at her was Jad-bal-ja, the golden lion.

"Tarzan!" shrieked La, taking a step toward the altar. "Cadj has had his way at last. God of my fathers have pity on me—Tarzan is dead."

"No," cried the ape-man; "far from dead. Come and release me. I am only bound, but had it not been for Jad-bal-ja I had been dead beneath your sacrificial knife."

"Thank God," cried La, and started to approach the altar, but paused before the menacing attitude of the growling lion.

"Down!" cried Tarzan, "let her approach;" and Jad-bal-ja lay down beside his master and stretched his whiskered chin across the ape-man's breast.

La came then, and picking up the sacrificial knife, cut the bonds that held the lord of the jungle captive, and then she saw beyond the altar the corpse of Cadj.

"Your worst enemy is dead," said Tarzan, "and for his death you may thank Jad-bal-ja, as I thank him for my life. You should rule now in peace and happiness and in friendship with the people of the Valley of the Palace of Diamonds."

That night Tarzan and the Bolgani and the head-men of the Gomangani, and the priests and priestesses of Opar, sat in the great banquet hall of the Palace of Opar, as the guests of La, the queen, and ate from the golden platters of the ancient Atlantians—platters that had been fashioned on a continent that exists today only in the legends of antiquity. And the following morning Tarzan and Jad-bal-ja set forth upon their return journey to the land of the Waziri and home.

THE TORTURE OF FIRE

Flora Hawkes and her four confederates, pursued by Luvini and his two hundred warriors, stumbled through the darkness of the jungle night. They had no objective, for, guided entirely as they had been by the blacks, they knew not where they were and were completely lost. The sole idea dominating the mind of each was to put as much distance between themselves and the camp of the ivory raiders as possible, for no matter what the outcome of the battle there might have been, their fate would be the same should the victorious party capture them. They had stumbled on for perhaps half an hour when, during a momentary rest, they heard plainly behind them the sound of pursuit, and again they plunged on in their aimless flight of terror.

Presently, to their surprise, they discerned the glow of a light ahead. What could it be? Had they made a complete circle, and was this again the camp they had been fleeing? They pushed on to reconnoiter, until at last they saw before them the outlines of a camp surrounded by a thorn boma, in the center of which was burning a small camp-fire. About the fire were congregated half-a-hundred black warriors, and as the fugitives crept closer they saw among the blacks a figure standing out clearly in the light of the camp-fire—a white woman—and behind them rose louder and louder the sound of pursuit.

From the gestures and gesticulations of the blacks around the camp-fire it was evident that they were discussing the sounds of the battle they had recently heard in the direction of the raiders' camp, for they often pointed in that direction, and now the woman raised her hand for silence and they all listened, and it was evident that they, too, heard the coming of the warriors who were pursuing Flora Hawkes and her confederates.

"There is a white woman there," said Flora to the others. "We do not know who she is, but she is our only hope, for those who are pursuing us will overtake us quickly. Perhaps this woman will protect us. Come, I am going to find out;" and without waiting for an answer she walked boldly toward the boma.

They had come but a short distance when the keen eyes of the Waziri discovered them, and instantly the boma wall was ringed with bristling spears.

"Stop!" cried one of the warriors. "We are the Waziri of Tarzan. Who are you?"

"I am an Englishwoman," called Flora in reply. "I and my companions are lost in the jungle. We have been betrayed by our safari—our head-man is pursuing us now with warriors. There are but five of us and we ask your protection."

"Let them come," said Jane to the Waziri.

As Flora Hawkes and the four men entered the boma beneath the scrutiny of Jane Clayton and the Waziri, another pair of eyes watched from the foliage of the great tree that overhung the camp upon the opposite side—gray eyes to which a strange light came as they recognized the girl and her companions.

As the newcomers approached Lady Greystoke the latter gave an exclamation of surprise. "Flora!" she exclaimed, in astonishment. "Flora Hawkes, what in the world are you doing here?"

The girl, startled too, came to a full stop. "Lady Greystoke!" she ejaculated.

"I do not understand," continued Lady Greystoke. "I did not know that you were in Africa."

For a moment the glib Flora was overcome by consternation, but presently her native wit came to her assistance. "I am here with Mr. Bluber and his friends," she said, "who came to make scientific researches, and brought me along because I had been to Africa with you and Lord Greystoke, and knew something of the manners and customs of the country, and now our boys have turned against us and unless you can help us we are lost."

"Are they west coast boys?" asked Jane.

"Yes," replied Flora.

"I think my Waziri can handle them. How many of them are there?"

"About two hundred," said Kraski.

Lady Greystoke shook her head. "The odds are pretty heavy," she commented, and then she called to Usula, who was in charge. "There are two hundred west coast boys coming after these people," she said; "we shall have to fight to defend them."

"We are Waziri," replied Usula, simply, and a moment later the van of Luvini's forces broke into view at the outer rim of the camp-fire's reach.

At sight of the glistening warriors ready to receive them the west coast boys halted. Luvini, taking in the inferior numbers of the enemy at a glance, stepped forward a few paces ahead of his men and commenced to shout taunts and insults, demanding the return of the whites to him. He accompanied his words with fantastic and grotesque steps, at the same time waving his rifle and shaking his fist. Presently his followers took up the refrain until the whole band of two hundred was shrieking and yelling and threatening, the while they leaped up and down as they worked themselves into a frenzy of excitement that would impart to them the courage necessary for the initiating of a charge.

The Waziri, behind the boma wall, schooled and disciplined by Tarzan of the Apes, had long since discarded the fantastic overture to battle so dear to the hearts of other warlike tribes and, instead, stood stolid and grim awaiting the coming of the foe.

"They have a number of rifles," commented Lady Greystoke; "that looks rather bad for us."

"There are not over half-a-dozen who can hit anything with their rifles," said Kraski.

"You men are all armed. Take your places among my Waziri. Warn your men to go away and leave us alone. Do not fire until they attack, but at the first overt act, commence firing, and keep it up—there is nothing that so discourages a west coast black as the rifle fire of white men. Flora and I will remain at the back of the camp, near that large tree." She spoke authoritatively, as one who is accustomed to command and knows whereof she speaks. The men obeyed her; even Bluber, though he trembled pitiably as he moved forward to take his place in the front ranks among the Waziri.

Their movements, in the light of the camp-fire, were all plainly discernible to Luvini, and also to that other who watched from the foliage of the tree beneath which Jane Clayton and Flora Hawkes took refuge. Luvini had not come to fight. He had come to capture Flora Hawkes. He turned to his men. "There are only fifty of them," he said. "We can kill them easily, but we did not come to make war. We came to get the white girl back again. Stay here and make a great show against those sons of jackals. Keep them always looking at you. Advance a little and then fall back again, and while you are thus keeping their attention attracted in this direction I will take fifty men and go to the rear of their camp and get the white girl, and when I have her I will send word to you and immediately you can return to the village, where, behind the palisade, we shall be safe against attack."

Now this plan well suited the west coast blacks, who had no stomach for the battle looming so imminent, and so they danced and yelled and menaced more vociferously than before, for they felt they were doing it all with perfect impunity, since presently they should retire, after a bloodless victory, to the safety of their palisade.

As Luvini, making a detour, crept through the concealment of the dense jungles to the rear of the camp while the din of the west coast blacks arose to almost deafening proportions, there dropped suddenly to the ground before the two white women from the tree above them, the figure of a white giant, naked except for loin cloth and leopard skin—his godlike contour picked out by the flickering light of the beast fire.

"John!" exclaimed Lady Greystoke. "Thank God it is you."

"S-s-sh!" cautioned the white giant, placing a forefinger to his lips, and then suddenly he wheeled upon Flora Hawkes. "It is you I want," he cried, and seizing the girl he threw her lightly across his shoulders, and before Lady Greystoke could interfere—before she half-realized what had occurred—he had lightly leaped the protecting boma in the rear of the camp and disappeared into the jungle beyond.

For a moment Jane Clayton stood reeling as one stunned by an unexpected blow, and then, with a stifled moan, she sank sobbing to the ground, her face buried in her arms.

It was thus that Luvini and his warriors found her as they crept stealthily over the boma and into the camp in the rear of the defenders upon the opposite side of the beast fire. They had come for a white woman and they had found one, and roughly dragging her to her feet, smothering her cries with rough and filthy palms, they bore her out into the jungle toward the palisaded village of the ivory raiders.

Ten minutes later the white men and the Waziri saw the west coast blacks retire slowly into the jungle, still yelling and threatening, as though bent on the total annihilation of their enemies—the battle was over without a shot fired or a spear hurled.

"Blime," said Throck, "what was all the bloomin' fuss about anyhow?"

"Hi thought they was goin' to heat hus hup, an' the blighters never done nothin' but yell, an' 'ere we are, 'n that's that."

The Jew swelled out his chest. "It takes more as a bunch of niggers to bluff Adolph Bluber," he said pompously.

Kraski looked after the departing blacks, and then, scratching his head, turned back toward the camp-fire. "I can't understand it," he said, and then, suddenly, "Where are Flora and Lady Greystoke?"

It was then that they discovered that the two women were missing.

The Waziri were frantic. They called the name of their mistress aloud, but there was no reply. "Come!" cried Usula, "we, the Waziri, shall fight, after all," and running to the boma he leaped it, and, followed by his fifty blacks, set out in pursuit of the west coast boys.

It was but a moment or two before they overtook them, and that which ensued resembled more a rout than a battle. Fleeing in terror toward their palisade with the Waziri at their heels the west coast blacks threw away their rifles that they might run the faster, but Luvini and his party had had sufficient start so that they were able to reach the village and gain the safety of the palisade before pursued and pursuers reached it. Once inside the gate the defenders made a stand for they realized that if the Waziri entered they should all be massacred, and so they fought as a cornered rat will fight, with the result that they managed to hold off the attackers until they could close and bar the gate. Built as it had been as a defense against far greater numbers the village was easy to defend, for there were less than fifty Waziri now, and nearly two hundred fighting men within the village to defend it against them.

Realizing the futility of blind attack Usula withdrew his forces a short distance from the palisade, and there they squatted, their fierce, scowling faces glaring at the gateway while Usula pondered schemes for outwitting the enemy, which he realized he could not overcome by force alone.

"It is only Lady Greystoke that we want," he said; "vengeance can wait until another day."

"But we do not even know that she is within the village," reminded one of his men.

"Where else could she be, then?" asked Usula. "It is true that you may be right—she may not be within the village, but that I intend to find out. I have a plan. See; the wind is from the opposite side of the village. Ten of you will accompany me, the others will advance again before the gate and make much noise, and pretend that you are about to attack. After awhile the gate will open and they will come out. That I promise you. I will try to be here before that happens, but if I am not, divide into two parties and stand upon either side of the gateway and let the west coast blacks escape; we do not care for them. Watch only for Lady Greystoke, and when you see her take her away from those who guard her. Do you understand?" His companions nodded. "Then come," he said, and selecting ten men disappeared into the jungle.

Luvini had carried Jane Clayton to a hut not far from the gateway to the village. Here he had bound her securely and tied her to a stake, still believing that she was Flora Hawkes, and then he had left her to hurry back toward the gate that he might take command of his forces in defense of the village.

So rapidly had the events of the past hour transpired that Jane Clayton was still half dazed from the series of shocks that she had been called upon to endure. Dwarfing to nothingness the menace of her present position was the remembrance that her Tarzan had deserted her in her hour of need, and carried off into the jungle another woman. Not even the remembrance of what Usula had told her concerning the accident that Tarzan had sustained, and which had supposedly again affected his memory, could reconcile her to the brutality of his desertion, and now she lay, face down, in the filth of the Arab hut, sobbing as she had not for many years.

As she lay there torn by grief, Usula and his ten crept stealthily and silently around the outside of the palisade to the rear of the village. Here they found great quantities of dead brush left from the clearing which the Arabs had made when constructing their village. This they brought and piled along the palisade, close against it, until nearly three-quarters of the palisade upon that side of the village was banked high with it. Finding that it was difficult to prosecute their work in silence, Usula despatched one of his men to the main body upon the opposite side of the village, with instructions that they were to keep up a continuous din of shouting to drown the sound of the operations of their fellows. The plan worked to perfection, yet even though it permitted Usula and his companions to labor with redoubled efforts, it was more than an hour before the brush pile was disposed to his satisfaction.

Luvini, from an aperture in the palisade, watched the main body of the Waziri who were now revealed by the rising of the moon, and finally he came to the conclusion that they did not intend to attack that night, and therefore he might relax his watchfulness and utilize the time in another and more agreeable manner. Instructing the bulk of his warriors to remain near the gate and ever upon the alert, with orders that he be summoned the moment that the Waziri showed any change in attitude, Luvini repaired to the hut in which he had left Lady Greystoke.

The black was a huge fellow, with low, receding forehead and prognathous jaw—a type of the lowest form of African negro. As he entered the hut with a lighted torch which he stuck in the floor, his bloodshot eyes gazed greedily at the still form of the woman lying prone before him. He licked his thick lips and, coming closer, reached out and touched her. Jane Clayton looked up, and recoiling in revulsion shrank away. At sight of the woman's face the black looked his surprise.

"Who are you?" he demanded in the pidgin English of the coast.

"I am Lady Greystoke, wife of Tarzan of the Apes," replied Jane Clayton. "If you are wise you will release me at once."

Surprise and terror showed in the eyes of Luvini, and another emotion as well, but which would dominate the muddy brain it was difficult, then, to tell. For a long time he sat gazing at her, and slowly the greedy, gloating expression upon his face dominated and expunged the fear that had at first been written there, and in the change Jane Clayton read her doom.

With fumbling fingers Luvini untied the knots of the bonds that held Jane Clayton's wrists and ankles. She felt his hot breath upon her and saw his bloodshot eyes and the red tongue that momentarily licked the thick lips. The instant that she felt the last thong with which she was tied fall away she leaped to her feet and sprang for the entrance to the hut, but a great hand reached forth and seized her, and as Luvini dragged her back toward him, she wheeled like a mad tigress and struck repeatedly at his grinning, ugly face. By brute force, ruthless and indomitable, he beat down her weak resistance and slowly and surely dragged her closer to him. Oblivious to aught else, deaf to the cries of the Waziri before the gate and to the sudden new commotion that arose in the village, the two struggled on, the woman, from the first, foredoomed to defeat.

Against the rear palisade Usula had already put burning torches to his brush pile at half-a-dozen different places. The flames, fanned by a gentle jungle breeze, had leaped almost immediately into a roaring conflagration, before which the dry wood of the palisade crumbled in a shower of ruddy sparks which the wind carried to the thatched roofs of the huts beyond, until in an incredibly short period of time the village was a roaring inferno of flames. And even as Usula had predicted the gate swung open and the west coast blacks swarmed forth in terror toward the jungle. Upon either side of the gateway the Waziri stood, looking for their mistress, but though they waited and watched in silence until no more came from the gateway of the village, and until the interior of the palisade was a seething hell of fire, they saw nothing of her.

Long after they were convinced that no human being could remain alive in the village they still waited and hoped; but at last Usula gave up the useless vigil.

"She was never there," he said, "and now we must pursue the blacks and capture some of them, from whom we may learn the whereabouts of Lady Greystoke."

It was daylight before they came upon a small band of stragglers, who were in camp a few miles toward the west. These they quickly surrounded, winning their immediate surrender by promises of immunity in the event that they would answer truthfully the questions that Usula should propound.

"Where is Luvini?" demanded Usula, who had learned the name of the leader of the west coast boys from the Europeans the evening before.

"We do not know; we have not seen him since We left the village," replied one of the blacks. "We were some of the slaves of the Arabs, and when we escaped the palisade last night we ran away from the others, for we thought that we should be safer alone than with Luvini, who is even crueller than the Arabs."

"Did you see the white women that he brought to the camp last night?" demanded Usula.

"He brought but one white woman," replied the other.

"What did he do with her? Where is she now?" asked Usula.

"I do not know. When he brought her he bound her hand and foot and put her in the hut which he occupied near the village gate. We have not seen her since."

Usula turned and looked at his companions. A great fear was in his eyes, a fear that was reflected in the countenances of the others.

"Come!" he said, "we shall return to the village. And you will go with us," he added, addressing the west coast blacks, "and if you have lied to us—" he made a significant movement with his forefinger across his throat.

"We have not lied to you," replied the others.

Quickly they retraced their steps toward the ruins of the Arab village, nothing of which was left save a few piles of smoldering embers.

"Where was the hut in which the white woman was confined?" demanded Usula, as they entered the smoking ruins.

"Here," said one of the blacks, and walked quickly a few paces beyond what had been the village gateway. Suddenly he halted and pointed at something which lay upon the ground.

"There," he said, "is the white woman you seek."

Usula and the others pressed forward. Rage and grief contended for mastery of them as they beheld, lying before them, the charred remnants of a human body.

"It is she," said Usula, turning away to hide his grief as the tears rolled down his ebon cheeks. The other Waziri were equally affected, for they all had loved the mate of the big Bwana.

"Perhaps it is not she," suggested one of them; "perhaps it is another."

"We can tell quickly," cried a third. "If her rings are among the ashes it is indeed she," and he knelt and searched for the rings which Lady Greystoke habitually wore.

Usula shook his head despairingly. "It is she," he said, "there is the very stake to which she was fastened"—he pointed to the blackened stub of a stake close beside the body—"and as for the rings, even if they are not there it will mean nothing, for Luvini would have taken them away from her as soon as he captured her. There was time for everyone else to leave the village except she, who was bound and could not leave—no, it cannot be another."

The Waziri scooped a shallow grave and reverently deposited the ashes there, marking the spot with a little cairn of stones.

THE SPOOR OF REVENGE

As Tarzan of the Apes, adapting his speed to that of Jad-bal-ja, made his comparatively slow way toward home, he reviewed with varying emotions the experiences of the past week. While he had been unsuccessful in raiding the treasure vaults of Opar, the sack of diamonds which he carried compensated several-fold for this miscarriage of his plans. His only concern now was for the safety of his Waziri, and, perhaps, a troublesome desire to seek out the whites who had drugged him and mete out to them the punishment they deserved. In view, however, of his greater desire to return home he decided to make no effort at apprehending them for the time being at least.

Hunting together, feeding together, and sleeping together, the man and the great lion trod the savage jungle trails toward home. Yesterday they shared the meat of Bara, the deer, today they feasted upon the carcass of Horta, the boar, and between them there was little chance that either would go hungry.

They had come within a day's march of the bungalow when Tarzan discovered the spoor of a considerable body of warriors. As some men devour the latest stock-market quotations as though their very existence depended upon an accurate knowledge of them, so Tarzan of the Apes devoured every scrap of information that the jungle held for him, for, in truth, an accurate knowledge of all that this information could impart to him had been during his lifetime a sine qua non to his existence. So now he carefully examined the spoor that lay before him, several days old though it was and partially obliterated by the passage of beasts since it had been made, but yet legible enough to the keen eyes and nostrils of the ape-man. His partial indifference suddenly gave way to keen interest, for among the footprints of the great warriors he saw now and again the smaller one of a white woman—a loved footprint that he knew as well as you know your mother's face.

"The Waziri returned and told her that I was missing," he soliloquized, "and now she has set out with them to search for me." He turned to the lion. "Well, Jad-bal-ja, once again we turn away from home—but no, where she is is home."

The direction that the trail led rather mystified Tarzan of the Apes, as it was not along the direct route toward Opar, but in a rather more southerly direction. On the sixth day his keen ears caught the sound of approaching men, and presently there was wafted to his nostrils the spoor of blacks. Sending Jad-bal-ja into a thicket to hide, Tarzan took to the trees and moved rapidly in the direction of the approaching negroes. As the distance between them lessened the scent became stronger, until, even before he saw them, Tarzan knew that they were Waziri, but the one effluvium that would have filled his soul with happiness was lacking.

It was a surprised Usula who, at the head of the sad and dejected Waziri, came at the turning of the trail suddenly face to face with his master.

"Tarzan of the Apes!" cried Usula. "Is it indeed you?"

"It is none other," replied the ape-man, "but where is Lady Greystoke?"

"Ah, master, how can we tell you!" cried Usula.

"You do not mean—" cried Tarzan. "It cannot be. Nothing could happen to her while she was guarded by my Waziri!"

The warriors hung their heads in shame and sorrow. "We offer our lives for hers," said Usula, simply. He threw down his spear and shield and, stretching his arms wide apart, bared his great breast to Tarzan. "Strike, Bwana," he said.

The ape-man turned away with bowed head. Presently he looked at Usula again. "Tell me how it happened," he said, "and forget your foolish speech as I have forgotten the suggestion which prompted it."

Briefly Usula narrated the events which had led up to the death of Jane, and when he was done Tarzan of the Apes spoke but three words, voicing a question which was typical of him.

"Where is Luvini?" he asked.

"Ah, that we do not know," replied Usula.

"But I shall know," said Tarzan of the Apes. "Go upon your way, my children, back to your huts, and your women and your children, and when next you see Tarzan of the Apes you will know that Luvini is dead."

They begged permission to accompany him, but he would not listen to them.

"You are needed at home at this time of year," he said. "Already have you been gone too long from the herds and fields. Return, then, and carry word to Korak, but tell him that it is my wish that he, too, remains at home—if I fail, then may he come and take up my unfinished work if he wishes to do so." As he ceased speaking he turned back in the direction from which he had come, and whistled once a single, low, long-drawn note, and a moment later Jad-bal-ja, the golden lion, bounded into view along the jungle trail.

"The golden lion!" cried Usula. "When he escaped from Keewazi it was to search for his beloved Bwana."

Tarzan nodded. "He followed many marches to a strange country until he found me," he said, and then he bid the Waziri good-bye and bent his steps once more away from home in search of Luvini and revenge.

John Peebles, wedged in the crotch of a large tree, greeted the coming dawn with weary eyes. Near him was Dick Throck, similarly braced in another crotch, while Kraski, more intelligent and therefore possessing more inventive genius, had rigged a small platform of branches across two parallel boughs, upon which he lay in comparative comfort. Ten feet above him Bluber swung, half exhausted and wholly terrified, to a smaller branch, supported in something that approximated safety by a fork of the branch to which he clung.

"Gord," groaned Peebles, "hi'll let the bloody lions 'ave me before hi'll spend another such a night as this, an' 'ere we are, 'n that's that!"

"And blime, too," said Throck, "hi sleeps on the ground hafter this, lions or no lions."

"If the combined intelligence of the three of you was equal to that of a walrus," remarked Kraski, "we might have slept in comparative safety and comfort last night on the ground."

"Hey there, Bluber, Mister Kraski is spikin' to yer," called Peebles in fine sarcasm, accenting the Mister.

"Oi! Oi! I don't care vot nobody says," moaned Bluber.

"'E wants us to build a 'ouse for 'im hevery night," continued Peebles, "while 'e stands abaht and tells us bloomin' well 'ow to do it, and 'im, bein' a fine gentleman, don't do no work."

"Why should I do any work with my hands when you two big beasts haven't got anything else to work with?" asked Kraski. "You would all have starved by this time if I hadn't found food for you. And you'll be lion meat in the end, or die of exhaustion if you don't listen to me—not that it would be much loss."

The others paid no attention to his last sally. As a matter of fact they had all been quarreling so much for such a long time that they really paid little attention to one another. With the exception of Peebles and Throck they all hated one another cordially, and only clung together because they were afraid to separate.

Slowly Peebles lowered his bulk to the ground. Throck followed him, and then came Kraski, and then, finally, Bluber, who stood for a moment in silence, looking down at his disreputable clothing.

"Mein Gott!" he exclaimed at last. "Look at me! Dis suit, vot it cost me twenty guineas, look at it. Ruined. Ruined. It vouldn't bring vun penny in der pound."

"The hell with your clothes!" exclaimed Kraski. "Here we are, lost, half starved, constantly menaced by wild animals, and maybe, for all we know, by cannibals, with Flora missing in the jungle, and you can stand there and talk about your 'twenty guinea' suit. You make me tired, Bluber. But come on, we might as well be moving."

"Which way?" asked Throck.

"Why, to the west, of course," replied Kraski. "The coast is there, and there is nothing else for us to do but try to reach it."

"We can't reach it by goin' east," roared Peebles, "an' 'ere we are, 'n that's that."

"Who said we could?" demanded Kraski.

"Well, we was travelin' east all day yesterday," said Peebles. "I knew all the time that there was somethin' wrong, and I just got it figured out."

Throck looked at his partner in stupid surprise. "What do you mean?" he growled. "What makes you think we was travelin' east?"

"It's easy enough," replied Peebles, "and I can prove it to you. Because this party here knows so much more than the rest of us we've been travelin' straight toward the interior ever since the niggers deserted us." He nodded toward the Russian, who stood with his hands on his hips, eyeing the other quizzically.

"If you think I'm taking you in the wrong direction, Peebles," said Kraski, "you just turn around and go the other way; but I'm going to keep on the way we've been going, which is the right way."

"It ain't the right way," retorted Peebles, "and I'll show yer. Listen here. When you travel west the sun is at your left side, isn't it—that is, all durin' the middle of the day. Well, ever since we've been travelin' without the niggers the sun has been on our right. I thought all the time there was somethin' wrong, but I could never figure it out until just now. It's plain as the face on your nose. We've been travelin' due east right along."

"Blime," cried Throck, "that we have, due east, and this blighter thinks as 'ow 'e knows it all."

"Oi!" groaned Bluber, "und ve got to valk it all back again yet, once more?"

Kraski laughed and turned away to resume the march in the direction he had chosen. "You fellows go on your own way if you want to," he said, "and while you're traveling, just ponder the fact that you're south of the equator and that therefore the sun is always in the north, which, however, doesn't change its old-fashioned habit of setting in the west."

Bluber was the first to grasp the truth of Kraski's statement. "Come on, boys," he said, "Carl vas right," and he turned and followed the Russian.

Peebles stood scratching his head, entirely baffled by the puzzling problem, which Throck, also, was pondering deeply. Presently the latter turned after Bluber and Kraski. "Come on, John," he said to Peebles, "hi don't hunderstand it, but hi guess they're right. They are headin' right toward where the sun set last night, and that sure must be west."

His theory tottering, Peebles followed Throck, though he remained unconvinced.

The four men, hungry and footsore, had dragged their weary way along the jungle trail toward the west for several hours in vain search for game. Unschooled in jungle craft they blundered on. There might have been on every hand fierce carnivore or savage warriors, but so dull are the perceptive faculties of civilized man, the most blatant foe might have stalked them unperceived.

And so it was that shortly after noon, as they were crossing a small clearing, the zip of an arrow that barely missed Bluber's head, brought them to a sudden, terrified halt. With a shrill scream of terror the Jew crumpled to the ground. Kraski threw his rifle to his shoulder and fired.

"There!" he cried, "behind those bushes," and then another arrow, from another direction, pierced his forearm. Peebles and Throck, beefy and cumbersome, got into action with less celerity than the Russian, but, like him, they showed no indication of fear.

"Down," cried Kraski, suiting the action to the word. "Lie down and let them have it."

Scarcely had the three men dropped among the long grass when a score of pigmy hunters came into the open, and a volley of arrows whizzed above the prone men, while from a nearby tree two steel-gray eyes looked down upon the ambush.

Bluber lay upon his belly with his face buried in his arms, his useless rifle lying at his side, but Kraski, Peebles, and Throck, fighting for their lives, pumped lead into the band of yelling pigmies.

Kraski and Peebles each dropped a native with his rifle and then the foe withdrew into the concealing safety of the surrounding jungle. For a moment there was a cessation of hostilities. Utter silence reigned, and then a voice broke the quiet from the verdure of a nearby forest giant.

"Do not fire until I tell you to," it said, in English, "and I will save you."

Bluber raised his head. "Come qvick! Come qvick!" he cried, "ve vill not shoot. Safe me, safe me, und I giff you five pounds."

From the tree from which the voice had issued there came a single, low, long-drawn, whistled note, and then silence for a time.

The pigmies, momentarily surprised by the mysterious voice emanating from the foliage of a tree, ceased their activities, but presently, hearing nothing to arouse their fear, they emerged from the cover of the bushes and launched another volley of arrows toward the four men lying among the grasses in the clearing. Simultaneously the figure of a giant white leaped from the lower branches of a patriarch of the jungle, as a great black-maned lion sprang from the thicket below.

"Oi!" shrieked Bluber, and again buried his face in his arms.

For an instant the pigmies stood terrified, and then their leader cried: "It is Tarzan!" and turned and fled into the jungle.

"Yes, it is Tarzan—Tarzan of the Apes," cried Lord Greystoke. "It is Tarzan and the golden lion," but he spoke in the dialect of the pigmies, and the whites understood no word of what he said. Then he turned to them. "The Gomangani have gone," he said; "get up."

The four men crawled to their feet. "Who are you, and what are you doing here?" demanded Tarzan of the Apes. "But I do not need to ask who you are. You are the men who drugged me, and left me helpless in your camp, a prey to the first passing lion or savage native."

Bluber stumbled forward, rubbing his palms together and cringing and smiling. "Oi! Oi! Mr. Tarzan, ve did not know you. Neffer vould ve did vat ve done, had ve known it vas Tarzan of the Apes. Safe me! Ten pounds—tventy pounds—anyt'ing. Name your own price. Safe me, und it is yours."

Tarzan ignored the Jew and turned toward the others. "I am looking for one of your men," he said; "a black named Luvini. He killed my wife. Where is he?"

"We know nothing of that," said Kraski. "Luvini betrayed us and deserted us. Your wife and another white woman were in our camp at the time. None of us knows what became of them. They were behind us when we took our post to defend the camp from our men and the slaves of the Arabs. Your Waziri were there. After the enemy had withdrawn we found that the two women had disappeared. We do not know what became of them. We are looking for them now."

"My Waziri told me as much," said Tarzan, "but have you seen aught of Luvini since?"

"No, we have not," replied Kraski.

"What are you doing here?" demanded Tarzan.

"We came with Mr. Bluber on a scientific expedition," replied the Russian. "We have had a great deal of trouble. Our head-men, askari, and porters have mutinied and deserted. We are absolutely alone and helpless."

"Oi! Oi!" cried Bluber. "Safe us! Safe us! But keep dot lion avay. He makes me nerfous."

"He will not hurt you—unless I tell him to," said Tarzan.

"Den please don't tell him to," cried Bluber.

"Where do you want to go?" asked Tarzan.

"We are trying to get back to the coast," replied Kraski, "and from there to London."

"Come with me," said Tarzan, "possibly I can help you. You do not deserve it, but I cannot see white men perish here in the jungle."

They followed him toward the west, and that night they made camp beside a small jungle stream.

It was difficult for the four Londoners to accustom themselves to the presence of the great lion, and Bluber was in a state of palpable terror.

As they squatted around the fire after the evening meal, which Tarzan had provided, Kraski suggested that they set to and build some sort of a shelter against the wild beasts.

"It will not be necessary," said Tarzan. "Jad-bal-ja will guard you. He will sleep here beside Tarzan of the Apes, and what one of us does not hear the other will."

Bluber sighed. "*Mein Gott!*" he cried. "I should giff ten pounds for vun night's sleep."

"You may have it tonight for less than that," replied Tarzan, "for nothing shall befall you while Jad-bal-ja and I are here."

"Vell, den I t'ink I say good night," said the Jew, and moving a few paces away from the fire he curled up and was soon asleep. Throck and Peebles followed suit, and shortly after Kraski, too.

As the Russian lay, half dozing, his eyes partially open, he saw the ape-man rise from the squatting position he had maintained before the fire, and turn toward a nearby tree. As he did so something fell from beneath his loin cloth—a little sack made of hides—a little sack, bulging with its contents.

Kraski, thoroughly awakened now, watched it as the ape-man moved off a short distance, accompanied by Jad-bal-ja, and lay down to sleep.

The great lion curled beside the prostrate man, and presently the Russian was assured that both slept. Immediately he commenced crawling, stealthily and slowly toward the little package lying beside the fire. With each forward move that he made he paused and looked at the recumbent figures of the two ferocious beasts before him, but both slept on peacefully. At last the Russian could reach out and grasp the sack, and drawing it toward him he stuffed it quickly inside his shirt. Then he turned and crawled slowly and carefully back to his place beyond the fire. There, lying with his head upon one arm as though in profound slumber, he felt carefully of the sack with the fingers of his left hand.

"They feel like pebbles," he muttered to himself, "and doubtless that is what they are, for the barbaric ornamentation of this savage barbarian who is a peer of England. It does not seem possible that this wild beast has sat in the House of Lords."

Noiselessly Kraski undid the knot which held the mouth of the sack closed, and a moment later he let a portion of the contents trickle forth into his open palm.

"My God!" he cried, "diamonds!"

Greedily he poured them all out and gloated over them—great scintillating stones of the first water—five pounds of pure, white diamonds, representing so fabulous a fortune that the very contemplation of it staggered the Russian.

"My God!" he repeated, "the wealth of Crœsus in my own hand."

Quickly he gathered up the stones and replaced them in the sack, always with one eye upon Tarzan and Jad-bal-ja; but neither stirred, and presently he had returned them all to the pouch and slipped the package inside his shirt.

"Tomorrow," he muttered, "tomorrow—would to God that I had the nerve to attempt it tonight."

In the middle of the following morning Tarzan, with the four Londoners, approached a good sized, stockaded village, containing many huts. He was received not only graciously, but with the deference due an emperor.

The whites were awed by the attitude of the black chief and his warriors as Tarzan was conducted into their presence.

After the usual ceremony had been gone through, Tarzan turned and waved his hand toward the four Europeans. "These are my friends," he said to the black chief, "and they wish to reach the coast in safety. Send with them, then, sufficient warriors to feed and guard them during the journey. It is I, Tarzan of the Apes, who requests this favor."

"Tarzan of the Apes, the great chief, Lord of the Jungle, has but to command," replied the black.

"Good!" exclaimed Tarzan, "feed them well and treat them well. I have other business to attend to and may not remain."

"Their bellies shall be filled, and they shall reach the coast unscathed," replied the chief.

Without a word of farewell, without even a sign that he realized their existence, Tarzan of the Apes passed from the sight of the four Europeans, while at his heels paced Jad-bal-ja, the golden lion.

A BARBED SHAFT KILLS

Kraski spent a sleepless night. He could not help but realize that sooner or later Tarzan would discover the loss of his pouch of diamonds, and that he would return and demand an accounting of the four Londoners he had befriended. And so it was that as the first streak of dawn lighted the eastern horizon, the Russian arose from his pallet of dried grasses within the hut that had been assigned him and Bluber by the chief, and crept stealthily out into the village street.

"God!" he muttered to himself. "There is only one chance in a thousand that I can reach the coast alone, but this," and he pressed his hand over the bag of diamonds that lay within his shirt—"but this, this is worth every effort, even to the sacrifice of life—the fortune of a thousand kings—my God, what could I not do with it in London, and Paris, and New York!"

Stealthily he slunk from the village, and presently the verdure of the jungle beyond closed about Carl Kraski, the Russian, as he disappeared forever from the lives of his companions.

Bluber was the first to discover the absence of Kraski, for, although there was no love between the two, they had been thrown together owing to the friendship of Peebles and Throck.

"Have you seen Carl this morning?" he asked Peebles as the three men gathered around the pot containing the unsavory stew that had been brought to them for their breakfast.

"No," said Peebles. "He must be asleep yet."

"He is not in the hut," replied Bluber. "He vas not dere ven I woke up."

"He can take care of himself," growled Throck, resuming his breakfast. "You'll likely find him with some of the ladies," and he grinned in appreciation of his little joke on Kraski's well-known weakness.

They had finished their breakfast and were attempting to communicate with some of the warriors, in an effort to learn when the chief proposed that they should set forth for the coast, and still Kraski had not made an appearance. By this time Bluber was considerably concerned, not at all for Kraski's safety, but for his own, since, if something could happen to Kraski in this friendly village in the still watches of the night, a similar fate might overtake him, and when he made this suggestion to the others it gave them food for thought, too, so that there were three rather apprehensive men who sought an audience with the chief.

By means of signs and pidgin English, and distorted native dialect, a word or two of which each of the three understood, they managed to convey to the chief the information that Kraski had disappeared, and that they wanted to know what had become of him.

The chief was, of course, as much puzzled as they, and immediately instituted a thorough search of the village, with the result that it was soon found that Kraski was not within the palisade, and shortly afterward footprints were discovered leading through the village gateway into the jungle.

"Mein Gott!" exclaimed Bluber, "he vent out dere, und he vent alone, in der middle of der night. He must have been crazy."

"Gord!" cried Throck, "what did he want to do that for?"

"You ain't missed nothin', have you?" asked Peebles of the other two. "'E might 'ave stolen somethin'."

"Oi! Oi! Vot have ve got to steal?" cried Bluber. "Our guns, our ammunition—dey are here beside us. He did not take them. Beside dose ve have nothing of value except my tventy guinea suit."

"But what did 'e do it for?" demanded Peebles.

"'E must 'ave been walkin' in 'is bloomin' sleep," said Throck. And that was as near to an explanation of Kraski's mysterious disappearance as the three could reach. An hour later they set out toward the coast under the protection of a company of the chief's warriors.

Kraski, his rifle slung over his shoulder, moved doggedly along the jungle trail, a heavy automatic pistol grasped in his right hand. His ears were constantly strained for the first intimation of pursuit as well as for whatever other dangers might lurk before or upon either side. Alone in the mysterious jungle he was experiencing a nightmare of terror, and with each mile that he traveled the value of the diamonds became less and less by comparison with the frightful ordeal that he realized he must pass through before he could hope to reach the coast.

Once Histah, the snake, swinging from a lowhung branch across the trail, barred his way, and the man dared not fire at him for fear of attracting the attention of possible pursuers to his position. He was forced, therefore, to make a detour through the tangled mass of underbrush which grew closely upon either side of the narrow trail. When he reached it again, beyond the snake, his clothing was more torn and tattered than before, and his flesh was scratched and cut and bleeding from the innumerable thorns past which he had been compelled to force his way. He was soaked with perspiration and panting from exhaustion, and his clothing was filled with ants whose vicious attacks upon his flesh rendered him half mad with pain.

Once again in the clear he tore his clothing from him and sought frantically to rid himself of the torturing pests.

So thick were the myriad ants upon his clothing that he dared not attempt to reclaim it. Only the sack of diamonds, his ammunition and his weapons did he snatch from the ravening horde whose numbers were rapidly increasing, apparently by millions, as they sought to again lay hold upon him and devour him.

Shaking the bulk of the ants from the articles he had retrieved, Kraski dashed madly along the trail as naked as the day he was born, and when, a half hour later, stumbling and at last falling exhausted, he lay panting upon the damp jungle earth, he realized the utter futility of his mad attempt to reach the coast alone, even more fully than he ever could have under any other circumstances, since there is nothing that so paralyzes the courage and self-confidence of a civilized man as to be deprived of his clothing.

However scant the protection that might have been afforded by the torn and tattered garments he had discarded, he could not have felt more helpless had he lost his weapons and ammunition instead, for, to such an extent are we the creatures of habit and environment. It was, therefore, a terrified Kraski, already foredoomed to failure, who crawled fearfully along the jungle trail.

That night, hungry and cold, he slept in the crotch of a great tree while the hunting carnivore roared, and coughed, and growled through the blackness of the jungle about him. Shivering with terror he started momentarily to fearful wakefulness, and when, from exhaustion, he would doze again it was not to rest but to dream of horrors that a sudden roar would merge into reality. Thus the long hours of a frightful night dragged out their tedious length, until it seemed that dawn would never come. But come it did, and once again he took up his stumbling way toward the west.

Reduced by fear and fatigue and pain to a state bordering upon half consciousness, he blundered on, with each passing hour becoming perceptibly weaker, for he had been without food or water since he had deserted his companions more than thirty hours before.

Noon was approaching. Kraski was moving but slowly now with frequent rests, and it was during one of these that there came to his numbed sensibilities an insistent suggestion of the voices of human beings not far distant. Quickly he shook himself and attempted to concentrate his waning faculties. He listened intently, and presently with a renewal of strength he arose to his feet.

There was no doubt about it. He heard voices but a short distance away and they sounded not like the tones of natives, but rather those of Europeans. Yet he was still careful, and so he crawled cautiously forward, until at a turning of the trail he saw before him a clearing dotted with trees which bordered the banks of a muddy stream. Near the edge of the river was a small hut thatched with grasses and surrounded by a rude palisade and further protected by an outer boma of thorn bushes.

It was from the direction of the hut that the voices were coming, and now he clearly discerned a woman's voice raised in protest and in anger, and replying to it the deep voice of a man.

Slowly the eyes of Carl Kraski went wide in incredulity, not unmixed with terror, for the tones of the voice of the man he heard were the tones of the dead Esteban Miranda, and the voice of the woman was that of the missing Flora Hawkes, whom he had long since given up as dead also. But Carl Kraski was no great believer in the supernatural. Disembodied spirits need no huts or palisades, or bomas of thorns. The owners of those voices were as live—as material—as he.

He started forward toward the hut, his hatred of Esteban and his jealousy almost forgotten in the relief he felt in the realization that he was to again have the companionship of creatures of his own kind. He had moved, however, but a few steps from the edge of the jungle when the woman's voice came again to his ear, and with it the sudden realization of his nakedness. He paused in thought, looking about him, and presently he was busily engaged gathering the long, broad-leaved jungle grasses, from which he fabricated a rude but serviceable skirt, which he fastened about his waist with a twisted rope of the same material. Then with a feeling of renewed confidence he moved forward toward the hut. Fearing that they might not recognize him at first, and, taking him for an enemy, attack him, Kraski, before he reached the entrance to the palisade, called Esteban by name. Immediately the Spaniard came from the hut, followed by the girl. Had Kraski not heard his voice and recognized him by it, he would have thought him Tarzan of the Apes, so close was the remarkable resemblance.

For a moment the two stood looking at the strange apparition before them.

"Don't you know me?" asked Kraski. "I am Carl—Carl Kraski. You know me, Flora."

"Carl!" exclaimed the girl, and started to leap forward, but Esteban grasped her by the wrist and held her back.

"What are you doing here, Kraski?" asked the Spaniard in a surly tone.

"I am trying to make my way to the coast," replied the Russian. "I am nearly dead from starvation and exposure."

"The way to the coast is there," said the Spaniard, and pointed down the trail toward the west. "Keep moving, Kraski, it is not healthy for you here."

"You mean to say that you will send me on without food or water?" demanded the Russian.

"There is water," said Esteban, pointing at the river, "and the jungle is full of food for one with sufficient courage and intelligence to gather it."

"You cannot send him away," cried the girl. "I did not think it possible that even you could be so cruel," and then, turning to the Russian, "O Carl," she cried, "do not go. Save me! Save me from this beast!"

"Then stand aside," cried Kraski, and as the girl wrenched herself free from the grasp of Miranda the Russian leveled his automatic and fired point-blank at the Spaniard. The bullet missed its target; the empty shell jammed in the breach and as Kraski pulled the trigger again with no result he glanced at his weapon

1000

and, discovering its uselessness, hurled it from him with an oath. As he strove frantically to bring his rifle into action Esteban threw back his spear hand with the short, heavy spear that he had learned by now so well to use, and before the other could press the trigger of his rifle the barbed shaft tore through his chest and heart. Without a sound Carl Kraski sank dead at the foot of his enemy and his rival, while the woman both had loved, each in his own selfish or brutal way, sank sobbing to the ground in the last and deepest depths of despair.

Seeing that the other was dead, Esteban stepped forward and wrenched his spear from Kraski's body and also relieved his dead enemy of his ammunition and weapons. As he did so his eyes fell upon a little bag made of skins which Kraski had fastened to his waist by the grass rope he had recently fashioned to uphold his primitive skirt.

The Spaniard felt of the bag and tried to figure out the nature of its contents, coming to the conclusion that it was ammunition, but he did not examine it closely until he had carried the dead man's weapons into his hut, where he had also taken the girl, who crouched in a corner, sobbing.

"Poor Carl! Poor Carl!" she moaned, and then to the man facing her: "You beast!"

"Yes," he cried, with a laugh, "I am a beast. I am Tarzan of the Apes, and that dirty Russian dared to call me Esteban. I am Tarzan! I am Tarzan of the Apes!" he repeated in a loud scream. "Who dares call me otherwise dies. I will show them. I will show them," he mumbled.

The girl looked at him with wide and flaming eyes and shuddered.

"Mad," she muttered. "Mad! My God—alone in the jungle with a maniac!" And, in truth, in one respect was Esteban Miranda mad—mad with the madness of the artist who lives the part he plays. And for so long, now, had Esteban Miranda played the part, and so really proficient had he become in his interpretation of the noble character, that he believed himself Tarzan, and in outward appearance he might have deceived the ape-man's best friend. But within that godlike form was the heart of a cur and the soul of a craven.

"He would have stolen Tarzan's mate," muttered Esteban. "Tarzan, Lord of the Jungle! Did you see how I slew him, with a single shaft? You could love a weakling, could you, when you could have the love of the great Tarzan!"

"I loathe you," said the girl. "You are indeed a beast. You are lower than the beasts."

"You are mine, though," said the Spaniard, "and you shall never be another's—first I would kill you—but let us see what the Russian had in his little bag of hides, it feels like ammunition enough to kill a regiment," and he untied the thongs that held the mouth of the bag closed and let some of the contents spill out upon the floor of the hut. As the sparkling stones rolled scintillant before their astonished eyes, the girl gasped in incredulity.

"Holy Mary!" exclaimed the Spaniard, "they are diamonds."

"Hundreds of them," murmured the girl. "Where could he have gotten them?"

"I do not know and I do not care," said Esteban. "They are mine. They are all mine—I am rich, Flora. I am rich, and if you are a good girl you shall share my wealth with me."

Flora Hawkes's eyes narrowed. Awakened within her breast was the always-present greed that dominated her being, and beside it, and equally as powerful now to dominate her, her hatred for the Spaniard. Could he have known it, possession of those gleaming baubles had crystallized at last in the mind of the woman a determination she had long fostered to slay the Spaniard while he slept. Heretofore she had been afraid of being left alone in the jungle, but now the desire to possess this great wealth overcame her terror.

Tarzan, ranging the jungle, picked up the trail of the various bands of west coast boys and the fleeing slaves of the dead Arabs, and overhauling each in turn he prosecuted his search for Luvini, awing the blacks into truthfulness and leaving them in a state of terror when he departed. Each and every one, they told him the same story. There was none who had seen Luvini since the night of the battle and the fire, and each was positive that he must have escaped with some other band.

So thoroughly occupied had the ape-man's mind been during the past few days with his sorrow and his search that lesser considerations had gone neglected, with the result that he had not noted that the bag containing the diamonds was missing. In fact, he had practically forgotten the diamonds when, by the merest vagary of chance his mind happened to revert to them, and then it was that he suddenly realized that they were missing, but when he had lost them, or the circumstances surrounding the loss, he could not recall.

"Those rascally Europeans," he muttered to Jad-bal-ja, "they must have taken them," and suddenly with the thought the scarlet scar flamed brilliantly upon his forehead, as just anger welled within him against the perfidy and ingratitude of the men he had succored. "Come," he said to Jad-bal-ja, "as we search for Luvini we shall search for these others also." And so it was that Peebles and Throck and Bluber had traveled but a short distance toward the coast when, during a noon-day halt, they were surprised to see the figure of the ape-man moving majestically toward them while, at his side, paced the great, black-maned lion.

Tarzan made no acknowledgment of their exuberant greeting, but came forward in silence to stand at last with folded arms before them. There was a grim, accusing expression upon his countenance that brought the chill of fear to Bluber's cowardly heart, and blanched the faces of the two hardened English pugs.

"What is it?" they chorused. "What is wrong? What has happened?"

"I have come for the bag of stones you took from me," said Tarzan simply.

Each of the three eyed his companion suspiciously.

"I do not understand vot you mean, Mr. Tarzan," purred Bluber, rubbing his palms together. "I am sure dere is some mistake, unless—" he cast a furtive and suspicious glance in the direction of Peebles and Throck.

"I don't know nothin' about no bag of stones," said Peebles, "but I will say as 'ow you can't trust no Jew."

"I don't trust any of you," said Tarzan. "I will give you five seconds to hand over the bag of stones, and if you don't produce it in that time I shall have you thoroughly searched."

"Sure," cried Bluber, "search me, search me, by all means. Vy, Mr. Tarzan, I vouldn't take notting from you for notting."

"There's something wrong here," growled Throck. "I ain't got nothin' of yours and I'm sure these two haven't neither."

"Where is the other?" asked Tarzan.

"Oh, Kraski? He disappeared the same night you brought us to that village. We hain't seen him since—that's it; I got it now—we wondered why he left, and now I see it as plain as the face on me nose. It was him that stole that bag of stones. That's what he done. We've been tryin' to figure out ever since he left what he stole, and now I see it plain enough."

"Sure," exclaimed Peebles. "That's it, and 'ere we are, 'n that's that."

"Ve might have knowed it, ve might have knowed it," agreed Bluber.

"But nevertheless I'm going to have you all searched," said Tarzan, and when the head-man came and Tarzan had explained what he desired, the three whites were quickly stripped and searched. Even their few belongings were thoroughly gone through, but no bag of stones was revealed.

Without a word Tarzan turned back toward the jungle, and in another moment the blacks and the three Europeans saw the leafy sea of foliage swallow the ape-man and the golden lion.

"Gord help Kraski!" exclaimed Peebles.

"Wot do yer suppose he wants with a bag o' stones?" inquired Throck. "'E must be a bit balmy, I'll say."

"Balmy nudding," exclaimed Bluber. "Dere is but vun kind of stones in Africa vot Kraski would steal and run off into der jungle alone mit—diamonds."

Peebles and Throck opened their eyes in surprise. "The damned Russian!" exclaimed the former. "He double-crossed us, that's what 'e did."

"He likely as not saved our lives, says hi," said Throck. "If this ape feller had found Kraski and the diamonds with us we'd of all suffered alike—you couldn't 'a' made 'im believe we didn't 'ave a 'and in it. And Kraski wouldn't 'a' done nothin' to help us out."

"I 'opes 'e catches the beggar!" exclaimed Peebles, fervently.

They were startled into silence a moment later by the sight of Tarzan returning to the camp, but he paid no attention to the whites, going instead directly to the head-man, with whom he conferred for several minutes. Then, once more, he turned and left.

Acting on information gained from the head-man, Tarzan struck off through the jungle in the general direction of the village where he had left the four whites in charge of the chief, and from which Kraski had later escaped alone. He moved rapidly, leaving Jad-bal-ja to follow behind, covering the distance to the village in a comparatively short time, since he moved almost in an air line through the trees, where there was no matted undergrowth to impede his progress.

Outside the village gate he took up Kraski's spoor, now almost obliterated, it is true, but still legible to the keen perceptive faculties of the ape-man. This he followed swiftly, since Kraski had clung tenaciously to the open trail that wound in a general westward direction.

The sun had dropped almost to the western tree-tops, when Tarzan came suddenly upon a clearing beside a sluggish stream, near the banks of which stood a small, rude hut, surrounded by a palisade and a thorn boma.

The ape-man paused and listened, sniffing the air with his sensitive nostrils, and then on noiseless feet he crossed the clearing toward the hut. In the grass outside the palisade lay the dead body of a white man, and a single glance told the ape-man that it was the fugitive whom he sought. Instantly he realized the futility of searching the corpse for the bag of diamonds, since it was a foregone conclusion that they were now in the possession of whoever had slain the Russian. A perfunctory examination revealed the fact that he was right in so far as the absence of the diamonds was concerned.

Both inside the hut and outside the palisade were indications of the recent presence of a man and woman, the spoor of the former tallying with that of the creature who had killed Gobu, the great ape, and hunted Bara, the deer, upon the preserves of the ape-man. But the woman—who was she? It was evident that she had been walking upon sore, tired feet, and that in lieu of shoes she wore bandages of cloth.

Tarzan followed the spoor of the man and the woman where it led from the hut into the jungle. As it progressed it became apparent that the woman had been lagging behind, and that she had commenced to limp more and more painfully. Her progress was very slow, and Tarzan could see that the man had not waited for her, but that he had been, in some places, a considerable distance ahead of her.

And so it was that Esteban had forged far ahead of Flora Hawkes, whose bruised and bleeding feet would scarce support her.

"Wait for me, Esteban," she had pleaded. "Do not desert me. Do not leave me alone here in this terrible jungle."

"Then keep up with me," growled the Spaniard. "Do you think that with this fortune in my possession I am going to wait here forever in the middle of the jungle for someone to come and take it away from me? No, I am going on to the coast as fast as I can. If you can keep up, well and good. If you cannot, that is your own lookout."

"But you could not desert me. Even you, Esteban, could not be such a beast after all that you have forced me to do for you."

The Spaniard laughed. "You are nothing more to me," he said, "than an old glove. With this," and he held the sack of diamonds before him, "I can purchase the finest gloves in the capitals of the world—new gloves," and he laughed grimly at his little joke.

"Esteban, Esteban," she cried, "come back, come back. I can go no farther. Do not leave me. Please come back and save me." But he only laughed at her, and as a turn of the trail shut him from her sight, she sank helpless and exhausted to the ground.

THE DEAD RETURN

That night Esteban made his lonely camp beside a jungle trail that wound through the dry wash of an old river bed, along which a tiny rivulet still trickled, affording the Spaniard the water which he craved.

The obsession which possessed him that he was in truth Tarzan of the Apes, imparted to him a false courage, so that he could camp alone upon the ground without recourse to artificial protection of any kind, and fortune had favored him in this respect in that it had sent no prowling beasts of prey to find him upon those occasions that he had dared too much. During the period that Flora Hawkes had been with him he had built shelters for her, but now that he had deserted her and was again alone, he could not, in the rôle that he had assumed, consider so effeminate an act as the building of even a thorn boma for protection during the darkness of the night.

He did, however, build a fire, for he had made a kill and had not yet reached a point of primitive savagery which permitted him even to imagine that he enjoyed raw meat.

Having devoured what meat he wanted and filled himself at the little rivulet, Esteban came back and squatted before his fire, where he drew the pouch of diamonds from his loin cloth and, opening it, spilled a handful of the precious gems into his palm. The flickering firelight playing upon them sent scintillant gleams shooting into the dark of the surrounding jungle night as the Spaniard let a tiny stream of the sparkling stones trickle from one hand to the other, and in the pretty play of light the Spaniard saw visions of the future—power, luxury, beautiful women—all that great wealth might purchase for a man. With half closed eyes he dreamed of the ideal that he should search the world over to obtain—the dream-woman for whom he had always searched—the dream-woman he had never found, the fit companion for such as Esteban Miranda imagined himself to be. Presently through the dark lashes that veiled his narrowed lids the Spaniard seemed to see before him in the flickering light of his campfire a vague materialization of the figure of his dream—a woman's figure, clothed in flowing diaphanous white which appeared to hover just above him at the outer rim of his firelight at the summit of the ancient river bank.

It was strange how the vision persisted. Esteban closed his eyes tightly, and then opened them ever so little, and there, as it had been before he closed them, the vision remained. And then he opened his eyes wide, and still the figure of the woman in white floated above him.

Esteban Miranda went suddenly pale. "Mother of God!" he cried. "It is Flora. She is dead and has come back to haunt me."

With staring eyes he slowly rose to his feet to confront the apparition, when in soft and gentle tones it spoke.

"Heart of my heart," it cried, "it is really you!"

Instantly Esteban realized that this was no disembodied spirit, nor was it Flora—but who was it? Who was this vision of beauty, alone in the savage African wilderness?

Very slowly now it was descending the embankment and coming toward him. Esteban returned the diamonds to the pouch and replaced it inside his loin cloth.

With outstretched arms the girl came toward him. "My love, my love," she cried, "do not tell me that you do not know me." She was close enough now for the Spaniard to see her rapidly rising and falling breasts and her lips trembling with love and passion. A sudden wave of hot desire swept over him, so with outstretched arms he sprang forward to meet her and crush her to his breast.

Tarzan, following the spoor of the man and the woman, moved in a leisurely manner along the jungle trail, for he realized that no haste was essential to overtake these two. Nor was he at all surprised when he came suddenly upon the huddled figure of a woman, lying in the center of the pathway. He knelt beside her and laid a hand upon her shoulder, eliciting a startled scream.

"God!" she cried, "this is the end!"

"You are in no danger," said the ape-man. "I will not harm you."

She turned her eyes and looked up at him. At first she thought he was Esteban. "You have come back to save me, Esteban?" she asked.

"Esteban!" he exclaimed. "I am not Esteban. That is not my name." And then she recognized him.

"Lord Greystoke!" she cried. "It is really you?"

"Yes," he said, "and who are you?"

"I am Flora Hawkes. I was Lady Greystoke's maid."

"I remember you," he said. "What are you doing here?"

"I am afraid to tell you," she said. "I am afraid of your anger."

"Tell me," he commanded. "You should know, Flora, that I do not harm women."

"We came to get gold from the vaults of Opar," she said. "But that you know."

"I know nothing of it," he replied. "Do you mean that you were with those Europeans who drugged me and left me in their camp?"

"Yes," she said, "we got the gold, but you came with your Waziri and took it from us."

"I came with no Waziri and took nothing from you," said Tarzan. "I do not understand you."

She raised her eyebrows in surprise, for she knew that Tarzan of the Apes did not lie.

"We became separated," she said, "after our men turned against us. Esteban stole me from the others, and then, after a while Kraski found us. He was the Russian. He came with a bagful of diamonds and then Esteban killed him and took the diamonds."

It was now Tarzan's turn to experience surprise.

"And Esteban is the man who is with you?" he asked.

"Yes," she said, "but he has deserted me. I could not walk farther on my sore feet. He has gone and left me here to die and he has taken the diamonds with him."

"We shall find him," said the ape-man. "Come."

"But I cannot walk," said the girl.

"That is a small matter," he said, and stooping lifted her to his shoulder.

Easily the ape-man bore the exhausted girl along the trail. "It is not far to water," he said, "and water is what you need. It will help to revive you and give you strength, and perhaps I shall be able to find food for you soon."

"Why are you so good to me?" asked the girl.

"You are a woman. I could not leave you alone in the jungle to die, no matter what you may have done," replied the ape-man. And Flora Hawkes could only sob a broken plea for forgiveness for the wrong she had done him.

It grew quite dark, but still they moved along the silent trail until presently Tarzan caught in the distance the reflection of firelight.

"I think we shall soon find your friend," he whispered. "Make no noise."

A moment later his keen ears caught the sound of voices. He halted and lowered the girl to her feet.

"If you cannot follow," he said, "wait here. I do not wish him to escape. I will return for you. If you can follow on slowly, do so." And then he left her and made his way cautiously forward toward the light and the voices. He heard Flora Hawkes moving directly behind him. It was evident that she could not bear the thought of being left alone again in the dark jungle. Almost simultaneously Tarzan heard a low whine a few paces to his right. "Jad-bal-ja," he whispered in a low voice, "heel," and the great black-maned lion crept close to him, and Flora Hawkes, stifling a scream, rushed to his side and grasped his arms.

"Silence," he whispered; "Jad-bal-ja will not harm you."

An instant later the three came to the edge of the ancient river bank, and through the tall grasses growing there looked down upon the little camp beneath.

Tarzan, to his consternation, saw a counterpart of himself standing before a little fire, while slowly approaching the man, with outstretched arms, was a woman, draped in flowing white. He heard her words;

soft words of love and endearment, and at the sound of the voice and the scent spoor that a vagrant wind carried suddenly to his nostrils, a strange complex of emotion overwhelmed him—happiness, despair, rage, love, and hate.

He saw the man at the fire step forward with open arms to take the woman to his breast, and then Tarzan separated the grasses and stepped to the very edge of the embankment, his voice shattering the jungle with a single word.

"Jane!" he cried, and instantly the man and woman turned and looked up at him, where his figure was dimly revealed in the light of the campfire. At sight of him the man wheeled and raced for the jungle on the opposite side of the river, and then Tarzan leaped to the bottom of the wash below and ran toward the woman.

"Jane," he cried, "it is you, it is you!"

The woman showed her bewilderment. She looked first at the retreating figure of the man she had been about to embrace and then turned her eyes toward Tarzan. She drew her fingers across her brow and looked back toward Esteban, but Esteban was no longer in sight. Then she took a faltering step toward the ape-man.

"My God," she cried, "what does it mean? Who are you, and if you are Tarzan who was he?"

"I am Tarzan, Jane," said the ape-man.

She looked back and saw Flora Hawkes approaching. "Yes," she said, "you are Tarzan. I saw you when you ran off into the jungle with Flora Hawkes. I cannot understand, John. I could not believe that you, even had you suffered an accident to your head, could have done such a thing."

"I, run off into the jungle with Flora Hawkes?" he asked, in unfeigned surprise.

"I saw you," said Jane.

The ape-man turned toward Flora. "I do not understand it," he said.

"It was Esteban who ran off into the jungle with me, Lady Greystoke," said the girl. "It was Esteban who was about to deceive you again. This is indeed Lord Greystoke. The other was an impostor, who only just deserted me and left me to die in the jungle. Had not Lord Greystoke come when he did I should be dead by now."

Lady Greystoke took a faltering step toward her husband. "Ah, John," she said, "I knew it could not have been you. My heart told me, but my eyes deceived me. Quick," she cried, "that impostor must be captured. Hurry, John, before he escapes."

"Let him go," said the ape-man. "As much as I want him, as much as I want that which he has stolen from me, I will not leave you alone again in the jungle, Jane, even to catch him."

"But Jad-bal-ja," she cried. "What of him?"

"Ah," cried the ape-man, "I had forgotten," and turning to the lion he pointed toward the direction that the Spaniard had escaped. "Fetch him, Jad-bal-ja," he cried; and, with a bound, the tawny beast was off upon the spoor of his quarry.

"He will kill him?" asked Flora Hawkes, shuddering. And yet at heart she was glad of the just fate that was overtaking the Spaniard.

"No, he will not kill him," said Tarzan of the Apes. "He may maul him a bit, but he will bring him back alive if it is possible." And then, as though the fate of the fugitive was already forgotten, he turned toward his mate.

"Jane," he said, "Usula told me that you were dead. He said that they found your burned body in the Arab village and that they buried it there. How is it, then, that you are here alive and unharmed? I have been searching the jungles for Luvini to avenge your death. Perhaps it is well that I did not find him."

"You would never have found him," replied Jane Clayton, "but I cannot understand why Usula should have told you that he had found my body and buried it."

"Some prisoners that he took," replied Tarzan, "told him that Luvini had taken you bound hand and foot into one of the Arab huts near the village gateway, and that there he had further secured you to a stake driven into the floor of the hut. After the village had been destroyed by fire Usula and the other Waziri returned to search for you with some of the prisoners they had taken who pointed out the location of the hut, where the charred remains of a human body were found beside a burned stake to which it had apparently been tied."

"Ah!" exclaimed the girl, "I see. Luvini did bind me hand and foot and tie me to the stake, but later he came back into the hut and removed the bonds. He attempted to attack me—how long we fought I do not know, but so engrossed were we in our struggle that neither one of us was aware of the burning of the village about us. As I persistently fought him off I caught a glimpse of a knife in his belt, and then I let him seize me and as his arms encircled me I grasped the knife and, drawing it from its sheath, plunged it into his back, below his left shoulder—that was the end. Luvini sank lifeless to the floor of the hut. Almost simultaneously the rear and roof of the structure burst into flames.

"I was almost naked, for he had torn nearly all my clothing from me in our struggles. Hanging upon the wall of the hut was this white burnoose, the property, doubtless, of one of the murdered Arabs. I seized it, and throwing it about me ran into the village street. The huts were now all aflame, and the last of the natives was disappearing through the gateway. To my right was a section of palisade that had not yet been attacked by the flames. To escape into the jungle by the gateway would have meant running into the arms of my enemies, and so, somehow, I managed to scale the palisade and drop into the jungle unseen by any.

"I have had considerable difficulty eluding the various bands of blacks who escaped the village. A part of the time I have been hunting for the Waziri and the balance I have had to remain in hiding. I was resting in the crotch of a tree, about half a mile from here, when I saw the light of this man's fire, and when I came to investigate I was almost stunned by joy to discover that I had, as I imagined, stumbled upon my Tarzan."

"It was Luvini's body, then, and not yours that they buried," said Tarzan.

"Yes," said Jane, "and it was this man who just escaped whom I saw run off into the jungle with Flora, and not you, as I believed."

Flora Hawkes looked up suddenly. "And it must have been Esteban who came with the Waziri and stole the gold from us. He fooled our men and he must have fooled the Waziri, too."

"He might have fooled anyone if he could deceive me," said Jane Clayton. "I should have discovered the deception in a few minutes I have no doubt, but in the flickering light of the campfire, and influenced as I was by the great joy of seeing Lord Greystoke again, I believed quickly that which I wanted to believe."

The ape-man ran his fingers through his thick shock of hair in a characteristic gesture of meditation. "I cannot understand how he fooled Usula in broad daylight," he said with a shake of his head.

"I can," said Jane. "He told him that he had suffered an injury to his head which had caused him to lose his memory partially—an explanation which accounted for many lapses in the man's interpretation of your personality."

"He was a clever devil," commented the ape-man.

"He was a devil, all right," said Flora.

It was more than an hour later that the grasses at the river bank suddenly parted and Jad-bal-ja emerged silently into their presence. Grasped in his jaws was a torn and bloody leopard skin which he brought and laid at the feet of his master.

The ape-man picked the thing up and examined it, and then he scowled. "I believe Jad-bal-ja killed him after all," he said.

"He probably resisted," said Jane Clayton, "in which event Jad-bal-ja could do nothing else in self-defense but slay him."

"Do you suppose he ate him?" cried Flora Hawkes, drawing fearfully away from the beast.

"No," said Tarzan, "he has not had time. In the morning we will follow the spoor and find his body. I should like to have the diamonds again." And then he told Jane the strange story connected with his acquisition of the great wealth represented by the little bag of stones.

The following morning they set out in search of Esteban's corpse. The trail led through dense brush and thorns to the edge of the river farther down stream, and there it disappeared, and though the ape-man searched both sides of the river for a couple of miles above and below the point at which he had lost the spoor, he found no further sign of the Spaniard. There was blood along the tracks that Esteban had made and blood upon the grasses at the river's brim.

At last the ape-man returned to the two women. "That is the end of the man who would be Tarzan," he said.

"Do you think he is dead?" asked Jane.

"Yes, I am sure of it," said the ape-man. "From the blood I imagine that Jad-bal-ja mauled him, but that he managed to break away and get into the river. The fact that I can find no indication of his having reached the bank within a reasonable distance of this spot leads me to believe that he has been devoured by crocodiles."

Again Flora Hawkes shuddered. "He was a wicked man," she said, "but I would not wish even the wickedest such a fate as that."

The ape-man shrugged. "He brought it upon himself, and, doubtless, the world is better off without him."

"It was my fault," said Flora. "It was my wickedness that brought him and the others here. I told them of what I had heard of the gold in the treasure vaults of Opar—it was my idea to come here and steal it and to find a man who could impersonate Lord Greystoke. Because of my wickedness many men have died, and you, Lord Greystoke, and your lady, have almost met your death—I do not dare to ask for forgiveness."

Jane Clayton put her arm about the girl's shoulder. "Avarice has been the cause of many crimes since the world began," she said, "and when crime is invoked in its aid it assumes its most repulsive aspect and brings most often its own punishment, as you, Flora, may well testify. For my part I forgive you. I imagine that you have learned your lesson."

"You have paid a heavy price for your folly," said the ape-man. "You have been punished enough. We will take you to your friends who are on their way to the coast under escort of a friendly tribe. They cannot be far distant, for, from the condition of the men when I saw them, long marches are beyond their physical powers."

The girl dropped to her knees at his feet. "How can I thank you for your kindness?" she said. "But I would rather remain here in Africa with you and Lady Greystoke, and work for you and show by my loyalty that I can redeem the wrong I did you."

Tarzan glanced at his wife questioningly, and Jane Clayton signified her assent to the girl's request.

"Very well, then," said the ape-man, "you may remain with us, Flora."

"You will never regret it," said the girl. "I will work my fingers off for you."

The three, and Jad-bal-ja, had been three days upon the march toward home when Tarzan, who was in the lead, paused, and, raising his head, sniffed the jungle air. Then he turned to them with a smile. "My Waziri are disobedient," he said. "I sent them home and yet here they are, coming toward us, directly away from home."

A few minutes later they met the van of the Waziri, and great was the rejoicing of the blacks when they found both their master and mistress alive and unscathed.

"And now that we have found you," said Tarzan, after the greetings were over, and innumerable questions had been asked and answered, "tell me what you did with the gold that you took from the camp of the Europeans."

"We hid it, O Bwana, where you told us to hide it," replied Usula.

"I was not with you, Usula," said the ape-man. "It was another, who deceived Lady Greystoke even as he deceived you—a bad man—who impersonated Tarzan of the Apes so cleverly that it is no wonder that you were imposed upon."

"Then it was not you who told us that your head had been injured and that you could not remember the language of the Waziri?" demanded Usula.

"It was not I," said Tarzan, "for my head has not been injured, and I remember well the language of my children."

"Ah," cried Usula, "then it was not our Big Bwana who ran from Buto, the rhinoceros?"

Tarzan laughed. "Did the other run from Buto?"

"That he did," cried Usula; "he ran in great terror."

"I do not know that I blame him," said Tarzan, "for Buto is no pleasant playfellow."

"But our Big Bwana would not run from him," said Usula, proudly.

"Even if another than I hid the gold it was you who dug the hole. Lead me to the spot then, Usula."

The Waziri constructed rude yet comfortable litters for the two white women, though Jane Clayton laughed at the idea that it was necessary that she be carried and insisted upon walking beside her bearers more often than she rode. Flora Hawkes, however, weak and exhausted as she was, could not have proceeded far without being carried, and was glad of the presence of the brawny Waziri who bore her along the jungle trail so easily.

It was a happy company that marched in buoyant spirits toward the spot where the Waziri had cached the gold for Esteban. The blacks were overflowing with good nature because they had found their master and their mistress, while the relief and joy of Tarzan and Jane were too deep for expression.

When at last they came to the place beside the river where they had buried the gold the Waziri, singing and laughing, commenced to dig for the treasure, but presently their singing ceased and their laughter was replaced by expressions of puzzled concern.

For a while Tarzan watched them in silence and then a slow smile overspread his countenance. "You must have buried it deep, Usula," he said.

The black scratched his head. "No, not so deep as this, Bwana," he cried. "I cannot understand it. We should have found the gold before this."

"Are you sure you are looking in the right place?" asked Tarzan.

"This is the exact spot, Bwana," the black assured him, "but the gold is not here. Someone has removed it since we buried it."

"The Spaniard again," commented Tarzan. "He was a slick customer."

"But he could not have taken it alone," said Usula. "There were many ingots of it."

"No," said Tarzan, "he could not, and yet it is not here."

The Waziri and Tarzan searched carefully about the spot where the gold had been buried, but so clever had been the woodcraft of Owaza that he had obliterated even from the keen senses of the ape-man every vestige of the spoor that he and the Spaniard had made in carrying the gold from the old hiding place to the new.

"It is gone," said the ape-man, "but I shall see that it does not get out of Africa," and he despatched runners in various directions to notify the chiefs of the friendly tribes surrounding his domain to watch carefully every safari crossing their territory, and to let none pass who carried gold.

"That will stop them," he said after the runners had departed.

That night as they made their camp upon the trail toward home, the three whites were seated about a small fire with Jad-bal-ja lying just behind the ape-man, who was examining the leopard skin that the golden lion had retrieved in his pursuit of the Spaniard, when Tarzan turned toward his wife.

"You were right, Jane," he said. "The treasure vaults of Opar are not for me. This time I have lost not only the gold but a fabulous fortune in diamonds as well, beside risking that greatest of all treasures—yourself."

"Let the gold and the diamonds go, John," she said; "we have one another, and Korak."

"And a bloody leopard skin," he supplemented, "with a mystery map painted upon it in blood."

Jad-bal-ja sniffed the hide and licked his chops in—anticipation or retrospection—which?

TARZAN SUPER PACK

AN ESCAPE AND A CAPTURE

At sight of the true Tarzan, Esteban Miranda turned and fled blindly into the jungle. His heart was cold with terror as he rushed on in blind fear. He had no objective in mind. He did not know in what direction he was going. His only thought—the thought which dominated him—was based solely upon a desire to put as much distance as possible between himself and the ape-man, and so he blundered on, forcing his way through dense thickets of thorns that tore and lacerated his flesh until, at every step he left a trail of blood behind him.

At the river's edge the thorns reached out and seized again, as they had several times before, the precious leopard skin to which he clung with almost the same tenacity as he clung to life itself. But this time the thorns would not leave go their hold, and as he struggled to tear it away from them his eyes turned back in the direction from which he had come. He heard the sound of a great body moving rapidly through the thicket toward him, and an instant later saw the baleful glare of two gleaming, yellow-green spots of flame. With a stifled cry of terror the Spaniard relinquished his hold upon the leopard skin and, wheeling, dived into the river.

As the black waters closed above his head Jad-bal-ja came to the edge of the bank and looked down upon the widening circles which marked the spot of his quarry's disappearance, for Esteban, who was a strong swimmer, struck boldly for the opposite side of the stream, keeping himself well submerged.

For a moment the golden lion scanned the surface of the river, and then he turned and sniffed at the hide the Spaniard had been forced to leave behind, and grasping it in his jaws tore it from the thorns that held it and carried it back to lay it at the feet of his master.

Forced at last to come to the surface for air the Spaniard arose amid a mass of tangled foliage and branches. For a moment he thought that he was lost, so tightly held was he by the entangling boughs, but presently he forced his way upward, and as his head appeared above the surface of the water amidst the foliage he discovered that he had arisen directly beneath a fallen tree that was floating down the center of the stream. After considerable effort he managed to draw himself up to the boughs and find a place astride the great bole, and thus he floated down stream in comparative safety.

He breathed a deep sigh of relief as he realized with what comparative ease he had escaped the just vengeance of the ape-man. It is true that he bemoaned the loss of the hide which carried the map to the location of the hidden gold, but he still retained in his possession a far greater treasure, and as he thought of it his hands gloatingly fondled the bag of diamonds fastened to his loin cloth. Yet, even though he possessed this great fortune in diamonds, his avaricious mind constantly returned to the golden ingots by the waterfall.

"Owaza will get it," he muttered to himself. "I never trusted the black dog, and when he deserted me I knew well enough what his plans were."

All night long Esteban Miranda floated down stream upon the fallen tree, seeing no sign of life, until shortly after daybreak, he passed a native village upon the shore.

It was the village of Obebe, the cannibal, and at sight of the strange figure of the white giant floating down the stream upon the bole of a tree, the young woman who espied him raised a great hue and cry until the population of the village lined the shore watching him pass.

"It is a strange god," cried one.

"It is the river devil," said the witch doctor. "He is a friend of mine. Now, indeed, shall we catch many fish if for each ten that you catch you give one to me."

"It is not the river devil," rumbled the deep voice of Obebe, the cannibal. "You are getting old," he said to the witch doctor, "and of late your medicine has been poor medicine, and now you tell me that Obebe's greatest enemy is the river devil. That is Tarzan of the Apes. Obebe knows him well." And in truth every cannibal chief in the vicinity knew Tarzan of the Apes well and feared and hated him, for relentless had been the ape-man's war against them.

"It is Tarzan of the Apes," repeated Obebe, "and he is in trouble. Perhaps it is our chance to capture him."

He called his warriors about him, and presently half a hundred brawny young bucks started at a jog trot down the trail that paralleled the river. For miles they followed the slowly moving tree which carried Esteban Miranda until at last at a bend in the river the tree was caught in the outer circle of a slow-moving eddy, which carried it beneath the overhanging limbs of trees growing close to the river's edge.

Cramped and chilled and hungry as he was, Esteban was glad of the opportunity to desert his craft and gain the shore. And so, laboriously, he drew himself up among the branches of the tree that momentarily offered him a haven of retreat from the river, and crawling to its stem lowered himself to the ground beneath, unconscious of the fact that in the grasses around him squatted half a hundred cannibal warriors.

Leaning against the bole of the tree the Spaniard rested for a moment. He felt for the diamonds and found that they were safe.

"I am a lucky devil, after all," he said aloud, and almost simultaneously the fifty blacks arose about him and leaped upon him. So sudden was the attack, so overwhelming the force, that the Spaniard had no opportunity to defend himself against them, with the result that he was down and securely bound almost before he could realize what was happening to him.

"Ah, Tarzan of the Apes, I have you at last," gloated Obebe, the cannibal, but Esteban did not understand a word the man said, and so he could make no reply. He talked to Obebe in English, but that language the latter did not understand.

Of only one thing was Esteban certain; that he was a prisoner and that he was being taken back toward the interior. When they reached Obebe's village there was great rejoicing on the part of the women and the children and the warriors who had remained behind. But the witch doctor shook his head and made wry faces and dire prophecies.

"You have seized the river devil," he said. "We shall catch no more fish, and presently a great sickness will fall upon Obebe's people and they will all die like flies." But Obebe only laughed at the witch doctor for, being an old man and a great king, he had accumulated much wisdom and, with the acquisition of wisdom man is more inclined to be skeptical in matters of religion.

"You may laugh now, Obebe," said the witch doctor, "but later you will not laugh. Wait and see."

"When, with my own hands, I kill Tarzan of the Apes, then indeed shall I laugh," replied the chief, "and when I and my warriors have eaten his heart and his flesh, then, indeed, shall we no longer fear any of your devils."

"Wait," cried the witch doctor angrily, "and you shall see."

They took the Spaniard, securely bound, and threw him into a filthy hut, through the doorway of which he could see the women of the village preparing cooking fires and pots for the feast of the coming night. A cold sweat stood out upon the brow of Esteban Miranda as he watched these gruesome preparations, the significance of which he could not misinterpret, when coupled with the gestures and the glances that were directed toward the hut where he lay, by the inhabitants of the village.

The afternoon was almost spent and the Spaniard felt that he could count the hours of life remaining to him upon possibly two fingers of one hand, when there came from the direction of the river a series of piercing screams which shattered the quiet of the jungle, and brought the inhabitants of the village to startled attention, and an instant later sent them in a mad rush in the direction of the fear-laden shrieks. But they were too late and reached the river only just in time to see a woman dragged beneath the surface by a huge crocodile.

"Ah, Obebe, what did I tell you?" demanded the witch doctor, exultantly. "Already has the devil god commenced his revenge upon your people."

The ignorant villagers, steeped in superstition, looked fearfully from their witch doctor to their chief. Obebe scowled, "He is Tarzan of the Apes," he insisted.

"He is the river devil who has taken the shape of Tarzan of the Apes," insisted the witch doctor.

"We shall see," replied Obebe. "If he is the river devil he can escape our bonds. If he is Tarzan of the Apes he cannot. If he is the river devil he will not die a natural death, like men die, but will live on forever. If he is Tarzan of the Apes some day he will die. We will keep him, then, and see, and that will prove whether or not he is Tarzan of the Apes or the river devil."

"How?" asked the witch doctor.

"It is very simple," replied Obebe. "If some morning we find that he has escaped we will know that he is the river devil, and because we have not harmed him but have fed him well while he has been here in our village, he will befriend us and no harm will come of it. But if he does not escape we will know that he is Tarzan of the Apes, provided he dies a natural death. And so, if he does not escape, we shall keep him until he dies and then we shall know that he was, indeed, Tarzan of the Apes."

"But suppose he does not die?" asked the witch doctor, scratching his woolly head.

"Then," exclaimed Obebe triumphantly, "we will know that you are right, and that he was, indeed, the river devil."

Obebe went and ordered women to take food to the Spaniard while the witch doctor stood, where Obebe had left him, in the middle of the street, still scratching his head in thought.

And thus was Esteban Miranda, possessor of the most fabulous fortune in diamonds that the world had ever known, condemned to life imprisonment in the village of Obebe, the cannibal.

While he had been lying in the hut his traitorous confederate, Owaza, from the opposite bank of the river from the spot where he and Esteban had hidden the golden ingots, saw Tarzan and his Waziri come and search for the gold and go away again, and the following morning Owaza came with fifty men whom he had recruited from a neighboring village and dug up the gold and started with it toward the coast.

That night Owaza made camp just outside a tiny village of a minor chief, who was weak in warriors. The old fellow invited Owaza into his compound, and there he fed him and gave him native beer, while the chief's people circulated among Owaza's boys plying them with innumerable questions until at last the truth leaked out and the chief knew that Owaza's porters were carrying a great store of yellow gold.

When the chief learned this for certain he was much perturbed, but finally a smile crossed his face as he talked with the half-drunken Owaza.

"You have much gold with you," said the old chief, "and it is very heavy. It will be hard to get your boys to carry it all the way back to the coast."

"Yes," said Owaza, "but I shall pay them well."

"If they did not have to carry it so far from home you would not have to pay them so much, would you?" asked the chief.

"No," said Owaza, "but I cannot dispose of it this side of the coast."

"I know where you can dispose of it within two days' march," replied the old chief.

"Where?" demanded Owaza. "And who here in the interior will buy it?"

"There is a white man who will give you a little piece of paper for it and you can take that paper to the coast and get the full value of your gold."

"Who is this white man?" demanded Owaza, "and where is he?"

"He is a friend of mine," said the chief, "and if you wish I will take you to him on the morrow, and you can bring with you all your gold and get the little piece of paper."

"Good," said Owaza, "and then I shall not have to pay the carriers but a very small amount."

The carriers were glad, indeed, to learn the next day that they were not to go all the way to the coast, for even the lure of payment was not sufficient to overcome their dislike to so long a journey, and their fear of being at so great a distance from home. They were very happy, therefore, as they set forth on a two days' march toward the northeast. And Owaza was happy and so was the old chief, who accompanied them himself, though why he was happy about it Owaza could not guess.

They had marched for almost two days when the chief sent one of his own men forward with a message.

"It is to my friend," he said, "to tell him to come and meet us and lead us to his village." And a few hours later, as the little caravan emerged from the jungle onto a broad, grassy plain, they saw not far from them, and approaching rapidly, a large band of warriors. Owaza halted.

"Who are those?" he demanded.

"Those are the warriors of my friend," replied the chief, "and he is with them. See?" and he pointed toward a figure at the head of the blacks, who were approaching at a trot, their spears and white plumes gleaming in the sunshine.

"They come for war and not for peace," said Owaza tearfully.

"That depends upon you, Owaza," replied the chief.

"I do not understand you," said Owaza.

"But you will in a few minutes after my friend has come."

As the advancing warriors approached more closely Owaza saw a giant white at their head—a white whom he mistook for Esteban—the confederate he had so traitorously deserted. He turned upon the chief. "You have betrayed me," he cried.

"Wait," said the old chief; "nothing that belongs to you shall be taken from you."

"The gold is not his," cried Owaza. "He stole it," and he pointed at Tarzan who had approached and halted before him, but who ignored him entirely and turned to the chief.

"Your runner came," he said to the old man, "and brought your message, and Tarzan and his Waziri have come to see what they could do for their old friend."

The chief smiled. "Your runner came to me, O Tarzan, four days since, and two days later came this man with his carriers, bearing golden ingots toward the coast. I told him that I had a friend who would buy them, giving him a little piece of paper for them, but that, of course, only in case the gold belonged to Owaza."

The ape-man smiled. "You have done well, my friend," he said. "The gold does not belong to Owaza."

"It does not belong to you, either," cried Owaza. "You are not Tarzan of the Apes. I know you. You came with the four white men and the white woman to steal the gold from Tarzan's country, and then you stole it from your own friends."

The chief and the Waziri laughed. The ape-man smiled one of his slow smiles.

"The other was an impostor, Owaza," he said, "but I am Tarzan of the Apes, and I thank you for bringing my gold to me. Come," he said, "it is but a few more miles to my home," and the ape-man compelled Owaza to direct his carriers to bear the golden ingots to the Greystoke bungalow. There Tarzan fed the carriers and paid them, and the next morning sent them back toward their own country, and he sent Owaza with them, but not without a gift of value, accompanied with an admonition that the black never again return to Tarzan's country.

When they had all departed, and Tarzan and Jane and Korak were standing upon the veranda of the bungalow with Jad-bal-ja lying at their feet, the ape-man threw an arm about his mate's shoulders.

"I shall have to retract what I said about the gold of Opar not being for me, for you see before you a new fortune that has come all the way from the treasure vaults of Opar without any effort on my part."

"Now, if someone would only bring your diamonds back," laughed Jane.

"No chance of that," said Tarzan. "They are unquestionably at the bottom of the Ugogo River," and far away, upon the banks of the Ugogo, in the village of Obebe, the cannibal, Esteban Miranda lay in the filth of the hut that had been assigned to him, gloating over the fortune that he could never utilize as he entered upon a life of captivity that the stubbornness and superstition of Obebe had doomed him to undergo.

TARZAN AND THE ANT-MEN

CHAPTER 1

In the filth of a dark hut, in the village of Obebe the cannibal, upon the banks of the Ugogo, Esteban Miranda squatted upon his haunches and gnawed upon the remnants of a half-cooked fish. About his neck was an iron slave-collar from which a few feet of rusty chain ran to a stout post set deep in the ground near the low entranceway that let upon the village street not far from the hut of Obebe himself.

For a year Esteban Miranda had been chained thus, like a dog, and like a dog he sometimes crawled through the low doorway of his kennel and basked in the sun outside. Two diversions had he; and only two. One was the persistent idea that he was Tarzan of the Apes, whom he had impersonated for so long and with such growing success that, like the good actor he was, he had come not only to act the part, but to live it—to be it. He was, as far as he was concerned, Tarzan of the Apes—there was no other—and he was Tarzan of the Apes to Obebe, too; but the village witch doctor still insisted that he was the river devil and as such, one to propitiate rather than to anger.

It had been this difference of opinion between the chief and the witch doctor that had kept Esteban Miranda from the fleshpots of the village, for Obebe had wanted to eat him, thinking him his old enemy the ape-man; but the witch doctor had aroused the superstitious fears of the villagers by half convincing them that their prisoner was the river devil masquerading as Tarzan, and, as such, dire disaster would descend upon the village were he harmed. The result of this difference between Obebe and the witch doctor had been to preserve the life of the Spaniard until the truth of one claim or the other was proved—if Esteban died a natural death he was Tarzan, the mortal, and Obebe the chief was vindicated; if he lived on forever, or mysteriously disappeared, the claim of the witch doctor would be accepted as gospel.

After he had learned their language and thus come to a realization of the accident of fate that had guided his destiny by so narrow a margin from the cooking pots of the cannibals he was less eager to proclaim himself Tarzan of the Apes. Instead he let drop mysterious suggestions that he was, indeed, none other than the river devil. The witch doctor was delighted, and everyone was fooled except Obebe, who was old and wise and did not believe in river devils, and the witch doctor who was old and wise and did not believe in them either, but realized that they were excellent things for his parishioners to believe in.

Esteban Miranda's other diversion, aside from secretly believing himself Tarzan, consisted in gloating over the bag of diamonds that Kraski the Russian had stolen from the ape-man, and that had fallen into the Spaniard's hands after he had murdered Kraski—the same bag of diamonds that the old man had handed to Tarzan in the vaults beneath The Tower of Diamonds, in the Valley of The Palace of Diamonds, when he had rescued the Gomangani of the valley from the tyrannical oppression of the Bolgani.

For hours at a time Esteban Miranda sat in the dim light of his dirty kennel counting and fondling the brilliant stones. A thousand times had he weighed each one in an appraising palm, computing its value and translating it into such pleasures of the flesh as great wealth might buy for him in the capitals of the world.

Mired in his own filth, feeding upon rotted scraps tossed to him by unclean hands, he yet possessed the wealth of a Croesus, and it was as Croesus he lived in his imaginings, his dismal hut changed into the pomp and circumstance of a palace by the scintillant gleams of the precious stones. At the sound of each approaching footstep he would hastily hide his fabulous fortune in the wretched loin cloth that was his only garment, and once again become a prisoner in a cannibal hut.

And now, after a year of solitary confinement, came a third diversion, in the form of Uhha, the daughter of Khamis the witch doctor. Uhha was fourteen, comely and curious. For a year now she had watched the mysterious prisoner from a distance until, at last, familiarity had overcome her fears and one day she approached him as he lay in the sun outside his hut. Esteban, who had been watching her half-timorous advance, smiled encouragingly. He had not a friend among the villagers. If he could make but one his lot would be much the easier and freedom a step nearer. At last Uhha came to a halt a few steps from him. She was a child, ignorant and a savage; but she was a woman-child and Esteban Miranda knew women.

"I have been in the village of the chief Obebe for a year," he said haltingly, in the laboriously acquired language of his captors, "but never before did I guess that its walls held one so beautiful as you. What is your name?"

Uhha was pleased. She smiled broadly. "I am Uhha," she told him. "My father is Khamis the witch doctor."

It was Esteban who was pleased now. Fate, after rebuffing him for long, was at last kind. She had sent him one who, with cultivation, might prove a flower of hope indeed.

"Why have you never come to see me before?" asked Esteban.

"I was afraid," replied Uhha simply.

"Why?"

"I was afraid—" she hesitated.

"Afraid that I was the river devil and would harm you?" demanded the Spaniard, smiling.

"Yes," she said.

"Listen!" whispered Esteban; "but tell no one. I am the river devil, but I shall not harm you."

"If you are the river devil why then do you remain chained to a stake?" inquired Uhha. "Why do you not change yourself to something else and return to the river?"

"You wonder about that, do you?" asked Miranda, sparring for time that he might concoct a plausible answer.

"It is not only Uhha who wonders," said the girl. "Many others have asked the same question of late. Obebe asked it first and there was none to explain. Obebe says that you are Tarzan, the enemy of Obebe and his people; but my father Khamis says that you are the river devil, and that if you wanted to get away you would change yourself into a snake and crawl through the iron collar that is about your neck. And the people wonder why you do not, and many of them are commencing to believe that you are not the river devil at all."

"Come closer, beautiful Uhha," whispered Miranda, "that no other ears than yours may hear what I am about to tell you."

The girl came a little closer and leaned toward him where he squatted upon the ground.

"I am indeed the river devil," said Esteban, "and I come and go as I wish. At night, when the village sleeps, I am wandering through the waters of the Ugogo, but always I come back again. I am waiting, Uhha, to try the people of the village of Obebe that I may know which are my friends and which my enemies. Already have I learned that Obebe is no friend of mine, and I am not sure of Khamis. Had Khamis been a good friend he would have brought me fine food and beer to drink. I could go when I pleased, but I wait to see if there be one in the village of Obebe who will set me free, thus may I learn which is my best friend. Should there be such a one, Uhha, fortune would smile upon him always, his every wish would be granted and he would live to a great age, for he would have nothing to fear from the river devil, who would help him in all his undertakings. But listen, Uhha, tell no one what I have told you! I shall wait a little longer and then if there be no such friend in the village of Obebe I shall return to my father and mother, the Ugogo, and destroy the people of Obebe. Not one shall remain alive."

The girl drew away, terrified. It was evident that she was much impressed.

"Do not be afraid," he reassured her. "I shall not harm you."

"But if you destroy all the people?" she demanded.

"Then, of course," he said, "I cannot help you; but let us hope that someone comes and sets me free so that I shall know that I have at least one good friend here. Now run along, Uhha, and remember that you must tell no one what I have told you."

She moved off a short distance and then returned.

"When will you destroy the village?" she asked.

"In a few days," he said.

Uhha, trembling with terror, ran quickly away in the direction of the hut of her father, Khamis, the witch doctor. Esteban Miranda smiled a satisfied smile and crawled back into his hole to play with his diamonds.

Khamis the witch doctor was not in his hut when Uhha his daughter, faint from fright, crawled into the dim interior. Nor were his wives. With their children, the latter were in the fields beyond the palisade, where Uhha should have been. And so it was that the girl had time for thought before she saw any of them again, with the result that she recalled distinctly, what she had almost forgotten in the first frenzy of fear, that the river devil had impressed upon her that she must reveal to no one the thing that he had told her.

And she had been upon the point of telling her father all! What dire calamity then would have befallen her? She trembled at the very suggestion of a fate so awful that she could not even imagine it. How close a call she had had! But what was she to do?

She lay huddled upon a mat of woven grasses, racking her poor, savage little brain for a solution of the immense problem that confronted her—the first problem that had ever entered her young life other than the constantly recurring one of how most easily to evade her share of the drudgery of the fields. Presently she sat suddenly erect, galvanized into statuesque rigidity by a thought engendered by the recollection of one of the river devil's remarks. Why had it not occurred to her before? Very plainly he had said, and he had repeated it, that if he were released he would know that he had at least one friend in the village of Obebe, and that whoever released him would live to a great age and have every thing he wished for; but after a few minutes of thought Uhha drooped again. How was she, a little girl, to compass the liberation of the river devil alone?

"How, baba," she asked her father, when he had returned to the hut, later in the day, "does the river devil destroy those who harm him?"

"As the fish in the river, so are the ways of the river devil—without number," replied Khamis. "He might send the fish from the river and the game from the jungle and cause our crops to die. Then we should starve. He might bring the fire out of the sky at night and strike dead all the people of Obebe."

"And you think he may do these things to us, baba?"

"He will not harm Khamis, who saved him from the death that Obebe would have inflicted," replied the witch doctor.

Uhha recalled that the river devil had complained that Khamis had not brought him good food nor beer, but she said nothing about that, although she realized that her father was far from being so high in the good graces of the river devil as he seemed to think he was. Instead, she took another tack.

"How can he escape," she asked "while the collar is about his neck—who will remove it for him?"

"No one can remove it but Obebe, who carries in his pouch the bit of brass that makes the collar open," replied Khamis; "but the river devil needs no help, for when the time comes that he wishes to be free he has but to become a snake and crawl forth from the iron band about his neck. Where are you going, Uhha?"

"I am going to visit the daughter of Obebe," she called back over her shoulder.

The chief's daughter was grinding maize, as Uhha should have been doing. She looked up and smiled as the daughter of the witch doctor approached.

"Make no noise, Uhha," she cautioned, "for Obebe, my father, sleeps within." She nodded toward the hut. The visitor sat down and the two girls chatted in low tones. They spoke of their ornaments, their coiffures, of the young men of the village, and often, when they spoke of these, they giggled. Their conversation was not unlike that which might pass between two young girls of any race or clime. As they talked, Uhha's eyes often wandered toward the entrance to Obebe's hut and many times her brows were contracted in much deeper thought than their idle passages warranted.

"Where," she demanded suddenly, "is the armlet of copper wire that your father's brother gave you at the beginning of the last moon?"

Obebe's daughter shrugged. "He took it back from me," she replied, "and gave it to the sister of his youngest wife."

Uhha appeared crestfallen. Could it be that she had coveted the copper bracelet? Her eyes closely scrutinized the person of her friend. Her brows almost met, so deeply was she thinking. Suddenly her face brightened.

"The necklace of many beads that your father took from the body of the warrior captured for the last feast!" she exclaimed. "You have not lost it?"

"No," replied her friend. "It is in the house of my father. When I grind maize it gets in my way and so I laid it aside."

"May I see it?" asked Uhha. "I will fetch it."

"No, you will awaken Obebe and he will be very angry," said the chief's daughter.

"I will not awaken him," replied Uhha, and started to crawl toward the hut's entrance.

Her friend tried to dissuade her. "I will fetch it as soon as baba has awakened," she told Uhha, but Uhha paid no attention to her and presently was crawling cautiously into the interior of the hut. Once within she waited silently until her eyes became accustomed to the dim light. Against the opposite wall of the hut Obebe lay sprawled upon a sleeping mat. He snored lustily. Uhha crept toward him. Her stealth was the stealth of Sheeta the leopard. Her heart was beating like the tom-tom when the dance is at its height. She feared that its noise and her rapid breathing would awaken the old chief, of whom she was as terrified as of the river devil; but Obebe snored on.

Uhha came close to him. Her eyes were accustomed now to the half-light of the hut's interior. At Obebe's side and half beneath his body she saw the chief's pouch. Cautiously she reached forth a trembling hand and laid hold upon it. She tried to draw it from beneath Obebe's weight. The sleeper stirred uneasily and Uhha drew back, terrified. Obebe changed his position and Uhha thought that he had awakened. Had she not been frozen with horror she would have rushed into headlong flight, but fortunately for her she could not move, and presently she heard Obebe resume his interrupted snoring; but her nerve was gone and she thought now only of escaping from the hut without being detected. She cast a last frightened glance at the chief to reassure herself that he still slept. Her eyes fell upon the pouch. Obebe had turned away from it and it now lay within her reach, free from the weight of his body.

She reached for it only to withdraw her hand suddenly. She turned away. Her heart was in her mouth. She swayed dizzily and then she thought of the river devil and of the possibilities for horrid death that lay within his power. Once more she reached for the pouch and this time she picked it up. Hurriedly opening it she examined the contents. The brass key was there. She recognized it because it was the only thing the purpose of which she was not familiar with. The collar, chain and key had been taken from an Arab slave raider that Obebe had killed and eaten and as some of the old men of Obebe's village had worn similar bonds in the past, there was no difficulty in adapting it to its intended purpose when occasion demanded.

Uhha hastily closed the pouch and replaced it at Obebe's side. Then, clutching the key in a clammy palm, she crawled hurriedly toward the doorway.

That night, after the cooking fires had died to embers and been covered with earth and the people of Obebe had withdrawn into their huts, Esteban Miranda heard a stealthy movement at the entrance to his kennel. He listened intently. Someone was creeping into the interior—someone or something.

"Who is it?" demanded the Spaniard in a voice that he tried hard to keep from trembling.

"Hush!" responded the intruder in soft tones. "It is I, Uhha, the daughter of Khamis the witch doctor. I have come to set you free that you may know that you have a good friend in the village of Obebe and will, therefore, not destroy us."

Miranda smiled. His suggestion had borne fruit more quickly than he had dared to hope, and evidently the girl had obeyed his injunction to keep silent. In that matter he had reasoned wrongly, but of what moment that, since his sole aim in life—freedom—was to be accomplished. He had cautioned the girl to silence believing this the surest way to disseminate the word he had wished spread through the village, where, he was positive, it would have come to the ears of some one of the superstitious savages with the means to free him now that the incentive was furnished.

"And how are you going to free me?" demanded Miranda.

"See!" exclaimed Uhha. "I have brought the key to the collar about your neck."

"Good," cried the Spaniard. "Where is it?"

Uhha crawled closer to the man and handed him the key. Then she would have fled.

"Wait!" demanded the prisoner. "When I am free you must lead me forth into the jungle. Whoever sets me free must do this if he would win the favor of the river god."

Uhha was afraid, but she did not dare refuse. Miranda fumbled with the ancient lock for several minutes before it at last gave to the worn key the girl had brought. Then he snapped the padlock again and carrying the key with him crawled toward the entrance.

"Get me weapons," he whispered to the girl and Uhha departed through the shadows of the village street. Miranda knew that she was terrified but was confident that this very terror would prove the means of bringing her back to him with the weapons. Nor was he wrong, for scarce five minutes had elapsed before Uhha had returned with a quiver of arrows, a bow and a stout knife.

"Now lead me to the gate," commanded Esteban.

Keeping out of the main street and as much in rear of the huts as possible Uhha led the fugitive toward the village gates. It surprised her a little that he, a river devil, should not know how to unlock and open them, for she had thought that river devils were all-wise; but she did as he bid and showed him how the great bar could be withdrawn, and helped him push the gates open enough to permit him to pass through. Beyond was the clearing that led to the river, on either hand rose the giants of the jungle. It was very dark out there and Esteban Miranda suddenly discovered that his new-found liberty had its drawbacks. To go forth alone at night into the dark, mysterious jungle filled him with a nameless dread.

Uhha drew back from the gates. She had done her part and saved the village from destruction. Now she wished to close the gates again and hasten back to the hut of her father, there to lie trembling in nervous excitement and terror against the morning that would reveal to the village the escape of the river devil.

Esteban reached forth and took her by the arm. "Come," he said, "and receive your reward."

Uhha shrank away from him. "Let me go!" she cried. "I am afraid."

But Esteban was afraid, too, and he had decided that the company of this little Negro girl would be better than no company at all in the depths of the lonely jungle. Possibly when daylight came he would let her go back to her people, but tonight he shuddered at the thought of entering the jungle without human companionship.

Uhha tried to tear herself free from his grasp. She struggled like a little lion cub, and at last would have raised her voice in a wild scream for help had not Miranda suddenly clapped his palm across her mouth, lifted her bodily from the ground and running swiftly across the clearing disappeared into the jungle.

Behind them the warriors of Obebe the cannibal slept in peaceful ignorance of the sudden tragedy that had entered the life of little Uhha and before them, far out in the jungle, a lion roared thunderously.

CHAPTER 2

Three persons stepped from the veranda of Lord Greystoke's African bungalow and walked slowly toward the gate along a rose-embowered path that swung in a graceful curve through the well-ordered, though unpretentious, grounds surrounding the ape-man's rambling, one-story home. There were two men and a woman, all in khaki, the older man carrying a flier's helmet and a pair of goggles in one hand. He was smiling quietly as he listened to the younger man.

"You wouldn't be doing this now if mother were here," said the latter, "she would never permit it."

"I'm afraid you are right, my son," replied Tarzan; "but only this one flight alone and then I'll promise not to go up again until she returns. You have said yourself that I am an apt pupil and if you are any sort of an instructor you should have perfect confidence in me after having said that I was perfectly competent to pilot a ship alone. Eh, Meriem, isn't that true?" he demanded of the young woman.

She shook her head. "Like My Dear, I am always afraid for you, mon père," she replied. "You take such risks that one would think you considered yourself immortal. You should be more careful."

The younger man threw his arm about his wife's shoulders. "Meriem is right," he said, "you should be more careful, Father."

Tarzan shrugged. "If you and mother had your way my nerves and muscles would have atrophied long since. They were given me to use and I intend using them—with discretion. Doubtless I shall be old and useless soon enough, and long enough, as it is."

A child burst suddenly from the bungalow, pursued by a perspiring governess, and raced to Meriem's side. "Muwer," he cried, "Dackie doe? Dackie doe?"

"Let him come along," urged Tarzan.

"Dare!" exclaimed the boy, turning triumphantly upon the governess; "Dackie do doe yalk!"

Out on the level plain, that stretched away from the bungalow to the distant jungle the verdant masses and deep shadows of which were vaguely discernible to the northwest, lay a biplane, in the shade of which lolled two Waziri warriors who had been trained by Korak, the son of Tarzan, in the duties of mechanicians, and, later, to pilot the ship themselves; a fact that had not been without weight in determining Tarzan of the Apes to perfect himself in the art of flying, since, as chief of the Waziri, it was not meet that the lesser warriors of his tribe should excel him in any particular. Adjusting his helmet and goggles Tarzan climbed into the cockpit.

"Better take me along," advised Korak.

Tarzan shook his head, smiling good-naturedly.

"Then one of the boys, here," urged his son. "You might develop some trouble that would force you to make a landing and if you have no mechanician along to make repairs what are you going to do?"

"Walk," replied the ape-man. "Turn her over, Andua!" he directed one of the blacks.

A moment later the ship was bumping over the veldt, from which, directly, it rose in smooth and graceful flight, circled, climbing to a greater altitude, and then sped away in an air line, while on the ground below the six strained their eyes until the wavering speck that it had dwindled to disappeared entirely from their view.

"Where do you suppose he is going?" asked Meriem.

Korak shook his head. "He isn't supposed to be going anywhere in particular," he replied, "just making his first practice flight alone; but, knowing him as I do, I wouldn't be surprised to learn that he had taken it into his head to fly to London and see mother."

"But he could never do it!" cried Meriem.

"No ordinary man could, with no more experience than he has had; but then, you will have to admit, father is no ordinary man."

For an hour and a half Tarzan flew without altering his course and without realizing the flight of time or the great distance he had covered, so delighted was he with the ease with which he controlled the ship, and so thrilled by this new power that gave him the freedom and mobility of the birds, the only denizens of his beloved jungle that he ever had had cause to envy.

Presently, ahead, he discerned a great basin, or what might better be described as a series of basins, surrounded by wooded hills, and immediately he recognized to the left of it the winding Ugogo; but the country of the basins was new to him and he was puzzled. He recognized, simultaneously, another fact; that he was over a hundred miles from home, and he determined to put back at once; but the mystery of the basins lured him on—he could not bring himself to return home without a closer view of them. Why was it that he had never come upon this country in his many wanderings? Why had he never even heard of it from the natives living within easy access to it. He dropped to a lower level the better to inspect the basins, which now appeared to him as a series of shallow craters of long extinct volcanoes.

He saw forests, lakes and rivers, the very existence of which he had never dreamed, and then quite suddenly he discovered a solution of the seeming mystery that there should exist in a country with which he was familiar so large an area of which he had been in total ignorance, in common with the natives of the country surrounding it. He recognized it now—the so-called Great Thorn Forest. For years he had been familiar with that impenetrable thicket that was supposed to cover a vast area of territory into which only the smallest of animals might venture, and now he saw it was but a relatively narrow fringe encircling a pleasant, habitable country, but a fringe so cruelly barbed as to have forever protected the secret that it held from the eyes of man.

Tarzan determined to circle the long hidden land of mystery before setting the nose of his ship toward home, and, to obtain a closer view, he accordingly dropped nearer the earth. Beneath him was a great forest and beyond that an open veldt that ended at the foot of precipitous, rocky hills. He saw that absorbed as he had been in the strange, new country he had permitted the plane to drop too low. Coincident with the realization and before he could move the control within his hand, the ship touched the leafy crown of some old monarch of the jungle, veered, swung completely around and crashed downward through the foliage amidst the snapping and rending of broken branches and the splintering of its own woodwork. Just for a second this noise, and then silence.

*

Along a forest trail slouched a mighty creature, manlike in its physical attributes, yet vaguely inhuman; a great brute that walked erect upon two feet and carried a club in one horny, calloused hand. Its long hair fell, unkempt, about its shoulders, and there was hair upon its chest and a little upon its arms and legs, though no more than is found upon many males of civilized races. A strip of hide about its waist supported the ends of a narrow G-string as well as numerous rawhide strands to the lower ends of which were fastened round stones from one to two inches in diameter. Close to each stone were attached several small feathers, for the most part of brilliant hues. The strands supporting the stones being fastened to the belt at intervals of one to two inches and the strands themselves being about eighteen inches long the whole formed a skeleton skirt, fringed with round stones and feathers, that fell almost to the creature's knees. Its large feet were bare and its white skin tanned to a light brown by exposure to the elements. The illusion of great size was suggested more by the massiveness of the shoulders and the development of the muscles of the back and arms than by height, though the creature measured close to six feet. Its face was massive, with a broad nose, and a wide, full-lipped mouth; the eyes, of normal size, were set beneath heavy, beetling brows, topped by a wide, low forehead. As it walked it flapped its large, flat ears and occasionally moved rapidly portions of its skin on various parts of its head and body to dislodge flies, as you have seen a horse do with the muscles along its sides and flanks.

It moved silently, its dark eyes constantly on the alert, while the flapping ears were often momentarily stilled as the woman listened for sounds of quarry or foe.

She stopped now, her ears bent forward, her nostrils, expanded, sniffing the air. Some scent or sound that our dead sensitory organs could not have perceived had attracted her attention. Warily she crept forward along the trail until, at a turning, she saw before her a figure lying face downward in the path. It was Tarzan of the Apes. Unconscious he lay while above him the splintered wreckage of his plane was wedged among the branches of the great tree that had caused its downfall.

The woman gripped her club more firmly and approached. Her expression reflected the puzzlement the discovery of this strange creature had engendered in her elementary mind, but she evinced no fear. She walked directly to the side of the prostrate man, her club raised to strike; but something stayed her hand. She knelt beside him and fell to examining his clothing. She turned him over on his back and placed one of her ears above his heart. Then, she fumbled with the front of his shirt for a moment and suddenly taking it in her two mighty hands tore it apart. Again she listened, her ear this time against his naked flesh. She arose and looked about, sniffing and listening, then she stooped and lifting the body of the ape-man she swung it lightly across one of her broad shoulders and continued along the trail in the direction she had been going. The trail, winding through the forest, broke presently from the leafy shade into an open, parklike strip of rolling land that stretched at the foot of rocky hills, and, crossing this, disappeared within the entrance of a narrow gorge, eroded by the elements from the native sandstone fancifully as the capricious architecture of a dream, among whose grotesque domes and miniature rocks the woman bore her burden.

A half mile from the entrance to the gorge the trail entered a roughly circular amphitheater, the precipitous walls of which were pierced by numerous cave-mouths before several of which squatted creatures similar to that which bore Tarzan into this strange, savage environment.

As she entered the amphitheater all eyes were upon her, for their large, sensitive ears had warned them of her approach long before she had arrived within scope of their vision. Immediately they beheld her and her burden several of them arose and came to meet her. All females, these, similar in physique and scant garb to the captor of the ape-man, though differing in proportions and physiognomy as do the individuals of all races differ from their fellows. They spoke no words nor uttered any sounds, nor did she whom they approached, as she moved straight along her way which was evidently directed toward one of the cave-mouths, but she gripped her bludgeon firmly and swung it to and fro, while her eyes, beneath their scowling brows, kept sullen surveillance upon the every move of her fellows.

She had approached close to the cave, which was quite evidently her destination, when one of those who followed her darted suddenly forward and clutched at Tarzan. With the quickness of a cat the woman dropped her burden, turned upon the temerarious one, and swinging her bludgeon with lightning-like celerity felled her with a heavy blow to the head, and then, standing astride the prostrate Tarzan, she glared about her like a lioness at bay, questioning dumbly who would be next to attempt to wrest her prize from her; but the others slunk back to their caves, leaving the vanquished one lying, unconscious, in the hot sand and the victor to shoulder her burden, undisputed, and continue her way to her cave, where she dumped the ape-man unceremoniously upon the ground just within the shadow of the entranceway, and, squatting beside him, facing outward that she might not be taken unaware by any of her fellows, she proceeded to examine her find minutely. Tarzan's clothing either piqued her curiosity or aroused her disgust, for she began almost immediately to divest him of it, and having had no former experience of buttons and buckles, she tore it away by main force. The heavy, cordovan boots troubled her for a moment, but finally their seams gave way to her powerful muscles.

Only the diamond-studded, golden locket that had been his mother's she left untouched upon its golden chain about his neck.

For a moment she sat contemplating him and then she arose and tossing him once more to her shoulder she walked toward the center of the amphitheater, the greater portion of which was covered by low buildings constructed of enormous slabs of stone, some set on edge to form the walls while others, lying across these, constituted the roofs. Joined end to end, with occasional wings at irregular intervals running out into the amphitheater, they enclosed a rough oval of open ground that formed a large courtyard.

The several outer entrances to the buildings were closed with two slabs of stone, one of which, standing on edge, covered the aperture, while the other, leaning against the first upon the outside, held it securely in place against any efforts that might be made to dislodge it from the interior of the building.

To one of these entrances the woman carried her unconscious captive, laid him on the ground, removed the slabs that closed the aperture and dragged him into the dim and gloomy interior, where she deposited him upon the floor and clapped her palms together sharply three times with the result that there presently slouched into the room six or seven children of both sexes, who ranged in age from one year to sixteen or seventeen. The very youngest of them walked easily and seemed as fit to care for itself as the young of most lower orders at a similar age. The girls, even the youngest, were armed with clubs, but the boys carried no weapons either of offense or defense. At sight of them the woman pointed to Tarzan, struck her head with her clenched fist and then gestured toward herself, touching her breast several times with a calloused thumb. She made several other motions with her hands, so eloquent of meaning that one entirely unfamiliar with her sign language could almost guess their purport, then she turned and left the building, replaced the stones before the entrance, and slouched back to her cave, passing, apparently without notice, the woman she had recently struck down and who was now rapidly regaining consciousness.

As she took her seat before her cave-mouth her victim suddenly sat erect, rubbed her head for a moment and then, after looking about dully, rose unsteadily to her feet. For just an instant she swayed and staggered, but presently she mastered herself, and with only a glance at the author of her hurt moved off in the direction of her own cave. Before she had reached it her attention, together with that of all the others of this strange community, or at least of all those who were in the open, was attracted by the sound of approaching footsteps. She halted in her tracks, her great ears up-pricked, listening, her eyes directed toward the trail leading up from the valley. The others were similarly watching and listening and a moment later their vigil was rewarded by sight of another of their kind as she appeared in the entrance of the amphitheater. A huge creature this, even larger than she who captured the ape-man, broader and heavier, though little, if any, taller—carrying upon one shoulder the carcass of an antelope and upon the other the body of a creature that might have been half-human and half-beast, yet, assuredly, not entirely either the one or the other.

The antelope was dead, but not so the other creature. It wriggled weakly—its futile movements could not have been termed struggles—as it hung, its middle across the bare brown shoulder of its captor, its arms and legs dangling limply before and behind, either in partial unconsciousness or in the paralysis of fear.

The woman who had brought Tarzan to the amphitheater rose and stood before the entrance of her cave. We shall have to call her The First Woman, for she had no name; in the muddy convolutions of her sluggish brain she never had sensed even the need for a distinctive specific appellation and among her fellows she was equally nameless, as were they, and so, that we may differentiate her from the others, we shall call her The First Woman, and, similarly, we shall know the creature that she felled with her bludgeon as The Second Woman, and she who now entered the amphitheater with a burden upon each shoulder, as The Third Woman. So The First Woman rose, her eyes fixed upon the newcomer, her ears up-pricked. And The Second Woman rose, and all the others that were in sight, and all stood glaring at The Third Woman who moved steadily along with her burden, her watchful eyes ever upon the menacing figures of her fellows. She was very large, this Third Woman, so for a while the others only stood and glared at her, but presently The First Woman took a step forward and turning, cast a long look at The Second Woman, and then she took another step forward and stopped and looked again at The Second Woman, and this time she pointed at herself, at The Second Woman and then at The Third Woman who now quickened her pace in the direction of her cave, for she understood the menace in the attitude of The First Woman. The Second Woman understood, too, and moved forward now with The First Woman. No word was spoken, no sound issued from those savage lips; lips that never had parted to a smile; lips that never had known laughter, nor ever would.

As the two approached her The Third Woman dropped her spoils in a heap at her feet, gripped her cudgel more firmly and prepared to defend her rights. The others, brandishing their own weapons, charged her. The remaining women were now but onlookers, their hands stayed, perhaps, by some ancient tribal custom that gauged the number of attackers by the quantity of spoil, awarding the right of contest to whoever initiated it. When The First Woman had been attacked by The Second Woman the others had all held aloof, for it had been The Second Woman that had advanced first to try conclusively for the possession of Tarzan. And now The Third Woman had come with two prizes, and since The First Woman and The Second Woman had stepped out to meet her the others had held back.

As the three women came together it seemed inevitable that The Third Woman would go down beneath the bludgeons of the others, but she warded both blows with the skill and celerity of a trained fencer and stepping quickly into the opening she had dealt The First Woman a terrific blow upon the head that stretched her motionless upon the ground, where a little pool of blood and brains attested the terrible strength of the wielder of the bludgeon the while it marked the savage, unmourned passing of The First Woman.

And now The Third Woman could devote her undivided attention to The Second Woman, but The Second Woman seeing the fate of her companion did not wait to discuss the matter further, and instead of remaining to continue the fight she broke and ran for the cave, while the creature that The Third Woman had been carrying along with the carcass of the antelope apparently believing that it saw a chance for escape while its captor was engaged with her assailants was crawling stealthily away in the opposite direction. Its attempt might have proved successful had the fight lasted longer; but the skill and ferocity of The Third Woman had terminated the whole thing in a matter of seconds, and now, turning about, she espied a portion of her prey seeking to escape and sprang quickly after it. As she did so The Second Woman wheeled and darted back to seize the carcass of the antelope, while the crawling fugitive leaped to its feet and raced swiftly down the trail that led through the mouth of the amphitheater toward the valley.

As the thing rose to its feet it became apparent that it was a man, or at least a male, and evidently of the same species as the women of this peculiar race, though much shorter and of proportionately lighter build. It stood about five feet in height, had a few hairs on its upper lip and chin, a much lower forehead than the women, and its eyes were set closer together. Its legs were much longer and more slender than those of the women, who seemed to have been designed for strength rather than speed, and the result was that it was apparent from the start that The Third Woman could have no hope of overhauling her escaping quarry, and then it was that the utility of the strange skirt of thongs and pebbles and feathers became apparent. Seizing one of the thongs she disengaged it easily and quickly from the girdle that supported them about her hips, and grasping the end of the thong between a thumb and forefinger she whirled it rapidly in a vertical plane until the feathered pebble at its end was moving with great rapidity—then she let go the thong. Like an arrow the missile sped toward the racing fugitive, the pebble, a fairly good-sized one as large as an English walnut, struck the man upon the back of his head dropping him, unconscious, to the ground. Then the Third Woman turned upon The Second Woman who, by this time, had seized the antelope, and brandishing her bludgeon bore down upon her. The Second Woman, possessing more courage than good sense, prepared to defend her stolen flesh and took her stand, her bludgeon ready. As The Third Woman bore down upon her, a veritable mountain of muscle, The Second Woman met her with threatening cudgel, but so terrific was the blow dealt by her mighty adversary that her weapon, splintered, was swept from her hands and she found herself at the mercy of the creature she would have robbed. Evidently she knew how much of mercy she might expect. She did not fall upon her knees in an attitude of supplication—not she. Instead she tore a handful of the pebble-missiles from her girdle in a vain attempt to defend herself. Futilest of futilities! The huge, destroying bludgeon had not even paused, but swinging in a great circle fell crushingly upon the skull of The Second Woman.

The Third Woman paused and looked about questioningly as if to ask: "Is there another who wishes to take from me my antelope or my man? If so, let her step forward." But no one accepted the gage and presently the woman turned and walked back to the prostrate man. Roughly she jerked him to his feet and shook him. Consciousness was returning slowly and he tried to stand. His efforts, however, were a failure and so she threw him across her shoulder again and walked back to the dead antelope, which she flung to the opposite shoulder and, continuing her interrupted way to her cave, dumped the two unceremoniously to the ground. Here, in the cave-mouth, she kindled a fire, twirling a fire stick dexterously amidst dry tinder in a bit of hollowed wood, and cutting generous strips from the carcass of the antelope ate ravenously. While she was thus occupied the man regained consciousness and sitting up looked about, dazed. Presently his nostrils caught the aroma of the cooking meat and he pointed at it. The woman handed him the rude stone knife that she had tossed back to the floor of the cave and motioned toward the meat. The man seized the implement and was soon broiling a generous cut above the fire. Half-burned and half-raw as it was he ate it with seeming relish, and as he ate the woman sat and watched him. He was not much to look at, yet she may have thought him handsome. Unlike the women, who wore no ornaments, the man had bracelets and anklets as well as a necklace of teeth and pebbles, while in his hair, which was wound into a small knot above his forehead, were thrust several wooden skewers ten or twelve inches long, which protruded in various directions in a horizontal plane.

When the man had eaten his fill the woman rose and seizing him by the hair dragged him into the cave. He scratched and bit at her, trying to escape, but he was no match for his captor.

Upon the floor of the amphitheater, before the entrances to the caves, lay the bodies of The First Woman and The Second Woman and black upon them swarmed the circling scavengers of the sky. Ska, the vulture, was first always to the feast.

CHAPTER 3

Within the dim interior of the strange rocky chamber where he had been so ruthlessly deposited, Tarzan immediately became the center of interest to the several Alali young that crowded about him. They examined him carefully, turned him over, pawed him, pinched him, and at last one of the young males, attracted by the golden locket removed it from the ape-man's neck and placed it about his own. Lowest, perhaps, in the order of human evolution nothing held their interest overlong, with the result that they soon tired of Tarzan and trooped out into the sunlit courtyard, leaving the ape-man to regain consciousness as best he could, or not at all. It was immaterial to them which he did. Fortunately for the Lord of the Jungle the fall through the roof of the forest had been broken by the fortuitous occurrence of supple branches directly in the path of his descent, with the happy result that he suffered only from a slight concussion of the brain. Already he was slowly regaining consciousness, and not long after the Alali young had left him his eyes opened, rolled dully inspecting the dim interior of his prison, and closed again. His breathing was normal and when again he opened his eyes it was as though he had emerged from a deep and natural slumber, the only reminder of his accident being a dull aching of the head.

Sitting up, he looked about him, his eyes gradually accustoming themselves to the dim light of the chamber. He found himself in a rude shelter constructed of great slabs of rock. A single opening led into what appeared to be another similar chamber the interior of which, however, was much lighter than that in which he lay. Slowly he rose to his feet and crossed to the opening. Across the second chamber he beheld another doorway leading into the fresh air and the sunshine. Except for filthy heaps of dead grasses on the floor both the rooms were unfurnished and devoid of any suggestion that they were utilized as places of human habitation. From the second doorway, to which he crossed, he looked out upon a narrow courtyard walled by great slabs of stone, the lower ends of which, embedded in the ground, caused them to remain erect. Here he saw the young Alali squatting about, some in the sun, others in the shadow. Tarzan looked at them in evident puzzlement. What were they? What was this place in which he was, all too evidently, incarcerated? Were these his keepers or were they his fellow prisoners? How had he come hither?

Running his fingers through his shock of black hair in a characteristic gesture of perplexity, he shook his head. He recalled the unfortunate termination of the flight; he even remembered falling through the foliage of the great tree; but beyond that all was blank. He stood for a moment examining the Alali, who were all unconscious of his near presence or his gaze upon them, and then he stepped boldly out into the courtyard before them, as a lion, fearless, ignores the presence of jackals.

Immediately they saw him, they rose and clustered about him, the girls pushing the boys aside and coming boldly close, and Tarzan spoke to them, first in one native dialect and then in another, but they seemed not to understand, for they made no reply, and then, as a last resort, he addressed them in the primitive language of the great apes, the language of Manu the monkey, the first language that Tarzan had learned when, as a babe, he suckled at the hairy breast of Kala, the she-ape, and listened to the gutturals of the savage members of the tribe of Kerchak; but again his auditors made no response—at least no audible response, though they moved their hands and shoulders and bodies, and jerked their heads in what the ape-man soon recognized as a species of sign language, nor did they utter any vocal sounds that might indicate that they were communicating with one another through the medium of a spoken language. Presently they again lost interest in the newcomer and resumed their indolent lounging about the walls of the courtyard while Tarzan paced to and fro its length, his keen eye searching for whatever avenue of escape chance might provide, and he saw it in the height of the walls, to the top of which a long, running jump would take his outstretched fingers, he was sure; but not yet—he must wait for darkness to shield his attempt from those within the enclosure and those without. And as darkness approached the actions of the other occupants of the courtyard became noticeably altered; they walked back and forth, constantly passing and re-passing the entrance to the shelter at the end of the courtyard, and occasionally entering the first room and often passing to the second room where they listened for a moment before the great slab that closed the outer aperture, then back into the courtyard again and back and forth in restless movement. Finally one stamped a foot upon the ground and this was taken up by the others until, in regular cadence the thud, thud, thud of their naked feet must have been audible for some distance beyond the confines of their narrow prison yard.

Whatever this procedure might have been intended to accomplish, nothing, apparently, resulted, and presently one of the girls, her sullen face snarling in anger, seized her bludgeon more firmly in her two hands and stepping close to one of the walls began pounding violently upon one of its huge stone slabs. Instantly the other girls followed her example, while the young males continued beating time with their heels.

For a while Tarzan was puzzled for an explanation of their behavior, but it was his own stomach that at last suggested an answer—the creatures were hungry and were attempting to attract the attention of their jailers; and their method of doing so suggested something else, as well, something of which his past brief experience with them had already partially convinced him—the creatures were without speech, even totally unvocal, perhaps.

The girl who had started the pounding upon the wall suddenly stopped and pointed at Tarzan. The others looked at him and then back at her, whereupon she pointed at her bludgeon and then at Tarzan again, after which she acted out a little pantomime, very quickly, very briefly, but none the less realistically. The pantomime depicted the bludgeon falling upon Tarzan's head, following which the pantomimist, assisted by her fellows, devoured the ape-man. The bludgeons ceased to fall upon the wall; the heels no longer smote the earth; the assemblage was interested in the new suggestion. They eyed Tarzan hungrily. The mother who should have brought them food, The First Woman, was dead. They did not know this; all they knew was that they were hungry and that The First Woman had brought them no food since the day before. They were not cannibals. Only in the last stages of hunger, would they have devoured one another, even as shipwrecked sailors of civilized races have been known to do; but they did not look upon the stranger as one of their own kind. He was as unlike them as some of the other creatures that The First Woman had brought them to feed upon. It was no more wrong to devour him than it would have been to devour an antelope. The thought, however, would not have occurred to most of them; the older girl it was who had suggested it to them, nor would it have occurred to her had there been other food, for she knew that he had not been brought here for that purpose—he had been brought as the mate of The First Woman, who in common with the other women of this primitive race hunted a new mate each season among the forests and the jungles where the timid males lived their solitary lives except for the brief weeks that they were held captive in the stone corrals of the dominant sex, and where they were treated with great brutality and contempt even by the children of their temporary spouses.

Sometimes they managed to escape, though rarely, but eventually they were turned loose, since it was easier to hunt a new one the following season than to feed one in captivity for a whole year. There was nothing approximating love in the family relations of these savage half-brutes. The young, conceived without love, knowing not their own fathers, possessed not even an elemental affection for one another, nor for any other living thing. A certain tie bound them to their savage mothers, at whose breasts they suckled for a few short months and to whom they looked for food until they were sufficiently developed to go forth into the forests and make their own kills or secure whatever other food bountiful Nature provided for them.

Somewhere between the ages of fifteen and seventeen the young males were liberated and chased into the forest, after which their mothers knew them not from any other male and at a similar age the females were taken to the maternal cave, where they lived, accompanying their mothers on the daily hunt, until they had succeeded in capturing a first mate. After that they took up their abodes in separate caves and the tie between parent and child was cut as cleanly as though it never had existed, and they might, the following season, even become rivals for the same man, or at any time quarrel to the death over the spoils of the chase.

The building of the stone shelters and corrals in which the children and the males were kept was the only community activity in which the women engaged and this work they were compelled to do alone, since the men would have escaped into the forest at the first opportunity had they been released from the corrals to take part in the work of construction, while the children as soon as they had become strong enough to be of any assistance would doubtless have done likewise; but the great shes were able to accomplish their titanic labors alone.

Equipped by nature with mighty frames and thews of steel they quarried the great slabs from a side hill overlooking the amphitheater, slid them to the floor of the little valley and pulled and pushed them into position by main strength and awkwardness, as the homely saying of our forefathers has it.

Fortunately for them it was seldom necessary to add to the shelters and corrals already built since the high rate of mortality among the females ordinarily left plenty of vacant enclosures for maturing girls. Jealousy, greed, the hazards of the hunt, the contingencies of intertribal wars all took heavy toll among the adult shes. Even the despised male, fighting for his freedom, sometimes slew his captor.

The hideous life of the Alalus was the natural result of the unnatural reversal of sex dominance. It is the province of the male to initiate love and by his masterfulness to inspire first respect, then admiration in the breast of the female he seeks to attract. Love itself developed after these other emotions. The gradually increasing ascendency of the female Alalus over the male eventually prevented the emotions of respect and admiration for the male from being aroused, with the result that love never followed.

Having no love for her mate and having become a more powerful brute, the savage Alalus woman soon came to treat the members of the opposite sex with contempt and brutality with the result that the power, or at least the desire, to initiate love ceased to exist in the heart of the male—he could not love a creature he feared and hated, he could not respect or admire the unsexed creatures that the Alali women had become, and so he fled into the forests and the jungles and there the dominant females hunted him lest their race perish from the earth.

It was the offspring of such savage and perverted creatures that Tarzan faced, fully aware of their cannibalistic intentions. The males did not attack him at once, but busily engaged themselves in fetching dry grass and small pieces of wood from one of the covered chambers, and while the three girls, one of them scarce seven years of age, approached the ape-man warily with ready bludgeons, they prepared a fire over which they expected soon to be broiling juicy cuts from the strange creature that their hairy dam had brought them.

One of the males, a lad of sixteen, held back, making excited signs with hands, head and body. He appeared to be trying to dissuade or prevent the girls from the carrying-out of their plan, he even appealed to the other boys for backing, but they merely glanced at the girls and continued their culinary preparations. At last however, as the girls were deliberately approaching the ape-man he placed himself directly in their path and attempted to stop them. Instantly the three little demons swung their bludgeons and sprang forward to destroy him. The boy dodged, plucked several of the feathered stones from his girdle and flung them at his assailants. So swift and so accurate did the missiles speed that two girls dropped, howling, to the ground. The third missed, striking one of the other boys on the temple, killing him instantly. He was the youth who had stolen Tarzan's locket, which, being like all his fellow males a timid creature, he had kept continually covered by a palm since the ape-man's return to consciousness had brought him out into the courtyard among them.

The older girl, nothing daunted, leaped forward, her face hideous in a snarl of rage. The boy cast another stone at her and then turned and ran toward the ape-man. What reception he expected he himself probably did not know. Perhaps it was the recrudescence of a long dead emotion of fellowship that prompted him to place himself at Tarzan's side—possibly Tarzan himself in whom loyalty to kind was strong had inspired this reawakening of an atrophied soul-sense. However that may be the fact remains that the boy came and stood at Tarzan's side while the girl, evidently sensing danger to herself in this strange, new temerity of her brother, advanced more cautiously.

In signs she seemed to be telling him what she would do to him if he did not cease to interpose his weak will between her and her gastronomic desires; but he signed back at her defiantly and stood his ground. Tarzan reached over and patted him on the back, smiling. The boy bared his teeth horribly, but it seemed evident that he was trying to return the ape-man's smile. And now the girl was almost upon them. Tarzan was quite at a loss as to how to proceed against her. His natural chivalry restrained him from attacking her and made it seem most repellent to injure her even in self-preservation; but he knew that before he was done with her he might even possibly have to kill her and so, while looking for an alternative, he steeled himself for the deed he loathed; but yet he hoped to escape without that.

*

The Third Woman, conducting her new mate from the cave to the corral where she would keep him imprisoned for a week or two, had heard the cadenced beating of naked heels and heavy bludgeons arising from the corral of The First Woman and immediately guessed their import. The welfare of the offspring of The First Woman concerned her not as an individual. Community instinct, however, prompted her to release them that they might search for food and their services not be lost to the tribe through starvation. She would not feed them, of course, as they did not belong to her, but she would open their prison gate and turn them loose to fend for themselves, to find food or not to find it, to survive or to perish according to the inexorable law of the survival of the fittest.

But the Third Woman took her time. Her powerful fingers entangled in the hair of her snarling spouse she dragged the protesting creature to her corral, removed the great slab from before the entrance, pushed the man roughly within, accelerating his speed with a final kick, replaced the slab and turned leisurely toward the nearby corral of The First Woman. Removing the stone door she passed through the two chambers and entered the corral at the moment that the oldest girl was advancing upon Tarzan. Pausing by the entranceway she struck her bludgeon against the stone wall of the shelter, evidently to attract the attention of those within the corral. Instantly all looked in her direction. She was the first adult female, other than their own dam, that the children of The First Woman had seen. They shrunk from her in evident terror. The youth at Tarzan's side slunk behind the ape-man, nor did Tarzan wonder at their fear. The Third Woman was the first adult Alalus he had seen, since all of the time that he had been in the hands of The First Woman he had been unconscious.

The girl who had been threatening him with her great club seemed now to have forgotten him, and instead stood with snarling face and narrowed eyes confronting the newcomer. Of all the children she seemed the least terrified.

The ape-man scrutinized the huge, brutish female standing at the far end of the corral with her savage eyes upon him. She had not seen him before as she had been in the forest hunting at the time that The First Woman had brought her prize back to the amphitheater. She had not known that The First Woman had any male in her corral other than her own spawn. Here, indeed, was a prize. She would remove him to her own corral. With this idea in mind, and knowing that, unless he succeeded in dodging past her and reaching the entranceway ahead of her, he could not escape her, she moved very slowly toward him, ignoring now the other occupants of the corral.

Tarzan, not guessing her real purpose, thought that she was about to attack him as a dangerous alien in the sacred precincts of her home. He viewed her great bulk, her enormous muscular development and the huge bludgeon swinging in her ham-like hand and compared them with his own defenseless nakedness.

To the jungle-born flight from useless and uneven combat carries with it no stigma of cowardice, and not only was Tarzan of the Apes jungle-born and jungle-raised, but the stripping of his clothes from him had now, as always before, stripped also away the thin and unnatural veneer of his civilization. It was, then, a savage beast that faced the oncoming Alalus woman—a cunning beast as well as a powerful one—a beast that knew when to fight and when to flee.

Tarzan cast a quick glance behind him. There crouched the Alalus lad, trembling in fear. Beyond was the rear wall of the corral, one of the great stone slabs of which tilted slightly outward. Slow is the mind of man, slower his eye by comparison with the eye and the mind of the trapped beast seeking escape. So quick was the ape-man that he was gone before The Third Woman had guessed that he was contemplating flight, and with him had gone the eldest Alalus boy.

Wheeling, all in a single motion Tarzan had swung the young male to his shoulder, leaped swiftly the few paces that had separated him from the rear wall of the corral, and, catlike, run up the smooth surface of the slightly tilted slab until his fingers closed upon the top, drawn himself over without a single backward glance, dropped the youth to the ground upon the opposite side, following him so quickly that they alighted almost together. Then he glanced about for the first time. He saw the natural amphitheater and the caves before several of which women still squatted. It would soon be dark. The sun was dropping behind the crest of the western hills. Tarzan saw but a single avenue of escape—the opening at the lower end of the amphitheater through which the trail led down into the valley and the forest below. Toward this he ran, followed by the youth.

Presently a woman, sitting before the entrance of her cave, saw him. Seizing her cudgel she leaped to her feet and gave immediate chase. Attracted by her another and another took up the pursuit, until five or six of them thundered along the trail.

The youth, pointing the way, raced swiftly ahead of the ape-man, but swift as he was, he could not outdistance the lithe muscles that had so often in the past carried their master safely from the swift rush of a maddened Numa, or won him a meal against the fleetness of Bara the deer. The heavy, lumbering women behind them had no chance of overhauling this swift pair if they were to depend entirely upon speed, but that they had no intention of doing. They had their stone missiles with which, almost from birth, they had practiced until approximate perfection was attained by each in casting them at either stationary or moving targets. But it was growing dark, the trail twisted and turned and the speed of the quarry made them elusive marks at which to cast an accurate missile that would be so timed as to stun rather than to kill. Of course more often than not a missile intended to stun did actually kill, but the quarry must take that chance. Instinct warned the women against killing the males, though it did not warn them against treating them with the utmost brutality. Had Tarzan realized why the women were pursuing him he would have run even faster than he did, and when the missiles began to fly past his head perhaps he did accelerate his speed a trifle.

Soon the ape-man reached the forest and as though he had dissolved into thin air disappeared from the astonished view of his pursuers, for now, indeed, was he in his own element. While they looked for him upon the ground he swung swiftly through the lower terraces, keeping in view the Alalus boy racing along the trail beneath him.

But with the man escaped, the women stopped and turned back toward the caves. The youth they did not want. For two or three years he would roam the forests unmolested by his own kind, and if he escaped the savage beasts and the spears and arrows of the ant people he would come to man's estate and be fair prey for any of the great shes during the mating season. For the time being, at least, he would lead a comparatively safe and happy existence.

His chances of survival had been materially lessened by his early escape into the forest. Had The First Woman lived she would have kept him safely within the walls of her corral for another year at least, when he would have been better fitted to cope with the dangers and emergencies of the savage life of the forest and the jungle.

The boy, his keen ears telling him that the women had given up the pursuit, halted and looked back for the strange creature that had freed him from the hated corral, but he could see only a short distance through the darkness of the growing forest night. The stranger was not in sight. The youth pricked up his great ears and listened intently. There was no sound of human footsteps other than the rapidly diminishing ones of the retreating women. There were other sounds, however, unfamiliar forest sounds that filled his muddy brain with vague terrors—sounds that came from the surrounding underbrush; sounds that came from the branches above his head, and, too, there were terrifying odors.

Darkness, complete and impenetrable, had closed in upon him with a suddenness that left him trembling. He could almost feel it weighing down upon him, crushing him and at the same time leaving him exposed to nameless terrors. He looked about him and could see naught, so that it seemed to him that he was without eyes, and being without a voice he could not call out either to frighten his enemies or attract the attention of the strange creature that had befriended him, and whose presence had so strangely aroused in his own breast an inexplicable emotion—a pleasurable emotion. He could not explain it; he had no word for it who had no word for anything, but he felt it and it still warmed his bosom and he wished in his muddy way that he could make a noise that would attract that strange creature to him again. He was lonely and much afraid.

A crackling of the bushes nearby aroused him to new and more intimate terror. Something large was approaching through the black night. The youth stood with his back against a great tree. He dared not move. He sniffed but what movement of the air there was took course from him in the direction of the thing that was creeping upon him out of the terrible forest, and so he could not identify it; but his instinct told him that the creature had identified him and was doubtless creeping closer to leap upon him and devour him.

He knew naught of lions, unless instinct carries with it a picture of the various creatures of which the denizens of the wild are instinctively afraid. In all his life he had never been outside the corral of The First Woman and as his people are without speech his dam could have told him nothing of the outside world, yet when the lion roared he knew that it was a lion.

CHAPTER 4

Esteban Miranda, clinging tightly to the wrist of little Uhha, crouched in the darkness of another forest twenty miles away and trembled as the thunderous notes of another lion reverberated through the jungle.

The girl felt the trembling of the body of the big man at her side and turned contemptuously upon him.

"You are not the river devil!" she cried. "You are afraid. You are not even Tarzan, for Khamis, my father, has told me that Tarzan is afraid of nothing. Let me go that I may climb a tree—only a coward or a fool would stand here dead with terror waiting for the lion to come and devour him. Let me go, I say!" and she attempted to wrench her wrist free from his grasp.

"Shut up!" he hissed. "Do you want to attract the lion to us?" But her words and struggles had aroused him from his paralysis and stooping he seized her and lifted her until she could grasp the lower branches of the tree beneath which they stood. Then, as she clambered to safety, he swung himself easily to her side.

Presently, higher up among the branches, he found a safer and more comfortable resting place, and there the two settled down to await the coming of the dawn, while below them Numa the lion prowled for a while, coughing and grunting, and occasionally voicing a deep roar that shook the jungle.

When daylight came at last the two, exhausted by a sleepless night, slipped to the ground. The girl would have delayed, hoping that the warriors of Obebe might overtake them; but the man harbored a fear rather than a hope of the same contingency and was, therefore, for hastening on as rapidly as possible that he might put the greatest possible distance between himself and the black cannibal chief.

EDGAR RICE BURROUGHS

He was completely lost, having not the remotest idea of where he should search for a reasonably good trail to the coast, nor, at present, did he care; his one wish being to escape recapture by Obebe, and so he elected to move northward, keeping always an eye open for any indication of a well-marked trail toward the west. Eventually, he hoped, he might discover a village of friendly natives who would aid him upon his journey toward the coast, and so the two moved as rapidly as they could in a northerly direction, their way skirting the Great Thorn Forest along the eastern edge of which they traveled.

*

The sun beating down upon the hot corral of The First Woman found it deserted of life. Only the corpse of a youth lay sprawled where it had fallen the previous evening. A speck appeared in the distant blue. It grew larger as it approached until it took upon itself the form of a bird gliding easily upon motionless wings. Nearer and nearer it came, now and again winging great, slow circles, until at last it swung above the corral of The First Woman. Once again it circled and then dropped to earth within the enclosure—Ska, the vulture, had come. Within the hour the body of the youth was hidden by a mantle of the great birds. It was a two-days feast, and when they left, only the clean picked bones remained, and entangled about the neck of one of the birds was a golden chain from which depended a diamond-encrusted locket. Ska fought the bauble that swung annoyingly beneath him when he flew and impeded his progress when he walked upon the ground, but it was looped twice about his neck and he was unable to dislodge it, and so he winged away across The Great Thorn Forest, the bright gems gleaming and scintillating in the sun.

*

Tarzan of the Apes, after eluding the women that had chased him and the Alalus youth into the forest, halted in the tree beneath which the frightened son of The First Woman had come to a terrified pause. He was there, close above him, when Numa charged, and reaching quickly down had seized the youth by the hair and dragged him to safety as the lion's raking talons embraced thin air beneath the feet of the Alalus.

The following day the ape-man concerned himself seriously in the hunt for food, weapons and apparel. Naked and unarmed as he was it might have gone hard with him had he been other than Tarzan of the Apes, and it might have gone hard with the Alalus had it not been for the ape-man. Fruits and nuts Tarzan found, and birds' eggs, but he craved meat and for meat he hunted assiduously, not alone because of the flesh of the kill, but for the skin and the gut and the tendons, that he could use in the fabrication of the things he required for the safety and comfort of his primitive existence.

As he searched for the spoor of his prey he searched also for the proper woods for a spear and for bow and arrows, nor were they difficult to find in this forest of familiar trees, but the day was almost done before the gentle wind, up which he had been hunting, carried to his sensitive nostrils the scent spoor of Bara the deer.

Swinging into a tree he motioned the Alalus to follow him, but so inept and awkward was the creature that Tarzan was compelled to drag him to a place among the branches, where, by signs, he attempted to impart to him the fact that he wished him to remain where he was, watching the materials that the ape-man had collected for his weapons, while the latter continued the hunt alone.

That the youth understood him he was not at all sure, but at least he did not follow when Tarzan swung off silently through the branches of the forest along the elusive trail of the ruminant, the scent of which was always translated to the foster son of Kala the she-ape as Bara the deer, though in fact, as practically always, the animal was an antelope. But strong are the impressions of childhood and since that long-gone day upon which he had pored over the colored alphabet primer in the far-off cabin of his dead father beside the landlocked harbor on the West Coast, and learned that "D stands for Deer," and had admired the picture of the pretty animal, the thing that most closely resembled it, with which he was familiar in his daily life, the antelope, became for him then, and always remained, Bara the deer.

To approach sufficiently close to Bara to bring him down with spear or arrow requires cunning and woodcraft far beyond the limited range of civilized man's ability. The native hunter loses more often than he wins in this game of wits and percipience. Tarzan, however, must excel them both and the antelope, too,

1031

in the keenness of his perceptive faculties and in coordination of mind and muscles if he were to lay Bara low with only the weapons with which nature had endowed him.

As Tarzan sped silently through the jungle, guided by his nostrils, in the direction of Bara the deer increasing strength of the familiar effluvium apprised him that not far ahead Bara foregathered in numbers, and the mouth of the savage ape-man watered in anticipation of the feast that but awaited his coming. And as the strength of the scent increased, more warily went the great beast, moving silently, a shadow among the shadows of the forest, until he came at last to the verge of an opening in which he saw a dozen antelope grazing.

Squatting motionless upon a low hanging limb the ape-man watched the movements of the herd against the moment that one might come close enough to the encircling trees to give a charge at least a shadow of a chance for success. To wait patiently, oftentimes hour upon hour, for the quarry to expose itself to more certain death is a part of the great game that the hunters of the wild must play. A single ill-timed or thoughtless movement may send the timorous prey scampering off into the far distance from which they may not return for days.

To avoid this Tarzan remained in statuesque immobility waiting for chance to send one of the antelope within striking distance, and while he waited there came to his nostrils, faintly, the scent of Numa the lion. Tarzan scowled. He was downwind from Bara and the lion was not between him and the antelope. It must, therefore, be upwind from the quarry as well as from himself; but why had not the sensitive nostrils of the herbivores caught the scent of their archenemy before it had reached the ape-man; that they had not was evidenced by their placidity as they grazed contentedly, their tails switching and occasionally a head raised to look about with up-pricked ears though with no symptom of the terror that would immediately follow the discovery of Numa in their vicinity.

The ape-man concluded that one of those freaks of the air currents that so often leave a motionless pocket of air directly in the path of the flow had momentarily surrounded the antelope, insulating them, as it were, from their immediate surroundings. And while he was thinking these things and wishing that Numa would go away he was shocked to hear a sudden crashing in the underbrush upon the opposite side of the clearing beyond the antelope, who were instantly upon the alert and poised for flight. Almost simultaneously there broke into view a young lion which, upon coming in sight of the antelope, set up a terrific roaring as it charged. Tarzan could have torn his hair in rage and disappointment. The blundering stupidity of a young lion had robbed him of his meat—the ruminants were scattering in all directions. The lion, charging futilely, had lost his own meat and Tarzan's too; but wait! What was this? A terrified buck, blind to all save the single thought of escape from the talons of the dread carnivore, was bolting straight for the tree in which Tarzan sat. As it came beneath him a sleek brown body shot head-foremost from the foliage, steel fingers gripped the throat of the buck, strong teeth fastened in its neck. The weight of the savage hunter carried the quarry to its knees and before it could stumble to its feet again a quick wrench with those powerful hands had twisted and broken its neck.

Without a backward glance the ape-man threw the carcass to his shoulder and leaped into the nearest tree. He had no need to waste time in looking back to know what Numa would be doing, for he realized that he had leaped upon Bara full in the sight of the king of beasts. Scarce had he drawn himself to safety ere the great cat crashed across the spot where he had stood.

Numa, baffled, roared terribly as he returned to glare up at the ape-man perched above him. Tarzan smiled.

"Son of Dango, the hyena," he taunted, "go hungry until you learn to hunt," and casting a broken branch contemptuously in the lion's face the ape-man vanished among the leafy branches bearing his kill lightly across one broad shoulder.

It was still daylight when Tarzan returned to where the Alalus was awaiting him. The youth had a small stone knife and with this the ape-man hacked off a generous portion of the antelope for the whelp of The First Woman and another for himself. Into the raw flesh, hungrily, sank the strong white teeth of the English lord, while the Alalus youth, gazing at him in surprise, sought materials for fire making. Amused, Tarzan watched him until the other had succeeded in preparing his food as he thought it should be prepared—the outside burned to a cinder, the inside raw, yet it was cooked food and doubtless imparted to its partaker a feeling of great superiority over the low beasts that devoured their meat raw, just as though he had been a civilized epicure eating decaying game and putrid cheeses at some fashionable club in London.

Tarzan smiled as he thought how vague, after all, the line that separates primitive from civilized man in matters pertaining to their instincts and their appetites. Some of his French friends, with whom he was dining upon a certain occasion, were horrified when they learned that in common with many of the African tribes and the apes he ate caterpillars, and they voiced their horror between mouthfuls of the snails they were eating with relish at the time. The provincial American scoffs at the French for eating frogs' legs, the while he munches upon the leg of a pig! The Esquimaux eat raw blubber, the Amazonians, both white and native, eat the contents of the stomachs of parrots and monkeys and consider them delicacies, the Chinese coolie asks not how his meat came by its death, nor how long since, and there is a man in New York, an estimable and otherwise harmless man, who eats Limburger cheese on Bartlett pears.

The following day, with sufficient meat to last them several days, Tarzan set to work upon his weapons and his loincloth. Showing the Alalus how to scrape the antelope hide with his stone knife, the ape-man set to work, with nothing more in the way of tools than bits of stone picked from the bed of a stream, to fashion weapons with which to cope successfully with the Alali women, the great carnivores and whatever other enemies time might reveal to him.

And as he worked he watched the Alalus youth and wondered of what use the poor creature could be to him in finding his way through the encircling thorn forest that he must pass to reach familiar country and the trail for home. That the poor thing was timid had been evidenced by its manner when fleeing from the Alali women and its terror when confronted by Numa. Its speechlessness made it useless as a companion and it was entirely without woodcraft other than a certain crude, instinctive kind that was of no use to Tarzan. But it had placed itself at his side during the altercation in the corral and although it could not have been of any help to him yet it had won a right to his consideration by its act. Moreover it was evident, quite evident, that the creature had attached itself to Tarzan and intended to remain with him.

An idea occurred to Tarzan as he worked upon his weapons and thought upon the Alalus—he would make similar weapons for the youth and teach him how to use them. He had seen that the crude weapons of the Alali would be no match against one armed with a bow and arrows, or even a good spear. Accurately they could not hope to throw their missiles as far as a good bowman could speed his shaft and their bludgeons were helpless in the face of a well-thrown spear.

Yes, he would make weapons for the youth and train him in their use and then he could be made of service in the hunt and, if necessary, in the fight, and as Tarzan of the Apes thought upon the matter the Alalus suddenly paused in his work and bent an ear close to the ground, then he lifted his head and turned his eyes upon Tarzan, pointing at him, at his ear, and then at the ground. The ape-man understood that he was to listen as the other had and when he did so he distinctly heard approaching footsteps resounding upon the hard-worn trail.

Gathering up his belongings he carried them high among the trees to a safe cache with the remnants of Bara the deer and then returning helped the youth into the tree beside him.

Slowly, already, the Alalus was becoming more at ease in the trees and could help himself to a greater extent in climbing into them, but he was still practically helpless in Tarzan's estimation.

The two had not long to wait before there swung down the trail one of the terrible women of the amphitheater, and behind her at ten or fifteen paces another, and behind the second a third. It was not often that they traveled thus, for theirs was a solitary existence, the Alali being almost devoid of gregarious instincts, yet they did occasionally start out upon their hunts together, especially when they were hunting some dangerous beast that had encroached upon their rights, or when, failing to collect sufficient men from the forest during the mating season, the unfortunate ones banded together to make a raid upon the corrals of a neighboring tribe.

The three, slouching along the trail, passed directly beneath the tree from which Tarzan and the youth watched them. The great, flat ears flapped lazily, the dark eyes wandered from side to side, and from time to time they moved rapidly the skin upon some portions of their bodies as they sought to dislodge annoying insects.

The two in the tree remained motionless while the three brute-women passed along down the trail to be presently lost to their view at a turning of the forest highway, then, after a short interval of listening, they descended to the ground and resumed their interrupted labors. The ape-man smiled as he idly pondered the events of the past few minutes—Tarzan of the Apes, Lord of the Jungle, hiding among the trees to escape the notice of three women! But such women! He knew little about them or their ways as yet, but what he did know was sufficient to convince him that they were as formidable foes as ever he had encountered and that while he remained weaponless he was no match against their great bludgeons and swift-thrown missiles.

The days passed; the ape-man and his silent companion perfected the weapons that would more easily give them food, the latter working mechanically, following the instructions of his master, until at last the time came when Tarzan and the Alalus were fully equipped and then they hunted together, the man training the youth in the use of bow and spear and the long grass rope that from boyhood had formed a unique feature of the ape-man's armament.

During these days of hunting there came over the Alalus youth, quite suddenly, a great change. It had been his habit to glide stealthily through the forest, stopping often to look this way and that, fearful, apparently, of every creature that roamed the shadowed trails; his one great fear the ferocious females of his kind; but suddenly all this changed as by magic. Slowly he was mastering the bow and the spear; with deep interest and a sense of awe and respect he had watched Tarzan bring down many animals, great and small, for food, and once he had seen him dispatch Sabor the lioness with a single thrust of his great spear when Sabor had caught the ape-man in a clearing too far from the sanctuary of his beloved trees, and then his own day came. He and Tarzan were hunting when the former disturbed a small herd of wild pigs, bringing down two with his arrows. The others scattered in all directions and one of these, a boar, sighting the Alalus, charged him. The youth was of a mind to flee, for ages of inherited instinct prompted him to flight. Always the male Alalus fled from danger, and between fleeing from carnivorous animals and from their own women they had become very swift, so swift that no dangerous enemy could overtake them—an Alalus man could be captured only by craft. He could have escaped the boar by flight and for an instant he was upon the verge of flight, but a sudden thought checked him—back flew his spear hand as the ape-man had taught him and then forward with all the weight of his body behind the cast. The boar was coming straight for him. The spear struck in front of the left shoulder and ranged downward through the heart. Horta the boar dropped in his tracks.

A new expression came into the eyes and spread over the countenance of the Alalus. He no longer wore that hunted expression; he no longer slunk through the forest casting fearful glances from side to side. Now he walked erect, boldly and with fearless mien, and, perhaps, instead of dreading the appearance of a female he rather courted the event. He was the personification of avenging manhood. Within him rankled countless ages of contemptuous treatment and abuse at the hands of his shes. Doubtless he never thought of the matter in this way at all, but the fact remained, and Tarzan realized it, that the first woman unfortunate enough to stumble upon this youth was going to get the surprise of her life.

*

And while Tarzan and the Alalus roamed the strange land hemmed in by The Great Thorn Forest and the ape-man sought for an avenue of escape, Esteban Miranda and little Uhha, daughter of Khamis the witch doctor, wandered along the forest's outer verge in search of a trail toward the west and the coast.

EDGAR RICE BURROUGHS

CHAPTER 5

With doglike devotion the Alalus youth clung to Tarzan. The latter had mastered the meager sign language of his protégé, giving them a means of communication that was adequate for all their needs. The former, gaining confidence with a growing familiarity with his new weapons, became more independent, with the result that the two more often separated for the hunt, thus insuring a more fully stocked larder.

It was upon one of these occasions that Tarzan came suddenly upon a strange sight. He had been following the scent spoor of Bara the deer when it was suddenly crossed by that of one of the great female Alali. That probably meant that another would attempt to rob him of his prey. The savage instinct of the jungle beast predominated in the guidance of the breech-clouted ape-man. It was not the polished Lord Greystoke of London whose snarling upper lip revealed two gleaming fighting fangs—it was a primordial hunting-brute about to be robbed of its quarry.

Taking to the trees he moved rapidly in the direction of the Alalus woman, but before he came within sight of her a new scent impinged upon his nostrils—a strange, new scent that puzzled him. It was the scent of man, yet strange and unfamiliar to a degree. Never before had anything like it arrested his attention. It was very faint and yet, somehow, he knew that it was close, and then, ahead of him, he heard voices, low musical voices, that came faintly to his ears; and though they were low and musical there was something in the quality and pitch of them that suggested excitement. Now Tarzan went more carefully, Bara, the deer, all but forgotten.

As he drew nearer he realized that there were many voices and much commotion and then he came upon a large plain that stretched away to distant hills, and in the foreground, not a hundred yards from him, he looked upon a sight that might well have caused him to doubt the veracity of his own eyes. The only familiar figure was a giant Alalus woman. Surrounding her was a horde of diminutive men—tiny white warriors—mounted upon what appeared to be a form of the Royal Antelope of the West Coast. Armed with lances and swords they repeatedly charged at the huge legs of the Alalus, who, backing slowly toward the forest, kicked viciously at her assailants and struck at them with her heavy bludgeon.

It quickly became evident to Tarzan that they were attempting to hamstring her and had they been successful they might easily have slain her then; but though there must have been fully a hundred of them their chances of success appeared small, since, with a single kick of her mighty foot the woman could lay low a dozen or more of her assailants at a time. Already fully half the force was hors de combat, their bodies with those of many of their mounts being scattered out onto the plain marking the trail of the combat up to the time that Tarzan had come upon the scene.

The courage of the survivors, however, filled Tarzan with admiration as he watched them hurl themselves upon almost certain death in their stubborn efforts to bring down the female, and then it was that the ape-man saw the reason, or the apparent reason, for the mad sacrifice of life—in her left hand the Alalus clutched one of the tiny warriors. It was to rescue him, evidently, that the others were maintaining this forlorn hope.

If the warriors filled Tarzan with admiration to scarcely a lesser extent did their courageous and agile mounts. Always had he thought of the Royal Antelope, the smallest known member of its family, as the most timid of creatures, but not so these cousins of theirs. Slightly larger, standing perhaps fifteen inches at the withers, they were in all other outward respects identical; yet, at the guidance of their riders, they leaped fearlessly into close range of those enormous feet and the great, slashing bludgeon. Perfectly reined were they, too; so perfectly that their muscles seemed to have coordinated with the minds of their riders. In and out they bounded, scarcely touching the ground before they were out of harm's way again. Ten or a dozen feet they covered at a leap, so that Tarzan wondered not only at their agility but at the almost marvelous riding ability of the warriors who could keep their seats so perfectly upon these leaping, bounding, turning, twisting mounts.

TARZAN SUPER PACK

It was a pretty sight and an inspiring one, and however unreal it had at first appeared to him he was not long in realizing that he was looking upon a race of real pygmies—not members of the black tribe with which all African explorers are more or less familiar, but with that lost white race of diminutive men reference to which is occasionally to be found in ancient manuscript of travel and exploration, of myth and legend.

While the encounter interested him and he viewed it at first as a disinterested neutral he soon found his sympathies gravitating to the tiny warriors and when it became evident that the Alalus woman was going to make good her escape into the forest with her captive, the ape-man decided to take a hand in the affair himself.

As he stepped from the concealment of the forest the little warriors were the first to see him. Evidently they mistook him at first for another of their giant enemies, for a great cry of disappointment rose from them, and they fell back for the first time since Tarzan had been watching the unequal struggle. Wishing to make his intentions clear before the little men set upon him he moved quickly in the direction of the woman, who, the instant that her eyes fell upon him, made imperative signs for him to join her in dispatching the balance of the pygmies. She was accustomed to being feared and obeyed by her mankind, when she had them in her power. Perhaps she wondered a little at the temerity of this he, for as a rule they all ran from her; but she needed him badly and that was the idea that dominated her thoughts.

As Tarzan advanced he commanded her in the sign language he had learned from the youth that she was to release her captive and go away, molesting the little men no more. At this she made an ugly grimace and raising her bludgeon came forward to meet him. The ape-man fitted an arrow to his bow.

"Go back!" he signed her. "Go back, or I will kill you. Go back, and put down the little man."

She snarled ferociously and increased her pace. Tarzan raised the arrow to the level of his eye and drew it back until the bow bent. The pygmies, realizing that for the moment at least this strange giant was their ally, sat their mounts and awaited the outcome of the duel. The ape-man hoped that the woman would obey his commands before he was compelled to take her life, but even a cursory glance at her face revealed anything but an intention to relinquish her purpose, which now seemed to be to annihilate this presumptuous meddler as well.

On she came. Already she was too close to make further delay safe and the ape-man released his shaft. Straight into her savage heart it drove and as she stumbled forward Tarzan leaped to meet her, seizing the warrior from her grasp before she might fall upon the tiny body and crush it, and as he did so the other warriors, evidently mistaking his intentions, spurred forward with loud shouts and brandishing weapons; but before they had reached him he had set the rescued man upon the ground and released him.

Instantly the attitude of the charging pygmies changed again and from war cries their tones turned to cheers. Riding forward they drew rein before the warrior that Tarzan had rescued and several of their number leaped from their mounts and, kneeling, raised his hand to their lips. It was evident then to the ape-man that he had rescued one who stood high among them, their chief, perhaps; and now he wondered what would be their attitude toward him, as, with a look of amused tolerance upon his grim features, he watched them as one might watch the interesting doings of a swarm of ants.

As they felicitated their fellow upon his miraculous escape Tarzan had an opportunity to inspect them more closely. The tallest of them stood about eighteen inches in height, their white skins were tanned by exposure to a shade a trifle darker than his own, yet there was no question but that they were white men; their features were regular and well proportioned, so that by any standards of our race they would have been considered handsome. There were, of course, variations and exceptions; but on the whole those that he saw before him were fine-looking men. All were smooth-faced and there seemed to be no very old men among them, while he whom Tarzan had saved from the Alalus woman was apparently younger than the average, and much younger than those who had dismounted to do him homage.

As Tarzan watched them the young man bade the others rise and then addressed them for a moment after which he turned toward the ape-man and directed his remarks to him, none of which, of course, Tarzan

EDGAR RICE BURROUGHS

could understand. By his manner, however, he guessed that the other was thanking him and possibly too asking his further intentions toward them and in reply the ape-man endeavored to assure them that he desired their friendship. Further to emphasize his peaceful intentions he cast his weapons aside and took a step toward them, his arms thrown slightly outward, his open palms in their direction.

The young man seemed to understand his friendly overtures, for he too advanced, offering his hand to Tarzan. The ape-man knew that the other meant that he should kiss it, but this he did not do, preferring to assume a role of equality with their highest. Instead, he kneeled upon one knee that he might more easily reach the proffered hand of the pygmy and pressing the tiny fingers gently, inclined his head slightly in a formal bow which carried no suggestion of servility. The other seemed satisfied, returned the bow with equal dignity and then attempted to convey to the ape-man that he and his party were about to ride off across the plain, inviting him to accompany them.

Rather curious to see more of these remarkable little people Tarzan was nothing loath to accept the invitation. Before the party set out, however, they dispersed to gather up their dead and wounded and to put out of their misery any of the injured antelope that were too severely hurt to travel. This they did with the relatively long, straight sword which was part of the armament of each. Their lances they left resting in cylindrical boots attached to the right side of their saddles. For other weapons Tarzan could discover nothing but a tiny knife carried in a scabbard at the right side by each warrior. The blade, like the blade of the rapier, was two edged but only about an inch and a half long, with a very sharp point.

Having gathered the dead and wounded, the latter were examined by the young leader of the party, who was accompanied by the five or six who had gathered about him at the time that Tarzan had released him. These Tarzan took to be lieutenants, or under-chiefs. He saw them question the wounded and in three cases, each evidently a hopeless one, the leader ran his sword quickly through the hearts of the unhappy men.

While this seemingly cruel, yet unquestionably sound, military measure was being carried out, the balance of the warriors, directed by under-officers, were excavating a long trench beside the dead, of which there were twenty, their tool being a stout shovel blade carried attached to the saddle and which could be quickly fitted to the butt of the spear or lance. The men worked with extreme rapidity and under a plan that seemed to abhor lost motion, of which there was the absolute minimum, until in an incredibly short time they had excavated a trench fifty inches in length, eighteen inches wide and nine inches deep, the equivalent of which to men of normal size would have been nearly seventeen feet long, six feet wide and three feet deep. Into this they packed the dead like sardines and in two layers. They then shoveled back sufficient earth to fill the interstices between the bodies and to come to a level with the top of the upper layer, after which loose stones were rolled in until the bodies were entirely covered by two inches of stones. The remaining earth from the excavation was then piled over all.

By the time this work was completed the loose antelope had been caught and the wounded strapped to their backs. At a word from their commander the party formed with military precision, a detail started ahead with the wounded and a moment later the balance of the troop was mounted and on the way. The method of mounting and taking up the march was unique and a source of considerable interest to Tarzan. The dismounted warriors were standing in line facing the young leader who was mounted, as were the several officers who accompanied him. Each warrior held his mount by the bridle. The commander made a rapid signal with the raised point of his sword—there was no spoken word of command—immediately after which he dropped the point quickly at his side simultaneously wheeling his mount, which leaped quickly off in the direction that the troop was facing, the mounts of his officers wheeling with him as though actuated by a single brain, and at the same instant the mount of each alternate warrior in the line leaped forward and as it leaped its rider swung to his saddle, vaulting to his seat as lightly as a feather. The instant the first line had cleared them the antelopes of the second line leaped in pursuit, their riders mounted as had the others before them and with a second and longer leap the intervals were closed and the whole troop raced forward in a compact line. It was a most clever and practical evolution and one that made it possible to put mounted troops in motion as rapidly as foot troops; there was no long delay caused by taking distance, mounting and closing ranks.

As the troop galloped away ten warriors wheeled from the left flank and, following one of the officers who had detached himself from the party of the commander of the troop, returned to Tarzan. By signs the officer conveyed to the ape-man the intelligence that he was to follow this party which would guide him to their destination. Already the main body was far away across the open plain, their lithe mounts clearing as many as five or six feet in a single bound. Even the swift Tarzan could not have kept pace with them.

As the ape-man started away under the guidance of the detachment his thoughts reverted for an instant to the Alalus youth who was hunting alone in the forest behind them, but he soon put the creature from his mind with the realization that it was better equipped to defend itself than any of its kind, and that when he had made his visit to the country of the pygmies he could doubtless return and find the Alalus, if he so desired.

Tarzan, inured to hardship and to long and rapid marches, fell into a dogtrot such as he could keep up for hours at a time without rest, while his guides, trotting their graceful mounts, kept just ahead of him. The plain was more rolling than it had appeared from the verge of the forest, with here and there a clump of trees; the grass was plentiful and there were occasional bands of the larger species of antelope grazing at intervals. At sight of the approaching riders and the comparatively giant-like figure of Tarzan they broke and ran. Once they passed a rhinoceros, the party making only a slight detour to avoid it, and later, in a clump of trees, the leader halted his detachment suddenly and seizing his lance advanced again slowly toward a clump of bushes at the same time transmitting an order to his men which caused them to spread and surround the thicket.

Tarzan halted and watched the proceedings. The wind was blowing from him in the direction of the thicket, so that he could not determine what manner of creature, if any, had attracted the attention of the officer; but presently, when the warriors had completely surrounded the bushes and those upon the other side had ridden into it, their spears couched and ready, he heard an ugly snarl issuing from the center of the thicket and an instant later an African wildcat sprang into view, leaping directly at the officer waiting with ready spear to receive it. The weight and momentum of the beast all but unseated the rider, the point of whose spear had met the cat full in the chest. There were a few spasmodic struggles before death ensued, during which, had the spear broken, the man would have been badly mauled and perhaps killed, for the cat was relatively as formidable a beast as is the lion to us. The instant that it died four warriors leaped forward and with their sharp knives removed the head and skin in an incredibly short time.

Tarzan could not but note that everything these people did was accomplished with maximum efficiency. Never did there seem to be any lost motion, never was one at a loss as to what to do, never did one worker get in the way of another. Scarcely ten minutes had elapsed from the moment that they had encountered the cat before the detachment was again moving, the head of the beast fastened to the saddle of one of the warriors, the skin to that of another.

The officer who commanded the detachment was a young fellow, not much, if any, older than the commander of the troop. That he was courageous Tarzan could bear witness from the manner in which he had faced what must have been, to so diminutive a people, a most deadly and ferocious beast; but then, the entire party's hopeless attack upon the Alalus woman had proved that they all were courageous, and the ape-man admired and respected courage. Already he liked these little men, though it was at times still difficult for him to accept them as a reality, so prone are we to disbelieve in the possibility of the existence of any form of life with which we are not familiar by association or credible repute.

They had been traveling for almost six hours across the plain, the wind had changed and there was borne to Tarzan's nostrils clearly the scent of Bara the deer, ahead. The ape-man, who had tasted no food that day, was ravenous, with the result that the odor of meat aroused all the savage instincts fostered by his strange upbringing. Springing forward abreast the leader of the detachment that was escorting him he signed them to halt and then as clearly as he could through the comparatively laborious and never quite satisfactory medium of further signs explained that he was hungry, that there was meat ahead and that they should remain in the rear until he had stalked his prey and made his kill.

The officer having understood and signified his assent Tarzan crept stealthily forward toward a small clump of trees beyond which his keen scent told him there were several antelope, and behind Tarzan followed the detachment, so noiselessly that even the keen ears of the ape-man heard them not.

Sheltered by the trees Tarzan saw a dozen or more antelope grazing a short distance beyond, the nearest being scarce a hundred feet from the small grove. Unslinging his bow and taking a handful of arrows from his quiver, the ape-man moved noiselessly to the tree nearest the antelope. The detachment was not far behind him, though it had stopped the moment the officer saw the game that Tarzan was stalking, lest it be frightened away.

The pygmies knew naught of bows and arrows and so they watched with deep interest every move of the ape-man. They saw him fit an arrow to his bow, draw it far back and release it almost all in a single movement, so quick with this weapon was he, and they saw the antelope leap to the impact of the missile which was followed in rapid succession by a second and a third, and as he shot his bolts Tarzan leaped forward in pursuit of his prey; but there was no danger that he would lose it. With the second arrow the buck was upon his knees and when Tarzan reached him he was already dead.

The warriors who had followed close behind Tarzan the instant that there was no further need for caution were already surrounding the antelope, where they were talking with much more excitement than Tarzan had seen them display upon any previous occasion, their interest seemingly centered about the death-dealing projectiles that had so easily laid the great animal low, for to them this antelope was as large as would be the largest elephant to us; and as they caught the ape-man's eye they smiled and rubbed their palms together very rapidly with a circular motion, an act which Tarzan assumed to be in the nature of applause.

Having withdrawn his arrows and returned them to his quiver Tarzan signed to the leader of the detachment that he would borrow his rapier. For an instant the man seemed to hesitate and all his fellows watched him intently, but he drew the sword and passed it hilt foremost to the ape-man. If you are going to eat flesh raw while it is still warm you do not bleed the carcass, nor did Tarzan in this instance. Instead he merely cut off a hind quarter, sliced off what he wanted and fell to devouring it hungrily.

The little men viewed his act with surprise not unmixed with horror and when he offered them some of the flesh they refused it and drew away. What their reaction was he could not know, but he guessed that they held a strong aversion to the eating of raw meat. Later he was to learn that their revulsion was due to the fact that within the entire range of their experience, heretofore, the only creatures that devoured raw meat devoured the pygmies as well. When, therefore, they saw this mighty giant eating the flesh of his kill raw they could not but draw the conclusion that should he become sufficiently hungry he would eat them.

Wrapping some of the meat of the antelope in its own skin Tarzan secured it to his back and the party resumed its journey. The warriors now seemed troubled and as they conversed in low tones they cast many backward glances in the direction of the ape-man. They were not afraid for themselves, for these warriors scarcely knew the meaning of fear. The question that caused them apprehension related to the wisdom of leading among their people such a huge devourer of raw flesh, who, at a single hurried meal, had eaten the equivalent of a grown man.

The afternoon was drawing to a close when Tarzan discerned in the far distance what appeared to be a group of symmetrical, dome-shaped hillocks and later, as they approached these, he saw a body of mounted warriors galloping to meet them. From his greater height he saw these before the others saw them, and attracting the officer's attention made signs apprising the latter of his discovery, but the oncoming warriors were hidden from the view of their fellows by the inequalities of the ground.

Realizing this Tarzan stooped and, before the officer could guess his intention, had gathered antelope and rider gently in his powerful hands and lifted them high above the ground. For an instant consternation held the remaining warriors. Swords flashed and a warning cry arose and even the plucky pygmy in his grasp drew his own diminutive weapon; but a smile from the ape-man reassured them all, and an instant later the officer saw why Tarzan had raised him aloft. He called down to the others below him then and from their manner as from that of him whom he held the ape-man guessed that the approaching party was composed of friends of his escort, and so, a few minutes later, it proved when he was surrounded by several hundreds of the pygmies, all friendly, eager and curious. Among them was the leader whom he had rescued from the Alalus woman and him he greeted with a handshake.

A consultation now took place between the leader of the detachment that had escorted the ape-man, the young commander of the larger party and several older warriors. By the expressions of their faces and the tone of their voices Tarzan judged that the matter was serious and that it concerned him he was sure from the numerous glances that were cast in his direction. He could not know, though, that the subject of their discussion was based upon the report of the commander of the escort that their mighty guest was an eater of raw flesh and the consequent danger of bringing him among their people.

The chief among them, the young commander, settled the question, however, by reminding them that though the giant must have been very hungry to have devoured as much flesh as they told him he had, nevertheless he had traveled for many hours with only a small number of their warriors always within easy reach of him and had not offered to molest them. This seemed a conclusive argument of his good intentions and consequently the cavalcade set forth without further delay in the direction of the hillocks that were now in plain view a mile or two away.

As they neared them Tarzan saw what appeared to be literally innumerable little men moving about among the hillocks, and as he came nearer still he realized that these seeming hillocks were symmetrical mounds of small stones quite evidently built by the pygmies themselves and that the hordes of pygmies moving about among them were workers, for here was a long line all moving in one direction, emerging from a hole in the ground and following a well-defined path to a half-completed hillock that was evidently in course of construction. Another line moved, empty-handed, in the opposite direction, entering the ground through a second hole, and upon the flanks of each line and at frequent intervals, marched armed warriors, while other similar lines of guarded workers moved in and out of openings in each of the other domelike structures, carrying to the mind of the ape-man a suggestion of ants laboring about their hills.

CHAPTER 6

Ska, the vulture, winged his way leisurely in great circles far above the right bank of the Ugogo. The pendant locket, sparkling in the sun light, had ceased to annoy him while on the wing, only when he alighted and walked upon the ground did it become an encumbrance; then he stepped upon it and tripped, but long since had he ceased to fight it, accepting it now as an inescapable evil. Beneath him he presently descried the still, recumbent form of Gorgo, the buffalo, whose posture proclaimed that he was already fit food for Ska. The great bird dropped, alighting in a nearby tree. All was well, no foes were in evidence. Satisfied of this, Ska flapped down to the fallen beast.

*

Miles away a giant white man crouched in the concealment of a dense thicket with a little black girl. The fingers of one of the man's hands were across her mouth, those of the other held a knife at her heart. The man's eyes were not upon the girl, but were straining through the dense foliage toward a game trail along which two ebon warriors were advancing. Succor was close at hand for Uhha, the daughter of Khamis the witch doctor, for the two approaching were hunters from the village of Obebe, the chief; but she dared not call aloud to attract them lest the sharp point of Miranda's knife slip into her young heart, and so she heard them come and go until, their voices lost in the distance, the Spaniard arose and dragged her back upon the trail, where they took up, what seemed to Uhha, their endless and fruitless wanderings through the jungle.

EDGAR RICE BURROUGHS

IN the village of the ant men Tarzan found a warm welcome and having decided to remain for a while that he might study them and their customs he set to work, as was his wont when thrown among strange peoples, to learn their language as quickly as possible. Having already mastered several languages and numerous dialects the ape-man never found it difficult to add to his linguistic attainments, and so it was only a matter of a comparatively short time before he found it possible to understand his hosts and to make himself understood by them. It was then that he learned that they had at first thought that he was some form of Alalus and had consequently believed that it ever would be impossible to communicate with him by other means than signs. They were greatly delighted therefore when it had become apparent that he could utter vocal sounds identical to theirs, and when they comprehended that he desired to learn their tongue, Adendrohahkis, the king, placed several instructors at his disposal and gave orders that all his people, with whom the giant stranger might come in contact, should aid him to an early understanding of their language.

Adendrohahkis was particularly well inclined toward the ape-man because of the fact that it had been the king's son, Komodoflorensal, whom Tarzan had rescued from the clutches of the Alalus woman, and so it was that everything was done to make the giant's stay among them a pleasant one. A hundred slaves brought his food to him where he had taken up his abode beneath the shade of a great tree that grew in lonely majesty just outside the city. When he walked among the group of dome-houses a troop of cavalry galloped ahead to clear a path for him, lest he trod upon some of the people of the city; but always was Tarzan careful of his hosts, so that no harm ever befell one of them because of him.

As he mastered the language he learned many things concerning these remarkable people. Prince Komodoflorensal almost daily took it upon himself to assist in the instruction of his colossal guest and it was from him that Tarzan learned most. Nor were his eyes idle as he strolled around the city. Particularly interesting was the method of construction used in erecting the comparatively gigantic dome-houses which towered high above even the great Tarzan. The first step in the construction was to outline the periphery of the base with boulders of uniform size and weighing, perhaps, fifty pounds each. Two slaves easily carried such a boulder when it was slung in a rope hammock and as thousands of slaves were employed the work progressed with rapidity. The circular base, with a diameter of one hundred and fifty to two hundred feet, having been outlined, another, smaller circle was laid about ten feet inside the first, four openings being left in each circle to mark the location of the four entrances to the completed building and corresponding to the four principal cardinal points of the compass. The walls of the entrances were then outlined upon the ground with similar large boulders, these being a little more carefully selected for uniformity, after which the four enclosures thus formed were packed closely with boulders. The corridors and chambers of the first floor were then outlined and the spaces between filled with boulders, each being placed with the utmost care and nicety in relation to those touching it and those that should rest upon it when the second course was laid, for these were to support a tremendous weight when the edifice was completed. The corridors were generally three feet wide, the equivalent of twelve feet by our standards, while the chambers, varied in dimensions according to the uses to which they were to be put. In the exact center of the building a circular opening was left that measured ten feet in diameter and this was carried upward as the building progressed until the whole formed an open shaft from ground floor to roof in the completed edifice.

The lower course having been built up in this manner to a height of six inches wooden arches were placed at intervals the lengths of the corridors which were now ceiled over by the simple expedient of fastening thin wooden strips lengthways of the corridors from arch to arch until the corridors were entirely roofed. The strips, or boards, which overlapped one another, were fastened in place by wooden dowels driven through them into the peripheries of the arches. As this work was progressing the walls of the various chambers and the outer wall of the building were raised to a height of twenty-four inches, bringing them to the level of the ceilings of the arched corridors, and the spaces between chambers and corridors were packed with boulders, the interstices between which were filled with smaller stones and gravel. The ceiling beams were then placed across the other chambers, timbers six inches square hewn from a hard, tough wood being used, and in the

1041

larger chambers these were further supported, at intervals, by columns of the same dimensions and material. The ceiling beams being in place they were covered over with tight-fitting boards, doweled to place. The ceilings of the chambers now projected six inches above the surrounding course of the structure, and at this juncture hundreds of cauldrons were brought in which a crude asphalt was heated until it became liquid and the interstices of the next six inch course were filled with it, bringing the entire completed course to the same level at a height of thirty inches, over all of which a second six inch course of rock and asphalt was laid, and the second story laid out and completed in a similar manner.

The palace of Adendrohahkis, constructed in this way, was two hundred twenty feet in diameter, and one hundred ten feet high, with thirty-six floors capable of housing eighty thousand people, a veritable anthill of humanity. The city consisted of ten similar domes, though each slightly smaller than the king's, housing a total of five hundred thousand people, two-thirds of whom were slaves; these being for the most part the artisans and body servants of the ruling class. Another half million slaves, the unskilled laborers of the city, dwelt in the subterranean chambers of the quarries from which the building material was obtained. The passageways and chambers of these mines were carefully shored and timbered as the work progressed, resulting in fairly commodious and comfortable quarters for the slaves upon the upper levels at least, and as the city was built upon the surface of an ancient ground moraine, on account of the accessibility of building material, the drainage was perfect, the slaves suffering no inconvenience because of their underground quarters.

The domes themselves were well ventilated through the large central air shaft and the numerous windows that pierced the outer walls at frequent intervals at each level above the ground floor, in which, as previously explained, there were but four openings. The windows, which were six and one-quarter inches wide by eighteen and a half inches high, admitted a certain amount of light as well as air; but the interior of the dome, especially the gloomy chambers midway between the windows and the central light and air shaft, was illuminated by immense, slow-burning, smokeless candles.

Tarzan watched the construction of the new dome with keenest interest, realizing that it was the only opportunity that he ever would have to see the interior of one of these remarkable, human hives, and as he was thus engaged Komodoflorensal and his friends hastened to initiate him into the mysteries of their language; and while he learned the language of his hosts he learned many other things of interest about them. The slaves, he discovered, were either prisoners of war or the descendants of prisoners of war. Some had been in bondage for so many generations that all trace of their origin had become lost and they considered themselves as much citizens of Trohanadalmakus, the city of King Adendrohahkis, as did any of the nobility. On the whole they were treated with kindness and were not overworked after the second generation. The recent prisoners and their children were, for the most part, included in the caste of unskilled labor from which the limit of human endurance was exacted. They were the miners, the quarriers and the builders and fully fifty per cent of them were literally worked to death. With the second generation the education of the children commenced, those who showed aptitude for any of the skilled crafts being immediately transferred from the quarries to the domes, where they took up the relatively easy life of a prosperous and indulged middle class. In another manner might an individual escape the quarries—by marriage, or rather by selection as they choose to call it, with a member of the ruling class. In a community where class consciousness was such a characteristic of the people and where caste was almost a fetish it was rather remarkable that such connections brought no odium upon the inferiors, but, on the contrary, automatically elevated the lesser to the caste of the higher contracting party.

"It is thus, Deliverer of the Son of Adendrohahkis," explained Komodoflorensal, in reply to Tarzan's inquiry relative to this rather peculiar exception to the rigid class distinctions the king's son had so often impressed upon him: "Ages ago, during the reign of Klamataamorosal in the city of Trohanadalmakus, the warriors of Veltopishago, king of the city of Veltopismakus, marched upon our fair Trohanadalmakus and in the battle that ensued the troops of our ancestors were all but annihilated. Thousands of our men and women were carried away into slavery and all that saved us from being totally wiped out was the courageous defense that our own slaves waged for their masters. Klamataamorosal, from whom I am descended, fighting in the thick of the fray noted the greater stamina of the slaves; they were stronger than the warriors of either city and seemed not to tire at all, while the high caste nobility of the fighting clans, though highly courageous, became completely exhausted after a few minutes of fighting.

"After the battle was over Klamataamorosal called together all the chief officers of the city, or rather all who had not been killed or taken prisoner, and pointed out to them that the reason our city had been defeated was not so much because of the greater numbers of the forces of the king Veltopishago as due to the fact that our own warriors were physical weaklings, and he asked them why this should be and what could be done to remedy so grievous a fault. The youngest man among them, wounded and weak from loss of blood, was the only one who could offer a reasonable explanation, or suggest a means of correcting the one obvious weakness of the city.

"He called their attention to the fact that of all the race of Minunians the people of the city of Trohanadalmakus were the most ancient and that for ages there had been no infusion of new blood, since they were not permitted to mate outside their own caste, while their slaves, recruited from all the cities of Minuni, had interbred, with the result that they had become strong and robust while their masters, through inbreeding, had grown correspondingly weaker.

"He exhorted Klamataamorosal to issue a decree elevating to the warrior class any slave that was chosen as mate by either a man or woman of that class, and further to obligate each and every warrior to select at least one mate from among their slaves. At first, of course, the objections to so iconoclastic a suggestion were loud and bitter; but Klamataamorosal was quick to sense the wisdom of the idea and not only did he issue the decree, but he was the first to espouse a slave woman, and what the king did all were anxious to do also.

"The very next generation showed the wisdom of the change and each succeeding generation has more than fulfilled the expectations of Klamataamorosal until now you see in the people of Trohanadalmakus the most powerful and warlike of the Minunians.

"Our ancient enemy, Veltopismakus, was the next city to adopt the new order, having learned of it through slaves taken in raids upon our own community, but they were several generations behind us. Now all the cities of Minuni wed their warriors with their slave women. And why not? Our slaves were all descended from the warrior class of other cities from which their ancestors were captured. We all are of the same race, we all have the same language and in all important respects the same customs.

"Time has made some slight changes in the manner of the selection of these new mates and now it is often customary to make war upon another city for the sole purpose of capturing their noblest born and most beautiful women.

"For us of the royal family it has been nothing less than salvation from extinction. Our ancestors were transmitting disease and insanity to their progeny. The new, pure, virile blood of the slaves has washed the taint from our veins and so altered has our point of view become that whereas, in the past, the child of a slave woman and a warrior was without caste the lowest of the low, now they rank highest of the high, since it is considered immoral for one of the royal family to wed other than a slave."

"And your wife?" asked Tarzan. "You took her in a battle with some other city?"

"I have no wife," replied Komodoflorensal. "We are preparing now to make war upon Veltopismakus the daughter of whose king, we are told by slaves from that city, is the most beautiful creature in the world. Her name is Janzara, and as she is not related to me, except possibly very remotely, she is a fit mate for the son of Adendrohahkis."

"How do you know she is not related to you?" asked the ape-man.

"We keep as accurate a record of the royal families of Veltopismakus and several others of the nearer cities of Minuni as we do of our own," replied Komodoflorensal, "obtaining our information from captives, usually from those who are chosen in marriage by our own people. For several generations the kings of

Veltopismakus have not been sufficiently powerful or fortunate to succeed in taking royal princesses from us by either force of arms or strategy, though they never have ceased attempting to do so, and the result has been that they have been forced to find their mates in other and oftentimes distant cities.

"The present king of Veltopismakus, Elkomoelhago, the father of the princess Janzara, took his mate, the mother of the princess, from a far distant city that has never, within historic times, taken slaves from Trohanadalmakus, nor have our warriors visited that city within the memory of any living man. Janzara, therefore, should make me an excellent mate."

"But what about love—suppose you should not care for one another?" asked Tarzan.

Komodoflorensal shrugged his shoulders. "She will bear me a son who will some day be king of Trohanadalmakus," he replied, "and that is all that can be asked."

While the preparations for the expedition against Veltopismakus were being carried on Tarzan was left much to his own devices. The activities of these diminutive people were a never ending source of interest to him. He watched the endless lines of slaves struggling with their heavy burdens toward the new dome that was rising with almost miraculous speed, or he strolled to the farmlands just beyond the city where other slaves tilled the rich soil, which they scratched with tiny plows drawn by teams of diadets, the diminutive antelope that was their only beast of burden. Always were the slaves accompanied by armed warriors if they were slaves of the first or second generation, lest they should attempt escape or revolution, as well as a protection against beasts of prey and human enemies, since the slaves were not permitted to bear arms and, consequently, could not protect themselves. These slaves of the first and second generations were always easily recognizable by the vivid green tunic, reaching almost to the knees, which was the single garment of their caste, and which carried upon both its front and back an emblem or character in black that denoted the city of the slave's birth and the individual to whom he now belonged. The slaves employed upon public works all belonged to the king, Adendrohahkis, but in the fields many families were represented by their chattels.

Moving about the city upon their various duties were thousands of white-tunicked slaves. They exercised the mounts of their masters, they oversaw much of the more menial and laborious work of the lower caste slaves, they plied their trades and sold their wares in perfect freedom; but like the other slaves they wore but a single garment, together with rough sandals which were common to both classes. On their breasts and backs in red were the emblems of their masters. The second generation slaves of the green tunics had a similar emblem, these having been born in the city and being consequently considered a part of it. There were other, though minor, distinguishing marks upon the tunics of the higher caste slaves; small insignia upon one shoulder or upon both, or upon a sleeve, denoting the occupation of the wearer. Groom, body servant, major-domo, cook, hairdresser, worker in gold and silver, potter—one could tell at a glance the vocation of each—and each belonged, body and soul, to his master, who was compelled to feed and dome these dependents, the fruits of whose labors belonged exclusively to him.

The wealth of one warrior family might lie in the beauty and perfection of the gold and silver ornaments it sold to its wealthy fellows and in such an instance all its skilled slaves, other than those required for personal and household duties, would be employed in the designing and fabrication of these articles. Another family might devote its attention to agriculture, another to the raising of diadets; but all the work was done by the slaves, with the single exception of the breaking of the diadets that were bred for riding, an occupation that was not considered beneath the dignity of the warrior class, but rather, on the contrary, looked upon as a fitting occupation for nobles. Even the king's son broke his own diadets.

As an interested spectator Tarzan whiled the lazy days away. To his repeated queries as to the possibility of a way out of this bizarre, thorn-infested world, his hosts replied that it was naught to penetrate the forest of thorn trees, but that as it continued indefinitely to the uttermost extremities of matter it was quite useless to attempt to penetrate it at all, their conception of the world being confined to what they actually had seen—a land of hills, valleys and forest, surrounded by thorn trees. To creatures of their size the thorn forest was far from impenetrable, but Tarzan was not their size. Still he never ceased to plan on a means of escape, though he was in no great haste to attempt it, since he found the Minunians interesting and it suited his present primitive mood to loll in lazy ease in the city of Trohanadalmakus.

But of a sudden a change came, early of a morning, just as the first, faint promise of dawn was tinging the eastern sky.

CHAPTER 7

The Alalus youth, son of The First Woman, ranged the forest in search of the ape-man, the only creature that ever had stirred within his savage, primitive breast any emotion even slightly akin to affection; but he did not find him. Instead he fell in with two older males of his own species, and these three hunted together, as was occasionally the custom of these inoffensive creatures. His new acquaintances showed little interest in his strange armament—they were quite content with a stick and a stone knife. To the former an occasional rodent fell and the latter discovered many a luscious grub and insect beneath the mold that floored the forest or hidden under the bark of a tree. For the most part, however, they fed upon fruits, nuts and tubers. Not so the son of The First Woman, however. He brought in many birds and an occasional antelope, for he was becoming daily more proficient with the bow and the spear, and as he often brought in more than he could eat and left the remainder to his two fellows, they were permanently attached to him, or at least until such time as some fearsome woman should appear upon the scene to shatter their idyllic existence and drag one of them away to her corral.

They wondered a little at him in their slow and stupid minds, for he seemed to differ in some vague, intangible way from them and all others of their sex that they had known. He held his chin higher for one thing and his gaze was far less shifty and apologetic. He strode with a firmer step and with less caution; but perhaps they smiled inwardly as they cogitated muddily upon that inevitable moment that would discover one of their coarse, brutal, hairy shes felling him with her bludgeon and dragging him off toward the caves by the hair of his head.

And then one day the thing happened, or at least a part of it happened—they met a huge she suddenly in an open place in the forest. The two who accompanied the son of The First Woman turned in flight, but when they had reached the vantage ground of close-growing timber they paused and looked back to see if the woman was pursuing them and what had become of their companion. To their relief they saw that the woman was not following them and to their consternation that their fellow had not fled, but was facing her defiantly, and motioning her to go away, or be killed. Such crass stupidity! He must have been whelped without brains. It never occurred to them to attribute his act to courage. Courage was for the shes; the male spent his life in fleeing danger and the female of his species.

But they were grateful to him, for his rash act would save them since the she would take but one of them and that one would be he who thus foolishly remained behind to defy her.

The woman, unaccustomed to having her rights challenged by mere man, was filled with surprise and righteous anger. Her surprise brought her to a sudden halt twenty paces from the man and her anger caused her to reach for one of the stone missiles hanging at her girdle. That was her undoing. The son of The First Woman, standing before her with an arrow already fitted to his bow, waited not to discover her further intentions, but even as the woman's fingers loosed the feathered messenger of defeat from the leather thong of her girdle, he drew the shaft to his cheek and released it.

His two companions, watching from the seclusion of the wood, saw the woman stiffen, her face contorted in a spasm of pain; they saw her clutch frantically at a feathered shaft protruding from her chest, sink to her knees and then sprawl to earth, where she lay kicking with her feet and clutching with her fingers for a brief moment before she relapsed into eternal quiet; then they emerged from their concealment, and as the son of The First Woman approached his victim and wrenched the arrow from her heart they joined him, half-stunned as they were by surprise, and gazed first at the corpse of the she with expressions of incredulity and then at him with what was closely akin to awe and reverence.

They examined his bow and arrows and again and again they returned to the wound in the woman's chest. It was all quite too amazing. And the son of The First Woman? He held his head high and his chest out and strutted proudly. Never before had he or any other man been cast in the role of hero and he enjoyed it. But he would impress them further. Seizing the corpse of the woman he dragged it to a nearby tree where he propped it in a sitting posture against the bole; then he walked away some twenty feet and, signing his fellows to observe him closely, he raised his heavy spear and hurled it at his realistic target, through which it passed to embed itself in the tree behind.

The others were greatly excited. One of them wanted to attempt this wondrous feat and when he had thrown, and missed, his fellow insisted upon having a turn. Later they craved practice with the bow and arrow. For hours the three remained before their grisly target, nor did they desist until hunger prompted them to move on and the son of The First Woman had promised to show them how to fashion weapons similar to his own—a momentous occurrence in the history of the Alali, though these three sensed it as little as did the hundreds of Alalus women repairing to their caves that night in blissful ignorance of the blow that had been struck at their supremacy by the militant suffragists of Minuni.

*

And as suddenly, with more immediate results, the even tenor of Tarzan's existence in the city of Trohanadalmakus was altered and a series of events initiated that were to lead to the maddest and most unbelievable denouement.

The ape-man lay upon a bed of grasses beneath a great tree that grew beside the city of King Adendrohahkis. Dawn was flushing the sky above the forest to the east of Trohanadalmakus, when Tarzan, his ear close to the ground, was suddenly awakened by a strange reverberation that seemed to come faintly from the bowels of the earth. It was such a dim and distant sound that it would scarce have been appreciable to you or to me had we placed an ear flat against the ground after having been told that the noise existed; but to Tarzan it was an interruption of the ordinary noises of the night and, therefore, however slight, of sufficient import to impinge upon his consciousness even in sleep.

Awakened, he still lay listening intently. He knew that the sound did not come from the bowels of the earth, but from the surface and he guessed that it originated at no great distance, and also, he knew, that it was coming closer rapidly. For just a moment it puzzled him and then a great light dawned upon him and he sprang to his feet. The dome of the king, Adendrohahkis, lay a hundred yards away and toward it he bent his steps. Just before the south entrance he was challenged by a tiny sentinel.

"Take word to your king," the ape-man directed him, "that Tarzan hears many diadets galloping toward Trohanadalmakus and that unless he is much mistaken each carries a hostile warrior upon its back."

The sentinel turned and hallooed down the corridor leading from the entrance, and a moment later an officer and several other warriors appeared. At sight of Tarzan they halted.

"What is wrong?" demanded the officer.

"The King's Guest says that he heard many diadets approaching," replied the sentinel.

"From what direction?" demanded the officer, addressing Tarzan.

"From that direction the sounds appeared to come," replied the ape-man, pointing toward the west.

"The Veltopismakusians!" exclaimed the officer, and then, turning to those who had accompanied him from the interior of the king's dome: "Quick! arouse Trohanadalmakus—I will warn the king's dome and the king," and he wheeled and ran quickly within, while the others sped away to awaken the city.

In an incredibly short space of time Tarzan saw thousands of warriors streaming from each of the ten domes. From the north and the south doors of each dome rode mounted men, and from the east and west marched the foot soldiers. There was no confusion; everything moved with military precision and evidently in accordance with a plan of defense in which each unit had been thoroughly drilled.

Small detachments of cavalry galloped quickly to the four points of the compass—these were scouts each detail of which spread fan wise just beyond the limits of the domes until the city was encircled by a thin line of mounted men that would halt when it had reached a predetermined distance from the city, and fall back with information before an advancing enemy. Following these, stronger detachments of mounted men moved out to north and south and east and west to take positions just inside the line of scouts. These detachments were strong enough to engage the enemy and impede his progress as they fell back upon the main body of the cavalry which might by this plan be summoned in time to the point at which the enemy was making his boldest effort to reach the city.

And then the main body of the cavalry moved out, and in this instance toward the west, from which point they were already assured the foe was approaching; while the infantry, which had not paused since it emerged from the domes, marched likewise toward the four points of the compass in four compact bodies of which by far the largest moved toward the west. The advance foot troops took their stations but a short distance outside the city, while within the area of the domes the last troops to emerge from them, both cavalry and infantry, remained evidently as a reserve force, and it was with these troops that Adendrohahkis took his post that he might be centrally located for the purpose of directing the defense of his city to better advantage.

Komodoflorensal, the prince, had gone out in command of the main body of cavalry that was to make the first determined stand against the oncoming foe. This body consisted of seven thousand five hundred men and its position lay two miles outside the city, half a mile behind a cavalry patrol of five hundred men, of which there were four, one at each point of the compass, and totaling two thousand men. The balance of the ten thousand advance troops consisted of the five hundred mounted scouts or vedettes who, in turn, were half a mile in advance of the picket patrols, at two hundred foot intervals, entirely surrounding the city at a distance of three miles. Inside the city fifteen thousand mounted men were held in reserve.

In the increasing light of dawn Tarzan watched these methodical preparations for defense with growing admiration for the tiny Minunians. There was no shouting and no singing, but on the face of every warrior who passed close enough for the ape-man to discern his features was an expression of exalted rapture. No need here for war cries or battle hymns to bolster the questionable courage of the weak—there were no weak.

The pounding of the hoofs of the advancing Veltopismakusian horde had ceased. It was evident that their scouts had discovered that the intended surprise had failed. Were they altering the plan or point of attack, or had they merely halted the main body temporarily to await the result of a reconnaissance? Tarzan asked a nearby officer if, perchance, the enemy had abandoned his intention of attacking at all. The man smiled and shook his head.

"Minunians never abandon an attack," he said.

As Tarzan's eyes wandered over the city's ten domes, illuminated now by the rays of the rising sun, he saw in each of the numerous window embrasures, that pierced the domes at regular intervals at each of their thirty odd floors, a warrior stationed at whose side lay a great bundle of short javelins, while just to his rear was piled a quantity of small, round stones. The ape-man smiled.

"They overlook no possible contingency," he thought. "But the quarry slaves! what of them? Would they not turn against their masters at the first opportunity for escape that an impending battle such as this would be almost certain to present to them?" He turned again to the officer and put the question to him.

The latter turned and pointed toward the entrance to the nearest quarry, where Tarzan saw hundreds of white-tunicked slaves piling rocks upon it while a detachment of infantry leaned idly upon their spears as their officers directed the labor of the slaves.

"There is another detachment of warriors bottled up inside the quarry entrance," explained the officer to Tarzan. "If the enemy gains the city and this outer guard is driven into the domes or killed or captured, the inner guard can hold off an entire army, as only one man can attack them at a time. Our slaves are safe, therefore, unless the city falls and that has not happened to any Minunian city within the memory of man. The best that the Veltopismakusians can hope for now is to pick up a few prisoners, but they will doubtless leave behind as many as they take. Had their surprise been successful they might have forced their way into one of the domes and made away with many women and much loot. Now, though, our forces are too well disposed to make it possible for any but a greatly superior force to seriously threaten the city itself. I even doubt if our infantry will be engaged at all."

"How is the infantry disposed?" asked Tarzan.

"Five thousand men are stationed within the windows of the domes," replied the officer; "five thousand more comprise the reserve which you see about you, and from which detachments have been detailed to guard the quarries. A mile from the city are four other bodies of infantry; those to the east, north and south having a strength of one thousand men each, while the one to the west, facing the probable point of attack, consists of seven thousand warriors."

"Then you think the fighting will not reach the city?" asked Tarzan.

"No. The lucky men today are in the advance cavalry—they will get whatever fighting there is. I doubt if an infantryman draws a sword or casts a spear; but that is usually the case—it is the cavalry that fights, always."

"I take it that you feel unfortunate in not being attached to a cavalry unit. Could you not be transferred?"

"Oh, we must all take our turns of duty in each branch," explained the officer. "We are all mounted except for defense of the city and for that purpose we are assigned to the foot troops for four moons, followed by five moons in the cavalry"—the word he used was diadetax—"five thousand men being transferred from one to the other the night of each new moon."

Tarzan turned and looked out across the plain toward the west. He could see the nearer troops standing at ease, awaiting the enemy. Even the main body of cavalry, two miles away, he could discern, because there were so many of them; but the distant pickets and vedettes were invisible. As he stood leaning upon his spear watching this scene, a scene such as no other man of his race ever had witnessed, and realized the seriousness of these little men in the business of war that confronted them, he could not but think of the people of his own world lining up their soldiers for purposes usually far less momentous to them than the call to arms that had brought the tough little warriors of Adendrohahkis swarming from their pallets in the defense of home and city.

No chicanery of politics here, no thinly veiled ambition of some potential tyrant, no mad conception of harebrained dreamers seized by the avaricious criminal for self-aggrandizement and riches; none of these, but patriotism of purest strain energized by the powerful urge of self-preservation. The perfect fighters, the perfect warriors, the perfect heroes these. No need for blaring trumpets; of no use to them the artificial aids to courage conceived by captains of the outer world who send unwilling men to battle for they know not what, deceived by lying propaganda, enraged by false tales of the barbarity of the foe, whose anger has been aroused against them by similar means.

During the lull that followed the departure from the city of the last of the advance troops Tarzan approached Adendrohahkis where he sat astride his diadet surrounded by a number of his high officers. The king was resplendent in golden jerkin, a leathern garment upon which small discs of gold were sewn, overlapping one another. About his waist was a wide belt of heavy leather, held in place by three buckles of gold, and of such dimensions as to have almost the appearance of a corset. This belt supported his rapier and knife, the scabbards of which were heavily inlaid with gold and baser metals in intricate and beautiful designs. Leather cuisses protected his upper legs in front covering the thighs to the knees, while his forearms were encased in metal armlets from wrists almost to elbows. Upon his feet were strapped tough sandals, with a circular golden plate protecting each ankle-bone. A well-shaped leather casque fitted his head closely.

As Tarzan stopped before him the king recognized the ape-man with a pleasant greeting. "The captain of the guard reports that it is to you we owe the first warning of the coming of the Veltopismakusians. Once again have you placed the people of Trohanadalmakus under deep obligations. However are we to repay our debt?"

Tarzan gestured deprecatively. "You owe me nothing, King of Trohanadalmakus," he replied. "Give me your friendship and tell me that I may go forward and join your noble son, the prince: then all the obligations shall be upon my head."

"Until the worms of death devour me I shall be your friend always, Tarzan," returned the king graciously. "Go where you will and that you choose to go where there should be fighting surprises me not."

It was the first time that any Minunian had addressed him by his name. Always had he been called Saviour of the Prince, Guest of the King, Giant of the Forest and by other similar impersonal appellations. Among the Minunians a man's name is considered a sacred possession, the use of which is permitted only his chosen friends and the members of his family, and to be called Tarzan by Adendrohahkis was equivalent to an invitation, or a command, to the closest personal friendship with the king.

The ape-man acknowledged the courtesy with a bow. "The friendship of Adendrohahkis is a sacred honor, ennobling those who wear it. I shall guard it always with my life, as my most treasured possession," he said in a low voice; nor was the Lord of the Jungle moved by any maudlin sentimentality as he addressed the king. For these little people he had long since acknowledged to himself a keen admiration and for the personal character of Adendrohahkis he had come to have the most profound respect. Never since he had learned their language had he ceased his inquiries concerning the manners and the customs of these people, and he had found the personality of Adendrohahkis so inextricably interwoven with the lives of his subjects that in receiving the answers to his questions he could not but absorb unquestionable evidence of the glories of the king's character.

Adendrohahkis seemed pleased with his words, which he acknowledged graciously, and then the ape-man withdrew and started toward the front. On the way he tore a leafy branch from a tree that grew beside his path for the thought had occurred to him that such a weapon might be useful against Minunians and he knew not what the day might hold.

He had just passed the advanced infantry when a courier sped by him on a mad race toward the city. Tarzan strained his eyes ahead, but he could see no sign of battle and when he reached the main cavalry advance there was still no indication of an enemy as far ahead as he could see.

Prince Komodoflorensal greeted him warmly and looked a little wonderingly, perhaps, at the leafy branch he carried across one shoulder.

"What news?" asked Tarzan.

"I have just sent a messenger to the king," replied the prince, "reporting that our scouts have come in touch with those of the enemy, who are, as we thought, the Veltopismakusians. A strong patrol from the outpost in our front pushed through the enemy's scout line and one courageous warrior even managed to penetrate as far as the summit of the Hill of Gartolas, from which he saw the entire main body of the enemy forming for attack. He says there are between twenty and thirty thousand of them."

As Komodoflorensal ceased speaking, a wave of sound came rolling toward them from the west.

"They are coming!" announced the prince.

CHAPTER 8

Ska, perched upon the horn of dead Gorgo, became suddenly aware of a movement in a nearby thicket. He turned his head in the direction of the sound and saw Sabor the lioness emerge from the foliage and walk slowly toward him. Ska was not terrified. He would leave, but he would leave with dignity. He crouched to spring upward, and extended his great wings to aid him in taking off. But Ska, the vulture, never rose. As he essayed to do so, something pulled suddenly upon his neck and held him down. He scrambled to his feet and, violently this time, strove to fly away. Again he was dragged back. Now Ska was terrified. The hateful thing that had been dangling about his neck for so long was holding him to earth—the swinging loop of the golden chain had caught around the horn of Gorgo, the buffalo. Ska was trapped.

He struggled, beating his wings. Sabor stopped to regard him and his wild antics. Ska was flopping around in a most surprising manner. Sabor had never seen Ska behave thus before, and lions are sensitive, temperamental animals; so Sabor was not surprised only, she was inclined to be frightened. For another moment she watched the unaccountable antics of Ska and then she turned tail and slunk back into the undergrowth, turning an occasional growling countenance back upon the vulture, as much as to say; "Pursue me at your peril!" But Ska had no thought of pursuing Sabor. Never again would Ska, the vulture, pursue aught.

*

"They are coming!" announced Komodoflorensal, prince of Trohanadalmakus.

As Tarzan looked out across the rolling country in the direction of the enemy, he presently saw, from his greater height, the advance of the Veltopismakusians.

"Our scouts are falling back," he announced to Komodoflorensal.

"You can see the enemy?" demanded the prince.

"Yes."

"Keep me advised as to their movements."

"They are advancing in several long lines, deployed over a considerable front," reported the ape-man. "The scouts are falling back upon the outpost which seems to be standing its ground to receive them. It will be overwhelmed—if not by the first line then by those that succeed it."

Komodoflorensal gave a short command. A thousand mounted men leaped forward, urging their diadets into bounding leaps that cleared five, six and even seven feet at a time. Straight for the outpost ahead of them they raced, deploying as they went.

Another thousand moved quickly toward the right and a third toward the left of the advance cavalry's position following Tarzan's announcement that the enemy had divided into two bodies just before it engaged the outpost, and that one of these was moving as though with the intention of turning the right flank of the main cavalry of Trohanadalmakus, while the other circled in the direction of the left flank.

"They are striking boldly and quickly for prisoners," said the prince to Tarzan.

"Their second and third lines are ploying upon the center and moving straight for us," said Tarzan. "They have reached the outpost, which is racing forward with them, giving battle vigorously with rapiers."

Komodoflorensal was dispatching messengers toward the rear. "It is thus that we fight," he said, evidently in explanation of the action of the outpost "It is time that you returned to the rear, for in another few moments you will be surrounded by the enemy if you remain. When they reach us we, too, will turn and fight them hand-to-hand back toward the city. If it still is their intention to enter the city the battle will resemble more a race than aught else, for the speed will be too great for effective fighting; but if they have abandoned that idea and intend contenting themselves with prisoners there will be plenty of fighting before we reach the infantry, past which I doubt if they will advance.

"With their greatly superior numbers they will take some prisoners, and we shall take some—but, quick! you must get back to the city, if already it is not too late."

"I think I shall remain here," replied the ape-man.

"But they will take you prisoner, or kill you."

Tarzan of the Apes smiled and shook his leafy branch. "I do not fear them," he said, simply.

"That is because you do not know them," replied the prince. "Your great size makes you overconfident, but remember that you are only four times the size of a Minunian and there may be thirty thousand seeking to overthrow you."

The Veltopismakusians were driving swiftly forward. The prince could give no more time to what he saw was but a futile attempt to persuade Tarzan to retreat, and while he admired the strange giant's courage he likewise deplored his ignorance. Komodoflorensal had grown fond of their strange guest and he would have saved him had it been possible, but now he must turn to the command of his troops, since the enemy was almost upon them.

Tarzan watched the coming of the little men on their agile, wiry mounts. Line after line poured across the rolling country toward him, carrying to his mind a suggestion of their similarity to the incoming rollers of the ocean's surf, each drop of which was soft and harmless, but in their countless numbers combined into a relentless and terrifying force of destruction, and the ape-man glanced at his leafy bough and smiled, albeit a trifle ruefully.

But now his whole attention was riveted by the fighting in the first two lines of the advancing horde. Racing neck and neck with the Veltopismakusian warriors were the men of Adendrohahkis' outpost and the thousands who had reinforced them. Each had selected an enemy rider whom he sought to strike from his saddle, and at top speed each duel was carried on with keen rapiers, though here and there was a man wielding his spear, and sometimes to good effect. A few riderless diadets leaped forward with the vanguard, while others, seeking to break back or to the flanks, fouled the racing ranks, often throwing beasts and riders to the ground; but more frequently the warriors leaped their mounts entirely over these terrified beasts. The riding of the Minunians was superb, and their apparently effortless control of their swift and nervous steeds bordered upon the miraculous. Now a warrior, lifting his mount high into the air, cleared an adversary and as he rose above him cut down viciously with his rapier at his foeman's head, striking him from the saddle; but there was scarce time to catch more than a fleeting, kaleidoscopic impression of the swift-moving spectacle before the great horde swarmed down upon him.

With his leafy bough, Tarzan had thought to sweep the little men from his path, but now friend and foe were so intermingled that he dared not attempt it for fear of unseating and injuring some of the warriors of his hosts. He raised the bough above their heads and waited until the first lines should have passed him and then, with only the enemies of Adendrohahkis about him, he would brush them aside and break the center of their charge.

He saw the surprised expressions upon the faces of the men of Veltopismakus as they passed near him—surprise, but no fear—and he heard their shouts as one more fortunate than his fellows was able to rein closer to him and cut viciously at his legs as he sped past. Then indeed it became naught other than a matter of self-preservation to attempt to fend these off with his bough, nor was this impossible as the first lines moved past in loose ranks; but presently the solid mass of the Veltopismakusian cavalry was upon him. There was no veering aside to avoid him. In unbroken ranks, file after file, they bore down upon him. He threw his useless bough before him to impede their progress and grappled them with his fingers, tearing the riders from their mounts and hurling them back upon their onrushing fellows; but still they came.

They jumped their diadets over every obstruction. One rider, leaping straight for him, struck him head on in the pit of the stomach, half winding him and sending him back a step. Another and another struck his legs and sides. Again and again the needlelike points of their rapiers pierced his brown hide until from hips to feet he was red with his own blood, and always there were more thousands bearing down upon him. His weapons, useless against them, he made no attempt to use and though he wrought havoc among them with his bare hands there were always a hundred to take the place of each that he disposed of.

He smiled grimly as he realized that in these little people, scarce one-fourth his size, he, the incomparable Tarzan, the Lord of the Jungle, had met his Wellington. He realized that he was entirely surrounded by the Veltopismakusians now, the warriors of Trohanadalmakus having engaged the advancing enemy were racing onward with them toward the seven thousand dismounted men who were to receive the brunt of that terrific charge. Tarzan wished that he might have witnessed this phase of the battle, but he had fighting enough and to spare to engage all his attention where he was.

Again he was struck in the stomach by a charging rider and again the blow staggered him. Before he could recover himself another struck him in the same place and this time he went down, and instantly he was covered, buried by warriors and diadets, swarming over him, like ants, in countless numbers. He tried to rise and that was the last he remembered before he sank into unconsciousness.

*

Uhha, daughter of Khamis the witch doctor of the tribe of Obebe the cannibal, lay huddled upon a little pile of grasses in a rude thorn shelter in an open jungle. It was night but she was not asleep. Through narrowed lids she watched a giant white man who squatted just outside the shelter before a tiny fire. The girl's lids were narrowed in hate as her smoldering eyes rested upon the man. There was no fear of the supernatural in her expression—just hate, undying hate.

Long since had Uhha ceased to think of Esteban Miranda as The River Devil. His obvious fear of the greater beasts of the jungle and of the black men-beasts had at first puzzled and later assured her that her companion was an impostor; River Devils do not fear anything. She was even commencing to doubt that the fellow was Tarzan, of whom she had heard so many fabulous stories during her childhood that she had come to look upon him as almost a devil himself—her people had no gods, only devils—which answer just as good a purpose among the ignorant and superstitious as do gods among the educated and superstitious.

And when Esteban Miranda quite conclusively proved by his actions that he feared lions and that he was lost in the jungle these things did not square at all with her preconceived estimate of the powers and attributes of the famous Tarzan.

With the loss of her respect for him she lost, also, nearly all her fear. He was stronger than she and brutal. He could and would hurt her if she angered him, but he could not harm her in any other way than physically and not at all if she could keep out of his clutches. Many times had she rehearsed plans for escape, but always she had hesitated because of the terrible fear she had of being alone in the jungle. Recently, however, she had been coming to realize more and more clearly that the white man was little or no protection to her. In fact, she might be better off without him, for at the first hint of danger it had been Miranda's habit to bolt for the nearest tree, and where trees were not numerous this habit of his had always placed Uhha under a handicap in the race for self-preservation, since Esteban, being stronger, could push her aside if she impeded his progress towards safety.

Yes, she would be as well off alone in the jungle as in the company of this man whom she thoroughly despised and hated, but before she left him she must, her savage little brain assured her, revenge herself upon him for having tricked her into aiding him in his escape from the village of Obebe the chief as well as for having forced her to accompany him.

Uhha was sure that she could find her way to the village, albeit they had traveled long and far, and she was sure too that she could find the means for subsistence along the way and elude the fiercer beasts of prey that might beset the way. Only man she feared; but in this she was not unlike all other created things. Man alone of all the creations of God is universally hunted and feared and not only by the lower orders but by his own kind, for of them all man alone joys in the death of others—the great coward who, of all creation, fears death the most.

And so the little Negro girl lay watching the Spaniard and her eyes glittered, for in his occupation she saw a means to her revenge. Squatting before his fire, leaning far forward, Esteban Miranda gloated over the contents of a small buckskin bag which he had partially emptied into the palm of one of his hands. Little Uhha knew how highly the white man prized these glittering stones, though she was entirely ignorant of their intrinsic worth. She did not even know them for diamonds. All she knew was that the white man loved them, that he valued them more highly than his other possessions and that he had repeatedly told her that he would die sooner than he would part with them.

For a long time Miranda played with the diamonds and for a long time Uhha watched him; but at last he returned them to their bag, which he fastened securely inside his loincloth. Then he crawled beneath the thorn shelter, dragged a pile of thorns into the entrance to close it against the inroads of prowling beasts, and lay down upon the grasses beside Uhha.

EDGAR RICE BURROUGHS

How was this little girl going to accomplish the theft of the diamonds from the huge, Amazonian Spaniard? She could not filch them by stealth, for the bag that contained them was so fastened inside his loincloth that it would be impossible to remove it without awakening him; and certainly this frail child could never wrest the jewels from Esteban by physical prowess. No, the whole scheme must die where it was born—inside Uhha's thick little skull.

Outside the shelter the fire flickered, lighting the jungle grasses about it and casting weird, fantastic shadows that leaped and danced in the jungle night. Something moved stealthily among the lush vegetation a score of paces from the tiny camp. It was something large, for the taller grasses spread to its advance. They parted and a lion's head appeared. The yellow-green eyes gazed uneasily at the fire. From beyond came the odor of man and Numa was hungry; too, upon occasion he had eaten of man and found him good—also of all his prey the slowest and the least able to protect himself; but Numa did not like the looks of things here and so he turned and disappeared from whence he had come. He was not afraid of the fire. Had he been he would have been afraid of the sun by day, for the sun he could not even look at without discomfort, and to Numa the fire and the sun might have been one, for he had no way of knowing which was sixty feet away and which ninety-three million miles. It was the dancing shadows that caused his nervous apprehension. Huge, grotesque creatures of which he had had no experience seemed to be leaping all about him, threatening him from every side.

But Uhha paid no attention to the dancing shadows and she had not seen Numa the lion. She lay very still now, listening. The fire flared less high as the slow minutes dragged their leaden feet along. It was not so very long that she lay thus, but it seemed long to Uhha, for she had her plan all matured and ready for execution. A civilized girl of twelve might have conceived it, but it is doubtful that she would have carried it to its conclusion. Uhha, however, was not civilized and being what she was she was not hampered by any qualms of conscience.

Presently the Spaniard's breathing indicated that he was asleep. Uhha waited a little longer to make assurance doubly sure, then she reached beneath the grasses just beside her and when she withdrew her hand again she brought forth a short, stout cudgel. Slowly and cautiously she rose until she kneeled beside the recumbent form of the sleeping Spaniard. Then she raised her weapon above her head and brought it down once, heavily, upon Esteban's skull. She did not continue to beat him—the one blow was enough. She hoped that she had not killed him, for he must live if her scheme of revenge was to be realized; he must live and know that Uhha had stolen the bag of pebbles that he so worshiped. Uhha appropriated the knife that swung at Miranda's hip and with it she cut away his loincloth and took possession of the buckskin bag and its contents. Then she removed the thorns from the entrance to the shelter, slipped out into the night and vanished into the jungle. During all her wanderings with the Spaniard she had not once lost her sense of the direction which pointed toward her home, and now, free, she set her face resolutely toward the southwest and the village of Obebe the cannibal. An elephant trail formed a jungle highway along which she moved at a swinging walk, her way lighted by the rays of a full moon that filtered through the foliage of a sparse forest. She feared the jungle night and the nocturnal beasts of prey, but she knew that she must take this chance that she might put as great a distance as possible between herself and the white man before he regained consciousness and started in pursuit.

A hundred yards ahead of her, in the dense thicket that bordered the trail, Numa the lion sniffed, and listened with up-pricked ears bent in her direction. No dancing shadows here to suggest menacing forms to Numa's high-strung nervous system—only the scent of man coming closer and closer—a young she-man, most tender of its kind. Numa licked his slavering jowls and waited.

The girl came rapidly along the trail. Now she was abreast the lion, but the king of beasts did not spring. There is something in the scent of the man-thing and the sight of the man-thing that awakens strange terrors in the breast of Numa. When he stalks Horta the boar or Bara the deer there is nothing in the near presence of either that arouses a similar sensation in the savage carnivore; then he knows no hesitancy when the instant comes to spring upon his prey. It is only the man-thing, helpless and leaden-footed, that causes him to pause in indecision at the crucial moment.

Uhha passed, ignorant of the fact that a great lion, hunting and hungry, stood within two paces of her. When she had passed Numa slunk into the trail behind her, and there he followed, stalking his tender quarry until the moment should come when the mists of his indecision should be dispelled. And so they went through the jungle night—the great lion, creeping on stealthy, noiseless pads, and just ahead of him the little black girl, unconscious of the grim death stalking her through the dappled moonlight.

CHAPTER 9

When Tarzan of the Apes regained consciousness he found himself lying upon an earthen floor in a large chamber. As he first opened his eyes, before complete consciousness returned, he noticed that the room was well, but not brilliantly, lighted, and that there were others there besides himself. Later, as he commenced to collect and dominate his faculties of thought he saw that the room was lighted by two immense candles that appeared to be fully three feet in diameter and, though evidently partially melted away, yet at least five feet tall. Each supported a wick fully as large as a man's wrist and though the manner of their burning was similar to the candles with which he was familiar, yet they gave off no smoke, nor were the beams and boards of the ceiling directly above them smoke-blackened.

The lights, being the most noticeable things in the room, had been the first to attract the ape-man's attention, but now his eyes wandered to the other occupants of the room. There were fifty or a hundred men of about his own height; but they were garbed and armed as had been the little men of Trohanadalmakus and Veltopismakus. Tarzan knit his brows and looked long and steadily at them. Who were they? Where was he?

As consciousness spread slowly throughout his body he realized that he was in pain and that his arms felt heavy and numb. He tried to move them, only to discover that he could not—they were securely bound behind his back. He moved his feet—they were not secured. At last, after considerable effort, for he found that he was very weak, he raised himself to a sitting posture and looked about him. The room was filled with warriors who looked precisely like the little Veltopismakusians, but they were as large as normal men, and the room itself was immense. There were a number of benches and tables standing about the floor and most of the men either were seated upon the benches or lay stretched upon the hard earth. A few men moved about among them and seemed to be working over them. Then it was that Tarzan saw that nearly all within the chamber were suffering from wounds, many of them severe ones. The men who moved about among them were evidently attending to the wounded, and those, who might have been the nurses, were garbed in white tunics like the high caste slaves of Trohanadalmakus. In addition to the wounded and the nurses there were a half dozen armed warriors who were uninjured. One of these was the first to espy Tarzan after he had raised himself to a sitting posture.

"Ho!" shouted he. "The giant has come to his senses," and crossing the room he approached the ape-man. Standing before him, his feet widespread, he eyed Tarzan with a broad grin upon his face. "Your great bulk availed you little," he taunted, "and now we are as large as you. We, too, are giants, eh?" and he turned to his fellows with a laugh in which they joined him.

Seeing that he was a prisoner, surrounded by enemies, the ape-man fell back upon that lifelong characteristic of the wild beast—sullen silence. He made no reply, but only sat there regarding them with the savage, level gaze of the brute at bay.

"He is dumb like the great beast-women of the caves," said the warrior to his fellows.

"Perhaps he is one of them," suggested another.

"Yes," seconded a third, "perhaps he is one of the Zertalacolols."

"But their men are all cowards," urged the first speaker; "and this one fought like a warrior born."

"Yes, with his bare hands he fought till he went down."

"You should have seen how he threw diadets and warriors as one might pick up tiny pebbles and hurl them afar."

"He would not give a step, or run; and always he smiled."

"He does not look like the men of the Zertalacolols; ask him if he is."

He who had first addressed him put the question to Tarzan, but the ape-man only continued to glare at them.

"He does not understand me," said the warrior. "I do not think that he is a Zertalacolol, though. What he is, however, I do not know."

He approached and examined Tarzan's wounds. "These will soon be healed. In seven days, or less, he will be fit for the quarries."

They sprinkled a brown powder upon his wounds and brought him food and water and the milk of antelopes, and when they found that his arms were swelling badly and becoming discolored they brought an iron chain and, fastening one end about his waist with a clumsy padlock, secured him to a ring in the stone wall of the chamber, and cut the bonds from his wrists.

As they believed that he did not understand their language they spoke freely before him, but as their tongue was almost identical with that employed by the Trohanadalmakusians Tarzan understood everything that they said, and thus he learned that the battle before the city of Adendrohahkis had not gone as well for the Veltopismakusians as Elkomoelhago, their king, had desired. They had lost many in killed and prisoners and in return had not killed near so many of the enemy and had taken comparatively few prisoners, though Elkomoelhago, he learned, considered him worth the entire cost of the brief war.

How they had changed themselves into men of his own stature Tarzan could not comprehend, nor did any of the remarks he overheard shed any light upon this mystery of mysteries. But the climax of improbability was attained a few days later when he saw pass through the corridor, upon which the room of his incarceration was located, a file of warriors as large as he, each of whom was mounted upon a huge antelope fully as tall at the shoulder as the great eland, though obviously, from its contour and markings, a Royal Antelope, which is the smallest known. Tarzan ran his brown fingers through his thatch of black hair and gave up attempting to solve the enigmas that surrounded him.

His wounds healed quickly, as did those of the Veltopismakusians who were convalescing about him, and upon the seventh day a half-dozen warriors came for him and the chain was removed from about his waist that he might accompany them. His captors had long since ceased to address him, believing that he was ignorant of their language, which meant to them that he was as speechless as an Alalus, since they could conceive of no language other than their own; but from their conversation, as they led him from the chamber and along a circular corridor, he discovered that he was being taken before their king, Elkomoelhago, who had expressed a desire to see this remarkable captive after he had recovered from his wounds.

The long corridor, through which they were proceeding, was lighted partially by small candles set in niches and by the light from illuminated chambers the doors of which opened upon it. Slaves and warriors moved in two continuous and opposing lines through this corridor and every one that crossed it. There were high caste slaves in white tunics with the red emblems of their owners and their own occupation insignia upon them; there were green-tunicked slaves of the second generation with their master's insignia upon breast and back in black, and green-tunicked slaves of the first generation with a black emblem upon their breasts denoting the city of their nativity and their master's emblem upon their backs; there were warriors of every rank and position; there were the plain leather trappings of the young and poor, and the jewel-studded harness of the rich; and passing all these in both directions and often at high speed were other warriors mounted upon the mighty antelopes that were still the greatest wonder that had confronted Tarzan since his incarceration in the city of Veltopismakus.

At intervals along the corridor Tarzan saw ladders extending to a floor above, but as he never saw one descending to a lower level he assumed that they were then upon the lowest floor of the structure.

From the construction that he noted he was convinced that the building was similar to the dome he had seen in the course of construction in the city of Adendrohahkis; but when he permitted his mind to dwell upon the tremendous proportions of such a dome capable of housing men of his own size he was staggered. Had Adendrohahkis' dome been duplicated in these greater dimensions, though in the same proportions, it would have been eight hundred eighty feet in diameter and four hundred forty feet high. It seemed preposterous to think that any race existed capable of accomplishing such an architectural feat with only the primitive means that these people might be able to command, yet here were the corridors with the arched roofs, the walls of neatly laid boulders and the great chambers with their heavy ceiling beams and stout columns, all exactly as he had seen the dome in Trohanadalmakus, but on a vastly larger scale.

As his eyes and mind dwelt upon these enigmas which confronted them his escort led him from the circular corridor into one that ran at right angles to it where presently they stopped at the entrance to a chamber filled with row upon row of shelving packed full with all manner of manufactured articles. There were large candles and small candles, candles of every conceivable size and shape; there were helmets, belts, sandals, tunics, bowls, jars, vases and the thousand other articles of the daily life of the Minunians with which Tarzan had become more or less familiar during his sojourn among the Trohanadalmakusians.

As they halted before the entrance to this room a white-tunicked slave came forward in response to the summons of one of the warriors of the escort.

"A green tunic for this fellow from Trohanadalmakus," he ordered.

"Whose insignia upon his back?" inquired the slave.

"He belongs to Zoanthrohago," replied the warrior.

The slave ran quickly to one of the shelves from which he selected a green tunic. From another he took two large, wooden blocks upon the face of each of which was carved a different device. These he covered evenly with some sort of paint or ink, slipped a smooth board inside the tunic, placed one of the dies face downward upon the cloth, tapped it smartly with a wooden mallet several times and then repeated the operation with the other die upon the reverse side of the tunic. When he handed the garment to Tarzan with the instructions to don it the ape-man saw that it bore a device in black upon the breast and another upon the back, but he could not read them—his education had not progressed thus far.

The slave then gave him a pair of sandals and when he had strapped these to his feet the warriors motioned him on down the corridor, which, as they proceeded, he was aware changed rapidly in appearance. The rough boulder walls were plastered now and decorated with colored paintings portraying, most often, battle scenes and happenings of the hunt, usually framed in panels bordered in intricate, formal designs. Vivid colorings predominated. Many-hued candles burned in frequent niches. Gorgeously trapped warriors were numerous. The green-tunicked slave almost disappeared, while the white tunics of the higher caste bondsmen were of richer material and the slaves themselves were often resplendently trapped with jewels and fine leather.

The splendor of the scene, the brilliancy of the lighting, increased until the corridor came to an abrupt end before two massive doors of hammered gold in front of which stood gorgeously trapped warriors who halted them and questioned the commander of the escort as to their business.

"By the king's command we bring the slave of Zoanthrohago," replied the commander, "the giant who was taken prisoner at Trohanadalmakus."

The warrior who had challenged them turned to one of his fellows. "Go with this message and deliver it to the king!" he said.

After the messenger had departed the warriors fell to examining Tarzan and asking many questions concerning him, to few of which could his guard give more than speculative answers, and then, presently, the messenger returned with word that the party was immediately to be admitted to the king's presence. The heavy doors were swung wide and Tarzan found himself upon the threshold of an enormous chamber, the walls of which converged toward the opposite end, where a throne stood upon a dais. Massive wooden columns supported the ceiling, which was plastered between its beams. The beams as well as the columns were ornamented with carving, while the plastered portions of the ceiling carried gorgeous arabesques in brilliant colors. The walls were paneled to half their height, and above the paneling of wood were painted panels which Tarzan assumed depicted historical events from the history of Veltopismakus and her kings.

The room was vacant except for two warriors who stood before doors that flanked the throne dais, and as the party moved down the broad center aisle toward the throne one of these warriors signaled the leader and motioned to the door which he was guarding and which he now threw open before them, revealing a small antechamber in which were half a dozen handsomely trapped warriors seated on small, carved benches, while a seventh lolled in a high-backed chair, his fingers tapping upon its broad arms as he listened to the conversation of the others, into which he threw an occasional word that always was received with deepest attention. If he scowled when he spoke, the others scowled still more deeply; if he smiled, they broke into laughter, and scarcely for an instant did their eyes leave his face, lest they miss some fleeting index of his changing moods.

Just inside the doorway the warriors who were conducting Tarzan halted, where they remained in silence until the man in the high-backed armchair deigned to notice them, then the leader knelt upon one knee, raised his arms, palms forward, high above his head, leaned as far back as he could and in a monotonous dead level intoned his salutation.

"O, Elkomoelhago, King of Veltopismakus, Ruler of All Men, Master of Created Things, All-Wise, All-Courageous, All-Glorious! We bring these, as thou hast commanded, the slave of Zoanthrohago."

"Arise and bring the slave closer," commanded the man in the high-backed armchair, and then to his companions: "This is the giant that Zoanthrohago brought back from Trohanadalmakus."

"We have heard of him, All-Glorious," they replied.

"And of Zoanthrohago's wager?" questioned the king.

"And of Zoanthrohago's wager, All-Wise!" replied one.

"What think you of it?" demanded Elkomoelhago.

"Even as you think, Ruler of All Men," quickly spoke another.

"And how is that?" asked the king.

The six looked quickly and uneasily, one at the others. "How does he think?" whispered he who was farthest from Elkomoelhago to his neighbor, who shrugged his shoulders hopelessly and looked to another.

"What was that, Gofoloso?" demanded the king. "What was that you said?"

"I was about to remark that unless Zoanthrohago first consulted our august and all-wise ruler and is now acting upon his judgment he must, almost of necessity, lose the wager," replied Gofoloso glibly.

"Of course," said the king, "there is something in what you say, Gofoloso. Zoanthrohago did consult me. It was I who discovered the vibratory principle which made the thing possible. It was I who decided just how the first experiments were to be carried out. Heretofore it has not been enduring; but we believe that the new formula will have a persistency of thirty-nine moons at least—it is upon this that Zoanthrohago has made his wager. If he is wrong he loses a thousand slaves to Dalfastomalo."

"Wonderful!" exclaimed Gofoloso. "Blessed indeed are we above all other peoples, with a king so learned and so wise as Elkomoelhago."

"You have much to be thankful for, Gofoloso," agreed the king; "but nothing compared to what will follow the success of my efforts to apply this principle of which we have been speaking, but with results diametrically opposite to those we have so far achieved; but we work upon it, we work upon it. Some day it will come and then I shall give to Zoanthrohago the formula that will revolutionize Minuni—then with a hundred men might we go forth and conquer the world!"

Elkomoelhago now turned his attention suddenly upon the green-tunicked slave standing a short distance before him. He scrutinized him closely and in silence for several minutes.

"From what city do you come?" demanded the king, at last

"O, All-Glorious Elkomoelhago," spoke up the leader of the escort, "the poor ignorant creature is without speech."

"Utters he any sound?" inquired the king.

"None since he was captured, Master of Men," replied the warrior.

"He is a Zertalacolol," stated Elkomoelhago. "Why all this silly excitement over one of these low, speechless creatures?"

"See now!" exclaimed Gofoloso, "how quickly and surely the father of wisdom grasps all things, probing to the bottom of all mysteries, revealing their secrets. Is it not marvelous!"

"Now that the Sun of Science has shone upon him even the dullest may see that the creature is indeed a Zertalacolol," cried another of the king's companions. "How simple, how stupid of us all! Ah, what would become of us were it not for the glorious intelligence of the All-Wise."

Elkomoelhago was examining Tarzan closely. He seemed not to have heard the eulogies of his courtiers. Presently he spoke again.

"He has not the features of the Zertalacolols," he pondered musingly. "See his ears. They are not the ears of the speechless ones, nor his hair. His body is not formed as theirs and his head is shaped for the storing of knowledge and the functioning of reason. No, he cannot be a Zertalacolol."

"Marvelous!" cried Gofoloso. "Did I not tell you! Elkomoelhago, our king, is always right?"

"The most stupid of us may easily see that he is not a Zertalacolol, now that the king's divine intelligence has made it go plain," exclaimed the second courtier.

At this juncture a door, opposite that through which Tarzan had been brought into the apartment, opened and a warrior appeared. "O, Elkomoelhago, King of Veltopismakus," he droned, "thy daughter, the Princess Janzara, has come. She would see the strange slave that Zoanthrohago brought from Trohanadalmakus and craves the royal permission to enter."

Elkomoelhago nodded his assent "Conduct the princess to us!" he commanded.

The princess must have been waiting within earshot immediately outside the door, for scarcely had the king spoken when she appeared upon the threshold, followed by two other young women, behind whom were a half dozen warriors. At sight of her the courtiers rose, but not the king.

"Come in, Janzara," he said, "and behold the strange giant who is more discussed in Veltopismakus than Veltopismakus' king."

The princess crossed the room and stood directly in front of the ape-man, who remained standing, as he had since he had entered the chamber, with arms folded across his broad chest, an expression of absolute indifference upon his face. He glanced at the princess as she approached him and saw that she was a very beautiful young woman. Except for an occasional distant glimpse of some of the women of Trohanadalmakus she was the first Minunian female Tarzan had seen. Her features were faultlessly chiseled, her soft, dark hair becomingly arranged beneath a gorgeous, jeweled headdress, her clear skin shaming the down of the peach in its softness. She was dressed entirely in white, befitting a virgin princess in the palace of her sire; her gown, of a soft, clinging stuff, fell in straight and simple lines to her arched insteps. Tarzan looked into her eyes. They were gray, but the shadows of her heavy lashes made them appear much darker than they were. He sought there an index to her character, for here was the young woman whom his friend, Komodoflorensal, hoped some day to espouse and make queen of Trohanadalmakus, and for this reason was the ape-man interested. He saw the beautiful brows knit into a sudden frown.

"What is the matter with the beast?" cried the princess. "Is it made of wood?"

"It speaks no language, nor understands any," explained her father. "It has uttered no sound since it was captured."

"It is a sullen, ugly brute," said the princess. "I'll wager to make it utter a sound, and that quickly," with which she snatched a thin dagger from her belt and plunged it into Tarzan's arm. With such celerity had she moved that her act had taken all who witnessed it by surprise; but she had given the Lord of the Jungle an instant's warning in the few words she had spoken before she struck and these had been sufficient for him. He could not avoid the blow, but he could and did avoid giving her the satisfaction of seeing her cruel experiment succeed, for he uttered no sound. Perhaps she would have struck again, for she was very angry now, but the king spoke sharply to her.

"Enough, Janzara!" he cried. "We would have no harm befall this slave upon whom we are conducting an experiment that means much to the future of Veltopismakus."

"He has dared to stare into my eyes," cried the princess, "and he has refused to speak when he knew that it would give me pleasure. He should be killed!"

"He is not yours to kill," returned the king. "He belongs to Zoanthrohago."

"I will buy him," and turning to one of her warriors, "Fetch Zoanthrohago!"

CHAPTER 10

When Esteban Miranda regained consciousness, the fire before his rude shelter was but a heap of cold ashes and dawn had almost come. He felt weak and dizzy and his head ached. He put his hand to it and found his thick hair matted with coagulated blood. He found something else as well—a great wound in his scalp, that made him shudder and turn sick, so that he fainted. When again he opened his eyes it was quite daylight. He looked about him questioning. Where was he? He called aloud in Spanish—called to a woman with a musical name. Not Flora Hawkes, but a soft, Spanish name that Flora never had heard.

He was sitting up now and presently he regarded his nakedness in evident surprise. He picked up the loincloth that had been cut from his body. Then he looked all about him on the ground—his eyes dull, stupid, wondering. He found his weapons and picking them up examined them. For a long time he sat fingering them and looking at them, his brows puckered in thought. The knife, the spear, the bow and arrows he went over time and time again.

He looked out upon the jungle scene before him and the expression of bewilderment on his face but increased. He half-rose, remaining upon his knees. A startled rodent scurried across the clearing. At sight of it the man seized his bow and fitted an arrow, but the animal was gone before he could loose his shaft Still kneeling, the bewildered expression upon his countenance deepening, he gazed in mute astonishment upon the weapon he held so familiarly in his hand. He arose, gathered up his spear and knife and the balance of his arrows and started off into the jungle.

A hundred yards from his shelter he came upon a lion feeding upon the carcass of its kill that it had dragged into the bushes beside the wide elephant trail along which the man made his way. The lion growled ominously. The man halted, listening intently. He was still bewildered; but only for an instant did he remain motionless in the trail. With the spring of a panther he gained the low swinging limb of the nearest tree. There he squatted for a few minutes. He could see Numa the lion feeding upon the carcass of some animal—what the animal had been he could not determine. After a while the man dropped silently from the tree and went off into the jungle in the opposite direction from that he had at first chanced upon. He was naked, but he did not know it. His diamonds were gone, but he would not have known a diamond had he seen one. Uhha had left him, but he did not miss her, for he knew not that she ever had existed.

Blindly and yet well, his muscles reacted to every demand made upon them in the name of the first law of nature. He had not known why he leaped to a tree at the sound of Numa's growl, nor could he have told why he walked in the opposite direction when he saw where Numa lay up with his kill. He did not know that his hand leaped to a weapon at each new sound or movement in the jungle about him.

Uhha had defeated her own ends. Esteban Miranda was not being punished for his sins for the very excellent reason that he was conscious of no sins nor of any existence. Uhha had killed his objective mind. His brain was but a storehouse of memories that would never again be raised above the threshold of consciousness. When acted upon by the proper force they stimulated the nerves that controlled his muscles, with results seemingly identical with those that would have followed had he been able to reason. An emergency beyond his experience would, consequently, have found him helpless, though ignorant of his helplessness. It was almost as though a dead man walked through the jungle. Sometimes he moved along in silence, again he babbled childishly in Spanish, or, perhaps, quoted whole pages of Shakespeare in English.

Could Uhha have seen him now, even she, savage little cannibal, might have felt remorse at the horror of her handiwork, which was rendered even more horrible because its miserable object was totally unconscious of it; but Uhha was not there to see, nor any other mortal; and the poor clay that once had been a man moved on aimlessly through the jungle, killing and eating when the right nerves were excited, sleeping, talking, walking as though he lived as other men live; and thus, watching him from afar, we see him disappear amidst the riotous foliage of a jungle trail.

*

The Princess Janzara of Veltopismakus did not purchase the slave of Zoanthrohago. Her father, the king, would not permit it, and so, very angry, she walked from the apartment where she had come to examine the captive and when she had passed into the next room and was out of her royal sire's range of vision, she turned and made a face in his direction, at which all her warriors and the two hand-maidens laughed.

"Fool!" she whispered in the direction of her unconscious father. "I shall own the slave yet and kill him, too, if I mind."

The warriors and the hand-maidens nodded their heads approvingly.

King Elkomoelhago arose languidly from his chair. "Take it to the quarries," he said, indicating Tarzan with a motion of his thumb, "but tell the officer in charge that it is the king's wish that it be not overworked, nor injured," and as the ape-man was led away through one doorway, the king quitted the chamber by another, his six courtiers bowing in the strange, Minunian way until he was gone. Then one of them tiptoed quickly to the doorway through which Elkomoelhago had disappeared, flattened himself against the wall beside the door and listened for a moment. Apparently satisfied, he cautiously insinuated his head beyond the doorframe until he could view the chamber adjoining with one eye, then he turned back toward his fellows.

"The old half-wit has gone," he announced, though in a whisper that would have been inaudible beyond the chamber in which it was breathed, for even in Minuni they have learned that the walls have ears, though they express it differently, saying, instead: Trust not too far the loyalty of even the stones of your chamber.

"Saw you ever a creature endowed with such inordinate vanity!" exclaimed one.

"He believes that he is wiser than, not any man, but all men combined," said another. "Sometimes I feel that I can abide his arrogance no longer."

"But you will, Gefasto," said Gofoloso. "To be Chief of Warriors of Veltopismakus is too rich a berth to be lightly thrown aside."

"When one might simultaneously throw away one's life at the same time," added Torndali, Chief of Quarries.

"But the colossal effrontery of the man!" ejaculated another, Makahago, Chief of Buildings. "He has had no more to do with Zoanthrohago's success than have I and yet he claims the successes all for himself and blames the failures upon Zoanthrohago."

"The glory of Veltopismakus is threatened by his egotism," cried Throwaldo, Chief of Agriculture. "He has chosen us as his advisers, six princes, whose knowledge of their several departments should be greater than that of any other individuals and whose combined knowledge of the needs of Veltopismakus and the affairs of state should form a bulwark against the egregious errors that he is constantly committing; but never will he heed our advice. To offer it he considers a usurpation of his royal prerogatives, to urge it, little short of treason. To question his judgment spells ruin. Of what good are we to Veltopismakus? What must the people of the state think of us?"

"It is well known what they think of us," snapped Gofoloso. "They say that we were chosen, not for what we know, but for what we do not know. Nor can you blame them. I, a breeder of diadets, master of ten thousand slaves who till the soil and raise a half of all the food that the city consumes, am chosen Chief of Chiefs, filling an office for which I have no liking and no training, while Throwaldo, who scarce knows the top of a vegetable from its roots, is Chief of Agriculture. Makahago worked the quarry slaves for a hundred moons and is made Chief of Buildings, while Torndali, who is acclaimed the greatest builder of our time, is Chief of Quarries. Gefasto and Vestako, alone, are masters of their bureaus. Vestako the king chose wisely as Chief of the Royal Dome, that his royal comfort and security might be assured; but in Gefasto behold his greatest blunder! He elevated a gay young pleasure-seeker to the command of the army of Veltopismakus and discovered in his new Chief of Warriors as great a military genius as Veltopismakus has ever produced."

Gefasto bowed his acknowledgment of the compliment.

"Had it not been for Gefasto the Trohanadalmakusians would have trapped us fairly the other day," continued Gofoloso.

"I advised the king against pushing the assault," interjected Gefasto, "as soon as it became evident that we had failed to surprise them. We should have withdrawn. It was only after we had advanced and I was free from him that I could direct the affair without interference, and then, as you saw, I quickly extricated our troops and withdrew them with as little loss of men and prestige as possible."

"It was nobly done, Gefasto," said Torndali. "The troops worship you. They would like a king who led them in battle as you might lead them."

"And let them have their wine as of old," interjected Makahago.

"We would all rally around a king who permitted us the innocent pleasure of our wine," said Gofoloso: "What say you, Vestako?"

The Chief of the Royal Dome, the king's major-domo, who had remained silent throughout the arraignment of his master, shook his head.

"It is not wise to speak treason now," he said.

The three looked sharply at him and glanced quickly at one another.

"Who has spoken treason, Vestako?" demanded Gofoloso.

"You have all come too close to it for safety," said the oily Vestako. He spoke in a much louder voice than the others had spoken, as though, far from being fearful of being overheard, he rather hoped that he would be. "Elkomoelhago has been good to us. He has heaped honors and riches upon us. We are very powerful. He is a wise ruler. Who are we to question the wisdom of his acts?"

The others looked uneasily about. Gofoloso laughed nervously. "You were ever slow to appreciate a joke, my good Vestako." he said. "Could you not see that we were hoaxing you?"

"I could not," replied Vestako, "but the king has a fine sense of humor. I will repeat the joke to him and if he laughs then I shall laugh, too, for I shall know that it was indeed a joke. But I wonder upon whom it will be!"

"Oh, Vestako, do not repeat what we have said—not to the king. He might not understand. We are good friends and it was said only among friends." Gofoloso was evidently perturbed in spirit—he spoke rapidly. "By the way, my good Vestako, I just happened to recall that the other day you admired one of my slaves. I have intended giving him to you. If you will accept him he is yours."

"I admire a hundred of your slaves," said Vestako, softly.

"They are yours, Vestako," said Gofoloso. "Come with me now and select them. It is a pleasure to make my friend so trifling a present."

Vestako looked steadily at the other four. They shifted uneasily in momentary silence, which was broken by Throwaldo, Chief of Agriculture. "If Vestako would accept a hundred of my poor slaves I should be overwhelmed with delight," he said.

"I hope they will be slaves of the white tunic," said Vestako.

"They will," said Throwaldo.

"I cannot be outdone in generosity," said Torndali; "you must accept a hundred slaves from me."

"And from me!" cried Makahago, Chief of Buildings.

"If you will send them to my head slave at my quarters before the Sun enters the Warriors' Corridor I shall be overwhelmed with gratitude," said Vestako, rubbing his palms and smiling unctuously. Then he looked quickly and meaningly at Gefasto, Chief of Warriors of Veltopismakus.

"Best can I show my friendship for the noble Vestako," said Gefasto, unsmiling, "by assuring him that I shall, if possible, prevent my warriors from slipping a dagger between his ribs. Should aught of harm befall me, however, I fear that I cannot be responsible for the acts of these men, who, I am told, love me." For a moment longer he stood looking straight into the eyes of Vestako, then he turned upon his heel and strode from the room.

Of the six men who composed the Royal Council, Gefasto and Gofoloso were the most fearless, though even they flattered the vain and arrogant Elkomoelhago, whose despotic powers rendered him a most dangerous enemy. Custom and inherent loyalty to the royal family, in addition to that most potent of human instrumentalities—self-interest, held them, to the service of their king, but so long had they been plotting against him and so rife was discontent throughout the city, that each now felt that he might become bolder with impunity.

Torndali, Makahago and Throwaldo having been chosen by the king for their supposed pliability and having, unlike Gefasto and Gofoloso, justified his expectations, counted for little one way or another. Like the majority of the Veltopismakusian nobles under the reign of Elkomoelhago they had become corrupt, and self-interest guided their every act and thought. Gefasto did not trust them, for he knew that they could be bought even while professing their virtue, and Gefasto had taken to the study of men since his success with the warriors of his city—a success that was fully as much a surprise to him as to others—and his knowledge of the mounting restlessness of the people had implanted in the fertile soil of a virile brain the idea that Veltopismakus was ripe for a new dynasty.

Vestako he knew for a self-acknowledged and shameless bribe-taker. He did not believe that there was an honest hair in the man's head, but he had been surprised at the veiled threat of exposure he had used to mulct his fellows.

"Low indeed have fallen the fortunes of Veltopismakus," he said to Gofoloso as the two walked along the Warriors' Corridor after quitting the council chamber of the king.

"As exemplified by—?" queried the Chief of Chiefs.

"By Vestako's infamy. He cares neither for king nor for people. For slaves or gold he would betray either, and Vestako is typical of the majority of us. No longer is friendship sacred, for even from Throwaldo he exacted the toll of his silence, and Throwaldo has ever been accounted his best friend."

"What has brought us to such a pass, Gefasto?" asked Gofoloso, thoughtfully. "Some attribute it to one cause and some to another, and though there should be no man in Veltopismakus better able than myself to answer my own question, I confess that I am at a loss. There are many theories, but I doubt me the right one has yet been expounded."

"If one should ask me, Gofoloso, and you have asked me, I should say to him as I am about to say to you that the trouble with Veltopismakus is too much peace. Prosperity follows peace—prosperity and plenty of idle time. Time must be occupied. Who would occupy it in labor, even the labor of preparing one's self to defend one's peace and prosperity, when it may so easily be occupied in the pursuit of pleasure? The material prosperity that has followed peace has given us the means to gratify our every whim. We have become satiated with the things we looked upon in the days of yesterday as luxuries to be sparingly enjoyed upon rare occasion. Consequently we have been forced to invent new whims to be gratified and you may rest assured that these have become more and more extravagant and exaggerated in form and idea until even our wondrous prosperity has been taxed to meet the demands of our appetites.

"Extravagance reigns supreme. It rests, like a malign incubus, upon the king and his government. To mend its inroads upon the treasury, the burden of the incubus is shifted from the back of the government to the back of the people in the form of outrageous taxes which no man can meet honestly and have sufficient remaining wherewith to indulge his appetites, and so by one means or another, he passes the burden on to those less fortunate or less shrewd."

"But the heaviest taxation falls upon the rich," Gofoloso reminded him.

"In theory, but not in fact," replied Gefasto. "It is true that the rich pay the bulk of the taxes into the treasury of the king, but first they collect it from the poor in higher prices and other forms of extortion, in the proportion of two jetaks for every one that they pay to the tax collector. The cost of collecting this tax added to the loss in revenue to the government by the abolition of wine and the cost of preventing the unscrupulous from making and selling wine illicitly would, if turned back into the coffers of the government, reduce our taxes so materially that they would fall as a burden upon none."

"And that, you think, would solve our problems and restore happiness to Veltopismakus?" asked Gofoloso.

"No," replied his fellow prince. "We must have war. As we have found that there is no enduring happiness in peace or virtue, let us have a little war and a little sin. A pudding that is all of one ingredient is nauseating—it must be seasoned, it must be spiced, and before we can enjoy the eating of it to the fullest we must be forced to strive for it. War and work, the two most distasteful things in the world, are, nevertheless, the most essential to the happiness and the existence of a people. Peace reduces the necessity for labor, and induces slothfulness. War compels labor, that her ravages may be effaced. Peace turns us into fat worms. War makes men of us."

"War and wine, then, would restore Veltopismakus to her former pride and happiness, you think?" laughed Gofoloso. "What a firebrand you have become since you came to the command of all the warriors of our city!"

"You misunderstand me, Gofoloso," said Gefasto, patiently. "War and wine alone will accomplish nothing but our ruin. I have no quarrel with peace or virtue or temperance. My quarrel is with the misguided theorists who think that peace alone, or virtue alone, or temperance alone will make a strong, a virile, a contented nation. They must be mixed with war and wine and sin and a great measure of hard work—especially hard work—and with nothing but peace and prosperity there is little necessity for hard work, and only the exceptional man works hard when he does not have to.

"But come, you must hasten to deliver the hundred slaves to Vestako before the Sun enters the Warriors' Corridor, or he will tell your little joke to Elkomoelhago."

Gofoloso smiled ruefully. "Some day he shall pay for these hundred slaves," he said, "and the price will be very high."

"If his master falls," said Gefasto.

"When his master falls!" Gofoloso corrected.

The Chief of Warriors shrugged his shoulders, but he smiled contentedly, and he was still smiling after his friend had turned into an intersecting corridor and gone his way.

CHAPTER 11

Tarzan of the Apes was led directly from the Royal Dome to the quarries of Veltopismakus, which lie a quarter of a mile from the nearer of the eight domes which constitute the city. A ninth dome was in course of construction and it was toward this that the line of burdened slaves wound from the entrance to the quarry to which the ape-man was conducted. Just below the surface, in a well-lighted chamber, he was turned over to the officer in charge of the quarry guard, to whom the king's instructions concerning him were communicated.

"Your name?" demanded the officer, opening a large book that lay upon the table at which he was seated.

"He is as dumb as the Zertalacolols," explained the commander of the escort that had brought him to the quarry. "Therefore he has no name."

"We will call him The Giant, then," said the officer, "for as such has he been known since his capture," and he wrote in his book, Zuanthrol, with Zoanthrohago as the owner, and Trohanadalmakus as the city of his origin, and then he turned to one of the warriors lolling upon a nearby bench. "Take him to the timbering crew in the extension of tunnel thirteen at the thirty-sixth level and tell the Vental in charge to give him light work and see that no harm befalls him, for such are the commands of the Thagostogol. But wait! Here is his number. Fasten it upon his shoulder."

The warrior took the circular piece of fabric with black hieroglyphics stamped upon it and affixed it with a metal clasp to the left shoulder of Tarzan's green tunic and then, motioning the ape-man to precede him, quit the chamber.

Tarzan now found himself in a short, dark corridor which presently opened into a wider and lighter one along which innumerable, unladen slaves were moving in the same direction that his guard now escorted him. He noticed that the floor of the corridor had a constant downward gradient and that it turned ever to the right, forming a great spiral leading downward into the earth. The walls and ceiling were timbered and the floor paved with flat stones, worn smooth by the millions of sandaled feet that had passed over them. At sufficiently frequent intervals candles were set in niches in the left-hand wall, and, also at regular intervals, other corridors opened out of it. Over each of these openings were more of the strange hieroglyphics of Minuni. As Tarzan was to learn later, these designated the levels at which the tunnels lay and led to circular corridors which surrounded the main spiral runway. From these circular corridors ran the numerous horizontal tunnels leading to the workings at each level. Shafts for ventilation and emergency exit pierced these tunnels at varying distances, running from the surface to the lowest levels of the quarry.

At almost every level a few slaves turned off into these lateral tunnels which were well lighted, though not quite as brilliantly as the spiral. Shortly after they had commenced the descent, Tarzan, accustomed from infancy to keen observation, had taken note of the numbers of tunnel entrances they passed, but he could only conjecture at the difference in the depths of the levels into which they opened. A rough guess placed them at fifteen feet, but before they reached the thirty-sixth, into which they turned, Tarzan felt that there must be an error in his calculations, for he was sure that they could not be five hundred and forty feet below the earth's surface with open flames and no forced ventilation.

The horizontal corridor they now entered after leaving the spiral curved sharply to the right and then back to the left. Shortly afterward it crossed a wide, circular corridor in which were both laden and unladen slaves, beyond which were two lines, those laden with rock moving back in the direction from which Tarzan had come, while others, bearing lumber moved in the same direction that he did. With both lines there were unladen slaves.

After traversing the horizontal tunnel for a considerable distance they came at last upon the working party, and here Tarzan was turned over to the Vental, a warrior who, in the military organizations of the Minunians, commands ten men.

"So this is The Giant!" exclaimed the Vental. "And we are not to work him too hard." His tone was sneering and disagreeable. "Such a giant!" he cried. "Why, he is no larger than I and they are afraid to let him do any work into the bargain. Mark you, he will work here or get the lash. Kalfastoban permits no sluggards," and the fellow struck his chest vauntingly.

He who had brought Tarzan appeared disgusted. "You will do well, Kalfastoban," he said, as he turned away to retrace his steps to the guard room, "to heed the king's commands. I should hate to be wearing your harness if aught befell this speechless slave that has set every tongue in Veltopismakus going and made Elkomoelhago so jealous of Zoanthrohago that he would slip steel between his ribs were it not that he could then no longer steal the great wizard's applause."

"Kalfastoban fears no king," blustered the Vental, "least of all the sorry specimen that befouls the throne of Veltopishago. He fools no one but himself. We all know that Zoanthrohago is his brain and Gefasto his sword."

"However," warned the other, "be careful of Zuanthrol," and he departed.

Kalfastoban Vental set the new slave to work upon the timbering of the tunnel as it was excavated from the great moraine that formed the quarry. The line of slaves coming from the surface empty-handed passed down one side of the tunnel to the end, loosened each a rock, or if heavy a rock to two men, and turned back up the tunnel's opposite side, carrying their burdens back to the spiral runway used by those leaving the workings and so up and out to the new dome. The earth, a light clay, that filled the interstices between the rocks in the moraine was tamped into the opening behind the wall timbers, the tunnel being purposely made sufficiently large to permit this. Certain slaves were detailed for this work, others carried timbers cut to the right dimensions down to the timbering crew, of which Tarzan was one. It was only necessary for this crew of three to scoop a narrow, shallow trench in which to place the foot of each wall board, set them in place and slip the ceiling board on top of them. At each end of the ceiling boards was a cleat, previously attached at the surface, which kept the wall boards from falling in after being set in place. The dirt tamped behind them fastened them solidly in their places, the whole making a quickly erected and substantial shoring.

The work was light for the ape-man, though he still was weak from the effects of his wounds, and he had opportunities constantly to observe all that went on around him and to gather new information relative to the people in whose power he found himself. Kalfastoban he soon set down as a loudmouthed braggart, from whom one need have nothing to fear during the routine of their everyday work, but who would bear watching if ever opportunity came for him to make a show of authority or physical prowess before the eyes of his superiors.

The slaves about him worked steadily, but seemed not to be overtaxed, while the guards, which accompanied them constantly, in the ratio of about one warrior to every fifty slaves, gave no indications of brutality in the treatment they accorded their charges, insofar as Tarzan was able to observe.

The fact that puzzled him most now as it had since the moment of his first return to consciousness, was the stature of these people. They were no pygmies, but men fully as large as the usual run of Europeans. There was none quite as tall as the ape-man, but there were many who missed it by but the scantiest fraction of an inch. He knew that they were Veltopismakusians, the same people he had seen battling with the Trohanadalmakusians; they spoke of having captured him in the battle that he had seen waged; and they called him Zuanthrol, The Giant, yet they were as large as he, and as he had passed from the Royal Dome to the quarry he had seen their gigantic dome dwellings rising fully four hundred feet above his head. It was all preposterous and impossible, yet he had the testimony of all his faculties that it was true. Contemplation of it but tended to confuse him more and so he gave over all attempts to solve the mystery and set himself to the gathering of information concerning his captors and his prison against that time which he well knew must some day come when the means of escape should offer itself to the alert and cunning instincts of the wild beast that, at heart, he always considered himself.

Wherever he had been in Veltopismakus, whoever he had heard refer to the subject, he had had it borne in upon him that the people were generally dissatisfied with their king and his government, and he knew that among a discontented people efficiency would be at low ebb and discipline demoralized to such an extent that, should he watch carefully, he must eventually discover the opportunity he sought, through the laxity of those responsible for his safekeeping. He did not expect it today or tomorrow, but today and tomorrow were the days upon which to lay the foundation of observation that would eventually reveal an avenue of escape.

When the long working day at last drew to a close the slaves were conducted to their quarters, which, as Tarzan discovered, were always on levels near to those in which they labored. He, with several other slaves, was conducted to the thirty-fifth level and into a tunnel the far end of which had been widened to the proportions of a large chamber, the narrow entrance to which had been walled up with stone except for a small aperture through which the slaves were forced to pass in and out of their chamber upon all fours, and when the last of them was within, this was closed and secured by a heavy door outside which two warriors watched throughout the night.

Once inside and standing upon his feet the ape-man looked about him to discover himself within a chamber so large that it seemed easy to accommodate the great throng of slaves that must have numbered fully five thousand souls of both sexes. The women were preparing food over small fires the smoke of which found its way from the chamber through openings in the ceiling. For the great number of fires the amount of smoke was noticeably little, a fact which was, however, accounted for by the nature of the fuel, a clean, hard charcoal; but why the liberated gases did not asphyxiate them all was quite beyond the ape-man, as was still the riddle of the open flames and the pure air at the depth where the workings lay. Candles burned in niches all about the walls and there were at least half-a-dozen large ones standing upon the floor.

The slaves were of all ages from infancy to middle age, but there were no aged venerables among them. The skins of the women and children were the whitest Tarzan had ever seen and he marveled at them until he came to know that some of the former and all of the latter had never seen daylight since birth. The children who were born here would go up into the daylight some time, when they were of an age that warranted beginning the training for the vocations their masters had chosen for them, but the women who had been captured from other cities would remain here until death claimed them, unless that rarest of miracles occurred—they should be chosen by a Veltopismakusian warrior as his mate; but that was scarce even a remote possibility, since the warriors almost invariably chose their mates from the slaves of the white tunic with whom they came in daily contact in the domes above ground.

The faces of the women bore the imprint of a sadness that brought a spontaneous surge of sympathy to the breast of the savage ape-man. Never in his life had he seen such abject hopelessness depicted upon any face.

As he crossed the room many were the glances that were cast upon him, for it was obvious from his deep tan that he was a newcomer, and, too, there was that about him that marked him of different clay from them, and soon there were whispers running through the throng, for the slaves who had entered with him had passed the word of his identity to the others, and who, even in the bowels of the earth, had not heard of the wondrous giant captured by Zoanthrohago during the battle with the Trohanadalmakusians?

Presently a young girl, kneeling above a brazier over which she was grilling a cut of flesh, caught his eye and motioned him to her. As he came he saw that she was very beautiful, with a pale, translucent skin the whiteness of which was accentuated by the blue-black of a wealth of lustrous hair.

"You are The Giant?" she asked.

"I am Zuanthrol," he replied.

"He has told me about you," said the girl. "I will cook for you, too. I cook for him. Unless," she added with a trace of embarrassment, "there is another you would rather have cook for you."

"There is no one I would rather have cook for me," Tarzan told her; "but who are you and who is he?"

"I am Talaskar," she replied; "but I know him only by his number. He says that while he remains a slave he has no name, but will go always by his number, which is Eight Hundred Cubed, Plus Nineteen. I see that you are Eight Hundred Cubed, Plus Twenty-one." She was looking at the hieroglyphics that had been fastened upon his shoulder. "Have you a name?"

"They call me Zuanthrol."

"Ah," she said, "you are a large man, but I should scarcely call you a giant. He, too, is from Trohanadalmakus and he is about your height. I never heard that there were any giants in Minuni except the people they call Zertalacolols."

"I thought you were a Zertalacolol," said a man's voice at Tarzan's ear.

The ape-man turned to see one of the slaves with whom he had been working eyeing him quizzically, and smiled.

"I am a Zertalacolol to my masters," he replied.

The other raised his brows. "I see," he said. "Perhaps you are wise. I shall not be the one to betray you," and passed on about his business.

"What did he mean?" asked the girl.

"I have never spoken, until now, since they took me prisoner," he explained, "and they think I am speechless, though I am sure that I do not look like a Zertalacolol, yet some of them insist that I am one."

"I have never seen one," said the girl.

"You are fortunate," Tarzan told her. "They are neither pleasant to see nor to meet."

"But I should like to see them," she insisted. "I should like to see anything that was different from these slaves whom I see all day and every day."

"Do not lose hope," he encouraged her, "for who knows but that it may be very soon that you will return to the surface."

"Return," she repeated. "I have never been there."

"Never been to the surface! You mean since you were captured."

"I was born in this chamber," she told him, "and never have I been out of it."

"You are a slave of the second generation and are still confined to the quarries—I do not understand it. In all Minunian cities, I have been told, slaves of the second generation are given the white tunic and comparative freedom above ground."

"It was not for me. My mother would not permit it. She would rather I had died than mated with a Veltopismakusian or another slave, as I must do if I go into the city above."

"But how do you avoid it? Your masters certainly do not leave such things to the discretion of their slaves."

"Where there are so many one or two may go unaccounted for indefinitely, and women, if they be ill-favored, cause no comment upon the part of our masters. My birth was never reported and so they have no record of me. My mother took a number for me from the tunic of one who died, and in this way I attract no attention upon the few occasions that our masters or the warriors enter our chamber."

"But you are not ill-favored—your face would surely attract attention anywhere," Tarzan reminded her.

For just an instant she turned her back upon him, putting her hands to her face and to her hair, and then she faced him again and the ape-man saw before him a hideous and wrinkled hag upon whose crooked features no man would look a second time.

"God!" ejaculated Tarzan.

Slowly the girl's face relaxed, assuming its normal lines of beauty, and with quick, deft touches she arranged her disheveled hair. An expression that was almost a smile haunted her lips.

"My mother taught me this," she said, "so that when they came and looked upon me they would not want me."

"But would it not be better to be mated with one of them and live a life of comfort above ground than to eke out a terrible existence below ground?" he demanded. "The warriors of Veltopismakus are, doubtless, but little different from those of your own country."

She shook her head. "It cannot be, for me," she said. "My father is of far Mandalamakus. My mother was stolen from him but a couple of moons before I was born in this horrid chamber, far from the air and sunlight that my mother never tired of telling me about."

"And your mother?" asked Tarzan. "Is she here?"

The girl shook her head sadly. "They came for her over twenty moons since and took her away. I do not know what became of her."

"And these others, they never betray you?" he inquired.

"Never! Whatever slave betrayed another would be torn to pieces by his fellows. But come, you must be hungry," and she offered him of the flesh she had been cooking.

Tarzan would have preferred his meat raw, but he did not wish to offend her and so he thanked her and ate that which she offered him, squatting on his haunches across the brazier from her.

"It is strange that Aoponato does not come," she remarked, using the Minunian form of Eight Hundred Cubed, Plus Nineteen. "Never before has he been so late."

A brawny slave, who had approached from behind her, had halted and was looking scowlingly at Tarzan.

"Perhaps this is he," said Tarzan to the girl, indicating the man with a gesture.

Talaskar turned quickly, an almost happy light in her eyes, but when she saw who it was that stood behind her she rose quickly and stepped back, her expression altered to one of disgust.

"No," she said, "it is not he."

"You are cooking for him?" demanded the fellow, pointing at Tarzan. "But you would not cook for me," he accused, not waiting for a reply to his question, the answer to which was all too obvious. "Who is he that you should cook for him? Is he better than I? You will cook for me, also."

"There are plenty to cook for you, Caraftap," replied Talaskar, "and I do not wish to. Go to some other woman. Until there are too many men we are permitted to choose those whom we shall cook for. I do not choose to cook for you."

"If you know what is well for you, you will cook for me," growled the man. "You will be my mate, too. I have a right to you, because I have asked you many times before these others came. Rather than let them have you I will tell the Vental tomorrow the truth about you and he will take you away. Have you ever seen Kalfastoban?"

The girl shuddered.

"I will see that Kalfastoban gets you," continued Caraftap. "They will not permit you to remain here when they find that you refuse to produce more slaves."

"I should prefer Kalfastoban to you," sneered the girl, "but neither one nor the other shall have me."

"Do not be too sure of that," he cried, and stepping forward, quickly, seized her by the arm before she could elude him. Dragging her toward him the man attempted to kiss her—but he did not succeed. Steel fingers closed upon his shoulder, he was torn roughly from his prey and hurled ruthlessly a dozen paces, stumbling and falling to the floor. Between him and the girl stood the gray-eyed stranger with the shock of black hair.

Almost roaring in his rage, Caraftap scrambled to his feet and charged Tarzan—charged as a mad bull charges, with lowered head and bloodshot eyes.

"For this you shall die," he screamed.

CHAPTER 12

The Son of The First Woman strode proudly through the forest. He carried a spear, jauntily, and there were a bow and arrows slung to his back. Behind him came ten other males of his species, similarly armed, and each walked as though he owned the earth he trod. Toward them along the trail, though still beyond their sight, or hearing, or smell, came a woman of their kind. She, too, walked with fearless step. Presently her eyes narrowed and she paused, up-pricking her great, flat ears to listen, sniffing the air. Men! She increased her gait to a trot, bearing down upon them. There was more than one—there were several. If she came upon them suddenly they would be startled, filled with confusion, and no doubt she could seize one of them before they took to flight. If not—the feathered pebbles at her girdle would seek one out.

For some time men had been scarce. Many women of her tribe who had gone out into the forest to capture mates had never returned. She had seen the corpses of several of these herself, lying in the forest. She had wondered what had killed them. But here were men at last, the first she had discovered in two moons, and this time she would not return empty-handed to her cave.

At a sudden turning of the forest trail she came within sight of them, but saw, to her dismay, that they were still a long way off. They would be sure to escape if they saw her, and she was upon the point of hiding when she realized that already it was too late. One of them was pointing at her. Loosing a missile from her girdle and grasping her cudgel more firmly she started toward them at a rapid, lumbering run. She was both surprised and pleased when she saw that they made no attempt to escape. How terrified they must be to stand thus docilely while she approached them. But what was this? They were advancing to meet her! And now she saw the expressions upon their faces. No fear there—only rage and menace. What were the strange things they carried in their hands? One who was running toward her, the nearest, paused and hurled a long pointed stick at her. It was sharp and when it grazed her shoulder it brought blood. Another paused and holding a little stick across a longer stick, the ends of which were bent back with a piece of gut, suddenly released the smaller stick, which leaped through the air and pierced the flesh beneath one of her arms. And behind these two the others were rushing upon her with similar weapons. She recalled the corpses of women she had seen in the forest and the dearth of men for the past several moons, and though she was dull of wit yet she was not without reasoning faculties and so she compared these facts with the occurrences of the past few seconds with a resultant judgment that sent her lumbering away, in the direction from which she had come, as fast as her hairy legs could carry her, nor did she once pause in her mad flight until she sank exhausted at the mouth of her own cave.

The men did not pursue her. As yet they had not reached that stage in their emancipation that was to give them sufficient courage and confidence in themselves to entirely overcome their hereditary fear of women. To chase one away was sufficient. To pursue her would have been tempting Providence.

When the other women of the tribe saw their fellow stagger to her cave and sensed that her condition was the result of terror and the physical strain of long flight they seized their cudgels and ran forth, prepared to meet and vanquish her pursuer, which they immediately assumed to be a lion. But no lion appeared and then some of them wandered to the side of the woman who lay panting on her threshold.

"From what did you run?" they asked her in their simple sign language.

"Men," she replied.

Disgust showed plainly upon every face, and one of them kicked her and another spat upon her.

"There were many," she told them, "and they would have killed me with flying sticks. Look!" and she showed them the spear wound, and the arrow still embedded in the flesh beneath her arm. "They did not run from me, but came forward to attack me. Thus have all the women been killed whose corpses we have seen in the forest during the past few moons."

This troubled them. They ceased to annoy the prostrate woman. Their leader, the fiercest of them, paced to and fro, making hideous faces. Suddenly she halted.

"Come!" she signaled. "We shall go forth together and find these men, and bring them back and punish them." She shook her cudgel above her head and grimaced horribly.

The others danced about her, imitating her expression and her actions, and when she started off toward the forest they trooped behind her, a savage, bloodthirsty company—all but the woman who still lay panting where she had fallen. She had had enough of man—she was through with him forever.

*

"For this you shall die!" screamed Caraftap, as he rushed upon Tarzan of the Apes in the long gallery of the slaves' quarters in the quarry of Elkomeolhago, king of Veltopismakus.

The ape-man stepped quickly aside, avoiding the other, and tripped him with a foot, sending him sprawling, face downward, upon the floor. Caraftap, before he arose, looked about as though in search of a weapon and, his eyes alighting upon the hot brazier, he reached forth to seize it. A murmur of disapproval rose from the slaves who, having been occupied nearby, had seen the inception of the quarrel.

"No weapons!" cried one. "It is not permitted among us. Fight with your bare hands or not at all."

But Caraftap was too drunk with hate and jealousy to hear them or to heed, and so he grasped the brazier and, rising, rushed at Tarzan to hurl it in his face. Now it was another who tripped him and this time two slaves leaped upon him and wrenched the brazier from his hand. "Fight fair!" they admonished him, and dragged him to his feet.

TARZAN SUPER PACK

Tarzan had stood smiling and indifferent, for the rage of others amused him where it was greater than circumstances warranted, and now he waited for Caraftap and when his adversary saw the smile upon his face it but increased his spleen, so that he fairly leaped upon the ape-man in his madness to destroy him, and Tarzan met him with the most surprising defense that Caraftap, who for long had been a bully among the slaves, ever had encountered. It was a doubled fist at the end of a straight arm and it caught Caraftap upon the point of his chin, stretching him upon his back. The slaves, who had by this time gathered in considerable numbers to watch the quarrel, voiced their approval in the shrill, "Ee-ah-ee-ah," that constituted one form of applause.

Dazed and groggy, Caraftap staggered to his feet once more and with lowered head looked about him as though in search of his enemy. The girl, Talaskar, had come to Tarzan's side and was standing there looking up into his face.

"You are very strong," she said, but the expression in her eyes said more, or at least it seemed to Caraftap to say more. It seemed to speak of love, whereas it was only the admiration that a normal woman always feels for strength exercised in a worthy cause.

Caraftap made a noise in his throat that sounded much like the squeal of an angry pig and once again he rushed upon the ape-man. Behind them some slaves were being let into the corridor and as the aperture was open one of the warriors beyond it, who chanced to be stooping down at the time, could see within. He saw but little, though what he saw was enough—a large slave with a shock of black hair raising another large slave high above his head and dashing him to the hard floor. The warrior, pushing the slaves aside, scrambled through into the corridor and ran forward toward the center. Before they were aware of his presence he stood facing Tarzan and Talaskar. It was Kalfastoban.

"What is the meaning of this?" he cried in a loud voice, and then: "Ah, ha! I see. It is The Giant. He would show the other slaves how strong he is, would he?" He glanced at Caraftap, struggling to rise from the floor, and his face grew very dark—Caraftap was a favorite of his. "Such things are not permitted here, fellow!" he cried, shaking his fist in the ape-man's face, and forgetting in his anger that the new slave neither spoke nor understood. But presently he recollected and motioned Tarzan to follow him. "A hundred lashes will explain to him that he must not quarrel," he said aloud to no one in particular, but he was looking at Talaskar.

"Do not punish him," cried the girl, still forgetful of herself. "It was all Caraftap's fault, Zuanthrol but acted in self-defense."

Kalfastoban could not take his eyes from the girl's face and presently she sensed her danger and flushed, but still she stood her ground, interceding for the ape-man. A crooked smile twisted Kalfastoban's mouth as he laid a familiar hand upon her shoulder.

"How old are you?" he asked.

She told him, shuddering.

"I shall see your master and purchase you," he announced. "Take no mate."

Tarzan was looking at Talaskar and it seemed that he could see her wilt, as a flower wilts in noxious air, and then Kalfastoban turned upon him.

"You cannot understand me, you stupid beast," he said, "but I can tell you, and those around you may listen and, perhaps, guide you from danger. This time I shall let you off, but let it happen again and you shall have a hundred lashes, or worse, maybe; and if I hear that you have had aught to do with this girl, whom I intend to purchase and take to the surface, it will go still harder with you," with which he strode to the entrance and passed through into the corridor beyond.

After the Vental had departed and the door of the chamber had been closed a hand was laid upon Tarzan's shoulder from behind and a man's voice called him by name: "Tarzan!" It sounded strange in his ears, far down in this buried chamber beneath the ground, in an alien city and among an alien people, not one of whom ever had heard his name, but as he turned to face the man who had greeted him a look of recognition and a smile of pleasure overspread his features.

"Kom—!" he started to ejaculate, but the other placed a finger to his lips. "Not here," he said. "Here I am Aoponato."

"But your stature! You are as large as I. It is beyond me. What has happened to swell the race of Minunians to such relatively gigantic proportions?"

Komodoflorensal smiled. "Human egotism would not permit you to attribute this change to an opposite cause from that to which you have ascribed it," he said.

Tarzan knit his brows and gazed long and thoughtfully at his royal friend. An expression that was of mingled incredulity and amusement crept gradually over his countenance.

"You mean," he asked slowly, "that I have been reduced in size to the stature of a Minunian?"

Komodoflorensal nodded. "Is it not easier to believe that than to think that an entire race of people and all their belongings, even their dwellings and the stones that they were built of, and all their weapons and their diadets, had been increased in size to your own stature?"

"But I tell you it is impossible!" cried the ape-man.

"I should have said the same thing a few moons ago," replied the prince. "Even when I heard the rumor here that they had reduced you I did not believe it, not for a long time, and I was still a bit skeptical until I entered this chamber and saw you with my own eyes."

"How was it accomplished?" demanded Tarzan.

"The greatest mind in Veltopismakus, and perhaps in all Minuni, is Zoanthrohago," explained Komodoflorensal. "We have recognized this for many moons, for, during the occasional intervals that we are at peace with Veltopismakus, there is some exchange of ideas as well as goods between the two cities, and thus we heard of many marvels attributed to this greatest of walmaks."

"I have never heard a wizard spoken of in Minuni until now," said Tarzan, for he thought that that was the meaning of the word walmak, and perhaps it is, as nearly as it can be translated into English. A scientist who works miracles would be, perhaps, a truer definition.

"It was Zoanthrohago who captured you," continued Aoponato, "encompassing your fall by means at once scientific and miraculous. After you had fallen he caused you to lose consciousness and while you were in that condition you were dragged hither by a score of diadets hitched to a hastily improvised litter built of small trees tied securely one to the other, after their branches had been removed. It was after they had you safely within Veltopismakus that Zoanthrohago set to work upon you to reduce your stature, using apparatus that he has built himself. I have heard them discussing it and they say that it did not take him long."

"I hope that Zoanthrohago has the power to undo that which he has done," said the ape-man.

"They say that that is doubtful. He has never been able to make a creature larger than it formerly was, though in his numerous experiments he has reduced the size of many of the lower animals. The fact of the matter is," continued Aoponato, "that he has been searching for a means to enlarge the Veltopismakusians so that they may overcome all the other peoples of Minuni, but he has only succeeded in developing a method that gives precisely opposite results from that which they seek, so, if he cannot make others larger, I doubt if he can make you any larger than you now are."

"I would be rather helpless among the enemies of my own world," said Tarzan, ruefully.

"You need not worry about that, my friend," said the prince gently.

"Why?" asked the ape-man.

"Because you have very little chance of reaching your own world again," said Komodoflorensal a trifle sadly. "I have no hope of ever seeing Trohanadalmakus again. Only by the utter overthrow of Veltopismakus by my father's warriors could I hope for rescue, since nothing less could overcome the guard in the quarry mouth. While we often capture slaves of the white tunic from the enemies' cities, it is seldom that we gather in any of the green tunic. Only in the rare cases of utter surprise attacks by daylight do any of us catch an enemies' green slaves above ground, and surprise day attacks may occur once in the lifetime of a man, or never."

"You believe that we will spend the rest of our lives in this underground hole?" demanded Tarzan.

"Unless we chance to be used for labor above ground during the daytime, occasionally," replied the prince of Trohanadalmakus, with a wry smile.

The ape-man shrugged. "We shall see," he said.

After Kalfastoban had left, Caraftap had limped away to the far end of the chamber, muttering to himself, his ugly face black and scowling.

"I am afraid that he will make you trouble," Talaskar said to Tarzan, indicating the disgruntled slave with a nod of her shapely head, "and I am sorry, for it is all my fault."

"Your fault?" demanded Komodoflorensal.

"Yes," said the girl. "Caraftap was threatening me when Aopontando interfered and punished him."

"Aopontando?" queried Komodoflorensal.

"That is my number," explained Tarzan.

"And it was on account of Talaskar that you were fighting? I thank you, my friend. I am sorry that I was not here to protect her. Talaskar cooks for me. She is a good girl." Komodoflorensal was looking at the girl as he spoke and Tarzan saw how her eyes lowered beneath his gaze and the delicate flush that mounted her cheeks, and he realized that he was downwind from an idea, and smiled.

"So this is the Aoponato of whom you told me?" he said to Talaskar.

"Yes, this is he."

"I am sorry that he was captured, but it is good to find a friend here," said the ape-man. "We three should be able to hit upon some plan of escape," but they shook their heads, smiling sadly.

For a while, after they had eaten, they sat talking together, being joined occasionally by other slaves, for Tarzan had many friends here now since he had chastised Caraftap and they would have talked all night had not the ape-man questioned Komodoflorensal as to the sleeping arrangements of the slaves.

Komodoflorensal laughed, and pointed here and there about the chamber at recumbent figures lying upon the hard earthen floor; men, women and children sleeping, for the most part, where they had eaten their evening meal.

"The green slaves are not pampered," he remarked laconically.

"I can sleep anywhere," said Tarzan, "but more easily when it is dark. I shall wait until the lights are extinguished."

"You will wait forever, then," Komodoflorensal told him.

"The lights are never extinguished?" demanded the ape-man.

"Were they, we should all be soon dead," replied the prince. "These flames serve two purposes—they dissipate the darkness and consume the foul gases that would otherwise quickly asphyxiate us. Unlike the ordinary flame, that consumes oxygen, these candles, perfected from the discoveries and inventions of an ancient Minunian scientist, consume the deadly gases and liberate oxygen. It is because of this even more than for the light they give that they are used exclusively throughout Minuni. Even our domes would be dark, ill-smelling, noxious places were it not for them, while the quarries would be absolutely unworkable."

"Then I shall not wait for them to be extinguished," said Tarzan, stretching himself at full length upon the dirt floor, with a nod and a "Tuano!"—a Minunian "Good night!"—to Talaskar and Komodoflorensal.

CHAPTER 13

As Talaskar was preparing their breakfast the following morning Komodoflorensal remarked to Tarzan that he wished they two could be employed upon the same work, that they might be always together.

"If there is ever the chance for escape that you seem to think will some day present itself," he said, "then it will be well if we are together."

"When we go," replied Tarzan, "we must take Talaskar with us."

Komodoflorensal shot a swift glance at the ape-man, but made no comment upon his suggestion.

EDGAR RICE BURROUGHS

"You would take me with you!" exclaimed Talaskar. "Ah, if such a dream could but be realized! I would go with you to Trohanadalmakus and be your slave, for I know that you would not harm me; but, alas, it can be nothing more than a pleasant daydream, enduring for a brief time, for Kalfastoban has spoken for me and doubtless my master will be glad to sell me to him, for I have heard it said among the slaves that he sells many of his each year to raise the money to pay his taxes."

"We will do what we can, Talaskar," said Tarzan, "and if Aoponato and I find a means of escape we will take you with us; but first he and I must find a way to be together more."

"I have a plan," said Komodoflorensal, "that might prove successful. They believe that you neither speak nor understand our language. To work a slave with whom they cannot communicate is, to say the least, annoying. I shall tell them that I can communicate with you, when it is quite probable that they will assign us to the same crew."

"But how will you communicate with me without using the Minunian language?" demanded the ape-man.

"Leave that to me," replied Komodoflorensal. "Until they discover in some other way that you speak Minunian I can continue to deceive them."

It was not long before the fruits of Komodoflorensal's plan ripened. The guards had come for the slaves and the various parties had gone forth from the sleeping chamber, joining in the corridors without the thousands of others wending their way to the scene of their daily labor. The ape-man joined the timbering crew at the extension of the thirteenth tunnel at the thirty-sixth level where he once more attacked the monotonous work of shoring the sides and roof of the shaft with an enthusiasm that elicited commendation from even the surly Kalfastoban, though Caraftap, who was removing rocks just ahead of Tarzan, often shot venomous looks at the ape-man.

The work had been progressing for perhaps two or three hours when two warriors descended the tunnel and halted beside Kalfastoban. They were escorting a green-tunicked slave, to whom Tarzan paid no more attention than he did to the warriors until a scrap of the conversation between the warriors and Kalfastoban reached his ears, then he shot a quick glance in the direction of the four and saw that the slave was Komodoflorensal, Prince of Trohanadalmakus, known in the quarries of Veltopismakus as Slave Aoponato, or 8003+19, which is written in Minunian hieroglyphics.

Tarzan's number Aopontando, 8003+21, appeared thus, upon the shoulder of his green tunic.

Although the Minunian form occupies less space than would our English equivalent of Tarzan's number, which is 512,000,021, it would be more difficult to read if expressed in English words, for it then would be, ten times ten times eight, cubed, plus seven times three; but the Minunians translate it in no such way. To them it is a whole number, Aopontando, which represents at first glance a single quantity as surely as do the digits 37 represent to our minds an invariable amount, a certain, definite measure of quantity which we never think of as three times ten plus seven, which, in reality, it is. The Minunian system of numerals, while unthinkably cumbersome and awkward from the European point of view, is, however, not without its merits.

As Tarzan looked up Komodoflorensal caught his eye and winked and then Kalfastoban beckoned to the ape-man, who crossed the corridor and stood in silence before the Vental.

"Let us hear you talk to him," cried Kalfastoban to Komodoflorensal. "I don't believe that he will understand you. How could he when he cannot understand us?" The fellow could not conceive of another language than his own.

"I will ask him in his own language," said Komodoflorensal, "if he understands me, and you will see that he nods his head affirmatively."

"Very good," cried Kalfastoban; "ask him."

Komodoflorensal turned toward Tarzan and voiced a dozen syllables of incomprehensible gibberish and when he was done the ape-man nodded his head.

"You see," demanded Komodoflorensal.

Kalfastoban scratched his head. "It is even as he says," he admitted, ruefully, "the Zertalacolol has a language."

Tarzan did not smile, though he should have liked to, at the clever manner in which Komodoflorensal had deceived the Veltopismakusians into believing that he had communicated with Tarzan in a strange language. As long as he could contrive to put all his communications into questions that could be answered by yes or no, the deception would be easily maintained; but under circumstances that made this impossible some embarrassments might be expected to arise, and he wondered how the resourceful Trohanadalmakusian would handle these.

"Tell him," said one of the warriors to Komodoflorensal, "that his master, Zoanthrohago, has sent for him, and ask him if he fully understands that he is a slave and that upon his good behavior depends his comfort; yes, even his life, for Zoanthrohago has the power of life and death over him; as much so as have the royal family. If he comes docilely to his master and is obedient he will not fare ill, but if he be lazy, impudent, or threatening he may expect to taste the point of a freeman's sword."

Komodoflorensal strung out, this time, a much longer series of senseless syllables, until he could scarce compose his features to comport with the seriousness of his mien.

"Tell them," said Tarzan, in English, which, of course, not one of them understood, "that at the first opportunity I shall break the neck of my master; that it would require but little incentive to cause me to seize one of these timbers and crack the skull of Kalfastoban and the rest of the warriors about us; and I shall run away at the first opportunity and take you and Talaskar with me."

Komodoflorensal listened intently until Tarzan had ceased speaking and then turned to the two warriors who had come with him to find the ape-man.

"Zuanthrol says that he fully understands his position and that he is glad to serve the noble and illustrious Zoanthrohago, from whom he claims but a single boon," translated the Trohanadalmakusian prince, rather freely.

"And what boon is that?" demanded one of the warriors.

"That I be permitted to accompany him that he may thus better fulfill the wishes of his master, since without me he could not even know what was desired of him," explained Aoponato.

Tarzan understood now how Komodoflorensal would surmount whatever difficulties of communication might arise and he felt that he would be safe in the hands of his quick-witted friend for as long a time as he cared to pretend ignorance of the Minunian tongue.

"The thought was even in our minds, slave, when we heard that you could communicate with this fellow," said the warrior to whom Komodoflorensal had addressed the suggestion. "You shall both be taken to Zoanthrohago, who will doubtless decide his wishes without consulting you or any other slave. Come! Kalfastoban Vental, we assume responsibility for the Slave Zuanthrol," and they handed the Vental a slip of paper upon which they had marked some curious hieroglyphics.

Then, with swords drawn, they motioned Komodoflorensal and Tarzan to precede them along the corridor, for the story of Tarzan's handling of Caraftap had reached even to the guard room of the quarry, and these warriors were taking no chances.

The way led through a straight corridor and up a winding spiral runway to the surface, where Tarzan greeted the sunlight and the fresh air almost with a sob of gratitude, for to be shut away from them for even a brief day was to the ape-man cruel punishment, indeed. Here he saw again the vast, endless multitude of slaves bearing their heavy burdens to and fro, the trim warriors who paced haughtily upon either flank of the long lines of toiling serfs, the richly trapped nobles of the higher castes and the innumerable white-tunicked slaves who darted hither and thither upon the errands of their masters, or upon their own business or pleasure, for many of these had a certain freedom and independence that gave them almost the standing of freemen. Always were these slaves of the white tunic owned by a master, but, especially in the case of skilled artisans, about the only allegiance they owed to this master was to pay to him a certain percentage of their incomes. They constituted the bourgeoisie of Minuni and also the higher caste serving class. Unlike the green-tunicked slaves, no guard was placed over them to prevent their escape, since there was no danger that they would attempt to escape, there being no city in Minuni where their estate would be improved, for any other city than that of their birth would treat them as alien prisoners, reducing them immediately to the green tunic and lifelong hard labor.

The domes of Veltopismakus were as imposing as those of Trohanadalmakus. In fact, to Tarzan, they appeared infinitely larger since he now was one-fourth the size he had been when he had left Trohanadalmakus. There were eight of them fully occupied and another in course of construction, for the surface population of Veltopismakus was already four hundred and eighty thousand souls, and as overcrowding was not permitted in the king's dome the remaining seven were packed densely with humanity.

It was to the royal dome that Tarzan and Komodoflorensal were conducted, but they did not enter by way of the King's Corridor, before the gates of which fluttered the white and gold of the royal standards. Instead they were escorted to the Warrior's Corridor, which opens toward the west. Unlike the city of Trohanadalmakus, Veltopismakus was beautiful in the areas between the domes with flowers and shrubbery and trees, among which wound graveled walks and broad roadways. The royal dome faced upon a large parade where a body of mounted warriors was at drill. There were a thousand of them, forming an amak, consisting of four novands of two hundred fifty men each, the larger body being commanded by a kamak and the smaller by a novand. Five entex of fifty men each compose a novand, there being five entals of ten men each to an entex; these latter units commanded by a Vental and a Ventex, respectively. The evolutions of the amak were performed with kaleidoscopic rapidity, so quick upon their feet and so well trained were the tiny diadets. There was one evolution in particular, performed while he was passing, that greatly interested the ape-man. Two novands formed line at one end of the parade and two at the other and at the command of the kamak the thousand men charged swiftly down the field in two solid ranks that approached one another with the speed of an express train. Just when it seemed impossible that a serious accident could be averted, when it seemed that in another instant diadets and riders must crash together in a bloody jumble of broken bones, the warriors rushing so swiftly toward the east raised their agile mounts, which fairly flew above the heads of the opposing force and alighting upon the other side in an unbroken line continued to the far end of the field.

Tarzan was commenting on this maneuver and upon the beauties of the landscaping of the city of Veltopismakus to Komodoflorensal as they proceeded along the Warrior's Corridor, sufficiently ahead of their escort that Tarzan might speak in a low tone without the guard being cognizant of the fact that he was using the language of Minuni.

"It is a beautiful evolution," replied Komodoflorensal, "and it was performed with a precision seldom attained. I have heard that Elkomoelhago's troops are famous for the perfection of their drill, and as justly so as is Veltopismakus for the beauty of her walks and gardens; but, my friend, these very things constitute the weakness of the city. While Elkomoelhago's warriors are practicing to perfect their appearance upon parade, the warriors of my father, Adendrohahkis, are far afield, out of sight of admiring women and spying slaves, practicing the art of war under the rough conditions of the field and camp. The amaks of Elkomoelhago might easily defeat those of Adendrohahkis in a contest for the most beautiful; but it was not long since you saw less than fifteen thousand Trohanadalmakusians repulse fully thirty thousand warriors of Veltopismakus, for they never passed the infantry line that day. Yet, they can drill beautifully upon parade and they are courageous, all Minunians are that, but they have not been trained in the sterner arts of war—it is not the way of Elkomoelhago. He is soft and effeminate. He cares not for war. He listens to the advice he likes best—the advice of the weaklings and the women who urge him to refrain from war entirely, which would be not altogether bad if he could persuade the other fellow to refrain, also.

"The beautiful trees and shrubs that almost make a forest of Veltopismakus, and which you so admire! I, too, admire them—especially do I admire them in the city of an enemy. How easy it would be for a

Trohanadalmakusian army to creep through the night, hidden by the beautiful trees and shrubs, to the very gateways of the domes of Veltopismakus! Do you understand now, my friend, why you saw less perfect maneuvers upon the parade grounds of my city than you have seen here, and why, though we love trees and shrubbery, we have none planted within the city of Trohanadalmakus?"

One of the guards who had approached him quickly from the rear touched Komodoflorensal upon the shoulder. "You said that Zuanthrol does not understand our language. Why then do you speak to him in this tongue which he cannot understand," the fellow demanded.

Komodoflorensal did not know how much the warrior had overheard. If he had heard Tarzan speak in Minuni it might be difficult to persuade the fellow that The Giant did not understand the language; but he must act on the assumption that he, alone, had been overheard.

"He wishes to learn it and I am trying to teach him," replied Komodoflorensal quickly.

"Has he learned anything of it?" asked the warrior.

"No," said Komodoflorensal, "he is very stupid."

And after this they went in silence, winding up long, gentle inclines, or again scaling the primitive ladders that the Minunians use to reach the upper levels of their dome-houses between the occasional levels that are not connected by the inclined runways, which are thus frequently broken for purposes of defense, the ladders being easily withdrawn upward behind hard-pressed defenders and the advance of the enemy thus more easily checked.

The royal dome of Elkomoelhago was of vast proportions, its summit rising to an equivalent of over four hundred feet, had it been built upon a scale corresponding to the relatively larger size of ordinary mankind. Tarzan ascended until he was almost as far above ground as he had been below ground in the quarry. Where the corridors on lower levels had been crowded with humanity, those which they now traversed were almost devoid of life. Occasionally they passed a tenanted chamber, but far more generally the rooms were utilized for storage purposes, especially for food, great quantities of which, cured, dried neatly wrapped, was packed ceiling-high in many large chambers.

The decorations of the walls were less ornate and the corridors narrower, on the whole, than those at lower levels. However, they passed through many large chambers, or halls, which were gorgeously decorated, and in several of which were many people of both sexes and all ages variously occupied, either with domestic activities or with the handiwork of one art or another.

Here was a man working in silver, perhaps fashioning a bracelet of delicate filigree, or another carving beautiful arabesques upon leather. There were makers of pottery, weavers of cloth, metal-stampers, painters, makers of candles, and these appeared to predominate, for the candle was in truth life to these people.

And then, at last, they reached the highest level, far above the ground, where the rooms were much closer to daylight because of the diminished thickness of the walls near the summit of the dome, but even here were the ever-present candles. Suddenly the walls of the corridor became gorgeously decorated, the number of candles increased, and Tarzan sensed that they were approaching the quarters of a rich or powerful noble. They halted, now, before a doorway where stood a sentinel, with whom one of the warriors conducting them communicated.

"Tell Zoanthrohago Zertol that we have brought Zuanthrol and another slave who can communicate with him in a strange tongue."

The sentinel struck a heavy gong with his lance and presently, from the interior of the chamber, a man appeared to whom the sentinel repeated the warrior's message.

"Let them enter," said the newcomer, who was a white-tunicked slave; "my glorious master, Zoanthrohago Zertol, expects his slave Zuanthrol! Follow me!"

They followed him through several chambers until at last he led them into the presence of a gorgeously garbed warrior who was seated behind a large table, or desk, upon which were numerous strange instruments, large, cumbersome looking volumes, pads of heavy Minunian writing paper and the necessary implements for writing. The man looked up as they entered the room.

"It is your slave, Zuanthrol, Zertol," announced the fellow who had led them hither.

"But the other?" Prince Zoanthrohago pointed at Komodoflorensal.

"He speaks the strange language that Zuanthrol speaks, and he was brought along that you might communicate with Zuanthrol if you so wished." Zoanthrohago nodded.

He turned to Komodoflorensal. "Ask him," he ordered, "if he feels any differently since I reduced his size."

When the question was put to Tarzan by Komodoflorensal in the imaginary language with which they were supposed to communicate the ape-man shook his head, at the same time speaking a few words in English.

"He says no, illustrious prince," translated Komodoflorensal out of his imagination, "and he asks when you will restore him to his normal size and permit him to return to his own country, which is far from Minuni."

"As a Minunian he should know," replied the Zertol, "that he never will be permitted to return to his own country—Trohanadalmakus never will see him again."

"But he is not of Trohanadalmakus, nor is he a Minunian," explained Komodoflorensal. "He came to us and we did not make a slave of him, but treated him as a friend, because he is from a far country with which we have never made war."

"What country is that?" demanded Zoanthrohago.

"That we do not know, but he says that there is a great country beyond the thorns where dwell many millions as large as was he. He says that his people would not be unfriendly to ours and for this reason we should not enslave him, but treat him as a guest."

Zoanthrohago smiled. "If you believe this you must be a simple fellow, Trohanadalmakusian," he said. "We all know that there is naught beyond Minuni but impenetrable forests of thorn to the very uttermost wall of the blue dome within which we all dwell. I can well believe that the fellow is no Trohanadalmakusian, but he most certainly is a Minunian, since all creatures of whatever kind dwell in Minuni. Doubtless he is a strange form of Zertalacolol, a member of a tribe inhabiting some remote mountain fastness, which we have never previously discovered; but be that as it may, he will never—"

At this juncture the prince was interrupted by the clanging of the great gong at the outer entrance to his apartments. He paused to count the strokes and when they reached five and ceased he turned to the warriors who had conducted Tarzan and Komodoflorensal to his presence.

"Take the slaves into that chamber," he instructed, pointing to a doorway in the rear of the apartment in which he had received them. "When the king has gone I will send for them."

As they were crossing toward the doorway Zoanthrohago had indicated a warrior halted in the main entrance to the chamber. "Elkomoelhago," he announced, "Thagosto of Veltopismakus, Ruler of All Men, Master of Created Things, All-Wise, All-Courageous, All-Glorious! Down before the thagosto!"

Tarzan glanced back as he was quitting the chamber to see Zoanthrohago and the others in the room kneel and lean far back with arms raised high above their heads as Elkomoelhago entered with a guard of a dozen gorgeous warriors, and he could not but compare this ruler with the simple and dignified soldier who ruled Trohanadalmakus and who went about his city without show or pomp, and oftentimes with no other escort than a single slave; a ruler to whom no man bent his knee, yet to whom was accorded the maximum of veneration and respect.

And Elkomoelhago had seen the slaves and the warriors leave the chamber as he had entered it. He acknowledged the salutes of Zoanthrohago and his people with a curt wave of the hand and commanded them to arise.

"Who quitted the apartment as I entered?" he demanded, looking suspiciously at Zoanthrohago.

"The slave Zuanthrol and another who interprets his strange language for me," explained the Zertol.

"Have them back," commanded the thagosto; "I would speak with you concerning Zuanthrol."

Zoanthrohago instructed one of his slaves to fetch them and, in the few moments that it required, Elkomoelhago took a chair behind the desk at which his host had been sitting. When Tarzan and Komodoflorensal entered the chamber the guard who accompanied them brought them to within a few paces of the desk behind which the king sat, and here he bade them kneel and make their obeisance to the thagosto.

Familiar since childhood, was every tradition of slavery to Komodoflorensal the Trohanadalmakusian. Almost in a spirit of fatalism had he accepted the conditions of this servitude that the fortunes of war had thrust him into and so it was that, without question or hesitation, he dropped to one knee in servile salute to this alien king; but not so Tarzan of the Apes. He was thinking of Adendrohahkis. He had bent no knee to him and he did not propose to do greater honor to Elkomoelhago, whose very courtiers and slaves despised him, than he had done to the really great king of Veltopismakus.

Elkomoelhago glared at him. "The fellow is not kneeling," he whispered to Zoanthrohago, who had been leaning back so far that he had not noticed the new slave's act of disrespect.

The Zertol glanced toward Tarzan. "Down, fellow!" he cried, and then recalling that he understood no Minunian, he commanded Komodoflorensal to order him to kneel, but when the Trohanadalmakusian Zertolosto pretended to do so Tarzan but shook his head.

Elkomoelhago signaled the others to rise. "We will let it pass this time," he said, for something in the attitude of the slave told him that Zuanthrol never would kneel to him and as he was valuable because of the experiment of which he was the subject, the king preferred to swallow his pride rather than risk having the slave killed in an effort to compel him to kneel. "He is but an ignorant Zertalacolol. See that he is properly instructed before we see him again."

CHAPTER 14

The Alali women, fifty strong, sallied forth into the forest to chastise their recalcitrant males. They carried their heavy bludgeons and many-feathered pebbles, but most formidable of all was their terrific rage. Never in the memory of one of them had man dared question their authority, never had he presumed to show aught but fear of them; but now, instead of slinking away at their approach, he had dared defy them, to attack them, to slay them! But such a condition was too preposterous, too unnatural, to exist, nor would it exist much longer. Had they had speech they would have said that and a number of other things. It was looking black for the men; the women were in an ugly mood—but what else could be expected of women who were denied the power of speech?

And in this temper they came upon the men in a large clearing where the renegades had built a fire and were cooking the flesh of a number of antelope. Never had the women seen their men so sleek and trim. Always before had they appeared skinny to the verge of cadaverousness, for in the past they had never fared so well as since the day that Tarzan of the Apes had given weapons to the son of The First Woman. Where before they had spent their lives fleeing in terror from their terrible women, with scarce time to hunt for decent food, now they had leisure and peace of mind and their weapons brought them flesh that otherwise they might not have tasted once in a year. From caterpillars and grubworms they had graduated to an almost steady diet of antelope meat.

But the women gave very little heed at the moment to the physical appearance of the men. They had found them. That was enough. They were creeping nearer when one of the men looked up and discovered them, and so insistent are the demands of habit that he forgot his new-found independence and leaping to his feet, bolted for the trees. The others, scarce waiting to know the cause of his precipitancy, followed close upon his heels. The women raced across the clearing as the men disappeared among the trees upon the opposite side. The former knew what the men would do. Once in the forest they would stop behind the nearest trees and look back to see if their pursuers were coming in their direction. It was this silly habit of the males that permitted their being easily caught by the less agile females.

But all the men had not disappeared. One had taken a few steps in the mad race for safety and had then halted and wheeled about, facing the oncoming women. He was the son of The First Woman, and to him Tarzan had imparted something more than knowledge of new weapons, for from the Lord of the Jungle, whom he worshipped with doglike devotion, he had acquired the first rudiments of courage, and so it now happened that when his more timorous fellows paused behind the trees and looked back they saw this one standing alone facing the charge of fifty infuriated shes. They saw him fit arrow to bow, and the women saw, too, but they did not understand—not immediately—and then the bow string twanged and the foremost woman collapsed with an arrow in her heart; but the others did not pause, because the thing had been done so quickly that the full purport of it had not as yet penetrated their thick skulls. The son of The First Woman fitted a second arrow and sped it. Another woman fell, rolling over and over, and now the others hesitated—hesitated and were lost, for that momentary pause gave courage to the other men peering from behind the trees. If one of their number could face fifty women and bring them to halt what might not eleven men accomplish? They rushed forth then with spears and arrows just as the women renewed their assault. The feathered pebbles flew thick and fast, but faster and more accurately flew the feathered arrows of the men. The leading women rushed courageously forward to close quarters where they might use their bludgeons and lay hold of the men with their mighty hands, but they learned then that spears were more formidable weapons than bludgeons, with the result that those who did not fall wounded, turned and fled.

It was then that the son of The First Woman revealed possession of a spark of generalship that decided the issue for that day, and, perhaps, for all time. His action was epochal in the existence of the Zertalacolols. Instead of being satisfied with repulsing the women, instead of resting upon laurels gloriously won, he turned the tables upon the hereditary foe and charged the women, signaling his fellows to accompany him, and when they saw the women running from them, so enthused were they by this reversal of a custom ages old, they leaped swiftly in pursuit.

They thought that the son of The First Woman intended that they should slay all of the enemy and so they were surprised when they saw him overhaul a comely, young female and, seizing her by the hair, disarm her. So remarkable did it seem to them that one of their number, having a woman in his power, did not immediately slay her, they were constrained to pause and gather around him, asking questions in their strange sign language.

"Why do you hold her?" "Why do you not kill her?" "Are you not afraid that she will kill you?" were some of the many that were launched at him.

"I am going to keep her," replied the son of The First Woman. "I do not like to cook. She shall cook for me. If she refuses I shall stick her with this," and he made a jab toward the young woman's ribs with his spear, a gesture that caused her to cower and drop fearfully upon one knee.

The men jumped up and down in excitement as the value of this plan and the evident terror of the woman for the man sank into their dull souls.

"Where are the women?" they signed to one another; but the women had disappeared.

One of the men started off in the direction they had gone. "I go!" he signaled. "I come back with a woman of my own, to cook for me!" In a mad rush the others followed him, leaving the son of The First Woman alone with his she. He turned upon her.

"You will cook for me?" he demanded.

To his signs she but returned a sullen, snarling visage. The son of The First Woman raised his spear and with the heavy shaft struck the girl upon the head, knocking her down, and he stood over her, himself snarling and scowling, menacing her with further punishment, while she cowered where she had fallen. He kicked her in the side.

"Get up!" he commanded.

Slowly she crawled to her knees and embracing his legs gazed up into his face with an expression of doglike adulation and devotion.

"You will cook for me!" he demanded again.

"Forever!" she replied in the sign language of their people.

*

Tarzan had remained but a short time in the little room adjoining that in which Zoanthrohago had received Elkomoelhago, when he was summoned to appear before them alone, and as he entered the room his master motioned him to approach the desk behind which the two men sat. There was no other person in the room, even the warriors having been dismissed.

"You are quite positive that he understands nothing of our language?" demanded the king.

"He has not spoken a word since he was captured," replied Zoanthrohago. "We had supposed him some new form of Zertalacolol until it was discovered that he possessed a language through which he was able to communicate with the other Trohanadalmakusian slave. It is perfectly safe to speak freely before him, All-Wise."

Elkomoelhago cast a quick, suspicious glance at his companion. He would have preferred that Zoanthrohago of all men address him as All-Glorious—it was less definite in its implication. He might deceive others, even himself, as to his wisdom, but he was perfectly aware that he could not fool Zoanthrohago.

"We have never discussed fully," said the king, "the details of this experiment. It was for this purpose that I came to the laboratory today. Now that we have the subject here let us go into the matter fully and determine what next step we should take."

"Yes, All-Wise," replied Zoanthrohago.

"Call me Thagosto," snapped Elkomoelhago.

"Yes, Thagosto," said the prince, using the Minunian word for Chief-Royal, or King, as Elkomoelhago had commanded. "Let us discuss the matter, by all means. It presents possibilities of great importance to your throne." He knew that what Elkomoelhago meant by discussing the matter consisted only in receiving from Zoanthrohago a detailed explanation of how he had reduced the stature of the slave Zuanthrol to one quarter its original proportions; but he proposed, if possible, to obtain value received for the information, which he knew the king would use for his own aggrandizement, giving Zoanthrohago no credit whatever for his discoveries or all the long moons he had devoted to accomplishing this marvelous, scientific miracle.

"Before we enter into this discussion, O, Thagosto," he said, "I beg that you will grant me one boon, which I have long desired and have hitherto hesitated to request, knowing that I did not deserve the recognition I crave for my poor talents and my mean service to thy illustrious and justly renowned rule."

"What boon do you wish?" demanded Elkomoelhago, crustily. At heart he feared this wisest of men, and, like the coward that he was, with him to fear was to hate. If he could have destroyed Zoanthrohago he would gladly have done so; but he could not afford to do this, since from this greatest of walmaks came whatever show of scientific ability the king could make, as well as all the many notable inventions for the safeguarding of the royal person.

"I would sit at the royal council," said Zoanthrohago, simply.

The king fidgeted. Of all the nobles of Veltopismakus here was the very last he would wish to see numbered among the royal councilors, whom he had chosen with especial reference to the obtuseness of their minds.

"There are no vacancies," he said, at last.

"The ruler of all men might easily make a vacancy," suggested Zoanthrohago, "or create a new post—Assistant Chief of Chiefs, for example, so that when Gofoloso was absent there would be one to take his place. Otherwise I should not have to attend upon your council meetings, but devote my time to the perfection of our discoveries and inventions."

Here was a way out and Elkomoelhago seized it. He had no objection to Zoanthrohago being a royal councilor and thus escaping the burdensome income tax, which the makers of the tax had been careful to see proved no burden to themselves, and he knew that probably that was the only reason that Zoanthrohago

1080

wished to be a councilor. No, the king had no objection to the appointment provided it could be arranged that the new minister was present at no council meetings, for even Elkomoelhago would have shrunk a bit from claiming as his own all the great discoveries of Zoanthrohago had Zoanthrohago been present.

"Very well," said the king, "you shall be appointed this very day—and when I want you at the council meetings I will send for you."

Zoanthrohago bowed. "And now," he said, "to the discussion of our experiments, which we hope will reveal a method for increasing the stature of our warriors when they go forth to battle with our enemies, and of reducing them to normal size once more when they return."

"I hate the mention of battles," cried the king, with a shudder.

"But we must be prepared to win them when they are forced upon us," suggested Zoanthrohago.

"I suppose so," assented the king; "but once we perfect this method of ours we shall need but a few warriors and the rest may be turned to peaceful and useful occupations. However, go on with the discussion."

Zoanthrohago concealed a smile, and rising, walked around the end of the table and stopped beside the ape-man. "Here," he said, placing a finger at the base of Tarzan's skull, "there lies, as you know, a small, oval, reddish gray body containing a liquid which influences the growth of tissues and organs. It long ago occurred to me that interference with the normal functioning of this gland would alter the growth of the subject to which it belonged. I experimented with small rodents and achieved remarkable results; but the thing I wished to accomplish, the increase of man's stature I have been unable to achieve. I have tried many methods and some day I shall discover the right one. I think I am on the right track, and that it is merely now a matter of experimentation. You know that stroking your face lightly with a smooth bit of stone produces a pleasurable sensation. Apply the same stone to the same face in the same manner, but with greatly increased force and you produce a diametrically opposite sensation. Rub the stone slowly across the face and back again many times, and then repeat the same motion rapidly for the same number of times and you will discover that the results are quite different. I am that close to a solution; I have the correct method but not quite, as yet, the correct application. I can reduce creatures in size, but I cannot enlarge them; and although I can reduce them with great ease, I cannot determine the period or endurance of their reduction. In some cases, subjects have not regained their normal size under thirty-nine moons, and in others, they have done so in as short a period as three moons. There have been cases where normal stature was regained gradually during a period of seven suns, and others where the subject passed suddenly from a reduced size to normal size in less than a hundred heartbeats; this latter phenomenon being always accompanied by fainting and unconsciousness when it occurred during waking hours."

"Of course," commented Elkomoelhago. "Now, let us see. I believe the thing is simpler than you imagine. You say that to reduce the size of this subject you struck him with a rock upon the base of the skull. Therefore, to enlarge his size, the most natural and scientific thing to do would be to strike him a similar blow upon the forehead. Fetch the rock and we will prove the correctness of my theory."

For a moment Zoanthrohago was at a loss as to how best to circumvent the stupid intention of the king without humiliating his pride and arousing his resentment; but the courtiers of Elkomoelhago were accustomed to think quickly in similar emergencies and Zoanthrohago speedily found an avenue of escape from his dilemma.

"You sagacity is the pride of your people, Thagosto," he said, "and your brilliant hyperbole the despair of your courtiers. In a clever figure of speech you suggest the way to achievement. By reversing the manner in which we reduced the stature of Zuanthrol we should be able to increase it; but, alas, I have tried this and failed. But wait, let us repeat the experiment precisely as it was originally carried out and then, by reversing it, we shall, perhaps, be enabled to determine why I have failed in the past."

He stepped quickly across the room to one of a series of large cupboards that lined the wall and opening the door of it revealed a cage in which were a number of rodents. Selecting one of these he returned to the table, where, with wooden pegs and bits of cord he fastened the rodent securely to a smooth board, its legs spread out and its body flattened, the under side of the lower jaw resting firmly upon a small metal plate set flush with the surface of the board. He then brought forth a small wooden box and a large metal disc, the latter mounted vertically between supports that permitted it to be revolved rapidly by means of a hand crank. Mounted rigidly upon the same axis as the revolving disc was another which remained stationary. The latter disc appeared to have been constructed of seven segments, each of a different material from all the others, and from each of these segments a pad, or brush, protruded sufficiently to press lightly against the revolving disc.

To the reverse side of each of the seven segments of the stationary disc a wire was attached, and these wires Zoanthrohago now connected to seven posts projecting from the upper surface of the wooden box. A single wire attached to a post upon the side of the box had at its other extremity a small, curved metal plate attached to the inside of a leather collar. This collar Zoanthrohago adjusted about the neck of the rodent so that the metal plate came in contact with its skin at the base of the skull and as close to the hypophysis gland as possible.

He then turned his attention once more to the wooden box, upon the top of which, in addition to the seven binding posts, was a circular instrument consisting of a dial about the periphery of which were a series of hieroglyphics. From the center of this dial projected seven tubular, concentric shafts, each of which supported a needle, which was shaped or painted in some distinguishing manner, while beneath the dial seven small metal discs were set in the cover of the box so that they lay in the arc of a circle from the center of which a revolving metal shaft was so arranged that its free end might be moved to any of the seven metal discs at the will of the operator.

The connections having all been made, Zoanthrohago moved the free end of the shaft from one of the metal discs to another, keeping his eyes at all times intently upon the dial, the seven needles of which moved variously as he shifted the shaft from point to point.

Elkomoelhago was an intent, if somewhat bewildered, observer, and the slave, Zuanthrol, unobserved, had moved nearer the table that he might better watch this experiment which might mean so much to him.

Zoanthrohago continued to manipulate the revolving shaft and the needles moved hither and thither from one series of hieroglyphics to another, until at last the walmak appeared satisfied.

"It is not always easy," he said, "to attune the instrument to the frequency of the organ upon which we are working. From all matter and even from such incorporeal a thing as thought there emanate identical particles, so infinitesimal as to be scarce noted by the most delicate of my instruments. These particles constitute the basic structure of all things whether animate or inanimate, corporeal or incorporeal. The frequency, quantity and rhythm of the emanations determine the nature of the substance. Having located upon this dial the coefficient of the gland under discussion it now becomes necessary, in order to so interfere with its proper functioning that the growth of the creature involved will be not only stopped but actually reversed, that we decrease the frequency, increase the quantity and compound the rhythm of these emanations. This I shall now proceed to do," and he forthwith manipulated several small buttons upon one side of the box, and grasping the crank handle of the free disc revolved it rapidly.

The result was instantaneous and startling. Before their eyes Elkomoelhago, the king, and Zuanthrol, the slave, saw the rodent shrink rapidly in size, while retaining its proportions unchanged. Tarzan, who had followed every move and every word of the walmak, leaned far over that he might impress indelibly upon his memory the position of the seven needles. Elkomoelhago glanced up and discovered his interest.

"We do not need this fellow now," he said, addressing Zoanthrohago. "Have him sent away."

"Yes, Thagosto," replied Zoanthrohago, summoning a warrior whom he directed to remove Tarzan and Komodoflorensal to a chamber where they could be secured until their presence was again required.

CHAPTER 15

Through several chambers and corridors they were conducted toward the center of the dome on the same level as the chamber in which they had left the king and the walmak until finally they were thrust into a small chamber and a heavy door was slammed and barred behind them.

There was no candle in the chamber. A faint light, however, relieved the darkness so that the interior of the room was discernible. The chamber contained two benches and a table—that was all. The light which faintly illuminated it entered through a narrow embrasure which was heavily barred, but it was evidently daylight.

"We are alone," whispered Komodoflorensal, "and at last we can converse; but we must be cautious," he added. "'Trust not too far the loyalty of even the stones of your chamber!'" he quoted.

"Where are we?" asked Tarzan. "You are more familiar with Minunian dwellings than I."

"We are upon the highest level of the Royal Dome of Elkomoelhago," replied the prince. "With no such informality does a king visit the other domes of his city. You may rest assured that this is Elkomoelhago's. We are in one of the innermost chambers, next the central shaft that pierces the dome from its lowest level to its roof. For this reason we do not need a candle to support life—we will obtain sufficient air through this embrasure. And now, tell me what happened within the room with Elkomoelhago and Zoanthrohago."

"I discovered how they reduced my stature," replied Tarzan, "and, furthermore, that at almost any time I may regain my full size—an occurrence that may eventuate from three to thirty-nine moons after the date of my reduction. Even Zoanthrohago cannot determine when this thing will happen."

"Let us hope that it does not occur while you are in this small chamber," exclaimed Komodoflorensal.

"I would have a devil of a time getting out," agreed Tarzan.

"You would never get out," his friend assured him. "While you might, before your reduction, have crawled through some of the larger corridors upon the first level, or even upon many of the lower levels, you could not squeeze into the smaller corridors of the upper levels, which are reduced in size as the necessity for direct supports for the roof increase as we approach the apex of the dome."

"Then it behooves me to get out of here as quickly as possible," said Tarzan.

Komodoflorensal shook his head. "Hope is a beautiful thing, my friend," he said, "but if you were a Minunian you would know that under such circumstances as we find ourselves it is a waste of mental energy. Look at these bars," and he walked to the window and shook the heavy irons that spanned the embrasure. "Think you that you could negotiate these?"

"I haven't examined them," replied the ape-man, "but I shall never give up hope of escaping; that your people do is doubtless the principal reason that they remain forever in bondage. You are too much a fatalist, Komodoflorensal."

As he spoke Tarzan crossed the room and standing at the prince's side took hold of the bars at the window. "They do not seem overheavy," he remarked, and at the same time exerted pressure upon them. They bent! Tarzan was interested now and Komodoflorensal, as well. The ape-man threw all his strength and weight into the succeeding effort with the result that two bars, bent almost double, were torn from their setting.

Komodoflorensal gazed at him in astonishment. "Zoanthrohago reduced your size, but left you with your former physical prowess," he cried.

"In no other way can it be accounted for," replied Tarzan, who now, one by one, was removing the remaining bars from the window embrasure. He straightened one of the shorter ones and handed it to Komodoflorensal. "This will make a good weapon," he said, "if we are forced to fight for our liberty," and then he straightened another for himself.

The Trohanadalmakusian gazed at him in wonder. "And you intend," he demanded, "to defy a city of four hundred and eighty thousand people, armed only with a bit of iron rod?"

"And my wits," added Tarzan.

"You will need them," said the prince.

"And I shall use them," Tarzan assured him.

"When shall you start?" asked Komodoflorensal, chaffingly.

"Tonight, tomorrow, next moon—who knows?" replied the ape-man. "Conditions must be ripe. All the time I shall be watching and planning. In that sense I started to escape the instant I regained consciousness and knew that I was a prisoner."

Komodoflorensal shook his head.

"You have no faith in me?" demanded Tarzan.

"That is precisely what I have—faith," replied Komodoflorensal. "My judgment tells me that you cannot succeed and yet I shall cast my lot with you, hoping for success, yes, believing in success. If that is not faith I do not know what it might be called."

The ape-man smiled. He seldom, if ever, laughed aloud. "Let us commence," he said. "First we will arrange these rods so that they will have the appearance, from the doorway, of not having been disturbed, for I take it we shall have an occasional visitor. Some one will bring us food, at least, and whoever comes must suspect nothing."

Together they arranged the rods so that they might be quickly removed and as quickly replaced. By that time it was getting quite dark within the chamber. Shortly after they had finished with the rods their door opened and two warriors, lighting their way with candles, appeared escorting a slave who bore food in bucket-like receptacles and water in bottles made of glazed pottery.

As they were going away again, after depositing the food and drink just inside the doorway, taking their candles with them, Komodoflorensal addressed them.

"We are without candles, warrior," he said to the nearer. "Will you not leave us one of yours?"

"You need no candle in this chamber," replied the man. "One night in darkness will do you good, and tomorrow you return to the quarry. Zoanthrohago is done with you. In the quarry you will have plenty of candles," and he passed out of the chamber, closing the door behind him.

The two slaves heard the heavy bolt shot into place upon the opposite side of the door. It was very dark now. With difficulty they found the receptacles containing the food and water.

"Well?" inquired Komodoflorensal, dipping into one of the food jars. "Do you think it is going to be so easy now, when tomorrow you will be back in the quarry, perhaps five hundred huals below ground?"

"But I shall not be," replied Tarzan, "and neither shall you."

"Why not?" asked the prince.

"Because, since they expect to remove us to the quarries tomorrow, it follows that we must escape tonight," explained Tarzan.

Komodoflorensal only laughed.

When Tarzan had eaten his fill he arose and walked to the window, where he removed the bars and, taking the one that he had selected for himself, crawled through the passage that led to the opposite end of the embrasure, for even so close to the apex of the dome the wall was quite thick, perhaps ten huals. The hual, which is about three inches in length by our standards, constitutes the Minunian basic unit of measure, corresponding most closely to our foot. At this high level the embrasure was much smaller than those opening at lower levels, practically all of which were of sufficient size to permit a warrior to walk erect within them; but here Tarzan was forced to crawl upon all fours.

At the far end he found himself looking out into a black void above which the stars were shining and about the sides of which were dotted vague reflections of inner lights, marking the lighted chambers within the dome. Above him it was but a short distance to the apex of the dome, below was a sheer drop of four hundred huals.

Tarzan, having seen all that could be seen from the mouth of the embrasure, returned to the chamber. "How far is it, Komodoflorensal," he asked, "from the floor of this embrasure to the roof of the dome?"

"Twelve huals, perhaps," replied the Trohanadalmakusian.

Tarzan took the longest of the bars from the embrasure and measured it as best he could. "Too far," he said.

"What is too far?" demanded Komodoflorensal.

"The roof," explained Tarzan.

"What difference does it make where the roof is—you did not expect to escape by way of the roof of the dome, did you?"

"Most certainly—had it been accessible," replied the ape-man; "but now we shall have to go by way of the shaft, which will mean crossing entirely through the dome from the interior shaft to the outer periphery. The other route would have entailed less danger of detection."

Komodoflorensal laughed aloud. "You seem to think that to escape a Minunian city it is only necessary to walk out and away. It cannot be done. What of the sentries? What of the outer patrols? You would be discovered before you were halfway down the outside of the dome, provided that you could get that far without falling to your death."

"Then perhaps the shaft would be safer," said Tarzan. "There would be less likelihood of discovery before we reached the bottom, for from what I could see it is as dark as pitch in the shaft."

"Clamber down the inside of the shaft!" exclaimed Komodoflorensal. "You are mad! You could not clamber from this level to the next without falling, and it must be a full four hundred huals to the bottom."

"Wait!" Tarzan admonished him.

Komodoflorensal could hear his companion moving around in the dark chamber. He heard the scraping of metal on stone and presently he heard a pounding, not loud, yet heavy.

"What are you doing?" he asked.

"Wait!" said Tarzan.

And Komodoflorensal waited, wondering. It was Tarzan who spoke next.

"Could you find the chamber in which Talaskar is confined in the quarry?" he asked.

"Why?" demanded the prince.

"We are going after her," explained Tarzan. "We promised that we would not leave without her."

"I can find it," said Komodoflorensal, rather sullenly Tarzan thought.

For some time the ape-man worked on in silence, except for the muffled pounding and the scraping of iron on stone, or of iron on iron.

"Do you know every one in Trohanadalmakus?" Tarzan asked, suddenly.

"Why, no," replied Komodoflorensal. "There are a million souls, including all the slaves. I could not know them all."

"Did you know by sight all those that dwelt in the royal dome?" continued the ape-man.

"No, not even those who lived in the royal dome," replied the Trohanadalmakusian; "though doubtless I knew practically all of the nobles, and the warrior class by sight if not by name."

"Did any one?" asked Tarzan,

"I doubt it," was the reply.

"Good!" exclaimed Tarzan.

Again there was a silence, broken again by the Englishman.

"Can a warrior go anywhere without question in any dome of his own city?" he inquired.

"Anywhere, under ordinary circumstances, except into the king's dome, in daytime."

"One could not go about at night, then?" asked Tarzan.

"No," replied his companion.

"By day, might a warrior go and come in the quarries as he pleased?"

"If he appeared to be employed he would not be questioned, ordinarily."

Tarzan worked a little longer in silence. "Come!" he said presently; "we are ready to go."

"I shall go with you," said Komodoflorensal, "because I like you and because I think it would be better to be dead than a slave. At least we shall have some pleasure out of what remains to us of life, even though it be not a long life."

"I think we shall have some pleasure, my friend," replied Zuanthrol. "We may not escape; but, like you, I should rather die now than remain a slave for life. I have chosen tonight for our first step toward freedom, because I realize that once returned to the quarry our chances for a successful break for liberty will be reduced to almost nothing, and tonight is our only night above ground."

"How do you propose that we escape from this chamber?"

"By way of the central shaft," replied Tarzan; "but first tell me, may a white-tunicked slave enter the quarries freely by day?"

Komodoflorensal wondered what bearing all these seemingly immaterial questions had upon the problem of their escape; but he answered patiently:

"No, white tunics are never seen in the quarries."

"Have you the iron bar I straightened for you?"

"Yes."

"Then follow me through the embrasure. Bring the other rods that I shall leave in the opening. I will carry the bulk of them. Come!"

Komodoflorensal heard Tarzan crawling into the embrasure, the iron rods that he carried breaking the silence of the little chamber. Then he followed. In the mouth of the embrasure he found the rods that Tarzan had left for him to carry. There were four rods, the ends of each bent into hooks. It had been upon this work that Tarzan had been engaged in the darkness—Komodoflorensal wondered to what purpose. Presently his further advance was halted by Tarzan's body.

"Just a moment," said the ape-man. "I am making a hole in the window ledge. When that is done we shall be ready." A moment later he turned his head back toward his companion. "Pass along the rods," he said.

After Komodoflorensal had handed the hooked rods to Tarzan he heard the latter working with them, very quietly, for several minutes, and then he heard him moving his body about in the narrow confines of the embrasure and presently when the ape-man spoke again the Trohanadalmakusian realized that he had turned around and that his head was close to that of his companion.

"I shall go first, Komodoflorensal," he said. "Come to the edge of the embrasure and when you hear me whistle once, follow me."

"Where?" asked the prince.

"Down the shaft to the first embrasure that will give us foot-hold, and let us pray that there is one directly below this within the next eighteen huals. I have hooked the rods together, the upper end hooked into the hole I made in the ledge, the lower end dangling down a distance of eighteen huals."

"Good-bye, my friend," said Komodoflorensal.

Tarzan smiled and slipped over the edge of the embrasure. In one hand he carried the rod that he had retained as a weapon, with the other he clung to the window ledge. Below him for eighteen huals dangled the slender ladder of iron hooks, and below this, four hundred huals of pitchy darkness hid the stone flagging of the inner courtyard. Perhaps it roofed the great central throne room of the king, as was true in the royal dome of Adendrohahkis; perhaps it was but an open court. The truth was immaterial if the frail support slipped from the shallow hole in the ledge above, or if one of the hooks straightened under the weight of the ape-man.

Now he grasped the upper section of his ladder with the hand that held his improvised weapon, removed the hand from the ledge and grasped the rod again, still lower down. In this way he lowered his body a few inches at a time. He moved very slowly for two reasons, the more important of which was that he feared that any sudden strains upon his series of hooks might straighten one of them and precipitate him into the abyss below; the other was the necessity for silence. It was very dark even this close to the summit of the dome, but that was rather an advantage than otherwise, for it hid his presence from any chance observer who might glance through one of the embrasures in the opposite wall of the shaft. As he descended he felt in both directions for an embrasure, but he was almost at the end of his ladder before he felt himself swing slightly into one. When he had lowered himself still farther and could look into the opening he saw that it was dark, an indication that it did not lead into an inhabited chamber, a fact for which he was thankful. He hoped, too, that the inner end of the embrasure was not barred, nor the door beyond bolted upon the outside.

He whistled once, very low, for Komodoflorensal, and an instant later he felt the movement of the iron ladder that told him his companion had commenced the descent. The embrasure in which he stood was higher than the one they had just quitted, permitting him to stand erect. There he waited for the Trohanadalmakusian who was soon standing upon the ledge beside him.

"Phew!" exclaimed the prince, in a whisper. "I should hate to have had to do that in the daytime when I could have seen all the way to the bottom. What next? We have come farther already than ever I dreamed would be possible. Now I am commencing to believe that escape may lie within the realm of possibilities."

"We haven't started yet," Tarzan assured him; "but we are going to now. Come!"

Grasping their rude weapons the two walked stealthily the length of the embrasure. There were no bars to impede their progress and they stepped to the floor of the chamber beyond. Very carefully, feeling each step before he planted a foot and with his weapon extended before him, Tarzan groped his way about the chamber, which he found was fairly well filled with casks and bottles, the latter in wooden and wicker cases. Komodoflorensal was directly behind him.

"We are in one of the rooms where the nobles charged with enforcing the laws against wine have hidden confiscated liquor," whispered the Trohanadalmakusian. "I have heard much talk concerning the matter since I was made prisoner—the warriors and the slaves, too, seem to talk of nothing else but this and the high taxes. The chances are that the door is heavily barred—they guard these forbidden beverages as never they guarded their gold or jewels."

"I have found the passageway leading to the door," whispered Tarzan, "and I can see a light beneath it."

They crept stealthily the length of the passage. Each grasped his weapon more firmly as Tarzan gently tried the latch. It gave! Slowly the ape-man pushed the door ajar. Through the tiny aperture thus opened he could see a portion of the room. Its floor was strewn with gorgeous carpets, thick and soft. That portion of the wall that was revealed to him was hung with heavy fabrics woven in many colors and strange patterns—splendid, barbaric. Directly in the line of his vision the body of a man lay sprawled, face down, upon the floor—a pool of red stained a white rug beneath his head.

Tarzan opened the door a little farther, revealing the bodies of three other men. Two lay upon the floor, the third upon a low divan. The scene, gorgeous in its coloring, tragic in its suggestion of mystery and violent death, held the eyes of the ape-man yet a moment longer before he opened the door still wider and leaped quickly to the center of the room, his weapon raised and ready, giving no possible skulking foe behind the door the opportunity to fell him that would have offered had he edged into the room slowly.

A quick glance about the apartment showed the bodies of six men that had not been visible from the partially opened door. These were lying in a pile in one corner of the room.

CHAPTER 16

Komodoflorensal stood at Tarzan's side, his weapon ready to take issue with any who might question their presence here; but presently the end of his iron rod dropped to the floor and a broad smile overspread his features.

Tarzan looked at him. "Who are they?" he demanded, "and why have they been killed?"

"They are not dead, my friend," replied Komodoflorensal. "They are the nobles whose duty it is to prevent the use of wine. They are not dead—they are drunk."

"But the blood beneath the head of this one at my feet!" demanded the ape-man.

"It is red wine, not blood," his companion assured him. Then Tarzan smiled.

"They could not have chosen a better night for their orgy," he said. "Had they remained sober the door through which we entered from the storeroom would have been securely fastened, I imagine."

"Assuredly, and we would have had a sober guard of warriors to deal with in this chamber, instead of ten drunken nobles. We are very fortunate, Zuanthrol."

He had scarcely ceased speaking when a door in the opposite side of the room swung open, revealing two warriors, who stepped immediately into the chamber. They eyed the two who faced them and then glanced about the room at the inert forms of its other occupants.

"What do you here, slaves?" demanded one of the newcomers.

"Sh-sh-sh!" cautioned Tarzan, placing a finger to his lips. "Enter and close the door, lest others hear."

"There is no one near to hear," snapped one of them, but they entered and he closed the door. "What is the meaning of this?"

"That you are our prisoners," cried the ape-man, leaping past them and placing himself before the door, his iron rod in readiness.

A sneer twisted the mouth of each of the two Veltopismakusians as they whipped out their rapiers and leaped toward the ape-man, ignoring for the moment the Trohanadalmakusian, who, seizing upon the opportunity thus afforded him, threw aside his iron rod and snatched a rapier from the side of one of the drunken nobles—a substitution of weapons that would render Komodoflorensal a dangerous opponent anywhere in Minuni, for there was no better swordsman among all the warlike clans of Trohanadalmakus, whose blades were famed throughout Minuni.

Facing, with only an iron rod, two skilled swordsmen placed Tarzan of the Apes at a disadvantage that might have proved his undoing had it not been for the presence of Komodoflorensal, who, no sooner than he had appropriated a weapon, leaped forward and engaged one of the warriors. The other pressed Tarzan fiercely.

"Your prisoner, eh, slave?" he sneered as he lunged for his opponent; but though less skilled, perhaps, in swordplay than his antagonist, the Lord of the Jungle had not faced Bolgani and Numa for nothing. His movements were as lightning, his strength as great as before Zoanthrohago had reduced his stature. At the first onslaught of the warriors he had leaped to one side to avoid the thrust of a blade, and as much to his own astonishment as to theirs, what he had intended for a nimble sidestep had carried him the length of the room, and then the man had been at him again, while the other was having his time well occupied with the Zertolosto of Trohanadalmakus.

Twice Tarzan parried cuts with his cumbersome bar and then a thrust but missed him by a hairsbreadth, his sidestep coming but in the nick of time. It was a close call, for the man had lunged at his abdomen—a close call for Tarzan and death for his opponent, for as the point slipped harmlessly by him the ape-man swung his rod upon the unguarded head of the Veltopismakusian, and with a grunt the fellow slumped to the floor, his skull crushed to the bridge of his nose.

Then Tarzan turned to aid Komodoflorensal, but the son of Adendrohahkis needed no aid. He had his man against the wall and was running him through the heart as Tarzan turned in their direction. As the man fell, Komodoflorensal swung toward the center of the room and as his eye fell upon the ape-man a smile crossed his face.

"With an iron bar you bested a swordsman of Minuni!" he cried. "I would not have believed it possible and so I hastened to dispatch my man that I might come to your rescue before it was too late."

Tarzan laughed. "I had the same thought in mind concerning you," he said.

"And you could have well held it had I not been able to secure this rapier," Komodoflorensal assured him. "But what now? We have again come much farther than it seems possible we can have. Naught will surprise me hereafter."

"We are going to trade apparel with these two unfortunate gentlemen," said Tarzan, divesting himself of the green tunic as he spoke.

Komodoflorensal chuckled as he followed the example of his companion.

"There are other peoples as great as the Minunians," he declared, "though until I met you, my friend, I should never have believed it."

A few moments later the two stood garbed in the habiliments of Veltopismakusian warriors and Tarzan was slipping his green tunic upon the corpse of him whom he had slain.

"But why are you doing that?" asked the prince.

"Do likewise with yours and you will see, presently," Tarzan replied.

Komodoflorensal did as the other bid him and when the change had been completed the ape-man threw one of the corpses across his shoulder and carried it into the storeroom, followed closely by Komodoflorensal with the other. Walking through the window embrasure to the edge of the shaft Tarzan hurled his burden out into space, and reaching back took Komodoflorensal's from him and pitched it after the first.

"If they do not examine them too closely," he said, "the ruse may serve to convince them that we died attempting to escape." As he spoke he detached two of the hooks from the ladder down which they had clambered from the window of their dungeon and dropped them after the corpses. "These will lend color to the suggestion," he added, in explanation.

Together they returned to the room where the drunken nobles lay, where Komodoflorensal began to rifle the fat money pouches of the unconscious men.

"We shall need all of this that we can get if we are to pose as Veltopismakusian warriors for any length of time," he said. "I know these people by reputation and that gold will buy many of the things that we may require—the blindness of guards and the complaisance of officials, if they do not guess too close to the truth concerning us."

"That part of it you must attend to, Komodoflorensal," said Tarzan, "for I am unfamiliar with the ways of your people; but we may not remain here. These gentlemen have served us well, and themselves, too, for their faithlessness and debauchery saved their lives, while the two who followed in sobriety the path of duty were destroyed."

"Matters are strangely ordered," commented Komodoflorensal.

"In Minuni as elsewhere," agreed Tarzan, leading the way to the door of the chamber which they found opened into a corridor instead of into another chamber as they had rather expected would be the fact at a point thus close to the central shaft.

In silence they proceeded along the passageway, which, at this hour of the morning, was deserted. They passed lighted chambers, where men and women were sleeping peacefully in the glare of many candles. They saw a sentry asleep before the door of a noble's quarters. No one discovered them and thus they passed down a series of inclined runways and along interminable corridors until they were far from that portion of the royal dome in which they had been incarcerated and where it would be most natural for the search for them to commence in the event that the bodies they had hurled into the shaft were not immediately discovered, or were identified for what they really were, rather than for what the two fugitives had tried to make them appear.

And now a white-tunicked slave was approaching them along the corridor. He passed without paying them any heed, and presently another and another appeared until the two realized that morning was approaching and the corridors would soon be filled with the inhabitants of the dome.

"It will be best," said Komodoflorensal, "to find a hiding place until there are more people abroad. We shall be safer in a crowd than among just a few where we shall be the more noticeable."

Nearly all the chambers they passed now were occupied by families, while those that were untenanted were without candles and therefore unsafe as hiding places for any length of time; but presently Komodoflorensal touched Tarzan's arm and pointed to a hieroglyphic beside a door they were approaching.

"Just the place," he said.

"What is it?" asked Tarzan, and as they came opposite the open door; "Why, it is filled with men! When they awake we shall be discovered."

"But not recognized," returned the Trohanadalmakusian; "or at least the chances are slight that we shall be. This is a common chamber where any man may purchase lodgings over night. Doubtless there are visitors from other domes and strangers will not be particularly remarked on this account."

He entered the room, followed by Tarzan. A white-tunicked slave approached them. "Candles for two," demanded Komodoflorensal, handing the slave one of the smaller golden coins he had filched from the sleeping nobles.

The fellow led them to a far corner of the room where there was plenty of space upon the floor, lit two candles and left them. A moment later they were stretched at full length, their faces toward the wall as a further protection against recognition, and were soon asleep.

When Tarzan awoke he saw that he and Komodoflorensal were the only remaining occupants of the chamber, other than the slave who had admitted them, and he awoke his companion, believing that they should do nothing that might even in a slight degree call more than ordinary attention to them. A bucket of water was brought them and they performed their ablutions at a gutter which encircled the chamber, passing along the foot of each wall, as was the custom throughout Minuni, the waste water being carried away in pipes to the fields beyond the cities, where it was used for irrigating the crops. As all the water had to be carried into the domes and to the different levels in buckets, the amount used for ablutions was reduced to the minimum, the warrior and noble class getting the bulk of it, while the white-tunicked slaves depended principally upon the rivers, near which domes are always erected, for their baths. The green slaves fare the worst, and suffer a real hardship through lack of bathing facilities, for the Minunians are a cleanly people; but they manage to alleviate their plight to some extent, where the quarry masters are more kindly disposed, by the use of stagnant seepage water that accumulates in every quarry at the lower levels and which, not being fit for drinking purposes, may be used by the slaves for bathing when they are permitted the time to obtain it.

Having washed, Tarzan and Komodoflorensal passed out into the corridor, a broad thoroughfare of the dome city, where there were now passing two solid lines of humanity moving in opposite directions, the very numbers of the people proving their greatest safeguard against detection. Candles at frequent intervals diffused a brilliant light and purified the air. Open doorways revealed shops of various descriptions within which men and women were bartering for goods, and now Tarzan had his first real glimpse of Veltopismakusian life. The shops were all conducted by white-tunicked slaves, but slaves and warriors intermingled as customers, both sexes of each class being represented. It was Tarzan's first opportunity, also, to see the women of the warrior class outside their own homes. He had seen the Princess Janzara in the palace quarters and, through the doorways in various portions of the dome, he had seen other women of varying stations in life; but these were the first that he had seen abroad at close hand. Their faces were painted deep vermilion, their ears blue, and their apparel so arranged that the left leg and left arm were bare, though if even so much as the right ankle or wrist became uncovered they hastily readjusted their garments to hide them, giving every evidence of confusion and embarrassment. As the ape-man watched them he was reminded of fat dowagers he had seen at home whose evening gowns left them naked to their kidneys, yet who would rather have died than to have exposed a knee.

The front of the shops were covered with brilliant paintings, usually depicting the goods that were on sale, together with hieroglyphics describing the wares and advertising the name of the proprietor. One of these finally held the attention of the Trohanadalmakusian, and he touched Tarzan's arm and pointed toward it.

"A place where food is served," he said. "Let us eat."

"Nothing would suit me better. I am famished," Tarzan assured him, and so the two entered the little shop where several customers were already sitting upon the floor with small benches pulled close to them, upon which food was being served in wooden dishes. Komodoflorensal found a space near the rear of the shop, not far from a doorway leading into another chamber, which was also a shop of a different character, not all the places of business being fortunately located upon a corridor, but having their entrances, like this one, through another place of business.

Having seated themselves and dragged a bench before them they looked about while waiting to be served. It was evidently a poor shop, Komodoflorensal told Tarzan, catering to the slave caste and the poorer warriors, of which there were several sitting at benches in different parts of the room. By their harness and apparel, which was worn and shabby, one might easily guess at their poverty. In the adjoining shop were several more of the same class of unfortunate warriors mending their own clothes with materials purchased from the poor shopkeeper.

The meal was served by a slave in a white tunic of very cheap material, who was much surprised when payment for the meal and the service was offered in gold.

"It is seldom," he said, "that warriors rich enough to possess gold come to our poor shop. Pieces of iron and bits of lead, with much wooden money, pass into my coffers; but rarely do I see gold. Once I did, and many of my customers were formerly of the richest of the city. Yonder see that tall man with the heavily wrinkled face. Once he was rich—the richest warrior in his dome. Look at him now! And see them in the next room performing menial services, men who once owned slaves so prosperous that they, in turn, hired other slaves to do the meaner duties for them. Victims, all of them, of the tax that Elkomoelhago has placed upon industry.

"To be poor," he continued, "assures one an easier life than being rich, for the poor have no tax to pay, while those who work hard and accumulate property have only their labor for their effort, since the government takes all from them in taxes.

"Over there is a man who was very rich. He worked hard all his life and accumulated a vast fortune. For several years after Elkomoelhago's new tax law was enforced, he struggled to earn enough to insure that his income would be at least equal to his taxes and the cost of his living; but he found that it was impossible. He had one enemy, a man who had wronged him grievously. This man was very poor, and to him he gave all of what remained of his great fortune and his property. It was a terrible revenge. From being a contented man, this victim of another's spleen is now a haggard wreck, laboring unceasingly eighteen hours each day in a futile attempt to insure himself an income that will defray his taxes."

Having finished their meal the two fugitives returned to the corridor and continued their way downward through the dome toward the first level, keeping always to the more crowded corridors, where detection seemed least likely. Now, mounted men were more frequently encountered and so rapidly and recklessly did the warriors ride along the narrow corridors that it was with difficulty that the pedestrians avoided being ridden down and trampled, and it seemed to Tarzan but little less than a miracle that any of them arrived at their destinations uninjured. Having at last come to the lowest level, they were engaged in searching for one of the four corridors that would lead them from the dome, when their way was completely blocked by a great throng that had congregated at the intersection of two corridors. Those in the rear were stretching their necks to observe what was going on in the center of the gathering. Everyone was asking questions of his neighbor, but as yet no one upon the outskirts of the mob appeared to know what had occurred, until at last fragments of rumors filtered back to the farthermost. Tarzan and Komodoflorensal dared ask no questions, but they kept their ears open and presently they were rewarded by overhearing repeated what seemed to be an authoritative account of what had transpired to cause this congestion. In answer to a question put by one of the throng a fellow who was elbowing his way out from the center of the jam explained that those in front had halted to view the remains of two slaves who had been killed while trying to escape.

"They were locked in one of Zoanthrohago's slave cells at the very highest level," he told his questioner, "and they tried to escape by climbing down an improvised ladder into the central shaft. Their ladder broke and they were precipitated to the roof of the throne room, where their bodies, terribly mangled, were but just found. They are being carried out to the beasts, now. One of them was a great loss to Zoanthrohago as it was the slave Zuanthrol, upon whom he was experimenting."

"Ah," exclaimed a listener, "I saw them but yesterday."

"You would not know them today," vouchsafed the informer, "so terribly are their faces disfigured."

When the press of humanity had been relieved Tarzan and Komodoflorensal continued their way, finding that the Slaves' Corridor lay just before them, and that it was down this avenue that the bodies of their victims of the previous night were being carried.

"What," asked the ape-man, "did he mean by saying that they were being carried to the beasts?"

"It is the way in which we dispose of the bodies of slaves," replied the Trohanadalmakusian. "They are carried to the edge of the jungle, where they are devoured by wild beasts. There are old and toothless lions near Trohanadalmakus that subsist entirely upon slave meat. They are our scavengers and so accustomed are they to being fed that they often come to meet the parties who bring out the corpses, pacing beside them, roaring and growling, until the spot is reached where the bodies are to be deposited."

"You dispose of all your dead in this manner?"

"Only the slave dead. The bodies of warriors and nobles are burned."

"In a short time, then," continued Tarzan, "there will be no danger of there ever being a correct identification of those two," he jerked his thumb along the corridor ahead, where the bodies of the two dead warriors were being bounced and jolted along upon the backs of diadets.

CHAPTER 17

"Where now?" demanded Komodoflorensal as the two emerged from the mouth of the Slaves' Corridor and stood for a moment in the brilliant sunlight without.

"Lead the way to the quarry where we were confined and to the chamber in which we slept."

"You must be weary of your brief liberty," remarked the Trohanadalmakusian.

"We are returning for Talaskar, as I promised," Tarzan reminded him.

"I know," said the Zertolosto, "and I commend your loyalty and valor while deprecating your judgment. It will be impossible to rescue Talaskar. Were it otherwise I should be the first to her assistance; but I know, and she knows, that, for her, escape is beyond hope. We will but succeed in throwing ourselves again into the hands of our masters."

"Let us hope not," said Tarzan; "but, if you feel as you say, that our effort is foredoomed to failure and that we shall but be recaptured, do not accompany me. My only real need of you is to guide me to the apartment where Talaskar is confined. If you can direct me to it that is all I ask."

"Think you I was attempting to evade the danger?" demanded Komodoflorensal. "No! Where you go, I will go. If you are captured I shall be captured. We shall fail, but let us not separate. I am ready to go wherever you go."

"Good," commented Tarzan. "Now lead the way to the quarry and use your knowledge of things Minunian and your best wits to gain us entrance without too much talking."

They passed, unchallenged, along the shaded walks between the domes of Veltopismakus and past the great parade where gorgeously caparisoned warriors were executing intricate evolutions with the nicest precision, and out beyond the domes along well-worn trails filled with toiling slaves and their haughty guards. Here they fell in beside the long column moving in the direction of the quarry in which they had been imprisoned, taking their places in the column of flanking guards, and thus they came to the entrance to the quarry.

Perfunctorily the numbers of the slaves were taken, as they passed in, and entered in a great book; but to Tarzan's relief he noted that no attention was paid to the guards, who moved along beside their charges and down into the interior without being checked or even counted, and with them went Komodoflorensal, Prince Royal of Trohanadalmakus, and Tarzan of the Apes.

Once inside the quarry and past the guard room the two fell gradually to the rear of the column, so that when it turned into a level above that which they wished to reach they were enabled to detach themselves from it without being noticed. To leave one column was but to join another, for there was no break in them and often there were several moving abreast; but when they reached the thirty-fifth level and entered the tunnel leading to the chamber in which Talaskar was confined they found themselves alone, since there is little or no activity in these corridors leading to slave quarters except early in the morning when the men are led forth to their labors and again at night when they are brought back.

Before the door of the chamber they found a single warrior on guard. He was squatting on the floor of the tunnel leaning against the wall, but at their approach he rose and challenged them.

Komodoflorensal, who was in the lead, approached him and halted. "We have come for the slave girl, Talaskar," he said.

Tarzan, who was just behind Komodoflorensal, saw a sudden light leap to the eyes of the warrior. Was it recognition?

"Who sent you?" demanded the warrior.

"Her master, Zoanthrohago," replied the Trohanadalmakusian.

The expression upon the face of the warrior changed to one of cunning.

"Go in and fetch her," he said, and unbolted the door, swinging it open.

Komodoflorensal dropped upon his hands and knees and crawled through the low aperture, but Tarzan stood where he was.

"Go in!" said the guard to him.

"I will remain where I am," replied the ape-man. "It will not require two of us to find a single slave girl and fetch her to the corridor."

For an instant the warrior hesitated, then he closed the door hurriedly and shot the heavy bolts. When he turned toward Tarzan again, who was now alone with him in the corridor, he turned with a naked sword in his hands; but he found Zuanthrol facing him with drawn rapier.

"Surrender!" cried the warrior. "I recognized you both instantly."

"I thought as much," said Zuanthrol. "You are clever, with the exception of your eyes—they are fools, for they betray you."

"But my sword is no fool," snapped the fellow, as he thrust viciously at the ape-man's breast.

Lieutenant Paul D'Arnot of the French navy had been recognized as one of the cleverest swordsmen in the service and to his friend Greystoke he had imparted a great measure of his skill during the many hours that the two had whiled away with the foils, and today Tarzan of the Apes breathed a prayer of gratitude to the far-distant friend whose careful training was, after many long years, to serve the ape-man in such good stead, for he soon realized that, though his antagonist was a master at the art of fence, he was not wholly outclassed, and to his skill was added his great strength and his agility.

They had fought for but a minute or two when the Veltopismakusian realized that he was facing no mean antagonist and that he was laboring at a disadvantage. He being unable to fall back when Tarzan rushed him, while his foeman had at his back the whole length of the tunnel. He tried then to force Tarzan back, but in this he failed, receiving a thrust in the shoulder for his pains, and then he commenced to call for help and the ape-man realized that he must silence him and that quickly. Awaiting the opportunity that was presently afforded by a feint that evoked a wild lunge, Tarzan stepped quickly in and passed his sword through the heart of the Veltopismakusian and as he withdrew his blade from the body of his antagonist he released the bolts that held the door and swung it open. Beyond it, white of face, crouched Komodoflorensal, but as his eyes fell upon Tarzan and the body of the guard behind him, a smile curved his lips and an instant later he was in the corridor beside his friend.

"How did it happen?" he demanded.

"He recognized us; but what of Talaskar? Is she not coming?"

"She is not here. Kalfastoban took her away. He has purchased her from Zoanthrohago."

Tarzan wheeled. "Rebolt the door and let us get out of here," he said.

Komodoflorensal closed and fastened the door. "Where now?" he asked.

"To find Kalfastoban's quarters," replied the ape-man.

Komodoflorensal shrugged his shoulders and followed on behind his friend. They retraced their steps toward the surface without incident until they were opposite the sixteenth level, when a face was suddenly turned toward them from a column of slaves crossing the runway from one lateral to another. Just for an instant did the eyes of the slave meet those of Tarzan, and then the fellow had passed into the mouth of the lateral and disappeared.

"We must hurry," whispered Tarzan to his companion.

"Why now more than before?" demanded Komodoflorensal.

"Did you not see the fellow who just passed us and turned to look a second time at me?"

"No; who was it?"

"Caraftap," replied Tarzan.

"Did he recognize you?"

"As to that I cannot say; but he evidently found something familiar in my appearance. Let us hope that he did not place me, though I fear that he did."

"Then we must lose no time in getting out of here, and out of Veltopismakus, as well."

They hurried on. "Where are Kalfastoban's quarters?" asked Tarzan.

"I do not know. In Trohanadalmakus warriors are detailed to the quarries for but short periods and do not transfer their quarters or their slaves during the time that they are there. I do not know the custom here. Kalfastoban may have finished his tour of duty in the quarries. On the other hand it may be for a long period that they are detailed for that service and his quarters may lie on the upper level of the quarry. We shall have to inquire."

Soon after this Tarzan stepped up to a warrior moving in the same direction as he and Komodoflorensal. "Where can I find Kalfastoban Vental?" he asked.

"They will tell you in the guard room, if it is any of your affair," he replied, shooting a quick glance at the two. "I do not know."

After that they passed the fellow and at the first turn that hid them from him they increased their speed, for both were becoming suspicious of every least untoward incident, and their one wish now was to escape the quarry in safety. Nearing the entrance they attached themselves to a column of slaves toiling upward with their heavy burdens of rocks for the new dome, and with them they came to the guard room where the slaves were checked out. The officer and the clerks labored in a mechanical manner, and it appeared that it was to be as easy to leave the quarry as it had been to enter it, when the officer suddenly drew his brow together and commenced to count.

"How many slaves in this crew?" he asked.

"One hundred," replied one of the warriors accompanying them.

"Then why four guards?" he demanded.

"There are but two of us," rejoined the warrior.

"We are not with them," Komodoflorensal spoke up quickly.

"What do you here?" demanded the officer.

"If we can see you alone we can explain that quickly," replied the Trohanadalmakusian.

The officer waved the crew of slaves upon their way and beckoned to Komodoflorensal and Tarzan to follow him into an adjoining chamber, where they found a small anteroom in which the commander of the guard slept.

"Now," he said, "let me see your passes."

"We have none," replied Komodoflorensal.

"No passes! That will be difficult to explain, will it not?"

"Not to one of your discrimination," replied the prince, accidentally jingling the golden coins in his pouch. "We are in search of Kalfastoban. We understand that he owns a slave we wish to purchase and not being able to obtain a pass to the quarry in the short time at our disposal we ventured to come, upon so simple an errand, without one. Could you direct us to Kalfastoban?" Again he jingled the coins.

"I shall be delighted," replied the officer. "His quarters are upon the fifth level of the Royal Dome upon the central corridor and about midway between the King's Corridor and the Warrior's Corridor. As he was relieved from duty in the quarry this very morning I have no doubt but that you will find him there."

"We thank you," said Komodoflorensal, leaning far back in the Minunian bow. "And now," he added, as though it was an afterthought, "if you will accept it we shall be filled with gratitude if you will permit us to leave this slight token of our appreciation," and he drew a large gold coin from the pouch and proffered it to the officer.

"Rather than seem ungrateful," replied the officer, "I must accept your gracious gift, with which I may alleviate the sufferings of the poor. May the shadow of disaster never fall upon you!"

The three then bowed and Tarzan and Komodoflorensal quitted the guard room and a moment later were in the free, fresh air of the surface.

"Even in Minuni!" breathed Tarzan.

"What was that?" asked his friend.

"I was just thinking of my simple, honest jungle and God's creatures that men call beasts."

"What should they call them?" demanded Komodoflorensal.

"If judged by the standards that men themselves make, and fail to observe, they should be called demigods," replied the ape-man.

"I believe I get your point," laughed the other, "but think! Had a lion guarded the entrance to this quarry no gold piece would have let us pass. The frailties of man are not without their virtues; because of them right has just triumphed over wrong and bribery has worn the vestments of virtue."

Returning to the Royal Dome they passed around the east side of the structure to the north front, where lies the Slaves' Corridor in every dome. In quitting the dome they had come from the Warriors' Corridor on the west and they felt that it would be but increasing the chances of detection were they to pass too often along the same route where someone, half-recognizing them in one instance, might do so fully after a second or third inspection.

To reach the fifth level required but a few minutes after they had gained entrance to the dome. With every appearance of boldness they made their way toward the point in the central corridor at which the officer of the guard had told them they would find Kalfastoban's quarters, and perhaps Kalfastoban himself; but they were constantly on the alert, for both recognized that the greatest danger of detection lay through the chance that Kalfastoban might recall their features, as he of all Veltopismakusians would be most apt to do so, since he had seen the most of them, or at least the most of Tarzan since he had donned the slave's green.

They had reached a point about midway between the Slaves' Corridor and the Warriors' Corridor when Komodoflorensal halted a young, female slave and asked her where the quarters of Kalfastoban were located.

"It is necessary to pass through the quarters of Hamadalban to reach those of Kalfastoban," replied the girl. "Go to the third entrance," and she pointed along the corridor in the direction they had been going.

After they had left her Tarzan asked Komodoflorensal if he thought there would be any difficulty in gaining entrance to Kalfastoban's quarters.

"No," he replied; "the trouble will arise in knowing what to do after we get there."

"We know what we have come for," replied the ape-man. "It is only necessary to carry out our design, removing all obstacles as they intervene."

"Quite simple," laughed the prince.

Tarzan was forced to smile. "To be candid," he admitted, "I haven't the remotest idea what we are going to do after we get in there, or after we get out either, if we are successful in finding Talaskar and bringing her away with us, but that is not strange, since I know nothing, or practically nothing, of what conditions I may expect to confront me from moment to moment in this strange city of a strange world. All that we can do is to do our best. We have come thus far much more easily than I expected—perhaps we will go the whole distance with no greater friction—or we may stop within the next dozen steps, forever."

Pausing before the third entrance they glanced in, discovering several women squatting upon the floor. Two of them were of the warrior class, the others slaves of the white tunic. Komodoflorensal entered boldly.

"These are the quarters of Hamadalban?" he asked.

"They are," replied one of the women.

"And Kalfastoban's are beyond?"

"Yes."

"And beyond Kalfastoban's?" inquired the Trohanadalmakusian.

"A long gallery leads to the outer corridor. Upon the gallery open many chambers where live hundreds of people. I do not know them all. Whom do you seek?"

"Palastokar," replied Komodoflorensal quickly, choosing the first name that presented itself to his memory.

"I do not recall the name," said the woman, knitting her brows in thought.

"But I shall find him now, thanks to you," said Komodoflorensal, "for my directions were to pass through the quarters of Hamadalban and Kalfastoban, when I should come upon a gallery into which opened the quarters of Palastokar; but perhaps if Kalfastoban is in, he will be able to direct me more exactly."

"Kalfastoban has gone out with Hamadalban," replied the woman; "but I expect them back momentarily. If you will wait, they will soon be here."

"Thank you," said Komodoflorensal, hastily; "but I am sure that we shall have no trouble finding the quarters of Palastokar. May your candles burn long and brilliantly!" and without waiting on further ceremony he crossed the room and entered the quarters of Kalfastoban, into which Tarzan of the Apes followed at his heels.

"I think, my friend," said the prince, "that we shall have to work rapidly."

Tarzan glanced quickly around the first chamber that they entered. It was vacant. Several doors opened from it. They were all closed either with wooden doors or with hangings. The ape-man stepped quickly to the nearer and tried the latch. It gave and he pushed the door ajar. All was darkness within.

"Bring a candle, Komodoflorensal," he said.

The prince brought two from their niches in the wall. "A storeroom," he said, as the rays of the candles illuminated the interior of the room. "Food and candles and raiment. Kalfastoban is no pauper. The tax collector has not ruined him yet."

Tarzan, standing in the doorway of the storeroom, just behind Komodoflorensal, turned suddenly and looked out across the other chamber. He had heard voices in the quarters of Hamadalban beyond—men's voices. One of them he recognized an instant later—it was the voice of Kalfastoban Vental.

"Come!" roared the bull voice of the Vental. "Come to my quarters, Hamadalban, and I will show you this new slave of mine."

Tarzan pushed Komodoflorensal into the storeroom and following him, closed the door. "Did you hear?" he whispered.

"Yes, it was Kalfastoban!"

The storeroom door was ornamented with a small, open grill covered with a hanging of some heavy stuff upon the inside. By drawing the hanging aside the two could obtain a view of most of the interior of the outer chamber, and they could hear all that was said by the two men who now entered from Hamadalban's quarters.

"I tell you she is the greatest bargain I have ever seen," cried Kalfastoban, "but wait, I'll fetch her," and he stepped to another door, which he unlocked with a key. "Come out!" he roared, flinging the door wide.

With the haughty bearing of a queen a girl stepped slowly into the larger room—no cowering servility of the slave here. Her chin was high, her gaze level. She glanced almost with contempt upon the Vental. And she was beautiful. It was Talaskar. Komodoflorensal realized that he had never before appreciated how really beautiful was the little slave girl, who had cooked for him. Kalfastoban had given her a white tunic of good quality, which set off the olive of her skin and the rich blackness of her hair to better effect than had the cheap green thing that he had always seen her in.

"She belonged to Zoanthrohago," Kalfastoban explained to his friend, "but I doubt that he ever saw her, else he never would have parted with her for the paltry sum I paid."

"You will take her for your own woman and raise her to our class?" asked Hamadalban.

"No," replied Kalfastoban, "for then she would no longer be a slave and I could not sell her. Women are too expensive. I shall keep her for a time and then sell her while her value is still high. I should make a pretty profit from her."

Tarzan's fingers closed tightly, as though upon the throat of an enemy, and the right hand of Komodoflorensal crept to the hilt of his rapier.

A woman came from the quarters of Hamadalban and stood in the doorway.

"Two of the guards from the quarry are here with a green slave inquiring for Kalfastoban," she said.

"Send them in," directed the Vental.

A moment later the three entered—the slave was Caraftap.

"Ah!" exclaimed Kalfastoban, "my good slave, Caraftap; the best in the quarry. Why is he brought here?"

"He says that he has information of great value," replied one of the guard; "but he will divulge it to none but you. He has staked his life against the worth of his information and the Novand of the guard ordered him brought hither."

"What information have you?" demanded Kalfastoban.

"It is of great moment," cried Caraftap. "Noble Zoanthrohago, and even the king, will be grateful for it; but were I to give it and have to return to the quarries the other slaves would kill me. You were always good to me, Kalfastoban Vental, and so I asked to be brought to you, for I know that if you promise that I shall be rewarded with the white tunic, if my service is considered worthy of it, I shall be safe."

"You know that I cannot do that," replied Kalfastoban.

"But the king can, and if you intercede with him he will not refuse."

"I can promise to intercede with the king in your behalf if the information you bring is of value; but that is all I can do."

"That is enough—if you promise," said Caraftap.

"Very well, I promise. What do you know that the king would like to know?"

"News travels fast in Veltopismakus," said Caraftap, "and so it was that we in the quarry heard of the death of the two slaves, Aoponato and Zuanthrol, within a short time after their bodies were discovered. As both had been slaves of Zoanthrohago we were all confined together in one chamber and thus I knew them both well. Imagine then my surprise when, while crossing one of the main spirals with a crew of other slaves, I beheld both Zuanthrol and Aoponato, in the habiliments of warriors, ascending toward the surface."

"What is the appearance of these two?" suddenly demanded one of the warriors who had accompanied Caraftap from the quarry.

The slave described them as fully as he could.

"The same!" cried the warrior. "These very two stopped me upon the spiral and inquired the whereabouts of Kalfastoban."

A crowd of women and men had gathered in the doorway of Kalfastoban's chamber, having been attracted by the presence of a green slave accompanied by members of the quarry guard. One of them was a young slave girl.

"I, too, was questioned by these very men," she exclaimed, "only a short time since, and they asked me the same question."

One of Hamadalban's women voiced a little scream. "They passed through our quarters but a moment since," she cried, "and entered Kalfastoban's, but they asked not where lay the quarters of Kalfastoban, the name they mentioned was unknown to me—a strange name."

"Palastokar," one of her companions reminded her.

"Yes, Palastokar, and they said he had his quarters upon the gallery leading from Kalfastoban's to the outer corridor."

"There is no one of such a name in the Royal Dome," said Kalfastoban. "It was but a ruse to enter my quarters."

"Or to pass through them," suggested one of the quarry guard.

"We must hurry after them," said the other.

"Keep Caraftap here until we return, Kalfastoban," said the first guard, "and also search your own quarters and those adjoining carefully. Come!" and motioning to the other guard he crossed the chamber and departed along the gallery that led to the outer corridor, followed not alone by his fellow but by Hamadalban and all the other men who had congregated in the chamber, leaving Kalfastoban and Caraftap, with the women, in the Vental's quarters.

CHAPTER 18

Kalfastoban turned immediately to a search of the various chambers of his quarters, but Caraftap laid a restraining hand upon his arm.

"Wait, Vental," he begged. "If they be here would it not be best to insure their capture by fastening the doors leading from your quarters?"

"A good thought, Caraftap," replied Kalfastoban, "and then we may take our time searching for them. Out of here, all you women!" he cried, waving the females back into Hamadalban's quarters. A moment later the two doors leading from the chamber to Hamadalban's quarters and the gallery were closed and locked.

"And now, master," suggested Caraftap, "as there be two of them would it not be well to supply me with a weapon."

Kalfastoban smote his chest. "A dozen such could Kalfastoban overcome alone," he cried; "but for your own protection get you a sword from yonder room while I lock this proud she-cat in her cell again."

As Kalfastoban followed Talaskar to the room in which she had been confined, Caraftap crossed to the door of the storeroom where the Vental had told him he would find a weapon.

The Vental reached the door of the room just behind the girl and reaching out caught her by the arm.

"Not so fast, my pretty!" he cried. "A kiss before you leave me; but fret not! The moment we are sure that those villainous slaves are not within these rooms I shall join you, so do not pine for your Kalfastoban."

Talaskar wheeled and struck the Vental in the face. "Lay not your filthy hands upon me, beast!" she cried, and struggled to free herself from his grasp.

"So-ho! a cat, indeed!" exclaimed the man, but he did not release her, and so they struggled until they disappeared from sight within the cell, and at the same moment Caraftap, the slave, laid his hand upon the latch of the storeroom door, and opening it stepped within.

As he did so steel fingers reached forth out of the darkness and closed upon his throat. He would have screamed in terror, but no sound could he force through his tight-closed throat. He struggled and struck at the thing that held him—a thing so powerful that he knew it could not be human, and then a low voice, cold and terrifying, whispered in his ear.

"Die, Caraftap!" it said. "Meet the fate that you deserve and that you well knew you deserved when you said that you dared not return to the quarters of the slaves of Zoanthrohago after betraying two of your number. Die, Caraftap! and know before you die that he whom you would have betrayed is your slayer. You searched for Zuanthrol and—you have found him!" With the last word the terrible fingers closed upon the man's neck. Spasmodically the slave struggled, fighting for air. Then the two hands that gripped him turned slowly in opposite directions and the head of the traitor was twisted from his body.

Throwing the corpse aside Tarzan sprang into the main chamber of the Vental's quarters and ran quickly toward the door of Talaskar's cell, Komodoflorensal but half a pace behind him. The door of the little room had been pushed to by the struggles of the couple within, and as Tarzan pushed it open he saw the girl in the clutches of the huge Vental, who, evidently maddened by her resistance, had lost his temper completely and was attempting to rain blows upon her face, which she sought to ward off, clutching at his arms and hands.

A heavy hand fell upon the shoulder of the Vental. "You seek us!" a low voice whispered in his ear. "Here we are!"

Kalfastoban released the girl and swung around, at the same time reaching for his sword. Facing him were the two slaves and both were armed, though only Aoponato had drawn his weapon. Zuanthrol, who held him, had not yet drawn.

"'A dozen such could Kalfastoban overcome alone,'" quoted Tarzan. "Here we are, braggart, and we are only two; but we cannot wait while you show us how mighty you be. We are sorry. Had you not molested this girl I should merely have locked you in your quarters, from which you would soon have been released; but your brutality deserves but one punishment—death."

"Caraftap!" screamed Kalfastoban. No longer was he a blusterer, deep-toned and swaggering. His voice was shrill with terror and he shook in the hands of the ape-man. "Caraftap! Help!" he cried.

"Caraftap is dead," said Tarzan. "He died because he betrayed his fellows. You shall die because you were brutal to a defenseless slave girl. Run him through, Komodoflorensal! We have no time to waste here."

As the Trohanadalmakusian withdrew his sword from the heart of Kalfastoban Vental and the corpse slid to the floor of the cell Talaskar ran forward and fell at the feet of the ape-man.

"Zuanthrol and Aoponato!" she cried. "Never did I think to see you again. What has happened? Why are you here? You have saved me, but now you will be lost. Fly—I know not where to you may fly—but go from here! Do not let them find you here. I cannot understand why you are here, anyway."

"We are trying to escape," explained Komodoflorensal, "and Zuanthrol would not go without you. He searched the quarry for you and now the Royal Dome. He has performed the impossible, but he has found you."

"Why did you do this for me?" asked Talaskar, looking wonderingly at Tarzan.

"Because you were kind to me when I was brought to the chamber of Zoanthrohago's slaves," replied the ape-man, "and because I promised that when the time for escape came we three should be together."

He had lifted her to her feet and led her into the main chamber. Komodoflorensal stood a little aside, his eyes upon the floor. Tarzan glanced at him and an expression of puzzlement came into the eyes of the ape-man, but whatever thought had caused it he must have put quickly aside for the consideration of more pressing matters.

"Komodoflorensal, you know best what avenues of escape should be the least beset by the dangers of discovery. Whether to go by way of Hamadalban's quarters or through the gallery they mentioned? These are questions I cannot answer to my own satisfaction; and look!" his eyes had been roving about the chamber, "there is an opening in the ceiling. Where might that lead?"

"It might lead almost anywhere, or nowhere at all!" replied the Trohanadalmakusian. "Many chambers have such openings. Sometimes they lead into small lofts that are not connected with any other chamber; again they lead into secret chambers, or even into corridors upon another level."

There came a pounding upon the door leading into Hamadalban's quarters and a woman's voice called aloud: "Kalfastoban, open!" she cried. "There has come an ental from the quarry guard in search of Caraftap. The sentry at the entrance to the quarters of the slaves of Zoanthrohago has been found slain and they wish to question Caraftap, believing that there is a conspiracy among the slaves."

"We must go by the gallery," whispered Komodoflorensal, stepping quickly to the door leading thereto.

As he reached it someone laid a hand upon the latch from the opposite side and attempted to open the door, which was locked.

"Kalfastoban!" cried a voice from the gallery beyond. "Let us in! The slaves went not this way. Come, open quickly!"

Tarzan of the Apes glanced quickly about. Upon his face was a half-snarl, for once again was he the cornered beast. He measured the distance from the floor to the trap in the ceiling, and then with a little run he sprang lightly upward. He had forgotten to what extent the reduction of his weight affected his agility. He had hoped to reach a handhold upon the upper edge of the opening, but instead he shot entirely through it, alighting upon his feet in a dark chamber. Turning he looked down at his friends below. Consternation was writ large upon the countenance of each; but at that he could not wonder. He was almost as much surprised himself.

"Is it too far for you to jump?" he asked.

"Too far!" they replied.

He swung, then, head downward through the opening, catching the edge of the trap in the hollow of his knees. At the gallery door the knocking was becoming insistent and now at that leading into the quarters of Hamadalban a man's voice had supplanted that of the woman. The fellow was demanding entrance, angrily.

"Open!" he shouted. "In the name of the king, open!"

"Open yourself!" shouted the fellow who had been hammering at the opposite door, thinking that the demand to open came from the interior of the chamber to which he sought admission.

"How can I open?" screamed back the other. "The door is locked upon your side!"

"It is not locked upon my side. It is locked upon yours," cried the other, angrily.

"You lie!" shouted he who sought entrance from Hamadalban's quarters, "and you will pay well when this is reported to the king."

Tarzan swung, head downward, into the chamber, his hands extended toward his companions. "Lift Talaskar to me," he directed Komodoflorensal, and as the other did so he grasped the girl's wrists and raised her as far as he could until she could seize upon a part of his leather harness and support herself alone without falling. Then he took another hold upon her, lower down, and lifted still higher, and in this way she managed to clamber into the chamber above.

The angry warriors at the two doors were now evidently engaged in an attempt to batter their way into the chamber. Heavy blows were falling upon the substantial panels that threatened to splinter them at any moment.

"Fill your pouch with candles, Komodoflorensal," said Tarzan, "and then jump for my hands."

"I took all the candles I could carry while we were in the storeroom," replied the other. "Brace yourself! I am going to jump."

A panel splintered and bits of wood flew to the center of the floor from the door at the gallery just as Tarzan seized the outstretched hands of Komodoflorensal and an instant later, as both men kneeled in the darkness of the loft and looked down into the chamber below the opposite door flew open and the ten warriors who composed the ental burst in at the heels of their Vental.

For an instant they looked about in blank surprise and then their attention was attracted by the pounding upon the other door. A smile crossed the face of the Vental as he stepped quickly to the gallery door and unlocked it. Angry warriors rushed in upon him, but when he had explained the misapprehension under which both parties had been striving for entrance to the chamber they all joined in the laughter, albeit a trifle shamefacedly.

"But who was in here?" demanded the Vental who had brought the soldiers from the quarry.

"Kalfastoban and the green slave Caraftap," proffered a woman belonging to Hamadalban.

"They must be hiding!" said a warrior.

"Search the quarters!" commanded the Vental.

"It will not take long to find one," said another warrior, pointing at the floor just inside the storeroom doorway.

The others looked and there they saw a human hand resting upon the floor. The fingers seemed frozen into the semblance of clutching claws. Mutely they proclaimed death. One of the warriors stepped quickly to the storeroom, opened the door and dragged forth the body of Caraftap, to which the head was clinging by a shred of flesh. Even the warriors stepped back, aghast. They looked quickly around the chamber.

"Both doors were barred upon the inside," said the Vental. "Whatever did this must still be here."

"It could have been nothing human," whispered a woman who had followed them from the adjoining quarters.

"Search carefully," said the Vental, and as he was a brave man, he went first into one chamber and then another. In the first one they found Kalfastoban, run through the heart.

"It is time we got out of here if there is any way out," whispered Tarzan to Komodoflorensal. "One of them will espy this hole directly."

Very cautiously the two men felt their way in opposite direction around the walls of the dark, stuffy loft. Deep dust, the dust of ages, rose about them, chokingly, evidencing the fact that the room had not been used for years, perhaps for ages. Presently Komodoflorensal heard a "H-s-s-t!" from the ape-man who called them to him. "Come here, both of you. I have found something."

"What have you found?" asked Talaskar, coming close.

"An opening near the bottom of the wall," replied Tarzan. "It is large enough for a man to crawl through. Think you, Komodoflorensal, that it would be safe to light a candle?"

"No, not now," replied the prince.

"I will go without it then," announced the ape-man, "for we must see where this tunnel leads, if anywhere."

He dropped upon his hands and knees, then, and Talaskar, who had been standing next him, felt him move away. She could not see him—it was too dark in the gloomy loft.

The two waited, but Zuanthrol did not return. They heard voices in the room below. They wondered if the searchers would soon investigate the loft but really there was no need for apprehension. The searchers had determined to invest the place—it would be safer than crawling into that dark hole after an unknown thing that could tear the head from a man's body. When it came down, as come down it would have to, they would be prepared to destroy or capture it; but in the meantime they were content to wait.

"What has become of him?" whispered Talaskar, anxiously.

"You care very much for him, do you not?" asked Komodoflorensal.

"Why should I not?" asked the girl. "You do, too, do you not?"

"Yes," replied Komodoflorensal.

"He is very wonderful," said the girl.

"Yes," said Komodoflorensal.

"I wish he would come back," said the girl.

"Yes," said Komodoflorensal.

As though in answer to their wish they heard a low whistle from the depths of the tunnel into which Tarzan had crawled. "Come!" whispered the ape-man.

Talaskar first, they followed him, crawling upon hands and knees through a winding tunnel, feeling their way through the darkness, until at last a light flared before them and they saw Zuanthrol lighting a candle in a small chamber, that was only just high enough to permit a tall man to sit erect within it.

"I got this far," he said to them, "and as it offered a fair hiding place where we might have light without fear of discovery I came back after you. Here we can stop a while in comparative comfort and safety until I can explore the tunnel further. From what I have been able to judge it has never been used during the lifetime of any living Veltopismakusian, so there is little likelihood that anyone will think of looking here for us."

"Do you think they will follow us?" asked Talaskar.

"I think they will," replied Komodoflorensal, "and as we cannot go back it will be better if we push on at once, as it is reasonable to assume that the opposite end of this tunnel opens into another chamber. Possibly there we shall find an avenue of escape."

"You are right, Komodoflorensal," agreed Tarzan. "Nothing can be gained by remaining here. I will go ahead. Let Talaskar follow me, and you bring up the rear. If the place proves a blind alley we shall be no worse off for having investigated it."

Lighting their way this time with candles the three crawled laboriously and painfully over the uneven, rock floor of the tunnel, which turned often, this way and that, as though passing around chambers, until, to their relief, the passageway abruptly enlarged, both in width and height, so that now they could proceed in an erect position. The tunnel now dropped in a steep declivity to a lower level and a moment later the three emerged into a small chamber, where Talaskar suddenly placed a hand upon Tarzan's arm, with a little intaking of her breath in a half gasp.

"What is that, Zuanthrol!" she whispered, pointing into the darkness ahead.

Upon the floor at one side of the room a crouching figure was barely discernible close to the wall.

"And that!" exclaimed the girl, pointing to another portion of the room.

The ape-man shook her hand from his arm and stepped quickly forward, his candle held high in his left hand, his right upon his sword. He came close to the crouching figure and bent to examine it. He laid his hand upon it and it fell into a heap of dust.

"What is it?" demanded the girl.

"It was a man," replied Tarzan; "but it has been dead many years. It was chained to this wall. Even the chain has rusted away."

"And the other, too?" asked Talaskar.

"There are several of them," said Komodoflorensal. "See? There and there."

"At least they cannot detain us," said Tarzan, and moved on again across the chamber toward a doorway on the opposite side.

"But they tell us something, possibly," ventured Komodoflorensal.

"What do they say?" asked the ape-man.

"That this corridor connected with the quarters of a very powerful Veltopismakusian," replied the prince. "So powerful was he that he might dispose of his enemies thus, without question; and it also tells us that all this happened long years ago."

"The condition of the bodies told us that," said Tarzan.

"Not entirely," replied Komodoflorensal. "The ants would have reduced them to that state in a short time. In past ages the dead were left within the domes, and the ants, who were then our scavengers, soon disposed of them, but the ants sometimes attacked the living. They grew from a nuisance to a menace, and then every precaution had to be taken to keep from attracting them. Also we fought them. There were great battles waged in Trohanadalmakus between the Minunians and the ants and thousands of our warriors were devoured alive, and though we slew billions of ants their queens could propagate faster than we could kill the sexless workers who attacked us with their soldiers. But at last we turned our attention to their nests.

Here the carnage was terrific, but we succeeded in slaying their queens and since then no ants have come into our domes. They live about us, but they fear us. However, we do not risk attracting them again by leaving our dead within the domes."

"Then you believe that this corridor leads to the quarters of some great noble?" inquired Tarzan.

"I believe that it once did. The ages bring change. Its end may now be walled up. The chamber to which it leads may have housed a king's son when these bones were quick; today it may be a barrack-room for soldiers, or a stable for diadets. About all that we know definitely about it," concluded Komodoflorensal, "is that it has not been used by man for a long time, and probably, therefore, is unknown to present-day Veltopismakusians."

Beyond the chamber of death the tunnel dropped rapidly to lower levels, entering, at last, a third chamber larger than either of the others. Upon the floor lay the bodies of many men.

"These were not chained to the walls," remarked Tarzan.

"No, they died fighting, as one may see by their naked swords and the position of their bones."

As the three paused a moment to look about the chamber there fell upon their ears the sound of a human voice.

CHAPTER 19

As the days passed and Tarzan did not return to his home his son became more and more apprehensive. Runners were sent to nearby villages, but each returned with the same report. No one had seen The Big Bwana. Korak dispatched messages, then, to the nearest telegraph inquiring from all the principal points in Africa, where the ape-man might have made a landing, if aught had been seen or heard of him; but always again were the answers in the negative.

And at last, stripped to a string and carrying naught but his primitive weapons, Korak the Killer took the trail with a score of the swiftest and bravest of the Waziri in search of his father. Long and diligently they searched the jungle and the forest, often enlisting the friendly services of the villages near which they chanced to be carrying on their quest, until they had covered as with a fine-toothed comb a vast area of country, covered it as could have no other body of men; but for all their care and all their diligence they uncovered no single clue as to the fate or whereabouts of Tarzan of the Apes, and so, disheartened yet indefatigable, they searched on and on through tangled miles of steaming jungle or across rocky uplands as inhospitable as the stunted thorns that dotted them.

*

And in the Royal Dome of Elkomoelhago, Thagosto of Veltopismakus, three people halted in a rock-walled, hidden chamber and listened to a human voice that appeared to come to them out of the very rock of the walls surrounding them. Upon the floor about them lay the bones of long-dead men. About them rose the impalpable dust of ages.

The girl pressed closer to Tarzan. "Who is it?" she whispered.

Tarzan shook his head.

"It is a woman's voice," said Komodoflorensal.

The ape-man raised his candle high above his head and took a step closer to the left-hand wall; then he stopped and pointed. The others looked in the direction indicated by Tarzan's finger and saw an opening in the wall a hual or two above his head. Tarzan handed his candle to Komodoflorensal, removed his sword and laid it on the floor, and then sprang lightly for the opening. For a moment he clung to its edge, listening, and then he dropped back into the chamber.

"It is pitch-black beyond," he said. "Whoever owns that voice is in another chamber beyond that into which I was just looking. There was no human being in the next apartment."

"If it was absolutely dark, how could you know that?" demanded Komodoflorensal.

"Had there been anyone there I should have smelled him," replied the ape-man.

TARZAN SUPER PACK

The others looked at him in astonishment. "I am sure of it," said Tarzan, "because I could plainly feel a draught sucking up from the chamber, through the aperture, and into this chamber. Had there been a human being there his effluvium would have been carried directly to my nostrils."

"And you could have detected it?" demanded Komodoflorensal. "My friend, I can believe much of you, but not that!"

Tarzan smiled. "I at least have the courage of my convictions," he said, "for I am going over there to investigate. From the clearness with which the voice comes to us I am certain that it comes through no solid wall. There must be an opening into the chamber where the woman is and as we should investigate every possible avenue of escape, I shall investigate this." He stepped again toward the wall below the aperture.

"Oh, let us not separate," cried the girl. "Where one goes, let us all go!"

"Two swords are better than one," said Komodoflorensal, though his tone was only halfhearted.

"Very well," replied Tarzan. "I will go first, and then you can pass Talaskar up to me."

Komodoflorensal nodded. A minute or two later the three stood upon the opposite side of the wall. Their candle revealed a narrow passage that showed indications of much more recent use than those through which they had passed from the quarters of Kalfastoban. The wall they had passed through to reach it was of stone, but that upon the opposite side was of studding and rough boards.

"This is a passage built along the side of a paneled room," whispered Komodoflorensal.

"The other side of these rough boards supports beautifully polished panels of brilliant woods or burnished metals."

"Then there should be a door, you think, opening from this passage into the adjoining chamber?" asked Tarzan.

"A secret panel, more likely," he replied.

They walked along the passage, listening intently. At first they had just been able to distinguish that the voice they heard was that of a woman; but now they heard the words.

"—had they let me have him," were the first that they distinguished.

"Most glorious mistress, this would not have happened then," replied another female voice.

"Zoanthrohago is a fool and deserves to die; but my illustrious father, the king, is a bigger fool," spoke the first voice. "He will kill Zoanthrohago and with him the chance of discovering the secret of making our warriors giants. Had they let me buy this Zuanthrol he would not have escaped. They thought that I would have killed him, but that was farthest from my intentions."

"What would you have done with him, wondrous Princess?"

"That is not for a slave to ask or know," snapped the mistress.

For a time there was silence.

"That is the Princess Janzara speaking," whispered Tarzan to Komodoflorensal. "It is the daughter of Elkomoelhago whom you would have captured and made your princess; but you would have had a handful."

"Is she as beautiful as they say?" asked Komodoflorensal.

"She is very beautiful, but she is a devil."

"It would have been my duty to take her," said Komodoflorensal.

Tarzan was silent. A plan was unfolding itself within his mind. The voice from beyond the partition spoke again.

"He was very wonderful," it said. "Much more wonderful than our warriors," and then, after a silence, "You may go, slave, and see to it that I am not disturbed before the sun stands midway between the Women's Corridor and the King's Corridor."

"May your candles burn as deathlessly as your beauty, Princess," said the slave, as she backed across the apartment.

An instant later the three behind the paneling heard a door close.

Tarzan crept stealthily along the passage, seeking the secret panel that connected the apartment where the Princess Janzara lay composed for the night; but it was Talaskar who found it.

"Here!" she whispered and together the three examined the fastening. It was simple and could evidently be opened from the opposite side by pressure upon a certain spot in the panel.

"Wait here!" said Tarzan to his companions. "I am going to fetch the Princess Janzara. If we cannot escape with her we should be able to buy our liberty with such a hostage."

Without waiting to discuss the advisability of his action with the others, Tarzan gently slid back the catch that held the panel and pushed it slightly ajar. Before him was the apartment of Janzara—a creation of gorgeous barbarity in the center of which, upon a marble slab, the princess lay upon her back, a gigantic candle burning at her head and another at her feet.

Regardless of the luxuriousness of their surroundings, of their wealth, or their positions in life, the Minunians never sleep upon a substance softer than a single thickness of fabric, which they throw upon the ground, or upon wooden, stone, or marble sleeping slabs, depending upon their caste and their wealth.

Leaving the panel open the ape-man stepped quietly into the apartment and moved directly toward the princess, who lay with closed eyes, either already asleep, or assiduously wooing Morpheus. He had crossed halfway to her cold couch when a sudden draught closed the panel with a noise that might well have awakened the dead.

Instantly the princess was on her feet and facing him. For a moment she stood in silence gazing at him and then she moved slowly toward him, the sinuous undulations of her graceful carriage suggesting to the Lord of the Jungle a similarity to the savage majesty of Sabor, the lioness.

"It is you, Zuanthrol!" breathed the princess. "You have come for me?"

"I have come for you, Princess," replied the ape-man. "Make no outcry and no harm will befall you."

"I will make no outcry," whispered Janzara as with half-closed lids she glided to him and threw her arms about his neck.

Tarzan drew back and gently disengaged himself. "You do not understand, Princess," he told her. "You are my prisoner. You are coming with me."

"Yes," she breathed, "I am your prisoner, but it is you who do not understand. I love you. It is my right to choose whatever slave I will to be my prince. I have chosen you."

Tarzan shook his head impatiently. "You do not love me," he said. "I am sorry that you think you do, for I do not love you. I have no time to waste. Come!" and he stepped closer to take her by the wrist.

Her eyes narrowed. "Are you mad?" she demanded. "Or can it be that you do not know who I am?"

"You are Janzara, daughter of Elkomoelhago," replied Tarzan. "I know well who you are."

"And you dare to spurn my love!" She was breathing heavily, her breasts rising and falling to the tumultuous urge of her emotions.

"It is no question of love between us," replied the ape-man. "To me it is only a question of liberty and life for myself and my companions."

"You love another?" questioned Janzara.

"Yes," Tarzan told her.

"Who is she?" demanded the princess.

"Will you come quietly, or shall I be compelled to carry you away by force?" asked the ape-man, ignoring her question.

For a moment the woman stood silently before him, her every muscle tensed, her dark eyes two blazing wells of fire, and then slowly her expression changed. Her face softened and she stretched one hand toward him.

"I will help you, Zuanthrol," she said. "I will help you to escape. Because I love you I shall do this. Come! Follow me!" She turned and moved softly across the apartment.

"But my companions," said the ape-man. "I cannot go without them."

"Where are they?"

He did not tell her, for as yet he was none too sure of her motives.

"Show me the way," he said, "and I can return for them."

"Yes," she replied, "I will show you and then perhaps you will love me better than you love the other."

In the passage behind the paneling Talaskar and Komodoflorensal awaited the outcome of Tarzan's venture. Distinctly to their ears came every word of the conversation between the ape-man and the princess.

"He loves you," said Komodoflorensal. "You see, he loves you."

"I see nothing of the kind," returned Talaskar. "Because he does not love the Princess Janzara is no proof that he loves me."

"But he does love you—and you love him! I have seen it since first he came. Would that he were not my friend, for then I might run him through."

"Why would you run him through because he loves me—if he does?" demanded the girl. "Am I so low that you would rather see your friend dead than mated with me?"

"I—" he hesitated. "I cannot tell you what I mean."

The girl laughed, and then suddenly sobered. "She is leading him from her apartment. We had better follow."

As Talaskar laid her fingers upon the spring that actuated the lock holding the panel in place, Janzara led Tarzan across her chamber toward a doorway in one of the side walls—not the doorway through which her slave had departed.

"Follow me," whispered the princess, "and you will see what the love of Janzara means."

Tarzan, not entirely assured of her intentions, followed her warily.

"You are afraid," she said. "You do not trust me! Well, come here then and look, yourself, into this chamber before you enter."

Komodoflorensal and Talaskar had but just stepped into the apartment when Tarzan approached the door to one side of which Janzara stood. They saw the floor give suddenly beneath his feet and an instant later Zuanthrol had disappeared. As he shot down a polished chute he heard a wild laugh from Janzara following him into the darkness of the unknown.

Komodoflorensal and Talaskar leaped quickly across the chamber, but too late. The floor that had given beneath Tarzan's feet had slipped quietly back into place. Janzara stood above the spot trembling with anger and staring down at the place where the ape-man had disappeared. She shook as an aspen shakes in the breeze—shook in the mad tempest of her own passions.

"If you will not come to me you shall never go to another!" she screamed, and then she turned and saw Komodoflorensal and Talaskar running toward her. What followed occurred so quickly that it would be impossible to record the facts in the brief time that they actually consumed. It was over almost before Tarzan reached the bottom of the chute and picked himself from the earthen floor upon which he had been deposited.

The room in which he found himself was lighted by several candles burning in iron-barred niches. Opposite him was a heavy gate of iron bars through which he could see another lighted apartment in which a man, his chin sagging dejectedly upon his breast, was seated upon a low bench. At the sound of Tarzan's precipitate entrance into the adjoining chamber the man looked up and at sight of Zuanthrol, leaped to his feet.

"Quick! To your left!" he cried, and Tarzan, turning, saw two huge, green-eyed beasts crouching to spring.

His first impulse was to rub his eyes as one might to erase the phantom figures of a disquieting dream, for what he saw were two ordinary African wildcats—ordinary in contour and markings, but in size gigantic. For an instant the ape-man forgot that he was but one-fourth his normal size, and that the cats, that appeared to him as large as full-grown lions, were in reality but average specimens of their kind.

As they came toward him he whipped out his sword, prepared to battle for his life with these great felines as he had so often before with their mighty cousins of his own jungle.

"If you can hold them off until you reach this gate," cried the man in the next chamber, "I can let you through. The bolt is upon this side," but even as he spoke one of the cats charged.

*

Komodoflorensal, brushing past Janzara, leaped for the spot upon the floor at which Tarzan had disappeared and as it gave beneath him he heard a savage cry break from the lips of the Princess of Veltopismakus.

"So it is you he loves?" she screamed. "But he shall not have you—no! not even in death!" and that was all that Komodoflorensal heard as the black chute swallowed him.

Talaskar, confronted by the infuriated Janzara, halted, and then stepped back, for the princess was rushing upon her with drawn dagger.

"Die, slave!" she screamed, as she lunged for the white breast of Talaskar, but the slave girl caught the other's wrist and a moment later they went down, locked in one another's embrace. Together they rolled about the floor, the daughter of Elkomoelhago seeking to drive her slim blade into the breast of the slave girl, while Talaskar fought to hold off the menacing steel and to close with her fingers upon the throat of her antagonist.

*

AS the first cat charged the other followed, not to be robbed of its share of the flesh of the kill, for both were half-starved and ravenous, and as the ape-man met the charge of the first, sidestepping its rush and springing in again to thrust at its side, Komodoflorensal, who had drawn his sword as he entered the apartment of Janzara, shot into the subterranean den almost into the teeth of the second beast, which was so disconcerted by the sudden appearance of this second human that it wheeled and sprang to the far end of the den before it could gather its courage for another attack.

*

In the chamber above, Talaskar and Janzara fought savagely, two she-tigers in human form. They rolled to and fro about the room, straining and striking, Janzara screaming: "Die, slave! You shall not have him!" But Talaskar held her peace and saved her breath, so that slowly she was overcoming the other when they chanced to roll upon the very spot that had let Tarzan and Komodoflorensal to the pit beneath.

As Janzara realized what had happened she uttered a scream of terror. "The cats! The cats!" she cried, and then the two disappeared into the black shaft.

*

Komodoflorensal did not follow the cat that had retreated to the far end of the pit, but sprang at once to Tarzan's aid, and together they drove off the first beast as they backed toward the gate where the man in the adjoining chamber stood ready to admit them to the safety of his own apartment.

The two cats charged and then retreated, springing in quickly and away again as quickly, for they had learned the taste of the sharp steel with which the humans were defending themselves. The two men were almost at the gate, another instant and they could spring through. The cats charged again and again were driven to the far corner of the pit. The man in the next chamber swung open the gate.

"Quick!" he cried, and at the same instant two figures shot from the mouth of the shaft and, locked tightly in one another's embrace, rolled to the floor of the pit directly in the path of the charging carnivores.

CHAPTER 20

As Tarzan and Komodoflorensal realized that Talaskar and Janzara lay exposed to the savage assault of the hungry beasts they both sprang quickly toward the two girls. As had been the case when Komodoflorensal had shot into the pit, the cats were startled by the sudden appearance of these two new humans, and in the first instant of their surprise had leaped again to the far end of the chamber.

1107

Janzara had lost her dagger as the two girls had fallen into the shaft and now Talaskar saw it lying on the floor beside her. Releasing her hold upon the princess she seized the weapon and leaped to her feet. Already Tarzan and Komodoflorensal were at her side and the cats were returning to the attack.

Janzara arose slowly and half-bewildered. She looked about, terror disfiguring her marvelous beauty, and as she did so the man in the adjoining chamber saw her.

"Janzara!" he cried. "My Princess, I come!" and seizing the bench upon which he had been sitting, and the only thing within the chamber that might be converted into a weapon, he swung wide the gate and leaped into the chamber where the four were now facing the thoroughly infuriated beasts.

Both animals, bleeding from many wounds, were mad with pain, rage and hunger. Screaming and growling they threw themselves upon the swords of the two men, who had pushed the girls behind them and were backing slowly toward the gate, and then the man with the bench joined Tarzan and Komodoflorensal and the three fought back the charges of the infuriated carnivores.

The bench proved fully as good a weapon of defense as the swords and so together the five drew slowly back, until, quite suddenly and without the slightest warning both cats leaped quickly to one side and darted behind the party as though sensing that the women would prove easier prey. One of them came near to closing upon Janzara had not the man with the bench, imbued apparently with demoniacal fury, leaped upon it with his strange weapon and beaten it back so desperately that it was forced to abandon the princess.

Even then the man did not cease to follow it but, brandishing the bench, pursued it and its fellow with such terrifying cries and prodigious blows that, to escape him, both cats suddenly dodged into the chamber that the man had occupied, and before they could return to the attack he with the bench had slammed the gate and fastened them upon its opposite side. Then he wheeled and faced the four.

"Zoanthrohago!" cried the princess.

"Your slave!" replied the noble, dropping to one knee and leaning far back, with outstretched arms.

"You have saved my life, Zoanthrohago," said Janzara, "and after all the indignities that I have heaped upon you! How can I reward you?"

"I love you, Princess, as you have long known," replied the man; "but now it is too late, for tomorrow I die by the king's will. Elkomoelhago has spoken, and, even though you be his daughter, I do not hesitate to say his very ignorance prevents him ever changing a decision once reached."

"I know," said Janzara. "He is my sire but I love him not. He killed my mother in a fit of unreasoning jealousy. He is a fool—the fool of fools."

Suddenly she turned upon the others. "These slaves would escape, Zoanthrohago," she cried. "With my aid they might accomplish it. With their company we might succeed in escaping, too, and in finding an asylum in their own land."

"If any one of them is of sufficient power in his native city," replied Zoanthrohago.

"This one," said Tarzan, seeing a miraculous opportunity for freedom, "is the son of Adendrohahkis, King of Trohanadalmakus—the eldest son, and Zertolosto."

Janzara looked at Tarzan a moment after he had done speaking. "I was wicked, Zuanthrol," she said, "but I thought that I wanted you and being the daughter of a king I have seldom been denied aught that I craved," and then to Talaskar: "Take your man, my girl, and may you be happy with him," and she pushed Talaskar gently toward the ape-man, but Talaskar drew back.

"You are mistaken, Janzara," she said, "I do not love Zuanthrol, nor does he love me."

Komodoflorensal looked quickly at Tarzan as though expecting that he would quickly deny the truth of Talaskar's statement, but the ape-man only nodded his head in assent.

"Do you mean," demanded Komodoflorensal, "that you do not love Talaskar?" and he looked straight into the eyes of his friend.

"On the contrary, I love her very much," replied Tarzan; "but not in the way that you have believed, or should I say feared? I love her because she is a good girl and a kind girl and a loyal friend, and also because she was in trouble and needed the love and protection which you and I alone could give her; but as a man loves his mate, I do not love her, for I have a mate of my own in my country beyond the thorns."

Komodoflorensal said no more, but he thought a great deal. He thought of what it would mean to return to his own city where he was the Zertolosto, and where, by all the customs of ages, he would be supposed to marry a princess from another city. But he did not want a princess—he wanted Talaskar, the little slave girl of Veltopismakus, who scarcely knew her own mother and most probably had never heard that of her father, if her mother knew it.

He wanted Talaskar, but he could only have her in Trohanadalmakus as a slave. His love for her was real and so he would not insult her by thinking such a thing as that. If he could not make her his princess he would not have her at all, and so Komodoflorensal, the son of Adendrohahkis, was sad.

But he had none too much time to dwell upon his sorrow now, for the others were planning the best means for escape.

"The keepers come down to feed the cats upon this side," said Zoanthrohago, indicating a small door in the wall of the pit opposite that which led into the chamber in which he had been incarcerated.

"Doubtless it is not locked, either," said Janzara, "for a prisoner could not reach it without crossing through this chamber where the cats were kept."

"We will see," said Tarzan, and crossed to the door.

A moment sufficed to force it open, revealing a narrow corridor beyond. One after another the five crawled through the small aperture and following the corridor ascended an acclivity, lighting their way with candles taken from the den of the carnivores. At the top a door opened into a wide corridor, a short distance down which stood a warrior, evidently on guard before a door.

Janzara looked through the tiny crack that Tarzan had opened the door and saw the corridor and the man. "Good!" she exclaimed. "It is my own corridor and the warrior is on guard before my door. I know him well. Through me he has escaped payment of his taxes for the past thirty moons. He would die for me. Come! We have nothing to fear," and stepping boldly into the corridor she approached the sentry, the others following behind her.

Until he recognized her there was danger that the fellow would raise an alarm, but the moment he saw who it was he was as wax in her hands.

"You are blind," she told him.

"If the Princess Janzara wishes it," he replied.

She told him what she wished—five diadets and some heavy warriors' wraps. He eyed those who were with her, and evidently recognized Zoanthrohago and guessed who the two other men were.

"Not only shall I be blind for my princess," he said, "but tomorrow I shall be dead for her."

"Fetch six diadets, then," said the princess.

Then she turned to Komodoflorensal "You are Prince Royal of Trohanadalmakus?" she asked.

"I am," he replied.

"And if we show you the way to liberty you will not enslave us?"

"I shall take you to the city as my own slaves and then liberate you," he replied.

"It is something that has seldom if ever been done," she mused; "not in the memory of living man in Veltopismakus. I wonder if your sire will permit it."

"The thing is not without precedent," replied Komodoflorensal "It has been done but rarely, yet it has been done. I think you may feel assured of a friendly welcome at the court of Adendrohahkis, where the wisdom of Zoanthrohago will not go unappreciated or unrewarded."

It was a long time before the warrior returned with the diadets. His face was covered with perspiration and his hands with blood.

"I had to fight for them," he said, "and we shall have to fight to use them if we do not hurry. Here, Prince, I brought you weapons," and he handed a sword and dagger to Zoanthrohago.

They mounted quickly. It was Tarzan's first experience upon one of the wiry, active, little mounts of the Minunians; but he found the saddle well designed and the diadet easily controlled.

"They will be following me from the King's Corridor," explained Oratharc, the warrior who had fetched the diadets. "It would be best, then, to leave by one of the others."

"Trohanadalmakus is east of Veltopismakus," said Zoanthrohago, "and if we leave by the Women's Corridor with two slaves from Trohanadalmakus they will assume that we are going there; but if we leave by another corridor they will not be sure and if they lose even a little time in starting the pursuit it will give us just that much of an advantage. If we go straight toward Trohanadalmakus we shall almost certainly be overtaken as the swiftest of diadets will be used in our pursuit. Our only hope lies in deceiving them as to our route or destination, and to accomplish this I believe that we should leave either by the Warriors' Corridor or the Slaves' Corridor, cross the hills north of the city, circle far out to the north and east, not turning south until we are well past Trohanadalmakus. In this way we can approach that city from the east while our pursuers are patrolling the country west of Trohanadalmakus to Veltopismakus."

"Let us leave by the Warriors' Corridor then," suggested Janzara.

"The trees and shrubbery will conceal us while we pass around to the north of the city," said Komodoflorensal.

"We should leave at once," urged Oratharc.

"Go first then, with the princess," said Zoanthrohago, "for there is a possibility that the guard at the entrance will let her pass with her party. We will muffle ourselves well with our warriors' cloaks. Come, lead the way!"

With Janzara and Oratharc ahead and the others following closely they moved at a steady trot along the circular corridor toward the Warriors' Corridor, and it was not until they had turned into the latter that any sign of pursuit developed. Even then, though they heard the voices of men behind them, they hesitated to break into a faster gait lest they arouse the suspicions of the warriors in the guard room which they must pass near the mouth of the corridor.

Never had the Warriors' Corridor seemed so long to any of the Veltopismakusians in the party as it did this night; never had they so wished to race their diadets as now; but they held their mounts to an even pace that would never have suggested to the most suspicious that here were six people seeking escape, most of them from death.

They had come almost to the exit when they were aware that the pursuit had turned into the Warriors' Corridor behind them and that their pursuers were advancing at a rapid gait.

Janzara and Oratharc drew up beside the sentry at the mouth of the corridor as he stepped out to bar their progress.

"The Princess Janzara!" announced Oratharc. "Aside for the Princess Janzara!"

The princess threw back the hood of the warrior's cloak she wore, revealing her features, well known to every warrior in the Royal Dome—and well feared. The fellow hesitated.

"Aside, man!" cried the princess, "or I ride you down."

A great shout arose behind them. Warriors on swiftly galloping diadets leaped along the corridor toward them. The warriors were shouting something, the sense of which was hidden by the noise; but the sentry was suspicious.

"Wait until I call the Novand of the guard, Princess," he cried. "Something is amiss and I dare let no one pass without authority; but wait! Here he is," and the party turned in their saddles to see a Novand emerging from the door of the guard room, followed by a number of warriors.

"Ride!" cried Janzara and spurred her diadet straight for the single sentry in their path.

The others lifted their mounts quickly in pursuit. The sentry went down, striking valiantly with his rapier at the legs and bellies of flying diadets. The Novand and his men rushed from the guard room just in time to collide with the pursuers, whom they immediately assumed were belated members of the fleeing party. The brief minutes that these fought, before explanations could be made and understood, gave the fugitives time to pass among the trees to the west side of the city, and, turning north, make for the hills that were dimly visible in the light of a clear, but moonless night.

Oratharc, who said that he knew the hill trails perfectly, led the way, the others following as closely as they could; Komodoflorensal and Tarzan bringing up the rear. Thus they moved on in silence through the night, winding along precipitous mountain trails, leaping now and again from rock to rock where the trail itself had been able to find no footing; sliding into dank ravines, clambering through heavy brush and timber along tunnel-like trails that followed their windings, or crept up their opposite sides to narrow ridge or broad plateau; and all night long no sign of pursuit developed.

Came the morning at last and with it, from the summit of a lofty ridge, a panorama of broad plain stretching to the north, of distant hills, of forests and of streams. They decided then to descend to one of the numerous park-like glades that they could see nestling in the hills below them, and there rest their mounts and permit them to feed, for the work of the night had been hard upon them.

They knew that in the hills they might hide almost indefinitely, so wild and so little traveled were they and so they went into camp an hour after sunrise in a tiny cuplike valley surrounded by great trees, and watered and fed their mounts with a sense of security greater than they had felt since they left Veltopismakus.

Oratharc went out on foot and killed a number of quail and Tarzan speared a couple of fish in the stream. These they prepared and ate, and then, the men taking turns on guard, they slept until afternoon, for none had had sleep the night before.

Taking up their flight again in mid-afternoon they were well out upon the plain when darkness overtook them. Komodoflorensal and Zoanthrohago were riding far out upon the flanks and all were searching for a suitable camping place. It was Zoanthrohago who found it and they all gathered about him. Tarzan saw nothing in the waning light of day that appeared any more like a good camping place than any other spot on the open plain. There was a little clump of trees, but they had passed many such clumps, and there was nothing about this one that seemed to offer any greater security than another. As a matter of fact, to Tarzan it appeared anything but a desirable camp-site. There was no water, there was little shelter from the wind and none from an enemy, but perhaps they were going into the trees. That would be better. He looked up at the lofty branches lovingly. How enormous these trees seemed! He knew them for what they were and that they were trees of but average size, yet to him now they reared their heads aloft like veritable giants.

"I will go in first," he heard Komodoflorensal say, and turned to learn what he referred to.

The other three men were standing at the mouth of a large hole, into which they were looking. Tarzan knew that the opening was the mouth of the burrow of a ratel, the African member of the badger family, and he wondered why any of them wished to enter it. Tarzan had never cared for the flesh of the ratel. He stepped over and joined the others, and as he did so he saw Komodoflorensal crawl into the opening, his drawn sword in his hand.

"Why is he doing that?" he asked Zoanthrohago.

"To drive out, or kill the cambon, if he is there," replied the prince, giving the ratel its Minunian name.

"And why?" asked Tarzan. "Surely, you do not eat its flesh!"

"No, but we want his home for the night," replied Zoanthrohago. "I had forgotten that you are not a Minunian. We will spend the night in the underground chambers of the cambon, safe from the attacks of the cat or the lion. It would be better were we there now—this is a bad hour of the night for Minunians to be abroad on the plain or in the forest, for it is at this hour that the lion hunts."

A few minutes later Komodoflorensal emerged from the hole. "The cambon is not there," he said. "The burrow is deserted. I found only a snake, which I killed. Go in, Oratharc, and Janzara and Talaskar will follow you. You have candles?"

They had, and one by one they disappeared into the mouth of the hole, until Tarzan, who had asked to remain until last, stood alone in the gathering night gazing at the mouth of the ratel's burrow, a smile upon his lips. It seemed ridiculous to him that Tarzan of the Apes should ever be contemplating hiding from Numa in the hole of a ratel, or, worse still, hiding from little Skree, the wildcat, and as he stood there smiling a bulk loomed dimly among the trees; the diadets, standing near it tethered, snorted and leaped away; and Tarzan wheeled to face the largest lion he ever had seen—a lion that towered over twice the ape-man's height above him.

How tremendous, how awe-inspiring Numa appeared to one the size of a Minunian!

The lion crouched, its tail extended, the tip moving ever so gently; but the ape-man was not deceived. He guessed what was coming and even as the great cat sprang he turned and dove head-foremost down the hole of the ratel and behind him rattled the loose earth pushed into the burrow's mouth by Numa as he alighted upon the spot where Tarzan had stood.

CHAPTER 21

For three days the six traveled toward the east, and then, upon the fourth, they turned south. A great forest loomed upon the distant southern horizon, sweeping also wide upon the east. To the southwest lay Trohanadalmakus, a good two-days' journey for their tired diadets. Tarzan often wondered what rest the little creatures obtained. At night they were turned loose to graze; but his knowledge of the habits of the carnivores assured him that the tiny antelope must spend the greater part of each night in terrified watching or in flight; yet every morning they were back at the camp awaiting the pleasure of their masters. That they did not escape, never to return, is doubtless due to two facts. One is that they have been for ages bred in the domes of the Minunians—they know no other life than with their masters, to whom they look for food and care—and the other is the extreme kindness and affection which the Minunians accord their beautiful beasts of burden, and which have won the love and confidence of the little animals to such an extent that the diadet is most contented when in the company of man.

It was during the afternoon of the fourth day of their flight that Talaskar suddenly called their attention to a small cloud of dust far to their rear. For a long time all six watched it intently as it increased in size and drew nearer.

"It may be the long-awaited pursuit," said Zoanthrohago.

"Or some of my own people from Trohanadalmakus," suggested Komodoflorensal.

"Whoever they are, they greatly outnumber us," said Janzara, "and I think we should find shelter until we know their identity."

"We can reach the forest before they overtake us," said Oratharc, "and in the forest we may elude them if it is necessary."

"I fear the forest," said Janzara.

"We have no alternative," said Zoanthrohago; "but even now I doubt that we can reach it ahead of them. Come! We must be quick!"

Never before had Tarzan of the Apes covered ground so rapidly upon the back of an animal. The diadets flew through the air in great bounds. Behind them the nucleus of the dust cloud had resolved itself into a dozen mounted warriors, against whom their four blades would be helpless. Their one hope, therefore, lay in reaching the forest ahead of their pursuers, and now it seemed that they would be successful and now it seemed that they would not.

The recently distant wood seemed rushing toward him as Tarzan watched ahead between the tiny horns of his graceful mount, and, behind, the enemy was gaining. They were Veltopismakusian—they were close enough now for the devices upon their helmets to be seen—and they had recognized their quarry, for they cried aloud upon them to stop, calling several of them by name.

One of the pursuers forged farther ahead than the others. He came now close behind Zoanthrohago, who rode neck and neck with Tarzan, in the rear of their party. A half-length ahead of Zoanthrohago, was Janzara. The fellow called aloud to her.

"Princess!" he cried. "The king's pardon for you all if you return the slaves to us. Surrender and all will be forgiven."

Tarzan of the Apes heard and he wondered what the Veltopismakusians would do. It must have been a great temptation and he knew it. Had it not been for Talaskar he would have advised them to fall back among their friends, but he would not see the slave girl sacrificed. He drew his sword then and dropped back beside Zoanthrohago, though the other never guessed his purpose.

"Surrender, and all will be forgiven!" shouted the pursuer again.

"Never!" cried Zoanthrohago.

"Never!" echoed Janzara.

"The consequences are yours," cried the messenger, and on they rushed, pursuers and pursued, toward the dark forest, while from just within its rim savage eyes watched the mad race and red tongues licked hungry lips in anticipation.

Tarzan had been glad to hear the reply given by both Zoanthrohago and Janzara whom he had found likable companions and good comrades. Janzara's whole attitude had changed since the very instant she had joined them in their attempted escape. No longer was she the spoiled daughter of a despot; but a woman seeking happiness through the new love that she had found, or the old love that she had just discovered, for she often told Zoanthrohago that she knew now that she always had loved him. And this new thing in her life made her more considerate and loving of others. She seemed now to be trying to make up to Talaskar for the cruelty of her attack upon her when she had first seen her. Her mad infatuation for Tarzan she now knew in its true light—because she had been refused him she wanted him, and she would have taken him as her prince to spite her father, whom she hated.

Komodoflorensal and Talaskar always rode together, but no words of love did the Trohanadalmakusian speak in the ear of the little slave girl. A great resolve was crystallizing in his mind, but it had as yet taken on no definite form. And Talaskar, seemingly happy just to be near him, rode blissfully through the first days of the only freedom she had ever known; but now all was forgotten except the instant danger of capture and its alternative concomitants, death and slavery.

The six urged their straining mounts ahead. The forest was so near now. Ah, if they could but reach it! There one warrior might be as good as three and the odds against them would be reduced, for in the forest the whole twelve could not engage them at once and by careful maneuvering they doubtless could separate them.

They were going to succeed! A great shout rose to the lips of Oratharc as his diadet leaped into the shadows of the first trees, and the others took it up, for a brief instant, and then it died upon their lips as they saw a giant hand reach down and snatch Oratharc from his saddle. They tried to stop and wheel their mounts, but it was too late. Already they were in the forest and all about them was a horde of the hideous Zertalacolols. One by one they were snatched from their diadets, while their pursuers, who must have seen what was taking place just inside the forest, wheeled and galloped away.

Talaskar, writhing in the grip of a she Alali, turned toward Komodoflorensal.

"Good-bye!" she cried. "This, at last, is the end; but I can die near you and so I am happier dying than I have been living until you came to Veltopismakus."

"Good-bye, Talaskar!" he replied. "Living, I dared not tell you; but dying, I can proclaim my love. Tell me that you loved me."

"With all my heart, Komodoflorensal!" They seemed to have forgotten that another existed but themselves. In death they were alone with their love.

Tarzan found himself in the hand of a male and he also found himself wondering, even as he faced certain death, how it occurred that this great band of male and female Alali should be hunting together, and then he noticed the weapons of the male. They were not the crude bludgeon and the slinging-stones that they had formerly carried, but long, trim spears, and bows and arrows.

And now the creature that held him had lifted him even with his face and was scrutinizing him and Tarzan saw a look of recognition and amazement cross the bestial features, and he, in turn, recognized his captor. It was the son of The First Woman. Tarzan did not wait to learn the temper of his old acquaintance. Possibly their relations were altered now. Possibly they were not. He recalled the doglike devotion of the creature when last he had seen him and he put him to the test at once.

"Put me down!" he signed, peremptorily; "and tell your people to put down all of my people. Harm them not!"

Instantly the great creature set Tarzan gently upon the ground and immediately signaled his fellows to do the same with their captives. The men did immediately as they were bid, and all of the women but one. She hesitated. The son of The First Woman leaped toward her, his spear raised like a whip, and the female cowered and set Talaskar down upon the ground.

Very proud, the son of the First Woman explained to Tarzan as best he could the great change that had come upon the Alali since the ape-man had given the men weapons and the son of The First Woman had discovered what a proper use of them would mean to the males of his kind. Now each male had a woman cooking for him—at least one, and some of them—the stronger—had more than one.

To entertain Tarzan and to show him what great strides civilization had taken in the land of the Zertalacolols, the son of The First Woman seized a female by the hair and dragging her to him struck her heavily about the head and face with his clenched fist, and the woman fell upon her knees and fondled his legs, looking wistfully into his face, her own glowing with love and admiration.

That night the six slept in the open surrounded by the great Zertalacolols and the next day they started across the plain toward Trohanadalmakus where Tarzan had resolved to remain until he regained his normal size, when he would make a determined effort to cut his way through the thorn forest to his own country.

The Zertalacolols went a short distance out into the plain with them, and both men and women tried in their crude, savage way, to show Tarzan their gratitude for the change that he had wrought among them, and the new happiness he had given them.

Two days later the six fugitives approached the domes of Trohanadalmakus. They had been seen by sentries when they were still a long way off, and a body of warriors rode forth to meet them, for it is always well to learn the nature of a visitor's business in Minuni before he gets too close to your home.

When the warriors discovered that Komodoflorensal and Tarzan had returned they shouted for joy and a number of them galloped swiftly back to the city to spread the news.

The fugitives were conducted at once to the throne room of Adendrohahkis and there that great ruler took his son in his arms and wept, so great was his happiness at having him returned safely to him. Nor did he forget Tarzan, though it was some time before he or the other Trohanadalmakusians could accustom themselves to the fact that this man, no bigger than they, was the great giant who had dwelt among them a few moons since.

Adendrohahkis called Tarzan to the foot of the throne and there, before the nobles and warriors of Trohanadalmakus, he made him a Zertol, or prince, and he gave him diadets and riches and allotted him quarters fitted to his rank, begging him to stay among them always.

Janzara, Zoanthrohago and Oratharc he gave their liberty and permission to remain in Trohanadalmakus, and then Komodoflorensal drew Talaskar to the foot of the throne.

"And now for myself I ask a boon, Adendrohahkis," he said. "As Zertolosto I am bound by custom to wed a prisoner princess taken from another city; but in this slave girl have I found the one I love. Let me renounce my rights to the throne and have her instead."

Talaskar raised her hand as though to demur, but Komodoflorensal would not let her speak, and then Adendrohahkis rose and descended the steps at the foot of which Talaskar stood and taking her by the hand led her to a place beside the throne.

"You are bound by custom only, Komodoflorensal," he said, "to wed a princess, but custom is not law. A Trohanadalmakusian may wed whom he pleases."

"And even though he were bound by law," said Talaskar, "to wed a princess, still might he wed me, for I am the daughter of Talaskhago, king of Mandalamakus. My mother was captured by the Veltopismakusians but a few moons before my birth, which took place in the very chamber in which Komodoflorensal found me. She taught me to take my life before mating with anyone less than a prince; but I would have forgotten her teachings had Komodoflorensal been but the son of a slave. That he was the son of a king I did not dream until the night we left Veltopismakus, and I had already given him my heart long before, though he did not know it."

Weeks passed and still no change came to Tarzan of the Apes. He was happy in his life with the Minunians, but he longed for his own people and the mate who would be grieving for him, and so he determined to set forth as he was, pass through the thorn forest and make his way toward home, trusting to chance that he might escape the countless dangers that would infest his way, and perhaps come to his normal size somewhere during the long journey.

His friends sought to dissuade him, but he was determined, and at last, brooking no further delay, he set out toward the southeast in the direction that he thought lay the point where he had entered the land of the Minuni. A kamak, a body consisting of one thousand mounted warriors, accompanied him to the great forest and there, after some days' delay, the son of The First Woman found him. The Minunians bade him good-bye, and as he watched them ride away upon their graceful mounts, something rose in his throat that only came upon those few occasions in his life that Tarzan of the Apes knew the meaning of homesickness.

The son of The First Woman and his savage band escorted Tarzan to the edge of the thorn forest. Further than that they could not go. A moment later they saw him disappear among the thorns, with a wave of farewell to them. For two days Tarzan, no larger than a Minunian, made his way through the thorn forest. He met small animals that were now large enough to be dangerous to him, but he met nothing that he could not cope with. By night he slept in the burrows of the larger burrowing animals. Birds and eggs formed his food supply.

During the second night he awoke with a feeling of nausea suffusing him. A premonition of danger assailed him. It was dark as the grave in the burrow he had selected for the night. Suddenly the thought smote him that he might be about to pass through the ordeal of regaining his normal stature. To have this thing happen while he lay buried in this tiny burrow would mean death, for he would be crushed, strangled, or suffocated before he regained consciousness.

Already he felt dizzy, as one might feel who was upon the verge of unconsciousness. He stumbled to his knees and clawed his way up the steep acclivity that led to the surface. Would he reach it in time? He stumbled on and then, suddenly, a burst of fresh night air smote his nostrils. He staggered to his feet. He was out! He was free!

Behind him he heard a low growl. Grasping his sword, he lunged forward among the thorn trees. How far he went, or in what direction he did not know. It was still dark when he stumbled and fell unconscious to the ground.

CHAPTER 22

Usula, returning from the village of Obebe the cannibal, saw a bone lying beside the trail. This, in itself, was nothing remarkable. Many bones lie along savage trails in Africa. But this bone caused him to pause. It was the bone of a child. Nor was that alone enough to give pause to a warrior hastening through an unfriendly country back toward his own people.

But Usula had heard strange tales in the village of Obebe the cannibal where rumor had brought him in search of his beloved master, The Big Bwana. Obebe had not seen nor heard anything of Tarzan of the Apes. Not for years had he seen the giant white. He assured Usula of this fact many times; but from other members of the tribe the Waziri learned that a white man had been kept a prisoner by Obebe for a year or more and that some time since he had escaped. At first Usula thought this white man might have been Tarzan but when he verified the statement of the time that had elapsed since the man was captured he knew that it could not have been his master, and so he turned back along the trail toward home; but when he saw the child's bone along the trail several days out he recalled the story of the missing Uhha and he paused, just for a moment, to look at the bone. And as he looked he saw something else—a small skin bag, lying among some more bones a few feet off the trail. Usula stooped and picked up the bag. He opened it and poured some of the contents into his palm. He knew what the things were and he knew that they had belonged to his master, for Usula was a headman who knew much about his master's affairs. These were the diamonds that had been stolen from The Big Bwana many moons before by the white men who had found Opar. He would take them back to The Big Bwana's lady.

Three days later as he moved silently along the trail close to The Great Thorn Forest he came suddenly to a halt, the hand grasping his heavy spear tensing in readiness. In a little open place he saw a man, an almost naked man, lying upon the ground. The man was alive—he saw him move—but what was he doing? Usula crept closer, making no noise. He moved around until he could observe the man from another angle and then he saw a horrid sight. The man was white and he lay beside the carcass of a long-dead buffalo, greedily devouring the remnants of hide that clung to the bleaching bones.

The man raised his head a little and Usula, catching a better view of his face, gave a cry of horror. Then the man looked up and grinned. It was The Big Bwana!

Usula ran to him and raised him upon his knees, but the man only laughed and babbled like a child. At his side, caught over one of the horns of the buffalo, was The Big Bwana's golden locket with the great diamonds set in it. Usula replaced it about the man's neck. He built a strong shelter for him nearby and hunted food, and for many days he remained until the man's strength came back, but his mind did not come back. And thus, in this condition, the faithful Usula led home his master.

They found many wounds and bruises upon his body and his head, some old, some new, some trivial, some serious; and they sent to England for a great surgeon to come out to Africa and seek to mend the poor thing that once had been Tarzan of the Apes.

The dogs that had once loved Lord Greystoke slunk from this brainless creature. Jad-bal-ja, the Golden Lion, growled when the man was wheeled near his cage.

Korak The Killer paced the floor in dumb despair, for his mother was on her way from England, and what would be the effect upon her of this awful blow? He hesitated even to contemplate it.

*

Khamis, the witch doctor, had searched untiringly for Uhha, his daughter, since The River Devil had stolen her from the village of Obebe the cannibal. He had made pilgrimages to other villages, some of them remote from his own country, but he had found no trace of her or her abductor.

He was returning from another fruitless search that had extended far to the east of the village of Obebe, skirting the Great Thorn Forest a few miles north of the Ugogo. It was early morning. He had just broken his lonely camp and set out upon the last leg of his homeward journey when his keen old eyes discovered something lying at the edge of a small open space a hundred yards to his right. He had just a glimpse of something that was not of the surrounding vegetation. He did not know what it was, but instinct bade him investigate. Moving cautiously nearer he presently identified the thing as a human knee just showing above the low grass that covered the clearing. He crept closer and suddenly his eyes narrowed and his breath made a single, odd little sound as it sucked idly between his lips in mechanical reaction to surprise, for what he saw was the body of The River Devil lying upon its back, one knee flexed—the knee that he had seen above the grasses.

His spear advanced and ready he approached until he stood above the motionless body. Was The River Devil dead, or was he asleep? Placing the point of his spear against the brown breast Khamis prodded. The

Devil did not awaken. He was not asleep, then! nor did he appear to be dead. Khamis knelt and placed an ear above the other's heart. He was not dead!

The witch doctor thought quickly. In his heart he did not believe in River Devils, yet there was a chance that there might be such things and perhaps this one was shamming unconsciousness, or temporarily absent from the flesh it assumed as a disguise that it might go among men without arousing suspicion. But, too, it was the abductor of his daughter. That thought filled him with rage and with courage. He must force the truth from those lips even though the creature were a Devil.

He unwound a bit of fiber rope from about his waist and, turning the body over upon its back, quickly bound the wrists behind it. Then he sat down beside it to wait. It was an hour before signs of returning consciousness appeared, then The River Devil opened his eyes.

"Where is Uhha, my daughter?" demanded the witch doctor.

The River Devil tried to free his arms, but they were too tightly bound. He made no reply to Khamis' question. It was as though he had not heard it. He ceased struggling and lay back again, resting. After a while he opened his eyes once more and lay looking at Khamis, but he did not speak.

"Get up!" commanded the witch doctor and prodded him with a spear.

The River Devil rolled over on his side, flexed his right knee, raised on one elbow and finally got to his feet. Khamis prodded him in the direction of the trail. Toward dusk they arrived at the village of Obebe.

When the warriors and the women and the children saw who it was that Khamis was bringing to the village they became very much excited, and had it not been for the witch doctor, of whom they were afraid, they would have knifed and stoned the prisoner to death before he was fairly inside the village gates; but Khamis did not want The River Devil killed—not yet. He wanted first to force from him the truth concerning Uhha. So far he had been unable to get a word out of his prisoner. Incessant questioning, emphasized by many prods of the spear point had elicited nothing.

Khamis threw his prisoner into the same hut from which The River Devil had escaped, but he bound him securely and placed two warriors on guard. He had no mind to lose him again. Obebe came to see him. He, too, questioned him; but The River Devil only looked blankly in the face of the chief.

"I will make him speak," said Obebe. "After we have finished eating we will have him out and make him speak. I know many ways."

"You must not kill him," said the witch doctor. "He knows what became of Uhha, and until he tells me no one shall kill him."

"He will speak before he dies," said Obebe.

"He is a River Devil and will never die," said Khamis, reverting to the old controversy.

"He is Tarzan," cried Obebe, and the two were still arguing after they had passed out of hearing of the prisoner lying in the filth of the hut.

After they had eaten he saw them heating irons in a fire near the hut of the witch doctor, who was squatting before the entrance working rapidly with numerous charms—bits of wood wrapped in leaves, pieces of stone, some pebbles, a zebra's tail.

Villagers were congregating about Khamis until presently the prisoner could no longer see him. A little later a black boy came and spoke to his guards, and he was taken out and pushed roughly toward the hut of the witch doctor.

Obebe was there, as he saw after the guards had opened a way through the throng and he stood beside the fire in the center of the circle. It was only a small fire; just enough to keep a couple of irons hot.

"Where is Uhha, my daughter?" demanded Khamis.

The River Devil did not answer. Not once had he spoken since Khamis had captured him.

"Burn out one of his eyes," said Obebe. "That will make him speak!"

"Cut out his tongue!" screamed a woman. "Cut out his tongue."

"Then he cannot speak at all, you fool," cried Khamis.

The witch doctor arose and put the question again, but received no reply. Then he struck The River Devil a heavy blow in the face. Khamis had lost his temper, so that he did not fear even a River Devil.

"You will answer me now!" he screamed, and stooping he seized a red-hot iron.

"The right eye first!" shrilled Obebe.

*

The doctor came to the bungalow of the ape-man—Lady Greystoke brought him with her. They were three tired and dusty travelers as they dismounted at last before the rose-embowered entrance—the famous London surgeon, Lady Greystoke, and Flora Hawkes, her maid. The surgeon and Lady Greystoke went immediately to the room where Tarzan sat in an improvised wheelchair. He looked up at them blankly as they entered.

"Don't you know me, John?" asked the woman.

Her son took her by the shoulders and led her away, weeping.

"He does not know any of us," he said. "Wait until after the operation, mother, before you see him again. You can do him no good and to see him this way is too hard upon you."

The great surgeon made his examination. There was pressure on the brain from a recent fracture of the skull. An operation would relieve the pressure and might restore the patient's mind and memory. It was worth attempting.

Nurses and two doctors from Nairobi, engaged the day they arrived there, followed Lady Greystoke and the London surgeon, reaching the bungalow the day after their arrival. The operation took place the following morning.

Lady Greystoke, Korak and Meriem were awaiting, in an adjoining room, the verdict of the surgeon. Was the operation a failure or a success? They sat mutely staring at the door leading into the improvised operating room. At last it opened, after what seemed ages, but was only perhaps, an hour. The surgeon entered the room where they sat. Their eyes, dumbly pleading, asked him the question that their lips dared not voice.

"I cannot tell you anything as yet," he said, "other than that the operation, as an operation, was successful. What the result of it will be only time will tell. I have given orders that no one is to enter his room, other than the nurses for ten days. They are instructed not to speak to him or allow him to speak for the same length of time; but he will not wish to speak, for I shall keep him in a semiconscious condition, by means of drugs, until the ten days have elapsed. Until then, Lady Greystoke, we may only hope for the best; but I can assure you that your husband has every chance for complete recovery. I think you may safely hope for the best."

*

The witch doctor laid his left hand upon the shoulder of The River Devil; in his right hand was clutched a red-hot iron.

"The right eye first," shrilled Obebe again.

Suddenly the muscles upon the back and shoulders of the prisoner leaped into action, rolling beneath his brown hide. For just an instant he appeared to exert terrific physical force, there was a snapping sound at his back as the strands about his wrists parted, and an instant later steel-thewed fingers fell upon the right wrist of the witch doctor. Blazing eyes burned into his. He dropped the red-hot rod, his fingers paralyzed by the pressure upon his wrist, and he screamed, for he saw death in the angry face of the god.

Obebe leaped to his feet. Warriors pressed forward, but not near enough to be within reach of The River Devil. They had never been certain of the safety of tempting Providence in any such manner as Khamis and Obebe had been about to do. Now here was the result! The wrath of The River Devil would fall upon them all. They fell back, some of them, and that was a cue for others to fall back. In the minds of all was the thought—if I have no hand in this The River Devil will not be angry with me. Then they turned and fled to their huts, stumbling over their women and their children who were trying to outdistance their lords and masters.

1118

TARZAN SUPER PACK

EDGAR RICE BURROUGHS

Obebe turned now to flee also, and The River Devil picked Khamis up, and held him in two hands high above his head, and ran after Obebe the chief. The latter dodged into his own hut. He had scarce reached the center of it when there came a terrific crash upon the light, thatched roof, which gave way beneath a heavy weight. A body descending upon the chief filled him with terror. The River Devil had leaped in through the roof of his hut to destroy him! The instinct of self-preservation rose momentarily above his fear of the supernatural, for now he was convinced that Khamis had been right and the creature they had so long held prisoner was indeed The River Devil. And Obebe drew the knife at his side and plunged it again and again into the body of the creature that had leaped upon him, and when he knew that life was extinct he rose and dragging the body after him stepped out of his hut into the light of the moon and the fires.

"Come, my people!" he cried. "You have nothing to fear, for I, Obebe, your chief, have slain The River Devil with my own hands," and then he looked down at the thing trailing behind him, and gave a gasp, and sat down suddenly in the dirt of the village street, for the body at his heels was that of Khamis, the witch doctor.

His people came and when they saw what had happened they said nothing, but looked terrified. Obebe examined his hut and the ground around it. He took several warriors and searched the village. The stranger had departed. He went to the gates. They were closed; but in the dust before them was the imprint of naked feet—the naked feet of a white man. Then he came back to his hut, where his frightened people stood waiting him.

"Obebe was right," he said. "The creature was not The River Devil—it was Tarzan of the Apes, for only he could hurl Khamis so high above his head that he would fall through the roof of a hut, and only he could pass unaided over our gates."

*

The tenth day had come. The great surgeon was still at the Greystoke bungalow awaiting the outcome of the operation. The patient was slowly emerging from under the influence of the last dose of drugs that had been given him during the preceding night, but he was regaining his consciousness more slowly than the surgeon had hoped. The long hours dragged by, morning ran into afternoon, and evening came, and still there was no word from the sickroom.

It was dark. The lamps were lighted. The family were congregated in the big living room. Suddenly the door opened and a nurse appeared. Behind her was the patient. There was a puzzled look upon his face; but the face of the nurse was wreathed in smiles. The surgeon came behind, assisting the man, who was weak from long inactivity.

"I think Lord Greystoke will recover rapidly now," he said. "There are many things that you may have to tell him. He did not know who he was, when he regained consciousness, but that is not unusual in such cases."

The patient took a few steps into the room, looking wonderingly about.

"There is your wife, Greystoke," said the surgeon, kindly.

Lady Greystoke rose and crossed the room toward her husband, her arms outstretched. A smile crossed the face of the invalid, as he stepped forward to meet her and take her in his arms, but suddenly someone was between them, holding them apart. It was Flora Hawkes.

"My Gawd, Lady Greystoke!" she cried. "He ain't your husband. It's Miranda, Esteban Miranda! Don't you suppose I'd know him in a million? I ain't seen him since we came back, never havin' been in the sick chamber, but I suspicioned something the minute he stepped into this room and when he smiled, I knew."

"Flora!" cried the distracted wife. "Are you sure? No! no! you must be wrong! God has not given me back my husband only to steal him away again. John! tell me, is it you? You would not lie to me?"

For a moment the man before them was silent. He swayed to and fro, as in weakness. The surgeon stepped forward and supported him.

TARZAN SUPER PACK

"I have been very sick," he said. "Possibly I have changed, but I am Lord Greystoke. I do not remember this woman," and he indicated Flora Hawkes.

"He lies!" cried the girl.

"Yes, he lies," said a quiet voice behind them, and they all turned to see the figure of a giant white standing in the open French windows leading to the veranda.

"John!" cried Lady Greystoke, running toward him, "how could I have been mistaken? I—" but the rest of the sentence was lost as Tarzan of the Apes sprang into the room and taking his mate in his arms covered her lips with kisses.

THE SUPER PACK EBOOK SERIES

If you enjoyed this Super Pack you may wish to find the other books in this series. We endeavor to provide you with a quality product. But since many of these stories have been scanned typos do occasionally creep in. If you spot one please share it with us at positronicpress@yahoo.com so that we can fix it. We occasionally add additional stories to some of our Super Packs so make sure that you download fresh copies of your Super Packs from time to time to get the latest edition.

Science Fiction Super Pack #1: ISBN 978-1-63384-240-3
Science Fiction Super Pack #2: ISBN 978-1-51540-477-4
Science Fiction Super Pack #3: (Forthcoming)
Fantasy Super Pack #1: ISBN 978-1-63384-282-3
Fantasy Super Pack #2: ISBN 9781-51543-932-5
Conan the Barbarian Super Pack: ISBN 978-1-63384-292-2
Lord Dunsany Super Pack: ISBN 978-1-63384-725-5
Philip K. Dick Super Pack: ISBN 978-1-63384-799-6
The Pirate Super Pack # 1: ISBN 978-1-51540-193-3
The Pirate Super Pack # 2: ISBN 978-1-51540-196-4
Harry Harrison Super Pack: ISBN 978-1-51540-217-6
Andre Norton Super Pack: ISBN 978-1-51540-262-6
Marion Zimmer Bradley Super Pack: ISBN 978-1-51540-287-9
Frederik Pohl Super Pack: ISBN 978-1-51540-289-3
King Arthur Super Pack: ISBN 978-1-51540-306-7
Alan E. Nourse Super Pack: ISBN 978-1-51540-393-7
Space Science Fiction Super Pack: ISBN 978-1-51540-440-8
Wonder Stories Super Pack: ISBN 978-1-51540-454-5
Galaxy Science Fiction Super Pack #1:ISBN 978-1-51540-524-5
Galaxy Science Fiction Super Pack #2: 978-1-5154-0577-1
Science Fiction Novel Super Pack #1: ISBN 978-1-51540-363-0
Science Fiction Novel Super Pack #2: (Forthcoming)
Dragon Super Pack: ISBN 978-1-5154-1124-6
Weird Tales Super Pack #1: ISBN 978-1-5154-0548-1
Weird Tales Super Pack #2: 978-1-5154-1107-9
Poul Anderson Super Pack: ISBN 978-1-5154-0609-9
Fantastic Universe Super Pack #1: ISBN 978-1-5154-0981-6
Fantastic Universe Super Pack #2: ISBN 978-1-5154-0654-9
Fantastic Universe Super Pack #3: ISBN 978-1-5154-0655-6
Imagination Super Pack: ISBN 978-1-5154-1089-8
Planet Stories Super Pack: ISBN 978-1-5154-1125-3
Worlds of If Super Pack #1: ISBN 978-1-5154-1148-2
Worlds of If Super Pack #2: ISBN 978-1-5154-1182-6
Worlds of If Super Pack #3: ISBN 978-1-5154-1234-2

Obebe turned now to flee also, and The River Devil picked Khamis up, and held him in two hands high above his head, and ran after Obebe the chief. The latter dodged into his own hut. He had scarce reached the center of it when there came a terrific crash upon the light, thatched roof, which gave way beneath a heavy weight. A body descending upon the chief filled him with terror. The River Devil had leaped in through the roof of his hut to destroy him! The instinct of self-preservation rose momentarily above his fear of the supernatural, for now he was convinced that Khamis had been right and the creature they had so long held prisoner was indeed The River Devil. And Obebe drew the knife at his side and plunged it again and again into the body of the creature that had leaped upon him, and when he knew that life was extinct he rose and dragging the body after him stepped out of his hut into the light of the moon and the fires.

"Come, my people!" he cried. "You have nothing to fear, for I, Obebe, your chief, have slain The River Devil with my own hands," and then he looked down at the thing trailing behind him, and gave a gasp, and sat down suddenly in the dirt of the village street, for the body at his heels was that of Khamis, the witch doctor.

His people came and when they saw what had happened they said nothing, but looked terrified. Obebe examined his hut and the ground around it. He took several warriors and searched the village. The stranger had departed. He went to the gates. They were closed; but in the dust before them was the imprint of naked feet—the naked feet of a white man. Then he came back to his hut, where his frightened people stood waiting him.

"Obebe was right," he said. "The creature was not The River Devil—it was Tarzan of the Apes, for only he could hurl Khamis so high above his head that he would fall through the roof of a hut, and only he could pass unaided over our gates."

*

The tenth day had come. The great surgeon was still at the Greystoke bungalow awaiting the outcome of the operation. The patient was slowly emerging from under the influence of the last dose of drugs that had been given him during the preceding night, but he was regaining his consciousness more slowly than the surgeon had hoped. The long hours dragged by, morning ran into afternoon, and evening came, and still there was no word from the sickroom.

It was dark. The lamps were lighted. The family were congregated in the big living room. Suddenly the door opened and a nurse appeared. Behind her was the patient. There was a puzzled look upon his face; but the face of the nurse was wreathed in smiles. The surgeon came behind, assisting the man, who was weak from long inactivity.

"I think Lord Greystoke will recover rapidly now," he said. "There are many things that you may have to tell him. He did not know who he was, when he regained consciousness, but that is not unusual in such cases."

The patient took a few steps into the room, looking wonderingly about.

"There is your wife, Greystoke," said the surgeon, kindly.

Lady Greystoke rose and crossed the room toward her husband, her arms outstretched. A smile crossed the face of the invalid, as he stepped forward to meet her and take her in his arms, but suddenly someone was between them, holding them apart. It was Flora Hawkes.

"My Gawd, Lady Greystoke!" she cried. "He ain't your husband. It's Miranda, Esteban Miranda! Don't you suppose I'd know him in a million? I ain't seen him since we came back, never havin' been in the sick chamber, but I suspicioned something the minute he stepped into this room and when he smiled, I knew."

"Flora!" cried the distracted wife. "Are you sure? No! no! you must be wrong! God has not given me back my husband only to steal him away again. John! tell me, is it you? You would not lie to me?"

For a moment the man before them was silent. He swayed to and fro, as in weakness. The surgeon stepped forward and supported him.

"I have been very sick," he said. "Possibly I have changed, but I am Lord Greystoke. I do not remember this woman," and he indicated Flora Hawkes.

"He lies!" cried the girl.

"Yes, he lies," said a quiet voice behind them, and they all turned to see the figure of a giant white standing in the open French windows leading to the veranda.

"John!" cried Lady Greystoke, running toward him, "how could I have been mistaken? I—" but the rest of the sentence was lost as Tarzan of the Apes sprang into the room and taking his mate in his arms covered her lips with kisses.

THE SUPER PACK EBOOK SERIES

If you enjoyed this Super Pack you may wish to find the other books in this series. We endeavor to provide you with a quality product. But since many of these stories have been scanned typos do occasionally creep in. If you spot one please share it with us at positronicpress@yahoo.com so that we can fix it. We occasionally add additional stories to some of our Super Packs so make sure that you download fresh copies of your Super Packs from time to time to get the latest edition.

Science Fiction Super Pack #1: ISBN 978-1-63384-240-3
Science Fiction Super Pack #2: ISBN 978-1-51540-477-4
Science Fiction Super Pack #3: (Forthcoming)
Fantasy Super Pack #1: ISBN 978-1-63384-282-3
Fantasy Super Pack #2: ISBN 9781-51543-932-5
Conan the Barbarian Super Pack: ISBN 978-1-63384-292-2
Lord Dunsany Super Pack: ISBN 978-1-63384-725-5
Philip K. Dick Super Pack: ISBN 978-1-63384-799-6
The Pirate Super Pack # 1: ISBN 978-1-51540-193-3
The Pirate Super Pack # 2: ISBN 978-1-51540-196-4
Harry Harrison Super Pack: ISBN 978-1-51540-217-6
Andre Norton Super Pack: ISBN 978-1-51540-262-6
Marion Zimmer Bradley Super Pack: ISBN 978-1-51540-287-9
Frederik Pohl Super Pack: ISBN 978-1-51540-289-3
King Arthur Super Pack: ISBN 978-1-51540-306-7
Alan E. Nourse Super Pack: ISBN 978-1-51540-393-7
Space Science Fiction Super Pack: ISBN 978-1-51540-440-8
Wonder Stories Super Pack: ISBN 978-1-51540-454-5
Galaxy Science Fiction Super Pack #1:ISBN 978-1-51540-524-5
Galaxy Science Fiction Super Pack #2: 978-1-5154-0577-1
Science Fiction Novel Super Pack #1: ISBN 978-1-51540-363-0
Science Fiction Novel Super Pack #2: (Forthcoming)
Dragon Super Pack: ISBN 978-1-5154-1124-6
Weird Tales Super Pack #1: ISBN 978-1-5154-0548-1
Weird Tales Super Pack #2: 978-1-5154-1107-9
Poul Anderson Super Pack: ISBN 978-1-5154-0609-9
Fantastic Universe Super Pack #1: ISBN 978-1-5154-0981-6
Fantastic Universe Super Pack #2: ISBN 978-1-5154-0654-9
Fantastic Universe Super Pack #3: ISBN 978-1-5154-0655-6
Imagination Super Pack: ISBN 978-1-5154-1089-8
Planet Stories Super Pack: ISBN 978-1-5154-1125-3
Worlds of If Super Pack #1: ISBN 978-1-5154-1148-2
Worlds of If Super Pack #2: ISBN 978-1-5154-1182-6
Worlds of If Super Pack #3: ISBN 978-1-5154-1234-2

TARZAN SUPER PACK

Argosy All-Story Weekly Super Pack: ISBN (Forthcoming)
Fritz Leiber Super Pack #1: ISBN 978-1-5154-1847-4
Fritz Leiber Super Pack #2: ISBN (Forthcoming)
Vampire Super Pack: ISBN 978-1-5154-3954-7
Max Brand Western Super-Pack: ISBN 978-1-6338-4841-2
Charles Boardman Hawes Super Pack: ISBN (Forthcoming)
The Edgar Wallace Super Pack ISBN: (Forthcoming)
The Doctor Dolittle Super Pack: ISBN (Forthcoming)
Tarzan Super Pack: ISBN (Forthcoming)
The Wizard of Oz Super Pack ISBN: 978-1-5154-1872-6